THE COMPLETE NOVELS OF
CHARLOTTE & EMILY
BRONTË

THE COMPLETE NOVELS OF
CHARLOTTE & EMILY BRONTË

Jane Eyre
by Charlotte Brontë

Wuthering Heights
by Emily Brontë

Shirley
by Charlotte Brontë

Villette
by Charlotte Brontë

The Professor
by Charlotte Brontë

AVENEL BOOKS · NEW YORK

This edition is published by Avenel Books,
distributed by Crown Publishers, Inc.
h g f e d c b a
AVENEL 1981 EDITION

Manufactured in the United States of America

Library of Congress Cataloging in Publication Data
Main entry under title:

The Complete novels of Charlotte and Emily Brontë.

 Contents: Jane Eyre / by Charlotte Brontë—Wuthering
Heights / by Emily Brontë—Shirley / by Charlotte
Brontë—[etc.]
 1. English fiction—19th century. [1. English fiction
—19th century] I. Brontë, Charlotte, 1816–1855.
II. Brontë, Emily, 1818–1848.
PR4166. 1981 823′.8′08 [Fic] 81-10808
ISBN: 0-517-348004 AACR2
ISBN: 0-517-351757 (lib. bdg.)

CONTENTS

Introduction

HERE ARE all five novels of the two most famous Brontë sisters, Charlotte and Emily. Thackeray, the novelist of *Vanity Fair*, said of Charlotte, "Which of her readers has not become her friend?" Millions have felt that way about Charlotte Brontë since *Jane Eyre* became an overnight sensation almost a century and a half ago. Emily Brontë's personality has always seemed more elusive, but the only novel from her pen, the somber *Wuthering Heights,* has its own equally wide and enthusiastic following.

Here is *Wuthering Heights,* set on the Yorkshire moors, the classic story of persistent and ruinous passion with its unforgettable tale of Heathcliff's obsession with Catherine and her family. Here too are all the novels of Charlotte Brontë. *Jane Eyre* tells of the penniless orphan who became a governess and her love for Mr. Rochester, the master of Thornfield Hall. *Shirley* is a tale of love and ambition and industrial unrest set among the wool mills of Yorkshire. In its title character, Charlotte gave a portrait of her sister Emily, who was dying as the book was being written. *Villette* is the story of Lucy Snowe's progress in love and self-knowledge at a school in Brussels. The Brontë sisters had actually studied and taught in Brussels, and the autobiographical element is strong. Also included is *The Professor,* Charlotte's first novel. Unpublished in her lifetime, it handles love themes similar to *Villette*'s, but from the man's point of view.

Charlotte and Emily were two of the six children of a country clergyman. Their mother died young, and the two elder sisters died in early childhood. The remaining four, Charlotte, Emily, sister Anne, and brother Branwell, were encouraged by their father in their precocity and lived in a world of literary fantasy. What they did, they did collectively. From childhood until they were fully adult, the four composed elaborate fantasy worlds in pairs: Charlotte with Branwell and Emily with Anne. They created these worlds at great length in tiny script on small sheets of paper which they bound into books.

The sisters' public literary career began when Charlotte decided to publish the poems that had been part of this childhood epic cycle in a collection which included poems by each of the three sisters. Then the sisters began to write a novel apiece in a kind of sisterly competition. They spent hours each evening walking around their parlor table and telling each other the plots and plans for the novels to come. Out of this competition came *Wuthering Heights* by Emily and *The Professor* by Charlotte.

The sisters lived lives so brief—only Charlotte lived long enough to enjoy her fame, and even she died at age thirty-nine, just a few months after marrying her father's curate. How did their private lives of relative isolation prepare them for the passionate expression of their novels? They were most at home in the world of the imagination. In their lives outside of their writing they met with one tragedy or failure after another. They took their education in bits and snatches between bouts of illness;

they failed to find students for the school they planned to open together—again a joint undertaking; their lives were brief, and Branwell, to whom they were devoted, failed most of all, dying from drink and drug addiction at age thirty-one.

But the paradox is that, despite the shortness of their lives, these sisters *were* "tenacious of life," as Rochester says of Jane Eyre. Charlotte described Jane Austen's writings as more real than her own, but not more true. This was the key. They had learned their ideas of life from romantic sources—Sir Walter Scott, Lord Byron, the Arabian Nights, and the lives of heroes like Wellington. Life demanded action, but this action was to be obedient to inner passions. Ignorance and suppression of these deep interior motivations were to the sisters the chief cause of personal trouble and even of social injustice. For Emily, who had a visionary and mystical intensity of mind, the heart's passion had an added inevitability. This is what gives her *Wuthering Heights* its demonic quality.

The Brontës were accused of immorality in their writings by some critics of their time. Romantic novels have always found criticism of this kind. When the authors were revealed to be women, the prejudiced criticism was added that they were unladylike. In person, however, Thackeray saw Charlotte as "an austere little Joan of Arc, marching in upon us, and rebuking our easy lives, our easy morals." The sisters' tales of the heart are indeed often in revolt against convention and show strong feelings for the plight of women. What Charlotte said of her sisters is true also of herself: "They always wrote from the impulse of nature, the dictates of intuition, and from such stores of observation as their limited experience had enabled them to amass." When you add unparalleled imagination, and the mark of genius and originality, then you have the Brontës.

THE COMPLETE NOVELS OF
CHARLOTTE & EMILY
BRONTË

Jane Eyre

by
Charlotte Brontë

Chapter I

THERE was no possibility of taking a walk that day. We had been wandering, indeed, in the leafless shrubbery an hour in the morning; but since dinner (Mrs. Reed, when there was no company, dined early) the cold winter wind had brought with it clouds so sombre, and a rain so penetrating, that further out-door exercise was now out of the question.

I was glad of it: I never liked long walks, especially on chilly afternoons: dreadful to me was the coming home in the raw twilight, with nipped fingers and toes, and a heart saddened by the chidings of Bessie, the nurse, and humbled by the consciousness of my physical inferiority to Eliza, John, and Georgiana Reed.

The said Eliza, John, and Georgiana were now clustered round their mama in the drawing-room: she lay reclined on a sofa by the fireside, and with her darlings about her (for the time neither quarrelling nor crying) looked perfectly happy. Me, she had dispensed from joining the group; saying, "She regretted to be under the necessity of keeping me at a distance; but that until she heard from Bessie, and could discover by her own observation that I was endeavouring in good earnest to acquire a more sociable and childlike disposition, a more attractive and sprightly manner,—something lighter, franker, more natural as it were—she really must exclude me from privileges intended only for contented, happy, little children."

"What does Bessie say I have done?" I asked.

"Jane, I don't like cavillers or questioners: besides, there is something truly forbidding in a child taking up her elders in that manner. Be seated somewhere; and until you can speak pleasantly, remain silent."

A small breakfast-room adjoined the drawing-room. I slipped in there. It contained a book-case: I soon possessed myself of a volume, taking care that it should be one stored with pictures. I mounted into the window-seat: gathering up my feet, I sat cross-legged, like a Turk; and, having drawn the red moreen curtain nearly close, I was shrined in double retirement.

Folds of scarlet drapery shut in my view to the right hand; to the left were the clear panes of glass, protecting, but not separating me from the drear November day. At intervals, while turning over the leaves of my book, I studied the aspect of that winter afternoon. Afar, it offered a pale blank of mist and cloud; near, a scene of wet lawn and storm-beat shrub, with ceaseless rain sweeping away wildly before a long and lamentable blast.

I returned to my book—Bewick's History of British Birds: the letter-press thereof I cared little for, generally speaking; and yet there were certain introductory pages that, child as I was, I could not pass quite as a blank. They were those which treat of the haunts of sea-fowl; of "the solitary rocks and promontories" by them only inhabited; of the coast of Norway, studded with isles from its southern extremity, the Lindeness, or Naze, to the North Cape—

"Where the Northern Ocean, in vast whirls,
Boils round the naked, melancholy isles
Of farthest Thule; and the Atlantic surge
Pours in among the stormy Hebrides."

Nor could I pass unnoticed the suggestion of the bleak shores of Lapland, Siberia, Spitzbergen, Nova Zembla, Iceland, Greenland, with "the vast sweep of the Arctic Zone, and those forlorn regions of dreary space,—that reservoir of frost and snow, where firm fields of ice, the accumulation of centuries of winters, glazed in Alpine heights above heights, surround the pole, and concentre the multiplied rigors of extreme cold." Of these death-white realms I formed an idea of my own: shadowy, like all the half-comprehended notions that float dim through children's brains, but strangely impressive. The words in these introductory pages connected themselves with the succeeding vignettes, and gave significance to the rock standing up alone in a sea of billow and spray; to the broken boat stranded on a desolate coast; to the cold and ghastly moon glancing through bars of cloud at a wreck just sinking.

I cannot tell what sentiment haunted the quiet solitary churchyard, with its inscribed headstone; its gate, its two trees, its low horizon, girdled by a broken wall, and its newly-risen crescent, attesting the hour of eventide.

The two ships becalmed on a torpid sea, I believed to be marine phantoms.

The fiend pinning down the thief's pack behind him, I passed over quickly: it was an object of terror.

So was the black, horned thing seated aloof on a rock, surveying a distant crowd surrounding a gallows.

Each picture told a story; mysterious often to my undeveloped understanding and imperfect feelings, yet ever profoundly interesting: as interesting as the tales Bessie sometimes narrated on winter evenings, when she chanced to be in good humour; and when, having brought her ironing-table to the nursery-hearth, she allowed us to sit about it, and while she got up Mrs. Reed's lace frills, and crimped her night-cap borders, fed our eager attention with passages of love and adventure taken from old fairy tales and older ballads; or (as at a later period I discovered) from the pages of Pamela, and Henry, Earl of Moreland.

With Bewick on my knee, I was then happy: happy at least in my way. I feared nothing but interruption, and that came too soon. The breakfast-room door opened.

"Boh! Madame Mope!" cried the voice of John Reed; then he paused: he found the room apparently empty.

"Where the dickens is she?" he continued. "Lizzy! Georgy! (calling to his sisters) Jane is not here: tell mama she is run out into the rain—bad animal!"

"It is well I drew the curtain," thought I; and I wished fervently he might not discover my hiding-place: nor would John Reed have found it out himself; he was not quick either of vision or conception; but Eliza just put her head in at the door, and said at once:—

"She is in the window-seat, to be sure, Jack."

And I came out immediately, for I trembled at the idea of being dragged forth by the said Jack.

"What do you want?" I asked, with awkward diffidence.

"Say, 'what do you want, Master Reed,' " was the answer. "I want you to come here;" and seating himself in an arm-chair, he intimated by a gesture that I was to approach and stand before him.

John Reed was a schoolboy of fourteen years old; four years older than I, for I was but ten; large and stout for his age, with a dingy and unwholesome skin; thick lineaments in a spacious visage, heavy limbs and large extremities. He gorged himself habitually at table, which made him bilious, and gave him a dim and bleared eye and flabby cheeks. He ought now to have been at school; but his mama had taken him home for a month or two, "on account of his delicate health." Mr.

Miles, the master, affirmed that he would do very well if he had fewer cakes and sweetmeats sent him from home; but the mother's heart turned from an opinion so harsh, and inclined rather to the more refined idea that John's sallowness was owing to over-application and, perhaps, to pining after home.

John had not much affection for his mother and sisters, and an antipathy to me. He bullied and punished me; not two or three times in the week, nor once or twice in the day, but continually: every nerve I had feared him, and every morsel of flesh on my bones shrank when he came near. There were moments when I was bewildered by the terror he inspired, because I had no appeal whatever against either his menaces or his inflictions; the servants did not like to offend their young master by taking my part against him, and Mrs. Reed was blind and deaf on the subject: she never saw him strike or heard him abuse me, though he did both now and then in her very presence; more frequently, however, behind her back.

Habitually obedient to John, I came up to his chair: he spent some three minutes in thrusting out his tongue at me as far as he could without damaging the roots: I knew he would soon strike, and while dreading the blow, I mused on the disgusting and ugly appearance of him who would presently deal it. I wonder if he read that notion in my face; for, all at once, without speaking, he struck suddenly and strongly. I tottered, and on regaining my equilibrium retired back a step or two from his chair.

"That is for your impudence in answering mama awhile since," said he, "and for your sneaking way of getting behind curtains, and for the look you had in your eyes two minutes since, you rat!"

Accustomed to John Reed's abuse, I never had an idea of replying to it; my care was how to endure the blow which would certainly follow the insult.

"What were you doing behind the curtain?" he asked.

"I was reading."

"Shew the book."

I returned to the window and fetched it thence.

"You have no business to take our books; you are a dependant, mama says; you have no money; your father left you none; you ought to beg, and not to live here with gentlemen's children like us, and eat the same meals we do, and wear clothes at our mama's expense. Now, I'll teach you to rummage my book-shelves: for they *are* mine; all the house belongs to me, or will do in a few years. Go and stand by the door, out of the way of the mirror and the windows."

I did so, not at first aware what was his intention; but when I saw him lift and poise the book and stand in act to hurl it, I instinctively started aside with a cry of alarm: not soon enough, however; the volume was flung, it hit me, and I fell, striking my head against the door and cutting it. The cut bled, the pain was sharp; my terror had passed its climax; other feelings succeeded.

"Wicked and cruel boy!" I said. "You are like a murderer—you are like a slave-driver—you are like the Roman emperors!"

I had read Goldsmith's History of Rome, and had formed my opinion of Nero, Caligula, etc. Also I had drawn parallels in silence, which I never thought thus to have declared aloud.

"What! what!" he cried. "Did you say that to me? Did you hear her, Eliza and Georgiana? Won't I tell mama? but first"—

He ran headlong at me: I felt him grasp my hair and my shoulder: he had closed with a desperate thing. I really saw in him a tyrant: a murderer. I felt a drop or two of blood from my head trickle down my neck, and was sensible of somewhat pungent sufferings: these sensations for the time predominated over fear, and I received him in frantic sort. I don't very well know what I did with my hands, but he called me "Rat! rat!" and bellowed out aloud. Aid was near him: Eliza and Georgiana had run for Mrs. Reed, who was gone upstairs; she now came upon the

scene, followed by Bessie and her maid Abbot. We were parted: I heard the words:—

"Dear! dear! What a fury to fly at Master John!"

"Did ever anybody see such a picture of passion!"

Then Mrs. Reed subjoined:—

"Take her away to the red-room, and lock her in there." Four hands were immediately laid upon me, and I was borne upstairs.

Chapter II

I RESISTED all the way: a new thing for me, and a circumstance which greatly strengthened the bad opinion Bessie and Miss Abbot were disposed to entertain of me. The fact is, I was a trifle beside myself; or rather *out* of myself, as the French would say: I was conscious that a moment's mutiny had already rendered me liable to strange penalties, and, like any other rebel slave, I felt resolved, in my desperation, to go all lengths.

"Hold her arms, Miss Abbot: she's like a mad cat."

"For shame! for shame!" cried the lady's-maid. "What shocking conduct, Miss Eyre, to strike a young gentleman, your benefactress's son! Your young master."

"Master! How is he my master? Am I a servant?"

"No; you are less than a servant, for you do nothing for your keep. There, sit down, and think over your wickedness."

They had got me by this time into the apartment indicated by Mrs. Reed, and had thrust me upon a stool: my impulse was to rise from it like a spring; their two pair of hands arrested me instantly.

"If you don't sit still, you must be tied down," said Bessie. "Miss Abbot, lend me your garters; she would break mine directly."

Miss Abbot turned to divest a stout leg of the necessary ligature. This preparation for bonds, and the additional ignominy it inferred, took a little of the excitement out of me.

"Don't take them off," I cried; "I will not stir."

In guarantee whereof, I attached myself to my seat by my hands.

"Mind you don't," said Bessie; and when she had ascertained that I was really subsiding, she loosened her hold of me; then she and Miss Abbot stood with folded arms, looking darkly and doubtfully on my face, as incredulous of my sanity.

"She never did so before," at last said Bessie, turning to the Abigail.

"But it was always in her," was the reply. "I've told Missis often my opinion about the child, and Missis agreed with me. She's an underhand little thing: I never saw a girl of her age with so much cover."

Bessie answered not; but ere long, addressing me, she said,—

"You ought to be aware, Miss, that you are under obligations to Mrs. Reed: she keeps you: if she were to turn you off, you would have to go to the poor-house."

I had nothing to say to these words: they were not new to me: my very first recollections of existence included hints of the same kind. This reproach of my dependence had become a vague sing-song in my ear; very painful and crushing, but only half intelligible. Miss Abbot joined in:—

"And you ought not to think yourself on an equality with the Misses Reed and Master Reed, because Missis kindly allows you to be brought up with them. They will have a great deal of money, and you will have none: it is your place to be humble, and to try to make yourself agreeable to them."

"What we tell you, is for your good," added Bessie, in no harsh voice: "you should try to be useful and pleasant, then, perhaps, you would have a home here; but if you become passionate and rude, Missis will send you away, I am sure."

"Besides," said Miss Abbot, "God will punish her: he might strike her dead in the midst of her tantrums, and then where would she go? Come, Bessie, we will leave her: I wouldn't have her heart for anything. Say your prayers, Miss Eyre, when you are by yourself; for if you don't repent, something bad might be permitted to come down the chimney and fetch you away."

They went, shutting the door, and locking it behind them.

The red-room was a spare chamber, very seldom slept in; I might say never, indeed, unless when a chance influx of visitors at Gateshead Hall rendered it necessary to turn to account all the accommodation it contained: yet it was one of the largest and stateliest chambers in the mansion. A bed supported on massive pillars of mahogany, hung with curtains of deep red damask, stood out like a tabernacle in the centre; the two large windows, with their blinds always drawn down, were half shrouded in festoons and falls of similar drapery; the carpet was red; the table at the foot of the bed was covered with a crimson cloth; the walls were a soft fawn colour, with a blush of pink in it; the wardrobe, the toilet-table, the chairs were of darkly polished old mahogany. Out of these deep surrounding shades rose high, and glared white, the piled-up mattresses and pillows of the bed, spread with a snowy Marseilles counterpane. Scarcely less prominent was an ample, cushioned easy-chair near the head of the bed, also white, with a footstool before it; and looking, as I thought, like a pale throne.

This room was chill, because it seldom had a fire; it was silent, because remote from the nursery and kitchens; solemn, because it was known to be so seldom entered. The housemaid alone came here on Saturdays, to wipe from the mirrors and the furniture a week's quiet dust: and Mrs. Reed herself, at far intervals, visited it to review the contents of a certain secret drawer in the wardrobe, where were stored divers parchments, her jewel-casket, and a miniature of her deceased husband; and in those last words lies the secret of the bed-room—the spell which kept it so lonely in spite of its grandeur.

Mr. Reed had been dead nine years: it was in this chamber he breathed his last; here he lay in state; hence his coffin was borne by the undertaker's men; and, since that day, a sense of dreary consecration had guarded it from frequent intrusion.

My seat, to which Bessie and the bitter Miss Abbot had left me riveted, was a low ottoman near the marble chimney-piece; the bed rose before me; to my right hand there was the high, dark wardrobe, with subdued, broken reflections varying the gloss of its panels; to my left were the muffled windows; a great looking-glass between them repeated the vacant majesty of the bed and room. I was not quite sure whether they had locked the door; and, when I dared move, I got up, and went to see. Alas! yes, no jail was ever more secure. Returning, I had to cross before the looking-glass; my fascinated glance involuntarily explored the depth it revealed. All looked colder and darker in that visionary hollow than in reality: and the strange little figure there gazing at me, with a white face and arms specking the gloom, and glittering eyes of fear moving where all else was still, had the effect of a real spirit: I thought it like one of the tiny phantoms, half fairy, half imp, Bessie's evening stories represented as coming up out of lone, ferny dells in moors, and appearing before the eyes of belated travellers. I returned to my stool.

Superstition was with me at that moment; but it was not yet her hour for complete victory: my blood was still warm; the mood of the revolted slave was still bracing me with its bitter vigour; I had to stem a rapid rush of retrospective thought before I quailed to the dismal present.

All John Reed's violent tyrannies, all his sisters' proud indifference, all his mother's aversion, all the servants' partiality, turned up in my disturbed mind like a dark deposit in a turbid well. Why was I always suffering, always brow-beaten, always accused, for ever condemned? Why could I never please? Why was it useless to try to win any one's favour? Eliza, who was headstrong and selfish, was respected. Georgiana, who had a spoiled temper, a very acrid spite, a captious and insolent

carriage, was universally indulged. Her beauty, her pink cheeks and golden curls, seemed to give delight to all who looked at her, and to purchase indemnity for every fault. John, no one thwarted, much less punished; though he twisted the necks of the pigeons, killed the little pea-chicks, set the dogs at the sheep, stripped the hothouse vines of their fruit, and broke the buds off the choicest plants in the conservatory: he called his mother "old girl," too; sometimes reviled her for her dark skin, similar to his own; bluntly disregarded her wishes; not unfrequently tore and spoiled her silk attire; and he was still "her own darling." I dared commit no fault: I strove to fulfil every duty; and I was termed naughty and tiresome, sullen and sneaking, from morning to noon, and from noon to night.

My head still ached and bled with the blow and fall I had received: no one had reproved John for wantonly striking me; and because I had turned against him to avert farther irrational violence, I was loaded with general opprobrium.

"Unjust!—unjust!" said my reason, forced by the agonising stimulus into precocious though transitory power; and Resolve, equally wrought up, instigated some strange expedient to achieve escape from insupportable oppression—as running away, or, if that could not be effected, never eating or drinking more, and letting myself die.

What a consternation of soul was mine that dreary afternoon! How all my brain was in tumult, and all my heart in insurrection! Yet in what darkness, what dense ignorance, was the mental battle fought! I could not answer the ceaseless inward question—*why* I thus suffered; now, at the distance of—I will not say how many years, I see it clearly.

I was a discord in Gateshead Hall; I was like nobody there; I had nothing in harmony with Mrs. Reed or her children, or her chosen vassalage. If they did not love me, in fact, as little did I love them. They were not bound to regard with affection a thing that could not sympathise with one amongst them; a heterogeneous thing, opposed to them in temperament, in capacity, in propensities; a useless thing, incapable of serving their interest, or adding to their pleasure; a noxious thing, cherishing the germs of indignation at their treatment, of contempt of their judgment. I know that had I been a sanguine, brilliant, careless, exacting, handsome, romping child—though equally dependent and friendless—Mrs. Reed would have endured my presence more complacently; her children would have entertained for me more of the cordiality of fellow-feeling; the servants would have been less prone to make me the scapegoat of the nursery.

Daylight began to forsake the red-room; it was past four o'clock, and the beclouded afternoon was tending to drear twilight. I heard the rain still beating continuously on the staircase window, and the wind howling in the grove behind the hall; I grew by degrees cold as a stone, and then my courage sank. My habitual mood of humiliation, self-doubt, forlorn depression, fell damp on the embers of my decaying ire. All said I was wicked, and perhaps I might be so; what thought had I been but just conceiving of starving myself to death? That certainly was a crime: and was I fit to die? Or was the vault under the chancel of Gateshead Church an inviting bourne? In such vault I had been told did Mr. Reed lie buried; and led by this thought to recall his idea, I dwelt on it with gathering dread. I could not remember him; but I knew that he was my own uncle—my mother's brother—that he had taken me when a parentless infant to his house; and that in his last moments he had required a promise of Mrs. Reed that she would rear and maintain me as one of her own children. Mrs. Reed probably considered she had kept this promise; and so she had, I dare say, as well as her nature would permit her; but how could she really like an interloper not of her race, and unconnected with her, after her husband's death, by any tie? It must have been most irksome to find herself bound by a hard-wrung pledge to stand in the stead of a parent to a strange child she could not love, and to see an uncongenial alien permanently intruded on her own family group.

A singular notion dawned upon me. I doubted not—never doubted—that if Mr. Reed had been alive he would have treated me kindly; and now, as I sat looking at the white bed and overshadowed walls—occasionally also turning a fascinated eye towards the dimly gleaming mirror—I began to recall what I had heard of dead men, troubled in their graves by the violation of their last wishes, revisiting the earth to punish the perjured and avenge the oppressed; and I thought Mr. Reed's spirit, harassed by the wrongs of his sister's child, might quit its abode—whether in the church vault or in the unknown world of the departed—and rise before me in this chamber. I wiped my tears and hushed my sobs, fearful lest any sign of violent grief might waken a preternatural voice to comfort me, or elicit from the gloom some haloed face, bending over me with strange pity. This idea, consolatory in theory, I felt would be terrible if realised: with all my might I endeavoured to stifle it—I endeavoured to be firm. Shaking my hair from my eyes, I lifted my head and tried to look boldly round the dark room: at this moment a light gleamed on the wall. Was it, I asked myself, a ray from the moon penetrating some aperture in the blind? No; moonlight was still, and this stirred; while I gazed, it glided up to the ceiling and quivered over my head. I can now conjecture readily that this streak of light was, in all likelihood, a gleam from a lantern, carried by some one across the lawn: but then, prepared as my mind was for horror, shaken as my nerves were by agitation, I thought the swift-darting beam was a herald of some coming vision from another world. My heart beat thick, my head grew hot; a sound filled my ears, which I deemed the rushing of wings: something seemed near me; I was oppressed, suffocated: endurance broke down; I rushed to the door and shook the lock in desperate effort. Steps came running along the outer passage; the key turned, Bessie and Abbot entered.

"Miss Eyre, are you ill?" said Bessie.

"What a dreadful noise! it went quite through me!" exclaimed Abbot.

"Take me out! Let me go into the nursery!" was my cry.

"What for! Are you hurt! Have you seen something?" again demanded Bessie.

"Oh! I saw a light, and I thought a ghost would come." I had now got hold of Bessie's hand, and she did not snatch it from me.

"She has screamed out on purpose," declared Abbot, in some disgust. "And what a scream! If she had been in great pain one would have excused it, but she only wanted to bring us all here. I know her naughty tricks."

"What is all this?" demanded another voice peremptorily; and Mrs. Reed came along the corridor, her cap flying wide, her gown rustling stormily. "Abbot and Bessie, I believe I gave orders that Jane Eyre should be left in the red-room till I came to her myself."

"Miss Jane screamed so loud, ma'am," pleaded Bessie.

"Let her go," was the only answer. "Loose Bessie's hand, child: you cannot succeed in getting out by these means, be assured. I abhor artifice, particularly in children; it is my duty to show you that tricks will not answer: you will now stay here an hour longer, and it is only on condition of perfect submission and stillness that I shall liberate you then."

"Oh aunt, have pity! Forgive me! I cannot endure it—let me be punished some other way! I shall be killed if"——

"Silence! This violence is all most repulsive:" and so, no doubt, she felt it. I was a precocious actress in her eyes: she sincerely looked on me as a compound of virulent passions, mean spirit, and dangerous duplicity.

Bessie and Abbot having retreated, Mrs. Reed, impatient of my now frantic anguish and wild sobs, abruptly thrust me back and locked me in, without farther parley. I heard her sweeping away; and soon after she was gone, I suppose I had a species of fit: unconsciousness closed the scene.

Chapter III

THE next thing I remember is, waking up with a feeling as if I had had a frightful night-mare, and seeing before me a terrible red glare, crossed with thick black bars. I heard voices, too, speaking with a hollow sound, and as if muffled by a rush of wind or water: agitation, uncertainty, and an all-predominating sense of terror confused my faculties. Ere long, I became aware that some one was handling me; lifting me up and supporting me in a sitting posture, and that more tenderly than I had ever been raised or upheld before. I rested my head against a pillow or an arm, and felt easy.

In five minutes more, the cloud of bewilderment dissolved: I knew quite well that I was in my own bed, and that the red glare was the nursery fire. It was night: a candle burnt on the table; Bessie stood at the bed-foot with a basin in her hand, and a gentleman sat in a chair near my pillow, leaning over me.

I felt an inexpressible relief, a soothing conviction of protection and security, when I knew that there was a stranger in the room, an individual not belonging to Gateshead, and not related to Mrs. Reed. Turning from Bessie (though her presence was far less obnoxious to me than that of Abbot, for instance, would have been), I scrutinised the face of the gentleman: I knew him; it was Mr. Lloyd, an apothecary, sometimes called in by Mrs. Reed when the servants were ailing: for herself and the children she employed a physician.

"Well, who am I?" he asked.

I pronounced his name, offering him at the same time my hand: he took it, smiling and saying, "We shall do very well by-and-by." Then he laid me down, and addressing Bessie, charged her to be very careful that I was not disturbed during the night. Having given some further directions, and intimated that he should call again the next day, he departed; to my grief: I felt so sheltered and befriended while he sat in the chair near my pillow; and as he closed the door after him, all the room darkened and my heart again sank: inexpressible sadness weighed it down.

"Do you feel as if you should sleep, Miss?" asked Bessie, rather softly.

Scarcely dared I answer her; for I feared the next sentence might be rough. "I will try."

"Would you like to drink, or could you eat anything?"

"No, thank you, Bessie."

"Then I think I shall go to bed, for it is past twelve o'clock; but you may call me if you want anything in the night."

Wonderful civility this! It emboldened me to ask a question.

"Bessie, what is the matter with me? Am I ill?"

"You fell sick, I suppose, in the red-room with crying; you'll be better soon, no doubt."

Bessie went into the housemaid's apartment which was near. I heard her say—

"Sarah, come and sleep with me in the nursery; I daren't for my life be alone with that poor child to-night; she might die; it's such a strange thing she should have that fit: I wonder if she saw anything. Missis was rather too hard."

Sarah came back with her; they both went to bed; they were whispering together for half an hour before they fell asleep. I caught scraps of their conversation, from which I was able only too distinctly to infer the main subject discussed.

"Something passed her, all dressed in white, and vanished"—"A great black dog behind him"—"Three loud raps on the chamber door"—"A light in the church-yard just over his grave"—etc., etc.

At last both slept: the fire and the candle went out. For me, the watches of that long night passed in ghastly wakefulness; ear, eye, and mind were alike strained by dread: such dread as children only can feel.

No severe or prolonged bodily illness followed this incident of the red-room: it only gave my nerves a shock, of which I feel the reverberation to this day. Yes, Mrs. Reed, to you I owe some fearful pangs of mental suffering. But I ought to forgive you, for you knew not what you did: while rending my heartstrings, you thought you were only up-rooting my bad propensities.

Next day, by noon, I was up and dressed, and sat wrapped in a shawl by the nursery hearth. I felt physically weak and broken down: but my worse ailment was an unutterable wretchedness of mind: a wretchedness which kept drawing from me silent tears; no sooner had I wiped one salt drop from my cheek than another followed. Yet I thought, I ought to have been happy, for none of the Reeds were there; they were all gone out in the carriage with their mama: Abbot, too, was sewing in another room, and Bessie, as she moved hither and thither, putting away toys and arranging drawers, addressed to me every now and then a word of unwonted kindness. This state of things should have been to me a paradise of peace, accustomed as I was to a life of ceaseless reprimand and thankless fagging; but, in fact, my racked nerves were now in such a state that no calm could soothe, and no pleasure excite them agreeably.

Bessie had been down into the kitchen, and she brought up with her a tart on a certain brightly painted china plate whose bird of paradise, nestling in a wreath of convolvuli and rosebuds, had been wont to stir in me a most enthusiastic sense of admiration; and which plate I had petitioned to be allowed to take in my hand in order to examine it more closely, but had always hitherto been deemed unworthy of such a privilege. This precious vessel was now placed on my knee, and I was cordially invited to eat the circlet of delicate pastry upon it. Vain favour! coming, like most other favours long deferred and often wished for, too late! I could not eat the tart: and the plumage of the bird, the tints of the flowers, seemed strangely faded: I put both plate and tart away. Bessie asked if I would have a book: the word *book* acted as a transient stimulus, and I begged her to fetch Gulliver's Travels from the library. This book I had again and again perused with delight. I considered it a narrative of facts, and discovered in it a vein of interest deeper than what I found in fairy tales: for as to the elves, having sought them in vain among foxglove leaves and bells, under mushrooms and beneath the ground-ivy mantling old wall-nooks, I had at length made up my mind to the sad truth, that they were all gone out of England to some savage country where the woods were wilder and thicker, and the population more scant; whereas, Lilliput and Brobdignag being, in my creed, solid parts of the earth's surface, I doubted not that I might one day, by taking a long voyage, see with my own eyes the little fields, houses, and trees, the diminutive people, the tiny cows, sheep, and birds of the one realm; and the corn-fields forest-high, the mighty mastiffs, the monster cats, the tower-like men and women, of the other. Yet, when this cherished volume was now placed in my hand—when I turned over its leaves, and sought in its marvellous pictures the charm I had, till now, never failed to find—all was eerie and dreary; the giants were gaunt goblins, the pigmies malevolent and fearful imps, Gulliver a most desolate wanderer in most dread and dangerous regions. I closed the book, which I dared no longer peruse, and put it on the table, beside the untasted tart.

Bessie had now finished dusting and tidying the room, and having washed her hands, she opened a certain little drawer, full of splendid shreds of silk and satin, and began making a new bonnet for Georgiana's doll. Meantime she sang: her song was—

> *"In the days when we went gipsying,*
> *A long time ago."*

I had often heard the song before, and always with lively delight; for Bessie had a sweet voice,—at least, I thought so. But now, though her voice was still sweet,

I found in its melody an indescribable sadness. Sometimes, pre-occupied with her work, she sang the refrain very low, very lingerly: "A long time ago" came out like the saddest cadence of a funeral hymn. She passed into another ballad, this time a really doleful one.

> *"My feet they are sore, and my limbs they are weary;*
> *Long is the way, and the mountains are wild;*
> *Soon will the twilight close moonless and dreary*
> *Over the path of the poor orphan child.*
>
> *"Why did they send me so far and so lonely,*
> *Up where the moors spread and grey rocks are piled?*
> *Men are hard-hearted, and kind angels only*
> *Watch'd o'er the steps of a poor orphan child.*
>
> *"Yet distant and soft the night-breeze is blowing,*
> *Clouds there are none, and clear stars beam mild.*
> *God, in His mercy, protection is showing,*
> *Comfort and hope to the poor orphan child.*
>
> *"Ev'n should I fall o'er the broken bridge passing,*
> *Or stray in the marshes, by false lights beguiled,*
> *Still will my Father, with promise and blessing,*
> *Take to His bosom the poor orphan child.*
>
> *"There is a thought that for strength should avail me,*
> *Though both of shelter and kindred despoiled;*
> *Heaven is a home, and a rest will not faill me;*
> *God is a friend to the poor orphan child."*

"Come, Miss Jane, don't cry," said Bessie, as she finished. She might as well have said to the fire, "don't burn!" but how could she divine the morbid suffering to which I was a prey? In the course of the morning, Mr. Lloyd came again.

"What, already up!" said he, as he entered the nursery. "Well, nurse, how is she?"

Bessie answered that I was doing very well.

"Then she ought to look more cheerful. Come here, Miss Jane: your name is Jane, is it not?"

"Yes, sir, Jane Eyre."

"Well, you have been crying, Miss Jane Eyre, can you tell me what about? Have you any pain?"

"No, sir."

"Oh! I daresay she is crying because she could not go out with Missis in the carriage," interposed Bessie.

"Surely not! why, she is too old for such pettishness."

I thought so too; and my self-esteem being wounded by the false charge, I answered promptly, "I never cried for such a thing in my life: I hate going out in the carriage. I cry because I am miserable."

"Oh fie, Miss!" said Bessie.

The good apothecary appeared a little puzzled. I was standing before him; he fixed his eyes on me very steadily: his eyes were small and grey; not very bright, but I daresay I should think them shrewd now: he had a hard-featured yet good-natured looking face. Having considered me at leisure, he said—

"What made you ill yesterday?"

"She had a fall," said Bessie, again putting in her word.

" Fall! why that is like a baby again! Can't she manage to walk at her age? She must be eight or nine years old."

"I was knocked down," was the blunt explanation jerked out of me by another pang of mortified pride: "but that did not make me ill," I added; while Mr. Lloyd helped himself to a pinch of snuff.

As he was returning the box to his waistcoat pocket, a loud bell rang for the servants' dinner; he knew what it was. "That's for you, nurse," said he; "you can go down; I'll give Miss Jane a lecture till you come back."

Bessie would rather have stayed, but she was obliged to go, because punctuality at meals was rigidly enforced at Gateshead Hall.

"The fall did not make you ill; what did, then?" pursued Mr. Lloyd, when Bessie was gone.

"I was shut up in a room where there is a ghost, till after dark."

I saw Mr. Lloyd smile and frown at the same time: "Ghost! What, you are a baby after all! You are afraid of ghosts?"

"Of Mr. Reed's ghost I am: he died in that room, and was laid out there. Neither Bessie nor any one else will go into it at night, if they can help it; and it was cruel to shut me up alone without a candle,—so cruel that I think I shall never forget it."

"Nonsense! And is it that makes you so miserable? Are you afraid now in daylight?"

"No: but night will come again before long: and besides,—I am unhappy,—very unhappy, for other things."

"What other things? Can you tell me some of them?"

How much I wished to reply fully to this question! How difficult it was to frame any answer! Children can feel, but they cannot analyse their feelings; and if the analysis is partially effected in thought, they know not how to express the result of the process in words. Fearful, however, of losing this first and only opportunity of relieving my grief by imparting it, I, after a disturbed pause, contrived to frame a meagre, though, as far as it went, true response.

"For one thing, I have no father or mother, brothers or sisters."

"You have a kind aunt and cousins."

Again I paused; then bunglingly enounced:

"But John Reed knocked me down, and my aunt shut me up in the red-room."

Mr. Lloyd a second time produced his snuff-box.

"Don't you think Gateshead Hall a very beautiful house?" asked he. "Are you not very thankful to have such a fine place to live at?"

"It is not my house, sir; and Abbot says I have less right to be here than a servant."

"Pooh! you can't be silly enough to wish to leave such a splendid place?"

"If I had anywhere else to go, I should be glad to leave it; but I can never get away from Gateshead till I am a woman."

"Perhaps you may—who knows? Have you any relations besides Mrs. Reed?"

"I think not, sir."

"None belonging to your father?"

"I don't know: I asked aunt Reed once, and she said possibly I might have some poor, low relations called Eyre, but she knew nothing about them."

"If you had such, would you like to go to them?"

I reflected. Poverty looks grim to grown people; still more so to children: they have not much idea of industrious, working, respectable poverty; they think of the word only as connected with ragged clothes, scanty food, fireless grates, rude manners, and debasing vices: poverty for me was synonymous with the degradation.

"No; I should not like to belong to poor people," was my reply.

"Not even if they were kind to you?"

I shook my head: I could not see how poor people had the means of being kind; and then to learn to speak like them, to adopt their manners, to be uneducated, to grow up like one of the poor women I saw sometimes nursing their children or washing their clothes at the cottage doors of the village of Gateshead: no, I was not heroic enough to purchase liberty at the price of caste.

"But are your relatives so very poor? Are they working people?"

"I cannot tell; aunt Reed says if I have any, they must be a beggarly set: I should not like to go a begging."

"Would you like to go to school?"

Again I reflected: I scarcely knew what school was; Bessie sometimes spoke of it as a place where young ladies sat in the stocks, wore backboards, and were expected to be exceedingly genteel and precise: John Reed hated his school, and abused his master; but John Reed's tastes were no rule for mine, and if Bessie's accounts of school-discipline (gathered from the young ladies of a family where she had lived before coming to Gateshead) were somewhat appalling, her details of certain accomplishments attained by these same young ladies were, I thought, equally attractive. She boasted of beautiful paintings of landscapes and flowers by them executed; of songs they could sing and pieces they could play, of purses they could net, of French books they could translate; till my spirit was moved to emulation as I listened. Besides, school would be a complete change: it implied a long journey, an entire separation from Gateshead, an entrance into a new life.

"I should indeed like to go to school," was the audible conclusion of my musings.

"Well, well; who knows what may happen?" said Mr. Lloyd, as he got up: "The child ought to have change of air and scene," he added, speaking to himself; "nerves not in a good state."

Bessie now returned; at the same moment the carriage was heard rolling up the gravel-walk.

"Is that your mistress, nurse?" asked Mr. Lloyd. "I should like to speak to her before I go."

Bessie invited him to walk into the breakfast-room, and led the way out. In the interview which followed between him and Mrs. Reed, I presume, from after-occurrences, that the apothecary ventured to recommend my being sent to school; and the recommendation was no doubt readily enough adopted; for as Abbot said, in discussing the subject with Bessie when both sat sewing in the nursery one night, after I was in bed, and, as they thought, asleep, "Missis was, she dared say, glad enough to get rid of such a tiresome, ill-conditioned child, who always looked as if she were watching everybody, and scheming plots underhand." Abbot, I think, gave me credit for being a sort of infantine Guy Fawkes.

On that same occasion I learned, for the first time, from Miss Abbot's communications to Bessie, that my father had been a poor clergyman; that my mother had married him against the wishes of her friends, who considered the match beneath her; that my grandfather Reed was so irritated at her disobedience, he cut her off without a shilling; that after my mother and father had been married a year, the latter caught the typhus fever while visiting among the poor of a large manufacturing town where his curacy was situated, and where that disease was then prevalent; that my mother took the infection from him, and both died within a month of each other.

Bessie, when she heard this narrative, sighed and said, "Poor Miss Jane is to be pitied, too, Abbot."

"Yes," responded Abbot; "if she were a nice, pretty child, one might compassionate her forlornness; but one really cannot care for such a little toad as that."

"Not a great deal to be sure," agreed Bessie: "at any rate, a beauty like Miss Georgiana would be more moving in the same condition."

"Yes, I doat on Miss Georgiana!" cried the fervent Abbot. "Little darling!—with her long curls and her blue eyes, and such a sweet colour as she has; just as if she were painted!—Bessie, I could fancy a Welsh rabbit for supper."

"So could I—with a roast onion. Come, we'll go down." They went.

Chapter IV

FROM my discourse with Mr. Lloyd, and from the above reported conference between Bessie and Abbot, I gathered enough of hope to suffice as a motive for wishing to get well: a change seemed near,—I desired and waited it in silence. It tarried, however: days and weeks passed: I had regained my normal state of health, but no new allusion was made to the subject over which I brooded. Mrs. Reed surveyed me at times with a severe eye, but seldom addressed me: since my illness, she had drawn a more marked line of separation than ever between me and her own children; appointing me a small closet to sleep in by myself, condemning me to take my meals alone, and pass all my time in the nursery, while my cousins were constantly in the drawing-room. Not a hint, however, did she drop about sending me to school: still I felt an instinctive certainty that she would not long endure me under the same roof with her; for her glance, now more than ever, when turned on me, expressed an insuperable and rooted aversion.

Eliza and Georgiana, evidently acting according to orders, spoke to me as little as possible: John thrust his tongue in his cheek whenever he saw me, and once attempted chastisement; but as I instantly turned against him, roused by the same sentiment of deep ire and desperate revolt which had stirred my corruption before, he thought it better to desist, and ran from me uttering execrations, and vowing I had burst his nose. I had indeed levelled at that prominent feature as hard a blow as my knuckles could inflict; and when I saw that either that or my look daunted him, I had the greatest inclination to follow up my advantage to purpose; but he was already with his mama. I heard him in a blubbering tone commence the tale of how "that nasty Jane Eyre" had flown at him like a mad cat: he was stopped rather harshly—

"Don't talk to me about her, John: I told you not to go near her; she is not worthy of notice; I do not choose that either you or your sisters should associate with her."

Here, leaning over the banister, I cried out suddenly, and without at all deliberating on my words,—

"They are not fit to associate with me."

Mrs. Reed was rather a stout woman; but, on hearing this strange and audacious declaration, she ran nimbly up the stair, swept me like a whirlwind into the nursery, and crushing me down on the edge of my crib, dared me in an emphatic voice to rise from that place, or utter one syllable during the remainder of the day.

"What would uncle Reed say to you, if he were alive?" was my scarcely voluntary demand. I say scarcely voluntary, for it seemed as if my tongue pronounced words without my will consenting to their utterance: something spoke out of me over which I had no control.

"What?" said Mrs. Reed under her breath: her usually cold composed grey eye became troubled with a look like fear; she took her hand from my arm, and gazed at me as if she really did not know whether I were child or fiend. I was now in for it.

"My uncle Reed is in heaven, and can see all you do and think; and so can papa and mama: they know how you shut me up all day long, and how you wish me dead."

Mrs. Reed soon rallied her spirits: she shook me most soundly, she boxed both my ears, and then left me without a word. Bessie supplied the hiatus by a homily of an hour's length, in which she proved beyond a doubt that I was the most wicked and abandoned child ever reared under a roof. I half believed her; for I felt indeed only bad feelings surging in my breast.

November, December, and half of January passed away. Christmas and the New Year had been celebrated at Gateshead with the usual festive cheer; presents had been interchanged, dinners and evening parties given. From every enjoyment I was, of course, excluded: my share of the gaiety consisted in witnessing the daily apparelling of Eliza and Georgiana, and seeing them descend to the drawing-room, dressed out in thin muslin frocks and scarlet sashes, with hair elaborately ringletted; and afterwards, in listening to the sound of the piano or the harp played below, to the passing to and fro of the butler and footman, to the jingling of glass and china as refreshments were handed, to the broken hum of conversation as the drawing-room doors opened and closed. When tired of this occupation, I would retire from the stair-head to the solitary and silent nursery: there, though somewhat sad, I was not miserable. To speak the truth, I had not the least wish to go into company, for in company I was very rarely noticed; and if Bessie had been kind and companionable, I should have deemed it a treat to spend the evenings quietly with her, instead of passing them under the formidable eye of Mrs. Reed, in a room full of ladies and gentlemen. But Bessie, as soon as she had dressed her young ladies, used to take herself off to the lively regions of the kitchen and housekeeper's room, generally bearing the candle along with her. I then sat with my doll on my knee, till the fire got low, glancing round occasionally to make sure that nothing worse than myself haunted the shadowy room; and when the embers sank to a dull red, I undressed hastily, tugging at knot and strings as I best might, and sought shelter from cold and darkness in my crib. To this crib I always took my doll; human beings must love something, and in the dearth of worthier objects of affection, I contrived to find a pleasure in loving and cherishing a faded graven image, shabby as a miniature scarecrow. It puzzles me now to remember with what absurd sincerity I doated on this little toy, half fancying it alive and capable of sensation. I could not sleep unless it was folded in my night-gown; and when it lay there safe and warm, I was comparatively happy, believing it to be happy likewise.

Long did the hours seem while I waited the departure of the company, and listened for the sound of Bessie's step on the stairs: sometimes she would come up in the interval to seek her thimble or her scissors, or perhaps to bring me something by way of supper—a bun or a cheese-cake—then she would sit on the bed while I ate it, and when I had finished, she would tuck the clothes round me, and twice she kissed me, and said, "Good-night, Miss Jane." When thus gentle, Bessie seemed to me the best, prettiest, kindest being in the world; and I wished most intensely that she would always be so pleasant and amiable, and never push me about, or scold, or task me unreasonably, as she was too often wont to do. Bessie Lee must, I think, have been a girl of good natural capacity, for she was smart in all she did, and had a remarkable knack of narrative; so, at least, I judge from the impression made on me by her nursery tales. She was pretty, too, if my recollections of her face and person are correct. I remember her as a slim young woman, with black hair, dark eyes, very nice features, and good, clear complexion; but she had a capricious and hasty temper, and indifferent ideas of principle or justice: still, such as she was, I preferred her to any one else at Gateshead Hall.

It was the fifteenth of January, about nine o'clock in the morning: Bessie was gone down to breakfast; my cousins had not yet been summoned to their mama; Eliza was putting on her bonnet and warm garden-coat to go and feed her poultry, an occupation of which she was fond: and not less so of selling the eggs to the housekeeper and hoarding up the money she thus obtained. She had a turn for traffic, and a marked propensity for saving; shown not only in the vending of eggs

and chickens, but also in driving hard bargains with the gardener about flower-roots, seeds, and slips of plants, that functionary having orders from Mrs. Reed to buy of his young lady all the products of her parterre she wished to sell: and Eliza would have sold the hair off her head if she could have made a handsome profit thereby. As to her money, she first secreted it in odd corners, wrapped in a rag or an old curl-paper; but some of these hoards having been discovered by the housemaid, Eliza, fearful of one day losing her valued treasure, consented to intrust it to her mother, at a usurious rate of interest—fifty or sixty per cent.; which interest she exacted every quarter, keeping her accounts in a little book with anxious accuracy.

Georgiana sat on a high stool, dressing her hair at the glass, and interweaving her curls with artificial flowers and faded feathers, of which she had found a store in a drawer in the attic. I was making my bed, having received strict orders from Bessie to get it arranged before she returned (for Bessie now frequently employed me as a sort of under-nurserymaid, to tidy the room, dust the chairs, etc.). Having spread the quilt and folded my night-dress, I went to the window-seat to put in order some picture-books and doll's house furniture scattered there; an abrupt command from Georgiana to let her playthings alone (for the tiny chairs and mirrors, the fairy plates and cups were her property) stopped my proceedings; and then, for lack of other occupation, I fell to breathing on the frost-flowers with which the window was fretted, and thus clearing a space in the glass through which I might look out on the grounds, where all was still and petrified under the influence of a hard frost.

From this window were visible the porter's lodge and the carriage-road, and just as I had dissolved so much of the silver-white foliage veiling the panes, as left room to look out, I saw the gates thrown open and a carriage roll through. I watched it ascending the drive with indifference: carriages often came to Gateshead, but none ever brought visitors in whom I was interested; it stopped in front of the house, the door-bell rang loudly, the new comer was admitted. All this being nothing to me, my vacant attention soon found livelier attraction in the spectacle of a little hungry robin, which came and chirruped on the twigs of the leafless cherry-tree nailed against the wall near the casement. The remains of my breakfast of bread and milk stood on the table, and having crumbled a morsel of roll, I was tugging at the sash to put out the crumbs on the window-sill, when Bessie came running upstairs into the nursery.

"Miss Jane, take off your pinafore: what are you doing there? Have you washed your hands and face this morning?" I gave another tug before I answered, for I wanted the bird to be secure of its bread: the sash yielded; I scattered the crumbs, some on the stone sill, some on the cherry-tree bough, then, closing the window, I replied:—

"No, Bessie; I have only just finished dusting."

"Troublesome, careless child! and what are you doing now? You look quite red, as if you had been about some mischief: what were you opening the window for?"

I was spared the trouble of answering, for Bessie seemed in too great a hurry to listen to explanations; she hauled me to the wash-stand, inflicted a merciless, but happily brief scrub on my face and hands with soap, water, and a coarse towel; disciplined my head with a bristly brush, denuded me of my pinafore, and then hurrying me to the top of the stairs, bid me go down directly, as I was wanted in the breakfast-room.

I would have asked who wanted me: I would have demanded if Mrs. Reed was there; but Bessie was already gone, and had closed the nursery-door upon me: I slowly descended. For nearly three months, I had never been called to Mrs. Reed's presence: restricted so long to the nursery, the breakfast, dining, and drawing-rooms were become for me awful regions, on which it dismayed me to intrude.

I now stood in the empty hall; before me was the breakfast-room door, and I stopped, intimidated and trembling. What a miserable little poltroon had fear,

engendered of unjust punishment, made of me in those days! I feared to return to the nursery, and feared to go forward to the parlour; ten minutes I stood in agitated hesitation: the vehement ringing of the breakfast-room bell decided me; I *must* enter.

"Who could want me?" I asked inwardly, as with both hands I turned the stiff door-handle which, for a second or two, resisted my efforts. "What should I see besides aunt Reed in the apartment?—a man or a woman?" The handle turned, the door unclosed, and passing through and curtseying low, I looked up at—a black pillar!—such, at least, appeared to me, at first sight, the straight, narrow, sable-clad shape standing erect on the rug: the grim face at the top was like a carved mask, placed above the shaft by way of capital.

Mrs. Reed occupied her usual seat by the fireside: she made a signal to me to approach: I did so, and she introduced me to the stony stranger with the words: "This is the little girl respecting whom I applied to you."

He, for it was a man, turned his head slowly towards where I stood, and having examined me with the two inquisitive-looking grey eyes which twinkled under a pair of bushy brows, said solemnly, and in a bass voice: "Her size is small: what is her age?"

"Ten years."

"So much?" was the doubtful answer; and he prolonged his scrutiny for some minutes. Presently he addressed me:—"Your name, little girl?"

"Jane Eyre, sir."

In uttering these words, I looked up: he seemed to me a tall gentleman; but then I was very little: his features were large, and they and all the lines of his frame were equally harsh and prim.

"Well, Jane Eyre, and are you a good child?"

Impossible to reply to this in the affirmative: my little world held a contrary opinion: I was silent. Mrs. Reed answered for me by an expressive shake of the head, adding soon, "Perhaps the less said on that subject the better, Mr. Brocklehurst."

"Sorry indeed to hear it! she and I must have some talk;" and bending from the perpendicular, he installed his person in the arm-chair, opposite Mrs. Reed's. "Come here," he said.

I stepped across the rug; he placed me square and straight before him. What a face he had, now that it was almost on a level with mine! what a great nose! and what a mouth! and what large prominent teeth!

"No sight so sad as that of a naughty child," he began, "especially a naughty little girl. Do you know where the wicked go after death?"

"They go to hell," was my ready and orthodox answer.

"And what is hell? Can you tell me that?"

"A pit full of fire."

"And should you like to fall into that pit, and to be burning there for ever?"

"No, sir."

"What must you do to avoid it?"

I deliberated a moment; my answer, when it did come, was objectionable: "I must keep in good health, and not die."

"How can you keep in good health? Children younger than you die daily. I buried a little child of five years old only a day or two since,—a good little child, whose soul is now in heaven. It is to be feared the same could not be said of you, were you to be called hence."

Not being in a condition to remove his doubts I only cast my eyes down on the two large feet planted on the rug, and sighed, wishing myself far enough away.

"I hope that sigh is from the heart, and that you repent of ever having been the occasion of discomfort to your excellent benefactress."

"Benefactress! benefactress!" said I, inwardly: "they all call Mrs. Reed my benefactress; if so, a benefactress is a disagreeable thing."

"Do you say your prayers night and morning?" continued my interrogator.

"Yes, sir."

"Do you read your Bible?"

"Sometimes."

"With pleasure? Are you fond of it?"

"I like Revelations, and the book of Daniel, and Genesis and Samuel, and a little bit of Exodus, and some parts of Kings and Chronicles, and Job and Jonah."

"And the Psalms? I hope you like them?"

"No, sir."

"No? oh, shocking! I have a little boy, younger than you, who knows six Psalms by heart: and when you ask him which he would rather have, a ginger-bread nut to eat, or a verse of a Psalm to learn, he says: 'Oh! the verse of a Psalm! angels sing Psalms;' says he, 'I wish to be a little angel here below;' he then gets two nuts in recompense for his infant piety."

"Psalms are not interesting," I remarked.

"That proves you have a wicked heart; and you must pray to God to change it: to give you a new and clean one: to take away your heart of stone and give you a heart of flesh."

I was about to propound a question, touching the manner in which that operation of changing my heart was to be performed, when Mrs. Reed interposed, telling me to sit down; she then proceeded to carry on the conversation herself.

"Mr. Brocklehurst, I believe I intimated in the letter which I wrote to you three weeks ago, that this little girl has not quite the character and disposition I could wish: should you admit her into Lowood school, I should be glad if the superintendent and teachers were requested to keep a strict eye on her, and above all, to guard against her worst fault, a tendency to deceit. I mention this in your hearing, Jane, that you may not attempt to impose on Mr. Brocklehurst."

Well might I dread, well might I dislike Mrs. Reed; for it was her nature to wound me cruelly: never was I happy in her presence: however carefully I obeyed, however strenuously I strove to please her, my efforts were still repulsed and repaid by such sentences as the above. Now, uttered before a stranger, the accusation cut me to the heart: I dimly perceived that she was already obliterating hope from the new phase of existence which she destined me to enter; I felt, though I could not have expressed the feeling, that she was sowing aversion and unkindness along my future path; I saw myself transformed under Mr. Brocklehurst's eye into an artful, noxious child, and what could I do to remedy the injury?

"Nothing, indeed!" thought I, as I struggled to repress a sob, and hastily wiped away some tears, the impotent evidences of my anguish.

"Deceit is, indeed, a sad fault in a child," said Mr. Brocklehurst; "it is akin to falsehood, and all liars will have their portion in the lake burning with fire and brimstone: she shall, however, be watched, Mrs. Reed; I will speak to Miss Temple and the teachers."

"I should wish her to be brought up in a manner suiting her prospects," continued my benefactress; "to be made useful, to be kept humble: as for the vacations, she will, with your permission, spend them always at Lowood."

"Your decisions are perfectly judicious, madam," returned Mr. Brocklehurst. "Humility is a Christian grace, and one peculiarly appropriate to the pupils of Lowood; I, therefore, direct that especial care shall be bestowed on its cultivation amongst them. I have studied how best to mortify in them the worldly sentiment of pride; and, only the other day, I had a pleasing proof of my success. My second daughter, Augusta, went with her mama to visit the school, and on her return she exclaimed: 'Oh, dear papa, how quiet and plain all the girls at Lowood look; with their hair combed behind their ears, and their long pinafores, and those little holland pockets outside their frocks—they are almost like poor people's children! and,' said she, 'they looked at my dress and mama's, as if they had never seen a silk gown before.' "

"This is the state of things I quite approve," returned Mrs. Reed; "had I sought all England over, I could scarcely have found a system more exactly fitting a child like Jane Eyre. Consistency, my dear Mr. Brocklehurst; I advocate consistency in all things."

"Consistency, madam, is the first of Christian duties; and it has been observed in every arrangement connected with the establishment of Lowood: plain fare, simple attire, unsophisticated accommodations, hardy and active habits; such is the order of the day in the house and its inhabitants."

"Quite right, sir. I may then depend upon this child being received as a pupil at Lowood, and there being trained in conformity to her position and prospects?"

"Madam, you may: she shall be placed in that nursery of chosen plants—and I trust she will show herself grateful for the inestimable privilege of her election."

"I will send her, then, as soon as possible, Mr. Brocklehurst; for, I assure you, I feel anxious to be relieved of a responsibility that was becoming too irksome."

"No doubt, no doubt, madam, and now I wish you good morning. I shall return to Brocklehurst Hall in the course of a week or two: my good friend, the Archdeacon, will not permit me to leave him sooner. I shall send Miss Temple notice that she is to expect a new girl, so that there will be no difficulty about receiving her. Good bye."

"Good bye, Mr. Brocklehurst; remember me to Mrs. and Miss Brocklehurst, and to Augusta and Theodore, and Master Broughton Brocklehurst."

"I will, madam. Little girl, here is a book entitled the 'Child's Guide'; read it with prayer, especially that part containing 'an account of the awfully sudden death of Martha G——, a naughty child addicted to falsehood and deceit.' "

With these words Mr. Brocklehurst put into my hand a thin pamphlet sewn in a cover, and having rung for his carriage, he departed.

Mrs. Reed and I were left alone: some minutes passed in silence; she was sewing, I was watching her. Mrs. Reed might be at that time some six or seven and thirty; she was a woman of robust frame, square-shouldered and strong-limbed, not tall, and, though stout, not obese: she had a somewhat large face, the under-jaw being much developed and very solid; her brow was low, her chin large and prominent, mouth and nose sufficiently regular; under her light eye-brows glimmered an eye devoid of ruth; her skin was dark and opaque, her hair nearly flaxen; her constitution was sound as a bell—illness never came near her; she was an exact, clever manager, her household and tenantry were thoroughly under her control; her children, only, at times defied her authority, and laughed it to scorn; she dressed well, and had a presence and port calculated to set off handsome attire.

Sitting on a low stool, a few yards from her arm-chair, I examined her figure; I perused her features. In my hand I held the tract, containing the sudden death of the Liar: to which narrative my attention had been pointed as to an appropriate warning. What had just passed; what Mrs. Reed had said concerning me to Mr. Brocklehurst; the whole tenor of their conversation, was recent, raw, and stinging in my mind; I had felt every word as acutely as I had heard it plainly, and a passion of resentment fomented now within me.

Mrs. Reed looked up from her work; her eye settled on mine, her fingers at the same time suspended their nimble movements.

"Go out of the room; return to the nursery," was her mandate. My look or something else must have struck her as offensive, for she spoke with extreme, though suppressed irritation. I got up, I went to the door; I came back again; I walked to the window, across the room, then close up to her.

Speak I must: I had been trodden on severely, and *must* turn: but how? What strength had I to dart retaliation at my antagonist? I gathered my energies and launched them in this blunt sentence:—

"I am not deceitful: if I were, I should say I loved *you;* but I declare I do not love you: I dislike you the worst of anybody in the world except John Reed; and

this book about the liar, you may give to your girl, Georgiana, for it is she who tells lies, and not I.''

Mrs. Reed's hands still lay on her work inactive: her eye of ice continued to dwell freezingly on mine.

''What more have you to say?'' she asked, rather in the tone in which a person might address an opponent of adult age than such as is ordinarily used to a child.

That eye of hers, that voice stirred every antipathy I had. Shaking from head to foot, thrilled with ungovernable excitement, I continued:—

''I am glad you are no relation of mine: I will never call you aunt again as long as I live. I will never come to see you when I am grown up; and if any one asks me how I liked you, and how you treated me, I will say the very thought of you makes me sick, and that you treated me with miserable cruelty.''

''How dare you affirm that, Jane Eyre?''

''How dare I, Mrs. Reed? How dare I? Because it is the *truth*. You think I have no feelings, and that I can do without one bit of love or kindness; but I cannot live so: and you have no pity. I shall remember how you thrust me back— roughly and violently thrust me back—into the red-room, and locked me up there, to my dying day; though I was in agony; though I cried out, while suffocating with distress, 'Have mercy! Have mercy, aunt Reed!' And that punishment you made me suffer because your wicked boy struck me—knocked me down for nothing. I will tell anybody who asks me questions, this exact tale. People think you a good woman, but you are bad; hard-hearted. *You* are deceitful!''

Ere I had finished this reply, my soul began to expand, to exult, with the strangest sense of freedom, of triumph, I ever felt. It seemed as if an invisible bond had burst, and that I had struggled out into unhoped-for liberty. Not without cause was this sentiment: Mrs. Reed looked frightened; her work had slipped from her knee; she was lifting up her hands, rocking herself to and fro, and even twisting her face as if she would cry.

''Jane, you are under a mistake: what is the matter with you? Why do you tremble so violently? Would you like to drink some water?''

''No, Mrs. Reed.''

''Is there anything else you wish for, Jane? I assure you, I desire to be your friend.''

''Not you. You told Mr. Brocklehurst I had a bad character, a deceitful disposition; and I'll let everybody at Lowood know what you are, and what you have done.''

''Jane, you don't understand these things: children must be corrected for their faults.''

''Deceit is not my fault!'' I cried out in a savage, high voice.

''But you are passionate, Jane, that you must allow; and now return to the nursery—there's a dear—and lie down a little.''

''I am not your dear; I cannot lie down: send me to school soon, Mrs. Reed, for I hate to live here.''

''I will indeed send her to school soon,'' murmured Mrs. Reed, *sotto voce;* and gathering up her work, she abruptly quitted the apartment.

I was left there alone—winner of the field. It was the hardest battle I had fought, and the first victory I had gained: I stood awhile on the rug, where Mr. Brocklehurst had stood, and I enjoyed my conqueror's solitude. First, I smiled to myself and felt elate; but this fierce pleasure subsided in me as fast as did the accelerated throb of my pulses. A child cannot quarrel with its elders, as I had done, cannot give its furious feelings uncontrolled play, as I had given mine, without experiencing afterwards the pang of remorse and the chill of reaction. A ridge of lighted heath, alive, glancing, devouring, would have been a meet emblem of my mind when I accused and menaced Mrs. Reed: the same ridge, black and blasted after the flames are dead, would have represented as meetly my subsequent condition, when half an

hour's silence and reflection had shown me the madness of my conduct, and the dreariness of my hated and hating position.

Something of vengeance I had tasted for the first time; as aromatic wine it seemed, on swallowing, warm and racy: its after-flavour, metallic and corroding, gave me a sensation as if I had been poisoned. Willingly would I now have gone and asked Mrs. Reed's pardon; but I knew, partly from experience and partly from instinct, that was the way to make her repulse me with double scorn, thereby re-exciting every turbulent impulse of my nature.

I would fain exercise some better faculty than that of fierce speaking; fain find nourishment for some less fiendish feeling than that of sombre indignation. I took a book—some Arabian tales; I sat down and endeavoured to read. I could make no sense of the subject; my own thoughts swam always between me and the page I had usually found fascinating. I opened the glass-door in the breakfast-room: the shrubbery was quite still: the black frost reigned, unbroken by sun or breeze, through the grounds. I covered my head and arms with the skirt of my frock, and went out to walk in a part of the plantation which was quite sequestered: but I found no pleasure in the silent trees, the falling fir-cones, the congealed relics of autumn, russet leaves, swept by past winds in heaps, and now stiffened together. I leaned against a gate, and looked into an empty field where no sheep were feeding, where the short grass was nipped and blanched. It was a very grey day; a most opaque sky, "onding on snaw" canopied all; thence flakes fell at intervals, which settled on the hard path and on the hoary lea without melting. I stood, a wretched child enough, whispering to myself over and over again, "What shall I do?—what shall I do?"

All at once I heard a clear voice call, "Miss Jane! where are you? Come to lunch!"

It was Bessie, I knew well enough; but I did not stir; her light step came tripping down the path.

"You naughty little thing!" she said. "Why don't you come when you are called?"

Bessie's presence, compared with the thoughts over which I had been brooding, seemed cheerful; even though, as usual she was somewhat cross. The fact is, after my conflict with and victory over Mrs. Reed, I was not disposed to care much for the nursemaid's transitory anger; and I *was* disposed to bask in her youthful lightness of heart. I just put my two arms round her, and said, "Come, Bessie! don't scold."

The action was more frank and fearless than any I was habituated to indulge in: somehow it pleased her.

"You are a strange child, Miss Jane," she said, as she looked down at me: "a little roving, solitary thing: and you are going to school, I suppose?"

I nodded.

"And won't you be sorry to leave poor Bessie?"

"What does Bessie care for me? She is always scolding me."

"Because you're such a queer, frightened, shy, little thing. You should be bolder."

"What! to get more knocks?"

"Nonsense! But you are rather put upon, that's certain. My mother said, when she came to see me last week, that she would not like a little one of her own to be in your place.—Now, come in, and I've some good news for you."

"I don't think you have, Bessie."

"Child! what do you mean? What sorrowful eyes you fix on me! Well! but Missis and the young ladies and Master John are going out to tea this afternoon, and you shall have tea with me. I'll ask cook to bake you a little cake, and then you shall help me to look over your drawers; for I am soon to pack your trunk. Missis intends you to leave Gateshead in a day or two, and you shall choose what toys you like to take with you."

"Bessie, you must promise not to scold me any more till I go."

"Well, I will: but mind you are a very good girl, and don't be afraid of me. Don't start when I chance to speak rather sharply: it's so provoking."

"I don't think I shall ever be afraid of you again, Bessie, because I have got used to you: and I shall soon have another set of people to dread."

"If you dread them, they'll dislike you."

"As you do, Bessie?"

"I don't dislike you, Miss; I believe I am fonder of you than of all the others."

"You don't show it."

"You sharp little thing! you've got quite a new way of talking. What makes you so venturesome and hardy?"

"Why, I shall soon be away from you, and besides——" I was going to say something about what had passed between me and Mrs. Reed; but on second thoughts I considered it better to remain silent on that head.

"And so you're glad to leave me?"

"Not at all, Bessie; indeed, just now I am rather sorry."

"Just now! and rather! How coolly my little lady says it! I daresay now if I were to ask you for a kiss you wouldn't give it to me: you'd say you'd *rather* not."

"I'll kiss you and welcome: bend your head down." Bessie stooped; we mutually embraced, and I followed her into the house quite comforted. That afternoon lapsed in peace and harmony; and in the evening Bessie told me some of her most enchanting stories, and sang me some of her sweetest songs. Even for me life had its gleams of sunshine.

Chapter V

FIVE o'clock had hardly struck on the morning of the 19th of January, when Bessie brought a candle into my closet and found me already up and nearly dressed. I had risen half an hour before her entrance, and had washed my face, and put on my clothes by the light of a half-moon just setting, whose rays streamed through the narrow window near my crib. I was to leave Gateshead that day by a coach which passed the lodge gates at 6 A.M. Bessie was the only person yet risen; she had lit a fire in the nursery, where she now proceeded to make my breakfast. Few children can eat when excited with the thoughts of a journey; nor could I. Bessie, having pressed me in vain to take a few spoonfuls of the boiled milk and bread she had prepared for me, wrapped up some biscuits in a paper and put them into my bag; then she helped me on with my pelisse and bonnet, and wrapping herself in a shawl, she and I left the nursery. As we passed Mrs. Reed's bed-room, she said, "Will you go in and bid Missis good-bye?"

"No, Bessie: she came to my crib last night when you were gone down to supper, and said I need not disturb her in the morning, or my cousins either; and she told me to remember that she had always been my best friend, and to speak of her and be grateful to her accordingly."

"What did you say, Miss?"

"Nothing: I covered my face with the bed-clothes, and turned from her to the wall."

"That was wrong, Miss Jane."

"It was quite right, Bessie: your Missis has not been my friend: she has been my foe."

"Oh, Miss Jane! don't say so!"

"Good-bye to Gateshead!" cried I, as we passed through the hall and went out at the front door.

The moon was set, and it was very dark; Bessie carried a lantern, whose light glanced on wet steps and gravel road soddened by a recent thaw. Raw and chill was the winter morning: my teeth chattered as I hastened down the drive. There was a light in the porter's lodge: when we reached it, we found the porter's wife just kindling her fire: my trunk, which had been carried down the evening before, stood corded at the door. It wanted but a few minutes of six, and shortly after that hour had struck, the distant roll of wheels announced the coming coach; I went to the door and watched its lamps approach rapidly through the gloom.

"Is she going by herself?" asked the porter's wife.

"Yes."

"And how far is it?"

"Fifty miles."

"What a long way! I wonder Mrs. Reed is not afraid to trust her so far alone."

The coach drew up; there it was at the gates with its four horses and its top laden with passengers: the guard and coachman loudly urged haste; my trunk was hoisted up; I was taken from Bessie's neck, to which I clung with kisses.

"Be sure and take good care of her," cried she to the guard, as he lifted me into the inside.

"Ay, ay!" was the answer: the door was slapped to, a voice exclaimed, "All right," and on we drove. Thus was I severed from Bessie and Gateshead: thus whirled away to unknown, and, as I then deemed, remote and mysterious regions.

I remember but little of the journey: I only know that the day seemed to me of a preternatural length, and that we appeared to travel over hundreds of miles of road. We passed through several towns, and in one, a very large one, the coach stopped; the horses were taken out, and the passengers alighted to dine. I was carried into an inn, where the guard wanted me to have some dinner; but, as I had no appetite, he left me in an immense room with a fireplace at each end, a chandelier pendent from the ceiling, and a little red gallery high up against the wall filled with musical instruments. Here I walked about for a long time, feeling very strange, and mortally apprehensive of some one coming in and kidnapping me; for I believed in kidnappers, their exploits having frequently figured in Bessie's fireside chronicles. At last the guard returned: once more I was stowed away in the coach, my protector mounted his own seat, sounded his hollow horn, and away we rattled over the "stony street" of L——.

The afternoon came on wet and somewhat misty: as it waned into dusk, I began to feel that we were getting very far indeed from Gateshead: we ceased to pass through towns; the country changed; great grey hills heaved up round the horizon: as twilight deepened, we descended a valley, dark with wood, and long after night had overclouded the prospect, I heard a wild wind rushing amongst trees.

Lulled by the sound, I at last dropped asleep: I had not long slumbered when the sudden cessation of motion awoke me; the coach-door was open, and a person like a servant was standing at it: I saw her face and dress by the light of the lamps.

"Is there a little girl called Jane Eyre here?" she asked. I answered "Yes," and was then lifted out; my trunk was handed down, and the coach instantly drove away.

I was stiff with long sitting, and bewildered with the noise and motion of the coach: gathering my faculties, I looked about me. Rain, wind, and darkness filled the air; nevertheless, I dimly discerned a wall before me and a door open in it. Through this door I passed with my new guide: she shut and locked it behind her. There was now visible a house or houses—for the building spread far—with many windows, and lights burning in some; we went up a broad pebbly path, splashing wet, and were admitted at a door; then the servant led me through a passage into a room with a fire, where she left me alone.

I stood and warmed my numbed fingers over the blaze, then I looked round; there was no candle, but the uncertain light from the hearth showed, by intervals,

papered walls, carpet, curtains, shining mahogany furniture: it was a parlour, not so spacious or splendid as the drawing-room at Gateshead, but comfortable enough. I was puzzling to make out the subject of a picture on the wall, when the door opened, and an individual carrying a light entered; another followed close behind.

The first was a tall lady with dark hair, dark eyes, and a pale and large forehead; her figure was partly enveloped in a shawl, her countenance was grave, her bearing erect.

"The child is very young to be sent alone," said she, putting her candle down on the table. She considered me attentively for a minute or two, then further added,—

"She had better be put to bed soon; she looks tired: are you tired?" she asked, placing her hand on my shoulder.

"A little, ma'am."

"And hungry too, no doubt: let her have some supper before she goes to bed, Miss Miller. Is this the first time you have left your parents to come to school, my little girl?"

I explained to her that I had no parents. She inquired how long they had been dead; then how old I was, what was my name, whether I could read, write, and sew a little: then she touched my cheek gently with her forefinger, and saying, "She hoped I should be a good child," dismissed me along with Miss Miller.

The lady I had left might be about twenty-nine; the one who went with me appeared some years younger: the first impressed me by her voice, look, and air. Miss Miller was more ordinary; ruddy in complexion, though of a careworn countenance; hurried in gait and action, like one who had always a multiplicity of tasks on hand: she looked, indeed, what I afterwards found she really was, an under-teacher. Led by her, I passed from compartment to compartment, from passage to passage, of a large and irregular building; till, emerging from the total and somewhat dreary silence pervading that portion of the house we had traversed, we came upon the hum of many voices, and presently entered a wide, long room, with great deal tables, two at each end, on each of which burnt a pair of candles, and seated all round on benches, a congregation of girls of every age, from nine or ten to twenty. Seen by the dim light of the dips, their number to me appeared countless, though not in reality exceeding eighty; they were uniformly dressed in brown stuff frocks of quaint fashion, and long holland pinafores. It was the hour of study; they were engaged in conning over their to-morrow's task, and the hum I had heard was the combined result of their whispered repetitions.

Miss Miller signed to me to sit on a bench near the door, then walking up to the top of the long room, she cried out,—

"Monitors, collect the lesson-books and put them away!"

Four tall girls arose from different tables, and going round, gathered the books and removed them. Miss Miller again gave the word of command,—

"Monitors, fetch the supper-trays!"

The tall girls went out and returned presently, each bearing a tray, with portions of something, I knew not what, arranged thereon, and a pitcher of water and mug in the middle of each tray. The portions were handed round; those who liked took a draught of the water, the mug being common to all. When it came to my turn, I drank, for I was thirsty, but did not touch the food, excitement and fatigue rendering me incapable of eating: I now saw, however, that it was a thin oaten cake, shared into fragments.

The meal over, prayers were read by Miss Miller, and the classes filed off, two and two, upstairs. Overpowered by this time with weariness, I scarcely noticed what sort of a place the bed-room was; except that, like the school-room, I saw it was very long. To-night I was to be Miss Miller's bed-fellow; she helped me to undress: when laid down I glanced at the long rows of beds, each of which was quickly filled with two occupants; in ten minutes the single light was extinguished; amid silence and complete darkness, I fell asleep.

The night passed rapidly: I was too tired even to dream; I only once awoke to hear the wind rave in furious gusts, and the rain fall in torrents, and to be sensible that Miss Miller had taken her place by my side. When I again unclosed my eyes, a loud bell was ringing: the girls were up and dressing; day had not yet begun to dawn, and a rushlight or two burnt in the room. I too rose reluctantly; it was bitter cold, and I dressed as well as I could for shivering, and washed when there was a basin at liberty, which did not occur soon, as there was but one basin to six girls, on the stands down the middle of the room. Again the bell rang: all formed in file, two and two, and in that order descended the stairs and entered the cold and dimly-lit school-room: here prayers were read by Miss Miller; afterwards she called out:—

"Form classes!"

A great tumult succeeded for some minutes, during which Miss Miller repeatedly exclaimed, "Silence!" and "Order!" When it subsided, I saw them all drawn up in four semi-circles, before four chairs, placed at the four tables; all held books in their hands, and a great book, like a Bible, lay on each table, before the vacant seat. A pause of some seconds succeeded, filled up by the low, vague hum of numbers; Miss Miller walked from class to class, hushing this indefinite sound.

A distant bell tinkled: immediately three ladies entered the room, each walked to a table and took her seat; Miss Miller assumed the fourth vacant chair, which was that nearest the door, and around which the smallest of the children were assembled: to this inferior class I was called, and placed at the bottom of it.

Business now began: the day's Collect was repeated, then certain texts of Scripture were said, and to these succeeded a protracted reading of chapters in the Bible, which lasted an hour. By the time that exercise was terminated, day had fully dawned. The indefatigable bell now sounded for the fourth time: the classes were marshalled and marched into another room to breakfast: how glad I was to behold a prospect of getting something to eat! I was now nearly sick from inanition, having taken so little the day before.

The refectory was a great, low-ceiled, gloomy room; on two long tables smoked basins of something hot, which, however, to my dismay, sent forth an odour far from inviting. I saw a universal manifestation of discontent when the fumes of the repast met the nostrils of those destined to swallow it; from the van of the procession, the tall girls of the first class, rose the whispered words:—

"Disgusting! The porridge is burnt again!"

"Silence!" ejaculated a voice; not that of Miss Miller, but one of the upper teachers, a little and dark personage, smartly dressed, but of somewhat morose aspect, who installed herself at the top of one table, while a more buxom lady presided at the other. I looked in vain for her I had first seen the night before; she was not visible: Miss Miller occupied the foot of the table where I sat, and a strange, foreign looking, elderly lady, the French teacher, as I afterwards found, took the corresponding seat at the other board. A long grace was said and a hymn sung; then a servant brought in some tea for the teachers, and the meal began.

Ravenous, and now very faint, I devoured a spoonful or two of my portion without thinking of its taste; but the first edge of hunger blunted, I perceived I had got in hand a nauseous mess: burnt porridge is almost as bad as rotten potatoes; famine itself soon sickens over it. The spoons were moved slowly: I saw each girl taste her food and try to swallow it; but in most cases the effort was soon relinquished. Breakfast was over, and none had breakfasted. Thanks being returned for what we had not got, and a second hymn chanted, the refectory was evacuated for the school-room. I was one of the last to go out, and in passing the tables, I saw one teacher take a basin of the porridge and taste it; she looked at the others; all their countenances expressed displeasure, and one of them, the stout one, whispered:—

"Abominable stuff! How shameful!"

A quarter of an hour passed before lessons again began, during which the school-room was in a glorious tumult; for that space of time, it seemed to be permitted to

talk loud and more freely, and they used their privilege. The whole conversation ran on the breakfast, which one and all abused roundly. Poor things! it was the sole consolation they had. Miss Miller was now the only teacher in the room: a group of great girls standing about her, spoke with serious and sullen gestures. I heard the name of Mr. Brocklehurst pronounced by some lips; at which Miss Miller shook her head disapprovingly; but she made no great effort to check the general wrath: doubtless she shared in it.

A clock in the school-room struck nine; Miss Miller left her circle, and standing in the middle of the room, cried:—

"Silence! To your seats!"

Discipline prevailed: in five minutes the confused throng was resolved into order, and comparative silence quelled the Babel clamour of tongues. The upper teachers now punctually resumed their posts: but still, all seemed to wait. Ranged on benches down the sides of the room, the eighty girls sat motionless and erect: a quaint assemblage they appeared, all with plain locks combed from their faces, not a curl visible; in brown dresses, made high and surrounded by a narrow tucker about the throat, with little pockets of holland (shaped something like a Highlander's purse) tied in front of their frocks, and designed to serve the purpose of a work-bag: all too wearing woollen stockings and country-made shoes, fastened with brass buckles. Above twenty of those clad in this costume were full-grown girls, or rather young women; it suited them ill, and gave an air of oddity even to the prettiest.

I was still looking at them, and also at intervals examining the teachers—none of whom precisely pleased me; for the stout one was a little coarse, the dark one not a little fierce, the foreigner harsh and grotesque, and Miss Miller, poor thing! looked purple, weather-beaten, and over-worked—when, as my eye wandered from face to face, the whole school rose simultaneously, as if moved by a common spring.

What was the matter? I had heard no order given: I was puzzled. Ere I had gathered my wits, the classes were again seated: but as all eyes were now turned to one point, mine followed the general direction, and encountered the personage who had received me last night. She stood at the bottom of the long room, on the hearth; for there was a fire at each end: she surveyed the two rows of girls silently and gravely. Miss Miller approaching, seemed to ask her a question, and having received her answer, went back to her place, and said aloud,—

"Monitor of the first class, fetch the globes!"

While the direction was being executed, the lady consulted moved slowly up the room. I suppose I have a considerable organ of Veneration, for I retain yet the sense of admiring awe with which my eyes traced her steps. Seen now, in broad daylight, she looked tall, fair, and shapely; brown eyes, with a benignant light in their irids, and a fine pencilling of long lashes round, relieved the whiteness of her large front; on each of her temples her hair, of a very dark brown, was clustered in round curls, according to the fashion of those times, when neither smooth bands nor long ringlets were in vogue; her dress, also in the mode of the day, was of purple cloth, relieved by a sort of Spanish trimming of black velvet; a gold watch (watches were not so common then as now) shone at her girdle. Let the reader add, to complete the picture, refined features; a complexion, if pale, clear; and a stately air and carriage, and he will have, at least, as clearly as words can give it, a correct idea of the exterior of Miss Temple—Maria Temple, as I afterwards saw the name written in a prayer-book entrusted to me to carry to church.

The superintendent of Lowood (for such was this lady) having taken her seat before a pair of globes placed on one of the tables, summoned the first class round her, and commenced giving a lesson in geography; the lower classes were called by the teachers: repetitions in history, grammar, etc., went on for an hour; writing and arithmetic succeeded, and music lessons were given by Miss Temple to some

of the elder girls. The duration of each lesson was measured by the clock, which at last struck twelve. The superintendent rose:—

"I have a word to address to the pupils," said she.

The tumult of cessation from lessons was already breaking forth, but it sank at her voice. She went on:—

"You had this morning a breakfast which you could not eat; you must be hungry:— I have ordered that a lunch of bread and cheese shall be served to all."

The teachers looked at her with a sort of surprise.

"It is to be done on my responsibility," she added, in an explanatory tone to them, and immediately afterwards left the room.

The bread and cheese was presently brought in and distributed, to the high delight and refreshment of the whole school. The order was now given "To the garden!" Each put on a coarse straw bonnet, with strings of coloured calico, and a cloak of grey frieze. I was similarly equipped, and, following the stream, I made my way into the open air.

The garden was a wide enclosure, surrounded with walls so high as to exclude every glimpse of prospect; a covered verandah ran down one side, and broad walks bordered a middle space divided into scores of little beds: these beds were assigned as gardens for the pupils to cultivate, and each bed had an owner. When full of flowers they would doubtless look pretty; but now, at the latter end of January, all was wintry blight and brown decay. I shuddered as I stood and looked round me: it was an inclement day for out-door exercise; not positively rainy, but darkened by a drizzling yellow fog; all underfoot was still soaking wet with the floods of yesterday. The stronger among the girls ran about and engaged in active games, but sundry pale and thin ones herded together for shelter and warmth in the verandah; and amongst these, as the dense mist penetrated to their shivering frames, I heard frequently the sound of a hollow cough.

As yet I had spoken to no one, nor did anybody seem to take notice of me; I stood lonely enough: but to that feeling of isolation I was accustomed; it did not oppress me much. I leant against a pillar of the verandah, drew my grey mantle close about me, and, trying to forget the cold which nipped me without, and the unsatisfied hunger which gnawed me within, delivered myself up to the employment of watching and thinking. My reflections were too undefined and fragmentary to merit record: I hardly yet knew where I was; Gateshead and my past life seemed floated away to an immeasurable distance; the present was vague and strange, and of the future I could form no conjecture. I looked round the convent-like garden, and then up at the house; a large building, half of which seemed grey and old, the other half quite new. The new part, containing the school-room and dormitory, was lit by mullioned and latticed windows, which gave it a church-like aspect; a stone tablet over the door, bore this inscription:—

"Lowood Institution.—This portion was rebuilt A.D.——, by Naomi Brocklehurst, of Brocklehurst Hall, in this county." "Let your light so shine before men that they may see your good works, and glorify your Father which is in heaven."—St. Matt. v. 16.

I read these words over and over again: I felt that an explanation belonged to them, and was unable fully to penetrate their import. I was still pondering the signification of "Institution," and endeavouring to make out a connection between the first words and the verse of Scripture, when the sound of a cough close behind me, made me turn my head. I saw a girl sitting on a stone bench near; she had bent over a book, on the perusal of which she seemed intent: from where I stood I could see the title—it was "Rasselas;" a name that struck me as strange, and consequently attractive. In turning a leaf she happened to look up, and I said to her directly:—

"Is your book interesting?" I had already formed the intention of asking her to lend it to me some day.

"I like it," she answered, after a pause of a second or two, during which she examined me.

"What is it about?" I continued. I hardly know where I found the hardihood thus to open a conversation with a stranger; the step was contrary to my nature and habits: but I think her occupation touched a chord of sympathy somewhere; for I too liked reading, though of a frivolous and childish kind; I could not digest or comprehend the serious or substantial.

"You may look at it," replied the girl, offering me the book.

I did so; a brief examination convinced me that the contents were less taking than the title: "Rasselas" looked dull to my trifling taste; I saw nothing about fairies, nothing about genii; no bright variety seemed spread over the closely-printed pages. I returned it to her; she received it quietly, and without saying anything she was about to relapse into her former studious mood: again I ventured to disturb her:—

"Can you tell me what the writing on that stone over the door means? What is Lowood Institution?"

"This house where you are come to live."

"And why do they call it Institution? Is it in any way different from other schools?"

"It is partly a charity-school: you and I, and all the rest of us, are charity-children. I suppose you are an orphan: are not either your father or your mother dead?"

"Both died before I can remember."

"Well, all the girls here have lost either one or both parents, and this is called an institution for educating orphans."

"Do we pay no money? Do they keep us for nothing?"

"We pay, or our friends pay, fifteen pounds a year for each."

"Then why do they call us charity-children?"

"Because fifteen pounds is not enough for board and teaching, and the deficiency is supplied by subscription."

"Who subscribes?"

"Different benevolent-minded ladies and gentlemen in this neighbourhood and in London."

"Who was Naomi Brocklehurst?"

"The lady who built the new part of this house as that tablet records, and whose son overlooks and directs everything here."

"Why?"

"Because he is treasurer and manager of the establishment."

"Then this house does not belong to that tall lady who wears a watch, and who said we were to have some bread and cheese."

"To Miss Temple? Oh, no! I wish it did: she has to answer to Mr. Brocklehurst for all she does. Mr. Brocklehurst buys all our food and all our clothes."

"Does he live here?"

"No—two miles off, at a large hall."

"Is he a good man?"

"He is a clergyman, and is said to do a great deal of good."

"Did you say that tall lady was called Miss Temple?"

"Yes."

"And what are the other teachers called?"

"The one with red cheeks is called Miss Smith; she attends to the work, and cuts out—for we make our own clothes, our frocks, and pelisses, and every thing; the little one with black hair is Miss Scatcherd; she teaches history and grammar, and hears the second class repetitions; and the one who wears a shawl, and has a pocket-handkerchief tied to her side with a yellow riband, is Madame Pierrot: she comes from Lisle, in France, and teaches French."

"Do you like the teachers?"

"Well enough."

"Do you like the little black one, and the Madame——? —I cannot pronounce her name as you do."

"Miss Scatcherd is hasty—you must take care not to offend her; Madame Pierrot is not a bad sort of person."

"But Miss Temple is the best—isn't she?"

"Miss Temple is very good, and very clever; she is above the rest, because she knows far more than they do."

"Have you been long here?"

"Two years."

"Are you an orphan?"

"My mother is dead."

"Are you happy here?"

"You ask rather too many questions. I have given you answers enough for the present: now I want to read."

But at that moment the summons sounded for dinner: all re-entered the house. The odour which now filled the refectory was scarcely more appetising than that which had regaled our nostrils at breakfast: the dinner was served in two huge tin-plated vessels, whence rose a strong steam redolent of rancid fat. I found the mess to consist of indifferent potatoes and strange shreds of rusty meat, mixed and cooked together. Of this preparation a tolerably abundant plateful was apportioned to each pupil. I ate what I could, and wondered within myself whether every day's fare would be like this.

After dinner, we immediately adjourned to the school-room: lessons recommenced, and were continued till five o'clock.

The only marked event of the afternoon was, that I saw the girl with whom I had conversed in the verandah, dismissed in disgrace, by Miss Scatcherd, from a history class, and sent to stand in the middle of the large school-room. The punishment seemed to me in a high degree ignominious, especially for so great a girl—she looked thirteen or upwards. I expected she would show signs of great distress and shame; but to my surprise she neither wept nor blushed: composed, though grave, she stood, the central mark of all eyes. "How can she bear it so quietly—so firmly?" I asked of myself. "Were I in her place, it seems to me I should wish the earth to open and swallow me up. She looks as if she were thinking of something beyond her punishment—beyond her situation: of something not round nor before her. I have heard of day-dreams—is she in a day-dream now? Her eyes are fixed on the floor, but I am sure they do not see it—her sight seems turned in, gone down into her heart: she is looking at what she can remember, I believe; not at what is really present. I wonder what sort of a girl she is—whether good or naughty."

Soon after five P.M. we had another meal, consisting of a small mug of coffee, and half a slice of brown bread. I devoured my bread and drank my coffee with relish; but I should have been glad of as much more—I was still hungry. Half an hour's recreation succeeded, then study; then the glass of water and the piece of oat-cake, prayers, and bed. Such was my first day at Lowood.

Chapter VI

THE next day commenced as before, getting up and dressing by rushlight: but this morning we were obliged to dispense with the ceremony of washing: the water in the pitchers was frozen. A change had taken place in the weather the preceding evening, and a keen north-east wind, whistling through the crevices of our bed-

room windows all night long, had made us shiver in our beds, and turned the contents of the ewers to ice.

Before the long hour and a half of prayers and Bible reading was over, I felt ready to perish with cold. Breakfast-time came at last, and this morning the porridge was not burnt; the quality was eatable, the quantity small; how small my portion seemed! I wished it had been doubled.

In the course of the day I was enrolled a member of the fourth class, and regular tasks and occupations were assigned me: hitherto, I had only been a spectator of the proceedings at Lowood, I was now to become an actor therein. At first, being little accustomed to learn by heart, the lessons appeared to me both long and difficult: the frequent change from task to task, too, bewildered me; and I was glad, when, about three o'clock in the afternoon, Miss Smith put into my hands a border of muslin two yards long, together with needle, thimble, etc., and sent me to sit in a quiet corner of the school-room, with direction to hem the same. At that hour most of the others were sewing likewise; but one class still stood round Miss Scatcherd's chair reading, and as all was quiet, the subject of their lessons could be heard, together with the manner in which each girl acquitted herself, and the animadversions or commendations of Miss Scatcherd on the performance. It was English history: among the readers, I observed my acquaintance of the verandah: at the commencement of the lesson, her place had been at the top of the class, but for some error of pronunciation or some inattention to stops, she was suddenly sent to the very bottom. Even in that obscure position, Miss Scatcherd continued to make her an object of constant notice: she was continually addressing to her such phrases as the following:—

"Burns" (such it seems was her name: the girls here were all called by their surnames, as boys are elsewhere), "Burns, you are standing on the side of your shoe, turn your toes out immediately." "Burns, you poke your chin most unpleasantly, draw it in." "Burns, I insist on your holding your head up; I will not have you before me in that attitude," etc., etc.

A chapter having been read through twice, the books were closed and the girls examined. The lesson had comprised part of the reign of Charles I., and there were sundry questions about tonnage and poundage, and ship-money, which most of them appeared unable to answer; still, every little difficulty was solved instantly when it reached Burns: her memory seemed to have retained the substance of the whole lesson, and she was ready with answers on every point. I kept expecting that Miss Scatcherd would praise her attention; but, instead of that, she suddenly cried out:—

"You dirty, disagreeable girl! you have never cleaned your nails this morning!"

Burns made no answer: I wondered at her silence.

"Why," thought I, "does she not explain that she could neither clean her nails nor wash her face, as the water was frozen?"

My attention was now called off by Miss Smith desiring me to hold a skein of thread: while she was winding it, she talked to me from time to time, asking whether I had ever been at school before, whether I could mark, stitch, knit, etc.; till she dismissed me, I could not pursue my observations on Miss Scatcherd's movements. When I returned to my seat, that lady was just delivering an order, of which I did not catch the import; but Burns immediately left the class, and, going into the small inner room where the books were kept, returned in half a minute, carrying in her hand a bundle of twigs tied together at one end. This ominous tool she presented to Miss Scatcherd with a respectful courtesy; then she quietly, and without being told, unloosed her pinafore, and the teacher instantly and sharply inflicted on her neck a dozen strokes with the bunch of twigs. Not a tear rose to Burns' eye; and, while I paused from my sewing, because my fingers quivered at this spectacle with a sentiment of unavailing and impotent anger, not a feature of her pensive face altered its ordinary expression.

"Hardened girl!" exclaimed Miss Scatcherd; "nothing can correct you of your slatternly habits: carry the rod away."

Burns obeyed; I looked at her narrowly as she emerged from the book-closet; she was just putting back her handkerchief into her pocket, and the trace of a tear glistened on her thin cheek.

The play-hour in the evening I thought the pleasantest fraction of the day at Lowood: the bit of bread, the draught of coffee swallowed at five o'clock had revived vitality, if it had not satisfied hunger; the long restraint of the day was slackened; the school-room felt warmer than in the morning—its fires being allowed to burn a little more brightly to supply, in some measure, the place of candles, not yet introduced: the ruddy gloaming, the licensed uproar, the confusion of many voices gave one a welcome sense of liberty.

On the evening of the day on which I had seen Miss Scatcherd flog her pupil, Burns, I wandered as usual among the forms and tables and laughing groups without a companion, yet not feeling lonely: when I passed the windows, I now and then lifted a blind and looked out; it snowed fast, a drift was already forming against the lower panes; putting my ear close to the window, I could distinguish from the gleeful tumult within, the disconsolate moan of the wind outside.

Probably, if I had lately left a good home and kind parents, this would have been the hour when I should most keenly have regretted the separation: that wind would then have saddened my heart; this obscure chaos would have disturbed my peace: as it was, I derived from both a strange excitement, and reckless and feverish, I wished the wind to howl more wildly, the gloom to deepen to darkness, and the confusion to rise to clamour.

Jumping over forms, and creeping under tables, I made my way to one of the fire-places; there, kneeling by the high wire fender, I found Burns, absorbed, silent, abstracted from all round her by the companionship of a book, which she read by the dim glare of the embers.

"It is still Rasselas?" I asked, coming behind her.

"Yes," she said, "and I have just finished it."

And in five minutes more she shut it up. I was glad of this.

"Now," thought I, "I can perhaps get her to talk."

I sat down by her on the floor.

"What is your name besides Burns?"

"Helen."

"Do you come a long way from here?"

"I come from a place further north; quite on the borders of Scotland."

"Will you ever go back?"

"I hope so; but nobody can be sure of the future."

"You must wish to leave Lowood?"

"No: why should I? I was sent to Lowood to get an education; and it would be of no use going away until I have attained that object."

"But that teacher, Miss Scatcherd, is so cruel to you?"

"Cruel? Not at all! She is severe: she dislikes my faults."

"And if I were in your place I should dislike her; I should resist her; if she struck me with that rod, I should get it from her hand; I should break it under her nose."

"Probably you would do nothing of the sort: but if you did, Mr. Brocklehurst would expel you from the school; that would be a great grief to your relations. It is far better to endure patiently a smart which nobody feels but yourself than to commit a hasty action whose evil consequences will extend to all connected with you; and, besides, the Bible bids us to return good for evil."

"But then it seems disgraceful to be flogged, and to be sent to stand in the middle of a room full of people; and you are such a great girl: I am far younger than you, and I could not bear it."

"Yet it would be your duty to bear it, if you could not avoid it: it is weak and silly to say you *cannot bear* what it is your fate to be required to bear."

I heard her with wonder: I could not comprehend this doctrine of endurance; and still less could I understand or sympathise with the forbearance she expressed for her chastiser. Still I felt that Helen Burns considered things by a light invisible to my eyes. I suspected she might be right and I wrong; but I would not ponder the matter deeply: like Felix, I put it off to a more convenient season.

"You say you have faults, Helen: what are they: To me you seem very good."

"Then learn from me, not to judge by appearances: I am, as Miss Scatcherd said, slatternly; I seldom put, and never keep, things in order; I am careless; I forget rules; I read when I should learn my lessons; I have no method; and sometimes I say, like you, I cannot *bear* to be subjected to systematic arrangements. This is all very provoking to Miss Scatcherd, who is naturally neat, punctual, and particular."

"And cross and cruel," I added; but Helen Burns would not admit my addition; she kept silence.

"Is Miss Temple as severe to you as Miss Scatcherd?"

At the utterance of Miss Temple's name, a soft smile flitted over her grave face.

"Miss Temple is full of goodness: it pains her to be severe to any one, even the worst in the school: she sees my errors, and tells me of them gently; and, if I do anything worthy of praise, she gives me my meed liberally. One strong proof of my wretchedly defective nature is, that even her expostulations, so mild, so rational, have no influence to cure me of my faults; and even her praise, though I value it most highly, cannot stimulate me to continued care and foresight."

"That is curious," said I: "it is so easy to be careful."

"For *you* I have no doubt it is. I observed you in your class this morning, and saw you were closely attentive: your thoughts never seemed to wander while Miss Miller explained the lesson and questioned you. Now, mine continually rove away: when I should be listening to Miss Scatcherd, and collecting all she says with assiduity, often I lose the very sound of her voice; I fall into a sort of dream. Sometimes I think I am in Northumberland, and that the noises I hear round me are the bubbling of a little brook which runs through Deepden, near our house;— then, when it comes to my turn to reply, I have to be wakened; and, having heard nothing of what was read for listening to the visionary brook, I have no answer ready."

"Yet how well you replied this afternoon."

"It was mere chance: the subject on which we had been reading had interested me. This afternoon, instead of dreaming of Deepden, I was wondering how a man who wished to do right could act so unjustly and unwisely as Charles the First sometimes did; and I thought what a pity it was that, with his integrity and conscientiousness, he could see no farther than the prerogatives of the crown. If he had but been able to look to a distance, and see how what they call the spirit of the age was tending! Still, I like Charles—I respect him—I pity him, poor murdered king! Yes, his enemies were the worst: they shed blood they had no right to shed. How dared they kill him!"

Helen was talking to herself now: she had forgotten I could not very well understand her—that I was ignorant, or nearly so, of the subject she discussed. I recalled her to my level.

"And when Miss Temple teaches you, do your thoughts wander then?"

"No, certainly, not often; because Miss Temple has generally something to say which is newer than my own reflections: her language is singularly agreeable to me, and the information she communicates is often just what I wished to gain."

"Well, then, with Miss Temple you are good?"

"Yes, in a passive way: I make no effort; I follow as inclination guides me. There is no merit in such goodness."

"A great deal: you are good to those who are good to you. It is all I ever desire to be. If people were always kind and obedient to those who are cruel and unjust, the wicked people would have it all their own way: they would never feel afraid, and so they would never alter, but would grow worse and worse. When we are struck at without a reason, we should strike back again very hard; I am sure we should—so hard as to teach the person who struck us never to do it again."

"You will change your mind, I hope, when you grow older: as yet you are but a little untaught girl."

"But I feel this, Helen: I must dislike those who, whatever I do to please them, persist in disliking me; I must resist those who punish me unjustly. It is as natural as that I should love those who show me affection, or submit to punishment when I feel it is deserved."

"Heathens and savage tribes hold that doctrine; but Christians and civilised nations disown it."

"How? I don't understand."

"It is not violence that best overcomes hate—nor vengeance that most certainly heals injury."

"What then?"

"Read the New Testament, and observe what Christ says, and how he acts; make his word your rule, and his conduct your example."

"What does he say?"

"Love your enemies; bless them that curse you; do good to them that hate you and despitefully use you."

"Then I should love Mrs. Reed, which I cannot do; I should bless her son John, which is impossible."

In her turn, Helen Burns asked me to explain; and I proceeded forthwith to pour out, in my own way, the tale of my sufferings and resentments. Bitter and truculent when excited, I spoke as I felt, without reserve or softening.

Helen heard me patiently to the end: I expected she would then make a remark, but she said nothing.

"Well," I asked impatiently, "is not Mrs. Reed a hard-hearted, bad woman?"

"She has been unkind to you, no doubt; because, you see, she dislikes your cast of character, as Miss Scatcherd does mine: but how minutely you remember all she has done and said to you! What a singularly deep impression her injustice seems to have made on your heart! No ill-usage so brands its record on my feelings. Would you not be happier if you tried to forget her severity, together with the passionate emotions it excited? Life appears to me too short to be spent in nursing animosity, or registering wrongs. We are, and must be, one and all, burdened with faults in this world: but the time will soon come when, I trust, we shall put them off in putting off our corruptible bodies; when debasement and sin will fall from us with this cumbrous frame of flesh, and only the spark of the spirit will remain,— the impalpable principle of life and thought, pure as when it left the Creator to inspire the creature: whence it came it will return; perhaps again to be communicated to some being higher than man—perhaps to pass through gradations of glory, from the pale human soul to brighten to the seraph! Surely it will never, on the contrary, be suffered to degenerate from man to fiend? No; I cannot believe that: I hold another creed; which no one ever taught me, and which I seldom mention; but in which I delight, and to which I cling: for it extends hope to all: it makes Eternity a rest—a mighty home, not a terror and an abyss. Besides, with this creed, I can so clearly distinguish between the criminal and his crime; I can so sincerely forgive the first while I abhor the last: with this creed revenge never worries my heart, degradation never too deeply disgusts me, injustice never crushes me too low: I live in calm, looking to the end."

Helen's head, always drooping, sank a little lower as she finished this sentence. I saw by her look she wished no longer to talk to me, but rather to converse with

her own thoughts. She was not allowed much time for meditation: a monitor, a great rough girl, presently came up, exclaiming in a strong Cumberland accent,—

"Helen Burns, if you don't go and put your drawer in order, and fold up your work this minute, I'll tell Miss Scatcherd to come and look at it!"

Helen sighed as her reverie fled, and getting up, obeyed the monitor without reply as without delay.

Chapter VII

MY first quarter at Lowood seemed an age; and not the golden age either: it comprised an irksome struggle with difficulties in habituating myself to new rules and unwonted tasks. The fear of failure in these points harassed me worse than the physical hardships of my lot; though these were no trifles.

During January, February, and part of March, the deep snows, and, after their melting, the almost impassable roads, prevented our stirring beyond the garden walls, except to go to church; but within these limits we had to pass an hour every day in the open air. Our clothing was insufficient to protect us from the severe cold: we had no boots, the snow got into our shoes and melted there; our ungloved hands became numbed and covered with chilblains, as were our feet: I remember well the distracting irritation I endured from this cause every evening, when my feet inflamed; and the torture of thrusting the swelled, raw, and stiff toes into my shoes in the morning. Then the scanty supply of food was distressing: with the keen appetites of growing children, we had scarcely sufficient to keep alive a delicate invalid. From this deficiency of nourishment resulted an abuse, which pressed hardly on the younger pupils: whenever the famished great girls had an opportunity, they would coax or menace the little ones out of their portion. Many a time I have shared between two claimants the precious morsel of brown bread distributed at tea-time; and after relinquishing to a third, half the contents of my mug of coffee, I have swallowed the remainder with an accompaniment of secret tears, forced from me by the exigency of hunger.

Sundays were dreary days in that wintry season. We had to walk two miles to Brocklebridge Church, where our patron officiated. We set out cold, we arrived at church colder: during the morning service we became almost paralysed. It was too far to return to dinner, and an allowance of cold meat and bread, in the same penurious proportion observed in our ordinary meals, was served round between the services.

At the close of the afternoon service we returned by an exposed and hilly road, where the bitter winter wind, blowing over a range of snowy summits to the north, almost flayed the skin from our faces.

I can remember Miss Temple walking lightly and rapidly along our drooping line, her plaid cloak, which the frosty wind fluttered, gathered close about her, and encouraging us, by precept, and example, to keep up our spirits, and march forward, as she said, "like stalwart soldiers." The other teachers, poor things, were generally themselves too much dejected to attempt the task of cheering others.

How we longed for the light and heat of a blazing fire when we got back! But, to the little ones at least, this was denied: each hearth in the school-room was immediately surrounded by a double row of great girls, and behind them the younger children crouched in groups, wrapping their starved arms in their pinafores.

A little solace came at tea-time, in the shape of a double ration of bread—a whole, instead of a half, slice—with the delicious addition of a thin scrape of butter: it was the hebdomadal treat to which we all looked forward from Sabbath to Sabbath.

I generally contrived to reserve a moiety of this bounteous repast for myself; but the remainder I was invariably obliged to part with.

The Sunday evening was spent in repeating, by heart, the Church Catechism, and the fifth, sixth, and seventh chapters of St. Matthew; and in listening to a long sermon, read by Miss Miller, whose irrepressible yawns attested her weariness. A frequent interlude of these performances was the enactment of the part of Eutychus by some half dozen of little girls; who, overpowered with sleep, would fall down, if not out of the third loft, yet off the fourth form, and be taken up half dead. The remedy was, to thrust them forward into the centre of the school-room, and oblige them to stand there till the sermon was finished. Sometimes, their feet failed them, and they sank together in a heap; they were then propped up with the monitors' high stools.

I have not yet alluded to the visits of Mr. Brocklehurst; and indeed that gentleman was from home during the greater part of the first month after my arrival; perhaps prolonging his stay with his friend the archdeacon: his absence was a relief to me. I need not say that I had my own reasons for dreading his coming: but come he did at last.

One afternoon (I had then been three weeks at Lowood), as I was sitting with a slate in my hand, puzzling over a sum in long division, my eyes, raised in abstraction to the window, caught sight of a figure just passing: I recognised almost instinctively that gaunt outline; and when, two minutes after, all the school, teachers included, rose *en masse,* it was not necessary for me to look up in order to ascertain whose entrance they thus greeted. A long stride measured the school-room, and presently beside Miss Temple, who herself had risen, stood the same black column which had frowned on me so ominously from the hearth-rug of Gateshead. I now glanced sideways at this piece of architecture. Yes, I was right: it was Mr. Brocklehurst, buttoned up in a surtout, and looking longer, narrower, and more rigid than ever.

I had my own reasons for being dismayed at this apparition: too well I remembered the perfidious hints given by Mrs. Reed about my disposition, etc.; the promise pledged by Mr. Brocklehurst to apprise Miss Temple and the teachers of my vicious nature. All along I had been dreading the fulfilment of this promise,—I had been looking out daily for the "Coming Man," whose information respecting my past life and conversation was to brand me as a bad child for ever: now there he was. He stood at Miss Temple's side; he was speaking low in her ear: I did not doubt he was making disclosures of my villainy; and I watched her eye with painful anxiety, expecting every moment to see its dark orb turn on me a glance of repugnance and contempt. I listened too; and as I happened to be seated quite at the top of the room, I caught most of what he said: its import relieved me from immediate apprehension.

"I suppose, Miss Temple, the thread I bought at Lowton will do; it struck me that it would be just of the quality for the calico chemises, and I sorted the needles to match. You may tell Miss Smith that I forgot to make a memorandum of the darning needles, but she shall have some papers sent in next week; and she is not, on any account, to give out more than one at a time to each pupil: if they have more, they are apt to be careless and lose them. And, oh ma'am! I wish the woollen stockings were better looked to!—when I was here last, I went into the kitchen-garden and examined the clothes drying on the line; there was a quantity of black hose in a very bad state of repair: from the size of the holes in them I was sure they had not been well-mended from time to time."

He paused.

"Your directions shall be attended to, sir," said Miss Temple.

"And, ma'am," he continued, "the laundress tells me some of the girls have two clean tuckers in the week: it is too much; the rules limit them to one."

"I think I can explain that circumstance, sir. Agnes and Catherine Johnstone were invited to take tea with some friends at Lowton last Thursday, and I gave them leave to put on clean tuckers for the occasion."

Mr. Brocklehurst nodded.

"Well, for once it may pass; but please not to let the circumstance occur too often. And there is another thing which surprised me: I find, in settling accounts with the housekeeper, that a lunch, consisting of bread and cheese, has twice been served out to the girls during the past fortnight. How is this? I look over the regulations, and I find no such meal as lunch mentioned. Who introduced this innovation! and by what authority?"

"I must be responsible for the circumstance, sir," replied Miss Temple: "the breakfast was so ill-prepared that the pupils could not possibly eat it; and I dared not allow them to remain fasting till dinner time."

"Madam, allow me an instant.—You are aware that my plan in bringing up these girls is, not to accustom them to habits of luxury and indulgence, but to render them hardy, patient, self-denying. Should any little accidental disappointment of the appetite occur, such as the spoiling of a meal, the under or the over dressing of a dish, the incident ought not to be neutralised by replacing with something more delicate the comfort lost, thus pampering the body and obviating the aim of this institution; it ought to be improved to the spiritual edification of the pupils, by encouraging them to evince fortitude under the temporary privation. A brief address on those occasions would not be mistimed, wherein a judicious instructor would take the opportunity of referring to the sufferings of the primitive Christians; to the torments of martyrs; to the exhortations of our blessed Lord himself, calling upon his disciples to take up their cross and follow him; to his warnings that man shall not live by bread alone, but by every word that proceedeth out of the mouth of God; to his divine consolations, 'if ye suffer hunger or thirst for my sake, happy are ye.' Oh, madam, when you put bread and cheese, instead of burnt porridge, into these children's mouths, you may indeed feed their vile bodies, but you little think how you starve their immortal souls!"

Mr. Brocklehurst again paused—perhaps overcome by his feelings. Miss Temple had looked down when he first began to speak to her; but she now gazed straight before her, and her face, naturally pale as marble, appeared to be assuming also the coldness and fixity of that material; especially her mouth, closed as if it would have required a sculptor's chisel to open it, and her brow settled gradually into petrified severity.

Meantime, Mr. Brocklehurst, standing on the hearth with his hands behind his back, majestically surveyed the whole school. Suddenly his eye gave a blink, as if it had met something that either dazzled or shocked its pupil; turning, he said in more rapid accents than he had hitherto used:—

"Miss Temple, Miss Temple, what—*what* is that girl with curled hair? Red hair, ma'am, curled—curled all over?" And extending his cane he pointed to the awful object, his hand shaking as he did so.

"It is Julia Severn," replied Miss Temple, very quietly.

"Julia Severn, ma'am! And why has she, or any other, curled hair? Why, in defiance of every precept and principle of this house, does she conform to the world so openly—here in an evangelical, charitable establishment—as to wear her hair one mass of curls?"

"Julia's hair curls naturally," returned Miss Temple, still more quietly.

"Naturally! Yes, but we are not to conform to nature: I wish these girls to be the children of Grace: and why that abundance? I have again and again intimated that I desire the hair to be arranged closely, modestly, plainly. Miss Temple, that girl's hair must be cut off entirely; I will send a barber to-morrow: and I see others who have far too much of the excrescence—that tall girl, tell her to turn round. Tell all the first form to rise up and direct their faces to the wall."

Miss Temple passed her handkerchief over her lips, as if to smooth away the involuntary smile that curled them; she gave the order, however, and when the first class could take in what was required of them, they obeyed. Leaning a little back on my bench, I could see the looks and grimaces with which they commented on this manœuvre: it was a pity Mr. Brocklehurst could not see them too; he would perhaps have felt that, whatever he might do with the outside of the cup and platter, the inside was further beyond his interference than he imagined.

He scrutinised the reverse of these living medals some five minutes, then pronounced sentence. These words fell like the knell of doom:—

"All these top-knots must be cut off."

Miss Temple seemed to remonstrate.

"Madam," he pursued," I have a Master to serve whose kingdom is not of this world: my mission is to mortify in these girls the lusts of the flesh; to teach them to clothe themselves with shame-facedness and sobriety, not with braided hair and costly apparel; and each of the young persons before us has a string of hair twisted in plaits which vanity itself might have woven: these, I repeat, must be cut off; think of the time wasted, of——"

Mr. Brocklehurst was here interrupted: three other visitors, ladies, now entered the room. They ought to have come a little sooner to have heard his lecture on dress, for they were splendidly attired in velvet, silk, and furs. The two younger of the trio (fine girls of sixteen and seventeen) had grey beaver hats, then in fashion, shaded with ostrich plumes, and from under the brim of this graceful head-dress fell a profusion of light tresses, elaborately curled; the elderly lady was enveloped in a costly velvet shawl, trimmed with ermine, and she wore a false front of French curls.

These ladies were deferentially received by Miss Temple, as Mrs. and Misses Brocklehurst, and conducted to seats of honour at the top of the room. It seems they had come in the carriage with their reverend relative, and had been conducting a rummaging scrutiny of the rooms upstairs, while he transacted business with the housekeeper, questioned the laundress, and lectured the superintendent. They now proceeded to address divers remarks and reproofs to Miss Smith, who was charged with the care of the linen and the inspection of the dormitories: but I had no time to listen to what they said; other matters called off and enchained my attention.

Hitherto, while gathering up the discourse of Mr. Brocklehurst and Miss Temple, I had not, at the same time, neglected precautions to secure my personal safety; which I thought would be effected, if I could only elude observation. To this end, I had sat well back on the form, and while seeming to be busy with my sum, had held my slate in such a manner as to conceal my face: I might have escaped notice, had not my treacherous slate somehow happened to slip from my hand, and falling with an obtrusive crash, directly drawn every eye upon me; I knew it was all over now, and, as I stooped to pick up the two fragments of slate, I rallied my forces for the worst. It came.

"A careless girl!" said Mr. Brocklehurst, and immediately after—"It is the new pupil, I perceive." And before I could draw breath, "I must not forget I have a word to say respecting her." Then aloud: how loud it seemed to "Let the child who broke her slate, come forward!"

Of my own accord, I could not have stirred; I was paralysed: but the two great girls who sat on each side of me, set me on my legs and pushed me towards the dread judge, and then Miss Temple gently assisted me to his very feet, and I caught her whispered counsel,—

"Don't be afraid, Jane, I saw it was an accident; you shall not be punished."

The kind whisper went to my heart like a dagger.

"Another minute, and she will despise me for a hypocrite," thought I; and an impulse of fury against Reed, Brocklehurst, and Co. bounded in my pulses at the conviction. I was no Helen Burns.

"Fetch that stool," said Mr. Brocklehurst, pointing to a very high one from which a monitor had just risen: it was brought.

"Place the child upon it."

And I was placed there, by whom I don't know: I was in no condition to note particulars; I was only aware that they had hoisted me up to the height of Mr. Brocklehurst's nose, that he was within a yard of me, and that a spread of shot orange and purple silk pelisses, and a cloud of silvery plumage extended and waved below me.

Mr. Brocklehurst hemmed.

"Ladies," said he, turning to his family; "Miss Temple, teachers, and children, you all see this girl?"

Of course they did; for I felt their eyes directed like burning-glasses against my scorched skin.

"You see she is yet young; you observe she possesses the ordinary form of childhood; God has graciously given her the shape that He has given to all of us; no signal deformity points her out as a marked character. Who would think that the Evil One had already found a servant and agent in her? Yet such, I grieve to say, is the case."

A pause—in which I began to steady the palsy of my nerves, and to feel that the Rubicon was passed; and that the trial, no longer to be shirked, must be firmly sustained.

"My dear children," pursued the black marble clergyman, with pathos, "this is a sad, a melancholy occasion; for it becomes my duty to warn you, that this girl, who might be one of God's own lambs, is a little castaway: not a member of the true flock, but evidently an interloper and an alien. You must be on your guard against her; you must shun her example: if necessary, avoid her company, exclude her from your sports, and shut her out from your converse. Teachers, you must watch her: keep your eyes on her movements, weigh well her words, scrutinise her actions, punish her body to save her soul: if, indeed, such salvation be possible, for (my tongue falters while I tell it) this girl, this child, the native of a Christian land, worse than many a little heathen who says its prayers to Brahma and kneels before Juggernaut—this girl is—a liar!"

Now came a pause of ten minutes; during which I, by this time in perfect possession of my wits, observed all the female Brocklehursts produce their pocket-handkerchiefs and apply them to their optics, while the elderly lady swayed herself to and fro, and the two younger ones whispered, "How shocking!"

Mr. Brocklehurst resumed.

"This I learned from her benefactress; from the pious and charitable lady who adopted her in her orphan state, reared her as her own daughter, and whose kindness, whose generosity the unhappy girl repaid by an ingratitude so bad, so dreadful, that at last her excellent patroness was obliged to separate her from her own young ones, fearful lest her vicious example should contaminate their purity: she has sent her here to be healed, even as the Jews of old sent their diseased to the troubled pool of Bethesda; and, teachers, superintendent, I beg of you not to allow the waters to stagnate round her."

With this sublime conclusion, Mr. Brocklehurst adjusted the top button of his surtout, muttered something to his family, who rose, bowed to Miss Temple, and then all the great people sailed in state from the room. Turning at the door, my judge said:—

"Let her stand half an hour longer on that stool, and let no one speak to her during the remainder of the day."

There was I, then, mounted aloft; I, who had said I could not bear the shame of standing on my natural feet in the middle of the room, was now exposed to general view on a pedestal of infamy. What my sensations were, no language can describe; but just as they all rose, stifling my breath and constricting my throat, a girl came

up and passed me: in passing, she lifted her eyes. What a strange light inspired them! What an extraordinary sensation that ray sent through me! How the new feeling bore me up! It was as if a martyr, a hero, had passed a slave or victim, and imparted strength in the transit. I mastered the rising hysteria, lifted up my head, and took a firm stand on the stool. Helen Burns asked some slight question about her work of Miss Smith, was chidden for the triviality of the inquiry, returned to her place, and smiled at me as she again went by. What a smile! I remember it now, and I know that it was the effluence of fine intellect, of true courage; it lit up her marked lineaments, her thin face, her sunken grey eye, like a reflection from the aspect of an angel. Yet at that moment Helen Burns wore on her arm ''the untidy badge''; scarcely an hour ago I had heard her condemned by Miss Scatcherd to a dinner of bread and water on the morrow, because she had blotted an exercise in copying it out. Such is the imperfect nature of man! such spots are there on the disc of the clearest planet; and eyes like Miss Scatcherd's can only see those minute defects, and are blind to the full brightness of the orb.

Chapter VIII

ERE the half-hour ended, five o'clock struck; school was dismissed, and all were gone into the refectory to tea. I now ventured to descend: it was deep dusk; I retired into a corner and sat down on the floor. The spell by which I had been so far supported began to dissolve; reaction took place, and soon, so overwhelming was the grief that seized me, I sank prostrate with my face to the ground. Now I wept: Helen Burns was not here; nothing sustained me; left to myself I abandoned myself, and my tears watered the boards. I had meant to be so good, and to do so much at Lowood: to make so many friends, to earn respect, and win affection. Already I had made visible progress: that very morning I had reached the head of my class; Miss Miller had praised me warmly; Miss Temple had smiled approbation; she had promised to teach me drawing, and to let me learn French, if I continued to make similar improvement two months longer: and then I was well-received by my fellow-pupils; treated as an equal by those of my own age and not molested by any; now, here I lay again crushed and trodden on; and could I ever rise more?

"Never," I thought; and ardently I wished to die. While sobbing out this wish in broken accents, some one approached: I started up—again Helen Burns was near me; the fading fires just showed her coming up the long, vacant room; she brought my coffee and bread.

"Come, eat something," she said; but I put both away from me, feeling as if a drop or a crumb would have choked me in my present condition. Helen regarded me, probably with surprise: I could not now abate my agitation, though I tried hard; I continued to weep aloud. She sat down on the ground near me, embraced her knees with her arms, and rested her head upon them; in that attitude she remained silent as an Indian. I was the first who spoke:—

"Helen, why do you stay with a girl whom everybody believes to be a liar?"

"Everybody, Jane? Why, there are only eighty people who have heard you called so, and the world contains hundreds of millions."

"But what have I to do with millions? The eighty I know despise me."

"Jane, you are mistaken: probably not one in the school either despises or dislikes you: many, I am sure, pity you much."

"How can they pity me after what Mr. Brocklehurst said?"

"Mr. Brocklehurst is not a god: nor is he even a great and admired man; he is little liked here; he never took steps to make himself liked. Had he treated you as an especial favourite, you would have found enemies, declared or covert, all around

you; as it is, the greater number would offer you sympathy if they dared. Teachers and pupils may look coldly on you for a day or two, but friendly feelings are concealed in their hearts; and if you persevere in doing well, these feelings will ere long appear so much the more evidently for their temporary suppression. Besides, Jane,''—she paused.

"Well, Helen?" said I, putting my hand into hers: she chafed my fingers gently to warm them, and went on:—

"If all the world hated you, and believed you wicked, while your own conscience approved you, and absolved you from guilt, you would not be without friends."

"No; I know I should think well of myself; but that is not enough: if others don't love me, I would rather die than live—I cannot bear to be solitary and hated, Helen. Look here; to gain some real affection from you, or Miss Temple, or any other whom I truly love, I would willingly submit to have the bone of my arm broken, or to let a bull toss me, or to stand behind a kicking horse, and let it dash its hoof at my chest,''——

"Hush, Jane! you think too much of the love of human beings: you are too impulsive, too vehement: the sovereign hand that created your frame, and put life into it, has provided you with other resources than your feeble self, or than creatures feeble as you. Besides this earth, and besides the race of men, there is an invisible world and a kingdom of spirits: that world is round us, for it is everywhere; and those spirits watch us, for they are commissioned to guard us; and if we were dying in pain and shame, if scorn smote us on all sides, and hatred crushed us, angels see our tortures, recognise our innocence (if innocent we be: as I know you are of this charge which Mr. Brocklehurst has weakly and pompously repeated at second-hand from Mrs. Reed; for I read a sincere nature in your ardent eyes and on your clear front), and God waits only the separation of spirit from flesh to crown us with a full reward. Why, then, should we ever sink overwhelmed with distress, when life is so soon over, and death is so certain an entrance to happiness—to glory?"

I was silent: Helen had calmed me; but in the tranquillity she imparted there was an alloy of inexpressible sadness. I felt the impression of woe as she spoke, but I could not tell whence it came; and when, having done speaking, she breathed a little fast and coughed a short cough, I momentarily forgot my own sorrows to yield to a vague concern for her.

Resting my head on Helen's shoulder, I put my arms round her waist; she drew me to her, and we reposed in silence. We had not sat long thus, when another person came in. Some heavy clouds, swept from the sky by a rising wind, had left the moon bare; and her light, streaming in through a window near, shone full both on us and on the approaching figure, which we at once recognised as Miss Temple.

"I came on purpose to find you, Jane Eyre," said she; "I want you in my room; and as Helen Burns is with you, she may come too."

We went; following the superintendent's guidance, we had to thread some intricate passages, and mount a staircase before we reached her apartment; it contained a good fire, and looked cheerful. Miss Temple told Helen Burns to be seated in a low arm-chair on one side of the hearth, and herself taking another, she called me to her side.

"Is it all over?" she asked, looking down at my face. "Have you cried your grief away?"

"I am afraid I never shall do that."

"Why?"

"Because I have been wrongly accused; and you, ma'am, and everybody else will now think me wicked."

"We shall think you what you prove yourself to be, my child. Continue to act as a good girl, and you will satisfy me."

"Shall I, Miss Temple?"

"You will," said she, passing her arm round me. "And now tell me who is the lady whom Mr. Brocklehurst called your benefactress?"

"Mrs. Reed, my uncle's wife. My uncle is dead, and he left me to her care."

"Did she not, then, adopt you of her own accord?"

"No, ma'am; she was sorry to have to do it: but my uncle, as I have often heard the servants say, got her to promise before he died, that she would always keep me."

"Well now, Jane, you know, or at least I will tell you, that when a criminal is accused, he is always allowed to speak in his own defence. You have been charged with falsehood; defend yourself to me as well as you can. Say whatever your memory suggests as true; but add nothing and exaggerate nothing."

I resolved, in the depth of my heart, that I would be most moderate—most correct; and, having reflected a few minutes in order to arrange coherently what I had to say, I told her all the story of my sad childhood. Exhausted by emotion, my language was more subdued than it generally was when it developed that sad theme; and mindful of Helen's warnings against the indulgence of resentment, I infused into the narrative far less of gall and wormwood than ordinary. Thus restrained and simplified, it sounded more credible: I felt as I went on that Miss Temple fully believed me.

In the course of the tale I had mentioned Mr. Lloyd as having come to see me after the fit: for I never forgot the, to me, frightful episode of the red-room; in detailing which, my excitement was sure, in some degree, to break bounds; for nothing could soften in my recollection the spasm of agony which clutched my heart when Mrs. Reed spurned my wild supplication for pardon, and locked me a second time in the dark and haunted chamber.

I had finished: Miss Temple regarded me a few minutes in silence; she then said—

"I know something of Mr. Lloyd; I shall write to him; if his reply agrees with your statement, you shall be publicly cleared from every imputation: to me, Jane, you are clear now."

She kissed me, and still keeping me at her side (where I was well contented to stand, for I derived a child's pleasure from the contemplation of her face, her dress, her one or two ornaments, her white forehead, her clustered and shining curls, and beaming dark eyes), she proceeded to address Helen Burns.

"How are you to-night, Helen? Have you coughed much to-day?"

"Not quite so much I think, ma'am."

"And the pain in your chest?"

"It is a little better."

Miss Temple got up, took her hand and examined her pulse; then she returned to her own seat: as she resumed it, I heard her sigh low. She was pensive a few minutes, then rousing herself, she said cheerfully:—

"But you two are my visitors to-night; I must treat you as such." She rang the bell.

"Barbara," she said to the servant who answered it, "I have not yet had tea; bring the tray, and place cups for these two young ladies."

And a tray was soon brought. How pretty, to my eyes, did the china and bright teapot look, placed on the little round table near the fire! How fragrant was the steam of the beverage, and the scent of the toast! of which, however, I, to my dismay (for I was beginning to be hungry), discerned only a very small portion: Miss Temple discerned it too:—

"Barbara," said she, "can you not bring a little more bread and butter? There is not enough for three."

Barbara went out: she returned soon:—

"Madam, Mrs. Harden says she has sent up the usual quantity."

Mrs. Harden, be it observed, was the housekeeper: a woman after Mr. Brocklehurst's own heart, made up of equal parts of whalebone and iron.

"Oh, very well!" returned Miss Temple; "we must make it do, Barbara, I suppose." And as the girl withdrew, she added, smiling, "Fortunately, I have it in my power to supply deficiencies for this once."

Having invited Helen and me to approach the table, and placed before each of us a cup of tea with one delicious but thin morsel of toast, she got up, unlocked a drawer, and taking from it a parcel wrapped in paper, disclosed presently to our eyes a good-sized seed-cake.

"I meant to give each of you some of this to take with you," said she; "but as there is so little toast, you must have it now," and she proceeded to cut slices with a generous hand.

We feasted that evening as on nectar and ambrosia; and not the least delight of the entertainment was the smile of gratification with which our hostess regarded us, as we satisfied our famished appetites on the delicate fare she liberally supplied. Tea over and the tray removed, she again summoned us to the fire; we sat one on each side of her, and now a conversation followed between her and Helen, which it was indeed a privilege to be admitted to hear.

Miss Temple had always something of serenity in her air, of state in her mien, of refined propriety in her language, which precluded deviation into the ardent, the excited, the eager: something which chastened the pleasure of those who looked on her and listened to her, by a controlling sense of awe; and such was my feeling now: but as to Helen Burns, I was struck with wonder.

The refreshing meal, the brilliant fire, the presence and kindness of her beloved instructress, or, perhaps, more than all these, something in her own unique mind, had roused her powers within her. They woke, they kindled: first, they glowed in the bright tint of her cheek, which till this hour I had never seen but pale and bloodless; then they shone in the liquid lustre of her eyes, which had suddenly acquired a beauty more singular than that of Miss Temple's—a beauty neither of fine colour nor long eyelash, nor pencilled brow, but of meaning, of movement, of radiance. Then her soul sat on her lips, and language flowed, from what source I cannot tell: has a girl of fourteen a heart large enough, vigorous enough to hold the swelling spring of pure, full, fervid eloquence? Such was the characteristic of Helen's discourse on that, to me, memorable evening; her spirit seemed hastening to live within a very brief span as much as many live during a protracted existence.

They conversed of things I had never heard of; of nations and times past; of countries far away: of secrets of nature discovered or guessed at: they spoke of books: how many they had read! What stores of knowledge they possessed! Then they seemed so familiar with French names and French authors: but my amazement reached its climax when Miss Temple asked Helen if she sometimes snatched a moment to recall the Latin her father had taught her, and taking a book from a shelf, bade her read and construe a page of "Virgil"; and Helen obeyed, my organ of Veneration expanding at every sounding line. She had scarcely finished ere the bell announced bedtime: no delay could be admitted; Miss Temple embraced us both, saying, as she drew us to her heart:—

"God bless you, my children!"

Helen she held a little longer than me: she let her go more reluctantly; it was Helen her eye followed to the door; it was for her she a second time breathed a sad sigh; for her she wiped a tear from her cheek.

On reaching the bed-room, we heard the voice of Miss Scatcherd: she was examining drawers; she had just pulled out Helen Burns's, and when we entered Helen was greeted with a sharp reprimand, and told that to-morrow she should have half a dozen of untidily folded articles pinned to her shoulder.

"My things were indeed in shameful disorder," murmured Helen to me, in a low voice: "I intended to have arranged them, but I forgot."

Next morning, Miss Scatcherd wrote in conspicuous characters on a piece of pasteboard the word "Slattern," and bound it like a phylactery round Helen's large, mild, intelligent, and benign-looking forehead. She wore it till evening, patient, unresentful, regarding it as a deserved punishment. The moment Miss Scatcherd withdrew after afternoon-school, I ran to Helen, tore it off, and thrust it into the fire: the fury of which she was incapable had been burning in my soul all day, and tears, hot and large, had continually been scalding my cheek; for the spectacle of her sad resignation gave me an intolerable pain at the heart.

About a week subsequently to the incidents above narrated, Miss Temple, who had written to Mr. Lloyd, received his answer: it appeared that what he said went to corroborate my account. Miss Temple, having assembled the whole school, announced that inquiry had been made into the charges alleged against Jane Eyre, and that she was most happy to be able to pronounce her completely cleared from every imputation. The teachers then shook hands with me and kissed me, and a murmur of pleasure ran through the ranks of my companions.

Thus relieved of a grievous load, I from that hour set to work afresh, resolved to pioneer my way through every difficulty: I toiled hard, and my success was proportionate to my efforts; my memory, not naturally tenacious, improved with practice; exercise sharpened my wits; in a few weeks I was promoted to a higher class; in less than two months I was allowed to commence French and drawing. I learned the first two tenses of the verb *Etre,* and sketched my first cottage (whose walls, by-the-by, outrivalled in slope those of the leaning tower of Pisa), on the same day. That night, on going to bed, I forgot to prepare in imagination the Barmecide supper of hot roast potatoes, or white bread and new milk, with which I was wont to amuse my inward cravings: I feasted instead on the spectacle of ideal drawings, which I saw in the dark; all the work of my own hands: freely pencilled houses and trees, picturesque rocks and ruins, Cuyp-like groups of cattle, sweet paintings of butterflies hovering over unblown roses, of birds picking at ripe cherries, of wrens' nests enclosing pearl-like eggs, wreathed about with young ivy sprays. I examined, too, in thought, the possibility of my ever being able to translate currently a certain little French story-book which Madame Pierrot had that day shown me; nor was that problem solved to my satisfaction ere I fell sweetly asleep.

Well has Solomon said—"Better is a dinner of herbs where love is, than a stalled ox and hatred therewith."

I would not now have exchanged Lowood with all its privations, for Gateshead and its daily luxuries.

Chapter IX

BUT the privations, or rather the hardships, of Lowood lessened. Spring drew on, she was indeed already come; the frosts of winter had ceased; its snows were melted, its cutting winds ameliorated. My wretched feet, flayed and swollen to lameness by the sharp air of January, began to heal and subside under the gentler breathings of April; the nights and mornings no longer by their Canadian temperature froze the very blood in our veins; we could now endure the play-hour in the garden: sometimes on a sunny day it began even to be pleasant and genial, and a greenness grew over those brown beds, which, freshening daily, suggested the thought that Hope traversed them at night, and left each morning brighter traces of her steps. Flowers peeped out amongst the leaves; snow-drops, crocuses, purple auriculas, and golden-eyed pansies. On Thursday afternoons (half-holidays) we now took walks, and found still sweeter flowers opening by the wayside, under the hedges.

I discovered, too, that a great pleasure, an enjoyment which the horizon only bounded, lay all outside the high and spike-guarded walls of our garden: this pleasure consisted in prospect of noble summits girdling a great hill-hollow, rich in verdure and shadow: in a bright beck, full of dark stones and sparkling eddies. How different had this scene looked when I viewed it laid out beneath the iron sky of winter, stiffened in frost, shrouded with snow!—when mists as chill as death wandered to the impulse of east winds along those purple peaks, and rolled down ''ing'' and holm till they blended with the frozen fog of the beck! That beck itself was then a torrent, turbid and curbless: it tore asunder the wood, and sent a raving sound through the air, often thickened with wild rain or whirling sleet; and for the forest on its banks, *that* showed only ranks of skeletons.

April advanced to May: a bright, serene May it was; days of blue sky, placid sunshine, and soft western or southern gales filled up its duration. And now vegetation matured with vigour; Lowood shook loose its tresses; it became all green, all flowery; its great elm, ash, and oak skeletons were restored to majestic life; woodland plants sprang up profusely in its recesses; unnumbered varieties of moss filled its hollows, and it made a strange ground-sunshine out of the wealth of its wild primrose plants: I have seen their pale gold gleam in overshadowed spots like scatterings of the sweetest lustre. All this I enjoyed often and fully, free, unwatched, and almost alone; for this unwonted liberty and pleasure there was a cause, to which it now becomes my task to advert.

Have I not described a pleasant site for a dwelling, when I speak of it as bosomed in hill and wood, and rising from the verge of a stream? Assuredly, pleasant enough: but whether healthy or not is another question.

That forest-dell, where Lowood lay, was the cradle of fog and fog-bred pestilence; which, quickening with the quickening spring, crept into the Orphan Asylum, breathed typhus through its crowded school-room and dormitory, and, ere May arrived, transformed the seminary into an hospital.

Semi-starvation and neglected colds had predisposed most of the pupils to receive infection: forty-five out of the eighty girls lay ill at one time. Classes were broken up, rules relaxed. The few who continued well were allowed almost unlimited licence; because the medical attendant insisted on the necessity of frequent exercise to keep them in health: and had it been otherwise, no one had leisure to watch or restrain them. Miss Temple's whole attention was absorbed by the patients: she lived in the sick-room, never quitting it except to snatch a few hours' rest at night. The teachers were fully occupied with packing up and making other necessary preparations for the departure of those girls who were fortunate enough to have friends and relations able and willing to remove them from the seat of contagion. Many, already smitten, went home only to die; some died at the school, and were buried quietly and quickly, the nature of the malady forbidding delay.

While disease had thus become an inhabitant of Lowood, and death its frequent visitor; while there was gloom and fear within its walls; while its rooms and passages steamed with hospital smells, the drug and the pastille striving vainly to overcome the effluvia of mortality, that bright May shone unclouded over the bold hills and beautiful woodland out of doors. Its garden, too, glowed with flowers: hollyhocks had sprung up tall as trees, lilies had opened, tulips and roses were in bloom; the borders of the little beds were gay with pink thrift and crimson double-daisies; the sweet-briars gave out, morning and evening, their scent of spice and apples; and these fragrant treasures were all useless for most of the inmates of Lowood, except to furnish now and then a handful of herbs and blossoms to put in a coffin.

But I, and the rest who continued well, enjoyed fully the beauties of the scene and season: they let us ramble in the wood, like gipsies, from morning till night; we did what we liked, went where we liked: we lived better too. Mr. Brocklehurst and his family never came near Lowood now: household matters were not scrutinised into: the cross housekeeper was gone, driven away by the fear of infection; her

successor, who had been matron at the Lowton Dispensary, unused to the ways of her new abode, provided with comparative liberality. Besides, there were fewer to feed: the sick could eat little; our breakfast-basins were better filled: when there was no time to prepare a regular dinner, which often happened, she would give us a large piece of cold pie, or a thick slice of bread and cheese, and this we carried away with us to the wood, where we each chose the spot we liked best, and dined sumptuously.

My favourite seat was a smooth and broad stone, rising white and dry from the very middle of the beck, and only to be got at by wading through the water; a feat I accomplished barefoot. The stone was just broad enough to accommodate, comfortably, another girl and me, at that time my chosen comrade—one Mary Ann Wilson; a shrewd observant personage, whose society I took pleasure in, partly because she was witty and original, and partly because she had a manner which set me at my ease. Some years older than I, she knew more of the world, and could tell me many things I liked to hear: with her my curiosity found gratification: to my faults also she gave ample indulgence, never imposing curb or rein on anything I said. She had a turn for narrative, I for analysis; she liked to inform, I to question; so we got on swimmingly together, deriving much entertainment, if not much improvement, from our mutual intercourse.

And where, meantime, was Helen Burns? Why did I not spend these sweet days of liberty with her? Had I forgotten her? or was I so worthless as to have grown tired of her pure society? Surely the Mary Ann Wilson I have mentioned was inferior to my first acquaintance: she could only tell me amusing stories, and reciprocate any racy and pungent gossip I chose to indulge in; while, if I have spoken truth of Helen, she was qualified to give those who enjoyed the privilege of her converse, a taste of far higher things.

True, reader; and I knew and felt this: and though I am a defective being, with many faults and few redeeming points, yet I never tired of Helen Burns; nor ever ceased to cherish for her a sentiment of attachment, as strong, tender, and respectful as any that ever animated my heart. How could it be otherwise, when Helen, at all times and under all circumstances, evinced for me a quiet and faithful friendship, which ill-humour never soured, nor irritation ever troubled? But Helen was ill at present: for some weeks she had been removed from my sight to I knew not what room upstairs. She was not, I was told, in the hospital portion of the house with the fever patients; for her complaint was consumption, not typhus: and by consumption I, in my ignorance, understood something mild, which time and care would be sure to alleviate.

I was confirmed in this idea by the fact of her once or twice coming downstairs on very warm sunny afternoons, and being taken by Miss Temple into the garden: but, on these occasions, I was not allowed to go and speak to her; I only saw her from the schoolroom window, and then not distinctly; for she was much wrapped up, and sat at a distance under the verandah.

One evening, in the beginning of June, I had stayed out very late with Mary Ann in the wood; we had, as usual, separated ourselves from the others, and had wandered far: so far that we lost our way, and had to ask it at a lonely cottage, where a man and woman lived, who looked after a herd of half-wild swine that fed on the mast in the wood. When we got back, it was after moon-rise: a pony, which we knew to be the surgeon's, was standing at the garden door. Mary Ann remarked that she supposed some one must be very ill, as Mr. Bates had been sent for at that time of the evening. She went into the house; I stayed behind a few minutes to plant in my garden a handful of roots I had dug up in the forest, and which I feared would wither if I left them till the morning. This done, I lingered yet a little longer: the flowers smelt so sweet as the dew fell; it was such a pleasant evening, so serene, so warm; the still glowing west promised so fairly another fine day on the morrow; the moon rose with such majesty in the grave east. I was noting

these things and enjoying them as a child might, when it entered my mind as it had never done before:—

"How sad to be lying now on a sick bed, and to be in danger of dying! This world is pleasant—it would be dreary to be called from it, and to have to go who knows where?"

And then my mind made its first earnest effort to comprehend what had been infused into it concerning heaven and hell: and for the first time it recoiled, baffled; and for the first time glancing behind, on each side, and before it, it saw all round an unfathomed gulf: it felt the one point where it stood—the present; all the rest was formless cloud and vacant depth: and it shuddered at the thought of tottering, and plunging amid that chaos. While pondering this new idea, I heard the front door open; Mr. Bates came out, and with him was a nurse. After she had seen him mount his horse and depart, she was about to close the door, but I ran up to her.

"How is Helen Burns?"

"Very poorly," was the answer.

"Is it her Mr. Bates has been to see?"

"Yes."

"And what does he say about her?"

"He says she'll not be here long."

This phrase, uttered in my hearing yesterday, would have only conveyed the notion that she was about to be removed to Northumberland, to her own home. I should not have suspected that it meant she was dying; but I knew instantly now; it opened clear on my comprehension that Helen Burns was numbering her last days in this world, and that she was going to be taken to the region of spirits, if such region there were. I experienced a shock of horror, then a strong thrill of grief, then a desire—a necessity to see her; and I asked in what room she lay.

"She is in Miss Temple's room," said the nurse.

"May I go up and speak to her?"

"Oh, no, child! It is not likely; and now it is time for you to come in; you'll catch the fever if you stop out when the dew is falling."

The nurse closed the front door; I went in by the side entrance which led to the school-room: I was just in time; it was nine o'clock, and Miss Miller was calling the pupils to go to bed.

It might be two hours later, probably near eleven, when I—not having been able to fall asleep, and deeming, from the perfect silence of the dormitory, that my companions were all wrapt in profound repose—rose softly, put on my frock over my night-dress, and, without shoes, crept from the apartment, and set off in quest of Miss Temple's room. It was quite at the other end of the house; but I knew my way; and the light of the unclouded summer moon, entering here and there at passage windows, enabled me to find it without difficulty. An odour of camphor and burnt vinegar warned me when I came near the fever room: and I passed its door quickly, fearful lest the nurse who sat up all night should hear me. I dreaded being discovered and sent back; for I *must* see Helen,—I must embrace her before she died,—I must give her one last kiss, exchange with her one last word.

Having descended a staircase, traversed a portion of the house below, and succeeded in opening and shutting, without noise, two doors, I reached another flight of steps; these I mounted, and then just opposite to me was Miss Temple's room. A light shone through the key-hole, and from under the door; a profound stillness pervaded the vicinity. Coming near, I found the door slightly ajar; probably to admit some fresh air into the close abode of sickness. Indisposed to hesitate, and full of impatient impulses—soul and senses quivering with keen throes—I put it back and looked in. My eye sought Helen, and feared to find death.

Close by Miss Temple's bed, and half covered, with its white curtains, there stood a little crib. I saw the outline of a form under the clothes, but the face was hid by the hangings: the nurse I had spoken to in the garden sat in an easy chair,

asleep; an unsnuffed candle burnt dimly on the table. Miss Temple was not to be seen: I knew afterwards that she had been called to a delirious patient in the fever room. I advanced; then paused by the crib side: my hand was on the curtain, but I preferred speaking before I withdrew it. I still recoiled at the dread of seeing a corpse.

"Helen?" I whispered softly; "are you awake?"

She stirred herself, put back the curtain, and I saw her face, pale, wasted, but quite composed: she looked so little changed that my fear was instantly dissipated.

"Can it be you, Jane?" she asked in her own gentle voice.

"Oh!" I thought, "she is not going to die; they are mistaken: she could not speak and look so calmly if she were."

I got on to her crib and kissed her; her forehead was cold, and her cheek both cold and thin, and so were her hand and wrist; but she smiled as of old.

"Why are you come here, Jane? It is past eleven o'clock: I heard it strike some minutes since."

"I came to see you, Helen: I heard you were very ill, and I could not sleep till I had spoken to you."

"You came to bid me good-bye, then: you are just in time probably."

"Are you going somewhere, Helen? Are you going home?"

"Yes; to my long home—my last home."

"No, no, Helen!" I stopped, distressed. While I tried to devour my tears, a fit of coughing seized Helen; it did not, however, wake the nurse; when it was over, she lay some minutes exhausted; then she whispered:—

"Jane, your little feet are bare; lie down and cover yourself with my quilt."

I did so: she put her arm over me, and I nestled close to her. After a long silence, she resumed; still whispering,—

"I am very happy, Jane; and when you hear that I am dead, you must be sure and not grieve: there is nothing to grieve about. We all must die one day, and the illness which is removing me is not painful; it is gentle and gradual: my mind is at rest. I leave no one to regret me much: I have only a father; and he is lately married, and will not miss me. By dying young, I shall escape great sufferings. I had not qualities or talents to make my way very well in the world: I should have been continually at fault."

"But where are you going to, Helen? Can you see? Do you know?"

"I believe; I have faith: I am going to God."

"Where is God? What is God?"

"My Maker and yours, who will never destroy what he created. I rely implicitly on his power, and confide wholly in his goodness: I count the hours till that eventful one arrives which shall restore me to him, reveal him to me."

"You are sure, then, Helen, that there is such a place as heaven; and that our souls can get to it when we die?"

"I am sure there is a future state; I believe God is good; I can resign my immortal part to him without any misgiving. God is my father; God is my friend: I love him; I believe he loves me."

"And shall I see you again, Helen, when I die?"

"You will come to the same region of happiness: be received by the same mighty, universal Parent, no doubt, dear Jane."

Again I questioned; but this time only in thought. "Where is that region? Does it exist?" And I clasped my arms closer round Helen; she seemed dearer to me than ever; I felt as if I could not let her go; I lay with my face hidden on her neck. Presently she said in the sweetest tone,—

"How comfortable I am! That last fit of coughing has tired me a little; I feel as if I could sleep: but don't leave me, Jane; I like to have you near me."

"I'll stay with you, *dear* Helen: no one shall take me away."

"Are you warm, darling?"

"Yes."

"Good-night, Jane."

"Good-night, Helen."

She kissed me, and I her; and we both soon slumbered.

When I awoke it was day; an unusual movement roused me; I looked up; I was in somebody's arms; the nurse held me; she was carrying me through the passage back to the dormitory. I was not reprimanded for leaving my bed; people had something else to think about: no explanation was afforded then to my many questions; but a day or two afterwards I learned that Miss Temple, on returning to her own room at dawn, had found me laid in a little crib; my face against Helen Burns's shoulder, my arms round her neck. I was asleep, and Helen was—dead.

Her grave is in Brocklebridge churchyard: for fifteen years after her death it was only covered by a grassy mound; but now a gray marble tablet marks the spot, inscribed with her name, and the word "Resurgam."

Chapter X

HITHERTO I have recorded in detail the events of my insignificant existence: to the first ten years of my life, I have given almost as many chapters. But this is not to be a regular autobiography: I am only bound to invoke memory where I know her responses will possess some degree of interest; therefore I now pass a space of eight years almost in silence: a few lines only are necessary to keep up the links of connection.

When the typhus fever had fulfilled its mission of devastation at Lowood, it gradually disappeared from thence; but not till its virulence and the number of its victims had drawn public attention on the school. Inquiry was made into the origin of the scourge, and by degrees various facts came out which excited public indignation in a high degree. The unhealthy nature of the site; the quantity and quality of the children's food; the brackish, fetid water used in its preparation; the pupils' wretched clothing and accommodations: all these things were discovered; and the discovery produced a result mortifying to Mr. Brocklehurst, but beneficial to the institution.

Several wealthy and benevolent individuals in the county subscribed largely for the erection of a more convenient building in a better situation; new regulations were made; improvements in diet and clothing introduced; the funds of the school were entrusted to the management of a committee. Mr. Brocklehurst, who, from his wealth and family connections, could not be overlooked, still retained the post of treasurer; but he was aided in the discharge of his duties by gentlemen of rather more enlarged and sympathising minds: his office of inspector, too, was shared by those who knew how to combine reason with strictness, comfort with economy, compassion with uprightness. The school, thus improved, became in time a truly useful and noble institution. I remained an inmate of its walls, after its regeneration, for eight years: six as pupil, and two as teacher; and in both capacities I bear my testimony to its value and importance.

During these eight years my life was uniform: but not unhappy, because it was not inactive. I had the means of an excellent education placed within my reach; a fondness for some of my studies, and a desire to excel in all, together with a great delight in pleasing my teachers, especially such as I loved, urged me on: I availed myself fully of the advantages offered me. In time I rose to be the first girl of the first class; then I was invested with the office of teacher; which I discharged with zeal for two years: but at the end of that time I altered.

Miss Temple, through all changes, had thus far continued superintendent of the seminary: to her instruction I owed the best part of my acquirements; her friendship

and society had been my continual solace; she had stood me in the stead of mother, governess, and, latterly, companion. At this period she married, removed with her husband (a clergyman, an excellent man, almost worthy of such a wife) to a distant county, and consequently was lost to me.

From the day she left I was no longer the same: with her was gone every settled feeling, every association that had made Lowood in some degree a home to me. I had imbibed from her something of her nature and much of her habits: more harmonious thoughts: what seemed better regulated feelings had become the inmates of my mind. I had given in allegiance to duty and order; I was quiet; I believed I was content: to the eyes of others, usually even to my own, I appeared a disciplined and subdued character.

But destiny, in the shape of the Rev. Mr. Nasmyth, came between me and Miss Temple: I saw her in her travelling dress step into a post-chaise, shortly after the marriage ceremony; I watched the chaise mount the hill and disappear beyond its brow; and then retired to my own room, and there spent in solitude the greatest part of the half-holiday granted in honour of the occasion.

I walked about the chamber most of the time. I imagined myself only to be regretting my loss, and thinking how to repair it; but when my reflections were concluded, and I looked up and found that the afternoon was gone, and evening far advanced, another discovery dawned on me, namely, that in the interval I had undergone a transforming process; that my mind had put off all it had borrowed of Miss Temple—or rather that she had taken with her the serene atmosphere I had been breathing in her vicinity—and that now I was left in my natural element, and beginning to feel the stirring of old emotions. It did not seem as if a prop were withdrawn, but rather as if a motive were gone: it was not the power to be tranquil which had failed me, but the reason for tranquillity was no more. My world had for some years been in Lowood: my experience had been of its rules and systems; now I remembered that the real world was wide, and that a varied field of hopes and fears, of sensations and excitements, awaited those who had courage to go forth into its expanse, to seek real knowledge of life amidst its perils.

I went to my window, opened it, and looked out. There were the two wings of the building; there was the garden; there were the skirts of Lowood; there was the hilly horizon. My eye passed all other objects to rest on those most remote, the blue peaks: it was those I longed to surmount; all within their boundary of rock and heath seemed prison-ground, exile limits. I traced the white road winding round the base of one mountain, and vanishing in a gorge between two: how I longed to follow it further! I recalled the time when I had travelled that very road in a coach; I remembered descending that hill at twilight: an age seemed to have elapsed since the day which brought me first to Lowood, and I had never quitted it since. My vacations had all been spent at school: Mrs. Reed had never sent for me to Gateshead; neither she nor any of her family had ever been to visit me. I had had no communication by letter or message with the outer world: school-rules, school-duties, school-habits and notions, and voices, and faces, and phrases, and costumes, and preferences, and antipathies: such was what I knew of existence. And now I felt that it was not enough: I tired of the routine of eight years in one afternoon. I desired liberty; for liberty I gasped; for liberty I uttered a prayer; it seemed scattered on the wind then faintly blowing. I abandoned it and framed a humbler supplication; for change, stimulus: that petition, too, seemed swept off into vague space: "Then," I cried, half desperate, "grant me at least a new servitude!"

Here a bell, ringing the hour of supper, called me downstairs.

I was not free to resume the interrupted chain of my reflections till bedtime: even then a teacher who occupied the same room with me kept me from the subject to which I longed to recur, by a prolonged effusion of small talk. How I wished sleep would silence her! It seemed as if, could I but go back to the idea which had last

entered my mind as I stood at the window, some inventive suggestion would rise for my relief.

Miss Gryce snored at last; she was a heavy Welshwoman, and till now her habitual nasal strains had never been regarded by me in any other light than as a nuisance; to-night I hailed the first deep notes with satisfaction; I was debarrassed of interruption; my half-effaced thought instantly revived.

"A new servitude! There is something in that," I soliloquised (mentally, be it understood; I did not talk aloud). "I know there is, because it does not sound too sweet; is it not like such words as Liberty, Excitement, Enjoyment: delightful sounds truly; but no more than sounds for me; and so hollow and fleeting that it is mere waste of time to listen to them. But Servitude! That must be matter of fact. Any one may serve: I have served here eight years; now all I want is to serve elsewhere. Can I not get so much of my own will? Is not the thing feasible? Yes—yes—the end is not so difficult; if I had only a brain active enough to ferret out the means of attaining it."

I sat up in bed by way of arousing this sad brain: it was a chilly night; I covered my shoulders with a shawl, and then I proceeded *to think* again with all my might.

"What do I want? A new place, in a new house, amongst new faces, under new circumstances: I want this because it is of no use wanting anything better. How do people do to get a new place? They apply to friends, I suppose: I have no friends. There are many others who have no friends, who must look about for themselves and be their own helpers; and what is their resource?"

I could not tell: nothing answered me; I then ordered my brain to find a response, and quickly. It worked and worked faster: I felt the pulses throb in my head and temples; but for nearly an hour it worked in chaos, and no result came of its efforts. Feverish with vain labour, I got up and took a turn in the room; undrew the curtain, and noted a star or two, shivered with cold, and again crept to bed.

A kind fairy, in my absence, had surely dropped the required suggestion on my pillow; for as I lay down it came quietly and naturally to my mind:—"Those who want situations advertise; you must advertise in the ——*shire Herald.*"

"How? I know nothing about advertising."

Replies rose smooth and prompt now:—

"You must inclose the advertisement and the money to pay for it under a cover directed to the Editor of the *Herald*; you must put it, the first opportunity you have, into the post at Lowton; answers must be addressed to J. E. at the post-office there: you can go and inquire in about a week after you send your letter, if any are come, and act accordingly."

This scheme I went over twice, thrice; it was then digested in my mind: I had it in a clear practical form; I felt satisfied, and fell asleep.

With earliest day, I was up: I had my advertisement written, enclosed, and directed before the bell rang to rouse the school; it ran thus:—

"A young lady accustomed to tuition" (had I not been a teacher two years?) "is desirous of meeting with a situation in a private family where the children are under fourteen (I thought that as I was barely eighteen, it would not do to undertake the guidance of pupils nearer my own age). She is qualified to teach the usual branches of a good English education, together with French, Drawing, and Music" (in those days, reader, this now narrow catalogue of accomplishments, would have been held tolerably comprehensive). "Address J. E., Post-office, Lowton, ——shire."

This document remained locked in my drawer all day: after tea, I asked leave of the new superintendent to go to Lowton, in order to perform some small commissions for myself and one or two of my fellow-teachers; permission was readily granted; I went. It was a walk of two miles, and the evening was wet, but the days were still long; I visited a shop or two, slipped the letter into the post-office, and came back through heavy rain, with streaming garments, but with a relieved heart.

The succeeding week seemed long: it came to an end at last, however, like all sublunary things, and once more, towards the close of a pleasant autumn day, I found myself afoot on the road to Lowton. A picturesque track it was, by the way; lying along the side of the beck and through the sweetest curves of the dale: but that day I thought more of the letter, that might or might not be awaiting me at the little burgh whither I was bound, than of the charms of lea and water.

My ostensible errand on this occasion was to get measured for a pair of shoes; so I discharged that business first, and when it was done, I stepped across the clean and quiet little street from the shoemaker's to the post-office: it was kept by an old dame, who wore horn spectacles on her nose, and black mittens on her hands.

"Are there any letters for J. E.?" I asked.

She peered at me over her spectacles, and then she opened a drawer and fumbled among its contents for a long time, so long that my hopes began to falter. At last, having held a document before her glasses for nearly five minutes, she presented it across the counter, accompanying the act by another inquisitive and mistrustful glance—it was for J. E.

"Is there only one?" I demanded.

"There are no more," said she; and I put it in my pocket and turned my face homeward: I could not open it then; rules obliged me to be back by eight, and it was already half-past seven.

Various duties awaited me on my arrival: I had to sit with the girls during their hour of study; then it was my turn to read prayers; to see them to bed: afterwards I supped with the other teachers. Even when we finally retired for the night, the inevitable Miss Gryce was still my companion: we had only a short end of a candle in our candlestick, and I dreaded lest she should talk till it was all burnt out; fortunately, however, the heavy supper she had eaten produced a soporific effect: she was already snoring, before I had finished undressing. There still remained an inch of candle: I now took out my letter; the seal was an initial F.; I broke it; the contents were brief.

"If J. E., who advertised in the ——*shire Herald* of last Thursday, possesses the acquirements mentioned; and if she is in a position to give satisfactory references as to character and competency; a situation can be offered her where there is but one pupil, a little girl, under ten years of age; and, where the salary is thirty pounds per annum. J. E. is requested to send references, name, address, and all particulars to the direction:—

"Mrs. Fairfax, Thornfield, near Millcote, ——shire."

I examined the document long; the writing was old-fashioned and rather uncertain, like that of an elderly lady. This circumstance was satisfactory: a private fear had haunted me, that in thus acting for myself, and by my own guidance, I ran the risk of getting into some scrape; and, above all things, I wished the result of my endeavours to be respectable, proper, *en règle*. I now felt that an elderly lady was no bad ingredient in the business I had on hand. Mrs. Fairfax! I saw her in a black gown and widow's cap; frigid, perhaps, but not uncivil: a model of elderly English respectability. Thornfield! that, doubtless, was the name of her house: a neat, orderly spot, I was sure; though I failed in my efforts to conceive a correct plan of the premises. Millcote, ——shire; I brushed up my recollections of the map of England; yes, I saw it; both the shire and the town. ——shire was seventy miles nearer London than the remote county where I now resided: that was a recommendation to me. I longed to go where there was life and movement: Millcote was a large manufacturing town on the banks of the A——; a busy place enough, doubtless: so much the better; it would be a complete change at least. Not that my fancy was much captivated by the idea of long chimneys and clouds of smoke—"but," I argued, "Thornfield will, probably, be a good way from the town."

Here the socket of the candle dropped, and the wick went out.

Next day new steps were to be taken: my plans could no longer be confined to my own breast; I must impart them in order to achieve their success. Having sought and obtained an audience of the superintendent, during the noon-tide recreation, I told her I had a prospect of getting a new situation where the salary would be double what I now received (for, at Lowood, I only got £15 per annum); and requested she would break the matter for me to Mr. Brocklehurst, or some of the committee, and ascertain whether they would permit me to mention them as references. She obligingly consented to act as mediatrix in the matter. The next day she laid the affair before Mr. Brocklehurst, who said that Mrs. Reed must be written to, as she was my natural guardian. A note was accordingly addressed to that lady, who returned for answer, that "I might do as I pleased: she had long relinquished all interference in my affairs." This note went the round of the committee, and at last, after what appeared to me most tedious delay, formal leave was given me to better my condition if I could; and an assurance added, that as I had always conducted myself well, both as teacher and pupil, at Lowood, a testimonial of character and capacity, signed by the inspectors of that institution, should forthwith be furnished me.

This testimonial I accordingly received in about a month, forwarded a copy of it to Mrs. Fairfax, and got that lady's reply, stating that she was satisfied, and fixing that day fortnight as the period for my assuming the post of governess in her house.

I now busied myself in preparations: the fortnight passed rapidly. I had not a very large wardrobe, though it was adequate to my wants; and the last day sufficed to pack my trunk,—the same I had brought with me eight years ago from Gateshead.

The box was corded, the card nailed on. In half an hour the carrier was to call for it to take it to Lowton, whither I myself was to repair at an early hour the next morning to meet the coach. I had brushed my black stuff travelling dress, prepared my bonnet, gloves, and muff; sought in all my drawers to see that no article was left behind; and now, having nothing more to do, I sat down and tried to rest. I could not; though I had been on foot all day, I could not now repose an instant; I was too much excited. A phase of my life was closing to-night, a new one opening to-morrow: impossible to slumber in the interval; I must watch feverishly while the change was being accomplished.

"Miss," said a servant who met me in the lobby, where I was wandering like a troubled spirit, "a person below wishes to see you."

"The carrier, no doubt," I thought, and ran downstairs without enquiry. I was passing the back parlour, or teachers' sitting-room, the door of which was half open, to go to the kitchen, when some one ran out:—

"It's her, I am sure!—I could have told her anywhere!" cried the individual who stopped my progress and took my hand.

I looked: I saw a woman attired like a well-dressed servant, matronly, yet still young; very good-looking, with black hair and eyes, and lively complexion.

"Well, who is it?" she asked in a voice and with a smile I half recognised; "you've not quite forgotten me, I think, Miss Jane?"

In another second I was embracing and kissing her rapturously: "Bessie! Bessie! Bessie!" that was all I said; whereat she half laughed, half cried, and we both went into the parlour. By the fire stood a little fellow of three years old, in plaid frock and trousers.

"That is my little boy," said Bessie, directly.

"Then you are married, Bessie?"

"Yes: nearly five years since, to Robert Leaven, the coachman; and I've a little girl besides Bobby there, that I've christened Jane."

"And you don't live at Gateshead?"

"I live at the lodge: the old porter has left."

"Well, and how do they all get on? Tell me everything about them, Bessie: but sit down first; and, Bobby, come and sit on my knee, will you?" but Bobby preferred sidling over to his mother.

"You're not grown so very tall, Miss Jane, nor so very stout," continued Mrs. Leaven. "I dare say they've not kept you too well at school; Miss Reed is the head and shoulders taller than you are; and Miss Georgiana would make two of you in breadth."

"Georgiana is handsome, I suppose, Bessie?"

"Very. She went up to London last winter with her mama, and there everybody admired her, and a young lord fell in love with her: but his relations were against the match; and—what do you think?—he and Miss Georgiana made it up to run away: but they were found out and stopped. It was Miss Reed that found them out: I believe she was envious; and now she and her sister lead a cat and dog life together; they are always quarrelling."

"Well, and what of John Reed?"

"Oh, he is not doing so well as his mama could wish. He went to college, and he got—plucked, I think they call it: and then his uncles wanted him to be a barrister, and study the law: but he is such a dissipated young man, they will never make much of him, I think."

"What does he look like?"

"He is very tall: some people call him a fine looking young man; but he has such thick lips."

"And Mrs. Reed?"

"Missis looks stout and well enough in the face, but I think she's not quite easy in her mind: Mr. John's conduct does not please her—he spends a deal of money."

"Did she send you here, Bessie?"

"No, indeed: but I have long wanted to see you, and when I heard that there had been a letter from you, and that you were going to another part of the country, I thought I'd just set off, and get a look at you before you were quite out of my reach."

"I am afraid you are disappointed in me, Bessie." I said this laughing: I perceived that Bessie's glance, though it expressed regard, did in no shape denote admiration.

"No, Miss Jane, not exactly: you are genteel enough; you look like a lady, and it is as much as ever I expected of you: you were no beauty as a child."

I smiled at Bessie's frank answer: I felt that it was correct, but I confess I was not quite indifferent to its import: at eighteen most people wish to please, and the conviction that they have not an exterior likely to second that desire brings anything but gratification.

"I dare say you are clever, though," continued Bessie, by way of solace. "What can you do? Can you play on the piano?"

"A little."

There was one in the room; Bessie went and opened it, and then asked me to sit down and give her a tune: I played a waltz or two, and she was charmed.

"The Miss Reeds could not play as well!" said she exultingly, "I always said you would surpass them in learning: and can you draw?"

"That is one of my paintings over the chimney-piece." It was a landscape in water colours, of which I had made a present to the superintendent, in acknowledgment of her obliging mediation with the committee on my behalf, and which she had framed and glazed.

"Well, that is beautiful, Miss Jane! It is as fine a picture as any Miss Reed's drawing-master could paint, let alone the young ladies themselves, who could not come near it: and have you learnt French?"

"Yes, Bessie, I can both read it and speak it."

"And you can work on muslin and canvass?"

"I can."

"Oh, you are quite a lady, Miss Jane! I knew you would be: you will get on whether your relations notice you or not. There was something I wanted to ask you. Have you ever heard anything from your father's kinsfolk, the Eyres?"

"Never in my life."

"Well, you know Missis always said they were poor and quite despicable: and they may be poor; but I believe they are as much gentry as the Reeds are; for one day, nearly seven years ago, a Mr. Eyre came to Gateshead and wanted to see you; Missis said you were at school fifty miles off; he seemed so much disappointed, for he could not stay: he was going on a voyage to a foreign country, and the ship was to sail from London in a day or two. He looked quite a gentleman, and I believe he was your father's brother."

"What foreign country was he going to, Bessie?"

"An island thousands of miles off, where they make wine—the butler did tell me"——

"Madeira!" I suggested.

"Yes, that is it—that is the very word."

"So he went?"

"Yes; he did not stay many minutes in the house: Missis was very high with him; she called him afterwards a 'sneaking tradesman.' My Robert believes he was a wine-merchant."

"Very likely," I returned; "or perhaps clerk or agent to a wine-merchant."

Bessie and I conversed about old times an hour longer, and then she was obliged to leave me: I saw her again for a few minutes the next morning at Lowton, while I was waiting for the coach. We parted finally at the door of the Brocklehurst Arms there: each went her separate way; she set off for the brow of Lowood Fell to meet the conveyance which was to take her back to Gateshead, I mounted the vehicle which was to bear me to new duties and a new life in the unknown environs of Millcote.

Chapter XI

A NEW chapter in a novel is something like a new scene in a play; and when I draw up the curtain this time, reader, you must fancy you see a room in the George Inn at Millcote, with such large figured papering on the walls as inn rooms have; such a carpet, such furniture, such ornaments on the mantel-piece, such prints; including a portrait of George the Third, and another of the Prince of Wales, and a representation of the death of Wolfe. All this is visible to you by the light of an oil lamp hanging from the ceiling, and by that of an excellent fire, near which I sit in my cloak and bonnet; my muff and umbrella lie on the table, and I am warming away the numbness and chill contracted by sixteen hours' exposure to the rawness of an October day: I left Lowton at four o'clock A.M., and the Millcote town clock is now just striking eight.

Reader, though I look comfortably accommodated, I am not very tranquil in my mind. I thought when the coach stopped here there would be some one to meet me; I looked anxiously round as I descended the wooden steps the "boots" placed for my convenience, expecting to hear my name pronounced, and to see some description of carriage waiting to convey me to Thornfield. Nothing of the sort was visible: and when I asked a waiter if any one had been to inquire after a Miss Eyre, I was answered in the negative: so I had no resource but to request to be shown into a private room: and here I am waiting, while all sorts of doubts and fears are troubling my thoughts.

It is a very strange sensation to inexperienced youth to feel itself quite alone in the world, cut adrift from every connection, uncertain whether the port to which it is bound can be reached, and prevented by many impediments from returning to that it has quitted. The charm of adventure sweetens that sensation, the glow of pride warms it; but then the throb of fear disturbs it; and fear with me became predominant, when half an hour elapsed and still I was alone. I bethought myself to ring the bell.

"Is there a place in this neighbourhood called Thornfield?" I asked of the waiter who answered the summons.

"Thornfield? I don't know, ma'am; I'll enquire at the bar." He vanished, but reappeared instantly:—

"Is your name Eyre, Miss?"

"Yes."

"Person here waiting for you."

I jumped up, took my muff and umbrella, and hastened into the inn-passage: a man was standing by the open door, and in the lamp-lit street I dimly saw a one-horse conveyance.

"This will be your luggage, I suppose?" said the man rather abruptly when he saw me, pointing to my trunk in the passage.

"Yes." He hoisted it on to the vehicle, which was a sort of car, and then I got in: before he shut me up, I asked him how far it was to Thornfield.

"A matter of six miles."

"How long shall we be before we get there?"

"Happen an hour and a half."

He fastened the car door, climbed to his own seat outside, and we set off. Our progress was leisurely, and gave me ample time to reflect: I was content to be at length so near the end of my journey; and as I leaned back in the comfortable though not elegant conveyance, I meditated much at my ease.

"I suppose," thought I, "judging from the plainness of the servant and carriage, Mrs. Fairfax is not a very dashing person: so much the better; I never lived amongst fine people but once, and I was very miserable with them. I wonder if she lives alone except this little girl; if so, and if she is in any degree amiable, I shall surely be able to get on with her; I will do my best: it is a pity that doing one's best does not always answer. At Lowood, indeed, I took that resolution, kept it, and succeeded in pleasing; but with Mrs. Reed, I remember my best was always spurned with scorn. I pray God Mrs. Fairfax may not turn out a second Mrs. Reed; but if she does, I am not bound to stay with her: let the worst come to the worst, I can advertise again. How far are we on our road now, I wonder?"

I let down the window and looked out: Millcote was behind us; judging by the number of its lights, it seemed a place of considerable magnitude, much larger than Lowton. We were now, as far as I could see, on a sort of common; but there were houses scattered all over the district; I felt we were in a different region to Lowood, more populous, less picturesque; more stirring, less romantic.

The roads were heavy, the night misty; my conductor let his horse walk all the way, and the hour and a half extended, I verily believe, to two hours; at last he turned in his seat and said:—

"You're noan so far fro' Thornfield now."

Again I looked out: we were passing a church: I saw its low broad tower against the sky, and its bell was tolling a quarter; I saw a narrow galaxy of lights too, on a hill-side, marking a village or hamlet. About ten minutes after, the driver got down and opened a pair of gates; we passed through, and they clashed to behind us. We now slowly ascended a drive, and came upon the long front of a house: candle-light gleamed from one curtained bow-window; all the rest were dark. The car stopped at the front door; it was opened by a maid-servant: I alighted and went in.

"Will you walk this way, ma'am," said the girl: and I followed her across a square hall with high doors all round: she ushered me into a room whose double illumination of fire and candle at first dazzled me, contrasting as it did with the darkness to which my eyes had been for two hours inured; when I could see, however, a cozy and agreeable picture presented itself to my view.

A snug, small room; a round table by a cheerful fire; an arm-chair high-backed and old-fashioned, wherein sat the neatest imaginable little elderly lady, in widow's cap, black silk gown and snowy muslin apron; exactly like what I had fancied Mrs. Fairfax, only less stately and milder looking. She was occupied in knitting; a large cat sat demurely at her feet; nothing in short was wanting to complete the beau-ideal of domestic comfort. A more reassuring introduction for a new governess could scarcely be conceived: there was no grandeur to overwhelm, no stateliness to embarrass; and then, as I entered, the old lady got up, and promptly and kindly came forward to meet me.

"How do you do, my dear? I am afraid you have had a tedious ride; John drives so slowly: you must be cold, come to the fire."

"Mrs. Fairfax, I suppose?" said I.

"Yes, you are right: do sit down."

She conducted me to her own chair, and then began to remove my shawl and untie my bonnet-strings: I begged she would not give herself so much trouble.

"Oh, it is no trouble; I dare say your own hands are almost numbed with cold. Leah, make a little hot negus and cut a sandwich or two: here are the keys of the store-room."

And she produced from her pocket a most housewifely bunch of keys, and delivered them to the servant.

"Now, then, draw nearer to the fire," she continued. "You've brought your luggage with you, haven't you, my dear?"

"Yes, ma'am."

"I'll see it carried into your room," she said, and bustled out.

"She treats me like a visitor," thought I. "I little expected such a reception; I anticipated only coldness and stiffness: this is not like what I have heard of the treatment of governesses; but I must not exult too soon."

She returned; with her own hands cleared her knitting apparatus and a book or two from the table, to make room for the tray which Leah now brought, and then herself handed me the refreshments. I felt rather confused at being the object of more attention than I had ever before received, and that, too, shown by my employer and superior; but as she did not herself seem to consider she was doing anything out of her place, I thought it better to take her civilities quietly.

"Shall I have the pleasure of seeing Miss Fairfax tonight?" I asked, when I had partaken of what she offered me.

"What did you say, my dear? I am a little deaf," returned the good lady, approaching her ear to my mouth.

I repeated the question more distinctly.

"Miss Fairfax? Oh, you mean Miss Varens! Varens is the name of your future pupil."

"Indeed! Then she is not your daughter?"

"No,—I have no family."

I should have followed up my first inquiry, by asking in what way Miss Varens was connected with her; but I recollected it was not polite to ask too many questions: besides, I was sure to hear in time.

"I am so glad," she continued, as she sat down opposite to me, and took the cat on her knee; "I am so glad you are come; it will be quite pleasant living here now with a companion. To be sure it is pleasant at any time; for Thornfield is a fine old hall, rather neglected of late years perhaps, but still it is a respectable place; yet you know in winter time one feels dreary quite alone, in the best quarters.

I say alone—Leah is a nice girl to be sure, and John and his wife are very decent people; but then you see they are only servants, and one can't converse with them on terms of equality: one must keep them at due distance, for fear of losing one's authority. I'm sure last winter (it was a very severe one, if you recollect, and when it did not snow, it rained and blew), not a creature but the butcher and postman came to the house, from November till February; and I really got quite melancholy with sitting night after night alone; I had Leah in to read to me sometimes; but I don't think the poor girl liked the task much: she felt it confining. In spring and summer one got on better: sunshine and long days make such a difference; and then, just at the commencement of this autumn, little Adela Varens came and her nurse: a child makes a house alive all at once; and now you are here I shall be quite gay.''

My heart really warmed to the worthy lady as I heard her talk; and I drew my chair a little nearer to her, and expressed my sincere wish that she might find my company as agreeable as she anticipated.

''But I'll not keep you sitting up late to-night,'' said she; ''it is on the stroke of twelve now, and you have been travelling all day: you must feel tired. If you have got your feet well warmed, I'll show you your bed-room. I've had the room next to mine prepared for you; it is only a small apartment, but I thought you would like it better than one of the large front chambers: to be sure they have finer furniture, but they are so dreary and solitary, I never sleep in them myself.''

I thanked her for her considerate choice, and as I really felt fatigued with my long journey, expressed my readiness to retire. She took her candle, and I followed her from the room. First she went to see if the hall-door was fastened; having taken the key from the lock, she led the way upstairs. The steps and banisters were of oak; the staircase window was high and latticed; both it and the long gallery into which the bed-room doors opened, looked as if they belonged to a church rather than a house. A very chill and vault-like air pervaded the stairs and gallery, suggesting cheerless ideas of space and solitude; and I was glad, when finally ushered into my chamber, to find it of small dimensions, and furnished in ordinary modern style.

When Mrs. Fairfax had bidden me a kind good-night, and I had fastened my door, gazed leisurely round, and in some measure effaced the eerie impression made by that wide hall, that dark and spacious staircase, and that long, cold gallery, by the livelier aspect of my little room, I remembered that after a day of bodily fatigue and mental anxiety, I was now at last in safe haven. The impulse of gratitude swelled my heart, and I knelt down at the bedside, and offered up thanks where thanks were due; not forgetting, ere I rose, to implore aid on my further path, and the power of meriting the kindness which seemed so frankly offered me before it was earned. My couch had no thorns in it that night; my solitary room no fears. At once weary and content, I slept soon and soundly: when I awoke it was broad day.

The chamber looked such a bright little place to me as the sun shone in between the gay blue chintz window curtains, showing papered walls and a carpeted floor, so unlike the bare planks and stained plaster of Lowood, that my spirits rose at the view. Externals have a great effect on the young: I thought that a fairer era of life was beginning for me, one that was to have its flowers and pleasures, as well as its thorns and toils. My faculties, roused by the change of scene, the new field offered to hope, seemed all astir. I cannot precisely define what they expected, but it was something pleasant: not perhaps that day or that month, but at an indefinite future period.

I rose; I dressed myself with care: obliged to be plain—for I had no article of attire that was not made with extreme simplicity—I was still by nature solicitous to be neat. It was not my habit to be disregardful of appearance, or careless of the impression I made: on the contrary, I ever wished to look as well as I could, and

to please as much as my want of beauty would permit. I sometimes regretted that I was not handsomer: I sometimes wished to have rosy cheeks, a straight nose, and small cherry mouth; I desired to be tall, stately, and finely developed in figure; I felt it a misfortune that I was so little, so pale, and had features so irregular and so marked. And why had I these aspirations and these regrets? It would be difficult to say: I could not then distinctly say it to myself; yet I had a reason, and a logical, natural reason too. However, when I had brushed my hair very smooth, and put on my black frock—which, Quakerlike as it was, at least had the merit of fitting to a nicety—and adjusted my clean white tucker, I thought I should do respectably enough to appear before Mrs. Fairfax; and that my new pupil would not at least recoil from me with antipathy. Having opened my chamber window, and seen that I left all things straight and neat on the toilet table, I ventured forth.

Traversing the long and matted gallery, I descended the slippery steps of oak; then I gained the hall: I halted there a minute; I looked at some pictures on the walls (one I remember represented a grim man in a cuirass, and one a lady with powdered hair and a pearl necklace), at a bronze lamp pendent from the ceiling, at a great clock whose case was of oak curiously carved, and ebon black with time and rubbing. Everything appeared very stately and imposing to me: but then I was so little accustomed to grandeur. The hall-door, which was half of glass, stood open; I stepped over the threshold. It was a fine autumn morning; the early sun shone serenely on embrowned groves and still green fields: advancing on to the lawn, I looked up and surveyed the front of the mansion. It was three stories high, of proportions not vast, though considerable: a gentleman's manorhouse, not a nobleman's seat: battlements round the top gave it a picturesque look. Its grey front stood out well from the background of a rookery, whose cawing tenants were now on the wing: they flew over the lawn and grounds to alight in a great meadow, from which these were separated by a sunk fence, and where an array of mighty old thorn trees, strong, knotty, and broad as oaks, at once explained the etymology of the mansion's designation. Farther off were hills: not so lofty as those round Lowood, nor so craggy, nor so like barriers of separation from the living world; but yet quiet and lonely hills enough, and seeming to embrace Thornfield with a seclusion I had not expected to find existent so near the stirring locality of Millcote. A little hamlet, whose roofs were blent with trees, straggled up the side of one of these hills; the church of the district stood nearer Thornfield: its old tower-top looked over a knoll between the house and gates.

I was yet enjoying the calm prospect and pleasant fresh air, yet listening with delight to the cawing of the rooks, yet surveying the wide, hoary front of the hall, and thinking what a great place it was for one lonely little dame like Mrs. Fairfax to inhabit, when that lady appeared at the door.

"What! out already?" said she. "I see you are an early riser." I went up to her, and was received with an affable kiss and shake of the hand.

"How do you like Thornfield?" she asked. I told her I liked it very much.

"Yes," she said, "it is a pretty place; but I fear it will be getting out of order, unless Mr. Rochester should take it into his head to come and reside here permanently; or, at least, visit it rather oftener: great houses and fine grounds require the presence of the proprietor."

"Mr. Rochester!" I exclaimed. "Who is he?"

"The owner of Thornfield," she responded quietly. "Did you not know he was called Rochester?"

Of course I did not—I had never heard of him before; but the old lady seemed to regard his existence as a universally understood fact, with which everybody must be acquainted by instinct.

"I thought," I continued, "Thornfield belonged to you."

"To me? Bless you, child; what an idea! To me? I am only the housekeeper—the manager. To be sure I am distantly related to the Rochesters by the mother's

side; or, at least, my husband was: he was a clergyman, incumbent of Hay—that little village yonder on the hill—and that church near the gates was his. The present Mr. Rochester's mother was a Fairfax, and second cousin to my husband; but I never presume on the connection—in fact it is nothing to me; I consider myself quite in the light of an ordinary housekeeper: my employer is always civil, and I expect nothing more.''

''And the little girl—my pupil?''

''She is Mr. Rochester's ward; he commissioned me to find a governess for her. He intends to have her brought up in ——shire, I believe. Here she comes, with her 'bonne,' as she calls her nurse.'' The enigma then was explained: this affable and kind little widow was no great dame, but a dependant like myself. I did not like her the worse for that; on the contrary, I felt better pleased than ever. The equality between her and me was real; not the mere result of condescension on her part: so much the better—my position was all the freer.

As I was meditating on this discovery, a little girl, followed by her attendant, came running up the lawn. I looked at my pupil, who did not at first appear to notice me: she was quite a child, perhaps seven or eight years old, slightly built, with a pale, small-featured face, and a redundancy of hair falling in curls to her waist.

''Good morning, Miss Adela,'' said Mrs. Fairfax. ''Come and speak to the lady who is to teach you, and to make you a clever woman some day.'' She approached.

''C'est là ma gouvernante?'' said she, pointing to me, and addressing her nurse; who answered:

''Mais oui, certainement.''

''Are they foreigners?'' I inquired, amazed at hearing the French language.

''The nurse is a foreigner, and Adela was born on the Continent; and, I believe, never left it till within six months ago. When she first came here she could speak no English; now she can make shift to talk it a little: I don't understand her, she mixes it so with French; but you will make out her meaning very well, I daresay.''

Fortunately I had had the advantage of being taught French by a French lady; and as I had always made a point of conversing with Madame Pierrot, as often as I could, and had, besides, during the last seven years, learnt a portion of French by heart daily—applying myself to take pains with my accent, and imitating as closely as possible the pronunciation of my teacher—I had acquired a certain degree of readiness and correctness in the language, and was not likely to be much at a loss with Mademoiselle Adela. She came and shook hands with me when she heard that I was her governess; and as I led her in to breakfast, I addressed some phrases to her in her own tongue: she replied briefly at first, but after we were seated at the table, and she had examined me some ten minutes with her large hazel eyes, she suddenly commenced chattering fluently.

''Ah,'' cried she, in French, ''you speak my language as well as Mr. Rochester does: I can talk to you as I can to him, and so can Sophie. She will be glad: nobody here understands her: Madame Fairfax is all English. Sophie is my nurse; she came with me over the sea in a great ship with a chimney that smoked—how it did smoke!—and I was sick, and so was Sophie, and so was Mr. Rochester. Mr. Rochester lay down on a sofa in a pretty room called the salon, and Sophie and I had little beds in another place. I nearly fell out of mine; it was like a shelf. And, Mademoiselle——what is your name?''

''Eyre—Jane Eyre.''

''Eyre? Bah! I cannot say it. Well: our ship stopped in the morning, before it was quite daylight, at a great city—a huge city, with very dark houses and all smoky; not at all like the pretty clean town I came from; and Mr. Rochester carried me in his arms over a plank to the land, and Sophie came after, and we all got into a coach, which took us to a beautiful large house, larger than this and finer, called an hotel. We stayed there nearly a week: I and Sophie used to walk every

day in a great green place full of trees, called the Park; and there were many children there besides me, and a pond with beautiful birds in it, that I fed with crumbs.''

"Can you understand her when she runs on so fast?'' asked Mrs. Fairfax.

I understood her very well, for I had been accustomed to the fluent tongue of Madame Pierrot.

"I wish,'' continued the good lady, "you would ask her a question or two about her parents: I wonder if she remembers them?''

"Adèle,'' I inquired, "with whom did you live when you were in that pretty clean town you spoke of?''

"I lived long ago with mama; but she is gone to the Holy Virgin. Mama used to teach me to dance and sing, and to say verses. A great many gentlemen and ladies came to see mama, and I used to dance before them, or to sit on their knees and sing to them: I liked it. Shall I let you hear me sing now?''

She had finished her breakfast, so I permitted her to give a specimen of her accomplishments. Descending from her chair, she came and placed herself on my knee; then, folding her little hands demurely before her, shaking back her curls and lifting her eyes to the ceiling, she commenced singing a song from some opera. It was the strain of a forsaken lady, who, after bewailing the perfidy of her lover, calls pride to her aid; desires her attendant to deck her in her brightest jewels and richest robes, and resolves to meet the false one that night at a ball, and prove to him, by the gaiety of her demeanour, how little his desertion had affected her.

The subject seemed strangely chosen for an infant singer; but I suppose the point of the exhibition lay in hearing the notes of love and jealousy warbled with the lisp of childhood; and in very bad taste that point was: at least I thought so.

Adèle sang the canzonette tunefully enough, and with the naïveté of her age. This achieved, she jumped from my knee and said, "Now, Mademoiselle, I will repeat you some poetry.''

Assuming an attitude, she began "La Ligue des Rats, fable de La Fontaine.'' She then declaimed the little piece with an attention to punctuation and emphasis, a flexibility of voice and an appropriateness of gesture, very unusual indeed at her age, and which proved she had been carefully trained.

"Was it your mama who taught you that piece?'' I asked.

"Yes, and she just used to say it in this way: 'Qu'avez vous donc? lui dit un de ces rats; parlez!' She made me lift my hand—so—to remind me to raise my voice at the question. Now shall I dance for you?''

"No, that will do: but after your mama went to the Holy Virgin, as you say, with whom did you live then?''

"With Madame Frédéric and her husband: she took care of me, but she is nothing related to me. I think she is poor, for she had not so fine a house as mama. I was not long there. Mr. Rochester asked me if I would like to go and live with him in England, and I said yes; for I knew Mr. Rochester before I knew Madame Frédéric, and he was always kind to me and gave me pretty dresses and toys: but you see he has not kept his word, for he has brought me to England, and now he has gone back again himself, and I never see him.''

After breakfast, Adèle and I withdrew to the library; which room, it appears, Mr. Rochester had directed should be used as the school-room. Most of the books were locked up behind glass doors; but there was one bookcase left open containing everything that could be needed in the way of elementary works, and several volumes of light literature, poetry, biography, travels, a few romances, etc. I suppose he had considered that these were all the governess would require for her private perusal; and, indeed, they contented me amply for the present; compared with the scanty pickings I had now and then been able to glean at Lowood, they seemed to offer an abundant harvest of entertainment and information. In this room, too, there was a cabinet piano, quite new and of superior tone; also an easel for painting, and a pair of globes.

I found my pupil sufficiently docile, though disinclined to apply: she had not been used to regular occupation of any kind. I felt it would be injudicious to confine her too much at first; so, when I had talked to her a great deal, and got her to learn a little, and when the morning had advanced to noon, I allowed her to return to her nurse. I then proposed to occupy myself till dinner-time in drawing some little sketches for her use.

As I was going upstairs to fetch my portfolio and pencils, Mrs. Fairfax called to me: "Your morning school-hours are over now, I suppose," said she. She was in a room the folding-doors of which stood open: I went in when she addressed me. It was a large, stately apartment, with purple chairs and curtains, a Turkey carpet, walnut-panelled walls, one vast window rich in stained glass, and a lofty ceiling, nobly moulded. Mrs. Fairfax was dusting some vases of fine purple spar, which stood on a sideboard.

"What a beautiful room!" I exclaimed, as I looked round; for I had never before seen any half so imposing.

"Yes; this is the dining-room. I have just opened the window, to let in a little air and sunshine; for everything gets so damp in apartments that are seldom inhabited: the drawing-room yonder feels like a vault."

She pointed to a wide arch corresponding to the window, and hung like it with a Tyrian-dyed curtain, now looped up. Mounting to it by two broad steps and looking through, I thought I caught a glimpse of a fairy place, so bright to my novice-eyes appeared the view beyond. Yet it was merely a very pretty drawing-room, and within it a boudoir, both spread with white carpets, on which seemed laid brilliant garlands of flowers; both ceiled with snowy mouldings of white grapes and vine-leaves, beneath which glowed in rich contrast crimson couches and ottomans; while the ornaments on the pale Parian mantel-piece were of sparkling Bohemian glass, ruby red; and between the windows large mirrors repeated the general blending of snow and fire.

"In what order you keep these rooms, Mrs. Fairfax!" said I. "No dust, no canvass coverings: except that the air feels chilly, one would think they were inhabited daily."

"Why, Miss Eyre, though Mr. Rochester's visits here are rare, they are always sudden and unexpected; and as I observed that it put him out to find everything swathed up, and to have a bustle of arrangement on his arrival, I thought it best to keep the rooms in readiness."

"Is Mr. Rochester an exacting, fastidious sort of man?"

"Not particularly so; but he has a gentleman's tastes and habits, and he expects to have things managed in conformity to them."

"Do you like him? Is he generally liked?"

"Oh, yes; the family have always been respected here. Almost all the land in this neighbourhood, as far as you can see, has belonged to the Rochesters time out of mind."

"Well, but, leaving his land out of the question, do you like him? Is he liked for himself?"

"*I* have no cause to do otherwise than like him; and I believe he is considered a just and liberal landlord by his tenants: but he has never lived much amongst them."

"But has he no peculiarities? What, in short, is his character?"

"Oh! his character is unimpeachable, I suppose. He is rather peculiar, perhaps: he has travelled a great deal, and seen a great deal of the world, I should think. I dare say he is clever: but I never had much conversation with him."

"In what way is he peculiar?"

"I don't know—it is not easy to describe—nothing striking, but you feel it when he speaks to you: you cannot be always sure whether he is in jest or earnest, whether

he is pleased or the contrary; you don't thoroughly understand him, in short—at least, I don't: but it is of no consequence, he is a very good master.''

This was all the account I got from Mrs. Fairfax, of her employer and mine. There are people who seem to have no notion of sketching a character, or observing and describing salient points, either in persons or things: the good lady evidently belonged to this class; my queries puzzled, but did not draw her out. Mr. Rochester was Mr. Rochester in her eyes; a gentleman, a landed proprietor—nothing more: she inquired and searched no further, and evidently wondered at my wish to gain a more definite notion of his identity.

When we left the dining-room, she proposed to show me over the rest of the house; and I followed her upstairs and downstairs, admiring as I went; for all was well-arranged and handsome. The large front chambers I thought especially grand; and some of the third story rooms, though dark and low, were interesting from their air of antiquity. The furniture once appropriated to the lower apartments had from time to time been removed here, as fashions changed: and the imperfect light entering by their narrow casements showed bedsteads of a hundred years old; chests in oak or walnut, looking, with their strange carvings of palm branches and cherubs' heads, like types of the Hebrew ark; rows of venerable chairs, high-backed and narrow; stools still more antiquated, on whose cushioned tops were yet apparent traces of half-effaced embroideries, wrought by fingers that for two generations had been coffin-dust. All these relics gave to the third story of Thornfield Hall the aspect of a home of the past: a shrine of memory. I liked the hush, the gloom, the quaintness of these retreats in the day; but I by no means coveted a night's repose on one of those wide and heavy beds: shut in, some of them with doors of oak; shaded, others with wrought old English hangings crusted with thick work, portraying effigies of strange flowers, and stranger birds, and strangest human beings,—all which would have looked strange, indeed, by the pallid gleam of moonlight.

"Do the servants sleep in these rooms?" I asked.

"No; they occupy a range of smaller apartments to the back; no one ever sleeps here: one would almost say that, if there were a ghost at Thornfield Hall, this would be its haunts.''

"So I think: you have no ghost, then?"

"None that I ever heard of," returned Mrs. Fairfax, smiling.

"Nor any traditions of one? no legends or ghost stories?"

"I believe not. And yet it is said, the Rochesters have been rather a violent than a quiet race in their time: perhaps, though, that is the reason they rest tranquilly in their graves now.''

"Yes—'after life's fitful fever they sleep well,' " I muttered. "Where are you going now, Mrs. Fairfax?" for she was moving away.

"On to the leads; will you come and see the view from thence?" I followed still, up a very narrow staircase to the attics, and thence by a ladder and through a trap-door to the roof of the hall. I was now on a level with the crow colony, and could see into their nests. Leaning over the battlements and looking far down, I surveyed the grounds laid out like a map: the bright and velvet lawn closely girding the grey base of the mansion; the field, wide as a park, dotted with its ancient timber; the wood, dun and sere, divided by a path visibly overgrown, greener with moss than the trees were with foliage; the church at the gates, the road, the tranquil hills, all reposing in the autumn day's sun; the horizon bounded by a propitious sky, azure, marbled with pearly white. No feature in the scene was extraordinary, but all was pleasing. When I turned from it and repassed the trap-door, I could scarcely see my way down the ladder; the attic seemed black as a vault compared with that arch of blue air to which I had been looking up, and to that sunlit scene of grove, pasture, and green hill of which the hall was the centre, and over which I had been gazing with delight.

Mrs. Fairfax stayed behind a moment to fasten the trap-door; I, by dint of groping, found the outlet from the attic, and proceeded to descend the narrow garret staircase. I lingered in the long passage to which this led, separating the front and back rooms of the third story: narrow, low, and dim, with only one little window at the far end, and looking, with its two rows of small black doors all shut, like a corridor in some Bluebeard's castle.

While I paced softly on, the last sound I expected to hear in so still a region, a laugh, struck my ear. It was a curious laugh; distinct, formal, mirthless. I stopped: the sound ceased, only for an instant; it began again, louder: for at first, though distinct, it was very low. It passed off in a clamorous peal that seemed to wake an echo in every lonely chamber; though it originated but in one, and I could have pointed out the door whence the accents issued.

"Mrs. Fairfax!" I called out: for I now heard her descending the great stairs. "Did you hear that loud laugh? Who is it?"

"Some of the servants, very likely," she answered: "perhaps Grace Poole."

"Did you hear it?" I again inquired.

"Yes, plainly: I often hear her; she sews in one of these rooms. Sometimes Leah is with her: they are frequently noisy together."

The laugh was repeated in its low, syllabic tone, and terminated in an odd murmur.

"Grace!" exclaimed Mrs. Fairfax.

I really did not expect any Grace to answer; for the laugh was as tragic, as preternatural a laugh as any I ever heard; and, but that it was high noon, and that no circumstance of ghostliness accompanied the curious cachinnation, but that neither scene nor season favoured fear, I should have been superstitiously afraid. However, the event showed me I was a fool for entertaining a sense even of surprise.

The door nearest me opened, and a servant came out,—a woman of between thirty and forty; a set, square-made figure, red-haired, and with a hard, plain face: any apparition less romantic or less ghostly could scarcely be conceived.

"Too much noise, Grace," said Mrs. Fairfax. "Remember directions!" Grace curtseyed silently and went in.

"She is a person we have to sew and assist Leah in her housemaid's work," continued the widow; "not altogether unobjectionable in some points, but she does well enough. By-the-bye, how have you got on with your new pupil this morning?"

The conversation, thus turned on Adèle, continued till we reached the light and cheerful region below. Adèle came running to meet us in the hall, exclaiming—

"Mesdames, vous êtes servies!" adding, "J'ai bien faim, moi!"

We found dinner ready, and waiting for us in Mrs. Fairfax's room.

Chapter XII

THE promise of a smooth career, which my first calm introduction to Thornfield Hall seemed to pledge, was not belied on a longer acquaintance with the place and its inmates. Mrs. Fairfax turned out to be what she appeared, a placid-tempered, kind-natured woman, of competent education and average intelligence. My pupil was a lively child, who had been spoilt and indulged, and therefore was sometimes wayward; but as she was committed entirely to my care, and no injudicious interference from any quarter ever thwarted my plans for her improvement, she soon forgot her little freaks, and became obedient and teachable. She had no great talents, no marked traits of character, no peculiar development of feeling or taste which raised her one inch above the ordinary level of childhood; but neither had she any deficiency or vice which sunk her below it. She made reasonable progress, entertained for me a vivacious, though perhaps not very profound, affection; and by her simplicity,

gay prattle, and efforts to please, inspired me, in return, with a degree of attachment sufficient to make us both content in each other's society.

This, *par parenthèse,* will be thought cool language by persons who entertain solemn doctrines about the angelic nature of children, and the duty of those charged with their education to conceive for them an idolatrous devotion: but I am not writing to flatter paternal egotism, to echo cant, or prop up humbug; I am merely telling the truth. I felt a conscientious solicitude for Adèle's welfare and progress, and a quiet liking to her little self; just as I cherished towards Mrs. Fairfax a thankfulness for her kindness, and a pleasure in her society proportionate to the tranquil regard she had for me, and the moderation of her mind and character.

Anybody may blame me who likes, when I add further, that, now and then, when I took a walk by myself in the grounds; when I went down to the gates and looked through them along the road; or when, while Adèle played with her nurse, and Mrs. Fairfax made jellies in the store-room, I climbed the three staircases, raised the trap-door of the attic, and having reached the leads, looked out afar over sequestered field and hill, and along dim sky-line—that then I longed for a power of vision which might overpass that limit; which might reach the busy world, towns, regions full of life I had heard of but never seen: that then I desired more of practical experience than I possessed; more of intercourse with my kind, of acquaintance with variety of character, than was here within my reach. I valued what was good in Mrs. Fairfax, and what was good in Adèle; but I believed in the existence of other and more vivid kinds of goodness, and what I believed in I wished to behold.

Who blames me? Many, no doubt; and I shall be called discontented. I could not help it: the restlessness was in my nature; it agitated me to pain sometimes. Then my sole relief was to walk along the corridor of the third story, backwards and forwards, safe in the silence and solitude of the spot, and allow my mind's eye to dwell on whatever bright visions rose before it—and, certainly, they were many and glowing; to let my heart be heaved by the exultant movement, which, while it swelled it in trouble, expanded it with life; and best of all, to open my inward ear to a tale that was never ended—a tale my imagination created, and narrated continuously; quickened with all of incident, life, fire, feeling, that I desired and had not in my actual existence.

It is in vain to say human beings ought to be satisfied with tranquillity: they must have action; and they will make it if they cannot find it. Millions are condemned to a stiller doom than mine, and millions are in silent revolt against their lot. Nobody knows how many rebellions besides political rebellions ferment in the masses of life which people earth. Women are supposed to be very calm generally: but women feel just as men feel; they need exercise for their faculties, and a field for their efforts as much as their brothers do; they suffer from too rigid a constraint, too absolute a stagnation, precisely as men would suffer; and it is narrow-minded in their more privileged fellow-creatures to say that they ought to confine themselves to making puddings and knitting stockings, to playing on the piano and embroidering bags. It is thoughtless to condemn them, or laugh at them, if they seek to do more or learn more than custom has pronounced necessary for their sex.

When thus alone, I not unfrequently heard Grace Poole's laugh: the same peal, the same low, slow ha! ha! which, when first heard, had thrilled me: I heard, too, her eccentric murmurs; stranger than her laugh. There were days when she was quite silent; but there were others when I could not account for the sounds she made. Sometimes I saw her: she would come out of her room with a basin, or a plate, or a tray in her hand, go down to the kitchen and shortly return, generally (oh, romantic reader, forgive me for telling the plain truth!) bearing a pot of porter. Her appearance always acted as a damper to the curiosity raised by her oral oddities: hard-featured and staid, she had no point to which interest could attach. I made some attempts to draw her into conversation, but she seemed a person of few words: a monosyllabic reply usually cut short every effort of that sort.

The other members of the household, viz., John and his wife, Leah the housemaid, and Sophie the French nurse, were decent people; but in no respect remarkable: with Sophie I used to talk French, and sometimes I asked her questions about her native country; but she was not of a descriptive or narrative turn, and generally gave such vapid and confused answers as were calculated rather to check than encourage inquiry.

October, November, December passed away. One afternoon in January, Mrs. Fairfax had begged a holiday for Adèle, because she had a cold; and, as Adèle seconded the request with an ardour that reminded me how precious occasional holidays had been to me in my own childhood, I accorded it, deeming that I did well in showing pliability on the point. It was a fine, calm day, though very cold; I was tired of sitting still in the library through a whole long morning: Mrs. Fairfax had just written a letter which was waiting to be posted, so I put on my bonnet and cloak and volunteered to carry it to Hay; the distance, two miles, would be a pleasant winter afternoon walk. Having seen Adèle comfortably seated in her little chair by Mrs. Fairfax's parlour fireside, and given her her best wax doll (which I usually kept enveloped in silver paper in a drawer) to play with, and a story-book for change of amusement, and having replied to her ''Revenez bientôt, ma bonne amie, ma chère Mdlle. Jeannette,'' with a kiss, I set out.

The ground was hard, the air was still, my road was lonely; I walked fast till I got warm, and then I walked slowly to enjoy and analyse the species of pleasure brooding for me in the hour and situation. It was three o'clock; the church bell tolled as I passed under the belfry; the charm of the hour lay in its approaching dimness, in the low-gliding and pale-beaming sun. I was a mile from Thornfield, in a lane noted for wild roses in summer, for nuts and blackberries in autumn, and even now possessing a few coral treasures in hips and haws, but whose best winter delight lay in its utter solitude and leafless repose. If a breath of air stirred, it made no sound here; for there was not a holly, not an evergreen to rustle, and the stripped hawthorn and hazel bushes were as still as the white, worn stones which causewayed the middle of the path. Far and wide, on each side, there were only fields, where no cattle now browsed; and the little brown birds, which stirred occasionally in the hedge, looked like single russet leaves that had forgotten to drop.

This lane inclined up-hill all the way to Hay: having reached the middle, I sat down on a stile which led thence into a field. Gathering my mantle about me, and sheltering my hands in my muff, I did not feel the cold, though it froze keenly; as was attested by a sheet of ice covering the causeway, where a little brooklet, now congealed, had overflowed after a rapid thaw some days since. From my seat I could look down on Thornfield: the grey and battlemented hall was the principal object in the vale below me; its woods and dark rookery rose against the west. I lingered till the sun went down amongst the trees, and sank crimson and clear behind them. I then turned eastward.

On the hill-top above me sat the rising moon; pale yet as a cloud, but brightening momently: she looked over Hay, which, half lost in trees, sent up a blue smoke from its few chimneys; it was yet a mile distant, but in the absolute hush I could hear plainly its thin murmurs of life. My ear too felt the flow of currents; in what dales and depths I could not tell: but there were many hills beyond Hay, and doubtless many becks threading their passes. That evening calm betrayed alike the tinkle of the nearest streams, the sough of the most remote.

A rude noise broke on these fine ripplings and whisperings, at once so far away and so clear: a positive tramp, tramp; a metallic clatter, which effaced the soft wave-wanderings; as, in a picture, the solid mass of a crag, or the rough boles of a great oak, drawn in dark and strong on the foreground, efface the aërial distance of azure hill, sunny horizon, and blended clouds, where tint melts into tint.

The din was on the causeway: a horse was coming; the windings of the lane yet hid it, but it approached. I was just leaving the stile; yet, as the path was narrow,

I sat still to let it go by. In those days I was young, and all sorts of fancies bright and dark tenanted my mind: the memories of nursery stories were there amongst other rubbish; and when they recurred, maturing youth added to them a vigour and vividness beyond what childhood could give. As this horse approached, and as I watched for it to appear through the dusk, I remembered certain of Bessie's tales, wherein figured a North-of-England spirit, called a "Gytrash"; which, in the form of horse, mule, or large dog, haunted solitary ways, and sometimes came upon belated travellers, as this horse was now coming upon me.

It was very near, but not yet in sight; when, in addition to the tramp, tramp, I heard a rush under the hedge, and close down by the hazel stems glided a great dog, whose black and white colour made him a distinct object against the trees. It was exactly one mask of Bessie's Gytrash,—a lion-like creature with long hair and a huge head: it passed me, however, quietly enough; not staying to look up, with strange pretercanine eyes, in my face, as I half expected it would. The horse followed,—a tall steed, and on its back a rider. The man, the human being, broke the spell at once. Nothing ever rode the Gytrash: it was always alone; and goblins, to my notions, though they might tenant the dumb carcasses of beasts, could scarce covet shelter in the commonplace human form. No Gytrash was this,—only a traveller taking the short cut to Millcote. He passed, and I went on; a few steps, and I turned: a sliding sound and an exclamation of "What the deuce is to do now?" and a clattering tumble, arrested my attention. Man and horse were down; they had slipped on the sheet of ice which glazed the causeway. The dog came bounding back, and seeing his master in a predicament, and hearing the horse groan, barked till the evening hills echoed the sound, which was deep in proportion to his magnitude. He snuffed round the prostrate group, and then he ran up to me; it was all he could do,—there was no other help at hand to summon. I obeyed him, and walked down to the traveller, by this time struggling himself free of his steed. His efforts were so vigorous, I thought he could not be much hurt; but I asked him the question:—

"Are you injured, sir?"

I think he was swearing, but am not certain; however, he was pronouncing some formula which prevented him from replying to me directly.

"Can I do anything?" I asked again.

"You must stand on one side," he answered as he rose, first to his knees, and then to his feet. I did; whereupon began a heaving, stamping, clattering process, accompanied by a barking and baying which removed me effectually some yards distance; but I would not be driven quite away till I saw the event. This was finally fortunate; the horse was re-established, and the dog was silenced with a "Down, Pilot!" The traveller now, stooping, felt his foot and leg, as if trying whether they were sound; apparently something ailed them, for he halted to the stile whence I had just risen, and sat down.

I was in the mood for being useful, or at least officious, I think, for I now drew near him again.

"If you are hurt, and want help, sir, I can fetch some one either from Thornfield Hall or from Hay."

"Thank you; I shall do: I have no broken bones,—only a sprain;" and again he stood up and tried his foot, but the result extorted an involuntary "Ugh!"

Something of daylight still lingered, and the moon was waxing bright: I could see him plainly. His figure was enveloped in a riding cloak, fur collared, and steel clasped; its details were not apparent, but I traced the general points of middle height, and considerable breadth of chest. He had a dark face, with stern features and a heavy brow; his eyes and gathered eyebrows looked ireful and thwarted just now; he was past youth, but had not reached middle age; perhaps he might be thirty-five. I felt no fear of him, and but little shyness. Had he been a handsome, heroic-looking young gentleman, I should not have dared to stand thus questioning

him against his will, and offering my services unasked. I had hardly ever seen a handsome youth; never in my life spoken to one. I had a theoretical reverence and homage for beauty, elegance, gallantry, fascination; but had I met those qualities incarnate in masculine shape, I should have known instinctively that they neither had nor could haye sympathy with anything in me, and should have shunned them as one would fire, lightning, or anything else that is bright but antipathetic.

If even this stranger had smiled and been good-humoured to me when I addressed him; if he had put off my offer of assistance gaily and with thanks, I should have gone on my way and not felt any vocation to renew inquiries: but the frown, the roughness of the traveller set me at my ease: I retained my station when he waved to me to go, and announced:—

"I cannot think of leaving you, sir, at so late an hour, in this solitary lane, till I see you are fit to mount your horse."

He looked at me when I said this: he had hardly turned his eyes in my direction before.

"I should think you ought to be at home yourself," said he, "if you have a home in this neighbourhood: where do you come from?"

"From just below; and I am not at all afraid of being out late when it is moonlight: I will run over to Hay for you with pleasure, if you wish it; indeed, I am going there to post a letter."

"You live just below—do you mean at that house with the battlements?"— pointing to Thornfield Hall, on which the moon cast a hoary gleam, bringing it out distinct and pale from the woods, that, by contrast with the western sky, now seemed one mass of shadow.

"Yes, sir."

"Whose house is it?"

"Mr. Rochester's."

"Do you know Mr. Rochester?"

"No, I have never seen him."

"He is not resident, then?"

"No."

"Can you tell me where he is?"

"I cannot."

"You are not a servant at the hall, of course. You are"——He stopped, ran his eye over my dress, which, as usual, was quite simple: a black merino cloak, a black beaver bonnet; neither of them half fine enough for a lady's maid. He seemed puzzled to decide what I was: I helped him.

"I am the governess."

"Ah, the governess!" he repeated; "deuce take me, if I had not forgotten! The governess!" and again my raiment underwent scrutiny. In two minutes he rose from the stile: his face expressed pain when he tried to move.

"I cannot commission you to fetch help," he said; "but you may help me a little yourself, if you will be so kind."

"Yes, sir."

"You have not an umbrella that I can use as a stick?"

"No."

"Try to get hold of my horse's bridle and lead him to me: you are not afraid?"

I should have been afraid to touch a horse when alone, but when told to do it, I was disposed to obey. I put down my muff on the stile, and went up to the tall steed; I endeavoured to catch the bridle, but it was a spirited thing, and would not let me come near its head; I made effort on effort, though in vain: meantime, I was mortally afraid of its trampling forefeet. The traveller waited and watched for some time, and at last he laughed.

"I see," he said, "the mountain will never be brought to Mahomet, so all you can do is to aid Mahomet to go to the mountain; I must beg of you to come here."

I came. "Excuse me," he continued; "necessity compels me to make you useful."
He laid a heavy hand on my shoulder, and leaning on me with some stress, limped
to his horse. Having once caught the bridle, he mastered it directly, and sprang to
his saddle; grimacing grimly as he made the effort, for it wrenched his sprain.

"Now," said he, releasing his under lip from a hard bite, "just hand me my
whip; it lies there under the hedge."

I sought it and found it.

"Thank you; now make haste with the letter to Hay, and return as fast as you
can."

A touch of a spurred heel made his horse first start and rear, and then bound
away; the dog rushed in his traces: all three vanished,

> *"Like heath that, in the wilderness,*
> *The wild wind whirls away."*

I took up my muff and walked on. The incident had occurred and was gone for
me: it *was* an incident of no moment, no romance, no interest in a sense; yet it
marked with change one single hour of a monotonous life. My help had been needed
and claimed; I had given it: I was pleased to have done something; trivial, transitory
though the deed was, it was yet an active thing, and I was weary of an existence
all passive. The new face, too, was like a new picture introduced to the gallery of
memory; and it was dissimilar to all the others hanging there: firstly, because it
was masculine; and, secondly, because it was dark, strong, and stern. I had it still
before me when I entered Hay, and slipped the letter into the post-office; I saw it
as I walked fast down hill all the way home. When I came to the stile, I stopped
a minute, looked round and listened, with an idea that a horse's hoofs might ring
on the causeway again, and that a rider in a cloak, and a Gytrash-like Newfoundland
dog, might be again apparent: I saw only the hedge and a pollard willow before
me, rising up still and straight to meet the moonbeams; I heard only the faintest
waft of wind roaming fitful among the trees round Thornfield, a mile distant; and
when I glanced down in the direction of the murmur, my eye, traversing the hall-
front, caught a light kindling in a window: it reminded me that I was late, and I
hurried on.

I did not like re-entering Thornfield. To pass its threshold was to return to
stagnation; to cross the silent hall, to ascend the darksome staircase, to seek my
own lonely little room, and then to meet tranquil Mrs. Fairfax, and spend the long
winter evening with her, and her only, was to quell wholly the faint excitement
wakened by my walk,—to slip again over my faculties the viewless fetters of an
uniform and too still existence; of an existence whose very privileges of security
and ease I was becoming incapable of appreciating. What good it would have done
me at that time to have been tossed in the storms of an uncertain struggling life,
and to have been taught by rough and bitter experience to long for the calm amidst
which I now repined! Yes, just as much good as it would do a man tired of sitting
still in a "too easy chair" to take a long walk: and just as natural was the wish to
stir, under my circumstances, as it would be under his.

I lingered at the gates; I lingered on the lawn; I paced backwards and forwards
on the pavement: the shutters of the glass door were closed; I could not see into
the interior; and both my eyes and spirit seemed drawn from the gloomy house—
from the grey hollow filled with rayless cells, as it appeared to me—to that sky
expanded before me,—a blue sea absolved from taint of cloud; the moon ascending
it in solemn march; her orb seeming to look up as she left the hill tops, from behind
which she had come, far and farther below her, and aspired to the zenith, midnight-
dark in its fathomless depth and measureless distance: and for those trembling stars
that followed her course; they made my heart tremble, my veins glow when I viewed

them. Little things recall us to earth: the clock struck in the hall; that sufficed; I turned from moon and stars, opened a side-door, and went in.

The hall was not dark, nor yet was it lit, only by the high-hung bronze lamp; a warm glow suffused both it and the lower steps of the oak staircase. This ruddy shine issued from the great dining-room, whose two-leaved door stood open, and showed a genial fire in the grate, glancing on marble hearth and brass fire-irons, and revealing purple draperies and polished furniture, in the most pleasant radiance. It revealed, too, a group near the mantelpiece: I had scarcely caught it, and scarcely become aware of a cheerful mingling of voices, amongst which I seemed to distinguish the tones of Adèle, when the door closed.

I hastened to Mrs. Fairfax's room: there was a fire there too, but no candle, and no Mrs. Fairfax. Instead, all alone, sitting upright on the rug, and gazing with gravity at the blaze, I beheld a great black and white long-haired dog, just like the Gytrash of the lane. It was so like it that I went forward and said,—

"Pilot," and the thing got up and came to me and snuffed me. I caressed him, and he wagged his great tail: but he looked an eerie creature to be alone with, and I could not tell whence he had come. I rang the bell, for I wanted a candle; and I wanted, too, to get an account of this visitant. Leah entered.

"What dog is this?"

"He came with master."

"With whom?"

"With master—Mr. Rochester—he is just arrived."

"Indeed! and is Mrs. Fairfax with him?"

"Yes, and Miss Adela; they are in the dining-room, and John is gone for a surgeon: for master has had an accident; his horse fell and his ankle is sprained."

"Did the horse fall in Hay Lane?"

"Yes, coming down hill; it slipped on some ice."

"Ah! Bring me a candle, will you, Leah?"

Leah brought it; she entered, followed by Mrs. Fairfax, who repeated the news; adding that Mr. Carter the surgeon was come, and was now with Mr. Rochester: then she hurried out to give orders about tea, and I went upstairs to take off my things.

Chapter XIII

MR. ROCHESTER, it seems, by the surgeon's orders, went to bed early that night; nor did he rise soon next morning. When he did come down, it was to attend to business: his agent and some of his tenants were arrived, and waiting to speak with him.

Adèle and I had now to vacate the library: it would be in daily requisition as a reception-room for callers. A fire was lit in an apartment upstairs, and there I carried our books, and arranged it for the future school-room. I discerned in the course of the morning that Thornfield Hall was a changed place: no longer silent as a church, it echoed every hour or two to a knock at the door, or a clang of the bell; steps, too, often traversed the hall, and new voices spoke in different keys below; a rill from the outer world was flowing through it; it had a master: for my part, I liked it better.

Adèle was not easy to teach that day; she could not apply: she kept running to the door and looking over the banisters to see if she could get a glimpse of Mr. Rochester; then she coined pretexts to go downstairs, in order, as I shrewdly suspected, to visit the library, where I knew she was not wanted; then, when I got a little angry, and made her sit still, she continued to talk incessantly of her "ami,

Monsieur Edouard Fairfax *de* Rochester,'' as she dubbed him (I had not before heard his prenomens), and to conjecture what presents he had brought her: for it appears he had intimated the night before, that when his luggage came from Millcote, there would be found amongst it a little box in whose contents she had an interest.

''Et cela doit signifier,'' said she, '' qu'il y aura là dedans un cadeau pour moi, et peutêtre pour vous aussi, mademoiselle. Monsieur a parlé de vous: il m'a demandé le nom de ma gouvernante, et si elle n'était pas une petite personne, assez mince et un peu pâle. J'ai dit qu'oui: car c'est vrai, n'est-ce pas, mademoiselle?''

I and my pupil dined as usual in Mrs. Fairfax's parlour; the afternoon was wild and snowy, and we passed it in the school-room. At dark I allowed Adèle to put away books and work, and to run downstairs; for, from the comparative silence below, and from the cessation of appeals to the door-bell, I conjectured that Mr. Rochester was now at liberty. Left alone, I walked to the window; but nothing was to be seen thence: twilight and snow-flakes together thickened the air, and hid the very shrubs on the lawn. I let down the curtain and went back to the fireside.

In the clear embers I was tracing a view, not unlike a picture I remembered to have seen of the castle of Heidelberg, on the Rhine, when Mrs. Fairfax came in, breaking up by her entrance the fiery mosaic I had been piecing together, and scattering too some heavy unwelcome thoughts that were beginning to throng on my solitude.

''Mr. Rochester would be glad if you and your pupil would take tea with him in the drawing-room this evening,'' said she: ''he has been so much engaged all day that he could not ask to see you before.''

''When is his tea-time?'' I inquired.

''Oh, at six o'clock: he keeps early hours in the country. You had better change your frock now; I will go with you and fasten it. Here is a candle.''

''Is it necessary to change my frock?''

''Yes, you had better: I always dress for the evening when Mr. Rochester is here.''

This additional ceremony seemed somewhat stately: however, I repaired to my room, and, with Mrs. Fairfax's aid, replaced my black stuff dress by one of black silk; the best and the only additional one I had, except one of light grey, which, in my Lowood notions of the toilette, I thought too fine to be worn, except on first-rate occasions.

''You want a brooch,'' said Mrs. Fairfax. I had a single little pearl ornament which Miss Temple gave me as a parting keepsake: I put it on, and then we went downstairs. Unused as I was to strangers, it was rather a trial to appear thus formally summoned in Mr. Rochester's presence. I let Mrs. Fairfax precede me into the dining-room, and kept in her shade as we crossed that apartment; and, passing the arch, whose curtain was now dropped, entered the elegant recess beyond.

Two wax candles stood lighted on the table, and two on the mantelpiece; basking in the light and heat of a superb fire, lay Pilot—Adèle knelt near him. Half reclined on a couch appeared Mr. Rochester, his foot supported by the cushion; he was looking at Adèle and the dog: the fire shone full on his face. I knew my traveller with his broad and jetty eyebrows; his square forehead, made squarer by the horizontal sweep of his black hair. I recognised his decisive nose, more remarkable for character than beauty; his full nostrils, denoting, I thought, choler; his grim mouth, chin, and jaw—yes, all three were very grim, and no mistake. His shape, now divested of cloak, I perceived harmonised in squareness with his physiognomy: I suppose it was a good figure in the athletic sense of the term—broad chested and thin flanked, though neither tall nor graceful.

Mr. Rochester must have been aware of the entrance of Mrs. Fairfax and myself; but it appeared he was not in the mood to notice us, for he never lifted his head as we approached.

"Here is Miss Eyre, sir," said Mrs. Fairfax, in her quiet way. He bowed, still not taking his eyes from the group of the dog and child.

"Let Miss Eyre be seated," said he: and there was something in the forced stiff bow, in the impatient yet formal tone, which seemed further to express, "What the deuce is it to me whether Miss Eyre be there or not? At this moment I am not disposed to accost her."

I sat down quite disembarrassed. A reception of finished politeness would probably have confused me: I could not have returned or repaid it by answering grace and elegance on my part; but harsh caprice laid me under no obligation; on the contrary, a decent quiescence, under the freak of manner, gave me the advantage. Besides, the eccentricity of the proceeding was piquant: I felt interested to see how he would go on.

He went on as a statue would, that is, he neither spoke nor moved. Mrs. Fairfax seemed to think it necessary that some one should be amiable, and she began to talk. Kindly, as usual—and, as usual, rather trite—she condoled with him on the pressure of business he had had all day; on the annoyance it must have been to him with that painful sprain: then she commended his patience and perseverance in going through with it.

"Madam, I should like some tea," was the sole rejoinder she got. She hastened to ring the bell; and, when the tray came, she proceeded to arrange the cups, spoons, etc., with assiduous celerity. I and Adèle went to the table; but the master did not leave his couch.

"Will you hand Mr. Rochester's cup?" said Mrs. Fairfax to me; "Adèle might perhaps spill it."

I did as requested. As he took the cup from my hand, Adèle, thinking the moment propitious for making a request in my favour, cried out:—

"N'est-ce pas, monsieur, qu'il y a un cadeau pour Mademoiselle Eyre, dans votre petit coffre?"

"Who talks of cadeaux?" said he, gruffly: "did you expect a present, Miss Eyre? Are you fond of presents?" and he searched my face with eyes that I saw were dark, irate, and piercing.

"I hardly know, sir; I have little experience of them: they are generally thought pleasant things."

"Generally thought? But what do *you* think?"

"I should be obliged to take time, sir, before I could give you an answer worthy of your acceptance: a present has many faces to it, has it not? and one should consider all, before pronouncing an opinion as to its nature."

"Miss Eyre, you are not so unsophisticated as Adèle: she demands a 'cadeau,' clamorously, the moment she sees me: you beat about the bush."

"Because I have less confidence in my deserts than Adèle has: she can prefer the claim of old acquaintance, and the right too of custom; for she says you have always been in the habit of giving her playthings; but if I had to make out a case I should be puzzled, since I am a stranger, and have done nothing to entitle me to an acknowledgment."

"Oh, don't fall back on over-modesty! I have examined Adèle, and find you have taken great pains with her: she is not bright, she has no talents; yet in a short time she has made much improvement."

"Sir, you have now given me my 'cadeau'; I am obliged to you; it is the meed teachers most covet; praise of their pupils' progress."

"Humph!" said Mr. Rochester, and he took his tea in silence.

"Come to the fire," said the master, when the tray was taken away, and Mrs. Fairfax had settled into a corner with her knitting; while Adèle was leading me by the hand round the room, showing me the beautiful books and ornaments on the consoles and chiffonnières. We obeyed, as in duty bound; Adèle wanted to take a seat on my knee, but she was ordered to amuse herself with Pilot.

"You have been resident in my house three months?"

"Yes, sir."

"And you came from——?"

"From Lowood school, in ——shire."

"Ah! a charitable concern.—How long were you there?"

"Eight years."

"Eight years! you must be tenacious of life. I thought half the time in such a place would have done up any constitution! No wonder you have rather the look of another world. I marvelled where you had got that sort of face. When you came on me in Hay Lane last night, I thought unaccountably of fairy tales, and had half a mind to demand whether you had bewitched my horse: I am not sure yet. Who are your parents?"

"I have none."

"Nor ever had, I suppose: do you remember them?"

"No."

"I thought not. And so you were waiting for your people when you sat on that stile?"

"For whom, sir?"

"For the men in green: it was a proper moonlight evening for them. Did I break through one of your rings, that you spread that damned ice on the causeway?"

I shook my head. "The men in green all forsook England a hundred years ago," said I, speaking as seriously as he had done. "And not even in Hay Lane, or the fields about it, could you find a trace of them. I don't think either summer or harvest, or winter moon, will ever shine on their revels more."

Mrs. Fairfax had dropped her knitting, and, with raised eyebrows, seemed wondering what sort of talk this was.

"Well," resumed Mr. Rochester, "if you disown parents, you must have some sort of kinsfolk: uncles and aunts?"

"No; none that I ever saw."

"And your home?"

"I have none."

"Where do your brothers and sisters live?"

"I have no brothers or sisters."

"Who recommended you to come here?"

"I advertised, and Mrs. Fairfax answered my advertisement."

"Yes," said the good lady, who now knew what ground we were upon, "and I am daily thankful for the choice Providence led me to make. Miss Eyre has been an invaluable companion to me, and a kind and careful teacher to Adèle."

"Don't trouble yourself to give her a character," returned Mr. Rochester: "eulogiums will not bias me; I shall judge for myself. She began by felling my horse."

"Sir?" said Mrs. Fairfax.

"I have to thank her for this sprain."

The widow looked bewildered.

"Miss Eyre, have you ever lived in a town?"

"No, sir."

"Have you seen much society?"

"None but the pupils and teachers of Lowood; and now the inmates of Thornfield."

"Have you read much?"

"Only such books as came in my way; and they have not been numerous, or very learned."

"You have lived the life of a nun: no doubt you are well drilled in religious forms;—Brocklehurst, who I understand directs Lowood, is a parson, is he not?"

"Yes, sir."

"And you girls probably worshipped him, as a convent full of religieuses would worship their director."

"Oh, no."

"You are very cool! No! What? a novice not worship her priest! That sounds blasphemous."

"I disliked Mr. Brocklehurst; and I was not alone in the feeling. He is a harsh man; at once pompous and meddling: he cut off our hair; and for economy's sake bought us bad needles and thread, with which we could hardly sew."

"That was very false economy," remarked Mrs. Fairfax, who now again caught the drift of the dialogue.

"And was that the head and front of his offending?" demanded Mr. Rochester.

"He starved us when he had the sole superintendence of the provision department, before the committee was appointed; and he bored us with long lectures once a week, and with evening readings from books of his own inditing, about sudden deaths and judgments, which made us afraid to go to bed."

"What age were you when you went to Lowood?"

"About ten."

"And you stayed there eight years: and are now, then, eighteen?"

I assented.

"Arithmetic, you see, is useful: without its aid, I should hardly have been able to guess your age. It is a point difficult to fix where the features and countenance are so much at variance as in your case. And now what did you learn at Lowood? Can you play?"

"A little."

"Of course: that is the established answer. Go into the library—I mean, if you please.—(Excuse my tone of command; I am used to say 'Do this,' and it is done: I cannot alter my customary habits for one new inmate.)—Go, then, into the library; take a candle with you; leave the door open; sit down to the piano, and play a tune."

I departed, obeying his directions.

"Enough!" he called out in a few minutes. "You play a *little*, I see; like any other English school-girl: perhaps rather better than some, but not well."

I closed the piano, and returned. Mr. Rochester continued.

"Adèle showed me some sketches this morning, which she said were yours. I don't know whether they were entirely of your doing: probably a master aided you?"

"No, indeed!" I interjected.

"Ah! that pricks pride. Well, fetch me your portfolio, if you can vouch for its contents being original; but don't pass your word unless you are certain: I can recognise patchwork."

"Then I will say nothing, and you shall judge for yourself, sir."

I brought the portfolio from the library.

"Approach the table," said he; and I wheeled it to his couch. Adèle and Mrs. Fairfax drew near to see the pictures.

"No crowding," said Mr. Rochester: " take the drawings from my hand as I finish with them; but don't push your faces up to mine."

He deliberately scrutinised each sketch and painting. Three he laid aside; the others, when he had examined them, he swept from him.

"Take them off to the other table, Mrs. Fairfax," said he, "and look at them with Adèle;—you" (glancing at me) "resume your seat, and answer my questions. I perceive these pictures were done by one hand: was that hand yours?"

"Yes."

"And when did you find time to do them? They have taken much time, and some thought."

"I did them in the last two vacations I spent at Lowood, when I had no other occupation."

"Where did you get your copies?"

"Out of my head."

"That head I see now on your shoulders?"

"Yes, sir."

"Has it other furniture of the same kind within?"

"I should think it may have: I should hope—better."

He spread the pictures before him, and again surveyed them alternately.

While he is so occupied, I will tell you, reader, what they are: and first, I must premise that they are nothing wonderful. The subjects had, indeed, risen vividly on my mind. As I saw them with the spiritual eye, before I attempted to embody them, they were striking; but my hand would not second my fancy, and in each case it had wrought out but a pale portrait of the thing I had conceived.

These pictures were in water colours. The first represented clouds low and livid, rolling over a swollen sea: all the distance was in eclipse; so, too, was the foreground; or, rather, the nearest billows, for there was no land. One gleam of light lifted into relief a half-submerged mast, on which sat a cormorant, dark and large, with wings flecked with foam; its beak held a gold bracelet, set with gems, that I had touched with as brilliant tints as my palette could yield, and as glittering distinctness as my pencil could impart. Sinking below the bird and mast, a drowned corpse glanced through the green water; a fair arm was the only limb clearly visible, whence the bracelet had been washed or torn.

The second picture contained for foreground only the dim peak of a hill, with grass and some leaves slanting as if by a breeze. Beyond and above spread an expanse of sky, dark blue as at twilight: rising into the sky was a woman's shape to the bust, portrayed in tints as dusk and soft as I could combine. The dim forehead was crowned with a star; the lineaments below were seen as through the suffusion of vapour; the eyes shone dark and wild; the hair streamed shadowy, like a beamless cloud torn by storm or by electric travail. On the neck lay a pale reflection like moonlight; the same faint lustre touched the train of thin clouds from which rose and bowed this vision of the Evening Star.

The third showed the pinnacle of an iceberg piercing a polar winter sky: a muster of northern lights reared their dim lances, close serried, along the horizon. Throwing these into distance, rose, in the foreground, a head,—a colossal head, inclined towards the iceberg, and resting against it. Two thin hands, joined under the forehead, and supporting it, drew up before the lower features a sable veil; a brow quite bloodless, white as bone, and an eye hollow and fixed, blank of meaning but for the glassiness of despair, alone were visible. Above the temples, amidst wreathed turban folds of black drapery, vague in its character and consistency as cloud, gleamed a ring of white flame, gemmed with sparkles of a more lurid tinge. This pale crescent was "The likeness of a Kingly Crown"; what it diademed was "the shape which shape had none."

"Were you happy when you painted these pictures?" asked Mr. Rochester, presently.

"I was absorbed, sir: yes, and I was happy. To paint them, in short, was to enjoy one of the keenest pleasures I have ever known."

"That is not saying much. Your pleasures, by your own account, have been few; but I daresay you did exist in a kind of artist's dreamland while you blent and arranged these strange tints. Did you sit at them long each day?"

"I had nothing else to do, because it was the vacation, and I sat at them from morning till noon, and from noon till night: the length of the midsummer days favoured my inclination to apply."

"And you felt self-satisfied with the result of your ardent labours?"

"Far from it. I was tormented by the contrast between my ideas and my handiwork: in each case I had imagined something which I was quite powerless to realize."

"Not quite: you have secured the shadow of your thought; but no more, probably. You had not enough of the artist's skill and science to give it full being: yet the

drawings are, for a school girl, peculiar. As to the thoughts, they are elfish. These eyes in the Evening Star you must have seen in a dream. How could you make them look so clear, and yet not at all brilliant? for the planet above quells their rays. And what meaning is that in their solemn depth? And who taught you to paint wind? There is a high gale in that sky, and on this hill-top. Where did you see Latmos? For that is Latmos. There,—put the drawings away!''

I had scarce tied the strings of the portfolio, when, looking at his watch, he said abruptly—

"It is nine o'clock: what are you about, Miss Eyre, to let Adèle sit up so long? Take her to bed.''

Adèle went to kiss him before quitting the room: he endured the caress, but scarcely seemed to relish it more than Pilot would have done, nor so much.

"I wish you all good-night, now," said he, making a movement of the hand towards the door, in token that he was tired of our company, and wished to dismiss us. Mrs. Fairfax folded up her knitting: I took my portfolio: we curtseyed to him, received a frigid bow in return, and so withdrew.

"You said Mr. Rochester was not strikingly peculiar, Mrs. Fairfax," I observed, when I rejoined her in her room, after putting Adèle to bed.

"Well, is he?''

"I think so: he is very changeful and abrupt.''

"True: no doubt he may appear so to a stranger, but I am so accustomed to his manner, I never think of it; and then, if he has peculiarities of temper, allowance should be made.''

"Why?''

"Partly because it is his nature—and we can none of us help our nature; and, partly, he has painful thoughts, no doubt, to harass him, and make his spirits unequal.''

"What about?''

"Family troubles, for one thing.''

"But he has no family.''

"Not now, but he has had—or, at least, relatives. He lost his elder brother a few years since.''

"His *elder* brother?''

"Yes. The present Mr. Rochester has not been very long in possession of the property; only about nine years.''

"Nine years is a tolerable time. Was he so very fond of his brother as to be still inconsolable for his loss?''

"Why, no—perhaps not. I believe there were some misunderstandings between them. Mr. Rowland Rochester was not quite just to Mr. Edward; and, perhaps, he prejudiced his father against him. The old gentleman was fond of money, and anxious to keep the family estate together. He did not like to diminish the property by division, and yet he was anxious that Mr. Edward should have wealth, too, to keep up the consequence of the name; and, soon after he was of age, some steps were taken that were not quite fair, and made a great deal of mischief. Old Mr. Rochester and Mr. Rowland combined to bring Mr. Edward into what he considered a painful position, for the sake of making his fortune: what the precise nature of that position was I never clearly knew, but his spirit could not brook what he had to suffer in it. He is not very forgiving: he broke with his family, and now for many years he has led an unsettled kind of life. I don't think he has ever been resident at Thornfield for a fortnight together, since the death of his brother without a will left him master of the estate; and, indeed, no wonder he shuns the old place.''

"Why should he shun it?''

"Perhaps he thinks it gloomy.''

The answer was evasive—I should have liked something clearer; but Mrs. Fairfax either could not, or would not, give me more explicit information of the origin and

nature of Mr. Rochester's trials. She averred they were a mystery to herself, and that what she knew was chiefly from conjecture. It was evident, indeed, that she wished me to drop the subject, which I did accordingly.

Chapter XIV

FOR several subsequent days I saw little of Mr. Rochester. In the mornings he seemed much engaged with business, and, in the afternoon, gentlemen from Millcote or the neighbourhood called, and sometimes stayed to dine with him. When his sprain was well enough to admit of horse exercise, he rode out a good deal; probably to return these visits, as he generally did not come back till late at night.

During this interval, even Adèle was seldom sent for to his presence, and all my acquaintance with him was confined to an occasional rencontre in the hall, on the stairs, or in the gallery, when he would sometimes pass me haughtily and coldly, just acknowledging my presence by a distant nod or a cool glance, and sometimes bow and smile with gentleman-like affability. His changes of mood did not offend me, because I saw that I had nothing to do with their alternation; the ebb and flow depended on causes quite disconnected with me.

One day he had had company to dinner, and had sent for my portfolio; in order, doubtless, to exhibit its contents: the gentlemen went away early, to attend a public meeting at Millcote, as Mrs. Fairfax informed me; but the night being wet and inclement, Mr. Rochester did not accompany them. Soon after they were gone, he rang the bell: a message came that I and Adèle were to go downstairs. I brushed Adèle's hair and made her neat, and having ascertained that I was myself in my usual Quaker trim, where there was nothing to retouch—all being too close and plain, braided locks included, to admit of disarrangement—we descended, Adèle wondering whether the *petit coffre* was at length come; for, owing to some mistake, its arrival had hitherto been delayed. She was gratified: there it stood, a little carton, on the table when we entered the dining-room. She appeared to know it by instinct.

"Ma boite! ma boite!" exclaimed she, running towards it.

"Yes—there is your 'boite' at last: take it into a corner, you genuine daughter of Paris, and amuse yourself with disembowelling it," said the deep and rather sarcastic voice of Mr. Rochester, proceeding from the depths of an immense easy chair at the fireside. "And mind," he continued, "don't bother me with any details of the anatomical process, or any notice of the condition of the entrails: let your operation be conducted in silence: tiens-toi tranquille, enfant; comprends-tu?"

Adèle seemed scarcely to need the warning; she had already retired to a sofa with her treasure, and was busy untying the cord which secured the lid. Having removed this impediment, and lifted certain silvery envelopes of tissue paper, she merely exclaimed:—

"Oh ciel! Que c'est beau!" and then remained absorbed in ecstatic contemplation.

"Is Miss Eyre there?" now demanded the master, half rising from his seat to look round to the door, near which I still stood.

"Ah! well; come forward: be seated here." He drew a chair near his own. "I am not fond of the prattle of children," he continued; "for, old bachelor as I am, I have no pleasant associations connected with their lisp. It would be intolerable to me to pass a whole evening *tête-à-tête* with a brat. Don't draw that chair further off, Miss Eyre; sit down exactly where I placed it—if you please, that is. Confound these civilities! I continually forget them. Nor do I particularly affect simple-minded old ladies. By-the-by, I must have mine in mind; it won't do to neglect her; she is a Fairfax, or wed to one; and blood is said to be thicker than water."

He rang and despatched an invitation to Mrs. Fairfax, who soon arrived, knitting-basket in hand.

"Good-evening, madam; I sent to you for a charitable purpose: I have forbidden Adèle to talk to me about her presents, and she is bursting with repletion; have the goodness to serve her as auditress and interlocutrice: it will be one of the most benevolent acts you ever performed."

Adèle, indeed, no sooner saw Mrs. Fairfax, than she summoned her to her sofa and there quickly filled her lap with the porcelain, the ivory, the waxen contents of her "boite"; pouring out, meantime, explanations and raptures in such broken English as she was mistress of.

"Now I have performed the part of a good host," pursued Mr. Rochester, "put my guests into the way of amusing each other, I ought to be at liberty to attend to my own pleasure. Miss Eyre, draw your chair still a little further forward: you are yet too far back; I cannot see you without disturbing my position in this comfortable chair, which I have no mind to do."

I did as I was bid, though I would much rather have remained somewhat in the shade: but Mr. Rochester had such a direct way of giving orders, it seemed a matter of course to obey him promptly.

We were, as I have said, in the dining-room: the lustre, which had been lit for dinner, filled the room with a festal breadth of light; the large fire was all red and clear; the purple curtains hung rich and ample before the lofty window and loftier arch; everything was still, save the subdued chat of Adèle (she dared not speak loud), and, filling up each pause, the beating of winter rain against the panes.

Mr. Rochester, as he sat in his damask-covered chair, looked different to what I had seen him look before; not quite so stern—much less gloomy. There was a smile on his lips, and his eyes sparkled, whether with wine or not, I am not sure; but I think it very probable. He was, in short, in his after-dinner mood; more expanded and genial, and also more self-indulgent than the frigid and rigid temper of the morning: still he looked preciously grim, cushioning his massive head against the swelling back of his chair, and receiving the light of the fire on his granite-hewn features, and in his great, dark eyes; for he had great, dark eyes, and very fine eyes, too—not without a certain change in their depths sometimes, which, if it was not softness, reminded you, at least of that feeling.

He had been looking two minutes at the fire, and I had been looking the same length of time at him, when, turning suddenly, he caught my gaze fastened on his physiognomy.

"You examine me, Miss Eyre," said he: "do you think me handsome?"

I should, if I had deliberated, have replied to this question by something conventionally vague and polite; but the answer somehow slipped from my tongue before I was aware:—" No, sir."

"Ah! By my word! there is something singular about you," said he: "you have the air of a little nonnette; quaint, quiet, grave, and simple, as you sit with your hands before you, and your eyes generally bent on the carpet (except, by-the-by, when they are directed piercingly to my face; as just now, for instance); and when one asks you a question, or makes a remark to which you are obliged to reply, you rap out a round rejoinder, which, if not blunt, is at least brusque. What do you mean by it?"

"Sir, I was too plain: I beg your pardon. I ought to have replied that it was not easy to give an impromptu answer to a question about appearances; that tastes differ; that beauty is of little consequence, or something of that sort."

"You ought to have replied no such thing. Beauty of little consequence, indeed! And so, under pretence of softening the previous outrage, of stroking and soothing me into placidity, you stick a sly penknife under my ear! Go on: what fault do you find with me, pray? I suppose I have all my limbs and all my features like any other man?"

"Mr. Rochester, allow me to disown my first answer: I intended no pointed repartee: it was only a blunder."

"Just so: I think so: and you shall be answerable for it. Criticise me: does my forehead not please you?"

He lifted up the sable waves of hair which lay horizontally over his brow, and showed a solid enough mass of intellectual organs, but an abrupt deficiency where the suave sign of benevolence should have risen.

"Now, ma'am, am I a fool?"

"Far from it, sir. You would, perhaps, think me rude if I inquired in return whether you are a philanthropist?"

"There again! Another stick of the penknife, when she pretended to pat my head: and that is because I said I did not like the society of children and old women (low be it spoken!). No, young lady, I am not a general philanthropist; but I bear a conscience;" and he pointed to the prominences which are said to indicate that faculty, and which, fortunately for him, were sufficiently conspicuous; giving, indeed, a marked breadth to the upper part of his head: "and, besides, I once had a kind of rude tenderness of heart. When I was as old as you, I was a feeling fellow enough; partial to the unfledged, unfostered, and unlucky; but fortune has knocked me about since: she has even kneaded me with her knuckles, and now I flatter myself I am hard and tough as an India-rubber ball; pervious, though, through a chink or two still, and with one sentient point in the middle of the lump. Yes: does that leave hope for me?"

"Hope of what, sir?"

"Of my final re-transformation from India-rubber back to flesh?"

"Decidedly he has had too much wine," I thought; and I did not know what answer to make to his queer question: how could I tell whether he was capable of being re-transformed?

"You look very much puzzled, Miss Eyre; and though you are not pretty any more than I am handsome, yet a puzzled air becomes you; besides, it is convenient, for it keeps those searching eyes of yours away from my physiognomy, and busies them with the worsted flowers of the rug; so puzzle on. Young lady, I am disposed to be gregarious and communicative to-night."

With this announcement he rose from his chair, and stood, leaning his arm on the marble mantelpiece: in that attitude his shape was seen plainly as well as his face; his unusual breadth of chest, disproportionate almost to his length of limb. I am sure most people would have thought him an ugly man; yet there was so much unconscious pride in his port: so much ease in his demeanour; such a look of complete indifference to his own external appearance; so haughty a reliance on the power of other qualities, intrinsic or adventitious, to atone for the lack of mere personal attractiveness, that, in looking at him, one inevitably shared the indifference, and, even in a blind, imperfect sense, put faith in the confidence.

"I am disposed to be gregarious and communicative to-night," he repeated; "and that is why I sent for you: the fire and the chandelier were not sufficient company for me; nor would Pilot have been, for none of these can talk. Adèle is a degree better, but still far below the mark; Mrs. Fairfax ditto; you, I am persuaded, can suit me if you will: you puzzled me the first evening I invited you down here. I have almost forgotten you since: other ideas have driven yours from my head; but to-night I am resolved to be at ease; to dismiss what importunes, and recall what pleases. It would please me now to draw you out—to learn more of you—therefore speak."

Instead of speaking, I smiled; and not a very complacent or submissive smile either.

"Speak," he urged.

"What about, sir?"

"Whatever you like. I leave both the choice of subject and the manner of treating it entirely to yourself."

Accordingly I sat and said nothing: "If he expects me to talk for the mere sake of talking and showing off, he will find he has addressed himself to the wrong person," I thought.

"You are dumb, Miss Eyre."

I was dumb still. He bent his head a little towards me, and with a single hasty glance seemed to dive into my eyes.

"Stubborn?" he said, "and annoyed. Ah, it is consistent. I put my request in an absurd, almost insolent form. Miss Eyre, I beg your pardon. The fact is, once for all, I don't wish to treat you like an inferior: that is (correcting himself), I claim only such superiority as must result from twenty years' difference in age and a century's advance in experience. This is legitimate, et j'y tiens, as Adèle would say; and it is by virtue of this superiority and this alone that I desire you to have the goodness to talk to me a little now, and divert my thoughts, which are galled with dwelling on one point—cankering as a rusty nail."

He had deigned an explanation; almost an apology: I did not feel insensible to his condescension, and would not seem so.

"I am willing to amuse you if I can, sir: quite willing; but I cannot introduce a topic, because how do I know what will interest you? Ask me questions, and I will do my best to answer them."

"Then, in the first place, do you agree with me that I have a right to be a little masterful, abrupt; perhaps exacting, sometimes, on the grounds I stated; namely, that I am old enough to be your father, and that I have battled through a varied experience with many men of many nations, and roamed over half the globe, while you have lived quietly with one set of people in one house?"

"Do as you please, sir."

"That is no answer; or rather it is a very irritating, because a very evasive one; reply clearly."

"I don't think, sir, you have a right to command me, merely because you are older than I, or because you have seen more of the world than I have; your claim to superiority depends on the use you have made of your time and experience."

"Humph! Promptly spoken. But I won't allow that, seeing that it would never suit my case; as I have made an indifferent, not to say a bad, use of both advantages. Leaving superiority out of the question then, you must still agree to receive my orders now and then, without being piqued or hurt by the tone of command—will you?"

I smiled: I thought to myself Mr. Rochester *is* peculiar—he seems to forget that he pays me £30 per annum for receiving his orders.

"The smile is very well," said he, catching instantly the passing expression; "but speak too."

"I was thinking, sir, that very few masters would trouble themselves to inquire whether or not their paid subordinates were piqued and hurt by their orders."

"Paid subordinates! What, you are my paid subordinate, are you? Oh yes, I had forgotten the salary! Well then, on that mercenary ground, will you agree to let me hector a little?"

"No, sir, not on that ground: but, on the ground that you did forget it, and that you care whether or not a dependent is comfortable in his dependency, I agree heartily."

"And will you consent to dispense with a great many conventional forms and phrases, without thinking that the omission arises from insolence?"

"I am sure, sir, I should never mistake informality for insolence: one I rather like, the other nothing free-born would submit to, even for a salary."

"Humbug! Most things free-born will submit to anything for a salary; therefore, keep to yourself, and don't venture on generalities of which you are intensely

ignorant. However, I mentally shake hands with you for your answer, despite its inaccuracy; and as much for the manner in which it was said, as for the substance of the speech: the manner was frank and sincere; one does not often see such a manner: no, on the contrary, affectation, or coldness, or stupid, coarse-minded misapprehension of one's meaning are the usual rewards of candour. Not three in three thousand raw school-girl governesses would have answered me as you have just done. But I don't mean to flatter you: if you are cast in a different mould to the majority, it is no merit of yours: Nature did it. And then, after all, I go too fast in my conclusions: for what I yet know, you may be no better than the rest; you may have intolerable defects to counterbalance your few good points.''

"And so may you," I thought. My eye met his as the idea crossed my mind: he seemed to read the glance, answering as if its import had been spoken as well as imagined:—

"Yes, yes, you are right," said he; " I have plenty of faults of my own: I know it, and I don't wish to palliate them, I assure you. God wot I need not be too severe about others; I have a past existence, a series of deeds, a colour of life to contemplate within my own breast, which might well call my sneers and censures from my neighbours to myself. I started, or rather (for, like other defaulters, I like to lay half the blame on ill fortune and adverse circumstances) was thrust on to a wrong tack at the age of one and twenty, and have never recovered the right course since: but I might have been very different; I might have been as good as you—wiser— almost as stainless. I envy you your peace of mind, your clean conscience, your unpolluted memory. Little girl, a memory without blot or contamination must be an exquisite treasure—an inexhaustible source of pure refreshment: is it not?''

"How was your memory when you were eighteen, sir?''

"All right then; limpid, salubrious: no gush of bilge water had turned it to fetid puddle. I was your equal at eighteen—quite your equal. Nature meant me to be, on the whole, a good man, Miss Eyre: one of the better end; and you see I am not so. You would say you don't see it: at least I flatter myself I read as much in your eye (beware, by-the-by, what you express with that organ, I am quick at interpreting its language). Then take my word for it,—I am not a villain: you are not to suppose that—not to attribute to me any such bad eminence; but, owing, I verily believe, rather to circumstances than to my natural bent, I am a trite common-place sinner, hackneyed in all the poor petty dissipations with which the rich and worthless try to put on life. Do you wonder that I avow this to you? Know, that in the course of your future life you will often find yourself elected the involuntary confidant of your acquaintances' secrets: people will instinctively find out, as I have done, that it is not your forte to tell of yourself, but to listen while others talk of themselves; they will feel, too, that you listen with no malevolent scorn of their indiscretion, but with a kind of innate sympathy; not the less comforting and encouraging because it is very unobtrusive in its manifestations.''

"How do you know?—how can you guess all this, sir?''

"I know it well; therefore I proceed almost as freely as if I were writing my thoughts in a diary. You would say, I should have been superior to circumstances: so I should—so I should; but you see I was not. When fate wronged me, I had not the wisdom to remain cool: I turned desperate; then I degenerated. Now, when any vicious simpleton excites my disgust by his paltry ribaldry, I cannot flatter myself that I am better than he: I am forced to confess that he and I are on a level. I wish I had stood firm—God knows I do! Dread remorse when you are tempted to err, Miss Eyre: remorse is the poison of life.''

"Repentance is said to be its cure, sir.''

"It is not its cure. Reformation may be its cure; and I could reform—I have strength yet for that—if—but where is the use of thinking of it, hampered, burdened, cursed as I am? Besides, since happiness is irrevocably denied me, I have a right to get pleasure out of life: and I *will* get it, cost what it may.''

"Then you will degenerate still more, sir."

"Possibly: yet why should I, if I can get sweet, fresh pleasure? And I may get it as sweet and fresh as the wild honey the bee gathers on the moor."

"It will sting—it will taste bitter, sir."

"How do you know?—you never tried it. How very serious—how very solemn you look; and you are as ignorant of the matter as this cameo head" (taking one from the mantelpiece). "You have no right to preach to me, you neophyte, that have not passed the porch of life, and are absolutely unacquainted with its mysteries."

"I only remind you of your own words, sir: you said error brought remorse, and you pronounced remorse the poison of existence."

"And who talks of error now? I scarcely think the notion that flittered across my brain was an error. I believe it was an inspiration rather than a temptation: it was very genial, very soothing,—I know that. Here it comes again! It is no devil, I assure you; or if it be, it has put on the robes of an angel of light. I think I must admit so fair a guest when it asks entrance to my heart."

"Distrust it, sir; it is not a true angel."

"Once more, how do you know? By what instinct do you pretend to distinguish between a fallen seraph of the abyss and a messenger from the eternal throne—between a guide and a seducer?"

"I judged by your countenance, sir; which was troubled: when you said the suggestion had returned upon you. I feel sure it will work you more misery if you listen to it."

"Not at all—it bears the most gracious message in the world: for the rest, you are not my conscience-keeper, so don't make yourself uneasy. Here, come in, bonny wanderer!"

He said this as if he spoke to a vision, viewless to any eye but his own; then, folding his arms, which he had half extended, on his chest, he seemed to enclose in their embrace the invisible being.

"Now," he continued, again addressing me, "I have received the pilgrim—a disguised deity, as I verily believe. Already it has done me good: my heart was a sort of charnel; it will now be a shrine."

"To speak truth, sir, I don't understand you at all: I cannot keep up the conversation, because it has got out of my depth. Only one thing I know: you said you were not as good as you should like to be, and that you regretted your own imperfection;—one thing I can comprehend: you intimated that to have a sullied memory was a perpetual bane. It seems to me, that if you tried hard, you would in time find it possible to become what you yourself would approve; and that if from this day you began with resolution to correct your thoughts and actions, you would in a few years have laid up a new and stainless store of recollections, to which you might revert with pleasure."

"Justly thought; rightly said, Miss Eyre; and, at this moment, I am paving hell with energy."

"Sir?"

"I am laying down good intentions, which I believe durable as flint. Certainly, my associates and pursuits shall be other than they have been."

"And better?"

"And better—so much better as pure ore is than foul dross. You seem to doubt me; I don't doubt myself: I know what my aim is, and what my motives are; and at this moment I pass a law, unalterable as that of the Medes and Persians, that both are right."

"They cannot be, sir, if they require a new statute to legalise them."

"They are, Miss Eyre, though they absolutely require a new statute: unheard-of combinations of circumstances demand unheard-of rules."

"That sounds a dangerous maxim, sir; because one can see at once that it is liable to abuse."

"Sententious sage! so it is: but I swear by my household gods not to abuse it."

"You are human and fallible."

"I am: so are you—what then?"

"The human and fallible should not arrogate a power with which the divine and perfect alone can be safely entrusted."

"What power?"

"That of saying of any strange, unsanctioned line of action,—'Let it be right.' "

" 'Let it be right'—the very words: you have pronounced them."

"*May* it be right, then," I said, as I rose, deeming it useless to continue a discourse which was all darkness to me; and, besides, sensible that the character of my interlocutor was beyond my penetration; at least, beyond its present reach; and feeling the uncertainty, the vague sense of insecurity, which accompanied a conviction of ignorance.

"Where are you going?"

"To put Adèle to bed: it is past her bedtime."

"You are afraid of me, because I talk like a Sphynx."

"Your language is enigmatical, sir: but though I am bewildered, I am certainly not afraid."

"You *are* afraid—your self-love dreads a blunder."

"In that sense I do feel apprehensive—I have no wish to talk nonsense."

"If you did, it would be in such a grave, quiet manner, I should mistake it for sense. Do you never laugh, Miss Eyre? Don't trouble yourself to answer—I see, you laugh rarely; but you can laugh very merrily: believe me, you are not naturally austere, any more than I am naturally vicious. The Lowood constraint still clings to you somewhat; controlling your features, muffling your voice, and restricting your limbs; and you fear in the presence of a man and a brother—or father, or master, or what you will—to smile too gaily, speak too freely, or move too quickly: but, in time, I think you will learn to be natural with me, as I find it impossible to be conventional with you; and then your looks and movements will have more vivacity and variety than they dare offer now. I see at intervals the glance of a curious sort of bird through the close-set bars of a cage: a vivid, restless, resolute captive is there; were it but free, it would soar cloud-high. You are still bent on going?"

"It has struck nine, sir."

"Never mind,—wait a minute: Adèle is not ready to go to bed yet. My position, Miss Eyre, with my back to the fire, and my face to the room, favours observation. While talking to you, I have also occasionally watched Adèle; (I have my own reasons for thinking her a curious study,—reasons that I may, nay that I shall, impart to you some day;) she pulled out of her box, about ten minutes ago, a little pink silk frock; rapture lit her face as she unfolded it; coquetry runs in her blood, blends with her brains, and seasons the marrow of her bones. 'Il faut que je l'essaie!' cried she; 'et à l'instant même!' and she rushed out of the room. She is now with Sophie, undergoing a robing process: in a few minutes she will re-enter; and I know what I shall see,—a miniature of Céline Varens, as she used to appear on the boards at the rising of——: but never mind that. However, my tenderest feelings are about to receive a shock: such is my presentiment; stay now, to see whether it will be realised."

Ere long, Adèle's little foot was heard tripping across the hall. She entered, transformed as her guardian had predicted. A dress of rose-coloured satin, very short, and as full in the skirt as it could be gathered, replaced the brown frock she had previously worn; a wreath of rosebuds circled her forehead: her feet were dressed in silk stockings and small white satin sandals.

"Est-ce que ma robe va bien?" cried she, bounding forwards; "et mes souliers? et mes bas? Tenez, je crois que je vais danser!"

And spreading out her dress, she chasséed across the room; till, having reached
Mr. Rochester, she wheeled lightly round before him on tip-toe, then dropped on
one knee at his feet, exclaiming:—

"Monsieur, je vous remercie mille fois de votre bonté;" then rising, she added,
"C'est comme cela que maman faisait, n'est-ce pas, monsieur?"

"Pre-cise-ly!" was the answer; "and, 'comme cela,' she charmed my English
gold out of my British breeches' pocket. I have been green, too, Miss Eyre,—ay,
grass green: not a more vernal tint freshens you now than once freshened me. My
Spring is gone, however: but it has left me that French floweret on my hands:
which, in some moods, I would fain be rid of. Not valuing now the root whence
it sprang; having found that it was of a sort which nothing but gold dust could
manure, I have but half a liking to the blossom: especially when it looks so artificial
as just now. I keep it and rear it rather on the Roman Catholic principle of expiating
numerous sins, great or small, by one good work. I'll explain all this some day.
Good-night."

Chapter XV

MR. ROCHESTER did, on a future occasion, explain it.

It was one afternoon, when he chanced to meet me and Adèle in the grounds;
and while she played with Pilot and her shuttlecock, he asked me to walk up and
down a long beech avenue within sight of her.

He then said that she was the daughter of a French opera-dancer, Céline Varens,
towards whom he had once cherished what he called a "grande passion." This
passion Céline had professed to return with even superior ardour. He thought
himself her idol; ugly as he was: he believed, as he said, that she preferred his
"taille d'athlète" to the elegance of the Apollo Belvidere.

"And, Miss Eyre, so much was I flattered by this preference of the Gallic sylph
for her British gnome, that I installed her in an hotel; gave her a complete establishment
of servants, a carriage, cashmeres, diamonds, dentelles, etc. In short, I began the
process of ruining myself in the received style, like any other spoony. I had not,
it seems, the originality to chalk out a new road to shame and destruction, but trode
the old track with stupid exactness not to deviate an inch from the beaten centre.
I had—as I deserved to have—the fate of all other spoonies. Happening to call one
evening, when Céline did not expect me, I found her out; but it was a warm night,
and I was tired with strolling through Paris, so I sat down in her boudoir; happy
to breathe the air consecrated so lately by her presence. No,—I exaggerate; I never
thought there was any consecrating virtue about her: it was rather a sort of pastille
perfume she had left; a scent of musk and amber, than an odour of sanctity. I was
just beginning to stifle with the fumes of conservatory flowers and sprinkled essences,
when I bethought myself to open the window and step out on to the balcony. It
was moonlight and gas-light besides, and very still and serene. The balcony was
furnished with a chair or two; I sat down, took out a cigar.—I will take one now,
if you will excuse me."

Here ensued a pause, filled up by the producing and lighting of a cigar; having
placed it to his lips and breathed a trail of Havannah incense on the freezing and
sunless air, he went on:—

"I liked bonbons too, in those days, Miss Eyre, and I was *croquant*— (overlook
the barbarism) *croquant* chocolate comfits, and smoking alternately, watching
meantime the equipages that rolled along the fashionable streets towards the neigh-
bouring opera-house, when in an elegant close carriage drawn by a beautiful pair
of English horses, and distinctly seen in the brilliant city-night, I recognised the

'voiture' I had given Céline. She was returning: of course my heart thumped with impatience against the iron rails I leant upon. The carriage stopped, as I had expected, at the hotel door; my flame (that is the very word for an opera inamorata) alighted: though muffled in a cloak—an unnecessary encumbrance, by-the-by, on so warm a June evening—I knew her instantly by her little foot, seen peeping from the skirt of her dress, as she skipped from the carriage-step. Bending over the balcony I was about to murmur, 'Mon ange'—in a tone, of course, which should be audible to the ear of love alone—when a figure jumped from the carriage after her; cloaked also; but that was a spurred heel which had rung on the pavement, and that was a hatted head which now passed under the arched *porte cochère* of the hotel.

"You never felt jealousy, did you, Miss Eyre? Of course not: I need not ask you; because you never felt love. You have both sentiments yet to experience; your soul sleeps: the shock is yet to be given which shall waken it. You think all existence lapses in as quiet a flow as that in which your youth has hitherto slid away. Floating on with closed eyes and muffled ears, you neither see the rocks bristling not far off in the bed of the flood, nor hear the breakers boil at their base. But I tell you— and you may mark my words—you will come some day to a craggy pass of the channel, where the whole of life's stream will be broken up into whirl and tumult, foam and noise: either you will be dashed to atoms on crag points, or lifted up and borne on by some master wave into a calmer current—as I am now.

"I like this day: I like that sky of steel; I like the sternness and stillness of the world under this frost. I like Thornfield; its antiquity; its retirement; its old crow-trees and thorn-trees; its grey façade, and lines of dark windows reflecting that metal welkin: and yet how long have I abhorred the very thought of it; shunned it like a great plague-house! How I do still abhor"——

He ground his teeth and was silent: he arrested his step and struck his boot against the hard ground. Some hated thought seemed to have him in its grip, and to hold him so tightly that he could not advance.

We were ascending the avenue when he thus paused; the hall was before us. Lifting his eye to its battlements, he cast over them a glare such as I never saw before or since. Pain, shame, ire—impatience, disgust, detestation—seemed momentarily to hold a quivering conflict in the large pupil dilating under his ebon eyebrow. Wild was the wrestle which should be paramount; but another feeling rose and triumphed: something hard and cynical; self-willed and resolute: it settled his passion and petrified his countenance: he went on:—

"During the moment I was silent, Miss Eyre, I was arranging a point with my destiny. She stood there, by that beech-trunk—a hag like one of those who appeared to Macbeth on the heath of Forres. 'You like Thornfield?' she said, lifting her finger; and then she wrote in the air a memento, which ran in lurid hieroglyphics all along the house-front, between the upper and lower row of windows. 'Like it if you can!' 'Like it if you dare!'

" 'I will like it,' said I. 'I dare like it;' and (he subjoined moodily) I will keep my word: I will break obstacles to happiness, to goodness—yes, goodness; I wish to be a better man than I have been; than I am—as Job's leviathan broke the spear, the dart and the habergeon, hinderances which others count as iron and brass, I will esteem but straw and rotten wood."

Adèle here ran before him with her shuttlecock. "Away!" he cried harshly; "keep at a distance, child; or go in to Sophie!" Continuing then to pursue his walk in silence, I ventured to recall him to the point whence he had abruptly diverged:—

"Did you leave the balcony, sir," I asked, "when Mdlle. Varens entered?"

I almost expected a rebuff for this hardly well-timed question; but, on the contrary, waking out of his scowling abstraction, he turned his eyes towards me, and the shade seemed to clear off his brow. "Oh, I had forgotten Céline! Well, to resume. When I saw my charmer thus come in accompanied by a cavalier, I seemed to hear

a hiss, and the green snake of jealousy, rising on undulating coils from the moonlit balcony, glided within my waistcoat, and ate its way in two minutes to my heart's core. Strange!'' he exclaimed, suddenly starting again from the point. "Strange that I should choose you for the confidant of all this, young lady: passing strange that you should listen to me quietly, as if it were the most usual thing in the world for a man like me to tell stories of his opera-mistresses to a quaint, inexperienced girl like you! But the last singularity explains the first, as I intimated once before: you, with your gravity, considerateness, and caution were made to be the recipient of secrets. Besides, I know what sort of a mind I have placed in communication with my own: I know it is not one liable to take infection: it is a peculiar mind; it is an unique one. Happily I do not mean to harm it: but, if I did, it would not take harm from me. The more you and I converse, the better; for while I cannot blight you, you may refresh me.'' After this digression he proceeded:—

"I remained in the balcony. 'They will come to her boudoir no doubt,' thought I: 'let me prepare an ambush.' So putting my hand in through the open window, I drew the curtain over it, leaving only an opening through which I could take observations; then I closed the casement, all but a chink just wide enough to furnish an outlet to lovers' whispered vows: then I stole back to my chair; and as I resumed it the pair came in. My eye was quickly at the aperture. Céline's chamber-maid entered, lit a lamp, left it on the table and withdrew. The couple were thus revealed to me clearly: both removed their cloaks, and there was 'the Varens' shining in satin and jewels,—my gifts of course,—and there was her companion in an officer's uniform; and I knew him for a young roué of a vicomte—a brainless and vicious youth whom I had sometimes met in society, and had never thought of hating because I despised him so absolutely. On recognising him, the fang of the snake, jealousy, was instantly broken; because at the same moment my love for Céline sank under an extinguisher. A woman who could betray me for such a rival was not worth contending for: she deserved only scorn; less, however, than I, who had been her dupe.

"They began to talk; their conversation eased me completely: frivolous, mercenary, heartless, and senseless, it was rather calculated to weary than enrage a listener. A card of mine lay on the table; this being perceived brought my name under discussion. Neither of them possessed energy or wit to belabour me soundly; but they insulted me as coarsely as they could in their little way: especially Céline; who even waxed rather brilliant on my personal defects—deformities she termed them. Now it had been her custom to launch out into fervent admiration of what she called my 'beauté mâle': wherein she differed diametrically from you, who told me point blank, at the second interview, that you did not think me handsome. The contrast struck me at the time, and''——

Adèle here came running up again.

"Monsieur, John has just been to say that your agent has called and wishes to see you.''

"Ah! in that case I must abridge. Opening the window, I walked in upon them; liberated Céline from my protection; gave her notice to vacate her hotel; offered her a purse for immediate exigencies; disregarded screams, hysterics, prayers, protestations, convulsions; made an appointment with the vicomte for a meeting at the Bois de Boulogne. Next morning I had the pleasure of encountering him; left a bullet in one of his poor, etiolated arms, feeble as the wing of a chicken in the pip, and then thought I had done with the whole crew. But unluckily the Varens, six months before, had given me this fillette Adèle; who she affirmed was my daughter; and perhaps she may be, though I see no proofs of such grim paternity written in her countenance: Pilot is more like me than she. Some years after I had broken with the mother, she abandoned her child and ran away to Italy with a musician or singer. I acknowledged no natural claim on Adèle's part to be supported by me; nor do I now acknowledge any, for I am not her father; but hearing that

she was quite destitute, I e'en took the poor thing out of the slime and mud of Paris, and transplanted it here, to grow up clean in the wholesome soil of an English country garden. Mrs. Fairfax found you to train it; but now you know that it is the illegitimate offspring of a French opera-girl, you will perhaps think differently of your post and protégée: you will be coming to me some day with notice that you have found another place—that you beg me to look out for a new governess, etc.— eh?''

"No: Adèle is not answerable for either her mother's faults or yours; I have a regard for her, and now that I know she is, in a sense, parentless—forsaken by her mother and disowned by you, sir—I shall cling closer to her than before. How could I possibly prefer the spoilt pet of a wealthy family, who would hate her governess as a nuisance, to a lonely little orphan, who leans towards her as a friend?''

"Oh, that is the light in which you view it! Well, I must go in now; and you too: it darkens.''

But I stayed out a few minutes longer with Adèle and Pilot—ran a race with her, and played a game of battledore and shuttlecock. When we went in and I had removed her bonnet and coat, I took her on my knee; kept her there an hour, allowing her to prattle as she liked: not rebuking even some little freedoms and trivialities into which she was apt to stray when much noticed: and which betrayed in her a superficiality of character, inherited probably from her mother, hardly congenial to an English mind. Still she had her merits; and I was disposed to appreciate all that was good in her to the utmost. I sought in her countenance and features a likeness to Mr. Rochester, but found none: no trait, no turn of expression announced relationship. It was a pity: if she could but have been proved to resemble him, he would have thought more of her.

It was not till after I had withdrawn to my own chamber for the night, that I steadily reviewed the tale Mr. Rochester had told me. As he had said, there was probably nothing at all extraordinary in the substance of the narrative itself: a wealthy Englishman's passion for a French dancer, and her treachery to him, were every-day matters enough, no doubt, in society; but there was something decidedly strange in the paroxysm of emotion which had suddenly seized him, when he was in the act of expressing the present contentment of his mood, and his newly revived pleasure in the old hall and its environs. I meditated wonderingly on this incident: but gradually quitting it, as I found it for the present inexplicable, I turned to the consideration of my master's manner to myself. The confidence he had thought fit to repose in me seemed a tribute to my discretion: I regarded and accepted it as such. His deportment had now for some weeks been more uniform towards me than at the first. I never seemed in his way; he did not take fits of chilling hauteur: when he met me unexpectedly, the encounter seemed welcome; he had always a word and sometimes a smile for me: when summoned by formal invitation to his presence, I was honoured by a cordiality of reception that made me feel I really possessed the power to amuse him, and that these evening conferences were sought as much for his pleasure as for my benefit.

I, indeed, talked comparatively little; but I heard him talk with relish. It was his nature to be communicative; he liked to open to a mind unacquainted with the world, glimpses of its scenes and ways (I do not mean its corrupt scenes and wicked ways, but such as derived their interest from the great scale on which they were acted, the strange novelty by which they were characterised); and I had a keen delight in receiving the new ideas he offered, in imagining the new pictures he portrayed, or followed him in thought through the new regions he disclosed, never startled or troubled by one noxious allusion.

The ease of his manner freed me from painful restraint: the friendly frankness, as correct as cordial, with which he treated me, drew me to him. I felt at times as if he were my relation, rather than my master: yet he was imperious sometimes

still; but I did not mind that; I saw it was his way. So happy, so gratified did I become with this new interest added to life, that I ceased to pine after kindred: my thin crescent-destiny seemed to enlarge; the blanks of existence were filled up; my bodily health improved; I gathered flesh and strength.

And was Mr. Rochester now ugly in my eyes? No, reader: gratitude, and many associations, all pleasurable and genial, made his face the object I best liked to see; his presence in a room was more cheering than the brightest fire. Yet I had not forgotten his faults: indeed, I could not, for he brought them frequently before me. He was proud, sardonic, harsh to inferiority of every description: in my secret soul I knew that his great kindness to me was balanced by unjust severity to many others. He was moody, too; unaccountably so: I more than once, when sent for to read to him, found him sitting in his library alone, with his head bent on his folded arms; and, when he looked up, a morose, almost a malignant scowl, blackened his features. But I believed that his moodiness, his harshness, and his former faults of morality (I say *former*, for now he seemed corrected of them) had their source in some cruel cross of fate. I believed he was naturally a man of better tendencies, higher principles, and purer tastes than such as circumstances had developed, education instilled, or destiny encouraged. I thought there were excellent materials in him; though for the present they hung together somewhat spoiled and tangled. I cannot deny that I grieved for his grief, whatever that was, and would have given much to assuage it.

Though I had now extinguished my candle and was laid down in bed, I could not sleep, for thinking of his look when he paused in the avenue, and told how his destiny had risen up before him, and dared him to be happy at Thornfield.

"Why not?" I asked myself. "What alienates him from the house? Will he leave it again soon? Mrs. Fairfax said he seldom stayed here longer than a fortnight at a time; and he has now been resident eight weeks. If he does go, the change will be doleful. Suppose he should be absent, spring, summer, and autumn: how joyless sunshine and fine days will seem!"

I hardly knew whether I had slept or not after this musing; at any rate, I started wide awake on hearing a vague murmur, peculiar and lugubrious, which sounded, I thought, just above me. I wished I had kept my candle burning: the night was drearily dark; my spirits were depressed. I rose and sat up in bed, listening. The sound was hushed.

I tried again to sleep; but my heart beat anxiously: my inward tranquillity was broken. The clock, far down in the hall, struck two. Just then it seemed my chamber-door was touched; as if fingers had swept the panels in groping a way along the dark gallery outside. I said, "Who is there?" Nothing answered. I was chilled with fear.

All at once I remembered that it might be Pilot: who, when the kitchen-door chanced to be left open, not unfrequently found his way up to the threshold of Mr. Rochester's chamber: I had seen him lying there myself, in the mornings. The idea calmed me somewhat: I lay down. Silence composes the nerves; and as an unbroken hush now reigned again through the whole house, I began to feel the return of slumber. But it was not fated that I should sleep that night. A dream had scarcely approached my ear, when it fled affrighted, scared by a marrow-freezing incident enough.

This was a demoniac laugh—low, suppressed, and deep—uttered, as it seemed, at the very key-hole of my chamber door. The head of my bed was near the door, and I thought at first the goblin-laughter stood at my bedside—or rather, crouched by my pillow: but I rose, looked round, and could see nothing; while, as I still gazed, the unnatural sound was reiterated: and I knew it came from behind the panels. My first impulse was to rise and fasten the bolt; my next, again to cry out, "Who is there?"

Something gurgled and moaned. Ere long, steps retreated up the gallery towards the third story staircase: a door had lately been made to shut in that staircase, I heard it open and close, and all was still.

"Was that Grace Poole? and is she possessed with a devil?" thought I. Impossible now to remain longer by myself: I must go to Mrs. Fairfax. I hurried on my frock and a shawl; I withdrew the bolt and opened the door with a trembling hand. There was a candle burning just outside, left on the matting in the gallery. I was surprised at this circumstance: but still more was I amazed to perceive the air quite dim, as if filled with smoke; and, while looking to the right hand and left, to find whence these blue wreaths issued, I became further aware of a strong smell of burning.

Something creaked: it was a door ajar, and that door was Mr. Rochester's, and the smoke rushed in a cloud from thence. I thought no more of Mrs. Fairfax; I thought no more of Grace Poole or the laugh: in an instant, I was within the chamber. Tongues of flame darted round the bed: the curtains were on fire. In the midst of blaze and vapour, Mr. Rochester lay stretched motionless, in deep sleep.

"Wake! wake!" I cried—I shook him, but he only murmured and turned: the smoke had stupefied him. Not a moment could be lost: the very sheets were kindling. I rushed to his basin and ewer; fortunately, one was wide and the other deep, and both were filled with water. I heaved them up, deluged the bed and its occupant, flew back to my own room, brought my own water jug, baptized the couch afresh, and, by God's aid, succeeded in extinguishing the flames which were devouring it.

The hiss of the quenched element, the breakage of a pitcher which I had flung from my hand when I had emptied it, and, above all, the splash of the shower-bath I had liberally bestowed, roused Mr. Rochester at last. Though it was now dark, I knew he was awake; because I heard him fulminating strange anathemas at finding himself lying in a pool of water.

"Is there a flood?" he cried.

"No, sir," I answered; "but there has been a fire: get up, do, you are quenched now; I will fetch you a candle."

"In the name of all the elves in Christendom, is that Jane Eyre?" he demanded. "What have you done with me, witch, sorceress? Who is in the room besides you? Have you plotted to drown me?"

"I will fetch you a candle, sir; and, in Heaven's name, get up. Somebody has plotted something: you cannot too soon find out who and what it is."

"There—I am up now; but at your peril you fetch a candle yet: wait two minutes till I get into some dry garments, if any dry there be—yes, here is my dressing-gown. Now run!"

I did run; I brought the candle which still remained in the gallery. He took it from my hand, held it up, and surveyed the bed, all blackened and scorched, the sheets drenched, the carpet round swimming in water.

"What is it? and who did it?" he asked.

I briefly related to him what had transpired: the strange laugh I had heard in the gallery; the step ascending to the third story; the smoke,—the smell of fire which had conducted me to his room; in what state I had found matters there, and how I had deluged him with all the water I could lay hands on.

He listened very gravely; his face, as I went on, expressed more concern than astonishment; he did not immediately speak when I had concluded.

"Shall I call Mrs. Fairfax?" I asked.

"Mrs. Fairfax? No: what the deuce would you call her for? What can she do? Let her sleep unmolested."

"Then I will fetch Leah, and wake John and his wife."

"Not at all: just be still. You have a shawl on? if you are not warm enough, you may take my cloak yonder; wrap it about you, and sit down in the arm-chair: there,—I will put it on. Now place your feet on the stool, to keep them out of the

wet. I am going to leave you a few minutes. I shall take the candle. Remain where you are till I return; be as still as a mouse. I must pay a visit to the second story. Don't move, remember, or call any one.''

He went: I watched the light withdraw. He passed up the gallery very softly, unclosed the staircase door with as little noise as possible, shut it after him, and the last ray vanished. I was left in total darkness. I listened for some noise, but heard nothing. A very long time elapsed. I grew weary: it was cold, in spite of the cloak; and then I did not see the use of staying, as I was not to rouse the house. I was on the point of risking Mr. Rochester's displeasure, by disobeying his orders, when the light once more gleamed dimly on the gallery-wall, and I heard his unshod feet tread the matting. "I hope it is he," thought I, "and not something worse."

He re-entered, pale and very gloomy. "I have found it all out," said he, setting his candle down on the washstand; "it is as I thought."

"How, sir?"

He made no reply, but stood with his arms folded, looking on the ground. At the end of a few minutes, he inquired in rather a peculiar tone:—

"I forget whether you said you saw anything when you opened your chamber door."

"No, sir, only the candlestick on the ground."

"But you heard an odd laugh? You have heard that laugh before, I should think, or something like it?"

"Yes, sir: there is a woman who sews here, called Grace Poole,—she laughs in that way. She is a singular person."

"Just so. Grace Poole—you have guessed it. She is, as you say, singular,—very. Well, I shall reflect on the subject. Meantime, I am glad that you are the only person, besides myself, acquainted with the precise details of tonight's incident. You are no talking fool: say nothing about it. I will account for this state of affairs (pointing to the bed): and now return to your own room. I shall do very well on the sofa in the library for the rest of the night. It is near four:—in two hours the servants will be up."

"Good-night, then, sir," said I, departing.

He seemed surprised—very inconsistently so, as he had just told me to go.

"What!" he exclaimed, "are you quitting me already: and in that way?"

"You said I might go, sir."

"But not without taking leave; not without a word or two of acknowledgment and good will: not, in short, in that brief, dry fashion. Why, you have saved my life!—snatched me from a horrible and excruciating death!—and you walk past me as if we were mutual strangers! At least shake hands."

He held out his hand; I gave him mine: he took it first in one, then in both his own.

"You have saved my life: I have a pleasure in owing you so immense a debt. I cannot say more. Nothing else that has being would have been tolerable to me in the character of creditor for such an obligation: but you: it is different;—I feel your benefits no burden, Jane."

He paused; gazed at me; words almost visible trembled on his lips,—but his voice was checked.

"Good-night again, sir. There is no debt, benefit, burden, obligation, in the case."

"I knew," he continued, "you would do me good in some way, at some time;—I saw it in your eyes when I first beheld you: their expression and smile did not—(again he stopped)—did not (he proceeded hastily) strike delight to my very inmost heart so for nothing. People talk of natural sympathies; I have heard of good genii:—there are grains of truth in the wildest fable. My cherished preserver, good-night!"

Strange energy was in his voice; strange fire in his look.

"I am glad I happened to be awake," I said: and then I was going.

"What! you *will* go?"

"I am cold, sir."

"Cold? Yes,—and standing in a pool! Go, then, Jane; go!" But he still retained my hand, and I could not free it. I bethought myself of an expedient.

"I think I hear Mrs. Fairfax move, sir," said I.

"Well, leave me:" he relaxed his fingers, and I was gone.

I regained my couch, but never thought of sleep. Till morning dawned I was tossed on a buoyant but unquiet sea, where billows of trouble rolled under surges of joy. I thought sometimes I saw beyond its wild waters a shore, sweet as the hills of Beulah; and now and then a freshening gale, wakened by hope, bore my spirit triumphantly towards the bourne: but I could not reach it, even in fancy,—a counteracting breeze blew off land, and continually drove me back. Sense would resist delirium: judgment would warn passion. Too feverish to rest, I rose as soon as day dawned.

Chapter XVI

I BOTH wished and feared to see Mr. Rochester on the day which followed this sleepless night: I wanted to hear his voice again, yet feared to meet his eye. During the early part of the morning, I momentarily expected his coming; he was not in the frequent habit of entering the school-room; but he did step in for a few minutes sometimes, and I had the impression that he was sure to visit it that day.

But the morning passed just as usual: nothing happened to interrupt the quiet course of Adèle's studies; only, soon after breakfast, I heard some bustle in the neighbourhood of Mr. Rochester's chamber, Mrs. Fairfax's voice, and Leah's, and the cook's—that is, John's wife—and even John's own gruff tones. There were exclamations of "What a mercy master was not burnt in his bed!" "It is always dangerous to keep a candle lit at night." "How providential that he had presence of mind to think of the water jug!" "I wonder he waked nobody!" "It is to be hoped he will not take cold with sleeping on the library sofa," etc.

To much confabulation succeeded a sound of scrubbing and setting to rights; and when I passed the room, in going downstairs to dinner, I saw through the open door that all was again restored to complete order; only the bed was stripped of its hangings. Leah stood up in the window-seat, rubbing the panes of glass dimmed with smoke. I was about to address her, for I wished to know what account had been given of the affair: but, on advancing, I saw a second person in the chamber—a woman sitting on a chair by the bedside, and sewing rings to new curtains. That woman was no other than Grace Poole.

There she sat, staid and taciturn-looking, as usual, in her brown stuff gown, her check apron, white handkerchief, and cap. She was intent on her work, in which her whole thoughts seemed absorbed: on her hard forehead, and in her commonplace features, was nothing either of the paleness or desperation one would have expected to see marking the countenance of a woman who had attempted murder; and whose intended victim had followed her last night to her lair, and (as I believed) charged her with the crime she wished to perpetrate. I was amazed—confounded. She looked up, while I still gazed at her: no start, no increase or failure of colour betrayed emotion, consciousness of guilt, or fear of detection. She said "Good morning, Miss," in her usual phlegmatic and brief manner; and taking up another ring and more tape, went on with her sewing.

"I will put her to some test," thought I: "such absolute impenetrability is past comprehension."

"Good morning, Grace," I said. "Has anything happened here? I thought I heard the servants all talking together a while ago."

"Only master had been reading in his bed last night; he fell asleep with his candle lit, and the curtains got on fire; but, fortunately, he awoke before the bed-clothes or the wood-work caught, and contrived to quench the flame with the water in the ewer."

"A strange affair!" I said, in a low voice: then, looking at her fixedly,—"Did Mr. Rochester wake nobody? Did no one hear him move?"

She again raised her eyes to me; and this time there was something of consciousness in their expression. She seemed to examine me warily; then she answered,—

"The servants sleep so far off, you know, Miss, they would not be likely to hear. Mrs. Fairfax's room and yours are the nearest to master's; but Mrs. Fairfax said she heard nothing: when people get elderly, they often sleep heavy." She paused, and then added, with a sort of assumed indifference, but still in a marked and significant tone, "But you are young, Miss; and I should say a light sleeper: perhaps you may have heard a noise?"

"I did," said I, dropping my voice, so that Leah, who was still polishing the panes, could not hear me, "and at first I thought it was Pilot: but Pilot cannot laugh; and I am certain I heard a laugh, and a strange one."

She took a new needleful of thread, waxed it carefully, threaded her needle with a steady hand, and then observed, with perfect composure,—

"It is hardly likely master would laugh, I should think, Miss, when he was in such danger: you must have been dreaming."

"I was not dreaming," I said, with some warmth, for her brazen coolness provoked me. Again she looked at me; and with the same scrutinising and conscious eye.

"Have you told master that you heard a laugh?" she inquired.

"I have not had the opportunity of speaking to him this morning."

"You did not think of opening your door and looking out into the gallery?" she further asked.

She appeared to be cross-questioning me; attempting to draw from me information unawares: the idea struck me that if she discovered I knew or suspected her guilt, she would be playing off some of her malignant pranks on me; I thought it advisable to be on my guard.

"On the contrary," said I, "I bolted my door."

"Then you are not in the habit of bolting your door every night before you get into bed?"

"Fiend! she wants to know my habits, that she may lay her plans accordingly!" Indignation again prevailed over prudence; I replied sharply, "Hitherto I have often omitted to fasten the bolt: I did not think it necessary. I was not aware any danger or annoyance was to be dreaded at Thornfield Hall: but in future" (and I laid marked stress on the words) "I shall take good care to make all secure before I venture to lie down."

"It will be wise so to do," was her answer: "this neighbourhood is as quiet as any I know, and I never heard of the hall being attempted by robbers since it was a house; though there are hundreds of pounds' worth of plate in the plate-closet, as is well known. And you see, for such a large house, there are very few servants, because master has never lived here much; and when he does come, being a bachelor, he needs little waiting on: but I always think it best to err on the safe side; a door is soon fastened, and it is as well to have a drawn bolt between one and any mischief that may be about. A deal of people, Miss, are for trusting all to Providence; but I say Providence will not dispense with the means, though he often blesses them when they are used discreetly." And here she closed her harangue: a long one for her, and uttered with the demureness of a Quakeress.

I still stood absolutely dumbfoundered at what appeared to me her miraculous self-possession and most inscrutable hypocrisy, when the cook entered.

"Mrs. Poole," said she, addressing Grace, "the servants' dinner will soon be ready: will you come down?"

"No; just put my pint of porter and bit of pudding on a tray, and I'll carry it upstairs."

"You'll have some meat?"

"Just a morsel, and a taste of cheese, that's all."

"And the sago?"

"Never mind it, at present: I shall be coming down before tea-time: I'll make it myself."

The cook here turned to me, saying that Mrs. Fairfax was waiting for me: so I departed.

I hardly heard Mrs. Fairfax's account of the curtain conflagration during dinner, so much was I occupied in puzzling my brains over the enigmatical character of Grace Poole; and still more in pondering the problem of her position at Thornfield: in questioning why she had not been given into custody that morning; or, at the very least, dismissed from her master's service. He had almost as much as declared his conviction of her criminality last night: what mysterious cause withheld him from accusing her? Why had he enjoined me, too, to secrecy? It was strange: a bold, vindictive, and haughty gentleman seemed somehow in the power of one of the meanest of his dependants; so much in her power, that even when she lifted her hand against his life, he dared not openly charge her with the attempt, much less punish her for it.

Had Grace been young and handsome, I should have been tempted to think that tenderer feelings than prudence or fear influenced Mr. Rochester in her behalf; but, hard-favoured and matronly as she was, the idea could not be admitted. "Yet," I reflected, "she has been young once; her youth would be contemporary with her master's: Mrs. Fairfax told me once, she had lived here many years. I don't think she can ever have been pretty; but, for aught I know, she may possess originality and strength of character to compensate for the want of personal advantages. Mr. Rochester is an amateur of the decided and eccentric: Grace is eccentric at least. What if a former caprice (a freak very possible to a nature so sudden and headstrong as his) has delivered him into her power, and she now exercises over his actions a secret influence, the result of his own indiscretion, which he cannot shake off, and dare not disregard?" But, having reached this point of conjecture, Mrs. Poole's square, flat figure, and uncomely, dry, even coarse face, recurred so distinctly to my mind's eye, that I thought, "No; impossible! my supposition cannot be correct. Yet," suggested the secret voice which talks to us in our hearts, "*you* are not beautiful either, and perhaps Mr. Rochester approves you: at any rate, you have often felt as if he did; and last night—remember his words; remember his look; remember his voice!"

I well remembered all: language, glance, and tone seemed at the moment vividly renewed. I was now in the school-room; Adèle was drawing; I bent over her and directed her pencil. She looked up with a sort of start.

"Qu'avez-vous, mademoiselle?" said she; "Vos doigts tremblent comme la feuille, et vos joues sont rouges: mais, rouges comme des cerises!"

"I am hot, Adèle, with stooping!" She went on sketching, I went on thinking.

I hastened to drive from my mind the hateful notion I had been conceiving respecting Grace Poole: it disgusted me. I compared myself with her, and found we were different. Bessie Leaven had said I was quite a lady; and she spoke truth: I was a lady. And now I looked much better than I did when Bessie saw me: I had more colour and more flesh; more life, more vivacity; because I had brighter hopes and keener enjoyments.

"Evening approaches," said I, as I looked towards the window. "I have never heard Mr. Rochester's voice or step in the house to-day; but surely I shall see him before night: I feared the meeting in the morning: now I desire it, because expectation has been so long baffled that it is grown impatient."

When dusk actually closed, and when Adèle left me to go and play in the nursery with Sophie, I did most keenly desire it. I listened for the bell to ring below; I listened for Leah coming up with a message; I fancied sometimes I heard Mr. Rochester's own tread, and I turned to the door, expecting it to open and admit him. The door remained shut: darkness only came in through the window. Still it was not late: he often sent for me at seven and eight o'clock, and it was yet but six. Surely I should not be wholly disappointed to-night, when I had so many things to say to him! I wanted again to introduce the subject of Grace Poole, and to hear what he would answer; I wanted to ask him plainly if he really believed it was she who had made last night's hideous attempt; and if so, why he kept her wickedness a secret. It little mattered whether my curiosity irritated him; I knew the pleasure of vexing and soothing him by turns; it was one I chiefly delighted in, and a sure instinct always prevented me from going too far: beyond the verge of provocation I never ventured; on the extreme brink I liked well to try my skill. Retaining every minute form of respect, every propriety of my station, I could still meet him in argument without fear of uneasy restraint: this suited both him and me.

A tread creaked on the stairs at last; Leah made her appearance; but it was only to intimate that tea was ready in Mrs. Fairfax's room. Thither I repaired, glad at least to go downstairs; for that brought me, I imagined, nearer to Mr. Rochester's presence.

"You must want your tea," said the good lady, as I joined her; "you ate so little at dinner. I am afraid," she continued, "you are not well to-day: you look flushed and feverish."

"Oh, quite well! I never felt better."

"Then you must prove it by evincing a good appetite; will you fill the tea-pot while I knit off this needle?" Having completed her task, she rose to draw down the blind which she had hitherto kept up; by way, I suppose, of making the most of daylight: though dusk was now fast deepening into total obscurity.

"It is fair to-night," said she, as she looked through the panes, "though not starlight; Mr. Rochester has, on the whole, had a favourable day for his journey."

"Journey!—Is Mr. Rochester gone anywhere? I did not know he was out."

"Oh, he set off the moment he had breakfasted! He is gone to the Leas; Mr. Eshton's place, ten miles on the other side Millcote; I believe there is quite a party assembled there; Lord Ingram, Sir George Lynn, Colonel Dent, and others."

"Do you expect him back to-night?"

"No—nor to-morrow either; I should think he is very likely to stay a week or more: when these fine, fashionable people get together, they are so surrounded by elegance and gaiety; so well provided with all that can please and entertain, they are in no hurry to separate. Gentlemen, especially, are often in request on such occasions; and Mr. Rochester is so talented and so lively in society, that I believe he is a general favourite: the ladies are very fond of him; though you would not think his appearance calculated to recommend him particularly in their eyes: but I suppose his acquirements and abilities, perhaps his wealth and good blood, make amends for any little fault of look."

"Are there ladies at the Leas?"

"There are Mrs. Eshton and her three daughters—very elegant young ladies, indeed; and there are the Honourable Blanche and Mary Ingram; most beautiful women, I suppose: indeed I have seen Blanche, six or seven years since, when she was a girl of eighteen. She came here to a Christmas ball and party Mr. Rochester gave. You should have seen the dining-room that day—how richly it was decorated, how brilliantly lit up! I should think there were fifty ladies and gentlemen present—

all of the first county-families; and Miss Ingram was considered the belle of the evening.''

"You saw her, you say, Mrs. Fairfax: what was she like?''

"Yes, I saw her. The dining-room doors were thrown open; and, as it was Christmas-time, the servants were allowed to assemble in the hall, to hear some of the ladies sing and play. Mr. Rochester would have me to come in, and I sat down in a quiet corner and watched them. I never saw a more splendid scene: the ladies were magnificently dressed; most of them—at least most of the younger ones—looked handsome; but Miss Ingram was certainly the queen.''

"And what was she like?''

"Tall, fine bust, sloping shoulders; long, graceful neck; olive complexion, dark and clear; noble features; eyes rather like Mr. Rochester's, large and black, and as brilliant as her jewels. And then she had such a fine head of hair; raven-black, and so becomingly arranged: a crown of thick plaits behind, and in front the longest, the glossiest curls I ever saw. She was dressed in pure white; an amber-coloured scarf was passed over her shoulder and across her breast, tied at the side, and descending in long, fringed ends below her knee. She wore an amber-coloured flower, too, in her hair: it contrasted well with the jetty mass of her curls.''

"She was greatly admired of course?''

"Yes, indeed: and not only for her beauty, but for her accomplishments. She was one of the ladies who sang: a gentleman accompanied her on the piano. She and Mr. Rochester sang a duet.''

"Mr. Rochester? I was not aware he could sing.''

"Oh! he has a fine bass voice, and an excellent taste for music.''

"And Miss Ingram: what sort of a voice had she?''

"A very rich and powerful one: she sang delightfully; it was a treat to listen to her;—and she played afterwards. I am no judge of music, but Mr. Rochester is; and I heard him say her execution was remarkably good.''

"And this beautiful and accomplished lady is not yet married?''

"It appears not: I fancy neither she nor her sister have very large fortunes. Old Lord Ingram's estates were chiefly entailed, and the eldest son came in for everything almost.''

"But I wonder no wealthy nobleman or gentleman has taken a fancy to her: Mr. Rochester, for instance. He is rich, is he not?''

"Oh! yes. But you see there is a considerable difference in age: Mr. Rochester is near forty; she is but twenty-five.''

"What of that? More unequal matches are made every day.''

"True: yet I should scarcely fancy Mr. Rochester would entertain an idea of the sort. But you eat nothing: you have scarcely tasted since you began tea.''

"No: I am too thirsty to eat. Will you let me have another cup?''

I was about again to revert to the probability of a union between Mr. Rochester and the beautiful Blanche; but Adèle came in, and the conversation was turned into another channel.

When once more alone, I reviewed the information I had got; looked into my heart, examined its thoughts and feelings, and endeavoured to bring back with a strict hand such as had been straying through imagination's boundless and trackless waste, into the safe fold of common sense.

Arraigned at my own bar, Memory having given her evidence of the hopes, wishes, sentiments I had been cherishing since last night—of the general state of mind in which I had indulged for nearly a fortnight past; Reason having come forward and told in her own quiet way, a plain, unvarnished tale, showing how I had rejected the real, and rabidly devoured the ideal;—I pronounced judgment to this effect:—

That a greater fool than Jane Eyre had never breathed the breath of life: that a more fantastic idiot had never surfeited herself on sweet lies, and swallowed poison as if it were nectar.

"*You,*" I said, "a favourite with Mr. Rochester? *You* gifted with the power of pleasing him? *You* of importance to him in any way? Go! your folly sickens me. And you have derived pleasure from occasional tokens of preference —equivocal tokens, shown by a gentleman of family, and a man of the world, to a dependant and a novice. How dared you? Poor stupid dupe!—Could not even self-interest make you wiser? You repeated to yourself this morning the brief scene of last night?—Cover your face and be ashamed! He said something in praise of your eyes, did he? Blind puppy! Open their bleared lids and look on your own accursed senselessness! It does good to no woman to be flattered by her superior, who cannot possibly intend to marry her; and it is madness in all women to let a secret love kindle within them, which, if unreturned and unknown, must devour the life that feeds it; and, if discovered and responded to, must lead, *ignis-fatuus*-like, into miry wilds whence there is no extrication.

"Listen, then, Jane Eyre, to your sentence: to-morrow, place the glass before you, and draw in chalk your own picture, faithfully; without softening one defect: omit no harsh line, smooth away no displeasing irregularity; write under it, 'Portrait of a Governess, disconnected, poor, and plain.'

"Afterwards, take a piece of smooth ivory—you have one prepared in your drawing-box: take your pallette, mix your freshest, finest, clearest tints; choose your most delicate camel-hair pencils; delineate carefully the loveliest face you can imagine; paint it in your softest shades and sweetest hues, according to the description given by Mrs. Fairfax of Blanche Ingram: remember the raven ringlets, the oriental eye;—what! you revert to Mr. Rochester as a model! Order! No snivel!—no sentiment!—no regret! I will endure only sense and resolution. Recall the august yet harmonious lineaments, the Grecian neck and bust: let the round and dazzling arm be visible, and the delicate hand; omit neither diamond ring nor gold bracelet; portray faithfully the attire, aërial lace and glistening satin, graceful scarf and golden rose: call it 'Blanche, an accomplished lady of rank.'

"Whenever, in future, you should chance to fancy Mr. Rochester thinks well of you, take out these two pictures and compare them: say, 'Mr. Rochester might probably win that noble lady's love, if he chose to strive for it; is it likely he would waste a serious thought on this indigent and insignificant plebeian?' "

"I'll do it," I resolved; and having framed this determination, I grew calm, and fell asleep.

I kept my word. An hour or two sufficed to sketch my own portrait in crayons; and in less than a fortnight I had completed an ivory miniature of an imaginary Blanche Ingram. It looked a lovely face enough, and when compared with the real head in chalk, the contrast was as great as self-control could desire. I derived benefit from the task: it had kept my head and hands employed, and had given force and fixedness to the new impressions I wished to stamp indelibly on my heart.

Ere long, I had reason to congratulate myself on the course of wholesome discipline to which I had thus forced my feelings to submit: thanks to it, I was able to meet subsequent occurrences with a decent calm; which, had they found me unprepared, I should probably have been unequal to maintain, even externally.

Chapter XVII

A WEEK passed, and no news arrived of Mr. Rochester: ten days; and still he did not come. Mrs. Fairfax said she should not be surprised if he were to go straight

from the Leas to London, and thence to the continent, and not show his face again at Thornfield for a year to come: he had not unfrequently quitted it in a manner quite as abrupt and unexpected. When I heard this I was beginning to feel a strange chill and failing at the heart. I was actually permitting myself to experience a sickening sense of disappointment: but rallying my wits, and recollecting my principles, I at once called my sensations to order; and it was wonderful how I got over the temporary blunder—how I cleared up the mistake of supposing Mr. Rochester's movements a matter in which I had any cause to take a vital interest. Not that I humbled myself by a slavish notion of inferiority: on the contrary, I just said—

"You have nothing to do with the master of Thornfield, further than to receive the salary he gives you for teaching his protégée, and to be grateful for such respectful and kind treatment as, if you do your duty, you have a right to expect at his hands. Be sure that is the only tie he seriously acknowledges between you and him: so don't make him the object of your fine feelings, your raptures, agonies, and so forth. He is not of your order: keep to your caste; and be too self-respecting to lavish the love of the whole heart, soul, and strength, where such a gift is not wanted and would be despised."

I went on with my day's business tranquilly; but ever and anon vague suggestions kept wandering across my brain of reasons why I should quit Thornfield; and I kept involuntarily framing advertisements and pondering conjectures about new situations: these thoughts I did not think it necessary to check; they might germinate and bear fruit if they could.

Mr. Rochester had been absent upwards of a fortnight, when the post brought Mrs. Fairfax a letter.

"It is from the master," said she, as she looked at the direction. "Now I suppose we shall know whether we are to expect his return or not."

And while she broke the seal and perused the document, I went on taking my coffee (we were at breakfast): it was hot, and I attributed to that circumstance a fiery glow which suddenly rose to my face. Why my hand shook, and why I involuntarily spilt half the contents of my cup into my saucer, I did not choose to consider.

"Well—I sometimes think we are too quiet; but we run a chance of being busy enough now: for a little while at least," said Mrs. Fairfax, still holding the note before her spectacles.

Ere I permitted myself to request an explanation, I tied the string of Adèle's pinafore, which happened to be loose: having helped her also to another bun and refilled her mug with milk, I said, nonchalantly:—

"Mr. Rochester is not likely to return soon, I suppose?"

"Indeed, he is—in three days, he says; that will be next Thursday; and not alone either. I don't know how many of the fine people at the Leas are coming with him: he sends directions for all the best bed-rooms to be prepared; and the library and drawing-rooms are to be cleaned out; and I am to get more kitchen hands from the George Inn, at Millcote, and from wherever else I can; and the ladies will bring their maids and the gentlemen their valets: so we shall have a full house of it." And Mrs. Fairfax swallowed her breakfast and hastened away to commence operations.

The three days were, as she had foretold, busy enough. I had thought all the rooms at Thornfield beautifully clean and well arranged: but it appears I was mistaken. Three women were got to help; and such scrubbing, such brushing, such washing of paint and beating of carpets, such taking down and putting up of pictures, such polishing of mirrors and lustres, such lighting of fires in bed-rooms, such airing of sheets and feather-beds on hearths, I never beheld, either before or since. Adèle ran quite wild in the midst of it: the preparations for company and the prospect of their arrival, seemed to throw her into ecstasies. She would have Sophie to look over all her "toilettes," as she called frocks; to furbish up any that were "passées," and to air and arrange the new. For herself, she did nothing but caper

about in the front chambers, jump on and off the bedsteads, and lie on the mattresses and piled-up bolsters and pillows before the enormous fires roaring in the chimneys. From school duties she was exonerated: Mrs. Fairfax had pressed me into her service, and I was all day in the store-room, helping (or hindering) her and the cook; learning to make custards and cheesecakes and French pastry, to truss game and garnish dessert-dishes.

The party were expected to arrive on Thursday afternoon, in time for dinner at six. During the intervening period I had no time to nurse chimeras; and I believe I was as active and gay as anybody—Adèle excepted. Still, now and then, I received a damping check to my cheerfulness; and was, in spite of myself, thrown back on the region of doubts and portents, and dark conjectures. This was when I chanced to see the third story staircase door (which of late had always been kept locked) open slowly, and give passage to the form of Grace Poole, in prim cap, white apron, and handkerchief; when I watched her glide along the gallery, her quiet tread muffled in a list slipper; when I saw her look into the bustling, topsy-turvy bed-rooms,—just say a word, perhaps, to the charwoman about the proper way to polish a grate, or clean a marble mantel-piece, or take stains from papered walls, and then pass on. She would thus descend to the kitchen once a day, eat her dinner, smoke a moderate pipe on the hearth, and go back, carrying her pot of porter with her, for her private solace, in her own gloomy, upper haunt. Only one hour in the twenty-four did she pass with her fellow-servants below; all the rest of her time was spent in some low-ceiled, oaken chamber of the third story: there she sat and sewed—and probably laughed drearily to herself,—as companionless as a prisoner in his dungeon.

The strangest thing of all was, that not a soul in the house, except me, noticed her habits, or seemed to marvel at them; no one discussed her position or employment; no one pitied her solitude or isolation. I once, indeed, overheard part of a dialogue between Leah and one of the charwomen, of which Grace formed the subject. Leah had been saying something I had not caught, and the charwoman remarked:—

"She gets good wages, I guess?"

"Yes," said Leah; "I wish I had as good; not that mine are to complain of,—there's no stinginess at Thornfield; but they're not one-fifth of the sum Mrs. Poole receives. And she is laying by: she goes every quarter to the bank at Millcote. I should not wonder but she has saved enough to keep her independent if she liked to leave; but I suppose she's got used to the place; and then she's not forty yet, and strong and able for anything. It is too soon for her to give up business."

"She is a good hand, I daresay," said the charwoman.

"Ah!—she understands what she has to do,—nobody better," rejoined Leah significantly; "and it is not every one could fill her shoes; not for all the money she gets."

"That it is not!" was the reply. "I wonder whether master"——

The charwoman was going on; but here Leah turned and perceived me, and she instantly gave her companion a nudge.

"Doesn't she know?" I heard the woman whisper.

Leah shook her head, and the conversation was of course dropped. All I had gathered from it amounted to this,— that there was a mystery at Thornfield; and that from participation in that mystery, I was purposely excluded.

Thursday came: all work had been completed the previous evening; carpets were laid down, bed-hangings festooned, radiant white counterpanes spread, toilet tables arranged, furniture rubbed, flowers piled in vases: both chambers and saloons looked as fresh and bright as hands could make them. The hall, too, was scoured; and the great carved clock, as well as the steps and banisters of the staircase, were polished to the brightness of glass; in the dining-room, the side-board flashed resplendent with plate; in the drawing-room and boudoir, vases of exotics bloomed on all sides.

Afternoon arrived: Mrs. Fairfax assumed her best black satin gown, her gloves, and her gold watch; for it was her part to receive the company,—to conduct the ladies to their rooms, etc. Adèle, too, would be dressed: though I thought she had little chance of being introduced to the party that day at least. However, to please her, I allowed Sophie to apparel her in one of her short, full muslin frocks. For myself, I had no need to make any change; I should not be called upon to quit my sanctum of the school-room; for a sanctum it was now become to me,—''a very pleasant refuge in time of trouble.''

It had been a mild, serene spring day; one of those days which, towards the end of March or the beginning of April, rise shining over the earth as heralds of summer. It was drawing to an end now; but the evening was even warm, and I sat at work in the school-room with the window open.

''It gets late,'' said Mrs. Fairfax, entering in rustling state. ''I am glad I ordered dinner an hour after the time Mr. Rochester mentioned; for it is past six now. I have sent John down to the gates to see if there is anything on the road: one can see a long way from thence in the direction of Millcote.'' She went to the window. ''Here he is!'' said she. ''Well John'' (leaning out) ''any news ?''

''They're coming, ma'am,'' was the answer. ''They'll be here in ten minutes.''

Adèle flew to the window. I followed; taking care to stand on one side, so that, screened by the curtain, I could see without being seen.

The ten minutes John had given seemed very long, but at last wheels were heard; four equestrians galloped up the drive, and after them came two open carriages. Fluttering veils and waving plumes filled the vehicles; two of the cavaliers were young, dashing-looking gentlemen; the third was Mr. Rochester, on his black horse, Mesrour; Pilot bounding before him: at his side rode a lady, and he and she were the first of the party. Her purple riding-habit almost swept the ground, her veil streamed long on the breeze; mingling with its transparent folds, and gleaming through them shone rich raven ringlets.

''Miss Ingram!'' exclaimed Mrs. Fairfax, and away she hurried to her post below.

The cavalcade, following the sweep of the drive, quickly turned the angle of the house, and I lost sight of it. Adèle now petitioned to go down; but I took her on my knee and gave her to understand that she must not on any account think of venturing in sight of the ladies, either now or at any other time, unless expressly sent for: that Mr. Rochester would be very angry, etc. ''Some natural tears she shed'' on being told this; but as I began to look very grave, she consented at last to wipe them.

A joyous stir was now audible in the hall: gentlemen's deep tones, and ladies' silvery accents blent harmoniously together, and distinguishable above all, though not loud, was the sonorous voice of the master of Thornfield Hall, welcoming his fair and gallant guests under its roof. Then light steps ascended the stairs; and there was a tripping through the gallery, and soft cheerful laughs, and opening and closing doors, and, for a time, a hush.

''Elles changent de toilettes,'' said Adèle; who, listening attentively, had followed every movement; and she sighed.

''Chez maman,'' said she, ''quand il y avait du monde, je le suivais partout, au salon et à leurs chambres; souvent je regardais les femmes de chambre coiffer et habiller les dames, et c'était si amusant: comme cela on apprend.''

''Don't you feel hungry, Adèle?''

''Mais oui, mademoiselle: voilà cinq ou six heures que nous n'avons pàs mangé.''

''Well now, while the ladies are in their rooms, I will venture down and get you something to eat.''

And issuing from my asylum with precaution, I sought a back-stairs which conducted directly to the kitchen. All in that region was fire and commotion; the soup and fish were in the last stage of projection, and the cook hung over her crucibles in a frame of mind and body threatening spontaneous combustion. In the

servants' hall two coachmen and three gentlemen's gentlemen stood or sat round the fire; the Abigails, I suppose, were upstairs with their mistresses: the new servants that had been hired from Millcote, were bustling about everywhere. Threading this chaos, I at last reached the larder; there I took possession of a cold chicken, a roll of bread, some tarts, a plate or two and a knife and fork: with this booty I made a hasty retreat. I had regained the gallery, and was just shutting the back-door behind me, when an accelerated hum warned me that the ladies were about to issue from their chambers. I could not proceed to the school-room without passing some of their doors, and running the risk of being surprised with my cargo of victualage; so I stood still at this end, which, being windowless, was dark: quite dark now, for the sun was set and twilight gathering.

Presently the chambers gave up their fair tenants one after another: each came out gaily and airily, with dress that gleamed lustrous through the dusk. For a moment they stood grouped together at the other extremity of the gallery, conversing in a key of sweet subdued vivacity; they then descended the staircase almost as noiselessly as a bright mist rolls down a hill. Their collective appearance had left on me an impression of high-born elegance, such as I had never before received.

I found Adèle peeping through the school-room door, which she held ajar. "What beautiful ladies!" cried she in English. "Oh, I wish I might go to them! Do you think Mr. Rochester will send for us by-and-by, after dinner?"

"No, indeed, I don't; Mr. Rochester has something else to think about. Never mind the ladies to-night; perhaps you will see them to-morrow: here is your dinner."

She was really hungry, so the chicken and tarts served to divert her attention for a time. It was well I secured this forage; or both she, I and Sophie, to whom I conveyed a share of our repast, would have run a chance of getting no dinner at all: every one downstairs was too much engaged to think of us. The dessert was not carried out till after nine; and at ten, footmen were still running to and fro with trays and coffee-cups. I allowed Adèle to sit up much later than usual; for she declared she could not possibly go to sleep while the doors kept opening and shutting below, and people bustling about. Besides, she added, a message might possibly come from Mr. Rochester when she was undressed; "et alors quel dommage!"

I told her stories as long as she would listen to them; and then for a change I took her out into the gallery. The hall lamp was now lit, and it amused her to look over the balustrade and watch the servants passing backwards and forwards. When the evening was far advanced, a sound of music issued from the drawing-room, whither the piano had been removed; Adèle and I sat down on the top step of the stairs to listen. Presently a voice blent with the rich tones of the instrument; it was a lady who sang, and very sweet her notes were. The solo over, a duet followed, and then a glee: a joyous conversational murmur filled up the intervals. I listened long: suddenly I discovered that my ear was wholly intent on analysing the mingled sounds, and trying to discriminate amidst the confusion of accents those of Mr. Rochester; and when it caught them, which it soon did, it found a further task in framing the tones, rendered by distance inarticulate, into words.

The clock struck eleven. I looked at Adèle, whose head leant against my shoulder; her eyes were waxing heavy, so I took her up in my arms and carried her off to bed. It was near one before the gentlemen and ladies sought their chambers.

The next day was as fine as its predecessor; it was devoted by the party to an excursion to some site in the neighbourhood. They set out early in the forenoon, some on horseback, the rest in carriages; I witnessed both the departure and the return. Miss Ingram, as before, was the only lady equestrian; and, as before, Mr. Rochester galloped at her side; the two rode a little apart from the rest. I pointed out this circumstance to Mrs. Fairfax, who was standing at the window with me:—

"You said it was not likely they should think of being married," said I, "but you see Mr. Rochester evidently prefers her to any of the other ladies."

"Yes; I daresay: no doubt he admires her."

"And she him," I added; "look how she leans her head towards him as if she were conversing confidentially; I wish I could see her face; I have never had a glimpse of it yet.

"You will see her this evening," answered Mrs. Fairfax. "I happened to remark to Mr. Rochester how much Adèle wished to be introduced to the ladies, and he said: 'Oh! let her come into the drawing-room after diimer; and request Miss Eyre to accompany her.' "

"Yes—he said that from mere politeness: I need not go, I am sure," I answered.

"Well—I observed to him that as you were unused to company, I did not think you would like appearing before so gay a party—all strangers; and he replied, in his quick way: 'Nonsense! If she objects, tell her it is my particular wish; and if she resists, say I shall come and fetch her in case of contumacy.' "

"I will not give him that trouble," I answered. "I will go, if no better may be: but I don't like it. Shall you be there, Mrs. Fairfax?"

"No; I pleaded off, and he admitted my plea. I'll tell you how to manage so as to avoid the embarrassment of making a formal entrance, which is the most disagreeable part of the business. You must go into the drawing-room while it is empty, before the ladies leave the dinner-table; choose your seat in any quiet nook you like; you need not stay long after the gentlemen come in, unless you please: just let Mr. Rochester see you are there and then slip away—nobody will notice you."

"Will these people remain long, do you think?"

"Perhaps two or three weeks; certainly not more. After the Easter recess, Sir George Lynn, who was lately elected member for Millcote, will have to go up to town and take his seat; I daresay Mr. Rochester will accompany him: it surprises me that he has already made so protracted a stay at Thornfield."

It was with some trepidation that I perceived the hour approach when I was to repair with my charge to the drawing-room. Adèle had been in a state of ecstasy all day, after hearing she was to be presented to the ladies in the evening; and it was not till Sophie commenced the operation of dressing her, that she sobered down. Then the importance of the process quickly steadied her; and by the time she had her curls arranged in well-smoothed, drooping clusters, her pink satin frock put on, her long sash tied, and her lace mittens adjusted, she looked as grave as any judge. No need to warn her not to disarrange her attire: when she was dressed, she sat demurely down in her little chair, taking care previously to lift up the satin skirt for fear she should crease it, and assured me she would not stir thence till I was ready. This I quickly was: my best dress (the silver-grey one, purchased for Miss Temple's wedding, and never worn since) was soon put on; my hair was soon smoothed; my sole ornament, the pearl brooch, soon assumed. We descended.

Fortunately there was another entrance to the drawing-room than that through the saloon where they were all seated at dinner. We found the apartment vacant; a large fire burning silently on the marble hearth, and wax candles shining in bright solitude, amid the exquisite flowers with which the tables were adorned. The crimson curtain hung before the arch: slight as was the separation this drapery formed from the party in the adjoining saloon, they spoke in so low a key that nothing of their conversation could be distinguished beyond a soothing murmur.

Adèle, who appeared to be still under the influence of a most solemnising impression, sat down, without a word, on the footstool I pointed out to her. I retired to a window-seat, and, taking a book from a table near, endeavoured to read. Adèle brought her stool to my feet; ere long she touched my knee.

"What is it, Adèle?"

"Est-ce que je ne puis pas prendre une seule de ces fleurs magnifiques, Mademoiselle? Seulement pour completer ma toilette."

"You think too much of your 'toilette,' Adèle: but you may have a flower." And I took a rose from a vase and fastened it in her sash. She sighed a sigh of ineffable satisfaction, as if her cup of happiness were now full. I turned my face

away to conceal a smile I could not suppress: there was something ludicrous as well as painful in the little Parisienne's earnest and innate devotion to matters of dress.

A soft sound of rising now became audible; the curtain was swept back from the arch; through it appeared the dining-room, with its lit lustre pouring down light on the silver and glass of a magnificent dessert-service covering a long table; a band of ladies stood in the opening; they entered, and the curtain fell behind them.

There were but eight; yet somehow as they flocked in, they gave the impression of a much larger number. Some of them were very tall, many were dressed in white, and all had a sweeping amplitude of array that seemed to magnify their persons as a mist magnifies the moon. I rose and curtseyed to them: one or two bent their heads in return; the others only stared at me.

They dispersed about the room; reminding me, by the lightness and buoyancy of their movements, of a flock of white plumy birds. Some of them threw themselves in half-reclining positions on the sofas and ottomans: some bent over the tables and examined the flowers and books: the rest gathered in a group round the fire: all talked in a low but clear tone which seemed habitual to them. I knew their names afterwards, and may as well mention them now.

First, there was Mrs. Eshton and two of her daughters. She had evidently been a handsome woman, and was well preserved still. Of her daughters, the eldest, Amy, was rather little; naïve, and child-like in face and manner, and piquant in form: her white muslin dress and blue sash became her well. The second, Louisa, was taller and more elegant in figure; with a very pretty face, of that order the French term "minois chiffonné": both sisters were fair as lilies.

Lady Lynn was a large and stout personage of about forty; very erect, very haughty-looking, richly dressed in a satin robe of changeful sheen: her dark hair shone glossily under the shade of an azure plume, and within the circlet of a band of gems.

Mrs. Colonel Dent was less showy; but, I thought, more lady-like. She had a slight figure, a pale, gentle face, and fair hair. Her black satin dress, her scarf of rich foreign lace, and her pearl ornaments, pleased me better than the rainbow radiance of the titled dame.

But the three most distinguished—partly, perhaps, because the tallest figures of the band—were the Dowager Lady Ingram and her daughters, Blanche and Mary. They were all three of the loftiest stature of woman. The dowager might be between forty and fifty: her shape was still fine; her hair (by candlelight at least) still black; her teeth, too, were still apparently perfect. Most people would have termed her a splendid woman of her age: and so she was, no doubt, physically speaking; but then there was an expression of almost insupportable haughtiness in her bearing and countenance. She had Roman features and a double chin, disappearing into a throat like a pillar: these features appeared to me not only inflated and darkened, but even furrowed with pride; and the chin was sustained by the same principle, in a position of almost preternatural erectness. She had, likewise, a fierce and a hard eye: it reminded me of Mrs. Reed's; she mouthed her words in speaking; her voice was deep, its inflections very pompous, very dogmatical,—very intolerable, in short. A crimson velvet robe, and a shawl turban of some gold-wrought Indian fabric, invested her (I suppose she thought) with a truly imperial dignity.

Blanche and Mary were of equal stature,—straight and tall as poplars. Mary was too slim for her height; but Blanche was moulded like a Dian. I regarded her, of course, with special interest. First, I wished to see whether her appearance accorded with Mrs. Fairfax's description; secondly, whether it at all resembled the fancy miniature I had painted of her; and thirdly—it will out!—whether it were such as I should fancy likely to suit Mr. Rochester's taste.

As far as person went, she answered point for point, both to my picture and Mrs. Fairfax's description. The noble bust, the sloping shoulders, the graceful neck,

the dark eyes and black ringlets were all there;—but her face? Her face was like her mother's; a youthful unfurrowed likeness: the same low brow, the same high features, the same pride. It was not, however, so saturnine a pride: she laughed continually; her laugh was satirical, and so was the habitual expression of her arched and haughty lip.

Genius is said to be self-conscious: I cannot tell whether Miss Ingram was a genius, but she was self-conscious—remarkably self-conscious indeed. She entered into a discourse on botany with the gentle Mrs. Dent. It seems Mrs. Dent had not studied that science: though, as she said, she liked flowers, "especially wild ones;" Miss Ingram had, and she ran over its vocabulary with an air. I presently perceived she was (what is vernacularly termed) *trailing* Mrs. Dent; that is, playing on her ignorance: her *trail* might be clever, but it was decidedly not good-natured. She played: her execution was brilliant; she sang: her voice was fine; she talked French apart to her mama; and she talked it well, with fluency and with a good accent.

Mary had a milder and more open countenance than Blanche; softer features too, and a skin some shades fairer (Miss Ingram was dark as a Spaniard)—but Mary was deficient in life: her face lacked expression, her eye lustre; she had nothing to say, and having once taken her seat, remained fixed like a statue in its niche. The sisters were both attired in spotless white.

And did I now think Miss Ingram such a choice as Mr. Rochester would be likely to make? I could not tell—I did not know his taste in female beauty. If he liked the majestic, she was the very type of majesty: then she was accomplished, sprightly. Most gentlemen would admire her, I thought; and that he *did* admire her, I already seemed to have obtained proof: to remove the last shade of doubt, it remained but to see them together.

You are not to suppose, reader, that Adèle has all this time been sitting motionless on the stool at my feet: no; when the ladies entered, she rose, advanced to meet them, made a stately reverence, and said, with gravity,—

"Bon jour, mesdames."

And Miss Ingram had looked down at her with a mocking air, and exclaimed, "Oh, what a little puppet!"

Lady Lynn had remarked, "It is Mr. Rochester's ward, I suppose—the little French girl he was speaking of."

Mrs. Dent had kindly taken her hand, and given her a kiss. Amy and Louisa Eshton had cried out simultaneously—

"What a love of a child!"

And then they had called her to a sofa, where she now sat, ensconced between them, chattering alternately in French and broken English; absorbing not only the young ladies' attention, but that of Mrs. Eshton and Lady Lynn, and getting spoilt to her heart's content.

At last coffee is brought in, and the gentlemen are summoned. I sit in the shade— if any shade there be in this brilliantly-lit apartment; the window-curtain half hides me. Again the arch yawns: they come. The collective appearance of the gentlemen, like that of the ladies, is very imposing: they are all costumed in black; most of them are tall, some young. Henry and Frederick Lynn are very dashing sparks, indeed; and Colonel Dent is a fine soldierly man. Mr. Eshton, the magistrate of the district, is gentleman-like: his hair is quite white, his eyebrows and whiskers still dark, which gives him something of the appearance of a "père noble de théâtre." Lord Ingram, like his sisters, is very tall; like them, also, he is handsome; but he shares Mary's apathetic and listless look: he seems to have more length of limb than vivacity of blood or vigour of brain.

And where is Mr. Rochester?

He comes in last: I am not looking at the arch, yet I see him enter. I try to concentrate my attention on those netting needles, on the meshes of the purse I am forming—I wish to think only of the work I have in my hands, to see only the

silver beads and silk threads that lie in my lap; whereas, I distinctly behold his figure, and I inevitably recall the moment when I last saw it: just after I had rendered him, what he deemed, an essential service—and he, holding my hand, and looking down on my face, surveyed me with eyes that revealed a heart full and eager to overflow; in whose emotions I had a part. How near had I approached him at that moment! What had occurred since, calculated to change his and my relative positions? Yet now, how distant, how far estranged we were! So far estranged, that I did not expect him to come and speak to me. I did not wonder, when, without looking at me, he took a seat at the other side of the room, and began conversing with some of the ladies.

No sooner did I see that his attention was riveted on them, and that I might gaze without being observed, than my eyes were drawn involuntarily to his face: I could not keep their lids under control: they would rise and the irids would fix on him. I looked, and had an acute pleasure in looking,—a precious, yet poignant pleasure; pure gold, with a steely point of agony: a pleasure like what the thirst-perishing man might feel who knows the well to which he has crept is poisoned, yet stoops and drinks divine draughts nevertheless.

Most true it is that "beauty is in the eye of the gazer." My master's colourless, olive face, square, massive brow, broad and jetty eyebrows, deep eyes, strong features, firm, grim mouth,—all energy, decision, will,—were not beautiful, according to rule; but they were more than beautiful to me: they were full of an interest, an influence that quite mastered me,—that took my feelings from my own power and fettered them in his. I had not intended to love him: the reader knows I had wrought hard to extirpate from my soul the germs of love there detected; and now, at the first renewed view of him, they spontaneously revived, green and strong! He made me love him without looking at me.

I compared him with his guests. What was the gallant grace of the Lynns, the languid elegance of Lord Ingram,—even the military distinction of Colonel Dent, contrasted with his look of native pith and genuine power? I had no sympathy in their appearance, their expression: yet I could imagine that most observers would call them attractive, handsome, imposing; while they would pronounce Mr. Rochester at once harsh-featured and melancholy-looking. I saw them smile, laugh—it was nothing: the light of the candles had as much soul in it as their smile; the tinkle of the bell as much significance as their laugh. I saw Mr. Rochester smile:—his stern features softened; his eye grew both brilliant and gentle, its ray both searching and sweet. He was talking, at the moment, to Louisa and Amy Eshton. I wondered to see them receive with calm that look which seemed to me so penetrating: I expected their eyes to fall, their colour to rise under it; yet I was glad when I found they were in no sense moved. "He is not to them what he is to me," I thought: "he is not of their kind. I believe he is of mine;—I am sure he is,—I feel akin to him,— I understand the language of his countenance and movements: though rank and wealth sever us widely, I have something in my brain and heart, in my blood and nerves, that assimilates me mentally to him. Did I say, a few days since, that I had nothing to do with him but to receive my salary at his hands? Did I forbid myself to think of him in any other light than as a paymaster? Blasphemy against nature! Every good, true, vigorous feeling I have, gathers impulsively round him. I know I must conceal my sentiments: I must smother hope; I must remember that he cannot care much for me. For when I say that I am of his kind, I do not mean that I have his force to influence, and his spell to attract: I mean only that I have certain tastes and feelings in common with him. I must, then, repeat continually that we are for ever sundered:—and yet, while I breathe and think I must love him."

Coffee is handed. The ladies, since the gentlemen entered, have become lively as larks; conversation waxes brisk and merry. Colonel Dent and Mr. Eshton argue on politics; their wives listen. The two proud dowagers, Lady Lynn and Lady

Ingram, confabulate together. Sir George—whom, by-the-by, I have forgotten to describe,—a very big, and very fresh-looking country gentleman, stands before their sofa, coffee-cup in hand, and occasionally puts in a word. Mr. Frederick Lynn had taken a seat beside Mary Ingram, and is showing her the engravings of a splendid volume: she looks, smiles now and then, but apparendy says little. The tall and phlegmatic Lord Ingram leans with folded arms on the chair-back of the little and lively Amy Eshton; she glances up at him, and chatters like a wren: she likes him better than she does Mr. Rochester. Henry Lynn has taken possession of an ottoman at the feet of Louisa; Adèle shares it with him: he is trying to talk French with her, and Louisa laughs at his blunders. With whom will Blanche Ingram pair? She is standing alone at the table, bending gracefully over an album. She seems waiting to be sought; but she will not wait too long: she herself selects a mate.

Mr. Rochester, having quitted the Eshtons, stands on the hearth as solitary as she stands by the table: she confronts him, taking her station on the opposite side of the mantel-piece.

"Mr. Rochester, I thought you were not fond of children?"

"Nor am I."

"Then, what induced you to take charge of such a little doll as that?" (pointing to Adèle). "Where did you pick her up?"

"I did not pick her up, she was left on my hands."

"You should have sent her to school."

"I could not afford it: schools are so dear."

"Why, I suppose you have a governess for her: I saw a person with her just now—is she gone? Oh, no! there she is still behind the window-curtain. You pay her, of course; I should think it quite as expensive,—more so; for you have them both to keep in addition."

I feared—or should I say, hoped?—the allusion to me would make Mr. Rochester glance my way; and I involuntarily shrank further into the shade: but he never turned his eyes.

"I have not considered the subject," said he indifferently, looking straight before him.

"No—you men never do consider economy and common-sense. You should hear mama on the chapter of governesses: Mary and I have had, I should think, a dozen at least in our day; half of them detestable and the rest ridiculous, and all incubi— were they not, mama?"

"Did you speak, my own?"

The young lady thus claimed as the dowager's special property, reiterated her question with an explanation.

"My dearest, don't mention governesses; the word makes me nervous. I have suffered a martyrdom from their incompetency and caprice; I thank Heaven I have now done with them!"

Mrs. Dent here bent over to the pious lady, and whispered something in her ear; I suppose from the answer elicited, it was a reminder that one of the anathematised race was present.

"Tant pis!" said her ladyship, "I hope it may do her good!" Then, in a lower tone, but still loud enough for me to hear, "I noticed her; I am a judge of physiognomy, and in hers I see all the faults of her class."

"What are they, madam?" inquired Mr. Rochester aloud.

"I will tell you in your private ear," replied she, wagging her turban three times with portentous significancy.

"But my curiosity will be past its appetite; it craves food now."

"Ask Blanche; she is nearer you than I."

"Oh, don't refer him to me, mama! I have just one word to say of the whole tribe; they are a nuisance. Not that I ever suffered much from them; I took care to

turn the tables. What tricks Theodore and I used to play on our Miss Wilsons, and Mrs. Greys, and Madame Jouberts! Mary was always too sleepy to join in a plot with spirit. The best fun was with Madame Joubert: Miss Wilson was a poor sickly thing, lachrymose and low-spirited: not worth the trouble of vanquishing, in short; and Mrs. Grey was coarse and insensible: no blow took effect on her. But poor Madame Joubert! I see her yet in her raging passions, when we had driven her to extremities—spilt our tea, crumbled our bread and butter, tossed our books up to the ceiling, and played a charivari with the ruler and desk, the fender and fire-irons. Theodore, do you remember those merry days?''

''Yaas, to be sure I do,'' drawled Lord Ingram; ''and the poor old stick used to cry out 'Oh you villains childs!'—and then we sermonised her on the presumption of attempting to teach such clever blades as we were, when she was herself so ignorant.''

''We did; and Tedo, you know, I helped you in prosecuting (or persecuting) your tutor, whey-faced Mr. Vining—the parson in the pip, as we used to call him. He and Miss Wilson took the liberty of falling in love with each other—at least Tedo and I thought so; we surprised sundry tender glances and sighs which we interpreted as tokens of 'la belle passion,' and I promise you the public soon had the benefit of our discovery: we employed it as a sort of lever to hoist our dead-weights from the house. Dear mama, there, as soon as she got an inkling of the business, found out that it was of an immoral tendency. Did you not, my lady-mother?''

''Certainly, my best. And I was quite right; depend on that: there are a thousand reasons why liaisons between governesses and tutors should never be tolerated a moment in any well-regulated house; firstly''——

''Oh gracious, mama! Spare us the enumeration! Au reste, we all know them: danger of bad example to innocence of childhood; distractions and consequent neglect of duty on the part of the attached—mutual alliance and reliance; confidence thence resulting—insolence accompanying—mutiny and general blow-up. Am I right, Baroness Ingram, of Ingram Park?''

''My lily-flower, you are right now, as always.''

''Then no more need be said: change the subject.''

Amy Eshton, not hearing or not heeding this dictum, joined in with her soft, infantine tone: ''Louisa and I used to quiz our governess too; but she was such a good creature, she would bear anything: nothing put her out. She was never cross with us; was she, Louisa?''

''No, never: we might do what we pleased; ransack her desk and her work-box, and turn her drawers inside out; and she was so good-natured, she would give us anything we asked for.''

''I suppose, now,'' said Miss Ingram, curling her lip sarcastically, ''we shall have an abstract of the memoirs of all the governesses extant: in order to avert such a visitation, I again move the introduction of a new topic. Mr. Rochester, do you second my motion?''

''Madam, I support you on this point as on every other.''

''Then on me be the onus of bringing it forward. Signior Eduardo, are you in voice to-night?''

''Donna Bianca, if you command it, I will be.''

''Then, signior, I lay on you my sovereign behest to furbish up your lungs and other vocal organs, as they will be wanted on my royal service.''

''Who would not be the Rizzio of so divine a Mary?''

''A fig for Rizzio!'' cried she, tossing her head with all its curls, as she moved to the piano. ''It is my opinion the fiddler David must have been an insipid sort of fellow: I like black Bothwell better: to my mind a man is nothing without a spice of the devil in him; and history may say what it will of James Hepburn, but I have

a notion, he was just the sort of wild, fierce, bandit hero whom I could have consented to gift with my hand.''

''Gentlemen, you hear! Now which of you most resembles Bothwell?'' cried Mr. Rochester.

''I should say the preference lies with you,'' responded Colonel Dent.

''On my honour, I am much obliged to you,'' was the reply.

Miss Ingram, who had now seated herself with proud grace at the piano, spreading out her snowy robes in queenly amplitude, commenced a brilliant prelude; talking meantime. She appeared to be on her high horse to-night; both her words and her air seemed intended to excite not only the admiration, but the amazement of her auditors: she was evidently bent on striking them as something very dashing and daring indeed.

''Oh, I am so sick of the young men of the present day!'' exclaimed she, rattling away at the instrument. ''Poor, puny things not fit to stir a step beyond papa's park-gates: nor to go even so far without mama's permission and guardianship! Creatures so absorbed in care about their pretty faces and their white hands, and their small feet; as if a man had anything to do with beauty! As if loveliness were not the special prerogative of woman—her legitimate appanage and heritage! I grant an ugly *woman* is a blot on the fair face of creation; but as to the *gentlemen,* let them be solicitous to possess only strength and valour: let their motto be:—Hunt, shoot, and fight: the rest is not worth a fillip. Such should be my device, were I a man.''

''Whenever I marry,'' she continued after a pause which none interrupted, ''I am resolved my husband shall not be a rival, but a foil to me. I will suffer no competitor near the throne; I shall exact an undivided homage: his devotions shall not be shared between me and the shape he sees in his mirror. Mr. Rochester, now sing, and I will play for you.''

''I am all obedience,'' was the response.

''Here then is a Corsair-song. Know that I doat on Corsairs; and for that reason, sing it 'con spirito.' ''

''Commands from Miss Ingram's lips would put spirit into a mug of milk and water.''

''Take care, then: if you don't please me, I will shame you by showing how such things *should* be done.''

''That is offering a premium on incapacity: I shall now endeavour to fail.''

''Gardez-vous en bien! If you err wilfully, I shall devise a proportionate punishment.''

''Miss Ingram ought to be clement, for she has it in her power to inflict a chastisement beyond mortal endurance.''

''Ha! explain!'' commanded the lady.

''Pardon me, madam: no need of explanation; your own fine sense must inform you that one of your frowns would be a sufficient substitute for capital punishment.''

''Sing!'' said she, and again touching the piano, she commenced an accompaniment in spirited style.

''Now is my time to slip away,'' thought I: but the tones that then severed the air arrested me. Mrs. Fairfax had said Mr. Rochester possessed a fine voice: he did—a mellow, powerful bass, into which he threw his own feeling, his own force; finding a way through the ear to the heart, and there waking sensation strangely. I waited till the last deep and full vibration had expired—till the tide of talk, checked an instant, had resumed its flow; I then quitted my sheltered corner and made my exit by the side-door, which was fortunately near. Thence a narrow passage led into the hall: in crossing it, I perceived my sandal was loose; I stopped to tie it, kneeling down for that purpose on the mat at the foot of the staircase. I heard the dining-room door unclose; a gentleman came out; rising hastily, I stood face to face with him: it was Mr. Rochester.

"How do you do?" he asked.

"I am very well, sir."

"Why did you not come and speak to me in the room?"

I thought I might have retorted the question on him who put it: but I would not take that freedom. I answered:—

"I did not wish to disturb you, as you seemed engaged, sir."

"What have you been doing during my absence?"

"Nothing particular; teaching Adèle as usual."

"And getting a good deal paler than you were—as I saw at first sight. What is the matter?"

"Nothing at all, sir."

"Did you take any cold that night you half drowned me?"

"Not the least."

"Return to the drawing-room: you are deserting too early."

"I am tired, sir."

He looked at me for a minute.

"And a little depressed," he said. "What about? Tell me."

"Nothing—nothing, sir. I am not depressed."

"But I affirm that you are: so much depressed that a few more words would bring tears to your eyes—indeed, they are there now, shining and swimming; and a bead has slipped from the lash and fallen on to the flag. If I had time, and was not in mortal dread of some prating prig of a servant passing, I would know what all this means. Well, to-night I excuse you; but understand that so long as my visitors stay, I expect you to appear in the drawing-room every evening; it is my wish; don't neglect it. Now go, and send Sophie for Adèle. Good-night, my"— He stopped, bit his lip, and abruptly left me.

Chapter XVIII

MERRY days were those at Thornfield Hall; and busy days too: how different from the first three months of stillness, monotony, and solitude I had passed beneath its roof! All sad feelings seemed now driven from the house, all gloomy associations forgotten: there was life everywhere, movement all day long. You could not now traverse the gallery, once so hushed, nor enter the front chambers, once so tenantless, without encountering a smart lady's maid or a dandy valet.

The kitchen, the butler's pantry, the servants' hall, the entrance hall, were equally alive; and the saloons were only left void and still, when the blue sky and halcyon sunshine of the genial spring weather called their occupants out into the grounds. Even when that weather was broken, and continuous rain set in for some days, no damp seemed cast over enjoyment: in-door amusements only became more lively and varied, in consequence of the stop put to out-door gaiety.

I wondered what they were going to do the first evening a change of entertainment was proposed: they spoke of "playing charades," but in my ignorance I did not understand the term. The servants were called in, the dining-room tables wheeled away, the lights otherwise disposed, the chairs placed in a semicircle opposite the arch. While Mr. Rochester and the other gentlemen directed these alterations, the ladies were running up and down stairs ringing for their maids. Mrs. Fairfax was summoned to give information respecting the resources of the house in shawls, dresses, draperies of any kind; and certain wardrobes of the third story were ransacked, and their contents, in the shape of brocaded and hooped petticoats, satin sacques, black modes, lace lappets, etc., were brought down in armfuls by the Abigails;

then a selection was made, and such things as were chosen were carried to the boudoir within the drawing-room.

Meantime, Mr. Rochester had again summoned the ladies round him, and was selecting certain of their number to be of his party. "Miss Ingram is mine, of course," said he: afterwards he named the two Misses Eshton, and Mrs. Dent. He looked at me: I happened to be near him, as I had been fastening the clasp of Mrs. Dent's bracelet, which had got loose.

"Will you play?" he asked. I shook my head. He did not insist, which I rather feared he would have done: he allowed me to return quietly to my usual seat.

He and his aids now withdrew behind the curtain: the other party, which was headed by Colonel Dent, sat down on the crescent of chairs. One of the gentlemen, Mr. Eshton, observing me, seemed to propose that I should be asked to join them; but Lady Ingram instantly negatived the notion.

"No," I heard her say: "she looks too stupid for any game of the sort."

Ere long, a bell tinkled, and the curtain drew up. Within the arch, the bulky figure of Sir George Lynn, whom Mr. Rochester had likewise chosen, was seen enveloped in a white sheet: before him, on a table, lay open a large book; and at his side stood Amy Eshton, draped in Mr. Rochester's cloak, and holding a book in her hand. Somebody, unseen, rang the bell merrily; then Adèle (who had insisted on being one of her guardian's party), bounded forward, scattering round her the contents of a basket of flowers she carried on her arm. Then appeared the magnificent figure of Miss Ingram, clad in white, a long veil on her head, and a wreath of roses round her brow: by her side walked Mr. Rochester, and together they drew near the table. They knelt; while Mrs. Dent and Louisa Eshton, dressed also in white, took up their stations behind them. A ceremony followed, in dumb show, in which it was easy to recognise the pantomime of a marriage. At its termination, Colonel Dent and his party consulted in whispers for two minutes, then the colonel called out,—

"Bride!" Mr. Rochester bowed, and the curtain fell.

A considerable interval elapsed before it again rose. Its second rising displayed a more elaborately prepared scene than the last. The drawing-room, as I have before observed, was raised two steps above the dining-room, and on the top of the upper step, placed a yard or two back within the room, appeared a large marble basin, which I recognised as an ornament of the conservatory—where it usually stood, surrounded by exotics, and tenanted by gold-fish—and whence it must have been transported with some trouble, on account of its size and weight.

Seated on the carpet, by the side of this basin, was seen Mr. Rochester, costumed in shawls, with a turban on his head. His dark eyes and swarth skin and Paynim features suited the costume exactly: he looked the very model of an eastern emir; an agent or a victim of the bowstring. Presently advanced into view Miss Ingram. She, too, was attired in oriental fashion: a crimson scarf tied sash-like round the waist: an embroidered handkerchief knotted about her temples; her beautifully-moulded arms bare, one of them up-raised in the act of supporting a pitcher, poised gracefully on her head. Both her cast of form and feature, her complexion and her general air, suggested the idea of some Israelitish princess of the patriarchal days; and such was doubtless the character she intended to represent.

She approached the basin, and bent over it as if to fill her pitcher; she again lifted it to her head. The personage on the well-brink now seemed to accost her; to make some request:—"She hasted, let down her pitcher on her hand and gave him to drink." From the bosom of his robe, he then produced a casket, opened it and showed magnificent bracelets and earrings: she acted astonishment and admiration; kneeling, he laid the treasure at her feet; incredulity and delight were expressed by her looks and gestures; the stranger fastened the bracelets on her arms, and the rings in her ears. It was Eliezer and Rebecca: the camels only were wanting.

The divining party again laid their heads together: apparently they could not agree about the word or syllable this scene illustrated. Colonel Dent, their spokesman, demanded "the tableau of the Whole"; whereupon the curtain again descended.

On its third rising only a portion of the drawing-room was disclosed; the rest being concealed by a screen, hung with some sort of dark and coarse drapery. The marble basin was removed; in its place stood a deal table and a kitchen chair: these objects were visible by a very dim light proceeding from a horn lantern, the wax candles being all extinguished.

Amidst this sordid scene, sat a man with his clenched hands resting on his knees, and his eyes bent on the ground. I knew Mr. Rochester; though the begrimed face, the disordered dress (his coat hanging loose from one arm, as if it had been almost torn from his back in a scuffle), the desperate and scowling countenance, the rough, bristling hair might well have disguised him. As he moved, a chain clanked; to his wrists were attached fetters.

"Bridewell!" exclaimed Colonel Dent, and the charade was solved.

A sufficient interval having elapsed for the performers to assume their ordinary costume, they re-entered the dining-room. Mr. Rochester led in Miss Ingram; she was complimenting him on his acting.

"Do you know," said she, "that, of the three characters, I liked you in the last best? Oh, had you but lived a few years earlier, what a gallant gentleman-highwayman you would have made!"

"Is all the soot washed from my face?" he asked, turning it towards her.

"Alas, yes; the more's the pity! Nothing could be more becoming to your complexion than that ruffian's rouge."

"You would like a hero of the road then?"

"An English hero of the road would be the next best thing to an Italian bandit; and that could only be surpassed by a Levantine pirate."

"Well, whatever I am, remember you are my wife; we were married an hour since, in the presence of all these witnesses." She giggled, and her colour rose.

"Now, Dent," continued Mr. Rochester, "it is your turn." And as the other party withdrew, he and his band took the vacated seats. Miss Ingram placed herself at her leader's right hand; the other diviners filled the chairs on each side of him and her. I did not now watch the actors; I no longer waited with interest for the curtain to rise; my attention was absorbed by the spectators; my eyes, erewhile fixed on the arch, were now irresistibly attracted to the semicircle of chairs. What charade Colonel Dent and his party played, what word they chose, how they acquitted themselves, I no longer remember! but I still see the consultation which followed each scene: I see Mr. Rochester turn to Miss Ingram, and Miss Ingram to him; I see her incline her head towards him, till the jetty curls almost touch his shoulder and wave against his cheek; I hear their mutual whisperings; I recall their interchanged glances; and something even of the feeling roused by the spectacle returns in memory at this moment.

I have told you, reader, that I had learnt to love Mr. Rochester: I could not unlove him now, merely because I found that he had ceased to notice me—because I might pass hours in his presence, and he would never once turn his eyes in my direction—because I saw all his attentions appropriated by a great lady, who scorned to touch me with the hem of her robes as she passed; who, if ever her dark and imperious eye fell on me by chance, would withdraw it instantly as from an object too mean to merit observation. I could not unlove him, because I felt sure he would soon marry this very lady—because I read daily in her a proud security in his intentions respecting her—because I witnessed hourly in him a style of courtship which, if careless and choosing rather to be sought than to seek, was yet, in its very carelessness, captivating, and in its very pride, irresistible.

There was nothing to cool or banish love in these circumstances; though much to create despair. Much too, you will think, reader, to engender jealousy: if a

woman, in my position, could presume to be jealous of a woman in Miss Ingram's. But I was not jealous: or very rarely;—the nature of the pain I suffered could not be explained by that word. Miss Ingram was a mark beneath jealousy: she was too inferior to excite that feeling. Pardon this seeming paradox: I mean what I say. She was very showy, but she was not genuine: she had a fine person, many brilliant attainments; but her mind was poor, her heart barren by nature: nothing bloomed spontaneously on that soil; no unforced natural fruit delighted by its freshness. She was not good; she was not original: she used to repeat sounding phrases from books: she never offered, nor had, an opinion of her own. She advocated a high tone of sentiment; but she did not know the sensations of sympathy and pity; tenderness and truth were not in her. Too often she betrayed this, by the undue vent she gave to a spiteful antipathy she had conceived against little Adèle: pushing her away with some contumelious epithet if she happened to approach her; sometimes ordering her from the room, and always treating her with coldness and acrimony. Other eyes besides mine watched these manifestations of character—watched them closely, keenly, shrewdly. Yes: the future bridegroom, Mr. Rochester himself, exercised over his intended a ceaseless surveillance: and it was from this sagacity—this guardedness of his—this perfect, clear consciousness of his fair one's defects—this obvious absence of passion in his sentiments towards her, that my ever-torturing pain arose.

I saw he was going to marry her, for family, perhaps political reasons; because her rank and connections suited him; I felt he had not given her his love, and that her qualifications were ill adapted to win from him that treasure. This was the point—this was where the nerve was touched and teased—this was where the fever was sustained and fed: *she could not charm him.*

If she had managed the victory at once, and he had yielded and sincerely laid his heart at her feet, I should have covered my face, turned to the wall, and (figuratively) have died to them. If Miss Ingram had been a good and noble woman, endowed with force, fervour, kindness, sense, I should have had one vital struggle with two tigers—jealousy and despair: then, my heart torn out and devoured, I should have admired her—acknowledged her excellence, and been quiet for the rest of my days: and the more absolute her superiority, the deeper would have been my admiration—the more truly tranquil my quiescence. But as matters really stood, to watch Miss Ingram's efforts at fascinating Mr. Rochester; to witness their repeated failure, herself unconscious that they did fail; vainly fancying that each shaft launched, hit the mark, and infatuatedly pluming herself on success, when her pride and self-complacency repelled further and further what she wished to allure—to witness *this,* was to be at once under ceaseless excitation and ruthless restraint.

Because, when she failed, I saw how she might have succeeded. Arrows that continually glanced off from Mr. Rochester's breast and fell harmless at his feet, might, I knew, if shot by a surer hand, have quivered keen in his proud heart—have called love into his stern eye, and softness into his sardonic face: or, better still, without weapons a silent conquest might have been won.

"Why can she not influence him more, when she is privileged to draw so near to him?" I asked myself. "Surely she cannot truly like him; or not like him with true affection! If she did, she need not coin her smiles so lavishly; flash her glances so unremittingly; manufacture airs so elaborate, graces so multitudinous. It seems to me, that she might, by merely sitting quietly at his side, saying little and looking less, get nigher his heart. I have seen in his face a far different expression from that which hardens it now while she is so vivaciously accosting him; but then it came of itself: it was not elicited by meretricious arts and calculated manœuvres; and one had but to accept it—to answer what he asked without pretension, to address him when needful without grimace—and it increased and grew kinder and more genial, and warmed one like a fostering sunbeam. How will she manage to please him when they are married? I do not think she will manage it; and yet it

might be managed; and his wife might, I verily believe, be the very happiest woman the sun shines on.''

I have not yet said anything condemnatory of Mr. Rochester's project of marrying for interest and connections. It surprised me when I first discovered that such was his intention: I had thought him a man unlikely to be influenced by motives so common-place in his choice of a wife; but the longer I considered the position, education, etc. of the parties, the less I felt justified in judging and blaming either him or Miss Ingram, for acting in conformity to ideas and principles instilled into them, doubtless, from their childhood. All their class held these principles: I supposed, then, they had reasons for holding them such as I could not fathom. It seemed to me that, were I a gentleman like him, I would take to my bosom only such a wife as I could love; but the very obviousness of the advantages to the husband's own happiness, offered by this plan, convinced me that there must be arguments against its general adoption of which I was quite ignorant: otherwise I felt sure all the world would act as I wished to act.

But in other points, as well as this, I was growing very lenient to my master: I was forgetting all his faults, for which I had once kept a sharp look-out. It had formerly been my endeavour to study all sides of his character: to take the bad with the good; and from the just weighing of both, to form an equitable judgment. Now I saw no bad. The sarcasm that had repelled, the harshness that had startled me once, were only like keen condiments in a choice dish: their presence was pungent, but their absence would be felt as comparatively insipid. And as for the vague something—was it a sinister or a sorrowful, a designing or a desponding expression?— that opened upon a careful observer, now and then, in his eye, and closed again before one could fathom the strange depth partially disclosed; that something which used to make me fear and shrink, as if I had been wandering amongst volcanic-looking hills, and had suddenly felt the ground quiver, and seen it gape: that something, I, at intervals, beheld still; and with throbbing heart, but not with palsied nerves. Instead of wishing to shun, I longed only to dare—to divine it; and I thought Miss Ingram happy, because one day she might look into the abyss at her leisure, explore its secrets and analyse their nature.

Meantime, while I thought only of my master and his future bride—saw only them, heard only their discourse, and considered only their movements of importance— the rest of the party were occupied with their own separate interests and pleasures. The ladies Lynn and Ingram continued to consort in solemn conferences; where they nodded their two turbans at each other, and held up their four hands in confronting gestures of surprise, or mystery, or horror, according to the theme on which their gossip ran, like a pair of magnified puppets. Mild Mrs. Dent talked with good-natured Mrs. Eshton; and the two sometimes bestowed a courteous word or smile on me. Sir George Lynn, Colonel Dent, and Mr. Eshton discussed politics, or county affairs, or justice business. Lord Ingram flirted with Amy Eshton; Louisa played and sang to and with one of the Messrs. Lynn, and Mary Ingram listened languidly to the gallant speeches of the other. Sometimes all, as with one consent, suspended their by-play to observe and listen to the principal actors: for, after all, Mr. Rochester, and—because closely connected with him—Miss Ingram, were the life and soul of the party. If he were absent from the room an hour, a perceptible dulness seemed to steal over the spirits of his guests; and his re-entrance was sure to give a fresh impulse to the vivacity of conversation.

The want of his animating influence appeared to be peculiarly felt one day that he had been summoned to Millcote on business, and was not likely to return till late. The afternoon was wet: a walk the party had proposed to take to see a gipsy camp, lately pitched on a common beyond Hay, was consequently deferred. Some of the gentlemen were gone to the stables: the younger ones, together with the younger ladies, were playing billiards in the billiard-room. The dowagers Ingram and Lynn sought solace in a quiet game at cards. Blanche Ingram, after having

repelled, by supercilious taciturnity, some efforts of Mrs. Dent and Mrs. Eshton to draw her into conversation, had first murmured over some sentimental tunes and airs on the piano, and then, having fetched a novel from the library, had flung herself in haughty listlessness on a sofa, and prepared to beguile, by the spell of fiction, the tedious hours of absence. The room and the house were silent: only now and then the merriment of the billiard players was heard from above.

It was verging on dusk, and the clock had already given warning of the hour to dress for dinner, when little Adèle, who knelt by me in the drawing-room window-seat, exclaimed:—

"Voilà Monsieur Rochester, qui revient!"

I turned, and Miss Ingram darted forwards from her sofa: the others, too, looked up from their several occupations; for at the same time a crunching of wheels, and a splashing tramp of horse-hoofs became audible on the wet gravel. A post-chaise was approaching.

"What can possess him to come home in that style?" said Miss Ingram. "He rode Mesrour (the black horse), did he not, when he went out? and Pilot was with him:—what has he done with the animals?"

As she said this, she approached her tall person and ample garments so near the window, that I was obliged to bend back almost to the breaking of my spine: in her eagerness she did not observe me at first, but when she did, she curled her lip and moved to another casement. The post-chaise stopped; the driver rang the door bell, and a gentleman alighted, attired in travelling garb; but it was not Mr. Rochester; it was a tall, fashionable-looking man, a stranger.

"Provoking!" exclaimed Miss Ingram: "you tiresome monkey!" (apostrophising Adèle) "who perched you up in the window to give false intelligence?" and she cast on me an angry glance, as if I were in fault.

Some parleying was audible in the hall, and soon the new comer entered. He bowed to Lady Ingram, as deeming her the eldest lady present.

"It appears I come at an inopportune time, madam," said he; "when my friend, Mr. Rochester, is from home; but I arrive from a very long journey, and I think I may presume so far on old and intimate acquaintance as to instal myself here till he returns."

His manner was polite; his accent, in speaking, struck me as being somewhat unusual,—not precisely foreign, but still not altogether English; his age might be about Mr. Rochester's,—between thirty and forty; his complexion was singularly sallow: otherwise he was a fine-looking man, at first sight especially. On closer examination, you detected something in his face that displeased; or rather, that failed to please. His features were regular, but too relaxed: his eye was large and well cut, but the life looking out of it was a tame, vacant life—at least so I thought.

The sound of the dressing-bell dispersed the party. It was not till after dinner that I saw him again: he then seemed quite at his ease. But I liked his physiognomy even less than before: it struck me as being, at the same time, unsettled, and inanimate. His eye wandered, and had no meaning in its wandering: this gave him an odd look, such as I never remembered to have seen. For a handsome and not an unamiable-looking man, he repelled me exceedingly: there was no power in that smooth-skinned face of a full oval shape; no firmness in that aquiline nose, and small, cherry mouth; there was no thought on the low, even forehead; no command in that blank, brown eye.

As I sat in my usual nook, and looked at him with the light of the girandoles on the mantel-piece beaming full over him—for he occupied an arm-chair, drawn close to the fire, and kept shrinking still nearer, as if he were cold—I compared him with Mr. Rochester. I think (with deference be it spoken) the contrast could not be much greater between a sleek gander and a fierce falcon: between a meek sheep and the rough-coated keen-eyed dog, its guardian.

He had spoken of Mr. Rochester as an old friend. A curious friendship theirs must have been: a pointed illustration indeed, of the old adage that "extremes meet."

Two or three of the gentlemen sat near him, and I caught at times scraps of their conversation across the room. At first I could not make much sense of what I heard; for the discourse of Louisa Eshton and Mary Ingram, who sat nearer to me, confused the fragmentary sentences that reached me at intervals. These last were discussing the stranger: they both called him "a beautiful man." Louisa said he was "a love of a creature," and she " adored him": and Mary instanced his "pretty little mouth, and nice nose," as her ideal of the charming.

"And what a sweet-tempered forehead he has!" cried Louisa,—"so smooth— none of those frowning irregularities I dislike so much: and such a placid eye and smile!"

And then, to my great relief, Mr. Henry Lynn summoned them to the other side of the room, to settle some point about the deferred excursion to Hay Common.

I was now able to concentrate my attention on the group by the fire, and I presently gathered that the new comer was called Mr. Mason: then I learned that he was but just arrived in England, and that he came from some hot country: which was the reason, doubtless, his face was so sallow, and that he sat so near the hearth, and wore a surtout in the house. Presently the words Jamaica, Kingston, Spanish Town, indicated the West Indies as his residence; and it was with no little surprise I gathered, ere long, that he had there first seen and become acquainted with Mr. Rochester. He spoke of his friend's dislike of the burning heats, the hurricanes, and rainy seasons of that region. I knew Mr. Rochester had been a traveller: Mrs. Fairfax had said so; but I thought the continent of Europe had bounded his wanderings: till now I had never heard a hint given of visits to more distant shores.

I was pondering these things, when an incident, and a somewhat unexpected one, broke the thread of my musings. Mr. Mason, shivering as some one chanced to open the door, asked for more coal to be put on the fire, which had burnt out its flame, though its mass of cinder still shone hot and red. The footman who brought the coal, in going out, stopped near Mr. Eshton's chair, and said something to him in a low voice, of which I heard only the words, "old woman,"—"quite troublesome."

"Tell her she shall be put in the stocks if she does not take herself off," replied the magistrate.

"No—stop!" interrupted Colonel Dent. "Don't send her away, Eshton; we might turn the thing to account; better consult the ladies." And speaking aloud, he continued, "Ladies, you talked of going to Hay Common to visit the gipsy camp; Sam, here, says that one of the old Mother Bunches is in the servants' hall at this moment, and insists upon being brought in before 'the quality,' to tell them their fortunes. Would you like to see her?"

"Surely, colonel," cried Lady Ingram, "you would not encourage such a low impostor? Dismiss her, by all means, at once!"

"But I cannot persuade her to go away, my lady," said the footman; "nor can any of the servants: Mrs. Fairfax is with her just now, entreating her to be gone; but she has taken a chair in the chimney-corner, and says nothing shall stir her from it till she gets leave to come in here."

"What does she want?" asked Mrs. Eshton.

" 'To tell the gentry their fortunes,' she says, ma'am; and she swears she must and will do it."

"What is she like?" inquired the Misses Eshton in a breath.

"A shockingly ugly old creature, miss; almost as black as a crock."

"Why, she's a real sorceress!" cried Frederick Lynn. "Let us have her in, of course."

"To be sure," rejoined his brother; "it would be a thousand pities to throw away such a chance of fun."

"My dear boys, what are you thinking about?" exclaimed Mrs. Lynn.

"I cannot possibly countenance any such inconsistent proceeding," chimed in the Dowager Ingram.

"Indeed, mamma, but you can—and will," pronounced the haughty voice of Blanche, as she turned round on the piano-stool; where till now she had sat silent, apparently examining sundry sheets of music. "I have a curiosity to hear my fortune told: therefore, Sam, order the beldame forwards."

"My darling Blanche! recollect"——

"I do—I recollect all you can suggest; and I must have my will—quick, Sam!"

"Yes—yes—yes!" cried all the juveniles, both ladies and gentlemen. "Let her come—it will be excellent sport!"

The footman still lingered. "She looks such a rough one," said he.

"Go!" ejaculated Miss Ingram, and the man went.

Excitement instantly seized the whole party: a running fire of raillery and jests was proceeding when Sam returned.

"She won't come now," said he. "She says it's not her mission to appear before the 'vulgar herd' (them's her words). I must show her into a room by herself, and then those who wish to consult her must go to her one by one."

"You see now, my queenly Blanche," began Lady Ingram, "she encroaches. Be advised, my angel girl—and"——

"Show her into the library, of course," cut in the "angel girl." "It is not my mission to listen to her before the vulgar herd either: I mean to have her all to myself. Is there a fire in the library?"

"Yes, ma'am—but she looks such a tinkler."

"Cease that chatter, blockhead! and do my bidding."

Again Sam vanished; and mystery, animation, expectation rose to full flow once more.

"She's ready now," said the footman, as he reappeared. "She wishes to know who will be her first visitor."

"I think I had better just look in upon her before any of the ladies go," said Colonel Dent.

"Tell her, Sam, a gentleman is coming."

Sam went and returned.

"She says, sir, that she'll have no gentlemen; they need not trouble themselves to come near her: nor," he added, with difficulty suppressing a titter, "any ladies either, except the young and single."

"By Jove, she has taste!" exclaimed Henry Lynn.

Miss Ingram rose solemnly: "I go first," she said, in a tone which might have befitted the leader of a forlorn hope, mounting a breach in the van of his men.

"Oh, my best! oh, my dearest! pause—reflect!" was her mama's cry; but she swept past her in stately silence, passed through the door which Colonel Dent held open, and we heard her enter the library.

A comparative silence ensued. Lady Ingram thought it "le cas" to wring her hands: which she did accordingly. Miss Mary declared she felt, for her part, she never dared venture. Amy and Louisa Eshton tittered under their breath, and looked a little frightened.

The minutes passed very slowly: fifteen were counted before the library-door again opened. Miss Ingram returned to us through the arch.

Would she laugh? Would she take it as a joke? All eyes met her with a glance of eager curiosity, and she met all eyes with one of rebuff and coldness: she looked neither flurried nor merry; she walked stiffly to her seat, and took it in silence.

"Well, Blanche?" said Lord Ingram.

"What did she say, sister?" asked Mary.

''What do you think? How do you feel? Is she a real fortune-teller?'' demanded the Misses Eshton.

''Now, now, good people,'' returned Miss Ingram, ''don't press upon me. Really your organs of wonder and credulity are easily excited: you seem by the importance you all—my good mama included—ascribe to this matter—absolutely to believe we have a genuine witch in the house, who is in close alliance with the old gentleman. I have seen a gipsy vagabond; she has practised in hackneyed fashion the science of palmistry, and told me what such people usually tell. My whim is gratified; and now I think Mr. Eshton will do well to put the hag in the stocks to-morrow morning, as he threatened.''

Miss Ingram took a book, leant back in her chair, and so declined further conversation. I watched her for nearly half an hour: during all that time she never turned a page, and her face grew momently darker, more dissatisfied, and more sourly expressive of disappointment. She had obviously not heard anything to her advantage: and it seemed to me, from her prolonged fit of gloom and taciturnity, that she herself, notwithstanding her professed indifference, attached undue importance to whatever revelations had been made her.

Meantime, Mary Ingram, Amy and Louisa Eshton, declared they dared not go alone; and yet they all wished to go. A negotiation was opened through the medium of the ambassador, Sam; and after much pacing to and fro, till, I think, the said Sam's calves must have ached with the exercise, permission was at last, with great difficulty, extorted from the rigorous Sybil, for the three to wait upon her in a body.

Their visit was not so still as Miss Ingram's had been: we heard hysterical giggling and little shrieks proceeding from the library; and at the end of about twenty minutes they burst the door open, and came running across the hall, as if they were half-scared out of their wits.

''I'm sure she is something not right!'' they cried, one and all. ''She told us such things! She knows all about us!'' and they sank breathless into the various seats the gentlemen hastened to bring them.

Pressed for further explanation, they declared she had told them of things they had said and done when they were mere children; described books and ornaments they had in their boudoirs at home: keepsakes that different relations had presented to them. They affirmed that she had even divined their thoughts, and had whispered in the ear of each the name of the person she liked best in the world, and informed them of what they most wished for.

Here the gentlemen interposed with earnest petitions to be further enlightened on these two last-named points; but they got only blushes, ejaculations, tremors, and titters, in return for their importunity. The matrons, meantime, offered vinaigrettes and wielded fans; and again and again reiterated the expression of their concern that their warning had not been taken in time; and the elder gentlemen laughed, and the younger urged their services on the agitated fair ones.

In the midst of the tumult, and while my eyes and ears were fully engaged in the scene before me, I heard a hem close at my elbow: I turned, and saw Sam.

''If you please, Miss, the gipsy declares that there is another young single lady in the room who has not been to her yet, and she swears she will not go till she has seen all. I thought it must be you: there is no one else for it. What shall I tell her?''

''Oh, I will go by all means,'' I answered; and I was glad of the unexpected opportunity to gratify my much-excited curiosity. I slipped out of the room, unobserved by any eye—for the company were gathered in one mass about the trembling trio just returned—and I closed the door quietly behind me.

''If you like, miss,'' said Sam, ''I'll wait in the hall for you; and if she frightens you, just call and I'll come in.''

"No, Sam, return to the kitchen: I am not in the least afraid." Nor was I; but I was a good deal interested and excited.

Chapter XIX

THE library looked tranquil enough as I entered it, and the Sybil—if Sybil she were, was seated snugly enough in an easy chair at the chimney-corner. She had on a red cloak and a black bonnet; or rather, a broad-brimmed gipsy hat, tied down with a striped handkerchief under the chin. An extinguished candle stood on the table; she was bending over the fire, and seemed reading in a little black book, like a prayer-book, by the light of the blaze: she muttered the words to herself, as most old women do, while she read; she did not desist immediately on my entrance: it appeared she wished to finish a paragraph.

I stood on the rug and warmed my hands, which were rather cold with sitting at a distance from the drawing-room fire. I felt now as composed as ever I did in my life: there was nothing indeed in the gipsy's appearance to trouble one's calm. She shut her book and slowly looked up; her hat-brim partially shaded her face, yet I could see, as she raised it, that it was a strange one. It looked all brown and black: elf-locks bristled out from beneath a white band which passed under her chin, and came half over her cheeks, or rather jaws; her eye confronted me at once, with a bold and direct gaze.

"Well, and you want your fortune told?" she said in a voice as decided as her glance, as harsh as her features.

"I don't care about it, mother; you may please yourself: but I ought to warn you, I have no faith."

"It's like your impudence to say so: I expected it of you; I heard it in your step as you crossed the threshold."

"Did you? You've a quick ear."

"I have; and a quick eye, and a quick brain."

"You need them all in your trade."

"I do; especially when I've customers like you to deal with. Why don't you tremble?"

"I'm not cold."

"Why don't you turn pale?"

"I am not sick."

"Why don't you consult my art?"

"I'm not silly."

The old crone "nichered" a laugh under her bonnet and bandage: she then drew out a short black pipe, and lighting it began to smoke. Having indulged a while in this sedative, she raised her bent body, took the pipe from her lips, and while gazing steadily at the fire, said very deliberately:—

"You are cold; you are sick; and you are silly."

"Prove it," I rejoined.

"I will; in few words. You are cold, because you are alone: no contact strikes the fire from you that is in you. You are sick: because the best of feelings, the highest and the sweetest given to man, keeps far away from you. You are silly, because, suffer as you may, you will not beckon it to approach; nor will you stir one step to meet it where it waits you."

She again put her short, black pipe to her lips, and renewed her smoking with vigour.

"You might say all that to almost any one who, you knew, lived as a solitary dependant in a great house."

"I might say it to almost any one; but would it be true of almost any one?"

"In my circumstances."

"Yes; just so, in *your* circumstances: but find me another precisely placed as you are."

"It would be easy to find you thousands."

"You could scarcely find me one. If you knew it, you are peculiarly situated: very near happiness; yes; within reach of it. The materials are all prepared; there only wants a movement to combine them. Chance laid them somewhat apart; let them be once approached and bliss results."

"I don't understand enigmas. I never could guess a riddle in my life."

"If you wish me to speak more plainly, show me your palm."

"And I must cross it with silver, I suppose?"

"To be sure."

I gave her a shilling: she put it into an old stocking-foot which she took out of her pocket, and having tied it round and returned it, she told me to hold out my hand. I did. She approached her face to the palm, and pored over it without touching it.

"It is too fine," said she. "I can make nothing of such a hand as that; almost without lines; besides, what is in a palm? Destiny is not written there."

"I believe you," said I.

"No," she continued, "it is in the face: on the forehead, about the eyes, in the eyes themselves, in the lines of the mouth. Kneel, and lift up your head."

"Ah! now you are coming to reality," I said as I obeyed her. "I shall begin to put some faith in you presently."

I knelt within half a yard of her. She stirred the fire, so that a ripple of light broke from the disturbed coal: the glare, however, as she sat, only threw her face into deeper shadow: mine, it illumined.

"I wonder with what feelings you came to me to-night," she said, when she had examined me a while. "I wonder what thoughts are busy in your heart during all the hours you sit in yonder room with the fine people flitting before you like shapes in a magic lantern: just as little sympathetic communion passing between you and them, as if they were really mere shadows of human forms, and not the actual substance."

"I feel tired often, sleepy sometimes; but seldom sad."

"Then you have some secret hope to buoy you up and please you with whispers of the future?"

"Not I. The utmost I hope is, to save money enough out of my earnings to set up a school some day in a little house rented by myself."

"A mean nutriment for the spirit to exist on: and sitting in that window-seat (you see I know your habits)"——

"You have learned them from the servants."

"Ah! you think yourself sharp. Well—perhaps I have: to speak truth, I have an acquaintance with one of them—Mrs. Poole"——

I started to my feet when I heard the name.

"You have—have you?" thought I; "there is diablerie in the business after all, then!"

"Don't be alarmed," continued the strange being; "she's a safe hand, is Mrs. Poole: close and quiet: any one may repose confidence in her. But, as I was saying: sitting in that window-seat, do you think of nothing but your future school? Have you no present interest in any of the company who occupy the sofas and chairs before you? Is there not one face you study? One figure whose movements you follow with, at least, curiosity?"

"I like to observe all the faces, and all the figures."

"But do you never single one from the rest—or it may be, two?"

"I do, frequently; when the gestures or looks of a pair seem telling a tale: it amuses me to watch them."

"What tale do you like best to hear?"

"Oh, I have not much choice! They generally run on the same theme—courtship; and promise to end in the same catastrophe—marriage."

"And do you like that monotonous theme?"

"Positively, I don't care about it: it is nothing to me."

"Nothing to you? When a lady, young and full of life and health, charming with beauty and endowed with the gifts of rank and fortune, sits and smiles in the eyes of a gentleman you"——

"I what?"

"You know—and, perhaps, think well of."

"I don't know the gentlemen here. I have scarcely interchanged a syllable with one of them; and as to thinking well of them, I consider some respectable and stately, and middle-aged, and others young, dashing, handsome and lively; but certainly they are all at liberty to be the recipients of whose smiles they please, without my feeling disposed to consider the transaction of any moment to me."

"You don't know the gentlemen here? You have not exchanged a syllable with one of them? Will you say that of the master of the house?"

"He is not at home."

"A profound remark! A most ingenious quibble! He went to Millcote this morning, and will be back here to-night, or to-morrow: does that circumstance exclude him from the list of your acquaintance—blot him, as it were, out of existence?"

"No; but I can scarcely see what Mr. Rochester has to do with the theme you had introduced."

"I was talking of ladies smiling in the eyes of gentlemen; and of late so many smiles have been shed into Mr. Rochester's eyes that they overflow like two cups filled above the brim: have you never remarked that?"

"Mr. Rochester has a right to enjoy the society of his guests."

"No question about his right: but have you never observed that, of all the tales told here about matrimony, Mr. Rochester has been favoured with the most lively and the most continuous?"

"The eagerness of a listener quickens the tongue of a narrator." I said this rather to myself than to the gipsy; whose strange talk, voice, manner, had by this time wrapped me in a kind of dream. One unexpected sentence came from her lips after another, till I got involved in a web of mystification; and wondered what unseen spirit had been sitting for weeks by my heart watching its workings, and taking record of every pulse.

"Eagerness of a listener;" repeated she: "yes; Mr. Rochester has sat by the hour, his ear inclined to the fascinating lips that took such delight in their task of communicating; and Mr. Rochester was so willing to receive and looked so grateful for the pastime given him: you have noticed this?"

"Grateful! I cannot remember detecting gratitude in his face."

"Detecting! You have analysed, then. And what did you detect, if not gratitude?" I said nothing.

"You have seen love: have you not?—and, looking forward, you have seen him married, and beheld his bride happy?"

"Humph! Not exactly. Your witch's skill is rather at fault sometimes."

"What the devil have you seen, then?"

"Never mind: I came here to inquire, not to confess. Is it known that Mr. Rochester is to be married?"

"Yes; and to the beautiful Miss Ingram."

"Shortly?"

"Appearances would warrant that conclusion; and, no doubt (though, with an audacity that wants chastising out of you, you seem to question it), they will be a

superlatively happy pair. He must love such a handsome, noble, witty, accomplished lady; and probably she loves him: or, if not his person, at least his purse. I know she considers the Rochester estate eligible to the last degree; though (God pardon me!) I told her something on that point about an hour ago, which made her look wondrous grave: the corners of her mouth fell half an inch. I would advise her black-aviced suitor to look out: if another comes, with a longer or clearer rent-roll,—he's dished''——

"But, mother, I did not come to hear Mr. Rochester's fortune: I came to hear my own; and you have told me nothing of it.''

"Your fortune is yet doubtful: when I examined your face, one trait contradicted another. Chance has meted you a measure of happiness: that I know. I knew it before I came here this evening. She has laid it carefully on one side for you. I saw her do it. It depends on yourself to stretch out your hand, and take it up: but whether you will do so, is the problem I study. Kneel again on the rug.''

"Don't keep me long; the fire scorches me.''

I knelt. She did not stoop towards me, but only gazed, leaning back in her chair. She began muttering,—

"The flame flickers in the eye; the eye shines like dew; it looks soft and full of feeling; it smiles at my jargon: it is susceptible; impression follows impression through its clear sphere; where it ceases to smile, it is sad; an unconscious lassitude weighs on the lid: that signifies melancholy resulting from loneliness. It turns from me; it will not suffer farther scrutiny; it seems to deny, by a mocking glance, the truth of the discoveries I have already made,—to disown the charge both of sensibility and chagrin: its pride and reserve only confirm me in my opinion. The eye is favourable.

"As to the mouth, it delights at times in laughter; it is disposed to impart all that the brain conceives; though I daresay it would be silent on much the heart experiences. Mobile and flexible, it was never intended to be compressed in the eternal silence of solitude: it is a mouth which should speak much and smile often, and have human affection for its interlocutor. That feature too is propitious.

"I see no enemy to a fortunate issue but in the brow; and that brow professes to say,—'I can live alone, if self-respect and circumstances require me so to do. I need not sell my soul to buy bliss. I have an inward treasure, born with me, which can keep me alive if all extraneous delights should be withheld; or offered only at a price I cannot afford to give.' The forehead declares, 'Reason sits firm and holds the reins, and she will not let the feelings burst away and hurry her to wild chasms. The passions may rage furiously, like true heathens, as they are; and the desires may imagine all sorts of vain things: but judgment shall still have the last word in every argument, and the casting vote in every decision. Strong wind, earthquake-shock, and fire may pass by: but I shall follow the guiding of that still small voice which interprets the dictates of conscience.'

"Well said, forehead; your declaration shall be respected. I have formed my plans—right plans I deem them—and in them I have attended to the claims of conscience, the counsels of reason. I know how soon youth would fade and bloom perish, if, in the cup of bliss offered, but one dreg of shame, or one flavour of remorse were detected; and I do not want sacrifice, sorrow, dissolution—such is not my taste. I wish to foster, not to blight—to earn gratitude, not to wring tears of blood—no, nor of brine: my harvest must be in smiles, in endearments, in sweet—That will do. I think I rave in a kind of exquisite delirium. I should wish now to protract this moment *ad infinitum;* but I dare not. So far I have governed myself thoroughly. I have acted as I inwardly swore I would act; but farther might try me beyond my strength. Rise, Miss Eyre: leave me; 'the play is played out.' ''

Where was I? Did I wake or sleep? Had I been dreaming? Did I dream still? The old woman's voice had changed: her accent, her gesture, and all were familiar to me as my own face in a glass—as the speech of my own tongue. I got up, but

did not go. I looked; I stirred the fire, and I looked again: but she drew her bonnet and her bandage closer about her face, and again beckoned me to depart. The flame illuminated her hand stretched out; roused now, and on the alert for discoveries, I at once noticed that hand. It was no more the withered limb of eld than my own; it was a rounded supple member, with smooth fingers, symmetrically turned; a broad ring flashed on the little finger, and stooping forward, I looked at it, and saw a gem I had seen a hundred times before. Again I looked at the face; which was no longer turned from me —on the contrary, the bonnet was doffed, the bandage displaced, the head advanced.

"Well, Jane, do you know me?" asked the familiar voice.

"Only take off the red cloak, sir, and then"——

"But the string is in a knot—help me."

"Break it, sir."

"There, then—'Off, ye lendings!' " And Mr. Rochester stepped out of his disguise.

"Now, sir, what a strange idea!"

"But well carried out, eh? Don't you think so?"

"With the ladies you must have managed well."

"But not with you?"

"You did not act the character of a gipsy with me."

"What character did I act? My own?"

"No; some unaccountable one. In short, I believe you have been trying to draw me out—or in; you have been talking nonsense to make me talk nonsense. It is scarcely fair, sir."

"Do you forgive me, Jane?"

"I cannot tell till I have thought it all over. If, on reflection, I find I have fallen into no great absurdity, I shall try to forgive you; but it was not right."

"Oh! you have been very correct—very careful, very sensible."

I reflected, and thought, on the whole, I had. It was a comfort; but, indeed, I had been on my guard almost from the beginning of the interview. Something of masquerade I suspected. I knew gipsies and fortune-tellers did not express themselves as this seeming old woman had expressed herself; besides, I had noted her feigned voice, her anxiety to conceal her features. But my mind had been running on Grace Poole—that living enigma, that mystery of mysteries, as I considered her. I had never thought of Mr. Rochester.

"Well," said he, "what are you musing about? What does that grave smile signify?"

"Wonder and self-congratulation, sir. I have your permission to retire now, I suppose?"

"No; stay a moment; and tell me what the people in the drawing-room yonder are doing."

"Discussing the gipsy, I daresay."

"Sit down!—Let me hear what they said about me."

"I had better not stay long, sir; it must be near eleven o'clock. Oh! are you aware, Mr. Rochester, that a stranger has arrived here since you left this morning?"

"A stranger!—no; who can it be? I expected no one; is he gone?"

"No; he said he had known you long, and that he could take the liberty of installing himself here till you returned."

"The devil he did! Did he give his name?"

"His name is Mason, sir; and he comes from the West Indies; from Spanish Town, in Jamaica, I think."

Mr. Rochester was standing near me; he had taken my hand, as if to lead me to a chair. As I spoke, he gave my wrist a convulsive grip; the smile on his lips froze: apparently a spasm caught his breath.

"Mason!—the West Indies!" he said, in the tone one might fancy a speaking automaton to enounce its single words; "Mason!—the West Indies!" he reiterated; and he went over the syllables three times, growing, in the intervals of speaking, whiter than ashes: he hardly seemed to know what he was doing.

"Do you feel ill, sir?" I inquired.

"Jane, I've got a blow;—I've got a blow, Jane!" He staggered.

"Oh!—lean on me, sir."

"Jane, you offered me your shoulder once before; let me have it now."

"Yes, sir, yes; and my arm."

He sat down, and made me sit beside him. Holding my hand in both his own, he chafed it; gazing on me, at the same time, with the most troubled and dreary look.

"My little friend!" said he, "I wish I were in a quiet island with only you; and trouble, and danger, and hideous recollections removed from me."

"Can I help you, sir?—I'd give my life to serve you."

"Jane, if aid is wanted, I'll seek it at your hands; I promise you that."

"Thank you, sir; tell me what to do,—I'll try, at least, to do it."

"Fetch me now, Jane, a glass of wine from the dining-room; they will be at supper there; and tell me if Mason is with them, and what he is doing."

I went. I found all the party in the dining-room at supper, as Mr. Rochester had said; they were not seated at table,—the supper was arranged on the side-board; each had taken what he chose, and they stood about here and there in groups, their plates and glasses in their hands. Every one seemed in high glee; laughter and conversation were general and animated. Mr. Mason stood near the fire, talking to Colonel and Mrs. Dent, and appeared as merry as any of them. I filled a wine-glass (I saw Miss Ingram watch me frowningly as I did so: she thought I was taking a liberty, I daresay), and I returned to the library.

Mr. Rochester's extreme pallor had disappeared, and he looked once more firm and stern. He took the glass from my hand.

"Here is to your health, ministrant spirit!" he said: he swallowed the contents and returned it to me. "What are they doing, Jane?"

"Laughing and talking, sir."

"They don't look grave and mysterious, as if they had heard something strange?"

"Not at all:—they are full of jests and gaiety."

"And Mason?"

"He was laughing too."

"If all these people came in a body and spat at me, what would you do, Jane?"

"Turn them out of the room, sir, if I could."

He half smiled. "But if I were to go to them, and they only looked at me coldly, and whispered sneeringly amongst each other, and then dropt off and left me one by one, what then? Would you go with them?"

"I rather think not, sir: I should have more pleasure in staying with you."

"To comfort me?"

"Yes, sir, to comfort you as well as I could."

"And if they laid you under a ban for adhering to me?"

"I, probably, should know nothing about their ban; and if I did, I should care nothing about it."

"Then, you could dare censure for my sake?"

"I could dare it for the sake of any friend who deserved my adherence; as you, I am sure, do."

"Go back now into the room; step quietly up to Mason, and whisper in his ear that Mr. Rochester is come and wishes to see him: show him in here and then leave me."

"Yes, sir."

I did his behest. The company all stared at me as I passed straight among them. I sought Mr. Mason, delivered the message, and preceded him from the room: I ushered him into the library, and then I went upstairs.

At a late hour, after I had been in bed some time, I heard the visitors repair to their chambers: I distinguished Mr. Rochester's voice, and heard him say, "This way, Mason; this is your room."

He spoke cheerfully: the gay tones set my heart at ease. I was soon asleep.

Chapter XX

I HAD forgotten to draw my curtain, which I usually did; and also to let down my window-blind. The consequence was, that when the moon, which was full and bright (for the night was fine), came in her course to that space in the sky opposite my casement, and looked in at me through the unveiled panes, her glorious gaze roused me. Awaking in the dead of night, I opened my eyes on her disk—silver-white and crystal-clear. It was beautiful, but too solemn: I half rose, and stretched my arm to draw the curtain.

Good God! What a cry!

The night—its silence—its rest, was rent in twain by a savage, a sharp, a shrilly sound that ran from end to end of Thornfield Hall.

My pulse stopped: my heart stood still; my stretched arm was paralysed. The cry died, and was not renewed. Indeed, whatever being uttered that fearful shriek could not soon repeat it: not the widest-winged condor on the Andes could, twice in succession, send out such a yell from the cloud shrouding his eyrie. The thing delivering such utterance must rest ere it could repeat the effort.

It came out of the third story; for it passed overhead. And overhead—yes, in the room just above my chamber-ceiling—I now heard a struggle: a deadly one it seemed from the noise; and a half-smothered voice shouted—

"Help! help! help!" three times rapidly.

"Will no one come?" it cried; and then, while the staggering and stamping went on wildly, I distinguished through plank and plaster:—

"Rochester! Rochester! for God's sake, come!"

A chamber-door opened: some one ran, or rushed, along the gallery. Another step stamped on the flooring above and something fell; and there was silence.

I put on some clothes, though horror shook all my limbs: I issued from my apartment. The sleepers were all aroused: ejaculations, terrified murmurs sounded in every room; door after door unclosed; one looked out and another looked out; the gallery filled. Gentlemen and ladies alike had quitted their beds; and "Oh! what is it?"—"Who is hurt?"—"What has happened?"—"Fetch a light!"—"Is it fire?"— "Are there robbers?"—"Where shall we run?" was demanded confusedly on all hands. But for the moonlight they would have been in complete darkness. They ran to and fro; they crowded together: some sobbed, some stumbled: the confusion was inextricable.

"Where the devil is Rochester?" cried Colonel Dent. "I cannot find him in his bed."

"Here! here!" was shouted in return. "Be composed, all of you: I'm coming."

And the door at the end of the gallery opened, and Mr. Rochester advanced with a candle: he had just descended from the upper story. One of the ladies ran to him directly; she seized his arm: it was Miss Ingram.

"What awful event has taken place?" said she. "Speak! let us know the worst at once!"

"But don't pull me down or strangle me," he replied: for the misses Eshton were clinging about him now; and the two dowagers, in vast white wrappers, were bearing down on him like ships in full sail.

"All's right!—all's right!" he cried. "It's a mere rehearsal of Much Ado About Nothing. Ladies, keep off; or I shall wax dangerous."

And dangerous he looked: his black eyes darted sparks. Calming himself by an effort, he added:—

"A servant has had the nightmare; that is all. She's an excitable, nervous person: she construed her dream into an apparition, or something of that sort, no doubt; and has taken a fit with fright. Now then, I must see you all back into your rooms; for, till the house is settled, she cannot be looked after. Gentlemen, have the goodness to set the ladies the example. Miss Ingram, I am sure you will not fail in evincing superiority to idle terrors. Amy and Louisa, return to your nests like a pair of doves, as you are. Mesdames" (to the dowagers), "you will take cold to a dead certainty, if you stay in this chill gallery any longer."

And so, by dint of alternate coaxing and commanding, he contrived to get them all once more enclosed in their separate dormitories. I did not wait to be ordered back to mine; but retreated unnoticed: as unnoticed as I had left it.

Not, however, to go to bed: on the contrary, I began and dressed myself carefully. The sounds I had heard after the scream, and the words that had been uttered, had probably been heard only by me; for they had proceeded from the room above mine: but they assured me that it was not a servant's dream which had thus struck horror through the house; and that the explanation Mr. Rochester had given was merely an invention framed to pacify his guests. I dressed, then, to be ready for emergencies. When dressed, I sat a long time by the window, looking out over the silent grounds and silvered fields, and waiting for I knew not what. It seemed to me that some event must follow the strange cry, struggle, and call.

No: stillness returned: each murmur and movement ceased gradually, and in about an hour Thornfield Hall was again as hushed as a desert. It seemed that sleep and night had resumed their empire. Meantime the moon declined: she was about to set. Not liking to sit in the cold and darkness, I thought I would lie down on my bed, dressed as I was. I left the window, and moved with little noise across the carpet; as I stooped to take off my shoes, a cautious hand tapped low at the door.

"Am I wanted?" I asked.

"Are you up?" asked the voice I expected to hear, viz., my master's.

"Yes, sir."

"And dressed?"

"Yes."

"Come out, then, quietly."

I obeyed. Mr. Rochester stood in the gallery, holding a light.

"I want you," he said: "come this way: take your time, and make no noise."

My slippers were thin: I could walk the matted floor as softly as a cat. He glided up the gallery and up the stairs, and stopped in the dark, low corridor of the fateful third story: I had followed and stood at his side.

"Have you a sponge in your room?" he asked in a whisper.

"Yes, sir."

"Have you any salts—volatile salts?"

"Yes."

"Go back and fetch both."

I returned, sought the sponge on the wash-stand, the salts in my drawer, and once more retraced my steps. He still waited; he held a key in his hand: approaching one of the small, black doors, he put it in the lock; he paused and addressed me again.

"You don't turn sick at the sight of blood?"

"I think I shall not: I have never been tried yet."

I felt a thrill while I answered him; but no coldness, and no faintness.

"Just give me your hand," he said; "it will not do to risk a fainting fit."

I put my fingers into his. "Warm and steady," was his remark: he turned the key and opened the door.

I saw a room I remembered to have seen before; the day Mrs. Fairfax showed me over the house: it was hung with tapestry; but the tapestry was now looped up in one part, and there was a door apparent, which had then been concealed. This door was open; a light shone out of the room within: I heard thence a snarling, snatching sound, almost like a dog quarrelling. Mr. Rochester, putting down his candle, said to me, "Wait a minute," and he went forward to the inner apartment. A shout of laughter greeted his entrance; noisy at first, and terminating in Grace Poole's own goblin ha! ha! *She* then was there. He made some sort of arrangement, without speaking: though I heard a low voice address him: he came out and closed the door behind him.

"Here, Jane!" he said; and I walked round to the other side of a large bed, which with its drawn curtains concealed a considerable portion of the chamber. An easy-chair was near the bed-head: a man sat in it, dressed with the exception of his coat; he was still; his head leant back; his eyes were closed. Mr. Rochester held the candle over him; I recognised in his pale and seemingly lifeless face—the stranger, Mason: I saw too that his linen on one side, and one arm, was almost soaked in blood.

"Hold the candle," said Mr. Rochester, and I took it; he fetched a basin of water from the wash-stand: "Hold that," said he. I obeyed. He took the sponge, dipped it in and moistened the corpse-like face: he asked for my smelling-bottle, and applied it to the nostrils. Mr. Mason shortly unclosed his eyes; he groaned. Mr. Rochester opened the shirt of the wounded man, whose arm and shoulder were bandaged: he sponged away blood, trickling fast down.

"Is there immediate danger?" murmured Mr. Mason.

"Pooh! No—a mere scratch. Don't be so overcome, man: bear up! I'll fetch a surgeon for you now, myself: you'll be able to be removed by morning, I hope. Jane," he continued.

"Sir?"

"I shall have to leave you in this room with this gentleman, for an hour, or perhaps two hours; you will sponge the blood as I do when it returns: if he feels faint, you will put the glass of water on that stand to his lips, and your salts to his nose. You will not speak to him on any pretext—and—Richard—it will be at the peril of your life if you speak to her: open your lips—agitate yourself—and I'll not answer for the consequences."

Again the poor man groaned: he looked as if he dared not move: fear, either of death or of something else, appeared almost to paralyse him. Mr. Rochester put the now bloody sponge into my hand, and I proceeded to use it as he had done. He watched me a second, then saying, "Remember!—No conversation," he left the room. I experienced a strange feeling as the key grated in the lock, and the sound of his retreating step ceased to be heard.

Here then I was in the third story, fastened into one of its mystic cells; night around me; a pale and bloody spectacle under my eyes and hands; a murderess hardly separated from me by a single door: yes—that was appalling—the rest I could bear; but I shuddered at the thought of Grace Poole bursting out upon me.

I must keep to my post, however. I must watch this ghastly countenance—these blue, still lips forbidden to unclose—these eyes now shut, now opening, now wandering through the room, now fixing on me, and ever glazed with the dulness of horror. I must dip my hand again and again in the basin of blood and water, and wipe away the trickling gore. I must see the light of the unsnuffed candle wane on my employment; the shadows darken on the wrought, antique tapestry round

me, and grow black under the hangings of the vast old bed, and quiver strangely over the doors of a great cabinet opposite—whose front, divided into twelve panels, bore, in grim design, the heads of the twelve apostles, each inclosed in its separate panel as in a frame; while above them at the top rose an ebon crucifix and a dying Christ.

According as the shifting obscurity and flickering gleam hovered here or glanced there, it was now the bearded physician, Luke, that bent his brow; now St. John's long hair that waved; and anon the devilish face of Judas, that grew out of the panel, and seemed gathering life and threatening a revelation of the arch-traitor—of Satan himself—in his subordinate's form.

Amidst all this, I had to listen as well as watch: to listen for the movements of the wild beast or the fiend in yonder side den. But since Mr. Rochester's visit it seemed spellbound: all the night I heard but three sounds at three long intervals,—a step creak, a momentary renewal of the snarling, canine noise, and a deep human groan.

Then my own thoughts worried me. What crime was this, that lived incarnate in this sequestered mansion, and could neither be expelled nor subdued by the owner?—What mystery, that broke out, now in fire and now in blood, at the deadest hours of night? What creature was it, that, masked in an ordinary woman's face and shape, uttered the voice, now of a mocking demon, and anon of a carrion-seeking bird of prey?

And this man I bent over—this common-place, quiet stranger—how had he become involved in the web of horror? and why had the Fury flown at him? What made him seek this quarter of the house at an untimely season, when he should have been asleep in bed? I had heard Mr. Rochester assign him an apartment below—what brought him here? And why, now, was he so tame under the violence or treachery done him? Why did he so quietly submit to the concealment Mr. Rochester enforced? Why *did* Mr. Rochester enforce this concealment? His guest had been outraged, his own life on a former occasion had been hideously plotted against; and both attempts he smothered in secrecy and sank in oblivion! Lastly, I saw Mr. Mason was submissive to Mr. Rochester; that the impetuous will of the latter held complete sway over the inertness of the former: the few words which had passed between them assured me of this. It was evident that in their former intercourse, the passive disposition of the one had been habitually influenced by the active energy of the other: whence then had arisen Mr. Rochester's dismay when he heard of Mr. Mason's arrival? Why had the mere name of this unresisting individual—whom his word now sufficed to control like a child—fallen on him, a few hours since, as a thunderbolt might fall on an oak?

Oh! I could not forget his look and his paleness when he whispered: "Jane, I have got a blow—I have got a blow, Jane." I could not forget how the arm had trembled which he rested on my shoulder: and it was no light matter which could thus bow the resolute spirit and thrill the vigorous frame of Fairfax Rochester.

"When will he come? When will he come?" I cried inwardly, as the night lingered and lingered—as my bleeding patient drooped, moaned, sickened: and neither day nor aid arrived. I had, again and again, held the water to Mason's white lips; again and again offered him the stimulating salts: my efforts seemed ineffectual: either bodily or mental suffering, or loss of blood, or all three combined, were fast prostrating his strength. He moaned so, and looked so weak, wild, and lost, I feared he was dying; and I might not even speak to him!

The candle, wasted at last, went out; as it expired, I perceived streaks of grey light edging the window curtains; dawn was approaching. Presently I heard Pilot bark far below, out of his distant kennel in the court-yard: hope revived. Nor was it unwarranted: in five minutes more the grating key, the yielding lock, warned me my watch was relieved. It could not have lasted more than two hours: many a week has seemed shorter.

Mr. Rochester entered, and with him the surgeon he had been to fetch.

"Now, Carter, be on the alert," he said to this last: "I give you but half an hour for dressing the wound, fastening the bandages, getting the patient downstairs and all."

"But is he fit to move, sir?"

"No doubt of it; it is nothing serious: he is nervous, his spirits must be kept up. Come, set to work."

Mr. Rochester drew back the thick curtain, drew up the holland blind, let in all the daylight he could; and I was surprised and cheered to see how far dawn was advanced: what rosy streaks were beginning to brighten the east. Then he approached Mason, whom the surgeon was already handling.

"Now, my good fellow, how are you?" he asked.

"She's done for me, I fear," was the faint reply.

"Not a whit!—courage! This day fortnight you'll hardly be a pin the worse of it: you've lost a little blood; that's all. Carter, assure him there's no danger."

"I can do that conscientiously," said Carter, who had now undone the bandages; "only I wish I could have got here sooner: he would not have bled so much—but how is this? The flesh on the shoulder is torn as well as cut. This wound was not done with a knife: there have been teeth here!"

"She bit me," he murmured. "She worried me like a tigress, when Rochester got the knife from her."

"You should not have yielded: you should have grappled with her at once," said Mr. Rochester.

"But under such circumstances what could one do?" returned Mason. "Oh, it was frightful!" he added, shuddering. "And I did not expect it: she looked so quiet at first."

"I warned you," was his friend's answer; "I said—be on your guard when you go near her. Besides, you might have waited till to-morrow, and had me with you: it was mere folly to attempt the interview to-night, and alone."

"I thought I could have done some good."

"You thought! you thought! Yes; it makes me impatient to hear you: but, however, you have suffered, and are likely to suffer enough for not taking my advice; so I'll say no more. Carter—hurry!—hurry! The sun will soon rise, and I must have him off."

"Directly, sir; the shoulder is just bandaged. I must look to this other wound in the arm: she has had her teeth here too, I think."

"She sucked the blood: she said she'd drain my heart," said Mason.

I saw Mr. Rochester shudder: a singularly marked expression of disgust, horror, hatred, warped his countenance almost to distortion; but he only said:—

"Come, be silent, Richard, and never mind her gibberish: don't repeat it."

"I wish I could forget it," was the answer.

"You will when you are out of the country: when you get back to Spanish Town, you may think of her as dead and buried—or rather, you need not think of her at all."

"Impossible to forget this night!"

"It is not impossible: have some energy, man. You thought you were as dead as a herring two hours since, and you are all alive and talking now. There!—Carter has done with you or nearly so; I'll make you decent in a trice. Jane" (he turned to me for the first time since his re-entrance) "take this key: go down into my bed-room, and walk straight forward into my dressing-room; open the top drawer of the wardrobe and take out a clean shirt and neck-handkerchief: bring them here; and be nimble."

I went; sought the repository he had mentioned, found the articles named, and returned with them.

"Now," said he, "go to the other side of the bed while I order his toilet; but don't leave the room: you may be wanted again."

I retired as directed.

"Was anybody stirring below when you went down, Jane?" inquired Mr. Rochester, presently.

"No, sir; all was very still."

"We shall get you off cannily, Dick: and it will be better, both for your sake, and for that of the poor creature in yonder. I have striven long to avoid exposure, and I should not like it to come at last. Here, Carter, help him on with his waistcoat. Where did you leave your furred cloak? You can't travel a mile without that, I know, in this damned cold climate. In your room?—Jane, run down to Mr. Mason's room,—the one next mine,—and fetch a cloak you will see there."

Again I ran, and again returned, bearing an immense mantle lined and edged with fur.

"Now, I've another errand for you," said my untiring master; "you must away to my room again. What a mercy you are shod with velvet, Jane!—a clod-hopping messenger would never do at this juncture. You must open the middle drawer of my toilet-table and take out a little phial and a little glass you will find there,— quick!" I flew thither and back, bringing the desired vessels.

"That's well! Now, doctor, I shall take the liberty of administering a dose myself; on my own responsibility. I got this cordial at Rome, of an Italian charlatan—a fellow you would have kicked, Carter. It is not a thing to be used indiscriminately, but it is good upon occasion: as now, for instance. Jane, a little water."

He held out the tiny glass, and I half filled it from the water bottle on the washstand.

"That will do:—now wet the lip of the phial."

I did so: he measured twelve drops of a crimson liquid, and presented it to Mason.

"Drink, Richard: it will give you the heart you lack, for an hour or so."

"But will it hurt me?—is it inflammatory?"

"Drink! drink! drink!"

Mr. Mason obeyed, because it was evidently useless to resist. He was dressed now: he still looked pale, but he was no longer gory and sullied. Mr. Rochester let him sit three minutes after he had swallowed the liquid; he then took his arm:—

"Now I am sure you can get on your feet," he said:—"try."

The patient rose.

"Carter, take him under the other shoulder. Be of good cheer, Richard; step out:—that's it!"

"I do feel better," remarked Mr. Mason.

"I am sure you do. Now, Jane, trip on before us away to the back-stairs; unbolt the side-passage door, and tell the driver of the post-chaise you will see in the yard—or just outside, for I told him not to drive his rattling wheels over the pavement—to be ready; we are coming: and, Jane, if any one is about, come to the foot of the stairs and hem."

It was by this time half-past five, and the sun was on the point of rising; but I found the kitchen still dark and silent. The side-passage door was fastened; I opened it with as little noise as possible: all the yard was quiet; but the gates stood wide open, and there was a post-chaise, with horses ready harnessed, and driver seated on the box, stationed outside. I approached him, and said the gentlemen were coming; he nodded: and then I looked carefully round and listened. The stillness of early morning slumbered everywhere; the curtains were yet drawn over the servants' chamber windows; little birds were just twittering in the blossom-blanched orchard trees, whose boughs drooped like white garlands over the wall enclosing one side of the yard; the carriage horses stamped from time to time in their closed stables: all else was still.

The gentlemen now appeared. Mason, supported by Mr. Rochester and the surgeon, seemed to walk with tolerable ease: they assisted him into the chaise; Carter followed.

"Take care of him," said Mr. Rochester to the latter, "and keep him at your house till he is quite well: I shall ride over in a day or two to see how he gets on. Richard, how is it with you?"

"The fresh air revives me, Fairfax."

"Leave the window open on his side, Carter; there is no wind—good-bye, Dick."

"Fairfax"——

"Well, what is it?"

"Let her be taken care of; let her be treated as tenderly as may be: let her"—he stopped and burst into tears.

"I do my best; and have done it, and will do it," was the answer: he shut up the chaise door, and the vehicle drove away.

"Yet would to God there was an end of all this!" added Mr. Rochester, as he closed and barred the heavy yard-gates. This done, he moved with slow step and abstracted air towards a door in the wall bordering the orchard. I, supposing he had done with me, prepared to return to the house; again, however, I heard him call "Jane!" He had opened the portal and stood at it, waiting for me.

"Come where there is some freshness, for a few moments," he said; "that house is a mere dungeon: don't you feel it so?"

"It seems to me a splendid mansion, sir."

"The glamour of inexperience is over your eyes," he answered; "and you see it through a charmed medium: you cannot discern that the gilding is slime and the silk draperies cobwebs; that the marble is sordid slate, and the polished woods mere refuse chips and scaly bark. Now *here* (he pointed to the leafy enclosure we had entered) all is real, sweet, and pure."

He strayed down a walk edged with box; with apple trees, pear trees, and cherry trees on one side, and a border on the other, full of all sorts of old-fashioned flowers, stocks, sweet-williams, primroses, pansies, mingled with southern-wood, sweet-briar, and various fragrant herbs. They were fresh now as a succession of April showers and gleams, followed by a lovely spring morning, could make them: the sun was just entering the dappled east, and his light illumined the wreathed and dewy orchard trees and shone down the quiet walks under them.

"Jane, will you have a flower?"

He gathered a half-blown rose, the first on the bush, and offered it to me.

"Thank you, sir."

"Do you like this sunrise, Jane? That sky with its high and light clouds which are sure to melt away as the day waxes warm—this placid and balmy atmosphere?"

"I do, very much."

"You have passed a strange night, Jane?"

"Yes, sir."

"And it has made you look pale—were you afraid when I left you alone with Mason?"

"I was afraid of some one coming out of the inner room."

"But I had fastened the door—I had the key in my pocket: I should have been a careless shepherd if I had left a lamb—my pet lamb—so near a wolf's den, unguarded: you were safe."

"Will Grace Poole live here still, sir?"

"Oh, yes! don't trouble your head about her—put the thing out of your thoughts."

"Yet it seems to me your life is hardly secure while she stays."

"Never fear—I will take care of myself."

"Is the danger you apprehended last night gone by now, sir?"

"I cannot vouch for that till Mason is out of England: nor even then. To live, for me, Jane, is to stand on a crater-crust which may crack and spue fire any day."

"But Mr. Mason seems a man easily led. Your influence, sir, is evidently potent with him: he will never set you at defiance, or wilfully injure you."

"Oh, no! Mason will not defy me; nor, knowing it, will he hurt me—but, unintentionally, he might in a moment, by one careless word, deprive me, if not of life, yet for ever of happiness."

"Tell him to be cautious, sir: let him know what you fear, and show him how to avert the danger."

He laughed sardonically, hastily took my hand, and as hastily threw it from him.

"If I could do that, simpleton, where would the danger be? Annihilated in a moment. Ever since I have known Mason, I have only had to say to him, 'Do that,' and the thing has been done. But I cannot give him orders in this case: I cannot say 'Beware of harming me, Richard;' for it is imperative that I should keep him ignorant that harm to me is possible. Now you look puzzled; and I will puzzle you farther. You are my little friend, are you not?"

"I like to serve you, sir, and to obey you in all that is right."

"Precisely: I see you do. I see genuine contentment in your gait, and mien, your eye and face, when you are helping me and pleasing me—working for me, and with me, in, as you characteristically say, '*all that is right:*' for if I bid you do what you thought wrong, there would be no light-footed running, no neat-handed alacrity, no lively glance and animated complexion. My friend would then turn to me, quiet and pale, and would say, 'No, sir; that is impossible: I cannot do it, because it is wrong;' and would become immutable as a fixed star. Well, you too have power over me, and may injure me: yet I dare not show you where I am vulnerable, lest, faithful and friendly as you are, you should transfix me at once."

"If you have no more to fear from Mr. Mason than you have from me, sir, you are very safe."

"God grant it may be so! Here, Jane, is an arbour; sit down."

The arbour was an arch in the wall, lined with ivy; it contained a rustic seat. Mr. Rochester took it, leaving room, however, for me: but I stood before him.

"Sit," he said; "the bench is long enough for two. You don't hesitate to take a place at my side, do you? Is that wrong, Jane?"

I answered him by assuming it: to refuse would, I felt have been unwise.

"Now, my little friend, while the sun drinks the dew—while all the flowers in this old garden awake and expand, and the birds fetch their young ones' breakfast out of the Thornfield, and the early bees do their first spell of work—I'll put a case to you; which you must endeavour to suppose your own: but first, look at me, and tell me you are at ease, and not fearing that I err in detaining you, or that you err in staying."

"No, sir; I am content."

"Well, then, Jane, call to aid your fancy:—suppose you were no longer a girl well reared and disciplined, but a wild boy indulged from childhood upwards; imagine yourself in a remote foreign land; conceive that you there commit a capital error, no matter of what nature or from what motives, but one whose consequences must follow you through life and taint all your existence. Mind, I don't say a *crime*; I am not speaking of shedding of blood or any other guilty act, which might make the perpetrator amenable to the law: my word is *error*. The results of what you have done become in time to you utterly insupportable; you take measures to obtain relief: unusual measures, but neither unlawful nor culpable. Still you are miserable; for hope has quitted you on the very confines of life: your sun at noon darkens in an eclipse, which you feel will not leave it till the time of setting. Bitter and base associations have become the sole food of your memory: you wander here and there, seeking rest in exile: happiness in pleasure—I mean in heartless, sensual pleasure—such as dulls intellect and blights feeling. Heart-weary and soul-withered, you come home after years of voluntary banishment; you make a new acquaintance— how or where no matter: you find in this stranger much of the good and bright

qualities which you have sought for twenty years, and never before encountered; and they are all fresh, healthy, without soil and without taint. Such society revives, regenerates: you feel better days come back—higher wishes, purer feelings; you desire to recommence your life, and to spend what remains to you of days in a way more worthy of an immortal being. To attain this end, are you justified in overleaping an obstacle of custom—a mere conventional impediment, which neither your conscience sanctifies nor your judgment approves?''

He paused for an answer: and what was I to say? Oh, for some good spirit to suggest a judicious and satisfactory response! Vain aspiration! The west wind whispered in the ivy round me; but no gentle Ariel borrowed its breath as a medium of speech: the birds sang in the tree-tops; but their song, however sweet, was inarticulate.

Again Mr. Rochester propounded his query:

''Is the wandering and sinful, but now rest-seeking and repentant, man justified in daring the world's opinion, in order to attach to him for ever this gentle, gracious, genial stranger; thereby securing his own peace of mind and regeneration of life?''

''Sir,'' I answered, ''a wanderer's repose or a sinner's reformation should never depend on a fellow-creature. Men and women die; philosophers falter in wisdom, and Christians in goodness: if any one you know has suffered and erred, let him look higher than his equals for strength to amend, and solace to heal.''

''But the instrument—the instrument! God, who does the work, ordains the instrument. I have myself—I tell it you without parable—been a worldly, dissipated, restless man; and I believe I have found the instrument for my cure, in''——

He paused: the birds went on carolling, the leaves lightly rustling. I almost wondered they did not check their songs and whispers to catch the suspended revelation: but they would have had to wait many minutes—so long was the silence protracted. At last I looked up at the tardy speaker: he was looking eagerly at me.

''Little friend,'' said he, in quite a changed tone—while his face changed too; losing all its softness and gravity, and becoming harsh and sarcastic—''you have noticed my tender penchant for Miss Ingram: don't you think if I married her she would regenerate me with a vengeance?''

He got up instantly, went quite to the other end of the walk, and when he came back he was humming a tune.

''Jane, Jane,'' said he, stopping before me, ''you are quite pale with your vigils: don't you curse me for disturbing your rest?''

''Curse you? No, sir.''

''Shake hands in confirmation of the word. What cold fingers! They were warmer last night when I touched them at the door of the mysterious chamber. Jane, when will you watch with me again?''

''Whenever I can be useful, sir.''

''For instance, the night before I am married! I am sure I shall not be able to sleep. Will you promise to sit up with me to bear me company? To you I can talk of my lovely one: for now you have seen her and know her.''

''Yes, sir.''

''She's a rare one, is she not, Jane?''

''Yes, sir.''

''A strapper—a real strapper, Jane: big, brown, and buxom; with hair just such as the ladies of Carthage must have had. Bless me! there's Dent and Lynn in the stables! Go in by the shrubbery, through that wicket.''

As I went one way, he went another, and I heard him in the yard, saying cheeringly:—

''Mason got the start of you all this morning; he was gone before sunrise: I rose at four to see him off.''

Chapter XXI

PRESENTIMENTS are strange things! and so are sympathies; and so are signs: and the three combined make one mystery to which humanity has not yet found the key. I never laughed at presentiments in my life; because I have had strange ones of my own. Sympathies, I believe, exist: (for instance, between far-distant, long-absent, wholly estranged relatives; asserting, notwithstanding their alienation, the unity of the source to which each traces his origin) whose workings baffle mortal comprehension. And signs, for aught we know, may be but the sympathies of Nature with man.

When I was a little girl, only six years old, I, one night, heard Bessie Leaven say to Martha Abbott that she had been dreaming about a little child; and that to dream of children was a sure sign of trouble, either to one's self or one's kin. The saying might have worn out of my memory, had not a circumstance immediately followed which served indelibly to fix it there. The next day Bessie was sent for home to the deathbed of her little sister.

Of late I had often recalled this saying and this incident; for during the past week scarcely a night had gone over my couch that had not brought with it a dream of an infant: which I sometimes hushed in my arms, sometimes dandled on my knee, sometimes watched playing with daisies on a lawn; or again, dabbling its hands in running water. It was a wailing child this night, and a laughing one the next: now it nestled close to me, and now it ran from me; but whatever mood the apparition evinced, whatever aspect it wore, it failed not for seven successive nights to meet me the moment I entered the land of slumber.

I did not like this iteration of one idea—this strange recurrence of one image; and I grew nervous as bedtime approached and the hour of the vision drew near. It was from companionship with this baby-phantom I had been roused on that moonlight night when I heard the cry; and it was on the afternoon of the day following I was summoned downstairs by a message that some one wanted me in Mrs. Fairfax's room. On repairing thither, I found a man waiting for me, having the appearance of a gentleman's servant: he was dressed in deep mourning, and the hat he held in his hand was surrounded with a crape band.

"I daresay you hardly remember me, miss," he said, rising as I entered; "but my name is Leaven; I lived coachman with Mrs. Reed when you were at Gateshead eight or nine years since, and I live there still."

"Oh, Robert! how do you do? I remember you very well: you used to give me a ride sometimes on Miss Georgiana's bay pony. And how is Bessie? You are married to Bessie?"

"Yes, miss: my wife is very hearty, thank you; she brought me another little one about two months since—we have three now—and both mother and child are thriving."

"And are the family well at the house, Robert?"

"I am sorry I can't give you better news of them, miss: they are very badly at present—in great trouble."

"I hope no one is dead," I said, glancing at his black dress. He too looked down at the crape round his hat and replied,—

"Mr. John died yesterday was a week, at his chambers in London."

"Mr. John?"

"Yes."

"And how does his mother bear it?"

"Why you see, Miss Eyre, it is not a common mishap: his life has been very wild: these last three years he gave himself up to strange ways; and his death was shocking."

"I heard from Bessie he was not doing well."

"Doing well! He could not do worse: he ruined his health and his estate amongst the worst men and the worst women. He got into debt and into jail: his mother helped him out twice, but as soon as he was free he returned to his old companions and habits. His head was not strong: the knaves he lived amongst fooled him beyond anything I ever heard. He came down to Gateshead about three weeks ago and wanted missis to give up all to him. Missis refused: her means have long been much reduced by his extravagance; so he went back again, and the next news was that he was dead. How he died, God knows!—they say he killed himself."

I was silent: the tidings were frightful. Robert Leaven resumed:—

"Missis had been out of health herself for some time: she had got very stout, but was not strong with it; and the loss of money and fear of poverty were quite breaking her down. The information about Mr. John's death and the manner of it came too suddenly: it brought on a stroke. She was three days without speaking; but last Tuesday she seemed rather better: she appeared as if she wanted to say something, and kept making signs to my wife and mumbling. It was only yesterday morning, however, that Bessie understood she was pronouncing your name; and at last she made out the words, 'Bring Jane—fetch Jane Eyre: I want to speak to her.' Bessie is not sure whether she is in her right mind, or means anything by the words; but she told Miss Reed and Miss Georgiana, and advised them to send for you. The young ladies put it off at first: but their mother grew so restless, and said, 'Jane, Jane,' so many times, that at last they consented. I left Gateshead yesterday; and if you can get ready, Miss, I should like to take you back with me early to-morrow morning."

"Yes, Robert, I shall be ready: it seems to me that I ought to go."

"I think so too, Miss. Bessie said she was sure you would not refuse: but I suppose you will have to ask leave before you can get off?"

"Yes; and I will do it now;" and having directed him to the servants' hall and recommended him to the care of John's wife, and the attentions of John himself, I went in search of Mr. Rochester.

He was not in any of the lower rooms; he was not in the yard, the stables, or the grounds. I asked Mrs. Fairfax if she had seen him;—yes: she believed he was playing billiards with Miss Ingram. To the billiard-room I hastened: the click of balls and the hum of voices resounded thence; Mr. Rochester, Miss Ingram, the two Misses Eshton, and their admirers, were all busied in the game. It required some courage to disturb so interesting a party; my errand, however, was one I could not defer, so I approached the master where he stood at Miss Ingram's side. She turned as I drew near, and looked at me haughtily: her eyes seemed to demand, "What can the creeping creature want now?" and when I said, in a low voice, "Mr. Rochester," she made a movement as if tempted to order me away. I remember her appearance at the moment,—it was very graceful and very striking: she wore a morning robe of sky-blue crape; a gauzy azure scarf was twisted in her hair. She had been all animation with the game, and irritated pride did not lower the expression of her haughty lineaments.

"Does that person want you?" she inquired of Mr. Rochester; and Mr. Rochester turned to see who the "person" was. He made a curious grimace,—one of his strange and equivocal demonstrations—threw down his cue and followed me from the room.

"Well, Jane?" he said, as he rested his back against the school-room door, which he had shut.

"If you please, sir, I want leave of absence for a week or two."

"What to do?—Where to go?"

"To see a sick lady who has sent for me."

"What sick lady?—Where does she live?"

"At Gateshead, in ——shire."

"——shire? That is a hundred miles off! Who may she be that sends for people to see her that distance?"

"Her name is Reed, sir,—Mrs. Reed."

"Reed of Gateshead? There was a Reed of Gateshead, a magistrate."

"It is his widow, sir."

"And what have you to do with her? How do you know her?"

"Mr. Reed was my uncle,—my mother's brother."

"The deuce he was! You never told me that before: you always said you had no relations."

"None that would own me, sir. Mr. Reed is dead, and his wife cast me off."

"Why?"

"Because I was poor, and burdensome, and she disliked me."

"But Reed left children?—you must have cousins? Sir George Lynn was talking of a Reed of Gateshead, yesterday—who, he said, was one of the veriest rascals on town; and Ingram was mentioning a Georgiana Reed of the same place, who was much admired for her beauty, a season or two ago, in London."

"John Reed is dead, too, sir: he ruined himself and half-ruined his family, and is supposed to have committed suicide. The news so shocked his mother that it brought on an apoplectic attack."

"And what good can you do her? Nonsense, Jane! I would never think of running a hundred miles to see an old lady who will, perhaps, be dead before you reach her: besides, you say she cast you off."

"Yes, sir, but that is long ago; and when her circumstances were very different: I could not be easy to neglect her wishes now."

"How long will you stay?"

"As short a time as possible, sir."

"Promise me only to stay a week"——

"I had better not pass my word: I might be obliged to break it."

"At all events you *will* come back: you will not be induced under any pretext to take up a permanent residence with her?"

"Oh no! I shall certainly return if all be well."

"And who goes with you? You don't travel a hundred miles alone."

"No, sir, she has sent her coachman."

"A person to be trusted?"

"Yes, sir, he has lived ten years in the family."

Mr. Rochester meditated. "When do you wish to go?"

"Early to-morrow morning, sir."

"Well, you must have some money; you can't travel without money, and I daresay you have not much: I have given you no salary yet. How much have you in the world, Jane?" he asked, smiling.

I drew out my purse; a meagre thing it was. "Five shillings, sir." He took the purse, poured the hoard into his palm and chuckled over it as if its scantiness pleased him. Soon he produced his pocket-book: "Here," said he, offering me a note: it was fifty pounds, and he owed me but fifteen. I told him I had no change.

"I don't want change: you know that. Take your wages."

I declined accepting more than was my due. He scowled at first; then, as if recollecting something, he said:—

"Right, right! Better not give you all now: you would, perhaps, stay away three months if you had fifty pounds. There are ten: is it not plenty?"

"Yes, sir, but now you owe five."

"Come back for it then: I am your banker for forty pounds."

"Mr. Rochester, I may as well mention another matter of business to you while I have the opportunity."

"Matter of business? I'm curious to hear it."

"You have as good as informed me, sir, that you are going shortly to be married?"

"Yes: what then?"

"In that case, sir, Adèle ought to go to school: I am sure you will perceive the necessity of it."

"To get her out of my bride's way; who might otherwise walk over her rather too emphatically. There's sense in the suggestion; not a doubt of it: Adèle, as you say, must go to school; and you, of course, must march straight to—the devil?"

"I hope not, sir: but I must seek another situation somewhere."

"In course!" he exclaimed, with a twang of voice and a distortion of features equally fantastic and ludicrous. He looked at me some minutes.

"And old Madam Reed, or the Misses, her daughters, will be solicited by you to seek a place, I suppose?"

"No, sir; I am not on such terms with my relatives as would justify me in asking favours of them—but I shall advertise."

"You shall walk up the pyramids of Egypt!" he growled. "At your peril you advertise! I wish I had only offered you a sovereign instead of ten pounds. Give me back nine pounds, Jane; I've a use for it."

"And so have I, sir," I returned, putting my hands and my purse behind me. "I could not spare the money on any account."

"Little niggard!" said he, "refusing me a pecuniary request! Give me five pounds, Jane."

"Not five shillings, sir; nor five pence."

"Just let me look at the cash."

"No, sir; you are not to be trusted."

"Jane!"

"Sir?"

"Promise me one thing."

"I'll promise you anything, sir, that I think I am likely to perform."

"Not to advertise: and to trust this quest of a situation to me. I'll find you one in time."

"I shall be glad so to do, sir, if you, in your turn, will promise that I and Adèle shall be both safe out of the house before your bride enters it."

"Very well! very well! I'll pledge my word on it. You go to-morrow, then?"

"Yes, sir; early."

"Shall you come down to the drawing-room after dinner?"

"No, sir, I must prepare for the journey."

"Then you and I must bid good-bye for a little while?"

"I suppose so, sir."

"And how do people perform that ceremony of parting, Jane? Teach me; I'm not quite up to it."

"They say, Farewell; or any other form they prefer."

"Then say it."

"Farewell, Mr. Rochester, for the present."

"What must I say?"

"The same, if you like, sir."

"Farewell, Miss Eyre, for the present: is that all?"

"Yes."

"It seems stingy, to my notions, and dry, and unfriendly. I should like something else: a little addition to the rite. If one shook hands, for instance; but no,—that would not content me either. So you'll do no more than say Farewell, Jane?"

"It is enough, sir: as much good-will may be conveyed in one hearty word as in many."

"Very likely; but it is blank and cool—'farewell.' "

"How long is he going to stand with his back against that door?" I asked myself; "I want to commence my packing." The dinner-bell rang, and suddenly away he

bolted, without another syllable: I saw him no more during the day, and was off before he had risen in the morning.

I reached the lodge at Gateshead about five o'clock in the afternoon of the first of May: I stepped in there before going up to the hall. It was very clean and neat: the ornamental windows were hung with little white curtains; the floor was spotless; the grate and fire-irons were burnished bright, and the fire burnt clear. Bessie sat on the hearth, nursing her last-born, and Robert and his sister played quietly in a corner.

"Bless you!—I knew you would come!" exclaimed Mrs. Leaven, as I entered.

"Yes, Bessie," said I, after I had kissed her; "and I trust I am not too late. How is Mrs. Reed?—Alive still, I hope."

"Yes, she is alive; and more sensible and collected than she was. The doctor says she may linger a week or two yet; but he hardly thinks she will finally recover."

"Has she mentioned me lately?"

"She was talking of you only this morning, and wishing you would come: but she is sleeping now; or was ten minutes ago, when I was up at the house. She generally lies in a kind of lethargy all the afternoon, and wakes up about six or seven. Will you rest yourself here an hour, miss, and then I will go up with you?"

Robert here entered, and Bessie laid her sleeping child in the cradle and went to welcome him: afterwards she insisted on my taking off my bonnet and having some tea; for she said I looked pale and tired. I was glad to accept her hospitality; and I submitted to be relieved of my travelling garb just as passively as I used to let her undress me when a child.

Old times crowded fast back on me as I watched her bustling about—setting out the tea-tray with her best china, cutting bread and butter, toasting a tea-cake, and, between whiles, giving little Robert or Jane an occasional tap or push, just as she used to give me in former days. Bessie had retained her quick temper as well as her light foot and good looks.

Tea ready, I was going to approach the table; but she desired me to sit still, quite in her old, peremptory tones. I must be served at the fireside, she said; and she placed before me a little round stand with my cup and a plate of toast, absolutely as she used to accommodate me with some privately purloined dainty on a nursery chair: and I smiled and obeyed her as in bygone days.

She wanted to know if I was happy at Thornfield Hall, and what sort of a person the mistress was; and when I told her there was only a master, whether he was a nice gentleman, and if I liked him. I told her he was rather an ugly man, but quite a gentleman; and that he treated me kindly, and I was content. Then I went on to describe to her the gay company that had lately been staying at the house; and to these details Bessie listened with interest: they were precisely of the kind she relished.

In such conversation an hour was soon gone: Bessie restored to me my bonnet, etc., and, accompanied by her, I quitted the lodge for the hall. It was also accompanied by her that I had, nearly nine years ago, walked down the path I was now ascending. On a dark, misty, raw morning in January, I had left a hostile roof with a desperate and embittered heart—a sense of outlawry and almost of reprobation—to seek the chilly harbourage of Lowood: that bourne so far away and unexplored. The same hostile roof now again rose before me: my prospects were doubtful yet; and I had yet an aching heart. I still felt as a wanderer on the face of the earth; but I experienced firmer trust in myself and my own powers, and less withering dread of oppression. The gaping wound of my wrongs, too, was now quite healed; and the flame of resentment extinguished.

"You shall go into the breakfast-room first," said Bessie, as she preceded me through the hall; "the young ladies will be there."

In another moment I was within that apartment. There was every article of furniture looking just as it did on the morning I was first introduced to Mr. Brocklehurst:

the very rug he had stood upon still covered the hearth. Glancing at the book-case, I thought I could distinguish the two volumes of Bewick's British Birds occupying their old place on the third shelf, and Gulliver's Travels and the Arabian Nights ranged just above. The inanimate objects were not changed: but the living things had altered past recognition.

Two young ladies appeared before me; one very tall, almost as tall as Miss Ingram,—very thin too, with a sallow face and severe mien. There was something ascetic in her look, which was augmented by the extreme plainness of a straight-skirted, black, stuff dress, a starched linen collar, hair combed away from the temples, and the nun-like ornament of a string of ebony beads and a crucifix. This I felt sure was Eliza, though I could trace little resemblance to her former self in that elongated and colourless visage.

The other was as certainly Georgiana: but not the Georgiana I remembered—the slim and fairy-like girl of eleven. This was a full-blown, very plump damsel, fair as waxwork; with handsome and regular features, languishing blue eyes, and ringleted yellow hair. The hue of her dress was black too; but its fashion was so different from her sister's—so much more flowing and becoming—it looked as stylish as the other's looked puritanical.

In each of the sisters there was one trait of the mother—and only one: the thin and pallid elder daughter had her parent's Cairngorm eye: the blooming and luxuriant younger girl had her contour of jaw and chin,—perhaps a little softened, but still imparting an indescribable hardness to the countenance, otherwise so voluptuous and buxom.

Both ladies, as I advanced, rose to welcome me, and both addressed me by the name of "Miss Eyre." Eliza's greeting was delivered in a short, abrupt voice, without a smile; and then she sat down again, fixed her eyes on the fire, and seemed to forget me. Georgiana added to her "How d'ye do?" several commonplaces about my journey, the weather and so on, uttered in rather a drawling tone: and accompanied by sundry side-glances that measured me from head to foot—now traversing the folds of my drab merino pelisse, and now lingering on the plain trimming of my cottage bonnet. Young ladies have a remarkable way of letting you know that they think you a "quiz," without actually saying the words. A certain superciliousness of look, coolness of manner, nonchalance of tone, express fully their sentiments on the point, without committing them by any positive rudeness in word or deed.

A sneer, however, whether covert or open, had now no longer that power over me it once possessed: as I sat between my cousins, I was surprised to find how easy I felt under the total neglect of the one and the semi-sarcastic attentions of the other—Eliza did not mortify, nor Georgiana ruffle me. The fact was, I had other things to think about; within the last few months feelings had been stirred in me so much more potent than any they could raise—pains and pleasures so much more acute and exquisite had been excited, than any it was in their power to inflict or bestow—that their airs gave me no concern either for good or bad.

"How is Mrs. Reed?" I asked soon, looking calmly at Georgiana; who thought fit to bridle at the direct address, as if it were an unexpected liberty.

"Mrs. Reed? Ah! mama you mean; she is extremely poorly: I doubt if you can see her to-night."

"If," said I, "you would just step upstairs and tell her I am come, I should be much obliged to you."

Georgiana almost started, and she opened her blue eyes wild and wide. "I know she had a particular wish to see me," I added, "and I would not defer attending to her desire longer than is absolutely necessary."

"Mama dislikes being disturbed in an evening," remarked Eliza. I soon rose, quietly took off my bonnet and gloves, uninvited, and said I would just step out to Bessie—who was, I dared say, in the kitchen—and ask her to ascertain whether Mrs. Reed was disposed to receive me or not to-night. I went, and having found

Bessie and despatched her on my errand, I proceeded to take further measures. It had heretofore been my habit always to shrink from arrogance: received as I had been to-day, I should, a year ago, have resolved to quit Gateshead the very next morning; now, it was disclosed to me all at once, that that would be a foolish plan. I had taken a journey of a hundred miles to see my aunt, and I must stay with her till she was better—or dead: as to her daughters' pride and folly, I must put it on one side; make myself independent of it. So I addressed the housekeeper; asked her to show me a room, told her I should probably be a visitor for a week or two, had my trunk conveyed to my chamber, and followed it thither myself: I met Bessie on the landing.

"Missis is awake," said she; "I have told her you are here: come and let us see if she will know you."

I did not need to be guided to the well-known room: to which I had so often been summoned for chastisement or reprimand in former days. I hastened before Bessie; I softly opened the door: a shaded light stood on the table, for it was now getting dark. There was the great four-post bed with amber hangings as of old; there the toilet-table, the arm-chair, and the foot-stool: at which I had a hundred times been sentenced to kneel, to ask pardon for offences, by me, uncommitted. I looked into a certain corner near, half-expecting to see the slim outline of a once-dreaded switch; which used to lurk there, waiting to leap out imp-like and lace my quivering palm or shrinking neck. I approached the bed; I opened the curtains and leant over the high-piled pillows.

Well did I remember Mrs. Reed's face, and I eagerly sought the familiar image. It is a happy thing that time quells the longings of vengeance, and hushes the promptings of rage and aversion: I had left this woman in bitterness and hate, and I came back to her now with no other emotion than a sort of ruth for her great sufferings, and a strong yearning to forget and forgive all injuries—to be reconciled and clasp hands in amity.

The well-known face was there: stern, relentless as ever—there was that peculiar eye which nothing could melt; and the somewhat raised, imperious, despotic eyebrow. How often had it lowered on me menace and hate! and how the recollection of childhood's terrors and sorrows revived as I traced its harsh line now! And yet I stooped down and kissed her: she looked at me.

"Is this Jane Eyre?" she said.

"Yes, aunt Reed. How are you, dear aunt?"

I had once vowed that I would never call her aunt again: I thought it no sin to forget and break that vow now. My fingers had fastened on her hand which lay outside the sheet: had she pressed mine kindly, I should at that moment have experienced true pleasure. But unimpressionable natures are not so soon softened, nor are natural antipathies so readily eradicated: Mrs. Reed took her hand away, and, turning her face rather from me, she remarked that the night was warm. Again she regarded me, so icily, I felt at once that her opinion of me—her feeling towards me—was unchanged, and unchangeable. I knew by her stony eye—opaque to tenderness, indissoluble to tears—that she was resolved to consider me bad to the last; because to believe me good, would give her no generous pleasure: only a sense of mortification.

I felt pain, and then I felt ire; and then I felt a determination to subdue her—to be her mistress in spite both of her nature and her will. My tears had risen, just as in childhood: I ordered them back to their source. I brought a chair to the bed-head: I sat down and leaned over the pillow.

"You sent for me," I said, "and I am here; and it is my intention to stay till I see how you get on."

"Oh, of course! You have seen my daughters?"

"Yes."

"Well, you may tell them I wish you to stay till I can talk some things over with you I have on my mind: tonight it is too late, and I have a difficulty in recalling them. But there was something I wished to say—let me see"——

The wandering look and changed utterance told what wreck had taken place in her once-vigorous frame. Turning restlessly, she drew the bed-clothes round her; my elbow, resting on a corner of the quilt, fixed it down: she was at once irritated.

"Sit up!" said she; "don't annoy me with holding the clothes fast—are you Jane Eyre?"

"I am Jane Eyre."

"I have had more trouble with that child than any one would believe. Such a burden to be left on my hands—and so much annoyance as she caused me, daily and hourly, with her incomprehensible dlsposition, and her sudden starts of temper, and her continual, unnatural watchings of one's movements! I declare she talked to me once like something mad, or like a fiend—no child ever spoke or looked as she did; I was glad to get her away from the house. What did they do with her at Lowood? The fever broke out there, and many of the pupils died. She, however, did not die: but I said she did—I wish she had died!"

"A strange wish, Mrs. Reed: why do you hate her so?"

"I had a dislike to her mother always; for she was my husband's only sister, and a great favourite with him: he opposed the family's disowning her when she made her low marriage; and when news came of her death, he wept like a simpleton. He would send for the baby; though I entreated him rather to put it out to nurse and pay for its maintenance. I hated it the first time I set my eyes on it—a sickly, whining, pining thing! It would wail in its cradle all night long—not screaming heartily like any other child, but whimpering and moaning. Reed pitied it; and he used to nurse it and notice it as if it had been his own: more, indeed, than he ever noticed his own at that age. He would try to make my children friendly to the little beggar: the darlings could not bear it, and he was angry with them when they showed their dislike. In his last illness, he had it brought continually to his bedside; and but an hour before he died, he bound me by vow to keep the creature. I would as soon have been charged with a pauper brat out of a workhouse: but he was weak, naturally weak. John does not at all resemble his father, and I'm glad of it: John is like me and like my brothers—he is quite a Gibson. Oh, I wish he would cease tormenting me with letters for money! I have no more money to give him: we are getting poor. I must send away half the servants and shut up part of the house; or let it off. I can never submit to do that—yet how are we to get on? Two-thirds of my income goes in paying the interest of mortgages. John gambles dreadfully, and always loses—poor boy! He is beset by sharpers: John is sunk and degraded—his look is frightful—I feel ashamed for him when I see him."

She was getting much excited. "I think I had better leave her now," said I to Bessie, who stood on the other side of the bed.

"Perhaps you had, Miss: but she often talks in this way towards night—in the morning she is calmer."

I rose. "Stop!" exclaimed Mrs. Reed, "There is another thing I wished to say. He threatens me—he continually threatens me with his own death, or mine: and I dream sometimes that I see him laid out with a great wound in his throat, or with a swollen and blackened face. I am come to a strange pass: I have heavy troubles. What is to be done? How is the money to be had?"

Bessie now endeavoured to persuade her to take a sedative draught: she succeeded with difficulty. Soon after, Mrs. Reed grew more composed, and sank into a dozing state. I then left her.

More than ten days elapsed before I had again any conversation with her. She continued either delirious or lethargic; and the doctor forbade everything which could painfully excite her. Meantime, I got on as well as I could with Georgiana and Eliza. They were very cold, indeed, at first. Eliza would sit half the day sewing,

reading, or writing, and scarcely utter a word either to me or her sister. Georgiana would chatter nonsense to her canary bird by the hour, and take no notice of me. But I was determined not to seem at a loss for occupation or amusement: I had brought my drawing materials with me, and they served me for both.

Provided with a case of pencils, and some sheets of paper, I used to take a seat apart from them, near the window, and busy myself in sketching fancy vignettes, representing any scene that happened momentarily to shape itself in the ever-shifting kaleidoscope of imagination: a glimpse of sea between two rocks; the rising moon, and a ship crossing its disk; a group of reeds and water-flags, and a naiad's head, crowned with lotus-flowers, rising out of them; an elf sitting in a hedge-sparrow's nest, under a wreath of hawthorn-bloom.

One morning I fell to sketching a face: what sort of a face it was to be, I did not care or know. I took a soft black pencil, gave it a broad point, and worked away. Soon I had traced on the paper a broad and prominent forehead, and a square lower outline of visage: that contour gave me pleasure; my fingers proceeded actively to fill it with features. Strongly-marked horizontal eyebrows must be traced under that brow; then followed, naturally, a well-defined nose, with a straight ridge and full nostrils; then a flexible-looking mouth, by no means narrow; then a firm chin, with a decided cleft down the middle of it: of course, some black whiskers were wanted, and some jetty hair, tufted on the temples, and waved above the forehead. Now for the eyes: I had left them to the last, because they required the most careful working. I drew them large; I shaped them well: the eyelashes I traced long and sombre; the irids lustrous and large. "Good! but not quite the thing," I thought, as I surveyed the effect: "They want more force and spirit;" and I wrought the shades blacker, that the lights might flash more brilliantly—a happy touch or two secured success. There, I had a friend's face under my gaze; and what did it signify that those young ladies turned their backs on me? I looked at it; I smiled at the speaking likeness: I was absorbed and content.

"Is that a portrait of some one you know?" asked Eliza, who had approached me unnoticed. I responded that it was merely a fancy head, and hurried it beneath the other sheets. Of course, I lied: it was, in fact, a very faithful representation of Mr. Rochester. But what was that to her, or to any one but myself? Georgiana also advanced to look. The other drawings pleased her much, but she called that "an ugly man." They both seemed surprised at my skill. I offered to sketch their portraits; and each, in turn, sat for a pencil outline. Then Georgiana produced her album. I promised to contribute a water-colour drawing: this put her at once into good humour. She proposed a walk in the grounds. Before we had been out two hours, we were deep in a confidential conversation: she had favoured me with a description of the brilliant winter she had spent in London two seasons ago—of the admiration she had there excited—the attention she had received; and I even got hints of the titled conquest she had made. In the course of the afternoon and evening these hints were enlarged on: various soft conversations were reported, and sentimental scenes represented; and, in short, a volume of a novel of fashionable life was that day improvised by her for my benefit. The communications were renewed from day to day: they always ran on the same theme—herself, her loves, and woes. It was strange she never once adverted either to her mother's illness, or her brother's death, or the present gloomy state of the family prospects. Her mind seemed wholly taken up with reminiscences of past gaiety, and aspirations after dissipations to come. She passed about five minutes each day in her mother's sick-room and no more.

Eliza still spoke little: she had evidently no time to talk. I never saw a busier person than she seemed to be; yet it was difficult to say what she did: or rather, to discover any result of her diligence. She had an alarum to call her up early. I know not how she occupied herself before breakfast, but after that meal she divided her time into regular portions; and each hour had its allotted task. Three times a

day she studied a little book, which I found, on inspection, was a Common Prayer Book. I asked her once what was the great attraction of that volume, and she said ''the Rubric.'' Three hours she gave to stitching, with gold thread, the border of a square crimson cloth, almost large enough for a carpet. In answer to my inquiries after the use of this article, she informed me it was a covering for the altar of a new church lately erected near Gateshead. Two hours she devoted to her diary; two to working by herself in the kitchen-garden; and one to the regulation of her accounts. She seemed to want no company; no conversation. I believe she was happy in her way: this routine sufficed to her; and nothing annoyed her so much as the occurrence of any incident which forced her to vary its clock-work regularity.

She told me one evening, when more disposed to be communicative than usual, that John's conduct, and the threatened ruin of the family, had been a source of profound affliction to her: but she had now, she said, settled her mind, and formed her resolution. Her own fortune she had taken care to secure; and when her mother died,—and it was wholly improbable, she tranquilly remarked, that she should either recover or linger long,—she would execute a long-cherished project: seek a retirement where punctual habits would be permanently secured from disturbance, and place safe barriers between herself and a frivolous world. I asked if Georgiana would accompany her.

''Of course not. Georgiana and she had nothing in common: they never had had. She would not be burdened with her society for any consideration. Georgiana should take her own course; and she, Eliza, would take hers.''

Georgiana, when not unburdening her heart to me, spent most of her time in lying on the sofa, fretting about the dulness of the house, and wishing over and over again that her aunt Gibson would send her an invitation up to town. ''It would be so much better,'' she said, ''if she could only get out of the way for a month or two, till all was over.'' I did not ask her what she meant by ''all being over,'' but I suppose she referred to the expected decease of her mother and the gloomy sequel of funeral rites. Eliza generally took no more notice of her sister's indolence and complaints than if no such murmuring, lounging object had been before her. One day, however, as she put away her account-book, and unfolded her embroidery, she suddenly took her up thus:—

''Georgiana, a more vain and absurd animal than you, was certainly never allowed to cumber the earth. You had no right to be born; for you make no use of life. Instead of living for, in, and with yourself, as a reasonable being ought, you seek only to fasten your feebleness on some other person's strength: if no one can be found willing to burden her or himself with such a fat, weak, puffy, useless thing, you cry out that you are ill-treated, neglected, miserable. Then, too, existence for you must be a scene of continual change and excitement, or else the world is a dungeon: you must be admired, you must be courted, you must be flattered—you must have music, dancing, and society—or you languish, you die away. Have you no sense to devise a system which will make you independent of all efforts, and all wills, but your own? Take one day; share it into sections; to each section apportion its task: leave no stray unemployed quarters of an hour, ten minutes, five minutes, include all; do each piece of business in its turn with method, with rigid regularity. The day will close almost before you are aware it has begun; and you are indebted to no one for helping you to get rid of one vacant moment: you have had to seek no one's company, conversation, sympathy, forbearance; you have lived, in short, as an independent being ought to do. Take this advice: the first and last I shall offer you; then you will not want me or any one else, happen what may. Neglect it—go on as heretofore, craving, whining, and idling—and suffer the results of your idiocy, however bad and insufferable they may be. I tell you this plainly; and listen: for though I shall no more repeat what I am now about to say, I shall steadily act on it. After my mother's death, I wash my hands of you: from the day her coffin is carried to the vault in Gateshead Church, you and I will be as separate as

if we had never known each other. You need not think that because we chanced
to be born of the same parents, I shall suffer you to fasten me down by even the
feeblest claim: I can tell you this—if the whole human race, ourselves excepted,
were swept away, and we two stood alone on the earth, I would leave you in the
old world, and betake myself to the new.''

She closed her lips.

''You might have spared yourself the trouble of delivering that tirade,'' answered
Georgiana. ''Everybody knows you are the most selfish heartless creature in existence:
and *I* know your spiteful hatred towards me: I have had a specimen of it before in
the trick you played me about Lord Edwin Vere: you could not bear me to be raised
above you, to have a title, to be received into circles where you dare not show
your face, and so you acted the spy and informer, and ruined my prospects for
ever.'' Georgiana took out her handkerchief and blew her nose for an hour afterwards;
Eliza sat cold, impassable, and assiduously industrious.

True, generous feeling is made small account of by some; but here were two
natures rendered, the one intolerably acrid, the other despicably savourless for the
want of it. Feeling without judgment is a washy draught indeed; but judgment
untempered by feeling is too bitter and husky a morsel for human deglutition.

It was a wet and windy afternoon: Georgiana had fallen asleep on the sofa over
the perusal of a novel; Eliza was gone to attend a saint's-day service at the new
church—for in matters of religion she was a rigid formalist: no weather ever prevented
the punctual discharge of what she considered her devotional duties; fair or foul,
she went to church thrice every Sunday, and as often on week-days as there were
prayers.

I bethought myself to go upstairs and see how the dying woman sped, who lay
there almost unheeded: the very servants paid her but a remittent attention: the hired
nurse, being little looked after, would slip out of the room whenever she could.
Bessie was faithful; but she had her own family to mind, and could only come
occasionally to the hall. I found the sick-room unwatched, as I had expected: no
nurse was there; the patient lay still, and seemingly lethargic; her livid face sunk
in the pillows: the fire was dying in the grate. I renewed the fuel, re-arranged the
bed-clothes, gazed awhile on her who could not now gaze on me, and then I moved
away to the window.

The rain beat strongly against the panes, the wind blew tempestuously: ''One
lies there,'' I thought, ''who will soon be beyond the war of earthly elements.
Whither will that spirit—now struggling to quit its material tenement—flit when at
length released?''

In pondering the great mystery, I thought of Helen Burns: recalled her dying
words—her faith—her doctrine of the equality of disembodied souls. I was still
listening in thought to her well-remembered tones—still picturing her pale and
spiritual aspect, her wasted face and sublime gaze, as she lay on her placid deathbed,
and whispered her longing to be restored to her divine Father's bosom—when a
feeble voice murmured from the couch behind: ''Who is that?''

I knew Mrs. Reed had not spoken for days: was she reviving? I went up to her.

''It is I, aunt Reed.''

''Who—I?'' was her answer. ''Who are you?'' looking at me with surprise and
a sort of alarm, but still not wildly. ''You are quite a stranger to me—where is
Bessie?''

''She is at the lodge, aunt.''

''Aunt,'' she repeated. ''Who calls me Aunt? You are not one of the Gibsons;
and yet I know you—that face, and the eyes and forehead are quite familiar to me:
you are like—why, you are like Jane Eyre!''

I said nothing: I was afraid of occasioning some shock by declaring my identity.

''Yet,'' said she, ''I am afraid it is a mistake: my thoughts deceive me. I wished
to see Jane Eyre, and I fancy a likeness where none exists: besides, in eight years

she must be so changed.'' I now gently assured her that I was the person she supposed and desired me to be: and seeing that I was understood, and that her senses were quite collected, I explained how Bessie had sent her husband to fetch me from Thornfield.

"I am very ill, I know,'' she said ere long. "I was trying to turn myself a few minutes since, and find I cannot move a limb. It is as well I should ease my mind before I die: what we think little of in health, burdens us at such an hour as the present is to me. Is the nurse here? or is there no one in the room but you?''

I assured her we were alone.

"Well, I have twice done you a wrong which I regret now. One was in breaking the promise which I gave my husband to bring you up as my own child; the other''— she stopped. "After all, it is of no great importance, perhaps,'' she murmured to herself: "and then I may get better; and to humble myself so to her is painful.''

She made an effort to alter her position, but failed: her face changed; she seemed to experience some inward sensation—the precursor, perhaps, of the last pang.

"Well: I must get it over. Eternity is before me: I had better tell her.—Go to my dressing-case, open it, and take out a letter you will see there.''

I obeyed her directions. "'Read the letter,'' she said. It was short, and thus conceived:—

> "MADAM,
> "Will you have the goodness to send me the address of my niece, Jane Eyre, and to tell me how she is: it is my intention to write shortly and desire her to come to me at Madeira. Providence has blessed my endeavours to secure a competency; and as I am unmarried and childless, I wish to adopt her during my life, and bequeath her at my death whatever I may have to leave.
> "I am, Madam, etc., etc.
> "JOHN EYRE, Madeira.''

It was dated three years back.

"Why did I never hear of this?'' I asked.

"Because I disliked you too fixedly and thoroughly ever to lend a hand in lifting you to prosperity. I could not forget your conduct to me, Jane—the fury with which you once turned on me; the tone in which you declared you abhorred me the worst of anybody in the world; the unchildlike look and voice with which you affirmed that the very thought of me made you sick, and asserted that I had treated you with miserable cruelty. I could not forget my own sensations when you thus started up and poured out the venom of your mind: I felt fear, as if an animal that I had struck or pushed had looked up at me with human eyes and cursed me in a man's voice.— Bring me some water! Oh! make haste!''

"Dear Mrs. Reed,'' said I, as I offered her the draught she required, "think no more of all this, let it pass away from your mind. Forgive me for my passionate language: I was a child then; eight, nine years have passed since that day.''

She heeded nothing of what I said; but when she had tasted the water and drawn breath, she went on thus:—

"I tell you I could not forget it; and I took my revenge: for you to be adopted by your uncle, and placed in a state of ease and comfort, was what I could not endure. I wrote to him; I said I was sorry for his disappointment, but Jane Eyre was dead: she had died of typhus fever at Lowood. Now act as you please: write and contradict my assertion—expose my falsehood as soon as you like. You were born, I think, to be my torment: my last hour is racked by the recollection of a deed, which, but for you, I should never have been tempted to commit.''

"If you could but be persuaded to think no more of it, aunt, and to regard me with kindness and forgiveness''——

"You have a very bad disposition," said she, "and one to this day I feel it impossible to understand: how for nine years you could be patient and quiescent under any treatment, and in the tenth break out all fire and violence, I can never comprehend."

"My disposition is not so bad as you think: I am passionate, but not vindictive. Many a time, as a little child, I should have been glad to love you if you would have let me; and I long earnestly to be reconciled to you now: kiss me, aunt."

I approached my cheek to her lips: she would not touch it. She said I oppressed her by leaning over the bed; and again demanded water. As I laid her down—for I raised her and supported her on my arm while she drank—I covered her ice-cold and clammy hand with mine: the feeble fingers shrank from my touch—the glazing eyes shunned my gaze.

"Love me, then, or hate me, as you will," I said at last, "you have my full and free forgiveness: ask now for God's; and be at peace."

Poor, suffering woman! it was too late for her to make now the effort to change her habitual frame of mind: living, she had ever hated me—dying, she must hate me still.

The nurse now entered, and Bessie followed. I yet lingered half an hour longer, hoping to see some sign of amity: but she gave none. She was fast relapsing into stupor; nor did her mind again rally: at twelve o'clock that night she died. I was not present to close her eyes; nor were either of her daughters. They came to tell us the next morning that all was over. She was by that time laid out. Eliza and I went to look at her: Georgiana, who had burst out into loud weeping, said she dared not go. There was stretched Sarah Reed's once robust and active frame, rigid and still: her eye of flint was covered with its cold lid; her brow and strong traits wore yet the impress of her inexorable soul. A strange and solemn object was that corpse to me. I gazed on it with gloom and pain: nothing soft, nothing sweet, nothing pitying, or hopeful, or subduing, did it inspire; only a grating anguish for *her* woes—not *my* loss—and a sombre tearless dismay at the fearfulness of death in such a form.

Eliza surveyed her parent calmly. After a silence of some minutes she observed,—

"With her constitution she should have lived to a good old age: her life was shortened by trouble." And then a spasm constricted her mouth for an instant: as it passed away she turned and left the room, and did I. Neither of us had dropt a tear.

Chapter XXII

MR. ROCHESTER had given me but one week's leave of absence: yet a month elapsed before I quitted Gateshead. I wished to leave immediately after the funeral; but Georgiana entreated me to stay till she could get off to London: whither she was now at last invited by her uncle, Mr. Gibson, who had come down to direct his sister's interment, and settle the family affairs. Georgiana said she dreaded being left alone with Eliza; from her she got neither sympathy in her dejection, support in her fears, nor aid in her preparations; so I bore with her feeble-minded quailings, and selfish lamentations, as well as I could, and did my best in sewing for her and packing her dresses. It is true, that while I worked, she would idle; and I thought to myself, "If you and I were destined to live always together, cousin, we would commence matters on a different footing. I should not settle tamely down into being the forbearing party; I should assign you your share of labour, and compel you to accomplish it, or else it should be left undone: I should insist, also, on your keeping some of those drawling, half-insincere complaints hushed in your own breast. It is

only because our connection happens to be very transitory, and comes at a peculiarly mournful season, that I consent thus to render it so patient and compliant on my part.''

At last I saw Georgiana off; but now it was Eliza's turn to request me to stay another week. Her plans required all her time and attention, she said: she was about to depart for some unknown bourne; and all day long she stayed in her own room, her door bolted within, filling trunks, emptying drawers, burning papers, and holding no communication with any one. She wished me to look after the house, to see callers, and answer notes of condolence.

One morning, she told me I was at liberty. ''And,'' she added, ''I am obliged to you for your valuable services and discreet conduct! There is some difference between living with such a one as you, and with Georgiana: you perform your own part in life, and burden no one. To-morrow,'' she continued, ''I set out for the Continent. I shall take up my abode in a religious house, near Lisle—a nunnery you would call it: there I shall be quiet and unmolested. I shall devote myself for a time to the examination of the Roman Catholic dogmas, and to a careful study of the workings of their system; if I find it to be, as I half suspect it is, the one best calculated to ensure the doing of all things decently and in order, I shall embrace the tenets of Rome and probably take the veil.''

I neither expressed surprise at this resolution nor attempted to dissuade her from it. ''The vocation will fit you to a hair,'' I thought: ''much good may it do you!''

When we parted, she said: ''Good-bye, cousin Jane Eyre; I wish you well: you have some sense.''

I then returned: ''You are not without sense, cousin Eliza; but what you have, I suppose in another year will be walled up alive in a French convent. However, it is not my business, and so it suits you—I don't much care.''

''You are in the right,'' said she: and with these words we each went our separate way. As I shall not have occasion to refer either to her or her sister again, I may as well mention here, that Georgiana made an advantageous match with a wealthy worn-out man of fashion; and that Eliza actually took the veil, and is at this day superior of the convent where she passed the period of her novitiate: and which she endowed with her fortune.

How people feel when they are returning home from an absence, long or short, I did not know: I had never experienced the sensation. I had known what it was to come back to Gateshead when a child, after a long walk—to be scolded for looking cold or gloomy; and later, what it was to come back from church to Lowood—to long for a plenteous meal and a good fire, and to be unable to get either. Neither of these returnings were very pleasant or desirable: no magnet drew me to a given point, increasing in its strength of attraction the nearer I came. The return to Thornfield was yet to be tried.

My journey seemed tedious—very tedious: fifty miles one day, a night spent at an inn; fifty miles the next day. During the first twelve hours I thought of Mrs. Reed in her last moments; I saw her disfigured and discoloured face, and heard her strangely altered voice. I mused on the funeral day, the coffin, the hearse, the black train of tenants and servants—few was the number of relatives—the gaping vault, the silent church, the solemn service. Then I thought of Eliza and Georgiana: I beheld one the cynosure of a ball-room, the other the inmate of a convent cell: and I dwelt on and analysed their separate peculiarities of person and character. The evening arrival at the great town of —— scattered these thoughts; night gave them quite another turn: laid down on my traveller's bed, I left reminiscence for anticipation.

I was going back to Thornfield: but how long was I to stay there? Not long; of that I was sure. I had heard from Mrs. Fairfax in the interim of my absence: the party at the hall was dispersed; Mr. Rochester had left for London three weeks ago, but he was then expected to return in a fortnight. Mrs. Fairfax surmised that he was gone to make arrangements for his wedding, as he had talked of purchasing

a new carriage: she said the idea of his marrying Miss Ingram still seemed strange to her; but from what everybody said, and from what she had herself seen, she could no longer doubt that the event would shortly take place. "You would be strangely incredulous if you did doubt it," was my mental comment. "I don't doubt it."

The question followed, "Where was I to go?" I dreamt of Miss Ingram all the night: in a vivid morning dream I saw her closing the gates of Thornfield against me and pointing me out another road; and Mr. Rochester looked on with his arms folded—smiling sardonically, as it seemed, at both her and me.

I had not notified to Mrs. Fairfax the exact day of my return; for I did not wish either car or carriage to meet me at Millcote. I proposed to walk the distance quietly by myself; and very quietly, after leaving my box in the ostler's care, did I slip away from the George Inn, about six o'clock of a June evening, and take the old road to Thornfield: a road which lay chiefly through fields, and was now little frequented.

It was not a bright or splendid summer evening, though fair and soft: the haymakers were at work all along the road; and the sky, though far from cloudless, was such as promised well for the future: its blue—where blue was visible—was mild and settled, and its cloud strata high and thin. The west, too, was warm: no watery gleam chilled it—it seemed as if there was a fire lit, an altar burning behind its screen of marbled vapour, and out of apertures shone a golden redness.

I felt glad as the road shortened before me: so glad that I stopped once to ask myself what that joy meant: and to remind reason that it was not to my home I was going, or to a permanent resting-place, or to a place where fond friends looked out for me and waited my arrival. "Mrs. Fairfax will smile you a calm welcome, to be sure," said I; "and little Adèle will clap her hands and jump to see you: but you know very well you are thinking of another than they; and that he is not thinking of you."

But what is so headstrong as youth? What so blind as inexperience? These affirmed that it was pleasure enough to have the privilege of again looking on Mr. Rochester, whether he looked on me or not; and they added—"Hasten! hasten! be with him while you may: but a few more days or weeks at most, and you are parted with him for ever!" And then I strangled a new-born agony—a deformed thing which I could not persuade myself to own and rear—and ran on.

They are making hay, too, in Thornfield meadows; or rather, the labourers are just quitting their work, and returning home with their rakes on their shoulders: now, at the hour I arrive. I have but a field or two to traverse, and then I shall cross the road and reach the gates. How full the hedges are of roses! But I have no time to gather any; I want to be at the house. I passed a tall briar, shooting leafy and flowery branches across the path; I see the narrow stile with stone steps; and I see—Mr. Rochester sitting there, a book and a pencil in his hand: he is writing.

Well, he is not a ghost; yet every nerve I have is unstrung: for a moment I am beyond my own mastery. What does it mean? I did not think I should tremble in this way when I saw him—or lose my voice or the power of motion in his presence. I will go back as soon as I can stir: I need not make an absolute fool of myself. I know another way to the house. It does not signify if I knew twenty ways; for he has seen me.

"Hillo!" he cries; and he puts up his book and his pencil. "There you are! Come on, if you please."

I suppose I do come on; though in what fashion I know not: being scarcely cognisant of my movements, and solicitous only to appear calm; and, above all, to control the working muscles of my face—which I feel rebel insolently against my will, and struggle to express what I had resolved to conceal. But I have a veil—it is down: I make shift yet to behave with decent composure.

"And this is Jane Eyre? Are you coming from Millcote, and on foot? Yes—just one of your tricks: not to send for a carriage, and come clattering over street and road like a common mortal, but to steal into the vicinage of your home along with twilight, just as if you were a dream or a shade. What the deuce have you done with yourself this last month?"

"I have been with my aunt, sir, who is dead."

"A true Janian reply! Good angels be my guard! She comes from the other world—from the abode of people who are dead; and tells me so when she meets me alone here in the gloaming! If I dared I'd touch you to see if you are substance or shadow, you elf!—but I'd as soon offer to take hold of a blue *ignis fatuus* light in a march. Truant! truant!" he added, when he had paused an instant. "Absent from me a whole month: and forgetting me quite, I'll be sworn!"

I knew there would be pleasure in meeting my master again; even though broken by the fear that he was so soon to cease to be my master, and by the knowledge that I was nothing to him: but there was ever in Mr. Rochester (so at least I thought) such a wealth of the power of communicating happiness, that to taste but of the crumbs he scattered to stray and stranger birds like me, was to feast genially. His last words were balm: they seemed to imply that it imported something to him whether I forgot him or not. And he had spoken of Thornfield as my home—would that it were my home!

He did not leave the stile, and I hardly liked to ask to go by. I inquired soon if he had not been to London.

"Yes: I suppose you found that out by second-sight?"

"Mrs. Fairfax told me in a letter."

"And did she inform you what I went to do?"

"Oh, yes, sir! Everybody knew your errand."

"You must see the carriage, Jane, and tell me if you don't think it will suit Mrs. Rochester exactly; and whether she won't look like Queen Boadicea, leaning back against those purple cushions. I wish, Jane, I were a trifle better adapted to match with her externally. Tell me, now, fairy as you are,—can't you give me a charm, or a philter, or something of that sort, to make me a handsome man?"

"It would be past the power of magic, sir;" and, in thought, I added, "a loving eye is all the charm needed: to such you are handsome enough; or rather, your sternness has a power beyond beauty."

Mr. Rochester had sometimes read my unspoken thoughts with an acumen to me incomprehensible: in the present instance he took no notice of my abrupt vocal response; but he smiled at me with a certain smile he had of his own, and which he used but on rare occasions. He seemed to think it too good for common purposes: it was the real sunshine of feeling—he shed it over me now.

"Pass, Janet," said he, making room for me to cross the stile: "go up home, and stay your weary little wandering feet at a friend's threshold."

All I had now to do was to obey him in silence: no need for me to colloquise further. I got over the stile without a word, and meant to leave him calmly. An impulse held me fast,—a force turned me round. I said—or something in me said for me, and in spite of me:—

"Thank you, Mr. Rochester, for your great kindness. I am strangely glad to get back again to you; and wherever you are is my home—my only home."

I walked on so fast that even he could hardly have overtaken me had he tried. Little Adèle was half wild with delight when she saw me. Mrs. Fairfax received me with her usual plain friendliness. Leah smiled; and even Sophie bid me "bon soir" with glee. This was very pleasant: there is no happiness like that of being loved by your fellow-creatures, and feeling that your presence is an addition to their comfort.

I, that evening, shut my eyes resolutely against the future: I stopped my ears against the voice that kept warning me of near separation and coming grief. When

tea was over and Mrs. Fairfax had taken her knitting, and I had assumed a low seat near her, and Adèle, kneeling on the carpet, had nestled close up to me, and a sense of mutual affection seemed to surround us with a ring of golden peace, I uttered a silent prayer that we might not be parted far or soon; but when, as we thus sat, Mr. Rochester entered, unannounced, and looking at us, seemed to take pleasure in the spectacle of a group so amicable—when he said he supposed the old lady was all right now that she had got her adopted daughter back again, and added that he saw Adèle was "prête à croquer sa petite maman Anglaise"—I half ventured to hope that he would, even after his marriage, keep us together somewhere under the shelter of his protection, and not quite exiled from the sunshine of his presence.

A fortnight of dubious calm succeeded my return to Thornfield Hall. Nothing was said of the master's marriage, and I saw no preparation going on for such an event. Almost every day I asked Mrs. Fairfax if she had yet heard anything decided: her answer was always in the negative. Once, she said, she had actually put the question to Mr. Rochester as to when he was going to bring his bride home; but he had answered her only by a joke, and one of his queer looks, and she could not tell what to make of him.

One thing specially surprised me, and that was, there were no journeyings backward and forward, no visits to Ingram Park: to be sure it was twenty miles off, on the borders of another county; but what was that distance to an ardent lover? To so practised and indefatigable a horseman as Mr. Rochester, it would be but a morning's ride. I began to cherish hopes I had no right to conceive: that the match was broken off; that rumour had been mistaken; that one or both parties had changed their minds. I used to look at my master's face to see if it were sad or fierce; but I could not remember the time when it had been so uniformly clear of clouds or evil feelings. If, in the moments I and my pupil spent with him, I lacked spirits and sank into inevitable dejection, he became even gay. Never had he called me more frequently to his presence; never been kinder to me when there—and, alas! never had I loved him so well.

Chapter XXIII

A SPLENDID Midsummer shone over England: skies so pure, suns so radiant as were then seen in long succession, seldom favour, even singly, our wave-girt land. It was as if a band of Italian days had come from the South, like a flock of glorious passenger birds, and lighted to rest them on the cliffs of Albion. The hay was all got in; the fields round Thornfield were green and shorn; the roads white and baked; the trees were in their dark prime; hedge and wood, full-leaved and deeply tinted, contrasted well with the sunny hue of the clear meadows between.

On Midsummer-eve, Adèle, weary with gathering wild strawberries in Hay Lane half the day, had gone to bed with the sun. I watched her drop asleep, and when I left her I sought the garden.

It was now the sweetest hour of the twenty-four:—"Day its fervid fires had wasted," and dew fell cool on panting plain and scorched summit. Where the sun had gone down in simple state—pure of the pomp of clouds—spread a solemn purple, burning with the light of red jewel and furnace flame at one point, on one hill-peak, and extending high and wide, soft and still softer, over half heaven. The east had its own charm of fine, deep blue, and its own modest gem, a rising and solitary star: soon it would boast the moon; but she was yet beneath the horizon.

I walked a while on the pavement; but a subtle, well-known scent—that of a cigar—stole from some window; I saw the library casement open a hand-breadth;

I knew I might be watched thence; so I went apart into the orchard. No nook in the grounds more sheltered and more Eden-like; it was full of trees, it bloomed with flowers: a very high wall shut it out from the court, on one side; on the other, a beech avenue screened it from the lawn. At the bottom was a sunk fence; its sole separation from lonely fields: a winding walk, bordered with laurels and terminating in a giant horse-chestnut, circled at the base by a seat, led down to the fence. Here one could wander unseen. While such honey-dew fell, such silence reigned, such gloaming gathered, I felt as if I could haunt such shade for ever: but in threading the flower and fruit-parterres at the upper part of the inclosure, enticed there by the light the now-risen moon casts on this more open quarter, my step is stayed—not by sound, not by sight, but once more by a warning fragrance.

Sweet briar and southernwood, jasmine, pink, and rose, have long been yielding their evening sacrifice of incense: this new scent is neither of shrub nor flower; it is—I know it well—it is Mr. Rochester's cigar. I look round and I listen. I see trees laden with ripening fruit. I hear a nightingale warbling in a wood half a mile off; no moving form is visible, no coming step audible; but that perfume increases: I must flee. I make for the wicket leading to the shrubbery, and I see Mr. Rochester entering. I step aside into the ivy recess, he will not stay long: he will soon return whence he came, and if I sit still he will never see me.

But no—eventide is as pleasant to him as to me, and this antique garden as attractive; and he strolls on, now lifting the gooseberry-tree branches to look at the fruit, large as plums, with which they are laden; now taking a ripe cherry from the wall; now stooping towards a knot of flowers, either to inhale their fragrance or to admire the dew-beads on their petals. A great moth goes humming by me: it alights on a plant at Mr. Rochester's foot: he sees it, and bends to examine it.

"Now, he has his back towards me," thought I, "and he is occupied too; perhaps, if I walk softly, I can slip away unnoticed."

I trode on an edging of turf that the crackle of the pebbly gravel might not betray me: he was standing among the beds at a yard or two distant from where I had to pass; the moth apparently engaged him. "I shall get by very well," I meditated. As I crossed his shadow, thrown long over the garden by the moon, not yet risen high, he said quietly without turning:—

"Jane, come and look at this fellow."

I had made no noise: he had not eyes behind—could his shadow feel? I started at first, and then I approached him.

"Look at his wings," said he, "he reminds me rather of a West Indian insect; one does not often see so large and gay a night-rover in England: there! he is flown."

The moth roamed away. I was sheepishly retreating also; but Mr. Rochester followed me, and when we reached the wicket, he said:—

"Turn back: on so lovely a night it is a shame to sit in the house; and surely no one can wish to go to bed while sunset is thus at meeting with moonrise."

It is one of my faults, that though my tongue is sometimes prompt enough at an answer, there are times when it sadly fails me in framing an excuse; and always the lapse occurs at some crisis, when a facile word or plausible pretext is specially wanted to get me out of painful embarrassment. I did not like to walk at this hour alone with Mr. Rochester in the shadowy orchard; but I could not find a reason to allege for leaving him. I followed with lagging step, and thoughts busily bent on discovering a means of extrication; but he himself looked so composed and so grave also, I became ashamed of feeling any confusion: the evil—if evil existent or prospective there was—seemed to lie with me only; his mind was unconscious and quiet.

"Jane," he recommenced, as we entered the laurel walk, and slowly strayed down in the direction of the sunk fence and the horse-chesnut, "Thornfield is a pleasant place in summer, is it not?"

"Yes, sir."

"You must have become in some degree attached to the house,—you, who have an eye for natural beauties, and a good deal of the organ of Adhesiveness?"

"I am attached to it, indeed."

"And though I don't comprehend how it is, I perceive you have acquired a degree of regard for that foolish little child Adèle, too; and even for simple dame Fairfax?"

"Yes, sir; in different ways, I have an affection for both."

"And would be sorry to part with them?"

"Yes."

"Pity!" he said, and sighed and paused. "It is always the way of events in this life," he continued presently: "no sooner have you got settled in a pleasant resting-place, than a voice calls out to you to rise and move on, for the hour of repose is expired."

"Must I move on, sir?" I asked. "Must I leave Thornfield?"

"I believe you must, Jane. I am sorry, Janet, but I believe indeed you must."

This was a blow: but I did not let it prostrate me.

"Well, sir, I shall be ready when the order to march comes."

"It is come now—I must give it to-night."

"Then you are going to be married, sir?"

"Ex-act-ly—pre-cise-ly: with your usual acuteness, you have hit the nail straight on the head."

"Soon, sir?"

"Very soon, my——that is, Miss Eyre: and you'll remember, Jane, the first time I, or Rumour, plainly intimated to you that it was my intention to put my old bachelor's neck into the sacred noose, to enter into the holy estate of matrimony— to take Miss Ingram to my bosom, in short (she's an extensive armful: but that's not to the point—one can't have too much of such a very excellent thing as my beautiful Blanche): well, as I was saying—listen to me, Jane! You're not turning your head to look after more moths, are you? That was only a lady-clock, child, 'flying away home.' I wish to remind you that it was you who first said to me, with that discretion I respect in you—with that foresight, prudence and humility which befit your responsible and dependent position—that in case I married Miss Ingram—both you and little Adèle had better trot forthwith. I pass over the sort of slur conveyed in this suggestion on the character of my beloved; indeed, when you are far away, Janet, I'll try to forget it: I shall notice only its wisdom; which is such that I have made it my law of action. Adèle must go to school; and you, Miss Eyre, must get a new situation."

"Yes, sir, I will advertise immediately: and meantime, I suppose"——I was going to say, "I suppose I may stay here, till I find another shelter to betake myself to:" but I stopped, feeling it would not do to risk a long sentence, for my voice was not quite under command.

"In about a month I hope to be a bridegroom," continued Mr. Rochester; "and in the interim I shall myself look out for employment and an asylum for you."

"Thank you, sir; I am sorry to give"——

"Oh, no need to apologise! I consider that when a dependent does her duty as well as you have done yours, she has a sort of claim upon her employer for any little assistance he can conveniently render her; indeed I have already, through my future mother-in-law, heard of a place that I think will suit: it is to undertake the education of the five daughters of Mrs. Dionysius O'Gall of Bitternutt Lodge, Connaught, Ireland. You'll like Ireland, I think: they're such warm-hearted people there, they say."

"It is a long way off, sir."

"No matter—a girl of your sense will not object to the voyage or the distance."

"Not the voyage, but the distance: and then the sea is a barrier"——

"From what, Jane?"

"From England and from Thornfield: and"——

"Well?"

"From *you*, sir."

I said this almost involuntarily; and, with as little sanction of free will, my tears gushed out. I did not cry so as to be heard, however; I avoided sobbing. The thought of Mrs. O'Gall and Bitternutt Lodge struck cold to my heart; and colder the thought of all the brine and foam, destined, as it seemed, to rush between me and the master at whose side I now walked; and coldest the remembrance of the wider ocean— wealth, caste, custom intervened between me and what I naturally and inevitably loved.

"It is a long way," I again said.

"It is, to be sure; and when you get to Bitternutt Lodge, Connaught, Ireland, I shall never see you again, Jane: that's morally certain. I never go over to Ireland, not having myself much of a fancy for the country. We have been good friends, Jane; have we not?"

"Yes, sir."

"And when friends are on the eve of separation, they like to spend the little time that remains to them close to each other. Come—we'll talk over the voyage and the parting quietly, half an hour or so, while the stars enter into their shining life up in heaven yonder: here is the chestnut tree: here is the bench at its old roots. Come, we will sit there in peace to-night, though we should never more be destined to sit there together." He seated me and himself.

"It is a long way to Ireland, Janet, and I am sorry to send my little friend on such weary travels: but if I can't do better, how is it to be helped? Are you anything akin to me, do you think, Jane?"

I could risk no sort of answer by this time: my heart was full.

"Because," he said, "I sometimes have a queer feeling with regard to you— especially when you are near me, as now: it is as if I had a string somewhere under my left ribs, tightly and inextricably knotted to a similar string situated in the corresponding quarter of your little frame. And if that boisterous channel, and two hundred miles or so of land come broad between us, I am afraid that cord of communion will be snapt; and then I've a nervous notion I should take to bleeding inwardly. As for you,—you'd forget me."

"That I *never* should, sir: you know"——impossible to proceed.

"Jane, do you hear that nightingale singing in the wood? Listen!"

In listening, I sobbed convulsively; for I could repress what I endured no longer; I was obliged to yield, and I was shaken from head to foot with acute distress. When I did speak, it was only to express an impetuous wish that I had never been born, or never come to Thornfield.

"Because you are sorry to leave it?"

The vehemence of emotion, stirred by grief and love within me, was claiming mastery, and struggling for full sway; and asserting a right to predominate: to overcome, to live, rise, and reign at last; yes,—and to speak.

"I grieve to leave Thornfield: I love Thornfield:—I love it, because I have lived in it a full and delightful life,—momentarily at least. I have not been trampled on. I have not been petrified. I have not been buried with inferior minds, and excluded from every glimpse of communion with what is bright and energetic, and high. I have talked, face to face, with what I reverence; with what I delight in,—with an original, a vigorous, an expanded mind. I have known you, Mr. Rochester; and it strikes me with terror and anguish to feel I absolutely must be torn from you for ever. I see the necessity of departure; and it is like looking on the necessity of death."

"Where do you see the necessity?" he asked, suddenly.

"Where? You, sir, have placed it before me."

"In what shape?"

"In the shape of Miss Ingram; a noble and beautiful woman,—your bride."

"My bride! What bride? I have no bride!"

"But you will have."

"Yes:—I will!—I will!" He set his teeth.

"Then I must go:—you have said it yourself."

"No: you must stay! I swear it—and the oath shall be kept."

"I tell you I must go!" I retorted, roused to something like passion. "Do you think I can stay to become nothing to you? Do you think I am an automaton?—a machine without feelings? and can bear to have my morsel of bread snatched from my lips, and my drop of living water dashed from my cup? Do you think, because I am poor, obscure, plain, and little, I am soulless and heartless? You think wrong!— I have as much soul as you,—and full as much heart! And if God had gifted me with some beauty, and much wealth, I should have made it as hard for you to leave me, as it is now for me to leave you. I am not talking to you now through the medium of custom, conventionalities, or even of mortal flesh:—it is my spirit that addresses your spirit; just as if both had passed through the grave, and we stood at God's feet, equal,—as we are!"

"As we are!" repeated Mr. Rochester—"so," he added, enclosing me in his arms, gathering me to his breast, pressing his lips on my lips: "so, Jane!"

"Yes, so, sir," I rejoined: "and yet not so; for you are a married man—or as good as a married man, and wed to one inferior to you—to one with whom you have no sympathy—whom I do not believe you truly love; for I have seen and heard you sneer at her. I would scorn such a union: therefore I am better than you— let me go!"

"Where, Jane? To Ireland?"

"Yes—to Ireland. I have spoken my mind, and can go anywhere now."

"Jane, be still; don't struggle so, like a wild, frantic bird that is rending its own plumage in its desperation."

"I am no bird; and no net ensnares me; I am a free human being with an independent will; which I now exert to leave you."

Another effort set me at liberty, and I stood erect before him.

"And your will shall decide your destiny," he said: "I offer you my hand, my heart, and a share of all my possessions."

"You play a farce, which I merely laugh at."

"I ask you to pass through life at my side—to be my second self and best earthly companion."

"For that fate you have already made your choice, and must abide by it."

"Jane, be still a few moments: you are over-excited: I will be still too."

A waft of wind came sweeping down the laurel-walk, and trembled through the boughs of the chestnut: it wandered away—away—to an indefinite distance—it died. The nightingale's song was then the only voice of the hour: in listening to it, I again wept. Mr. Rochester sat quiet, looking at me gently and seriously. Some time passed before he spoke: he at last said:—

"Come to my side, Jane, and let us explain and understand one another."

"I will never again come to your side: I am torn away now, and cannot return."

"But, Jane, I summon you as my wife: it is you only I intend to marry."

I was silent: I thought he mocked me.

"Come, Jane—come hither."

"Your bride stands between us."

He rose, and with a stride reached me.

"My bride is here," he said, again drawing me to him, "because my equal is here, and my likeness. Jane, will you marry me?"

Still I did not answer, and still I writhed myself from his grasp: for I was still incredulous.

"Do you doubt me, Jane?"

"Entirely."

"You have no faith in me?"

"Not a whit."

"Am I a liar in your eyes?" he asked passionately. "Little sceptic, you *shall* be convinced. What love have I for Miss Ingram? None: and that you know. What love has she for me? None: as I have taken pains to prove: I caused a rumour to reach her that my fortune was not a third of what was supposed, and after that I presented myself to see the result; it was coldness both from her and her mother. I would not—I could not—marry Miss Ingram. You—you strange—you almost unearthly thing!—I love as my own flesh. You—poor and obscure, and small and plain as you are—I entreat to accept me as a husband."

"What, me!" I ejaculated: beginning in his earnestness—and especially in his incivility—to credit his sincerity: "me who have not a friend in the world but you—if you are my friend: not a shilling but what you have given me?"

"You, Jane. I must have you for my own—entirely my own. Will you be mine? Say yes, quickly."

"Mr. Rochester, let me look at your face: turn to the moonlight."

"Why?"

"Because I want to read your countenance; turn!"

"There: you will find it scarcely more legible than a crumpled, scratched page. Read on: only make haste, for I suffer."

His face was very much agitated and very much flushed, and there were strong workings in the features, and strange gleams in the eyes.

"Oh, Jane, you torture me!" he exclaimed. "With that searching and yet faithful and generous look, you torture me!"

"How can I do that? If you are true and your offer real, my only feelings to you must be gratitude and devotion—they cannot torture."

"Gratitude!" he ejaculated; and added wildly—"Jane, accept me quickly. Say Edward—give me my name—Edward—I will marry you."

"Are you in earnest?—Do you truly love me?—Do you sincerely wish me to be your wife?"

"I do; and if an oath is necessary to satisfy you, I swear it."

"Then, sir, I will marry you."

"Edward—my little wife!"

"Dear Edward!"

"Come to me—come to me entirely now," said he: and added, in his deepest tone, speaking in my ear as his cheek was laid on mine, "Make my happiness—I will make yours.

"God pardon me!" he subjoined ere long, "and man meddle not with me: I have her, and will hold her."

"There is no one to meddle, sir. I have no kindred to interfere."

"No—that is the best of it," he said. And if I had loved him less I should have thought his accent and look of exultation savage: but sitting by him, roused from the nightmare of parting—called to the paradise of union—I thought only of the bliss given me to drink in so abundant a flow. Again and again he said, "Are you happy, Jane?" and again and again I answered, "Yes." After which he murmured, "It will atone—it will atone. Have I not found her friendless, and cold, and comfortless? Will I not guard, and cherish, and solace her? Is there not love in my heart, and constancy in my resolves? It will expiate at God's tribunal. I know my Maker sanctions what I do. For the world's judgment—I wash my hands thereof. For man's opinion—I defy it."

But what had befallen the night? The moon was not yet set, and we were all in shadow: I could scarcely see my master's face, near as I was. And what ailed the

chestnut tree? it writhed and groaned; while wind roared in the laurel walk, and
came sweeping over us.

"We must go in," said Mr. Rochester: "the weather changes. I could have sat
with thee till morning, Jane."

"And so," thought I, "could I with you." I should have said so, perhaps, but
a livid, vivid spark leapt out of a cloud at which I was looking, and there was a
crack, a crash, and a close rattling peal; and I thought only of hiding my dazzled
eyes against Mr. Rochester's shoulder.

The rain rushed down. He hurried me up the walk, through the grounds, and
into the house; but we were quite wet before we could pass the threshold. He was
taking off my shawl in the hall, and shaking the water out of my loosened hair,
when Mrs. Fairfax emerged from her room. I did not observe her at first, nor did
Mr. Rochester. The lamp was lit. The clock was on the stroke of twelve.

"Hasten to take off your wet things," said he: "and before you go, good-night—
good-night, my darling!"

He kissed me repeatedly. When I looked up, on leaving his arms, there stood
the widow, pale, grave, and amazed. I only smiled at her, and ran upstairs. "Ex-
planation will do for another time," thought I. Still, when I reached my chamber,
I felt a pang at the idea she should even temporarily misconstrue what she had
seen. But joy soon effaced every other feeling; and loud as the wind blew, near
and deep as the thunder crashed, fierce and frequent as the lightning gleamed,
cataract-like as the rain fell during a storm of two hours' duration, I experienced
no fear, and little awe. Mr. Rochester came thrice to my door in the course of it,
to ask if I was safe and tranquil: and that was comfort, that was strength for anything.

Before I left my bed in the morning, little Adèle came running in to tell me that
the great horse-chestnut at the bottom of the orchard had been struck by lightning
in the night, and half of it split away.

Chapter XXIV

As I rose and dressed, I thought over what had happened, and wondered if it were
a dream. I could not be certain of the reality till I had seen Mr. Rochester again,
and heard him renew his words of love and promise.

While arranging my hair, I looked at my face in the glass, and felt it was no
longer plain: there was hope in its aspect, and life in its colour: and my eyes seemed
as if they had beheld the fount of fruition, and borrowed beams from the lustrous
ripple. I had often been unwilling to look at my master, because I feared he could
not be pleased at my look; but I was sure I might lift my face to his now, and not
cool his affection by its expression. I took a plain but clean and light summer dress
from my drawer and put it on: it seemed no attire had ever so well become me;
because none had I ever worn in so blissful a mood.

I was not surprised, when I ran down into the hall, to see that a brilliant June
morning had succeeded to the tempest of the night; and to feel, through the open
glass door, the breathing of a fresh and fragrant breeze. Nature must be gladsome
when I was so happy. A beggar-woman and her little boy—pale, ragged objects
both—were coming up the walk, and I ran down and gave them all the money I
happened to have in my purse—some three or four shillings: good or bad, they
must partake of my jubilee. The rooks cawed, and blither birds sang; but nothing
was so merry or so musical as my own rejoicing heart.

Mrs. Fairfax surprised me by looking out of the window with a sad countenance,
and saying gravely:—"Miss Eyre, will you come to breakfast?" During the meal
she was quiet and cool: but I could not undeceive her then. I must wait for my

master to give explanations; and so must she. I ate what I could, and then I hastened upstairs. I met Adèle leaving the school-room.

"Where are you going? It is time for lessons."

"Mr. Rochester has sent me away to the nursery."

"Where is he?"

"In there," pointing to the apartment she had left; and I went in, and there he stood.

"Come and bid me good-morning," said he. I gladly advanced; and it was not merely a cold word now, or even a shake of the hand that I received, but an embrace and a kiss. It seemed natural: it seemed genial to be so well-loved, so caressed by him.

"Jane, you look blooming, and smiling, and pretty," said he: "truly pretty this morning. Is this my pale little elf? Is this my mustard-seed? This little sunny-faced girl with the dimpled cheek and rosy lips; the satin-smooth hazel hair, and the radiant hazel eyes?" (I had green eyes, reader; but you must excuse the mistake: for him they were new-dyed, I suppose.)

"It is Jane Eyre, sir."

"Soon to be Jane Rochester," he added: "in four weeks, Janet; not a day more. Do you hear that?"

I did, and I could not quite comprehend it: it made me giddy. The feeling, the announcement sent through me, was something stronger than was consistent with joy— something that smote and stunned: it was, I think, almost fear.

"You blushed, and now you are white, Jane: what is that for?"

"Because you gave me a new name—Jane Rochester; and it seems so strange."

"Yes; Mrs. Rochester," said he; "young Mrs. Rochester—Fairfax Rochester's girl-bride."

"It can never be, sir; it does not sound likely. Human beings never enjoy complete happiness in this world. I was not born for a different destiny to the rest of my species; to imagine such a lot befalling me is a fairy tale—a day-dream."

"Which I can and will realise. I shall begin to-day. This morning I wrote to my banker in London to send me certain jewels he has in his keeping,—heirlooms for the ladies of Thornfield. In a day or two I hope to pour them into your lap: for every privilege, every attention shall be yours, that I would accord a peer's daughter if I about to marry her."

"Oh, sir!—never mind jewels! I don't like to hear them spoken of. Jewels for Jane Eyre sounds unnatural and strange: I would rather not have them."

"I will myself put the diamond charm round your neck, and the circlet on your forehead,—which it will become: for nature, at least, has stamped her patent of nobility on this brow, Jane; and I will clasp the bracelets on these fine wrists, and load these fairy-like fingers with rings."

"No, no, sir! think of other subjects, and speak of other things, and in another strain. Don't address me as if I were a beauty; I am your plain, Quakerish governess."

"You are a beauty, in my eyes; and a beauty just after the desire of my heart,— delicate and aërial."

"Puny and insignificant, you mean. You are dreaming, sir,—or you are sneering. For God's sake, don't be ironical!"

"I will make the world acknowledge you a beauty, too," he went on, while I really became uneasy at the strain he had adopted; because I felt he was either deluding himself, or trying to delude me. "I will attire my Jane in satin and lace, and she shall have roses in her hair; and I will cover the head I love best with a priceless veil."

"And then you won't know me, sir; and I shall not be your Jane Eyre any longer, but an ape in a harlequin's jacket,—a jay in borrowed plumes. I would as soon see you, Mr. Rochester, tricked out in stage-trappings, as myself clad in a court-lady's

robe; and I don't call you handsome, sir, though I love you most dearly: far too dearly to flatter you. Don't flatter me.''

He pursued his theme, however, without noticing my deprecation. ''This very day I shall take you in the carriage to Millcote, and you must choose some dresses for yourself. I told you we shall be married in four weeks. The wedding is to take place quietly, in the church down below yonder; and then I shall waft you away at once to town. After a brief stay there, I shall bear my treasure to regions nearer the sun: to French vineyards and Italian plains; and she shall see whatever is famous in old story and in modern record: she shall taste, too, of the life of cities; and she shall learn to value herself by just comparison with others.''

''Shall I travel?—and with you, sir?''

''You shall sojourn at Paris, Rome, and Naples: at Florence, Venice, and Vienna: all the ground I have wandered over shall be re-trodden by you: wherever I stamped my hoof, your sylph's foot shall step also. Ten years since, I flew through Europe half mad; with disgust, hate, and rage, as my companions: now I shall revisit it healed and cleansed, with a very angel as my comforter.''

I laughed at him as he said this. ''I am not an angel,'' I asserted; ''and I will not be one till I die: I will be myself, Mr. Rochester, you must neither expect nor exact anything celestial of me—for you will not get it, any more than I shall get it of you: which I do not at all anticipate.''

''What do you anticipate of me?''

''For a little while you will perhaps be as you are now,—a very little while; and then you will turn cool; and then you will be capricious; and then you will be stern, and I shall have much ado to please you: but when you get well used to me, you will perhaps like me again,—*like* me, I say, not *love* me. I suppose your love will effervesce in six months, or less. I have observed in books written by men, that period assigned as the farthest to which a husband's ardour extends. Yet, after all, as a friend and companion, I hope never to become quite distasteful to my dear master.''

''Distasteful! and like you again! I think I shall like you again and yet again: and I will make you confess I do not only *like,* but *love* you—with truth, fervour, constancy.''

''Yet are you not capricious, sir?''

''To women who please me only by their faces, I am the very devil when I find out they have neither souls nor hearts—when they open to me a perspective of flatness, triviality, and perhaps imbecility, coarseness, and ill-temper: but to the clear eye and eloquent tongue, to the soul made of fire, and the character that bends but does not break—at once supple and stable, tractable and consistent—I am ever tender and true.''

''Had you ever experience of such a character, sir? Did you ever love such an one?''

''I love it now.''

''But before me: if I, indeed, in any respect come up to your difficult standard?''.

''I never met your likeness. Jane: you please me, and you master me—you seem to submit, and I like the sense of pliancy you impart; and while I am twining the soft, silken skein round my finger, it sends a thrill up my arm to my heart. I am influenced—conquered; and the influence is sweeter than I can express; and the conquest I undergo has a witchery beyond any triumph *I* can win. Why do you smile, Jane? What does that inexplicable, that uncanny turn of countenance mean?''

''I was thinking, sir (you will excuse the idea; it was involuntary), I was thinking of Hercules and Samson with their charmers''——

''You were, you little elfish''——

''Hush, sir! You don't talk very wisely just now; any more than those gentlemen acted very wisely. However, had they been married, they would no doubt by their severity as husbands have made up for their softness as suitors; and so will you, I

fear. I wonder how you will answer me a year hence, should I ask a favour it does not suit your convenience or pleasure to grant.''

"Ask me something now, Janet—the least thing: I desire to be entreated"——

"Indeed, I will, sir; I have my petition all ready.''

"Speak! But if you look up and smile with that countenance, I shall swear concession before I know to what, and that will make a fool of me.''

"Not at all, sir; I ask only this: don't send for the jewels, and don't crown me with roses: you might as well put a border of gold lace round that plain pocket handkerchief you have there.''

"I might as well 'gild refined gold.' I know it: your request is granted then—for the time. I will remand the order I despatched to my banker. But you have not yet asked for anything: you have prayed a gift to be withdrawn: try again.''

"Well, then, sir, have the goodness to gratify my curiosity, which is much piqued on one point.''

He looked disturbed. "What? what?'' he said hastily. "Curiosity is a dangerous petition: it is well I have not taken a vow to accord every request"——

"But there can be no danger in complying with this, sir.''

"Utter it, Jane: but I wish that instead of a mere inquiry into, perhaps, a secret, it was a wish for half my estate.''

"Now, king Ahasuerus! What do I want with half your estate? Do you think I am a Jew-usurer, seeking good investment in land? I would much rather have all your confidence. You will not exclude me from your confidence, if you admit me to your heart?''

"You are welcome to all my confidence that is worth having, Jane: but for God's sake, don't desire a useless burden! Don't long for poison—don't turn out a downright Eve on my hands!''

"Why not, sir? You have just been telling me how much you liked to be conquered, and how pleasant over-persuasion is to you. Don't you think I had better take advantage of the confession, and begin and coax and entreat—even cry and be sulky if necessary—for the sake of a mere essay of my power?''

"I dare you to any such experiment. Encroach, presume, and the game is up.''

"Is it, sir? You soon give in. How stern you look now! Your eyebrows have become as thick as my finger, and your forehead resembles, what, in some very astonishing poetry, I once saw styled, 'a blue-piled thunderloft.' That will be your married look, sir, I suppose?''

"If that will be *your* married look, I, as a Christian, will soon give up the notion of consorting with a mere sprite or salamander. But what had you to ask, thing?—out with it!''

"There, you are less than civil now; and I like rudeness a great deal better than flattery. I had rather be a *thing* than an angel. This is what I have to ask,—Why did you take such pains to make me believe you wished to marry Miss Ingram?''

"Is that all! Thank God, it is no worse!'' And now he unknit his black brows; looked down, smiling at me, and stroked my hair, as if well pleased at seeing a danger averted. "I think I may confess,'' he continued, "even although I should make you a little indignant, Jane—and I have seen what a fire-spirit you can be when you are indignant. You glowed in the cool moonlight last night, when you mutinied against fate, and claimed your rank as my equal. Janet, by-the-by, it was you who made me the offer.''

"Of course, I did. But to the point if you please, sir—Miss Ingram?''

"Well, I feigned courtship of Miss Ingram, because I wished to render you as madly in love with me as I was with you; and I knew jealousy would be the best ally I could call in for the furtherance of that end.''

"Excellent!—Now you are small—not one whit bigger than the end of my little finger. It was a burning shame, and a scandalous disgrace to act in that way. Did you think nothing of Miss Ingram's feelings, sir!''

"Her feelings are concentrated in one—pride; and that needs humbling. Were you jealous, Jane?"

"Never mind, Mr. Rochester: it is in no way interesting to you to know that. Answer me truly once more. Do you think Miss Ingram will not suffer from your dishonest coquetry? Won't she feel forsaken and deserted?"

"Impossible!—when I told you how she, on the contrary, deserted me: the idea of my insolvency cooled, or rather extinguished, her flame in a moment."

"You have a curious, designing mind, Mr. Rochester. I am afraid your principles on some points are eccentric."

"My principles were never trained, Jane: they may have grown a little awry for want of attention."

"Once again, seriously; may I enjoy the great good that has been vouchsafed to me, without fearing that any one else is suffering the bitter pain I myself felt a while ago?"

"That you may, my good little girl: there is not another being in the world has the same pure love for me as yourself—for I lay that pleasant unction to my soul, Jane, a belief in your affection."

I turned my lips to the hand that lay on my shoulder. I loved him very much—more than I could trust myself to say—more than words had power to express.

"Ask something more," he said presently; "it is my delight to be entreated, and to yield."

I was again ready with my request. "Communicate your intentions to Mrs. Fairfax, sir: she saw me with you last night in the hall, and she was shocked. Give her some explanation before I see her again. It pains me to be misjudged by so good a woman."

"Go to your room, and put on your bonnet," he replied. "I mean you to accompany me to Millcote this morning; and while you prepare for the drive, I will enlighten the old lady's understanding. Did she think, Janet, you had given the world for love, and considered it well lost?"

"I believe she thought I had forgotten my station, and yours, sir."

"Station! station!—your station is in my heart, and on the necks of those who would insult you, now or hereafter.—Go."

I was soon dressed; and when I heard Mr. Rochester quit Mrs. Fairfax's parlour, I hurried down to it. The old lady had been reading her morning portion of Scripture—the lesson for the day; her Bible lay open before her, and her spectacles were upon it. Her occupation, suspended by Mr. Rochester's announcement, seemed now forgotten: her eyes, fixed on the blank wall opposite, expressed the surprise of a quiet mind, stirred by unwonted tidings. Seeing me, she roused herself: she made a sort of effort to smile, and framed a few words of congratulation; but the smile expired, and the sentence was abandoned unfinished. She put up her spectacles, shut the Bible, and pushed her chair back from the table.

"I feel so astonished," she began, "I hardly know what to say to you, Miss Eyre. I have surely not been dreaming, have I? Sometimes I half fall asleep when I am sitting alone, and fancy things that have never happened. It has seemed to me more than once when I have been in a doze, that my dear husband, who died fifteen years since, has come in and sat down beside me; and that I have even heard him call me by my name, Alice, as he used to do. Now, can you tell me whether it is actually true that Mr. Rochester has asked you to marry him? Don't laugh at me. But I really thought he came in here five minutes ago, and said, that in a month you would be his wife."

"He has said the same thing to me," I replied.

"He has! Do you believe him? Have you accepted him?"

"Yes." She looked at me bewildered.

"I could never have thought it. He is a proud man: all the Rochesters were proud: and his father, at least, liked money. He, too, has always been careful. He means to marry you?''

"He tells me so.''

She surveyed my whole person: in her eyes I read that they had there found no charm powerful enough to solve the enigma.

"It passes me!'' she continued: "but no doubt it is true since you say so. How it will answer, I cannot tell: I really don't know. Equality of position and fortune is often advisable in such cases; and there are twenty years of difference in your ages. He might almost be your father.''

"No, indeed, Mrs. Fairfax!'' exclaimed I, nettled: "he is nothing like my father! No one, who saw us together, would suppose it for an instant. Mr. Rochester looks as young, and is as young as some men at five-and-twenty.''

"Is it really for love he is going to marry you?'' she asked.

I was so hurt by her coldness and scepticism, that the tears rose to my eyes.

"I am sorry to grieve you,'' pursued the widow; "but you are so young, and so little acquainted with men, I wished to put you on your guard. It is an old saying that 'all is not gold that glitters'; and in this case I do fear there will be something found to be different to what either you or I expect.''

"Why!—am I a monster?'' I said: "is it impossible that Mr. Rochester should have a sincere affection for me?''

"No: you are very well; and much improved of late; and Mr. Rochester, I daresay, is fond of you. I have always noticed that you were a sort of pet of his. There are times when, for your sake, I have been a little uneasy at his marked preference, and have wished to put you on your guard: but I did not like to suggest even the possibility of wrong. I knew such an idea would shock, perhaps offend you; and you were so discreet, and so thoroughly modest and sensible, I hoped you might be trusted to protect yourself. Last night I cannot tell you what I suffered when I sought all over the house, and could find you nowhere, nor the master either; and then, at twelve o'clock, saw you come in with him.''

"Well, never mind that now,'' I interrupted impatiently: "it is enough that all was right.''

"I hope all will be right in the end,'' she said: "but, believe me, you cannot be too careful. Try and keep Mr. Rochester at a distance: distrust yourself as well as him. Gentlemen in his station are not accustomed to marry their governesses.''

I was growing truly irritated: happily, Adèle ran in.

"Let me go,—let me go to Millcote too!'' she cried. "Mr. Rochester won't; though there is so much room in the new carriage. Beg him to let me go, mademoiselle.''

"That I will, Adèle;'' and I hastened away with her, glad to quit my gloomy monitress. The carriage was ready; they were bringing it round to the front, and my master was pacing the pavement, Pilot following him backwards and forwards.

"Adèle may accompany us, may she not, sir?''

"I told her no. I'll have no brats!—I'll have only you.''

"Do let her go, Mr. Rochester, if you please: it would be better.''

"Not it: she will be a restraint.''

He was quite peremptory, both in look and voice. The chill of Mrs. Fairfax's warnings, and the damp of her doubts were upon me: something of unsubstantiality and uncertainty had beset my hopes. I half lost the sense of power over him. I was about mechanically to obey him, without further remonstrance: but as he helped me into the carriage, he looked at my face.

"What is the matter?'' he asked; "all the sunshine is gone. Do you really wish the bairn to go? Will it annoy you if she is left behind?''

"I would far rather she went, sir.''

"Then off for your bonnet, and back, like a flash of lightning!'' cried he to Adèle.

She obeyed him with what speed she might.

"After all, a single morning's interruption will not matter much," said he, "when I mean shortly to claim you—your thoughts, conversation, and company—for life."

Adèle, when lifted in, commenced kissing me, by way of expressing her gratitude for my intercession; she was instantly stowed away into a corner on the other side of him. She then peeped round to where I sat; so stern a neighbour was too restrictive: to him, in his present fractious mood, she dared whisper no observations, nor ask, of him any information.

"Let her come to me," I entreated: "she will, perhaps, trouble you, sir: there is plenty of room on this side."

He handed her over as if she had been a lap-dog: "I'll send her to school yet," he said, but now he was smiling.

Adèle heard him, and asked if she was to go to school "sans mademoiselle?"

"Yes," he replied, "absolutely sans mademoiselle; for I am to take mademoiselle to the moon, and there I shall seek a cave in one of the white valleys among the volcano-tops, and mademoiselle shall live with me there and only me."

"She will have nothing to eat: you will starve her," observed Adèle.

"I shall gather manna for her morning and night: the plains and hill-sides in the moon are bleached with manna, Adèle."

"She will want to warm herself: what will she do for a fire?"

"Fire rises out of the lunar mountains: when she is cold, I'll carry her up to a peak and lay her down on the edge of a crater."

"Oh, qu'elle y sera mal—peu comfortable! And her clothes, they wil wear out: how can she get new ones?"

Mr. Rochester professed to be puzzled. "Hem!" said he. "What would you do, Adèle? Cudgel your brains for an expedient. How would a white or a pink cloud answer for a gown, do you think? And one could cut a pretty enough scarf out of a rainbow."

"She is far better as she is," concluded Adèle, after musing some time: "besides, she would get tired of living with only you in the moon. If I were mademoiselle, I would never consent to go with you."

"She has consented: she has pledged her word."

"But you can't get her there: there is no road to the moon: it is all air; and neither you nor she can fly."

"Adèle, look at that field." We were now outside Thornfield gates, and bowling lightly along the smooth road to Millcote, where the dust was well laid by the thunder-storm, and where the low hedges and lofty timber trees on each side glistened green, and rain-refreshed.

"In that field, Adèle, I was walking late one evening about a fortnight since— the evening of the day you helped me to make hay in the orchard meadows; and as I was tired with raking swaths, I sat down to rest me on a stile; and there I took out a little book and a pencil, and began to write about a misfortune that befell me long ago, and a wish I had for happy days to come: I was writing away very fast, though daylight was fading from the leaf, when something came up the path and stopped two yards off me. I looked at it. It was a little thing with a veil of gossamer on its head. I beckoned it to come near me: it stood soon at my knee. I never spoke to it, and it never spoke to me in words: but I read its eyes, and it read mine; and our speechless colloquy was to this effect:—

"It was a fairy, and come from Elf-land, it said; and its errand was to make me happy: I must go with it out of the common world to a lonely place—such as the moon, for instance—and it nodded its head towards her horn, rising over Hay-hill: it told me of the alabaster cave and silver vale where we might live. I said I should like to go: but reminded it, as you did me, that I had no wings to fly.

" 'Oh,' returned the fairy, 'that does not signify! Here is a talisman will remove all difficulties;' and she held out a pretty gold ring. 'Put it,' she said, 'on the fourth

finger of my left hand, and I am yours, and you are mine; and we shall leave earth, and make our own heaven yonder.' She nodded again at the moon. The ring, Adèle, is in my breeches-pocket, under the disguise of a sovereign: but I mean soon to change it to a ring again.''

"But what has mademoiselle to do with it? I don't care for the fairy: you said it was mademoiselle you would take to the moon?''——

"Mademoiselle is a fairy,'' he said, whispering mysteriously. Whereupon I told her not to mind his badinage; and she, on her part, evinced a fund of genuine French scepticism: denominating Mr. Rochester "un vrai menteur,'' and assuring him that she made no account whatever of his "Contes de fée,'' and that "du reste, il n'y avait pas de fées, et quand même il y en avait:'' she was sure they would never appear to him, nor ever give him rings, or offer to live with him in the moon.

The hour spent at Millcote was a somewhat harassing one to me. Mr. Rochester obliged me to go to a certain silk warehouse: there I was ordered to choose half a dozen dresses. I hated the business, I begged leave to defer it: no—it should be gone through with now. By dint of entreaties expressed in energetic whispers, I reduced the half-dozen to two: these, however, he vowed he would select himself. With anxiety I watched his eye rove over the gay stores: he fixed on a rich silk of the most brilliant amethyst dye, and a superb pink satin. I told him in a new series of whispers, that he might as well buy me a gold gown and a silver bonnet at once: I should certainly never venture to wear his choice. With infinite difficulty, for he was stubborn as a stone, I persuaded him to make an exchange in favour of a sober black satin and pearl-grey silk. "It might pass for the present,'' he said; "but he would yet see me glittering like a parterre.''

Glad was I to get him out of the silk warehouse, and then out of a jeweller's shop: the more he bought me, the more my cheek burned with a sense of annoyance and degradation. As we re-entered the carriage, and I sat back feverish and fagged, I remembered what in the hurry of events, dark and bright, I had wholly forgotten— the letter of my uncle, John Eyre, to Mrs. Reed: his intention to adopt me and make me his legatee. "It would, indeed, be a relief,'' I thought, "if I had ever so small an independency; I never can bear being dressed like a doll by Mr. Rochester, or sitting like a second Danae with the golden shower falling daily round me. I will write to Madeira the moment I get home, and tell my uncle John I am going to be married, and to whom: if I had but a prospect of one day bringing Mr. Rochester an accession of fortune, I could better endure to be kept by him now.'' And somewhat relieved by this idea (which I failed not to execute that day), I ventured once more to meet my master's and lover's eye; which most pertinaciously sought mine, though I averted both face and gaze. He smiled; and I thought his smile was such as a sultan might, in a blissful and fond moment, bestow on a slave his gold and gems had enriched: I crushed his hand, which was ever hunting mine, vigorously, and thrust it back to him red with the passionate pressure—

"You need not look in that way,'' I said: "if you do, I'll wear nothing but my old Lowood frocks to the end of the chapter. I'll be married in this lilac gingham— you may make a dressing-gown for yourself out of the pearl-grey silk, and an infinite series of waistcoats out of the black satin.''

He chuckled; he rubbed his hands: "Oh, it is rich to see and hear her!'' he exclaimed. "Is she original? Is she piquant? I would not exchange this one little English girl for the grand Turk's whole seraglio; gazelle-eyes, houri forms and all!''

The eastern allusion bit me again: "I'll not stand you an inch in the stead of a seraglio,'' I said; "so don't consider me an equivalent for one; if you have a fancy for anything in that line, away with you, sir, to the bazars of Stamboul without delay; and lay out in extensive slave-purchases some of that spare cash you seem at a loss to spend satisfactorily here.''

"And what will you do, Janet, while I am bargaining for so many tons of flesh and such an assortment of black eyes?"

"I'll be preparing myself to go out as a missionary to preach liberty to them that are enslaved—your harem inmates amongst the rest. I'll get admitted there, and I'll stir up mutiny; and you, three-tailed bashaw as you are, sir, shall in a trice find yourself fettered amongst our hands: nor will I, for one, consent to cut your bonds till you have signed a charter, the most liberal that despot ever yet conferred."

"I would consent to be at your mercy, Jane."

"I would have no mercy, Mr. Rochester, if you supplicated for it with an eye like that. While you looked so, I should be certain that whatever charter you might grant under coercion, your first act, when released, would be to violate its conditions."

"Why, Jane, what would you have? I fear you will compel me to go through a private marriage ceremony, besides that performed at the altar. You will stipulate, I see, for peculiar terms—what will they be?"

"I only want an easy mind, sir; not crushed by crowded obligations. Do you remember what you said of Céline Varens?—of the diamonds, the cashmeres you gave her? I will not be your English Céline Varens. I shall continue to act as Adèle's governess; by that I shall earn my board and lodging, and thirty pounds a year besides. I'll furnish my own wardrobe out of that money, and you shall give me nothing but"——

"Well, but what?"

"Your regard: and if I give you mine in return, that debt will be quit."

"Well, for cool native impudence, and pure innate pride, you haven't your equal," said he. We were now approaching Thornfield. "Will it please you to dine with me to-day?" he asked, as we re-entered the gates.

"No, thank you, sir."

"And what for 'no, thank you'? if one may inquire."

"I never have dined with you, sir: and I see no reason why I should now: till"——

"Till what? You delight in half-phrases."

"Till I can't help it."

"Do you suppose I eat like an ogre, or a ghoul, that you dread being the companion of my repast?"

"I have formed no supposition on the subject, sir; but I want to go on as usual for another month."

"You will give up your governessing slavery at once."

"Indeed! begging your pardon, sir, I shall not. I shall just go on with it as usual. I shall keep out of your way all day, as I have been accustomed to do: you may send for me in the evening, when you feel disposed to see me, and I'll come then, but at no other time."

"I want a smoke, Jane, or a pinch of snuff, to comfort me under all this 'pour me donner une contenance,' as Adèle would say; and unfortunately I have neither my cigar-case, nor my snuff-box. But listen—whisper—it is your time now, little tyrant, but it will be mine presently: and when once I have fairly seized you, to have and to hold, I'll just—figuratively speaking—attach you to a chain like this" (touching his watch-guard). "Yes, bonny wee thing, I'll wear you in my bosom, lest my jewel I should tyne."

He said this as he helped me to alight from the carriage: and while he afterwards lifted out Adèle, I entered the house, and made good my retreat upstairs.

He duly summoned me to his presence in the evening. I had prepared an occupation for him; for I was determined not to spend the whole time in a *tête-à-tête* conversation. I remembered his fine voice: I knew he liked to sing—good singers generally do. I was no vocalist myself, and, in his fastidious judgment, no musician, either; but I delighted in listening when the performance was good. No sooner had twilight, that hour of romance, began to lower her blue and starry banner over the lattice, than I rose, opened the piano, and entreated him, for the love of heaven,

to give me a song. He said I was a capricious witch, and that he would rather sing another time; but I averred that no time was like the present.

"Did I like his voice?" he asked.

"Very much." I was not fond of pampering that susceptible vanity of his; but for once, and from motives of expediency, I would e'en soothe and stimulate it.

"Then, Jane, you must play the accompaniment."

"Very well, sir, I will try."

I did try, but was presently swept off the stool and denominated, "a little bungler." Being pushed unceremoniously to one side—which was precisely what I wished—he usurped my place, and proceeded to accompany himself: for he could play as well as sing. I hied me to the window-recess; and while I sat there and looked out on the still trees and dim lawn, to a sweet air was sung in mellow tones the following strain:—

> The truest love that ever heart
> Felt at its kindled core
> Did through each vein, in quickened start,
> The tide of being pour.
>
> Her coming was my hope each day,
> Her parting was my pain;
> The chance that did her steps delay
> Was ice in every vein.
>
> I dreamed it would be nameless bliss,
> As I loved, loved to be;
> And to this object did I press
> As blind as eagerly.
>
> But wide as pathless was the space
> That lay, our lives, between,
> And dangerous as the foamy race
> Of ocean-surges green.
>
> And haunted as a robber path
> Through wilderness or wood;
> For Might and Right, and Woe and Wrath,
> Between our spirits stood.
>
> I dangers dared; I hind'rance scorned;
> I omens did defy;
> Whatever menaced, harassed, warned,
> I passed impetuous by.
>
> On sped my rainbow, fast as light;
> I flew as in a dream;
> For glorious rose upon my sight
> That child of Shower and Gleam.
>
> Still bright on clouds of suffering dim
> Shines that soft, solemn joy;
> Nor care I now, how dense and grim
> Disasters gather nigh.

I care not in this moment sweet,
 Though all I have rushed o'er
Should come on pinion, strong and fleet,
 Proclaiming vengeance sore:

Though haughty Hate should strike me down,
 Right, bar approach to me,
And grinding Might, with furious frown,
 Swear endless enmity.

My love has placed her little hand
 With noble faith in mine,
And vowed that wedlock's sacred band
 Our nature shall entwine.

My love has sworn, with sealing kiss,
 With me to live—to die;
I have at last my nameless bliss:
 As I love.—loved am I!

He rose and came towards me, and I saw his face all kindled, and his full falcon-eye flashing, and tenderness and passion in every lineament. I quailed momentarily—then I rallied. Soft scene, daring demonstration, I would not have; and I stood in peril of both: a weapon of defence must be prepared—I whetted my tongue; as he reached me, I asked with asperity, ''whom he was going to marry now?''

''That was a strange question to be put by his darling Jane.''

''Indeed! I considered it a very natural and necessary one: he had talked of his future wife dying with him. What did he mean by such a pagan idea? *I* had no intention of dying with him—he might depend on that.''

''Oh, all he longed, all he prayed for, was that I might live with him! Death was not for such as I.''

''Indeed it was: I had as good a right to die when my time came as he had: but I should bide that time, and not be hurried away in a suttee.''

''Would I forgive him for the selfish idea, and prove my pardon by a reconciling kiss?''

''No: I would rather be excused.''

Here I heard myself apostrophised as a ''hard little thing''; and it was added, ''any other woman would have been melted to marrow at hearing such stanzas crooned in her praise.''

I assured him I was naturally hard—very flinty, and that he would often find me so; and that, moreover, I was determined to show him divers rugged points in my character before the ensuing four weeks elapsed: he should know fully what sort of a bargain he had made, while there was yet time to rescind it.

''Would I be quiet, and talk rationally?''

''I would be quiet if he liked; and as to talking rationally, I flattered myself I was doing that now.''

He fretted, pished, and pshawed. ''Very good,'' I thought; ''you may fume and fidget as you please: but this is the best plan to pursue with you, I am certain. I like you more than I can say; but I'll not sink into a bathos of sentiment; and with this needle of repartee I'll keep you from the edge of the gulph too; and, moreover, maintain by its pungent aid that distance between you and myself most conducive to our real mutual advantage.''

From less to more, I worked him up to considerable irritation; then, after he had retired, in dudgeon, quite to the other end of the room, and I got up, saying, ''I

wish you good-night, sir,'' in my natural and wonted respectful manner, I slipped out by the side-door and got away.

The system thus entered on, I pursued during the whole season of probation; and with the best success. He was kept, to be sure, rather cross and crusty: but on the whole I could see he was excellently entertained; and that a lamb-like submission and turtle-dove sensibility, while fostering his despotism more, would have pleased his judgment, satisfied his common-sense, and even suited his taste, less.

In other people's presence I was, as formerly, deferential and quiet; any other line of conduct being uncalled for: it was only in the evening conferences I thus thwarted and afflicted him. He continued to send for me punctually the moment the clock struck seven; though when I appeared before him now, he had no such honeyed terms as ''love'' and ''darling'' on his lips: the best words at my service were ''provoking puppet,'' ''malicious elf,'' ''sprite,'' ''changeling,'' etc. For caresses, too, I now got grimaces; for a pressure of the hand, a pinch on the arm; for a kiss on the cheek, a severe tweak of the ear. It was all right: at present I decidedly preferred these fierce favours to anything more tender. Mrs. Fairfax, I saw, approved me: her anxiety on my account vanished; therefore I was certain I did well. Meantime, Mr. Rochester affirmed I was wearing him to skin and bone, and threatened awful vengeance for my present conduct at some period fast coming. I laughed in my sleeve at his menaces: ''I can keep you in reasonable check now,'' I reflected; ''and I don't doubt to be able to do it hereafter: if one expedient loses its virtue, another must be devised.''

Yet after all my task was not an easy one; often I would rather have pleased than teased him. My future husband was becoming to me my whole world; and more than the world: almost my hope of heaven. He stood between me and every thought of religion, as an eclipse intervenes between man and the broad sun. I could not, in those days, see God for his creature: of whom I had made an idol.

Chapter XXV

THE month of courtship had wasted: its very last hours were being numbered. There was no putting off the day that advanced—the bridal day; and all preparations for its arrival were complete. *I*, at least, had nothing more to do: there were my trunks, packed, locked, corded, ranged in a row along the wall of my little chamber; to-morrow, at this time, they would be far on their road to London: and so should I (D.V.),—or rather, not I, but one Jane Rochester, a person whom as yet I knew not. The cards of address alone remained to nail on: they lay, four little squares on the drawer. Mr. Rochester had himself written the direction, ''Mrs. Rochester, —— Hotel, London,'' on each: I could not persuade myself to affix them, or to have them affixed. Mrs. Rochester! She did not exist: she would not be born till to-morrow, some time after eight o'clock A.M.: and I would wait to be assured she had come into the world alive, before I assigned to her all that property. It was enough that in yonder closet, opposite my dressing-table, garments said to be hers had already displaced my black stuff Lowood frock and straw bonnet: for not to me appertained that suit of wedding raiment; the pearl-coloured robe, the vapoury veil, pendent from the usurped portmanteau. I shut the closet, to conceal the strange, wraith-like apparel it contained; which, at this evening hour—nine o'clock—gave out certainly a most ghostly shimmer through the shadow of my apartment. ''I will leave you by yourself, white dream,'' I said. ''I am feverish: I heard the wind blowing: I will go out of doors and feel it.''

It was not only the hurry of preparation that made me feverish; not only the anticipation of the great change—the new life which was to commence to-morrow;

both these circumstances had their share, doubtless, in producing that restless, excited mood which hurried me forth at this late hour into the darkening grounds: but a third cause influenced my mind more than they.

I had at heart a strange and anxious thought. Something had happened which I could not comprehend; no one knew of or had seen the event but myself: it had taken place the preceding night. Mr. Rochester that night was absent from home; nor was he yet returned: business had called him to a small estate of two or three farms he possessed thirty miles off—business it was requisite he should settle in person, previously to his meditated departure from England. I waited now his return; eager to disburthen my mind, and to seek of him the solution of the enigma that perplexed me. Stay till he comes, reader; and, when I disclose my secret to him, you shall share the confidence.

I sought the orchard: driven to its shelter by the wind, which all day had blown strong and full from the south; without, however, bringing a speck of rain. Instead of subsiding as night drew on, it seemed to augment its rush and deepen its roar: the trees blew stedfastly one way, never writhing round, and scarcely tossing back their boughs once in an hour; so continuous was the strain bending their branchy heads northward—the clouds drifted from pole to pole, fast following, mass on mass: no glimpse of blue sky had been visible that July day.

It was not without a certain wild pleasure I ran before the wind delivering my trouble of mind to the measureless air-torrent thundering through space. Descending the laurel walk, I faced the wreck of the chestnut-tree; it stood up, black and riven: the trunk, split down the centre, gasped ghastly. The cloven halves were not broken from each other, for the firm base and strong roots kept them unsundered below; though community of vitality was destroyed—the sap could flow no more: their great boughs on each side were dead, and next winter's tempests would be sure to fell one or both to earth: as yet, however, they might be said to form one tree—a ruin, but an entire ruin.

"You did right to hold fast to each other," I said: as if the monster-splinters were living things, and could hear me. "I think, scathed as you look, and charred and scorched, there must be a little sense of life in you yet: rising out of that adhesion at the faithful, honest roots: you will never have green leaves more— never more see birds making nests and singing idylls in your boughs; the time of pleasure and love is over with you: but you are not desolate: each of you has a comrade to sympathise with him in his decay." As I looked up at them, the moon appeared momentarily in that part of the sky which filled their fissure; her disk was blood-red, and half overcast; she seemed to throw on me one bewildered, dreary glance, and buried herself again instantly in the deep drift of cloud. The wind fell, for a second, round Thornfield; but far away over wood and water, poured a wild, melancholy wail: it was sad to listen to, and I ran off again.

Here and there I strayed through the orchard, gathered up the apples with which the grass round the tree roots was thickly strewn: then I employed myself in dividing the ripe from the unripe; I carried them into the house and put them away in the store-room. Then I repaired to the library to ascertain whether the fire was lit; for, though summer, I knew on such a gloomy evening, Mr. Rochester would like to see a cheerful hearth when he came in: yes, the fire had been kindled some time, and burnt well. I placed his arm-chair by the chimney-corner: I wheeled the table near it: I let down the curtain, and had the candles brought in ready for lighting. More restless than ever, when I had completed these arrangements I could not sit still, nor even remain in the house: a little time-piece in the room and the old clock in the hall simultaneously struck ten.

"How late it grows!" I said: "I will run down to the gates: it is moonlight at intervals: I can see a good way on the road. He may be coming now, and to meet him will save some minutes of suspense."

The wind roared high in the great trees which embowered the gates; but the road as far as I could see, to the right hand and the left, was all still and solitary: save for the shadows of clouds crossing it at intervals, as the moon looked out, it was but a long pale line, unvaried by one moving speck.

A puerile tear dimmed my eye while I looked—a tear of disappointment and impatience: ashamed of it, I wiped it away. I lingered; the moon shut herself wholly within her chamber, and drew close her curtain of dense cloud: the night grew dark; rain came driving fast on the gale.

"I wish he would come! I wish he would come!" I exclaimed, seized with hypochondriac foreboding. I had expected his arrival before tea; now it was dark: what could keep him? Had an accident happened? The event of last night again recurred to me. I interpreted it as a warning of disaster. I feared my hopes were too bright to be realised; and I had enjoyed so much bliss lately that I imagined my fortune had passed its meridian, and must now decline.

"Well, I cannot return to the house," I thought; "I cannot sit by the fireside, while he is abroad in inclement weather: better tire my limbs than strain my heart; I will go forward and meet him."

I set out; I walked fast, but not far: ere I had measured a quarter of a mile, I heard the tramp of hoofs; a horseman came on, full gallop; a dog ran by his side. Away with evil presentiment! It was he: here he was, mounted on Mesrour, followed by Pilot. He saw me; for the moon had opened a blue field in the sky, and rode in it watery bright: he took his hat off, and waved it round his head. I now ran to meet him.

"There!" he exclaimed, as he stretched out his hand and bent from the saddle: "You can't do without me, that is evident. Step on my boot-toe; give me both hands: mount!"

I obeyed; joy made me agile: I sprang up before him. A hearty kissing I got for a welcome; and some boastful triumph, which I swallowed as well as I could. He checked himself in his exultation to demand, "But is there anything the matter, Janet, that you come to meet me at such an hour: Is there anything wrong?"

"No; but I thought you would never come. I could not bear to wait in the house for you, especially with this rain and wind."

"Rain and wind, indeed! Yes, you are dripping like a mermaid; pull my cloak round you: but I think you are feverish, Jane: both your cheek and hand are burning hot. I ask again, is there anything the matter?"

"Nothing, now: I am neither afraid nor unhappy."

"Then you have been both?"

"Rather: but I'll tell you all about it by-and-by, sir; and I daresay you will only laugh at me for my pains."

"I'll laugh at you heartily when to-morrow is past; till then I dare not: my prize is not certain. This is you; who have been as slippery as an eel this last month, and as thorny as a briar-rose? I could not lay a finger anywhere but I was pricked; and now I seem to have gathered up a stray lamb in my arms: you wandered out of the fold to seek your shepherd, did you, Jane?"

"I wanted you, but don't boast. Here we are at Thornfield: now let me get down."

He landed me on the pavement. As John took his horse, and he followed me into the hall, he told me to make haste and put something dry on, and then return to him in the library; and he stopped me, as I made for the staircase, to extort a promise that I would not be long: nor was I long; in five minutes I rejoined him. I found him at supper.

"Take a seat and bear me company, Jane: please God, it is the last meal but one you will eat at Thornfield Hall for a long time."

I sat down near him; but told him I could not eat.

"Is it because you have the prospect of a journey before you, Jane? Is it the thoughts of going to London that takes away your appetite?"

"I cannot see my prospects clearly to-night, sir: and I hardly know what thoughts I have in my head. Everything in life seems unreal."

"Except me: I am substantial enough:—touch me."

"You, sir, are the most phantom-like of all: you are a mere dream."

He held out his hand, laughing: "Is that a dream?" said he, placing it close to my eyes. He had a rounded, muscular, and vigorous hand, as well as a long, strong arm.

"Yes; though I touch it, it is a dream," said I, as I put it down from before my face. "Sir, have you finished supper?"

"Yes, Jane."

I rang the bell, and ordered away the tray. When we were again alone, I stirred the fire, and then took a low seat at my master's knee.

"It is near midnight," I said.

"Yes: but remember, Jane, you promised to wake with me the night before my wedding."

"I did; and I will keep my promise, for an hour or two at least; I have no wish to go to bed."

"Are all your arrangements complete?"

"All, sir."

"And on my part, likewise," he returned, "I have settled everything; and we leave Thornfield to-morrow, within half an hour after our return from church."

"Very well, sir."

"With what an extraordinary smile you uttered that word—'very well,' Jane! What a bright spot of colour you have on each cheek! and how strangely your eyes glitter! Are you well?"

"I believe I am."

"Believe! What is the matter?—Tell me what you feel."

"I could not, sir: no words could tell you what I feel. I wish this present hour would never end: who knows with what fate the next may come charged?"

"This is hypochondria, Jane. You have been over-excited or over-fatigued."

"Do you, sir, feel calm and happy?"

"Calm?—no: but happy—to the heart's core."

I looked up at him to read the signs of bliss in his face: it was ardent and flushed.

"Give me your confidence, Jane," he said: "relieve your mind of any weight that oppresses it, by imparting it to me. What do you fear?—that I shall not prove a good husband?"

"It is the idea farthest from my thoughts."

"Are you apprehensive of the new sphere you are about to enter?—of the new life into which you are passing?"

"No."

"You puzzle me, Jane: your look and tone of sorrowful audacity perplex and pain me. I want an explanation."

"Then, sir,—listen. You were from home last night?"

"I was:—I know that; and you hinted a while ago at something which had happened in my absence:—nothing, probably, of consequence; but, in short, it has disturbed you. Let me hear it. Mrs. Fairfax has said something, perhaps? or you have overheard the servants talk?—your sensitive self-respect has been wounded?"

"No, sir." It struck twelve—I waited till the time-piece had concluded its silver chime, and the clock its hoarse, vibrating stroke, and then I proceeded.

"All day, yesterday, I was very busy, and very happy in my ceaseless bustle: for I am not, as you seem to think, troubled by any haunting fears about the new sphere, et cetera: I think it a glorious thing to have the hope of living with you, because I love you. No, sir, don't caress me now—let me talk undisturbed. Yesterday

I trusted well in Providence, and believed that events were working together for your good and mine: it was a fine day, if you recollect—the calmness of the air and sky forbade apprehensions regarding your safety or comfort on your journey. I walked a little while on the pavement after tea, thinking of you; and I beheld you in imagination so near me, I scarcely missed your actual presence. I thought of the life that lay before me—*your* life, sir—an existence more expansive and stirring than my own: as much more so as the depths of the sea to which the brook runs, are than the shallows of its own strait channel. I wondered why moralists call this world a dreary wilderness: for me it blossomed like a rose. Just at sunset, the air turned cold and the sky cloudy: I went in. Sophie called me upstairs to look at my wedding-dress, which they had just brought; and under it in the box I found your present—the veil which, in your princely extravagance, you sent for from London: resolved, I suppose, since I would not have jewels, to cheat me into accepting something as costly. I smiled as I unfolded it, and devised how I would tease you about your aristocratic tastes, and your efforts to masque your plebeian bride in the attributes of a peeress. I thought how I would carry down to you the square of unembroidered blond I had myself prepared as a covering for my low-born head, and ask if that was not good enough for a woman who could bring her husband neither fortune, beauty, nor connections. I saw plainly how you would look; and heard your impetuous republican answers, and your haughty disavowal of any necessity on your part to augment your wealth, or elevate your standing, by marrying either a purse or a coronet.''

"How well you read me, you witch!'' interposed Mr. Rochester: "but what did you find in the veil besides its embroidery? Did you find poison or a dagger that you look so mournful now?''

"No, no, sir; besides the delicacy and richness of the fabric, I found nothing save Fairfax Rochester's pride; and that did not scare me, because I am used to the sight of the demon. But, sir, as it grew dark, the wind rose: it blew yesterday evening, not as it blows now—wild and high—but 'with a sullen, moaning sound' far more eerie. I wished you were at home. I came into this room, and the sight of the empty chair and fireless hearth chilled me. For some time after I went to bed, I could not sleep—a sense of anxious excitement distressed me. The gale still rising, seemed to my ear to muffle a mournful under-sound; whether in the house or abroad I could not at first tell, but it recurred, doubtful yet doleful at every lull: at last I made out it must be some dog howling at a distance. I was glad when it ceased. On sleeping, I continued in dreams the idea of a dark and gusty night. I continued also the wish to be with you, and experienced a strange, regretful consciousness, of some barrier dividing us. During all my first sleep, I was following the windings of an unknown road; total obscurity environed me; rain pelted me; I was burdened with the charge of a little child: a very small creature, too young and feeble to walk, and which shivered in my cold arms, and wailed piteously in my ear. I thought, sir, that you were on the road a long way before me; and I strained every nerve to overtake you, and made effort on effort to utter your name and entreat you to stop—but my movements were fettered; and my voice still died away inarticulate; while you, I felt, withdrew farther and farther every moment.''

"And these dreams weigh on your spirits now, Jane, when I am close to you? Little nervous subject! Forget visionary woe, and think only of real happiness! You say you love me, Janet: yes—I will not forget that; and you cannot deny it. *Those* words did not die inarticulate on your lips. I heard them clear and soft: a thought too solemn perhaps, but sweet as music—'I think it is a glorious thing to have the hope of living with you, Edward, because I love you.'—Do you love me, Jane? repeat it.''

"I do, sir.—I do, with my whole heart.''

"Well,'' he said, after some minutes' silence, "it is strange; but that sentence has penetrated my breast painfully. Why? I think because you said it with such an

earnest, religious energy; and because your upward gaze at me now is the very sublime of faith, truth, and devotion: it is too much as if some spirit were near me. Look wicked, Jane; as you know well how to look: coin one of your wild, shy, provoking smiles; tell me you hate me—tease me, vex me: do anything but move me: I would rather be incensed than saddened.''

"I will tease you and vex you to your heart's content, when I have finished my tale: but hear me to the end.''

"I thought, Jane, you had told me all. I thought I had found the source of your melancholy in a dream!''

I shook my head. "What! is there more? But I will not believe it to be anything important. I warn you of incredulity beforehand. Go on.''

The disquietude of his air, and somewhat apprehensive impatience of his manner, surprised me: but I proceeded.

"I dreamt another dream, sir: that Thornfield Hall was a dreary ruin, the retreat of bats and owls. I thought that of all the stately front nothing remained but a shell-like wall, very high, and very fragile-looking. I wandered, on a moon-light night, through the grass-grown enclosure within: here I stumbled over a marble hearth, and there over a fallen fragment of cornice. Wrapped up in a shawl, I still carried the unknown little child: I might not lay it down anywhere, however tired were my arms—however much its weight impeded my progress, I must retain it. I heard a gallop of a horse at a distance on the road: I was sure it was you; and you were departing for many years, and for a distant country. I climbed the thin wall with frantic perilous haste, eager to catch one glimpse of you from the top: the stones rolled from under my feet, the ivy branches I grasped gave way, the child clung round my neck in terror, and almost strangled me: at last I gained the summit. I saw you like a speck on a white track, lessening every moment. The blast blew so strong I could not stand. I sat down on the narrow ledge; I hushed the scared infant in my lap: you turned an angle in the road; I bent forward to take a last look; the wall crumbled; I was shaken; the child rolled from my knee, I lost my balance, fell, and woke.''

"Now, Jane, that is all.''

"All the preface, sir; the tale is yet to come. On waking, a gleam dazzled my eyes: I thought—oh, it is daylight! But I was mistaken: it was only candle-light. Sophie, I supposed, had come in. There was a light on the dressing table, and the door of the closet, where, before going to bed, I had hung my wedding dress and veil, stood open: I heard a rustling there. I asked, 'Sophie, what are you doing?' No one answered; but a form emerged from the closet: it took the light, held it aloft and surveyed the garments pendent from the portmanteau. 'Sophie! Sophie!' I again cried: and still it was silent. I had risen up in bed, I bent forward: first, surprise, then bewilderment, came over me; and then my blood crept cold through my veins. Mr. Rochester, this was not Sophie, it was not Leah, it was not Mrs. Fairfax: it was not—no, I was sure of it, and am still—it was not even that strange woman, Grace Poole.''

"It must have been one of them,'' interrupted my master.

"No, sir, I solemnly assure you to the contrary. The shape standing before me had never crossed my eyes within the precincts of Thornfield Hall before; the height, the contour were new to me.''

"Describe it, Jane.''

"It seemed, sir, a woman, tall and large, with thick and dark hair hanging long down her back. I know not what dress she had on: it was white and straight; but whether gown, sheet, or shroud, I cannot tell.''

"Did you see her face?''

"Not at first. But presently she took my veil from its place; she held it up; gazed at it long, and then she threw it over her own head, and turned to the mirror. At

that moment I saw the reflection of the visage and features quite distinctly in the dark oblong glass.''

''And how were they?''

''Fearful and ghastly to me—oh, sir, I never saw a face like it! It was a discoloured face—it was a savage face. I wish I could forget the roll of the red eyes and the fearful blackened inflation of the lineaments!''

''Ghosts are usually pale, Jane.''

''This, sir, was purple: the lips were swelled and dark; the brow furrowed; the black eyebrows widely raised over the blood-shot eyes. Shall I tell you of what it reminded me?''

''You may.''

''Of the foul German spectre—the Vampyre.''

''Ah!—what did it do?''

''Sir, it removed my veil from its gaunt head, rent it in two parts, and flinging both on the floor, trampled on them.''

''Afterwards?''

''It drew aside the window-curtain and looked out: perhaps it saw dawn approaching, for, taking the candle, it retreated to the door. Just at my bedside the figure stopped: the fiery eye glared upon me—she thrust up her candle close to my face, and extinguished it under my eyes. I was aware her lurid visage flamed over mine, and I lost consciousness: for the second time in my life—only the second time—I became insensible from terror.''

''Who was with you when you revived?''

''No one, sir; but the broad day. I rose, bathed my head and face in water, drank a long draught; felt that though enfeebled I was not ill, and determined that to none but you would I impart this vision. Now, sir, tell me who and what that woman was?''

''The creature of an over-stimulated brain; that is certain. I must be careful of you, my treasure: nerves like yours were not made for rough handling.''

''Sir, depend upon it, my nerves were not in fault; the thing was real: the transaction actually took place.''

''And your previous dreams: were they real too? Is Thornfield Hall a ruin? Am I severed from you by insuperable obstacles? Am I leaving you without a tear—without a kiss—without a word?''

''Not yet.''

''Am I about to do it?—Why, the day is already commenced which is to bind us indissolubly; and when we are once united, there shall be no recurrence of these mental terrors: I guarantee that.''

''Mental terrors, sir! I wish I could believe them to be only such: I wish it more than ever; since even you cannot explain to me the mystery of that awful visitant.''

''And since I cannot do it, Jane, it must have been unreal.''

''But, sir, when I said so to myself on rising this morning, and when I looked round the room to gather courage and comfort from the cheerful aspect of each familiar object in full daylight, there—on the carpet—I saw what gave the distinct lie to my hypothesis,—the veil, torn from top to bottom in two halves!''

I felt Mr. Rochester start and shudder; he hastily flung his arms round me: ''Thank God!'' he exclaimed, ''that if anything malignant did come near you last night, it was only the veil that was harmed.—Oh, to think what might have happened!''

He drew his breath short, and strained me so close to him, I could scarcely pant. After some minutes' silence, he continued, cheerily:—

''Now, Janet, I'll explain to you all about it. It was half dream, half reality: a woman did, I doubt not, enter your room: and that woman was—must have been—Grace Poole. You call her a strange being yourself: from all you know, you have reason so to call her—what did she do to me? what to Mason? In a state between sleeping and waking, you noticed her entrance and her actions; but feverish, almost

delirious as you were, you ascribed to her a goblin appearance different from her own: the long dishevelled hair, the swelled black face, the exaggerated stature, were figments of imagination; results of nightmare: the spiteful tearing of the veil was real: and it is like her. I see you would ask why I keep such a woman in my house: when we have been married a year and a day, I will tell you: but not now. Are you satisfied, Jane? Do you accept my solution of the mystery?''

I reflected, and in truth it appeared to me the only possible one: satisfied I was not, but to please him I endeavoured to appear so—relieved, I certainly did feel; so I answered him with a contented smile. And now, as it was long past one, I prepared to leave him.

"Does not Sophie sleep with Adèle in the nursery?" he asked, as I lit my candle.

"Yes, sir."

"And there is room enough in Adèle's little bed for you. You must share it with her to-night, Jane: it is no wonder that the incident you have related should make you nervous, and I would rather you did not sleep alone: promise me to go to the nursery."

"I shall be very glad to do so, sir."

"And fasten the door securely on the inside. Wake Sophie when you go upstairs, under pretence of requesting her to rouse you in good time to-morrow; for you must be dressed and have finished breakfast before eight. And now, no more sombre thoughts: chase dull care away, Janet. Don't you hear to what soft whispers the wind has fallen? and there is no more beating of rain against the window-panes: look here" (he lifted up the curtain)—"it is a lovely night!"

It was. Half heaven was pure and stainless: the clouds, now trooping before the wind, which had shifted to the west, were filing off eastward, in long, silvered columns. The moon shone peacefully.

"Well," said Mr. Rochester, gazing inquiringly into my eyes, "how is my Janet now?"

"The night is serene, sir; and so am I."

"And you will not dream of separation and sorrow to-night; but of happy love and blissful union."

This prediction was but half fulfilled: I did not indeed dream of sorrow, but as little did I dream of joy; for I never slept at all. With little Adèle in my arms, I watched the slumber of childhood—so tranquil, so passionless, so innocent—and waited for the coming day: all my life was awake and astir in my frame: and as soon as the sun rose I rose too. I remember Adèle clung to me as I left her: I remember I kissed her as I loosened her little hands from my neck; and I cried over her with strange emotion, and quitted her because I feared my sobs would break her still sound repose. She seemed the emblem of my past life; and he, I was now to array myself to meet, the dread, but adored, type of my unknown future day.

Chapter XXVI

SOPHIE came at seven to dress me; she was very long indeed in accomplishing her task; so long that Mr. Rochester, grown, I suppose, impatient of my delay, sent up to ask why I did not come. She was just fastening my veil (the plain square of blond after all) to my hair with a brooch; I hurried from under her hands as soon as I could.

"Stop!" she cried in French. "Look at yourself in the mirror: you have not taken one peep."

So I turned at the door: I saw a robed and veiled figure, so unlike my usual self that it seemed almost the image of a stranger. "Jane!" called a voice, and I hastened down. I was received at the foot of the stairs by Mr. Rochester.

"Lingerer," he said, "my brain is on fire with impatience; and you tarry so long!"

He took me into the dining-room, surveyed me keenly all over, pronounced me "fair as a lily, and not only the pride of his life, but the desire of his eyes," and then telling me he would give me but ten minutes to eat some breakfast, he rang the bell. One of his lately hired servants, a footman, answered it.

"Is John getting the carriage ready?"

"Yes, sir."

"Is the luggage brought down?"

"They are bringing it down, sir."

"Go you to the church: see if Mr. Wood (the clergyman) and the clerk are there: return and tell me."

The church, as the reader knows, was but just beyond the gates; the footman soon returned.

"Mr. Wood is in the vestry, sir, putting on his surplice."

"And the carriage?"

"The horses are harnessing."

"We shall not want it to go to church; but it must be ready the moment we return: all the boxes and luggage arranged and strapped on, and the coachman in his seat."

"Yes, sir."

"Jane, are you ready?"

I rose. There were no groomsmen, no bridesmaids, no relatives to wait for or marshal: none but Mr. Rochester and I. Mrs. Fairfax stood in the hall as we passed. I would fain have spoken to her, but my hand was held by a grasp of iron: I was hurried along by a stride I could hardly follow; and to look at Mr. Rochester's face was to feel that not a second of delay would be tolerated for any purpose. I wonder what other bridegroom ever looked as he did—so bent up to a purpose, so grimly resolute: or who, under such stedfast brows, ever revealed such flaming and flashing eyes.

I know not whether the day was fair or foul; in descending the drive, I gazed neither on sky nor earth: my heart was with my eyes; and both seemed migrated into Mr. Rochester's frame. I wanted to see the invisible thing on which, as we went along, he appeared to fasten a glance fierce and fell. I wanted to feel the thoughts whose force he seemed breasting and resisting.

At the churchyard wicket he stopped: he discovered I was quite out of breath. "Am I cruel in my love?" he said. "Delay an instant: lean on me, Jane."

And now I can recall the picture of the grey old house of God rising calm before me, of a rook wheeling round the steeple, of a ruddy morning sky beyond. I remember something, too, of the green grave-mounds; and I have not forgotten, either, two figures of strangers, straying amongst the low hillocks, and reading the mementoes graven on the few mossy head-stones. I noticed them, because, as they saw us, they passed round to the back of the church; and I doubted not they were going to enter by the side-aisle door, and witness the ceremony. By Mr. Rochester they were not observed; he was earnestly looking at my face, from which the blood had, I daresay, momentarily fled: for I felt my forehead dewy, and my cheeks and lips cold. When I rallied, which I soon did, he walked gently with me up the path to the porch.

We entered the quiet and humble temple; the priest waited in his white surplice at the lowly altar, the clerk beside him. All was still: two shadows only moved in a remote corner. My conjecture had been correct: the strangers had slipped in before us, and they now stood by the vault of the Rochesters, their backs towards us,

viewing through the rails the old time-stained marble tomb, where a kneeling angel guarded the remains of Damer de Rochester, slain at Marston Moor in the time of the civil wars; and of Elizabeth, his wife.

Our place was taken at the communion rails. Hearing a cautious step behind me, I glanced over my shoulder: one of the strangers—a gentleman, evidently—was advancing up the chancel. The service began. The explanation of the intent of matrimony was gone through; and then the clergyman came a step further forward, and, bending slightly towards Mr. Rochester, went on.

"I require and charge you both (as ye will answer at the dreadful day of judgment, when the secrets of all hearts shall be disclosed), that if either of you know any impediment why ye may not lawfully be joined together in matrimony, ye do now confess it; for be ye well assured that so many as are coupled together otherwise than God's word doth allow, are not joined together by God, neither is their matrimony lawful."

He paused, as the custom is. When is the pause after that sentence ever broken by reply? Not, perhaps, once in a hundred years. And the clergyman, who had not lifted his eyes from his book, and had held his breath but for a moment, was proceeding: his hand was already stretched towards Mr. Rochester, as his lips unclosed to ask, "Wilt thou have this woman for thy wedded wife?"—when a distinct and near voice said:—

"The marriage cannot go on: I declare the existence of an impediment."

The clergyman looked up at the speaker, and stood mute; the clerk did the same; Mr. Rochester moved slightly, as if an earthquake had rolled under his feet: taking a firmer footing, and not turning his head or eyes, he said, "Proceed."

Profound silence fell when he had uttered that word, with deep but low intonation. Presently Mr. Wood said:—

"I cannot proceed without some investigation into what has been asserted, and evidence of its truth or falsehood."

"The ceremony is quite broken off," subjoined the voice behind us. "I am in a condition to prove my allegation: an insuperable impediment to this marriage exists."

Mr. Rochester heard, but heeded not: he stood stubborn and rigid: making no movement, but to possess himself of my hand. What a hot and strong grasp he had!—and how like quarried marble was his pale, firm, massive front at this moment! How his eye shone, still, watchful, and yet wild beneath!

Mr. Wood seemed at a loss. "What is the nature of the impediment?" he asked. "Perhaps it may be got over—explained away?"

"Hardly," was the answer: "I have called it insuperable, and I speak advisedly."

The speaker came forwards, and leaned on the rails. He continued, uttering each word distinctly, calmly, steadily, but not loudly.

"It simply consists in the existence of a previous marriage. Mr. Rochester has a wife now living."

My nerves vibrated to those low-spoken words as they had never vibrated to thunder—my blood felt their subtle violence as it had never felt frost or fire: but I was collected, and in no danger of swooning. I looked at Mr. Rochester: I made him look at me. His whole face was colourless rock: his eye was both spark and flint. He disavowed nothing; he seemed as if he would defy all things. Without speaking; without smiling; without seeming to recognise in me a human being, he only twined my waist with his arm, and riveted me to his side.

"Who are you?" he asked of the intruder.

"My name is Briggs—a solicitor of —— Street, London."

"And you would thrust on me a wife?"

"I would remind you of your lady's existence, sir; which the law recognises, if you do not."

"Favour me with an account of her—with her name, her parentage, her place of abode."

"Certainly." Mr. Briggs calmly took a paper from his pocket, and read out in a sort of official, nasal voice:—

" 'I affirm and can prove that on the 20th of October, A.D., ——, (a date of fifteen years back) Edward Fairfax Rochester, of Thornfield Hall, in the county of ——, and of Ferndean Manor, in ——shire, England, was married to my sister, Bertha Antoinetta Mason, daughter of Jonas Mason, merchant, and of Antoinetta his wife, a Creole—at —— church, Spanish Town, Jamaica. The record of the marriage will be found in the register of that church—a copy of it is now in my possession. Signed, Richard Mason.' "

"That—if a genuine document—may prove I have been married, but it does not prove that the woman mentioned therein as my wife is still living."

"She was living three months ago," returned the lawyer.

"How do you know?"

"I have a witness to the fact; whose testimony even you, sir, will scarcely controvert."

"Produce him—or go to hell."

"I will produce him first—he is on the spot: Mr. Mason, have the goodness to step forward."

Mr. Rochester, on hearing the name, set his teeth; he experienced, too, a sort of strong convulsive quiver; near to him as I was, I felt the spasmodic movement of fury or despair run through his frame. The second stranger, who had hitherto lingered in the background, now drew near; a pale face looked over the solicitor's shoulder—yes, it was Mason himself. Mr. Rochester turned and glared at him. His eye, as I have often said, was a black eye: it had now a tawny, nay a bloody light in its gloom; and his face flushed—olive cheek, and hueless forehead received a glow, as from spreading, ascending heart-fire: and he stirred, lifted his strong arm— he could have struck Mason—dashed him on the church-floor—shocked by ruthless blow the breath from his body—but Mason shrank away, and cried faintly, "Good God!" Contempt fell cool on Mr. Rochester—his passion died as if a blight had shrivelled it up: he only asked, "What have *you* to say?"

An inaudible reply escaped Mason's white lips.

"The devil is in it if you cannot answer distinctly. I again demand, what have *you* to say?"

"Sir—sir"—interrupted the clergyman, "do not forget you are in a sacred place." Then addressing Mason, he inquired gently, "Are you aware, sir, whether or not this gentleman's wife is still living?"

"Courage," urged the lawyer,—"speak out."

"She is now living at Thornfield Hall;" said Mason, in more articulate tones: "I saw her there last April. I am her brother."

"At Thornfield Hall!" ejaculated the clergyman. "Impossible! I am an old resident in this neighbourhood, sir, and I never heard of a Mrs. Rochester at Thornfield Hall."

I saw a grim smile contort Mr. Rochester's lip, and he muttered:—

"No—by God! I took care that none should hear of it—or of her under that name." He mused—for ten minutes he held counsel with himself: he formed his resolve, and announced it:—

"Enough—all shall bolt out at once, like the bullet from the barrel.—Wood, close your book, and take off your surplice; John Green (to the clerk), leave the church: there will be no wedding to-day:" the man obeyed.

Mr. Rochester continued, hardily and recklessly: "Bigamy is an ugly word!—I meant, however, to be a bigamist: but fate has out-manœuvred me; or Providence has checked me, perhaps the last. I am little better than a devil at this moment; and, as my pastor there would tell me, deserve no doubt the sternest judgments of

God,—even to the quenchless fire and deathless worm. Gentlemen, my plan is broken up!—what this lawyer and his client say is true: I have been married: and the woman to whom I was married lives! You say you never heard of a Mrs. Rochester at the house up yonder, Wood: but I daresay you have many a time inclined your ear to gossip about the mysterious lunatic kept there under watch and ward. Some have whispered to you that she is my bastard half-sister: some, my cast-off mistress; I now inform you that she is my wife, whom I married fifteen years ago,—Bertha Mason by name; sister of this resolute personage, who is now, with his quivering limbs and white cheeks, showing you what a stout heart men may bear. Cheer up, Dick!—never fear me!—I'd almost as soon strike a woman as you. Bertha Mason is mad; and she came of a mad family;—idiots and maniacs through three generations! Her mother, the Creole, was both a mad woman and a drunkard!—as I found out after I had wed the daughter: for they were silent on family secrets before. Bertha, like a dutiful child, copied her parent in both points. I had a charming partner—pure, wise, modest: you can fancy I was a happy man.— I went through rich scenes! Oh! my experience has been heavenly, if you only knew it! But I owe you no further explanation. Briggs, Wood, Mason,—I invite you all to come up to the house and visit Mrs. Poole's patient, and *my wife*!—You shall see what sort of a being I was cheated into espousing, and judge whether or not I had a right to break the compact, and seek sympathy with something at least human. This girl," he continued, looking at me, "knew no more than you, Wood, of the disgusting secret: she thought all was fair and legal; and never dreamt she was going to be entrapped into a feigned union with a defrauded wretch, already bound to a bad, mad, and embruted partner! Come all of you, follow!"

Still holding me fast, he left the church: the three gentlemen came after. At the front door of the hall we found the carriage.

"Take it back to the coach-house, John," said Mr. Rochester, coolly; "it will not be wanted to-day."

At our entrance, Mrs. Fairfax, Adèle, Sophie, Leah, advanced to meet and greet us.

"To the right about—every soul!" cried the master: "away with your congratulations! Who wants them?—Not I!—they are fifteen years too late!"

He passed on and ascended the stairs, still holding my hand, and still beckoning the gentlemen to follow him; which they did. We mounted the first staircase, passed up the gallery, proceeded to the third story: the low, black door, opened by Mr. Rochester's master key, admitted us to the tapestried room, with its great bed, and its pictorial cabinet.

"You know this place, Mason," said our guide; "she bit and stabbed you here."

He lifted the hangings from the wall, uncovering the second door: this, too, he opened. In a room without a window, there burnt a fire, guarded by a high and strong fender, and a lamp suspended from the ceiling by a chain. Grace Poole bent over the fire, apparently cooking something in a saucepan. In the deep shade, at the further end of the room, a figure ran backwards and forwards. What it was, whether beast or human being, one could not, at first sight, tell: it grovelled, seemingly, on all fours; it snatched and growled like some strange wild animal: but it was covered with clothing; and a quantity of dark, grizzled hair, wild as a mane, hid its head and face.

"Good-morrow, Mrs. Poole!" said Mr. Rochester. "How are you? and how is your charge to-day?"

"We're tolerable, sir, I thank you," replied Grace, lifting the boiling mess carefully on to the hob: "rather snappish, but not 'rageous."

A fierce cry seemed to give the lie to her favourable report: the clothed hyena rose up, and stood tall on its hind feet.

"Ah, sir, she sees you!" exclaimed Grace: "you'd better not stay."

"Only a few moments, Grace: you must allow me a few moments."

"Take care then, sir!—for God's sake, take care!"

The maniac bellowed: she parted her shaggy locks from her visage, and gazed wildly at her visitors. I recognised well that purple face,—those bloated features. Mrs. Poole advanced.

"Keep out of the way," said Mr. Rochester, thrusting her aside: "she has no knife, now, I suppose? and I'm on my guard."

"One never knows what she has, sir: she is so cunning: it is not in mortal discretion to fathom her craft."

"We had better leave her," whispered Mason.

"Go to the devil!" was his brother-in-law's recommendation.

"'Ware!" cried Grace. The three gentlemen retreated simultaneously. Mr. Rochester flung me behind him: the lunatic sprang and grappled his throat viciously, and laid her teeth to his cheek: they struggled. She was a big woman, in statue almost equalling her husband, and corpulent besides: she showed virile force in the contest—more than once she almost throttled him, athletic as he was. He could have settled her with a well-planted blow; but he would not strike: he would only wrestle. At last he mastered her arms; Grace Poole gave him a cord, and he pinioned them behind her: with more rope, which was at hand, he bound her to a chair. The operation was performed amidst the fiercest yells, and the most convulsive plunges. Mr. Rochester then turned to the spectators: he looked at them with a smile both acrid and desolate.

"That is *my wife*," said he. "Such is the sole conjugal embrace I am ever to know—such are the endearments which are to solace my leisure hours! And *this* is what I wished to have" (laying his hand on my shoulder): "this young girl, who stands so grave and quiet at the mouth of hell, looking collectedly at the gambols of a demon. I wanted her just as a change after that fierce ragout. Wood and Briggs, look at the difference! Compare these clear eyes with the red balls yonder—this face with that mask—this form with that bulk; then judge me, priest of the gospel and man of the law, and remember, with what judgment ye judge ye shall be judged! Off with you now. I must shut up my prize."

We all withdrew. Mr. Rochester stayed a moment behind us, to give some further order to Grace Poole. The solicitor addressed me as he descended the stair.

"You, madam," said he, "are cleared from all blame: your uncle will be glad to hear it—if, indeed, he should be still living—when Mr. Mason returns to Madeira."

"My uncle! What of him? Do you know him?"

"Mr. Mason does: Mr. Eyre has been the Funchal correspondent of his house for some years. When your uncle received your letter intimating the contemplated union between yourself and Mr. Rochester, Mr. Mason, who was staying at Madeira to recruit his health, on his way back to Jamaica, happened to be with him. Mr. Eyre mentioned the intelligence; for he knew that my client here was acquainted with a gentleman of the name of Rochester. Mr. Mason, astonished and distressed as you may suppose, revealed the real state of matters. Your uncle, I am sorry to say, is now on a sick bed; from which, considering the nature of his disease—decline—and the stage it has reached, it is unlikely he will ever rise. He could not then hasten to England himself, to extricate you from the snare into which you had fallen, but he implored Mr. Mason to lose no time in taking steps to prevent the false marriage. He referred him to me for assistance. I used all despatch, and am thankful I was not too late: as you, doubtless, must be also. Were I not morally certain that your uncle will be dead ere you reach Madeira, I would advise you to accompany Mr. Mason back: but as it is, I think you had better remain in England till you can hear further, either from or of Mr. Eyre. Have we anything else to stay for?" he inquired of Mr. Mason.

"No, no—let us be gone," was the anxious reply; and without waiting to take leave of Mr. Rochester, they made their exit at the hall door. The clergyman stayed

to exchange a few sentences, either of admonition or reproof, with his haughty parishioner; this duty done, he too departed.

I heard him go as I stood at the half open door of my own room, to which I had now withdrawn. The house cleared, I shut myself in, fastened the bolt that none might intrude, and proceeded—not to weep, not to mourn, I was yet too calm for that, but—mechanically to take off the wedding dress, and replace it by the stuff gown I had worn yesterday, as I thought for the last time. I then sat down: I felt weak and tired. I leaned my arms on a table, and my head dropped on them. And now I thought: till now I had only heard, seen, moved—followed up and down where I was led or dragged—watched event rush on event, disclosure open beyond disclosure: but *now, I thought*.

The morning had been a quiet morning enough—all except the brief scene with the lunatic: the transaction in the church had not been noisy; there was no explosion of passion, no loud altercation, no dispute, no defiance or challenge, no tears, no sobs: a few words had been spoken, a calmly pronounced objection to the marriage made; some stern short questions put by Mr. Rochester; answers, explanations given, evidence adduced; an open admission of the truth had been uttered by my master; then the living proof had been seen: the intruders were gone, and all was over.

I was in my own room as usual—just myself, without obvious change: nothing had smitten me, or scathed me, or maimed me. And yet where was the Jane Eyre of yesterday?—where was her life?—where were her prospects?

Jane Eyre, who had been an ardent, expectant woman—almost a bride—was a cold, solitary girl again: her life was pale, her prospects were desolate. A Christmas frost had come at midsummer; a white December storm had whirled over June; ice glazed the ripe apples, drifts crushed the blowing roses; on hay-field and corn-field lay a frozen shroud: lanes which last night blushed full of flowers, to-day were pathless with untrodden snow; and the woods which twelve hours since waved leafy and fragrant as groves between the tropics, now spread, waste, wild and white as pine-forests in wintry Norway. My hopes were all dead—struck with a subtle doom, such as, in one night, fell on all the first-born in the land of Egypt. I looked on my cherished wishes, yesterday so blooming and glowing; they lay stark, chill, livid corpses, that could never revive. I looked at my love: that feeling which was my master's—which he had created; it shivered in my heart, like a suffering child in a cold cradle; sickness and anguish had seized it; it could not seek Mr. Rochester's arms—it could not derive warmth from his breast. Oh, never more could it turn to him; for faith was blighted—confidence destroyed! Mr. Rochester was not to me what he had been; for he was not what I had thought him. I would not ascribe vice to him; I would not say he had betrayed me: but the attribute of stainless truth was gone from his idea; and from his presence I must go: *that* I perceived well. When—how—whither, I could not yet discern: but he himself, I doubted not, would hurry me from Thornfield. Real affection, it seemed, he could not have for me; it had been only fitful passion, that was balked; he would want me no more. I should fear even to cross his path now: my view must be hateful to him. Oh, how blind had been my eyes! How weak my conduct!

My eyes were covered and closed: eddying darkness seemed to swim round me, and reflection came in as black and confused a flow. Self-abandoned, relaxed, and effortless, I seemed to have laid me down in the dried-up bed of a great river; I heard a flood loosened in remote mountains, and felt the torrent come: to rise I had no will, to flee I had no strength. I lay faint; longing to be dead. One idea only still throbbed life-like within me—a remembrance of God: it begot an unuttered prayer: these words went wandering up and down in my rayless mind, as something that should be whispered; but no energy was found to express them:—

"Be not far from me, for trouble is near: there is none to help."

It was near: and as I had lifted no petition to Heaven to avert it—as I had neither joined my hands, nor bent my knees, nor moved my lips—it came: in full, heavy swing the torrent poured over me. The whole consciousness of my life lorn, my love lost, my hope quenched, my faith death-struck, swayed full and mighty above me in one sullen mass. That bitter hour cannot be described: in truth, "the waters came into my soul; I sank in deep mire: I felt no standing; I came into deep waters; the floods overflowed me."

Chapter XXVII

SOME time in the afternoon I raised my head, and looking round and seeing the western sun gilding the sign of its decline on the wall, I asked, "What am I to do?"

But the answer my mind gave—"Leave Thornfield at once"—was so prompt, so dread, that I stopped my ears: I said, I could not bear such words now. "That I am not Edward Rochester's bride is the least part of my woe," I alleged: "that I have wakened out of most glorious dreams, and found them all void and vain, is a horror I could bear and master; but that I must leave him decidedly, instantly, entirely, is intolerable. I cannot do it."

But, then, a voice within me averred that I could do it; and foretold that I should do it. I wrestled with my own resolution: I wanted to be weak that I might avoid the awful passage of further suffering I saw laid out for me; and conscience, turned tyrant, held passion by the throat, told her tauntingly, she had yet but dipped her dainty foot in the slough, and swore that with that arm of iron, he would thrust her down to unsounded depths of agony.

"Let me be torn away, then!" I cried. "Let another help me!"

"No; you shall tear yourself away, none shall help you: you shall, yourself, pluck out your right eye: yourself cut off your right hand: your heart shall be the victim; and you, the priest, to transfix it."

I rose up suddenly, terror-struck at the solitude which so ruthless a judge haunted,—at the silence which so awful a voice filled. My head swam as I stood erect: I perceived that I was sickening from excitement and inanition; neither meat nor drink had passed my lips that day, for I had taken no breakfast. And, with a strange pang, I now reflected that, long as I had been shut up here, no message had been sent to ask how I was, or to invite me to come down: not even little Adèle had tapped at the door; not even Mrs. Fairfax had sought me. "Friends always forget those whom fortune forsakes," I murmured, as I undrew the bolt and passed out. I stumbled over an obstacle: my head was still dizzy, my sight was dim, and my limbs were feeble. I could not soon recover myself. I fell, but not on to the ground: an out-stretched arm caught me; I looked up—I was supported by Mr. Rochester, who sat in a chair across my chamber threshold.

"You have come out at last," he said. "Well, I have been waiting for you long, and listening: yet not one movement have I heard, nor one sob: five minutes more of that death-like hush, and I should have forced the lock like a burglar. So, you shun me?—you shut yourself up and grieve alone! I would rather you had come and upbraided me with vehemence. You are passionate: I expected a scene of some kind. I was prepared for the hot rain of tears; only I wanted them to be shed on my breast: now a senseless floor has received them, or your drenched handkerchief. But I err: you have not wept at all! I see a white cheek and a faded eye, but no trace of tears. I suppose, then, your heart has been weeping blood?

"Well, Jane; not a word of reproach? Nothing bitter—nothing poignant? Nothing to cut a feeling or sting a passion? You sit quietly where I have placed you, and regard me with a weary, passive look.

"Jane, I never meant to wound you thus. If the man who had but one little ewe lamb that was dear to him as a daughter, that ate of his bread and drank of his cup, and lay in his bosom, had by some mistake slaughtered it at the shambles, he would not have rued his bloody blunder more than I now rue mine. Will you ever forgive me?"

Reader!—I forgave him at the moment, and on the spot. There was such deep remorse in his eye, such true pity in his tone, such manly energy in his manner; and, besides, there was such unchanged love in his whole look and mien—I forgave him all: yet not in words, not outwardly; only at my heart's core.

"You know I am a scoundrel, Jane?" ere long he inquired wistfully—wondering, I suppose, at my continued silence and tameness: the result rather of weakness than of will.

"Yes, sir."

"Then tell me so roundly and sharply—don't spare me."

"I cannot: I am tired and sick. I want some water." He heaved a sort of shuddering sigh, and taking me in his arms, carried me downstairs. At first I did not know to what room he had borne me; all was cloudy to my glazed sight: presently I felt the reviving warmth of a fire; for, summer as it was, I had become icy cold in my chamber. He put wine to my lips; I tasted it and revived; then I ate something he offered me, and was soon myself. I was in the library—sitting in his chair—he was quite near. "If I could go out of life now, without too sharp a pang, it would be well for me," I thought; "then I should not have to make the effort of cracking my heart-strings in rending them from among Mr. Rochester's. I must leave him, it appears. I do not want to leave him—I cannot leave him."

"How are you now, Jane?"

"Much better, sir: I shall be well soon."

"Taste the wine again, Jane."

I obeyed him; then he put the glass on the table, stood before me, and looked at me attentively. Suddenly he turned away, with an inarticulate exclamation, full of passionate emotion of some kind; he walked fast through the room and came back: he stooped towards me as if to kiss me; but I remembered caresses were now forbidden. I turned my face away, and put his aside.

"What!—how is this?" he exclaimed hastily. "Oh, I know! you won't kiss the husband of Bertha Mason? You consider my arms filled, and my embraces appropriated?"

"At any rate, there is neither room nor claim for me, sir."

"Why, Jane? I will spare you the trouble of much talking: I will answer for you—because I have a wife already, you would reply.—I guess rightly?"

"Yes."

"If you think so, you must have a strange opinion of me; you must regard me as a plotting profligate—a base and low rake who has been simulating disinterested love in order to draw you into a snare deliberately laid, and strip you of honour, and rob you of self-respect. What do you say to that? I see you can say nothing: in the first place, you are faint, still, and have enough to do to draw your breath; in the second place, you cannot yet accustom yourself to accuse and revile me; and, besides, the flood-gates of tears are opened, and they would rush out if you spoke much; and you have no desire to expostulate, to upbraid, to make a scene: you are thinking how *to act*—*talking*, you consider, is of no use. I know you—I am on my guard."

"Sir, I do not wish to act against you," I said; and my unsteady voice warned me to curtail my sentence.

"Not in *your* sense of the word but in *mine*, you are scheming to destroy me. You have as good as said that I am a married man—as a married man you will shun me, keep out of my way: just now you have refused to kiss me. You intend to make yourself a complete stranger to me; to live under this roof only as Adèle's governess; if ever I say a friendly word to you; if ever a friendly feeling inclines you again to me, you will say,—'That man had nearly made me his mistress: I must be ice and rock to him;' and ice and rock you will accordingly become."

I cleared and steadied my voice to reply: "All is changed about me, sir; I must change too—there is no doubt of that: and to avoid fluctuations of feeling, and continual combats with recollections and associations, there is only one way— Adèle must have a new governess, sir."

"Oh, Adèle will go to school—I have settled that already; nor do I mean to torment you with the hideous associations and recollections of Thornfield Hall— this accursed place—this tent of Achan—this insolent vault, offering the ghastliness of living death to the light of the open sky—this narrow stone hell, with its one real fiend, worse than a legion of such as we imagine.—Jane, you shall not stay here, nor will I. I was wrong ever to bring you to Thornfield Hall, knowing as I did how it was haunted. I charged them to conceal from you, before I ever saw you, all knowledge of the curse of the place; merely because I feared Adèle never would have a governess to stay if she knew with what inmate she was housed, and my plans would not permit me to remove the maniac elsewhere—though I possess an old house, Ferndean Manor, even more retired and hidden than this, where I could have lodged her safely enough, had not a scruple about the unhealthiness of the situation, in the heart of a wood, made my conscience recoil from the arrangement. Probably those damp walls would soon have eased me of her charge: but to each villain his own vice; and mine is not a tendency to indirect assassination, even of what I most hate.

"Concealing the mad-woman's neighbourhood, from you, however, was something like covering a child with a cloak, and laying it down near a upas-tree: that demon's vicinage is poisoned, and always was. But I'll shut up Thornfield Hall: I'll nail up the front door, and board the lower windows; I'll give Mrs. Poole two hundred a year to live here with *my wife,* as you term that fearful hag: Grace will do much for money, and she shall have her son, the keeper at Grimsby Retreat, to bear her company and be at hand to give her aid, in the paroxysms, when *my wife* is prompted by her familiar to burn people in their beds at night, to stab them, to bite their flesh from their bones, and so on"——

"Sir," I interrupted him, "you are inexorable for that unfortunate lady: you speak of her with hate—with vindictive antipathy. It is cruel—she cannot help being mad."

"Jane, my little darling (so I will call you, for so you are), you don't know what you are talking about; you misjudge me again: it is not because she is mad I hate her. If you were mad, do you think I should hate you?"

"I do indeed, sir."

"Then you are mistaken, and you know nothing about me, and nothing about the sort of love of which I am capable. Every atom of your flesh is as dear to me as my own: in pain and sickness it would still be dear. Your mind is my treasure, and if it were broken, it would be my treasure still: if you raved, my arms should confine you, and not a strait waistcoat—your grasp, even in fury, would have a charm for me: if you flew at me as wildly as that woman did this morning, I should receive you in an embrace, at least as fond as it would be restrictive. I should not shrink from you with disgust as I did from her: in your quiet moments you should have no watcher and no nurse but me; and I could hang over you with untiring tenderness, though you gave me no smile in return; and never weary of gazing into your eyes, though they had no longer a ray of recognition for me.—But why do I follow that train of ideas? I was talking of removing you from Thornfield. All, you

know, is prepared for prompt departure: to-morrow you shall go. I only ask you to endure one more night under this roof, Jane: and then, farewell to its miseries and terrors for ever! I have a place to repair to, which will be a secure sanctuary from hateful reminiscences, from unwelcome intrusion—even from falsehood and slander.''

''And take Adèle with you, sir,'' I interrupted; ''she will be a companion for you.''

''What do you mean, Jane? I told you I would send Adèle to school: and what do I want with a child for a companion? and not my own child,—a French dancer's bastard. Why do you importune me about her? I say, why do you assign Adèle to me for a companion?''

''You spoke of a retirement, sir; and retirement and solitude are dull: too dull for you.''

''Solitude! solitude!'' he reiterated, with irritation. ''I see I must come to an explanation. I don't know what sphynx-like expression is forming in your countenance. *You* are to share my solitude. Do you understand?''

I shook my head: it required a degree of courage, excited as he was becoming, even to risk that mute sign of dissent. He had been walking fast about the room, and he stopped, as if suddenly rooted to one spot. He looked at me long and hard: I turned my eyes from him, fixed them on the fire, and tried to assume and maintain a quiet, collected aspect.

''Now for the hitch in Jane's character,'' he said at last, speaking more calmly than from his look I had expected him to speak. ''The reel of silk has run smoothly enough so far; but I always knew there would come a knot and a puzzle: here it is. Now for vexation, and exasperation, and endless trouble! By God! I long to exert a fraction of Samson's strength, and break the entanglement like tow!''

He recommenced his walk: but soon again stopped, and this time just before me.

''Jane! will you hear reason?'' (he stooped and approached his lips to my ear) ''because, if you won't, I'll try violence.'' His voice was hoarse; his look that of a man who is just about to burst an insufferable bond and plunge headlong into wild licence. I saw that in another moment, and with one impetus of frenzy more, I should be able to do nothing with him. The present—the passing second of time —was all I had in which to control and restrain him: a movement of repulsion, flight, fear, would have sealed my doom,—and his. But I was not afraid: not in the least. I felt an inward power; a sense of influence, which supported me. The crisis was perilous; but not without its charm: such as the Indian, perhaps, feels when he slips over the rapid in his canoe. I took hold of his clenched hand; loosened the contorted fingers; and said to him, soothingly,—

''Sit down; I'll talk to you as long as you like, and hear all you have to say, whether reasonable or unreasonable.''

He sat down: but he did not get leave to speak directly. I had been struggling with tears for some time: I had taken great pains to repress them, because I knew he would not like to see me weep. Now, however, I considered it well to let them flow as freely and as long as they liked. If the flood annoyed him, so much the better. So I gave way and cried heartily.

Soon I heard him earnestly entreating me to be composed. I said I could not while he was in such a passion.

''But I am not angry, Jane: I only love you too well; and you had steeled your little pale face with such a resolute, frozen look, I could not endure it. Hush, now, and wipe your eyes.''

His softened voice announced that he was subdued; so I, in my turn, became calm. Now he made an effort to rest his head on my shoulder: but I would not permit it. Then he would draw me to him: no.

''Jane! Jane!'' he said—in such an accent of bitter sadness it thrilled along every nerve I had; ''you don't love me, then? It was only my station, and the rank of

my wife that you valued? Now that you think me disqualified to become your husband, you recoil from my touch as if I were some toad or ape.''

These words cut me: yet what could I do or say? I ought probably to have done or said nothing: but I was so tortured by a sense of remorse at thus hurting his feelings, I could not control the wish to drop balm where I had wounded.

"I *do* love you," I said, "more than ever: but I must not show or indulge the feeling: and this is the last time I must express it.''

"The last time, Jane! What! do you think you can live with me, and see me daily, and yet, if you still love me, be always cold and distant?''

"No, sir; that I am certain I could not; and therefore I see there is but one way: but you will be furious if I mention it.''

"Oh, mention it! If I storm, you have the art of weeping.''

"Mr. Rochester, I must leave you.''

"For how long, Jane? For a few minutes, while you smooth your hair—which is somewhat dishevelled; and bathe your face—which looks feverish?''

"I must leave Adèle and Thornfield. I must part with you for my whole life: I must begin a new existence amongst strange faces and strange scenes.''

"Of course: I told you you should. I pass over the madness about parting from me. You mean you must become a part of me. As to the new existence, it is all right: you shall yet be my wife: I am not married. You shall be Mrs. Rochester— both virtually and nominally. I shall keep only to you so long as you and I live. You shall go to a place I have in the south of France: a white-washed villa on the shores of the Mediterranean. There you shall live a happy, and guarded, and most innocent life. Never fear that I wish to lure you into error—to make you my mistress. Why do you shake your head? Jane, you must be reasonable; or in truth I shall again become frantic.''

His voice and hand quivered: his large nostrils dilated: his eye blazed: still I dared to speak:—

"Sir, your wife is living: that is a fact acknowledged this morning by yourself. If I lived with you as you desire, I should then be your mistress: to say otherwise is sophistical—is false.''

"Jane, I am not a gentle-tempered man—you forget that: I am not long-enduring; I am not cool and dispassionate. Out of pity to me and yourself, put your finger on my pulse, feel how it throbs, and—beware!''

He bared his wrist, and offered it to me: the blood was forsaking his cheek and lips, they were growing livid; I was distressed on all hands. To agitate him thus deeply, by a resistance he so abhorred, was cruel: to yield was out of the question. I did what human beings do instinctively when they are driven to utter extremity— looked for aid to one higher than man: the words "God help me!" burst involuntarily from my lips.

"I am a fool!" cried Mr. Rochester, suddenly. "I keep telling her I am not married, and do not explain to her why. I forget she knows nothing of the character of that woman, or of the circumstances attending my infernal union with her. Oh, I am certain Jane will agree with me in opinion, when she knows all that I know! Just put your hand in mine, Janet—that I may have the evidence of touch as well as sight, to prove you are near me—and I will in a few words show you the real state of the case. Can you listen to me?''

"Yes, sir; for hours if you will.''

"I ask only minutes. Jane, did you ever hear, or know that I was not the eldest son of my house: that I had once a brother older than I?''

"I remember Mrs. Fairfax told me so once.''

"And did you ever hear that my father was an avaricious, grasping man?''

"I have understood something to that effect.''

"Well, Jane, being so, it was his resolution to keep the property together; he could not bear the idea of dividing his estate and leaving me a fair portion: all, he

resolved, should go to my brother, Rowland. Yet as little could he endure that a son of his should be a poor man. I must be provided for by a wealthy marriage. He sought me a partner betimes. Mr. Mason, a West India planter and merchant, was his old acquaintance. He was certain his possessions were real and vast: he made inquiries. Mr. Mason, he found, had a son and daughter; and he learned from him that he could and would give the latter a fortune of thirty thousand pounds: that sufficed. When I left college, I was sent out to Jamaica, to espouse a bride already courted for me. My father said nothing about her money; but he told me Miss Mason was the boast of Spanish Town for her beauty: and this was no lie. I found her a fine woman, in the style of Blanche Ingram; tall, dark, majestic. Her family wished to secure me because I was of a good race; and so did she. They showed her to me in parties, splendidly dressed. I seldom saw her alone, and had very little private conversation with her. She flattered me, and lavishly displayed for my pleasure her charms and accomplishments. All the men in her circle seemed to admire her and envy me. I was dazzled, stimulated: my senses were excited; and being ignorant, raw, and inexperienced, I thought I loved her. There is no folly so besotted that the idiotic rivalries of society, the prurience, the rashness, the blindness of youth, will not hurry a man to its commission. Her relatives encouraged me; competitors piqued me; she allured me: a marriage was achieved almost before I knew where I was. Oh, I have no respect for myself when I think of that act!— an agony of inward contempt masters me. I never loved, I never esteemed, I did not even know her. I was not sure of the existence of one virtue in her nature: I had marked neither modesty, nor benevolence, nor candour, nor refinement in her mind or manners—and, I married her:—gross, grovelling, mole-eyed blockhead that I was! With less sin I might have—but let me remember to whom I am speaking.

"My bride's mother I had never seen: I understood she was dead. The honey-moon over, I learned my mistake; she was only mad, and shut up in a lunatic asylum. There was a younger brother, too; a complete dumb idiot. The elder one, whom you have seen (and whom I cannot hate, whilst I abhor all his kindred, because he has some grains of affection in his feeble mind; shown in the continued interest he takes in his wretched sister and also in a dog-like attachment he once bore me), will probably be in the same state one day. My father and my brother Rowland, knew all this; but they thought only of the thirty thousand pounds, and joined in the plot against me.

"These were vile discoveries; but, except for the treachery of concealment, I should have made them no subject of reproach to my wife: even when I found her nature wholly alien to mine; her tastes obnoxious to me; her cast of mind common, low, narrow, and singularly incapable of being led to anything higher, expanded to anything larger—when I found that I could not pass a single evening nor a single hour of the day with her in comfort; that kindly conversation could not be sustained between us, because whatever topic I started, immediately received from her a turn at once coarse and trite, perverse and imbecile—when I perceived that I should never have a quiet or settled household, because no servant would bear the continued outbreaks of her violent and unreasonable temper, or the vexations of her absurd, contradictory, exacting orders—even then I restrained myself: I eschewed upbraiding, I curtailed remonstrance; I tried to devour my repentance and disgust in secret; I repressed the deep antipathy I felt.

"Jane, I will not trouble you with abominable details: some strong words shall express what I have to say. I lived with that woman upstairs four years, and before that time she had tried me indeed: her character ripened and developed with frightful rapidity; her vices sprang up fast and rank: they were so strong, only cruelty could check them; and I would not use cruelty. What a pigmy intellect she had—and what giant propensities! How fearful were the curses those propensities entailed on me! Bertha Mason,—the true daughter of an infamous mother,—dragged me through

all the hideous and degrading agonies which must attend a man bound to a wife at once intemperate and unchaste.

"My brother in the interval was dead; and at the end of the four years my father died too. I was rich enough now—yet poor to hideous indigence: a nature the most gross, impure, depraved I ever saw, was associated with mine, and called by the law and by society a part of me. And I could not rid myself of it by any legal proceedings: for the doctors now discovered that *my wife* was mad—her excesses had prematurely developed the germs of insanity: Jane, you don't like my narrative; you look almost sick—shall I defer the rest to another day?"

"No, sir, finish it now: I pity you—I do earnestly pity you."

"Pity, Jane, from some people is a noxious and insulting sort of tribute, which one is justified in hurling back in the teeth of those who offer it; but that is a sort of pity native to callous, selfish hearts: it is a hybrid, egotistical pain at hearing of woes, crossed with ignorant contempt for those who have endured them. But that is not your pity, Jane: it is not the feeling of which your whole face is full at this moment—with which your eyes are now almost overflowing—with which your heart is heaving—with which your hand is trembling in mine. Your pity, my darling, is the suffering mother of love: its anguish is the very natal pang of the divine passion. I accept it, Jane; let the daughter have free advent—my arms wait to receive her."

"Now, sir, proceed: what did you do when you found she was mad?"

"Jane—I approached the verge of despair: a remnant of self-respect was all that intervened between me and the gulf. In the eyes of the world, I was doubtless covered with grimy dishonour: but I resolved to be clean in my own sight—and to the last I repudiated the contamination of her crimes, and wrenched myself from connection with her mental defects. Still, society associated my name and person with hers; I yet saw her and heard her daily: something of her breath (faugh!) mixed with the air I breathed; and, besides, I remembered I had once been her husband—that recollection was then, and is now, inexpressibly odious to me; moreover, I knew that while she lived I could never be the husband of another and better wife; and, though five years my senior (her family and her father had lied to me even in the particular of her age), she was likely to live as long as I, being as robust in frame as she was infirm in mind. Thus, at the age of twenty-six, I was hopeless.

"One night I had been awakened by her yells—(since the medical men had pronounced her mad, she had of course been shut up)—it was a fiery West Indian night; one of the description that frequently precedes the hurricanes of those climates; being unable to sleep in bed, I got up and opened the window. The air was like sulphur-steams—I could find no refreshment anywhere. Mosquitoes came buzzing in and hummed sullenly round the room; the sea, which I could hear from thence, rumbled dull like an earthquake—black clouds were casting up over it; the moon was setting in the waves, broad and red, like a hot cannon-ball—she threw her last bloody glance over a world quivering with the ferment of tempest. I was physically influenced by the atmosphere and scene, and my ears were filled with the curses the maniac still shrieked out; wherein she momentarily mingled my name with such a tone of demon-hate, with such language!—no professed harlot ever had a fouler vocabulary than she: though two rooms off, I heard every word—the thin partitions of the West India house opposing but slight obstruction to her wolfish cries.

" 'This life,' said I at last, 'is hell! this is the air—those are the sounds of the bottomless pit! I have a right to deliver myself from it if I can. The sufferings of this mortal state will leave me with the heavy flesh that now cumbers my soul. Of the fanatic's burning eternity I have no fear: there is not a future state worse than this present one—let me break away and go home to God!'

"I said this whilst I knelt down at, and unlocked a trunk which contained a brace of loaded pistols: I meant to shoot myself. I only entertained the intention for a

moment; for, not being insane, the crisis of exquisite and unalloyed despair which
had originated the wish and design of self-destruction, was past in a second.

"A wind fresh from Europe blew over the ocean and rushed through the open
casement: the storm broke, streamed, thundered, blazed, and the air grew pure. I
then framed and fixed a resolution. While I walked under the dripping orange-trees
of my wet garden, and amongst its drenched pomegranates and pine-apples, and
while the refulgent dawn of the tropics kindled round me—I reasoned thus, Jane:—
and now listen; for it was true Wisdom that consoled me in that hour, and showed
me the right path to follow.

"The sweet wind from Europe was still whispering in the refreshed leaves, and
the Atlantic was thundering in glorious liberty; my heart, dried up and scorched
for a long time, swelled to the tone, and filled with living blood—my being longed
for renewal—my soul thirsted for a pure draught. I saw Hope revive—and felt
Regeneration possible. From a flowery arch at the bottom of my garden I gazed
over the sea—bluer than the sky; the old world was beyond; clear prospects opened
thus:—

" 'Go,' said Hope, 'and live again in Europe: there it is not known what a sullied
name you bear, nor what a filthy burden is bound to you. You may take the maniac
with you to England; confine her with due attendance and precautions at Thornfield:
then travel yourself to what clime you will, and form what new tie you like. That
woman, who has so abused your long-suffering—so sullied your name; so outraged
your honour; so blighted your youth—is not your wife; nor are you her husband.
See that she is cared for as her condition demands, and you have done all that God
and Humanity require of you. Let her identity, her connection with yourself, be
buried in oblivion: you are bound to impart them to no living being. Place her in
safety and comfort: shelter her degradation with secrecy, and leave her.'

"I acted precisely on this suggestion. My father and brother had not made my
marriage known to their acquaintance; because, in the very first letter I wrote to
apprise them of the union—having already begun to experience extreme disgust of
its consequences; and from the family character and constitution, seeing a hideous
future opening to me—I added an urgent charge to keep it secret: and very soon,
the infamous conduct of the wife my father had selected for me, was such as to
make him blush to own her as his daughter-in-law. Far from desiring to publish
the connection, he became as anxious to conceal it as myself.

"To England, then, I conveyed her; a fearful voyage I had with such a monster
in the vessel. Glad was I when I at last got her to Thornfield, and saw her safely
lodged in that third story room, of whose secret inner cabinet she has now for ten
years made a wild beast's den—a goblin's cell. I had some trouble in finding an
attendant for her: as it was necessary to select one on whose fidelity dependence
could be placed; for her ravings would inevitably betray my secret: besides, she
had lucid intervals of days—sometimes weeks—which she filled up with abuse of
me. At last I hired Grace Poole, from the Grimsby Retreat. She and the surgeon,
Carter (who dressed Mason's wounds that night he was stabbed and worried), are
the only two I have ever admitted to my confidence. Mrs. Fairfax may indeed have
suspected something; but she could have gained no precise knowledge as to facts.
Grace has, on the whole, proved a good keeper; though, owing partly to a fault of
her own, of which it appears nothing can cure her, and which is incident to her
harassing profession, her vigilance has been more than once lulled and baffled. The
lunatic is both cunning and malignant; she has never failed to take advantage of
her guardian's temporary lapses; once to secrete the knife with which she stabbed
her brother, and twice to possess herself of the key of her cell, and issue therefrom
in the night-time. On the first of these occasions, she perpetrated the attempt to
burn me in my bed; on the second she paid that ghastly visit to you. I thank
Providence, who watched over you, that she then spent her fury on your wedding
apparel; which perhaps brought back vague reminiscences of her own bridal days:

but on what might have happened, I cannot endure to reflect. When I think of the thing which flew at my throat this morning, hanging its black and scarlet visage over the nest of my dove, my blood curdles''——

"And what, sir," I asked, while he paused, "did you do when you had settled her here? Where did you go?"

"What did I do, Jane? I transformed myself into a Will-o'-the-wisp. Where did I go? I pursued wanderings as wild as those of the March-spirit. I sought the Continent, and went devious through all its lands. My fixed desire was to seek and find a good and intelligent woman, whom I could love: a contrast to the fury I left at Thornfield''——

"But you could not marry, sir."

"I had determined, and was convinced that I could and ought. It was not my original intention to deceive, as I have deceived you. I meant to tell my tale plainly, and make my proposals openly: and it appeared to me so absolutely rational that I should be considered free to love and be loved, I never doubted some woman might be found willing and able to understand my case and accept me, in spite of the curse with which I was burdened.''

"Well, sir?"

"When you are inquisitive, Jane, you always make me smile. You open your eyes like an eager bird, and make every now and then a restless movement; as if answers in speech did not flow fast enough for you, and you wanted to read the tablet of one's heart. But before I go on, tell me what you mean by your 'Well, sir?' It is a small phrase very frequent with you; and which many a time has drawn me on and on through interminable talk: I don't very well know why.''

"I mean,—What next? How did you proceed? What came of such an event?"

"Precisely: and what do you wish to know now?"

"Whether you found any one you liked: whether you asked her to marry you; and what she said.''

"I can tell you whether I found any one I liked, and whether I asked her to marry me: but what she said is yet to be recorded in the book of Fate. For ten long years I roved about, living first in one capital, then another: sometimes in St. Petersburgh; oftener in Paris; occasionally in Rome, Naples, and Florence. Provided with plenty of money, and the passport of an old name, I could choose my own society: no circles were closed against me. I sought my ideal of a woman amongst English ladies, French countesses, Italian signoras, and German gräfinnen. I could not find her. Sometimes, for a fleeting moment, I thought I caught a glance, heard a tone, beheld a form, which announced the realisation of my dream: but I was presently undeceived. You are not to suppose that I desired perfection, either of mind or person. I longed only for what suited me—for the antipodes of the Creole: and I longed vainly. Amongst them all I found not one, whom, had I been ever so free, I—warned as I was of the risks, the horrors, the loathings of incongruous unions—would have asked to marry me. Disappointment made me reckless. I tried dissipation—never debauchery: that I hated, and hate. That was my Indian Messalina's attribute: rooted disgust at it and her restrained me much, even in pleasure. Any enjoyment that bordered on riot seemed to approach me to her and her vices, and I eschewed it.

"Yet I could not live alone; so I tried the companionship of mistresses. The first I chose was Céline Varens—another of those steps which make a man spurn himself when he recalls them. You already know what she was, and how my liaison with her terminated. She had two successors: an Italian, Giacinta, and a German, Clara; both considered singularly handsome. What was their beauty to me in a few weeks? Giacinta was unprincipled and violent: I tired of her in three months. Clara was honest and quiet; but heavy, mindless, unimpressible: not one whit to my taste. I was glad to give her a sufficient sum to set her up in a good line of business, and so get decently rid of her. But, Jane, I see by your face you are not forming a very

favourable opinion of me just now. You think me an unfeeling, loose-principled rake: don't you?''

"I don't like you so well as I have done sometimes, indeed, sir. Did it not seem to you in the least wrong to live in that way: first with one mistress and then another? You talk of it as a mere matter of course.''

"It was with me; and I did not like it. It was a grovelling fashion of existence: I should never like to return to it. Hiring a mistress is the next worse thing to buying a slave: both are often by nature, and always by position, inferior: and to live familiarly with inferiors is degrading. I now hate the recollection of the time I passed with Céline, Giacinta, and Clara.''

I felt the truth of these words; and I drew from them the certain inference, that if I were so far to forget myself and all the teaching that had ever been instilled into me, as—under any pretext—with any justification—through any temptation— to become the successor of these poor girls, he would one day regard me with the same feeling which now in his mind desecrated their memory. I did not give utterance to this conviction: it was enough to feel it. I impressed it on my heart, that it might remain there to serve me as aid in the time of trial.

"Now, Jane, why don't you say 'Well, sir?' I have not done. You are looking grave. You disapprove of me still, I see. But let me come to the point. Last January, rid of all mistresses—in a harsh, bitter, frame of mind, the result of a useless, roving, lonely life—corroded with disappointment, sourly disposed against all men, and especially against all *woman*kind (for I began to regard the notion of an intellectual, faithful, loving woman as a mere dream), recalled by business, I came back to England.

"On a frosty winter afternoon, I rode in sight of Thornfield Hall. Abhorred spot! I expected no peace—no pleasure there. On a stile in Hay Lane I saw a quiet little figure sitting by itself. I passed it as negligently as I did the pollard willow opposite to it: I had no presentiment of what it would be to me; no inward warning that the arbitress of my life—my genius for good or evil—waited there in humble guise. I did not know it, even when, on the occasion of Mesrour's accident, it came up and gravely offered me help. Childish and slender creature! It seemed as if a linnet had hopped to my foot and proposed to bear me on its tiny wing. I was surly; but the thing would not go: it stood by me with strange perseverance, and looked and spoke with a sort of authority. I must be aided, and by that hand: and aided I was.

"When once I had pressed the frail shoulder, something new—a fresh sap and sense—stole into my frame. It was well I had learnt that this elf must return to me—that it belonged to my house down below—or I could not have felt it pass away from under my hand, and seen it vanish behind the dim hedge, without singular regret. I heard you come home that night, Jane: though probably you were not aware that I thought of you, or watched for you. The next day I observed you— myself unseen—for half an hour, while you played with Adèle in the gallery. It was a snowy day, I recollect, and you could not go out of doors. I was in my room; the door was ajar: I could both listen and watch. Adèle claimed your outward attention for a while; yet I fancied your thoughts were elsewhere: but you were very patient with her, my little Jane; you talked to her and amused her a long time. When at last she left you, you lapsed at once into deep reverie: you betook yourself slowly to pace the gallery. Now and then, in passing a casement, you glanced out at the thick-falling snow; you listened to the sobbing wind, and again you paced gently on and dreamed. I think those day visions were not dark: there was a pleasurable illumination in your eye occasionally, a soft excitement in your aspect, which told of no bitter, bilious, hypochondriac brooding: your look revealed rather the sweet musings of youth, when its spirit follows on willing wings the flight of Hope, up and on to an ideal heaven. The voice of Mrs. Fairfax, speaking to a servant in the hall, wakened you: and how curiously you smiled to and at yourself, Jane! There was much sense in your smile: It was very shrewd, and seemed to

make light of your own abstraction. It seemed to say—'My fine visions are all very well, but I must not forget they are absolutely unreal. I have a rosy sky, and a green flowery Eden in my brain; but without, I am perfectly aware, lies at my feet a rough tract to travel, and around me gather black tempests to encounter.' You ran downstairs and demanded of Mrs. Fairfax some occupation: the weekly house accounts to make up, or something of that sort, I think it was. I was vexed with you for getting out of my sight.

"Impatiently I waited for evening, when I might summon you to my presence. An unusual—to me—a perfectly new character I suspected was yours: I desired to search it deeper, and know it better. You entered the room with a look and air at once shy and independent: you were quaintly dressed—much as you are now. I made you talk: ere long I found you full of strange contrasts. Your garb and manner were restricted by rule; your air was often diffident, and altogether that of one refined by nature, but absolutely unused to society, and a good deal afraid of making herself disadvantageously conspicuous by some solecism or blunder; yet when addressed, you lifted a keen, a daring and a glowing eye to your interlocutor's face: there was penetration and power in each glance you gave; when plied by close questions, you found ready and round answers. Very soon, you seemed to get used to me: I believe you felt the existence of sympathy between you and your grim and cross master, Jane; for it was astonishing to see how quickly a certain pleasant ease tranquillised your manner: snarl as I would, you showed no surprise, fear, annoyance, or displeasure at my moroseness; you watched me, and now and then smiled at me with a simple yet sagacious grace I cannot describe. I was at once content and stimulated with what I saw: I liked what I had seen, and wished to see more. Yet, for a long time, I treated you distantly, and sought your company rarely. I was an intellectual epicure, and wished to prolong the gratification of making this novel and piquant acquaintance: besides, I was for a while troubled with a haunting fear that if I handled the flower freely its bloom would fade—the sweet charm of freshness would leave it. I did not then know that it was no transitory blossom; but rather the radiant resemblance of one, cut in an indestructible gem. Moreover, I wished to see whether you would seek me if I shunned you—but you did not; you kept in the school-room as still as your own desk and easel; if by chance I met you, you passed me as soon, and with as little token of recognition, as was consistent with respect. Your habitual expression in those days, Jane, was a thoughtful look; not despondent, for you were not sickly; but not buoyant, for you had little hope, and no actual pleasure. I wondered what you thought of me—or if you ever thought of me; to find this out, I resumed my notice of you. There was something glad in your glance, and genial in your manner, when you conversed: I saw you had a social heart; it was the silent school-room—it was the tedium of your life—that made you mournful. I permitted myself the delight of being kind to you; kindness stirred emotion soon: your face became soft in expression, your tones gentle: I liked my name pronounced by your lips in a grateful happy accent. I used to enjoy a chance meeting with you, Jane, at this time: there was a curious hesitation in your manner: you glanced at me with a slight trouble—a hovering doubt: you did not know what my caprice might be—whether I was going to play the master and be stern, or the friend and be benignant. I was now too fond of you often to simulate the first whim; and, when I stretched my hand out cordially, such bloom and light and bliss rose to your young, wistful features, I had much ado often to avoid straining you then and there to my heart."

"Don't talk any more of those days, sir," I interrupted, furtively dashing away some tears from my eyes; his language was torture to me; for I knew what I must do—and do soon—and all these reminiscences, and these revelations of his feelings only made my work more difficult.

"No, Jane," he returned: "what necessity is there to dwell on the Past, when the Present is so much surer—the Future so much brighter?"

I shuddered to hear the infatuated assertion.

"You see now how the case stands—do you not?" he continued. "After a youth and manhood passed half in unutterable misery and half in dreary solitude, I have for the first time found what I can truly love—I have found *you*. You are my sympathy—my better self—my good angel—and I am bound to you with a strong attachment. I think you good, gifted, lovely: a fervent, a solemn passion is conceived in my heart; it leans to you, draws you to my centre and spring of life, wraps my existence about you—and, kindling in pure, powerful flame, fuses you and me in one.

"It was because I felt and knew this, that I resolved to marry you. To tell me that I had already a wife is empty mockery: you know now that I had but a hideous demon. I was wrong to attempt to deceive you; but I feared a stubbornness that exists in your character. I feared early instilled prejudice: I wanted to have you safe before hazarding confidences. This was cowardly: I should have appealed to your nobleness and magnanimity at first, as I do now—opened to you plainly my life of agony—described to you my hunger and thirst after a higher and worthier existence—shown to you, not my *resolution* (that word is weak), but my resistless *bent* to love faithfully and well, where I am faithfully and well loved in return. Then I should have asked you to accept my pledge of fidelity, and to give me yours: Jane—give it me now."

A pause.

"Why are you silent, Jane?"

I was experiencing an ordeal: a hand of fiery iron grasped my vitals. Terrible moment: full of struggle, blackness, burning! Not a human being that ever lived could wish to be loved better than I was loved; and him who thus loved me I absolutely worshipped: and I must renounce love and idol. One drear word comprised my intolerable duty—"Depart!"

"Jane, you understand what I want of you? Just this promise—'I will be yours, Mr. Rochester.' "

"Mr. Rochester, I will *not* be yours."

Another long silence.

"Jane!" recommenced he, with a gentleness that broke me down with grief, and turned me stone-cold with ominous terror—for this still voice was the pant of a lion rising—"Jane, do you mean to go one way in the world, and to let me go another?"

"I do."

"Jane" (bending towards and embracing me), "do you mean it now?"

"I do."

"And now?" softly kissing my forehead and cheek.

"I do"—extricating myself from restraint rapidly and completely.

"Oh, Jane, this is bitter! This—this is wicked. It would not be wicked to love me."

"It would to obey you."

A wild look raised his brows—crossed his features: he rose; but he forbore yet. I laid my hand on the back of a chair for support: I shook, I feared—but I resolved.

"One instant, Jane. Give one glance to my horrible life when you are gone. All happiness will be torn away with you. What then is left? For a wife I have but the maniac upstairs: as well might you refer me to some corpse in yonder churchyard. What shall I do, Jane? Where turn for a companion, and for some hope?"

"Do as I do: trust in God and yourself. Believe in heaven. Hope to meet again there."

"Then you will not yield?"

"No."

"Then you condemn me to live wretched, and to die accursed?" His voice rose.

"I advise you to live sinless: and I wish you to die tranquil."

"Then you snatch love and innocence from me? You fling me back on lust for a passion—vice for an occupation?"

"Mr. Rochester, I no more assign this fate to you than I grasp at it for myself. We were born to strive and endure—you as well as I: do so. You will forget me before I forget you."

"You make me a liar by such language: you sully my honour. I declared I could not change: you tell me to my face I shall change soon. And what a distortion in your judgment, what a perversity in your ideas, is proved by your conduct! Is it better to drive a fellow-creature to despair than to transgress a mere human law— no man being injured by the breach? for you have neither relatives nor acquaintances whom you need fear to offend by living with me."

This was true: and while he spoke my very conscience and reason turned traitors against me, and charged me with crime in resisting him. They spoke almost as loud as Feeling: and that clamoured wildly. "Oh, comply!" it said. "Think of his misery; think of his danger—look at his state when left alone; remember his headlong nature; consider the recklessness following on despair—soothe him; save him; love him; tell him you love him and will be his. Who in the world cares for *you*? or who will be injured by what you do?"

Still indomitable was the reply—"*I* care for myself. The more solitary, the more friendless, the more unsustained I am, the more I will respect myself. I will keep the law given by God; sanctioned by man. I will hold to the principles received by me when I was sane, and not mad—as I am now. Laws and principles are not for the times when there is no temptation: they are for such moments as this, when body and soul rise in mutiny against their rigour; stringent are they; inviolate they shall be. If at my individual convenience I might break them, what would be their worth? They have a worth—so I have always believed; and if I cannot believe it now, it is because I am insane—quite insane: with my veins running fire, and my heart beating faster than I can count its throbs. Preconceived opinions, foregone determinations, are all I have at this hour to stand by: there I plant my foot."

I did. Mr. Rochester, reading my countenance, saw I had done so. His fury was wrought to the highest: he must yield to it for a moment, whatever followed; he crossed the floor and seized my arm, and grasped my waist. He seemed to devour me with his flaming glance: physically, I felt, at the moment, powerless as stubble exposed to the draught and glow of a furnace—mentally, I still possessed my soul, and with it the certainty of ultimate safety. The soul, fortunately, has an interpreter— often an unconscious, but still a truthful interpreter—in the eye. My eye rose to his; and while I looked in his fierce face, I gave an involuntary sigh: his gripe was painful, and my over-tasked strength almost exhausted.

"Never," said he, as he ground his teeth, "never was anything at once so frail and so indomitable. A mere reed she feels in my hand!" (And he shook me with the force of his hold.) "I could bend her with my finger and thumb: and what good would it do if I bent, if I uptore, if I crushed her? Consider that eye: consider the resolute, wild, free thing looking out of it, defying me, with more than courage— with a stern triumph. Whatever I do with its cage, I cannot get at it—the savage, beautiful creature! If I tear, if I rend the slight prison, my outrage will only let the captive loose. Conqueror I might be of the house; but the inmate would escape to heaven before I could call myself possessor of its clay dwelling-place. And it is you, spirit—with will and energy, and virtue and purity—that I want: not alone your brittle frame. Of yourself, you could come with soft flight and nestle against my heart, if you would: seized against your will you will elude the grasp like an essence—you will vanish ere I inhale your fragrance. Oh! come, Jane, come!"

As he said this, he released me from his clutch, and only looked at me. The look was far worse to resist than the frantic strain: only an idiot, however, would have succumbed now. I had dared and baffled his fury; I must elude his sorrow: I retired to the door.

"You are going, Jane?"

"I am going, sir."

"You are leaving me?"

"Yes."

"You will not come?—You will not be my comforter, my rescuer?—My deep love, my wild woe, my frantic prayer, are all nothing to you?"

What unutterable pathos was in his voice! How hard it was to reiterate firmly, "I am going."

"Jane!"

"Mr. Rochester!"

"Withdraw, then,—I consent—but remember, you leave me here in anguish. Go up to your own room; think over all I have said, Jane, cast a glance on my sufferings— think of me."

He turned away; he threw himself on his face on the sofa. "Oh, Jane! my hope— my love—my life!" broke in anguish from his lips. Then came a deep, strong sob.

I had already gained the door: but, reader, I walked back—walked back as determinedly as I had retreated. I knelt down by him; I turned his face from the cushion to me; I kissed his cheek; I smoothed his hair with my hand.

"God bless you, my dear master!" I said. "God keep you from harm and wrong— direct you, solace you—reward you well for your past kindness to me."

"Little Jane's love would have been my best reward," he answered: "without it, my heart is broken. But Jane will give me her love: yes—nobly, generously."

Up the blood rushed to his face; forth flashed the fire from his eyes; erect he sprang; he held his arms out; but I evaded the embrace, and at once quitted the room.

"Farewell!" was the cry of my heart as I left him. Despair added, "Farewell, for ever!"

* * * * * * *

That night I never thought to sleep; but a slumber fell on me as soon as I lay down in bed. I was transported in thought to the scenes of childhood: I dreamt I lay in the red-room at Gateshead; that the night was dark, and my mind impressed with strange fears. The light that long ago had struck me into syncope, recalled in this vision, seemed glidingly to mount the wall, and tremblingly to pause in the centre of the obscured ceiling. I lifted up my head to look: the roof resolved to clouds, high and dim; the gleam was such as the moon imparts to vapours she is about to sever. I watched her come—watched with the strangest anticipation; as though some word of doom were to be written on her disk. She broke forth as never moon yet burst from cloud: a hand first penetrated the sable folds and waved them away; then, not a moon, but a white human form shone in the azure, inclining a glorious brow earthward. It gazed and gazed on me. It spoke to my spirit: immeasurably distant was the tone, yet so near, it whispered in my heart—

"My daughter, flee temptation!"

"Mother, I will."

So I answered after I had waked from the trance-like dream. It was yet night, but July nights are short: soon after midnight, dawn comes. "It cannot be too early to commence the task I have to fulfil," thought I. I rose: I was dressed; for I had taken off nothing but my shoes. I knew where to find in my drawers some linen, a locket, a ring. In seeking these articles, I encountered the beads of a pearl necklace Mr. Rochester had forced me to accept a few days ago. I left that; it was not mine: it was the visionary bride's, who had melted in air. The other articles I made up in a parcel; my purse, containing twenty shillings (it was all I had), I put in my pocket: I tied on my straw bonnet, pinned my shawl, took the parcel and my slippers, which I would not put on yet, and stole from my room.

"Farewell, kind Mrs. Fairfax!" I whispered, as I glided past her door. "Farewell, my darling Adèle!" I said as I glanced towards the nursery. No thought could be admitted of entering to embrace her. I had to deceive a fine ear: for aught I knew, it might now be listening.

I would have got past Mr. Rochester's chamber without a pause; but my heart momentarily stopping its beat at that threshold, my foot was forced to stop also. No sleep was there: the inmate was walking restlessly from wall to wall; and again and again he sighed while I listened. There was a heaven—a temporary heaven—in this room for me, if I chose: I had but to go in and to say—

"Mr. Rochester, I will love you and live with you through life till death," and a fount of rapture would spring to my lips. I thought of this.

That kind master, who could not sleep now, was waiting with impatience for day. He would send for me in the morning; I should be gone. He would have me sought for: vainly. He would feel himself forsaken; his love rejected: he would suffer; perhaps grow desperate. I thought of this too. My hand moved towards the lock: I caught it back, and glided on.

Drearily I wound my way downstairs: I knew what I had to do, and I did it mechanically. I sought the key of the side-door in the kitchen; I sought, too, a phial of oil and a feather; I oiled the key and the lock. I got some water, I got some bread: for perhaps I should have to walk far; and my strength, sorely shaken of late, must not break down. All this I did without one sound. I opened the door, passed out, shut it softly. Dim dawn glimmered in the yard. The great gates were closed and locked; but a wicket in one of them was only latched. Through that I departed: it, too, I shut; and now I was out of Thornfield.

A mile off, beyond the fields, lay a road which stretched in the contrary direction to Millcote; a road I had never travelled, but often noticed, and wondered where it led: thither I bent my steps. No reflection was to be allowed now: not one glance was to be cast back; not even one forward. Not one thought was to be given either to the past or the future. The first was a page so heavenly sweet—so deadly sad—that to read one line of it would dissolve my courage and break down my energy. The last was an awful blank: something like the world when the deluge was gone by.

I skirted fields, and hedges, and lanes, till after sunrise. I believe it was a lovely summer morning: I knew my shoes, which I had put on when I left the house, were soon wet with dew. But I looked neither to rising sun, nor smiling sky, nor wakening nature. He who is taken out to pass through a fair scene to the scaffold, thinks not of the flowers that smile on his road, but of the block and axe-edge; of the disseverment of bone and vein; of the grave gaping at the end: and I thought of drear flight and homeless wandering—and oh! with agony I thought of what I left. I could not help it. I thought of him now—in his room—watching the sunrise; hoping I should soon come to say I would stay with him, and be his. I longed to be his; I panted to return: it was not too late; I could yet spare him the bitter pang of bereavement. As yet my flight, I was sure, was undiscovered. I could go back and be his comforter—his pride; his redeemer from misery; perhaps from ruin. Oh, that fear of his self-abandonment—far worse than my abandonment—how it goaded me! It was a barbed arrow-head in my breast; it tore me when I tried to extract it; it sickened me when remembrance thrust it further in. Birds began singing in brake and copse: birds were faithful to their mates; birds were emblems of love. What was I? In the midst of my pain of heart, and frantic effort of principle, I abhorred myself. I had no solace from self-approbation: none even from self-respect. I had injured—wounded—left my master. I was hateful in my own eyes. Still I could not turn, nor retrace one step. God must have led me on. As to my own will or conscience, impassioned grief had trampled one and stifled the other. I was weeping wildly as I walked along my solitary way: fast, fast I went like one delirious. A weakness, beginning inwardly, extending to the limbs, seized me, and I fell: I lay

on the ground some minutes, pressing my face to the wet turf. I had some fear—
or hope—that here I should die: but I was soon up; crawling forward on my hands
and knees, and then again raised to my feet—as eager and as determined as ever
to reach the road.

When I got there I was forced to sit to rest me under the hedge; and while I sat,
I heard wheels, and saw a coach come on. I stood up and lifted my hand; it stopped.
I asked where it was going: the driver named a place a long way off, and where I
was sure Mr. Rochester had no connections. I asked for what sum he would take
me there; he said thirty shillings; I answered I had but twenty; well, he would try
to make it do. He further gave me leave to get into the inside, as the vehicle was
empty: I entered, was shut in, and it rolled on its way.

Gentle reader, may you never feel what I then felt! May your eyes never shed
such stormy, scalding, heart-wrung tears as poured from mine. May you never
appeal to Heaven in prayers so hopeless and so agonised as in that hour left my
lips: for never may you, like me, dread to be the instrument of evil to what you
wholly love.

Chapter XXVIII

Two days are passed. It is a summer evening; the coachman has set me down at
a place called Whitcross; he could take me no farther for the sum I had given, and
I was not possessed of another shilling in the world. The coach is a mile off by
this time; I am alone. At this moment I discover that I forgot to take my parcel out
of the pocket of the coach, where I had placed it for safety; there it remains, there
it must remain; and now, I am absolutely destitute.

Whitcross is no town, nor even a hamlet; it is but a stone pillar set up where
four roads meet: white-washed, I suppose to be more obvious at a distance and in
darkness. Four arms spring from its summit: the nearest town to which these point
is, according to the inscription, distant ten miles; the farthest, above twenty. From
the well known names of these towns I learn in what county I have lighted; a north-
midland shire, dusk with moorland, ridged with mountain: this I see. There are
great moors behind and on each hand of me; there are waves of mountains far
beyond that deep valley at my feet. The population here must be thin, and I see
no passengers on these roads: they stretch out east, west, north, and south—white,
broad, lonely; they are all cut in the moor, and the heather grows deep and wild
to their very verge. Yet a chance traveller might pass by; and I wish no eye to see
me now: strangers would wonder what I am doing, lingering here at the sign-post,
evidently objectless and lost. I might be questioned: I could give no answer but
what would sound incredible, and excite suspicion. Not a tie holds me to human
society at this moment—not a charm or hope calls me where my fellow-creatures
are—none that saw me would have a kind thought or good wish for me. I have no
relative but the universal mother, Nature: I will seek her breast and ask repose.

I struck straight into the heath; I held on to a hollow I saw deeply furrowing the
brown moorside; I waded knee-deep in its dark growth; I turned with its turnings,
and finding a moss-blackened granite crag in a hidden angle, I sat down under it.
High banks of moor were about me; the crag protected my head: the sky was over
that.

Some time passed before I felt tranquil even here: I had a vague dread that wild
cattle might be near, or that some sportsman or poacher might discover me. If a
gust of wind swept the waste, I looked up, fearing it was the rush of a bull; if a
plover whistled, I imagined it a man. Finding my apprehensions unfounded, however,
and calmed by the deep silence that reigned as evening declined at nightfall, I took

confidence. As yet I had not thought; I had only listened, watched, dreaded; now I regained the faculty of reflection.

What was I to do? Where to go? Oh, intolerable questions, when I could do nothing and go nowhere!—when a long way must yet be measured by my weary, trembling limbs, before I could reach human habitation—when cold charity must be entreated before I could get a lodging: reluctant sympathy importuned: almost certain repulse incurred: before my tale could be listened to, or one of my wants relieved!

I touched the heath: it was dry, and yet warm with the heat of the summer-day. I looked at the sky; it was pure: a kindly star twinkled just above the chasm ridge. The dew fell, but with propitious softness; no breeze whispered. Nature seemed to me benign and good; I thought she loved me, outcast as I was; and I, who from man could anticipate only mistrust, rejection, insult, clung to her with filial fondness. To-night, at least, I would be her guest—as I was her child: my mother would lodge me without money and without price. I had one morsel of bread yet: the remnant of a roll I had bought in a town we passed through at noon with a stray penny—my last coin. I saw ripe bilberries gleaming here and there, like jet beads in the heath: I gathered a handful and ate them with the bread. My hunger, sharp before, was, if not satisfied, appeased by this hermit's meal. I said my evening prayers at its conclusion, and then chose my couch.

Beside the crag, the heath was very deep: when I lay down my feet were buried in it; rising high on each side, it left only a narrow space for the night-air to invade. I folded my shawl double, and spread it over me for a coverlet; a low, mossy swell was my pillow. Thus lodged, I was not, at least at the commencement of the night, cold.

My rest might have been blissful enough, only a sad heart broke it. It plained of its gaping wounds, its inward bleeding, its riven chords. It trembled for Mr. Rochester and his doom: it bemoaned him with bitter pity; it demanded him with ceaseless longing: and, impotent as a bird with both wings broken, it still quivered its shattered pinions in vain attempts to seek him.

Worn out with this torture of thought, I rose to my knees. Night was come, and her planets were risen: a safe, still night; too serene for the companionship of fear. We know that God is everywhere; but certainly we feel His presence most when His works are on the grandest scale spread before us: and it is in the unclouded night-sky, where His worlds wheel their silent course, that we read clearest His infinitude, His omnipotence, His omnipresence. I had risen to my knees to pray for Mr. Rochester. Looking up, I, with tear-dimmed eyes, saw the mighty Milky-way. Remembering what it was—what countless systems swept space like a soft trace of light—I felt the might and strength of God. Sure was I of His efficiency to save what He had made: convinced I grew that neither earth should perish, nor one of the souls it treasured. I turned my prayer to thanks-giving: the Source of Life was also the Saviour of spirits. Mr. Rochester was safe: he was God's and by God would he be guarded. I again nestled to the breast of the hill; and ere long, in sleep, forgot sorrow.

But next day, Want came to me, pale and bare. Long after the little birds had left their nests; long after bees had come in the sweet prime of day to gather the heath honey before the dew was dried—when the long morning shadows were curtailed, and the sun filled earth and sky—I got up, and I looked round me.

What a still, hot, perfect day! What a golden desert this spreading moor! Everywhere sunshine. I wished I could live in it and on it. I saw a lizard run over the crag; I saw a bee busy among the sweet bilberries. I would fain at the moment have become bee or lizard, that I might have found fitting nutriment, permanent shelter here. But I was a human being, and had a human being's wants: I must not linger where there was nothing to supply them. I rose; I looked back at the bed I had left. Hopeless of the future, I wished but this—that my Maker had that night thought

good to require my soul of me while I slept; and that this weary frame, absolved by death from further conflict with fate, had now but to decay quietly, and mingle in peace with the soil of this wilderness. Life, however, was yet in my possession: with all its requirements, and pains, and responsibilities. The burden must be carried; the want provided for; the suffering endured; the responsibility fulfilled. I set out.

Whitcross regained, I followed a road which led from the sun, now fervent and high. By no other circumstance had I will to decide my choice. I walked a long time, and when I thought I had nearly done enough, and might conscientiously yield to the fatigue that almost overpowered me—might relax this forced action, and, sitting down on a stone I saw near, submit restlessly to the apathy that clogged heart and limb—I heard a bell chime—a church bell.

I turned in the direction of the sound, and there, amongst the romantic hills, whose changes and aspect I had ceased to note an hour ago, I saw a hamlet and a spire. All the valley at my right hand was full of pasture-fields, and corn-fields, and wood; and a glittering stream ran zig-zag through the varied shades of green, the mellowing grain, the sombre wood-land, the clear and sunny lea. Recalled by the rumbling of wheels to the road before me, I saw a heavily-laden waggon labouring up the hill; and not far beyond were two cows and their drover. Human life and human labour were near. I must struggle on: strive to live and bend to toil like the rest.

About two o'clock, P.M., I entered the village. At the bottom of its one street, there was a little shop with some cakes of bread in the window. I coveted a cake of bread. With that refreshment I could perhaps regain a degree of energy; without it, it would be difficult to proceed. The wish to have some strength and some vigour returned to me as soon as I was amongst my fellow-beings. I felt it would be degrading to faint with hunger on the causeway of a hamlet. Had I nothing about me I could offer in exchange for one of these rolls? I considered. I had a small silk handkerchief tied round my throat; I had my gloves. I could hardly tell how men and women in extremities of destitution proceeded. I did not know whether either of these articles would be accepted: probably they would not; but I must try.

I entered the shop: a woman was there. Seeing a respectably-dressed person, a lady as she supposed, she came forward with civility. How could she serve me? I was seized with shame: my tongue would not utter the request I had prepared. I dared not offer her the half-worn gloves, the creased handkerchief: besides, I felt it would be absurd. I only begged permission to sit down a moment, as I was tired. Disappointed in the expectation of a customer, she coolly acceded to my request. She pointed to a seat; I sank into it. I felt sorely urged to weep; but conscious how unseasonable such a manifestation would be, I restrained it. Soon I asked her, "if there were any dressmaker or plain-work-woman in the village?"

"Yes; two or three. Quite as many as there was employment for."

I reflected. I was driven to the point now. I was brought face to face with Necessity. I stood in the position of one without a resource: without a friend; without a coin. I must do something. What? I must apply somewhere. Where?

"Did she know of any place in the neighbourhood where a servant was wanted?"

"Nay; she couldn't say."

"What was the chief trade in this place? What did most of the people do?"

"Some were farm labourers; a good deal worked at Mr. Oliver's needle-factory, and at the foundry."

"Did Mr. Oliver employ women?"

"Nay; it was men's work."

"And what do the women do?"

"I knawn't," was the answer. "Some does one thing, and some another. Poor folk mun get on as they can."

She seemed to be tired of my questions: and, indeed, what claim had I to importune her? A neighbour or two came in; my chair was evidently wanted. I took leave.

I passed up the street, looking as I went at all the houses to the right hand and to the left: but I could discover no pretext, nor see an inducement, to enter any. I rambled round the hamlet, going sometimes to a little distance and returning again, for an hour or more. Much exhausted, and suffering greatly now for want of food, I turned aside into a lane and sat down under the hedge. Ere many minutes had elapsed, I was again on my feet, however, and again searching something—a resource, or at least an informant. A pretty little house stood at the top of the lane, with a garden before it; exquisitely neat, and brilliantly blooming. I stopped at it. What business had I to approach the white door, or touch the glittering knocker? In what way could it possibly be the interest of the inhabitants of that dwelling to serve me? Yet I drew near and knocked. A mild-looking, cleanly-attired young woman opened the door. In such a voice as might be expected from a hopeless heart and fainting frame—a voice wretchedly low and faltering—I asked if a servant was wanted here?

"No," said she; "we do not keep a servant."

"Can you tell me where I could get employment of any kind?" I continued. "I am a stranger, without acquaintance, in this place. I want some work: no matter what."

But it was not her business to think for me, or to seek a place for me: besides, in her eyes, how doubtful must have appeared my character, position, tale. She shook her head, she "was sorry she could give me no information," and the white door closed, quite gently and civilly: but it shut me out. If she had held it open a little longer, I believe I should have begged a piece of bread; for I was now brought low.

I could not bear to return to the sordid village; where, besides, no prospect of aid was visible. I should have longed rather to deviate to a wood I saw not far off, which appeared in its thick shade to offer inviting shelter; but I was so sick, so weak, so gnawed with nature's cravings, instinct kept me roaming round abodes where there was a chance of food. Solitude would be no solitude—rest no rest— while the vulture, hunger, thus sank beak and talons in my side.

I drew near houses; I left them, and came back again, and again I wandered away: always repelled by the consciousness of having no claim to ask—no right to expect interest in my isolated lot. Meantime, the afternoon advanced, while I thus wandered about like a lost and starving dog. In crossing a field, I saw the church spire before me: I hastened towards it. Near the churchyard, and in the middle of a garden, stood a well-built though small house, which I had no doubt was the parsonage. I remembered that strangers who arrive at a place where they have no friends, and who want employment, sometimes apply to the clergyman for introduction and aid. It is the clergyman's function to help—at least with advice— those who wished to help themselves. I seemed to have something like a right to seek counsel here. Renewing then, my courage, and gathering my feeble remains of strength, I pushed on. I reached the house, and knocked at the kitchen-door. An old woman opened: I asked was this the parsonage?

"Yes."

"Was the clergyman in?"

"No."

"Would he be in soon?"

"No, he was gone from home."

"To a distance?"

"Not so far—happen three mile. He had been called away by the sudden death of his father: he was at Marsh End now, and would very likely stay there a fortnight longer."

"Was there any lady of the house?"

"Nay, there was naught but her, and she was housekeeper;" and of her, reader, I could not bear to ask the relief for want of which I was sinking; I could not yet beg; and again I crawled away.

Once more I took off my handkerchief—once more I thought of the cakes of bread in the little shop. Oh, for but a crust! for but one mouthful to allay the pang of famine! Instinctively I turned my face again to the village; I found the shop again, and I went in; and though others were there besides the woman, I ventured the request: "Would she give me a roll for this handkerchief?"

She looked at me with evident suspicion: "Nay, she never sold stuff i' that way."

Almost desperate, I asked for half a cake; she again refused. "How could she tell where I had got the handkerchief," she said.

"Would she take my gloves?"

"No! what could she do with them?"

Reader, it is not pleasant to dwell on these details. Some say there is enjoyment in looking back to painful experience past; but at this day I can scarcely bear to review the times to which I allude: the moral degradation, blent with the physical suffering, form too distressing a recollection ever to be willingly dwelt on. I blamed none of those who repulsed me. I felt it was what was to be expected, and what could not be helped: an ordinary beggar is frequently an object of suspicion; a well-dressed beggar inevitably so. To be sure what I begged was employment: but whose business was it to provide me with employment? Not, certainly, that of persons who saw me then for the first time, and who knew nothing about my character. And as to the woman who would not take my handkerchief in exchange for her bread, why, she was right; if the offer appeared to her sinister, or the exchange unprofitable. Let me condense now. I am sick of the subject.

A little before dark I passed a farm-house, at the open door of which the farmer was sitting, eating his supper of bread and cheese; I stopped, and said:—

"Will you give me a piece of bread? for I am very hungry." He cast on me a glance of surprise; but without answering, he cut a thick slice from his loaf, and gave it to me. I imagine he did not think I was a beggar, but only an eccentric sort of lady, who had taken a fancy to his brown loaf. As soon as I was out of sight of his house, I sat down and ate it.

I could not hope to get a lodging under a roof, and sought it in the wood I have before alluded to. But my night was wretched, my rest broken: the ground was damp, the air cold: besides, intruders passed near me more than once, and I had again and again to change my quarters: no sense of safety or tranquillity befriended me. Towards morning it rained; the whole of the following day was wet. Do not ask me, reader, to give a minute account of that day; as before, I sought work; as before, I was repulsed; as before, I starved; but once did food pass my lips. At the door of a cottage I saw a little girl about to throw a mess of cold porridge into a pig trough. "Will you give me that?" I asked.

She stared at me. "Mother!" she exclaimed; "there is a woman wants me to give her these porridge."

"Well, lass," replied a voice within, "give it her if she's a beggar. T' pig doesn't want it."

The girl emptied the stiffened mould into my hand, and I devoured it ravenously.

As the wet twilight deepened, I stopped in a solitary bridle path, which I had been pursuing an hour or more.

"My strength is quite failing me," I said, in soliloquy. "I feel I cannot go much further. Shall I be an outcast again this night? While the rain descends so, must I lay my head on the cold, drenched ground! I fear I cannot do otherwise: for who will receive me? But it will be very dreadful: with this feeling of hunger, faintness, chill, and this sense of desolation—this total prostration of hope. In all likelihood, though, I should die before morning. And why cannot I reconcile myself to the

prospect of death? Why do I struggle to retain a valueless life? Because I know, or believe, Mr. Rochester is still living: and then, to die of want and cold, is a fate to which nature cannot submit passively. Oh, Providence! sustain me a little longer! Aid—direct me!''

My glazed eye wandered over the dim and misty landscape. I saw I had strayed far from the village: it was quite out of sight. The very cultivation surrounding it had disappeared. I had, by cross-ways and by-paths, once more drawn near the tract of moorland; and now, only a few fields, almost as wild and unproductive as the heath from which they were scarcely reclaimed, lay between me and the dusky hill.

''Well, I would rather die yonder than in a street, or on a frequented road,'' I reflected. ''And far better that crows and ravens—if any ravens there be in these regions—should pick my flesh from my bones, than that they should be prisoned in a workhouse coffin and moulder in a pauper's grave.''

To the hill, then, I turned. I reached it. It remained now only to find a hollow where I could lie down, and feel at least hidden, if not secure: but all the surface of the waste looked level. It showed no variation but of tint: green, where rush and moss overgrew the marshes; black, where the dry soil bore only heath. Dark as it was getting, I could still see these changes: though but as mere alterations of light and shade: for colour had faded with the daylight.

My eye still roved over the sullen swell, and along the moor-edge, vanishing amidst the wildest scenery; when at one dim point, far in among the marshes and the ridges, a light sprang up. ''That is an *ignis fatuus*,'' was my first thought; and I expected it would soon vanish. It burnt on, however, quite steadily; neither receding nor advancing. ''Is it, then, a bonfire just kindled?'' I questioned. I watched to see whether it would spread: but no; as it did not diminish, so it did not enlarge. ''It may be a candle in a house,'' I then conjectured: ''but if so, I can never reach it. It is much too far away: and were it within a yard of me, what would it avail? I should but knock at the door to have it shut in my face.''

And I sank down where I stood, and hid my face against the ground. I lay still a while: the night-wind swept over the hill and over me, and died moaning in the distance; the rain fell fast, wetting me afresh to the skin. Could I but have stiffened to the still frost—the friendly numbness of death—it might have pelted on: I should not have felt it; but my yet living flesh shuddered to its chilling influence. I rose ere long.

The light was yet there: shining dim, but constant, through the rain. I tried to walk again: I dragged my exhausted limbs slowly towards it. It led me aslant over the hill, through a wide bog; which would have been impassable in winter, and was splashy and shaking even now, in the height of summer. Here I fell twice; but as often I rose and rallied my faculties. This light was my forlorn hope: I must gain it.

Having crossed the marsh, I saw a trace of white over the moor. I approached it; it was a road or a track: it led straight up to the light, which now beamed from a sort of knoll, amidst a clump of trees—firs, apparently, from what I could distinguish of the character of their forms and foliage through the gloom. My star vanished as I drew near: some obstacle had intervened between me and it. I put out my hand to feel the dark mass before me; I discriminated the rough stones of a low wall—above it, something like palisades, and within, a high and prickly hedge. I groped on. Again a whitish object gleamed before me: it was a gate—a wicket; it moved on its hinges as I touched it. On each side stood a sable bush—holly or yew.

Entering the gate and passing the shrubs, the silhouette of a house rose to view; black, low, and rather long; but the guiding light shone nowhere. All was obscurity. Were the inmates retired to rest? I feared it must be so. In seeking the door, I turned an angle: there shot out the friendly gleam again, from the lozenged panes

of a very small latticed window, within a foot of the ground; made still smaller by the growth of ivy or some other creeping plant, whose leaves clustered thick over the portion of the house wall in which it was set. The aperture was so screened and narrow, that curtain or shutter had been deemed unnecessary; and when I stooped down and put aside the spray of foliage shooting over it, I could see all within. I could see clearly a room with a sanded floor, clean scoured; a dresser of walnut, with pewter plates ranged in rows, reflecting the redness and radiance of a glowing peat-fire. I could see a clock, a white deal table, some chairs. The candle, whose ray had been my beacon, burnt on the table; and by its light an elderly woman, somewhat rough-looking, but scrupulously clean, like all about her, was knitting a stocking.

I noted these objects cursorily only—in them there was nothing extraordinary. A group of more interest appeared near the hearth, sitting still amidst the rosy peace and warmth suffusing it. Two young, graceful women—ladies in every point—sat, one on a low rocking-chair, the other on a lower stool; both wore deep mourning of crape and bombazeen, which sombre garb singularly set off very fair necks and faces: a large old pointer dog rested its massive head on the knee of one girl—in the lap of the other was cushioned a black cat.

A strange place was this humble kitchen for such occupants! Who were they? They could not be the daughters of the elderly person at the table; for she looked like a rustic, and they were all delicacy and cultivation. I had nowhere seen such faces as theirs: and yet, as I gazed on them, I seemed intimate with every lineament. I cannot call them handsome—they were too pale and grave for the word: as they each bent over a book, they looked thoughtful almost to severity. A stand between them supported a second candle and two great volumes, to which they frequently referred; comparing them seemingly with the smaller books they held in their hands, like people consulting a dictionary to aid them in the task of translation. This scene was as silent as if all the figures had been shadows, and the fire-lit apartment a picture: so hushed was it, I could hear the cinders fall from the grate, the clock tick in its obscure corner; and I even fancied I could distinguish the click-click of the woman's knitting-needles. When, therefore, a voice broke the strange stillness at last, it was audible enough to me.

"Listen, Diana," said one of the absorbed students: "Franz and old Daniel are together in the night-time, and Franz is telling a dream from which he has awakened in terror—listen!" And in a low voice she read something, of which not one word was intelligible to me; for it was in an unknown tongue—neither French nor Latin. Whether it were Greek or German I could not tell.

"That is strong," she said, when she had finished: "I relish it." The other girl, who had lifted her head to listen to her sister, repeated, while she gazed at the fire, a line of what had been read. At a later day, I knew the language and the book; therefore I will here quote the line: though when I first heard it, it was only like a stroke on sounding brass to me—conveying no meaning:—

" 'Da trat hervor Einer, anzusehen wie die Sternen Nacht.' Good! good!" she exclaimed, while her dark and deep eye sparkled. "There you have a dim and mighty archangel, fitly set before you! The line is worth a hundred pages of fustian. 'Ich wäge die Gedanken in der Schale meines Zornes und die Werke mit dem Gewichte meines Grimms.' I like it!"

Both were again silent.

"Is there ony country where they talk i' that way?" asked the old woman, looking up from her knitting.

"Yes, Hannah—a far larger country than England; where they talk in no other way."

"Well, for sure case, I knawn't how they can understand t' one t' other: and if either o' ye went there, ye could tell what they said, I guess?"

"We could probably tell something of what they said, but not all—for we are not as clever as you think us, Hannah. We don't speak German, and we cannot read it without a dictionary to help us."

"And what good does it do you?"

"We mean to teach it some time—or at least the elements, as they say; and then we shall get more money than we do now."

"Varry like: but give ower studying: ye've done enough for to-night."

"I think we have: at least I'm tired. Mary, are you?"

"Mortally: after all, it's tough work fagging away at a language with no master but a lexicon."

"It is: especially such a language as this crabbed but glorious Deutsch. I wonder when St. John will come home."

"Surely he will not be long now: it is just ten" (looking at a little gold watch she drew from her girdle). "It rains fast. Hannah, will you have the goodness to look at the fire in the parlour?"

The woman rose: she opened a door, through which I dimly saw a passage: soon I heard her stir a fire in an inner room; she presently came back.

"Ah, childer!" said she, "it fair troubles me to go into yond' room now; it looks so lonesome wi' the chair empty and set back in a corner."

She wiped her eyes with her apron: the two girls, grave before, looked sad now.

"But he is in a better place," continued Hannah: "we shouldn't wish him here again. And then, nobody need to have a quieter death nor he had."

"You say he never mentioned us?" inquired one of the ladies.

"He hadn't time, bairn: he was gone in a minute—was your father. He had been a bit ailing like the day before, but naught to signify; and when Mr. St. John asked if he would like either o' ye to be sent for, he fair laughed at him. He began again with a bit of a heaviness in his head the next day—that is, a fortnight sin'—and he went to sleep and niver wakened; he wor a'most stark when your brother went into t' chamber and fand him. Ah, childer! that's t' last o' t' old stock—for ye and Mr. St. John is like of a different soart to them 'at's gone; for all your mother wor mich i' your way; and a'most as book-learned. She wor the pictur' o' ye, Mary: Diana is more like your father."

I thought them so similar I could not tell where the old servant (for such I now concluded her to be) saw the difference. Both were fair complexioned and slenderly made; both possessed faces full of distinction and intelligence. One, to be sure, had hair a shade darker than the other, and there was a difference in their style of wearing it: Mary's pale brown locks were parted and braided smooth; Diana's duskier tresses covered her neck with thick curls. The clock struck ten.

"You'll want your supper, I am sure," observed Hannah; "and so will Mr. St. John when he comes in."

And she proceeded to prepare the meal. The ladies rose; they seemed about to withdraw to the parlour. Till this moment, I had been so intent on watching them, their appearance and conversation had excited in me so keen an interest, I had half-forgotten my own wretched position: now it recurred to me. More desolate, more desperate than ever, it seemed from contrast. And how impossible did it appear to touch the inmates of this house with concern on my behalf; to make them believe in the truth of my wants and woes—to induce them to vouchsafe a rest for my wanderings! As I groped out the door, and knocked at it hesitatingly, I felt that last idea to be a mere chimera. Hannah opened.

"What do you want?" she inquired, in a voice of surprise, as she surveyed me by the light of the candle she held.

"May I speak to your mistresses?" I said.

"You had better tell me what you have to say to them. Where do you come from?"

"I am a stranger."

"What is your business here at this hour?"

"I want a night's shelter in an out-house or anywhere, and a morsel of bread to eat."

Distrust, the very feeling I dreaded, appeared in Hannah's face. "I'll give you a piece of bread," she said, after a pause; "but we can't take in a vagrant to lodge. It isn't likely."

"Do let me speak to your mistresses."

"No; not I. What can they do for you? You should not be roving about now; it looks very ill."

"But where shall I go if you drive me away? What shall I do?"

"Oh, I'll warrant you know where to go, and what to do. Mind you don't do wrong, that's all. Here is a penny; now go"——

"A penny cannot feed me, and I have no strength to go farther. Don't shut the door:—oh, don't, for God's sake!"

"I must; the rain is driving in"——

"Tell the young ladies.—Let me see them"——

"Indeed, I will not. You are not what you ought to be, or you wouldn't make such a noise. Move off."

"But I must die if I am turned away."

"Not you. I'm fear'd you have some ill plans agate, that bring you about folk's houses at this time o' night. If you've any followers—housebreakers or such like—anywhere near, you may tell them we are not by ourselves in the house; we have a gentleman, and dogs, and guns." Here the honest but inflexible servant clapped the door to and bolted it within.

This was the climax. A pang of exquisite suffering—a throe of true despair—rent and heaved my heart. Worn out, indeed, I was; not another step could I stir. I sank on the wet door-step: I groaned—I wrung my hands—I wept in utter anguish. Oh, this spectre of death! Oh, this last hour, approaching in such horror! Alas, this isolation—this banishment from my kind! Not only the anchor of home, but the footing of fortitude was gone—at least for a moment: but the last I soon endeavoured to regain.

"I can but die," I said, "and I believe in God. Let me try to wait His will in silence."

These words I not only thought, but uttered; and thrusting back all my misery into my heart, I made an effort to compel it to remain there—dumb and still.

"All men must die," said a voice quite close at hand; "but all are not condemned to meet a lingering and premature doom, such as yours would be if you perished here of want."

"Who or what speaks?" I asked, terrified at the unexpected sound, and incapable now of deriving from any occurrence a hope of aid. A form was near—what form, the pitch-dark night and my enfeebled vision prevented me from distinguishing. With a loud long knock, the new comer appealed to the door.

"Is it you, Mr. St. John?" cried Hannah.

"Yes—yes; open quickly."

"Well, how wet and cold you must be, such a wild night as it is! Come in—your sisters are quite uneasy about you, and I believe there are bad folks about. There has been a beggar-woman—I declare she is not gone yet!—laid down there. Get up! for shame! Move off, I say!"

"Hush, Hannah! I have a word to say to the woman. You have done your duty in excluding, now let me do mine in admitting her. I was near, and listened to both you and her. I think this is a peculiar case—I must at least examine into it. Young woman, rise, and pass before me into the house."

With difficulty I obeyed him. Presently I stood within that clean, bright kitchen—on the very hearth—trembling, sickening; conscious of an aspect in the last degree

ghastly, wild, and weather-beaten. The two ladies, their brother, Mr. St. John, the old servant, were all gazing at me.

"St. John, who is it?" I heard one ask.

"I cannot tell: I found her at the door," was the reply.

"She does look white," said Hannah.

"As white as clay or death," was responded. "She will fall: let her sit."

And indeed my head swam: I dropped; but a chair received me. I still possessed my senses; though just now I could not speak.

"Perhaps a little water would restore her. Hannah, fetch some. But she is worn to nothing. How very thin, and how very bloodless!"

"A mere spéctre!"

"Is she ill, or only famished?"

"Famished, I think. Hannah, is that milk? Give it me, and a piece of bread."

Diana (I knew her by the long curls which I saw drooping between me and the fire as she bent over me) broke some bread, dipped it in milk, and put it to my lips. Her face was near mine: I saw there was pity in it, and I felt sympathy in her hurried breathing. In her simple words, too, the same balm-like emotion spoke: "Try to eat."

"Yes—try," repeated Mary gently; and Mary's hand removed my sodden bonnet and lifted my head. I tasted what they offered me: feebly at first, eagerly soon.

"Not too much at first—restrain her," said the brother; "she has had enough." And he withdrew the cup of milk and the plate of bread.

"A little more, St. John—look at the avidity in her eyes."

"No more at present, sister. Try if she can speak now—ask her her name."

I felt I could speak, and I answered—"My name is Jane Elliott." Anxious as ever to avoid discovery, I had before resolved to assume an *alias*.

"And where do you live? Where are your friends?"

I was silent.

"Can we send for any one you know?"

I shook my head.

"What account can you give of yourself?"

Somehow, now that I had once crossed the threshold of this house, and once was brought face to face with its owners, I felt no longer outcast, vagrant, and disowned by the wide world. I dared to put off the mendicant—to resume my natural manner and character. I began once more to know myself; and when Mr. St. John demanded an account—which at present I was far too weak to render—I said after a brief pause,—

"Sir, I can give you no details to-night."

"But what, then," said he, "do you expect me to do for you?"

"Nothing," I replied. My strength sufficed for but short answers. Diana took the word:—

"Do you mean," she asked, "that we have now given you what aid you require? and that we may dismiss you to the moor and the rainy night?"

I looked at her. She had, I thought, a remarkable countenance; instinct both with power and goodness. I took sudden courage. Answering her compassionate gaze with a smile, I said: "I will trust you. If I were a masterless and stray dog, I know that you would not turn me from your hearth to-night: as it is, I really have no fear. Do with me and for me as you like; but excuse me from much discourse— my breath is short—I feel a spasm when I speak." All three surveyed me, and all three were silent.

"Hannah," said Mr. St. John, at last, "let her sit there at present, and ask her no questions; in ten minutes more, give her the remainder of that milk and bread. Mary and Diana, let us go into the parlour and talk the matter over."

They withdrew. Very soon one of the ladies returned—I could not tell which. A kind of pleasant stupor was stealing over me as I sat by the genial fire. In an

under tone she gave some directions to Hannah. Ere long, with the servant's aid, I contrived to mount a staircase; my dripping clothes were removed; soon, a warm, dry bed received me. I thanked God—experienced amidst unutterable exhaustion a glow of grateful joy—and slept.

Chapter XXIX

THE recollection of about three days and nights succeeding this is very dim in my mind. I can recall some sensations felt in the interval; but few thoughts framed, and no actions performed. I knew I was in a small room, and in a narrow bed. To that bed I seemed to have grown; I lay on it motionless as a stone; and to have torn me from it would have been almost to kill me. I took no note of the lapse of time—of the change from morning to noon, from noon to evening. I observed when any one entered or left the apartment; I could even tell who they were; I could understand what was said when the speaker stood near to me; but I could not answer; to open my lips or move my limbs was equally impossible. Hannah, the servant, was my most frequent visitor. Her coming disturbed me. I had a feeling that she wished me away: that she did not understand me or my circumstances: that she was prejudiced against me. Diana and Mary appeared in the chamber once or twice a day. They would whisper sentences of this sort at my bedside:—

"It is very well we took her in."

"Yes; she would certainly have been found dead at the door in the morning, had she been left out all night. I wonder what she has gone through?"

"Strange hardships, I imagine—poor, emaciated, pallid wanderer!"

"She is not an uneducated person, I should think, by her manner of speaking; her accent was quite pure; and the clothes she took off, though splashed and wet, were little worn and fine."

"She has a peculiar face; fleshless and haggard as it is, I rather like it; and when in good health and animated, I can fancy her physiognomy would be agreeable."

Never once in their dialogues did I hear a syllable of regret at the hospitality they had extended to me; or of suspicion of, or aversion to, myself. I was comforted.

Mr. St. John came but once: he looked at me, and said my state of lethargy was the result of reaction from excessive and protracted fatigue. He pronounced it needless to send for a doctor: nature, he was sure, would manage best, left to herself. He said every nerve had been overstrained in some way, and the whole system must sleep torpid a while. There was no disease. He imagined my recovery would be rapid enough when once commenced. These opinions he delivered in a few words, in a quiet, low voice; and added, after a pause, in the tone of a man little accustomed to expansive comment, "rather an unusual physiognomy; certainly, not indicative of vulgarity or degradation."

"Far otherwise," responded Diana. "To speak truth, St. John, my heart rather warms to the poor little soul. I wish we may be able to benefit her permanently."

"That is hardly likely," was the reply. "You will find she is some young lady who has had a misunderstanding with her friends and has probably injudiciously left them. We may, perhaps, succeed in restoring her to them, if she is not obstinate: but I trace lines of force in her face which make me sceptical of her tractability." He stood considering me some minutes; then added, "She looks sensible, but not at all handsome."

"She is so ill, St. John."

"Ill or well, she would always be plain. The grace and harmony of beauty are quite wanting in those features."

On the third day, I was better; on the fourth, I could speak, move, rise in bed, and turn. Hannah had brought me some gruel and dry toast, about, as I supposed, the dinner hour. I had eaten with relish: the food was good—void of the feverish flavour which had hitherto poisoned what I had swallowed. When she left me, I felt comparatively strong and revived: ere long satiety of repose, and desire for action stirred me. I wished to rise; but what could I put on? Only my damp and bemired apparel; in which I had slept on the ground and fallen in the marsh. I felt ashamed to appear before my benefactors so clad. I was spared the humiliation.

On a chair by the bedside were all my own things, clean and dry. My black silk frock hung against the wall. The traces of the bog were removed from it; the creases left by the wet smoothed out: it was quite decent. My very shoes and stockings were purified and rendered presentable. There were the means of washing in the room, and a comb and brush to smooth my hair. After a weary process, and resting every five minutes, I succeeded in dressing myself. My clothes hung loose on me; for I was much wasted, but I covered deficiencies with a shawl, and once more, clean and respectable-looking—no speck of the dirt, no trace of the disorder I so hated, and which seemed so to degrade me, left—I crept down a stone staircase with the aid of the banisters, to a narrow low passage, and found my way presently to the kitchen.

It was full of the fragrance of new bread, and the warmth of a generous fire. Hannah was baking. Prejudices, it is well known, are most difficult to eradicate from the heart whose soil has never been loosened or fertilised by education: they grow there, firm as weeds among stones. Hannah had been cold and stiff, indeed, at the first: latterly she had begun to relent a little; and when she saw me come in tidy and well-dressed, she even smiled.

"What, you have got up?" she said. "You are better, then. You may sit you down in my chair on the hearth-stone, if you will."

She pointed to the rocking chair: I took it. She bustled about, examining me every now and then with the corner of her eye. Turning to me, as she took some loaves from the oven, she asked, bluntly—

"Did you ever go a-begging afore you came here?"

I was indignant for a moment; but remembering that anger was out of the question, and that I had indeed appeared as a beggar to her, I answered quietly; but still not without a certain marked firmness—

"You are mistaken in supposing me a beggar. I am no beggar; any more than yourself or your young ladies."

After a pause, she said, "I dunnut understand that: you've no house, nor no brass, I guess?"

"The want of house or brass (by which I suppose you mean money) does not make a beggar in your sense of the word."

"Are you book-learned?" she inquired, presently.

"Yes, very."

"But you've never been to a boarding-school!"

"I was at a boarding-school eight years."

She opened her eyes wide. "Whatever cannot ye keep yourself for, then?"

"I have kept myself; and, I trust, shall keep myself again. What are you going to do with these gooseberries?" I inquired, as she brought out a basket of the fruit.

"Mak'em into pies."

"Give them to me and I'll pick them."

"Nay; I dunnut want ye to do nought."

"But I must do something. Let me have them."

She consented; and she even brought me a clean towel to spread over my dress, "lest," as she said, "I should mucky it."

"Ye've not been used to sarvant's wark, I see by your hands," she remarked. "Happen ye've been a dressmaker."

"No, you are wrong. And, now, never mind what I have been: don't trouble your head further about me; but tell me the name of the house where we are."

"Some calls it Marsh End, and some calls it Moor House."

"And the gentleman who lives here is called Mr. St. John?"

"Nay; he doesn't live here: he is only staying a while. When he is at home, he is in his own parish at Morton."

"That village a few miles off?"

"Aye."

"And what is he?"

"He is a parson."

I remembered the answer of the old housekeeper at the parsonage, when I had asked to see the clergyman. "This, then, was his father's residence?"

"Aye; old Mr. Rivers lived here, and his father, and grandfather, and gurt (great) grandfather afore him."

"The name, then, of that gentleman, is Mr. St. John Rivers?"

"Aye; St. John is like his kirstened name."

"And his sisters are called Diana and Mary Rivers?"

"Yes."

"Their father is dead?"

"Dead three weeks sin' of a stroke."

"They have no mother?"

"The mistress has been dead this mony a year."

"Have you lived with the family long?"

"I've lived here thirty year. I nursed them all three."

"That proves you must have been an honest and faithful servant. I will say so much for you, though you have had the incivility to call me a beggar."

She again regarded me with a surprised stare. "I believe," she said, "I was quite mista'en in my thoughts of you: but there is so mony cheats goes about, you mun forgie me."

"And though," I continued, rather severely, "you wished to turn me from the door, on a night when you should not have shut out a dog."

"Well, it was hard: but what can a body do? I thought more o' the childer nor of mysel: poor things! They've like nobody to tak' care on'em but me. I'm like to look sharpish."

I maintained a grave silence for some minutes.

"You munnut think too hardly of me," she again remarked.

"But I do think hardly of you," I said; "and I'll tell you why—not so much because you refused to give me shelter, or regarded me as an impostor, as because you just now made it a species of reproach that I had no 'brass,' and no house. Some of the best people that ever lived have been as destitute as I am; and if you are a Christian, you ought not to consider poverty a crime."

"No more I ought," said she: "Mr. St. John tells me so too; and I see I wor wrang—but I've clear a different notion on you now to what I had. You look a raight down dacent little crater."

"That will do—I forgive you now. Shake hands."

She put her floury and horny hand into mine; another and heartier smile illumined her rough face; and from that moment we were friends.

Hannah was evidently fond of talking. While I picked the fruit, and she made the paste for the pies, she proceeded to give me sundry details about her deceased master and mistress, and "the childer," as she called the young people.

Old Mr. Rivers, she said, was a plain man enough; but a gentleman, and of as ancient a family as could be found. Marsh End had belonged to the Rivers' ever since it was a house: and it was, she affirmed, "aboon two hundred year old—for all it looked but a small, humble place, naught to compare wi' Mr. Oliver's grand hall down i' Morton Vale. But she could remember Bill Oliver's father a journeyman

needle-maker; and th' Rivers wor gentry i' th' owd days o' th' Henrys, as onybody might see by looking into th' registers i' Morton Church vestry.'' Still, she allowed, ''the owd maister was like other folk—naught mich out o' t' common way: stark mad o' shooting, and farming, and sich like.'' The mistress was different. She was a great reader, and studied a deal; and the ''bairns'' had taken after her. There was nothing like them in these parts, nor ever had been; they had liked learning, all three, almost from the time they could speak; and they had always been ''of a mak' of their own.'' Mr. St. John, when he grew up, would go to college and be a parson; and the girls, as soon as they left school, would seek places as governesses: for they had told her their father had some years ago lost a great deal of money, by a man he had trusted turning bankrupt; and as he was now not rich enough to give them fortunes, they must provide for themselves. They had lived very little at home for a long while, and were only come now to stay a few weeks on account of their father's death: but they did so like Marsh End and Morton, and all these moors and hills about. They had been in London, and many other grand towns; but they always said there was no place like home; and then they were so agreeable with each other—never fell out nor ''threaped.'' She did not know where there was such a family for being united.

Having finished my task of gooseberry picking, I asked where the two ladies and their brother were now.

''Gone over to Morton for a walk; but they would be back in half an hour to tea.''

They returned within the time Hannah had allotted them: they entered by the kitchen door. Mr. St. John, when he saw me, merely bowed and passed through; the two ladies stopped: Mary, in a few words, kindly and calmly expressed the pleasure she felt in seeing me well enough to be able to come down; Diana took my hand: she shook her head at me.

''You should have waited for my leave to descend,'' she said. ''You still look very pale—and so thin! Poor child!—poor girl!''

Diana had a voice toned, to my ear, like the cooing of a dove. She possessed eyes whose gaze I delighted to encounter. Her whole face seemed to me full of charm. Mary's countenance was equally intelligent—her features equally pretty: but her expression was more reserved; and her manners, though gentle, more distant. Diana looked and spoke with a certain authority: she had a will, evidently. It was my nature to feel pleasure in yielding to authority supported like hers; and to bend, where my conscience and self-respect permitted, to an active will.

''And what business have you here?'' she continued. ''It is not your place. Mary and I sit in the kitchen sometimes, because at home we like to be free, even to licence—but you are a visitor, and must go into the parlour.''

''I am very well here.''

''Not at all—with Hannah bustling about and covering you with flour.''

''Besides, the fire is too hot for you,'' interposed Mary.

''To be sure,'' added her sister. ''Come, you must be obedient.'' And still holding my hand she made me rise, and led me into the inner room.

''Sit there,'' she said, placing me on the sofa, ''while we take our things off and get the tea ready; it is another privilege we exercise in our little moorland home—to prepare our own meals when we are so inclined; or when Hannah is baking, brewing, washing, or ironing.''

She closed the door, leaving me solus with Mr. St. John, who sat opposite; a book or newspaper in his hand. I examined, first, the parlour, and then its occupant.

The parlour was rather a small room, very plainly furnished; yet comfortable, because clean and neat. The old-fashioned chairs were very bright, and the walnut-wood table was like a looking-glass. A few strange, antique portraits of the men and women of other days decorated the stained walls; a cupboard with glass doors contained some books and an ancient set of china. There was no superfluous

ornament in the room—not one modern piece of furniture, save a brace of work-boxes and a lady's desk in rosewood, which stood on a side-table: everything—including the carpet and curtains—looked at once well worn and well saved.

Mr. St. John—sitting as still as one of the dusky pictures on the walls; keeping his eyes fixed on the page he perused and his lips mutely sealed—was easy enough to examine. Had he been a statue instead of a man, he could not have been easier. He was young—perhaps from twenty-eight to thirty—tall, slender; his face riveted the eye; it was like a Greek face, very pure in outline: quite a straight, classic nose; quite an Athenian mouth and chin. It is seldom, indeed, an English face comes so near the antique models as did his. He might well be a little shocked at the irregularity of my lineaments, his own being so harmonious. His eyes were large and blue, with brown lashes; his high forehead, colourless as ivory, was partially streaked over by careless locks of fair hair.

This is a gentle delineation, is it not, reader? Yet he whom it describes scarcely impressed one with the idea of a gentle, a yielding, an impressible, or even of a placid nature. Quiescent as he now sat, there was something about his nostril, his mouth, his brow, which, to my perceptions, indicated elements within either restless, or hard, or eager. He did not speak to me one word nor even direct to me one glance, till his sisters returned. Diana, as she passed in and out, in the course of preparing tea, brought me a little cake, baked on the top of the oven.

"Eat that now," she said: "you must be hungry. Hannah says you have had nothing but some gruel since breakfast."

I did not refuse it, for my appetite was awakened and keen. Mr. Rivers now closed his book, approached the table, and, as he took a seat, fixed his blue pictorial-looking eyes full on me. There was an unceremonious directness, a searching, decided steadfastness in his gaze now, which told that intention, and not diffidence, had hitherto kept it averted from the stranger.

"You are very hungry," he said.

"I am, sir." It is my way—it always was my way, by instinct—ever to meet the brief with brevity, the direct with plainness.

"It is well for you that a low fever has forced you to abstain for the last three days: there would have been danger in yielding to the cravings of your appetite at first. Now you may eat; though still not immoderately."

"I trust I shall not eat long at your expense, sir," was my very clumsily-contrived, unpolished answer.

"No," he said, coolly: "when you have indicated to us the residence of your friends, we can write to them, and you may be restored to home."

"That, I must plainly tell you, is out of my power to do; being absolutely without home and friends."

The three looked at me; but not distrustfully; I felt there was no suspicion in their glances: there was more of curiosity. I speak particularly of the young ladies. St. John's eyes, though clear enough in a literal sense, in a figurative one were difficult to fathom. He seemed to use them rather as instruments to search other people's thoughts, than as agents to reveal his own: the which combination of keenness and reserve was considerably more calculated to embarrass than to encourage.

"Do you mean to say," he asked, "that you are completely isolated from every connection?"

"I do. Not a tie links me to any living thing: not a claim do I possess to admittance under any roof in England."

"A most singular position at your age!"

Here I saw his glance directed to my hands, which were folded on the table before me. I wondered what he sought there: his words soon explained the quest.

"You have never been married? You are a spinster?"

Diana laughed. "Why, she can't be above seventeen or eighteen years old, St. John," she said.

"I am near nineteen; but I am not married. No."

I felt a burning glow mount to my face; for bitter and agitating recollections were awakened by the allusion to marriage. They all saw the embarrassment, and the emotion. Diana and Mary relieved me by turning their eyes elsewhere than to my crimsoned visage; but the colder and sterner brother continued to gaze, till the trouble he had excited forced out tears as well as colour.

"Where did you last reside?" he now asked.

"You are too inquisitive, St. John," murmured Mary, in a low voice; but he leaned over the table and required an answer, by a second firm and piercing look.

"The name of the place where, and of the person with whom I lived, is my secret," I replied, concisely.

"Which, if you like, you have, in my opinion, a right to keep, both from St. John and every other questioner," remarked Diana.

"Yet if I know nothing about you or your history, I cannot help you," he said. "And you need help: do you not?"

"I need it, and I seek it; so far, sir, that some true philanthropist will put me in the way of getting work which I can do, and the remuneration for which will keep me: if but in the barest necessaries of life."

"I know not whether I am a true philanthropist; yet I am willing to aid you to the utmost of my power, in a purpose so honest. First, then, tell me what you have been accustomed to do, and what you *can* do."

I had now swallowed my tea. I was mightily refreshed by the beverage; as much so as a giant with wine: it gave new tone to my unstrung nerves, and enabled me to address this penetrating young judge steadily.

"Mr. Rivers," I said, turning to him, and looking at him, as he looked at me, openly and without diffidence, "you and your sisters have done me a great service—the greatest man can do his fellow-being; you have rescued me, by your noble hospitality, from death. This benefit conferred gives you an unlimited claim on my gratitude; and a claim to a certain extent, on my confidence. I will tell you as much of the history of the wanderer you have harboured, as I can tell without compromising my own peace of mind—my own security, moral and physical, and that of others.

"I am an orphan; the daughter of a clergyman. My parents died before I could know them. I was brought up a dependant; educated in a charitable institution. I will even tell you the name of the establishment, where I passed six years as a pupil, and two as a teacher—Lowood Orphan Asylum, ——shire: you will have heard of it, Mr. Rivers?—the Rev. Robert Brocklehurst is the treasurer."

"I have heard of Mr. Brocklehurst, and I have seen the school."

"I left Lowood nearly a year since to become a private governess. I obtained a good situation, and was happy. This place I was obliged to leave four days before I came here. The reason of my departure I cannot and ought not to explain: it would be useless—dangerous; and would sound incredible. No blame attached to me: I am as free from culpability as any one of you three. Miserable I am, and must be for a time; for the catastrophe which drove me from the house I had found a paradise was of a strange and direful nature. I observed but two points in planning my departure—speed, secrecy: to secure these, I had to leave behind me everything I possessed except a small parcel; which, in my hurry and trouble of mind, I forgot to take out of the coach that brought me to Whitcross. To this neighbourhood, then, I came, quite destitute. I slept two nights in the open air, and wandered about two days without crossing a threshold: but twice in that space of time did I taste food; and it was when brought by hunger, exhaustion, and despair, almost to the last gasp, that you, Mr. Rivers, forbade me to perish of want at your door, and took me under the shelter of your roof. I know all your sisters have done for me since—for I have not been insensible during my seeming torpor—and I owe to their spontaneous, genuine, genial compassion, as large a debt as to your evangelical charity."

"Don't make her talk any more now, St. John," said Diana, as I paused; "she is evidently not yet fit for excitement. Come to the sofa, and sit down now, Miss Elliott."

I gave an involuntary half-start at hearing the *alias:* I had forgotten my new name. Mr. Rivers, whom nothing seemed to escape, noticed it at once.

"You said your name was Jane Elliott?" he observed.

"I did say so; and it is the name by which I think it expedient to be called at present: but it is not my real name, and when I hear it, it sounds strange to me."

"Your real name you will not give?"

"No: I fear discovery above all things; and whatever disclosure would lead to it, I avoid."

"You are quite right, I am sure," said Diana. "Now do, brother, let her be at peace awhile."

But when St. John had mused a few moments, he recommenced, as imperturbably, and with as much acumen as ever.

"You would not like to be long dependent on our hospitality—you would wish, I see, to dispense as soon as may be with my sisters' compassion; and, above all, with my *charity* (I am quite sensible of the distinction drawn, nor do I resent it— it is just): you desire to be independent of us?"

"I do: I have already said so. Show me how to work, or how to seek work: that is all I now ask; then let me go, if it be but to the meanest cottage—but *till then*, allow me to stay here: I dread another essay of the horrors of homeless destitution."

"Indeed, you *shall* stay here," said Diana, putting her white hand on my head. "You *shall*,", repeated Mary, in the tone of undemonstrative sincerity, which seemed natural to her.

"My sisters, you see, have a pleasure in keeping you," said Mr. St. John, "as they would have a pleasure in keeping and cherishing a half-frozen bird, some wintry wind might have driven through their casement. *I* feel more inclination to put you in the way of keeping yourself: and shall endeavour to do so: but observe, my sphere is narrow. I am but the incumbent of a poor country parish: my aid must be of the humblest sort. And if you are inclined to despise the day of small things, seek some more efficient succour than such as I can offer."

"She has already said that she is willing to do anything honest she *can* do," answered Diana, for me; "and you know, St. John, she has no choice of helpers: she is forced to put up with such crusty people as you."

"I will be a dressmaker: I will be a plain work-woman; I will be a servant, a nurse-girl, if I can be no better," I answered.

"Right," said Mr. St. John, quite coolly. "If such is your spirit, I promise to aid you; in my own time and way."

He now resumed the book with which he had been occupied before tea. I soon withdrew; for I had talked as much, and sat up as long, as my present strength would permit.

Chapter XXX

THE more I knew of the inmates of Moor House, the better I liked them. In a few days I had so far recovered my health that I could sit up all day, and walk out sometimes. I could join with Diana and Mary in all their occupations; converse with them as much as they wished, and aid them when and where they would allow me. There was a reviving pleasure in this intercourse, of a kind now tasted by me for the first time—the pleasure arising from perfect congeniality of tastes, sentiments, and principles.

I liked to read what they liked to read: what they enjoyed, delighted me; what they approved, I reverenced. They loved their sequestered home. I, too, in the grey, small, antique structure, with its low roof, its latticed casements, its mouldering walls, its avenue of aged firs—all grown aslant under the stress of mountain winds; its garden, dark with yew and holly—and where no flowers but of the hardiest species would bloom—found a charm both potent and permanent. They clung to the purple moors behind and around their dwelling—to the hollow vale into which the pebbly bridle-path leading from their gate descended; and which wound between fern-banks first, and then amongst a few of the wildest little pasture-fields that ever bordered a wilderness of heath, or gave sustenance to a flock of grey moorland sheep, with their little mossy-faced lambs:—they clung to this scene, I say, with a perfect enthusiasm of attachment. I could comprehend the feeling, and share both its strength and truth. I saw the fascination of the locality. I felt the consecration of its loneliness: my eye feasted on the outline of swell and sweep—on the wild colouring communicated to ridge and dell, by moss, by heath-bell, by flower-sprinkled turf, by brilliant bracken, and mellow granite crag. These details were just to me what they were to them—so many pure and sweet sources of pleasure. The strong blast and the soft breeze; the rough and the halcyon day; the hours of sunrise and sunset; the moonlight and the clouded night, developed for me, in these regions, the same attraction as for them—wound round my faculties the same spell that entranced theirs.

In-doors we agreed equally well. They were both more accomplished and better read than I was: but with eagerness I followed in the path of knowledge they had trodden before me. I devoured the books they lent me: then it was full satisfaction to discuss with them in the evening what I had perused during the day. Thought fitted thought; opinion met opinion: we coincided, in short, perfectly.

If in our trio there was a superior and a leader, it was Diana. Physically, she far excelled me: she was handsome; she was vigorous. In her animal spirits, there was an affluence of life, and certainty of flow, such as excited my wonder, while it baffled my comprehension. I could talk a while when the evening commenced: but the first gush of vivacity and fluency gone, I was fain to sit on a stool at Diana's feet, to rest my head on her knee, and listen alternately to her and Mary; while they sounded thoroughly the topic on which I had but touched. Diana offered to teach me German. I liked to learn of her; I saw the part of instructress pleased and suited her; that of scholar pleased and suited me no less. Our natures dovetailed: mutual affection—of the strongest kind—was the result. They discovered I could draw: their pencils and colour-boxes were immediately at my service. My skill, greater in this one point than theirs, surprised and charmed them. Mary would sit and watch me by the hour together: then she would take lessons; and a docile, intelligent, assiduous pupil, she made. Thus occupied, and mutually entertained, days passed like hours, and weeks like days.

As to Mr. St. John, the intimacy which had arisen so naturally and rapidly between me and his sisters, did not extend to him. One reason of the distance yet observed between us was, that he was comparatively seldom at home: a large proportion of his time appeared devoted to visiting the sick and poor among the scattered population of his parish.

No weather seemed to hinder him in these pastoral excursions: rain or fair, he would, when his hours of morning study were over, take his hat, and followed by his father's old pointer, Carlo, go out on his mission of love or duty—I scarcely know in which light he regarded it. Sometimes, when the day was very unfavourable, his sisters would expostulate. He would then say, with a peculiar smile, more solemn than cheerful,—

"And if I let a gust of wind or a sprinkling of rain turn me aside from these easy tasks, what preparation would such sloth be for the future I propose to myself?"

Diana and Mary's general answer to this question was a sigh, and some minutes of apparently mournful meditation.

But besides his frequent absences, there was another barrier to friendship with him: he seemed of a reserved, an abstracted, and even of a brooding nature. Zealous in his ministerial labours, blameless in his life and habits, he yet did not appear to enjoy that mental serenity, that inward content, which should be the reward of every sincere Christian and practical philanthropist. Often, of an evening, when he sat at the window, his desk and papers before him, he would cease reading or writing, rest his chin on his hand, and deliver himself up to I know not what course of thought: but that it was perturbed and exciting might be seen in the frequent flash and changeful dilation of his eye.

I think, moreover, that Nature was not to him that treasury of delight it was to his sisters. He expressed once, and but once in my hearing, a strong sense of the rugged charm of the hills, and an inborn affection for the dark roof and hoary walls he called his home: but there was more of gloom than pleasure in the tone and words in which the sentiment was manifested; and never did he seem to roam the moors for the sake of their soothing silence—never seek out or dwell upon the thousand peaceful delights they could yield.

Incommunicative as he was, some time elapsed before I had an opportunity of gauging his mind. I first got an idea of its calibre when I heard him preach in his own church at Morton. I wish I could describe that sermon: but it is past my power. I cannot even render faithfully the effect it produced on me.

It began calm—and indeed, as far as delivery and pitch of voice went, it was calm to the end: an earnestly felt, yet strictly restrained zeal breathed soon in the distinct accents, and prompted the nervous language. This grew to force—compressed, condensed, controlled. The heart was thrilled, the mind astonished, by the power of the preacher: neither were softened. Throughout there was a strange bitterness; an absence of consolatory gentleness; stern allusions to Calvinistic doctrines— election, predestination, reprobation—were frequent; and each reference to these points sounded like a sentence pronounced for doom. When he had done, instead of feeling better, calmer, more enlightened by his discourse, I experienced an inexpressible sadness; for it seemed to me—I know not whether equally so to others—that the eloquence to which I had been listening had sprung from a depth where lay turbid dregs of disappointment—where moved troubling impulses of insatiate yearnings and disquieting aspirations. I was sure St. John Rivers—pure-lived, conscientious, zealous as he was—had not yet found that peace of God which passeth all understanding: he had no more found it, I thought, than had I; with my concealed and racking regrets for my broken idol and lost elysium—regrets to which I have latterly avoided referring; but which possessed me and tyrannised over me ruthlessly.

Meantime a month was gone. Diana and Mary were soon to leave Moor House, and return to the far different life and scene which awaited them, as governesses in a large, fashionable, south-of-England city; where each held a situation in families, by whose wealthy and haughty members they were regarded only as humble dependants, and who neither knew nor sought one of their innate excellences, and appreciated only their acquired accomplishments as they appreciated the skill of their cook, or the taste of their waiting-woman. Mr. St. John had said nothing to me yet about the employment he had promised to obtain for me; yet it became urgent that I should have a vocation of some kind. One morning, being left alone with him a few minutes in the parlour, I ventured to approach the window-recess—which his table, chair, and desk consecrated as a kind of study—and I was going to speak; though not very well knowing in what words to frame my inquiry—for it is at all times difficult to break the ice of reserve glassing over such natures as his—when he saved me the trouble, by being the first to commence a dialogue.

Looking up as I drew near—"You have a question to ask of me?" he said.

"Yes; I wish to know whether you have heard of any service I can offer myself to undertake."

"I found or devised something for you three weeks ago; but as you seemed both useful and happy here—as my sisters had evidently become attached to you, and your society gave them unusual pleasure—I deemed it inexpedient to break in on your mutual comfort, till their approaching departure from Marsh End should render yours necessary."

"And they will go in three days now?" I said.

"Yes; and when they go, I shall return to the parsonage at Morton: Hannah will accompany me; and this old house will be shut up."

I waited a few moments, expecting he would go on with the subject first broached: but he seemed to have entered another train of reflection: his look denoted abstraction from me and my business. I was obliged to recall him to a theme which was of necessity one of close and anxious interest to me.

"What is the employment you had in view, Mr. Rivers? I hope this delay will not have increased the difficulty of securing it."

"Oh, no; since it is an employment which depends only on me to give, and you to accept."

He again paused: there seemed a reluctance to continue. I grew impatient: a restless movement or two, and an eager and exacting glance fastened on his face, conveyed the feeling to him as effectually as words could have done, and with less trouble.

"You need be in no hurry to hear," he said: "let me frankly tell you, I have nothing eligible or profitable to suggest. Before I explain, recall, if you please, my notice, clearly given, that if I helped you, it must be as the blind man would help the lame. I am poor; for I find that, when I have paid my father's debts, all the patrimony remaining to me will be this crumbling grange, the row of scathed firs behind, and the patch of moorish soil, with the yew-trees and holly-bushes in front. I am obscure: Rivers is an old name; but of the three sole descendants of the race, two earn the dependant's crust among strangers, and the third considers himself an alien from his native country—not only for life, but in death. Yes, and deems, and is bound to deem, himself honoured by the lot, and aspires but after the day when the cross of separation from fleshly ties shall be laid on his shoulders, and when the Head of that church-militant of whose humblest members he is one, shall give the word, 'Rise, follow me!' "

St. John said these words as he pronounced his sermons, with a quiet, deep voice; with an unflushed cheek, and a coruscating radiance of glance. He resumed:—

"And since I am myself poor and obscure, I can offer you but a service of poverty and obscurity. *You* may even think it degrading—for I see now your habits have been what the world calls refined: your tastes lean to the ideal; and your society has at least been amongst the educated—but *I* consider that no service degrades which can better our race. I hold that the more arid and unreclaimed the soil where the Christian labourer's task of tillage is appointed him—the scantier the meed his toil brings—the higher the honour. His, under such circumstances, is the destiny of the pioneer; and the first pioneers of the Gospel were the Apostles—their captain was Jesus, the Redeemer himself."

"Well?" I said, as he again paused—"proceed."

He looked at me before he proceeded: indeed, he seemed leisurely to read my face, as if its features and lines were characters on a page. The conclusions drawn from this scrutiny he partially expressed in his succeeding observations.

"I believe you will accept the post I offer you," said he; "and hold it for a while: not permanently, though: any more than I could permanently keep the narrow and narrowing—the tranquil, hidden office of English country incumbent: for in your nature is an alloy as detrimental to repose as that in mine; though of a different kind."

"Do explain," I urged, when he halted once more.

"I will; and you shall hear how poor the proposal is,— how trivial—how cramping. I shall not stay long at Morton, now that my father is dead, and that I am my own master. I shall leave the place probably in the course of a twelvemonth: but while I do stay, I will exert myself to the utmost for its improvement. Morton, when I came to it two years ago, had no school: the children of the poor were excluded from every hope of progress. I established one for boys: I mean now to open a second school for girls. I have hired a building for the purpose, with a cottage of two rooms attached to it for the mistress's house. Her salary will be thirty pounds a year: her house is already furnished, very simply, but sufficiently, by the kindness of a lady, Miss Oliver; the only daughter of the sole rich man in my parish—Mr. Oliver, the proprietor of a needle-factory and iron-foundry in the valley. The same lady pays for the education and clothing of an orphan from the workhouse; on condition that she shall aid the mistress in such menial offices connected with her own house and the school, as her occupation of teaching will prevent her having time to discharge in person. Will you be this mistress?"

He put the question rather hurriedly; he seemed half to expect an indignant, or at least a disdainful rejection of the offer: not knowing all my thoughts and feelings, though guessing some, he could not tell in what light the lot would appear to me. In truth it was humble—but then it was sheltered, and I wanted a safe asylum: it was plodding—but then, compared with that of a governess in a rich house, it was independent; and the fear of servitude with strangers entered my soul like iron: it was not ignoble—not unworthy—not mentally degrading. I made my decision.

"I thank you for the proposal, Mr. Rivers; and I accept it with all my heart."

"But you comprehend me?" he said. "It is a village school: your scholars will be only poor girls—cottagers' children—at the best, farmers' daughters. Knitting, sewing, reading, writing, cyphering, will be all you will have to teach. What will you do with your accomplishments? What, with the largest portion of your mind—sentiments— tastes?"

"Save them till they are wanted. They will keep."

"You know what you undertake, then?"

"I do."

He now smiled: not a bitter or a sad smile; but one well pleased and deeply gratified.

"And when will you commence the exercise of your function?"

"I will go to my house to-morrow; and open the school, if you like, next week."

"Very well: so be it."

He rose and walked through the room. Standing still, he again looked at me. He shook his head.

"What do you disapprove of, Mr. Rivers?" I asked.

"You will not stay at Morton long: no, no!"

"Why! What is your reason for saying so?"

"I read it in your eye; it is not of that description which promises the maintenance of an even tenor in life."

"I am not ambitious."

He started at the word "ambitious." He repeated, "No. What made you think of ambition? Who is ambitious? I know I am: but how did you find it out?"

"I was speaking of myself."

"Well, if you are not ambitious, you are"—— He paused.

"What?"

"I was going to say, impassioned: but perhaps you would have misunderstood the word, and been displeased. I mean that human affections and sympathies have a most powerful hold on you. I am sure you cannot long be content to pass your leisure in solitude, and to devote your working hours to a monotonous labour wholly void of stimulus; any more than I can be content," he added, with emphasis, "to

live here buried in morass, pent in with mountain—my nature, that God gave me, contravened; my faculties, heaven-bestowed, paralysed—made useless. You hear now how I contradict myself. I, who preached contentment with a humble lot, and justified the vocation even of hewers of wood, and drawers of water, in God's service—I, his ordained minister, almost rave in my restlessness. Well, propensities and principles must be reconciled by some means.''

He left the room. In this brief hour I had learnt more of him than in the whole previous month: yet still he puzzled me.

Diana and Mary Rivers became more sad and silent as the day approached for leaving their brother, and their home. They both tried to appear as usual; but the sorrow they had to struggle against was one that could not be entirely conquered or concealed. Diana intimated that this would be a different parting from any they had ever yet known. It would probably, as far as St. John was concerned, be a parting for years: it might be a parting for life.

"He will sacrifice all to his long-framed resolves," she said: "natural affection and feelings more potent still. St. John looks quiet, Jane; but he hides a fever in his vitals. You would think him gentle, yet in some things he is inexorable as death; and the worst of it is, my conscience will hardly permit me to dissuade him from his severe decision: certainly, I cannot for a moment blame him for it. It is right, noble, Christian: yet it breaks my heart.'' And the tears gushed to her fine eyes. Mary bent her head low over her work.

"We are now without father: we shall soon be without home and brother," she murmured.

At that moment a little accident supervened, which seemed decreed by fate, purposely to prove the truth of the adage, that "misfortunes never come singly:" and to add to their distresses the vexing one of the slip between the cup and the lip. St. John passed the window reading a letter. He entered.

"Our uncle John is dead," said he.

Both the sisters seemed struck: not shocked or appalled; the tidings appeared in their eyes rather momentous than afflicting.

"Dead?" repeated Diana.

"Yes."

She riveted a searching gaze on her brother's face. "And what then?" she demanded, in a low voice.

"What then, Die?" he replied, maintaining a marble immobility of feature. "What then? Why—nothing. Read."

He threw the letter into her lap. She glanced over it, and handed it to Mary. Mary perused it in silence, and returned it to her brother. All three looked at each other, and all three smiled—a dreary, pensive smile enough.

"Amen! We can yet live," said Diana, at last.

"At any rate, it makes us no worse off than we were before," remarked Mary.

"Only it forces rather strongly on the mind the picture of what *might have been*," said Mr. Rivers; "and contrasts it somewhat too vividly with what *is*."

He folded the letter, and locked it in his desk, and again went out.

For some minutes no one spoke. Diana then turned to me.

"Jane, you will wonder at us and our mysteries," she said; "and think us hard-hearted beings not to be more moved at the death of so near a relation as an uncle; but we have never seen him or known him. He was my mother's brother. My father and he quarrelled long ago. It was by his advice that my father risked most of his property in the speculation that ruined him. Mutual recrimination passed between them: they parted in anger, and were never reconciled. My uncle engaged afterwards in more prosperous undertakings: it appears he realised a fortune of twenty thousand pounds. He was never married and had no near kindred but ourselves, and one other person, not more closely related than we. My father always cherished the idea that he would atone for his error, by leaving his possessions to us; that letter

informs us that he has bequeathed every penny to the other relation; with the exception of thirty guineas, to be divided between St. John, Diana, and Mary Rivers, for the purchase of three mourning rings. He had a right, of course, to do as he pleased: and yet a momentary damp is on the spirits by the receipt of such news. Mary and I would have esteemed ourselves rich with a thousand pounds each; and to St. John such a sum would have been valuable, for the good it would have enabled him to do.''

This explanation given, the subject was dropped, and no further reference made to it, by either Mr. Rivers or his sisters. The next day, I left Marsh End for Morton. The day after, Diana and Mary quitted it for distant B——. In a week, Mr. Rivers and Hannah repaired to the parsonage: and so the old grange was abandoned.

Chapter XXXI

MY home, then,—when I at last find a home,—is a cottage: a little room with white-washed walls, and a sanded floor; containing four painted chairs and a table, a clock, a cupboard, with two or three plates and dishes, and a set of tea-things in delf. Above, a chamber of the same dimensions as the kitchen, with a deal bedstead, and chest of drawers; small, yet too large to be filled with my scanty wardrobe: though the kindness of my gentle and generous friends has increased that, by a modest stock of such things as are necessary.

It is evening. I have dismissed, with the fee of an orange, the little orphan who serves me as a handmaid. I am sitting alone on the hearth. This morning, the village school opened. I had twenty scholars. But three of the number can read: none write or cypher. Several knit, and a few sew a little. They speak with the broadest accent of the district. At present, they and I have a difficulty in understanding each other's language. Some of them are unmannered, rough, intractable, as well as ignorant; but others are docile, have a wish to learn, and evince a disposition that pleases me. I must not forget that these coarsely-clad little peasants are of flesh and blood as good as the scions of gentlest genealogy; and that the germs of native excellence, refinement, intelligence, kind feeling, are as likely to exist in their hearts as in those of the best-born. My duty will be to develop these germs: surely I shall find some happiness in discharging that office. Much enjoyment I do not expect in the life opening before me: yet it will, doubtless, if I regulate my mind, and exert my powers as I ought, yield me enough to live on from day to day.

Was I very gleeful, settled, content, during the hours I passed in yonder bare, humble school-room this morning and afternoon? Not to deceive myself, I must reply—No: I felt desolate to a degree. I felt—yes, idiot that I am—I felt degraded. I doubted I had taken a step which sank instead of raising me in the scale of social existence. I was weakly dismayed at the ignorance, the poverty, the coarseness of all I heard and saw round me. But let me not hate and despise myself too much for these feelings: I know them to be wrong—that is a great step gained; I shall strive to overcome them. To-morrow, I trust, I shall get the better of them partially; and in a few weeks, perhaps, they will be quite subdued. In a few months, it is possible, the happiness of seeing progress, and a change for the better in my scholars, may substitute gratification for disgust.

Meantime, let me ask myself one question—Which is better?—To have surrendered to temptation; listened to passion; made no painful effort—no struggle;—but to have sunk down in the silken snare; fallen asleep on the flowers covering it; wakened in a southern clime, amongst the luxuries of a pleasure villa: to have been now living in France, Mr. Rochester's mistress; delirious with his love half my time— for he would—oh, yes, he would have loved me well for a while. He *did* love

me—no one will ever love me so again. I shall never more know the sweet homage given to beauty, youth, and grace—for never to any one else shall I seem to possess these charms. He was fond and proud of me—it is what no man besides will ever be.—But where am I wandering, and what am I saying; and, above all, feeling? Whether is it better, I ask, to be a slave in a fool's paradise at Marseilles—fevered with delusive bliss one hour—suffocating with the bitterest tears of remorse and shame the next—or to be a village-schoolmistress, free and honest, in a breezy mountain nook in the healthy heart of England?

Yes; I feel now that I was right when I adhered to principle and law, and scorned and crushed the insane promptings of a frenzied moment. God directed me to a correct choice: I thank His providence for the guidance!

Having brought my eventide musings to this point, I rose, went to my door, and looked at the sunset of the harvest-day, and at the quiet fields before my cottage; which, with the school, was distant half a mile from the village. The birds were singing their last strains—

"The air was mild; the dew was balm."

While I looked, I thought myself happy, and was surprised to find myself ere long weeping—and why? For the doom which had reft me from adhesion to my master: for him I was no more to see; for the desperate grief and fatal fury—consequences of my departure—which might now, perhaps, be dragging him from the path of right, too far to leave hope of ultimate restoration thither. At this thought, I turned my face aside from the lovely sky of eve and lonely vale of Morton—I say *lonely*, for in that bed of it visible to me, there was no building apparent save the church and the parsonage, half-hid in trees; and, quite at the extremity, the roof of Vale Hall, where the rich Mr. Oliver and his daughter lived. I hid my eyes, and leant my head against the stone frame of my door; but soon a slight noise near the wicket which shut in my tiny garden from the meadow beyond it, made me look up. A dog—old Carlo, Mr. Rivers' pointer, as I saw in a moment—was pushing the gate with his nose, and St. John himself leant upon it with folded arms; his brow knit, his gaze, grave almost to displeasure, fixed on me. I asked him to come in.

"No, I cannot stay; I have only brought you a little parcel my sisters left for you. I think it contains a colour-box, pencils, and paper."

I approached to take it: a welcome gift it was. He examined my face, I thought, with austerity, as I came near: the traces of tears were doubtless very visible upon it.

"Have you found your first day's work harder than you expected?" he asked.

"Oh, no! On the contrary, I think in time I shall get on with my scholars very well."

"But perhaps your accommodations—your cottage—your furniture—have disappointed your expectations? They are, in truth, scanty enough; but"——I interrupted:

"My cottage is clean and weather-proof; my furniture sufficient and commodious. All I see has made me thankful, not despondent. I am not absolutely such a fool and sensualist as to regret the absence of a carpet, a sofa, and silver plate: besides, five weeks ago I had nothing—I was an outcast, a beggar, a vagrant; now I have acquaintance, a home, a business. I wonder at the goodness of God; the generosity of my friends; the bounty of my lot. I do not repine."

"But you feel solitude an oppression? The little house there behind you is dark and empty."

"I have hardly had time yet to enjoy a sense of tranquillity, much less to grow impatient under one of loneliness."

"Very well; I hope you feel the content you express: at any rate, your good sense will tell you that it is too soon yet to yield to the vacillating fears of Lot's wife. What you had left before I saw you, of course I do not know; but I counsel

you to resist, firmly, every temptation which would incline you to look back: pursue your present career steadily, for some months at least.''

''It is what I mean to do,'' I answered. St. John continued:—

''It is hard work to control the workings of inclination, and turn the bent of nature: but that it may be done, I know from experience. God has given us, in a measure, the power to make our own fate; and when our energies seem to demand a sustenance they cannot get—when our will strains after a path we may not follow— we need neither starve from inanition, nor stand still in despair: we have but to seek another nourishment for the mind, as strong as the forbidden food it longed to taste—and perhaps purer; and to hew out for the adventurous foot a road as direct and broad as the one Fortune has blocked up against us, if rougher than it.

''A year ago, I was myself intensely miserable, because I thought I had made a mistake in entering the ministry: its uniform duties wearied me to death. I burnt for the more active life of the world—for the more exciting toils of a literary career—for the destiny of an artist, author, orator; anything rather than that of a priest: yes, the heart of a politician, of a soldier, of a votary of glory, a lover of renown, a luster after power, beat under my curate's surplice. I considered; my life was so wretched, it must be changed, or I must die. After a season of darkness and struggling, light broke and relief fell: my cramped existence all at once spread out to a plain without bounds—my powers heard a call from heaven to rise, gather their full strength, spread their wings, and mount beyond ken. God had an errand for me; to bear which afar, to deliver it well, skill and strength, courage and eloquence, the best qualifications of soldier, statesman, and orator, were all needed: for these all centre in the good missionary.

''A missionary I resolved to be. From that moment my state of mind changed; the fetters dissolved and dropped from every faculty, leaving nothing of bondage but its galling soreness—which time only can heal. My father, indeed, opposed the determination, but since his death, I have not a legitimate obstacle to contend with; some affairs settled, a successor for Morton provided, an entanglement or two of the feelings broken through or cut asunder—a last conflict with human weakness, in which I know I shall overcome, because I have vowed that I *will* overcome— and I leave Europe for the East.''

He said this, in his peculiar, subdued, yet emphatic voice; looking, when he had ceased speaking, not at me, but at the setting sun, at which I looked too. Both he and I had our backs towards the path leading up the field to the wicket. We had heard no step on that grass-grown track; the water running in the vale was the one lulling sound of the hour and scene; we might well then start, when a gay voice, sweet as a silver bell, exclaimed:—

''Good evening, Mr. Rivers. And good evening, old Carlo. Your dog is quicker to recognise his friends than you are, sir; he pricked his ears and wagged his tail when I was at the bottom of the field, and you have your back towards me now.''

It was true. Though Mr. Rivers had started at the first of those musical accents, as if a thunderbolt had split a cloud over his head, he stood yet, at the close of the sentence, in the same attitude in which the speaker had surprised him—his arm resting on the gate, his face directed towards the west. He turned at last, with measured deliberation. A vision, as it seemed to me, had risen at his side. There appeared, within three feet of him, a form clad in pure white—a youthful, graceful form: full, yet fine in contour; and when, after bending to caress Carlo, it lifted up its head, and threw back a long veil, there bloomed under his glance a face of perfect beauty. Perfect beauty is a strong expression; but I do not retrace or qualify it: as sweet features as ever the temperate clime of Albion moulded; as pure hues of rose and lily as ever her humid gales and vapoury skies generated and screened, justified, in this instance, the term. No charm was wanting, no defect was perceptible; the young girl had regular and delicate lineaments; eyes shaped and coloured as we see them in lovely pictures, large, and dark, and full; the long and shadowy

eyelash which encircles a fine eye with so soft a fascination; the pencilled brow which gives such clearness; the white, smooth forehead, which adds such repose to the livelier beauties of tint and ray; the cheek, oval, fresh and smooth; the lips, fresh too, ruddy, healthy, sweetly formed; the even and gleaming teeth without flaw; the small dimpled chin; the ornament of rich, plenteous tresses—all advantages, in short, which, combined, realise the ideal of beauty, were fully hers. I wondered, as I looked at this fair creature: I admired her with my whole heart. Nature had surely formed her in a partial mood; and, forgetting her usual stinted step-mother dole of gifts, had endowed this, her darling, with a granddame's bounty.

What did St. John Rivers think of this earthly angel? I naturally asked myself that question as I saw him turn to her and look at her; and, as naturally, I sought the answer to the inquiry in his countenance. He had already withdrawn his eye from the Peri, and was looking at a humble tuft of daisies which grew by the wicket.

"A lovely evening, but late for you to be out alone," he said, as he crushed the snowy heads of the closed flowers with his foot.

"Oh, I only came home from S——" (she mentioned the name of a large town some twenty miles distant) "this afternoon. Papa told me you had opened your school, and that the new mistress was come; and so I put on my bonnet after tea, and ran up the valley to see her: this is she?" pointing to me.

"It is," said St. John.

"Do you think you shall like Morton?" she asked of me, with a direct and naïve simplicity of tone and manner, pleasing, if child-like.

"I hope I shall. I have many inducements to do so."

"Did you find your scholars as attentive as you expected?"

"Quite."

"Do you like your house?"

"Very much."

"Have I furnished it nicely?"

"Very nicely, indeed."

"And made a good choice of an attendant for you in Alice Wood?"

"You have, indeed. She is teachable and handy." (This, then, I thought, is Miss Oliver, the heiress; favoured, it seems, in the gifts of fortune, as well as in those of nature! What happy combination of the planets presided over her birth, I wonder?)

"I shall come up and help you to teach sometimes," she added. "It will be a change for me to visit you now and then; and I like a change. Mr. Rivers, I have been *so* gay during my stay at S——. Last night, or rather this morning, I was dancing till two o'clock. The ——th regiment are stationed there since the riots; and the officers are the most agreeable men in the world: they put all our young knife-grinders and scissor merchants to shame."

It seemed to me that Mr. St. John's under lip protruded, and his upper lip curled a moment. His mouth certainly looked a good deal compressed, and the lower part of his face unusually stern and square, as the laughing girl gave him this information. He lifted his gaze, too, from the daisies, and turned it on her. An unsmiling, a searching, a meaning gaze it was. She answered it with a second laugh, and laughter well became her youth, her roses, her dimples, her bright eyes.

As he stood, mute and grave, she again fell to caressing Carlo. "Poor Carlo loves me," said she. "*He* is not stern and distant to his friends; and if he could speak, he would not be silent."

As she patted the dog's head, bending with native grace before his young and austere master, I saw a glow rise to that master's face. I saw his solemn eye melt with sudden fire, and flicker with resistless emotion. Flushed and kindled thus, he looked nearly as beautiful for a man as she for a woman. His chest heaved once, as if his large heart, weary of despotic constriction, had expanded, despite the will, and made a vigorous bound for the attainment of liberty. But he curbed it, I think,

as a resolute rider would curb a rearing steed. He responded neither by word nor movement to the gentle advances made him.

"Papa says you never come to see us now," continued Miss Oliver, looking up. "You are quite a stranger at Vale Hall. He is alone this evening, and not very well: will you return with me and visit him?"

"It is not a seasonable hour to intrude on Mr. Oliver," answered St. John.

"Not a seasonable hour! But, I declare, it is. It is just the hour when papa most wants company: when the works are closed, and he has no business to occupy him. Now, Mr. Rivers, *do* come. Why are you so very shy, and so very sombre?" She filled up the hiatus his silence left by a reply of her own.

"I forgot!" she exclaimed, shaking her beautiful curled head, as if shocked at herself. "I am so giddy and thoughtless! *Do* excuse me. It had slipped my memory that you have good reasons to be indisposed for joining in my chatter. Diana and Mary have left you, and Moor House is shut up, and you are so lonely. I am sure I pity you. Do come and see papa."

"Not to-night, Miss Rosamond, not to-night."

Mr. St. John spoke almost like an automaton: himself only knew the effect it cost him thus to refuse.

"Well, if you are so obstinate, I will leave you; for I dare not stay any longer: the dew begins to fall. Good evening!"

She held out her hand. He just touched it. "Good evening!" he repeated, in a voice low and hollow as an echo. She turned; but in a moment returned.

"Are you well?" she asked. Well might she put the question: his face was blanched as her gown.

"Quite well," he enunciated; and, with a bow, she left the gate. She went one way; he another. She turned twice to gaze after him, as she tripped fairy-like down the field; he, as he strode firmly across, never turned at all.

This spectacle of another's suffering and sacrifice, rapt my thoughts from exclusive meditation on my own. Diana Rivers had designated her brother "inexorable as death." She had not exaggerated.

Chapter XXXII

I CONTINUED the labours of the village-school as actively and faithfully as I could. It was truly hard work at first. Some time elapsed before, with all my efforts, I could comprehend my scholars and their nature. Wholly untaught, with faculties quite torpid, they seemed to me hopelessly dull; and, at first sight, all dull alike: but I soon found I was mistaken. There was a difference amongst them as amongst the educated; and when I got to know them, and they me, this difference rapidly developed itself. Their amazement at me, my language, my rules, and ways, once subsided, I found some of these heavy-looking, gaping rustics wake up into sharp-witted girls enough. Many showed themselves obliging, and amiable too; and I discovered amongst them not a few examples of natural politeness, and innate self-respect, as well as of excellent capacity, that won my good-will and my admiration. These soon took a pleasure in doing their work well; in keeping their persons neat; in learning their tasks regularly; in acquiring quiet and orderly manners. The rapidity of their progress, in some instances, was even surprising; and an honest and happy pride I took in it: besides, I began personally to like some of the best girls; and they liked me. I had amongst my scholars several farmers' daughters: young women grown, almost. These could already read, write, and sew; and to them I taught the elements of grammar, geography, history, and the finer kinds of needlework. I found estimable characters amongst them—characters desirous of information, and

disposed for improvement—with whom I passed many a pleasant evening hour in their own homes. Their parents then (the farmer and his wife) loaded me with attentions. There was an enjoyment in accepting their simple kindness, and in repaying it by a consideration—a scrupulous regard to their feelings—to which they were not, perhaps, at all times accustomed, and which both charmed and benefited them; because, while it elevated them in their own eyes, it made them emulous to merit the deferential treatment they received.

I felt I became a favourite in the neighbourhood. Whenever I went out, I heard on all sides cordial salutations, and was welcomed with friendly smiles. To live amidst general regard, though it be but the regard of working-people, is like "sitting in sunshine, calm and sweet:" serene inward feelings bud and bloom under the ray. At this period of my life, my heart far oftener swelled with thankfulness than sank with dejection: and yet, reader, to tell you all, in the midst of this calm, this useful existence—after a day passed in honourable exertion amongst my scholars, an evening spent in drawing or reading contentedly alone—I used to rush into strange dreams at night: dreams many-coloured, agitated, full of the ideal, the stirring, the stormy—dreams where, amidst unusual scenes, charged with adventure, with agitating risk and romantic chance, I still again and again met Mr. Rochester, always at some exciting crisis; and then the sense of being in his arms, hearing his voice, meeting his eye, touching his hand and cheek, loving him, being loved by him—the hope of passing a lifetime at his side, would be renewed, with all its first force and fire. Then I awoke. Then I recalled where I was, and how situated. Then I rose up on my curtainless bed, trembling and quivering; and then the still, dark night witnessed the convulsion of despair, and heard the burst of passion. By nine o'clock the next morning I was punctually opening the school; tranquil, settled, prepared for the steady duties of the day.

Rosamond Oliver kept her word in coming to visit me. Her call at the school was generally made in the course of her morning ride. She would canter up to the door on her pony, followed by a mounted livery servant. Anything more exquisite than her appearance, in her purple habit, with her Amazon's cap of black velvet placed gracefully above the long curls that kissed her cheek and floated to her shoulders, can scarcely be imagined: and it was thus she would enter the rustic building, and glide through the dazzled ranks of the village children. She generally came at the hour when Mr. Rivers was engaged in giving his daily catechising lesson. Keenly, I fear, did the eye of the visitress pierce the young pastor's heart. A sort of instinct seemed to warn him of her entrance, even when he did not see it; and when he was looking quite away from the door, if she appeared at it, his cheek would glow, and his marble-seeming features, though they refused to relax, changed indescribably; and in their very quiescence became expressive of a repressed fervour, stronger than working muscle or darting glance could indicate.

Of course, she knew her power: indeed, he did not, because he could not, conceal it from her. In spite of his Christian stoicism, when she went up and addressed him, and smiled gaily, encouragingly, even fondly in his face, his hand would tremble, and his eye burn. He seemed to say, with his sad and resolute look, if he did not say it with his lips, "I love you, and I know you prefer me. It is not despair of success that keeps me dumb. If I offered my heart, I believe you would accept it. But that heart is already laid on a sacred altar: the fire is arranged round it. It will soon be no more than a sacrifice consumed."

And then she would pout like a disappointed child; a pensive cloud would soften her radiant vivacity; she would withdraw her hand hastily from his, and turn in transient petulance from his aspect at once so heroic and so martyr-like. St. John, no doubt, would have given the world to follow, recall, retain her, when she thus left him; but he would not give one chance of Heaven; nor relinquish, for the elysium of her love, one hope of the true, eternal Paradise. Besides, he could not bound all that he had in his nature—the rover, the aspirant, the poet, the priest—

in the limits of a single passion. He could not—he would not—renounce his wild field of mission warfare for the parlours and the peace of Vale Hall. I learnt so much from himself, in an inroad I once, despite his reserve, had the daring to make on his confidence.

Miss Oliver already honoured me with frequent visits to my cottage. I had learnt her whole character; which was without mystery or disguise: she was coquettish, but not heartless; exacting, but not worthlessly selfish. She had been indulged from her birth, but was not absolutely spoilt. She was hasty, but good-humoured; vain (she could not help it, when every glance in the glass showed her such a flush of loveliness), but not affected; liberal-handed; innocent of the pride of wealth; ingenuous; sufficiently intelligent; gay, lively, and unthinking: she was very charming, in short, even to a cool observer of her own sex like me; but she was not profoundly interesting or thoroughly impressive. A very different sort of mind was hers from that, for instance, of the sisters of St. John. Still, I liked her almost as I liked my pupil Adèle; except that, for a child whom we have watched over and taught, a closer affection is engendered than we can give an equally attractive adult acquaintance.

She had taken an amiable caprice to me. She said I was like Mr. Rivers (only, certainly, she allowed, "not one-tenth so handsome, though I was a nice neat little soul enough, but he was an angel"). I was, however, good, clever, composed, and firm, like him. I was a *lusus naturæ*, she affirmed, as a village schoolmistress: she was sure my previous history, if known, would make a delightful romance.

One evening, while, with her usual child-like activity, and thoughtless yet not offensive inquisitiveness, she was rummaging the cupboard and the table-drawer of my little kitchen, she discovered first two French books, a volume of Schiller, a German grammar and dictionary; and then my drawing-materials and some sketches, including a pencil-head of a pretty, little cherub-like girl, one of my scholars, and sundry views from nature, taken in the Vale of Morton and on the surrounding moors. She was first transfixed with surprise, and then electrified with delight.

"Had I done these pictures? Did I know French and German? What a love—what a miracle I was! I drew better than her master in the first school in S——. Would I sketch a portrait of her, to show to papa?"

"With pleasure," I replied; and I felt a thrill of artist-delight at the idea of copying from so perfect and radiant a model. She had then on a dark-blue silk dress; her arms and her neck were bare; her only ornament was her chestnut tresses, which waved over her shoulders with all the wild grace of natural curls. I took a sheet of fine cardboard, and drew a careful outline. I promised myself the pleasure of colouring it; and, as it was getting late then, I told her she must come and sit another day.

She made such a report of me to her father, that Mr. Oliver himself accompanied her next evening—a tall, massive-featured, middle-aged, and grey-headed man, at whose side his lovely daughter looked like a bright flower near a hoary turret. He appeared a taciturn, and perhaps a proud personage; but he was very kind to me. The sketch of Rosamond's portrait pleased him highly, he said I must make a finished picture of it. He insisted, too, on my coming the next day to spend the evening at Vale Hall.

I went. I found it a large, handsome residence, showing abundant evidences of wealth in the proprietor. Rosamond was full of glee and pleasure all the time I stayed. Her father was affable; and when he entered into conversation with me after tea, he expressed in strong terms his approbation of what I had done in Morton school; and said he only feared, from what he saw and heard, I was too good for the place, and would soon quit it for one more suitable.

"Indeed!" cried Rosamond, "she is clever enough to be a governess in a high family, papa."

I thought—I would far rather be where I am than in any high family in the land. Mr. Oliver spoke of Mr. Rivers—of the Rivers family—with great respect. He said

it was a very old name in that neighbourhood; that the ancestors of the house were wealthy; that all Morton had once belonged to them; that even now he considered the representative of that house might, if he liked, make an alliance with the best. He accounted it a pity that so fine and talented a young man should have formed the design of going out as a missionary; it was quite throwing a valuable life away. It appeared, then, that her father would throw no obstacle in the way of Rosamond's union with St. John. Mr. Oliver evidently regarded the young clergyman's good birth, old name, and sacred profession, as sufficient compensation for the want of fortune.

It was the 5th of November, and a holiday. My little servant, after helping me to clean my house, was gone, well satisfied with the fee of a penny for her aid. All about me was spotless and bright—scoured floor, polished grate, and well rubbed chairs. I had also made myself neat, and had now the afternoon before me to spend as I would.

The translation of a few pages of German occupied an hour; then I got my palette and pencils, and fell to the more soothing, because easier occupation, of completing Rosamond Oliver's miniature. The head was finished already; there was but the background to tint, and the drapery to shade off; a touch of carmine, too, to add to the ripe lips—a soft curl here and there to the tresses—a deeper tinge to the shadow of the lash under the azure eyelid. I was absorbed in the execution of these nice details, when, after one rapid tap, my door unclosed, admitting St. John Rivers.

"I am come to see how you are spending your holiday," he said. "Not, I hope, in thought? No, that is well: while you draw you will not feel lonely. You see, I mistrust you still: though you have borne up wonderfully so far. I have brought you a book for evening solace," and he laid on the table a new publication—a poem: one of those genuine productions so often vouchsafed to the fortunate public of those days—the golden age of modern literature. Alas! the readers of our era are less favoured. But, courage! I will not pause either to accuse or repine. I know poetry is not dead, nor genius lost; nor has Mammon gained power over either, to bind or slay: they will both assert their existence, their presence, their liberty and strength again one day. Powerful angels, safe in heaven! they smile when sordid souls triumph, and feeble ones weep over their destruction. Poetry destroyed? Genius banished? No! Mediocrity, no: do not let envy prompt you to the thought. No; they not only live, but reign, and redeem: and without their divine influence spread everywhere, you would be in hell—the hell of your own meanness.

While I was eagerly glancing at the bright pages of Marmion (for Marmion it was), St. John stooped to examine my drawing. His tall figure sprang erect again with a start: he said nothing. I looked up at him: he shunned my eye. I knew his thoughts well, and could read his heart plainly; at the moment I felt calmer and cooler than he: I had then temporarily the advantage of him; and I conceived an inclination to do him some good, if I could.

"With all his firmness and self-control," thought I, "he tasks himself too far: locks every feeling and pang within—expresses, confesses, imparts nothing. I am sure it would benefit him to talk a little about this sweet Rosamond, whom he thinks he ought not to marry: I will make him talk."

I said first: "Take a chair, Mr. Rivers." But he answered, as he always did, that he could not stay. "Very well," I responded mentally, "stand if you like; but you shall not go just yet, I am determined: solitude is at least as bad for you as it is for me. I'll try if I cannot discover the secret spring of your confidence, and find an aperture in that marble breast through which I can shed one drop of the balm of sympathy."

"Is this portrait like?" I asked bluntly.

"Like! Like whom! I did not observe it closely."

"You did, Mr. Rivers."

He almost started at my sudden and strange abruptness: he looked at me astonished. "Oh, that is nothing yet," I muttered within. "I don't mean to be baffled by a little stiffness on your part; I'm prepared to go to considerable lengths." I continued, "You observed it closely and distinctly: but I have no objection to your looking at it again," and I rose and placed it in his hand.

"A well-executed picture," he said; "very, soft, clear colouring; very graceful and correct drawing."

"Yes, yes; I know all that. But what of the resemblance? Who is it like?"

Mastering some hesitation, he answered, "Miss Oliver, I presume."

"Of course. And now, sir, to reward you for the accurate guess, I will promise to paint you a careful and faithful duplicate of this very picture, provided you admit that the gift would be acceptable to you. I don't wish to throw away my time and trouble on an offering you would deem worthless."

He continued to gaze at the picture: the longer he looked, the firmer he held it, the more he seemed to covet it. "It is like!" he murmured; "the eye is well managed: the colour, light, expression, are perfect. It smiles!"

"Would it comfort, or would it wound you to have a similar painting? Tell me that. When you are at Madagascar, or at the Cape, or in India, would it be a consolation to have that memento in your possession? or would the sight of it bring recollections calculated to enervate and distress?"

He now furtively raised his eyes: he glanced at me, irresolute, disturbed: he again surveyed the picture.

"That I should like to have it, is certain: whether it would be judicious or wise is another question."

Since I had ascertained that Rosamond really preferred him, and that her father was not likely to oppose the match, I—less exalted in my views than St. John— had been strongly disposed in my own heart to advocate their union. It seemed to me that, should he become the possessor of Mr. Oliver's large fortune, he might do as much good with it as if he went and laid his genius out to wither, and his strength to waste, under a tropical sun. With this persuasion I now answered:—

"As far as I can see, it would be wiser and more judicious if you were to take to yourself the original at once."

By this time he had sat down: he had laid the picture on the table before him, and with his brow supported on both hands, hung fondly over it. I discerned he was now neither angry nor shocked at my audacity. I saw even that to be thus frankly addressed on a subject he had deemed unapproachable—to hear it thus freely handled—was beginning to be felt by him as a new pleasure—an unhoped-for relief. Reserved people often really need the frank discussion of their sentiments and griefs more than the expansive. The sternest-seeming stoic is human after all; and to "burst" with boldness and good will into "the silent sea" of their souls, is often to confer on them the first of obligations.

"She likes you, I am sure," said I, as I stood behind his chair, "and her father respects you. Moreover, she is a sweet girl—rather thoughtless; but you would have sufficient thought for both yourself and her. You ought to marry her."

"*Does* she like me?" he asked.

"Certainly; better than she likes any one else. She talks of you continually: there is no subject she enjoys so much, or touches upon so often."

"It is very pleasant to hear this," he said—"very: go on for another quarter of an hour." And he actually took out his watch and laid it upon the table to measure the time.

"But where is the use of going on," I asked, "when you are probably preparing some iron blow of contradiction, or forging a fresh chain to fetter your heart?"

"Don't imagine such hard things. Fancy me yielding and melting, as I am doing: human love rising like a freshly opened fountain in my mind and overflowing with sweet inundation all the field I have so carefully, and with such labour prepared—

so assiduously sown with the seeds of good intentions, of self-denying plans. And now it is deluged with a nectarous flood—the young germs swamped—delicious poison cankering them: now I see myself stretched on an ottoman in the drawing-room at Vale Hall, at my bride Rosamond Oliver's feet: she is talking to me with her sweet voice—gazing down on me with those eyes your skilful hand has copied so well—smiling at me with these coral lips. She is mine—I am hers—this present life and passing world suffice to me. Hush! say nothing—my heart is full of delight—my senses are entranced—let the time I marked pass in peace."

I humoured him: the watch ticked on: he breathed fast and low: I stood silent. Amidst this hush the quarter sped; he replaced the watch, laid the picture down, rose, and stood on the hearth.

"Now," said he, "that little space was given to delirium and delusion. I rested my temples on the breast of temptation, and put my neck voluntarily under her yoke of flowers; I tasted her cup. The pillow was burning: there is an asp in the garland: the wine has a bitter taste: her promises are hollow—her offers false: I see and know all this."

I gazed at him in wonder.

"It is strange," pursued he, "that while I love Rosamond Oliver so wildly—with all the intensity, indeed, of a first passion, the object of which is exquisitely beautiful, graceful, and fascinating—I experience at the same time a calm, unwarped consciousness, that she would not make me a good wife; that she is not the partner suited to me; that I should discover this within a year after marriage; and that to twelve months' rapture would succeed a lifetime of regret. This I know."

"Strange, indeed!" I could not help ejaculating.

"While something in me," he went on, "is acutely sensible to her charms, something else is as deeply impressed with her defects: they are such that she could sympathise in nothing I aspired to—co-operate in nothing I undertook. Rosamond a sufferer, a labourer, a female apostle? Rosamond a missionary's wife? No!"

"But you need not be a missionary. You might relinquish that scheme."

"Relinquish! What! my vocation? My great work? My foundation laid on earth for a mansion in heaven? My hopes of being numbered in the band who have merged all ambitions in the glorious one of bettering their race—of carrying knowledge into the realms of ignorance—of substituting peace for war—freedom for bondage—religion for superstition—the hope of heaven for the fear of hell? Must I relinquish that? It is dearer than the blood in my veins. It is what I have to look forward to, and to live for."

After a considerable pause, I said,—"And Miss Oliver? Are her disappointment and sorrow of no interest to you?"

"Miss Oliver is ever surrounded by suitors and flatterers: in less than a month, my image will be effaced from her heart. She will forget me; and will marry, probably, some one who will make her far happier than I should do."

"You speak coolly enough; but you suffer in the conflict. You are wasting away."

"No. If I get a little thin, it is with anxiety about my prospects, yet unsettled—my departure, continually procrastinated. Only this morning, I received intelligence that the successor, whose arrival I have been so long expecting, cannot be ready to replace me for three months to come yet; and perhaps the three months may extend to six."

"You tremble and become flushed whenever Miss Oliver enters the school-room."

Again the surprised expression crossed his face. He had not imagined that a woman would dare to speak so to a man. For me, I felt at home in this sort of discourse. I could never rest in communication with strong, discreet, and refined minds, whether male or female, till I had passed the outworks of conventional reserve, and crossed the threshold of confidence, and won a place by their heart's very hearthstone.

"You *are* original," said he, "and not timid. There is something brave in your spirit, as well as penetrating in your eye: but allow me to assure you that you partially misinterpret my emotions. You think them more profound and potent than they are. You give me a larger allowance of sympathy than I have a just claim to. When I colour, and when I shake before Miss Oliver, I do not pity myself. I scorn the weakness. I know it is ignoble; a mere fever of the flesh: not, I declare, the convulsion of the soul. *That* is just as fixed as a rock, firm set in the depths of a restless sea. Know me to be what I am—a cold hard man."

I smiled incredulously.

"You have taken my confidence by storm," he continued: "and now it is much at your service. I am simply, in my original state—stripped of that blood-bleached robe with which Christianity covers human deformity—a cold, hard, ambitious man. Natural affection only, of all the sentiments, has permanent power over me. Reason, and not Feeling, is my guide; my ambition is unlimited; my desire to rise higher, to do more than others insatiable. I honour endurance, perseverance, industry, talent; because these are the means by which men achieve great ends, and mount to lofty eminence. I watch your career with interest, because I consider you a specimen of a diligent, orderly, energetic woman: not because I deeply compassionate what you have gone through, or what you still suffer."

"You would describe yourself as a mere pagan philosopher," I said.

"No. There is this difference between me and deistic philosophers: I believe; and I believe the Gospel. You missed your epithet. I am not a pagan, but a Christian philosopher—a follower of the sect of Jesus. As his disciple I adopt his pure, his merciful, his benignant doctrines. I advocate them: I am sworn to spread them. Won in youth to religion, she has cultivated my original qualities thus:—From the minute germ, natural affection, she has developed the over-shadowing tree, philanthropy. From the wild, stringy root of human uprightness, she has reared a due sense of the Divine justice. Of the ambition to win power and renown for my wretched self, she has formed the ambition to spread my Master's kingdom; to achieve victories for the standard of the cross. So much has religion done for me; turning the original materials to the best account; pruning and training nature. But she could not eradicate nature: nor will it be eradicated 'till this mortal shall put on immortality.' "

Having said this, he took his hat, which lay on the table beside my palette. Once more he looked at the portrait.

"She *is* lovely," he murmured. "She is well named the Rose of the World, indeed!"

"And may I not paint one like it for you?"

"*Cui bono?* No."

He drew over the picture the sheet of thin paper on which I was accustomed to rest my hand in painting, to prevent the card-board from being sullied. What he suddenly saw on this blank paper, it was impossible for me to tell: but something had caught his eye. He took it up with a snatch; he looked at the edge; then shot a glance at me, inexpressibly peculiar, and quite incomprehensible: a glance that seemed to take and make note of every point in my shape, face, and dress; for it traversed all, quick, keen as lightning. His lips parted, as if to speak: but he checked the coming sentence, whatever it was.

"What is the matter?" I asked.

"Nothing in the world," was the reply: and, replacing the paper, I saw him dexterously tear a narrow slip from the margin. It disappeared in his glove; and, with one hasty nod and "good-afternoon," he vanished.

"Well!" I exclaimed, using an expression of the district; "that caps the globe, however!"

I, in my turn, scrutinised the paper; but saw nothing on it save a few dingy stains of paint where I had tried the tint in my pencil. I pondered the mystery a minute

or two; but finding it insolvable, and being certain it could not be of much moment, I dismissed, and soon forgot it.

Chapter XXXIII

WHEN Mr. St. John went, it was beginning to snow; the whirling storm continued all night. The next day a keen wind brought fresh and blinding falls; by twilight the valley was drifted up and almost impassable. I had closed my shutter, laid a mat to the door to prevent the snow from blowing in under it, trimmed my fire, and after sitting nearly an hour on the hearth listening to the muffled fury of the tempest, I lit a candle, took down Marmion, and beginning—

> *"Day set on Norham's castled steep,*
> *And Tweed's fair river broad and deep,*
> *And Cheviot's mountains lone;*
> *The massive towers, the donjon keep,*
> *The flanking walls that round them sweep,*
> *In yellow lustre shone."*

I soon forgot storm in music.

I heard a noise: the wind, I thought, shook the door. No; it was St. John Rivers, who, lifting the latch, came in out of the frozen hurricane—the howling darkness—and stood before me: the cloak that covered his tall figure all white as a glacier. I was almost in consternation; so little had I expected any guest from the blocked-up vale that night.

"Any ill news?" I demanded. "Has anything happened?"

"No. How very easily alarmed you are!" he answered, removing his cloak and hanging it up against the door, towards which he again coolly pushed the mat which his entrance had deranged. He stamped the snow from his boots.

"I shall sully the purity of your floor," said he, "but you must excuse me for once." Then he approached the fire: "I have had hard work to get here, I assure you," he observed, as he warmed his hands over the flame. "One drift took me up to the waist; happily the snow is quite soft yet."

"But why are you come?" I could not forbear saying.

"Rather an inhospitable question to put to a visitor; but since you ask it, I answer simply to have a little talk with you; I got tired of my mute books and empty rooms. Besides, since yesterday, I have experienced the excitement of a person to whom a tale has been half-told, and who is impatient to hear the sequel."

He sat down. I recalled his singular conduct of yesterday, and really I began to fear his wits were touched. If he were insane, however, his was a very cool and collected insanity: I had never seen that handsome-featured face of his look more like chiselled marble than it did just now, as he put aside his snow-wet hair from his forehead and let the firelight shine free on his pale brow and cheek as pale, where it grieved me to discover the hollow trace of care or sorrow now so plainly graved. I waited, expecting he would say something I could at least comprehend; but his hand was now at his chin, his finger on his lip: he was thinking. It struck me that his hand looked wasted like his face. A perhaps uncalled-for gush of pity came over my heart: I was moved to say:—

"I wish Diana or Mary would come and live with you: it is too bad that you should be quite alone; and you are recklessly rash about your own health."

"Not at all," said he: "I care for myself when necessary. I am well now. What do you see amiss in me?"

This was said with a careless, abstracted indifference, which showed that my solicitude was, at least in his opinion, wholly superfluous. I was silenced.

He still slowly moved his finger over his upper lip, and still his eye dwelt dreamily on the glowing grate; thinking it urgent to say something, I asked him presently if he felt any cold draught from the door, which was behind him.

"No, no;" he responded, shortly and somewhat testily.

"Well," I reflected, "if you won't talk, you may be still; I'll let you alone now, and return to my book."

So I snuffed the candle, and resumed the perusal of Marmion. He soon stirred; my eye was instantly drawn to his movements; he only took out a morocco pocketbook, thence produced a letter, which he read in silence, folded it, put it back, relapsed into meditation. It was vain to try to read with such an inscrutable fixture before me; nor could I, in my impatience, consent to be dumb; he might rebuff me if he liked, but talk I would.

"Have you heard from Diana and Mary lately?"

"Not since the letter I showed you a week ago."

"There has not been any change made about your own arrangements? You will not be summoned to leave England sooner than you expected?"

"I fear not, indeed: such chance is too good to befall me." Baffled so far I changed my ground—I bethought myself to talk about the school and my scholars.

"Mary Garrett's mother is better, and Mary came back to the school this morning, and I shall have four new girls next week from the Foundry Close—they would have come to-day but for the snow."

"Indeed!"

"Mr. Oliver pays for two."

"Does he?"

"He means to give the whole school a treat at Christmas."

"I know."

"Was it your suggestion?"

"No."

"Whose then?"

"His daughter's, I think."

"It is like her: she is so good-natured."

"Yes."

Again came the blank of a pause: the clock struck eight strokes. It aroused him; he uncrossed his legs, sat erect, turned to me.

"Leave your book a moment, and come a little nearer the fire," he said.

Wondering, and of my wonder finding no end, I complied.

"Half an hour ago," he pursued, "I spoke of my impatience to hear the sequel of a tale: on reflection, I find the matter will be better managed by my assuming the narrator's part, and converting you into a listener. Before commencing, it is but fair to warn you that the story will sound somewhat hackneyed in your ears: but stale details often regain a degree of freshness when they pass through new lips. For the rest, whether trite or novel, it is short.

"Twenty years ago, a poor curate—never mind his name at this moment—fell in love with a rich man's daughter; she fell in love with him, and married him, against the advice of all her friends; who consequently disowned her immediately after the wedding. Before two years passed, the rash pair were both dead, and laid quietly side by side under one slab. (I have seen their grave; it formed part of the pavement of a huge churchyard surrounding the grim, soot-black old cathedral of an overgrown manufacturing town in ——shire.) They left a daughter, which, at its very birth, Charity received in her lap—cold as that of the snow-drift I almost stuck fast in to-night. Charity carried the friendless thing to the house of its rich, maternal relations; it was reared by an aunt-in-law, called (I come to names now) Mrs. Reed of Gateshead—you start—did you hear a noise? I daresay it is only a

rat scrambling along the rafters of the adjoining schoolroom: it was a barn before I had it repaired and altered, and barns are generally haunted by rats.—To proceed. Mrs. Reed kept the orphan ten years: whether it was happy or not with her, I cannot say, never having been told; but at the end of that time she transferred it to a place you know—being no other than Lowood School, where you so long resided yourself. It seems her career there was very honourable: from a pupil, she became a teacher, like yourself—really it strikes me there are parallel points in her history and yours—she left it to be a governess: there, again, your fates were analogous; she undertook the education of the ward of a certain Mr. Rochester."

"Mr. Rivers!" I interrupted.

"I can guess your feelings," he said, "but restrain them for a while: I have nearly finished; hear me to the end. Of Mr. Rochester's character I know nothing, but the one fact that he professed to offer honourable marriage to this young girl, and that at the very altar she discovered he had a wife yet alive, though a lunatic. What his subsequent conduct and proposals were is a matter of pure conjecture; but when an event transpired which rendered inquiry after the governess necessary, it was discovered she was gone—no one could tell when, where, or how. She had left Thornfield Hall in the night; every research after her course had been vain: the country had been scoured far and wide; no vestige of information could be gathered respecting her. Yet that she should be found is become a matter of serious urgency: advertisements have been put in all the papers; I myself have received a letter from one Mr. Briggs, a solicitor, communicating the details I have just imparted. Is it not an odd tale?"

"Just tell me this," said I, "and since you know so much, you surely *can* tell it me—what of Mr. Rochester? How and where is he? What is he doing? Is he well?"

"I am ignorant of all concerning Mr. Rochester: the letter never mentions him but to narrate the fraudulent and illegal attempt I have adverted to. You should rather ask the name of the governess—the nature of the event which requires her appearance."

"Did no one go to Thornfield Hall then? Did no one see Mr. Rochester?"

"I suppose not."

"But they wrote to him?"

"Of course."

"And what did he say? Who has his letters?"

"Mr. Briggs intimates that the answer to his application was not from Mr. Rochester, but from a lady: it is signed 'Alice Fairfax.' "

I felt cold and dismayed: my worst fears then were probably true: he had in all probability left England and rushed in reckless desperation to some former haunt on the Continent. And what opiate for his severe sufferings—what object for his strong passions—had he sought there? I dared not answer the question. Oh, my poor master—once almost my husband—whom I had often called "my dear Edward!"

"He must have been a bad man," observed Mr. Rivers.

"You don't know him—don't pronounce an opinion upon him," I said, with warmth.

"Very well," he answered, quietly: "and indeed my head is otherwise occupied than with him: I have my tale to finish. Since you won't ask the governess's name, I must tell it of my own accord—stay—I have it here—it is always more satisfactory to see important points written down, fairly committed to black and white."

And the pocket-book was again deliberately produced, opened, sought through; from one of its compartments was extracted a shabby slip of paper, hastily torn off: I recognised in its texture and its stains of ultra-marine, and lake, and vermilion, the ravished margin of the portrait-cover. He got up, held it close to my eyes: and I read, traced in Indian ink, in my own hand-writing, the words "JANE EYRE"—the work doubtless of some moment of abstraction.

"Briggs wrote to me of a Jane Eyre:" he said, "the advertisements demanded a Jane Eyre: I knew a Jane Elliott.—I confess I had my suspicions, but it was only yesterday afternoon they were at once resolved into certainty. You own the name and renounce the *alias*?"

"Yes—yes—but where is Mr. Briggs? He perhaps knows more of Mr. Rochester than you do."

"Briggs is in London; I should doubt his knowing anything at all about Mr. Rochester; it is not in Mr. Rochester he is interested. Meantime, you forget essential points in pursuing trifles: you do not inquire why Mr. Briggs sought after you—what he wanted with you."

"Well, what did he want?"

"Merely to tell you that your uncle, Mr. Eyre of Madeira, is dead; that he has left you all his property, and that you are now rich—merely that—nothing more."

"I! rich?"

"Yes, you, rich—quite an heiress."

Silence succeeded.

"You must prove your identity of course," resumed St. John, presently: "a step which will offer no difficulties; you can then enter on imediate possession. Your fortune is vested in the English funds; Briggs has the will and the necessary documents."

Here was a new card turned up! It is a fine thing, reader, to be lifted in a moment from indigence to wealth—a very fine thing: but not a matter one can comprehend, or consequently enjoy, all at once. And then there are other chances in life far more thrilling and rapture-giving: *this* is solid, an affair of the actual world, nothing ideal about it: all its associations are solid and sober, and its manifestations are the same. One does not jump, and spring, and shout hurrah! at hearing one has got a fortune, one begins to consider responsibilities, and to ponder business; on a base of steady satisfaction rise certain grave cares—and we contain ourselves, and brood over our bliss with a solemn brow.

Besides, the words Legacy, Bequest, go side by side with the words Death, Funeral. My uncle I had heard was dead—my only relative; ever since being made aware of his existence, I had cherished the hope of one day seeing him: now, I never should. And then this money came only to me: not to me and a rejoicing family, but to my isolated self. It was a grand boon doubtless; and independence would be glorious—yes, I felt that—*that* thought swelled my heart.

"You unbend your forehead at last," said Mr. Rivers: "I thought Medusa had looked at you, and that you were turning to stone—perhaps now you will ask how much you are worth?"

"How much am I worth?"

"Oh, a trifle! Nothing of course to speak of—twenty thousand pounds, I think they say—but what is that?"

"Twenty thousand pounds?"

Here was a new stunner—I had been calculating on four or five thousand. This news actually took my breath for a moment: Mr. St. John, whom I had never heard laugh before, laughed now.

"Well," said he, "if you had committed a murder, and I had told you your crime was discovered, you could scarcely look more aghast."

"It is a large sum—don't you think there is a mistake?"

"No mistake at all."

"Perhaps you have read the figures wrong—it may be 2,000!"

"It is written in letters, not figures,—twenty thousand."

I again felt rather like an individual of but average gastronomical powers, sitting down to feast alone at a table spread with provisions for a hundred. Mr. Rivers rose now and put his cloak on.

"If it were not such a very wild night," he said, "I would send Hannah down to keep you company: you look too desperately miserable to be left alone. But

Hannah, poor woman! could not stride the drifts so well as I: her legs are not quite so long: so I must e'en leave you to your sorrows. Good-night.''

He was lifting the latch: a sudden thought occurred to me.

"Stop one minute!" I cried.

"Well?"

"It puzzles me to know why Mr. Briggs wrote to you about me; or how he knew you, or could fancy that you, living in such an out-of-the-way place, had the power to aid in my discovery.''

"Oh! I am a clergyman," he said; "and the clergy are often appealed to about odd matters.'' Again the latch rattled.

"No: that does not satisfy me!" I exclaimed: and, indeed, there was something in the hasty and unexplanatory reply, which, instead of allaying, piqued my curiosity more than ever.

"It is a very strange piece of business," I added. "I must know more about it.''

"Another time.''

"No: to-night!—to-night!" and as he turned from the door, I placed myself between it and him. He looked rather embarrassed.

"You certainly shall not go till you have told me all!" I said.

"I would rather not, just now.''

"You shall!—you must!''

"I would rather Diana or Mary informed you.''

Of course these objections wrought my eagerness to a climax: gratified it must be, and that without delay; and I told him so.

"But I apprised you that I was a hard man," said he; "difficult to persuade.''

"And I am a hard woman,—impossible to put off.''

"And then," he pursued, "I am cold: no fervour infects me.''

"Whereas I am hot, and fire dissolves ice. The blaze there has thawed all the snow from your cloak; by the same token, it has streamed on to my floor, and made it like a trampled street. As you hope ever to be forgiven, Mr. Rivers, the high crime and misdemeanour of spoiling a sanded kitchen, tell me what I wish to know.''

"Well, then," he said, "I yield; if not to your earnestness, to your perseverance: as stone is worn by continual dropping. Besides, you must know some day,—as well now as later. Your name is Jane Eyre?''

"Of course: that was all settled before.''

"You are not, perhaps, aware that I am your namesake?—that I was christened St. John Eyre Rivers?''

"No, indeed! I remember now seeing the letter E. comprised in your initials written in books you have at different times lent me; but I never asked for what name it stood. But what then? Surely''——

I stopped: I could not trust myself to entertain, much less to express, the thought that rushed upon me—that embodied itself,—that, in a second, stood out a strong, solid probability. Circumstances knit themselves, fitted themselves, shot into order: the chain that had been lying hitherto a formless lump of links, was drawn out straight,—every ring was perfect, the connection complete. I knew, by instinct, how the matter stood, before St. John had said another word: but I cannot expect the reader to have the same intuitive perception, so I must repeat his explanation.

"My mother's name was Eyre; she had two brothers; one a clergyman, who married Miss Jane Reed, of Gateshead; the other, John Eyre, Esq., merchant, late of Funchal, Madeira. Mr. Briggs, being Mr. Eyre's solicitor, wrote to us last August to inform us of our uncle's death; and to say that he had left his property to his brother the clergyman's orphan daughter; overlooking us, in consequence of a quarrel, never forgiven, between him and my father. He wrote again a few weeks since, to intimate that the heiress was lost; and asking if we knew anything of her.

A name casually written on a slip of paper has enabled me to find her out. You know the rest.'' Again he was going, but I set my back against the door.

"Do let me speak,'' I said; "let me have one moment to draw breath and reflect.'' I paused—he stood before me, hat in hand, looking composed enough. I resumed:—

"Your mother was my father's sister.''

"Yes.''

"My aunt, consequently?''

He bowed.

"My uncle John was your uncle John? You, Diana and Mary, are his sister's children; as I am his brother's child?''

"Undeniably.''

"You three, then, are my cousins; half our blood on each side flows from the same source?''

"We are cousins; yes.''

I surveyed him. It seemed I had found a brother: one I could be proud of,—one I could love; and two sisters, whose qualities were such, that, when I knew them but as mere strangers, they had inspired me with genuine affection and admiration. The two girls, on whom, kneeling down on the wet ground, and looking through the low, latticed window of Moor House kitchen, I had gazed with so bitter a mixture of interest and despair, were my dear kinswomen; and the young and stately gentleman who had found me almost dying at his threshold, was my blood relation. Glorious discovery to a lonely wretch! This was wealth indeed!—wealth to the heart!—a mine of pure, genial affections. This was a blessing, bright, vivid, and exhilarating;—not like the ponderous gift of gold: rich and welcome enough in its way, but sobering from its weight. I now clapped my hands in sudden joy—my pulse bounded, my veins thrilled.

"Oh, I am glad!—I am glad!'' I exclaimed.

St. John smiled. "Did I not say you neglected essential points to pursue trifles?'' he asked. "You were serious when I told you you had got a fortune; and now, for a matter of no moment, you are excited.''

"What *can* you mean? It may be of no moment to you; you have sisters, and don't care for a cousin; but I had nobody; and now three relations,—or two, if you don't choose to be counted,—are born into my world full grown. I say again, I am glad!''

I walked fast through the room: I stopped, half suffocated with the thoughts that rose faster than I could receive, comprehend, settle them:—thoughts of what might, could, would, and should be, and that ere long. I looked at the blank wall: it seemed a sky, thick with ascending stars,—every one lit me to a purpose or delight. Those who had saved my life, whom, till this hour, I had loved barrenly, I could now benefit. They were under a yoke: I could free them: they were scattered,—I could reunite them—the independence, the affluence which was mine, might be theirs too. Were we not four? Twenty thousand pounds shared equally, would be five thousand each,—enough and to spare: justice would be done,—mutual happiness secured. Now the wealth did not weigh on me: now it was not a mere bequest of coin,—it was a legacy of life, hope, enjoyment.

How I looked while these ideas were taking my spirit by storm, I cannot tell; but I perceived soon that Mr. Rivers had placed a chair behind me, and was gently attempting to make me sit down on it. He also advised me to be composed: I scorned the insinuation of helplessness and distraction, shook off his hand, and began to walk about again.

"Write to Diana and Mary to-morrow,'' I said, "and tell them to come home directly; Diana said they would both consider themselves rich with a thousand pounds, so with five thousand, they will do very well.''

"Tell me where I can get a glass of water,'' said St. John; "you must really make an effort to tranquillise your feelings.''

"Nonsense! and what sort of an effect will the bequest have on you? Will it keep you in England, induce you to marry Miss Oliver, and settle down like an ordinary mortal?"

"You wander: your head becomes confused, I have been too abrupt in communicating the news; it has excited you beyond your strength."

"Mr. Rivers! you quite put me out of patience; I am rational enough; it is you who misunderstand; or rather who affect to misunderstand."

"Perhaps if you explained yourself a little more fully, I should comprehend better."

"Explain! What is there to explain? You cannot fail to see that twenty thousand pounds, the sum in question, divided equally between the nephew and three nieces of our uncle, will give five thousand to each? What I want is, that you should write to your sisters and tell them of the fortune that has accrued to them."

"To you, you mean."

"I have intimated my view of the case: I am incapable of taking any other. I am not brutally selfish, blindly unjust, or fiendishly ungrateful. Besides, I am resolved I will have a home and connections. I like Moor House, and I will live at Moor House; I like Diana and Mary, and I will attach myself for life to Diana and Mary. It would please and benefit me to have five thousand pounds; it would torment and oppress me to have twenty thousand; which, moreover, could never be mine in justice, though it might in law. I abandon to you, then, what is absolutely superfluous to me. Let there be no opposition, and no discussion about it; let us agree amongst each other, and decide the point at once."

"This is acting on first impulses; you must take days to consider such a matter, ere your word can be regarded as valid."

"Oh! if all you doubt is my sincerity, I am easy: you see the justice of the case?"

"I *do* see a certain justice; but it is contrary to all custom. Besides, the entire fortune is your right: my uncle gained it by his own efforts; he was free to leave it to whom he would: he left it to you. After all, justice permits you to keep it: you may, with a clear conscience, consider it absolutely your own."

"With me," said I, "it is fully as much a matter of feeling as of conscience: I must indulge my feelings; I so seldom have had an opportunity of doing so. Were you to argue, object, and annoy me for a year, I could not forego the delicious pleasure of which I have caught a glimpse—that of repaying, in part, a mighty obligation, and winning to myself life-long friends."

"You think so now," rejoined St. John; "because you do not know what it is to possess, nor consequently to enjoy wealth: you cannot form a notion of the importance twenty thousand pounds would give you; of the place it would enable you to take in society; of the prospects it would open to you: you cannot"——

"And you," I interrupted, "cannot at all imagine the craving I have for fraternal and sisterly love. I never had a home, I never had brother or sisters; I must and will have them now: you are not reluctant to admit me and own me, are you?"

"Jane: I will be your brother—my sisters will be your sisters—without stipulating for this sacrifice of your just rights."

"Brother? Yes; at the distance of a thousand leagues! Sisters? Yes; slaving amongst strangers! I, wealthy—gorged with gold I never earned and do not merit! You, penniless! Famous equality and fraternisation! Close union! Intimate attachment!"

"But, Jane, your aspirations after family ties and domestic happiness may be realised otherwise than by the means you contemplate: you may marry."

"Nonsense, again! Marry! I don't want to marry, and never shall marry."

"That is saying too much: such hazardous affirmations are a proof of the excitement under which you labour."

"It is not saying too much: I know what I feel, and how averse are my inclinations to the bare thought of marriage. No one would take me for love; and I will not be regarded in the light of a mere money-speculation. And I do not want a stranger—

unsympathising alien, different from me; I want my kindred: those with whom I have full fellow-feeling. Say again you will be my brother: when you uttered the words I was satisfied, happy; repeat them, if you can, repeat them sincerely.''

"I think I can. I know I have always loved my own sisters; and I know on what my affection for them is grounded,—respect for their worth, and admiration of their talents. You too have principle and mind: your tastes and habits resemble Diana's and Mary's; your presence is always agreeable to me; in your conversation I have already for some time found a salutary solace. I feel I can easily and naturally make room in my heart for you, as my third and youngest sister.''

"Thank you: that contents me for to-night. Now you had better go; for if you stay longer, you will perhaps irritate me afresh by some mistrustful scruple.''

"And the school, Miss Eyre? It must now be shut up, I suppose?''

"No. I will retain my post of mistress till you get a substitute.''

He smiled approbation: we shook hands, and he took leave.

I need not narrate in detail the further struggles I had, and arguments I used, to get matters regarding the legacy settled as I wished. My task was a very hard one: but, as I was absolutely resolved—as my cousins saw at length that my mind was really and immutably fixed on making a just division of the property—as they must in their own hearts have felt the equity of the intention; and must, besides, have been innately conscious that in my place they would have done precisely what I wished to do—they yielded at length so far as to consent to put the affair to arbitration. The judges chosen were Mr. Oliver and an able lawyer: both coincided in my opinion: I carried my point. The instruments of transfer were drawn out: St. John, Diana, Mary, and I, each became possessed of a competency.

Chapter XXXIV

IT was near Christmas by the time all was settled: the season of general holiday approached. I now closed Morton school; taking care that the parting should not be barren on my side. Good fortune opens the hand as well as the heart wonderfully; and to give somewhat when we have largely received, is but to afford a vent to the unusual ebullition of the sensations. I had long felt with pleasure that many of my rustic scholars liked me, and when we parted, that consciousness was confirmed: they manifested their affection plainly and strongly. Deep was my gratification to find I had really a place in their unsophisticated hearts: I promised them that never a week should pass in future that I did not visit them, and give them an hour's teaching in their school.

Mr. Rivers came up, as—having seen the classes, now numbering sixty girls, file out before me, and locked the door—I stood with the key in my hand, exchanging a few words of special farewell with some half-dozen of my best scholars: as decent, respectable, modest, and well-informed young women as could be found in the ranks of the British peasantry. And that is saying a great deal; for after all, the British peasantry are the best taught, best mannered, most self-respecting of any in Europe: since those days I have seen paysannes and Bäuerinnen; and the best of them seemed to me ignorant, coarse, and besotted, compared with my Morton girls.

"Do you consider you have got your reward for a season of exertion?'' asked Mr. Rivers, when they were gone. "Does not the consciousness of having done some real good in your day and generation give pleasure?''

"Doubtless.''

"And you have only toiled a few months! Would not a life devoted to the task of regenerating your race be well spent?''

"Yes," I said; "but I could not go on for ever so: I want to enjoy my own faculties as well as to cultivate those of other people. I must enjoy them now; don't recall either my mind or body to the school; I am out of it and disposed for full holiday."

He looked grave. "What now? What sudden eagerness is this you evince? What are you going to do?"

"To be active: as active as I can. And first I must beg you to set Hannah at liberty, and get somebody else to wait on you."

"Do you want her?"

"Yes, to go with me to Moor House: Diana and Mary will be at home in a week, and I want to have everything in order against their arrival."

"I understand: I thought you were for flying off on some excursion. It is better so: Hannah shall go with you."

"Tell her to be ready by to-morrow then; and here is the schoolroom key: I will give you the key of my cottage in the morning."

He took it. "You give it up very gleefully," said he: "I don't quite understand your light-heartedness; because I cannot tell what employment you propose to yourself as a substitute for the one you are relinquishing. What aim, what purpose, what ambition in life have you now?"

"My first aim will be to *clean down* (do you comprehend the full force of the expression?)—to *clean down* Moor House from chamber to cellar; my next to rub it up with bees-wax, oil, and an indefinite number of cloths, till it glitters again; my third, to arrange every chair, table, bed, carpet, with mathematical precision; afterwards I shall go near to ruin you in coals and peat to keep up good fires in every room; and lastly, the two days preceding that on which your sisters are expected, will be devoted by Hannah and me to such a beating of eggs, sorting of currants, grating of spices, compounding of Christmas cakes, chopping up of materials for mince-pies, and solemnising of other culinary rites, as words can convey but an inadequate notion of to the uninitiated like you. My purpose, in short, is to have all things in an absolutely perfect state of readiness for Diana and Mary, before next Thursday; and my ambition is to give them a beau-ideal of a welcome when they come."

St. John smiled slightly: still he was dissatisfied.

"It is all very well for the present," said he: "but seriously, I trust that when the first flush of vivacity is over, you will look a little higher than domestic endearments and household joys."

"The best things the world has!" I interrupted.

"No, Jane, no: this world is not the scene of fruition; do not attempt to make it so: nor of rest; do not turn slothful."

"I mean, on the contrary, to be busy."

"Jane, I excuse you for the present: two months' grace I allow you for the full enjoyment of your new position, and for pleasing yourself with this late-found charm of relationship; but *then*, I hope you will begin to look beyond Moor House and Morton, and sisterly society, and the selfish calm and sensual comfort of civilised affluence. I hope your energies will then once more trouble you with their strength."

I looked at him with surprise. "St. John," I said, "I think you are almost wicked to talk so. I am disposed to be as content as a queen, and you try to stir me up to restlessness! To what end?"

"To the end of turning to profit the talents which God has committed to your keeping; and of which he will surely one day demand a strict account. Jane, I shall watch you closely and anxiously—I warn you of that. And try to restrain the disproportionate fervour with which you throw yourself into common-place home pleasures. Don't cling so tenaciously to ties of the flesh; save your constancy and

ardour for an adequate cause; forbear to waste them on trite transient objects. Do you hear, Jane?''

"Yes; just as if you were speaking Greek. I feel I have adequate cause to be happy, and I *will* be happy. Good-bye!''

Happy at Moor House I was, and hard I worked; and so did Hannah: she was charmed to see how jovial I could be amidst the bustle of a house turned topsy-turvy—how I could dust, and brush, and clean, and cook. And really after a day or two of confusion worse confounded, it was delightful, by degrees, to invoke order from the chaos ourselves had made. I had previously taken a journey to S—, to purchase some new furniture: my cousins having given me carte blanche to effect what alterations I pleased, and a sum having been set aside for that purpose. The ordinary sitting-rooms and bedrooms I left much as they were: for I knew Diana and Mary would derive more pleasure from seeing again the old homely tables, and chairs, and beds, than from the spectacle of the smartest innovations. Still some novelty was necessary, to give to their return the piquancy with which I wished it to be invested. Dark handsome new carpets and curtains, an arrangement of some carefully selected antique ornaments in porcelain and bronze, new coverings, and mirrors, and dressing-cases for the toilet tables, answered the end: they looked fresh without being glaring. A spare parlour and bedroom I refurnished entirely, with old mahogany and crimson upholstery: I laid canvas on the passage, and carpets on the stairs. When all was finished, I thought Moor House as complete a model of bright modest snugness within, as it was, at this season, a specimen of wintry waste and desert dreariness without.

The eventful Thursday at length came. They were expected about dark, and ere dusk, fires were lit upstairs and below; the kitchen was in perfect trim; Hannah and I were dressed and all was in readiness.

St. John arrived first. I had entreated him to keep quite clear of the house till everything was arranged: and, indeed, the bare idea of the commotion, at once sordid and trivial, going on within its walls sufficed to scare him to estrangement. He found me in the kitchen, watching the progress of certain cakes for tea, then baking. Approaching the hearth, he asked, "If I was at last satisfied with housemaid's work?'' I answered by inviting him to accompany me on a general inspection of the result of my labours. With some difficulty, I got him to make the tour of the house. He just looked in at the doors I opened: and when he had wandered upstairs and downstairs, he said I must have gone through a great deal of fatigue and trouble to have effected such considerable changes in so short a time: but not a syllable did he utter indicating pleasure in the improved aspect of his abode.

This silence damped me. I thought perhaps the alterations had disturbed some old associations he valued. I inquired whether this was the case: no doubt in a somewhat crest-fallen tone.

"Not at all; he had, on the contrary, remarked that I had scrupulously respected every association: he feared, indeed, I must have bestowed more thought on the matter than it was worth. How many minutes, for instance, had I devoted to studying the arrangement of this very room?—By-the-by, could I tell him where such a book was?''

I showed him the volume on the shelf: he took it down, and withdrawing to his accustomed window recess, he began to read it.

Now, I did not like this, reader. St. John was a good man; but I began to feel he had spoken truth of himself, when he said he was hard and cold. The humanities and amenities of life had no attraction for him—its peaceful enjoyments no charm. Literally, he lived only to aspire—after what was good and great, certainly: but still he would never rest; nor approve of others resting round him. As I looked at his lofty forehead, still and pale as a white stone—at his fine lineaments fixed in study—I comprehended all at once that he would hardly make a good husband: that it would be a trying thing to be his wife. I understood, as by inspiration, the

nature of his love for Miss Oliver; I agreed with him that it was but a love of the senses. I comprehended how he should despise himself for the feverish influence it exercised over him; how he should wish to stifle and destroy it; how he should mistrust its ever conducing permanently to his happiness, or hers. I saw he was of the material from which nature hews her heroes—Christian and Pagan—her lawgivers, her statesmen, her conquerors: a steadfast bulwark for great interests to rest upon; but, at the fireside, too often a cold cumbrous column, gloomy and out of place.

"This parlour is not his sphere," I reflected: "the Himalayan ridge, or Caffre bush, even the plague-cursed Guinea Coast swamp, would suit him better. Well may he eschew the calm of domestic life; it is not his element: there his faculties stagnate—they cannot develop or appear to advantage. It is in scenes of strife and danger—where courage is proved, and energy exercised, and fortitude tasked—that he will speak and move, the leader and superior. A merry child would have the advantage of him on this hearth. He is right to choose a missionary's career—I see it now."

"They are coming! they are coming!" cried Hannah, throwing open the parlour door. At the same moment old Carlo barked joyfully. Out I ran. It was now dark; but a rumbling of wheels was audible. Hannah soon had a lantern lit. The vehicle had stopped at the wicket: the driver opened the door: first one well-known form, then another, stepped out. In a minute I had my face under their bonnets, in contact first with Mary's soft cheek, then with Diana's flowing curls. They laughed—kissed me—then Hannah: patted Carlo, who was half wild with delight, asked eagerly if all was well; and being assured in the affirmative, hastened into the house.

They were stiff with their long and jolting drive from Whitcross, and chilled with the frosty night air; but their pleasant countenances expanded to the cheerful firelight. While the driver and Hannah brought in the boxes, they demanded St. John. At this moment he advanced from the parlour. They both threw their arms round his neck at once. He gave each one quiet kiss, said in a low tone a few words of welcome, stood a while to be talked to, and then, intimating that he supposed they would soon rejoin him in the parlour, withdrew there as to a place of refuge.

I had lit their candles to go upstairs, but Diana had first to give hospitable orders respecting the driver; this done, both followed me. They were delighted with the renovation and decoration of their rooms; with the new drapery, and fresh carpets, and rich tinted china vases: they expressed their gratification ungrudgingly. I had the pleasure of feeling that my arrangements met their wishes exactly; and that what I had done added a vivid charm to their joyous return home.

Sweet was that evening. My cousins, full of exhilaration, were so eloquent in narrative and comment, that their fluency covered St. John's taciturnity: he was sincerely glad to see his sisters; but in their glow of fervour and flow of joy he could not sympathise. The event of the day—that is, the return of Diana and Mary—pleased him; but the accompaniments of that event, the glad tumult, the garrulous glee of reception, irked him: I saw he wished the quieter morrow was come. In the very meridian of the night's enjoyment, about an hour after tea, a rap was heard at the door. Hannah entered with the intimation that "a poor lad was come, at that unlikely time, to fetch Mr. Rivers to see his mother, who was drawing away."

"Where does she live, Hannah?"

"Clear up at Whitcross Brow, almost four miles off; and moor and moss all the way."

"Tell him I will go."

"I'm sure, sir, you had better not. It's the worst road to travel after dark that can be: there's no track at all over the bog. And then it is such a bitter night—the keenest wind you ever felt. You had better send word, sir, that you will be there in the morning."

But he was already in the passage, putting on his cloak; and without one objection, one murmur, he departed. It was then nine o'clock: he did not return till midnight. Starved and tired enough he was: but he looked happier than when he set out. He had performed an act of duty; made an exertion; felt his own strength to do and deny, and was on better terms with himself.

I am afraid the whole of the ensuing week tried his patience. It was Christmas week: we took to no settled employment, but spent it in a sort of merry domestic dissipation. The air of the moors, the freedom of home, the dawn of prosperity, acted on Diana and Mary's spirits like some life-giving elixir: they were gay from morning till noon, and from noon till night. They could always talk; and their discourse, witty, pithy, original, had such charms for me, that I preferred listening to, and sharing in it, to doing anything else. St. John did not rebuke our vivacity; but he escaped from it: he was seldom in the house; his parish was large, the population scattered, and he found daily business in visiting the sick and poor in its different districts.

One morning, at breakfast, Diana, after looking a little pensive for some minutes, asked him, "If his plans were yet unchanged?"

"Unchanged and unchangeable," was the reply. And he proceeded to inform us that his departure from England was now definitely fixed for the ensuing year.

"And Rosamond Oliver?" suggested Mary: the words seeming to escape her lips involuntarily: for no sooner had she uttered them, than she made a gesture as if wishing to recall them. St. John had a book in his hand—it was his unsocial custom to read at meals—he closed it, and looked up.

"Rosamond Oliver," said he, "is about to be married to Mr. Granby; one of the best connected and most estimable residents in S——, grandson and heir to Sir Frederic Granby: I had the intelligence from her father yesterday."

His sisters looked at each other, and at me; we all three looked at him: he was serene as glass.

"The match must have been got up hastily," said Diana: "they cannot have known each other long."

"But two months: they met in October at the county ball at S——. But where there are no obstacles to a union as in the present case, where the connection is in every point desirable, delays are unnecessary: they will be married as soon as S—— Place, which Sir Frederic gives up to them, can be refitted for their reception."

The first time I found St. John alone after this communication, I felt tempted to inquire if the event distressed him: but he seemed so little to need sympathy, that, so far from venturing to offer him more, I experienced some shame at the recollection of what I had already hazarded. Besides, I was out of practice in talking to him: his reserve was again frozen over, and my frankness was congealed beneath it. He had not kept his promise of treating me like his sisters; he continually made little, chilling differences between us, which did not at all tend to the development of cordiality: in short, now that I was acknowledged his kinswoman, and lived under the same roof with him, I felt the distance between us to be far greater than when he had known me only as the village schoolmistress. When I remembered how far I had once been admitted to his confidence, I could hardly comprehend his present frigidity.

Such being the case, I felt not a little surprised when he raised his head suddenly from the desk over which he was stooping, and said:—

"You see, Jane, the battle is fought and the victory won."

Startled at being thus addressed, I did not immediately reply: after a moment's hesitation I answered:—

"But are you sure, you are not in the position of those conquerors whose triumphs have cost them too dear? Would not such another ruin you?"

"I think not; and if I were, it does not much signify; I shall never be called upon to contend for such another. The event of the conflict is decisive: my way is now clear; I thank God for it!" So saying, he returned to his papers and his silence.

As our mutual happiness (*i.e.*, Diana's, Mary's, and mine) settled into a quieter character, and we resumed our usual habits and regular studies, St. John stayed more at home: he sat with us in the same room, sometimes for hours together. While Mary drew, Diana pursued a course of encyclopædic reading she had (to my awe and amazement) undertaken, and I fagged away at German, he pondered a mystic lore of his own: that of some Eastern tongue, the acquisition of which he thought necessary to his plans.

Thus engaged, he appeared, sitting in his own recess, quiet and absorbed enough; but that blue eye of his had a habit of leaving the outlandish-looking grammar, and wandering over, and sometimes fixing upon us, his fellow-students, with a curious intensity of observation: if caught, it would be instantly withdrawn; yet ever and anon, it returned searchingly to our table. I wondered what it meant: I wondered, too, at the punctual satisfaction he never failed to exhibit on an occasion that seemed to me of small moment, namely,—my weekly visit to Morton School; and still more was I puzzled when, if the day was unfavourable, if there was snow, or rain, or high wind, and his sisters urged me not to go, he would invariably make light of their solicitude, and encourage me to accomplish the task without regard to the elements.

"Jane is not such a weakling as you would make her," he would say: "she can bear a mountain blast, or a shower, or a few flakes of snow, as well as any of us. Her constitution is both sound and elastic:—better calculated to endure variations of climate than many more robust."

And when I returned, sometimes a good deal tired, and not a little weather-beaten, I never dared complain, because I saw that to murmur would be to vex him: on all occasions fortitude pleased him: the reverse was a special annoyance.

One afternoon, however, I got leave to stay at home, because I really had a cold. His sisters were gone to Morton in my stead: I sat reading Schiller; he, deciphering his crabbed Oriental scrolls. As I exchanged a translation for an exercise, I happened to look his way: there I found myself under the influence of the ever-watchful blue eye. How long it had been searching me through and through, and over and over, I cannot tell: so keen was it, and yet so cold, I felt for the moment superstitious—as if I were sitting in the room with something uncanny.

"Jane, what are you doing?"

"Learning German."

"I want you to give up German, and learn Hindostanee."

"You are not in earnest?"

"In such earnest that I must have it so: and I will tell you why."

He then went on to explain that Hindostanee was the language he himself was at present studying: that, as he advanced, he was apt to forget the commencement: that it would assist him greatly to have a pupil with whom he might again and again go over the elements, and so fix them thoroughly in his mind; that his choice had hovered for some time between me and his sisters; but that he had fixed on me, because he saw I could sit at a task the longest of the three. Would I do him this favour? I should not, perhaps, have to make the sacrifice long; as it wanted now barely three months to his departure.

St. John was not a man to be lightly refused: you felt that every impression made on him, either for pain or pleasure, was deep-graved and permanent. I consented. When Diana and Mary returned, the former found her scholar transferred from her to her brother: she laughed; and both she and Mary agreed that St. John should never have persuaded them to such a step. He answered, quietly:—

"I know it."

I found him a very patient, very forbearing, and yet an exacting master: he expected me to do a great deal; and when I fulfilled his expectations, he, in his own way, fully testified his approbation. By degrees, he acquired a certain influence over me that took away my liberty of mind: his praise and notice were more restraining than his indifference. I could no longer talk or laugh freely when he was by; because a tiresomely importunate instinct reminded me that vivacity (at least in me) was distasteful to him. I was so fully aware that only serious moods and occupations were acceptable, that in his presence every effort to sustain or follow any other became vain: I fell under a freezing spell. When he said "go," I went: "come," I came; "do this," I did it. But I did not love my servitude: I wished, many a time, he had continued to neglect me.

One evening, when, at bedtime, his sisters and I stood round him, bidding him good-night, he kissed each of them, as was his custom; and, as was equally his custom, he gave me his hand. Diana, who chanced to be in a frolicsome humour (*she* was not painfully controlled by his will; for hers, in another way, was as strong), exclaimed:—

"St. John! you used to call Jane your third sister, but you don't treat her as such: you should kiss her too."

She pushed me towards him. I thought Diana very provoking, and felt uncomfortably confused; and while I was thus thinking and feeling, St. John bent his head; his Greek face was brought to a level with mine, his eyes questioned my eyes piercingly—he kissed me. There are no such things as marble kisses, or ice kisses, or I should say, my ecclesiastical cousin's salute belonged to one of these classes; but there may be experiment kisses, and his was an experiment kiss. When given, he viewed me to learn the result; it was not striking: I am sure I did not blush; perhaps I might have turned a little pale, for I felt as if the kiss were a seal affixed to my fetters. He never omitted the ceremony afterwards, and the gravity and quiescence with which I underwent it, seemed to invest it for him with a certain charm.

As for me, I daily wished more to please him: but to do so, I felt daily more and more that I must disown half my nature, stifle half my faculties, wrest my tastes from their original bent, force myself to the adoption of pursuits for which I had no natural vocation. He wanted to train me to an elevation I could never reach; it racked me hourly to aspire to the standard he uplifted. The thing was as impossible as to mould my irregular features to his correct and classic pattern, to give to my changeable green eyes the sea-blue tint and solemn lustre of his own.

Not his ascendancy, alone, however, held me in thrall at present. Of late it had been easy enough for me to look sad: a cankering evil sat at my heart and drained my happiness at its source—the evil of suspense.

Perhaps you think I had forgotten Mr. Rochester, reader, amidst these changes of place and fortune. Not for a moment. His idea was still with me; because it was not a vapour sunshine could disperse; nor a sand-traced effigy storms could wash away: it was a name graven on a tablet, fated to last as long as the marble it inscribed. The craving to know what had become of him followed me everywhere; when I was at Morton, I re-entered my cottage every evening to think of that; and now at Moor House, I sought my bed-room each night to brood over it.

In the course of my necessary correspondence with Mr. Briggs about the will, I had inquired if he knew anything of Mr. Rochester's present residence and state of health; but, as St. John had conjectured, he was quite ignorant of all concerning him. I then wrote to Mrs. Fairfax, entreating information on the subject. I had calculated with certainty on this step answering my end: I felt sure it would elicit an early answer. I was astonished when a fortnight passed without reply; but when two months wore away, and day after day the post arrived and brought nothing for me, I fell a prey to the keenest anxiety.

I wrote again: there was a chance of my first letter having missed. Renewed hope followed renewed effort: it shone like the former for some weeks, then, like it,

faded, flickered: not a line, not a word reached me. When half a year wasted in vain expectancy my hope died out: and then I felt dark indeed.

A fine spring shone round me, which I could not enjoy. Summer approached; Diana tried to cheer me: she said I looked ill, and wished to accompany me to the sea-side. This St. John opposed; he said I did not want dissipation, I wanted employment; my present life was too purposeless, I required an aim: and, I suppose, by way of supplying deficiencies, he prolonged still further my lessons in Hindostanee, and grew more urgent in requiring their accomplishment: and I, like a fool, never thought of resisting him—I could not resist him.

One day I had come to my studies in lower spirits than usual; the ebb was occasioned by a poignantly felt disappointment: Hannah had told me in the morning there was a letter for me, and when I went down to take it, almost certain that the long looked-for tidings were vouchsafed me at last, I found only an unimportant note from Mr. Briggs on business. The bitter check had wrung from me some tears; and now as I sat poring over the crabbed characters and flourishing tropes of an Indian scribe, my eyes filled again.

St. John called me to his side to read; in attempting to do this my voice failed me: words were lost in sobs. He and I were the only occupants of the parlour: Diana was practising her music in the drawing-room, Mary was gardening—it was a very fine May-day, clear, sunny, and breezy. My companion expressed no surprise at this emotion, nor did he question me as to its cause; he only said:—

"We will wait a few minutes, Jane, till you are more composed." And while I smothered the paroxysm with all haste, he sat calm and patient, leaning on his desk and looking like a physician watching with the eye of science an expected and fully-understood crisis in a patient's malady. Having stifled my sobs, wiped my eyes, and muttered something about not being very well that morning, I resumed my task, and succeeded in completing it. St. John put away my books and his, locked his desk, and said:—

"Now, Jane, you shall take a walk; and with me."

"I will call Diana and Mary."

"No. I want only one companion this morning, and that must be you: put on your things; go out by the kitchen door: take the road towards the head of Marsh Glen: I will join you in a moment."

I know no medium: I never in my life have known any medium in my dealings with positive, hard characters, antagonistic to my own, between absolute submission and determined revolt. I have always faithfully observed the one, up to the very moment of bursting, sometimes with volcanic vehemence, into the other; and as neither present circumstances warranted, nor my present mood inclined me to mutiny, I observed careful obedience to St. John's directions; and in ten minutes I was treading the wild track of the glen, side by side with him.

The breeze was from the west: it came over the hills, sweet with scents of heath and rush; the sky was of stainless blue; the stream descending the ravine, swelled with past spring rains, poured along plentiful and clear, catching golden gleams from the sun, and sapphire tints from the firmament. As we advanced and left the track, we trod a soft turf, mossy fine and emerald green, minutely enamelled with a tiny white flower, and spangled with a star-like yellow blossom: the hills, meantime, shut us quite in; for the glen, towards its head, wound to their very core.

"Let us rest here," said St. John, as we reached the first stragglers of a battalion of rocks, guarding a sort of pass, beyond which the beck rushed down a waterfall; and where, still a little further, the mountain shook off turf and flower, had only heath for raiment, and crag for gem—where it exaggerated the wild to the savage, and exchanged the fresh for the frowning—where it guarded the forlorn hope of solitude, and a last refuge for silence.

I took a seat: St. John stood near me. He looked up the pass and down the hollow; his glance wandered away with the stream, and returned to traverse the

unclouded heaven which coloured it: he removed his hat, let the breeze stir his hair and kiss his brow. He seemed in communion with the genius of the haunt: with his eye he bade farewell to something.

"And I shall see it again," he said aloud, "in dreams, when I sleep by the Ganges: and again, in a more remote hour—when another slumber overcomes me—on the shore of a darker stream."

Strange words of a strange love! An austere patriot's passion for his fatherland! He sat down; for half an hour we never spoke; neither he to me nor I to him: that interval passed, he recommenced:—

"Jane, I go in six weeks: I have taken my berth in an East Indiaman which sails on the twentieth of June."

"God will protect you; for you have undertaken His work," I answered.

"Yes," said he, "there is my glory and joy. I am the servant of an infallible master. I am not going out under human guidance, subject to the defective laws and erring control of my feeble fellow-worms: my king, my lawgiver, my captain, is the All-perfect. It seems strange to me that all round me do not burn to enlist under the same banner,—to join in the same enterprise."

"All have not your powers: and it would be folly for the feeble to wish to march with the strong."

"I do not speak to the feeble, or think of them: I address only such as are worthy of the work, and competent to accomplish it."

"Those are few in number, and difficult to discover."

"You say truly: but when found, it is right to stir them up—to urge and exhort them to the effort—to show them what their gifts are, and why they were given—to speak Heaven's message in their ear,—to offer them, direct from God, a place in the ranks of His chosen."

"If they are really qualified for the task, will not their own hearts be the first to inform them of it?"

I felt as if an awful charm was framing round and gathering over me: I trembled to hear some fatal word spoken which would at once declare and rivet the spell.

"And what does *your* heart say?" demanded St. John.

"My heart is mute,—my heart is mute," I answered, struck and thrilled.

"Then I must speak for it," continued the deep, relentless voice. "Jane, come with me to India: come as my helpmeet and fellow-labourer."

The glen and sky spun round: the hills heaved! It was as if I had heard a summons from Heaven—as if a visionary messenger, like him of Macedonia, had enounced, "Come over and help us!" But I was no apostle,—I could not behold the herald,—I could not receive his call.

"Oh, St. John!" I cried, "have some mercy!"

I appealed to one who, in the discharge of what he believed his duty, knew neither mercy nor remorse. He continued:—

"God and nature intended you for a missionary's wife. It is not personal, but mental endowments they have given you: you are formed for labour, not for love. A missionary's wife you must—shall be. You shall be mine: I claim you—not for my pleasure, but for my Sovereign's service."

"I am not fit for it: I have no vocation," I said.

He had calculated on these first objections: he was not irritated by them. Indeed, as he leaned back against the crag behind him, folded his arms on his chest, and fixed his countenance, I saw he was prepared for a long and trying opposition, and had taken in a stock of patience to last him to its close—resolved, however, that that close should be conquest for him.

"Humility, Jane," said he, "is the groundwork of Christian virtues: you say right that you are not fit for the work. Who is fit for it? Or who, that ever was truly called, believed himself worthy of the summons? I, for instance, am but dust and ashes. With St. Paul, I acknowledge myself the chiefest of sinners: but I do

not suffer this sense of my personal vileness to daunt me. I know my Leader: that He is just as well as mighty; and while He has chosen a feeble instrument to perform a great task, He will, from the boundless stores of His providence, supply the inadequacy of the means to the end. Think like me, Jane—trust like me. It is the Rock of Ages I ask you to lean on: do not doubt but it will bear the weight of your human weakness.''

"I do not understand a missionary life: I have never studied missionary labours.''

"There, I, humble as I am, can give you the aid you want: I can set your task from hour to hour; stand by you always; help you from moment to moment. This I could do in the beginning: soon (for I know your powers) you would be as strong and apt as myself, and would not require my help.''

"But my powers—where are they for this undertaking? I do not feel them. Nothing speaks or stirs in me while you talk. I am sensible of no light kindling— no life quickening—no voice counselling or cheering. Oh, I wish I could make you see how much my mind is at this moment like a rayless dungeon, with one shrinking fear fettered in its depths—the fear of being persuaded by you to attempt what I cannot accomplish!''

"I have an answer for you—hear it. I have watched you ever since we first met: I have made you my study for ten months. I have proved you in that time by sundry tests: and what have I seen and elicited? In the village school I found you could perform well, punctually, uprightly, labour uncongenial to your habits and inclinations; I saw you could perform it with capacity and tact: you could win while you controlled. In the calm with which you learnt you had become suddenly rich, I read a mind clear of the vice of Demas:—lucre had no undue power over you. In the resolute readiness with which you cut your wealth into four shares, keeping but one to yourself, and relinquishing the three others to the claim of abstract justice, I recognised a soul that revelled in the flame and excitement of sacrifice. In the tractability with which, at my wish, you forsook a study in which you were interested, and adopted another because it interested me; in the untiring assiduity with which you have since persevered in it—in the unflagging energy and unshaken temper with which you have met its difficulties—I acknowledge the complement of the qualities I seek. Jane, you are docile, diligent, disinterested, faithful, constant, and courageous; very gentle, and very heroic: cease to mistrust yourself—I can trust you unreservedly. As a conductress of Indian schools, and a helper amongst Indian women, your assistance will be to me invaluable.''

My iron shroud contracted round me; persuasion advanced with slow sure step. Shut my eyes as I would, these last words of his succeeded in making the way, which had seemed blocked up, comparatively clear. My work, which had appeared so vague, so hopelessly diffuse, condensed itself as he proceeded, and assumed a definite form under his shaping hand. He waited for an answer. I demanded a quarter of an hour to think, before I again hazarded a reply.

"Very willingly,'' he rejoined: and rising, he strode a little distance up the pass, threw himself down on a swell of heath, and there lay still.

"I *can* do what he wants me to do: I am forced to see and acknowledge that,'' I meditated—"That is, if life be spared me. But I feel mine is not the existence to be long protracted under an Indian sun.—What then? He does not care for that: when my time came to die he would resign me, in all serenity and sanctity, to the God who gave me. The case is very plain before me. In leaving England, I should leave a loved but empty land—Mr. Rochester is not there: and if he were, what is, what can that ever be to me? My business is to live without him now: nothing so absurd, so weak as to drag on from day to day, as if I were waiting some impossible change in circumstances, which might reunite me to him. Of course (as St. John once said) I must seek another interest in life to replace the one lost: is not the occupation he now offers me truly the most glorious man can adopt or God assign? Is it not, by its noble cares and sublime results, the one best calculated to

fill the void left by uptorn affections and demolished hopes? I believe I must say,
Yes—and yet I shudder. Alas! If I join St. John, I abandon half myself: if I go to
India, I go to premature death. And how will the interval between leaving England
for India, and India for the grave, be filled? Oh, I know well! That, too, is very
clear to my vision. By straining to satisfy St. John till my sinews ache, I *shall*
satisfy him—to the finest central point and farthest outward circle of his expectations.
If I *do* go with him—if I *do* make the sacrifice he urges, I will make it absolutely:
I will throw all on the altar—heart, vitals, the entire victim. He will never love
me; but he shall approve me; I will show him energies he has not seen, resources
he has never suspected. Yes: I can work as hard as he can; and with as little
grudging.

"Consent, then, to his demand is possible: but for one item—one dreadful item.
It is—that he asks me to be his wife, and has no more of a husband's heart for me
than that frowning giant of a rock, down which the stream is foaming in yonder
gorge. He prizes me as a soldier would a good weapon; and that is all. Unmarried
to him, this would never grieve me; but can I let him complete his calculations—
coolly put into practice his plans—go through the wedding ceremony? Can I receive
from him the bridal ring, endure all the forms of love (which I doubt not he would
scrupulously observe) and know that the spirit was quite absent? Can I bear the
consciousness that every endearment he bestows is a sacrifice made on principle?
No: such a martyrdom would be monstrous. I will never undergo it. As his sister,
I might accompany him—not as his wife: I will tell him so."

I looked towards the knoll: there he lay, still as a prostrate column; his face
turned to me: his eye beaming watchful, and keen. He started to his feet, and
approached me.

"I am ready to go to India, if I may go free."

"Your answer requires a commentary," he said; "it is not clear."

"You have hitherto been my adopted brother: I, your adopted sister; let us
continue as such: you and I had better not marry."

He shook his head. "Adopted fraternity will not do in this case. If you were my
real sister it would be different: I should take you, and seek no wife. But as it is,
either our union must be consecrated and sealed by marriage, or it cannot exist:
practical obstacles oppose themselves to any other plan. Do you not see it, Jane?
Consider a moment—your strong sense will guide you."

I did consider: and still my sense, such as it was, directed me only to the fact
that we did not love each other as man and wife should; and therefore it inferred
we ought not to marry. I said so. "St. John," I returned, "I regard you as a
brother—you, me as a sister: so let us continue."

"We cannot—we cannot," he answered, with short, sharp determination: "it
would not do. You have said you will go with me to India: remember—you have
said that."

"Conditionally."

"Well—well. To the main point—the departure with me from England, the co-
operation with me in my future labours—you do not object. You have already as
good as put your hand to the plough: you are too consistent to withdraw it. You
have but one end to keep in view—how the work you have undertaken can best be
done. Simplify your complicated interests, feelings, thoughts, wishes, aims; merge
all considerations in one purpose: that of fulfilling with effect—with power—the
mission of your great Master. To do so, you must have a coadjutor—not a brother;
that is a loose tie; but a husband. I, too, do not want a sister; a sister might any
day be taken from me. I want a wife: the sole helpmeet I can influence efficiently
in life, and retain absolutely till death."

I shuddered as he spoke: I felt his influence in my marrow—his hold on my
limbs.

"Seek one elsewhere than in me, St. John: seek one fitted to you."

"One fitted to my purpose, you mean—fitted to my vocation. Again I tell you it is not the insignificant private individual—the mere man, with the man's selfish senses—I wish to mate: it is a missionary."

"And I will give the missionary my energies—it is all he wants—but not myself: that would be only adding the husk and shell to the kernel. For them he has no use: I retain them."

"You cannot—you ought not. Do you think God will be satisfied with half an oblation? Will he accept a mutilated sacrifice? It is the cause of God I advocate: it is under his standard I enlist you. I cannot accept on His behalf a divided allegiance: it must be entire."

"Oh! I will give my heart to God," I said. "*You* do not want it."

I will not swear, reader, that there was not something of repressed sarcasm both in the tone in which I uttered this sentence, and in the feeling that accompanied it. I had silently feared St. John till now, because I had not understood him. He had held me in awe, because he had held me in doubt. How much of him was saint, how much mortal, I could not heretofore tell: but revelations were being made in this conference: the analysis of his nature was proceeding before my eyes. I saw his fallibilities: I comprehended them. I understood that, sitting there where I did, on the bank of heath, and with that handsome form before me, I sat at the feet of a man, erring as I. The veil fell from his hardness and despotism. Having felt in him the presence of these qualities, I felt his imperfection, and took courage. I was with an equal—one with whom I might argue—one whom, if I saw good, I might resist.

He was silent after I had uttered the last sentence, and I presently risked an upward glance at his countenance. His eye, bent on me, expressed at once stern surprise and keen inquiry. "Is she sarcastic, and sarcastic to *me!*" it seemed to say.

"What does this signify?"

"Do not let us forget that this is a solemn matter," he said ere long; "one of which we may neither think nor talk lightly without sin. I trust, Jane, you are in earnest when you say you will give your heart to God: it is all I want. Once wrench your heart from man, and fix it on your Maker, the advancement of that Maker's spiritual kingdom on earth will be your chief delight and endeavour; you will be ready to do at once whatever furthers that end. You will see what impetus would be given to your efforts and mine by our physical and mental union in marriage: the only union that gives a character of permanent conformity to the destinies and designs of human beings: and, passing over all minor caprices—all trivial difficulties and delicacies of feeling—all scruple about the degree, kind, strength, or tenderness of mere personal inclination—you will hasten to enter into that union at once."

"Shall I?" I said, briefly; and I looked at his features, beautiful in their harmony, but strangely formidable in their still severity; at his brow, commanding but not open; at his eyes, bright and deep, and searching, but never soft; at his tall, imposing figure; and fancied myself in idea *his wife*. Oh! it would never do! As his curate, his comrade, all would be right: I would cross oceans with him in that capacity; toil under eastern suns, in Asian deserts with him in that office; admire and emulate his courage, and devotion, and vigour; accommodate quietly to his masterhood; smile undisturbed at his ineradicable ambition; discriminate the Christian from the man; profoundly esteem the one, and freely forgive the other. I should suffer often, no doubt, attached to him only in this capacity: my body would be under rather a stringent yoke, but my heart and mind would be free. I should still have my unblighted self to turn to: my natural unenslaved feelings with which to communicate in moments of loneliness. There would be recesses in my mind which would be only mine, to which he never came; and sentiments growing there fresh and sheltered, which his austerity could never blight, nor his measured warrior-march trample down: but as his wife—at his side always, and always restrained, and always

checked—forced to keep the fire of my nature continually low, to compel it to burn inwardly and never utter a cry, though the imprisoned flame consumed vital after vital—*this* would be unendurable.

"St. John!" I exclaimed, when I had got so far in my meditation.

"Well?" he answered, icily.

"I repeat: I freely consent to go with you as your fellow-missionary; but not as your wife; I cannot marry you and become part of you."

"A part of me you must become," he answered steadily; "otherwise the whole bargain is void. How can I, a man not yet thirty, take out with me to India a girl of nineteen, unless she be married to me? How can we be for ever together—sometimes in solitudes, sometimes amidst savage tribes—and unwed?"

"Very well," I said shortly; "under the circumstances, quite as well as if I were either your real sister, or a man and a clergyman like yourself."

"It is known that you are not my sister; I cannot introduce you as such: to attempt it would be to fasten injurious suspicions on us both. And for the rest, though you have a man's vigorous brain, you have a woman's heart, and—it would not do."

"It would do," I affirmed with some disdain, "perfectly well. I have a woman's heart; but not where you are concerned; for you I have only a comrade's constancy; a fellow-soldier's frankness, fidelity, fraternity, if you like; a neophyte's respect and submission to his hierophant: nothing more—don't fear."

"It is what I want," he said, speaking to himself; "it is just what I want. And there are obstacles in the way: they must be hewn down. Jane, you would not repent marrying me; be certain of that; we *must* be married. I repeat it: there is no other way; and undoubtedly enough of love would follow upon marriage to render the union right even in your eyes."

"I scorn your idea of love," I could not help saying; as I rose up and stood before him, leaning my back against the rock. "I scorn the counterfeit sentiment you offer: yes, St. John, and I scorn you when you offer it."

He looked at me fixedly: compressing his well-cut lips while he did so. Whether he was incensed or surprised, or what, it was not easy to tell: he could command his countenance thoroughly.

"I scarcely expected to hear that expression from you," he said: "I think I have done and uttered nothing to deserve scorn."

I was touched by his gentle tone, and overawed by his high, calm mien.

"Forgive me the words, St. John: but it is your own fault that I have been roused to speak so unguardedly. You have introduced a topic on which our natures are at variance—a topic we should never discuss: the very name of love is an apple of discord between us—if the reality were required what should we do? How should we feel? My dear cousin, abandon your scheme of marriage—forget it."

"No," said he; "it is a long-cherished scheme, and the only one which can secure my great end: but I shall urge you no further at present. To-morrow, I leave home for Cambridge: I have many friends there to whom I should wish to say farewell. I shall be absent a fortnight—take that space of time to consider my offer: and do not forget that if you reject it, it is not me you deny, but God. Through my means, He opens to you a noble career; as my wife only can you enter upon it. Refuse to be my wife, and you limit yourself for ever to a track of selfish ease and barren obscurity. Tremble lest in that case you should be numbered with those who have denied the faith, and are worse than infidels!"

He had done. Turning from me, he once more—

> *"Looked to river, looked to hill:"*

But this time his feelings were all pent in his heart: I was not worthy to hear them uttered. As I walked by his side homeward, I read well in his iron silence all he felt towards me: the disappointment of an austere and despotic nature, which has

met resistance where it expected submission—the disapprobation of a cool, inflexible judgment, which has detected in another feelings and views in which it has no power to sympathise: in short, as a man, he would have wished to coerce me into obedience: it was only as a sincere Christian he bore so patiently with my perversity, and allowed so long a space for reflection and repentance.

That night, after he had kissed his sisters, he thought proper to forget even to shake hands with me; but left the room in silence. I—who, though I had no love, had much friendship for him—was hurt by the marked omission: so much hurt that tears started to my eyes.

"I see you and St. John have been quarrelling, Jane," said Diana, "during your walk on the moor. But go after him; he is now lingering in the passage, expecting you—he will make it up."

I have not much pride under such circumstances: I would always rather be happy than dignified; and I ran after him—he stood at the foot of the stairs.

"Good-night, St. John," said I.

"Good-night, Jane," he replied calmly.

"Then shake hands," I added.

What a cold, loose touch he impressed on my fingers! He was deeply displeased by what had occurred that day: cordiality would not warm, nor tears move him. No happy reconciliation was to be had with him—no cheering smile or generous word: but still the Christian was patient and placid; and when I asked him if he forgave me, he answered that he was not in the habit of cherishing the remembrance of vexation; that he had nothing to forgive: not having been offended.

And with that answer he left me. I would much rather he had knocked me down.

Chapter XXXV

HE did not leave for Cambridge the next day, as he had said he would. He deferred his departure a whole week; and during that time he made me feel what severe punishment, a good, yet stern, a conscientious, yet implacable man can inflict on one who has offended him. Without one overt act of hostility, one upbraiding word, he contrived to impress me momently with the conviction that I was put beyond the pale of his favour.

Not that St. John harboured a spirit of unchristian vindictiveness—not that he would have injured a hair of my head, if it had been fully in his power to do so. Both by nature and principle, he was superior to the mean gratification of vengeance: he had forgiven me for saying I scorned him and his love, but he had not forgotten the words; and as long as he and I lived he never would forget them. I saw by his look, when he turned to me, that they were always written on the air between me and him; whenever I spoke, they sounded in my voice to his ear; and their echo toned every answer he gave me.

He did not abstain from conversing with me: he even called me as usual each morning to join him at his desk; and I fear the corrupt man within him had a pleasure unimparted to, and unshared by, the pure Christian, in evincing with what skill he could, while acting and speaking apparently just as usual, extract from every deed and every phrase the spirit of interest and approval which had formerly communicated a certain austere charm to his language and manner. To me, he was in reality become no longer flesh, but marble; his eye was a cold, bright, blue gem; his tongue, a speaking instrument—nothing more.

All this was torture to me—refined, lingering torture. It kept up a slow fire of indignation, and a trembling trouble of grief, which harassed and crushed me altogether. I felt how—if I were his wife, this good man, pure as the deep sunless

source, could soon kill me: without drawing from my veins a single drop of blood, or receiving on his own crystal conscience the faintest stain of crime. Especially I felt this, when I made any attempt to propitiate him. No ruth met my ruth. *He* experienced no suffering from estrangement—no yearning after reconciliation; and though, more than once, my fast falling tears blistered the page over which we both bent, they produced no more effect on him than if his heart had been really a matter of stone or metal. To his sisters, meantime, he was somewhat kinder than usual: as if afraid that mere coldness would not sufficiently convince me how completely I was banished and banned, he added the force of contrast: and this I am sure he did, not by malice, but on principle.

The night before he left home, happening to see him walking in the garden about sunset, and remembering, as I looked at him, that this man, alienated as he now was, had once saved my life, and that we were near relations, I was moved to make a last attempt to regain his friendship. I went out and approached him, as he stood leaning over the little gate: I spoke to the point at once.

"St. John, I am unhappy, because you are still angry with me. Let us be friends."

"I hope we are friends," was the unmoved reply; while he still watched the rising of the moon, which he had been contemplating as I approached.

"No, St. John, we are not friends as we were. You know that."

"Are we not? That is wrong. For my part, I wish you no ill and all good."

"I believe you, St. John; for I am sure you are incapable of wishing any one ill: but, as I am your kinswoman, I should desire somewhat more of affection than that sort of general philanthropy you extend to mere strangers."

"Of course," he said. "Your wish is reasonable; and I am far from regarding you as a stranger."

This, spoken in a cool, tranquil tone, was mortifying and baffling enough. Had I attended to the suggestions of pride and ire, I should immediately have left him: but something worked within me more strongly than those feelings could. I deeply venerated my cousin's talent and principle. His friendship was of value to me: to lose it tried me severely. I would not so soon relinquish the attempt to reconquer it.

"Must we part in this way, St. John? And when you go to India, will you leave me so, without a kinder word than you have yet spoken?"

He now turned quite from the moon, and faced me.

"When I go to India, Jane, will I leave you? What! do you not go to India?"

"You said I could not, unless I married you."

"And you will not marry me? You adhere to that resolution?"

Reader, do you know, as I do, what terror those cold people can put into the ice of their questions? How much of the fall of the avalanche is in their anger? of the breaking up of the frozen sea in their displeasure?

"No, St. John, I will not marry you. I adhere to my resolution."

The avalanche had shaken and slid a little forward; but it did not yet crash down.

"Once more, why this refusal?" he asked.

"Formerly," I answered, "because you did not love me; now, I reply, because you almost hate me. If I were to marry you, you would kill me. You are killing me now."

His lips and cheeks turned white—quite white.

"*I should kill you—I am killing you?* Your words are such as ought not to be used: violent, unfeminine, and untrue. They betray an unfortunate state of mind: they merit severe reproof: they would seem inexcusable; but that it is the duty of man to forgive his fellow, even until seventy-and-seven times."

I had finished the business now. While earnestly wishing to erase from his mind the trace of my former offence, I had stamped on that tenacious surface, another and far deeper impression: I had burnt it in.

"Now, you will indeed hate me," I said. "It is useless to attempt to conciliate you: I see I have made an eternal enemy of you."

A fresh wrong did these words inflict: the worse, because they touched on the truth. That bloodless lip quivered to a temporary spasm. I knew the steely ire I had whetted. I was heart-wrung.

"You utterly misinterpret my words," I said, at once seizing his hand: "I have no intention to grieve or pain you—indeed, I have not."

Most bitterly he smiled—most decidedly he withdrew his hand from mine. "And now you recall your promise, and will not go to India at all, I presume?" said he, after a considerable pause.

"Yes I will, as your assistant," I answered.

A very long silence succeeded. What struggle there was in him between Nature and Grace in this interval, I cannot tell: only singular gleams scintillated in his eyes, and strange shadows passed over his face. He spoke at last.

"I before proved to you the absurdity of a single woman of your age proposing to accompany abroad a single man of mine. I proved it to you in such terms as, I should have thought, would have prevented your ever again alluding to the plan. That you have done so, I regret—for your sake."

I interrupted him. Anything like a tangible reproach gave me courage at once. "Keep to common sense, St. John: you are verging on nonsense. You pretend to be shocked by what I have said. You are not really shocked; for, with your superior mind, you cannot be either so dull or so conceited as to misunderstand my meaning. I say again, I will be your curate, if you like, but never your wife."

Again he turned lividly pale; but, as before, controlled his passion perfectly. He answered emphatically, but calmly:—

"A female curate, who is not my wife, would never suit me. With me, then, it seems, you cannot go: but if you are sincere in your offer, I will, while in town, speak to a married missionary, whose wife needs a coadjutor. Your own fortune will make you independent of the Society's aid; and thus you may still be spared the dishonour of breaking your promise, and deserting the band you engaged to join."

Now I never had, as the reader knows, either given any formal promise, or entered into any engagement; and this language was much too hard, and much too despotic for the occasion. I replied:—

"There is no dishonour; no breach of promise; no desertion in the case. I am not under the slightest obligation to go to India: especially with strangers. With you I would have ventured much; because I admire, confide in, and, as a sister, I love you: but I am convinced that, go when and with whom I would, I should not live long in that climate."

"Ah! you are afraid of yourself," he said, curling his lip.

"I am. God did not give me my life to throw away; and to do as you wish me would, I begin to think, be almost equivalent to committing suicide. Moreover, before I definitely resolve on quitting England, I will know for certain, whether I cannot be of greater use by remaining in it than by leaving it."

"What do you mean?"

"It would be fruitless to attempt to explain: but there is a point on which I have long endured painful doubt; and I can go nowhere till by some means that doubt is removed."

"I know where your heart turns, and to what it clings. The interest you cherish is lawless and unconsecrated. Long since you ought to have crushed it: now you should blush to allude to it. You think of Mr. Rochester?"

It was true. I confessed it by silence.

"Are you going to seek Mr. Rochester?"

"I must find out what has become of him."

"It remains for me, then," he said, "to remember you in my prayers; and to entreat God for you, in all earnestness, that you may not indeed become a castaway. I had thought I recognised in you one of the chosen. But God sees not as man sees: *His* will be done."

He opened the gate, passed through it, and strayed away down the glen. He was soon out of sight.

On re-entering the parlour, I found Diana standing at the window, looking very thoughtful. Diana was a great deal taller than I: she put her hand on my shoulder, and, stooping, examined my face.

"Jane," she said, "you are always agitated and pale now. I am sure there is something the matter. Tell me what business St. John and you have on hands. I have watched you this half hour from the window: you must forgive my being such a spy, but for a long time I have fancied I hardly know what. St. John is a strange being"——

She paused—I did not speak: soon she resumed:—

"That brother of mine cherishes peculiar views of some sort respecting you, I am sure: he has long distinguished you by a notice and interest he never showed to anyone else—to what end? I wish he loved you—does he, Jane?"

I put her cool hand to my hot forehead: "No, Die, not one whit."

"Then why does he follow you so with his eyes—and get you so frequently alone with him, and keep you so continually at his side? Mary and I had both concluded he wished you to marry him."

"He does—he has asked me to be his wife."

Diana clapped her hands. "That is just what we hoped and thought! And you will marry him, Jane, won't you? And then he will stay in England."

"Far from that, Diana; his sole idea in proposing to me is to procure a fitting fellow-labourer in his Indian toils."

"What! He wishes you to go to India?"

"Yes."

"Madness!" she exclaimed. "You would not live three months there, I am certain. You never shall go: you have not consented—have you, Jane?"

"I have refused to marry him"——

"And have consequently displeased him?" she suggested.

"Deeply: he will never forgive me, I fear: yet I offered to accompany him as his sister."

"It was frantic folly to do so, Jane. Think of the task you undertook—one of incessant fatigue: where fatigue kills even the strong; and you are weak. St. John—you know him—would urge you to impossibilities—with him there would be no permission to rest during the hot hours; and unfortunately, I have noticed, whatever he exacts, you force yourself to perform. I am astonished you found courage to refuse his hand. You do not love him then, Jane?"

"Not as a husband."

"Yet he is a handsome fellow."

"And I am so plain you see, Die. We should never suit."

"Plain! You? Not at all. You are much too pretty, as well as too good, to be grilled alive in Calcutta." And again she earnestly conjured me to give up all thoughts of going out with her brother.

"I must, indeed," I said: "for when just now I repeated the offer of serving him for a deacon, he expressed himself shocked at my want of decency. He seemed to think I had committed an impropriety in proposing to accompany him unmarried: as if I had not from the first hoped to find in him a brother; and habitually regarded him as such."

"What makes you say he does not love you, Jane?"

"You should hear himself on the subject. He has again and again explained that it is not himself, but his office he wishes to mate. He has told me I am formed for

labour— not for love: which is true, no doubt. But, in my opinion, if I am not formed for love, it follows that I am not formed for marriage. Would it not be strange, Die, to be chained for life to a man who regarded one but as a useful tool?''

"Insupportable—unnatural—out of the question!''

"And then,'' I continued, "though I have only sisterly affection for him now, yet, if forced to be his wife, I can imagine the possibility of conceiving an inevitable, strange, torturing kind of love for him: because he is so talented; and there is often a certain heroic grandeur in his look, manner, and conversation. In that case, my lot would become unspeakably wretched. He would not want me to love him; and if I showed the feeling, he would make me sensible that it was a superfluity unrequired by him, unbecoming in me. I know he would.''

"And yet, St. John is a good man,'' said Diana.

"He is a good and a great man: but he forgets, pitilessly, the feelings and claims of little people, in pursuing his own large views. It is better, therefore, for the insignificant to keep out of his way; lest, in his progress, he should trample them down. Here he comes! I will leave you, Diana.'' And I hastened upstairs, as I saw him entering the garden.

But I was forced to meet him again at supper. During that meal he appeared just as composed as usual. I had thought he would hardly speak to me, and I was certain he had given up the pursuit of his matrimonial scheme: the sequel showed I was mistaken on both points. He addressed me precisely in his ordinary manner; or what had, of late, been his ordinary manner; one scrupulously polite. No doubt he had invoked the help of the Holy Spirit to subdue the anger I had roused in him, and now believed he had forgiven me once more.

For the evening reading before prayers, he selected the twenty-first chapter of Revelation. It was at all times pleasant to listen, while from his lips fell the words of the Bible: never did his fine voice sound at once so sweet and full—never did his manner become so impressive in its noble simplicity, as when he delivered the oracles of God: and to-night that voice took a more solemn tone—that manner a more thrilling meaning—as he sat in the midst of his household circle (the May moon shining in through the uncurtained window, and rendering almost unnecessary the light of the candle on the table): as he sat there, bending over the great old Bible, and described from its page the vision of the new heaven and the new earth— told how God would come to dwell with men, how he would wipe away all tears from their eyes, and promised that there should be no more death, neither sorrow nor crying, nor any more pain, because the former things were passed away.

The succeeding words thrilled me strangely as he spoke them: especially as I felt, by the slight, indescribable alteration in sound, that in uttering them, his eye had turned on me.

"He that overcometh shall inherit all things; and I will be his God, and he shall be my son. But,'' was slowly, distinctly read, "the fearful, the unbelieving, etc., shall have their part in the lake which burneth with fire and brimstone, which is the second death.''

Henceforward, I knew what fate St. John feared for me.

A calm, subdued triumph, blent with a longing earnestness, marked his enunciation of the last glorious verses of that chapter. The reader believed his name was already written in the Lamb's book of life, and he yearned after the hour which should admit him to the city to which the kings of the earth bring their glory and honour; which has no need of sun or moon to shine in it, because the glory of God lightens it, and the Lamb is the light thereof.

In the prayer following the chapter, all his energy gathered—all his stern zeal woke: he was in deep earnest, wrestling with God, and resolved on a conquest. He supplicated strength for the weak-hearted; guidance for wanderers from the fold: a return, even at the eleventh hour, for those whom the temptations of the world and

the flesh were luring from the narrow path. He asked, he urged, he claimed the
boon of a brand snatched from the burning. Earnestness is ever deeply solemn:
first, as I listened to that prayer, I wondered at his; then, when it continued and
rose, I was touched by it, and at last awed. He felt the greatness and goodness of
his purpose so sincerely: others who heard him plead for it, could not but feel it
too.

The prayer over, we took leave of him: he was to go at a very early hour in the
morning. Diana and Mary having kissed him, left the room—in compliance, I think,
with a whispered hint from him: I tendered my hand, and wished him a pleasant journey.

"Thank you, Jane. As I said, I shall return from Cambridge in a fortnight: that
space, then, is yet left you for reflection. If I listened to human pride, I should say
no more to you of marriage with me; but I listen to my duty, and keep steadily in
view my first aim—to do all things to the glory of God. My Master was long-
suffering: so will I be. I cannot give you up to perdition as a vessel of wrath:
repent—resolve; while there is yet time. Remember, we are bid to work while it
is day—warned that 'the night cometh when no man shall work.' Remember the
fate of Dives, who had his good things in this life. God give you strength to choose
that better part which shall not be taken from you!"

He laid his hand on my head as he uttered the last words. He had spoken earnestly,
mildly: his look was not, indeed, that of a lover beholding his mistress; but it was
that of a pastor recalling his wandering sheep—or better, of a guardian angel
watching the soul for which he is responsible. All men of talent, whether they be
men of feeling or not; whether they be zealots, or aspirants, or despots—provided
only they be sincere—have their sublime moments: when they subdue and rule. I
felt veneration for St.John—veneration so strong that its impetus thrust me at once
to the point I had so long shunned. I was tempted to cease struggling with him—
to rush down the torrent of his will into the gulf of his existence, and there lose
my own. I was almost as hard beset by him now as I had been once before, in a
different way, by another. I was a fool both times. To have yielded then would
have been an error of principle; to have yielded now would have been an error of
judgment. So I think at this hour, when I look back to the crisis through the quiet
medium of time: I was unconscious of folly at the instant.

I stood motionless under my hierophant's touch. My refusals were forgotten—
my fears overcome—my wrestlings paralysed. The Impossible—*i.e.*, my marriage
with St. John—was fast becoming the Possible. All was changing utterly, with a
sudden sweep. Religion called—Angels beckoned—God commanded—life rolled
together like a scroll—death's gates opening, showed eternity beyond: it seemed,
that for safety and bliss there, all here might be sacrificed in a second. The dim
room was full of visions.

"Could you decide now?" asked the missionary. The inquiry was put in gentle
tones: he drew me to him gently. Oh, that gentleness! how far more potent is it
than force! I could resist St. John's wrath: I grew pliant as a reed under his kindness.
Yet I knew all the time, if I yielded now, I should not the less be made to repent,
some day, of my former rebellion. His nature was not changed by one hour of
solemn prayer: it was only elevated.

"I could decide if I were but certain," I answered: "were I but convinced that
it is God's will I should marry you, I could vow to marry you here and now—
come afterwards what would!"

"My prayers are heard!" ejaculated St. John. He pressed his hand firmer on my
head, as if he claimed me: he surrounded me with his arm, *almost* as if he loved
me (I say *almost*—I knew the difference—for I had felt what it was to be loved;
but, like him, I had now put love out of the question, and thought only of duty):
I contended with my inward dimness of vision, before which clouds yet rolled. I
sincerely, deeply, fervently longed to do what was right; and only that. "Show
me, show me the path!" I entreated of Heaven. I was excited more than I had ever

been; and whether what followed was the effect of excitement, the reader shall judge.

All the house was still; for I believe all, except St. John and myself, were now retired to rest. The one candle was dying out: the room was full of moonlight. My heart beat fast and thick: I heard its throb. Suddenly it stood still to an inexpressible feeling that thrilled it through, and passed at once to my head and extremities. The feeling was not like an electric shock; but it was quite as sharp, as strange, as startling: it acted on my senses as if their utmost activity hitherto had been but torpor; from which they were now summoned, and forced to wake. They rose expectant: eye and ear waited, while the flesh quivered on my bones.

"What have you heard? What do you see?" asked St. John. I saw nothing: but I heard a voice somewhere cry—

"Jane! Jane! Jane!" nothing more.

"Oh God!what is it?" I gasped.

I might have said, "Where is it?" for it did not seem in the room—nor in the house—nor in the garden: it did not come out of the air—nor from under the earth—nor from overhead. I had heard it—where, or whence, for ever impossible to know! And it was the voice of a human being—a known, loved, well-remembered voice—that of Edward Fairfax Rochester; and it spoke in pain and woe wildly, eerily, urgently.

"I am coming!" I cried. "Wait for me! Oh, I will come!" I flew to the door, and looked into the passage: it was dark. I ran out into the garden: it was void.

"Where are you?" I exclaimed.

The hills beyond Marsh Glen sent the answer faintly back—"Where are you?" I listened. The wind sighed low in the firs: all was moorland loneliness and midnight hush.

"Down superstition!" I commented, as that spectre rose up black by the black yew at the gate. "This is not thy deception, not thy witchcraft: it is the work of nature. She was roused, and did—no miracle—but her best."

I broke from St. John; who had followed, and would have detained me. It was *my* time to assume ascendancy. *My* powers were in play, and in force. I told him to forbear question or remark; I desired him to leave me: I must, and would be alone. He obeyed at once. Where there is energy to command well enough, obedience never fails. I mounted to my chamber; locked myself in; fell on my knees; and prayed in my way—a different way to St. John's, but effective in its own fashion. I seemed to penetrate very near a Mighty Spirit; and my soul rushed out in gratitude at His feet. I rose from the thanksgiving—took a resolve—and lay down, unscared, enlightened—eager but for the daylight.

Chapter XXXVI

THE daylight came. I rose at dawn. I busied myself for an hour or two with arranging my things in my chamber, drawers and wardrobe, in the order wherein I should wish to leave them during a brief absence. Meantime, I heard St. John quit his room. He stopped at my door: I feared he would knock—no, but a slip of paper was passed under the door. I took it up. It bore these words—

"You left me too suddenly last night. Had you stayed but a little longer, you would have laid your hand on the Christian's cross and the angel's crown. I shall expect your clear decision when I return this day fortnight. Meantime, watch and pray that you enter not into temptation: the spirit, I trust, is willing, but the flesh, I see, is weak. I shall pray for you hourly,—Yours, St. John."

"My spirit," I answered, mentally, "is willing to do what is right; and my flesh, I hope, is strong enough to accomplish the will of Heaven, when once that will is distinctly known to me. At any rate, it shall be strong enough to search—inquire—to grope an outlet from this crowd of doubt, and find the open day of certainty."

It was the first of June; yet the morning was overcast and chilly: rain beat fast on my casement. I heard the front-door open, and St. John pass out. Looking through the window, I saw him traverse the garden. He took the way over the misty moors in the direction of Whitcross—there he would meet the coach.

"In a few more hours I shall succeed you in that track, cousin," thought I: "I too have a coach to meet at Whitcross. I too have some to see and ask after in England, before I depart for ever."

It wanted yet two hours of breakfast-time. I filled the interval in walking softly about my room, and pondering the visitation which had given my plans their present bent. I recalled that inward sensation I had experienced: for I could recall it, with all its unspeakable strangeness. I recalled the voice I had heard; again I questioned whence it came, as vainly as before: it seemed in *me*—not in the external world. I asked, was it a mere nervous impression—a delusion? I could not conceive or believe: it was more like an inspiration. The wondrous shock of feeling had come like the earthquake which shook the foundations of Paul and Silas's prison; it had opened the doors of the soul's cell, and loosed its bands—it had wakened it out of its sleep, whence it sprang trembling, listening, aghast; then vibrated thrice a cry on my startled ear, and in my quaking heart, and through my spirit; which neither feared nor shook, but exulted as if in joy over the success of one effort it had been privileged to make, independent of the cumbrous body.

"Ere many days," I said, as I terminated my musings, "I will know something of him whose voice seemed last night to summon me. Letters have proved of no avail—personal inquiry shall replace them."

At breakfast I announced to Diana and Mary that I was going a journey, and should be absent at least four days.

"Alone, Jane?" they asked.

"Yes; it was to see, or hear news of, a friend about whom I had for some time been uneasy."

They might have said, as I have no doubt they thought, that they had believed me to be without any friends save them: for, indeed, I had often said so; but with their true natural delicacy, they abstained from comment: except that Diana asked me if I was sure I was well enough to travel. I looked very pale, she observed. I replied, that nothing ailed me save anxiety of mind, which I hoped soon to alleviate.

It was easy to make my further arrangements; for I was troubled with no inquiries—no surmises. Having once explained to them that I could not now be explicit about my plans, they kindly and wisely acquiesced in the silence with which I pursued them; according to me the privilege of free action I should, under similar circumstances, have accorded them.

I left Moor House at three o'clock P.M., and soon after four, I stood at the foot of the sign-post of Whitcross, waiting the arrival of the coach which was to take me to distant Thornfield. Amidst the silence of those solitary roads and desert hills, I heard it approach from a great distance. It was the same vehicle whence, a year ago, I had alighted one summer evening on this very spot—how desolate, and hopeless, and objectless! It stopped as I beckoned. I entered—not now obliged to part with my whole fortune as the price of its accommodation. Once more on the road to Thornfield, I felt like the messenger-pigeon flying home.

It was a journey of six-and-thirty hours. I had set out from Whitcross on a Tuesday afternoon, and early on the succeeding Thursday morning the coach stopped to water the horses at a wayside inn, situated in the midst of scenery whose green hedges and large fields, and low pastoral hills (how mild of feature and verdant of hue compared with the stern north-midland moors of Morton!) met my eye like the

lineaments of a once familiar face. Yes, I knew the character of this landscape: I was sure we were near my bourne.

"How far is Thornfield Hall from here?" I asked of the ostler.

"Just two miles, ma'am, across the fields."

"My journey is closed," I thought to myself. I got out of the coach, gave a box I had into the ostler's charge, to be kept till I called for it; paid my fare; satisfied the coachman, and was going: the brightening day gleamed on the sign of the inn, and I read in gilt letters, "The Rochester Arms." My heart leapt up: I was already on my master's very lands. It fell again: the thought struck it:—

"Your master himself may be beyond the British Channel, for aught you know: and then, if he is at Thornfield Hall, towards which you hasten, who besides him is there? His lunatic wife: and you have nothing to do with him: you dare not speak to him or seek his presence. You have lost your labour—you had better go no farther," urged the monitor. "Ask information of the people at the inn; they can give you all you seek: they can solve your doubts at once. Go up to that man, and inquire if Mr. Rochester be at home."

The suggestion was sensible; and yet I could not force myself to act on it. I so dreaded a reply that would crush me with despair. To prolong doubt was to prolong hope. I might yet once more see the Hall under the ray of her star. There was the stile before me—the very fields through which I had hurried, blind, deaf, distracted, with a revengeful fury tracking and scourging me, on the morning I fled from Thornfield: ere I well knew what course I had resolved to take, I was in the midst of them. How fast I walked! How I ran sometimes! How I looked forward to catch the first view of the well-known woods! With what feelings I welcomed single trees I knew, and familiar glimpses of meadow and hill between them!

At last the woods rose; the rookery clustered dark; a loud cawing broke the morning stillness. Strange delight inspired me: on I hastened. Another field crossed—a lane threaded—and there were the courtyard walls—the back offices: the house itself, the rookery still hid. "My first view of it shall be in front," I determined, "where its bold battlements will strike the eye nobly at once, and where I can single out my master's very window: perhaps he will be standing at it—he rises early: perhaps he is now walking in the orchard, or on the pavement in front. Could I but see him!—but a moment! Surely, in that case, I should not be so mad as to run to him? I cannot tell—I am not certain. And if I did—what then? God bless him! What then? Who would be hurt by my once more tasting the life his glance can give me—I rave: perhaps at this moment he is watching the sun rise over the Pyrenees, or on the tideless sea of the south."

I had coasted along the lower wall of the orchard—turned its angle: there was a gate just there, opening into the meadow, between two stone pillars, crowned by stone balls. From behind one pillar, I could peep round quietly at the full front of the mansion. I advanced my head with precaution, desirous to ascertain if any bedroom window-blinds were yet drawn up: battlements, windows, long front—all from this sheltered station were at my command.

The crows sailing overhead perhaps watched me while I took this survey. I wonder what they thought: they must have considered I was very careful and timid at first, and that gradually I grew very bold and reckless. A peep, and then a long stare; and then a departure from my niche and a straying out into the meadow; and a sudden stop full in front of the great mansion, and a protracted, hardy gaze towards it. "What affectation of diffidence was this at first?" they might have demanded, "What stupid regardlessness now?"

Hear an illustration, reader.

A lover finds his mistress asleep on a mossy bank; he wishes to catch a glimpse of her fair face without waking her. He steals softly over the grass, careful to make no sound; he pauses—fancying she has stirred: he withdraws; not for worlds would he be seen. All is still: he again advances: he bends over her; a light veil rests on

her features: he lifts it, bends lower; now his eyes anticipate the vision of beauty—warm, and blooming, and lovely, in rest. How hurried was their first glance! But how they fix! How he starts! How he suddenly and vehemently clasps in both arms the form he dared not, a moment since, touch with his finger! How he calls aloud a name, and drops his burden, and gazes on it wildly! He thus grasps and cries, and gazes, because he no longer fears to waken by any sound he can utter—by any movement he can make. He thought his love slept sweetly: he finds she is stone-dead.

I looked with timorous joy towards a stately house: I saw a blackened ruin.

No need to cower behind a gate-post, indeed!—to peep up at chamber lattices, fearing life was astir behind them! No need to listen for doors opening—to fancy steps on the pavement or the gravel-walk! The lawn, the grounds were trodden and waste: the portal yawned void. The front was, as I had once seen it in a dream, but a shell-like wall, very high and very fragile looking, perforated with paneless windows: no roof, no battlements, no chimneys—all had crashed in.

And there was the silence of death about it: the solitude of a lonesome wild. No wonder that letters addressed to people here had never received an answer: as well despatch epistles to a vault in a church aisle. The grim blackness of the stones told by what fate the Hall had fallen—by conflagration: but how kindled? What story belonged to this disaster? What loss, besides mortar and marble, and woodwork, had followed upon it? Had life been wrecked, as well as property? If so, whose? Dreadful question: there was no one here to answer it—not even dumb sign, mute token.

In wandering round the shattered walls and through the devastated interior, I gathered evidence that the calamity was not of late occurrence. Winter snows, I thought, had drifted through that void arch; winter rains beaten in at those hollow casements; for, amidst the drenched piles of rubbish, spring had cherished vegetation: grass and weed grew here and there between the stones and fallen rafters. And oh! where, meantime, was the hapless owner of this wreck? In what land? Under what auspices? My eye involuntarily wandered to the grey church tower near the gates, and I asked, "Is he with Damer de Rochester, sharing the shelter of his narrow marble house?"

Some answer must be had to these questions. I could find it nowhere but at the inn, and thither, ere long, I returned. The host himself brought my breakfast into the parlour. I requested him to shut the door and sit down: I had some questions to ask him. But when he complied, I scarcely knew how to begin; such horror had I of the possible answers. And yet the spectacle of desolation I had just left, prepared me in a measure for a tale of misery. The host was a respectable-looking, middle-aged man.

"You know Thornfield Hall, of course?" I managed to say at last.

"Yes, ma'am; I lived there once."

"Did you?" Not in my time, I thought; you are a stranger to me.

"I was the late Mr. Rochester's butler," he added.

The late! I seemed to have received with full force, the blow I had been trying to evade.

"The late!" I gasped. "Is he dead?"

"I mean the present gentleman, Mr. Edward's father," he explained. I breathed again: my blood resumed its flow. Fully assured by these words that Mr. Edward—*my* Mr. Rochester (God bless him, wherever he was!) was at least alive: was, in short, "the present gentleman." Gladdening words! It seemed I could hear all that was to come—whatever the disclosures might be—with comparative tranquillity. Since he was not in the grave, I could bear, I thought, to learn that he was at the Antipodes.

"Is Mr. Rochester living at Thornfield now?" I asked, knowing, of course, what the answer would be, but yet desirous of deferring the direct question as to where he really was.

"No, ma'am—oh, no! No one is living there. I suppose you are a stranger in these parts, or you would have heard what happened last autumn,—Thornfield Hall is quite a ruin: it was burnt down just about harvest time. A dreadful calamity! such an immense quantity of valuable property destroyed: hardly any of the furniture could be saved. The fire broke out at dead of night, and before the engines arrived from Millcote, the building was one mass of flame. It was a terrible spectacle: I witnessed it myself."

"At dead of night!" I muttered. Yes, that was ever the hour of fatality at Thornfield. "Was it known how it originated?" I demanded.

"They guessed, ma'am: they guessed. Indeed, I should say it was ascertained beyond a doubt. You are not perhaps aware," he continued, edging his chair a little nearer the table, and speaking low, "that there was a lady,—a—a lunatic, kept in the house?"

"I have heard something of it."

"She was kept in very close confinement, ma'am; people even for years was not absolutely certain of her existence. No one saw her: they only knew by rumour that such a person was at the Hall; and who or what she was it was difficult to conjecture. They said Mr. Edward had brought her from abroad; and some believed she had been his mistress. But a queer thing happened a year since—a very queer thing."

I feared now to hear my own story. I endeavoured to recall him to the main fact.

"And this lady?"

"This lady, ma'am," he answered, "turned out to be Mr. Rochester's wife! The discovery was brought about in the strangest way. There was a young lady, a governess at the Hall, that Mr. Rochester fell in"——

"But the fire," I suggested.

"I'm coming to that, ma'am—that Mr. Edward fell in love with. The servants say they never saw anybody so much in love as he was: he was after her continually. They used to watch him—servants will, you know, ma'am—and he set store on her past everything: for all, nobody but him thought her so very handsome. She was a little small thing, they say, almost like a child. I never saw her myself; but I've heard Leah, the housemaid, tell of her. Leah liked her well enough. Mr. Rochester was about forty, and this governess not twenty; and you see, when gentlemen of his age fall in love with girls, they are often like as if they were bewitched: well, he would marry her."

"You shall tell me this part of the story another time," I said; "but now I have a particular reason for wishing to hear all about the fire. Was it suspected that this lunatic, Mrs. Rochester, had any hand in it?"

"You've hit it, ma'am: it's quite certain that it was her and nobody but her, that set it going. She had a woman to take care of her called Mrs. Poole—an able woman in her line, and very trustworthy, but for one fault—a fault common to a deal of them nurses and matrons—*she kept a private bottle of gin by her,* and now and then took a drop over much. It is excusable, for she had a hard life of it: but still it was dangerous; for when Mrs. Poole was fast asleep, after the gin and water, the mad lady, who was as cunning as a witch, would take the keys out of her pocket, let herself out of her chamber, and go roaming about the house, doing any wild mischief that came into her head. They say she had nearly burnt her husband in his bed once: but I don't know about that. However, on this night, she set fire first to the hangings of the room next to her own; and then she got down to a lower story, and made her way to the chamber that had been the governess's—(she was like as if she knew somehow matters had gone on, and had a spite at her)—and she kindled the bed there; but there was nobody sleeping in it fortunately. The

governess had run away two months before; and for all Mr. Rochester sought her as if she had been the most precious thing he had in the world, he never could hear a word of her; and he grew savage—quite savage on his disappointment: he never was a wild man, but he got dangerous after he lost her. He would be alone, too. He sent Mrs. Fairfax, the housekeeper, away to her friends at a distance; but he did it handsomely, for he settled an annuity on her for life: and she deserved it— she was a very good woman. Miss Adèle, a ward he had, was put to school. He broke off acquaintance with all the gentry, and shut himself up, like a hermit, at the Hall.''

"What! did he not leave England?''

"Leave England? Bless you, no! He would not cross the door-stones of the house; except at night, when he walked just like a ghost about the grounds and in the orchard as if he had lost his senses—which it is my opinion he had; for a more spirited, bolder, keener gentleman than he was before that midge of a governess crossed him, you never saw, ma'am. He was not a man given to wine, or cards, or racing, as some are, and he was not so very handsome; but he had a courage and a will of his own, if ever man had. I knew him from a boy, you see: and for my part I have often wished that Miss Eyre had been sunk in the sea before she came to Thornfield Hall.''

"Then Mr. Rochester was at home when the fire broke out?''

"Yes, indeed was he; and he went up to the attics when all was burning above and below, and got the servants out of their beds and helped them down himself— and went back to get his mad wife out of her cell. And then they called out to him that she was on the roof; where she was standing, waving her arms, above the battlements, and shouting out till they could hear her a mile off: I saw her and heard her with my own eyes. She was a big woman, and had long, black hair: we could see it streaming against the flames as she stood. I witnessed, and several more witnessed Mr. Rochester ascend through the skylight on to the roof: we heard him call 'Bertha!' We saw him approach her; and then, ma'am, she yelled, and gave a spring, and the next minute she lay smashed on the pavement.''

"Dead?''

"Dead? Ay, dead as the stones on which her brains and blood were scattered.''

"Good God!''

"You may well say so, ma'am: it was frightful!''

He shuddered.

"And afterwards?'' I urged.

"Well, ma'am, afterwards the house was burnt to the ground: there are only some bits of walls standing now.''

"Were any other lives lost?''

"No—perhaps it would have been better if there had.''

"What do you mean?''

"Poor Mr. Edward!'' he ejaculated, "I little thought ever to have seen it! Some say it was a just judgment on him for keeping his first marriage secret, and wanting to take another wife while he had one living: but I pity him, for my part.''

"You said he was alive?'' I exclaimed.

"Yes, yes: he is alive; but many think he had better be dead.''

"Why? How?'' My blood was again running cold.

"Where is he?'' I demanded. "Is he in England?''

"Ay—ay—he's in England; he can't get out of England, I fancy—he's a fixture now.''

What agony was this! And the man seemed resolved to protract it.

"He is stone-blind,'' he said at last. "Yes—he is stone-blind—is Mr. Edward.''

I had dreaded worse. I had dreaded he was mad. I summoned strength to ask what had caused this calamity.

"It was all his own courage, and a body may say, his kindness, in a way, ma'am: he wouldn't leave the house till every one else was out before him. As he came down the great staircase at last, after Mrs. Rochester had flung herself from the battlements, there was a great crash—all fell. He was taken out from under the ruins, alive, but sadly hurt: a beam had fallen in such a way as to protect him partly; but one eye was knocked out, and one hand so crushed that Mr. Carter, the surgeon, had to amputate it directly. The other eye inflamed: he lost the sight of that also. He is now helpless, indeed—blind and a cripple."

"Where is he? Where does he now live?"

"At Ferndean, a manor-house on a farm he has, about thirty miles off: quite a desolate spot."

"Who is with him?"

"Old John and his wife: he would have none else. He is quite broken down, they say."

"Have you any sort of conveyance?"

"We have a chaise, ma'am, a very handsome chaise."

"Let it be got ready instantly; and if your post-boy can drive me to Ferndean before dark this day, I'll pay both you and him twice the hire you usually demand."

Chapter XXXVII

THE manor-house of Ferndean was a building of considerable antiquity, moderate size, and no architectural pretensions, deep buried in a wood. I had heard of it before. Mr. Rochester often spoke of it, and sometimes went there. His father had purchased the estate for the sake of the game covers. He would have let the house: but could find no tenant, in consequence of its ineligible and insalubrious site. Ferndean then remained uninhabited and unfurnished; with the exception of some two or three rooms fitted up for the accommodation of the squire when he went there in the season to shoot.

To this house I came, just ere dark, on an evening marked by the characteristics of sad sky, cold gale, and continued small, penetrating rain. The last mile I performed on foot, having dismissed the chaise and driver with the double remuneration I had promised. Even when within a very short distance of the manor-house, you could see nothing of it; so thick and dark grew the timber of the gloomy wood about it. Iron gates between granite pillars showed me where to enter, and passing through them, I found myself at once in the twilight of close-ranked trees. There was a grass-grown track descending the forest aisle, between hoar and knotty shafts and under branched arches. I followed it, expecting soon to reach the dwelling; but it stretched on and on, it wound far and farther: no sign of habitation or grounds was visible.

I thought I had taken a wrong direction and lost my way. The darkness of natural as well as of sylvan dusk gathered over me. I looked round in search of another road. There was none: all was interwoven stem, columnar trunk, dense, summer foliage—no opening anywhere.

I proceeded: at last my way opened, the trees thinned a little; presently I beheld a railing, then the house—scarce, by this dim light, distinguishable from the trees; so dank and green were its decaying walls. Entering a portal, fastened only by a latch, I stood amidst a space of enclosed ground, from which the wood swept away in a semicircle. There were no flowers, no garden-beds; only a broad gravel-walk girdling a grass-plat, and this set in the heavy frame of the forest. The house presented two pointed gables in its front: the windows were latticed and narrow: the front-door was narrow too, one step led up to it. The whole looked, as the host

of the Rochester Arms had said, "quite a desolate spot." It was as still as a church
on a week-day: the pattering rain on the forest leaves was the only sound audible
in its vicinage.

"Can there be life here?" I asked.

Yes: life of some kind there was; for I heard a movement—that narrow front-
door was unclosing, and some shape was about to issue from the grange.

It opened slowly; a figure came out into the twilight and stood on the step; a
man without a hat: he stretched forth his hand as if to feel whether it rained. Dusk
as it was, I had recognised him—it was my master, Edward Fairfax Rochester, and
no other.

I stayed my step, almost my breath, and stood to watch him—to examine him,
myself unseen, and alas! to him invisible. It was a sudden meeting, and one in
which rapture was kept well in check by pain. I had no difficulty in restraining my
voice from exclamation, my step from hasty advance.

His form was of the same strong and stalwart contour as ever: his port was still
erect, his hair was still raven-black; nor were his features altered or sunk: not in
one year's space, by any sorrow, could his athletic strength be quelled, or his
vigorous prime blighted. But in his countenance, I saw a change: that looked
desperate and brooding—that reminded me of some wronged and fettered wild beast
or bird, dangerous to approach in his sullen woe. The caged eagle, whose gold-
ringed eyes cruelty has extinguished, might look as looked that sightless Samson.

And, reader, do you think I feared him in his blind ferocity?—if you do, you
little know me. A soft hope blent with my sorrow that soon I should dare to drop
a kiss on that brow of rock, and on those lips so sternly sealed beneath it: but not
yet. I would not accost him yet.

He descended the one step, and advanced slowly and gropingly towards the grass-
plat. Where was his daring stride now? Then he paused, as if he knew not which
way to turn. He lifted his hand and opened his eyelids; gazed blank, and with a
straining effort, on the sky, and towards the amphitheatre of trees: one saw that all
to him was void darkness. He stretched his right hand (the left arm, the mutilated
one, he kept hidden in his bosom); he seemed to wish by touch to gain an idea of
what lay around him: he met but vacancy still; for the trees were some yards off
where he stood. He relinquished the endeavour, folded his arms, and stood quiet
and mute in the rain, now falling fast on his uncovered head. At this moment John
approached him from some quarter.

"Will you take my arm, sir?" he said; "there is a heavy shower coming on;
had you not better go in?"

"Let me alone," was the answer.

John withdrew, without having observed me. Mr. Rochester now tried to walk
about: vainly,—all was too uncertain. He groped his way back to the house, and,
re-entering it, closed the door.

I now drew near and knocked: John's wife opened for me. "Mary," I said,
"how are you?"

She started as if she had seen a ghost: I calmed her. To her hurried "Is it really
you, miss, come at this late hour to this 'only place?" I answered by taking her
hand; and then I followed her into the kitchen, where John now sat by a good fire.
I explained to them, in a few words, that I had heard all which had happened since
I left Thornfield, and that I was come to see Mr. Rochester. I asked John to go
down to the turnpike-house, where I had dismissed the chaise, and bring my trunk,
which I had left there: and then, while I removed my bonnet and shawl, I questioned
Mary as to whether I could be accommodated at the Manor House for the night;
and finding that arrangements to that effect, though difficult, would not be impossible,
I informed her I should stay. Just at this moment the parlour-bell rang.

"When you go in," said I, "tell your master that a person wishes to speak to
him, but do not give my name."

"I don't think he will see you," she answered; "he refuses every body."

When she returned, I inquired what he had said.

"You are to send in your name and your business," she replied. She then proceeded to fill a glass with water, and place it on a tray, together with candles.

"Is that what he rang for?" I asked.

"Yes: he always has candles brought in at dark, though he is blind."

"Give the tray to me, I will carry it in."

I took it from her hand: she pointed me out the parlour door. The tray shook as I held it; the water spilt from the glass; my heart struck my ribs loud and fast. Mary opened the door for me, and shut it behind me.

This parlour looked gloomy: a neglected handful of fire burnt low in the grate; and, leaning over it, with his head supported against the high, old-fashioned mantel-piece, appeared the blind tenant of the room. His old dog, Pilot, lay on one side, removed out of the way, and coiled up as if afraid of being inadvertently trodden upon. Pilot pricked up his ears when I came in: then he jumped up with a yelp and a whine, and bounded towards me: he almost knocked the tray from my hands. I set it on the table; then patted him, and said softly, "Lie down!" Mr. Rochester turned mechanically to *see* what the commotion was: but as he *saw* nothing, he returned and sighed.

"Give me the water, Mary," he said.

I approached him with the now only half-filled glass. Pilot followed me, still excited.

"What is the matter?" he inquired.

"Down, Pilot!" I again said. He checked the water on its way to his lips, and seemed to listen: he drank, and put the glass down. "This is you, Mary, is it not?"

"Mary is in the kitchen," I answered.

He put out his hand with a quick gesture, but not seeing where I stood, he did not touch me. "Who is this? Who is this?" he demanded, trying, as it seemed, to *see* with those sightless eyes—unavailing and distressing attempt! "Answer me—speak again!" he ordered, imperiously and aloud.

"Will you have a little more water, sir? I spilt half of what was in the glass," I said.

"*Who* is it? *What* is it? Who speaks?"

"Pilot knows me, and John and Mary know I am here. I came only this evening," I answered.

"Great God!—what delusion has come over me? What sweet madness has seized me?"

"No delusion—no madness: your mind, sir, is too strong for delusion, your health too sound for frenzy."

"And where is the speaker? Is it only a voice? Oh! I *cannot* see, but I must feel, or my heart will stop and my brain burst. Whatever—whoever you are—be perceptible to the touch or I cannot live!"

He groped; I arrested his wandering hand, and prisoned it in both mine.

"Her very fingers!" he cried; "her small, slight fingers! If so, there must be more of her."

The muscular hand broke from my custody; my arm was seized, my shoulder—neck—waist—I was entwined and gathered to him.

"Is it Jane? *What* is it? This is her shape—this is her size"——

"And this her voice," I added. "She is all here: her heart, too. God bless you, sir! I am glad to be so near you again."

"Jane Eyre!—Jane Eyre," was all he said.

"My dear master," I answered, "I am Jane Eyre: I have found you out—I am come back to you."

"In truth?—in the flesh? My living Jane?"

"You touch me, sir,—you hold me, and fast enough: I am not like a corpse, nor vacant like air, am I?"

"My living darling! These are certainly her limbs, and these her features; but I cannot be so blest, after all my misery. It is a dream; such dreams as I have had at night when I have clasped her once more to my heart, as I do now; and kissed her, as thus—and felt that she loved me, and trusted that she would not leave me."

"Which I never will, sir, from this day."

"Never will, says the vision? But I always woke and found it an empty mockery; and I was desolate and abandoned—my life dark, lonely, hopeless—my soul athirst and forbidden to drink—my heart famished and never to be fed. Gentle, soft dream, nestling in my arms now, you will fly, too, as your sisters have all fled before you: but kiss me before you go—embrace me, Jane."

"There, sir—and there!"

I pressed my lips to his once brilliant and now rayless eyes—I swept his hair from his brow, and kissed that too. He suddenly seemed to arouse himself: the conviction of the reality of all this seized him.

"It is you—is it, Jane? You are come back to me, then?"

"I am."

"And you do not lie dead in some ditch under some stream? And you are not a pining outcast amongst strangers?"

"No, sir; I am an independent woman now."

"Independent! What do you mean, Jane?"

"My uncle in Madeira is dead, and he left me five thousand pounds."

"Ah, this is practical—this is real!" he cried: "I should never dream that. Besides, there is that peculiar voice of hers, so animating and piquant, as well as soft: it cheers my withered heart; it puts life into it.—What, Janet! Are you an independent woman? A rich woman?"

"Quite rich, sir. If you won't let me live with you, I can build a house of my own close up to your door, and you may come and sit in my parlour when you want company of an evening."

"But as you are rich, Jane, you have now, no doubt, friends who will look after you, and not suffer you to devote yourself to a blind lameter like me?"

"I told you I am independent, sir, as well as rich: I am my own mistress."

"And you will stay with me?"

"Certainly—unless you object. I will be your neighbour, your nurse, your house-keeper. I find you lonely: I will be your companion—to read to you, to walk with you, to sit with you, to wait on you, to be eyes and hands to you. Cease to look so melancholy, my dear master; you shall not be left desolate, so long as I live."

He replied not: he seemed serious—abstracted; he sighed; he half-opened his lips as if to speak: he closed them again. I felt a little embarrassed. Perhaps I had too rashly overleaped conventionalities; and he, like St. John, saw impropriety in my inconsiderateness. I had indeed made my proposal from the idea that he wished and would ask me to be his wife: an expectation, not the less certain because unexpressed, had buoyed me up, that he would claim me at once as his own. But no hint to that effect escaping him and his countenance becoming more overcast, I suddenly remembered that I might have been all wrong, and was perhaps playing the fool unwittingly; and I began gently to withdraw myself from his arms—but he eagerly snatched me closer.

"No—no—Jane; you must not go. No—I have touched you, heard you, felt the comfort of your presence—the sweetness of your consolation: I cannot give up these joys. I have little left in myself—I must have you. The world may laugh—may call me absurd, selfish—but it does not signify. My very soul demands you: it will be satisfied: or it will take deadly vengeance on its frame."

"Well, sir, I will stay with you: I have said so."

"Yes—but you understand one thing by staying with me: and I understand another. You, perhaps, could make up your mind to be about my hand and chair—to wait on me as a kind little nurse (for you have an affectionate heart and a generous spirit, which prompt you to make sacrifices for those you pity), and that ought to suffice for me no doubt. I suppose I should now entertain none but fatherly feelings for you; do you think so? Come—tell me."

"I will think what you like, sir: I am content to be only your nurse, if you think it better."

"But you cannot always be my nurse, Janet: you are young—you must marry one day."

"I don't care about being married."

"You should care, Janet: if I were what I once was, I would try to make you care—but—a sightless block!"

He relapsed again into gloom. I, on the contrary, became more cheerful, and took fresh courage: these last words gave me an insight as to where the difficulty lay; and as it was no difficulty with me, I felt quite relieved from my previous embarrassment. I resumed a livelier vein of conversation.

"It is time some one undertook to rehumanise you," said I, parting his thick and long uncut locks; "for I see you are being metamorphosed into a lion, or something of that sort. You have a 'faux air' of Nebuchadnezzar in the fields about you, that is certain: your hair reminds me of eagles' feathers; whether your nails are grown like birds' claws or not, I have not yet noticed."

"On this arm, I have neither hand nor nails," he said, drawing the mutilated limb from his breast, and showing it to me. "It is a mere stump—a ghastly sight! Don't you think so, Jane?"

"It is a pity to see it; and a pity to see your eyes—and the scar of fire on your forehead: and the worst of it is, one is in danger of loving you too well for all this; and making too much of you."

"I thought you would be revolted, Jane, when you saw my arm, and my cicatrised visage."

"Did you? Don't tell me so—lest I should say something disparaging to your judgment. Now, let me leave you an instant, to make a better fire, and have the hearth swept up. Can you tell when there is a good fire?"

"Yes; with the right eye I see a glow—a ruddy haze."

"And you see the candles?"

"Very dimly—each is a luminous cloud."

"Can you see me?"

"No, my fairy: but I am only too thankful to hear and feel you."

"When do you take supper?"

"I never take supper."

"But you shall have some to-night. I am hungry: so are you, I daresay, only you forget."

Summoning Mary, I soon had the room in more cheerful order: I prepared him, likewise, a comfortable repast. My spirits were excited, and with pleasure and ease I talked to him during supper, and for a long time after. There was no harassing restraint, no repressing of glee and vivacity with him; for with him I was at perfect ease, because I knew I suited him: all I said or did seemed either to console or revive him. Delightful consciousness! It brought to life and light my whole nature: in his presence I thoroughly lived; and he lived in mine. Blind as he was, smiles played over his face, joy dawned on his forehead: his lineaments softened and warmed.

After supper, he began to ask me many questions, of where I had been, what I had been doing, how I had found him out; but I gave him only very partial replies: it was too late to enter into particulars that night. Besides, I wished to touch no deep-thrilling chord—to open no fresh well of emotion in his heart: my sole present

aim was to cheer him. Cheered, as I have said, he was: and yet but by fits. If a moment's silence broke the conversation, he would turn restless, touch me, then say, ''Jane.''

''You are altogether a human being, Jane? You are certain of that?''

''I conscientiously believe so, Mr. Rochester.''

''Yet how, on this dark and doleful evening, could you so suddenly rise on my lone hearth? I stretched my hand to take a glass of water from a hireling, and it was given me by you: I asked a question, expecting John's wife to answer me, and your voice spoke at my ear.''

''Because I had come in, in Mary's stead, with the tray.''

''And there is enchantment in the very hour I am now spending with you. Who can tell what a dark, dreary, hopeless life I have dragged on for months past? Doing nothing, expecting nothing; merging night in day; feeling but the sensation of cold when I let the fire go out, of hunger when I forgot to eat: and then a ceaseless sorrow, and, at times, a very delirium of desire to behold my Jane again. Yes: for her restoration I longed, far more than for that of my lost sight. How can it be that Jane is with me, and says she loves me? Will she not depart as suddenly as she came? To-morrow, I fear I shall find her no more.''

A common-place, practical reply, out of the train of his own disturbed ideas, was, I was sure, the best and most reassuring for him in this frame of mind. I passed my finger over his eyebrows, and remarked that they were scorched, and that I would apply something which should make them grow as broad and black as ever.

''What is the use of doing me good in any way, beneficent spirit, when, at some fatal moment, you will again desert me—passing like a shadow, whither and how to me unknown; and for me, remaining afterwards undiscoverable?''

''Have you a pocket-comb about you, sir?''

''What for, Jane?''

''Just to comb out this shaggy black mane. I find you rather alarming, when I examine you close at hand: you talk of my being a fairy; but I am sure, you are more like a brownie.''

''Am I hideous, Jane?''

''Very, sir: you always were, you know.''

''Humph! The wickedness has not been taken out of you, wherever you have sojourned.''

''Yet I have been with good people; far better than you: a hundred times better people; possessed of ideas and views you never entertained in your life: quite more refined and exalted.''

''Who the deuce have you been with?''

''If you twist in that way you will make me pull the hair out of your head; and then I think you will cease to entertain doubts of my substantiality.''

''Who have you been with, Jane?''

''You shall not get it out of me to-night, sir; you must wait till to-morrow; to leave my tale half-told, will, you know, be a sort of security that I shall appear at your breakfast-table to finish it. By-the-by, I must mind not to rise on your hearth with only a glass of water, then: I must bring an egg at the least, to say nothing of fried ham.''

''You mocking changeling—fairy-born and human-bred! You make me feel as I have not felt these twelve months. If Saul could have had you for his David, the evil spirit would have been exorcised without the aid of the harp.''

''There, sir, you are redd up and made decent. Now I'll leave you: I have been travelling these last three days, and I believe I am tired. Good-night.''

''Just one word, Jane: were there only ladies in the house where you have been?''

I laughed and made my escape, still laughing as I ran upstairs. "A good idea!" I thought, with glee. "I see I have the means of fretting him out of his melancholy for some time to come."

Very early the next morning, I heard him up and astir, wandering from one room to another. As soon as Mary came down I heard the question: "Is Miss Eyre here?" Then: "Which room did you put her into? Was it dry? Is she up? Go and ask if she wants anything: and when she will come down."

I came down as soon as I thought there was a prospect of breakfast. Entering the room very softly, I had a view of him before he discovered my presence. It was mournful, indeed, to witness the subjugation of that vigorous spirit to a corporeal infirmity. He sat in his chair,—still, but not at rest: expectant evidently; the lines of now habitual sadness marking his strong features. His countenance reminded one of a lamp quenched, waiting to be relit—and alas! it was not himself that could now kindle the lustre of animated expression: he was dependent on another for that office! I had meant to be gay and careless, but the powerlessness of the strong man touched my heart to the quick: still I accosted him with what vivacity I could:—

"It is a bright, sunny morning, sir," I said. "The rain is over and gone, and there is a tender shining after it: you shall have a walk soon."

I had wakened the glow: his features beamed.

"Oh, you are indeed there, my skylark! Come to me. You are not gone: not vanished? I heard one of your kind an hour ago, singing high over the wood: but its song had no music for me, any more than the rising sun had rays. All the melody on earth is concentrated in my Jane's tongue to my ear (I am glad it is not naturally a silent one): all the sunshine I can feel is in her presence."

The water stood in my eyes to hear this avowal of his dependence: just as if a royal eagle, chained to a perch, should be forced to entreat a sparrow to become its purveyor. But I would not be lachrymose: I dashed off the salt drops, and busied myself with preparing breakfast.

Most of the morning was spent in the open air. I led him out of the wet and wild wood into some cheerful fields: I described to him how brilliantly green they were; how the flowers and hedges looked refreshed; how sparklingly blue was the sky. I sought a seat for him in a hidden and lovely spot: a dry stump of a tree; nor did I refuse to let him, when seated, place me on his knee: why should I, when both he and I were happier near than apart? Pilot lay beside us: all was quiet. He broke out suddenly while clasping me in his arms:—

"Cruel, cruel deserter! Oh, Jane, what did I feel when I discovered you had fled from Thornfield, and when I could nowhere find you; and, after examining your apartment, ascertained that you had taken no money, nor anything which could serve as an equivalent! A pearl necklace I had given you lay untouched in its little casket; your trunks were left corded and locked as they had been prepared for the bridal tour. What could my darling do, I asked, left destitute and penniless? And what did she do? Let me hear now."

Thus urged, I began the narrative of my experience for the last year. I softened considerably what related to the three days of wandering and starvation, because to have told him all would have been to inflict unnecessary pain: the little I did say lacerated his faithful heart deeper than I wished.

I should not have left him thus, he said, without any means of making my way: I should have told him my intention. I should have confided in him: he would never have forced me to be his mistress. Violent as he had seemed in his despair, he, in truth, loved me far too well and too tenderly to constitute himself my tyrant: he would have given me half his fortune, without demanding so much as a kiss in return, rather than I should have flung myself friendless on the wide world. I had endured, he was certain, more than I had confessed to him.

"Well, whatever my sufferings had been, they were very short," I answered: and then I proceeded to tell him how I had been received at Moor House; how I

had obtained the office of schoolmistress, etc. The accession of fortune, the discovery of my relations, followed in due order. Of course, St. John Rivers' name came in frequently in the progress of my tale. When I had done, that name was immediately taken up.

"This St. John, then, is your cousin?"

"Yes."

"You have spoken of him often: did you like him?"

"He was a very good man, sir; I could not help liking him."

"A good man? Does that mean a respectable, well-conducted man of fifty? Or what does it mean?"

"St. John was only twenty-nine, sir."

" '*Jeune encore,*' as the French say. Is he a person of low stature, phlegmatic, and plain? A person whose goodness consists rather in his guiltlessness of vice, than in his prowess in virtue?"

"He is untiringly active. Great and exalted deeds are what he lives to perform."

"But his brain? That is probably rather soft? He means well: but you shrug your shoulders to hear him talk?"

"He talks little, sir: what he does say is ever to the point. His brain is first-rate, I should think not impressible, but vigorous."

"Is he an able man, then?"

"Truly able."

"A thoroughly educated man?"

"St. John is an accomplished and profound scholar."

"His manners, I think, you said are not to your taste?—priggish and parsonic?"

"I never mentioned his manners; but, unless I had a very bad taste, they must suit it; they are polished, calm, and gentlemanlike."

"His appearance,—I forget what description you gave of his appearance;—a sort of raw curate, half strangled with his white neckcloth, and stilted up on his thick-soled high-lows, eh?"

"St. John dresses well. He is a handsome man: tall, fair with blue eyes, and a Grecian profile."

(*Aside.*) "Damn him!"—(*To me.*) "Did you like him, Jane?"

"Yes, Mr. Rochester, I liked him: but you asked me that before."

I perceived, of course, the drift of my interlocutor. Jealousy had got hold of him: she stung him; but the sting was salutary: it gave him respite from the gnawing fang of melancholy. I would not, therefore, immediately charm the snake.

"Perhaps you would rather not sit any longer on my knee, Miss Eyre?" was the next somewhat unexpected observation.

"Why not, Mr. Rochester?"

"The picture you have just drawn is suggestive of a rather too overwhelming contrast. Your words have delineated very prettily a graceful Apollo: he is present to your imagination,—tall, fair, blue-eyed, and with a Grecian profile. Your eyes dwell on a Vulcan,—a real blacksmith, brown, broad-shouldered; and blind and lame into the bargain."

"I never thought of it before; but you certainly are rather like Vulcan, sir."

"Well,—you can leave me, ma'am: but before you go" (and he retained me by a firmer grasp than ever), "you will be pleased just to answer me a question or two." He paused.

"What questions, Mr. Rochester?"

Then followed this cross-examination.

"St. John made you schoolmistress of Morton before he knew you were his cousin?"

"Yes."

"You would often see him? He would visit the school sometimes?"

"Daily."

"He would approve of your plans, Jane? I know they would be clever, for you are a talented creature."

"He approved of them—yes."

"He would discover many things in you he could not have expected to find? Some of your accomplishments are not ordinary."

"I don't know about that."

"You had a little cottage near the school, you say: did he ever come there to see you?"

"Now and then."

"Of an evening?"

"Once or twice."

A pause.

"How long did you reside with him and his sisters after the cousinship was discovered?"

"Five months."

"Did Rivers spend much time with the ladies of his family?"

"Yes; the back parlour was both his study and ours: he sat near the window, and we by the table."

"Did he study much?"

"A good deal."

"What?"

"Hindostanee."

"And what did you do meantime?"

"I learnt German, at first."

"Did he teach you?"

"He did not understand German."

"Did he teach you nothing?"

"A little Hindostanee."

"Rivers taught you Hindostanee?"

"Yes, sir."

"And his sisters also?"

"No."

"Only you?"

"Only me."

"Did you ask to learn?"

"No."

"He wished to teach you?"

"Yes."

A second pause.

"Why did he wish it? Of what use could Hindostanee be to you?"

"He intended me to go with him to India."

"Ah! here I reach the root of the matter. He wanted you to marry him?"

"He asked me to marry him."

"That is a fiction—an impudent invention to vex me."

"I beg your pardon, it is the literal truth: he asked me more than once, and was as stiff about urging his point as ever you could be."

"Miss Eyre, I repeat it, you can leave me. How often am I to say the same thing? Why do you remain pertinaciously perched on my knee, when I have given you notice to quit?"

"Because I am comfortable there."

"No, Jane, you are not comfortable there, because your heart is not with me: it is with this cousin—this St. John. Oh, till this moment, I thought my little Jane was all mine! I had a belief she loved me even when she left me: that was an atom of sweet in much bitter. Long as we have been parted, hot tears as I have wept

over our separation, I never thought that while I was mourning her, she was loving another! But it is useless grieving. Jane, leave me: go and marry Rivers.''

"Shake me off, then, sir,—push me away, for I'll not leave you of my own accord.''

"Jane, I ever like your tone of voice: it still renews hope, it sounds so truthful. When I hear it, it carries me back a year. I forget that you have formed a new tie. But I am not a fool—go''——

"Where must I go, sir?''

"Your own way—with the husband you have chosen.''

"Who is that?''

"You know—this St. John Rivers.''

"He is not my husband, nor ever will be. He does not love me: I do not love him. He loves (as he *can* love, and that is not as you love) a beautiful young lady called Rosamond. He wanted to marry me only because he thought I should make a suitable missionary's wife, which she would not have done. He is good and great, but severe; and, for me, cold as an iceberg. He is not like you, sir: I am not happy at his side, nor near him, nor with him. He has no indulgence for me—no fondness. He sees nothing attractive in me; not even youth—only a few useful mental points.— Then I must leave you, sir, to go to him?''

I shuddered involuntarily, and clung instinctively closer to my blind but beloved master. He smiled.

"What Jane! Is this true? Is such really the state of matters between you and Rivers?''

"Absolutely, sir. Oh, you need not be jealous! I wanted to tease you a little to make you less sad: I thought anger would be better than grief. But if you wish me to love you, could you but see how much I *do* love you, you would be proud and content. All my heart is yours, sir: it belongs to you; and with you it would remain, were fate to exile the rest of me from your presence for ever.''

Again, as he kissed me, painful thoughts darkened his aspect.

"My seared vision! My crippled strength!'' he murmured regretfully.

I caressed, in order to soothe him. I knew of what he was thinking, and wanted to speak for him; but dared not. As he turned aside his face a minute, I saw a tear slide from under the sealed eyelid, and trickle down the manly cheek. My heart swelled.

"I am no better than the old lightning-struck chestnut-tree in Thornfield orchard,'' he remarked, ere long. "And what right would that ruin have to bid a budding woodbine cover its decay with freshness?''

"You are no ruin, sir—no lightning-struck tree: you are green and vigorous. Plants will grow about your roots, whether you ask them or not, because they take delight in your bountiful shadow; and as they grow they will lean towards you, and wind round you, because your strength offers them so safe a prop.''

Again he smiled: I gave him comfort.

"You speak of friends, Jane?'' he asked.

"Yes; of friends,'' I answered, rather hesitatingly: for I knew I meant more than friends, but could not tell what other word to employ. He helped me!

"Ah! Jane. But I want a wife.''

"Do you, sir?''

"Yes: is it news to you?''

"Of course: you said nothing about it before.''

"Is it unwelcome news?''

"That depends on circumstances, sir—on your choice.''

"Which you shall make for me, Jane. I will abide by your decision.''

"Choose then, sir—*her who loves you best.*''

"I will at least choose—*her I love best.* Jane, will you marry me?''

"Yes, sir.''

"A poor blind man, whom you will have to lead about by the hand?"

"Yes, sir."

"A crippled man, twenty years older than you, whom you will have to wait on?"

"Yes, sir."

"Truly, Jane?"

"Most truly, sir."

"Oh! my darling! God bless you and reward you!"

"Mr. Rochester, if ever I did a good deed in my life—if ever I thought a good thought—if ever I prayed a sincere and blameless prayer—if ever I wished a righteous wish,—I am rewarded now. To be your wife is, for me, to be as happy as I can be on earth."

"Because you delight in sacrifice."

"Sacrifice! What do I sacrifice? Famine for food, expectation for content. To be privileged to put my arms round what I value—to press my lips to what I love— to repose on what I trust: is that to make a sacrifice? If so, then certainly I delight in sacrifice."

"And to bear with my infirmities, Jane: to overlook my deficiencies."

"Which are none, sir, to me. I love you better now, when I can really be useful to you, than I did in your state of proud independence, when you disdained every part but that of the giver and protector."

"Hitherto I have hated to be helped—to be led: henceforth, I feel, I shall hate it no more. I did not like to put my hand into a hireling's, but it is pleasant to feel it circled by Jane's little fingers. I preferred utter loneliness to the constant attendance of servants; but Jane's soft ministry will be a perpetual joy. Jane suits me: do I suit her?"

"To the finest fibre of my nature, sir."

"The case being so, we have nothing in the world to wait for: we must be married instantly."

He looked and spoke with eagerness: his old impetuosity was rising.

"We must become one flesh without any delay, Jane: there is but the licence to get—then we marry."

"Mr. Rochester, I have just discovered the sun is far declined from its meridian, and Pilot is actually gone home to his dinner. Let me look at your watch."

"Fasten it into your girdle, Janet, and keep it henceforward: I have no use for it."

"It is nearly four o'clock in the afternoon, sir. Don't you feel hungry?"

"The third day from this must be our wedding-day, Jane. Never mind fine clothes and jewels, now: all that is not worth a fillip."

"The sun has dried up all the rain-drops, sir. The breeze is still: it is quite hot."

"Do you know, Jane, I have your little pearl necklace at this moment fastened round my bronze scrag under my cravat? I have worn it since the day I lost my only treasure: as a memento of her."

"We will go home through the wood: that will be the shadiest way."

He pursued his own thoughts without heeding me.

"Jane! you think me, I daresay, an irreligious dog: but my heart swells with gratitude to the beneficent God of this earth just now. He sees not as man sees, but far clearer: judges not as man judges, but far more wisely. I did wrong: I would have sullied my innocent flower—breathed guilt on its purity: the Omnipotent snatched it from me. I, in my stiff-necked rebellion, almost cursed the dispensation: instead of bending to the decree, I defied it. Divine justice pursued its course; disasters came thick on me: I was forced to pass through the valley of the shadow of death. *His* chastisements are mighty; and one smote me which has humbled me for ever. You know I was proud of my strength: but what is it now, when I must give it over to foreign guidance, as a child does its weakness? Of late, Jane—

only—only of late—I began to see and acknowledge the hand of God in my doom. I began to experience remorse, repentance; the wish for reconcilement to my Maker. I began sometimes to pray: very brief prayers they were, but very sincere.

"Some days since: nay, I can number them—four; it was last Monday night, a singular mood came over me: one in which grief replaced frenzy—sorrow, sullenness. I had long had the impression that since I could nowhere find you, you must be dead. Late that night—perhaps it might be between eleven and twelve o'clock— ere I retired to my dreary rest, I supplicated God, that, if it seemed good to Him, I might soon be taken from this life, and admitted to that world to come, where there was still hope of rejoining Jane.

"I was in my own room, and sitting by the window, which was open: it soothed me to feel the balmy night-air; though I could see no stars, and only by a vague, luminous haze, knew the presence of a moon. I longed for thee, Janet! Oh, I longed for thee both with soul and flesh! I asked of God, at once in anguish and humility, if I had not been long enough desolate, afflicted, tormented; and might not soon taste bliss and peace once more. That I merited all I endured, I acknowledged— that I could scarcely endure more, I pleaded; and the alpha and omega of my heart's wishes broke involuntarily from my lips in the words—'Jane! Jane! Jane!' "

"Did you speak these words aloud?"

"I did, Jane. If any listener had heard me, he would have thought me mad: I pronounced them with such frantic energy."

"And it was last Monday night: somewhere near midnight?"

"Yes; but the time is of no consequence: what followed is the strange point. You will think me superstitious,—some superstition I have in my blood, and always had: nevertheless, this is true—true at least it is that I heard what I now relate.

"As I exclaimed 'Jane! Jane! Jane!' a voice—I cannot tell whence the voice came, but I know whose voice it was— replied, 'I am coming: wait for me;' and a moment after, went whispering on the wind, the words—'Where are you?'

"I'll tell you, if I can, the idea, the picture these words opened to my mind: yet it is difficult to express what I want to express. Ferndean is buried, as you see, in a heavy wood, where sound falls dull, and dies unreverberating. 'Where are you?' seemed spoken amongst mountains; for I heard a hill-sent echo repeat the words. Cooler and fresher at the moment the gale seemed to visit my brow: I could have deemed that in some wild, lone scene, I and Jane were meeting. In spirit, I believe we must have met. You no doubt were, at that hour, in unconscious sleep, Jane: perhaps your soul wandered from its cell to comfort mine; for those were your accents—as certain as I live—they were yours!"

Reader, it was on Monday night—near midnight—that I too had received the mysterious summons: those were the very words by which I replied to it. I listened to Mr. Rochester's narrative; but made no disclosure in return. The coincidence struck me as too awful and inexplicable to be communicated or discussed. If I told anything, my tale would be such as must necessarily make a profound impression on the mind of my hearer: and that mind, yet from its sufferings too prone to gloom, needed not the deeper shade of the supernatural. I kept these things then, and pondered them in my heart.

"You cannot now wonder," continued my master, "that when you rose upon me so unexpectedly last night, I had difficulty in believing you any other than a mere voice and vision: something that would melt to silence and annihilation, as the midnight whisper and mountain echo had melted before. Now, I thank God! I knew it to be otherwise. Yes, I thank God!"

He put me off his knee, rose, and reverently lifting his hat from his brow, and bending his sightless eyes to the earth, he stood in mute devotion. Only the last words of the worship were audible.

"I thank my Maker, that in the midst of judgment he has remembered mercy. I humbly entreat my Redeemer to give me strength to lead henceforth a purer life than I have done hitherto!"

Then he stretched his hand out to be led. I took that dear hand, held it a moment to my lips, then let it pass round my shoulder: being so much lower of stature than he, I served both for his prop and guide. We entered the wood, and wended homeward.

Chapter XXXVIII

CONCLUSION

READER, I married him. A quiet wedding we had: he and I, the parson and clerk, were alone present. When we got back from church, I went into the kitchen of the manor-house, where Mary was cooking the dinner, and John cleaning the knives, and I said:—

"Mary, I have been married to Mr. Rochester this morning." The housekeeper and her husband were both of that decent phlegmatic order of people, to whom one may at any time safely communicate a remarkable piece of news without incurring the danger of having one's ears pierced by some shrill ejaculation, and subsequently stunned by a torrent of wordy wonderment. Mary did look up, and she did stare at me: the ladle with which she was basting a pair of chickens roasting at the fire, did for some three minutes hang suspended in the air; and for the same space of time John's knives also had a rest from the polishing process: but Mary, bending again over the roast, said only—

"Have you, Miss? Well, for sure!"

A short time after she pursued: "I seed you go out with the master, but I didn't know you were gone to church to be wed;" and she basted away. John, when I turned to him, was grinning from ear to ear.

"I told Mary how it would be," he said: "I knew what Mr. Edward" (John was an old servant, and had known his master when he was the cadet of the house, therefore, he often gave him his Christian name)—"I knew what Mr. Edward would do; and I was certain he would not wait long neither: and he's done right, for aught I know. I wish you joy, Miss!" and he politely pulled his forelock.

"Thank you, John. Mr. Rochester told me to give you and Mary this." I put into his hand a five-pound note. Without waiting to hear more, I left the kitchen. In passing the door of that sanctum some time after, I caught the words,—

"She'll happen do better for him nor ony o' t' grand ladies." And again, "If she ben't one o' th' handsomest, she's noan faâl and varry good-natured; and i' his een she's fair beautiful, onybody may see that."

I wrote to Moor House and to Cambridge immediately, to say what I had done: fully explaining also why I had thus acted. Diana and Mary approved the step unreservedly. Diana announced that she would just give me time to get over the honey-moon, and then she would come and see me.

"She had better not wait till then, Jane," said Mr. Rochester, when I read her letter to him; "if she does, she will be too late, for our honey-moon will shine our life-long: its beams will only fade over your grave or mine."

How St. John received the news, I don't know; he never answered the letter in which I communicated it: yet six months after he wrote to me; without, however, mentioning Mr. Rochester's name, or alluding to my marriage. His letter was then calm; and, though very serious, kind. He has maintained a regular, though not

frequent correspondence ever since: he hopes I am happy, and trusts I am not of those who live without God in the world, and only mind earthly things.

You have not quite forgotten little Adèle, have you, reader? I had not; I soon asked and obtained leave of Mr. Rochester, to go and see her at the school where he had placed her. Her frantic joy at beholding me again moved me much. She looked pale and thin: she said she was not happy. I found the rules of the establishment were too strict, its course of study too severe, for a child of her age: I took her home with me. I meant to become her governess once more; but I soon found this impracticable; my time and cares were now required by another—my husband needed them all. So I sought out a school conducted on a more indulgent system; and near enough to permit of my visiting her often, and bringing her home sometimes. I took care she should never want for anything that could contribute to her comfort: she soon settled in her new abode, became very happy there, and made fair progress in her studies. As she grew up, a sound English education corrected in a great measure her French defects; and when she left school, I found in her a pleasing and obliging companion: docile, good-tempered, and well-principled. By her grateful attention to me and mine, she has long since well repaid any little kindness I ever had it in my power to offer her.

My tale draws to its close: one word respecting my experience of married life, and one brief glance at the fortunes of those whose names have most frequently recurred in this narrative, and I have done.

I have now been married ten years. I know what it is to live entirely for and with what I love best on earth. I hold myself supremely blest—blest beyond what language can express; because I am my husband's life as fully as he is mine. No woman was ever nearer to her mate than I am: ever more absolutely bone of his bone, and flesh of his flesh. I know no weariness of my Edward's society: he knows none of mine, any more than we each do of the pulsation of the heart that beats in our separate bosoms; consequently, we are ever together. To be together is for us to be at once, as free as in solitude, as gay as in company. We talk, I believe, all day long: to talk to each other is but a more animated and an audible thinking. All my confidence is bestowed on him, all his confidence is devoted to me; we are precisely suited in character—perfect concord is the result.

Mr. Rochester continued blind the first two years of our union: perhaps it was that circumstance that drew us so very near—that knit us so very close! for I was then his vision, as I am still his right hand. Literally, I was (what he often called me) the apple of his eye. He saw nature—he saw books through me; and never did I weary of gazing for his behalf, and of putting into words the effect of field, tree, town, river, cloud, sunbeam—of the landscape before us; of the weather round us—and impressing by sound on his ear what light could no longer stamp on his eye. Never did I weary of reading to him; never did I weary of conducting him where he wished to go: of doing for him what he wished to be done. And there was a pleasure in my services, most full, most exquisite, even though sad—because he claimed these services without painful shame or damping humiliation. He loved me so truly, that he knew no reluctance in profiting by my attendance: he felt that I loved him so fondly, that to yield that attendance was to indulge my sweetest wishes.

One morning at the end of the two years, as I was writing a letter to his dictation, he came and bent over me, and said—

"Jane, have you a glittering ornament round your neck?"

I had a gold watch-chain: I answered "Yes."

"And have you a pale blue dress on?"

I had. He informed me then, that for some time he had fancied the obscurity clouding one eye was becoming less dense; and that now he was sure of it.

He and I went up to London. He had the advice of an eminent oculist; and he eventually recovered the sight of that one eye. He cannot now see very distinctly:

he cannot read or write much; but he can find his way without being led by the hand: the sky is no longer a blank to him—the earth no longer a void. When his first-born was put into his arms, he could see that the boy had inherited his own eyes, as they once were—large, brilliant, and black. On that occasion, he again, with a full heart, acknowledged that God had tempered judgment with mercy.

My Edward and I, then, are happy: and the more so, because those we most love are happy likewise. Diana and Mary Rivers are both married: alternately, once every year, they come to see us, and we go to see them. Diana's husband is a captain in the navy; a gallant officer, and a good man. Mary's is a clergyman; a college friend of her brother's; and, from his attainments and principles, worthy of the connection. Both Captain Fitzjames and Mr. Wharton love their wives, and are loved by them.

As to St. John Rivers, he left England: he went to India. He entered on the path he had marked for himself; he pursues it still. A more resolute, indefatigable pioneer never wrought amidst rocks and dangers. Firm, faithful, and devoted; full of energy, and zeal, and truth, he labours for his race: he clears their painful way to improvement: he hews down like a giant the prejudices of creed and caste that encumber it. He may be stern; he may be exacting; he may be ambitious yet; but his is the sternness of the warrior Great-heart, who guards his pilgrim convoy from the onslaught of Apollyon. His is the exaction of the apostle, who speaks but for Christ, when he says—''Whosoever will come after me, let him deny himself, and take up his cross and follow me.'' His is the ambition of the high master-spirit, which aims to fill a place in the first rank of those who are redeemed from the earth—who stand without fault before the throne of God; who share the last mighty victories of the Lamb; who are called, and chosen, and faithful.

St. John is unmarried: he never will marry now. Himself has hitherto sufficed to the toil; and the toil draws near its close: his glorious sun hastens to its setting. The last letter I received from him drew from my eyes human tears, and yet filled my heart with Divine joy: he anticipated his sure reward, his incorruptible crown. I know that a stranger's hand will write to me next, to say that the good and faithful servant has been called at length into the joy of his Lord. And why weep for this? No fear of death will darken St. John's last hour: his mind will be unclouded; his heart will be undaunted; his hope will be sure; his faith steadfast. His own words are a pledge of this:—

''My Master,'' he says, ''has forewarned me. Daily he announces more distinctly,— 'Surely I come quickly!' and hourly I more eagerly respond,—'Amen; even so come, Lord Jesus!' ''

Wuthering Heights

by Emily Brontë

Chapter I

1801.—

I HAVE just returned from a visit to my landlord—the solitary neighbour that I shall be troubled with. This is certainly a beautiful country! In all England, I do not believe that I could have fixed on a situation so completely removed from the stir of society. A perfect misanthropist's heaven: and Mr Heathcliff and I are such a suitable pair to divide the desolation between us. A capital fellow! He little imagined how my heart warmed towards him when I beheld his black eyes withdraw so suspiciously under their brows, as I rode up, and when his fingers sheltered themselves, with a jealous resolution, still farther in his waistcoat, as I announced my name.

'Mr Heathcliff!' I said.

A nod was the answer.

'Mr Lockwood, your new tenant, sir. I do myself the honour of calling as soon as possible after my arrival, to express the hope that I have not inconvenienced you by my perseverance in soliciting the occupation of Thrushcross Grange: I heard yesterday you had had some thoughts——'

'Thrushcross Grange is my own, sir,' he interrupted, wincing. 'I should not allow anyone to inconvenience me, if I could hinder it—walk in!'

The 'walk in' was uttered with closed teeth, and expressed the sentiment, 'Go to the deuce': even the gate over which he leant manifested no sympathizing movement to the words; and I think that circumstance determined me to accept the invitation: I felt interested in a man who seemed more exaggeratedly reserved than myself.

When he saw my horse's breast fairly pushing the barrier, he did put out his hand to unchain it, and then sullenly preceded me up the causeway, calling, as we entered the court: 'Joseph, take Mr Lockwood's horse; and bring up some wine.'

'Here we have the whole establishment of domestics, I suppose,' was the reflection suggested by this compound order. 'No wonder the grass grows up between the flags, and cattle are the only hedge-cutters.'

Joseph was an elderly, nay, an old man: very old, perhaps, though hale and sinewy. 'The Lord help us!' he soliloquized in an undertone of peevish displeasure, while relieving me of my horse: looking, meantime, in my face so sourly that I charitably conjectured he must have need of divine aid to digest his dinner, and his pious ejaculation had no reference to my unexpected advent.

Wuthering Heights is the name of Mr Heathcliff's dwelling. 'Wuthering' being a significant provincial adjective, descriptive of the atmospheric tumult to which its station is exposed in stormy weather. Pure, bracing ventilation they must have up there at all times, indeed; one may guess the power of the north wind blowing over the edge, by the excessive slant of a few stunted firs at the end of the house; and by a range of gaunt thorns all stretching their limbs one way, as if craving alms of the sun. Happily, the architect had foresight to build it strong: the narrow

windows are deeply set in the wall, and the corners defended with large jutting stones.

Before passing the threshold, I paused to admire a quantity of grotesque carving lavished over the front, and especially about the principal door; above which, among a wilderness of crumbling griffins and shameless little boys, I detected the date '1500', and the name 'Hareton Earnshaw'. I would have made a few comments, and requested a short history of the place from the surly owner; but his attitude at the door appeared to demand my speedy entrance, or complete departure, and I had no desire to aggravate his impatience previous to inspecting the penetralium.

One step brought us into the family sitting-room, without any introductory lobby or passage: they call it here 'the house' pre-eminently. It includes kitchen and parlour, generally; but I believe at Wuthering Heights the kitchen is forced to retreat altogether into another quarter: at least I distinguished a chatter of tongues, and a clatter of culinary utensils, deep within; and I observed no signs of roasting, boiling, or baking, about the huge fireplace; nor any glitter of copper saucepans and tin cullenders on the walls. One end, indeed, reflected splendidly both light and heat from ranks of immense pewter dishes, interspersed with silver jugs and tankards, towering row after row, on a vast oak dresser, to the very roof. The latter had never been underdrawn: its entire anatomy lay bare to an inquiring eye, except where a frame of wood laden with oatcakes and clusters of legs of beef, mutton, and ham, concealed it. Above the chimney were sundry villainous old guns, and a couple of horse-pistols: and, by way of ornament, three gaudily painted canisters disposed along its ledge. The floor was of smooth, white stone; the chairs, high-backed, primitive structures, painted green: one or two heavy black ones lurking in the shade. In an arch under the dresser, reposed a huge, liver-coloured bitch pointer, surrounded by a swarm of squealing puppies; and other dogs haunted other recesses.

The apartment and furniture would have been nothing extraordinary as belonging to a homely, northern farmer, with a stubborn countenance, and stalwart limbs set out to advantage in knee breeches and gaiters. Such an individual seated in his armchair, his mug of ale frothing on the round table before him, is to be seen in any circuit of five or six miles among these hills, if you go at the right time after dinner. But Mr Heathcliff forms a singular contrast to his abode and style of living. He is a dark-skinned gipsy in aspect, in dress and manners a gentleman: that is, as much a gentleman as many a country squire: rather slovenly, perhaps, yet not looking amiss with his negligence, because he has an erect and handsome figure; and rather morose. Possibly, some people might suspect him of a degree of under-bred pride; I have a sympathetic chord within that tells me it is nothing of the sort: I know, by instinct, his reserve springs from an aversion to showy displays of feeling—to manifestations of mutual kindliness. He'll love and hate equally under cover, and esteem it a species of impertinence to be loved or hated again. No, I'm running on too fast: I bestow my own attributes over liberally on him. Mr Heathcliff may have entirely dissimilar reasons for keeping his hand out of the way when he meets a would-be acquaintance, to those which actuate me. Let me hope my constitution is almost peculiar: my dear mother used to say I should never have a comfortable home; and only last summer I proved myself perfectly unworthy of one.

While enjoying a month of fine weather at the sea coast, I was thrown into the company of a most fascinating creature: a real goddess in my eyes, as long as she took no notice of me. I 'never told my love' vocally; still, if looks have language, the merest idiot might have guessed I was over head and ears: she understood me at last, and looked a return—the sweetest of all imaginable looks. And what did I do? I confess it with shame—shrunk icily into myself, like a snail; at every glance retired colder and further; till finally the poor innocent was led to doubt her own senses, and, overwhelmed with confusion at her supposed mistake, persuaded her

mamma to decamp. By this curious turn of disposition I have gained the reputation of deliberate heartlessness; how undeserved, I alone can appreciate.

I took a seat at the end of the hearthstone opposite that towards which my landlord advanced, and filled up an interval of silence by attempting to caress the canine mother, who had left her nursery, and was sneaking wolfishly to the back of my legs, her lip curled up, and her white teeth watering for a snatch. My caress provoked a long, guttural gnarl.

'You'd better let the dog alone,' growled Mr Heathcliff in unison, checking fiercer demonstrations with a punch of his foot. 'She's not accustomed to be spoiled—not kept for a pet.' Then, striding to a side door, he shouted again, 'Joseph!'

Joseph mumbled indistinctly in the depths of the cellar, but gave no intimation of ascending; so his master dived down to him, leaving me *vis-à-vis* the ruffianly bitch and a pair of grim shaggy sheep-dogs, who shared with her a jealous guardianship over all my movements. Not anxious to come in contact with their fangs, I sat still; but, imagining they would scarcely understand tacit insults, I unfortunately indulged in winking and making faces at the trio, and some turn of my physiognomy so irritated madam, that she suddenly broke into a fury and leapt on my knees. I flung her back, and hastened to interpose the table between us. This proceeding roused the whole hive: half a dozen four-footed fiends, of various sizes and ages, issued from hidden dens to the common centre. I felt my heels and coat-laps peculiar subjects of assault; and parrying off the larger combatants as effectually as I could with the poker, I was constrained to demand, aloud, assistance from some of the household in re-establishing peace.

Mr Heathcliff and his man climbed the cellar steps with vexatious phlegm: I don't think they moved one second faster than usual, though the hearth was an absolute tempest of worrying and yelping. Happily, an inhabitant of the kitchen made more dispatch: a lusty dame, with tucked-up gown, bare arms, and fire-flushed cheeks, rushed into the midst of us flourishing a frying-pan: and used that weapon, and her tongue, to such purpose, that the storm subsided magically, and she only remained, heaving like a sea after a high wind, when her master entered on the scene.

'What the devil is the matter?' he asked, eyeing me in a manner that I could ill endure after this inhospitable treatment.

'What the devil, indeed!' I muttered. 'The herd of possessed swine could have had no worse spirits in them than those animals of yours, sir. You might as well leave a stranger with a brood of tigers!'

'They won't meddle with persons who touch nothing,' he remarked, putting the bottle before me, and restoring the displaced table. 'The dogs do right to be vigilant. Take a glass of wine?'

'No, thank you.'

'Not bitten, are you?'

'If I had been, I would have set my signet on the biter.'

Heathcliff's countenance relaxed into a grin.

'Come, come,' he said, 'you are flurried, Mr Lockwood. Here, take a little wine. Guests are so exceedingly rare in this house that I and my dogs, I am willing to own, hardly know how to receive them. Your health, sir!'

I bowed and returned the pledge; beginning to perceive that it would be foolish to sit sulking for the misbehaviour of a pack of curs: besides, I felt loath to yield the fellow further amusement at my expense; since the humour took that turn. He—probably swayed by prudential consideration of the folly of offending a good tenant—relaxed a little in the laconic style of chipping off his pronouns and auxiliary verbs, and introduced what he supposed would be a subject of interest to me—a discourse on the advantages and disadvantages of my present place of retirement. I found him very intelligent on the topics we touched; and before I went home, I

was encouraged so far as to volunteer another visit tomorrow. He evidently wished no repetition of my intrusion. I shall go, notwithstanding. It is astonishing how sociable I feel myself compared with him.

Chapter II

YESTERDAY afternoon set in misty and cold. I had half a mind to spend it by my study fire, instead of wading through heath and mud to Wuthering Heights. On coming up from dinner, however (N.B. I dine between twelve and one o'clock; the housekeeper, a matronly lady, taken as a fixture along with the house, could not, or would not, comprehend my request that I might be served at five), on mounting the stairs with this lazy intention, and stepping into the room, I saw a servant girl on her knees surrounded by brushes and coal-scuttles, and raising an infernal dust as she extinguished the flames with heaps of cinders. This spectacle drove me back immediately; I took my hat, and, after a four-miles' walk, arrived at Heathcliff's garden gate just in time to escape the first feathery flakes of a snow shower.

On that bleak hill top the earth was hard with a black frost, and the air made me shiver through every limb. Being unable to remove the chain, I jumped over, and, running up the flagged causeway bordered with straggling gooseberry bushes, knocked vainly for admittance, till my knuckles tingled and the dogs howled.

'Wretched inmates!' I ejaculated mentally, 'you deserve perpetual isolation from your species for your churlish inhospitality. At least, I would not keep my doors barred in the day time. I don't care—I will get in!' So resolved, I grasped the latch and shook it vehemently. Vinegar-faced Joseph projected his head from a round window of the barn.

'Whet are ye for?' he shouted. 'T' maister's dahn i' t' fowld. Go rahnd by th' end ut' laith, if yah went tuh spake tull him.'

'Is there nobody inside to open the door?' I hallooed, responsively.

'They's nobbut t' missis; and shoo'll nut oppen't an ye mak yer flaysome dins till neeght.'

'Why? Cannot you tell her who I am, eh, Joseph?'

'Nor-ne me! Aw'll hae noa hend wi't,' muttered the head, vanishing.

The snow began to drive thickly. I seized the handle to essay another trial; when a young man without coat, and shouldering a pitchfork, appeared in the yard behind. He hailed me to follow him, and, after marching through a wash-house, and a paved area containing a coal shed, pump, and pigeon cot, we at length arrived in the huge, warm, cheerful apartment, where I was formerly received. It glowed delightfully in the radiance of an immense fire, compounded of coal, peat, and wood; and near the table, laid for a plentiful evening meal, I was pleased to observe the 'missis', an individual whose existence I had never previously suspected. I bowed and waited, thinking she would bid me take a seat. She looked at me, leaning back in her chair, and remained motionless and mute.

'Rough weather!' I remarked. 'I'm afraid, Mrs Heathcliff, the door must bear the consequence of your servants' leisure attendance: I had hard work to make them hear me.'

She never opened her mouth. I stared—she stared also: at any rate, she kept her eyes on me in a cool, regardless manner, exceedingly embarrassing and disagreeable.

'Sit down,' said the young man gruffly. 'He'll be in soon.'

I obeyed; and hemmed, and called the villain Juno, who deigned, at this second interview, to move the extreme tip of her tail, in token of owning my acquaintance.

'A beautiful animal!' I commenced again. 'Do you intend parting with the little ones, madam?'

'They are not mine,' said the amiable hostess, more repellingly than Heathcliff himself could have replied.

'Ah, your favourites are among these?' I continued, turning to an obscure cushion full of something like cats.

'A strange choice of favourites!' she observed scornfully.

Unluckily, it was a heap of dead rabbits. I hemmed once more, and drew closer to the hearth, repeating my comment on the wildness of the evening.

'You should not have come out,' she said, rising and reaching from the chimney-piece two of the painted canisters.

Her position before was sheltered from the light; now, I had a distinct view of her whole figure and countenance. She was slender, and apparently scarcely past girlhood: an admirable form, and the most exquisite little face that I have ever had the pleasure of beholding; small features, very fair; flaxen ringlets, or rather golden, hanging loose on her delicate neck; and eyes, had they been agreeable in expression, they would have been irresistible: fortunately for my susceptible heart, the only sentiment they evinced hovered between scorn, and a kind of desperation, singularly unnatural to be detected there. The canisters were almost out of her reach; I made a motion to aid her; she turned upon me as a miser might turn if anyone attempted to assist him in counting his gold.

'I don't want your help,' she snapped; 'I can get them for myself.'

'I beg your pardon!' I hastened to reply.

'Were you asked to tea?' she demanded, tying an apron over her neat black frock, and standing with a spoonful of the leaf poised over the pot.

'I shall be glad to have a cup,' I answered.

'Were you asked?' she repeated.

'No,' I said, half smiling. 'You are the proper person to ask me.'

She flung the tea back, spoon and all, and resumed her chair in a pet; her forehead corrugated, and her red under lip pushed out, like a child's ready to cry.

Meanwhile, the young man had slung on to his person a decidedly shabby upper garment, and, erecting himself before the blaze, looked down on me from the corner of his eyes, for all the world as if there were some mortal feud unavenged between us. I began to doubt whether he were a servant or not: his dress and speech were both rude, entirely devoid of the superiority observable in Mr and Mrs Heathcliff; his thick brown curls were rough and uncultivated, his whiskers encroached bearishly over his cheeks, and his hands were embrowned like those of a common labourer: still his bearing was free, almost haughty, and he showed none of a domestic's assiduity in attending on the lady of the house. In the absence of clear proofs of his condition, I deemed it best to abstain from noticing his curious conduct; and, five minutes afterwards, the entrance of Heathcliff relieved me, in some measure, from my uncomfortable state.

'You see, sir, I am come, according to promise!' I exclaimed, assuming the cheerful; 'and I fear I shall be weatherbound for half an hour, if you can afford me shelter during that space.'

'Half an hour?' he said, shaking the white flakes from his clothes; 'I wonder you should select the thick of a snowstorm to ramble about in. Do you know that you run a risk of being lost in the marshes? People familiar with these moors often miss their road on such evenings; and I can tell you there is no chance of a change at present.'

'Perhaps I can get a guide among your lads, and he might stay at the Grange till morning—could you spare me one?'

'No, I could not.'

'Oh, indeed! Well, then, I must trust to my own sagacity.'

'Umph!'

'Are you going to mak th' tea?' demanded he of the shabby coat, shifting his ferocious gaze from me to the young lady.

'Is *he* to have any?' she asked, appealing to Heathcliff.

'Get it ready, will you?' was the answer, uttered so savagely that I started. The tone in which the words were said revealed a genuine bad nature. I no longer felt inclined to call Heathcliff a capital fellow. When the preparations were finished, he invited me with—'Now, sir, bring forward your chair.' And we all, including the rustic youth, drew round the table: an austere silence prevailing while we discussed our meal.

I thought, if I had caused the cloud, it was my duty to make an effort to dispel it. They could not every day sit so grim and taciturn; and it was impossible, however ill-tempered they might be, that the universal scowl they wore was their everyday countenance.

'It is strange,' I began, in the interval of swallowing one cup of tea and receiving another—'it is strange how custom can mould our tastes and ideas: many could not imagine the existence of happiness in a life of such complete exile from the world as you spend, Mr Heathcliff; yet I'll venture to say, that, surrounded by your family, and with your amiable lady as the presiding genius over your home and heart—'

'My amiable lady!' he interrupted, with an almost diabolical sneer on his face. 'Where is she—my amiable lady?'

'Mrs Heathcliff, your wife, I mean.'

'Well, yes—Oh, you would intimate that her spirit has taken the post of ministering angel, and guards the fortunes of Wuthering Heights even when her body is gone. Is that it?'

Perceiving myself in a blunder, I attempted to correct it. I might have seen there was too great a disparity between the ages of the parties to make it likely that they were man and wife. One was about forty: a period of mental vigour at which men seldom cherish the delusion of being married for love by girls: that dream is reserved for the solace of our declining years. The other did not look seventeen.

Then it flashed upon me—'The clown at my elbow, who is drinking his tea out of a basin and eating his bread with unwashed hands, may be her husband: Heathcliff, junior, of course. Here is the consequence of being buried alive: she has thrown herself away upon that boor from sheer ignorance that better individuals existed! A sad pity—I must beware how I cause her to regret her choice.' The last reflection may seem conceited; it was not. My neighbour struck me as bordering on repulsive; I knew, through experience, that I was tolerably attractive.

'Mrs Heathcliff is my daughter-in-law,' said Heathcliff, corroborating my surmise. He turned, as he spoke, a peculiar look in her direction: a look of hatred; unless he has a most perverse set of facial muscles that will not, like those of other people, interpret the language of his soul.

'Ah, certainly—I see now: you are the favoured possessor of the beneficent fairy,' I remarked, turning to my neighbour.

This was worse than before: the youth grew crimson, and clenched his fist, with every appearance of a meditated assault. But he seemed to recollect himself presently, and smothered the storm in a brutal curse, muttered on my behalf: which, however, I took care not to notice.

'Unhappy in your conjectures, sir,' observed my host; 'we neither of us have the privilege of owning your good fairy; her mate is dead. I said she was my daughter-in-law, therefore, she must have married my son.'

'And this young man is——'

'Not my son, assuredly.'

Heathcliff smiled again, as if it were rather too bold a jest to attribute the paternity of that bear to him.

'My name is Hareton Earnshaw,' growled the other; 'and I'd counsel you to respect it!'

'I've shown no disrespect,' was my reply, laughing internally at the dignity with which he announced himself.

He fixed his eye on me longer than I cared to return the stare, for fear I might be tempted either to box his ears or render my hilarity audible. I began to feel unmistakably out of place in that pleasant family circle. The dismal spiritual atmosphere overcame, and more than neutralized, the glowing physical comforts round me; and I resolved to be cautious how I ventured under those rafters a third time.

The business of eating being concluded, and no one uttering a word of sociable conversation, I approached a window to examine the weather. A sorrowful sight I saw: dark night coming down prematurely, and sky and hills mingled in one bitter whirl of wind and suffocating snow.

'I don't think it possible for me to get home now without a guide,' I could not help exclaiming. 'The roads will be buried already; and, if they were bare, I could scarcely distinguish a foot in advance.'

'Hareton, drive those dozen sheep into the barn porch. They'll be covered if left in the fold all night: and put a plank before them,' said Heathcliff.

'How must I do?' I continued, with rising irritation.

There was no reply to my question; and on looking round I saw only Joseph bringing in a pail of porridge for the dogs, and Mrs Heathcliff leaning over the fire, diverting herself with burning a bundle of matches which had fallen from the chimney-piece as she restored the tea canister to its place. The former, when he had deposited his burden, took a critical survey of the room, and in cracked tones, grated out:

'Aw woonder hagh yah can faishion tuh stand thear i' idleness un war, when all on 'em's goan aght! Bud yah're a nowt, and it's noa use talking—yah'll niver mend uh yer ill ways, bud goa raight tuh t' divil, like yer mother afore ye!'

I imagined, for a moment, that this piece of eloquence was addressed to me; and, sufficiently enraged, stepped towards the aged rascal with an intention of kicking him out of the door. Mrs Heathcliff, however, checked me by her answer.

'You scandalous old hypocrite!' she replied. 'Are you not afraid of being carried away bodily, whenever you mention the devil's name? I warn you to refrain from provoking me, or I'll ask your abduction as a special favour. Stop! look here, Joseph,' she continued, taking a long, dark book from a shelf; 'I'll show you how far I've progressed in the Black Art: I shall soon be competent to make a clear house of it. The red cow didn't die by chance; and your rheumatism can hardly be reckoned among providential visitations!'

'Oh, wicked, wicked!' gasped the elder; 'may the Lord deliver us from evil!'

'No, reprobate! you are a castaway—be off, or I'll hurt you seriously! I'll have you all modelled in wax and clay; and the first who passes the limits I fix, shall—I'll not say what he shall be done to—but, you'll see! Go, I'm looking at you!'

The little witch put a mock malignity into her beautiful eyes, and Joseph, trembling with sincere horror, hurried out praying and ejaculating 'wicked' as he went. I thought her conduct must be prompted by a species of dreary fun; and, now that we were alone, I endeavoured to interest her in my distress.

'Mrs Heathcliff,' I said earnestly, 'you must excuse me for troubling you. I presume, because, with that face, I'm sure you cannot help being good-hearted. Do point out some landmarks by which I may know my way home: I have no more idea how to get there than you would have how to get to London!'

'Take the road you came,' she answered, ensconcing herself in a chair, with a candle, and the long book open before her. 'It is brief advice, but as sound as I can give.'

'Then, if you hear of me being discovered dead in a bog or a pit full of snow, your conscience won't whisper that it is partly your fault?'

'How so? I cannot escort you. They wouldn't let me go to the end of the garden wall.'

'*You!* I should be sorry to ask you to cross the threshold, for my convenience, on such a night,' I cried. 'I want you to *tell* me my way, not to *show* it; or else to persuade Mr Heathcliff to give me a guide.'

'Who? There is himself, Earnshaw, Zillah, Joseph, and I. Which would you have?'

'Are there no boys at the farm?'

'No, those are all.'

'Then, it follows that I am compelled to stay.'

'That you may settle with your host. I have nothing to do with it.'

'I hope it will be a lesson to you to make no more rash journeys on these hills,' cried Heathcliff's stern voice from the kitchen entrance. 'As to staying here, I don't keep accommodations for visitors: you must share a bed with Hareton or Joseph, if you do.'

'I can sleep on a chair in this room,' I replied.

'No, no! A stranger is a stranger, be he rich or poor: it will not suit me to permit anyone the range of the place while I am off guard!' said the unmannerly wretch.

With this insult, my patience was at an end. I uttered an expression of disgust, and pushed past him into the yard, running against Earnshaw in my haste. It was so dark that I could not see the means of exit; and, as I wandered round, I heard another specimen of their civil behaviour amongst each other. At first the young man appeared about to befriend me.

'I'll go with him as far as the park,' he said.

'You'll go with him to hell!' exclaimed his master, or whatever relation he bore. 'And who is to look after the horses, eh?'

'A man's life is of more consequence than one evening's neglect of the horses: somebody must go,' murmured Mrs Heathcliff, more kindly than I expected.

'Not at your command!' retorted Hareton. 'If you set store on him, you'd better be quiet.'

'Then I hope his ghost will haunt you; and I hope Mr Heathcliff will never get another tenant till the Grange is a ruin!' she answered sharply.

'Hearken, hearken, shoo's cursing on 'em!' muttered Joseph, towards whom I had been steering.

He sat within earshot, milking the cows by the light of a lantern, which I seized unceremoniously, and, calling out that I would send it back on the morrow, rushed to the nearest postern.

'Maister, maister, he's stealing t' lantern!' shouted the ancient, pursuing my retreat. 'Hey, Gnasher! Hey, dog! Hey, Wolf, holld him, holld him!'

On opening the little door, two hairy monsters flew at my throat, bearing me down and extinguishing the light; while a mingled guffaw from Heathcliff and Hareton, put the copestone on my rage and humiliation. Fortunately, the beasts seemed more bent on stretching their paws and yawning, and flourishing their tails, than devouring me alive; but they would suffer no resurrection, and I was forced to lie till their malignant master pleased to deliver me: then, hatless and trembling with wrath, I ordered the miscreants to let me out—on their peril to keep me one minute longer—with several incoherent threats of retaliation that, in their indefinite depth of virulency, smacked of King Lear.

The vehemence of my agitation brought on a copious bleeding at the nose, and still Heathcliff laughed, and still I scolded. I don't know what would have concluded the scene, had there not been one person at hand rather more rational than myself, and more benevolent than my entertainer. This was Zillah, the stout housewife; who at length issued forth to inquire into the nature of the uproar. She thought that some of them had been laying violent hands on me; and, not daring to attack her master, she turned her vocal artillery against the young scoundrel.

'Well, Mr Earnshaw,' she cried, 'I wonder what you'll have agait next! Are we

going to murder folk on our very doorstones? I see this house will never do for me—look at t' poor lad, he's fair choking! Wisht, wisht! you mun'n't go on so. Come in, and I'll cure that: there now, hold ye still.'

With these words she suddenly splashed a pint of icy water down my neck, and pulled me into the kitchen. Mr Heathcliff followed, his accidental merriment expiring quickly in his habitual moroseness.

I was sick exceedingly, and dizzy and faint; and thus compelled perforce to accept lodgings under his roof. He told Zillah to give me a glass of brandy, and then passed on to the inner room; while she condoled with me on my sorry predicament, and having obeyed his orders, whereby I was somewhat revived, ushered me to bed.

Chapter III

WHILE leading the way upstairs, she recommended that I should hide the candle, and not make a noise; for her master had an odd notion about the chamber she would put me in, and never let anybody lodge there willingly. I asked the reason. She did not know, she answered: she had only lived there a year or two; and they had so many queer goings on, she could not begin to be curious.

Too stupefied to be curious myself, I fastened my door and glanced round for the bed. The whole furniture consisted of a chair, a clothes-press, and a large oak case, with squares cut out near the top resembling coach windows. Having approached this structure I looked inside, and perceived it to be a singular sort of old-fashioned couch, very conveniently designed to obviate the necessity for every member of the family having a room to himself. In fact it formed a little closet, and the ledge of a window, which it enclosed, served as a table. I slid back the panelled sides, got in with my light, pulled them together again, and felt secure against the vigilance of Heathcliff, and everyone else.

The ledge, where I placed my candle, had a few mildewed books piled up in one corner; and it was covered with writing scratched on the paint. This writing, however, was nothing but a name repeated in all kinds of characters, large and small—*Catherine Earnshaw*, here and there varied to *Catherine Heathcliff*, and again to *Catherine Linton*.

In vapid listlessness I leant my head against the window, and continued spelling over Catherine Earnshaw—Heathcliff—Linton, till my eyes closed; but they had not rested five minutes when a glare of white letters started from the dark as vivid as spectres—the air swarmed with Catherines; and rousing myself to dispel the obtrusive name, I discovered my candle wick reclining on one of the antique volumes, and perfuming the place with an odour of roasted calfskin. I snuffed it off, and, very ill at ease under the influence of cold and lingering nausea, sat up and spread open the injured tome on my knee. It was a Testament, in lean type, and smelling dreadfully musty: a fly-leaf bore the inscription—'Catherine Earnshaw, her book', and a date some quarter of a century back. I shut it, and took up another, and another, till I had examined all. Catherine's library was select, and its state of dilapidation proved it to have been well used; though not altogether for a legitimate purpose: scarcely one chapter had escaped a pen-and-ink commentary—at least, the appearance of one—covering every morsel of blank that the printer had left. Some were detached sentences; other parts took the form of a regular diary, scrawled in an unformed childish hand. At the top of an extra page (quite a treasure, probably, when first lighted on) I was greatly amused to behold an excellent caricature of my friend Joseph,—rudely, yet powerfully sketched. An immediate interest kindled

within me for the unknown Catherine, and I began forthwith to decipher her faded hieroglyphics.

'An awful Sunday!' commenced the paragraph beneath. 'I wish my father were back again. Hindley is a detestable substitute—his conduct to Heathcliff is atrocious—H. and I are going to rebel—we took our initiatory step this evening.

'All day had been flooding with rain; we could not go to church, so Joseph must needs get up a congregation in the garret; and, while Hindley and his wife basked downstairs before a comfortable fire—doing anything but reading their Bibles, I'll answer for it—Heathcliff, myself, and the unhappy plough-boy, were commanded to take our prayer books, and mount: we were ranged in a row, on a sack of corn, groaning and shivering, and hoping that Joseph would shiver too, so that he might give us a short homily for his own sake. A vain idea! The service lasted precisely three hours; and yet my brother had the face to exclaim, when he saw us descending, "What, done already?" On Sunday evenings we used to be permitted to play, if we did not make much noise; now a mere titter is sufficient to send us into corners!

' "You forget you have a master here," says the tyrant. "I'll demolish the first who puts me out of temper! I insist on perfect sobriety and silence. Oh, boy! was that you? Frances, darling, pull his hair as you go by: I heard him snap his fingers." Frances pulled his hair heartily, and then went and seated herself on her husband's knee; and there they were, like two babies, kissing and talking nonsense by the hour—foolish palaver that we should be ashamed of. We made ourselves as snug as our means allowed in the arch of the dresser. I had just fastened our pinafores together, and hung them up for a curtain, when in comes Joseph on an errand from the stables. He tears down my handiwork, boxes my ears, and croaks—

' "T' maister nobbut just buried, and Sabbath nut o'ered, und t' sahnd uh t' gospel still i' yer lugs, and yah darr be laiking! Shame on ye! sit ye dahn, ill childer! they's good books eneugh if ye'll read 'em! sit ye dahn, and think uh yer sowls!"

'Saying this, he compelled us so to square our positions that we might receive from the far-off fire a dull ray to show us the text of the lumber thrust upon us. I could not bear the employment. I took my dingy volume by the scroop, and hurled it into the dog kennel, vowing I hated a good book. Heathcliff kicked his to the same place. Then there was a hubbub!

' "Maister Hindley!" shouted our chaplain. "Maister, coom hither! Miss Cathy's riven th' back off 'Th' Helmet uh Salvation,' un' Heathcliff's pawsed his fit intuh t' first part uh 'T' Brooad Way to Destruction!' It's fair flaysome ut yah let 'em goa on this gait. Ech! th' owd man ud uh laced 'em properly—but he's goan!"

'Hindley hurried up from his paradise on the hearth, and seizing one of us by the collar, and the other by the arm, hurled both into the back kitchen; where, Joseph asseverated, "owd Nick" would fetch us as sure as we were living: and, so comforted, we each sought a separate nook to await his advent. I reached this book, and a pot of ink from a shelf, and pushed the house door ajar to give me light, and I have got the time on with writing for twenty minutes; but my companion is impatient, and proposes that we should appropriate the dairywoman's cloak, and have a scamper on the moors, under its shelter. A pleasant suggestion—and then, if the surly old man come in, he may believe his prophecy verified—we cannot be damper, or colder, in the rain than we are here.'

*　　*　　*　　*　　*　　*　　*

I suppose Catherine fulfilled her project, for the next sentence took up another subject: she waxed lachrymose.

'How little did I dream that Hindley would ever make me cry so!' she wrote. 'My head aches, till I cannot keep it on the pillow; and still I can't give over. Poor Heathcliff! Hindley calls him a vagabond, and won't let him sit with us, nor eat

with us any more; and, he says, he and I must not play together, and threatens to turn him out of the house if we break his orders. He has been blaming our father (how dared he?) for treating H. too liberally; and swears he will reduce him to his right place——'

* * * * * * *

I began to nod drowsily over the dim page: my eye wandered from manuscript to print, I saw a red ornamented title—'Seventy Times Seven, and the First of the Seventy-First. A Pious Discourse delivered by the Reverend Jabes Branderham, in the Chapel of Gimmerden Sough.' And while I was, half consciously, worryng my brain to guess what Jabes Branderham would make of his subject, I sank back in bed, and fell asleep. Alas, for the effects of bad tea and bad temper! what else could it be that made me pass such a terrible night? I don't remember another that I can at all compare with it since I was capable of suffering.

I began to dream, almost before I ceased to be sensible of my locality. I thought it was morning; and I had set out on my way home, with Joseph for a guide. The snow lay yards deep in our road; and, as we floundered on, my companion wearied me with constant reproaches that I had not brought a pilgrim's staff: telling me that I could never get into the house without one, and boastfully flourishing a heavy-headed cudgel, which I understood to be so denominated. For a moment I considered it absurd that I should need such a weapon to gain admittance into my own residence. Then a new idea flashed across me. I was not going there: we were journeying to hear the famous Jabes Branderham preach from the text—'Seventy Times Seven'; and either Joseph, the preacher, or I had committed the 'First of the Seventy-First', and were to be publicly exposed and excommunicated.

We came to the chapel. I have passed it really in my walks, twice or thrice; it lies in a hollow, between two hills; an elevated hollow, near a swamp, whose peaty moisture is said to answer all the purposes of embalming on the few corpses deposited there. The roof has been kept whole hitherto; but as the clergyman's stipend is only twenty pounds per annum, and a house with two rooms, threatening speedily to determine into one, no clergyman will undertake the duties of pastor: especially as it is currently reported that his flock would rather let him starve than increase the living by one penny from their own pockets. However, in my dream, Jabes had a full and attentive congregation; and he preached—good God! what a sermon: divided into *four hundred and ninety* parts, each fully equal to an ordinary address from the pulpit, and each discussing a separate sin! Where he searched for them, I cannot tell. He had his private manner of interpreting the phrase, and it seemed necessary the brother should sin different sins on every occasion. They were of the most curious character: odd transgressions that I never imagined previously.

Oh, how weary I grew. How I writhed, and yawned, and nodded, and revived! How I pinched and pricked myself, and rubbed my eyes, and stood up, and sat down again, and nudged Joseph to inform me if he would *ever* have done. I was condemned to hear all out: finally, he reached the *'First of the Seventy-First'*. At that crisis, a sudden inspiration descended on me; I was moved to rise and denounce Jabes Branderham as the sinner of the sin that no Christian need pardon.

'Sir,' I exclaimed, 'sitting here within these four walls, at one stretch, I have endured and forgiven the four hundred and ninety heads of your discourse. Seventy times seven times have I plucked up my hat and been about to depart—seventy times seven times have you preposterously forced me to resume my seat. The four hundred and ninety-first is too much. Fellow-martyrs, have at him! Drag him down, and crush him to atoms, that the place which knows him may know him no more!'

'Thou art the Man!' cries Jabes, after a solemn pause, leaning over his cushion. 'Seventy times seven times didst thou gapingly contort thy visage—seventy times seven did I take counsel with my soul—Lo, this is human weakness: this also may

be absolved! The First of the Seventy-First is come. Brethren, execute upon him the judgment written. Such honour have all His saints!'

With that concluding word, the whole assembly, exalting their pilgrim's staves, rushed round me in a body; and I, having no weapon to raise in self-defence, commenced grappling with Joseph, my nearest and most ferocious assailant, for his. In the confluence of the multitude, several clubs crossed; blows, aimed at me, fell on other sconces. Presently the whole chapel resounded with rappings and counter-rappings: every man's hand was against his neighbour; and Branderham, unwilling to remain idle, poured forth his zeal in a shower of loud taps on the boards of the pulpit, which responded so smartly that, at last, to my unspeakable relief, they woke me. And what was it that had suggested the tremendous tumult? What had played Jabes's part in the row? Merely, the branch of a fir tree that touched my lattice, as the blast wailed by, and rattled its dry cones against the panes! I listened doubtingly an instant; detected the disturber, then turned and dozed, and dreamt again: if possible, still more disagreeably than before.

This time, I remembered I was lying in the oak closet, and I heard distinctly the gusty wind, and the driving of the snow; I heard, also, the fir bough repeat its teasing sound, and ascribed it to the right cause: but it annoyed me so much, that I resolved to silence it, if possible; and, I thought, I rose and endeavoured to unhasp the casement. The hook was soldered into the staple: a circumstance observed by me when awake, but forgotten. 'I must stop it, nevertheless!' I muttered, knocking my knuckles through the glass, and stretching an arm out to seize the importunate branch; instead of which, my fingers closed on the fingers of a little, ice-cold hand! The intense horror of nightmare came over me: I tried to draw back my arm, but the hand clung to it, and a most melancholy voice sobbed, 'Let me in—let me in!' 'Who are you?' I asked, struggling, meanwhile, to disengage myself. 'Catherine Linton,' it replied, shiveringly (why did I think of *Linton*? I had read *Earnshaw* twenty times for Linton); 'I'm come home: I'd lost my way on the moor!' As it spoke, I discerned, obscurely, a child's face looking through the window. Terror made me cruel; and, finding it useless to attempt shaking the creature off, I pulled its wrist on to the broken pane, and rubbed it to and fro till the blood ran down and soaked the bedclothes: still it wailed, 'Let me in!' and maintained its tenacious gripe, almost maddening me with fear. 'How can I?' I said at length. 'Let *me* go, if you want me to let you in!' The fingers relaxed, I snatched mine through the hole, hurriedly piled the books up in a pyramid against it, and stopped my ears to exclude the lamentable prayer. I seemed to keep them closed above a quarter of an hour; yet, the instant I listened again, there was the doleful cry moaning on! 'Begone!' I shouted, 'I'll never let you in, not if you beg for twenty years.' 'It is twenty years,' mourned the voice: 'twenty years. I've been a waif for twenty years!' Thereat began a feeble scratching outside, and the pile of books moved as if thrust forward. I tried to jump up; but could not stir a limb; and so yelled aloud, in a frenzy of fright. To my confusion, I discovered the yell was not ideal: hasty footsteps approached my chamber door; somebody pushed it open, with a vigorous hand, and a light glimmering through the squares at the top of the bed. I sat shuddering yet, and wiping the perspiration from my forehead: the intruder appeared to hesitate, and muttered to himself. At last, he said in a half-whisper, plainly not expecting an answer, 'Is any one here?' I considered it best to confess my presence, for I knew Heathcliff's accents, and feared he might search further, if I kept quiet. With this intention, I turned and opened the panels. I shall not soon forget the effect my action produced.

Heathcliff stood near the entrance, in his shirt and trousers: with a candle dripping over his fingers, and his face as white as the wall behind him. The first creak of the oak startled him like an electric shock! the light leaped from his hold to a distance of some feet, and his agitation was so extreme, that he could hardly pick it up.

'It is only your guest, sir,' I called out, desirous to spare him the humiliation of exposing his cowardice further. 'I had the misfortune to scream in my sleep, owing to a frightful nightmare. I'm sorry I disturbed you.'

'Oh God confound you, Mr Lockwood! I wish you were at the——' commenced my host, setting the candle on a chair, because he found it impossible to hold it steady. 'And who showed you up into this room?' he continued, crushing his nails into his palms, and grinding his teeth to subdue the maxillary convulsions. 'Who was it? I've a good mind to turn them out of the house this moment!'

'It was your servant, Zillah,' I replied, flinging myself on to the floor, and rapidly resuming my garments. 'I should not care if you did, Mr Heathcliff; she richly deserves it. I suppose that she wanted to get another proof that the place was haunted, at my expense. Well, it is—swarming with ghosts and goblins! You have reason in shutting it up, I assure you. No one will thank you for a doze in such a den!'

'What do you mean?' asked Heathcliff, 'and what are you doing? Lie down and finish out the night, since you *are* here; but, for heaven's sake! don't repeat that horrid noise; nothing could excuse it, unless you were having your throat cut!'

'If the little fiend had got in at the window, she probably would have strangled me!' I returned. 'I'm not going to endure the persecutions of your hospitable ancestors again. Was not the Reverend Jabes Branderham akin to you on the mother's side? And that minx, Catherine Linton, or Earnshaw, or however she was called—she must have been a changeling—wicked little soul! She told me she had been walking the earth those twenty years: a just punishment for her mortal transgressions, I've no doubt!'

Scarcely were these words uttered, when I recollected the association of Heathcliff's with Catherine's name in the book, which had completely slipped from my memory, till thus awakened. I blushed at my inconsideration; but, without showing further consciousness of the offence, I hastened to add—'The truth is, sir, I passed the first part of the night in'—Here I stopped afresh—I was about to say 'perusing those old volumes', then it would have revealed my knowledge of their written, as well as their printed, contents: so, correcting myself, I went on, 'in spelling over the name scratched on that window-ledge. A monotonous occupation, calculated to set me asleep, like counting, or——'

'What *can* you mean by talking in this way to *me*?' thundered Heathcliff with savage vehemence. 'How—how *dare* you, under my roof?—God! he's mad to speak so!' And he struck his forehead with rage.

I did not know whether to resent this language or pursue my explanation; but he seemed so powerfully affected that I took pity and proceeded with my dreams; affirming I had never heard the appellation of 'Catherine Linton' before, but reading it often over produced an impression which personified itself when I had no longer my imagination under control. Heathcliff gradually fell back into the shelter of the bed, as I spoke; finally sitting down almost concealed behind it. I guessed, however, by his irregular and intercepted breathing, that he struggled to vanquish an excess of violent emotion. Not liking to show him that I had heard the conflict, I continued my toilette rather noisily, looking at my watch, and soliloquized on the length of the night: 'Not three o'clock yet! I could have taken oath it had been six. Time stagnates here: we must surely have retired to rest at eight!'

'Always at nine in winter, and always rise at four,' said my host, suppressing a groan: and, as I fancied, by the motion of his shadow's arm, dashing a tear from his eyes. 'Mr Lockwood,' he added, 'you may go into my room: you'll only be in the way, coming downstairs so early; and your childish outcry has sent sleep to the devil for me.'

'And for me, too,' I replied. 'I'll walk in the yard till daylight, and then I'll be off; and you need not dread a repetition of my intrusion. I'm now quite cured of

seeking pleasure in society, be it country or town. A sensible man ought to find sufficient company in himself.'

'Delightful company!' muttered Heathcliff. 'Take the candle, and go where you please. I shall join you directly. Keep out of the yard, though, the dogs are unchained; and the house—Juno mounts sentinel there, and—nay, you can only ramble about the steps and passages. But, away with you! I'll come in two minutes!'

I obeyed, so far as to quit the chamber; when, ignorant where the narrow lobbies led, I stood still, and was witness, involuntarily, to a piece of superstition on the part of my landlord, which belied, oddly, his apparent sense. He got on to the bed, and wrenched open the lattice, bursting, as he pulled at it, into an uncontrollable passion of tears. 'Come in! come in!' he sobbed. 'Cathy, do come. Oh do—*once* more! Oh! my heart's darling! hear me *this* time, Catherine, at last!' The spectre showed a spectre's ordinary caprice: it gave no sign of being; but the snow and wind whirled wildly through, even reaching my station, and blowing out the light.

There was such anguish in the gust of grief that accompanied this raving, that my compassion made me overlook its folly, and I drew off, half angry to have listened at all, and vexed at having related my ridiculous nightmare, since it produced that agony; though *why*, was beyond my comprehension. I descended cautiously to the lower regions, and landed in the back kitchen, where a gleam of fire, raked compactly together, enabled me to rekindle my candle. Nothing was stirring except a bridled, grey cat, which crept from the ashes, and saluted me with a querulous mew.

Two benches, shaped in sections of a circle, nearly enclosed the hearth; on one of these I stretched myself, and Grimalkin mounted the other. We were both of us nodding, ere anyone invaded our retreat, and then it was Joseph, shuffling down a wooden ladder that vanished in the roof, through a trap: the ascent to his garret, I suppose. He cast a sinister look at the little flame which I had enticed to play between the ribs, swept the cat from its elevation, and bestowing himself in the vacancy, commenced the operation of stuffing a three-inch pipe with tobacco. My presence in his sanctum was evidently esteemed a piece of impudence too shameful for remark: he silently applied the tube to his lips, folded his arms, and puffed away. I let him enjoy the luxury unannoyed; and after sucking out his last wreath, and heaving a profound sigh, he got up, and departed as solemnly as he came.

A more elastic footstep entered next; and now I opened my mouth for a 'good morning', but closed it again, the salutation unachieved; for Hareton Earnshaw was performing his orisons *sotto voce*, in a series of curses directed against every object he touched, while he rummaged a corner for a spade or shovel to dig through the drifts. He glanced over the back of the bench, dilating his nostrils, and thought as little of exchanging civilities with me as with my companion the cat. I guessed, by his preparations, that egress was allowed, and, leaving my hard couch, made a movement to follow him. He noticed this, and thrust at an inner door with the end of his spade, intimating by an inarticulate sound that there was the place where I must go, if I changed my locality.

It opened into the house, where the females were already astir. Zillah urging flakes of flame up the chimney with a colossal bellows; and Mrs Heathcliff, kneeling on the hearth, reading a book by the aid of the blaze. She held her hand interposed between the furnace heat and her eyes, and seemed absorbed in her occupation; desisting from it only to chide the servant for covering her with sparks, or to push away a dog, now and then, that snoozled its nose over-forwardly into her face. I was surprised to see Heathcliff there also. He stood by the fire, his back towards me, just finishing a stormy scene to poor Zillah; who ever and anon interrupted her labour to pluck up the corner of her apron, and heave an indignant groan.

'And you, you worthless'—he broke out as I entered, turning to his daughter-in-law, and employing an epithet as harmless as duck, or sheep, but generally represented by a dash ——. 'There you are, at your idle tricks again! The rest of

them do earn their bread—you live on my charity! Put your trash away, and find something to do. You shall pay me for the plague of having you eternally in my sight—do you hear, damnable jade?'

'I'll put my trash away, because you can make me, if I refuse,' answered the young lady, closing her book, and throwing it on a chair. 'But I'll not do anything, though you should swear your tongue out, except what I please!'

Heathcliff lifted his hand, and the speaker sprang to a safer distance, obviously acquainted with its weight. Having no desire to be entertained by a cat-and-dog combat, I stepped foward briskly, as if eager to partake the warmth of the hearth, and innocent of any knowledge of the interrupted dispute. Each had enough decorum to suspend further hostilities: Heathcliff placed his fist, out of temptation, in his pocket; Mrs Heathcliff curled her lip, and walked to a seat far off, where she kept her word by playing the part of a statue during the remainder of my stay. That was not long. I declined joining their breakfast, and, at the first gleam of dawn, took an opportunity of escaping into the free air, now clear, and still, and cold as impalpable ice.

My landlord hallooed for me to stop, ere I reached the bottom of the garden, and offered to accompany me across the moor. It was well he did, for the whole hill-back was one billowy, white ocean; the swells and falls not indicating corresponding rises and depressions in the ground: many pits, at least, were filled to a level; and entire ranges of mounds, the refuse of the quarries, blotted from the chart which my yesterday's walk left pictured in my mind. I had remarked on one side of the road, at intervals of six or seven yards, a line of upright stones, continued through the whole length of the barren: these were erected, and daubed with lime on purpose to serve as guides in the dark; and also when a fall, like the present, confounded the deep swamps on either hand with the firmer path: but, excepting a dirty dot pointing up here and there, all traces of their existence had vanished: and my companion found it necessary to warn me frequently to steer to the right or left, when I imagined I was following, correctly, the windings of the road. We exchanged little conversation, and he halted at the entrance of Thrushcross Park, saying, I could make no error there. Our adieux were limited to a hasty bow, and then I pushed forward, trusting to my own resources; for the porter's lodge is untenanted as yet. The distance from the gate to the Grange is two miles: I believe I managed to make it four; what with losing myself among the trees, and sinking up to the neck in snow: a predicament which only those who have experienced it can appreciate. At any rate, whatever were my wanderings, the clock chimed twelve as I entered the house; and that gave exactly an hour for every mile of the usual way from Wuthering Heights.

My human fixture and her satellites rushed to welcome me; exclaiming, tumultuously, they had completely given me up; everybody conjectured that I perished last night; and they were wondering how they must set about the search for my remains. I bid them be quiet, now that they saw me returned, and, benumbed to my very heart, I dragged upstairs; whence, after putting on dry clothes, and pacing to and fro thirty or forty minutes, to restore the animal heat, I am adjourned to my study, feeble as a kitten: almost too much so to enjoy the cheerful fire and smoking coffee which the servant has prepared for my refreshment.

Chapter IV

WHAT vain weather-cocks we are! I, who had determined to hold myself independent of all social intercourse, and thanked my stars that, at length, I had lighted on a spot where it was next to impracticable—I, weak wretch, after maintaining till dusk

a struggle with low spirits and solitude, was finally compelled to strike my colours; and, under pretence of gaining information concerning the necessities of my establishment, I desired Mrs Dean, when she brought in supper, to sit down while I ate it; hoping sincerely she would prove a regular gossip, and either rouse me to animation or lull me to sleep by her talk.

'You have lived here a considerable time,' I commenced; 'did you not say sixteen years?'

'Eighteen, sir: I came, when the mistress was married, to wait on her; after she died, the master retained me for his housekeeper.'

'Indeed.'

There ensued a pause. She was not a gossip, I feared; unless about her own affairs, and those could hardly interest me. However, having studied for an interval, with a fist on either knee, and a cloud of meditation over her ruddy countenance, she ejaculated:

'Ah, times are greatly changed since then!'

'Yes,' I remarked, 'you've seen a good many alterations, I suppose?'

'I have: and troubles too,' she said.

'Oh, I'll turn the talk on my landlord's family!' I thought to myself. 'A good subject to start—and that pretty girl-widow, I should like to know her history: whether she be a native of the country, or, as is more probable, an exotic that the surly *indigenae* will not recognize for kin.' With this intention I asked Mrs Dean why Heathcliff let Thrushcross Grange, and preferred living in a situation and residence so much inferior. 'Is he not rich enough to keep the estate in good order?' I inquired.

'Rich, sir!' she returned. 'He has, nobody knows what money, and every year it increases. Yes, yes, he's rich enough to live in a finer house than this: but he's very near—close-handed; and, if he had meant to flit to Thrushcross Grange, as soon as he heard of a good tenant he could not have borne to miss the chance of getting a few hundreds more. It is strange people should be so greedy, when they are alone in the world!'

'He had a son, it seems?'

'Yes, he had one—he is dead.'

'And that young lady, Mrs Heathcliff, is his widow?'

'Yes.'

'Where did she come from originally?'

'Why, sir, she is my late master's daughter: Catherine Linton was her maiden name. I nursed her, poor thing! I did wish Mr Heathcliff would remove here, and then we might have been together again.'

'What! Catherine Linton?' I exclaimed, astonished. But a minute's reflection convinced me it was not my ghostly Catherine. 'Then,' I continued, 'my predecessor's name was Linton?'

'It was.'

'And who is that Earnshaw, Hareton Earnshaw, who lives with Mr Heathcliff? are they relations?'

'No; he is the late Mrs Linton's nephew.'

'The young lady's cousin, then?'

'Yes; and her husband was her cousin also: one on the mother's, the other on the father's side: Heathcliff married Mr Linton's sister.'

'I see the house at Wuthering Heights has "Earnshaw" carved over the front door. Are they an old family?'

'Very old, sir; and Hareton is the last of them, as our Miss Cathy is of us—I mean of the Lintons. Have you been to Wuthering Heights? I beg pardon for asking; but I should like to hear how she is!'

'Mrs Heathcliff? She looked very well, and very handsome; yet, I think, not very happy.'

'Oh dear, I don't wonder! And how did you like the master?'

'A rough fellow, rather, Mrs Dean. Is not that his character?'

'Rough as a saw edge, and hard as whinstone! The less you meddle with him the better.'

'He must have had some ups and downs in life to make him such a churl. Do you know anything of his history?'

'It's a cuckoo's, sir—I know all about it: except where he was born, and who were his parents, and how he got his money, at first. And Hareton has been cast out like an unfledged dunnock! The unfortunate lad is the only one in all this parish that does not guess how he has been cheated.'

'Well, Mrs Dean, it will be a charitable deed to tell me something of my neighbours: I feel I shall not rest, if I go to bed; so be good enough to sit and chat an hour.'

'Oh, certainly, sir! I'll just fetch a little sewing, and then I'll sit as long as you please. But you've caught cold: I saw you shivering, and you must have some gruel to drive it out.'

The worthy woman bustled off, and I crouched nearer the fire; my head felt hot, and the rest of me chill: moreover, I was excited, almost to a pitch of foolishness, through my nerves and brain. This caused me to feel, not uncomfortable, but rather fearful (as I am still) of serious effects from the incidents of today and yesterday. She returned presently, bringing a smoking basin and a basket of work; and, having placed the former on the hob, drew in her seat, evidently pleased to find me so companionable.

Before I came to live here, she commenced—waiting no further invitation to her story—I was almost always at Wuthering Heights; because my mother had nursed Mr Hindley Earnshaw, that was Hareton's father, and I got used to playing with the children: I ran errands too, and helped to make hay, and hung about the farm ready for anything that anybody would set me to. One fine summer morning—it was the begining of harvest, I remember—Mr Earnshaw, the old master, came downstairs, dressed for a journey; and after he had told Joseph what was to be done during the day, he turned to Hindley, and Cathy, and me—for I sat eating my porridge with them—and he said, speaking to his son, 'Now my bonny man, I'm going to Liverpool today, what shall I bring you? You may choose what you like: only let it be little, for I shall walk there and back: sixty miles each way, that is a long spell!' Hindley named a fiddle, and then he asked Miss Cathy; she was hardly six years old, but she could ride any horse in the stable, and she chose a whip. He did not forget me; for he had a kind heart, though he was rather severe sometimes. He promised to bring me a pocketful of apples and pears, and then he kissed his children goodbye and set off.

It seemed a long while to us all—the three days of his absence—and often did little Cathy ask when he would be home. Mrs Earnshaw expected him by supper time on the third evening, and she put the meal off hour after hour; there were no signs of his coming, however, and at last the children got tired of running down to the gate to look. Then it grew dark; she would have had them to bed, but they begged sadly to be allowed to stay up; and, just about eleven o'clock, the door latch was raised quietly and in stepped the master. He threw himself into a chair, laughing and groaning, and bid them all stand off, for he was nearly killed—he would not have such another walk for the three kingdoms.

'And at the end of it, to be flighted to death!' he said, opening his greatcoat, which he held bundled up in his arms. 'See here, wife! I was never so beaten with anything in my life: but you must e'en take it as a gift of God; though it's as dark almost as if it came from the devil.'

We crowded round, and over Miss Cathy's head, I had a peep at a dirty, ragged, black-haired child; big enough both to walk and talk: indeed, its face looked older than Catherine's; yet, when it was set on its feet, it only stared round, and repeated

over and over again some gibberish, that nobody could understand. I was frightened, and Mrs Earnshaw was ready to fling it out of doors: she did fly up, asking how he could fashion to bring that gipsy brat into the house, when they had their own bairns to feed and fend for? What he meant to do with it, and whether he were mad? The master tried to explain the matter; but he was really half dead with fatigue, and all that I could make out, amongst her scolding, was a tale of his seeing it starving, and houseless, and as good as dumb, in the streets of Liverpool; where he picked it up and inquired for its owner. Not a soul knew to whom it belonged, he said; and his money and time being both limited, he thought it better to take it home with him at once, than run into vain expenses there: because he was determined he would not leave it as he found it. Well, the conclusion was that my mistress grumbled herself calm; and Mr Earnshaw told me to wash it, and give it clean things, and let it sleep with the children.

Hindley and Cathy contented themselves with looking and listening till peace was restored: then, both began searching their father's pockets for the presents he had promised them. The former was a boy of fourteen, but when he drew out what had been a fiddle crushed to morsels in the greatcoat, he blubbered aloud; and Cathy, when she learned the master had lost her whip in attending on the stranger, showed her humour by grinning and spitting at the stupid little thing; earning for her pains a sound blow from her father to teach her cleaner manners. They entirely refused to have it in bed with them, or even in their room; and I had no more sense, so I put it on the landing of the stairs, hoping it might be gone on the morrow. By chance, or else attracted by hearing his voice, it crept to Mr Earnshaw's door, and there he found it on quitting his chamber. Inquiries were made as to how it got there; I was obliged to confess, and in recompense for my cowardice and inhumanity was sent out of the house.

This was Heathcliff's first introduction to the family. On coming back a few days afterwards (for I did not consider my banishment perpetual) I found they had christened him 'Heathcliff': it was the name of a son who died in childhood, and it has served him ever since, both for Christian and surname. Miss Cathy and he were now very thick; but Hindley hated him! and to say the truth I did the same; and we plagued and went on with him shamefully: for I wasn't reasonable enough to feel my injustice, and the mistress never put in a word on his behalf when she saw him wronged.

He seemed a sullen, patient child; hardened, perhaps, to ill-treatment: he would stand Hindley's blows without winking or shedding a tear, and my pinches moved him only to draw in a breath and open his eyes, as if he had hurt himself by accident and nobody was to blame. This endurance made old Earnshaw furious, when he discovered his son persecuting the poor, fatherless child, as he called him. He took to Heathcliff strangely, believing all he said (for that matter, he said precious little, and generally the truth), and petting him up far above Cathy, who was too mischievous and wayward for a favourite.

So, from the very beginning, he bred bad feeling in the house; and at Mrs Earnshaw's death, which happened in less than two years after, the young master had learned to regard his father as an oppressor rather than a friend, and Heathcliff as a usurper of his parent's affections and his privileges; and he grew bitter with brooding over these injuries. I sympathized awhile; but when the children fell ill of the measles, and I had to tend them, and take on me the cares of a woman at once, I changed my ideas. Heathcliff was dangerously sick: and while he lay at the worst he would have me constantly by his pillow: I suppose he felt I did a good deal for him, and he hadn't wit to guess that I was compelled to do it. However, I will say this, he was the quietest child that ever nurse watched over. The difference between him and the others forced me to be less partial. Cathy and her brother harassed me terribly: *he* was as uncomplaining, as a lamb; though hardness, not gentleness, made him give little trouble.

He got through, and the doctor affirmed it was in a great measure owing to me, and praised me for my care. I was vain of his commendations, and softened towards the being by whose means I earned them, and thus Hindley lost his last ally: still I couldn't dote on Heathcliff, and I wondered often what my master saw to admire so much in the sullen boy, who never, to my recollection, repaid his indulgence by any sign of gratitude. He was not insolent to his benefactor, he was simply insensible; though knowing perfectly the hold he had on his heart, and conscious he had only to speak and all the house would be obliged to bend to his wishes. As an instance, I remember Mr Earnshaw once bought a couple of colts at the parish fair, and gave the lads each one. Heathcliff took the handsomest, but it soon fell lame, and when he discovered it, he said to Hindley—

'You must exchange horses with me: I don't like mine; and if you won't I shall tell your father of the three thrashings you've given me this week, and show him my arm, which is black to the shoulder.' Hindley put out his tongue and cuffed him over the ears. 'You'd better do it at once,' he persisted, escaping to the porch (they were in the stable): 'you will have to; and if I speak of these blows, you'll get them again with interest.' 'Off, dog!' cried Hindley, threatening him with an iron weight used for weighing potatoes and hay. 'Throw it,' he replied, standing still, 'and then I'll tell how you boasted that you would turn me out of doors as soon as he died, and see whether he will not turn you out directly.' Hindley threw it, hitting him on the breast, and down he fell, but staggered up immediately, breathless and white; and, had not I prevented it, he would have gone just so to the master, and got full revenge by letting his condition plead for him, intimating who had caused it. 'Take my colt, gipsy, then!' said young Earnshaw. 'And I pray that he may break your neck: take him, and be damned, you beggarly interloper! and wheedle my father out of all he has: only afterwards show him what you are, imp of Satan.—And take that, I hope he'll kick out your brains!'

Heathcliff had gone to loose the beast, and shift it to his own stall; he was passing behind it, when Hindley finished his speech by knocking him under its feet, and without stopping to examine whether his hopes were fulfilled, ran away as fast as he could. I was surprised to witness how coolly the child gathered himself up, and went on with his intention; exchanging saddles and all, and then sitting down on a bundle of hay to overcome the qualm which the violent blow occasioned, before he entered the house. I persuaded him easily to let me lay the blame of his bruises on the horse: he minded little what tale was told since he had what he wanted. He complained so seldom, indeed, of such stirs as these, that I really thought him not vindictive: I was deceived completely, as you will hear.

Chapter V

IN the course of time, Mr Earnshaw began to fail. He had been active and healthy, yet his strength left him suddenly; and when he was confined to the chimney corner he grew grievously irritable. A nothing vexed him; and suspected slights of his authority nearly threw him into fits. This was especially to be remarked if anyone attempted to impose upon, or domineer over, his favourite: he was painfully jealous lest a word should be spoken amiss to him; seeming to have got into his head the notion that, because he liked Heathcliff, all hated, and longed to do him an ill turn. It was a disadvantage to the lad; for the kinder among us did not wish to fret the master, so we humoured his partiality; and that humouring was rich nourishment to the child's pride and black tempers. Still it became in a manner necessary; twice, or thrice, Hindley's manifestation of scorn, while his father was near, roused the

old man to a fury: he seized his stick to strike him, and shook with rage that he could not do it.

At last, our curate (we had a curate then who made the living answer by teaching the little Lintons and Earnshaws, and farming his bit of land himself), he advised that the young man should be sent to college; and Mr Earnshaw agreed, though with a heavy spirit, for he said—'Hindley was nought, and would never thrive as where he wandered.'

I hoped heartily we should have peace now. It hurt me to think the master should be made uncomfortable by his own good deed. I fancied the discontent of age and disease arose from his family disagreements: as he would have it that it did: really, you know, sir, it was in his sinking frame. We might have got on tolerably, notwithstanding, but for two people, Miss Cathy and Joseph, the servant: you saw him, I dare say, up yonder. He was, and is yet most likely, the wearisomest self-righteous Pharisee that ever ransacked a Bible to rake the promises to himself and fling the curses on his neighbours. By his knack of sermonizing and pious discoursing, he contrived to make a great impression on Mr Earnshaw; and the more feeble the master became, the more influence he gained. He was relentless in worrying him about his soul's concerns, and about ruling his children rigidly. He encouraged him to regard Hindley as a reprobate; and, night after night, he regularly grumbled out a long string of tales against Heathcliff and Catherine: always minding to flatter Earnshaw's weakness by heaping the heaviest blame on the last.

Certainly, she had ways with her such as I never saw a child take up before; and she put all of us past our patience fifty times and oftener in a day: from the hour she came downstairs till the hour she went to bed, we had not a minute's security that she wouldn't be in mischief. Her spirits were always at high-water mark, her tongue always going—singing, laughing, and plaguing everybody who would not do the same. A wild, wicked slip she was—but she had the bonniest eye, the sweetest smile, and lightest foot in the parish; and, after all, I believe she meant no harm; for when once she made you cry in good earnest, it seldom happened that she would not keep you company, and oblige you to be quiet that you might comfort her. She was much too fond of Heathcliff. The greatest punishment we could invent for her was to keep her separate from him: yet she got chided more than any of us on his account. In play, she liked exceedingly to act the little mistress; using her hands freely, and commanding her companions: she did so to me, but I would not bear shopping and ordering; and so I let her know.

Now, Mr Earnshaw did not understand jokes from his children: he had always been strict and grave with them; and Catherine, on her part, had no idea why her father should be crosser and less patient in his ailing condition, than he was in his prime. His peevish reproofs wakened in her a naughty delight to provoke him: she was never so happy as when we were all scolding her at once, and she defying us with her bold, saucy look, and her ready words; turning Joseph's religious curses into ridicule, baiting me, and doing just what her father hated most—showing how her pretended insolence, which he thought real, had more power over Heathcliff than his kindness: how the boy would do *her* bidding in anything, and *his* only when it suited his own inclination. After behaving as badly as possible all day, she sometimes came fondling to make it up at night. 'Nay, Cathy,' the old man would say, 'I cannot love thee; thou'rt worse than thy brother. Go, say thy prayers, child, and ask God's pardon. I doubt thy mother and I must rue that we ever reared thee!' That made her cry, at first: and then being repulsed continually hardened her, and she laughed if I told her to say she was sorry for her faults, and beg to be forgiven.

But the hour came, at last, that ended Mr Earnshaw's troubles on earth. He died quietly in his chair one October evening, seated by the fireside. A high wind blustered round the house, and roared in the chimney: it sounded wild and stormy, yet it was not cold, and we were all together—I, a little removed from the hearth, busy at my knitting, and Joseph reading his Bible near the table (for the servants

generally sat in the house then, after their work was done). Miss Cathy had been sick, and that made her still; she leant against her father's knee, and Heathcliff was lying on the floor with his head in her lap. I remember the master, before he fell into a doze, stroking her bonny hair—it pleased him rarely to see her gentle—and saying—'Why canst thou not always be a good lass, Cathy?' And she turned her face up to his, and laughed, and answered, 'Why cannot you always be a good man, father?' But as soon as she saw him vexed again, she kissed his hand, and said she would sing him to sleep. She began singing very low, till his fingers dropped from hers, and his head sank on his breast. Then I told her to hush, and not stir, for fear she should wake him. We all kept as mute as mice a full half-hour, and should have done longer, only Joseph, having finished his chapter, got up and said that he must rouse the master for prayers and bed. He stepped forward, and called him by name, and touched his shoulder; but he would not move, so he took the candle and looked at him. I thought there was something wrong as he set down the light; and seizing the children each by an arm, whispered them to 'frame upstairs, and make little din—they might pray alone that evening—he had summut to do'.

'I shall bid father good night first,' said Catherine, putting her arms round his neck, before we could hinder her. The poor thing discovered her loss directly— she screamed out—'Oh, he's dead, Heathcliff! he's dead!' And they both set up a heart-breaking cry.

I joined my wail to theirs, loud and bitter; but Joseph asked what we could be thinking of to roar in that way over a saint in heaven. He told me to put on my cloak and run to Gimmerton for the doctor and the parson. I could not guess the use that either would be of, then. However, I went, through wind and rain, and brought one, the doctor, back with me; the other said he would come in the morning. Leaving Joseph to explain matters, I ran to the children's room: their door was ajar, I saw they had never laid down, though it was past midnight; but they were calmer, and did not need me to console them. The little souls were comforting each other with better thoughts than I could have hit on: no parson in the world ever pictured heaven so beautifully as they did, in their innocent talk: and, while I sobbed and listened, I could not help wishing we were all there safe together.

Chapter VI

MR HINDLEY came home to the funeral; and—a thing that amazed us, and set the neighbours gossiping right and left—he brought a wife with him. What she was, and where she was born, he never informed us: probably she had neither money nor name to recommend her, or he would scarcely have kept the union from his father.

She was not one that would have disturbed the house much on her own account. Every object she saw, the moment she crossed the threshold, appeared to delight her; and every circumstance that took place about her: except the preparing the burial, and the presence of the mourners. I thought she was half silly, from her behaviour while that went on: she ran into her chamber, and made me come with her, though I should have been dressing the children; and there she sat shivering and clasping her hands, and asking repeatedly: 'Are they gone yet?' Then she began describing with hysterical emotion the effect it produced on her to see black; and started, and trembled, and, at last, fell a-weeping—and when I asked what was the matter? answered, she didn't know; but she felt so afraid of dying! I imagined her as little likely to die as myself. She was rather thin, but young, and fresh-complexioned, and her eyes sparkled as bright as diamonds. I did remark, to be sure, that mounting

the stairs made her breathe very quick: that the least sudden noise set her all in a quiver, and that she coughed troublesomely sometimes: but I knew nothing of what these symptoms portended, and had no impulse to sympathize with her. We don't in general take to foreigners here, Mr Lockwood, unless they take to us first.

Young Earnshaw was altered considerably in the three years of his absence. He had grown sparer, and lost his colour, and spoke and dressed quite differently; and, on the very day of his return, he told Joseph and me we must thenceforth quarter ourselves in the back kitchen, and leave the house for him. Indeed, he would have carpeted and papered a small spare room for a parlour; but his wife expressed such pleasure at the white floor and huge glowing fireplace, at the pewter dishes and delf case, and dog kennel, and the wide space there was to move about in where they usually sat, that he thought it unnecessary to her comfort, and so dropped the intention.

She expressed pleasure, too, at finding a sister among her new acquaintance; and she prattled to Catherine, and kissed her, and ran about with her, and gave her quantities of presents, at the beginning. Her affection tired very soon, however, and when she grew peevish, Hindley became tyrannical. A few words from her, evincing a dislike to Heathcliff, were enough to rouse in him all his old hatred of the boy. He drove him from their company to the servants, deprived him of the instructions of the curate, and insisted that he should labour out of doors instead; compelling him to do so as hard as any other lad on the farm.

Heathcliff bore his degradation pretty well at first, because Cathy taught him what she learnt, and worked or played with him in the fields. They both promised fair to grow up as rude as savages; the young master being entirely negligent how they behaved, and what they did, so they kept clear of him. He would not even have seen after their going to church on Sundays, only Joseph and the curate reprimanded his carelessness when they absented themselves; and that reminded him to order Heathcliff a flogging, and Catherine a fast from dinner or supper. But it was one of their chief amusements to run away to the moors in the morning and remain there all day, and the after punishment grew a mere thing to laugh at. The curate might set as many chapters as he pleased for Catherine to get by heart, and Joseph might thrash Heathcliff till his arm ached; they forgot everything the minute they were together again: at least the minute they had contrived some naughty plan of revenge; and many a time I've cried to myself to watch them growing more reckless daily, and I not daring to speak a syllable, for fear of losing the small power I still retained over the unfriended creatures. One Sunday evening, it chanced that they were banished from the sitting-room, for making a noise, or a light offence of the kind; and when I went to call them to supper, I could discover them nowhere. We searched the house, above and below, and the yard and stables; they were invisible: and at last, Hindley in a passion told us to bolt the doors, and swore nobody should let them in that night. The household went to bed; and I, too anxious to lie down, opened my lattice and put my head out to hearken, though it rained: determined to admit them in spite of the prohibition, should they return. In a while, I distinguished steps coming up the road, and the light of a lantern glimmered through the gate. I threw a shawl over my head and ran to prevent them from waking Mr Earnshaw by knocking. There was Heathcliff, by himself: it gave me a start to see him alone.

'Where is Miss Catherine?' I cried hurriedly. 'No accident, I hope?' 'At Thrushcross Grange,' he answered; 'and I would have been there too, but they had not the manners to ask me to stay.' 'Well, you will catch it!' I said: 'you'll never be content till you're sent about your business. What in the world led you wandering to Thrushcross Grange?' 'Let me get off my wet clothes, and I'll tell you all about it, Nelly,' he replied. I bid him beware of rousing the master, and while he undressed and I waited to put out the candle, he continued—'Cathy and I escaped from the wash-house to have a ramble at liberty, and getting a glimpse of the Grange lights,

we thought we would just go and see whether the Lintons passed their Sunday evenings standing shivering in corners, while their father and mother sat eating and drinking, and singing and laughing, and burning their eyes out before the fire. Do you think they do? Or reading sermons, and being catechized by their manservant, and set to learn a column of Scripture names, if they don't answer properly?' 'Probably not,' I responded. 'They are good children, no doubt, and don't deserve the treatment you receive, for your bad conduct.' 'Don't you cant, Nelly,' he said: 'nonsense! We ran from the top of the Heights to the park, without stopping— Catherine completely beaten in the race, because she was barefoot. You'll have to seek for her shoes in the bog tomorrow. We crept through a broken hedge, groped our way up the path, and planted ourselves on a flower plot under the drawing-room window. The light came from thence; they had not put up the shutters, and the curtains were only half closed. Both of us were able to look in by standing on the basement, and clinging to the ledge, and we saw—ah! it was beautiful—a splendid place carpeted with crimson, and crimson-covered chairs and tables, and a pure white ceiling bordered by gold, a shower of glass drops hanging in silver chains from the centre, and shimmering with little soft tapers. Old Mr and Mrs Linton were not there; Edgar and his sister had it entirely to themselves. Shouldn't they have been happy? We should have thought ourselves in heaven! And now, guess what your good children were doing? Isabella—I believe she is eleven, a year younger than Cathy—lay screaming at the farther end of the room, shrieking as if witches were running red-hot needles into her. Edgar stood on the hearth weeping silently, and in the middle of the table sat a little dog, shaking its paw and yelping; which, from their mutual accusations, we understood they had nearly pulled in two between them. The idiots! That was their pleasure! to quarrel who should hold a heap of warm hair, and each begin to cry because both, after struggling to get it, refused to take it. We laughed outright at the petted things; we did despise them! When would you catch me wishing to have what Catherine wanted? or find us by ourselves, seeking entertainment in yelling, and sobbing, and rolling on the ground, divided by the whole room? I'd not exchange, for a thousand lives, my condition here, for Edgar Linton's at Thrushcross Grange—not if I might have the privilege of flinging Joseph off the highest gable, and painting the house-front with Hindley's blood!'

'Hush, hush!' I interrupted. 'Still you have not told me, Heathcliff, how Catherine is left behind?'

'I told you we laughed,' he answered. 'The Lintons heard us, and with one accord, they shot like arrows to the door; there was silence, and then a cry, "Oh, mamma, mamma! Oh, papa! Oh, mamma, come here. Oh, papa, oh!" They really did howl out something in that way. We made frightful noises to terrify them still more, and then we dropped off the ledge, because somebody was drawing the bars, and we felt we had better flee. I had Cathy by the hand, and was urging her on, when all at once she fell down. "Run, Heathcliff, run!" she whispered. "They have let the bulldog loose, and he holds me!" The devil had seized her ankle, Nelly: I heard his abominable snorting. She did not yell out—no! she would have scorned to do it, if she had been spitted on the horns of a mad cow. I did, though! I vociferated curses enough to annihilate any fiend in Christendom; and I got a stone and thrust it between his jaws, and tried with all my might to cram it down his throat. A beast of a servant came up with a lantern, at last, shouting—"Keep fast, Skulker, keep fast!" He changed his note, however, when he saw Skulker's game. The dog was throttled off; his huge, purple tongue hanging half a foot out of his mouth, and his pendent lips streaming with bloody slaver. The man took Cathy up: she was sick: not from fear, I'm certain, but from pain. He carried her in; I followed, grumbling execrations and vengeance. "What prey, Robert?" hallooed Linton from the entrance. "Skulker has caught a little girl, sir," he replied; "and there's a lad here", he added, making a clutch at me, "who looks an out-and-

outer! Very like, the robbers were for putting them through the window to open the doors to the gang after all were asleep, that they might murder us at their ease. Hold your tongue, you foul-mouthed thief, you! you shall go to the gallows for this. Mr Linton, sir, don't lay by your gun.'' ''No, no, Robert,'' said the old fool. ''The rascals knew that yesterday was my rent day: they thought to have me cleverly. Come in; I'll furnish them a reception. There, John, fasten the chain. Give Skulker some water, Jenny. To beard a magistrate in his stronghold, and on the Sabbath, too! Where will their insolence stop? Oh, my dear Mary, look here! Don't be afraid, it is but a boy—yet the villain scowls so plainly in his face; would it not be a kindness to the country to hang him at once, before he shows his nature in acts as well as features?'' He pulled me under the chandelier, and Mrs Linton placed her spectacles on her nose and raised her hands in horror. The cowardly children crept nearer also, Isabella lisping—''Frightful thing! Put him in the cellar, papa. He's exactly like the son of the fortune-teller that stole my tame pheasant. Isn't he, Edgar?''

'While they examined me, Cathy came round; she heard the last speech, and laughed. Edgar Linton, after an inquisitive stare, collected sufficient wit to recognize her. They see us at church, you know, though we seldom meet them elsewhere. ''That's Miss Earnshaw!'' he whispered to his mother, ''and look how Skulker has bitten her—how her foot bleeds!''

' ''Miss Earnshaw? Nonsense!'' cried the dame! ''Miss Earnshaw scouring the country with a gipsy! And yet, my dear, the child is in mourning—surely it is— and she may be lamed for life!''

' ''What culpable carelessness in her brother!'' exclaimed Mr Linton, turning from me to Catherine. ''I've understood from Shielders'' (that was the curate, sir) ''that he lets her grow up in absolute heathenism. But who is this? Where did she pick up this companion? Oho! I declare he is that strange acquisition my late neighbour made, in his journey to Liverpool—a little Lascar, or an American or Spanish castaway.''

' ''A wicked boy, at all events,'' remarked the old lady, ''and quite unfit for a decent house! Did you notice his language, Linton? I'm shocked that my children should have heard it.''

'I recommenced cursing—don't be angry, Nelly—and so Robert was ordered to take me off. I refused to go without Cathy; he dragged me into the garden, pushed the lantern into my hand, assured me that Mr Earnshaw should be informed of my behaviour, and, bidding me march directly, secured the door again. The curtains were still looped up at one corner, and I resumed my station as spy; because, if Catherine had wished to return, I intended shattering their great glass panes to a million of fragments, unless they let her out. She sat on the sofa quietly. Mrs Linton took off the grey cloak of the dairymaid which we had borrowed for our excursion, shaking her head and expostulating with her, I suppose: she was a young lady, and they made a distinction between her treatment and mine. Then the woman-servant brought a basin of warm water, and washed her feet; and Mr Linton mixed a tumbler of negus, and Isabella emptied a plateful of cakes into her lap, and Edgar stood gaping at a distance. Afterwards, they dried and combed her beautiful hair, and gave her a pair of enormous slippers, and wheeled her to the fire; and I left her, as merry as she could be, dividing her food between the little dog and Skulker, whose nose she pinched as he ate; and kindling a spark of spirit in the vacant blue eyes of the Lintons—a dim reflection from her own enchanting face. I saw they were full of stupid admiration; she is so immeasurably superior to them—to everybody on earth, is she not, Nelly?'

'There will more come of this business than you reckon on,' I answered, covering him up and extinguishing the light. 'You are incurable, Heathcliff; and Mr Hindley will have to proceed to extremities, see if he won't.' My words came truer than I desired. The luckless adventure made Earnshaw furious. And then Mr Linton, to

mend matters, paid us a visit himself on the morrow; and read the young master such a lecture on the road he guided his family, that he was stirred to look about him, in earnest. Heathcliff received no flogging, but he was told that the first word he spoke to Miss Catherine should ensure a dismissal; and Mrs Earnshaw undertook to keep her sister-in-law in due restraint when she returned home; employing art, not force: with force she would have found it impossible.

Chapter VII

CATHY stayed at Thrushcross Grange five weeks: till Christmas. By that time her ankle was thoroughly cured, and her manners much improved. The mistress visited her often in the interval, and commenced her plan of reform by trying to raise her self-respect with fine clothes and flattery, which she took readily; so that, instead of a wild, hatless little savage jumping into the house, and rushing to squeeze us all breathless, there alighted from a handsome black pony a very dignified person, with brown ringlets falling from the cover of a feathered beaver, and a long cloth habit, which she was obliged to hold up with both hands that she might sail in. Hindley lifted her from her horse, exclaiming delightedly, 'Why, Cathy, you are quite a beauty! I should scarcely have known you: you look like a lady now. Isabella Linton is not to be compared with her, is she, Frances?' 'Isabella has not her natural advantages,' replied his wife: 'but she must mind and not grow wild again here. Ellen, help Miss Catherine off with her things—stay, dear, you will disarrange your curls—let me untie your hat.'

I removed the habit, and there shone forth, beneath a grand plaid silk frock, white trousers, and burnished shoes; and, while her eyes sparkled joyfully when the dogs came bounding up to welcome her, she dare hardly touch them lest they should fawn upon her splendid garments. She kissed me gently: I was all flour making the Christmas cake, and it would not have done to give me a hug; and, then, she looked round for Heathcliff. Mr and Mrs Earnshaw watched anxiously their meeting; thinking it would enable them to judge, in some measure, what grounds they had for hoping to succeed in separating the two friends.

Heathcliff was hard to discover, at first. If he were careless, and uncared for, before Catherine's absence, he had been ten times more so, since. Nobody but I even did him the kindness to call him a dirty boy, and bid him wash himself, once a week; and children of his age seldom have a natural pleasure in soap and water. Therefore, not to mention his clothes, which had seen three months' service in mire and dust, and his thick uncombed hair, the surface of his face and hands was dismally beclouded. He might well skulk behind the settle, on beholding such a bright, graceful damsel enter the house, instead of a rough-headed counterpart of himself, as he expected. 'Is Heathcliff not here?' she demanded, pulling off her gloves, and displaying fingers wonderfully whitened with doing nothing and staying indoors.

'Heathcliff, you may come forward,' cried Mr Hindley, enjoying his discomfiture, and gratified to see what a forbidding young blackguard he would be compelled to present himself. 'You may come and wish Miss Catherine welcome, like the other servants.'

Cathy, catching a glimpse of her friend in his concealment, flew to embrace him; she bestowed seven or eight kisses on his cheek within the second, and then stopped, and drawing back, burst into a laugh, exclaiming, 'Why, how very black and cross you look! and how—how funny and grim! But that's because I'm used to Edgar and Isabella Linton. Well, Heathcliff, have you forgotten me?'

She had some reason to put the question, for shame and pride threw double gloom over his countenance, and kept him immovable.

'Shake hands, Heathcliff,' said Mr Earnshaw, condescendingly; 'once in a way, that is permitted.'

'I shall not,' replied the boy, finding his tongue at last; 'I shall not stand to be laughed at. I shall not bear it!'

And he would have broken from the circle, but Miss Cathy seized him again.

'I did not mean to laugh at you,' she said; 'I could not hinder myself: Heathcliff, shake hands at least! What are you sulky for? It was only that you looked odd. If you wash your face and brush your hair, it will be all right: but you are so dirty!'

She gazed concernedly at the dusky fingers she held in her own, and also at her dress; which she feared had gained no embellishment from its contact with his.

'You needn't have touched me!' he answered, following her eye and snatching away his hand. 'I shall be as dirty as I please: and I like to be dirty, and I will be dirty.'

With that he dashed head foremost out of the room, amid the merriment of the master and mistress, and to the serious disturbance of Catherine; who could not comprehend how her remarks should have produced such an exhibition of bad temper.

After playing lady's-maid to the newcomer, and putting my cakes in the oven, and making the house and kitchen cheerful with great fires, befitting Christmas eve, I prepared to sit down and amuse myself by singing carols, all alone; regardless of Joseph's affirmations that he considered the merry tunes I chose as next door to songs. He had retired to private prayer in his chamber, and Mr and Mrs Earnshaw were engaging Missy's attention by sundry gay trifles bought for her to present to the little Lintons, as an acknowledgment of their kindness. They had invited them to spend the morrow at Wuthering Heights, and the invitation had been accepted, on one condition: Mrs Linton begged that her darlings must be kept carefully apart from that 'naughty swearing boy'.

Under these circumstances I remained solitary. I smelt the rich scent of the heating spices; and admired the shining kitchen utensils, the polished clock, decked in holly, the silver mugs ranged on a tray ready to be filled with mulled ale for supper; and above all, the speckless purity of my particular care—the scoured and well-swept floor. I gave due inward applause to every object, and then I remembered how old Earnshaw used to come in when all was tidied, and call me a cant lass, and slip a shilling into my hand as a Christmas box; and from that I went on to think of his fondness for Heathcliff, and his dread lest he should suffer neglect after death had removed him; and that naturally led me to consider the poor lad's situation now, and from singing I changed my mind to crying. It struck me soon, however, there would be more sense in endeavouring to repair some of his wrongs than shedding tears over them: I got up and walked into the court to seek him. He was not far; I found him smoothing the glossy coat of the new pony in the stable, and feeding the other beasts, according to custom.

'Make haste, Heathcliff!' I said, 'the kitchen is so comfortable; and Joseph is upstairs: make haste, and let me dress you smart before Miss Cathy comes out, and then you can sit together, with the whole hearth to yourselves, and have a long chatter till bedtime.'

He proceeded with his task and never turned his head towards me.

'Come—are you coming?' I continued. 'There's a little cake for each of you, nearly enough; and you'll need half an hour's donning.'

I waited five minutes, but getting no answer, left him. Catherine supped with her brother and sister-in-law: Joseph and I joined in an unsociable meal, seasoned with reproofs on one side and sauciness on the other. His cake and cheese remained on the table all night for the fairies. He managed to continue work till nine o'clock, and then marched dumb and dour to his chamber. Cathy sat up late, having a world

of things to order for the reception of her new friends: she came into the kitchen once to speak to her old one; but he was gone, and she only stayed to ask what was the matter with him, and then went back. In the morning he rose early; and as it was a holiday carried his ill humour on to the moors; not reappearing till the family were departed for church. Fasting and reflection seemed to have brought him to a better spirit. He hung about me for a while, and having screwed up his courage, exclaimed abruptly:

'Nelly, make me decent, I'm going to be good.'

'High time, Heathcliff,' I said; 'you *have* grieved Catherine: she's sorry she ever came home, I dare say! It looks as if you envied her, because she is more thought of than you.'

The notion of *envying* Catherine was incomprehensible to him, but the notion of grieving her he understood clearly enough.

'Did she say she was grieved?' he inquired, looking very serious.

'She cried when I told her you were off again this morning.'

'Well, *I* cried last night,' he returned, 'and I had more reason to cry than she.'

'Yes: you had the reason of going to bed with a proud heart and an empty stomach,' said I. 'Proud people breed sad sorrows for themselves. But, if you be ashamed of your touchiness, you must ask pardon, mind, when she comes in. You must go up and offer to kiss her, and say—you know best what to say; only do it heartily, and not as if you thought her converted into a stranger by her grand dress. And now, though I have dinner to get ready, I'll steal time to arrange you so that Edgar Linton shall look quite a doll beside you: and that he does. You are younger, and yet, I'll be bound, you are taller and twice as broad across the shoulders: you could knock him down in a twinkling? don't you feel that you could?'

Heathcliff's face brightened a moment; then it was overcast afresh, and he sighed.

'But, Nelly, if I knocked him down twenty times, that wouldn't make him less handsome or me more so. I wish I had light hair and a fair skin, and was dressed and behaved as well, and had a chance of being as rich as he will be!'

'And cried for mamma at every turn,' I added, 'and trembled if a country lad heaved his fist against you, and sat at home all day for a shower of rain. Oh, Heathcliff, you are showing a poor spirit! Come to the glass, and I'll let you see what you should wish. Do you mark those two lines between your eyes; and those thick brows, that instead of rising arched, sink in the middle; and that couple of black fiends, so deeply buried, who never open their windows boldy, but lurk glinting under them, like devil's spies? Wish and learn to smooth away the surly wrinkles, to raise your lids frankly, and change the fiends to confident, innocent angels, suspecting and doubting nothing, and always seeing friends where they are not sure of foes. Don't get the expression of a vicious cur that appears to know the kicks it gets are its desert, and yet hates all the world as well as the kicker, for what it suffers.'

'In other words, I must wish for Edgar Linton's great blue eyes and even forehead,' he replied. 'I do—and that won't help me to them.'

'A good heart will help you to a bonny face, my lad,' I continued, 'if you were a regular black; and a bad one will turn the bonniest into something worse than ugly. And now that we've done washing, and combing, and sulking—tell me whether you don't think yourself rather handsome? I'll tell you, I do. You're fit for a prince in disguise. Who knows but your father was Emperor of China, and your mother an Indian queen, each of them able to buy up, with one week's income, Wuthering Heights and Thrushcross Grange together? And you were kidnapped by wicked sailors and brought to England. Were I in your place, I would frame high notions of my birth; and the thoughts of what I was should give me courage and dignity to support the oppressions of a little farmer!'

So I chattered on; and Heathcliff gradually lost his frown and began to look quite pleasant, when all at once our conversation was interrupted by a rumbling sound

moving up the road and entering the court. He ran to the window and I to the door, just in time to behold the two Lintons descend from the family carriage, smothered in cloaks and furs, and the Earnshaws dismount from their horses: they often rode to church in winter. Catherine took a hand of each of the children, and brought them into the house and set them before the fire, which quickly put colour into their white faces.

I urged my companion to hasten now and show his amiable humour, and he willingly obeyed; but ill luck would have it that, as he opened the door leading from the kitchen on one side, Hindley opened it on the other. They met, and the master, irritated at seeing him clean and cheerful; or, perhaps, eager to keep his promise to Mrs Linton, shoved him back with a sudden thrust, and angrily bade Joseph 'keep the fellow out of the room—send him into the garret till dinner is over. He'll be cramming his fingers in the tarts and stealing the fruit, if left alone with them a minute.'

'Nay, sir,' I could not avoid answering, 'he'll touch nothing, not he: and I suppose he must have his share of the dainties as well as we.'

'He shall have his share of my hand, if I catch him downstairs again till dark,' cried Hindley. 'Begone, you vagabond! What! you are attempting the coxcomb, are you? Wait till I get hold of those elegant locks—see if I won't pull them a bit longer.'

'They are long enough, already,' observed Master Linton, peeping from the doorway; 'I wonder they don't make his head ache. It's like a colt's mane over his eyes!'

He ventured his remark without any intention to insult; but Heathcliff's violent nature was not prepared to endure the appearance of impertinence from one whom he seemed to hate, even then, as a rival. He seized a tureen of hot apple sauce (the first thing that come under his gripe) and dashed it full against the speaker's face and neck; who instantly commenced a lament that brought Isabella and Catherine hurrying to the place. Mr Earnshaw snatched up the culprit directly and conveyed him to his chamber; where, doubtless, he administered a rough remedy to cool the fit of passion, for he reappeared red and breathless. I got the dish-cloth and rather spitefully scrubbed Edgar's nose and mouth, affirming it served him right for meddling. His sister began weeping to go home, and Cathy stood by confounded, blushing for all.

'You should not have spoken to him!' she expostulated with Master Linton. 'He was in a bad temper, and now you've spoilt your visit; and he'll be flogged: I hate him to be flogged! I can't eat my dinner. Why did you speak to him, Edgar?'

'I didn't,' sobbed the youth, escaping from my hands, and finishing the remainder of the purification with his cambric pocket handkerchief. 'I promised mamma that I wouldn't say one word to him, and I didn't.'

'Well, don't cry,' replied Catherine, contemptuously, 'you're not killed. Don't make more mischief; my brother is coming: be quiet! Give over, Isabella! Has anybody hurt *you*?'

'There, there, children—to your seats!' cried Hindley, bustling in. 'That brute of a lad has warmed me nicely. Next time, Master Edgar, take the law into your own fists —it will give you an appetite!'

The little party recovered its equanimity at sight of the fragrant feast. They were hungry after their ride, and easily consoled, since no real harm had befallen them. Mr Earnshaw carved bountiful platefuls, and the mistress made them merry with lively talk. I waited behind her chair, and was pained to behold Catherine, with dry eyes and an indifferent air, commence cutting up the wing of a goose before her. 'An unfeeling child,' I thought to myself; 'how lightly she dismisses her old playmate's troubles. I could not have imagined her to be so selfish.' She lifted a mouthful to her lips; then she set it down again: her cheeks flushed, and the tears gushed over them. She slipped her fork to the floor, and hastily dived under the

cloth to conceal her emotion. I did not call her unfeeling long; for I perceived she was in purgatory throughout the day, and wearying to find an opportunity of getting by herself, or paying a visit to Heathcliff, who had been locked up by the master: as I discovered, on endeavouring to introduce to him a private mess of victuals.

In the evening we had a dance. Cathy begged that he might be liberated then, as Isabella Linton had no partner; her entreaties were vain, and I was appointed to supply the deficiency. We got rid of all gloom in the excitement of the exercise, and our pleasure was increased by the arrival of the Gimmerton band, mustering fifteen strong: a trumpet, a trombone, clarionets, bassoons, French horns, and a bass viol, besides singers. They go the rounds of all the respectable houses, and receive contributions every Christmas, and we esteemed it a first-rate treat to hear them. After the usual carols had been sung, we set them to songs and glees. Mrs Earnshaw loved the music, and so they gave us plenty.

Catherine loved it too; but she said it sounded sweetest at the top of the steps, and she went up in the dark; I followed. They shut the house door below, never noting our absence, it was so full of people. She made no stay at the stair's head, but mounted farther, to the garret where Heathcliff was confined, and called him. He stubbornly declined answering for a while; she persevered, and finally persuaded him to hold communion with her through the boards. I let the poor things converse unmolested, till I supposed the songs were going to cease, and the singers to get some refreshment; then, I clambered up the ladder to warn her. Instead of finding her outside, I heard her voice within. The little monkey had crept by the skylight of one garret, along the roof, into the skylight of the other, and it was with the utmost difficulty I could coax her out again. When she did come Heathcliff came with her, and she insisted that I should take him into the kitchen, as my fellow-servant had gone to a neighbour's to be removed from the sound of our 'devil's psalmody', as it pleased him to call it. I told them I intended by no means to encourage their tricks; but as the prisoner had never broken his fast since yesterday's dinner, I would wink at his cheating Mr Hindley that once. He went down; I set him a stool by the fire, and offered him a quantity of good things; but he was sick and could eat little, and my attempts to entertain him were thrown away. He leant his two elbows on his knees, and his chin on his hands, and remained wrapt in dumb meditation. On my inquiring the subject of his thoughts, he answered gravely:

'I'm trying to settle how I shall pay Hindley back. I don't care how long I wait, if I can only do it at last. I hope he will not die before I do!'

'For shame, Heathcliff!' said I. 'It is for God to punish wicked people; we should learn to forgive.'

'No, God won't have the satisfaction that I shall,' he returned. 'I only wish I knew the best way! Let me alone, and I'll plan it out: while I'm thinking of that I don't feel pain.'

But, Mr Lockwood, I forget these tales cannot divert you. I'm annoyed how I should dream of chattering on at such a rate; and your gruel cold, and you nodding for bed! I could have told Heathcliff's history, all that you need hear, in half a dozen words.

Thus interrupting herself, the housekeeper rose, and proceeded to lay aside her sewing; but I felt incapable of moving from the hearth, and I was very far from nodding. 'Sit still, Mrs Dean,' I cried, 'do sit still, another half-hour! You've done just right to tell the story leisurely. That is the method I like; and you must finish it in the same style. I am interested in every character you have mentioned, more or less.'

'The clock is on the stroke of eleven, sir.'

'No matter—I'm not accustomed to go to bed in the long hours. One or two is early enough for a person who lies till ten.'

'You shouldn't lie till ten. There's the very prime of the morning gone long before that time. A person who has not done one half his day's work by ten o'clock, runs a chance of leaving the other half undone.'

'Nevertheless, Mrs Dean, resume your chair; because tomorrow I intend lengthening the night till afternoon. I prognosticate for myself an obstinate cold, at least.'

'I hope not, sir. Well, you must allow me to leap over some three years; during that space Mrs Earnshaw——'

'No, no, I'll allow nothing of the sort! Are you acquainted with the mood of mind in which, if you were seated alone, and the cat licking its kitten on the rug before you, you would watch the operation so intently that puss's neglect of one ear would put you seriously out of temper?'

'A terribly lazy mood, I should say.'

'On the contrary, a tiresomely active one. It is mine, at present; and, therefore, continue minutely. I perceive that people in these regions acquire over people in towns the value that the spider in a dungeon does over a spider in a cottage, to their various occupants; and yet the deepened attraction is not entirely owing to the situation of the looker-on. They *do* live more in earnest, more in themselves, and less in surface change, and frivolous external things. I could fancy a love for life here almost possible; and I was a fixed unbeliever in any love of a year's standing. One state resembles setting a hungry man down to a single dish, on which he may concentrate his entire appetite and do it justice; the other, introducing him to a table laid out by French cooks: he can perhaps extract as much enjoyment from the whole; but each part is a mere atom in his regard and remembrance.'

'Oh! here we are the same as anywhere else, when you get to know us,' observed Mrs Dean, somewhat puzzled at my speech.

'Excuse me,' I responded; 'you, my good friend, are a striking evidence against that assertion. Excepting a few provincialisms of slight consequence, you have no marks of the manners which I am habituated to consider as peculiar to your class. I am sure you have thought a great deal more than the generality of servants think. You have been compelled to cultivate your reflective faculties for want of occasions for frittering your life away in silly trifles.'

Mrs Dean laughed.

'I certainly esteem myself a steady, reasonable kind of body,' she said; 'not exactly from living among the hills and seeing one set of faces, and one series of actions, from year's end to year's end; but I have undergone sharp discipline, which has taught me wisdom; and then, I have read more than you would fancy, Mr Lockwood. You could not open a book in this library that I have not looked into, and got something out of also: unless it be that range of Greek and Latin and that of French; and those I know one from another: it is as much as you can expect of a poor man's daughter. However, if I am to follow my story in true gossip's fashion, I had better go on; and instead of leaping three years, I will be content to pass to the next summer—the summer of 1778, that is, nearly twenty-three years ago.'

Chapter VIII

ON the morning of a fine June day, my first bonny little nursling, and the last of the ancient Earnshaw stock, was born. We were busy with the hay in a far away field, when the girl that usually brought our breakfasts, came running an hour too soon, across the meadow and up the lane, calling me as she ran.

'Oh, such a grand bairn!' she panted out. 'The finest lad that ever breathed! But the doctor says missis must go: he says she's been in a consumption these many months. I heard him tell Mr Hindley: and now she has nothing to keep her, and

she'll be dead before winter. You must come home directly. You're to nurse it, Nelly: to feed it with sugar and milk, and take care of it day and night. I wish I were you, because it will be all yours when there is no missis!'

'But is she very ill?' I asked, flinging down my rake, and tying my bonnet.

'I guess she is; yet she looks bravely,' replied the girl, 'and she talks as if she thought of living to see it grow a man. She's out of her head for joy, it's such a beauty! If I were her, I'm certain I should not die: I should get better at the bare sight of it, in spite of Kenneth. I was fairly mad at him. Dame Archer brought the cherub down to master, in the house, and his face just began to light up, then the old croaker steps forward, and says he: "Earnshaw, it's a blessing your wife has been spared to leave you this son. When she came, I felt convinced we shouldn't keep her long; and now, I must tell you, the winter will probably finish her. Don't take on, and fret about it too much! it can't be helped. And besides, you should have known better than to choose such a rush of a lass!'

'And what did the master answer?' I inquired.

'I think he swore: but I didn't mind him, I was straining to see the bairn,' and she began again to describe it rapturously. I, as zealous as herself, hurried eagerly home to admire, on my part; though I was very sad for Hindley's sake. He had room in his heart only for two idols—his wife and himself: he doted on both, and adored one, and I couldn't conceive how he would bear the loss.

When we got to Wuthering Heights, there he stood at the front door; and, as I passed in, I asked, 'How was the baby?'

'Nearly ready to run about, Nell;' he replied, putting on a cheerful smile.

'And the mistress?' I ventured to inquire; 'the doctor says she's——'

'Damn the doctor!' he interrupted, reddening. 'Frances is quite right; she'll be perfectly well by this time next week. Are you going upstairs? will you tell her that I'll come, if she'll promise not to talk. I left her because she would not hold her tongue; and she must—tell her Mr Kenneth says she must be quiet.'

I delivered this message to Mrs Earnshaw; she seemed in flighty spirits, and replied merrily:

'I hardly spoke a word, Ellen, and there he has gone out twice, crying. Well, say I promise I won't speak: but that does not bind me not to laugh at him!'

Poor soul! Till within a week of her death that gay heart never failed her, and her husband persisted doggedly, nay, furiously, in affirming her health improved every day. When Kenneth warned him that his medicines were useless at that stage of the malady, and he needn't put him to further expense by attending her, he retorted:

'I know you need not—she's well—she does not want any more attendance from you! She never was in a consumption. It was a fever; and it is gone: her pulse is as slow as mine now, and her cheek as cool.'

He told his wife the same story, and she seemed to believe him; but one night, while leaning on his shoulder, in the act of saying she thought she should be able to get up tomorrow, a fit of coughing took her—a very slight one—he raised her in his arms; she put her two hands about his neck, her face changed, and she was dead.

As the girl had anticipated, the child Hareton fell wholly into my hands. Mr Earnshaw, provided he saw him healthy and never heard him cry, was contented, as far as regarded him. For himself, he grew desperate: his sorrow was of that kind that will not lament. He neither wept nor prayed: he cursed and defied: execrated God and man, and gave himself up to reckless dissipation. The servants could not bear his tyrannical and evil conduct long: Joseph and I were the only two that would stay. I had not the heart to leave my charge; and besides, you know I had been his foster-sister, and excused his behaviour more readily than a stranger would. Joseph remained to hector over tenants and labourers; and because it was his vocation to be where he had plenty of wickedness to reprove.

The master's bad ways and bad companions formed a pretty example for Catherine and Heathcliff. His treatment of the latter was enough to make a fiend of a saint. And, truly, it appeared as if the lad *were* possessed of something diabolical at that period. He delighted to witness Hindley degrading himself past redemption; and became daily more notable for savage sullenness and ferocity. I could not half tell what an infernal house we had. The curate dropped calling, and nobody decent came near us, at last; unless Edgar Linton's visits to Miss Cathy might be an exception. At fifteen she was the queen of the countryside; she had no peer; and she did turn out a haughty, headstrong creature! I own I did not like her, after her infancy was past; and I vexed her frequently by trying to bring down her arrogance: she never took an aversion to me, though. She had a wondrous constancy to old attachments: even Heathcliff kept his hold on her affections unalterably; and young Linton, with all his superiority, found it difficult to make an equally deep impression. He was my late master: that is his portrait over the fireplace. It used to hang on one side, and his wife's on the other; but hers has been removed, or else you might see something of what she was. Can you make that out?

Mrs Dean raised the candle, and I discerned a soft-featured face, exceedingly resembling the young lady at the Heights, but more pensive and amiable in expression. It formed a sweet picture. The long light hair curled slightly on the temples; the eyes were large and serious; the figure almost too graceful. I did not marvel how Catherine Earnshaw could forget her first friend for such an individual. I marvelled much how he, with a mind to correspond with his person, could fancy my idea of Catherine Earnshaw.

'A very agreeable portrait,' I observed to the housekeeper. 'Is it like?'

'Yes,' she answered; 'but he looked better when he was animated; that is his everyday countenance: he wanted spirit in general.'

Catherine had kept up her acquaintance with the Lintons since her five weeks' residence among them; and as she had no temptation to show her rough side in their company, and had the sense to be ashamed of being rude where she experienced such invariable courtesy, she imposed unwittingly on the old lady and gentleman, by her ingenious cordiality; gained the admiration of Isabella, and the heart and soul of her brother: acquisitions that flattered her from the first, for she was full of ambition, and led her to adopt a double character without exactly intending to deceive anyone. In the place where she heard Heathcliff termed a 'vulgar young ruffian', and 'worse than a brute', she took care not to act like him; but at home she had small inclination to practise politeness that would only be laughed at, and restrain an unruly nature when it would bring her neither credit nor praise.

Mr Edgar seldom mustered courage to visit Wuthering Heights openly. He had a terror of Earnshaw's reputation, and shrunk from encountering him; and yet he was always received with our best attempts at civility: the master himself avoided offending him, knowing why he came; and if he could not be gracious, kept out of the way. I rather think his appearance there was distasteful to Catherine: she was not artful, never played the coquette, and had evidently an objection to her two friends meeting at all; for when Heathcliff expressed contempt of Linton in his presence, she could not half coincide, as she did in his absence; and when Linton evinced disgust and antipathy to Heathcliff, she dared not treat his sentiments with indifference, as if depreciation of her playmate were of scarcely any consequence to her. I've had many a laugh at her perplexities and untold troubles, which she vainly strove to hide from my mockery. That sounds ill-natured: but she was so proud, it became really impossible to pity her distresses, till she should be chastened into more humility. She did bring herself, finally, to confess, and confide in me: there was not a soul else that she might fashion into an adviser.

Mr Hindley had gone from home one afternoon, and Heathcliff presumed to give himself a holiday on the strength of it. He had reached the age of sixteen then, I think, and without having bad features, or being deficient in intellect, he contrived

to convey an impression of inward and outward repulsiveness that his present aspect retains no traces of. In the first place, he had by that time lost the benefit of his early education: continual hard work, begun soon and concluded late, had extinguished any curiosity he once possessed in pursuit of knowledge, and any love for books or learning. His childhood's sense of superiority, instilled into him by the favours of old Mr Earnshaw, was faded away. He struggled long to keep up an equality with Catherine in her studies, and yielded with poignant though silent regret: but he yielded completely; and there was no prevailing on him to take a step in the way of moving upward, when he found he must, necessarily, sink beneath his former level. Then personal appearance sympathized with mental deterioration: he acquired a slouching gait, and ignoble look; his naturally reserved disposition was exaggerated into an almost idiotic excess of unsociable moroseness; and he took a grim pleasure, apparently, in exciting the aversion rather than the esteem of his few acquaintance.

Catherine and he were constant companions still at his seasons of respite from labour; but he had ceased to express his fondness for her in words, and recoiled with angry suspicion from her girlish caresses, as if conscious there could be no gratification in lavishing such marks of affection on him. On the before-named occasion he came into the house to announce his intention of doing nothing, while I was assisting Miss Cathy to arrange her dress: she had not reckoned on his taking it into his head to be idle; and imagining she would have the whole place to herself, she managed, by some means, to inform Mr Edgar of her brother's absence, and was then preparing to receive him.

'Cathy, are you busy, this afternoon?' asked Heathcliff. 'Are you going anywhere?'

'No, it is raining,' she answered.

'Why have you that silk frock on, then?' he said. 'Nobody coming here, I hope?'

'Not that I know of,' stammered Miss: 'but you should be in the field now, Heathcliff. It is an hour past dinner time: I thought you were gone.'

'Hindley does not often free us from his accursed presence,' observed the boy. 'I'll not work any more today: I'll stay with you.'

'Oh, but Joseph will tell,' she suggested; 'you'd better go!'

'Joseph is loading lime on the farther side of Pennistow Crag; it will take him till dark, and he'll never know.'

So saying, he lounged to the fire, and sat down. Catherine reflected an instant, with knitted brows—she found it needful to smooth the way for an intrusion. 'Isabella and Edgar Linton talked of calling this afternoon,' she said, at the conclusion of a minute's silence. 'As it rains, I hardly expect them; but they may come, and if they do, you run the risk of being scolded for no good.'

'Order Ellen to say you are engaged, Cathy,' he persisted; 'don't turn me out for those pitiful, silly friends of yours! I'm on the point, sometimes, of complaining that they—but I'll not——'

'That they what?' cried Catherine, gazing at him with a troubled countenance. 'Oh, Nelly!' she added petulantly, jerking her head away from my hands, 'you've combed my hair quite out of curl! That's enough; let me alone. What are you on the point of complaining about, Heathcliff?'

'Nothing—only look at the almanac on that wall;' he pointed to a framed sheet hanging near the window, and continued—'The crosses are for the evenings you have spent with the Lintons, the dots for those spent with me. Do you see? I've marked every day.'

'Yes—very foolish: as if I took notice!' replied Catherine in a peevish tone. 'And where is the sense of that?'

'To show that I *do* take notice,' said Heathcliff.

'And should I always be sitting with you?' she demanded, growing more irritated. 'What good do I get? What do you talk about? You might be dumb, or a baby, for anything you say to amuse me, or for anything you do, either!'

'You never told me before that I talked too little, or that you disliked my company, Cathy!' exclaimed Heathcliff, in much agitation.

'It's no company at all, when people know nothing and say nothing,' she muttered.

Her companion rose up, but he hadn't time to express his feelings further, for a horse's feet were heard on the flags, and having knocked gently, young Linton entered, his face brilliant with delight at the unexpected summons he had received. Doubtless Catherine marked the difference between her friends, as one came in and the other went out. The contrast resembled what you see in exchanging a bleak, hilly, coal country for a beautiful fertile valley; and his voice and greeting were as opposite as his aspect. He had a sweet, low manner of speaking, and pronounced his words as you do: that's less gruff than we talk here, and softer.

'I'm not come too soon, am I?' he said, casting a look at me: I had begun to wipe the plate, and tidy some drawers at the far end in the dresser.

'No,' answered Catherine. 'What are you doing there, Nelly?'

'My work, miss,' I replied. (Mr Hindley had given me directions to make a third party in any private visits Linton chose to pay.)

She stepped behind me and whispered crossly, 'Take yourself and your dusters off; when company are in the house, servants don't commence scouring and cleaning in the room where they are!'

'It's a good opportunity, now that the master is away,' I answered aloud: 'he hates me to be fidgeting over these things in his presence. I'm sure Mr Edgar will excuse me.'

'I hate you to be fidgeting in *my* presence,' exclaimed the young lady imperiously, not allowing her guest time to speak: she had failed to recover her equanimity since the little dispute with Heathcliff.

'I'm sorry for it, Miss Catherine,' was my response; and I proceeded assiduously with my occupation.

She, supposing Edgar could not see her, snatched the cloth from my hand, and pinched me, with a prolonged wrench, very spitefully on the arm. I've said I did not love her, and rather relished mortifying her vanity now and then: besides, she hurt me extremely; so I started up from my knees, and screamed out, 'Oh, miss, that's a nasty trick! You have no right to nip me, and I'm not going to bear it.'

'I didn't touch you, you lying creature!' cried she, her fingers tingling to repeat the act, and her ears red with rage. She never had power to conceal her passion, it always set her whole complexion in a blaze.

'What's that, then?' I retorted, showing a decided purple witness to refute her.

She stamped her foot, wavered a moment, and then irresistibly impelled by the naughty spirit within her, slapped me on the cheek a stinging blow that filled both eyes with water.

'Catherine, love! Catherine!' interposed Linton, greatly shocked at the double fault of falsehood and violence which his idol had committed.

'Leave the room, Ellen!' she repeated, trembling all over.

Little Hareton, who followed me everywhere, and was sitting near me on the floor, at seeing my tears commenced crying himself, and sobbed out complaints against 'wicked aunt Cathy', which drew her fury on to his unlucky head: she seized his shoulders, and shook him till the poor child waxed livid, and Edgar thoughtlessly laid hold of her hands to deliver him. In an instant one was wrung free, and the astonished young man felt it applied over his own ear in a way that could not be mistaken for jest. He drew back in consternation. I lifted Hareton in my arms, and walked off to the kitchen with him, leaving the door of communication open, for I was curious to watch how they would settle their disagreement. The insulted visitor moved to the spot where he had laid his hat, pale and with a quivering lip.

'That's right!' I said to myself. 'Take warning and begone! It's a kindness to let you have a glimpse of her genuine disposition.'

'Where are you going?' demanded Catherine, advancing to the door.

He swerved aside, and attempted to pass.

'You must not go!' she exclaimed energetically.

'I must and shall!' he replied in a subdued voice.

'No,' she persisted, grasping the handle; 'not yet, Edgar Linton: sit down; you shall not leave me in that temper. I should be miserable all night, and I won't be miserable for you!'

'Can I stay after you have struck me?' asked Linton.

Catherine was mute.

'You've made me afraid and ashamed of you,' he continued; 'I'll not come here again!'

Her eyes began to glisten, and her lids to twinkle.

'And you told a deliberate untruth!' he said.

'I didn't!' she cried, recovering her speech; 'I did nothing deliberately. Well, go, if you please—get away! And now I'll cry—I'll cry myself sick!'

She dropped down on her knees by a chair, and set to weeping in serious earnest. Edgar persevered in his resolution as far as the court; there he lingered. I resolved to encourage him.

'Miss is dreadfully wayward, sir,' I called out. 'As bad as any marred child: you'd better be riding home, or else she will be sick only to grieve us.'

The soft thing looked askance through the window: he possessed the power to depart, as much as a cat possesses the power to leave a mouse half killed, or a bird half eaten. Ah, I thought, there will be no saving him: he's doomed, and flies to his fate! And so it was: he turned abruptly, hastened into the house again, shut the door behind him; and when I went in a while after to inform them that Earnshaw had come home rabid drunk, ready to pull the whole place about our ears (his ordinary frame of mind in that condition), I saw the quarrel had merely effected a closer intimacy—had broken the outworks of youthful timidity, and enabled them to forsake the disguise of friendship, and confess themselves lovers.

Intelligence of Mr Hindley's arrival drove Linton speedily to his horse, and Catherine to her chamber. I went to hide little Hareton, and to take the shot out of the master's fowling-piece, which he was fond of playing with in his insane excitement, to the hazard of the lives of any who provoked, or even attracted his notice too much; and I had hit upon the plan of removing it, that he might do less mischief if he did go the length of firing the gun.

Chapter IX

HE entered, vociferating oaths dreadful to hear; and caught me in the act of stowing his son away in the kitchen cupboard. Hareton was impressed with a wholesome terror of encountering either his wild beast's fondness or his madman's rage; for in one he ran a chance of being squeezed and kissed to death, and in the other of being flung into the fire, or dashed against the wall; and the poor thing remained perfectly quiet wherever I chose to put him.

'There, I've found it out at last!' cried Hindley, pulling me back by the skin of my neck, like a dog. 'By heaven and hell, you've sworn between you to murder that child! I know how it is, now, that he is always out of my way. But, with the help of Satan, I shall make you swallow the carving-knife, Nelly! You needn't laugh; for I've just crammed Kenneth, head downmost, in the Blackhorse marsh; and two is the same as one—and I want to kill some of you: I shall have no rest till I do!'

'But I don't like the carving-knife, Mr Hindley,' I answered: 'it has been cutting red herrings. I'd rather be shot, if you please.'

'You'd rather be damned!' he said; 'and so you shall. No law in England can hinder a man from keeping his house decent, and mine's abominable ! open your mouth.'

He held the knife in his hand, and pushed its point between my teeth: but, for my part, I was never much afraid of his vagaries. I spat out, and affirmed it tasted detestably—I would not take it on any account.

'Oh!' said he, releasing me, 'I see that hideous little villain is not Hareton: I beg your pardon, Nell. If it be, he deserves flaying alive for not running to welcome me, and for screaming as if I were a goblin. Unnatural cub, come hither! I'll teach thee to impose on a good-hearted, deluded father. Now, don't you think the lad would be handsomer cropped? It makes a dog fiercer, and I love something fierce—get me a scissors—something fierce and trim! Besides, it's infernal affectation—devilish conceit it is, to cherish our ears—we're asses enough without them. Hush, child, hush! Well then, it is my darling! wisht, dry thy eyes—there's a joy; kiss me. What! it won't? Kiss me, Hareton! Damn thee, kiss me! By God, as if I would rear such a monster! As sure as I'm living, I'll break the brat's neck.'

Poor Hareton was squalling and kicking in his father's arms with all his might, and redoubled his yells when he carried him upstairs and lifted him over the banister. I cried out that he would frighten the child into fits, and ran to rescue him. As I reached them, Hindley leant forward on the rails to listen to a noise below; almost forgetting what he had in his hands. 'Who is that?' he asked, hearing someone approaching the stair's foot. I leant forward also, for the purpose of signing to Heathcliff, whose step I recognized, not to come farther; and, at the instant when my eye quitted Hareton, he gave a sudden spring, delivered himself from the careless grasp that held him, and fell.

There was scarcely time to experience a thrill of horror before we saw that the little wretch was safe. Heathcliff arrived underneath just at the critical moment; by a natural impulse, he arrested his descent, and setting him on his feet, looked up to discover the author of the accident. A miser who has parted with a lucky lottery ticket for five shillings, and finds next day he has lost in the bargain five thousand pounds, could not show a blanker countenance than he did on beholding the figure of Mr Earnshaw above. It expressed, plainer than words could do, the intense anguish at having made himself the instrument of thwarting his own revenge. Had it been dark, I dare say, he would have tried to remedy the mistake by smashing Hareton's skull on the steps; but we witnessed his salvation; and I was presently below with my precious charge pressed to my heart. Hindley descended more leisurely, sobered and abashed.

'It is your fault, Ellen,' he said; 'you should have kept him out of sight: you should have taken him from me! Is he injured anywhere?'

'Injured!' I cried angrily; 'if he's not killed, he'll be an idiot! Oh! I wonder his mother does not rise from her grave to see how you use him. You're worse than a heathen—treating your own flesh and blood in that manner!'

He attempted to touch the child, who, on finding himself with me, sobbed off his terror directly. At the first finger his father laid on him, however, he shrieked again louder than before, and struggled as if he would go into convulsions.

'You shall not meddle with him!' I continued. 'He hates you—they all hate you—that's the truth! A happy family you have: and a pretty state you're come to!'

'I shall come to a prettier, yet, Nelly,' laughed the misguided man, recovering his hardness. 'At present, convey yourself and him away. And, hark you, Heathcliff! clear you too, quite from my reach and hearing. I wouldn't murder you tonight; unless, perhaps, I set the house on fire: but that's as my fancy goes.'

While saying this he took a pint bottle of brandy from the dresser, and poured some into a tumbler.

'Nay, don't!' I entreated. 'Mr Hindley, do take warning. Have mercy on this unfortunate boy, if you care nothing for yourself!'

'Anyone will do better for him than I shall,' he answered.

'Have mercy on your own soul!' I said, endeavouring to snatch the glass from his hand.

'Not I! On the contrary, I shall have great pleasure in sending it to perdition to punish its Maker,' exclaimed the blasphemer. 'Here's to its hearty damnation!'

He drank the spirits and impatiently bade us go; terminating his command with a sequel of horrid imprecations, too bad to repeat or remember.

'It's a pity he cannot kill himself with drink,' observed Heathcliff, muttering an echo of curses back when the door was shut. 'He's doing his very utmost; but his constitution defies him. Mr Kenneth says he would wager his mare, that he'll outlive any man on this side Gimmerton, and go to the grave a hoary sinner; unless some happy chance out of the common course befall him.'

I went into the kitchen, and sat down to lull my little lamb to sleep. Heathcliff, as I thought, walked through to the barn. It turned out afterwards that he only got as far as the other side the settle, when he flung himself on a bench by the wall, removed from the fire, and remained silent.

I was rocking Hareton on my knee, and humming a song that began:

> It was far in the night, and the bairnies grat,
> The mither beneath the mools heard that—

when Miss Cathy, who had listened to the hubbub from her room, put her head in, and whispered:

'Are you alone, Nelly?'

'Yes, miss,' I replied.

She entered and approached the hearth. I, supposing she was going to say something, looked up. The expression of her face seemed disturbed and anxious. Her lips were half asunder, as if she meant to speak, and she drew a breath; but it escaped in a sigh instead of a sentence. I resumed my song; not having forgotten her recent behaviour.

'Where's Heathcliff?' she said, interrupting me.

'About his work in the stable,' was my answer.

He did not contradict me; perhaps he had fallen into a doze. There followed another long pause, during which I perccived a drop or two trickle from Catherine's cheek to the flags. Is she sorry for her shameful conduct? I asked myself. That will be a novelty: but she may come to the point as she will—I shan't help her! No, she felt small trouble regarding any subject, save her own concerns.

'Oh, dear!' she cried at last. 'I'm very unhappy!'

'A pity,' observed I. 'You're hard to please: so many friends and so few cares, and can't make yourself content!'

'Nelly, will you keep a secret for me?' she pursued, kneeling down by me, and lifting her winsome eyes to my face with that sort of look which turns off bad temper, even when one has all the right in the world to indulge it.

'Is it worth keeping?' I inquired, less sulkily.

'Yes, and it worries me, and I must let it out! I want to know what I should do. Today, Edgar Linton has asked me to marry him, and I've given him an answer. Now, before I tell you whether it was a consent or denial, you tell me which it ought to have been.'

'Really, Miss Catherine, how can I know?' I replied. 'To be sure, considering the exhibition you performed in his presence this afternoon, I might say it would be wise to refuse him: since he asked you after that, he must either be hopelessly stupid or a venturesome fool.'

'If you talk so, I won't tell you any more,' she returned peevishly, rising to her feet. 'I accepted him, Nelly. Be quick, and say whether I was wrong!'

'You accepted him! then what good is it discussing the matter? You have pledged your word, and cannot retract.'

'But, say whether I should have done so—do!' she exclaimed in an irritated tone; chafing her hands together, and frowning.

'There are many things to be considered before that question can be answered properly,' I said sententiously. 'First and foremost, do you love Mr Edgar?'

'Who can help it? Of course I do,' she answered.

Then I put her through the following catechism: for a girl of twenty-two it was not injudicious.

'Why do you love him, Miss Cathy?'

'Nonsense, I do—that's sufficient.'

'By no means; you must say why?'

'Well, because he is handsome, and pleasant to be with.'

'Bad!' was my commentary.

'And because he is young and cheerful.'

'Bad, still.'

'And because he loves me.'

'Indifferent, coming there.'

'And he will be rich, and I shall like to be the greatest woman of the neighbourhood, and I shall be proud of having such a husband.'

'Worst of all. And now, say how you love him?'

'As everybody loves—You're silly, Nelly.'

'Not at all—Answer.'

'I love the ground under his feet, and the air over his head, and everything he touches, and every word he says. I love all his looks, and all his actions, and him entirely and altogether. There now!'

'And why?'

'Nay; you are making a jest of it; it is exceedingly ill-natured! It's no jest to me!' said the young lady, scowling, and turning her face to the fire.

'I'm very far from jesting, Miss Catherine,' I replied. 'You love Mr Edgar because he is handsome, and young, and cheerful, and rich, and loves you. The last, however, goes for nothing: you would love him without that, probably; and with it you wouldn't, unless he possessed the four former attractions.'

'No, to be sure not: I should only pity him—hate him, perhaps, if he were ugly, and a clown.'

'But there are several other handsome, rich young men in the world: handsomer, possibly, and richer than he is. What should hinder you from loving them?'

'If there be any, they are out of my way! I've seen none like Edgar.'

'You may see some; and he won't always be handsome, and young, and may not always be rich.'

'He is now; and I have only to do with the present. I wish you would speak rationally.'

'Well, that settles it: if you have only to do with the present, marry Mr Linton.'

'I don't want your permission for that—I *shall* marry him: and yet you have not told me whether I'm right.'

'Perfectly right; if people be right to marry only for the present. And now, let us hear what you are unhappy about. Your brother will be pleased; the old lady and gentleman will not object, I think; you will escape from a disorderly, comfortless home into a wealthy, respectable one; and you love Edgar, and Edgar loves you. All seems smooth and easy: where is the obstacle?'

'*Here!* and *here!*' replied Catherine, striking one hand on her forehead, and the other on her breast: 'in whichever place the soul lives. In my soul and in my heart, I'm convinced I'm wrong!'

'That's very strange! I cannot make it out.'

'It's my secret. But if you will not mock at me, I'll explain it: I can't do it distinctly: but I'll give you a feeling of how I feel.'

She seated herself by me again: her countenance grew sadder and graver, and her clasped hands trembled.

'Nelly, do you never dream queer dreams?' she said, suddenly, after some minutes' reflection.

'Yes, now and then,' I answered.

'And so do I. I've dreamt in my life dreams that have stayed with me ever after, and changed my ideas: they've gone through and through me, like wine through water, and altered the colour of my mind. And this is one; I'm going to tell it— but take care not to smile at any part of it.'

'Oh! don't, Miss Catherine!' I cried. 'We're dismal enough without conjuring up ghosts and visions to perplex us. Come, come, be merry and like yourself! Look at little Hareton! *he's* dreaming nothing dreary. How sweetly he smiles in his sleep!'

'Yes; and how sweetly his father curses in his solitude! You remember him, I dare say, when he was just such another as that chubby thing: nearly as young and innocent. However, Nelly, I shall oblige you to listen: it's not long; and I've no power to be merry tonight.'

'I won't hear it, I won't hear it!' I repeated hastily.

I was superstitious about dreams then, and am still; and Catherine had an unusual gloom in her aspect, that made me dread something from which I might shape a prophecy, and foresee a fearful catastrophe. She was vexed, but she did not proceed. Apparently taking up another subject, she recommenced in a short time.

'If I were in heaven, Nelly, I should be extremely miserable.'

'Because you are not fit to go there,' I answered. 'All sinners would be miserable in heaven.'

'But it is not for that. I dreamt once that I was there.'

'I tell you I won't hearken to your dreams, Miss Catherine! I'll go to bed,' I interrupted again.

She laughed, and held me down; for I made a motion to leave my chair.

'This is nothing,' cried she: 'I was only going to say that heaven did not seem to be my home; and I broke my heart with weeping to come back to earth; and the angels were so angry that they flung me out into the middle of the heath on the top of Wuthering Heights; where I woke sobbing for joy. That will do to explain my secret, as well as the other. I've no more business to marry Edgar Linton than I have to be in heaven; and if the wicked man in there had not brought Heathcliff so low, I shouldn't have thought of it. It would degrade me to marry Heathcliff now; so he shall never know how I love him: and that, not because he's handsome, Nelly, but because he's more myself than I am. Whatever our souls are made of, his and mine are the same; and Linton's is as different as a moonbeam from lightning, or frost from fire.'

Ere this speech ended, I became sensible of Heathcliff's presence. Having noticed a slight movement, I turned my head, and saw him rise from the bench, and steal out noiselessly. He had listened till he heard Catherine say it would degrade her to marry him, and then he stayed to hear no further. My companion, sitting on the ground, was prevented by the back of the settle from remarking his presence or departure; but I started, and bade her hush!

'Why?' she asked, gazing nervously round.

'Joseph is here,' I answered, catching opportunely the roll of his cart-wheels up the road; 'and Heathcliff will come in with him. I'm not sure whether he were not at the door this moment.'

'Oh, he couldn't overhear me at the door!' said she. 'Give me Hareton, while you get the supper, and when it is ready ask me to sup with you. I want to cheat

my uncomfortable conscience, and be convinced that Heathcliff has no notion of these things. He has not, has he? He does not know what being in love is?'

'I see no reason that he should not know, as well as you,' I returned; 'and if *you* are his choice, he will be the most unfortunate creature that ever was born! As soon as you become Mrs Linton, he loses friend, and love, and all! Have you considered how you'll bear the separation, and how he'll bear to be quite deserted in the world? Because, Miss Catherine——'

'He quite deserted! we separated!' she exclaimed, with an accent of indignation. 'Who is to separate us, pray? They'll meet the fate of Milo! Not as long as I live, Ellen: for no mortal creature. Every Linton on the face of the earth might melt into nothing, before I could consent to forsake Heathcliff. Oh, that's not what I intend— that's not what I mean! I shouldn't be Mrs Linton were such a price demanded! He'll be as much to me as he has been all his lifetime. Edgar must shake off his antipathy, and tolerate him, at least. He will, when he learns my true feelings towards him. Nelly, I see now, you think me a selfish wretch; but did it never strike you that if Heathcliff and I married, we should be beggars? whereas, if I marry Linton, I can aid Heathcliff to rise, and place him out of my brother's power.'

'With your husband's money, Miss Catherine?' I asked. 'You'll find him not so pliable as you calculate upon: and, though I'm hardly a judge, I think that's the worst motive you've given yet for being the wife of young Linton.'

'It is not,' retorted she; 'it is the best! The others were the satisfaction of my whims: and for Edgar's sake, too, to satisfy him. This is for the sake of one who comprehends in his person my feelings to Edgar and myself. I cannot express it; but surely you and everybody have a notion that there is or should be an existence of yours beyond you. What were the use of my creation, if I were entirely contained here? My great miseries in this world have been Heathcliff's miseries, and I watched and felt each from the beginning: my great thought in living is himself. If all else perished, and *he* remained, *I* should still continue to be; and if all else remained, and he were annihilated, the universe would turn to a mighty stranger: I should not seem a part of it. My love for Linton is like the foliage in the woods: time will change it, I'm well aware, as winter changes the trees. My love for Heathcliff resembles the eternal rocks beneath: a source of little visible delight, but necessary. Nelly, I *am* Heathcliff! He's always, always in my mind: not as a pleasure, any more than I am always a pleasure to myself, but as my own being. So don't talk of our separation again: it is impracticable; and——'

She paused, and hid her face in the folds of my gown; but I jerked it forcibly away. I was out of patience with her folly!

'If I can make any sense of your nonsense, miss,' I said, 'it only goes to convince me that you are ignorant of the duties you undertake in marrying; or else that you are a wicked, unprincipled girl. But trouble me with no more secrets: I'll not promise to keep them.'

'You'll keep that?' she asked eagerly.

'No, I'll not promise,' I repeated.

She was about to insist, when the entrance of Joseph finshed our conversation; and Catherine removed her seat to a corner, and nursed Hareton, while I made the supper. After it was cooked, my fellow-servant and I began to quarrel who should carry some to Mr Hindley; and we didn't settle it till all was nearly cold. Then we came to the agreement that we would let him ask, if he wanted any; for we feared particularly to go into his presence when he had been some time alone.

'Und hah isn't that nowt comed in frough th' field, be this time? What is he abaht? girt eedle seeght!' demanded the old man, looking round for Heathcliff.

'I'll call him,' I replied. 'He's in the barn, I've no doubt.'

I went and called, but got no answer. On returning, I whispered to Catherine that he had heard a good part of what she said, I was sure; and told how I saw him quit the kitchen just as she complained of her brother's conduct regarding him. She

jumped up in a fine fright, flung Hareton on to the settle, and ran to seek for her friend herself; not taking leisure to consider why she was so flurried, or how her talk would have affected him. She was absent such a while that Joseph proposed we should wait no longer. He cunningly conjectured they were staying away in order to avoid hearing his protracted blessing. They were 'ill eneugh for ony fahl manners', he affirmed. And on their behalf he added that night a special prayer to the usual quarter of an hour's supplication before meat, and would have tacked another to the end of the grace, had not his young mistress broken in upon him with a hurried command that he must run down the road, and wherever Heathcliff had rambled, find and make him re-enter directly!

'I want to speak to him, and I *must,* before I go upstairs,' she said. 'And the gate is open: he is somewhere out of hearing; for he would not reply, though I shouted at the top of the fold as loud as I could.'

Joseph objected at first; she was too much in earnest, however, to suffer contradiction; and at last he placed his hat on his head, and walked grumbling forth. Meantime, Catherine paced up and down the floor, exclaiming:

'I wonder where he is—I wonder where he *can* be? What did I say, Nelly? I've forgotten. Was he vexed at my bad humour this afternoon? Dear! tell me what I've said to grieve him? I do wish he'd come. I do wish he would!'

'What a noise for nothing!' I cried, though rather uneasy myself. 'What a trifle scares you! It's surely no great cause of alarm that Heathcliff should take a moonlight saunter on the moors, or even lie too sulky to speak to us in the hay-loft. I'll engage he's lurking there. See if I don't ferret him out!'

I departed to renew my search; its result was disappointment, and Joseph's quest ended in the same.

'Yon lads gets war un war!' observed he on re-entering. 'He's left th' yate ut t' full swing, and Miss's pony has trodden dahn two rigs uh corn, un plottered through, raight o'er intuh t' meadow! Hahsomdiver, t' maister 'ull play t' devil tomorn, and he'll do weel. He's patience itsseln wi' sich careless, offald craters—patience itsseln he is! Bud he'll nut be soa allus—yah's see, all on ye! Yah mum'nt drive him aht uf his heead for nowt!'

'Have you found Heathcliff, you ass?' interrupted Catherine. 'Have you been looking for him, as I ordered?'

'Aw sud more likker look for th' horse,' he replied. 'It 'ud be tuh more sense. Bud, Aw can look for norther horse nur man uf a neeght loike this—as black as t' chimbley! und Hathecliff's noan t' chap to coom at *maw* whistle—happen he'll be less hard uh hearing wi' *ye*!'

It *was* a very dark evening for summer: the clouds appeared inclined to thunder, and I said we had better all sit down; the approaching rain would be certain to bring him home without further trouble. However, Catherine would not be persuaded into tranquility. She kept wandering to and fro, from the gate to the door, in a state of agitation which permitted no repose; and at length took up a permanent situation on one side of the wall, near the road: where, heedless of my expostulations and the growling thunder, and the great drops that began to plash around her, she remained, calling at intervals, and then listening, and then crying outright. She beat Hareton, or any child, at a good passionate fit of crying.

About midnight, while we still sat up, the storm came rattling over the Heights in full fury. There was a violent wind, as well as thunder, and either one or the other split a tree off at the corner of the building: a huge bough fell across the roof, and knocked down a portion of the east chimney-stack, sending a clatter of stones and soot into the kitchen fire. We thought a bolt had fallen in the middle of us; and Joseph swung on to his knees beseeching the Lord to remember the patriarchs Noah and Lot, and, as in former times, spare the righteous, though He smote the ungodly. I felt some sentiment that it must be a judgment on us also. The Jonah, in my mind, was Mr Earnshaw; and I shook the handle of his den that I might

ascertain if he were yet living. He replied audibly enough, in a fashion which made my companion vociferate, more clamorously than before, that a wide distinction might be drawn between saints like himself and sinners like his master. But the uproar passed away in twenty minutes, leaving us all unharmed; excepting Cathy, who got thoroughly drenched for her obstinacy in refusing to take shelter, and standing bonnetless and shawl-less to catch as much water as she could with her hair and clothes. She came in and lay down on the settle, all soaked as she was, turning her face to the back, and putting her hands before it.

'Well, miss!' I exclaimed, touching her shoulder; 'you are not bent on getting your death, are you? Do you know what o'clock it is? Half past twelve. Come, come to bed! there's no use waiting longer on that foolish boy: he'll be gone to Gimmerton, and he'll stay there now. He guesses we shouldn't wait for him till this late hour: at least, he guesses that only Mr Hindley would be up; and he'd rather avoid having the door opened by the master.'

'Nay, nay, he's noan at Gimmerton,' said Joseph. 'Aw's niver wonder, bud he's at t' bothom uf a bog-hoile. This visitation worn't for nowt, and I wod hev ye to look out, miss—yah muh be t' next. Thank Hiven for all! All warks togither for gooid to them as is chozzen, and piked out fro' th' rubbidge! Yah knaw whet t' Scripture ses.' And he began quoting several texts, referring us to the chapters and verses where we might find them.

I, having vainly begged the wilful girl to rise and remove her wet things, left him preaching and her shivering, and betook myself to bed with little Hareton, who slept as fast as if everyone had been sleeping round him. I heard Joseph read on a while afterwards; then I distinguished his slow step on the ladder, and then I dropped asleep.

Coming down somewhat later than usual, I saw, by the sunbeams piercing the chinks of the shutters, Miss Catherine still seated near the fireplace. The house door was ajar, too; light entered from its unclosed windows; Hindley had come out, and stood on the kitchen hearth, haggard and drowsy.

'What ails you, Cathy?' he was saying when I entered: 'you look as dismal as a drowned whelp. Why are you so damp and pale, child?'

'I've been wet,' she answered reluctantly, 'and I'm cold, that's all.'

'Oh, she is naughty!' I cried, perceiving the master to be tolerably sober. 'She got steeped in the shower of yesterday evening, and there she has sat the night through, and I couldn't prevail on her to stir.'

Mr Earnshaw stared at us in surprise. 'The night through,' he repeated. 'What kept her up? not fear of the thunder, surely? That was over hours since.'

Neither of us wished to mention Heathcliff's absence, as long as we could conceal it; so I replied, I didn't know how she took it into her head to sit up; and she said nothing. The morning was fresh and cool; I threw back the lattice, and presently the room filled with sweet scents from the garden; but Catherine called peevishly to me, 'Ellen, shut the window. I'm starving!' And her teeth chattered as she shrunk closer to the almost extinguished embers.

'She's ill,' said Hindley, taking her wrist; 'I suppose that's the reason she would not go to bed. Damn it! I don't want to be troubled with more sickness here. What took you into the rain!'

'Running after t' lads, as usuald!' croaked Joseph, catching an opportunity, from our hesitation, to thrust in his evil tongue. 'If I war yah, maister, I'd just slam t' boards i' their faces all on 'em, gentle and simple! Never a day ut yah're off, but yon cat o' Linton comes sneaking hither; and Miss Nelly, shoo's a fine lass! shoo sits watching for ye i' t' kitchen; and as yah're in at one door, he's out at t'other; and, then, wer grand lady goes a coorting of her side! It's bonny behaviour, lurking amang t' fields, after twelve o' t' night, wi' that fahl, flaysome divil of a gipsy, Heathcliff! They think *I'm* blind; but I'm noan: nowt ut t' soart!—I seed young Linton boath coming and going, and I seed *yah*' (directing his discourse to me),

'yah gooid fur nowt, slattenly witch! nip up and bolt into th' house, t' minute yah heard t' maister's horse fit clatter up t' road.'

'Silence, eavesdropper!' cried Catherine; 'none of your insolence before me! Edgar Linton came yesterday by chance, Hindley; and it was *I* who told him to be off: because I knew you would not like to have met him as you were.'

'You lie, Cathy, no doubt,' answered her brother, 'and you are a confounded simpleton! But never mind Linton at present: tell me, were you not with Heathcliff last night? Speak the truth, now. You need not be afraid of harming him: though I hate him as much as ever, he did me a good turn a short time since, that will make my conscience tender of breaking his neck. To prevent it, I shall send him about his business, this very morning; and after he's gone, I'd advise you all to look sharp: I shall only have the more humour for you.'

'I never saw Heathcliff last night,' answered Catherine, beginning to sob bitterly: 'and if you do turn him out of doors, I'll go with him. But, perhaps, you'll never have an opportunity: perhaps he's gone.' Here she burst into uncontrollable grief, and the remainder of her words were inarticulate.

Hindley lavished on her a torrent of scornful abuse, and bade her get to her room immediately, or she shouldn't cry for nothing! I obliged her to obey; and I shall never forget what a scene she acted when we reached her chamber: it terrified me. I thought she was going mad, and I begged Joseph to run for the doctor. It proved the commencement of delirium: Mr Kenneth, as soon as he saw her, pronounced her dangerously ill; she had a fever. He bled her, and he told me to let her live on whey and water gruel, and take care she did not throw herself downstairs or out of the window; and then he left: for he had enough to do in the parish, where two or three miles was the ordinary distance between cottage and cottage.

Though I cannot say I made a gentle nurse, and Joseph and the master were no better; and though our patient was as wearisome and headstrong as a patient could be, she weathered it through. Old Mrs Linton paid us several visits, to be sure, and set things to rights, and scolded and ordered us all; and when Catherine was convalescent, she insisted on conveying her to Thrushcross Grange: for which deliverance we were very grateful. But the poor dame had reason to repent of her kindness: she and her husband both took the fever, and died within a few days of each other.

Our young lady returned to us, saucier and more passionate, and haughtier than ever. Heathcliff had never been heard of since the evening of the thunder-storm; and one day I had the misfortune, when she had provoked me exceedingly, to lay the blame of his disappearance on her: where indeed it belonged, as she well knew. From that period, for several months, she ceased to hold any communication with me, save in the relation of a mere servant. Joseph fell under a ban also: he *would* speak his mind, and lecture her all the same as if she were a little girl; and she esteemed herself a woman, and our mistress, and thought that her recent illness gave her a claim to be treated with consideration. Then the doctor had said that she would not bear crossing much; she ought to have her own way; and it was nothing less than murder in her eyes for anyone to presume to stand up and contradict her. From Mr Earnshaw and his companions she kept aloof; and tutored by Kenneth, and serious threats of a fit that often attended her rages, her brother allowed her whatever she pleased to demand, and generally avoided aggravating her fiery temper. He was rather *too* indulgent in humouring her caprices; not from affection, but from pride: he wished earnestly to see her bring honour to the family by an alliance with the Lintons, and as long as she let him alone she might trample us like slaves, for aught he cared! Edgar Linton, as multitudes have been before and will be after him, was infatuated; and believed himself the happiest man alive on the day he led her to Gimmerton Chapel, three years subsequent to his father's death.

Much against my inclination, I was persuaded to leave Wuthering Heights and accompany her here. Little Hareton was nearly five years old, and I had just begun

to teach him his letters. We made a sad parting; but Catherine's tears were more powerful than ours. When I refused to go, and when she found her entreaties did not move me, she went lamenting to her husband and brother. The former offered me munificent wages; the latter ordered me to pack up: he wanted no women in the house, he said, now that there was no mistress; and as to Hareton, the curate should take him in hand, by and by. And so I had but one choice left: to do as I was ordered. I told the master he got rid of all decent people only to run to ruin a little faster; I kissed Hareton goodbye; and since then he has been a stranger: and it's very queer to think it, but I've no doubt he has completely forgotten all about Ellen Dean, and that he was ever more than all the world to her, and she to him!

At this point of the housekeeper's story, she chanced to glance towards the timepiece over the chimney; and was in amazement on seeing the minute hand measure half past one. She would not hear of staying a second longer: in truth, I felt rather disposed to defer the sequel of her narrative, myself. And now that she is vanished to her rest, and I have meditated for another hour or two, I shall summon courage to go, also, in spite of aching laziness of head and limbs.

Chapter X

A CHARMING introduction to a hermit's life! Four weeks' torture, tossing, and sickness! Oh! these bleak winds and bitter northern skies, and impassable roads, and dilatory country surgeons! And, oh, this dearth of the human physiognomy! and, worse than all, the terrible intimation of Kenneth that I need not expect to be out of doors till spring!

Mr Heathcliff has just honoured me with a call. About seven days ago he sent me a brace of grouse—the last of the season. Scoundrel! He is not altogether guiltless in this illness of mine; and that I had a great mind to tell him. But, alas! how could I offend a man who was charitable enough to sit at my bedside a good hour, and talk on some other subject than pills and draughts, blisters and leeches? This is quite an easy interval. I am too weak to read; yet I feel as if I could enjoy something interesting. Why not have up Mrs Dean to finsh her tale? I can recollect its chief incidents as far as she had gone. Yes: I remember her hero had run off, and never been heard of for three years; and the heroine was married. I'll ring: she'll be delighted to find me capable of talking cheerfully. Mrs Dean came.

'It wants twenty minutes, sir, to taking the medicine,' she commenced.

'Away, away with it!' I replied; 'I desire to have——'

'The doctor says you must drop the powders.'

'With all my heart! Don't interrupt me. Come and take your seat here. Keep your fingers from that bitter phalanx of vials. Draw your knitting out of your pocket—that will do—now continue the history of Mr Heathcliff, from where you left off, to the present day. Did he finish his education on the Continent, and come back a gentleman? or did he get a sizar's place at college, or escape to America, and earn honours by drawing blood from his foster-country? or make a fortune more promptly on the English highways?'

'He may have done a little in all these vocations, Mr Lockwood; but I couldn't give my word for any. I stated before that I didn't know how he gained his money; neither am I aware of the means he took to raise his mind from the savage ignorance into which it was sunk: but, with your leave, I'll proceed in my own fashion, if you think it will amuse and not weary you. Are you feeling better this morning?'

'Much.'

'That's good news. I got Miss Catherine and myself to Thrushcross Grange; and, to my agreeable disappointment, she behaved infinitely better than I dared expect. She seemed almost over fond of Mr Linton; and even to his sister she showed plenty of affection. They were both very attentive to her comfort, certainly. It was not the thorn bending to the honeysuckles, but the honeysuckles embracing the thorn. There were no mutual concessions; one stood erect, and the others yielded: and who *can* be ill-natured and bad-tempered when they encounter neither opposition nor indifference? I observed that Mr Edgar had a deep-rooted fear of ruffling her humour. He concealed it from her; but if ever he heard me answer sharply, or saw any other servant grow cloudy at some imperious order of hers, he would show his trouble by a frown of displeasure that never darkened on his own account. He many a time spoke sternly to me about my pertness; and averred that the stab of a knife could not inflict a worse pang than he suffered at seeing his lady vexed. Not to grieve a kind master, I learned to be less touchy; and, for the space of half a year, the gunpowder lay as harmless as sand, because no fire came near to explode it. Catherine had seasons of gloom and silence now and then: they were respected with sympathizing silence by her husband, who ascribed them to an alteration in her constitution, produced by her perilous illness; as she was never subject to depression of spirits before. The return of sunshine was welcomed by answering sunshine from him. I believe I may assert that they were really in possession of deep and growing happiness.

It ended. Well, we *must* be for ourselves in the long run; the mild and generous are only more justly selfish than the domineering; and it ended when circumstances caused each to feel that the one's interest was not the chief consideration in the other's thoughts. On a mellow evening in September, I was coming from the garden with a heavy basket of apples which I had been gathering. It had got dusk, and the moon looked over the high wall of the court, causing undefined shadows to lurk in the corners of the numerous projecting portions of the building. I set my burden on the house steps by the kitchen door, and lingered to rest, and drew in a few more breaths of the soft, sweet air; my eyes were on the moon, and my back to the entrance, when I heard a voice behind me say—

'Nelly, is that you?'

It was a deep voice, and foreign in tone; yet there was something in the manner of pronouncing my name which made it sound familiar. I turned about to discover who spoke, fearfully; for the doors were shut, and I had seen nobody on approaching the steps. Something stirred in the porch; and, moving nearer, I distinguished a tall man dressed in dark clothes, with dark face and hair. He leant against the side, and held his fingers on the latch as if intending to open for himself. 'Who can it be?' I thought. 'Mr Earnshaw? Oh, no! The voice has no resemblance to his.'

'I have waited here an hour,' he resumed, while I continued staring; 'and the whole of that time all round has been as still as death. I dared not enter. You do not know me? Look, I'm not a stranger!'

A ray fell on his features; the cheeks were sallow, and half covered with black whiskers; the brows lowering, the eyes deep set and singular. I remembered the eyes.

'What!' I cried, uncertain whether to regard him as a worldly visitor, and I raised my hands in amazement. 'What! you come back? Is it really you? Is it?'

'Yes, Heathcliff,' he replied, glancing from me up to the windows, which reflected a score of glittering moons, but showed no lights from within. 'Are they at home? where is she? Nelly, you are not glad! you needn't be so disturbed. Is she here? Speak! I want to have one word with her— your mistress. Go, and say some person from Gimmerton desires to see her.'

'How will she take it?' I exclaimed. 'What will she do? The surprise bewilders me—it will put her out of her head! And you *are* Heathcliff! But altered! Nay, there's no comprehending it. Have you been for a soldier?'

'Go and carry my message,' he interrupted impatiently. 'I'm in hell till you do!'

He lifted the latch, and I entered; but when I got to the parlour where Mr and Mrs Linton were, I could not persuade myself to proceed. At length, I resolved on making an excuse to ask if they would have the candles lighted, and I opened the door.

They sat together in a window whose lattice lay back against the wall, and displayed, beyond the garden trees and the wild green park, the valley of Gimmerton, with a long line of mist winding nearly to its top (for very soon after you pass the chapel, as you may have noticed, the sough that runs from the marshes joins a beck which follows the bend of the glen). Wuthering Heights rose above this silvery vapour; but our old house was invisible; it rather dips down on the other side. Both the room and its occupants, and the scene they gazed on, looked wondrously peaceful. I shrank reluctantly from performing my errand; and was actually going away leaving it unsaid, after having put my question about the candles, when a sense of my folly compelled me to return, and mutter—'A person from Gimmerton wishes to see you, ma'am.'

'What does he want?' asked Mrs Linton.

'I did not question him,' I answered.

'Well, close the curtains, Nelly,' she said; 'and bring up tea. I'll be back again directly.'

She quitted the apartment; Mr Edgar inquired, carelessly, who it was.

'Someone mistress does not expect,' I replied. 'That Heathcliff—you recollect him, sir,—who used to live at Mr Earnshaw's.'

'What! the gipsy—the ploughboy?' he cried. 'Why did you not say so to Catherine?'

'Hush! you must not call him by those names, master,' I said. 'She'd be sadly grieved to hear you. She was nearly heartbroken when he ran off. I guess his return will make a jubilee to her.'

Mr Linton walked to a window on the other side of the room that overlooked the court. He unfastened it and leant out. I suppose they were below, for he exclaimed quickly—'Don't stand there, love! Bring the person in, if it be anyone particular.' Ere long I heard the click of the latch, and Catherine flew upstairs, breathless and wild; too excited to show gladness: indeed, by her face, you would rather have surmised an awful calamity.

'Oh, Edgar, Edgar!' she panted, flinging her arms round his neck. 'Oh Edgar, darling! Heathcliff's come back—he is!' And she tightened her embrace to a squeeze.

'Well, well,' cried her husband crossly, 'don't strangle me for that! He never struck me as such a marvellous treasure. There is no need to be frantic!'

'I know you didn't like him,' she answered, repressing a little the intensity of her delight. 'Yet, for my sake, you must be friends now. Shall I tell him to come up?'

'Here?' he said, 'into the parlour?'

'Where else?' she asked.

He looked vexed, and suggested the kitchen as a more suitable place for him. Mrs Linton eyed him with a droll expression—half angry, half laughing at his fastidiousness.

'No,' she added after a while; 'I cannot sit in the kitchen. Set two tables here, Ellen: one for your master and Miss Isabella, being gentry; the other for Heathcliff and myself, being of the lower orders. Will that please you, dear? Or must I have a fire lighted elsewhere? If so, give directions. I'll run down and secure my guest. I'm afraid the joy is too great to be real!'

She was about to dart off again; but Edgar arrested her.

'*You* bid him step up,' he said, addressing me! 'and, Catherine, try to be glad, without being absurd! the whole household need not witness the sight of your welcoming a runaway servant as a brother.'

I descended and found Heathcliff waiting under the porch, evidently anticipating an invitation to enter. He followed my guidance without waste of words, and I ushered him into the presence of the master and mistress, whose flushed cheeks betrayed signs of warm talking. But the lady's glowed with another feeling when her friend appeared at the door: she sprang forward, took both his hands, and led him to Linton; and then she seized Linton's reluctant fingers and crushed them into his. Now fully revealed by the fire and candlelight, I was amazed, more than ever, to behold the transformation of Heathcliff. He had grown a tall, athletic, well-formed man; beside whom, my master seemed quite slender and youth-like. His upright carriage suggested the idea of his having been in the army. His countenance was much older in expression and decision of feature than Mr Linton's; it looked intelligent, and retained no marks of former degradation. A half-civilized ferocity lurked yet in the depressed brows and eyes full of black fire, but it was subdued; and his manner was even dignified: quite divested of roughness, though too stern for grace. My master's surprise equalled or exceeded mine: he remained for a minute at a loss how to address the ploughboy, as he had called him. Heathcliff dropped his slight hand, and stood looking at him coolly till he chose to speak.

'Sit down, sir,' he said, at length. 'Mrs Linton, recalling old times, would have me give you a cordial reception; and, of course, I am gratified when anything occurs to please her.'

'And I also,' answered Heathcliff, 'especially if it be anything in which I have a part. I shall stay an hour or two willingly.'

He took a seat opposite Catherine, who kept her gaze fixed on him as if she feared he would vanish were she to remove it. He did not raise his to her often: a quick glance now and then sufficed; but it flashed back, each time more confidently, the undisguised delight he drank from hers. They were too much absorbed in their mutual joy to suffer embarrassment. Not so Mr Edgar: he grew pale with pure annoyance: a feeling that reached its climax when his lady rose, and stepping across the rug, seized Heathcliff's hands again, and laughed like one beside herself.

'I shall think it a dream tomorrow!' she cried. 'I shall not be able to believe that I have seen, and touched, and spoken to you once more. And yet, cruel Heathcliff! you don't deserve this welcome. To be absent and silent for three years, and never to think of me!'

'A little more than you have thought of me,' he murmured. 'I heard of your marriage, Cathy, not long since; and, while waiting in the yard below, I meditated this plan:—just to have one glimpse of your face, a stare of surprise, perhaps, and pretended pleasure; afterwards settle my score with Hindley; and then prevent the law by doing execution on myself. Your welcome has put these ideas out of my mind; but beware of meeting me with another aspect next time! Nay, you'll not drive me off again. You were really sorry for me, were you? Well, there was cause. I've fought through a bitter life since I last heard your voice; and you must forgive me, for I struggled only for you!'

'Catherine, unless we are to have cold tea, please to come to the table,' interrupted Linton, striving to preserve his ordinary tone, and a due measure of politeness. 'Mr Heathcliff will have a long walk, wherever he may lodge tonight; and I'm thirsty.'

She took her post before the urn; and Miss Isabella came, summoned by the bell; then, having handed their chairs forward, I left the room. The meal hardly endured ten minutes. Catherine's cup was never filled: she could neither eat nor drink. Edgar had made a slop in his saucer, and scarcely swallowed a mouthful. Their guest did not protract his stay that evening above an hour longer. I asked, as he departed, if he went to Gimmerton?

'No, to Wuthering Heights,' he answered: 'Mr Earnshaw invited me, when I called this morning.'

Mr Earnshaw invited *him*! and *he* called on Mr Earnshaw! I pondered this sentence painfully, after he was gone. Is he turning out a bit of a hypocrite, and coming

into the country to work mischief under a cloak? I mused: I had a presentiment in the bottom of my heart that he had better have remained away.

About the middle of the night, I was wakened from my first nap by Mrs Linton gliding into my chamber, taking a seat on my bedside, and pulling me by the hair to rouse me.

'I cannot rest, Ellen,' she said, by way of apology. 'And I want some living creature to keep me company in my happiness! Edgar is sulky, because I'm glad of a thing that does not interest him: he refuses to open his mouth, except to utter pettish, silly speeches; and he affirmed I was cruel and selfish for wishing to talk when he was so sick and sleepy. He always contrives to be sick at the least cross! I gave a few sentences of commendation to Heathcliff, and he, either for a headache or a pang of envy, began to cry: so I got up and left him.'

'What use is it praising Heathcliff to him?' I answered. 'As lads they had an aversion to each other, and Heathcliff would hate just as much to hear him praised: it's human nature. Let Mr Linton alone about him, unless you would like an open quarrel between them.'

'But does it not show great weakness?' pursued she. 'I'm not envious: I never feel hurt at the brightness of Isabella's yellow hair and the whiteness of her skin, at her dainty elegance, and the fondness all the family exhibit for her. Even you, Nelly, if we have a dispute sometimes, you back Isabella at once; and I yield like a foolish mother: I call her a darling, and flatter her into a good temper. It pleases her brother to see us cordial, and that pleases me. But they are very much alike: they are spoiled children, and fancy the world was made for their accommodation; and though I humour both, I think a smart chastisement might improve them, all the same.'

'You're mistaken, Mrs Linton,' said I. 'They humour you: I know what there would be to do if they did not. You can well afford to indulge their passing whims as long as their business is to anticipate all your desires. You may, however, fall out, at last, over something of equal consequence to both sides; and then those you term weak are very capable of being as obstinate as you.'

'And then we shall fight to the death, shan't we, Nelly?' she returned, laughing. 'No! I tell you, I have such faith in Linton's love, that I believe I might kill him, and he wouldn't wish to retaliate.'

I advised her to value him the more for his affection.

'I do:' she answered, 'but he needn't resort to whining for trifles. It is childish; and, instead of melting into tears because I said that Heathcliff was now worthy of anyone's regard, and it would honour the first gentleman in the country to be his friend, he ought to have said it for me, and been delighted from sympathy. He must get accustomed to him, and he may as well like him: considering how Heathcliff has reason to object to him, I'm sure he behaved excellently!'

'What do you think of his going to Wuthering Heights?' I inquired. 'He is reformed in every respect apparently: quite a Christian: offering the right hand of fellowship to his enemies all around!'

'He explained it,' she replied. 'I wondered as much as you. He said he called to gather information concerning me from you, supposing you resided there still; and Joseph told Hindley, who came out and fell to questioning him of what he had been doing, and how he had been living; and finally, desired him to walk in. There were some persons sitting at cards; Heathcliff joined them; my brother lost some money to him, and, finding him plentifully supplied, he requested that he would come again in the evening: to which he consented. Hindley is too reckless to select his acquaintance prudently: he doesn't trouble himself to reflect on the causes he might have for mistrusting one whom he has basely injured. But Heathcliff affirms his principal reason for resuming a connection with his ancient persecutor is a wish to install himself in quarters at walking distance from the Grange, and an attachment to the house where we lived together; and likewise a hope that I shall have more

opportunities of seeing him there than I could have if he settled in Gimmerton. He means to offer liberal payment for permission to lodge at the Heights; and doubtless my brother's covetousness will prompt him to accept the terms: he was always greedy; though what he grasps with one hand he flings away with the other.'

'It's a nice place for a young man to fix his dwelling in!' said I. 'Have you no fear of the consequences, Mrs Linton?'

'None for my friend,' she replied: 'his strong head will keep him from danger; a little for Hindley: but he can't be made morally worse than he is; and I stand between him and bodily harm. The event of this evening has reconciled me to God and humanity! I had risen in angry rebellion against Providence. Oh, I've endured very, very bitter misery, Nelly! If that creature knew how bitter, he'd be ashamed to cloud its removal with idle petulance. It was kindness for him which induced me to bear it alone: had I expressed the agony I frequently felt, he would have been taught to long for its alleviation as ardently as I. However, it's over, and I'll take no revenge on his folly; I can afford to suffer anything hereafter! Should the meanest thing alive slap me on the cheek, I'd not only turn the other, but, I'd ask pardon for provoking it; and, as a proof, I'll go make my peace with Edgar instantly. Good night! I'm an angel!'

In this self-complacent conviction she departed; and the success of her fulfilled resolution was obvious on the morrow: Mr Linton had not only abjured his peevishness (though his spirits seemed still subdued by Catherine's exuberance of vivacity), but he ventured no objection to her taking Isabella with her to Wuthering Heights in the afternoon; and she rewarded him with such a summer of sweetness and affection in return, as made the house a paradise for several days; both master and servants profiting from the perpetual sunshine.

Heathcliff—Mr Heathcliff I should say in future—used the liberty of visiting at Thrushcross Grange cautiously, at first: he seemed estimating how far its owner would bear his intrusion. Catherine, also, deemed it judicious to moderate her expressions of pleasure in receiving him; and he gradually established his right to be expected. He retained a great deal of the reserve for which his boyhood was remarkable; and that served to repress all startling demonstrations of feeling. My master's uneasiness experienced a lull, and further circumstances diverted it into another channel for a space.

His new source of trouble sprang from the not anticipated misfortune of Isabella Linton evincing a sudden and irresistible attraction towards the tolerated guest. She was at that time a charming young lady of eighteen; infantile in manners, though possessed of keen wit, keen feelings, and a keen temper, too, if irritated. Her brother, who loved her tenderly, was appalled at this fantastic preference. Leaving aside the degradation of an alliance with a nameless man, and the possible fact that his property, in default of heirs male, might pass into such a one's power, he had sense to comprehend Heathcliff's disposition: to know that, though his exterior was altered, his mind was unchangeable and unchanged. And he dreaded that mind: it revolted him: he shrank forebodingly from the idea of committing Isabella to his keeping. He would have recoiled still more had he been aware that her attachment rose unsolicited, and was bestowed where it awakened no reciprocation of sentiment; for the minute he discovered its existence, he laid the blame on Heathcliff's deliberate designing.

We had all remarked, during some time, that Miss Linton fretted and pined over something. She grew cross and wearisome; snapping at and teasing Catherine continually, at the imminent risk of exhausting her limited patience. We excused her, to a certain extent, on the plea of ill-health: she was dwindling and fading before our eyes. But one day, when she had been peculiarly wayward, rejecting her breakfast, complaining that the servants did not do what she told them; that the mistress would allow her to be nothing in the house, and Edgar neglected her; that she had caught a cold with the doors being left open, and we let the parlour fire

go out on purpose to vex her, with a hundred yet more frivolous accusations, Mrs Linton peremptorily insisted that she should get to bed; and, having scolded her heartily, threatened to send for the doctor. Mention of Kenneth caused her to exclaim, instantly, that her health was perfect, and it was only Catherine's harshness which made her unhappy.

'How can you say I am harsh, you naughty fondling?' cried the mistress, amazed at the unreasonable assertion. 'You are surely losing your reason. When have I been harsh, tell me?'

'Yesterday,' sobbed Isabella, 'and now!'

'Yesterday!' said her sister-in-law. 'On what occasion?'

'In our walk along the moor: you told me to ramble where I pleased, while you sauntered on with Mr Heathcliff!'

'And that's your notion of harshness?' said Catherine, laughing. 'It was no hint that your company was superfluous: we didn't care whether you kept with us or not; I merely thought Heathcliff's talk would have nothing entertaining for your ears.'

'Oh no,' wept the young lady; 'you wished me away, because you knew I liked to be there!'

'Is she sane?' asked Mrs Linton, appealing to me. 'I'll repeat our conversation, word for word, Isabella; and you point out any charm it could have had for you.'

'I don't mind the conversation,' she answered: 'I wanted to be with——'

'Well!' said Catherine, perceiving her hesitate to complete the sentence.

'With him: and I won't be always sent off!' she continued, kindling up. 'You are a dog in the manger, Cathy, and desire no one to be loved but yourself!'

'You are an impertinent little monkey!' exclaimed Mrs Linton, in surprise. 'But I'll not believe this idiocy! It is impossible that you can covet the admiration of Heathcliff—that you consider him an agreeable person! I hope I have misunderstood you, Isabella?'

'No, you have not,' said the infatuated girl. 'I love him more than ever you loved Edgar; and he might love me, if you would let him!'

'I wouldn't be you for a kingdom, then!' Catherine declared emphatically: and she seemed to speak sincerely. 'Nelly, help me to convince her of her madness. Tell her what Heathcliff is: an unreclaimed creature, without refinement, without cultivation: an arid wilderness of furze and whinstone. I'd as soon put that little canary into the park on a winter's day, as recommend you to bestow your heart on him! It is deplorable ignorance of his character, child, and nothing else, which makes that dream enter your head. Pray, don't imagine that he conceals depths of benevolence and affection beneath a stern exterior! He's not a rough diamond—a pearl-containing oyster of a rustic: he's a fierce, pitiless, wolfish man. I never say to him, "Let this or that enemy alone, because it would be ungenerous or cruel to harm them"; I say, "Let them alone, because *I* should hate them to be wronged": and he'd crush you like a sparrow's egg, Isabella, if he found you a troublesome charge. I know he couldn't love a Linton; and yet he'd be quite capable of marrying your fortune and expectations! avarice is growing with him a besetting sin. There's my picture: and I'm his friend—so much so, that had he thought seriously to catch you, I should, perhaps, have held my tongue, and let you fall into his trap.'

Miss Linton regarded her sister-in-law with indignation.

'For shame! for shame!' she repeated angrily, 'you are worse than twenty foes, you poisonous friend!'

'Ah! you won't believe me, then?' said Catherine. 'You think I speak from wicked selfishness?'

'I'm certain you do,' retorted Isabella; 'and I shudder at you!'

'Good!' cried the other. 'Try for yourself, if that be your spirit: I have done, and yield the argument to your saucy insolence.'

'And I must suffer for her egotism!' she sobbed, as Mrs Linton left the room. 'All, all is against me; she has blighted my single consolation. But she uttered falsehoods, didn't she? Mr Heathcliff is not a fiend: he has an honourable soul, and a true one, or how could he remember her?'

'Banish him from your thoughts, miss,' I said. 'He's a bird of bad omen: no mate for you. Mrs Linton spoke strongly, and yet I can't contradict her. She is better acquainted with his heart than I, or anyone besides; and she would never represent him as worse than he is. Honest people don't hide their deeds. How has he been living? how has he got rich? why is he staying at Wuthering Heights, the house of a man whom he abhors? They say Mr Earnshaw is worse and worse since he came. They sit up all night together continually, and Hindley has been borrowing money on his land, and does nothing but play and drink: I heard only a week ago—it was Joseph who told me—I met him at Gimmerton: "Nelly," he said, "we's hae a crahnr's 'quest enah, at ahr folks. One on 'em's a'most getten his finger cut off wi' hauding t'other froo' sticking hisseln loike a cawlf. That's maister, yah knaw, 'ut's soa up uh going tuh t' grand 'sizes. He's noan feard uh t' bench uh judges, norther Paul, nur Peter, nur John, nur Matthew, nor noan on 'em, nut he! He fair likes—he langs to set his brazened face agean 'em! And yon bonny lad Heathcliff, yah mind, he's a rare 'un! He can girn a laugh as weel's onybody at a raight divil's jest. Does he niver say nowt of his fine living amang us, when he goas tuh t' Grange? This is t' way on't:—up at sundahn; dice, brandy, cloised shutters, und can'le-lught till next day at nooin: then, t' fooil gangs banning un raving to his cham'er, makking dacent fowks dig thur fingers i' thur lugs fur varry shaume; un' the knave, wah he carn cahnt his brass, un' ate, un' sleep, un' off to his neighbour's tuh gossip wi' t' wife. I' course, he tells Dame Catherine hah hor father's goold runs intuh his pocket, and her father's son gallops dahn t' Broad road, while he flees afore to oppen t' pikes?" Now, Miss Linton, Joseph is an old rascal, but no liar; and, if his account of Heathcliff's conduct be true, you would never think of desiring such a husband, would you?'

'You are leagued with the rest, Ellen!' she replied. 'I'll not listen to your slanders. What malevolence you must have to wish to convince me that there is no happiness in the world!'

Whether she would have got over this fancy if left to herself or persevered in nursing it perpetually, I cannot say: she had little time to reflect. The day after, there was a justice-meeting at the next town; my master was obliged to attend; and Mr Heathcliff, aware of his absence, called rather earlier than usual. Catherine and Isabella were sitting in the library, on hostile terms, but silent. The latter alarmed at her recent indiscretion, and the disclosure she had made of her secret feelings in a transient fit of passion; the former, on mature consideration, really offended with her companion; and, if she laughed again at her pertness, inclined to make it no laughing matter to *her*. She did laugh as she saw Heathcliff pass the window. I was sweeping the hearth, and I noticed a mischievous smile on her lips. Isabella, absorbed in her meditations, or a book, remained till the door opened; and it was too late to attempt an escape, which she would gladly have done had it been practicable.

'Come in, that's right!' exclaimed the mistress gaily, pulling a chair to the fire. 'Here are two people sadly in need of a third to thaw the ice between them; and you are the very one we should both of us choose. Heathcliff, I'm proud to show you, at last, somebody that dotes on you more than myself. I expect you to feel flattered. Nay, it's not Nelly; don't look at her! My poor little sister-in-law is breaking her heart by mere contemplation of your physical and moral beauty. It lies in your own power to be Edgar's brother! No, no, Isabella, you shan't run off,' she continued, arresting, with feigned playfulness, the confounded girl, who had risen indignantly. 'We were quarrelling like cats about you, Heathcliff; and I was fairly beaten in protestations of devotion and admiration: and, moreover, I was

informed that if I would but have the manners to stand aside, my rival, as she will have herself to be, would shoot a shaft into your soul that would fix you for ever, and send my image into eternal oblivion!'

'Catherine!' said Isabella, calling up her dignity, and disdaining to struggle from the tight grasp that held her. 'I'd thank you to adhere to the truth and not slander me, even in joke! Mr Heathcliff, be kind enough to bid this friend of yours release me: she forgets that you and I are not intimate acquaintances; and what amuses her is painful to me beyond expression.'

As the guest answered nothing, but took his seat, and looked thoroughly indifferent what sentiments she cherished concerning him, she turned and whispered an earnest appeal for liberty to her tormentor.

'By no means!' cried Mrs Linton in answer. 'I won't be named a dog in the manger again. You *shall* stay: now then! Heathcliff, why don't you evince satisfaction at my pleasant news? Isabella swears that the love Edgar has for me is nothing to that she entertains for you. I'm sure she made some speech of the kind; did she not, Ellen? And she has fasted ever since the day before yesterday's walk, from sorrow and rage that I dispatched her out of your society under the idea of its being unacceptable.'

'I think you belie her,' said Heathcliff, twisting his chair to face them. 'She wishes to be out of my society now, at any rate!'

And he stared hard at the object of discourse, as one might do at a strange repulsive animal: a centipede from the Indies, for instance, which curiosity leads one to examine in spite of the aversion it raises. The poor thing couldn't bear that: she grew white and red in rapid succession, and, while tears beaded her lashes, bent the strength of her small fingers to loosen the firm clutch of Catherine; and perceiving that as fast as she raised one finger off her arm another closed down, and she could not remove the whole together, she began to make use of her nails; and their sharpness presently ornamented the detainer's with crescents of red.

'There's a tigress!' exclaimed Mrs Linton, setting her free, and shaking her hand with pain. 'Begone, for God's sake, and hide your vixen face! How foolish to reveal those talons to *him*. Can't you fancy the conclusions he'll draw? Look, Heathcliff! they are instruments that will do execution—you must beware of your eyes.'

'I'd wrench them off her fingers, if they ever menaced me,' he answered brutally, when the door had closed after her. 'But what did you mean by teasing the creature in that manner, Cathy? You were not speaking the truth, were you?'

'I assure you I was,' she returned. 'She has been pining for your sake several weeks; and raving about you this morning, and pouring forth a deluge of abuse, because I represented your failings in a plain light, for the purpose of mitigating her adoration. But don't notice it further: I wished to punish her sauciness, that's all. I like her too well, my dear Heathcliff, to let you absolutely seize and devour her up.'

'And I like her too ill to attempt it,' said he, 'except in a very ghoulish fashion. You'd hear of odd things if I lived alone with that mawkish, waxen face: the most ordinary would be painting on its white the colours of the rainbow, and turning the blue eyes black, every day or two: they detestably resemble Linton's.'

'Delectably!' observed Catherine. 'They are dove's eyes—angel's!'

'She's her brother's heir, is she not?' he asked, after a brief silence.

'I should be sorry to think so,' returned his companion. 'Half a dozen nephews shall erase her title, please Heaven! Abstract your mind from the subject at present: you are too prone to covet your neighbour's goods; remember *this* neighbour's goods are mine.'

'If they were *mine*, they would be none the less that,' said Heathcliff; 'but though Isabella Linton may be silly, she is scarcely mad; and, in short, we'll dismiss the matter, as you advise.'

From their tongues they did dismiss it; and Catherine, probably, from her thoughts. The other, I felt certain, recalled it often in the course of the evening. I saw him smile to himself—grin rather—and lapse into ominous musing whenever Mrs Linton had occasion to be absent from the apartment.

I determined to watch his movements. My heart invariably cleaved to the master's, in preference to Catherine's side: with reason I imagined, for he was kind, and trustful, and honourable; and she—she could not be called the *opposite*, yet she seemed to allow herself such wide latitude, that I had little faith in her principles, and still less sympathy for her feelings. I wanted something to happen which might have the effect of freeing both Wuthering Heights and the Grange of Mr Heathcliff, quietly; leaving us as we had been prior to his advent. His visits were a continual nightmare to me; and, I suspected, to my master also. His abode at the Heights was an oppression past explaining. I felt that God had forsaken the stray sheep there to its own wicked wanderings, and an evil beast prowled between it and the fold, waiting his time to spring and destroy.

Chapter XI

SOMETIMES, while meditating on these things in solitude, I've got up in a sudden terror, and put on my bonnet to go see how all was at the farm. I've persuaded my conscience that it was a duty to warn him how people talked regarding his ways; and then I've recollected his confirmed bad habits, and, hopeless of benefiting him, have flinched from re-entering the dismal house, doubting if I could bear to be taken at my word.

One time I passed the old gate, going out of my way, on a journey to Gimmerton. It was about the period that my narrative has reached: a bright frosty afternoon; the ground bare, and the road hard and dry. I came to a stone where the highway branches off on to the moor at your left hand; a rough sand pillar, with the letters W.H. cut on its north side, on the east, G., and on the south-west, T.G. It serves as guide-post to the Grange, the Heights, and village. The sun shone yellow on its grey head, reminding me of summer; and I cannot say why, but all at once, a gush of child's sensations flowed into my heart. Hindley and I held it a favourite spot twenty years before. I gazed long at the weather-worn block, and, stooping down, perceived a hole near the bottom still full of snail-shells and pebbles, which we were fond of storing there with more perishable things; and, as fresh as reality, it appeared that I beheld my early playmate seated on the withered turf: his dark, square head bent forward, and his little hand scooping out the earth with a piece of slate. 'Poor Hindley!' I exclaimed involuntarily. I started: my bodily eye was cheated into a momentary belief that the child lifted its face and stared straight into mine! It vanished in a twinkling; but immediately I felt an irresistible yearning to be at the Heights. Superstition urged me to comply with this impulse: supposing he should be dead! I thought—or should die soon!—supposing it were a sign of death! The nearer I got to the house the more agitated I grew; and on catching sight of it I trembled in every limb. The apparition had outstripped me: it stood looking through the gate. That was my first idea on observing an elf-locked, brown-eyed boy setting his ruddy countenance against the bars. Further reflection suggested this must be Hareton, *my* Hareton, not altered greatly since I left him, ten months since.

'God bless thee, darling!' I cried, forgetting instantaneously my foolish fears. 'Hareton, it's Nelly! Nelly, thy nurse.'

He retreated out of arm's length, and picked up a large flint.

'I am come to see thy father, Hareton,' I added, guessing from the action that Nelly, if she lived in his memory at all, was not recognized as one with me.

He raised his missile to hurl it; I commenced a soothing speech, but could not stay his hand: the stone struck my bonnet; and then ensued, from the stammering lips of the little fellow, a string of curses, which, whether he comprehended them or not, were delivered with practised emphasis, and distorted his baby features into a shocking expression of malignity. You may be certain this grieved more than angered me. Fit to cry, I took an orange from my pocket, and offered it to propitiate him. He hesitated, and then snatched it from my hold; as if he fancied I only intended to tempt and disappoint him. I showed another, keeping it out of his reach.

'Who has taught you those fine words, my bairn?' I inquired. 'The curate?'

'Damn the curate, and thee! Gie me that,' he replied.

'Tell us where you got your lessons, and you shall have it,' said I. 'Who's your master?'

'Devil daddy,' was his answer.

'And what do you learn from daddy?' I continued.

He jumped at the fruit; I raised it higher. 'What does he teach you?' I asked.

'Naught,' said he, 'but to keep out of his gait. Daddy cannot bide me, because I swear at him.'

'Ah! and the devil teaches you to swear at daddy?' I observed.

'Ah—nay,' he drawled.

'Who then?'

'Heathcliff.'

I asked if he liked Mr Heathcliff.

'Ay!' he answered again.

Desiring to have his reasons for liking him, I could only gather the sentences— 'I known't: he pays dad back what he gies to me—he curses daddy for cursing me. He says I mun do as I will.'

'And the curate does not teach you to read and write then?' I pursued.

'No, I was told the curate should have his — teeth dashed down his — throat, if he stepped over the threshold—Heathcliff had promised that!'

I put the orange in his hand, and bade him tell his father that a woman called Nelly Dean was waiting to speak with him, by the garden gate. He went up the walk, and entered the house; but, instead of Hindley, Heathcliff appeared on the doorstones; and I turned directly and ran down the road as hard as ever I could race, making no halt till I gained the guide-post, and feeling as scared as if I had raised a goblin. This is not much connected with Miss Isabella's affair: except that it urged me to resolve further on mounting vigilant guard, and doing my utmost to check the spread of such bad influence at the Grange: even though I should wake a domestic storm, by thwarting Mrs Linton's pleasure.

The next time Heathcliff came, my young lady chanced to be feeding some pigeons in the court. She had never spoken a word to her sister-in-law for three days; but she had likewise dropped her fretful complaining, and we found it a great comfort. Heathcliff had not the habit of bestowing a single unnecessary civility on Miss Linton, I knew. Now, as soon as he beheld her, his first precaution was to take a sweeping survey of the house front. I was standing by the kitchen window, but I drew out of sight. He then stepped across the pavement to her, and said something: she seemed embarrassed, and desirous of getting away; to prevent it, he laid his hand on her arm. She averted her face: he apparently put some question which she had no mind to answer. There was another rapid glance at the house, and supposing himself unseen, the scoundrel had the impudence to embrace her.

'Judas! traitor!' I ejaculated. 'You are a hypocrite, too, are you? A deliberate deceiver.'

'Who is, Nelly?' said Catherine's voice at my elbow: I had been over intent on watching the pair outside to mark her entrance.

'Your worthless friend!' I answered warmly: 'the sneaking rascal yonder. Ah, he has caught a glimpse of us—he is coming in! I wonder will he have the art to find a plausible excuse for making love to Miss, when he told you he hated her?'

Mrs Linton saw Isabella tear herself free, and run into the garden; and a minute after, Heathcliff opened the door. I couldn't withhold giving some loose to my indignation; but Catherine angrily insisted on silence, and threatened to order me out of the kitchen, if I dared to be so presumptuous as to put in my insolent tongue.

'To hear you, people might think you were the mistress!' she cried. 'You want setting down in your right place! Heathcliff, what are you about, raising this stir? I said you must let Isabella alone!—I beg you will, unless you are tired of being received here, and wish Linton to draw the bolts against you!'

'God forbid that he should try!' answered the black villain. I detested him just then. 'God keep him meek and patient! Every day I grow madder after sending him to heaven!'

'Hush!' said Catherine, shutting the inner door. 'Don't vex me. My have you disregarded my request? Did she come across you on purpose?'

'What is it to you?' he growled. 'I have a right to kiss her, if she chooses; and you have no right to object. I'm not *your* husband: *you* needn't be jealous of me!'

'I'm not jealous *of* you,' replied the mistress, 'I'm jealous *for* you. Clear your face: you shan't scowl at me! If you like Isabella, you shall marry her. But do you like her? Tell the truth, Heathcliff! There, you won't answer. I'm certain you don't!'

'And would Mr Linton approve of his sister marrying that man?' I inquired.

'Mr Linton should approve,' returned my lady, decisively.

'He might spare himself the trouble,' said Heathcliff: 'I could do as well without his approbation. And as to you, Catherine, I have a mind to speak a few words now, while we are at it. I want you to be aware that I *know* you have treated me infernally—infernally! Do you hear? And if you flatter yourself that I don't perceive it, you are a fool; and if you think I can be consoled by sweet words, you are an idiot; and if you fancy I'll suffer unrevenged, I'll convince you of the contrary, in a very little while! Meantime, thank you for telling me your sister-in-law's secret: I swear I'll make the most of it. And stand you aside!'

'What new phase of his character is this?' exclaimed Mrs Linton, in amazement. 'I've treated you infernally—and you'll take your revenge! How will you take it, ungrateful brute? How have I treated you infernally?'

'I seek no revenge on you,' replied Heathcliff less vehemently. 'That's not the plan. The tyrant grinds down his slaves and they don't turn against him; they crush those beneath them. You are welcome to torture me to death for your amusement, only allow me to amuse myself a little in the same style, and refrain from insult as much as you are able. Having levelled my palace, don't erect a hovel and complacently admire your own charity in giving me that for a home. If I imagined you really wished me to marry Isabel, I'd cut my throat!'

'Oh, the evil is that I am *not* jealous, is it?' cried Catherine. 'Well, I won't repeat my offer of a wife: it is as bad as offering Satan a lost soul. Your bliss lies, like his, in inflicting misery. You prove it. Edgar is restored from the ill-temper he gave way to at your coming; I begin to be secure and tranquil; and you, restless to know us at peace, appear resolved on exciting a quarrel. Quarrel with Edgar, if you please, Heathcliff, and deceive his sister: you'll hit on exactly the most efficient method of revenging yourself on me.'

The conversation ceased. Mrs Linton sat down by the fire, flushed and gloomy. The spirit which served her was growing intractable: she could neither lay nor control it. He stood on the hearth with folded arms, brooding on his evil thoughts; and in this position I left them to seek the master, who was wondering what kept Catherine below so long.

'Ellen,' said he, when I entered, 'have you seen your mistress?'

'Yes; she's in the kitchen, sir,' I answered. 'She's sadly put out by Mr Heathcliff's behaviour: and, indeed, I do think it's time to arrange his visits on another footing. There's harm in being too soft, and now it's come to this——' And I related the scene in the court, and, as near as I dared, the whole subsequent dispute. I fancied it could not be very prejudicial to Mrs Linton; unless she made it so afterwards, by assuming the defensive for her guest. Edgar Linton had difficulty in hearing me to the close. His first words revealed that he did not clear his wife of blame.

'This is insufferable!' he exclaimed. 'It is disgraceful that she should own him for a friend, and force his company on me! Call me two men out of the hall, Ellen. Catherine shall linger no longer to argue with the low ruffian—I have humoured her enough.'

He descended, and bidding the servants wait in the passage, went, followed by me, to the kitchen. Its occupants had recommenced their angry discussion: Mrs Linton, at least, was scolding with renewed vigour; Heathcliff had moved to the window, and hung his head, somewhat cowed by her violent rating apparently. He saw the master first, and made a hasty motion that she should be silent; which she obeyed, abruptly, on discovering the reason of his intimation.

'How is this?' said Linton, addressing her; 'what notion of propriety must you have to remain here, after the language which has been held to you by that blackguard? I suppose, because it is his ordinary talk, you think nothing of it; you are habituated to his baseness, and, perhaps, imagine I can get used to it too!'

'Have you been listening at the door, Edgar?' asked the mistress, in a tone particularly calculated to provoke her husband, implying both carelessness and contempt of his irritation. Heathcliff, who had raised his eyes at the former speech, gave a sneering laugh at the latter; on purpose, it seemed, to draw Mr Linton's attention to him. He succeeded; but Edgar did not mean to entertain him with any high flights of passion.

'I have been so far forbearing with you, sir,' he said quietly; 'not that I was ignorant of your miserable, degraded character, but I felt you were only partly responsible for that; and Catherine wishing to keep up your acquaintance, I acquiesced—foolishly. Your presence is a moral poison that would contaminate the most virtuous: for that cause, and to prevent worse consequences, I shall deny you hereafter admission into this house, and give notice now that I require your instant departure. Three minutes' delay will render it involuntary and ignominious.'

Heathcliff measured the height and breadth of the speaker with an eye full of derision.

'Cathy, this lamb of yours threatens like a bull!' he said. 'It is in danger of splitting its skull against my knuckles. By God! Mr Linton, I'm mortally sorry that you are not worth knocking down!'

My master glanced towards the passage, and signed me to fetch the men: he had no intention of hazarding a personal encounter. I obeyed the hint; but Mrs Linton, suspecting something, followed; and when I attempted to call them, she pulled me back, slammed the door to, and locked it.

'Fair means!' she said, in answer to her husband's look of angry surprise. 'If you have not courage to attack him, make an apology, or allow yourself to be beaten. It will correct you of feigning more valour than you possess. No, I'll swallow the key before you shall get it! I'm delightfully rewarded for my kindness to each! After constant indulgence of one's weak nature, and the other's bad one, I earn for thanks two samples of blind ingratitude, stupid to absurdity! Edgar, I was defending you and yours; and I wish Heathcliff may flog you sick, for daring to think an evil thought of me!'

It did not need the medium of a flogging to produce that effect on the master. He tried to wrest the key from Catherine's grasp, and for safety she flung it into the hottest part of the fire; whereupon Mr Edgar was taken with a nervous trembling, and his countenance grew deadly pale. For his life he could not avert that

access of emotion; mingled anguish and humiliation overcame him completely. He leant on the back of a chair, and covered his face.

'Oh, heavens! In old days, this would win you knighthood!' exclaimed Mrs Linton. 'We are vanquished! we are vanquished! Heathcliff would as soon lift a finger at you as a king would march his army against a colony of mice. Cheer up! you shan't be hurt! Your type is not a lamb, it's a sucking leveret.'

'I wish you joy of the milk-blooded coward, Cathy!' said her friend. 'I compliment you on your taste. And that is the slavering, shivering thing you preferred to me! I would not strike him with my fist, but I'd kick him with my foot, and experience considerable satisfaction. Is he weeping, or is he going to faint for fear?'

The fellow approached and gave the chair on which Linton rested a push. He'd better have kept his distance; my master quickly sprang erect, and struck him full on the throat a blow that would have levelled a slighter man. It took his breath for a minute; and while he choked, Mr Linton walked out by the back door into the yard, and from thence to the front entrance.

'There! you've done with coming here,' cried Catherine. 'Get away, now; he'll return with a brace of pistols, and half a dozen assistants. If he did overhear us, of course he'd never forgive you. You've played him an ill turn, Heathcliff! But go—make haste! I'd rather see Edgar at bay than you.'

'Do you suppose I'm going with that blow burning in my gullet?' he thundered. 'By hell, no! I'll crush his ribs in like a rotten hazel nut before I cross the threshold! If I don't floor him now, I shall murder him some time; so, as you value his existence, let me get at him!'

'He's not coming,' I interposed, framing a bit of a lie. 'There's the coachman and the two gardeners; you'll surely not wait to be thrust into the road by them! Each has a bludgeon; and master will, very likely, be watching from the parlour windows, to see that they fulfil his orders.'

The gardeners and coachman *were* there; but Linton was with them. They had already entered the court. Heathcliff, on second thoughts, resolved to avoid a struggle against the three underlings; he seized the poker, smashed the lock from the inner door, and made his escape as they tramped in.

Mrs Linton, who was very much excited, bade me accompany her upstairs. She did not know my share in contributing to the disturbance, and I was anxious to keep her in ignorance.

'I'm nearly distracted, Nelly!' she exclaimed, throwing herself on the sofa. 'A thousand smiths' hammers are beating in my head! Tell Isabella to shun me; this uproar is owing to her; and should she or anyone else aggravate my anger at present, I shall get wild. And, Nelly, say to Edgar, if you see him again tonight, that I'm in danger of being seriously ill. I wish it may prove true. He has startled and distressed me shockingly! I want to frighten him. Besides, he might come and begin a string of abuse or complainings; I'm certain I should recriminate, and God knows where we should end! Will you do so, my good Nelly? You are aware that I am in no way blamable in this matter. What possessed him to turn listener? Heathcliff's talk was outrageous, after you left us; but I could soon have diverted him from Isabella, and the rest meant nothing. Now all is dashed wrong by the fool's craving to hear evil of self, that haunts some people like a demon! Had Edgar never gathered our conversation, he would never have been the worse for it. Really, when he opened on me in that unreasonable tone of displeasure after I had scolded Heathcliff till I was hoarse for *him*, I did not care, hardly, what they did to each other; especially as I felt that, however the scene closed, we should all be driven asunder for nobody knows how long! Well, if I cannot keep Heathcliff for my friend—if Edgar will be mean and jealous, I'll try to break their hearts by breaking my own. That will be a prompt way of finshing all, when I am pushed to extremity! But it's a deed to be reserved for a forlorn hope; I'd not take Linton by surprise with it. To this point he has been discreet in dreading to provoke me; you must

represent the peril of quitting that policy, and remind him of my passionate temper, verging, when kindled, on frenzy. I wish you could dismiss that apathy out of your countenance, and look rather more anxious about me.'

The stolidity with which I received these instructions was, no doubt, rather exasperating: for they were delivered in perfect sincerity; but I believed a person who could plan the turning of her fits of passion to account, beforehand, might, by exerting her will, manage to control herself tolerably, even while under their influence; and I did not wish to 'frighten' her husband, as she said, and multiply his annoyances for the purpose of serving her selfishness. Therefore I said nothing when I met the master coming towards the parlour; but I took the liberty of turning back to listen whether they would resume their quarrel together. He began to speak first.

'Remain where you are, Catherine,' he said; without any anger in his voice, but with much sorrowful despondency. 'I shall not stay. I am neither come to wrangle nor be reconciled; but I wish just to learn whether, after this evening's events, you intend to continue your intimacy with——'

'Oh, for mercy's sake,' interrupted the mistress, stamping her foot, 'for mercy's sake, let us hear no more of it now! Your cold blood cannot be worked into a fever: your veins are full of ice-water; but mine are boiling, and the sight of such chillness makes them dance.'

'To get rid of me, answer my question,' persevered Mr Linton. 'You *must* answer it; and that violence does not alarm me. I have found that you can be as stoical as anyone, when you please. Will you give up Heathcliff hereafter, or will you give up me? It is impossible for you to be *my* friend and *his* at the same time; and I absolutely *require* to know which you choose.'

'I require to be let alone!' exclaimed Catherine furiously. 'I demand it! Don't you see I can scarcely stand? Edgar, you—you leave me!'

She rang the bell till it broke with a twang; I entered leisurely. It was enough to try the temper of a saint, such senseless, wicked rages! There she lay dashing her head against the arm of the sofa, and grinding her teeth, so that you might fancy she would crash them to splinters! Mr Linton stood looking at her in sudden compunction and fear. He told me to fetch some water. She had no breath for speaking. I brought a glass full; and as she would not drink, I sprinkled it on her face. In a few seconds she stretched herself out stiff, and turned up her eyes, while her cheeks, at once blanched and livid, assumed the aspect of death. Linton looked terrified.

'There is nothing in the world the matter,' I whispered. I did not want him to yield, though I could not help being afraid in my heart.

'She has blood on her lips!' he said, shuddering.

'Never mind!' I answered tartly. And I told him how she had resolved, previous to his coming, on exhibiting a fit of frenzy. I incautiously gave the account aloud, and she heard me; for she started up—her hair flying over her shoulders, her eyes flashing, the muscles of her neck and arms standing out preternaturally. I made up my mind for broken bones, at least; but she only glared about her for an instant, and then rushed from the room. The master directed me to follow; I did, to her chamber door: she hindered me from going farther by securing it against me.

As she never offered to descend to breakfast next morning, I went to ask whether she would have some carried up. 'No!' she replied peremptorily. The same question was repeated at dinner and tea; and again on the morrow after, and received the same answer. Mr Linton, on his part, spent his time in the library, and did not inquire concerning his wife's occupations. Isabella and he had had an hour's interview, during which he tried to elicit from her some sentiment of proper horror for Heathcliff's advances: but he could make nothing of her evasive replies, and was obliged to close the examination unsatisfactorily; adding, however, a solemn warning, that if she were so insane as to encourage that worthless suitor, it would dissolve all bonds of relationship between herself and him.

Chapter XII

WHILE Miss Linton moped about the park and garden, always silent, and almost always in tears; and her brother shut himself up among books that he never opened—wearying, I guessed, with a continual vague expectation that Catherine, repenting her conduct, would come of her own accord to ask pardon, and seek a reconciliation—and *she* fasted pertinaciously, under the idea, probably, that at every meal, Edgar was ready to choke for her absence, and pride alone held him from running to cast himself at her feet: I went about my household duties, convinced that the Grange had but one sensible soul in its walls, and that lodged in my body. I wasted no condolences on Miss, nor any expostulations on my mistress; nor did I pay much attention to the sighs of my master, who yearned to hear his lady's name, since he might not hear her voice. I determined they should come about as they pleased for me; and though it was a tiresomely slow process, I began to rejoice at length in a faint dawn of its progress: as I thought at first.

Mrs Linton, on the third day, unbarred her door, and having finished the water in her pitcher and decanter, desired a renewed supply, and a basin of gruel, for she believed she was dying. That I set down as a speech meant for Edgar's ears; I believed no such thing, so I kept it to myself and brought her some tea and dry toast. She ate and drank eagerly; and sank back on her pillow again clenching her hands and groaning. 'Oh, I will die,' she exclaimed, 'since no one cares anything about me. I wish I had not taken that.' Then a good while after I heard her murmur, 'No, I'll not die—he'd be glad—he does not love me at all—he would never miss me!'

'Did you want anything, ma'am?' I inquired, still preserving my external composure, in spite of her ghastly countenance, and strange exaggerated manner.

'What is that apathetic being doing?' she demanded, pushing her thick entangled locks from her wasted face. 'Has he fallen into a lethargy, or is he dead?'

'Neither,' replied I; 'if you mean Mr Linton. He's tolerably well, I think, though his studies occupy him rather more than they ought: he is continually among his books, since he has no other society.'

I should not have spoken so, if I had known her true condition, but I could not get rid of the notion that she acted a part of her disorder.

'Among his books!' she cried, confounded. 'And I dying! I on the brink of the grave! My God! does he know how I'm altered?' continued she, staring at her reflection in a mirror hanging against the opposite wall. 'Is that Catherine Linton! He imagines me in a pet—in play, perhaps. Cannot you inform him that it is frightful earnest? Nelly, if it be not too late, as soon as I learn how he feels, I'll choose between these two; either to starve at once—that would be no punishment unless he had a heart—or to recover, and leave the country. Are you speaking the truth about him now? Take care. Is he actually so utterly indifferent for my life?'

'Why, ma'am,' I answered, 'the master has no idea of your being deranged; and of course he does not fear that you will let yourself die of hunger.'

'You think not? Cannot you tell him I will?' she returned. 'Persuade him! speak of your own mind: say you are certain I will!'

'No, you forget, Mrs Linton,' I suggested, 'that you have eaten some food with a relish this evening, and tomorrow you will perceive its good effects.'

'If I were only sure it would kill him,' she interrupted, 'I'd kill myself directly! These three awful nights, I've never closed my lids—and oh, I've been tormented! I've been haunted, Nelly! But I begin to fancy you don't like me. How strange! I thought, though everybody hated and despised each other, they could not avoid loving me. And they have all turned to enemies in a few hours: *they* have, I'm positive; the people *here*. How dreary to meet death, surrounded by their cold faces!

Isabella terrified and repelled, afraid to enter the room, it would be so dreadful to watch Catherine go. And Edgar standing solemnly by to see it over; then offering prayers of thanks to God for restoring peace to his house, and going back to his *books*! What in the name of all that feels has he to do with *books,* when I am dying?'

She could not bear the notion which I had put into her head of Mr Linton's philosophical resignation. Tossing about, she increased her feverish bewilderment to madness, and tore the pillow with her teeth; then raising herself up all burning, desired that I would open the window. We were in the middle of winter, the wind blew strong from the north-east, and I objected. Both the expressions flitting over her face, and the changes of her moods, began to alarm me terribly; and brought to my recollection her former illness, and the doctor's injunction that she should not be crossed. A minute previously she was violent; now, supported on one arm, and not noticing my refusal to obey her, she seemed to find childish diversion in pulling the feathers from the rents she had just made, and ranging them on the sheet according to their different species: her mind had strayed to other associations.

'That's a turkey's,' she murmured to herself; 'and this is a wild duck's; and this is a pigeon's. Ah, they put pigeons' feathers in the pillows—no wonder I couldn't die! Let me take care to throw it on the floor when I lie down. And here is a moor-cock's; and this—I should know it among a thousand—it's a lapwing's. Bonny bird; wheeling over our heads in the middle of the moor. It wanted to get to its nest, for the clouds had touched the swells, and it felt rain coming. This feather was picked up from the heath, the bird was not shot: we saw its nest in the winter, full of little skeletons. Heathcliff set a trap over it, and the old ones dare not come. I made him promise he'd never shoot a lapwing after that, and he didn't. Yes, here are more! Did he shoot my lapwings, Nelly? Are they red, any of them! Let me look.'

'Give over with that baby-work!' I interrupted, dragging the pillow away, and turning the holes towards the mattress, for she was removing its contents by handfuls. 'Lie down and shut your eyes: you're wandering. There's a mess! The down is flying about like snow.'

I went here and there collecting it.

'I see in you, Nelly,' she continued dreamily, 'an aged woman: you have grey hair and bent shoulders. This bed is the fairy cave under Peniston Crag, and you are gathering elf-bolts to hurt our heifers; pretending, while I am near, that they are only locks of wool. That's what you'll come to fifty years hence: I know you are not so now. I'm not wandering: you're mistaken, or else I should believe you really *were* that withered hag, and I should think I *was* under Peniston Crag; and I'm conscious it's night, and there are two candles on the table making the black press shine like jet.'

'The black press? where is that?' I asked. 'You are talking in your sleep!'

'It's against the wall, as it always is,' she replied. 'It *does* appear odd—I see a face in it!'

'There's no press in the room, and never was,' said I, resuming my seat, and looping up the curtain that I might watch her.

'Don't *you* see that face?' she inquired, gazing earnestly at the mirror.

And say what I could, I was incapable of making her comprehend it to be her own; so I rose and covered it with a shawl.

'It's behind there still!' she pursued anxiously. 'And it stirred. Who is it? I hope it will not come out when you are gone! Oh! Nelly, the room is haunted! I'm afraid of being alone!'

I took her hand in mine, and bid her be composed: for a succession of shudders convulsed her frame, and she *would* keep straining her gaze towards the glass.

'There's nobody here!' I insisted. 'It was *yourself*, Mrs Linton: you knew it a while since.'

'Myself!' she gasped, 'and the clock is striking twelve! It's true, then! that's dreadful!'

Her fingers clutched the clothes, and gathered them over her eyes. I attempted to steal to the door with an intention of calling her husband; but I was summoned back by a piercing shriek—the shawl had dropped from the frame.

'Why, what *is* the matter?' cried I. 'Who is coward now? Wake up! That is the glass—the mirror, Mrs Linton; and you see yourself in it, and there am I too, by your side.'

Trembling and bewildered, she held me fast, but the horror gradually passed from her countenance; its paleness gave place to a glow of shame.

'Oh, dear! I thought I was at home,' she sighed. 'I thought I was lying in my chamber at Wuthering Heights. Because I'm weak, my brain got confused, and I screamed unconsciously. Don't say anything; but stay with me. I dread sleeping: my dreams appal me.'

'A sound sleep would do you good, ma'am,' I answered; 'and I hope this suffering will prevent your trying starving again.'

'Oh, if I were but in my own bed in the old house!' she went on bitterly, wringing her hands, 'And that wind sounding in the firs by the lattice. Do let me feel it— it comes straight down the moor—do let me have one breath!'

To pacify her, I held the casement ajar a few seconds. A cold blast rushed through; I closed it, and returned to my post. She lay still now, her face bathed in tears. Exhaustion of body had entirely subdued her spirit: our fiery Catherine was no better than a wailing child.

'How long is it since I shut myself in here?' she asked, suddenly reviving.

'It was Monday evening,' I replied, 'and this is Thursday night, or rather Friday morning, at present.'

'What! of the same week?' she exclaimed. 'Only that brief time?'

'Long enough to live on nothing but cold water and ill-temper,' observed I.

'Well, it seems a weary number of hours,' she muttered doubtfully: 'it must be more. I remember being in the parlour after they had quarrelled, and Edgar being cruelly provoking, and me running into this room desperate. As soon as ever I had barred the door, utter blackness overwhelmed me, and I fell on the floor. I couldn't explain to Edgar how certain I felt of having a fit, or going raging mad, if he persisted in teasing me! I had no command of tongue, or brain, and he did not guess my agony, perhaps: it barely left me sense to try to escape from him and his voice. Before I recovered sufficiently to see and hear, it began to be dawn, and, Nelly, I'll tell you what I thought, and what has kept recurring and recurring till I feared for my reason. I thought as I lay there, with my head against that table leg, and my eyes dimly discerning the grey square of the window, that I was enclosed in the oak-panelled bed at home; and my heart ached with some great grief which, just waking, I could not recollect. I pondered, and worried myself to discover what it could be, and, most strangely, the whole last seven years of my life grew a blank! I did not recall that they had been at all. I was a child; my father was just buried, and my misery arose from the separation that Hindley had ordered between me and Heathcliff. I was laid alone, for the first time; and, rousing from a dismal doze after a night of weeping, I lifted my hand to push the panels aside: it struck the table top! I swept it along the carpet, and then memory burst in: my late anguish was swallowed in a paroxysm of despair. I cannot say why I felt so wildly wretched: it must have been temporary derangement, for there is scarcely cause. But, supposing at twelve years old I had been wrenched from the Heights, and every early association, and my all in all, as Heathcliff was at that time, and been converted at a stroke into Mrs Linton, the lady of Thrushcross Grange, and the wife of a stranger: an exile, and outcast, thenceforth, from what had been my world. You may fancy a glimpse of the abyss where I grovelled! Shake your head as you will, Nelly, *you* have helped to unsettle me! You should have spoken to Edgar, indeed you should,

and compelled him to leave me quiet! Oh, I'm burning! I wish I were out of doors!
I wish I were a girl again, half savage and hardy, and free; and laughing at injuries,
not maddening under them! Why am I so changed? why does my blood rush into
a hell of tumult at a few words? I'm sure I should be myself were I once among
the heather on those hills. Open the window again wide: fasten it open! Quick,
why don't you move?'

'Because I won't give you your death of cold,' I answered.

'You won't give me a chance of life, you mean,' she said sullenly. 'However,
I'm not helpless, yet: I'll open it myself.'

And sliding from the bed before I could hinder her, she crossed the room, walking
very uncertainly, threw it back, and bent out, careless of the frosty air that cut
about her shoulders as keen as a knife. I entreated, and finally attempted to force
her to retire. But I soon found her delirious strength much surpassed mine (she *was*
delirious, I became convinced by her subsequent actions and ravings). There was
no moon, and everything beneath lay in misty darkness: not a light gleamed from
any house, far or near—all had been extinguished long ago; and those at Wuthering
Heights were never visible—still she asserted she caught their shining.

'Look!' she cried eagerly, 'that's my room with the candle in it, and the trees
swaying before it: and the other candle is in Joseph's garret. Joseph sits up late,
doesn't he? He's waiting till I come home that he may lock the gate. Well, he'll
wait a while yet. It's a rough journey, and a sad heart to travel it; and we must
pass by Gimmerton Kirk, to go that journey! We've braved its ghosts often together,
and dared each other to stand among the graves and ask them to come. But,
Heathcliff, if I dare you now, will you venture? If you do, I'll keep you. I'll not
lie there by myself: they may bury me twelve feet deep, and throw the church down
over me, but I won't rest till you are with me. I never will!'

She paused, and resumed with a strange smile. 'He's considering—he'd rather
I'd come to him! Find a way, then! not through that kirkyard. You are slow! Be
content, you always followed me!'

Perceiving it vain to argue against her insanity, I was planning how I could reach
something to wrap about her, without quitting my hold of herself (for I could not
trust her alone by the gaping lattice), when, to my consternation, I heard the rattle
of the door handle, and Mr Linton entered. He had only then come from the library;
and, in passing through the lobby, had noticed our talking and been attracted by
curiosity, or fear, to examine what it signified, at that late hour.

'Oh, sir!' I cried, checking the exclamation risen to his lips at the sight which
met him, and the bleak atmosphere of the chamber. 'My poor mistress is ill, and
she quite masters me: I cannot manage her at all; pray, come and persuade her to
go to bed. Forget your anger, for she's hard to guide any way but her own.'

'Catherine ill?' he said, hastening to us. 'Shut the window, Ellen! Catherine!
why——'

He was silent. The haggardness of Mrs Linton's appearance smote him speechless,
and he could only glance from her to me in horrified astonishment.

'She's been fretting here,' I continued, 'and eating scarcely anything, and never
complaining; she would admit none of us till this evening, and so we couldn't
inform you of her state as we were not aware of it ourselves; but it is nothing.'

I felt I uttered my explanations awkwardly; the master frowned. 'It is nothing,
is it, Ellen Dean?' he said sternly. 'You shall account more clearly for keeping me
ignorant of this!' And he took his wife in his arms, and looked at her with anguish.

At first she gave him no glance of recognition; he was invisible to her abstracted
gaze. The delirium was not fixed, however; having weaned her eyes from contemplating
the outer darkness, by degrees she centred her attention on him, and discovered
who it was that held her.

'Ah! you are come, are you, Edgar Linton?' she said, with angry animation.
'You are one of those things that are ever found when least wanted, and when you

are wanted, never! I suppose we shall have plenty of lamentations now—I see we shall—but they can't keep me from my narrow home out yonder: my resting-place, where I'm bound before spring is over! There it is: not among the Lintons, mind, under the chapel roof, but in the open air, with a headstone; and you may please yourself, whether you go to them or come to me!'

'Catherine, what have you done?' commenced the master. 'Am I nothing to you any more? Do you love that wretch Heath—'

'Hush!' cried Mrs Linton. 'Hush, this moment ! You mention that name and I end the matter instantly, by a spring from the window! What you touch at present you may have; but my soul will be on that hill top before you lay hands on me again. I don't want you, Edgar: I'm past wanting you. Return to your books. I'm glad you possess a consolation, for all you had in me is gone.'

'Her mind wanders, sir,' I interposed. 'She has been talking nonsense the whole evening; but let her have quiet, and proper attendance, and she'll rally. Hereafter, we must be cautious how we vex her.'

'I desire no further advice from you,' answered Mr Linton. 'You know your mistress's nature, and you encouraged me to harass her. And not to give me one hint of how she has been these three days! It was heartless! Months of sickness could not cause such a change!'

I began to defend myself, thinking it too bad to be blamed for another's wicked waywardness. 'I knew Mrs Linton's nature to be headstrong and domineering,' cried I; 'but I didn't know that you wished to foster her fierce temper! I didn't know that, to humour her, I should wink at Mr Heathcliff. I performed the duty of a faithful servant in telling you, and I have got a faithful servant's wages! Well, it will teach me to be careful next time. Next time you may gather intelligence for yourself!'

'The next time you bring a tale to me, you shall quit my service, Ellen Dean,' he replied.

'You'd rather hear nothing about it, I suppose, then, Mr Linton?' said I. 'Heathcliff has your permission to come a courting to miss, and to drop in at every opportunity your absence offers, on purpose to poison the mistress against you?'

Confused as Catherine was, her wits were alert at applying our conversation.

'Ah! Nelly has played traitor,' she exclaimed passionately. 'Nelly is my hidden enemy. You witch! So you do seek elf-bolts to hurt us! Let me go, I'll make her rue! I'll make her howl a recantation!'

A maniac's fury kindled under her brows; she struggled desperately to disengage herself from Linton's arms. I felt no inclination to tarry the event; and, resolving to seek medical aid on my own responsibility, I quitted the chamber.

In passing the garden to reach the road, at a place where a bridle hook is driven into the wall, I saw something white moved irregularly, evidently by another agent than the wind. Notwithstanding my hurry, I stayed to examine it, lest ever after I should have the conviction impressed on my imagination that it was a creature of the other world. My surprise and perplexity were great to discover, by touch more than vision, Miss Isabella's springer, Fanny, suspended by a handkerchief, and nearly at its last gasp. I quickly released the animal, and lifted it into the garden. I had seen it follow its mistress upstairs when she went to bed; and wondered much how it could have got out there, and what mischievous person had treated it so. While untying the knot round the hook, it seemed to me that I repeatedly caught the beat of horses' feet galloping at some distance; but there were such a number of things to occupy my reflections that I hardly gave the circumstance a thought: though it was a strange sound, in that place, at two o'clock in the morning.

Mr Kenneth was fortunately just issuing from his house to see a patient in the village as I came up the street; and my account of Catherine Linton's malady induced him to accompany me back immediately. He was a plain rough man; and

he made no scruple to speak his doubts of her surviving this second attack; unless she were more submissive to his directions than she had shown herself before.

'Nelly Dean,' said he, 'I can't help fancying there's an extra cause for this. What has there been to do at the Grange? We've odd reports up here. A stout, hearty lass like Catherine, does not fall ill for a trifle; and that sort of people should not either. It's hard work bringing them through fevers, and such things. How did it begin?'

'The master will inform you,' I answered; 'but you are acquainted with the Earnshaws' violent dispositions, and Mrs Linton caps them all. I may say this: it commenced in a quarrel. She was struck during a tempest of passion with a kind of fit. That's her account, at least; for she flew off in the height of it, and locked herself up. Afterwards, she refused to eat, and now she alternately raves and remains in a half-dream; knowing those about her, but having her mind filled with all sorts of strange ideas and illusions.'

'Mr Linton will be sorry?' observed Kenneth, interrogatively.

'Sorry? he'll break his heart should anything happen!' I replied. 'Don't alarm him more than necessary.'

'Well, I told him to beware,' said my companion; 'and he must bide the consequences of neglecting my warning! Hasn't he been thick with Mr Heathcliff, lately?'

'Heathcliff frequently visits at the Grange,' answered I, 'though more on the strength of the mistress having known him when a boy, than because the master likes his company. At present, he's discharged from the trouble of calling; owing to some presumptuous aspirations after Miss Linton which he manifested. I hardly think he'll be taken in again.'

'And does Miss Linton turn a cold shoulder on him?' was the doctor's next question.

'I'm not in her confidence,' returned I, reluctant to continue the subject.

'No, she's a sly one,' he remarked, shaking his head. 'She keeps her own counsel! But she's a real little fool. I have it from good authority, that, last night (and a pretty night it was!) she and Heathcliff were walking in the plantation at the back of your house, above two hours; and he pressed her not to go in again, but just mount his horse and away with him! My informant said she could only put him off by pledging her word of honour to be prepared on their first meeting after that: when it was to be, he didn't hear; but you urge Mr Linton to look sharp!'

This news filled me with fresh fears; I outstripped Kenneth, and ran most of the way back. The little dog was yelping in the garden yet. I spared a minute to open the gate for it, but instead of going to the house door, it coursed up and down snuffing the grass, and would have escaped to the road, had I not seized and conveyed it in with me. On ascending to Isabella's room, my suspicions were confirmed: it was empty. Had I been a few hours sooner, Mrs Linton's illness might have arrested her rash step. But what could be done now? There was a bare possibility of overtaking them if pursued instantly. *I* could not pursue them, however; and I dare not rouse the family, and fill the place with confusion; still less unfold the business to my master, absorbed as he was in his present calamity, and having no heart to spare for a second grief! I saw nothing for it but to hold my tongue, and suffer matters to take their course; and Kenneth being arrived, I went with a badly composed countenance to announce him. Catherine lay in a troubled sleep: her husband had succeeded in soothing the access of frenzy: he now hung over her pillow, watching every shade, and every change of her painfully expressive features.

The doctor, on examining the case for himself, spoke hopefully to him of its having a favourable termination, if we could only preserve around her perfect and constant tranquillity. To me, he signified the threatening danger was not so much death, as permanent alienation of intellect.

I did not close my eyes that night, nor did Mr Linton: indeed, we never went to bed; and the servants were all up long before the usual hour, moving through the

house with stealthy tread, and exchanging whispers as they encountered each other in their vocations. Everyone was active, but Miss Isabella; and they began to remark how sound she slept: her brother, too, asked if she had risen, and seemed impatient for her presence, and hurt that she showed so little anxiety for her sister-in-law. I trembled lest he should send me to call her; but I was spared the pain of being the first proclaimant of her flight. One of the maids, a thoughtless girl, who had been on an early errand to Gimmerton, came panting upstairs, open-mouthed, and dashed into the chamber, crying:

Oh, dear, dear! What mun we have next? Master, master, our young lady—'

'Hold your noise!' cried I hastily, enraged at her clamorous manner.

'Speak lower, Mary—What is the matter?' said Mr Linton. 'What ails your young lady?'

'She's gone, she's gone! Yon' Heathcliff's run off wi' her!' gasped the girl.

'That is not true!' exclaimed Linton, rising in agitation. 'It cannot be: how has the idea entered your head? Ellen Dean, go and seek her. It is incredible: it cannot be.'

As he spoke he took the servant to the door, and then repeated his demand to know her reasons for such an assertion.

'Why, I met on the road a lad that fetches milk here,' she stammered, 'and he asked whether we weren't in trouble at the Grange. I thought he meant for missis's sickness, so I answered, yes. Then says he, "They's somebody gone after 'em, I guess?" I stared. He saw I knew nought about it, and he told how a gentleman and lady had stopped to have a horse's shoe fastened at a blacksmith's shop, two miles out of Gimmerton, not very long after midnight! and how the blacksmith's lass had got up to spy who they were: she knew them both directly. And she noticed the man—Heathcliff it was, she felt certain: nob'dy could mistake him, besides—put a sovereign in her father's hand for payment. The lady had a cloak about her face; but having desired a sup of water, while she drank, it fell back, and she saw her very plain. Heathcliff held both bridles as they rode on, and they set their faces from the village, and went as fast as the rough roads would let them. The lass said nothing to her father, but she told it all over Gimmerton this morning.'

I ran and peeped, for form's sake, into Isabella's room; confirming, when I returned, the servant's statement. Mr Linton had resumed his seat by the bed; on my re-entrance, he raised his eyes, read the meaning of my blank aspect, and dropped them without giving an order, or uttering a word.

'Are we to try any measures for overtaking and bringing her back?' I inquired. 'How should we do?'

'She went of her own accord,' answered the master; 'she had a right to go if she pleased. Trouble me no more about her. Hereafter she is only my sister in name: not because I disown her, but because she has disowned me.'

And that was all he said on the subject: he did not make a single inquiry further, or mention her in any way, except directing me to send what property she had in the house to her fresh home, wherever it was, when I knew it.

Chapter XIII

FOR two months the fugitives remained absent; in those two months, Mrs Linton encountered and conquered the worst shock of what was denominated a brain fever. No mother could have nursed an only child more devotedly than Edgar tended her. Day and night he was watching, and patiently enduring all the annoyances that irritable nerves and a shaken reason could inflict; and, though Kenneth remarked that what he saved from the grave would only recompense his care by forming the

source of constant future anxiety—in fact, that his health and strength were being sacrificed to preserve a mere ruin of humanity—he knew no limits in gratitude and joy when Catherine's life was declared out of danger; and hour after hour he would sit beside her, tracing the gradual return to bodily health, and flattering his too sanguine hopes with the illusion that her mind would settle back to its right balance also, and she would soon be entirely her former self.

The first time she left her chamber was at the commencement of the following March. Mr Linton had put on her pillow, in the morning, a handful of golden crocuses; her eye, long stranger to any gleam of pleasure, caught them in waking, and shone delighted as she gathered them eagerly together.

'These are the earliest flowers at the Heights,' she exclaimed. 'They remind me of soft thaw winds, and warm sunshine, and nearly melted snow. Edgar, is there not a south wind, and is not the snow almost gone?'

'The snow is quite gone down here, darling,' replied her husband; 'and I only see two white spots on the whole range of moors: the sky is blue, and the larks are singing, and the becks and brooks are all brim full. Catherine, last spring at this time, I was longing to have you under this roof, now, I wish you were a mile or two up those hills: the air blows so sweetly, I feel that it would cure you.'

'I shall never be there but once more,' said the invalid; 'and then you'll leave me, and I shall remain for ever. Next spring you'll long again to have me under this roof, and you'll look back and think you were happy today.'

Linton lavished on her the kindest caresses, and tried to cheer her by the fondest words; but, vaguely regarding the flowers, she let the tears collect on her lashes and stream down her cheeks unheeding. We knew she was really better, and, therefore, decided that long confinement to a single place produced much of this despondency, and it might be partially removed by a change of scene. The master told me to light a fire in the many-weeks-deserted parlour, and to set an easy chair in the sunshine by the window; and then he brought her down, and she sat a long while enjoying the genial heat, and, as we expected, revived by the objects round her: which, though familiar, were free from the dreary associations investing her hated sick chamber. By evening, she seemed greatly exhausted; yet no arguments could persuade her to return to that apartment, and I had to arrange the parlour sofa for her bed, till another room could be prepared. To obviate the fatigue of mounting and descending the stairs, we fitted up this, where you lie at present: on the same floor with the parlour; and she was soon strong enough to move from one to the other, leaning on Edgar's arm. Ah, I thought myself she might recover, so waited on as she was. And there was double cause to desire it, for on her existence depended that of another: we cherished the hope that in a little while, Mr Linton's heart would be gladdened, and his lands secured from a stranger's gripe, by the birth of an heir.

I should mention that Isabella sent to her brother, some six weeks from her departure, a short note, announcing her marriage with Heathcliff. It appeared dry and cold; but at the bottom was dotted in with pencil an obscure apology, and an entreaty for kind remembrance and reconciliation, if her proceeding had offended him: asserting that she could not help it then, and being done, she had now no power to repeal it. Linton did not reply to this, I believe; and, in a fortnight more, I got a long letter which I considered odd, coming from the pen of a bride just out of the honeymoon. I'll read it: for I keep it yet. Any relic of the dead is precious, if they were valued living.

DEAR ELLEN, it begins:—
 I came last night to Wuthering Heights, and heard, for the first time, that Catherine has been, and is yet, very ill. I must not write to her, I suppose, and my brother is either too angry or too distressed to answer

what I sent him. Still, I must write to somebody, and the only choice left me is you.

Inform Edgar that I'd give the world to see his face again—that my heart returned to Thrushcross Grange in twenty-four hours after I left it, and is there at this moment, full of warm feelings for him, and Catherine! *I can't follow it, though*—(those words are underlined) they need not expect me, and they may draw what conclusions they please; taking care, however, to lay nothing at the door of my weak will or deficient affection.

The remainder of the letter is for yourself alone. I want to ask you two questions: the first is—How did you contrive to preserve the common sympathies of human nature when you resided here? I cannot recognize any sentiment which those around share with me.

The second question, I have great interest in; it is this—is Mr Heathcliff a man? If so, is he mad? And if not, is he a devil? I shan't tell my reasons for making this inquiry; but, I beseech you to explain, if you can, what I have married: that is, when you call to see me; and you must call, Ellen, very soon. Don't write, but come, and bring me something from Edgar.

Now, you shall hear how I have been received in my new home, as I am led to imagine the Heights will be. It is to amuse myself that I dwell on such subjects as the lack of external comforts: they never occupy my thoughts, except at the moment when I miss them. I should laugh and dance for joy, if I found their absence was the total of my miseries, and the rest was an unnatural dream!

The sun set behind the Grange, as we turned on to the moors; by that, I judged it to be six o'clock; and my companion halted half an hour, to inspect the park, and the gardens, and, probably, the place itself, as well as he could; so it was dark when we dismounted in the paved yard of the farmhouse, and your old fellow-servant, Joseph, issued out to receive us by the light of a dip candle. He did it with a courtesy that redounded to his credit. His first act was to elevate his torch to a level with my face, squint malignantly, project his under lip, and turn away. Then he took the two horses, and led them into the stables; reappearing for the purpose of locking the outer gate, as if we lived in an ancient castle.

Heathcliff stayed to speak to him, and I entered the kitchen—a dingy, untidy hole; I dare say you would not know it, it is so changed since it was in your charge. By the fire stood a ruffianly child, strong in limb and dirty in garb, with a look of Catherine in his eyes and about his mouth.

'This is Edgar's legal nephew,' I reflected—'mine in a manner; I must shake hands, and—yes—I must kiss him. It is right to establish a good understanding at the beginning.'

I approached, and, attempting to take his chubby fist, said:

'How do you do, my dear?'

He replied in a jargon I did not comprehend.

'Shall you and I be friends, Hareton?' was my next essay at conversation.

An oath, and a threat to set Throttler on me if I did not 'frame off', rewarded my perseverance.

'Hey, Throttler, lad!' whispered the little wretch, rousing a half-bred bulldog from its lair in a corner. 'Now, wilt tuh be ganging?' he asked authoritatively.

Love for my life urged a compliance; I stepped over the threshold to wait till the others should enter. Mr Heathcliff was nowhere visible; and Joseph, whom I followed to the stables, and requested to accompany me

in, after staring and muttering to himself, screwed up his nose, and replied:

'Mim! mim! mim! Did iver Christian body hear aught like it? Minching un' munching! How can Aw tell whet ye say?'

'I say, I wish you to come with me into the house!' I cried, thinking him deaf, yet highly disgusted at his rudeness.

'Nor nuh me! I getten summat else to do,' he answered, and continued his work; moving his lantern jaws meanwhile, and surveying my dress and countenance (the former a great deal too fine, but the latter, I'm sure, as sad as he could desire) with sovereign contempt.

I walked round the yard, and through a wicket, to another door, at which I took the liberty of knocking, in hopes some more civil servant might show himself. After a short suspense, it was opened by a tall, gaunt man, without neckerchief, and otherwise extremely slovenly; his features were lost in masses of shaggy hair that hung on his shoulders; and *his* eyes, too, were like a ghostly Catherine's with all their beauty annihilated.

'What's your business here?' he demanded grimly. 'Who are you?'

'My name *was* Isabella Linton,' I replied. 'You've seen me before, sir. I'm lately married to Mr Heathcliff, and he has brought me here— I suppose by your permission.'

'Is he come back, then?' asked the hermit, glaring like a hungry wolf.

'Yes—we came just now,' I said; 'but he left me by the kitchen door; and when I would have gone in, your little boy played sentinel over the place, and frightened me off by the help of a bulldog.'

'It's well the hellish villain has kept his word!' growled my future host, searching the darkness beyond me in expectation of discovering Heathcliff; and then he indulged in a soliloquy of execrations, and threats of what he would have done had the 'fiend' deceived him.

I repented having tried this second entrance, and was almost inclined to slip away before he finshed cursing, but ere I could execute that intention, he ordered me in, and shut and refastened the door. There was a great fire, and that was all the light in the huge apartment, whose floor had grown a uniform grey; and the once brilliant pewter dishes, which used to attract my gaze when I was a girl, partook of a similar obscurity, created by tarnish and dust. I inquired whether I might call the maid, and be conducted to a bedroom? Mr Earnshaw vouchsafed no answer. He walked up and down, with his hands in his pockets, apparently quite forgetting my presence; and his abstraction was evidently so deep, and his whole aspect so misanthropical, that I shrank from disturbing him again.

You'll not be surprised, Ellen, at my feeling particularly cheerless, seated in worse than solitude on that inhospitable hearth, and remembering that four miles distant lay my delightful home, containing the only people I loved on earth; and there might as well be the Atlantic to part us, instead of those four miles: I could not overpass them! I questioned with myself—where must I turn for comfort? and—mind you don't tell Edgar, or Catherine—above every sorrow beside, this rose pre-eminent: despair at finding nobody who could or would be my ally against Heathcliff! I had sought shelter at Wuthering Heights, almost gladly, because I was secured by that arrangement from living alone with him; but he knew the people we were coming amongst, and he did not fear their intermeddling.

I sat and thought a doleful time: the clock struck eight, and nine, and still my companion paced to and fro, his head bent on his breast, and perfectly silent, unless a groan or a bitter ejaculation forced itself out at

intervals. I listened to detect a woman's voice in the house, and filled the interim with wild regrets and dismal anticipations, which, at last, spoke audibly in irrepressible sighing and weeping. I was not aware how openly I grieved, till Earnshaw halted opposite, in his measured walk, and gave me a stare of newly-awakened surprise. Taking advantage of his recovered attention, I exclaimed:

'I'm tired with my journey, and I want to go to bed! Where is the maidservant? Direct me to her, as she won't come to me!'

'We have none,' he answered; 'you must wait on yourself!'

'Where must I sleep, then?' I sobbed: I was beyond regarding self-respect, weighed down by fatigue and wretchedness.

'Joseph will show you Heathcliff's chamber,' said he; 'open that door—he's in there.'

I was going to obey, but he suddenly arrested me, and added in the strangest tone:

'Be so good as to turn your lock, and draw your bolt—don't omit it!'

'Well!' I said. 'But why, Mr Earnshaw?' I did not relish the notion of deliberately fastening myself in with Heathcliff.

'Look here!' he replied, pulling from his waistcoat a curiously constructed pistol, having a double-edged spring knife attached to the barrel. 'That's a great tempter to a desperate man, is it not? I cannot resist going up with this every night, and trying his door. If once I find it open he's done for! I do it invariably, even though the minute before I have been recalling a hundred reasons that should make me refrain: it is some devil that urges me to thwart my own schemes by killing him. You fight against that devil for love as long as you may; when the time comes, not all the angels in heaven shall save him!'

I surveyed the weapon inquisitively. A hideous notion struck me: how powerful I should be possessing such an instrument! I took it from his hand, and touched the blade. He looked astonished at the expression my face assumed during a brief second: it was not horror, it was covetousness. He snatched the pistol back, jealously; shut the knife, and returned it to its concealment.

'I don't care if you tell him,' said he. 'Put him on his guard, and watch for him. You know the terms we are on, I see: his danger does not shock you.'

'What has Heathcliff done to you?' I asked. 'In what has he wronged you, to warrant this appalling hatred? Wouldn't it be wiser to bid him quit the house?'

'No!' thundered Earnshaw, 'should he offer to leave me, he's a dead man: persuade him to attempt it, and you are a murderess! Am I to lose *all,* without a chance of retrieval? Is Hareton to be a beggar? Oh, damnation! I *will* have it back; and I'll have *his* gold too; and then his blood; and hell shall have his soul! It will be ten times blacker with that guest than ever it was before!'

You've acquainted me, Ellen, with your old master's habits. He is clearly on the verge of madness: he was so last night at least. I shuddered to be near him, and thought on the servant's ill-bred moroseness as comparatively agreeable. He now recommenced his moody walk, and I raised the latch, and escaped into the kitchen. Joseph was bending over the fire, peering into a large pan that swung above it; and a wooden bowl of oatmeal stood on the settle close by. The contents of the pan began to boil, and he turned to plunge his hand into the bowl; I conjectured that this preparation was probably for our supper, and, being hungry, I resolved it should be eatable; so, crying out sharply, '*I'll* make the

porridge!' I removed the vessel out of his reach, and proceeded to take
off my hat and riding habit. 'Mr Earnshaw', I continued, 'directs me to
wait on myself: I will. I'm not going to act the lady among you, for fear
I should starve.'

'Gooid Lord!' he muttered, sitting down, and stroking his ribbed stockings
from the knee to the ankle. 'If they's tuh be fresh ortherings—just when
Aw gettin used tuh two maisters, if Aw mun hev a *mistress* set o'er my
heead, it's loike time tuh be flitting. Aw niver *did* think tuh say t' day
ut Aw mud lave th' owld place—but Aw daht it's nigh at hend!'

This lamentation drew no notice from me: I went briskly to work,
sighing to remember a period when it would have been all merry fun;
but compelled speedily to drive off the remembrance. It racked me to
recall past happiness, and the greater peril there was of conjuring up its
apparition, the quicker the thible ran round, and the faster the handfuls
of meal fell into the water. Joseph beheld my style of cookery with
growing indignation.

'Thear!' he ejaculated, 'Hareton, thah willut sup thy porridge tuh
neight; they'll be nowt bud lumps as big as maw nave. Thear, agean!
Aw'd fling in bowl un all, if Aw wer yah! There, pale t' guilp off, un'
then yah'll hae done wi't. Bang, bang. It's a marcy t' bothom isn't
deaved aht!'

It *was* rather a rough mess, I own, when poured into the basins; four
had been provided, and a gallon pitcher of new milk was brought from
the dairy, which Hareton seized and commenced drinking and spilling
from the expansive lip. I expostulated, and desired that he should have
his in a mug; affirming that I could not taste the liquid treated so dirtily.
The old cynic chose to be vastly offended at this nicety; assuring me,
repeatedly, that 'the barn was every bit as good' as I, 'and every bit as
wollsome', and wondering how I could fashion to be so conceited. Mean-
while, the infant ruffian continued sucking; and glowered at me defyingly,
as he slavered into the jug.

'I shall have my supper in another room,' I said. 'Have you no place
you call a parlour?'

'*Parlour!*' he echoed sneeringly, '*parlour!* Nay, we've noa *parlours*.
If yah dunnut loike wer company, there's maister's; un' if yah dunnut
loike maister, there's us.'

'Then I shall go upstairs!' I answered; 'show me a chamber.'

I put my basin on a tray, and went myself to fetch some more milk.
With great grumblings, the fellow rose, and preceded me in my ascent:
we mounted to the garrets; he opening a door, now and then, to look
into the apartments we passed.

'Here's a rahm,' he said, at last, flinging back a cranky board on
hinges. 'It's weel eneugh tuh ate a few porridge in. They's a pack o'
corn i' t' corner, thear, meeterly clane; if yah're feared uh muckying yer
grand silk cloes, spread yer hankerchir o' t' top on't.'

The 'rahm' was a kind of lumber-hole smelling strong of malt and
grain; various sacks of which articles were piled around, leaving a wide,
bare space in the middle.

'Why, man!' I exclaimed, facing him angrily, 'this is not a place to
sleep in. I wish to see my bedroom.'

'*Bed-rume!*' he repeated, in a tone of mockery. 'Yah's see all t' *bed-
rumes* thear is—yon's mine.'

He pointed into the second garret, only differing from the first in being
more naked about the walls, and having a large low, curtainless bed,
with an indigo-coloured quilt at one end.

'What do I want with yours?' I retorted. 'I suppose Mr Heathcliff does not lodge at the top of the house, does he?'

'Oh! it's Maister *Hathecliff's* yah're wenting!' cried he, as if making a new discovery. 'Couldn't ye uh said soa, at onst? un then, Aw mud uh tell'd ye, baht all this wark, ut that's just one yah cannut sea—he allas keeps it locked, un nob'dy iver mells on't but hisseln.'

'You've a nice house, Joseph,' I could not refrain from observing, 'and pleasant inmates; and I think the concentrated essence of all the madness in the world took up its abode in my brain the day I linked my fate with theirs! However, that is not to the present purpose—there are other rooms. For heaven's sake be quick, and let me settle somewhere!'

He made no reply to this adjuration; only plodding doggedly down the wooden steps, and halting before an apartment which, from that halt and the superior quality of its furniture, I conjectured to be the best one. There was a carpet: a good one, but the pattern was obliterated by dust; a fireplace hung with cut paper, dropping to pieces; a handsome oak bedstead with ample crimson curtains of rather expensive material and modern make; but they had evidently experienced rough usage: the valances hung in festoons, wrenched from their rings, and the iron rod supporting them was bent in an arc on one side, causing the drapery to trail upon the floor. The chairs were also damaged, many of them severely; and deep indentations deformed the panels of the walls. I was endeavouring to gather resolution for entering and taking possession, when my fool of a guide announced, 'This here is t' maister's.' My supper by this time was cold, my appetite gone, and my patience exhausted. I insisted on being provided instantly with a place of refuge, and means of repose.

'Whear the divil?' began the religious elder. 'The Lord bless us! The Lord forgie us! Whear the *hell* wold ye gang? ye marred, wearisome nowt! Yah seen all bud Hareton's bit uf a cham'er. They's not another hoile tuh lig dahn in i' th' hahse!'

I was so vexed, I flung my tray and its contents on the ground; and then seated myself at the stairs-head, hid my face in my hands, and cried.

'Ech! ech!' exclaimed Joseph. 'Weel done, Miss Cathy! weel done, Miss Cathy! Hahsiver, t' maister sall just tum'le o'er them brocken pots; un' then we's hear summut; we's hear hah it's tuh be. Gooid-for-nowt madling! yah desarve pining froo this to Churstmas, flinging t' precious gifts uh God under fooit i' yer flaysome rages! Bud Aw'm mista'en if yah shew yer sperrit lang. Will Hathecliff bide sich bonny ways, think ye? Aw nobbut wish he muh cotch ye i' that plisky. Aw nobbut wish he may.'

And so he went on scolding to his den beneath, taking the candle with him; and I remained in the dark. The period of reflection succeeding this silly action, compelled me to admit the necessity of smothering my pride and choking my wrath, and bestirring myself to remove its effects. An unexpected aid presently appeared in the shape of Throttler, whom I now recognized as a son of our old Skulker: it had spent its whelphood at the Grange, and was given by my father to Mr Hindley. I fancy it knew me: it pushed its nose against mine by way of salute, and then hastened to devour the porridge; while I groped from step to step, collecting the shattered earthenware, and drying the spatters of milk from the banister with my pocket handkerchief. Our labours were scarcely over when I heard Earnshaw's tread in the passage; my assistant tucked in his tail, and pressed to the wall; I stole into the nearest doorway. The dog's endeavour to avoid him was unsuccessful; as I guessed by a scutter downstairs, and a prolonged, piteous yelping. I had better luck! he passed

on, entered his chamber, and shut the door. Directly after Joseph came
up with Hareton, to put him to bed. I had found shelter in Hareton's
room, and the old man, on seeing me, said:

'They's rahm for boath ye un yer pride, now, I sud think, i' the hahse.
It's empty; ye may hev it all to yerseln, un Him as allas maks a third,
i' such ill company!'

Gladly did I take advantage of this intimation; and the minute I flung
myself into a chair, by the fire, I nodded, and slept. My slumber was
deep and sweet, though over far too soon. Mr Heathcliff awoke me; he
had just come in, and demanded, in his loving manner, what I was doing
there? I told him the cause of my staying up so late—that he had the key
of our room in his pocket. The adjective *our* gave mortal offence. He
swore it was not, nor ever should be, mine; and he'd—But I'll not repeat
his language, nor describe his habitual conduct: he is ingenious and
unresting in seeking to gain my abhorrence! I sometimes wonder at him
with an intensity that deadens my fear: yet, I assure you, a tiger or a
venomous serpent could not rouse terror in me equal to that which he
wakens. He told me of Catherine's illness, and accused my brother of
causing it; promising that I should be Edgar's proxy in suffering, till he
could get hold of him.

I do hate him—I am wretched—I have been a fool! Beware of uttering
one breath of this to anyone at the Grange. I shall expect you every
day—don't disappoint me!

ISABELLA.

Chapter XIV

As soon as I had perused this epistle, I went to the master, and informed him that
his sister had arrived at the Heights, and sent me a letter expressing her sorrow for
Mrs Linton's situation, and her ardent desire to see him; with a wish that he would
transmit to her, as early as possible, some token of forgiveness by me.

'Forgiveness!' said Linton. 'I have nothing to forgive her, Ellen. You may call
at Wuthering Heights this afternoon, if you like, and say that I am not *angry*, but
I'm *sorry* to have lost her; especially as I can never think she'll be happy. It is out
of the question my going to see her, however: we are eternally divided; and should
she really wish to oblige me, let her persuade the villain she has married to leave
the country.'

'And you won't write her a little note, sir?' I asked imploringly.

'No,' he answered. 'It is needless. My communication with Heathcliff's family
shall be as sparing as his with mine. It shall not exist!'

Mr Edgar's coldness depressed me exceedingly; and all the way from the Grange
I puzzled my brains how to put more heart into what he said, when I repeated it;
and how to soften his refusal of even a few lines to console Isabella. I dare say
she had been on the watch for me since morning: I saw her looking through the
lattice, as I came up the garden causeway, and I nodded to her; but she drew back,
as if afraid of being observed. I entered without knocking. There never was such
a dreary, dismal scene as the formerly cheerful house presented! I must confess,
that if I had been in the young lady's place, I would, at least, have swept the hearth,
and wiped the tables with a duster. But she already partook of the pervading spirit
of neglect which encompassed her. Her pretty face was wan and listless; her hair
uncurled: some locks hanging lankly down, and some carelessly twisted round her
head. Probably she had not touched her dress since yester evening. Hindley was

not there. Mr Heathcliff sat at a table, turning over some papers in his pocket-book; but he rose when I appeared, asked me how I did, quite friendly, and offered me a chair. He was the only thing there that seemed decent: and I thought he never looked better. So much had circumstances altered their positions, that he would certainly have struck a stranger as a born and bred gentleman; and his wife as a thorough little slattern! She came forward eagerly to greet me; and held out one hand to take the expected letter. I shook my head. She wouldn't understand the hint, but followed me to a sideboard, where I went to lay my bonnet, and importuned me in a whisper to give her directly what I had brought. Heathcliff guessed the meaning of her manœuvres, and said:

'If you have got anything for Isabella (as no doubt you have, Nelly), give it to her. You needn't make a secret of it! we have no secrets between us.'

'Oh, I have nothing,' I replied, thinking it best to speak the truth at once. 'My master bid me tell his sister that she must not expect either a letter or a visit from him at present. He sends his love, ma'am, and his wishes for your happiness, and his pardon for the grief you have occasioned; but he thinks that after this time, his household and the household here should drop intercommunication, as nothing good could come of keeping it up.'

Mrs Heathcliff's lip quivered slightly, and she returned to her seat in the window. Her husband took his stand on the hearthstone, near me, and began to put questions concerning Catherine. I told him as much as I thought proper of her illness, and he extorted from me, by cross-examination, most of the facts connected with its origin. I blamed her, as she deserved, for bringing it all on herself; and ended by hoping that he would follow Mr Linton's example and avoid future interference with his family, for good or evil.

'Mrs Linton is now just recovering,' I said; 'she'll never be like she was, but her life is spared; and if you really have a regard for her, you'll shun crossing her way again: nay, you'll move out of this country entirely; and that you may not regret it, I'll inform you Catherine Linton is as different now from your old friend Catherine Earnshaw, as that young lady is different from me. Her appearance is changed greatly, her character much more so; and the person who is compelled, of necessity, to be her companion, will only sustain his affection hereafter by the remembrance of what she once was, by common humanity, and a sense of duty!'

'That is quite possible,' remarked Heathcliff, forcing himself to seem calm: 'quite possible that your master should have nothing but common humanity and a sense of duty to fall back upon. But do you imagine that I shall leave Catherine to his *duty* and *humanity*? and can you compare my feelings respecting Catherine to his? Before you leave this house, I must exact a promise from you, that you'll get me an interview with her: consent or refuse, I *will* see her! What do you say?'

'I say, Mr Heathcliff,' I replied, 'you must not: you never shall, through my means. Another encounter between you and the master would kill her altogether.'

'With your aid, that may be avoided,' he continued; 'and should there be danger of such an event—should he be the cause of adding a single trouble more to her existence—why, I think I shall be justified in going to extremes! I wish you had sincerity enough to tell me whether Catherine would suffer greatly from his loss: the fear that she would restrains me. And there you see the distinctions between our feelings: had he been in my place, and I in his, though I hated him with a hatred that turned my life to gall, I never would have raised a hand against him. You may look incredulous, if you please! I never would have banished him from her society as long as she desired his. The moment her regard ceased, I would have torn his heart out, and drunk his blood! But, till then—if you don't believe me, you don't know me—till then, I would have died by inches before I touched a single hair of his head!'

'And yet,' I interrupted, 'you have no scruples in completely ruining all hopes of her perfect restoration, by thrusting yourself into her remembrance now, when

she has nearly forgotten you, and involving her in a new tumult of discord and distress.'

'You suppose she has nearly forgotten me?' he said. 'Oh, Nelly! you know she has not! You know as well as I do, that for every thought she spends on Linton, she spends a thousand on me! At a most miserable period of my life, I had a notion of the kind: it haunted me on my return to the neighbourhood last summer; but only her own assurance could make me admit the horrible idea again. And then, Linton would be nothing, nor Hindley, nor all the dreams that ever I dreamt. Two words would comprehend my future—*death* and *hell*: existence, after losing her, would be hell. Yet I was a fool to fancy for a moment that she valued Edgar Linton's attachment more than mine. If he loved with all the powers of his puny being, he couldn't love as much in eighty years as I could in a day. And Catherine has a heart as deep as I have: the sea could be as readily contained in that horse-trough, as her whole affection be monopolized by him! Tush! He is scarcely a degree dearer to her than her dog, or her horse. It is not in him to be loved like me: how can she love in him what he has not?'

'Catherine and Edgar are as fond of each other as any two people can be,' cried Isabella, with sudden vivacity. 'No one has a right to talk in that manner, and I won't hear my brother depreciated in silence!'

'Your brother is wondrous fond of you too, isn't he?' observed Heathcliff scornfully. 'He turns you adrift on the world with surprising alacrity.'

'He is not aware of what I suffer,' she replied. 'I didn't tell him that.'

'You have been telling him something, then: you have written, have you?'

'To say that I was married, I did write—you saw the note.'

'And nothing since?'

'No.'

'My young lady is looking sadly the worse for her change of condition,' I remarked. 'Somebody's love comes short in her case, obviously: whose, I may guess; but, perhaps, I shouldn't say.'

'I should guess it was her own,' said Heathcliff. 'She degenerates into a mere slut! She is tired of trying to please me uncommonly early. You'd hardly credit it, but the very morrow of our wedding, she was weeping to go home. However, she'll suit this house so much the better for not being over nice, and I'll take care she does not disgrace me by rambling abroad.'

'Well, sir,' returned I, 'I hope you'll consider that Mrs Heathcliff is accustomed to be looked after and waited on; and that she has been brought up like an only daughter, whom everyone was ready to serve. You must let her have a maid to keep things tidy about her, and you must treat her kindly. Whatever be your notion of Mr Edgar, you cannot doubt that she has a capacity for strong attachments, or she wouldn't have abandoned the elegances, and comforts, and friends of her former home, to fix contentedly, in such a wilderness as this, with you.'

'She abandoned them under a delusion,' he answered; 'picturing in me a hero of romance, and expecting unlimited indulgences from my chivalrous devotion. I can hardly regard her in the light of a rational creature, so obstinately has she persisted in forming a fabulous notion of my character and acting on the false impressions she cherished. But, at last, I think she begins to know me: I don't perceive the silly smiles and grimaces that provoked me at first; and the senseless incapability of discerning that I was in earnest when I gave her my opinion of her infatuation and herself. It was a marvellous effort of perspicacity to discover that I did not love her. I believed, at one time, no lessons could teach her that! And yet it is poorly learnt; for this morning she announced, as a piece of appalling intelligence, that I had actually succeeded in making her hate me! A positive labour of Hercules, I assure you! If it be achieved, I have cause to return thanks. Can I trust your assertion, Isabella? Are you sure you hate me? If I let you alone for half a day, won't you come sighing and wheedling to me again? I dare say she would

rather I had seemed all tenderness before you: it wounds her vanity to have the truth exposed. But I don't care who knows that the passion was wholly on one side; and I never told her a lie about it. She cannot accuse me of showing a bit of deceitful softness. The first thing she saw me do, on coming out of the Grange, was to hang up her little dog; and when she pleaded for it, the first words I uttered were a wish that I had the hanging of every being belonging to her, except one: possibly she took that exception for herself. But no brutality disgusted her: I suppose she has an innate admiration of it, if only her precious person were secure from injury! Now, was it not the depth of absurdity—of genuine idiocy, for that pitiful, slavish, mean-minded brach to dream that I could love her? Tell your master, Nelly, that I never, in all my life, met with such an abject thing as she is. She even disgraces the name of Linton; and I've sometimes relented, from pure lack of invention, in my experiments on what she could endure, and still creep shamefully cringing back! But tell him, also, to set his fraternal and magisterial heart at ease: that I keep strictly within the limits of the law. I have avoided, up to this period, giving her the slightest right to claim a separation; and, what's more, she'd thank nobody for dividing us. If she desired to go, she might: the nuisance of her presence outweighs the gratification to be derived from tormenting her!'

'Mr Heathcliff,' said I, 'this is the talk of a madman, and your wife, most likely, is convinced you are mad; and, for that reason, she has borne with you hitherto: but now that you say she may go, she'll doubtless avail herself of the permission. You are not so bewitched, ma'am, are you, as to remain with him of your own accord?'

'Take care, Ellen!' answered Isabella, her eyes sparkling irefully; there was no misdoubting by their expression the full success of her partner's endeavours to make himself detested. 'Don't put faith in a single word he speaks. He's a lying fiend! a monster, and not a human being! I've been told I might leave him before; and I've made the attempt, but I dare not repeat it! Only, Ellen, promise you'll not mention a syllable of his infamous conversation to my brother or Catherine. Whatever he may pretend, he wishes to provoke Edgar to desperation: he says he has married me on purpose to obtain power over him; and he shan't obtain it—I'll die first! I just hope, I pray, that he may forget his diabolical prudence and kill me! The single pleasure I can imagine is to die or see him dead!'

'There—that will do for the present!' said Heathcliff. 'If you are called upon in a court of law, you'll remember her language, Nelly! And take a good look at that countenance: she's near the point which would suit me. No; you're not fit to be your own guardian, Isabella, now; and I, being your legal protector, must detain you in my custody, however distasteful the obligation may be. Go upstairs; I have something to say to Ellen Dean in private. That's not the way: upstairs, I tell you! Why, this is the road upstairs, child!'

He seized, and thrust her from the room: and returned muttering:

'I have no pity! I have no pity! The more the worms writhe, the more I yearn to crush out their entrails! It is a moral teething; and I grind with greater energy, in proportion to the increase of pain.'

'Do you understand what the word pity means?' I said, hastening to resume my bonnet. 'Did you ever feel a touch of it in your life?'

'Put that down!' he interrupted, perceiving my intention to depart. 'You are not going yet. Come here now, Nelly: I must either persuade or compel you to aid me in fulfilling my determination to see Catherine, and that without delay. I swear that I meditate no harm: I don't desire to cause any disturbance, or to exasperate or insult Mr Linton; I only wish to hear from herself how she is, and why she has been ill; and to ask if anything that I could do would be of use to her. Last night, I was in the Grange garden six hours, and I'll return there tonight; and every night I'll haunt the place, and every day, till I find an opportunity of entering. If Edgar Linton meets me, I shall not hesitate to knock him down, and give him enough to

insure his quiescence while I stay. If his servants oppose me, I shall threaten them off with these pistols. But wouldn't it be better to prevent my coming in contact with them, or their master? And you could do it so easily. I'd warn you when I came, and then you might let me in unobserved, as soon as she was alone, and watch till I departed, your conscience quite calm: you would be hindering mischief.'

I protested against playing that treacherous part in my employer's house: and, besides, I urged the cruelty and selfishness of his destroying Mrs Linton's tranquillity for his satisfaction. 'The commonest occurrence startles her painfully,' I said. 'She's all nerves, and she couldn't bear the surprise, I'm positive. Don't persist, sir! or else, I shall be obliged to inform my master of your designs; and he'll take measures to secure his house and its inmates from any such unwarrantable intrusions!'

'In that case, I'll take measures to secure you, woman!' exclaimed Heathcliff; 'you shall not leave Wuthering Heights till tomorrow morning. It is a foolish story to assert that Catherine could not bear to see me; and as to surprising her, I don't desire it: you must prepare her—ask her if I may come. You say she never mentions my name, and that I am never mentioned to her. To whom should she mention me if I am a forbidden topic in the house? She thinks you are all spies for her husband. Oh, I've no doubt she's in hell among you! I guess by her silence, as much as anything, what she feels. You say she is often restless, and anxious-looking; is that a proof of tranquillity? You talk of her mind being unsettled. How the devil could it be otherwise in her frightful isolation? And that insipid, paltry creature attending her from *duty* and *humanity*! From *pity* and *charity*! He might as well plant an oak in a flowerpot, and expect it to thrive, as imagine he can restore her to vigour in the soil of his shallow cares! Let us settle it at once: will you stay here, and am I to fight my way to Catherine over Linton and his footmen? Or will you be my friend, as you have been hitherto, and do what I request? Decide! because there is no reason for my lingering another minute, if you persist in your stubborn ill-nature!'

Well, Mr Lockwood, I argued and complained, and flatly refused him fifty times; but in the long run he forced me to an agreement. I engaged to carry a letter from him to my mistress; and should she consent, I promised to let him have intelligence of Linton's next absence from home, when he might come, and get in as he was able: I wouldn't be there, and my fellow-servants should be equally out of the way. Was it right or wrong? I fear it was wrong, though expedient. I thought I prevented another explosion by my compliance; and I thought, too, it might create a favourable crisis in Catherine's mental illness: and then I remembered Mr Edgar's stern rebuke of my carrying tales; and I tried to smooth away all disquietude on the subject, by affirming, with frequent iteration, that that betrayal of trust, if it merited so harsh an appellation, should be the last. Notwithstanding, my journey homeward was sadder than my journey thither; and many misgivings I had, ere I could prevail on myself to put the missive into Mrs Linton's hand.

But here is Kenneth; I'll go down, and tell him how much better you are. My history is *dree*, as we say, and will serve to while away another morning.

Dree, and dreary! I reflected as the good woman descended to receive the doctor; and not exactly of the kind which I should have chosen to amuse me. But never mind! I'll extract wholesome medicines from Mrs Dean's bitter herbs; and firstly, let me beware of the fascination that lurks in Catherine Heathcliff's brilliant eyes. I should be in a curious taking if I surrendered my heart to that young person, and the daughter turned out a second edition of the mother!

Chapter XV

ANOTHER week over—and I am so many days nearer health, and spring! I have now heard all my neighbour's history, at different sittings, as the housekeeper could

spare time from more important occupations. I'll continue it in her own words, only a little condensed. She is, on the whole, a very fair narrator, and I don't think I could improve her style.

In the evening, she said, the evening of my visit to the Heights, I knew, as well as if I saw him, that Mr Heathcliff was about the place; and I shunned going out, because I still carried his letter in my pocket, and didn't want to be threatened or teased any more. I had made up my mind not to give it till my master went somewhere, as I could not guess how its receipt would affect Catherine. The consequence was, that it did not reach her before the lapse of three days. The fourth was Sunday, and I brought it into her room after the family were gone to church. There was a manservant left to keep the house with me, and we generally made a practice of locking the doors during the hours of service; but on that occasion the weather was so warm and pleasant that I set them wide open, and, to fulfil my engagement, as I knew who would be coming, I told my companion that the mistress wished very much for some oranges, and he must run over to the village and get a few, to be paid for on the morrow. He departed, and I went upstairs.

Mrs Linton sat in a loose, white dress, with a light shawl over her shoulders, in the recess of the open window, as usual. Her thick, long hair had been partly removed at the beginning of her illness, and now she wore it simply combed in its natural tresses over her temples and neck. Her appearance was altered, as I had told Heathcliff; but when she was calm, there seemed unearthly beauty in the change. The flash of her eyes had been succeeded by a dreamy and melancholy softness; they no longer gave the impression of looking at the objects around her: they appeared always to gaze beyond, and far beyond—you would have said out of this world. Then the paleness of her face—its haggard aspect having vanished as she recovered flesh—and the peculiar expression arising from her mental state, though painfully suggestive of their causes, added to the touching interest which she awakened; and—invariably to me, I know, and to any person who saw her, I should think— refuted more tangible proofs of convalescence, and stamped her as one doomed to decay.

A book lay spread on the sill before her, and the scarcely perceptible wind fluttered its leaves at intervals. I believe Linton had laid it there: for she never endeavoured to divert herself with reading, or occupation of any kind, and he would spend many an hour in trying to entice her attention to some subject which had formerly been her amusement. She was conscious of his aim, and in her better moods endured his efforts placidly, only showing their uselessness by now and then suppressing a wearied sigh, and checking him at last with the saddest of smiles and kisses. At other times, she would turn petulantly away, and hide her face in her hands, or even push him off angrily; and then he took care to let her alone, for he was certain of doing no good.

Gimmerton chapel bells were still ringing; and the full, mellow flow of the beck in the valley came soothingly on the ear. It was a sweet substitute for the yet absent murmur of the summer foliage, which drowned that music about the Grange when the trees were in leaf. At Wuthering Heights it always sounded on quiet days following a great thaw or a season of steady rain. And of Wuthering Heights Catherine was thinking as she listened: that is, if she thought or listened at all; but she had the vague, distant look I mentioned before, which expressed no recognition of material things either by ear or eye.

'There's a letter for you, Mrs Linton,' I said, gently inserting it in one hand that rested on her knee. 'You must read it immediately, because it wants an answer. Shall I break the seal?' 'Yes,' she answered, without altering the direction of her eyes. I opened it—it was very short. 'Now', I continued, 'read it.' She drew away her hand, and let it fall. I replaced it in her lap, and stood waiting till it should please her to glance down; but that movement was so long delayed that at last I resumed:

'Must I read it, ma'am? It is from Mr Heathcliff.'

There was a start and a troubled gleam of recollection, and a struggle to arrange her ideas. She lifted the letter, and seemed to peruse it; and when she came to the signature she sighed: yet still I found she had not gathered its import, for, upon my desiring to hear her reply, she merely pointed to the name, and gazed at me with mournful and questioning eagerness.

'Well, he wishes to see you,' said I, guessing her need of an interpreter. 'He's in the garden by this time, and impatient to know what answer I shall bring.'

As I spoke, I observed a large dog lying on the sunny grass beneath raise its ears as if about to bark, and then smoothing them back, announce, by a wag of the tail, that someone approached whom it did not consider a stranger. Mrs Linton bent forward, and listened breathlessly. The minute after a step traversed the hall; the open house was too tempting for Heathcliff to resist walking in: most likely he supposed that I was inclined to shirk my promise, and so resolved to trust to his own audacity. With straining eagerness Catherine gazed towards the entrance of her chamber. He did not hit the right room directly, she motioned me to admit him, but he found it out ere I could reach the door, and in a stride or two was at her side, and had her grasped in his arms.

He neither spoke nor loosed his hold for some five minutes, during which period he bestowed more kisses than ever he gave in his life before, I dare say: but then my mistress had kissed him first, and I plainly saw that he could hardly bear, for downright agony, to look into her face! The same conviction had stricken him as me, from the instant he beheld her, that there was no prospect of ultimate recovery there—she was fated, sure to die.

'Oh, Cathy! Oh, my life! how can I bear it?' was the first sentence he uttered, in a tone that did not seek to disguise his despair. And now he stared at her so earnestly that I thought the very intensity of his gaze would bring tears into his eyes; but they burned with anguish: they did not melt.

'What now?' said Catherine, leaning back, and returning his look with a suddenly clouded brow: her humour was a mere vane for constantly varying caprices. 'You and Edgar have broken my heart, Heathcliff! And you both came to bewail the deed to me, as if you were the people to be pitied! I shall not pity you, not I. You have killed me—and thriven on it, I think. How strong you are! How many years do you mean to live after I am gone?'

Heathcliff had knelt on one knee to embrace her; he attempted to rise, but she seized his hair, and kept him down.

'I wish I could hold you,' she continued bitterly, 'till we were both dead! I shouldn't care what you suffered. I care nothing for your sufferings. Why shouldn't you suffer? I do! Will you forget me? Will you be happy when I am in the earth? Will you say twenty years hence, "That's the grave of Catherine Earnshaw. I loved her long ago, and was wretched to lose her; but it is past. I've loved many others since: my children are dearer to me than she was; and at death, I shall not rejoice that I am going to her: I shall be sorry that I must leave them!" Will you say so, Heathcliff?'

'Don't torture me till I am as mad as yourself,' cried he, wrenching his head free, and grinding his teeth.

The two, to a cool spectator, made a strange and fearful picture. Well might Catherine deem that heaven would be a land of exile to her, unless with her mortal body she cast away her moral character also. Her present countenance had a wild vindictiveness in its white cheek, and a bloodless lip and scintillating eye; and she retained in her closed fingers a portion of the locks she had been grasping. As to her companion, while raising himself with one hand, he had taken her arm with the other; and so inadequate was his stock of gentleness to the requirements of her condition, that on his letting go I saw four distinct impressions left blue in the colourless skin.

'Are you possessed with a devil,' he pursued savagely, 'to talk in that manner to me when you are dying? Do you reflect that all those words will be branded on my memory, and eating deeper eternally after you have left me? You know you lie to say I have killed you: and, Catherine, you know that I could as soon forget you as my existence! Is it not sufficient for your infernal selfishness, that while you are at peace I shall writhe in the torments of hell?'

'I shall not be at peace,' moaned Catherine, recalled to a sense of physical weakness by the violent, unequal throbbing of her heart, which beat visibly and audibly under this excess of agitation. She said nothing further till the paroxysm was over; then she continued, more kindly—

'I'm not wishing you greater torment than I have, Heathcliff. I only wish us never to be parted: and should a word of mine distress you hereafter, think I feel the same distress underground, and for my own sake, forgive me! Come here and kneel down again! You never harmed me in your life. Nay, if you nurse anger, that will be worse to remember than my harsh words! Won't you come here again? Do!'

Heathcliff went to the back of her chair, and leant over, but not so far as to let her see his face, which was livid with emotion. She bent round to look at him; he would not permit it: turning abruptly, he walked to the fireplace, where he stood, silent, with his back towards us. Mrs Linton's glance followed him suspiciously: every movement woke a new sentiment in her. After a pause and a prolonged gaze, she resumed; addressing me in accents of indignant disappointment—

'Oh, you see, Nelly, he would not relent a moment to keep me out of the grave. *That* is how I'm loved! Well, never mind. That is not *my* Heathcliff. I shall love mine yet; and take him with me: he's in my soul. And', added she, musingly, 'the thing that irks me most in this shattered prison, after all. I'm tired, tired of being enclosed here. I'm wearying to escape into that glorious world, and to be always there: not seeing it dimly through tears, and yearning for it through the walls of an aching heart; but really with it, and in it. Nelly, you think you are better and more fortunate than I; in full health and strength: you are sorry for me—very soon that will be altered. I shall be sorry for *you*. I shall be incomparably beyond and above you all. I *wonder* he won't be near me!' She went on to herself. 'I thought he wished it. Heathcliff, dear! you should not be sullen now. Do come to me, Heathcliff.'

In her eagerness she rose and supported herself on the arm of the chair. At that earnest appeal he turned to her, looking absolutely desperate. His eyes, wide and wet, at last flashed fiercely on her; his breast heaved convulsively. An instant they held asunder, and then how they met I hardly saw, but Catherine made a spring, and he caught her, and they were locked in an embrace from which I thought my mistress would never be released alive: in fact, to my eyes, she seemed directly insensible. He flung himself into the nearest seat, and on my approaching hurriedly to ascertain if she had fainted, he gnashed at me, and foamed like a mad dog, and gathered her to him with greedy jealousy. I did not feel as if I were in the company of a creature of my own species: it appeared that he would not understand, though I spoke to him; so I stood off, and held my tongue, in great perplexity.

A movement of Catherine's relieved me a little presently: she put up her hand to clasp his neck, and bring her cheek to his as he held her; while he, in return, covering her with frantic caresses, said wildly—

'You teach me now how cruel you've been—cruel and false. *Why* did you despise me? *Why* did you betray your own heart, Cathy? I have not one word of comfort. You deserve this. You have killed yourself. Yes, you may kiss me, and cry; and ring out my kisses and tears: they'll blight you—they'll damn you. You loved me— then what *right* had you to leave me? What right—answer me—for the poor fancy you felt for Linton? Because misery and degradation, and death, and nothing that God or Satan could inflict would have parted us, *you*, of your own will, did it. I have not broken your heart—*you* have broken it; and in breaking it, you have broken

mine. So much the worse for me, that I am strong. Do I want to live? What kind of living will it be when you—oh, God! would *you* like to live with your soul in the grave?'

'Let me alone. Let me alone,' sobbed Catherine. 'If I have done wrong, I'm dying for it. It is enough! You left me too: but I won't upbraid you! I forgive you. Forgive me!'

'It is hard to forgive, and to look at those eyes, and feel those wasted hands,' he answered. 'Kiss me again; and don't let me see your eyes! I forgive what you have done to me. I love *my* murderer—but *yours*! How can I?'

They were silent—their faces hid against each other, and washed by each other's tears. At least, I suppose the weeping was on both sides; as it seemed Heathcliff *could* weep on a great occasion like this.

I grew very uncomfortable, meanwhile; for the afternoon wore fast away, the man whom I had sent off returned from his errand, and I could distinguish, by the shine of the westering sun up the valley, a concourse thickening outside Gimmerton chapel porch.

'Service is over,' I announced. 'My master will be here in half an hour.'

Heathcliff groaned a curse, and strained Catherine closer: she never moved.

Ere long I perceived a group of the servants passing up the road towards the kitchen wing. Mr Linton was not far behind; he opened the gate himself and sauntered slowly up, probably enjoying the lovely afternoon that breathed as soft as summer.

'Now he is here,' I exclaimed. 'For Heaven's sake, hurry down! You'll not meet anyone on the front stairs. Do be quick; and stay among the trees till he is fairly in.'

'I must go, Cathy,' said Heathcliff, seeking to extricate himself from his companion's arms. 'But if I live, I'll see you again before you are asleep. I won't stray five yards from your window.'

'You must not go!' she answered, holding him as firmly as her strength allowed. 'You shall not, I tell you.'

'For one hour,' he pleaded earnestly.

'Not for one minute,' she replied.

'I *must*—Linton will be up immediately,' persisted the alarmed intruder.

He would have risen, and unfixed her fingers by the act—she clung fast, gasping: there was mad resolution in her face.

'No!' she shrieked. 'Oh, don't, don't go. It is the last time! Edgar will not hurt us. Heathcliff, I shall die! I shall die!'

'Damn the fool! There he is,' cried Heathcliff, sinking back into his seat. 'Hush, my darling! Hush, hush, Catherine! I'll stay. If he shot me so, I'd expire with a blessing on my lips.'

And there they were fast again. I heard my master mounting the stairs—the cold sweat ran from my forehead: I was horrified.

'Are you going to listen to her ravings?' I said passionately. 'She does not know what she says. Will you ruin her, because she has not wit to help herself? Get up! You could be free instantly. That is the most diabolical deed that ever you did. We are all done for—master, mistress, and servant.'

I wrung my hands, and cried out; Mr Linton hastened his step at the noise. In the midst of my agitation, I was sincerely glad to observe that Catherine's arms had fallen relaxed, and her head hung down.

'She's fainted or dead,' I thought: 'so much the better. Far better that she should be dead, than lingering a burden and a misery-maker to all about her.'

Edgar sprang to his unbidden guest, blanched with astonishment and rage. What he meant to do, I cannot tell; however, the other stopped all demonstrations, at once, by placing the lifeless looking form in his arms.

'Look there!' he said; 'unless you be a fiend, help her first—then you shall speak to me!'

He walked into the parlour, and sat down. Mr Linton summoned me, and with great difficulty, and after resorting to many means, we managed to restore her to sensation; but she was all bewildered; she sighed, and moaned, and knew nobody. Edgar, in his anxiety for her, forgot her hated friend. I did not. I went, at the earliest opportunity, and besought him to depart; affirming that Catherine was better, and he should hear from me in the morning how she passed the night.

'I shall not refuse to go out of doors,' he answered; 'but I shall stay in the garden: and, Nelly, mind you keep your word tomorrow. I shall be under those larch trees. Mind! or I pay another visit, whether Linton be in or not.'

He sent a rapid glance through the half-open door of the chamber, and, ascertaining that what I stated was apparently true, delivered the house of his luckless presence.

Chapter XVI

ABOUT twelve o'clock that night, was born the Catherine you saw at Wuthering Heights: a puny, seven months' child; and two hours after the mother died, having never recovered sufficient consciousness to miss Heathcliff, or know Edgar. The latter's distraction at his bereavement is a subject too painful to be dwelt on; its after effects showed how deep the sorrow sunk. A great addition, in my eyes, was his being left without an heir. I bemoaned that, as I gazed on the feeble orphan; and I mentally abused old Linton for (what was only natural partiality) the securing his estate to his own daughter, instead of his son's. An unwelcomed infant it was, poor thing! It might have wailed out of life, and nobody cared a morsel, during those first hours of existence. We redeemed the neglect afterwards; but its beginning was as friendless as its end is likely to be.

Next morning—bright and cheerful out of doors—stole softened in through the blinds of the silent room, and suffused the couch and its occupant with a mellow, tender glow. Edgar Linton had his head laid on the pillow, and his eyes shut. His young and fair features were almost as deathlike as those of the form beside him, and almost as fixed: but *his* was the hush of exhausted anguish, and *hers* of perfect peace. Her brow smooth, her lids closed, her lips wearing the expression of a smile; no angel in heaven could be more beautiful than she appeared. And I partook of the infinite calm in which she lay: my mind was never in a holier frame than while I gazed on that untroubled image of divine rest. I instinctively èchoed the words she had uttered a few hours before: 'Incomparably beyond and above us all! Whether still on earth or now in heaven, her spirit is at home with God!'

I don't know if it be a peculiarity in me, but I am seldom otherwise than happy while watching in the chamber of death, should no frenzied or despairing mourner share the duty with me. I see a repose that neither earth nor hell can break, and I feel an assurance of the endless and shadowless hereafter—the Eternity they have entered—where life is boundless in its duration, and love in its sympathy, and joy in its fulness. I noticed on that occasion how much selfishness there is even in a love like Mr Linton's, when he so regretted Catherine's blessed release! To be sure, one might have doubted, after the wayward and impatient existence she had led, whether she merited a haven of peace at last. One might doubt in seasons of cold reflection; but not then, in the presence of her corpse. It asserted its own tranquillity, which seemed a pledge of equal quiet to its former inhabitant.

Do you believe such people *are* happy in the other world, sir? I'd give a great deal to know.

I declined answering Mrs Dean's question, which struck me as something heterodox. She proceeded—

Retracing the course of Catherine Linton, I fear we have no right to think she is; but we'll leave her with her Maker.

The master looked asleep, and I ventured soon after sunrise to quit the room and steal out to the pure refreshing air. The servants thought me gone to shake off the drowsiness of my protracted watch; in reality, my chief motive was seeing Mr Heathcliff. If he had remained among the larches all night, he would have heard nothing of the stir at the Grange; unless, perhaps, he might catch the gallop of the messenger going to Gimmerton. If he had come nearer, he would probably be aware, from the lights flitting to and fro, and the opening and shutting of the outer doors, that all was not right within. I wished, yet feared, to find him. I felt the terrible news must be told, and I longed to get it over; but *how* to do it, I did not know. He was there—at least a few yards farther in the park; leant against an old ash tree, his hat off, and his hair soaked with the dew that had gathered on the budded branches, and fell pattering round him. He had been standing a long time in that position, for I saw a pair of ousels passing and repassing scarcely three feet from him, busy in building their nest, and regarding his proximity no more than that of a piece of timber. They flew off at my approach, and he raised his eyes and spoke—

'She's dead!' he said; 'I've not waited for you to learn that. Put your handkerchief away—don't snivel before me. Danm you all! she wants none of *your* tears!'

I was weeping as much for him as her; we do sometimes pity creatures that have none of the feeling either for themselves or others; and when I first looked into his face, I perceived that he had got intelligence of the catastrophe; and a foolish notion struck me that his heart was quelled and he prayed, because his lips moved and his gaze was bent on the ground.

'Yes, she's dead!' I answered, checking my sobs and drying my cheeks. 'Gone to heaven, I hope; where we may, everyone, join her, if we take due warning and leave our evil ways to follow good!'

'Did *she* take due warning, then?' asked Heathcliff, attempting a sneer. 'Did she die like a saint? Come, give me a true history of the event. How did——'

He endeavoured to pronounce the name, but could not manage it; and compressing his mouth he held a silent combat with his inward agony, defying, meanwhile, my sympathy with an unflinching ferocious stare. 'How did she die?' he resumed at last—fain, notwithstanding his hardihood, to have a support behind him; for, after the struggle, he trembled, in spite of himself, to his very finger-ends.

'Poor wretch!' I thought; 'you have a heart and nerves the same as your brother men! Why should you be anxious to conceal them? Your pride cannot blind God! You tempt Him to wring them, till He forces a cry of humiliation.'

'Quietly as a lamb!' I answered aloud. 'She drew a sigh, and stretched herself, like a child reviving, and sinking again to sleep; and five minutes after I felt one little pulse at her heart, and nothing more!'

'And—did she ever mention me?' he asked, hesitating, as if he dreaded the answer to his question would introduce details that he could not bear to hear.

'Her senses never returned; she recognized nobody from the time you left her,' I said. 'She lies with a sweet smile on her face; and her latest ideas wandered back to pleasant early days. Her life closed in a gentle dream—may she wake as kindly in the other world!'

'May she wake in torment!' he cried, with frightful vehemence, stamping his foot, and groaning in a sudden paroxysm of ungovernable passion. 'Why, she's a liar to the end! Where is she? Not *there*—not in heaven—not perished—where? Oh! you said you cared nothing for my sufferings! And I pray one prayer—I repeat it till my tongue stiffens—Catherine Earnshaw, may you not rest as long as I am living! You said I killed you—haunt me, then! The murdered *do* haunt their murderers,

I believe. I know that ghosts *have* wandered on earth. Be with me always—take any form—drive me mad! only *do* not leave me in this abyss, where I cannot find you! Oh, God! it is unutterable! I *cannot* live without my life! I *cannot* live without my soul!'

He dashed his head against the knotted trunk; and, lifting up his eyes, howled, not like a man, but like a savage beast getting goaded to death with knives and spears. I observed several splashes of blood about the bark of the tree, and his hand and forehead were both stained; probably the scene I witnessed was a repetition of others acted during the night. It hardly moved my compassion—it appalled me: still, I felt reluctant to quit him so. But the moment he recollected himself enough to notice me watching, he thundered a command for me to go, and I obeyed. He was beyond my skill to quiet or console!

Mrs Linton's funeral was appointed to take place on the Friday following her decease; and till then her coffin remained uncovered, and strewn with flowers and scented leaves, in the great drawing-room. Linton spent his days and nights there, a sleepless guardian; and—a circumstance concealed from all but me—Heathcliff spent his nights, at least, outside, equally a stranger to repose. I held no communication with him; still, I was conscious of his design to enter, if he could; and on the Tuesday, a little after dark, when my master, from sheer fatigue, had been compelled to retire a couple of hours, I went and opened one of the windows; moved by his perseverance, to give him a chance of bestowing on the faded image of his idol one final adieu. He did not omit to avail himself of the opportunity, cautiously and briefly: too cautiously to betray his presence by the slightest noise. Indeed, I shouldn't have discovered that he had been there, except for the disarrangement of the drapery about the corpse's face, and for observing on the floor a curl of light hair, fastened with a silver thread; which, on examination, I ascertained to have been taken from a locket hung round Catherine's neck. Heathcliff had opened the trinket and cast out its contents, replacing them by a black lock of his own. I twisted the two, and enclosed them together.

Mr Earnshaw was, of course, invited to attend the remains of his sister to the grave; and he sent no excuse, but he never came; so that, besides her husband, the mourners were wholly composed of tenants and servants. Isabella was not asked.

The place of Catherine's interment, to the surprise of the villagers, was neither in the chapel under the carved monument of the Lintons, nor yet by the tombs of her own relations, outside. It was dug on a green slope in a corner of the kirkyard, where the wall is so low that heath and bilberry plants have climbed over it from the moor; and peat mould almost buries it. Her husband lies in the same spot now; and they have each a simple headstone above, and a plain grey block at their feet, to mark the graves.

Chapter XVII

THAT Friday made the last of our fine days for a month. In the evening, the weather broke: the wind shifted from south to north-east, and brought rain first, and then sleet and snow. On the morrow one could hardly imagine that there had been three weeks of summer: the primroses and crocuses were hidden under wintry drifts; the larks were silent, the young leaves of the early trees smitten and blackened. And dreary, and chill, and dismal, that morrow did creep over! My master kept his room; I took possession of the lonely parlour, converting it into a nursery: and there I was, sitting with the moaning doll of a child laid on my knee; rocking it to and fro, and watching, meanwhile, the still driving flakes build up the uncurtained window, when the door opened, and some person entered, out of breath and laughing!

My anger was greater than my astonishment for a minute. I supposed it one of the
maids, and I cried—

'Have done! How dare you show your giddiness here? What would Mr Linton
say if he heard you?'

'Excuse me!' answered a familiar voice; 'but I know Edgar is in bed, and I
cannot stop myself.'

With that the speaker came forward to the fire, panting and holding her hand to
her side.

'I have ran the whole way from Wuthering Heights!' she continued, after a pause;
'except where I've flown. I couldn't count the number of falls I've had. Oh, I'm
aching all over! Don't be alarmed! There shall be an explanation as soon as I can
give it; only just have the goodness to step out and order the carriage to take me
on to Gimmerton, and tell a servant to seek up a few clothes in my wardrobe.'

The intruder was Mrs Heathcliff. She certainly seemed in no laughing predicament:
her hair streamed on her shoulders, dripping with snow and water; she was dressed
in the girlish dress she commonly wore, befitting her age more than her position:
a low frock with short sleeves, and nothing on either head or neck. The frock was
of light silk, and clung to her with wet, and her feet were protected merely by thin
slippers; add to this a deep cut under one ear, which only the cold prevented from
bleeding profusely, a white face scratched and bruised, and a frame hardly able to
support itself, through fatigue; and you may fancy my first fright was not much
allayed when I had had leisure to examine her.

'My dear young lady,' I exclaimed, 'I'll stir nowhere, and hear nothing, till you
have removed every article of your clothes, and put on dry things; and certainly
you shall not go to Gimmerton tonight, so it is needless to order the carriage.'

'Certainly, I shall,' she said; 'walking or riding: yet I've no objection to dress
myself decently. And—ah, see how it flows down my neck now! The fire does
make it smart.'

She insisted on my fulfilling her directions, before she would let me touch her;
and not till after the coachman had been instructed to get ready, and a maid set to
pack up some necessary attire, did I obtain her consent for binding the wound and
helping to change her garments.

'Now, Ellen,' she said, when my task was finished and she was seated in an
easy chair on the hearth, with a cup of tea before her, 'you sit down opposite me,
and put poor Catherine's baby away: I don't like to see it! You mustn't think I care
little for Catherine, because I behaved so foolishly on entering: I've cried, too,
bitterly—yes, more than anyone else has reason to cry. We parted unreconciled,
you remember, and I shan't forgive myself. But, for all that, I was not going to
sympathize with him—the brute beast! Oh, give me the poker! This is the last thing
of his I have about me:' she slipped the gold ring from her third finger, and threw
it on the floor. 'I'll smash it!' she continued, striking it with childish spite, 'and
then I'll burn it!' and she took and dropped the misused article among the coals.
'There! he shall buy another, if he gets me back again. He'd be capable of coming
to seek me, to tease Edgar. I dare not stay, lest that notion should possess his
wicked head! And besides, Edgar has not been kind, has he? And I won't come
suing for his assistance; nor will I bring him into more trouble. Necessity compelled
me to seek shelter here; though, if I had not learned he was out of the way, I'd
have halted at the kitchen, washed my face, warmed myself, got you to bring what
I wanted, and departed again to anywhere out of the reach of my accursed—of that
incarnate goblin! Ah! he was in such a fury! If he had caught me! It's a pity
Earnshaw is not his match in strength: I wouldn't have run till I'd seen him all but
demolished, had Hindley been able to do it!'

'Well, don't talk so fast, miss!' I interrupted; 'you'll disorder the handkerchief
I have tied round your face, and make the cut bleed again. Drink your tea, and

take breath, and give over laughing: laughter is sadly out of place under this roof, and in your condition!'

'An undeniable truth,' she replied. 'Listen to that child! It maintains a constant wail—send it out of my hearing for an hour; I shan't stay any longer.'

I rang the bell, and committed it to a servant's care; and then I inquired what had urged her to escape from Wuthering Heights in such an unlikely plight, and where she meant to go, as she refused remaining with us.

'I ought, and I wish to remain,' answered she, 'to cheer Edgar and take care of the baby, for two things, and because the Grange is my right home. But I tell you he wouldn't let me! Do you think he could bear to see me grow fat and merry; and could bear to think that we were tranquil, and not resolve on poisoning our comfort? Now, I have the satisfaction of being sure that he detests me, to the point of its annoying him seriously to have me within earshot or eyesight: I notice, when I enter his presence, the muscles of his countenance are involuntarily distorted into an expression of hatred; partly arising from his knowledge of the good causes I have to feel that sentiment for him, and partly from original aversion. It is strong enough to make me feel pretty certain that he would not chase me over England, supposing I contrived a clear escape; and therefore I must get quite away. I've recovered from my first desire to be killed by him: I'd rather he'd kill himself! He has extinguished my love effectually, and so I'm at my ease. I can recollect yet how I loved him; and can dimly imagine that I could still be loving him, if—no, no! Even if he had doted on me, the devilish nature would have revealed its existence somehow. Catherine had an awfully perverted taste to esteem him so dearly, knowing him so well. Monster! would that he could be blotted out of creation, and out of my memory!'

'Hush, hush! He's a human being,' I said. 'Be more charitable: there are worse men than he is yet!'

'He's not a human being,' she retorted; 'and he has no claim on my charity. I gave him my heart, and he took and pinched it to death, and flung it back to me. People feel with their hearts, Ellen: and since he has destroyed mine, I have not power to feel for him: and I would not, though he groaned from this to his dying day, and wept tears of blood for Catherine! No, indeed, indeed, I wouldn't!' And here Isabella began to cry; but, immediately dashing the water from her lashes, she recommenced. 'You asked, what has driven me to flight at last? I was compelled to attempt it, because I had succeeded in rousing his rage a pitch above his malignity. Pulling out the nerves with red-hot pincers requires more coolness than knocking on the head. He was worked up to forget the fiendish prudence he boasted of, and proceeded to murderous violence. I experienced pleasure in being able to exasperate him; the sense of pleasure woke my instinct of self-preservation, so I fairly broke free; and if ever I come into his hands again he is welcome to a signal revenge.

'Yesterday, you know, Mr Earnshaw should have been at the funeral. He kept himself sober for the purpose—tolerably sober: not going to bed mad at six o'clock and getting up drunk at twelve. Consequently he rose, in suicidal low spirits, as fit for the church as for a dance; and instead, he sat down by the fire and swallowed gin or brandy by tumblerfuls.

'Heathcliff—I shudder to name him! has been a stranger in the house from last Sunday till today. Whether the angels have fed him, or his kin beneath, I cannot tell; but he has not eaten a meal with us for nearly a week. He has just come home at dawn, and gone upstairs to his chamber; locking himself in—as if anybody dreamt of coveting his company! There he has continued, praying like a Methodist: only the deity he implored in senseless dust and ashes; and God, when addressed, was curiously confounded with his own black father! After concluding these precious orisons—and they lasted generally till he grew hoarse and his voice was strangled in his throat—he would be off again; always straight down to the Grange! I wonder Edgar did not send for a constable, and give him into custody! For me, grieved as

I was about Catherine, it was impossible to avoid regarding this season of deliverance from degrading oppression as a holiday.

'I recovered spirits sufficient to hear Joseph's eternal lectures without weeping, and to move up and down the house less with the foot of a frightened thief than formerly. You wouldn't think that I should cry at anything Joseph could say; but he and Hareton are detestable companions. I'd rather sit with Hindley, and hear his awful talk, than with "t' little maister" and his staunch supporter, that odious old man! When Heathcliff is in, I'm often obliged to seek the kitchen and their society, or starve among the damp uninhabited chambers; when he is not, as was the case this week, I establish a table and chair at one corner of the house fire, and never mind how Mr Earnshaw may occupy himself; and he does not interfere with my arrangements. He is quieter now than he used to be, if no one provokes him: more sullen and depressed, and less furious. Joseph affirms he's sure he's an altered man: that the Lord has touched his heart, and he is saved "so as by fire". I'm puzzled to detect signs of the favourable change: but it is not my business.

'Yester-evening I sat in my nook reading some old books till late on towards twelve. It seemed so dismal to go upstairs, with the wild snow blowing outside, and my thoughts continually reverting to the kirkyard and the new-made grave! I dared hardly lift my eyes from the page before me, that melancholy scene so instantly usurped its place. Hindley sat opposite, his head leant on his hand; perhaps meditating on the same subject. He had ceased drinking at a point below irrationality, and had neither stirred nor spoken during two or three hours. There was no sound through the house but the moaning wind, which shook the windows every now and then, the faint crackling of the coals, and the click of my snuffers as I removed at intervals the long wick of the candle. Hareton and Joseph were probably fast asleep in bed. It was very, very sad: and while I read I sighed, for it seemed as if all joy had vanished from the world, never to be restored.

'The doleful silence was broken at length by the sound of the kitchen latch: Heathcliff had returned from his watch earlier than usual; owing, I suppose, to the sudden storm. That entrance was fastened, and we heard him coming round to get in by the other. I rose with an irrepressible expression of what I felt on my lips, which induced my companion, who had been staring towards the door, to turn and look at me.

' "I'll keep him out five minutes," he exclaimed. "You won't object?"

' "No, you may keep him out the whole night for me," I answered. "Do! put the key in the lock, and draw the bolts."

'Earnshaw accomplished this ere his guest reached the front; he then came and brought his chair to the other side of my table, leaning over it, and searching in my eyes, a sympathy with the burning hate that gleamed from his: as he both looked and felt like an assassin, he couldn't exactly find that; but he discovered enough to encourage him to speak.

' "You and I", he said, "have each a great debt to settle with the man out yonder! If we were neither of us cowards, we might combine to discharge it. Are you as soft as your brother? Are you willing to endure to the last, and not once attempt a repayment?"

' "I'm weary of enduring now," I replied; "and I'd be glad of a retaliation that wouldn't recoil on myself; but treachery and violence are spears pointed at both ends: they wound those who resort to them worse than their enemies."

' "Treachery and violence are a just return for treachery and violence!" cried Hindley. "Mrs Heathcliff, I'll ask you to do nothing; but sit still and be dumb. Tell me now, can you? I'm sure you would have as much pleasure as I in witnessing the conclusion of the fiend's existence; he'll be *your* death unless you overreach him; and he'll be *my* ruin. Damn the hellish villain! He knocks at the door as if he were master here already! Promise to hold your tongue, and before that clock strikes—it wants three minutes of one—you're a free woman!"

'He took the implements which I described to you in my letter from his breast, and would have turned down the candle. I snatched it away, however, and seized his arm.

' "I'll not hold my tongue!" I said; "you mustn't touch him. Let the door remain shut, and be quiet!"

' "No! I've formed my resolution, and by God I'll execute it!" cried the desperate being. "I'll do you a kindness in spite of yourself, and Hareton justice! And you needn't trouble your head to screen me; Catherine is gone. Nobody alive would regret me, or be ashamed, though I cut my throat this minute—and it's time to make an end!"

'I might as well have struggled with a bear, or reasoned with a lunatic. The only resource left me was to run to a lattice and warn his intended victim of the fate which awaited him.

' "You'd better seek shelter somewhere else tonight!" I exclaimed in a rather triumphant tone. "Mr Earnshaw has a mind to shoot you, if you persist in endeavouring to enter."

' "You'd better open the door, you ——" he answered, addressing me by some elegant term that I don't care to repeat.

' "I shall not meddle in the matter," I retorted again. "Come in and get shot, if you please! I've done my duty."

'With that I shut the window and returned to my place by the fire; having too small a stock of hypocrisy at my command to pretend any anxiety for the danger that menaced him. Earnshaw swore passionately at me: affirming that I loved the villain yet; and calling me all sorts of names for the base spirit I evinced. And I, in my secret heart (and conscience never reproached me), thought what a blessing it would be for *him* should Heathcliff put him out of misery; and what a blessing for *me* should he send Heathcliff to his right abode! As I sat nursing these reflections, the casement behind me was banged on to the floor by a blow from the latter individual, and his black countenance looked blightingly through. The stanchions stood too close to suffer his shoulders to follow, and I smiled, exulting in my fancied security. His hair and clothes were whitened with snow, and his sharp cannibal teeth, revealed by cold and wrath, gleamed through the dark.

' "Isabella, let me in, or I'll make you repent!" he "girned", as Joseph calls it.

' "I cannot commit murder," I replied. "Mr Hindley stands sentinel with a knife and loaded pistol."

' "Let me in by the kitchen door," he said.

' "Hindley will be there before you," I answered: "and that's a poor love of yours that cannot bear a shower of snow! We were left at peace on our beds as long as the summer moon shone, but the moment a blast of winter returns, you must run for shelter! Heathcliff, if I were you, I'd go stretch myself over her grave and die like a faithful dog. The world is surely not worth living in now, is it? You had distinctly impressed on me the idea that Catherine was the whole joy of your life: I can't imagine how you think of surviving her loss."

' "He's there, is he?" exclaimed my companion, rushing to the gap. "If I can get my arm out I can hit him!"

'I'm afraid, Ellen, you'll set me down as really wicked; but you don't know all, so don't judge. I wouldn't have aided or abetted an attempt on even *his* life for anything. Wish that he were dead, I must; and therefore I was fearfully disappointed, and unnerved by terror for the consequences of my taunting speech, when he flung himself on Earnshaw's weapon and wrenched it from his grasp.

'The charge exploded, and the knife, in springing back, closed into it's owner's wrist. Heathcliff pulled it away by main force, slitting up the flesh as it passed on, and thrust it dripping into his pocket. He then took a stone, struck down the division between two windows, and sprang in. His adversary had fallen senseless with

excessive pain and the flow of blood, that gushed from an artery or a large vein. The ruffian kicked and trampled on him, and dashed his head repeatedly against the flags, holding me with one hand, meantime, to prevent me summoning Joseph. He exerted preterhuman self-denial in abstaining from finishing him completely; but getting out of breath he finally desisted, and dragged the apparently inanimate body on to the settle. There he tore off the sleeve of Earnshaw's coat, and bound up the wound with brutal roughness; spitting and cursing during the operation as energetically as he had kicked before. Being at liberty, I lost no time in seeking the old servant; who, having gathered by degrees the purport of my hasty tale, hurried below, gasping, as he descended the steps two at once.

' "What is ther to do, now? what is ther to do, now?''

' "There's this to do,'' thundered Heathcliff, "that your master's mad; and should he last another month, I'll have him to an asylum. And how the devil did you come to fasten me out, you toothless hound? Don't stand muttering and mumbling there. Come, I'm not going to nurse him. Wash that stuff away; and mind the sparks of your candle—it is more than half brandy!''

' "And so, ye've been murthering on him?'' exclaimed Joseph, lifting his hands and eyes in horror. "If iver I seed a seeght loike this! May the Lord——''

'Heathcliff gave him a push on to his knees in the middle of the blood, and flung a towel to him; but instead of proceeding to dry it up, he joined his hands and began a prayer, which excited my laughter from its odd phraseology. I was in the condition of mind to be shocked at nothing: in fact, I was as reckless as some malefactors show themselves at the foot of the gallows.

' "Oh, I forgot you,'' said the tyrant. "You shall do that. Down with you. And you conspire with him against me, do you, viper? There, that is work fit for you!''

'He shook me till my teeth rattled, and pitched me beside Joseph, who steadily concluded his supplications and then rose, vowing he would set off for the Grange directly. Mr Linton was a magistrate, and though he had fifty wives dead, he should inquire into this. He was so obstinate in his resolution, that Heathcliff deemed it expedient to compel from my lips a recapitulation of what had taken place; standing over me, heaving with malevolence, as I reluctantly delivered the account in answer to his questions. It required a great deal of labour to satisfy the old man that Heathcliff was not the aggressor; especially with my hardly wrung replies. However, Mr Earnshaw soon convinced him that he was alive still; Joseph hastened to administer a dose of spirits, and by their succour his master presently regained motion and consciousness. Heathcliff, aware that his opponent was ignorant of the treatment received while insensible, called him deliriously intoxicated; and said he should not notice his atrocious conduct further, but advised him to get to bed. To my joy, he left us, after giving this judicious counsel, and Hindley stretched himself on the hearthstone. I departed to my own room, marvelling that I had escaped so easily.

'This morning, when I came down, about half an hour before noon, Mr Earnshaw was sitting by the fire, deadly sick; his evil genius, almost as gaunt and ghastly, leant against the chimney. Neither appeared inclined to dine, and, having waited till all was cold on the table, I commenced alone. Nothing hindered me from eating heartily, and I experienced a certain sense of satisfaction and superiority, as, at intervals, I cast a look towards my silent companions, and felt the comfort of a quiet conscience within me. After I had done, I ventured on the unusual liberty of drawing near the fire, going round Earnshaw's seat, and kneeling in the corner beside him.

'Heathcliff did not glance my way, and I gazed up, and contemplated his features almost as confidently as if they had been turned to stone. His forehead, that I once thought so manly, and that I now think so diabolical, was shaded with a heavy cloud; his basilisk eyes were nearly quenched by sleeplessness, and weeping, perhaps, for the lashes were wet then; his lips devoid of their ferocious sneer, and sealed in an expression of unspeakable sadness. Had it been another, I would have covered

my face in the presence of such grief. In *his* case, I was gratified; and, ignoble as it seems to insult a fallen enemy, I couldn't miss this chance of sticking in a dart: his weakness was the only time when I could taste the delight of paying wrong for wrong.'

'Fie, fie, miss!' I interrupted. 'One might suppose you had never opened a Bible in your life. If God afflict your enemies, surely that ought to suffice you. It is both mean and presumptuous to add your torture to His!'

'In general I'll allow that it would be, Ellen,' she continued; 'but what misery laid on Heathcliff could content me, unless I have a hand in it? I'd rather he suffered *less*, if I might cause his sufferings and he might *know* that I was the cause. O, I owe him so much. On only one condition can I hope to forgive him. It is, if I may take an eye for an eye, a tooth for a tooth; for every wrench of agony return a wrench: reduce him to my level. As he was the first to injure, make him the first to implore pardon; and then—why then, Ellen, I might show you some generosity. But it is utterly impossible I can ever be revenged, and therefore I cannot forgive him. Hindley wanted some water, and I handed him a glass, and asked him how he was.

' "Not as ill as I wish," he replied. "But leaving out my arm, every inch of me is as sore as if I had been fighting with a legion of imps!"

' "Yes, no wonder," was my next remark. "Catherine used to boast that she stood between you and bodily harm: she meant that certain persons would not hurt you for fear of offending her. It's well people don't *really* rise from their grave, or, last night, she might have witnessed a repulsive scene! Are not you bruised and cut over your chest and shoulders?"

' "I can't say," he answered: "but what do you mean? Did he dare to strike me when I was down?"

' "He trampled on you and kicked you, and dashed you on the ground," I whispered. "And his mouth watered to tear you with his teeth; because he's only half a man—not so much."

'Mr Earnshaw looked up, like me, to the countenance of our mutual foe; who, absorbed in his anguish, seemed insensible to anything around him: the longer he stood, the plainer his reflections revealed their blackness through his features.

' "Oh, if God would but give me strength to strangle him in my last agony, I'd go to hell with joy," groaned the impatient man, writhing to rise, and sinking back in despair, convinced of his inadequacy for the struggle.

' "Nay, it's enough that he has murdered one of you," I observed aloud. "At the Grange, everyone knows your sister would have been living now, had it not been for Mr Heathcliff. After all, it is preferable to be hated than loved by him. When I recollect how happy we were—how happy Catherine was before he came—I'm fit to curse the day."

'Most likely, Heathcliff noticed more the truth of what was said, than the spirit of the person who said it. His attention was roused, I saw, for his eyes rained down tears among the ashes, and he drew his breath in suffocating sighs. I stared full at him, and laughed scornfully. The clouded windows of hell flashed a moment towards me; the fiend which usually looked out, however, was so dimmed and drowned that I did not fear to hazard another sound of derision.

' "Get up, and begone out of my sight," said the mourner.

'I guessed he uttered those words, at least, though his voice was hardly intelligible.

' "I beg your pardon," I replied. "But I loved Catherine too; and her brother requires attendance, which, for her sake, I shall supply. Now that she's dead, I see her in Hindley: Hindley has exactly her eyes, if you had not tried to gouge them out, and made them black and red; and her——"

' "Get up, wretched idiot, before I stamp you to death!" he cried, making a movement that caused me to make one also.

' "But then," I continued, holding myself ready to flee; "if poor Catherine had trusted you, and assumed the ridiculous, contemptible, degrading title of Mrs Heathcliff, she would soon have presented a similar picture! *She* wouldn't have borne your abominable behaviour quietly: her detestation and disgust must have found voice."

'The back of the settle and Earnshaw's person interposed between me and him: so instead of endeavouring to reach me, he snatched a dinner knife from the table and flung it at my head. It struck beneath my ear, and stopped the sentence I was uttering; but, pulling it out, I sprang to the door and delivered another; which I hope went a little deeper than his missile. The last glimpse I caught of him was a furious rush on his part, checked by the embrace of his host; and both fell locked together on the hearth. In my flight through the kitchen I bid Joseph speed to his master; I knocked over Hareton, who was hanging a litter of puppies from a chair back in the doorway; and, blest as a soul escaped from purgatory, I bounded, leaped, and flew down the steep road; then, quitting its windings, shot direct across the moor, rolling over banks, and wading through marshes: precipitating myself, in fact, towards the beacon light of the Grange. And far rather would I be condemned to a perpetual dwelling in the infernal regions, than, even for one night, abide beneath the roof of Wuthering Heights again.'

Isabella ceased speaking, and took a drink of tea; then she rose, and bidding me put on her bonnet, and a great shawl I had brought, and turning a deaf ear to my entreaties for her to remain another hour, she stepped on to a chair, kissed Edgar's and Catherine's portraits, bestowed a similar salute on me, and descended to the carriage, accompanied by Fanny, who yelped wild with joy at recovering her mistress. She was driven away, never to revisit this neighbourhood: but a regular correspondence was established between her and my master when things were more settled. I believe her new abode was in the south, near London; there she had a son born, a few months subsequent to her escape. He was christened Linton, and, from the first, she reported him to be an ailing, peevish creature.

Mr Heathcliff, meeting me one day in the village, inquired where she lived. I refused to tell. He remarked that it was not of any moment, only she must beware of coming to her brother: she should not be with him, if he had to keep her himself. Though I would give no information, he discovered, through some of the other servants, both her place of residence and the existence of the child. Still he didn't molest her: for which forbearance she might thank his aversion, I suppose. He often asked about the infant, when he saw me; and on hearing its name, smiled grimly, and observed:

'They wish me to hate it too, do they?'

'I don't think they wish you to know anything about it,' I answered.

'But I'll have it,' he said, 'when I want it. They may reckon on that!'

Fortunately, its mother died before the time arrived; some thirteen years after the decease of Catherine, when Linton was twelve, or a little more.

On the day succeeding Isabella's unexpected visit, I had no opportunity of speaking to my master: he shunned conversation, and was fit for discussing nothing. When I could get him to listen, I saw it pleased him that his sister had left her husband; whom he abhorred with an intensity which the mildness of his nature would scarcely seem to allow. So deep and sensitive was his aversion, that he refrained from going anywhere where he was likely to see or hear of Heathcliff. Grief, and that together, transformed him into a complete hermit: he threw up his office of magistrate, ceased even to attend church, avoided the village on all occasions, and spent a life of entire seclusion within the limits of his park and grounds; only varied by solitary rambles on the moors, and visits to the grave of his wife, mostly at evening, or early morning before other wanderers were abroad. But he was too good to be thoroughly unhappy long. *He* didn't pray for Catherine's soul to haunt him. Time brought resignation, and a melancholy sweeter than common joy. He recalled her

memory with ardent, tender love, and hopeful aspiring to the better world; where he doubted not she was gone.

And he had earthly consolation and affections also. For a few days, I said, he seemed regardless of the puny successor to the departed: the coldness melted as fast as snow in April, and ere the tiny thing could stammer a word or totter a step, it wielded a despot's sceptre in his heart. It was named Catherine; but he never called it the name in full, as he had never called the first Catherine short; probably because Heathcliff had a habit of doing so. The little one was always Cathy; it formed to him a distinction from the mother, and yet a connection with her; and his attachment sprang from its relation to her, far more than from its being his own.

I used to draw a comparison between him and Hindley Earnshaw, and perplex myself to explain satisfactorily why their conduct was so opposite in similar circumstances. They had both been fond husbands, and were both attached to their children; and I could not see how they shouldn't both have taken the same road, for good or evil. But, I thought in my mind, Hindley, with apparently the stronger head, has shown himself sadly the worse and the weaker man. When his ship struck, the captain abandoned his post; and the crew, instead of trying to save her, rushed into riot and confusion, leaving no hope for their luckless vessel. Linton, on the contrary, displayed the true courage of a loyal and faithful soul: he trusted God; and God comforted him. One hoped, and the other despaired: they chose their own lots, and were righteously doomed to endure them. But you'll not want to hear my moralizing, Mr Lockwood: you'll judge as well as I can, all these things: at least, you'll think you will, and that's the same. The end of Earnshaw was what might have been expected; it followed fast on his sister's: there was scarcely six months between them. We, at the Grange, never got a very succinct account of his state preceding it; all that I did learn, was on occasion of going to aid in the preparations for the funeral. Mr Kenneth came to announce the event to my master.

'Well, Nelly,' said he, riding into the yard one morning, too early not to alarm me with an instant presentiment of bad news, 'it's yours and my turn to go into mourning at present. Who's given us the slip now, do you think?'

'Who?' I asked in a flurry.

'Why, guess!' he returned, dismounting, and slinging his bridle on a hook by the door. 'And nip up the corner of your apron: I'm certain you'll need it.'

'Not Mr Heathcliff, surely?' I exclaimed.

'What! would you have tears for him?' said the doctor. 'No, Heathcliff's a tough young fellow: he looks blooming today. I've just seen him. He's rapidly regaining flesh since he lost his better half.'

'Who is it then, Mr Kenneth?' I repeated impatiently.

'Hindley Earnshaw! Your old friend Hindley,' he replied, 'and my wicked gossip: though he's been too wild for me this long while. There! I said we should draw water. But cheer up. He died true to his character: drunk as a lord. Poor lad! I'm sorry, too. One can't help missing an old companion: though he had the worst tricks with him that ever man imagined, and has done me many a rascally turn. He's barely twenty-seven, it seems; that's your own age: who would have thought you were born in one year?'

I confess this blow was greater to me than the shock of Mrs Linton's death: ancient associations lingered round my heart; I sat down in the porch and wept as for a blood relation, desiring Kenneth to get another servant to introduce him to the master. I could not hinder myself from pondering on the question—'Had he had fair play?' Whatever I did, that idea would bother me: it was so tiresomely pertinacious that I resolved on requesting leave to go to Wuthering Heights, and assist in the last duties to the dead. Mr Linton was extremely reluctant to consent, but I pleaded eloquently for the friendless condition in which he lay; and I said my old master and foster-brother had a claim on my services as strong as his own. Besides, I reminded him that the child Hareton was his wife's nephew, and, in the

absence of nearer kin, he ought to act as its guardian; and he ought to and must inquire how the property was left, and look over the concerns of his brother-in-law. He was unfit for attending to such matters then, but he bid me speak to his lawyer; and at length permitted me to go. His lawyer had been Earnshaw's also: I called at the village, and asked him to accompany me. He shook his head, and advised that Heathcliff should be let alone; affirming, if the truth were known, Hareton would be found little else than a beggar.

'His father died in debt,' he said; 'the whole property is mortgaged, and the sole chance for the natural heir is to allow him an opportunity of creating some interest in the creditor's heart, that he may be inclined to deal leniently towards him.'

When I reached the Heights, I explained that I had come to see everything carried on decently; and Joseph, who appeared in sufficient distress, expressed satisfaction at my presence. Mr Heathcliff said he did not perceive that I was wanted; but I might stay and order the arrangements for the funeral, if I chose.

'Correctly,' he remarked, 'that fool's body should be buried at the crossroads, without ceremony of any kind. I happen to leave him ten minutes yesterday afternoon, and in that interval he fastened the two doors of the house against me, and he has spent the night in drinking himself to death deliberately! We broke in this morning, for we heard him snorting like a horse; and there he was, laid over the settle; flaying and scalping would not have wakened him. I sent for Kenneth, and he came; but not till the beast had changed into carrion: he was both dead and cold, and stark; and so you'll allow it was useless making more stir about him!'

The old servant confirmed this statement, but muttered:

'Aw'd rayther he'd goan hisseln fur t' doctor! Aw sud uh taen tent uh t' maister better nur him—un he warn't deead when Aw left, nowt uh t' soart!'

I insisted on the funeral being respectable. Mr Heathcliff said I might have my own way there too; only, he desired me to remember that the money for the whole affair came out of his pocket. He maintained a hard, careless deportment, indicative of neither joy nor sorrow; if anything, it expressed a flinty gratification at a piece of difficult work successfully executed. I observed once, indeed, something like exultation in his aspect: it was just when the people were bearing the coffin from the house. He had the hypocrisy to represent a mourner: and previous to following with Hareton, he lifted the unfortunate child on to the table and muttered, with peculiar gusto, 'Now, my bonny lad, you are *mine*! And we'll see if one tree won't grow as crooked as another, with the same wind to twist it!' The unsuspecting thing was pleased at this speech: he played with Heathcliff's whiskers, and stroked his cheek; but I divined its meaning, and observed tartly, 'That boy must go back with me to Thrushcross Grange, sir. There is nothing in the world less yours than he is!'

'Does Linton say so?' he demanded.

'Of course—he has ordered me to take him,' I replied.

'Well,' said the scoundrel, 'we'll not argue the subject now: but I have a fancy to try my hand at rearing a young one; so intimate to your master that I must supply the place of this with my own, if he attempt to remove it. I don't engage to let Hareton go undisputed; but I'll be pretty sure to make the other come! Remember to tell him.'

This hint was enough to bind our hands. I repeated its substance on my return; and Edgar Linton, little interested at the commencement, spoke no more of interfering. I'm not aware that he could have done it to any purpose, had he been ever so willing.

The guest was now the master of Wuthering Heights: he held firm possession, and proved to the attorney—who, in his turn, proved it to Mr Linton—that Earnshaw had mortgaged every yard of land he owned, for cash to supply his mania for gaming; and he, Heathcliff, was the mortgagee. In that manner Hareton, who should now be the first gentleman in the neighbourhood, was reduced to a state of complete

dependence on his father's inveterate enemy; and lives in his own house as a servant, deprived of the advantage of wages, and quite unable to right himself, because of his friendlessness, and his ignorance that he has been wronged.

Chapter XVIII

THE twelve years, continued Mrs Dean, following that dismal period, were the happiest of my life: my greatest troubles in their passage rose from our little lady's trifling illnesses, which she had to experience in common with all children, rich and poor. For the rest, after the first six months, she grew like a larch, and could walk and talk too, in her own way, before the heath blossomed a second time over Mrs Linton's dust. She was the most winning thing that ever brought sunshine into a desolate house: a real beauty in face, with the Earnshaws' handsome dark eyes, but the Lintons' fair skin and small features, and yellow curling hair. Her spirit was high, though not rough, and qualified by a heart sensitive and lively to excess in its affections. That capacity for intense attachments reminded me of her mother: still she did not resemble her; for she could be soft and mild as a dove, and she had a gentle voice and pensive expression: her anger was never furious; her love never fierce: it was deep and tender. However, it must be acknowledged, she had faults to foil her gifts. A propensity to be saucy was one; and a perverse will, that indulged children invariably acquire, whether they be good-tempered or cross. If a servant chanced to vex her, it was always—'I shall tell papa!' And if he reproved her, even by a look, you would have thought it a heart-breaking business: I don't believe he ever did speak a harsh word to her. He took her education entirely on himself, and made it an amusement. Fortunately, curiosity and a quick intellect urged her into an apt scholar: she learned rapidly and eagerly, and did honour to his teaching.

Till she reached the age of thirteen, she had not once been beyond the range of the park by herself. Mr Linton would take her with him a mile or so outside, on rare occasions; but he trusted her to no one else. Gimmerton was an unsubstantial name in her ears; the chapel, the only building she had approached or entered, except her own home. Wuthering Heights and Mr Heathcliff did not exist for her: she was a perfect recluse; and, apparently, perfectly contented. Sometimes, indeed, while surveying the country from her nursery window, she would observe:

'Ellen, how long will it be before I can walk to the top of those hills? I wonder what lies on the other side—is it the sea?'

'No, Miss Cathy,' I would answer; 'it is hills again, just like these.'

'And what are those golden rocks like when you stand under them?' she once asked.

The abrupt descent of Penistone Crags particularly attracted her notice; especially when the setting sun shone on it and the topmost heights, and the whole extent of landscape besides lay in shadow. I explained that they were bare masses of stone, with hardly enough earth in their clefts to nourish a stunted tree.

'And why are they bright so long after it is evening here?' she pursued.

'Because they are a great deal higher up than we are,' replied I; 'you could not climb them, they are too high and steep. In winter the frost is always there before it comes to us; and deep into summer I have found snow under that black hollow on the north-east side!'

'Oh, you have been on them!' she cried gleefully. 'Then I can go, too, when I am a woman. Has papa been, Ellen?'

'Papa would tell you, miss,' I answered hastily, 'that they are not worth the trouble of visiting. The moors, where you ramble with him, are much nicer; and Thrushcross Park is the finest place in the world.'

'But I know the park, and I don't know those,' she murmured to herself. 'And I should delight to look round me from the brow of that tallest point: my little pony Minny shall take me some time.'

One of the maids mentioning the Fairy Cave, quite turned her head with a desire to fulfil this project: she teased Mr Linton about it; and he promised she should have the journey when she got older. But Miss Catherine measured her age by months, and, 'Now, am I old enough to go to Penistone Crags?' was the constant question in her mouth. The road thither wound close by Wuthering Heights. Edgar had not the heart to pass it; so she received as constantly the answer, 'Not yet, love: not yet.'

I said Mrs Heathcliff lived above a dozen years after quitting her husband. Her family were of a delicate constitution: she and Edgar both lacked the ruddy health that you will generally meet in these parts. What her last illness was, I am not certain: I conjecture, they died of the same thing, a kind of fever, slow at its commencement, but incurable, and rapidly consuming life towards the close. She wrote to inform her brother of the probable conclusion of a four months' indisposition under which she had suffered, and entreated him to come to her, if possible; for she had much to settle, and she wished to bid him adieu, and deliver Linton safely into his hands. Her hope was, that Linton might be left with him, as he had been with her: his father, she would fain convince herself, had no desire to assume the burden of his maintenance or education. My master hesitated not a moment in complying with her request: reluctant as he was to leave home at ordinary calls, he flew to answer this; commending Catherine to my peculiar vigilance, in his absence, with reiterated orders that she must not wander out of the park, even under my escort: he did not calculate on her going unaccompanied.

He was away three weeks. The first day or two, my charge sat in a corner of the library, too sad for either reading or playing: in that quiet state she caused me little trouble; but it was succeeded by an interval of impatient fretful weariness; and being too busy, and too old then, to run up and down amusing her, I hit on a method by which she might entertain herself. I used to send her on her travels round the grounds—now on foot, and now on a pony; indulging her with a patient audience of all her real and imaginary adventures, when she returned.

The summer shone in full prime; and she took such a taste for this solitary rambling that she often contrived to remain out from breakfast till tea; and then the evenings were spent in recounting her fanciful tales. I did not fear her breaking bounds; because the gates were generally locked, and I thought she would scarcely venture forth alone, if they had stood wide open. Unluckily, my confidence proved misplaced. Catherine came to me, one morning, at eight o'clock, and said she was that day an Arabian merchant, going to cross the desert with his caravan; and I must give her plenty of provision for herself and beasts: a horse, and three camels, personated by a large hound and a couple of pointers. I got together good store of dainties, and slung them in a basket on one side of the saddle; and she sprang up as gay as a fairy, sheltered by her wide-brimmed hat and gauze veil from the July sun, and trotted off with a merry laugh, mocking my cautious counsel to avoid galloping, and come back early. The naughty thing never made her appearance at tea. One traveller, the hound, being an old dog and fond of its ease, returned; but neither Cathy, nor the pony, nor the two pointers were visible in any direction: I dispatched emissaries down this path, and that path, and at last went wandering in search of her myself. There was a labourer working at a fence round a plantation, on the borders of the grounds. I inquired of him if he had seen our young lady.

'I saw her at morn,' he replied; 'she would have me to cut her a hazel switch, and then she leapt her Galloway over the hedge yonder, where it is lowest, and galloped out of sight.'

You may guess how I felt at hearing this news. It struck me directly she must have started for Penistone Crags. 'What will become of her?' I ejaculated, pushing through a gap which the man was repairing, and making straight to the high road. I walked as if for a wager, mile after mile, till a turn brought me in view of the Heights; but no Catherine could I detect far or near. The Crags lie about a mile and a half beyond Mr Heathcliff's place, and that is four from the Grange, so I began to fear night would fall ere I could reach them. 'And what if she should have slipped in clambering among them?' I reflected, 'and been killed, or broken some of her bones?' My suspense was truly painful; and, at first, it gave me delightful relief to observe, in hurrying by the farmhouse, Charlie, the fiercest of the pointers, lying under a window, with swelled head and bleeding ear. I opened the wicket and ran to the door, knocking vehemently for admittance. A woman whom I knew, and who formerly lived at Gimmerton, answered: she had been servant there since the death of Mr Earnshaw.

'Ah,' said she, 'you are come a seeking your little mistress! don't be frightened. She's here safe: but I'm glad it isn't the master.'

'He is not at home then, is he?' I panted, quite breathless with quick walking and alarm.

'No, no,' she replied: 'both he and Joseph are off, and I think they won't return this hour or more. Step in and rest you a bit.'

I entered, and beheld my stray lamb seated on the hearth, rocking herself in a little chair that had been her mother's when a child. Her hat was hung against the wall, and she seemed perfectly at home, laughing and chattering, in the best spirits imaginable, to Hareton—now a great, strong lad of eighteen—who stared at her with considerable curiosity and astonishment: comprehending precious little of the fluent succession of remarks and questions which her tongue never ceased pouring forth.

'Very well, miss!' I exclaimed, concealing my joy under an angry countenance. 'This is your last ride, till papa comes back. I'll not trust you over the threshold again, you naughty, naughty girl!'

'Aha, Ellen!' she cried gaily, jumping up and running to my side. 'I shall have a pretty story to tell tonight: and so you've found me out. Have you ever been here in your life before?'

'Put that hat on, and home at once,' said I. 'I'm dreadfully grieved at you, Miss Cathy: you've done extremely wrong. It's no use pouting and crying: that won't repay the trouble I've had, scouring the country after you. To think how Mr Linton charged me to keep you in; and you stealing off so! it shows you are a cunning little fox, and nobody will put faith in you any more.'

'What have I done?' sobbed she, instantly checked. 'Papa charged me nothing: he'll not scold me, Ellen—he's never cross, like you!'

'Come, come!' I repeated. 'I'll tie the riband. Now, let us have no petulance. Oh, for shame! You thirteen years old, and such a baby!'

This exclamation was caused by her pushing the hat from her head, and retreating to the chimney out of my reach.

'Nay,' said the servant, 'don't be hard on the bonny lass, Mrs Dean. We made her stop: she'd fain have ridden forwards, afeard you should be uneasy. But Hareton offered to go with her, and I thought he should: it's a wild road over the hills.'

Hareton, during the discussion, stood with his hands in his pockets, too awkward to speak; though he looked as if he did not relish my intrusion.

'How long am I to wait?' I continued, disregarding the woman's interference. 'It will be dark in ten minutes. Where is the pony, Miss Cathy? And where is Phoenix? I shall leave you, unless you be quick; so please yourself.'

'The pony is in the yard,' she replied, 'and Phoenix is shut in there. He's bitten—and so is Charlie. I was going to tell you all about it; but you are in a bad temper, and don't deserve to hear.'

I picked up her hat, and approached to reinstate it; but perceiving that the people of the house took her part, she commenced capering round the room; and on my giving chase, ran like a mouse over and under and behind the furniture, rendering it ridiculous for me to pursue. Hareton and the woman laughed, and she joined them, and waxed more impertinent still; till I cried, in great irritation:

'Well, Miss Cathy, if you were aware whose house this is, you'd be glad enough to get out.'

'It's *your* father's, isn't it?' said she, turning to Hareton.

'Nay,' he replied, looking down, and blushing bashfully.

He could not stand a steady gaze from her eyes, though they were just his own.

'Whose then—your master's?' she asked.

He coloured deeper, with a different feeling, muttered an oath, and turned away.

'Who is his master?' continued the tiresome girl, appealing to me. 'He talked about "our house", and "our folk". I thought he had been the owner's son. And he never said, Miss; he should have done, shouldn't he, if he's a servant?'

Hareton grew black as a thunder cloud, at this childish speech. I silently shook my questioner, and at last succeeded in equipping her for departure.

'Now, get my horse,' she said, addressing her unknown kinsman as she would one of the stable-boys at the Grange. 'And you may come with me. I want to see where the goblin-hunter rises in the marsh, and to hear about the *fairishes,* as you call them: but make haste! What's the matter? Get my horse, I say.'

'I'll see thee damned before I be *thy* servant!' growled the lad.

'You'll see me *what?*' asked Catherine in surprise.

'Damned—thou saucy witch!' he replied.

'There, Miss Cathy! you see you have got into pretty company,' I interposed. 'Nice words to be used to a young lady! Pray don't begin to dispute with him. Come, let us seek for Minny ourselves, and begone.'

'But, Ellen,' cried she, staring, fixed in astonishment, 'how dare he speak so to me? Mustn't he be made to do as I ask him? You wicked creature, I shall tell papa what you said.—Now, then!'

Hareton did not appear to feel this threat; so the tears sprang into her eyes with indignation. 'You bring the pony,' she exclaimed, turning to the woman, 'and let my dog free this moment!'

'Softly, miss,' answered the addressed: 'you'll lose nothing by being civil. Though Mr Hareton, there, be not the master's son, he's your cousin; and I was never hired to serve you.'

'*He* my cousin!' cried Cathy, with a scornful laugh.

'Yes, indeed,' responded her reprover.

'Oh, Ellen! don't let them say such things,' she pursued, in great trouble. 'Papa is gone to fetch my cousin from London: my cousin is a gentleman's son. That my'—she stopped, and wept outright; upset at the bare notion of relationship with such a clown.

'Hush, hush!' I whispered, 'people can have many cousins, and of all sorts, Miss Cathy, without being any the worse for it; only they needn't keep their company, if they be disagreeable and bad.'

'He's not—he's not my cousin, Ellen!' she went on, gathering fresh grief from reflection, and flinging herself into my arms for refuge from the idea.

I was much vexed at her and the servant for their mutual revelations; having no doubt of Linton's approaching arrival, communicated by the former, being reported to Mr Heathcliff; and feeling as confident that Catherine's first thought on her father's return, would be to seek an explanation of the latter's assertion concerning her rude-bred kindred. Hareton, recovering from his disgust at being taken for a

servant, seemed moved by her distress; and, having fetched the pony round to the door, he took, to propitiate her, a fine crooked-legged terrier whelp from the kennel, and putting it into her hand bid her wisht! for he meant nought. Pausing in her lamentations, she surveyed him with a glance of awe and horror, then burst forth anew.

I could scarcely refrain from smiling at this antipathy to the poor fellow; who was a well-made, athletic youth, good-looking in features, and stout and healthy, but attired in garments befitting his daily occupations of working on the farm, and lounging among the moors after rabbits and game. Still, I thought I could detect in his physiognomy a mind owning better qualities than his father ever possessed. Good things lost amid a wilderness of weeds, to be sure, whose rankness far overtopped their neglected growth; yet, notwithstanding, evidence of a wealthy soil, that might yield luxuriant crops under other and favourable circumstances. Mr Heathcliff, I believe, had not treated him physically ill, thanks to his fearless nature, which offered no temptation to that course of oppression: it had none of the timid susceptibility that would have given zest to ill-treatment, in Heathcliff's judgment. He appeared to have bent his malevolence on making him a brute: he was never taught to read or write; never rebuked for any bad habit which did not annoy his keeper; never led a single step towards virtue, or guarded by a single precept against vice. And from what I heard, Joseph contributed much to his deterioration, by a narrow-minded partiality which prompted him to flatter and pet him, as a boy, because he was the head of the old family. And as he had been in the habit of accusing Catherine Earnshaw and Heathcliff, when children, of putting the master past his patience, and compelling him to seek solace in drink by what he termed their 'offalld ways', so at present he laid the whole burden of Hareton's faults on the shoulders of the usurper of his property. If the lad swore, he wouldn't correct him: nor however culpably he behaved. It gave Joseph satisfaction, apparently, to watch him go the worst lengths: he allowed that he was ruined: that his soul was abandoned to perdition; but then, he reflected that Heathcliff must answer for it. Hareton's blood would be required at his hands; and there lay immense consolation in that thought. Joseph had instilled into him a pride of name, and of his lineage; he would, had he dared, have fostered hate between him and the present owner of the Heights: but his dread of that owner amounted to superstition; and he confined his feelings regarding him to muttered innuendoes and private comminations. I don't pretend to be intimately acquainted with the mode of living customary in those days at Wuthering Heights: I only speak from hearsay; for I saw little. The villagers affirmed Mr Heathcliff was *near,* and a cruel hard landlord to his tenants; but the house, inside, had regained its ancient aspect of comfort under female management, and the scenes of riot common in Hindley's time were not now enacted within its walls. The master was too gloomy to seek companionship with any people, good or bad; and he is yet.

This, however, is not making progress with my story. Miss Cathy rejected the peace offering of the terrier, and demanded her own dogs, Charlie and Phoenix. They came limping, and hanging their heads; and we set out for home, sadly out of sorts, every one of us. I could not wring from my little lady how she had spent the day; except that, as I supposed, the goal of her pilgrimage was Penistone Crags; and she arrived without adventure to the gate of the farmhouse, when Hareton happened to issue forth, attended by some canine followers, who attacked her train. They had a smart battle, before their owners could separate them: that formed an introduction. Catherine told Hareton who she was, and where she was going; and asked him to show her the way: finally, beguiling him to accompany her. He opened the mysteries of the Fairy Cave, and twenty other queer places. But, being in disgrace, I was not favoured with a description of the interesting objects she saw. I could gather, however, that her guide had been a favourite till she hurt his feelings by addressing him as a servant; and Heathcliff's housekeeper hurt hers by calling

him her cousin. Then the language he had held to her rankled in her heart; she who was always 'love', and 'darling', and 'queen', and 'angel', with everybody at the Grange, to be insulted so shockingly by a stranger! She did not comprehend it; and hard work I had to obtain a promise that she would not lay the grievance before her father. I explained how he objected to the whole household at the Heights, and how sorry he would be to find she had been there; but I insisted most on the fact, that if she revealed my negligence of his orders, he would perhaps be so angry, that I should have to leave; and Cathy couldn't bear that prospect: she pledged her word, and kept it, for my sake. After all, she was a sweet little girl.

Chapter XIX

A LETTER, edged with black, announced the day of my master's return. Isabella was dead; and he wrote to bid me get mourning for his daughter, and arrange a room, and other accommodations, for his youthful nephew. Catherine ran wild with joy at the idea of welcoming her father back; and indulged most sanguine anticipations of the innumerable excellences of her 'real' cousin. The evening of their expected arrival came. Since early morning, she had been busy ordering her own small affairs; and now, attired in her new black frock—poor thing! her aunt's death impressed her with no definite sorrow—she obliged me, by constant worrying, to walk with her down through the grounds to meet them.

'Linton is just six months younger than I am,' she chattered, as we strolled leisurely over the swells and hollows of mossy turf, under shadow of the trees. 'How delightful it will be to have him for a playfellow! Aunt Isabella sent papa a beautiful lock of his hair; it was lighter than mine—more flaxen, and quite as fine. I have it carefully preserved in a little glass box: and I've often thought what pleasure it would be to see its owner. Oh! I am happy—and papa, dear, dear papa! Come, Ellen, let us run! come, run.'

She ran, and returned and ran again, many times before my sober footsteps reached the gate, and then she seated herself on the grassy bank beside the path, and tried to wait patiently; but that was impossible: she couldn't be still a minute.

'How long they are!' she exclaimed. 'Ah, I see some dust on the road—they are coming? No! When will they be here? May we not go a little way—half a mile, Ellen: only just half a mile? Do say yes: to that clump of birches at the turn!'

I refused staunchly. At length her suspense was ended: the travelling carriage rolled in sight. Miss Cathy shrieked and stretched out her arms, as soon as she caught her father's face looking from the window. He descended, nearly as eager as herself: and a considerable interval elapsed ere they had a thought to spare for any but themselves. While they exchanged caresses, I took a peep in to see after Linton. He was asleep in a corner, wrapped in a warm, fur-lined cloak, as if it had been winter. A pale, delicate, effeminate boy, who might have been taken for my master's younger brother, so strong was the resemblance: but there was a sickly peevishness in his aspect, that Edgar Linton never had. The latter saw me looking; and having shaken hands, advised me to close the door, and leave him undisturbed; for the journey had fatigued him. Cathy would fain have taken one glance, but her father told her to come on, and they walked together up the park, while I hastened before to prepare the servants.

'Now, darling,' said Mr Linton, addressing his daughter, as they halted at the bottom of the front steps; 'your cousin is not so strong or so merry as you are, and he has lost his mother, remember, a very short time since; therefore, don't expect him to play and run about with you directly. And don't harass him much by talking: let him be quiet this evening, at least, will you?'

'Yes, yes, papa,' answered Catherine: 'but I do want to see him; and he hasn't once looked out.'

The carriage stopped; and the sleeper being roused, was lifted to the ground by his uncle.

'This is your cousin Cathy, Linton,' he said, putting their little hands together. 'She's fond of you already; and mind you don't grieve her by crying tonight. Try to be cheerful now; the travelling is at an end, and you have nothing to do but rest and amuse yourself as you please.'

'Let me go to bed, then,' answered the boy, shrinking from Catherine's salute; and he put his fingers to his eyes to remove incipient tears.

'Come, come, there's a good child,' I whispered, leading him in. 'You'll make her weep too—see how sorry she is for you!'

I do not know whether it were sorrow for him, but his cousin put on as sad a countenance as himself, and returned to her father. All three entered, and mounted to the library, where tea was laid ready. I proceeded to remove Linton's cap and mantle, and placed him on a chair by the table; but he was no sooner seated than he began to cry afresh. My master inquired what was the matter.

'I can't sit on a chair,' sobbed the boy.

'Go to the sofa, then, and Ellen shall bring you some tea,' answered his uncle patiently.

He had been greatly tried during the journey, I felt convinced, by his fretful ailing charge. Linton slowly trailed himself off, and lay down. Cathy carried a footstool and her cup to his side. At first she sat silent; but that could not last: she had resolved to make a pet of her little cousin, as she would have him to be; and she commenced stroking his curls, and kissing his cheek, and offering him tea in her saucer, like a baby. This pleased him, for he was not much better: he dried his eyes, and lightened into a faint smile.

'Oh, he'll do very well,' said the master to me, after watching them a minute. 'Very well, if we can keep him, Ellen. The company of a child of his own age will instil new spirit into him soon, and by wishing for strength he'll gain it.'

'Ay, if we can keep him!' I mused to myself; and sore misgivings came over me that there was slight hope of that. And then, I thought, however will that weakling live at Wuthering Heights, between his father and Hareton, what playmates and instructors they'll be. Our doubts were presently decided—even earlier than I expected. I had just taken the children upstairs, after tea was finished, and seen Linton asleep—he would not suffer me to leave him till that was the case—I had come down, and was standing by the table in the hall, lighting a bedroom candle for Mr Edgar, when a maid stepped out of the kitchen and informed me that Mr Heathcliff's servant Joseph was at the door, and wished to speak with the master.

'I shall ask him what he wants first,' I said, in considerable trepidation. 'A very unlikely hour to be troubling people, and the instant they have returned from a long journey. I don't think the master can see him.'

Joseph had advanced through the kitchen as I uttered these words, and now presented himself in the hall. He was donned in his Sunday garments, with his most sanctimonious and sourest face, and, holding his hat in one hand and his stick in the other, he proceeded to clean his shoes on the mat.

'Good evening, Joseph,' I said coldly. 'What business brings you here tonight?'

'It's Maister Linton Aw mun spake tull,' he answered, waving me disdainfully aside.

'Mr Linton is going to bed; unless you have something particular to say, I'm sure he won't hear it now,' I continued. 'You had better sit down in there, and entrust your message to me.'

'Which is his rahm?' pursued the fellow, surveying the range of closed doors.

I perceived he was bent on refusing my mediation, so very reluctantly I went up to the library, and announced the unseasonable visitor, advising that he should be

dismissed till next day. Mr Linton had no time to empower me to do so, for Joseph mounted close at my heels, and, pushing into the apartment, planted himself at the far side of the table, with his two fists clapped on the head of his stick, and began in an elevated tone, as if anticipating opposition:

'Hathecliff has send me for his lad, and Aw munn't goa back 'bout him.'

Edgar Linton was silent a minute; an expression of exceeding sorrow overcast his features: he would have pitied the child on his own account; but, recalling Isabella's hopes and fears, and anxious wishes for her son, and her commendations of him to his care, he grieved bitterly at the prospect of yielding him up, and searched in his heart how it might be avoided. No plan offered itself: the very exhibition of any desire to keep him would have rendered the claimant more peremptory: there was nothing left but to resign him. However, he was not going to rouse him from his sleep.

'Tell Mr Heathcliff,' he answered calmly, 'that his son shall come to Wuthering Heights tomorrow. He is in bed, and too tired to go the distance now. You may also tell him that the mother of Linton desired him to remain under my guardianship; and, at present, his health is very precarious.'

'Noa!' said Joseph, giving a thud with his prop on the floor, and assuming an authoritative air; 'noa! that manes nowt. Hathecliff maks noa 'cahnt uh t' mother, nur yah norther; bud he'll hev his lad; und Aw mun tak him—soa nah yah knaw!'

'You shall not tonight!' answered Linton decisively. 'Walk downstairs at once, and repeat to your master what I have said. Ellen, show him down. Go——'

And, aiding the indignant elder with a lift by the arm, he rid the room of him, and closed the door.

'Varrah weell!' shouted Joseph, as he slowly drew off. 'Tuh-morn, he's come hisseln, un thrust *him* aht, if yah darr!'

Chapter XX

To obviate the danger of this threat being fulfilled, Mr Linton commissioned me to take the boy home early, on Catherine's pony; and, said he: 'As we shall now have no influence over his destiny, good or bad, you must say nothing of where he is gone, to my daughter: she cannot associate with him hereafter, and it is better for her to remain in ignorance of his proximity; lest she should be restless, and anxious to visit the Heights. Merely tell her his father sent for him suddenly, and he has been obliged to leave us.'

Linton was very reluctant to be roused from his bed at five o'clock, and astonished to be informed that he must prepare for further travelling; but I softened off the matter by stating that he was going to spend some time with his father, Mr Heathcliff, who wished to see him so much, he did not like to defer the pleasure till he should recover from his late journey.

'My father!' he cried, in strange perplexity. 'Mamma never told me I had a father. Where does he live? I'd rather stay with uncle.'

'He lives a little distance from the Grange,' I replied; 'just beyond those hills: not so far, but you may walk over here when you get hearty. And you should be glad to go home, and to see him. You must try to love him, as you did your mother, and then he will love you.'

'But why have I not heard of him before?' asked Linton, 'Why didn't mamma and he live together, as other people do?'

'He had business to keep him in the north,' I answered, 'and your mother's health required her to reside in the south.'

'And why didn't mamma speak to me about him?' persevered the child. 'She often talked of uncle, and I learnt to love him long ago. How am I to love papa? I don't know him.'

'Oh, all children love their parents,' I said. 'Your mother, perhaps, thought you would want to be with him if she mentioned him often to you. Let us make haste. An early ride on such a beautiful morning is much preferable to an hour's more sleep.'

'Is *she* to go with us,' he demanded: 'the little girl I saw yesterday?'

'Not now,' replied I.

'Is uncle?' he continued.

'No, I shall be your companion there,' I said.

Linton sank back on his pillow and fell into a brown study.

'I won't go without uncle,' he cried at length: 'I can't tell where you mean to take me.'

I attempted to persuade him of the naughtiness of showing reluctance to meet his father; still he obstinately resisted any progress towards dressing, and I had to call for my master's assistance in coaxing him out of bed. The poor thing was finally got off, with several delusive assurances that his absence should be short; that Mr Edgar and Cathy would visit him, and other promises, equally ill-founded, which I invented and reiterated at intervals throughout the way. The pure heather-scented air, and the bright sunshine, and the gentle canter of Minny, relieved his despondency after a while. He began to put questions concerning his new home, and its inhabitants, with greater interest and liveliness.

'Is Wuthering Heights as pleasant a place as Thrushcross Grange?' he inquired, turning to take a last glance into the valley, whence a light mist mounted and formed a fleecy cloud on the skirts of the blue.

'It is not so buried in trees,' I replied, 'and it is not quite so large, but you can see the country beautifully all round; and the air is healthier for you—fresher and dryer. You will, perhaps, think the building old and dark at first; though it is a respectable house: the next best in the neighbourhood. And you will have such nice rambles on the moors. Hareton Earnshaw—that is Miss Cathy's other cousin, and so yours in a manner—will show you all the sweetest spots; and you can bring a book in fine weather, and make a green hollow your study; and, now and then, your uncle may join you in a walk: he does, frequently, walk out on the hills.'

'And what is my father like?' he asked. 'Is he as young and handsome as uncle?'

'He's as young,' said I; 'but he has black hair and eyes, and looks sterner; and he is taller and bigger altogether. He'll not seem to you so gentle and kind at first, perhaps, because it is not his way: still, mind you, be frank and cordial with him; and naturally he'll be fonder of you than any uncle, for you are his own.'

'Black hair and eyes!' mused Linton. 'I can't fancy him. Then I am not like him, am I?'

'Not much,' I answered: not a morsel, I thought, surveying with regret the white complexion and slim frame of my companion, and his large languid eyes—his mother's eyes, save that, unless a morbid touchiness kindled them a moment, they had not a vestige of her sparkling spirit.

'How strange that he should never come to see mamma and me!' he murmured. 'Has he ever seen me? If he have, I must have been a baby. I remember not a single thing about him!'

'Why, Master Linton,' said I, 'three hundred miles is a great distance; and ten years seem very different in length to a grown-up person compared with what they do to you. It is probable Mr Heathcliff proposed going from summer to summer, but never found a convenient opportunity; and now it is too late. Don't trouble him with questions on the subject: it will disturb him, for no good.'

The boy was fully occupied with his own cogitations for the remainder of the ride, till we halted before the farmhouse garden gate. I watched to catch his impressions

in his countenance. He surveyed the carved front and low-browed lattices, the straggling gooseberry bushes and crooked firs, with solemn intentness, and then shook his head: his private feelings entirely disapproved of the exterior of his new abode. But he had sense to postpone complaining: there might be compensation within. Before he dismounted, I went and opened the door. It was half past six; the family had just finished breakfast; the servant was clearing and wiping down the table. Joseph stood by his master's chair telling some tale concerning a lame horse; and Hareton was preparing for the hay field.

'Hallo, Nelly!' cried Mr Heathcliff, when he saw me. 'I feared I should have to come down and fetch my property myself. You've brought it, have you? Let us see what we can make of it.'

He got up and strode to the door. Hareton and Joseph followed in gaping curiosity. Poor Linton ran a frightened eye over the faces of the three.

'Sure-ly,' said Joseph, after a grave inspection, 'he's swopped wi' ye, maister, an' yon's his lass!'

Heathcliff, having stared his son into an ague of confusion, uttered a scornful laugh.

'God! what a beauty! what a lovely, charming thing!' he exclaimed. 'Haven't they reared it on snails and sour milk, Nelly? Oh, damn my soul! but that's worse than I expected—and the devil knows I was not sanguine!'

I bid the trembling and bewildered child get down, and enter. He did not thoroughly comprehend the meaning of his father's speech, or whether it were intended for him: indeed, he was not yet certain that the grim, sneering stranger was his father. But he clung to me with growing trepidation; and on Mr Heathcliff's taking a seat and bidding him 'come hither', he hid his face on my shoulder and wept.

'Tut, tut!' said Heathcliff, stretching out a hand and dragging him roughly between his knees, and then holding up his head by the chin. 'None of that nonsense! We're not going to hurt thee, Linton—isn't that thy name? Thou art thy mother's child, entirely! Where is *my* share in thee, puling chicken?'

He took off the boy's cap and pushed back his thick flaxen curls, felt his slender arms and his small fingers; during which examination, Linton ceased crying, and lifted his great blue eyes to inspect the inspector.

'Do you know me?' asked Heathcliff, having satisfied himself that the limbs were all equally frail and feeble.

'No,' said Linton, with a gaze of vacant fear.

'You've heard of me, I dare say?'

'No,' he replied again.

'No? What a shame of your mother, never to waken your filial regard for me! You are my son, then, I'll tell you; and your mother was a wicked slut to leave you in ignorance of the sort of father you possessed. Now, don't wince, and colour up! Though it *is* something to see you have not white blood. Be a good lad; and I'll do for you. Nelly, if you be tired you may sit down; if not, get home again. I guess you'll report what you hear and see to the cipher at the Grange; and this thing won't be settled while you linger about it.'

'Well,' replied I, 'I hope you'll be kind to the boy, Mr Heathcliff, or you'll not keep him long; and he's all you have akin in the wide world, that you will ever know—remember.'

'I'll be *very* kind to him, you needn't fear,' he said, laughing. 'Only nobody else must be kind to him: I'm jealous of monopolizing his affection. And, to begin my kindness, Joseph, bring the lad some breakfast. Hareton, you infernal calf, begone to your work. Yes, Nell,' he added, when they had departed, 'my son is prospective owner of your place, and I should not wish him to die till I was certain of being his successor. Besides, he's *mine*, and I want the triumph of seeing *my* descendant fairly lord of their estates: my child hiring their children to till their father's lands for wages. That is the sole consideration which can make me endure

the whelp: I despise him for himself, and hate him for the memories he revives! But that consideration is sufficient: he's as safe with me, and shall be tended as carefully as your master tends his own. I have a room upstairs, furnished for him in handsome style: I've engaged a tutor, also, to come three times a week, from twenty miles distance, to teach him what he pleases to learn. I've ordered Hareton to obey him; and in fact I've arranged everything with a view to preserve the superior and the gentleman in him, above his associates. I do regret, however, that he so little deserves the trouble; if I wished any blessing in the world, it was to find him a worthy object of pride; and I'm bitterly disappointed with the whey-faced whining wretch!'

While he was speaking, Joseph returned bearing a basin of milk porridge, and placed it before Linton. He stirred round the homely mess with a look of aversion, and affirmed he could not eat it. I saw the old manservant shared largely in his master's scorn of the child; though he was compelled to retain the sentiment in his heart, because Heathcliff plainly meant his underlings to hold him in honour.

'Cannot ate it?' repeated he, peering in Linton's face, and subduing his voice to a whisper, for fear of being overheard. 'But Maister Hareton nivir ate naught else, when he wer a little un; and what were gooid eneugh for him's gooid eneugh for ye, Aw's rayther think!'

'I *shan't* eat it!' answered Linton snappishly. 'Take it away.'

Joseph snatched up the food indignantly, and brought it to us.

'Is there aught ails th' yictuals?' he asked thrusting the tray under Heathcliff's nose.

'What should ail them?' he said.

'Wah!' answered Joseph, 'yon dainty chap says he cannut ate 'em. But Aw guess it's raight! His mother wer just soa—we wer a'most too mucky to sow t' corn for makking her breead.' ◆

'Don't mention his mother to me,' said the master angrily. 'Get him something that he can eat, that's all. What is his usual food, Nelly?'

I suggested boiled milk or tea; and the housekeeper received instructions to prepare some. Come, I reflected, his father's selfishness may contribute to his comfort. He perceives his delicate constitution, and the necessity of treating him tolerably. I'll console Mr Edgar by acquainting him with the turn Heathcliff's humour has taken. Having no excuse for lingering longer I slipped out, while Linton was engaged in timidly rebuilding the advances of a friendly sheepdog. But he was too much on the alert to be cheated: as I closed the door, I heard a cry, and a frantic repetition of the words:

'Don't leave me! I'll not stay here! I'll not stay here!'

Then the latch was raised and fell: they did not suffer him to come forth. I mounted Minny, and urged her to a trot; and so my brief guardianship ended.

Chapter XXI

WE had sad work with little Cathy that day; she rose in high glee, eager to join her cousin, and such passionate tears and lamentations followed the news of his departure, that Edgar himself was obliged to soothe her, by affirming he should come back soon: he added, however, 'if I can get him'; and there were no hopes of that. This promise poorly pacified her: but time was more potent; and though still at intervals she inquired of her father when Linton would return, before she did see him again his features had waxed so dim in her memory that she did not recognize him.

When I chanced to encounter the housekeeper of Wuthering Heights in paying business visits to Gimmerton, I used to ask how the young master got on; for he lived almost as secluded as Catherine herself, and was never to be seen. I could gather from her that he continued in weak health, and was a tiresome inmate. She said Mr Heathcliff seemed to dislike him ever longer and worse, though he took some trouble to conceal it: he had an antipathy to the sound of his voice, and could not do at all with his sitting in the same room with him many minutes together. There seldom passed much talk between them: Linton learnt his lessons and spent his evenings in a small apartment they called the parlour: or else lay in bed all day: for he was constantly getting coughs, and colds, and aches, and pains of some sort.

'And I never knew such a faint-hearted creature,' added the woman; 'nor one so careful of hisseln. He *will* go on, if I leave the window open a bit late in the evening. Oh! it's killing! a breath of night air! And he must have a fire in the middle of summer; and Joseph's bacca pipe is poison; and he must always have sweets and dainties, and always milk, milk for ever—heeding naught how the rest of us are pinched in winter; and there he'll sit, wrapped in his furred cloak in his chair by the fire, some toast and water or other slop on the hob to sip at; and if Hareton, for pity, comes to amuse him—Hareton is not bad-natured, though he's rough—they're sure to part, one swearing and the other crying. I believe the master would relish Earnshaw's thrashing him to a mummy, if he were not his son; and I'm certain he would be fit to turn him out of doors, if he knew half the nursing he gives hisseln. But then, he won't go into danger of temptation: he never enters the parlour, and should Linton show those ways in the house where he is, he sends him upstairs directly.'

I divined, from this account, that utter lack of sympathy had rendered young Heathcliff selfish and disagreeable, if he were not so originally; and my interest in him, consequently, decayed: though still I was moved with a sense of grief at his lot, and a wish that he had been left with us. Mr Edgar encouraged me to gain information: he thought a great deal about him, I fancy, and would have run some risk to see him; and he told me once to ask the housekeeper whether he ever came into the village? She said he had only been twice, on horseback, accompanying his father, and both times he pretended to be quite knocked up for three or four days afterwards. The housekeeper left, if I recollect rightly, two years after he came; and another, whom I did not know, was her successor: she lives there still.

Time wore on at the Grange in its former pleasant way, till Miss Cathy reached sixteen. On the anniversary of her birth we never manifested any signs of rejoicing, because it was also the anniversary of my late mistress's death. Her father invariably spent that day alone in the library; and walked, at dusk, as far as Gimmerton kirkyard, where he would frequently prolong his stay beyond midnight. Therefore Catherine was thrown on her own resources for amusement. This 20th of March was a beautiful spring day, and when her father had retired, my young lady came down dressed for going out, and said she had asked to have a ramble on the edge of the moors with me; and Mr Linton had given her leave, if we went only a short distance and were back within the hour.

'So make haste, Ellen!' she cried. 'I know where I wish to go; where a colony of moor game are settled: I want to see whether they have made their nests yet.'

'That must be a good distance up,' I answered; 'they don't breed on the edge of the moor.'

'No, it's not,' she said. 'I've gone very near with papa.'

I put on my bonnet and sallied out, thinking nothing more of the matter. She bounded before me, and returned to my side, and was off again like a young greyhound; and, at first, I found plenty of entertainment in listening to the larks singing far and near, and enjoying the sweet, warm sunshine; and watching her, my pet, and my delight, with her golden ringlets flying loose behind, and her bright cheek, as soft and pure in its bloom as a wild rose, and her eyes radiant with

cloudless pleasure. She was a happy creature, and an angel, in those days. It's a pity she could not be content.

'Well,' said I, 'where are your moor game, Miss Cathy? We should be at them: the Grange park fence is a great way off now.'

'Oh, a little farther—only a little farther, Ellen,' was her answer continually. 'Climb to that hillock, pass that bank, and by the time you reach the other side I shall have raised the birds.'

But there were so many hillocks and banks to climb and pass, that, at length, I began to be weary, and told her we must halt, and retrace our steps. I shouted to her, as she had outstripped me a long way; she either did not hear or did not regard, for she still sprang on, and I was compelled to follow. Finally, she dived into a hollow; and before I came in sight of her again, she was two miles nearer Wuthering Heights than her own home; and I beheld a couple of persons arrest her, one of whom I felt convinced was Mr Heathcliff himself.

Cathy had been caught in the fact of plundering, or, at least, hunting out the nests of the grouse. The Heights were Heathcliff's land, and he was reproving the poacher.

'I've neither taken any nor found any,' she said, as I toiled to them, expanding her hands in corroboration of the statement. 'I didn't mean to take them; but papa told me there were quantities up here, and I wished to see the eggs.'

Heathcliff glanced at me with an ill-meaning smile, expressing his acquaintance with the party, and, consequently, his malevolence towards it, and demanded who 'papa' was?

'Mr Linton of Thrushcross Grange,' she replied. 'I thought you did not know me, or you wouldn't have spoken in that way.'

'You suppose papa is highly esteemed and respected then?' he said sarcastically.

'And what are you?' inquired Catherine, gazing curiously on the speaker. 'That man I've seen before. Is he your son?'

She pointed to Hareton, the other individual, who had gained nothing but increased bulk and strength by the addition of two years to his age: he seemed as awkward and rough as ever.

'Miss Cathy,' I interrupted, 'it will be three hours instead of one that we are out, presently. We really must go back.'

'No, that man is not my son,' answered Heathcliff, pushing me aside. 'But I have one, and you have seen him before too; and, though your nurse is in a hurry, I think both you and she would be the better for a little rest. Will you just turn this nab of heath, and walk into my house? You'll get home earlier for the ease; and you shall receive a kind welcome.'

I whispered Catherine that she mustn't, on any account, accede to the proposal: it was entirely out of the question.

'Why?' she asked, aloud. 'I'm tired of running, and the ground is dewy: I can't sit here. Let us go, Ellen. Besides, he says I have seen his son. He's mistaken, I think; but I guess where he lives: at the farmhouse I visited in coming from Penistone Crags. Don't you?'

'I do. Come, Nelly, hold your tongue—it will be a treat for her to look in on us. Hareton, get forwards with the lass. You shall walk with me, Nelly.'

'No, she's not going to any such place,' I cried, struggling to release my arm, which he had seized: but she was almost at the doorstones already, scampering round the brow at full speed. Her appointed companion did not pretend to escort her: he shied off by the roadside, and vanished.

'Mr Heathcliff, it's very wrong,' I continued: 'you know you mean no good. And there she'll see Linton, and all will be told as soon as ever we return; and I shall have the blame.'

'I want her to see Linton,' he answered; 'he's looking better these few days: it's not often he's fit to be seen. And we'll soon persuade her to keep the visit secret: where is the harm of it?'

'The harm of it is, that her father would hate me if he found I suffered her to enter your house; and I am convinced you have a bad design in encouraging her to do so,' I replied.

'My design is as honest as possible. I'll inform you of its whole scope,' he said. 'That the two cousins may fall in love, and get married. I'm acting generously to your master: his young chit has no expectations, and should she second my wishes, she'll be provided for at once as joint successor with Linton.'

'If Linton died,' I answered, 'and his life is quite uncertain, Catherine would be the heir.'

'No, she would not,' he said. 'There is no clause in the will to secure it so: his property would go to me; but, to prevent disputes, I desire their union, and am resolved to bring it about.'

'And I'm resolved she shall never approach your house with me again,' I returned, as we reached the gate, where Miss Cathy waited our coming.

Heathcliff bid me be quiet; and, preceding us up the path, hastened to open the door. My young lady gave him several looks, as if she could not exactly make up her mind what to think of him; but now he smiled when he met her eye, and softened his voice in addressing her; and I was foolish enough to imagine the memory of her mother might disarm him from desiring her injury. Linton stood on the hearth. He had been out walking in the fields, for his cap was on, and he was calling to Joseph to bring him dry shoes. He had grown tall of his age, still wanting some months of sixteen. His features were pretty yet, and his eye and complexion brighter than I remembered them, though with merely temporary lustre borrowed from the salubrious air and genial sun.

'Now, who is that?' asked Mr Heathcliff, turning to Cathy. 'Can you tell?'

'Your son?' she said, having doubtfully surveyed, first one and then the other.

'Yes, yes,' answered he: 'but is this the only time you have beheld him? Think! Ah! you have a short memory. Linton, don't you recall your cousin, that you used to tease us so with wishing to see?'

'What, Linton!' cried Cathy, kindling into joyful surprise at the name. 'Is that little Linton? He's taller than I am! Are you, Linton?'

The youth stepped forward, and acknowledged himself: she kissed him fervently, and they gazed with wonder at the change time had wrought in the appearance of each. Catherine had reached her full height; her figure was both plump and slender, elastic as steel, and her whole aspect sparkling with health and spirits. Linton's looks and movements were very languid, and his form extremely slight; but there was a grace in his manner that mitigated these defects, and rendered him not unpleasing. After exchanging numerous marks of fondness with him, his cousin went to Mr Heathcliff, who lingered by the door, dividing his attention between the objects inside and those that lay without: pretending, that is, to observe the latter, and really noting the former alone.

'And you are my uncle, then!' she cried, reaching up to salute him. 'I thought I liked you, though you were cross at first. Why don't you visit at the Grange with Linton? To live all these years such close neighbours, and never see us, is odd: what have you done so for?'

'I visited it once or twice too often before you were born,' he answered. 'There— damn it! If you have any kisses to spare, give them to Linton: they are thrown away on me.'

'Naughty Ellen!' exclaimed Catherine, flying to attack me next with her lavish caresses. 'Wicked Ellen! to try to hinder me from entering. But I'll take this walk every morning in future: may I, uncle? and sometimes bring papa. Won't you be glad to see us?'

'Of course!' replied the uncle, with a hardly suppressed grimace, resulting from his deep aversion to both the proposed visitors. 'But stay,' he continued, turning towards the young lady. 'Now I think of it, I'd better tell you. Mr Linton has a prejudice against me: we quarrelled at one time of our lives, with unchristian ferocity; and, if you mention coming here to him, he'll put a veto on your visits altogether. Therefore, you must not mention it, unless you be careless of seeing your cousin hereafter: you may come, if you will, but you must not mention it.'

'Why did you quarrel?' asked Catherine, considerably crestfallen.

'He thought me too poor to wed his sister,' answered Heathcliff, 'and was grieved that I got her: his pride was hurt, and he'll never forgive it.'

'That's wrong!' said the young lady: 'some time, I'll tell him so. But Linton and I have no share in your quarrel. I'll not come here, then; he shall come to the Grange.'

'It will be too far for me,' murmured her cousin: 'to walk four miles would kill me. No, come here, Miss Catherine, now and then: not every morning, but once or twice a week.'

The father launched towards his son a glance of bitter contempt.

'I am afraid, Nelly, I shall lose my labour,' he muttered to me. 'Miss Catherine, as the ninny calls her, will discover his value, and send him to the devil. Now, if it had been Hareton!—Do you know that, twenty times a day, I covet Hareton, with all his degradation? I'd have loved the lad had he been someone else. But I think he's safe from *her* love. I'll pit him against that paltry creature, unless it bestir itself briskly. We calculate it will scarcely last till it is eighteen. Oh, confound the vapid thing! He's absorbed in drying his feet, and never looks at her.—Linton!'

'Yes, father,' answered the boy.

'Have you nothing to show your cousin anywhere about? not even a rabbit or a weasel's nest? Take her into the garden, before you change your shoes; and into the stable to see your horse.'

'Wouldn't you rather sit here?' asked Linton, addressing Cathy in a tone which expressed reluctance to move again.

'I don't know,' she replied, casting a longing look to the door, and evidently eager to be active.

He kept his seat, and shrank closer to the fire. Heathcliff rose, and went into the kitchen, and from thence to the yard, calling out for Hareton. Hareton responded, and presently the two re-entered. The young man had been washing himself, as was visible by the glow on his cheeks and his wetted hair.

'Oh, I'll ask *you,* uncle,' cried Miss Cathy, recollecting the housekeeper's assertion. 'That is not my cousin, is he?'

'Yes,' he replied, 'your mother's nephew. Don't you like him?'

Catherine looked queer.

'Is he not a handsome lad?' he continued.

The uncivil little thing stood on tiptoe, and whispered a sentence in Heathcliff's ear. He laughed; Hareton darkened: I perceived he was very sensitive to suspected slights, and had obviously a dim notion of his inferiority. But his master or guardian chased the frown by exclaiming:

'You'll be the favourite among us, Hareton! She says you are a—What was it? Well, something very flattering. Here! you go with her round the farm. And behave like a gentleman, mind! Don't use any bad words; and don't stare when the young lady is not looking at you, and be ready to hide your face when she is; and, when you speak, say your words slowly, and keep your hands out of your pockets. Be off, and entertain her as nicely as you can.'

He watched the couple walking past the window. Earnshaw had his countenance completely averted from his companion. He seemed studying the familiar landscape with a stranger's and an artist's interest. Catherine took a sly look at him, expressing

small admiration. She then turned her attention to seeking out objects of amusement for herself, and tripped merrily on, lilting a tune to supply the lack of conversation.

'I've tied his tongue,' observed Heathcliff. 'He'll not venture a single syllable, all the time! Nelly, you recollect me at his age—nay, some years younger. Did I ever look so stupid: so "gaumless", as Joseph calls it?'

'Worse,' I replied, 'because more sullen with it.'

'I've a pleasure in him,' he continued, reflecting aloud. 'He has satisfied my expectations. If he were a born fool I should not enjoy it half so much. But he's no fool; and I can sympathize with all his feelings, having felt them myself. I know what he suffers now, for instance, exactly: it is merely a beginning of what he shall suffer, though. And he'll never be able to emerge from his bathos of coarseness and ignorance. I've got him faster than his scoundrel of a father secured me, and lower; for he takes a pride in his brutishness. I've taught him to scorn everything extra-animal as silly and weak. Don't you think Hindley would be proud of his son, if he could see him? almost as proud as I am of mine. But there's this difference; one is gold put to the use of paving-stones, and the other is tin polished to ape a service of silver. *Mine* has nothing valuable about it; yet I shall have the merit of making it go as far as such poor stuff can go. *His* had first-rate qualities, and they are lost: rendered worse than unavailing. I have nothing to regret; he would have more than any but I are aware of. And the best of it is, Hareton is damnably fond of me! You'll own that I've outmatched Hindley there. If the dead villain could rise from his grave to abuse me for his offspring's wrongs, I should have the fun of seeing the said offspring fight him back again, indignant that he should dare to rail at the one friend he has in the world!'

Heathcliff chuckled a fiendish laugh at the idea. I made no reply, because I saw that he expected none. Meantime, our young companion, who sat too removed from us to hear what was said, began to evince symptoms of uneasiness, probably repenting that he had denied himself the treat of Catherine's society for fear of a little fatigue. His father remarked the restless glances wandering to the window, and the hand irresolutely extended towards his cap.

'Get up, you idle boy!' he exclaimed, with assumed heartiness. 'Away after them! they are just at the corner, by the stand of hives.'

Linton gathered his energies, and left the hearth. The lattice was open, and, as he stepped out, I heard Cathy inquiring of her unsociable attendant, what was that inscription over the door? Hareton stared up, and scratched his head like a true clown.

'It's some damnable writing,' he answered. 'I cannot read it.'

'Can't read it?' cried Catherine; 'I can read it: it's English. But I want to know why it is there.'

Linton giggled: the first appearance of mirth he had exhibited.

'He does not know his letters,' he said to his cousin. 'Could you believe in the existence of such a colossal dunce?'

'Is he all as he should be?' asked Miss Cathy seriously; 'or is he simple: not right? I've questioned him twice now, and each time he looked so stupid I think he does not understand me. I can hardly understand *him*, I'm sure!'

Linton repeated his laugh, and glanced at Hareton tauntingly; who certainly did not seem quite clear of comprehension at that moment.

'There's nothing the matter but laziness; is there, Earnshaw?' he said. 'My cousin fancies you are an idiot. There you experience the consequence of scorning "book-larning", as you would say. Have you noticed, Catherine, his frightful Yorkshire pronunciation?'

'Why, where the devil is the use on't?' growled Hareton, more ready in answering his daily companion. He was about to enlarge further, but the two youngsters broke into a noisy fit of merriment; my giddy miss being delighted to discover that she might turn his strange talk to matter of amusement.

'Where is the use of the devil in that sentence?' tittered Linton. 'Papa told you not to say any bad words, and you can't open your mouth without one. Do try to behave like a gentleman, now do!'

'If thou weren't more a lass than a lad, I'd fell thee this minute, I would; pitiful lath of a crater!' retorted the angry boor, retreating, while his face burnt with mingled rage and mortification; for he was conscious of being insulted, and embarrassed how to resent it.

Mr Heathcliff having overheard the conversation, as well as I, smiled when he saw him go; but immediately afterwards cast a look of singular aversion on the flippant pair, who remained chattering in the doorway: the boy finding animation enough while discussing Hareton's faults and deficiencies, and relating anecdotes of his goings-on; and the girl relishing his pert and spiteful sayings, without considering the ill nature they evinced: but I began to dislike, more than to compassionate Linton, and to excuse his father, in some measure, for holding him cheap.

We stayed till afternoon: I could not tear Miss Cathy away, before; but happily my master had not quitted his apartment, and remained ignorant of our prolonged absence. As we walked home, I would fain have enlightened my charge on the characters of the people we had quitted; but she got it into her head that I was prejudiced against them.

'Aha!' she cried, 'you take papa's side, Ellen: you are partial, I know; or else you wouldn't have cheated me so many years into the notion that Linton lived a long way from here. I'm really extremely angry; only I'm so pleased I can't show it! But you must hold your tongue about my uncle; he's *my* uncle, remember; and I'll scold papa for quarrelling with him.'

And so she ran on, till I dropped endeavouring to convince her of her mistake. She did not mention the visit that night, because she did not see Mr Linton. Next day it all came out, sadly to my chagrin; and still I was not altogether sorry: I thought the burden of directing and warning would be more efficiently borne by him than me. But he was too timid in giving satisfactory reasons for his wish that she should shun connection with the household of the Heights, and Catherine liked good reasons for every restraint that harassed her petted will.

'Papa!' she exclaimed, after the morning's salutations, 'guess whom I saw yesterday, in my walk on the moors. Ah, papa, you started! you've not done right, have you, now? I saw—But listen, and you shall hear how I found you out; and Ellen, who is in league with you, and yet pretended to pity me so, when I kept hoping, and was always disappointed about Linton's coming back!'

She gave a faithful account of her excursion and its consequences; and my master, though he cast more than one reproachful look at me, said nothing till she had concluded. Then he drew her to him, and asked if she knew why he had concealed Linton's near neighbourhood from her. Could she think it was to deny her a pleasure that she might harmlessly enjoy?

'It was because you disliked Mr Heathcliff,' she answered.

'Then you believe I care more for my own feelings than yours, Cathy?' he said. 'No, it was not because I disliked Mr Heathcliff, but because Mr Heathcliff dislikes me; and is a most diabolical man, delighting to wrong and ruin those he hates, if they give him the slightest opportunity. I knew that you could not keep up an acquaintance with your cousin, without being brought into contact with him; and I knew he would detest you on my account; so for your own good, and nothing else, I took precautions that you should not see Linton again. I meant to explain this some time as you grew older, and I'm sorry I delayed it.'

'But Mr Heathcliff was quite cordial, papa,' observed Catherine, not at all convinced; 'and *he* didn't object to our seeing each other: he said I might come to his house when I pleased; only I must not tell you, because you had quarrelled with him, and would not forgive him for marrying aunt Isabella. And you won't. *You*

are the one to be blamed: he is willing to let *us* be friends, at least; Linton and I; and you are not.'

My master, perceiving that she would not take his word for her uncle-in-law's evil disposition, gave a hasty sketch of his conduct to Isabella, and the manner in which Wuthering Heights became his property. He could not bear to discourse long upon the topic; for though he spoke little of it, he still felt the same horror and detestation of his ancient enemy that had occupied his heart ever since Mrs Linton's death. 'She might have been living yet, if it had not been for him!' was his constant bitter reflection; and, in his eyes, Heathcliff seemed a murderer. Miss Cathy— conversant with no bad deeds except her own slight acts of disobedience, injustice, and passion, rising from hot temper and thoughtlessness, and repented of on the day they were committed—was amazed at the blackness of spirit that could brood on and cover revenge for years, and deliberately prosecute its plans without a visitation of remorse. She appeared so deeply impressed and shocked at this new view of human nature—excluded from all her studies and all her ideas till now— that Mr Edgar deemed it unnecessary to pursue the subject. He merely added:

'You will know hereafter, darling, why I wish you to avoid his house and family; now return to your old employments and amusements, and think no more about them.'

Catherine kissed her father and sat down quietly to her lessons for a couple of hours, according to custom; then she accompanied him into the grounds, and the whole day passed as usual: but in the evening, when she had retired to her room, and I went to help her to undress, I found her crying, on her knees by the bedside.

'Oh, fie, silly child!' I exclaimed. 'If you had any real griefs, you'd be ashamed to waste a tear on this little contrariety. You never had one shadow of substantial sorrow, Miss Catherine. Suppose, for a minute, that master and I were dead, and you were by yourself in the world: how would you feel then? Compare the present occasion with such an affliction as that, and be thankful for the friends you have, instead of coveting more.'

'I'm not crying for myself, Ellen,' she answered, 'it's for him. He expected to see me again tomorrow, and there he'll be so disappointed: and he'll wait for me, and I shan't come!'

'Nonsense,' said I, 'do you imagine he has thought as much of you as you have of him? Hasn't he Hareton for a companion? Not one in a hundred would weep at losing a relation they had just seen twice, for two afternoons. Linton will conjecture how it is, and trouble himself no further about you.'

'But may I not write a note to tell him why I cannot come?' she asked, rising to her feet. 'And just send those books I promised to lend him? His books are not as nice as mine, and he wanted to have them extremely, when I told him how interesting they were. May I not, Ellen?'

'No, indeed! no, indeed!' replied I, with decision. 'Then he would write to you, and there'd never be an end of it. No, Miss Catherine, the acquaintance must be dropped entirely: so papa expects, and I shall see that it is done.'

'But how can one little note——' she recommenced, putting on an imploring countenance.

'Silence!' I interrupted. 'We'll not begin with your little notes. Get into bed.'

She threw at me a very naughty look, so naughty that I would not kiss her good night at first: I covered her up, and shut her door, in great displeasure; but, repenting half way, I returned softly, and lo! there was miss standing at the table with a bit of blank paper before her and a pencil in her hand, which she guiltily slipped out of sight, on my entrance.

'You'll get nobody to take that, Catherine,' I said, 'if you write it; and at present I shall put out your candle.'

I set the extinguisher on the flame, receiving as I did so a slap on my hand, and petulant 'Cross thing!' I then quitted her again, and she drew the bolt in one of her

worst, most peevish humours. The letter was finished and forwarded to its destination by a milk-fetcher who came from the village: but that I didn't learn till some time afterwards. Weeks passed on, and Cathy recovered her temper; though she grew wondrous fond of stealing off to corners by herself; and often, if I came near her suddenly while reading, she would start and bend over the book, evidently desirous to hide it; and I detected edges of loose paper sticking out beyond the leaves. She also got a trick of coming down early in the morning and lingering about the kitchen, as if she were expecting the arrival of something: and she had a small drawer in a cabinet in the library, which she would trifle over for hours, and whose key she took special care to remove when she left it.

One day, as she inspected this drawer, I observed that the playthings, and trinkets which recently formed its contents, were transmuted into bits of folded paper. My curiosity and suspicions were aroused; I determined to take a peep at her mysterious treasures; so, at night, as soon as she and my master were safe upstairs, I searched and readily found among my house keys one that would fit the lock. Having opened, I emptied the whole contents into my apron, and took them with me to examine at leisure in my own chamber. Though I could not but suspect, I was still surprised to discover that they were a mass of correspondence—daily almost, it must have been—from Linton Heathcliff: answers to documents forwarded by her. The earlier dated were embarrassed and short; gradually, however, they expanded into copious love letters, foolish, as the age of the writer rendered natural, yet with touches here and there which I thought were borrowed from a more experienced source. Some of them struck me as singularly odd compounds of ardour and flatness; commencing in strong feeling, and concluding in the affected, wordy way that a schoolboy might use to a fancied, incorporeal sweetheart. Whether they satisfied Cathy, I don't know; but they appeared very worthless trash to me. After turning over as many as I thought proper, I tied them in a handkerchief and set them aside, relocking the vacant drawer.

Following her habit, my young lady descended early, and visited the kitchen: I watched her go to the door, on the arrival of a certain little boy; and, while the dairymaid filled his can, she tucked something into his jacket pocket, and plucked something out. I went round by the garden, and laid wait for the messenger; who fought valorously to defend his trust, and we spilt the milk between us; but I succeeded in abstracting the epistle; and, threatening serious consequences if he did not look sharp home, I remained under the wall and perused Miss Cathy's affectionate composition. It was more simple and more eloquent than her cousin's; very pretty and very silly. I shook my head, and went meditating into the house. The day being wet, she could not divert herself with rambling about the park; so, at the conclusion of her morning studies, she resorted to the solace of the drawer. Her father sat reading at the table; and I, on purpose, had sought a bit of work in some unripped fringes of the window curtain, keeping my eye steadily fixed on her proceedings. Never did any bird flying back to a plundered nest which it had left brimful of chirping young ones, express more complete despair in its anguished cries and flutterings, than she by her single 'Oh!' and the change that transfigured her late happy countenance. Mr Linton looked up.

'What is the matter, love? Have you hurt yourself?' he said.

His tone and look assured her *he* had not been the discoverer of the hoard.

'No, papa!' she gasped. 'Ellen! Ellen! come upstairs—I'm sick!'

I obeyed her summons, and accompanied her out.

'Oh, Ellen! you have got them,' she commenced immediately, dropping on her knees, when we were enclosed alone. 'Oh, give them to me, and I'll never, never do so again! Don't tell papa. You have not told papa, Ellen? say you have not? I've been exceedingly naughty, but I won't do it any more!'

With a grave severity in my manner, I bid her stand up.

'So,' I exclaimed, 'Miss Catherine, you are tolerably far on, it seems: you may well be ashamed of them! A fine bundle of trash you study in your leisure hours, to be sure: why, it's good enough to be printed! And what do you suppose the master will think when I display it before him? I haven't shown it yet, but you needn't imagine I shall keep your ridiculous secrets. For shame! and you must have led the way in writing such absurdities: he would not have thought of beginning, I'm certain.'

'I didn't! I didn't!' sobbed Cathy fit to break her heart. 'I didn't once think of loving him till——'

'*Loving!*' cried I, as scornfully as I could utter the word. '*Loving!* Did anybody ever hear the like! I might just as well talk of loving the miller who comes once a year to buy our corn. Pretty loving, indeed! and both times together you have seen Linton hardly four hours in your life! Now here is the babyish trash. I'm going with it to the library; and we'll see what your father says to such *loving.*'

She sprang at her precious epistles, but I held them above my head; and then she poured out further frantic entreaties that I would burn them—do anything rather than show them. And being really fully as inclined to laugh as scold—for I esteemed it all girlish vanity—I at length relented in a measure, and asked:

'If I consent to burn them, will you promise faithfully neither to send nor receive a letter again, nor a book (for I perceive you have sent him books), nor locks of hair, nor rings, nor playthings?'

'We don't send playthings!' cried Catherine, her pride overcoming her shame.

'Nor anything at all, then, my lady,' I said. 'Unless you will, here I go.'

'I promise, Ellen!' she cried, catching my dress. 'Oh, put them in the fire, do, do!'

But when I proceeded to open a place with the poker, the sacrifice was too painful to be borne. She earnestly supplicated that I would spare her one or two.

'One or two, Ellen, to keep for Linton's sake!'

I unknotted the handkerchief, and commenced dropping them in from an angle, and the flame curled up the chimney.

'I will have one, you cruel wretch!' she screamed, darting her hand into the fire, and drawing forth some half consumed fragments, at the expense of her fingers.

'Very well—and I will have some to exhibit to papa!' I answered, shaking back the rest into the bundle, and turning anew to the door.

She emptied her blackened pieces into the flames, and motioned me to finish the immolation. It was done; I stirred up the ashes, and interred them under a shovelful of coals; and she mutely, and with a sense of intense injury, retired to her private apartment. I descended to tell my master that the young lady's qualm of sickness was almost gone, but I judged it best for her to lie down a while. She wouldn't dine; but she reappeared at tea, pale, and red about the eyes, and marvellously subdued in outward aspect. Next morning, I answered the letter by a slip of paper, inscribed, 'Master Heathcliff is requested to send no more notes to Miss Linton, as she will not receive them.' And, thenceforth, the little boy came with vacant pockets.

Chapter XXII

SUMMER drew to an end, and early autumn: it was past Michaelmas, but the harvest was late that year, and a few of our fields were still uncleared. Mr Linton and his daughter would frequently walk out among the reapers; at the carrying of the last sheaves, they stayed till dusk, and the evening happening to be chill and damp,

my master caught a bad cold, that settling obstinately on his lungs, confined him indoors throughout the whole of the winter, nearly without intermission.

Poor Cathy, frightened from her little romance, had been considerably sadder and duller since its abandonment; and her father insisted on her reading less, and taking more exercise. She had his companionship no longer; I esteemed it a duty to supply its lack, as much as possible, with mine: an inefficient substitute; for I could only spare two or three hours, from my numerous diurnal occupations, to follow her footsteps, and then my society was obviously less desirable than his.

On an afternoon in October, or the beginning of November—a fresh watery afternoon, when the turf and paths were rustling with moist, withered leaves, and the cold, blue sky was half hidden by clouds—dark grey streamers, rapidly mounting from the west, and boding abundant rain—I requested my young lady to forego her ramble, because I was certain of showers. She refused; and I unwillingly donned a cloak, and took my umbrella to accompany her on a stroll to the bottom of the park: a formal walk which she generally affected if low-spirited—and that she invariably was when Mr Edgar had been worse than ordinary, a thing never known from his confession, but guessed both by her and me, from his increased silence and the melancholy of his countenance. She went sadly on: there was no running or bounding now, though the chill wind might well have tempted her to a race. And often, from the side of my eye, I could detect her raising a hand, and brushing something off her cheek. I gazed round for a means of diverting her thoughts. On one side of the road rose a high, rough bank, where hazels and stunted oaks, with their roots half exposed, held uncertain tenure: the soil was too loose for the latter; and strong winds had blown some nearly horizontal. In summer, Miss Catherine delighted to climb along these trunks, and sit in the branches, swinging twenty feet above the ground; and I, pleased with her agility and her light, childish heart, still considered it proper to scold every time I caught her at such an elevation, but so that she knew there was no necessity for descending. From dinner to tea she would lie in her breeze-rocked cradle, doing nothing except singing old songs—my nursery lore—to herself, or watching the birds, joint tenants, feed and entice their young ones to fly: or nestling with closed lids, half thinking, half dreaming, happier than words can express.

'Look, miss!' I exclaimed, pointing to a nook under the roots of one twisted tree. 'Winter is not here yet. There's a little flower up yonder, the last bud from the multitude of bluebells that clouded those turf steps in July with a lilac mist. Will you clamber up, and pluck it to show to papa?'

Cathy stared a long time at the lonely blossom trembling in its earthy shelter, and replied, at length:

'No, I'll not touch it: but it looks melancholy, does it not, Ellen?'

'Yes,' I observed, 'about as starved and sackless as you: your cheeks are bloodless; let us take hold of hands and run. You're so low, I dare say I shall keep up with you.'

'No,' she repeated, and continued sauntering on, pausing, at intervals, to muse over a bit of moss, or a tuft of blanched grass, or a fungus spreading its bright orange among the heaps of brown foliage; and, ever and anon, her hand was lifted to her averted face.

'Catherine, why are you crying, love?' I asked, approaching and putting my arm over her shoulder. 'You mustn't cry because papa has a cold; be thankful it is nothing worse.'

She now put no further restraint on her tears; her breath was stifled by sobs.

'Oh, it *will* be something worse,' she said. 'And what shall I do when papa and you leave me, and I am by myself? I can't forget your words, Ellen; they are always in my ear. How life will be changed, how dreary the world will be, when papa and you are dead.'

'None can tell, whether you won't die before us,' I replied. 'It's wrong to anticipate evil. We'll hope there are years and years to come before any of us go: master is young, and I am strong, and hardly forty-five. My mother lived till eighty, a canty dame to the last. And suppose Mr Linton were spared till he saw sixty, that would be more years than you have counted, miss. And would it not be foolish to mourn a calamity above twenty years beforehand?'

'But Aunt Isabella was younger than papa,' she remarked, gazing up with timid hope to seek further consolation.

'Aunt Isabella had not you and me to nurse her,' I replied. 'She wasn't as happy as master: she hadn't as much to live for. All you need do, is to wait well on your father, and cheer him by letting him see you cheerful; and avoid giving him anxiety on any subject: mind that, Cathy! I'll not disguise but you might kill him, if you were wild and reckless, and cherished a foolish, fanciful affection for the son of a person who would be glad to have him in his grave; and allowed him to discover that you fretted over the separation he has judged it expedient to make.'

'I fret about nothing on earth except papa's illness,' answered my companion 'I care for nothing in comparison with papa. And I'll never—never—oh, never, while I have my senses, do an act or say a word to vex him. I love him better than myself, Ellen; and I know it by this: I pray every night that I may live after him; because I would rather be miserable than that he should be: that proves I love him better than myself.'

'Good words,' I replied. 'But deeds must prove it also; and after he is well, remember you don't forget resolutions formed in the hour of fear.'

As we talked, we neared a door that opened on the road; and my young lady, lightening into sunshine again, climbed up and seated herself on the top of the wall, reaching over to gather some hips that bloomed scarlet on the summit branches of the wild rose trees, shadowing the highway side: the lower fruit had disappeared, but only birds could touch the upper, except from Cathy's present station. In stretching to pull them, her hat fell off; and as the door was locked, she proposed scrambling down to recover it. I bid her be cautious lest she got a fall, and she nimbly disappeared. But the return was no such easy matter: the stones were smooth and neatly cemented, and the rose-bushes and blackberry stragglers could yield no assistance in re-ascending. I, like a fool, didn't recollect that, till I heard her laughing and exclaiming:

'Ellen, you'll have to fetch the key, or else I must run round to the porter's lodge. I can't scale the ramparts on this side!'

'Stay where you are,' I answered, 'I have my bundle of keys in my pocket: perhaps I may manage to open it; if not I'll go.'

Catherine amused herself with dancing to and fro before the door, while I tried all the large keys in succession. I had applied the last, and found that none would do; so, repeating my desire that she would remain there, I was about to hurry home as fast as I could, when an approaching sound arrested me. It was the trot of a horse; Cathy's dance stopped, and in a minute the horse stopped also.

'Who is that?' I whispered.

'Ellen, I wish you could open the door,' whispered back my companion anxiously.

'Ho, Miss Linton!' cried a deep voice (the rider's), 'I'm glad to meet you. Don't be in haste to enter, for I have an explanation to ask and obtain.'

'I shan't speak to you, Mr Heathcliff,' answered Catherine. 'Papa says you are a wicked man, and you hate both him and me; and Ellen says the same.'

'That is nothing to the purpose,' said Heathcliff. (He it was.) 'I don't hate my son, I suppose; and it is concerning him that I demand your attention. Yes; you have cause to blush. Two or three months since, were you not in the habit of writing to Linton? making love in play, eh? You deserved, both of you, flogging for that! You especially, the elder; and less sensitive, as it turns out. I've got your letters, and if you give me any pertness I'll send them to your father. I presume you grew

weary of the amusement and dropped it, didn't you? Well, you dropped Linton with it into a slough of despond. He was in earnest: in love, really. As true as I live, he's dying for you; breaking his heart at your fickleness: not figuratively, but actually. Though Hareton has made him a standing jest for six weeks, and I have used more serious measures, and attempted to frighten him out of his idiotcy, he gets worse daily; and he'll be under the sod before summer, unless you restore him!'

'How can you lie so glaringly to the poor child?' I called from the inside. 'Pray ride on! How can you deliberately get up such paltry falsehoods? Miss Cathy, I'll knock the lock off with a stone: you won't believe that vile nonsense. You can feel in yourself, it is impossible that a person should die for love of a stranger.'

'I was not aware there were eavesdroppers,' muttered the detected villain. 'Worthy Mrs Dean, I like you, but I don't like your double-dealing,' he added aloud. 'How could *you* lie so glaringly, as to affirm I hated the ''poor child''? and invent bugbear stories to terrify her from my doorstones? Catherine Linton (the very name warms me), my bonnie lass, I shall be from home all this week; go and see if I have not spoken truth: do, there's a darling! Just imagine your father in my place, and Linton in yours; then think how you would value your careless lover if he refused to stir a step to comfort you, when your father himself entreated him; and don't, from pure stupidity, fall into the same error. I swear, on my salvation, he's going to his grave, and none but you can save him!'

The lock gave way and I issued out.

'I swear Linton is dying,' repeated Heathcliff, looking hard at me. 'And grief and disappointment are hastening his death. Nelly, if you won't let her go, you can walk over yourself. But I shall not return till this time next week; and I think your master himself would scarcely object to her visiting her cousin!'

'Come in,' said I, taking Cathy by the arm and half-forcing her to re-enter; for she lingered, viewing with troubled eyes the features of the speaker, too stern to express his inward deceit.

He pushed his horse close, and, bending down, observed:

'Miss Catherine, I'll owe to you that I have little patience with Linton; and Hareton and Joseph have less. I'll own that he's with a harsh set. He pines for kindness, as well as love; and a kind word from you would be his best medicine. Don't mind Mrs Dean's cruel cautions; but be generous, and contrive to see him. He dreams of you day and night, and cannot be persuaded that you don't hate him, since you neither write nor call.'

I closed the door, and rolled a stone to assist the loosened lock in holding it; and spreading my umbrella, I drew my charge underneath: for the rain began to drive through the moaning branches of the trees, and warned us to avoid delay. Our hurry prevented any comment on the encounter with Heathcliff, as we stretched towards home; but I divined instinctively that Catherine's heart was clouded now in double darkness. Her features were so sad, they did not seem hers: she evidently regarded what she had heard as every syllable true.

The master had retired to rest before we came in. Cathy stole to his room to inquire how he was; he had fallen asleep. She returned, and asked me to sit with her in the library. We took our tea together; and afterwards she lay down on the rug, and told me not to talk, for she was weary. I got a book, and pretended to read. As soon as she supposed me absorbed in my occupation, she recommenced her silent weeping: it appeared, at present, her favourite diversion. I suffered her to enjoy it a while; then I expostulated: deriding and ridiculing all Mr Heathcliff's assertions about his son, as if I were certain she would coincide. Alas! I hadn't skill to counteract the effect his account had produced: it was just what he intended.

'You may be right, Ellen,' she answered; 'but I shall never feel at ease till I know. And I must tell Linton it is not my fault that I don't write, and convince him that I shall not change.'

What use were anger and protestations against her silly credulity? We parted that night—hostile; but next day beheld me on the road to Wuthering Heights, by the side of my wilful young mistress's pony. I couldn't bear to witness her sorrow: to see her pale dejected countenance, and heavy eyes; and I yielded, in the faint hope that Linton himself might prove, by his reception of us, how little of the tale was founded on fact.

Chapter XXIII

THE rainy night had ushered in a misty morning—half frost, half drizzle—and temporary brooks crossed our path—gurgling from the uplands. My feet were thoroughly wetted; I was cross and low; exactly the humour suited for making the most of these disagreeable things. We entered the farmhouse by the kitchen way, to ascertain whether Mr Heathcliff were really absent; because I put slight faith in his own affirmation.

Joseph seemed sitting in a sort of elysium alone, beside a roaring fire; a quart of ale on the table near him, bristling with large pieces of toasted oatcake; and his black, short pipe in his mouth. Catherine ran to the hearth to warm herself. I asked if the master was in? My question remained so long unanswered, that I thought the old man had grown deaf, and repeated it louder.

'Na—ay!' he snarled, or rather screamed through his nose. 'Na—ay! yah muh goa back whear yah coom frough.'

'Joseph!' cried a peevish voice, simultaneously with me, from the inner room. 'How often am I to call you? There are only a few red ashes now. Joseph! come this moment.'

Vigorous puffs, and a resolute stare into the grate declared he had no ear for this appeal. The housekeeper and Hareton were invisible; one gone on an errand, and the other at his work, probably. We knew Linton's tones, and entered.

'Oh, I hope you'll die in a garret! starved to death,' said the boy, mistaking our approach for that of his negligent attendant.

He stopped, on observing his error; his cousin flew to him.

'Is that you, Miss Linton?' he said, raising his head from the arm of the great chair, in which he reclined. 'No—don't kiss me: it takes my breath. Dear me! Papa said you would call,' continued he, after recovering a little from Catherine's embrace; while she stood by looking very contrite. 'Will you shut the door, if you please? you left it open; and those—those *detestable* creatures won't bring coals to the fire. It's so cold!'

I stirred up the cinders, and fetched a scuttleful myself. The invalid complained of being covered with ashes; but he had a tiresome cough, and looked feverish and ill, so I did not rebuke his temper.

'Well, Linton,' murmured Catherine, when his corrugated brow relaxed. 'Are you glad to see me? Can I do you any good?'

'Why didn't you come before?' he asked. 'You should have come, instead of writing. It tired me dreadfully, writing those long letters. I'd far rather have talked to you. Now, I can neither bear to talk, nor anything else. I wonder where Zillah is! Will you (looking at me) step into the kitchen and see?'

I had received no thanks for my other service; and being unwilling to run out to and fro at his behest, I replied:

'Nobody is out there but Joseph.'

'I want to drink,' he exclaimed fretfully, turning away. 'Zillah is constantly gadding off to Gimmerton since papa went: it's miserable! And I'm obliged to come down here—they resolved never to hear me upstairs.'

'Is your father attentive to you, Master Heathcliff?' I asked, perceiving Catherine to be checked in her friendly advances.

'Attentive? He makes *them* a little more attentive at least,' he cried. 'The wretches! Do you know, Miss Linton, that brute Hareton laughs at me! I hate him! indeed, I hate them all: they are odious beings.'

Cathy began searching for some water; she lighted on a pitcher in the dresser, filled a tumbler, and brought it. He bid her add a spoonful of wine from a bottle on the table; and having swallowed a small portion, appeared more tranquil, and said she was very kind.

'And are you glad to see me?' asked she, reiterating her former question, and pleased to detect the faint dawn of a smile.

'Yes, I am. It's something new to hear a voice like yours!' he replied. 'But I *have* been vexed, because you wouldn't come. And papa swore it was owing to me: he called me a pitiful, shuffling, worthless thing; and said you despised me; and if he had been in my place, he would be more the master of the Grange than your father, by this time. But you don't despise me, do you, Miss——'

'I wish you would say Catherine, or Cathy,' interrupted my young lady. 'Despise you? No! Next to papa and Ellen, I love you better than anybody living. I don't love Mr Heathcliff, though; and I dare not come when he returns; will he stay away many days?'

'Not many,' answered Linton; 'but he goes on to the moors frequently, since the shooting season commenced; and you might spend an hour or two with me in his absence. Do say you will. I think I should not be peevish with you: you'd not provoke me, and you'd always be ready to help me, wouldn't you?'

'Yes,' said Catherine, stroking his long soft hair; 'if I could only get papa's consent, I'd spend half my time with you. Pretty Linton! I wish you were my brother.'

'And then you would like me as well as your father?' observed he, more cheerfully. 'But papa says you would love me better than him and all the world, if you were my wife; so I'd rather you were that.'

'No, I should never love anybody better than papa,' she returned gravely. 'And people hate their wives, sometimes; but not their sisters and brothers: and if you were the latter you would live with us, and papa would be as fond of you as he is of me.'

Linton denied that people ever hated their wives; but Cathy affirmed they did, and, in her wisdom, instanced his own father's aversion to her aunt. I endeavoured to stop her thoughtless tongue. I couldn't succeed till everything she knew was out. Master Heathcliff, much irritated, asserted her relation was false.

'Papa told me; and papa does not tell falsehoods,' she answered pertly.

'*My* papa scorns yours!' cried Linton. 'He calls him a sneaking fool!'

'Yours is a wicked man,' retorted Catherine, 'and you are very naughty to dare to repeat what he says. He must be wicked to have made Aunt Isabella leave him as she did!'

'She didn't leave him,' said the boy; 'you shan't contradict me!'

'She did!' cried my young lady.

'Well, I'll tell *you* something!' said Linton. 'Your mother hated your father: now then.'

'Oh!' exclaimed Catherine, too enraged to continue.

'And she loved mine!' added he.

'You little liar! I hate you now,' she panted, and her face grew red with passion.

'She did! she did!' sang Linton, sinking into the recess of his chair, and leaning back his head to enjoy the agitation of the other disputant, who stood behind.

'Hush, Master Heathcliff!' I said; 'that's your father's tale, too, I suppose.'

'It isn't: you hold your tongue!' he answered. 'She did, she did, Catherine! she did, she did!'

Cathy, beside herself, gave the chair a violent push, and caused him to fall against one arm. He was immediately seized by a suffocating cough that soon ended his triumph. It lasted so long that it frightened even me. As to his cousin, she wept, with all her might; aghast at the mischief she had done: though she said nothing. I held him till the fit exhausted itself. Then he thrust me away, and leant his head down silently. Catherine quelled her lamentations also, took a seat opposite, and looked solemnly into the fire.

'How do you feel now, Master Heathcliff?' I inquired, after waiting ten minutes.

'I wish *she* felt as I do,' he replied: 'spiteful, cruel thing! Hareton never touches me: he never struck me in his life. And I was better today: and there——' his voice died in a whimper.

'*I* didn't strike you!' muttered Cathy, chewing her lip to prevent another burst of emotion.

He sighed and moaned like one under great suffering, and kept it up for a quarter of an hour; on purpose to distress his cousin apparently, for whenever he caught a stifled sob from her he put renewed pain and pathos into the inflections of his voice.

'I'm sorry I hurt you, Linton,' she said at length, racked beyond endurance. 'But *I* couldn't have been hurt by that little push, and I had no idea that you could, either: you're not much, are you, Linton? Don't let me go home thinking I've done you harm. Answer! speak to me.'

'I can't speak to you,' he murmured; 'you've hurt me so, that I shall lie awake all night choking with this cough. If you had it you'd know what it was; but *you'll* be comfortably asleep while I'm in agony, and nobody near me. I wonder how you would like to pass those fearful nights!' And he began to wail aloud, for very pity of himself.

'Since you are in the habit of passing dreadful nights,' I said, 'it won't be miss who spoils your ease: you'd be the same had she never come. However, she shall not disturb you again; and perhaps you'll get quieter when we leave you.'

'Must I go?' asked Catherine dolefully, bending over him. 'Do you want me to go, Linton?'

'You can't alter what you've done,' he replied pettishly, shrinking from her, 'unless you alter it for the worse by teasing me into a fever.'

'Well, then, I must go?' she repeated.

'Let me alone, at least,' said he; 'I can't bear your talking.'

She lingered, and resisted my persuasions to departure a tiresome while; but as he neither looked up nor spoke, she finally made a movement to the door and I followed. We were recalled by a scream. Linton had slid from his seat on to the hearthstone, and lay writhing in the mere perverseness of an indulged plague of a child, determined to be as grievous and harassing as it can. I thoroughly gauged his disposition from his behaviour, and saw at once it would be folly to attempt humouring him. Not so my companion: she ran back in terror, knelt down, and cried, and soothed, and entreated, till he grew quiet from lack of breath: by no means from compunction at distressing her.

'I shall lift him on the settle,' I said, 'and he may roll about as he pleases: we can't stop to watch him. I hope you are satisfied, Miss Cathy, that *you* are not the person to benefit him; and that his condition of health is not occasioned by attachment to you. Now, then, there he is! Come away: as soon as he knows there is nobody by to care for his nonsense, he'll be glad to lie still.'

She placed a cushion under his head, and offered him some water; he rejected the latter, and tossed uneasily on the former, as if it were a stone or a block of wood. She tried to put it more comfortably.

'I can't do with that,' he said; 'it's not high enough.'

Catherine brought another to lay above it.

'That's *too* high,' murmured the provoking thing.

'How must I arrange it, then?' she asked despairingly.

He twined himself up to her, as she half knelt by the settle, and converted her shoulder into a support.

'No, that won't do,' I said. 'You'll be content with the cushion, Master Heathcliff. Miss has wasted too much time on you already: we cannot remain five minutes longer.'

'Yes, yes, we can!' replied Cathy. 'He's good and patient now. He's beginning to think I shall have far greater misery than he will tonight, if I believe he is the worse for my visit; and then I dare not come again. Tell the truth about it, Linton; for I mustn't come, if I have hurt you.'

'You must come, to cure me,' he answered. 'You ought to come, because you have hurt me: you know you have extremely! I was not as ill when you entered as I am at present—was I?'

'But you've made yourself ill by crying and being in a passion.'

'I didn't do it at all,' said his cousin. 'However, we'll be friends now. And you want me: you would wish to see me sometimes, really?'

'I told you I did,' he replied impatiently. 'Sit on the settle and let me lean on your knee. That's as mamma used to do, whole afternoons together. Sit quite still and don't talk: but you may sing a song, if you can sing; or you may say a nice long interesting ballad—one of those you promised to teach me: or a story. I'd rather have a ballad, though: begin.'

Catherine repeated the longest she could remember. The employment pleased both mightily. Linton would have another; and after that another, notwithstanding my strenuous objections; and so they went on until the clock struck twelve, and we heard Hareton in the court, returning for his dinner.

'And tomorrow, Catherine, will you be here tomorrow?' asked young Heathcliff, holding her frock as she rose reluctantly.

'No,' I answered, 'nor next day neither.' She, however, gave a different response evidently, for his forehead cleared as she stooped and whispered in his ear.

'You won't go tomorrow, recollect, miss!' I commenced, when we were out of the house. 'You are not dreaming of it, are you?'

She smiled.

'Oh, I'll take good care,' I continued: 'I'll have that lock mended, and you can escape by no way else.'

'I can get over the wall,' she said, laughing. 'The Grange is not a prison, Ellen, and you are not my jailer. And besides, I'm almost seventeen: I'm a woman. And I'm certain Linton would recover quickly if he had me to look after him. I'm older than he is, you know, and wiser: less childish, am I not? And he'll soon do as I direct him, with some slight coaxing. He's a pretty little darling when he's good. I'd make such a pet of him, if he were mine. We should never quarrel, should we, after we were used to each other? Don't you like him, Ellen?'

'Like him?' I exclaimed. 'The worst-tempered bit of a sickly slip that ever struggled into its teens. Happily, as Mr Heathcliff conjectured, he'll not win twenty. I doubt whether he'll see spring, indeed. And small loss to his family whenever he drops off. And lucky it is for us that his father took him: the kinder he was treated, the more tedious and selfish he'd be. I'm glad you have no chance of having him for a husband, Miss Catherine.'

My companion waxed serious at hearing this speech. To speak of his death so regardlessly, wounded her feelings.

'He's younger than I,' she answered, after a protracted pause of meditation, 'and he ought to live the longest: he will—he must live as long as I do. He's as strong now as when he first came into the north; I'm positive of that. It's only a cold that ails him, the same as papa has. You say papa will get better, and why shouldn't he?'

'Well, well,' I cried, 'after all, we needn't trouble ourselves; for listen, miss, and mind, I'll keep my word,—if you attempt going to Wuthering Heights again,

with or without me, I shall inform Mr Linton, and, unless he allow it, the intimacy with your cousin must not be revived.'

'It has been revived,' muttered Cathy sulkily.

'Must not be continued, then,' I said.

'We'll see,' was her reply, and she set off at a gallop, leaving me to toil in the rear.

We both reached home before our dinner time; my master supposed we had been wandering through the park, and therefore he demanded no explanation of our absence. As soon as I entered, I hastened to change my soaked shoes and stockings; but sitting such a while at the Heights had done the mischief. On the succeeding morning I was laid up, and during three weeks I remained incapacitated for attending to my duties: a calamity never experienced prior to that period, and never, I am thankful to say, since.

My little mistress behaved like an angel, in coming to wait on me, and cheer my solitude: the confinement brought me exceedingly low. It is wearisome, to a stirring active body: but few have slighter reasons for complaint than I had. The moment Catherine left Mr Linton's room, she appeared at my bedside. Her day was divided between us; no amusement usurped a minute: she neglected her meals, her studies, and her play; and she was the fondest nurse that ever watched. She must have had a warm heart, when she loved her father so, to give so much to me. I said her days were divided between us; but the master retired early, and I generally needed nothing after six o'clock; thus the evening was her own. Poor thing! I never considered what she did with herself after tea. And though frequently, when she looked in to bid me good night, I remarked a fresh colour in her cheeks and a pinkness over her slender fingers; instead of fancying the hue borrowed from a cold ride across the moors, I laid it to the charge of a hot fire in the library.

Chapter XXIV

AT the close of three weeks, I was able to quit my chamber, and move about the house. And on the first occasion of my sitting up in the evening, I asked Catherine to read to me, because my eyes were weak. We were in the library, the master having gone to bed: she consented, rather unwillingly, I fancied; and imagining my sort of books did not suit her, I bid her please herself in the choice of what she perused. She selected one of her own favourites, and got forward steadily about an hour; then came frequent questions.

'Ellen, are not you tired? Hadn't you better lie down now? You'll be sick, keeping up so long, Ellen.'

'No, no, dear, I'm not tired,' I returned continually.

Perceiving me immovable, she essayed another method of showing her disrelish for her occupation. It changed to yawning, and stretching, and:

'Ellen, I'm tired.'

'Give over then and talk,' I answered.

That was worse: she fretted and sighed, and looked at her watch till eight, and finally went to her room, completely overdone with sleep; judging by her peevish, heavy look, and the constant rubbing she inflicted on her eyes. The following night she seemed more impatient still; and on the third from recovering my company, she complained of a headache, and left me. I thought her conduct odd; and having remained alone a long while, I resolved on going and inquiring whether she were better, and asking her to come and lie on the sofa, instead of upstairs in the dark. No Catherine could I discover upstairs, and none below. The servants affirmed

they had not seen her. I listened at Mr Edgar's door; all was silence. I returned to her apartment, extinguished my candle, and seated myself in the window.

The moon shone bright; a sprinkling of snow covered the ground, and I reflected that she might, possibly, have taken it into her head to walk about the garden, for refreshment. I did detect a figure creeping along the inner fence of the park; but it was not my young mistress: on its merging into the light, I recognized one of the grooms. He stood a considerable period, viewing the carriage-road through the grounds; then started off at a brisk pace, as if he had detected something, and reappeared presently, leading miss's pony; and there she was, just dismounted, and walking by its side. The man took his charge stealthily across the grass towards the stable. Cathy entered by the casement window of the drawing-room, and glided noiselessly up to where I awaited her. She put the door gently to, slipped off her snowy shoes, untied her hat, and was proceeding, unconscious of my espionage, to lay aside her mantle, when I suddenly rose and revealed myself. The surprise petrified her an instant: she uttered an inarticulate exclamation, and stood fixed.

'My dear Miss Catherine,' I began, too vividly impressed by her recent kindness to break into a scold, 'where have you been riding out at this hour? And why should you try to deceive me, by telling a tale? Where have you been? Speak.'

'To the bottom of the park,' she stammered. 'I didn't tell a tale.'

'And nowhere else?' I demanded.

'No,' was the muttered reply.

'Oh, Catherine!' I cried sorrowfully. 'You know you have been doing wrong, or you wouldn't be driven to uttering an untruth to me. That does grieve me. I'd rather be three months ill, than hear you frame a deliberate lie.'

She sprang forward, and bursting into tears, threw her arms round my neck.

'Well, Ellen, I'm so afraid of you being angry,' she said. 'Promise not to be angry, and you shall know the very truth: I hate to hide it.'

We sat down in the window-seat; I assured her I would not scold, whatever her secret might be, and I guessed it of course; so she commenced:

'I've been to Wuthering Heights, Ellen, and I've never missed going a day since you fell ill; except thrice before, and twice after you left your room. I gave Michael books and pictures to prepare Minny every evening, and to put her back in the stable: you mustn't scold *him* either, mind. I was at the Heights by half past six, and generally stayed till half past eight, and then galloped home. It was not to amuse myself that I went: I was often wretched all the time. Now and then I was happy; once in a week perhaps. At first, I expected there would be sad work persuading you to let me keep my word to Linton: for I had engaged to call again next day, when we quitted him; but, as you stayed upstairs on the morrow, I escaped that trouble; and while Michael was refastening the lock of the park door in the afternoon, I got possession of the key, and told him how my cousin wished me to visit him, because he was sick, and couldn't come to the Grange; and how papa would object to my going: and then I negotiated with him about the pony. He is fond of reading, and he thinks of leaving soon to get married; so he offered, if I would lend him books out of the library, to do what I wished: but I preferred giving him my own, and that satisfied him better.

'On my second visit, Linton seemed in lively spirits; and Zillah (that is their housekeeper) made us a clean room and a good fire, and told us that, as Joseph was out at a prayer meeting and Hareton Earnshaw was off with his dogs—robbing our woods of pheasants, as I heard afterwards—we might do what we liked. She brought me some warm wine and gingerbread, and appeared exceedingly good-natured; and Linton sat in the armchair, and I in the little rocking-chair on the hearthstone, and we laughed and talked so merrily, and found so much to say: we planned where we would go, and what we would do in summer. I needn't repeat that, because you would call it silly.

'One time, however, we were near quarrelling. He said the pleasantest manner of spending a hot July day was lying from morning till evening on a bank of heath in the middle of the moors, with the bees humming dreamily about among the bloom, and the larks singing high up overhead, and the blue sky and bright sun shining steadily and cloudlessly. That was his most perfect idea of heaven's happiness: mine was rocking in a rustling green tree, with a west wind blowing, and bright white clouds flitting rapidly above; and not only larks, but throstles, and blackbirds, and linnets, and cuckoos pouring out music on every side, and the moors seen at a distance, broken into cool dusky dells; but close by great swells of long grass undulating in waves to the breeze; and woods and sounding water, and the whole world awake and wild with joy. He wanted all to lie in an ecstasy of peace; I wanted all to sparkle and dance in a glorious jubilee. I said his heaven would be only half alive; and he said mine would be drunk: I said I should fall asleep in his; and he said he could not breathe in mine, and began to grow very snappish. At last, we agreed to try both, as soon as the right weather came; and then we kissed each other and were friends.

'After sitting still an hour, I looked at the great room with its smooth uncarpeted floor, and thought how nice it would be to play in, if we removed the table; and I asked Linton to call Zillah in to help us, and we'd have a game at blind-man's buff; she should try to catch us: you used to, you know, Ellen. He wouldn't: there was no pleasure in it, he said; but he consented to play at ball with me. We found two in a cupboard, among a heap of old toys, tops, and hoops, and battledores, and shuttlecocks. One was marked C., and the other H.; I wished to have the C., because that stood for Catherine, and the H. might be for Heathcliff, his name; but the bran came out of H., and Linton didn't like it. I beat him constantly, and he got cross again, and coughed, and returned to his chair. That night, though, he easily recovered his good humour: he was charmed with two or three pretty songs—*your* songs, Ellen; and when I was obliged to go, he begged and entreated me to come the following evening; and I promised. Minny and I went flying home as light as air; and I dreamt of Wuthering Heights and my sweet, darling cousin, till morning.

'On the morrow I was sad; partly because you were poorly, and partly that I wished my father knew, and approved of my excursions: but it was beautiful moonlight after tea; and, as I rode on, the gloom cleared. I shall have another happy evening, I thought to myself: and what delights me more, my pretty Linton will. I trotted up their garden, and was turning round to the back, when that fellow Earnshaw met me, took my bridle, and bid me go in by the front entrance. He patted Minny's neck, and said she was a bonny beast, and appeared as if he wanted me to speak to him. I only told him to leave my horse alone, or else it would kick him. He answered in his vulgar accent, "It wouldn't do mitch hurt if it did''; and surveyed its legs with a smile. I was half inclined to make it try; however, he moved off to open the door, and, as he raised the latch, he looked up to the inscription above, and said, with a stupid mixture of awkwardness and elation:

' "Miss Catherine! I can read yon, nah.''

' "Wonderful,'' I exclaimed. "Pray let us hear you—you *are* grown clever!''

'He spelt, and drawled over by syllables, the name—"Hareton Earnshaw''.

' "And the figures?'' I cried encouragingly, perceiving that he came to a dead halt.

' "I cannot tell them yet,'' he answered.

' "Oh, you dunce!'' I said, laughing heartily at his failure.

'The fool stared, with a grin hovering about his lips, and a scowl gathering over his eyes, as if uncertain whether he might not join in my mirth: whether it were not pleasant familiarity, or what it really was, contempt. I settled his doubts, by suddenly retrieving my gravity and desiring him to walk away, for I came to see Linton, not him. He reddened—I saw that by the moonlight—dropped his hand

from the latch, and skulked off, a picture of mortified vanity. He imagined himself to be as accomplished as Linton, I suppose, because he could spell his own name; and was marvellously discomfited that I didn't think the same.'

'Stop, Miss Catherine, dear!' I interrupted. 'I shall not scold, but I don't like your conduct there. If you had remembered that Hareton was your cousin as much as Master Heathcliff, you would have felt how improper it was to behave in that way. At least, it was praiseworthy ambition for him to desire to be as accomplished as Linton; and probably he did not learn merely to show off: you had made him ashamed of his ignorance before, I have no doubt; and he wished to remedy it and please you. To sneer at his imperfect attempt was very bad breeding. Had *you* been brought up in his circumstances, would you be less rude? He was as quick and as intelligent a child as ever you were; and I'm hurt that he should be despised now, because that base Heathcliff has treated him so unjustly.'

'Well, Ellen, you won't cry about it, will you?' she exclaimed, surprised at my earnestness. 'But wait, and you shall hear if he conned his A B C to please me; and if it were worth while being civil to the brute. I entered; Linton was lying on the settle, and half got up to welcome me.

' "I'm ill tonight, Catherine, love," he said; "and you must have all the talk, and let me listen. Come, and sit by me. I was sure you wouldn't break your word, and I'll make you promise again, before you go."

'I knew now that I mustn't tease him, as he was ill; and I spoke softly and put no questions, and avoided irritating him in any way. I had brought some of my nicest books for him; he asked me to read a little of one, and I was about to comply, when Earnshaw burst the door open: having gathered venom with reflection. He advanced direct to us, seized Linton by the arm, and swung him off the seat.

' "Get to thy own room!" he said, in a voice almost inarticulate with passion; and his face looked swelled and furious. "Take her there if she comes to see thee: thou shalln't keep me out of this. Begone wi' ye both!"

'He swore at us, and left Linton no time to answer, nearly throwing him into the kitchen; and he clenched his fist as I followed, seemingly longing to knock me down. I was afraid for a moment, and I let one volume fall; he kicked it after me, and shut us out. I heard a malignant, crackly laugh by the fire, and turning, beheld that odious Joseph standing rubbing his bony hands, and quivering.

' "Aw wer sure he'd sarve ye eht! He's a grand lad! He's getten t' raight sperrit in him! *He* knaws—Aye, he knaws, as weel as Aw do, who sud be t'maister yonder—Ech, ech, ech! He mad ye skift properly! Ech, ech, ech!"

' "Where must we go?" I said to my cousin, disregarding the old wretch's mockery.

'Linton was white and trembling. He was not pretty then, Ellen: oh no! he looked frightful; for his thin face and large eyes were wrought into an expression of frantic, powerless fury. He grasped the handle of the door, and shook it: it was fastened inside.

' "If you don't let me in I'll kill you!—If you don't let me in, I'll kill you!" he rather shrieked than said. "Devil! devil!—I'll kill you—I'll kill you!"

'Joseph uttered his croaking laugh again.

' "Thear, that's t' father!" he cried. "That's father! We've allas summut uh orther side in us. Niver heed Hareton, lad—dunnut be 'feard—he cannot get at thee!"

'I took hold of Linton's hands, and tried to pull him away; but he shrieked so shockingly that I dared not proceed. At last his cries were choked by a dreadful fit of coughing; blood gushed from his mouth, and he fell on the ground. I ran into the yard, sick with terror; and called for Zillah, as loud as I could. She soon heard me: she was milking the cows in a shed behind the barn, and hurrying from her work, she inquired what there was to do? I hadn't breath to explain; dragging her in, I looked about for Linton. Earnshaw had come out to examine the mischief he

had caused, and he was then conveying the poor thing upstairs. Zillah and I ascended after him; but he stopped me at the top of the steps, and said I shouldn't go in: I must go home. I exclaimed that he had killed Linton, and I *would* enter. Joseph locked the door, and declared I should do ''no sich stuff'', and asked me whether I were ''bahn to be as mad as him''. I stood crying, till the housekeeper reappeared. She affirmed he would be better in a bit, but he couldn't do with that shrieking and din; and she took me, and nearly carried me into the house.

'Ellen, I was ready to tear my hair off my head! I sobbed and wept so that my eyes were almost blind; and the ruffian you have such sympathy with stood opposite: presuming every now and then to bid me ''wisht'', and denying that it was his fault; and, finally, frightened by my assertions that I would tell papa, and that he should be put in prison and hanged, he commenced blubbering himself, and hurried out to hide his cowardly agitation. Still, I was not rid of him: when at length they compelled me to depart, and I had got some hundred yards off the premises, he suddenly issued from the shadow of the roadside, and checked Minny and took hold of me.

' ''Miss Catherine, I'm ill grieved,'' he began, ''but it's rayther too bad——''

'I gave him a cut with my whip, thinking perhaps he would murder me. He let go, thundering one of his horrid curses, and I galloped home more than half out of my senses.

'I didn't bid you good night that evening, and I didn't go to Wuthering Heights the next: I wished to, exceedingly; but I was strangely excited, and dreaded to hear that Linton was dead, sometimes; and sometimes shuddered at the thought of encountering Hareton. On the third day I took courage: at least, I couldn't bear longer suspense, and stole off once more. I went at five o'clock, and walked; fancying I might manage to creep into the house, and up to Linton's room, unobserved. However, the dogs gave notice of my approach. Zillah received me, and saying, ''the lad was mending nicely'', showed me into a small, tidy, carpeted apartment, where, to my inexpressible joy, I beheld Linton laid on a little sofa, reading one of my books. But he would neither speak to me nor look at me, through a whole hour, Ellen: he has such an unhappy temper. And what quite confounded me, when he did open his mouth, it was to utter the falsehood that I had occasioned the uproar, and Hareton was not to blame! Unable to reply, except passionately, I got up and walked from the room. He sent after me a faint ''Catherine!'' He did not reckon on being answered so: but I wouldn't turn back; and the morrow was the second day on which I stayed at home, nearly determined to visit him no more. But it was so miserable going to bed and getting up, and never hearing anything about him, that my resolution melted into air before it was properly formed. It *had* appeared wrong to take the journey once; now it seemed wrong to refrain. Michael came to ask if he must saddle Minny; I said ''Yes'', and considered myself doing a duty as she bore me over the hills. I was forced to pass the front windows to get to the court: it was no use trying to conceal my presence.

' ''Young master is in the house,'' said Zillah, as she saw me making for the parlour. I went in; Earnshaw was there also, but he quitted the room directly. Linton sat in the great armchair half asleep; walking up to the fire, I began in a serious tone, partly meaning it to be true:

' ''As you don't like me, Linton, and as you think I come on purpose to hurt you, and pretend that I do so every time, this is our last meeting: let us say goodbye; and tell Mr Heathcliff that you have no wish to see me, and that he mustn't invent any more falsehoods on the subject.'

' ''Sit down and take your hat off, Catherine,'' he answered. ''You are so much happier than I am, you ought to be better. Papa talks enough of my defects, and shows enough scorn of me, to make it natural I should doubt myself. I doubt whether I am not altogether as worthless as he calls me, frequently; and then I feel so cross and bitter, I hate everybody! I *am* worthless, and bad in temper, and bad

in spirit, almost always; and, if you choose, you *may* say goodbye: you'll get rid of an annoyance. Only, Catherine, do me this justice: believe that if I might be as sweet, and as kind, and as good as you are, I would be; as willingly, and more so, than as happy and as healthy. And believe that your kindness has made me love you deeper than if I deserved your love: and though I couldn't, and cannot help showing my nature to you, I regret it and repent it; and shall regret and repent it till I die!''

'I felt he spoke the truth; and I felt I must forgive him: and, though he should quarrel the next moment, I must forgive him again. We were reconciled; but we cried, both of us, the whole time I stayed: not entirely for sorrow; yet I *was* sorry Linton had that distorted nature. He'll never let his friends be at ease, and he'll never be at ease himself! I have always gone to his little parlour, since that night; because his father returned the day after.

'About three times, I think, we have been merry and hopeful, as we were the first evening; the rest of my visits were dreary and troubled: now with his selfishness and spite, and now with his sufferings: but I've learned to endure the former with nearly as little resentment as the latter. Mr Heathcliff purposely avoids me: I have hardly seen him at all. Last Sunday, indeed, coming earlier than usual, I heard him abusing poor˙Linton, cruelly, for his conduct of the night before. I can't tell how he knew of it, unless he listened. Linton had certainly behaved provokingly: however, it was the business of nobody but me, and I interrupted Mr Heathcliff's lecture by entering and telling him so. He burst into a laugh, and went away, saying he was glad I took that view of the matter. Since then, I've told Linton he must whisper his bitter things. Now Ellen, you have heard all; and I can't be prevented from going to Wuthering Heights except by inflicting misery on two people; whereas, if you'll only not tell papa, my going need disturb the tranquillity of none. You'll not tell, will you? It will be very heartless if you do.

'I'll make up my mind on that point by tomorrow, Miss Catherine,' I replied. 'It requires some study; and so I'll leave you to your rest, and go think it over.'

I thought it over aloud, in my master's presence; walking straight from her room to his, and relating the whole story: with the exception of her conversations with her cousin, and any mention of Hareton. Mr Linton was alarmed and distressed, more than he would acknowledge to me. In the morning, Catherine learnt my betrayal of her confidence, and she learnt also that her secret visits were to end. In vain she wept and writhed against the interdict, and implored her father to have pity on Linton: all she got to comfort her was a promise that he would write and give him leave to come to the Grange when he pleased; but explaining that he must no longer expect to see Catherine at Wuthering Heights. Perhaps, had he been aware of his nephew's disposition and state of health, he would have seen fit to withhold even that slight consolation.

Chapter XXV

'THESE things happened last winter, sir,' said Mrs Dean; 'hardly more than a year ago. Last winter, I did not think, at another twelve months' end, I should be amusing a stranger to the family with relating them! Yet, who knows how long you'll be a stranger? You're too young to rest always contented, living by yourself; and I some way fancy no one could see Catherine Linton and not love her. You smile; but why do you look so lively and interested, when I talk about her? and why have you asked me to hang her picture over your fireplace? and why——'

'Stop, my good friend!' I cried. 'It may be very possible that *I* should love her; but would she love me? I doubt it too much to venture my tranquillity by running

into temptation: and then my home is not here. I'm of the busy world, and to its arms I must return. Go on. Was Catherine obedient to her father's commands?'

'She was,' continued the housekeeper. 'Her affection for him was still the chief sentiment in her heart; and he spoke without anger: he spoke in the deep tenderness of one about to leave his treasure amid perils and foes, where his remembered words would be the only aid that he could bequeath to guide her. He said to me, a few days afterwards:

' "I wish my nephew would write, Ellen, or call. Tell me, sincerely, what you think of him: is he changed for the better, or is there a prospect of improvement, as he grows a man?"

' "He's very delicate, sir," I replied; "and scarcely likely to reach manhood; but this I can say, he does not resemble his father; and if Miss Catherine had the misfortune to marry him, he would not be beyond her control: unless she were extremely and foolishly indulgent. However, master, you'll have plenty of time to get acquainted with him, and see whether he would suit her: it wants four years and more to his being of age." '

Edgar sighed; and walking to the window, looked out towards Gimmerton Kirk. It was a misty afternoon, but the February sun shone dimly, and we could just distinguish the two fir trees in the yard, and the sparely scattered gravestones.

'I've prayed often', he half soliloquized, 'for the approach of what is coming; and now I begin to shrink, and fear it. I thought the memory of the hour I came down that glen a bridegroom would be less sweet than the anticipation that I was soon, in a few months, or, possibly, weeks, to be carried up, and laid in its lonely hollow! Ellen, I've been very happy with my little Cathy: through winter nights and summer days she was a living hope at my side. But I've been as happy musing by myself among those stones, under that old church: lying, through the long June evenings, on the green mound of her mother's grave and wishing—yearning for the time when I might lie beneath it. What can I do for Cathy? How must I quit her? I'd not care one moment for Linton being Heathcliff's son; nor for his taking her from me, if he could console her for my loss. I'd not care that Heathcliff gained his ends, and triumphed in robbing me of my last blessing! But should Linton be unworthy—only a feeble tool to his father—I cannot abandon her to him! And, hard though it be to crush her buoyant spirit, I must persevere in making her sad while I live, and leaving her solitary when I die. Darling! I'd rather resign her to God, and lay her in the earth before me.'

'Resign her to God, as it is, sir,' I answered, 'and if we should lose you—which may He forbid—under His providence, I'll stand her friend and counsellor to the last. Miss Catherine is a good girl: I don't fear that she will go wilfully wrong; and people who do their duty are always finally rewarded.'

Spring advanced; yet my master gathered no real strength, though he resumed his walks in the grounds with his daughter. To her inexperienced notions, this itself was a sign of convalescence; and then his cheek was often flushed, and his eyes were bright: she felt sure of his recovering. On her seventeenth birthday, he did not visit the churchyard: it was raining, and I observed:

'You'll surely not go out tonight, sir?'

He answered:

'No, I'll defer it this year a little longer.'

He wrote again to Linton, expressing his great desire to see him; and, had the invalid been presentable, I've no doubt his father would have permitted him to come. As it was, being instructed, he returned an answer, intimating that Mr Heathcliff objected to his calling at the Grange; but his uncle's kind remembrance delighted him, and he hoped to meet him, sometimes, in his rambles, and personally to petition that his cousin and he might not remain long so utterly divided.

That part of his letter was simple, and probably his own. Heathcliff knew he could plead eloquently enough for Catherine's company, then.

'I do not ask', he said, 'that she may visit here; but, am I never to see her, because my father forbids me to go to her home, and you forbid her to come to mine? Do now and then, ride with her towards the Heights; and let us exchange a few words, in your presence! We have done nothing to deserve this separation; and you are not angry with me; you have no reason to dislike me, you allow, yourself. Dear uncle! send me a kind note tomorrow, and leave to join you anywhere you please, except at Thrushcross Grange. I believe an interview would convince you that my father's character is not mine: he affirms I am more your nephew than his son; and though I have faults which render me unworthy of Catherine, she has excused them, and for her sake, you should also. You inquire after my health—it is better; but while I remain cut off from all hope, and doomed to solitude, or the society of those who never did and never will like me, how can I be cheerful and well?'

Edgar, though he felt for the boy, could not consent to grant his request; because he could not accompany Catherine. He said, in summer, perhaps, they might meet: meantime, he wished him to continue writing at intervals, and engaged to give him what advice and comfort he was able by letter; being well aware of his hard position in his family. Linton complied; and had he been unrestrained, would probably have spoiled all by filling his epistles with complaints and lamentations: but his father kept a sharp watch over him; and, of course, insisted on every line that my master sent being shown; so, instead of penning his peculiar personal sufferings and distresses, the themes constantly uppermost in his thoughts, he harped on the cruel obligation of being held asunder from his friend and love; and gently intimated that Mr Linton must allow an interview soon, or he should fear he was purposely deceiving him with empty promises.

Cathy was a powerful ally at home; and, between them, they at length persuaded my master to acquiesce in their having a ride or a walk together about once a week, under my guardianship, and on the moors nearest the Grange: for June found him still declining; and though he had set aside yearly a portion of his income for my young lady's fortune, he had a natural desire that she might retain—or at least return in a short time to—the house of her ancestors; and he considered her only prospect of doing that was by a union with his heir; he had no idea that the latter was failing almost as fast as himself; nor had anyone; I believe: no doctor visited the Heights, and no one saw Master Heathcliff to make report of his condition among us. I, for my part, began to fancy my forebodings were false, and that he must be actually rallying, when he mentioned riding and walking on the moors, and seemed so earnest in pursuing his object. I could not picture a father treating a dying child as tyrannically and wickedly as I afterwards learned Heathcliff had treated him, to compel this apparent eagerness: his efforts redoubling the more imminently his avaricious and unfeeling plans were threatened with defeat by death.

Chapter XXVI

SUMMER was already past its prime, when Edgar reluctantly yielded his assent to their entreaties, and Catherine and I set out on our first ride to join her cousin. It was a close, sultry day: devoid of sunshine, but with a sky too dappled and hazy to threaten rain; and our place of meeting had been fixed at the guide-stone, by the crossroads. On arriving there, however, a little herd-boy, dispatched as a messenger, told us that:

'Maister Linton wer just ut this side th' Heights: and he'd be mitch obleeged to us to gang on a bit farther.'

'Then Master Linton has forgot the first injunction of his uncle,' I observed: 'he bid us keep on the Grange land, and here we are off at once.'

'Well, we'll turn our horses' heads round, when we reach him,' answered my companion, 'our excursion shall lie towards home.'

But when we reached him, and that was scarcely a quarter of a mile from his own door, we found he had no horse; and we were forced to dismount, and leave ours to graze. He lay on the heath, awaiting our approach, and did not rise till we came within a few yards. Then he walked so feebly, and looked so pale, that I immediately exclaimed:

'Why, Master Heathcliff, you are not fit for enjoying a ramble, this morning. How ill you do look!'

Catherine surveyed him with grief and astonishment; and changed the ejaculation of joy on her lips, to one of alarm; and the congratulation on their long-postponed meeting, to an anxious inquiry, whether he were worse than usual?

'No—better—better!' he panted, trembling, and retaining her hand as if he needed its support, while his large blue eyes wandered timidly over her; the hollowness round them transforming to haggard wildness the languid expression they once possessed.

'But you have been worse,' persisted his cousin; 'worse than when I saw you last; you are thinner, and——'

'I'm tired,' he interrupted hurriedly. 'It is too hot for walking, let us rest here. And, in the morning, I often feel sick—papa says I grow so fast.'

Badly satisfied, Cathy sat down, and he reclined beside her.

'This is something like your paradise,' said she, making an effort at cheerfulness. 'You recollect the two days we agreed to spend in the place and way each thought pleasantest? This is surely yours, only there are clouds: but then they are so soft and mellow: it is nicer than sunshine. Next week, if you can, we'll ride down to the Grange Park, and try mine.'

Linton did not appear to remember what she talked of; and he had evidently great difficulty in sustaining any kind of conversation. His lack of interest in the subjects she started, and his equal incapacity to contribute to her entertainment, were so obvious that she could not conceal her disappointment. An indefinite alteration had come over his whole person and manner. The pettishness that might be caressed into fondness, had yielded to a listless apathy; there was less of the peevish temper of a child which frets and teases on purpose to be soothed, and more of the self-absorbed moroseness of a confirmed invalid, repelling consolation, and ready to regard the good-humoured mirth of others as an insult. Catherine perceived, as well as I did, that he held it rather a punishment, than a gratification, to endure our company; and she made no scruple of proposing, presently, to depart. That proposal, unexpectedly, roused Linton from his lethargy, and threw him into a strange state of agitation. He glanced fearfully towards the Heights, begging she would remain another half-hour at least.

'But I think', said Cathy, 'you'd be more comfortable at home than sitting here; and I cannot amuse you today, I see, by my tales, and songs, and chatter: you have grown wiser than I, in these six months; you have little taste for my diversions now: or else, if I could amuse you, I'd willingly stay.'

'Stay to rest yourself,' he replied. 'And Catherine, don't think, or say that I'm *very* unwell: it is the heavy weather and heat that make me dull; and I walked about, before you came, a great deal for me. Tell uncle I'm in tolerable health, will you?'

'I'll tell him that *you* say so, Linton. I couldn't affirm that you are,' observed my young lady, wondering at his pertinacious assertion of what was evidently an untruth.

'And be here again next Thursday,' continued he, shunning her puzzled gaze. 'And give him my thanks for permitting you to come—my best thanks, Catherine.

And—and, if you *did* meet my father, and he asked you about me, don't lead him to suppose that I've been extremely silent and stupid: don't look sad and downcast, as you *are* doing—he'll be angry.'

'I care nothing for his anger,' exclaimed Cathy, imagining she would be its object.

'But I do,' said her cousin, shuddering. *'Don't* provoke him against me, Catherine, for he is very hard.'

'Is he severe to you, Master Heathcliff?' I inquired. 'Has he grown weary of indulgence, and passed from passive to active hatred?'

Linton looked at me, but did not answer; and, after keeping her seat by his side another ten minutes, during which his head fell drowsily on his breast, and he uttered nothing except suppressed moans of exhaustion or pain, Cathy began to seek solace in looking for bilberries, and sharing the produce of her researches with me: she did not offer them to him, for she saw further notice would only weary and annoy.

'Is it half an hour now, Ellen?' she whispered in my ear, at last. 'I can't tell why we should stay. He's asleep, and papa will be wanting us back.'

'Well, we must not leave him asleep,' I answered; 'wait till he wakes, and be patient. You were mighty eager to set off, but your longing to see poor Linton has soon evaporated!'

'Why did *he* wish to see me?' returned Catherine. 'In his crossest humours, formerly, I liked him better than I do in his present curious mood. It's just as if it were a task he was compelled to perform—this interview—for fear his father should scold him. But I'm hardly going to come to give Mr Heathcliff pleasure; whatever reason he may have for ordering Linton to undergo this penance. And, though I'm glad he's better in health, I'm sorry he's so much less pleasant, and so much less affectionate to me.'

'You think *he is* better in health then?' I said.

'Yes,' she answered; 'because he always made such a great deal of his sufferings, you know. He is not tolerably well, as he told me to tell papa; but he's better, very likely.'

'There you differ with me, Miss Cathy,' I remarked; 'I should conjecture him to be far worse.'

Linton here started from his slumber in bewildered terror, and asked if anyone had called his name.

'No,' said Catherine; 'unless in dreams. I cannot conceive how you manage to doze out of doors, in the morning.'

'I thought I heard my father,' he gasped, glancing up to the frowning nab above us. 'You are sure nobody spoke?'

'Quite sure,' replied his cousin. 'Only Ellen and I were disputing concerning your health. Are you truly stronger, Linton, than when we separated in winter? If you be I'm certain one thing is not stronger—your regard for me: speak,—are you?'

The tears gushed from Linton's eyes as he answered, 'Yes, yes, I am!' And, still under the spell of the imaginary voice, his gaze wandered up and down to detect its owner. Cathy rose. 'For today we must part,' she said. 'And I won't conceal that I have been sadly disappointed with our meeting; though I'll mention it to nobody but you: not that I stand in awe of Mr Heathcliff.'

'Hush,' murmured Linton: 'for God's sake, hush! He's coming.' And he clung to Catherine's arm, striving to detain her; but at that announcement she hastily disengaged herself, and whistled to Minny, who obeyed her like a dog.

'I'll be here next Thursday,' she cried, springing to the saddle. 'Goodbye. Quick, Ellen!'

And so we left him, scarcely conscious of our departure, so absorbed was he in anticipating his father's approach.

Before we reached home, Catherine's displeasure softened into a perplexed sensation of pity and regret, largely blended with vague, uneasy doubts about Linton's actual circumstances, physical and social; in which I partook, though I counselled her not to say much; for a second journey would make us better judges. My master requested an account of our ongoings. His nephew's offering of thanks was duly delivered, Miss Cathy gently touching on the rest: I also threw little light on his inquiries, for I hardly knew what to hide, and what to reveal.

Chapter XXVII

SEVEN days glided away, every one marking its course by the henceforth rapid alteration of Edgar Linton's state. The havoc that months had previously wrought was now emulated by the inroads of hours. Catherine, we would fain have deluded yet: but her own quick spirit refused to delude her: it divined in secret, and brooded on the dreadful probability, gradually ripening into certainty. She had not the heart to mention her ride, when Thursday came round; I mentioned it for her, and obtained permission to order her out of doors: for the library, where her father stopped a short time daily—the brief period he could bear to sit up—and his chamber, had become her whole world. She grudged each moment that did not find her bending over his pillow, or seated by his side. Her countenance grew wan with watching and sorrow, and my master gladly dismissed her to what he flattered himself would be a happy change of scene and society; drawing comfort from the hope that she would not now be left entirely alone after his death.

He had a fixed idea, I guessed by several observations he let fall, that, as his nephew resembled him in person, he would resemble him in mind; for Linton's letters bore few or no indications of his defective character. And I, through pardonable weakness, refrained from correcting the error; asking myself what good there would be in disturbing his last moments with information that he had neither power nor opportunity to turn to account.

We deferred our excursion till the afternoon; a golden afternoon of August: every breath from the hills so full of life, that it seemed whoever respired it, though dying, might revive. Catherine's face was just like the landscape—shadows and sunshine flitting over it in rapid succession; but the shadows rested longer, and the sunshine was more transient; and her poor little heart reproached itself for even that passing forgetfulness of its cares.

We discerned Linton watching at the same spot he had selected before. My young mistress alighted, and told me that, as she was resolved to stay a very little while, I had better hold the pony and remain on horseback; but I dissented: I wouldn't risk losing sight of the charge committed to me a minute; so we climbed the slope of heath together. Master Heathcliff received us with greater animation on this occasion: not the animation of high spirits though, nor yet of joy; it looked more like fear.

'It is late!' he said, speaking short and with difficulty. 'Is not your father very ill? I thought you wouldn't come.'

'*Why* won't you be candid?' cried Catherine, swallowing her greeting. 'Why cannot you say at once you don't want me? It is strange, Linton, that for the second time you have brought me here on purpose, apparently, to distress us both, and for no reason besides!'

Linton shivered, and glanced at her, half supplicating, half ashamed; but his cousin's patience was not sufficient to endure this enigmatical behaviour.

'My father *is* very ill,' she said; 'and why am I called from his bedside? Why didn't you send to absolve me from my promise, when you wished I wouldn't keep

it? Come! I desire an explanation: playing and trifling are completely banished out of my mind; and I can't dance attendance on your affectations now!'

'My affections!' he murmured; 'what are they? For Heaven's sake, Catherine, don't look so angry! Despise me as much as you please; I am a worthless, cowardly wretch: I can't be scorned enough; but I'm too mean for your anger. Hate my father, and spare me for contempt.'

'Nonsense!' cried Catherine, in a passion. 'Foolish, silly boy! And there! he trembles, as if I were really going to touch him! You needn't bespeak contempt, Linton: anybody will have it spontaneously at your service. Get off! I shall return home: it is folly dragging you from the hearthstone, and pretending—what do we pretend? Let go my frock! If I pitied you for crying and looking so very frightened, you should spurn such pity. Ellen, tell him how disgraceful this conduct is. Rise, and don't degrade yourself into an abject reptile—*don't*!'

With streaming face and an expression of agony, Linton had thrown his nerveless frame along the ground: he seemed convulsed with exquisite terror.

'Oh!' he sobbed, 'I cannot bear it! Catherine, Catherine, I'm a traitor, too, and I dare not tell you! But leave me, and I shall be killed! *Dear* Catherine, my life is in your hands: and you have said you loved me, and if you did, it wouldn't harm you. You'll not go, then? kind, sweet, good Catherine! And perhaps you *will* consent—and he'll let me die with you!'

My young lady, on witnessing his intense anguish, stooped to raise him. The old feeling of indulgent tenderness overcame her vexation, and she grew thoroughly moved and alarmed.

'Consent to what?' she asked. 'To stay? Tell me the meaning of this strange talk, and I will. You contradict your own words, and distract me! Be calm and frank, and confess at once all that weighs on your heart. You wouldn't injure me, Linton, would you? You wouldn't let any enemy hurt me, if you could prevent it? I'll believe you are a coward for yourself, but not a cowardly betrayer of your best friend.'

'But my father threatened me,' gasped the boy, clasping his attenuated fingers, 'and I dread him—I dread him! I *dare* not tell!'

'Oh, well!' said Catherine, with scornful compassion, 'keep your secret: *I'm* no coward. Save yourself: I'm not afraid!'

Her magnanimity provoked his tears: he wept wildly, kissing her supporting hands, and yet could not summon courage to speak out. I was cogitating what the mystery might be, and determined Catherine should never suffer, to benefit him or anyone else, by my goodwill; when hearing a rustle among the ling, I looked up and saw Mr Heathcliff almost close upon us, descending the Heights. He didn't cast a glance towards my companions, though they were sufficiently near for Linton's sobs to be audible; but hailing me in the almost hearty tone he assumed to none besides, and the sincerity of which I couldn't avoid doubting, he said:

'It is something to see you so near to my house, Nelly. How are you at the Grange? Let us hear. The rumour goes', he added in a lower tone, 'that Edgar Linton is on his deathbed: perhaps they exaggerate his illness!'

'No; my master is dying,' I replied: 'it is true enough. A sad thing it will be for us all, but a blessing for him!'

'How long will he last, do you think?' he asked.

'I don't know,' I said.

'Because,' he continued, looking at the two young people, who were fixed under his eye—Linton appeared as if he could not venture to stir or raise his head, and Catherine could not move, on his account—'because that lad yonder seems determined to beat me; and I'd thank his uncle to be quick, and go before him. Hallo! has the whelp been playing that game long? I *did* give him some lessons about snivelling. Is he pretty lively with Miss Linton generally?'

'Lively? no—he has shown the greatest distress,' I answered. 'To see him, I should say, that instead of rambling with his sweetheart on the hills, he ought to be in bed, under the hands of a doctor.'

'He shall be in a day or two,' muttered Heathcliff. 'But first—get up, Linton! Get up!' he shouted. 'Don't grovel on the ground there: up, this moment!'

Linton had sunk prostrate again in another paroxysm of helpless fear, caused by his father's glance towards him, I suppose: there was nothing else to produce such humiliation. He made several efforts to obey, but his little strength was annihilated for the time, and he fell back again with a moan. Mr Heathcliff advanced, and lifted him to lean against a ridge of turf.

'Now,' said he, with curbed ferocity, 'I'm getting angry; and if you don't command that paltry spirit of yours—*Damn* you! get up directly!'

'I will, Father,' he panted. 'Only, let me alone, or I shall faint. I've done as you wished, I'm sure. Catherine will tell you that I—that I—have been cheerful. Ah! keep by me, Catherine: give me your hand.'

'Take mine,' said his father; 'stand on your feet. There now—she'll lend you her arm: that's right, look at *her*. You would imagine I was the devil himself, Miss Linton, to excite such horror. Be so kind as to walk home with him, will you? He shudders if I touch him.'

'Linton, dear!' whispered Catherine, 'I can't go to Wuthering Heights: papa has forbidden me. He'll not harm you: why are you so afraid?'

'I can never re-enter that house,' he answered. 'I'm *not* to re-enter it without you!'

'Stop!' cried his father. 'We'll respect Catherine's filial scruples. Nelly, take him in, and I'll follow your advice concerning the doctor, without delay.'

'You'll do well,' replied I. 'But I must remain with my mistress: to mind your son is not my business.'

'You are very stiff,' said Heathcliff, 'I know that: but you'll force me to pinch the baby and make it scream before it moves your charity. Come, then, my hero. Are you willing to return, escorted by me?'

He approached once more, and made as if he would seize the fragile being; but, shrinking back, Linton clung to his cousin, and implored her to accompany him, with a frantic importunity that admitted no denial. However I disapproved, I couldn't hinder her: indeed, how could she have refused him herself? What was filling him with dread we had no means of discerning: but there he was, powerless under its grip, and any addition seemed capable of shocking him into idiotcy. We reached the threshold: Catherine walked in, and I stood waiting till she had conducted the invalid to a chair, expecting her out immediately; when Mr Heathcliff, pushing me forward, exclaimed:

'My house is not stricken with the plague, Nelly; and I have a mind to be hospitable today: sit down, and allow me to shut the door.'

He shut and locked it also. I started.

'You shall have tea before you go home,' he added. 'I am by myself. Hareton is gone with some cattle to the Lees, and Zillah and Joseph are off on a journey of pleasure; and, though I'm used to being alone, I'd rather have some interesting company, if I can get it. Miss Linton, take your seat by *him*. I give you what I have: the present is hardly worth accepting; but I have nothing else to offer. It is Linton, I mean. How she does stare! It's odd what a savage feeling I have to anything that seems afraid of me! Had I been born where laws are less strict and tastes less dainty, I should treat myself to a slow vivisection of those two, as an evening's amusement.'

He drew in his breath, struck the table, and swore to himself, 'By hell! I hate them.'

'I'm not afraid of you!' exclaimed Catherine, who could not hear the latter part of his speech. She stepped close up; her black eyes flashing with passion and

resolution. 'Give me that key: I will have it!' she said. 'I wouldn't eat or drink here, if I were starving.'

Heathcliff had the key in his hand that remained on the table. He looked up, seized with a sort of surprise at her boldness; or, possibly, reminded by her voice and glance, of the person from whom she inherited it. She snatched at the instrument, and half succeeded in getting it out of his loosened fingers: but her action recalled him to the present; he recovered it speedily.

'Now, Catherine Linton,' he said, 'stand off, or I shall knock you down; and that will make Mrs Dean mad.'

Regardless of this warning, she captured his closed hand and its contents again. 'We *will* go!' she repeated, exerting her utmost efforts to cause the iron muscles to relax; and finding that her nails made no impression, she applied her teeth pretty sharply. Heathcliff glanced at me a glance that kept me from interfering a moment. Catherine was too intent on his fingers to notice his face. He opened them suddenly, and resigned the object of dispute; but, ere she had well secured it, he seized her with the liberated hand, and, pulling her on his knee, administered with the other a shower of terrific slaps on the side of the head, each sufficient to have fulfilled his threat, had she been able to fall.

At this diabolical violence I rushed on him furiously. 'You villain!' I began to cry, 'you villain!' A touch on the chest silenced me: I am stout, and soon put out of breath; and, what with that and the rage, I staggered dizzily back, and felt ready to suffocate, or to burst a blood vessel. The scene was over in two minutes; Catherine, released, put her two hands to her temples, and looked just as if she were not sure whether her ears were off or on. She trembled like a reed, poor thing, and leant against the table perfectly bewildered.

'I know how to chastise children, you see,' said the scoundrel grimly, as he stooped to repossess himself of the key, which had dropped to the floor. 'Go to Linton now, as I told you; and cry at your ease! I shall be your father, tomorrow— all the father you'll have in a few days—and you shall have plenty of that. You can bear plenty; you're no weakling: you shall have a daily taste, if I catch such a devil of a temper in your eyes again!'

Cathy ran to me instead of Linton, and knelt down and put her burning cheek on my lap, weeping aloud. Her cousin had shrunk into a corner of the settle, as quiet as a mouse, congratulating himself, I dare say, that the correction had lighted on another than him. Mr Heathcliff, perceiving us all confounded, rose, and expeditiously made the tea himself. The cups and saucers were laid ready. He poured it out, and handed me a cup.

'Wash away your spleen,' he said. 'And help your own naughty pet and mine. It is not poisoned, though I prepared it. I'm going out to seek your horses.'

Our first thought, on his departure, was to force an exit somewhere. We tried the kitchen door, but that was fastened outside: we looked at the windows—they were too narrow for even Cathy's little figure.

'Master Linton,' I cried, seeing we were regularly imprisoned: 'you know what your diabolical father is after, and you shall tell us, or I'll box your ears, as he has done your cousin's.'

'Yes, Linton, you must tell,' said Catherine. 'It was for your sake I came; and it will be wickedly ungrateful if you refuse.'

'Give me some tea, I'm thirsty, and then I'll tell you,' he answered. 'Mrs Dean, go away. I don't like you standing over me. Now, Catherine, you are letting your tears fall into my cup. I won't drink that. Give me another.'

Catherine pushed another to him, and wiped her face. I felt disgusted at the little wretch's composure, since he was no longer in terror for himself. The anguish he had exhibited on the moor subsided as soon as ever he entered Wuthering Heights; so I guessed he had been menaced with an awful visitation of wrath if he failed in decoying us there; and, that accomplished, he had no further immediate fears.

'Papa wants us to be married,' he continued, after sipping some of the liquid. 'And he knows your papa wouldn't let us marry now; and he's afraid of my dying, if we wait; so we are to be married in the morning, and you are to stay here all night; and if you do as he wishes, you shall return home next day, and take me with you.'

'Take you with her, pitiful changeling?' I exclaimed. '*You* marry? Why, the man is mad; or he thinks us fools, every one. And do you imagine that beautiful young lady, that healthy, hearty girl, will tie herself to a little perishing monkey like you! Are you cherishing the notion that *anybody,* let alone Miss Catherine Linton, would have you for a husband? You want whipping for bringing us in here at all, with your dastardly puling tricks; and—don't look so silly, now! I've a very good mind to shake you severely, for your contemptible treachery, and your imbecile conceit.'

I did give him a slight shaking; but it brought on the cough, and he took to his ordinary resource of moaning and weeping, and Catherine rebuked me.

'Stay all night? No,' she said, looking slowly round. 'Ellen, I'll burn that door down, but I'll get out.'

And she would have commenced the execution of her threat directly, but Linton was up in alarm for his dear self again. He clasped her in his two feeble arms, sobbing:

'Won't you have me, and save me? not let me come to the Grange? Oh! darling Catherine! you mustn't go and leave me, after all. You *must* obey my father—you *must*!'

'I must obey my own,' she replied, 'and relieve him from this cruel suspense. The whole night! What would he think? he'll be distressed already. I'll either break or burn a way out of the house. Be quiet! You're in no danger; but if you hinder me—Linton, I love papa better than you!'

The mortal terror he felt of Mr Heathcliff's anger, restored to the boy his coward's eloquence. Catherine was near distraught: still, she persisted that she must go home, and tried entreaty in her turn, persuading him to subdue his selfish agony. While they were thus occupied, our gaoler re-entered.

'Your beasts have trotted off,' he said, 'and—now, Linton! snivelling again? What has she been doing to you? Come, come—have done, and get to bed. In a month or two, my lad, you'll be able to pay her back her present tyrannies with a vigorous hand. You're pining for pure love, are you not? nothing else in the world: and she shall have you! There, to bed! Zillah won't be here tonight; you must undress yourself. Hush! hold your noise! Once in your own room, I'll not come near you: you needn't fear. By chance you've managed tolerably. I'll look to the rest.'

He spoke these words, holding the door open for his son to pass; and the latter achieved his exit exactly as a spaniel might, which suspected the person who attended on it of designing a spiteful squeeze. The lock was re-secured. Heathcliff approached the fire, where my mistress and I stood silent. Catherine looked up, and instinctively raised her hand to her cheek: his neighbourhood revived a painful sensation. Anybody else would have been incapable of regarding the childish act with sternness, but he scowled on her, and muttered:

'Oh! you are not afraid of me? Your courage is well disguised: you *seem* damnably afraid!'

'I *am* afraid now,' she replied, 'because, if I stay, papa will be miserable; and how can I endure making him miserable;—when he—when he—Mr Heathcliff, *let* me go home! I promise to marry Linton: papa would like me to, and I love him—why should you wish to force me to do what I'll willingly do of myself?'

'Let him dare to force you!' I cried. 'There's law in the land, thank God there is; though we *be* in an out-of-the-way place. I'd inform if he were my own son: and it's felony without benefit of clergy!'

'Silence!' said the ruffian. 'To the devil with your clamour! I don't want *you* to speak. Miss Linton, I shall enjoy myself remarkably in thinking your father will be miserable: I shall not sleep for satisfaction. You could have hit on no surer way of fixing your residence under my roof for the next twenty-four hours, than informing me that such an event would follow. As to your promise to marry Linton, I'll take care you shall keep it; for you shall not quit this place till it is fulfilled.'

'Send Ellen, then, to let papa know I'm safe!' exclaimed Catherine, weeping bitterly. 'Or marry me now. Poor papa! Ellen, he'll think we're lost. What shall we do?'

'Not he! He'll think you are tired of waiting on him, and run off for a little amusement,' answered Heathcliff. 'You cannot deny that you entered my house of your own accord, in contempt of his injunctions to the contrary. And it is quite natural that you should desire amusement at your age; and that you would weary of nursing a sick man, and that man *only* your father. Catherine, his happiest days were over when your days began. He cursed you, I dare say, for coming into the world (I did, at least); and it would just do if he cursed you as *he* went out of it. I'd join him. I don't love you! How should I? Weep away. As far as I can see, it will be your chief diversion hereafter; unless Linton make amends for other losses: and your provident parent appears to fancy he may. His letters of advice and consolation entertained me vastly. In his last he recommended my jewel to be careful of his; and kind to her when he got her. Careful and kind—that's paternal. But Linton requires his whole stock of care and kindness for himself. Linton can play the little tyrant well. He'll undertake to torture any number of cats, if their teeth be drawn and their claws pared. You'll be able to tell his uncle fine tales of his *kindness,* when you get home again, I assure you.'

'You're right there!' I said; 'explain your son's character. Show his resemblance to yourself; and then, I hope, Miss Cathy will think twice before she takes the cockatrice!'

'I don't much mind speaking of his amiable qualities now,' he answered; 'because she must either accept him or remain a prisoner, and you along with her, till your master dies. I can detain you both, quite concealed, here. If you doubt, encourage her to retract her word, and you'll have an opportunity of judging!'

'I'll not retract my word,' said Catherine. 'I'll marry him within this hour, if I may go to Thrushcross Grange afterwards. Mr Heathcliff, you're a cruel man, but you're not a fiend; and you won't, from *mere* malice, destroy irrevocably all my happiness. If papa thought I had left him on purpose, and if he died before I returned, could I bear to live? I've given over crying: but I'm going to kneel here, at your knee; and I'll not get up, and I'll not take my eyes from your face till you look back at me! No, don't turn away! *do* look! You'll see nothing to provoke you. I don't hate you. I'm not angry that you struck me. Have you never loved *anybody* in all your life, uncle? *never?* Ah! you must look once. I'm so wretched, you can't help being sorry and pitying me.'

'Keep your eft's fingers off; and move, or I'll kick you!' cried Heathcliff, brutally repulsing her. 'I'd rather be hugged by a snake. How the devil can you dream of fawning on me? I *detest* you!'

He shrugged his shoulders: shook himself, indeed, as if his flesh crept with aversion; and thrust back his chair; while I got up, and opened my mouth, to commence a downright torrent of abuse. But I was rendered dumb in the middle of the first sentence, by a threat that I should be shown into a room by myself the very next syllable I uttered. It was growing dark—we heard a sound of voices at the garden gate. Our host hurried out instantly: *he* had his wits about him; *we* had not. There was a talk of two or three minutes, and he returned alone.

'I thought it had been your cousin Hareton,' I observed to Catherine. 'I wish he would arrive! Who knows but he might take our part?'

'It was three servants sent to seek you from the Grange,' said Heathcliff, overhearing me. 'You should have opened a lattice and called out: but I could swear that chit is glad you didn't. She's glad to be obliged to stay, I'm certain.'

At learning the chance we had missed, we both gave vent to our grief without control; and he allowed us to wail on till nine o'clock. Then he bid us go upstairs, through the kitchen, to Zillah's chamber; and I whispered my companion to obey: perhaps we might contrive to get through the window there, or into a garret, and out by its skylight. The window, however, was narrow, like those below, and the garret trap was safe from our attempts; for we were fastened in as before. We neither of us lay down: Catherine took her station by the lattice, and watched anxiously for morning; a deep sigh being the only answer I could obtain to my frequent entreaties that she would try to rest. I seated myself in a chair, and rocked to and fro, passing harsh judgment on my many derelictions of duty; from which, it struck me then, all the misfortunes of all my employers sprang. It was not the case, in reality, I am aware; but it was, in my imagination, that dismal night; and I thought Heathcliff himself less guilty than I.

At seven o'clock he came, and inquired if Miss Linton had risen. She ran to the door immediately, and answered, 'Yes.' 'Here, then,' he said, opening it, and pulling her out. I rose to follow, but he turned the lock again. I demanded my release.

'Be patient,' he replied; 'I'll send up your breakfast in a while.'

I thumped on the panels, and rattled the latch angrily; and Catherine asked why I was still shut up? He answered, I must try to endure it another hour, and they went away. I endured it two or three hours; at length, I heard a footstep: not Heathcliff's.

'I've brought you something to eat,' said a voice; 'oppen t' door!'

Complying eagerly, I beheld Hareton, laden with food enough to last me all day. 'Tak it,' he added, thrusting the tray into my hand.

'Stay one minute,' I began.

'Nay,' cried he, and retired, regardless of any prayers I could pour forth to detain him.

And there I remained enclosed the whole day, and the whole of the next night; and another, and another. Five nights and four days I remained, altogether, seeing nobody but Hareton, once every morning; and he was a model of a jailer: surly, and dumb, and deaf to every attempt at moving his sense of justice or compassion.

Chapter XXVIII

ON the fifth morning, or rather afternoon, a different step approached—lighter and shorter; and, this time, the person entered the room. It was Zillah; donned in her scarlet shawl, with a black silk bonnet on her head, and a willow basket swung to her arm.

'Eh, dear! Mrs Dean!' she exclaimed. 'Well! there is a talk about you at Gimmerton. I never thought but you were sunk in the Blackhorse marsh, and missy with you till master told me you'd been found, and he'd lodged you here! What! and you must have got on an island, sure? And how long were you in the hole? Did master save you, Mrs Dean? But you're not so thin—you've not been so poorly, have you?'

'Your master is a true scoundrel!' I replied. 'But he shall answer for it. He needn't have raised that tale: it shall all be laid bare!'

'What do you mean?' asked Zillah. 'It's not his tale: they tell that in the village—about your being lost in the marsh: and I calls to Earnshaw, when I come in—

"Eh, they's queer things, Mr Hareton, happened since I went off. It's a sad pity of that likely young lass, and cant Nelly Dean." He stared. I thought he had not heard aught, so I told him the rumour. The master listened, and he just smiled to himself, and said, "If they have been in the marsh, they are out now, Zillah. Nelly Dean is lodged, at this minute, in your room. You can tell her to flit, when you go up; here is the key. The bog water got into her head, and she would have run home quite flighty; but I fixed her till she came round to her senses. You can bid her go to the Grange at once, if she be able, and carry a message from me, that her young lady will follow in time to attend the squire's funeral." '

'Mr Edgar is not dead?' I gasped. 'Oh! Zillah, Zillah!'

'No, no; sit you down, my good mistress,' she replied, 'you're right sickly yet. He's not dead; Doctor Kenneth thinks he may last another day. I met him on the road and asked.'

Instead of sitting down, I snatched my outdoor things, and hastened below, for the way was free. On entering the house, I looked about for someone to give information of Catherine. The place was filled with sunshine, and the door stood wide open; but nobody seemed at hand. As I hesitated whether to go off at once, or return and seek my mistress, a slight cough drew my attention to the hearth. Linton lay on the settle, sole tenant, sucking a stick of sugar-candy, and pursuing my movements with apathetic eyes. 'Where is Miss Catherine?' I demanded sternly, supposing I could frighten him into giving intelligence, by catching him thus, alone. He sucked on like an innocent.

'Is she gone?' I said.

'No,' he replied; 'she's upstairs: she's not to go; we won't let her.'

'You won't let her, little idiot!' I exclaimed. 'Direct me to her room immediately, or I'll make you sing out sharply.'

'Papa would make you sing out, if you attempted to get there,' he answered. 'He says I'm not to be soft with Catherine: she's my wife, and it's shameful that she should wish to leave me. He says, she hates me and wants me to die, that she may have my money; but she shan't have it: and she shan't go home! She never shall!—she may cry, and be sick as much as she pleases!'

He resumed his former occupation, closing his lids, as if he meant to drop asleep.

'Master Heathcliff,' I resumed, 'have you forgotten all Catherine's kindness to you last winter, when you affirmed you loved her, and when she brought you books and sung you songs, and came many a time through wind and snow to see you? She wept to miss one evening, because you would be disappointed; and you felt then that she was a hundred times too good to you: and now you believe the lies your father tells, though you know he detests you both. And you join him against her. That's fine gratitude, is it not?'

The corner of Linton's mouth fell, and he took the sugar-candy from his lips.

'Did she come to Wuthering Heights, because she hated you?' I continued. 'Think for yourself! As to your money, she does not even know that you will have any. And you say she's sick; and yet, you leave her alone, up there in a strange house! *You* who have felt what it is to be so neglected! You could pity your own sufferings; and she pitied them too; but you won't pity hers! I shed tears, Master Heathcliff, you see—an elderly woman, and a servant merely—and you, after pretending such affection, and having reason to worship her almost, store every tear you have for yourself, and lie there quite at ease. Ah! you're a heartless, selfish boy!'

'I can't stay with her,' he answered crossly. 'I'll not stay by myself. She cries so I can't bear it. And she won't give over, though I say I'll call my father. I did call him once, and he threatened to strangle her, if she was not quiet; but she began again the instant he left the room, moaning and grieving all night long, though I screamed for vexation that I couldn't sleep.'

'Is Mr Heathcliff out?' I inquired, perceiving that the wretched creature had no power to sympathize with his cousin's mental tortures.

'He's in the court,' he replied, 'talking to Dr Kenneth; who says uncle is dying, truly, at last. I'm glad, for I shall be master of the Grange after him—and Catherine always spoke of it as *her* house. It isn't hers! It's mine: papa says everything she has is mine. All her nice books are mine; she offered to give me them, and her pretty birds, and her pony Minny, if I would get the key of our room, and let her out; but I told her she had nothing to give, they were all, all mine. And then she cried, and took a little picture from her neck, and said I should have that; two pictures in a gold case, on one side her mother, and on the other, uncle, when they were young. That was yesterday—I said *they* were mine, too; and tried to get them from her. The spiteful thing wouldn't let me: she pushed me off, and hurt me. I shrieked out—that frightens her—she heard papa coming, and she broke the hinges and divided the case, and gave me her mother's portrait; the other she attempted to hide: but papa asked what was the matter, and I explained it. He took the one I had away, and ordered her to resign hers to me; she refused, and he—he struck her down, and wrenched it off the chain, and crushed it with his foot.'

'And were you pleased to see her struck?' I asked: having my designs in encouraging his talk.

'I winked,' he answered: 'I wink to see my father strike a dog or a horse, he does it so hard. Yet I was glad at first—she deserved punishing for pushing me: but when papa was gone, she made me come to the window and showed me her cheek cut on the inside, against her teeth, and her mouth filling with blood; and then she gathered up the bits of the picture, and went and sat down with her face to the wall, and she has never spoken to me since: and I sometimes think she can't speak for pain. I don't like to think so; but she's a naughty thing for crying continually; and she looks so pale and wild, I'm afraid of her.'

'And you can get the key if you choose?' I said.

'Yes, when I'm upstairs,' he answered; 'but I can't walk upstairs now.'

'In what apartment is it?' I asked.

'Oh,' he cried, 'I shan't tell *you* where it is! It is our secret. Nobody, neither Hareton nor Zillah, is to know. There! you've tired me—go away, go away!' And he turned his face on to his arm, and shut his eyes again.

I considered it best to depart without seeing Mr Heathcliff, and bring a rescue for my young lady from the Grange. On reaching it, the astonishment of my fellow-servants to see me, and their joy also, was intense; and when they heard that their little mistress was safe, two or three were about to hurry up and shout the news at Mr Edgar's door: but I bespoke the announcement of it, myself. How changed I found him, even in those few days! He lay an image of sadness and resignation waiting his death. Very young he looked; though his actual age was thirty-nine, one would have called him ten years younger, at least. He thought of Catherine; for he murmured her name. I touched his hand, and spoke.

'Catherine is coming, dear master!' I whispered; 'she is alive and well; and will be here, I hope, tonight.'

I trembled at the first effects of this intelligence: he half rose up, looked eagerly round the apartment, and then sank back in a swoon. As soon as he recovered, I related our compulsory visit, and detention at the Heights. I said Heathcliff forced me to go in: which was not quite true. I uttered as little as possible against Linton; nor did I describe all his father's brutal conduct—my intentions being to add no bitterness, if I could help it, to his already overflowing cup.

He divined that one of his enemy's purposes was to secure the personal property, as well as the estate, to his son: or rather himself; yet why he did not wait till his decease was a puzzle to my master, because ignorant how nearly he and his nephew would quit the world together. However, he felt that his will had better be altered: instead of leaving Catherine's fortune at her own disposal, he determined to put it in the hands of trustees for her use during life, and for her children, if she had any, after her. By that means, it could not fall to Mr Heathcliff should Linton die.

Having received his orders, I dispatched a man to fetch the attorney, and four more, provided with serviceable weapons, to demand my young lady of her jailer. Both parties were delayed very late. The single servant returned first. He said Mr Green, the lawyer, was out when he arrived at his house, and he had to wait two hours for his re-entrance; and then Mr Green told him he had a little business in the village that must be done; but he would be at Thrushcross Grange before morning. The four men came back unaccompanied also. They brought word that Catherine was ill: too ill to quit her room; and Heathcliff would not suffer them to see her. I scolded the stupid fellows well for listening to that tale, which I would not carry to my master; resolving to take a whole bevy up to the Heights, at daylight, and storm it literally, unless the prisoner were quietly surrendered to us. Her father *shall* see her, I vowed, and vowed again, if that devil be killed on his own doorstones in trying to prevent it!

Happily, I was spared the journey and the trouble. I had gone downstairs at three o'clock to fetch a jug of water; and was passing through the hall with it in my hand, when a sharp knock at the front door made me jump. 'Oh! it is Green,' I said, recollecting myself—'only Green,' and I went on, intending to send somebody else to open it; but the knock was repeated: not loud, and still importunately. I put the jug on the banister and hastened to admit him myself. The harvest moon shone clear outside. It was not the attorney. My own sweet little mistress sprang on my neck, sobbing:

'Ellen! Ellen! is papa alive?'

'Yes,' I cried: 'yes, my angel, he is. God be thanked, you are safe with us again!'

She wanted to run, breathless as she was, upstairs to Mr Linton's room; but I compelled her to sit down on a chair, and made her drink, and washed her pale face, chafing it into a faint colour with my apron. Then I said I must go first, and tell of her arrival; imploring her to say, she should be happy with young Heathcliff. She stared, but soon comprehending why I counselled her to utter the falsehood, she assured me she would not complain.

I couldn't abide to be present at their meeting. I stood outside the chamber door a quarter of an hour, and hardly ventured near the bed, then. All was composed, however: Catherine's despair was as silent as her father's joy. She supported him calmly, in appearance; and he fixed on her features his raised eyes, that seemed dilating with ecstasy.

He died blissfully, Mr Lockwood: he died so. Kissing her cheek, he murmured. 'I am going to her; and you, darling child, shall come to us!' and never stirred or spoke again; but continued that rapt, radiant gaze, till his pulse imperceptibly stopped and his soul departed. None could have noticed the exact minute of his death, it was so entirely without a struggle.

Whether Catherine had spent her tears, or whether the grief were too weighty to let them flow, she sat there dry-eyed till the sun rose: she sat till noon, and would still have remained brooding over that deathbed, but I insisted on her coming away and taking some repose. It was well I succeeded in removing her; for at dinner time appeared the lawyer, having called at Wuthering Heights to get his instructions how to behave. He had sold himself to Mr Heathcliff, and that was the cause of his delay in obeying my master's summons. Fortunately, no thought of worldly affairs crossed the latter's mind, to disturb him, after his daughter's arrival.

Mr Green took upon himself to order everything and everybody about the place. He gave all the servants, but me, notice to quit. He would have carried his delegated authority to the point of insisting that Edgar Linton should not be buried beside his wife, but in the chapel, with his family. There was the will, however, to hinder that, and my loud protestations against any infringement of its directions. The funeral was hurried over; Catherine, Mrs Linton Heathcliff now, was suffered to stay at the Grange till her father's corpse had quitted it.

She told me that her anguish had at last spurred Linton to incur the risk of liberating her. She heard the men I sent disputing at the door, and she gathered the sense of Heathcliff's answer. It drove her desperate. Linton, who had been conveyed up to the little parlour soon after I left, was terrified into fetching the key before his father re-ascended. He had the cunning to unlock and relock the door, without shutting it; and when he should have gone to bed, he begged to sleep with Hareton, and his petition was granted for once. Catherine stole out before break of day. She dare not try the doors, lest the dogs should raise an alarm; she visited the empty chambers and examined their windows; and, luckily, lighting on her mother's, she got easily out of its lattice, and on to the ground, by means of the fir tree close by. Her accomplice suffered for his share in the escape, notwithstanding his timid contrivances.

Chapter XXIX

THE evening after the funeral, my young lady and I were seated in the library; now musing mournfully—one of us despairingly—on our loss, now venturing conjectures as to the gloomy future.

We had just agreed the best destiny which could await Catherine, would be a permission to continue resident at the Grange; at least, during Linton's life: he being allowed to join her there, and I to remain as housekeeper. That seemed rather too favourable an arrangement to be hoped for: and yet I did hope, and began to cheer up under the prospect of retaining my home and my employment, and, above all, my beloved young mistress; when a servant—one of the discarded ones, not yet departed—rushed hastily in, and said 'that devil Heathcliff' was coming through the court: should he fasten the door in his face?

If we had been mad enough to order that proceeding, we had not time. He made no ceremony of knocking or announcing his name: he was master, and availed himself of the master's privilege to walk straight in, without saying a word. The sound of our informant's voice directed him to the library: he entered, and motioning him out, shut the door.

It was the same room into which he had been ushered, as a guest, eighteen years before: the same moon shone through the window; and the same autumn landscape lay outside. We had not yet lighted a candle, but all the apartment was visible, even to the portraits on the wall: the splendid head of Mrs Linton, and the graceful one of her husband. Heathcliff advanced to the hearth. Time had little altered his person either. There was the same man: his dark face rather sallower and more composed, his frame a stone or two heavier, perhaps, and no other difference. Catherine had risen, with an impulse to dash out, when she saw him.

'Stop!' he said, arresting her by the arm. 'No more runnings away! Where would you go? I'm come to fetch you home; and I hope you'll be a dutiful daughter, and not encourage my son to further disobedience. I was embarrassed how to punish him when I discovered his part in the business: he's such a cobweb, a pinch would annihilate him; but you'll see by his look that he has received his due! I brought him down one evening, the day before yesterday, and just set him in a chair, and never touched him afterwards. I sent Hareton out, and we had the room to ourselves. In two hours, I called Joseph to carry him up again; and since then my presence is as potent on his nerves as a ghost; and I fancy he sees me often, though I am not near. Hareton says he wakes and shrieks in the night by the hour together, and calls you to protect him from me; and, whether you like your precious mate or not, you must come: he's your concern now; I yield all my interest in him to you.

'Why not let Catherine continue here?' I pleaded, 'and send Master Linton to her. As you hate them both, you'd not miss them: they *can* only be a daily plague to your unnatural heart.'

'I'm seeking a tenant for the Grange,' he answered; 'and I want my children about me, to be sure. Besides, that lass owes me her services for her bread. I'm not going to nurture her in luxury and idleness after Linton has gone. Make haste and get ready, now; and don't oblige me to compel you.'

'I shall,' said Catherine. 'Linton is all I have to love in the world, and though you have done what you could to make him hateful to me, and me to him, you *cannot* make us hate each other. And I defy you to hurt him when I am by, and I defy you to frighten me!'

'You are a boastful champion,' replied Heathcliff; 'but I don't like you well enough to hurt him: you shall get the full benefit of the torment, as long as it lasts. It is not I who will make him hateful to you—it is his own sweet spirit. He's as bitter as gall at your desertion and its consequences: don't expect thanks for this noble devotion. I heard him draw a pleasant picture to Zillah of what he would do if he were as strong as I: the inclination is there, and his very weakness will sharpen his wits to find a substitute for strength.'

'I know he has a bad nature,' said Catherine: 'he's your son. But I'm glad I've a better, to forgive it; and I know he loves me, and for that reason I love him. Mr Heathcliff, *you* have *nobody* to love you; and, however miserable you make us, we shall still have the revenge of thinking that your cruelty arises from your greater misery. You *are* miserable, are you not? Lonely, like the devil, and envious like him? *Nobody* loves you—*nobody* will cry for you when you die! I wouldn't be you!'

Catherine spoke with a kind of dreary triumph: she seemed to have made up her mind to enter into the spirit of her future family, and draw pleasure from the griefs of her enemies.

'You shall be sorry to be yourself presently', said her father-in-law, 'if you stand there another minute. Begone, witch, and get your things!'

She scornfully withdrew. In her absence, I began to beg for Zillah's place at the Heights, offering to resign mine to her; but he would suffer it on no account. He bid me be silent; and then, for the first time, allowed himself a glance round the room and a look at the pictures. Having studied Mrs Linton, he said:

'I shall have that home. Not because I need it, but——' He turned abruptly to the fire, and continued, with what, for lack of a better word, I must call a smile— 'I'll tell you what I did yesterday! I got the sexton, who was digging Linton's grave, to remove the earth off her coffin-lid, and I opened it. I thought, once, I would have stayed there: when I saw her face again—it is hers yet!—he had hard work to stir me; but he said it would change if the air blew on it, and so I struck one side of the coffin loose, and covered it up: not Linton's side, damn him! I wish he'd been soldered in lead. And I bribed the sexton to pull it away when I'm laid there, and slide mine out too; I'll have it made so: and then, by the time Linton gets to us he'll not know which is which!'

'You were very wicked, Mr Heathcliff!' I exclaimed, 'were you not ashamed to disturb the dead?'

'I disturbed nobody, Nelly,' he replied; 'and I gave some ease to myself. I shall be a great deal more comfortable now; and you'll have a better chance of keeping me underground, when I get there. Disturbed her? No! she has disturbed me, night and day, through eighteen years—incessantly—remorselessly—till yesternight; and yesternight I was tranquil. I dreamt I was sleeping the last sleep by that sleeper, with my heart stopped and my cheek frozen against hers.'

'And if she had been dissolved into earth, or worse, what would you have dreamt of then?' I said.

'Of dissolving with her, and being more happy still!' he answered. 'Do you suppose I dread any change of that sort? I expected such a transformation on raising the lid: but I'm better pleased that it should not commence till I share it. Besides, unless I had received a distinct impression of her passionless features, that strange feeling would hardly have been removed. It began oddly. You know I was wild after she died; and eternally, from dawn to dawn, praying her to return to me her spirit! I have a strong faith in ghosts: I have a conviction that they can, and do, exist among us! The day she was buried there came a fall of snow. In the evening I went to the churchyard. It blew bleak as winter—all round was solitary. I didn't fear that her fool of a husband would wander up the den so late; and no one else had business to bring them there. Being alone, and conscious two yards of loose earth was the sole barrier between us, I said to myself—"I'll have her in my arms again! If she be cold, I'll think it is this north wind that chills *me;* and if she be motionless, it is sleep." I got a spade from the tool-house, and began to delve with all my might—it scraped the coffin; I fell to work with my hands; the wood commenced cracking about the screws; I was on the point of attaining my object, when it seemed that I heard a sigh from someone above, close at the edge of the grave, and bending down. "If I can only get this off," I muttered, "I wish they may shovel in the earth over us both!" and I wrenched at it more desperately still. There was another sigh, close at my ear. I appeared to feel the warm breath of it displacing the sleet-laden wind. I knew no living thing in flesh and blood was by; but, as certainly as you perceive the approach to some substantial body in the dark, though it cannot be discerned, so certainly I felt that Cathy was there: not under me, but on the earth. A sudden sense of relief flowed from my heart through every limb. I relinquished my labour of agony, and turned consoled at once: unspeakably consoled. Her presence was with me: it remained while I refilled the grave, and led me home. You may laugh, if you will; but I was sure I should see her there. I was sure she was with me, and I could not help talking to her. Having reached the Heights, I rushed eagerly to the door. It was fastened; and, I remember, that accursed Earnshaw and my wife opposed my entrance. I remember stopping to kick the breath out of him, and then hurrying upstairs, to my room and hers. I looked round impatiently—I felt her by me—I could *almost* see her, and yet I *could not!* I ought to have sweat blood then, from the anguish of my yearning—from the fervour of my supplications to have but one glimpse! I had not one. She showed herself, as she often was in life, a devil to me! And, since then, sometimes more and sometimes less, I've been the sport of that intolerable torture! Infernal! keeping my nerves at such a stretch, that, if they had not resembled catgut, they would long ago have relaxed to the feebleness of Linton's. When I sat in the house with Hareton, it seemed that on going out, I should meet her; when I walked on the moors I should meet her coming in. When I went from home, I hastened to return: she *must* be somewhere at the Heights, I was certain! And when I slept in her chamber—I was beaten out of that. I couldn't lie there; for the moment I closed my eyes, she was either outside the window, or sliding back the panels, or entering the room, or even resting her darling head on the same pillow as she did when a child; and I must open my lids to see. And so I opened and closed them a hundred times a night—to be always disappointed! It racked me! I've often groaned aloud, till that old rascal Joseph no doubt believed that my conscience was playing the fiend inside of me. Now, since I've seen her, I'm pacified—a little. It was a strange way of killing! not by inches, but by fractions and hairbreadths, to beguile me with the spectre of a hope, through eighteen years!'

Mr Heathcliff paused and wiped his forehead; his hair clung to it, wet with perspiration; his eyes were fixed on the red embers of the fire, the brows not contracted, but raised next the temples; diminishing the grim aspect of his countenance, but imparting a peculiar look of trouble, and a painful appearance of mental tension towards one absorbing subject. He only half addressed me, and I maintained silence.

I didn't like to hear him talk! After a short period he resumed his meditation on the picture, took it down and leant it against the sofa to contemplate it at better advantage; and while so occupied Catherine entered, announcing that she was ready, when her pony should be saddled.

'Send that over tomorrow,' said Heathcliff to me; then turning to her, he added— 'You may do without your pony: it is a fine evening, and you'll need no ponies at Wuthering Heights; for what journeys you take, your own feet will serve you. Come along.'

'Goodbye, Ellen!' whispered my dear little mistress. As she kissed me, her lips felt like ice. 'Come and see me, Ellen; don't forget.'

'Take care you do no such thing, Mrs Dean!' said her new father. 'When I wish to speak to you I'll come here. I want none of your prying at my house!'

He signed her to precede him; and casting back a look that cut my heart, she obeyed. I watched them from the window, walk down the garden. Heathcliff fixed Catherine's arm under his: though she disputed the act at first evidently; and with rapid strides he hurried her into the alley, whose trees concealed them.

Chapter XXX

I HAVE paid a visit to the Heights, but I have not seen her since she left: Joseph held the door in his hand when I called to ask after her, and wouldn't let me pass. He said Mrs Linton was 'thrang', and the master was not in. Zillah has told me something of the way they go on, otherwise I should hardly know who was dead and who living. She thinks Catherine haughty, and does not like her, I can guess by her talk. My young lady asked some aid of her when she first came; but Mr Heathcliff told her to follow her own business, and let his daughter-in-law look after herself; and Zillah willingly acquiesced, being a narrow-minded, selfish woman. Catherine evinced a child's annoyance at this neglect; repaid it with contempt, and thus enlisted my informant among her enemies, as securely as if she had done her some great wrong. I had a long talk with Zillah about six weeks ago, a little before you came, one day when we foregathered on the moor; and this is what she told me.

'The first thing Mrs Linton did', she said, 'on her arrival at the Heights, was to run upstairs, without even wishing good evening to me and Joseph; she shut herself into Linton's room, and remained till morning. Then, while the master and Earnshaw were at breakfast, she entered the house, and asked all in a quiver if the doctor might be sent for? her cousin was very ill.

' "We know that!" answered Heathcliff; "but his life is not worth a farthing, and I won't spend a farthing on him."

' "But I cannot tell how to do," she said; "and if nobody will help me, he'll die!"

' "Walk out of the room," cried the master, "and let me never hear a word more about him! None here care what becomes of him; if you do, act the nurse; if you do not, lock him up and leave him."

'Then she began to bother me, and I said I'd had enough plague with the tiresome thing; we each had our tasks, and hers was to wait on Linton, Mr Heathcliff bid me leave that labour to her.

'How they managed together, I can't tell. I fancy he fretted a great deal, and moaned hisseln night and day; and she had precious little rest: one could guess by her white face and heavy eyes. She sometimes came into the kitchen all wildered like, and looked as if she would fain beg assistance; but I was not going to disobey the master: I never dare disobey him, Mrs Dean; and, though I thought it wrong

that Kenneth should not be sent for, it was no concern of mine either to advise or
complain, and I always refused to meddle. Once or twice, after we had gone to
bed, I've happened to open my door again and seen her sitting crying on the stairs'
top; and then I've shut myself in quick, for fear of being moved to interfere. I did
pity her then, I'm sure: still I didn't wish to lose my place, you know.

'At last, one night she came boldly into my chamber, and frightened me out of
my wits, by saying:

' "Tell Mr Heathcliff that his son is dying—I'm sure he is, this time. Get up,
instantly, and tell him."

'Having uttered this speech, she vanished again. I lay a quarter of an hour listening
and trembling. Nothing stirred—the house was quiet.

'She's mistaken, I said to myself. He's got over it. I needn't disturb them; and
I began to doze. But my sleep was marred a second time by a sharp ringing of the
bell—the only bell we have, put up on purpose for Linton; and the master called
to me to see what was the matter, and inform them that he wouldn't have that noise
repeated.

'I delivered Catherine's message. He cursed to himself, and in a few minutes
came out with a lighted candle, and proceeded to their room. I followed. Mrs
Heathcliff was seated by the bedside, with her hands folded on her knees. Her
father-in-law went up, held the light to Linton's face, looked at him, and touched
him; afterwards he turned to her.

' "Now—Catherine," he said, "how do you feel?"

'She was dumb.

' "How do you feel, Catherine?" he repeated.

' "He's safe, and I'm free," she answered: "I should feel well—but", she
continued, with a bitterness she couldn't conceal, "you have left me so long to
struggle against death alone, that I feel and see only death! I feel like death!"

'And she looked like it, too! I gave her a little wine. Hareton and Joseph, who
had been wakened by the ringing and the sound of feet, and heard our talk from
outside, now entered. Joseph was fain, I believe, of the lad's removal; Hareton
seemed a thought bothered: though he was more taken up with staring at Catherine
than thinking of Linton. But the master bid him get off to bed again: we didn't
want his help. He afterwards made Joseph remove the body to his chamber, and
told me to return to mine, and Mrs Heathcliff remained by herself.

'In the morning, he sent me to tell her she must come down to breakfast: she
had undressed, and appeared going to sleep, and said she was ill; at which I hardly
wondered. I informed Mr Heathcliff, and he replied:

' "Well, let her be till after the funeral; and go up now and then to get her what
is needful; and, as soon as she seems better, tell me." '

Cathy stayed upstairs a fortnight, according to Zillah; who visited her twice a
day, and would have been rather more friendly, but her attempts at increasing
kindness were proudly and promptly repelled.

Heathcliff went up once, to show her Linton's will. He had bequeathed the whole
of his, and what had been her, movable property to his father: the poor creature
was threatened, or coaxed, into that act during her week's absence, when his uncle
died. The lands, being a minor, he could not meddle with. However, Mr Heathcliff
has claimed and kept them in his wife's right and his also: I suppose legally: at
any rate, Catherine, destitute of cash and friends, cannot disturb his possession.

'Nobody', said Zillah, 'ever approached her door, except that once, but I; and
nobody asked anything about her. The first occasion of her coming down into the
house was on a Sunday afternoon. She had cried out, when I carried up her dinner,
that she couldn't bear any longer being in the cold: and I told her the master was
going to Thrushcross Grange, and Earnshaw and I needn't hinder her from descending;
so, as soon as she heard Heathcliff's horse trot off, she made her appearance donned

in black, and her yellow curls combed back behind her ears as plain as a Quaker: she couldn't comb them out.

'Joseph and I generally go to chapel on Sundays'; the kirk, you know, has no minister now, explained Mrs Dean; and they call the Methodists' or Baptists' place (I can't say which it is), at Gimmerton, a chapel. 'Joseph had gone,' she continued, 'but I thought proper to bide at home. Young folks are always the better for an elder's overlooking; and Hareton, with all his bashfulness, isn't a model of nice behaviour. I let him know that his cousin would very likely sit with us, and she had been always used to see the Sabbath respected; so he had as good leave his guns and bits of indoor work alone, while she stayed. He coloured up at the news, and cast his eyes over his hands and clothes. The train-oil and gunpowder were shoved out of sight in a minute. I saw he meant to give her his company; and I guessed, by his way, he wanted to be presentable; so, laughing, as I durst not laugh when the master is by, I offered to help him, if he would, and joked at his confusion. He grew sullen, and began to swear.

'Now, Mrs Dean,' Zillah went on, seeing me not pleased by her manner, 'you happen think your young lady too fine for Mr Hareton; and happen you're right: but I own I should love well to bring her pride a peg lower. And what will all her learning and her daintiness do for her, now? She's as poor as you or I: poorer I'll be bound: you're saving, and I'm doing my little all that road.'

Hareton allowed Zillah to give him her aid; and she flattered him into a good humour: so, when Catherine came, half forgetting her former insults, he tried to make himself agreeable, by the housekeeper's account.

'Missis walked in', she said, 'as chill as an icicle, and as high as a princess. I got up and offered her my seat in the armchair. No, she turned up her nose at my civility. Earnshaw rose, too, and bid her come to the settle, and sit close by the fire: he was sure she was starved.

' "I've been starved a month and more," she answered, resting on the word as scornful as she could.

'And she got a chair for herself, and placed it at a distance from both of us. Having sat till she was warm, she began to look round, and discovered a number of books in the dresser; she was instantly upon her feet again, stretching to reach them: but they were too high up. Her cousin, after watching her endeavours a while, at last summoned courage to help her; she held her frock, and he filled it with the first that came to hand.

'That was a great advance for the lad. She didn't thank him; still, he felt gratified that she had accepted his assistance, and ventured to stand behind as she examined them, and even to stoop and point out what struck his fancy in certain old pictures which they contained; nor was he daunted by the saucy style in which she jerked the page from his finger: he contented himself with going a bit farther back, and looking at her instead of the book. She continued reading, or seeking for something to read. His attention became, by degrees, quite centred in the study of her thick, silky curls: her face he couldn't see, and she couldn't see him. And, perhaps, not quite awake to what he did, but attracted like a child to a candle, at last he proceeded from staring to touching; he put out his hand and stroked one curl, as gently as if it were a bird. He might have stuck a knife into her neck, she started round in such a taking.

' "Get away, this moment! How dare you touch me? Why are you stopping there?" she cried, in a tone of disgust. "I can't endure you! I'll go upstairs again, if you come near me."

'Mr Hareton recoiled, looking as foolish as he could do: he sat down in the settle very quiet, and she continued turning over her volumes another half-hour; finally, Earnshaw crossed over, and whispered to me:

' "Will you ask her to read to us, Zillah? I'm stalled of doing naught; and I do like—I could like to hear her! Dunnot say I wanted it, but ask of yourseln."

' "Mr Hareton wishes you would read to us, ma'am," I said immediately. "He'd take it very kind—he'd be much obliged."

'She frowned; and looking up, answered:

' "Mr Hareton, and the whole set of you, will be good enough to understand that I reject any pretence at kindness you have the hypocrisy to offer! I despise you, and will have nothing to say to any of you! When I would have given my life for one kind word, even to see one of your faces, you all kept off. But I won't complain to you! I'm driven down here by the cold; not either to amuse you or enjoy your society."

' "What could I ha' done?" began Earnshaw. "How was I to blame?"

' "Oh! you are an exception," answered Mrs Heathcliff. "I never missed such a concern as you."

' "But I offered more than once, and asked," he said, kindling up at her pertness, "I asked Mr Heathcliff to let me wake for you——"

' "Be silent! I'll go out of doors, or anywhere, rather than have your disagreeable voice in my ear!" said my lady.

'Hareton muttered she might go to hell, for him! and unslinging his gun, restrained himself from his Sunday occupations no longer. He talked now, freely enough; and she presently saw fit to retreat to her solitude: but the frost had set in, and, in spite of her pride, she was forced to condescend to our company, more and more. However, I took care there should be no further scorning at my good nature: ever since, I've been as stiff as herself; and she has no lover or liker among us: and she does not deserve one; for, let them say the least word to her, and she'll curl back without respect of anyone! She'll snap at the master himself, and as good as dares him to thrash her; and the more hurt she gets, the more venomous she grows.'

At first, on hearing this account from Zillah, I determined to leave my situation, take a cottage, and get Catherine to come and live with me: but Mr Heathcliff would as soon permit that as he would set up Hareton in an independent house; and I can see no remedy, at present, unless she could marry again: and that scheme it does not come within my province to arrange.

Thus ended Mrs Dean's story. Notwithstanding the doctor's prophecy, I am rapidly recovering strength; and though it be only the second week in January, I propose getting out on horseback in a day or two, and riding over to Wuthering Heights, to inform my landlord that I shall spend the next six months in London; and, if he likes, he may look out for another tenant to take the place after October. I would not pass another winter here for much.

Chapter XXXI

YESTERDAY was bright, calm, and frosty. I went to the Heights as I proposed; my housekeeper entreated me to bear a little note from her to her young lady, and I did not refuse, for the worthy woman was not conscious of anything odd in her request. The front door stood open, but the jealous gate was fastened, as at my last visit; I knocked, and invoked Earnshaw from among the garden beds; he unchained it, and I entered. The fellow is as handsome a rustic as need be seen. I took particular notice of him this time; but then he does his best, apparently, to make the least of his advantages.

I asked if Mr Heathcliff were at home? He answered, No; but he would be in at dinner time. It was eleven o'clock, and I announced my intention of going in and waiting for him, at which he immediately flung down his tools and accompanied me, in the office of watchdog, not as a substitute for the host.

We entered together; Catherine was there, making herself useful in preparing some vegetables for the approaching meal; she looked more sulky and less spirited than when I had seen her first. She hardly raised her eyes to notice me, and continued her employment with the same disregard to common forms of politeness as before; never returning my bow and good morning by the slightest acknowledgment.

'She does not seem so amiable', I thought, 'as Mrs Dean would persuade me to believe. She's a beauty, it is true; but not an angel.'

Earnshaw surlily bid her remove her things to the kitchen. 'Remove them yourself,' she said, pushing them from her as soon as she had done; and retiring to a stool by the window, where she began to carve figures of birds and beasts out of the turnip parings in her lap. I approached her, pretending to desire a view of the garden; and, as I fancied, adroitly dropped Mrs Dean's note on to her knee, unnoticed by Hareton—but she asked aloud, 'What is that?' and chucked it off.

'A letter from your old acquaintance, the housekeeper at the Grange,' I answered; annoyed at her exposing my kind deed, and fearful lest it should be imagined a missive of my own. She would gladly have gathered it up at this information, but Hareton beat her; he seized and put it in his waistcoat, saying Mr Heathcliff should look at it first. Thereat, Catherine silently turned her face from us, and, very stealthily, drew out her pocket handkerchief and applied it to her eyes; and her cousin, after struggling a while to keep down his softer feelings, pulled out the letter and flung it on the floor beside her, as ungraciously as he could. Catherine caught and perused it eagerly; then she put a few questions to me concerning the inmates, rational and irrational, of her former home; and gazing towards the hills, murmured in soliloquy:

'I should like to be riding Minny down there! I should like to be climbing up there! Oh! I'm tired—I'm *stalled*, Hareton!' And she leant her pretty head back against the sill, with half a yawn and half a sigh, and lapsed into an aspect of abstracted sadness: neither caring nor knowing whether we remarked her.

'Mrs Heathcliff,' I said, after sitting some time mute, 'you are not aware that I am an acquaintance of yours? so intimate that I think it strange you won't come and speak to me. My housekeeper never wearies of talking about and praising you; and she'll be greatly disappointed if I return with no news of or from you, except that you received her letter and said nothing!'

She appeared to wonder at this speech, and asked:

'Does Ellen like you?'

'Yes, very well,' I replied unhesitatingly.

'You must tell her,' she continued, 'that I would answer her letter, but I have no materials for writing: not even a book from which I might tear a leaf.'

'No books!' I exclaimed. 'How do you contrive to live here without them? if I may take the liberty to inquire. Though provided with a large library, I'm frequently very dull at the Grange; take my books away, and I should be desperate!'

'I was always reading, when I had them,' said Catherine; 'and Mr Heathcliff never reads; so he took it into his head to destroy my books. I have not had a glimpse of one for weeks. Only once, I searched through Joseph's store of theology, to his great irritation; and once, Hareton, I came upon a secret stock in your room— some Latin and Greek, and some tales and poetry: all old friends. I brought the last here—and you gathered them, as a magpie gathers silver spoons, for the mere love of stealing! They are of no use to you; or else you concealed them in the bad spirit that as you cannot enjoy them nobody else shall. Perhaps *your* envy counselled Mr Heathcliff to rob me of my treasures? But I've most of them written on my brain and printed in my heart, and you cannot deprive me of those!'

Earnshaw blushed crimson when his cousin made this revelation of his private literary accumulations, and stammered an indignant denial of her accusations.

'Mr Hareton is desirous of increasing his amount of knowledge,' I said, coming to his rescue. 'He is not *envious* but *emulous* of your attainments. He'll be a clever scholar in a few years.'

'And he wants *me* to sink into a dunce, meantime,' answered Catherine. 'Yes, I hear him trying to spell and read to himself, and pretty blunders he makes! I wish you would repeat Chevy Chase as you did yesterday: it was extremely funny. I heard you; and I heard you turning over the dictionary to seek out the hard words, and then cursing because you couldn't read their explanations!'

The young man evidently thought it too bad that he should be laughed at for his ignorance, and then laughed at for trying to remove it. I had a similar notion; and, remembering Mrs Dean's anecdote of his first attempt at enlightening the darkness in which he had been reared, I observed:

'But, Mrs Heathcliff, we have each had a commencement, and each stumbled and tottered on the threshold; had our teachers scorned instead of aiding us, we should stumble and totter yet.'

'Oh!' she replied, 'I don't wish to limit his acquirements: still, he has no right to appropriate what is mine, and make it ridiculous to me with his vile mistakes and mispronunciations! Those books, both prose and verse, were consecrated to me by other associations; and I hate to have them debased and profaned in his mouth! Besides, of all, he has selected my favourite pieces that I love the most to repeat, as if out of deliberate malice.'

Hareton's chest heaved in silence a minute: he laboured under a severe sense of mortification and wrath, which it was no easy task to suppress. I rose, and, from a gentlemanly idea of relieving his embarrassment, took up my station in the doorway, surveying the external prospect as I stood. He followed my example, and left the room; but presently reappeared, bearing half a dozen volumes in his hands, which he threw into Catherine's lap, exclaiming:

'Take them! I never want to hear, or read, or think of them again!'

'I won't have them now,' she answered. 'I shall connect them with you, and hate them.'

She opened one that had obviously been often turned over, and read a portion in the drawling tone of a beginner; then laughed, and threw it from her. 'And listen,' she continued provokingly, commencing a verse of an old ballad in the same fashion.

But his self-love would endure no further torment: I heard, and not altogether disapprovingly, a manual check given to her saucy tongue. The little wretch had done her utmost to hurt her cousin's sensitive though uncultivated feelings, and a physical argument was the only mode he had of balancing the account, and repaying its effects on the inflicter. He afterwards gathered the books and hurled them on the fire. I read in his countenance what anguish it was to offer that sacrifice to spleen. I fancied that as they consumed, he recalled the pleasure they had already imparted, and the triumph and ever-increasing pleasur̤ ̤e had anticipated from them; and I fancied I guessed the incitement to his secret studies also. He had been content with daily labour and rough animal enjoyments, till Catherine crossed his path. Shame at her scorn, and hope of her approval, were his first prompters to higher pursuits; and, instead of guarding him from one and winning him to the other, his endeavours to rise himself had produced just the contrary result.

'Yes; that's all the good that such a brute as you can get from them!' cried Catherine, sucking her damaged lip, and watching the conflagration with indignant eyes.

'You'd *better* hold your tongue, now,' he answered fiercely.

And his agitation precluding further speech, he advanced hastily to the entrance, where I made way for him to pass. But ere he had crossed the doorstones, Mr Heathcliff, coming up the causeway, encountered him, and laying hold of his shoulder, asked:

'What's to do now, my lad?'

'Naught, naught,' he said, and broke away to enjoy his grief and anger in solitude. Heathcliff gazed after him, and sighed.

'It will be odd if I thwart myself,' he muttered, unconscious that I was behind him. 'But when I look for his father in his face, I find *her* every day more. How the devil is he so like? I can hardly bear to see him.'

He bent his eyes to the ground, and walked moodily in. There was a restless, anxious expression in his countenance I had never remarked there before; and he looked sparer in person. His daughter-in-law, on perceiving him through the window, immediately escaped to the kitchen, so that I remained alone.

'I'm glad to see you out of doors again, Mr Lockwood,' he said, in reply to my greeting; 'from selfish motives partly: I don't think I could readily supply your loss in this desolation. I've wondered more than once what brought you here.'

'An idle whim, I fear, sir,' was my answer; 'or else an idle whim is going to spirit me away. I shall set out for London, next week; and I must give you warning that I feel no disposition to retain Thrushcross Grange beyond the twelve months I agreed to rent it. I believe I shall not live there any more.'

'Oh, indeed; you're tired of being banished from the world, are you?' he said. 'But if you be coming to plead off paying for a place you won't occupy, your journey is useless: I never relent in exacting my due from anyone.'

'I'm coming to plead off nothing about it,' I exclaimed, considerably irritated. 'Should you wish it, I'll settle with you now,' and I drew my notebook from my pocket.

'No, no,' he replied coolly; 'you'll leave sufficient behind to cover your debts, if you fail to return: I'm not in such a hurry. Sit down and take your dinner with us; a guest that is safe from repeating his visit can generally be made welcome. Catherine, bring the things in: where are you?'

Catherine reappeared, bearing a tray of knives and forks.

'You may get your dinner with Joseph,' muttered Heathcliff aside, 'and remain in the kitchen till he is gone.'

She obeyed his directions very punctually: perhaps she had no temptation to transgress. Living among clowns and misanthropists, she probably cannot appreciate a better class of people when she meets them.

With Mr Heathcliff, grim and saturnine, on the one hand, and Hareton, absolutely dumb, on the other, I made a somewhat cheerless meal, and bid adieu early. I would have departed by the back way, to get a last glimpse of Catherine and annoy old Joseph; but Hareton received orders to lead up my horse, and my host himself escorted me to the door, so I could not fulfil my wish.

'How dreary life gets over in that house!' I reflected, while riding down the road. 'What a realization of something more romantic than a fairy tale it would have been for Mrs Linton Heathcliff, had she and I struck up an attachment, as her good nurse desired, and migrated together into the stirring atmosphere of the town!'

Chapter XXXII

1802.—

THIS September I was invited to devastate the moors of a friend in the north, and on my journey to his abode, I unexpectedly came within fifteen miles of Gimmerton. The ostler at a roadside public house was holding a pail of water to refresh my horses, when a cart of very green oats, newly reaped, passed by, and he remarked:

'Yon's frough Gimmerton, nah! They're allas three wick after other folk wi' ther harvest.'

'Gimmerton?' I repeated—my residence in that locality had already grown dim and dreamy. 'Ah! I know. How far is it from this?'

'Happen fourteen mile o'er th' hills; and a rough road,' he answered.

A sudden impulse seized me to visit Thrushcross Grange. It was scarcely noon, and I conceived that I might as well pass the night under my own roof as in an inn. Besides, I could spare a day easily to arrange matters with my landlord, and thus save myself the trouble of invading the neighbourhood again. Having rested a while, I directed my servant to inquire the way to the village; and, with great fatigue to our beasts, we managed the distance in some three hours.

I left him there, and proceeded down the valley alone. The grey church looked greyer, and the lonely churchyard lonelier. I distinguished a moor sheep cropping the short turf on the graves. It was sweet, warm weather—too warm for travelling; but the heat did not hinder me from enjoying the delightful scenery above and below: had I seen it nearer August, I'm sure it would have tempted me to waste a month among its solitudes. In winter nothing more dreary, in summer nothing more divine, than those glens shut in by hills, and those bluff, bold swells of heath.

I reached the Grange before sunset, and knocked for admittance; but the family had retreated into the back premises, I judged, by one thin, blue wreath curling from the kitchen chimney, and they did not hear. I rode into the court. Under the porch, a girl of nine or ten sat knitting, and an old woman reclined on the house steps, smoking a meditative pipe.

'Is Mrs Dean within?' I demanded of the dame.

'Mistress Dean? Nay!' she answered, 'shoo doesn't bide here: shoo's up at th' Heights.'

'Are you the housekeeper, then?' I continued.

'Ea, Aw keep th' house,' she replied.

'Well, I'm Mr Lockwood, the master. Are there any rooms to lodge me in, I wonder? I wish to stay here all night.'

'T' maister!' she cried in astonishment. 'Whet, whoiver knew yah wur coming? Yah sud ha' send word. They's nowt norther dry nor mensful abaht t' place: nowt there isn't!'

She threw down her pipe and bustled in, the girl followed, and I entered too; soon perceiving that her report was true, and, moreover, that I had almost upset her wits by my unwelcome apparition, I bid her be composed. I would go out for a walk; and, meantime, she must try to prepare a corner of a sitting-room for me to sup in, and a bedroom to sleep in. No sweeping and dusting, only good fire and dry sheets were necessary. She seemed willing to do her best; though she thrust the hearth-brush into the grates in mistake for the poker, and malappropriated several other articles of her craft: but I retired, confiding in her energy for a resting-place against my return. Wuthering Heights was the goal of my proposed excursion. An afterthought brought me back, when I had quitted the court.

'All well at the Heights?' I inquired of the woman.

'Eea, f'r owt Ee knaw,' she answered, skurrying away with a pan of hot cinders.

I would have asked why Mrs Dean had deserted the Grange, but it was impossible to delay her at such a crisis, so I turned away and made my exit, rambling leisurely along with the glow of a sinking sun behind, and the mild glory of a rising moon in front—one fading, and the other brightening—as I quitted the park, and climbed the stony by-road branching off to Mr Heathcliff's dwelling. Before I arrived in sight of it, all that remained of day was a beamless amber light along the west: but I could see every pebble on the path, and every blade of grass, by that splendid moon. I had neither to climb the gate nor to knock—it yielded to my hand. That is an improvement, I thought. And I noticed another, by the aid of my nostrils; a fragrance of stocks and wallflowers wafted on the air from amongst the homely fruit trees.

Both doors and lattices were open; and yet, as is usually the case in a coal district, a fine, red fire illumined the chimney: the comfort which the eye derives from it renders the extra heat endurable. But the house of Wuthering Heights is so large, that the inmates have plenty of space for withdrawing out of its influence; and accordingly, what inmates there were had stationed themselves not far from one of the windows. I could both see them and hear them talk before I entered, and looked and listened in consequence; being moved thereto by a mingled sense of curiosity and envy, that grew as I lingered.

'Con-*trary!*' said a voice as sweet as a silver bell—'That for the third time, you dunce! I'm not going to tell you again. Recollect, or I'll pull your hair!'

'Contrary, then,' answered another, in deep but softened tones. 'And now, kiss me, for minding so well.'

'No, read it over first correctly, without a single mistake.'

The male speaker began to read: he was a young man, respectably dressed and seated at a table, having a book before him. His handsome features glowed with pleasure, and his eyes kept impatiently wandering from the page to a small white hand over his shoulder, which recalled him by a smart slap on the cheek, whenever its owner detected such signs of inattention. Its owner stood behind; her light, shining ringlets blending, at intervals, with his brown locks, as she bent to superintend his studies; and her face—it was lucky he could not see her face, or he would never have been so steady. I could; and I bit my lip in spite, at having thrown away the chance I might have had of doing something besides staring at its smiling beauty.

The task was done, not free from further blunders; but the pupil claimed a reward, and received at least five kisses: which, however, he generously returned. Then they came to the door, and from their conversation I judged they were about to issue out and have a walk on the moors. I supposed I should be condemned in Hareton Earnshaw's heart, if not by his mouth, to the lowest pit in the infernal regions, if I showed my unfortunate person in his neighbourhood then; and feeling very mean and malignant, I skulked round to seek refuge in the kitchen. There was unobstructed admittance on that side also, and at the door sat my old friend Nelly Dean, sewing and singing a song; which was often interrupted from within by harsh words of scorn and intolerance, uttered in far from musical accents.

'Aw'd rayther, by th' hauf, hev 'em swearing i' my lugs frough morn to neeght, nur hearken yah, hahsiver!' said the tenant of the kitchen, in answer to an unheard speech of Nelly's. 'It's a blazing shaime, ut Aw cannut oppen t' blessed Book, bud yah set up them glories tuh Sattan, un' all t' flaysome wickednesses ut iver wer born intuh t' warld! Oh! yah'er a raight nowt; un' shoo's another; un' that poor lad'll be lost atween ye. Poor lad!' he added, with a groan; 'he's witched: Aw'm sartin on't! O Lord, judge 'em, fur they's norther law nur justice amang wer rullers!'

'No! or we should be sitting in flaming fagots, I suppose,' retorted the singer. 'But wisht, old man, and read your Bible like a Christian, and never mind me. This is "Fairy Annie's Wedding"—a bonny tune—it goes to a dance.'

Mrs Dean was about to recommence, when I advanced; and recognizing me directly, she jumped to her feet, crying:

'Why, bless you, Mr Lockwood! How could you think of returning in this way? All's shut up at Thrushcross Grange. You should have given us notice!'

'I've arranged to be accommodated there, for as long as I shall stay,' I answered. 'I depart again tomorrow. And how are you transplanted here, Mrs Dean? tell me that.'

'Zillah left, and Mr Heathcliff wished me to come, soon after you went to London, and stay till you returned. But, step in, pray! Have you walked from Gimmerton this evening?'

'From the Grange,' I replied; 'and while they make me lodging room there, I want to finish my business with your master; because I don't think of having another opportunity in a hurry.'

'What business, sir?' said Nelly, conducting me into the house. 'He's gone out at present, and won't return soon.'

'About the rent,' I answered.

'Oh! then it is with Mrs Heathcliff you must settle,' she observed; 'or rather with me. She has not learnt to manage her affairs yet, and I act for her: there's nobody else.'

I looked surprised.

'Ah! you have not heard of Heathcliff's death, I see,' she continued.

'Heathcliff dead!' I exclaimed, astonished. 'How long ago?'

'Three months since: but sit down and let me take your hat, and I'll tell you all about it. Stop, you have had nothing to eat, have you?'

'I want nothing: I have ordered supper at home. You sit down too. I never dreamt of his dying! Let me hear how it came to pass. You say you don't expect them back for some time—the young people?'

'No—I have to scold them every evening for their late rambles: but they don't care for me. At least have a drink of our old ale; it will do you good: you seem weary.'

She hastened to fetch it before I could refuse, and I heard Joseph asking whether 'it warn't a crying scandal that she should have fellies at her time of life? And then, to get them jocks out uh' t' maister's cellar! He fair shaamed to 'bide still and see it.'

She did not stay to retaliate, but re-entered in a minute, bearing a reaming silver pint, whose contents I lauded with becoming earnestness. And afterwards she furnished me with the sequel of Heathcliff's history. He had a 'queer' end, as she expressed it.

I was summoned to Wuthering Heights, within a fortnight of your leaving us, she said; and I obeyed joyfully, for Catherine's sake. My first interview with her grieved and shocked me: she had altered so much since our separation. Mr Heathcliff did not explain his reasons for taking a new mind about my coming here; he only told me he wanted me, and he was tired of seeing Catherine: I must make the little parlour my sitting-room, and keep her with me. It was enough if he were obliged to see her once or twice a day. She seemed pleased at this arrangement; and, by degrees, I smuggled over a great number of books, and other articles, that had formed her amusement at the Grange; and flattered myself we should get on in tolerable comfort. The delusion did not last long. Catherine, contented at first, in a brief space grew irritable and restless. For one thing, she was forbidden to move out of the garden, and it fretted her sadly to be confined to its narrow bounds as spring drew on; for another, in following the house, I was forced to quit her frequently, and she complained of loneliness: she preferred quarrelling with Joseph in the kitchen to sitting at peace in her solitude. I did not mind their skirmishes: but Hareton was often obliged to seek the kitchen also, when the master wanted to have the house to himself; and though in the beginning she either left it at his approach, or quietly joined in my occupations, and shunned remarking or addressing him—and though he was always as sullen and silent as possible—after a while she changed her behaviour, and became incapable of letting him alone: talking at him; commenting on his stupidity and idleness; expressing her wonder how he could endure the life he lived—how he could sit a whole evening staring into the fire and dozing.

'He's just like a dog, is he not, Ellen?' she once observed, 'or a carthorse? He does his work, eats his food, and sleeps eternally! What a blank, dreary mind he must have! Do you ever dream, Hareton? And, if you do, what is it about? But you can't speak to me!'

Then she looked at him; but he would neither open his mouth nor look again.

'He's, perhaps, dreaming now,' she continued. 'He twitched his shoulder as Juno twitches hers. Ask him, Ellen.'

'Mr Hareton will ask the master to send you upstairs, if you don't behave!' I said. He had not only twitched his shoulder but clenched his fist, as if tempted to use it.

'I know why Hareton never speaks, when I am in the kitchen,' she exclaimed, on another occasion. 'He is afraid I shall laugh at him. Ellen, what do you think? He began to teach himself to read once; and because I laughed, he burned his books, and dropped it: was he not a fool?'

'Were not you naughty?' I said; 'answer me that.'

'Perhaps I was,' she went on; 'but I did not expect him to be so silly. Hareton, if I gave you a book, would you take it now? I'll try!'

She placed one she had been perusing on his hand; he flung it off, and muttered, if she did not give over, he would break her neck.

'Well, I shall put it here,' she said, 'in the table drawer; and I'm going to bed.'

Then she whispered me to watch whether he touched it, and departed. But he would not come near it; and so I informed her in the morning, to her great disappointment. I saw she was sorry for his persevering sulkiness and indolence: her conscience reproved her for frightening him off improving himself: she had done it effectually. But her ingenuity was at work to remedy the injury: while I ironed, or pursued other stationary employments I could not well do in the parlour, she would bring some pleasant volume and read it aloud to me. When Hareton was there, she generally paused in an interesting part, and left the book lying about: that she did repeatedly; but he was as obstinate as a mule, and, instead of snatching at her bait, in wet weather he took to smoking with Joseph; and they sat like automatons, one on each side of the fire, the elder happily too deaf to understand her wicked nonsense, as he would have called it, the younger doing his best to seem to disregard it. On fine evenings the latter followed his shooting expeditions, and Catherine yawned and sighed, and teased me to talk to her, and ran off into the court or garden, the moment I began; and, as a last resource, cried, and said she was tired of living: her life was useless.

Mr Heathcliff, who grew more and more disinclined to society, had almost banished Earnshaw out of his apartment. Owing to an accident at the commencement of March, he became for some days a fixture in the kitchen. His gun burst while out on the hills by himself; a splinter cut his arm, and he lost a good deal of blood before he could reach home. The consequence was that, perforce, he was condemned to the fireside and tranquillity, till he made it up again. It suited Catherine to have him there: at any rate, it made her hate her room upstairs more than ever: and she would compel me to find out business below, that she might accompany me.

On Easter Monday, Joseph went to Gimmerton fair with some cattle; and, in the afternoon, I was busy getting up linen in the kitchen. Earnshaw sat, morose as usual, at the chimney-corner, and my little mistress was beguiling an idle hour with drawing pictures on the window panes; varying her amusement by smothered bursts of songs, and whispered ejaculations, and quick glances of annoyance and impatience in the direction of her cousin, who steadfastly smoked, and looked into the grate. At a notice that I could do with her no longer intercepting my light, she removed to the hearthstone. I bestowed little attention on her proceedings, but, presently, I heard her begin:

'I've found out, Hareton, that I want—that I'm glad—that I should like you to be my cousin now, if you had not grown so cross to me, and so rough.'

Hareton returned no answer.

'Hareton, Hareton, Hareton! do you hear?' she continued.

'Get off wi' ye!' he growled, with uncompromising gruffness.

'Let me take that pipe,' she said, cautiously advancing her hand and abstracting it from his mouth.

Before he could attempt to recover it, it was broken, and behind the fire. He swore at her and seized another.

'Stop,' she cried, 'you must listen to me first; and I can't speak while those clouds are floating in my face.'

'Will you go to the devil!' he exclaimed ferociously, 'and let me be!'

'No,' she persisted, 'I won't: I can't tell what to do to make you talk to me; and you are determined not to understand. When I call you stupid, I don't mean anything: I don't mean that I despise you. Come, you shall take notice of me, Hareton! you are my cousin, and you shall own me.'

'I shall have naught to do wi' you and your mucky pride, and your damned mocking tricks!' he answered. 'I'll go to hell, body and soul, before I look sideways after you again. Side out o' t' gait, now; this minute!'

Catherine frowned, and retreated to the window-seat chewing her lip, and endeavouring, by humming an eccentric tune, to conceal a growing tendency to sob.

'You should be friends with your cousin, Mr Hareton,' I interrupted, 'since she repents of her sauciness. It would do you a great deal of good: it would make you another man to have her for a companion.'

'A companion?' he cried; 'when she hates me, and does not think me fit to wipe her shoon! Nay! if it made me a king, I'd not be scorned for seeking her goodwill any more.'

'It is not I who hate you, it is you who hate me!' wept Cathy, no longer disguising her trouble. 'You hate me as much as Mr Heathcliff does, and more.'

'You're a damned liar,' began Earnshaw: 'why have I made him angry, by taking your part, then, a hundred times? and that when you sneered at and despised me, and—Go on plaguing me, and I'll step in yonder, and say you worried me out of the kitchen!'

'I didn't know you took my part,' she answered, drying her eyes; 'and I was miserable and bitter at everybody; but now I thank you, and beg you to forgive me: what can I do besides?'

She returned to the hearth, and frankly extended her hand. He blackened and scowled like a thunder cloud, and kept his fists resolutely clenched, and his gaze fixed on the ground. Catherine, by instinct, must have divined it was obdurate perversity, and not dislike, that prompted this dogged conduct; for, after remaining an instant undecided, she stooped and impressed on his cheek a gentle kiss. The little rogue thought I had not seen her, and, drawing back, she took her former station by the window, quite demurely. I shook my head reprovingly, and then she blushed and whispered:

'Well! what should I have done, Ellen? He wouldn't shake hands, and he wouldn't look: I must show him some way that I like him—that I want to be friends.'

Whether the kiss convinced Hareton, I cannot tell: he was very careful, for some minutes, that his face should not be seen, and when he did raise it, he was sadly puzzled where to turn his eyes.

Catherine employed herself in wrapping a handsome book neatly in white paper, and having tied it with a bit of ribband, and addressed it to 'Mr Hareton Earnshaw', she desired me to be her ambassadress, and convey the present to its destined recipient.

'And tell him, if he'll take it I'll come and teach him to read it right,' she said; 'and, if he refuse it, I'll go upstairs, and never tease him again.'

I carried it, and repeated the message; anxiously watched by my employer. Hareton would not open his fingers, so I laid it on his knee. He did not strike off, either. I returned to my work. Catherine leaned her head and arms on the table, till she heard the slightest rustle of the covering being removed; then she stole away, and quietly seated herself beside her cousin. He trembled, and his face glowed: all his rudeness and all his surly harshness had deserted him: he could not summon courage, at first, to utter a syllable in reply to her questioning look, and her murmured petition.

'Say you forgive me, Hareton, do? You can make me so happy by speaking that little word.'

He muttered something inaudible.

'And you'll be my friend?' added Catherine interrogatively.

'Nay, you'll be ashamed of me every day of your life,' he answered; 'and the more, the more you know me; and I cannot bide it.'

'So you won't be my friend?' she said, smiling as sweet as honey, and creeping close up.

I overheard no further distinguishable talk, but, on looking round again, I perceived two such radiant countenances bent over the page of the accepted book, that I did not doubt the treaty had been ratified on both sides; and the enemies were, thenceforth, sworn allies.

The work they studied was full of costly pictures; and those and their position had charm enough to keep them unmoved till Joseph came home. He, poor man, was perfectly aghast at the spectacle of Catherine seated on the same bench with Hareton Earnshaw, leaning her hand on his shoulder; and confounded at his favourite's endurance of her proximity: it affected him too deeply to allow an observation on the subject that night. His emotion was only revealed by the immense sighs he drew, as he solemnly spread his large Bible on the table, and overlaid it with dirty bank-notes from his pocket-book, the produce of the day's transactions. At length, he summoned Hareton from his seat.

'Tak' these in tuh t' maister, lad,' he said, 'un' bide thar. Aw's gang up tuh my awn rahm. This hoile's norther mensful nor seemly fur us: we mun side aht and seearch another.'

'Come, Catherine,' I said, 'we must "side out" too; I've done my ironing, are you ready to go?'

'It is not eight o'clock!' she answered, rising unwillingly. 'Hareton, I'll leave this book upon the chimney-piece, and I'll bring some more tomorrow.'

'Ony books ut yah leave, Aw suall tak' intuh th' hahse,' said Joseph, 'un it'll be mitch if yah find em agean; soa, yah muh plase yourseln!'

Cathy threatened that his library should pay for hers; and, smiling as she passed Hareton, went singing upstairs: lighter of heart, I venture to say, than ever she had been under that roof before; except, perhaps, during her earliest visits to Linton.

The intimacy thus commenced, grew rapidly; though it encountered temporary interruptions. Earnshaw was not to be civilized with a wish, and my young lady was no philosopher, and no paragon of patience; but both their minds tending to the same point—one loving and desiring to esteem, and the other loving and desiring to be esteemed—they contrived in the end to reach it.

You see, Mr Lockwood, it was easy enough to win Mrs Heathcliff's heart. But now, I'm glad you did not try. The crown of all my wishes will be the union of those two. I shall envy no one on their wedding day: there won't be a happier woman than myself in England!

Chapter XXXIII

ON the morrow of that Monday, Earnshaw being still unable to follow his ordinary employments, and therefore remaining about the house, I speedily found it would be impracticable to retain my charge beside me, as heretofore. She got downstairs before me, and out into the garden, where she had seen her cousin performing some easy work; and when I went to bid them come to breakfast, I saw she had persuaded him to clear a large space of ground from currant and gooseberry bushes; and they were busy planning together an importation of plants from the Grange.

I was terrified at the devastation which had been accomplished in a brief half-hour; the black-currant trees were the apple of Joseph's eye, and she had just fixed her choice of a flower bed in the midst of them.

'There! That will be all shown to the master,' I exclaimed, 'the minute it is discovered. And what excuse have you to offer for taking such liberties with the garden? We shall have a fine explosion on the head of it: see if we don't! Mr Hareton, I wonder you should have no more wit, than to go and make that mess at her bidding!'

'I'd forgotten they were Joseph's,' answered Earnshaw, rather puzzled; 'but I'll tell him I did it.'

We always ate our meals with Mr Heathcliff. I held the mistress's post in making tea and carving; so I was indispensable at table. Catherine usually sat by me, but today she stole nearer to Hareton; and I presently saw she would have no more discretion in her friendship than she had in her hostility.

'Now, mind you don't talk with and notice your cousin too much,' were my whispered instructions as we entered the room. 'It will certainly annoy Mr Heathcliff, and he'll be mad at you both.'

'I'm not going to,' she answered.

The minute after, she had sidled to him, and was sticking primroses in his plate of porridge.

He dared not speak to her there: he dared hardly look; and yet she went on teasing, till he was twice on the point of being provoked to laugh; and I frowned, and then she glanced towards the master: whose mind was occupied on other subjects than his company, as his countenance evinced; and she grew serious for an instant, scrutinizing him with deep gravity. Afterwards she turned, and recommenced her nonsense; at last, Hareton uttered a smothered laugh. Mr Heathcliff started; his eye rapidly surveyed our faces. Catherine met it with her accustomed look of nervousness and yet defiance, which he abhorred.

'It is well you are out of my reach,' he exclaimed. 'What fiend possesses you to stare back at me, continually, with those infernal eyes? Down with them! and don't remind me of your existence again. I thought I had cured you of laughing.'

'It was me,' muttered Hareton.

'What do you say?' demanded the master.

Hareton looked at his plate, and did not repeat the confession. Mr Heathcliff looked at him a bit, and then silently resumed his breakfast and his interrupted musing. We had nearly finished, and the two young people prudently shifted wider asunder, so I anticipated no further disturbance during that sitting: when Joseph appeared at the door, revealing by his quivering lip and furious eyes, that the outrage committed on his precious shrubs was detected. He must have seen Cathy and her cousin about the spot before he examined it, for while his jaws worked like those of a cow chewing its cud, and rendered his speech difficult to understand, he began:

'Aw mun hev my wage, and Aw mun goa! Aw *hed* aimed tuh dee, wheare Aw'd sarved fur sixty year; 'un Aw thowt Aw'd lug my books up intuh t' garret, un' all my bits uh stuff, un' they sud hev t' kitchen tuh theirseln; fur t' sake uh quietness. It wur hard tuh gie up my awn hearthstun, bud Aw thowt Aw *could* do that! Bud, nah, shoo's taan my garden frough me, un' by th' heart, maister, Aw cannot stand it! Yah muh bend tuh th' yoak, an ye will—*Aw* noan used to 't, and an ow'd man dosen't sooin get used tuh new barthens. Aw'd rayther arn my bite an' my sup wi' a hammer in th' road!'

'Now, now, idiot!' interrupted Heathcliff, 'cut it short! What's your grievance? I'll interfere in no quarrels between you and Nelly. She may thrust you into the coal-hole for anything I care.'

'It's noan Nelly!' answered Joseph. 'Aw sudn't shift fur Nellie—nasty ill nowt as shoo is. Thank God! *shoo* cannot stale t' sowl o' nob'dy! Shoo wer niver soa

handsome, bud whet a body mud look at her 'baht winking. It's yon flaysome, graceless quean, ut's witched ahr lad, wi' her bold een un' her forrard ways—till— Nay! it fair brusts my heart! He's forgetten all Ee done for him, un' made on him, un' goan un' riven up a whole row ut t' grandest currant trees, i' t' garden!' And here he lamented outright; unmanned by a sense of his bitter injuries, and Earnshaw's ingratitude and dangerous condition.

'Is the fool drunk?' asked Mr Heathcliff. 'Hareton, is it you he's finding fault with?'

'I've pulled up two or three bushes,' replied the young man; 'but I'm going to set 'em again.'

'And why have you pulled them up?' said the master.

Catherine unwisely put in her tongue.

'We wanted to plant some flowers there,' she cried. 'I'm the only person to blame, for I wished him to do it.'

'And who the devil gave *you* leave to touch a stick about the place?' demanded her father-in-law, much surprised. 'And who ordered *you* to obey her?' he added, turning to Hareton.

The latter was speechless; his cousin replied:

'You shouldn't grudge a few yards of earth for me to ornament, when you have taken all my land!'

'Your land, insolent slut! You never had any,' said Heathcliff.

'And my money,' she continued; returning his angry glare, and meantime biting a piece of crust, the remnant of her breakfast.

'Silence!' he exclaimed. 'Get done, and begone!'

'And Hareton's land, and his money,' pursued the reckless thing. 'Hareton and I are friends now; and I shall tell him all about you!'

The master seemed confounded a moment: he grew pale, and rose up, eyeing her all the while, with an expression of mortal hate.

'If you strike me, Hareton will strike you,' she said; 'so you may as well sit down.'

'If Hareton does not turn you out of the room, I'll strike him to hell,' thundered Heathcliff. 'Damnable witch! dare you pretend to rouse him against me? Off with her! Do you hear? Fling her into the kitchen! I'll kill her, Ellen Dean, if you let her come into my sight again!'

Hareton tried, under his breath, to persuade her to go.

'Drag her away!' he cried savagely. 'Are you staying to talk?' And he approached to execute his own command.

'He'll not obey you, wicked man, any more,' said Catherine; 'and he'll soon detest you as much as I do.'

'Wisht! wisht!' muttered the young man reproachfully. 'I will not hear you speak so to him. Have done.'

'But you won't let him strike me?' she cried.

'Come, then,' he whispered earnestly.

It was too late: Heathcliff had caught hold of her.

'Now *you* go!' he said to Earnshaw. 'Accursed witch! this time she has provoked me when I could not bear it; and I'll make her repent it for ever!'

He had his hand in her hair; Hareton attempted to release the locks, entreating him not to hurt her that once. Heathcliff's black eyes flashed; he seemed ready to tear Catherine in pieces, and I was just worked up to risk coming to the rescue, when of a sudden his fingers relaxed; he shifted his grasp from her head to her arm, and gazed intently in her face. Then he drew his hand over his eyes, stood a moment to collect himself apparently, and turning anew to Catherine, said with assumed calmness: 'You must learn to avoid putting me in a passion, or I shall really murder you some time! Go with Mrs Dean, and keep with her; and confine your insolence to her ears. As to Hareton Earnshaw, if I see him listen to you, I'll

send him seeking his bread where he can get it! Your love will make him an outcast and a beggar. Nelly, take her; and leave me, all of you! Leave me!'

I led my young lady out: she was too glad of her escape to resist; the other followed, and Mr Heathcliff had the room to himself till dinner. I had counselled Catherine to get hers upstairs; but, as soon as he perceived her vacant seat, he sent me to call her. He spoke to none of us, ate very little, and went out directly afterwards, intimating that he should not return before evening.

The two new friends established themselves in the house during his absence; when I heard Hareton sternly check his cousin, on her offering a revelation of her father-in-law's conduct to his father. He said he wouldn't suffer a word to be uttered to him, in his disparagement: if he were the devil, it didn't signify: he would stand by him; and he'd rather she would abuse himself, as she used to, than begin on Mr Heathcliff. Catherine was waxing cross at this; but he found means to make her hold her tongue, by asking how she would like *him* to speak ill of her father? and then she comprehended that Earnshaw took the master's reputation home to himself; and was attached by ties stronger than reason could break—chains, forged by habit, which it would be cruel to attempt to loosen. She showed a good heart, thenceforth, in avoiding both complaints and expressions of antipathy concerning Heathcliff; and confessed to me her sorrow that she had endeavoured to raise a bad spirit between him and Hareton: indeed, I don't believe she has ever breathed a syllable, in the latter's hearing, against her oppressor since.

When this slight disagreement was over, they were thick again, and as busy as possible in their several occupations of pupil and teacher. I came in to sit with them, after I had done my work; and I felt so soothed and comforted to watch them, that I did not notice how time got on. You know, they both appeared in a measure my children: I had long been proud of one; and now, I was sure, the other would be a source of equal satisfaction. His honest, warm, and intelligent nature shook off rapidly the clouds of ignorance and degradation in which it had been bred; and Catherine's sincere commendations acted as a spur to his industry. His brightening mind brightened his features, and added spirit and nobility to their aspect: I could hardly fancy it the same individual I had beheld on the day I discovered my little lady at Wuthering Heights, after her expedition to the Crags. While I admired and they laboured, dusk grew on, and with it returned the master. He came upon us quite unexpectedly, entering by the front way, and had a full view of the whole three, ere we could raise our heads to glance at him. Well, I reflected, there was never a pleasanter, or more harmless sight; and it will be a burning shame to scold them. The red firelight glowed on their two bonny heads, and revealed their faces animated with the eager interest of children; for, though he was twenty-three and she eighteen, each had so much of novelty to feel and learn, that neither experienced nor evinced the sentiments of sober disenchanted maturity.

They lifted their eyes together, to encounter Mr Heathcliff: perhaps you have never remarked that their eyes are precisely similar, and they are those of Catherine Earnshaw. The present Catherine has no other likeness to her, except a breadth of forehead, and a certain arch of the nostril that makes her appear rather haughty, whether she will or not. With Hareton the resemblance is carried further: it is singular at all times, then it was particularly striking; because his senses were alert, and his mental faculties wakened to unwonted activity. I suppose this resemblance disarmed Mr Heathcliff: he walked to the hearth in evident agitation; but it quickly subsided as he looked at the young man: or, I should say, altered its character; for it was there yet. He took the book from his hand, and glanced at the open page, then returned it without any observation; merely signing Catherine away: her companion lingered very little behind her, and I was about to depart also, but he bid me sit still.

'It is a poor conclusion, is it not?' he observed, having brooded a while on the scene he had just witnessed: 'an absurd termination to my violent exertions? I get levers and mattocks to demolish the two houses, and train myself to be capable of working like Hercules, and when everything is ready and in my power, I find the will to lift a slate off either roof has vanished! My old enemies have not beaten me; now would be the precise time to revenge myself on their representatives: I could do it; and none could hinder me. But where is the use? I don't care for striking; I can't take the trouble to raise my hand! That sounds as if I had been labouring the whole time only to exhibit a fine trait of magnanimity. It is far from being the case: I have lost the faculty of enjoying their destruction, and I am too idle to destroy for nothing.

'Nelly, there is a strange change approaching: I'm in its shadow at present. I take so little interest in my daily life, that I hardly remember to eat and drink. Those two who have left the room are the only objects which retain a distinct material appearance to me; and that appearance causes me pain, amounting to agony. About *her* I won't speak; and I don't desire to think; but I earnestly wish she were invisible: her presence invokes only maddening sensations. *He* moves me differently: and yet if I could do it without seeming insane, I'd never see him again. You'll perhaps think me rather inclined to become so,' he added, making an effort to smile, 'if I try to describe the thousand forms of past associations and ideas he awakens or embodies. But you'll not talk of what I tell you; and my mind is so eternally secluded in itself, it is tempting at last to turn it out to another.

'Five minutes ago, Hareton seemed a personification of my youth, not a human being: I felt to him in such a variety of ways, that it would have been impossible to have accosted him rationally. In the first place, his startling llkeness to Catherine connected him fearfully with her. That, however, which you may suppose the most potent to arrest my imagination, is actually the least: for what is not connected with her to me? and what does not recall her? I cannot look down to this floor, but her features are shaped in the flags! In every cloud, in every tree—filling the air at night, and caught by glimpses in every object by day—I am surrounded with her image! The most ordinary faces of men and women—my own features—mock me with a resemblance. The entire world is a dreadful collection of memoranda that she did exist, and that I have lost her! Well, Hareton's aspect was the ghost of my immortal love; of my wild endeavours to hold my right; my degradation, my pride, my happiness, and my anguish:

'But it is frenzy to repeat these thoughts to you: only it will let you know why, with a reluctance to be always alone, his society is no benefit; rather an aggravation of the constant torment I suffer; and it partly contributes to render me regardless how he and his cousin go on together. I can give them no attention, any more.'

'But what do you mean by a *change*, Mr Heathcliff?' I said, alarmed at his manner: though he was neither in danger of losing his senses, nor dying, according to my judgment; he was quite strong and healthy: and, as to his reason, from childhood he had a delight in dwelling on dark things, and entertaining odd fancies. He might have had a monomania on the subject of his departed idol; but on every other point his wits were as sound as mine.

'I shall not know that till it comes,' he said, 'I'm only half conscious of it now.'

'You have no feelings of illness, have you?' I asked.

'No, Nelly, I have not,' he answered.

'Then you are not afraid of death?' I pursued.

'Afraid? No!' he replied. 'I have neither a fear, nor a presentiment, nor a hope of death. Why should I? With my hard constitution and temperate mode of living, and unperilous occupations, I ought to, and probably *shall,* remain above ground till there is scarcely a black hair on my head. And yet I cannot continue in this condition! I have to remind myself to breathe—almost to remind my heart to beat! And it is like bending back a stiff spring; it is by compulsion that I do the slightest

act not prompted by one thought; and by compulsion that I notice anything alive or dead, which is not associated with one universal idea. I have a single wish, and my whole being and faculties are yearning to attain it. They have yearned towards it so long, and so unwaveringly, that I'm convinced it *will* be reached—and *soon*—because it has devoured my existence: I am swallowed up in the anticipation of its fulfilment. My confessions have not relieved me; but they may account for·some otherwise unaccountable phases of humour which I show. O God! It is a long fight, I wish it were over!'

He began to pace the room, muttering terrible things to himself, till I was inclined to believe, as he said Joseph did, that conscience had turned his heart to an earthly hell. I wondered greatly how it would end. Though he seldom before had revealed this state of mind, even by looks, it was his habitual mood, I had no doubt: he asserted it himself; but not a soul, from his general bearing, would have conjectured the fact. You did not when you saw him, Mr Lockwood: and at the period of which I speak he was just the same as then; only fonder of continued solitude, and perhaps still more laconic in company.

Chapter XXXIV

FOR some days after that evening, Mr Heathcliff shunned meeting us at meals; yet he would not consent formally to exclude Hareton and Cathy. He had an aversion to yielding so completely to his feelings, choosing rather to absent himself; and eating once in twenty-four hours seemed sufficient sustenance for him.

One night, after the family were in bed, I heard him go downstairs, and out at the front door. I did not hear him re-enter, and in the morning I found he was still away. We were in April then: the weather was sweet and warm, the grass as green as showers and sun could make it, and the two dwarf apple trees near the southern wall in full bloom. After breakfast, Catherine insisted on my bringing a chair and sitting with my work under the fir trees at the end of the house; and she beguiled Hareton, who had perfectly recovered from his accident, to dig and arrange her little garden, which was shifted to that corner by the influence of Joseph's complaints. I was comfortably revelling in the spring fragrance around, and the beautiful soft blue overhead, when my young lady, who had run down near the gate to procure some primrose roots for a border, returned only half laden, and informed us that Mr Heathcliff was coming in. 'And he spoke to me,' she added, with a perplexed countenance.

'What did he say?' asked Hareton.

'He told me to begone as fast as I could,' she answered. 'But he looked so different from his usual look that I stopped a moment to stare at him.'

'How?' he inquired.

'Why, almost bright and cheerful. No, *almost* nothing—*very much* excited, and wild and glad!' she replied.

'Night walking amuses him, then,' I remarked, affecting a careless manner: in reality as surprised as she was, and anxious to ascertain the truth of her statement; for to see the master looking glad would not be an everyday spectacle. I framed an excuse to go in. Heathcliff stood at the open door, he was pale, and he trembled: yet, certainly, he had a strange, joyful glitter in his eyes, that altered the aspect of his whole face.

'Will you have some breakfast?' I said. 'You must be hungry, rambling about all night!' I wanted to discover where he had been, but I did not like to ask directly.

'No, I'm not hungry,' he answered, averting his head, and speaking rather contemptuously, as if he guessed I was trying to divine the occasion of his good humour.

I felt perplexed: I didn't know whether it were not a proper opportunity to offer a bit of admonition.

'I don't think it right to wander out of doors,' I observed, 'instead of being in bed: it is not wise, at any rate, this moist season. I dare say you'll catch a bad cold, or a fever: you have something the matter with you now!'

'Nothing but what I can bear,' he replied; 'and with the greatest pleasure, provided you'll leave me alone; get in, and don't annoy me.'

I obeyed: and, in passing, I noticed he breathed as fast as a cat.

'Yes!' I reflected to myself, 'we shall have a fit of illness. I cannot conceive what he has been doing.'

That noon he sat down to dinner with us, and received a heaped-up plate from my hands, as if he intended to make amends for previous fasting.

'I've neither cold nor fever, Nelly,' he remarked, in allusion to my morning's speech; 'and I'm ready to do justice to the food you give me.'

He took his knife and fork, and was going to commence eating, when the inclination appeared to become suddenly extinct. He laid them on the table, looked eagerly towards the window, then rose and went out. We saw him walking to and fro in the garden while we concluded our meal, and Earnshaw said he'd go and ask why he would not dine: he thought we had grieved him some way.

'Well, is he coming?' cried Catherine, when her cousin returned.

'Nay,' he answered; 'but he's not angry: he seemed rare and pleased indeed; only I made him impatient by speaking to him twice; and then he bid me be off to you: he wondered how I could want the company of anybody else.'

I set his plate to keep warm on the fender; and after an hour or two he re-entered, when the room was clear, in no degree calmer: the same unnatural—it was unnatural—appearance of joy under his black brows; the same bloodless hue, and his teeth visible, now and then, in a kind of smile; his frame shivering, not as one shivers with chill or weakness, but as a tight-stretched cord vibrates—a strong thrilling, rather than trembling.

I will ask what is the matter, I thought; or who should? And I exclaimed:

'Have you heard any good news, Mr Heathcliff? You look uncommonly animated.'

'Where should good news come from to me?' he said. 'I'm animated with hunger; and, seemingly, I must not eat.'

'Your dinner is here,' I returned; 'why won't you get it?'

'I don't want it now,' he muttered hastily; 'I'll wait till supper. And, Nelly, once for all, let me beg you to warn Hareton and the other away from me. I wish to be troubled by nobody: I wish to have this place to myself.'

'Is there some new reason for this banishment?' I inquired. 'Tell me why you are so queer, Mr Heathcliff? Where were you last night? I'm not putting the question through idle curiosity, but——'

'You are putting the question through very idle curiosity,' he interrupted, with a laugh. 'Yet I'll answer it. Last night I was on the threshold of hell. Today, I am within sight of my heaven. I have my eyes on it: hardly three feet to sever me! And now you'd better go! You'll neither see nor hear anything to frighten you, if you refrain from prying.'

Having swept the hearth and wiped the table, I departed; more perplexed than ever.

He did not quit the house again that afternoon, and no one intruded on his solitude; till, at eight o'clock, I deemed it proper, though unsummoned, to carry a candle and his supper to him. He was leaning against the ledge of an open lattice, but not looking out: his face was turned to the interior gloom. The fire had smouldered to ashes; the room was filled with the damp mild air of the cloudy evening; and so

still, that not only the murmur of the beck down Gimmerton was distinguishable, but its ripples and its gurgling over the pebbles, or through the large stones which it could not cover. I uttered an ejaculation of discontent at seeing the dismal grate, and commenced shutting the casements one after another, till I came to his.

'Must I close this?' I asked, in order to rouse him; for he would not stir.

The light flashed on his features as I spoke. Oh, Mr Lockwood, I cannot express what a terrible start I got by the momentary view! Those deep black eyes! That smile, and ghastly paleness! It appeared to me, not Mr Heathcliff, but a goblin; and, in my terror, I let the candle bend towards the wall, and it left me in darkness.

'Yes, close it,' he replied, in his familiar voice. 'There, that is pure awkwardness! Why did you hold the candle horizontally? Be quick, and bring another.'

I hurried out in a foolish state of dread, and said to Joseph:

'The master wishes you to take him a light and rekindle the fire.' For I dare not go in myself again just then.

Joseph rattled some fire into the shovel, and went; but he brought it back immediately, with the supper tray in his other hand, explaining that Mr Heathcliff was going to bed, and he wanted nothing to eat till morning. We heard him mount the stairs directly; he did not proceed to his ordinary chamber, but turned into that with the panelled bed: its window, as I mentioned before, is wide enough for anybody to get through; and it struck me that he plotted another midnight excursion, of which he had rather we had no suspicion.

'Is he a ghoul or a vampire?' I mused. I had read of such hideous incarnate demons. And then I set myself to reflect how I had tended him in infancy, and watched him grow to youth, and followed him almost through his whole course; and what absurd nonsense it was to yield to that sense of horror. 'But where did he come from, the little dark thing, harboured by a good man to his bane?' muttered Superstition, as I dozed into unconsciousness. And I began, half dreaming, to weary myself with imagining some fit parentage for him; and, repeating my waking meditations, I tracked his existence over again, with grim variations; at last, picturing his death and funeral: of which, all I can remember is, being exceedingly vexed at having the task of dictating an inscription for his monument, and consulting the sexton about it; and, as he had no surname, and we could not tell his age, we were obliged to content ourselves with the single word, 'Heathcliff'. That came true: we were. If you enter the kirkyard, you'll read on his headstone, only that, and the date of his death.

Dawn restored me to common sense. I rose, and went into the garden, as soon as I could see, to ascertain if there were any footmarks under his window. There were none. 'He has stayed at home,' I thought, 'and he'll be all right today.' I prepared breakfast for the household, as was my usual custom, but told Hareton and Catherine to get theirs ere the master came down, for he lay late. They preferred taking it out of doors, under the trees, and I set a little table to accommodate them.

On my re-entrance, I found Mr Heathcliff below. He and Joseph were conversing about some farming business; he gave clear, minute directions concerning the matter discussed, but he spoke rapidly, and turned his head continually aside, and had the same excited expression, even more exaggerated. When Joseph quitted the room he took his seat in the place he generally chose, and I put a basin of coffee before him. He drew it nearer, and then rested his arms on the table, and looked at the opposite wall, as I supposed, surveying one particular portion, up and down, with glittering, restless eyes, and with such eager interest that he stopped breathing during half a minute together.

'Come now,' I exclaimed, pushing some bread against his hand, 'eat and drink that, while it is hot: it has been waiting near an hour.'

He didn't notice me, and yet he smiled. I'd rather have seen him gnash his teeth than smile so.

'Mr Heathcliff! master!' I cried, 'don't, for God's sake, stare as if you saw an unearthly vision.'

'Don't, for God's sake, shout so loud,' he replied. 'Turn round, and tell me, are we by ourselves?'

'Of course,' was my answer; 'of course we are.'

Still I involuntarily obeyed him, as if I were not quite sure. With a sweep of his hand he cleared a vacant space in front among the breakfast things, and leant forward to gaze more at his ease.

Now, I perceived he was not looking at the wall; for when I regarded him alone, it seemed exactly that he gazed at something within two yards' distance. And whatever it was, it communicated, apparently, both pleasure and pain in exquisite extremes: at least the anguished, yet raptured, expression of his countenance suggested that idea. The fancied object was not fixed: either his eyes pursued it with unwearied diligence, and, even in speaking to me, were never weaned away. I vainly reminded him of his protracted abstinence from food: if he stirred to touch anything in compliance with my entreaties, if he stretched his hand out to get a piece of bread, his fingers clenched before they reached it, and remained on the table, forgetful of their aim.

I sat, a model of patience, trying to attract his absorbed attention from its engrossing speculation; till he grew irritable, and got up, asking why I would not allow him to have his own time in taking his meals? and saying that on the next occasion, I needn't wait: I might set the things down and go. Having uttered these words he left the house, slowly sauntered down the garden path, and disappeared through the gate.

The hours crept anxiously by: another evening came. I did not retire to rest till late, and when I did, I could not sleep. He returned after midnight, and, instead of going to bed, shut himself into the room beneath. I listened, and tossed about, and, finally, dressed and descended. It was too irksome to lie up there, harassing my brain with a hundred idle misgivings.

I distinguished Mr Heathcliff's step, restlessly measuring the floor, and he frequently broke the silence by a deep inspiration, resembling a groan. He muttered detached words also; the only one I could catch was the name of Catherine, coupled with some wild term of endearment or suffering; and spoken as one would speak to a person present: low and earnest, and wrung from the depth of his soul. I had not courage to walk straight into the apartment; but I desired to divert him from his reverie, and therefore fell foul of the kitchen fire, stirred it, and began to scrape the cinders. It drew him forth sooner than I expected. He opened the door immediately, and said:

'Nelly, come here—is it morning? Come in with your light.'

'It is striking four,' I answered. 'You want a candle to take upstairs: you might have lit one at this fire.'

'No, I don't wish to go upstairs,' he said. 'Come in, and kindle *me* a fire, and do anything there is to do about the room.'

'I must blow the coals red first, before I can carry any,' I replied, getting a chair and the bellows.

He roamed to and fro, meantime, in a state approaching distraction; his heavy sighs succeeding each other so thick as to leave no space for common breathing between.

'When day breaks I'll send for Green,' he said; 'I wish to make some legal inquiries of him while I can bestow a thought on those matters, and while I can act calmly. I have not written my will yet; and how to leave my property I cannot determine. I wish I could annihilate it from the face of the earth.'

'I would not talk so, Mr Heathcliff,' I interposed. 'Let your will be a while: you'll be spared to repent of your many injustices yet. I never expected that your nerves would be disordered: they are, at present, marvellously so, however; and

almost entirely through your own fault. The way you've passed these three last days might knock up a Titan. Do take some food, and some repose. You need only look at yourself in a glass to see how you require both. Your cheeks are hollow, and your eyes bloodshot, like a person starving with hunger and going blind with loss of sleep.'

'It is not my fault that I cannot eat or rest,' he replied. 'I assure you it is through no settled designs. I'll do both as soon as I possibly can. But you might as well bid a man struggling in the water rest within arm's length of the shore! I must reach it first, and then I'll rest. Well, never mind Mr Green: as to repenting of my injustices, I've done no injustice, and I repent of nothing. I'm too happy; and yet I'm not happy enough. My soul's bliss kills my body, but does not satisfy itself.'

'Happy, master?' I cried. 'Strange happiness! If you would hear me without being angry, I might offer some advice that would make you happier.'

'What is that?' he asked. 'Give it.'

'You are aware, Mr Heathcliff,' I said, 'that from the time you were thirteen years old, you have lived a selfish, unchristian life; and probably hardly had a Bible in your hands during all that period. You must have forgotten the contents of the book, and you may not have space to search it now. Could it be hurtful to send for someone—some minister of any denomination, it does not matter which—to explain it, and show you how very far you have erred from its precepts; and how unfit you will be for its heaven, unless a change takes place before you die?'

'I'm rather obliged than angry, Nelly,' he said, 'for you remind me of the manner that I desire to be buried in. It is to be carried to the churchyard in the evening. You and Hareton may, if you please, accompany me: and mind, particularly, to notice that the sexton obeys my directions concerning the two coffins! No minister need come; nor need anything be said over me.—I tell you I have nearly attained *my* heaven; and that of others is altogether unvalued and uncoveted by me.'

'And supposing you persevered in your obstinate fast, and died by that means, and they refused to bury you in the precincts of the kirk?' I said, shocked at his godless indifference. 'How would you like it?'

'They won't do that,' he replied: 'if they did, you must have me removed secretly: and if you neglect it you shall prove, practically, that the dead are not annihilated!'

As soon as he heard the other members of the family stirring he retired to his den, and I breathed freer. But in the afternoon, while Joseph and Hareton were at their work, he came into the kitchen again, and, with a wild look, bid me come and sit in the house: he wanted somebody with him. I declined: telling him plainly that his strange talk and manner frightened me, and I had neither the nerve nor the will to be his companion alone.

'I believe you think me a fiend,' he said, with his dismal laugh: 'something too horrible to live under a decent roof.' Then turning to Catherine, who was there, and who drew behind me at his approach, he added, half sneeringly—'Will *you* come, chuck? I'll not hurt you. No! to you I've made myself worse than the devil. Well, there is *one* who won't shrink from my company! By God! she's relentless. Oh, damn it! It's unutterably too much for flesh and blood to bear—even mine.'

He solicited the society of no one more. At dusk, he went into his chamber. Through the whole night, and far into the morning, we heard him groaning and murmuring to himself. Hareton was anxious to enter; but I bade him fetch Mr Kenneth, and he should go in and see him. When he came, and I requested admittance and tried to open the door, I found it locked; and Heathcliff bid us be damned. He was better, and would be left alone; so the doctor went away.

The following evening was very wet: indeed it poured down till day-dawn; and, as I took my morning walk round the house, I observed the master's window swinging open, and the rain driving straight in. He cannot be in bed, I thought: those showers would drench him through. He must either be up or out. But I'll make no more ado, I'll go boldly and look.

Having succeeded in obtaining entrance with another key, I ran to unclose the panels, for the chamber was vacant; quickly pushing them aside, I peeped in. Mr Heathcliff was there—laid on his back. His eyes met mine so keen and fierce, I started; and then he seemed to smile. I could not think him dead: but his face and throat were washed with rain; the bedclothes dripped, and he was perfectly still. The lattice, flapping to and fro, had grazed one hand that rested on the sill; no blood trickled from the broken skin, and when I put my fingers to it, I could doubt no more: he was dead and stark!

I hasped the window; I combed his black long hair from his forehead; I tried to close his eyes: to extinguish, if possible, that frightful, lifelike gaze of exultation before anyone else beheld it. They would not shut: they seemed to sneer at my attempts: and his parted lips and sharp white teeth sneered too! Taken with another fit of cowardice, I cried out for Joseph. Joseph shuffled up and made a noise; but resolutely refused to meddle with him.

'Th' divil's harried off his soul,' he cried, 'and he muh hev his carcass intuh t' bargain, for ow't Aw care! Ech! what a wicked un he looks girning at death!' and the old sinner grinned in mockery. I thought he intended to cut a caper round the bed; but, suddenly composing himself, he fell on his knees, and raised his hands, and returned thanks that the lawful master and the ancient stock were restored to their rights.

I felt stunned by the awful event; and my memory unavoidably recurred to former times with a sort of oppressive sadness. But poor Hareton, the most wronged, was the only one that really suffered much. He sat by the corpse all night, weeping in bitter earnest. He pressed its hand, and kissed the sarcastic savage face that everyone else shrank from contemplating; and bemoaned him with that strong grief which springs naturally from a generous heart, though it be tough as tempered steel.

Mr Kenneth was perplexed to pronounce of what disorder the master died. I concealed the fact of his having swallowed nothing for four days, fearing it might lead to trouble, and then, I am persuaded, he did not abstain on purpose: it was the consequence of his strange illness, not the cause.

We buried him, to the scandal of the whole neighbourhood, as he wished. Earnshaw and I, the sexton, and six men to carry the coffin, comprehended the whole attendance. The six men departed when they had let it down into the grave: we stayed to see it covered. Hareton, with a streaming face, dug green sods, and laid them over the brown mould himself: at present it is as smooth and verdant as its companion mounds—and I hope its tenant sleeps as soundly. But the country folk, if you ask them, would swear on the Bible that he *walks*: there are those who speak to having met him near the church, and on the moor, and even in this house. Idle tales, you'll say, and so say I. Yet that old man by the kitchen fire affirms he has seen two on 'em, looking out of his chamber window, on every rainy night since his death: and an odd thing happened to me about a month ago. I was going to the Grange one evening—a dark evening, threatening thunder—and, just at the turn of the Heights, I encountered a little boy with a sheep and two lambs before him; he was crying terribly; and I supposed the lambs were skittish, and would not be guided.

'What's the matter, my little man?' I asked.

'There's Heathcliff and a woman, yonder, under t' nab,' he blubbered, 'un' I darnut pass 'em.'

I saw nothing; but neither the sheep nor he would go on; so I bid him take the road lower down. He probably raised the phantoms from thinking, as he traversed the moors alone, on the nonsense he had heard his parents and companions repeat. Yet, still, I don't like being out in the dark now; and I don't like being left by myself in this grim house: I cannot help it; I shall be glad when they leave it, and shift to the Grange.

'They are going to the Grange, then,' I said.

'Yes,' answered Mrs Dean, 'as soon as they are married, and that will be on New Year's Day.'

'And who will live here, then?'

'Why, Joseph will take care of the house, and, perhaps, a lad to keep him company. They will live in the kitchen, and the rest will be shut up.'

'For the use of such ghosts as choose to inhabit it,' I observed.

'No, Mr Lockwood,' said Nelly, shaking her head. 'I believe the dead are at peace: but it is not right to speak of them with levity.'

At that moment the garden gate swung to; the ramblers were returning.

'*They* are afraid of nothing,' I grumbled, watching their approach through the window. 'Together they would brave Satan and all his legions.'

As they stepped on to the doorstones, and halted to take a last look at the moon—or, more correctly, at each other by her light—I felt irresistibly impelled to escape them again; and, pressing a remembrance into the hand of Mrs Dean, and disregarding her expostulations at my rudeness, I vanished through the kitchen as they opened the house-door; and so should have confirmed Joseph in his opinion of his fellow-servant's gay indiscretions, had he not fortunately recognized me for a respectable character by the sweet ring of a sovereign at his feet.

My walk home was lengthened by a diversion in the direction of the kirk. When beneath its walls, I perceived decay had made progress, even in seven months: many a window showed black gaps deprived of glass; and slates jutted off, here and there, beyond the right line of the roof, to be gradually worked off in coming autumn storms.

I sought, and soon discovered, the three headstones on the slope next the moor: the middle one grey, and half buried in heath: Edgar Linton's only harmonized by the turf and moss creeping up its foot: Heathcliff's still bare.

I lingered round them, under that benign sky; watched the moths fluttering among the heath and harebells, listened to the soft wind breathing through the grass, and wondered how anyone could ever imagine unquiet slumbers for the sleepers in that quiet earth.

Shirley

by
Charlotte Brontë

Chapter I

OF late years, an abundant shower of curates has fallen upon the north of England: they lie very thick on the hills; every parish has one or more of them; they are young enough to be very active, and ought to be doing a great deal of good. But not of late years are we about to speak; we are going back to the beginning of this century: late years—present years are dusty, sun-burnt, hot, arid; we will evade the noon, forget it in siesta, pass the mid-day in slumber, and dream of dawn.

If you think, from this prelude, that anything like a romance is preparing for you, reader, you never were more mistaken. Do you anticipate sentiment, and poetry, and reverie? Do you expect passion, and stimulus, and melodrama? Calm your expectations; reduce them to a lowly standard. Something real, cool, and solid, lies before you; something unromantic as Monday morning, when all who have work wake with the consciousness that they must rise and betake themselves thereto. It is not positively affirmed that you shall not have a taste of the exciting, perhaps towards the middle and close of the meal, but it is resolved that the first dish set upon the table shall be one that a Catholic—ay, even an Anglo-Catholic—might eat on Good Friday in Passion Week: it shall be cold lentils and vinegar without oil; it shall be unleavened bread with bitter herbs, and no roast lamb.

Of late years, I say, an abundant shower of curates has fallen upon the north of England; but in eighteen-hundred-eleven-twelve that affluent rain had not descended: curates were scarce then: there was no Pastoral Aid—no Additional Curates' Society to stretch a helping hand to worn-out old rectors and incumbents, and give them the wherewithal to pay a vigorous young colleague from Oxford or Cambridge. The present successors of the apostles, disciples of Dr. Pusey and tools of the Propaganda, were at that time being hatched under cradle-blankets, or undergoing regeneration by nursery-baptism in wash-hand-basins, You could not have guessed by looking at any one of them that the Italian-ironed double frills of its net-cap surrounded the brows of a pre-ordained, specially sanctified successor of St. Paul, St. Peter, or St. John; nor could you have foreseen in the folds of its long night-gown the white surplice in which it was hereafter cruelly to exercise the souls of its parishioners, and strangely to nonplus its old-fashioned vicar by flourishing aloft in a pulpit the shirt-like raiment which had never before waved higher than the reading-desk.

Yet even in those days of scarcity there were curates: the precious plant was rare, but it might be found. A certain favoured district in the West Riding of Yorkshire could boast three rods of Aaron blossoming within a circuit of twenty miles. You shall see them, reader. Step into this neat garden-house on the skirts of Whinbury, walk forward into the little parlour—there they are at dinner. Allow me to introduce them to you:—Mr. Donne, curate of Whinbury; Mr. Malone, curate of Briarfield; Mr. Sweeting, curate of Nunnely. These are Mr. Donne's lodgings,

being the habitation of one John Gale, a small clothier. Mr. Donne has kindly invited his brethren to regale with him. You and I will join the party, see what is to be seen, and hear what is to be heard. At present, however, they are only eating; and while they eat we will talk aside.

These gentlemen are in the bloom of youth; they possess all the activity of that interesting age—an activity which their moping old vicars would fain turn into the channel of their pastoral duties, often expressing a wish to see it expended in a diligent superintendence of the schools, and in frequent visits to the sick of their respective parishes. But the youthful Levites feel this to be dull work; they prefer lavishing their energies on a course of proceeding, which, though to other eyes it appear more heavy with ennui, more cursed with monotony, than the toil of the weaver at his loom, seems to yield them an unfailing supply of enjoyment and occupation.

I allude to a rushing backwards and forwards, amongst themselves, to and from their respective lodgings: not a round—but a triangle of visits, which they keep up all the year through, in winter, spring, summer, and autumn. Season and weather make no difference; with unintelligible zeal they dare snow and hail, wind and rain, mire and dust, to go and dine, or drink tea, or sup with each other. What attracts them, it would be difficult to say. It is not friendship; for whenever they meet they quarrel. It is not religion; the thing is never named amongst them: theology they may discuss occasionally, but piety—never. It is not the love of eating and drinking: each might have as good a joint and pudding, tea as potent, and toast as succulent, at his own lodgings, as is served to him at his brother's. Mrs. Gale, Mrs. Hogg, and Mrs. Whipp—their respective landladies—affirm that "it is just for nought else but to give folk trouble." By "folk," the good ladies of course mean themselves; for indeed they are kept in a continual "fry" by this system of mutual invasion.

Mr. Donne and his guests, as I have said, are at dinner; Mrs. Gale waits on them, but a spark of the hot kitchen fire is in her eye. She considers that the privilege of inviting a friend to a meal occasionally, without additional charge (a privilege included in the terms on which she lets her lodgings), has been quite sufficiently exercised of late. The present week is yet but at Thursday, and on Monday, Mr. Malone, the curate of Briarfield, came to breakfast and stayed dinner; on Tuesday, Mr. Malone and Mr. Sweeting of Nunnely, came to tea, remained to supper, occupied the spare bed, and favoured her with their company to breakfast on Wednesday morning; now, on Thursday, they are both here at dinner, and she is almost certain they will stay all night. "C'en est trop," she would say, if she could speak French.

Mr. Sweeting is mincing the slice of roast-beef on his plate, and complaining that it is very tough; Mr. Donne says the beer is flat. Ay! that is the worst of it: if they would only be civil, Mrs. Gale wouldn't mind it so much; if they would only seem satisfied with what they get, she wouldn't care, but "these young parsons is so high and so scornful, they set everybody beneath their 'fit': they treat her with less than civility, just because she does not keep a servant, but does the work of the house herself, as her mother did afore her: then they are always speaking against Yorkshire ways and Yorkshire folk," and by that very token Mrs. Gale does not believe one of them to be a real gentleman, or come of gentle kin. "The old parsons is worth the whole lump of college lads; they know what belongs to good manners, and is kind to high and low."

"More bread!" cries Mr. Malone, in a tone which, though prolonged but to utter two syllables, proclaims him at once a native of the land of shamrocks and potatoes. Mrs. Gale hates Mr. Malone more than either of the other two; but she fears him also, for he is a tall, strongly-built personage, with real Irish legs and arms, and a face as genuinely national: not the Milesian face—not Daniel O'Connell's style, but the high-featured, North-American-Indian sort of visage, which belongs to a

certain class of the Irish gentry, and has a petrified and proud look, better suited to the owner of an estate of slaves, than to the landlord of a free peasantry. Mr. Malone's father termed himself a gentleman: he was poor and in debt, and besottedly arrogant; and his son was like him.

Mrs. Gale offered the loaf.

"Cut it, woman," said her guest; and the "woman" cut it accordingly. Had she followed her inclinations, she would have cut the parson also; her Yorkshire soul revolted absolutely from his manner of command.

The curates had good appetites, and though the beef was "tough," they ate a great deal of it. They swallowed, too, a tolerable allowance of the "flat beer," while a dish of Yorkshire pudding, and two tureens of vegetables, disappeared like leaves before locusts. The cheese, too, received distinguished marks of their attention; and a "spice-cake," which followed by way of dessert, vanished like a vision, and was no more found. Its elegy was chanted in the kitchen by Abraham, Mrs. Gale's son and heir, a youth of six summers: he had reckoned upon the reversion thereof, and when his mother brought down the empty platter, he lifted up his voice and wept sore.

The curates, meantime, sat and sipped their wine; a liquor of unpretending vintage, moderately enjoyed. Mr. Malone, indeed, would much rather have had whisky; but Mr. Donne, being an Englishman, did not keep the beverage. While they sipped, they argued; not on politics, nor on philosophy, nor on literature— these topics were now as ever totally without interest for them—not even on theology, practical or doctrinal; but on minute points of ecclesiastical discipline, frivolities which seemed empty as bubbles to all save themselves. Mr. Malone, who contrived to secure two glasses of wine, when his brethren contented themselves with one, waxed by degrees hilarious after his fashion; that is, he grew a little insolent, said rude things in a hectoring tone, and laughed clamorously at his own brilliancy.

Each of his companions became in turn his butt. Malone had a stock of jokes at their service, which he was accustomed to serve out regularly on convivial occasions like the present, seldom varying his wit; for which, indeed, there was no necessity, as he never appeared to consider himself monotonous, and did not at all care what others thought. Mr. Donne, he favoured with hints about his extreme meagreness, allusions to his turned-up nose, cutting sarcasms on a certain threadbare chocolate surtout, which that gentleman was accustomed to sport whenever it rained, or seemed likely to rain, and criticisms on a choice set of cockney phrases, and modes of pronunciation, Mr. Donne's own property, and certainly deserving of remark for the elegance and finish they communicated to his style.

Mr. Sweeting was bantered about his stature—he was a little man, a mere boy in height and breadth compared with the athletic Malone—rallied on his musical accomplishments—he played the flute and sang hymns like a seraph (some young ladies of his parish thought), sneered at as "the ladies' pet," teased about his mamma and sisters; for whom poor Mr. Sweeting had some lingering regard, and of whom he was foolish enough now and then to speak in the presence of the priestly Paddy, from whose anatomy the bowels of natural affection had somehow been omitted.

The victims met these attacks each in his own way; Mr. Donne with a stilted self-complacency, and half-sullen phlegm, the sole props of his otherwise somewhat rickety dignity; Mr. Sweeting with the indifference of a light, easy disposition, which never professed to have any dignity to maintain.

When Malone's raillery became rather too offensive, which it soon did, they joined in an attempt to turn the tables on him by asking him how many boys had shouted "Irish Peter!" after him as he came along the road that day (Malone's name was Peter—the Rev. Peter Augustus Malone); requesting to be informed whether it was the mode in Ireland for clergymen to carry loaded pistols in their pockets, and a shillelagh in their hands, when they made pastoral visits: inquiring

the signification of such words as vele, firrum, hellum, storrum (so Mr. Malone invariably pronounced veil, firm, helm, storm), and employing such other methods of retaliation as the innate refinement of their minds suggested.

This, of course, would not do. Malone, being neither good-natured nor phlegmatic, was presently in a towering passion. He vociferated, gesticulated; Donne and Sweeting laughed. He reviled them as Saxons and snobs at the very top pitch of his high Celtic voice; they taunted him with being the native of a conquered land. He menaced rebellion in the name of his ''counthry,'' vented bitter hatred against English rule; they spoke of rags, beggary, and pestilence. The little parlour was in an uproar; you would have thought a duel must follow such virulent abuse; it seemed a wonder that Mr. and Mrs. Gale did not take alarm at the noise, and send for a constable to keep the peace. But they were accustomed to such demonstrations; they well knew that the curates never dined or took tea together without a little exercise of the sort, and were quite easy as to consequences; knowing that these clerical quarrels were as harmless as they were noisy; that they resulted in nothing; and that, on whatever terms the curates might part to-night, they would be sure to meet the best friends in the world to-morrow morning.

As the worthy pair were sitting by their kitchen fire, listening to the repeated and sonorous contact of Malone's fist with the mahogany plane of the parlour table, and to the consequent start and jingle of decanters and glasses following each assault, to the mocking laughter of the allied English disputants, and the stuttering declamation of the isolated Hibernian,—as they thus sat, a foot was heard at the outer door-step, and the knocker quivered to a sharp appeal.

Mr. Gale went and opened.

''Whom have you upstairs in the parlour?'' asked a voice; a rather remarkable voice, nasal in tone, abrupt in utterance.

''Oh! Mr. Helstone, is it you, sir? I could hardly see you for the darkness; it is so soon dark now. Will you walk in, sir?''

''I want to know first whether it is worth my while walking in. Whom have you upstairs?''

''The curates, sir.''

''What! all of them?''

''Yes, sir.''

''Been dining here?''

''Yes, sir.''

''That will do.''

With these words a person entered—a middle-aged man, in black. He walked straight across the kitchen to an inner door, opened it, inclined his head forward, and stood listening. There was something to listen to, for the noise above was just then louder than ever.

''Hey!'' he ejaculated to himself: then turning to Mr. Gale—''Have you often this sort of work?''

Mr. Gale had been a churchwarden, and was indulgent to the clergy.

''They're young, you know, sir—they're young,'' said he deprecatingly.

''Young! They want caning. Bad boys—bad boys! and if you were a Dissenter, John Gale, instead of being a good Churchman, they'd do the like—they'd expose themselves: but I'll''——

By way of finish to this sentence, he passed through the inner door, drew it after him, and mounted the stair. Again he listened a few minutes when he arrived at the upper room. Making entrance without warning, he stood before the curates.

And they were silent; they were transfixed; and so was the invader. He—a personage short of stature, but straight of port, and bearing on broad shoulders a hawk's head, beak, and eye, the whole surmounted by a Rehoboam, or shovel hat, which he did not seem to think it necessary to lift or remove before the presence

in which he then stood—*he* folded his arms on his chest and surveyed his young friends—if friends they were—much at his leisure.

"What!" he began, delivering his words in a voice no longer nasal, but deep—more than deep—a voice made purposely hollow and cavernous; "What! has the miracle of Pentecost been renewed? Have the cloven tongues come down again? Where are they? The sound filled the whole house just now. I heard the seventeen languages in full action: Parthians, and Medes, and Elamites, the dwellers in Mesopotamia, and in Judea, and Cappadocia, in Pontus and Asia, Phrygia and Pamphylia, in Egypt and in the parts of Libya about Cyrene, strangers of Rome, Jews and proselytes, Cretes and Arabians; every one of these must have had its representative in this room two minutes since."

"I beg your pardon, Mr. Helstone," began Mr. Donne; "take a seat, pray, sir. Have a glass of wine?"

His civilities received no answer: the falcon in the black coat proceeded:—

"What do I talk about the gift of tongues? Gift, indeed! I mistook the chapter, and book, and testament: Gospel for law, Acts for Genesis, the city of Jerusalem for the plain of Shinar. It was no gift, but the confusion of tongues which has gabbled me deaf as a post. *You,* apostles? What! you three? Certainly not: three presumptuous Babylonish masons—neither more nor less!"

"I assure you, sir, we were only having a little chat together over a glass of wine after a friendly dinner: settling the Dissenters!"

"Oh! settling the Dissenters—were you? Was Malone settling the Dissenters? It sounded to me much more like settling his co-apostles. You were quarrelling together; making almost as much noise—you three alone—as Moses Barraclough, the preaching tailor, and all his hearers, are making in the Methodist chapel down yonder, where they are in the thick of a revival. I know whose fault it is—it is yours, Malone."

"Mine, sir?"

"Yours, sir. Donne and Sweeting were quiet before you came, and would be quiet if you were gone. I wish when you crossed the Channel you had left your Irish habits behind you. Dublin student ways won't do here: the proceedings which might pass unnoticed in a wild bog and mountain district in Connaught will, in a decent English parish, bring disgrace on those who indulge in them, and, what is far worse, on the sacred institution of which they are merely the humble appendages."

There was a certain dignity in the little elderly gentleman's manner of rebuking these youths; though it was not, perhaps, quite the dignity most appropriate to the occasion. Mr. Helstone—standing straight as a ramrod—looking keen as a kite, presented, despite his clerical hat, black coat, and gaiters, more the air of a veteran officer chiding his subalterns, than of a venerable priest exhorting his sons in the faith. Gospel mildness—apostolic benignity, never seemed to have breathed their influence over that keen brown visage; but firmness had fixed the features, and sagacity had carved her own lines about them.

"I met Supplehough," he continued, "plodding through the mud this wet night, going to preach at Milldean opposition shop. As I told you, I heard Barraclough bellowing in the midst of a conventicle like a possessed bull; and I find *you,* gentlemen, tarrying over your half-pint of muddy port-wine, and scolding like angry old women. No wonder Supplehough should have dipped sixteen adult converts in a day—which he did a fortnight since; no wonder Barraclough, scamp and hypocrite as he is, should attract all the weaver-girls in their flowers and ribbons, to witness how much harder are his knuckles than the wooden brim of his tub; as little wonder that *you,* when you are left to yourselves, without your rectors—myself, and Hall, and Boultby—to back you, should too often perform the holy service of our church to bare walls, and read your bit of a dry discourse to the clerk, and the organist, and the beadle. But enough of the subject: I came to see Malone—I have an errand unto thee, O captain!"

"What is it?" inquired Malone discontentedly; "there can be no funeral to take at this time of day."

"Have you any arms about you?"

"Arms, sir?—yes, and legs": and he advanced the mighty members.

"Bah! weapons, I mean."

"I have the pistols you gave me yourself; I never part with them: I lay them ready cocked on a chair by my bedside at night. I have my blackthorn."

"Very good. Will you go to Hollow's Mill?"

"What is stirring at Hollow's Mill?"

"Nothing as yet, nor perhaps will be; but Moore is alone there: he has sent all the workmen he can trust to Stilbro'; there are only two women left about the place. It would be a nice opportunity for any of his well-wishers to pay him a visit, if they knew how straight the path was made before them."

"I am none of his well-wishers, sir: I don't care for him."

"Soh! Malone, you are afraid."

"You know me better than that. If I really thought there was a chance of a row, I would go: but Moore is a strange, shy man, whom I never pretend to understand; and for the sake of his sweet company only, I would not stir a step."

"But there *is* a chance of a row; if a positive riot does not take place—of which, indeed, I see no signs—yet it is unlikely this night will pass quite tranquilly. You know Moore has resolved to have the new machinery, and he expects two waggon loads of frames and shears from Stilbro' this evening. Scott, the overlooker, and a few picked men, are gone to fetch them."

"They will bring them in safely and quietly enough, sir."

"Moore says so, and affirms he wants nobody: some one, however, he must have, if it were only to bear evidence in case anything should happen. I call him very careless. He sits in the counting-house with the shutters unclosed; he goes out here and there after dark, wanders right up the hollow, down Fieldhead Lane, among the plantations, just as if he were the darling of the neighbourhood, or—being, as he is, its detestation—bore a 'charmed life' as they say in tale-books. He takes no warning from the fate of Pearson, nor from that of Armitage—shot, one in his own house and the other on the moor."

"But he should take warning, sir, and use precautions too," interposed Mr. Sweeting; "and I think he would if he heard what I heard the other day."

"What did you hear, Davy?"

"You know Mike Hartley, sir?"

"The Antinomian weaver. Yes."

"When Mike has been drinking for a few weeks together, he generally winds up by a visit to Nunnely vicarage, to tell Mr. Hall a piece of his mind about his sermons, to denounce the horrible tendency of his doctrine of works, and warn him that he and all his hearers are sitting in outer darkness."

"Well—that has nothing to do with Moore."

"Besides being an Antinomian, he is a violent Jacobin and leveller, sir."

"I know. When he is very drunk, his mind is always running on regicide. Mike is not unacquainted with history, and it is rich to hear him going over the list of tyrants of whom, as he says, 'the revenger of blood has obtained satisfaction.' The fellow exults strangely in murder done on crowned heads, or on any head for political reasons. I have already heard it hinted that he seems to have a queer hankering after Moore: is that what you allude to, Sweeting?"

"You use the proper term, sir. Mr. Hall thinks Mike has no personal hatred of Moore; Mike says he even likes to talk to him, and run after him, but he has a *hankering* that Moore should be made an example of: he was extolling him to Mr. Hall the other day as the mill-owner with the most brains in Yorkshire, and for that reason he affirms Moore should be chosen as a sacrifice, an oblation of a sweet

savour. Is Mike Hartley in his right mind, do you think, sir?'' inquired Sweeting simply.

"Can't tell, Davy: he may be crazed or he may be only crafty—or, perhaps, a little of both.''

"He talks of seeing visions, sir.''

"Ay! He is a very Ezekiel or Daniel for visions. He came just when I was going to bed, last Friday night, to describe one that had been revealed to him in Nunnely Park that very afternoon.''

"Tell it, sir—what was it?'' urged Sweeting.

"Davy, thou hast an enormous organ of Wonder in thy cranium; Malone, you see, has none; neither murders nor visions interest him: see what a big vacant Saph he looks at this moment.''

"Saph! Who was Saph, sir?''

"I thought you would not know: you may find it out: it is biblical. I know nothing more of him than his name and race; but from a boy upwards, I have always attached a personality to Saph. Depend on it he was honest, heavy, and luckless; he met his end at Gob, by the hand of Sibbechai.''

"But the vision, sir?''

"Davy, thou shalt hear. Donne is biting his nails, and Malone yawning; so I will tell it but to thee. Mike is out of work, like many others, unfortunately; Mr. Grame, Sir Philip Nunnely's steward, gave him a job about the priory: according to his account, Mike was busy hedging rather late in the afternoon, but before dark, when he heard what he thought was a band at a distance, bugles, fifes, and the sound of a trumpet; it came from the forest, and he wondered that there should be music there. He looked up: all amongst the trees he saw moving objects, red, like poppies, or white, like May-blossom; the wood was full of them, they poured out and filled the park. He then perceived they were soldiers—thousands and tens of thousands; but they made no more noise than a swarm of midges on a summer evening. They formed in order, he affirmed, and marched, regiment after regiment, across the park; he followed them to Nunnely Common; the music still played soft and distant. On the common he watched them go through a number of evolutions, a man clothed in scarlet stood in the centre and directed them; they extended, he declared, over fifty acres; they were in sight half-an-hour; then they marched away quite silently: the whole time he heard neither voice nor tread—nothing but the faint music playing a solemn march.''

"Where did they go, sir?''

"Towards Briarfield. Mike followed them; they seemed passing Fieldhead, when a column of smoke, such as might be vomited by a park of artillery, spread noiseless over the fields, the road, the common, and rolled, he said, blue and dim, to his very feet. As it cleared away he looked again for the soldiers, but they were vanished; he saw them no more. Mike, like a wise Daniel as he is, not only rehearsed the vision, but gave the interpretation thereof: it signifies, he intimated, bloodshed and civil conflict.''

"Do you credit it, sir?'' asked Sweeting.

"Do you, Davy? But come, Malone, why are you not off?''

"I am rather surprised, sir, you did not stay with Moore yourself: you like this kind of thing.''

"So I should have done, had I not unfortunately happened to engage Boultby to sup with me on his way home from the Bible Society meeting at Nunnely. I promised to send you as my substitute; for which, by-the-bye, he did not thank me: he would much rather have had me than you, Peter. Should there be any real need of help, I shall join you: the mill-bell will give warning. Meantime, go; unless (turning suddenly to Messrs. Sweeting and Donne)—unless Davy Sweeting or Joseph Donne prefers going. What do you say, gentlemen? The commission is an honourable one, not without the seasoning of a little real peril; for the country is in a queer state,

as you all know, and Moore and his mill, and his machinery, are held in sufficient odium. There are chivalric sentiments, there is high-beating courage under those waistcoats of yours, I doubt not. Perhaps I am too partial to my favourite, Peter; little David shall be the champion, or spotless Joseph. Malone, you are but a great floundering Saul after all, good only to lend your armour: out with your fire-arms, fetch your shillelagh; it is there—in the corner.''

With a significant grin, Malone produced his pistols, offering one to each of his brethren. They were not readily seized on: with graceful modesty, each gentleman retired a step from the presented weapon.

''I never touch them; I never did touch anything of the kind,'' said Mr. Donne.

''I am almost a stranger to Mr. Moore,'' murmured Sweeting.

''If you never touched a pistol, try the feel of it now, great satrap of Egypt. As to the little minstrel, he probably prefers encountering the Philistines with no other weapon than his flute. Get their hats, Peter; they'll both of 'em go.''

''No, sir; no, Mr. Helstone: my mother wouldn't like it,'' pleaded Sweeting.

''And I make it a rule never to get mixed up in affairs of the kind,'' observed Donne.

Helstone smiled sardonically; Malone laughed a horse-laugh. He then replaced his arms, took his hat and cudgel, and saying that ''he never felt more in tune for a shindy in his life, and that he wished a score of greasy cloth-dressers might beat up Moore's quarters that night,'' he made his exit; clearing the stairs at a stride or two, and making the house shake with the bang of the front-door behind him.

Chapter II

THE WAGGONS

THE evening was pitch-dark: star and moon were quenched in grey rain-clouds— grey they would have been by day, by night they looked sable. Malone was not a man given to close observation of Nature; her changes passed, for the most part, unnoticed by him: he could walk miles on the most varying April day, and never see the beautiful dallying of earth and heaven; never mark when a sunbeam kissed the hilltops, making them smile clear in green light, or when a shower wept over them, hiding their crests with the low-hanging, dishevelled tresses of a cloud. He did not, therefore, care to contrast the sky as it now appeared—a muffled, streaming vault, all black, save where, towards the east, the furnaces of Stilbro' iron-works threw a tremulous lurid shimmer on the horizon—with the same sky on an unclouded frosty night. He did not trouble himself to ask where the constellations and the planets were gone, or to regret the ''black-blue'' serenity of the air-ocean which those white islets stud; and which another ocean, of heavier and denser element, now rolled below and concealed. He just doggedly pursued his way, leaning a little forward as he walked, and wearing his hat on the back of his head, as his Irish manner was. ''Tramp, tramp,'' he went along the causeway, where the road boasted the privilege of such an accommodation; ''splash, splash,'' through the mire-filled cart-ruts, where the flags were exchanged for soft mud. He looked but for certain land-marks: the spire of Briarfield church; further on, the lights of Redhouse. This was an inn; and when he reached it, the glow of a fire through a half-curtained window, a vision of glasses on a round table, and of revellers on an oaken settle, had nearly drawn aside the curate from his course. He thought longingly of a tumbler of whisky-and-water; in a strange place, he would instantly have realised the dream; but the company assembled in that kitchen were Mr. Helstone's own parishioners; they all knew him. He sighed, and passed on.

The high road was now to be quitted, as the remaining distance to Hollow's Mill might be considerably reduced by a short cut across fields. These fields were level and monotonous; Malone took a direct course through them, jumping hedge and wall. He passed but one building here, and that seemed large and hall-like, though irregular: you could see a high gable, then a long front, then a low gable, then a thick, lofty stack of chimneys: there were some trees behind it. It was dark; not a candle shone from any window; it was absolutely still: the rain running from the eaves, and the rather wild, but very low whistle of the wind round the chimneys and through the boughs, were the sole sounds in its neighbourhood.

This building passed, the fields, hitherto flat, declined in a rapid descent: evidently a vale lay below, through which you could hear the water run. One light glimmered in the depth: for that beacon Malone steered.

He came to a little white house—you could see it was white even through this dense darkness—and knocked at the door. A fresh-faced servant opened it; by the candle she held was revealed a narrow passage, terminating in a narrow stair. Two doors covered with crimson baize, a strip of crimson carpet down the steps, contrasted with light-coloured walls and white floor, made the little interior look clean and fresh.

"Mr. Moore is at home, I suppose?"

"Yes, sir, but he is not in."

"Not in! Where is he then?"

"At the mill—in the counting-house."

Here one of the crimson doors opened.

"Are the waggons come, Sarah?" asked a female voice, and a female head at the same time was apparent. It might not be the head of a goddess—indeed a screw of curl-paper on each side the temples quite forbade that supposition—but neither was it the head of a Gorgon; yet Malone seemed to take it in the latter light. Big as he was, he shrank bashfully back into the rain at the view thereof; and saying, "I'll go to him," hurried in seeming trepidation down a short lane, across an obscure yard, towards a huge black mill.

The work-hours were over; the "hands" were gone; the machinery was at rest; the mill shut up. Malone walked round it; somewhere in its great sooty flank he found another chink of light; he knocked at another door, using for the purpose the thick end of his shillelagh, with which he beat a rousing tattoo. A key turned; the door unclosed.

"Is it Joe Scott? What news of the waggons, Joe?"

"No—it's myself. Mr. Helstone would send me."

"Oh! Mr. Malone." The voice in uttering this name had the slightest possible cadence of disappointment. After a moment's pause, it continued, politely, but a little formally—

"I beg you will come in, Mr. Malone. I regret extremely Mr. Helstone should have thought it necessary to trouble you so far; there was no necessity:—I told him so;—and on such a night—but walk forwards."

Through a dark apartment, of aspect undistinguishable, Malone followed the speaker into a light and bright room within: very light and bright indeed it seemed to eyes which, for the last hour, had been striving to penetrate the double darkness of night and fog; but except for its excellent fire and for a lamp of elegant design and vivid lustre burning on a table, it was a very plain place. The boarded floor was carpetless; the three or four stiff-backed green-painted chairs seemed once to have furnished the kitchen of some farmhouse; a desk of strong, solid formation, the table aforesaid, and some framed sheets on the stone-coloured walls, bearing plans for building, for gardening, designs of machinery, etc., completed the furniture of the place.

Plain as it was, it seemed to satisfy Malone; who, when he had removed and hung up his wet surtout and hat, drew one of the rheumatic-looking chairs to the hearth, and set his knees almost within the bars of the red grate.

"Comfortable quarters you have here, Mr. Moore; and all snug to yourself."

"Yes; but my sister would be glad to see you, if you would prefer stepping into the house."

"Oh, no! the ladies are best alone. I never was a lady's man. You don't mistake me for my friend Sweeting, do you, Mr. Moore?"

"Sweeting!—which of them is that? The gentleman in the chocolate overcoat, or the little gentleman?"

"The little one;—he of Nunnely; the cavalier of the Misses Sykes, with the whole six of whom he is in love, ha! ha!"

"Better be generally in love with all than specially with one, I should think, in that quarter."

"But he *is* specially in love with one besides, for when I and Donne urged him to make a choice amongst the fair bevy, he named—which do you think?"

With a queer, quiet smile, Mr. Moore replied, "Dora, of course, or Harriet."

"Ha! ha! you've an excellent guess; but what made you hit on those two?"

"Because they are the tallest, the handsomest: and Dora, at least, is the stoutest; and as your friend Mr. Sweeting is but a little, slight figure, I concluded that, according to a frequent rule in such cases, he preferred his contrast."

"You are right; Dora it is: but he has no chance, has he, Moore?"

"What has Mr. Sweeting, besides his curacy?"

This question seemed to tickle Malone amazingly; he laughed for full three minutes before he answered it.

"What has Sweeting? Why, David has his harp, or flute, which comes to the same thing. He has a sort of pinchbeck watch; ditto, ring; ditto, eyeglass: that's what he has."

"How would he propose to keep Miss Sykes in gowns only?"

"Ha! ha! Excellent! I'll ask him that next time I see him. I'll roast him for his presumption: but no doubt he expects old Christopher Sykes would do something handsome. He is rich, is he not? They live in a large house."

"Sykes carries on an extensive concern."

"Therefore he must be wealthy, eh?"

"Therefore he must have plenty to do with his wealth; and in these times would be about as likely to think of drawing money from the business to give dowries to his daughters as I should be to dream of pulling down the cottage there, and constructing on its ruins a house as large as Fieldhead."

"Do you know what I heard, Moore, the other day?"

"No: perhaps that I *was* about to effect some such change. Your Briarfield gossips are capable of saying that or sillier things."

"That you were going to take Fieldhead on a lease—I thought it looked a dismal place, by-the-bye, to-night, as I passed it—and that it was your intention to settle a Miss Sykes there as mistress; to be married, in short, ha! ha! Now, which is it? Dora—I am sure: you said she was the handsomest."

"I wonder how often it has been settled that I was to be married since I came to Briarfield! They have assigned me every marriageable single woman by turns in the district. Now it was the two Misses Wynns—first the dark, then the light one. Now the red-haired Miss Armitage, then the mature Ann Pearson; at present you throw on my shoulders all the tribe of the Misses Sykes. On what grounds this gossip rests, God knows. I visit nowhere—I seek female society about as assiduously as you do, Mr. Malone. If ever I go to Whinbury, it is only to give Sykes or Pearson a call in their counting-house; where our discussions run on other topics than matrimony, and our thoughts are occupied with other things than courtships, establishments, dowries: the cloth we can't sell, the hands we can't employ, the

mills we can't run, the perverse course of events generally, which we cannot alter, fill our hearts, I take it, pretty well at present, to the tolerably complete exclusion of such figments as love-making, etc.''

"I go along with you completely, Moore. If there is one notion I hate more than another, it is that of marriage: I mean marriage in the vulgar weak sense, as a mere matter of sentiment; two beggarly fools agreeing to unite their indigence by some fantastic tie of feeling—humbug! But an advantageous connection, such as can be formed in consonance with dignity of views, and permanency of solid interests, is not so bad—eh?''

"No," responded Moore, in an absent manner; the subject seemed to have no interest for him: he did not pursue it. After sitting for some time gazing at the fire with a preoccupied air, he suddenly turned his head.

"Hark!" said he; "did you hear wheels?"

Rising, he went to the window, opened it, and listened. He soon closed it. "It is only the sound of the wind rising," he remarked, "and the rivulet a little swollen, rushing down the hollow. I expected those waggons at six; it is near nine now."

"Seriously, do you suppose that the putting up of this new machinery will bring you into danger?'' inquired Malone. "Helstone seems to think it will.''

"I only wish the machines—the frames were safe here, and lodged within the walls of this mill. Once put up I defy the framebreakers: let them only pay me a visit, and take the consequences; my mill is my castle.''

"One despises such low scoundrels," observed Malone, in a profound vein of reflection. "I almost wish a party would call upon you to-night; but the road seemed extremely quiet as I came along: I saw nothing astir.''

"You came by the Redhouse?''

"Yes.''

"There would be nothing on that road; it is in the direction of Stilbro' the risk lies.''

"And do you think there is risk?''

"What these fellows have done to others, they may do to me. There is only this difference; most of the manufacturers seem paralysed when they are attacked. Sykes, for instance, when his dressing-shop was set on fire and burned to the ground, when the cloth was torn from his tenters and left in shreds in the field, took no steps to discover or punish the miscreants: he gave up as tamely as a rabbit under the jaws of a ferret. Now I, if I know myself, should stand by my trade, my mill, and my machinery.''

"Helstone says these three are your gods; that the 'Orders in Council' are with you another name for the seven deadly sins; that Castlereagh is your Antichrist, and the war-party his legions.''

"Yes; I abhor all these things because they ruin me: they stand in my way: I cannot get on. I cannot execute my plans because of them: I see myself baffled at every turn by their untoward effects.''

"But you are rich and thriving, Moore?''

"I am very rich in cloth I cannot sell: you should step into my warehouse yonder, and observe how it is piled to the roof with pieces. Roakes and Pearson are in the same condition: America used to be their market, but the Orders in Council have cut that off.''

Malone did not seem prepared to carry on briskly a conversation of this sort; he began to knock the heels of his boots together, and to yawn.

"And then to think," continued Mr. Moore, who seemed too much taken up with the current of his own thoughts to note the symptoms of his guest's *ennui*,— "to think that these ridiculous gossips of Whinbury and Briarfield will keep pestering one about being married! As if there was nothing to be done in life but to 'pay attention,' as they say, to some young lady, and then to go to church with her, and then to start on a bridal tour, and then to run through a round of visits, and then,

I suppose, to be 'having a family,'—Oh, que le diable emporte!''—He broke off
the aspiration into which he was launching with a certain energy, and added, more
calmly—''I believe women talk and think only of these things, and they naturally
fancy men's minds similarly occupied.''

''Of course—of course,'' assented Malone; ''but never mind them.'' And he
whistled, looked impatiently round, and seemed to feel a great want of something.
This time Moore caught, and, it appeared, comprehended his demonstrations.

''Mr. Malone,'' said he, ''you must require refreshment after your wet walk: I
forget hospitality.''

''Not at all,'' rejoined Malone; but he looked as if the right nail was at last hit
on the head, nevertheless. Moore rose and opened a cupboard.

''It is my fancy,'' said he, ''to have every convenience within myself, and not
to be dependent on the femininity in the cottage yonder for every mouthful I eat
or every drop I drink. I often spend the evening and sup here alone, and sleep with
Joe Scott in the mill. Sometimes I am my own watchman; I require little sleep,
and it pleases me on a fine night to wander for an hour or two with my musket
about the hollow. Mr. Malone, can you cook a mutton-chop?''

''Try me: I've done it hundreds of times at college.''

''There's a dishful, then, and there's the gridiron. Turn them quickly; you know
the secret of keeping the juices in?''

''Never fear me—you shall see. Hand a knife and fork, please.''

The curate turned up his coat-cuffs, and applied himself to the cookery with
vigour. The manufacturer placed on the table plates, a loaf of bread, a black bottle,
and two tumblers. He then produced a small copper kettle—still from the same
well-stored recess, his cupboard—filled it with water from a large stone jar in a
corner, set it on the fire beside the hissing gridiron, got lemons, sugar, and a small
china punch-bowl; but while he was brewing the punch, a tap at the door called
him away.

''Is it you, Sarah?''

''Yes, sir. Will you come to supper, please, sir?''

''No; I shall not be in to-night: I shall sleep in the mill. So lock the doors, and
tell your mistress to go to bed.'' He returned.

''You have your household in proper order,'' observed Malone approvingly, as,
with his fine face ruddy as the embers over which he bent, he assiduously turned
the mutton-chops. ''You are not under petticoat government, like poor Sweeting;
a man—whew!—how the fat spits!—it has burnt my hand—destined to be ruled
by women. Now you and I, Moore—there's a fine brown one for you, and full of
gravy—you and I will have no grey mares in our stables when we marry.''

''I don't know—I never think about it: if the grey mare is handsome and tractable,
why not?''

''The chops are done: is the punch brewed?''

''There is a glassful; taste it. When Joe Scott and his minions return they shall
have a share of this, provided they bring home the frames intact.''

Malone waxed very exultant over the supper: he laughed aloud at trifles; made
bad jokes and applauded them himself; and, in short, grew unmeaningly noisy. His
host, on the contrary, remained quiet as before. It is time, reader, that you should
have some idea of the appearance of this same host: I must endeavour to sketch
him as he sits at table.

He is what you would probably call, at first view, rather a strange-looking man;
for he is thin, dark, sallow; very foreign of aspect, with shadowy hair carelessly
streaking his forehead: it appears that he spends but little time at his toilette, or he
would arrange it with more taste. He seems unconscious that his features are fine,
that they have a southern symmetry, clearness, regularity in their chiselling; nor
does a spectator become aware of this advantage till he has examined him well,
for an anxious countenance, and a hollow, somewhat haggard, outline of face disturb

the idea of beauty with one of care. His eyes are large, and grave, and grey; their expression is intent and meditative, rather searching than soft, rather thoughtful than genial. When he parts his lips in a smile his physiognomy is agreeable—not that it is frank or cheerful even then, but you feel the influence of a certain sedate charm, suggestive, whether truly or delusively, of a considerate, perhaps a kind nature; of feelings that may wear well at home; patient, forbearing, possibly faithful feelings. He is still young—not more than thirty; his stature is tall, his figure slender. His manner of speaking displeases: he has an outlandish accent, which, notwithstanding a studied carelessness of pronunciation and diction, grates on a British, and especially on a Yorkshire ear.

Mr. Moore, indeed, was but half a Briton, and scarcely that. He came of a foreign ancestry by the mother's side, and was himself born and partly reared on a foreign soil. A hybrid in nature, it is probable he had a hybrid's feeling on many points—patriotism for one; it is likely that he was unapt to attach himself to parties, to sects, even to climes and customs; it is not impossible that he had a tendency to isolate his individual person from any community amidst which his lot might temporarily happen to be thrown, and that he felt it to be his best wisdom to push the interests of Robert Gérard Moore to the exclusion of philanthropic consideration for general interests: with which he regarded the said Gérard Moore as in a great measure disconnected. Trade was Mr. Moore's hereditary calling: the Gérards of Antwerp had been merchants for two centuries back. Once they had been wealthy merchants; but the uncertainties, the involvements of business had come upon them; disastrous speculations had loosened by degrees the foundations of their credit; the house had stood on a tottering base for a dozen years; and at last, in the shock of the French Revolution, it had rushed down a total ruin. In its fall was involved the English and Yorkshire firm of Moore, closely connected with the Antwerp house; and of which one of the partners, resident in Antwerp, Robert Moore, had married Hortense Gérard, with the prospect of his bride inheriting her father Constantine Gérard's share in the business. She inherited, as we have seen, but his share in the liabilities of the firm; and these liabilities, though duly set aside by a composition with creditors, some said her son Robert accepted, in his turn, as a legacy; and that he aspired one day to discharge them, and to rebuild the fallen house of Gérard and Moore on a scale at least equal to its former greatness. It was even supposed that he took by-past circumstances much to heart; and if a childhood passed at the side of a saturnine mother, under foreboding of coming evil, and a manhood drenched and blighted by the pitiless descent of the storm, could painfully impress the mind, *his* probably was impressed in no golden characters.

If, however, he had a great end of restoration in view, it was not in his power to employ great means for its attainment; he was obliged to be content with the day of small things. When he came to Yorkshire, he—whose ancestors had owned warehouses in this seaport, and factories in that inland town, had possessed their town-house and their country-seat—saw no way open to him but to rent a cloth-mill, in an out-of-the-way nook of an out-of-the-way district; to take a cottage adjoining it for his residence, and to add to his possessions, as pasture for his horse, and space for his cloth-tenters, a few acres of the steep rugged land that lined the hollow through which his millstream brawled. All this he held at a somewhat high rent (for these war times were hard, and everything was dear), of the trustees of the Fieldhead estate, then the property of a minor.

At the time this history commences, Robert Moore had lived but two years in the district; during which period he had at least proved himself possessed of the quality of activity. The dingy cottage was converted into a neat, tasteful residence. Of part of the rough land he had made garden-ground, which he cultivated with singular, even with Flemish, exactness and care. As to the mill, which was an old structure, and fitted up with old machinery, now become inefficient and out of date, he had from the first evinced the strongest contempt for all its arrangements

and appointments: his aim had been to effect a radical reform, which he had executed as fast as his very limited capital would allow; and the narrowness of that capital, and consequent check on his progress, was a restraint which galled his spirit sorely. Moore ever wanted to push on: "Forward" was the device stamped upon his soul; but poverty curbed him: sometimes (figuratively) he foamed at the mouth when the reins were drawn very tight.

In this state of feeling, it is not to be expected that he would deliberate much as to whether his advance was or was not prejudicial to others. Not being a native, nor for any length of time a resident of the neighbourhood, he did not sufficiently care when the new inventions threw the old workpeople out of employ: he never asked himself where those to whom he no longer paid weekly wages found daily bread; and in this negligence he only resembled thousands besides, on whom the starving poor of Yorkshire seemed to have a closer claim.

The period of which I write was an overshadowed one in British history, and especially in the history of the northern provinces. War was then at its height. Europe was all involved therein. England, if not weary, was worn with long resistance: yes, and half her people were weary too, and cried out for peace on any terms. National honour was become a mere empty name, of no value in the eyes of many, because their sight was dim with famine; and for a morsel of meat they would have sold their birthright.

The "Orders in Council," provoked by Napoleon's Milan and Berlin decrees, and forbidding neutral powers to trade with France, had, by offending America, cut off the principal market of the Yorkshire woollen trade, and brought it consequently to the verge of ruin. Minor foreign markets were glutted, and would receive no more: the Brazils, Portugal, Sicily, were all overstocked by nearly two years' consumption. At this crisis, certain inventions in machinery were introduced into the staple manufactures of the north, which, greatly reducing the number of hands necessary to be employed, threw thousands out of work, and left them without legitimate means of sustaining life. A bad harvest supervened. Distress reached its climax. Endurance, overgoaded, stretched the hand of fraternity to sedition. The throes of a sort of moral earthquake were felt heaving under the hills of the northern counties. But, as is usual in such cases, nobody took much notice. When a food-riot broke out in a manufacturing town, when a gig-mill was burnt to the ground, or a manufacturer's house was attacked, the furniture thrown into the streets, and the family forced to flee for their lives, some local measures were or were not taken by the local magistracy; a ringleader was detected, or more frequently suffered to elude detection; newspaper paragraphs were written on the subject, and there the thing stopped. As to the sufferers, whose sole inheritance was labour, and who had lost that inheritance—who could not get work, and consequently could not get wages, and consequently could not get bread—they were left to suffer on; perhaps inevitably left: it would not do to stop the progress of invention, to damage science by discouraging its improvements; the war could not be terminated, efficient relief could not be raised: there was no help then; so the unemployed underwent their destiny—ate the bread and drank the waters of affliction.

Misery generates hate: these sufferers hated the machines which they believed took their bread from them: they hated the buildings which contained those machines; they hated the manufacturers who owned those buildings. In the parish of Briarfield, with which we have at present to do, Hollow's Mill was the place held most abominable; Gérard Moore, in his double character of semi-foreigner and thoroughgoing progressist, the man most abominated. And it perhaps rather agreed with Moore's temperament than otherwise to be generally hated; especially when he believed the thing for which he was hated a right and an expedient thing; and it was with a sense of warlike excitement he, on this night, sat in his counting-house waiting the arrival of his frame-laden waggons. Malone's coming and company were, it may be, most unwelcome to him: he would have preferred sitting alone;

for he liked a silent, sombre, unsafe solitude: his watchman's musket would have been company enough for him; the full-flowing beck in the den would have delivered continuously the discourse most genial to his ear.

With the queerest look in the world, had the manufacturer for some ten minutes been watching the Irish curate, as the latter made free with the punch; when suddenly that steady grey eye changed, as if another vision came between it and Malone. Moore raised his head.

"Chut!" he said, in his French fashion, as Malone made a noise with his glass. He listened a moment, then rose, put his hat on, and went out at the counting-house door.

The night was still, dark, and stagnant: the water yet rushed on full and fast: its flow almost seemed a flood in the utter silence. Moore's ear, however, caught another sound—very distant, but yet dissimilar—broken and rugged: in short, a sound of heavy wheels crunching a stony road. He returned to the counting-house and lit a lantern, with which he walked down the mill-yard, and proceeded to open the gates. The big waggons were coming on; the dray-horses' huge hoofs were heard splashing in the mud and water. Moore hailed them.

"Hey, Joe Scott! Is all right?"

Probably Joe Scott was yet at too great a distance to hear the inquiry; he did not answer it.

"Is all right, I say?" again asked Moore when the elephant-like leader's nose almost touched his.

Some one jumped out from the foremost waggon into the road; a voice cried aloud, "Ay, ay, divil, all's raight! We've smashed 'em."

And there was a run. The waggons stood still: they were now deserted.

"Joe Scott!" No Joe Scott answered. "Murgatroyd ! Pighills! Sykes!" No reply. Mr. Moore lifted his lantern, and looked into the vehicles; there was neither man nor machinery: they were empty and abandoned.

Now Mr. Moore loved his machinery: he had risked the last of his capital on the purchase of these frames and shears which to-night had been expected; speculations most important to his interests depended on the results to be wrought by them: where were they?

The words "we've smashed 'em!" rung in his ears. How did the catastrophe affect him? By the light of the lantern he held, were his features visible, relaxing to a singular smile: the smile the man of determined spirit wears when he reaches a juncture in his life where this determined spirit is to feel a demand on its strength: when the strain is to be made, and the faculty must bear or break. Yet he remained silent, and even motionless: for at the instant he neither knew what to say nor what to do. He placed the lantern on the ground, and stood with his arms folded, gazing down and reflecting.

An impatient trampling of one of the horses made him presently look up; his eye in the moment caught the gleam of something white attached to a part of the harness. Examined by the light of the lantern, this proved to be a folded paper—a billet. It bore no address without; within was the superscription—

"To the Divil of Hollow's Miln."

We will not copy the rest of the orthography, which was very peculiar, but translate it into legible English. It ran thus—

"Your hellish machinery is shivered to smash on Stilbro' Moor, and your men are lying bound hand and foot in a ditch by the roadside. Take this as a warning from men that are starving, and have starving wives and children to go home to when they have done this deed. If you get new machines, or if you otherwise go on as you have done, you shall hear from us again. Beware!"

"Hear from you again? Yes; I'll hear from you again, and you shall hear from me. I'll speak to you directly: on Stilbro' Moor you shall hear from me in a moment."

Having led the waggons within the gates, he hastened towards the cottage. Opening the door, he spoke a few words quickly but quietly to two females who ran to meet him in the passage. He calmed the seeming alarm of one by a brief palliative account of what had taken place; to the other he said, "Go into the mill, Sarah—there is the key—and ring the mill-bell as loud as you can: afterwards you will get another lantern and help me to light up the front."

Returning to his horses, he unharnessed, fed, and stabled them with equal speed and care, pausing occasionally while so occupied, as if to listen for the mill-bell. It clanged out presently, with irregular but loud and alarming din: the hurried agitated peal seemed more urgent than if the summons had been steadily given by a practised hand. On that still night, at that unusual hour, it was heard a long way round: the guests in the kitchen of the Redhouse were startled by the clangour; and declaring that "there must be summat more nor common to do at Hollow's Miln," they called for lanterns, and hurried to the spot in a body. And scarcely had they thronged into the yard with their gleaming lights, when the tramp of horses was heard, and a little man in a shovel hat, sitting erect on the back of a shaggy pony, "rode lightly in," followed by an aide-de-camp mounted on a larger steed.

Mr. Moore, meantime, after stabling his dray-horses, had saddled his hackney: and, with the aid of Sarah, the servant, lit up his mill; whose wide and long front now glared one great illumination, throwing a sufficient light on the yard to obviate all fear of confusion arising from obscurity. Already a deep hum of voices became audible. Mr. Malone had at length issued from the counting-house, previously taking the precaution to dip his head and face in the stone water-jar; and this precaution, together with the sudden alarm, had nearly restored to him the possession of those senses which the punch had partially scattered. He stood with his hat on the back of his head, and his shillelagh grasped in his dexter fist, answering much at random the questions of the newly-arrived party from the Redhouse. Mr. Moore now appeared, and was immediately confronted by the shovel hat and the shaggy pony.

"Well, Moore, what is your business with us! I thought you would want us to-night: me and the hetman here (patting his pony's neck), and Tom and his charger. When I heard your mill-bell, I could sit still no longer, so I left Boultby to finish his supper alone: but where is the enemy? I do not see a mask or a smutted face present; and there is not a pane of glass broken in your windows. Have you had an attack, or do you expect one?"

"Oh, not at all! I have neither had one nor expect one," answered Moore coolly. "I only ordered the bell to be rung because I want two or three neighbours to stay here in the Hollow while I and a couple or so more go over to Stilbro' Moor."

"To Stilbro' Moor! What to do? To meet the waggons?"

"The waggons are come home an hour ago."

"Then all's right. What more would you have?"

"They came home empty: and Joe Scott and company are left on the moor, and so are the frames. Read that scrawl."

Mr. Helstone received and perused the document of which the contents have before been given.

"Hum! They've only served you as they serve others. But, however, the poor fellows in the ditch will be expecting help with some impatience: this is a wet night for such a berth. I and Tom will go with you; Malone may stay behind and take care of the mill: what is the matter with him? His eyes seem starting out of his head."

"He has been eating a mutton-chop."

"Indeed! Peter Augustus, be on your guard. Eat no more mutton-chops to-night. You are left here in command of these premises: an honourable post!"

"Is anybody to stay with me?"

"As many of the present assemblage as choose. My lads, how many of you will remain here, and how many will go a little way with me and Mr. Moore on the Stilbro' road, to meet some men who have been waylaid and assaulted by frame-breakers?"

The small number of three volunteered to go; the rest preferred staying behind. As Mr. Moore mounted his horse, the Rector asked him in a low voice whether he had locked up the mutton-chops, so that Peter Augustus could not get at them? The manufacturer nodded an affirmative, and the rescue-party set out.

Chapter III

MR. YORKE

CHEERFULNESS, it would appear, is a matter which depends fully as much on the state of things within, as on the state of things without and around us. I make this trite remark, because I happen to know that Messrs. Helstone and Moore trotted forth from the mill-yard gates, at the head of their very small company, in the best possible spirits. When a ray from a lantern (the three pedestrians of the party carried each one) fell on Mr. Moore's face, you could see an unusual, because a lively spark, dancing in his eyes, and a new-found vivacity mantling on his dark physiognomy; and when the Rector's visage was illuminated, his hard features were revealed all agrin and ashine with glee. Yet a drizzling night, a somewhat perilous expedition, you would think were not circumstances calculated to enliven those exposed to the wet and engaged in the adventure. If any member or members of the crew who had been at work on Stilbro' Moor had caught a view of this party, they would have had great pleasure in shooting either of the leaders from behind a wall: and the leaders knew this; and, the fact is, being both men of steely nerves and steady-beating hearts, were elate with the knowledge.

I am aware, reader, and you need not remind me, that it is a dreadful thing for a parson to be warlike: I am aware that he should be a man of peace. I have some faint outline of an idea of what a clergyman's mission is amongst mankind, and I remember distinctly whose servant he is: whose message he delivers, whose example he should follow: yet, with all this, if you are a parson-hater, you need not expect me to go along with you every step of your dismal, downward-tending, unchristian road; you need not expect me to join in your deep anathemas, at once so narrow and so sweeping—in your poisonous rancour, so intense and so absurd, against "the cloth"; to lift up my eyes and hands with a Supplehough, or to inflate my lungs with a Barraclough, in horror and denunciation of the diabolical rector of Briarfield.

He was not diabolical at all. The evil simply was—he had missed his vocation: he should have been a soldier, and circumstances had made him a priest. For the rest, he was a conscientious, hard-headed, hard-handed, brave, stern, implacable, faithful little man: a man almost without sympathy, ungentle, prejudiced, and rigid: but a man true to principle—honourable, sagacious, and sincere. It seems to me, reader, that you cannot always cut out men to fit their profession, and that you ought not to curse them because that profession sometimes hangs on them ungracefully: nor will I curse Helstone, clerical cossack as he was. Yet he *was* cursed, and by many of his own parishioners, as by others he was adored: which is the frequent fate of men who show partiality in friendship and bitterness in enmity; who are equally attached to principles and adherent to prejudices.

Helstone and Moore, being both in excellent spirits, and united for the present in one cause, you would expect that, as they rode side by side, they would converse amicably. Oh, no! These two men, of hard bilious natures both, rarely came into contact but they chafed each other's moods. Their frequent bone of contention was the war. Helstone was a high Tory (there were Tories in those days), and Moore was a bitter Whig—a Whig, at least, as far as opposition to the war-party was concerned; that being the question which affected his own interest; and only on that question did he profess any British politics at all. He liked to infuriate Helstone by declaring his belief in the invincibility of Bonaparte; by taunting England and Europe with the impotence of their efforts to withstand him; and by coolly advancing the opinion that it was as well to yield to him soon as late, since he must in the end crush every antagonist, and reign supreme.

Helstone could not bear these sentiments: it was only on the consideration of Moore being a sort of outcast and alien, and having but half measure of British blood to temper the foreign gall which corroded his veins, that he brought himself to listen to them without indulging the wish he felt to cane the speaker. Another thing, too, somewhat allayed his disgust; namely, a fellow-feeling for the dogged tone with which these opinions were asserted, and a respect for the consistency of Moore's crabbed contumacy.

As the party turned into the Stilbro' road, they met what little wind there was; the rain dashed in their faces. Moore had been fretting his companion previously, and now, braced up by the raw breeze, and perhaps irritated by the sharp drizzle, he began to goad him.

"Does your Peninsular news please you still?" he asked.

"What do you mean?" was the surly demand of the Rector.

"I mean have you still faith in that Baal of a Lord Wellington?"

"And what do you mean now?"

"Do you still believe that this wooden-faced and pebble-hearted idol of England has power to send fire down from heaven to consume the French holocaust you want to offer up?"

"I believe Wellington will flog Bonaparte's marshals into the sea, the day it pleases him to lift his arm."

"But, my dear sir, you can't be serious in what you say. Bonaparte's marshals are great men, who act under the guidance of an omnipotent master-spirit; your Wellington is the most hum-drum of commonplace martinets, whose slow mechanical movements are further cramped by an ignorant home government."

"Wellington is the soul of England. Wellington is the right champion of a good cause; the fit representative of a powerful, a resolute, a sensible, and an honest nation."

"Your good cause, as far as I understand it, is simply the restoration of that filthy, feeble Ferdinand to a throne which he disgraced; your fit representative of an honest people is a dull-witted drover, acting for a duller-witted farmer; and against these are arrayed victorious supremacy and invincible genius."

"Against legitimacy is arrayed usurpation: against modest, single-minded, righteous, and brave resistance to encroachment, is arrayed boastful, double-tongued, selfish, and treacherous ambition to possess. God defend the right!"

"God often defends the powerful."

"What! I suppose the handful of Israelites standing dryshod on the Asiatic side of the Red Sea, was more powerful than the host of the Egyptians drawn up on the African side? Were they more numerous? Were they better appointed? Were they more mighty, in a word—eh? Don't speak, or you'll tell a lie, Moore; you know you will. They were a poor overwrought band of bondsmen. Tyrants had oppressed them through four hundred years; a feeble mixture of women and children diluted their thin ranks; their masters, who roared to follow them through the divided flood, were a set of pampered Ethiops, about as strong and brutal as the lions of

Libya. They were armed, horsed, and charioted, the poor Hebrew wanderers were afoot; few of them, it is likely, had better weapons than their shepherds' crooks, or their masons' building-tools; their meek and mighty leader himself had only his rod. But bethink you, Robert Moore, right was with them; the God of battles was on their side. Crime and the lost archangel generalled the ranks of Pharaoh, and which triumphed? We know that well: 'The Lord saved Israel that day out of the hand of the Egyptians, and Israel saw the Egyptians dead upon the sea-shore'; yea, 'the depths covered them, they sank to the bottom as a stone.' The right hand of the Lord became glorious in power; the right hand of the Lord dashed in pieces the enemy!''

''You are all right; only you forget the true parallel: France is Israel, and Napoleon is Moses. Europe, with her old over-gorged empires and rotten dynasties, is corrupt Egypt: gallant France is the Twelve Tribes, and her fresh and vigorous Usurper the Shepherd of Horeb.''

''I scorn to answer you.''

Moore accordingly answered himself; at least he subjoined to what he had just said an additional observation in a lower voice.

''Oh, in Italy he was as great as any Moses! He was the right thing there; fit to head and organise measures for the regeneration of nations. It puzzles me to this day how the conqueror of Lodi should have condescended to become an emperor, a vulgar, a stupid humbug; and still more how a people, who had once called themselves republicans, should have sunk again to the grade of mere slaves. I despise France! If England had gone as far on the march of civilisation as France did, she would hardly have retreated so shamelessly.''

''You don't mean to say that besotted Imperial France is any worse than bloody republican France?'' demanded Helstone fiercely.

''I mean to say nothing: but I can think what I please, you know, Mr. Helstone, both about France and England; and about revolutions, and regicides, and restorations in general; and about the divine right of kings, which you often stickle for in your sermons, and the duty of non-resistance, and the sanity of war, and''——

Mr. Moore's sentence was here cut short by the rapid rolling up of a gig, and its sudden stoppage in the middle of the road; both he and the Rector had been too much occupied with their discourse to notice its approach till it was close upon them.

''Nah, maister, did th' waggons hit home?'' demanded a voice from the vehicle.

''Can that be Joe Scott?''

''Ay, ay!'' returned another voice; for the gig contained two persons, as was seen by the glimmer of its lamp: the men with the lanterns had now fallen into the rear, or rather, the equestrians of the rescue-party had outridden the pedestrians. ''Ay, Mr. Moore, it's Joe Scott. I'm bringing him back to you in a bonny pickle. I fand him on the top of the moor yonder, him and three others. What will you give me for restoring him to you?''

''Why, my thanks, I believe: for I could better have afforded to lose a better man. That is you, I suppose, Mr. Yorke, by your voice?''

''Ay, lad, it's me. I was coming home from Stilbro' market, and just as I got to the middle of the moor, and was whipping on as swift as the wind (for these, they say, are not safe times, thanks to a bad goverment!), I heard a groan. I pulled up: some would have whipt on faster; but I've naught to fear, that I know of. I don't believe there's a lad in these parts would harm me; at least I'd give them as good as I got if they offered to do it. I said, 'Is there aught wrong anywhere?'— 'Deed is there,' somebody says, speaking out of the ground, like. 'What's to do? be sharp, and tell me,' I ordered.—'Nobbut four on us ligging in a ditch,' says Joe, as quiet as could be. I tell'd 'em, more shame to 'em, and bid them get up and move on, or I'd lend them a lick of the gig-whip; for my notion was, they were all fresh.—'We'd ha' done that an hour sin'; but we're teed wi' a bit o' band,'

says Joe. So in a while I got down and loosed 'em wi' my penknife, and Scott
would ride wi' me, to tell me all how it happened; and t' others are coming on as
fast as their feet will bring them.''

"Well, I am greatly obliged to you, Mr. Yorke.''

"Are you, my lad? you know you're not. However, here are the rest approaching.
And here, by the Lord! is another set with lights in their pitchers, like the army of
Gideon; and as we've th' parson wi' us—good evening, Mr. Helstone—we'se do.''

Mr. Helstone returned the salutation of the individual in the gig very stiffly
indeed. That individual proceeded—

"We're eleven strong men, and there's both horses and chariots amang us. If
we could only fall in wi' some of these starved ragamuffins of frame-breakers, we
could win a grand victory; we could iv'ry one be a Wellington—that would please
ye, Mr. Helstone; and sich paragraphs as we could contrive for t' papers! Briarfield
suld be famous: but we'se hev a column and a half i' th' *Stilbro' Courier* ower
this job, as it is, I daresay: I'se expect no less.''

"And I'll promise you no less, Mr. Yorke, for I'll write the article myself,''
returned the Rector.

"To be sure! sartainly! And mind ye recommend weel that them 'at brake t' bits
o' frames, and teed Joe Scott's legs wi' band, suld be hung without benefit o'
clergy. It's a hanging matter, or suld be; no doubt o' that.''

"If I judged them, I'd give them short shrift!'' cried Moore; "but I mean to let
them quite alone this bout, to give them rope enough, certain that in the end they
will hang themselves.''

"Let them alone, will ye, Moore? Do you promise that?''

"Promise? No. All I mean to say is, I shall give myself no particular trouble to
catch them; but if one falls in my way''—

"You'll snap him up, of course: only you would rather they would do something
worse than merely stop a waggon before you reckon with them. Well, we'll say
no more on the subject at present. Here we are at my door, gentlemen, and I hope
you and the men will step in: you will none of you be the worse of a little
refreshment.''

Moore and Helstone opposed this proposition as unnecessary; it was, however,
pressed on them so courteously, and the night, besides, was so inclement, and the
gleam from the muslin-curtained windows of the house before which they had halted
looked so inviting, that at length they yielded. Mr. Yorke, after having alighted
from his gig, which he left in charge of a man who issued from an outbuilding on
his arrival, led the way in.

It will have been remarked that Mr. Yorke varied a little in his phraseology; now
he spoke broad Yorkshire, and anon he expressed himself in very pure English.
His manner seemed liable to equal alternations; he could be polite and affable, and
he could be blunt and rough. His station then you could not easily determine by
his speech and demeanour; perhaps the appearance of his residence may decide it.

The men he recommended to take the kitchen way, saying that he would "see
them served wi'summat to taste presently.'' The gentlemen were ushered in at the
front entrance. They found themselves in a matted hall, lined almost to the ceiling
with pictures, through this they were conducted to a large parlour, with a magnificent
fire in the grate; the most cheerful of rooms it appeared as a whole, and when you
came to examine details, the enlivening effect was not diminished. There was no
splendour, but there was taste everywhere,—unusual taste,—the taste, you would
have said, of a travelled man, a scholar, and a gentleman. A series of Italian views
decked the walls; each of these was a specimen of true art; a connoisseur had
selected them: they were genuine and valuable. Even by candlelight, the bright
clear skies, the soft distances, with blue air quivering between the eye and the hills,
the fresh tints, and well-massed lights and shadows, charmed the view. The subjects
were all pastoral, the scenes were all sunny. There was a guitar and some music

on a sofa; there were cameos, beautiful miniatures; a set of Grecian-looking vases on the mantelpiece; there were books well arranged in two elegant bookcases.

Mr. Yorke bade his guests be seated; he then rang for wine; to the servant who brought it he gave hospitable orders for the refreshment of the men in the kitchen. The Rector remained standing; he seemed not to like his quarters; he would not touch the wine his host offered him.

"E'en as you will," remarked Mr. Yorke. "I reckon you're thinking of Eastern customs, Mr. Helstone, and you'll not eat nor drink under my roof, feard we suld be forced to be friends; but I am not so particular or superstitious. You might sup the contents of that decanter, and you might give me a bottle of the best in your own cellar, and I'd hold myself free to oppose you at every turn still,—in every vestry-meeting and justice-meeting where we encounter one another."

"It is just what I should expect of you, Mr. Yorke."

"Does it agree wi' ye now, Mr. Helstone, to be riding out after rioters, of a wet night, at your age?"

"It always agrees with me to be doing my duty; and in this case my duty is a thorough pleasure. To hunt down vermin is a noble occupation,—fit for an archbishop."

"Fit for ye, at ony rate: but where's t' curate? He's happen gone to visit some poor body in a sick gird, or he's happen hunting down vermin in another direction."

"He is doing garrison-duty at Hollow's Mill."

"You left him a sup o' wine, I hope, Bob (turning to Mr. Moore), to keep his courage up?"

He did not pause for an answer, but continued, quickly—still addressing Moore, who had thrown himself into an old-fashioned chair by the fireside—"Move it, Robert ! Get up, my lad! That place is mine. Take the sofa, or three other chairs, if you will, but not this; it belangs to me, and nob'dy else."

"Why are you so particular to that chair, Mr. Yorke?" asked Moore, lazily vacating the place in obedience to orders.

"My father war afore me, and that's all t' answer I sall gie thee; and it's as good a reason as Mr. Helstone can give for the main feck o' his notions."

"Moore, are you ready to go?" inquired the Rector.

"Nay; Robert's not ready; or rather, I'm not ready to part wi' him: he's an ill lad, and wants correcting."

"Why, sir? What have I done?"

"Made thyself enemies on every hand."

"What do I care for that? What diference does it make to me whether your Yorkshire louts hate me or like me?"

"Ay, there it is. The lad is a mak' of an alien amang us: his father would never have talked i' that way. Go back to Antwerp, where you were born and bred, mauvaise tête!"

"Mauvaise tête vous-même; je ne fais que mon devoir: quant à vos lourdauds de paysans, je m'en moque!"

"En ravanche mon garçon, nos lourdauds de paysans se moqueront de toi; sois en certain," replied Yorke, speaking with nearly as pure a French accent as Gérard Moore.

"C'est bon! c'est bon! Et puisque cela m'est égal, que mes amis ne s'en inquiètent pas."

"Tes amis! Où sont-ils, tes amis?"

"Je fais écho où sont-ils? et je suis fort aise que l'écho seul y répond. Au diable les amis! Je me souviens encore du moment où mon père et mes oncles Gérard appellèrent autour d'eux leurs amis, et Dieu sait si les amis se sont empressés d'accourir à leur secours! Tenez, M. Yorke, ce mot, ami, m'irrite trop; ne m'en parlez plus."

"Comme tu voudras."

And here Mr. Yorke held his peace; and while he sits leaning back in his three-cornered, carved oak chair, I will snatch my opportunity to sketch the portrait of this French-speaking Yorkshire gentleman.

Chapter IV

MR. YORKE (continued)

A YORKSHIRE gentleman he was, par excellence, in every point. About fifty-five years old, but looking at first sight still older, for his hair was silver white. His forehead was broad, not high; his face fresh and hale; the harshness of the north was seen in his features, as it was heard in his voice; every trait was thoroughly English, not a Norman line anywhere; it was an inelegant, unclassic, unaristocratic mould of visage. Fine people would perhaps have called it vulgar; sensible people would have termed it characteristic; shrewd people would have delighted in it for the pith, sagacity, intelligence—the rude, yet real originality marked in every lineament, latent in every furrow. But it was an indocile, a scornful, and a sarcastic face; the face of a man difficult to lead, and impossible to drive. His stature was rather tall, and he was well-made and wiry, and had a stately integrity of port; there was not a suspicion of the clown about him anywhere.

I did not find it easy to sketch Mr. Yorke's person, but it is more difficult to indicate his mind. If you expect to be treated to a Perfection, reader, or even to a benevolent, philanthropic old gentleman in him, you are mistaken. He has spoken with some sense, and with some good feeling, to Mr. Moore; but you are not thence to conclude that he always spoke and thought justly and kindly.

Mr. Yorke, in the first place, was without the organ of Veneration—a great want, and which throws a man wrong on every point where veneration is required. Secondly, he was without the organ of Comparison—a deficiency which strips a man of sympathy; and, thirdly, he had too little of the organs of Benevolence and Ideality, which took the glory and softness from his nature, and for him diminished those divine qualities throughout the universe.

The want of veneration made him intolerant to those above him: kings and nobles and priests, dynasties and parliaments and establishments, with all their doings, most of their enactments, their forms, their rights, their claims, were to him an abomination—all rubbish; he found no use or pleasure in them, and believed it would be clear gain, and no damage to the world, if its high places were razed, and their occupants crushed in the fall. The want of veneration, too, made him dead at heart to the electric delight of admiring what is admirable; it dried up a thousand pure sources of enjoyment; it withered a thousand vivid pleasures. He was not irreligious, though a member of no sect; but his religion could not be that of one who knows how to venerate. He believed in God and heaven; but his God and heaven were those of a man in whom awe, imagination, and tenderness lack.

The weakness of his powers of comparison made him inconsistent; while he professed some excellent general doctrines of mutual toleration and forbearance, he cherished towards certain classes a bigoted antipathy: he spoke of "parsons" and all who belonged to parsons, of "lords" and the appendages of lords, with a harshness, sometimes an insolence, as unjust as it was insufferable. He could not place himself in the position of those he vituperated; he could not compare their errors with their temptations, their defects with their disadvantages; he could not realise the effect of such and such circumstances on himself similarly situated, and he would often express the most ferocious and tyrannical wishes regarding those who had acted, as he thought, ferociously and tyrannically. To judge by his threats, he would have employed arbitrary, even cruel, means to advance the cause of

freedom and equality. Equality—yes, Mr. Yorke talked about equality, but at heart he was a proud man: very friendly to his workpeople, very good to all who were beneath him, and submitted quietly to be beneath him, but haughty as Beelzebub to whomsoever the world deemed (for he deemed no man) his superior. Revolt was in his blood: he could not bear control; his father, his grandfather before him, could not bear it, and his children after him never could.

The want of general benevolence made him very impatient of imbecility, and of all faults which grated on his strong, shrewd nature: it left no check to his cutting sarcasm. As he was not merciful, he would sometimes wound and wound again, without noticing how much he hurt, or caring how deep he thrust.

As to the paucity of ideality in his mind, that can scarcely be called a fault: a fine ear for music, a correct eye for colour and form, left him the quality of taste; and who cares for imagination? Who does not think it a rather dangerous, senseless attribute—akin to weakness—perhaps partaking of frenzy—a disease rather than a gift of the mind?

Probably all think it so, but those who possess—or fancy they possess—it. To hear them speak, you would believe that their hearts would be cold if that elixir did not flow about them; that their eyes would be dim if that flame did not refine their vision; that they would be lonely if this strange companion abandoned them. You would suppose that it imparted some glad hope to spring, some fine charm to summer, some tranquil joy to autumn, some consolation to winter, which you do not feel. An illusion, of course; but the fanatics cling to their dream, and would not give it for gold.

As Mr. Yorke did not possess poetic imagination himself, he considered it a most superfluous quality in others. Painters and musicians he could tolerate, and even encourage, because he could relish the results of their art; he could see the charm of a fine picture, and feel the pleasure of good music; but a quiet poet—whatever force struggled, whatever fire glowed, in his breast—if he could not have played the man in the counting-house, or the tradesman in the Piece Hall, might have lived despised, and died scorned, under the eyes of Hiram Yorke.

And as there are many Hiram Yorkes in the world, it is well that the true poet, quiet externally though he may be, has often a truculent spirit under his placidity, and is full of shrewdness in his meekness, and can measure the whole stature of those who look down on him, and correctly ascertain the weight and value of the pursuits they disdain him for not having followed. It is happy that he can have his own bliss, his own society with his great friend and goddess, Nature, quite independent of those who find little pleasure in him, and in whom he finds no pleasure at all. It is just, that while the world and circumstances often turn a dark, cold side to him—and properly, too, because he first turns a dark, cold, careless side to them—he should be able to maintain a festal brightness and cherishing glow in his bosom, which makes all bright and genial for him; while strangers, perhaps, deem his existence a Polar winter never gladdened by a sun. The true poet is not one whit to be pitied; and he is apt to laugh in his sleeve, when any misguided sympathiser whines over his wrongs. Even when utilitarians sit in judgment on him, and pronounce him and his art useless, he hears the sentence with such a hard derision, such a broad, deep, comprehensive, and merciless contempt of the unhappy Pharisees who pronounce it, that he is rather to be chidden than condoled with. These, however, are not Mr. Yorke's reflections; and it is with Mr. Yorke we have at present to do.

I have told you some of his faults, reader; as to his good points, he was one of the most honourable and capable men in Yorkshire; even those who disliked him were forced to respect him. He was much beloved by the poor, because he was thoroughly kind and very fatherly to them. To his workmen he was considerate and cordial: when he dismissed them from an occupation, he would try to set them on to something else; or, if that was impossible, help them to remove with their families to a district where work might possibly be had. It must also be remarked

that if, as sometimes chanced, any individual amongst his "hands" showed signs of insubordination, Yorke—who, like many who abhor being controlled, knew how to control with vigour—had the secret of crushing rebellion in the germ, of eradicating it like a bad weed, so that it never spread or developed within the sphere of his authority. Such being the happy state of his own affairs, he felt himself at liberty to speak with the utmost severity of those who were differently situated; to ascribe whatever was unpleasant in their position entirely to their own fault, to sever himself from the masters, and advocate freely the cause of the operatives.

Mr. Yorke's family was the first and oldest in the district; and he, though not the wealthiest, was one of the most influential men. His education had been good; in his youth, before the French Revolution, he had travelled on the Continent: he was an adept in the French and Italian languages. During a two years' sojourn in Italy, he had collected many good paintings and tasteful rarities, with which his residence was now adorned. His manners, when he liked, were those of a finished gentleman of the old school; his conversation, when he was disposed to please, was singularly interesting and original; and if he usually expressed himself in the Yorkshire dialect, it was because he chose to do so, preferring his native Doric to a more refined vocabulary. "A Yorkshire burr," he affirmed, "was as much better than a Cockney's lisp, as a bull's bellow than a ratton's squeak."

Mr. Yorke knew every one, and was known by every one for miles round; yet his intimate acquaintances were very few. Himself thoroughly original, he had no taste for what was ordinary; a racy, rough character, high or low, ever found acceptance with him; a refined, insipid personage, however exalted in station, was his aversion. He would spend an hour any time in talking freely with a shrewd workman of his own, or with some queer, sagacious old woman amongst his cottagers, when he would have grudged a moment to a commonplace fine gentleman, or to the most fashionable and elegant, if frivolous, lady. His preferences on these points he carried to an extreme forgetting that there may be amiable, and even admirable characters amongst those who cannot be original. Yet he made exceptions to his own rule; there was a certain order of mind, plain, ingenuous, neglecting refinement, almost devoid of intellectuality, and quite incapable of appreciating what was intellectual in him; but which, at the same time, never felt disgust at his rudeness, was not easily wounded by his sarcasm, did not closely analyse his sayings, doings, or opinions; with which he was peculiarly at ease, and, consequently, which he peculiarly preferred. He was lord amongst such characters. They, while submitting implicitly to his influence, never acknowledged, because they never reflected on, his superiority; they were quite tractable, therefore, without running the smallest danger of being servile; and their unthinking, easy, artless insensibility was as acceptable, because as convenient, to Mr. Yorke, as that of the chair he sat on, or of the floor he trod.

It will have been observed that he was not quite uncordial with Mr. Moore; he had two or three reasons for entertaining a faint partiality to that gentleman. It may sound odd, but the first of these was that Moore spoke English with a foreign, and French with a perfectly pure, accent; and that his dark, thin face, with its fine though rather wasted lines, had a most anti-British and anti-Yorkshire look. These points seem frivolous, unlikely to influence a character like Yorke's; but the fact is, they recalled old, perhaps pleasurable associations: they brought back his travelling, his youthful days. He had seen, amidst Italian cities and scenes, faces like Moore's; he had heard, in Parisian cafés and theatres, voices like his; he was young then, and when he looked at and listened to the alien, he seemed young again.

Secondly, he had known Moore's father, and had had dealings with him; that was a more substantial, though by no means a more agreeable tie; for, as his firm had been connected with Moore's in business, it had also, in some measure, been implicated in its losses.

Thirdly, he had found Robert himself a sharp man of business. He saw reason to anticipate that he would, in the end, by one means or another, make money; and he respected both his resolution and acuteness, perhaps also his hardness. A fourth circumstance which drew them together was that of Mr. Yorke being one of the guardians of the minor on whose estate Hollow's Mill was situated; consequently Moore, in the course of his alterations and improvements, had frequent occasion to consult him.

As to the other guest now present in Mr. Yorke's parlour, Mr. Helstone, between him and his host there existed a double antipathy: the antipathy of nature and that of circumstances. The free-thinker hated the formalist; the lover of liberty detested the disciplinarian: besides it was said that in former years they had been rival suitors of the same lady.

Mr. Yorke, as a general rule, was, when young, noted for his preference of sprightly and dashing women: a showy shape and air, a lively wit, a ready tongue, chiefly seemed to attract him. He never, however, proposed to any of these brilliant belles, whose society he sought; and all at once he seriously fell in love with, and eagerly wooed a girl who presented a complete contrast to those he had hitherto noticed: a girl with the face of a Madonna; a girl of living marble; stillness personified. No matter that, when he spoke to her, she only answered him in monosyllables; no matter that his sighs seemed unheard, that his glances were unreturned, that she never responded to his opinions, rarely smiled at his jests, paid him no respect and no attention; no matter that she seemed the opposite of everything feminine he had ever, in his whole life, been known to admire; for him Mary Cave was perfect, because somehow, for some reason—no doubt he had a reason—he loved her.

Mr. Helstone, at that time curate of Briarfield, loved Mary too; or, at any rate, he fancied her. Several others admired her, for she was beautiful as a monumental angel; but the clergyman was preferred for his office's sake: that office probably investing him with some of the illusion necessary to allure to the commission of matrimony, and which Miss Cave did not find in any of the young wool-staplers, her other adorers. Mr. Helstone neither had, nor professed to have, Mr. Yorke's absorbing passion for her: he had none of the humble reverence which seemed to subdue most of her suitors; he saw her more as she really was than the rest did; he was consequently more master of her and himself. She accepted him at the first offer, and they were married.

Nature never intended Mr. Helstone to make a very good husband, especially to a quiet wife. He thought, so long as a woman was silent, nothing ailed her, and she wanted nothing. If she did not complain of solitude, solitude, however continued, could not be irksome to her. If she did not talk and put herself forward, express a partiality for this, an aversion to that, she had no partialities or aversions, and it was useless to consult her tastes. He made no pretence of comprehending women, or comparing them with men; they were a different, probably a very inferior order of existence; a wife could not be her husband's companion, much less his confidant, much less his stay. *His* wife, after a year or two, was of no great importance to him in any shape; and when she one day, as he thought, suddenly—for he had scarcely noticed her decline—but, as others thought, gradually, took her leave of him and of life, and there was only a still beautiful-featured mould of clay left, cold and white in the conjugal couch, he felt his bereavement—who shall say how little? Yet, perhaps, more than he seemed to feel it; for he was not a man from whom grief easily wrung tears.

His dry-eyed and sober mourning scandalised an old housekeeper, and likewise a female attendant, who had waited upon Mrs. Helstone in her sickness: and who, perhaps, had had opportunities of learning more of the deceased lady's nature, of her capacity for feeling and loving, than her husband knew: they gossiped together over the corpse, related anecdotes with embellishments of her lingering decline, and its real or supposed cause; in short, they worked each other up to some indignation

against the austere little man, who sat examining papers in an adjoining room, unconscious of what opprobrium he was the object.

Mrs. Helstone was hardly under the sod when rumours began to be rife in the neighbourhood that she had died of a broken heart; these magnified quickly into reports of hard usage, and, finally, details of harsh treatment on the part of her husband: reports grossly untrue, but not the less eagerly received on that account. Mr. Yorke heard them, partly believed them. Already, of course, he had no friendly feeling to his successful rival; though himself a married man now, and united to a woman who seemed a complete contrast to Mary Cave in all respects, he could not forget the great disappointment of his life; and when he heard that what would have been so precious to him had been neglected, perhaps abused by another, he conceived for that other a rooted and bitter animosity.

Of the nature and strength of this animosity, Mr. Helstone was but half aware: he neither knew how much Yorke had loved Mary Cave, what he had felt on losing her, nor was he conscious of the calumnies concerning his treatment of her, familiar to every ear in the neighbourhood but his own. He believed political and religious differences alone separated him and Mr. Yorke; had he known how the case really stood, he would hardly have been induced by any persuasion to cross his former rival's threshold.

Mr. Yorke did not resume his lecture of Robert Moore; the conversation erelong recommenced in a more general form, though still in a somewhat disputative tone. The unquiet state of the country, the various depredations lately committed on mill-property in the district, supplied abundant matter for disagreement; especially as each of the three gentlemen present differed more or less in his views on these subjects. Mr. Helstone thought the masters aggrieved, the workpeople unreasonable: he condemned sweepingly the widespread spirit of disaffection against constituted authorities, the growing indisposition to bear with patience evils he regarded as inevitable: the cures he prescribed were vigorous government interference, strict magisterial vigilance; when necessary, prompt military coercion.

Mr. Yorke wished to know whether this interference, vigilance, and coercion would feed those who were hungry, give work to those who wanted work, and whom no man would hire. He scouted the idea of inevitable evils; he said public patience was a camel, on whose back the last atom that could be borne had already been laid, and that resistance was now a duty: the wide-spread spirit of disaffection against constituted authorities he regarded as the most promising sign of the times; the masters, he allowed, were truly aggrieved, but their main grievances had been heaped on them by a "corrupt, base, and bloody" government (these were Mr. Yorke's epithets). Madmen like Pitt, demons like Castlereagh, mischievous idiots like Perceval, were the tyrants, the curses of the country, the destroyers of her trade. It was their infatuated perseverance in an unjustifiable, a hopeless, a ruinous war, which had brought the nation to its present pass. It was their monstrously oppressive taxation, it was the infamous "Orders in Council"—the originators of which deserved impeachment and the scaffold, if ever public men did—that hung a millstone about England's neck.

"But where was the use of talking?" he demanded—"What chance was there of reason being heard in a land that was king-ridden, priest-ridden, peer-ridden— where a lunatic was the nominal monarch, an unprincipled debauchee the real ruler; where such an insult to common sense as hereditary legislators was tolerated— where such a humbug as a bench of bishops—such an arrogant abuse as a pampered, persecuting established Church was endured and venerated—where a standing army was maintained, and a host of lazy parsons and their pauper families were kept on the fat of the land?"

Mr. Helstone, rising up and putting on his shovel-hat, observed in reply, "That in the course of his life he had met with two or three instances where sentiments

of this sort had been very bravely maintained so long as health, strength, and worldly prosperity had been the allies of him who professed them; but there came a time,'' he said, ''to all men, 'when the keepers of the house should tremble; when they should be afraid of that which is high, and fear should be in the way'; and that time was the test of the advocate of anarchy and rebellion, the enemy of religion and order. Ere now,'' he affirmed, ''he had been called upon to read those prayers our Church has provided for the sick, by the miserable dying-bed of one of her most rancorous foes; he had seen such a one stricken with remorse, solicitous to discover a place for repentance, and unable to find any, though he sought it carefully with tears. He must forewarn Mr. Yorke, that blasphemy against God and the king was a deadly sin, and that there was such a thing as 'judgment to come.' ''

Mr. Yorke ''believed fully that there was such a thing as judgment to come. If it were otherwise, it would be difficult to imagine how all the scoundrels who seemed triumphant in this world, who broke innocent hearts with impunity, abused unmerited privileges, were a scandal to honourable callings, took the bread out of the mouths of the poor, browbeat the humble, and truckled meanly to the rich and proud—were to be properly paid off, in such coin as they had earned. But,'' he added, ''whenever he got low-spirited about such-like goings-on, and their seeming success in this mucky lump of a planet, he just reached down t' owd book'' (pointing to a great Bible in the bookcase), ''opened it like at a chance, and he was sure to light of a verse blazing wi' a blue brimstone low that set all straight. He knew,'' he said, ''where some folk war bound for, just as weel as if an angel wi' great white wings had come in ower t' door-stone and told him.''

''Sir,'' said Mr. Helstone, collecting all his dignity, ''Sir—the great knowledge of man is to know himself, and the bourne whither his own steps tend.''

''Ay, ay! you'll recollect, Mr. Helstone, that Ignorance was carried away from the very gates of heaven, borne through the air, and thrust in at a door in the side of the hill which led down to hell.''

''Nor have I forgotten, Mr. Yorke, that Vain-Confidence, not seeing the way before him, fell into a deep pit, which was on purpose there made by the prince of the grounds, to catch vainglorious fools withal, and was dashed to pieces with his fall.''

''Now,'' interposed Mr. Moore, who had hitherto sat a silent but amused spectator of this wordy combat, and whose indifference to the party politics of the day, as well as to the gossip of the neighbourhood, made him an impartial, if apathetic, judge of the merits of such an encounter—''you have both sufficiently black-balled each other, and proved how cordially you detest each other, and how wicked you think each other. For my part, my hate is still running in such a strong current against the fellows who have broken my frames, that I have none to spare for my private acquaintance, and still less for such a vague thing as a sect or a government: but really, gentlemen, you both seem very bad by your own showing; worse than ever I suspected you to be. I dare not stay all night with a rebel and blasphemer, like you, Yorke; and I hardly dare ride home with a cruel and tyrannical ecclesiastic, like Mr. Helstone.''

''I am going, however, Mr. Moore,'' said the Rector sternly: ''come with me or not, as you please.''

''Nay, he shall not have the choice—he *shall* go with you,'' responded Yorke. ''It's midnight, and past; and I'll have nob'dy staying up i' my house any longer. Ye mun all go.''

He rang the bell.

''Deb,'' said he to the servant who answered it, ''clear them folk out o' t' kitchen, and lock t' doors, and be off to bed. Here is your way, gentlemen,'' he continued to his guests; and, lighting them through the passage, he fairly put them out at his front-door.

They met their party hurrying out pell-mell by the back way; their horses stood at the gate; they mounted, and rode off—Moore laughing at their abrupt dismissal, Helstone deeply indignant thereat.

Chapter V

HOLLOW'S COTTAGE

MOORE'S good spirits were still with him when he rose next morning. He and Joe Scott had both spent the night in the mill, availing themselves of certain sleeping accommodations producible from recesses in the front and back counting-houses; the master, always an early riser, was up somewhat sooner even than usual; he awoke his man by singing a French song as he made his toilet.

"Ye're not custen dahm, then, maister?" cried Joe.

"Not a stiver, mon garçon—which means, my lad. Get up, and we'll take a turn through the mill before the hands come in, and I'll explain my future plans. We'll have the machinery yet, Joseph; you never heard of Bruce, perhaps?"

"And th' arrand (spider)? Yes, but I hev: I've read th' history o' Scotland, and happen knaw as mich on't as ye; and I understand ye to mean to say ye'll persevere."

"I do."

"Is there mony o' your mak i' your country?" inquired Joe as he folded up his temporary bed, and put it away.

"In my country! Which is my country?"

"Why, France—isn't it?"

"Not it, indeed! The circumstance of the French having seized Antwerp, where I was born, does not make me a Frenchman."

"Holland, then?"

"I am not a Dutchman: now you are confounding Antwerp with Amsterdam!"

"Flanders?"

"I scorn the insinuation, Joe! I, a Flamand! Have I a Flemish face?—the clumsy nose standing out—the mean forehead falling back—the pale blue eyes 'à fleur de tête'? Am I all body and no legs, like a Flamand? But you don't know what they are like—those Netherlanders. Joe, I'm an Anversois: my mother was an Anversoise, though she came of French lineage, which is the reason I speak French."

"But your father war Yorkshire, which maks ye a bit Yorkshire too: and onybody may see ye're akin to us, ye're so keen o' making brass, and getting forrards."

"Joe, you're an impudent dog; but I've always been accustomed to a boorish sort of insolence from my youth up: the 'classe ouvrière'—that is, the working people in Belgium—bear themselves brutally towards their employers; and by *brutally,* Joe, I mean *brutalement*—which, perhaps, when properly translated, should be *roughly.*"

"We allus speak our minds i' this country; and them young parsons and grand folk fro' London is shocked at wer '*incivility*,' and we like weel enough to gi'e 'em summat to be shocked at, 'cause it's sport to us to watch 'em turn up the whites o' their een, and spreed out their bits o' hands, like as they're flayed wi' bogards, and then to hear 'em say, nipping off their words short like—'Dear! dear! Whet seveges! How very corse!' "

"You *are* savages, Joe; you don't suppose you're civilised, do you?"

"Middling, middling, maister. I reckon 'at us manufacturing lads i' th' north is a deal more intelligent, and knaws a deal more nor th' farming folk i' th' south. Trade sharpens wer wits; and them that's mechanics, like me, is forced to think. Ye know, what wi' looking after machinery and sich like, I've getten into that way that when I see an effect, I look straight out for a cause, and I oft lig hold on't to

purpose; and then I like reading, and I'm curious to knaw what them that reckons to govern us aims to do for us and wi' us: and there's many 'cuter nor me; there's many a one among them greasy chaps 'at smells o' oil, and amang them dyers wi' blue and black skins, that has a long head, and that can tell what a fooil of a law is, as well as ye or old Yorke, and a deal better nor soft uns like Christopher Sykes o' Whinbury, and greet hectoring nowts like yond' Irish Peter, Helstone's curate.''

"You think yourself a clever fellow, I know, Scott.''

"Ay! I'm fairish; I can tell cheese fro' chalk, and I'm varry weel aware that I've improved sich opportunities as I have had, a deal better nor some 'at reckons to be aboon me; but there's thousands i' Yorkshire that's as good as me, and a two-three that's better.''

"You're a great man—you're a sublime fellow; but you're a prig, a conceited noodle with it all, Joe! You need not to think that because you've picked up a little knowledge of practical mathematics, and because you have found some scantling of the elements of chemistry at the bottom of a dyeing vat, that therefore you're a neglected man of science; and you need not to suppose that because the course of trade does not always run smooth, and you, and such as you, are sometimes short of work and of bread, that therefore your class are martyrs, and that the whole form of government under which you live is wrong. And, moreover, you need not for a moment to insinuate that the virtues have taken refuge in cottages and wholly abandoned slated houses. Let me tell you, I particularly abominate that sort of trash, because I know so well that human nature is human nature everywhere, whether under tile or thatch, and that in every specimen of human nature that breathes, vice and virtue are ever found blended, in smaller or greater proportions, and that the proportion is not determined by station. I have seen villains who were rich, and I have seen villains who were poor, and I have seen villains who were neither rich nor poor, but who had realised Agar's wish, and lived in fair and modest competency. The clock is going to strike six: away with you, Joe, and ring the mill-bell.''

It was now the middle of the month of February; by six o'clock, therefore, dawn was just beginning to steal on night, to penetrate with a pale ray its brown obscurity, and give a demi-translucence to its opaque shadows. Pale enough that ray was on this particular morning; no colour tinged the east, no flush warmed it. To see what a heavy lid day slowly lifted, what a wan glance she flung along the hills, you would have thought the sun's fire quenched in last night's floods. The breath of this morning was chill as its aspect; a raw wind stirred the mass of night-cloud, and showed, as it slowly rose—leaving a colourless, silver-gleaming ring all round the horizon—not blue sky, but a stratum of paler vapour beyond. It had ceased to rain, but the earth was sodden, and the pools and rivulets were full.

The mill-windows were alight, the bell still rung loud, and now the little children came running in, in too great a hurry, let us hope, to feel very much nipped by the inclement air; and, indeed, by contrast, perhaps the morning appeared rather favourable to them than otherwise; for they had often come to their work that winter through snow-storms, through heavy rain, through hard frost.

Mr. Moore stood at the entrance to watch them pass: he counted them as they went by; to those who came rather late he said a word of reprimand, which was a little more sharply repeated by Joe Scott when the lingerers reached the workrooms. Neither master nor overlooker spoke savagely; they were not savage men either of them, though it appeared both were rigid, for they fined a delinquent who came considerably too late: Mr. Moore made him pay his penny down ere he entered, and informed him that the next repetition of the fault would cost him twopence.

Rules, no doubt, are necessary in such cases, and coarse and cruel masters will make coarse and cruel rules, which, at the time we treat of at least, they used sometimes to enforce tyrannically; but, though I describe imperfect characters (every character in this book will be found to be more or less imperfect, my pen refusing

to draw anything in the model line), I have not undertaken to handle degraded or utterly infamous ones. Child-torturers, slave masters and drivers, I consign to the hands of jailers; the novelist may be excused from sullying his page with the record of their deeds.

Instead, then, of harrowing up my reader's soul, and delighting his organ of Wonder, with effective descriptions of stripes and scourgings, I am happy to be able to inform him that neither Mr. Moore nor his overlooker ever struck a child in their mill. Joe had, indeed, once very severely flogged a son of his own for telling a lie and persisting in it; but, like his employer, he was too phlegmatic, too calm, as well as too reasonable a man, to make corporal chastisement other than the exception to his treatment of the young.

Mr. Moore haunted his mill, his mill-yard, his dye-house, and his warehouse, till the sickly dawn strengthened into day. The sun even rose,—at least a white disk, clear, tintless, and almost chill-looking as ice,—peeped over the darkness of a hill, changed to silver the livid edge of the cloud above it, and looked solemnly down the whole length of the den, or narrow dale, to whose strait bounds we are at present limited. It was eight o'clock; the mill lights were all extinguished; the signal was given for breakfast; the children, released for half an hour from toil, betook themselves to the little tin cans which held their coffee, and to the small baskets which contained their allowance of bread. Let us hope they have enough to eat; it would be a pity were it otherwise.

And now, at last, Mr. Moore quitted the mill-yard, and bent his steps to his dwelling-house. It was only a short distance from the factory, but the hedge and high bank on each side of the lane which conducted to it seemed to give it something of the appearance and feeling of seclusion. It was a small, white-washed place, with a green porch over the door; scanty brown stalks showed in the garden soil near this porch, and likewise beneath the windows,—stalks budless and flowerless now, but giving dim prediction of trained and blooming creepers for summer days. A grass plot and borders fronted the cottage; the borders presented only black mould yet, except where, in sheltered nooks, the first shoots of snowdrop or crocus peeped, green as emerald, from the earth. The spring was late; it had been a severe and long winter; the last deep snow had but just disappeared before yesterday's rains; on the hills, indeed, white remnants of it yet gleamed, flecking the hollows and crowning the peaks: the lawn was not verdant, but bleached, as was the grass on the bank, and under the hedge in the lane. Three trees, gracefully grouped, rose beside the cottage: they were not lofty, but having no rivals near, they looked well and imposing where they grew. Such was Mr. Moore's home: a snug nest for content and contemplation, but one within which the wings of action and ambition could not long lie folded.

Its air of modest comfort seemed to possess no particular attraction for its owner; instead of entering the house at once, he fetched a spade from a little shed, and began to work in the garden. For about an hour he dug on uninterrupted: at length, however, a window opened, and a female voice called to him—

"Eh, bien! Tu ne déjeûnes pas ce matin?"

The answer and the rest of the conversation was in French; but, as this is an English book, I shall translate it into English.

"Is breakfast ready, Hortense?"

"Certainly; it has been ready half-an-hour."

"Then I am ready too: I have a canine hunger."

He threw down his spade and entered the house: the narrow passage conducted him to a small parlour, where a breakfast of coffee and bread and butter, with the somewhat un-English accompaniment of stewed pears, was spread on the table. Over these viands presided the lady who had spoken from the window. I must describe her before I go any further.

She seemed a little older than Mr. Moore, perhaps she was thirty-five, tall, and proportionately stout; she had very black hair, for the present twisted up in curl-papers; a high colour in her cheeks, a small nose, a pair of little black eyes. The lower part of her face was large in proportion to the upper; her forehead was small and rather corrugated; she had a fretful, though not an ill-natured expression of countenance; there was something in her whole appearance one felt inclined to be half provoked with and half amused at. The strangest point was her dress; a stuff petticoat and a striped cotton camisole. The petticoat was short, displaying well a pair of feet and ankles which left much to be desired in the article of symmetry.

You will think I have depicted a remarkable slattern, reader;—not at all. Hortense Moore (she was Mr. Moore's sister) was a very orderly, economical person; the petticoat, camisole, and curl-papers were her morning costume, in which, of forenoons, she had always been accustomed to "go her household ways" in her own country. She did not choose to adopt English fashions because she was obliged to live in England; she adhered to her old Belgian modes, quite satisfied that there was a merit in so doing.

Mademoiselle had an excellent opinion of herself, an opinion not wholly undeserved; for she possessed some good and sterling qualities; but she rather over-estimated the kind and degree of these qualities, and quite left out of the account sundry little defects which accompanied them. You could never have persuaded her that she was a prejudiced aud narrow-minded person, that she was too susceptible on the subject of her own dignity and importance, and too apt to take offence about trifles; yet all this was true. However, where her claims to distinction were not opposed, and where her prejudices were not offended, she could be kind and friendly enough. To her two brothers (for there was another Gérard Moore besides Robert) she was very much attached. As the sole remaining representatives of their decayed family, the persons of both were almost sacred in her eyes: of Louis, however, she knew less than of Robert; he had been sent to England when a mere boy, and had received his education at an English school. His education not being such as to adapt him for trade, perhaps, too, his natural bent not inclining him to mercantile pursuits, he had, when the blight of hereditary prospects rendered it necessary for him to push his own fortune, adopted the very arduous and very modest career of a teacher; he had been usher in a school, and was said now to be tutor in a private family. Hortense, when she mentioned Louis, described him as having what she called "des moyens," but as being too backward and quiet: her praise of Robert was in a different strain, less qualified; she was very proud of him; she regarded him as the greatest man in Europe; all he said and did was remarkable in her eyes, and she expected others to behold him from the same point of view; nothing could be more irrational, monstrous, and infamous, than opposition from any quarter to Robert, unless it were opposition to herself.

Accordingly, as soon as the said Robert was seated at the breakfast table, and she had helped him to a portion of stewed pears, and cut him a good-sized Belgian tartine, she began to pour out a flood of amazement and horror at the transaction of last night, the destruction of the frames.

"Quelle idée? to destroy them. Quelle action honteuse! On voyait bien que les ouvriers de ce pays étaient à la fois bêtes et méchants. C'était absolument comme les domestiques Anglais, les servantes surtout: rien d'insupportable comme cette Sara, par exemple!"

"She looks clean and industrious," Mr. Moore remarked.

"Looks! I don't know how she looks; and I do not say that she is altogether dirty or idle: mais elle est d'une insolence! She disputed with me a quarter of an hour yesterday about the cooking of the beef; she said I boiled it to rags, that English people would never be able to eat such a dish as our bouilli, that the bouillon was no better than greasy warm water, and as to the choucroute, she affirms she cannot touch it. That barrel we have in the cellar—delightfully prepared by my

own hands—she termed a tub of hog-wash, which means food for pigs. I am harassed with the girl, and yet I cannot part with her lest I should get a worse. You are in the same position with your workmen,—pauvre cher frère!''

''I am afraid you are not very happy in England, Hortense.''

''It is my duty to be happy where you are, brother; but otherwise, there are certainly a thousand things which make me regret our native town. All the world here appears to me ill-bred (mal-élevé). I find my habits considered ridiculous: if a girl out of your mill chances to come into the kitchen and find me in my jupon and camisole preparing dinner (for you know I cannot trust Sarah to cook a single dish), she sneers. If I accept an invitation out to tea, which I have done once or twice, I perceive I am put quite into the background; I have not that attention paid me which is decidedly my due. Of what an excellent family are the Gérards, as we know, and the Moores also! They have a right to claim a certain respect, and to feel wounded when it is withheld from them. In Antwerp I was always treated with distinction; here, one would think that when I open my lips in company, I speak English with a ridiculous accent, whereas I am quite assured that I pronounce it perfectly.''

''Hortense, in Antwerp we were known rich; in England we were never known but poor.''

''Precisely, and thus mercenary are mankind. Again, dear brother, last Sunday, if you recollect, was very wet: accordingly, I went to church in my neat black sabots, objects one would not indeed wear in a fashionable city; but which in the country I have ever been accustomed to use for walking in dirty roads. Believe me, as I paced up the aisle, composed and tranquil, as I am always, four ladies, and as many gentlemen, laughed and hid their faces behind their prayer-books.''

''Well, well! don't put on the sabots again. I told you before I thought they were not quite the thing for this country.''

''But, brother, they are not the common sabots such as the peasantry wear. I tell you they are sabots noirs, très propres, très convenables. At Mons and Leuze— cities not very far removed from the elegant capital of Brussels—it is very seldom that the respectable people wear anything else for walking in winter. Let any one try to wade the mud of the Flemish chaussées in a pair of Paris brodequins, on m'en dirait des nouvelles!''

''Never mind Mons and Leuze, and the Flemish chaussées; do at Rome as the Romans do! and as to the camisole and jupon, I am not quite sure about them either. I never see an English lady dressed in such garments. Ask Caroline Helstone.''

''Caroline! *I* ask Caroline? *I* consult her about my dress? It is *she* who on all points should consult *me;* she is a child.''

''She is eighteen, or at the least seventeen; old enough to know all about gowns, petticoats, and chaussures.''

''Do not spoil Caroline, I entreat you, brother; do not make her of more consequence than she ought to be. At present she is modest and unassuming, let us keep her so.''

''With all my heart. Is she coming this morning?''

''She will come at ten, as usual, to take her French lesson.''

''You don't find that she sneers at you, do you?''

''She does not, she appreciates me better than any one else here; but then she has more intimate opportunities of knowing me: she sees that I have education, intelligence, manner, principles; all, in short, which belongs to a person well born and well bred.''

''Are you at all fond of her?''

''For *fond*—I cannot say: I am not one who is prone to take violent fancies, and, consequently, my friendship is the more to be depended on. I have a regard for her as my relative; her position also inspires interest, and her conduct as my pupil

has hitherto been such as rather to enhance than diminish the attachment that springs from other causes.''

"She behaves pretty well at lessons?"

"To *me* she behaves very well; but you are conscious, brother, that I have a manner calculated to repel over-familiarity, to win esteem, and to command respect. Yet, possessed of penetration, I perceive clearly that Caroline is not perfect; that there is much to be desired in her.''

"Give me a last cup of coffee, and while I am drinking it amuse me with an account of her faults."

"Dear brother, I am happy to see you eat your breakfast with relish, after the fatiguing night you have passed. Caroline, then, is defective; but, with my forming hand and almost motherly care, she may improve. There is about her an occasional something—a reserve, I think—which I do not quite like, because it is not sufficiently girlish and submissive; and there are glimpses of an unsettled hurry in her nature, which put me out. Yet she is usually most tranquil, too dejected and thoughtful indeed sometimes. In time, I doubt not, I shall make her uniformly sedate and decorous, without being unaccountably pensive. I ever disapprove what is not intelligible.''

"I don't understand your account in the least; what do you mean by 'unsettled hurries,' for instance?"

"An example will, perhaps, be the most satisfactory explanation. I sometimes, you are aware, make her read French poetry by way of practice in pronunciation. She has, in the course of her lessons, gone through much of Corneille and Racine, in a very steady, sober spirit, such as I approve. Occasionally she showed, indeed, a degree of languor in the perusal of those esteemed authors, partaking rather of apathy than sobriety, and apathy is what I cannot tolerate in those who have the benefit of my instructions; besides, one should not be apathetic in studying standard works. The other day I put into her hands a volume of short fugitive pieces. I sent her to the window to learn one by heart, and when I looked up I saw her turning the leaves over impatiently, and curling her lip, absolutely with scorn, as she surveyed the little poems cursorily. I chid her. 'Ma cousine,' said she, 'tout cela m'ennuie à la mort.' I told her this was improper language.—'Dieu!' she exclaimed. 'Il n'y a donc pas deux lignes de poésie dans toute la littérature française?' I inquired what she meant. She begged my pardon with proper submission. Erelong she was still; I saw her smiling to herself over the book; she began to learn assiduously. In half-an-hour she came and stood before me, presented the volume, folded her hands, as I always require her to do, and commenced the repetition of that short thing by Chénier, 'La Jeune Captive.' If you had heard the manner in which she went through this, and in which she uttered a few incoherent comments when she had done, you would have known what I meant by the phrase 'unsettled hurry.' One would have thought Chénier was more moving than all Racine and all Corneille. You, brother, who have so much sagacity, will discern that this disproportionate preference argues an ill-regulated mind; but she is fortunate in a preceptress. I will give her a system, a method of thought, a set of opinions: I will give her the perfect control and guidance of her feelings.''

"Be sure you do, Hortense; here she comes. That was her shadow passed the window, I believe.''

"Ah! truly. She is too early—half-an-hour before her time.—My child, what brings you here before I have breakfasted?''

This question was addressed to an individual who now entered the room, a young girl, wrapped in a winter mantle, the folds of which were gathered with some grace round an apparently slender figure.

"I came in haste to see how you were, Hortense, and how Robert was, too. I was sure you would both be grieved by what happened last night. I did not hear till this morning; my uncle told me at breakfast.''

"Ah! it is unspeakable. You sympathise with us? Your uncle sympathises with us?"

"My uncle is very angry; but he was with Robert, I believe: was he not? Did he not go with you to Stilbro' Moor?"

"Yes: we set out in very martial style, Caroline: but the prisoners we went to rescue met us half-way."

"Of course, nobody was hurt?"

"Why, no; only Joe Scott's wrists were a little galled with being pinioned too tightly behind his back."

"You were not there? You were not with the waggons when they were attacked?"

"No: one seldom has the fortune to be present at occurrences at which one would particularly wish to assist."

"Where are you going this morning? I saw Murgatroyd saddling your horse in the yard."

"To Whinbury: it is market day."

"Mr. Yorke is going too: I met him in his gig. Come home with him."

"Why?"

"Two are better than one, and nobody dislikes Mr. Yorke; at least, poor people do not dislike him."

"Therefore he would be a protection to me, who am hated?"

"Who are *misunderstood;* that, probably, is the word. Shall you be late?—Will he be late, cousin Hortense?"

"It is too probable: he has often much business to transact at Whinbury. Have you brought your exercise-book, child?"

"Yes. What time will you return, Robert?"

"I generally return at seven. Do you wish me to be at home earlier?"

"Try rather to be back by six. It is not absolutely dark at six now; but by seven daylight is quite gone."

"And what danger is to be apprehended, Caroline, when daylight *is* gone? What peril do you conceive comes as the companion of darkness, for me?"

"I am not sure that I can define my fears; but we all have a certain anxiety at present about our friends. My uncle calls these times dangerous: he says, too, that mill-owners are unpopular."

"And I one of the most unpopular? Is not that the fact? You are reluctant to speak out plainly, but at heart you think me liable to Pearson's fate, who was shot at—not, indeed, from behind a hedge, but in his own house, through his staircase-window, as he was going to bed."

"Anne Pearson showed me the bullet in the chamber-door," remarked Caroline gravely, as she folded her mantle, and arranged it and her muff on a side-table. "You know," she continued, "there is a hedge all the way along the road from here to Whinbury, and there are the Fieldhead plantations to pass; but you will be back by six—or before?"

"Certainly he will," affirmed Hortense. "And now, my child, prepare your lessons for repetition, while I put the peas to soak for the purée at dinner."

With this direction, she left the room.

"You suspect I have many enemies, then, Caroline," said Mr. Moore; "and doubtless you know me to be destitute of friends?"

"Not destitute, Robert. There is your sister, your brother Louis—whom I have never seen—there is Mr. Yorke, and there is my uncle; besides, of course, many more."

Robert smiled. "You would be puzzled to name your 'many more,' " said he. "But show me your exercise-book. What extreme pains you take with the writing. My sister, I suppose, exacts this care: she wants to form you in all things after the model of a Flemish school-girl. What life are you destined for, Caroline? What

will you do with your French, drawing, and other accomplishments when they are acquired?''

"You may well say, when they are acquired; for, as you are aware, till Hortense began to teach me, I knew precious little. As to the life I am destined for, I cannot tell: I suppose, to keep my uncle's house, till''——She hesitated.

"Till what? Till he dies?"

"No. How harsh to say that! I never think of his dying: he is only fifty-five. But till—in short, till events offer other occupations for me.''

"A remarkably vague prospect! Are you content with it?"

"I used to be, formerly. Children, you know, have little reflection, or rather their reflections run on ideal themes. There are moments *now* when I am not quite satisfied.''

"Why?"

"I am making no money—earning nothing.''

"You come to the point, Lina; you too, then, wish to make money?''

"I do: I should like an occupation; and if I were a boy, it would not be so difficult to find one. I see such an easy, pleasant way of learning a business, and making my way in life.''

"Go on: let us hear what way.''

"I could be apprenticed to your trade—the cloth-trade: I could learn it of you, as we are distant relations. I would do the counting-house work, keep the books, and write the letters, while you went to market. I know you greatly desire to be rich, in order to pay your father's debts; perhaps I could help you to get rich.''

"Help *me?* You should think of yourself.''

"I do think of myself; but must one for ever think only of oneself?''

"Of whom else do I think? Of whom else *dare* I think? The poor ought to have no large sympathies; it is their duty to be narrow.''

"No, Robert''——

"Yes, Caroline. Poverty is necessarily selfish, contracted, grovelling, anxious. Now and then a poor man's heart, when certain beams and dews visit it, may swell like the budding vegetation in yonder garden on this spring-day, may feel ripe to evolve in foliage—perhaps blossom; but he must not encourage the pleasant impulse; he must invoke Prudence to check it, with that frosty breath of hers, which is as nipping as any north wind.''

"No cottage would be happy then.''

"When I speak of poverty, I do not so much mean the natural, habitual poverty of the working-man, as the embarrassed penury of the man in debt; my grub-worm is always a straitened, struggling, care-worn tradesman.''

"Cherish hope, not anxiety. Certain ideas have become too fixed on your mind. It may be presumptuous to say it, but I have the impression that there is something wrong in your notions of the best means of attaining happiness; as there is in''——
——Second hesitation.

"I am all ear, Caroline.''

"In—(courage! let me speak the truth)—in your manner—mind, I say only *manner*—to these Yorkshire workpeople.''

"You have often wanted to tell me that, have you not?''

"Yes; often—very often.''

"The faults of my manner are, I think, only negative. I am not proud: what has a man in my position to be proud of? I am only taciturn, phlegmatic, and joyless.''

"As if your living cloth-dressers were all machines like your frames and shears: in your own house you seem different.''

"To those of my own house I am no alien, which I am to these English clowns. I might act the benevolent with them, but acting is not my *forte*. I find them irrational, perverse; they hinder me when I long to hurry forward. In treating them justly, I fulfil my whole duty towards them.''

"You don't expect them to love you, of course?"

"Nor wish it."

"Ah!" said the monitress, shaking her head and heaving a deep sigh. With this ejaculation, indicative that she perceived a screw to be loose somewhere, but that it was out of her reach to set it right, she bent over her grammar, and sought the rule and exercise for the day.

"I suppose I am not an affectionate man, Caroline; the attachment of a very few suffices me."

"If you please, Robert, will you mend me a pen or two before you go?"

"First, let me rule your book, for you always contrive to draw the lines aslant. . . . There now. . . . And now for the pens: you like a fine one, I think?"

"Such as you generally make for me and Hortense; not your own broad points."

"If I were of Louis's calling, I might stay at home and dedicate this morning to you and your studies; whereas I must spend it in Sykes's wool-warehouse."

"You will be making money."

"More likely losing it."

As he finished mending the pens, a horse, saddled and bridled, was brought up to the garden-gate.

"There, Fred is ready for me; I must go. I'll take one look to see what the spring has done in the south border, too, first."

He quitted the room, and went out into the garden-ground behind the mill. A sweet fringe of young verdure and opening flowers—snowdrop, crocus, even primrose—bloomed in the sunshine under the hot wall of the factory. Moore plucked here and there a blossom and leaf, till he had collected a little bouquet; he returned to the parlour, pilfered a thread of silk from his sister's work-basket, tied the flowers, and laid them on Caroline's desk.

"Now, good-morning."

"Thank you, Robert: it is pretty; it looks, as it lies there, like sparkles of sunshine, and blue sky: good-morning."

He went to the door—stopped—opened his lips as if to speak—said nothing, and moved on. He passed through the wicket, and mounted his horse: in a second, he had flung himself from the saddle again, transferred the reins to Murgatroyd, and re-entered the cottage.

"I forgot my gloves," he said, appearing to take something from the side-table; then, as an impromptu thought, he remarked, "You have no binding engagement at home perhaps, Caroline?"

"I never have: some children's socks, which Mrs. Ramsden has ordered, to knit for the Jew's basket; but they will keep."

"Jew's basket be——sold! Never was utensil better named. Anything more Jewish than it—its contents, and their prices—cannot be conceived: but I see something, a very tiny curl, at the corners of your lip, which tells me that you know its merits as well as I do. Forget the Jew's basket, then, and spend the day here as a change. Your uncle won't break his heart at your absence?"

She smiled. "No."

"The old Cossack! I daresay not," muttered Moore. "Then stay and dine with Hortense; she will be glad of your company; I shall return in good time. We will have a little reading in the evening: the moon rises at half-past eight, and I will walk up to the rectory with you at nine. Do you agree?"

She nodded her head, and her eyes lit up.

Moore lingered yet two minutes: he bent over Caroline's desk and glanced at her grammar, he fingered her pen, he lifted her bouquet and played with it; his horse stamped impatient: Fred Murgatroyd hemmed and coughed at the gate, as if he wondered what in the world his master was doing. "Good-morning," again said Moore, and finally vanished.

Hortense, coming in ten minutes after, found to her surprise that Caroline had not yet commenced her exercise.

Chapter VI
CORIOLANUS

MADEMOISELLE MOORE had that morning a somewhat absent-minded pupil. Caroline forgot, again and again, the explanations which were given to her; however, she still bore with unclouded mood the chidings her inattention brought upon her. Sitting in the sunshine, near the window, she seemed to receive with its warmth a kind influence, which made her both happy and good. Thus disposed, she looked her best, and her best was a pleasing vision.

To her had not been denied the gift of beauty; it was not absolutely necessary to know her in order to like her; she was fair enough to please, even at the first view. Her shape suited her age: it was girlish, light and pliant; every curve was neat, every limb proportionate: her face was expressive and gentle; her eyes were handsome, and gifted at times with a winning beam that stole into the heart, with a language that spoke softly to the affections. Her mouth was very pretty; she had a delicate skin, and a fine flow of brown hair, which she knew how to arrange with taste; curls became her, and she possessed them in picturesque profusion. Her style of dress announced taste in the wearer; very unobtrusive in fashion, far from costly in material, but suitable in colour to the fair complexion with which it contrasted, and in make to the slight form which it draped. Her present winter garb was of merino, the same soft shade of brown as her hair; the little collar round her neck lay over a pink ribbon, and was fastened with a pink knot: she wore no other decoration.

So much for Caroline Helstone's appearance; as to her character or intellect, if she had any, they must speak for themselves in due time.

Her connections are soon explained. She was the child of parents separated soon after her birth, in consequence of disagreement of disposition. Her mother was the half-sister of Mr. Moore's father; thus—though there was no mixture of blood—she was, in a distant sense, the cousin of Robert, Louis, and Hortense. Her father was the brother of Mr. Helstone—a man of the character friends desire not to recall, after death has once settled all earthly accounts. He had rendered his wife unhappy: the reports which were known to be true concerning him had given an air of probability to those which were falsely circulated respecting his better-principled brother. Caroline had never known her mother, as she was taken from her in infancy, and had not since seen her; her father died comparatively young, and her uncle, the Rector, had for some years been her sole guardian. He was not, as we are aware, much adapted, either by nature or habits, to have the charge of a young girl: he had taken little trouble about her education; probably, he would have taken none if she, finding herself neglected, had not grown anxious on her own account, and asked, every now and then, for a little attention, and for the means of acquiring such amount of knowledge as could not be dispensed with. Still, she had a depressing feeling that she was inferior, that her attainments were fewer than were usually possessed by girls of her age and station; and very glad was she to avail herself of the kind offer made by her cousin Hortense, soon after the arrival of the latter at Hollow's Mill, to teach her French and fine needlework. Mlle. Moore, for her part, delighted in the task, because it gave her importance; she liked to lord it a little over a docile yet quick pupil. She took Caroline precisely at her own estimate, as an irregularly-taught, even ignorant girl; and when she found that she made rapid and eager progress, it was to no talent, no application in the scholar, she ascribed

the improvement, but entirely to her own superior method of teaching; when she found that Caroline, unskilled in routine, had a knowledge of her own, desultory but varied, the discovery caused her no surprise, for she still imagined that from her conversation had the girl unawares gleaned these treasures: she thought it even when forced to feel that her pupil knew much on subjects whereof she knew little: the idea was not logical, but Hortense had perfect faith in it.

Mademoiselle, who prided herself on possessing "un esprit positif," and on entertaining a decided preference for dry studies, kept her young cousin to the same as closely as she could. She worked her unrelentingly at the grammar of the French language, assigning her, as the most improving exercise she could devise, interminable "analyses logiques." These "analyses" were by no means a source of particular pleasure to Caroline; she thought she could have learned French just as well without them, and grudged excessively the time spent in pondering over "propositions, principales, et incidents"; in deciding the "incidente determinative," and the "incidente applicative"; in examining whether the proposition was "pleine," "elliptique," or "implicite." Sometimes she lost herself in the maze, and when so lost, she would, now and then (while Hortense was rummaging her drawers upstairs,—an unaccountable occupation in which she spent a large portion of each day, arranging, disarranging, rearranging and counter-arranging) carry her book to Robert in the counting-house, and get the rough place made smooth by his aid. Mr. Moore possessed a clear, tranquil brain of his own; almost as soon as he looked at Caroline's little difficulties they seemed to dissolve beneath his eye; in two minutes he would explain all—in two words give the key to the puzzle. She thought if Hortense could only teach like him, how much faster she might learn! Repaying him by an admiring and grateful smile, rather shed at his feet than lifted to his face, she would leave the mill reluctantly to go back to the cottage, and then, while she completed the exercise, or worked out the sum (for Mlle. Moore taught her arithmetic, too), she would wish nature had made her a boy instead of a girl, that she might ask Robert to let her be his clerk, and sit with him in the counting-house, instead of sitting with Hortense in the parlour.

Occasionally—but this happened very rarely—she spent the evening at Hollow's Cottage. Sometimes during these visits Moore was away, attending a market; sometimes he was gone to Mr. Yorke's; often he was engaged with a male visitor in another room; but sometimes, too, he was at home, disengaged, free to talk with Caroline. When this was the case, the evening hours passed on wings of light; they were gone before they were counted. There was no room in England so pleasant as that small parlour when the three cousins occupied it. Hortense, when she was not teaching, or scolding, or cooking, was far from ill-humoured; it was her custom to relax towards evening, and to be kind to her young English kinswoman. There was a means, too, of rendering her delightful, by inducing her to take her guitar and sing and play; she then became quite good-natured; and as she played with skill, and had a well-toned voice, it was not disagreeable to listen to her: it would have been absolutely agreeable, except that her formal and self-important character modulated her strains, as it impressed her manners and moulded her countenance.

Mr. Moore, released from the business-yoke, was, if not lively himself, a willing spectator of Caroline's liveliness, a complacent listener to her talk, a ready respondent to her questions. He was something agreeable to sit near, to hover round, to address and look at. Sometimes he was better than this,—almost animated, quite gentle and friendly.

The drawback was, that by the next morning he was sure to be frozen up again; and however much he seemed, in his quiet way, to enjoy these social evenings, he rarely contrived their recurrence. This circumstance puzzled the inexperienced head of his cousin. "If I had a means of happiness at my command," she thought, "I would employ that means often; I would keep it bright with use, and not let it lie for weeks aside, till it gets rusty."

Yet she was careful not to put in practice her own theory. Much as she liked an evening visit to the cottage, she never paid one unasked. Often, indeed, when pressed by Hortense to come, she would refuse, because Robert did not second, or but slightly seconded the request. This morning was the first time he had ever, of his own unprompted will, given her an invitation; and then he had spoken so kindly, that in hearing him she had received a sense of happiness sufficient to keep her glad for the whole day.

The morning passed as usual. Mademoiselle, ever breathlessly busy, spent it in bustling from kitchen to parlour—now scolding Sarah, now looking over Caroline's exercise or hearing her repetition-lesson. However faultlessly these tasks were achieved, she never commended: it was a maxim with her that praise is inconsistent with a teacher's dignity, and that blame, in more or less unqualified measure, is indispensable to it. She thought incessant reprimand, severe or slight, quite necessary to the maintenance of her authority; and if no possible error was to be found in the lesson, it was the pupil's carriage, or air, or dress, or mien, which required correction.

The usual affray took place about the dinner, which meal, when Sarah at last brought it into the room, she almost flung upon the table, with a look that expressed quite plainly—"I never dished such stuff i' my life afore; it's not fit for dogs." Notwithstanding Sarah's scorn, it was a savoury repast enough. The soup was a sort of purée of dried peas, which Mademoiselle had prepared amidst bitter lamentations that in this desolate country of England no haricot beans were to be had. Then came a dish of meat—nature unknown, but supposed to be miscellaneous—singularly chopped up with crumbs of bread, seasoned uniquely though not unpleasantly, and baked in a mould; a queer, but by no means unpalatable dish. Greens, oddly bruised, formed the accompanying vegetable; and a pâté of fruit, conserved after a receipt devised by Madame Gérard Moore's "grand'mère," and from the taste of which it appeared probable that "mélasse" had been substituted for sugar, completed the dinner.

Caroline had no objection to this Belgian cookery: indeed, she rather liked it for a change, and it was well she did so, for had she evinced any disrelish thereof, such manifestation would have injured her in Mademoiselle's good graces for ever; a positive crime might have been more easily pardoned than a symptom of distaste for the foreign comestibles.

Soon after dinner Caroline coaxed her governess-cousin upstairs to dress: this manœuvre required management. To have hinted that the jupon, camisole, and curl-papers were odious objects, or indeed other than quite meritorious points, would have been a felony. Any premature attempt to urge their disappearance was therefore unwise, and would be likely to issue in the persevering wear of them during the whole day. Carefully avoiding rocks and quicksands, however, the pupil, on pretence of requiring a change of scene, contrived to get the teacher aloft, and, once in the bed-room, she persuaded her that it was not worth while returning thither, and that she might as well make her toilette now; and while Mademoiselle delivered a solemn homily on her own surpassing merit in disregarding all frivolities of fashion, Caroline denuded her of the camisole, invested her with a decent gown, arranged her collar, hair, etc., and made her quite presentable. But Hortense would put the finishing touches herself, and these finishing touches consisted in a thick handkerchief tied round the throat, and a large, servant-like black apron, which spoiled everything. On no account would Mademoiselle have appeared in her own house without the thick handkerchief and the voluminous apron: the first was a positive matter of morality—it was quite improper not to wear a fichu; the second was the ensign of a good housewife—she appeared to think that by means of it she somehow effected a large saving in her brother's income. She had, with her own hands, made and presented to Caroline similar equipments; and the only serious quarrel they ever had, and which still left a soreness in the elder cousin's soul, had

arisen from the refusal of the younger one to accept of and profit by these elegant presents.

"I wear a high dress and a collar," said Caroline, "and I should feel suffocated with a handkerchief in addition; and my short aprons do quite as well as that very long one: I would rather make no change."

Yet Hortense, by dint of perseverance, would probably have compelled her to make a change, had not Mr. Moore chanced to overhear a dispute on the subject, and decided that Caroline's little aprons would suffice, and that, in his opinion, as she was still but a child, she might for the present dispense with the fichu, especially as her curls were long, and almost touched her shoulders.

There was no appeal against Robert's opinion, therefore his sister was compelled to yield; but she disapproved entirely of the piquant neatness of Caroline's costume, and the ladylike grace of her appearance: something more solid and homely she would have considered "beaucoup plus convenable."

The afternoon was devoted to sewing. Mademoiselle, like most Belgian ladies, was specially skilful with her needle. She by no means thought it waste of time to devote unnumbered hours to fine embroidery, sight-destroying lace-work, marvellous netting and knitting, and, above all, to most elaborate stocking-mending. She would give a day to the mending of two holes in a stocking any time, and think her "mission" nobly fulfilled when she had accomplished it. It was another of Caroline's troubles to be condemned to learn this foreign style of darning, which was done stitch by stitch, so as exactly to imitate the fabric of the stocking itself; a wearifu' process, but considered by Hortense Gérard, and by her ancestresses before her for long generations back, as one of the first "duties of women." She herself had had a needle, cotton, and a fearfully torn stocking put into her hand while she yet wore a child's coif on her little black head: her "hauts faits" in the darning line had been exhibited to company ere she was six years old, and when she first discovered that Caroline was profoundly ignorant of this most essential of attainments, she could have wept with pity over her miserably neglected youth.

No time did she lose in seeking up a hopeless pair of hose, of which the heels were entirely gone, and in setting the ignorant English girl to repair the deficiency: this task had been commenced two years ago, and Caroline had the stockings in her work-bag yet. She did a few rows every day, by way of penance for the expiation of her sins: they were a grievous burden to her; she would much have liked to put them in the fire; and once Mr. Moore, who had observed her sitting and sighing over them, had proposed a private incremation in the counting-house, but to this proposal Caroline knew it would have been impolitic to accede—the result could only be a fresh pair of hose, probably in worse condition: she adhered, therefore, to the ills she knew.

All the afternoon the two ladies sat and sewed, till the eyes and fingers, and even the spirits of one of them were weary. The sky since dinner had darkened; it had begun to rain again, to pour fast; secret fears began to steal on Caroline that Robert would be persuaded by Mr. Sykes or Mr. Yorke to remain at Whinbury till it cleared, and of that there appeared no present chance. Five o'clock struck, and time stole on; still the clouds streamed; a sighing wind whispered in the roof-trees of the cottage; day seemed already closing; the parlour-fire shed on the clear hearth a glow ruddy as at twilight.

"It will not be fair till the moon rises," pronounced Mademoiselle Moore; "consequently, I feel assured that my brother will not return till then: indeed, I should be sorry if he did. We will have coffee: it would be vain to wait for him."

"I am tired—may I leave my work now, cousin?"

"You may, since it grows too dark to see to do it well. Fold it up; put it carefully in your bag; then step into the kitchen, and desire Sarah to bring in the goûter, or tea, as you call it."

"But it has not yet struck six: he may still come."

"He will not, I tell you. I can calculate his movements. I understand my brother."

Suspense is irksome, disappointment bitter. All the world has, some time or other, felt that. Caroline, obedient to orders, passed into the kitchen. Sarah was making a dress for herself at the table.

"You are to bring in coffee," said the young lady, in a spiritless tone; and then she leaned her arm and head against the kitchen mantelpiece, and hung listlessly over the fire.

"How low you seem, miss! But it's all because your cousin keeps you so close to work. It's a shame!"

"Nothing of the kind, Sarah," was the brief reply.

"Oh! but I know it is. You're fit to cry just this minute, for nothing else but because you've sat still the whole day. It would make a kitten dull to be mewed up so."

"Sarah, does your master often come home early from market when it is wet?"

"Never, hardly; but just to-day, for some reason, he has made a difference."

"What do you mean?"

"He is come: I am certain I saw Murgatroyd lead his horse into the yard by the back-way, when I went to get some water at the pump five minutes since. He was in the counting-house with Joe Scott, I believe."

"You are mistaken."

"What should I be mistaken for? I know his horse surely?"

"But you did not see himself?"

"I heard him speak, though. He was saying something to Joe Scott about having settled all concerning ways and means, and that there would be a new set of frames in the mill before another week passed; and that this time he would get four soldiers from Stilbro' barracks to guard the waggon."

"Sarah, are you making a gown?"

"Yes: is it a handsome one?"

"Beautiful! Get the coffee ready. I'll finish cutting out that sleeve for you; and I'll give you some trimming for it. I have some narrow satin ribbon of a colour that will just match it."

"You're very kind, miss."

"Be quick, there's a good girl; but first put your master's shoes on the hearth: he will take his boots off when he comes in. I hear him—he is coming."

"Miss! you're cutting the stuff wrong."

"So I am; but it is only a snip: there is no harm done."

The kitchen-door opened; Mr. Moore entered, very wet and cold. Caroline half turned from her dressmaking occupation, but renewed it for a moment, as if to gain a minute's time for some purpose. Bent over the dress, her face was hidden; there was an attempt to settle her features and veil their expression, which failed: when she at last met Mr. Moore, her countenance beamed.

"We had ceased to expect you: they asserted you would not come," she said.

"But I promised to return soon: *you* expected me, I suppose?"

"No, Robert: I dared not when it rained so fast. And you are wet and chilled—change everything! if you took cold, I should—we should blame ourselves in some measure."

"I am not wet through: my riding-coat is waterproof. Dry shoes are all I require.—There . . . the fire is pleasant after facing the cold wind and rain for a few miles."

He stood on the kitchen hearth; Caroline stood beside him. Mr. Moore, while enjoying the genial glow, kept his eyes directed towards the glittering brasses on the shelf above. Chancing for an instant to look down, his glance rested on an upturned face, flushed, smiling, happy, shaded with silky curls, lit with fine eyes. Sarah was gone into the parlour with the tray: a lecture from her mistress detained her there. Moore placed his hand a moment on his young cousin's shoulder, stooped, and left a kiss on her forehead.

"Oh!" said she, as if the action had unsealed her lips, "I was miserable when I thought you would not come: I am almost too happy now. Are you happy, Robert? Do you like to come home?"

"I think I do; to-night, at least."

"Are you certain you are not fretting about your frames, and your business, and the war?"

"Not just now."

"Are you positive you don't feel Hollow's Cottage too small for you, and narrow and dismal?"

"At this moment, no."

"Can you affirm that you are not bitter at heart because rich and great people forget you?"

"No more questions. You are mistaken if you think I am anxious to curry favour with rich and great people. I only want means—a position—a career."

"Which your own talent and goodness shall win you. You were made to be great—you *shall* be great."

"I wonder now, if you spoke honestly out of your heart, what receipt you would give me for acquiring this same greatness; but I know it—better than you know it yourself. Would it be efficacious? would it work? Yes—poverty, misery, bankruptcy. Oh! life is not what you think it, Lina!"

"But you are what I think you."

"I am not."

"You are better, then?"

"Far worse."

"No; far better. I know you are good."

"How do you know it?"

"You look so; and I feel you *are* so."

"Where do you feel it?"

"In my heart."

"Ah! you judge me with your heart, Lina: you should judge me with your head."

"I do; and then I am quite proud of you. Robert, you cannot tell all my thoughts about you."

Mr. Moore's dark face mustered colour; his lips smiled, and yet were compressed; his eyes laughed, and yet he resolutely knit his brow.

"Think meanly of me, Lina," said he. "Men, in general, are a sort of scum, very different to anything of which you have an idea; I make no pretension to be better than my fellows."

"If you did, I should not esteem you so much; it is because you are modest that I have such confidence in your merit."

"Are you flattering me?" he demanded, turning sharply upon her, and searching her face with an eye of acute penetration.

"No," she said softly, laughing at his sudden quickness. She seemed to think it unnecessary to proffer any eager disavowal of the charge.

"You don't care whether I think you flatter me or not?"

"No."

"You are so secure of your own intentions?"

"I suppose so."

"What are they, Caroline?"

"Only to ease my mind by expressing for once part of what I think; and then to make you better satisfied with yourself."

"By assuring me that my kinswoman is my sincere friend?"

"Just so; I am your sincere friend, Robert."

"And I am—what chance and change shall make me, Lina."

"Not my enemy, however?"

The answer was cut short by Sarah and her mistress entering the kitchen together in some commotion. They had been improving the time which Mr. Moore and Miss Helstone had spent in dialogue by a short dispute on the subject of "café au lait," which Sarah said was the queerest mess she ever saw, and a waste of God's good gifts, as it was "the nature of coffee to be boiled in water"; and which Mademoiselle affirmed to be "un breuvage royal," a thousand times too good for the mean person who objected to it.

The former occupants of the kitchen now withdrew into the parlour. Before Hortense followed them thither, Caroline had only time again to question, "Not my enemy, Robert?" And Moore, Quaker-like, had replied with another query, "Could I be?" and then, seating himself at the table, had settled Caroline at his side.

Caroline scarcely heard Mademoiselle's explosion of wrath when she rejoined them; the long declamation about the "conduite indigne de cette méchante créature" sounded in her ear as confusedly as the agitated rattling of the china. Robert laughed a little at it, in very subdued sort, and then, politely and calmly entreating his sister to be tranquil, assured her that if it would yield her any satisfaction, she should have her choice of an attendant among all the girls in his mill; only he feared they would scarcely suit her, as they were most of them, he was informed, completely ignorant of household work: and pert and self-willed as Sarah was, she was, perhaps, no worse than the majority of the women of her class.

Mademoiselle admitted the truth of this conjecture: according to her, "ces paysannes Anglaises étaient tout insupportables." What would she not give for some "bonne cuisinière Anversoise," with the high cap, short petticoat, and decent sabots proper to her class: something better, indeed, than an insolent coquette in a flounced gown and absolutely without cap! (for Sarah, it appears, did not partake the opinion of St. Paul, that "it is a shame for a woman to go with her head uncovered"; but, holding rather a contrary doctrine, resolutely refused to imprison in linen or muslin the plentiful tresses of her yellow hair, which it was her wont to fasten up smartly with a comb behind, and on Sundays to wear curled in front).

"Shall I try and get you an Antwerp girl?" asked Mr. Moore, who—stern in public—was on the whole very kind in private.

"Merci du cadeau!" was the answer. "An Antwerp girl would not stay here ten days, sneered at as she would be by all the young coquines in your factory"; then softening, "You are very good, dear brother—excuse my petulance—but truly, my domestic trials are severe, yet they are probably my destiny; for I recollect that our revered mother experienced similar sufferings, though she had the choice of all the best servants in Antwerp; domestics are in all countries a spoiled and unruly set."

Mr. Moore had also certain reminiscences about the trials of his revered mother. A good mother she had been to him, and he honoured her memory, but he recollected that she kept a hot kitchen of it in Antwerp, just as his faithful sister did here in England. Thus, therefore, he let the subject drop, and when the coffee-service was removed, proceeded to console Hortense by fetching her music-book and guitar; and, having arranged the ribbon of the instrument round her neck with a quiet fraternal kindness he knew to be all-powerful in soothing her most ruffled moods, he asked her to give him some of their mother's favourite songs.

Nothing refines like affection. Family jarring vulgarises—family union elevates. Hortense, pleased with her brother, and grateful to him, looked, as she touched her guitar, almost graceful, almost handsome; her every-day fretful look was gone for a moment, and was replaced by a "sourire plein de bonté." She sang the songs he asked for, with feeling; they reminded her of a parent to whom she had been truly attached; they reminded her of her young days. She observed, too, that Caroline listened with naïve interest; this augmented her good-humour; and the exclamation at the close of the song, "I wish I could sing and play like Hortense!" achieved the business, and rendered her charming for the evening.

It is true, a little lecture to Caroline followed, on the vanity of *wishing,* and the duty of *trying.* "As Rome," it was suggested, "had not been built in a day, so neither had Mademoiselle Gérard Moore's education been completed in a week, or by merely *wishing* to be clever. It was effort that had accomplished that great work: she was ever remarkable for her perseverance, for her industry: her masters had remarked that it was as delightful as it was uncommon to find so much talent united with so much solidity, and so on." Once on the theme of her own merits, Mademoiselle was fluent.

Cradled at last in blissful self-complacency, she took her knitting, and sat down tranquil. Drawn curtains, a clear fire, a softly shining lamp, gave now to the little parlour its best—its evening charm. It is probable that the three there present felt this charm: they all looked happy.

"What shall we do now, Caroline?" asked Mr. Moore, returning to his seat beside his cousin.

"What shall we do, Robert?" repeated she playfully. "You decide."

"Not play at chess?"

"No."

"Nor draughts, nor backgammon?"

"No—no; we both hate silent games that only keep one's hands employed, don't we?"

"I believe we do; then, shall we talk scandal?"

"About whom? Are we sufficiently interested in anybody to take a pleasure in pulling their character to pieces?"

"A question that comes to the point. For my part—unamiable as it sounds—I must say, no."

"And I, too. But it is strange—though we want no third—fourth, I mean" (she hastily and with contrition glanced at Hortense), "living person among us—so selfish we are in our happiness—though we don't want to think of the present existing world, it would be pleasant to go back to the past; to hear people that have slept for generations in graves that are perhaps no longer graves now, but gardens and fields, speak to us and tell us their thoughts, and impart their ideas."

"Who shall be the speaker? What language shall he utter? French?"

"Your French forefathers don't speak so sweetly, nor so solemnly, nor so impressively as your English ancestors, Robert. To-night you shall be entirely English: you shall read an English book."

"An old English book?"

"Yes, an old English book, one that you like; and I will choose a part of it that is toned quite in harmony with something in you. It shall waken your nature, fill your mind with music: it shall pass like a skilful hand over your heart, and make its strings sound. Your heart is a lyre, Robert; but the lot of your life has not been a minstrel to sweep it, and it is often silent. Let glorious William come near and touch it: you will see how he will draw the English power and melody out of its chords."

"I must read Shakespeare?"

"You must have his spirit before you; you must hear his voice with your mind's ear; you must take some of his soul into yours."

"With a view to making me better; is it to operate like a sermon?"

"It is to stir you; to give you new sensations. It is to make you feel your life strongly, not only your virtues, but your vicious, perverse points."

"Dieu! que dit-elle?" cried Hortense, who hitherto had been counting stitches in her knitting, and had not much attended to what was said, but whose ear these two strong words caught with a tweak.

"Never mind her, sister: let her talk; now just let her say anything she pleases to-night. She likes to come down hard upon your brother sometimes; it amuses me, so let her alone."

Caroline, who, mounted on a chair, had been rummaging the book-case, returned with a book.

"Here's Shakespeare," she said, "and there's Coriolanus. Now, read, and discover by the feelings the reading will give you at once how low and how high you are."

"Come then, sit near me, and correct when I mispronounce."

"I am to be the teacher then, and you my pupil?"

"Ainsi, soit-il!"

"And Shakespeare is our science, since we are going to study?"

"It appears so."

"And you are not going to be French, sceptical, and sneering? You are not going to think it a sign of wisdom to refuse to admire?"

"I don't know."

"If you do, Robert, I'll take Shakespeare away; and I'll shrivel up within myself, and put on my bonnet and go home."

"Sit down; here I begin."

"One minute, if you please, brother," interrupted Mademoiselle, "when the gentleman of a family reads, the ladies should always sew. Caroline, dear child, take your embroidery: you may get three sprigs done to-night."

Caroline looked dismayed. "I can't see by lamp-light; my eyes are tired, and I can't do two things well at once. If I sew, I cannot listen; if I listen, I cannot sew."

"Fi, donc! Quel enfantillage!" began Hortense. Mr. Moore, as usual, suavely interposed.

"Permit her to neglect the embroidery for this evening. I wish her whole attention to be fixed on my accent, and to ensure this, she must follow the reading with her eyes; she must look at the book."

He placed it between them, reposed his arm on the back of Caroline's chair, and thus began to read.

The very first scene in *Coriolanus* came with smart relish to his intellectual palate, and still as he read he warmed. He delivered the haughty speech of Caius Marcius to the starving citizens with unction; he did not say he thought his irrational pride right, but he seemed to feel it so. Caroline looked up at him with a singular smile.

"There's a vicious point hit already," she said; "you sympathise with that proud patrician who does not sympathise with his famished fellow-men, and insults them: there, go on." He proceeded. The warlike portions did not rouse him much; he said all that was out of date, or should be; the spirit displayed was barbarous, yet the encounter single-handed between Marcius and Tullus Aufidius he delighted in. As he advanced, he forgot to criticise; it was evident he appreciated the power, the truth of each portion; and, stepping out of the narrow line of private prejudices, began to revel in the large picture of human nature, to feel the reality stamped upon the characters who were speaking from that page before him.

He did not read the comic scenes well, and Caroline, taking the book out of his hand, read these parts for him. From her he seemed to enjoy them, and indeed she gave them with a spirit no one could have expected of her, with a pithy expression with which she seemed gifted on the spot, and for that brief moment only. It may be remarked, in passing, that the general character of her conversation that evening, whether serious or sprightly, grave or gay, was as of something untaught, unstudied, intuitive, fitful; when once gone, no more to be reproduced as it had been, than the glancing ray of the meteor, than the tints of the dew-gem, than the colour or form of the sunset cloud, than the fleeting and glittering ripple varying the flow of a rivulet.

Coriolanus in glory; Coriolanus in disaster; Coriolanus banished, followed like giant shades one after the other. Before the vision of the banished man, Moore's spirit seemed to pause. He stood on the hearth of Aufidius's hall, facing the image of greatness fallen, but greater than ever in that low estate. He saw "the grim

appearance,'' the dark face ''bearing command in it,'' ''the noble vessel with its tackle torn.'' With the revenge of Caius Marcius, Moore perfectly sympathised; he was not scandalised by it; and again Caroline whispered, ''There I see another glimpse of brotherhood in error.''

The march on Rome, the mother's supplication, the long resistance, the final yielding of bad passions to good, which ever must be the case in a nature worthy the epithet of noble, the rage of Aufidius at what he considered his ally's weakness, the death of Coriolanus, the final sorrow of his great enemy; all scenes made of condensed truth and strength, came on in succession and carried with them in their deep, fast flow the heart and mind of reader and listener.

''Now, have you felt Shakespeare?'' asked Caroline, some ten minutes after her cousin had closed the book.

''I think so.''

''And have you felt anything in Coriolanus like you?''

''Perhaps I have.''

''Was he not faulty as well as great?''

Moore nodded. ''And what was his fault? What made him hated by the citizens? What caused him to be banished by his countrymen?''

''What do you think it was?''

''I ask again—

> *Whether was it pride,*
> *Which out of daily fortune ever taints*
> *The happy man? whether defect of judgment,*
> *To fail in the disposing of those chances*
> *Which he was lord of? or whether nature,*
> *Not to be other than one thing; not moving*
> *From the casque to the cushion, but commanding peace*
> *Even with the same austerity and garb*
> *As he controlled the war?''*

''Well, answer yourself, Sphynx.''

''It was a spice of all; and you must not be proud to your workpeople; you must not neglect chances of soothing them, and you must not be of an inflexible nature, uttering a request as austerely as if it were a command.''

''That is the moral you tack to the play. What puts such notions into your head?''

''A wish for your good, a care for your safety, dear Robert, and a fear caused by many things which I have heard lately, that you will come to harm.''

''Who tells you these things?''

''I hear my uncle talk about you: he praises your hard spirit, your determined cast of mind, your scorn of low enemies, your resolution not 'to truckle to the mob,' as he says.''

''And would you have me truckle to them?''

''No, not for the world: I never wish you to lower yourself; but somehow, I cannot help thinking it unjust to include all poor working people under the general and insulting name of 'the mob,' and continually to think of them and treat them haughtily.''

''You are a little democrat, Caroline: if your uncle knew, what would he say?''

''I rarely talk to my uncle, as you know, and never about such things: he thinks everything but sewing and cooking above women's comprehension, and out of their line.''

''And do you fancy you comprehend the subjects on which you advise me?''

''As far as they concern you, I comprehend them. I know it would be better for you to be loved by your workpeople than to be hated by them, and I am sure that kindness is more likely to win their regard than pride. If you were proud and cold

to me and Hortense, should we love you? When you are cold to me, as you *are* sometimes, can I venture to be affectionate in return?''

"Now, Lina, I've had my lesson both in languages and ethics, with a touch on politics; it is your turn. Hortense tells me you were much taken by a little piece of poetry you learned the other day, a piece by poor André Chénier—'La Jeune Captive'; do you remember it still?''

''I think so.''

"Repeat it, then. Take your time and mind your accent: especially let us have no English *u*'s.''

Caroline, beginning in a low, rather tremulous voice, but gaining courage as she proceeded, repeated the sweet verses of Chénier; the last three stanzas she rehearsed well.

> *Mon beau voyage encore est si loin de sa fin!*
> *Je pars, et des ormeaux qui bordent le chemin*
> *J'ai passé le premiers à peine.*
> *Au banquet de la vie à peine commencé,*
> *Un instant seulement mes lèvres ont pressé*
> *La coupe en mes mains encore pleine.*
>
> *Je ne suis qu'au printemps—je veux voir la moisson*
> *Et comme le soleil, de saison en saison,*
> *Je veux achever mon année.*
> *Brillante sur ma tige, et l'honneur du jardin*
> *Je n'ai vu luire encore que les feux du matin,*
> *Je veux achever ma journée!*

Moore listened at first with his eyes cast down, but soon he furtively raised them: leaning back in his chair, he could watch Caroline without her perceiving where his gaze was fixed. Her cheek had a colour, her eyes a light, her countenance an expression, this evening, which would have made even plain features striking: but there was not the grievous defect of plainness to pardon in her case. The sunshine was not shed on rough barrenness; it fell on soft bloom. Each lineament was turned with grace; the whole aspect was pleasing. At the present moment—animated, interested, touched—she might be called beautiful. Such a face was calculated to awaken not only the calm sentiment of esteem, the distant one of admiration; but some feeling more tender, genial, intimate; friendship, perhaps—affection, interest. When she had finished, she turned to Moore, and met his eye.

"Is that pretty well repeated?'' she inquired, smiling like any happy, docile child.

"I really don't know.''

"Why don't you know? Have you not listened?''

"Yes—and looked. You are fond of poetry, Lina?''

"When I meet with *real* poetry, I cannot rest till I have learned it by heart, and so made it partly mine.''

Mr. Moore now sat silent for several minutes. It struck nine o'clock: Sarah entered, and said that Mr. Helstone's servant was come for Miss Caroline.

"Then the evening is gone already,'' she observed; "and it will be long, I suppose, before I pass another here.''

Hortense had been for some time nodding over her knitting; fallen into a doze now, she made no response to the remark.

"You would have no objections to come here oftener of an evening?'' inquired Robert, as he took her folded mantle from the side-table, where it still lay, and carefully wrapped it round her.

"I like to come here; but I have no desire to be intrusive. I am not hinting to be asked: you must understand that.''

"Oh! I understand thee, child. You sometimes lecture me for wishing to be rich, Lina; but if I *were* rich, you should live here always: at any rate, you should live with me wherever my habitation might be."

"That would be pleasant; and if you were poor—ever so poor—it would still be pleasant. Good-night, Robert."

"I promised to walk with you up to the Rectory."

"I know you did; but I thought you had forgotten, and I hardly knew how to remind you, though I wished to do it. But would you like to go? It is a cold night; and, as Fanny is come, there is no necessity"——

"Here is your muff—don't wake Hortense—come."

The half-mile to the Rectory was soon traversed. They parted in the garden without a kiss, scarcely with a pressure of hands: yet Robert sent his cousin in excited and joyously troubled. He had been singularly kind to her that day: not in phrase, compliment, profession; but in manner, in look, and in soft and friendly tones.

For himself, he came home grave, almost morose. As he stood leaning on his own yard-gate, musing in the watery moonlight all alone—the hushed, dark mill before him, the hill-environed hollow round—he exclaimed, abruptly—

"This won't do! There's weakness—there's downright ruin in all this. However," he added, dropping his voice, "the frenzy is quite temporary. I know it very well: I have had it before. It will be gone to-morrow."

Chapter VII

THE CURATES AT TEA

CAROLINE HELSTONE was just eighteen years old; and at eighteen the true narrative of life is yet to be commenced. Before that time, we sit listening to a tale, a marvellous fiction; delightful sometimes, and sad sometimes; almost always unreal. Before that time, our world is heroic; its inhabitants half-divine or semi-demon; its scenes are dream-scenes: darker woods and stranger hills; brighter skies, more dangerous waters; sweeter flowers, more tempting fruits: wider plains, drearier deserts, sunnier fields than are found in nature, over-spread our enchanted globe. What a moon we gaze on before that time! How the trembling of our hearts at her aspect bears witness to its unutterable beauty! As to our sun, it is a burning heaven— the world of gods.

At that time—at eighteen, drawing near the confines of illusive, void dreams, Elf-land lies behind us, the shores of Reality rise in front. These shores are yet distant: they look so blue, soft, gentle, we long to reach them. In sunshine we see a greenness beneath the azure, as of spring meadows; we catch glimpses of silver lines, and imagine the roll of living waters. Could we but reach this land, we think to hunger and thirst no more: whereas many a wilderness, and often the flood of Death, or some stream of sorrow as cold and almost as black as Death, is to be crossed ere true bliss can be tasted. Every joy that life gives must be earned ere it is secured; and how hardly earned, those only know who have wrestled for great prizes. The heart's blood must gem with red beads the brow of the combatant, before the wreath of victory rustles over it.

At eighteen, we are not aware of this. Hope, when she smiles on us, and promises happiness to-morrow, is implicitly believed;—Love, when he comes wandering like a lost angel to our door, is at once admitted, welcomed, embraced: his quiver is not seen; if his arrows penetrate, their wound is like a thrill of new life: there are no fears of poison, none of the barb which no leech's hand can extract: that perilous passion—an agony ever in some of its phases; with many, an agony

throughout—is believed to be an unqualified good: in short, at eighteen, the school of Experience is to be entered, and her humbling, crushing, grinding, but yet purifying and invigorating lessons are yet to be learnt.

Alas, Experience! No other mentor has so wasted and frozen a face as yours: none wears a robe so black, none bears a rod so heavy, none with hand so inexorable draws the novice so sternly to his task, and forces him with authority so resistless to its acquirement. It is by your instructions alone that man or woman can ever find a safe track through life's wilds; without it, how they stumble, how they stray! On what forbidden grounds do they intrude, down what dread declivities are they hurled!

Caroline, having been convoyed home by Robert, had no wish to pass what remained of the evening with her uncle: the room in which he sat was very sacred ground to her; she seldom intruded on it, and to-night she kept aloof till the bell rung for prayers. Part of the evening Church service was the form of worship observed in Mr. Helstone's household: he read it in his usual nasal voice, clear, loud, and monotonous. The rite over, his niece, according to her wont, stepped up to him.

"Good-night, uncle."

"Hey! You've been gadding abroad all day—visiting, dining out, and what not!"

"Only at the cottage."

"And have you learnt your lessons?"

"Yes."

"And made a shirt?"

"Only part of one."

"Well, that will do: stick to the needle—learn shirt-making and gown-making, and pie-crust-making, and you'll be a clever woman some day. Go to bed now; I'm busy with a pamphlet here."

Presently the niece was enclosed in her small bed-room; the door bolted, her white dressing-gown assumed, her long hair loosened and falling thick, soft, and wavy to her waist; and as, resting from the task of combing it out, she leaned her cheek on her hand and fixed her eyes on the carpet, before her rose, and close around her drew, the visions we see at eighteen years.

Her thoughts were speaking with her: speaking pleasantly, as it seemed, for she smiled as she listened. She looked pretty, meditating thus: but a brighter thing than she was in that apartment—the spirit of youthful Hope. According to this flattering prophet, she was to know disappointment, to feel chill no more: she had entered on the dawn of a summer day—no false dawn, but the true spring of morning— and her sun would quickly rise. Impossible for her now to suspect that she was the sport of delusion: her expectations seemed warranted, the foundation on which they rested appeared solid.

"When people love, the next step is they marry," was her argument. "Now, I love Robert, and I feel sure that Robert loves me: I have thought so many a time before; to-day I *felt* it. When I looked up at him after repeating Chénier's poem, his eyes (what handsome eyes he has!) sent the truth through my heart. Sometimes I am afraid to speak to him, lest I should be too frank, lest I should seem forward: for I have more than once regretted bitterly overflowing, superfluous words, and feared I had said more than he expected me to say, and that he would disapprove what he might deem my indiscretion; now, to-night, I could have ventured to express any thought, he was so indulgent. How kind he was, as we walked up the lane! He does not flatter or say foolish things; his love-making (friendship, I mean: of course I don't yet account him my lover, but I hope he will be so some day) is not like what we read of in books—it is far better—original, quiet, manly, sincere. I *do* like him: I would be an excellent wife to him if he did marry me: I would tell him of his faults (for he has a few faults), but I would study his comfort, and cherish him, and do my best to make him happy. Now, I am sure he will not be

cold to-morrow: I feel almost certain that to-morrow evening he will either come here, or ask me to go there.''

She recommenced combing her hair, long as a mermaid's; turning her head, as she arranged it, she saw her own face and form in the glass. Such reflections are soberising to plain people: their own eyes are not enchanted with the image; they are confident then that the eyes of others can see in it no fascination; but the fair must naturally draw other conclusions: the picture is charming, and must charm. Caroline saw a shape, a head, that daguerreotyped in that attitude and with that expression would have been lovely: she could not choose but derive from the spectacle confirmation to her hopes: it was then in undiminished gladness she sought her couch.

And in undiminished gladness she rose the next day: as she entered her uncle's breakfast-room, and with soft cheerfulness wished him good-morning, even that little man of bronze himself thought, for an instant, his niece was growing ''a fine girl.'' Generally she was quiet and timid with him; very docile, but not communicative: this morning, however, she found many things to say. Slight topics alone might be discussed between them; for with a woman—a girl—Mr. Helstone would touch on no other. She had taken an early walk in the garden, and she told him what flowers were beginnimg to spring there; she inquired when the gardener was to come and trim the borders; she informed him that certain starlings were beginning to build their nests in the church-tower (Briarfield church was close to Briarfield rectory); she wondered the tolling of the bells in the belfry did not scare them.

Mr. Helstone opined that ''they were like other fools who had just paired; insensible to inconvenience just for the moment.'' Caroline, made perhaps a little too courageous by her temporary good spirits, here hazarded a remark of a kind she had never before ventured to make on observations dropped by her revered relative.

''Uncle,'' said she, ''whenever you speak of marriage, you speak of it scornfully: do you think people shouldn't marry?''

''It is decidedly the wisest plan to remain single, especially for women.''

''Are all marriages unhappy?''

''Millions of marriages are unhappy: if everybody confessed the truth, perhaps all are more or less so.''

''You are always vexed when you are asked to come and marry a couple—why?''

''Because one does not like to act as accessory to the commission of a piece of pure folly.''

Mr. Helstone spoke so readily, he seemed rather glad of the opportunity to give his niece a piece of his mind on this point. Emboldened by the impunity which had hitherto attended her questions, she went a little further—

''But why,'' said she, ''should it be pure folly? If two people like each other, why shouldn't they consent to live together?''

''They tire of each other—they tire of each other in a month. A yokefellow is not a companion; he or she is a fellow-sufferer.''

It was by no means naïve simplicity which inspired Caroline's next remark: it was a sense of antipathy to such opinions, and of displeasure at him who held them.

''One would think you had never been married, uncle: one would think you were an old bachelor.''

''Practically, I am so.''

''But you have been married. Why were you so inconsistent as to marry?''

''Every man is mad once or twice in his life.''

''So you tired of my aunt, and my aunt of you, and you were miserable together?''

Mr. Helstone pushed out his cynical lip, wrinkled his brown forehead and gave an inarticulate grunt.

"Did she not suit you? Was she not good-tempered? Did you not get used to her? Were you not sorry when she died?"

"Caroline," said Mr. Helstone, bringing his hand slowly down to within an inch or two of the table, and then smiting it suddenly on the mahogany, "understand this: it is vulgar and puerile to confound generals with particulars: in every case, there is the rule, and there are the exceptions. Your questions are stupid and babyish. Ring the bell, if you have done breakfast."

The breakfast was taken away, and that meal over, it was the general custom of uncle and niece to separate, and not to meet again till dinner; but to-day the niece, instead of quitting the room, went to the window-seat, and sat down there. Mr. Helstone looked round uneasily once or twice, as if he wished her away, but she was gazing from the window, and did not seem to mind him; so he continued the perusal of his morning paper—a particularly interesting one it chanced to be, as new movements had just taken place in the Peninsula, and certain columns of the journal were rich in long despatches from General Lord Wellington. He little knew, meantime, what thoughts were busy in his niece's mind—thoughts the conversation of the past half-hour had revived, but not generated; tumultuous were they now, as disturbed bees in a hive, but it was years since they had first made their cells in her brain.

She was reviewing his character, his disposition, repeating his sentiments on marriage. Many a time had she reviewed them before, and sounded the gulf between her own mind and his; and then, on the other side of the wide and deep chasm, she had seen, and she now saw, another figure standing beside her uncle's—a strange shape; dim, sinister, scarcely earthly: the half-remembered image of her own father, James Helstone, Matthewson Helstone's brother.

Rumours had reached her ear of what that father's character was; old servants had dropped hints: she knew, too, that he was not a good man, and that he was never kind to her. She recollected—a dark recollection it was—some weeks that she had spent with him in a great town somewhere, when she had had no maid to dress her or take care of her; when she had been shut up, day and night, in a high garret-room, without a carpet, with a bare uncurtained bed, and scarcely any other furniture; when he went out early every morning, and often forgot to return and give her her dinner during the day, and at night, when he came back, was like a madman, furious, terrible; or—still more painful—like an idiot, imbecile, senseless. She knew she had fallen ill in this place, and that one night when she was very sick, he had come raving into the room, and said he would kill her, for she was a burden to him; her screams had brought aid, and from the moment she was then rescued from him she had never seen him, except as a dead man in his coffin.

That was her father: also she had a mother; though Mr. Helstone never spoke to her of that mother; though she could not remember having seen her: but that she was alive she knew. This mother was then the drunkard's wife: what had *their* marriage been? Caroline, turning from the lattice whence she had been watching the starlings (though without seeing them), in a low voice, and with a sad bitter tone, thus broke the silence of the room—

"You term marriage miserable, I suppose, from what you saw of my father and mother's. If my mother suffered what I suffered when I was with papa, she must have had a dreadful life."

Mr. Helstone, thus addressed, wheeled about in his chair, and looked over his spectacles at his niece: he was taken aback.

Her father and mother! What had put it into her head to mention her father and mother, of whom he had never, during the twelve years she had lived with him, spoken to her? That the thoughts were self-matured; that she had any recollections or speculations about her parents, he could not fancy.

"Your father and mother? Who has been talking to you about them?"

"Nobody; but I remember something of what papa was, and I pity mamma. Where is she?"

This "Where is she?" had been on Caroline's lips hundreds of times before; but till now she had never uttered it.

"I hardly know," returned Mr. Helstone; "I was little acquainted with her. I have not heard from her for years: but wherever she is, she thinks nothing of you; she never inquires about you; I have reason to believe she does not wish to see you. Come, it is school-time: you go to your cousin at ten, don't you? The clock has struck."

Perhaps Caroline would have said more; but Fanny coming in, informed her master that the churchwardens wanted to speak to him in the vestry. He hastened to join them, and his niece presently set out for the cottage.

The road from the Rectory to Hollow's Mill inclined downwards; she ran, therefore, almost all the way. Exercise, the fresh air, the thought of seeing Robert, at least of being on his premises, in his vicinage, revived her somewhat depressed spirits quickly. Arriving in sight of the white house, and within hearing of the thundering mill and its rushing watercourse, the first thing she saw was Moore at his garden-gate. There he stood; in his belted Holland blouse, a light cap covering his head, which undress costume suited him: he was looking down the lane, not in the direction of his cousin's approach. She stopped, withdrawing a little behind a willow, and studied his appearance.

"He has not his peer," she thought; "he is as handsome as he is intelligent. What a keen eye he has! What clearly cut, spirited features—thin and serious, but graceful! I do like his face—I do like his aspect—I do like him so much! Better than any of these shuffling curates, for instance—better than anybody: bonnie Robert!"

She sought "bonnie Robert's" presence speedily. For his part, when she challenged his sight, I believe he would have passed from before her eyes like a phantom, if he could; but being a tall fact, and no fiction, he was obliged to stand the greeting. He made it brief: it was cousin-like, brother-like, friend-like, anything but lover-like. The nameless charm of last night had left his manner: he was no longer the same man; or, at any rate, the same heart did not beat in his breast.

Rude disappointment! sharp cross! At first the eager girl would not believe in the change, though she saw and felt it. It was difficult to withdraw her hand from his, till he had bestowed at least something like a kind pressure; it was difficult to turn her eyes from his eyes, till his looks had expressed something more and fonder than that cool welcome.

A lover masculine so disappointed can speak and urge explanation; a lover feminine can say nothing; if she did, the result would be shame and anguish, inward remorse for self-treachery. Nature would brand such demonstration as a rebellion against her instincts, and would vindictively repay it afterwards by the thunderbolt of self-contempt smiting suddenly in secret. Take the matter as you find it; ask no questions; utter no remonstrances: it is your best wisdom. You expected bread, and you have got a stone; break your teeth on it, and don't shriek because the nerves are martyrised: do not doubt that your mental stomach—if you have such a thing—is strong as an ostrich's: the stone will digest. You held out your hand for an egg, and fate put into it a scorpion. Show no consternation: close your fingers firmly upon the gift; let it sting through your palm. Never mind: in time, after your hand and arm have swelled and quivered long with torture, the squeezed scorpion will die, and you will have learned the great lesson how to endure without a sob. For the whole remnant of your life, if you survive the test—some, it is said, die under it—you will be stronger, wiser, less sensitive. This you are not aware of, perhaps, at the time, and so cannot borrow courage of that hope. Nature, however, as has been intimated, is an excellent friend in such cases; sealing the lips, interdicting utterance, commanding a placid dissimulation: a dissimulation often wearing an

easy and gay mien at first, settling down to sorrow and paleness in time, then passing away, and leaving a convenient stoicism, not the less fortifying because it is half-bitter.

Half-bitter! Is that wrong? No—it should be bitter: bitterness is strength—it is a tonic. Sweet mild force following acute suffering, you find nowhere: to talk of it is delusion. There may be apathetic exhaustion after the rack; if energy remains, it will be rather a dangerous energy—deadly when confronted with injustice.

Who has read the ballad of *Puir Mary Lee*?—that old Scotch ballad, written I know not in what generation nor by what hand. Mary had been ill-used—probably in being made to believe that truth which was falsehood: she is not complaining, but she is sitting alone in the snow-storm, and you hear her thoughts. They are not the thoughts of a model-heroine under her circumstances, but they are those of a deeply-feeling, strongly-resentful peasant-girl. Anguish has driven her from the ingle-nook of home, to the white-shrouded and icy hills: crouched under the "cauld drift," she recalls every image of horror,—"the yellow-wymed ask," "the hairy adder," "the auld moon-bowing tyke," "the ghaist at e'en," "the sour bullister," "the milk on the taed's back": she hates these, "but waur she hates Robin-a-Ree!"

> *Oh! ance I lived happily by yon bonny burn—*
> *The warld was in love wi' me;*
> *But now I maun sit 'neath the cauld drift and mourn,*
> *And curse black Robin-a-Ree!*
>
> *Then whudder awa', thou bitter biting blast,*
> *And sough through the scrunty tree,*
> *And smoor me up in the snaw fu' fast,*
> *And ne'er let the sun me see!*
>
> *Oh, never melt awa' thou wreath o' snaw*
> *That's sae kind in graving me;*
> *But hide me frae the scorn and guffaw*
> *O' villains like Robin-a-Ree!*

But what has been said in the last page or two is not germane to Caroline Helstone's feelings, or to the state of things between her and Robert Moore. Robert had done her no wrong; he had told her no lie; it was she that was to blame, if any one was: what bitterness her mind distilled should and would be poured on her own head. She had loved without being asked to love,—a natural, sometimes an inevitable chance, but big with misery.

Robert, indeed, had sometimes seemed to be fond of her—but why? Because she had made herself so pleasing to him, he could not, in spite of all his efforts, help testifying a state of feeling his judgment did not approve, nor his will sanction. He was about to withdraw decidedly from intimate communication with her, because he did not choose to have his affections inextricably entangled, nor to be drawn, despite his reason, into a marriage he believed imprudent. Now, what was she to do?—to give way to her feelings, or to vanquish them? To pursue him, or to turn upon herself? If she is weak, she will try the first expedient,—will lose his esteem and win his aversion: if she has sense, she will be her own governor, and resolve to subdue and bring under guidance the disturbed realm of her emotions. She will determine to look on life steadily, as it is; to begin to learn its severe truths seriously, and to study its knotty problems closely, conscientiously.

It appeared she had a little sense, for she quitted Robert quietly, without complaint or question—without the alteration of a muscle or the shedding of a tear—betook herself to her studies under Hortense as usual, and at dinner-time went home without lingering.

When she had dined, and found herself in the Rectory drawing-room alone, having left her uncle over his temperate glass of port wine, the difficulty that occurred to and embarrassed her, was—"How am I to get through this day?"

Last night she had hoped it would be spent as yesterday was,—that the evening would be again passed with Happiness and Robert: she had learned her mistake this morning, and yet she could not settle down, convinced that no chance would occur to recall her to Hollow's Cottage, or to bring Moore again into her society.

He had walked up after tea, more than once, to pass an hour with her uncle: the door-bell had rung, his voice had been heard in the passage just at twilight, when she little expected such a pleasure; and this had happened twice after he had treated her with peculiar reserve; and, though he rarely talked to her in her uncle's presence, he had looked at her relentingly as he sat opposite her work-table during his stay: the few words he had spoken to her were comforting; his manner on bidding her good-night was genial. Now, he might come this evening, said False Hope: she almost knew it was False Hope which breathed the whisper, and yet she listened.

She tried to read—her thoughts wandered; she tried to sew—every stitch she put in was an ennui, the occupation was insufferably tedious; she opened her desk, and attempted to write a French composition,—she wrote nothing but mistakes.

Suddenly the door-bell sharply rang—her heart leaped—she sprang to the drawing-room door, opened it softly, peeped through the aperture: Fanny was admitting a visitor—a gentleman—a tall man—just the height of Robert. For one second she thought it was Robert—for one second she exulted; but the voice asking for Mr. Helstone undeceived her: that voice was an Irish voice, consequently not Moore's but the curate's—Malone's. He was ushered into the dining-room, where, doubtless, he speedily helped his Rector to empty the decanters.

It was a fact to be noted that at whatever house in Briarfield, Whinbury, or Nunnely one curate dropped in to a meal—dinner or tea, as the case might be—another presently followed; often two more. Not that they gave each other the rendezvous, but they were usually all on the run at the same time; and when Donne, for instance, sought Malone at his lodgings and found him out, he inquired whither he had posted, and having learned of the landlady his destination, hastened with all speed after him: the same causes operated in the same way with Sweeting. Thus it chanced on that afternoon that Caroline's ears were three times tortured with the ringing of the bell, and the advent of undesired guests: for Donne followed Malone, and Sweeting followed Donne; and more wine was ordered up from the cellar into the dining-room (for though old Helstone chid the inferior priesthood when he found them "carousing," as he called it, in their own tents, yet at his hierarchical table he ever liked to treat them to a glass of his best), and through the closed doors Caroline heard their boyish laughter, and the vacant cackle of their voices. Her fear was lest they should stay to tea; for she had no pleasure in making tea for that particular trio. What distinctions people draw! These three were men—young men—educated men, like Moore, yet, for her, how great the diference! Their society was a bore—his a delight.

Not only was she destined to be favoured with their clerical company, but Fortune was at this moment bringing her four other guests—lady-guests, all packed in a pony-phaeton now rolling somewhat heavily along the road from Whinbury: an elderly lady, and three of her buxom daughters, were coming to see her "in a friendly way," as the custom of that neighbourhood was. Yes, a fourth time the bell clanged: Fanny brought the present announcement to the drawing-room—

"Mrs. Sykes and the three Misses Sykes."

When Caroline was going to receive company, her habit was to wring her hands very nervously, to flush a little, and come forward hurriedly yet hesitatingly, wishing herself meantime at Jericho. She was, at such crises, sadly deficient in finished manner, though she had once been at school a year. Accordingly, on this occasion,

her small white hands sadly maltreated each other, while she stood up, waiting the entrance of Mrs. Sykes.

In stalked that lady, a tall bilious gentlewoman, who made an ample and not altogether insincere profession of piety, and was greatly given to hospitality towards the clergy; in sailed her three daughters, a showy trio, being all three well-grown, and more or less handsome.

In English country ladies there is this point to be remarked. Whether young or old, pretty or plain, dull or sprightly, they all (or almost all) have a certain expression stamped on their features, which seems to say, "I know—I do not boast of it—but I *know* that I am the standard of what is proper; let every one therefore whom I approach, or who approaches me, keep a sharp look-out, for wherein they differ from me—be the same in dress, manner, opinion, principle, or practice—therein they are wrong."

Mrs. and Misses Sykes, far from being exceptions to this observation, were pointed illustrations of its truth. Miss Mary—a well-looked, well-meant, and, on the whole, well-dispositioned girl—wore her complacency with some state, though without harshness; Miss Harriet—a beauty—carried it more overbearingly: she looked high and cold; Miss Hannah, who was conceited, dashing, pushing, flourished hers consciously and openly; the mother evinced it with the gravity proper to her age and religious fame.

The reception was got through somehow. Caroline "was glad to see them" (an unmitigated fib), hoped they were well, hoped Mrs. Sykes's cough was better (Mrs. Sykes had had a cough for the last twenty years), hoped the Misses Sykes had left their sisters at home well; to which inquiry the Misses Sykes, sitting on three chairs opposite the music-stool, whereon Caroline had undesignedly come to anchor, after wavering for some seconds between it and a large arm-chair, into which she at length recollected she ought to induct Mrs. Sykes: and indeed that lady saved her the trouble by depositing herself therein: the Misses Sykes replied to Caroline by one simultaneous bow, very majestic and mighty awful. A pause followed: this bow was of a character to ensure silence for the next five minutes, and it did. Mrs. Sykes then inquired after Mr. Helstone, and whether he had had any return of rheumatism, and whether preaching twice on a Sunday fatigued him, and if he was capable of taking a full service now; and on being assured he was, she and all her daughters, combining in chorus, expressed their opinion that he was "a wonderful man of his years."

Pause second.

Miss Mary, getting up the steam in her turn, asked whether Caroline had attended the Bible Society meeting which had been held at Nunnely last Thursday night: the negative answer which truth compelled Caroline to utter—for last Thursday evening she had been sitting at home, reading a novel which Robert had lent her—elicited a simultaneous expression of surprise from the lips of the four ladies.

"We were all there," said Miss Mary; "mamma and all of us; we even persuaded papa to go: Hannah would insist upon it: but he fell asleep while Mr. Langweilig, the German Moravian minister, was speaking: I felt quite ashamed, he nodded so."

"And there was Dr. Broadbent," cried Hannah, "such a beautiful speaker! You couldn't expect of him, for he is almost a vulgar-looking man."

"But such a dear man," interrupted Mary.

"And such a good man, such a useful man," added her mother.

"Only like a butcher in appearance," interposed the fair proud Harriet. "I couldn't bear to look at him: I listened with my eyes shut."

Miss Helstone felt her ignorance and incompetency; not having seen Dr. Broadbent, she could not give her opinion. Pause third came on. During its continuance, Caroline was feeling at her heart's core what a dreaming fool she was; what an unpractical life she led; how little fitness there was in her for ordinary intercourse with the ordinary world. She was feeling how exclusively she had attached herself

to the white cottage in the Hollow; how in the existence of one inmate of that cottage she had pent all her universe: she was sensible that this would not do, and that some day she would be forced to make an alteration: it could not be said that she exactly wished to resemble the ladies before her, but she wished to become superior to her present self, so as to feel less scared by their dignity.

The sole means she found of reviving the flagging discourse, was by asking them if they would all stay to tea; and a cruel struggle it cost her to perform this piece of civility. Mrs. Sykes had begun—''We are much obliged to you, but''——when in came Fanny once more.

''The gentlemen will stay the evening, ma'am,'' was the message she brought from Mr. Helstone.

''What gentlemen have you?'' now inquired Mrs. Sykes. Their names were specified; she and her daughters interchanged glances: the curates were not to them what they were to Caroline. Mr. Sweeting was quite a favourite with them; even Mr. Malone rather so, because he was a clergyman. ''Really, since you have company already, I think we will stay,'' remarked Mrs. Sykes. ''We shall be quite a pleasant little party: I always like to meet the clergy.''

And now Caroline had to usher them upstairs, to help them to unshawl, smooth their hair, and make themselves smart; to re-conduct them to the drawing-room, to distribute amongst them books of engravings, or odd things purchased from the Jew-basket: she was obliged to be a purchaser, though she was but a slack contributor: and if she had possessed plenty of money, she would rather, when it was brought to the Rectory—an awful incubus!—have purchased the whole stock, than contributed a single pincushion.

It ought perhaps to be explained in passing, for the benefit of those who are not ''au fait'' with the mysteries of the ''Jew-basket'' and ''Missionary-basket,'' that these ''meubles'' are willow-repositories, of the capacity of a good-sized family clothes-basket, dedicated to the purpose of conveying from house to house a monster collection of pincushions, needlebooks, cardracks, work-bags, articles of infant wear, etc., etc., etc., made by the willing or reluctant hands of the Christian ladies of a parish, and sold perforce to the heathenish gentlemen thereof, at prices unblushingly exorbitant. The proceeds of such compulsory sales are applied to the conversion of the Jews, the seeking up of the ten missing tribes, or to the regeneration of the interesting coloured population of the globe. Each lady contributor takes it in her turn to keep the basket a month, to sew for it, and to foist off its contents on a shrinking male public. An exciting time it is when that turn comes round: some active-minded women, with a good trading spirit, like it, and enjoy exceedingly the fun of making hard-handed worsted-spinners cash up, to the tune of four or five hundred per cent. above cost price, for articles quite useless to them; other— feebler souls object to it, and would rather see the prince of darkness himself at their door any morning, than that phantom-basket, brought with ''Mrs. Rouse's compliments, and please, ma'am, she says it's your turn now.''

Miss Helstone's duties of hostess performed, more anxiously than cheerily, she betook herself to the kitchen, to hold a brief privy-council with Fanny and Eliza about the tea.

''What a lot on 'em!'' cried Eliza, who was cook. ''And I put off the baking to-day because I thought there would be bread plenty to fit while morning: we shall never have enow.''

''Are there any tea-cakes?'' asked the young mistress.

''Only three and a loaf. I wish these fine folk would stay at home till they're asked: and I want to finish trimming my hat'' (bonnet she meant).

''Then,'' suggested Caroline, to whom the importance of the emergency gave a certain energy, ''Fanny must run down to Briarfield and buy some muffins and crumpets, and some biscuits: and don't be cross, Eliza, we can't help it now.''

''And which tea-things are we to have?''

"Oh, the best, I suppose: I'll get out the silver service," and she ran upstrirs to the plate-closet, and presently brought down tea-pot, cream-ewer, and sugar-basin.

"And mun we have th' urn?"

"Yes; and now get it ready as quickly as you can, for the sooner we have tea over, the sooner they will go—at least, I hope so. Heigho! I wish they were gone," she sighed as she returned to the drawing-room. "Still," she thought as she paused at the door ere opening it, "if Robert would but come even now how bright all would be!—How comparatively easy the task of amusing these people, if he were present! There would be an interest in hearing him talk (though he never says much in company) and in talking in his presence: there can be no interest in hearing any of them, or in speaking to them. How they will gabble when the curates come in, and how weary I shall grow with listening to them! But I suppose I am a selfish fool: these are very respectable gentlefolks; I ought no doubt to be proud of their countenance; I don't say they are not as good as I am—far from it—but they are different from me."

She went in.

Yorkshire people, in those days, took their tea round the table; sitting well into it, with their knees duly introduced under the mahogany. It was essential to have a multitude of plates of bread and butter, varied in sorts and plentiful in quantity: it was thought proper, too, that on the centre-plate should stand a glass dish of marmalade; among the viands was expected to be found a small assortment of cheesecakes and tarts: if there was also a plate of thin slices of pink ham garnished with green parsley, so much the better.

Eliza, the Rector's cook, fortunately knew her business as provider: she had been put out of humour a little at first, when the invaders came so unexpectedly in such strength; but it appeared that she regained her cheerfulness with action, for in due time the tea was spread forth in handsome style; and neither ham, tarts, nor marmalade were wanting among its accompaniments.

The curates, summoned to this bounteous repast, entered joyous; but at once, on seeing the ladies, of whose presence they had not been forewarned, they came to a stand in the doorway. Malone headed the party; he stopped short and fell back, almost capsizing Donne, who was behind him. Donne, staggering three paces in retreat, sent little Sweeting into the arms of old Helstone, who brought up the rear. There was some expostulation, some tittering: Malone was desired to mind what he was about, and urged to push forward; which at last he did, though colouring to the top of his peaked forehead a bluish purple. Helstone, advancing, set the shy curates aside, welcomed all his fair guests, shook hands and passed a jest with each, and seated himself snugly between the lovely Harriet and the dashing Hannah; Miss Mary he requested to move to the seat opposite to him, that he might see her if he couldn't be near her. Perfectly easy and gallant, in his way, were his manners always to young ladies; and most popular was he amongst them: yet, at heart, he neither respected nor liked the sex, and such of them as circumstances had brought into intimate relation with him had ever feared rather than loved him.

The curates were left to shift for themselves. Sweeting, who was the least embarrassed of the three, took refuge beside Mrs. Sykes; who, he knew, was almost as fond of him as if he had been her son. Donne, after making his general bow with a grace all his own, and saying in a high pragmatical voice, "How d'ye do, Miss Helstone?" dropped into a seat at Caroline's elbow: to her unmitigated annoyance, for she had a peculiar antipathy to Donne, on account of his stultified and unmovable self-conceit, and his incurable narrowness of mind. Malone, grinning most unmeaningly, inducted himself into the corresponding seat on the other side: she was thus blessed in a pair of supporters; neither of whom, she knew, would be of any mortal use, whether for keeping up the conversation, handing cups, circulating the muffins, or even lifting the plate from the slop-basin. Little Sweeting, small and boyish as he was, would have been worth twenty of them.

Malone, though a ceaseless talker when there were only men present, was usually tongue-tied in the presence of ladies: three phrases, however, he had ready cut and dried, which he never failed to produce—

1stly. "Have you had a walk to-day, Miss Helstone?"

2ndly. "Have you seen your cousin, Moore, lately?"

3rdly. "Does your class at the Sunday-school keep up number?"

These three questions being put and responded to, between Caroline and Malone reigned silence.

With Donne it was otherwise: he was troublesome, exasperating. He had a stock of small-talk on hand, at once the most trite and perverse that can well be imagined: abuse of the people of Briarfield; of the natives of Yorkshire generally; complaints of the want of high society; of the backward state of civilisation in these districts; murmurings against the disrespectful conduct of the lower orders in the north toward their betters; silly ridicule of the manner of living in these parts,—the want of style, the absence of elegance, as if he, Donne, had been accustomed to very great doings indeed: an insinuation which his somewhat underbred manner and aspect failed to bear out. These strictures he seemed to think must raise him in the estimation of Miss Helstone, or of any other lady who heard him; whereas with her, at least, they brought him to a level below contempt: though sometimes, indeed, they incensed her; for, a Yorkshire girl herself, she hated to hear Yorkshire abused by such a pitiful prater; and when brought up to a certain pitch, she would turn and say something of which neither the matter nor the manner recommended her to Mr. Donne's good-will. She would tell him it was no proof of refinement to be ever scolding others for vulgarity; and no sign of a good pastor to be eternally censuring his flock. She would ask him what he had entered the Church for, since he complained there were only cottages to visit, and poor people to preach to?—whether he had been ordained to the ministry merely to wear soft clothing and sit in kings' houses? These questions were considered by all the curates as, to the last degree, audacious and impious.

Tea was a long time in progress: all the guests gabbled as their hostess had expected they would. Mr. Helstone, being in excellent spirits,—when, indeed, was he ever otherwise in society, attractive female society?—it being only with the one lady of his own family that he maintained a grim taciturnity,—kept up a brilliant flow of easy prattle with his right-hand and left-hand neighbours, and even with his *vis-à-vis,* Miss Mary: though as Mary was the most sensible, the least coquettish of the three, to her the elderly widower was the least attentive. At heart, he could not abide sense in women: he liked to see them as silly, as light-headed, as vain, as open to ridicule as possible; because they were then in reality what he held them to be, and wished them to be,—inferior: toys to play with, to amuse a vacant hour and to be thrown away.

Hannah was his favourite. Harriet, though beautiful, egotistical, and self-satisfied, was not quite weak enough for him: she had some genuine self-respect amidst much false pride, and if she did not talk like an oracle, neither would she babble like one crazy: she would not permit herself to be treated quite as a doll, a child, a plaything: she expected to be bent to like a queen.

Hannah, on the contrary, demanded no respect; only flattery: if her admirers only *told* her that she was an angel, she would let them *treat* her like an idiot. So very credulous and frivolous was she; so very silly did she become when besieged with attention, flattered and admired to the proper degree, that there were moments when Helstone actually felt tempted to commit matrimony a second time, and to try the experiment of taking her for his second helpmeet: but, fortunately, the salutary recollection of the ennuis of his first marriage, the impression still left on him of the weight of the millstone he had once worn round his neck, the fixity of his feelings respecting the insufferable evils of conjugal existence, operated as a check to his tenderness, suppressed the sigh heaving his old iron lungs, and restrained

him from whispering to Hannah proposals it would have been high fun and great satisfaction to her to hear.

It is probable she would have married him if he had asked her; her parents would have quite approved the match: to them his fifty-five years, his bend-leather heart, could have presented no obstacles; and, as he was a rector, held an excellent living, occupied a good house, and was supposed even to have private property (though in that the world was mistaken: every penny of the £5000 inherited by him from his father had been devoted to the building and endowing of a new church at his native village in Lancashire—for he could show a lordly munificence when he pleased, and if the end was to his liking, never hesitated about making a grand sacrifice to attain it), her parents I say would have delivered Hannah over to his loving-kindness and his tender mercies without one scruple; and the second Mrs. Helstone, inversing the natural order of insect existence, would have fluttered through the honeymoon a bright, admired butterfly, and crawled the rest of her days a sordid trampled worm.

Little Mr. Sweeting, sitting between Mrs. Sykes and Miss Mary, both of whom were very kind to him, and having a dish of tarts before him, and marmalade and crumpet upon his plate, looked and felt more content than any monarch. He was fond of all the Misses Sykes; they were all fond of him: he thought them magnificent girls, quite proper to mate with one of his inches. If he had a cause of regret at this blissful moment, it was that Miss Dora happened to be absent; Dora being the one whom he secretly hoped one day to call Mrs. David Sweeting, with whom he dreamt of taking stately walks, leading her like an empress through the village of Nunnely: and an empress she would have been, if size could make an empress. She was vast, ponderous: seen from behind, she had the air of a very stout lady of forty; but withal she possessed a good face, and no unkindly character.

The meal at last drew to a close: it would have been over long ago, if Mr. Donne had not persisted in sitting with his cup half full of cold tea before him, long after the rest had finished and after he himself had discussed such allowance of viands as he felt competent to swallow—long, indeed, after signs of impatience had been manifested all round the board: till chairs were pushed back; till the talk flagged; till silence fell. Vainly did Caroline inquire repeatedly if he would have another cup; if he would take a little hot tea, as that must be cold, etc.: he would neither drink it nor leave it. He seemed to think that this isolated position of his gave him somehow a certain importance: that it was dignified and stately to be the last; that it was grand to keep all the others waiting. So long did he linger, that the very urn died: it ceased to hiss. At length, however, the old Rector himself, who had hitherto been too pleasantly engaged with Hannah to care for the delay, got impatient.

"For whom are we waiting?" he asked.

"For me, I believe," returned Donne complacently; appearing to think it much to his credit that a party should thus be kept dependent on his movements.

"Tut!" cried Helstone: then standing up, "Let us return thanks," said he: which he did forthwith, and all quitted the table. Donne, nothing abashed, still sat ten minutes quite alone, whereupon Mr. Helstone rang the bell for the things to be removed; the curate at length saw himself forced to empty his cup, and to relinquish the *rôle* which, he thought, had given him such a felicitous distinction, drawn upon him such flattering general notice.

And now, in the natural course of events (Caroline, knowing how it would be, had opened the piano, and produced music-books in readiness), music was asked for. This was Mr. Sweeting's chance for showing off: he was eager to commence; he undertook, therefore, the arduous task of persuading the young ladies to favour the company with an air—a song. *Con amore,* he went through the whole business of begging, praying, resisting excuses, explaining away difficulties, and at last succeeded in persuading Miss Harriet to allow herself to be led to the instrument. Then out came the pieces of his flute (he always carried them in his pocket, as

unfailingly as he carried his handkerchief). They were screwed and arranged; Malone and Donne meantime herding together, and sneering at him, which the little man, glancing over his shoulder, saw, but did not heed at all: he was persuaded their sarcasm all arose from envy; they could not accompany the ladies as he could; he was about to enjoy a triumph over them.

The triumph began. Malone, much chagrined at hearing him pipe up in most superior style, determined to earn distinction, too, if possible, and all at once assuming the character of a swain (which character he had endeavoured to enact once or twice before, but in which he had not hitherto met with the success he doubtless opined his merits deserved), approached a sofa on which Miss Helstone was seated, and depositing his great Irish frame near her, tried his hand (or rather tongue) at a fine speech or two, accompanied by grins the most extraordinary and incomprehensible. In the course of his efforts to render himself agreeable, he contrived to possess himself of the two long sofa cushions and a square one; with which, after rolling them about for some time with strange gestures, he managed to erect a sort of barrier between himself and the object of his attentions. Caroline, quite willing that they should be sundered, soon devised an excuse for stepping over to the opposite side of the room, and taking up a position beside Mrs. Sykes; of which good lady she entreated some instruction in a new stitch in ornamental knitting, a favour readily granted; and thus Peter Augustus was thrown out.

Very sullenly did his countenance lower when he saw himself abandoned,—left entirely to his own resources, on a large sofa, with the charge of three small cushions on his hands. The fact was, he felt disposed seriously to cultivate acquaintance with Miss Helstone; because he thought, in common with others, that her uncle possessed money, and concluded, that since he had no children, he would probably leave it to his niece. Gérard Moore was better instructed on this point; he had seen the neat church that owed its origin to the Rector's zeal and cash, and more than once, in his inmost soul, had cursed an expensive caprice which crossed his wishes.

The evening seemed long to one person in that room. Caroline at intervals dropped her knitting on her lap, and gave herself up to a sort of brain-lethargy—closing her eyes and depressing her head—caused by what seemed to her the unmeaning hum around her: the inharmonious, tasteless rattle of the piano keys, the squeaking and gasping notes of the flute, the laughter and mirth of her uncle, and Hannah, and Mary, she could not tell whence originating, for she heard nothing comic or gleeful in their discourse; and more than all, by the interminable gossip of Mrs. Sykes murmured close at her ear; gossip which rang the changes on four subjects: her own health and that of the various members of her family; the Missionary and Jew baskets and their contents; the late meeting at Nunnely, and one which was expected to come off next week at Whinbury.

Tired at length to exhaustion, she embraced the opportunity of Mr. Sweeting coming up to speak to Mrs. Sykes, to slip quietly out of the apartment, and seek a moment's respite in solitude. She repaired to the dining-room, where the clear but now low remnant of a fire still burnt in the grate. The place was empty and quiet, glasses and decanters were cleared from the table, the chairs were put back in their places, all was orderly. Caroline sank into her uncle's large easy-chair, half shut her eyes, and rested herself—rested at least her limbs, her senses, her hearing, her vision—weary with listening to nothing, and gazing on vacancy. As to her mind, that flew directly to the Hollow: it stood on the threshold of the parlour there, then it passed to the counting-house, and wondered which spot was blessed by the presence of Robert. It so happened that neither locality had that honour; for Robert was half a mile away from both, and much nearer to Caroline than her deadened spirit suspected: he was at this moment crossing the churchyard, approaching the Rectory garden-gate: not, however, coming to see his cousin, but intent solely on communicating a brief piece of intelligence to the Rector.

Yes, Caroline; you hear the wire of the bell vibrate: it rings again for the fifth time this afternoon: you start, and you are certain now that this must be him of whom you dream. Why you are so certain you cannot explain to yourself, but you know it. You lean forward, listening eagerly as Fanny opens the door: right! that is *the* voice—low—with the slight foreign accent, but so sweet, as you fancy: you half rise: "Fanny will tell him Mr. Helstone is with company and then he will go away." Oh! she cannot let him go: in spite of herself—in spite of her reason she walks half across the room; she stands ready to dart out in case the step should retreat: but he enters the passage. "Since your master is engaged," he says, "just show me into the dining-room; bring me pen and ink: I will write a short note and leave it for him."

Now, having caught these words, and hearing him advance, Caroline, if there was a door within the dining-room, would glide through it and disappear. She feels caught, hemmed in; she dreads her unexpected presence may annoy him. A second since, she would have flown to him; that second past, she would flee from him. She cannot; there is no way of escape: the dining-room has but one door, through which now enters her cousin. The look of troubled surprise she expected to see in his face has appeared there, has shocked her, and is gone. She has stammered a sort of apology—

"I only left the drawing-room a minute for a little quiet."

There was something so diffident and downcast in the air and tone with which she said this, that any one might perceive that some saddening change had lately passed over her prospects, and that the faculty of cheerful self-possession had left her. Mr. Moore, probably, remembered how she had formerly been accustomed to meet him with gentle ardour and hopeful confidence; he must have seen how the check of this morning had operated: here was an opportunity for carrying out his new system with effect, if he chose to improve it. Perhaps he found it easier to practise that system in broad daylight, in his mill-yard, amidst busy occupations, than in a quiet parlour, disengaged, at the hour of eventide. Fanny lit the candles, which before had stood unlit on the table, brought writing materials, and left the room: Caroline was about to follow her. Moore, to act consistently, should have let her go; whereas he stood in the doorway, and, holding out his hand, gently kept her back: he did not ask her to stay, but he would not let her go.

"Shall I tell my uncle you are here?" asked she, still in the same subdued voice.

"No: I can say to you all I had to say to him. You will be my messenger?"

"Yes, Robert."

"Then you may just inform him that I have got a clue to the identity of one, at least, of the men who broke my frames; that he belongs to the same gang who attacked Sykes and Pearson's dressing-shop; and that I hope to have him in custody to-morrow. You can remember that?"

"Oh! yes." These two monosyllables were uttered in a sadder tone than ever; and, as she said them, she shook her head slightly, and sighed. "Will you prosecute him?"

"Doubtless."

"No, Robert."

"And why no, Caroline?"

"Because it will set all the neighbourhood against you more than ever."

"That is no reason why I should not do my duty, and defend my property. This fellow is a great scoundrel, and ought to be incapacitated from perpetrating further mischief."

"But his accomplices will take revenge on you. You do not know how the people of this country bear malice: it is the boast of some of them that they can keep a stone in their pocket seven years, turn it at the end of that time, keep it seven years longer, and hurl it and hit their mark 'at last.' "

Moore laughed.

''A most pithy vaunt,'' said he; ''one that redounds vastly to the credit of your dear Yorkshire friends. But don't fear for me, Lina: I am on my guard against these lamb-like compatriots of yours: don't make yourself uneasy about me.''

''How can I help it? You are my cousin. If anything happened''——she stopped.

''Nothing will happen, Lina. To speak in your own language, there is a Providence above all—is there not?''

''Yes, dear Robert. May He guard you!''

''And if prayers have efficacy, yours will benefit me: you pray for me sometimes?''

''Not *sometimes,* Robert: you, and Louis, and Hortense are *always* remembered.''

''So I have often imagined: it has occurred to me, when, weary and vexed, I have myself gone to bed like a heathen, that another had asked forgiveness for my day and safety for my night. I don't suppose such vicarial piety will avail much; but the petitions come out of a sincere breast, from innocent lips: they should be acceptable as Abel's offering; and doubtless would be if the object deserved them.''

''Annihilate that doubt: it is groundless.''

''When a man has been brought up only to make money, and lives to make it, and for nothing else, and scarcely breathes any other air than that of mills and markets, it seems odd to utter his name in a prayer, or to mix his idea with anything divine; and very strange it seems, that a good, pure heart should take him in and harbour him, as if he had any claim to that sort of nest. If I could guide that benignant heart, I believe I should counsel it to exclude one who does not profess to have any higher aim in life than that of patching up his broken fortune, and wiping clean from his bourgeois scutcheon the foul stain of bankruptcy.''

The hint, though conveyed thus tenderly and modestly (as Caroline thought), was felt keenly and comprehended clearly.

''Indeed, I only think—or I *will only* think—of you as my cousin,'' was the quick answer. ''I am beginning to understand things better than I did, Robert, when you first came to England: better than I did, a week—a day ago. I know it is your duty to try to get on, and that it won't do for you to be romantic; but in future you must not misunderstand me if I seem friendly. You misunderstood me this morning, did you not?''

''What made you think so?''

''Your look—your manner.''

''But look at me now''——

''Oh! you are different now: at present I dare speak to you.''

''Yet I am the same, except that I have left the tradesman behind me in the Hollow: your kinsman alone stands before you.''

''My cousin, Robert; not Mr. Moore.''

''Not a bit of Mr. Moore. Caroline''——

Here the company was heard rising in the other room; the door was opened; the pony-carriage was ordered; shawls and bonnets were demanded; Mr. Helstone called for his niece.

''I must go, Robert.''

''Yes, you must go, or they will come in, and find us here; and I, rather than meet all that host in the passage, will take my departure through the window: luckily, it opens like a door. One minute only—put down the candle an instant— good-night. I kiss you because we are cousins; and, being cousins—one—two— three kisses are allowable. Caroline, good-night!''

Chapter VIII

NOAH AND MOSES

THE next day, Moore had risen before the sun, and had taken a ride to Whinbury and back ere his sister had made the café au lait, or cut the tartines for his breakfast.

What business he transacted there, he kept to himself. Hortense asked no questions: it was not her wont to comment on his movements, nor his to render an account of them. The secrets of business—complicated and often dismal mysteries—were buried in his breast, and never came out of their sepulchre, save now and then to scare Joe Scott, or give a start to some foreign correspondent: indeed, a general habit of reserve on whatever was important seemed bred in his mercantile blood.

Breakfast over, he went to his counting-house. Henry, Joe Scott's boy, brought in the letters and the daily papers; Moore seated himself at his desk, broke the seals of the documents, and glanced them over. They were all short, but not—it seemed—sweet; probably rather sour on the contrary, for as Moore laid down the last, his nostrils emitted a derisive and defiant snuff; and, though he burst into no soliloquy, there was a glance in his eye which seemed to invoke the devil, and lay charges on him to sweep the whole concern to Gehenna. However, having chosen a pen and stripped away the feathered top in a brief spasm of finger-fury—only finger-fury, his face was placid—he dashed off a batch of answers, sealed them, and then went out and walked through the mill: on coming back, he sat down to read his newspaper.

The contents seemed not absorbingly interesting: he more than once laid it across his knee, folded his arms, and gazed into the fire; he occasionally turned his head towards the window: he looked at intervals at his watch: in short, his mind appeared preoccupied. Perhaps he was thinking of the beauty of the weather—for it was a fine and mild morning for the season—and wishing to be out in the fields enjoying it. The door of his counting-house stood wide open, the breeze and sunshine entered freely; but the first visitant brought no spring perfume on its wings, only an occasional sulphur-puff from the soot-thick column of smoke rushing sable from the gaunt mill-chimney.

A dark blue apparition (that of Joe Scott, fresh from a dyeing vat) appeared momentarily at the open door, uttered the words "He's comed, sir," and vanished.

Mr. Moore raised not his eyes from the paper. A large man, broad-shouldered and massive-limbed, clad in fustian garments and grey-worsted stockings, entered, who was received with a nod, and desired to take a seat, which he did, making the remark—as he removed his hat (a very bad one), stowed it away under his chair, and wiped his forehead with a spotted cotton handkerchief extracted from the hat-crown—that it was "raight dahn warm for Febewerry." Mr. Moore assented: at least he uttered some slight sound, which, though inarticulate, might pass for an assent. The visitor now carefully deposited in the corner beside him an official-looking staff which he bore in his hand; this done, he whistled, probably by way of appearing at his ease.

"You have what is necessary, I suppose?" said Mr. Moore.

"Ay! ay! all's right."

He renewed his whistling, Mr. Moore his reading: the paper apparently had become more interesting. Presently, however, he turned to his cupboard, which was within reach of his long arm, opened it without rising, took out a black bottle—the same he had produced for Malone's benefit—a tumbler, and a jug, placed them on the table, and said to his guest—

"Help yourself; there's water in that jar in the corner."

"I dunnut knaw that there's mich need, for all a body is dry (thirsty) in a morning," said the fustian gentleman, rising and doing as requested.

"Will you tak' naught yourseln, Mr. Moore?" he inquired as with skilled hand he mixed a portion, and having tested it by a deep draught, sank back satisfied and bland in his seat. Moore—chary of words—replied by a negative movement and murmur.

"Yah'd as good," continued his visitor; "it'uld set ye up, wald a sup o' this stuff. Uncommon good Hollands! ye get it fro' furrin' parts, I'se think?"

"Ay!"

"Tak' my advice, and try a glass on't; them lads 'at's coming 'll keep ye talking, nob'dy knows how long: ye'll need propping."

"Have you seen Mr. Sykes this moring?" inquired Moore.

"I seed him a hauf an hour—nay—happen a quarter of an hour sin', just afore I set off: he said he aimed to come here, and I sudn't wonder but ye'll have old Helstone too; I seed 'em saddling his little nag as I passed at back o' t' Rectory."

The speaker was a true prophet, for the trot of a little nag's hoofs was, five minutes after, heard in the yard; it stopped, and a well-known nasal voice cried aloud—"Boy" (probably addressing Harry Scott, who usually hung about the premises from nine A.M. to five P.M.), "take my horse and lead him into the stable."

Helstone came in marching nimbly and erect, looking browner, keener, and livelier than usual.

"Beautiful morning, Moore: how do, my boy? Ha! Whom have we here?" (turning to the personage with the staff). "Sugden! What! you're going to work directly? On my word, you lose no time: but I come to ask explanations: your message was delivered to me; are you sure you are on the right scent? How do you mean to set about the business? Have you got a warrant?"

"Sugden has."

"Then you are going to seek him now? I'll accompany you."

"You will be spared that trouble, sir; he is coming to seek me. I'm just now sitting in state, waiting his arrival."

"And who is it? One of my parishioners?"

Joe Scott had entered unobserved; he now stood, a most sinister phantom, half his person being dyed of the deepest tint of indigo, leaning on the desk. His master's answer to the Rector's question was a smile; Joe took the word; putting on a quiet but pawky look, he said—

"It's a friend of yours, Mr. Helstone; a gentleman you often speak of."

"Indeed! His name, Joe?—You look well this morning."

"Only the Rev. Moses Barraclough: 't tub orator you call him sometimes, I think."

"Ah!" said the Rector, taking out his snuff-box, and administering to himself a very long pinch—"Ah! couldn't have supposed it. Why, the pious man never was a workman of yours, Moore? He's a tailor by trade."

"And so much the worse grudge I owe him, for interfering, and setting my discarded men against me."

"And Moses was actually present at the battle of Stilbro' Moor? He went there—wooden leg and all?"

"Ay, sir," said Joe; "he went there on horseback, that his leg mightn't be noticed: he was the captain and wore a mask; the rest only had their faces blacked."

"And how was he found out?"

"I'll tell you, sir," said Joe: "t' maister's not so fond of talking; I've no objections. He courted Sarah, Mr. Moore's sarvant lass, and so it seems she would have nothing to say to him; she either didn't like his wooden leg, or she'd some notion about his being a hypocrite. Happen (for women is queer hands—we may say that amang werseln when there's none of 'em nigh) she'd have encouraged him, in spite of his leg and his deceit—just to pass time like; I've known some on 'em do as mich, and some o' t' bonniest and mimmest-looking too—ay! I've seen clean, trim young things, that looked as denty and pure as daisies, and wi' time a body fun' 'em out to be nowt but stinging, venomed nettles."

"Joe's a sensible fellow," interjected Helstone.

"Howsiver, Sarah had another string to her bow: Fred Murgatroyd, one of our lads, is for her, and as women judge men by their faces—and Fred has a middling face, while Moses is none so handsome, as we all knaw—the lass took on wi' Fred. A two-three months sin', Murgatroyd and Moses chanced to meet one Sunday night; they'd both come lurking about these premises wi' the notion of counselling

Sarah to tak' a bit of a walk wi' them; they fell out, had a tussle, and Fred was worsted; for he's young and small, and Barraclough, for all he has only one leg, is almost as strong as Sugden there; indeed, anybody that hears him roaring at a revival or a love-feast, may be sure he's no weakling.''

"Joe, you're insupportable,'' here broke in Mr. Moore. "You spin out your explanation as Moses spins out his sermons. The long and short of it is, Murgatroyd was jealous of Barraclough; and last night, as he and a friend took shelter in a barn from a shower, they heard and saw Moses conferring with some associates within. From their discourse, it was plain he had been the leader, not only at Stilbro' Moor, but in the attack on Sykes's property: moreover they planned a deputation to wait on me this morning, which the tailor is to head, and which, in the most religious and peaceful spirit, is to entreat me to put the accursed thing out of my tent. I rode over to Whinbury this morning, got a constable and a warrant, and I am now waiting to give my friend the reception he deserves; here, meantime, comes Sykes; Mr. Helstone, you must spirit him up; he feels timid at the thoughts of prosecuting.''

A gig was heard to roll into the yard: Mr. Sykes entered; a tall stout man of about fifty, comely of feature, but feeble of physiognomy: he looked anxious.

"Have they been? Are they gone? Have you got him? Is it over?'' he asked.

"Not yet,'' returned Moore with phlegm. "We are waiting for them.''

"They'll not come; it's near noon: better give it up; it will excite bad feeling—make a stir—cause perhaps fatal consequences.''

"*You* need not appear,'' said Moore. "I shall meet them in the yard when they come; *you* can stay here.''

"But my name must be seen in the law proceedings: a wife and family, Mr. Moore—a wife and family make a man cautious.''

Moore looked disgusted. "Give way, if you please,'' said he; "leave me to myself; I have no objection to act alone: only be assured you will not find safety in submission: your partner, Pearson, gave way, and conceded, and forebore—well, that did not prevent them from attempting to shoot him in his own house.''

"My dear sir, take a little wine and water,'' recommended Mr. Helstone. The wine and water was Hollands and water, as Mr. Sykes discovered when he had compounded and swallowed a brimming tumbler thereof; it transfigured him in two minutes, brought the colour back to his face, and made him at least *word*-valiant. He now announced that he hoped he was above being trampled on by the common people; he was determined to endure the insolence of the working-classes no longer; he had considered of it and made up his mind to go all lengths; if money and spirit could put down these rioters, they should be put down; Mr. Moore might do as he liked, but *he*—Christie Sykes—would spend his last penny in law before he would be beaten: he'd settle them, or he'd see.

"Take another glass,'' urged Moore.

Mr. Sykes didn't mind if he did; this was a cold morning (Sugden had found it a warm one); it was necessary to be careful at this season of the year—it was proper to take something to keep the damp out; he had a little cough already (here he coughed in attestation of the fact); something of this sort (lifting the black bottle) was excellent, taken medicinally (he poured the physic into his tumbler); he didn't make a practice of drinking spirits in a morning, but occasionally it really was prudent to take precautions.

"Quite prudent, and take them by all means,'' urged the host.

Mr. Sykes now addressed Mr. Helstone, who stood on the hearth, his shovel-hat on his head, watching him significantly with his little, keen eyes.

"You, sir, as a clergyman,'' said he, "may feel it disagreeable to be present amidst scenes of hurry and flurry, and, I may say, peril: I dare say your nerves won't stand it; you're a man of peace, sir, but we manufacturers, living in the world, and always in turmoil, get quite belligerent. Really, there's an ardour excited by the thoughts of danger that makes my heart pant. When Mrs. Sykes is afraid of

the house being attacked and broke open—as she is every night—I get quite excited. I couldn't describe to you, sir, my feelings: really, if anybody was to come— thieves or anything—I believe I should enjoy it, such is my spirit.''

The hardest of laughs, though brief and low, and by no means insulting, was the response of the Rector. Moore would have pressed upon the heroic mill-owner a third tumbler, but the clergyman, who never transgressed, nor would suffer others in his presence to transgress the bounds of decorum, checked him.

"Enough is as good as a feast, is it not, Mr. Sykes?'' he said, and Mr. Sykes assented; and then sat and watched Joe Scott remove the bottle at a sign from Helstone, with a self-satisfied simper on his lips, and a regretful glisten in his eye. Moore looked as if he should have liked to fool him to the top of his bent. What would a certain young kinswoman of his have said could she have seen her dear, good, great Robert—her Coriolanus—just now? Would she have acknowledged in that mischievous, sardonic visage the same face to which she had looked up with such love, which had bent over her with such gentleness last night? Was that the man who had spent so quiet an evening with his sister and his cousin—so suave to one, so tender to the other—reading Shakespeare and listening to Chénier?

Yes, it was the same man, only seen on a different side; a side Caroline had not yet fairly beheld, though perhaps she had enough sagacity faintly to suspect its existence. Well, Caroline had, doubtless, her defective side too: she was human, she must, then, have been very imperfect, and had she seen Moore on his very worst side, she would probably have said this to herself and excused him. Love can excuse anything except Meanness; but Meanness kills Love, cripples even Natural Affection; without Esteem, True Love cannot exist. Moore with all his faults might be esteemed; for he had no moral scrofula in his mind, no hopeless polluting taint, such, for instance, as that of falsehood; neither was he the slave of his appetites; the active life to which he had been born and bred had given him something else to do than to join the futile chase of the pleasure-hunter: he was a man undegraded, the disciple of Reason, *not* the votary of Sense. The same might be said of old Helstone: neither of these two would look, think, or speak a lie; for neither of them had the wretched black bottle, which had just been put away, any charms; both might boast a valid claim to the proud title of "lord of the creation,'' for no animal vice was lord of them: they looked and were superior beings to poor Sykes.

A sort of gathering and trampling sound was heard in the yard, and then a pause. Moore walked to the window, Helstone followed; both stood on one side, the tall junior behind the under-sized senior, looking forth carefully, so that they might not be visible from without; their sole comment on what they saw was a cynical smile flashed into each other's stern eyes.

A flourishing oratorical cough was now heard, followed by the interjection "Wisht!'' designed, as it seemed, to still the hum of several voices. Moore opened his casement an inch or two to admit sound more freely.

"Joseph Scott,'' began a snuffing voice—Scott was standing sentinel at the counting-house door—"might we inquire if your master be within, and is to be spoken to?''

"He's within, ay!'' said Joe nonchalantly.

"Would you, then, if *you* please'' (emphasis on "you''), "have the goodness to tell *him* that twelve gentlemen wants to see him.''

"He'd happen to ax what for,'' suggested Joe. "I mught as weel tell him at t' same time.''

"For a purpose,'' was the answer. Joe entered.

"Please, sir, there's twelve gentlemen wants to see ye, 'for a purpose.' ''

"Good, Joe; I'm their man. Sugden, come when I whistle.''

Moore went out, chuckling drily. He advanced into the yard, one hand in his pocket, the other in his waistcoat, his cap brim over his eyes, shading in some

measure their deep dancing ray of scorn. Twelve men waited in the yard, some in their shirt-sleeves, some in blue aprons: two figured conspicuously in the van of the party. One, a little dapper strutting man, with a turued-up nose: the other, a broad-shouldered fellow, distinguished no less by his demure face and cat-like, trustless eyes, than by a wooden leg and stout crutch: there was a kind of leer about his lips, he seemed laughing in his sleeve at some person or thing, his whole air was anything but that of a true man.

"Good-morning, Mr. Barraclough," said Moore debonairly, for him.

"Peace be unto you!" was the answer: Mr. Barraclough entirely closing his naturally half-shut eyes as he delivered it.

"I'm obliged to you: peace is an excellent thing; there's nothing I more wish for myself; but that is not all you have to say to me, I suppose? I imagine peace is not your purpose?"

"As to our purpose," began Barraclough, "it's one that may sound strange, and perhaps foolish to ears like yours, for the childer of this world is wiser in their generation than the childer of light."

"To the point, if you please, and let me hear what it is."

"Ye'se hear, sir; if I cannot get it off, there's eleven behint can help me. It is a grand purpose, and" (changing his voice from a half-sneer to a whine) "it's the Looard's own purpose, and that's better."

"Do you want a subscription to a new Ranter's chapel, Mr. Barraclough? Unless your errand be something of that sort, I cannot see what you have to do with it."

"I hadn't that duty on my mind, sir; but as Providence has led ye to mention the subject, I'll make it i' my way to tak' ony trifle ye may have to spare; the smallest contribution will be acceptable."

With that he doffed his hat, and held it out as a begging-box; a brazen grin at the same time crossing his countenance.

"If I gave you sixpence, you would drink it."

Barraclough uplifted the palms of his hands and the whites of his eyes, evincing in the gesture a mere burlesque of hypocrisy.

"You seem a fine fellow," said Moore, quite coolly and drily; "you don't care for showing me that you are a double-dyed hypocrite, that your trade is fraud: you expect indeed to make me laugh at the cleverness with which you play your coarsely farcical part, while at the same time you think you are deceiving the men behind you."

Moses's countenance lowered; he saw he had gone too far: he was going to answer, when the second leader, impatient of being hitherto kept in the background, stepped forward. This man did not look like a traitor, though he had an exceedingly self-confident and conceited air.

"Mr. Moore," commenced he, speaking also in his throat and nose, and enunciating each word very slowly, as if with a view to giving his audience time to appreciate fully the uncommon elegance of the phraseology; "it might, perhaps, justly be said that reason rather than peace is our purpose. We come, in the first place, to request you to hear reason, and should *you* refuse, it is my duty to warn *you*, in very decided terms, that measures will be had resort to" (he meant recourse), "which will probably terminate in—in bringing *you* to a sense of the unwisdom, of the— the foolishness, which seems to guide and guard your perceedings as a tradesman in this manufacturing part of the country. Hem! . . . Sir, I would beg to allude that as a furriner, coming from a distant coast, another quarter and hemisphere of this globe, thrown, as I may say, a perfect outcast on these shores—the cliffs of Albion— you have not that understanding of huz and wer ways which might conduce to the benefit of the working classes. If, to come at once to partic'lars, you'd consider to give up this here miln, and go without further protractions straight home to where you belong, it 'ud happen be as well. I can see naught ageean such a plan. What

hev ye to say tull't, lads?'' turning round to the other members of the deputation, who responded unanimously, ''Hear, hear!''

''Brayvo, Noah o' Tim's!'' murmured Joe Scott, who stood behind Mr. Moore. ''Moses'll never beat that—Cliffs o' Albion, and t' other hemisphere! my certy! Did ye come fro' th' Antarctic Zone, maister? Moses is dished.''

Moses, however, refused to be dished; he thought he would try again. Casting a somewhat ireful glance at ''Noah o' Tim's,'' he launched out in his turn: and now he spoke in a serious tone, relinquishing the sarcasm which he found had not answered.

''Or iver you set up the pole o' your tent amang us, Mr. Moore, we lived i' peace and quietness; yea, I may say, in all loving-kindness. I am not myself an aged person as yet, but I can remember as far back as maybe some twenty year, when hand-labour were encouraged and respected, and no mischief-maker had ventured to introduce these here machines, which is so pernicious. Now, I am not a cloth-dresser myself, but by trade a tailor; howsiver, my heart is of a softish natur': I'm a very feeling man, and when I see my brethren oppressed, like my great namesake of old, I stand up for 'em; for which intent, I this day speak with you face to face, and advises you to part wi' your infernal machinery and tak' on more hands.''

''What if I don't follow your advice, Mr. Barraclough?''

''The Looard pardon you! The Looard soften your heart, sir!''

''Are you in connection with the Wesleyans now, Mr. Barraclough?''

''Praise God! Bless His name! I'm a joined Methody!''

''Which in no respect prevents you from being at the same time a drunkard and a swindler. I saw you one night a week ago laid dead-drunk by the road-side, as I returned from Stilbro' market; and while you preach peace, you make it the business of your life to stir up dissension. You no more sympathise with the poor who are in distress, than you sympathise with me: you incite them to outrage for bad purposes of your own; so does the individual called Noah o' Tim's. You two are restless, meddling, impudent scoundrels, whose chief motive principle is a selfish ambition, as dangerous as it is puerile. The persons behind you are some of them honest though misguided men; but you two I count altogether bad.''

Barraclough was going to speak.

''Silence! You have had your say, and now I will have mine. As to being dictated to by you or any Jack, Jem, or Jonathan on earth, I shall not suffer it for a moment. You desire me to quit the country: you request me to part with my machinery; in case I refuse, you threaten me. I *do* refuse—point-blank! Here I stay; and by this mill I stand; and into it will I convey the best machinery inventors can furnish. What will you do? The utmost you *can* do—and this you will never *dare* to do— is to burn down my mill, destroy its contents, and shoot me. What then? Suppose that building was a ruin and I was a corpse, what then?—you lads behind these two scamps, would that stop invention or exhaust science?—Not for the fraction of a second of time! Another and better gig mill would rise on the ruins of this, and perhaps a more enterprising owner come in my place. Hear me!—I'll make my cloth as I please, and according to the best lights I have. In its manufacture I will employ what means I choose. Whoever, after hearing this, shall dare to interfere with me, may just take the consequences. An example shall prove I'm in earnest.''

He whistled shrill and loud. Sugden, his staff and warrant, came on to the scene.

Moore turned sharply to Barraclough: ''You were at Stilbro','' said he; ''I have proof of that. You were on the moor,—you wore a mask,—you knocked down one of my men with your own hand,—you! a preacher of the Gospel! Sugden, arrest him!''

Moses was captured. There was a cry and a rush to rescue, but the right hand which all this while had lain hidden in Moore's breast, reappearing, held out a pistol.

"Both barrels are loaded," said he. "I'm quite determined!—keep off!"

Stepping backwards, facing the foe as he went, he guarded his prey to the counting-house. He ordered Joe Scott to pass in with Sugden and the prisoner, and to bolt the door inside. For himself, he walked backwards and forwards along the front of the mill, looking meditatively on the ground, his hand hanging carelessly by his side, but still holding the pistol. The eleven remaining deputies watched him some time, talking under their breath to each other: at length one of them approached. This man looked very different from either of the two who had previously spoken: he was hard-favoured, but modest, and manly-looking.

"I've not much faith i' Moses Barraclough," said he, "and I would speak a word to you myseln, Mr. Moore. It's out o' no ill-will that I am here, for my part; it's just to mak' an effort to get things straightened, for they're sorely a crooked. Ye see we're ill off—varry ill off: wer families is poor and pined. We're thrown out o' work wi' these frames: we can get nought to do: we can earn nought. What is to be done? Mun we say, wisht! and lig us down and dee? Nay: I've no grand words at my tongue's end, Mr. Moore, but I feel that it would be a low principle for a reasonable man to starve to death like a dumb creatur':—I will n't do't. I'm not for shedding blood: I'd neither kill a man nor hurt a man; and I'm not for pulling down mills and breaking machines: for, as ye say, that way o' going on'll niver stop invention; but I'll talk—I'll mak' as big a din as ever I can. Invention may be all right, but I know it isn't right for poor folks to starve. Them that governs mun find a way to help us: they mun mak' fresh orderations. Ye'll say that's hard to do:—so mich louder mun we shout out then, for so much slacker will t' Parliament-men be to set on to a tough job."

"Worry the Parliament-men as much as you please," said Moore; "but to worry the mill-owners is absurd; and I, for one, won't stand it."

"Ye're a raight hard'un!" returned the workman. "Will n't ye gie us a bit o' time?—Will n't ye consent to mak' your changes rather more slowly?"

"Am I the whole body of clothiers in Yorkshire? Answer me that!"

"Ye're yourseln."

"And only myself! and if I stopped by the way an instant, while others are rushing on, I should be trodden down. If I did as you wish me to do, I should be bankrupt in a month: and would my bankruptcy put bread into your hungry children's mouths? William Farren, neither to your dictation, nor to that of any other, will I submit, Talk to me no more about machinery; I will have my own way. I shall get new frames in to-morrow:—If you broke these, I would still get more. *I'll never give in.*"

Here the mill-bell rang twelve o'clock: it was the dinner-hour. Moore abruptly turned from the deputation and reentered his counting-house.

His last words had left a bad, harsh impression: he, at least, had "failed in the disposing of a chance he was lord of." By speaking kindly to William Farren—who was a very honest man, without envy or hatred of those more happily circumstanced than himself; thinking it no hardship and no injustice to be forced to live by labour; disposed to be honourably content if he could but get work to do—Moore might have made a friend. It seemed wonderful how he could turn from such a man without a conciliatory or a sympathising expression. The poor fellow's face looked haggard with want: he had the aspect of a man who had not known what it was to live in comfort and plenty for weeks, perhaps months past: and yet there was no ferocity, no malignity in his countenance: it was worn, dejected, austere, but still patient. How could Moore leave him thus, with the words "I'll never give in," and not a whisper of good-will, or hope, or aid?

Farren, as he went home to his cottage—once, in better times, a decent, clean, pleasant place, but now, though still clean, very dreary, because so poor—asked himself this question. He concluded that the foreign mill-owner was a selfish, an unfeeling, and, he thought, too, a foolish man. It appeared to him that emigration,

had he only the means to emigrate, would be preferable to service under such a master. He felt much cast down—almost hopeless.

On his entrance, his wife served out, in orderly sort, such dinner as she had to give him and the bairns: it was only porridge, and too little of that. Some of the younger children asked for more when they had done their portion—an application which disturbed William much: while his wife quieted them as well as she could, he left his seat and went to the door. He whistled a cheery stave, which did not, however, prevent a broad drop or two (much more like the "first of a thunder-shower" than those which oozed from the wound of the gladiator) from gathering on the lids of his grey eyes, and plashing thence to the threshold. He cleared his vision with his sleeve, and the melting mood over, a very stern one followed.

He still stood brooding in silence, when a gentleman in black came up—a clergyman, it might be seen at once; but neither Helstone, nor Malone, nor Donne, nor Sweeting. He might be forty years old: he was plain-looking, dark-complexioned, and already rather grey-haired. He stooped a little in walking. His countenance, as he came on, wore an abstracted and somewhat doleful air; but, in approaching Farren, he looked up, and then a hearty expression illuminated the preoccupied, serious face.

"Is it you, William? How are you?" he asked.

"Middling, Mr. Hall; how are *ye? Will* ye step in and rest ye?"

Mr. Hall, whose name the reader has seen mentioned before (and who, indeed, was vicar of Nunnely, of which parish Farren was a native, and from whence he had removed but three years ago to reside in Briarfield, for the convenience of being near Hollow's Mill, where he had obtained work), entered the cottage, and, having greeted the good wife and the children, sat down. He proceeded to talk very cheerfully about the length of time that had elapsed since the family quitted his parish, the changes which had occurred since; he answered questions touching his sister Margaret, who was inquired after with much interest; he asked questions in his turn, and at last, glancing hastily and anxiously round through his spectacles (he wore spectacles, for he was short-sighted) at the bare room, and at the meagre and wan faces of the circle about him—for the children had come round his knee, and the father and mother stood before him—he said abruptly—"And how are you all? How do you get on?"

Mr. Hall, be it remarked, though an accomplished scholar, not only spoke with a strong northern accent, but, on occasion, used freely north-country expressions.

"We get on poorly," said William: "we're all out of work. I've selled most o' t' household stuff, as you may see; and what we're to do next, God knows."

"Has Mr. Moore turned you off?"

"He has turned us off; and I've sich an opinion of him now, that I think, if he'd tak' me on again to-morrow, I wouldn't work for him."

"It is not like you to say so, William."

"I know it isn't; but I'm getting different to mysel': I feel I am changing. I wadn't heed, if t' bairns and t' wife had enough to live on; but they're pinched—they're pined"——

"Well, my lad, and so are you; I see you are. These are grievous times; I see suffering wherever I turn. William, sit down; Grace, sit down; let us talk it over."

And in order the better to talk it over, Mr. Hall lifted the least of the children on to his knee, and placed his hand on the head of the next least; but when the small things began to chatter to him he bid them "Wisht!" and, fixing his eyes on the grate, he regarded the handful of embers which burnt there very gravely.

"Sad times!" he said, "and they last long. It is the will of God: His will be done! but He tries us to the utmost."

Again he reflected.

"You've no money, William, and you've nothing you could sell to raise a small sum?"

"No; I've selled t' chest o' drawers, and t' clock, and t' bit of a mahogany stand, and t' wife's bonny tea-tray and set o' cheeney 'at she brought for a portion when we were wed."

"And if somebody lent you a pound or two, could you make any good use of it? Could you get into a new way of doing something?"

Farren did not answer; but his wife said quickly, "Ay, I'm sure he could, sir; he's a very contriving chap, is our William. If he'd two or three pounds, he could begin selling stuff."

"Could you, William?"

"Please God," returned William deliberately, "I could buy groceries, and bits o' tapes, and thread, and what I thought would sell, and I could begin hawking at first."

"And you know, sir," interposed Grace, "you're sure William would neither drink, nor idle, nor waste, in any way. He's my husband, and I shouldn't praise him; but I *will* say there's not a soberer, honester man i' England nor he is."

"Well, I'll speak to one or two friends, and I think I can promise to let him have £5 in a day or two: as a loan, ye mind, not a gift: he must pay it back."

"I understand, sir: I'm quite agreeable to that."

"Meantime, there's a few shillings for you, Grace, just to keep the pot boiling till custom comes. Now, bairns, stand up in a row and say your catechism, while your mother goes and buys some dinner: for you've not had much to-day, I'll be bound. You begin, Ben. What is your name?"

Mr. Hall stayed till Grace came back; then he hastily took his leave, shaking hands with both Farren and his wife: just at the door, he said to them a few brief but very earnest words of religious consolation and exhortation: with a mutual "God bless you, sir!" "God bless you, my friends!" they separated.

Chapter IX

BRIARMAINS

MESSRS. Helstone and Sykes began to be extremely jocose and congratulatory with Mr. Moore when he returned to them after dismissing the deputation; he was so quiet, however, under their compliments upon his firmness, etc., and wore a countenance so like a still, dark day, equally beamless and breezeless, that the Rector, after glancing shrewdly into his eyes, buttoned up his felicitations with his coat, and said to Sykes, whose senses were not acute enough to enable him to discover unassisted where his presence and conversation were a nuisance—"Come, sir; your road and mine lie partly together: had we not better bear each other company? We'll bid Moore good-morning, and leave him to the happy fancies he seems disposed to indulge."

"And where is Sugden?" demanded Moore, looking up.

"Ah, ha!" cried Helstone. "I've not been quite idle while you were busy. I've been helping you a little: I flatter myself, not injudiciously. I thought it better not to lose time; so, while you were parleying with that down-looking gentleman— Farren, I think his name is,—I opened this back window, shouted to Murgatroyd, who was in the stable, to bring Mr. Sykes's gig round; then I smuggled Sugden and brother Moses—wooden leg and all—through the aperture, and saw them mount the gig (always with our good friend Sykes's permission, of course). Sugden took the reins—he drives like Jehu, and in another quarter of an hour Barraclough will be safe in Stilbro' jail."

"Very good: thank you," said Moore, "and good-morning, gentlemen," he added, and so politely conducted them to the door and saw them clear of his premises.

He was a taciturn, serious man the rest of the day: he did not even bandy a repartee with Joe Scott; who, for his part, said to his master only just what was absolutely necessary to the progress of business, but looked at him a good deal out of the corners of his eyes, frequently came to poke the counting-house fire for him, and once, as he was locking up for the day (the mill was then working short time, owing to the slackness of trade), observed that it was a grand evening, and he "could wish Mr. Moore to take a bit of a walk up th' Hollow; it would do him good."

At this recommendation Mr. Moore burst into a short laugh, and after demanding of Joe what all this solicitude meant, and whether he took him for a woman or a child, seized the keys from his hand, and shoved him by the shoulders out of his presence. He called him back, however, ere he had reached the yard-gate.

"Joe, do you know those Farrens? They are not well off, I suppose?"

"They cannot be well off, sir, when they've not had work as a three month. Ye'd see yoursel' 'at William's sorely changed,—fair pared: they've selled most o' t' stuff out o' th' house."

"He was not a bad workman?"

"Ye never had a better, sir, sin' ye began trade."

"And decent people—the whole family?"

"Niver dacenter: th' wife's a raight cant body, and as clean——! ye mught eat your porridge off th' house floor: they're sorely comed down. I wish William could get a job as gardener or summat i' that way; he understands gardening weel. He once lived wi' a Scotchman that tached him the mysteries o' that craft, as they say."

"Now, then, you can go, Joe; you need not stand there staring at me."

"Ye've no orders to give, sir?"

"None, but for you to take yourself off."

Which Joe did accordingly.

Spring evenings are often cold and raw, and though this had been a fine day, warm even in the morning and meridian sunshine, the air chilled at sunset, the ground crisped, and ere dusk a hoar frost was insidiously stealing over growing grass and unfolding bud. It whitened the pavement in front of Briarmains (Mr. Yorke's residence), and made silent havoc among the tender plants in his garden, and on the mossy level of his lawn. As to that great tree, strong-trunked and broad-armed, which guarded the gable nearest the road, it seemed to defy a spring-night frost to harm its still bare boughs; and so did the leafless grove of walnut-trees rising tall behind the house.

In the dusk of the moonless if starry night, lights from windows shone vividly; this was no dark or lonely scene, nor even a silent one. Briarmains stood near the highway, it was rather an old place, and had been built ere that highway was cut, and when a lane winding up through fields was the only path conducting to it. Briarfield lay scarce a mile off; its hum was heard, its glare distinctly seen. Briar Chapel, a large, new, raw, Wesleyan place of worship, rose but a hundred yards distant; and, as there was even now a prayer-meeting being held within its walls, the illumination of its windows cast a bright reflection on the road, while a hymn of a most extraordinary description, such as a very Quaker might feel himself moved by the spirit to dance to, roused cheerily all the echoes of the vicinage. The words were distinctly audible by snatches: here is a quotation or two from different strains; for the singers passed jauntily from hymn to hymn and from tune to tune, with an ease and buoyancy all their own.

> *Oh! who can explain*
> *This struggle for life,*

> *This travail and pain,*
> *This trembling and strife?*
> *Plague, earthquake, and famine,*
> *And tumult and war,*
> *The wonderful coming*
> *Of Jesus declare!*

> *For every fight*
> *Is dreadful and loud,—*
> *The warrior's delight*
> *Is slaughter and blood;*
> *His foes overturning,*
> *Till all shall expire,—*
> *And this is with burning,*
> *And fuel, and fire!*

Here followed an interval of clamorous prayer, accompanied by fearful groans. A shout of "I've found liberty!" "Doad o'Bill's has fun' liberty!" rung from the chapel, and out all the assembly broke again.

> *What a mercy is this!*
> *What a heaven of bliss!*
> *How unspeakable happy am I.*
> *Gather'd into the fold,*
> *With thy people enroll'd,*
> *With thy people to live and to die!*

> *Oh, the goodness of God*
> *In employing a clod*
> *His tribute of glory to raise;*
> *His standard to bear,*
> *And with triumph declare*
> *His unspeakable riches of grace!*

> *Oh, the fathomless love,*
> *That has deign'd to approve*
> *And prosper the work of my hands,*
> *With my pastoral crook,*
> *I went over the brook,*
> *And behold I am spread into bands!*

> *Who, I ask in amaze,*
> *Hath begotten me these?*
> *And inquire from what quarter they came;*
> *My full heart it replies,*
> *They are born from the skies,*
> *And gives glory to God and the Lamb!*

The stanza which followed this, after another and longer interregnum of shouts, yells, ejaculations, frantic cries, agonised groans, seemed to cap the climax of noise and zeal.

> *Sleeping on the brink of sin,*
> *Tophet gaped to take us in;*

> *Mercy to our rescue flew,—*
> *Broke the snare, and brought us through.*

> *Here, as in a lion's den,*
> *Undevour'd we still remain;*
> *Pass secure the watery flood,*
> *Hanging on the arm of God.*

> *Here—*

(Terrible, most distracting to the ear was the strained shout in which the last stanza was given.)

> *Here we raise our voices higher,*
> *Shout in the refiner's fire;*
> *Clap our hands amidst the flame,*
> *Glory give to Jesus' name!*

The roof of the chapel did *not* fly off; which speaks volumes in praise of its solid slating.

But if Briar chapel seemed alive, so also did Briarmains: though certainly the mansion appeared to enjoy a quieter phase of existence than the temple; some of its windows too were aglow: the lower casements opened upon the lawn, curtains concealed the interior, and partly obscured the ray of the candles which lit it, but they did not entirely muffle the sound of voice and laughter. We are privileged to enter that front-door, and to penetrate to the domestic sanctum.

It is not the presence of company which makes Mr. Yorke's habitation lively, for there is none within it save his own family, and they are assembled in that farthest room to the right, the back parlour.

This is the usual sitting room of an evening. Those windows would be seen by daylight to be of brilliantly-stained glass—purple and amber the predominant hues, glittering round a gravely tinted medallion in the centre of each, representing the suave head of William Shakespeare, and the serene one of John Milton. Some Canadian views hang on the walls—green forest and blue water scenery—and in the midst of them blazes a night-eruption of Vesuvius; very ardently it glows, contrasted with the cool foam and azure of cataracts, and the dusky depths of woods.

The fire illuminating this room, reader, is such as, if you be a southern, you do not often see burning on the hearth of a private apartment; it is a clear, hot, coal fire, heaped high in the ample chimney. Mr. Yorke *will* have such fires even in warm summer weather: he sits beside it with a book in his hand, a little round stand at his elbow supporting a candle—but he is not reading, he is watching his children. Opposite to him sits his lady—a personage whom I might describe minutely, but I feel no vocation to the task. I see her, though, very plainly before me: a large woman of the gravest aspect, care on her front and on her shoulders—but not overwhelming, inevitable care—rather the sort of voluntary, exemplary cloud and burden people ever carry who deem it their duty to be gloomy. Ah, well-a-day! Mrs. Yorke had that notion, and grave as Saturn she was, morning, noon, and night; and hard things she thought of any unhappy wight—especially of the female sex—who dared in her presence to show the light of a gay heart on a sunny countenance. In her estimation, to be mirthful was to be profane; to be cheerful was to be frivolous: she drew no distinctions. Yet she was a very good wife, a very careful mother, looked after her children unceasingly, was sincerely attached to her husband; only the worst of it was, if she could have had her will, she would

not have permitted him to have any friend in the world beside herself: all his relations were insupportable to her, and she kept them at arm's length.

Mr. Yorke and she agreed perfectly well; yet he was naturally a social, hospitable man—an advocate for family unity—and in his youth, as has been said, he liked none but lively, cheerful women. Why he chose her—how they contrived to suit each other, is a problem puzzling enough, but which might soon be solved if one had time to go into the analysis of the case. Suffice it here to say, that Yorke had a shadowy as well as a sunny side to his character, and that his shadowy side found sympathy and affinity in the whole of his wife's uniformly overcast nature. For the rest, she was a strong-minded woman; never said a weak or a trite thing; took stern, democratic views of society, and rather cynical ones of human nature; considered herself perfect and safe, and the rest of the world all wrong. Her main fault was a brooding, eternal, immitigable suspicion of all men, things, creeds, and parties: this suspicion was a mist before her eyes, a false guide in her path, wherever she looked, wherever she turned.

It may be supposed that the children of such a pair were not likely to turn out quite ordinary, commonplace beings; and they were not. You see six of them, reader: the youngest is a baby on the mother's knee; it is all her own yet—and that one she has not yet begun to doubt, suspect, condemn; it derives its sustenance from her, it hangs on her, it clings to her, it loves her above everything else in the world: she is sure of that, because, as it lives by her, it cannot be otherwise, therefore she loves it.

The two next are girls, Rose and Jessy; they are both now at their father's knee; they seldom go near their mother, except when obliged to do so. Rose, the elder, is twelve years old; she is like her father—the most like him of the whole group— but it is a granite head copied in ivory; all is softened in colour and line. Yorke himself has a harsh face; his daughter's is not harsh, neither is it quite pretty; it is simple—childlike in feature; the round cheeks bloom: as to the grey eyes, they are otherwise than childlike—a serious soul lights them—a young soul yet, but it will mature, if the body lives; and neither father nor mother have a spirit to compare with it. Partaking of the essence of each, it will one day be better than either— stronger, much purer, more aspiring. Rose is a still, sometimes a stubborn girl now: her mother wants to make of her such a woman as she is herself—a woman of dark and dreary duties—and Rose has a mind full-set, thick-sown with the germs of ideas her mother never knew. It is agony to her often to have these ideas trampled on and repressed. She has never rebelled yet; but if hard driven, she will rebel one day, and then it will be once for all. Rose loves her father: her father does not rule her with a rod of iron; he is good to her. He sometimes fears she will not live, so bright are the sparks of intelligence which, at moments, flash from her glance, and gleam in her language. This idea makes him often sadly tender to her.

He has no idea that little Jessy will die young, she is so gay and chattering, arch—original even now: passionate when provoked, but most affectionate if caressed; by turns gentle and rattling; exacting yet generous; fearless—of her mother, for instance, whose irrationally hard and strict rule she has often defied—yet reliant on any who will help her. Jessy, with her little piquant face, engaging prattle, and winning ways, is made to be a pet; and her father's pet she accordingly is. It is odd that the doll should resemble her mother feature by feature, as Rose resembles her father, and yet the physiognomy—how different!

Mr. Yorke, if a magic mirror were now held before you, and if therein were shown you your two daughters as they will be twenty years from this night, what would you think? The magic mirror is here: you shall learn their destinies—and first that of your little life, Jessy.

Do you know this place? No, you never saw it; but you recognise the nature of these trees, this foliage—the cypress, the willow, the yew. Stone crosses like these are not unfamiliar to you, nor are these dim garlands of everlasting flowers. Here

is the place; green sod and a grey marble headstone—Jessy sleeps below. She lived through an April day; much loved was she, much loving. She often, in her brief life, shed tears, she had frequent sorrows; she smiled between, gladdening whatever saw her. Her death was tranquil and happy in Rose's guardian arms, for Rose had been her stay and defence through many trials: the dying and the watching English girls were at that hour alone in a foreign country, and the soil of that country gave Jessy a grave.

Now, behold Rose, two years later. The crosses and garlands looked strange, but the hills and the woods of this landscape look still stranger. This, indeed, is far from England; remote must be the shores which wear that wild, luxuriant aspect. This is some virgin solitude: unknown birds flutter round the skirts of that forest; no European river this, on whose banks Rose sits thinking. The little quiet Yorkshire girl is a lonely emigrant in some region of the southern hemisphere. Will she ever come back?

The three eldest of the family are all boys: Matthew, Mark, and Martin. They are seated together in that corner, engaged in some game. Observe their three heads: much alike at a first glance; at a second, different; at a third, contrasted. Dark-haired, dark-eyed, red-cheeked, are the whole trio; small English features they all possess; all own a blended resemblance to sire and mother, and yet a distinctive physiognomy, mark of a separate character, belongs to each.

I shall not say much about Matthew, the first-born of the house; though it is impossible to avoid gazing at him long, and conjecturing what qualities that visage hides or indicates. He is no plain-looking boy: that jet-black hair, white brow, high-coloured cheek, those quick, dark eyes, are good points in their way. How is it that, look as long as you will, there is but one object in the room, and that the most sinister, to which Matthew's face seems to bear an affinity, and of which, ever and anon, it reminds you strangely—the eruption of Vesuvius? Flame and shadow seem the component parts of that lad's soul: no daylight in it, and no sunshine, and no pure, cool moonbeam ever shone there. He has an English frame, but, apparently, not an English mind: you would say, an Italian stiletto in a sheath of British workmanship. He is crossed in the game—look at his scowl. Mr. Yorke sees it, and what does he say? In a low voice, he pleads: ''Mark and Martin, don't anger your brother.'' And this is ever the tone adopted by both parents. Theoretically, they decry partiality; no rights of primogeniture are to be allowed in that house; but Matthew is never to be vexed, never to be opposed: they avert provocation from him assiduously as they would avert fire from a barrel of gunpowder. ''Concede, conciliate,'' is their motto wherever he is concerned. The republicans are fast making a tyrant of their own flesh and blood. This the younger scions know and feel, and at heart they all rebel against the injustice: they cannot read their parents' motives; they only see the difference of treatment. The dragon's teeth are already sown amongst Mr. Yorke's young olive-branches: discord will one day be the harvest.

Mark is a bonnie-looking boy, the most regular-featured of the family; he is exceedingly calm; his smile is shrewd; he can say the driest, most cutting things in the quietest of tones. Despite his tranquillity, a somewhat heavy brow speaks temper, and reminds you that the smoothest waters are not always the safest. Besides, he is too still, unmoved, phlegmatic, to be happy. Life will never have much joy in it for Mark: by the time he is five-and-twenty, he will wonder why people ever laugh, and think all fools who seem merry. Poetry will not exist for Mark, either in literature or in life; its best effusions will sound to him mere rant and jargon: enthusiasm will be his aversion and contempt. Mark will have no youth: while he looks juvenile and blooming, he will be already middle-aged in mind. His body is now fourteen years of age, but his soul is already thirty.

Martin, the youngest of the three, owns another nature. Life may, or may not, be brief for him; but it will certainly be brilliant: he will pass through all its illusions, half believe in them, wholly enjoy them, then outlive them. That boy is not handsome—

not so handsome as either of his brothers: he is plain; there is a husk upon him, a dry shell, and he will wear it till he is near twenty; then he will put it off: about that period he will make himself handsome. He will wear uncouth manners till that age, perhaps homely garments; but the chrysalis will retain the power of transfiguring itself into the butterfly, and such transfiguration will, in due season, take place. For a space he will be vain, probably a downright puppy, eager for pleasure and desirous of admiration; athirst, too, for knowledge. He will want all that the world can give him, both of enjoyment and lore; he will, perhaps, take deep draughts at each fount. That thirst satisfied—what next? I know not. Martin might be a remarkable man: whether he will or not, the seer is powerless to predict: on that subject there has been no open vision.

Take Mr. Yorke's family in the aggregate, there is as much mental power in those six young heads, as much originality, as much activity and vigour of brain, as—divided amongst half-a-dozen commonplace broods—would give to each rather more than an average amount of sense and capacity. Mr. Yorke knows this, and is proud of his race. Yorkshire has such families here and there amongst her hills and wolds—peculiar, racy, vigorous; of good blood and strong brain; turbulent somewhat in the pride of their strength, and intractable in the force of their native powers; wanting polish, wanting consideration, wanting docility, but sound, spirited, and true-bred as the eagle on the cliff or the steed in the steppe.

A low tap is heard at the parlour door; the boys have been making such a noise over their game, and little Jessy, besides, has been singing so sweet a Scotch song to her father—who delights in Scotch and Italian songs, and has taught his musical little daughter some of the best—that the ring at the outer door was not observed.

"Come in," says Mrs. Yorke, in that conscientiously constrained and solemnised voice of hers, which ever modulates itself to a funereal dreariness of tone, though the subject it is exercised upon be but to give orders for the making of a pudding in the kitchen, to bid the boys hang up their caps in the hall, or to call the girls to their sewing: "Come in!" And in came Robert Moore.

Moore's habitual gravity, as well as his abstemiousness (for the case of spirit-decanters is never ordered up when he pays an evening visit), has so far recommended him to Mrs. Yorke, that she has not yet made him the subject of private animadversions with her husband: she has not yet found out that he is hampered by a secret intrigue which prevents him from marrying, or that he is a wolf in sheep's clothing; discoveries which she made at an early date after marriage concerning most of her husband's bachelor friends, and excluded them from her board accordingly; which part of her conduct, indeed, might be said to have its just and sensible, as well as its harsh side.

"Well, is it you?" she says to Mr. Moore, as he comes up to her and gives his hand. "What are you roving about at this time of night for? You should be at home."

"Can a single man be said to have a home, madam?" he asks.

"Pooh!" says Mrs. Yorke, who despises conventional smoothness quite as much as her husband does, and practises it as little, and whose plain speaking on all occasions is carried to a point calculated, sometimes, to awaken admiration, but oftener alarm—"Pooh! you need not talk nonsense to me; a single man can have a home if he likes. Pray, does not your sister make a home for you?"

"Not she," joined in Mr. Yorke. "Hortense is an honest lass; but when I was Robert's age, I had five or six sisters, all as decent and proper as she is; but you see, Hesther, for all that, it did not hinder me from looking out for a wife."

"And sorely he has repented marrying me," added Mrs. Yorke, who liked occasionally to crack a dry jest against matrimony, even though it should be at her own expense. "He has repented it in sackcloth and ashes, Robert Moore, as you may well believe when you see his punishment" (here she pointed to her children). "Who would burden themselves with such a set of great, rough lads as those, if

they could help it? It is not only bringing them into the world, though that is bad enough, but they are all to feed, to clothe, to rear, to settle in life. Young sir, when you feel tempted to marry, think of our four sons and two daughters, and look twice before you leap.''

''I am not tempted now, at any rate: I think these are not times for marrying or giving in marriage.''

A lugubrious sentiment of this sort was sure to obtain Mrs. Yorke's approbation: she nodded and groaned acquiescence; but in a minute she said—''I make little account of the wisdom of a Solomon of your age; it will be upset by the first fancy that crosses you. Meantime, sit down, sir: you can talk, I suppose, as well sitting as standing?''

This was her way of inviting her guest to take a chair; he had no sooner obeyed her, than little Jessy jumped from her father's knee and ran into Mr. Moore's arms, which were very promptly held out to receive her.

''You talk of marrying him,'' said she to her mother, quite indignantly, as she was lifted lightly to his knee, ''and he is married now, or as good: he promised that I should be his wife last summer, the first time he saw me in my new white frock and blue sash. Didn't he, father?'' (These children were not accustomed to say papa and mamma; their mother would allow no such ''namby-pamby.'')

''Ay, my little lassie, he promised; I'll bear witness. But make him say it over again now, Jessy: such as he are only false loons.''

''He is not false: he is too bonnie to be false,'' said Jessy, looking up to her tall sweetheart with the fullest confidence in his faith.

''Bonnie!'' cried Mr. Yorke; ''that's the reason that he should be, and proof that he is—a scoundrel.''

''But he looks too sorrowful to be false,'' here interposed a quiet voice from behind the father's chair. ''If he were always laughing, I should think he forgot promises soon, but Mr. Moore never laughs.''

''Your sentimental buck is the greatest cheat of all, Rose,'' remarked Mr. Yorke.

''He's not sentimental,'' said Rose.

Mr. Moore turned to her with a little surprise, smiling at the same time.

''How do you know I am not sentimental, Rose?''

''Because I heard a lady say you were not.''

''Voilà, qui devient intéressant!'' exclaimed Mr. Yorke, hitching his chair nearer the fire. ''A lady! That has quite a romantic twang: we must guess who it is. Rosy, whisper the name low to your father: don't let *him* hear.''

''Rose, don't be too forward to talk,'' here interrupted Mrs, Yorke, in her usual kill-joy fashion; ''nor Jessy either: it becomes all children, especially girls, to be silent in the presence of their elders.''

''Why have we tongues, then?'' asked Jessy pertly; while Rose only looked at her mother with an expression that seemed to say, she should take that maxim in, and think it over at her leisure. After two minutes' grave deliberation, she asked— ''And why especially girls, mother?''

''Firstly, because I say so: and, secondly, because discretion and reserve is a girl's best wisdom.''

''My dear madam,'' observed Moore, ''what you say is excellent: it reminds me, indeed, of my dear sister's observations; but really it is not applicable to these little ones. Let Rose and Jessy talk to me freely, or my chief pleasure in coming here is gone. I like their prattle: it does me good.''

''Does it not?'' asked Jessy. ''More good than if the rough lads came round you: you call them rough, mother, yourself.''

''Yes, mignonne, a thousand times more good: I have rough lads enough about me all day long, poulet.''

''There are plenty of people,'' continued she, ''who take notice of the boys: all my uncles and aunts seem to think their nephews better than their nieces; and when

gentlemen come here to dine, it is always Matthew, and Mark, and Martin, that are talked to, and never Rose and me. Mr. Moore is *our* friend, and we'll keep him: but mind, Rose, he's not so much your friend as he is mine; he is my *particular acquaintance;* remember that!'' And she held up her small hand with an admonitory gesture.

Rose was quite accustomed to be admonished by that small hand: her will daily bent itself to that of the impetuous little Jessy: she was guided—overruled by Jessy in a thousand things. On all occasions of show and pleasure, Jessy took the lead, and Rose fell quietly into the background; whereas, when the disagreeables of life— its work and privations were in question, Rose instinctively took upon her, in addition to her own share, what she could of her sister's. Jessy had already settled it in her mind that she, when she was old enough, was to be married; Rose, she decided, must be an old maid, to live with her, look after her children, keep her house. This state of things is not uncommon between two sisters, where one is plain and the other pretty; but in this case, if there *was* a difference in external appearance, Rose had the advantage: her face was more regular-featured than that of the piquant little Jessy. Jessy, however, was destined to possess, along with sprightly intelligence and vivacious feeling, the gift of fascination, the power to charm when, where, and whom she would. Rose was to have a fine, generous soul, a noble intellect profoundly cultivated, a heart as true as steel, but the manner to attract was not to be hers.

"Now, Rose, tell me the name of this lady who denied that I was sentimental,'' urged Mr. Moore.

Rose had no idea of tantalisation, or she would have held him a while in doubt: she answered briefly—"I can't: I don't know her name.''

"Describe her to me: what was she like? Where did you see her?''

"When Jessy and I went to spend the day at Whinbury with Kate and Susan Pearson, who were just come home from school, there was a party at Mrs. Pearson's, and some grown-up ladies were sitting in a corner of the drawing-room talking about you.''

"Did you know none of them?''

"Hannah, and Harriet, and Dora, and Mary Sykes.''

"Good. Were they abusing me, Rosy?''

"Some of them were: they called you a misanthrope: I remember the word—I looked for it in the dictionary when I came home: it means a man-hater.''

"What besides?''

"Hannah Sykes said you were a solemn puppy.''

"Better!'' cried Mr. Yorke, laughing. "Oh! excellent! Hannah—that's the one with the red hair: a fine girl, but half-witted.''

"She has wit enough for me, it appears,'' said Moore. "A solemn puppy, indeed! Well, Rose, go on.''

"Miss Pearson said she believed there was a good deal of affectation about you, and that with your dark hair and pale face, you looked to her like some sort of a sentimental noodle.''

Again Mr. Yorke laughed: Mrs. Yorke even joined in this time. "You see in what esteem you are held behind your back,'' said she; "yet I believe *that* Miss Pearson would like to catch you: she set her cap at you when you first came into the country, old as she is.''

"And who contradicted her, Rosy?'' inquired Moore.

"A lady whom I don't know, because she never visits here, though I see her every Sunday at church; she sits in the pew near the pulpit. I generally look at her, instead of looking at my prayer-book; for she is like a picture in our dining-room, that woman with the dove in her hand: at least she has eyes like it, and a nose too, a straight nose, that makes all her face look, somehow, what I call clear.''

"And you don't know her!" exclaimed Jessy, in a tone of exceeding surprise. "That's so like Rose. Mr. Moore, I often wonder in what sort of a world my sister lives; I am sure she does not live all her time in this: one is continually finding out that she is quite ignorant of some little matter which everybody else knows. To think of her going solemnly to church every Sunday, and looking all service-time at one particular person, and never so much as asking that person's name. She means Caroline Helstone, the Rector's niece: I remember all about it. Miss Helstone was quite angry with Anne Pearson: she said, 'Robert Moore is neither affected nor sentimental; you mistake his character utterly, or rather not one of you here knows anything about it.' Now, shall I tell you what she is like? I can tell what people are like, and how they are dressed, better than Rose can."

"Let us hear."

"She is nice; she is fair; she has a pretty white slender throat; she has long curls, not stiff ones, they hang loose and soft, their colour is brown but not dark: she speaks quietly, with a clear tone; she never makes a bustle in moving; she often wears a grey silk dress; she is neat all over: her gowns, and her shoes, and her gloves always fit her. She is what I call a lady, and when I am as tall as she is, I mean to be like her. Shall I suit you if I am? Will you really marry me?"

Moore stroked Jessy's hair: for a minute he seemed as if he would draw her nearer to him, but instead he put her a little farther off.

"Oh! you won't have me? You push me away."

"Why, Jessy, you care nothing about me: you never come to see me now at the Hollow."

"Because you don't ask me."

Hereupon, Mr. Moore gave both the little girls an invitation to pay him a visit next day, promising that, as he was going to Stilbro' in the morning, he would buy them each a present, of what nature he would not then declare, but they must come and see. Jessy was about to reply, when one of the boys unexpectedly broke in.

"I know that Miss Helstone you have all been palavering about: she's an ugly girl. I hate her! I hate all womenites. I wonder what they were made for."

"Martin!" said his father—for Martin it was—the lad only answered by turning his cynical young face, half-arch, half-truculent, towards the paternal chair. "Martin, my lad, thou'rt a swaggering whelp now; thou wilt some day be an outrageous puppy: but stick to those sentiments of thine. See, I'll write down the words now i' my pocket-book." (The senior took out a morocco-covered book, and deliberately wrote therein.) "Ten years hence, Martin, if thou and I be both alive at that day, I'll remind thee of that speech."

"I'll say the same then: I mean always to hate women; they're such dolls: they do nothing but dress themselves finely, and go swimming about to be admired. I'll never marry; I'll be a bachelor."

"Stick to it! stick to it! Hesther" (addressing his wife), "I was like him when I was his age, a regular misogamist; and, behold! by the time I was three-and-twenty—being then a tourist in France and Italy, and the Lord knows where!—I curled my hair every night before I went to bed, and wore a ring i' my ear, and would have worn one i' my nose if it had been the fashion—and all that I might make mysel' pleasing and charming to the ladies. Martin will do the like."

"Will I? Never! I've more sense. What a Guy you were, father! As to dressing I make this vow: I'll never dress more finely than as you see me at present. Mr. Moore, I'm clad in blue cloth from top to toe, and they laugh at me, and call me sailor at the grammar-school. I laugh louder at them, and say they are all magpies and parrots, with their coats one colour, and their waistcoats another, and their trousers a third. I'll always wear blue cloth, and nothing but blue cloth: it is beneath a human being's dignity to dress himself in parti-coloured garments.

"Ten years hence, Martin, no tailor's shop will have choice of colours varied enough for thy exacting taste; no perfumer's stores essences exquisite enough for thy fastidious senses."

Martin looked disdain, but vouchsafed no further reply. Meantime Mark, who for some minutes had been rummaging amongst a pile of books on a side-table, took the word. He spoke in a peculiarly slow, quiet voice, and with an expression of still irony in his face not easy to describe.

"Mr. Moore," said he, "you think perhaps it was a compliment on Miss Caroline Helstone's part to say you were not sentimental. I thought you appeared confused when my sisters told you the words, as if you felt flattered; you turned red, just like a certain vain little lad at our school, who always thinks proper to blush when he gets a rise in the class. For your benefit, Mr. Moore, I've been looking up the word 'sentimental' in the dictionary, and I find it to mean 'tinctured with sentiment.' On examining further, 'sentiment' is explained to be, thought, idea, notion. A sentimental man, then, is one who has thoughts, ideas, notions; an unsentimental man is one destitute of thought, idea, or notion."

And Mark stopped: he did not smile, he did not look round for admiration: he had said his say, and was silent.

"Ma foi! mon ami," observed Mr. Moore to Yorke; "ce sont vraiment des enfants terribles, que les vôtres!"

Rose, who had been listening attentively to Mark's speech, replied to him— "There are different kinds of thoughts, ideas, and notions," said she, "good and bad: sentimental must refer to the bad, or Miss Helstone must have taken it in that sense, for she was not blaming Mr. Moore; she was defending him."

"That's my kind little advocate!" said Moore, taking Rose's hand.

"She was defending him," repeated Rose, "as I should have done had I been in her place, for the other ladies seemed to speak spitefully."

"Ladies always do speak spitefully," observed Martin; "it is the nature of womenites to be spiteful."

Matthew now, for the first time, opened his lips—"What a fool Martin is, to be always gabbling about what he does not understand."

"It is my privilege, as a freeman, to gabble on whatever subject I like," responded Martin.

"You use it, or rather abuse it, to such an extent," rejoined the elder brother, "that you prove you ought to have been a slave."

"A slave! a slave! That to a Yorke, and from a Yorke! This fellow," he added, standing up at the table, and pointing across it to Matthew—"this fellow forgets, what every cottier in Briarfield knows, that all born of our house have that arched instep under which water can flow—proof that there has not been a slave of the blood for three hundred years."

"Mountebank!" said Matthew.

"Lads, be silent!" exclaimed Mr. Yorke. "Martin, you are a mischief-maker: there would have been no disturbance, but for you."

"Indeed! Is that correct? Did I begin, or did Matthew? Had I spoken to him when he accused me of gabbling like a fool?"

"A presumptuous fool!" repeated Matthew.

Here Mrs. Yorke commenced rocking herself—rather a portentous movement with her, as it was occasionally followed, especially when Matthew was worsted in a conflict, by a fit of hysterics.

"I don't see why I should bear insolence from Matthew Yorke, or what right he has to use bad language to me," observed Martin.

"He has no right, my lad; but forgive your brother until seventy and seven times," said Mr. Yorke soothingly.

"Always alike, and theory and practice always adverse!" murmured Martin as he turned to leave the room.

"Where art thou going, my son?" asked the father.

"Somewhere where I shall be safe from insult: if in this house I can find any such place."

Matthew laughed very insolently: Martin threw a strange look at him, and trembled through all his slight lad's frame, but he restrained himself.

"I suppose there is no objection to my withdrawing?" he inquired.

"No; go, my lad: but remember not to bear malice."

Martin went, and Matthew sent another insolent laugh after him. Rose, lifting her fair head from Moore's shoulder, against which, for a moment, it had been resting, said, as she directed a steady gaze to Matthew—"Martin is grieved, and you are glad; but I would rather be Martin than you: I dislike your nature."

Here Mr. Moore, by way of averting, or at least escaping, a scene—which a sob from Mrs. Yorke warned him was likely to come on—rose, and putting Jessy off his knee, he kissed her and Rose; reminding them, at the same time, to be sure and come to the Hollow in good time to-morrow afternoon: then, having taken leave of his hostess, he said to Mr. Yorke—"May I speak a word with you?" and was followed by him from the room. Their brief conference took place in the hall.

"Have you employment for a good workman?" asked Moore.

"A nonsense question in these times, when you know that every master has many good workmen to whom he cannot give full employment."

"You must oblige me by taking on this man, if possible."

"My lad, I can take on no more hands to oblige all England."

"It does not signify; I must find him a place somewhere."

"Who is he?"

"William Farren."

"I know William; a right-down honest man is William."

"He has been out of work three months; he has a large family: we are sure they cannot live without wages: he was one of a deputation of cloth-dressers who came to me this morning to complain and threaten. William did not threaten: he only asked me to give them rather more time—to make my changes more slowly. You know I cannot do that: straitened on all sides as I am, I have nothing for it but to push on. I thought it would be idle to palaver long with them. I sent them away, after arresting a rascal amongst them, whom I hope to transport—a fellow who preaches at the chapel yonder sometimes."

"Not Moses Barraclough?"

"Yes."

"Ah! you've arrested him? Good! Then out of a scoundrel you're going to make a martyr: you've done a wise thing."

"I've done a right thing. Well, the short and the long of it is, I'm determined to get Farren a place, and I reckon on you to give him one."

"This is cool, however!" exclaimed Mr. Yorke. "What right have you to reckon on me to provide for your dismissed workmen? What do I know about your Farrens and your Williams? I've heard he's an honest man; but am I to support all the honest men in Yorkshire? You may say that would be no great charge to undertake; but great or little, I'll none of it."

"Come, Mr. Yorke, what can you find for him to do?"

"*I* find! You'll make me use language I'm not accustomed to use. I wish you would go home—here is the door—set off."

Moore sat down on one of the hall chairs.

"You can't give him work in your mill—good—but you have land: find him some occupation on your land, Mr. Yorke."

"Bob, I thought you cared nothing about our 'lourdauds de paysans': I don't understand this change."

"I do: the fellow spoke to me nothing but truth and sense. I answered him just as roughly as I did the rest, who jabbered mere gibberish. I couldn't make distinctions

there and then: his appearance told what he had gone through lately clearer than his words: but where is the use of explaining? Let him have work.''

"Let him have it yourself. If you are so very much in earnest, strain a point.''

"If there was a point left in my affairs to strain, I would strain it till it cracked again; but I received letters this morning which show me pretty nearly where I stand, and it is not far off the end of the plank. My foreign market, at any rate, is gorged. If there is no change—if there dawns no prospect of peace—if the Orders in Council are not, at least, suspended, so as to open our way in the West—I do not know where I am to turn. I see no more light than if I were sealed in a rock; so that for me to pretend to offer a man a livelihood would be to do a dishonest thing.''

"Come, let us take a turn on the front: it is a starlight night,'' said Mr. Yorke.

They passed out, closing the front-door after them, and, side by side, paced the frost-white pavement to and fro.

"Settle about Farren at once,'' urged Mr. Moore. "You have large fruit-gardens at York Mills: he is a good gardener: give him work there.''

"Well, so be it. I'll send for him to-morrow, and we'll see. And now, my lad, you're concerned about the condition of your affairs?''

"Yes: a second failure—which I may delay, but which, at this moment, I see no way finally to avert—would blight the name of Moore completely; and you are aware I had fine intentions of paying off every debt, and re-establishing the old firm on its former basis.''

"You want capital—that's all you want.''

"Yes; but you might as well say that breath is all a dead man wants to live.''

"I know—I know capital is not to be had for the asking; and if you were a married man, and had a family, like me, I should think your case pretty nigh desperate; but the young and unencumbered have chances peculiar to themselves. I hear gossip now and then about your being on the eve of marriage with this miss and that; but I suppose it is none of it true?''

"You may well suppose that: I think I am not in a position to be dreaming of marriage. Marriage! I cannot bear the word: it sounds so silly and utopian. I have settled it decidedly that marriage and love are superfluities, intended only for the rich, who live at ease, and have no need to take thought for the morrow; or desperations, the last and reckless joy of the deeply wretched, who never hope to rise out of the slough of their utter poverty.''

"I should not think so if I were circumstanced as you are: I should think I could very likely get a wife with a few thousands, who would suit both me and my affairs.''

"I wonder where?''

"Would you try, if you had a chance?''

"I don't know: it depends on—in short, it depends on many things.''

"Would you take an old woman?''

"I'd rather break stones on the road.''

"So would I. Would you take an ugly one?''

"Bah! I hate ugliness and delight in beauty: my eyes and heart, Yorke, take pleasure in a sweet, young, fair face, as they are repelled by a grim, rugged, meagre one: soft delicate lines and hues please—harsh ones prejudice me. I won't have an ugly wife.''

"Not if she were rich?''

"Not if she were dressed in gems. I could not love—I could not fancy—I could not endure her. My taste must have satisfaction, or disgust would break out in despotism—or worse—freeze to utter iciness.''

"What, Bob, if you married an honest, good-natured, and wealthy lass, though a little hard-favoured, couldn't you put up with the high cheek-bones, the rather wide mouth, and reddish hair?''

"I'll never try, I tell you. Grace at least I *will* have, and youth and symmetry—
yes, and what I call beauty."

"And poverty, and a nursery full of bairns you can neither clothe nor feed, and
very soon an anxious faded mother—and then bankruptcy, discredit—a life-long
struggle."

"Let me alone, Yorke."

"If you are romantic, Robert, and especially if you are already in love, it is of
no use talking."

"I am not romantic. I am stript of romance as bare as the white tenters in that
field are of cloth."

"Always use such figures of speech, lad; I can understand them: and there is no
love-affair to disturb your judgment?"

"I thought I had said enough on that subject before. Love for me? Stuff!"

"Well, then; if you are sound both in heart and head, there is no reason why
you should not profit by a good chance if it offers: therefore, wait and see."

"You are quite oracular, Yorke."

"I think I am a bit i' that line. I promise ye naught and I advise ye naught; but
I bid ye keep your heart up, and be guided by circumstances."

"My namesake the physician's almanack could not speak more guardedly."

"In the meantime, I care naught about ye, Robert Moore: ye are nothing akin
to me or mine, and whether ye lose or find a fortune it mak's no difference to me.
Go home, now: it has stricken ten, Miss Hortense will be wondering where ye are."

Chapter X

OLD MAIDS

TIME wore on, and spring matured. The surface of England began to look pleasant:
her fields grew green, her hills fresh, her gardens blooming; but at heart she was
no better: still her poor were wretched, still their employers were harassed: commerce,
in some of its branches, seemed threatened with paralysis, for the war continued;
England's blood was shed and her wealth lavished: all, it seemed, to attain most
inadequate ends. Some tidings there were indeed occasionally of successes in the
Peninsula, but these came in slowly; long intervals occurred between, in which no
note was heard but the insolent self-felicitations of Bonaparte on his continued
triumphs. Those who suffered from the results of the war felt this tedious, and—
as they thought—hopeless, struggle against what their fears or their interests taught
them to regard as an invincible power, most insufferable: they demanded peace on
any terms: men like Yorke and Moore—and there were thousands whom the war
placed where it placed them, shuddering on the verge of bankruptcy—insisted on
peace with the energy of desperation.

They held meetings; they made speeches; they got up petitions to extort this
boon: on what terms it was made they cared not.

All men, taken singly, are more or less selfish; and taken in bodies they are
intensely so. The British merchant is no exception to this rule: the mercantile classes
illustrate it strikingly. These classes certainly think too exclusively of making
money: they are too oblivious of every national consideration but that of extending
England's (*i.e.*, their own) commerce. Chivalrous feeling, disinterestedness, pride
in honour, is too dead in their hearts. A land ruled by them alone would too often
make ignominious submission—not at all from the motives Christ teaches, but
rather from those Mammon instils. During the late war, the tradesmen of England
would have endured buffets from the French on the right cheek and on the left;
their cloak they would have given to Napoleon, and then have politely offered him

their coat also, nor would they have withheld their waistcoat if urged: they would have prayed permission only to retain their one other garment, for the sake of the purse in its pocket. Not one spark of spirit, not one symptom of resistance would they have shown till the hand of the Corsican bandit had grasped that beloved purse: *then*, perhaps, transfigured at once into British bull-dogs, they would have sprung at the robber's throat, and there they would have fastened, and there hung— inveterate, insatiable, till the treasure had been restored. Tradesmen, when they speak against war, always profess to hate it because it is a bloody and barbarous proceeding: you would think, to hear them talk, that they are peculiarly civilised— especially gentle and kindly of disposition to their fellow-men. This is not the case. Many of them are extremely narrow and cold-hearted, have no good feeling for any class but their own, are distant—even hostile to all others; call them useless; seem to question their right to exist; seem to grudge them the very air they breathe, and to think the circumstance of their eating, drinking, and living in decent houses, quite unjustifiable. They do not know what others do in the way of helping, pleasing, or teaching their race; they will not trouble themselves to inquire; whoever is not in trade is accused of eating the bread of idleness, of passing a useless existence. Long may it be ere England really becomes a nation of shopkeepers!

We have already said that Moore was no self-sacrificing patriot, and we have also explained what circumstances rendered him specially prone to confine his attention and efforts to the furtherance of his individual interest; accordingly, when he felt himself urged a second time to the brink of ruin, none struggled harder than he against the influences which would have thrust him over. What he *could* do towards stirring agitation in the North against the war, he did, and he instigated others whose money and connections gave them more power than he possessed. Sometimes, by flashes, he felt there was little reason in the demands his party made on Government: when he heard of all Europe threatened by Bonaparte, and of all Europe arming to resist him; when he saw Russia menaced, and beheld Russia rising, incensed and stern, to defend her frozen soil, her wild provinces of serfs, her dark native despotism, from the tread, the yoke, the tyranny of a foreign victor, he knew that England, a free realm, could not *then* depute her sons to make concessions and propose terms to the unjust, grasping French leader. When news came from time to time of the movements of that MAN then representing England in the Peninsula; of his advance from success to success—that advance so deliberate but so unswerving, so circumspect but so certain, so "unhasting" but so "unresting"; when he read Lord Wellington's own despatches in the columns of the newspapers, documents written by Modesty to the dictation of Truth—Moore confessed at heart that a power was with the troops of Britain, of that vigilant, enduring, genuine, unostentatious sort, which must win victory to the side it led, in the end. In the end! but that end, he thought, was yet far off; and meantime he, Moore, as an individual, would be crushed, his hopes ground to dust: it was himself he had to care for, his hopes he had to pursue, and he would fulfil his destiny.

He fulfilled it so vigorously, that ere long he came to a decisive rupture with his old Tory friend the Rector. They quarrelled at a public meeting, and afterwards exchanged some pungent letters in the newspapers. Mr. Helstone denounced Moore as a Jacobin, ceased to see him, would not even speak to him when they met: he intimated also to his niece, very distinctly, that her communications with Hollow's Cottage must for the present cease; she must give up taking French lessons. The language, he observed, was a bad and frivolous one at the best, and most of the works it boasted were bad and frivolous, highly injurious in their tendency to weak female minds. He wondered (he remarked parenthetically) what noodle first made it the fashion to teach women French: nothing was more improper for them; it was like feeding a rickety child on chalk and water-gruel; Caroline must give it up, and give up her cousins too: they were dangerous people.

Mr. Helstone quite expected opposition to this order; he expected tears. Seldom did he trouble himself about Caroline's movements, but a vague idea possessed him that she was fond of going to Hollow's Cottage: also he suspected that she liked Robert Moore's occasional presence at the Rectory. The Cossack had perceived that whereas if Malone stepped in of an evening to make himself sociable and charming, by pinching the ears of an aged black cat, which usually shared with Miss Helstone's feet the accommodation of her footstool, or by borrowing a fowling-piece, and banging away at a tool-shed door in the garden while enough of daylight remained to show that conspicuous mark—keeping the passage and sitting-room doors meantime uncomfortably open for the convenience of running in and out to announce his failures and successes with noisy brusquerie—he had observed that under such entertaining circumstances Caroline had a trick of disappearing, tripping noiselessly upstairs, and remaining invisible till called down to supper. On the other hand, when Robert Moore was the guest, though he elicited no vivacities from the cat, did nothing to it, indeed, beyond occasionally coaxing it from the stool to his knee, and there letting it purr, climb to his shoulder, and rub its head against his cheek; though there was no ear-splitting cracking off of firearms, no diffusion of sulphurous gunpowder perfume, no noise, no boasting during his stay, that still Caroline sat in the room, and seemed to find wondrous content in the stitching of Jew-basket pin-cushions, and the knitting of Missionary-basket socks.

She was very quiet, and Robert paid her little attention, scarcely ever addressing his discourse to her; but Mr. Helstone, not being one of those elderly gentlemen who are easily blinded, on the contrary, finding himself on all occasions extremely wide-awake, had watched them when they bade each other good-night: he had just seen their eyes meet once—only once. Some natures would have taken pleasure in the glance then surprised, because there was no harm and some delight in it. It was by no means a glance of mutual intelligence, for mutual love-secrets existed not between them: there was nothing then of craft and concealment to offend; only Mr. Moore's eyes, looking into Caroline's, felt they were clear and gentle, and Caroline's eyes encountering Mr. Moore's, confessed they were manly and searching: each acknowledged the charm in his or her own way. Moore smiled slightly, and Caroline coloured as slightly. Mr. Helstone could, on the spot, have rated them both: they annoyed him; why?—impossible to say. If you had asked him what Moore merited at that moment, he would have said "a horsewhip"; if you had inquired into Caroline's deserts, he would have adjudged her a box on the ear; if you had further demanded the reason of such chastisements, he would have stormed against flirtation and love-making, and vowed he would have no such folly going on under his roof.

These private considerations, combined with political reasons, fixed his resolution of separating the cousins. He announced his will to Caroline one evening, as she was sitting at work near the drawing-room window: her face was turned towards him, and the light fell full upon it. It had struck him a few minutes before that she was looking paler and quieter than she used to look; it had not escaped him either that Robert Moore's name had never, for some three weeks past, dropped from her lips; nor during the same space of time had that personage made his appearance at the Rectory. Some suspicion of clandestine meetings haunted him; having but an indifferent opinion of women, he always suspected them: he thought they needed constant watching. It was in a tone drily significant he desired her to cease her daily visits to the Hollow; he expected a start, a look of deprecation: the start he saw, but it was a very slight one; no look whatever was directed to him.

"Do you hear me?" he asked.

"Yes, uncle."

"Of course you mean to attend to what I say?"

" Yes, certainly."

"And there must be no letter-scribbling to your cousin Hortense: no intercourse whatever. I do not approve of the principles of the family: they are Jacobinical."

"Very well," said Caroline quietly. She acquiesced then: there was no vexed flushing of the face, no gathering tears: the shadowy thoughtfulness which had covered her features ere Mr. Helstone spoke remained undisturbed: she was obedient.

Yes, perfectly; because the mandate coincided with her own previous judgment; because it was now become pain to her to go to Hollow's Cottage; nothing met her there but disappointment: hope and love had quitted that little tenement, for Robert seemed to have deserted its precincts. Whenever she asked after him—which she very seldom did since the mere utterance of his name made her face grow hot—the answer was, he was from home, or he was quite taken up with business: Hortense feared he was killing himself by application: he scarcely ever took a meal in the house; he lived in the counting-house.

At church only Caroline had the chance of seeing him, and there she rarely looked at him: it was both too much pain and too much pleasure to look: it excited too much emotion; and that it was all wasted emotion, she had learned well to comprehend.

Once, on a dark, wet Sunday, when there were few people at church, and when especially certain ladies were absent, of whose observant faculties and tomahawk tongues Caroline stood in awe, she had allowed her eye to seek Robert's pew, and to rest a while on its occupant. He was there alone: Hortense had been kept at home by prudent considerations relative to the rain and a new spring "chapeau." During the sermon, he sat with folded arms and eyes cast down, looking very sad and abstracted. When depressed, the very hue of his face seemed more dusk than when he smiled, and to-day cheek and forehead wore their most tintless and sober olive. By instinct Caroline knew, as she examined that clouded countenance, that his thoughts were running in no familiar or kindly channel; that they were far away, not merely from her, but from all which she could comprehend, or in which she could sympathise. Nothing that they had ever talked of together was now in his mind: he was wrapped from her by interests and responsibilities in which it was deemed such as she could have no part.

Caroline meditated in her own way on the subject; speculated on his feelings, on his life, on his fears, on his fate; mused over the mystery of "business," tried to comprehend more about it than had ever been told her—to understand its perplexities, liabilities, duties, exactions; endeavoured to realise the state of mind of man of a "man of business," to enter into it, feel what he would feel, aspire to what he would aspire. Her earnest wish was to see things as they were, and not to be romantic. By dint of effort she contrived to get a glimpse of the light of truth here and there, and hoped that scant ray might suffice to guide her.

"Different, indeed," she concluded, "is Robert's mental condition to mine: I think only of him; he has no room, no leisure to think of me. The feeling called love is and has been for two years the predominant emotion of my heart: always there, always awake, always astir: quite other feelings absorb his reflections, and govern his faculties. He is rising now, going to leave the church, for service is over. Will he turn his head towards this pew?—no—not once—he has not one look for me: that is hard: a kind glance would have made me happy till to-morrow. I have not got it; he would not give it; he is gone. Strange that grief should now almost choke me, because another human being's eye has failed to greet mine."

That Sunday evening, Mr. Malone coming, as usual, to pass it with his Rector, Caroline withdrew after tea to her chamber. Fanny, knowing her habits, had lit her a cheerful little fire, as the weather was so gusty and chill. Closeted there, silent and solitary, what could she do but think? She noiselessly paced to and fro the carpeted floor, her head drooped, her hands folded: it was irksome to sit: the current of reflection ran rapidly through her mind: to-night she was mutely excited.

Mute was the room,—mute the house. The double door of the study muffled the voices of the gentlemen: the servants were quiet in the kitchen, engaged with books their young mistress had lent them; books which she had told them were "fit for

Sunday reading.'' And she herself had another of the same sort open on the table, but she could not read it: its theology was incomprehensible to her, and her own mind was too busy, teeming, wandering, to listen to the language of another mind.

Then, too, her imagination was full of pictures; images of Moore; scenes where he and she had been together; winter fireside sketches; a glowing landscape of a hot summer afternoon passed with him in the bosom of Nunnely Wood: divine vignettes of mild spring or mellow autumn moments, when she had sat at his side in Hollow's Copse, listening to the call of the May cuckoo, or sharing the September treasure of nuts and ripe blackberries—a wild dessert which it was her morning's pleasure to collect in a little basket, and cover with green leaves and fresh blossoms, and her afternoon's delight to administer to Moore, berry by berry, and nut by nut, like a bird feeding its fledgling.

Robert's features and form were with her; the sound of his voice was quite distinct in her ear; his few caresses seemed renewed. But these joys being hollow, were, ere long, crushed in: the pictures faded, the voice failed, the visionary clasp melted chill from her hand, and where the warm seal of lips had made impress on her forehead, it felt now as if a sleety rain-drop had fallen. She returned from an enchanted region to the real world: for Nunnely Wood in June, she saw her narrow chamber; for the songs of birds in alleys, she heard the rain on her casement; for the sigh of the south wind, came the sob of the mournful east; and for Moore's manly companionship, she had the thin illusion of her own dim shadow on the wall. Turning from the pale phantom which reflected herself in its outline, and her reverie in the drooped attitude of its dim head and colourless tresses, she sat down— inaction would suit the frame of mind into which she was now declining—she said to herself—''I have to live, perhaps, till seventy years. As far as I know, I have good health: half a century of existence may lie before me. How am I to occupy it? What am I to do to fill the interval of time which spreads between me and the grave?''

She reflected.

''I shall not be married, it appears,'' she continued. ''I suppose, as Robert does not care for me, I shall never have a husband to love, nor little children to take care of. Till lately I had reckoned securely on the duties and affections of wife and mother to occupy my existence. I considered, somehow, as a matter of course, that I was growing up to the ordinary destiny, and never troubled myself to seek any other; but now, I perceive plainly, I may have been mistaken. Probably I shall be an old maid. I shall live to see Robert married to some one else, some rich lady: I shall never marry. What was I created for, I wonder? Where is my place in the world?''

She mused again.

''Ah! I see,'' she pursued presently: ''that is the question which most old maids are puzzled to solve; other people solve it for them by saying, 'Your place is to do good to others, to be helpful whenever help is wanted.' That is right in some measure, and a very convenient doctrine for the people who hold it; but I perceive that certain sets of human beings are very apt to maintain that other sets should give up their lives to them and their service, and then they requite them by praise: they call them devoted and virtuous. Is this enough? Is it to live? Is there not a terrible hollowness, mockery, want, craving, in that existence which is given away to others, for want of something of your own to bestow it on? I suspect there is. Does virtue lie in abnegation of self? I do not believe it. Undue humility makes tyranny; weak concession creates selfishness. The Romish religion especially teaches renunciation of self, submission to others, and nowhere are found so many grasping tyrants as in the ranks of the Romish priesthood. Each human being has his share of rights. I suspect it would conduce to the happiness and welfare of all, if each knew his allotment, and held to it as tenaciously as the martyr to his creed. Queer thoughts these, that surge in my mind: are they right thoughts? I am not certain.

"Well, life is short at the best: seventy years, they say, pass like a vapour, like a dream when one awaketh; and every path trod by human feet terminates in one bourne—the grave: the little chink in the surface of this great globe—the furrow where the mighty husbandman with the scythe deposits the seed he has shaken from the ripe stem; and there it falls, decays, and thence it springs again, when the world has rolled round a few times more. So much for the body: the soul meantime wings its long flight upward, folds its wings on the brink of the sea of fire and glass, and gazing down through the burning clearness, finds there mirrored the vision of the Christian's triple Godhead: the Sovereign Father; the mediating Son; the Creator Spirit. Such words, at least, have been chosen to express what is inexpressible, to describe what baffles description. The soul's real hereafter, who shall guess?''

Her fire was decayed to its last cinder; Malone had departed; and now the study bell rang for prayers.

The next day Caroline had to spend altogether alone, her uncle being gone to dine with his friend Dr. Boultby, vicar of Whinbury. The whole time she was talking inwardly in the same strain; looking forwards, asking what she was to do with life. Fanny, as she passed in and out of the room occasionally, intent on housemaid errands, perceived that her young mistress sat very still. She was always in the same place, always bent industriously over a piece of work: she did not lift her head to speak to Fanny, as her custom was; and when the latter remarked that the day was fine, and she ought to take a walk, she only said—"It is cold.''

"You are very diligent at that sewing, Miss Caroline,'' continued the girl, approaching her little table.

"I am tired of it, Fanny.''

"Then why do you go on with it? Put it down: read, or do something to amuse you.''

"It is solitary in this house, Fanny: don't you think so?''

"I don't find it so, miss. Me and Eliza are company for one another; but you are quite too still—you should visit more. Now, be persuaded; go upstairs and dress yourself smart, and go and take tea, in a friendly way, with Miss Mann or Miss Ainley: I am certain either of those ladies would be delighted to see you.''

"But their houses are dismal: they are both old maids. I am certain old maids are a very unhappy race.''

"Not they, miss: they can't be unhappy; they take such care of themselves. They are all selfish.''

"Miss Ainley is not selfish, Fanny: she is always doing good. How devotedly kind she was to her stepmother, as long as the old lady lived; and now when she is quite alone in the world, without brother or sister, or any one to care for her, how charitable she is to the poor, as far as her means permit! Still nobody thinks much of her, or has pleasure in going to see her: and how gentlemen always sneer at her!''

"They shouldn't, miss; I believe she is a good woman: but gentlemen think only of ladies' looks.''

"I'll go and see her,'' exclaimed Caroline, starting up: "and if she asks me to stay to tea, I'll stay. How wrong it is to neglect people because they are not pretty, and young, and merry! Aud I will certainly call to see Miss Mann, too: she may not be amiable; but what has made her unamiable? What has life been to her?''

Fanny helped Miss Helstone to put away her work, and afterwards assisted her to dress.

"*You'll* not be an old maid, Miss Caroline,'' she said, as she tied the sash of her brown-silk frock, having previously smoothed her soft, full, and shining curls; "there are no signs of an old maid about you.''

Caroline looked at the little mirror before her, and she thought there were some signs. She could see that she was altered within the last month; that the hues of her complexion were paler, her eyes changed—a wan shade seemed to circle them,

her countenance was dejected: she was not, in short, so pretty or so fresh as she used to be. She distantly hinted this to Fanny, from whom she got no direct answer, only a remark that people did vary in their looks; but that at her age a little falling away signified nothing,—she would soon come round again, and be plumper and rosier than ever. Having given this assurance, Fanny showed singular zeal in wrapping her up in warm shawls and handkerchiefs, till Caroline, nearly smothered with the weight, was fain to resist further additions.

She paid her visits: first to Miss Mann, for this was the most difficult point: Miss Mann was certainly not quite a lovable person. Till now, Caroline had always unhesitatingly declared she disliked her, and more than once she had joined her cousin Robert in laughing at some of her peculiarities. Moore was not habitually given to sarcasm, especially on anything humbler or weaker than himself; but he had once or twice happened to be in the room when Miss Mann had made a call on his sister, and after listening to her conversation and viewing her features for a time, he had gone out into the garden where his little cousin was tending some of his favourite flowers, and while standing near and watching her, he had amused himself with comparing fair youth—delicate and attractive—with shrivelled eld, livid and loveless, and in jestingly repeating to a smiling girl the vinegar discourse of a cankered old maid. Once on such an occasion, Caroline had said to him, looking up from the luxuriant creeper she was binding to its frame, "Ah! Robert, you do not like old maids. I, too, should come under the lash of your sarcasm, if I were an old maid."

"You an old maid!" he had replied. "A piquant notion suggested by lips of that tint and form. I can fancy you, though, at forty, quietly dressed, pale and sunk, but still with that straight nose, white forehead, and those soft eyes. I suppose, too, you will keep your voice, which has another 'timbre' than that hard, deep organ of Miss Mann's. Courage, Cary!—even at fifty you will not be repulsive."

"Miss Mann did not make herself, or tune her voice, Robert."

"Nature made her in the mood in which she makes her briars and thorns; whereas for the creation of some women, she reserves the May morning hours, when with light and dew she woos the primrose from the turf, and the lily from the wood-moss."

Ushered into Miss Mann's little parlour, Caroline found her, as she always found her, surrounded by perfect neatness, cleanliness, and comfort (after all, is it not a virtue in old maids that solitude rarely makes them negligent or disorderly?); no dust on her polished furniture, none on her carpet, fresh flowers in the vase on her table, a bright fire in the grate. She herself sat primly and somewhat grimly-tidy in a cushioned rocking-chair, her hands busied with some knitting: this was her favourite work, as it required the least exertion. She scarcely rose as Caroline entered; to avoid excitement was one of Miss Mann's aims in life: she had been composing herself ever since she came down in the morning, and had just attained a certain lethargic state of tranquillity when the visitor's knock at the door startled her, and undid her day's work. She was scarcely pleased, therefore, to see Miss Helstone: she received her with reserve, bade her be seated with austerity, and when she got her placed opposite, she fixed her with her eye.

This was no ordinary doom—to be fixed with Miss Mann's eye. Robert Moore had undergone it once, and had never forgotten the circumstance.

He considered it quite equal to anything Medusa could do: he professed to doubt whether, since that infliction, his flesh had been quite what it was before—whether there was not something stony in its texture. The gaze had had such an effect on him as to drive him promptly from the apartment and house; it had even sent him straightway up to the Rectory, where he had appeared in Caroline's presence with a very queer face, and amazed her by demanding a cousinly salute on the spot, to rectify a damage that had been done him.

Certainly Miss Mann had a formidable eye for one of the softer sex: it was prominent, and showed a great deal of the white, and looked as steadily, as unwinkingly, at you as if it were a steel ball soldered in her head; and when, while looking, she began to talk in an indescribably dry monotonous tone—a tone without vibration or inflection—you felt as if a graven image of some bad spirit were addressing you. But it was all a figment of fancy, a matter of surface. Miss Mann's goblin-grimness scarcely went deeper than the angel-sweetness of hundreds of beauties. She was a perfectly honest, conscientious woman, who had performed duties in her day from whose severe anguish many a human Peri, gazelle-eyed, silken-tressed, and silver-tongued, would have shrunk appalled: she had passed alone through protracted scenes of suffering, exercised rigid self-denial, made large sacrifices of time, money, health, for those who had repaid her only by ingratitude, and now her main—almost her sole—fault was, that she was censorious.

Censorious she certainly was. Caroline had not sat five minutes ere her hostess, still keeping her under the spell of that dread and Gorgon gaze, began flaying alive certain of the families in the neighbourhood. She went to work at this business in a singularly cool, deliberate manner, like some surgeon practising with his scalpel on a lifeless subject: she made few distinctions; she allowed scarcely any one to be good; she dissected impartially almost all her acquaintance. If her auditress ventured now and then to put in a palliative word, she set it aside with a certain disdain. Still, though thus pitiless in moral anatomy, she was no scandal-monger: she never disseminated really malignant or dangerous reports: it was not her heart so much as her temper that was wrong.

Caroline made this discovery for the first time to-day; and moved thereby to regret divers unjust judgments she had more than once passed on the crabbed old maid, she began to talk to her softly, not in sympathising words, but with a sympathising voice. The loneliness of her condition struck her visitor in a new light; as did also the character of her ugliness—a bloodless pallor of complexion, and deeply worn lines of feature. The girl pitied the solitary and afflicted woman; her looks told what she felt: a sweet countenance is never so sweet as when the moved heart animates it with compassionate tenderness. Miss Mann, seeing such a countenance raised to her, was touched in her turn: she acknowledged her sense of the interest thus unexpectedly shown in her, who usually met with only coldness and ridicule, by replying to her candidly. Communicative on her own affairs she usually was not, because no one cared to listen to her; but to-day she became so, and her confidant shed tears as she heard her speak: for she told of cruel, slow-wasting, obstinate sufferings. Well might she be corpse-like; well might she look grim, and never smile; well might she wish to avoid excitement, to gain and retain composure! Caroline, when she knew all, acknowledged that Miss Mann was rather to be admired for fortitude than blamed for moroseness. Reader! when you behold an aspect for whose constant gloom and frown you cannot account, whose unvarying cloud exasperates you by its apparent causelessness, be sure that there is a canker somewhere, and a canker not the less deeply corroding because concealed.

Miss Mann felt that she was understood partly, and wished to be understood further; for however old, plain, humble, desolate, afflicted we may be, so long as our hearts preserve the feeblest spark of life, they preserve also, shivering near that pale ember, a starved, ghostly longing for appreciation and affection. To this extenuated spectre, perhaps, a crumb is not thrown once a year; but when ahungered and athirst to famine—when all humanity has forgotten the dying tenant of a decaying house—Divine Mercy remembers the mourner, and a shower of manna falls for lips that earthly nutriment is to pass no more. Biblical promises, heard first in health, but then unheeded, come whispering to the couch of sickness: it is felt that a pitying God watches what all mankind have forsaken; the tender compassion of Jesus is recalled and relied on: the faded eye, gazing beyond Time, sees a Home, a Friend, a Refuge in Eternity.

Miss Mann, drawn on by the still attention of her listener, proceeded to allude to circumstances in her past life. She spoke like one who tells the truth—simply, and with a certain reserve: she did not boast, nor did she exaggerate. Caroline found that the old maid had been a most devoted daughter and sister, an unwearied watcher by lingering deathbeds; that to prolonged and unrelaxing attendance on the sick, the malady that now poisoned her own life owed its origin; that to one wretched relative she had been a support and succour in the depths of self-earned degradation, and that it was still her hand which kept him from utter destitution. Miss Helstone stayed the whole evening, omitting to pay her other intended visit; and when she left Miss Mann, it was with the determination to try in future to excuse her faults, never again to make light of her peculiarities or to laugh at her plainness; and, above all things, not to neglect her, but to come once a week, and to offer her, from one human heart at least, the homage of affection and respect: she felt she could now sincerely give her a small tribute of each feeling.

Caroline, on her return, told Fanny she was very glad she had gone out, as she felt much better for the visit. The next day she failed not to seek Miss Ainley. This lady was in narrower circumstances than Miss Mann, and her dwelling was more humble: it was, however, if possible, yet more exquisitely clean; though the decayed gentlewoman could not afford to keep a servant, but waited on herself, and had only the occasional assistance of a little girl who lived in a cottage near.

Not only was Miss Ainley poorer, but she was even plainer than the other old maid. In her first youth she must have been ugly; now, at the age of fifty, she was *very* ugly. At first sight, all but peculiarly well-disciplined minds were apt to turn from her with annoyance: to conceive against her a prejudice, simply on the ground of her unattractive look. Then she was prim in dress and manner: she looked, spoke, and moved the complete old maid.

Her welcome to Caroline was formal, even in its kindness—for it was kind; but Miss Helstone excused this. She knew something of the benevolence of the heart which beat under that starched kerchief; all the neighbourhood—at least all the female neighbourhood—knew something of it: no one spoke against Miss Ainley except lively young gentlemen, and inconsiderate old ones, who declared her hideous.

Caroline was soon at home in that tiny parlour; a kind hand took from her her shawl and bonnet, and installed her in the most comfortable seat near the fire. The young and the antiquated woman were presently deep in kindly conversation, and soon Caroline became aware of the power a most serene, unselfish, and benignant mind could exercise over those to whom it was developed. She talked never of herself—always of others, Their faults she passed over; her theme was their wants, which she sought to supply; their sufferings, which she longed to alleviate. She was religious—a professor of religion—what some would call "a saint," and she referred to religion often in sanctioned phrase—in phrase which those who possess a perception of the ridiculous, without owning the power of exactly testing and truly judging character, would certainly have esteemed a proper subject for satire—a matter for mimicry and laughter. They would have been hugely mistaken for their pains. Sincerity is never ludicrous; it is always respectable. Whether truth—be it religious or moral truth—speak eloquently and in well-chosen language or not, its voice should be heard with reverence. Let those who cannot nicely, and with certainty, discern the difference between the tones of hypocrisy and those of sincerity, never presume to laugh at all, lest they should have the miserable misfortune to laugh in the wrong place, and commit impiety when they think they are achieving wit.

Not from Miss Ainley's own lips did Caroline hear of her good works; but she knew much of them nevertheless; her beneficence was the familiar topic of the poor in Briarfield. They were not works of almsgiving: the old maid was too poor to give much, though she straitened herself to privation that she might contribute her mite when needful: they were the works of a Sister of Charity, far more difficult

to perform than those of a Lady Bountiful. She would watch by any sick-bed: she seemed to fear no disease; she would nurse the poorest whom none else would nurse: she was serene, humble, kind, and equable through everything.

For this goodness she got but little reward in this life. Many of the poor became so accustomed to her services that they hardly thanked her for them: the rich heard them mentioned with wonder, but were silent, from a sense of shame at the difference between her sacrifices and their own. Many ladies, however, respected her deeply: they could not help it; one gentleman—one only—gave her his friendship and perfect confidence: this was Mr. Hall, the vicar of Nunnely. He said, and said truly, that her life came nearer the life of Christ than that of any other human being he had ever met with. You must not think, reader, that in sketching Miss Ainley's character, I depict a figment of imagination—no—we seek the originals of such portraits in real life only.

Miss Helstone studied well the mind and heart now revealed to her. She found no high intellect to admire: the old maid was merely sensible; but she discovered so much goodness, so much usefulness, so much mildness, patience, truth, that she bent her own mind before Miss Ainley's in reverence. What was her love of nature, what was her sense of beauty, what were her more varied and fervent emotions, what was her deeper power of thought, what her wider capacity to comprehend, compared to the practical excellence of this good woman? Momently, they seemed only beautiful forms of selfish delight; mentally, she trod them under foot.

It is true, she still felt with pain that the life which made Miss Ainley happy could not make her happy: pure and active as it was, in her heart she deemed it deeply dreary because it was so loveless—to her ideas, so forlorn. Yet, doubtless, she reflected, it needed only habit to make it practicable and agreeable to any one: it was despicable, she felt, to pine sentimentally, to cherish secret griefs, vain memories; to be inert, to waste youth in aching languor, to grow old doing nothing.

"I will bestir myself," was her resolution, "and try to be wise if I cannot be good."

She proceeded to make inquiry of Miss Ainley if she could help her in anything. Miss Ainley, glad of an assistant, told her that she could, and indicated some poor families in Briarfield that it was desirable she should visit; giving her likewise, at her further request, some work to do for certain poor women who had many children, and who were unskilled in using the needle for themselves.

Caroline went home, laid her plans, and took a resolve not to swerve from them. She allotted a certain portion of her time for her various studies, and a certain portion for doing anything Miss Ainley might direct her to do; the remainder was to be spent in exercise; not a moment was to be left for the indulgence of such fevered thoughts as had poisoned last Sunday evening.

To do her justice, she executed her plans conscientiously, perseveringly. It was very hard work at first—it was even hard work to the end, but it helped her to stem and keep down anguish: it forced her to be employed; it forbade her to brood; and gleams of satisfaction chequered her grey life here and there when she found she had done good, imparted pleasure, or allayed suffering.

Yet I must speak truth; these efforts brought her neither health of body nor continued peace of mind: with them all, she wasted, grew more joyless and more wan; with them all, her memory kept harping on the name of Robert Moore; an elegy over the past still rung constantly in her ear; a funereal inward cry haunted and harassed her: the heaviness of a broken spirit, and of pining and palsying faculties, settled slow on her buoyant youth. Winter seemed conquering her spring: the mind's soil and its treasures were freezing gradually to barren stagnation.

Chapter XI

FIELDHEAD

YET Caroline refused tamely to succumb: she had native strength in her girl's heart, and she used it. Men and women never struggle so hard as when they struggle alone, without witness, counsellor, or confidant; unencouraged, unadvised, and unpitied.

Miss Helstone was in this position. Her sufferings were her only spur; and being very real and sharp, they roused her spirit keenly. Bent on victory over a mortal pain, she did her best to quell it. Never had she been seen so busy, so studious, and, above all, so active. She took walks in all weathers—long walks in solitary directions. Day by day she came back in the evening, pale and wearied-looking, yet seemingly not fatigued; for still, as soon as she had thrown off her bonnet and shawl, she would, instead of resting, begin to pace her apartment: sometimes she would not sit down till she was literally faint. She said she did this to tire herself well, that she might sleep soundly at night. But if that was her aim it was unattained, for at night, when others slumbered, she was tossing on her pillow, or sitting at the foot of her couch in the darkness, forgetful, apparently, of the necessity of seeking repose. Often, unhappy girl! she was crying—crying in a sort of intolerable despair; which, when it rushed over her, smote down her strength, and reduced her to childlike helplessness.

When thus prostrate, temptations besieged her: weak suggestions whispered in her weary heart to write to Robert, and say that she was unhappy because she was forbidden to see him and Hortense, and that she feared he would withdraw his friendship (not love) from her, and forget her entirely, and begging him to remember her, and sometimes to write to her. One or two such letters she actually indited, but she never sent them: shame and good sense forbade.

At last the life she led reached the point when it seemed she could bear it no longer; that she must seek and find a change somehow, or her heart and head would fail under the pressure which strained them. She longed to leave Briarfield, to go to some very distant place. She longed for something else: the deep, secret, anxious yearning to discover and know her mother strengthened daily; but with the desire was coupled a doubt, a dread—if she knew her, could she love her? There was cause for hesitation, for apprehension on this point: never in her life had she heard that mother praised: whoever mentioned her, mentioned her coolly. Her uncle seemed to regard his sister-in-law with a sort of tacit antipathy; an old servant, who had lived with Mrs. James Helstone for a short time after her marriage, whenever she referred to her former mistress, spoke with chilling reserve: sometimes she called her "queer," sometimes she said she did not understand her. These expressions were ice to the daughter's heart; they suggested the conclusions that it was perhaps better never to know her parent, than to know her and not like her.

But one project could she frame whose execution seemed likely to bring her a hope of relief; it was to take a situation, to be a governess—she could do nothing else. A little incident brought her to the point when she found courage to break her design to her uncle.

Her long and late walks lay always, as has been said, on lonely roads; but in whatever direction she had rambled, whether along the drear skirts of Stilbro' Moor, or over the sunny stretch of Nunnely Common, her homeward path was still so contrived as to lead her near the Hollow. She rarely descended the den, but she visited its brink at twilight almost as regularly as the stars rose over the hill-crests. Her resting-place was at a certain stile under a certain old thorn: thence she could look down on the cottage, the mill, the dewy garden-ground, the still, deep dam; thence was visible the well-known counting-house window, from whose panes at

a fixed hour shot, suddenly bright, the ray of the well-known lamp. Her errand was to watch for this ray: her reward to catch it, sometimes sparkling bright in clear air, sometimes shimmering dim through mist, and anon flashing broken between slant lines of rain—for she came in all weathers.

There were nights when it failed to appear: she knew then that Robert was from home, and went away doubly sad; whereas its kindling rendered her elate, as though she saw in it the promise of some indefinite hope. If, while she gazed, a shadow bent between the light and lattice, her heart leaped—that eclipse was Robert: she had seen him. She would return home comforted, carrying in her mind a clearer vision of his aspect, a distincter recollection of his voice, his smile, his bearing; and, blent with these impressions, was often a sweet persuasion that, if she could get near him, his heart might welcome her presence yet: that at this moment he might be willing to extend his hand and draw her to him, and shelter her at his side as he used to do. That night, though she might weep as usual, she would fancy her tears less scalding; the pillow they watered seemed a little softer; the temples pressed to that pillow ached less.

The shortest path from the Hollow to the Rectory wound near a certain mansion, the same under whose lone walls Malone passed on that night-journey mentioned in an early chapter of this work—the old and tenantless dwelling yclept Fieldhead. Tenantless by the proprietor it had been for ten years, but it was no ruin: Mr. Yorke had seen it kept in good repair, and an old gardener and his wife had lived in it, cultivated the grounds, and maintained the house in habitable condition.

If Fieldhead had few other merits as a building, it might at least be termed picturesque: its irregular architecture, and the grey and mossy colouring communicated by time, gave it a just claim to this epithet. The old latticed windows, the stone porch, the walls, the roof, the chimney-stacks, were rich in crayon touches and sepia lights and shades. The trees behind were fine, bold, and spreading; the cedar on the lawn in front was grand, and the granite urns on the garden wall, the fretted arch of the gateway, were, for an artist, as the very desire of the eye.

One mild May evening, Caroline passing near about moonrise, and feeling, though weary, unwilling yet to go home, where there was only the bed of thorns and the night of grief to anticipate, sat down on the mossy ground near the gate, and gazed through towards cedar and mansion. It was a still night—calm, dewy, cloudless: the gables, turned to the west, reflected the clear amber of the horizon they faced; the oaks behind were black; the cedar was blacker; under its dense, raven boughs a glimpse of sky opened gravely blue: it was full of the moon, which looked solemnly and mildly down on Caroline from beneath that sombre canopy.

She felt this night and prospect mournfully lovely. She wished she could be happy: she wished she could know inward peace: she wondered Providence had no pity on her, and would not help or console her. Recollections of happy trysts of lovers commemorated in old ballads returned on her mind: she thought such tryst in such scene would be blissful. Where now was Robert? she asked: not at the Hollow: she had watched for his lamp long, and had not seen it. She questioned within herself whether she and Moore were ever destined to meet and speak again. Suddenly the door within the stone porch of the hall opened, and two men came out: one elderly and white-headed, the other young, dark-haired, and tall. They passed across the lawn, out through a portal in the garden wall: Caroline saw them cross the road, pass the stile, descend the fields; she saw them disappear. Robert Moore had passed before her with his friend Mr. Yorke: neither had seen her.

The apparition had been transient—scarce seen ere gone; but its electric passage left her veins kindled, her soul insurgent. It found her despairing: it left her desperate— two different states.

"Oh! had he but been alone! Had he but seen me!" was her cry, "he would have said something; he would have given me his hand. He *does*, he *must* love me a little: he would have shown some token of affection: in his eye, on his lips, I

should have read comfort: but the chance is lost. The wind—the cloud's shadow does not pass more silently, more emptily than he. I have been mocked, and Heaven is cruel!''

Thus, in the utter sickness of longing and disappointment, she went home.

The next morning at breakfast, when she appeared white-cheeked and miserable-looking as one who had seen a ghost, she inquired of Mr. Helstone—''Have you any objection, uncle, to my inquiring for a situation in a family?''

Her uncle, ignorant as the table supporting his coffee-cup of all his niece had undergone and was undergoing, scarcely believed his ears.

''What whim now?'' he asked. ''Are you bewitched? What can you mean?''

''I am not well, and need a change,'' she said.

He examined her. He discovered she had *experienced* a change, at any rate. Without his being aware of it, the rose had dwindled and faded to a mere snowdrop: bloom had vanished, flesh wasted; she sat before him drooping, colourless, and thin. But for the soft expression of her brown eyes, the delicate lines of her features, and the flowing abundance of her hair, she would no longer have possessed a claim to the epithet—pretty.

''What on earth is the matter with you?'' he asked. ''What is wrong? How are you ailing?''

No answer, only the brown eyes filled, the faintly-tinted lips trembled.

''Look out for a situation, indeed! For what situation are you fit? What have you been doing with yourself? You are not well.''

''I should be well if I went from home.''

''These women are incomprehensible. They have the strangest knack of startling you with unpleasant surprises. To-day you see them bouncing, buxom, red as cherries, and round as apples; to-morrow they exhibit themselves effete as dead weeds blanched and broken down. And the reason of it all? that's the puzzle. She has her meals, her liberty, a good house to live in, and good clothes to wear, as usual: a while since that sufficed to keep her handsome and cheery, and there she sits now, a poor little, pale, puling chit enough. Provoking! Then comes the question, what is to be done? I suppose I must send for advice. Will you have a doctor, child?''

''No, uncle: I don't want one: a doctor could do me no good. I merely want change of air and scene.''

''Well, if that be the caprice, it shall be gratified. You shall go to a watering-place. I don't mind the expense: Fanny shall accompany you.''

''But, uncle, some day I must do something for myself; I have no fortune. I had better begin now.''

''While I live, you shall not turn out as a governess, Caroline. I will not have it said that my niece is a governess.''

''But the later in life one makes a change of that sort, uncle, the more difficult and painful it is. I should wish to get accustomed to the yoke before any habits of ease and independence are formed.''

''I beg you will not harass me, Caroline. I mean to provide for you. I have always meant to provide for you: I will purchase an annuity. Bless me; I am but fifty-five; my health and constitution are excellent: there is plenty of time to save and take measures. Don't make yourself anxious respecting the future: is that what frets you?''

''No, uncle; but I long for a change.''

He laughed. ''There speaks the woman!'' cried he, ''the very woman! A change! a change! Always fantastical and whimsical? Well, it's in her sex.''

''But it is not fantasy and whim, uncle.''

''What is it, then?''

''Necessity, I think. I feel weaker than formerly; I believe I should have more to do.''

"Admirable! She feels weak, and *therefore* she should be set to hard labour—'clair comme le jour'—as Moore—confound Moore! You shall go to Cliff Bridge; and there are two guineas to buy a new frock. Come, Cary, never fear: we'll find balm in Gilead."

"Uncle, I wish you were less generous, and more"——

"More what?"

Sympathising was the word on Caroline's lips, but it was not uttered: she checked herself in time: her uncle would indeed have laughed if that namby-pamby word had escaped her. Finding her silent, he said—"The fact is, you don't know precisely what you want."

"Only to be a governess."

"Pooh! mere nonsense! I'll not hear of governessing. Don't mention it again. It is rather too feminine a fancy. I have finished breakfast, ring the bell: put all crotchets out of your head, and run away and amuse yourself."

"What with? My doll?" asked Caroline to herself as she quitted the room.

A week or two passed; her bodily and mental health neither grew worse nor better. She was now precisely in that state, when, if her constitution had contained the seeds of consumption, decline, or slow fever, those diseases would have been rapidly developed, and would soon have carried her quietly from the world. People never die of love or grief alone; though some die of inherent maladies, which the tortures of those passions prematurely force into destructive action. The sound by nature undergo these tortures, and are racked, shaken, shattered: their beauty and bloom perish, but life remains untouched. They are brought to a certain point of dilapidation; they are reduced to pallor, debility, and emaciation. People think, as they see them gliding languidly about, that they will soon withdraw to sick-beds, perish there, and cease from among the healthy and happy. This does not happen: they live on; and though they cannot regain youth and gaiety, they may regain strength and serenity. The blossom which the March wind nips, but fails to sweep away, may survive to hang a withered apple on the tree late into autumn: having braved the last frosts of spring, it may also brave the first of winter.

Every one noticed the change in Miss Helstone's appearance, and most people said she was going to die. She never thought so herself: she felt in no dying case; she had neither pain nor sickness. Her appetite was diminished; she knew the reason: it was because she wept so much at night. Her strength was lessened; she could account for it; sleep was coy and hard to be won; dreams were distressing and baleful. In the far future she still seemed to anticipate a time when this passage of misery should be got over, and when she should once more be calm, though perhaps never again happy.

Meanwhile her uncle urged her to visit; to comply with the frequent invitations of their acquaintance: this she evaded doing; she could not be cheerful in company: she felt she was observed there with more curiosity than sympathy. Old ladies were always offering her their advice, recommending this or that nostrum; young ladies looked at her in a way she understood, and from which she shrank. Their eyes said they knew she had been "disappointed," as custom phrases it: by whom, they were not certain.

Commonplace young ladies can be quite as hard as commonplace young gentlemen—quite as worldly and selfish. Those who suffer should always avoid them; grief and calamity they despise: they seem to regard them as the judgments of God on the lowly. With them, to "love" is merely to contrive a scheme for achieving a good match: to be "disappointed" is to have their scheme seen through and frustrated. They think the feelings and projects of others on the subject of love similar to their own, and judge them accordingly.

All this Caroline knew, partly by instinct, partly by observation: she regulated her conduct by her knowledge, keeping her pale face and wasted figure as much

out of sight as she could. Living thus in complete seclusion, she ceased to receive intelligence of the little transactions of the neighbourhood.

One morning her uncle came into the parlour, where she sat endeavouring to find some pleasure in painting a little group of wild flowers, gathered under a hedge at the top of the Hollow fields, and said to her in his abrupt manner—''Come, child, you are always stooping over palette, or book, or sampler: leave that tinting work. By-the-bye, do you put your pencil to your lips when you paint?''

''Sometimes, uncle, when I forget.''

''Then it is that which is poisoning you. The paints are deleterious, child: there is white lead and red lead, and verdigris, and gamboge, and twenty other poisons in those colour cakes. Lock them up! lock them up! Get your bonnet on. I want you to make a call with me.''

''With *you*, uncle?''

This question was asked in a tone of surprise. She was not accustomed to make calls with her uncle: she never rode or walked out with him on any occasion.

''Quick! quick! I am always busy, you know: I have no time to lose.''

She hurriedly gathered up her materials, asking, meantime, where they were going.

''To Fieldhead.''

''Fieldhead! What, to see old James Booth, the gardener? Is he ill?''

''We are going to see Miss Shirley Keeldar.''

''Miss Keeldar! Is she come to Yorkshire? Is she at Fieldhead?''

''She is. She has been there a week. I met her at a party last night;—that party to which you would not go. I was pleased with her: I choose that you shall make her acquaintance: it will do you good.''

''She is now come of age, I suppose?''

''She is come of age, and will reside for a time on her property. I lectured her on the subject: I showed her her duty: she is not intractable; she is rather a fine girl; she will teach you what it is to have a sprightly spirit: nothing lackadaisical about *her*.''

''I don't think she will want to see me, or to have me introduced to her. What good can I do her? How can I amuse her?''

''Pshaw! Put your bonnet on.''

''Is she proud, uncle?''

''Don't know. You hardly imagine she would show her pride to me, I suppose? A chit like that would scarcely presume to give herself airs with the Rector of her parish, however rich she might be.''

''No—but how did she behave to other people?''

''Didn't observe. She holds her head high, and probably can be saucy enough where she dare—she wouldn't be a woman otherwise. There,—away now for your bonnet at once!''

Not naturally very confident, a failure of physical strength and a depression of spirits had not tended to increase Caroline's presence of mind and ease of manner, or to give her additional courage to face strangers, and she quailed, in spite of self-remonstrance, as she and her uncle walked up the broad, paved approach leading from the gateway of Fieldhead to its porch. She followed Mr. Helstone reluctantly through that porch into the sombre old vestibule beyond.

Very sombre it was; long, vast, and dark: one latticed window lit it but dimly; the wide old chimney contained now no fire, for the present warm weather needed it not; it was filled instead with willow-boughs. The gallery on high, opposite the entrance, was seen but in outline, so shadowy became this hall towards its ceiling; carved stags' heads, with real antlers, looked down grotesquely from the walls. This was neither a grand nor a comfortable house: within as without it was antique, rambling, and incommodious. A property of a thousand a year belonged to it; which property had descended, for lack of male heirs, on a female. There were mercantile

families in the district boasting twice the income, but the Keeldars, by virtue of their antiquity, and their distinction of lords of the manor, took the precedence of all.

Mr. and Miss Helstone were ushered into a parlour: of course, as was to be expected in such a Gothic old barrack, this parlour was lined with oak: fine dark, glossy panels compassed the walls gloomily and grandly. Very handsome, reader, these shining brown panels are: very mellow in colouring and tasteful in effect, but—if you know what a "Spring-clean" is—very execrable and inhuman. Whoever, having the bowels of humanity, has seen servants scrubbing at these polished wooden walls with bees-waxed cloths on a warm May day, must allow that they are "intolerable and not to be endured"; and I cannot but secretly applaud the benevolent barbarian who had painted another and larger apartment of Fieldhead— the drawing-room to wit, formerly also an oak-room—of a delicate pinky white; thereby earning for himself the character of a Hun, but mightily enhancing the cheerfulness of that portion of his abode, and saving future housemaids a world of toil.

The brown-panelled parlour was furnished all in old style, and with real old furniture. On each side of the high mantelpiece stood two antique chairs of oak, solid as sylvan thrones, and in one of these sat a lady. But if this were Miss Keeldar, she must have come of age at least some twenty years ago: she was of matronly form, and though she wore no cap, and possessed hair of quite an undimmed auburn, shading small and naturally young-looking features, she had no youthful aspect, nor apparently the wish to assume it. You could have wished her attire of a newer fashion: in a well-cut, well-made gown, hers would have been no uncomely presence. It puzzled you to guess why a garment of handsome materials should be arranged in such scanty folds, and devised after such an obsolete mode: you felt disposed to set down the wearer as somewhat eccentric at once.

This lady received the visitors with a mixture of ceremony and diffidence quite English: no middle-aged matron who was not an Englishwoman *could* evince precisely the same manner; a manner so uncertain of herself, of her own merits, of her power to please; and yet so anxious to be proper, and if possible, rather agreeable than otherwise. In the present instance, however, more embarrassment was shown than is usual even with diffident Englishwomen: Miss Helstone felt this, sympathised with the stranger, and knowing by experience what was good for the timid, took a seat quietly near her, and began to talk to her with a gentle ease, communicated for the moment by the presence of one less self-possessed than herself.

She and this lady would, if alone, have at once got on extremely well together. The lady had the clearest voice imaginable: infinitely softer and more tuneful than could have been reasonably expected from forty years, and a form decidedly inclined to embonpoint. This voice Caroline liked: it atoned for the formal, if correct, accent and language: the lady would soon have discovered she liked it and her, and in ten minutes they would have been friends. But Mr. Helstone stood on the rug looking at them both; looking especially at the strange lady with his sarcastic, keen eye, that clearly expressed impatience of her chilly ceremony, and annoyance at her want of aplomb. His hard gaze and rasping voice discomfited the lady more and more; she tried, however, to get up little speeches about the weather, the aspect of the country, etc., but the impracticable Mr. Helstone presently found himself somewhat deaf: whatever she said, he affected not to hear distinctly, and she was obliged to go over each elaborately constructed nothing twice. The effort soon became too much for her; she was just rising in a perplexed flutter, nervously murmuring that she knew not what detained Miss Keeldar—that she would go and look for her, when Miss Keeldar saved her the trouble by appearing: it was to be presumed at least that she who now came in through a glass-door from the garden owned that name.

There is real grace in ease of manner, and so old Helstone felt when an erect, slight girl walked up to him, retaining with her left hand her little silk apron full of flowers, and, giving him her right hand, said pleasantly—"I knew you would come to see me, though you *do* think Mr. Yorke has made me a Jacobin. Good-morning."

"But we'll not have you a Jacobin," returned he. "No, Miss Shirley, they shall not steal the flower of my parish from me: now that you are amongst us, you shall be my pupil in politics and religion: I'll teach you sound doctrine on both points."

"Mrs. Pryor has anticipated you," she replied, turning to the elder lady. "Mrs. Pryor, you know, was my governess, and is still my friend; and of all the high and rigid Tories, she is queen; of all the stanch churchwomen, she is chief. I have been well drilled both in theology and history, I assure you, Mr. Helstone."

The Rector immediately bowed very low to Mrs. Pryor, and expressed himself obliged to her.

The ex-governess disclaimed skill either in political or religious controversy, explained that she thought such matters little adapted for female minds, but avowed herself in general terms the advocate of order and loyalty, and, of course, truly attached to the Establishment. She added, she was ever averse to change under any circumstances; and something scarcely audible about the extreme danger of being too ready to take up new ideas, closed her sentence.

"Miss Keeldar thinks as you think, I hope, madam."

"Difference of age and difference of temperament occasion difference of sentiment," was the reply. "It can scarcely be expected that the eager and young should hold the opinions of the cool and middle-aged."

"Oh! oh! we are independent: we think for ourselves!" cried Mr. Helstone. "We are a little Jacobin, for anything I know: a little free-thinker, in good earnest. Let us have a confession of faith on the spot."

And he took the heiress's two hands—causing her to let fall her whole cargo of flowers—and seated her by him on the sofa.

"Say your creed," he ordered.

"The Apostles' creed?"

"Yes."

She said it like a child.

"Now for St. Athanasius's: that's the test!"

"Let me gather up my flowers: here is Tartar coming, he will tread upon them."

Tartar was a rather large, strong, and fierce-looking dog, very ugly, being of a breed between mastiff and bull-dog, who at this moment entered through the glass-door, and posting directly to the rug, snuffed the fresh flowers scattered there. He seemed to scorn them as food; but probably thinking their velvety petals might be convenient as litter, he was turning round preparatory to depositing his tawny bulk upon them, when Miss Helstone and Miss Keeldar simultaneously stooped to the rescue.

"Thank you," said the heiress, as she again held out her little apron for Caroline to heap the blossoms into it. "Is this your daughter, Mr. Helstone?" she asked.

"My niece, Caroline,"

Miss Keeldar shook hands with her, and then looked at her. Caroline also looked at her hostess.

Shirley Keeldar (she had no Christian name but Shirley: her parents, who had wished to have a son, finding that, after eight years of marriage, Providence had granted them only a daughter, bestowed on her the same masculine family cognomen they would have bestowed on a boy, if with a boy they had been blessed)—Shirley Keeldar was no ugly heiress: she was agreeable to the eye. Her height and shape were not unlike Miss Helstone's: perhaps in stature she might have the advantage by an inch or two; she was gracefully made, and her face, too, possessed a charm as well described by the word grace as any other. It was pale naturally, but intelligent,

and of varied expression. She was not a blonde, like Caroline: clear and dark were the characteristics of her aspect as to colour: her face and brow were clear, her eyes of the darkest grey: no green lights in them,—transparent, pure, neutral grey: and her hair of the darkest brown. Her features were distinguished: by which I do not mean that they were high, bony, and Roman, being indeed rather small and slightly marked than otherwise; but only that they were, to use a few French words, "fins, gracieux, spirituels": mobile they were and speaking; but their changes were not to be understood, nor their language interpreted all at once. She examined Caroline seriously, inclining her head a little to one side, with a thoughtful air.

"You see she is only a feeble chick," observed Mr. Helstone.

"She looks young—younger than I. How old are you?" she inquired, in a manner that would have been patronising if it had not been extremely solemn and simple.

"Eighteen years and six months."

"And I am twenty-one."

She said no more; she had now placed her flowers on the table, and was busied in arranging them.

"And St. Athanasius's creed?" urged the Rector; "you believe it all—don't you?"

"I can't remember it quite all. I will give you a nosegay, Mr. Helstone, when I have given your niece one."

She had selected a little bouquet of one brilliant and two or three delicate flowers, relieved by a spray of dark verdure: she tied it with silk from her work-box, and placed it on Caroline's lap; and then she put her hands behind her, and stood bending slightly towards her guest, still regarding her, in the attitude and with something of the aspect of a grave but gallant little cavalier. This temporary expression of face was aided by the style in which she wore her hair, parted on one temple, and brushed in a glossy sweep above the forehead, whence it fell in curls that looked natural, so free were their wavy undulations.

"Are you tired with your walk?" she inquired.

"No—not in the least; it is but a short distance—but a mile."

"You look pale. Is she always so pale?" she asked, turning to the Rector.

"She used to be as rosy as the reddest of your flowers."

"Why is she altered? What has made her pale? Has she been ill?"

"She tells me she wants a change."

"She ought to have one: you ought to give her one: you should send her to the sea-coast."

"I will, ere summer is over. Meantime, I intend her to make acquaintance with you, if you have no objection."

"I am sure Miss Keeldar will have no objection," here observed Mrs. Pryor. "I think I may take it upon me to say that Miss Helstone's frequent presence at Fieldhead will be esteemed a favour."

"You speak my sentiments precisely, ma'am," said Shirley, "and I thank you for anticipating me. Let me tell you," she continued, turning again to Caroline, "that you also ought to thank my governess; it is not every one she would welcome as she has welcomed you: you are distinguished more than you think. This morning, as soon as you are gone, I shall ask Mrs. Pryor's opinion of you. I am apt to rely on her judgment of character, for hitherto I have found it wondrous accurate. Already I foresee a favourable answer to my inquiries: do I not guess rightly, Mrs. Pryor?"

"My dear—you said but now you would ask my opinion when Miss Helstone was gone; I am scarcely likely to give it in her presence."

"No—and perhaps it will be long enough before I obtain it. I am sometimes sadly tantalised, Mr. Helstone, by Mrs. Pryor's extreme caution: her judgments ought to be correct when they come, for they are often as tardy of delivery as a Lord Chancellor's: on some people's characters I cannot get her to pronounce sentence, entreat as I may."

Mrs. Pryor here smiled.

"Yes," said her pupil, "I know what that smile means: you are thinking of my gentleman-tenant. Do you know Mr. Moore of the Hollow?" she asked Mr. Helstone.

"Ay! ay! your tenant—so he is: you have seen a good deal of him, no doubt, since you came?"

"I have been obliged to see him: there was business to transact. Business! Really the word makes me conscious I am indeed no longer a girl, but quite a woman and something more. I am an esquire! Shirley Keeldar, Esquire, ought to be my style and title. They gave me a man's name; I hold a man's position: it is enough to inspire me with a touch of manhood, and when I see such people as that stately Anglo-Belgian—that Gérard Moore before me, gravely talking to me of business, really I feel quite gentleman-like. You must choose me for your church-warden, Mr. Helstone, the next time you elect new ones: they ought to make me a magistrate and a captain of yeomanry: Tony Lumpkin's mother was a colonel, and his aunt a justice of the peace—why shouldn't I be?"

"With all my heart. If you choose to get up a requisition on the subject, I promise to head the list of signatures with my name. But you were speaking of Moore?"

"Ah! yes. I find it a little difficult to understand Mr. Moore—to know what to think of him: whether to like him or not. He seems a tenant of whom any proprietor might be proud—and proud of him I am, in that sense—but as a neighbour, what is he? Again and again I have entreated Mrs. Pryor to say what she thinks of him, but she still evades returning a direct answer. I hope you will be less oracular, Mr. Helstone, and pronounce at once: do you like him?"

"Not at all, just now: his name is entirely blotted from my good books."

"What is the matter? What has he done?"

"My uncle and he disagree on politics," interposed the low voice of Caroline. She had better not have spoken just then: having scarcely joined in the conversation before, it was not apropos to do it now: she felt this with nervous acuteness as soon as she had spoken, and coloured to the eyes.

"What are Moore's politics?" inquired Shirley.

"Those of a tradesman," returned the Rector; "narrow, selfish, and unpatriotic. The man is eternally writing and speaking against the continuance of the war: I have no patience with him."

"The war hurts his trade. I remember he remarked that only yesterday. But what other objection have you to him?"

"That is enough."

"He looks the gentleman, in my sense of the term," pursued Shirley, "and it pleases me to think he is such."

Caroline rent the Tyrian petals of the one brilliant flower in her bouquet, and answered in distinct tones—"Decidedly he is." Shirley, hearing this courageous affirmation, flashed an arch, searching glance at the speaker from her deep, expressive eyes.

"*You* are his friend, at any rate," she said; "you defend him in his absence."

"I am both his friend and his relative," was the prompt reply. "Robert Moore is my cousin."

"Oh, then, you can tell me all about him. Just give me a sketch of his character."

Insuperable embarrassment seized Caroline when this demand was made: she could not, and did not attempt to comply with it. Her silence was immediately covered by Mrs. Pryor, who proceeded to address sundry questions to Mr. Helstone regarding a family or two in the neighbourhood, with whose connections in the south she said she was acquainted. Shirley soon withdrew her gaze from Miss Helstone's face. She did not renew her interrogations, but returning to her flowers, proceeded to choose a nosegay for the Rector. She presented it to him as he took leave, and received the homage of a salute on the hand in return.

"Be sure you wear it for my sake," said she.

"Next my heart, of course," responded Helstone. "Mrs. Pryor, take care of this future magistrate, this churchwarden in perspective, this captain of yeomanry, this young squire of Briarfield, in a word: don't let him exert himself too much: don't let him break his neck in hunting: especially, let him mind how he rides down that dangerous hill near the Hollow."

"I like a descent," said Shirley—"I like to clear it rapidly; and especially I like that romantic Hollow, with all my heart."

"Romantic—with a mill in it?"

"Romantic with a mill in it. The old mill and the white cottage are each admirable in its way."

"And the counting-house, Mr. Keeldar?"

"The counting-house is better than my bloom-coloured drawing-room: I adore the counting-house."

"And the trade? The cloth—the greasy wool—the polluting dyeing-vats?"

"The trade is to be thoroughly respected."

"And the tradesman is a hero? Good!"

"I am glad to hear you say so: I thought the tradesman looked heroic."

Mischief, spirit, and glee sparkled all over her face as she thus bandied words with the old Cossack, who almost equally enjoyed the tilt.

"Captain Keeldar, you have no mercantile blood in your veins: why are you so fond of trade?"

"Because I am a mill-owner, of course. Half my income comes from the works in that Hollow."

"Don't enter into partnership, that's all."

"You've put it into my head! you've put it into my head!" she exclaimed, with a joyous laugh. "It will never get out: thank you." And waving her hand, white as a lily and fine as a fairy's, she vanished within the porch, while the Rector and his niece passed out through the arched gateway.

Chapter XII

SHIRLEY AND CAROLINE

SHIRLEY showed she had been sincere in saying she should be glad of Caroline's society, by frequently seeking it: and, indeed, if she had not sought it, she would not have had it; for Miss Helstone was slow to make fresh acquaintance. She was always held back by the idea that people could not want her,—that she could not amuse them; and a brilliant, happy, youthful creature, like the heiress of Fieldhead, seemed to her too completely independent of society so uninteresting as hers, ever to find it really welcome.

Shirley might be brilliant, and probably happy likewise, but no one is independent of genial society; and though in about a month she had made the acquaintance of most of the families round, and was on quite free and easy terms with all the Misses Sykes, and all the Misses Pearson, and the two superlative Misses Wynne of Walden Hall; yet, it appeared, she found none amongst them very genial: she fraternised with none of them, to use her own words. If she had had the bliss to be really Shirley Keeldar, Esq., Lord of the Manor of Briarfield, there was not a single fair one in this and the two neighbouring parishes, whom she should have felt disposed to request to become Mrs. Keeldar, lady of the manor. This declaration she made to Mrs. Pryor, who received it very quietly, as she did most of her pupil's off-hand speeches, responding—"My dear, do not allow that habit of alluding to yourself as a gentleman to be confirmed: it is a strange one. Those who do not know you, hearing you speak thus, would think you affected masculine manners."

Shirley never laughed at her former governess: even the little formalities and harmless peculiarities of that lady were respectable in her eyes: had it been otherwise, she would have proved herself a weak character at once: for it is only the weak who make a butt of quiet worth; therefore she took her remonstrance in silence. She stood quietly near the window, looking at the grand cedar on her lawn, watching a bird on one of its lower boughs. Presently she began to chirrup to the bird: soon her chirrup grew clearer; erelong she was whistling; the whistle struck into a tune, and very sweetly and deftly it was executed.

"My dear!" expostulated Mrs. Pryor.

"Was I whistling?" said Shirley; "I forgot. I beg your pardon, ma'am. I had resolved to take care not to whistle before you."

"But, Miss Keeldar, where did you learn to whistle? You must have got the habit since you came down into Yorkshire. I never knew you guilty of it before."

"Oh! I learned to whistle a long while ago."

"Who taught you?"

"No one: I took it up by listening, and I had laid it down again; but lately, yesterday evening, as I was coming up our lane, I heard a gentleman whistling that very tune in the field on the other side of the hedge, and that reminded me."

"What gentleman was it?"

"We have only one gentleman in this region, ma'am, and that is Mr. Moore: at least he is the only gentleman who is not grey-haired: my two venerable favourites, Mr. Helstone and Mr. Yorke, it is true, are fine old beaux; infinitely better than any of the stupid young ones."

Mrs. Pryor was silent.

"You do not like Mr. Helstone, ma'am?"

"My dear, Mr. Helstone's office secures him from criticism."

"You generally contrive to leave the room when he is announced."

"Do you walk out this morning, my dear?"

"Yes, I shall go to the Rectory, and seek and find Caroline Helstone, and make her take some exercise: she shall have a breezy walk over Nunnely Common."

"If you go in that direction, my dear, have the goodness to remind Miss Helstone to wrap up well, as there is a fresh wind, and she appears to me to require care."

"You shall be minutely obeyed, Mrs. Pryor: meantime, will you not accompany us yourself?"

"No, my love; I should be a restraint upon you: I am stout, and cannot walk so quickly as you would wish to do."

Shirley easily persuaded Caroline to go with her: and when they were fairly out on the quiet road, traversing the extensive and solitary sweep of Nunnely Common, she as easily drew her into conversation. The first feelings of diffidence overcome, Caroline soon felt glad to talk with Miss Keeldar. The very first interchange of slight observations sufficed to give each an idea of what the other was. Shirley said she liked the green sweep of the common turf, and, better still, the heath on its ridges, for the heath reminded her of moors: she had seen moors when she was travelling on the borders near Scotland. She remembered particularly a district traversed one long afternoon, on a sultry but sunless day in summer: they journeyed from noon till sunset, over what seemed a boundless waste of deep heath, and nothing had they seen but wild sheep; nothing heard but the cries of wild birds.

"I know how the heath would look on such a day," said Caroline; "purple-black: a deeper shade of the sky-tint, and that would be livid."

"Yes—quite livid, with brassy edges to the clouds, and here and there a white gleam, more ghastly than the lurid tinge, which, as you looked at it, you momentarily expected would kindle into blinding lightning."

"Did it thunder?"

"It muttered distant peals, but the storm did not break till evening, after we had reached our inn: that inn being an isolated house at the foot of a range of mountains."

"Did you watch the clouds come down over the mountains?"

"I did: I stood at the window an hour watching them. The hills seemed rolled in a sullen mist, and when the rain fell in whitening sheets, suddenly they were blotted from the prospect: they were washed from the world."

"I have seen such storms in hilly districts in Yorkshire; and at their riotous climax, while the sky was all cataract, the earth all flood, I have remembered the Deluge."

"It is singularly reviving after such hurricanes to feel calm return, and from the opening clouds to receive a consolatory gleam, softly testifying that the sun is not quenched."

"Miss Keeldar, just stand still now, and look down at Nunnely dale and wood."

They both halted on the green brow of the Common: they looked down on the deep valley robed in May raiment; on varied meads, some pearled with daisies, and some golden with king-cups: to-day all this young verdure smiled clear in sunlight; transparent emerald and amber gleams played over it. On Nunnwood—the sole remnant of antique British forest in a region whose lowlands were once all sylvan chase, as its highlands were breast-deep heather—slept the shadow of a cloud; the distant hills were dappled, the horizon was shaded and tinted like mother-of-pearl; silvery blues, soft purples, evanescent greens and rose-shades, all melting into fleeces of white cloud, pure as azury snow, allured the eye as with a remote glimpse of heaven's foundations. The air blowing on the brow was fresh, and sweet, and bracing.

"Our England is a bonnie island," said Shirley, "and Yorkshire is one of her bonniest nooks."

"You are a Yorkshire girl too?"

"I am—Yorkshire in blood and birth. Five generations of my race sleep under the aisles of Briarfield Church: I drew my first breath in the old black hall behind us."

Hereupon Caroline presented her hand, which was accordingly taken and shaken. "We are compatriots," said she.

"Yes," agreed Shirley, with a grave nod.

"And that," asked Miss Keeldar, pointing to the forest—"that is Nunnwood?"

"It is."

"Were you ever there?"

"Many a time."

"In the heart of it?"

"Yes."

"What is it like?"

"It is like an encampment of forest sons of Anak. The trees are huge and old. When you stand at their roots, the summits seem in another region: the trunks remain still and firm as pillars, while the boughs sway to every breeze. In the deepest calm their leaves are never quite hushed, and in high wind a flood rushes—a sea thunders above you."

"Was it not one of Robin Hood's haunts?"

"Yes, and there are mementoes of him still existing. To penetrate into Nunnwood, Miss Keeldar, is to go far back into the dim days of old. Can you see a break in the forest, about the centre?"

"Yes, distinctly."

"That break is a dell; a deep, hollow cup, lined with turf as green and short as the sod of this common: the very oldest of the trees, gnarled mighty oaks crowd about the brink of this dell: in the bottom lie the ruins of a nunnery."

"We will go—you and I alone, Caroline—to that wood, early some fine summer morning, and spend a long day there. We can take pencils and sketch-books, and any interesting readingbook we like; and of course we shall take something to eat. I have two little baskets, in which Mrs. Gill, my housekeeper, might pack our

provisions, and we could each carry our own. It would not tire you too much to walk so far?''

"Oh, no; especially if we rested the whole day in the wood, and I know all the pleasantest spots: I know where we could get nuts in nutting time; I know where wild strawberries abound: I know certain lonely, quite untrodden glades, carpeted with strange mosses, some yellow as if gilded, some a sober grey, some gem-green. I know groups of trees that ravish the eye with their perfect, picture-like effects: rude oak, delicate birch, glossy beech, clustered in contrast; and ash trees stately as Saul, standing isolated, and superannuated wood-giants clad in bright shrouds of ivy. Miss Keeldar, I could guide you.''

"You would be dull with me alone?''

"I should not. I think we should suit: and what third person is there whose presence would not spoil our pleasure?''

"Indeed, I know of none about our own ages—no lady at least, and as to gentlemen''——

"An excursion becomes quite a different thing when there are gentlemen of the party,'' interrupted Caroline.

"I agree with you—quite a different thing to what we were proposing.''

"We were going simply to see the old trees, the old ruins; to pass a day in old times, surrounded by olden silence, and above all by quietude.''

"You are right; and the presence of gentlemen dispels the last charm, I think. If they are of the wrong sort, like your Malones, and your young Sykes, and Wynnes, irritation takes the place of serenity. If they are of the right sort, there is still a change—I can hardly tell what change, one easy to feel, difficult to describe.''

"We forget Nature, imprimis.''

"And then Nature forgets us; covers her vast calm brow with a dim veil, conceals her face, and withdraws the peaceful joy with which, if we had been content to worship her only, she would have filled our hearts.''

"What does she give us instead?''

"More elation and more anxiety: an excitement that steals the hours away fast, and a trouble that ruffles their course.''

"Our power of being happy lies a good deal in ourselves, I believe,'' remarked Caroline sagely. "I have gone to Nunnwood with a large party, all the curates and some other gentry of these parts, together with sundry ladies; and I found the affair insufferably tedious and absurd: and I have gone quite alone, or accompanied but by Fanny, who sat in the woodman's hut and sewed, or talked to the good wife, while I roamed about and made sketches, or read; and I have enjoyed much happiness of a quiet kind all day long. But that was when I was young—two years ago.''

"Did you ever go with your cousin, Robert Moore?''

"Yes; once.''

"What sort of a companion is he on these occasions?''

"A cousin, you know, is different to a stranger.''

"I am aware of that; but cousins, if they are stupid, are still more insupportable than strangers, because you cannot so easily keep them at a distance. But your cousin is not stupid?''

"No; but——''

"Well?''

"If the company of fools irritates, as you say, the society of clever men leaves its own peculiar pain also. Where the goodness or talent of your friend is beyond and above all doubt, your own worthiness to be his associate often becomes a matter of question.''

"Oh! there I cannot follow you: that crotchet is not one I should choose to entertain for an instant. I consider myself not unworthy to be the associate of the best of them—of gentlemen, I mean: though that is saying a great deal. Where they are good, they are very good, I believe. Your uncle, by-the-bye, is not a bad

specimen of the elderly gentleman: I am always glad to see his brown, keen, sensible old face, either in my own house or any other. Are you fond of him? Is he kind to you? Now speak the truth.''

"He has brought me up from childhood, I doubt not, precisely as he would have brought up his own daughter, if he had had one; and that is kindness; but I am not fond of him: I would rather be out of his presence than in it.''

"Strange! when he has the art of making himself so agreeable.''

"Yes, in company; but he is stern and silent at home. As he puts away his cane and shovel-hat in the Rectory-hall, so he locks his liveliness in his book-case and study-desk: the knitted brow and brief word for the fire-side; the smile, the jest, the witty sally, for society.''

"Is he tyrannical?''

"Not in the least: he is neither tyrannical nor hypocritical: he is simply a man who is rather liberal than good-natured, rather brilliant than genial, rather scrupulously equitable than truly just,—if you can understand such superfine distinctions?''

"Oh! yes: good-nature implies indulgence, which he has not; geniality, warmth of heart, which he does not own; and genuine justice is the offspring of sympathy and considerateness, of which, I can well conceive, my bronzed old friend is quite innocent.''

"I often wonder, Shirley, whether most men resemble my uncle in their domestic relations; whether it is necessary to be new and unfamiliar to them, in order to seem agreeable or estimable in their eyes; and whether it is impossible to their natures to retain a constant interest and affection for those they see every day.''

"I don't know: I can't clear up your doubts. I ponder over similar ones myself sometimes. But, to tell you a secret, if I were convinced that they are necessarily and universally different from us—fickle, soon petrifying, unsympathising—I would never marry. I should not like to find out that what I loved did not love me, that it was weary of me, and that whatever effort I might make to please would hereafter be worse than useless, since it was inevitably in its nature to change and become indifferent. That discovery once made, what should I long for? To go away—to remove from a presence where my society gave no pleasure.''

"But you could not, if you were married.''

"No, I could not,—there it is. I could never be my own mistress more. A terrible thought!—it suffocates me! Nothing irks me like the idea of being a burden and a bore,—an inevitable burden,—a ceaseless bore! Now, when I feel my company superfluous, I can comfortably fold my independence round me like a mantle, and drop my pride like a veil, and withdraw to solitude. If married, that could not be.''

"I wonder we don't all make up our minds to remain single,'' said Caroline: "we should if we listened to the wisdom of experience. My uncle always speaks of marriage as a burden; and I believe whenever he hears of a man being married, he invariably regards him as a fool, or at any rate, as doing a foolish thing.''

"But, Caroline, men are not all like your uncle: surely not—I hope not.''

She paused and mused.

"I suppose we each find an exception in the one we love, till we *are* married,'' suggested Caroline.

"I suppose so: and this exception we believe to be of sterling materials; we fancy it like ourselves; we imagine a sense of harmony. We think his voice gives the softest, truest promise of a heart that will never harden against us: we read in his eyes that faithful feeling—affection. I don't think we should trust to what they call passion at all, Caroline. I believe it is a mere fire of dry sticks, blazing up and vanishing: but we watch him, and see him kind to animals, to little children, to poor people. He is kind to us likewise—good—considerate: he does not flatter women, but he is patient with them, and he seems to be easy in their presence, and to find their company genial. He likes them not only for vain and selfish reasons, but as *we* like him—because we like him. Then we observe that he is

just—that he always speaks the truth—that he is conscientious. We feel joy and peace when he comes into a room: we feel sadness and trouble when he leaves it. We know that this man has been a kind son, that he is a kind brother: will any one dare to tell me that he will not be a kind husband?''

"My uncle would affirm it unhesitatingly. 'He will be sick of you in a month,' he would say."

"Mrs. Pryor would seriously intimate the same."

"Miss Yorke and Miss Mann would darkly suggest ditto."

"If they are true oracles, it is good never to fall in love."

"Very good, if you can avoid it."

"I choose to doubt their truth."

"I am afraid that proves you are already caught."

"Not I: but if I were, do you know what soothsayers I would consult?"

"Let me hear."

"Neither man nor woman, elderly nor young:—the little Irish beggar that comes barefoot to my door; the mouse that steals out of the cranny in the wainscot; the bird that in frost and snow pecks at my window for a crumb; the dog that licks my hand and sits beside my knee."

"Did you ever see any one who was kind to such things?"

"Did you ever see any one whom such things seemed instinctively to follow, like, rely on?"

"We have a black cat and an old dog at the Rectory. I know somebody to whose knee that black cat loves to climb; against whose shoulder and cheek it likes to purr. The old dog always comes out of his kennel and wags his tail, and whines affectionately when somebody passes."

"And what does that somebody do?"

"He quietly strokes the cat, and lets her sit while he conveniently can, and when he must disturb her by rising, he puts her softly down, and never flings her from him roughly; he always whistles to the dog and gives him a caress."

"Does he? It is not Robert?"

"But it is Robert."

"Handsome fellow!" said Shirley, with enthusiasm: her eyes sparkled.

"Is he not handsome? Has he not fine eyes and well-cut features, and a clear, princely forehead?"

"He has all that, Caroline. Bless him! he is both graceful and good."

"I was sure you would see that he was: when I first looked at your face I knew you would."

"I was well inclined to him before I saw him. I liked him when I did see him: I admire him now. There is charm in beauty for itself, Caroline; when it is blent with goodness, there is a powerful charm."

"When mind is added, Shirley?"

"Who can resist it?"

"Remember my uncle, Mesdames Pryor, Yorke, and Mann."

"Remember the croaking of the frogs of Egypt! He is a noble being. I tell you when they *are* good, they are the lords of the creation,—they are the sons of God. Moulded in their Maker's image, the minutest spark of His spirit lifts them almost above mortality. Indisputably, a great, good, handsome man is the first of created things."

"Above us?"

"I would scorn to contend for empire with him,—I would scorn it. Shall my left hand dispute for precedence with my right?—shall my heart quarrel with my pulse?—shall my veins be jealous of the blood which fills them?"

"Men and women, husbands and wives quarrel horribly, Shirley."

"Poor things!—poor, fallen, degenerate things! God made them for another lot—for other feelings."

"But are we men's equals, or are we not?"

"Nothing ever charms me more than when I meet my superior—one who makes me sincerely feel that he is my superior."

"Did you ever meet him?"

"I should be glad to see him any day: the higher above me, so much the better: it degrades to stoop—it is glorious to look up. What frets me is, that when I try to esteem, I am baffled: when religiously inclined, there are but false gods to adore. I disdain to be a Pagan."

"Miss Keeldar, will you come in? We are here at the Rectory gates."

"Not to-day; but to-morrow I shall fetch you to spend the evening with me. Caroline Helstone—if you really are what at present to me you seem—you and I will suit. I have never in my whole life been able to talk to a young lady as I have talked to you this morning. Kiss me—and good-bye."

* * * * * * *

Mrs. Pryor seemed as well-disposed to cultivate Caroline's acquaintance as Shirley. She, who went nowhere else, called on an early day at the Rectory. She came in the afternoon, when the Rector happened to be out. It was rather a close day; the heat of the weather had flushed her, and she seemed fluttered, too, by the circumstance of entering a strange house; for it appeared her habits were most retiring and secluded. When Miss Helstone went to her in the dining-room she found her seated on the sofa, trembling, fanning herself with her handkerchief, and seeming to contend with a nervous discomposure that threatened to become hysterical.

Caroline marvelled somewhat at this unusual want of self-command in a lady of her years, and also at the lack of real strength in one who appeared almost robust: for Mrs. Pryor hastened to allege the fatigue of her walk, the heat of the sun, etc., as reasons for her temporary indisposition; and still as, with more hurry than coherence, she again and again enumerated these causes of exhaustion, Caroline gently sought to relieve her by opening her shawl and removing her bonnet. Attentions of this sort, Mrs. Pryor would not have accepted from everyone: in general, she recoiled from touch or close approach, with a mixture of embarrassment and coldness far from flattering to those who offered her aid: to Miss Helstone's little light hand, however, she yielded tractably, and seemed soothed by its contact. In a few minutes she ceased to tremble, and grew quiet and tranquil.

Her usual manner being resumed, she proceeded to talk of ordinary topics. In a miscellaneous company, Mrs. Pryor rarely opened her lips; or, if obliged to speak, she spoke under restraint, and consequently not well; in dialogue, she was a good converser: her language, always a little formal, was well chosen; her sentiments were just; her information was varied and correct. Caroline felt it pleasant to listen to her: more pleasant than she could have anticipated.

On the wall opposite the sofa where they sat, hung three pictures: the centre one, above the mantel-piece, that of a lady; the two others, male portraits.

"That is a beautiful face," said Mrs. Pryor, interrupting a brief pause which had followed half-an-hour's animated conversation: "the features may be termed perfect; no statuary's chisel could improve them: it is a portrait from the life, I presume?"

"It is a portrait of Mrs. Helstone."

"Of Mrs. Matthewson Helstone? Of your uncle's wife?"

"It is, and is said to be a good likeness: before her marriage, she was accounted the beauty of the district."

"I should say she merited the distinction: what accuracy in all the lineaments! It is, however, a passive face: the original could not have been what is generally termed 'a woman of spirit.' "

"I believe she was a remarkably still, silent person."

"One would scarcely have expected, my dear, that your uncle's choice should have fallen on a partner of that description. Is he not fond of being amused by lively chat?"

"In company he is; but he always says he could never do with a talking wife: he must have quiet at home. You go out to gossip, he affirms; you come home to read and reflect."

"Mrs. Matthewson lived but a few years after her marriage, I think I have heard?"

"About five years."

"Well, my dear," pursued Mrs. Pryor, rising to go, "I trust it is understood that you will frequently come to Fieldhead: I hope you will. You must feel lonely here, having no female relative in the house: you must necessarily pass much of your time in solitude."

"I am inured to it: I have grown up by myself. May I arrange your shawl for you?"

Mrs. Pryor submitted to be assisted.

"Should you chance to require help in your studies," she said, "you may command me."

Caroline expressed her sense of such kindness.

"I hope to have frequent conversations with you. I should wish to be of use to you."

Again Miss Helstone returned thanks. She thought what a kind heart was hidden under her visitor's seeming chilliness. Observing that Mrs. Pryor again glanced with an air of interest towards the portraits, as she walked down the room, Caroline casually explained—"The likeness that hangs near the window, you will see, is my uncle, taken twenty years ago; the other, to the left of the mantelpiece, is his brother James, my father."

"They resemble each other in some measure," said Mrs. Pryor; "yet a difference of character may be traced in the different mould of the brow and mouth."

"What difference?" inquired Caroline, accompanying her to the door. "James Helstone—that is, my father—is generally considered the best-looking of the two: strangers, I remark, always exclaim, 'What a handsome man!' Do you think his picture handsome, Mrs. Pryor?"

"It is much softer or finer featured than that of your uncle."

"But where or what is the difference of character to which you alluded? Tell me: I wish to see if you guess right."

"My dear, your uncle is a man of principle: his forehead and his lips are firm, and his eye is steady."

"Well, and the other? Do not be afraid of offending me: I always like the truth."

"Do you like the truth? It is well for you: adhere to that preference—never swerve thence. The other, my dear, if he had been living now, would probably have furnished little support to his daughter. It is, however, a graceful head—taken in youth, I should think. My dear" (turning abruptly), "you acknowledge an inestimate value in principle?"

"I am sure no character can have true worth without it."

"You feel what you say? You have considered the subject?"

"Often. Circumstances early forced it upon my attention."

"The lesson was not lost, then, though it came so prematurely. I suppose the soil is not light nor stony, otherwise seed falling in that season never would have borne fruit. My dear, do not stand in the air of the door, you will take cold: good afternoon."

Miss Helstone's new acquaintance soon became of value to her: their society was acknowledged a privilege. She found she would have been in error indeed to have let slip this chance of relief—to have neglected to avail herself of this happy change: a turn was thereby given to her thoughts; a new channel was opened for them, which, diverting a few of them at least from the one direction in which all

had hitherto tended, abated the impetuosity of their rush, and lessened the force of their pressure on one worn-down point.

Soon she was content to spend whole days at Fieldhead, doing by turns whatever Shirley or Mrs. Pryor wished her to do: and now one would claim her, now the other. Nothing could be less demonstrative than the friendship of the elder lady; but also nothing could be more vigilant, assiduous, untiring. I have intimated that she was a peculiar personage; and in nothing was her peculiarity more shown than in the nature of the interest she evinced for Caroline. She watched all her movements: she seemed as if she would have guarded all her steps: it gave her pleasure to be applied to by Miss Helstone for advice and assistance; she yielded her aid, when asked, with such quiet yet obvious enjoyment, that Caroline ere long took delight in depending on her.

Shirley Keeldar's complete docility with Mrs. Pryor had at first surprised Miss Helstone, and not less the fact of the reserved ex-governess being so much at home and at ease in the residence of her young pupil, where she filled with such quiet independency a very dependent post; but she soon found that it needed but to know both ladies to comprehend fully the enigma. Every one, it seemed to her, must like, must love, must prize Mrs. Pryor when they knew her. No matter that she perseveringly wore old-fashioned gowns; that her speech was formal, and her manner cool; that she had twenty little ways such as nobody else had—she was still such a stay, such a counsellor, so truthful, so kind in her way, that, in Caroline's idea, none once accustomed to her presence could easily afford to dispense with it.

As to dependency or humiliation, Caroline did not feel it in her intercourse with Shirley, and why should Mrs. Pryor? The heiress was rich—very rich—compared with her new friend: one possessed a clear thousand a year—the other not a penny; and yet there was a safe sense of equality experienced in her society, never known in that of the ordinary Briarfield and Whinbury gentry.

The reason was, Shirley's head ran on other things than money and position. She was glad to be independent as to property: by fits she was even elated at the notion of being lady of the manor, and having tenants and an estate: she was especially tickled with an agreeable complacency when reminded of "all that property" down in the Hollow, "comprising an excellent cloth-mill, dyehouse, warehouse, together with the messuage, gardens, and outbuildings, termed Hollow's Cottage"; but her exultation being quite undisguised was singularly inoffensive; and, for her serious thoughts, they tended elsewhere. To admire the great, reverence the good, and be joyous with the genial, was very much the bent of Shirley's soul: she mused therefore on the means of following this bent far oftener than she pondered on her social superiority.

In Caroline Miss Keeldar had first taken an interest because she was quiet, retiring, looked delicate, and seemed as if she needed some one to take care of her. Her predilection increased greatly when she discovered that her own way of thinking and talking was understood and responded to by this new acquaintance. She had hardly expected it. Miss Helstone, she fancied, had too pretty a face, manners and voice too soft, to be anything out of the common way in mind and attainments; and she very much wondered to see the gentle features light up archly to the reveillé of a dry sally or two risked by herself; and more did she wonder to discover the self-won knowledge treasured, and the untaught speculations working in that girlish, curl-veiled head. Caroline's instinct of taste, too, was like her own: such books as Miss Keeldar had read with the most pleasure, were Miss Helstone's delight also. They held many aversions too in common, and could have the comfort of laughing together over works of false sentimentality and pompous pretension.

Few, Shirley conceived, men or women have the right taste in poetry: the right sense for discriminating between what is real and what is false. She had again and again heard very clever people pronounce this or that passage, in this or that versifier,

altogether admirable, which, when she read, her soul refused to acknowledge as anything but cant, flourish, and tinsel, or at the best, elaborate wordiness; curious, clever, learned perhaps; haply even tinged with the fascinating hues of fancy, but, God knows, as different from real poetry as the gorgeous and massy vase of mosaic is from the little cup of pure metal; or, to give the reader a choice of similes, as the milliner's artificial wreath is from the fresh-gathered lily of the field.

Caroline, she found, felt the value of the true ore, and knew the deception of the flashy dross. The minds of the two girls being toned in harmony, often chimed very sweetly together.

One evening, they chanced to be alone in the oak-parlour. They had passed a long wet day together without ennui; it was now on the edge of dark; candles were not yet brought in; both, as twilight deepened, grew meditative and silent. A western wind roared high round the hall, driving wild clouds and stormy rain up from the far-remote ocean: all was tempest outside the antique lattices, all deep peace within. Shirley sat at the window, watching the rack in heaven, the mist on earth, listening to certain notes of the gale that plained like restless spirits—notes which, had she not been so young, gay, and healthy, would have swept her trembling nerves like some omen, some anticipatory dirge: in this her prime of existence and bloom of beauty, they but subdued vivacity to pensiveness. Snatches of sweet ballads haunted her ear; now and then she sang a stanza: her accents obeyed the fitful impulse of the wind; they swelled as its gusts rushed on, and died as they wandered away. Caroline, withdrawn to the farthest and darkest end of the room, her figure just discernible by the ruby shine of the flameless fire, was pacing to and fro, murmuring to herself fragments of well-remembered poetry. She spoke very low, but Shirley heard her; and while singing softly, she listened, This was the strain:

> Obscurist night involved the sky,
> The Atlantic billows roar'd,
> When such a destined wretch as I,
> Washed headlong from on board,
> Of friends, of hope, of all bereft,
> His floating home for ever left.

Here the fragment stopped; because Shirley's song, erewhile somewhat full and thrilling, had become delicately faint.

"Go on," said she.

"Then you go on, too. I was only repeating *The Castaway*."

"I know: if you can remember it all, say it all."

And as it was nearly dark, and, after all, Miss Keeldar was no formidable auditor, Caroline went through it. She went through it as she should have gone through it. The wild sea, the drowning mariner, the reluctant ship swept on in the storm, you heard were realised by her; and more vividly was realised the heart of the poet, who did not weep for The Castaway, but who, in an hour of tearless anguish, traced a semblance to his own God-abandoned misery in the fate of that man-forsaken sailor, and cried from the depths where he struggled:

> No voice divine the storm allayed,
> No light propitious shone,
> When, snatch'd from all effectual aid,
> We perish'd—each alone!
> But I—beneath a rougher sea,
> And whelm'd in deeper gulfs than he.

"I hope William Cowper is safe and calm in heaven now," said Caroline.

"Do you pity what he suffered on earth?" asked Miss Keeldar.

"Pity him, Shirley? What can I do else? He was nearly broken-hearted when he wrote that poem, and it almost breaks one's heart to read it. But he found relief in writing it—I know he did; and that gift of poetry—the most divine bestowed on man—was, I believe, granted to allay emotions when their strength threatens harm. It seems to me, Shirley, that nobody should write poetry to exhibit intellect or attainment. Who cares for that sort of poetry? Who cares for learning—who cares for fine words in poetry? And who does not care for feeling—real feeling—however simply, even rudely expressed?"

"It seems you care for it, at all events: and certainly, in hearing that poem, one discovers that Cowper was under an impulse strong as that of the wind which drove the ship—an impulse which, while it would not suffer him to stop to add ornament to a single stanza, filled him with force to achieve the whole with consummate perfection. You managed to recite it with a steady voice, Caroline: I wonder thereat."

"Cowper's hand did not tremble in writing the lines; why should my voice falter in repeating them? Depend on it, Shirley, no tear blistered the manuscript of *The Castaway*, I hear in it no sob of sorrow, only the cry of despair; but, that cry uttered, I believe the deadly spasm passed from his heart; that he wept abundantly, and was comforted."

Shirley resumed her ballad minstrelsy. Stopping short, she remarked ere long— "One could have loved Cowper, if it were only for the sake of having the privilege of comforting him."

"You never would have loved Cowper," rejoined Caroline promptly: "he was not made to be loved by woman."

"What do you mean?"

"What I say. I know there is a kind of natures in the world—and very noble, elevated natures, too—whom love never comes near. You might have sought Cowper with the intention of loving him; and you would have looked at him, pitied him, and left him: forced away by a sense of the impossible, the incongruous, as the crew were borne from their drowning comrade by 'the furious blast.' "

"You may be right. Who told you this?"

"And what I say of Cowper, I should say of Rousseau. Was Rousseau ever loved? He loved passionately; but was his passion ever returned? I am certain, never. And if there were any female Cowpers and Rousseaus, I should assert the same of them."

"Who told you this, I ask? Did Moore?"

"Why should anybody have told me? Have I not an instinct? Can I not divine by analogy? Moore never talked to me either about Cowper, or Rousseau, or love. The voice we hear in solitude told me all I know on these subjects."

"Do you like characters of the Rousseau order, Caroline?"

"Not at all, as a whole. I sympathise intensely with certain qualities they possess: certain divine sparks in their nature dazzle my eyes, and make my soul glow. Then, again, I scorn them. They are made of clay and gold. The refuse and the ore make a mass of weakness: taken altogether, I feel them unnatural, unhealthy, repulsive."

"I dare say I should be more tolerant of a Rousseau than you would, Cary: submissive and contemplative yourself, you like the stern and the practical. By the way, you must miss that Cousin Robert of yours very much, now that you and he never meet."

"I do."

"And he must miss you?"

"That he does not."

"I cannot imagine," pursued Shirley, who had lately got a habit of introducing Moore's name into the conversation, even when it seemed to have no business there,—"I cannot imagine but that he was fond of you, since he took so much notice of you, talked to you, and taught you so much."

"He never was fond of me: he never professed to be fond of me. He took pains to prove that he only just tolerated me."

Caroline, determined not to err on the flattering side in estimating her cousin's regard for her, always now habitually thought of it and mentioned it in the most scanty measure. She had her own reasons for being less sanguine than ever in hopeful views of the future: less indulgent to pleasurable retrospections of the past.

"Of course, then," observed Miss Keeldar, "you only just tolerated him, in return?"

"Shirley, men and women are so different: they are in such a different position. Women have so few things to think about—men so many: you may have a friendship for a man, while he is almost indifferent to you. Much of what cheers your life may be dependent on him, while not a feeling or interest of moment in his eyes may have reference to you. Robert used to be in the habit of going to London, sometimes for a week or a fortnight together; well, while he was away, I found his absence a void: there was something wanting; Briarfield was duller. Of course, I had my usual occupations; still I missed him. As I sat by myself in the evenings, I used to feel a strange certainty of conviction I cannot describe: that if a magician or a genius had, at that moment, offered me Prince Ali's tube (you remember it in the *Arabian Nights*?), and if, with its aid, I had been enabled to take a view of Robert—to see where he was, how occupied—I should have learned, in a startling manner, the width of the chasm which gaped between such as he and such as I. I knew that, however my thoughts might adhere to him, his were effectually sundered from me."

"Caroline," demanded Miss Keeldar abruptly, "don't you wish you had a profession—a trade?"

"I wish it fifty times a day. As it is, I often wonder what I came into the world for. I long to have something absorbing and compulsory to fill my head and hands, and to occupy my thoughts."

"Can labour alone make a human being happy?"

"No; but it can give varieties of pain, and prevent us from breaking our hearts with a single tyrant master-torture. Besides, successful labour has its recompense; a vacant, weary, lonely, hopeless life has none."

"But hard labour and learned professions, they say, make women masculine, coarse, unwomanly."

"And what does it signify, whether unmarried and never-to-be-married women are unattractive and inelegant, or not?—provided only they are decent, decorous, and neat, it is enough. The utmost which ought to be required of old maids, in the way of appearance, is that they should not absolutely offend men's eyes as they pass them in the street; for the rest, they should be allowed, without too much scorn, to be as absorbed, grave, plain-looking, and plain-dressed as they please."

"You might be an old maid yourself, Caroline, you speak so earnestly."

"I shall be one: it is my destiny. I will never marry a Malone or a Sykes—and no one else will ever marry me."

Here fell a long pause. Shirley broke it. Again the name by which she seemed bewitched was almost the first on her lips.

"Lina—did not Moore call you Lina sometimes?"

"Yes: it is sometimes used as the abbreviation of Caroline in his native country."

"Well, Lina, do you remember my one day noticing an inequality in your hair—a curl wanting on that right side—and your telling me that it was Robert's fault, as he had once cut therefrom a long lock?"

"Yes."

"If he is, and always was, as indifferent to you as you say, why did he steal your hair?"

"I don't know—yes, I do: it was my doing, not his. Everything of that sort always was my doing. He was going from home, to London, as usual; and the

night before he went, I had found in his sister's workbox a lock of black hair—a short, round curl: Hortense told me it was her brother's and a keepsake. He was sitting near the table; I looked at his head—he has plenty of hair; on the temples were many such round curls. I thought he could spare me one: I knew I should like to have it, and I asked for it. He said, on condition that he might have his choice of a tress from my head; so he got one of my long locks of hair, and I got one of his short ones. I keep his, but, I dare say, he has lost mine. It was my doing, and one of those silly deeds it distresses the heart and sets the face on fire to think of: one of those small but sharp recollections that return, lacerating your self-respect like tiny penknives, and forcing from your lips, as you sit alone, sudden, insane-sounding interjections.''

"Caroline!"

"I *do* think myself a fool, Shirley, in some respects: I *do* despise myself. But I said I would not make you my confessor; for you cannot reciprocate foible for foible: you are not weak. How steadily you watch me now! Turn aside your clear, strong, she-eagle eye: it is an insult to fix it on me thus.''

"What a study of character you are! Weak, certainly; but not in the sense you think.—Come in!"

This was said in answer to a tap at the door. Miss Keeldar happened to be near it at the moment, Caroline at the other end of the room; she saw a note put into Shirley's hands, and heard the words—"From Mr. Moore, ma'am:''

"Bring candles," said Miss Keeldar.

Caroline sat expectant.

"A communication on business," said the heiress; but when candles were brought, she neither opened nor read it. The Rector's Fanny was presently announced, and the Rector's niece went home.

Chapter XIII

FURTHER COMMUNICATIONS ON BUSINESS

IN Shirley's nature prevailed at times an easy indolence: there were periods when she took delight in perfect vacancy of hand and eye—moments when her thoughts, her simple existence, the fact of the world being around—and heaven above her, seemed to yield her such fulness of happiness, that she did not need to lift a finger to increase the joy. Often, after an active morning, she would spend a sunny afternoon in lying stirless on the turf, at the foot of some tree of friendly umbrage: no society did she need but that of Caroline, and it sufficed if she were within call; no spectacle did she ask but that of the deep blue sky, and such cloudlets as sailed afar and aloft across its span; no sound but that of the bee's hum, the leaf's whisper. Her sole book in such hours was the dim chronicle of memory, or the sibyl page of anticipation: from her young eyes fell on each volume a glorious light to read by; round her lips at moments played a smile which revealed glimpses of the tale or prophecy: it was not sad, not dark. Fate had been benign to the blissful dreamer, and promised to favour her yet again. In her past were sweet passages; in her future rosy hopes.

Yet one day when Caroline drew near to rouse her, thinking she had lain long enough, behold, as she looked down, Shirley's cheek was wet as if with dew: those fine eyes of hers shone humid and brimming.

"Shirley, why do *you* cry?" asked Caroline, involuntarily laying stress on *you*.

Miss Keeldar smiled, and turned her picturesque head towards the questioner. "Because it pleases me mightily to cry," she said; "my heart is both sad and glad:

but why, you good, patient child—why do you not bear me company? I only weep tears, delightful and soon wiped away: you might weep gall, if you choose.''

"Why should I weep gall?"

"Mateless, solitary bird!" was the only answer.

"And are not you, too, mateless, Shirley?"

"At heart—no."

"Oh! who nestles there, Shirley?"

But Shirley only laughed gaily at this question, and alertly started up.

"I have dreamed," she said: "a mere day-dream; certainly bright, probably baseless!"

$$* * * * * * *$$

Miss Helstone was by this time free enough from illusions: she took a sufficiently grave view of the future, and fancied she knew pretty well how her own destiny and that of some others were tending. Yet old associations retained their influence over her, and it was these, and the power of habit, which still frequently drew her of an evening to the field-stile and the old thorn overlooking the Hollow.

One night, the night after the incident of the note, she had been at her usual post, watching for her beacon—watching vainly; that evening no lamp was lit. She waited till the rising of certain constellations warned her of lateness, and signed her away. In passing Fieldhead, on her return, its moonlight beauty attracted her glance, and stayed her step an instant. Tree and hall rose peaceful under the night sky and clear full orb; pearly paleness gilded the building; mellow brown gloom bosomed it round; shadows of deep green brooded above its oak-wreathed roof. The broad pavement in front shone pale also; it gleamed as if some spell had transformed the dark granite to glistering Parian: on the silvery space slept two sable shadows, thrown sharply defined from two human figures. These figures when first seen were motionless and mute; presently they moved in harmonious step, and spoke low in harmonious key. Earnest was the gaze that scrutinised them as they emerged from behind the trunk of the cedar. "Is it Mrs. Pryor and Shirley?"

Certainly it is Shirley. Who else has a shape so lithe, and proud and graceful? And her face, too, is visible: her countenance careless and pensive, and musing and mirthful, and mocking and tender. Not fearing the dew, she has not covered her head; her curls are free: they veil her neck and caress her shoulder with their tendril rings. An ornament of gold gleams through the half-closed folds of the scarf she has wrapped across her bust, and a large bright gem glitters on the white hand which confines it. Yes, that is Shirley.

Her companion then is, of course, Mrs. Pryor?

Yes, if Mrs. Pryor owns six feet of stature, and if she has changed her decent widow's weeds for masculine disguise. The figure walking at Miss Keeldar's side is a man—a tall, young, stately man—it is her tenant, Robert Moore.

The pair speak softly, their words are not distinguishable: to remain a moment to gaze is not to be an eavesdropper; and as the moon shines so clearly and their countenances are so distinctly apparent, who can resist the attraction of such interest; Caroline it seems cannot, for she lingers.

There was a time when, on summer nights, Moore had been wont to walk with his cousin, as he was now walking with the heiress. Often had she gone up the Hollow with him after sunset, to scent the freshness of the earth, where a growth of fragrant herbage carpeted a certain narrow terrace, edging a deep ravine, from whose rifted gloom was heard a sound like the spirit of the lonely watercourse, moaning amongst its wet stones, and between its weedy banks, and under its dark bower of alders.

"But I used to be closer to him," thought Caroline: "he felt no obligation to treat me with homage; I needed only kindness. He used to hold my hand: he does

not touch hers. Aud yet Shirley is not proud where she loves. There is no haughtiness in her aspect now, only a little in her port; what is natural to and inseparable from her; what she retains in her most careless as in her most guarded moments. Robert must think as I think, that he is at this instant looking down on a fine face; and he must think it with a man's brain, not with mine. She has such generous, yet soft fire in her eyes. She smiles—what makes her smile so sweet? I saw that Robert felt its beauty, and he must have felt it with his man's heart, not with my dim woman's perceptions. They look to me like two great happy spirits; yonder silver pavement reminds me of that white shore we believe to be beyond the death-flood: they have reached it, they walk there united. And what am I—standing here in shadow, shrinking into concealment, my mind darker than my hiding-place? I am one of this world, no spirit—a poor, doomed mortal, who asks, in ignorance and hopelessness, wherefore she was born, to what end she lives; whose mind for ever runs on the question, how she shall at last encounter, and by whom be sustained through death?

"This is the worst passage I have come to yet: still I was quite prepared for it. I gave Robert up, and gave him up to Shirley, the first day I heard she was come: the first moment I saw her—rich, youthful, and lovely. She has him now: he is her lover; she is his darling: she will be far more his darling yet when they are married: the more Robert knows of Shirley, the more his soul will cleave to her. They will both be happy, and I do not grudge them their bliss; but I groan under my own misery: some of my suffering is very acute. Truly, I ought not to have been born: they should have smothered me at the first cry."

Here, Shirley stepping aside to gather a dewy flower, she and her companion turned into a path that lay nearer the gate: some of their conversation became audible. Caroline would not stay to listen: she passed away noiselessly, and the moonlight kissed the wall which her shadow had dimmed. The reader is privileged to remain, and try what he can make of the discourse.

"I cannot conceive why Nature did not give you a bulldog's head, for you have all a bulldog's tenacity," said Shirley.

"Not a flattering idea: am I so ignoble?"

"And something also you have of the same animal's silent ways of going about its work: you give no warning; you come noiselessly behind, seize fast, and hold on."

"This is guess-work; you have witnessed no such feat on my part: in your presence I have been no bulldog."

"Your very silence indicates your race. How little you talk in general, yet how deeply you scheme! You are far-seeing; you are calculating."

"I know the ways of these people. I have gathered information of their intentions. My note last night informed you that Barraclough's trial had ended in his conviction and sentence to transportation: his associates will plot vengeance. I shall lay my plans so as to counteract, or, at least, be prepared for theirs; that is all. Having now given you as clear an explanation as I can, am I to understand that for what I propose doing I have your approbation?"

"I shall stand by you so long as you remain on the defensive. Yes."

"Good! Without any aid—even opposed or disapproved by you—I believe I should have acted precisely as I now intend to act; but in another spirit. I now feel satisfied. On the whole, I relish the position."

"I dare say you do; that is evident: you relish the work which lies before you still better than you would relish the execution of a government order for army-cloth."

"I certainly feel it congenial."

"So would old Helstone. It is true there is a shade of difference in your motives: many shades, perhaps. Shall I speak to Mr. Helstone? I will, if you like."

"Act as you please: your judgment, Miss Keeldar, will guide you accurately. I could rely on it myself, in a more difficult crisis; but I should inform you, Mr. Helstone is somewhat prejudiced against me at present."

"I am aware, I have heard all about your differences: depend upon it they will melt away: he cannot resist the temptation of an alliance under present circumstances."

"I should be glad to have him: he is of true metal."

"I think so also."

"An old blade, and rusted somewhat; but the edge and temper still excellent."

"Well, you shall have him, Mr, Moore; that is, if I can win him."

"Whom can you not win?"

"Perhaps not the Rector; but I will make the effort."

"Effort! He will yield for a word—a smile."

"By no means. It will cost me several cups of tea, some toast and cake, and an ample measure of remonstrances, expostulations, and persuasions. It grows rather chill."

"I perceive you shiver. Am I acting wrongly to detain you here? Yet it is so calm: I even feel it warm; and society such as yours is a pleasure to me so rare.— If you were wrapped in a thicker shawl——"

"I might stay longer, and forget how late it is, which would chagrin Mrs. Pryor. We keep early and regular hours at Fieldhead, Mr. Moore; and so, I am sure, does your sister at the cottage."

"Yes; but Hortense and I have an understanding the most convenient in the world, that we shall each do as we please."

"How do you please to do?"

"Three nights in the week I sleep in the mill: but I require little rest; and when it is moonlight and mild, I often haunt the Hollow till daybreak."

"When I was a very little girl, Mr. Moore, my nurse used to tell me tales of fairies being seen in that Hollow. That was before my father built the mill, when it was a perfectly solitary ravine: you will be falling under enchantment."

"I fear it is done," said Moore, in a low voice.

"But there are worse things than fairies to be guarded against," pursued Miss Keeldar.

"Things more perilous," he subjoined.

"Far more so. For instance, how would you like to meet Michael Hartley, that mad Calvinist and Jacobin weaver? They say he is addicted to poaching, and often goes abroad at night with his gun."

"I have already had the luck to meet him. We held a long argument together one night. A strange little incident it was: I liked it."

"Liked it? I admire your taste! Michael is not sane. Where did you meet him?"

"In the deepest, shadiest spot in the glen, where the water runs low, under brushwood. We sat down near that plank bridge. It was moonlight, but clouded, and very windy. We had a talk."

"On politics?"

"And religion. I think the moon was at the full, and Michael was as near crazed as possible: he uttered strange blasphemy in his Antinomian fashion."

"Excuse me, but I think you must have been nearly as mad as he, to sit listening to him."

"There is a wild interest in his ravings. The man would be half a poet, if he were not wholly a maniac; and perhaps a prophet, if he were not a profligate. He solemnly informed me that hell was foreordained my inevitable portion; that he read the mark of the beast on my brow; that I had been an outcast from the beginning. God's vengeance, he said, was preparing for me, and affirmed that in a vision of the night he had beheld the manner and the instrument of my doom. I wanted to know further, but he left me with these words, 'The end is not yet.' "

"Have you ever seen him since?"

"About a month afterwards, in returing from market, I encountered him and Moses Barraclough both in an advanced stage of inebriation: they were praying in frantic sort at the roadside. They accosted me as Satan, bid me avaunt, and clamoured to be delivered from temptation. Again, but a few days ago, Michael took the trouble of appearing at the counting-house door, hatless, in his shirt-sleeves,—his coat and castor having been detained at the public-house in pledge; he delivered himself of the comfortable message that he could wish Mr. Moore to set his house in order, as his soul was likely shortly to be required of him."

"Do you make light of these things?"

"The poor man had been drinking for weeks, and was in a state bordering on delirium tremens."

"What then? He is the more likely to attempt the fulfilment of his own prophecies."

"It would not do to permit incidents of this sort to affect one's nerves."

"Mr. Moore, go home!"

"So soon?"

"Pass straight down the fields, not round by the lane and plantations."

"It is early yet."

"It is late: for my part I am going in. Will you promise me not to wander in the Hollow to-night?"

"If you wish it."

"I do wish it. May I ask whether you consider life valueless?"

"By no means: on the contrary, of late I regard my life as invaluable."

"Of late?"

"Existence is neither aimless nor hopeless to me now; and it was both three months ago. I was then drowning, and rather wished the operation over. All at once a hand was stretched to me,—such a delicate hand, I scarcely dared trust it:— its strength, however, has rescued me from ruin."

"Are you really rescued?"

"For the time: your assistance has given me another chance."

"Live to make the best of it. Don't offer yourself as a target to Michael Hartley, and good-night!"

* * * * * * *

Miss Helstone was under a promise to spend the evening of the next day at Fieldhead: she kept her promise. Some gloomy hours had she spent in the interval. Most of the time had been passed shut up in her own apartment; only issuing from it, indeed, to join her uncle at meals, and anticipating inquiries from Fanny by telling her that she was busy altering a dress, and preferred sewing upstairs, to avoid interruption.

She did sew: she plied her needle continuously, ceaselessly; but her brain worked faster than her fingers. Again, and more intensely than ever, she desired a fixed occupation,—no matter how onerous, how irksome. Her uncle must be once more entreated, but first she would consult Mrs. Pryor. Her head laboured to frame projects as diligently as her hands to plait and stitch the thin texture of the muslin summer dress spread on the little white couch at the foot of which she sat. Now and then, while thus doubly occupied, a tear would fill her eyes and fall on her busy hands; but this sign of emotion was rare and quickly effaced: the sharp pang passed, the dimness cleared from her vision; she would re-thread her needle, rearrange tuck and trimming, and work on.

Late in the afternoon she dressed herself: she reached Fieldhead, and appeared in the oak parlour just as tea was brought in. Shirley asked her why she came so late.

"Because I have been making my dress," said she. "These fine sunny days began to make me ashamed of my winter merino; so I have furbished up a lighter garment."

"In which you look as I like to see you," said Shirley. "You are a lady-like little person, Caroline: is she not, Mrs, Pryor?"

Mrs. Pryor never paid compliments, and seldom indulged in remarks, favourable or otherwise, on personal appearance. On the present occasion she only swept Caroline's curls from her cheek as she took a seat near her, caressed the oval outline, and observed—"You get somewhat thin, my love, and somewhat pale. Do you sleep well? Your eyes have a languid look"; and she gazed at her anxiously.

"I sometimes dream melancholy dreams," answered Caroline; "and if I lie awake for an hour or two in the night, I am continually thinking of the Rectory as a dreary old place. You know it is very near the churchyard: the back part of the house is extremely ancient, and it is said that the out-kitchens there were once enclosed in the churchyard, and that there are graves under them. I rather long to leave the Rectory."

"My dear! You are surely not superstitious?"

"No, Mrs. Pryor; but I think I grow what is called nervous. I see things under a darker aspect than I used to do. I have fears I never used to have—not of ghosts, but of omens and disastrous events; and I have an inexpressible weight on my mind which I would give the world to shake off, and I cannot do it."

"Strange!" cried Shirley. "I never feel so." Mrs. Pryor said nothing.

"Fine weather, pleasant days, pleasant scenes are powerless to give me pleasure," continued Caroline. "Calm evenings are not calm to me: moonlight, which I used to think mild, now only looks mournful. Is this weakness of mind, Mrs. Pryor, or what is it? I cannot help it: I often struggle against it: I reason: but reason and effort make no difference."

"You should take more exercise," said Mrs. Pryor.

"Exercise! I exercise sufficiently: I exercise till I am ready to drop."

"My dear, you should go from home."

"Mrs. Pryor, I should like to go from home, but not on any purposeless excursion or visit. I wish to be a governess as you have been. It would oblige me greatly if you would speak to my uncle on the subject."

"Nonsense!" broke in Shirley. "What an idea! Be a governess! Better be a slave at once. Where is the necessity of it? Why should you dream of such a painful step?"

"My dear," said Mrs. Pryor, "you are very young to be a governess, and not sufficiently robust: the duties a governess undertakes are often severe."

"And I believe I want severe duties to occupy me."

"Occupy you!" cried Shirley. "When are you idle? I never saw a more industrious girl than you: you are always at work. Come," she continued—"come and sit by my side, and take some tea to refresh you. You don't care much for my friendship, then, that you wish to leave me?"

"Indeed, I do, Shirley; and I don't wish to leave you. I shall never find another friend so dear."

At which words Miss Keeldar put her hand into Caroline's with an impulsively affectionate movement, which was well seconded by the expression of her face.

"If you think so, you had better make much of me," she said, "and not run away from me. I hate to part with those to whom I am become attached. Mrs. Pryor there sometimes talks of leaving me, and says I might make a more advantageous connection than herself. I should as soon think of exchanging an old-fashioned mother for something modish and stylish. As for you—why, I began to flatter myself we were thoroughly friends; that you liked Shirley almost as well as Shirley likes you: and she does not stint her regard."

"I *do* like Shirley: I like her more and more every day; but that does not make me strong or happy."

"And would it make you strong or happy to go and live as a dependent amongst utter strangers? It would not; and the experiment must not be tried. I tell you it

would fail: it is not in your nature to bear the desolate life governesses generally lead: you would fall ill: I won't hear of it.''

And Miss Keeldar paused, having uttered this prohibition very decidedly. Soon she recommenced, still looking somewhat *courroucée*—''Why, it is my daily pleasure now to look out for the little cottage bonnet and the silk scarf glancing through the trees in the lane, and to know that my quiet, shrewd, thoughtful companion and monitress is coming back to me: that I shall have her sitting in the room to look at, to talk to, or to let alone, as she and I please. This may be a selfish sort of language—I know it is; but it is the language which naturally rises to my lips; therefore I utter it.''

''I would write to you, Shirley.''

''And what are letters? Only a sort of *pis-aller*. Drink some tea, Caroline: eat something—you eat nothing; laugh and be cheerful, and stay at home.''

Miss Helstone shook her head and sighed. She felt what difficulty she would have to persuade any one to assist or sanction her in making that change in her life which she believed desirable. Might she only follow her own judgment, she thought she should be able to find, perhaps a harsh, but an effectual cure for her sufferings. But this judgment, founded on circumstances she could fully explain to none, least of all to Shirley, seemed, in all eyes but her own, incomprehensible and fantastic, and was opposed accordingly.

There really was no present pecuniary need for her to leave a comfortable home and ''take a situation''; and there was every probability that her uncle might in some way permanently provide for her. So her friends thought, and, as far as their lights enabled them to see, they reasoned correctly: but of Caroline's strange sufferings, which she desired so eagerly to overcome or escape, they had no idea,—of her racked nights and dismal days, no suspicion. It was at once impossible and hopeless to explain: to wait and endure was her only plan. Many that want food and clothing have cheerier lives and brighter prospects than she had; many, harassed by poverty, are in a strait less afflictive.

''Now, is your mind quieted?'' inquired Shirley. ''Will you consent to stay at home?''

''I shall not leave it against the approbation of my friends,'' was the reply; ''but I think in time they will be obliged to think as I do.''

During this conversation Mrs. Pryor looked far from easy. Her extreme habitual reserve would rarely permit her to talk freely, or to interrogate others closely. She could think a multitude of questions she never ventured to put; give advice in her mind which her tongue never delivered. Had she been alone with Caroline, she might possibly have said something to the point: Miss Keeldar's presence, accustomed as she was to it, sealed her lips. Now, as on a thousand other occasions, inexplicable nervous scruples kept her back from interfering. She merely showed her concern for Miss Helstone in an indirect way, by asking her if the fire made her too warm, placing a screen between her chair and the hearth, closing a window whence she imagined a draught proceeded, and often and restlessly glancing at her. Shirley resumed—''Having destroyed your plan,'' she said, ''which I hope I have done, I shall construct a new one of my own. Every summer I make an excursion. This season I propose spending two months either at the Scotch lochs or the English lakes: that is, I shall go there, provided you consent to accompany me: if you refuse, I shall not stir a foot.''

''You are very good, Shirley.''

''I would be very good if you would let me: I have every disposition to be good. It is my misfortune and habit, I know, to think of myself paramount to anybody else: but who is not like me in that respect? However, when Captain Keeldar is made comfortable, accommodated with all he wants, including a sensible genial comrade, it gives him a thorough pleasure to devote his spare efforts to making that comrade happy. And should we not be happy, Caroline, in the Highlands? We

will go to the Highlands. We will, if you can bear a sea-voyage, go to the Isles,—the Hebrides, the Shetland, the Orkney Islands. Would you not like that? I see you would: Mrs. Pryor, I call you to witness; her face is all sunshine at the bare mention of it.''

"I should like it much," returned Caroline; to whom, indeed, the notion of such a tour was not only pleasant, but gloriously reviving. Shirley rubbed her hands.

"Come, I can bestow a benefit," she exclaimed. "I can do a good deed with my cash. My thousand a year is not merely a matter of dirty bank-notes and jaundiced guineas (let me speak respectfully of both though, for I adore them); but, it may be, health to the drooping, strength to the weak, consolation to the sad. I was determined to make something of it better than a fine old house to live in, than satin gowns to wear; better than deference from acquaintance, and homage from the poor. Here is to begin. This summer—Caroline, Mrs. Pryor, and I go out into the North Atlantic, beyond the Shetland—perhaps to the Faroe Isles. We will see seals in Suderoe, and, doubtless, mermaids in Stromoe. Caroline is laughing, Mrs. Pryor: *I* made her laugh; *I* have done her good.''

"I shall like to go, Shirley," again said Miss Helstone. "I long to hear the sound of waves—ocean-waves, and to see them as I have imagined them in dreams, like tossing banks of green light, strewed with vanishing and re-appearing wreaths of foam, whiter than lilies. I shall delight to pass the shores of those lone rock-islets where the sea-birds live and breed unmolested. We shall be on the track of the old Scandinavians—of the Norsemen; we shall almost see the shores of Norway. This is a very vague delight that I feel, communicated by your proposal, but it *is* a delight.''

"Will you think of Fitful Head now, when you lie awake at night; of gulls shrieking round it, and waves tumbling in upon it, rather than of the graves under the Rectory back-kitchen?''

"I will try; and instead of musing about remnants of shrouds, and fragments of coffins, and human bones and mould, I will fancy seals lying in the sunshine on solitary shores, where neither fisherman nor hunter ever come: of rock-crevices full of pearly eggs bedded in sea-weed; of unscared birds covering white sands in happy flocks.''

"And what will become of that inexpressible weight you said you had on your mind?''

"I will try to forget it in speculation on the sway of the whole Great Deep above a herd of whales rushing through the livid and liquid thunder down from the frozen zone: a hundred of them, perhaps, wallowing, flashing, rolling in the wake of a patriarch bull, huge enough to have been spawned before the Flood: such a creature as poor Smart had in his mind when he said:

> Strong against tides, the enormous whale
> Emerges as he goes.''

"I hope our bark will meet with no such shoal, or herd, as you term it, Caroline. (I suppose you fancy the sea-mammoths pasturing about the bases of the 'everlasting hills,' devouring strange provender in the vast valleys through and above which sea-billows roll.) I should not like to be capsized by the patriarch bull.''

"I suppose you expect to see mermaids, Shirley?''

"One of them at any rate: I do not bargain for less: and she is to appear in some such fashion as this. I am to be walking by myself on deck, rather late of an August evening, watching and being watched by a full harvest-moon: something is to rise white on the surface of the sea, over which that moon mounts silent, and hangs glorious: the object glitters and sinks. It rises again. I think I hear it cry with an articulate voice: I call you up from the cabin: I show you an image, fair as alabaster, emerging from the dim wave. We both see the long hair, the lifted and foam-white

arm, the oval mirror brilliant as a star. It glides nearer: a human face is plainly
visible; a face in the style of yours, whose straight, pure (excuse the word, it is
appropriate),—whose straight, pure lineaments, paleness does not disfigure. It looks
at us, but not with your eyes. I see a preternatural lure in its wily glance: it beckons.
Were we men, we should spring at the sign, the cold billow would be dared for
the sake of the colder enchantress; being women, we stand safe, though not dreadless.
She comprehends our unmoved gaze; she feels herself powerless; anger crosses her
front; she cannot charm, but she will appal us: she rises high, and glides all revealed,
on the dark wave-ridge. Temptress-terror! monstrous likeness of ourselves! Are you
not glad, Caroline, when at last, and with a wild shriek, she dives?''

"But, Shirley, she is not like us: we are neither temptresses, nor terrors, nor
monsters.''

"Some of our kind, it is said, are all three. There are men who ascribe to 'woman,'
in general, such attributes.''

"My dears,'' here interrupted Mrs. Pryor, "does it not strike you that your
conversation for the last ten minutes has been rather fanciful?''

"But there is no harm in our fancies: is there, ma'am?''

"We are aware that mermaids do not exist: why speak of them as if they did?
How can you find interest in speaking of a nonentity?''

"I don't know,'' said Shirley.

"My dear, I think there is an arrival. I heard a step in the lane, while you were
talking; and is not that the garden-gate which creaks?''

Shirley stepped to the window.

"Yes, there is some one,'' said she, turning quietly away; and, as she resumed
her seat, a sensitive flush animated her face, while a trembling ray at once kindled
and softened her eye. She raised her hand to her chin, cast her gaze down, and
seemed to think as she waited.

The servant announced Mr. Moore, and Shirley turned round when Mr. Moore
appeared at the door. His figure seemed very tall as he entered, and stood in contrast
with the three ladies, none of whom could boast a stature much beyond the average.
He was looking well, better than he had been known to look for the past twelve
months: a sort of renewed youth glowed in his eye and colour, and an invigorated
hope and settled purpose sustained his bearing: firmness his countenance still indicated,
but not austerity: it looked as cheerful as it was earnest.

"I am just returned from Stilbro','' he said to Miss Keeldar, as he greeted her;
"and I thought I would call to impart to you the result of my mission.''

"You did right not to keep me in suspense,'' she said; "and your visit is well-
timed. Sit down: we have not finished tea. Are you English enough to relish tea;
or do you faithfully adhere to coffee?''

Moore accepted tea.

"I am learning to be a naturalised Englishman,'' said he; "my foreign habits
are leaving me one by one.''

And now he paid his respects to Mrs. Pryor, and paid them well, with a grave
modesty that became his age, compared with hers. Then he looked at Caroline—
not, however, for the first time—his glance had fallen upon her before: he bent
towards her as she sat, gave her his hand, and asked her how she was. The light
from the window did not fall upon Miss Helstone, her back was turned towards it:
a quiet though rather low reply, a still demeanour, and the friendly protection of
early twilight, kept out of view each traitorous symptom. None could affirm that
she had trembled or blushed, that her heart had quaked, or her nerves thrilled: none
could prove emotion: a greeting showing less effusion was never interchanged.
Moore took the empty chair near her, opposite Miss Keeldar. He had placed himself
well: his neighbour, screened by the very closeness of his vicinage from his scrutiny,
and sheltered further by the dusk which deepened each moment, soon regained not

merely *seeming,* but *real* mastery of the feelings which had started into insurrection at the first announcement of his name.

He addressed his conversation to Miss Keeldar.

"I went to the barracks," he said, "and had an interview with Colonel Ryde: he approved my plans, and promised the aid I wanted: indeed, he offered a more numerous force than I require—half-a-dozen will suffice. I don't intend to be swamped by redcoats: they are needed for appearance rather than anything else: my main reliance is on my own civilians."

"And on their Captain," interposed Shirley.

"What, Captain Keeldar?" inquired Moore, slightly smiling, and not lifting his eyes: the tone of raillery in which he said this was very respectful and suppressed.

"No," returned Shirley, answering the smile; "Captain Gérard Moore, who trusts much to the prowess of his own right arm, I believe."

"Furnished with his counting-house ruler," added Moore. Resuming his usual gravity, he went on: "I received by this evening's post a note from the Home Secretary in answer to mine: it appears they are uneasy at the state of matters here in the north; they especially condemn the supineness and pusillanimity of the mill-owners; they say, as I have always said, that inaction, under present circumstances, is criminal, and that cowardice is cruelty, since both can only encourage disorder, and lead finally to sanguinary outbreaks. There is the note: I brought it for your perusal; and there is a batch of newspapers, containing further accounts of proceedings in Nottingham, Manchester, and elsewhere."

He produced letters and journals, and laid them before Miss Keeldar. While she perused them, he took his tea quietly; but, though his tongue was still, his observant faculties seemed by no means off duty. Mrs. Pryor, sitting in the background, did not come within the range of his glance, but the two younger ladies had the full benefit thereof.

Miss Keeldar, placed directly opposite, was seen without effort: she was the object his eyes, when lifted, naturally met first; and, as what remained of daylight—the gilding of the west—was upon her, her shape rose in relief from the dark panelling behind. Shirley's clear cheek was tinted yet with the colour which had risen into it a few minutes since: the dark lashes of her eyes looking down as she read, the dusk yet delicate line of her eyebrows, the almost sable gloss of her curls, made her heightened complexion look fine as the bloom of a red wild-flower by contrast. There was natural grace in her attitude, and there was artistic effect in the ample and shining folds of her silk dress—an attire simply fashioned, but almost splendid from the shifting brightness of its dye, warp and woof being of tints deep and changing as the hue on a pheasant's neck. A glancing bracelet on her arm produced the contrast of gold and ivory: there was something brilliant in the whole picture. It is to be supposed that Moore thought so, as his eye dwelt long on it, but he seldom permitted his feelings or his opinions to exhibit themselves in his face: his temperament boasted a certain amount of phlegm, and he preferred an undemonstrative, not ungentle, but serious aspect, to any other.

He could not, by looking straight before him, see Caroline, as she was close at his side; it was necessary, therefore, to manœuvre a little to get her well within the range of his observation: he leaned back in his chair, and looked down on her. In Miss Helstone, neither he nor any one else could discover brilliancy. Sitting in the shade, without flowers or ornaments, her attire the modest muslin dress, colourless but for its narrow stripe of pale azure, her complexion unflushed, unexcited, the very brownness of her hair and eyes invisible by this faint light, she was, compared with the heiress, as a graceful pencil-sketch compared with a vivid painting. Since Robert had seen her last, a great change had been wrought in her; whether he perceived it, might not be ascertained: he said nothing to that effect.

"How is Hortense?" asked Caroline softly.

"Very well; but she complains of being unemployed; she misses you."

"Tell her that I miss her, and that I write and read a portion of French every day."

"She will ask if you sent your love: she is always particular on that point. You know she likes attention."

"My best love—my very best; and say to her, that whenever she has time to write me a little note, I shall be glad to hear from her."

"What if I forget? I am not the surest messenger of compliments."

"No, don't forget, Robert: it is no compliment—it is in good earnest."

"And must therefore be delivered punctually?"

"If you please."

"Hortense will be ready to shed tears. She is tender-hearted on the subject of her pupil; yet she reproaches you sometimes for obeying your uncle's injunctions too literally. Affection, like love, will be unjust now and then."

And Caroline made no answer to this observation; for indeed her heart was troubled, and to her eyes she would have raised her handkerchief, if she had dared. If she had dared, too, she would have declared how the very flowers in the garden of Hollow's Cottage were dear to her; how the little parlour of that house was her earthly paradise; how she longed to return to it, as much almost as the First Woman, in her exile, must have longed to revisit Eden. Not daring, however, to say these things, she held her peace: she sat quiet at Robert's side, waiting for him to say something more. It was long since this proximity had been hers—long since his voice had addressed her; could she, with any show of probability, even of possibility, have imagined that the meeting gave him pleasure, to her it would have given deep bliss. Yet, even in doubt that it pleased—in dread that it might annoy him—she received the boon of the meeting as an imprisoned bird would the admission of sunshine to its cage: it is of no use arguing—contending against the sense of present happiness: to be near Robert was to be revived.

Miss Keeldar laid down the papers.

"And are you glad or sad for all these menacing tidings?" she inquired of her tenant.

"Not precisely either; but I certainly am instructed. I see that our only plan is to be firm. I see that efficient preparation and a resolute attitude are the best means of averting bloodshed."

He then inquired if she had observed some particular paragraph, to which she replied in the negative, and he rose to show it to her: he continued the conversation standing before her. From the tenor of what he said, it appeared evident that they both apprehended disturbances in the neighbourhood of Briarfield, though in what form they expected them to break out was not specified. Neither Caroline nor Mrs. Pryor asked questions: the subject did not appear to be regarded as one ripe for free discussion; therefore the lady and her tenant were suffered to keep details to themselves, unimportuned by the curiosity of their listeners.

Miss Keeldar, in speaking to Mr. Moore, took a tone at once animated and dignified, confidential and self-respecting. When, however, the candles were brought in, and the fire was stirred up, and the fulness of light thus produced rendered the expression of her countenance legible, you could see that she was all interest, life, and earnestness: there was nothing coquettish in her demeanour: whatever she felt for Moore, she felt it seriously. And serious, too, were his feelings, and settled were his views, apparently; for he made no petty effort to attract, dazzle, or impress. He contrived, notwithstanding, to command a little; because the deeper voice, however mildly modulated, the somewhat harder mind, now and then, though involuntarily and unintentionally, bore down by some peremptory phrase or tone the mellow accents and susceptible, if high, nature of Shirley. Miss Keeldar looked happy in conversing with him, and her joy seemed twofold,—a joy of the past and present, of memory and of hope.

What I have just said are Caroline's ideas of the pair: she felt what has just been described. In thus feeling, she tried not to suffer; but suffered sharply, nevertheless. She suffered, indeed, miserably: a few minutes before, her famished heart had tasted a drop and crumb of nourishment, that, if freely given, would have brought back abundance of life where life was failing; but the generous feast was snatched from her, spread before another, and she remained but a bystander at the banquet.

The clock struck nine: it was Caroline's time for going home: she gathered up her work, put the embroidery, the scissors, the thimble into her bag: she bade Mrs. Pryor a quiet good-night, receiving from that lady a warmer pressure of the hand than usual: she stepped up to Miss Keeldar.

"Good-night, Shirley!"

Shirley started up: "What!—so soon? Are you going already?"

"It is past nine."

"I never heard the clock. You will come again to-morrow, and you will be happy to-night, will you not? Remember our plans."

"Yes," said Caroline: "I have not forgotten."

Her mind misgave her that neither those plans nor any other could permanently restore her mental tranquillity. She turned to Robert, who stood close behind her: as he looked up, the light of the candles on the mantelpiece fell full on her face: all its paleness, all its change, all its forlorn meaning were clearly revealed. Robert had good eyes, and might have seen it, if he would: whether he did see it, nothing indicated.

"Good-night!" she said, shaking like a leaf, offering her thin hand hastily, anxious to part from him quickly.

"You are going home?" he asked, not touching her hand.

"Yes."

"Is Fanny come for you?"

"Yes."

"I may as well accompany you a step of the way: not up to the Rectory, though, lest my old friend, Helstone, should shoot me from the window."

He laughed and took his hat. Caroline spoke of unnecessary trouble: he told her to put on her bonnet and shawl. She was quickly ready, and they were soon both in the open air. Moore drew her hand under his arm, just in his old manner,—that manner which she ever felt to be so kind.

"You may run on, Fanny," he said to the house-maid: "we shall overtake you": and when the girl had got a little in advance, he enclosed Caroline's hand in his, and said he was glad to find she was a familiar guest at Fieldhead: he hoped her intimacy with Miss Keeldar would continue; such society would be both pleasant and improving.

Caroline replied that she liked Shirley.

"And there is no doubt the liking is mutual," said Moore: "if she professes friendship, be certain she is sincere: she cannot feign; she scorns hypocrisy. And, Caroline, are we never to see you at Hollow's Cottage again?"

"I suppose not, unless my uncle should change his mind."

"Are you much alone now?"

"Yes; a good deal. I have little pleasure in any society but Miss Keeldar's."

"Have you been quite well lately?"

"Quite."

"You must take care of yourself. Be sure not to neglect exercise. Do you know I fancied you somewhat altered;—a little fallen away, and pale. Is your uncle kind to you?"

"Yes; he is just as he always is."

"Not too tender, that is to say; not too protective and attentive. And what ails you, then?—tell me, Lina."

"Nothing, Robert"; but her voice faltered.

"That is to say, nothing that you will tell me: I am not to be taken into confidence. Separation is then quite to estrange us, is it?"

"I do not know: sometimes I almost fear it is."

"But it ought not to have that effect. 'Should auld acquaintance be forgot, and days o' lang syne?' "

"Robert, I don't forget."

"It is two months, I should think, Caroline, since you were at the cottage."

"Since I was *within* it—yes."

"Have you ever passed that way in your walk?"

"I have come to the top of the fields sometimes of an evening, and looked down. Once I saw Hortense in the garden watering her flowers, and I know at what time you light your lamp in the counting-house: I have waited for it to shine out now and then; and I have seen you bend between it and the window: I knew it was you—I could almost trace the outline of your form."

"I wonder I never encountered you: I occasionally walk to the top of the Hollow's fields after sunset."

"I know you do: I had almost spoken to you one night, you passed so near me."

"Did I? I passed near you, and did not see you! Was I alone?"

"I saw you twice, and neither time were you alone."

"Who was my companion? Probably nothing but Joe Scott, or my own shadow by moonlight."

"No; neither Joe Scott nor your shadow, Robert. The first time you were with Mr. Yorke; and the second time what you call your shadow was a shape with a white forehead and dark curls, and a sparkling necklace round its neck; but I only just got a glimpse of you and that fairy shadow: I did not wait to hear you converse."

"It appears you walk invisible. I noticed a ring on your hand this evening; can it be the ring of Gyges? Henceforth, when sitting in the counting-house by myself, perhaps at dead of night, I shall permit myself to imagine that Caroline may be leaning over my shoulder reading with me from the same book, or sitting at my side engaged in her own particular task, and now and then raising her unseen eyes to my face to read there my thoughts."

"You need fear no such infliction: I do not come near you: I only stand afar off, watching what may become of you."

"When I walk out along the hedgerows in the evening after the mill is shut—or at night, when I take the watchman's place—I shall fancy the flutter of every little bird over its nest, the rustle of every leaf, a movement made by you; tree-shadows will take your shape: in the white sprays of hawthorn, I shall imagine glimpses of you. Lina, you will haunt me."

"I will never be where you would not wish me to be, nor see nor hear what you would wish unseen and unheard."

"I shall see you in my very mill in broad daylight: indeed, I have seen you there once. But a week ago, I was standing at the top of one of my long rooms, girls were working at the other end, and amongst half-a-dozen of them, moving to and fro, I seemed to see a figure resembling yours. It was some effect of doubtful light or shade, or of dazzling sunbeam. I walked up to this group; what I sought had glided away: I found myself between two buxom lasses in pinafores."

"I shall not follow you into your mill, Robert, unless you call me there."

"Nor is that the only occasion on which imagination has played me a trick. One night, when I came home late from market, I walked into the cottage parlour thinking to find Hortense; but instead of her, I thought I found you. There was no candle in the room: my sister had taken the light upstairs with her; the window-blind was not drawn, and broad moonbeams poured through the panes: there you were, Lina, at the casement, shrinking a little to one side in an attitude not unusual with you. You were dressed in white, as I have seen you dressed at an evening party. For half a second, your fresh, living face seemed turned towards me, looking at me;

for half a second, my idea was to go and take your hand, to chide you for your long absence, and welcome your present visit. Two steps forward broke the spell: the drapery of the dress changed outline; the tints of the complexion dissolved, and were formless: positively, as I reached the spot, there was nothing left but the sweep of a white muslin curtain, and a balsam plant in a flower-pot, covered with a flush of bloom—'sic transit,' et cetera.''

"It was not my wraith, then? I almost thought it was."

"No; only gauze, crockery, and pink blossom: a sample of earthly illusions."

"I wonder you have time for such illusions, occupied as your mind must be."

"So do I. But I find in myself, Lina, two natures; one for the world and business, and one for home and leisure. Gérard Moore is a hard dog, brought up to mill and market: the person you call your cousin Robert is sometimes a dreamer, who lives elsewhere than in Cloth-hall and counting-house."

"Your two natures agree with you: I think you are looking in good spirits and health: you have quite lost the harassed air which it often pained one to see in your face a few months ago."

"Do you observe that? Certainly, I am disentangled of some difficulties: I have got clear of some shoals, and have more sea-room."

"And, with a fair wind, you may now hope to make a prosperous voyage?"

"I may *hope* it—yes—but hope is deceptive: there is no controlling wind or wave: gusts and swells perpetually trouble the mariner's course; he dare not dismiss from his mind the expectation of tempest."

"But you are ready for a breeze—you are a good seaman—an able commander: you are a skilful pilot, Robert; you will weather the storm."

"My kinswoman always thinks the best of me, but I will take her words for a propitious omen; I will consider that in meeting her to-night, I have met with one of those birds whose appearance is to the sailor the harbinger of good-luck."

"A poor harbinger of good-luck is she who can do nothing—who has no power. I feel my incapacity: it is of no use saying I have the will to serve you, when I cannot prove it; yet I have the will. I wish you success; I wish you high fortune and true happiness."

"When did you ever wish me anything else? What is Fanny waiting for—I told her to walk on? Oh! we have reached the churchyard: then, we are to part here, I suppose: we might have sat a few minutes in the church-porch, if the girl had not been with us. It is so fine a night, so summer-mild and still, I have no particular wish yet to return to the Hollow."

"But we cannot sit in the porch now, Robert."

Caroline said this because Moore was turning her round towards it.

"Perhaps not, but tell Fanny to go in; say we are coming, a few minutes will make no difference."

The church-clock struck ten.

"My uncle will be coming out to take his usual sentinel round, and he always surveys the church and churchyard."

"And if he does? If it were not for Fanny, who knows we are here, I should find pleasure in dodging and eluding him. We could be under the east window when he is at the porch; as he came round to the north side we could wheel off to the south; we might at a pinch hide behind some of the monuments: that tall erection of the Wynnes would screen us completely."

"Robert, what good spirits you have! Go—go!" added Caroline hastily, "I hear the front door——"

"I don't want to go; on the contrary, I want to stay."

"You know my uncle will be terribly angry: he forbade me to see you because you are a Jacobin."

"A queer Jacobin!"

"Go, Robert, he is coming; I hear him cough."

"Diable! It is strange—what a pertinacious wish I feel to stay!"

"You remember what he did to Fanny's——" began Caroline, and stopped abruptly short. Sweetheart was the word that ought to have followed, but she could not utter it; it seemed calculated to suggest ideas she had no intention to suggest; ideas delusive and disturbing. Moore was less scrupulous; "Fanny's sweetheart?" he said at once. "He gave him a shower-bath under the pump—did he not? He'd do as much for me, I daresay, with pleasure. I should like to provoke the old Turk—not however against *you:* but he would make a distinction between a cousin and a lover, would he not?"

"Oh! he would not think of you in that way, of course not; his quarrel with you is entirely political; yet I should not like the breach to be widened, and he is so testy. Here he is at the garden gate—for your own sake and mine, Robert, go!"

The beseeching words were aided by a beseeching gesture and a more beseeching look. Moore covered her clasped hands an instant with his, answered her upward by a downward gaze, said "Good-night!" and went.

Caroline was in a moment at the kitchen-door behind Fanny; the shadow of the shovel-hat at that very instant fell on a moonlit tomb; the Rector emerged erect as a cane, from his garden, and proceeded in slow march, his hands behind him, down the cemetery. Moore was almost caught: he had to "dodge" after all, to coast round the church, and finally to bend his tall form behind the Wynnes' ambitious monument. There he was forced to hide full ten minutes, kneeling with one knee on the turf, his hat off, his curls bare to the dew, his dark eye shining, and his lips parted with inward laughter at his position; for the Rector meantime stood coolly star-gazing, and taking snuff within three feet of him.

It happened, however, that Mr. Helstone had no suspicion whatever on his mind; for being usually but vaguely informed of his niece's movements, not thinking it worth while to follow them closely, he was not aware that she had been out at all that day, and imagined her then occupied with book or work in her chamber: where, indeed, she was by this time; though not absorbed in the tranquil employment he ascribed to her, but standing at her window with fast-throbbing heart, peeping anxiously from behind the blind, watching for her uncle to re-enter and her cousin to escape; and at last she was gratified; she heard Mr. Helstone come in; she saw Robert stride the tombs and vault the wall; she then went down to prayers. When she returned to her chamber, it was to meet the memory of Robert. Slumber's visitation was long averted: long she sat at her lattice, long gazed down on the old garden and older church, on the tombs laid out all grey and calm, and clear in moonlight. She followed the steps of the night, on its pathway of stars, far into the "wee sma' hours ayont the twal':" she was with Moore, in spirit, the whole time: she was at his side: she heard his voice: she gave her hand into his hand; it rested warm in his fingers. When the church-clock struck, when any other sound stirred, when a little mouse familiar to her chamber, an intruder for which she would never permit Fanny to lay a trap, came rattling amongst the links of her locket chain, her one ring, and another trinket or two on the toilet-table, to nibble a bit of biscuit laid ready for it, she looked up, recalled momentarily to the real. Then she said half aloud, as if deprecating the accusation of some unseen and unheard monitor, "I am not cherishing love-dreams: I am only thinking because I cannot sleep; of course, I know he will marry Shirley."

With returning silence, with the lull of the chime, and the retreat of her small untamed and unknown protégé, she still resumed the dream, nestling to the vision's side,—listening to, conversing with it. It paled at last: as dawn approached, the setting stars and breaking day dimmed the creation of Fancy: the wakened song of birds hushed her whispers. The tale full of fire, quick with interest, borne away by the morning wind, became a vague murmur. The shape that, seen in a moonbeam, lived, had a pulse, had movement, wore health's glow and youth's freshness, turned

cold and ghostly grey, confronted with the red of sunrise. It wasted. She was left solitary at last: she crept to her couch, chill and dejected.

Chapter XIV

SHIRLEY SEEKS TO BE SAVED BY WORKS

"OF course, I know he will marry Shirley," were her first words when she rose in the morning. "And he ought to marry her: she can help him," she added firmly. "But I shall be forgotten when they *are* married," was the cruel succeeding thought. "Oh! I shall be wholly forgotten! And what—*what* shall I do when Robert is taken quite from me? Where shall I turn? *My* Robert! I wish I could justly call him mine: but I am poverty and incapacity; Shirley is wealth and power: and she is beauty too, and love—I cannot deny it. This is no sordid suit: she loves him—not with inferior feelings: she loves, or *will* love, as he must feel proud to be loved. Not a valid objection can be made. Let them be married then: but afterwards I shall be nothing to him. As for being his sister, and all that stuff, I despise it. I will either be all or nothing to a man like Robert: no feeble shuffling or false cant is endurable. Once let that pair be united, and I will certainly leave them. As for lingering about, playing the hypocrite, and pretending to calm sentiments of friendship, when my soul will be wrung with other feelings, I shall not descend to such degradation. As little could I fill the place of their mutual friend as that of their deadly foe: as little could I stand between them as trample over them. Robert is a first-rate man—in my eyes: I *have* loved, *do* love, and *must* love him. I would be his wife, if I could; as I cannot, I must go where I shall never see him. There is but one alternative—to cleave to him as if I were a part of him, or to be sundered from him wide as the two poles of a sphere. Sunder me then, Providence. Part us speedily."

Some such aspirations as these were again working in her mind late in the afternoon, when the apparition of one of the personages haunting her thoughts passed the parlour window. Miss Keeldar sauntered slowly by: her gait, her countenance wearing that mixture of wistfulness and carelessness which, when quiescent, was the wonted cast of her look, and character of her bearing. When animated, the carelessness quite vanished, the wistfulness became blent with a genial gaiety, seasoning the laugh, the smile, the glance, with an unique flavour of sentiment, so that mirth from her never resembled "the crackling of thorns under a pot."

"What do you mean by not coming to see me this afternoon, as you promised?" was her address to Caroline as she entered the room.

"I was not in the humour," replied Miss Helstone, very truly.

Shirley had already fixed on her a penetrating eye.

"No," she said; "I see you are not in the humour for loving me: you are in one of your sunless, inclement moods, when one feels a fellow-creature's presence is not welcome to you. You have such moods: are you aware of it?"

"Do you mean to stay long, Shirley?"

"Yes; I am come to have my tea, and must have it before I go. I shall take the liberty then of removing my bonnet, without being asked."

And this she did, and then stood on the rug with her hands behind her.

"A pretty expression you have in your countenance," she went on, still gazing keenly, though not inimically, rather indeed pityingly at Caroline. "Wonderfully self-supported you look, you solitude-seeking, wounded deer. Are you afraid Shirley will worry you, if she discovers that you are hurt, and that you bleed?"

"I never do fear Shirley."

"But sometimes you dislike her: often you avoid her. Shirley can feel when she is slighted and shunned. If you had not walked home in the company you did last

night, you would have been a different girl to-day. What time did you reach the Rectory?''

''By ten.''

''Humph! You took three-quarters of an hour to walk a mile. Was it you, or Moore, who lingered so?''

''Shirley, you talk nonsense.''

''*He* talked nonsense—that I doubt not; or he looked it, which is a thousand times worse: I see the reflection of his eyes on your forehead at this moment. I feel disposed to call him out, if I could only get a trustworthy second: I feel desperately irritated: I felt so last night, and have felt it all day.''

''You don't ask me why,'' she proceeded, after a pause, ''you little silent, over-modest thing; and you don't deserve that I should pour out my secrets into your lap without an invitation. Upon my word, I could have found it in my heart to have dogged Moore yesterday evening with dire intent: I have pistols, and can use them.''

''Stuff, Shirley! Which would you have shot—me or Robert?''

''Neither, perhaps—perhaps myself—more likely a bat or a tree-bough. He is a puppy—your cousin: a quiet, serious, sensible, judicious, ambitious puppy. I see him standing before me, talking his half-stern, half-gentle talk, bearing me down (as I am very conscious he does) with his fixity of purpose, etc.; and then——I have no patience with him!''

Miss Keeldar started off on a rapid walk through the room, repeating energetically that she had no patience with men in general, and with her tenant in particular.

''You are mistaken,'' urged Caroline, in some anxiety: ''Robert is no puppy or male flirt; I can vouch for that.''

''*You* vouch for it! Do you think I'll take your word on the subject? There is no one's testimony I would not credit sooner than yours. To advance Moore's fortune, you would cut off your right hand.''

''But not tell lies; and if I speak the truth, I must assure you that he was just civil to me last night—that was all.''

''I never asked what he was—I can guess: I saw him from the window take your hand in his long fingers, just as he went out at my gate.''

''That is nothing. I am not a stranger, you know: I am an old acquaintance, and his cousin.''

''I feel indignant; and that is the long and short of the matter,'' responded Miss Keeldar. ''All my comfort,'' she added presently, ''is broken up by his manœuvres. He keeps intruding between you and me: without him we should be good friends; but that six feet of puppy-hood makes a perpetually-recurring eclipse of our friendship. Again and again he crosses and obscures the disk I want always to see clear: ever and anon he renders me to you a mere bore and nuisance.''

''No, Shirley; no.''

''He does. You did not want my society this afternoon, and I feel it hard: you are naturally somewhat reserved, but I am a social personage, who cannot live alone. If we were but left unmolested, I have that regard for you that I could bear you in my presence for ever, and not for the fraction of a second do I ever wish to be rid of you. You cannot say as much respecting me.''

''Shirley, I can say anything you wish: Shirley, I like you.''

''You will wish me at Jericho to-morrow, Lina.''

''I shall not. I am every day growing more accustomed to—fonder of you. You know I am too English to get up a vehement friendship all at once; but you are so much better than common—you are so different to everyday young ladies—I esteem you—I value you: you are never a burden to me—never. Do you believe what I say?''

''Partly,'' replied Miss Keeldar, smiling rather incredulously; ''but you are a peculiar personage: quiet as you look, there is both a force and a depth somewhere within, not easily reached or appreciated: then you certainly are not happy.''

"And unhappy people are rarely good—is that what you mean?"

"Not at all: I mean rather that unhappy people are often pre-occupied, and not in the mood for discoursing with companions of my nature. Moreover, there is a sort of unhappiness which not only depresses, but corrodes—and that, I fear, is your portion. Will pity do you any good, Lina? If it will, take some from Shirley: she offers largely, and warrants the article genuine."

"Shirley, I never had a sister—you never had a sister; but it flashes on me at this moment how sisters feel towards each other. Affection twined with their life, which no shocks of feeling can uproot, which little quarrels only trample an instant that it may spring more freshly when the pressure is removed: affection that no passion can ultimately outrival, with which even love itself cannot do more than compete in force and truth. Love hurts us so, Shirley: it is so tormenting, so racking, and it burns away our strength with its flame; in affection is no pain and no fire, only sustenance and balm. I am supported and soothed when you—that is, *you only*—are near, Shirley. Do you believe me now?"

"I am always easy of belief when the creed pleases me. We really are friends then, Lina, in spite of the black eclipse?"

"We really are," returned the other, drawing Shirley towards her, and making her sit down, "chance what may."

"Come, then, we will talk of something else than the Troubler." But at this moment the Rector came in, and the "something else" of which Miss Keeldar was about to talk was not again alluded to till the moment of her departure; she then delayed a few minutes in the passage to say.—"Caroline, I wish to tell you that I have a great weight on my mind: my conscience is quite uneasy, as if I had committed, or was going to commit, a crime. It is not my *private* conscience, you must understand, but my landed-proprietor and lord-of-the-manor conscience. I have got into the clutch of an eagle with iron talons. I have fallen under a stern influence, which I scarcely approve, but cannot resist. Something will be done ere long, I fear, which it by no means pleases me to think of. To ease my mind, and to prevent harm as far as I can, I mean to enter on a series of good works. Don't be surprised, therefore, if you see me all at once turn outrageously charitable. I have no idea how to begin, but you must give me some advice: we will talk more on the subject to-morrow; and just ask that excellent person, Miss Ainley, to step up to Fieldhead: I have some notion of putting myself under her tuition—won't she have a precious pupil? Drop a hint to her, Lina, that, though a well-meaning, I am rather a neglected character, and then she will feel less scandalised at my ignorance about clothing societies, and such things."

On the morrow, Caroline found Shirley sitting gravely at her desk, with an account-book, a bundle of bank-notes, and a well-filled purse before her. She was looking mighty serious, but a little puzzled. She said she had been "casting an eye" over the weekly expenditure in housekeeping at the Hall, trying to find out where she could retrench; that she had also just given audience to Mrs. Gill, the cook, and had sent that person away with a notion that her (Shirley's) brain was certainly crazed. "I have lectured her on the duty of being careful," said she, "in a way quite new to her. So eloquent was I on the text of economy, that I surprised myself; for, you see, it is altogether a fresh idea: I never thought, much less spoke, on the subject till lately. But it is all theory; for when I came to the practical part I could retrench nothing. I had not firmness to take off a single pound of butter, or to prosecute to any clear result an inquest into the destiny of either dripping, lard, bread, cold meat, or other kitchen perquisite whatever. I know we never get up illuminations at Fieldhead, but I could not ask the meaning of sundry quite unaccountable pounds of candles: we do not wash for the parish, yet I viewed in silence items of soap and bleaching-powder calculated to satisfy the solicitude of the most anxious inquirer after our position in reference to those articles: carnivorous I am not, nor is Mrs. Pryor, nor is Mrs. Gill herself, yet I only hemmed and opened

my eyes a little wide when I saw butchers' bills whose figures seemed to prove that fact—falsehood, I mean. Caroline, you may laugh at me, but you can't change me. I am a poltroon on certain points—I feel it. There is a base alloy of moral cowardice in my composition. I blushed and hung my head before Mrs. Gill, when she ought to have been faltering confessions to me. I found it impossible to get up the spirit even to hint, much less to prove, to her that she was a cheat. I have no calm dignity—no true courage about me."

"Shirley, what fit of self-injustice is this? My uncle, who is not given to speak well of women, says there are not ten thousand men in England as genuinely fearless as you."

"I am fearless, physically: I am never nervous about danger. I was not startled from self-possession when Mr. Wynne's great red bull rose with a bellow before my face, as I was crossing the cowslip-lea alone, stooped his begrimed, sullen head, and made a run at me: but I was afraid of seeing Mrs. Gill brought to shame and confusion of face. You have twice—ten times my strength of mind on certain subjects, Caroline: you, whom no persuasions can induce to pass a bull, however quiet he looks, would have firmly shown my housekeeper she had done wrong; then you would have gently and wisely admonished her; and at last, I daresay, provided she had seemed penitent, you would have very sweetly forgiven her. Of this conduct I am incapable. However, in spite of exaggerated imposition, I still find we live within our means: I have money in hand, and I really must do some good with it. The Briarfield poor are badly off: they must be helped. What ought I to do, think you, Lina? Had I not better distribute the cash at once?"

"No, indeed, Shirley: you will not manage properly. I have often noticed that your only notion of charity is to give shillings and half-crowns in a careless, freehanded sort of way, which is liable to continual abuse. You must have a prime minister, or you will get yourself into a series of scrapes. You suggested Miss Ainley yourself: to Miss Ainley I will apply; and, meantime, promise to keep quiet, and not begin throwing away your money. What a great deal you have, Shirley!—you must feel very rich with all that?"

"Yes; I feel of consequence. It is not an immense sum, but I feel responsible for its disposal; and really this responsibility weighs on my mind more heavily than I could have expected. They say that there are some families almost starving to death in Briarfield: some of my own cottagers are in wretched circumstances: I must and will help them."

"Some people say we shouldn't give alms to the poor, Shirley."

"They are great fools for their pains. For those who are not hungry, it is easy to palaver about the degradation of charity, and so on; but they forget the brevity of life, as well as its bitterness. We have none of us long to live: let us help each other through seasons of want and woe, as well as we can, without heeding in the least the scruples of vain philosophy."

"But you do help others, Shirley: you give a great deal as it is."

"Not enough: I must give more, or, I tell you, my brother's blood will some day be crying to Heaven against me. For, after all, if political incendiaries come here to kindle conflagration in the neighbourhood, and my property is attacked, I shall defend it like a tigress—I know I shall. Let me listen to Mercy as long as she is near me: her voice once drowned by the shout of ruffian defiance, and I shall be full of impulses to resist and quell. If once the poor gather and rise in the form of the mob, I shall turn against them as an aristocrat: if they bully me, I must defy; if they attack, I must resist,—and I will."

"You talk like Robert."

"I feel like Robert, only more fierily. Let them meddle with Robert, or Robert's mill, or Robert's interests, and I shall hate them. At present I am no patrician, nor do I regard the poor around me as plebeians; but if once they violently wrong me or mine, and then presume to dictate to us, I shall quite forget pity for their

wretchedness and respect for their poverty, in scorn of their ignorance and wrath at their insolence.''

''Shirley—how your eyes flash!''

''Because my soul burns. Would you, any more than me, let Robert be borne down by numbers?''

''If I had your power to aid Robert, I would use it as you mean to use it. If I could be such a friend to him as you can be, I would stand by him, as you mean to stand by him—till death.''

''And now, Lina, though your eyes don't flash, they glow. You drop your lids; but I saw a kindled spark. However, it is not yet come to fighting. What I want to do is to *prevent* mischief. I cannot forget, either day or night, that these embittered feelings of the poor against the rich have been generated in suffering: they would neither hate nor envy us if they did not deem us so much happier than themselves. To allay this suffering, and thereby lessen this hate, let me, out of my abundance, give abundantly: and that the donation may go farther, let it be made wisely. To that intent, we must introduce some clear, calm, practical sense into our councils: so go, and fetch Miss Ainley.''

Without another word, Caroline put on her bonnet and departed. It may, perhaps, appear strange that neither she nor Shirley thought of consulting Mrs. Pryor on their scheme; but they were wise in abstaining. To have consulted her—and this they knew by instinct—would only have been to involve her in painful embarrassment. She was far better informed, better read, a deeper thinker than Miss Ainley, but of administrative energy, of executive activity, she had none. She would subscribe her own modest mite to a charitable object willingly,—secret almsgiving suited her; but in public plans, on a large scale, she could take no part: as to originating them, that was out of the question. This Shirley knew, and therefore she did not trouble Mrs. Pryor by unavailing conferences, which could only remind her of her own deficiencies, and do no good.

It was a bright day for Miss Ainley when she was summoned to Fieldhead to deliberate on projects so congenial to her; when she was seated with all honour and deference at a table with paper, pen, ink and—what was best of all—cash before her, and requested to draw up a regular plan for administering relief to the destitute poor of Briarfield. She, who knew them all, had studied their wants, had again and again felt in what way they might best be succoured, could the means of succour only be found, was fully competent to the undertaking, and a meek exultation gladdened her kind heart as she felt herself able to answer clearly and promptly the eager questions put by the two young girls; as she showed them in her answers how much and what serviceable knowledge she had acquired of the condition of her fellow-creatures round her.

Shirley placed at her disposal £300, and at sight of the money Miss Ainley's eyes filled with joyful tears; for she already saw the hungry fed, the naked clothed, the sick comforted thereby. She quickly drew up a simple, sensible plan for its expenditure; and she assured them brighter times would now come round, for she doubted not the lady of Fieldhead's example would be followed by others: she should try to get additional subscriptions, and to form a fund; but first she must consult the clergy: yes, on that point, she was peremptory: Mr. Helstone, Dr. Boultby, Mr. Hall, *must* be consulted—(for not only must Briarfield be relieved, but Whinbury and Nunnely)—it would, she averred, be presumption in her to take a single step unauthorised by them.

The clergy were sacred beings in Miss Ainley's eyes: no matter what might be the insignificance of the individual, his station made him holy. The very curates—who, in their trivial arrogance, were hardly worthy to tie her patten strings, or carry her cotton umbrella, or check woollen-shawl—she, in her pure, sincere enthusiasm, looked upon as sucking saints. No matter how clearly their little vices and enormous

absurdities were pointed out to her, she could not see them: she was blind to ecclesiastical defects: the white surplice covered a multitude of sins.

Shirley, knowing this harmless infatuation on the part of her recently chosen prime minister, stipulated expressly that the curates were to have no voice in the disposal of the money; that their meddling fingers were not to be inserted into the pie. The rectors, of course, must be paramount, and they might be trusted: they had some experience, some sagacity, and Mr. Hall, at least, had sympathy and loving-kindness for his fellow-men; but as for the youth under them, they must be set aside, kept down, and taught that subordination and silence best became their years and capacity.

It was with some horror Miss Ainley heard this language: Caroline, however, interposing with a mild word or two in praise of Mr. Sweeting, calmed her again. Sweeting was, indeed, her own favourite: she endeavoured to respect Messrs. Malone and Donne; but the slices of sponge-cake, and glasses of cowslip or primrose wine, she had at different times administered to Sweeting when he came to see her in her little cottage, were ever offered with sentiments of truly motherly regard. The same innocuous collation she had once presented to Malone; but that personage evinced such open scorn of the offering, she had never ventured to renew it. To Donne she always served the treat, and was happy to see his approbation of it proved beyond a doubt, by the fact of his usually eating two pieces of cake, and putting a third in his pocket.

Indefatigable in her exertions where good was to be done, Miss Ainley would immediately have set out on a walk of ten miles round to the three rectors, in order to show her plan, and humbly solicit their approval: but Miss Keeldar interdicted this, and proposed, as an amendment, to collect the clergy in a small select reunion that evening at Fieldhead. Miss Ainley was to meet them, and the plan was to be discussed in full privy council.

Shirley managed to get the senior priesthood together accordingly; and before the old maid's arrival she had, further, talked all the gentlemen into the most charming mood imaginable. She herself had taken in hand Dr. Boultby and Mr. Helstone. The first was a stubborn old Welshman, hot, opinionated, and obstinate, but withal a man who did a great deal of good, though not without making some noise about it: the latter we know. She had rather a friendly feeling for both; especially for old Helstone; and it cost her no trouble to be quite delightful to them. She took them round the garden; she gathered them flowers; she was like a kind daughter to them. Mr. Hall she left to Caroline—or rather, it was to Caroline's care Mr. Hall consigned himself.

He generally sought Caroline in every party where she and he happened to be. He was not generally a lady's man, though all ladies liked him: something of a book-worm he was, near-sighted, spectacled, now and then abstracted. To old ladies he was kind as a son. To men of every occupation and grade he was acceptable: the truth, simplicity, frankness of his manners, the nobleness of his integrity, the reality and elevation of his piety, won him friends in every grade: his poor clerk and sexton delighted in him; the noble patron of his living esteemed him highly. It was only with young, handsome, fashionable, and stylish ladies he felt a little shy: being himself a plain man—plain in aspect, plain in manners, plain in speech—he seemed to fear their dash, elegance, and airs. But Miss Helstone had neither dash nor airs, and her native elegance was of a very quiet order—quiet as the beauty of a ground-loving hedge-flower. He was a fluent, cheerful, agreeable talker. Caroline could talk, too, in a *tête-à-tête:* she liked Mr. Hall to come and take the seat next her in a party, and thus secure her from Peter Augustus Malone, Joseph Donne, or John Sykes; and Mr. Hall never failed to avail himself of this privilege when he possibly could. Such preference shown by a single gentleman to a single lady would certainly, in ordinary cases, have set in motion the tongues of the gossips; but Cyril Hall was forty-five years old, slightly bald and slightly grey, and nobody

ever said or thought he was likely to be married to Miss Helstone. Nor did he think so himself: he was wedded already to his books and his parish: his kind sister Margaret, spectacled and learned like himself, made him happy in his single state; he considered it too late to change. Besides, he had known Caroline as a pretty little girl: she had sat on his knee many a time; he had bought her toys and given her books; he felt that her friendship for him was mixed with a sort of filial respect; he could not have brought himself to attempt to give another colour to her sentiments, and his serene mind could glass a fair image without feeling its depths troubled by the reflection.

When Miss Ainley arrived, she was made kindly welcome by every one: Mrs. Pryor and Margaret Hall made room for her on the sofa between them; and when the three were seated, they formed a trio which the gay and thoughtless would have scorned, indeed, as quite worthless and unattractive—a middle-aged widow and two plain spectacled old maids—yet which had its own quiet value, as many a suffering and friendless human being knew.

Shirley opened the business and showed the plan.

"I know the hand which drew up that," said Mr. Hall, glancing at Miss Ainley, and smiling benignantly: his approbation was won at once. Boultby heard and deliberated with bent brow and protruded under lip: his consent he considered too weighty to be given in a hurry. Helstone glanced sharply round with an alert, suspicious expression, as if he apprehended that female craft was at work, and that something in petticoats was somehow trying underhand to acquire too much influence, and make itself of too much importance. Shirley caught and comprehended the expression—"This scheme is nothing," said she carelessly; "it is only an outline—a mere suggestion; you, gentlemen, are requested to draw up rules of your own."

And she directly fetched her writing-case, smiling queerly to herself as she bent over the table where it stood: she produced a sheet of paper, a new pen, drew an arm-chair to the table, and presenting her hand to old Helstone, begged permission to instal him in it. For a minute he was a little stiff, and stood wrinkling his copper-coloured forehead strangely. At last he muttered—"Well, you are neither my wife nor my daughter, so I'll be led for once; but mind—I know I *am* led: your little female manœuvres don't blind me."

"Oh!" said Shirley, dipping the pen in the ink, and putting it into his hand, "you must regard me as Captain Keeldar to-day. This is quite a gentleman's affair—yours and mine entirely, Doctor" (so she had dubbed the Rector). "The ladies there are only to be our aides-de-camp, and at their peril they speak, till we have settled the whole business."

He smiled a little grimly, and began to write. He soon interrupted himself to ask questions, and consult his brethren, disdainfully lifting his glance over the curly heads of the two girls, and the demure caps of the elder ladies, to meet the winking glasses and grey pates of the priests. In the discussion which ensued, all three gentlemen, to their infinite credit, showed a thorough acquaintance with the poor of their parishes,—an even minute knowledge of their separate wants. Each rector knew where clothing was needed, where food would be most acceptable, where money could be bestowed with a probability of it being judiciously laid out. Wherever their memories fell short, Miss Ainley or Miss Hall, if applied to, could help them out; but both ladies took care not to speak unless spoken to. Neither of them wanted to be foremost, but each sincerely desired to be useful, and useful the clergy consented to make them: with which boon they were content.

Shirley stood behind the rectors, leaning over their shoulders now and then to glance at the rules drawn up, and the list of cases making out, listening to all they said, and still at intervals smiling her queer smile—a smile not ill-natured, but significant: too significant to be generally thought amiable. Men rarely like such of their fellows as read their inward nature too clearly and truly. It is good for women, especially, to be endowed with a soft blindness: to have mild, dim eyes,

that never penetrate below the surface of things—that take all for what it seems: thousands, knowing this, keep their eyelids drooped, on system; but the most downcast glance has its loophole, through which it can, on occasion, take its sentinel-survey of life. I remember once seeing a pair of blue eyes, that were usually thought sleepy, secretly on the alert, and I knew by their expression—an expression which chilled my blood, it was in that quarter so wondrously unexpected—that for years they had been accustomed to silent soul-reading. The world called the owner of these blue eyes "bonne petite femme" (she was not an Englishwoman): I learned her nature afterwards—got it off by heart—studied it in its farthest, most hidden recesses—she was the finest, deepest, subtlest schemer in Europe.

When all was at length settled to Miss Keeldar's mind, and the clergy had entered so fully into the spirit of her plans as to head the subscription-list with their signatures for £50 each, she ordered supper to be served; having previously directed Mrs. Gill to exercise her utmost skill in the preparation of this repast. Mr. Hall was no bon-vivant: he was naturally an abstemious man, indifferent to luxury; but Boultby and Helstone both liked good cookery; the recherché supper consequently put them into excellent humour: they did justice to it, though in a gentlemanly way—not in the mode Mr. Donne would have done, had he been present. A glass of fine wine was likewise tasted, with discerning though most decorous relish. Captain Keeldar was complimented on his taste; the compliment charmed him: it had been his aim to gratify and satisfy his priestly guests: he had succeeded, and was radiant with glee.

Chapter XV

MR. DONNE'S EXODUS

THE next day Shirley expressed to Caroline how delighted she felt that the little party had gone off so well.

"I rather like to entertain a circle of gentlemen," said she; "it is amusing to observe how they enjoy a judiciously concocted repast. For ourselves, you see, these choice wines and these scientific dishes are of no importance to us; but gentlemen seem to retain something of the naïveté of children about food, and one likes to please them: that is, when they show the becoming, decent self-government of our admirable rectors. I watch Moore sometimes, to try and discover how he can be pleased; but he has not that child's simplicity about him. Did you ever find out his accessible point, Caroline? You have seen more of him than I."

"It is not, at any rate, that of my uncle and Dr. Boultby," returned Caroline, smiling. She always felt a sort of shy pleasure in following Miss Keeldar's lead respecting the discussion of her cousin's character: left to herself, she would never have touched on the subject; but when invited, the temptation of talking about him of whom she was ever thinking was irresistible. "But," she added, "I really don't know what it is; for I never watched Robert in my life but my scrutiny was presently baffled by finding he was watching me."

"There it is!" exclaimed Shirley: "you can't fix your eyes on him but his presently flash on you. He is never off his guard: he won't give you an advantage: even when he does not look at you, his thoughts seem to be busy amongst your own thoughts, tracing your words and actions to their source, contemplating your motives at his ease. Oh! I know that sort of character, or something in the same style: it is one that piques me singularly—how does it affect you?"

This question was a specimen of one of Shirley's sharp, sudden turns: Caroline used to be fluttered by them at first, but she had now got into the way of parrying these home-thrusts like a little Quakeress.

"Pique you? In what way does it pique you?" she said.

"Here he comes!" suddenly exclaimed Shirley, breaking off, starting up and running to the window. "Here comes a diversion. I never told you of a superb conquest I have made lately—made at those parties to which I can never persuade you to accompany me; and the thing has been done without effort or intention on my part: that I aver. There is the bell—and, by all that's delicious! there are two of them. Do they never hunt, then, except in couples? You may have one, Lina, and you may take your choice: I hope I am generous enough. Listen to Tartar!"

The black-muzzled, tawny dog, a glimpse of which was seen in the chapter which first introduced its mistress to the reader, here gave tongue in the hall, amidst whose hollow space the deep bark resounded formidably. A growl, more terrible than the bark—menacing as muttered thunder—succeeded.

"Listen!" again cried Shirley, laughing. "You would think that the prelude to a bloody onslaught: they will be frightened: they don't know old Tartar as I do: they are not aware his uproars are all sound and fury, signifying nothing."

Some bustle was heard. "Down, sir!—down!" exclaimed a high-toned, imperious voice, and then came a crack of a cane or whip. Immediately there was a yell—a scutter—a run—a positive tumult.

"Oh! Malone! Malone!"

"Down! down! down!" cried the high voice.

"He really is worrying them!" exclaimed Shirley. "They have struck him: a blow is what he is not used to, and will not take."

Out she ran—a gentleman was fleeing up the oak staircase, making for refuge in the gallery or chambers in hot haste; another was backing fast to the stair-foot, wildly flourishing a knotty stick, at the same time reiterating, "Down! down! down!" while the tawny dog bayed, bellowed, howled at him, and a group of servants came bundling from the kitchen. The dog made a spring: the second gentleman turned tail and rushed after his comrade: the first was already safe in a bed-room: he held the door against his fellow;—nothing so merciless as terror;—but the other fugitive struggled hard: the door was about to yield to his strength.

"Gentlemen," was uttered in Miss Keeldar's silvery but vibrating tones, "spare my locks, if you please. Calm yourselves!—come down! Look at Tartar,—he won't harm a cat."

She was caressing the said Tartar: he lay crouched at her feet, his fore-paws stretched out, his tail still in threatening agitation, his nostrils snorting, his bulldog eyes conscious of a dull fire. He was an honest, phlegmatic, stupid, but stubborn canine character: he loved his mistress, and John—the man who fed him—but was mostly indifferent to the rest of the world: quiet enough he was, unless struck or threatened with a stick, and that put a demon into him at once.

"Mr. Malone, how do you do?" continued Shirley, lifting up her mirth-lit face to the gallery. "That is not the way to the oak-parlour: that is Mrs. Pryor's apartment. Request your friend Mr. Donne to evacuate: I shall have the greatest pleasure in receiving him in a lower room."

"Ha! ha!" cried Malone, in hollow laughter, quitting the door, and leaning over the massive balustrade. "Really that animal alarmed Donne. He is a little timid," he proceeded, stiffening himself, and walking trimly to the stairhead. "I thought it better to follow, in order to reassure him."

"It appears you did: well, come down, if you please. John" (turning to her manservant), "go upstairs and liberate Mr. Donne. Take care, Mr. Malone, the stairs are slippery."

In truth they were; being of polished oak. The caution came a little late for Malone: he had slipped already in his stately descent, and was only saved from falling by a clutch at the banisters, which made the whole structure creak again.

Tartar seemed to think the visitor's descent effected with unwarranted éclat, and accordingly he growled once more. Malone, however, was no coward: the spring

of the dog had taken him by surprise: but he passed him now in suppressed fury rather than fear: if a look could have strangled Tartar, he would have breathed no more. Forgetting politeness, in his sullen rage, Malone pushed into the parlour before Miss Keeldar. He glanced at Miss Helstone; he could scarcely bring himself to bend to her. He glared on both the ladies: he looked as if, had either of them been his wife, he would have made a glorious husband at the moment: in each hand he seemed as if he would have liked to clutch one and gripe her to death.

However, Shirley took pity: she ceased to laugh; and Caroline was too true a lady to smile even at any one under mortification. Tartar was dismissed; Peter Augustus was soothed: for Shirley had looks and tones that might soothe a very bull: he had sense to feel that, since he could not challenge the owner of the dog, he had better be civil; and civil he tried to be; and his attempts being well received, he grew presently *very* civil and quite himself again. He had come, indeed, for the express purpose of making himself charming and fascinating: rough portents had met him on his first admission to Fieldhead; but that passage got over, charming and fascinating he resolved to be. Like March, having come in like a lion, he purposed to go out like a lamb.

For the sake of air, as it appeared, or perhaps for that of ready exit in case of some new emergency arising, he took his seat—not on the sofa, where Miss Keeldar offered him enthronisation, nor yet near the fireside, to which Caroline, by a friendly sign, gently invited him,—but on a chair close to the door. Being no longer sullen or furious, he grew, after his fashion, constrained and embarrassed. He talked to the ladies by fits and starts, choosing for topics whatever was most intensely commonplace: he sighed deeply, significantly, at the close of every sentence; he sighed in each pause; he sighed ere he opened his mouth. At last, finding it desirable to add ease to his other charms, he drew forth to aid him an ample silk pocket-handkerchief. This was to be the graceful toy with which his unoccupied hands were to trifle. He went to work with a certain energy: he folded the red and yellow square cornerwise; he whipped it open with a waft: again he folded it in narrower compass: he made of it a handsome band. To what purpose would he proceed to apply the ligature? Would he wrap it about his throat—his head? Should it be a comforter or a turban? Neither. Peter Augustus had an inventive—an original genius: he was about to show the ladies graces of action possessing at least the charm of novelty. He sat on the chair with his athletic Irish legs crossed, and these legs, in that attitude, he circled with the bandanna and bound firmly together. It was evident he felt this device to be worth an encore: he repeated it more than once. The second performance sent Shirley to the window to laugh her silent but irrepressible laugh unseen: it turned Caroline's head aside, that her long curls might screen the smile mantling on her features. Miss Helstone, indeed, was amused by more than one point in Peter's demeanour: she was edified at the complete though abrupt diversion of his homage from herself to the heiress: the £5000 he supposed her likely one day to inherit, were not to be weighed in the balance against Miss Keeldar's estate and hall. He took no pains to conceal his calculations and tactics: he pretended to no gradual change of views: he wheeled about at once: the pursuit of the lesser fortune was openly relinquished for that of the greater. On what grounds he expected to succeed in his chase, himself best knew: certainly not by skilful management.

From the length of time that elapsed, it appeared that John had some difficulty in persuading Mr. Donne to descend. At length, however, that gentleman appeared: nor, as he presented himself at the oak-parlour door, did he seem in the slightest degree ashamed or confused—not a whit. Donne, indeed, was of that coldly phlegmatic, immovably complacent, densely self-satisfied nature which is insensible to shame. He had never blushed in his life: no humiliation could abash him: his nerves were not capable of sensation enough to stir his life, and make colour mount to his cheek: he had no fire in his blood, and no modesty in his soul: he was a frontless, arrogant, decorous slip of the commonplace; conceited, inane, insipid: and this gentleman

had a notion of wooing Miss Keeldar! He knew no more, however, how to set about the business than if he had been an image carved in wood: he had no idea of a taste to be pleased, a heart to be reached in courtship: his notion was, when he should have formally visited her a few times, to write a letter proposing marriage; then he calculated she would accept him for love of his office, then they would be married, then he should be master of Fieldhead, and he should live very comfortably, have servants at his command, eat and drink of the best, and be a great man. You would not have suspected his intentions when he addressed his intended bride in an impertinent, injured tone—"A very dangerous dog that, Miss Keeldar. I wonder you should keep such an animal."

"Do you, Mr. Donne? Perhaps you will wonder more when I tell you I am very fond of him."

"I should say you are not serious in the assertion. Can't fancy a lady fond of that brute—'tis so ugly—a mere carter's dog—pray hang him."

"Hang what I am fond of!"

"And purchase in his stead some sweetly pooty pug or poodle: something appropriate to the fair sex: ladies generally like lapdogs."

"Perhaps I am an exception."

"Oh! you can't be, you know. All ladies are alike in those matters: that is universally allowed."

"Tartar frightened you terribly, Mr. Donne. I hope you won't take any harm."

"That I shall, no doubt. He gave me a turn I shall not soon forget. When I *sor* him" (such was Mr. Donne's pronunciation) "about to spring, I thought I should have fainted."

"Perhaps you did faint in the bed-room—you were a long time there?"

"No; I bore up that I might hold the door fast: I was determined not to let any one enter: I thought I would keep a barrier between me and the enemy."

"But what if your friend Mr. Malone had been worried?"

"Malone must take care of himself. Your man persuaded me to come out at last by saying the dog was chained up in his kennel: if I had not been assured of this, I would have remained all day in the chamber. But what is that? I declare the man has told a falsehood! The dog is there!"

And indeed Tartar walked past the glass-door opening to the garden, stiff, tawny, and black-muzzled as ever. He still seemed in bad humour; he was growling again, and whistling a half-strangled whistle, being an inheritance from the bull-dog side of his ancestry.

"There are other visitors coming," observed Shirley, with that provoking coolness which the owners of formidable-looking dogs are apt to show while their animals are all bristle and bay. Tartar sprang down the pavement towards the gate, bellowing "avec explosion." His mistress quietly opened the glass-door, and stepped out chirruping to him. His bellow was already silenced, and he was lifting up his huge, blunt, stupid head to the new callers to be patted.

"What—Tartar, Tartar!" said a cheery, rather boyish voice, "don't you know us? Good-morning, old boy!"

And little Mr. Sweeting, whose conscious good-nature made him comparatively fearless of man, woman, child, or brute, came through the gate, caressing the guardian. His vicar, Mr. Hall, followed: he had no fear of Tartar either, and Tartar had no ill-will to him: he snuffed both the gentlemen round, and then, as if concluding that they were harmless, and might be allowed to pass, he withdrew to the sunny front of the hall, leaving the archway free. Mr. Sweeting followed, and would have played with him, but Tartar took no notice of his caresses: it was only his mistress's hand whose touch gave him pleasure; to all others he showed himself obstinately insensible.

Shirley advanced to meet Messrs. Hall and Sweeting, shaking hands with them cordially: they were come to tell her of certain successes they had achieved that

morning in applications for subscriptions to the fund. Mr. Hall's eyes beamed benignantly through his spectacles: his plain face looked positively handsome with goodness, and when Caroline, seeing who was come, ran out to meet him, and put both her hands into his, he gazed down on her with a gentle, serene, affectionate expression, that gave him the aspect of a smiling Melanchthon.

Instead of re-entering the house, they strayed through the garden, the ladies walking one on each side of Mr. Hall. It was a breezy sunny day; the air freshened the girls' cheeks, and gracefully dishevelled their ringlets: both of them looked pretty,—one, gay: Mr. Hall spoke oftenest to his brilliant companion, looked most frequently at the quiet one. Miss Keeldar gathered handfuls of the profusely blooming flowers, whose perfume filled the enclosure; she gave some to Caroline, telling her to choose a nosegay for Mr. Hall; and with her lap filled with delicate and splendid blossoms, Caroline sat down on the steps of a summer-house: the Vicar stood near her, leaning on his cane.

Shirley, who could not be inhospitable, now called out the neglected pair in the oak-parlour: she convoyed Donne past his dread enemy Tartar, who, with his nose on his fore-paws, lay snoring under the meridian sun. Donne was not grateful: he never *was* grateful for kindness and attention; but he was glad of the safeguard. Miss Keeldar, desirous of being impartial, offered the curates flowers: they accepted them with native awkwardness. Malone seemed specially at a loss, when a bouquet filled one hand, while his shillelagh occupied the other. Donne's "Thank you!" was rich to hear: it was the most fatuous and arrogant of sounds, implying that he considered this offering an homage to his merits, and an attempt on the part of the heiress to ingratiate herself into his priceless affections. Sweeting alone received the posy like a smart, sensible little man, as he was; putting it gallantly and nattily into his button-hole.

As a reward for his good manners, Miss Keeldar beckoning him apart, gave him some commission, which made his eyes sparkle with glee. Away he flew, round by the courtyard to the kitchen: no need to give him directions; he was always at home everywhere. Erelong he re-appeared, carrying a round table, which he placed under the cedar; then he collected six garden-chairs from various nooks and bowers in the grounds, and placed them in a circle. The parlour-maid—Miss Keeldar kept no footman—came out, bearing a napkin-covered tray. Sweeting's nimble fingers aided in disposing glasses, plates, knives and forks: he assisted her too in setting forth a neat luncheon, consisting of cold chicken, ham, and tarts.

This sort of impromptu regale, it was Shirley's delight to offer any chance guests: and nothing pleased her better than to have an alert, obliging little friend, like Sweeting, to run about her hand, cheerily receive and briskly execute her hospitable hints. David and she were on the best terms in the world; and his devotion to the heiress was quite disinterested, since it prejudiced in nothing his faithful allegiance to the magnificent Dora Sykes.

The repast turned out a very merry one. Donne and Malone, indeed, contributed but little to its vivacity, the chief part they played in it being what concerned the knife, fork, and wine-glass; but where four such natures as Mr. Hall, David Sweeting, Shirley, and Caroline, were assembled in health and amity, on a green lawn, under a sunny sky, amidst a wilderness of flowers, there could not be ungenial dullness.

In the course of conversation, Mr. Hall reminded the ladies that Whitsuntide was approaching, when the grand United Sunday-School tea-drinking and procession of the three parishes of Briarfield, Whinbury, and Nunnely were to take place. Caroline he knew would be at her post as teacher, he said, and he hoped Miss Keeldar would not be wanting: he hoped she would make her first public appearance amongst them at that time. Shirley was not the person to miss an occasion of this sort; she liked festive excitement, a gathering of happiness, a concentration and combination of pleasant details, a throng of glad faces, a muster of elated hearts:

she told Mr. Hall they might count on her with security: she did not know what she would have to do, but they might dispose of her as they pleased.

"And," said Caroline, "you will promise to come to my table, and to sit near me, Mr. Hall?"

"I shall not fail, Deo volente," said he. "I have occupied the place on her right hand at these monster tea-drinkings for the last six years," he proceeded, turning to Miss Keeldar. "They made her a Sunday-school teacher when she was a little girl of twelve: she is not particularly self-confident by nature, as you may have observed; and the first time she had to 'take a tray,' as the phrase is, and make tea in public, there was some piteous trembling and flushing. I observed the speechless panic, the cups shaking in the little hand, and the over-flowing tea-pot filled too full from the urn. I came to her aid, took a seat near her, managed the urn and the slop-basin, and in fact made the tea for her like any old woman."

"I was very grateful to you," interposed Caroline.

"You were: you told me so with an earnest sincerity that repaid me well; inasmuch as it was not like the majority of little ladies of twelve, whom you may help and caress for ever without their evincing any quicker sense of the kindness done and meant than if they were made of wax and wood, instead of flesh and nerves. She kept close to me, Miss Keeldar, the rest of the evening, walking with me over the grounds where the children were playing; she followed me into the vestry when all were summoned into church: she would, I believe, have mounted with me to the pulpit, had I not taken the previous precaution of conducting her to the Rectory-pew."

"And he has been my friend ever since," said Caroline.

"And always sat at her table, near her tray, and handed the cups,—that is the extent of my services. The next thing I do for her will be to marry her some day to some curate or mill-owner: but mind, Caroline, I shall inquire about the bridegroom's character, and if he is not a gentleman likely to render happy the little girl who walked with me hand in hand over Nunnely Common, I will not officiate: so take care."

"The caution is useless: I am not going to be married. I shall live single like your sister Margaret, Mr. Hall."

"Very well—you might do worse—Margaret is not unhappy: she has her books for a pleasure, and her brother for a care, and is content. If ever you want a home; if the day should come when Briarfield Rectory is yours no longer, come to Nunnely Vicarage. Should the old maid and bachelor be still living, they will make you tenderly welcome."

"There are your flowers. Now," said Caroline, who had kept the nosegay she had selectcd for him till this moment, "*you* don't care for a bouquet, but you must give it to Margaret: only—to be sentimental for once—keep that little forget-me-not, which is a wild-flower I gathered from the grass; and—to be still more sentimental—let me take two or three of the blue blossoms and put them in my souvenir."

And she took out a small book with enamelled cover and silver clasp, wherein, having opened it, she inserted the flowers, writing round them in pencil—"To be kept for the sake of the Rev. Cyril Hall, my friend. May —, 18—."

The Rev. Cyril Hall, on his part also, placed a sprig in safety between the leaves of a pocket Testament: he only wrote on the margin—"Caroline."

"Now," said he, smiling, "I trust we are romantic enough. Miss Keeldar," he continued (the curates, by-the-bye, during this conversation, were too much occupied with their own jokes to notice what passed at the other end of the table), "I hope you are laughing at this trait of '*exaltation*' in tbe old grey-headed Vicar; but the fact is, I am so used to comply with the requests of this young friend of yours, I don't know how to refuse her when she tells me to do anything. You would say it

is not much in my way to traffic with flowers and forget-me-nots: but, you see, when requested to be sentimental, I am obedient.''

"He is naturally rather sentimental," remarked Caroline; "Margaret told me so, and I know what pleases him."

"That you should be good and happy? Yes; that is one of my greatest pleasures. May God long preserve to you the blessings of peace and innocence! By which phrase, I mean *comparative* innocence; for in His sight, I am well aware, *none* are pure. What, to our human perceptions, looks spotless as we fancy angels, is to Him but frailty, needing the blood of His Son to cleanse, and the strength of His Spirit to sustain. Let us each and all cherish humility—I, as you, my young friends; and we may well do it when we look into our own hearts, and see there temptations, inconsistencies, propensities, even we blush to recognise. And it is not youth, nor good looks, nor grace, nor any gentle outside charm which makes either beauty or goodness in God's eyes. Young ladies, when your mirror or men's tongues flatter you, remember that, in the sight of her Maker, Mary Ann Ainley—a woman whom neither glass nor lips have ever panegyrised—is fairer and better than either of you. She is, indeed," he added, after a pause—"she is, indeed. You young things— wrapt up in yourselves and in earthly hopes—scarcely live as Christ lived: perhaps you cannot do it yet, while existence is so sweet and earth so smiling to you; it would be too much to expect: she, with meek heart and due reverence, treads close in her Redeemer's steps.''

Here the harsh voice of Donne broke in on the mild tones of Mr. Hall—"Ahem!" he began, clearing his throat evidently for a speech of some importance. "Ahem! Miss Keeldar, your attention an instant, if you please."

"Well," said Shirley nonchalantly. "What is it? I listen: all of me is ear that is not eye."

"I hope part of you is hand also," returned Donne, in his vulgarly presumptuous and familiar style, "and part purse: it is to the hand and purse I propose to appeal. I came here this morning with a view to beg of you——"

"You should have gone to Mrs. Gill: she is my almoner."

"To beg of you a subscription to a school. I and Dr. Boultby intend to erect one in the hamlet of Ecclefigg, which is under our vicarage of Whinbury. The Baptists have got possession of it: they have a chapel there, and we want to dispute the ground.''

"But I have nothing to do with Ecclefigg: I possess no property there."

"What does that signify? You're a Churchwoman, ain't you?"

"Admirable creature!" muttered Shirley, under her breath: "exquisite address: fine style! What raptures he excites in me!" Then aloud, "I am a Churchwoman, certainly.''

"Then you can't refuse to contribute in this case. The population of Ecclefigg are a parcel of brutes—we want to civilise them.''

"Who is to be the missionary?"

"Myself, probably."

"You won't fail through lack of sympathy with your flock."

"I hope not—I expect success; but we must have money. There is the paper— pray give a handsome sum.''

When asked for money, Shirley rarely held back. She put down her name for £5: after the £300 she had lately given, and the many smaller sums she was giving constantly, it was as much as she could at present afford. Donne looked at it, declared the subscription "shabby," and clamorously demanded more. Miss Keeldar flushed up with some indignation and more astonishment.

"At present I shall give no more," said she.

"Not give more! Why, I expected you to head the list with a cool hundred. With your property, you should never put down a signature for less.''

She was silent.

"In the south," went on Donne, "a lady with a thousand a year would be ashamed to give five pounds for a public object."

Shirley, so rarely haughty, looked so now. Her slight frame became nerved; her distinguished face quickened with scorn.

"Strange remarks!" said she: "most inconsiderate! Reproach in return for bounty is misplaced."

"Bounty! Do you call five pounds bounty?"

"I do: and bounty which, had I not given it to Dr. Boultby's intended school, of the erection of which I approve, and in no sort to his curate, who seems ill-advised in his manner of applying for— or rather extorting—subscriptions,—bounty, I repeat, which, but for this consideration, I should instantly reclaim."

Donne was thick-skinned: he did not feel all or half that the tone, air, glance of the speaker expressed: he knew not on what ground he stood.

"Wretched place—this Yorkshire," he went on. "I could never have formed an ide*ar* of the country had I not seen it; and the people—rich and poor—what a set! How *corse* and uncultivated! They would be scouted in the south."

Shirley leaned forwards on the table, her nostrils dilating a little, her taper fingers interlaced and compressing each other hard.

"The rich," pursued the infatuated and unconscious Donne, "are a parcel of misers—never living as persons with their incomes ought to live: you scarsley"— (you must excuse Mr. Donne's pronunciation, reader; it was very choice; he considered it genteel, and prided himself on his southern accent; northern ears received with singular sensations his utterance of certain words); "you scarsley ever see a fam'ly where a propa carriage or a reg'la butla is kep; and as to the poor—just look at them when they come crowding about the church-doors on the occasion of a marriage or a funeral, clattering in clogs; the men in their shirt-sleeves and wool-combers' aprons, the women in mob-caps and bed-gowns. They pos'tively deserve that one should turn a mad cow in amongst them to rout their rabble-rank—he! he! What fun it would be!"

"There,—you have reached the climax," said Shirley quietly. "You have reached the climax," she repeated, turning her glowing glance towards him. "You cannot go beyond it, and," she added with emphasis, "you *shall* not, in my house."

Up she rose: nobody could control her now, for she was exasperated; straight she walked to her garden-gates, wide she flung them open.

"Walk through," she said austerely, "and pretty quickly, and set foot on this pavement no more."

Donne was astounded. He had thought all the time he was showing himself off to high advantage, as a lofty-souled person of the first "ton"; he imagined he was producing a crushing impression. Had he not expressed disdain of everything in Yorkshire? What more conclusive proof could be given that he was better than anything there? And yet here was he about to be turned like a dog out of a Yorkshire garden! Where, under such circumstances, was the "concatenation accordingly"?

"Rid me of you instantly—instantly!" reiterated Shirley, as he lingered.

"Madam—a clergyman! Turn out a clergyman?"

"Off! Were you an archbishop you have proved yourself no gentleman, and must go. Quick!"

She was quite resolved: there was no trifling with her: besides, Tartar was again rising; he perceived symptoms of a commotion: he manifested a disposition to join in; there was evidently nothing for it but to go, and Donne made his Exodus; the heiress sweeping him a deep curtsey as she closed the gates on him.

"How dare the pompous priest abuse his flock? How dare the lisping cockney revile Yorkshire?" was her sole observation on the circumstance, as she returned to the table.

Ere long, the little party broke up: Miss Keeldar's ruffled and darkened brow, curled lip, and incensed eye, gave no invitation to further social enjoyment.

Chapter XVI

WHITSUNTIDE

THE fund prospered. By dint of Miss Keeldar's example, the three rectors' vigorous exertions, and the efficient though quiet aid of their spinster and spectacled lieutenants, Mary Ann Ainley and Margaret Hall, a handsome sum was raised; and this being judiciously managed, served for the present greatly to alleviate the distress of the unemployed poor. The neighbourhood seemed to grow calmer: for a fortnight past no cloth had been destroyed; no outrage on mill or mansion had been committed in the three parishes. Shirley was sanguine that the evil she wished to avert was almost escaped; that the threatened storm was passing over: with the approach of summer she felt certain that trade would improve—it always did; and then this weary war could not last for ever: peace must return one day: with peace what an impulse would be given to commerce!

Such was the usual tenor of her observations to her tenant, Gérard Moore, whenever she met him where they could converse, and Moore would listen very quietly—too quietly to satisfy her. She would then by her impatient glance demand something more from him—some explanation, or at least some additional remark. Smiling in his way, with that expression which gave a remarkable cast of sweetness to his mouth, while his brow remained grave, he would answer to the effect, that himself, too, trusted in the finite nature of the war; that it was indeed on that ground the anchor of his hopes was fixed: thereon his speculations depended. "For you are aware," he would continue, "that I now work Hollow's Mill entirely on speculation: I sell nothing; there is no market for my goods. I manufacture for a future day: I make myself ready to take advantage of the first opening that shall occur. Three months ago this was impossible to me; I had exhausted both credit and capital: you well know who came to my rescue; from what hand I received the loan which saved me. It is on the strength of that loan I am enabled to continue the bold game which, a while since, I feared I should never play more. Total ruin I know will follow loss, and I am aware that gain is doubtful; but I am quite cheerful: so long as I can be active, so long as I can strive, so long, in short, as my hands are not tied, it is impossible for me to be depressed. One year, nay, but six months of the reign of the olive, and I am safe; for, as you say, peace will give an impulse to commerce. In this you are right; but as to the restored tranquillity of the neighbourhood—as to the permanent good effect of your charitable fund—I doubt. Eleemosynary relief never yet tranquillised the working-classes—it never made them grateful; it is not in human nature that it should. I suppose, were all things ordered aright, they ought not to be in a position to need that humiliating relief; and this they feel: we should feel it were we so placed. Besides, to whom should they be grateful? To you—to the clergy perhaps, but not to us mill-owners. They hate us worse than ever. Then, the disaffected here are in correspondence with the disaffected elsewhere: Nottingham is one of their headquarters, Manchester another, Birmingham a third. The subalterns receive orders from their chiefs; they are in a good state of discipline: no blow is struck without mature deliberation. In sultry weather, you have seen the sky threaten thunder day by day, and yet night after night the clouds have cleared, and the sun has set quietly; but the danger was not gone, it was only delayed: the long-threatening storm is sure to break at last. There is analogy between the moral and physical atmosphere."

"Well, Mr. Moore" (so these conferences always ended), "take care of yourself. If you think that I have ever done you any good, reward me by promising to take care of yourself."

"I do: I will take close and watchful care. I wish to live, not to die: the future opens like Eden before me; and still, when I look deep into the shades of my

paradise, I see a vision, that I like better than seraph or cherub, glide across remote vistas.''

"Do you? Pray, what vision?"

"I see—"

The maid came bustling in with the tea-things.

The early part of that May, as we have seen, was fine, the middle was wet; but in the last week, at change of moon, it cleared again. A fresh wind swept off the silver-white, deep-piled rain-clouds, bearing them, mass on mass, to the eastern horizon; on whose verge they dwindled, and behind whose rim they disappeared, leaving the vault behind all pure blue space, ready for the reign of the summer sun. That sun rose broad on Whitsuntide: the gathering of the schools was signalised by splendid weather.

Whit-Tuesday was the great day, in preparation for which the two large schoolrooms of Briarfield, built by the present rector, chiefly at his own expense, were cleaned out, white-washed, repainted, and decorated with flowers and evergreens—some from the Rectory-garden, two cart-loads from Fieldhead, and a wheel-barrowful from the more stingy domain of De Walden, the residence of Mr. Wynne. In these schoolrooms twenty tables, each calculated to accommodate twenty guests, were laid out, surrounded with benches, and covered with white cloths: above them were suspended at least some twenty cages, containing as many canaries, according to a fancy of the district, specially cherished by Mr. Helstone's clerk, who delighted in the piercing song of these birds, and knew that amidst confusion of tongues they always carolled loudest. These tables, be it understood, were not spread for the twelve hundred scholars to be assembled from the three parishes, but only for the patrons and teachers of the schools: the children's feast was to be spread in the open air. At one o'clock the troops were to come in; at two they were to be marshalled; till four they were to parade the parish; then came the feast, and afterwards the meeting, with music and speechifying in the church.

Why Briarfield was chosen for the point of rendezvous—the scene of the fête—should be explained. It was not because it was the largest or most populous parish—Whinbury far outdid it in that respect; nor because it was the oldest—antique as were the hoary Church and Rectory, Nunnely's low-roofed Temple and mossy Parsonage, buried both in coeval oaks, outstanding sentinels of Nunnwood, were older still: it was simply because Mr. Helstone willed it so, and Mr. Helstone's will was stronger than that of Boultby or Hall; the former *could* not, the latter *would* not, dispute a point of precedence with their resolute and imperious brother: they let him lead and rule.

This notable anniversary had always hitherto been a trying day to Caroline Helstone, because it dragged her perforce into public, compelling her to face all that was wealthy, respectable, influential in the neighbourhood; in whose presence, but for the kind countenance of Mr. Hall, she would have appeared unsupported. Obliged to be conspicuous; obliged to walk at the head of her regiment as the Rector's niece, and first teacher of the first class; obliged to make tea at the first table for a mixed multitude of ladies and gentlemen; and to do all this without the countenance of mother, aunt, or other chaperon—she, meantime, being a nervous person, who mortally feared publicity—it will be comprehended that, under these circumstances, she trembled at the approach of Whitsuntide.

But this year Shirley was to be with her, and that changed the aspect of the trial singularly—it changed it utterly: it was a trial no longer—it was almost an enjoyment. Miss Keeldar was better in her single self than a host of ordinary friends. Quite self-possessed, and always spirited and easy; conscious of her social importance, yet never presuming upon it, it would be enough to give one courage only to look at her. The only fear was, lest the heiress should not be punctual to tryst: she often had a careless way of lingering behind time, and Caroline knew her uncle would not wait a second for any one: at the moment of the church-clock tolling two, the

bells would clash out and the march begin. She must look after Shirley, then, in this matter, or her expected companion would fail her.

Whit-Tuesday saw her rise almost with the sun. She, Fanny, and Eliza were busy the whole morning arranging the Rectory-parlours in first-rate company order, and setting out a collation of cooling refreshments—wine, fruit, cakes—on the dining-room sideboard. Then she had to dress in her freshest and fairest attire of white muslin; the perfect fineness of the day and the solemnity of the occasion warranted, and even exacted, such costume. Her new sash—a birthday present from Margaret Hall, which she had reason to believe Cyril himself had bought, and in return for which she had indeed given him a set of cambric bands in a handsome case—was tied by the dexterous fingers of Fanny, who took no little pleasure in arraying her fair young mistress for the occasion; her simple bonnet had been trimmed to correspond with her sash; her pretty but inexpensive scarf of white crape suited her dress. When ready she formed a picture, not bright enough to dazzle, but fair enough to interest; not brilliantly striking, but very delicately pleasing; a picture in which sweetness of tint, purity of air, and grace of mien, atoned for the absence of rich colouring and magnificent contour. What her brown eye and clear forehead showed of her mind, was in keeping with her dress and face—modest, gentle, and, though pensive, harmonious. It appeared that neither lamb nor dove need fear her, but would welcome rather, in her look of simplicity and softness, a sympathy with their own natures, or with the natures we ascribe to them.

After all, she was an imperfect, faulty human being; fair enough of form, hue, and array; but, as Cyril Hall said, neither so good nor so great as the withered Miss Ainley, now putting on her best black gown and Quaker-drab shawl and bonnet in her own narrow cottage-chamber.

Away Caroline went, across some very sequestered fields and through some quite hidden lanes, to Fieldhead. She glided quickly under the green hedges and across the greener leas. There was no dust—no moisture—to soil the hem of her stainless garment, or to damp her slender sandal: after the late rains all was clean, and under the present glowing sun all was dry: she walked fearlessly, then on daisy and turf, and through thick plantations; she reached Fieldhead and penetrated to Miss Keeldar's dressing-room.

It was well she had come, or Shirley would have been too late. Instead of making ready with all speed, she lay stretched on a couch, absorbed in reading: Mrs. Pryor stood near, vainly urging her to rise and dress. Caroline wasted no words: she immediately took the book from her, and with her own hands commenced the business of disrobing and re-robing her. Shirley, indolent with the heat, and gay with her youth and pleasurable nature, wanted to talk, laugh and linger; but Caroline, intent on being in time, persevered in dressing her as fast as fingers could fasten strings or insert pins. At length, as she united a final row of hooks and eyes, she found leisure to chide her, saying she was very naughty to be so unpunctual; that she looked even now the picture of incorrigible carelessness: and so Shirley did— but a very lovely picture of that tiresome quality.

She presented quite a contrast to Caroline: there was style in every fold of her dress and every line of her figure: the rich silk suited her better than a simpler costume; the deep embroidered scarf became her: she wore it negligently, but gracefully; the wreath on her bonnet crowned her well: the attention to fashion, the tasteful appliance of ornament in each portion of her dress, were quite in place with her: all this suited her, like the frank light in her eyes, the rallying smile about her lips, like her shaft-straight carriage and lightsome step. Caroline took her hand when she was dressed, hurried her downstairs, out of doors, and thus they sped through the fields, laughing as they went, and looking very much like a snow-white dove and gem-tinted bird-of-paradise joined in social flight.

Thanks to Miss Helstone's promptitude, they arrived in good time. While yet trees hid the church, they heard the bell tolling a measured but urgent summons

for all to assemble; the trooping in of numbers, the trampling of many steps, and murmuring of many voices were likewise audible. From a rising ground they presently saw, on the Whinbury road, the Whinbury school approaching: it numbered five hundred souls. The Rector and Curate, Boultby and Donne, headed it: the former, looming large in full canonicals, walking as became a beneficed priest, under the canopy of a shovel-hat, with the dignity of an ample corporation, the embellishment of the squarest and vastest of black coats, and the support of the stoutest of gold-headed canes. As the Doctor walked, he now and then slightly flourished his cane, and inclined his shovel-hat with a dogmatical wag towards his aide-de-camp. That aide-de-camp—Donne, to wit—narrow as the line of his shape was compared to the broad bulk of his principal, contrived, notwithstanding, to look every inch a curate: all about him was pragmatical and self-complacent, from his turned-up nose and elevated chin to his clerical black gaiters, his somewhat short, strapless trousers, and his square-toed shoes.

Walk on, Mr. Donne! You have undergone scrutiny. You think you look well—whether the white and purple figures watching you from yonder hill think so, is another question.

These figures come running down when the regiment has marched by: the churchyard is full of children and teachers, all in their very best holiday attire: and—distressed as is the district, bad as are the times—it is wonderful to see how respectably—how handsomely even—they have contrived to clothe themselves. That British love of decency will work miracles: the poverty which reduces an Irish girl to rags is impotent to rob the English girl of the neat wardrobe she knows necessary to her self-respect. Besides, the lady of the manor—that Shirley, now gazing with pleasure on this well-dressed and happy-looking crowd—has really done them good: her seasonable bounty consoled many a poor family against the coming holiday, and supplied many a child with a new frock or bonnet for the occasion; she knows it, and is elate with the consciousness: glad that her money, example, and influence have really—substantially—benefited those around her. She cannot be charitable like Miss Ainley—it is not in her nature: it relieves her to feel that there is another way of being charitable, practicable for other characters, and under other circumstances.

Caroline, too, is pleased; for she also has done good in her small way; robbed herself of more than one dress, ribbon, or collar she could ill spare, to aid in fitting out the scholars of her class; and as she could not give money, she has followed Miss Ainley's example, in giving her time and her industry to sew for the children.

Not only is the churchyard full, but the Rectory-garden is also thronged: pairs and parties of ladies and gentlemen are seen walking amongst the waving lilacs and laburnums. The house also is occupied: at the wide-open parlour-windows gay groups are standing. These are the patrons and teachers, who are to swell the procession. In the parson's croft, behind the Rectory, are the musicians of the three parish bands, with their instruments. Fanny and Eliza, in the smartest of caps and gowns, and the whitest of aprons, move amongst them, serving out quarts of ale; whereof a stock was brewed very sound and strong some weeks since, by the Rector's orders, and under his special superintendence. Whatever he had a hand in, must be managed handsomely: "shabby doings," of any description, were not endured under his sanction: from the erection of a public building, a church, school, or courthouse, to the cooking of a dinner, he still advocated the lordly, liberal, and effective. Miss Keeldar was like him in this respect, and they mutually approved each other's arrangements.

Caroline and Shirley were soon in the midst of the company; the former met them very easily for her: instead of sitting down in a retired corner, or stealing away to her own room till the procession should be marshalled, according to her wont, she moved through the three parlours, conversed and smiled, absolutely spoke once or twice ere she was spoken to, and, in short, seemed a new creature. It was Shirley's presence which thus transformed her: the view of Miss Keeldar's

air and manner did her a world of good. Shirley had no fear of her kind; no tendency to shrink from, to avoid it. All human beings, men, women, or children, whom low breeding or coarse presumption did not render positively offensive, were welcome enough to her: some much more so than others, of course; but, generally speaking, till a man had indisputably proved himself bad and a nuisance, Shirley was willing to think him good and an acquisition, and to treat him accordingly. This disposition made her a general favourite, for it robbed her very raillery of its sting, and gave her serious or smiling conversation a happy charm: nor did it diminish the value of her intimate friendship, which was a distinct thing from this social benevolence, depending, indeed, on quite a different part of her character. Miss Helstone was the choice of her affection and intellect; the Misses Pearson, Sykes, Wynne, etc., etc., only the profiters by her good-nature and vivacity.

Donne happened to come into the drawing-room while Shirley, sitting on the sofa, formed the centre of a tolerably wide circle. She had already forgotten her exasperation against him, and she bowed and smiled good-humouredly. The disposition of the man was then seen. He knew neither how to decline the advance with dignity, as one whose just pride has been wounded, nor how to meet it with frankness, as one who is glad to forget and forgive; his punishment had impressed him with no sense of shame, and he did not experience that feeling on encountering his chastiser: he was not vigorous enough in evil to be actively malignant—he merely passed by sheepishly with a rated, scowling look. Nothing could ever again reconcile him to his enemy; while no passion of resentment, for even sharper and more ignominious inflictions, could his lymphatic nature know.

"He was not worth a scene!" said Shirley to Caroline. "What a fool I was! To revenge on poor Donne his silly spite at Yorkshire, is something like crushing a gnat for attacking the hide of a rhinoceros. Had I been a gentleman, I believe I should have helped him off the premises by dint of physical force: I am glad now I only employed the moral weapon. But he must come near me no more: I don't like him: he irritates me: there is not even amusement to be had out of him: Malone is better sport."

It seemed as if Malone wished to justify the preference; for the words were scarcely out of the speaker's mouth, when Peter Augustus came up, all in "grande tenue," gloved and scented, with his hair oiled and brushed to perfection, and bearing in one hand a huge bunch of cabbage roses, five or six in full blow: these he presented to the heiress with a grace to which the most cunning pencil could do but defective justice. And who, after this, could dare to say that Peter was not a lady's man? He had gathered and he had given flowers: he had offered a sentimental— a poetic tribute at the shrine of Love or Mammon. Hercules holding the distaff was but a faint type of Peter bearing the roses. He must have thought this himself, for he seemed amazed at what he had done: he backed without a word; he was going away with a husky chuckle of self-felicitation; then he bethought himself to stop and turn, to ascertain by ocular testimony that he really had presented a bouquet: yes—there were the six red cabbages on the purple satin lap, a very white hand, with some gold rings on the fingers, slightly holding them together, and streaming ringlets, half hiding a laughing face, drooped over them: only *half* hiding: Peter saw the laugh—it was unmistakable—he was made a joke of—his gallantry, his chivalry were the subject of a jest for a petticoat—for two petticoats—Miss Helstone too was smiling. Moreover, he felt he was seen through, and Peter grew black as a thundercloud. When Shirley looked up, a fell eye was fastened on her: Malone, at least, had energy enough in hate: she saw it in his glance.

"Peter *is* worth a scene, and shall have it, if he likes, one day," she whispered to her friend.

And now—solemn and sombre as to their colour, though bland enough as to their faces—appeared at the dining-room door the three rectors: they had hitherto been busy in the church, and were now coming to take some little refreshment for

the body, ere the march commenced. The large morocco-covered easy chair had been left vacant for Dr. Boultby; he was put into it, and Caroline, obeying the instigations of Shirley, who told her now was the time to play the hostess, hastened to hand to her uncle's vast, revered, and, on the whole, worthy friend, a glass of wine and a plate of macaroons. Boultby's churchwardens, patrons of the Sunday-school both, as he insisted on their being, were already beside him; Mrs. Sykes and the other ladies of his congregation were on his right hand and on his left, expressing their hopes that he was not fatigued, their fears that the day would be too warm for him. Mrs. Boultby, who held an opinion that when her lord dropped asleep after a good dinner his face became as the face of an angel, was bending over him, tenderly wiping some perspiration, real or imaginary, from his brow: Boultby, in short, was in his glory, and in a round sound "voix de poitrine," he rumbled out thanks for attentions, and assurances of his tolerable health. Of Caroline he took no manner of notice as she came near, save to accept what she offered; he did not see her, he never did see her: he hardly knew that such a person existed. He saw the macaroons, however, and being fond of sweets, possessed himself of a small handful thereof. The wine Mrs. Boultby insisted on mingling with hot water, and qualifying with sugar and nutmeg.

Mr. Hall stood near an open window, breathing the fresh air and scent of flowers, and talking like a brother to Miss Ainley. To him Caroline turned her attention with pleasure. "What should she bring him? He must not help himself—he must be served by her"; and she provided herself with a little salver, that she might offer him variety. Margaret Hall joined them; so did Miss Keeldar: the four ladies stood round their favourite pastor: they also had an idea that they looked on the face of an earthly angel: Cyril Hall was their pope, infallible to them as Dr. Thomas Boultby to his admirers. A throng, too, enclosed the Rector of Briarfield: twenty or more pressed round him; and no parson was ever more potent in a circle than old Helstone. The curates, herding together after their manner, made a constellation of three lesser planets: divers young ladies watched them afar off, but ventured not nigh.

Mr. Helstone produced his watch. "Ten minutes to two," he announced aloud. "Time for all to fall into line. Come." He seized his shovel-hat and marched away; all rose and followed *en masse*.

The twelve hundred children were drawn up in three bodies of four hundred souls each: in the rear of each regiment was stationed a band; between every twenty there was an interval, wherein Helstone posted the teachers in pairs: to the van of the armies he summoned—

"Grace Boultby and Mary Sykes lead out Whinbury."

"Margaret Hall and Mary Ann Ainley conduct Nunnely."

"Caroline Helstone and Shirley Keeldar head Briarfield."

Then again he gave command—

"Mr. Donne to Whinbury: Mr, Sweeting to Nunnely; Mr, Malone to Briarfield."

And these gentlemen stepped up before the lady-generals.

The rectors passed to the full front—the parish clerks fell to the extreme rear; Helstone lifted his shovel-hat; in an instant out clashed the eight bells in the tower, loud swelled the sounding bands, flute spoke and clarion answered, deep rolled the drums, and away they marched.

The broad white road unrolled before the long procession, the sun and sky surveyed it cloudless, the wind tossed the tree-boughs above it, and the twelve hundred children, and one hundred and forty adults, of which it was composed, trod on in time and tune, with gay faces and glad hearts. It was a joyous scene, and a scene to do good: it was a day of happiness for rich and poor: the work, first of God, and then of the clergy. Let England's priests have their due: they are a faulty set in some respects, being only of common flesh and blood, like us all; but

the land would be badly off without them: Britain would miss her church, if that church fell. God save it! God also reform it!

Chapter XVII

THE SCHOOL-FEAST

NOT on combat bent, nor of foemen in search, was this priest-led and women-officered company: yet their music played martial tunes, and—to judge by the eyes and carriage of some, Miss Keeldar, for instance—these sounds awoke, if not a martial, yet a longing spirit. Old Helstone, turning by chance, looked into her face, and he laughed, and she laughed at him.

"There is no battle in prospect," he said; "our country does not want us to fight for it: no foe or tyrant is questioning or threatening our liberty: there is nothing to be done: we are only taking a walk. Keep your hand on the reins, Captain, and slack the fire of that spirit: it is not wanted; the more's the pity."

"Take your own advice, Doctor," was Shirley's response. To Caroline she murmured, "I'll borrow of imagination what reality will not give me. We are not soldiers—bloodshed is not my desire; or, if we are, we are soldiers of the Cross. Time has rolled back some hundreds of years, and we are bound on a pilgrimage to Palestine. But no,—that is too visionary. I need a sterner dream: we are Lowlanders of Scotland, following a covenanting captain up into the hills to hold a meeting out of the reach of persecuting troopers. We know that battle may follow prayer; and, as we believe that in the worst issue of battle, heaven must be our reward, we are ready and willing to redden the peat-moss with our blood. That music stirs my soul; it wakens all my life; it makes my heart beat: not with its temperate daily pulse, but with a new, thrilling vigour. I almost long for danger; for a faith—a land—or, at least, a lover to defend."

"Look, Shirley!" interrupted Caroline. "What is that red speck above Stilbro' Brow? You have keener sight than I; just turn your eagle eye to it."

Miss Keeldar looked. "I see," she said: then added presently, "there is a line of red. They are soldiers—cavalry soldiers," she subjoined quickly: "they ride fast: there are six of them: they will pass us: no—they have turned off to the right: they saw our procession, and avoid it by making a circuit. Where are they going?"

"Perhaps they are only exercising their horses."

"Perhaps so. We see them no more now."

Mr. Helstone here spoke.

"We shall pass through Royd Lane, to reach Nunnely Common by a short cut," said he.

And into the straits of Royd Lane they accordingly defiled. It was very narrow,—so narrow that only two could walk abreast without falling into the ditch which ran along each side. They had gained the middle of it, when excitement became obvious in the clerical commanders: Boultby's spectacles and Helstone's Rehoboam were agitated: the curates nudged each other: Mr. Hall turned to the ladies and smiled.

"What is the matter?" was the demand.

He pointed with his staff to the end of the lane before them. Lo and behold! another,—an opposition procession was there entering, headed also by men in black, and followed also, as they could now hear, by music.

"Is it our double?" asked Shirley: "our manifold wraith? Here is a card turned up."

"If you wanted a battle, you are likely to get one,—at least of looks," whispered Caroline, laughing.

"They shall not pass us!" cried the curates unanimously: "we'll not give way!"

"Give way!" retorted Helstone sternly, turning round; "who talks of giving way? You, boys, mind what you are about: the ladies, I know, will be firm; I can trust them. There is not a churchwoman here but will stand her ground against these folks, for the honour of the Establishment. What does Miss Keeldar say?"

"She asks what is it?"

"The Dissenting and Methodist schools, the Baptists, Independents, and Wesleyans, joined in unholy alliance, and turning purposely into this lane with the intention of obstructing our march and driving us back."

"Bad manners!" said Shirley; "and I hate bad manners. Of course, they must have a lesson."

"A lesson in politeness," suggested Mr. Hall, who was ever for peace: "not an example of rudeness."

Old Helstone moved on. Quickening his step, he marched some yards in advance of his company. He had nearly reached the other sable leaders, when he who appeared to act as the hostile commander-in-chief—a large, greasy man, with black hair combed flat on his forehead—called a halt. The procession paused: he drew forth a hymn-book, gave out a verse, set a tune, and they all struck up the most dolorous of canticles.

Helstone signed to his bands: they clashed out with all the power of brass. He desired them to play "Rule, Britannia," and ordered the children to join in vocally, which they did with enthusiastic spirit. The enemy was sung and stormed down; his psalm quelled: as far as noise went, he was conquered.

"Now, follow me!" exclaimed Helstone; "not at a run, but at a firm, smart pace. Be steady, every child and woman of you:—keep together:—hold on by each other's skirts, if necessary,"

And he strode on with such a determined and deliberate gait, and was, besides, so well seconded by his scholars and teachers—who did exactly as he told them, neither running nor faltering, but marching with cool, solid impetus: the curates, too, being compelled to do the same, as they were between two fires,—Helstone and Miss Keeldar, both of whom watched any deviation with lynx-eyed vigilance, and were ready, the one with his cane, the other with her parasol, to rebuke the slightest breach of orders, the least independent or irregular demonstration,—that the body of Dissenters were first amazed, then alarmed, then borne down and pressed back, and at last forced to turn tail and leave the outlet from Royd Lane free. Boultby suffered in the onslaught, but Helstone and Malone, between them, held him up, and brought him through the business, whole in limb, though sorely tried in wind.

The fat Dissenter who had given out the hymn was left sitting in the ditch. He was a spirit merchant by trade, a leader of the Nonconformists, and, it was said, drank more water in that one afternoon than he had swallowed for a twelvemonth before. Mr. Hall had taken care of Caroline, and Caroline of him: he and Miss Ainley made their own quiet comments to each other afterwards on the incident. Miss Keeldar and Mr. Helstone shook hands heartily when they had fairly got the whole party through the lane. The curates began to exult, but Mr. Helstone presently put the curb on their innocent spirits: he remarked that they never had sense to know what to say, and had better hold their tongues; and he reminded them that the business was none of their managing.

About half-past three the procession turned back, and at four once more regained the starting-place. Long lines of benches were arranged in the close-shorn fields round the school: there the children were seated, and huge baskets, covered up with white cloths, and great smoking tin vessels were brought out. Ere the distribution of good things commenced, a brief grace was pronounced by Mr. Hall, and sung by the children: their young voices sounded melodious, even touching, in the open air. Large currant buns, and hot, well-sweetened tea, were then administered in the proper spirit of liberality: no stinting was permitted on this day, at least; the rule

for each child's allowance being that it was to have about twice as much as it could possibly eat, thus leaving a reserve to be carried home for such as age, sickness, or other impediment, prevented from coming to the feast. Buns and beer circulated, meantime, amongst the musicians and church-singers: afterwards the benches were removed, and they were left to unbend their spirits in licensed play.

A bell summoned the teachers, patrons, and patronesses to the schoolroom; Miss Keeldar, Miss Helstone, and many other ladies were already there, glancing over the arrangement of their separate trays and tables. Most of the female servants of the neighbourhood, together with the clerks', the singers', and the musicians' wives, had been pressed into the service of the day as waiters: each vied with the other in smartness and daintiness of dress, and many handsome forms were seen amongst the younger ones. About half a score were cutting bread and butter; another half-score supplying hot water, brought from the coppers of the Rector's kitchen. The profusion of flowers and evergreens decorating the white walls, the show of silver teapots and bright porcelain on the tables, the active figures, blithe faces, gay dresses flitting about everywhere, formed altogether a refreshing and lively spectacle. Everybody talked, not very loudly, but merrily, and the canary birds sang shrill in their high-hung cages.

Caroline, as the Rector's niece, took her place at one of the three first tables; Mrs. Boultby and Margaret Hall officiated at the others. At these tables the élite of the company were to be entertained; strict rules of equality not being more in fashion at Briarfield than elsewhere. Miss Helstone removed her bonnet and scarf, that she might be less oppressed with the heat; her long curls, falling on her neck, served almost in place of a veil, and for the rest, her muslin dress was fashioned modestly as a nun's robe, enabling her thus to dispense with the encumbrance of a shawl.

The room was filling: Mr. Hall had taken his post beside Caroline, who now, as she re-arranged the cups and spoons before her, whispered to him in a low voice remarks on the events of the day. He looked a little grave about what had taken place in Royd Lane, and she tried to smile him out of his seriousness. Miss Keeldar sat near; for a wonder, neither laughing nor talking; on the contrary, very still, and gazing round her vigilantly: she seemed afraid lest some intruder should take a seat she apparently wished to reserve next her own: ever and anon she spread her satin dress over an undue portion of the bench, or laid her gloves or her embroidered handkerchief upon it. Caroline noticed this *manège* at last, and asked her what friend she expected. Shirley bent towards her, almost touched her ear with her rosy lips, and whispered with a musical softness that often characterised her tones, when what she said tended even remotely to stir some sweet secret source of feeling in her heart—"I expect Mr. Moore: I saw him last night, and I made him promise to come with his sister, and to sit at our table: he won't fail me, I feel certain, but I apprehend his coming too late, and being separated from us. Here is a fresh batch arriving; every place will be taken: provoking!"

In fact Mr. Wynne the magistrate, his wife, his son, and his two daughters, now entered in high state. They were Briarfield gentry: of course their place was at the first table, and being conducted thither, they filled up the whole remaining space. For Miss Keeldar's comfort, Mr. Sam Wynne inducted himself into the very vacancy she had kept for Moore, planting himself solidly on her gown, her gloves, and her handkerchief. Mr. Sam was one of the objects of her aversion; and the more so because he showed serious symptoms of an aim at her hand. The old gentleman, too, had publicly declared that the Fieldhead estate and the De Walden estate were delightfully *contagious*—a malapropism which rumour had not failed to repeat to Shirley.

Caroline's ears yet rung with that thrilling whisper, "I expect Mr. Moore," her heart yet beat and her cheek yet glowed with it, when a note from the organ pealed above the confused hum of the place. Dr. Boultby, Mr. Helstone, and Mr. Hall

rose, so did all present, and grace was sung to the accompaniment of the music; and then tea began. She was kept too busy with her office for a while to have leisure for looking round, but the last cup being filled, she threw a restless glance over the room. There were some ladies and several gentlemen standing about yet unaccommodated with seats; amidst a group she recognised her spinster friend, Miss Mann, whom the fine weather had tempted, or some urgent friend had persuaded, to leave her drear solitude for one hour of social enjoyment. Miss Mann looked tired of standing: a lady in a yellow bonnet brought her a chair. Caroline knew well that "chapeau en satin jaune"; she knew the black hair, and the kindly though rather opinionated and froward-looking face under it; she knew that "robe de soie noire"; she knew even that "schal gris de lin"; she knew, in short, Hortense Moore, and she wanted to jump up and run to her and kiss her—to give her one embrace for her own sake, and two for her brother's. She half rose, indeed, with a smothered exclamation, and perhaps—for the impulse was very strong—she would have run across the room, and actually saluted her, but a hand replaced her in her seat, and a voice behind her whispered—"Wait till after tea, Lina, and then I'll bring her to you."

And when she *could* look up she did, and there was Robert himself close behind, smiling at her eagerness, looking better than she had ever seen him look—looking, indeed, to her partial eyes, so very handsome, that she dared not trust herself to hazard a second glance; for his image struck on her vision with painful brightness, and pictured itself on her memory as vividly as if there daguerreotyped by a pencil of keen lightning.

He moved on, and spoke to Miss Keeldar. Shirley, irritated by some unwelcome attentions from Sam Wynne, and by the fact of that gentleman being still seated on her gloves and handkerchief—and probably, also, by Moore's want of punctuality— was by no means in good humour. She first shrugged her shoulder at him, and then she said a bitter word or two about his "insupportable tardiness." Moore neither apologised nor retorted: he stood near her quietly, as if waiting to see whether she would recover her temper; which she did in little more than three minutes, indicating the change by offering him her hand. Moore took it with a smile, half corrective, half grateful: the slightest possible shake of the head delicately marked the former quality; it is probable a gentle pressure indicated the latter.

"You may sit where you can now, Mr. Moore," said Shirley, also smiling: "you see there is not an inch of room for you here; but I discern plenty of space at Mrs. Boultby's table, between Miss Armitage and Miss Birtwhistle; go: John Sykes will be your *vis-à-vis*, and you will sit with your back towards us."

Moore, however, preferred lingering about where he was: he now and then took a turn down the long room, pausing in his walk to interchange greetings with other gentlemen in his own placeless predicament: but still he came back to the magnet, Shirley, bringing with him, each time he returned, observations it was necessary to whisper in her ear.

Meantime, poor Sam Wynne looked far from comfortable; his fair neighbour, judging from her movements, appeared in a mood the most unquiet and unaccommodating: she would not sit still two seconds: she was hot; she fanned herself; complained of want of air and space. She remarked, that, in her opinion, when people had finished their tea they ought to leave the tables, and announced distinctly that she expected to faint if the present state of things continued. Mr. Sam offered to accompany her into the open air; just the way to give her her death of cold, she alleged: in short, his post became untenable; and having swallowed his quantum of tea, he judged it expedient to evacuate.

Moore should have been at hand, whereas he was quite at the other extremity of the room, deep in conference with Christopher Sykes. A large corn-factor, Timothy Ramsden, Esq., happened to be nearer, and feeling himself tired of standing, he advanced to fill the vacant seat. Shirley's expedients did not fail her: a sweep

of her scarf upset her teacup, its contents were shared between the bench and her own satin dress. Of course, it became necessary to call a waiter to remedy the mischief: Mr. Ramsden, a stout, puffy gentleman, as large in person as he was in property, held aloof from the consequent commotion. Shirley, usually almost culpably indifferent to slight accidents affecting dress, etc., now made a commotion that might have become the most delicate and nervous of her sex; Mr. Ramsden opened his mouth, withdrew slowly, and, as Miss Keeldar again intimated her intention to "give way" and swoon on the spot, he turned on his heel, and beat a heavy retreat.

Moore at last returned: calmly surveying the bustle, and somewhat quizzically scanning Shirley's enigmatical-looking countenance, he remarked, that in truth this was the hottest end of the room; that he found a climate there calculated to agree with none but cool temperaments like his own; and, putting the waiters, the napkins, the satin robe, the whole turmoil, in short, to one side, he installed himself where destiny evidently decreed he should sit. Shirley subsided; her features altered their lines: the raised knit brow and inexplicable curve of the mouth became straight again: wilfulness and roguery gave place to other expressions; and all the angular movements with which she had vexed the soul of Sam Wynne were conjured to rest as by a charm. Still, no gracious glance was cast on Moore: on the contrary, he was accused of giving her a world of trouble, and roundly charged with being the cause of depriving her of the esteem of Mr. Ramsden, and the invaluable friendship of Mr. Samuel Wynne.

"Wouldn't have offended either gentleman, for the world," she averred: "I have always been accustomed to treat both with the most respectful consideration, and there, owing to you, how they have been used! I shall not be happy till I have made it up: I never am happy till I am friends with my neighbours; so to-morrow I must make a pilgrimage to Royd corn-mill, soothe the miller, and praise the grain; and next day I must call at De Walden—where I hate to go—and carry in my reticule half an oat-cake to give to Mr. Sam's favourite pointers."

"You know the surest path to the heart of each swain, I doubt not," said Moore quietly. He looked very content to have at last secured his present place; but he made no fine speech expressive of gratification, and offered no apology for the trouble he had given. His phlegm became him wonderfully: it made him look handsomer, he was so composed: it made his vicinage pleasant, it was so peace-restoring. You would not have thought, to look at him, that he was a poor, struggling man seated beside a rich woman; the calm of equality stilled his aspect: perhaps that calm, too, reigned in his soul. Now and then, from the way in which he looked down on Miss Keeldar as he addressed her, you would have fancied his station towered above hers as much as his stature did. Almost stern lights sometimes crossed his brow and gleamed in his eyes: their conversation had become animated, though it was confined to a low key; she was urging him with questions—evidently he refused to her curiosity all the gratification it demanded. She sought his eye once with hers: you read, in its soft yet eager expression, that it solicited clearer replies. Moore smiled pleasantly, but his lips continued sealed. Then she was piqued and turned away, but he recalled her attention in two minutes: he seemed making promises, which he soothed her into accepting, in lieu of information.

It appeared that the heat of the room did not suit Miss Helstone: she grew paler and paler as the process of tea-making was protracted. The moment thanks were returned, she quitted the table, and hastened to follow her cousin Hortense, who, with Miss Mann, had already sought the open air. Robert Moore had risen when she did—perhaps he meant to speak to her; but there was yet a parting word to exchange with Miss Keeldar, and while it was being uttered, Caroline had vanished.

Hortense received her former pupil with a demeanour of more dignity than warmth: she had been seriously offended by Mr. Helstone's proceedings, and had all along considered Caroline to blame in obeying her uncle too literally.

"You are a very great stranger," she said austerely, as her pupil held and pressed her hand. The pupil knew her too well to remonstrate or complain of coldness; she let the punctilious whim pass, sure that her natural *bonté* (I use this French word, because it expresses just what I mean; neither goodness nor good-nature, but something between the two) would presently get the upper hand. It did: Hortense had no sooner examined her face well, and observed the change its somewhat wasted features betrayed, than her mien softened. Kissing her on both cheeks, she asked anxiously after her health: Caroline answered gaily. It would, however, have been her lot to undergo a long cross-examination, followed by an endless lecture on this head, had not Miss Mann called off the attention of the questioner, by requesting to be conducted home. The poor invalid was already fatigued: her weariness made her cross—too cross almost to speak to Caroline; and besides, that young person's white dress and lively look were displeasing in the eyes of Miss Mann: the everyday garb of brown stuff or grey gingham, and the everyday air of melancholy, suited the solitary spinster better: she would hardly know her young friend to-night, and quitted her with a cool nod. Hortense having promised to accompany her home, they departed together.

Caroline now looked round for Shirley. She saw the rainbow scarf and purple dress in the centre of a throng of ladies, all well known to herself, but all of the order whom she systematically avoided whenever avoidance was possible. Shyer at some moments than at others, she felt just now no courage at all to join this company: she could not, however, stand alone where all others went in pairs or parties, so she approached a group of her own scholars, great girls, or rather young women, who were standing watching some hundreds of the younger children playing at blind-man's buff.

Miss Helstone knew these girls liked her, yet she was shy even with them out of school: they were not more in awe of her than she of them: she drew near them now, rather to find protection in their company than to patronise them with her presence. By some instinct they knew her weakness, and with natural politeness they respected it. Her knowledge commanded their esteem when she taught them; her gentleness attracted their regard; and because she was what they considered wise and good when *on* duty, they kindly overlooked her evident timidity when off: they did not take advantage of it. Peasant girls as they were, they had too much of her own English sensibility to be guilty of the coarse error: they stood round her still, civil, friendly, receiving her slight smiles, and rather hurried efforts to converse, with a good feeling and good breeding: the last quality being the result of the first, which soon set her at her ease.

Mr. Sam Wynne coming up with great haste, to insist on the elder girls joining in the game as well as the younger ones, Caroline was again left alone. She was meditating a quiet retreat to the house, when Shirley, perceiving from afar her isolation, hastened to her side.

"Let us go to the top of the fields," she said: "I know you don't like crowds, Caroline."

"But it will be depriving you of a pleasure, Shirley, to take you from all these fine people, who court your society so assiduously, and to whom you can, without art or effort, make yourself so pleasant."

"Not quite without effort: I am already tired of the exertion: it is but insipid, barren work, talking and laughing with the good gentlefolks of Briarfield. I have been looking out for your white dress for the last ten minutes: I like to watch those I love in a crowd, and to compare them with others: I have thus compared you. You resemble none of the rest, Lina: there are some prettier faces than yours here; you are not a model-beauty like Harriet Sykes, for instance; beside her, your person appears almost insignificant; but you look agreeable—you look reflective—you look what I call interesting."

"Hush, Shirley! You flatter me."

"I don't wonder that your scholars like you."

"Nonsense, Shirley: talk of something else."

"We will talk of Moore, then, and we will watch him: I see him even now."

"Where?" And as Caroline asked the question, she looked not over the fields, but into Miss Keeldar's eyes, as was her wont whenever Shirley mentioned any object she descried afar. Her friend had quicker vision than herself; and Caroline seemed to think that the secret of her eagle acuteness might be read in her dark grey irids: or rather, perhaps, she only sought guidance by the direction of those discriminating and brilliant spheres.

"There is Moore," said Shirley, pointing right across the wide field where a thousand children were playing, and now nearly a thousand adult spectators walking about. "There—can you miss the tall stature and straight port? He looks amidst the set that surround him like Eliab amongst humbler shepherds—like Saul in a war-council: and a war-council it is, if I am not mistaken."

"Why so, Shirley?" asked Caroline, whose eye had at last caught the object it sought. "Robert is just now speaking to my uncle, and they are shaking hands; they are then reconciled."

"Reconciled not without good reason, depend on it: making common cause against some common foe. And why, think you, are Messrs. Wynne and Sykes, and Armitage and Ramsden, gathered in such a close circle round them? And why is Malone beckoned to join them? When *he* is summoned, be sure a strong arm is needed."

Shirley, as she watched, grew restless: her eyes flashed.

"They won't trust me," she said: "that is always the way when it comes to the point."

"What about?"

"Cannot you feel? There is some mystery afloat: some event is expected; some preparation is to be made, I am certain: I saw it all in Mr. Moore's manner this evening: he was excited, yet hard."

"Hard to *you*, Shirley!"

"Yes, to *me*. He often is hard to me. We seldom converse *tête-à-tête*, but I am made to feel that the basis of his character is not of eider-down."

"Yet he seemed to talk to you softly."

"Did he not? Very gentle tones and quiet manner; yet the man is peremptory and secret: his secrecy vexes me."

"Yes—Robert is secret."

"Which he has scarcely a right to be with me; especially as he commenced by giving me his confidence. Having done nothing to forfeit that confidence, it ought not to be withdrawn: but I suppose I am not considered iron-souled enough to be trusted in a crisis."

"He fears, probably, to occasion you uneasiness."

"An unnecessary precaution: I am of elastic materials, not soon crushed: he ought to know that: but the man is proud: he has his faults, say what you will, Lina. Observe how engaged that group appear: they do not know we are watching them."

"If we keep on the alert, Shirley, we shall perhaps find the clue to their secret."

"There will be some unusual movements ere long—perhaps to-morrow—possibly to-night. But my eyes and ears are wide open: Mr. Moore, you shall be under surveillance. Be you vigilant also, Lina."

"I will: Robert is going, I saw him turn—I believe he noticed us—they are shaking hands."

"Shaking hands, with emphasis," added Shirley; "as if they were ratifying some solemn league and covenant."

They saw Robert quit the group, pass through a gate, and disappear.

"And he has not bid us good-bye," murmured Caroline.

Scarcely had the words escaped her lips, when she tried by a smile to deny the confession of disappointment they seemed to imply. An unbidden suffusion for one moment both softened and brightened her eyes.

"Oh, that is soon remedied!" exclaimed Shirley. "We'll *make* him bid us good-bye."

"*Make* him! that is not the same thing," was the answer.

"It *shall* be the same thing."

"But he is gone: you can't overtake him."

"I know a shorter way than that he has taken: we will intercept him."

"But, Shirley, I would rather not go."

Caroline said this as Miss Keeldar seized her arm, and hurried her down the fields. It was vain to contend: nothing was so wilful as Shirley, when she took a whim into her head: Caroline found herself out of sight of the crowd almost before she was aware, and ushered into a narrow shady spot, embowered above with hawthorns, and enamelled under foot with daisies. She took no notice of the evening sun chequering the turf, nor was she sensible of the pure incense exhaling at this hour from tree and plant; she only heard the wicket opening at one end, and knew Robert was approaching. The long sprays of the hawthorns, shooting out before them, served as a screen; they saw him before he observed them. At a glance Caroline perceived that his social hilarity was gone: he had left it behind him in the joy-echoing fields round the school; what remained now was his dark, quiet, business countenance. As Shirley had said, a certain hardness characterised his air, while his eye was excited, but austere. So much the worse-timed was the present freak of Shirley's: if he had looked disposed for holiday mirth, it would not have mattered much, but now——

"I told you not to come," said Caroline, somewhat bitterly, to her friend. She seemed truly perturbed: to be intruded on Robert thus, against her will and his expectation, and when he evidently would rather not be delayed, keenly annoyed her. It did not annoy Miss Keeldar in the least: she stepped forward and faced her tenant, barring his way—"You omitted to bid us good-bye," she said.

"Omitted to bid you good-bye! Where did you come from? Are you fairies? I left two like you, one in purple and one in white, standing at the top of a bank, four fields off, but a minute ago."

"You left us there and find us here. We have been watching you; and shall watch you still: you must be questioned one day, but not now: at present, all you have to do is to say good-night, and then pass."

Moore glanced from one to the other, without unbending his aspect. "Days of fête have their privileges, and so have days of hazard," observed he gravely.

"Come—don't moralise: say good-night, and pass," urged Shirley.

"Must I say good-night to you, Miss Keeldar?"

"Yes, and to Caroline likewise. It is nothing new, I hope: you have bid us both good-night before."

He took her hand, held it in one of his, and covered it with the other: he looked down at her gravely, kindly, yet commandingly. The heiress could not make this man her subject: in his gaze on her bright face there was no servility, hardly homage; but there was interest and affection, heightened by another feeling: something in his tone when he spoke, as well as in his words, marked that last sentiment to be gratitude.

"Your debtor bids you good-night!—May you rest safely and serenely till morning!"

"And you, Mr. Moore,—what are you going to do? What have you been saying to Mr. Helstone, with whom I saw you shake hands? Why did all those gentlemen gather round you? Put away reserve for once: be frank with me."

"Who can resist you? I will be frank: to-morrow, if there is anything to relate, you shall hear it."

"Just now," pleaded Shirley: "don't procrastinate."

"But I could only tell half a tale; and my time is limited,—I have not a moment to spare: hereafter I will make amends for delay by candour.''

"But are you going home?''

"Yes.''

"Not to leave it any more to-night?''

"Certainly not. At present, farewell to both of you!''

He would have taken Caroline's hand and joined it in the same clasp in which he held Shirley's, but somehow it was not ready for him; she had withdrawn a few steps apart: her answer to Moore's adieu was only a slight bend of the head, and a gentle, serious smile. He sought no more cordial token: again he said "Farewell!'' and quitted them both.

"There!—it is over!'' said Shirley, when he was gone. "We have made him bid us good-night, and yet not lost ground in his esteem, I think, Cary.''

"I hope not,'' was the brief reply.

"I consider you very timid and undemonstrative,'' remarked Miss Keeldar. "Why did you not give Mr. Moore your hand when he offered you his? He is your cousin: you like him. Are you ashamed to let him perceive your affection?''

"He perceives all of it that interests him: no need to make a display of feeling.''

"You are laconic: you would be stoical if you could. Is love, in your eyes, a crime, Caroline?''

"Love a crime! No, Shirley:—love is a divine virtue; but why drag that word into the conversation? it is singularly irrelevant!''

"Good!'' pronounced Shirley.

The two girls paced the green lane in silence. Caroline first resumed.

"Obtrusiveness is a crime; forwardness is a crime; and both disgust: but love!— no purest angel need blush to love! And when I see or hear either man or woman couple shame with love, I know their minds are coarse, their associations debased. Many who think themselves refined ladies and gentlemen, and on whose lips the word ' vulgarity' is for ever hovering, cannot mention ' love' without betraying their own innate and imbecile degradation: it is a low feeling in their estimation, connected only with low ideas for them.''

"You describe three-fourths of the world, Caroline.''

"They are cold—they are cowardly—they are stupid on the subject, Shirley! They never loved—they never were loved!''

"Thou art right, Lina! And in their dense ignorance they blaspheme living fire, seraph-brought from a divine altar.''

"They confound it with sparks mounting from Tophet!''

The sudden and joyous clash of bells here stopped the dialogue by summoning all to the church.

Chapter XVIII

WHICH THE GENTEEL READER IS RECOMMENDED TO SKIP, LOW PERSONS BEING HERE INTRODUCED

THE evening was still and warm; close and sultry it even promised to become. Round the descending sun the clouds glowed purple; summer tints, rather Indian than English, suffused the horizon, and cast rosy reflections on hill-side, house-front, tree-bole; on winding road, and undulating pasture-ground. The two girls came down from the fields slowly: by the time they reached the churchyard the bells were hushed; the multitudes were gathered into the church: the whole scene was solitary.

"How pleasant and calm it is!'' said Caroline.

"And how hot it will be in the church!'' responded Shirley; "and what a dreary

long speech Dr. Boultby will make! and how the curates will hammer over their prepared orations! For my part, I would rather not enter.''

"But my uncle will be angry, if he observes our absence."

"I will bear the brunt of his wrath: he will not devour me. I shall be sorry to miss his pungent speech. I know it will be all sense for the Church, and all causticity for Schism: he'll not forget the battle of Royd Lane. I shall be sorry also to deprive you of Mr. Hall's sincere friendly homily, with all its racy Yorkshireisms; but here I must stay. The grey church and greyer tombs look divine with this crimson gleam on them. Nature is now at her evening prayers: she is kneeling before those red hills. I see her prostrate on the great steps of her altar, praying for a fair night for mariners at sea, for travellers in deserts, for lambs on moors, and unfledged birds in woods. Caroline, I see her! and I will tell you what she is like: she is like what Eve was when she and Adam stood alone on earth."

"And that is not Milton's Eve, Shirley."

"Milton's Eve! Milton's Eve! I repeat. No, by the pure Mother of God, she is not! Cary, we are alone: we may speak what we think. Milton was great; but was he good? His brain was right; how was his heart? He saw heaven: he looked down on hell. He saw Satan, and Sin his daughter, and Death their horrible offspring. Angels serried before him their battalions: the long lines of adamantine shields flashed back on his blind eyeballs the unutterable splendour of heaven. Devils gathered their legions in his sight: their dim, discrowned, and tarnished armies passed rank and file before him. Milton tried to see the first woman; but, Cary, he saw her not."

"You are bold to say so, Shirley."

"Not more bold than faithful. It was his cook that he saw; or it was Mrs. Gill, as I have seen her, making custards, in the heat of summer, in the cool dairy, with rose-trees and nasturtiums about the latticed window, preparing a cold collation for the rectors,—preserves, and 'dulcet creams'—puzzled 'what choice to choose for delicacy best; what order so contrived as not to mix tastes, not well-joined, inelegant; but bring taste after taste, upheld with kindliest change.' ''

"All very well too, Shirley."

"I would beg to remind him that the first men of the earth were Titans, and that Eve was their mother: from her sprang Saturn, Hyperion, Oceanus; she bore Prometheus"——

"Pagan that you are! what does that signify?"

"I say, there were giants on the earth in those days: giants that strove to scale heaven. The first woman's breast that heaved with life on this world yielded the daring which could contend with Omnipotence: the strength which could bear a thousand years of bondage,—the vitality which could feed that vulture death through uncounted ages,—the unexhausted life and uncorrupted excellence, sisters to immortality, which, after millenniums of crimes, struggles, and woes, could conceive and bring forth a Messiah. The first woman was heaven-born: vast was the heart whence gushed the well-spring of the blood of nations; and grand the undegenerate head where rested the consort-crown of creation."

"She coveted an apple, and was cheated by a snake: but you have got such a hash of Scripture and mythology into your head that there is no making any sense of you. You have not yet told me what you saw kneeling on those hills."

"I saw—I now see—a woman-Titan: her robe of blue air spreads to the outskirts of the heath, where yonder flock is grazing; a veil white as an avalanche sweeps from her head to her feet, and arabesques of lightning flame on its borders. Under her breast I see her zone, purple like that horizon: through its blush shines the star of evening. Her steady eyes I cannot picture; they are clear—they are deep as lakes—they are lifted and full of worship—they tremble with the softness of love and the lustre of prayer. Her forehead has the expanse of a cloud, and is paler than the early moon, risen long before dark gathers: she reclines her bosom on the ridge

of Stilbro' Moor; her mighty hands are joined beneath it. So kneeling, face to face she speaks with God. That Eve is Jehovah's daughter, as Adam was His son.''

"She is very vague and visionary! Come, Shirley, we ought to go into church.''

"Caroline, I will not: I will stay out here with my mother Eve, in these days called Nature. I love her, undying, mighty being! Heaven may have faded from her brow when she fell in paradise; but all that is glorious on earth shines there still. She is taking me to her bosom, and showing me her heart. Hush, Caroline! you will see her and feel her as I do, if we are both silent.''

"I will humour your whim; but you will begin talking again, ere ten minutes are over.''

Miss Keeldar, on whom the soft excitement of the warm summer evening seemed working with unwonted power, leaned against an upright headstone: she fixed her eyes on the deep-burning west, and sank into a pleasurable trance. Caroline, going a little apart, paced to and fro beneath the Rectory garden-wall, dreaming, too, in her way. Shirley had mentioned the word "mother": that word suggested to Caroline's imagination not the mighty and mystical parent of Shirley's visions, but a gentle human form—the form she ascribed to her own mother; unknown, unloved, but not unlonged for.

"Oh, that the day would come when she would remember her child! Oh, that I might know her, and knowing, love her!''

Such was her aspiration.

The longing of her childhood filled her soul again. The desire which many a night had kept her awake in her crib, and which fear of its fallacy had of late years almost extinguished, relit suddenly, and glowed warm in her heart: that her mother might come some happy day, and send for her to her presence—look upon her fondly with loving eyes, and say to her tenderly, in a sweet voice—"Caroline, my child I have a home for you: you shall live with me. All the love you have needed, and not tasted, from infancy, I have saved for you carefully. Come! it shall cherish you now.''

A noise on the road roused Caroline from her filial hopes, and Shirley from her Titan visions. They listened, and heard the tramp of horses: they looked, and saw a glitter through the trees: they caught through the foliage glimpses of martial scarlet; helm shone, plume waved. Silent and orderly, six soldiers rode softly by.

"The same we saw this afternoon,'' whispered Shirley: "they have been halting somewhere till now. They wish to be as little noticed as possible, and are seeking their rendezvous at this quiet hour, while the people are at church. Did I not say we should see unusual things ere long?''

Scarcely were sight and sound of the soldiers lost, when another and somewhat different disturbance broke the night-hush—a child's impatient scream. They looked: a man issued from the church, carrying in his arms an infant—a robust, ruddy little boy, of some two years old—roaring with all the power of his lungs; he had probably just awaked from a church-sleep: two little girls, of nine and ten, followed. The influence of the fresh air, and the attraction of some flowers gathered from a grave, soon quieted the child; the man sat down with him, dandling him on his knee as tenderly as any woman; the two little girls took their places one on each side.

"Good evening, William,'' said Shirley, after due scrutiny of the man. He had seen her before, and apparently was waiting to be recognised; he now took off his hat, and grinned a smile of pleasure. He was a rough-headed, hard-featured personage, not old, but very weather-beaten; his attire was decent and clean, that of his children singularly neat; it was our old friend, Farren. The young ladies approached him.

"You are not going into the church?'' he inquired, gazing at them complacently, yet with a mixture of bashfulness in his look: a sentiment not by any means the result of awe of their station, but only of appreciation of their elegance and youth. Before gentlemen—such as Moore or Helstone, for instance—William was often a little dogged; with proud or insolent ladies, too, he was quite unmanageable,

sometimes very resentful; but he was most sensible of, most tractable to, good-humour and civility. His nature—a stubborn one—was repelled by inflexibility in other natures; for which reason, he had never been able to like his former master, Moore; and unconscious of that gentleman's good opinion of himself, and of the service he had secretly rendered him in recommending him as gardener to Mr. Yorke, and by this means to other families in the neighbourhood, he continued to harbour a grudge against his austerity. Latterly, he had often worked at Fieldhead; Miss Keeldar's frank, hospitable manners were perfectly charming to him. Caroline he had known from her childhood: unconsciously she was his ideal of a lady. Her gentle mien, step, gestures, her grace of person and attire, moved some artist-fibres about his peasant heart: he had a pleasure in looking at her, as he had in examining rare flowers, or in seeing pleasant landscapes. Both the ladies liked William: it was their delight to lend him books, to give him plants; and they preferred his conversation far before that of many coarse, hard, pretentious people, immeasurably higher in station.

"Who was speaking, William, when you came out?" asked Shirley.

"A gentleman ye set a deal of store on, Miss Shirley—Mr. Donne."

"You look knowing, William. How did you find out my regard for Mr. Donne?"

"Ay, Miss Shirley, there's a gleg light i' your een sometimes which betrays you. You look raight down scornful sometimes, when Mr. Donne is by."

"Do you like him yourself, William?"

"Me? I'm stalled o' t' curates, and so is t' wife: they've no manners; they talk to poor folk fair as if they thought they were beneath them. They're allus magnifying their office: it is a pity but their office could magnify them; but it does nought o' t' soart. I fair hate pride."

"But you are proud in your own way yourself," interposed Caroline: "you are what you call house-proud; you like to have everything handsome about you: sometimes you look as if you were almost too proud to take your wages. When you were out of work, you were too proud to get anything on credit; but for your children, I believe you would rather have starved than gone to the shops without money; and when I wanted to give you something, what a difficulty I had in making you take it!"

"It is partly true, Miss Caroline: ony day I'd rather give than take, especially from sich as ye. Look at t' difference between us: ye're a little, young, slender lass, and I'm a great strong man: I'm rather more nor twice your age. It is not *my* part then, I think, to tak' fro' *ye*—to be under obligations (as they say) to *ye;* and that day ye came to our house, and called me to t' door, and offered me five shillings, which I doubt ye could ill spare,—for ye've no fortin', I know,—that day I war fair a rebel—a radical—an insurrectionist; and *ye* made me so. I thought it shameful that, willing and able as I was to work, I suld be i' such a condition that a young cratur about the age o' my own eldest lass suld think it needful to come and offer me her bit o' brass."

"I suppose you were angry with me, William?"

"I almost was, in a way; but I forgave ye varry soon: ye meant well. Ay, *I am* proud, and so are *ye;* but your pride and mine is t' raight mak'—what we call i' Yorkshire clean pride—such as Mr. Malone and Mr. Donne knows nought about: theirs is mucky pride. Now, I shall teach my lasses to be as proud as Miss Shirley there, and my lads to be as proud as myseln; but I dare ony o' 'em to be like t' curates: I'd lick little Michael, if I seed him show any signs o' that feeling."

"What is the difference, William?"

"Ye know t' difference weel enow, but ye want me to get a gate o' talking. Mr. Malone and Mr. Donne is almost too proud to do aught for theirsel'n; *we* are almost too proud to let anybody do aught for us. T' curates can hardly bide to speak a civil word to them they think beneath them; *we* can hardly bide to tak' an uncivil word fro' them that thinks themsel'n aboon us."

"Now, William, be humble enough to tell me truly how you are getting on in the world. Are you well off?"

"Miss Shirley—I am varry well off. Since I got into t' gardening line, wi' Mr. Yorke's help, and since Mr. Hall (another o' t' raight sort) helped my wife to set up a bit of a shop, I've nought to complain of. My family has plenty to eat and plenty to wear: my pride makes me find means to save an odd pound now and then against rainy days; for I think I'd die afore I'd come to t' parish: and me and mine is content; but th' neighbours is poor yet: I see a great deal of distress."

"And, consequently, there is still discontent, I suppose?" inquired Miss Keeldar.

"*Consequently*—ye say right—*consequently*. In course, starving folk cannot be satisfied or settled folk. The country's not in a safe condition;—I'll say so mich!"

"But what can be done? What more can I do, for instance?"

"Do?—ye can do not mich, poor young lass! Ye've gi'en your brass: ye've done well. If ye could transport your tenant, Mr. Moore, to Botany Bay, ye'd happen do better. Folks hate him."

"William, for shame!" exclaimed Caroline warmly. "If folks *do* hate him, it is to their disgrace, not his. Mr. Moore himself hates nobody; he only wants to do his duty, and maintain his rights: you are wrong to talk so!"

"I talk as I think. He has a cold, unfeeling heart, yond' Moore."

"But," interposed Shirley, "supposing Moore was driven from the country, and his mill razed to the ground, would people have more work?"

"They'd have less. I know that, and they know that; and there is many an honest lad driven desperate by the certainty that, whichever way he turns, he cannot better himself, and there is dishonest men plenty to guide them to the devil: scoundrels that reckons to be the ' people's friends,' and that knows naught about the people, and is as insincere as Lucifer. I've lived aboon forty year in the world, and I believe that 'the people' will never have any true friends but theirsel'n, and them two or three good folk i' different stations that is friends to all the world. Human natur', taking it i' th' lump, is naught but selfishness. It is but excessive few, it is but just an exception here and there, now and then, sich as ye two young uns and me, that being in a different sphere, can understand t' one t' other, and be friends wi'out slavishness o' one hand, or pride o' t' other. Them that reckons to be friends to a lower class than their own fro' political motives is never to be trusted: they always try to make their inferiors tools. For my own part, I will neither be patronised nor misled for no man's pleasure. I've had overtures made to me lately that I saw were treacherous, and I flung 'em back i' the faces o' them that offered 'em."

"You won't tell us what overtures?"

"I will not: it would do no good; it would mak' no difference: them they concerned can look after theirsel'n."

"Ay, we'se look after wersel'n," said another voice. Joe Scott had sauntered forth from the church to get a breath of fresh air, and there he stood.

"I'll warrant *ye,* Joe," observed William, smiling.

"And I'll warrant my maister," was the answer. "Young ladies," continued Joe, assuming a lordly air, "ye'd better go into th' house."

"I wonder what for?" inquired Shirley, to whom the overlooker's somewhat pragmatical manners were familiar, and who was often at war with him; for Joe, holding supercilious theories about women in general, resented greatly, in his secret soul, the fact of his master and his master's mill being, in a manner, under petticoat government, and had felt as wormwood and gall certain business-visits of the heiress to the Hollow's counting-house.

"Because there is naught agate that fits women to be consarned in."

"Indeed! There is prayer and preaching agate in that church: are we not concerned in that?"

"Ye have been present neither at the prayer nor preaching, ma'am, if I have observed aright. What I alluded to was politics: William Farren, here, was touching on that subject, if I'm not mista'en."

"Well, what then? Politics are our habitual study, Joe. Do you know I see a newspaper every day, and two of a Sunday?"

"I should think you'll read the marriages, probably, Miss, and the murders, and the accidents, and sich like?"

"I read the leading articles, Joe, and the foreign intelligence, and I look over the market prices: in short, I read just what gentlemen read."

Joe looked as if he thought this talk was like the chattering of a pie. He replied to it by a disdainful silence.

"Joe," continued Miss Keeldar, "I never yet could ascertain properly whether you are a Whig or a Tory: pray which party has the honour of your alliance?"

"It is rayther difficult to explain where you are sure not to be understood," was Joe's haughty response; "but, as to being a Tory, I'd as soon be an old woman, or a young one, which is a more flimsier article still. It is the Tories that carries on the war and ruins trade; and, if I be of any party—though political parties is all nonsense—I'm of that which is most favourable to peace, and, by consequence, to the mercantile interests of this here land."

"So am I, Joe," replied Shirley, who had rather a pleasure in teasing the overlooker, by persisting in talking on subjects with which he opined she—as a woman—had no right to meddle: "partly, at least. I have rather a leaning to the agricultural interest, too; as good reason is, seeing that I don't desire England to be under the feet of France, and that if a share of my income comes from Hollow's Mill, a larger share comes from the landed estate around it. It would not do to take any measure injurious to the farmers, Joe, I think?"

"The dews at this hour is unwholesome for females," observed Joe.

"If you make that remark out of interest in me, I have merely to assure you that I am impervious to cold. I should not mind taking my turn to watch the mill one of these summer nights, armed with your musket, Joe."

Joe Scott's chin was always rather prominent: he poked it out, at this speech, some inches farther than usual.

"But—to go back to my sheep," she proceeded—"clothier and mill-owner as I am, besides farmer, I cannot get out of my head a certain idea that we manufacturers and persons of business are sometimes a little—a *very little* selfish and shortsighted in our views, and rather *too* regardless of human suffering, rather heartless in our pursuit of gain: don't you agree with me, Joe?"

"I cannot argue, where I cannot be comprehended," was again the answer.

"Man of mystery! Your master will argue with me sometimes, Joe; he is not so stiff as you are."

"May be not: we've all our own ways."

"Joe, do you seriously think all the wisdom in the world is lodged in male skulls?"

"I think that women are a kittle and a froward generation; and I've a great respect for the doctrines delivered in the second chapter of St. Paul's first Epistle to Timothy."

"What doctrines, Joe?"

" 'Let the woman learn in silence, with all subjection. I suffer not a woman to teach, nor to usurp authority over the man; but to be in silence. For Adam was first formed, then Eve.' "

"What has that to do with the business?" interjected Shirley: "that smacks of rights of primogeniture. I'll bring it up to Mr. Yorke the first time he inveighs against those rights."

" 'And,' " continued Joe Scott, " 'Adam was not deceived; but the woman, being deceived, was in the transgression.' "

"More shame to Adam to sin with his eyes open!" cried Miss Keeldar. "To confess the honest truth, Joe, I never was easy in my mind concerning that chapter: it puzzles me."

"It is very plain, Miss: he that runs may read."

"He may read it in his own fashion," remarked Caroline, now joining in the dialogue for the first time. "You allow the right of private judgment, I suppose, Joe?"

"My certy, that I do! I allow and claim it for every line of the holy Book."

"Women may exercise it as well as men?"

"Nay: women is to take their husbands' opinion, both in politics and religion: it's wholesomest for them."

"Oh! oh!" exclaimed both Shirley and Caroline.

"To be sure; no doubt on't," persisted the stubborn overlooker.

"Consider yourself groaned down, and cried shame over, for such a stupid observation," said Miss Keeldar. "You might as well say men are to take the opinions of their priests without examination. Of what value would a religion so adopted be? It would be mere blind, besotted superstition."

"And what is *your* reading, Miss Helstone, o' these words o' St. Paul's?"

"Hem! I—I account for them in this way: he wrote that chapter for a particular congregation of Christians, under peculiar circumstances; and besides, I dare say, if I could read the original Greek, I should find that many of the words have been wrongly translated, perhaps misapprehended altogether. It would be possible, I doubt not, with a little ingenuity, to give the passage quite a contrary turn: to make it say, 'Let the woman speak out whenever she sees fit to make an objection;'— 'it is permitted to a woman to teach and to exercise authority as much as may be. Man, meantime, cannot do better than hold his peace,' and so on."

"That willn't wash, Miss."

"I dare say it will. My notions are dyed in faster colours than yours, Joe. Mr. Scott, you are a thoroughly dogmatical person, and always were: I like William better than you."

"Joe is well enough in his own house," said Shirley: "I have seen him as quiet as a lamb at home. There is not a better nor a kinder husband in Briarfield. He does not dogmatise to his wife."

"My wife is a hard-working, plain woman: time and trouble has ta'en all the conceit out of her; but that is not the case with you, young misses. And then you reckon to have so much knowledge; and i' my thoughts it's only superficial sort o' vanities you're acquainted with. I can tell—happen a year sin'—one day Miss Caroline coming into our counting-house when I war packing up summat behind t' great desk, and she didn't see me, and she brought a slate wi' a sum on it to t' maister: it were only a bit of a sum in practice, that our Harry would have settled i' two minutes. She couldn't do it; Mr. Moore had to show her how; and when he did show her, she couldn't understand him."

"Nonsense, Joe!"

"Nay, it's no nonsense: and Miss Shirley there reckons to hearken to t' maister when he's talking ower trade, so attentive like, as if she followed him word for word, and all war as clear as a lady's looking-glass to her een; and all t' while she's peeping and peeping out o' t' window to see if t' mare stands quiet; and then looking at a bit of a splash on her riding-skirt; and then glancing glegly round at wer counting-house cobwebs and dust, and thinking what mucky folk we are, and what a grand ride she'll have just i' now ower Nunnely Common. She hears no more o' Mr. Moore's talk nor if he spake Hebrew."

"Joe, you are a real slanderer. I would give you your answer, only the people are coming out of church: we must leave you. Man of prejudice, good-bye: William, good-bye. Children, come up to Fieldhead to-morrow, and you shall choose what you like best out of Mrs. Gill's store-room."

Chapter XIX

A SUMMER NIGHT

THE hour was now that of dusk. A clear air favoured the kindling of the stars.

"There will be just light enough to show me the way home," said Miss Keeldar, as she prepared to take leave of Caroline at the Rectory garden-door.

"You must not go alone, Shirley. Fanny shall accompany you."

"That she shall not. Of what need I be afraid in my own parish? I would walk from Fieldhead to the church any fine midsummer night, three hours later than this, for the mere pleasure of seeing the stars, and the chance of meeting a fairy."

"But just wait till the crowd is cleared away."

"Agreed. There are the five Misses Armitage streaming by. Here comes Mrs. Sykes's phaeton, Mr. Wynne's close carriage, Mrs. Birtwhistle's car: I don't wish to go through the ceremony of bidding them all good-bye, so we will step into the garden and take shelter amongst the laburnums for an instant."

The rectors, their curates and their churchwardens, now issued from the church-porch. There was a great confabulation, shaking of hands, congratulation on speeches, recommendation to be careful of the night air, etc. By degrees the throng dispersed; the carriages drove off. Miss Keeldar was just emerging from her flowery refuge, when Mr. Helstone entered the garden and met her.

"Oh! I want you!" he said: "I was afraid you were already gone. Caroline, come here!"

Caroline came, expecting, as Shirley did, a lecture on not having been visible at church. Other subjects, however, occupied the Rector's mind.

"I shall not sleep at home to-night," he continued. "I have just met with an old friend, and promised to accompany him. I shall return probably about noon to-morrow. Thomas, the clerk, is engaged, and I cannot get him to sleep in the house, as I usually do when I am absent for a night; now——"

"Now," interrupted Shirley, "you want me as a gentleman—the first gentleman in Briarfield, in short, to supply your place, be master of the Rectory, and guardian of your niece and maids while you are away?"

"Exactly, Captain: I thought the post would suit you. Will you favour Caroline so far as to be her guest for one night? Will you stay here instead of going back to Fieldhead?"

"And what will Mrs. Pryor do? She expects me home."

"I will send her word. Come, make up your mind to stay. It grows late; the dew falls heavily: you and Caroline will enjoy each other's society, I doubt not."

"I promise you then to stay with Caroline," replied Shirley. "As you say, we shall enjoy each other's society: we will not be separated to-night. Now, rejoin your old friend, and fear nothing for us."

"If there should chance to be any disturbance in the night, Captain—if you should hear the picking of a lock, the cutting out of a pane of glass, a stealthy tread of steps about the house (and I need not fear to tell *you*, who bear a well-tempered, mettlesome heart under your girl's ribbon-sash, that such little incidents are very possible in the present time), what would you do?"

"Don't know—faint, perhaps—fall down, and have to be picked up again. But, doctor, if you assign me the post of honour, you must give me arms. What weapons are there in your stronghold?"

"You could not wield a sword?"

"No; I could manage the carving-knife better."

"You will find a good one in the dining-room sideboard: a lady's knife, light to handle, and as sharp-pointed as a poignard."

"It will suit Caroline; but you must give me a brace of pistols: I know you have pistols."

"I have two pairs; one pair I can place at your disposal. You will find them suspended over the mantelpiece of my study in cloth cases."

"Loaded?"

"Yes, but not on the cock. Cock them before you go to bed. It is paying you a great compliment, Captain, to lend you these; were you one of the awkward squad you should not have them."

"I will take care. You need delay no longer, Mr. Helstone: you may go now. He is gracious to me to lend me his pistols," she remarked, as the rector passed out at the garden-gate. "But come, Lina," she continued; "let us go in and have some supper: I was too much vexed at tea with the vicinage of Mr. Sam Wynne to be able to eat, and now I am really hungry."

Entering the house, they repaired to the darkened dining-room, through the open windows of which apartment stole the evening air, bearing the perfume of flowers from the garden, the very distant sound of far-retreating steps from the road, and a soft vague murmur, whose origin Caroline explained by the remark, uttered as she stood listening at the casement—"Shirley, I hear the beck in the Hollow."

Then she rung the bell, asked for a candle and some bread and milk—Miss Keeldar's usual supper and her own. Fanny, when she brought in the tray, would have closed the windows and the shutters, but was requested to desist for the present: the twilight was too calm, its breath too balmy to be yet excluded. They took their meal in silence: Caroline rose once, to remove to the window-sill a glass of flowers which stood on the side-board; the exhalation from the blossoms being somewhat too powerful for the sultry room: in returning, she half opened a drawer, and took from it something that glittered clear and keen in her hand.

"You assigned this to me, then, Shirley—did you? It is bright, keen-edged, finely-tapered: it is dangerous-looking, I never yet felt the impulse which could move me to direct this against a fellow-creature. It is difficult to fancy what circumstances could nerve my arm to strike home with this long knife."

"I should hate to do it," replied Shirley; "but I think I could do it, if goaded by certain exigencies which I can imagine." And Miss Keeldar quietly sipped her glass of new milk, looking somewhat thoughtful, and a little pale: though, indeed, when did she not look pale? She was never florid.

The milk sipped and the bread eaten, Fanny was again summoned: she and Eliza were recommended to go to bed, which they were quite willing to do, being weary of the day's exertions, of much cutting of currant-buns, and filling of urns and teapots, and running backwards and forwards with trays. Erelong the maids' chamber-door was heard to close; Caroline took a candle, and went quietly all over the house, seeing that every window was fast and every door barred. She did not even evade the haunted back-kitchen, nor the vault-like cellars. These visited, she returned.

"There is neither spirit nor flesh in the house at present," she said, "which should not be there. It is now near eleven o'clock, fully bed-time, yet I would rather sit up a little longer, if you do not object, Shirley. Here," she continued, "I have brought the brace of pistols from my uncle's study: you may examine them at your leisure."

She placed them on the table before her friend.

"Why would you rather sit up longer?" asked Miss Keeldar, taking up the firearms, examining them, and again laying them down.

"Because I have a strange excited feeling in my heart."

"So have I."

"Is this state of sleeplessness and restlessness caused by something electrical in the air, I wonder?"

"No: the sky is clear, the stars numberless: it is a fine night."

"But very still. I hear the water fret over its stony bed in Hollow's Copse as distinctly as if it ran below the churchyard wall."

"I am glad it is so still a night: a moaning wind or rushing rain would vex me to fever just now."

"Why, Shirley?"

"Because it would baffle my efforts to listen."

"Do you listen towards the Hollow?"

"Yes; it is the only quarter whence we can hear a sound just now."

"The only one, Shirley."

They both sat near the window, and both leaned their arms on the sill, and both inclined their heads towards the open lattice. They saw each other's young faces by the starlight, and that dim June twilight which does not wholly fade from the west till dawn begins to break in the east.

"Mr. Helstone thinks we have no idea which way he is gone," murmured Miss Keeldar, "nor on what errand, nor with what expectations, nor how prepared; but I guess much—do not you?"

"I guess something."

"All those gentlemen—your cousin Moore included—think that you and I are now asleep in our beds, unconscious."

"Caring nothing about them—hoping and fearing nothing for them," added Caroline.

Both kept silence for full half-an-hour. The night was silent, too; only the church-clock measured its course by quarters. Some words were interchanged about the chill of the air: they wrapped their scarves closer round them, resumed their bonnets which they had removed, and again watched.

Towards midnight the teasing, monotonous bark of the house-dog disturbed the quietude of their vigil. Caroline rose, and made her way noiselessly through the dark passages to the kitchen, intending to appease him with a piece of bread: she succeeded. On returning to the dining-room, she found it all dark, Miss Keeldar having extinguished the candle: the outline of her shape was visible near the still open window, leaning out. Miss Helstone asked no questions: she stole to her side. The dog recommenced barking furiously; suddenly he stopped, and seemed to listen. The occupants of the dining-room listened too, and not merely now to the flow of the mill-stream: there was a nearer, though a muffled sound on the road below the churchyard; a measured, beating, approaching sound; a dull tramp of marching feet.

It drew near. Those who listened by degrees comprehended its extent. It was not the tread of two, nor of a dozen, nor of a score of men: it was the tread of hundreds. They could see nothing: the high shrubs of the garden formed a leafy screen between them and the road. To hear, however, was not enough; and this they felt as the troop trod forwards, and seemed actually passing the Rectory. They felt it more when a human voice—though that voice spoke but one word—broke the hush of the night.

"Halt."

A halt followed: the march was arrested. Then came a low conference, of which no word was distinguishable from the dining-room.

"We *must* hear this," said Shirley.

She turned, took her pistols from the table, silently passed out through the middle window of the dining-room, which was, in fact, a glass door, stole down the walk to the garden wall, and stood listening under the lilacs. Caroline would not have quitted the house had she been alone, but where Shirley went she would go. She glanced at the weapon on the side-board, but left it behind her, and presently stood at her friend's side. They dared not look over the wall, for fear of being seen: they were obliged to crouch behind it: they heard these words—

"It looks a rambling old building. Who lives in it besides the damned parson?"

"Only three women: his niece and two servants."

"Do you know where they sleep?"

"The lasses behind: the niece in a front room."

"And Helstone?"

"Yonder is his chamber. He uses burning a light: but I see none now."

"Where would you get in?"

"If I were ordered to do his job—and he desarves it—I'd try yond' long window: it opens to the dining-room: I could grope my way upstairs, and I know his chamber."

"How would you manage about the women-folk?"

"Let'em alone except they shrieked, and then I'd soon quieten 'em. I could wish to find the old chap asleep: if he waked, he'd be dangerous."

"Has he arms?"

"Fire-arms, allus—and allus loadened."

"Then you're a fool to stop us here; a shot would give the alarm: Moore would be on us before we could turn round. We should miss our main object."

"You might go on, I tell you. I'd engage Helstone alone."

A pause. One of the party dropped some weapon, which rang on the stone causeway: at this sound the Rectory dog barked again furiously—fiercely.

"That spoils all!" said the voice; "he'll awake: a noise like that might rouse the dead. You did not say there was a dog. Damn you! Forward!"

Forward they went,—tramp, tramp,—with mustering manifold, slow-filing tread. They were gone.

Shirley stood erect; looked over the wall, along the road.

"Not a soul remains," she said.

She stood and mused. "Thank God!" was the next observation.

Caroline repeated the ejaculation, not in so steady a tone: she was trembling much; her heart was beating fast and thick: her face was cold; her forehead damp.

"Thank God for us!" she reiterated; "but what will happen elsewhere? They have passed us by that they may make sure of others."

"They have done well," returned Shirley with composure: "the others will defend themselves,—they can do it,—they are prepared for them: with us it is otherwise. My finger was on the trigger of this pistol. I was quite ready to give that man, if he had entered, such a greeting as he little calculated on; but behind him followed three hundred: I had neither three hundred hands nor three hundred weapons. I could not have effectually protected either you, myself, or the two poor women asleep under that roof; therefore I again earnestly thank God for insult and peril escaped."

After a second pause, she continued—"What is it my duty and wisdom to do next? Not to stay here inactive, I am glad to say, but of course to walk over to the Hollow."

"To the Hollow, Shirley?"

"To the Hollow. Will you go with me?"

"Where those men are gone?"

"They have taken the highway: we should not encounter them: the road over the fields is as safe, silent, and solitary as a path through the air would be. Will you go?"

"Yes," was the answer, given mechanically, not because the speaker wished, or was prepared to go; or, indeed, was otherwise than scared at the prospect of going, but because she felt she could not abandon Shirley.

"Then we must fasten up these windows, and leave all as secure as we can behind us. Do you know what we are going for, Cary?"

"Yes—no—because you wish it."

"Is that all? And you are so obedient to a mere caprice of mine? What a docile wife you would make to a stern husband. The moon's face is not whiter than yours at this moment; and the aspen at the gate does not tremble more than your busy fingers; and so tractable and terror-struck, and dismayed and devoted, you would follow me into the thick of real danger! Cary, let me give your fidelity a motive:

we are going for Moore's sake; to see if we can be of use to him: to make an effort
to warn him of what is coming.''

"To be sure! I am a blind, weak fool, and you are acute and sensible, Shirley!
I will go with you! I will gladly go with you!''

"I do not doubt it. You would die blindly and meekly for me, but you would
intelligently and gladly die for Moore; but in truth there is no question of death to-
night,—we run no risk at all.''

Caroline rapidly closed shutter and lattice. "Do not fear that I shall not have
breath to run as fast as you can possibly run, Shirley. Take my hand: let us go
straight across the fields.''

"But you cannot climb walls?''

"To-night I can.''

"You are afraid of hedges, and the beck which we shall be forced to cross.''

"I can cross it.''

They started: they ran. Many a wall checked but did not baffle them. Shirley
was sure-footed and agile: she could spring like a deer when she chose. Caroline,
more timid and less dexterous, fell once or twice, and bruised herself; but she rose
again directly, saying she was not hurt. A quickset hedge bounded the last field:
they lost time in seeking a gap in it: the aperture, when found, was narrow, but
they worked their way through: the long hair, the tender skin, the silks and the
muslins suffered; but what was chiefly regretted was the impediment this difficulty
had caused to speed. On the other side they met the beck, flowing deep in a rough
bed: at this point a narrow plank formed the only bridge across it. Shirley had
trodden the plank successfully and fearlessly many a time before: Caroline had
never yet dared to risk the transit.

"I will carry you across,'' said Miss Keeldar: "you are light, and I am not weak:
let me try.''

"If I fall in you may fish me out,'' was the answer, as a grateful squeeze
compressed her hand. Caroline, without pausing, trod forward on the trembling
plank as if it were a continuation of the firm turf: Shirley, who followed, did not
cross it more resolutely or safely. In their present humour, on their present errand,
a strong and foaming channel would have been a barrier to neither. At the moment
they were above the control either of fire or water: all Stilbro' Moor, alight and
alow with bonfires, would not have stopped them, nor would Calder or Aire thundering
in flood. Yet one sound made them pause. Scarce had they set foot on the solid
opposite bank, when a shot split the air from the north. One second elapsed. Further
off, burst a like note in the south. Within the space of three minutes, similar signals
boomed in the east and west.

"I thought we were dead at the first explosion,'' observed Shirley, drawing a
long breath. "I felt myself hit in the temples, and I concluded your heart was
pierced; but the reiterated voice was an explanation: those are signals—it is their
way—the attack must be near. We should have had wings: our feet have not borne
us swiftly enough.''

A portion of the copse was now to clear: when they emerged from it, the mill
lay just below them: they could look down upon the buildings, the yard; they could
see the road beyond. And the first glance in that direction told Shirley she was
right in her conjecture: they were already too late to give warning: it had taken
more time than they calculated on to overcome the various obstacles which embarrassed
the short cut across the fields.

The road, which should have been white, was dark with a moving mass: the
rioters were assembled in front of the closed yard gates, and a single figure stood
within, apparently addressing them: the mill itself was perfectly black and still;
there was neither life, light, nor motion around it.

"Surely he is prepared: surely that is not Moore meeting them alone?'' whispered
Shirley.

"It is—we must go to him! I *will* go to him."

"*That* you will not."

"Why did I come then? I came only for him. I shall join him."

"Fortunately, it is out of your power: there is no entrance to the yard."

"There *is* a small entrance at the back, besides the gates in front: it opens by a secret method which I know—I will try it."

"Not with my leave."

Miss Keeldar clasped her round the waist with both arms and held her back. "Not one step shall you stir," she went on authoritatively. "At this moment, Moore would be both shocked and embarrassed, if he saw either you or me. Men never want women near them in time of real danger."

"I would not trouble—I would help him," was the reply.

"How? By inspiring him with heroism? Pooh! These are not the days of chivalry: it is not a tilt at a tournament we are going to behold, but a struggle about money, and food, and life."

"It is natural that I should be at his side."

"As queen of his heart? His mill is his lady-love, Cary! Backed by his factory and his frames, he has all the encouragement he wants or can know. It is not for love or beauty, but for ledger and broadcloth, he is going to break a spear. Don't be sentimental; Robert is not so."

"I *could* help him—I *will* seek him."

"Off then—I let you go—seek Moore: you'll not find him."

She loosened her hold. Caroline sped like levelled shaft from bent bow; after her rang a jesting, gibing laugh. "Look well there is no mistake!" was the warning given.

But there *was* a mistake. Miss Helstone paused, hesitated, gazed. The figure had suddenly retreated from the gate, and was running back hastily to the mill.

"Make haste, Lina!" cried Shirley: "meet him before he enters."

Caroline slowly returned. "It is not Robert," she said: "it has neither his height, form, nor bearing."

"I saw it was not Robert when I let you go. How could you imagine it? It is a shabby little figure of a private soldier: they have posted him as sentinel. He is safe in the mill now: I saw the door open and admit him. My mind grows easier; Robert is prepared: our warning would have been superfluous, and now I am thankful we came too late to give it: it has saved us the trouble of a scene. How fine to have entered the counting-house 'toute éperdue,' and to have found oneself in presence of Messrs. Armitage and Ramsden smoking, Malone swaggering, your uncle sneering, Mr. Sykes sipping a cordial, and Moore himself in his cold man-of-business vein: I am glad we missed it all."

"I wonder if there are many in the mill, Shirley!"

"Plenty to defend it. The soldiers we have twice seen to-day were going there no doubt, and the group we noticed surrounding your cousin in the fields will be with him."

"What are they doing now, Shirley? What is that noise?"

"Hatchets and crowbars against the yard-gates: they are forcing them. Are you afraid?"

"No; but my heart throbs fast; I have a difficulty in standing: I will sit down. Do you feel unmoved?"

"Hardly that—but I am glad I came: we shall see what transpires with our own eyes: we are here on the spot, and none know it. Instead of amazing the curate, the clothier, and the corn-dealer with a romantic rush on the stage, we stand alone with the friendly night, its mute stars, and these whispering trees, whose report our friends will not come to gather."

"Shirley—Shirley, the gates are down! That crash was like the felling of great trees. Now they are pouring through. They will break down the mill doors as they

have broken the gate: what can Robert do against so many? Would to God I were a little nearer him—could hear him speak—could speak to him! With my will—my longing to serve him—I could not be a useless burden in his way: I could be turned to some account.''

"They come on!'' cried Shirley. "How steadily they march in! There is discipline in their ranks—I will not say there is courage: hundreds against tens are no proof of that quality; but'' (she dropped her voice) "there is suffering and desperation enough amongst them—these goads will urge them forwards.''

"Forwards against Robert—and they hate him. Shirley, is there much danger they will win the day?''

"We shall see. Moore and Helstone are of 'earth's first blood'—no bunglers—no cravens''——

A crash—smash—shiver—stopped their whispers. A simultaneously-hurled volley of stones had saluted the broad front of the mill, with all its windows; and now every pane of every lattice lay in shattered and pounded fragments. A yell followed this demonstration—a rioters' yell—a North-of-England—a Yorkshire—a West-Riding—a West-Riding-clothing-district-of-Yorkshire rioters' yell. You never heard that sound, perhaps, reader? So much the better for your ears—perhaps for your heart; since, if it rends the air in hate to yourself, or to the men or principles you approve, the interests to which you wish well. Wrath wakens to the cry of Hate: the Lion shakes his mane, and rises to the howl of the Hyena: Caste stands up ireful against Caste; and the indignant, wronged spirit of the Middle Rank bears down in zeal and scorn on the famished and furious mass of the Operative class. It is difficult to be tolerant—difficult to be just—in such moments.

Caroline rose, Shirley put her arm round her: they stood together as still as the straight stems of two trees. That yell was a long one, and when it ceased, the night was yet full of the swaying and murmuring of a crowd.

"What next?'' was the question of the listeners. Nothing came yet. The mill remained mute as a mausoleum.

"He *cannot* be alone!'' whispered Caroline.

"I would stake all I have, that he is as little alone as he is alarmed,'' responded Shirley.

Shots were discharged by the rioters. Had the defenders waited for this signal? It seemed so. The hitherto inert and passive mill woke: fire flashed from its empty window-frames; a volley of musketry pealed sharp through the Hollow.

"Moore speaks at last!'' said Shirley, "and he seems to have the gift of tongues; that was not a single voice.''

"He has been forbearing; no one can accuse him of rashness,'' alleged Caroline: "their discharge preceded his: they broke his gates and his windows; they fired at his garrison before he repelled them.''

What was going on now? It seemed difficult, in the darkness, to distinguish, but something terrible, a still-renewing tumult, was obvious: fierce attacks, desperate repulses; the mill-yard, the mill itself, was full of battle movements: there was scarcely any cessation now of the discharge of firearms; and there was struggling, rushing, trampling, and shouting between. The aim of the assailants seemed to be to enter the mill, that of the defendants to beat them off. They heard the rebel leader cry, "To the back, lads!'' They heard a voice retort, "Come round, we will meet you!''

"To the counting-house!'' was the order again.

"Welcome!—We shall have you there!'' was the response. And accordingly, the fiercest blaze that had yet glowed, the loudest rattle that had yet been heard, burst from the counting-house front, when the mass of rioters rushed up to it.

The voice that had spoken was Moore's own voice. They could tell by its tones that his soul was now warm with the conflict: they could guess that the fighting

animal was roused in every one of those men there struggling together, and was for the time quite paramount above the rational human being.

Both the girls felt their faces glow and their pulses throb: both knew they would do no good by rushing down into the mêlée: they desired neither to deal nor to receive blows; but they could not have run away—Caroline no more than Shirley; they could not have fainted; they could not have taken their eyes from the dim, terrible scene—from the mass of cloud, of smoke—the musket-lightning—for the world.

"How and when would it end?" was the demand throbbing in their throbbing pulses. "Would a juncture arise in which they could be useful?" was what they waited to see; for, though Shirley put off their too-late arrival with a jest, and was ever ready to satirise her own or any other person's enthusiasm, she would have given a farm of her best land for a chance of rendering good service.

The chance was not vouchsafed her; the looked-for juncture never came: it was not likely. Moore had expected this attack for days, perhaps weeks: he was prepared for it at every point. He had fortified and garrisoned his mill, which in itself was a strong building: he was a cool, brave man: he stood to the defence with unflinching firmness; those who were with him caught his spirit, and copied his demeanour. The rioters had never been so met before. At other mills they had attacked, they had found no resistance; an organised, resolute defence was what they never dreamed of encountering. When their leaders saw the steady fire kept up from the mill, witnessed the composure and determination of its owner, heard themselves coolly defied and invited on to death, and beheld their men falling wounded round them, they felt that nothing was to be done here. In haste, they mustered their forces, drew them away from the building: a roll was called over, in which the men answered to figures instead of names: they dispersed wide over the fields, leaving silence and ruin behind them. The attack, from its commencement to its termination, had not occupied an hour.

Day was by this time approaching: the west was dim, the east beginning to gleam. It would have seemed that the girls who had watched this conflict would now wish to hasten to the victors, on whose side all their interest had been enlisted; but they only very cautiously approached the now battered mill, and, when suddenly a number of soldiers and gentlemen appeared at the great door opening into the yard, they quickly stepped aside into a shed, the deposit of old iron and timber, whence they could see without being seen.

It was no cheering spectacle: these premises were now a mere blot of desolation on the fresh front of the summer-dawn. All the copse up the Hollow was shady and dewy, the hill at its head was green; but just here in the centre of the sweet glen, Discord, broken loose in the night from control, had beaten the ground with his stamping hoofs, and left it waste and pulverised. The mill yawned all ruinous with unglazed frames; the yard was thickly bestrewn with stones and brickbats, and, close under the mill, with the glittering fragments of the shattered windows, muskets and other weapons lay here and there; more than one deep crimson stain was visible on the gravel; a human body lay quiet on its face near the gates; and five or six wounded men writhed and moaned in the bloody dust.

Miss Keeldar's countenance changed at this view: it was the after-taste of the battle, death and pain replacing excitement and exertion: it was the blackness the bright fire leaves when its blaze is sunk, its warmth failed, and its glow faded.

"That is what I wished to prevent," she said, in a voice whose cadence betrayed the altered impulse of her heart.

"But you could not prevent it; you did your best; it was in vain," said Caroline comfortingly. "Don't grieve, Shirley."

"I am sorry for those poor fellows," was the answer, while the spark in her glance dissolved to dew. "Are any within the mill hurt, I wonder? Is that your uncle?"

"It is, and there is Mr. Malone, and, O Shirley! there is Robert!"

"Well" (resuming her former tone), "don't squeeze your fingers quite into my hand: I see, there is nothing wonderful in that. We knew he, at least, was here, whoever might be absent."

"He is coming here towards us, Shirley!"

"Towards the pump, that is to say, for the purpose of washing his hands and his forehead, which has got a scratch, I perceive."

"He bleeds, Shirley: don't hold me; I must go."

"Not a step."

"He is hurt, Shirley!"

"Fiddlestick!"

"But I *must* go to him: I wish to go so much: I cannot bear to be restrained."

"What for?"

"To speak to him, to ask how he is, and what I can do for him?"

"To teaze and annoy him; to make a spectacle of yourself and him before those soldiers, Mr. Malone, your uncle, et cetera. Would he like it, think you? Would you like to remember it a week hence?"

"Am I always to be curbed and kept down?" demanded Caroline, a little passionately.

"For his sake, yes. And still more for your own. I tell you, if you showed yourself now, you would repent it an hour hence, and so would Robert."

"You think he would not like it, Shirley?"

"Far less than he would like our stopping him to say good-night, which you were so sore about."

"But that was all play; there was no danger."

"And this is serious work: he must be unmolested."

"I only wish to go to him because he is my cousin—you understand?"

"I quite understand. But now, watch him. He has bathed his forehead, and the blood has ceased trickling; his hurt is really a mere graze: I can see it from hence: he is going to look after the wounded men."

Accordingly Mr. Moore and Mr. Helstone went round the yard, examining each prostrate form. They then gave directions to have the wounded taken up and carried into the mill. This duty being performed, Joe Scott was ordered to saddle his master's horse and Mr. Helstone's pony, and the two gentlemen rode away full gallop, to seek surgical aid in different directions.

Caroline was not yet pacified.

"Shirley, Shirley, I should have liked to speak one word to him before he went," she murmured, while the tears gathered glittering in her eyes.

"Why do you cry, Lina?" asked Miss Keeldar a little sternly. "You ought to be glad instead of sorry. Robert has escaped any serious harm; he is victorious; he has been cool and brave in combat; he is now considerate in triumph: is this a time—are these causes for weeping?"

"You do not know what I have in my heart," pleaded the other: "what pain, what distraction; nor whence it arises. I can understand that you should exult in Robert's greatness and goodness; so do I, in one sense, but, in another, I feel so miserable. I am too far removed from him: I used to be nearer. Let me alone, Shirley: do let me cry a few minutes; it relieves me."

Miss Keeldar, feeling her tremble in every limb, ceased to expostulate with her: she went out of the shed, and left her to weep in peace. It was the best plan: in a few minutes Caroline rejoined her, much calmer: she said with her natural, docile, gentle manner—"Come, Shirley, we will go home now. I promise not to try to see Robert again till he asks for me. I never will try to push myself on him. I thank you for restraining me just now."

"I did it with a good intention," retured Miss Keeldar.

"Now, dear Lina," she continued, "let us turn our faces to the cool morning breeze, and walk very quietly back to the Rectory. We will steal in as we stole out; none shall know where we have been, or what we have seen to-night: neither taunt nor misconstruction can consequently molest us. To-morrow, we will see Robert, and be of good cheer; but I will say no more, lest I should begin to cry too. I seem hard towards you, but I am not so."

Chapter XX

TO-MORROW

THE two girls met no living soul on their way back to the Rectory: they let themselves in noiselessly; they stole upstairs unheard: the breaking morning gave them what light they needed. Shirley sought her couch immediately; and, though the room was strange—for she had never slept at the Rectory before—and though the recent scene was one unparalleled for excitement and terror by any it had hitherto been her lot to witness, yet, scarce was her head laid on the pillow, ere a deep, refreshing sleep closed her eyes, and calmed her senses.

Perfect health was Shirley's enviable portion; though warm-hearted and sympathetic, she was not nervous: powerful emotions could rouse and sway, without exhausting her spirit: the tempest troubled and shook her while it lasted; but it left her elasticity unbent, and her freshness quite unblighted. As every day brought her stimulating emotion, so every night yielded her recreating rest. Caroline now watched her sleeping, and read the serenity of her mind in the beauty of her happy countenance.

For herself, being of a different temperament, she could not sleep. The commonplace excitement of the tea-drinking and school-gathering would alone have sufficed to make her restless all night: the effect of the terrible drama which had just been enacted before her eyes was not likely to quit her for days. It was vain even to try to retain a recumbent posture: she sat up by Shirley's side, counting the slow minutes, and watching the June sun mount the heavens.

Life wastes fast in such vigils as Caroline had of late but too often kept; vigils during which the mind—having no pleasant food to nourish it—no manna of hope—no hived-honey of joyous memories—tries to live on the meagre diet of wishes, and failing to derive thence either delight or support, and feeling itself ready to perish with craving want, turns to philosophy, to resolution, to resignation; calls on all these gods for aid, calls vainly—is unheard, unhelped, and languishes.

Caroline was a Christian; therefore in trouble she framed many a prayer after the Christian creed; preferred it with deep earnestness; begged for patience, strength, relief. This world, however, we all know, is the scene of trial and probation; and, for any favourable result her petitions had yet wrought, it seemed to her that they were unheard and unaccepted. She believed, sometimes, that God had turned His face from her. At moments she was a Calvinist, and, sinking into the gulf of religious despair, she saw darkening over her the doom of reprobation.

Most people have had a period or periods in their lives when they have felt thus forsaken; when, having long hoped against hope, and still seen the day of fruition deferred, their hearts have truly sickened within them. This is a terrible hour, but it is often that darkest point which precedes the rise of day; that turn of the year when the icy January wind carries over the waste at once the dirge of departing winter, and the prophecy of coming spring. The perishing birds, however, cannot thus understand the blast before which they shiver; and as little can the suffering soul recognise, in the climax of its affliction, the dawn of its deliverance. Yet, let whoever grieves still cling fast to love and faith in God: God will never deceive,

never finally desert him. "Whom He loveth, He chasteneth." These words are true, and should not be forgotten.

The household was astir at last: the servants were up; the shutters were opened below. Caroline, as she quitted the couch, which had been but a thorny one to her, felt that revival of spirits which the return of day, of action, gives to all but the wholly despairing or actually dying: she dressed herself, as usual, carefully, trying so to arrange her hair and attire that nothing of the forlornness she felt at heart should be visible externally: she looked as fresh as Shirley when both were dressed, only that Miss Keeldar's eyes were lively, and Miss Helstone's languid.

"To-day I shall have much to say to Moore," were Shirley's first words; and you could see in her face that life was full of interest, expectation, and occupation for her. "He will have to undergo cross-examination," she added: "I dare say he thinks he has outwitted me cleverly. Aud this is the way men deal with women; still concealing danger from them: thinking, I suppose, to spare them pain. They imagined we little knew where they were to-night: we *know* they little conjectured where we were. Men, I believe, fancy women's minds something like those of children. Now, that is a mistake."

This was said as she stood at the glass, training her naturally waved hair into curls by twining it round her fingers. She took up the theme again five minutes after, as Caroline fastened her dress and clasped her girdle.

"If men could see us as we really are, they would be a little amazed; but the cleverest, the acutest men are often under an illusion about women: they do not read them in a true light: they misapprehend them, both for good and evil: their good woman is a queer thing, half doll, half angel; their bad woman almost always a fiend. Then to hear them fall into ecstasies with each other's creations, worshipping the heroine of such a poem—novel—drama, thinking it fine—divine! Fine and divine it may be, but often quite artificial—false as the rose in my best bonnet there. If I spoke all I think on this point; if I gave my real opinion of some first-rate female characters in first-rate works, where should I be? Dead under a cairn of avenging stones in half-an-hour."

"Shirley, you chatter so, I can't fasten you: be still. And after all, authors' heroines are almost as good as authoress's heroes."

"Not at all: women read men more truly than men read women. I'll prove that in a magazine paper some day when I've time; only it will never be inserted: it will be 'declined with thanks,' and left for me at the publisher's."

"To be sure: you could not write cleverly enough; you don't know enough; you are not learned, Shirley."

"God knows, I can't contradict you, Cary: I'm as ignorant as a stone. There's one comfort, however, you are not much better."

They descended to breakfast.

"I wonder how Mrs. Pryor and Hortense Moore have passed the night," said Caroline, as she made the coffee. "Selfish being that I am! I never thought of either of them till just now: they will have heard all the tumult, Fieldhead and the Cottage are so near; and Hortense is timid in such matters: so no doubt is Mrs. Pryor."

"Take my word for it, Lina, Moore will have contrived to get his sister out of the way: she went home with Miss Mann; he will have quartered her there for the night. As to Mrs. Pryor, I own I am uneasy about her; but in another half-hour we will be with her."

By this time the news of what had happened at the Hollow was spread all over the neighbourhood. Fanny, who had been to Fieldhead to fetch the milk, returned in panting haste, with tidings that there had been a battle in the night at Mr. Moore's mill, and that some said twenty men were killed. Eliza, during Fanny's absence, had been apprised by the butcher's boy that the mill was burnt to the ground. Both women rushed into the parlour to announce these terrible facts to the ladies, terminating

their clear and accurate narrative by the assertion that they were sure master must have been in it all. He and Thomas, the clerk, they were confident, must have gone last night to join Mr. Moore and the soldiers: Mr. Malone, too, had not been heard of at his lodgings since yesterday afternoon; and Joe Scott's wife and family were in the greatest distress, wondering what had become of their head.

Scarcely was this information imparted when a knock at the kitchen-door announced the Fieldhead errand-boy, arrived in hot haste, bearing a billet from Mrs. Pryor. It was hurriedly written, and urged Miss Keeldar to return directly, as the neighbourhood and the house seemed likely to be all in confusion, and orders would have to be given which the mistress of the hall alone could regulate. In a postscript it was entreated that Miss Helstone might not be left alone at the Rectory: she had better, it was suggested, accompany Miss Keeldar.

"There are not two opinions on that head," said Shirley, as she tied on her own bonnet, and then ran to fetch Caroline's.

"But what will Fanny and Eliza do? And if my uncle returns?"

"Your uncle will not return yet; he has other fish to fry; he will be galloping backwards and forwards from Briarfield to Stilbro' all day, rousing the magistrates in the court-house, and the officers at the barracks; and Fanny and Eliza can have in Joe Scott's and the clerk's wives to bear them company. Besides, of course, there is no real danger to be apprehended now: weeks will elapse before the rioters can again rally, or plan any other attempt; and I am much mistaken if Moore and Mr. Helstone will not take advantage of last night's outbreak to quell them altogether: they will frighten the authorities of Stilbro' into energetic measures. I only hope they will not be too severe—not pursue the discomfited too relentlessly."

"Robert will not be cruel: we saw that last night," said Caroline.

"But he will be hard," retorted Shirley; "and so will your uncle."

As they hurried along the meadow and plantation-path to Fieldhead, they saw the distant highway already alive with an unwonted flow of equestrians and pedestrians, tending in the direction of the usually solitary Hollow. On reaching the hall, they found the back-yard gates open, and the court and kitchen seemed crowded with excited milk-fetchers—men, women, and children, whom Mrs. Gill, the housekeeper, appeared vainly persuading to take their milk-cans and depart. (It *is*, or *was*, by-the-bye, the custom in the north of England for the cottagers on a country squire's estate to receive their supplies of milk and butter from the dairy of the Manor-House, on whose pastures a herd of milch kine was usually fed for the convenience of the neighbourhood. Miss Keeldar owned such a herd—all deep-dewlapped, Craven cows, reared on the sweet herbage and clear waters of bonnie Airedale; and very proud she was of their sleek aspect and high condition.) Seeing now the state of matters, and that it was desirable to effect a clearance of the premises, Shirley stepped in amongst the gossiping groups. She bade them good-morning with a certain frank, tranquil ease—the natural characteristic of her manner when she addressed numbers; especially if those numbers belonged to the working-class; she was cooler amongst her equals, and rather proud to those above her. She then asked them if they had all got their milk measured out, and understanding that they had, she further observed that she "wondered what they were waiting for, then."

"We're just talking a bit over this battle there has been at your mill, Mistress," replied a man.

"Talking a bit! Just like you!" said Shirley. "It is a queer thing all the world is so fond of *talking* over events: you *talk* if anybody dies suddenly; you *talk* if a fire breaks out; you *talk* if a mill-owner fails; you *talk* if he's murdered. What good does your talking do?"

There is nothing the lower orders like better than a little downright good-humoured rating. Flattery they scorn very much: honest abuse they enjoy. They call it speaking plainly, and take a sincere delight in being the objects thereof. The homely harshness of Miss Keeldar's salutation won her the ear of the whole throng in a second.

"We're no war nor some 'at is aboon us; are we?'' asked a man smiling.

"Nor a whit better: you that should be models of industry are just as gossip-loving as the idle. Fine, rich people that have nothing to do, may be partly excused for trifling their time away: you who have to earn your bread with the sweat of your brow are quite inexcusable.''

"That's queer, Mistress: suld we never hae a holiday because we work hard?''

"*Never,*'' was the prompt answer; "unless,'' added the 'mistress,' with a smile that half-belied the severity of her speech, "unless you knew how to make a better use of it than to get together over rum and tea, if you are women—or over beer and pipes, if you are men, and *talk* scandal at your neighbours' expense. Come, friends,'' she added, changing at once from bluntness to courtesy, "oblige me by taking your cans and going home. I expect several persons to call to-day, and it will be inconvenient to have the avenues to the house crowded.''

Yorkshire people are as yielding to persuasion as they are stubborn against compulsion: the yard was clear in five minutes.

"Thank you, and good-bye to you, friends,'' said Shirley, as she closed the gates on a quiet court.

Now, let me hear the most refined of Cockneys presume to find fault with Yorkshire manners! Taken as they ought to be, the majority of the lads and lasses of the West-Riding are gentlemen and ladies, every inch of them: it is only against the weak affectation and futile pomposity of a would-be aristocrat they turn mutinous.

Entering by the back-way, the young ladies passed through the kitchen (or *house,* as the inner kitchen is called) to the hall. Mrs. Pryor came running down the oak staircase to meet them. She was all unnerved: her naturally sanguine complexion was pale; her usually placid, though timid, blue eye was wandering, unsettled, alarmed. She did not, however, break out into any exclamations, or hurried narrative of what had happened. Her predominant feeling had been in the course of the night, and was now this morning, a sense of dissatisfaction with herself that she could not feel firmer, cooler, more equal to the demands of the occasion.

"You are aware,'' she began with a trembling voice, and yet the most conscientious anxiety to avoid exaggeration in what she was about to say,—"that a body of rioters has attacked Mr. Moore's mill to-night: we heard the firing and confusion very plainly here; we none of us slept: it was a sad night: the house has been in great bustle all the morning with people coming and going: the servants have applied to me for orders and directions, which I really did not feel warranted in giving. Mr. Moore has, I believe, sent up for refreshments for the soldiers and others engaged in the defence; for some conveniences also for the wounded. I could not undertake the responsibility of giving orders or taking measures. I fear delay may have been injurious in some instances; but this is not my house: you were absent, my dear Miss Keeldar—what could I do?''

"Were no refreshments sent?'' asked Shirley, while her countenance, hitherto so clear, propitious, and quiet, even while she was rating the milk-fetchers, suddenly turned dark and warm.

"I think not, my dear.''

"And nothing for the wounded? no linen—no wine—no bedding?''

"I think not. I cannot tell what Mrs. Gill did: but it seemed impossible to me, at the moment, to venture to dispose of your property by sending supplies to soldiers—provisions for a company of soldiers sounds formidable: how many there are I did not ask; but I could not think of allowing them to pillage the house, as it were. I intended to do what was right; yet I did not see the case quite clearly, I own.''

"It lies in a nutshell, notwithstanding. These soldiers have risked their lives in defence of my property—I suppose they have a right to my gratitude: the wounded are our fellow-creatures—I suppose we should aid them. Mrs. Gill!''

She turned, and called in a voice more clear than soft. It rung through the thick oak of the hall and kitchen doors more effectually than a bell's summons. Mrs. Gill, who was deep in bread-making, came with hands and apron in culinary case, not having dared to stop to rub the dough from the one, or to shake the flour from the other. Her mistress had never called a servant in that voice save once before, and that was when she had seen from the window Tartar in full tug with two carriers' dogs, each of them a match for him in size, if not in courage, and their masters standing by, encouraging their animals, while hers was unbefriended: then, indeed, she had summoned John as if the Day of Judgment were at hand: nor had she waited for the said John's coming, but had walked out into the lane bonnetless; and after informing the carriers that she held them far less of men than the three brutes whirling and worrying in the dust before them, had put her hands round the thick neck of the largest of the curs and given her whole strength to the essay of choking it from Tartar's torn and bleeding eye, just above and below which organ the vengeful fangs were inserted. Five or six men were presently on the spot to help her, but she never thanked one of them: "They might have come before, if their will had been good," she said. She had not a word for anybody during the rest of the day; but sat near the hall fire till evening watching and tending Tartar, who lay all gory, stiff, and swelled on a mat at her feet. She wept furtively over him sometimes, and murmured the softest words of pity and endearment, in tones whose music the old, scarred, canine warrior acknowledged by licking her hand or her sandal alternately with his own red wounds. As to John, his lady turned a cold shoulder on him for a week afterwards.

Mrs. Gill, remembering this little episode, came "all of a tremble," as she said herself. In a firm, brief voice, Miss Keeldar proceeded to put questions and give orders. That at such a time Fieldhead should have evinced the inhospitality of a miser's hovel, stung her haughty spirit to the quick; and the revolt of its pride was seen in the heaving of her heart; stirred stormily under the lace and silk which veiled it.

"How long is it since that message came from the mill?"

"Not an hour yet, ma'am," answered the housekeeper soothingly.

"Not an hour! You might almost as well have said not a day. They will have applied elsewhere by this time. Send a man instantly down to tell them that everything this house contains is at Mr. Moore's, Mr. Helstone's, and the soldiers' service. Do that first!"

While the order was being executed, Shirley moved away from her friends, and stood at the hall-window, silent, unapproachable. When Mrs. Gill came back, she turned: the purple flush which painful excitement kindles on a pale cheek, glowed on hers: the spark which displeasure lights in a dark eye fired her glance.

"Let the contents of the larder and the wine-cellar be brought up, put into the hay-carts, and driven down to the Hollow. If there does not happen to be much bread or much meat in the house, go to the butcher and baker, and desire them to send what they have: but I will see for myself."

She moved off.

"All will be right soon: she will get over it in an hour," whispered Caroline to Mrs. Pryor. "Go upstairs, dear madam," she added affectionately, "and try to be as calm and easy as you can. The truth is, Shirley will blame herself more than you before the day is over."

By dint of a few more gentle assurances and persuasions, Miss Helstone contrived to soothe the agitated lady. Having accompanied her to her apartment, and promised to rejoin her there when things were settled, Caroline left her to see, as she said, "if she could be useful." She presently found that she could be very useful; for the retinue of servants at Fieldhead was by no means numerous, and just now their mistress found plenty of occupation for all the hands at her command, and for her own also. The delicate good-nature and dexterous activity which Caroline brought

to the aid of the housekeeper and maids—all somewhat scared by their lady's unwonted mood—did a world of good at once: it helped the assistants and appeased the directress. A chance glance and smile from Caroline moved Shirley to an answering smile directly. The former was carrying a heavy basket up tbe cellar-stairs.

"This is a shame," cried Shirley, running to her. "It will strain your arm."

She took it from her, and herself bore it out into the yard. The cloud of temper was dispelled when she came back; the flash in her eye was melted; the shade on her forehead vanished: she resumed her usual cheerful and cordial manner to those about her, tempering her revived spirits with a little of the softness of shame at her previous unjust anger.

She was still superintending the lading of the cart, when a gentleman entered the yard and approached her ere she was aware of his presence.

"I hope I see Miss Keeldar well this morning?" he said, examining with rather significant scrutiny her still flushed face.

She gave him a look, and then again bent to her employment, without reply. A pleasant enough smile played on her lips, but she hid it. The gentleman repeated his salutation, stooping, that it might reach her ear with more facility.

"Well enough, if she be good enough," was the answer; "and so is Mr. Moore too, I dare say. To speak truth, I am not anxious about him; some slight mischance would be only his just due: his conduct has been—we will say *strange,* just now, till we have time to characterise it by a more exact epithet. Meantime, may I ask what brings him here?"

"Mr. Helstone and I have just received your message, that everything at Fieldhead was at our service. We judged, by the unlimited wording of the gracious intimation, that you would be giving yourself too much trouble: I perceive our conjecture was correct. We are not a regiment, remember: only about half-a-dozen soldiers, and as many civilians. Allow me to retrench something from these too abundant supplies."

Miss Keeldar blushed, while she laughed at her own over-eager generosity, and most disproportionate calculations. Moore laughed too—very quietly, though; and as quietly, he ordered basket after basket to be taken from the cart, and remanded vessel after vessel to the cellar.

"The Rector must hear of this," he said: "he will make a good story of it. What an excellent army contractor Miss Keeldar would have been!" again he laughed, adding—"It is precisely as I conjectured."

"You ought to be thankful," said Shirley, "and not mock me. What could I do? How could I gauge your appetites, or number your band? For aught I knew, there might have been fifty of you at least to victual. You told me nothing; and then, an application to provision soldiers naturally suggests large ideas."

"It appears so," remarked Moore, levelling another of his keen, quiet glances at the discomfited Shirley. "Now," he continued, addressing the carter, "I think you may take what remains to the Hollow. Your load will be somewhat lighter than the one Miss Keeldar destined you to carry."

As the vehicle rumbled out of the yard, Shirley, rallying her spirits, demanded what had become of the wounded.

"There was not a single man hurt on our side," was the answer.

"You were hurt yourself, on the temples," interposed a quick, low voice—that of Caroline, who, having withdrawn within the shade of the door, and behind the large person of Mrs. Gill, had till now escaped Moore's notice: when she spoke, his eye searched the obscurity of her retreat.

"Are you much hurt?" she inquired.

"As you might scratch your finger with a needle in sewing."

"Lift your hair, and let us see."

He took his hat off, and did as he was bid, disclosing only a narrow slip of court-plaster. Caroline indicated, by a slight movement of the head, that she was satisfied, and disappeared within the clear obscure of the interior.

"How did she know I was hurt?" asked Moore.

"By rumour, no doubt. But it is too good in her to trouble herself about you. For my part, it was of your victims I was thinking when I inquired after the wounded: what damage have your opponents sustained?"

"One of the rioters, or victims, as you call them, was killed, and six were hurt."

"What have you done with them?"

"What you will perfectly approve. Medical aid was procured immediately; and as soon as we can get a couple of covered waggons, and some clean straw, they will be removed to Stilbro'."

"Straw! you must have beds and bedding. I will send my waggon directly, properly furnished; and Mr. Yorke, I am sure, will send his."

"You guess correctly: he has volunteered already; and Mrs. Yorke—who, like you, seems disposed to regard the rioters as martyrs, and me, and especially Mr. Helstone, as murderers—is at this moment, I believe, most assiduously engaged in fitting it up with feather-beds, pillows, bolsters, blankets, etc. The *victims* lack no attentions—I promise you. Mr. Hall—your favourite parson—has been with them ever since six o'clock, exhorting them, praying with them, and even waiting on them like any nurse; and Caroline's good friend, Miss Ainley, that *very* plain old maid, sent in a stock of lint and linen, something in the proportion of another lady's allowance of beef and wine.

"That will do. Where is your sister?"

"Well cared for. I had her securely domiciled with Miss Mann. This very morning the two set out for Wormwood Wells (a noted watering-place), and will stay there some weeks."

"So Mr. Helstone domiciled me at the Rectory! Mighty clever you gentlemen think you are! I make you heartily welcome to the idea, and hope its savour, as you chew the cud of reflection upon it, gives you pleasure. Acute and astute, why are you not also omniscient? How is it that events transpire, under your very noses, of which you have no suspicion? It should be so, otherwise the requisite gratification of out-manœuvring you would be unknown. Ah! friend, you may search my countenance, but you cannot read it."

Moore, indeed, looked as if he could not.

"You think me a dangerous specimen of my sex. Don't you, now?"

"A peculiar one, at least."

"But Caroline—is she peculiar?"

"In her way—yes."

"Her way! What is her way?"

"You know her as well as I do."

"And knowing her I assert that she is neither eccentric nor difficult of control: is she?"

"That depends—"

"However, there is nothing masculine about *her*?"

"Why lay such emphasis on *her*? Do you consider her a contrast, in that respect, to yourself?"

"You do, no doubt; but that does not signify. Caroline is neither masculine, nor of what they call the spirited order of women."

"I have seen her flash out."

"So have I—but not with manly fire: it was a short, vivid, trembling glow, that shot up, shone, vanished——"

"And left her scared at her own daring. You describe others besides Caroline."

"The point I wish to establish is, that Miss Helstone, though gentle, tractable, and candid enough, is still perfectly capable of defying even Mr. Moore's penetration."

"What have you and she been doing?" asked Moore suddenly.

"Have you had any breakfast?"

"What is your mutual mystery?"

"If you are hungry, Mrs. Gill will give you something to eat here. Step into the oak-parlour, and ring the bell—you will be served as if at an inn; or, if you like better, go back to the Hollow."

"The alternative is not open to me: I *must* go back. Good-morning: the first leisure I have, I will see you again."

Chapter XXI

MRS. PRYOR

WHILE Shirley was talking with Moore, Caroline rejoined Mrs. Pryor upstairs. She found that lady deeply depressed. She would not say that Miss Keeldar's hastiness had hurt her feelings; but it was evident an inward wound galled her. To any but a congenial nature, she would have seemed insensible to the quiet, tender attentions by which Miss Helstone sought to impart solace; but Caroline knew that, unmoved or slightly moved as she looked, she felt, valued, and was healed by them.

"I am deficient in self-confidence and decision," she said at last. "I always have been deficient in those qualities: yet I think Miss Keeldar should have known my character well enough by this time, to be aware that I always feel an even painful solicitude to do right, to act for the best. The unusual nature of the demand on my judgment puzzled me, especially following the alarms of the night. I could not venture to act promptly for another: but I trust no serious harm will result from my lapse of firmness."

A gentle knock was here heard at the door: it was half-opened.

"Caroline, come here," said a low voice.

Miss Helstone went out: there stood Shirley in the gallery, looking contrite, ashamed, sorry as any repentant child.

"How is Mrs. Pryor?" she asked.

"Rather out of spirits," said Caroline.

"I have behaved very shamefully, very ungenerously, very ungratefully to her," said Shirley. "How insolent in me to turn on her thus, for what after all was no fault, only an excess of conscientiousness on her part. But I regret my error most sincerely: tell her so, and ask if she will forgive me."

Caroline discharged the errand with heartfelt pleasure. Mrs. Pryor rose, came to the door: she did not like scenes; she dreaded them as all timid people do: she said falteringly—"Come in, my dear."

Shirley did come in with some impetuosity: she threw her arms round her governess, and while she kissed her heartily, she said—"You know you *must* forgive me, Mrs. Pryor. I could not get on at all if there was a misunderstanding between you and me."

"I have nothing to forgive," was the reply. "We will pass it over now, if you please. The final result of the incident is that it proves more plainly than ever how unequal I am to certain crises."

And that was the painful feeling which *would* remain on Mrs. Pryor's mind: no effort of Shirley's or Caroline's could efface it thence: she could forgive her offending pupil, not her innocent self.

Miss Keeldar, doomed to be in constant request during the morning, was presently summoned downstairs again. The Rector called first: a lively welcome and livelier reprimand were at his service; he expected both, and, being in high spirits, took them in equally good part.

In the course of his brief visit, he quite forgot to ask after his niece: the riot, the rioters, the mill, the magistrates, the heiress, absorbed all his thoughts to the exclusion of family ties. He alluded to the part himself and curate had taken in the defence of the Hollow.

"The vials of pharisaical wrath will be emptied on our heads, for our share in this business," he said; "but I defy every calumniator. I was there only to support the law, to play my part as a man and a Briton; which characters I deem quite compatible with those of the priest and Levite, in their highest sense. Your tenant, Moore," he went on, "has won my approbation. A cooler commander I would not wish to see, nor a more determined. Besides, the man has shown sound judgment and good sense; first, in being thoroughly prepared for the event which has taken place, and subsequently, when his well-concerted plans had secured him success, in knowing how to use without abusing his victory. Some of the magistrates are now well frightened, and, like all cowards, show a tendency to be cruel; Moore restrains them with admirable prudence. He has hitherto been very unpopular in the neighbourhood; but, mark my words, the tide of opinion will now take a turn in his favour: people will find out that they have not appreciated him, and will hasten to remedy their error; and he, when he perceives the public disposed to acknowledge his merits, will show a more gracious mien than that with which he has hitherto favoured us."

Mr. Helstone was about to add to this speech some half-jesting, half-serious warnings to Miss Keeldar, on the subject of her rumoured partiality for her talented tenant, when a ring at the door, announcing another caller, checked his raillery; and as that other caller appeared in the form of a white-haired, elderly gentleman, with a rather truculent countenance and disdainful eye—in short, our old acquaintance, and the Rector's old enemy, Mr. Yorke—the priest and Levite seized his hat, and with the briefest of adieux to Miss Keeldar, and the sternest of nods to her guest, took an abrupt leave.

Mr. Yorke was in no mild mood, and in no measured terms did he express his opinion on the transaction of the night: Moore, the magistrates, the soldiers, the mob-leaders, each and all came in for a share of his invectives; but he reserved his strongest epithets—and real racy Yorkshire Doric adjectives they were—for the benefit of the fighting parsons, the "sanguinary, demoniac" rector and curate. According to him, the cup of ecclesiastical guilt was now full indeed.

"The Church," he said, "was in a bonnie pickle now: it was time it came down when parsons took to swaggering amang soldiers, blazing away wi' bullet and gunpowder, taking the lives of far honester men than themselves."

"What would Moore have done, if nobody had helped him?" asked Shirley.

"Drunk as he'd brewed—eaten as he'd baked."

"Which means, you would have left him by himself to face that mob. Good. He has plenty of courage; but the greatest amount of gallantry that ever garrisoned one human breast could scarce avail against two hundred."

"He had the soldiers; those poor slaves who hire out their own blood and spill other folk's for money."

"You abuse soldiers almost as much as you abuse clergymen. All who wear red coats are national refuse in your eyes, and all who wear black are national swindlers. Mr. Moore, according to you, did wrong to get military aid, and he did still worse to accept of any other aid. Your way of talking amounts to this:—he should have abandoned his mill and his life to the rage of a set of misguided madmen, and Mr. Helstone and every other gentleman in the parish should have looked on, and seen the building razed and its owner slaughtered, and never stirred a finger to save either."

"If Moore had behaved to his men from the beginning as a master ought to behave, they never would have entertained their present feelings towards him."

"Easy for you to talk," exclaimed Miss Keeldar, who was beginning to wax warm in her tenant's cause: "you, whose family have lived at Briarmains for six generations, to whose person the people have been accustomed for fifty years, who know all their ways, prejudices, and preferences. Easy, indeed, for *you* to act so as to avoid offending them; but Mr. Moore came a stranger into the district: he came here poor and friendless, with nothing but his own energies to back him; nothing but his honour, his talent, and his industry to make his way for him. A monstrous crime indeed that, under such circumstances, he could not popularise his naturally grave, quiet manners, all at once: could not be jocular, and free, and cordial with a strange peasantry, as you are with your fellow-townsmen! An unpardonable transgression, that when he introduced improvements he did not go about the business in quite the most politic way; did not graduate his changes as delicately as a rich capitalist might have done! For errors of this sort is he to be the victim of mob-outrage? Is he to be denied even the privilege of defending himself? Are those who have the hearts of men in their breasts (and Mr. Helstone— say what you will of him—has such a heart) to be reviled like malefactors because they stand by him—because they venture to espouse the cause of one against two hundred?"

"Come—come now—be cool," said Mr. Yorke, smiling at the earnestness with which Shirley multiplied her rapid questions.

"Cool! Must I listen coolly to downright nonsense—to dangerous nonsense? No. I like you very well, Mr. Yorke, as you know; but I thoroughly dislike some of your principles. All that cant—excuse me, but I repeat the word—all that *cant* about soldiers and parsons is most offensive in my ears. All ridiculous, irrational crying up of one class, whether the same be aristocrat or democrat—all howling down of another class, whether clerical or military—all exacting injustice to individuals, whether monarch or mendicant—is really sickening to me: all arraying of ranks against ranks, all party hatreds, all tyrannies disguised as liberties, I reject and wash my hands of. *You* think you are a philanthropist; *you* think you are an advocate of liberty; but I will tell you this—Mr. Hall, the parson of Nunnely, is a better friend both of man and freedom than Hiram Yorke, the Reformer of Briarfield."

From a man, Mr. Yorke would not have borne this language very patiently, nor would he have endured it from some women; but he accounted Shirley both honest and pretty, and her plain-spoken ire amused him: besides, he took a secret pleasure in hearing her defend her tenant, for we have already intimated he had Robert Moore's interest very much at heart: moreover, if he wished to avenge himself for her severity, he knew the means lay in his power: a word, he believed, would suffice to tame and silence her, to cover her frank forehead with the rosy shadow of shame, and veil the glow of her eye under down-drooped lid and lash.

"What more hast thou to say?" he inquired, as she paused, rather it appeared to take breath, than because her subject or her zeal was exhausted.

"Say, Mr. Yorke!" was the answer, the speaker meantime walking fast from wall to wall of the oak-parlour. "Say? I have a great deal to say, if I could get it out in lucid order which I never *can* do. I have to say that your views, and those of most extreme politicians, are such as none but men in an irresponsible position *can* advocate; that they are purely opposition views, meant only to be talked about, and never intended to be acted on. Make you Prime Minister of England to-morrow, and you would have to abandon them. You abuse Moore for defending his mill: had you been in Moore's place you could not with honour or sense have acted otherwise than he acted. You abuse Mr. Helstone for everything he does: Mr. Helstone has his faults: he sometimes does wrong, but oftener right. Were you ordained vicar of Briarfield, you would find it no easy task to sustain all the active schemes for the benefit of the parish planned and persevered in by your predecessor. wonder people cannot judge more fairly of each other and themselves. When I hear Messrs. Malone and Donne chatter about the authority of the Church, the dignity

and claims of the priesthood, the deference due to them as clergymen; when I hear the outbreaks of their small spite against Dissenters; when I witness their silly narrow jealousies and assumptions; when their palaver about forms, and traditions, and superstitions, is sounding in my ear; when I behold their insolent carriage to the poor, their often base servility to the rich, I think the Establishment is indeed in a poor way, and both she and her sons appear in the utmost need of reformation. Turning away distressed from minster-tower and village-spire—ay, as distressed as a churchwarden who feels the exigence of white-wash, and has not wherewithal to purchase lime—I recall your senseless sarcasms on the ' fat bishops,' the 'pampered parsons,' ' old mother church,' etc. I remember your strictures on all who differ from you, your sweeping condemnation of classes and individuals, without the slightest allowance made for circumstances or temptations; and then, Mr. Yorke, doubt clutches my inmost heart as to whether men exist clement, reasonable, and just enough to be entrusted with the task of reform. don't believe *you* are of the number.''

"You have an ill opinion of me, Miss Shirley: you never told me so much of your mind before.''

"I never had an opening; but I have sat on Jessy's stool by your chair in the back-parlour at Briarmains, for evenings together, listening excitedly to your talk, half-admiring what you said, and half-rebelling against it. I think you a fine old Yorkshireman, sir: I am proud to have been born in the same county and parish as yourself—truthful, upright, independent you are, as a rock based below seas; but also you are harsh, rude, narrow, and merciless.''

"Not to the poor, lass—nor to the meek of the earth—only to the proud and high-minded.''

"And what right have you, sir, to make such distinctions? A prouder—a higher-minded man than yourself does not exist. You find it easy to speak comfortably to your inferiors—you are too haughty, too ambitious, too jealous to be civil to those above you. But you are all alike. Helstone also is proud and prejudiced. Moore, though juster and more considerate than either you or the Rector, is still haughty, stern, and in a public sense, selfish. It is well there are such men as Mr. Hall to be found occasionally: men of large and kind hearts, who can love their whole race, who can forgive others for being richer, more prosperous, or more powerful than they are. Such men may have less originality, less force of character than you, but they are better friends to mankind.''

"And when is it to be?'' said Mr. Yorke, now rising.

"When is what to be?''

"The wedding.''

"Whose wedding?''

"Only that of Robert Gérard Moore, Esq., of Hollow's Cottage, with Miss Keeldar, daughter and heiress of the late Charles Cave Keeldar of Fieldhead Hall.''

Shirley gazed at the questioner with rising colour; but the light in her eye was not faltering: it shone steadily—yes—it burned deeply.

"That is your revenge,'' she said slowly: then added; "Would it be a bad match, unworthy of the late Charles Cave Keeldar's representative?''

"My lass, Moore is a gentleman: his blood is pure and ancient as mine or thine.''

"And we too set store by ancient blood? We have family pride, though one of us at least is a Republican?''

Yorke bowed as he stood before her. His lips were mute, but his eye confessed the impeachment. Yes—he had family pride—you saw it in his whole bearing.

"Moore *is* a gentleman,'' echoed Shirley, lifting her head with glad grace. She checked herself—words seemed crowding to her tongue, she would not give them utterance; but her look spoke much at the moment: what—Yorke tried to read, but could not—the language was there—visible, but untranslatable—a poem—a fervid lyric in an unknown tongue. It was not a plain story, however—no simple gush of

feeling—no ordinary love-confession—that was obvious; it was something other, deeper, more intricate than he guessed at: he felt his revenge had not struck home; he felt that Shirley triumphed—she held him at fault, baffled, puzzled; *she* enjoyed the moment—not *he*.

"And if Moore is a gentleman, you *can* be only a lady, therefore——"

"Therefore there would be no inequality in our union?"

"None."

"Thank you for your approbation. Will you give me away when I relinquish the name of Keeldar for that of Moore?"

Mr. Yorke, instead of replying, gazed at her much puzzled. He could not divine what her look signified; whether she spoke in earnest or in jest: there was purpose and feeling, banter and scoff, playing, mingled, on her mobile lineaments.

"I don't understand thee," he said, turning away.

She laughed: "Take courage, sir; you are not singular in your ignorance: but I suppose if Moore understands me, that will do—will it not?"

"Moore may settle his own matters henceforward for me; I'll neither meddle nor make with them further."

A new thought crossed her: her countenance changed magically; with a sudden darkening of the eye, and austere fixing of the features, she demanded—"Have you been asked to interfere. Are you questioning me as another's proxy?"

"The Lord save us! Whoever weds thee must look about him! Keep all your questions for Robert; I'll answer no more on 'em. Good-day, lassie!"

The day being fine, or at least fair—for soft clouds curtained the sun, and a dim but not chill or waterish haze slept blue on the hills—Caroline, while Shirley was engaged with her callers, had persuaded Mrs. Pryor to assume her bonnet and summer shawl, and to take a walk with her up towards the narrow end of the Hollow.

Here, the opposing sides of the glen approaching each other, and becoming clothed with brushwood and stunted oaks, formed a wooded ravine; at the bottom of which ran the mill-stream, in broken unquiet course, struggling with many stones, chafing against rugged banks, fretting with gnarled tree-roots, foaming, gurgling, battling as it went. Here, when you had wandered half-a-mile from the mill, you found a sense of deep solitude: found it in the shade of unmolested trees; received it in the singing of many birds, for which that shade made a home. This was no trodden way: the freshness of the wood-flowers attested that foot of man seldom pressed them: abounding wild-roses looked as if they budded, bloomed, and faded under the watch of solitude, as in a Sultan's harem. Here you saw the sweet azure of blue-bells, and recognised in pearl-white blossoms, spangling the grass, an humble type of some star-lit spot in space.

Mrs. Pryor liked a quiet walk: she ever shunned highroads, and sought byways and lonely lanes: one companion she preferred to total solitude, for in solitude she was nervous; a vague fear of annoying encounters broke the enjoyment of quite lonely rambles; but she feared nothing with Caroline: when once she got away from human habitations, and entered the still demesne of nature accompanied by this one youthful friend, a propitious change seemed to steal over her mind and beam in her countenance. When with Caroline—and Caroline only—her heart, you would have said, shook off a burden, her brow put aside a veil, her spirits too escaped from a restraint: with her she was cheerful; with her, at times, she was tender: to her she would impart her knowledge, reveal glimpses of her experience, give her opportunities for guessing what life she had lived, what cultivation her mind had received, of what calibre was her intelligence, how and where her feelings were vulnerable.

To-day, for instance, as they walked along, Mrs. Pryor talked to her companion about the various birds singing in the trees, discriminated their species, and said

something about their habits and peculiarities. English natural history seemed familiar to her. All the wild flowers round their path were recognised by her: tiny plants springing near stones and peeping out of chinks in old walls—plants such as Caroline had scarcely noticed before—received a name and an intimation of their properties: it appeared that she had minutely studied the botany of English fields and woods. Having reached the head of the ravine, they sat down together on a ledge of grey and mossy rock jutting from the base of a steep green hill, which towered above them: she looked round her, and spoke of the neighbourhood as she had once before seen it long ago. She alluded to its changes, and compared its aspect with that of other parts of England; revealing in quiet, unconscious touches of description, a sense of the picturesque, an appreciation of the beautiful or commonplace, a power of comparing the wild with the cultured, the grand with the tame, that gave to her discourse a graphic charm as pleasant as it was unpretending.

The sort of reverent pleasure with which Caroline listened—so sincere, so quiet, yet so evident, stirred the elder lady's faculties to a gentle animation. Rarely, probably, had she, with her chill, repellent outside—her diffident mien and incommunicative habits, known what it was to excite in one whom she herself could love, feelings of earnest affection and admiring esteem. Delightful, doubtless, was the consciousness that a young girl towards whom it seemed—judging by the moved expression of her eyes and features—her heart turned with almost a fond impulse, looked up to her as an instructor, and clung to her as a friend. With a somewhat more marked accent of interest than she often permitted herself to use, she said, as she bent towards her youthful companion, and put aside from her forehead a pale brown curl which had strayed from the confining comb—"I do hope this sweet air blowing from the hill will do you good, my dear Caroline: I wish I could see something more of colour in these cheeks—but perhaps you were never florid?"

"I had red cheeks once," returned Miss Helstone, smiling. "I remember a year—two years ago, when I used to look in the glass, I saw a different face there to what I see now—rounder and rosier. But when we are young," added the girl of eighteen, "our minds are careless and our lives easy."

"Do you"—continued Mrs. Pryor, mastering by an effort that tyrant timidity which made it difficult for her, even under present circumstances, to attempt the scrutiny of another's heart—"Do you, at your age, fret yourself with cares for the future? Believe me, you had better not: let the morrow take thought for the things of itself."

"True, dear madam: it is not over the future I pine. The evil of the day is sometimes oppressive—*too* oppressive, and I long to escape it."

"That is—the evil of the day—that is—your uncle perhaps is not—you find it difficult to understand—he does not appreciate——"

Mrs. Pryor could not complete her broken sentences: she could not manage to put the question whether Mr. Helstone was too harsh with his niece, but Caroline comprehended.

"Oh, that is nothing," she replied; "my uncle and I get on very well: we never quarrel—I don't call him harsh—he never scolds me. Sometimes I wish somebody in the world loved me; but I cannot say that I particularly wish him to have more affection for me than he has. As a child, I should perhaps have felt the want of attention, only the servants were very kind to me; but when people are long indifferent to us, we grow indifferent to their indifference. It is my uncle's way not to care for women and girls—unless they be ladies that he meets in company: he could not alter, and I have no wish that he should alter, as far as I am concerned. I believe it would merely annoy and frighten me were he to be affectionate towards me now. But you know, Mrs. Pryor, it is scarcely *living* to measure time as I do at the Rectory. The hours pass, and I get them over somehow, but I do not *live*. I endure existence, but I rarely enjoy it. Since Miss Keeldar and you came, I have been—I was going to say—happier, but that would be untrue." She paused.

"How, untrue? You are fond of Miss Keeldar, are you not, my dear?"

"Very fond of Shirley: I both like and admire her: but I am painfully circumstanced: for a reason I cannot explain, I want to go away from this place, and to forget it."

"You told me before you wished to be a governess; but, my dear, if you remember, I did not encourage the idea. I have been a governess myself great part of my life. In Miss Keeldar's acquaintance, I esteem myself most fortunate: her talents and her really sweet disposition have rendered my office easy to me; but when I was young, before I married, my trials were severe, poignant. I should not like a—— I should not like you to endure similar ones. It was my lot to enter a family of considerable pretensions to good birth and mental superiority, and the members of which also believed that 'on them was perceptible' an usual endowment of the 'Christian graces'; that all their hearts were regenerate, and their spirits in a peculiar state of discipline. I was early given to understand that 'as I was not their equal,' so I could not expect 'to have their sympathy.' It was in no sort concealed from me that I was held a 'burden and a restraint in society.' The gentlemen, I found, regarded me as a 'tabooed woman,' to whom 'they were interdicted from granting the usual privileges of the sex,' and yet who 'annoyed them by frequently crossing their path.' The ladies too made it plain that they thought me 'a bore.' The servants, it was signified, 'detested me'; *why*, I could never clearly comprehend. My pupils, I was told, 'however much they might love me, and how deep soever the interest I might take in them, could not be my friends.' It was intimated that I must 'live alone, and never transgress the invisible but rigid line which established the difference between me and my employers.' My life in this house was sedentary, solitary, constrained, joyless, toilsome. The dreadful crushing of the animal spirits, the ever-prevailing sense of friendlessness and homelessness consequent on this state of things, began ere long to produce mortal effects on my constitution—I sickened. The lady of the house told me coolly I was the victim of 'wounded vanity.' She hinted, that if I did not make an effort to quell my 'ungodly discontent,' to cease 'murmuring against God's appointment,' and to cultivate the profound humility befitting my station, my mind would very likely 'go to pieces' on the rock that wrecked most of my sisterhood—morbid self-esteem; and that I should die an inmate of a lunatic asylum.

"I said nothing to Mrs. Hardman; it would have been useless: but to her eldest daughter I one day dropped a few observations, which were answered thus:—There were hardships, she allowed, in the position of a governess: 'doubtless they had their trials: but,' she averred, with a manner it makes me smile now to recall— 'but it must be so. *She* (Miss H.) had neither view, hope, nor *wish* to see these things remedied: for, in the inherent constitution of English habits, feelings, and prejudices, there was no possibility that they should be. Governesses,' she observed, 'must ever be kept in a sort of isolation: it is the only means of maintaining that distance which the reserve of English manners and the decorum of English families exact.'

"I remember I sighed as Miss Hardman quitted my bedside: she caught the sound, and turning, said severely—'I fear, Miss Grey, you have inherited in fullest measure the worst sin of our fallen nature—the sin of pride. You are proud, and therefore you are ungrateful too. Mamma pays you a handsome salary; and, if you had average sense, you would thankfully put up with much that is fatiguing to do and irksome to bear, since it is so well made worth your while.'

"Miss Hardman, my love, was a very strong-minded young lady, of most distinguished talents: the aristocracy are decidedly a very superior class, you know— both physically, and morally, and mentally—as a high Tory I acknowledge that;— I could not describe the dignity of her voice and mien as she addressed me thus: still, I fear, she was selfish, my dear. I would never wish to speak ill of my superiors in rank; but I think she was a little selfish."

"I remember," continued Mrs. Pryor, after a pause, "another of Miss H.'s observations, which she would utter with quite a grand air. 'WE,' she would say,— 'WE need the imprudences, extravagances, mistakes, and crimes of a certain number of fathers to sow the seed from which WE reap the harvest of governesses. The daughters of tradespeople, however well-educated, must necessarily be underbred, and as such unfit to be inmates of OUR dwellings, or guardians of OUR children's minds and persons. WE shall ever prefer to place those about OUR offspring, who have been born and bred with somewhat of the same refinement as OURSELVES' ''.

"Miss Hardman must have thought herself something better than her fellow-creatures, ma'am, since she held that their calamities, and even crimes, were necessary to minister to her convenience. You say she was religious: her religion must have been that of the Pharisee, who thanked God that he was not as other men are, nor even as that publican.''

"My dear, we will not discuss the point: I should be the last person to wish to instil into your mind any feeling of dissatisfaction with your lot in life, or any sentiment of envy or insubordination towards your superiors. Implicit submission to authorities, scrupulous deference to our betters (under which term I, of course, include the higher classes of society) are in my opinion, indispensable to the well-being of every community. All I mean to say, my dear, is, that you had better not attempt to be a governess, as the duties of the position would be too severe for your constitution. Not one word of disrespect would I breathe towards either Mrs. or Miss Hardman; only, recalling my own experience, I cannot but feel that, were you to fall under auspices such as theirs, you would contend a while courageously with your doom: then you would pine and grow too weak for your work; you would come home—if you still had a home—broken down. Those languishing years would follow, of which none but the invalid and her immediate friends feel the heart-sickness and know the burden: consumption or decline would close the chapter. Such is the history of many a life: I would not have it yours. My dear, we will now walk about a little, if you please.''

They both rose, and slowly paced a green natural terrace bordering the chasm.

"My dear," erelong again began Mrs. Pryor, a sort of timid, embarrassed abruptness marking her manner as she spoke, "the young, especially those to whom nature has been favourable—often—frequently—anticipate—look forward to—to marriage as the end, the goal of their hopes.''

And she stopped. Caroline came to her relief with promptitude, showing a great deal more self-possession and courage than herself on the formidable topic now broached.

"They do; and naturally," she replied, with a calm emphasis that startled Mrs. Pryor. "They look forward to marriage with some one they love as the brightest,— the only bright destiny that can await them. Are they wrong?''

"Oh, my dear!'' exclaimed Mrs. Pryor, clasping her hands: and again she paused. Caroline turned a searching, an eager eye on the face of her friend: that face was much agitated. "My dear," she murmured, "life is an illusion.''

"But not love! Love is real: the most real, the most lasting—the sweetest and yet the bitterest thing we know.''

"My dear—it is very bitter. It is said to be strong—strong as death! Most of the cheats of existence are strong. As to their sweetness—nothing is so transitory: its date is a moment,—the twinkling of an eye: the sting remains for ever: it may perish with the dawn of eternity, but it tortures through time into its deepest night.''

"Yes, it tortures through time," agreed Caroline, "except when it is mutual love.''

"Mutual love! My dear, romances are pernicious. You do not read them, I hope?''

"Sometimes—whenever I can get them, indeed; but romance-writers might know nothing of love, judging by the way in which they treat of it.''

"Nothing whatever, my dear!" assented Mrs. Pryor eagerly; "nor of marriage; and the false pictures they give of those subjects cannot be too strongly condemned. They are not like reality: they show you only the green tempting surface of the marsh, and give not one faithful or truthful hint of the slough underneath."

"But it is not always slough," objected Caroline: "there are happy marriages. Where affection is reciprocal and sincere, and minds are harmonious, marriage *must* be happy."

"It is never wholly happy. Two people can never literally be as one: there is, perhaps, a possibility of content under peculiar circumstances, such as are seldom combined; but it is as well not to run the risk: you may make fatal mistakes. Be satisfied, my dear: let all the single be satisfied with their freedom."

"You echo my uncle's words!" exclaimed Caroline, in a tone of dismay: "you speak like Mrs. Yorke, in her most gloomy moments;—like Miss Mann, when she is most sourly and hypochondriacally disposed. This is terrible!"

"No, it is only true. Oh, child! you have only lived the pleasant morning time of life: the hot, weary noon, the sad evening, the sunless night, are yet to come for you! Mr. Helstone, you say, talks as I talk; and I wonder how Mrs. Matthewson Helstone would have talked had she been living. She died! She died!"

"And, alas! my own mother and father . . ." exclaimed Caroline, struck by a sombre recollection.

"What of them?"

"Did I never tell you that they were separated?"

"I have heard it."

"They must then have been very miserable."

"You see all *facts* go to prove what I say."

"In this case there ought to be no such thing as marriage."

"There ought, my dear, were it only to prove that this life is a mere state of probation, wherein neither rest nor recompense is to be vouchsafed."

"But your own marriage, Mrs. Pryor?"

Mrs. Pryor shrunk and shuddered as if a rude finger had pressed a naked nerve: Caroline felt she had touched what would not bear the slightest contact.

"My marriage was unhappy," said the lady, summoning courage at last; "but yet——" she hesitated.

"But yet," suggested Caroline, "not immitigably wretched?"

"Not in its results, at least. No," she added, in a softer tone; "God mingles something of the balm of mercy even in vials of the most corrosive woe. He can so turn events, that from the very same blind, rash act whence sprang the curse of half our life, may flow the blessing of the remainder. Then, I am of a peculiar disposition, I own that: far from facile, without address, in some points eccentric. I ought never to have married: mine is not the nature easily to find a duplicate, or likely to assimilate with a contrast. I was quite aware of my own ineligibility; and if I had not been so miserable as a governess, I never should have married; and then——"

Caroline's eyes asked her to proceed: they entreated her to break the thick cloud of despair which her previous words had seemed to spread over life.

"And then, my dear, Mr.——that is, the gentleman I married, was, perhaps, rather an exceptional than an average character. I hope, at least, the experience of few has been such as mine was, or that few have felt their sufferings as I felt mine. They nearly shook my mind: relief was so hopeless, redress so unattainable: but, my dear, I do not wish to dishearten, I only wish to warn you, and to prove that the single should not be too anxious to change their state, as they may change for the worse."

"Thank you, my dear madam, I quite understand your kind intentions; but there is no fear of my falling into the error to which you allude. I, at least, have no

thoughts of marriage and, for that reason, I want to make myself a position by some other means.''

''My dear, listen to me. On what I am going to say, I have carefully deliberated; having, indeed, revolved the subject in my thoughts ever since you first mentioned your wish to obtain a situation. You know I at present reside with Miss Keeldar in the capacity of companion: should she marry (and that she *will* marry ere long, many circumstances induce me to conclude), I shall cease to be necessary to her in that capacity. I must tell you that I possess a small independency, arising partly from my own savings, and partly from a legacy left me some years since; whenever I leave Fieldhead, I shall take a house of my own: I could not endure to live in solitude: I have no relations whom I care to invite to close intimacy; for, as you must have observed, and as I have already avowed, my habits and tastes have their peculiarities: to you, my dear, I need not say I am attached; with you I am happier than I have ever been with any living thing'' (this was said with marked emphasis). ''Your society I should esteem a very dear privilege—an inestimable privilege, a comfort, a blessing. You shall come to me then. Caroline, do you refuse me? I hope you can love me?''

And with these two abrupt questions she stopped.

''Indeed, I *do* love you,'' was the reply. ''I should like to live with you: but you are too kind.''

''All I have,'' went on Mrs. Pryor, ''I would leave to you: you should be provided for, but never again say I am *too kind*. You pierce my heart, child!''

''But, my dear madam—this generosity—I have no claim—''

''Hush! you must not talk about it: there are some things we cannot bear to hear. Oh! it is late to begin, but I may yet live a few years: I can never wipe out the past, but perhaps a brief space in the future may yet be mine!''

Mrs. Pryor seemed deeply agitated: large tears trembled in her eyes and rolled down her cheeks. Caroline kissed her, in her gentle caressing way, saying softly— ''I love you dearly. Don't cry.''

But the lady's whole frame seemed shaken: she sat down, bent her head to her knee, and wept aloud. Nothing could console her till the inward storm had had its way. At last the agony subsided of itself.

''Poor thing!'' she murmured, returning Caroline's kiss: ''poor lonely lamb! But come,'' she added abruptly: ''come, we must go home.''

For a short distance Mrs. Pryor walked very fast: by degrees, however, she calmed down to her wonted manner, fell into her usual characteristic pace—a peculiar one, like all her movements—and by the time they reached Fieldhead, she had re-entered into herself: the outside was, as usual, still and shy.

Chapter XXII

TWO LIVES

ONLY half of Moore's activity and resolution had been seen in his defence of the mill: he showed the other half (and a terrible half it was) in the indefatigable, the relentless assiduity, with which he pursued the leaders of the riot. The mob, the mere followers, he let alone: perhaps an innate sense of justice told him that men misled by false counsel, goaded by privations, are not fit objects of vengeance, and that he who would visit an even violent act on the bent head of suffering, is a tyrant, not a judge. At all events, though he knew many of the number, having recognised them during the latter part of the attack when day began to dawn, he let them daily pass him on street and road without notice or threat.

The leaders he did not know. They were strangers: emissaries from the large towns. Most of these were not members of the operative class: they were chiefly "downdraughts," bankrupts, men always in debt and often in drink—men who had nothing to lose, and much—in the way of character, cash, and cleanliness— to gain. These persons Moore hunted like any sleuth-hound; and well he liked the occupation: its excitement was of a kind pleasant to his nature: he liked it better than making cloth.

His horse must have hated these times, for it was ridden both hard and often: he almost lived on the road, and the fresh air was as welcome to his lungs as the policeman's quest to his mood: he preferred it to the steam of dye-houses. The magistrates of the district must have dreaded him: they were slow, timid men; he liked both to frighten and to rouse them. He liked to force them to betray a certain fear, which made them alike falter in resolve and recoil in action—the fear, simply, of assassination. This, indeed, was the dread which had hitherto hampered every manufacturer—and almost every public man in the district. Helstone alone had ever repelled it. The old Cossack knew well he might be shot: he knew there was risk; but such a death had for his nerves no terrors: it would have been his chosen— might he have had a choice.

Moore likewise knew his danger: the result was an unquenchable scorn of the quarter whence such danger was to be apprehended. The consciousness that he hunted assassins was the spur in his high-mettled temper's flank. As for fear, he was too proud—too hard-natured—(if you will)—too phlegmatic a man to fear. Many a time he rode belated over moors, moonlit or moonless as the case might be, with feelings far more elate, faculties far better refreshed, than when safety and stagnation environed him in the counting-house. Four was the number of the leaders to be accounted for: two, in the course of a fortnight, were brought to bay near Stilbro'; the remaining two it was necessary to seek further off: their haunts were supposed to lie near Birmingham.

Meantime the clothier did not neglect his battered mill: its reparation was esteemed a light task; carpenters' and glaziers' work alone being needed. The rioters not having succeeded in effecting an entrance, his grim, metal darlings—the machines —had escaped damage.

Whether, during this busy life—whether, while stern justice and exacting business claimed his energies and harassed his thoughts—he now and then gave one moment, dedicated one effort, to keep alive gentler fires than those which smoulder in the fane of Nemesis, it was not easy to discover. He seldom went near Fieldhead; if he did, his visits were brief: if he called at the Rectory, it was only to hold conferences with the Rector in his study. He maintained his rigid course very steadily. Meantime the history of the year continued troubled; there was no lull in the tempest of war; her long hurricane still swept the Continent. There was not the faintest sign of serene weather: no opening amid "the clouds of battle-dust and smoke"; no fall of pure dews genial to the olive; no cessation of the red rain which nourishes the baleful and glorious laurel. Meantime, Ruin had her sappers and miners at work under Moore's feet, and whether he rode or walked—whether he only crossed his counting-house hearth, or galloped over sullen Rushedge—he was aware of a hollow echo, and felt the ground shake to his tread.

While the summer thus passed with Moore, how did it lapse with Shirley and Caroline? Let us first visit the heiress. How does she look? Like a love-lorn maiden, pale and pining for a neglectful swain? Does she sit the day long bent over some sedentary task? Has she for ever a book in her hand, or sewing on her knee, and eyes only for that, and words for nothing, and thoughts unspoken?

By no means. Shirley is all right. If her wistful cast of physiognomy is not gone, no more is her careless smile. She keeps her dark old manor-house light and bright with her cheery presence: the gallery, and the low-ceiled chambers that open into it, have learned lively echoes from her voice: the dim entrance-hall, with its one

window, has grown pleasantly accustomed to the frequent rustle of a silk dress, as its wearer sweeps across from room to room, now carrying flowers to the barbarous peach-bloom *salon,* now entering the dining-room to open its casements and let in the scent of mignonette and sweet-briar, anon bringing plants from the staircase-window to place in the sun at the open porch-door.

She takes her sewing occasionally: but, by some fatality, she is doomed never to sit steadily at it for above five minutes at a time: her thimble is scarcely fitted on, her needle scarce threaded, when a sudden thought calls her upstairs: perhaps she goes to seek some just-then-remembered old ivory-backed needle-book, or older china-topped workbox, quite unneeded, but which seems at the moment indispensable; perhaps to arrange her hair, or a drawer which she recollects to have seen that morning in a state of curious confusion; perhaps only to take a peep from a particular window at a particular view, whence Briarfield Church and Rectory are visible, pleasantly bowered in trees. She has scarcely returned, and again taken up the slip of cambric, or square of half-wrought canvas, when Tartar's bold scrape and strangled whistle are heard at the porch-door, and she must run to open it for him; it is a hot day; he comes in panting; she must convoy him to the kitchen, and see with her own eyes that his water-bowl is replenished. Through the open kitchen-door the court is visible, all sunny and gay, and peopled with turkeys and their poults, peahens and their chicks, pearl-flecked Guinea fowls, and a bright variety of pure white, and purple-necked, and blue and cinnamon-plumed pigeons. Irresistible spectacle to Shirley! She runs to the pantry for a roll, and she stands on the door-step scattering crumbs: around her throng her eager, plump, happy, feathered vassals. John is about the stables, and John must be talked to, and her mare looked at. She is still petting and patting it, when the cows come in to be milked: this is important: Shirley must stay and take a review of them all. There are perhaps some little calves, some little new-yeaned lambs—it may be twins, whose mothers have rejected them: Miss Keeldar must be introduced to them by John—must permit herself the treat of feeding them with her own hand, under the direction of her careful foreman. Meantime, John moots doubtful questions about the farming of certain "crofts," and "ings," and "holms," and his mistress is necessitated to fetch her garden-hat—a gipsy-straw—and accompany him, over stile and along hedgerow, to hear the conclusion of the whole agricultural matter on the spot, and with the said "crofts," "ings," and "holms" under her eye. Bright afternoon thus wears into soft evening, and she comes home to a late tea, and after tea she never sews.

After tea Shirley reads, and she is just about as tenacious of her book as she is lax of her needle. Her study is the rug, her seat a footstool, or perhaps only the carpet at Mrs. Pryor's feet—there she always learned her lessons when a child, and old habits have a strong power over her. The tawny and lion-like bulk of Tartar is ever stretched beside her; his negro muzzle laid on his fore-paws, straight, strong, and shapely as the limbs of an Alpine wolf. One hand of the mistress generally reposes on the loving serf's rude head, because if she takes it away he groans and is discontented. Shirley's mind is given to her book; she lifts not her eyes; she neither stirs nor speaks; unless, indeed, it be to return a brief respectful answer to Mrs. Pryor, who addresses deprecatory phrases to her now and then.

"My dear, you had better not have that great dog so near you: he is crushing the border of your dress."

"Oh, it is only muslin: I can put a clean one on to-morrow."

"My dear, I wish you could acquire the habit of sitting to a table when you read."

"I will try, ma'am, some time; but it is so comfortable to do as one has always been accustomed to do."

"My dear, let me beg of you to put that book down: you are trying your eyes by the doubtful firelight."

"No, ma'am, not at all: my eyes are never tired."

At last, however, a pale light falls on the page from the window: she looks, the moon is up; she closes the volume, rises, and walks through the room. Her book has perhaps been a good one; it has refreshed, refilled, rewarmed her heart; it has set her brain astir, furnished her mind with pictures. The still parlour, the clean hearth, the window opening on the twilight sky, and showing its "sweet regent," new throned and glorious, suffice to make earth an Eden, life a poem, for Shirley. A still, deep, inborn delight glows in her young veins; unmingled—untroubled, not to be reached or ravished by human agency, because by no human agency bestowed: the pure gift of God to His creature, the free dower of Nature to her child. This joy gives her experience of a genii-life. Buoyant, by green steps, by glad hills, all verdure and light, she reaches a station scarcely lower than that whence angels looked down on the dreamer of Bethel, and her eye seeks, and her soul possesses, the vision of life as she wishes it. No—not as she wishes it; she has not time to wish: the swift glory spreads out, sweeping and kindling, and multiplies its splendour faster than Thought can effect his combinations, faster than Aspiration can utter her longings. Shirley says nothing while the trance is upon her—she is quite mute; but if Mrs. Pryor speaks to her now, she goes out quietly, and continues her walk upstairs in the dim gallery.

If Shirley were not an indolent, a reckless, an ignorant being, she would take a pen at such moments; or at least while the recollection of such moments was yet fresh on her spirit: she would seize, she would fix the apparition, tell the vision revealed. Had she a little more of the organ of acquisitiveness in her head—a little more of the love of property in her nature, she would take a good-sized sheet of paper and write plainly out, in her own queer but clear and legible hand, the story that has been narrated, the song that has been sung to her, and thus possess what she was enabled to create. But indolent she is, reckless she is, and most ignorant, for she does not know her dreams are rare—her feelings peculiar: she does not know, has never known, and will die without knowing, the full value of that spring whose bright fresh bubbling in her heart keeps it green.

Shirley takes life easily: is not that fact written in her eye? In her good-tempered moments, is it not as full of lazy softness as in her brief fits of anger it is fulgent with quick-flashing fire? Her nature is in her eye: so long as she is calm, indolence, indulgence, humour, and tenderness possess that large grey sphere: incense her,—a red ray pierces the dew,—it quickens instantly to flame.

Ere the month of July was passed, Miss Keeldar would probably have started with Caroline on that northern tour they had planned; but just at that epoch an invasion befell Fieldhead: a genteel foraging party besieged Shirley in her castle and compelled her to surrender at discretion. An uncle, an aunt, and two cousins from the south, a Mr., Mrs., and two Misses Sympson, of Sympson Grove, ——shire, came down upon her in state. The laws of hospitality obliged her to give in, which she did with a facility which somewhat surprised Caroline, who knew her to be prompt in action and fertile in expedient, where a victory was to be gained for her will. Miss Helstone even asked her how it was she submitted so readily?—she answered, old feelings had their power—she had passed two years of her early youth at Sympson Grove.

"How did she like her relatives?"

She had nothing in common with them, she replied: little Harry Sympson, indeed, the sole son of the family, was very unlike his sisters, and of him she had formerly been fond; but he was not coming to Yorkshire: at least, not yet.

The next Sunday the Fieldhead pew in Briarfield Church appeared peopled with a prim, trim, fidgety, elderly gentleman, who shifted his spectacles and changed his position every three minutes; a patient, placid-looking elderly lady, in brown satin, and two pattern young ladies, in pattern attire, with pattern deportment. Shirley had the air of a black swan, or a white crow, in the midst of this party;

and very forlorn was her aspect. Having brought her into respectable society, we will leave her there a while, and look after Miss Helstone.

Separated from Miss Keeldar for the present, as she could not seek her in the midst of her fine relatives; scared away from Fieldhead by the visiting commotion which the new arrivals occasioned in the neighbourhood, Caroline was limited once more to the grey Rectory; the solitary morning walk in remote by-paths; the long, lonely afternoon sitting in a quiet parlour which the sun forsook at noon, or in the garden alcove where it shone bright, yet sad, on the ripening red currants trained over the trellis, and on the fair monthly roses entwined between, and through them fell chequered on Caroline sitting in her white summer dress, still as a garden statue. There she read old books, taken from her uncle's library; the Greek and Latin were of no use to her; and its collection of light literature was chiefly contained on a shelf which had belonged to her aunt Mary: some venerable Lady's Magazines, that had once performed a sea voyage with their owner, and undergone a storm, and whose pages were stained with salt water; some mad Methodist Magazines, full of miracles and apparitions, of preternatural warnings, ominous dreams, and frenzied fanaticism; the equally mad Letters of Mrs. Elizabeth Rowe from the Dead to the Living; a few old English Classics:—from these faded flowers Caroline had in her childhood extracted the honey,—they were tasteless to her now. By way of change, and also of doing good, she would sew; make garments for the poor, according to good Miss Ainley's direction. Sometimes, as she felt and saw her tears fall slowly on her work, she would wonder how the excellent woman who had cut it out and arranged it for her, managed to be so equally serene in *her* solitude.

"I never find Miss Ainley oppressed with despondency, or lost in grief," she thought; "yet her cottage is a still, dim little place, and she is without a bright hope or near friend in the world. I remember, though, she told me once, she had tutored her thoughts to tend upwards to Heaven. She allowed there was, and ever had been, little enjoyment in this world for her, and she looks, I suppose, to the bliss of the world to come. So do nuns—with their close cell, their iron lamp, their robe straight as a shroud, their bed narrow as a coffin. She says, often, she has no fear of death—no dread of the grave: no more, doubtless, had St. Simeon Stylites, lifted up terrible on his wild column in the wilderness: no more has the Hindoo votary stretched on his couch of iron spikes. Both these having violated nature, their natural likings and antipathies are reversed: they grow altogether morbid. I do fear death as yet, but I believe it is because I am young: poor Miss Ainley would cling closer to life, if life had more charms for her. God surely did not create us, and cause us to live, with the sole end of wishing always to die. I believe, in my heart, we were intended to prize life and enjoy it, so long as we retain it. Existence never was originally meant to be that useless, blank, pale, slow-trailing thing it often becomes to many, and is becoming to me, among the rest.

"Nobody," she went on—"nobody in particular is to blame, that I can see, for the state in which things are: and I cannot tell, however much I puzzle over it, how they are to be altered for the better; but I feel there is something wrong somewhere. I believe single women should have more to do—better chances of interesting and profitable occupation than they possess now. And when I speak thus, I have no impression that I displease God by my words; that I am either impious or impatient, irreligious or sacrilegious. My consolation is, indeed, that God hears many a groan, and compassionates much grief which man stops his ears against, or frowns on with impotent contempt. I say *impotent,* for I observe that to such grievances as society cannot readily cure, it usually forbids utterance, on pain of its scorn: this scorn being only a sort of tinselled cloak to its deformed weakness. People hate to be reminded of ills they are unable or unwilling to remedy: such reminder, in forcing on them a sense of their own incapacity, or a more painful sense of an obligation to make some unpleasant effort, troubles their ease and shakes their self-complacency.

Old maids, like the houseless and unemployed poor, should not ask for a place and an occupation in the world: the demand disturbs the happy and rich: it disturbs parents. Look at the numerous families of girls in this neighbourhood: the Armitages, the Birtwistles, the Sykes. The brothers of these girls are every one in business or in professions; they have something to do: their sisters have no earthly employment, but household work and sewing; no earthly pleasure, but an unprofitable visiting; and no hope, in all their life to come, of anything better. This stagnant state of things makes them decline in health: they are never well; and their minds and views shrink to wondrous narrowness. The great wish—the sole aim of every one of them is to be married, but the majority will never marry: they will die as they now live. They scheme, they plot, they dress to ensnare husbands. The gentlemen turn them into ridicule: they don't want them; they hold them very cheap: they say—I have heard them say it with sneering laughs many a time—the matrimonial market is overstocked. Fathers say so likewise, and are angry with their daughters when they observe their manœuvres: they order them to stay at home. What do they expect them to do at home? If you ask,—they would answer, sew and cook. They expect them to do this, and this only, contentedly, regularly, uncomplainingly all their lives long, as if they had no germs of faculties for anything else: a doctrine as reasonable to hold, as it would be that the fathers have no faculties but for eating what their daughters cook, or for wearing what they sew. Could men live so themselves? Would they not be very weary? And, when there came no relief to their weariness, but only reproaches at its slightest manifestation, would not their weariness ferment in time to frenzy? Lucretia, spinning at midnight in the midst of her maidens, and Solomon's virtuous woman, are often quoted as patterns of what 'the sex' (as they say) ought to be. I don't know: Lucretia, I dare say, was a most worthy sort of person, much like my cousin Hortense Moore; but she kept her servants up very late. I should not have liked to be amongst the number of the maidens. Hortense would just work me and Sarah in that fashion, if she could, and neither of us would bear it. The 'virtuous woman,' again, had her household up in the very middle of the night; she 'got breakfast over' (as Mrs. Sykes says) before one o'clock A.M.; but *she* had something more to do than spin and give out portions: she was a manufacturer—she made fine linen and sold it: she was an agriculturist— she bought estates and planted vineyards. *That* woman was a manager: she was what the matrons hereabouts call 'a clever woman.' On the whole, I like her a good deal better than Lucretia; but I don't believe either Mr. Armitage or Mr. Sykes could have got the advantage of her in a bargain: yet, I like her. 'Strength and honour were her clothing: the heart of her husband safely trusted in her. She opened her mouth with wisdom; in her tongue was the law of kindness: her children rose up and called her blessed; her husband also praised her.' King of Israel! your model of a woman is a worthy model! But are we, in these days, brought up to be like her? Men of Yorkshire! do your daughters reach this royal standard? Can they reach it? Can you help them to reach it? Can you give them a field in which their faculties may be exercised and grow? Men of England! look at your poor girls, many of them fading round you, dropping off in consumption or decline; or, what is worse, degenerating to sour old maids,—envious, back-biting, wretched, because life is a desert to them: or, what is worst of all, reduced to strive, by scarce modest coquetry and debasing artifice, to gain that position and consideration by marriage which to celibacy is denied. Fathers! cannot you alter these things? Perhaps not all at once; but consider the matter well when it is brought before you, receive it as a theme worthy of thought: do not dismiss it with an idle jest or an unmanly insult. You would wish to be proud of your daughters and not to blush for them—then seek for them an interest and an occupation which shall raise them above the flirt, the manœuvrer, the mischief-making tale-bearer. Keep your girls' minds narrow and fettered—they will still be a plague and a care, sometimes a disgrace to you: cultivate

them—give them scope and work—they will be your gayest companions in health; your tenderest nurses in sickness; your most faithful prop in age.''

Chapter XXIII

AN EVENING OUT

ONE fine summer day that Caroline had spent entirely alone (her uncle being at Whinbury), and whose long, bright, noiseless, breezeless, cloudless hours (how many they seemed since sunrise!) had been to her as desolate as if they had gone over her head in the shadowless and trackless wastes of Sahara, instead of in the blooming garden of an English home, she was sitting in the alcove,—her task of work on her knee, her fingers assiduously plying the needle, her eyes following and regulating their movements, her brain working restlessly,—when Fanny came to the door, looked round over the lawn and borders, and not seeing her whom she sought, called out—''Miss Caroline!''

A low voice answered—''Fanny!'' It issued from the alcove, and thither Fanny hastened—a note in her hand, which she delivered to fingers that hardly seemed to have nerve to hold it. Miss Helstone did not ask whence it came, and she did not look at it: she let it drop amongst the folds of her work.

''Joe Scott's son, Harry, brought it,'' said Fanny.

The girl was no enchantress, and knew no magic-spell, yet what she said took almost magical effect on her young mistress: she lifted her head with the quick motion of revived sensation; she shot—not a languid, but a lifelike, questioning glance at Fanny.

''Harry Scott! Who sent him?''

''He came from the Hollow.''

The dropped note was snatched up eagerly—the seal was broken; it was read in two seconds. An affectionate billet from Hortense, informing her young cousin that she was returned from Wormwood Wells; that she was alone to-day, as Robert was gone to Whinbury market; that nothing would give her greater pleasure than to have Caroline's company to tea; and—the good lady added—she was sure such a change would be most acceptable and beneficial to Caroline, who must be sadly at a loss both for safe guidance and improving society since the misunderstanding between Robert and Mr. Helstone had occasioned a separation from her ''*meilleure amie*, Hortense Gérard Moore.'' In a postscript, she was urged to put on her bonnet and run down directly.

Caroline did not need the injunction: glad was she to lay by the child's brown holland slip she was trimming with braid for the Jew's basket, to hasten upstairs, cover her curls with her straw bonnet, and throw round her shoulders the black silk scarf, whose simple drapery suited as well her shape as its dark hue set off the purity of her dress and the fairness of her face; glad was she to escape for a few hours the solitude, the sadness, the nightmare of her life; glad to run down the green lane sloping to the Hollow, to scent the fragrance of hedge-flowers sweeter than the perfume of moss-rose or lily. True, she knew Robert was not at the cottage; but it was delight to go where he had lately been: so long, so totally separated from him, merely to see his home, to enter the room where he had that morning sat, felt like a reunion. As such it revived her; and then Illusion was again following her in Perimask: the soft agitation of wings caressed her cheek, and the air, breathing from the blue summer sky, bore a voice which whispered—''Robert may come home while you are in his house; and then, at least, you may look in his face,— at least you may give him your hand: perhaps, for a minute, you may sit beside him.''

"Silence!" was her austere response: but she loved the comforter and the consolation.

Miss Moore probably caught from the window the gleam and flutter of Caroline's white attire through the branchy garden-shrubs, for she advanced from the cottage porch to meet her. Straight, unbending, phlegmatic as usual, she came on: no haste or ecstasy was ever permitted to disorder the dignity of *her* movements; but she smiled, well pleased to mark the delight of her pupil, to feel her kiss, and the gentle, genial strain of her embrace. She led her tenderly in—half deceived and wholly flattered. Half deceived! had it not been so, she would in all probability have put her to the wicket, and shut her out. Had she known clearly to whose account the chief share of this child-like joy was to be placed, Hortense would most likely have felt both shocked and incensed. Sisters do not like young ladies to fall in love with their brothers: it seems, if not presumptuous, silly, weak, a delusion, an absurd mistake. *They* do not love these gentlemen—whatever sisterly affection they may cherish towards them—and that others should, repels them with a sense of crude romance. The first movement, in short, excited by such discovery (as with many parents on finding their children to be in love), is one of mixed impatience and contempt. Reason—if they be rational people—corrects the false feeling in time; but if they be irrational, it is never corrected and the daughter or sister-in-law is disliked to the end.

"You would expect to find me alone, from what I said in my note," observed Miss Moore, as she conducted Caroline towards the parlour; "but it was written this morning: since dinner, company has come in."

And, opening the door, she made visible an ample spread of crimson skirts overflowing the elbow-chair at the fireside, and above them, presiding with dignity, a cap more awful than a crown. That cap had never come to the cottage under a bonnet; no, it had been brought, in a vast bag, or rather a middle-sized balloon of black silk, held wide with whalebone. The screed, or frill of the cap, stood a quarter of a yard broad round the face of the wearer: the ribbon, flourishing in puffs and bows about the head, was of the sort called love ribbon: there was a good deal of it,—I may say, a very great deal. Mrs. Yorke wore the cap—it became her: she wore the gown also—it suited her no less.

That great lady was come in a friendly way to take tea with Miss Moore. It was almost as great and as rare a favour as if the Queen were to go uninvited to share pot-luck with one of her subjects: a higher mark of distinction she could not show,— she who, in general, scorned visiting and tea-drinking, and held cheap and stigmatised as "gossips" every maid and matron of the vicinage.

There was no mistake, however; Miss Moore was a favourite with her: she had evinced the fact more than once; evinced it by stopping to speak to her in the churchyard on Sundays; by inviting her, almost hospitably, to come to Briarmains; evinced it to-day by the grand condescension of a personal visit. Her reasons for the preference, as assigned by herself, were, that Miss Moore was a woman of steady deportment, without the least levity of conversation or carriage; also, that, being a foreigner, she must feel the want of a friend to countenance her. She might have added, that her plain aspect, homely precise dress, and phlegmatic unattractive manner were to her so many additional recommendations. It is certain, at least, that ladies remarkable for the opposite qualities of beauty, lively bearing, and elegant taste in attire, were not often favoured with her approbation. Whatever gentlemen are apt to admire in women, Mrs. Yorke condemned; and what they overlook or despise, she patronised.

Caroline advanced to the mighty matron with some sense of diffidence: she knew little of Mrs. Yorke; and, as a parson's niece, was doubtful what sort of a reception she might get. She got a very cool one, and was glad to hide her discomfiture by turning away to take off her bonnet. Nor, upon sitting down, was she displeased to be immediately accosted by a little personage in a blue frock and sash, who started up like some fairy from the side of the great dame's chair, where she had

been sitting on a footstool, screened from view by the folds of the wide red gown, and running to Miss Helstone, unceremoniously threw her arms round her neck and demanded a kiss.

"My mother is not civil to you," said the petitioner, as she received and repaid a smiling salute; "and Rose, there, takes no notice of you: it is their way. If, instead of you, a white angel, with a crown of stars, had come into the room, mother would nod stiffly, and Rose never lift her head at all: but I will be your friend: I have always liked you!"

"Jessy, curb that tongue of yours, and repress your forwardness!" said Mrs. Yorke.

"But, mother, you are so frozen!" expostulated Jessy. "Miss Helstone has never done you any harm: why can't you be kind to her? You sit so stiff, and look so cold, and speak so dry—what for? That's just the fashion in which you treat Miss Shirley Keeldar, and every other young lady who comes to our house. And Rose, there, is such an aut—aut——I have forgotten the word, but it means a machine in the shape of a human being. However, between you, you will drive every soul away from Briarmains—Martin often says so!"

"I am an automaton? Good! Let me alone then," said Rose, speaking from a corner where she was sitting on the carpet at the foot of a bookcase, with a volume spread open on her knee. "Miss Helstone—how do you do?" she added, directing a brief glance to the person addressed, and then again casting down her grey, remarkable eyes on the book, and returning to the study of its pages.

Caroline stole a quiet gaze towards her, dwelling on her young, absorbed countenance, and observing a certain unconscious movement of the mouth as she read—a movement full of character. Caroline had tact, and she had fine instinct: she felt that Rose Yorke was a peculiar child—one of the unique; she knew how to treat her. Approaching quietly, she knelt on the carpet at her side, and looked over her little shoulder at her book. It was a romance of Mrs. Radcliffe's—*The Italian*.

Caroline read on with her, making no remark: presently Rose showed her the attention of asking, ere she turned a leaf—"Are you ready?"

Caroline only nodded.

"Do you like it?" inquired Rose, ere long.

"Long since, when I read it as a child, I was wonderfully taken with it."

"Why?"

"It seemed to open with such promise—such foreboding of a most strange tale to be unfolded."

"And in reading it, you feel as if you were far away from England—really in Italy—under another sort of sky—that blue sky of the south which travellers describe."

"You are sensible of that, Rose?"

"It makes me long to travel, Miss Helstone."

"When you are a woman, perhaps, you may be able to gratify your wish."

"I mean to make a way to do so, if one is not made for me. l cannot live always in Briarfield. The whole world is not very large compared with creation: I must see the outside of our own round planet at least."

"How much of its outside?"

"First this hemisphere where we live; then the other. I am resolved that my life shall be a life: not a black trance like the toad's, buried in marble; nor a long, slow death like yours in Briarfield Rectory."

"Like mine! What can you mean, child?"

"Might you not as well be tediously dying, as for ever shut up in that glebe-house—a place that, when I pass it, always reminds me of a windowed grave? I never see any movement about the door: I never hear a sound from the wall: I believe smoke never issues from the chimneys. What do you do there?"

"I sew, I read, I learn lessons."

"Are you happy?"

"Should I be happier wandering alone in strange countries as you wish to do?"

"Much happier, even if you did nothing but wander. Remember, however, that I shall have an object in view: but if you only went on and on, like some enchanted lady in a fairy tale, you might be happier than now. In a day's wandering, you would pass many a hill, wood, and watercourse, each perpetually altering in aspect as the sun shone out or was overcast; as the weather was wet or fair, dark or bright. Nothing changes in Briarfield Rectory: the plaster of the parlour-ceilings, the paper on the walls, the curtains, carpets, chairs, are still the same."

"Is change necessary to happiness?"

"Yes."

"Is it synonymous with it?"

"I don't know; but I feel monotony and death to be almost the same."

Here Jessy spoke.

"Isn't she mad?" she asked.

"But Rose," pursued Caroline, "I fear a wanderer's life, for me at least, would end like that tale you are reading—in disappointment, vanity, and vexation of spirit."

"Does *The Italian* so end?"

"I thought so when I read it."

"Better to try all things and find all empty, than to try nothing and leave your life a blank. To do this is to commit the sin of him who buried his talent in a napkin—despicable sluggard!"

"Rose," observed Mrs. Yorke, "solid satisfaction is only to be realised by doing one's duty."

"Right, mother! And if my Master has given me ten talents, my duty is to trade with them, and make them ten talents more. Not in the dust of household drawers shall the coin be interred. I will *not* deposit it in a broken-spouted tea-pot, and shut it up in a china-closet among tea-things. I will *not* commit it to your work-table to be smothered in piles of woollen hose. I will *not* prison it in the linen press to find shrouds among the sheets: and least of all, mother"—(she got up from the floor)— "least of all will I hide it in a tureen of cold potatoes, to be ranged with bread, butter, pastry, and ham on the shelves of the larder."

She stopped—then went on:—"Mother, the Lord who gave each of us our talents will come home some day, and will demand from all an account. The tea-pot, the old stocking-foot, the linen rag, the willow-pattern tureen, will yield up their barren deposit in many a house: suffer your daughters, at least, to put their money to the exchangers, that they may be enabled at the Master's coming to pay Him His own with usury."

"Rose, did you bring your sampler with you, as I told you?"

"Yes, mother."

"Sit down, and do a line of marking."

Rose sat down promptly, and wrought according to orders. After a busy pause of ten minutes, her mother asked—"Do you think yourself oppressed now? A victim?"

"No, mother."

"Yet, as far as I understood your tirade, it was a protest against all womanly and domestic employment."

You misunderstood it, mother. I should be sorry not to learn to sew; you do right to teach me, and to make me work."

"Even to the mending of your brothers' stockings and the making of sheets?"

"Yes."

"Where is the use of ranting and spouting about it, then?"

"Am I to do nothing but that? I will do that, and then I will do more. Now, mother, I have said my say. I am twelve years old at present, and not till I am

sixteen will I speak again about talents: for four years, I bind myself an industrious apprentice to all you can teach me.''

''You see what my daughters are, Miss Helstone,'' observed Mrs. Yorke: ''how precociously wise in their own conceits! 'I would rather this—I prefer that'; such is Jessy's cuckoo-song: while Rose utters the bolder cry, 'I *will*, and I will *not!'* ''

''I render a reason, mother: besides, if my cry is bold, it is only heard once in a twelvemonth. About each birthday, the spirit moves me to deliver one oracle respecting my own instruction and management: I utter it and leave it; it is for you, mother, to listen or not.''

''I would advise all young ladies,'' pursued Mrs. Yorke, ''to study the characters of such children as they chance to meet with before they marry, and have any of their own; to consider well how they would like the responsibility of guiding the careless, the labour of persuading the stubborn, the constant burden and task of training the best.''

''But with love it need not be so very difficult,'' interposed Caroline. ''Mothers love their children most dearly—almost better than they love themselves.''

''Fine talk! Very sentimental! There is the rough, practical part of life yet to come for you, young Miss!''

''But, Mrs. Yorke, if I take a little baby into my arms—any poor woman's infant for instance,—I feel that I love that helpless thing quite peculiarly, though I am not its mother. I could do almost anything for it willingly, if it were delivered over entirely to my care—if it were quite dependent on me.''

''You *feel!* Yes! yes! I daresay, now: you are led a great deal by your *feelings*, and you think yourself a very sensitive, refined personage, no doubt. Are you aware that, with all these romantic ideas, you have managed to train your features into an habitually lackadaisical expression, better suited to a novel-heroine than to a woman who is to make her way in the real world by dint of common sense?''

''No; I am not at all aware of that, Mrs. Yorke.''

''Look in the glass just behind you. Compare the face you see there with that of any early-rising, hard-working milkmaid.''

''My face is a pale one, but it is *not* sentimental, and most milkmaids, however red and robust they may be, are more stupid and less practically fitted to make their way in the world than I am. I think more and more correctly than milkmaids in general do; consequently, where they would often, for want of reflection, act weakly, I, by dint of reflection, should act judiciously.''

''Oh, no! you would be influenced by your feelings. You would be guided by impulse.''

''Of course, I should often be influenced by my feelings: they were given me to that end. Whom my feelings teach me to love, I *must* and *shall* love; and I hope, if ever I have a husband and children, my feelings will induce me to love them. I hope, in that case, all my impulses will be strong in compelling me to love.''

Caroline had a pleasure in saying this with emphasis: she had a pleasure in daring to say it in Mrs. Yorke's presence. She did not care what unjust sarcasm might be hurled at her in reply: she flushed, not with anger, but excitement, when the ungenial matron answered coolly—''Don't waste your dramatic effects. That was well said,— it was quite fine; but it is lost on two women—an old wife and an old maid; there should have been a disengaged gentleman present. Is Mr. Robert nowhere hid behind the curtains, do you think, Miss Moore?''

Hortense, who during the chief part of the conversation had been in the kitchen superintending the preparations for tea, did not yet quite comprehend the drift of the discourse. She answered with a puzzled air that Robert was at Whinbury. Mrs. Yorke laughed her own peculiar short laugh.

''Straightforward Miss Moore!'' said she patronisingly. ''It is like you to understand my question so literally, and answer it so simply. *Your* mind comprehends nothing

of intrigue. Strange things might go on around you without your being the wiser: you are not of the class the world calls sharp-witted.''

These equivocal compliments did not seem to please Hortense. She drew herself up, puckered her black eyebrows, but still looked puzzled.

''I have ever been noted for sagacity and discernment from childhood,'' she returned: for, indeed, on the possession of these qualities she peculiarly piqued herself.

''You never plotted to win a husband, I'll be bound,'' pursued Mrs. Yorke; ''and you have not the benefit of previous experience to aid you in discovering when others plot.''

Caroline felt this kind language where the benevolent speaker intended she should feel it—in her very heart. She could not even parry the shafts: she was defenceless for the present: to answer would have been to avow that the cap fitted. Mrs. Yorke, looking at her as she sat with troubled downcast eyes, and cheek burning painfully, and figure expressing in its bent attitude and unconscious tremor all the humiliation and chagrin she experienced, felt the sufferer was fair game. The strange woman had a natural antipathy to a shrinking, sensitive character—a nervous temperament: nor was a pretty, delicate, and youthful face a passport to her affections. It was seldom she met with all these obnoxious qualities combined in one individual: still more seldom she found that individual at her mercy, under circumstances in which she could crush her well. She happened, this afternoon, to be specially bilious and morose: as much disposed to gore as any vicious ''mother of the herd'': lowering her large head, she made a new charge.

''Your cousin Hortense is an excellent sister, Miss Helstone: such ladies as come to try their life's luck here, at Hollow's Cottage, may, by a very little clever female artifice, cajole the mistress of the house, and have the game all in their own hands. You are fond of your cousin's society, I daresay, Miss?''

''Of which cousin's?''

''Oh, of the lady's, *of course.*''

''Hortense is, and always has been, most kind to me.''

''Every sister, with an eligible single brother, is considered most kind by her spinster friends.''

''Mrs. Yorke,'' said Caroline, lifting her eyes slowly, their blue orbs at the same time clearing from trouble, and shining steady and full, while the glow of shame left her cheek, and its hue turned pale and settled: ''Mrs. Yorke, may I ask what you mean?''

''To give you a lesson on the cultivation of rectitude: to disgust you with craft and false sentiment.''

''Do I need this lesson?''

''Most young ladies of the present day need it. You are quite a modern young lady—morbid, delicate, professing to like retirement; which implies, I suppose, that you find little worthy of your sympathies in the ordinary world. The ordinary world—every-day, honest folks—are better than you think them: much better than any bookish, romancing chit of a girl can be, who hardly ever puts her nose over her uncle's, the parson's garden wall.''

''Consequently, of whom you know nothing. Excuse me—indeed, it does not matter whether you excuse me or not—you have attacked me without provocation: I shall defend myself without apology. Of my relations with my two cousins, you are ignorant: in a fit of ill-humour you have attempted to poison them by gratuitous insinuations, which are far more crafty and false than anything with which you can justly charge me. That I happen to be pale, and sometimes to look diffident, is no business of yours. That I am fond of books, and indisposed for common gossip, is still less your business. That I am a 'romancing chit of a girl' is a mere conjecture on your part: I never romanced to you, nor to anybody you know. That I am the parson's niece is not a crime, though you may be narrow-minded enough to think

it so. You dislike me: you have no just reason for disliking me; therefore keep the expression of your aversion to yourself. If at any time, in future, you evince it annoyingly, I shall answer even less scrupulously than I have done now."

She ceased, and sat in white and still excitement. She had spoken in the clearest of tones, neither fast nor loud; but her silver accent thrilled the ear. The speed of the current in her veins was just then as swift as it was viewless.

Mrs. Yorke was not irritated at the reproof, worded with a severity so simple, dictated by a pride so quiet. Turning coolly to Miss Moore, she said, nodding her cap approvingly—"She has spirit in her, after all. Always speak as honestly as you have done just now," she continued, "and you'll do."

"I repel a recommendation so offensive," was the answer, delivered in the same pure key, with the same clear look. "I reject counsel poisoned by insinuation. It is my right to speak as I think proper: nothing binds me to converse as you dictate. So far from always speaking as I have done just now, I shall never address any one in a tone so stern, or in language so harsh, unless in answer to unprovoked insult."

"Mother, you have found your match," pronounced little Jessy, whom the scene appeared greatly to edify. Rose had heard the whole with an unmoved face. She now said, "No: Miss Helstone is not my mother's match—for she allows herself to be vexed: my mother would wear her out in a few weeks. Shirley Keeldar manages better. Mother, you have never hurt Miss Keeldar's feelings yet. She wears armour under her silk dress that you cannot penetrate."

Mrs. Yorke often complained that her children were mutinous. It was strange, that with all her strictness, with all her "strong-mindedness," she could gain no command over them: a look from their father had more influence with them than a lecture from her.

Miss Moore—to whom the position of witness to an altercation in which she took no part was highly displeasing, as being an unimportant secondary post— now, rallying her dignity, prepared to utter a discourse which was to prove both parties in the wrong, and to make it clear to each disputant that she had reason to be ashamed of herself, and ought to submit humbly to the superior sense of the individual then addressing her. Fortunately for her audience, she had not harangued above ten minutes, when Sarah's entrance with the tea-tray called her attention, first, to the fact of that damsel having a gilt comb in her hair, and a red necklace round her throat, and secondly, and subsequently to a pointed remonstrance, to the duty of making tea. After the meal, Rose restored her to good humour by bringing her guitar and asking for a song, and afterwards engaging her in an intelligent and sharp cross-examination about guitar-playing and music in general.

Jessy, meantime, directed her assiduities to Caroline. Sitting on a stool at her feet, she talked to her, first about religion and then about politics. Jessy was accustomed at home to drink in a great deal of what her father said on these subjects, and afterwards in company to retail, with more wit and fluency than consistency or discretion, his opinions, antipathies, and preferences. She rated Caroline soundly for being a member of the Established Church, and for having an uncle a clergyman. She informed her that she lived on the country, and ought to work for her living honestly, instead of passing a useless life, and eating the bread of idleness in the shape of tithes. Thence Jessy passed to a review of the Ministry at that time in office, and a consideration of its deserts. She made familiar mention of the names of Lord Castlereagh and Mr. Perceval. Each of these personages she adorned with a character that might have separately suited Moloch and Belial. She denounced the war as wholesale murder, and Lord Wellington as a "hired butcher."

Her auditress listened with exceeding edification. Jessy had something of the genius of humour in her nature: it was inexpressibly comic to hear her repeating her sire's denunciations in her nervous northern Doric; as hearty a little Jacobin as ever pent a free mutinous spirit in a muslin frock and sash. Not malignant by nature,

her language was not so bitter as it was racy, and the expressive little face gave a piquancy to every phrase which held a beholder's interest captive.

Caroline chid her when she abused Lord Wellington; but she listened delighted to a subsequent tirade against the Prince Regent. Jessy quickly read in the sparkle of her hearer's eye, and the laughter hovering round her lips, that at last she had hit on a topic that pleased. Many a time had she heard the fat "Adonis of fifty" discussed at her father's breakfast-table, and she now gave Mr. Yorke's comments on the theme—genuine as uttered by his Yorkshire lips.

But, Jessy, I will write about you no more. This is an autumn evening, wet and wild. There is only one cloud in the sky; but it curtains it from pole to pole. The wind cannot rest: it hurries sobbing over hills of sullen outline, colourless with twilight and mist. Rain has beat all day on that church tower: it rises dark from the stony enclosure of its graveyard: the nettles, the long grass, and the tombs all drip with wet. This evening reminds me too forcibly of another evening some years ago: a howling, rainy autumn evening too—when certain who had that day performed a pilgrimage to a grave new-made in a heretic cemetery sat near a wood-fire on the hearth of a foreign dwelling. They were merry and social, but they each knew that a gap, never to be filled, had been made in their circle. They knew they had lost something whose absence could never be quite atoned for so long as they lived: and they knew that heavy falling rain was soaking into the wet earth which covered their lost darling; and that the sad, sighing gale was mourning above her buried head. The fire warmed them; Life and Friendship yet blessed them; but Jessy lay cold, coffined, solitary—only the sod screening her from the storm.

Mrs. Yorke folded up her knitting, cut short the music-lesson and the lecture on politics, and concluded her visit to the cottage, at an hour early enough to ensure her return to Briarmains before the blush of sunset should quite have faded in heaven, or the path up the fields have become thoroughly moist with evening dew.

The lady and her daughters being gone, Caroline felt that she also ought to resume her scarf, kiss her cousin's cheek, and trip away homeward. If she lingered much later, dusk would draw on, and Fanny would be put to the trouble of coming to fetch her: it was both baking and ironing day at the Rectory, she remembered— Fanny would be busy. Still, she could not quit her seat at the little parlour-window. From no point of view could the West look so lovely as from that lattice with the garland of jessamine round it, whose white stars and green leaves seemed now but grey pencil outlines—graceful in form, but colourless in tint—against the gold incarnadined of a summer evening—against the fire-tinged blue of an August sky, at eight o'clock P.M.

Caroline looked at the wicket-gate, beside which holly-oaks spired up tall; she looked at the close hedge of privet and laurel fencing in the garden; her eyes longed to see something more than the shrubs, before they turned from that limited prospect: they longed to see a human figure, of a certain mould and height, pass the hedge and enter the gate. A human figure she at last saw—nay, two: Frederick Murgatroyd went by, carrying a pail of water; Joe Scott followed, dangling on his forefinger the keys of the mill. They were going to lock up mill and stables for the night, and then betake themselves home.

"So must I," thought Caroline, as she half rose and sighed.

"This is all folly—heart-breaking folly," she added. "In the first place, though I should stay till dark, there will be no arrival; because I feel in my heart, Fate has written it down in to-day's page of her eternal book, that I am not to have the pleasure I long for. In the second place, if he stepped in this moment, my presence here would be a chagrin to him, and the consciousness that it must be so would turn half my blood to ice. His hand would, perhaps, be loose and chill, if I put mine into it: his eye would be clouded if I sought its beam. I should look up for that kindling something I have seen in past days, when my face, or my language,

or my disposition had at some happy moment pleased him—I should discover only darkness. I had better go home.''

She took her bonnet from the table where it lay, and was just fastening the ribbon, when Hortense, directing her attention to a splendid bouquet of flowers in a glass on the same table, mentioned that Miss Keeldar had sent them that morning from Fieldhead; and went on to comment on the guests that lady was at present entertaining, on the bustling life she had lately been leading; adding divers conjectures that she did not very well like it, and much wonderment that a person who was so fond of her own way as the heiress, did not find some means of sooner getting rid of this cortège of relatives.

"But they say she actually will not let Mr. Sympson and his family go," she added: "they wanted much to return to the south last week, to be ready for the reception of the only son, who is expected home from a tour. She insists that her cousin Henry shall come and join his friends here in Yorkshire. I daresay she partly does it to oblige Robert and myself.''

"How to oblige Robert and you?" inquired Caroline.

"Why, my child, you are dull. Don't you know—you must often have heard——''

"Please, ma'am," said Sarah, opening the door, "the preserves that you told me to boil in treacle—the congfiters, as you call them—is all burnt to the pan.''

"Les confitures! Elles sont brûlées? Ah, quelle négligence coupable! Coquine de cuisinière—fille insupportable!''

And Mademoiselle, hastily taking from a drawer a large linen apron, and tying it over her black apron, rushed "éperdue" into the kitchen, whence—to speak truth—exhaled an odour of calcined sweets rather strong than savoury.

The mistress and maid had been in full feud the whole day, on the subject of preserving certain black cherries, hard as marbles, sour as sloes. Sarah held that sugar was the only orthodox condiment to be used in that process; Mademoiselle maintained—and proved it by the practice and experience of her mother, grandmother, and great-grandmother—that treacle, "mélasse," was infinitely preferable. She had committed an imprudence in leaving Sarah in charge of the preserving-pan, for her want of sympathy in the nature of its contents had induced a degree of carelessness in watching their confection, whereof the result was—dark and cindery ruin. Hubbub followed: high upbraiding, and sobs rather loud than deep or real.

Caroline, once more turning to the little mirror, was shading her ringlets from her cheek to smooth them under her cottage bonnet, certain that it would not only be useless but unpleasant to stay longer; when, on the sudden opening of the back-door, there fell an abrupt calm in the kitchen: the tongues were checked, pulled up as with bit and bridle. "Was it—was it—Robert?" He often—almost always—entered by the kitchen-way on his return from market. No: it was only Joe Scott, who, having hemmed significantly thrice—every hem being meant as a lofty rebuke to the squabbling womankind—said, "Now, I thowt I heerd a crack?''

None answered.

"And," he continued pragmatically, "as t' maister's comed, and as he'll enter through this hoyle, I *con*sidered it desirable to step in and let ye know. A household o' women is nivver fit to be comed on wi'out warning. Here he is; walk forrard sir. They war playing up queerly, but I think I've quieted 'em.''

Another person—it was now audible—entered. Joe Scott proceeded with his rebukes.

"What d'ye mean by being all i' darkness? Sarah, thou quean, canst t' not light a candle? It war sundown an hour syne. He'll brak' his shins agean some o' yer pots, and tables, and stuff. Tak' tent o' this baking-bowl, sir, they've set it i' yer way, fair as if they did it i' malice.''

To Joe's observations succeeded a confused sort of pause, which Caroline, though she was listening with both her ears, could not understand. It was very brief: a cry

broke it—a sound of surprise, followed by the sound of a kiss: ejaculations, but half articulate, succeeded.

"Mon Dieu! mon Dieu! Est-ce que je m'y attendais?" were the words chiefly to be distinguished.

"Et tu te portes toujours bien, bonne sœur?" inquired another voice—Robert's, certainly.

Caroline was puzzled. Obeying an impulse, the wisdom of which she had not time to question, she escaped from the little parlour, by way of leaving the coast clear, and running upstairs took up a position at the head of the banisters, whence she could make further observations ere presenting herself. It was considerably past sunset now: dusk filled the passage, yet not such deep dusk but that she could presently see Robert and Hortense traverse it.

"Caroline! Caroline!" called Hortense, a moment afterwards, "venez voir mon frère!"

"Strange!" commented Miss Helstone, "passing strange! What does this unwonted excitement about such an everyday occurrence as a return from market portend? She has not lost her senses, has she? Surely the burnt treacle has not crazed her?"

She descended in a subdued flutter: yet more was she fluttered when Hortense seized her hand at the parlour-door, and leading her to Robert, who stood in bodily presence, tall and dark against the one window, presented her with a mixture of agitation and formality, as though they had been utter strangers, and this was their first mutual introduction.

Increasing puzzle! He bowed rather awkwardly, and turning from her with a stranger's embarrassment, he met the doubtful light from a window: it fell on his face, and the enigma of the dream (a dream it seemed) was at its height: she saw a visage like and unlike,—Robert, and no Robert.

"What is the matter?" said Caroline. "Is my sight wrong? Is it my cousin?"

"Certainly, it is your cousin," asserted Hortense.

Then who was this now coming through the passage—now entering the room? Caroline, looking round, met a new Robert—the real Robert, as she felt at once.

"Well," said he, smiling at her questioning, astonished face, "which is which?"

"Ah! this is *you!*" was the answer.

He laughed. "I believe it is *me:* and do you know who *he* is? You never saw him before; but you have heard of him."

She had gathered her senses now.

"It *can* be only one person: your brother, since it is so like you: my other cousin, Louis."

"Clever little Œdipus!—you would have baffled the Sphynx!—but now, see us together. Change places. Change again, to confuse her, Louis. Which is the old love now, Lina?"

"As if it were possible to make a mistake when you speak! You should have told Hortense to ask. But you are not so much alike: it is only your height, your figure, and complexion that are so similar."

"And I am Robert, am I not?" asked the newcomer, making a first effort to overcome what seemed his natural shyness.

Caroline shook her head gently. A soft, expressive ray from her eye beamed on the real Robert: it said much.

She was not permitted to quit her cousins soon: Robert himself was peremptory in obliging her to remain. Glad, simple, and affable in her demeanour (glad for this night, at least), in light, bright spirits for the time, she was too pleasant an addition to the cottage circle to be willingly parted with by any of them. Louis seemed naturally rather a grave, still, retiring man, but the Caroline of this evening, which was not (as you know, reader) the Caroline of every day, thawed his reserve, and cheered his gravity soon. He sat near her, and talked to her. She already knew

his vocation was that of tuition; she learned now he had for some years been the tutor of Mr. Sympson's son; that he had been travelling with him, and had accompanied him to the north. She inquired if he liked his post, but got a look in reply which did not invite or license further question. The look woke Caroline's ready sympathy: she thought it a very sad expression to pass over so sensible a face as Louis's: for he *had* a sensible face,—though not handsome, she considered, when seen near Robert's. She turned to make the comparison. Robert was leaning against the wall, a little behind her, turning over the leaves of a book of engravings, and probably listening, at the same time, to the dialogue between her and Louis.

"How could I think them alike?" she asked herself: "I see now it is Hortense Louis resembles, not Robert."

And this was in part true: he had the shorter nose and longer upper-lip of his sister, rather than the fine traits of his brother: he had her mould of mouth and chin—all less decisive, accurate, and clear than those of the young mill-owner. His air, though deliberate and reflective, could scarcely be called prompt and acute. You felt, in sitting near and looking up at him, that a slower and probably a more benignant nature than that of the elder Moore shed calm on your impressions.

Robert—perhaps aware that Caroline's glance had wandered towards and dwelt upon him, though he had neither met nor answered it—put down the book of engravings, and approaching, took a seat at her side. She resumed her conversation with Louis, but, while she talked to him, her thoughts were elsewhere: her heart beat on the side from which her face was half-averted. She acknowledged a steady, manly, kindly air in Louis; but she bent before the secret power of Robert. To be so near him—though he was silent—though he did not touch so much as her scarf-fringe, or the white hem of her dress—affected her like a spell. Had she been obliged to speak to him *only,* it would have quelled—but, at liberty to address another, it excited her. Her discourse flowed freely: it was gay, playful, eloquent. The indulgent look and placid manner of her auditor encouraged her to ease; the sober pleasure expressed by his smile drew out all that was brilliant in her nature. She felt that this evening she appeared to advantage, and, as Robert was a spectator, the consciousness contented her: had he been called away, collapse would at once have succeeded stimulus.

But her enjoyment was not long to shine full-orbed: a cloud soon crossed it.

Hortense, who for some time had been on the move ordering supper, and was now clearing the little table of some books, etc., to make room for the tray, called Robert's attention to the glass of flowers, the carmine, and snow, and gold of whose petals looked radiant indeed by candlelight.

"They came from Fieldhead," she said, "intended as a gift to you, no doubt: we know who is the favourite there—not I, I'm sure."

It was a wonder to hear Hortense jest; a sign that her spirits were at high-water mark indeed.

"We are to understand, then, that Robert is the favourite?" observed Louis.

"Mon cher," replied Hortense, "Robert—c'est tout ce qu'il y a de plus précieux au monde: à côté de lui, le reste du genre humain n'est que du rebut. N'ai-je pas raison, mon enfant?" she added, appealing to Caroline.

Caroline was obliged to reply, "Yes"—and her beacon was quenched: her star withdrew as she spoke.

"Et toi, Robert?" inquired Louis.

"When you shall have an opportunity, ask herself," was the quiet answer. Whether he reddened or paled Caroline did not examine: she discovered it was late, and she must go home. Home she would go: not even Robert could detain her now.

Chapter XXIV

THE VALLEY OF THE SHADOW OF DEATH

THE future sometimes seems to sob a low warning of the events it is bringing us, like some gathering though yet remote storm, which, in tones of the wind, in flushings of the firmament, in clouds strangely torn, announces a blast strong to strew the sea with wrecks; or commissioned to bring in fog the yellow taint of pestilence, covering white Western isles with the poisoned exhalations of the East, dimming the lattices of English homes with the breath of Indian plague. At other times this Future bursts suddenly, as if a rock had rent, and in it a grave had opened, whence issues the body of one that slept. Ere you are aware you stand face to face with a shrouded and unthought-of Calamity—a new Lazarus.

Caroline Helstone went home from Hollow's Cottage in good health, as she imagined. On waking the next morning she felt oppressed with unwonted languor: at breakfast, at each meal of the following day, she missed all sense of appetite: palatable food was as ashes and sawdust to her.

"Am I ill?" she asked, and looked at herself in the glass. Her eyes were bright, their pupils dilated, her cheeks seemed rosier and fuller than usual. "I look well; why can I not eat?"

She felt a pulse beat fast in her temples: she felt, too, her brain in strange activity: her spirits were raised; hundreds of busy and broken, but brilliant thoughts engaged her mind: a glow rested on them, such as tinged her complexion.

Now followed a hot, parched, thirsty, restless night. Towards morning one terrible dream seized her like a tiger: when she woke, she felt and knew she was ill.

How she had caught the fever (fever it was), she could not tell. Probably in her late walk home, some sweet, poisoned breeze, redolent of honey-dew and miasma, had passed into her lungs and veins, and finding there already a fever of mental excitement, and a languor of long conflict and habitual sadness, had fanned the spark of flame, and left a well-lit fire behind it.

It seemed, however, but a gentle fire: after two hot days and worried nights, there was no violence in the symptoms, and neither her uncle, nor Fanny, nor the doctor, nor Miss Keeldar, when she called, had any fear for her: a few days would restore her, every one believed.

The few days passed, and—though it was still thought it could not long delay— the revival had not begun. Mrs. Pryor, who had visited her daily—being present in her chamber one morning when she had been ill a fortnight—watched her very narrowly for some minutes: she took her hand, and placed her finger on her wrist; then, quietly leaving the chamber, she went to Mr. Helstone's study. With him she remained closeted a long time—half the morning. On returning to her sick young friend, she laid aside shawl and bonnet: she stood a while at the bedside, one hand placed in the other, gently rocking herself to and fro, in an attitude and with a movement habitual to her. At last she said—"I have sent Fanny to Fieldhead to fetch a few things for me, such as I shall want during a short stay here: it is my wish to remain with you till you are better. Your uncle kindly permits my attendance: will it to yourself be acceptable, Caroline?"

"I am sorry you should take such needless trouble. I do not feel very ill, but I cannot refuse resolutely: it will be such comfort to know you are in the house, to see you sometimes in the room; but don't confine yourself on my account, dear Mrs. Pryor. Fanny nurses me very well."

Mrs. Pryor—bending over the pale little sufferer—was now smoothing the hair under her cap, and gently raising her pillow. As she performed these offices, Caroline, smiling, lifted her face to kiss her.

"Are you free from pain? Are you tolerably at ease?" was inquired in a low, earnest voice, as the self-elected nurse yielded to the caress.

"I think I am almost happy."

"You wish to drink? Your lips are parched."

She held a glass filled with some cooling beverage to her mouth.

"Have you eaten anything to-day, Caroline?"

"I cannot eat."

"But soon your appetite will return: it *must* return: that is, I pray God it may!"

In laying her again on the couch, she encircled her in her arms; and while so doing, by a movement which seemed scarcely voluntary, she drew her to her heart, and held her close gathered an instant.

"I shall hardly wish to get well, that I may keep you always," said Caroline.

Mrs. Pryor did not smile at this speech: over her features ran a tremor, which for some minutes she was absorbed in repressing.

"You are more used to Fanny than to me," she remarked, ere long. "I should think my attendance must seem strange, officious?"

"No: quite natural, and very soothing. You must have been accustomed to wait on sick people, ma'am. You move about the room so softly, and you speak so quietly, and touch me so gently."

"I am dexterous in nothing, my dear. You will often find me awkward, but never negligent."

Negligent, indeed, she was not. From that hour, Fanny and Eliza became ciphers in the sick room: Mrs. Pryor made it her domain: she performed all its duties; she lived in it day and night. The patient remonstrated—faintly, however, from the first, and not at all ere long: loneliness and gloom were now banished from her bedside; protection and solace sat there instead. She and her nurse coalesced in wondrous union. Caroline was usually pained to require or receive much attendance: Mrs. Pryor, under ordinary circumstances, had neither the habit nor the art of performing little offices of service; but all now passed with such ease—so naturally, that the patient was as willing to be cherished as the nurse was bent on cherishing; no sign of weariness in the latter ever reminded the former that she ought to be anxious. There was, in fact, no very hard duty to perform; but a hireling might have found it hard.

With all this care, it seemed strange the sick girl did not get well; yet such was the case: she wasted like any snow-wreath in thaw; she faded like any flower in drought. Miss Keeldar, on whose thoughts danger or death seldom intruded, had at first entertained no fears at all for her friend; but seeing her change and sink from time to time when she paid her visits, alarm clutched her heart. She went to Mr. Helstone and expressed herself with so much energy that that gentleman was at last obliged, however unwillingly, to admit the idea that his niece was ill of something more than a migraine; and when Mrs. Pryor came and quietly demanded a physician, he said she might send for two if she liked. One came, but that one was an oracle: he delivered a dark saying of which the future was to solve the mystery, wrote some prescriptions, gave some directions—the whole with an air of crushing authority—pocketed his fee, and went. Probably, he knew well enough he could do no good; but didn't like to say so.

Still, no rumour of serious illness got wind in the neighbourhood. At Hollow's Cottage it was thought that Caroline had only a severe cold, she having written a note to Hortense to that effect; and Mademoiselle contented herself with sending two pots of currant jam, a receipt for a tisane, and a note of advice.

Mrs. Yorke being told that a physician had been summoned, sneered at the hypochondriac fancies of the rich and idle, who, she said, having nothing but themselves to think about, must needs send for a doctor if only so much as their little finger ached.

The "rich and idle," represented in the person of Caroline, were meantime falling fast into a condition of prostration, whose quickly consummated debility

puzzled all who witnessed it, except one; for that one alone reflected how liable is the undermined structure to sink in sudden ruin.

Sick people often have fancies inscrutable to ordinary attendants, and Caroline had one which even her tender nurse could not at first explain. On a certain day in the week, at a certain hour, she would—whether worse or better—entreat to be taken up and dressed, and suffered to sit in her chair near the window. This station she would retain till noon was past: whatever degree of exhaustion or debility her wan aspect betrayed, she still softly put off all persuasion to seek repose until the church-clock had duly tolled mid-day: the twelve strokes sounded, she grew docile, and would meekly lie down. Returned to the couch, she usually buried her face deep in the pillow, and drew the coverlets close round her, as if to shut out the world and sun, of which she was tired: more than once, as she thus lay, a slight convulsion shook the sick-bed, and a faint sob broke the silence round it. These things were not unnoted by Mrs. Pryor.

One Tuesday morning, as usual, she had asked leave to rise, and now she sat wrapped in her white dressing-gown, leaning forward in the easy-chair, gazing steadily and patiently from the lattice. Mrs. Pryor was seated a little behind, knitting as it seemed, but, in truth, watching her. A change crossed her pale mournful brow, animating its languor; a light shot into her faded eyes, reviving their lustre; she half rose and looked earnestly out. Mrs. Pryor, drawing softly near, glanced over her shoulder. From this window was visible the churchyard, beyond it the road, and there, riding sharply by, appeared a horseman. The figure was not yet too remote for recognition; Mrs. Pryor had long sight; she knew Mr. Moore. Just as an intercepting rising ground concealed him from view, the clock struck twelve.

"May I lie down again?" asked Caroline.

Her nurse assisted her to bed: having laid her down and drawn the curtain, she stood listening near. The little couch trembled, the suppressed sob stirred the air. A contraction as of anguish altered Mrs. Pryor's features; she wrung her hands; half a groan escaped her lips. She now remembered that Tuesday was Whinbury market-day: Mr. Moore must always pass the Rectory on his way thither, just ere noon of that day.

Caroline wore continually round her neck a slender braid of silk, attached to which was some trinket. Mrs. Pryor had seen the bit of gold glisten; but had not yet obtained a fair view of it. Her patient never parted with it: when dressed it was hidden in her bosom; as she lay in bed she always held it in her hand. That Tuesday afternoon the transient doze—more like lethargy than sleep—which sometimes abridged the long days, had stolen over her: the weather was hot: while turning in febrile restlessness, she had pushed the coverlets a little aside; Mrs. Pryor bent to replace them; the small, wasted hand, lying nerveless on the sick girl's breast, clasped as usual her jealously-guarded treasure: those fingers whose attenuation it gave pain to see, were now relaxed in sleep: Mrs. Pryor gently disengaged the braid, drawing out a tiny locket—a slight thing it was, such as it suited her small purse to purchase: under its crystal face appeared a curl of black hair—too short and crisp to have been severed from a female head.

Some agitated movement occasioned a twitch of the silken chain: the sleeper started and woke. Her thoughts were usually now somewhat scattered on waking; her look generally wandering. Half-rising, as if in terror, she exclaimed—"Don't take it from me, Robert! Don't! It is my last comfort—let me keep it. I never tell any one whose hair it is—I never show it."

Mrs. Pryor had already disappeared behind the curtain: reclining far back in a deep arm-chair by the bedside, she was withdrawn from view. Caroline looked abroad into the chamber: she thought it empty. As her stray ideas returned slowly, each folding its weak wings on the mind's sad shore, like birds exhausted,—beholding void, and perceiving silence round her, she believed herself alone. Collected, she was not yet: perhaps healthy self-possession and self-control were to be hers

no more; perhaps that world the strong and prosperous live in had already rolled from beneath her feet for ever: so, at least, it often seemed to herself. In health, she had never been accustomed to think aloud; but now words escaped her lips unawares.

"Oh! I *should* see him once more before all is over! Heaven *might* favour me thus far?" she cried. "God grant me a little comfort before I die!" was her humble petition.

"But he will not know I am ill till I am gone; and he will come when they have laid me out, and I am senseless, cold, and stiff.

"What can my departed soul feel then? Can it see or know what happens to the clay? Can spirits, through any medium, communicate with living flesh? Can the dead at all revisit those they leave? Can they come in the elements? Will wind, water, fire, lend me a path to Moore?

"Is it for nothing the wind sounds almost articulately sometimes—sings as I have lately heard it sing at night—or passes the casement sobbing, as if for sorrow to come? Does nothing, then, haunt it—nothing inspire it?

"Why, it suggested to me words one night: it poured a strain which I could have written down, only I was appalled, and dared not rise to seek pencil and paper by the dim watch-light.

"What is that electricity they speak of, whose changes make us well or ill; whose lack or excess blasts; whose even balance revives? What are all those influences that are about us in the atmosphere, that keep playing over our nerves like fingers on stringed instruments, and call forth now a sweet note, and now a wail—now an exultant swell, and, anon, the saddest cadence?

"*Where is* the other world? In *what* will another life consist? Who do I ask? Have I not cause to think that the hour is hasting but too fast when the veil must be rent for me? Do I not know the Grand Mystery is likely to burst prematurely on me? Great Spirit! in whose goodness I confide; whom, as my Father, I have petitioned night and morning from early infancy, help the weak creation of Thy hands! Sustain me through the ordeal I dread and must undergo! Give me strength! Give me patience! Give me—oh! *give me* FAITH!"

She fell back on her pillow. Mrs. Pryor found means to steal quietly from the room: she re-entered it soon after, apparently as composed as if she had really not overheard this strange soliloquy.

The next day several callers came. It had become known that Miss Helstone was worse. Mr. Hall and his sister Margaret arrived: both, after they had been in the sick-room, quitted it in tears; they had found the patient more altered than they expected. Hortense Moore came. Caroline seemed stimulated by her presence: she assured her, smiling, she was not dangerously ill; she talked to her in a low voice, but cheerfully: during her stay, excitement kept up the flush of her complexion: she looked better.

"How is Mr. Robert?" asked Mrs. Pryor, as Hortense was preparing to take leave.

"He was very well when he left."

"Left! Is he gone from home?"

It was then explained that some police intelligence about the rioters of whom he was in pursuit, had, that morning, called him away to Birmingham, and probably a fortnight might elapse ere he returned.

"He is not aware that Miss Helstone is very ill?"

"Oh! no. He thought, like me, that she had only a bad cold."

After this visit, Mrs. Pryor took care not to approach Caroline's couch for above an hour: she heard her weep, and dared not look on her tears.

As evening closed in, she brought her some tea. Caroline, opening her eyes from a moment's slumber, viewed her nurse with an unrecognising glance.

"I smelt the honeysuckles in the glen this summer morning," she said, "as I stood at the counting-house window."

Strange words like these from pallid lips pierce a loving listener's heart more poignantly than steel. They sound romantic, perhaps, in books: in real life, they are harrowing.

"My darling, do you know me?" said Mrs. Pryor.

"I went in to call Robert to breakfast: I have been with him in the garden: he asked me to go: a heavy dew has refreshed the flowers: the peaches are ripening."

"My darling! my darling!" again and again repeated the nurse.

"I thought it was daylight—long after sunrise: it looks dark—is the moon now set?"

That moon, lately risen, was gazing full and mild upon her: floating in deep blue space, it watched her unclouded.

"Then it is not morning? I am not at the cottage? Who is this?—I see a shape at my bedside."

"It is myself—it is your friend—your nurse—your—— Lean your head on my shoulder: collect yourself." (In a lower tone.) "O God, take pity! Give *her* life, and *me* strength! Send me courage—teach me words!"

Some minutes passed in silence. The patient lay mute and passive in the trembling arms—on the throbbing bosom of the nurse.

"I am better now," whispered Caroline at last, "much better—I feel where I am: this is Mrs. Pryor near me: I was dreaming—I talk when I wake up from dreams: people often do in illness. How fast your heart beats, ma'am! Do not be afraid."

"It is not fear, child; only a little anxiety, which will pass. I have brought you some tea, Cary; your uncle made it himself. You know he says he can make a better cup of tea than any housewife can. Taste it. He is concerned to hear that you eat so little: he would be glad if you had a better appetite."

"I am thirsty: let me drink."

She drank eagerly.

"What o'clock is it, ma'am?" she asked.

"Past nine."

"Not later? Oh! I have yet a long night before me: but the tea has made me strong: I will sit up."

Mrs. Pryor raised her, and arranged her pillows.

"Thank Heaven! I am not always equally miserable, and ill, and hopeless. The afternoon has been bad since Hortense went: perhaps the evening may be better. It is a fine night, I think? The moon shines clear."

"Very fine: a perfect summer night. The old church-tower gleams white almost as silver."

"And does the churchyard look peaceful?"

"Yes, and the garden also: dew glistens on the foliage."

"Can you see many long weeds and nettles amongst the graves; or do they look turfy and flowery?"

"I see closed daisy-heads, gleaming like pearls on some mounds. Thomas has mown down the dock-leaves and rank grass, and cleared all away."

"I always like that to be done: it soothes one's mind to see the place in order: and, I dare say, within the church just now that moonlight shines as softly as in my room. It will fall through the east window full on the Helstone monument. When I close my eyes I seem to see poor papa's epitaph in black letters on white marble. There is plenty of room for other inscriptions underneath."

"William Farren came to look after your flowers this morning: he was afraid, now you cannot tend them yourself, they would be neglected. He has taken two of your favourite plants home to nurse for you."

"If I were to make a will, I would leave William all my plants; Shirley my trinkets—except one, which must not be taken off my neck: and you, ma'am, my books." (After a pause.) "Mrs. Pryor, I feel a longing wish for something."

"For what, Caroline?"

"You know I always delight to hear you sing: sing me a hymn just now: sing that hymn which begins:

> *Our God, our help in ages past,—*
> *Our hope for years to come;*
> *Our shelter from the stormy blast;*
> *Our refuge, haven, home!"*

Mrs. Pryor at once complied.

No wonder Caroline liked to hear her sing: her voice, even in speaking, was sweet and silver clear; in song it was almost divine: neither flute nor dulcimer has tones so pure. But the tone was secondary compared to the expression which trembled through: a tender vibration from a feeling heart.

The servants in the kitchen, hearing the strain, stole to the stair-foot to listen: even old Helstone, as he walked in the garden, pondering over the unaccountable and feeble nature of women, stood still amongst his borders to catch the mournful melody more distinctly. Why it reminded him of his forgotten dead wife, he could not tell; nor why it made him more concerned than he had hitherto been for Caroline's fading girlhood. He was glad to recollect that he had promised to pay Wynne, the magistrate, a visit that evening. Low spirits and gloomy thoughts were very much his aversions: when they attacked him he usually found means to make them march in double-quick time. The hymn followed him faintly as he crossed the fields: he hastened his customary sharp pace, that he might get beyond its reach.

> *Thy word commands our flesh to dust,—*
> *"Return, ye sons of men";*
> *All nations rose from earth at first*
> *And turn to earth again.*
>
> *A thousand ages in Thy sight*
> *Are like an evening gone;*
> *Short as the watch that ends the night*
> *Before the rising sun.*
>
> *Time, like an ever-rolling stream,*
> *Bears all its sons away;*
> *They fly, forgotten, as a dream*
> *Dies at the opening day.*
>
> *Like flowery fields, the nations stand,*
> *Fresh in the morning light;*
> *The flowers beneath the mower's hand*
> *Lie withering ere 'tis night.*
>
> *Our God, our help in ages past,—*
> *Our hope for years to come;*
> *Be Thou our guard while troubles last,—*
> *O Father, be our home!*

"Now sing a song—a Scottish song," suggested Caroline when the hymn was over,—" 'Ye banks and braes o' bonny Doon.' "

Again Mrs. Pryor obeyed, or essayed to obey. At the close of the first stanza she stopped: she could get no further: her full heart flowed over.

"You are weeping at the pathos of the air: come here, and I will comfort you," said Caroline, in a pitying accent. Mrs. Pryor came: she sat down on the edge of her patient's bed, and allowed the wasted arms to encircle her.

"You often soothe me, let me soothe you," murmured the young girl, kissing her cheek, "I hope," she added, "it is not for me you weep?"

No answer followed.

"Do you think I shall not get better? I do not feel *very* ill—only weak."

"But your mind, Caroline: your mind is crushed: your heart is almost broken, you have been so neglected, so repulsed, left so desolate."

"I believe grief is, and always has been, my worst ailment. I sometimes think, if an abundant gush of happiness came on me, I could revive yet."

"Do you wish to live?"

"I have no object in life."

"You love me, Caroline?"

"Very much,—very truly,—inexpressibly sometimes: just now I feel as if I could almost grow to your heart."

"I will return directly, dear," remarked Mrs. Pryor, as she laid Caroline down.

Quitting her, she glided to the door, softly turned the key in the lock, ascertained that it was fast, and came back. She bent over her. She threw back the curtain to admit the moonlight more freely. She gazed intently on her face.

"Then, if you love me," said she, speaking quickly, with an altered voice: "if you feel as if—to use your own words—you could 'grow to my heart,' it will be neither shock nor pain for you to know that *that* heart is the source whence yours was filled: that from *my* veins issued the tide which flows in *yours;* that you are *mine*—my daughter—my own child."

"Mrs. Pryor——"

"My own child!"

"That is—that means—you have adopted me?"

"It means that, if I have given you nothing else, I at least gave you life; that I bore you—nursed you; that I am your true mother; no other woman can claim the title—it is *mine*."

"But Mrs. James Helstone—but my father's wife, whom I do not remember ever to have seen, she is my mother?"

"She *is* your mother: James Helstone was *my* husband. I say you are *mine*. I have proved it. I thought perhaps you were all his, which would have been a cruel dispensation for me: I find it is *not* so. God permitted me to be the parent of my child's mind; it belongs to me: it is my property—my *right*. These features are James's own. He had a fine face when he was young, and not altered by error. Papa, my darling, gave you your blue eyes and soft brown hair: he gave you the oval of your face and the regularity of your lineaments; the outside *he* conferred; but the heart and the brain are *mine*: the germs are from *me*, and they are improved, they are developed to excellence. I esteem and approve my child as highly as I do most fondly love her."

"Is what I hear true? Is it no dream?"

"I wish it were as true that the substance and colour of health were restored to your cheek."

"My own mother! is she one I can be so fond of as I can of you? People generally did not like her, so I have been given to understand."

"They told you that? Well, your mother now tells you, that, not having the gift to please people generally, for their approbation she does not care: her thoughts are centred in her child: does that child welcome or reject her?"

"But if you *are* my mother, the world is all changed to me. Surely I can live— I should like to recover——"

"You *must* recover. You drew life and strength from my breast when you were a tiny, fair infant, over whose blue eyes I used to weep, fearing I beheld in your very beauty the sign of qualities that had entered my heart like iron, and pierced through my soul like a sword. Daughter! we have been long parted: I return now to cherish you again."

She held her to her bosom: she cradled her in her arms: she rocked her softly, as if lulling a young child to sleep.

"My mother! My own mother!"

The offspring nestled to the parent; that parent, feeling the endearment and hearing the appeal, gathered her closer still. She covered her with noiseless kisses: she murmured love over her, like a cushat fostering its young.

There was silence in the room for a long while.

* * * * * * *

"Does my uncle know?"

"Your uncle knows: I told him when I first came to stay with you here."

"Did you recognise me when we first met at Fieldhead?"

"How could it be otherwise? Mr. and Miss Helstone being announced, I was prepared to see my child."

"It was that then which moved you: I saw you disturbed."

"You saw nothing, Caroline, I can cover my feelings. You can never tell what an age of strange sensation I lived, during the two minutes that elapsed between the report of your name and your entrance. You can never tell how your look, mien, carriage, shook me."

"Why? Were you disappointed?"

"What will she be like? I had asked myself; and when I saw what you were like, I could have dropped."

"Mamma, why?"

"I trembled in your presence. I said I will never own her; she shall never know me."

"But I said and did nothing remarkable. I felt a little diffident at the thought of an introduction to strangers, that was all."

"I soon saw you were diffident; that was the first thing which reassured me: had you been rustic, clownish, awkward, I should have been content."

"You puzzle me."

"I had reason to dread a fair outside, to mistrust a popular bearing, to shudder before distinction, grace, and courtesy. Beauty and affability had come in my way when I was recluse, desolate, young, and ignorant: a toil-worn governess perishing of uncheered labour, breaking down before her time. These, Caroline, when they smiled on me, I mistook for angels! I followed them home, and when into their hands I had given without reserve my whole chance of future happiness, it was my lot to witness a transfiguration on the domestic hearth: to see the white mask lifted, the bright disguise put away, and opposite me sat down—O God! I *have* suffered!"

She sank on the pillow.

"I *have* suffered! None saw—none knew: there was no sympathy—no redemption—no redress!"

"Take comfort, mother: it is over now."

"It is over and not fruitlessly. I tried to keep the word of His patience: He kept me in the days of my anguish. I was afraid with terror—I was troubled: through great tribulation He brought me through to a salvation revealed in this last time. My fear had torment—He has cast it out: He has given me in its stead perfect love. . . . But, Caroline——"

Thus she invoked her daughter after a pause.

"Mother!"

"I charge you, when you next look on your father's monument, to respect the name chiselled there. To you he did only good. On you he conferred his whole treasure of beauties; nor added to them one dark defect. All *you* derived from him is excellent. You owe him gratitude. Leave, between him and me, the settlement of our mutual account: meddle not: God is the arbiter. This world's laws never came near us—never! They were powerless as a rotten bulrush to protect me!—impotent as idiot babblings to restrain him! As you said, it is all over now: the grave lies between us. There he sleeps—in that church! To his dust I say this night, what I have never said before, 'James, slumber peacefully! See! your terrible debt is cancelled! Look! I wipe out the long, black account with my own hand! James, your child atones: this living likeness of you—this thing with your perfect features—this one good gift you gave me has nestled affectionately to my heart, and tenderly called me "mother." Husband! rest forgiven!' "

"Dearest mother, that is right! Can papa's spirit hear us? Is he comforted to know that we still love him?"

"I said nothing of love: I spoke of forgiveness. Mind the truth, child—I said nothing of love! On the threshold of eternity, should he be there to see me enter, will I maintain that."

"Oh, mother! you must have suffered!"

"Oh, child! the human heart *can* suffer. It can hold more tears than the ocean holds waters. We never know how deep—how wide it is, till misery begins to unbind her clouds, and fill it with rushing blackness."

"Mother, forget."

"Forget!" she said, with the strangest spectre of a laugh. "The north pole will rush to the south, and the headlands of Europe be locked into the bays of Australia ere I forget."

"Hush, mother! rest!—be at peace!"

And the child lulled the parent, as the parent had erst lulled the child. At last Mrs. Pryor wept: she then grew calmer. She resumed those tender cares agitation had for a moment suspended. Replacing her daughter on the couch, she smoothed the pillow, and spread the sheet. The soft hair whose locks were loosened, she rearranged, the damp brow she refreshed with a cool, fragrant essence.

"Mamma, let them bring a candle, that I may see you; and tell my uncle to come into this room by-and-by: I want to hear him say that I am your daughter: and, mamma, take your supper here; don't leave me for one minute to-night."

"Oh, Caroline! it is well you are gentle. You will say to me go, and I shall go; come, and I shall come; do this, and I shall do it. You inherit a certain manner as well as certain features. It will be always 'mamma' prefacing a mandate: softly spoken though from you, thank God! Well" (she added, under her breath), "he spoke softly too, once,—like a flute breathing tenderness; and then, when the world was not by to listen, discords that split the nerves and curdled the blood—sounds to inspire insanity."

"It seems so natural, mamma, to ask you for this and that. I shall want nobody but you to be near me, or to do anything for me; but do not let me be troublesome: check me, if I encroach."

"You must not depend on me to check you: you must keep guard over yourself. I have little moral courage: the want of it is my bane. It is that which has made me an unnatural parent—which has kept me apart from my child during the ten years which have elapsed since my husband's death left me at liberty to claim her: it was that which first unnerved my arms and permitted the infant I might have retained a while longer to be snatched prematurely from their embrace."

"How, mamma?"

"I let you go as a babe, because you were pretty, and I feared your loveliness; deeming it the stamp of perversity. They sent me your portrait, taken at eight years old; that portrait confirmed my fears. Had it shown me a sunburnt little rustic—a

heavy, blunt-featured, commonplace child—I should have hastened to claim you; but there, under the silver paper, I saw blooming the delicacy of an aristocratic flower—'little lady' was written on every trait. I had too recently crawled from under the yoke of the fine gentleman—escaped, galled, crushed, paralysed, dying—to dare to encounter his still finer and most fairy-like representative. My sweet little lady overwhelmed me with dismay: her air of native elegance froze my very marrow. In my experience I had not met with truth, modesty, good principle as the concomitants of beauty. A form so straight and fine, I argued, must conceal a mind warped and cruel. I had little faith in the power of education to rectify such a mind; or rather, I entirely misdoubted my own ability to influence it. Caroline, I dared not undertake to rear you: I resolved to leave you in your uncle's hands. Matthewson Helstone I knew, if an austere, was an upright man. He and all the world thought hardly of me for my strange, unmotherly resolve, and I deserved to be misjudged.''

''Mamma, why did you call yourself Mrs. Pryor?''

''It was a name in my mother's family. I adopted it that I might live unmolested. My married name recalled too vividly my married life: I could not bear it. Besides, threats were uttered of forcing me to return to bondage: it could not be; rather a bier for a bed—the grave for a home. My new name sheltered me: I resumed under its screen my old occupation of teaching. At first, it scarcely procured me the means of sustaining life; but how savoury was hunger when I fasted in peace! How safe seemed the darkness and chill of an unkindled hearth, when no lurid reflection from terror crimsoned its desolation! How serene was solitude, when I feared not the irruption of violence and vice.''

''But, mamma, you have been in this neighbourhood before. How did it happen, that when you re-appeared here with Miss Keeldar, you were not recognised?''

''I only paid a short visit, as a bride, twenty years ago; and then I was very different to what I am now—slender, almost as slender as my daughter is at this day: my complexion—my very features are changed; my hair, my style of dress—everything is altered. You cannot fancy me a slim young person, attired in scanty drapery of white muslin, with bare arms, bracelets and necklace of beads, and hair disposed in round Grecian curls above my forehead?''

''You must, indeed, have been different. Mamma, I heard the front door open: if it is my uncle coming in, just ask him to step upstairs, and let me hear his assurance that I am truly awake and collected, and not dreaming or delirious.''

The Rector, of his own accord, was mounting the stairs; and Mrs. Pryor summoned him to his niece's apartment,

''She's not worse, I hope?'' he inquired hastily.

''I think her better; she is disposed to converse—she seems stronger.''

''Good!'' said he, brushing quickly into the room. ''Ha, Cary! how do? Did you drink my cup of tea? I made it for you just as I like it myself.''

''I drank it every drop, uncle: it did me good—it has made me quite alive. I have a wish for company, so I begged Mrs. Pryor to call you in.''

The respected ecclesiastic looked pleased, and yet embarrassed. He was willing enough to bestow his company on his sick niece for ten minutes, since it was her whim to wish it; but what means to employ for her entertainment, he knew not: he hemmed—he fidgeted.

''You'll be up in a trice,'' he observed, by way of saying something. ''The little weakness will soon pass off; and then you must drink port-wine—a pipe, if you can—and eat game and oysters: I'll get them for you, if they are to be had anywhere. Bless me! we'll make you as strong as Samson before we've done with you.''

''Who is that lady, uncle, standing beside you at the bed-foot?''

''Good God!'' he ejaculated. ''She's not wandering—is she, ma'am?''

Mrs. Pryor smiled.

"I am wandering in a pleasant world," said Caroline, in a soft, happy voice, "and I want you to tell me whether it is real or visionary. What lady is that? Give her a name, uncle?"

"We must have Dr. Rile again, ma'am, or better still, MacTurk: he's less of a humbug. Thomas must saddle the pony, and go for him."

"No: I don't want a doctor; mamma shall be my only physician. Now, do you understand, uncle?"

Mr. Helstone pushed up his spectacles from his nose to his forehead, handled his snuff-box, and administered to himself a portion of the contents. Thus fortified, he answered briefly—"I see daylight. You've told her then, ma'am?"

"And is it *true*?" demanded Caroline, rising on her pillow, "Is she *really* my mother?"

"You won't cry, or make any scene, or turn hysterical, if I answer Yes?"

"Cry? I'd cry if you said *No*. It would be terrible to be disappointed now. But give her a name: how do you call her?"

"I call this stout lady in a quaint black dress, who looks young enough to wear much smarter raiment, if she would—I call her Agnes Helstone: she married my brother James, and is his widow."

"And my mother?"

"What a little sceptic it is! Look at her small face, Mrs. Pryor, scarcely larger than the palm of my hand, alive with acuteness and eagerness." (To Caroline.) "She had the trouble of bringing you into the world at any rate: mind you show your duty to her by quickly getting well, and repairing the waste of these cheeks. Heigho! she used to be plump: what she has done with it all, I can't, for the life of me, divine."

"If *wishing* to get well will help me, I shall not be long sick. This morning, I had no reason and no strength to wish it."

Fanny here tapped at the door, and said that supper was ready.

"Uncle, if you please, you may send me a little bit of supper—anything you like, from your own plate. That is wiser than going into hysterics,—is it not?"

"It is spoken like a sage, Cary: see if I don't cater for you judiciously. When women are sensible—and, above all, intelligible—I can get on with them. It is only the vague, superfine sensations, and extremely wire-drawn notions, that put me about. Let a woman ask me to give her an edible or a wearable—be the same a roc's egg or the breastplate of Aaron, a share of St. John's locusts and honey or the leathern girdle about his loins—I can, at least, understand the demand: but when they pine for they know not what—sympathy—sentiment—some of these indefinite abstractions—I can't do it: I don't know it; I haven't got it. Madam, accept my arm."

Mrs. Pryor signified that she should stay with her daughter that evening. Helstone, accordingly, left them together. He soon returned, bringing a plate in his own consecrated hand.

"This is chicken," he said; "but we'll have partridge to-morrow. Lift her up, and put a shawl over her. On my word, I understand nursing. Now, here is the very same little silver fork you used when you first came to the Rectory: that strikes me as being what you may call a happy thought—a delicate attention. Take it, Cary, and munch away cleverly."

Caroline did her best. Her uncle frowned to see that her powers were so limited: he prophesied, however, great things for the future; and as she praised the morsel he had brought, and smiled gratefully in his face, he stooped over her pillow, kissed her, and said, with a broken, rugged accent—"Good night, bairnie! God bless thee!"

Caroline enjoyed such peaceful rest that night, circled by her mother's arms, and pillowed on her breast, that she forgot to wish for any other stay; and though more than one feverish dream came to her in slumber, yet, when she woke up panting,

so happy and contented a feeling returned with returning consciousness, that her agitation was soothed almost as soon as felt.

As to the mother, she spent the night like Jacob at Peniel. Till break of day, she wrestled with God in earnest prayer.

Chapter XXV

THE WEST WIND BLOWS

NOT always do those who dare such divine conflict prevail. Night after night the sweat of agony may burst dark on the forehead; the supplicant may cry for mercy with that soundless voice the soul utters when its appeal is to the Invisible. "Spare my beloved," it may implore. "Heal my life's life. Rend not from me what long affection entwines with my whole nature. God of heaven—bend—hear—be clement!" And after this cry and strife, the sun may rise and see him worsted. That opening morn, which used to salute him with the whisper of zephyrs, the carol of skylarks, may breathe, as its first accents, from the dear lips which colour and heat have quitted—"Oh! I have had a suffering night. This morning I am worse. I have tried to rise. I cannot. Dreams I am unused to have troubled me."

Then the watcher approaches the patient's pillow, and sees a new and strange moulding of the familiar features, feels at once that the insufferable moment draws nigh, knows that it is God's will his idol shall be broken, and bends his head, and subdues his soul to the sentence he cannot avert, and scarce can bear.

Happy Mrs. Pryor! She was still praying, unconscious that the summer sun hung above the hills, when her child softly woke in her arms. No piteous, unconscious moaning—sound which so wastes our strength that, even if we have sworn to be firm, a rush of unconquerable tears sweeps away the oath—preceded her waking. No space of deaf apathy followed. The first words spoken were not those of one becoming estranged from this world, and already permitted to stray at times into realms foreign to the living. Caroline evidently remembered with clearness what had happened.

"Mamma, I have slept *so* well, I only dreamed and woke twice."

Mrs. Pryor rose with a start, that her daughter might not see the joyful tears called into her eyes by that affectionate word "mamma," and the welcome assurance that followed it.

For many days the mother dared rejoice only with trembling. That first revival seemed like the flicker of a dying lamp: if the flame streamed up bright one moment, the next it sank dim in the socket. Exhaustion followed close on excitement.

There was always a touching endeavour to *appear* better, but too often ability refused to second will; too often the attempt to bear up failed: the effort to eat, to talk, to look cheerful, was unsuccessful. Many an hour passed, during which Mrs. Pryor feared that the chords of life could never more be strengthened, though the time of their breaking might be deferred.

During this space the mother and daughter seemed left almost alone in the neighbourhood. It was the close of August: the weather was fine—that is to say, it was very dry and very dusty, for an arid wind had been blowing from the east this month past: very cloudless, too, though a pale haze, stationary in the atmosphere, seemed to rob of all depth of tone the blue of heaven, of all freshness the verdure of earth, and of all glow the light of day. Almost every family in Briarfield was absent on an excursion. Miss Keeldar and her friends were at the sea-side; so were Mrs. Yorke's household. Mr. Hall and Louis Moore, between whom a spontaneous intimacy seemed to have arisen, the result, probably, of harmony of views and temperament, were gone "up north" on a pedestrian excursion to the Lakes. Even

Hortense, who would fain have stayed at home and aided Mrs. Pryor in nursing Caroline, had been so earnestly entreated by Miss Mann to accompany her once more to Wormwood Wells, in the hope of alleviating sufferings greatly aggravated by the insalubrious weather, that she felt obliged to comply; indeed, it was not in her nature to refuse a request that at once appealed to her goodness of heart,— and—by a confession of dependency—flattered her *amour-propre*. As for Robert, from Birmingham he had gone on to London, where he still sojourned.

So long as the breath of Asiatic deserts parched Caroline's lips and fevered her veins, her physical convalescence could not keep pace with her returning mental tranquillity: but there came a day when the wind ceased to sob at the eastern gable of the Rectory, and at the oriel window of the church. A little cloud like a man's hand arose in the west: gusts from the same quarter drove it on and spread it wide; wet and tempest prevailed a while. When that was over the sun broke out genially, heaven regained its azure, and earth its green; the livid cholera-tint had vanished from the face of nature: the hills rose clear round the horizon, absolved from that pale malaria-haze.

Caroline's youth could now be of some avail to her, and so could her mother's nurture: both—crowned by God's blessing, sent in the pure west wind blowing soft as fresh through the ever-open chamber lattice—rekindled her long-languishing energies. At last Mrs. Pryor saw that it was permitted to hope—a genuine, material convalescence had commenced. It was not merely Caroline's smile which was brighter, or her spirits which were cheered, but a certain look had passed from her face and eye—a look dread and indescribable, but which will easily be recalled by those who have watched the couch of dangerous disease. Long before the emaciated outlines of her aspect began to fill, or its departed colour to return, a more subtle change took place: all grew softer and warmer. Instead of a marble mask and glassy eye, Mrs. Pryor saw laid on the pillow a face pale and wasted enough, perhaps more haggard than the other appearance, but less awful; for it was a sick, living girl—not a mere white mould, or rigid piece of statuary.

Now, too, she was not always petitioning to drink. The words "I am *so* thirsty" ceased to be her plaint. Sometimes, when she had swallowed a morsel, she would say it had revived her: all descriptions of food were no longer equally distasteful; she could be induced, sometimes, to indicate a preference. With what trembling pleasure and anxious care did not her nurse prepare what was selected! How she watched her as she partook of it!

Nourishment brought strength. She could sit up. Then she longed to breathe the fresh air, to revisit her flowers, to see how the fruit had ripened. Her uncle, always liberal, had bought a garden-chair for her express use: he carried her down in his own arms, and placed her in it himself, and William Farren was there to wheel her round the walks, to show her what he had done amongst her plants, to take her directions for further work.

William and she found plenty to talk about: they had a dozen topics in common; interesting to them, unimportant to the rest of the world. They took a similar interest in animals, birds, insects, and plants: they held similar doctrines about humanity to the lower creation; and had a similar turn for minute observation on points of natural history. The nest and proceedings of some ground-bees, which had burrowed in the turf under an old cherry-tree, was one subject of interest: the haunts of certain hedge-sparrows, and the welfare of certain pearly eggs and callow fledglings, another.

Had *Chambers's Journal* existed in those days, it would certainly have formed Miss Helstone's and Farren's favourite periodical. She would have subscribed for it; and to him each number would duly have been lent: both would have put implicit faith, and found great savour in its marvellous anecdotes of animal sagacity.

This is a digression; but it suffices to explain why Caroline would have no other hand than William's to guide her chair, and why his society and conversation sufficed to give interest to her garden-airings.

Mrs. Pryor, walking near, wondered how her daughter could be so much at ease with a "man of the people." *She* found it impossible to speak to him otherwise than stiffly. She felt as if a great gulf lay between her caste and his; and that to cross it, or meet him half-way, would be to degrade herself. She gently asked Caroline—"Are you not afraid, my dear, to converse with that person so unreservedly? He may presume, and become troublesomely garrulous."

"William presume, mamma? You don't know him. He never presumes: he is altogether too proud and sensitive to do so. William has very fine feelings."

And Mrs. Pryor smiled sceptically at the naïve notion of that rough-handed, rough-headed, fustian-clad clown having "fine feelings."

Farren, for his part, showed Mrs. Pryor only a very sulky brow. He knew when he was misjudged, and was apt to turn unmanageable with such as failed to give him his due.

The evening restored Caroline entirely to her mother, and Mrs. Pryor liked the evening; for then, alone with her daughter, no human shadow came between her and what she loved. During the day, she would have her stiff demeanour and cool moments, as was her wont. Between her and Mr. Helstone a very respectful but most rigidly ceremonious intercourse was kept up: anything like familiarity would have bred contempt at once in one or both these personages: but by dint of strict civility and well-maintained distance, they got on very smoothly.

Towards the servants, Mrs. Pryor's bearing was not uncourteous, but shy, freezing, ungenial. Perhaps it was diffidence rather than pride which made her appear so haughty; but, as was to be expected, Fanny and Eliza failed to make the distinction, and she was unpopular with them accordingly. She felt the effect produced: it rendered her at times dissatisfied with herself for faults she could not help; and with all else, dejected, chill, and taciturn.

This mood changed to Caroline's influence, and to that influence alone. The dependent fondness of her nursling, the natural affection of her child, came over her suavely: her frost fell away; her rigidity unbent: she grew smiling and pliant. Not that Caroline made any wordy profession of love—that would ill have suited Mrs. Pryor: she would have read therein the proof of insincerity; but she hung on her with easy dependence; she confided in her with fearless reliance: these things contented the mother's heart.

She liked to hear her daughter say "Mamma, do this." "Please, mamma, fetch me that." "Mamma, read to me." "Sing a little, mamma."

Nobody else—not one living thing—had ever so claimed her services, so looked for help at her hand. Other people were always more or less reserved and stiff with her, as she was reserved and stiff with them; other people betrayed consciousness of and annoyance at her weak points: Caroline no more showed such wounding sagacity or reproachful sensitiveness now, than she had done when a suckling of three months old.

Yet Caroline could find fault. Blind to the constitutional defects that were incurable, she had her eyes wide open to the acquired habits that were susceptible of remedy. On certain points she would quite artlessly lecture her parent; and that parent, instead of being hurt, felt a sensation of pleasure in discovering that the girl *dared* lecture her; that she was so much at home with her.

"Mamma, I am determined you shall not wear that old gown any more; its fashion is not becoming: it is too strait in the skirt. You shall put on your black silk every afternoon; in that you look nice: it suits you; and you shall have a black satin dress for Sundays—a real satin—not a satinet or any of the shams. And, mamma, when you get the new one, mind you must wear it."

"My dear, I thought of the black silk serving me as a best dress for many years yet, and I wished to buy you several things."

"Nonsense, mamma: my uncle gives me cash to get what I want: you know he is generous enough; and I have set my heart on seeing you in a black satin. Get it soon, and let it be made by a dressmaker of my recommending: let me choose the pattern. You always want to disguise yourself like a grandmother: you would persuade one that you are old and ugly,—not at all! On the contrary, when well dressed and cheerful, you are very comely indeed. Your smile is so pleasant, your teeth are so white, your hair is still such a pretty light colour. And then you speak like a young lady, with such a clear, fine tone, and you sing better than any young lady I ever heard. Why do you wear such dresses and bonnets, mamma, such as nobody else ever wears?"

"Does it annoy you, Caroline?"

"Very much: it vexes me even. People say you are miserly; and yet you are not, for you give liberally to the poor and to religious societies: though your gifts are conveyed so secretly and quietly, that they are known to few except the receivers. But I will be your maid myself: when I get a little stronger I will set to work, and you must be good, mamma, and do as I bid you."

And Caroline, sitting near her mother, re-arranged her muslin handkerchief, and re-smoothed her hair.

"My own mamma," then she went on, as if pleasing herself with the thought of their relationship, "who belongs to me, and to whom I belong! I am a rich girl now: I have something I can love well, and not be afraid of loving. Mamma, who gave you this little brooch? Let me unpin it and look at it."

Mrs. Pryor, who usually shrank from meddling fingers and near approach, allowed the license complacently.

"Did papa give you this, mamma?"

"My sister gave it me—my only sister, Cary. Would that your aunt Caroline had lived to see her niece!"

"Have you nothing of papa's?—no trinket, no gift of his?"

"I have one thing."

"That you prize?"

"That I prize."

"Valuable and pretty?"

"Invaluable and sweet to me."

"Show it, mamma. Is it here or at Fieldhead?"

"It is talking to me now, leaning on me: its arms are round me."

"Ah! mamma! you mean your teasing daughter, who will never let you alone; who, when you go into your room, cannot help running to seek for you; who follows you upstairs and down, like a dog."

"Whose features still give me such a strange thrill sometimes. I half fear your fair looks yet, child."

"You don't; you can't. Mamma, I'm sorry papa was not good: I do so wish he had been. Wickedness spoils and poisons all pleasant things: it kills love. If you and I thought each other wicked, we could not love each other, could we?"

"And if we could not trust each other, Cary?"

"How miserable we should be! Mother, before I knew you, I had an apprehension that you were not good, that I could not esteem you: that dread damped my wish to see you; and now my heart is elate because I find you perfect,—almost; kind, clever, nice. Your sole fault is that you are old-fashioned, and of that I shall cure you. Mamma, put your work down: read to me. I like your southern accent: it is so pure, so soft. It has no rugged burr, no nasal twang, such as almost every one's voice here in the north has. My uncle and Mr. Hall say that you are a fine reader, mamma. Mr. Hall said he never heard any lady read with such propriety of expression, or purity of accent."

"I wish I could reciprocate the compliment, Cary; but really the first time I heard your truly excellent friend read and preach, I could not understand his broad, northern tongue."

"Could you understand me, mamma? Did I seem to speak roughly?"

"No: I almost wished you had, as I wished you had looked unpolished. Your father, Caroline, naturally spoke well; quite otherwise than your worthy uncle: correctly, gently, smoothly. You inherit the gift."

"Poor papa! When he was so agreeable, why was he not good?"

"Why he was *as* he was—and, happily, of that you, child, can form no conception— I cannot tell: it is a deep mystery. The key is in the hands of his Maker: there I leave it."

"Mamma, you will keep stitching, stitching away: put down the sewing; I am an enemy to it. It cumbers your lap, and I want it for my head: it engages your eyes, and I want them for a book. Here is your favourite—Cowper."

These importunities were the mother's pleasure. If ever she delayed compliance, it was only to hear them repeated, and to enjoy her child's soft, half-playful, half-petulant urgency. And then, when she yielded, Caroline would say archly—"You will spoil me, mamma. I always thought I should like to be spoiled, and I find it very sweet."

So did Mrs. Pryor.

Chapter XXVI

OLD COPY-BOOKS

BY the time the Fieldhead party returned to Briarfield, Caroline was nearly well. Miss Keeldar, who had received news by post of her friend's convalescence, hardly suffered an hour to elapse between her arrival at home and her first call at the Rectory.

A shower of rain was falling gently, yet fast, on the late flowers and russet autumn shrubs, when the garden-wicket was heard to swing open, and Shirley's well-known form passed the window. On her entrance, her feelings were evinced in her own peculiar fashion. When deeply moved, by serious fears or joys, she was not garrulous. The strong emotion was rarely suffered to influence her tongue; and even her eye refused it more than a furtive and fitful conquest. She took Caroline in her arms, gave her one look, one kiss, then said—"You are better."

And a minute after—"I see you are safe now, but take care. God grant your health may be called on to sustain no more shocks!"

She proceeded to talk fluently about the journey. In the midst of vivacious discourse, her eye still wandered to Caroline: there spoke in its light a deep solicitude, some trouble, and some amaze.

"She may be better," it said: "but how weak she still is! What peril she has come through!"

Suddenly her glance reverted to Mrs. Pryor: it pierced her through.

"When will my governess return to me?" she asked.

"May I tell her all?" demanded Caroline of her mother. Leave being signified by a gesture, Shirley was presently enlightened on what had happened in her absence.

"Very good!" was the cool comment. "Very good! But it is no news to me."

"What! Did you know?"

"I guessed long since the whole business. I have heard somewhat of Mrs. Pryor's history—not from herself, but from others. With every detail of Mr. James Helstone's career and character I was acquainted: an afternoon's sitting and conversation with

Miss Mann had rendered me familiar therewith; also he is one of Mrs. Yorke's warning-examples—one of the blood-red lights she hangs out to scare young ladies from matrimony. I believe I should have been sceptical about the truth of the portrait traced by such fingers—both these ladies take a dark pleasure in offering to view the dark side of life—but I questioned Mr. Yorke on the subject, and he said— 'Shirley, my woman, if you want to know aught about yond' James Helstone, I can only say he was a man-tiger. He was handsome, dissolute, soft, treacherous, courteous, cruel'— Don't cry, Cary; we'll say no more about it.''

"I am not crying, Shirley; or if I am, it is nothing—go on: you are no friend if you withhold from me the truth: I hate that false plan of disguising, mutilating the truth.''

"Fortunately, I have said pretty nearly all that I have to say, except that your uncle himself confirmed Mr. Yorke's words: for he too scorns a lie, and deals in none of those conventional subterfuges that are shabbier than lies.''

"But papa is dead: they should let him alone now.''

"They should—and we *will* let him alone. Cry away, Cary, it will do you good: it is wrong to check natural tears; besides, I choose to please myself by sharing an idea that at this moment beams in your mother's eye while she looks at you: every drop blots out a sin. Weep—your tears have the virtue which the rivers of Damascus lacked: like Jordan, they can cleanse a leprous memory.''

"Madam,'' she continued, addressing Mrs. Pryor, "did you think I could be daily in the habit of seeing you and your daughter together—marking your marvellous similarity in many points—observing, pardon me—your irrepressible emotions in the presence and still more in the absence of your child, and not form my own conjectures? I formed them, and they are literally correct. I shall begin to think myself shrewd.''

"And you said nothing?'' observed Caroline, who soon regained the quiet control of her feelings.

"Nothing. I had no warrant to breathe a word on the subject. *My* business it was not: I abstained from making it such.''

"You guessed so deep a secret, and did not hint that you guessed it?''

"Is that so difficult?''

"It is not like you.''

"How do you know?''

"You are not reserved. You are frankly communicative.''

"I may be communicative, yet know where to stop. In showing my treasure, I may withhold a gem or two—a curious unbought, graven stone—an amulet, of whose mystic glitter I rarely permit even myself a glimpse. Good-day.''

Caroline thus seemed to get a view of Shirley's character under a novel aspect. Erelong, the prospect was renewed: it opened upon her.

No sooner had she regained sufficient strength to bear a change of scene—the excitement of a little society—than Miss Keeldar sued daily for her presence at Fieldhead. Whether Shirley had become wearied of her honoured relatives is not known: she did not say she was; but she claimed and retained Caroline with an eagerness which proved that an addition to that worshipful company was not unwelcome.

The Sympsons were Church people: of course, the Rectors' niece was received by them with courtesy. Mr. Sympson proved to be a man of spotless respectability, worrying temper, pious principles, and worldly views; his lady was a very good woman, patient, kind, well-bred. She had been brought up on a narrow system of views—starved on a few prejudices: a mere handful of bitter herbs; a few preferences, soaked till their natural flavour was extracted, and with no seasoning added in the cooking; some excellent principles, made up in a stiff raised-crust of bigotry, difficult to digest: far too submissive was she to complain of this diet, or to ask for a crumb beyond it.

The daughters were an example to their sex. They were tall, with a Roman nose apiece. They had been educated faultlessly. All they did was well done. History, and the most solid books, had cultivated their minds. Principles and opinions they possessed which could not be mended. More exactly-regulated lives, feelings, manners, habits, it would have been difficult to find anywhere. They knew by heart a certain young-ladies'-school-room code of laws on language, demeanour, etc.; themselves never deviated from its curious little pragmatical provisions; and they regarded with secret, whispered horror, all deviations in others. The Abomination of Desolation was no mystery to them: they had discovered that unutterable Thing in the characteristic others call Originality. Quick were they to recognise the signs of this evil; and wherever they saw its trace—whether in look, word, or deed; whether they read it in the fresh vigorous style of a book, or listened to it in interesting, unhackneyed, pure, expressive language—they shuddered—they recoiled: danger was above their heads—peril about their steps. What was this strange thing? Being unintelligible, it must be bad. Let it be denounced and chained up.

Henry Sympson—the only son, and youngest child of the family—was a boy of fifteen. He generally kept with his tutor; when he left him, he sought his cousin Shirley. This boy differed from his sisters; he was little, lame, and pale; his large eyes shone somewhat languidly in a wan orbit: they were, indeed, usually rather dim—but they were capable of illumination: at times, they could not only shine, but blaze: inward emotion could likewise give colour to his cheek and decision to his crippled movements. Henry's mother loved him; she thought his peculiarities were a mark of election: he was not like other children, she allowed; she believed him regenerate—a new Samuel—called of God from his birth: he was to be a clergyman. Mr. and the Misses Sympson, not understanding the youth, let him much alone. Shirley made him her pet; and he made Shirley his playmate.

In the midst of this family circle—or rather outside it—moved the tutor—the satellite.

Yes: Louis Moore was a satellite of the house of Sympson: connected, yet apart; ever attendant—ever distant. Each member of that correct family treated him with proper dignity. The father was austerely civil, sometimes irritable; the mother, being a kind woman, was attentive, but formal; the daughters saw in him an abstraction, not a man. It seemed, by their manner, that their brother's tutor did not live for them. They were learned: so was he—but not for them. They were accomplished: he had talents too, imperceptible to their senses. The most spirited sketch from his fingers was a blank to their eyes; the most original observation from his lips fell unheard on their ears. Nothing could exceed the propriety of their behaviour.

I should have said, nothing could have equalled it; but I remember a fact which strangely astonished Caroline Helstone. It was—to discover that her cousin had absolutely *no* sympathising friend at Fieldhead: that to Miss Keeldar he was as much a mere teacher, as little gentleman, as little a man, as to the estimable Misses Sympson.

What had befallen the kind-hearted Shirley that she should be so indifferent to the dreary position of a fellow-creature thus isolated under her roof? She was not, perhaps, haughty to him, but she never noticed him: she let him alone. He came and went, spoke or was silent, and she rarely recognised his existence.

As to Louis Moore himself, he had the air of a man used to this life, and who had made up his mind to bear it for a time. His faculties seemed walled up in him, and were unmurmuring in their captivity. He never laughed; he seldom smiled; he was uncomplaining. He fulfilled the round of his duties scrupulously. His pupil loved him; he asked nothing more than civility from the rest of the world. It even appeared that he would accept nothing more: in that abode at least; for when his cousin Caroline made gentle overtures of friendship, he did not encourage them; he rather avoided than sought her. One living thing alone, besides his pale, crippled

scholar, he fondled in the house, and that was the ruffianly Tartar; who, sullen and impracticable to others, acquired a singular partiality for him: a partiality so marked that sometimes, when Moore, summoned to a meal, entered the room and sat down unwelcomed, Tartar would rise from his lair at Shirley's feet, and betake himself to the taciturn tutor. Once—but once—she noticed the desertion; and holding out her white hand, and speaking softly, tried to coax him back. Tartar looked, slavered, and sighed, as his manner was, but yet disregarded the invitation, and coolly settled himself on his haunches at Louis Moore's side. That gentleman drew the dog's big, black-muzzled head on to his knee, patted him, and smiled one little smile to himself.

An acute observer might have remarked, in the course of the same evening, that after Tartar had resumed his allegiance to Shirley, and was once more couched near her foot-stool, the audacious tutor by one word and gesture fascinated him again. He pricked up his ears at the word; he started erect at the gesture, and came, with head lovingly depressed, to receive the expected caress: as it was given, the significant smile again rippled across Moore's quiet face.

"Shirley," said Caroline one day, as they two were sitting alone in the summer-house, "did you know that my cousin Louis was tutor in your uncle's family before the Sympsons came down here?"

Shirley's reply was not so prompt as her responses usually were, but at last she answered—"Yes,—of course: I knew it well."

"I thought you must have been aware of the circumstance."

"Well! what then?"

"It puzzles me to guess how it chances that you never mentioned it to me."

"Why should it puzzle you?"

"It seems odd. I cannot account for it. You talk a great deal,—you talk freely. How was that circumstance never touched on?"

"Because it never was." and Shirley laughed.

"You are a singular being!" observed her friend: "I thought I knew you quite well: I begin to find myself mistaken. You were silent as the grave about Mrs. Pryor; and now, again, here is another secret. But why you made it a secret is the mystery to me."

"I never made it a secret: I had no reason for so doing. If you had asked me who Henry's tutor was, I would have told you: besides, I thought you knew."

"I am puzzled about more things than one in this matter: you don't like poor Louis,—why? Are you impatient at what you perhaps consider his *servile* position? Do you wish that Robert's brother were more highly placed?"

"Robert's brother, indeed!" was the exclamation, uttered in a tone like the accents of scorn; and, with a movement of proud impatience, Shirley snatched a rose from a branch peeping through the open lattice.

"Yes," repeated Caroline, with mild firmness; "Robert's brother. He *is* thus closely related to Gérard Moore of the Hollow, though nature has not given him features so handsome, or an air so noble as his kinsman; but his blood is as good, and he is as much a gentleman, were he free."

"Wise, humble, pious Caroline!" exclaimed Shirley ironically. "Men and angels, hear her! We should not despise plain features, nor a laborious yet honest occupation, should we? Look at the subject of your panegyric,—he is there in the garden," she continued, pointing through an aperture in the clustering creepers; and by that aperture Louis Moore was visible, coming slowly down the walk.

"He is not ugly, Shirley," pleaded Caroline; "he is not ignoble; he is sad: silence seals his mind; but I believe him to be intelligent, and be certain, if he had not something very commendable in his disposition, Mr. Hall would never seek his society as he does."

Shirley laughed: she laughed again; each time with a slightly sarcastic sound. "Well, well," was her comment. "On the plea of the man being Cyril Hall's friend and Robert Moore's brother, we'll just tolerate his existence—won't we, Cary? You believe him to be intelligent, do you? Not quite an idiot—eh? Something commendable in his disposition! *id est,* not an absolute ruffian. Good! Your representations have weight with me; and to prove that they have, should he come this way I will speak to him."

He approached the summer-house: unconscious that it was tenanted, he sat down on the step. Tartar, now his customary companion, had followed him, and he crouched across his feet.

"Old boy!" said Louis, pulling his tawny ear, or rather the mutilated remains of that organ, torn and chewed in a hundred battles, "the autumn sun shines as pleasantly on us as on the fairest and richest. This garden is none of ours, but we enjoy its greenness and perfume, don't we?"

He sat silent, still caressing Tartar, who slobbered with exceeding affection. A faint twittering commenced among the trees round: something fluttered down as light as leaves: they were little birds, which, lighting on the sward at shy distance, hopped as if expectant.

"The small brown elves actually remember that I fed them the other day," again soliloquised Louis. "They want some more biscuit: to-day, I forgot to save a fragment. Eager little sprites, I have not a crumb for you."

He put his hand in his pocket and drew it out empty.

"A want easily supplied," whispered the listening Miss Keeldar.

She took from her reticule a morsel of sweet-cake: for that repository was never destitute of something available to throw to the chickens, young ducks, or sparrows; she crumbled it, and bending over his shoulder, put the crumbs into his hand.

"There," said she; "there is a Providence for the improvident."

"This September afternoon is pleasant," observed Louis Moore, as—not at all discomposed—he calmly cast the crumbs on to the grass.

"Even for you?"

"As pleasant for me as for any monarch."

"You take a sort of harsh, solitary triumph in drawing pleasure out of the elements, and the inanimate and lower animate creation."

"Solitary, but not harsh. With animals I feel I am Adam's son: the heir of him to whom dominion was given over 'every living thing that moveth upon the earth.' Your dog likes and follows me; when I go into that yard, the pigeons from your dove-cot flutter at my feet; your mare in the stable knows me as well as it knows you, and obeys me better."

"And my roses smell sweet to you, and my trees give you shade."

"And," continued Louis, "no caprice can withdraw these pleasures from me: they are *mine.*"

He walked off: Tartar followed him, as if in duty and affection bound, and Shirley remained standing on the summer-house step. Caroline saw her face as she looked after the rude tutor: it was pale, as if her pride bled inwardly.

"You see," remarked Caroline apologetically, "his feelings are so often hurt, it makes him morose."

"You see," returned Shirley, with ire, "he is a topic on which you and I shall quarrel if we discuss it often; so drop it hence-forward and for ever."

"I suppose he has more than once behaved in this way," thought Caroline to herself; "and that renders Shirley so distant to him: yet I wonder she cannot make allowance for character and circumstances: I wonder the general modesty, manliness, sincerity of his nature, do not plead with her in his behalf. She is not often so inconsiderate—so irritable."

The verbal testimony of two friends of Caroline's to her cousin's character augmented her favourable opinion of him. William Farren, whose cottage he had visited in company with Mr. Hall, pronounced him a "real gentleman": there was not such another in Briarfield: he—William—"could do aught for that man. And then to see how t' bairns liked him, and how t' wife took to him first minute she saw him: he never went into a house but t' childer wor about him directly: them little things wor like as if they'd a keener sense nor grown-up folks i' finding out folk's natures."

Mr. Hall, in answer to a question of Miss Helstone's, as to what he thought of Louis Moore, replied promptly that he was the best fellow he had met with since he left Cambridge.

"But he is so grave," objected Caroline.

"Grave! The finest company in the world! Full of odd, quiet, out of the way humour. Never enjoyed an excursion so much in my life as the one I took with him to the Lakes. His understanding and tastes are so superior, it does a man good to be within their influence; and as to his temper and nature, I call them fine."

"At Fieldhead he looks gloomy, and, I believe, has the character of being misanthropical."

"Oh! I fancy he is rather out of place there—in a false position. The Sympsons are most estimable people, but not the folks to comprehend him: they think a great deal about form and ceremony, which are quite out of Louis's way."

"I don't think Miss Keeldar likes him."

"She doesn't know him—she doesn't know him; otherwise, she has sense enough to do justice to his merits."

"Well, I suppose she doesn't know him," mused Caroline to herself, and by this hypothesis she endeavoured to account for what seemed else unaccountable. But such simple solution of the difficulty was not left her long: she was obliged to refuse Miss Keeldar even this negative excuse for her prejudice.

One day she chanced to be in the schoolroom with Henry Sympson, whose amiable and affectionate disposition had quickly recommended him to her regard. The boy was busied about some mechanical contrivance: his lameness made him fond of sedentary occupation: he began to ransack his tutor's desk for a piece of wax, or twine, necessary to his work. Moore happened to be absent. Mr. Hall, indeed, had called for him to take a long walk. Henry could not immediately find the object of his search: he rummaged compartment after compartment; and, at last opening an inner drawer, he came upon—not a ball of cord, or a lump of bees' wax—but a little bundle of small marble-coloured *cahiers*, tied with tape. Henry looked at them—"What rubbish Mr. Moore stores up in his desk!" he said: "I hope he won't keep my old exercises so carefully."

"What is it?"

"Old copy-books."

He threw the bundle to Caroline. The packet looked so neat externally, her curiosity was excited to see its contents.

"If they are only copy-books, I suppose I may open them?"

"Oh! yes; quite freely. Mr. Moore's desk is half mine—for he lets me keep all sorts of things in it—and I give you leave."

On scrutiny they proved to be French compositions, written in a hand peculiar but compact, and exquisitely clean and clear. The writing was recognisable: she scarcely needed the further evidence of the name signed at the close of each theme to tell her whose they were. Yet that name astonished her: "Shirley Keeldar, Sympson Grove, ——shire" (a southern county), and a date four years back.

She tied up the packet, and held it in her hand, meditating over it. She half felt as if, in opening it, she had violated a confidence.

"They are Shirley's, you see," said Henry carelessly.

"Did *you* give them to Mr. Moore? She wrote them with Mrs. Pryor, I suppose?"

"She wrote them in my schoolroom at Sympson Grove, when she lived with us there. Mr. Moore taught her French; it is his native language."

"I know. . . . Was she a good pupil, Henry?"

"She was a wild, laughing thing, but pleasant to have in the room: she made lesson-time charming. She leared fast—you could hardly tell when or how. French was nothing to her: she spoke it quick—quick; as quick as Mr. Moore himself."

"Was she obedient? Did she give trouble?"

"She gave plenty of trouble in a way: she was giddy, but I liked her. I'm desperately fond of Shirley."

"*Desperately* fond—you small simpleton: you don't know what you say."

"I am *desperately* fond of her; she is the light of my eyes: I said so to Mr. Moore last night."

"He would reprove you for speaking with exaggeration."

"He didn't. He never reproves and reproves, as girls' governesses do. He was reading, and he only smiled into his book, and said that if Miss Keeldar was no more than that, she was less than he took her to be; for I was but a dim-eyed, short-sighted little chap. I'm afraid I am a poor unfortunate, Miss Caroline Helstone. I am a cripple, you know."

"Never mind, Henry, you are a very nice little fellow; and if God has not given you health and strength, He has given you a good disposition, and an excellent heart and brain."

"I shall be despised. I sometimes think both Shirley and you despise me."

"Listen, Henry. Generally, I don't like schoolboys: I have a great horror of them. They seem to me little ruffians, who take an unnatural delight in killing and tormenting birds, and insects, and kittens, and whatever is weaker than themselves; but you are so different, I am quite fond of you. You have almost as much sense as a man (far more, God wot," she muttered to herself, "than many men); you are fond of reading, and you can talk sensibly about what you read."

"I *am* fond of reading. I know I have sense, and I know I have feeling."

Miss Keeldar here entered.

"Henry," she said, "I have brought your lunch here: I shall prepare it for you myself."

She placed on the table a glass of new milk, a plate of something which looked not unlike leather, and a utensil which resembled a toasting-fork.

"What are you two about," she continued, "ransacking Mr, Moore's desk?"

"Looking at your old copy-books," returned Caroline.

"My old copy-books?"

"French exercise-books. Look here! They must be held precious: they are kept carefully."

She showed the bundle. Shirley snatched it up—"Did not know one was in existence," she said. "I thought the whole lot had long since lit the kitchen-fire, or curled the maid's hair at Sympson Grove. What made you keep them, Henry?"

"It is not my doing: I should not have thought of it: it never entered my head to suppose copy-books of value. Mr. Moore put them by in the inner drawer of his desk: perhaps he forgot them."

"*C'est cela*: he forgot them, no doubt," echoed Shirley. "They are extremely well written," she observed complacently.

"What a giddy girl you were, Shirley, in those days! I remember you so well: a slim, light creature whom, though you were so tall, I could lift off the floor. I see you with your long, countless curls on your shoulders, and your streaming sash. You used to make Mr. Moore lively, that is, at first: I believe you grieved him after a while."

Shirley turned the closely-written pages and said nothing. Presently she observed, "That was written one winter afternoon. It was a description of a snow-scene."

"I remember," said Henry; "Mr. Moore, when he read it, cried 'Voilà le Français gagné!' He said it was well done. Afterwards, you made him draw, in sepia, the landscape you described."

"You have not forgotten then, Hal?"

"Not at all. We were all scolded that day for not coming down to tea when called. I can remember my tutor sitting at his easel, and you standing behind him, holding the candle, and watching him draw the snowy cliff, the pine, the deer couched under it, and the half-moon hung above."

"Where are his drawings, Henry? Caroline should see them."

"In his portfolio: but it is padlocked: he has the key."

"Ask him for it when he comes in."

"You should ask him, Shirley; you are shy of him now: you are grown a proud lady to him, I notice that."

"Shirley, you are a real enigma," whispered Caroline in her ear. "What queer discoveries I make day by day now! I, who thought I had your confidence. Inexplicable creature! even this boy reproves you."

"I have forgotten 'Auld lang syne,' you see, Harry," said Miss Keeldar, answering young Sympson, and not heeding Caroline.

"Which you never should have done. You don't deserve to be a man's morning star, if you have so short a memory."

"A man's morning star, indeed! and by 'a man' is meant your worshipful self, I suppose? Come, drink your new milk while it is warm."

The young cripple rose and limped towards the fire; he had left his crutch near the mantelpiece.

"My poor lame darling!" murmured Shirley, in her softest voice, aiding him.

"Whether do you like me or Mr. Sam Wynne best, Shirley?" inquired the boy, as she settled him in an arm-chair.

"O Harry! Sam Wynne is my aversion! you are my pet."

"Me or Mr. Malone?"

"You again, a thousand times."

"Yet they are great whiskered fellows, six feet high each."

"Whereas, as long as you live, Harry, you will never be anything more than a little pale lameter."

"Yes, I know."

"You need not be sorrowful. Have I not often told you who was almost as little, as pale, as suffering as you, and yet potent as a giant, and brave as a lion?"

"Admiral Horatio?"

"Admiral Horatio, Viscount Nelson, and Duke of Bronti; great at heart as a Titan; gallant and heroic as all the world and age of chivalry; leader of the might of England; commander of her strength on the deep; hurler of her thunder over the flood."

"A great man: but I am not warlike, Shirley: and yet my mind is so restless, I burn day and night—for what—I can hardly tell—to be—to do—to suffer, I think."

"Harry, it is your mind, which is stronger and older than your frame, that troubles you. It is a captive. It lies in physical bondage. But it will work its own redemption yet. Study carefully, not only books but the world. You love nature; love her without fear. Be patient—wait the course of time. You will not be a soldier or a sailor, Henry: but, if you live, you will be—listen to my prophecy—you will be an author—perhaps, a poet."

"An author! It is a flash—a flash of light to me! I will—I *will!* I'll write a book that I may dedicate it to you."

"You will write it, that you may give your soul its natural release. Bless me! what am I saying? more than I understand, I believe, or can make good. Here, Hal; here is your toasted oat-cake—eat and live!"

"Willingly!" here cried a voice outside the open window; "I know that fragrance of meal bread. Miss Keeldar, may I come in and partake?"

"Mr. Hall" (it was Mr. Hall, and with him was Louis Moore, returned from their walk), "there is a proper luncheon laid out in the dining-room, and there are proper people seated round it: you may join that society and share that fare if you please; but if your ill-regulated tastes lead you to prefer ill-regulated proceedings, step in here, and do as we do."

"I approve the perfume, and therefore shall suffer myself to be led by the nose," returned Mr. Hall, who presently entered accompanied by Louis Moore. That gentleman's eye fell on his desk, pillaged.

"Burglars!" said he. "Henry, you merit the ferule."

"Give it to Shirley and Caroline—they did it," was alleged with more attention to effect than truth.

"Traitor and false witness!" cried both the girls. "We never laid hands on a thing, except in the spirit of laudable inquiry!"

"Exactly so," said Moore, with his rare smile. "And what have you ferreted out, in your 'spirit of laudable inquiry'?"

He perceived the inner drawer open.

"This is empty," said he. "Who has taken——"

"Here! here!" Caroline hastened to say; and she restored the little packet to its place. He shut it up; he locked it in with a small key attached to his watch-guard; he restored the other papers to order, closed the repository, and sat down without further remark.

"I thought you would have scolded much more, sir," said Henry. "The girls deserve reprimand."

"I leave them to their own consciences."

"It accuses them of crimes intended as well as perpetrated, sir. If I had not been here, they would have treated your portfolio as they have done your desk; but I told them it was padlocked."

"And will you have lunch with us?" here interposed Shirley, addressing Moore, and desirous, as it seemed, to turn the conversation.

"Certainly, if I may."

"You will be restricted to new milk and Yorkshire oat-cake."

"Va—pour le lait frais!" said Louis, "But for your oat-cake!"—and he made a grimace.

"He cannot eat it," said Henry: "he thinks it is like bran, raised with sour yeast."

"Come, then, by special dispensation, we will allow him a few cracknels; but nothing less homely."

The hostess rang the bell and gave her frugal orders, which were presently executed. She herself measured out the milk, and distributed the bread round the cosy circle now enclosing the bright little schoolroom fire. She then took the post of toaster-general; and kneeling on the rug, fork in hand, fulfilled her office with dexterity. Mr. Hall, who relished any homely innovation on ordinary usages, and to whom the husky oat cake was from custom suave as manna—seemed in his best spirits. He talked and laughed gleefully—now with Caroline, whom he had fixed by his side, now with Shirley, and again with Louis Moore. And Louis met him in congenial spirit: he did not laugh much, but he uttered in the quietest tone the wittiest things. Gravely spoken sentences, marked by unexpected turns and a quite fresh flavour and poignancy, fell easily from his lips. He proved himself to be—what Mr. Hall had said he was—excellent company. Caroline marvelled at his humour, but still more at his entire self-possession. Nobody there present seemed to impose on him a sensation of unpleasant restraint: nobody seemed a bore—a check—a chill to him; and yet there was the cool and lofty Miss Keeldar kneeling before the fire, almost at his feet.

But Shirley was cool and lofty no longer—at least not at this moment. She appeared unconscious of the humility of her present position—or if conscious, it was only to taste a charm in its lowliness. It did not revolt her pride that the group to whom she voluntarily officiated as handmaid should include her cousin's tutor: it did not scare her that while she handed the bread and milk to the rest, she had to offer it to him also; and Moore took his portion from her hand as calmly as if he had been her equal.

"You are overheated now," he said, when she had retained the fork for some time: "let me relieve you."

And he took it from her with a sort of quiet authority, to which she submitted passively—neither resisting him nor thanking him.

"I should like to see your pictures, Louis," said Caroline, when the sumptuous luncheon was discussed. "Would not you, Mr. Hall?"

"To please you, I should; but, for my own part, I have cut him as an artist. I had enough of him in that capacity in Cumberland and Westmoreland. Many a wetting we got amongst the mountains because he would persist in sitting on a camp-stool, catching effects of rain-clouds, gathering mists, fitful sunbeams, and what not."

"Here is the portfolio," said Henry, bringing it in one hand, and leaning on his crutch with the other.

Louis took it, but he still sat as if he wanted another to speak. It seemed as if he would not open it unless the proud Shirley deigned to show herself interested in the exhibition.

"He makes us wait to whet our curiosity," she said.

"You understand opening it," observed Louis, giving her the key. "You spoiled the lock for me once—try now."

He held it: she opened it; and, monopolising the contents, had the first view of every sketch herself. She enjoyed the treat—if treat it were—in silence, without a single comment. Moore stood behind her chair and looked over her shoulder, and when she had done, and the others were still gazing, he left his post and paced through the room.

A carriage was heard in the lane—the gate-bell rang; Shirley started.

"There are callers," she said, "and I shall be summoned to the room. A pretty figure—as they say—I am to receive company: I and Henry have been in the garden gathering fruit half the morning. Oh, for rest under my own vine and my own fig-tree! Happy is the slave-wife of the Indian chief, in that she has no drawing-room duty to perform, but can sit at ease weaving mats, and stringing beads, and peacefully flattening her picaninny's head in an unmolested corner of her wigwam. I'll emigrate to the western woods."

Louis Moore laughed.

"To marry a White Cloud or a Big Buffalo; and after wedlock to devote yourself to the tender task of digging your lord's maize-field, while he smokes his pipe or drinks fire-water."

Shirley seemed about to reply, but here the schoolroom door unclosed, admitting Mr. Sympson. That personage stood aghast when he saw the group around the fire.

"I thought you alone, Miss Keeldar," he said. "I find quite a party."

And evidently from his shocked, scandalised air—had he not recognised in one of the party a clergyman—he would have delivered an extempore philippic on the extraordinary habits of his niece: respect for the cloth arrested him.

"I merely wished to announce," he proceeded coldly, "that the family from De Walden Hall, Mr., Mrs., the Misses, and Mr. Sam Wynne, are in the drawing-room." And he bowed and withdrew.

"The family from De Walden Hall! Couldn't be a worse set," murmured Shirley.

She sat still, looking a little contumacious, and very much indisposed to stir. She was flushed with the fire: her dark hair had been more than once dishevelled

by the morning wind that day; her attire was a light, neatly-fitting, but amply flowing dress of muslin; the shawl she had worn in the garden was still draped in a careless fold round her. Indolent, wilful, picturesque, and singularly pretty was her aspect—prettier than usual, as if some soft inward emotion—stirred who knows how?—had given new bloom and expression to her features.

"Shirley, Shirley, you ought to go," whispered Caroline.

"I wonder why?"

She lifted her eyes, and saw in the glass over the fireplace both Mr. Hall and Louis Moore gazing at her gravely.

"If," she said, with a yielding smile—"if a majority of the present company maintain that the De Walden Hall people have claims on my civility, I will subdue my inclinations to my duty. Let those who think I ought to go, hold up their hands."

Again consulting the mirror, it reflected an unanimous vote against her.

"You must go," said Mr. Hall, "and behave courteously, too. You owe many duties to society. It is not permitted you to please only yourself."

Louis Moore assented with a low "Hear! hear!"

Caroline, approaching her, smoothed her wavy curls, gave to her attire a less artistic and more domestic grace, and Shirley was put out of the room, protesting still, by a pouting lip, against her dismissal.

"There is a curious charm about her," observed Mr. Hall, when she was gone. "And now," he added, "I must away, for Sweeting is off to see his mother, and there are two funerals."

"Henry, get your books; it is leason-time," said Moore, sitting down to his desk.

"A curious charm!" repeated the pupil, when he and his master were left alone. "True. Is she not a kind of white witch?" he asked.

"Of whom are you speaking, sir?"

"Of my cousin Shirley."

"No irrelevant questions. Study in silence."

Mr. Moore looked and spoke sternly—sourly. Henry knew this mood: it was a rare one with his tutor; but when it came he had an awe of it: he obeyed.

Chapter XXVII

THE FIRST BLUE-STOCKING

MISS KEELDAR and her uncle had characters that would not harmonise,—that never had harmonised. He was irritable, and she was spirited: he was despotic, and she liked freedom; he was worldly, and she, perhaps, romantic.

Not without purpose had he come down to Yorkshire: his mission was clear, and he intended to discharge it conscientiously: he anxiously desired to have his niece married; to make for her a suitable match: give her in charge to a proper husband, and wash his hands of her for ever.

The misfortune was, from infancy upwards, Shirley and he had disagreed on the meaning of the words "suitable" and "proper." She never yet had accepted his definition; and it was doubtful whether, in the most important step of her life, she would consent to accept it.

The trial soon came.

Mr. Wynne proposed in form for his son, Samuel Fawthrop Wynne.

"Decidedly suitable! Most proper!" pronounced Mr. Sympson. "A fine unencumbered estate: real substance: good connections. *It must be done!*"

He sent for his niece to the oak parlour; he shut himself up there with her alone; he communicated the offer; he gave his opinion; he claimed her consent.

It was withheld.

"No: I shall not marry Samuel Fawthrop Wynne."

"I ask why? I must have a reason. In all respects he is more than worthy of you."

She stood on the hearth; she was pale as the white marble slab and cornice behind her; her eyes flashed large, dilated, unsmiling.

"And *I* ask in what sense that young man is worthy of *me*?"

"He has twice your money,—twice your common sense;—equal connections,—equal respectability."

"Had he my money counted five score times, I would take no vow to love him."

"Please to state your objections."

"He has run a course of despicable, commonplace profligacy. Accept that as the first reason why I spurn him."

"Miss Keeldar, you shock me!"

"That conduct alone sinks him in a gulf of immeasurable inferiority. His intellect reaches no standard I can esteem:—there is a second stumbling-block. His views are narrow; his feelings are blunt; his tastes are coarse; his manners vulgar."

"The man is a respectable, wealthy man. To refuse him is presumption on your part."

"I refuse, point-blank! Cease to annoy me with the subject: I forbid it!"

"Is it your intention ever to marry, or do you prefer celibacy?"

"I deny your right to claim an answer to that question."

"May I ask if you expect some man of title—some peer of the realm—to demand your hand?"

"I doubt if the peer breathes on whom I would confer it."

"Were there insanity in the family, I should believe you mad. Your eccentricity and conceit touch the verge of frenzy."

"Perhaps, ere I have finished, you will see me overleap it."

"I anticipate no less. Frantic and impracticable girl! Take warning!—I dare you to sully our name by a *mésalliance*!"

"*Our* name! Am *I* called Sympson?"

"God be thanked that you are not! But be on your guard! I will not be trifled with!"

"What, in the name of common law and common sense, would you, or could you do, if my pleasure led me to a choice you disapproved?"

"Take care! take care!" (warning her with voice and hand that trembled alike).

"Why? What shadow of power have *you* over me? Why should I fear you?"

"Take care, madam!"

"Scrupulous care I will take, Mr. Sympson. Before I marry, I am resolved to esteem—to admire—to *love*."

"Preposterous stuff!—indecorous!—unwomanly!"

"To love with my whole heart. I know I speak in an unknown tongue; but I feel indifferent whether I am comprehended or not."

"And if this love of yours should fall on a beggar?"

"On a beggar it will never fall. Mendicancy is not estimable."

"On a low clerk, a play actor, a play-writer, or—or——"

"Take courage, Mr. Sympson! Or what?"

"Any literary scrub, or shabby, whining artist."

"For the scrubby, shabby, whining, I have no taste: for literature and the arts, I have. And there I wonder how your Fawthrop Wynne would suit me? He cannot write a note without orthographical errors; he reads only a sporting paper: he was the booby of Stilbro' grammar school!"

"Unladylike language! Great God!—to what will she come?" He lifted hands and eyes.

"Never to the altar of Hymen with Sam Wynne."

"To what will she come? Why are not the laws more stringent, that I might compel her to hear reason?"

"Console yourself, uncle. Were Britain a serfdom, and you the Czar, you could not *compel* me to this step. *I* will write to Mr. Wynne. Give yourself no further trouble on the subject."

Fortune is proverbially called changeful, yet her caprice often takes the form of repeating again and again a similar stroke of luck in the same quarter. It appeared that Miss Keeldar—or her fortune—had by this time made a sensation in the district, and produced an impression in quarters by her unthought of. No less than three offers followed Mr. Wynne's—all more or less eligible. All were in succession pressed on her by her uncle, and all in succession she refused. Yet amongst them was more than one gentleman of unexceptional character, as well as ample wealth. Many besides her uncle asked what she meant, and whom she expected to entrap, that she was so insolently fastidious.

At last, the gossips thought they had found the key to her conduct, and her uncle was sure of it; and, what is more, the discovery showed his niece to him in quite a new light, and he changed his whole deportment to her accordingly.

Fieldhead had, of late, been fast growing too hot to hold them both; the suave aunt could not reconcile them; the daughters froze at the view of their quarrels: Gertrude and Isabella whispered by the hour together in their dressing-room, and became chilled with decorous dread if they chanced to be left alone with their audacious cousin. But, as I have said, a change supervened: Mr. Sympson was appeased and his family tranquillised.

The village of Nunnely has been alluded to: its old church, its forest, its monastic ruins. It had also its Hall, called the Priory—an older, a larger, a more lordly abode than any Briarfield or Whinbury owned; and, what is more, it had its man of title—its baronet, which neither Briarfield nor Whinbury could boast. This possession—its proudest and most prized—had for years been nominal only: the present baronet, a young man hitherto resident in a distant province, was unknown on his Yorkshire estate.

During Miss Keeldar's stay at the fashionable watering-place of Cliffbridge, she and her friends had met with and been introduced to Sir Philip Nunnely. They encountered him again and again on the sands, the cliffs, in the various walks, sometimes at the public balls of the place. He seemed solitary; his manner was very unpretending—too simple to be termed affable; rather timid than proud: he did not *condescend* to their society—he seemed *glad* of it.

With any unaffected individual, Shirley could easily and quickly cement an acquaintance. She walked and talked with Sir Philip; she, her aunt, and cousins, sometimes took a sail in his yacht. She liked him because she found him kind and modest, and was charmed to feel she had the power to amuse him.

One slight drawback there was—where is the friendship without it?—Sir Philip had a literary turn: he wrote poetry, sonnets, stanzas, ballads. Perhaps Miss Keeldar thought him a little too fond of reading and reciting these compositions; perhaps she wished the rhyme had possessed more accuracy—the measure more music—the tropes more freshness—the inspiration more fire; at any rate, she always winced when he recurred to the subject of his poems, and usually did her best to divert the conversation into another channel.

He would beguile her to take moonlight walks with him on the bridge, for the sole purpose, as it seemed, of pouring into her ear the longest of his ballads: he would lead her away to sequestered rustic seats, whence the rush of the surf to the sands was heard soft and soothing; and when he had her all to himself, and the sea lay before them, and the scented shade of gardens spread round, and the tall shelter of cliffs rose behind them, he would pull out his last batch of sonnets, and read them in a voice tremulous with emotion. He did not seem to know, that though

they might be rhyme, they were not poetry. It appeared by Shirley's downcast eye and disturbed face that she knew it, and felt heartily mortified by the single foible of this good and amiable gentleman.

Often she tried, as gently as might be, to wean him from this fanatic worship of the Muses: it was his monomania—on all ordinary subjects he was sensible enough; and fain was she to engage him in ordinary topics. He questioned her sometimes about his place at Nunnely; she was but too happy to answer his interrogatories at length: she never wearied of describing the antique Priory, the wild sylvan park, the hoary church and hamlet; nor did she fail to counsel him to come down and gather his tenantry about him in his ancestral halls.

Somewhat to her surprise Sir Philip followed her advice to the letter; and actually, towards the close of September, arrived at the Priory.

He soon made a call at Fieldhead, and his first visit was not his last: he said—when he had achieved the round of the neighbourhood—that under no roof had he found such pleasant shelter as beneath the massive oak beams of the grey manor house of Briarfield: a cramped, modest dwelling enough, compared with his own—but he liked it.

Presently, it did not suffice to sit with Shirley in her panelled parlour, where others came and went, and where he could rarely find a quiet moment to show her the latest production of his fertile muse; he must have her out amongst the pleasant pastures, and lead her by the still waters. *Tête-à-tête* ramblings she shunned; so he made parties for her to his own grounds, his glorious forest; to remoter scenes—woods severed by the Wharfe, vales watered by the Aire.

Such assiduity covered Miss Keeldar with distinction. Her uncle's prophetic soul anticipated a splendid future: he already scented the time afar off when, with nonchalant air, and left foot nursed on his right knee, he should be able to make dashingly-familiar allusions to his "nephew the baronet." Now, his niece dawned upon him no longer "a mad girl," but a "most sensible woman." He termed her, in confidential dialogues with Mrs. Sympson, "a truly superior person: peculiar, but very clever." He treated her with exceeding deference; rose reverently to open and shut doors for her; reddened his face, and gave himself headaches, with stooping to pick up gloves, handkerchiefs, and other loose property, whereof Shirley usually held but insecure tenure. He would cut mysterious jokes about the superiority of woman's wit over man's wisdom; commence obscure apologies for the blundering mistake he had committed respecting the generalship, the tactics, of "a personage not a hundred miles from Fieldhead": in short, he seemed elate as any "midden cock on pattens."

His niece viewed his manœuvres, and received his innuendoes, with phlegm: apparently, she did not above half-comprehend to what aim they tended. When plainly charged with being the preferred of the baronet, she said, she believed he did like her, and for her part she liked him: she had never thought a man of rank—the only son of a proud, fond mother—the only brother of doting sisters—could have so much goodness, and, on the whole, so much sense.

Time proved, indeed, that Sir Philip liked her. Perhaps he had found in her that "curious charm" noticed by Mr. Hall. He sought her presence more and more; and, at last, with a frequency that attested it had become to him an indispensable stimulus. About this time, strange feelings hovered round Fieldhead; restless hopes and haggard anxieties haunted some of its rooms. There was an unquiet wandering of some of the inmates among the still fields round the mansion; there was a sense of expectancy that kept the nerves strained.

One thing seemed clear. Sir Philip was not a man to be despised: he was amiable; if not highly intellectual, he was intelligent. Miss Keeldar could not affirm of him—what she had so bitterly affirmed of Sam Wynne—that his feelings were blunt, his tastes coarse and his manners vulgar. There was sensibility in his nature: there was a very real, if not a very discriminating, love of the arts; there was the English

gentleman in all his deportment: as to his lineage and wealth, both were, of course, far beyond her claims.

His appearance had at first elicited some laughing, though not ill-natured, remarks from the merry Shirley. It was boyish: his features were plain and slight; his hair sandy: his stature insignificant. But she soon checked her sarcasm on this point; she would even fire up if any one else made uncomplimentary allusion thereto. He had "a pleasing countenance," she affirmed; "and there was that in his heart which was better than three Roman noses, than the locks of Absalom, or the proportions of Saul." A spare and rare shaft she still reserved for his unfortunate poetic propensity: but, even here, she would tolerate no irony save her own.

In short, matters had reached a point which seemed fully to warrant an observation made about this time by Mr. Yorke, to the tutor, Louis.

"Yond' brother Robert of yours seems to me to be either a fool or a madman. Two months ago, I could have sworn he had the game all in his own hands; and there he runs the country, and quarters himself up in London for weeks together, and by the time he comes back, he'll find himself checkmated. Louis, 'there is a tide in the affairs of men, which, taken at the flood, leads on to fortune; but, once let slip, never returns again.' I'd write to Robert, if I were you, and remind him of that."

"Robert had views on Miss Keeldar?" inquired Louis, as if the idea were new to him.

"Views I suggested to him myself, and views he might have realised, for she liked him."

"As a neighbour?"

"As more than that. I have seen her change countenance and colour at the mere mention of his name. Write to the lad, I say, and tell him to come home. He is a finer gentleman than this bit of a baronet, after all."

"Does it not strike you, Mr. Yorke, that for a mere penniless adventurer to aspire to a rich woman's hand is presumptuous—contemptible?"

"Oh! if you are for high notions, and double-refined sentiment, I've naught to say. I'm a plain, practical man myself; and if Robert is willing to give up that royal prize to a lad-rival—a puling slip of aristocracy—I am quite agreeable. At *his* age, in *his* place, with *his* inducements, I would have acted differently. Neither baronet, nor duke, nor prince, should have snatched my sweetheart from me without a struggle. But you tutors are such solemn chaps: it is almost like speaking to a parson to consult with you."

Flattered and fawned upon as Shirley was just now, it appeared she was not absolutely spoiled—that her better nature did not quite leave her. Universal report had indeed ceased to couple her name with that of Moore, and this silence seemed sanctioned by her own apparent oblivion of the absentee; but that she had not *quite* forgotten him—that she still regarded him, if not with love yet with interest— seemed proved by the increased attention which at this juncture of affairs a sudden attack of illness induced her to show that tutor-brother of Robert's, to whom she habitually bore herself with strange alternations of cool reserve and docile respect: now sweeping past him in all the dignity of the moneyed heiress and prospective Lady Nunnely, and anon accosting him as abashed schoolgirls are wont to accost their stern professors: bridling her neck of ivory, and curling her lip of carmine, if he encountered her glance, one minute; and the next submitting to the grave rebuke of his eye, with as much contrition as if he had the power to inflict penalties in case of contumacy.

Louis Moore had perhaps caught the fever, which for a few days laid him low, in one of the poor cottages of the district, which he, his lame pupil, and Mr. Hall, were in the habit of visiting together. At any rate he sickened, and after opposing to the malady a taciturn resistance for a day or two, was obliged to keep his chamber.

He lay tossing on his thorny bed one evening, Henry, who would not quit him, watching faithfully beside him, when a tap—too light to be that of Mrs. Gill or the housemaid—summoned young Sympson to the door.

"How is Mr. Moore to-night?" asked a low voice from the dark gallery.

"Come in and see him yourself."

"Is he asleep?"

"I wish he could sleep. Come and speak to him, Shirley."

"He would not like it."

But the speaker stepped in, and Henry, seeing her hesitate on the threshold, took her hand and drew her to the couch.

The shaded light showed Miss Keeldar's form but imperfectly, yet it revealed her in elegant attire. There was a party assembled below, including Sir Philip Nunnely; the ladies were now in the drawing-room, and their hostess had stolen from them to visit Henry's tutor. Her pure white dress, her fair arms and neck, the trembling chainlet of gold circling her throat, and quivering on her breast, glistened strangely amid the obscurity of the sick-room. Her mien was chastened and pensive: she spoke gently.

"Mr. Moore, how are you to-night?"

"I have not been very ill, and am now better."

"I heard that you complained of thirst: I have brought you some grapes: can you taste one?"

"No: but I thank you for remembering me."

"Just one."

From the rich cluster that filled a small basket held in her hand, she severed a berry and offered it to his lips. He shook his head, and turned aside his flushed face.

"But what then can I bring you instead? You have no wish for fruit; yet I see that your lips are parched. What beverage do you prefer?"

"Mrs. Gill supplies me with toast and water: I like it best."

Silence fell for some minutes.

"Do you suffer? Have you pain?"

"Very little."

"What made you ill?"

Silence.

"I wonder what caused this fever? To what do you attribute it?"

"Miasma, perhaps—malaria. This is autumn, a season fertile in fevers."

"I hear you often visit the sick in Briarfield, and Nunnely too, with Mr. Hall: you should be on your guard: temerity is not wise."

"That reminds me, Miss Keeldar, that perhaps you had better not enter this chamber, or come near this couch. I do not believe my illness is infectious: I scarcely fear" (with a sort of smile) "*you* will take it; but why should you run even the shadow of a risk? Leave me."

"Patience: I will go soon; but I should like to do something for you before I depart—any little service——"

"They will miss you below."

"No, the gentlemen are still at table."

"They will not linger long: Sir Philip Nunnely is no wine-bibber, and I hear him just now pass from the dining-room to the drawing-room."

"It is a servant."

"It is Sir Philip, I know his step."

"Your hearing is acute."

"It is never dull, and the sense seems sharpened at present. Sir Philip was here to tea last night. I heard you sing to him some song which he had brought you. I heard him, when he took his departure at eleven o'clock, call you out on to the pavement, to look at the evening star."

"You must be nervously sensitive."

"I heard him kiss your hand."

"Impossible!"

"No; my chamber is over the hall, the window just above the front door, the sash was a little raised, for I felt feverish: you stood ten minutes with him on the steps: I heard your discourse, every word, and I heard the salute. Henry, give me some water."

"Let me give it him."

But he half rose to take the glass from young Sympson, and declined her attendance.

"And can I do nothing?"

"Nothing: for you cannot guarantee me a night's peaceful rest, and it is all I at present want."

"You do not sleep well?"

"Sleep has left me."

"Yet you said you were not very ill?"

"I am often sleepless when in high health."

"If I had power, I would lap you in the most placid slumber; quite deep and hushed, without a dream."

"Blank annihilation! I do not ask that."

"With dreams of all you most desire."

"Monstrous delusions! The sleep would be delirium, the waking death."

"Your wishes are not so chimerical: you are no visionary?"

"Miss Keeldar, I suppose you think so: but my character is not, perhaps, quite as legible to you as a page of the last new novel might be."

"That is possible. . . . But this sleep: I *should* like to woo it to your pillow—to win for you its favour. If I took a book and sat down, and read some pages——? I can well spare half an hour."

"Thank you, but I will not detain you."

"I would read softly."

"It would not do. I am too feverish and excitable to bear a soft, cooing, vibrating voice close at my ear. You had better leave me."

"Well, I will go."

"And no good-night?"

"Yes, sir, yes. Mr. Moore, good-night." (Exit Shirley.)

"Henry, my boy, go to bed now: it is time you had some repose."

"Sir, it would please me to watch at your bedside all night."

"Nothing less called for: I am getting better: there, go."

"Give me your blessing, sir."

"God bless you, my best pupil!"

"You never call me your dearest pupil!"

"No, nor ever shall."

Possibly Miss Keeldar resented her former teacher's rejection of her courtesy: it is certain she did not repeat the offer of it. Often as her light step traversed the gallery in the course of a day, it did not again pause at his door; nor did her "cooing, vibrating voice" disturb a second time the hush of the sick-room. A sick-room, indeed, it soon ceased to be; Mr. Moore's good constitution quickly triumphed over his indisposition: in a few days he shook it off, and resumed his duties as tutor.

That "Auld Lang Syne" had still its authority both with preceptor and scholar, was proved by the manner in which he sometimes promptly passed the distance she usually maintained between them, and put down her high reserve with a firm, quiet hand.

One afternoon the Sympson family were gone out to take a carriage airing. Shirley, never sorry to snatch a reprieve from their society, had remained behind,

detained by business, as she said. The business—a little letter-writing—was soon despatched after the yard-gates had closed on the carriage: Miss Keeldar betook herself to the garden.

It was a peaceful autumn day. The gilding of the Indian summer mellowed the pastures far and wide. The russet woods stood ripe to be stript, but were yet full of leaf. The purple of heath-bloom, faded but not withered, tinged the hills. The beck wandered down to the Hollow, through a silent district; no wind followed its course, or haunted its woody borders. Fieldhead gardens bore the seal of gentle decay. On the walks, swept that morning, yellow leaves had fluttered down again. Its time of flowers, and even of fruits, was over; but a scantling of apples enriched the trees; only a blossom here and there expanded pale and delicate amidst a knot of faded leaves.

These single flowers—the last of their race—Shirley culled as she wandered thoughtfully amongst the beds. She was fastening into her girdle a hueless and scentless nosegay, when Henry Sympson called to her as he came limping from the house.

"Shirley, Mr. Moore would be glad to see you in the schoolroom and to hear you read a little French, if you have no more urgent occupation."

The messenger delivered his commission very simply, as if it were a mere matter of course.

"Did Mr. Moore tell you to say that?"

"Certainly: why not? And now, do come, and let us once more be as we were at Sympson Grove. We used to have pleasant school-hours in those days."

Miss Keeldar, perhaps, thought that circumstances were changed since then; however, she made no remark, but after a little reflection quietly followed Henry.

Entering the schoolroom, she inclined her head with a decent obeisance, as had been her wont in former times; she removed her bonnet, and hung it up beside Henry's cap. Louis Moore sat at his desk, turning the leaves of a book, open before him, and marking passages with his pencil; he just moved, in acknowledgment of her curtsey, but did not rise.

"You proposed to read to me a few nights ago," said he. "I could not hear you then; my attention is now at your service. A little renewed practice in French may not be unprofitable: your accent, I have observed, begins to rust."

"What book shall I take?"

"Here are the posthumous works of St. Pierre. Read a few pages of the *Fragments de l'Amazone*."

She accepted the chair which he had placed in readiness near his own—the volume lay on his desk—there was but one between them; her sweeping curls drooped so low as to hide the page from him.

"Put back your hair," he said.

For one moment, Shirley looked not quite certain whether she would obey the request or disregard it: a flicker of her eye beamed furtive on the professor's face; perhaps if he had been looking at her harshly or timidly, or if one undecided line had marked his countenance, she would have rebelled, and the lesson had ended there and then; but he was only awaiting her compliance—as calm as marble, and as cool. She threw the veil of tresses behind her ear. It was well her face owned an agreeable outline, and that her cheek possessed the polish and the roundness of early youth, or, thus robbed of a softening shade, the contours might have lost their grace. But what mattered that in the present society? Neither Calypso nor Eucharis cared to fascinate Mentor.

She began to read. The language had become strange to her tongue; it faltered; the lecture flowed unevenly, impeded by hurried breath, broken by Anglicised tones. She stopped.

"I can't do it. Read me a paragraph, if you please, Mr. Moore."

What *he* read, *she* repeated: she caught his accent in three minutes.

"Très bien," was the approving comment at the close of the piece.
"C'est presque le Français rattrapé, n'est-ce pas?"
"You could not write French as you once could, I dare say?"
"Oh! no. I should make strange work of my concords now."
"You could not compose the *devoir* of *La Première Femme Savante*?"
"Do you still remember that rubbish?"
"Every line."
"I doubt you."
"l will engage to repeat it word for word."
"You would stop short at the first line."
"Challenge me to the experiment."
"I challenge you."

He proceeded to recite the following: he gave it in French, but we must translate, on pain of being unintelligible to some readers.

> And it came to pass when men began to multiply on the face of the earth, and daughters were born unto them, that the sons of God saw the daughters of men that they were fair; and they took them wives of all they chose.

This was in the dawn of time, before the morning stars were set, and while they yet sang together.

The epoch is so remote, the mists and dewy grey of matin twilight veil it with so vague an obscurity, that all distinct feature of custom, all clear line of locality, evade perception and baffle research. It must suffice to know that the world then existed; that men peopled it; that man's nature, with its passions, sympathies, pains, and pleasures, informed the planet and gave it soul.

A certain tribe colonised a certain spot on the globe; of what race this tribe—unknown: in what region that spot—untold. We usually think of the East when we refer to transactions of that date; but who shall declare that there was no life in the West, the South, the North? What is to disprove that this tribe, instead of camping under palm-groves in Asia, wandered beneath island oak-woods rooted in our own seas of Europe?

It is no sandy plain, nor any circumscribed and scant oasis I seem to realise. A forest valley, with rocky sides and brown profundity of shade, formed by tree crowding on tree, descends deep before me. Here, indeed, dwell human beings, but so few, and in alleys so thick branched and over-arched, they are neither heard nor seen. Are they savage?—doubtless. They live by the crook and the bow: half shepherds, half hunters, their flocks wander wild as their prey. Are they happy?—no: not more happy than we are at this day. Are they good?—no: not better than ourselves: their nature is our nature—human both. There is one in this tribe too often miserable—a child bereaved of both parents. None cares for this child: she is fed sometimes, but oftener forgotten: a hut rarely receives her: the hollow tree and chill cavern are her home. Forsaken, lost, and wandering, she lives more with the wild beast and bird than with her own kind. Hunger and cold are her comrades: sadness hovers over, and solitude besets her round. Unheeded and unvalued, she should die: but she both lives and grows: the green wilderness nurses her, and becomes to her a mother: feeds her on juicy berry, on saccharine root and nut.

There is something in the air of this clime which fosters life kindly: there must be something, too, in its dews, which heals with sovereign balm. Its gentle seasons exaggerate no passion, no sense; its temperature tends to harmony; its breezes, you would say, bring down from heaven the germ of pure thought, and purer feeling. Not grotesquely fantastic are the forms of cliff and foliage; not violently vivid the colouring of flower and bird: in all the grandeur of these forests there is repose; in all their freshness there is tenderness.

The gentle charm vouchsafed to flower and tree,—bestowed on deer and dove,—has not been denied to the human nursling. All solitary, she has sprung up straight and graceful. Nature cast her features in a fine mould; they have matured in their pure, accurate first lines, unaltered by the shocks of disease. No fierce dry blast has dealt rudely with the surface of her frame; no burning sun has crisped or withered her tresses: her form gleams ivory-white through the trees; her hair flows plenteous, long, and glossy; her eyes, not dazzled by vertical fires, beam in the shade large and open, and full and dewy: above those eyes, when the breeze bares her forehead, shines an expanse fair and ample,—a clear, candid page, whereon knowledge, should knowledge ever come, might write a golden record. You see in the desolate young savage nothing vicious or vacant; she haunts the wood harmless and thoughtful: though of what one so untaught can think, it is not easy to divine.

On the evening of one summer day, before the Flood, being utterly alone—for she had lost all trace of her tribe, who had wandered leagues away, she knew not where,—she went up from the vale, to watch Day take leave and Night arrive. A crag, overspread by a tree, was her station: the oak-roots, turfed and mossed, gave a seat: the oak-boughs, thick-leaved, wove a canopy.

Slow and grand the Day withdrew, passing in purple fire, and parting to the farewell of a wild, low chorus from the woodlands. Then Night entered, quiet as death: the wind fell, the birds ceased singing. Now every nest held happy mates, and hart and hind slumbered blissfully safe in their lair.

The girl sat, her body still, her soul astir; occupied, however, rather in feeling than in thinking,—in wishing, than hoping,—in imagining, than projecting. She felt the world, the sky, the night, boundlessly mighty. Of all things, herself seemed to herself the centre,—a small, forgotten atom of life, a spark of soul emitted inadvertent from the great creative source, and now burning unmarked to waste in the heart of a black hollow. She asked, was she thus to burn out and perish, her living light doing no good, never seen, never needed,—a star in an else starless firmament,—which nor shepherd, nor wanderer, nor sage, nor priest, tracked as a guide, or read as a prophecy? Could this be, she demanded, when the flame of her intelligence burned so vivid; when her life beat so true, and real, and potent; when something within her stirred disquieted, and restlessly asserted a God-given strength, for which it insisted she should find exercise?

She gazed abroad on Heaven and Evening: Heaven and Evening gazed back on her. She bent down, searching bank, hill, river, spread dim below. All she questioned responded by oracles: she heard,—she was impressed; but she could not understand. Above her head she raised her hands joined together.

"Guidance—help—comfort—come!" was her cry.

There was no voice, nor any that answered.

She waited, kneeling, steadfastly looking up. Yonder sky was sealed: the solemn stars shone alien and remote.

At last, one over-stretched chord of her agony slacked: she thought Something above relented: she felt as if Something far round drew nigher: she heard as if Silence spoke. There was no language, no word, only a tone.

Again—a fine, full, lofty tone, a deep, soft sound, like a storm whispering, made twilight undulate.

Once more, profounder, nearer, clearer, it rolled harmonious.

Yet, again—a distinct voice passed between Heaven and Earth.

"Eva!"

If Eva were not this woman's name, she had none. She rose.

"Here am I."

"Eva!"

"Oh, Night! (it can be but Night that speaks) I am here!"

The voice, descending, reached Earth.

"Eva!"

"Lord!" she cried, "behold thine handmaid!"

She had her religion: all tribes held some creed.

"I come: a Comforter!"

"Lord, come quickly!"

The Evening flushed full of hope: the Air panted; the Moon—rising before—ascended large, but her light showed no shape.

"Lean towards me, Eva. Enter my arms; repose thus."

"Thus I lean, O Invisible, but felt! And what art thou?"

"Eva, I have brought a living draught from heaven. Daughter of Man, drink of my cup!"

"I drink—it is as if sweetest dew visited my lips in a full current. My arid heart revives: my affliction is lightened: my strait and struggle are gone. And the night changes! the wood, the hill, the moon, the wide sky—all change!"

"All change, and for ever. I take from thy vision, darkness: I loosen from thy faculties, fetters! I level in thy path, obstacles: I, with my presence, fill vacancy: I claim as mine the lost atom of life: I take to myself the spark of soul—burning, heretofore, forgotten!"

"Oh, take me! Oh, claim me! This is a god."

"This is a son of God: one who feels himself in the portion of life that stirs you: he is suffered to reclaim his own, and so to foster and aid that it shall not perish hopeless."

"A son of God! Am I indeed chosen?"

"Thou only in this land. I saw thee that thou wert fair: I knew thee that thou wert mine. To me it is given to rescue, to sustain, to cherish, mine own. Acknowledge in me that Seraph on earth, named Genius."

"My glorious Bridegroom! True Dayspring from on high! All I would have, at last I possess. I receive a revelation. The dark hint, the obscure whisper, which have haunted me from childhood, are interpreted. Thou art He I sought. God-born, take me, thy bride!"

"Unhumbled, I can take what is mine. Did I not give from the altar the very flame which lit Eva's being? Come again into the heaven whence thou wert sent."

That Presence, invisible, but mighty, gathered her in like a lamb to the fold; that voice, soft, but all-pervading, vibrated through her heart like music. Her eye received no image: and yet a sense visited her vision and her brain as of the serenity of stainless air, the power of sovereign seas, the majesty of marching stars, the energy of colliding elements, the rooted endurance of hills wide based, and, above all, as of the lustre of heroic beauty rushing victorious on the Night, vanquishing its shadows like a diviner sun.

Such was the bridal-hour of Genius and Humanity. Who shall rehearse the tale of their after-union? Who shall depict its bliss and bale? Who shall tell how He, between whom and the Woman God put enmity, forged deadly plots to break the bond or defile its purity? Who shall record the long strife between Serpent and Seraph? How still the Father of Lies insinuated evil into good—pride into wisdom—grossness into glory—pain into bliss—poison into passion? How the "dreadless Angel" defied, resisted, and repelled? How, again and again, he refined the polluted cup, exalted the debased emotion, rectified the perverted impulse, detected the lurking venom, baffled the frontless temptation—purified, justified, watched, and withstood? How, by his patience, by his strength, by that unutterable excellence he held from God—his Origin—this faithful Seraph fought for Humanity a good fight through time; and, when Time's course closed, and Death was encountered at the end, barring with fleshless arms the portals of Eternity, how Genius still held close his dying bride, sustained her through the agony of the passage, bore her triumphant into his own home—Heaven; restored her, redeemed, to Jehovah—her Maker; and at last, before Angel and Archangel, crowned her with the crown of Immortality.

Who shall, of these things, write the chronicle?

"I never could correct that composition," observed Shirley, as Moore concluded.
"Your censor-pencil scored it with condemnatory lines, whose signification I strove
vainly to fathom."

She had taken a crayon from the tutor's desk, and was drawing little leaves,
fragments of pillars, broken crosses, on the margin of the book.

"French may be half-forgotten, but the habits of the French lesson are retained,
I see," said Louis: "my books would now, as erst, be unsafe with you. My newly
bound St. Pierre would soon be like my Racine: Miss Keeldar, her mark—traced
on every page.

Shirley dropped her crayon as if it burned her fingers.

"Tell me what were the faults of that *devoir?*" she asked. "Were they grammatical
errors, or did you object to the substance?"

"I never said that the lines I drew were indications of faults at all. You would
have it that such was the case, and I refrained from contradiction."

"What else did they denote?"

"No matter now."

"Mr. Moore," cried Henry, "make Shirley repeat some of the pieces she used
to say so well by heart."

"If I ask for any, it will be *Le Cheval Dompté*," said Moore, trimming with
his pen-knife the pencil Miss Keeldar had worn to a stump.

She turned aside her head; the neck, the clear cheek, forsaken by their natural
veil, were seen to flush warm.

"Ah! she has not forgotten, you see, sir," said Henry, exultant. "She knows
how naughty she was."

A smile, which Shirley would not permit to expand, made her lip tremble; she
bent her face, and hid it half with her arms, half in her curls, which, as she stooped,
fell loose again.

"Certainly, I was a rebel!" she answered.

"A rebel!" repeated Henry. "Yes: you and papa had quarrelled terribly, and
you set both him and mamma, and Mrs. Pryor, and everybody, at defiance: you
said he had insulted you——"

"He *had* insulted me," interposed Shirley.

"And you wanted to leave Sympson Grove directly. You packed your things up,
and papa threw them out of your trunk; mamma cried—Mrs. Pryor cried; they both
stood wringing their hands begging you to be patient, and you knelt on the floor
with your things and your upturned box before you, looking, Shirley—looking—
why, in one of *your* passions. Your features, in such passions, are not distorted;
they are fixed, but quite beautiful: you scarcely look angry, only resolute, and in
a certain haste; yet one feels that, at such times, an obstacle cast across your path
would be split as with lightning. Papa lost heart, and called Mr. Moore."

"Enough, Henry."

"No: it is not enough. I hardly know how Mr. Moore managed, except that I
recollect he suggested to papa that agitation would bring on his gout; and then he
spoke quietly to the ladies, and got them away; and afterwards he said to you, Miss
Shirley, that it was of no use talking or lecturing now, but that the tea-things were
just brought into the schoolroom, and he was very thirsty, and he would be glad
if you would leave your packing for the present and come and make a cup of tea
for him and me. You came: you would not talk at first; but soon you softened and
grew cheerful. Mr. Moore began to tell us about the Continent, the war, and
Bonaparte; subjects we were both fond of listening to. After tea he said we should
neither of us leave him that evening: he would not let us stray out of his sight, lest
we should again get into mischief. We sat one on each side of him: we were so
happy. I never passed so pleasant an evening. The next day he gave you, missy,

a lecture of an hour, and wound it up by marking you a piece to learn in Bossuet as a punishment-lesson—*Le Cheval Dompté*. You learned it instead of packing up, Shirley. We heard no more of your running away. Mr. Moore used to tease you on the subject for a year afterwards.''

''She never said a lesson with greater spirit,'' subjoined Moore. ''She then, for the first time, gave me the treat of hearing my native tongue spoken without accent by an English girl.''

''She was as sweet as summer-cherries for a month afterwards,'' struck in Henry: ''a good hearty quarrel always left Shirley's temper better than it found it.''

''You talk of me as if I were not present,'' observed Miss Keeldar, who had not yet lifted her face.

''Are you sure you *are* present?'' asked Moore: ''there have been moments since my arrival here, when I have been tempted to inquire of the lady of Fieldhead if she knew what had become of my former pupil?''

''She is here now.''

''I see her, and humble enough; but I would neither advise Harry, nor others, to believe too implicitly in the humility which one moment can hide its blushing face like a modest little child, and the next lift it pale and lofty as a marble Juno.''

''One man in times of old, it is said, imparted vitality to the statue he had chiselled. Others may have the contrary gift of turning life to stone.''

Moore paused on this observation before he replied to it. His look, at once struck and meditative, said, ''A strange phrase: what may it mean?'' He turned it over in his mind, with thought deep and slow, as some German pondering metaphysics.

''You mean,'' he said at last, ''that some men inspire repugnance, and so chill the kind heart.''

''Ingenious!'' responded Shirley. ''If the interpretation pleases you, you are welcome to hold it valid. *I* don't care.''

And with that she raised her head, lofty in look, and statue-like in hue, as Louis had described it.

''Behold the metamorphosis!'' he said: ''scarce imagined ere it is realised: a lowly nymph develops to an inaccessible goddess. But Henry must not be disappointed of his recitation, and Olympia will deign to oblige him. Let us begin.''

''I have forgotten the very first line.''

''Which I have not. *My* memory, if a slow, is a retentive one. I acquire deliberately both knowledge and liking: the acquisition grows into my brain, and the sentiment into my breast; and it is not as the rapid springing produce which, having no root in itself, flourishes verdurous enough for a time, but too soon falls withered away. Attention, Henry! Miss Keeldar consents to favour you. 'Voyez ce Cheval ardent et impétueux,' so it commences.''

Miss Keeldar did consent to make the effort; but she soon stopped.

''Unless I heard the whole repeated, I cannot continue it,'' she said.

''Yet it was quickly learned, 'soon gained, soon gone,' '' moralised the tutor. He recited the passage deliberately, accurately, with slow, impressive emphasis.

Shirley, by degrees, inclined her ear as he went on. Her face, before turned from him, *re*turned towards him. When he ceased, she took the word up as if from his lips: she took his very tone; she seized his very accent; she delivered the periods as he had delivered them: she reproduced his manner, his pronunciation, his expression.

It was now her turn to petition.

''Recall *Le Songe d'Athalie*,'' she entreated, ''and say it.''

He said it for her; she took it from him; she found lively excitement in the pleasure of making his language her own: she asked for further indulgence; all the old school-pieces were revived, and with them Shirley's old school-days.

He had gone through some of the best passages of Racine and Corneille, and then had heard the echo of his own deep tones in the girl's voice, that modulated itself faithfully on his:—*Le Chêne et le Roseau,* that most beautiful of La Fontaine's

fables, had been recited, well recited by the tutor, and the pupil had animatedly availed herself of the lesson. Perhaps a simultaneous feeling seized them now, that their enthusiasm had kindled to a glow, which the slight fuel of French poetry no longer sufficed to feed; perhaps they longed for a trunk of English oak to be thrown as a Yule log to the devouring flame. Moore observed—"And these are our best pieces! And we have nothing more dramatic, nervous, natural!"

And then he smiled and was silent. His whole nature seemed serenely alight: he stood on the hearth, leaning his elbow on the mantelpiece, musing not unblissfully. Twilight was closing on the diminished autumn day: the schoolroom windows— darkened with creeping plants, from which no high October winds had as yet swept the sere foliage—admitted scarce a gleam of sky; but the fire gave light enough to talk by.

And now Louis Moore addressed his pupil in French; and she answered, at first, with laughing hesitation and in broken phrase: Moore encouraged while he corrected her; Henry joined in the lesson; the two scholars stood opposite the master, their arms round each other's waists: Tartar, who long since had craved and obtained admission, sat sagely in the centre of the rug, staring at the blaze which burst fitful from morsels of coal among the red cinders: the group were happy enough, but—

> *Pleasures are like poppies spread;*
> *You seize the flower—its bloom is shed.*

The dull, rumbling sound of wheels was heard on the pavement in the yard.

"It is the carriage returned," said Shirley; "and dinner must be just ready, and I am not dressed."

A servant came in with Mr. Moore's candle and tea: for the tutor and his pupil usually dined at luncheon time.

"Mr. Sympson and the ladies are returned," she said, "and Sir Philip Nunnely is with them."

"How you did start, and how your hand trembled, Shirley!" said Henry, when the maid had closed the shutter and was gone. "But I know why—don't you, Mr. Moore? I know what papa intends. He is a little ugly man, that Sir Philip. I wish he had not come: I wish sisters and all of them had stayed at De Walden Hall to dine. Shirley should once more have made tea for you and me, Mr. Moore, and we would have had a happy evening of it."

Moore was locking up his desk, and putting away his St. Pierre—"That was *your* plan—was it, my boy?"

"Don't you approve it, sir?"

"I approve nothing Utopian. Look Life in its iron face: stare Reality out of its brassy countenance. Make the tea, Henry; I shall be back in a minute."

He left the room: so did Shirley, by another door.

Chapter XXVIII

PHŒBE

SHIRLEY probably got on pleasantly with Sir Philip that evening, for the next morning she came down in one of her best moods.

"Who will take a walk with me?" she asked, after breakfast. "Isabella and Gertrude— will you?"

So rare was such an invitation from Miss Keeldar to her female cousins that they hesitated before they accepted it. Their mamma, however, signifying acquiescence in the project, they fetched their bonnets, and the trio set out.

It did not suit these three persons to be thrown much together: Miss Keeldar liked the society of few ladies: indeed, she had a cordial pleasure in that of none except Mrs. Pryor and Caroline Helstone. She was civil, kind, attentive even to her cousins; but still she usually had little to say to them. In the sunny mood of this particular morning, she contrived to entertain even the Misses Sympson. Without deviating from her wonted rule of discussing with them only ordinary themes, she imparted to these themes an extraordinary interest: the sparkle of her spirit glanced along her phrases.

What made her so joyous? All the cause must have been in herself. The day was not bright; it was dim—a pale, waning autumn day: the walks through the dun woods were damp; the atmosphere was heavy, the sky overcast; and yet, it seemed that in Shirley's heart lived all the light and azure of Italy, as all its fervour laughed in her grey English eye.

Some directions necessary to be given to her foreman, John, delayed her behind her cousins as they neared Fieldhead on their return; perhaps an interval of twenty minutes elapsed between her separation from them and her re-entrance into the house: in the meantime she had spoken to John, and then she had lingered in the lane at the gate. A summons to luncheon called her in: she excused herself from the meal, and went upstairs.

"Is not Shirley coming to luncheon?" asked Isabella: "she said she was not hungry."

An hour after, as she did not quit her chamber, one of her cousins went to seek her there. She was found sitting at the foot of the bed, her head resting on her hand: she looked quite pale, very thoughtful, almost sad.

"You are not ill?" was the question put.

"A little sick," replied Miss Keeldar.

Certainly she was not a little changed from what she had been two hours before.

This change, accounted for only by those three words, explained no otherwise; this change—whencesoever springing, effected in a brief ten minutes—passed like no light summer cloud. She talked when she joined her friends at dinner, talked as usual; she remained with them during the evening; when again questioned respecting her health, she declared herself perfectly recovered: it had been a mere passing faintness: a momentary sensation, not worth a thought: yet it was felt there was a difference in Shirley.

The next day—the day—the week—the fortnight after—this new and peculiar shadow lingered on the countenance, in the manner of Miss Keeldar. A strange quietude settled over her look, her movements, her very voice. The alteration was not so marked as to court or permit frequent questioning, yet it *was* there, and it would not pass away: it hung over her like a cloud which no breeze could stir or disperse. Soon it became evident that to notice this change was to annoy her. First she shrunk from remark; and, if persisted in, she, with her own peculiar hauteur, repelled it. "Was she ill?" The reply came with decision.

"I *am not.*"

"Did anything weigh on her mind? Had anything happened to affect her spirits?"

She scornfully ridiculed the idea. "What did they mean by spirits? She had no spirits, black or white, blue or grey, to affect."

"Something must be the matter—she was so altered."

"She supposed she had a right to alter at her ease. She knew she was plainer: if it suited her to grow ugly, why need others fret themselves on the subject."

"There must be a cause for the change—what was it?"

She peremptorily requested to be let alone.

Then she would make every efort to appear quite gay, and she seemed indignant at herself that she could not perfectly succeed: brief, self-spurning epithets burst from her lips when alone. "Fool! coward!" she would term herself. "Poltroon!"

she would say: "if you must tremble—tremble in secret! Quail where no eye sees you!"

"How dare you"—she would ask herself—"how dare you show your weakness and betray your imbecile anxieties? Shake them off: rise above them: if you cannot do this, hide them."

And to hide them she did her best. She once more became resolutely lively in company. When weary of effort and forced to relax, she sought solitude: not the solitude of her chamber—she refused to mope, shut up between four walls—but that wilder solitude which lies out of doors, and which she could chase, mounted on Zoë, her mare. She took long rides of half a day. Her uncle disapproved, but he dared not remonstrate: it was never pleasant to face Shirley's anger, even when she was healthy and gay; but now that her face showed thin, and her large eye looked hollow, there was something in the darkening of that face and kindling of that eye which touched as well as alarmed.

To all comparative strangers who, unconscious of the alterations in her spirits, commented on the alteration in her looks, she had one reply—

"I am perfectly well: I have not an ailment."

And health, indeed, she must have had, to be able to bear the exposure to the weather she now encountered. Wet or fair, calm or storm, she took her daily ride over Stilbro' Moor, Tartar keeping up at her side, with his wolf-like gallop, long and untiring.

Twice—three times, the eyes of gossips—those eyes which are everywhere: in the closet and on the hill-top—noticed that instead of turning on Rushedge, the top-ridge of Stilbro' Moor, she rode forwards all the way to the town. Scouts were not wanting to mark her destination there; it was ascertained that she alighted at the door of one Mr. Pearson Hall, a solicitor, related to the Vicar of Nunnely: this gentleman and his ancestors had been the agents of the Keeldar family for generations back: some people affirmed that Miss Keeldar was become involved in business speculations connected with Hollow's Mill; that she had lost money, and was constrained to mortgage her land: others conjectured that she was going to be married, and that the settlements were preparing.

Mr. Moore and Henry Sympson were together in the schoolroom: the tutor was waiting for a lesson which the pupil seemed busy in preparing.

"Henry, make haste! the afternoon is getting on."

"Is it, sir?"

"Certainly. Are you nearly ready with that lesson?"

"No."

"Not *nearly* ready?"

"I have not construed a line."

Mr. Moore looked up: the boy's tone was rather peculiar.

"The task presents no difficulties, Henry; or, if it does, bring them to me: we will work together."

"Mr. Moore, I can do no work."

"My boy, you are ill."

"Sir, I am not worse in bodily health than usual, but my heart is full."

"Shut the book. Come hither, Harry. Come to the fireside."

Harry limped forward; his tutor placed him in a chair: his lips were quivering, his eyes brimming. He laid his crutch on the floor, bent down his head, and wept.

"This distress is not occasioned by physical pain, you say, Harry? You have a grief—tell it me."

"Sir, I have such a grief as I never had before. I wish it could be relieved in some way: I can hardly bear it."

"Who knows but, if we talk it over, we may relieve it? What is the cause? Whom does it concern?"

"The cause, sir, is Shirley: it concerns Shirley."

"Does it? . . . You think her changed?"

"All who know her think her changed: you too, Mr. Moore."

"Not seriously,—no. I see no alteration but such as a favourable turn might repair in a few weeks: besides, her own word must go for something: she says she is well."

"There it is, sir: as long as she maintained she was well, I believed her. When I was sad out of her sight, I soon recovered spirits in her presence. Now . . ."

"Well, Harry, now . . . ? Has she said anything to you? You and she were together in the garden two hours this morning: I saw her talking, and you listening. Now, my dear Harry! if Miss Keeldar has said she is ill, and enjoined you to keep her secret, do not obey her. For her life's sake, avow everything. Speak, my boy!"

"*She* say she is ill! I believe, sir, if she were dying, she would smile, and aver 'Nothing ails me.' "

"What have you learned, then? What new circumstance . . . ?"

"I have learned that she has just made her will."

"Made her will?"

The tutor and pupil were silent.

"She told you that?" asked Moore, when some minutes had elapsed.

"She told me quite cheerfully: not as an ominous circumstance, which I felt it to be. She said I was the only person besides her solicitor, Pearson Hall, and Mr. Helstone and Mr. Yorke, who knew anything about it; and to me, she intimated, she wished specially to explain its provisions."

"Go on, Harry."

" 'Because,' she said, looking down on me with her beautiful eyes,—oh! they *are* beautiful, Mr. Moore! I love them,—I love her! She is my star! Heaven must not claim her! She is lovely in this world, and fitted for this world. Shirley is not an angel; she is a woman, and she shall live with men. Seraphs shall not have her! Mr. Moore—if one of the 'sons of God,' with wings wide and bright as the sky, blue and sounding as the sea, having seen that she was fair, descended to claim her, his claim should be withstood—withstood by me—boy and cripple as I am!"

"Henry Sympson, go on, when I tell you."

" 'Because,' she said, 'if I made no will, and died before you, Harry, all my property would go to you; and I do not intend that it should be so, though your father would like it. But you,' she said, 'will have his whole estate, which is large—larger than Fieldhead; your sisters will have nothing, so I have left them some money: though I do not love them, both together, half so much as I love one lock of your fair hair.' She said these words, and she called me her 'darling,' and let me kiss her. She went on to tell me that she had left Caroline Helstone some money too; that this manor-house, with its furniture and books, she had bequeathed to me, as she did not choose to take the old family place from her own blood; and that all the rest of her property, amounting to about twelve thousand pounds, exclusive of the legacies to my sisters and Miss Helstone, she had willed, not to me, seeing I was already rich, but to a good man, who would make the best use of it that any human being could do: a man, she said, that was both gentle and brave, strong and merciful; a man that might not profess to be pious, but she knew he had the secret of religion pure and undefiled before God. The spirit of love and peace was with him; he visited the fatherless and widows in their affliction, and kept himself unspotted from the world. Then she asked, 'Do you approve what I have done, Harry?' I could not answer,—my tears choked me, as they do now."

Mr. Moore allowed his pupil a moment to contend with and master his emotion: he then demanded—"What else did she say?"

"When I had signified my full consent to the conditions of her will, she told me I was a generous boy, and she was proud of me: 'And now,' she added, 'in case anything should happen, you will know what to say to Malice when she comes

whispering hard things in your ear, insinuating that Shirley has wronged you; that she did not love you. You will know that I *did* love you, Harry; that no sister could have loved you better, my own treasure.' Mr. Moore, sir, when I remember her voice, and recall her look, my heart beats as if it would break its strings. She *may* go to heaven before me—if God commands it, she *must;* but the rest of my life— and my life will not be long—I am glad of that now—shall be a straight, quick, thoughtful journey in the path her step has pressed. I thought to enter the vault of the Keeldars before her: should it be otherwise, lay my coffin by Shirley's side.''

Moore answered him with a weighty calm, that offered a strange contrast to the boy's perturbed enthusiasm.

''You are wrong, both of you—you harm each other. If youth once falls under the influence of a shadowy terror, it imagines there will never be full sunlight again, its first calamity it fancies will last a lifetime. What more did she say? Anything more?''

''We settled one or two family points between ourselves.''

''I should rather like to know what——''

''But, Mr. Moore, you smile—*I* could not smile to see Shirley in such a mood.''

''My boy, I am neither nervous, nor poetic, nor inexperienced. I see things as they are: you don't as yet. Tell me these family points.''

''Only, sir, she asked me whether I considered myself most of a Keeldar or a Sympson; and I answered I was Keeldar to the core of the heart, and to the marrow of the bones. She said she was glad of it; for, besides her, I was the only Keeldar left in England: and then we agreed on some matters.''

''Well?''

''Well, sir, that if I lived to inherit my father's estate, and her house, I was to take the name of Keeldar, and to make Fieldhead my residence. Henry Shirley Keeldar I said I would be called: and I will. Her name and her manor-house are ages old, and Sympson and Sympson Grove are of yesterday.''

''Come, you are neither of you going to heaven yet. I have the best hopes of you both, with your proud distinctions—a pair of half-fledged eaglets. Now, what is your inference from all you have told me? Put it into words.''

''That Shirley thinks she is going to die.''

''She referred to her health?''

''Not once; but I assure you she is wasting: her hands are growing quite thin, and so is her cheek.''

''Does she ever complain to your mother or sisters?''

''Never. She laughs at them when they question her. Mr. Moore, she is a strange being—so fair and girlish: not a man-like woman at all—not an Amazon, and yet lifting her head above both help and sympathy.''

''Do you know where she is now, Henry? Is she in the house, or riding out?''

''Surely not out, sir—it rains fast.''

''True: which, however, is no guarantee that she is not at this moment cantering over Rushedge. Of late she has never permitted weather to be a hindrance to her rides.''

''You remember, Mr. Moore, how wet and stormy it was last Wednesday? so wild, indeed, that she would not permit Zoë to be saddled; yet the blast she thought too tempestuous for her mare, she herself faced on foot; that afternoon she walked nearly as far as Nunnely. I asked her, when she came in, if she was not afraid of taking cold. 'Not I,' she said, 'it would be too much good luck for me. I don't know, Harry; but the best thing that could happen to me would be to take a good cold and fever, and so pass off like other Christians.' She is reckless, you see, sir.''

''Reckless indeed! Go and find out where she is; and if you can get an opportunity of speaking to her, without attracting attention, request her to come here a minute.''

''Yes, sir.''

He snatched his crutch, and started up to go.

"Harry!"

He returned.

"Do not deliver the message formally. Word it as, in former days, you would have worded an ordinary summons to the schoolroom."

"I see, sir; she will be more likely to obey."

"And Harry——"

"Sir?"

"I will call you when I want you: till then, you are dispensed from lessons."

He departed. Mr. Moore, left alone, rose from his desk.

"I can be very cool and very supercilious with Henry," he said. "I can seem to make light of his apprehensions, and look down 'du haut de ma grandeur' on his youthful ardour. To *him* I can speak as if, in my eyes, they were both children. Let me see if I can keep up the same rôle with her. I have known the moment when I seemed about to forget it; when Confusion and Submission seemed about to crush me with their soft tyranny; when my tongue faltered, and I have almost let the mantle drop, and stood in her presence, not master—no—but something else. I trust I shall never so play the fool: it is well for a Sir Philip Nunnely to redden when he meets her eye: he may permit himself the indulgence of submission— he may even without disgrace suffer his hand to tremble when it touches hers; but if one of her farmers were to show himself susceptible and sentimental, he would merely prove his need of a strait waistcoat. So far I have always done very well. She has sat near me, and I have not shaken—more than my desk. I have encountered her looks and smiles like—why, like a tutor, as I am. Her hand I never yet touched— never underwent that test. Her farmer or her footman I am not—no serf nor servant of hers have I ever been: but I am poor, and it behoves me to look to my self-respect—not to compromise an inch of it. What did she mean by that allusion to the cold people who petrify flesh to marble? It pleased me—I hardly know why— I would not permit myself to inquire—I never do indulge in scrutiny either of her language or countenance; for if I did, I should sometimes forget Common Sense and believe in Romance. A strange, secret ecstasy steals through my veins at moments: I'll not encourage—I'll not remember it. I am resolved, as long as may be, to retain the right to say with Paul—'I am not mad, but speak forth the words of truth and soberness.' "

He paused—listening.

"Will she come, or will she not come?" he inquired, "How will she take the message? naïvely or disdainfully? like a child or like a queen? Both characters are in her nature.

"If she comes, what shall I say to her? How account, firstly, for the freedom of the request? Shall I apologise to her? I could in all humility; but would an apology tend to place us in the positions we ought relatively to occupy in this matter? I *must* keep up the professor, otherwise—I hear a door——" He waited. Many minutes passed.

"She will refuse me. Henry is entreating her to come: she declines. My petition is presumption in her eyes: let her *only* come, I can teach her to the contrary. I would rather she were a little perverse—it will steel me. I prefer her, cuirassed in pride, armed with a taunt. Her scorn startles me from my dreams—I stand up myself. A sarcasm from her eyes or lips puts strength into every nerve and sinew I have. Some step approaches, and not Henry's. . . ."

The door unclosed; Miss Keeldar came in. The message, it appeared, had found her at her needle: she brought her work in her hand. That day she had not been riding out: she had evidently passed it quietly. She wore her neat indoor dress and silk apron. This was no Thalestris from the fields, but a quiet domestic character from the fireside. Mr. Moore had her at advantage; he should have addressed her at once in solemn accents, and with rigid mien; perhaps he would, had she looked

saucy; but her air never showed less of *crânerie*; a soft kind of youthful shyness depressed her eyelid and mantled on her cheek. The tutor stood silent.

She made a full stop between the door and his desk.

"Did you want me, sir?" she asked.

"I ventured, Miss Keeldar, to send for you—that is, to ask an interview of a few minutes."

She waited: she plied her needle.

"Well, sir" (not lifting her eyes)—"what about?"

"Be seated first. The subject I would broach is one of some moment: perhaps I have hardly a right to approach it: it is possible I ought to frame an apology: it is possible no apology can excuse me. The liberty I have taken arises from a conversation with Henry. The boy is unhappy about your health: all your friends are unhappy on that subject. It is of your health I would speak."

"I am quite well," she said briefly.

"Yet changed."

"That matters to none but myself. We all change."

"Will you sit down? Formerly, Miss Keeldar, I had some influence with you— have I any now? May I feel that what I am saying is not accounted positive presumption?"

"Let me read some French, Mr. Moore, or I will even take a spell at the Latin grammar, and let us proclaim a truce to all sanitary discussions."

"No—no: it is time there were discussions."

"Discuss away, then, but do not choose me for your text; I am a healthy subject."

"Do you not think it wrong to affirm and reaffirm what is substantially untrue?"

"I say I am well: I have neither cough, pain, nor fever."

"Is there no equivocation in that assertion? Is it the direct truth?"

"The direct truth."

Louis Moore looked at her earnestly.

"I can myself," he said, "trace no indications of actual disease; but why, then, are you altered?"

"*Am* I altered?"

"We will try: we will seek a proof."

"How?"

"I ask, in the first place, do you sleep as you used to?"

"I do not: but it is not because I am ill."

"Have you the appetite you once had?"

"No: but it is not because I am ill."

"You remember this little ring fastened to my watch-chain? It was my mother's, and is too small to pass the joint of my little finger. You have many a time sportively purloined it: it fitted your fore-finger. Try now."

She permitted the test: the ring dropped from the wasted little hand. Louis picked it up, and re-attached it to the chain. An uneasy flush coloured his brow. Shirley again said—"It is not because I am ill."

"Not only have you lost sleep, appetite, and flesh," proceeded Moore, "but your spirits are always at ebb: besides, there is a nervous alarm in your eye—a nervous disquiet in your manner: these peculiarities were not formerly yours."

"Mr. Moore, we will pause here. You have exactly hit it: I am nervous. Now, talk of something else. What wet weather we have! Steady, pouring rain!"

"*You* nervous? Yes: and if Miss Keeldar is nervous, it is not without a cause. Let me reach it. Let me look nearer. The ailment is not physical: I have suspected that. It came in one moment. I know the day. I noticed the change. Your pain is mental."

"Not at all: it is nothing so dignified—merely nervous. Oh! dismiss the topic."

"When it is exhausted: not till then. Nervous alarms should always be communicated, that they may be dissipated. I wish I had the gift of persuasion, and could incline

you to speak willingly. I believe confession, in your case, would be half equivalent to cure.''

"No,'' said Shirley abruptly: "I wish that were at all probable: but I am afraid it is not.''

She suspended her work a moment. She was now seated. Resting her elbow on the table, she leaned her head on her hand. Mr. Moore looked as if he felt he had at last gained some footing in this difficult path. She was serious, and in her wish was implied an important admission; after that, she could no longer affirm that *nothing* ailed her.

The tutor allowed her some minutes for repose and reflection, ere he returned to the charge: once, his lips moved to speak; but he thought better of it, and prolonged the pause. Shirley lifted her eye to his: had he betrayed injudicious emotion, perhaps obstinate persistence in silence would have been the result; but he looked calm, strong, trustworthy.

"I had better tell *you* than my aunt,'' she said, "or than my cousins, or my uncle: they would all make such a bustle—and it is that very bustle I dread; the alarm, the flurry, the éclat: in short, I never liked to be the centre of a small domestic whirlpool. You can bear a little shock—eh?''

"A great one, if necessary.''

Not a muscle of the man's frame moved, and yet his large heart beat fast in his deep chest. What was she going to tell him? Was irremediable mischief done?

"Had I thought it right to go to you, I would never have made a secret of the matter one moment,'' she continued: "I would have told you at once, and asked advice.''

"Why was it not right to come to me?''

"It might be *right*—I do not mean that; but I could not do it. I seemed to have no title to trouble you: the mishap concerned me only—I wanted to keep it to myself, and people will not let me. I tell you, I hate to be an object of worrying attention, or a theme for village gossip. Besides, it may pass away without result—God knows!''

Moore, though tortured with suspense, did not demand a quick explanation; he suffered neither gesture, glance, nor word, to betray impatience. His tranquillity tranquillised Shirley; his confidence reassured her.

"Great effects may spring from trivial causes,'' she remarked, as she loosened a bracelet from her wrist; then, unfastening her sleeve, and partially turning it up—"Look here, Mr. Moore.''

She showed a mark on her white arm; rather a deep though healed-up indentation: something between a burn and a cut.

"I would not show that to any one in Briarfield but you, because you can take it quietly.''

"Certainly there is nothing in the little mark to shock: its history will explain.''

"Small as it is, it has taken my sleep away, and made me nervous, thin, and foolish; because, on account of that little mark, I am obliged to look forward to a possibility that has its terrors.''

The sleeve was readjusted; the bracelet replaced.

"Do you know that you try me?'' he said, smiling. "I am a patient sort of man, but my pulse is quickening.''

"Whatever happens, you will befriend me, Mr. Moore. You will give me the benefit of your self-possession, and not leave me at the mercy of agitated cowards?''

"I make no promise now. Tell me the tale, and then exact what pledge you will.''

"It is a very short tale. I took a walk with Isabella and Gertrude one day, about three weeks ago. They reached home before me: I stayed behind to speak to John. After leaving him, I pleased myself with lingering in the lane, where all was very still and shady: I was tired of chattering to the girls, and in no hurry to rejoin them.

As I stood leaning against the gate-pillar, thinking some very happy thoughts about my future life—for that morning I imagined that events were beginning to turn as I had long wished them to turn——''

"Ah! Nunnely had been with her the evening before!" thought Moore parenthetically.

"I heard a panting sound; a dog came running up the lane. I know most of the dogs in this neighbourhood; it was Phœbe, one of Mr. Sam Wynne's pointers. The poor creature ran with her head down, her tongue hanging out; she looked as if bruised and beaten all over. I called her; I meant to coax her into the house, and give her some water and dinner; I felt sure she had been ill-used: Mr. Sam often flogs his pointers cruelly. She was too flurried to know me; and when I attempted to pat her head, she turned and snatched at my arm. She bit it so as to draw blood, then ran panting on. Directly after, Mr. Wynne's keeper came up, carrying a gun. He asked if I had seen a dog; I told him I had seen Phœbe.

" 'You had better chain up Tartar, ma'am,' he said, 'and tell your people to keep within the house; I am after Phœbe to shoot her, and the groom is gone another way. She is raging mad.' ''

Mr. Moore leaned back in his chair, and folded his arms across his chest; Miss Keeldar resumed her square of silk canvas, and continued the creation of a wreath of Parmese violets.

"And you told no one, sought no help, no cure: you would not come to me?"

"I got as far as the schoolroom door; there my courage failed: I preferred to cushion the matter."

"Why! What can I demand better in this world than to be of use to you?"

"I had no claim."

"Monstrous! And you did nothing?"

"Yes: I walked straight into the laundry, where they are ironing most of the week, now that I have so many guests in the house. While the maid was busy crimping or starching, I took an Italian iron from the fire, and applied the light scarlet glowing tip to my arm: I bored it well in: it cauterised the little wound. Then I went upstairs."

"I dare say you never once groaned?"

"I am sure I don't know. I was very miserable. Not firm or tranquil at all, I think: there was no calm in my mind."

"There was calm in your person. I remember listening the whole time we sat at luncheon, to hear if you moved in the room above: all was quiet."

"I was sitting at the foot of the bed, wishing Phœbe had not bitten me."

"And alone! You like solitude."

"Pardon me."

"You disdain sympathy."

"Do I, Mr. Moore?"

"With your powerful mind, you must feel independent of help, of advice, of society."

"So be it—since it pleases you."

She smiled. She pursued her embroidery carefully and quickly; but her eyelash twinkled, and then it glittered, and then a drop fell.

Mr. Moore leaned forward on his desk, moved his chair, altered his attitude.

"If it is not so," he asked, with a peculiar, mellow change in his voice, "how is it, then?"

"I don't know."

"You do know, but you won't speak: all must be locked up in yourself."

"Because it is not worth sharing."

"Because nobody can give the high price you require for your confidence. Nobody is rich enough to purchase it. Nobody has the honour, the intellect, the power you demand in your adviser. There is not a shoulder in England on which

you would rest your hand for support—far less a bosom which you would permit to pillow your head. Of course you must live alone.''

"I *can* live alone, if need be. But the question is not how to live—but how to die alone. That strikes me in a more grisly light.''

"You apprehend the effects of the virus? You anticipate an indefinitely threatening, dreadful doom?''

She bowed.

"You are very nervous and womanish.''

"You complimented me two minutes since on my powerful mind.''

"You are very womanish. If the whole affair were coolly examined and discussed, I feel assured it would turn out that there is no danger of your dying at all.''

"Amen! I am very willing to live, if it please God. I have felt life sweet.''

"How can it be otherwise than sweet with your endowments and nature? Do you truly expect that you will be seized with hydrophobia, and die raving mad?''

"I *expect* it, and have *feared* it. Just now, I fear nothing.''

"Nor do I, on your account. I doubt whether the smallest particle of virus mingled with your blood: and if it did, let me assure you that—young, healthy, faultlessly sound as you are—no harm will ensue. For the rest, I shall inquire whether the dog was really mad. I hold she was not mad.''

"Tell nobody that she bit me.''

"Why should I, when I believe the bite innocuous as a cut of this penknife? Make yourself easy: *I* am easy, though I value your life as much as I do my own chance of happiness in eternity. Look up.''

"Why, Mr. Moore?''

"I wish to see if you are cheered. Put your work down, raise your head.''

"There——''

"Look at me. Thank you! And is the cloud broken?''

"I fear nothing.''

"Is your mind restored to its own natural sunny clime?''

"I am very content: but I want your promise.''

"Dictate.''

"You know, in case the worst I *have* feared should happen, they will smother me. You need not smile: they will—they always do. My uncle will be full of horror, weakness, precipitation; and that is the only expedient which will suggest itself to him. Nobody in the house will be self-possessed but you: now promise to befriend me—to keep Mr. Sympson away from me—not to let Henry come near, lest I should hurt him. Mind—*mind* that you take care of yourself, too: but I shall not injure you, I know I shall not. Lock the chamber-door against the surgeons—turn them out, if they get in. Let neither the young nor the old MacTurk lay a finger on me; nor Mr. Greaves, their colleague; and, lastly, if I give trouble, with your own hand administer to me a strong narcotic: such a sure dose of laudanum as shall leave no mistake. *Promise to do this*.''

Moore left his desk, and permitted himself the recreation of one or two turns round the room. Stopping behind Shirley's chair, he bent over her, and said, in a low emphatic voice—"I promise all you ask—without comment, without reservation.''

"If female help is needed, call in my housekeeper, Mrs. Gill: let her lay me out, if I die. She is attached to me. She wronged me again and again, and again and again I forgave her. She now loves me, and would not defraud me of a pin: confidence has made her honest; forbearance has made her kind-hearted. At this day, I can trust both her integrity, her courage, and her affection. Call her; but keep my good aunt and my timid cousins away. Once more, promise.''

"I promise.''

"That is good in you," she said, looking up at him as he bent over her, and smiling.

"Is it good? Does it comfort?''

"Very much."

"I will be with you—I and Mrs. Gill only—in any, in every extremity where calm and fidelity are needed. No rash or coward hand shall meddle."

"Yet you think me childish?"

"I do."

"Ah! you despise me."

"Do we despise children?"

"In fact, I am neither so strong, nor have I such pride in my strength, as people think, Mr. Moore; nor am I so regardless of sympathy; but when I have any grief, I fear to impart it to those I love, lest it should pain them; and to those whom I view with indifference, I cannot condescend to complain. After all, you should not taunt me with being childish; for if you were as unhappy as I have been for the last three weeks, you too would want some friend."

"We all want a friend, do we not?"

"All of us that have anything good in our natures,"

"Well, you have Caroline Helstone."

"Yes. . . . And you have Mr. Hall."

"Yes. . . . Mrs. Pryor is a wise, good woman: she can counsel you when you need counsel."

"For your part, you have your brother Robert."

"For any right-hand defections, there is the Rev. Matthewson Helstone, M.A., to lean upon; for any left-hand fallings off, there is Hiram Yorke, Esq. Both elders pay you homage."

"I never saw Mrs. Yorke so motherly to any young man as she is to you. I don't know how you have won her heart; but she is more tender to you than she is to her own sons. You have, besides, your sister, Hortense."

"It appears we are both well provided."

"It appears so."

"How thankful we ought to be!"

"Yes."

"How contented!"

"Yes."

"For my part, I am almost contented just now, and very thankful. Gratitude is a divine emotion: it fills the heart, but not to bursting: it warms it, but not to fever. I like to taste leisurely of bliss: devoured in haste, I do not know its flavour."

Still leaning on the back of Miss Keeldar's chair, Moore watched the rapid motion of her fingers, as the green and purple garland grew beneath them. After a prolonged pause, he again asked, "Is the shadow *quite* gone?"

"Wholly. As I *was* two hours since, and as I *am* now, are two different states of existence. I believe, Mr. Moore, griefs and fears nursed in silence grow like Titan infants."

"You will cherish such feelings no more in silence?"

"Not if I dare speak."

"In using the word '*dare*,' to whom do you allude?"

"To you."

"How is it applicable to me?"

"On account of your austerity and shyness."

"Why am I austere and shy?"

"Because you are proud."

"Why am I proud?"

"I should like to know; will you be good enough to tell me?

"Perhaps, because I am poor, for one reason: poverty and pride often go together."

"That is such a nice reason: I should be charmed to discover another that would pair with it. Mate that turtle, Mr. Moore."

"Immediately. What do you think of marrying to sober Poverty many-tinted Caprice?"

"Are you capricious?"

"*You* are."

"A libel. I am steady as a rock: fixed as the Polar Star."

"I look out at some early hour of the day, and see a fine, perfect rainbow, bright with promise, gloriously spanning the beclouded welkin of life. An hour afterwards I look again—half the arch is gone, and the rest is faded. Still later, the stern sky denies that it ever wore so benign a symbol of hope."

"Well, Mr. Moore, you should contend against these changeful humours: they are your besetting sin. One never knows where to have you."

"Miss Keeldar, I had once—for two years—a pupil who grew very dear to me. Henry is dear, but she was dearer. Henry never gives me trouble; she—well—she did. I think she vexed me twenty-three hours out of the twenty-four——"

"She was never with you above three hours, or at the most six at a time."

"She sometimes spilled the draught from my cup, and stole the food from my plate; and when she had kept me unfed for a day (and that did not suit me, for I am a man accustomed to take my meals with reasonable relish, and to ascribe due importance to the rational enjoyment of creature comforts)——"

"I know you do. I can tell what sort of dinners you like best—perfectly well. I know precisely the dishes you prefer——"

"She robbed these dishes of flavour, and made a fool of me besides. I like to sleep well. In my quiet days, when I was my own man, I never quarrelled with the night for being long, nor cursed my bed for its thorns. She changed all this."

"Mr. Moore——"

"And having taken from me peace of mind, and ease of life, she took from me herself; quite coolly—just as if, when she was gone, the world would be all the same to me. I knew I should see her again at some time. At the end of two years, it fell out that we encountered again under her own roof, where she was mistress. How do you think she bore herself towards me, Miss Keeldar?"

"Like one who had profited well by lessons learned from yourself."

"She received me haughtily: she meted out a wide space between us, and kept me aloof by the reserved gesture, the rare and alienated glance, the word calmly civil."

"She was an excellent pupil! Having seen you distant, she at once learned to withdraw. Pray, sir, admire in her hauteur a careful improvement on your own coolness."

"Conscience, and honour, and the most despotic necessity, dragged me apart from her, and kept me sundered with ponderous fetters. She was free: she might have been clement."

"Never free to compromise her self-respect: to seek where she had been shunned."

"Then she was inconsistent: she tantalised as before. When I thought I had made up my mind to seeing in her only a lofty stranger, she would suddenly show me such a glimpse of loving simplicity—she would warm me with such a beam of reviving sympathy, she would gladden an hour with converse so gentle, gay, and kindly—that I could no more shut my heart on her image, than I could close that door against her presence. Explain why she distressed me so."

"She could not bear to be quite outcast; and then she would sometimes get a notion into her head, on a cold, wet day, that the schoolroom was no cheerful place, and feel it incumbent on her to go and see if you and Henry kept up a good fire; and once there she liked to stay."

"But she should not be changeful: if she came at all, she should come oftener."

"There is such a thing as intrusion."

"To-morrow, you will not be as you are to-day."

"I don't know. Will you?"

"I am not mad, most noble Berenice! We may give one day to dreaming, but the next we must awake; and I shall awake to purpose the morning you are married to Sir Philip Nunnely. The fire shines on you and me, and shows us very clearly in the glass, Miss Keeldar; and I have been gazing on the picture all the time I have been talking. Look up! What a difference between your head and mine!—I look old for thirty!"

"You are so grave; you have such a square brow; and your face is sallow. I never regard you as a young man, nor as Robert's junior."

"Don't you? I thought not. Imagine Robert's clear-cut, handsome face looking over my shoulder. Does not the apparition make vividly manifest the obtuse mould of my heavy traits? There!" (he started) "I have been expecting that wire to vibrate this last half-hour."

The dinner-bell rang, and Shirley rose.

"Mr. Moore," she said, as she gathered up her silks, "have you heard from your brother lately? Do you know what he means by staying in town so long? Does he talk of returning?"

"He talks of returning; but what has caused his long absence I cannot tell. To speak the truth, I thought none in Yorkshire knew better than yourself why he was reluctant to come home."

A crimson shadow passed across Miss Keeldar's cheek.

"Write to him and urge him to come," she said. "I know there has been no impolicy in protracting his absence thus far: it is good to let the mill stand, while trade is so bad; but he must not abandon the county."

"I am aware," said Louis, "that he had an interview with you the evening before he left, and I saw him quit Fieldhead afterwards. I read his countenance, or *tried* to read it. He turned from me. I divined that he would be long away. Some fine, slight fingers have a wondrous knack at pulverising a man's brittle pride. I suppose Robert put too much trust in his manly beauty and native gentlemanhood. Those are better off who, being destitute of advantage, cannot cherish delusion. But I will write, and say you advise his return."

"Do not say *I* advise his return, but that his return is advisable."

The second bell rang, and Miss Keeldar obeyed its call.

Chapter XXIX

LOUIS MOORE

LOUIS MOORE was used to a quiet life: being a quiet man, he endured it better than most men would: having a large world of his own in his own head and heart, he tolerated confinement to a small, still corner of the real world very patiently.

How hushed is Fieldhead this evening! All but Moore—Miss Keeldar, the whole family of the Sympsons, even Henry—are gone to Nunnely. Sir Philip would have them come: he wished to make them acquainted with his mother and sisters, who are now at the Priory. Kind gentleman as the Baronet is, he asked the tutor too; but the tutor would much sooner have made an appointment with the ghost of the Earl of Huntingdon to meet him, and a shadowy ring of his merry men, under the canopy of the thickest, blackest, oldest oak in Nunnely Forest. Yes, he would rather have appointed tryst with a phantom abbess, or mist-pale nun, among the wet and weedy relics of that ruined sanctuary of theirs, mouldering in the core of the wood. Louis Moore longs to have something near him to-night: but not the boy-baronet, nor his benevolent but stern mother, nor his patrician sisters, nor one soul of the Sympsons.

This night is not calm: the equinox still struggles in its storms. The wild rains of the day are abated: the great single cloud disparts and rolls away from heaven, not passing and leaving a sea all sapphire, but tossed buoyant before a continued, long-sounding, high-rushing moonlight tempest. The Moon reigns glorious, glad of the gale; as glad as if she gave herself to his fierce caress with love. No Endymion will watch for his goddess to-night: there are no flocks out on the mountains; and it is well, for to-night she welcomes Æolus.

Moore—sitting in the schoolroom—heard the storm roar round the other gable, and along the hall-front: this end was sheltered. He wanted no shelter; he desired no subdued sounds or screened position.

"All the parlours are empty," said he: "I am sick at heart of this cell."

He left it, and went where the casements, larger and freer than the branch-screened lattice of his own apartment, admitted unimpeded the dark-blue, the silver-fleeced, the stirring and sweeping vision of the autumn night-sky. He carried no candle: unneeded was lamp or fire: the broad and clear, though cloud-crossed and fluctuating beam of the moon shone on every floor and wall.

Moore wanders through all the rooms: he seems following a phantom from parlour to parlour. In the oak-room he stops; this is not chill, and polished, and fireless like the salon: the hearth is hot and ruddy; the cinders tinkle in the intense heat of their clear glow; near the rug is a little work-table, a desk upon it, a chair near it.

Does the vision Moore has tracked occupy that chair? You would think so, could you see him standing before it. There is as much interest now in his eye, and as much significance in his face, as if in this household solitude he had found a living companion, and was going to speak to it.

He makes discoveries. A bag, a small satin bag, hangs on the chair-back. The desk is open, the keys are in the lock; a pretty seal, a silver pen, a crimson berry or two of ripe fruit on a green leaf, a small, clean, delicate glove—these trifles at once decorate and disarrange the stand they strew. Order forbids details in a picture: she puts them tidily away; but details give charm.

Moore spoke.

"Her mark," he said: "here she has been—careless, attractive thing!—called away in haste, doubtless, and forgetting to return and put all to rights. Why does she leave fascination in her footprints? Whence did she acquire the gift to be heedless, and never offend? There is always something to chide in her, and the reprimand never settles in displeasure on the heart; but, for her lover or her husband, when it had trickled a while in words, would naturally melt from his lips in a kiss. Better pass half-an-hour in remonstrating with her, than a day in admiring or praising any other woman alive. Am I muttering?—soliloquising? Stop that."

He did stop it. He stood thinking; and then he made an arrangement for his evening's comfort.

He dropped the curtains over the broad window and regal moon: he shut out Sovereign and Court and Starry Armies; he added fuel to the hot but fast-wasting fire; he lit a candle, of which there were a pair on the table; he placed another chair opposite that near the work-stand, and then he sat down. His next movement was to take from his pocket a small, thick book of blank paper; to produce a pencil; and to begin to write in a cramp, compact hand. Come near, by all means, reader: do not be shy: stoop over his shoulder fearlessly, and read as he scribbles.

"It is nine o'clock; the carriage will not return before eleven, I am certain. Freedom is mine till then: till then, I may occupy her room; sit opposite her chair; rest my elbow on her table; have her little mementoes about me.

"I used rather to like Solitude—to fancy her a somewhat quiet and serious, yet fair nymph; an Oread, descending to me from lone mountain-passes; something of the blue mist of hills in her array and of their chill breeze in her breath—but much, also, of their solemn beauty in her mien. I once could court her serenely, and imagine my heart easier when I held her to it—all mute, but majestic.

"Since that day I called S. to me in the schoolroom, and she came and sat so near my side; since she opened the trouble of her mind to me—asked my protection—appealed to my strength: since that hour I abhor Solitude. Cold abstraction—fleshless skeleton—daughter—mother—and mate of Death!

"It is pleasant to write about what is near and dear as the core of my heart: none can deprive me of this little book, and through this pencil, I can say to it what I will—say what I dare utter to nothing living—say what I dare not *think* aloud.

"We have scarcely encountered each other since that evening. Once, when I was alone in the drawing-room, seeking a book of Henry's, she entered, dressed for a concert at Stilbro'. Shyness—*her* shyness, not mine—drew a silver veil between us. Much cant have I heard and read about 'maiden modesty'; but, properly used, and not hackneyed, the words are good and appropriate words: as she passed to the window, after tacitly but gracefully recognising me, I could call her nothing in my own mind save 'stainless virgin': to my perception, a delicate splendour robed her, and the modesty of girlhood was her halo. I may be the most fatuous, as I am one of the plainest, of men; but, in truth, that shyness of hers touched me exquisitely: it flattered my finest sensations. I looked a stupid block, I dare say: I was alive with a life of Paradise, as she tured *her* glance from *my* glance, and softly averted her head to hide the suffusion of her cheek.

"I know this is the talk of a dreamer—of a rapt, romantic lunatic: I *do* dream: I *will* dream now and then; and if she has inspired romance into my prosaic composition, how can I help it?

"What a child she is sometimes! What an unsophisticated, untaught thing! I see her now, looking up into my face, and entreating me to prevent them from smothering her, and to be sure and give her a strong narcotic: I see her confessing that she was not so self-sufficing, so independent of sympathy, as people thought: I see the secret tear drop quietly from her eyelash. She said I thought her childish—and I did. She imagined I despised her.—Despised her! it was unutterably sweet to feel myself at once near her and above her: to be conscious of a natural right and power to sustain her, as a husband should sustain his wife.

"I worship her perfections; but it is her faults, or at least her foibles, that bring her near to me—that nestle her to my heart—that fold her about with my love—and that for a most selfish, but deeply-natural reason; these faults are the steps by which I mount to ascendancy over her. If she rose a trimmed, artificial mound, without inequality, what vantage would she offer the foot? It is the natural hill, with its mossy breaks and hollows, whose slope invites ascent—whose summit it is pleasure to gain.

"To leave metaphor. It delights my eye to look on her: she suits me: if I were a king, and she the housemaid that swept my palace-stairs—across all that space between us—my eye would recognise her qualities; a true pulse would beat for her in my heart, though an unspanned gulf made acquaintance impossible. If I were a gentleman, and she waited on me as a servant, I could not help liking that Shirley. Take from her her education—take her ornaments, her sumptuous dress—all extrinsic advantages—take all grace, but such as the symmetry of her form renders inevitable; present her to me at a cottage-door, in a stuff-gown: let her offer me there a draught of water, with that smile—with that warm goodwill with which she now dispenses manorial hospitality—I should like her. I should wish to stay an hour: I should linger to talk with that rustic. I should not feel as I *now* do. I should find in her nothing divine; but whenever I met the young peasant, it would be with pleasure—whenever I left her, it would be with regret.

"How culpably careless in her to leave her desk open, where I know she has money! In the lock hang the keys of all her repositories, of her very jewel-casket. There is a purse in that little satin bag: I see the tassel of silver beads hanging out. That spectacle would provoke my brother Robert: all her little failings would, I know, be a source of irritation to him; if they vex me it is a most pleasurable

vexation: I delight to find her at fault, and were I always resident with her, I am aware she would be no niggard in thus ministering to my enjoyment. She would just give me something to do; to rectify: a theme for my tutor-lectures. I never lecture Henry: never feel disposed to do so: if he does wrong,—and that is very seldom, dear excellent lad!—a word suffices: often I do no more than shake my head; but the moment her 'minois mutin' meets my eye, expostulatory words crowd to my lips: from a taciturn man, I believe she would transform me into a talker. Whence comes the delight I take in that talk? It puzzles myself sometimes; the more *crâne, malin, taquin* is her mood, consequently the clearer occasion she gives me for disapprobation, the more I seek her, the better I like her. She is never wilder than when equipped in her habit and hat: never less manageable than when she and Zoë come in fiery from a race with the wind on the hills: and I confess it—to this mute page I may confess it—I have waited an hour in the court, for the chance of witnessing her return, and for the dearer chance of receiving her in my arms from the saddle. I have noticed (again, it is to this page only I would make the remark) that she will never permit any man but myself to render her that assistance. I have seen her politely decline Sir Philip Nunnely's aid: she is always mighty gentle with her young baronet; mighty tender of his feelings, forsooth, and of his very thin-skinned amour-propre: I have marked her haughtily reject Sam Wynne's. Now I know—my heart knows it, for it has felt it—that she resigns herself to me unreluctantly: is she conscious how my strength rejoices to serve her? I myself am not her slave—I declare it,—but my faculties gather to her beauty, like the genii to the glisten of the Lamp. All my knowledge, all my prudence, all my calm, and all my power, stand in her presence humbly waiting a task. How glad they are when a mandate comes! What joy they take in the toils she assigns. Does she know it?

"I have called her careless: it is remarkable that her carelessness never compromises her refinement; indeed, through this very loophole of character, the reality, depth, genuineness of that refinement may be ascertained: a whole garment sometimes covers meagreness and malformation; through a rent sleeve, a fair round arm may be revealed. I have seen and handled many of her possessions, because they are frequently astray. I never saw anything that did not proclaim the lady: nothing sordid, nothing soiled; in one sense she is as scrupulous as, in another, she is unthinking: as a peasant girl, she would go ever trim and cleanly. Look at the pure kid of this little glove,—at the fresh, unsullied satin of the bag.

"What a difference there is between S. and that pearl C. H.! Caroline, I fancy, is the soul of conscientious punctuality and nice exactitude; she would precisely suit the domestic habits of a certain fastidious kinsman of mine: so delicate, dexterous, quaint, quick, quiet; all done to a minute, all arranged to a straw-breadth: she would suit Robert; but what could *I* do with anything so nearly faultless? *She* is my equal; poor as myself; she is certainly pretty: a little Raffaelle head hers; Raffaelle in feature, quite English in expression: all insular grace and purity; but where is there anything to alter, anything to endure, anything to reprimand, to be anxious about? There she is, a lily of the valley, untinted, needing no tint. What change could improve her? What pencil dare to paint? *My* sweetheart, if I ever have one, must bear nearer affinity to the rose: a sweet, lively delight guarded with prickly peril. *My* wife, if I ever marry, must stir my great frame with a sting now and then; she must furnish use to her husband's vast mass of patience. I was not made so enduring to be mated with a lamb: I should find more congenial responsibility in the charge of a young lioness or leopardess. I like few things sweet, but what are likewise pungent; few things bright, but what are likewise hot. I like the summer-day, whose sun makes fruit blush and corn blanch. Beauty is never so beautiful as when, if I tease it, it wreathes back on me with spirit. Fascination is never so imperial as when, roused and half ireful, she threatens transformation to fierceness. I fear I should tire of the mute, monotonous innocence of the lamb; I should erelong feel

as burdensome the nestling dove which never stirred in my bosom: but my patience would exult in stilling the flutterings and training the energies of the restless merlin. In managing the wild instincts of the scarce manageable 'bête fauve,' my powers would revel.

"Oh, my pupil! Oh, Peri! too mutinous for heaven—too innocent for hell! never shall I do more than see, and worship, and wish for thee. Alas! knowing I could make thee happy, will it be my doom to see thee possessed by those who have not that power?

"However kindly the hand—if it is feeble, it cannot bend Shirley; and she must be bent: it cannot curb her; and she must be curbed.

"Beware! Sir Philip Nunnely! I never see you walking or sitting at her side, and observe her lips compressed, or her brow knit, in resolute endurance of some trait of your character which she neither admires nor likes; in determined toleration of some weakness she believes atoned for by a virtue, but which annoys her, despite that belief: I never mark the grave glow of her face, the unsmiling sparkle of her eye, the slight recoil of her whole frame when you draw a little too near, and gaze a little too expressively, and whisper a little too warmly: I never witness these things, but I think of the fable of Semele reversed.

"It is not the daughter of Cadmus I see: nor do I realise her fatal longing to look on Jove in the majesty of his godhead. It is a priest of Juno that stands before me, watching late and lone at a shrine in an Argive temple. For years of solitary ministry, he has lived on dreams: there is divine madness upon him: he loves the idol he serves, and prays day and night that his frenzy may be fed, and that the Ox-eyed may smile on her votary. She has heard; she will be propitious. All Argos slumbers. The doors of the temple are shut: the priest waits at the altar.

"A shock of heaven and earth is felt—not by the slumbering city; only by that lonely watcher, brave and unshaken in his fanaticism. In the midst of silence, with no preluding sound, he is wrapt in sudden light. Through the roof—through the rent, wide-yawning, vast, white-blazing blue of heaven above, pours a wondrous descent—dread as the down-rushing of stars. He has what he asked: withdraw—forbear to look—I am blinded. I hear in that fane an unspeakable sound—would that I could not hear it! I see an insufferable glory burning terribly between the pillars. Gods be merciful and quench it!

"A pious Argive enters to make an early offering in the cool dawn of morning. There was thunder in the night: the bolt fell here. The shrine is shivered: the marble pavement round, split and blackened. Saturnia's statue rises chaste, grand, untouched: at her feet, piled ashes lie pale. No priest remains: he who watched will be seen no more.

*　　*　　*　　*　　*　　*　　*

"There is the carriage! Let me lock up the desk and pocket the keys: she will be seeking them to-morrow: she will have to come to me. I hear her—'Mr. Moore, have you seen my keys?'

"So she will say, in her clear voice, speaking with reluctance, looking ashamed, conscious that this is the twentieth time of asking. I will tantalise her: keep her with me, expecting, doubting; and when I *do* restore them, it shall not be without a lecture. Here is the bag, too, and the purse; the glove—pen—seal. She shall wring them all out of me slowly and separately: only by confession, penitence, entreaty. I never can touch her hand, or a ringlet of her head, or a ribbon of her dress, but I will make privileges for myself: every feature of her face, her bright eyes, her lips, shall go through each change they know, for my pleasure: display each exquisite variety of glance and curve, to delight—thrill—perhaps, more hopelessly to enchain me. If I must be her slave, I wil not lose my freedom for nothing."

He locked the desk, pocketed all the property, and went.

Chapter XXX

RUSHEDGE, A CONFESSIONAL

EVERYBODY said it was high time for Mr. Moore to return home: all Briarfield wondered at his strange absence, and Whinbury and Nunnely brought each its separate contribution of amazement.

Was it known why he stayed away? Yes: it was known twenty—forty times over; there being, at least, forty plausible reasons adduced to account for the unaccountable circumstance. Business it was not—*that* the gossips agreed: he had achieved the business on which he departed long ago: his four ringleaders he had soon scented out and run down: he had attended their trial, heard their conviction and sentence, and seen them safely shipped prior to transportation.

This was known at Briarfield: the newspapers had reported it: the *Stilbro' Courier* had given every particular, with amplifications. None applauded his perseverance, or hailed his success; though the mill-owners were glad of it, trusting that the terrors of Law vindicated would henceforward paralyse the sinister valour of disaffection. Disaffection, however, was still heard muttering to himself. He swore ominous oaths over the drugged beer of ale-houses, and drank strange toasts in fiery British gin.

One report affirmed that Moore *dared* not come to Yorkshire; he knew his life was not worth an hour's purchase, if he did.

"I'll tell him that," said Mr. Yorke, when his foreman mentioned the rumour; "and if *that* does not bring him home full-gallop—nothing will."

Either that or some other motive prevailed, at last, to recall him. He announced to Joe Scott the day he should arrive at Stilbro', desiring his hackney to be sent to the "George" for his accommodation; and Joe Scott having informed Mr. Yorke, that gentleman made it in his way to meet him.

It was market-day: Moore arrived in time to take his usual place at the market-dinner. As something of a stranger—and as a man of note and action—the assembled manufacturers received him with a certain distinction. Some—who in public would scarcely have dared to acknowledge his acquaintance, lest a little of the hate and vengeance laid up in store for him should perchance have fallen on them—in private hailed him as in some sort their champion. When the wine had circulated, their respect would have kindled to enthusiasm, had not Moore's unshaken nonchalance held it in a damp, low, smouldering state.

Mr. Yorke—the permanent president of these dinners—witnessed his young friend's bearing with exceeding complacency. If one thing could stir his temper or excite his contempt more than another, it was to see a man befooled by flattery, or elate with popularity. If one thing smoothed, soothed, and charmed him especially, it was the spectacle of a public character incapable of relishing his publicity: *incapable*, I say; disdain would but have incensed—it was indifference that appeased his rough spirit.

Robert, leaning back in his chair, quiet and almost surly, while the clothiers and blanket-makers vaunted his prowess and rehearsed his deeds—many of them interspersing their flatteries with coarse invectives against the operative class—was a delectable sight for Mr. Yorke. His heart tingled with the pleasing conviction that these gross eulogiums shamed Moore deeply, and made him half-scorn himself and his work. On abuse, on reproach, on calumny, it is easy to smile; but painful indeed is the panegyric of those we contemn. Often had Moore gazed with a brilliant countenance over howling crowds from a hostile hustings: he had breasted the storm of unpopularity with gallant bearing and soul elate; but he drooped his head under the half-bred tradesmen's praise, and shrank chagrined before their congratulations.

Yorke could not help asking him how he liked his supporters, and whether he did not think they did honour to his cause. "But it is a pity, lad," he added, "that

you did not hang these four samples of the Unwashed. If you had managed *that* feat, the gentry here would have riven the horses out of the coach, yoked to a score of asses, and drawn you into Stilbro' like a conquering general.''

Moore soon forsook the wine, broke from the party, and took the road. In less than five minutes Mr. Yorke followed him: they rode out of Stilbro' together.

It was early to go home, but yet it was late in the day: the last ray of the sun had already faded from the cloud-edges, and the October night was casting over the moorlands the shadow of her approach.

Mr. Yorke—moderately exhilarated with his moderate libations, and not displeased to see young Moore again in Yorkshire, and to have him for his comrade during the long ride home—took the discourse much to himself. He touched briefly, but scoffingly, on the trials and the conviction: he passed thence to the gossip of the neighbourhood, and, ere long, he attacked Moore on his own personal concerns.

''Bob, I believe you are worsted; and you deserve it. All was smooth. Fortune had fallen in love with you: she had decreed you the first prize in her wheel—twenty thousand pounds: she only required that you should hold your hand out and take it. And what did you do? You called for a horse and rode a-hunting to Warwickshire. Your sweetheart—Fortune, I mean—was perfectly indulgent. She said, 'I'll excuse him: he's young.' She waited like 'Patience on a monument,' till the chase was over, and the vermin-prey run down. She expected you would come back then, and be a good lad: you might still have had her first prize.

''It capped her beyond expression, and me too, to find that, instead of thundering home in a breakneck gallop, and laying your assize-laurels at her feet, you coolly took coach up to London. What you have done there, Satan knows: nothing in this world, I believe, but sat and sulked: your face was never lily-fair, but it is olive-green now. You're not as bonnie as you were, man.''

''And who is to have this prize you talk so much about?''

''Only a baronet: that is all. I have not a doubt in my own mind you've lost her: she will be Lady Nunnely before Christmas.''

''Hem! Quite probable.''

''But she need not to have been. Fool of a lad! I swear you might have had her!''

''By what token, Mr. Yorke?''

''By every token. By the light of her eyes, the red of her cheeks: red they grew when your name was mentioned, though of custom they are pale.''

''My chance is quite over, I suppose?''

''It ought to be; but try: it is worth trying. I call this Sir Philip milk and water. And then he writes verses, they say—tags rhymes. *You* are above that, Bob, at all events.''

''Would you advise me to propose, late as it is, Mr. Yorke? at the eleventh hour?''

''You can but make the experiment, Robert. If she has a fancy for you—and, on my conscience, I believe she has, or had—she will forgive much. But, my lad, you are laughing: is it at me? You had better grin at your own perverseness. I see, however, you laugh at the wrong side of your mouth: you have as sour a look at this moment as one need wish to see.''

''I have so quarrelled with myself, Yorke. I have so kicked against the pricks, and struggled in a strait waistcoat, and dislocated my wrists with wrenching them in handcuffs, and battered my hard head, by driving it against a harder wall.''

''Ha! I'm glad to hear that. Sharp exercise yon! I hope it has done you good; ta'en some of the self-conceit out of you?''

''Self-conceit! What is it? Self-respect, self-tolerance, even what are they? Do you sell the articles? Do you know anybody who does? Give an indication: they would find in me a liberal chapman. I would part with my last guinea this minute to buy.''

"Is it so with you, Robert? I find that spicy. I like a man to speak his mind. What has gone wrong?"

"The machinery of all my nature; the whole enginery of this human mill: the boiler, which I take to be the heart, is fit to burst."

"That suld be putten i' print: it's striking. It's almost blank verse. Ye'll be jingling into poetry just e'now. If the afflatus comes, give way, Robert; never heed me: I'll bear it this whet (time)."

"Hideous, abhorrent, base blunder! You may commit in a moment, what you may rue for years—what life cannot cancel."

"Lad, go on. I call it pie, nuts, sugar-candy. I like the taste uncommonly. Go on: it will do you good to talk: the moor is before us now, and there is no life for many a mile round."

"I *will* talk. I am not ashamed to tell. There is a sort of wild cat in my breast, and I choose that you shall hear how it can yell."

"To me it is music. What grand voices you and Louis have! When Louis sings— tones off like a soft, deep bell, I've felt myself tremble again. The night is still: it listens: it is just leaning down to you, like a black priest to a blacker penitent. Confess, lad: smooth naught down: be candid as a convicted, justified, sanctified Methody at an experience-meeting. Make yourself as wicked as Beelzebub: it will ease your mind."

"As mean as Mammon, you would say. Yorke, if I got off horseback and laid myself down across the road, would you have the goodness to gallop over me— backwards and forwards—about twenty times?"

"Wi' all the pleasure in life, if there were no such thing as a coroner's inquest."

"Hiram Yorke, I certainly believed she loved me. I have seen her eyes sparkle radiantly when she has found me out in a crowd: she has flushed up crimson when she has offered me her hand, and said, 'How do you do, Mr. Moore?'

"My name had a magical influence over her: when others uttered it, she changed countenance,—I know she did. She pronounced it herself in the most musical of her many musical tones. She was cordial to me; she took an interest in me; she was anxious about me; she wished me well; she sought, she seized every opportunity to benefit me. I considered, paused, watched, weighed, wondered: I could come to but one conclusion—this is love.

"I looked at her, Yorke: I saw, in her, youth and a species of beauty. I saw power in her. Her wealth offered me the redemption of my honour and my standing. I owed her gratitude. She had aided me substantially and effectually by a loan of five thousand pounds. Could I remember these things? Could I believe she loved me? Could I hear wisdom urge me to marry her, and disregard every dear advantage, disbelieve every flattering suggestion, disdain every well-weighed counsel, turn and leave her? Young, graceful, gracious,—my benefactress, attached to me, en- amoured of me,—I used to say so to myself; dwell on the word; mouth it over and over again; swell over it with a pleasant, pompous complacency,—with an admiration dedicated entirely to myself, and unimpaired even by esteem for her; indeed, I smiled in deep secrecy at her naïveté and simplicity, in being the first to love, and to show it. That whip of yours seems to have a good heavy handle, Yorke: you can swing it about your head and knock me out of the saddle, if you choose. I should rather relish a loundering whack."

"Tak' patience, Robert, till the moon rises, and I can see you. Speak plain out,— did you love her or not? I could like to know: I feel curious."

"Sir . . . Sir—I say—she is very pretty, in her own style, and very attractive. She has a look, at times, of a thing made out of fire and air, at which I stand and marvel, without a thought of clasping and kissing it. I felt in her a powerful magnet to my interest and vanity: I never felt as if nature meant her to be my other and better self. When a question on that head rushed upon me, I flung it off, saying

brutally, I should be rich with her, and ruined without her: vowing I would be practical, and not romantic.''

"A very sensible resolve. What mischief came of it, Bob?''

"With this sensible resolve, I walked up to Fieldhead one night last August: it was the very eve of my departure for Birmingham—for—you see—I wanted to secure fortune's splendid prize: I had previously despatched a note, requesting a private interview. I found her at home, and alone.

"She received me without embarrassment, for she thought I came on business: *I* was embarrassed enough, but determined. I hardly know how I got the operation over; but I went to work in a hard, firm fashion,—frightful enough, I dare say. I sternly offered myself—my fine person—with my debts, of course, as a settlement.

"It vexed me; it kindled my ire, to find that she neither blushed, trembled, nor looked down. She responded—'I doubt whether I have understood you, Mr. Moore.'

"And I had to go over the whole proposal twice, and word it as plainly as A B C, before she would fully take it in. And then, what did she do? Instead of faltering a sweet Yes, or maintaining a soft, confused silence (which would have been as good) she started up, walked twice fast through the room, in the way that *she* only does, and no other woman, and ejaculated—'God bless me!'

"Yorke, I stood on the hearth, backed by the mantelpiece; against it I leaned, and prepared for anything—everything. I knew my doom, and I knew myself. There was no misunderstanding her aspect and voice. She stopped and looked at me.

" 'God bless me!' she piteously repeated, in that shocked, indignant, yet saddened accent. 'You have made a strange proposal—strange from *you;* and if you knew how strangely you worded it, and looked it, you would be startled at yourself. You spoke like a brigand who demanded my purse, rather than like a lover who asked my heart.'

"A queer sentence, was it not, Yorke? and I knew, as she uttered it, it was true as queer. Her words were a mirror in which I saw myself.

"I looked at her, dumb and wolfish: she at once enraged and shamed me.

" 'Gérard Moore, you know you don't love Shirley Keeldar.' I might have broken out into false swearing: vowed that I did love her; but I could not lie in her pure face: I could not perjure myself in her truthful presence. Besides, such hollow oaths would have been vain as void: she would no more have believed me than she would have believed the ghost of Judas, had he broken from the night and stood before her. Her female heart had finer perceptions than to be cheated into mistaking my half-coarse, half-cold admiration, for true-throbbing, manly love.

"What next happened? you will say, Mr. Yorke.

"Why, she sat down in the window-seat and cried. She cried passionately: her eyes not only rained, but lightened. They flashed, open, large, dark, haughty, upon me: they said—'You have pained me: you have outraged me: you have deceived me.'

"She added words soon to looks.

" 'I *did* respect—I *did* admire—I *did* like you,' she said: 'yes—as much as if you were my brother: and *you*—*you* want to make a speculation of me. You would immolate me to that mill—your Moloch!'

"I had the common sense to abstain from any word of excuse—any attempt at palliation: I stood to be scorned.

"Sold to the devil for the time being, I was certainly infatuated: when I did speak, what do you think I said?

" 'Whatever my own feelings were, I was persuaded *you* loved *me,* Miss Keeldar.'

"Beautiful!—was it not? She sat quite confounded. 'Is it Robert Moore that speaks?' I heard her mutter. 'Is it a man—or something lower?'

" 'Do you mean,' she asked aloud—'do you mean you thought I loved you as we love those we wish to marry?'

"It *was* my meaning; and I said so.

" 'You conceived an idea obnoxious to a woman's feelings,' was her answer: 'you have announced it in a fashion revolting to a woman's soul. You insinuate that all the frank kindness I have shown you has been a complicated, a bold, and an immodest manœuvre to ensnare a husband: you imply that at last you come here out of pity to offer me your hand, because I have courted you. Let me say this:— Your sight is jaundiced: you have seen wrong. Your mind is warped: you have judged wrong. Your tongue betrays you: you now speak wrong. I never loved you. Be at rest there. My heart is as pure of passion for you as yours is barren of affection for me.'

"I hope I was answered, Yorke?

" 'I seem to be a blind besotted sort of person,' was my remark.

" '*Loved* you!' she cried. 'Why, I have been as frank with you as a sister— never shunned you—never feared you. You cannot,' she affirmed triumphantly— 'you cannot make me tremble with your coming, nor accelerate my pulse by your influence.'

"I alleged that often, when she spoke to me, she blushed, and that the sound of my name moved her.

" 'Not for *your* sake!' she declared briefly: I urged explanation, but could get none.

" 'When I sat beside you at the school-feast, did you think I loved you then? When I stopped you in Maythorn Lane, did you think I loved you then? When I called on you in the counting-house—when I walked with you on the pavement— did you think I loved you then?'

"So she questioned me; and I said I did.

"By the Lord! Yorke—she rose—she grew tall—she expanded and refined almost to flame: there was a trembling all through her, as in live coal, when its vivid vermilion is hottest.

" ' That is to say, that you have the worst opinion of me: that you deny me the possession of all I value most. That is to say, that I am a traitor to all my sisters: that I have acted as no woman can act, without degrading herself and her sex: that I have sought where the incorrupt of my kind naturally scorn and abhor to seek.' She and I were silent for many a minute. 'Lucifer—Star of the Morning!' she went on, 'thou art fallen. You—once high in my esteem—are hurled down: you—once intimate in my friendship—are cast out. Go!'

"I went not: I had heard her voice tremble—seen her lip quiver: I knew another storm of tears would fall; and then, I believed, some calm and some sunshine must come, and I would wait for it.

"As fast, but more quietly than before, the warm rain streamed down: there was another sound in her weeping—a softer, more regretful sound. While I watched, her eyes lifted to me a gaze more reproachful than haughty—more mournful than incensed.

" 'Oh, Moore!' said she: it was worse than 'Et tu, Brute!'

"I relieved myself by what should have been a sigh, but it became a groan. A sense of Cain-like desolation made my breast ache.

" 'There has been error in what I have done,' I said, 'and it has won me bitter wages: which I will go and spend far from her who gave them.'

"I took my hat. All the time, I could not have borne to depart so; and I believed she would not let me. Nor would she, but for the mortal pang I had given her pride, that cowed her compassion and kept her silent.

"I was obliged to turn back of my own accord when I reached the door, to approach her and to say, 'Forgive me.'

" 'I could, if there was not myself to forgive, too,' was her reply; 'but to mislead a sagacious man so far, I must have done wrong.'

"I broke out suddenly with some declamation I do not remember: I know that it was sincere, and that my wish and aim were to absolve her to herself: in fact, in her case, self-accusation was a chimera.

"At last, she extended her hand. For the first time I wished to take her in my arms and kiss her. I *did* kiss her hand many times.

" 'Some day we shall be friends again,' she said, 'when you have had time to read my actions and motives in a true light, and not so horribly to misinterpret them. Time may give you the right key to all: then, perhaps, you will comprehend me; and then we shall be reconciled.'

"Farewell drops rolled slow down her cheeks: she wiped them away.

" 'I am sorry for what has happened—deeply sorry,' she sobbed. So was I, God knows! Thus were we severed."

"A queer tale!" commented Mr. Yorke.

"I'll do it no more," vowed his companion: "never more will I mention marriage to a woman, unless I feel love. Henceforth, Credit and Commerce may take care of themselves. Bankruptcy may come when it lists. I have done with slavish fear of disaster. I mean to work diligently, wait patiently, bear steadily. Let the worst come—I will take an axe and an emigrant's berth, and go out with Louis to the West—he and I have settled it. No woman shall ever again look at me as Miss Keeldar looked—ever again feel towards me as Miss Keeldar felt: in no woman's presence will I ever again stand at once such a fool and such a knave—such a brute and such a puppy."

"Tut!" said the imperturbable Yorke, "you make too much of it; but still, I say, I am capped: firstly, that she did not love you; and, secondly, that you did not love her. You are both young; you are both handsome; you are both well enough for wit, and even for temper—take you on the right side: what ailed you, that you could not agree?"

"We never *have* been—never *could* be *at home* with each other, Yorke. Admire each other as we might at a distance, still we jarred when we came very near. I have sat at one side of a room and observed her at the other; perhaps in an excited, genial moment, when she had some of her favourites round her—her old beaux, for instance, yourself and Helstone, with whom she is so playful, pleasant, and eloquent. I have watched her when she was most natural, most lively, and most lovely: my judgment has pronounced her beautiful: beautiful she is, at times, when her mood and her array partake of the splendid. I have drawn a little nearer, feeling that our terms of acquaintance gave me the right of approach; I have joined the circle round her seat, caught her eye, and mastered her attention; then we have conversed; and others—thinking me, perhaps, peculiarly privileged—have withdrawn by degrees, and left us alone. Were we happy thus left? For myself, I must say, No. Always a feeling of constraint came over me; always I was disposed to be stern and strange. We talked politics and business: no soft sense of domestic intimacy ever opened our hearts, or thawed our language, and made it flow easy and limpid. If we had confidences, they were confidences of the counting-house, not of the heart. Nothing in her cherished affection in me—made me better, gentler: she only stirred my brain and whetted my acuteness: she never crept into my heart or influenced its pulse; and for this good reason, no doubt, because I had not the secret of making her love me."

"Well, lad, it is a queer thing. I might laugh at thee, and reckon to despise thy refinements; but as it is dark night and we are by ourselves, I don't mind telling thee that thy talk brings back a glimpse of my own past life. Twenty-five years ago, I tried to persuade a beautiful woman to love me, and she would not. I had not the key to her nature: she was a stone wall to me, doorless and windowless."

"But you loved *her*, Yorke: you worshipped Mary Cave: your conduct, after all, was that of a man—never of a fortune-hunter."

"Ay! I *did* love her: but then she was beautiful as the moon we do *not* see to-night; there is nought like her in these days: Miss Helstone, maybe, has a look of her, but nobody else."

"Who has a look of her?"

"That black-coated tyrant's niece; that quiet, delicate Miss Helstone. Many a time I have put on my spectacles to look at the lassie in church, because she has gentle blue een, wi' long lashes; and, when she sits in shadow, and is very still and very pale, and is, happen, about to fall asleep wi' the length of the sermon and the heat of the biggin'—she is as like one of Canova's marbles as aught else."

"Was Mary Cave in that style?"

"Far grander! Less lass-like and flesh-like. You wondered why she hadn't wings and a crown. She was a stately, peaceful angel—was Mary."

"And you could not persuade her to love you?"

"Not with all I could do; though I prayed Heaven many a time, on my bended knees, to help me."

"Mary Cave was not what you think her, Yorke—I have seen her picture at the Rectory. She is no angel, but a fair, regular-featured, taciturn-looking woman—rather too white and lifeless for my taste. But—supposing she had been something better than she was——"

"Robert," interrupted Yorke, "I could fell you off your horse at this moment. However, I'll hold my hand. Reason tells me you are right, and I am wrong. I know well enough that the passion I still have is only the remnant of an illusion. If Miss Cave had possessed either feeling or sense, she could not have been so perfectly impassible to my regard as she showed herself—she must have preferred me to that copper-faced despot."

"Supposing, Yorke, she had been educated (no women were educated in those days); supposing she had possessed a thoughtful, original mind, a love of knowledge, a wish for information, which she took an artless delight in receiving from your lips, and having measured out to her by your hand; supposing her conversation—when she sat at your side—was fertile, varied, imbued with a picturesque grace and genial interest, quiet flowing but clear and bounteous; supposing that when you stood near her by chance, or when you sat near her by design, comfort at once became your atmosphere, and content your element; supposing that whenever her face was under your gaze, or her idea filled your thoughts, you gradually ceased to be hard and anxious, and pure affection, love of home, thirst for sweet discourse, unselfish longing to protect and cherish, replaced the sordid, cankering calculations of your trade; supposing—with all this—that many a time, when you had been so happy as to possess your Mary's little hand, you had felt it tremble as you held it—just as a warm little bird trembles when you take it from its nest; supposing you had noticed her shrink into the background on your entrance into a room, yet if you sought her in her retreat she welcomed you with the sweetest smile that ever lit a fair virgin face, and only turned her eyes from the encounter of your own, lest their clearness should reveal too much; supposing, in short, your Mary had been—not cold, but modest; not vacant, but reflective; not obtuse, but sensitive; not inane, but innocent; not prudish, but pure—would you have left her to court another woman for her wealth?"

Mr. Yorke raised his hat, wiped his forehead with his handkerchief.

"The moon is up," was his first not quite relevant remark, pointing with his whip across the moor. "There she is, rising into the haze, staring at us wi' a strange red glower. She is no more silver than old Helstone's brow is ivory. What does she mean by leaning her cheek on Rushedge i' that way, and looking at us wi' a scowl and a menace?"

"Yorke, if Mary had loved you silently, yet faithfully—chastely, yet fervently—as you would wish your wife to love, would you have left her?"

"Robert!" he lifted his arm: he held it suspended, and paused. "Robert! this is a queer world, and men are made of the queerest dregs that Chaos churned up in her ferment. I might swear sounding oaths—oaths that would make the poachers think there was a bittern booming in Bilberry Moss—that, in the case you put, Death only should have parted me from Mary. But I have lived in the world fifty-five years; I have been forced to study human nature; and—to speak a dark truth—the odds are, if Mary had loved and not scorned me; if I had been secure of her affection, certain of her constancy, been irritated by no doubts, stung by no humiliations—the odds are" (he let his hand fall heavy on the saddle)—"the odds are, I should have left her!"

They rode side by side in silence. Ere either spoke again, they were on the other side of Rushedge: Briarfield lights starred the purple skirt of the moor. Robert, being the youngest, and having less of the past to absorb him than his comrade, recommenced first.

"I believe—I daily find it proved—that we can get nothing in this world worth keeping, not so much as a principle or a conviction, except out of purifying flame, or through strengthening peril. We err; we fall; we are humbled—then we walk more carefully. We greedily eat and drink poison out of the gilded cup of vice, or from the beggar's wallet of avarice; we are sickened, degraded; everything good in us rebels against us; our souls rise bitterly indignant against our bodies; there is a period of civil war; if the soul has strength, it conquers and rules thereafter."

"What art thou going to do, Robert? What are thy plans?"

"For my private plans, I'll keep them to myself; which is very easy, as at present I have none: no private life is permitted a man in my position, a man in debt. For my public plans, my views are a little altered. While I was in Birmingham, I looked a little into reality, considered closely, and at their source, the causes of the present troubles of this country; I did the same in London. Unknown, I could go where I pleased, mix with whom I would. I went where there was want of food, of fuel, of clothing; where there was no occupation and no hope. I saw some, with naturally elevated tendencies and good feelings, kept down amongst sordid privations and harassing griefs. I saw many originally low, and to whom lack of education left scarcely anything but animal wants, disappointed in those wants, ahungered, athirst, and desperate as famished animals: I saw what taught my brain a new lesson, and filled my breast with fresh feelings. I have no intention to profess more softness or sentiment than I have hitherto professed; mutiny and ambition I regard as I have always regarded them: I should resist a riotous mob, just as heretofore; I should open on the scent of a runaway ringleader as eagerly as ever, and run him down as relentlessly, and follow him up to condign punishment as rigorously; but I should do it now chiefly for the sake and the security of those he misled. Something there is to look to, Yorke, beyond a man's personal interest: beyond the advancement of well-laid schemes; beyond even the discharge of dishonouring debts. To respect himself, a man must believe he renders justice to his fellow-men. Unless I am more considerate to ignorance, more forbearing to suffering, than I have hitherto been, I shall scorn myself as grossly unjust. What now?" he said, addressing his horse, which, hearing the ripple of water, and feeling thirsty, turned to a wayside trough, where the moonbeam was playing in a crystal eddy.

"Yorke," pursued Moore, "ride on: I must let him drink."

Yorke accordingly rode slowly forwards, occupying himself as he advanced, in discriminating, amongst the many lights now spangling the distance, those of Briarmains. Stilbro' Moor was left behind; plantations rose dusk on either hand; they were descending the hill; below them lay the valley with its populous parish: they felt already at home.

Surrounded no longer by heath, it was not startling to Mr. Yorke to see a hat rise, and to hear a voice speak behind the wall. The words, however, were peculiar.

"When the wicked perisheth, there is shouting," it said; and added, "As the whirlwind passeth, so is the wicked no more" (with a deeper growl); "terrors take hold of him as waters; hell is naked before him. He shall die without knowledge."

A fierce flash and sharp crack violated the calm of night. Yorke, ere he turned, knew the four convicts of Birmingham were avenged.

Chapter XXXI

UNCLE AND NIECE

THE die was cast. Sir Philip Nunnely knew it: Shirley knew it: Mr. Sympson knew it. That evening, when all the Fieldhead family dined at Nunnely Priory, decided the business.

Two or three things conduced to bring the Baronet to a point. He had observed that Miss Keeldar looked pensive and delicate. This new phase in her demeanour smote him on his weak or poetic side: a spontaneous sonnet brewed in his brain; and while it was still working there, one of his sisters persuaded his lady-love to sit down to the piano and sing a ballad—one of Sir Philip's own ballads. It was the least elaborate, the least affected—out of all comparison the best of his numerous efforts.

It chanced that Shirley, the moment before, had been gazing from a window down on the park; she had seen that stormy moonlight which "le Professeur Louis" was perhaps at the same instant contemplating from her own oak-parlour lattice; she had seen the isolated trees of the domain—broad, strong, spreading oaks, and high-towering heroic beeches—wrestling with the gale. Her ear had caught the full roar of the forest lower down; the swift rushing of clouds, the moon, to the eye, hasting swifter still, had crossed her vision: she turned from sight and sound—touched, if not rapt,—wakened, if not inspired.

She sang, as requested. There was much about love in the ballad: faithful love that refused to abandon its object; love that disaster could not shake; love that, in calamity, waxed fonder, in poverty clung closer. The words were set to a fine old air—in themselves they were simple and sweet: perhaps, when read, they wanted force; when *well* sung, they wanted nothing. Shirley sang them well: she breathed into the feeling, softness; she poured round the passion, force: her voice was fine that evening; its expression dramatic: she impressed all, and charmed one.

On leaving the instrument, she went to the fire, and sat down on a seat—semi-stool, semi-cushion: the ladies were round her—none of them spoke. The Misses Sympson and the Misses Nunnely looked upon her, as quiet poultry might look on an egret, an ibis, or any other strange fowl. What made her sing so? *They* never sang so. Was it proper to sing with such expression, with such originality—so unlike a school-girl? Decidedly not: it was strange, it was unusual. What was *strange* must be *wrong;* what was *unusual* must be *improper*. Shirley was judged.

Moreover, old Lady Nunnely eyed her stonily from her great chair by the fireside: her gaze said—"This woman is not of mine or my daughters' kind: I object to her as my son's wife."

Her son's catching the look, read its meaning: he grew alarmed: what he so wished to win, there was danger he might lose. He must make haste.

The room they were in had once been a picture-gallery. Sir Philip's father—Sir Monckton—had converted it into a saloon; but still it had a shadowy, long-withdrawing look. A deep recess with a window—a recess that held one couch, one table, and a fairy cabinet, formed a room within a room. Two persons standing there might interchange a dialogue, and, so it were neither long nor loud, none be the wiser.

Sir Philip induced two of his sisters to perpetrate a duet; he gave occupation to the Misses Sympson: the elder ladies were conversing together. He was pleased to remark that, meantime, Shirley rose to look at the pictures. He had a tale to tell about one ancestress, whose dark beauty seemed as that of a flower of the south: he joined her, and began to tell it.

There were mementos of the same lady in the cabinet adorning the recess; and while Shirley was stooping to examine the missal and the rosary on the inlaid shelf, and while the Misses Nunnely indulged in a prolonged screech, guiltless of expression, pure of originality, perfectly conventional and absolutely unmeaning, Sir Philip stooped too, and whispered a few hurried sentences. At first, Miss Keeldar was struck so still, you might have fancied that whisper a charm which had changed her to a statue; but she presently looked up and answered. They parted. Miss Keeldar returned to the fire, and resumed her seat: the Baronet gazed after her, then went and stood behind his sisters. Mr. Sympson—Mr. Sympson only—had marked the pantomime.

That gentleman drew his own conclusions. Had he been as acute as he was meddling, as profound as he was prying, he might have found that in Sir Philip's face whereby to correct his inference. Ever shallow, hasty, and positive, he went home quite cock-a-hoop.

He was not a man that kept secrets well: when elate on a subject, he could not avoid talking about it. The next morning, having occasion to employ his son's tutor as his secretary, he must needs announce to him, in mouthing accents, and with much flimsy pomp of manner, that he had better hold himself prepared for a return to the south, at an early day, as the important business which had detained him (Mr. Sympson) so long in Yorkshire, was now on the eve of fortunate completion: his anxious and laborious efforts were likely, at last, to be crowned with the happiest success: a truly eligible addition was about to be made to the family connections.

"In Sir Philip Nunnely?" Louis Moore conjectured.

Whereupon Mr. Sympson treated himself simultaneously to a pinch of snuff and a chuckling laugh, checked only by a sudden choke of dignity, and an order to the tutor to proceed with business.

For a day or two, Mr. Sympson continued as bland as oil, but also he seemed to sit on pins, and his gait, when he walked, emulated that of a hen treading a hot girdle. He was for ever looking out of the window, and listening for chariot-wheels: Bluebeard's wife—Sisera's mother—were nothing to him. He waited when the matter should be opened in form; when himself should be consulted; when lawyers should be summoned; when settlement discussions, and all the delicious worldly fuss, should pompously begin.

At last there came a letter: he himself handed it to Miss Keeldar out of the bag: he knew the handwriting; he knew the crest on the seal. He did not see it opened and read, for Shirley took it to her own room; nor did he see it answered, for she wrote her reply shut up,—and was very long about it,—the best part of a day. He questioned her whether it was answered; she responded, "Yes."

Again he waited—waited in silence—absolutely not daring to speak: kept mute by something in Shirley's face,—a very awful something—inscrutable to him as the writing on the wall to Belshazzar. He was moved more than once to call Daniel, in the person of Louis Moore, and to ask an interpretation: but his dignity forbade the familiarity. Daniel himself, perhaps, had his own private difficulties connected with that baffling bit of translation: he looked like a student for whom grammars are blank, and dictionaries dumb.

Mr. Sympson had been out, to while away an anxious hour in the society of his friends at De Walden Hall. He returned a little sooner than was expected; his family and Miss Keeldar were assembled in the oak-parlour; addressing the latter, he

requested her to step with him into another room: he wished to have with her a "*strictly* private interview."

She rose, asking no questions, and professing no surprise.

"Very well, sir," she said in the tone of a determined person, who is informed that the dentist is come to extract that large double tooth of his, from which he has suffered such a purgatory this month past. She left her sewing and her thimble in the window-seat, and followed her uncle where he led.

Shut into the drawing-room, the pair took seats, each in an arm-chair, placed opposite, a few yards between them.

"I have been to De Walden Hall," said Mr. Sympson. He paused. Miss Keeldar's eyes were on the pretty white and green carpet. *That* information required no response: she gave none.

"I have learned," he went on slowly,—"I have learned a circumstance which surprises me."

Resting her cheek on her forefinger, she waited to be told *what* circumstance.

"It seems that Nunnely Priory is shut up; that the family are gone back to their place in ——shire. It seems that the baronet—that the baronet—that Sir Philip himself has accompanied his mother and sisters."

"Indeed!" said Shirley.

"May I ask if you share the amazement with which I received this news?"

"No, sir."

"*Is* it news to you?"

"Yes, sir."

"I mean—I mean"—pursued Mr. Sympson, now fidgeting in his chair, quitting his hitherto brief and tolerably clear phraseology, and returning to his customary wordy, confused, irritable style; "I mean to have a *thorough* explanation. I will *not* be put off. I—I—shall *insist* on being heard; and on—on having my own way. My questions *must* be answered. I will have clear, satisfactory replies. I am not to be trifled with. (Silence.)

"It is a strange and an extraordinary thing—a very singular—a most odd thing! I thought all was right; knew no other: and there—the family are gone!"

"I suppose, sir, they had a right to go."

"*Sir Philip is gone!*" (with emphasis).

Shirley raised her brows: "Bon voyage!" said she.

"This will not do: this must be altered, ma'am."

He drew his chair forward; he pushed it back; he looked perfectly incensed, and perfectly helpless.

"Come, come, now, uncle," expostulated Shirley, "do not begin to fret and fume, or we shall make no sense of the business. Ask me what you want to know: I am as willing to come to an explanation as you: I promise you truthful replies."

"I want—I demand to know, Miss Keeldar, whether Sir Philip has made you an offer?"

"He has."

"You avow it?"

"I avow it. But now, go on: consider that point settled."

"He made you an offer that night we dined at the Priory?"

"It is enough to say that he made it. Go on."

"He proposed in the recess—in the room that used to be a picture gallery—that Sir Monckton converted into a saloon?"

No answer.

"You were both examining a cabinet: I saw it all: my sagacity was not at fault— it never is. Subsequently, you received a letter from him. On what subject—of what nature were the contents?"

"No matter."

"Ma'am, is that the way in which you speak to me?"

Shirley's foot tapped quick on the carpet.

"There you sit, silent and sullen—*you* who promised truthful replies!"

"Sir, I have answered you thus far: proceed."

"I should like to see that letter."

"You *cannot* see it."

"I *must* and *shall*, ma'am. I am your guardian."

"Having ceased to be a ward, I have no guardian."

"Ungrateful being! Reared by me as my own daughter—"

"Once more, uncle, have the kindness to keep to the point. Let us both remain cool. For my part, I do not wish to get into a passion; but, you know, once drive me beyond certain bounds, I care little what I say: I am not then soon checked. Listen! You have asked me whether Sir Philip made me an offer: that question is answered. What do you wish to know next?"

"I desire to know whether you accepted or refused him? and know it I will."

"Certainly: you ought to know it. I refused him."

"Refused him! You—*you*, Shirley Keeldar, *refused* Sir Philip Nunnely?"

"I did."

The poor gentleman bounced from his chair, and first rushed, and then trotted, through the room.

"There it is! There it is! There it is!"

"Sincerely speaking, I am sorry, uncle, you are so disappointed."

Concession—contrition, never do any good with some people. Instead of softening and conciliating, they but embolden and harden them: of that number was Mr. Sympson.

"*I* disappointed? What is it to me? Have *I* an interest in it? You would insinuate, perhaps, that I have motives?"

"Most people have motives, of some sort, for their actions."

"She accuses me to my face! I—that have been a parent to her—she charges with bad motives!"

"*Bad* motives, I did not say."

"And now you prevaricate. You have no principles!"

"Uncle, you tire me: I want to go away."

"Go you shall not! I will be answered. What are your intentions, Miss Keeldar?"

"In what respect?"

"In respect of matrimony."

"To be quiet—and to do just as I please."

"Just as you please! The words are to the last degree indecorous."

"Mr. Sympson, I advise you not to become insulting: you know I will not bear that."

"You read French. Your mind is poisoned with French novels. You have imbibed French principles."

"The ground you are treading now returns a mighty hollow sound under your feet. Beware!"

"It will end in infamy, sooner or later: I have foreseen it all along."

"Do you assert, sir, that something in which *I* am concerned will end in infamy?"

"That it will—that it will. You said just now you would act as you please. You acknowledge no rules—no limitations."

"Silly stuff! and vulgar as silly!"

"Regardless of decorum, you are prepared to fly in the face of propriety."

"You tire me, uncle."

"What, madam—*what* could be your reasons for refusing Sir Philip?"

"At last, there is another sensible question: I shall be glad to reply to it. Sir Philip is too young for me: I regard him as a boy: all his relations—his mother especially—would be annoyed if he married me: such a step would embroil him with them: I am not his equal in the world's estimation."

"Is that all?"

"Our dispositions are not compatible."

"Why, a more amiable gentleman never breathed."

"He is very amiable—very excellent—truly estimable, but *not my master;* not in one point. I could not trust myself with his happiness: I would not undertake the keeping of it for thousands: I will accept no hand which cannot hold me in check."

"I thought you liked to do as you please: you are vastly inconsistent."

"When I promise to obey, it shall be under the conviction that I can keep that promise: I could not obey a youth like Sir Philip. Besides, he would never command me: he would expect me always to rule—to guide, and I have no taste whatever for the office."

"*You* no taste for swaggering, and subduing, and ordering, and ruling?"

"Not my husband: only my uncle."

"Where is the difference?"

"There *is* a slight difference: that is certain. And I know full well, any man who wishes to live in decent comfort with me as a husband must be able to control me."

"I wish you had a real tyrant."

"A tyrant would not hold me for a day—not for an hour. I would rebel—break from him—defy him."

"Are you not enough to bewilder one's brain with your self-contradiction?"

"It is evident I bewilder your brain."

"You talk of Sir Philip being young: he is two-and-twenty."

"My husband must be thirty, with the sense of forty."

"You had better pick out some old man—some white-headed or bald-headed swain."

"No, thank you."

"You could lead some doting fool: you might pin him to your apron."

"I might do that with a boy: but it is not my vocation. Did I not say I prefer a *master*? One in whose presence I shall feel obliged and disposed to be good. One whose control my impatient temper must acknowledge. A man whose approbation can reward—whose displeasure punish me. A man I shall feel it impossible not to love, and very possible to fear."

"What is there to hinder you from doing all this with Sir Philip? He is a baronet; a man of rank, property, connections, far above yours. If you talk of intellect, he is a poet: he writes verses: which you, I take it, cannot do, with all your cleverness."

"Neither his title, wealth, pedigree, nor poetry, avail to invest him with the power I describe. These are featherweights: they want ballast: a measure of sound, solid practical sense would have stood him in better stead with me."

"You and Henry rave about poetry! you used to catch fire like tinder on the subject when you were a girl."

"Oh! uncle, there is nothing really valuable in this world, there is nothing glorious in the world to come, that is not poetry!"

"Marry a poet, then, in God's name!"

"Show him me, and I will."

"Sir Philip."

"Not at all. You are almost as good a poet as he."

"Madam, you are wandering from the point."

"Indeed, uncle, I wanted to do so; and I shall be glad to lead you away with me. Do not let us get out of temper with each other: it is not worth while."

"Out of temper, Miss Keeldar! I should be glad to know who is out of temper?"

"*I* am not, yet."

"If you mean to insinuate that *I* am, I consider that you are guilty of impertinence."

"You will be soon, if you go on at that rate."

"There it is! With your pert tongue, you would try the patience of a Job."

"I know I should."

"No levity, miss! This is not a laughing matter. It is an affair I am resolved to probe thoroughly, convinced that there is mischief at the bottom. You described just now, with far too much freedom for your years and sex, the sort of individual you would prefer as a husband. Pray, did you paint from the life?"

Shirley opened her lips; but instead of speaking she only glowed rose-red.

"I shall have an answer to that question," affirmed Mr. Sympson, assuming vast courage and consequence on the strength of this symptom of confusion.

"It was an historical picture, uncle, from several originals."

"Several originals! Bless my heart!"

"I have been in love several times."

"This is cynical."

"With heroes of many nations,"

"What next——"

"And philosophers."

"She is mad——"

"Don't ring the bell, uncle; you will alarm my aunt."

"Your poor dear aunt, what a niece she has!"

"Once I loved Socrates."

"Pooh! No trifling, ma'am."

"I admired Themistocles, Leonidas, Epaminondas."

"Miss Keeldar——"

"To pass over a few centuries, Washington was a plain man, but I liked him: but, to speak of the actual present——"

"Ah! the actual present."

"To quit crude school-girl fancies, and come to realities."

"Realities! That is the test to which you shall be brought, ma'am."

"To avow before what altar I now kneel—to reveal the present idol of my soul——"

"You will make haste about it, if you please; it is near luncheon time, and confess *you shall.*"

"Confess, I must: my heart is full of the secret; it must be spoken: I only wish you were Mr. Helstone instead of Mr. Sympson, you would sympathise with me better."

"Madam—it is a question of common sense and common prudence, not of sympathy and sentiment, and so on. Did you say it was Mr. Helstone?"

"Not precisely, but as near as may be: they are rather alike."

"I will know the name—I will have particulars."

"They positively *are* rather alike; their very faces are not dissimilar—a pair of human falcons—and dry, direct, decided both. But my hero is the mightier of the two: his mind has the clearness of the deep sea, the patience of its rocks, the force of its billows."

"Rant and fustian!"

"I daresay he can be harsh as a saw-edge, and gruff as a hungry raven."

"Miss Keeldar, does the person reside in Briarfield? answer me that."

"Uncle—I am going to tell you—his name is trembling on my tongue."

"Speak, girl!"

"That was well said, uncle. 'Speak, girl!' it is quite tragic. England has howled savagely against this man, uncle; and she will one day roar exultingly over him. He has been unscared by the howl, and he will be unelated by the shout."

"I said she was mad—she is."

"This country will change and change again in her demeanour to him: he will never change in his duty to her. Come, cease to chafe, uncle, I'll tell you his name."

"You shall tell me, or——"

"Listen! Arthur Wellesley, Lord Wellington."

Mr. Sympson rose up furious: he bounced out of the room, but immediately bounced back again, shut the door, and resumed his seat.

"Ma'am, you *shall* tell me *this:* will your principles permit you to marry a man without money—a man below you?"

"Never a man below me."

(In a high voice.) "Will you, Miss Keeldar, marry a poor man?"

"What right have you, Mr. Sympson, to ask me?"

"I insist upon knowing."

"You don't go the way to know."

"My family respectability shall not be compromised."

"A good resolution: keep it."

"Madam, it is you who shall keep it."

"Impossible, sir, since I form no part of your family."

"Do you disown us?"

"I disdain your dictatorship."

"Whom *will* you marry, Miss Keeldar?"

"Not Mr. Sam Wynne, because I scorn him: not Sir Philip Nunnely, because I *only* esteem him."

"Whom have you in your eye?"

"Four rejected candidates."

"Such obstinacy could not be, unless you were under improper influence."

"What do you mean? There are certain phrases potent to make my blood boil— improper influence! What old woman's cackle is that?"

"Are you a young lady?"

"I am a thousand times better: I am an honest woman, and as such I will be treated."

"Do you know" (leaning mysteriously forward, and speaking with ghastly solemnity), "do you know the whole neighbourhood teems with rumours respecting you and a bankrupt tenant of yours—the foreigner Moore?"

"Does it?"

"It does. Your name is in every mouth."

"It honours the lips it crosses, and I wish to the gods it may purify them."

"Is it *that* person who has power to influence you?"

"Beyond any whose cause you have advocated."

"Is it he you will marry?"

"He is handsome, and manly, and commanding."

"You declare it to my face! The Flemish knave! The low trader!"

"He is talented, and venturous, and resolute. Prince is on his brow, and ruler in his bearing."

"She glories in it! She conceals nothing! No shame, no fear!"

"When we speak the name of Moore, shame should be forgotten and fear discarded: the Moores know only honour and courage."

"I say she is mad."

"You have taunted me till my blood is up. You have worried me till I turn again."

"That Moore is the brother of my son's tutor. Would you let the Usher call you Sister?"

Bright and broad shone Shirley's eye, as she fixed it on her questioner now.

"No: no. Not for a province of possession—not for a century of life."

"You cannot separate the husband from his family."

"What then?"

"Mr. Louis Moore's sister you will be."

"Mr. Sympson . . . I am sick at heart with all this weak trash: I will bear no more. Your thoughts are not my thoughts, your aims are not my aims, your gods

are not my gods. We do not view things in the same light; we do not measure them by the same standard; we hardly speak in the same tongue. Let us part.

"It is not," she resumed, much excited—"It is not that I hate you; you are a good sort of man: perhaps you mean well in your way; but we cannot suit: we are ever at variance. You annoy me with small meddling, with petty tyranny; you exasperate my temper, and make and keep me passionate. As to your small maxims, your narrow rules, your little prejudices, aversions, dogmas, bundle them off: Mr. Sympson—go, offer them a sacrifice to the deity you worship; I'll none of them: I wash my hands of the lot. I walk by another creed, light, faith, and hope than you."

"Another creed! I believe she is an infidel."

"An infidel to *your* religion; an atheist to *your* god."

"*An—atheist!!!*"

"Your god, sir, is the World. In my eyes, you too, if not an infidel, are an idolater. I conceive that you ignorantly worship: in all things you appear to me too superstitious. Sir, your god, your great Bel, your fish-tailed Dagon, rises before me as a demon. You, and such as you, have raised him to a throne, put on him a crown, given him a sceptre. Behold how hideously he governs! See him busied at the work he likes best—making marriages. He binds the young to the old, the strong to the imbecile. He stretches out the arm of Mezentius and fetters the dead to the living. In his realm there is hatred—secret hatred: there is disgust—unspoken disgust: there is treachery—family treachery: there is vice—deep, deadly, domestic vice. In his dominions, children grow unloving between parents who have never loved: infants are nursed on deception from their very birth; they are reared in an atmosphere corrupt with lies. Your god rules at the bridal of kings—look at your royal dynasties! your deity is the deity of foreign aristocracies—analyse the blue blood of Spain! Your god is the Hymen of France—what is French domestic life? All that surrounds him hastens to decay: all declines and degenerates under his sceptre. *Your* god is a masked Death."

"This language is terrible! My daughters and you must associate no longer, Miss Keeldar: there is danger in such companionship. Had I known you a little earlier— but, extraordinary as I thought you, I could not have believed——"

"Now, sir, do you begin to be aware that it is useless to scheme for me? That, in doing so, you but sow the wind to reap the whirlwind? I sweep your cobweb projects from my path, that I may pass on unsullied. I am anchored on a resolve you cannot shake. My heart, my conscience shall dispose of my hand—*they only*. Know this at last."

Mr. Sympson was becoming a little bewildered.

"Never heard such language!" he muttered again and again. "Never was so addressed in my life—never was so used."

"You are quite confused, sir. You had better withdraw, or I will."

He rose hastily.

"We must leave this place: they must pack up at once."

"Do not hurry my aunt and cousins: give them time."

"No more intercourse: she's not proper."

He made his way to the door; he came back for his handkerchief; he dropped his snuff-box; leaving the contents scattered on the carpet, he stumbled out; Tartar lay outside across the mat—Mr. Sympson almost fell over him: in the climax of his exasperation he hurled an oath at the dog, and a coarse epithet at his mistress.

"Poor Mr. Sympson! He is both feeble and vulgar," said Shirley to herself. "My head aches, and I am tired," she added; and leaning her head upon a cushion, she softly subsided from excitement to repose. One, entering the room a quarter of an hour afterwards, found her asleep. When Shirley had been agitated, she generally took this natural refreshment. It would come at her call.

The intruder paused in her unconscious presence, and said—"Miss Keeldar."

Perhaps his voice harmonised with some dream into which she was passing—it did not startle, it hardly roused her, without opening her eyes, she but turned her head a little, so that her cheek and profile, before hidden by her arm, became visible: she looked rosy, happy, half-smiling, but her eyelashes were wet: she had wept in slumber; or perhaps, before dropping asleep, a few natural tears had fallen after she had heard that epithet; no man—no woman is always strong, always able to bear up against the unjust opinion—the vilifying word: calumny, even from the mouth of a fool, will sometimes cut into unguarded feelings. Shirley looked like a child that had been naughty and punished, but was now forgiven and at rest.

"Miss Keeldar," again said the voice: this time it woke her; she looked up and saw at her side Louis Moore—not close at her side, but standing, with arrested step, two or three yards from her.

"Oh, Mr. Moore!" she said; "I was afraid it was my uncle again: he and I have quarelled."

"Mr. Sympson should let you alone," was the reply: "can he not see that you are yet far from strong?"

"I assure you he did not find me weak: I did not cry when he was here."

"He is about to evacuate Fieldhead—so he says. He is now giving orders to his family: he has been in the schoolroom issuing commands in a manner which, I suppose, was a continuation of that which he has harassed you."

"Are you and Henry to go?"

"I believe, as far as Henry is concerned, that was the tenor of his scarcely-intelligible directions; but he may change all to-morrow: he is just in that mood when you cannot depend on his consistency for two consecutive hours: I doubt whether he will leave you for weeks yet. To myself he addressed some words which will require a little attention and comment by-and-by, when I have time to bestow on them. At the moment he came in, I was busied with a note I have got from Mr. Yorke—so fully busied that I cut short the interview with him somewhat abruptly: I left him raving: here is the note—I wish you to see it—it refers to my brother Robert." And he looked at Shirley.

"I shall be glad to hear news of him: is he coming home?"

"He is come: he is in Yorkshire: Mr. Yorke went yesterday to Stilbro' to meet him."

"Mr. Moore—something is wrong——"

"Did my voice tremble? He is now at Briarmains—and I am going to see him."

"What has occurred?"

"If you turn so pale I shall be sorry I have spoken. It might have been worse: Robert is not dead, but much hurt."

"Oh! sir; it is you who are pale. Sit down near me."

"Read the note—let me open it."

Miss Keeldar read the note: it briefly signified that last night Robert Moore had been shot at from behind the wall of Milldean Plantation, at the foot of the Brow; that he was wounded severely, but it was hoped not fatally: of the assassin, or assassins, nothing was known—they had escaped. "No doubt," Mr. Yorke observed, "it was done in revenge: it was a pity ill-will had ever been raised; but that could not be helped now."

"He is my only brother," said Louis, as Shirley returned the note. "I cannot hear unmoved that ruffians have laid in wait for him, and shot him down like some wild beast from behind a wall."

"Be comforted: be hopeful. He will get better—I know he will."

Shirley, solicitous to soothe, held her hand over Mr. Moore's, as it lay on the arm of the chair: she just touched it lightly, scarce palpably.

"Well, give me your hand," he said; "it will be for the first time: it is in a moment of calamity—give it me."

Awaiting neither consent nor refusal, he took what he asked.

"I am going to Briarmains now," he went on. "I want you to step over to the Rectory, and tell Caroline Helstone what has happened: will you do this? she will hear it best from you."

"Immediately," said Shirley, with docile promptitude. "Ought I to say that there is no danger?"

"Say so."

"You will come back soon, and let me know more?"

"I will either come or write."

"Trust me for watching over Caroline. I will communicate with your sister, too; but, doubtless, she is already with Robert?"

"Doubtless; or will be soon. Good morning, now."

"You will bear up, come what may?"

"We shall see that."

Shirley's fingers were obliged to withdraw from the tutor's: Louis was obliged to relinquish that hand folded, clasped, hidden in his own.

"I thought I should have had to support her," he said, as he walked towards Briarmains, "and it is she who has made me strong. That look of pity—that gentle touch! No down was ever softer—no elixir more potent! It lay like a snowflake: it thrilled like lightning. A thousand times I have longed to possess that hand—to have it in mine. I *have* possessed it—for five minutes I held it. Her fingers and mine can never be strangers more—having met once, they must meet again."

Chapter XXXII

THE SCHOOLBOY AND THE WOOD-NYMPH

BRIARMAINS being nearer than the Hollow, Mr. Yorke had conveyed his young comrade there. He had seen him laid in the best bed of the house, as carefully as if he had been one of his own sons. The sight of his blood, welling from the treacherously-inflicted wound, made him indeed the son of the Yorkshire gentleman's heart. The spectacle of the sudden event: of the tall, straight shape prostrated in its pride across the road: of the fine southern head laid low in the dust; of that youth in prime flung at once before him pallid, lifeless, helpless—this was the very combination of circumstances to win for the victim Mr. Yorke's liveliest interest.

No other hand was there to raise—to aid; no other voice to question kindly; no other brain to concert measures: he had to do it all himself. This utter dependence of the speechless, bleeding youth (as a youth he regarded him) on his benevolence, secured that benevolence most effectually. Well did Mr. Yorke like to have power, and to use it: he had now between his hands power over a fellow-creature's life: it suited him.

No less perfectly did it suit his saturnine better-half: the incident was quite in her way, and to her taste. Some women would have been terror-struck to see a gory man brought in over their threshold, and laid down in their hall in the "howe of the night." There, you would suppose, was subject-matter for hysterics. No: Mrs. Yorke went into hysterics when Jessy would not leave the garden to come to her knitting, or when Martin proposed starting for Australia, with a view to realise freedom, and escape the tyranny of Matthew; but an attempted murder near her door—a half-murdered man in her best bed—set her straight, cheered her spirits, gave her cap the dash of a turban.

Mrs. Yorke was just the woman who, while rendering miserable the drudging life of a simple maid-servant, would nurse like a heroine an hospital full of plague patients. She almost loved Moore: her tough heart almost yearned towards him, when she found him committed to her charge,—left in her arms, as dependent on

her as her youngest-born in the cradle. Had she seen a domestic, or one of her daughters, give him a draught of water, or smooth his pillow, she would have boxed the intruder's ears. She chased Jessy and Rose from the upper realm of the house: she forbade the housemaids to set their foot in it.

Now, if the accident had happened at the Rectory gates, and old Helstone had taken in the martyr, neither Yorke nor his wife would have pitied him: they would have adjudged him right served for his tyranny and meddling: as it was, he became, for the present, the apple of their eye.

Strange! Louis Moore was permitted to come,—to sit down on the edge of the bed, and lean over the pillow,—to hold his brother's hand, and press his pale forehead with his fraternal lips; and Mrs. Yorke bore it well. She suffered him to stay half the day there; she once sufffered him to sit up all night in the chamber; she rose herself at five o'clock of a wet November morning, and with her own hands lit the kitchen fire, and made the brothers a breakfast, and served it to them herself. Majestically arrayed in a boundless flannel wrapper, a shawl, and her nightcap, she sat and watched them eat, as complacently as a hen beholds her chickens feed. Yet she gave the cook warning that day for venturing to make and carry up to Mr. Moore a basin of sago-gruel; and the housemaid lost her favour because, when Mr. Louis was departing, she brought him his surtout aired from the kitchen, and, like a "forward piece," as she was, helped him on with it, and accepted, in return, a smile, a "thank you, my girl," and a shilling. Two ladies called one day, pale and anxious, and begged earnestly, humbly, to be allowed to see Mr. Moore one instant: Mrs. Yorke hardened her heart, and sent them packing,— not without opprobrium.

But how was it when Hortense Moore came?—Not so bad as might have been expected: the whole family of the Moores really seemed to suit Mrs. Yorke so as no other family had ever suited her. Hortense and she possessed an exhaustless mutual theme of conversation in the corrupt propensities of servants. Their views of this class were similar: they watched them with the same suspicion, and judged them with the same severity. Hortense, too, from the very first showed no manner of jealousy of Mrs. Yorke's attentions to Robert; she let her keep the post of nurse with little interference: and, for herself, found ceaseless occupation in fidgeting about the house, holding the kitchen under surveillance, reporting what passed there, and, in short, making herself generally useful. Visitors, they both of them agreed in excluding sedulously from the sick-room. They held the young millowner captive, and hardly let the air breathe or the sun shine on him.

Mr. MacTurk, the surgeon to whom Moore's case had been committed, pronounced his wound of a dangerous, but, he trusted, not of a hopeless character. At first he wished to place with him a nurse of his own selection; but this neither Mrs. Yorke nor Hortense would hear of: they promised faithful observance of directions. He was left, therefore, for the present, in their hands.

Doubtless, they executed the trust to the best of their ability; but something got wrong: the bandages were displaced, or tampered with; great loss of blood followed. MacTurk, being summoned, came with steed afoam. He was one of those surgeons whom it is dangerous to vex: abrupt in his best moods; in his worst, savage. On seeing Moore's state, he relieved his feelings by a little flowery language, with which it is not neccssary to strew the present page. A bouquet or two of the choicest blossoms fell on the unperturbed head of one Mr. Graves, a stony young assistant he usually carried about with him; with a second nosegay he gifted another young gentleman in his train—an interesting facsimile of himself, being, indeed, his own son; but the full *corbeille* of blushing bloom fell to the lot of meddling womankind, *en masse*.

For the best part of one winter night, himself and satellites were busied about Moore. There, at his bedside, shut up alone with him in his chamber, they wrought and wrangled over his exhausted frame. They three were on one side of the bed,

and Death on the other. The conflict was sharp: it lasted till day broke, when the balance between the belligerents seemed so equal that both parties might have claimed the victory.

At dawn, Graves and young MacTurk were left in charge of the patient, while the senior went himself in search of additional strength, and secured it in the person of Mrs. Horsfall, the best nurse on his staff. To this woman he gave Moore in charge, with the sternest injunctions respecting the responsibility laid on her shoulders. She took this responsibility stolidly, as she did also the easy chair at the bed-head. That moment she began her reign.

Mrs. Horsfall had one virtue,—orders received from MacTurk she obeyed to the letter: the Ten Commandments were less binding in her eyes than her surgeon's dictum. In other respects, she was no woman, but a dragon. Hortense Moore fell effaced before her; Mrs. Yorke withdrew—crushed; yet both these women were personages of some dignity in their own estimation, and of some bulk in the estimation of others. Perfectly cowed by the breadth, the height, the bone, and the brawn of Mrs. Horsfall, they retreated to the back-parlour. She, for her part, sat upstairs when she liked, and downstairs when she preferred it: she took her dram three times a day, and her pipe of tobacco four times.

As to Moore, no one now ventured to inquire about him: Mrs. Horsfall had him at dry-nurse: it was she who was to do for him; and the general conjecture now ran that she did for him accordingly.

Morning and evening MacTurk came to see him: his case, thus complicated by a new mischance, was become one of interest in the surgeon's eyes: he regarded him as a damaged piece of clock-work, which it would be creditable to his skill to set a-going again. Graves and young MacTurk—Moore's sole other visitors—contemplated him in the light in which they were wont to contemplate the occupant for the time being of the dissecting-room at Stilbro' Infirmary.

Robert Moore had a pleasant time of it: in pain; in danger; too weak to move; almost too weak to speak; a sort of giantess his keeper; the three surgeons his sole society. Thus he lay through the diminishing days and lengthening nights of the whole drear month of November.

In the commencement of his captivity, Moore used feebly to resist Mrs. Horsfall: he hated the sight of her rough bulk, and dreaded the contact of her hard hands; but she taught him docility in a trice. She made no account whatever of his six feet—his manly thews and sinews: she turned him in his bed as another woman would have turned a babe in its cradle. When he was good, she addressed him as "my dear," and "honey"; and when he was bad, she sometimes shook him. Did he attempt to speak when MacTurk was there, she lifted her hand and bade him "hush!" like a nurse checking a forward child. If she had not smoked—if she had not taken gin, it would have been better, he thought; but she did both. Once—in her absence—he intimated to MacTurk, that "that woman was a dram-drinker."

"Pooh! my dear sir; they are all so," was the reply he got for his pains. "But Horsfall has this virtue," added the surgeon,—"drunk or sober, she always remembers to obey *me*."

At length the latter autumn passed; its fogs, its rains withdrew from England their mourning and their tears; its winds swept on to sigh over lands far away. Behind November came deep winter; clearness, stillness, frost accompanying.

A calm day had settled into a crystalline evening: the world wore a North Pole colouring: all its lights and tints looked like the "reflets"[1] of white, or violet, or pale green gems. The hills wore a lilac blue; the setting sun had purple in its red; the sky was ice, all silvered azure; when the stars rose, they were of white crystal—not gold; grey, or cerulean, or faint emerald hues—cool, pure, and transparent—tinged the mass of the landscape.

[1] Find me an English word as good, reader, and I will gladly dispense with the French word. Reflections won't do.

What is this by itself in a wood no longer green, no longer even russet; a wood, neutral tint—this dark blue moving object? Why, it is a schoolboy—a Briarfield grammar-schoolboy—who has left his companions, now trudging home by the high road, and is seeking a certain tree, with a certain mossy mound at its root—convenient as a seat. Why is he lingering here?—the air is cold, and the time wears late. He sits down: what is he thinking about? Does he feel the chaste charm Nature wears to-night? A pearl-white moon smiles through the green trees: does he care for her smile?

Impossible to say; for he is silent, and his countenance does not speak: as yet, it is no mirror to reflect sensation, but rather a mask to conceal it. This boy is a stripling of fifteen—slight, and tall of his years; in his face there is as little of amenity as of servility: his eye seems prepared to note any incipient attempt to control or overreach him, and the rest of his features indicate faculties alert for resistance. Wise ushers avoid unnecessary interference with that lad. To break him in by severity would be a useless attempt; to win him by flattery would be an effort worse than useless. He is best let alone. Time will educate, and experience train him.

Professedly, Martin Yorke (it is a young Yorke, of course) tramples on the name of poetry: talk sentiment to him, and you would be answered by sarcasm. Here he is, wandering alone, waiting duteously on Nature, while she unfolds a page of stern, of silent, and of solemn poetry, beneath his attentive gaze.

Being seated, he takes from his satchel a book—not the Latin grammar, but a contraband volume of fairy tales; there will be light enough yet for an hour to serve his keen young vision: besides, the moon waits on him—her beam, dim and vague as yet, fills the glade where he sits.

He reads: he is led into a solitary mountain region; all round him is rude and desolate, shapeless, and almost colourless. He hears bells tinkle on the wind: forthriding from the formless folds of the mist, dawns on him the brightest vision—a green-robed lady, on a snow-white palfrey; he sees her dress, her gems, and her steed; she arrests him with some mysterious questions: he is spell-bound, and must follow her into Fairyland.

A second legend bears him to the sea-shore: there tumbles in a strong tide, boiling at the base of dizzy cliffs: it rains and blows. A reef of rocks, black and rough, stretches far into the sea; all along, and among, and above these crags, dash and flash, sweep and leap, swells, wreaths, drifts of snowy spray. Some lone wanderer is out on these rocks, treading, with cautious step, the wet, wild sea-weed; glancing down into hollows where the brine lies fathoms deep and emerald-clear, and seeing there wilder and stranger, and huger vegetation, than is found on land, with treasure of shells—some green, some purple, some pearly—clustered in the curls of the snaky plants. He hears a cry. Looking up, and forward, he sees, at the bleak point of the reef, a tall, pale thing—shaped like man, but made of spray—transparent, tremulous, awful: it stands not alone: they are all human figures that wanton in the rocks—a crowd of foam-women—a band of white, evanescent Nereides.

Hush:—shut the book: hide it in the satchel:—Martin hears a tread. He listens: No—yes: once more the dead leaves, lightly crushed, rustle on the wood-path. Martin watches: the trees part: the trees part, and a woman issues forth.

She is a lady dressed in dark silk, a veil covering her face. Martin never met a lady in this wood before—nor any female, save, now and then, a village-girl come to gather nuts. To-night, the apparition does not displease him. He observes, as she approaches, that she is neither old nor plain, but, on the contrary, very youthful; and, but that he now recognises her for one whom he has often wilfully pronounced ugly, he would deem that he discovered traits of beauty behind the thin gauze of that veil.

She passes him, and says nothing. He knew she would: all women are proud monkeys—and he knows no more conceited doll than that Caroline Helstone. The

thought is hardly hatched in his mind, when the lady retraces those two steps she had got beyond him, and raising her veil, reposes her glance on his face, while she softly asks—''Are you one of Mr. Yorke's sons?''

No human evidence would ever have been able to persuade Martin Yorke that he blushed when thus addressed; yet blush he did, to the ears.

''I am,'' he said bluntly; and encouraged himself to wonder, superciliously, what would come next.

''You are Martin, I think?'' was the observation that followed.

It could not have been more felicitous: it was a simple sentence—very artlessly, a little timidly, pronounced; but it chimed in harmony to the youth's nature: it stilled him like a note of music.

Martin had a keen sense of his personality: he felt it right and sensible that the girl should discriminate him from his brothers. Like his father, he hated ceremony: it was acceptable to hear a lady address him as ''Martin,'' and not Mr. Martin or Master Martin, which form would have lost her good graces for ever. Worse, if possible, than ceremony, was the other extreme of slipshod familiarity: the slight tone of bashfulness—the scarcely perceptible hesitation—was considered perfectly in place.

''I am Martin,'' he said.

''Are your father and mother well?''—(it was lucky she did not say *papa* and *mamma*: that would have undone all)—''and Rose and Jessy?''

''I suppose so.''

''My cousin Hortense is still at Briarmains?''

''Oh, yes!''

Martin gave a comic half-smile and demi-groan: the half-smile was responded to by the lady, who could guess in what sort of odour Hortense was likely to be held by the young Yorkes.

''Does your mother like her?''

''They suit so well about the servants, they can't help liking each other!''

''It is cold to-night.''

''Why are you out so late?''

''I lost my way in this wood.''

Now, indeed, Martin allowed himself a refreshing laugh of scorn.

''Lost your way in the mighty forest of Briarmains! You deserve never more to find it.''

''I never was here before, and I believe I am trespassing now: you might inform against me if you chose, Martin, and have me fined: it is your father's wood.''

''I should think I knew that; but since you are so simple as to lose your way, I will guide you out.''

''You need not: I have got into the track now: I shall be right. Martin'' (a little quickly), ''how is Mr. Moore?''

Martin had heard certain rumours: it struck him that it might be amusing to make an experiment.

''Going to die. Nothing can save him. All hope flung overboard!''

She put her veil aside. She looked into his eyes, and said—''To die!''

''To die. All along of the women, my mother and the rest: they did something about his bandages that finished everything: he would have got better but for them. I am sure they should be arrested, cribbed, tried, and brought in for Botany Bay, at the very least.''

The questioner, perhaps, did not hear this judgment: she stood motionless. In two minutes, without another word, she moved forwards: no good-night, no further inquiry. This was not amusing, nor what Martin had calculated on: he expected something dramatic and demonstrative: it was hardly worth while to frighten the girl, if she would not entertain him in return. He called—''Miss Helstone!''

She did not hear or turn. He hastened after and overtook her.

"Come. Are you uneasy about what I said?"

"You know nothing about death, Martin: you are too young for me to talk to concerning such a thing."

"Did you believe me? It's all flummery! Moore eats like three men: they are always making sago or tapioca, or something good for him: I never go into the kitchen, but there is a saucepan on the fire, cooking him some dainty. I think I will play the old soldier, and be fed on the fat of the land like him."

"Martin! Martin!" Here her voice trembled, and she stopped.

"It is exceedingly wrong of you, Martin: you have almost killed me."

Again she stopped; she leaned against a tree, trembling, shuddering, and as pale as death.

Martin contemplated her with inexpressible curiosity. In one sense it was, as he would have expressed it, "nuts" to him to see this: it told him so much, and he was beginning to have a great relish for discovering secrets; in another sense, it reminded him of what he had once felt when he had heard a blackbird lamenting for her nestlings, which Matthew had crushed with a stone, and that was not a pleasant feeling. Unable to find anything very appropriate to *say,* in order to comfort her, he began to cast about in his mind what he could *do:* he smiled: the lad's smile gave wondrous transparency to his physiognomy.

"Eureka!" he cried. "I'll set all straight by-and-by. You are better now, Miss Caroline; walk forward," he urged.

Not reflecting that it would be more difficult for Miss Helstone than for himself to climb a wall or penetrate a hedge, he piloted her by a short cut which led to no gate. The consequence was he had to help her over some formidable obstacles, and, while he railed at her for helplessness, he perfectly liked to feel himself of use.

"Martin, before we separate, assure me seriously, and on your word of honour, that Mr. Moore is better."

"How very much you think of that Moore!"

"No—but—many of his friends may ask me, and I wish to be able to give an authentic answer."

"You may tell them he is well enough, only idle: you may tell them that he takes mutton-chops for dinner, and the best of arrowroot for supper. I intercepted a basin myself one night on its way upstairs, and ate half of it."

"And who waits on him, Martin? Who nurses him?"

"Nurses him?—the great baby! Why, a woman as round and big as our largest water-butt—a rough, hard-favoured old girl. I make no doubt she leads him a rich life: nobody else is let near him: he is chiefly in the dark. It is my belief she knocks him about terribly in that chamber. I listen at the wall sometimes when I am in bed, and I think I hear her thumping him. You should see her fist: she could hold half-a-dozen hands like yours in her one palm. After all, notwithstanding the chops and jellies he gets, I would not be in his shoes. In fact, it is my private opinion that she eats most of what goes up on the tray to Mr. Moore. I wish she may not be starving him."

Profound silence and meditation on Caroline's part, and a sly watchfulness on Martin's.

"You never see him, I suppose, Martin?"

"I? No: I don't care to see him, for my own part."

Silence again.

"Did not you come to our house once with Mrs. Pryor, about five weeks since, to ask after him?" again inquired Martin.

"Yes."

"I daresay you wished to be shown upstairs?"

"We *did* wish it: we entreated it; but your mother declined."

"Aye! she declined. I heard it all: she treated you as it is her pleasure to treat visitors now and then: she behaved to you rudely and harshly."

"She was not kind; for, you know, Martin, we are relations, and it is natural we should take an interest in Mr. Moore. But here we must part: we are at your father's gate."

"Very well—what of that? I shall walk home with you?"

"They will miss you, and wonder where you are."

"Let them. . . . I can take care of myself, I suppose."

Martin knew that he had already incurred the penalty of a lecture, and dry bread for his tea. No matter, the evening had furnished him with an adventure: it was better than muffins and toast.

He walked home with Caroline. On the way he promised to see Mr. Moore, in spite of the dragon who guarded his chamber, and appointed an hour on the next day, when Caroline was to come to Briarmains Wood and get tidings of him: he would meet her at a certain tree. The scheme led to nothing: still he liked it.

Having reached home, the dry bread and the lecture were duly administered to him, and he was dismissed to bed at an early hour. He accepted his punishment with the toughest stoicism.

Ere ascending to his chamber he paid a secret visit to the dining-room, a still, cold, stately apartment, seldom used; for the family customarily dined in the back-parlour. He stood before the mantelpiece, and lifted his candle to two pictures hung above—female heads: one, a type of serene beauty—happy and innocent; the other, more lovely—but forlorn and desperate.

"She looked like *that*," he said, gazing on the latter sketch, "when she sobbed, turned white, and leaned against the tree."

"I suppose," he pursued, when he was in his room, and seated on the edge of his pallet-bed—"I suppose she is what they call, *'in love'*; yes, *in love* with that long thing in the next chamber. Whist! is that Horsfall clattering him? I wonder he does not yell out. It really sounds as if she had fallen on him tooth and nail; but I suppose she is making the bed. I saw her at it once—she hit into the mattresses as if she was boxing. It is queer, Zillah (they call her Zillah)—Zillah Horsfall is a woman, and Caroline Helstone is a woman: they are two individuals of the same species—not much alike though. Is she a pretty girl, that Caroline? I suspect she is—very nice to look at—something so clear in her face—so soft in her eyes. I approve of her looking at me; it does me good. She has long eyelashes: their shadow seems to rest where she gazes, and to instil peace and thought. If she behaves well, and continues to suit me, as she has suited me to-day, I may do her a good turn. I rather relish the notion of circumventing my mother and that ogress, old Horsfall. Not that I like humouring Moore; but whatever I do I'll be paid for, and in coin of my own choosing: I know what reward I will claim—one displeasing to Moore, and agreeable to myself."

He turned into bed.

Chapter XXXIII

MARTIN'S TACTICS

It was necessary to the arrangement of Martin's plan, that he should stay at home that day. Accordingly, he found no appetite for breakfast; and, just about school-time, took a severe pain about his heart, which rendered it advisable that, instead of setting out to the grammar-school with Mark, he should succeed to his father's arm-chair by the fireside, and also to his morning-paper. This point being satisfactorily settled, and Mark being gone to Mr. Summer's class, and Matthew and Mr. Yorke

withdrawn to the counting-house, three other exploits, nay four, remained to be achieved.

The first of these was to realise the breakfast he had not yet tasted, and with which his appetite of fifteen could ill afford to dispense; the second, third, fourth, to get his mother, Miss Moore and Mrs. Horsfall successively, out of the way before four o'clock that afternoon.

The first was, for the present, the most pressing, since the work before him demanded an amount of energy which the present empty condition of his youthful stomach did not seem likely to supply.

Martin knew the way to the larder; and knowing this way, he took it. The servants were in the kitchen, breakfasting solemnly with closed doors; his mother and Miss Moore were airing themselves on the lawn, and discussing the closed doors aforesaid: Martin, safe in the larder, made fastidious selection from its stores. His breakfast had been delayed—he was determined it should be recherché: it appeared to him that a variety on his usual somewhat insipid fare of bread and milk was both desirable and advisable: the savoury and the salutary he thought might be combined. There was store of rosy apples laid in straw upon a shelf; he picked out three. There was pastry upon a dish; he selected an apricot-puff and a damson tart. On the plain household bread his eye did not dwell; but he surveyed with favour some currant tea-cakes, and condescended to make choice of one. Thanks to his clasp-knife, he was able to appropriate a wing of fowl and a slice of ham; a cantlet of cold custard-pudding he thought would harmonise with these articles; and having made this final addition to his booty, he at length sallied forth into the hall.

He was already half-way across—three steps more would have anchored him in the harbour of the back-parlour—when the front door opened, and there stood Matthew. Better far had it been the Old Gentleman, in full equipage of horns, hoofs, and tail.

Matthew, sceptic and scoffer, had already failed to subscribe a prompt belief in that pain about the heart: he had muttered some words, amongst which the phrase "shamming Abraham" had been very distinctly audible; and the succession to the arm-chair and newspaper had appeared to affect him with mental spasms: the spectacle now before him, the apples, the tarts, the tea-cake, the fowl, ham, and pudding, offered evidence but too well calculated to inflate his opinion of his own sagacity.

Martin paused "interdit" one minute, one instant; the next he knew his ground, and pronounced all well. With the true perspicacity "des âmes élites," he at once saw how this—at first sight untoward event—might be turned to excellent account: he saw how it might be so handled as to secure the accomplishment of his second task, viz., the disposal of his mother. He knew that a collision between him and Matthew always suggested to Mrs. Yorke the propriety of a fit of hysterics; he further knew that, on the principle of calm succeeding to storm, after a morning of hysterics his mother was sure to indulge in an afternoon of bed. This would accommodate him perfectly.

The collision duly took place in the hall. A dry laugh, an insulting sneer, a contemptuous taunt, met by a nonchalant but most cutting reply, were the signals. They rushed at it. Martin, who usually made little noise on these occasions, made a great deal now. In flew the servants, Mrs. Yorke, Miss Moore: no female hand could separate them. Mr. Yorke was summoned.

"Sons," said he, "one of you must leave my roof if this occurs again: I will have no Cain and Abel strife here."

Martin now allowed himself to be taken off: he had been hurt; he was the youngest and slightest: he was quite cool, in no passion: he even smiled, content that the most difficult part of the labour he had set himself was over.

Once he seemed to flag in the course of the morning.

"It is not worth while to bother myself for that Caroline," he remarked. But, a quarter of an hour afterwards, he was again in the dining-room, looking at the head with dishevelled tresses, and eyes turbid with despair.

"Yes," he said, "I made her sob, shudder, almost faint: I'll see her smile before I've done with her: besides, I want to outwit all these womenites."

Directly after dinner, Mrs. Yorke fulfilled her son's calculation, by withdrawing to her chamber. Now for Hortense.

That lady was just comfortably settled to stocking-mending in the back parlour, when Martin—laying down a book which, stretched on the sofa (he was still indisposed, according to his own account), he had been perusing in all the voluptuous ease of a yet callow pacha—lazily introduced some discourse about Sarah, the maid at the Hollow. In the course of much verbal meandering, he insinuated information that this damsel was said to have three suitors, Frederic Murgatroyd, Jeremiah Pighills, and John-of-Mally's-of-Hannah's-of-Deb's; and that Miss Mann had affirmed she knew for a fact, that, now the girl was left in sole charge of the cottage, she often had her swains to meals, and entertained them with the best the house afforded.

It needed no more. Hortense could not have lived another hour without betaking herself to the scene of these nefarious transactions, and inspecting the state of matters in person. Mrs. Horsfall remained.

Martin, master of the field now, extracted from his mother's work-basket a bunch of keys; with these he opened the sideboard cupboard, produced thence a black bottle and a small glass, placed them on the table, nimbly mounted the stairs, made for Mr. Moore's door, tapped, the nurse opened.

"If you please, ma'am, you are invited to step into the back-parlour, and take some refreshment: you will not be disturbed: the family are out."

He watched her down; he watched her in; himself shut the door: he knew she was safe.

The hard work was done; now for the pleasure. He snatched his cap, and away for the wood.

It was yet but half-past three; it had been a fine morning, but the sky looked dark now: it was beginning to snow; the wind blew cold; the wood looked dismal; the old tree grim. Yet Martin approved the shadow on his path: he found a charm in the spectral aspect of the doddered oak.

He had to wait; to and fro he walked, while the flakes fell faster; and the wind, which at first had but moaned, pitifully howled.

"She is long in coming," he muttered, as he glanced along the narrow track. "I wonder," he subjoined, "what I wish to see her so much for? She is not coming for me. But I have power over her, and I want her to come that I may use that power."

He continued his walk.

"Now," he resumed, when a further period had elapsed, "if she fails to come, I shall hate and scorn her."

It struck four: he heard the church-clock far away. A step so quick, so light, that, but for the rustling of leaves, it would scarcely have sounded on the wood-walk, checked his impatience. The wind blew fiercely now, and the thickened white storm waxed bewildering: but on she came, and not dismayed.

"Well, Martin," she said eagerly, "how is he?"

"It is queer how she thinks of *him*," reflected Martin: "the blinding snow and bitter cold are nothing to her, I believe: yet she is but a 'chitty-faced creature,' as my mother would say. I could find in my heart to wish I had a cloak to wrap her in."

Thus meditating to himself, he neglected to answer Miss Helstone.

"You have seen him?"

"No."

"Oh! You promised you would."

"I mean to do better by you than that. Didn't I say *I* don't care to see him?"

"But now it will be so long before I get to know anything certain about him, and I am sick of waiting. Martin, *do* see him, and give him Caroline Helstone's regards, and say she wished to know how he was, and if anything could be done for his comfort."

"I won't."

"You are changed: you were so friendly last night."

"Come: we must not stand in this wood; it is too cold."

"But, before I go, promise me to come again to-morrow with news."

"No such thing; I am much too delicate to make and keep such appointments in the winter season: if you knew what a pain I had in my chest this morning, and how I went without breakfast, and was knocked down besides, you'd feel the impropriety of bringing me here in the snow. Come, I say."

"Are you really delicate, Martin?"

"Don't I look so?"

"You have rosy cheeks."

"That's hectic. Will you come—or you won't?"

"Where?"

"With me. I was a fool not to bring a cloak: I would have made you cosy."

"You are going home! my nearest road lies in the opposite direction."

"Put your arm through mine. I'll take care of you."

"But, the wall—the hedge—it is such hard work climbing, and you are too slender and young to help me without hurting yourself."

"You shall go through the gate."

"But——"

"But!—but! Will you trust me or not?"

She looked into his face.

"I think I will. Anything rather than return as anxious as I came."

"I can't answer for that. This, however, I promise you; be ruled by me, and you shall see Moore yourself."

"See him myself?"

"Yourself."

"But, dear Martin, does he know?"

"Ah! I'm dear now. No: he doesn't know."

"And your mother and the others?"

"All is right."

Caroline fell into a long silent fit of musing, but still she walked on with her guide: they came in sight of Briarmains.

"Have you made up your mind?" he asked.

She was silent.

"Decide. We are just on the spot. I *won't* see him—that I tell you—except to announce your arrival."

"Martin, you are a strange boy, and this is a strange step; but all I feel *is* and *has* been, for a long time, strange. I will see him."

"Having said that, you will neither hesitate nor retract?"

"No."

"Here we are, then. Do not be afraid of passing the parlour-window: no one will see you. My father and Matthew are at the mill; Mark is at school; the servants are in the back-kitchen; Miss Moore is at the cottage; my mother in her bed; and Mrs. Horsfall in Paradise. Observe—I need not ring: I open the door; the hall is empty; the staircase quiet; so is the gallery: the whole house and all its inhabitants are under a spell, which I will not break till you are gone."

"Martin, I trust you."

"You never said a better word. Let me take your shawl: I will shake off the snow and dry it for you. You are cold and wet: never mind; there is a fire upstairs. Are you ready?"

"Yes."

"Follow me."

He left his shoes on the mat; mounted the stair unshod; Caroline stole after, with noiseless step: there was a gallery, and there was a passage; at the end of that passage Martin paused before a door and tapped: he had to tap twice—thrice: a voice, known to one listener, at last said—"Come in."

The boy entered briskly.

"Mr. Moore, a lady called to inquire after you: none of the women were about: it is washing day, and the maids are over the crown of the head in soap-suds in the back-kitchen; so I asked her to step up."

"Up here, sir?"

"Up here, sir: but if you object, she shall go down again."

"Is this a place, or am I a person to bring a lady to, you absurd lad?"

"No: so I'll take her off."

"Martin, you will stay here. Who is she?"

"Your grandmother from that château on the Scheldt Miss Moore talks about."

"Martin," said the softest whisper at the door, "don't be foolish."

"Is she there?" inquired Moore hastily. He had caught an imperfect sound.

"She is there, fit to faint: she is standing on the mat, shocked at your want of filial affection."

"Martin, you are an evil cross between an imp and a page. What is she like?"

"More like me than you; for she is young and beautiful."

"You are to show her forward. Do you hear?"

"Come, Miss Caroline."

"Miss Caroline!" repeated Moore.

And when Miss Caroline entered, she was encountered in the middle of the chamber by a tall, thin, wasted figure, who took both her hands.

"I give you a quarter of an hour," said Martin as he withdrew: "no more. Say what you have to say in that time: till it is past, I will wait in the gallery: nothing shall approach: I'll see you safe away. Should you persist in staying longer, I leave you to your fate."

He shut the door. In the gallery he was as elate as a king: he had never been engaged in an adventure he liked so well; for no adventure had ever invested him with so much importance or inspired him with so much interest.

"You are come at last," said the meagre man, gazing on his visitress with hollow eyes.

"Did you expect me before?"

"For a month—near two months, we have been very near; and I have been in sad pain, and danger, and misery, Cary."

"I could not come."

"Couldn't you? But the Rectory and Briarmains are very near: not two miles apart."

There was pain—there was pleasure in the girl's face as she listened to these implied reproaches: it was sweet—it was bitter to defend herself.

"When I say I could not come, I mean I could not see you; for I came with mamma the very day we heard what had happened. Mr. MacTurk then told us it was impossible to admit any stranger."

"But afterwards—every fine afternoon these many weeks past I have waited and listened. Something here, Cary" (laying his hand on his breast), "told me it was impossible but that you should think of me. Not that I merit thought; but we are old acquaintance; we are cousins."

"I came again, Robert: mamma and I came again."

"Did you? Come, that is worth hearing: since you came again, we will sit down and talk about it."

They sat down. Caroline drew her chair up to his. The air was now dark with snow: an Iceland blast was driving it wildly. This pair neither heard the long "wuthering" rush, nor saw the white burden it drifted: each seemed conscious but of one thing—the presence of the other.

"And so mamma and you came again?"

"And Mrs. Yorke did treat us strangely. We asked to see you. 'No,' said she; 'not in my house. I am at present responsible for his life: it shall not be forfeited for half-an-hour's idle gossip.' But I must not tell you all she said: it was very disagreeable. However, we came yet again—mamma, Miss Keeldar, and I. This time we thought we should conquer, as we were three against one, and Shirley was on our side. But Mrs. Yorke opened such a battery."

Moore smiled. "What did she say?"

"Things that astonished us. Shirley laughed at last; I cried; mamma was seriously annoyed; we were all three driven from the field. Since that time I have only walked once a day past the house, just for the satisfaction of looking up at your window, which I could distinguish by the drawn curtains. I really dared not come in."

"I *have* wished for you, Caroline."

"I did not know that. I never dreamt one instant that you thought of me. If I had but most distantly imagined such a possibility——"

"Mrs. Yorke would still have beaten you."

"She would not. Stratagem should have been tried, if persuasion failed. I would have come to the kitchen-door; the servant should have let me in; and I would have walked straight upstairs. In fact, it was far more the fear of intrusion—the fear of yourself, that baffled me, than the fear of Mrs. Yorke."

"Only last night, I despaired of ever seeing you again. Weakness has wrought terrible depression in me—terrible depression."

"And you sit alone?"

"Worse than alone."

"But you must be getting better, since you can leave your bed?"

"I doubt whether I shall live: I see nothing for it, after such exhaustion, but decline."

"You—you shall go home to the Hollow."

"Dreariness would accompany—nothing cheerful come near me."

"I *will* alter this: this *shall* be altered, were there ten Mrs. Yorkes to do battle with."

"Cary, you make me smile."

"Do smile: smile again. Shall I tell you what I should like?"

"Tell me anything—only keep talking. I am Saul: but for music I should perish."

"I should like you to be brought to the Rectory, and given to me and mamma."

"A precious gift! I have not laughed since they shot me till now."

"Do you suffer pain, Robert?"

"Not so much pain now; but I am hopelessly weak, and the state of my mind is inexpressible—dark, barren, impotent. Do you not read it all in my face? I look a mere ghost."

"Altered, yet I should have known you anywhere: but I understand your feelings: I experienced something like it. Since we met, I too have been very ill."

"*Very* ill?"

"I thought I should die. The tale of my life seemed told. Every night, just at midnight, I used to wake from awful dreams—and the book lay open before me at the last page, where was written 'Finis.' I had strange feelings."

"You speak my experience."

"I believed I should never see you again; and I grew so thin—as thin as you are now: I could do nothing for myself—neither rise nor lie down; and I could not eat—yet, you see I am better."

"Comforter! sad as sweet: I am too feeble to say what I feel; but, while you speak, I *do* feel."

"Here, I am at your side, where I thought never more to be; here I speak to you—I see you listen to me willingly—look at me kindly. Did I count on that? I despaired."

Moore sighed—a sigh so deep, it was nearly a groan: he covered his eyes with his hand.

"May I be spared to make some atonement."

Such was his prayer.

"And for what?"

"We will not touch on it now, Cary; unmanned as I am, I have not the power to cope with such a topic. Was Mrs. Pryor with you during your illness?"

"Yes" (Caroline smiled brightly)—"you know she is mamma?"

"I have heard: Hortense told me; but that tale, too, I will receive from yourself. Does she add to your happiness?"

"What! mamma? She is *dear* to me; *how* dear I cannot say. I was altogether weary, and she held me up."

"I deserve to hear that in a moment when I can scarce lift my hand to my head. I deserve it."

"It is no reproach against you."

"It is a coal of fire heaped on my head; and so is every word you address to me, and every look that lights your sweet face. Come still nearer, Lina; and give me your hand—if my thin fingers do not scare you."

She took those thin fingers between her two little hands—she bent her head "et les effleura de ses lèvres" (I put that in French, because the word "effleurer" is an exquisite word). Moore was much moved: a large tear or two coursed down his hollow cheek.

"I'll keep these things in my heart, Cary; that kiss I will put by, and you shall hear of it again some day."

"Come out!" cried Martin, opening the door. "Come away—you have had twenty minutes instead of a quarter of an hour."

"She will not stir yet—you hempseed."

"I dare not stay longer, Robert."

"Can you promise to return?"

"No, she can't," responded Martin. "The thing mustn't become customary: I can't be troubled. It's very well for once: I'll not have it repeated."

"*You'll* not have it repeated."

"Hush! don't vex him—we could not have met to-day but for him: but I will come again, if it is your wish that I should come."

"It *is* my wish—my *one* wish—almost the only wish I can feel."

"Come this minute: my mother has coughed, got up, set her feet on the floor. Let her only catch you on the stairs, Miss Caroline: you're not to bid him good-bye" (stepping between her and Moore),—"you are to march."

"My shawl, Martin."

"I have it. I'll put it on for you when you are in the hall."

He made them part: he would suffer no farewell but what could be expressed in looks: he half carried Caroline down the stairs. In the hall he wrapped her shawl round her, and—but that his mother's tread then creaked in the gallery, and but that a sentiment of diffidence—the proper, natural, therefore the noble impulse of his boy's heart, held him back, he would have claimed his reward—he would have said, "Now, Miss Caroline, for all this give me one kiss." But ere the words had

passed his lips, she was across the snowy road, rather skimming than wading the drifts.

"She is my debtor, and I *will* be paid."

He flattered himself that it was opportunity, not audacity, which had failed him: he misjudged the quality of his own nature, and held it for something lower than it was.

Chapter XXXIV

CASE OF DOMESTIC PERSECUTION—REMARKABLE INSTANCE OF PIOUS PERSEVERANCE IN THE DISCHARGE OF RELIGIOUS DUTIES

MARTIN, having known the taste of excitement, wanted a second draught; having felt the dignity of power, he loathed to relinquish it. Miss Helstone—that girl he had always called ugly, and whose face was now perpetually before his eyes, by day and by night, in dark and in sunshine—had once come within his sphere: it fretted him to think the visit might never be repeated.

Though a schoolboy, he was no ordinary schoolboy: he was destined to grow up an original. At a few years later date, he took great pains to pare and polish himself down to the pattern of the rest of the world, but he never succeeded: an unique stamp marked him always. He now sat idle at his desk in the grammar-school, casting about in his mind for the means of adding another chapter to his commenced romance: he did not yet know how many commenced life-romances are doomed never to get beyond the first—or, at most, the second chapter. His Saturday half-holiday he spent in the wood with his book of fairy legends, and that other unwritten book of his imagination.

Martin harboured an irreligious reluctance to see the approach of Sunday. His father and mother—while disclaiming community with the Establishment—failed not duly, once on the sacred day, to fill their large pew in Briarfield church with the whole of their blooming family. Theoretically, Mr. Yorke placed all sects and churches on a level: Mrs. Yorke awarded the palm to Moravians and Quakers, on account of that crown of humility by these worthies worn: neither of them were ever known, however, to set foot in a conventicle.

Martin, I say, disliked Sunday, because the morning service was long, and the sermon usually little to his taste: this Saturday afternoon, however, his woodland musings disclosed to him a new-found charm in the coming day.

It proved a day of deep snow: so deep, that Mrs. Yorke, during breakfast, announced her conviction that the children, both boys and girls, would be better at home; and her decision that, instead of going to church, they should sit silent for two hours in the back-parlour, while Rose and Martin alternately read a succession of sermons—John Wesley's Sermons: John Wesley, being a Reformer and an Agitator, had a place both in her own and her husband's favour.

"Rose will do as she pleases," said Martin, not looking up from the book which, according to his custom then and in after life, he was studying over his bread and milk.

"Rose will do as she is told, and Martin too," observed the mother.

"I am going to church."

So her son replied, with the ineffable quietude of a true Yorke, who knows his will and means to have it, and who, if pushed to the wall, will let himself be crushed to death, provided no way of escape can be found—but will never capitulate.

"It is not fit weather," said the father.

No answer: the youth read studiously; he slowly broke his bread and sipped his milk.

"Martin hates to go to church, but he hates still more to obey," said Mrs. Yorke.

"I suppose I am influenced by pure perverseness?"

"Yes—you are."

"Mother—*I am not.*"

"By what, then, are you influenced?"

"By a complication of motives; the intricacies of which I should as soon think of explaining to you as I should of turning myself inside out to exhibit the internal machinery of my frame."

"Hear Martin! Hear him!" cried Mr. Yorke. "I must see and have this lad of mine brought up to the Bar: Nature meant him to live by his tongue. Hesther, your third son must certainly be a lawyer: he has the stock in trade—brass, self-conceit, and words—words—words."

"Some bread, Rose, if you please," requested Martin with intense gravity, serenity, phlegm: the boy had naturally a low, plaintive voice, which, in his "dour moods," rose scarcely above a lady's whisper: the more inflexibly stubborn the humour, the softer, the sadder the tone. He rang the bell, and gently asked for his walking-shoes.

"But, Martin," urged his sire, "there is drift all the way—a man could hardly wade through it. However, lad," he continued, seeing that the boy rose as the church-bell began to toll, "this is a case wherein I would by no means balk the obdurate chap of his will. Go to church by all means. There is a pitiless wind, and a sharp, frozen sleet, besides the depth under foot. Go out into it, since thou prefers it to a warm fireside."

Martin quietly assumed his cloak, comforter, and cap, and deliberately went out.

"My father has more sense than my mother," he pronounced. "How women miss it! They drive the nail into the flesh, thinking they are hammering away at insensate stone."

He reached church early.

"Now, if the weather frightens her (and it is a real December tempest), or if that Mrs. Pryor objects to her going out, and I should miss her after all, it will vex me: but, tempest or tornado, hail or ice, she *ought* to come; and, if she has a mind worthy of her eyes and features, she *will* come: she will be here for the chance of seeing me, as I am here for the chance of seeing her: she will want to get a word respecting her confounded sweetheart, as I want to get another flavour of what I think the essence of life: a taste of existence, with the spirit preserved in it, and not evaporated. Adventure is to stagnation what champagne is to flat porter."

He looked round. The church was cold, silent, empty, but for one old woman. As the chimes subsided, and the single bell tolled slowly, another and another elderly parishioner came dropping in, and took a humble station in the free sittings. It is always the frailest, the oldest, and the poorest that brave the worst weather, to prove and maintain their constancy to dear old mother Church: this wild morning not one affluent family attended, not one carriage party appeared—all the lined and cushioned pews were empty; only on the bare oaken seats sat ranged the grey-haired elders and feeble paupers.

"I'll scorn her, if she doesn't come," muttered Martin shortly and savagely to himself. The Rector's shovel-hat had passed the porch: Mr. Helstone and his clerk were in the vestry.

The bells ceased—the reading-desk was filled—the doors were closed—the service commenced: void stood the Rectory pew—she was not there: Martin scorned her.

"Worthless thing! Vapid thing! Commonplace humbug! Like all other girls—weakly, selfish, shallow!"

Such was Martin's liturgy.

"She is not like our picture: her eyes are not large and expressive: her nose is not straight, delicate, Hellenic: her mouth has not that charm I thought it had—

which, I imagined, could beguile me of sullenness in my worst moods. What is she? A thread-paper, a doll, a toy—a *girl,* in short.''

So absorbed was the young cynic, he forgot to rise from his knees at the proper place, and was still in an exemplary attitude of devotion when—the litany over— the first hymn was given out. To be so caught did not contribute to soothe him: he started up red (for he was as sensitive to ridicule as any girl). To make the matter worse, the church-door had re-opened, and the aisles were filling: patter, patter, patter, a hundred little feet trotted in. It was the Sunday-scholars. According to Briarfield winter custom, these children had till now been kept where there was a warm stove, and only led into church just before the Communion and Sermon.

The little ones were settled first, and at last, when the boys and the younger girls were all arranged—when the organ was swelling high, and the choir and congregation were rising to uplift a spiritual song—a tall class of young women came quietly in, closing the procession. Their teacher, having seen them seated, passed into the Rectory-pew. The French-grey cloak and small beaver bonnet were known to Martin: it was the very costume his eyes had ached to catch. Miss Helstone had not suffered the storm to prove an impediment: after all, she was come to church. Martin probably whispered his satisfaction to his hymn-book; at any rate, he therewith hid his face two minutes.

Satisfied or not, he had time to get very angry with her again before the sermon was over; she had never once looked his way: at least, he had not been so lucky as to encounter a glance.

"If," he said—"if she takes no notice of me; if she shows I am not in her thoughts, I shall have a worse, a meaner opinion of her than ever. Most despicable would it be to come for the sake of those sheep-faced Sunday scholars, and not for my sake, or that long skeleton Moore's.''

The sermon found an end; the benediction was pronounced; the congregation dispersed: she had not been near him.

Now, indeed, as Martin set his face homeward, he felt that the sleet was sharp, and the east wind cold.

His nearest way lay through some fields: it was a dangerous, because an untrodden way: he did not care; he would take it. Near the second stile rose a clump of trees: was that an umbrella waiting there? Yes: an umbrella held with evident difficulty against the blast: behind it fluttered a French-grey cloak. Martin grinned as he toiled up the steep encumbered field, difficult to the foot as a slope in the upper realms of Etna. There was an inimitable look in his face when, having gained the stile, he seated himself coolly thereupon, and thus opened a conference which, for his own part, he was willing to prolong indefinitely.

"I think you had better strike a bargain: exchange me for Mrs. Pryor.''

"I was not sure whether you would come this way, Martin; but I thought I would run the chance: there is no such thing as getting a quiet word spoken in the church or churchyard.''

"Will you agree? Make over Mrs. Pryor to my mother, and put me in her skirts?''

"As if I could understand you! What puts Mrs. Pryor into your head?''

"You call her 'mamma,' don't you?''

"She *is* my mamma.''

"Not possible—or so inefficient, so careless a mamma—I should make a five times better one. You *may* laugh: I have no objection to see you laugh: your teeth— I hate ugly teeth; but yours are as pretty as a pearl necklace, and a necklace, of which the pearls are very fair, even, and well matched too.''

"Martin, what now? I thought the Yorkes never paid compliments?''

"They have not done till this generation; but I feel as if it were my vocation to turn out a new variety of the Yorke species. I am rather tired of my own ancestors: we have traditions going back for four ages—tales of Hiram, which was the son of Hiram which was the son of Samuel, which was the son of John, which was

the son of Zerubbabel Yorke. All, from Zerubbabel down to the last Hiram, were such as you see my father. Before that, there was a Godfrey: we have his picture; it hangs in Moore's bedroom: it is like me. Of his character we know nothing; but I am sure it was different to his descendants: he has long curling dark hair; he is carefully and cavalierly dressed. Having said that he is like me, I need not add that he is handsome.''

''You are not handsome, Martin.''

''No; but wait a while: just let me take my time: I mean to begin from this day to cultivate, to polish,—and we shall see.''

''You are a very strange—a very unaccountable boy, Martin; but don't imagine you ever will be handsome: you cannot.''

''I mean to try. But we were talking about Mrs. Pryor: she must be the most unnatural mamma in existence, coolly to let her daughter come out in this weather. Mine was in such a rage, because I would go to church: she was fit to fling the kitchen-brush after me.''

''Mamma was very much concerned about me; but I am afraid I was obstinate: I *would* go.''

''To see me?''

''Exactly: I thought of nothing else. I greatly feared the snow would hinder you from coming: you don't know how pleased I was to see you all by yourself in the pew.''

''*I* came to fulfil my duty, and set the parish a good example. And so you were obstinate, were you? I should like to see you obstinate, I should. Wouldn't I have you in good discipline if I owned you? Let me take the umbrella.''

''I can't stay two minutes: our dinner will be ready.''

''And so will ours; and we have always a hot dinner on Sundays. Roast goose to-day, with apple-pie and rice-pudding. I always contrive to know the bill of fare: well, I like these things uncommonly: but I'll make the sacrifice, if you will.''

''We have a cold dinner: my uncle will allow no unnecessary cooking on the Sabbath. But I must return: the house would be in commotion, if I failed to appear.''

''So will Briarmains, bless you! I think I hear my father sending out the overlooker and five of the dyers, to look in six directions for the body of his prodigal son in the snow; and my mother repenting her of her many misdeeds towards me, now I am gone.''

''Martin, how is Mr. Moore?''

''*That* is what you came for—just to say that word.''

''Come, tell me quickly.''

''Hang him! he is no worse; but as ill-used as ever—mewed up, kept in solitary confinement. They mean to make either an idiot or a maniac of him, and take out a commission of lunacy. Horsfall starves him: you saw how thin he was.''

''You were very good the other day, Martin.''

''What day? I am always good—a model.''

''When will you be so good again?''

''I see what you are after; but you'll not wheedle me: I am no cat's-paw.''

''But it must be done: it is quite a right thing, and a necessary thing.''

''How you encroach! Remember, I managed the matter of my own free will before.''

''And you will again.''

''I won't: the business gave me far too much trouble; I like my ease.''

''Mr. Moore wishes to see me, Martin; and I wish to see him.''

''I dare say'' (coolly).

''It is too bad of your mother to exclude his friends.''

''Tell her so.''

''His own relations.''

''Come and blow her up.''

"You know that would advance nothing. Well, I shall stick to my point. See him I will. If you won't help me, I'll manage without help."

"I have no time to reason with you now; but I consider you provoking. Good-morning."

Away she went—the umbrella shut; for she could not carry it against the wind.

"She is not vapid; she is not shallow," said Martin. "I shall like to watch, and mark how she will work her way without help. If the storm were not of snow, but of fire—such as came refreshingly down on the cities of the plain—she would go through it to procure five minutes' speech with that Moore. Now, I consider I have had a pleasant morning: the disappointments got time on: the fears and fits of anger only made that short discourse pleasanter, when it came at last. She expected to coax me at once: she'll not manage that in one effort: she shall come again, again, and yet again. It would please me to put her in a passion—to make her cry: I want to discover how far she will go—what she will do and dare—to get her will. It seems strange and new to find one human being thinking so much about another as she thinks about Moore. But it is time to go home; my appetite tells me the hour: won't I walk into that goose?—and we'll try whether Matthew or I shall get the largest cut of the apple-pie to-day."

Chapter XXXV

WHEREIN MATTERS MAKE SOME PROGRESS, BUT NOT MUCH

MARTIN had planned well: he had laid out a dexterously concerted scheme for his private amusement; but older and wiser schemers than he are often doomed to see their finest-spun projects swept to annihilation by the sudden broom of Fate—that fell housewife, whose red arm none can control. In the present instance, this broom was manufactured out of the tough fibres of Moore's own stubborn purpose, bound tight with his will. He was now resuming his strength, and making strange head against Mrs. Horsfall. Each morning he amazed that matron with a fresh astonishment. First, he discharged her from her valet-duties; he would dress himself. Then, he refused the coffee she brought him: he would breakfast with the family. Lastly, he forbade her his chamber. On the same day, amidst the outcries of all the women in the place, he put his head out of doors. The morning after, he followed Mr. Yorke to his counting-house, and requested an envoy to fetch a chaise from the Red-House Inn. He was resolved, he said, to return home to the Hollow that very afternoon. Mr. Yorke, instead of opposing, aided and abetted him: the chaise was sent for, though Mrs. Yorke declared the step would be his death. It came. Moore, little disposed to speak, made his purse do duty for his tongue: he expressed his gratitude to the servants and to Mrs. Horsfall, by the chink of his coin. The latter personage approved and understood this language perfectly; it made amends for all previous contumacy: she and her patient parted the best friends in the world.

The kitchen visited and soothed, Moore betook himself to the parlour; he had Mrs. Yorke to appease; not quite so easy a task as the pacification of her housemaids. There she sat plunged in sullen dudgeon; the gloomiest speculations on the depths of man's ingratitude absorbing her thoughts. He drew near and bent over her; she was obliged to look up, if it were only to bid him "avaunt." There was beauty still in his pale wasted features; there was earnestness, and a sort of sweetness—for he was smiling—in his hollow eyes.

"Good-bye!" he said; and, as he spoke, the smile glittered and melted. He had no iron mastery of his sensations now: a trifling emotion made itself apparent in his present weak state.

"And what are you going to leave us for?" she asked; "we will keep you, and do anything in the world for you, if you will only stay till you are stronger."

"Good-bye!" he again said: and added, "you have been a mother to me: give your wilful son one embrace."

Like a foreigner, as he was, he offered her first one cheek, then the other: she kissed him.

"What a trouble—what a burden I have been to you!" he muttered.

"You are the worst trouble now, headstrong youth!" was the answer. "I wonder who is to nurse you at Hollow's Cottage? your sister Hortense knows no more about such matters than a child."

"Thank God! for I have had nursing enough to last me my life."

Here the little girls came in; Jessy crying, Rose quiet, but grave. Moore took them out into the hall to soothe, pet, and kiss them. He knew it was not in their mother's nature to bear to see any living thing caressed but herself: she would have felt annoyed had he fondled a kitten in her presence.

The boys were standing about the chaise as Moore entered it; but for them he had no farewell. To Mr. Yorke he only said—"You have a good riddance of me: that was an unlucky shot for you, Yorke; it tured Briarmains into an hospital. Come and see me at the cottage soon."

He drew up the glass; the chaise rolled away. In half-an-hour he alighted at his own garden-wicket. Having paid the driver and dismissed the vehicle, he leaned on that wicket an instant, at once to rest and to muse.

"Six months ago I passed out of this gate," said he, "a proud, angry, disappointed man: I come back sadder and wiser: weakly enough, but not worried. A cold, grey, yet quiet world lies around—a world where, if I hope little, I fear nothing. All slavish terrors of embarrassment have left me: let the worst come, I can work, as Joe Scott does, for an honourable living: in such doom I yet see some hardship, but no degradation. Formerly, pecuniary ruin was equivalent in my eyes to personal dishonour. It is not so now: I know the difference. Ruin *is* an evil; but one for which I am prepared; the day of whose coming I know, for I have calculated. I can yet put it off six months—not an hour longer; if things by that time alter— which is not probable; if fetters, which now seem indissoluble, should be loosened from our trade (of all things the most unlikely to happen)—I might conquer in this long struggle yet—I might——Good God! what might I not do? But the thought is a brief madness: let me see things with sane eyes. Ruin will come, lay her axe to my fortune's roots, and hew them down. I shall snatch a sapling, I shall cross the sea, and plant it in American woods. Louis will go with me. Will none but Louis go? I cannot tell—I have no right to ask."

He entered the house.

It was afternoon, twilight yet out of doors: starless and moonless twilight; for, though keenly freezing with a dry, black frost, heaven wore a mask of clouds congealed and fast-locked. The mill-dam too was frozen: the Hollow was very still: indoors it was already dark. Sarah had lit a good fire in the parlour; she was preparing tea in the kitchen.

"Hortense," said Moore, as his sister bustled up to help him off with his cloak, "I am pleased to come home."

Hortense did not feel the peculiar novelty of this expression coming from her brother, who had never before called the cottage his home, and to whom its narrow limits had always heretofore seemed rather restrictive than protective: still, whatever contributed to his happiness pleased her; and she expressed herself to that effect.

He sat down, but soon rose again: he went to the window; he came back to the fire.

"Hortense!"

"Mon frère?"

"This little parlour looks very clean and pleasant: unusually bright, somehow."

"It is true, brother: I have had the whole house thoroughly and scrupulously cleaned in your absence."

"Sister, I think on this first day of my return home, you ought to have a friend or so to tea; if it were only to see how fresh and spruce you have made the little place."

"True, brother: if it were not late I might send for Miss Mann."

"So you might; but it really is too late to disturb that good lady; and the evening is much too cold for her to come out."

"How thoughtful in you, dear Gérard! We must put it off till another day."

"I want some one to-day, dear sister; some quiet guest, who would tire neither of us."

"Miss Ainley?"

"An excellent person, they say; but she lives too far off. Tell Harry Scott to step up to the Rectory with a request from you that Caroline Helstone should come and spend the evening with you."

"Would it not be better to-morrow, dear brother?"

"I should like her to see the place as it is just now; its brilliant cleanliness and perfect neatness are so much to your credit."

"It might benefit her in the way of example."

"It might and must: she ought to come."

He went into the kitchen.

"Sarah, delay tea half-an-hour." He then commissioned her to despatch Harry Scott to the Rectory, giving her a twisted note hastily scribbled in pencil by himself, and addressed "Miss Helstone."

Scarcely had Sarah time to get impatient under the fear of damage to her toast already prepared, when the messenger returned; and with him the invited guest.

She entered through the kitchen, quietly tripped up Sarah's stairs to take off her bonnet and furs, and came down as quietly, with her beautiful curls nicely smoothed; her graceful merino dress and delicate collar all trim and spotless; her gay little work-bag in her hand. She lingered to exchange a few kindly words with Sarah; and to look at the new tortoise-shell kitten basking on the kitchen hearth; and to speak to the canary-bird, which a sudden blaze from the fire had startled on its perch; and then she betook herself to the parlour.

The gentle salutation, the friendly welcome, were interchanged in such tranquil sort as befitted cousins meeting; a sense of pleasure, subtle and quiet as a perfume, diffused itself through the room; the newly-kindled lamp burnt up bright; the tray and the singing urn were brought in.

"I am pleased to come home," repeated Mr. Moore.

They assembled round the table. Hortense chiefly talked. She congratulated Caroline on the evident improvement in her health: her colour and her plump cheeks were returning, she remarked. It was true. There was an obvious change in Miss Helstone: all about her seemed elastic; depression, fear, forlornness, were withdrawn: no longer crushed, and saddened, and slow, and drooping, she looked like one who had tasted the cordial of heart's ease, and been lifted on the wing of hope.

After tea, Hortense went upstairs: she had not rummaged her drawers for a month past, and the impulse to perform that operation was now become resistless. During her absence, the talk passed into Caroline's hands: she took it up with ease; she fell into her best tone of conversation. A pleasing facility and elegance of language gave fresh charm to familiar topics; a new music in the always soft voice gently surprised and pleasingly captivated the listener; unwonted shades and lights of expression elevated the young countenance with character, and kindled it with animation.

"Caroline, you look as if you had heard good tidings," said Moore, after earnestly gazing at her for some minutes.

"Do I?"

"I sent for you this evening that I might be cheered; but you cheer me more than I had calculated."

"I am glad of that. And I *really* cheer you?"

"You look brightly, move buoyantly, speak musically."

"It is pleasant to be here again."

"Truly it is pleasant: I feel it so. And to see health on your cheek, and hope in your eye, is pleasant, Cary; but what is this hope, and what is the source of this sunshine I perceive about you?"

"For one thing, I am happy in mamma: I love her so much, and she loves me. Long and tenderly she nursed me; now, when her care has made me well, I can occupy myself for and with her all the day. I say it is my turn to attend to her; and I *do* attend to her: I am her waiting woman, as well as her child: I like—you would laugh if you knew what pleasure I have in making dresses and sewing for her. She looks so nice now, Robert: I will not let her be old-fashioned. And then, she is charming to talk to: full of wisdom; ripe in judgment; rich in information; exhaustless in stores her observant faculties have quietly amassed. Every day that I live with her, I like her better; I esteem her more highly; I love her more tenderly."

"*That* for one thing, then, Cary: you talk in such a way about 'mamma,' it is enough to make one jealous of the old lady."

"She is not old, Robert."

"Of the young lady, then."

"She does not pretend to be young."

"Well—of the matron. But you said, 'mamma's' affection was *one* thing that made you happy; now for the other thing."

"I am glad you are better."

"What besides?"

"I am glad we are friends."

"You and I?"

"Yes: I once thought we never should be."

"Cary, some day I mean to tell you a thing about myself that is not to my credit, and, consequently, will not please you."

"Ah!—don't! I cannot bear to think ill of you."

"And I cannot bear that you should think better of me than I deserve."

"Well, but I half know your 'thing': indeed, I believe I know all about it."

"You do not."

"I believe I do."

"Whom does it concern besides me?"

She coloured; she hesitated; she was silent.

"Speak, Cary!—whom does it concern?"

She tried to utter a name and could not.

"Tell me: there is none present but ourselves: be frank."

"But if I guess wrong?"

"I will forgive. Whisper, Cary."

He bent his ear to her lips: still she would not, or could not, speak clearly to the point. Seeing that Moore waited, and was resolved to hear something, she at last said—"Miss Keeldar spent a day at the Rectory about a week since. The evening came on very wintry, and we persuaded her to stay all night."

"And you and she curled your hair together?"

"How do you know that?"

"And then you chatted; and she told you——"

"It was not at curling-hair time; so you are not as wise as you think: and besides, she didn't tell me."

"You slept together afterwards?"

"We occupied the same room and bed. We did not sleep much: we talked the whole night through."

"I'll be sworn you did! and then it all came out—*tant pis*. I would rather you had heard it from myself."

"You are quite wrong: she did not tell me what you suspect: she is not the person to proclaim such things; but yet I inferred something from parts of her discourse: I gathered more from rumour, and I made out the rest by instinct."

"But if she did not tell you that I wanted to marry her for the sake of her money, and that she refused me indignantly and scornfully (you need neither start nor blush; nor yet need you prick your trembling fingers with your needle: that is the plain truth, whether you like it or not)—if such was not the subject of her august confidences, on what point did they turn? You say you talked the whole night through: what about?"

"About things we never thoroughly discussed before, intimate friends as we have been; but you hardly expect I should tell you?"

"Yes, yes, Cary—you will tell me: you said we were friends; and friends should always confide in each other."

"But are you sure you won't repeat it?"

"Quite sure."

"Not to Louis?"

"Not even to Louis? What does Louis care for young ladies' secrets?"

"Robert—Shirley is a curious, magnanimous being."

"I dare say: I can imagine there are both odd points and grand points about her."

"I have found her chary in showing her feelings; but when they rush out, river-like, and pass full and powerful before you—almost without leave from her—you gaze, wonder, you admire, and—I think—love her."

"You saw this spectacle?"

"Yes: at dead of night; when all the house was silent, and starlight, and the cold reflection from the snow glimmered in our chamber,—then I saw Shirley's heart."

"Her heart's core? Do you think she showed you that?"

"Her heart's core."

"And how was it?"

"Like a shrine,—for it was holy; like snow,—for it was pure; like flame,—for it was warm; like death,—for it was strong."

"Can she love? Tell me that."

"What think you?"

"She has loved none that have loved her yet."

"Who are those that have loved her?"

He named a list of gentlemen, closing with Sir Philip Nunnely.

"She has loved none of these."

"Yet some of them were worthy of a woman's affection."

"Of some women's; but not of Shirley's."

"Is she better than others of her sex?"

"She is peculiar, and more dangerous to take as a wife—rashly."

"I can imagine that."

"She spoke of you——"

"Oh! she did! I thought you denied it."

"She did not speak in the way you fancy; but I asked her, and I would make her tell me what she thought of you, or rather, how she felt towards you. I wanted to know: I had long wanted to know."

"So had I; but let us hear: she thinks meanly—she feels contemptuously, doubtless?"

"She thinks of you almost as highly as a woman can think of a man. You know she can be eloquent: I yet feel in fancy the glow of the language in which her opinion was conveyed."

"But how does she feel?"

"Till you shocked her (she said you had shocked her, but she would not tell me how), she felt as a sister feels towards a brother of whom she is at once fond and proud."

"I'll shock her no more, Cary, for the shock rebounded on myself till I staggered again: but that comparison about sister and brother is all nonsense: she is too rich and proud to entertain fraternal sentiments for me."

"You don't know her, Robert; and somehow, I fancy *now* (I had other ideas formerly), that you cannot know her: you and she are not so constructed as to be able thoroughly to understand each other."

"It may be so. I esteem her; I admire her; and yet my impressions concerning her are harsh—perhaps uncharitable. I believe, for instance, that she is incapable of love——"

"Shirley incapable of love!"

"That she will never marry: I imagine her jealous of compromising her pride, of relinquishing her power, of sharing her property."

"Shirley has hurt your amour-propre."

"She did hurt it—though I had not an emotion of tenderness, not a spark of passion for her."

"Then, Robert, it was very wicked in you to want to marry her."

"And very mean, my little pastor, my pretty priestess. I never wanted to kiss Miss Keeldar in my life, though she has fine lips, scarlet and round, as ripe cherries; or, if I did wish it, it was the mere desire of the eye."

"I doubt, now, whether you are speaking the truth: the grapes or the cherries are sour—'hung too high.'"

"She has a pretty figure, a pretty face, beautiful hair; I acknowledge all her charms and feel none of them; or only feel them in a way she would disdain. I suppose I was truly tempted, by the mere gilding of the bait. Caroline, what a noble fellow your Robert is—great, good, disinterested, and then so pure!"

"But not perfect: he made a great blunder once, and we will hear no more about it."

"And shall we think no more about it, Cary? Shall we not despise him in our heart, gentle but just, compassionate but upright?"

"Never! We will remember that with what measure we mete it shall be measured unto us, and so we will give no scorn—only affection."

"Which won't satisfy, I warn you of that. Something besides affection—something far stronger, sweeter, warmer—will be demanded one day: is it there to give?"

Caroline was moved—much moved.

"Be calm, Lina," said Moore soothingly; "I have no intention, because I have no right, to perturb your mind now, nor for months to come: don't look as if you would leave me: we will make no more agitating allusions: we will resume our gossip. Do not tremble: look me in the face: see what a poor grim phantom I am—more pitiable than formidable."

She looked shyly. "There is something formidable still, pale as you are," she said, as her eye fell under his.

"To return to Shirley," pursued Moore; "is it your opinion that she is ever likely to marry?"

"She loves."

"Platonically—theoretically—all humbug!"

"She loves, what I call, sincerely."

"Did she say so?"

"I cannot affirm that she said so: no such confession as, I love this man or that, passed her lips."

"I thought not."

"But the feeling made its way in spite of her, and I saw it. She spoke of one man in a strain not to be misunderstood: her voice alone was sufficient testimony.

Having wrung from her an opinion on your character, I demanded a second opinion of—another person about whom I had my conjectures; though they were the most tangled and puzzled conjectures in the world. I would *make* her speak: I shook her, I chid her, I pinched her fingers when she tried to put me off with gibes and jests in her queer, provoking way, and at last, out it came: the voice, I say, was enough; hardly raised above a whisper, and yet such a soft vehemence in its tones. There was no confession—no confidence in the matter: to these things she cannot condescend; but I am sure that man's happiness is dear to her as her own life.''

"Who is it?"

"I charged her with the fact; she did not deny; she did not avow, but looked at me: I saw her eyes by the snow-gleam. It was quite enough: I triumphed over her mercilessly."

"What right had *you* to triumph? Do you mean to say *you* are fancy-free?"

"Whatever *I* am, Shirley is a bondswoman. Lioness! she has found her captor. Mistress she may be of all round her—but her own mistress she is not."

"So you exulted at recognising a fellow-slave in one so fair and imperial?"

"I did; Robert, you say right, in one so fair and imperial."

"You confess it—a *fellow*-slave?"

"I confess nothing; but I say that haughty Shirley is no more free than was Hagar."

"And who, pray, is the Abraham; the hero of a patriarch who has achieved such a conquest?"

"You still speak scornfully, and cynically, and sorely; but I will make you change your note before I have done with you."

"We will see that: can she marry this Cupidon?"

"Cupidon! he is just about as much a Cupidon as you are a Cyclops."

"Can she marry him?"

"You will see."

"I want to know his name, Cary."

"Guess it."

"Is it any one in this neighbourhood?"

"Yes, in Briarfield parish."

"Then it is some person unworthy of her. I don't know a soul in Briarfield parish her equal."

"Guess."

"Impossible. I suppose she is under a delusion, and will plunge into some absurdity after all."

Caroline smiled.

"Do *you* approve the choice?" asked Moore.

"Quite, *quite*."

"Then I *am* puzzled; for the head which owns this bounteous fall of hazel curls is an excellent little thinking machine, most accurate in its working: it boasts a correct, steady judgment, inherited from 'mamma,' I suppose."

"And I *quite* approve, and mamma was charmed."

" 'Mamma' charmed! Mrs. Pryor. It can't be romantic then?"

"It *is* romantic, but it is also right."

"Tell me, Cary. Tell me out of pity: I am too weak to be tantalised."

"You shall be tantalised: it will do you no harm: you are not so weak as you pretend."

"I have twice this evening had some thought of falling on the floor at your feet."

"You had better not: I shall decline to help you up."

"And worshipping you downright. My mother was a Roman Catholic; you look like the loveliest of her pictures of the Virgin: I think I will embrace her faith, and kneel and adore."

"Robert, Robert, sit still; don't be absurd: I will go to Hortense, if you commit extravagances."

"You have stolen my senses: just now nothing will come into my mind but 'les litanies de la sainte Vierge. Rose céleste, reine des Anges!' "

" 'Tour d'ivoire, maison d'or': is not that the jargon? Well, sit down quietly, and guess your riddle."

"But, 'mamma' charmed! There's the puzzle."

"I'll tell you what mamma said when I told her: 'Depend upon it, my dear, such a choice will make the happiness of Miss Keeldar's life.' "

"I'll guess once, and no more. It is old Helstone. She is going to be your aunt."

"I'll tell my uncle, I'll tell Shirley!" cried Caroline, laughing gleefully. "Guess again, Robert; your blunders are charming."

"It is the parson, Hall."

"Indeed, no: he is mine, if you please."

"Yours! Ay! the whole generation of women in Briarfield seem to have made an idol of that priest: I wonder why; he is bald, sand-blind, grey-haired."

"Fanny will be here to fetch me, before you have solved the riddle, if you don't make haste."

"I'll guess no more, I am tired: and then I don't care. Miss Keeldar may marry 'le grand Turc' for me."

"Must I whisper?"

"That you must, and quickly: here comes Hortense; come near, a little nearer, my own Lina: I care for the whisper more than the words."

She whispered: Robert gave a start, a flash of the eye, a brief laugh: Miss Moore entered, and Sarah followed behind, with information that Fanny was come. The hour of converse was over.

Robert found a moment to exchange a few more whispered sentences: he was waiting at the foot of the staircase, as Caroline descended after putting on her shawl.

"Must I call Shirley a noble creature now?" he asked.

"If you wish to speak the truth, certainly."

"Must I forgive her?"

"Forgive her? Naughty Robert! Was she in the wrong, or were you?"

"Must I at length love her downright, Cary?"

Caroline looked keenly up, and made a movement towards him, something between the loving and the petulant.

"Only give the word, and I'll try to obey you."

"Indeed, you must not love her: the bare idea is perverse."

"But then she is handsome, peculiarly handsome: hers is a beauty that grows on you: you think her but graceful, when you first see her; you discover her to be beautiful when you have known her for a year."

"It is not you who are to say these things. Now, Robert, be good."

"O Cary, I have no love to give. Were the goddess of beauty to woo me, I could not meet her advances: there is no heart which I can call mine in this breast."

"So much the better: you are a great deal safer without: good-night."

"Why must you always go, Lina, at the very instant when I most want you to stay?"

"Because you most wish to retain when you are most certain to lose."

"Listen; one other word. Take care of your own heart: do you hear me?"

"There is no danger."

"I am not convinced of that: the Platonic parson, for instance."

"Who? Malone?"

"Cyril Hall: I owe more than one twinge of jealousy to that quarter."

"As to you, you have been flirting with Miss Mann: she showed me the other day a plant you had given her.—Fanny, I am ready."

Chapter XXXVI

WRITTEN IN THE SCHOOLROOM

LOUIS MOORE'S doubts, respecting the immediate evacuation of Fieldhead by Mr. Sympson, turned out to be perfectly well founded. The very next day after the grand quarrel about Sir Philip Nunnely, a sort of reconciliation was patched up between uncle and niece: Shirley, who could never find it in her heart to be or to seem inhospitable (except in the single instance of Mr. Donne), begged the whole party to stay a little longer: she begged in such earnest, it was evident she wished it for some reason. They took her at her word: indeed, the uncle could not bring himself to leave her quite unwatched—at full liberty to marry Robert Moore, as soon as that gentleman should be able (Mr. Sympson piously prayed this might never be the case) to reassert his supposed pretensions to her hand. They all stayed.

In his first rage against all the house of Moore, Mr. Sympson had so conducted himself towards Mr. Louis, that that gentleman—patient of labour or suffering, but intolerant of coarse insolence—had promptly resigned his post, and could now be induced to resume and retain it only till such time as the family should quit Yorkshire: Mrs. Sympson's entreaties prevailed with him thus far; his own attachment to his pupil constituted an additional motive for concession; and probably he had a third motive, stronger than either of the other two: probably he would have found it very hard indeed to leave Fieldhead just now.

Things went on, for some time, pretty smoothly; Miss Keeldar's health was re-established; her spirits resumed their flow: Moore had found means to relieve her from every nervous apprehension; and, indeed, from the moment of giving him her confidence, every fear seemed to have taken wing: her heart became as lightsome, her manner as careless, as those of a little child, that, thoughtless of its own life or death, trusts all responsibility to its parents. He and William Farren—through whose medium he made inquiries concerning the state of Phœbe—agreed in asserting that the dog was not mad: that it was only ill-usage which had driven her from home: for it was proved that her master was in the frequent habit of chastising her violently. Their assertion might, or might not, be true: the groom and gamekeeper affirmed to the contrary; both asserting that, if hers was not a clear case of hydrophobia, there was no such disease. But to this evidence Louis Moore turned an incredulous ear: he reported to Shirley only what was encouraging: she believed him: and, right or wrong, it is certain that in her case the bite proved innocuous.

November passed: December came: the Sympsons were now really departing; it was incumbent on them to be at home by Christmas; their packages were preparing; they were to leave in a few days. One winter evening, during the last week of their stay, Louis Moore again took out his little blank book, and discoursed with it as follows:

"She is lovelier than ever. Since that little cloud was dispelled, all the temporary waste and wanness have vanished. It was marvellous to see how soon the magical energy of youth raised her elastic, and revived her blooming.

"After breakfast this morning, when I had seen her, and listened to her, and—so to speak—felt her, in every sentient atom of my frame, I passed from her sunny presence into the chill drawing-room. Taking up a little gilt volume, I found it to contain a selection of lyrics. I read a poem or two: whether the spell was in me or in the verse, I know not, but my heart filled genially—my pulse rose: I glowed, notwithstanding the frost air. I, too, am young as yet: though she said she never considered me young, I am barely thirty; there are moments when life—for no other reason than my own youth—beams with sweet hues upon me.

"It was time to go to the schoolroom: I went. That same schoolroom is rather pleasant in a morning; the sun then shines through the low lattice; the books are

in order; there are no papers strewn about; the fire is clear and clean; no cinders have fallen, no ashes accumulated. I found Henry there, and he had brought with him Miss Keeldar: they were together.

"I said she was lovelier than ever: she is. A fine rose, not deep but delicate, opens on her cheek; her eye, always dark, clear, and speaking, utters now a language I cannot render—it is the utterance, seen not heard, through which angels must have communed when there was 'silence in heaven.' Her hair was always dusk as night, and fine as silk; her neck was always fair, flexible, polished—but both have now a new charm: the tresses are soft as shadow, the shoulders they fall on wear a goddess-grace. Once I only *saw* her beauty, now I *feel* it.

"Henry was repeating his lesson to her before bringing it to me—one of her hands was occupied with the book, he held the other: that boy gets more than his share of privileges; he dares caress and is caressed. What indulgence and compassion she shows him! Too much: if this went on, Henry, in a few years, when his soul was formed, would offer it on her altar, as I have offered mine.

"I saw her eyelid flitter when I came in, but she did not look up: *now* she hardly ever gives me a glance. She seems to grow silent too—to *me* she rarely speaks, and, when I am present, she says little to others. In my gloomy moments, I attribute this change to indifference,—aversion,—what not? In my sunny intervals I give it another meaning. I say, were I her equal, I could find in this shyness—coyness, and in that coyness—love. As it is, dare I look for it? What could I do with it, if found?

"This morning I dared, at least, contrive an hour's communion for her and me; I dared not only *wish*—but *will* an interview with her: I dared summon solitude to guard us. Very decidedly I called Henry to the door; without hesitation, I said, 'Go where you will, my boy, but, till I call you, return not here.'

"Henry, I could see, did not like his dismissal: that boy is young, but a thinker; his meditative eye shines on me strangely sometimes: he half feels what links me to Shirley; he half guesses that there is a dearer delight in the reserve with which I am treated, than in all the endearments he is allowed. The young, lame, half-grown lion would growl at me now and then, because I have tamed his lioness and am her keeper, did not the habit of discipline and the instinct of affection hold him subdued. Go, Henry; you must learn to take your share of the bitter of life with all of Adam's race that have gone before, or will come after you; your destiny can be no exception to the common lot: be grateful that your love is overlooked thus early, before it can claim any affinity to passion: an hour's fret, a pang of envy, suffice to express what you feel: Jealousy, hot as the sun above the line, Rage, destructive as the tropic storm, the clime of your sensations ignores—as yet.

"I took my usual seat at the desk, quite in my usual way: I am blessed in that power to cover all inward ebullition with outward calm. No one who looks at my slow face can guess the vortex sometimes whirling in my heart, and engulfing thought, and wrecking prudence. Pleasant is it to have the gift to proceed peacefully and powerfully in your course without alarming by one eccentric movement. It was not my present intention to utter one word of love to her, or to reveal one glimpse of the fire in which I wasted. Presumptuous, I never have been; presumptuous, I never will be: rather than even *seem* selfish and interested, I would resolutely rise, gird my loins, part and leave her, and seek, on the other side of the globe, a new life, cold and barren as the rock the salt tide daily washes. My design this morning was to take of her a near scrutiny—to read a line in the page of her heart: before I left I determined to know *what* I was leaving.

"I had some quills to make into pens: most men's hands would have trembled when their hearts were so stirred; mine went to work steadily, and my voice, when I called it into exercise, was firm.

" 'This day week you will be alone at Fieldhead, Miss Keeldar.'

" 'Yes: I rather think my uncle's intention to go is a settled one now.'

" 'He leaves you dissatisfied.'

" 'He is not pleased with me.'

" 'He departs as he came—no better for his journey: this is mortifying.'

" 'I trust the failure of his plans will take from him all inclination to lay new ones.'

" 'In his way, Mr. Sympson honestly wished you well. All he has done, or intended to do, he believed to be for the best.'

" 'You are kind to undertake the defence of a man who has permitted himself to treat you with so much insolence.'

" 'I never feel shocked at, or bear malice for, what is spoken in character; and most perfectly in character was that vulgar and violent onset against me, when he had quitted you worsted.'

" 'You cease now to be Henry's tutor?'

" 'I shall be parted from Henry for a while—(if he and I live we shall meet again somehow, for we love each other)—and be ousted from the bosom of the Sympson family for ever. Happily this change does not leave me stranded: it but hurries into premature execution designs long formed.'

" 'No change finds you off your guard: I was sure, in your calm way, you would be prepared for sudden mutation. I always think you stand in the world like a solitary but watchful, thoughtful archer in a wood; and the quiver on your shoulder holds more arrows than one; your bow is provided with a second string. Such too is your brother's wont. You two might go forth homeless hunters to the loneliest western wilds; all would be well with you. The hewn tree would make you a hut, the cleared forest yield you fields from its stripped bosom, the buffalo would feel your rifle-shot, and with lowered horns and hump pay homage at your feet.'

" 'And any Indian tribe of Black-feet, or Flat-heads, would afford us a bride, perhaps?'

" 'No' (hesitatingly): 'I think not. The savage is sordid: I think,—that is, I *hope*,—you would neither of you share your hearth with that to which you could not give your heart.'

" 'What suggested the wild West to your mind, Miss Keeldar? Have you been with me in spirit when I did not see you? Have you entered into my day-dreams, and beheld my brain labouring at its scheme of a future?'

"She had separated a slip of paper for lighting papers—a spill, as it is called—into fragments: she threw morsel by morsel into the fire, and stood pensively watching them consume. She did not speak.

" 'How did you learn what you seem to know about my intentions?'

" 'I know nothing: I am only discovering them now: I spoke at hazard.'

" 'Your hazard sounds like divination. A tutor I will never be again: never take a pupil after Henry and yourself: not again will I sit habitually at another man's table—no more be the appendage of a family. I am now a man of thirty: I have never been free since I was a boy of ten. I have such a thirst for freedom—such a deep passion to know her and call her mine—such a day-desire and night-longing to win her and possess her, I will not refuse to cross the Atlantic for her sake: her I will follow deep into virgin woods. Mine it shall not be to accept a savage girl as a slave—she could not be a wife. I know no white woman whom I love that would accompany me; but I am certain Liberty will await me, sitting under a pine: when I call her she will come to my loghouse, and she shall fill my arms.'

"She could not hear me speak so unmoved, and she *was* moved. It was right—I meant to move her. She could not answer me, nor could she look at me: I should have been sorry if she could have done either. Her cheek glowed as if a crimson flower, through whose petals the sun shone, had cast its light upon it. On the white lid and dark lashes of her downcast eye, trembled all that is graceful in the sense of half-painful half-pleasing shame.

"Soon she controlled her emotion, and took all her feelings under command. I saw she had felt insurrection, and was waking to empire—she sat down. There was that in her face which I could read: it said, I see the line which is my limit—nothing shall make me pass it. I feel—I know how far I may reveal my feelings, and when I must clasp the volume. I have advanced to a certain distance, as far as the true and sovereign and undegraded nature of my kind permits—now here I stand rooted. My heart may break if it is baffled: let it break—it shall never dishonour me—it shall never dishonour my sisterhood in me. Suffering before degradation! death before treachery!

"I, for my part, said, 'If she were poor, I would be at her feet. If she were lowly, I would take her in my arms. Her Gold and her Station are two griffins, that guard her on each side. Love looks and longs, and dares not: Passion hovers round, and is kept at bay: Truth and Devotion are scared. There is nothing to lose in winning her—no sacrifice to make—it is all clear gain, and therefore unimaginably difficult.'

"Difficult or not, something must be done; something must be said. I could not, and would not, sit silent with all that beauty modestly mute in my presence. I spoke thus; and still I spoke with calm: quiet as my words were, I could hear they fell in a tone distinct, round, and deep.

" 'Still, I know I shall be strangely placed with that mountain nymph, Liberty. She is, I suspect, akin to that Solitude which I once wooed, and from which I now seek a divorce. These Oreads are peculiar: they come upon you with an unearthly charm, like some starlight evening; they inspire a wild but not warm delight; their beauty is the beauty of spirits: their grace is not the grace of life, but of seasons or scenes in nature: theirs is the dewy bloom of morning—the languid flush of evening—the peace of the moon—the changefulness of clouds. I want and will have something different. This elfish splendour looks chill to my vision, and feels frozen to my touch. I am not a poet: I cannot live on abstractions. You, Miss Keeldar, have sometimes, in your laughing satire, called me a material philosopher, and implied that I live sufficiently for the substantial. Certain I feel material from head to foot; and glorious as Nature is, and deeply as I worship her with the solid powers of a solid heart, I would rather behold her through the soft human eyes of a loved and lovely wife, than through the wild orbs of the highest goddess of Olympus.'

" 'Juno could not cook a buffalo steak as you like it,' said she.

" 'She could not: but I will tell you who could—some young, penniless, friendless orphan-girl. I wish I could find such a one: pretty enough for me to love, with something of the mind and heart suited to my taste: not uneducated—honest and modest. I care nothing for attainments; but I would fain have the germ of those sweet natural powers which nothing acquired can rival; any temper Fate wills,—I can manage the hottest. To such a creature as this, I should like to be first tutor and then husband. I would teach her my language, my habits, and my principles, and then I would reward her with my love.'

" '*Reward* her! lord of the creation! *Reward* her!' ejaculated she, with a curled lip.

" 'And be repaid a thousandfold.'

" 'If she willed it, Monseigneur.'

" 'And she *should* will it.'

" 'You have stipulated for any temper Fate wills. Compulsion is flint and a blow to the metal of some souls.'

" 'And love the spark it elicits.'

" 'Who cares for the love that is but a spark—seen, flown upward, and gone?'

" 'I must find my orphan-girl. Tell me how, Miss Keeldar.'

" 'Advertise; and be sure you add, when you describe the qualifications, she must be a good plain cook.'

" 'I must find her; and when I do find her, I shall marry her.'

" 'Not you!' and her voice took a sudden accent of peculiar scorn.

"I liked this: I had roused her from the pensive mood in which I had first found her: I would stir her further.

" 'Why doubt it?'

" '*You* marry!'

" 'Yes—of course: nothing more evident than that I can, and shall.'

" 'The contrary is evident, Mr. Moore.'

"She charmed me in this mood: waxing disdainful, half insulting, pride, temper, derision, blent in her large fine eye, that had, just now, the look of a merlin's.

" 'Favour me with your reasons for such an opinion, Miss Keeldar.'

" 'How will *you* manage to marry, I wonder?'

" 'I shall manage it with ease and speed when I find the proper person.'

" 'Accept celibacy!' (and she made a gesture with her hand as if she gave me something) 'take it as your doom!'

" 'No: you cannot give what I already have. Celibacy has been mine for thirty years. If you wish to offer me a gift, a parting present, a keepsake, you must change the boon.'

" 'Take worse, then!'

" 'How? What?'

"I now felt, and looked, and spoke eagerly. I was unwise to quit my sheet-anchor of calm even for an instant: it deprived me of an advantage and transferred it to her. The little spark of temper dissolved in sarcasm, and eddied over her countenance in the ripples of a mocking smile.

" 'Take a wife that has paid you court to save your modesty, and thrust herself upon you to spare your scruples.'

" 'Only show me where.'

" 'Any stout widow that has had a few husbands already, and can manage these things.'

" 'She must not be rich then. Oh these riches!'

" 'Never would you have gathered the produce of the gold-bearing garden. You have not courage to confront the sleepless dragon! you have not craft to borrow the aid of Atlas!'

" 'You look hot and haughty.'

" 'And you far haughtier. Yours is the monstrous pride which counterfeits humility.'

" 'I am a dependent: I know my place.'

" 'I am a woman: I know mine.'

" 'I am poor: I must be proud.'

" 'I have received ordinances, and own obligations stringent as yours.'

"We had reached a critical point now, and we halted and looked at each other. *She* would not give in, I felt. Beyond this, I neither felt nor saw. A few moments yet were mine: the end was coming—I heard its rush—but not come; I would dally, wait, talk, and when impulse urged, I would act. I am never in a hurry: I never was in a hurry in my whole life. Hasty people drink the nectar of existence scalding hot: I taste it cool as dew. I proceeded—'Apparently, Miss Keeldar, you are as little likely to marry as myself: I know you have refused three, nay, four advantageous offers, and, I believe, a fifth. Have you rejected Sir Philip Nunnely?'

"I put this question suddenly and promptly.

" 'Did you think I should take him?'

" 'I thought you might.'

" 'On what grounds, may I ask?'

" 'Conformity of rank; age; pleasing contrast of temper, for *he* is mild and amiable; harmony of intellectual tastes.'

" 'A beautiful sentence! Let us take it to pieces. "Conformity of rank."'—He is quite above me: compare my grange with his palace, if you please: I am disdained by his kith and kin. "Suitability of age."—We were born in the same year; consequently, he still a boy, while I am a woman: ten years his senior to all intents and purposes. "Contrast of temper."—Mild and amiable, is he: I——what? Tell me.'

" 'Sister of the spotted, bright, quick, fiery leopard.'

" 'And you would mate me with a kid—the Millennium being yet millions of centuries from mankind; being yet, indeed, an archangel high in the seventh heaven, uncommissioned to descend——? Unjust barbarian! "Harmony of intellectual tastes."—He is fond of poetry, and I hate it——'

" 'Do you? That is news.'

" 'I absolutely shudder at the sight of metre or at the sound of rhyme, whenever I am at the Priory or Sir Philip at Fieldhead. Harmony, indeed! When did I whip up syllabub sonnets, or string stanzas fragile as fragments of glass? and when did I betray a belief that those penny-beads were genuine brilliants?'

" 'You might have the satisfaction of leading him to a higher standard—of improving his tastes.'

" 'Leading and improving! teaching and tutoring! bearing and forbearing! Pah! My husband is not to be my baby. I am not to set him his daily lesson and see that he learns it, and give him a sugar-plum if he is good, and a patient, pensive, pathetic lecture if he is bad. But it is like a tutor to talk of the "satisfaction of teaching."—I suppose *you* think it the finest employment in the world. I don't—I reject it. Improving a husband! No. I shall insist upon my husband improving me, or else we part.'

" 'God knows it is needed!'

" 'What do you mean by that, Mr. Moore?'

" 'What I say. Improvement is imperatively needed.'

" 'If you were a woman you would school Monsieur, *votre mari,* charmingly: it would just suit you; schooling is your vocation.'

" 'May I ask, whether, in your present just and gentle mood, you mean to taunt me with being a tutor?'

" 'Yes—bitterly; and with anything else you please: any defect of which you are painfully conscious.'

" 'With being poor, for instance?'

" 'Of course; that will sting you; you are sore about your poverty: you brood over that.'

" 'With having nothing but a very plain person to offer the woman who may master my heart?'

" 'Exactly. You have a habit of calling yourself plain. You are sensitive about the cut of your features, because they are not quite on an Apollo-pattern. You abuse them more than is needful, in the faint hope that others may say a word in their behalf—which won't happen. Your face is nothing to boast of, certainly: not a pretty line, nor a pretty tint, to be found therein.'

" 'Compare it with your own.'

" 'It looks like a god of Egypt: a great sand-buried stone head; or rather I will compare it to nothing so lofty: it looks like Tartar: you are my mastiff's cousin: I think you as much like him as a man can be like a dog.'

" 'Tartar is your dear companion. In summer, when you rise early, and run out into the fields to wet your feet with the dew, and freshen your cheek and uncurl your hair with the breeze, you always call him to follow you: you call him sometimes with a whistle that you learned from me. In the solitude of your wood, when you think nobody but Tartar is listening, you whistle the very tunes you imitated from my lips, or sing the very songs you have caught up by ear from my voice; I do not ask whence flows the feeling which you pour into these songs, for I know it flows

out of your heart, Miss Keeldar. In the winter evenings, Tartar lies at your feet: you suffer him to rest his head on your perfumed lap; you let him couch on the borders of your satin raiment: his rough hide is familiar with the contact of your hand; I once saw you kiss him on that snow-white beauty-spot which stars his broad forehead. It is dangerous to say I am like Tartar; it suggests to me a claim to be treated like Tartar.'

" 'Perhaps, sir, you can extort as much from your penniless and friendless young orphan-girl, when you find her.'

" 'Oh! could I find her such as I image her. Something to tame first, and teach afterwards: to break in and then to fondle. To lift the destitute proud thing out of poverty; to establish power over, and then to be indulgent to the capricious moods that never were influenced and never indulged before; to see her alternately irritated and subdued about twelve times in the twenty-four hours; and perhaps, eventually, when her training was accomplished, to behold her the exemplary and patient mother of about a dozen children, only now and then lending little Louis a cordial cuff by way of paying the interest of the vast debt she owes his father. Oh!' (I went on) 'my orphan-girl would give me many a kiss; she would watch on the threshold for my coming home of an evening; she would run into my arms; should keep my hearth as bright as she would make it warm. God bless the sweet idea! Find her I must.'

"Her eyes emitted an eager flash, her lips opened; but she reclosed them, and impetuously turned away.

" 'Tell me, tell me where she is, Miss Keeldar!'

"Another movement: all haughtiness, and fire, and impulse.

" 'I must know. You *can* tell me. You *shall* tell me.'

" 'I *never will.*'

"She turned to leave me. Could I now let her part as she had always parted from me? No: I had gone too far not to finish. I had come too near the end not to drive home to it. All the encumbrance of doubt, all the rubbish of indecision must be removed at once, and the plain truth must be ascertained. She must take her part, and tell me what it was. I must take mine and adhere to it.

" 'A minute, madam,' I said, keeping my hand on the door-handle before I opened it. 'We have had a long conversation this morning, but the last word has not been spoken yet: it is yours to speak it.'

" 'May I pass?'

" 'No. I guard the door. I would almost rather die than let you leave me just now, without speaking the word I demand.'

" 'What dare you expect me to say?'

" 'What I am dying and perishing to hear; what I *must* and *will* hear; what you dare not now suppress.'

" 'Mr. Moore, I hardly know what you mean: you are not like yourself.'

"I suppose I hardly was like my usual self, for I scared her; that I could see: it was right; she must be scared to be won.

" 'You *do* know what I mean, and for the first time I stand before you *myself*. I have flung off the tutor, and beg to introduce you to the man: and remember, he is a gentleman.'

"She trembled. She put her hand to mine as if to remove it from the lock; she might as well have tried to loosen, by her soft touch, metal welded to metal. She felt she was powerless, and receded; and again she trembled.

"What change I underwent I cannot explain; but out of her emotion passed into me a new spirit. I neither was crushed nor elated by her lands and gold; I thought not of them, cared not for them: they were nothing: dross that could not dismay me. I saw only herself; her young beautiful form; the grace, the majesty, the modesty of her girlhood.

" 'My pupil,' I said.

" 'My master,' was the low answer.

" 'I have a thing to tell you.'

"She waited with declined brow, and ringlets drooped.

" 'I have to tell you, that for four years you have been growing into your tutor's heart, and that you are rooted there now. I have to declare that you have bewitched me, in spite of sense and experience, and difference of station and estate: you have so looked, and spoken, and moved; so shown me your faults and your virtues—beauties rather; they are hardly so stern as virtues—that I love you—love you with my life and strength. It is out now.'

"She sought what to say, but could not find a word: she tried to rally, but vainly. I passionately repeated that I loved her.

" 'Well, Mr. Moore, what then?' was the answer I got, uttered in a tone that would have been petulant if it had not faltered.

" 'Have you nothing to say to me: Have you no love for me?'

" 'A little bit.'

" 'I am not to be tortured: I will not even play at present.'

" 'I don't want to play; I want to go.'

" 'I wonder you dare speak of going at this moment. *You* go! What! with my heart in your hand, to lay it on your toilet and pierce it with your pins! From my presence you do not stir; out of my reach you do not stray, till I receive a hostage—pledge for pledge—your heart for mine.'

" 'The thing you want is mislaid—lost some time since: let me go and seek it.'

" 'Declare that it is where your keys often are—in my possession.'

" 'You ought to know. And where are my keys, Mr. Moore? indeed and truly I have lost them again; and Mrs. Gill wants some money, and I have none, except this sixpence.'

"She took the coin out of her apron-pocket, and showed it in her palm. I could have trifled with her; but it would not do: life and death were at stake. Mastering at once the sixpence, and the hand that held it, I demanded—'Am I to die without you, or am I to live for you?'

" 'Do as you please: far be it from me to dictate your choice.'

" 'You shall tell me with your own lips, whether you doom me to exile, or call me to hope.'

" 'Go. I can bear to be left.'

" 'Perhaps, I too *can* bear to leave you: but reply, Shirley, my pupil, my sovereign—reply.'

" 'Die without me if you will. Live for me if you dare.'

" 'I am not afraid of you, my leopardess: I *dare* live for and with you, from this hour till my death. Now, then, I have you: you are mine: I will never let you go. Wherever my home be, I have chosen my wife. If I stay in England, in England you will stay; if I cross the Atlantic, you will cross it also: our lives are riveted; our lots intertwined.'

" 'And are we equal then, sir? Are we equal at last?'

" 'You are younger, frailer, feebler, more ignorant than I.'

" 'Will you be good to me, and never tyrannise?'

" 'Will you let me breathe, and not bewilder me? You must not smile at present. The world swims and changes round me. The sun is a dizzying scarlet blaze, the sky a violet vortex whirling over me.'

"I am a strong man, but I staggered as I spoke. All creation was exaggerated: colour grew more vivid: motion more rapid; life itself more vital. I hardly saw her for a moment; but I heard her voice—pitilessly sweet. She would not subdue one of her charms in compassion: perhaps she did not know what I felt.

" 'You name me leopardess: remember, the leopardess is tameless,' said she.

" 'Tame or fierce, wild or subdued, you are *mine*.'

" 'I am glad I know my keeper, and am used to him. Only his voice will I follow; only his hand shall manage me; only at his feet will I repose.'

"I took her back to her seat, and sat down by her side: I wanted to hear her speak again: I could never have enough of her voice and her words.

" 'How much do you love me?' I asked.

" 'Ah! you know: I will not gratify you: I will not flatter.'

" 'I don't know half enough: my heart craves to be fed. If you knew how hungry and ferocious it is, you would hasten to stay it with a kind word or two.'

" 'Poor Tartar!' said she, touching and patting my hand: 'poor fellow; stalwart friend; Shirley's pet and favourite, lie down!'

" 'But I will not lie down till I am fed with one sweet word.'

"And at last she gave it.

" 'Dear Louis, be faithful to me: never leave me. I don't care for life, unless I may pass it at your side.'

" 'Something more.'

"She gave me a change: it was not her way to offer the same dish twice.

" 'Sir!' she said, starting up, 'at your peril you ever again name such sordid things as money, or poverty, or inequality. It will be absolutely dangerous to torment me with these maddening scruples. I defy you to do it.'

"My face grew hot. I did once more wish I were not so poor, or she were not so rich. She saw the transient misery; and then, indeed, she caressed me. Blent with torment, I experienced rapture.

" 'Mr. Moore,' said she, looking up with a sweet, open, earnest countenance, 'teach me and help me to be good. I do not ask you to take off my shoulders all the cares and duties of property; but I ask you to share the burden, and to show me how to sustain my part well. Your judgment is well balanced; your heart is kind; your principles are sound. I know you are wise; I feel you are benevolent; I believe you are conscientious. Be my companion through life; be my guide where I am ignorant: be my master where I am faulty; be my friend always!'

" 'So help me God, I will!' "

Yet again, a passage from the blank book, if you like, reader; if you don't like it, pass it over:

"The Sympsons are gone; but not before discovery and explanation. My manner must have betrayed something, or my looks: I was quiet, but I forgot to be guarded sometimes. I stayed longer in the room than usual; I could not bear to be out of her presence; I returned to it, and basked in it, like Tartar in the sun. If she left the oak-parlour, instinctively I rose, and left it too. She chid me for this procedure more than once: I did it with a vague, blundering idea of getting a word with her in the hall or elsewhere. Yesterday towards dusk, I had her to myself for five minutes, by the hall-fire: we stood side by side; she was railing at me, and I was enjoying the sound of her voice: the young ladies passed, and looked at us; we did not separate: ere long, they repassed, and again looked. Mrs. Sympson came; we did not move: Mr. Sympson opened the dining-room door; Shirley flashed him back full payment for his spying gaze: she curled her lip, and tossed her tresses. The glance she gave was at once explanatory and defiant; it said—'I like Mr. Moore's society, and I dare you to find fault with my taste.'

"I asked, 'Do you mean him to understand how matters are?'

" 'I do,' said she; 'but I leave the development to chance. There will be a scene. I neither invite it nor fear it—only, you must be present; for I am inexpressibly tired of facing him solus. I don't like to see him in a rage; he then puts off all his fine proprieties and conventional disguises, and the real human being below is what you would call "commun, plat, bas—vilain et un peu méchant." His ideas are not clean, Mr. Moore; they want scouring with soft soap and fuller's earth. I think,

if he could add his imagination to the contents of Mrs. Gill's bucking-basket, and let her boil it in her copper, with rain-water and bleaching-powder (I hope you think me a tolerable laundress), it would do him incalculable good.'

"This morning, fancying I heard her descend somewhat early, I was down instantly. I had not been deceived: there she was, busy at work in the breakfast-parlour, of which the housemaid was completing the arrangement and dusting. She had risen betimes to finish some little keepsake she intended for Henry. I got only a cool reception; which I accepted till the girl was gone, taking my book to the window-seat very quietly. Even when we were alone, I was slow to disturb her: to sit with her in sight was happiness, and the proper happiness, for early morning—serene, incomplete, but progressive. Had I been obtrusive, I knew I should have encountered rebuff. 'Not at home to suitors,' was written on her brow; therefore, I read on—stole, now and then, a look; watched her countenance soften and open, and she felt I respected her mood, and enjoyed the gentle content of the moment.

"The distance between us shrank, and the light hoar-frost thawed insensibly: ere an hour elapsed, I was at her side, watching her sew, gathering her sweet smiles and her merry words, which fell for me abundantly. We sat as we had a right to sit, side by side: my arm rested on her chair; I was near enough to count the stitches of her work, and to discern the eye of her needle. The door suddenly opened.

"I believe, if I had just then started from her, she would have despised me: thanks to the phlegm of my nature, I rarely start. When I am well off, *bien*, comfortable, I am not soon stirred: *bien* I was—*très bien*—consequently, immutable: no muscle moved. I hardly looked to the door.

" 'Good morning, uncle,'' said she, addressing that personage; who paused on the threshold in a state of petrifaction.

" 'Have you been long downstairs, Miss Keeldar, and alone with Mr. Moore?'

" 'Yes, a very long time: we both came down early; it was scarcely light.'

" 'The proceeding is improper——'

" 'It was at first: I was rather cross, and not civil; but you will perceive that we are now friends.'

" 'I perceive more than you would wish me to perceive.'

" 'Hardly, sir,' said I: 'we have no disguises. Will you permit me to intimate, that any further observations you have to make may as well be addressed to me. Henceforward, I stand between Miss Keeldar and all annoyance.'

" '*You!* What have *you* to do with Miss Keeldar?'

" 'To protect, watch over, serve her.'

" 'You, sir?—you, the tutor?'

" 'Not one word of insult, sir,' interposed she: 'not one syllable of disrespect to Mr. Moore, in this house.'

" 'Do you take his part?'

" '*His* part? Oh, yes!'

"She turned to me with a sudden, fond movement, which I met by circling her with my arm. She and I both rose.

" 'Good Ged!' was the cry from the morning-gown standing quivering at the door. *Ged*, I think, must be the cognomen of Mr. Sympson's Lares: when hard pressed, he always invokes this idol.

" 'Come forward, uncle: you shall hear all. Tell him all, Louis.'

" 'I dare him to speak! The beggar! the knave! the specious hypocrite! the vile, insinuating, infamous menial! Stand apart from my niece, sir: let her go!'

"She clung to me with energy. 'I am near my future husband,' she said: 'who dares touch him or me?'

" 'Her husband!' he raised and spread his hands: he dropped into a seat.

" 'A while ago you wanted much to know whom I meant to marry: my intention was then formed, but not mature for communication; now it is ripe, sun-mellowed, perfect: take the crimson-peach—take Louis Moore!'

" 'But' (savagely) 'you *shall not* have him—he *shall not* have you.'

" 'I would die before I would have another. I would die if I might not have him.'

"He uttered words with which this page shall never be polluted.

"She turned white as death: she shook all over: she lost her strength. I laid her down on the sofa: just looked to ascertain that she had not fainted—of which, with a divine smile, she assured me; I kissed her, and then, if I were to perish, I cannot give a clear account of what happened in the course of the next five minutes: she has since—through tears, laughter, and trembling—told me that I turned terrible, and gave myself to the demon; she says I left her, made one bound across the room—that Mr. Sympson vanished through the door as if shot from a cannon—I also vanished, and she heard Mrs. Gill scream.

"Mrs. Gill was still screaming when I came to my senses; I was then in another apartment—the oak-parlour, I think: I held Sympson before me crushed into a chair, and my hand was on his cravat: his eyes rolled in his head—I was strangling him, I think: the housekeeper stood wringing her hands, entreating me to desist; I desisted that moment, and felt at once as cool as stone. But I told Mrs. Gill to fetch the Red-House Inn chaise instantly, and informed Mr. Sympson he must depart from Fieldhead the instant it came: though half frightened out of his wits, he declared he would not. Repeating the former order, I added a commission to fetch a constable. I said—'you *shall* go—by fair means or foul.'

"He threatened prosecution—I cared for nothing: I had stood over him once before, not quite so fiercely as now, but full as austerely. It was one night when burglars attempted the house at Sympson Grove; and in his wretched cowardice he would have given a vain alarm, without daring to offer defence: I had then been obliged to protect his family and his abode by mastering himself—and I had succeeded. I now remained with him till the chaise came: I marshalled him to it, he scolding all the way. He was terribly bewildered, as well as enraged; he would have resisted me, but knew not how: he called for his wife and daughters to come. I said they should follow him as soon as they could prepare: the smoke, the fume, the fret of his demeanour was inexpressible, but it was a fury incapable of producing a deed: that man, properly handled, must ever remain impotent. I know he will never touch me with the law: I know his wife, over whom he tyrannises in trifles, guides him in matters of importance. I have long since earned her undying mother's gratitude by my devotion to her boy: in some of Henry's ailments I have nursed him—better, she said, than any woman could nurse: she will never forget that. She and her daughters quitted me to-day, in mute wrath and consternation—but she respects me. When Henry clung to my neck, as I lifted him into the carriage and placed him by her side—when I arranged her own wrapping to make her warm, though she turned her head from me, I saw the tears start to her eyes. She will but the more zealously advocate my cause, because she has left me in anger. I am glad of this: not for my own sake, but for that of my life and idol—my Shirley.''

Once again he writes—a week after: "I am now at Stilbro': I have taken up my temporary abode with a friend—a professional man—in whose business I can be useful. Every day I ride over to Fieldhead. How long will it be before I can call that place my home, and its mistress mine? I am not easy—not tranquil: I am tantalised—sometimes tortured. To see her now, one would think she had never pressed her cheek to my shoulder, or clung to me with tenderness or trust. I feel unsafe: she renders me miserable: I am shunned when I visit her: she withdraws from my reach. Once, this day, I lifted her face, resolved to get a full look down her deep, dark eyes: difficult to describe what I read there! Pantheress!—beautiful forest-born!—wily, tameless, peerless nature! She gnaws her chain: I see the white teeth working at the steel! She has dreams of her wild woods, and pinings after virgin freedom. I wish Sympson would come again, and oblige her again to entwine

her arms about me. I wish there was danger she should lose me, as there is risk I shall lose her. No: final loss I do not fear; but long delay——

"It is now night—midnight. I have spent the afternoon and evening at Fieldhead. Some hours ago she passed me, coming down the oak-staircase to the hall: she did not know I was standing in the twilight, near the staircase-window, looking at the frost-bright constellations. How closely she glided against the banisters! How shyly shone her large eyes upon me! How evanescent, fugitive, fitful, she looked,—slim and swift as a Northern Streamer!

"I followed her into the drawing-room: Mrs. Pryor and Caroline Helstone were both there: she has summoned them to bear her company awhile. In her white evening dress; with her long hair flowing full and wavy; with her noiseless step, her pale cheek, her eye full of night and lightning, she looked I thought, spirit-like,—a thing made of an element,—the child of a breeze and a flame,—the daughter of ray and rain-drop,—a thing never to be overtaken, arrested, fixed. I wished I could avoid following her with my gaze, as she moved here and there, but it was impossible. I talked with the other ladies as well as I could, but still I looked at her. She was very silent: I think she never spoke to me,—not even when she offered me tea. It happened that she was called out a minute by Mrs. Gill. I passed into the moon-lit hall, with the design of getting a word as she returned; nor in this did I fail.

" 'Miss Keeldar, stay one instant!' said I, meeting her.

" 'Why?—the hall is too cold.'

" 'It is not cold for me: at my side, it should not be cold for you.'

" 'But I shiver.'

" 'With fear, I believe. What makes you fear me? You are quiet and distant: why?'

" 'I may well fear what looks like a great dark goblin meeting me in the moonlight.'

" '*Do not—do not* pass!—stay with me awhile: let us exchange a few quiet words. It is three days since I spoke to you alone: such changes are cruel.'

" 'I have no wish to be cruel,' she responded, softly enough; indeed, there was softness in her whole deportment—in her face, in her voice: but there was also reserve, and an air fleeting, evanishing, intangible.

" 'You certainly give me pain,' said I. 'It is hardly a week since you called me your future husband, and treated me as such; now I am once more the tutor for you: I am addressed as Mr. Moore, and Sir; your lips have forgotten Louis.'

" 'No, Louis, no: it is an easy, liquid name; not soon forgotten.'

" 'Be cordial to Louis, then: approach him—let him approach.'

" 'I *am* cordial,' said she, hovering aloof like a white shadow.

" 'Your voice is very sweet and very low,' I answered, quietly advancing: 'you seem subdued, but still startled.'

" 'No—quite calm, and afraid of nothing,' she assured me.

" 'Of nothing but your votary.'

"I bent a knee to the flags at her feet.

" 'You see I am in a new world, Mr. Moore. I don't know myself,—I don't know you: but rise; when you do so, I feel troubled and disturbed.'

"I obeyed; it would not have suited me to retain that attitude long. I courted serenity and confidence for her, and not vainly: she trusted, and clung to me again.

" 'Now, Shirley,' I said, 'you can conceive I am far from happy in my present uncertain, unsettled state.'

" 'Oh, yes; you *are* happy!' she cried hastily: 'you don't know how happy you are!—any change will be for the worse!'

" 'Happy or not, I cannot bear to go on so much longer: you are too generous to require it.'

" 'Be reasonable, Louis,—be patient! I like you because you are patient.'

" 'Like me no longer, then,—love me instead: fix our marriage-day. Think of it to-night, and decide.'

"She breathed a murmur, inarticulate yet expressive: darted or melted from my arms—and I lost her.''

Chapter XXXVII

THE WINDING-UP

YES, reader, we must settle accounts now. I have only briefly to narrate the final fates of some of the personages whose acquaintance we have made in this narrative, and then you and I must shake hands, and for the present separate.

Let us turn to the Curates,—to the much-loved, though long-neglected. Come forward, modest merit! Malone, I see, promptly answers the invocation: he knows his own description when he hears it.

No, Peter Augustus, we can have nothing to say to you: it won't do. Impossible to trust ourselves with the touching tale of your deeds and destinies. Are you not aware, Peter, that a discriminating public has its crotchets: that the unvarnished truth does not answer; that plain facts will not digest? Do you not know that the squeak of the real pig is no more relished now than it was in days of yore? Were I to give the catastrophe of your life and conversation, the public would sweep off in shrieking hysterics, and there would be a wild cry for sal-volatile and burnt feathers. ''Impossible!'' would be pronounced here: ''untrue!'' would be responded there. ''Inartistic!'' would be solemnly decided. Note well! Whenever you present the actual, simple truth, it is, somehow, always denounced as a lie: they disown it, cast it off, throw it on the parish; whereas the product of your own imagination, the mere figment, the sheer fiction, is adopted, petted, termed pretty, proper, sweetly natural: the little spurious wretch gets all the comfits,—the honest, lawful bantling all the cuffs. Such is the way of the world, Peter; and, as you are the legitimate urchin, rude, unwashed, and naughty, you must stand down.

Make way for Mr. Sweeting.

Here he comes, with his lady on his arm; the most splendid and the weightiest woman in Yorkshire: Mrs. Sweeting, formerly Miss Dora Sykes. They were married under the happiest auspices; Mr. Sweeting having been just inducted to a comfortable living, and Mr. Sykes being in circumstances to give Dora a handsome portion. They lived long and happily together, beloved by their parishioners and by a numerous circle of friends.

There! I think the varnish has been put on very nicely.

Advance, Mr. Donne.

This gentleman turned out admirably: far better than either you or I could possibly have expected, reader. He, too, married a most sensible, quiet, lady-like little woman: the match was the making of him: he became an exemplary domestic character, and a truly active parish-priest (as a pastor, he, to his dying day, conscientiously refused to act). The outside of the cup and platter he burnished up with the best polishing-powder; the furniture of the altar and temple he looked after with the zeal of an upholsterer—the care of a cabinet-maker. His little school, his little church, his little parsonage, all owed their erection to him; and they did him credit: each was a model in its way: if uniformity and taste in architecture had been the same thing as consistency and earnestness in religion, what a shepherd of a Christian flock Mr. Donne would have made! There was one art in the mastery of which nothing mortal ever surpassed Mr. Donne—it was that of begging. By his own unassisted efforts, he begged all the money for all his erections. In this matter he had a grasp of plan, a scope of action quite unique: he begged of high and low—

of the shoeless cottage-brat and the coroneted duke: he sent out begging-letters far and wide—to old Queen Charlotte, to the princesses her daughters, to her sons the royal dukes, to the Prince Regent, to Lord Castlereagh, to every member of the Ministry then in office; and, what is more remarkable, he screwed something out of every one of these personages. It is on record that he got five pounds from the close-fisted old lady, Queen Charlotte, and two guineas from the royal profligate, her eldest son. When Mr. Donne set out on begging expeditions, he armed himself in a complete suit of brazen mail: that you had given a hundred pounds yesterday, was, with him, no reason why you should not give two hundred to-day: he would tell you so to your face, and, ten to one, get the money out of you: people gave to get rid of him. After all, he did some good with the cash; he was useful in his day and generation.

Perhaps I ought to remark, that on the premature and sudden vanishing of Mr. Malone from the stage of Briarfield parish (you cannot know how it happened, reader; your curiosity must be robbed to pay your elegant love of the pretty and pleasing), there came as his successor another Irish curate, Mr. Macarthey. I am happy to be able to inform you, *with truth,* that this gentleman did as much credit to his country as Malone had done it discredit: he proved himself as decent, decorous, and conscientious, as Peter was rampant, boisterous, and——(this last epithet I choose to suppress, because it would let the cat out of the bag). He laboured faithfully in the parish: the schools, both Sunday and day-schools, flourished under his sway like green bay-trees. Being human, of course he had his faults; these, however, were proper, steady-going, clerical faults; what many would call virtues: the circumstance of finding himself invited to tea with a dissenter would unhinge him for a week; the spectacle of a Quaker wearing his hat in the church, the thought of an unbaptised fellow-creature being interred with Christian rites—these things could make strange havoc in Mr. Macarthey's physical and mental economy; otherwise he was sane and rational, diligent and charitable.

I doubt not a justice-loving public will have remarked, ere this, that I have thus far shown a criminal remissness in pursuing, catching, and bringing to condign punishment the would-be assassin of Mr. Robert Moore: here was a fine opening to lead my willing readers a dance, at once decorous and exciting: a dance of law and gospel, of the dungeon, the dock, and the "dead-thraw." You might have liked it, reader, but *I* should not: I and my subject would presently have quarrelled, and then I should have broken down: I was happy to find that facts perfectly exonerated me from the attempt. The murderer was never punished; for the good reason that he was never caught; the result of the further circumstance that he was never pursued. The magistrates made a shuffling, as if they were going to rise and do valiant things; but, since Moore himself, instead of urging and leading them as heretofore, lay still on his little cottage-couch, laughing in his sleeve and sneering with every feature of his pale, foreign face, they considered better of it; and, after fulfilling certain indispensable forms, prudently resolved to let the matter quietly drop, which they did.

Mr. Moore knew who had shot him, and all Briarfield knew; it was no other than Michael Hartley, the half-crazed weaver once before alluded to, a frantic Antinomian in religion, and a mad leveller in politics; the poor soul died of delirium tremens, a year after the attempt on Moore, and Robert gave his wretched widow a guinea to bury him.

The winter is over and gone: spring has followed with beamy and shadowy, with flowery and showery flight: we are now in the heart of summer—in mid-June,—the June of 1812.

It is burning weather: the air is deep azure and red gold: it fits the time; it fits the age; it fits the present spirit of the nations. The nineteenth century wantons in its giant adolescence: the Titan-boy uproots mountains in his game, and hurls rocks

in his wild sport. This summer, Bonaparte is in the saddle: he and his host scour Russian deserts: he has with him Frenchmen and Poles, Italians and children of the Rhine, six hundred thousand strong. He marches on old Moscow: under old Moscow's walls the rude Cossack waits him. Barbarian stoic! he waits without fear of the boundless ruin rolling on. He puts his trust in a snow-cloud: the Wilderness, the Wind, the Hail-Storm are his refuge: his allies are the elements—Air, Fire, Water. And what are these? Three terrible archangels ever stationed before the throne of Jehovah. They stand clothed in white, girdled with golden girdles; they uplift vials, brimming with the wrath of God. Their time is the day of vengeance; their signal, the word of the Lord of Hosts, "thundering with the voice of His excellency."

"Hast thou entered into the treasures of the snow? or hast thou seen the treasures of the hail, which I have reserved against the time of trouble, against the day of battle and war?

"Go your ways: pour out the vials of the wrath of God upon the earth."

It is done: the earth is scorched with fire: the sea becomes "as the blood of a dead man": the islands flee away; the mountains are not found.

In this year Lord Wellington assumed the reins in Spain: they made him Generalissimo, for their own salvation's sake. In this year he took Badajos, he fought the field of Vittoria, he captured Pampeluna, he stormed St. Sebastian; in this year, he won Salamanca.

Men of Manchester! I beg your pardon for this slight résumé of warlike facts: but it is of no consequence. Lord Wellington is, for you, only a decayed old gentleman now: I rather think some of you have called him a "dotard"—you have taunted him with his age, and the loss of his physical vigour. What fine heroes what you are yourselves! Men like you have a right to trample on what is mortal in a demigod. Scoff at your ease—your scorn can never break his grand, old heart.

But come, friends, whether Quakers or Cotton-printers, let us hold a Peace-Congress, and let out our venom quietly. We have been talking with unseemly zeal about bloody battles and butchering generals; we arrive now at a triumph in your line. On the 18th of June, 1812, the Orders in Council were repealed, and the blockaded ports thrown open. You know very well—such of you as are old enough to remember—you made Yorkshire and Lancashire shake with your shout on that occasion: the ringers cracked a bell in Briarfield belfry; it is dissonant to this day. The Association of Merchants and Manufacturers dined together at Stilbro', and one and all went home in such a plight as their wives would never wish to witness more. Liverpool started and snorted like a river-horse roused amongst his reeds by thunder. Some of the American merchants felt threatenings of apoplexy, and had themselves bled: all, like wise men, at this first moment of prosperity, prepared to rush into the bowels of speculation, and to delve new difficulties, in whose depths they might lose themselves at some future day. Stocks, which had been accumulating for years, now went off in a moment, in the twinkling of an eye; warehouses were lightened, ships were laden; work abounded, wages rose; the good time seemed come. These prospects might be delusive, but they were brilliant—to some they were even true. At that epoch, in that single month of June, many a solid fortune was realised.

When a whole province rejoices, the humblest of its inhabitants tastes a festal feeling: the sound of public bells rouses the most secluded abode, as if with a call to be gay. And so Caroline Helstone thought, when she dressed herself more carefully than usual on the day of this trading triumph, and went, attired in her neatest muslin, to spend the afternoon at Fieldhead, there to superintend certain millinery preparations for a great event: the last appeal in these matters being reserved for her unimpeachable taste. She decided on the wreath, the veil, the dress to be worn at the altar: she chose various robes and fashions for more ordinary occasions, without much reference to the bride's opinion; that lady, indeed, being in a somewhat impracticable mood.

Louis had presaged difficulties, and he had found them: in fact, his mistress had shown herself exquisitely provoking; putting off her marriage day by day, week by week, month by month. At first coaxing him with soft pretences of procrastination, and in the end rousing his whole deliberate but determined nature to revolt against her tyranny, at once so sweet and so intolerable.

It had needed a sort of tempest-shock to bring her to the point; but there she was at last, fettered to a fixed day: there she lay, conquered by love, and bound with a vow.

Thus vanquished and restricted, she pined, like any other chained denizen of deserts. Her captor alone could cheer her; his society only could make amends for the lost privilege of liberty: in his absence, she sat or wandered alone; spoke little, and ate less.

She furthered no preparations for her nuptials; Louis was himself obliged to direct all arrangements: he was virtually master of Fieldhead, weeks before he became so nominally: the least presumptuous, the kindest master that ever was; but with his lady absolute. She abdicated without a word or a struggle. "Go to Mr. Moore; ask Mr. Moore," was her answer when applied to for orders. Never was wooer of wealthy bride so thoroughly absolved from the subaltern part; so inevitably compelled to assume a paramount character.

In all this, Miss Keeldar partly yielded to her disposition; but a remark she made a year afterwards proved that she partly also acted on system. "Louis," she said, "would never have learned to rule, if she had not ceased to govern: the incapacity of the sovereign had developed the powers of the premier."

It had been intended that Miss Helstone should act as bridesmaid at the approaching nuptials; but Fortune had destined her another part.

She came home in time to water her plants. She had performed this little task. The last flower attended to was a rose-tree, which bloomed in a quiet green nook at the back of the house. This plant had received the refreshing shower: she was now resting a minute. Near the wall stood a fragment of sculptured stone—a monkish relic; once, perhaps, the base of a cross: she mounted it, that she might better command the view. She had still the watering-pot in one hand; with the other, her pretty dress was held lightly aside, to avoid trickling drops: she gazed over the wall, along some lonely fields; beyond three dusk trees, rising side by side against the sky; beyond a solitary thorn, at the head of a solitary lane far off: she surveyed the dusk moors, where bonfires were kindling: the summer-evening was warm; the bell-music was joyous; the blue smoke of the fires looked soft; their red flame bright; above them, in the sky whence the sun had vanished, twinkled a silver point—the Star of Love.

Caroline was not unhappy that evening; far otherwise: but as she gazed she sighed, and as she sighed a hand circled her, and rested quietly on her waist. Caroline thought she knew who had drawn near: she received the touch unstartled.

"I am looking at Venus, mamma: see, she is beautiful. How white her lustre is, compared with the deep red of the bonfires!"

The answer was a closer caress; and Caroline turned, and looked, not into Mrs. Pryor's matron face, but up at a dark manly visage. She dropped her watering-pot, and stepped down from the pedestal.

"I have been sitting with 'mamma' an hour," said the intruder. "I have had a long conversation with her. Where, meantime, have you been?"

"To Fieldhead. Shirley is as naughty as ever, Robert: she will neither say Yes nor No to any question put. She sits alone: I cannot tell whether she is melancholy or nonchalant: if you rouse her, or scold her, she gives you a look half wistful, half reckless, which sends you away as queer and crazed as herself. What Louis will make of her, I cannot tell: for my part, if I were a gentleman, I think I would not dare undertake her."

"Never mind them: they were cut out for each other. Louis, strange to say, likes her all the better for these freaks: he will manage her, if any one can. She tries him, however: he has had a stormy courtship for such a calm character; but you see it all ends in victory for him. Caroline, I have sought you to ask an audience. Why are those bells ringing?"

"For the repeal of your terrible law; the Orders you hate so much. You are pleased, are you not?"

"Yesterday evening at this time, I was packing some books for a sea-voyage: they were the only possessions, except some clothes, seeds, roots, and tools, which I felt free to take with me to Canada. I was going to leave you."

"To leave me? To leave *me*?"

Her little fingers fastened on his arm: she spoke and looked affrighted.

"Not now—not now. Examine my face; yes, look at me well; is the despair of parting legible thereon?"

She looked into an illuminated countenance, whose characters were all beaming, though the page itself was dusk: this face, potent in the majesty of its traits, shed down on her hope, fondness, delight.

"Will the repeal do you good; *much* good—*immediate* good?" she inquired.

"The repeal of the Orders in Council saves me. Now I shall not turn bankrupt; now I shall not give up business; now I shall not leave England; now I shall be no longer poor; now I can pay my debts; now all the cloth I have in my warehouses will be taken off my hands, and commissions given me for much more; this day lays for my fortunes abroad, firm foundation; on which, for the first time in my life, I can securely build."

Caroline devoured his words: she held his hand in hers; she drew a long breath.

"You are saved? Your heavy difficulties are lifted?"

"They are lifted: I breathe: I can act."

"At last! Oh! Providence is kind. Thank Him, Robert."

"I do thank Providence."

"And I also, for your sake!" She looked up devoutly.

"Now, I can take more workmen; give better wages; lay wiser and more liberal plans; do some good; be less selfish: *now,* Caroline, I can have a house—a home which I can truly call mine—and *now*"——

He paused; for his deep voice was checked.

"And *now*," he resumed—"now I can think of marriage, *now* I can seek a wife."

This was no moment for her to speak: she did not speak.

"Will Caroline, who meekly hopes to be forgiven as she forgives—will she pardon all I have made her suffer—all that long pain I have wickedly caused her— all that sickness of body and mind she owed to me? Will she forget what she knows of my poor ambition—my sordid schemes? Will she let me expiate these things? Will she suffer me to prove that, as I once deserted cruelly, trifled wantonly, injured basely, I can now love faithfully, cherish fondly, treasure tenderly?"

His hand was in Caroline's still: a gentle pressure answered him.

"Is Caroline mine?"

"Caroline is yours."

"I will prize her: the sense of her value is here, in my heart; the necessity for her society is blended with my life: not more jealous shall I be of the blood whose flow moves my pulses, than of her happiness and well-being."

"I love you, too, Robert, and will take faithful care of you."

"Will you take faithful care of me?—faithful care! as if that rose should promise to shelter from tempest this hard, grey stone? But she *will* care for me, in her way: these hands will be the gentle ministrants of every comfort I can taste. I know the being I seek to entwine with my own will bring me a solace—a charity—a purity— to which, of myself, I am a stranger."

Suddenly, Caroline was troubled; her lip quivered.

"What flutters my dove?" asked Moore, as she nestled to, and then uneasily shrank from him.

"Poor mamma! I am all mamma has: must I leave her?"

"Do you know, I thought of that difficulty: I and 'mamma' have discussed it."

"Tell me what you wish—what you would like—and I will consider if it is possible to consent; but I cannot desert her, even for you: I cannot break her heart, even for your sake."

"She was faithful when I was false—was she not? I never came near your sick-bed, and she watched it ceaselessly."

"What must I do? Anything but leave her."

"At my wish, you never shall leave her."

"She may live very near us?"

"With us—only she will have her own rooms and servant: for this she stipulates herself."

"You know she has an income, that, with her habits, makes her quite independent?"

"She told me that, with a gentle pride that reminded me of somebody else."

"She is not at all interfering, and incapable of gossip."

"I know her, Cary: but if—instead of being the personification of reserve and discretion—she were something quite opposite, I should not fear her."

"Yet she will be your mother-in-law?" The speaker gave an arch little nod: Moore smiled.

"Louis and I are not of the order of men who fear their mothers-in-law, Cary: our foes never have been, nor will be, those of our own household. I doubt not, my mother-in-law will make much of me."

"That she will—in her quiet way, you know. She is not demonstrative; and when you see her silent, or even cool, you must not fancy her displeased—it is only a manner she has. Be sure to let me interpret for her, whenever she puzzles you; always believe my account of the matter, Robert."

"Oh, implicitly! Jesting apart, l feel that she and I will suit—*on ne peut mieux*. Hortense, you know, is exquisitely susceptible—in our French sense of the word— and not, perhaps, always reasonable in her requirements; yet—dear, honest girl— I never painfully wounded her feelings, or had a serious quarrel with her, in my life."

"No: you are most generously considerate—indeed, most tenderly indulgent to her; and you will be considerate with mamma. You are a gentleman all through, to the bone, and nowhere so perfect a gentleman as at your own fireside."

"An eulogium I like: it is very sweet. I am well pleased my Caroline should view me in this light."

"Mamma just thinks of you as I do."

"Not quite, I hope?"

"She does not want to marry you—don't be vain; but she said to me the other day, 'My dear, Mr. Moore has pleasing manners; he is one of the few gentlemen I have seen who combine politeness with an air of sincerity.' "

" 'Mamma' is rather a misanthropist, is she not? Not the best opinion of the sterner sex?"

"She forbears to judge them as a whole, but she has her exceptions whom she admires. Louis and Mr. Hall, and, of late—yourself. She did not like you once: I knew that because she would never speak of you. But, Robert——"

"Well, what now? What is the new thought?"

"You have not seen my uncle yet?"

"I have: 'mamma' called him into the room. He consents conditionally: if I prove that I can keep a wife, I may have her; and I *can* keep her better than he thinks—better than I choose to boast."

"If you get rich, you will do good with your money, Robert?"

"I *will* do good; you shall tell me how: indeed, I have some schemes of my own, which you and I will talk about on our own hearth one day. I have seen the necessity of doing good: I have learned the downright folly of being selfish. Caroline, I foresee what I will now foretell. This war *must* ere long draw to a close: Trade is likely to prosper for some years to come: there may be a brief misunderstanding between England and America, but that will not last. What would you think if, one day—perhaps ere another ten years elapse—Louis and I divide Briarfield parish betwixt us? Louis, at any rate, is certain of power and property: he will not bury his talents: he is a benevolent fellow, and has, besides, an intellect of his own of no trifling calibre. His mind is slow but strong: it must work: it may work deliberately, but it will work well. He will be made magistrate of the district—Shirley says he shall: she would proceed impetuously and prematurely to obtain for him this dignity, if he would let her, but he will not; as usual, he will be in no haste: ere he has been master of Fieldhead a year, all the district will feel his quiet influence, and acknowledge his unassuming superiority: a magistrate is wanted—they will, in time, invest him with the office voluntarily and unreluctantly. Everybody admires his future wife: and everybody will, in time, like him: he is of the 'pâte' generally approved, 'bon comme le pain'—daily bread for the most fastidious; good for the infant and the aged, nourishing for the poor, wholesome for the rich. Shirley, in spite of her whims and oddities, her dodges and delays, has an infatuated fondness for him: she will one day see him as universally beloved as even *she* could wish: he will also be universally esteemed, considered, consulted, depended on—too much so: his advice will be always judicious, his help always good-natured—ere long, both will be in inconvenient request: he will have to impose restrictions. As for me, if I succeed as I intend to do, my success will add to his and Shirley's income: I can double the value of their mill-property: I can line yonder barren Hollow with lines of cottages, and rows of cottage-gardens——"

"Robert? And root up the copse?"

"The copse shall be firewood ere five years elapse: the beautiful wild ravine shall be a smooth descent; the green natural terrace shall be a paved street: there shall be cottages in the dark ravine, and cottages on the lonely slopes: the rough pebbled track shall be an even, firm, broad, black, sooty road, bedded with the cinders from my mill: and my mill, Caroline—my mill shall fill its present yard."

"Horrible! You will change our blue hill-country air into the Stilbro' smoke atmosphere."

"I will pour the waters of Pactolus through the valley of Briarfield."

"I like the beck a thousand times better."

"I will get an act for enclosing Nunnely Common, and parcelling it out into farms."

"Stilbro' Moor, however, defies you, thank Heaven! What can you grow in Bilberry Moss? What will flourish on Rushedge?"

"Caroline, the houseless, the starving, the unemployed, shall come to Hollow's Mill from far and near; and Joe Scott shall give them work, and Louis Moore, Esq., shall let them a tenement, and Mrs. Gill shall mete them a portion till the first pay-day."

She smiled up in his face.

"Such a Sunday-school as you will have, Cary! such collections as you will get! such a day-school as you and Shirley, and Miss Ainley, will have to manage between you! The mill shall find salaries for a master and mistress, and the Squire or the Clothier shall give a treat once a quarter."

She mutely offered a kiss, an offer taken unfair advantage of, to the extortion of about a hundred kisses.

"Extravagant day-dreams!" said Moore, with a sigh and smile, "yet perhaps we may realise some of them. Meantime, the dew is falling: Mrs. Moore, I shall take you in."

It is August: the bells clash out again, not only through Yorkshire but through England: from Spain, the voice of a trumpet has sounded long: it now waxes louder and louder; it proclaims Salamanca won. This night is Briarfield to be illuminated. On this day the Fieldhead tenantry dine together; the Hollow's Mill workpeople will be assembled for a like festal purpose; the schools have a grand treat. This morning there were two marriages solemnised in Briarfield church.—Louis Gérard Moore, Esq., late of Antwerp, to Shirley, daughter of the late Charles Cave Keeldar, Esq., of Fieldhead. Robert Gérard Moore, Esq., of Hollow's Mill, to Caroline, niece of the Rev. Matthewson Helstone, M.A., Rector of Briarfield.

The ceremony, in the first instance, was performed by Mr. Helstone; Hiram Yorke, Esq., of Briarmains, giving the bride away. In the second instance, Mr. Hall, Vicar of Nunnely, officiated. Amongst the bridal train, the two most noticeable personages were the youthful bridesmen, Henry Sympson, and Martin Yorke.

I suppose Robert Moore's prophecies were, partially, at least, fulfilled. The other day I passed up the Hollow, which tradition says was once green, and lone, and wild; and there I saw the manufacturer's day-dreams embodied in substantial stone and brick and ashes—the cinder-black highway, the cottages, and the cottage gardens; there I saw a mighty mill, and a chimney, ambitious as the tower of Babel. I told my old housekeeper when I came home where I had been.

"Ay!" said she; "this world has queer changes. I can remember the old mill being built—the very first it was in all the district; and then, I can remember it being pulled down, and going with my lake-lasses (companions) to see the foundation-stone of the new one laid: the two Mr. Moores made a great stir about it; they were there, and a deal of fine folk beside, and both their ladies; very bonnie and grand they looked; but Mrs. Louis was the grandest, she always wore such handsome dresses: Mrs. Robert was quieter like. Mrs. Louis smiled when she talked: she had a real, happy, glad, good-natured look; but she had een that pierced a body through: there is no such ladies now-a-days."

"What was the Hollow like then, Martha?"

"Different to what it is now; but I can tell of it clean different again: when there was neither mill, nor cot, nor hall, except Fieldhead, within two miles of it. I can tell, one summer evening, fifty years syne, my mother coming running in just at the edge of dark, almost fleyed out of her wits, saying she had seen a fairish (fairy) in Fieldhead Hollow; and that was the last fairish that ever was seen on this country side (though they've been heard within these forty years). A lonesome spot it was—and a bonnie spot—full of oak trees and nut trees. It is altered now."

The story is told. I think I now see the judicious reader putting on his spectacles to look for the moral. It would be an insult to his sagacity to offer directions. I only say, God speed him in the quest!

Villette

by
Charlotte Brontë

Chapter I

BRETTON

MY godmother lived in a handsome house in the clean and ancient town of Bretton. Her husband's family had been residents there for generations, and bore, indeed, the name of their birthplace—Bretton of Bretton: whether by coincidence, or because some remote ancestor had been a personage of sufficient importance to leave his name to his neighbourhood, I know not.

When I was a girl I went to Bretton about twice a year, and well I liked the visit. The house and its inmates specially suited me. The large peaceful rooms, the well-arranged furniture, the clear wide windows, the balcony outside, looking down on a fine antique street, where Sundays and holidays seemed always to abide—so quiet was its atmosphere, so clean its pavement—these things pleased me well.

One child in a household of grown people is usually made very much of, and in a quiet way I was a good deal taken notice of by Mrs. Bretton, who had been left a widow, with one son, before I knew her; her husband, a physician, having died while she was yet a young and handsome woman.

She was not young, as I remember her, but she was still handsome, tall, well-made, and though dark for an English-woman, yet wearing always the clearness of health in her brunette cheek, and its vivacity in a pair of fine, cheerful black eyes. People esteemed it a grievous pity that she had not conferred her complexion on her son, whose eyes were blue—though, even in boyhood, very piercing—and the colour of his long hair such as friends did not venture to specify, except as the sun shone on it, when they called it golden. He inherited the lines of his mother's features, however; also her good teeth, her stature (or the promise of her stature, for he was not yet full-grown), and, what was better, her health without flaw, and her spirits of that tone and equality which are better than a fortune to the possessor.

In the autumn of the year —— I was staying at Bretton, my godmother having come in person to claim me of the kinsfolk with whom was at that time fixed my permanent residence. I believe she then plainly saw events coming, whose very shadow I scarce guessed; yet of which the faint suspicion sufficed to impart unsettled sadness, and made me glad to change scene and society.

Time always flowed smoothly for me at my godmother's side; not with tumultuous swiftness, but blandly, like the gliding of a full river through a plain. My visits to her resembled the sojourn of Christian and Hopeful beside a certain pleasant stream, with ''green trees on each bank, and meadows beautified with lilies all the year round.'' The charm of variety there was not, nor the excitement of incident; but I liked peace so well, and sought stimulus so little, that when the latter came I almost felt it a disturbance, and wished rather it had still held aloof.

One day a letter was received of which the contents evidently caused Mrs. Bretton surprise and some concern. I thought at first it was from home, and trembled, expecting I know not what disastrous communication: to me, however, no reference was made, and the cloud seemed to pass.

The next day, on my return from a long walk, I found, as I entered my bedroom, an unexpected change. In addition to my own French bed in its shady recess, appeared in a corner a small crib, draped with white; and in addition to my mahogany chest of drawers, I saw a tiny rosewood chest. I stood still, gazed, and considered.

"Of what are these things the signs and tokens?" I asked. The answer was obvious. "A second guest is coming; Mrs. Bretton expects other visitors."

On descending to dinner, explanations ensued. A little girl, I was told, would shortly be my companion: the daughter of a friend and distant relation of the late Dr. Bretton's. This little girl, it was added, had recently lost her mother; though, indeed, Mrs. Bretton ere long subjoined, the loss was not so great as might at first appear. Mrs. Home (Home it seems was the name) had been a very pretty, but a giddy, careless woman, who had neglected her child, and disappointed and disheartened her husband. So far from congenial had the union proved, that separation at last ensued—separation by mutual consent, not after any legal process. Soon after this event, the lady having over-exerted herself at a ball, caught cold, took a fever, and died after a very brief illness. Her husband, naturally a man of very sensitive feelings, and shocked inexpressibly by too sudden communication of the news, could hardly, it seems, now be persuaded but that some over-severity on his part— some deficiency in patience and indulgence—had contributed to hasten her end. He had brooded over this idea till his spirits were seriously affected; the medical men insisted on travelling being tried as a remedy, and meanwhile Mrs. Bretton had offered to take charge of his little girl. "And I hope," added my godmother in conclusion, "the child will not be like her mamma; as silly and frivolous a little flirt as ever sensible man was weak enough to marry. For," said she, "Mr. Home *is* a sensible man in his way, though not very practical: he is fond of science, and lives half his life in a laboratory trying experiments—a thing his butterfly wife could neither comprehend nor endure; and indeed," confessed my godmother, "I should not have liked it myself."

In answer to a question of mine, she further informed me that her late husband used to say, Mr. Home had derived this scientific turn from a maternal uncle, a French savant: for he came, it seems, of mixed French and Scottish origin, and had connections now living in France, of whom more than one wrote *de* before his name, and called himself noble.

That same evening at nine o'clock, a servant was despatched to meet the coach by which our little visitor was expected. Mrs. Bretton and I sat alone in the drawing-room waiting her coming; John Graham Bretton being absent on a visit to one of his schoolfellows who lived in the country. My godmother read the evening paper while she waited; I sewed. It was a wet night; the rain lashed the panes, and the wind sounded angry and restless.

"Poor child!" said Mrs. Bretton from time to time. "What weather for her journey! I wish she were safe here."

A little before ten the door-bell announced Warren's return. No sooner was the door opened than I ran down into the hall; there lay a trunk and some bandboxes, beside them stood a person like a nurse girl, and at the foot of the staircase was Warren with a shawled bundle in his arms.

"Is that the child?" I asked.

"Yes, miss."

I would have opened the shawl, and tried to get a peep at the face, but it was hastily turned from me to Warren's shoulder.

"Put me down, please," said a small voice when Warren opened the drawing-room door, "and take off this shawl," continued the speaker, extracting with its minute hand the pin, and with a sort of fastidious haste doffing the clumsy wrapping. The creature which now appeared made a deft attempt to fold the shawl; but the drapery was much too heavy and large to be sustained or wielded by those hands

and arms. "Give it to Harriet, please," was then the direction, "and she can put it away." This said, it turned and fixed its eyes on Mrs. Bretton.

"Come here, little dear," said that lady. "Come and let me see if you are cold and damp: come and let me warm you at the fire."

The child advanced promptly. Relieved of her wrapping, she appeared exceedingly tiny; but was a neat, completely-fashioned little figure, light, slight, and straight. Seated on my godmother's ample lap, she looked a mere doll; her neck, delicate as wax, her head of silky curls, increased, I thought, the resemblance.

Mrs. Bretton talked in little fond phrases as she chafed the child's hands, arms, and feet; first she was considered with a wistful gaze, but soon a smile answered her. Mrs. Bretton was not generally a caressing woman: even with her deeply-cherished son, her manner was rarely sentimental, often the reverse; but when the small stranger smiled at her, she kissed it, asking—"What is my little one's name?"

"Missy."

"But besides Missy?"

"Polly, papa calls her."

"Will Polly be content to live with me?"

"Not *always;* but till papa comes home. Papa is gone away." She shook her head expressively.

"He will return to Polly, or send for her."

"Will he, ma'am? Do you know he will?"

"I think so."

"But Harriet thinks not: at least not for a long while. He is ill."

Her eyes filled. She drew her hand from Mrs. Bretton's, and made a movement to leave her lap; it was at first resisted, but she said—"Please, I wish to go: I can sit on a stool."

She was allowed to slip down from the knee, and taking a footstool, she carried it to a corner where the shade was deep, and there seated herself. Mrs. Bretton, though a commanding, and in grave matters even a peremptory woman, was often passive in trifles: she allowed the child her way. She said to me, "Take no notice at present." But I did take notice: I watched Polly rest her small elbow on her small knee, her head on her hand; I observed her draw a square inch or two of pocket-handkerchief from the doll-pocket of her doll-skirt, and then I heard her weep. Other children in grief or pain cry aloud, without shame or restraint; but this being wept: the tiniest occasional sniff testified to her emotion. Mrs. Bretton did not hear it: which was quite as well. Ere long, a voice, issuing from the corner, demanded—"May the bell be rung for Harriet?"

I rang; the nurse was summoned and came.

"Harriet, I must be put to bed," said her little mistress. "You must ask where my bed is."

Harriet signified that she had already made that inquiry.

"Ask if you sleep with me, Harriet."

"No, Missy," said the nurse: "you are to share this young lady's room," designating me.

Missy did not leave her seat, but I saw her eyes seek me. After some minutes' silent scrutiny, she emerged from her corner.

"I wish you, ma'am, good-night," said she to Mrs. Bretton; but she passed me mute.

"Good-night, Polly," I said.

"No need to say good-night, since we sleep in the same chamber," was the reply with which she vanished from the drawing-room. We heard Harriet propose to carry her upstairs. "No need," was again her answer—"No need, no need": and her small step toiled wearily up the staircase.

On going to bed an hour afterwards, I found her still wide awake. She had arranged her pillows so as to support her little person in a sitting posture: her hands,

placed one within the other, rested quietly on the sheet, with an old-fashioned calm most unchildlike. I abstained from speaking to her for some time, but just before extinguishing the light, I recommended her to lie down.

''By-and-by,'' was the answer.

''But you will take cold, Missy.''

She took some tiny article of raiment from the chair at her crib side, and with it covered her shoulders. I suffered her to do as she pleased. Listening a while in the darkness, I was aware that she still wept,—wept under restraint, quietly and cautiously.

On awaking with daylight, a trickling of water caught my ear. Behold! there she was risen and mounted on a stool near the washstand, with pains and difficulty inclining the ewer (which she could not lift) so as to pour its contents into the basin. It was curious to watch her as she washed and dressed, so small, busy, and noiseless. Evidently she was little accustomed to perform her own toilet; and the buttons, strings, hooks and eyes, offered difficulties which she encountered with a perseverance good to witness. She folded her night-dress, she smoothed the drapery of her couch quite neatly; withdrawing into a corner, where the sweep of the white curtain concealed her, she became still. I half rose, and advanced my head to see how she was occupied. On her knees, with her forehead bent on her hands, I perceived that she was praying.

Her nurse tapped at the door. She started up.

''I am dressed, Harriet,'' said she: ''I have dressed myself, but I do not feel neat. Make me neat!''

''Why did you dress yourself, Missy?''

''Hush! speak low, Harriet, for fear of waking *the girl*'' (meaning me, who now lay with my eyes shut). ''I dressed myself to learn, against the time you leave me.''

''Do you want me to go?''

''When you are cross, I have many a time wanted you to go, but not now. Tie my sash straight; make my hair smooth, please.''

''Your sash is straight enough. What a particular little body you are!''

''It must be tied again. Please to tie it.''

''There, then. When I am gone you must get that young lady to dress you.''

''On no account.''

''Why? She is a very nice young lady. I hope you mean to behave prettily to her, Missy, and not show your airs.''

''She shall dress me on no account.''

''Comical little thing!''

''You are not passing the comb straight through my hair, Harriet; the line will be crooked.''

''Ay, you are ill to please. Does that suit?''

''Pretty well. Where should I go now that I am dressed?''

''I will take you into the breakfast-room.''

''Come then.''

They proceeded to the door. She stopped.

''Oh! Harriet, I wish this was papa's house! I don't know these people.''

''Be a good child, Missy.''

''I am good, but I ache here''; putting her hand to her heart, and moaning while she reiterated ''Papa! papa!''

I roused myself and started up, to check this scene while it was yet within bounds.

''Say good morning to the young lady,'' dictated Harriet.

She said ''good morning,'' and then followed her nurse from the room. Harriet temporarily left that same day, to go to her own friends, who lived in the neighbourhood.

On descending, I found Paulina (the child called herself Polly, but her full name was Paulina Mary) seated at the breakfast-table, by Mrs. Bretton's side; a mug of

milk stood before her, a morsel of bread filled her hand, which lay passive on the table-cloth: she was not eating.

"How we shall conciliate this little creature," said Mrs. Bretton to me, "I don't know: she tastes nothing, and, by her looks, she has not slept."

I expressed my confidence in the effects of time and kindness.

"If she were to take a fancy to anybody in the house, she would soon settle; but not till then," replied Mrs. Bretton.

Chapter II
PAULINA

SOME days elapsed, and it appeared she was not likely to take much of a fancy to anybody in the house. She was not exactly naughty or wilful: she was far from disobedient; but an object less conducive to comfort—to tranquillity even—than she presented, it was scarcely possible to have before one's eyes. She moped: no grown person could have performed that uncheering business better: no furrowed face of adult exile, longing for Europe at Europe's antipodes, ever bore more legibly the signs of home sickness than did her infant visage. She seemed growing old and unearthly. I, Lucy Snowe, plead guiltless of that curse, an overheated and discursive imagination; but whenever, opening a room-door, I found her seated in a corner alone, her head in her pigmy hand, that room seemed to me not inhabited, but haunted.

And again, when of moonlight nights, on waking, I beheld her figure, white and conspicuous in its night-dress, kneeling upright in bed, and praying like some Catholic or Methodist enthusiast—some precocious fanatic or untimely saint—I scarcely know what thoughts I had; but they ran risk of being hardly more rational and healthy than that child's mind must have been.

I seldom caught a word of her prayers, for they were whispered low: sometimes, indeed, they were not whispered at all, but put up unuttered; such rare sentences as reached my ear still bore the burden, "Papa; my dear papa!" This, I perceived was a one-idead nature; betraying that monomaniac tendency I have ever thought the most unfortunate with which man or woman can be cursed.

What might have been the end of this fretting, had it continued unchecked, can only be conjectured; it received, however, a sudden turn.

One afternoon, Mrs. Bretton, coaxing her from her usual station in a corner, had lifted her into the window-seat, and, by way of occupying her attention, told her to watch the passengers and count how many ladies should go down the street in a given time. She had sat listlessly, hardly looking, and not counting, when—my eye being fixed on hers—I witnessed in its irid and pupil a startling transfiguration. These sudden, dangerous natures—*sensitive* as they are called—offer many a curious spectacle to those whom a cooler temperament has secured from participation in their angular vagaries. The fixed and heavy gaze swam, trembled, then glittered in fire; the small, overcast brow cleared; the trivial and dejected features lit up; the sad countenance vanished, and in its place appeared a sudden eagerness, an intense expectancy.

"It *is*!" were her words.

Like a bird or a shaft, or any other swift thing, she was gone from the room. How she got the house-door open I cannot tell; probably it might be ajar; perhaps Warren was in the way and obeyed her behest, which would be impetuous enough. I—watching calmly from the window—saw her, in her black frock and tiny braided apron (to pinafores she had an antipathy), dart half the length of the street; and, as I was on the point of turning, and quietly announcing to Mrs. Bretton that the child

was run out mad, and ought instantly to be pursued, I saw her caught up, and wrapt at once from my cool observation, and from the wondering stare of the passengers. A gentleman had done this good turn, and now, covering her with his cloak, advanced to restore her to the house whence he had seen her issue.

I concluded he would leave her in a servant's charge and withdraw; but he entered: having tarried a little while below, he came upstairs.

His reception immediately explained that he was known to Mrs. Bretton. She recognised him; she greeted him, and yet she was fluttered, surprised, taken unawares. Her look and manner were even expostulatory; and in reply to these, rather than her words, he said—"I could not help it, madam: I found it impossible to leave the country without seeing with my own eyes how she settled."

"But you will unsettle her."

"I hope not. And how is papa's little Polly?"

This question he addressed to Paulina, as he sat down and placed her gently on the ground before him.

"How is Polly's papa?" was the reply, as she leaned on his knee, and gazed up into his face.

It was not a noisy, not a wordy scene: for that I was thankful; but it was a scene of feeling too brimful, and which, because the cup did not foam up high or furiously overflow, only oppressed one the more. On all occasions of vehement, unrestrained expansion, a sense of disdain or ridicule comes to the weary spectator's relief; whereas I have ever felt most burdensome that sort of sensibility which bends of its own will, a giant slave under the sway of good sense.

Mr. Home was a stern-featured—perhaps I should rather say, a hard-featured man: his forehead was knotty, and his cheekbones were marked and prominent. The character of his face was quite Scotch; but there was feeling in his eye, and emotion in his now agitated countenance. His northern accent in speaking harmonised with his physiognomy. He was at once proud-looking and homely-looking.

He laid his hand on the child's uplifted head. She said—"Kiss Polly."

He kissed her. I wished she would utter some hysterical cry, so that I might get relief and be at ease. She made wonderfully little noise: she seemed to have got what she wanted—*all* she wanted, and to be in a trance of content. Neither in mien nor in features was this creature like her sire, and yet she was of his strain: her mind had been filled from his, as the cup from the flagon.

Indisputably, Mr. Home owned manly self-control, however he might secretly feel on some matters. "Polly," he said, looking down on his little girl, "go into the hall; you will see papa's great-coat lying on a chair; put your hand into the pockets, you will find a pocket-handkerchief there; bring it to me."

She obeyed; went and returned deftly and nimbly. He was talking to Mrs. Bretton when she came back, and she waited with the handkerchief in her hand. It was a picture, in its way, to see her, with her tiny stature, and trim, neat shape, standing at his knee. Seeing that he continued to talk, apparently unconscious of her return, she took his hand, opened the unresisting fingers, insinuated into them the handkerchief, and closed them upon it one by one. He still seemed not to see or to feel her; but by-and-by, he lifted her to his knee; she nestled against him, and though neither looked at nor spoke to the other for an hour following, I suppose both were satisfied.

During tea, the minute thing's movements and behaviour gave, as usual, full occupation to the eye. First she directed Warren, as he placed the chairs.

"Put papa's chair here, and mine near it, between papa and Mrs. Bretton: *I* must hand his tea."

She took her own seat, and beckoned with her hand to her father.

"Be near me, as if we were at home, papa."

And again, as she intercepted his cup in passing, and would stir the sugar and put in the cream herself, "I always did it for you at home, papa: nobody could do it as well, not even your own self."

Throughout the meal she continued her attentions: rather absurd they were. The sugar-tongs were too wide for one of her hands, and she had to use both in wielding them; the weight of the silver cream-ewer, the bread-and-butter plates, the very cup and saucer, tasked her insufficient strength and dexterity; but she would lift this, hand that, and luckily contrived through it all to break nothing. Candidly speaking, I thought her a little busy-body; but her father, blind like other parents, seemed perfectly content to let her wait on him, and even wonderfully soothed by her offices.

"She is my comfort!" he could not help saying to Mrs. Bretton. That lady had her own "comfort" and nonpareil on a much larger scale, and, for the moment, absent; so she sympathised with his foible.

This second "comfort" came on the stage in the course of the evening. I knew this day had been fixed for his return, and was aware that Mrs. Bretton had been expecting him through all its hours. We were seated round the fire, after tea, when Graham joined our circle: I should rather say, broke it up—for, of course, his arrival made a bustle; and then, as Mr. Graham was fasting, there was refreshment to be provided. He and Mr. Home met as old acquaintance; of the little girl he took no notice for a time.

His meal over, and numerous questions from his mother answered, he turned from the table to the hearth. Opposite where he had placed himself was seated Mr. Home, and at his elbow, the child. When I say *child* I use an inappropriate and undescriptive term—a term suggesting any picture rather than that of the demure little person in a mourning frock and white chemisette, that might just have fitted a good-sized doll—perched now on a high chair beside a stand, whereon was her toy work-box of white varnished wood, and holding in her hands a shred of a handkerchief which she was professing to hem, and at which she bored perseveringly with a needle, that in her fingers seemed almost a skewer, pricking herself ever and anon, marking the cambric with a track of minute red dots; occasionally starting when the perverse weapon—swerving from her control—inflicted a deeper stab than usual; but still silent, diligent, absorbed, womanly.

Graham was at that time a handsome, faithless-looking youth of sixteen. I say faithless-looking, not because he was really of a very perfidious disposition, but because the epithet strikes me as proper to describe the fair, Celtic (not Saxon) character of his good looks; his waved light auburn hair, his supple symmetry, his smile frequent, and destitute neither of fascination nor of subtlety (in no bad sense). A spoiled, whimsical boy he was in those days.

"Mother," he said, after eyeing the little figure before him in silence for some time, and when the temporary absence of Mr. Home from the room relieved him from the half-laughing bashfulness, which was all he knew of timidity—"Mother, I see a young lady in the present society to whom I have not been introduced."

"Mr. Home's little girl, I suppose you mean," said his mother.

"Indeed, ma'am," replied her son, "I consider your expression of the least ceremonious: Miss Home *I* should certainly have said, in venturing to speak of the gentlewoman to whom I allude."

"Now Graham, I will not have that child teased. Don't flatter yourself that I shall suffer you to make her your butt."

"Miss Home," pursued Graham, undeterred by his mother's remonstrance, "might I have the honour to introduce myself, since no one else seems willing to render you and me that service? Your slave, John Graham Bretton."

She looked at him; he rose and bowed quite gravely. She deliberately put down thimble, scissors, work; descended with precaution from her perch, and curtseying with unspeakable seriousness, said, "How do you do?"

"I have the honour to be in fair health, only in some measure fatigued with a hurried journey. I hope, ma'am, I see you well."

"Tor-rer-ably well," was the ambitious reply of the little woman; and she now essayed to regain her former elevation, but finding this could not be done without some climbing and straining—a sacrifice of decorum not to be thought of—and being utterly disdainful of aid in the presence of a strange young gentleman, she relinquished the high chair for a low stool: towards that low stool Graham drew in his chair.

"I hope, ma'am, the present residence, my mother's house, appears to you a convenient place of abode?"

"Not par-tic-er-er-ly; I want to go home."

"A natural and laudable desire, ma'am; but one which, notwithstanding, I shall do my best to oppose. I reckon on being able to get out of you a little of that precious commodity called amusement, which mamma and Mistress Snowe there fail to yield me."

"I shall have to go with papa soon: I shall not stay long at your mother's."

"Yes, yes; you will stay with me, I am sure. I have a pony on which you shall ride, and no end of books with pictures to show you."

"Are *you* going to live here now?"

"I am. Does that please you? Do you like me?"

"No."

"Why?"

"I think you queer."

"My face, ma'am?"

"Your face and all about you. You have long red hair."

"Auburn hair, if you please: mamma calls it auburn, or golden, and so do all her friends. But even with my 'long red hair' " (and he waved his mane with a sort of triumph—tawny he himself well knew that it was, and he was proud of the leonine hue), "I cannot possibly be queerer than is your ladyship."

"You call me queer?"

"Certainly."

(After a pause) "I think I shall go to bed."

"A little thing like you ought to have been in bed many hours since; but you probably sat up in the expectation of seeing me?"

"No, indeed."

"You certainly wished to enjoy the pleasure of my society. You knew I was coming home, and would wait to have a look at me."

"I sat up for papa, and not for you."

"Very good, Miss Home. I am going to be a favourite: preferred before papa soon, I dare say."

She wished Mrs. Bretton and myself good-night; she seemed hesitating whether Graham's deserts entitled him to the same attention, when he caught her up with one hand, and with that one hand held her poised aloft above his head. She saw herself thus lifted up on high, in the glass over the fireplace. The suddenness, the freedom, the disrespect of the action were too much.

"For shame, Mr. Graham!" was her indignant cry, "put me down!"—and when again on her feet, "I wonder what you would think of me if I were to treat you in that way, lifting you with my hand" (raising that mighty member) "as Warren lifts the little cat."

So saying, she departed.

Chapter III
THE PLAYMATES

MR. HOME stayed two days. During his visit he could not be prevailed on to go out: he sat all day long by the fireside, sometimes silent, sometimes receiving and

answering Mrs. Bretton's chat, which was just of the proper sort for a man in his morbid mood—not over-sympathetic, yet not too uncongenial, sensible; and even with a touch of the motherly—she was sufficiently his senior to be permitted this touch.

As to Paulina, the child was at once happy and mute, busy and watchful. Her father frequently lifted her to his knee; she would sit there till she felt or fancied he grew restless; then it was—"Papa, put me down; I shall tire you with my weight."

And the mighty burden slid to the rug, and establishing itself on carpet or stool just at "papa's" feet, the white work-box and the scarlet-speckled handkerchief came into play. This handkerchief, it seems, was intended as a keepsake for "papa," and must be finished before his departure; consequently the demand on the sempstress's industry (she accomplished about a score of stitches in half-an-hour) was stringent.

The evening, by restoring Graham to the maternal roof (his days were passed at school), brought us an accession of animation—a quality not diminished by the nature of the scenes pretty sure to be enacted between him and Miss Paulina.

A distant and haughty demeanour had been the result of the indignity put upon her the first evening of his arrival: her usual answer, when he addressed her, was— "I can't attend to you; I have other things to think about." Being implored to state *what* things: "Business."

Graham would endeavour to seduce her attention by opening his desk and displaying its multifarious contents: seals, bright sticks of wax, pen-knives, with a miscellany of engravings—some of them gaily coloured—which he had amassed from time to time. Nor was this powerful temptation wholly unavailing: her eyes, furtively raised from her work, cast many a peep towards the writing-table, rich in scattered pictures. An etching of a child playing with a Blenheim spaniel happened to flutter to the floor.

"Pretty little dog!" said she, delighted.

Graham prudently took no notice. Ere long, stealing from her corner, she approached to examine the treasure more closely. The dog's great eyes and long ears, and the child's hat and feathers, were irresistible.

"Nice picture!" was her favourable criticism.

"Well—you may have it," said Graham.

She seemed to hesitate. The wish to possess was strong, but to accept would be a compromise of dignity. No. She put it down and turned away.

"You won't have it, then, Polly?"

"I would rather not, thank you."

"Shall I tell you what I will do with the picture if you refuse it?"

She half turned to listen.

"Cut it into strips for lighting the taper."

"No!"

"But I shall."

"Please—don't."

Graham waxed inexorable on hearing the pleading tone; he took the scissors from his mother's work-basket.

"Here goes!" said he making a menacing flourish. "Right through Fido's head, and splitting little Harry's nose."

"No! *No!* NO!"

"Then come to me. Come quickly, or it is done."

She hesitated, lingered, but complied.

"Now, will you have it?" he asked, as she stood before him.

"Please."

"But I shall want payment."

"How much?"

"A kiss."

"Give the picture first into my hand."

Polly, as she said this, looked rather faithless in her turn. Graham gave it. She absconded a debtor, darted to her father, and took refuge on his knee. Graham rose in mimic wrath and followed. She buried her face in Mr. Home's waistcoat.

"Papa—papa—send him away!"

"I'll not be sent away," said Graham.

With face still averted, she held out her hand to keep him off.

"Then, I shall kiss the hand," said he; but that moment it became a miniature fist, and dealt him payment in a small coin that was not kisses.

Graham—not failing in his way to be as wily as his little playmate—retreated apparently quite discomfited; he flung himself on a sofa, and resting his head against the cushion, lay like one in pain. Polly, finding him silent, presently peeped at him. His eyes and face were covered with his hands. She turned on her father's knee, and gazed at her foe anxiously and long. Graham groaned.

"Papa, what is the matter?" she whispered.

"You had better ask him, Polly."

"Is he hurt?" (Groan second.)

"He makes a noise as if he were," said Mr. Home.

"Mother," suggested Graham feebly, "I think you had better send for the doctor. Oh my eye!" (Renewed silence, broken only by sighs from Graham.)

"If I were to become blind"——suggested this last.

His chastiser could not bear the suggestion. She was beside him directly.

"Let me see your eye: I did not mean to touch it, only your mouth; and I did not think I hit so *very* hard."

Silence answered her. Her features worked,—"I am sorry; I am sorry!"

Then succeeded emotion, faltering, weeping.

"Have done trying that child, Graham," said Mrs. Bretton.

"It is all nonsense, my pet," cried Mr. Home.

And Graham once more snatched her aloft, and she again punished him; and while she pulled his lion's locks, termed him—"The naughtiest, rudest, worst, untruest person that ever was."

On the morning of Mr. Home's departure, he and his daughter had some conversation in a window-recess by themselves; I heard part of it.

"Couldn't I pack my box and go with you, papa?" she whispered earnestly.

He shook his head.

"Should I be a trouble to you?"

"Yes, Polly."

"Because I am little?"

"Because you are little and tender. It is only great, strong people that should travel. But don't look sad, my little girl; it breaks my heart. Papa will soon come back to his Polly."

"Indeed, indeed, I am not sad, scarcely at all."

"Polly would be sorry to give papa pain; would she not?"

"Sorrier than sorry."

"Then Polly must be cheerful: not cry at parting; not fret afterwards. She must look forward to meeting again, and try to be happy meanwhile. Can she do this?"

"She will try."

"I see she will. Farewell, then. It is time to go."

"*Now?*—just *now?*"

"Just now."

She held up quivering lips. Her father sobbed, but she, I remarked, did not. Having put her down, he shook hands with the rest present, and departed.

When the street-door closed, she dropped on her knees at a chair with a cry—"Papa!"

It was low and long; a sort of "Why hast thou forsaken me?" During an ensuing space of some minutes, I perceived she endured agony. She went through, in that brief interval of her infant life, emotions such as some never feel; it was in her constitution: she would have more of such instants if she lived. Nobody spoke. Mrs. Bretton, being a mother, shed a tear or two. Graham, who was writing, lifted up his eyes and gazed at her. I, Lucy Snowe, was calm.

The little creature, thus left unharassed, did for herself what none other could do—contended with an intolerable feeling; and, ere long, in some degree, repressed it. That day she would accept solace from none; nor the next day: she grew more passive afterwards.

On the third evening, as she sat on the floor, worn and quiet, Graham, coming in, took her up gently, without a word. She did not resist: she rather nestled in his arms, as if weary. When he sat down, she laid her head against him; in a few minutes she slept; he carried her upstairs to bed. I was not surprised that, the next morning, the first thing she demanded was—"Where is Mr. Graham?"

It happened that Graham was not coming to the breakfast-table; he had some exercises to write for that morning's class, and had requested his mother to send a cup of tea into the study. Polly volunteered to carry it: she must be busy about something, look after somebody. The cup was entrusted to her; for, if restless, she was also careful. As the study was opposite the breakfast-room, the doors facing across the passage, my eye followed her.

"What are you doing?" she asked, pausing on the threshold.

"Writing," said Graham.

"Why don't you come to take breakfast with your mamma?"

"Too busy."

"Do you want any breakfast?"

"Of course."

" There, then."

And she deposited the cup on the carpet, like a jailer putting a prisoner's pitcher of water through his cell-door, and retreated. Presently she returned.

"What will you have besides tea—what to eat?"

"Anything good. Bring me something particularly nice; that's a kind little woman."

She came back to Mrs. Bretton.

"Please, ma'am, send your boy something good."

"You shall choose for him, Polly; what shall my boy have?"

She selected a portion of whatever was best on the table, and, ere long, came back with a whispered request for some marmalade, which was not there. Having got it, however (for Mrs. Bretton refused the pair nothing), Graham was shortly after heard lauding her to the skies; promising that, when he had a house of his own, she should be his housekeeper, and perhaps—if she showed any culinary genius—his cook; and, as she did not return, and I went to look after her, I found Graham and her breakfasting *tête-à-tête*—she standing at his elbow, and sharing his fare: excepting the marmalade, which she delicately refused to touch, lest, I suppose, it should appear that she had procured it as much on her own account as his. She constantly evinced these nice perceptions and delicate instincts.

The league of acquaintanceship thus struck up was not hastily dissolved; on the contrary, it appeared that time and circumstances served rather to cement than loosen it. Ill-assimilated as the two were in age, sex, pursuits, etc., they somehow found a great deal to say to each other. As to Paulina, I observed that her little character never properly came out, except with young Bretton. As she got settled, and accustomed to the house, she proved tractable enough with Mrs. Bretton; but she would sit on a stool at that lady's feet all day long, learning her task, or sewing, or drawing figures with a pencil on a slate, and never kindling once to originality, or showing a single gleam of the peculiarities of her nature. I ceased to watch her under such circumstances: she was not interesting. But the moment Graham's knock

sounded of an evening, a change occurred; she was instantly at the head of the staircase. Usually her welcome was a reprimand or a threat.

"You have not wiped your shoes properly on the mat. I shall tell your mamma."

"Little busybody! Are you there?"

"Yes—and you can't reach me: I am higher up than you" (peeping between the rails of the banisters; she could not look over them).

"Polly!"

"My dear boy!" (such was one of her terms for him, adopted in imitation of his mother).

"I am fit to faint with fatigue," declared Graham, leaning against the passage-wall in seeming exhaustion. "Dr. Digby" (the headmaster) "has quite knocked me up with overwork. Just come down and help me to carry up my books."

"Ah! you're cunning!"

"Not at all, Polly—it is positive fact. I'm as weak as a rush. Come down."

"Your eyes are quiet like the cat's, but you'll spring."

"Spring? Nothing of the kind: it isn't in me. Come down."

"Perhaps I may—if you'll promise not to touch—not to snatch me up, and not to whirl me round."

"I? I couldn't do it!" (sinking into a chair).

"Then put the books down on the first step, and go three yards off."

This being done, she descended warily, and not taking her eyes from the feeble Graham. Of course her approach always galvanised him to new and spasmodic life: the game of romps was sure to be exacted. Sometimes she would be angry; sometimes the matter was allowed to pass smoothly, and we could hear her say as she led him upstairs—"Now, my dear boy, come and take your tea—I am sure you must want something."

It was sufficiently comical to observe her as she sat beside Graham, while he took that meal. In his absence she was a still personage, but with him the most officious, fidgety little body possible. I often wished she would mind herself and be tranquil; but no—herself was forgotten in him: he could not be sufficiently well waited on, nor carefully enough looked after; he was more than the Grand Turk in her estimation. She would gradually assemble the various plates before him, and, when one would suppose all he could possibly desire was within his reach, she would find out something else—

"Ma'am," she would whisper to Mrs. Bretton,—"perhaps your son would like a little cake—sweet cake, you know—there is some in there" (pointing to the sideboard cupboard). Mrs. Bretton, as a rule, disapproved of sweet cake at tea, but still the request was urged,—"One little piece—only for him—as he goes to school: girls—such as me and Miss Snowe—don't need treats, but *he* would like it."

Graham did like it very well, and almost always got it. To do him justice, he would have shared his prize with her to whom he owed it; but that was never allowed: to insist, was to ruffle her for the evening. To stand by his knee, and monopolise his talk and notice, was the reward she wanted—not a share of the cake.

With curious readiness did she adapt herself to such schemes as interested him. One would have thought the child had no mind or life of her own, but must necessarily live, move, and have her being in another: now that her father was taken from her, she nestled to Graham, and seemed to feel by his feelings: to exist in his existence. She learned the names of all his schoolfellows in a trice; she got by heart their characters as given from his lips: a single description of an individual seemed to suffice. She never forgot, or confused identities: she would talk with him the whole evening about people she had never seen, and appear completely to realise their aspect, manners, aud dispositions. Some she learned to mimic: an under-master, who was an aversion of young Bretton's, had, it seems, some pe-

culiarities, which she caught up in a moment from Graham's representation, and rehearsed for his amusement; this, however, Mrs. Bretton disapproved and forbade.

The pair seldom quarrelled; yet once a rupture occurred, in which her feelings received a severe shock.

One day Graham, on the occasion of his birthday, had some friends—lads of his own age—to dine with him. Paulina took much interest in the coming of these friends; she had frequently heard of them; they were amongst those of whom Graham oftenest spoke. After dinner, the young gentlemen were left by themselves in the dining-room, where they soon became very merry and made a good deal of noise. Chancing to pass through the hall, I found Paulina sitting alone on the lowest step of the staircase, her eyes fixed on the glossy panels of the dining-room door, where the reflection of the hall-lamp was shining; her little brow knit in anxious meditation.

"What are you thinking about, Polly?"

"Nothing particular; only I wish that door was clear glass—that I might see through it. The boys seem very cheerful, and I want to go to them: I want to be with Graham, and watch his friends."

"What hinders you from going?"

"I feel afraid: but may I try, do you think? May I knock at the door, and ask to be let in?"

I thought perhaps they might not object to have her as a playmate, and therefore encouraged the attempt.

She knocked—too faintly at first to be heard, but on a second essay the door unclosed; Graham's head appeared; he looked in high spirits, but impatient.

"What do you want, you little monkey?"

"To come to you."

"Do you indeed? As if I would be troubled with you! Away to mamma and Mistress Snowe, and tell them to put you to bed." The auburn head and bright flushed face vanished,—the door shut peremptorily. She was stunned.

"Why does he speak so? He never spoke so before," she said in consternation. "What have I done?"

"Nothing, Polly; but Graham is busy with his school-friends."

"And he likes them better than me! He turns me away now they are here!"

I had some thoughts of consoling her, and of improving the occasion by inculcating some of those maxims of philosophy whereof I had ever a tolerable stock ready for application. She stopped me, however, by putting her fingers in her ears at the first words I uttered, and then lying down on the mat with her face against the flags; nor could either Warren or the cook root her from that position: she was allowed to lie, therefore, till she chose to rise of her own accord.

Graham forgot his impatience the same evening, and would have accosted her as usual when his friends were gone, but she wrenched herself from his hand; her eye quite flashed; she would not bid him good night; she would not look in his face. The next day he treated her with indifference, and she grew like a bit of marble. The day after, he teased her to know what was the matter; her lips would not unclose. Of course he could not feel real anger on his side: the match was too unequal in every way; he tried soothing and coaxing. "Why was she so angry? What had he done?" By-and-by tears answered him; he petted her, and they were friends. But she was one on whom such incidents were not lost: I remarked that never after this rebuff did she seek him, or follow him, or in any way solicit his notice. I told her once to carry a book or some other article to Graham when he was shut up in his study.

"I shall wait till he comes out," said she proudly; "I don't choose to give him the trouble of rising to open the door."

Young Bretton had a favourite pony on which he often rode out; from the window she always watched his departure and return. It was her ambition to be permitted to have a ride round the courtyard on this pony; but far be it from her to ask such

a favour. One day she descended to the yard to watch him dismount; as she leaned against the gate, the longing wish for the indulgence of a ride glittered in her eye.

"Come, Polly, will you have a canter?" asked Graham, half carelessly. I suppose she thought he was *too* careless.

"No, thank you," said she, turning away with the utmost coolness.

"You'd better," pursued he. "You will like it, I am sure."

"Don't think I should care a fig about it," was the response.

"That is not true. You told Lucy Snowe you longed to have a ride."

"Lucy Snowe is a *tatter*-box," I heard her say (her imperfect articulation was the least precocious thing she had about her): and with this she walked into the house. Graham, coming in soon after, observed to his mother—"Mamma, I believe that creature is a changeling: she is a perfect cabinet of oddities; but I should be dull without her: she amuses me a great deal more than you or Lucy Snowe."

"Miss Snowe," said Paulina to me (she had now got into the habit of occasionally chatting with me when we were alone in our room at night), "do you know on what day in the week I like Graham best?"

"How can I possibly know anything so strange? Is there one day out of the seven when he is otherwise than on the other six?"

"To be sure! Can't you see? Don't you know? I find him the most excellent on a Sunday; then we have him the whole day, and he is quiet, and, in the evening, *so* kind."

This observation was not altogether groundless: going to church, etc., kept Graham quiet on the Sunday, and the evening he generally dedicated to a serene, though rather indolent sort of enjoyment by the parlour fireside. He would take possession of the couch, and then he would call Polly.

Graham was a boy not quite as other boys are; all his delight did not lie in action: he was capable of some intervals of contemplation; he could take a pleasure too in reading, nor was his selection of books wholly indiscriminate: there were glimmerings of characteristic preference, and even of instinctive taste in the choice. He rarely, it is true, remarked on what he read, but I have seen him sit and think of it.

Polly being near him, kneeling on a little cushion or the carpet, a conversation would begin in murmurs, not inaudible, though subdued. I caught a snatch of their tenor now and then; and, in truth, some influence better and finer than that of every day seemed to soothe Graham at such times into no ungentle mood.

"Have you learned any hymns this week, Polly?"

"I have learned a very pretty one, four verses long. Shall I say it?"

"Speak nicely, then: don't be in a hurry."

The hymn being rehearsed, or rather half-chanted, in a little singing-voice, Graham would take exceptions at the manner, and proceed to give a lesson in recitation. She was quick in learning, apt in imitating; and, besides, her pleasure was to please Graham: she proved a ready scholar. To the hymn would succeed some reading—perhaps a chapter in the Bible; correction was seldom required here, for the child could read any simple narrative chapter very well; and, when the subject was such as she could understand and take an interest in, her expression and emphasis were something remarkable. Joseph cast into the pit; the calling of Samuel; Daniel in the lion's den;—these were favourite passages: of the first especially she seemed perfectly to feel the pathos.

"Poor Jacob!" she would sometimes say, with quivering lips. "How he loved his son Joseph! As much," she once added—"as much, Graham, as I love you: if you were to die" (and she re-opened the book, sought the verse, and read), "I should 'refuse to be comforted, and go down into the grave to you mourning.' "

With these words she gathered Graham in her little arms, drawing his long-tressed head towards her. The action, I remember, struck me as strangely rash; exciting the feeling one might experience on seeing an animal dangerous by nature, and but

half-tamed by art, too heedlessly fondled. Not that I feared Graham would hurt, or very roughly check her; but I thought she ran risk of incurring such a careless, impatient repulse, as would be worse almost to her than a blow. On the whole, however, these demonstrations were borne passively: sometimes even a sort of complacent wonder at her earnest partiality would smile not unkindly in his eyes. Once he said—"You like me almost as well as if you were my little sister, Polly."

"Oh! I *do* like you," said she; "I *do* like you very much."

I was not long allowed the amusement of this study of character. She had scarcely been at Bretton two months, when a letter came from Mr. Home, signifying that he was now settled amongst his maternal kinsfolk on the Continent; that, as England was become wholly distasteful to him, he had no thoughts of returning thither, perhaps, for years; and that he wished his little girl to join him immediately.

"I wonder how she will take this news?" said Mrs. Bretton, when she had read the letter. *I* wondered, too, and I took upon myself to communicate it.

Repairing to the drawing-room—in which calm and decorated apartment she was fond of being alone, and where she could be implicitly trusted, for she fingered nothing, or rather soiled nothing she fingered—I found her seated, like a little Odalisque, on a couch, half shaded by the drooping draperies of the window near. She seemed happy; all her appliances for occupation were about her; the white wood work-box, a shred or two of muslin, an end or two of ribbon, collected for conversion into doll-millinery. The doll, duly night-capped and night-gowned, lay in its cradle; she was rocking it to sleep, with an air of the most perfect faith in its possession of sentient and somnolent faculties; her eyes, at the same time, being engaged with a picture-book which lay open on her lap.

"Miss Snowe," said she in a whisper, "this is a wonderful book. Candace" (the doll, christened by Graham; for, indeed, its begrimed complexion gave it much of an Ethiopian aspect)—"Candace is asleep now, and I may tell you about it; only we must both speak low, lest she should waken. This book was given me by Graham; it tells about distant countries, a long, long way from England, which no traveller can reach without sailing thousands of miles over the sea. Wild men live in these countries, Miss Snowe, who wear clothes different from ours: indeed, some of them wear scarcely any clothes, for the sake of being cool, you know; for they have very hot weather. Here is a picture of thousands gathered in a desolate place—a plain, spread with sand—round a man in black,—a good, *good* Englishman— a missionary, who is preaching to them under a palm-tree." (She showed a little coloured cut to that effect.) "And here are pictures" (she went on) "more stranger" (grammar was occasionally forgotten) "than that. There is the wonderful Great Wall of China; here is a Chinese lady, with a foot littler than mine. There is a wild horse of Tartary; and here, most strange of all—is a land of ice and snow, without green fields, woods, or gardens. In this land, they found some mammoth bones: there are no mammoths now. You don't know what it was; but I can tell you, because Graham told me. A mighty, goblin creature, as high as this room, and as long as the hall; but not a fierce, flesh-eating thing, Graham thinks. He believes, if I met one in a forest, it would not kill me, unless I came quite in its way; when it would trample me down amongst the bushes, as I might tread on a grasshopper in a hayfield without knowing it."

Thus she rambled on.

"Polly," I interrupted, "should you like to travel?"

"Not just yet," was the prudent answer; "but perhaps in twenty years, when I am grown a woman, as tall as Mrs. Bretton, I may travel with Graham. We intend going to Switzerland, and climbing Mount Blanc; and some day we shall sail over to South America, and walk to the top of Kim—kim—borazo."

"But how would you like to travel now, if your papa was with you?"

Her reply—not given till after a pause—evinced one of those unexpected turns of temper peculiar to her—"Where is the good of talking in that silly way?" said she. "Why do you mention papa? What is papa to you? I was just beginning to be happy, and not think about him so much; and there it will be all to do over again!"

Her lip trembled. I hastened to disclose the fact of a letter having been received, and to mention the directions given that she and Harriet should immediately rejoin this dear papa. "Now, Polly, are you not glad?" I added.

She made no answer. She dropped her book, and ceased to rock her doll; she gazed at me with gravity and earnestness.

"Shall not you like to go to papa?"

"Of course," she said at last in that trenchant manner she usually employed in speaking to me; and which was quite different from that she used with Mrs. Bretton, and different again from the one dedicated to Graham. I wished to ascertain more of what she thought; but no: she would converse no more. Hastening to Mrs. Bretton, she questioned her, and received the confirmation of my news. The weight and importance of these tidings kept her perfectly serious the whole day. In the evening, at the moment Graham's entrance was heard below, I found her at my side. She began to arrange a locket-ribbon about my neck, she displaced and replaced the comb in my hair; while thus busied, Graham entered.

"Tell him by-and-by," she whispered: "tell him I am going."

In the course of tea-time I made the desired communication. Graham, it chanced, was at that time greatly preoccupied about some school-prize, for which he was competing. The news had to be told twice before it took proper hold of his attention, and even then he dwelt on it but momently.

"Polly going? What a pity! Dear little Mousie, I shall be sorry to lose her: she must come to us again, mamma."

And hastily swallowing his tea, he took a candle and a small table to himself and his books, and was soon buried in study.

"Little Mousie" crept to his side, and lay down on the carpet at his feet, her face to the floor; mute and motionless she kept that post and position till bed-time. Once I saw Graham—wholly unconscious of her proximity—push her with his restless foot. She receded an inch or two. A minute after one little hand stole out from beneath her face, to which it had been pressed, and softly caressed the heedless foot. When summoned by her nurse she rose and departed very obediently, having bid us all a subdued good-night.

I will not say that I dreaded going to bed, an hour later; yet I certainly went with an unquiet anticipation that I should find that child in no peaceful sleep. The forewarning of my instinct was but fulfilled, when I discovered her, all cold and vigilant, perched like a white bird on the outside of the bed. I scarcely knew how to accost her; she was not to be managed like another child. She, however, accosted me. As I closed the door, and put the light on the dressing-table, she turned to me with these words—"I cannot—*cannot* sleep; and in this way I cannot—*cannot* live!"

I asked what ailed her.

"Dedful miz-er-y!" said she, with her piteous lisp.

"Shall I call Mrs. Bretton?"

"That is downright silly," was her impatient reply; and, indeed, I well knew that if she had heard Mrs. Bretton's foot approach, she would have nestled quiet as a mouse under the bedclothes. Whilst lavishing her eccentricities regardlessly before me—for whom she professed scarcely the semblance of affection—she never showed my godmother one glimpse of her inner self; for her, she was nothing but a docile, somewhat quaint little maiden. I examined her; her cheek was crimson; the dilated eye was both troubled and glowing, and painfully restless: in this state it was obvious she must not be left till morning. I guessed how the case stood.

"Would you like to bid Graham good-night again?" I asked, "He is not gone to his room yet."

She at once stretched out her little arms to be lifted. Folding a shawl round her, I carried her back to the drawing-room. Graham was just coming out.

"She cannot sleep without seeing and speaking to you once more," I said. "She does not like the thought of leaving you."

"I've spoilt her," said he, taking her from me with good humour, and kissing her little hot face and burning lips. "Polly, you care for me more than for papa, now"——

"I *do* care for you, but you care nothing for me," was her whisper.

She was assured to the contrary, again kissed, restored to me, and I carried her away; but, alas! not soothed.

When I thought she could listen to me, I said—"Paulina, you should not grieve that Graham does not care for you so much as you care for him. It must be so."

Her lifted and questioning eyes asked why.

"Because he is a boy and you are a girl; he is sixteen and you are only six; his nature is strong and gay, and yours is otherwise."

"But I love him so much; he *should* love me a little."

"He does. He is fond of you. You are his favourite."

"Am I Graham's favourite?"

"Yes, more than any little child I know."

The assurance soothed her; she smiled in her anguish.

"But," I continued, "don't fret, and don't expect too much of him, or else he will feel you to be troublesome, and then it is all over."

"All over," she echoed softly, "then I'll be good. I'll try to be good, Lucy Snowe."

I put her to bed.

"Will he forgive me this one time?" she asked, as I undressed myself. I assured her that he would; that as yet he was by no means alienated; that she had only to be careful for the future.

"There is no future," said she: "I am going. Shall I ever—ever—see him again, after I leave England?"

I returned an encouraging response. The candle being extinguished, a still half-hour elapsed. I thought her asleep, when the little white shape once more lifted itself in the crib, and the small voice asked—"Do you like Graham, Miss Snowe?"

"Like him! Yes, a little."

"Only a little! Do you like him as I do?"

"I think not. No: not as you do."

"Do you like him much?"

"I told you I liked him a little. Where is the use of caring for him so very much: he is full of faults."

"Is he?"

"All boys are."

"More than girls?"

"Very likely. Wise people say it is folly to think anybody perfect; and as to likes and dislikes, we should be friendly to all, and worship none."

"Are you a wise person?"

"I mean to try to be so. Go to sleep."

"I *cannot* go to sleep. Have you no pain just here" (laying her elfish hand on her elfish breast), "when you think *you* shall have to leave Graham; for *your* home is not here?"

"Surely, Polly," said I, "you should not feel so much pain when you are very soon going to rejoin your father. Have you forgotten him? Do you no longer wish to be his little companion?"

Dead silence succeeded this question.

"Child, lie down and sleep," I urged.

"My bed is cold," said she. "I can't warm it."

I saw the little thing shiver. "Come to me," I said, wishing, yet scarcely hoping, that she would comply: for she was a most strange, capricious little creature, and especially whimsical with me. She came, however, instantly, like a small ghost gliding over the carpet. I took her in. She was chill: I warmed her in my arms. She trembled nervously; I soothed her. Thus tranquillised and cherished she at last slumbered.

"A very unique child," thought I, as I viewed her sleeping countenance by the fitful moonlight, and cautiously and softly wiped her glittering eyelids and her wet cheeks with my handkerchief. "How will she get through this world, or battle with this life? How will she bear the shocks and repulses, the humiliations and desolations, which books, and my own reason, tell me are prepared for all flesh?"

She departed the next day; trembling like a leaf when she took leave, but exercising self-command.

Chapter IV

MISS MARCHMONT

ON quitting Bretton, which I did a few weeks after Paulina's departure—little thinking then I was never again to visit it; never more to tread its calm old streets— I betook myself home, having been absent six months. It will be conjectured that I was of course glad to return to the bosom of my kindred. Well! the amiable conjecture does no harm, and may therefore be safely left uncontradicted. Far from saying nay, indeed, I will permit the reader to picture me, for the next eight years, as a bark slumbering through halcyon weather, in a harbour still as glass—the steersman stretched on the little deck, his face up to heaven, his eyes closed: buried, if you will, in a long prayer. A great many women and girls are supposed to pass their lives something in that fashion; why not I with the rest?

Picture me then idle, basking, plump, and happy, stretched on a cushioned deck, warmed with constant sunshine, rocked by breezes indolently soft. However, it cannot be concealed that, in that case, I must somehow have fallen overboard, or that there must have been wreck at last. I too well remember a time—a long time— of cold, of danger, of contention. To this hour, when I have the nightmare, it repeats the rush and saltness of briny waves in my throat, and their icy pressure on my lungs. I even know there was a storm, and that not of one hour nor one day. For many days and nights neither sun nor stars appeared; we cast with our own hands the tackling out of the ship; a heavy tempest lay on us; all hope that we should be saved was taken away. In fine, the ship was lost, the crew perished.

As far as I recollect, I complained to no one about these troubles. Indeed, to whom could I complain? Of Mrs. Bretton I had long lost sight. Impediments, raised by others, had, years ago, come in the way of our intercourse, and cut it off. Besides, time had brought changes for her too: the handsome property of which she was left guardian for her son, and which had been chiefly invested in some joint-stock undertaking, had melted, it was said, to a fraction of its original amount. Graham, I learned from incidental rumours, had adopted a profession; both he and his mother were gone from Bretton, and were understood to be now in London. Thus, there remained no possibility of dependence on others; to myself alone could I look. I know not that I was of a self-reliant or active nature; but self-reliance and exertion were forced upon me by circumstances, as they are upon thousands besides; and when Miss Marchmont, a maiden lady of our neighbourhood, sent for me, I obeyed her behest, in the hope that she might assign me some task I could undertake.

Miss Marchmont was a woman of fortune, and lived in a handsome residence; but she was a rheumatic cripple, impotent, foot and hand, and had been so for twenty years. She always sat upstairs: her drawing-room adjoined her bed-room. I had often heard of Miss Marchmont, and of her peculiarities (she had the character of being very eccentric), but till now had never seen her. I found her a furrowed, grey-haired woman, grave with solitude, stern with long affliction, irritable also, and perhaps exacting. It seemed that a maid, or rather companion, who had waited on her for some years, was about to be married; and she, hearing of my bereaved lot, had sent for me, with the idea that I might supply this person's place. She made the proposal to me after tea, as she and I sat alone by her fireside.

"It will not be an easy life," said she candidly, "for I require a good deal of attention, and you will be much confined; yet perhaps, contrasted with the existence you have lately led, it may appear tolerable."

I reflected. Of course it ought to appear tolerable, I argued inwardly; but somehow, by some strange fatality, it would not. To live here, in this close room, the watcher of suffering—sometimes, perhaps, the butt of temper—through all that was to come of my youth; while all that was gone had passed, to say the least, not blissfully! My heart sunk one moment, then it revived; for though I forced myself to *realise* evils, I think I was too prosaic to *idealise,* and consequently to exaggerate them.

"My doubt is whether I should have strength for the undertaking," I observed.

"That is my own scruple," said she; "for you look a worn-out creature!"

So I did. I saw myself in the glass, in my mourning-dress, a faded, hollow-eyed vision. Yet I thought little of the wan spectacle. The blight, I believed, was chiefly external: I still felt life at life's sources.

"What else have you in view—anything?"

"Nothing clear as yet: but I may find something."

"So you imagine: perhaps you are right. Try your own method, then; and if it does not succeed, test mine. The chance I have offered shall be left open to you for three months."

That was kind. I told her so, and expressed my gratitude. While I was speaking, a paroxysm of pain came on. I ministered to her; made the necessary applications, according to her directions, and, by the time she was relieved, a sort of intimacy was already formed between us. I, for my part, had learned from the manner in which she bore this attack, that she was a firm, patient woman (patient under physical pain, though sometimes perhaps excitable under long mental canker); and she, from the good-will with which I succoured her, discovered that she could influence my sympathies (such as they were). She sent for me the next day; for five or six successive days she claimed my company. Closer acquaintance, while it developed both faults and eccentricities, opened, at the same time, a view of a character I could respect. Stern and even morose as she sometimes was, I could wait on her and sit beside her with that calm which always blesses us when we are sensible that our manners, presence, contact, please and soothe the persons we serve. Even when she scolded me—which she did, now and then, very tartly—it was in such a way as did not humiliate, and left no sting; it was rather like an irascible mother rating her daughter, than a harsh mistress lecturing a dependent: lecture, indeed, she could not, though she could occasionally storm. Moreover, a vein of reason ever ran through her passion: she was logical even when fierce. Ere long a growing sense of attachment began to present the thought of staying with her as companion in quite a new light; in another week I had agreed to remain.

Two hot, close rooms thus became my world; and a crippled old woman my mistress, my friend, my all. Her service was my duty—her pain, my suffering— her relief, my hope—her anger, my punishment—her regard, my reward. I forgot that there were fields, woods, rivers, seas, an ever-changing sky outside the steam-dimmed lattice of this sick-chamber; I was almost content to forget it. All within me became narrowed to my lot. Tame and still by habit, disciplined by destiny, I

demanded no walks in the fresh air; my appetite needed no more than the tiny messes served for the invalid. In addition she gave me the originality of her character to study: the steadiness of her virtues, I will add, the power of her passions, to admire; the truth of her feelings to trust. All these things she had, and for these things I clung to her.

For these things I would have crawled on with her for twenty years, if for twenty years longer her life of endurance had been protracted. But another decree was written. It seemed I must be stimulated into action. I must be goaded, driven, stung, forced to energy. My little morsel of human affection, which I prized as if it were a solid pearl, must melt in my fingers and slip thence like a dissolving hailstone. My small adopted duty must be snatched from my easily contented conscience. I had wanted to compromise with Fate: to escape occasional great agonies by submitting to a whole life of privation and small pains. Fate would not so be pacified; nor would Providence sanction this shrinking sloth and cowardly indolence.

One February night—I remember it well—there came a voice near Miss Marchmont's house, heard by every inmate, but translated, perhaps, only by one. After a calm winter, storms were ushering in the spring. I had put Miss Marchmont to bed; I sat at the fireside sewing. The wind was wailing at the windows: it had wailed all day; but, as night deepened, it took a new tone—an accent keen, piercing, almost articulate to the ear; a plaint, piteous and disconsolate to the nerves, trilled in every gust.

"Oh, hush! hush!" I said in my disturbed mind, dropping my work, and making a vain effort to stop my ears against that subtle, searching cry. I had heard that very voice ere this, and compulsory observation had forced on me a theory as to what it boded. Three times in the course of my life, events had taught me that these strange accents in the storm—this restless, hopeless cry—denote a coming state of the atmosphere unpropitious to life. Epidemic diseases, I believed, were often heralded by a gasping, sobbing, tormented, long-lamenting east wind. Hence, I inferred, arose the legend of the Banshee. I fancied, too, I had noticed—but was not philosopher enough to know whether there was any connection between the circumstances—that we often at the same time hear of disturbed volcanic action in distant parts of the world; of rivers suddenly rushing above their banks; and of strange high tides flowing furiously in on low sea-coasts. "Our globe," I had said to myself, "seems at such periods torn and disordered; the feeble amongst us wither in her distempered breath, rushing hot from steaming volcanoes."

I listened and trembled; Miss Marchmont slept.

About midnight, the storm in one half-hour fell to a dead calm. The fire, which had been burning dead, glowed up vividly. I felt the air change, and become keen. Raising blind and curtain, I looked out, and saw in the stars the keen sparkle of a sharp frost.

Turning away, the object that met my eyes was Miss Marchmont awake, lifting her head from the pillow, and regarding me with unusual earnestness.

"Is it a fine night?" she asked.

I replied in the affirmative.

"I thought so," she said; "for I feel so strong, so well. Raise me. I feel young to-night," she continued; "young, light-hearted, and happy. What if my complaint be about to take a turn, and I am yet destined to enjoy health? It would be a miracle!"

"And these are not the days of miracles," I thought to myself, and wondered to hear her talk so. She went on directing her conversation to the past, and seeming to recall its incidents, scenes, and personages, with singular vividness.

"I love memory to-night," she said: "I prize her as my best friend. She is just now giving me a deep delight: she is bringing back to my heart, in warm and beautiful life, realities—not mere empty ideas, but what were once realities, and

that I long have thought decayed, dissolved, mixed in with grave-mould. I possess just now the hours, the thoughts, the hopes of my youth. I renew the love of my life—its only love—almost its only affection; for I am not a particularly good woman: I am not amiable. Yet I have had my feelings, strong and concentrated; and these feelings had their object; which, in its single self, was dear to me, as, to the majority of men and women, are all the unnumbered points on which they dissipate their regard. While I loved, and while I was loved, what an existence I enjoyed! What a glorious year I can recall—how bright it comes back to me! What a living spring—what a warm, glad summer—what soft moonlight, silvering the autumn evenings—what strength of hope under the ice-bound waters and frost-hoar fields of that year's winter! Through that year my heart lived with Frank's heart. O my noble Frank—my faithful Frank—my *good* Frank! so much better than myself—his standard in all things so much higher! This I can now see and say: if few women have suffered as I did in his loss, few have enjoyed what I did in his love. It was a far better kind of love than common; I had no doubts about it or him: it was such a love as honoured, protected, and elevated, no less than it gladdened her to whom it was given. Let me now ask, just at this moment, when my mind is so strangely clear,—let me reflect why it was taken from me? For what crime was I condemned, after twelve months of bliss, to undergo thirty years of sorrow?''

"I do not know," she continued, after a pause: "I cannot—*cannot* see the reason; yet at this hour I can say with sincerity, what I never tried to say before—Inscrutable God, Thy will be done! And at this moment I can believe that death will restore me to Frank. I never believed it till now.''

"He is dead, then?'' I inquired in a low voice.

"My dear girl,'' she said, "one happy Christmas Eve I dressed and decorated myself, expecting my lover, very soon to be my husband, would come that night to visit me. I sat down to wait. Once more I see that moment—I see the snow-twilight stealing through the window over which the curtain was not dropped, for I designed to watch him ride up the white walk; I see and feel the soft firelight warming me, playing on my silk dress, and fitfully showing me my own young figure in a glass. I see the moon of a calm winter night float full, clear, and cold, over the inky mass of shrubbery, and the silvered turf of my grounds. I wait, with some impatience in my pulse, but no doubt in my breast. The flames had died in the fire, but it was a bright mass yet; the moon was mounting high, but she was still visible from the lattice; the clock neared ten; he rarely tarried later than this, but once or twice he had been delayed so long.

"Would he for once fail me? No—not even for once; and now he was coming—and coming fast—to atone for lost time. 'Frank! you furious rider,' I said inwardly, listening gladly, yet anxiously, to his approaching gallop, 'you shall be rebuked for this: I will tell you it is *my* neck you are putting in peril; for whatever is yours is, in a dearer and tenderer sense, mine.' There he was: I saw him; but I think tears were in my eyes, my sight was so confused. I saw the horse; I heard it stamp—I saw at least a mass; I heard a clamour. *Was* it a horse? or what heavy, dragging thing was it, crossing, strangely dark, the lawn? How could I name that thing in the moonlight before me? or how could I utter the feeling which rose in my soul?

"I could only run out. A great animal—truly Frank's black horse—stood trembling, panting, snorting before the door; a man held it: Frank, as I thought.

" 'What is the matter?' I demanded. Thomas, my own servant, answered by saying sharply, 'Go into the house, madam.' And then calling to another servant, who came hurrying from the kitchen as if summoned by some instinct, 'Ruth, take missis into the house directly.' But I was kneeling down in the snow beside something that lay there—something that I had seen dragged along the ground—something that sighed, that groaned on my breast, as I lifted and drew it to me. He was not dead; he was not quite unconscious. I had him carried in; I refused to be ordered

about and thrust from him. I was quite collected enough, not only to be my own mistress but the mistress of others. They had begun by trying to treat me like a child, as they always do with people struck by God's hand; but I gave place to none except the surgeon; and when he had done what he could, I took my dying Frank to myself. He had strength to fold me in his arms; he had power to speak my name; he heard me as I prayed over him very softly; he felt me as I tenderly and fondly comforted him.

" 'Maria,' he said, 'I am dying in Paradise.' He spent his last breath in faithful words for me. When the dawn of Christmas morning broke, my Frank was with God.

"And that," she went on, "happened thirty years ago. I have suffered since. I doubt if I have made the best use of all my calamities. Soft, amiable natures they would have refined to saintliness; of strong, evil spirits they would have made demons; as for me, I have only been a woe-struck and selfish woman."

"You have done much good," I said; for she was noted for her liberal almsgiving.

"I have not withheld money, you mean, where it could assuage affliction. What of that? It cost me no effort or pang to give. But I think from this day I am about to enter a better frame of mind, to prepare myself for reunion with Frank. You see I still think of Frank more than of God; and unless it be counted that in thus loving the creature so much, so long, and so exclusively, I have not at least blasphemed the Creator, small is my chance of salvation. What do you think, Lucy, of these things? Be my chaplain, and tell me."

This question I could not answer: I had no words. It seemed as if she thought I *had* answered it.

"Very right, my child. We should acknowledge God merciful, but not always for us comprehensible. We should accept our own lot, whatever it be, and try to render happy that of others. Should we not? Well, to-morrow I will begin by trying to make you happy. I will endeavour to do something for you, Lucy: something that will benefit you when I am dead. My head aches now with talking too much; still I am happy. Go to bed. The clock strikes two. How late you sit up; or rather how late I, in my selfishness, keep you up. But go now; have no more anxiety for me: I feel I shall rest well."

She composed herself as if to slumber. I, too, retired to my crib in a closet within her room. The night passed in quietness; quietly her doom must at last have come: peacefully and painlessly: in the morning she was found without life, nearly cold, but all calm and undisturbed. Her previous excitement of spirits and change of mood had been the prelude of a fit; one stroke sufficed to sever the thread of an existence so long fretted by affliction.

Chapter V

TURNING A NEW LEAF

MY mistress being dead, and I once more alone, I had to look out for a new place. About this time I might be a little—a very little—shaken in nerves. I grant I was not looking well, but, on the contrary, thin, haggard, and hollow-eyed; like a sitter-up at night, like an overwrought servant, or a placeless person in debt. In debt, however, I was not; nor quite poor; for though Miss Marchmont had not had time to benefit me, as, on that last night, she said she intended, yet, after the funeral, my wages were duly paid by her second cousin, the heir, an avaricious-looking man, with pinched nose and narrow temples, who, indeed, I heard long afterwards, turned out a thorough miser: a direct contrast to his generous kinswoman, and a foil to her memory, blessed to this day by the poor and needy. The possessor, then,

of fifteen pounds; of health, though worn, not broken, and of a spirit in similar condition; I might still, in comparison with many people, be regarded as occupying an enviable position. An embarrassing one it was, however, at the same time; as I felt with some acuteness on a certain day, of which the corresponding one in the next week was to see my departure from my present abode, while with another I was not provided.

In this dilemma I went, as the last and sole resource, to see and consult an old servant of our family; once my nurse, now housekeeper at a grand mansion not far from Miss Marchmont's. I spent some hours with her; she comforted, but knew not how to advise me. Still all inward darkness, I left her about twilight: a walk of two miles lay before me; it was a clear, frosty night. In spite of my solitude, my poverty, and my perplexity, my heart, nourished and nerved with the vigour of a youth that had not yet counted twenty-three summers, beat light and not feebly. Not feebly, I am sure, or I should have trembled in that lonely walk, which lay through still fields, and passed neither village nor farmhouse, nor cottage; I should have quailed in the absence of moonlight, for it was by the leading of stars only I traced the dim path; I should have quailed still more in the unwonted presence of that which to-night shone in the north, a moving mystery—the Aurora Borealis. But this solemn stranger influenced me otherwise than through my fears. Some new power it seemed to bring. I drew in energy with the keen, low breeze that blew on its path. A bold thought was sent to my mind; my mind was made strong to receive it.

"Leave this wilderness," it was said to me, "and go out hence."

"Where?" was the query.

I had not very far to look; gazing from this country parish in that flat, rich middle of England—I mentally saw within reach what I had never yet beheld with my bodily eyes; I saw London.

The next day I returned to the hall, and asking once more to see the housekeeper, I communicated to her my plan.

Mrs. Barrett was a grave, judicious woman, though she knew little more of the world than myself; but grave and judicious as she was, she did not charge me with being out of my senses: and, indeed, I had a staid manner of my own which ere now had been as good to me as cloak and hood of hodden grey; since under its favour I had been enabled to achieve with impunity, and even approbation, deeds that, if attempted with an excited and unsettled air, would in some minds have stamped me as a dreamer and zealot.

The housekeeper was slowly propounding some difficulties, while she prepared orange-rind for marmalade, when a child ran past the window and came bounding into the room. It was a pretty child, and as it danced, laughing, up to me—for we were not strangers (nor, indeed, was its mother—a young married daughter of the house—a stranger)—I took it on my knee. Different as were our social positions now, this child's mother and I had been schoolfellows, when I was a girl of ten and she a young lady of sixteen; and I remembered her—good-looking, but dull—in a lower class than mine.

I was admiring the boy's handsome dark eyes, when the mother, young Mrs. Leigh, entered. What a beautiful and kind-looking woman was the good-natured and comely, but unintellectual girl become! Wifehood and maternity had changed her thus, as I have since seen them change others even less promising than she. Me she had forgotten. I was changed, too, though not, I fear, for the better. I made no attempt to recall myself to her memory; why should I? She came for her son to accompany her in a walk, and behind her followed a nurse, carrying an infant. I only mention the incident because, in addressing the nurse, Mrs. Leigh spoke French (very bad French, by the way, and with an incorrigibly bad accent, again forcibly reminding me of our school-days): and I found the woman was a foreigner. The little boy chattered volubly in French too. When the whole party were withdrawn,

Mrs. Barrett remarked that her young lady had brought that foreign nurse home with her two years ago, on her return from a Continental excursion; that she was treated almost as well as a governess, and had nothing to do but walk out with the baby and chatter French with Master Charles; "and," added Mrs. Barrett, "she says there are many Englishwomen in foreign families as well placed as she."

I stored up this piece of casual information, as careful housewives store seemingly worthless shreds and fragments for which their prescient minds anticipate a possible use some day. Before I left my old friend, she gave me the address of a respectable old-fashioned inn in the city, which, she said, my uncles used to frequent in former days.

In going to London, I ran less risk and evinced less enterprise than the reader may think. In fact, the distance was only fifty miles. My means would suffice both to take me there, to keep me a few days, and also to bring me back if I found no inducement to stay. I regarded it as a brief holiday, permitted for once to work-weary faculties, rather than as an adventure of life and death. There is nothing like taking all you do at a moderate estimate: it keeps mind and body tranquil; whereas grandiloquent notions are apt to hurry both into fever.

Fifty miles were then a day's journey (for I speak of a time gone by: my hair, which, till a late period, withstood the frosts of time, lies now, at last white, under a white cap, like snow beneath snow). About nine o'clock of a wet February night I reached London.

My reader, I know, is one who would not thank me for an elaborate reproduction of poetic first impressions; and it is well, inasmuch as I had neither time nor mood to cherish such: arriving as I did late, on a dark, raw, and rainy evening, in a Babylon and a wilderness, of which the vastness and the strangeness tried to the utmost any powers of clear thought and steady self-possession with which, in the absence of more brilliant faculties, Nature might have gifted me.

When I left the coach, the strange speech of the cabmen and others waiting round, seemed to me odd as a foreign tongue. I had never before heard the English language chopped up in that way. However, I managed to understand and to be understood, so far as to get myself and trunk safely conveyed to the old inn whereof I had the address. How difficult, how oppressive, how puzzling seemed my flight! In London for the first time; at an inn for the first time; tired with travelling; confused with darkness; palsied with cold; unfurnished with either experience or advice to tell me how to act, and yet—to act obliged.

Into the hands of common-sense I confided the matter. Common-sense, however was as chilled and bewildered as all my other faculties, and it was only under the spur of an inexorable necessity that she spasmodically executed her trust. Thus urged, she paid the porter: considering the crisis, I did not blame her too much that she was hugely cheated; she asked the waiter for a room; she timorously called for the chambermaid; what is far more, she bore, without being wholly overcome, a highly supercilious style of demeanour from that young lady, when she appeared.

I recollect this same chambermaid was a pattern of town prettiness and smartness. So trim her waist, her cap, her dress—I wondered how they had all been manufactured. Her speech had an accent which in its mincing glibness seemed to rebuke mine as by authority; her spruce attire flaunted an easy scorn to my plain country garb.

"Well, it can't be helped," I thought, "and then the scene is new, and the circumstances; I shall gain good."

Maintaining a very quiet manner towards this arrogant little maid, and subsequently observing the same towards the parsonic-looking, black-coated, white-neckclothed waiter, I got civility from them ere long. I believe at first they thought I was a servant; but in a little while they changed their minds, and hovered in a doubtful state between patronage and politeness.

I kept up well till I had partaken of some refreshment, warmed myself by a fire, and was fairly shut into my own room; but, as I sat down by the bed and rested

my head and arms on the pillow, a terrible oppression overcame me. All at once my position rose on me like a ghost. Anomalous, desolate, almost blank of hope, it stood. What was I doing here alone in great London? What should I do on the morrow? What prospects had I in life? What friends had I on earth? Whence did I come? Whither should I go? What should I do?

I wet the pillow, my arms, and my hair, with rushing tears. A dark interval of most bitter thought followed this burst; but I did not regret the step taken, nor wish to retract it. A strong, vague persuasion that it was better to go forward than backward, and that I *could* go forward—that a way, however narrow and difficult, would in time open—predominated over other feelings: its influence hushed them so far, that at last I became sufficiently tranquil to be able to say my prayers and seek my couch. I had just extinguished my candle and lain down, when a deep, low, mighty tone swung through the night. At first I knew it not; but it was uttered twelve times, and at the twelfth colossal hum and trembling knell, I said—"I lie in the shadow of St. Paul's."

Chapter VI

LONDON

THE next day was the first of March, and when I awoke, rose, and opened my curtain, I saw the risen sun struggling through fog. Above my head, above the house-tops, co-elevate almost with the clouds, I saw a solemn, orbed mass, dark-blue and dim—THE DOME. While I looked, my inner self moved; my spirit shook its always-fettered wings half loose; I had a sudden feeling as if I, who never yet truly lived, were at last about to taste life. In that morning my soul grew as fast as Jonah's gourd.

"I did well to come," I said, proceeding to dress with speed and care. "I like the spirit of this great London which I feel around me. Who but a coward would pass his whole life in hamlets, and for ever abandon his faculties to the eating rust of obscurity?"

Being dressed, I went down; not travel-worn and exhausted, but tidy and refreshed. When the waiter came in with my breakfast, I managed to accost him sedately, yet cheerfully; we had ten minutes' discourse, in the course of which we became usefully known to each other.

He was a grey-haired, elderly man; and, it seemed, had lived in his present place twenty years. Having ascertained this, I was sure he must remember my two uncles, Charles and Wilmot, who, fifteen years ago, were frequent visitors here. I mentioned their names; he recalled them perfectly and with respect. Having intimated my connection, my position in his eyes was henceforth clear, and on a right footing. He said I was like my uncle Charles: I suppose he spoke truth, because Mrs. Barrett was accustomed to say the same thing. A ready and obliging courtesy now replaced his former uncomfortably doubtful manner; henceforth I need no longer be at a loss for a civil answer to a sensible question.

The street on which my little sitting-room window looked was narrow, perfectly quiet, and not dirty: the few passengers were just such as one sees in provincial towns: here was nothing formidable; I felt sure I might venture out alone.

Having breakfasted, out I went. Elation and pleasure were in my heart: to walk alone in London seemed of itself an adventure. Presently I found myself in Paternoster Row—classic ground this. I entered a bookseller's shop, kept by one Jones: I bought a little book—a piece of extravagance I could ill afford; but I thought I would one day give or send it to Mrs. Barrett. Mr. Jones, a dried-in man of business, stood behind his desk; he seemed one of the greatest, and I one of the happiest of beings.

Prodigious was the amount of life I lived that morning. Finding myself before St. Paul's, I went in; I mounted to the dome: I saw thence London, with its river, and its bridges, and its churches; I saw antique Westminster, and the green Temple Gardens, with sun upon them, and a glad, blue sky, of early spring above; and, between them and it, not too dense a cloud of haze.

Descending, I went wandering whither chance might lead, in a still ecstasy of freedom and enjoyment; and I got—I know not how—I got into the heart of city life. I saw and felt London at last: I got into the Strand; I went up Cornhill; I, mixed with the life passing along; I dared the perils of crossings. To do this, and to do it utterly alone, gave me, perhaps an irrational, but a real pleasure. Since those days, I have seen the West End, the parks, the fine squares; but I love the city far better. The city seems so much more in earnest: its business, its rush, its roar, are such serious things, sights, and sounds. The city is getting its living—the West End but enjoying its pleasure. At the West End you may be amused, but in the city you are deeply excited.

Faint, at last, and hungry (it was years since I had felt such healthy hunger), I returned, about two o'clock, to my dark, old, and quiet inn. I dined on two dishes— a plain joint, and vegetables; both seemed excellent: how much better than the small, dainty messes Miss Marchmont's cook used to send up to my kind, dead mistress and me, and to the discussion of which we could not bring half an appetite between us! Delightfully tired, I lay down on three chairs for an hour (the room did not boast a sofa). I slept, then I woke and thought for two hours.

My state of mind, and all accompanying circumstances, were just now such as most to favour the adoption of a new, resolute, and daring—perhaps desperate— line of action. I had nothing to lose. Unutterable loathing of a desolate existence past, forbade return. If I failed in what I now designed to undertake, who, save myself, would suffer? If I died far away from—home, I was going to say, but I had no home—from England, then, who would weep?

I might suffer; I was inured to suffering: death itself had not, I thought, those terrors for me which it has for the softly reared. I had, ere this, looked on the thought of death with a quiet eye. Prepared, then, for any consequences, I formed a project.

That same evening I obtained from my friend, the waiter, information respecting the sailing of vessels for a certain continental port, Boue-Marine. No time, I found, was to be lost: that very night I must take my berth. I might, indeed, have waited till the morning before going on board, but would not run the risk of being too late.

"Better take your berth at once, ma'am," counselled the waiter. I agreed with him, and having discharged my bill, and acknowledged my friend's services at a rate which I now know was princely, and which in his eyes must have seemed absurd—and indeed, while pocketing the cash, he smiled a faint smile which intimated his opinion of the donor's *savoir-faire*—he proceeded to call a coach. To the driver he also recommended me, giving at the same time an injunction about taking me, I think, to the wharf, and not leaving me to the watermen; which that functionary promised to observe, but failed in keeping his promise: on the contrary, he offered me up as an oblation, served me as a dripping roast, making me alight in the midst of a throng of watermen.

This was an uncomfortable crisis. It was a dark night. The coachman instantly drove off as soon as he had got his fare; the watermen commenced a struggle for me and my trunk, Their oaths I hear at this moment: they shook my philosophy more than did the night, or the isolation, or the strangeness of the scene. One laid hands on my trunk. I looked on and waited quietly; but when another laid hands on me, I spoke up, shook off his touch, stepped at once into a boat, desired austerely that the trunk should be placed beside me—"just there,"—which was instantly done; for the owner of the boat I had chosen became now an ally: I was rowed off.

Black was the river as a torrent of ink; lights glanced on it from the piles of building round, ships rocked on its bosom. They rowed me up to several vessels; I read by lantern-light their names painted in great, white letters on a dark ground: the *Ocean*, the *Phœnix*, the *Consort*, the *Dolphin*, were passed in turns; but the *Vivid* was my ship, and it seemed she lay further down.

Down the sable flood we glided; I thought of the Styx, and of Charon rowing some solitary soul to the Land of Shades. Amidst the strange scene, with a chilly wind blowing in my face and midnight-clouds dropping rain above my head; with two rude rowers for companions, whose insane oaths still tortured my ear, I asked myself if I was wretched or terrified. I was neither. Often in my life have I been far more so under comparatively safe circumstances. "How is this?" said I. "Methinks I am animated and alert, instead of being depressed and apprehensive!" I could not tell how it was.

"THE VIVID" started out, white and glaring, from the black night at last. "Here you are!" said the waterman, and instantly demanded six shillings.

"You ask too much," I said. He drew off from the vessel, and swore he would not embark me till I paid it. A young man, the steward as I found afterwards, was looking over the ship's side; he grinned a smile in anticipation of the coming contest; to disappoint him, I paid the money. Three times that afternoon I had given crowns where I should have given shillings; but I consoled myself with the reflection, "It is the price of experience."

"They've cheated you!" said the steward exultingly when I got on board. I answered phlegmatically that "I knew it," and went below.

A stout, handsome, and showy woman was in the ladies' cabin. I asked to be shown my berth; she looked hard at me, muttered something about its being unusual for passengers to come on board at that hour, and seemed disposed to be less than civil. What a face she had—so comely—so insolent and so selfish!

"Now that I am on board, I shall certainly stay here," was my answer. "I will trouble you to show me my berth."

She complied, but sullenly. I took off my bonnet, arranged my things, and lay down. Some difficulties had been passed through; a sort of victory was won: my homeless, anchorless, unsupported mind had again leisure for a brief repose. Till the *Vivid* arrived in harbour, no further action would be required of me; but then. . . . Oh! I could not look forward. Harassed, exhausted, I lay in a half-trance.

The stewardess talked all night; not to me but to the young steward, her son and her very picture. He passed in and out of the cabin continually: they disputed, they quarrelled, they made it up again twenty times in the course of the night. She professed to be writing a letter home—she said to her father; she read passages of it aloud, heeding me no more than a stock—perhaps she believed me asleep. Several of these passages appeared to comprise family secrets, and bore special reference to one "Charlotte," a younger sister, who, from the bearing of the epistle, seemed to be on the brink of perpetrating a romantic and imprudent match; loud was the protest of this elder lady against the distasteful union. The dutiful son laughed his mother's correspondence to scorn. She defended it, and raved at him. They were a strange pair. She might be thirty-nine or forty, and was buxom and blooming as a girl of twenty. Hard, loud, vain and vulgar, her mind and body alike seemed brazen and imperishable. I should think, from her childhood, she must have lived in public stations; and in her youth might very likely have been a barmaid.

Towards morning her discourse ran on a new theme: "the Watsons," a certain expected family-party of passengers, known to her, it appeared, and by her much esteemed on account of the handsome profit realised in their fees. She said, "it was as good as a little fortune to her whenever this family crossed."

At dawn all were astir, and by sunrise the passengers came on board. Boisterous was the welcome given by the stewardess to "the Watsons," and great was the bustle made in their honour. They were four in number, two males and two females.

Besides them, there was but one other passenger—a young lady, whom a gentlemanly, though languid-looking man escorted. The two groups offered a marked contrast. The Watsons were doubtless rich people, for they had the confidence of conscious wealth in their bearing; the women—youthful both of them, and one perfectly handsome, as far as physical beauty went—were dressed richly, gaily, and absurdly out of character for the circumstances. Their bonnets with bright flowers, their velvet cloaks and silk dresses, seemed better suited for park or promenade than for a damp packet-deck. The men were of low stature, plain, fat, and vulgar; the oldest, plainest, greasiest, broadest, I soon found was the husband—the bridegroom I suppose, for she was very young—of the beautiful girl. Deep was my amazement at this discovery; and deeper still when I perceived that, instead of being desperately wretched in such a union, she was gay even to giddiness. ''Her laughter,'' I reflected, ''must be the mere frenzy of despair.'' And even while this thought was crossing my mind, as I stood leaning quiet and solitary against the ship's side, she came tripping up to me, an utter stranger, with a camp stool in her hand, and smiling a smile of which the levity puzzled and startled me, though it showed a perfect set of perfect teeth, she offered me the accommodation of this piece of furniture. I declined it, of course, with all the courtesy I could put into my manner; she danced off heedless and lightsome. She must have been good-natured; but what had made her marry that individual, who was at least as much like an oil-barrel as a man?

The other lady-passenger, with the gentleman-companion, was quite a girl, pretty and fair: her simple print dress, untrimmed straw-bonnet, and large shawl, gracefully worn, formed a costume plain to quakerism: yet, for her, becoming enough. Before the gentleman quitted her, I observed him throwing a glance of scrutiny over all the passengers, as if to ascertain in what company his charge would be left. With a most dissatisfied air did his eye turn from the ladies with the gay flowers; he looked at me, and then he spoke to his daughter, niece, or whatever she was: she also glanced in my direction, and slightly curled her short, pretty lip. It might be myself, or it might be my homely mourning habit, that elicited this mark of contempt; more likely, both. A bell rang; her father (I afterwards knew that it was her father) kissed her, and returned to land. The packet sailed.

Foreigners say that it is only English girls who can thus be trusted to travel alone, and deep is their wonder at the daring confidence of English parents and guardians. As for the ''jeunes Miss,'' by some their intrepidity is pronounced masculine and ''inconvenant,'' others regard them as the passive victims of an educational and theological system which wantonly dispenses with proper ''surveillance.'' Whether this particular young lady was of the sort that can the most safely be left unwatched, I do not know: or rather did not *then* know; but it soon appeared that the dignity of solitude was not to her taste. She paced the deck once or twice backwards and forwards; she looked with a little sour air of disdain at the flaunting silks and velvets, and the bears which thereon danced attendance, and eventually she approached me and spoke.

''Are you fond of a sea-voyage?'' was her question.

I explained that my *fondness* for a sea-voyage had yet to undergo the test of experience; I had never made one.

''Oh, how charming!'' cried she. ''I quite envy you the novelty: first impressions, you know, are so pleasant. Now I have made so many, I quite forget the first: I am quite *blasée* about the sea and all that.''

I could not help smiling.

''Why do you laugh at me?'' she inquired, with a frank testiness that pleased me better than her other talk.

''Because you are so young to be *blasée* about anything.''

''I am seventeen'' (a little piqued).

''You hardly look sixteen. Do you like travelling alone?''

"Bah! I care nothing about it. I have crossed the Channel ten times, alone; but then I take care never to be long alone: I always make friends."

"You will scarcely make many friends this voyage, I think" (glancing at the Watson group, who were now laughing and making a great deal of noise on deck).

"Not of those odious men and women," said she: "such people should be steerage passengers. Are you going to school?"

"No."

"Where are you going?"

"I have not the least idea—beyond, at least, the Port of Boue-Marine."

She stared, then carelessly ran on—

"I am going to school. Oh, the number of foreign schools I have been at in my life! And yet I am quite an ignoramus. I know nothing—nothing in the world—I assure you; except that I play and dance beautifully,—and French and German of course I know, to speak; but I can't read or write them very well. Do you know they wanted me to translate a page of an easy German book into English the other day, and I couldn't do it. Papa was so mortified: he says it looks as if M. de Bassompierre—my godpapa, who pays all my school-bills—had thrown away all his money. And then, in matters of information—in history, geography, arithmetic, and so on, I am quite a baby; and I write English so badly—such spelling and grammar, they tell me. Into the bargain I have quite forgotten my religion: they call me a Protestant, you know, but really I am not sure whether I am one or not: I don't well know the difference between Romanism and Protestantism. However, I don't in the least care for that. I was a Lutheran once at Bonn—dear Bonn!—charming Bonn!—where there were so many handsome students. Every nice girl in our school had an admirer; they knew our hours for walking out, and almost always passed us on the promenade: 'Schönes Mädchen,' we used to hear them say. I was excessively happy at Bonn!"

"And where are you going now?" I inquired.

"Oh! at—*chose,*" said she.

Now, Miss Ginevra Fanshawe (such was this young person's name) only substituted this word "chose" in temporary oblivion of the real name. It was a habit she had: "chose" came in at every turn in her conversation—the convenient substitute for any missing word in any language she might chance at the time to be speaking. French girls often do the like; from them she had caught the custom. "Chose," however, I found in this instance, stood for Villette—the great capital of the great kingdom of Labassecour.

"Do you like Villette?" I asked.

"Pretty well. The natives, you know, are intensely stupid and vulgar; but there are some nice English families."

"Are you in a school?"

"Yes."

"A good one?"

"Oh no! horrid: but I go out every Sunday, and care nothing about the maîtresses or the professeurs, or the élèves, and send lessons *au diable* (one daren't say that in English, you know, but it sounds quite right in French); and thus I get on charmingly. . . . You are laughing at me again?"

"No—I am only smiling at my own thoughts."

"What are they?"(without waiting for an answer)—"Now, *do* tell me where you are going."

"Where Fate may lead me. My business is to earn a living where I can find it."

"To earn!" (in consternation). "Are you poor, then?"

"As poor as Job."

(After a pause) "Bah! how unpleasant! But *I* know what it is to be poor: they are poor enough at home—papa and mamma, and all of them. Papa is called Captain Fanshawe; he is an officer on half-pay, but well-descended, and some of our

connections are great enough; but my uncle and godpapa De Bassompierre, who lives in France, is the only one that helps us: he educates us girls. I have five sisters and three brothers. By-and-by we are to marry—rather elderly gentlemen, I suppose, with cash: papa and mamma manage that. My sister Augusta is married now to a man much older-looking than papa. Augusta is very beautiful—not in my style— but dark; her husband, Mr. Davies, had the yellow fever in India, and he is still the colour of a guinea; but then he is rich, and Augusta has her carriage and establishment, and we all think she has done perfectly well. Now, this is better than 'earning a living,' as you say. By the way, are you clever?''

''No—not at all.''

''You can play, sing, speak three or four languages?''

''By no means.''

''Still I think you are clever'' (a pause and a yawn).

''Shall you be sea-sick?''

''Shall you?''

''Oh, immensely! as soon as ever we get in sight of the sea: I begin, indeed, to feel it already. I shall go below; and won't I order about that fat odious stewardess! Heureusement je sais faire aller mon monde.'' Down she went.

It was not long before the other passengers followed her: throughout the afternoon I remained on deck alone. When I recall the tranquil, and even happy mood in which I passed those hours, and remember, at the same time, the position in which I was placed: its hazardous—some would have said its hopeless—character; I feel that, as—

> Stone walls do not a prison make,
> Nor iron bars—a cage,

so peril, loneliness, an uncertain future, are not oppressive evils, so long as the frame is healthy and the faculties are employed; so long, especially, as Liberty lends us her wings and Hope guides us by her star.

I was not sick till long after we passed Margate, and deep was the pleasure I drank in with the sea breeze; divine the delight I drew from the heaving Channel waves, from the sea-birds on their ridges, from the white sails on their dark distance, from the quiet yet beclouded sky, overhanging all. In my reverie, methought I saw the continent of Europe, like a wide dreamland, far away. Sunshine lay on it, making the long coast one line of gold; tiniest tracery of clustered town and snow-gleaming tower, of woods deep massed, of heights serrated, of smooth pasturage and veiny stream, embossed the metal-bright prospect. For background, spread a sky, solemn and dark blue, and—grand with imperial promise, soft with tints of enchantment—strode from north to south a God-bent bow, an arch of hope.

Cancel the whole of that, if you please, reader—or rather let it stand, and draw thence a moral—an alliterative, text-hand copy—

> Day-dreams are delusions of the demon.

Becoming excessively sick, I faltered down into the cabin.

Miss Fanshawe's berth chanced to be next mine; and, I am sorry to say, she tormented me with an unsparing selfishness during the whole time of our mutual distress. Nothing could exceed her impatience and fretfulness. The Watsons, who were very sick too, and on whom the stewardess attended with shameless partiality, were stoics compared with her. Many a time since have I noticed, in persons of Ginevra Fanshawe's light, careless temperament, and fair, fragile style of beauty, an entire incapacity to endure: they seem to sour in adversity, like small beer in thunder. The man who takes such a woman for his wife, ought to be prepared to guarantee her an existence all sunshine. Indignant at last with her teasing peevishness,

I curtly requested her "to hold her tongue." The rebuff did her good, and it was observable that she liked me no worse for it.

As dark night drew on, the sea roughened: larger waves swayed strong against the vessel's side. It was strange to reflect that blackness and water were round us, and to feel the ship ploughing straight on her pathless way, despite noise, billow, and rising gale. Articles of furniture began to fall about, and it became needful to lash them to their places; the passengers grew sicker than ever; Miss Fanshawe declared, with groans, that she must die.

"Not just yet, honey," said the stewardess. "We're just in port." Accordingly, in another quarter of an hour, a calm fell upon us all; and about midnight the voyage ended.

I was sorry: yes, I was sorry. My resting-time was past; my difficulties—my stringent difficulties—recommenced. When I went on deck, the cold air and black scowl of the night seemed to rebuke me for my presumption in being where I was: the lights of the foreign seaport town, glimmering round the foreign harbour, met me like unnumbered threatening eyes. Friends came on board to welcome the Watsons; a whole family of friends surrounded and bore away Miss Fanshawe; I——but I dared not for one moment dwell on a comparison of positions.

Yet where should I go? I must go somewhere. Necessity dare not be nice. As I gave the stewardess her fee—and she seemed surprised at receiving a coin of more value than, from such a quarter, her coarse calculations had probably reckoned on—I said—

"Be kind enough to direct me to some quiet, respectable inn, where I can go for the night."

She not only gave me the required direction, but called a commissionaire, and bid him take charge of me, and—*not* my trunk, for that was gone to the custom-house.

I followed this man along a rudely-paved street, lit now by a fitful gleam of moonlight; he brought me to the inn. I offered him sixpence, which he refused to take; supposing it not enough, I changed it for a shilling; but this also he declined, speaking rather sharply, in a language to me unknown. A waiter, coming forward into the lamp-lit inn-passage, reminded me, in broken English, that my money was foreign money, not current here. I gave him a sovereign to change. This little matter settled, I asked for a bedroom; supper I could not take: I was still sea-sick and unnerved, and trembling all over. How deeply glad I was when the door of a very small chamber at length closed on me and my exhaustion. Again I might rest: though the cloud of doubt would be as thick to-morrow as ever; the necessity for exertion more urgent, the peril (of destitution) nearer, the conflict (for existence) more severe.

Chapter VII

VILLETTE

I AWOKE next morning with courage revived and spirits refreshed: physical debility no longer enervated my judgment; my mind felt prompt and clear.

Just as I finished dressing, a tap came to the door; I said "Come in," expecting the chambermaid, whereas a rough man walked in and said—

"Gif me your keys, Meess."

"Why?" I asked.

"Gif!" said he impatiently; and as he half-snatched them from my hand, he added, "All right! haf your tronc soon."

Fortunately it did turn out all right: he was from the custom-house. Where to go to get some breakfast I could not tell; but I proceeded, not without hesitation, to descend.

I now observed, what I had not noticed in my extreme weariness last night, viz., that this inn was, in fact, a large hotel; and as I slowly descended the broad staircase, halting on each step (for I was in wonderfully little haste to get down), I gazed at the high ceiling above me, at the painted walls around, at the wide windows which filled the house with light, at the veined marble I trod (for the steps were all of marble, though uncarpeted and not very clean), and contrasting all this with the dimensions of the closet assigned to me as a chamber, with the extreme modesty of its appointments, I fell into a philosophising mood.

Much I marvelled at the sagacity evinced by waiters and chambermaids in proportioning the accommodation to the guest. How could inn-servants and ship-stewardesses everywhere tell at a glance that I, for instance, was an individual of no social significance and little burdened by cash? They *did* know it evidently: I saw quite well that they all, in a moment's calculation, estimated me at about the same fractional value. The fact seemed to me curious and pregnant: I would not disguise from myself what it indicated, yet managed to keep up my spirits pretty well under its pressure.

Having at last landed in a great hall, full of skylight glare, I made my way somehow to what proved to be the coffee-room. It cannot be denied that on entering this room I trembled somewhat; felt uncertain, solitary, wretched; wished to Heaven I knew whether I was doing right or wrong; felt convinced that it was the last, but could not help myself. Acting in the spirit and with the calm of a fatalist, I sat down at a small table, to which a waiter presently brought me some breakfast; and I partook of that meal in a frame of mind not greatly calculated to favour digestion. There were many other people breakfasting at other tables in the room; I should have felt rather more happy if amongst them all I could have seen any women; however, there was not one—all present were men. But nobody seemed to think I was doing anything strange; one or two gentlemen glanced at me occasionally, but none stared obtrusively: I suppose if there was anything eccentric in the business, they accounted for it by this word "Anglaise!"

Breakfast over, I must again move—in what direction? "Go to Villette," said an inward voice; prompted doubtless by the recollection of this slight sentence uttered carelessly and at random by Miss Fanshawe, as she bid me good-bye—

"I wish you would come to Madame Beck's; she has some marmots whom you might look after: she wants an English gouvernante, or was wanting one two months ago."

Who Madame Beck was, where she lived, I knew not; I had asked, but the question passed unheard: Miss Fanshawe, hurried away by her friends, left it unanswered. I presumed Villette to be her residence—to Villette I would go. The distance was forty miles. I knew I was catching at straws; but in the wide and weltering deep where I found myself, I would have caught at cobwebs. Having inquired about the means of travelling to Villette, and secured a seat in the diligence, I departed on the strength of this outline—this shadow of a project. Before you pronounce on the rashness of the proceeding, reader, look back to the point whence I started; consider the desert I had left, note how little I perilled: mine was the game where the player cannot lose and may win.

Of an artistic temperament, I deny that I am; yet I must possess something of the artist's faculty of making the most of present pleasure: that is to say, when it is of the kind to my taste. I enjoyed that day, though we travelled slowly, though it was cold, though it rained. Somewhat bare, flat, and treeless was the route along which our journey lay; and slimy canals crept, like half-torpid green snakes, beside the road; and formal pollard willows edged level fields, tilled like kitchen-garden beds. The sky, too, was monotonously grey; the atmosphere was stagnant and

humid; yet amidst all these deadening influences, my fancy budded fresh and my heart basked in sunshine. These feelings, however, were well kept in check by the secret but ceaseless consciousness of anxiety lying in wait on enjoyment, like a tiger crouched in a jungle. The breathing of that beast of prey was in my ear always; his fierce heart panted close against mine; he never stirred in his lair but I felt him; I knew he waited only for sun-down to bound ravenous from his ambush.

I had hoped we might reach Villette ere night set in, and that thus I might escape the deeper embarrassment which obscurity seems to throw round a first arrival at an unknown bourne; but, what with our slow progress and long stoppages—what with a thick fog and small, dense rain—darkness, that might almost be felt, had settled on the city by the time we gained its suburbs.

I know we passed through a gate where soldiers were stationed—so much I could see by lamplight; then, having left behind us the miry Chaussée, we rattled over a pavement of strangely rough and flinty surface. At a bureau, the diligence stopped, and the passengers alighted. My first business was to get my trunk: a small matter enough, but important to me. Understanding that it was best not to be importunate or over-eager about luggage, but to wait and watch quietly the delivery of other boxes till I saw my own, and then promptly claim and secure it, I stood apart; my eye fixed on that part of the vehicle in which I had seen my little portmanteau safely stowed, and upon which piles of additional bags and boxes were now heaped. One by one, I saw these removed, lowered, and seized on. I was sure mine ought to be by this time visible: it was not. I had tied on the direction-card with a piece of green ribbon, that I might know it at a glance: not a fringe or fragment of green was perceptible. Every package was removed; every tin-case and brown paper parcel: the oil-cloth cover was lifted; I saw with distinct vision that not an umbrella, cloak, cane, hat-box or band-box remained.

And my portmanteau, with my few clothes and little pocketbook enclasping the remnant of my fifteen pounds, where were they?

I ask this question now, but I could not ask it then. I could say nothing whatever; not possessing a phrase of *speaking* French: and it was French, and French only, the whole world seemed now gabbling around me. *What* should I do? Approaching the conductor, I just laid my hand on his arm, pointed to a trunk, thence to the diligence-roof, and tried to express a question with my eyes. He misunderstood me, seized the trunk indicated, and was about to hoist it on the vehicle.

"Let that alone—will you?" said a voice in good English; then, in correction, "Qu'est ce que vous faîtes donc? Cette malle est à moi."

But I had heard the Fatherland accents; they rejoiced my heart; I turned.

"Sir," said I, appealing to the stranger, without in my distress noticing what he was like, "I cannot speak French. May I entreat you to ask this man what he has done with my trunk?"

Without discriminating, for the moment, what sort of face it was to which my eyes were raised and on which they were fixed, I felt in its expression half-surprise at my appeal and half-doubt of the wisdom of interference.

"*Do* ask him; I would do as much for you," said I.

I don't know whether he smiled, but he said in a gentlemanly tone, that is to say, a tone not hard nor terrifying—

"What sort of trunk was yours?"

I described it, including in my description the green ribbon. And forthwith he took the conductor under hand, and I felt through all the storm of French which followed, that he raked him fore and aft. Presently he returned to me.

"The fellow avers he was overloaded, and confesses that he removed your trunk after you saw it put on, and has left it behind at Boue-Marine with other parcels; he has promised, however, to forward it to-morrow; the day after, therefore, you will find it safe at this bureau."

"Thank you," said I: but my heart sank.

Meantime what should I do? Perhaps this English gentleman saw the failure of courage in my face; he inquired kindly—

"Have you any friends in this city?"

"No, and I don't know where to go."

There was a little pause, in the course of which, as he turned more fully to the light of a lamp above him, I saw that he was a young, distinguished, and handsome man; he might be a lord, for anything I knew: nature had made him good enough for a prince, I thought. His face was very pleasant; he looked high but not arrogant, manly but not overbearing. I was turning away, in the deep consciousness of all absence of claim to look for further help from such a one as he.

"Was all your money in your trunk?" he asked, stopping me.

How thankful was I to be able to answer with truth—

"No. I have enough in my purse" (for I had near twenty francs) "to keep me at a quiet inn till the day after to-morrow; but I am quite a stranger in Villette, and don't know the streets and the inns."

"I can give you the address of such an inn as you want," said he; "and it is not far off: with my direction you will easily find it."

He tore a leaf from his pocket-book, wrote a few words, and gave it to me. I *did* think him kind; and as to distrusting him, or his advice, or his address, I should almost as soon have thought of distrusting the Bible. There was goodness in his countenance, and honour in his bright eyes.

"Your shortest way will be to follow the Boulevard and cross the park," he continued; "but it is too late and too dark for a woman to go through the park alone; I will step with you thus far."

He moved on, and I followed him, through the darkness and the small soaking rain. The Boulevard was all deserted, its path miry, the water dripping from its trees; the park was black as midnight. In the double gloom of trees and fog, I could not see my guide; I could only follow his tread. Not the least fear had I: I believe I would have followed that frank tread, through continual night, to the world's end.

"Now," said he, when the park was traversed, "you will go along this broad street till you come to steps; two lamps will show you where they are: these steps you will descend: a narrower street lies below; following that, at the bottom you will find your inn. They speak English there, so your difficulties are now pretty well over. Good-night."

"Good-night, sir," said I: "accept my sincerest thanks." And we parted.

The remembrance of his countenance, which I am sure wore a light not unbenignant to the friendless—the sound in my ear of his voice, which spoke a nature chivalric to the needy and feeble, as well as the youthful and fair—were a sort of cordial to me long after. He was a true young English gentleman.

On I went, hurrying fast through a magnificent street and square, with the grandest houses round, and amidst them the huge outline of more than one overbearing pile; which might be palace or church—I could not tell. Just as I passed a portico, two moustachioed men came suddenly from behind the pillars; they were smoking cigars, their dress implied pretensions to the rank of gentlemen, but, poor things! they were very plebeian in soul. They spoke with insolence, and, fast as I walked, they kept pace with me a long way. At last I met a sort of patrol, and my dreaded hunters were turned from the pursuit; but they had driven me beyond my reckoning: when I could collect my faculties, I no longer knew where I was; the staircase I must long since have passed. Puzzled, out of breath, all my pulses throbbing in inevitable agitation, I knew not where to turn. It was terrible to think of again encountering those bearded, sneering simpletons; yet the ground must be retraced, and the steps sought out.

I came at last to an old and worn flight, and, taking it for granted that this must be the one indicated, I descended them. The street into which they led was indeed narrow, but it contained no inn. On I wandered. In a very quiet and comparatively

clean and well-paved street, I saw a light burning over the door of a rather large house, loftier by a storey than those round it. *This* might be the inn at last. I hastened on: my knees now trembled under me: I was getting quite exhausted.

No inn was this. A brass-plate embellished the great porte-cochère: "Pensionnat de Demoiselles" was the inscription; and beneath, a name, "Madame Beck."

I started. About a hundred thoughts volleyed through my mind in a moment. Yet I planned nothing, and considered nothing: I had not time. Providence said, "Stop here; this is *your* inn." Fate took me in her strong hand; mastered my will: directed my actions: I rang the door-bell.

While I waited, I would not reflect. I fixedly looked at the street-stones, where the door-lamp shone, and counted them and noted their shapes, and the glitter of wet on their angles. I rang again. They opened at last. A bonne in a smart cap stood before me.

"May I see Madame Beck?" I inquired.

I believe if I had spoken French she would not have admitted me: but, as I spoke English, she concluded I was a foreign teacher come on business connected with the pensionnat, and, even at that late hour, she let me in, without a word of reluctance or a moment of hesitation.

The next moment I sat in a cold, glittering salon, with porcelain stove unlit, and gilded ornaments and polished floor. A pendule on the mantelpiece struck nine o'clock.

A quarter of an hour passed. How fast beat every pulse in my frame! How I turned cold and hot by turns! I sat with my eyes fixed on the door—a great white folding-door, with gilt mouldings: I watched to see a leaf move and open. All had been quiet: not a mouse had stirred; the white doors were closed and motionless.

"You ayre Engliss?" said a voice at my elbow. I almost bounded, so unexpected was the sound; so certain had I been of solitude.

No ghost stood beside me, nor anything of spectral aspect; merely a motherly, dumpy little woman, in a large shawl, a wrapping-gown, and a clean, trim night-cap.

I said I was English, and immediately, without further prelude, we fell to a most remarkable conversation. Madame Beck (for Madame Beck it was—she had entered by a little door behind me, and, being shod with the shoes of silence, I had heard neither her entrance nor approach)—Madame Beck had exhausted her command of insular speech when she said "You ayre Engliss," and she now proceeded to work away volubly in her own tongue. I answered in mine. She partly understood me, but as I did not at all understand her—though we made together an awful clamour (anything like Madame's gift of utterance I had not hitherto heard or imagined)— we achieved little progress. She rang, ere long, for aid; which arrived in the shape of a "maîtresse," who had been partly educated in an Irish convent, and was esteemed a perfect adept in the English language. A bluff little personage this maîtresse was—Labassecourienne from top to toe: and how she did slaughter the speech of Albion! However, I told her a plain tale, which she translated. I told her how I had left my own country, intent on extending my knowledge, and gaining my bread; how I was ready to turn my hand to any useful thing, provided it was not wrong or degrading; how I would be a child's-nurse, or a lady's-maid, and would not refuse even housework adapted to my strength. Madame heard this; and, questioning her countenance, I almost thought the tale won her ear.

"Il n'y a que les Anglaises pour ces sortes d'entreprises," said she: "sont-elles donc intrépides ces femmes là!"

She asked my name, my age; she sat and looked at me—not pityingly, not with interest: never a gleam of sympathy, or a shade of compassion, crossed her countenance during the interview. I felt she was not one to be led an inch by her feelings: grave and considerate, she gazed, consulting her judgment and studying my narrative. A bell rang.

"Voilà pour la prière du soir!" said she, and rose. Through her interpreter, she desired me to depart now, and come back on the morrow; but this did not suit me: I could not bear to return to the perils of darkness and the street. With energy, yet with a collected and controlled manner, I said, addressing her personally, and not the maîtresse—

"Be assured, Madame, that by instantly securing my services, your interests will be served and not injured: you will find me one who will wish to give, in her labour, a full equivalent for her wages; and if you hire me, it will be better that I should stay here this night. Having no acquaintance in Villette, and not possessing the language of the country, how can I secure a lodging?"

"It is true," said she; "but at least you can give a reference?"

" None."

She inquired after my luggage: I told her when it would arrive. She mused. At that moment a man's step was heard in the vestibule, hastily proceeding to the outer door. (I shall go on with this part of my tale as if I had understood all that passed; for though it was then scarce intelligible to me, I heard it translated afterwards.)

"Who goes out now?" demanded Madame Beck, listening to the tread.

"M. Paul," replied the teacher. "He came this evening to give a reading to the first class."

"The very man I should at this moment most wish to see. Call him."

The teacher ran to the salon door. M. Paul was summoned. He entered: a small, dark, and spare man, in spectacles.

"Mon cousin," began Madame, "I want your opinion. We know your skill in physiognomy; use it now. Read that countenance."

The little man fixed on me his spectacles. A resolute compression of the lips and gathering of the brow seemed to say that he meant to see through me, and that a veil would be no veil for him.

"I read it," he pronounced.

"Et qu'en dites vous?"

"Mais—bien des choses," was the oracular answer.

"Bad or good?"

"Of each kind, without doubt," pursued the diviner.

"May one trust her word?"

"Are you negotiating a matter of importance?"

"She wishes me to engage her as bonne or gouvernante; tells a tale full of integrity, but gives no reference."

"She is a stranger?"

"An Englishwoman, as one may see."

"She speaks French?"

"Not a word."

"She understands it?"

"No."

"One may then speak plainly in her presence?"

"Doubtless."

He gazed steadily. "Do you need her services?"

"I could do with them. You know I am disgusted with Madame Svini."

Still he scrutinised. The judgment, when it at last came, was as indefinite as what had gone before it.

"Engage her. If good predominates in that nature, the action will bring its own reward; if evil—eh bien! ma cousine, ce sera toujours une bonne œuvre." And with a bow and a "bon soir," this vague arbiter of my destiny vanished.

And Madame did engage me that very night—by God's blessing I was spared the necessity of passing forth again into the lonesome, dreary, hostile street.

Chapter VIII

MADAME BECK

BEING delivered into the charge of the maîtresse, I was led through a long narrow passage into a foreign kitchen, very clean but very strange. It seemed to contain no means of cooking—neither fireplace nor oven; I did not understand that the great black furnace which filled one corner was an efficient substitute for these. Surely pride was not already beginning its whispers in my heart; yet I felt a sense of relief when, instead of being left in the kitchen, as I half anticipated, I was led forward to a small inner room termed a "cabinet." A cook in a jacket, a short petticoat and sabots, brought my supper: to wit—some meat, nature unknown, served in an odd and acid, but pleasant sauce; some chopped potatoes, made savoury with I know not what—vinegar and sugar, I think: a tartine, or slice of bread and butter, and a baked pear. Being hungry, I ate and was grateful.

After the "Prière du Soir," Madame herself came to have another look at me. She desired me to follow her upstairs. Through a series of the queerest little dormitories—which, I heard afterwards, had once been nuns' cells: for the premises were in part of ancient date—and through the oratory—a long, low, gloomy room, where a crucifix hung, pale, against the wall, and two tapers kept dim vigils—she conducted me to an apartment where three children were asleep in three tiny beds. A heated stove made the air of this room oppressive; and, to mend matters, it was scented with an odour rather strong than delicate: a perfume, indeed, altogether surprising and unexpected under the circumstances, being like the combination of smoke with some spirituous essence—a smell, in short, of whisky.

Beside a table, on which flared the remnant of a candle guttering to waste in the socket, a coarse woman, heterogeneously clad in a broad striped showy silk dress and a stiff apron, sat in a chair fast asleep. To complete the picture, and leave no doubt as to the state of matters, a bottle and an empty glass stood at the sleeping beauty's elbow.

Madame contemplated this remarkable tableau with great calm; she neither smiled nor scowled; no impress of anger, disgust, or surprise ruffled the equality of her grave aspect; she did not even wake the woman. Serenely pointing to a fourth bed, she intimated that it was to be mine; then, having extinguished the candle and substituted for it a night-lamp, she glided through an inner door, which she left ajar—the entrance to her own chamber, a large, well-furnished apartment, as was discernible through the aperture.

My devotions that night were all thanksgiving. Strangely had I been led since morning—unexpectedly had I been provided for. Scarcely could I believe that not forty-eight hours had elapsed since I left London, under no other guardianship than that which protects the passenger-bird—with no prospects but the dubious cloud-tracery of hope.

I was a light sleeper; in the dead of night I suddenly awoke. All was hushed, but a white figure stood in the room—Madame in her night-dress. Moving without perceptible sound, she visited the three children in the three beds; she approached me: I feigned sleep, and she studied me long. A small pantomime ensued, curious enough. I dare say she sat a quarter of an hour on the edge of my bed, gazing at my face. She then drew nearer, bent close over me; slightly raised my cap, and turned back the border so as to expose my hair; she looked at my hand lying on the bedclothes. This done, she turned to the chair where my clothes lay: it was at the foot of the bed. Hearing her touch and lift them, I opened my eyes with precaution, for I own I felt curious to see how far her taste for research would lead her. It led her a good way: every article did she inspect. I divined her motive for this proceeding, viz., the wish to form from the garments a judgment respecting the wearer, her station, means, neatness, etc. The end was not bad, but the means

were hardly fair or justifiable. In my dress was a pocket; she fairly turned it inside out: she counted the money in my purse; she opened a little memorandum-book, coolly perused its contents, and took from between the leaves a small plaited lock of Miss Marchmont's grey hair. To a bunch of three keys, being those of my trunk, desk, and workbox, she accorded special attention: with these, indeed, she withdrew a moment to her own room. I softly rose in my bed and followed her with my eye: these keys, reader, were not brought back till they had left on the toilet of the adjoining room the impress of their wards in wax. All being thus done decently and in order, my property was returned to its place, my clothes were carefully refolded. Of what nature were the conclusions deduced from this scrutiny? Were they favourable or otherwise? Vain question. Madame's face of stone (for of stone in its present night aspect it looked: it had been human, and, as I said before, motherly, in the salon) betrayed no response.

Her duty done—I felt that in her eyes this business was a duty—she rose, noiseless as a shadow: she moved towards her own chamber; at the door, she turned, fixing her eye on the heroine of the bottle, who still slept and loudly snored. Mrs. Svini (I presume this was Mrs. Svini, *Anglicè* or *Hibernicè* Sweeny)—Mrs. Sweeny's doom was in Madame Beck's eye—an immutable purpose that eye spoke: Madame's visitations for shortcomings might be slow, but they were sure. All this was very un-English: truly I was in a foreign land.

The morrow made me further acquainted with Mrs. Sweeny. It seems she had introduced herself to her present employer as an English lady in reduced circumstances: a native, indeed, of Middlesex, professing to speak the English tongue with the purest metropolitan accent. Madame—reliant on her own infallible expedients for finding out the truth in time—had a singular intrepidity in hiring service off-hand (as indeed seemed abundantly proved in my own case). She received Mrs. Sweeny as nursery-governess to her three children. I need hardly explain to the reader that this lady was in effect a native of Ireland; her station I do not pretend to fix: she boldly declared that she had "had the bringing-up of the son and daughter of a marquis." I think, myself, she might possibly have been a hanger-on, nurse, fosterer, or washerwoman, in some Irish family: she spoke a smothered tongue, curiously overlaid with mincing cockney inflections. By some means or other she had acquired, and now held in possession, a wardrobe of rather suspicious splendour— gowns of stiff and costly silk, fitting her indifferently, and apparently made for other proportions than those they now adorned; caps with real lace borders, and— the chief item in the inventory, the spell by which she struck a certain awe through the household, quelling the otherwise scornfully-disposed teachers and servants, and, so long as her broad shoulders *wore* the folds of that majestic drapery, even influencing Madame herself—*a real Indian shawl*—"un véritable Cachmire," as Madame Beck said, with unmixed reverence and amaze. I feel quite sure that without this "Cachmire" she would not have kept her footing in the pensionnat for two days: by virtue of it, and it only, she maintained the same a month.

But when Mrs. Sweeny knew that I was come to fill her shoes, then it was that she declared herself—then did she rise on Madame Beck in her full power—then come down on me with her concentrated weight. Madame bore this revelation and visitation so well, so stoically, that I for very shame could not support it otherwise than with composure. For one little moment Madame Beck absented herself from the room: ten minutes after, an agent of the police stood in the midst of us. Mrs. Sweeny and her effects were removed. Madame's brow had not been ruffled during the scene—her lips had not dropped one sharply-accented word.

This brisk little affair of the dismissal was all settled before breakfast: order to march given, policemen called, mutineer expelled, "chambre d'enfants" fumigated and cleansed, windows thrown open, and every trace of the accomplished Mrs. Sweeny—even to the fine essence and spiritual fragrance which gave token so subtle and so fatal of the head and front of her offending—was annihilated from the Rue

Fossette: all this, I say, was done between the moment of Madame Beck's issuing like Aurora from her chamber and that in which she coolly sat down to pour out her first cup of coffee.

About noon, I was summoned to dress Madame. (It appeared my place was to be a hybrid between gouvernante and lady's-maid.) Till noon, she haunted the house in her wrapping-gown, shawl, and soundless slippers. How would the lady-chief of an English school approve this custom?

The dressing of her hair puzzled me; she had plenty of it: auburn, unmixed with grey: though she was forty years old. Seeing my embarrassment, she said, "You have not been a femme de chambre in your own country?" And taking the brush from my hand, and setting me aside, not ungently or disrespectfully, she arranged it herself. In performing other offices of the toilet, she half-directed, half-aided me, without the least display of temper or impatience. (N.B., that was the first and last time I was required to dress her. Henceforth, on Rosine, the portress, devolved that duty.)

When attired, Madame Beck appeared a personage of a figure rather short and stout, yet still graceful in its own peculiar way; that is, with the grace resulting from proportion of parts. Her complexion was fresh and sanguine, not too rubicund; her eye, blue and serene; her dark silk dress fitted her as a French sempstress alone can make a dress fit: she looked well, though a little bourgeoise; as bourgeoise, indeed, she was. I know not what of harmony pervaded her whole person; and yet her face offered contrast, too: its features were by no means such as are usually seen in conjunction with a complexion of such blended freshness and repose: their outline was stern: her forehead was high but narrow; it expressed capacity and some benevolence, but no expanse; nor did her peaceful yet watchful eye ever know the fire which is kindled in the heart or the softness which flows thence. Her mouth was hard: it could be a little grim; her lips were thin. For sensibility and genius, with all their tenderness and temerity, I felt somehow that Madame would be the right sort of Minos in petticoats.

In the long run, I found she was something else in petticoats too. Her name was Modeste Maria Beck, *née* Kint: it ought to have been Ignacia. She was a charitable woman, and did a great deal of good. There never was a mistress whose rule was milder. I was told that she never once remonstrated with the intolerable Mrs. Sweeny, despite her tipsiness, disorder, and general neglect; yet Mrs. Sweeny had to go the moment her departure became convenient. I was told, too, that neither masters nor teachers were found fault with in that establishment; yet both masters and teachers were often changed: they vanished and others filled their places, none could well explain how.

The establishment was both a pensionnat and an externat: the externes, or day-pupils, exceeded one hundred in number; the boarders were about a score. Madame must have possessed high administrative powers; she ruled all these, together with four teachers, eight masters, six servants, and three children, managing at the same time to perfection the pupils' parents and friends; and that without apparent effort; without bustle, fatigue, fever, or any symptom of undue excitement: occupied she always was—busy, rarely. It is true that Madame had her own system for managing and regulating this mass of machinery; and a very pretty system it was: the reader has seen a specimen of it in that small affair of turning my pocket inside out, and reading my private memoranda. "Surveillance," "espionage,"—these were her watchwords.

Still, Madame knew what honesty was, and liked it—that is, when it did not obtrude its clumsy scruples in the way of her will and interest. She had a respect for "Angleterre"; and as to "les Anglaises," she would have the women of no other country about her own children, if she could help it.

Often in the evening, after she had been plotting and counter-plotting, spying and receiving the reports of spies all day, she would come up to my room—a trace

of real weariness on her brow—and she would sit down and listen while the children said their little prayers to me in English: the Lord's Prayer, and the hymn beginning "Gentle Jesus," these little Catholics were permitted to repeat at my knee; and, when I had put them to bed, she would talk to me (I soon gained enough French to be able to understand, and even answer her) about England and Englishwomen, and the reasons for what she was pleased to term their superior intelligence, and more real and reliable probity. Very good sense she often showed; very sound opinions she often broached: she seemed to know that keeping girls in distrustful restraint, in blind ignorance, and under a surveillance that left them no moment and no corner for retirement, was not the best way to make them grow up honest and modest women; but she averred that ruinous consequences would ensue if any other method were tried with continental children: they were so accustomed to restraint, that relaxation, however guarded, would be misunderstood and fatally presumed on. She was sick, she would declare, of the means she had to use, but use them she must; and after discoursing, often with dignity and delicacy, to me, she would move away on her "souliers de silence," and glide ghost-like through the house, watching and spying everywhere, peering through every keyhole, listening behind every door.

After all, Madame's system was not bad—let me do her justice. Nothing could be better than all her arrangements for the physical well-being of her scholars. No minds were overtasked; the lessons were well distributed and made incomparably easy to the learner; there was a liberty of amusement, and a provision for exercise which kept the girls healthy; the food was abundant and good: neither pale nor puny faces were anywhere to be seen in the Rue Fossette. She never grudged a holiday; she allowed plenty of time for sleeping, dressing, washing, eating; her method in all these matters was easy, liberal, salutary, and rational: many an austere English schoolmistress would do vastly well to imitate her—and I believe many would be glad to do so, if exacting English parents would let them.

As Madame Beck ruled by espionage, she of course had her staff of spies: she perfectly knew the quality of the tools she used, and while she would not scruple to handle the dirtiest for a dirty occasion—flinging this sort from her like refuse rind, after the orange has been duly squeezed—I have known her fastidious in seeking pure metal for clean uses; and when once a bloodless and rustless instrument was found, she was careful of the prize, keeping it in silk and cotton-wool. Yet, woe be to that man or woman who relied on her one inch beyond the point where it was her interest to be trustworthy: interest was the master-key of Madame's nature—the mainspring of her motives—the alpha and omega of her life. I have seen her *feelings* appealed to, and I have smiled in half-pity, half-scorn at the appellants. None ever gained her ear through that channel, or swayed her purpose by that means. On the contrary, to attempt to touch her heart was the surest way to rouse her antipathy, and to make of her a secret foe. It proved to her that she had no heart to be touched: it reminded her where she was impotent and dead. Never was the distinction between charity and mercy better exemplified than in her. While devoid of sympathy, she had a sufficiency of rational benevolence: she would give in the readiest manner to people she had never seen—rather, however, to classes than to individuals. "Pour les pauvres" she opened her purse freely—against *the poor man,* as a rule, she kept it closed. In philanthropic schemes for the benefit of society at large she took a cheerful part; no private sorrow touched her: no force or mass of suffering concentrated in one heart had power to pierce hers. Not the agony in Gethsemane, not the death on Calvary, could have wrung from her eyes one tear.

I say again, Madame was a very great and a very capable woman. That school offered her for her powers too limited a sphere; she ought to have swayed a nation: she should have been the leader of a turbulent legislative assembly. Nobody could have browbeaten her, none irritated her nerves, exhausted her patience, or over-

reached her astuteness. In her own single person, she could have comprised the duties of a first minister and a superintendent of police. Wise, firm, faithless; secret, crafty, passionless; watchful and inscrutable; acute and insensate—withal perfectly decorous—what more could be desired?

The sensible reader will not suppose that I gained all the knowledge here condensed for his benefit in one month, or in one half-year. No! what I saw at first was the thriving outside of a large and flourishing educational establishment. Here was a great house, full of healthy, lively girls, all well-dressed and many of them handsome, gaining knowledge by a marvellously easy method, without painful exertion or useless waste of spirits; not, perhaps, making very rapid progress in anything; taking it easy, but still always employed, and never oppressed. Here was a corps of teachers and masters more stringently tasked, as all the real head-labour was to be done by them, in order to save the pupils, yet having their duties so arranged that they relieved each other in quick succession whenever the work was severe: here, in short, was a foreign school; of which the life, movement, and variety made it a complete and most charming contrast to many English institutions of the same kind.

Behind the house was a large garden, and in summer the pupils almost lived out of doors amongst the rose-bushes and the fruit-trees. Under the vast and vine-draped berceau, Madame would take her seat on summer afternoons, and send for the classes, in turns, to sit round her and sew and read. Meantime, masters came and went, delivering short and lively lectures, rather than lessons, and the pupils made notes of their instructions, or did *not* make them—just as inclination prompted; secure that, in case of neglect, they could copy the notes of their companions. Besides the regular monthly *jours de sortie,* the Catholic fête-days brought a succession of holidays all the year round; and sometimes on a bright summer morning, or soft summer evening, the boarders were taken out for a long walk into the country, regaled with *gaufres* and *vin blanc,* or new milk and *pain bis,* or *pistolets au beurre* (rolls) and coffee. All this seemed very pleasant, and Madame appeared goodness itself; and the teachers not so bad but they might be worse; and the pupils perhaps a little noisy and rough, but types of health and glee.

Thus did the view appear, seen through the enchantment of distance; but there came a time when distance was to melt for me—when I was to be called down from my watch-tower of the nursery, whence I had hitherto made my observations, and was to be compelled into closer intercourse with this little world of the Rue Fossette.

I was one day sitting upstairs, as usual, hearing the children their English lessons, and at the same time turning a silk dress for Madame, when she came sauntering into the room with that absorbed air and brow of hard thought she sometimes wore, and which made her look so little genial. Dropping into a seat opposite mine, she remained some minutes silent. Désirée, the eldest girl, was reading to me some little essay of Mrs. Barbauld's, and I was making her translate currently from English to French as she proceeded, by way of ascertaining that she comprehended what she read: Madame listened.

Presently, without preface or prelude, she said, almost in the tone of one making an accusation, ''Meess, in England you were a governess.''

''No, Madame,'' said I, smiling, ''you are mistaken.''

''Is this your first essay at teaching—this attempt with my children?''

I assured her it was. Again she became silent; but looking up, as I took a pin from the cushion, I found myself an object of study: she held me under her eye; she seemed turning me round in her thoughts—measuring my fitness for a purpose, weighing my value in a plan. Madame had, ere this, scrutinised all I had, and I believe she esteemed herself cognisant of much that I was; but from that day, for the space of about a fortnight, she tried me by new tests. She listened at the nursery door when I was shut in with the children; she followed me at a cautious distance when I walked out with them, stealing within ear-shot whenever the trees of park

or boulevard afforded a sufficient screen: a strict preliminary process having thus been observed, she made a move forward.

One morning, coming on me abruptly, and with the semblance of hurry, she said she found herself placed in a little dilemma; Mr. Wilson, the English master, had failed to come at his hour; she feared he was ill; the pupils were waiting in classe; there was no one to give a lesson; should I, for once, object to giving a short dictation exercise, just that the pupils might not have it to say they had missed their English lesson?

"In classe, Madame?" I asked.

"Yes, in classe: in the second division."

"Where there are sixty pupils," said I; for I knew the number, and with my usual base habit of cowardice I shrank into my sloth like a snail into a shell, and alleged incapacity and impracticability as a pretext to escape action. If left to myself, I should infallibly have let this chance slip. Inadventurous, unstirred by impulses of practical ambition, I was capable of sitting twenty years teaching infants the hornbook, turning silk dresses, and making children's frocks. Not that true contentment dignified this infatuated resignation: my work had neither charm for my taste, nor hold on my interest; but it seemed to me a great thing to be without heavy anxiety, and relieved from intimate trial: the negation of severe suffering was the nearest approach to happiness I expected to know. Besides, I seemed to hold two lives— the life of thought, and that of reality; and, provided the former was nourished with a sufficiency of the strange necromantic joys of fancy, the privileges of the latter might remain limited to daily bread, hourly work, and a roof of shelter.

"Come," said Madame, as I stooped more busily than ever over the cutting-out of a child's pinafore, "leave that work."

"But Fifine wants it, Madame."

"Fifine must want it, then, for *I* want *you*."

And as Madame Beck did really want and was resolved to have me—as she had long been dissatisfied with the English master, with his shortcomings in punctuality, and his careless method of tuition—as, too, *she* did not lack resolution and practical activity, whether *I* lacked them or not—she, without more ado, made me relinquish thimble and needle; my hand was taken into hers, and I was conducted downstairs. When we reached the carré, a large square hall between the dwelling-house and the pensionnat, she paused, dropped my hand, faced and scrutinised me. I was flushed, and tremulous from head to foot: tell it not in Gath, I believe I was crying. In fact, the difficulties before me were far from being wholly imaginary; some of them were real enough; and not the least substantial lay in my want of mastery over the medium through which I should be obliged to teach. I had, indeed, studied French closely since my arrival in Villette; learning its practice by day, and its theory in every leisure moment at night, to as late an hour as the rule of the house would allow candle-light; but I was far from yet being able to trust my powers of correct oral expression.

"Dites donc," said Madame, sternly, "vous sentez vous réellement trop faible?"

I might have said "Yes," and gone back to nursery obscurity, and there, perhaps, mouldered for the rest of my life; but looking up at Madame, I saw in her countenance a something that made me think twice ere I decided. At that instant she did not wear a woman's aspect, but rather a man's. Power of a particular kind strongly limned itself in all her traits, and that power was not *my* kind of power: neither sympathy, nor congeniality, nor submission, were the emotions it awakened. I stood—not soothed, nor won, nor overwhelmed. It seemed as if a challenge of strength between opposing gifts was given, and I suddenly felt all the dishonour of my diffidence, all the pusillanimity of my slackness to aspire.

"Will you," she said, "go backward or forward?" indicating with her hand, first, the small door of communication with the dwelling-house, and then the great double portals of the classes or schoolrooms.

"En avant," I said.

"But," pursued she, cooling as I warmed, and continuing the hard look, from very antipathy to which I drew strength and determination, "can you face the classes, or are you over excited?"

She sneered slightly in saying this: nervous excitability was not much to Madame's taste.

"I am no more excited than this stone," I said, tapping the flag with my toe: "or than you," I added, returning her look.

"Bon! But let me tell you these are not quiet, decorous English girls you are going to encounter. Ce sont des Labassecouriennes, rondes, franches, brusques, et tant soit peu rebelles."

I said: "I know; and I know, too, that though I have studied French hard since I came here, yet I still speak it with far too much hesitation—too little accuracy to be able to command their respect: I shall make blunders that will lay me open to the scorn of the most ignorant. Still, I mean to give the lesson."

"They always throw over timid teachers," said she.

"I know that too, Madame; I have heard how they rebelled against and persecuted Miss Turner"—a poor friendless English teacher, whom Madame had employed, and lightly discarded; and to whose piteous history I was no stranger.

"C'est vrai," said she coolly. "Miss Turner had no more command over them than a servant from the kitchen would have had. She was weak and wavering; she had neither tact nor intelligence, decision nor dignity, Miss Turner would not do for these girls at all."

I made no reply, but advanced to the closed schoolroom door.

"You will not expect aid from me, or from any one," said Madame. "That would at once set you down as incompetent for your office."

I opened the door, let her pass with courtesy, and followed her. There were three schoolrooms, all large. That dedicated to the second division, where I was to figure, was considerably the largest, and accommodated an assemblage more numerous, more turbulent, and infinitely more unmanageable than the other two. In after days, when I knew the ground better, I used to think sometimes (if such a comparison may be permitted) that the quiet, polished, tame first division was to the robust, riotous, demonstrative second division what the English House of Lords is to the House of Commons.

The first glance informed me that many of the pupils were more than girls—quite young women; I knew that some of them were of noble family (as nobility goes in Labassecour), and I was well convinced that not one amongst them was ignorant of my position in Madame's household. As I mounted the estrade (a low platform, raised a step above the flooring), where stood the teacher's chair and desk, I beheld opposite to me a row of eyes and brows that threatened stormy weather—eyes full of insolent light, and brows hard and unblushing as marble. The continental "female" is quite a different being to the insular "female" of the same age and class: I never saw such eyes and brows in England. Madame Beck introduced me in one cool phrase, sailed from the room, and left me alone in my glory.

I shall never forget that first lesson, nor all the under-current of life and character it opened up to me. Then first did I begin rightly to see the wide difference that lies between the novelist's and poet's ideal "jeune fille" and the said "jeune fille" as she really is.

It seems that three titled belles in the first row had sat down predetermined that a bonne d'enfants should not give them lessons in English. They knew they had succeeded in expelling obnoxious teachers before now; they knew that Madame would at any time throw overboard a professeur or maîtresse who became unpopular with the school—that she never assisted a weak official to retain his place—that if he had not strength to fight, or tact to win his way, down he went: looking at "Miss Snowe" they promised themselves an easy victory.

Mesdemoiselles Blanche, Virginie, and Angélique opened the campaign by a series of titterings and whisperings; these soon swelled into murmurs and short laughs, which the remoter benches caught up and echoed more loudly. This growing revolt of sixty against one soon became oppressive enough; my command of French being so limited, and exercised under such cruel constraint.

Could I have but spoken in my own tongue, I felt as if I might have gained a hearing; for, in the first place, though I knew I looked a poor creature, and in many respects actually was so, yet nature had given me a voice that could make itself heard, if lifted in excitement or deepened by emotion. In the second place, while I had no flow, only a hesitating trickle of language, in ordinary circumstances, yet—under stimulus such as was now rife through the mutinous mass—I could, in English, have rolled out readily phrases stigmatising their proceedings as such proceedings deserved to be stigmatised; and then with some sarcasm, flavoured with contemptuous bitterness for the ringleaders, and relieved with easy banter for the weaker but less knavish followers, it seemed to me that one might possibly get command over this wild herd and bring them into training, at least. All I could now do was to walk up to Blanche—Mademoiselle de Melcy, a young baronne—the eldest, tallest, handsomest, and most vicious—stand before her desk, take from under her hand her exercise-book, remount the estrade, deliberately read the composition, which I found very stupid, and as deliberately, and in the face of the whole school, tear the blotted page in two.

This action availed to draw attention and check noise. One girl alone, quite in the background, persevered in the riot with undiminished energy. I looked at her attentively. She had a pale face, hair like night, broad strong eyebrows, decided features, and a dark, mutinous, sinister eye: I noted that she sat close by a little door, which door, I was well aware, opened into a small closet where books were kept. She was standing up for the purpose of conducting her clamour with freer energies. I measured her stature and calculated her strength. She seemed both tall and wiry; but, if the conflict were brief and the attack unexpected, I thought I might manage her.

Advancing up the room, looking as cool and careless as I possibly could, in short, *ayant l'air de rien*; I slightly pushed the door and found it was ajar. In an instant, and with sharpness, I had turned on her. In another instant she occupied the closet, the door was shut, and the key in my pocket.

It so happened that this girl, Dolores by name, and a Catalonian by race, was the sort of character at once dreaded and hated by all her associates; the act of summary justice above noted proved popular: there was not one present but, in her heart, liked to see it done. They were stilled for a moment; then a smile—not a laugh—passed from desk to desk: then—when I had gravely and tranquilly returned to the estrade, courteously requested silence, and commenced a dictation as if nothing at all had happened—the pens travelled peacefully over the pages, and the remainder of the lesson passed in order and industry.

"C'est bien," said Madame Beck, when I came out of class, hot and a little exhausted. "Ça ira."

She had been listening and peeping through a spy-hole the whole time.

From that day I ceased to be nursery governess, and became English teacher. Madame raised my salary; but she got thrice the work out of me she had extracted from Mr. Wilson, at half the expense.

Chapter IX

ISIDORE

MY time was now well and profitably filled up. What with teaching others and studying closely myself, I had hardly a spare moment. It was pleasant. I felt I was

getting on; not lying the stagnant prey of mould and rust, but polishing my faculties and whetting them to a keen edge with constant use. Experience of a certain kind lay before me on no narrow scale. Villette is a cosmopolitan city, and in this school were girls of almost every European nation, and likewise of very varied rank in life. Equality is much practised in Labassecour; though not republican in form, it is nearly so in substance, and at the desks of Madame Beck's establishment the young countess and the young bourgeoise sat side by side. Nor could you always by outward indications decide which was noble and which plebeian; except that, indeed, the latter had often franker and more courteous manners, while the former bore away the bell for a delicately-balanced combination of insolence and deceit. In the former there was often quick French blood mixed with the marsh-phlegm: I regret to say that the effect of this vivacious fluid chiefly appeared in the oilier glibness with which flattery and fiction ran from the tongue, and in a manner lighter and livelier, but quite heartless and insincere.

To do all parties justice, the honest aboriginal Labassecouriennes had an hypocrisy of their own, too; but it was of a coarse order, such as could deceive few. Whenever a lie was necessary for their occasions, they brought it out with a careless ease and breadth altogether untroubled by the rebuke of conscience. Not a soul in Madame Beck's house, from the scullion to the directress herself, but was above being ashamed of a lie; they thought nothing of it: to invent might not be precisely a virtue, but it was the most venial of faults. "J'ai menti plusieurs fois" formed an item of every girl's and woman's monthly confession; the priest heard unshocked, and absolved unreluctant. If they had missed going to mass, or read a chapter of a novel, that was another thing: these were crimes whereof rebuke and penance were the unfailing meed.

While yet but half-conscious of this state of things, and unlearned in its results, I got on in my new sphere very well. After the first few difficult lessons, given amidst peril and on the edge of a moral volcano that rumbled under my feet and sent sparks and hot fumes into my eyes, the eruptive spirit seemed to subside, as far as I was concerned. My mind was a good deal bent on success: I could not bear the thought of being baffled by mere undisciplined disaffection and wanton indocility in this first attempt to get on in life. Many hours of the night I used to lie awake, thinking what plan I had best adopt to get a reliable hold on these mutineers, to bring this stiff-necked tribe under permanent influence. In the first place, I saw plainly that aid in no shape was to be expected from Madame: her righteous plan was to maintain an unbroken popularity with the pupils, at any and every cost of justice or comfort to the teachers. For a teacher to seek her alliance in any crisis of insubordination was equivalent to securing her own expulsion. In intercourse with her pupils, Madame only took to herself what was pleasant, amiable, and recommendatory; rigidly requiring of her lieutenants sufficiency for every annoying crisis, where to act with adequate promptitude was to be unpopular. Thus, I must look only to myself.

Imprimis—it was clear as the day that this swinish multitude were not to be driven by force. They were to be humoured, borne with very patiently; a courteous though sedate manner impressed them: a very rare flash of raillery did good. Severe or continuous mental application they could not, or would not, bear: heavy demand on the memory, the reason, the attention, they rejected point-blank. Where an English girl of not more than average capacity and docility would quietly take a theme and bind herself to the task of comprehension and mastery, a Labassecourienne would laugh in your face, and throw it back to you with the phrase,—"Dieu que c'est difficile! Je n'en veux pas. Cela m'ennuie trop."

A teacher who understood her business would take it back at once, without hesitation, contest, or expostulation—proceed with even exaggerated care to smooth every difficulty, to reduce it to the level of their understandings, return it to them thus modified, and lay on the lash of sarcasm with unsparing hand. They would

feel the sting, perhaps wince a little under it; but they bore no malice against this sort of attack, provided the sneer was not *sour,* but *hearty,* and that it held well up to them, in a clear, light, and bold type, so that she who ran might read, their incapacity, ignorance, and sloth. They would riot for three additional lines to a lesson; but I never knew them rebel against a wound given to their self-respect: the little they had of that quality was trained to be crushed, and it rather liked the pressure of a firm heel than otherwise.

By degrees, as I acquired fluency and freedom in their language, and could make such application of its more nervous idioms as suited their case, the elder and more intelligent girls began rather to like me in their way: I noticed that whenever a pupil had been roused to feel in her soul the stirring of worthy emulation, or the quickening of honest shame, from that date she was won. If I could but once make their (usually large) ears burn under their thick glossy hair, all was comparatively well. By-and-by bouquets began to be laid on my desk in the morning; by way of acknowledgment for this little foreign attention, I used sometimes to walk with a select few during recreation. In the course of conversation it befell once or twice that I made an unpremeditated attempt to rectify some of their singularly distorted notions of principle; especially I expressed my ideas of the evil and baseness of a lie. In an unguarded moment, I chanced to say that, of the two errors, I considered falsehood worse than an occasional lapse in church attendance. The poor girls were tutored to report in Catholic ears whatever the Protestant teacher said. An edifying consequence ensued. Something—an unseen, an indefinite, a nameless something—stole between myself and these my best pupils: the bouquets continued to be offered, but conversation thenceforth became impracticable. As I paced the alleys or sat in the berceau, a girl never came to my right hand but a teacher, as if by magic, appeared on my left. Also, wonderful to relate, Madame's shoes of silence brought her continually to my back, as quick, as noiseless and unexpected, as some wandering zephyr.

The opinion of my Catholic acquaintance concerning my spiritual prospects was somewhat naïvely expressed to me on one occasion. A pensionnaire, to whom I had rendered some little service, exclaimed one day as she sat beside me—

"Mademoiselle, what a pity you are a Protestant!"

"Why, Isabelle?"

"Parceque, quand vous serez morte—vous brûlerez tout de suite dans l'Enfer."

"Croyez-vouz?"

"Certainement que j'y crois: tout le monde le sait; et d'ailleurs le prêtre me l'a dit."

Isabelle was an odd, blunt little creature. She added, *sotto voce*—

"Pour assurer votre salut là-haut, on ferait bien de vous brûler toute vie ici-bas."

I laughed, as, indeed, it was impossible to do otherwise.

Has the reader forgotten Miss Ginevra Fanshawe? If so, I must be allowed to re-introduce that young lady as a thriving pupil of Madame Beck's; for such she was. On her arrival in the Rue Fossette, two or three days after my sudden settlement there, she encountered me with very little surprise. She must have had good blood in her veins, for never was any duchess more perfectly, radically, unaffectedly nonchalante than she: a weak, transient amaze was all she knew of the sensation of wonder. Most of her other faculties seemed to be in the same flimsy condition: her liking and disliking, her love and hate, were mere cobweb and gossamer; but she had one thing about her that seemed strong and durable enough, and that was—her selfishness.

She was not proud; and—bonne d'enfants as I was—she would forthwith have made of me a sort of friend and confidant. She teased me with a thousand vapid complaints about school-quarrels and household economy: the cookery was not to her taste; the people about her, teachers and pupils, she held to be despicable,

because they were foreigners. I bore with her abuse of the Friday's salt fish and hard eggs—with her invective against the soup, the bread, the coffee—with some patience for a time; but at last, wearied by iteration, I turned crusty, and put her to rights: a thing I ought to have done in the very beginning, for a salutary setting down always agreed with her.

Much longer had I to endure her demands on me in the way of work. Her wardrobe, so far as concerned articles of external wear, was well and elegantly supplied; but there were other habiliments not so carefully provided: what she had, needed frequent repair. She hated needle-drudgery herself, and she would bring her hose, etc., to me in heaps, to be mended. A compliance of some weeks threatening to result in the establishment of an intolerable bore—I at last distinctly told her she must make up her mind to mend her own garments. She cried on receiving this information, and accused me of having ceased to be her friend; but I held by my decision, and let the hysterics pass as they could.

Notwithstanding these foibles, and various others needless to mention—but by no means of a refined or elevating character—how pretty she was! How charming she looked, when she came down on a sunny Sunday morning, well-dressed, and well-humoured, robed in pale lilac silk, and with her fair long curls reposing on her white shoulders. Sunday was a holiday which she always passed with friends resident in town; and amongst these friends she speedily gave me to understand was one who would fain become something more. By glimpses and hints it was shown me, and by the general buoyancy of her look and manner it was ere long proved, that ardent admiration—perhaps genuine love—was at her command. She called her suitor "Isidore": this, however, she intimated was not his real name, but one by which it pleased her to baptise him—his own, she hinted, not being "very pretty." Once, when she had been bragging about the vehemence of "Isidore's" attachment, I asked if she loved him in return.

"Comme cela," said she: "he is handsome, and he loves me to distraction, so that I am well amused. Ça suffit."

Finding that she carried the thing on longer than, from her very fickle tastes, I had anticipated, I one day took it upon me to make serious inquiries as to whether the gentleman was such as her parents, and especially her uncle—on whom, it appeared, she was dependent—would be likely to approve. She allowed that this was very doubtful, as she did not believe "Isidore" had much money.

"Do you encourage him?" I asked.

"Furieusement, sometimes," said she.

"Without being certain that you will be permitted to marry him?"

"Oh, how dowdyish you are! I don't want to be married. I am too young."

"But if he loves you as much as you say, and yet it comes to nothing in the end, he will be made miserable."

"Of course he will break his heart. I should be shocked and disappointed if he didn't."

"I wonder whether this M. Isidore is a fool?" said I.

"He is, about me; but he is wise in other things, à ce qu'on dit. Mrs. Cholmondeley considers him extremely clever: she says he will push his way by his talents; all I know is, that he does little more than sigh in my presence, and that I can wind him round my little finger."

Wishing to get a more definite idea of this love-stricken M. Isidore, whose position seemed to me of the least secure, I requested her to favour me with a personal description; but she could not describe: she had neither words nor the power of putting them together so as to make graphic phrases. She even seemed not properly to have noticed him: nothing of his looks, of the changes in his countenance, had touched her heart or dwelt in her memory—that he was "beau, mais plutôt bel homme que joli garçon," was all she could assert. My patience would often have failed, and my interest flagged, in listening to her, but for one

thing. All the hints she dropped, all the details she gave, went unconsciously to prove, to my thinking, that M. Isidore's homage was offered with great delicacy and respect. I informed her very plainly that I believed him much too good for her, and intimated with equal plainness my impression that she was but a vain coquette. She laughed, shook her curls from her eyes, and danced away as if I had paid her a compliment.

Miss Ginevra's school-studies were little better than nominal; there were but three things she practised in earnest, viz., music, singing, and dancing; also embroidering the fine cambric handkerchiefs which she could not afford to buy ready worked: such mere trifles as lessons in history, geography, grammar, and arithmetic, she left undone, or got others to do for her. Very much of her time was spent in visiting. Madame, aware that her stay at school was now limited to a certain period which would not be extended whether she made progress or not, allowed her great licence in this particular. Mrs. Cholmondeley—her chaperon—a gay, fashionable lady, invited her whenever she had company at her own house, and sometimes took her to evening parties at the houses of her acquaintance. Ginevra perfectly approved this mode of procedure: it had but one inconvenience; she was obliged to be well dressed, and she had not money to buy variety of dresses. All her thoughts turned on this difficulty; her whole soul was occupied with expedients for effecting its solution. It was wonderful to witness the activity of her otherwise indolent mind on this point, and to see the much-daring intrepidity to which she was spurred by a sense of necessity, and the wish to shine.

She begged boldly of Mrs. Cholmondeley—boldly, I say: not with an air of reluctant shame, but in this strain—

"My darling Mrs. C., I have nothing in the world fit to wear for your party next week; you *must* give me a book-muslin dress, and then a *ceinture bleu celeste: do*—there's an angel! will you?"

The "darling Mrs. C." yielded at first; but finding that applications increased as they were complied with, she was soon obliged, like all Miss Fanshawe's friends, to oppose resistance to encroachment. After a while I heard no more of Mrs. Cholmondeley's presents; but still, visiting went on, and absolutely necessary dresses continued to be supplied: also many little expensive etcetera—gloves, bouquets, even trinkets. These things, contrary to her custom, and even nature—for she was not secretive—were most sedulously kept out of sight for a time; but one evening, when she was going to a large party for which particular care and elegance of costume were demanded, she could not resist coming to my chamber to show herself in all her splendour.

Beautiful she looked: so young, so fresh, and with a delicacy of skin and flexibility of shape altogether English, and not found in the list of continental female charms. Her dress was new, costly, and perfect. I saw at a glance that it lacked none of those finishing details which cost so much, and give to the general effect such an air of tasteful completeness.

I viewed her from top to toe. She turned airily round that I might survey her on all sides. Conscious of her charms, she was in her best humour: her rather small blue eyes sparkled gleefully. She was going to bestow on me a kiss, in her schoolgirl fashion of showing her delight: but I said, "Steady! Let us be steady, and know what we are about, and find out the meaning of our magnificence"—and so put her off at arm's length, to undergo cooler inspection.

"Shall I do?" was her question.

"Do?" said I. "There are different ways of doing; and, by my word, I don't understand yours."

"But how do I look?"

"You look well dressed."

She thought the praise not warm enough, and proceeded to direct attention to the various decorative points of her attire. "Look at this parure," said she. "The

brooch, the earrings, the bracelets: no one in the school has such a set—not Madame herself.''

''I see them all.'' (Pause.) ''Did M. de Bassompierre give you those jewels?''

''My uncle knows nothing about them.''

''Were they presents from Mrs. Cholmondeley?''

''Not they, indeed. Mrs. Cholmondeley is a mean, stingy creature; she never gives me anything now.''

I did not choose to ask any further questions, but turned abruptly away.

''Now, old Crusty—old Diogenes'' (these were her familiar terms for me when we disagreed), ''what is the matter now?''

''Take yourself away. I have no pleasure in looking at you or your parure.''

For an instant, she seemed taken by surprise.

''What now, Mother Wisdom? I have not got into debt for it—that is, not for the jewels, nor the gloves, nor the bouquet. My dress is certainly not paid for, but uncle de Bassompierre will pay it in the bill: he never notices items, but just looks at the total; and he is so rich, one need not care about a few guineas more or less.''

''Will you go? I want to shut the door. . . . Ginevra, people may tell you you are very handsome in that ball-attire; but, in *my* eyes, you will never look so pretty as you did in the gingham gown and plain straw bonnet you wore when I first saw you.''

''Other people have not your puritanical tastes,'' was her angry reply. ''And, besides, I see no right you have to sermonise me.''

''Certainly! I have little right; and you, perhaps, have still less to come flourishing and fluttering into my chamber—a mere jay in borrowed plumes. I have not the least respect for your feathers, Miss Fanshawe; and especially the peacock's eyes, you call a parure: very pretty things, if you had bought them with money which was your own, and which you could well spare, but not at all pretty under present circumstances.''

''On est là pour Mademoiselle Fanshawe!'' was announced by the portress, and away she tripped.

This semi-mystery of the parure was not solved till two or three days afterwards, when she came to make a voluntary confession.

''You need not be sulky with me,'' she began, ''in the idea that I am running somebody, papa or M. de Bassompierre, deeply into debt. I assure you nothing remains unpaid for, but the few dresses I have lately had: all the rest is settled.''

''There,'' I thought, ''lies the mystery; considering that they were not given you by Mrs. Cholmondeley, and that your own means are limited to a few shillings, of which I know you to be excessively careful.''

''Écoutez;'' she went on, drawing near and speaking in her most confidential and coaxing tone; for my ''sulkiness'' was inconvenient to her: she liked me to be in a talking and listening mood, even if I only talked to chide and listened to rail. ''Écoutez, chère grogneuse! I will tell you all how and about it; and you will then see, not only how right the whole thing is, but how cleverly managed. In the first place, I *must* go out. Papa himself said that he wished me to see something of the world; he particularly remarked to Mrs. Cholmondeley that, though I was a sweet creature enough, I had rather a bread-and-butter-eating, school-girl air; of which it was his special desire that I should get rid, by an introduction to society here, before I make my regular début in England. Well, then, if I go out, I *must* dress. Mrs. Cholmondeley is turned shabby, and will give nothing more; it would be too hard upon uncle to make him pay for *all* the things I need: *that* you can't deny—*that* agrees with your own preachments. Well, but SOMEBODY who heard me (quite by chance, I assure you) complaining to Mrs. Cholmondeley of my distressed circumstances, and what straits I was put to for an ornament or two—*somebody*, far from grudging one a present, was quite delighted at the idea of being permitted to offer some trifle. You should have seen what a blanc-bec he looked when he

first spoke of it: how he hesitated and blushed, and positively trembled from fear of a repulse.''

"That will do, Miss Fanshawe. I suppose I am to understand that M. Isidore is the benefactor: that it is from him you have accepted that costly parure; that he supplies your bouquets and your gloves?''

"You express yourself so disagreeably,'' said she, "one hardly knows how to answer; what I mean to say is, that I occasionally allow Isidore the pleasure and honour of expressing his homage by the offer of a trifle.''

"It comes to the same thing. . . . Now, Ginevra, to speak the plain truth, I don't very well understand these matters; but I believe you are doing very wrong—seriously wrong. Perhaps, however, you now feel certain that you will be able to marry M. Isidore; your parents and uncle have given their consent, and, for your part, you love him entirely?''

"Mais pas du tout!'' (she always had recourse to French when about to say something specially heartless and perverse). "Je suis sa reine, mais il n'est pas mon roi.''

"Excuse me, I must believe this language is mere nonsense and coquetry. There is nothing great about you, yet you are above profiting by the good-nature and purse of a man to whom you feel absolute indifference. You love M. Isidore far more than you think, or will avow.''

"No. I danced with a young officer the other night, whom I love a thousand times more than he. I often wonder why I feel so very cold to Isidore, for everybody says he is handsome, and other ladies admire him; but, somehow, he bores me: let me see now how it is . . .''

And she seemed to make an effort to reflect. In this I encouraged her. "Yes!'' I said, "try to get a clear idea of the state of your mind. To me it seems in a great mess—chaotic as a rag-bag.''

"It is something in this fashion,'' she cried out ere long: "the man is too romantic and devoted, and he expects something more of me than I find it convenient to be. He thinks I am perfect: furnished with all sorts of sterling qualities and solid virtues, such as I never had, nor intend to have. Now, one can't help, in his presence, rather trying to justify his good opinion; and it does so tire one to be goody, and to talk sense,—for he really thinks I am sensible. I am far more at my ease with you, old lady—you, you dear crosspatch—who take me at my lowest, and know me to be coquettish, and ignorant, and flirting, and fickle, and silly, and selfish, and all the other sweet things you and I have agreed to be a part of my character.''

"This is all very well,'' I said, making a strenuous effort to preserve that gravity and severity which ran risk of being shaken by this whimsical candour, "but it does not alter that wretched business of the presents. Pack them up, Ginevra, like a good, honest girl, and send them back.''

"Indeed, I won't,'' said she stoutly.

"Then you are deceiving M. Isidore. It stands to reason that by accepting his presents you give him to understand he will one day receive an equivalent, in your regard . . .''

"But he won't,'' she interrupted: "he has his equivalent now, in the pleasure of seeing me wear them—quite enough for him: he is only bourgeois.''

This phrase, in its senseless arrogance, quite cured me of the temporary weakness which had made me relax my tone and aspect. She rattled on—

"My present business is to enjoy youth, and not to think of fettering myself, by promise or vow, to this man or that. When first I saw Isidore, I believed he would help me to enjoy it. I believed he would be content with my being a pretty girl; and that we should meet and part and flutter about like two butterflies, and be happy. Lo and behold! I find him at times as grave as a judge, and deep-feeling and thoughtful. Bah! Les penseurs, les hommes profonds et passionés, ne sont pas à mon goût. Le Colonel Alfred de Hamal suits me far better. Va pour les beaux

fats et les jolis fripons! Vive les joies et les plaisirs! A bas les grandes passions et les sévères vertus!''

She looked for an answer to this tirade. I gave none.

''J'aime mon beau Colonel,'' she went on: ''je n'aimerai jamais son rival. Je ne serai jamais femme de bourgeois, moi!''

I now signified that it was imperatively necessary my apartment should be relieved of the honour of her presence: she went away laughing.

Chapter X

DR. JOHN

MADAME BECK was a most consistent character; forbearing with all the world, and tender to no part of it. Her own children drew her into no deviation from the even tenor of her stoic calm. She was solicitous about her family, vigilant for their interests and physical well-being; but she never seemed to know the wish to take her little children upon her lap, to press their rosy lips with her own, to gather them in a genial embrace, to shower on them softly the benignant caress, the loving word.

I have watched her sometimes sitting in the garden, viewing the little ones afar off, as they walked in a distant alley with Trinette, their *bonne*; in her mien spoke care and prudence. I know she often pondered anxiously what she called ''leur avenir''; but if the youngest, a puny and delicate but engaging child, chancing to spy her, broke from its nurse, and toddling down the walk, came all eager and laughing and panting to clasp her knee, Madame would just calmly put out one hand, so as to prevent inconvenient concussion from the child's sudden onset: ''Prends garde, mon enfant!'' she would say unmoved, patiently permit it to stand near her a few moments, and then, without smile or kiss, or endearing syllable, rise and lead it back to Trinette.

Her demeanour to the elder girl was equally characteristic in another way. This was a vicious child. ''Quelle peste que cette Désirée! Quel poison que cet enfant là!'' were the expressions dedicated to her, alike in kitchen and in schoolroom. Amongst her other endowments she boasted an exquisite skill in the art of provocation, sometimes driving her bonne and the servants almost wild. She would steal to their attics, open their drawers and boxes, wantonly tear their best caps and soil their best shawls; she would watch her opportunity to get at the beaufet of the salle à manger, where she would smash articles of porcelain or glass—or to the cupboard of the store-room, where she would plunder the preserves, drink the sweet wine, break jars and bottles, and so contrive as to throw the onus of suspicion on the cook and the kitchen-maid. All this when Madame saw, and of which when she received report, her sole observation, uttered with matchless serenity, was—

''Désirée a besoin d'une surveillance toute particulière.'' Accordingly she kept this promising olive-branch a good deal at her side. Never once, I believe, did she tell her faithfully of her faults, explain the evil of such habits, and show the results which must thence ensue. Surveillance must work the whole cure. It failed of course. Désirée was kept in some measure from the servants, but she teased and pillaged her mamma instead. Whatever belonging to Madame's work-table or toilet she could lay her hands on, she stole and hid. Madame saw all this, but she still pretended not to see: she had not rectitude of soul to confront the child with her vices. When an article disappeared whose value rendered restitution necessary, she would profess to think that Désirée had taken it away in play, and beg her to restore it. Désirée was not to be so cheated: she had learned to bring falsehood to the aid of theft, and would deny having touched the brooch, ring, or scissors.

Carrying on the hollow system, the mother would calmly assume an air of belief, and afterwards ceaselessly watch and dog the child till she tracked her to her hiding-places—some hole in the garden-wall, some chink or cranny in garret or out-house. This done, Madame would send Désirée out for a walk with her bonne, and profit by her absence to rob the robber. Désirée proved herself the true daughter of her astute parent by never suffering either her countenance or manner to betray the least sign of mortification on discovering the loss.

The second child, Fifine, was said to be like its dead father. Certainly, though the mother had given it her healthy frame, her blue eye and ruddy cheek, not from her was derived its moral being. It was an honest, gleeful little soul: a passionate, warm-tempered, bustling creature it was too, and of the sort likely to blunder often into perils and difficulties. One day it bethought itself to fall from top to bottom of a steep flight of stone steps; and when Madame, hearing the noise (she always heard every noise), issued from the salle à manger and picked it up, she said quietly—

"Cet enfant a un os de cassé."

At first we hoped this was not the case. It was, however, but too true: one little plump arm hung powerless.

"Let Meess" (meaning me) "take her," said Madame; "et qu'on aille tout de suite chercher un fiacre."

In a fiacre she promptly, but with admirable coolness and self-possession, departed to fetch a surgeon.

It appeared she did not find the family surgeon at home; but that mattered not: she sought until she laid her hand on a substitute to her mind, and brought him back with her. Meantime I had cut the child's sleeve from its arm, undressed and put it to bed.

We none of us, I suppose (by *we* I mean the bonne, the cook, the portress, and myself, all which personages were now gathered in the small and heated chamber), looked very scrutinisingly at the new doctor when he came into the room. I, at least, was taken up with endeavouring to soothe Fifine; whose cries (for she had good lungs) were appalling to hear. These cries redoubled in intensity as the stranger approached her bed. When he took her up, "Let alone!" she cried passionately, in her broken English (for she spoke English, as did the other children). "I will not you: I will Dr. Pillule!"

"And Dr. Pillule is my very good friend," was the answer, in perfect English; "but he is busy at a place three leagues off, and I am come in his stead. So now, when we get a little calmer, we must commence business; and we will soon have that unlucky little arm bandaged and in right order."

Hereupon he called for a glass of *eau sucrée,* fed her with some teaspoonful of the sweet liquid (Fifine was a frank gourmande; anybody could win her heart through her palate), promised her more when the operation should be over, and promptly went to work. Some assistance being needed, he demanded it of the cook, a robust, strong-armed woman; but she, the portress, and the nurse instantly fled. I did not like to touch that small, tortured limb, but, thinking there was no alternative, my hand was already extended to do what was requisite. I was anticipated; Madame Beck had put out her own hand: hers was steady, while mine trembled.

"Ça vaudra mieux," said the doctor, turning from me to her.

He showed wisdom in his choice. Mine would have been feigned stoicism, forced fortitude. Hers was neither forced nor feigned.

"Merci Madame; très bien, fort bien!" said the operator, when he had finished. "Voilà un sang-froid bien opportun, et qui vaut mille élans de sensibilité déplacée."

He was pleased with her firmness, she with his compliment. It is likely, too, that his whole general appearance, his voice, mien, and manner, wrought impressions in his favour. Indeed, when you looked well at him, and when a lamp was brought in—for it was evening and now waxing dusk—you saw that, unless Madame Beck

had been less than woman, it could not well be otherwise. This young doctor (he *was* young) had no common aspect. His stature looked imposingly tall in that little chamber, and amidst that group of Dutch-made women; his profile was clear, fine, and expressive: perhaps his eye glanced from face to face rather too vividly, too quickly, and too often; but it had a most pleasant character, and so had his mouth; his chin was full, cleft, Grecian, and perfect. As to his smile, one could not in a hurry make up one's mind as to the descriptive epithet it merited; there was something in it that pleased, but something, too, that brought surging up into the mind all one's foibles and weak points: all that could lay one open to a laugh. Yet Fifine liked this doubtful smile, and thought the owner genial: much as he had hurt her, she held out her hand to bid him a friendly good-night. He patted the little hand kindly, and then he and Madame went downstairs together; she talking in her highest tide of spirits and volubility, he listening with an air of good-natured amenity, dashed with that unconscious roguish archness I find it difficult to describe.

I noticed that though he spoke French well, he spoke English better; he had, too, an English complexion, eyes, and form. I noticed more. As he passed me in leaving the room, turning his face in my direction one moment—not to address me, but to speak to Madame, yet so standing, that I almost necessarily looked up at him—a recollection which had been struggling to form in my memory, since the first moment I heard his voice, started up perfected. This was the very gentleman to whom I had spoken at the bureau; who had helped me in the matter of the trunk; who had been my guide through the dark wet park. Listening, as he passed down the long vestibule out into the street, I recognised his very tread; it was the same firm and equal stride I had followed under the dripping trees.

It was to be concluded that this young surgeon-physician's first visit to the Rue Fossette would be the last. The respectable Dr. Pillule being expected home the next day, there appeared no reason why his temporary substitute should again represent him; but the Fates had written their decree to the contrary.

Dr. Pillule had been summoned to see a rich old hypochondriac at the antique university town of Bouquin-Moisi, and upon his prescribing change of air and travel as remedies, he was retained to accompany the timid patient on a tour of some weeks; it but remained, therefore, for the new doctor to continue his attendance at the Rue Fossette.

I often saw him when he came; for Madame would not trust the little invalid to Trinette, but required me to spend much of my time in the nursery. I think he was skilful. Fifine recovered rapidly under his care, yet even her convalescence did not hasten his dismissal. Destiny and Madame Beck seemed in league, and both had ruled that he should make deliberate acquaintance with the vestibule, the private staircase, and upper chambers of the Rue Fossette.

No sooner did Fifine emerge from his hands than Désirée declared herself ill. That possessed child had a genius for simulation, and captivated by the attentions and indulgences of a sick-room, she came to the conclusion that an illness would perfectly accommodate her tastes, and took her bed accordingly. She acted well, and her mother still better; for while the whole case was transparent to Madame Beck as the day, she treated it with an astonishingly well-assured air of gravity and good faith.

What surprised me was, that Dr. John (so the young Englishman had taught Fifine to call him, and we all took from her the habit of addressing him by this name, till it became an established custom, and he was known by no other in the Rue Fossette)—that Dr. John consented tacitly to adopt Madame's tactics, and to fall in with her manœuvres. He betrayed, indeed, a period of comic doubt, cast one or two rapid glances from the child to the mother, indulged in an interval of self-consultation, but finally resigned himself with a good grace to play his part in the farce. Désirée ate like a raven, gambolled day and night in her bed, pitched

tents with the sheets and blankets, lounged like a Turk amidst pillows and bolsters, diverted herself with throwing her shoes at her bonne and grimacing at her sisters—overflowed, in short, with unmerited health and evil spirits; only languishing when her mamma and the physician paid their diurnal visit. Madame Beck, I knew, was glad, at any price, to have her daughter in bed out of the way of mischief; but I wondered that Dr. John did not tire of the business.

Every day, on this mere pretext of a motive, he gave punctual attendance; Madame always received him with the same empressement, the same sunshine for himself, the same admirably counterfeited air of concern for her child. Dr. John wrote harmless prescriptions for the patient, and viewed her mother with a shrewdly sparkling eye. Madame caught his rallying looks without resenting them—she had too much good sense for that. Supple as the young doctor seemed, one could not despise him—this pliant part was evidently not adopted in the design to curry favour with his employer: while he liked his office at the pensionnat, and lingered strangely about the Rue Fossette, he was independent, almost careless in his carriage there; and yet, too, he was often thoughtful and preoccupied.

It was not perhaps my business to observe the mystery of his bearing, or search out its origin or aim; but, placed as I was, I could hardly help it. He laid himself open to my observation, according to my presence in the room just that degree of notice and consequence a person of my exterior habitually expects; that is to say, about what is given to unobtrusive articles of furniture, chairs of ordinary joiner's work, and carpets of no striking pattern. Often, while waiting for Madame, he would muse, smile, watch, or listen like a man who thinks himself alone. I, meantime, was free to puzzle over his countenance and movements, and wonder what could be the meaning of that peculiar interest and attachment—all mixed up with doubt and strangeness, and inexplicably ruled by some presiding spell—which wedded him to this demi-convent, secluded in the built-up core of a capital. He, I believe, never remembered that I had eyes in my head, much less a brain behind them.

Nor would he ever have found this out, but that one day, while he sat in the sunshine and I was observing the colouring of his hair, whiskers, and complexion—the whole being of such a tone as a strong light brings out with somewhat perilous force (indeed I recollect I was driven to compare his beamy head in my thoughts to that of the "golden image" which Nebuchadnezzar, the king, had set up), an idea new, sudden, and startling, riveted my attention with an overmastering strength and power of attraction. I know not to this day how I looked at him: the force of surprise, and also of conviction, made me forget myself; and I only recovered wonted consciousness when I saw that his notice was arrested, and that it had caught my movement in a clear little oval mirror fixed in the side of the window recess—by the aid of which reflector Madame often secretly spied persons walking in the garden below. Though of so gay and sanguine a temperament, he was not without a certain nervous sensitiveness which made him ill at ease under a direct, inquiring gaze. On surprising me thus, he turned and said, in a tone which, though courteous, had just so much dryness in it as to mark a shade of annoyance, as well as to give to what was said the character of rebuke—

"Mademoiselle does not spare me: I am not vain enough to fancy that it is my merits which attract her attention; it must then be some defect. Dare I ask—what?"

I was confounded, as the reader may suppose, yet not with an irrecoverable confusion; being conscious that it was from no emotion of incautious admiration, nor yet in a spirit of unjustifiable inquisitiveness, that I had incurred this reproof. I might have cleared myself on the spot, but would not. I did not speak. I was not in the habit of speaking to him. Suffering him, then, to think what he chose and accuse me of what he would, I resumed some work I had dropped, and kept my head bent over it during the remainder of his stay. There is a perverse mood of the mind which is rather soothed than irritated by misconstruction; and in quarters

where we can never be rightly known, we take pleasure, I think, in being consummately ignored. What honest man, on being casually taken for a house-breaker, does not feel rather tickled than vexed at the mistake?

Chapter XI

THE PORTRESSE'S CABINET

IT was summer and very hot. Georgette, the youngest of Madame Beck's children, took a fever. Désirée, suddenly cured of her ailments, was, together with Fifine, packed off to Bonne-Maman in the country, by way of precaution against infection. Medical aid was now really needed, and Madame, choosing to ignore the return of Dr. Pillule, who had been at home a week, conjured his English rival to continue his visits. One or two of the pensionnaires complained of headache, and in other respects seemed slightly to participate in Georgette's ailment. "Now, at last," I thought, "Dr. Pillule must be recalled: the prudent directress will never venture to permit the attendance of so young a man on the pupils."

The directress was very prudent, but she could also be intrepidly venturous. She actually introduced Dr. John to the school-division of the premises, and established him in attendance on the proud and handsome Blanche de Melcy, and the vain, flirting Angélique, her friend. Dr. John, I thought, testified a certain gratification at this mark of confidence; and if discretion of bearing could have justified the step, it would by him have been amply justified. Here, however, in this land of convents and confessionals, such a presence as his was not to be suffered with impunity in a "pensionnat de demoiselles." The school gossiped, the kitchen whispered, the town caught the rumour, parents wrote letters and paid visits of remonstrance. Madame, had she been weak, would now have been lost; a dozen rival educational houses were ready to improve this false step—if false it were—to her ruin; but Madame was not weak, and little Jesuit though she might be, yet I clapped the hands of my heart, and with its voice cried "Brava!" as I watched her able bearing, her skilled management, her temper and her firmness on this occasion.

She met the alarmed parents with a good-humoured, easy grace: for nobody matched her in, I know not whether to say the possession or the assumption of a certain "rondeur et franchise de bonne femme"; which on various occasions gained the point aimed at with instant and complete success, where severe gravity and serious reasoning would probably have failed.

"Ce pauvre Docteur Jean!" she would say, chuckling and rubbing joyously her fat little white hands; "ce cher jeune homme! le meilleur créature du monde!" and go on to explain how she happened to be employing him for her own children, who were so fond of him they would scream themselves into fits at the thought of another doctor; how where she had confidence for her own, she thought it natural to repose trust for others, and au reste it was only the most temporary expedient in the world: Blanche and Angélique had the migraine; Dr. John had written a prescription; voila tout!

The parents' mouths were closed. Blanche and Angélique saved all her remaining trouble by chanting loud duets in their physician's praise; the other pupils echoed them, unanimously declaring that when they were ill they would have Dr. John and nobody else; and Madame laughed, and the parents laughed, too. The Labas-secouriens must have a large organ of philoprogenitiveness: at least the indulgence of offspring is carried by them to excessive lengths; the law of most households being the children's will. Madame now got credit for having acted on this occasion in a spirit of motherly partiality: she came off with flying colours; people liked her as a directress better than ever.

To this day I never fully understood why she thus risked her interest for the sake of Dr. John. What people said, of course I know well: the whole house—pupils, teachers, servants included—affirmed that she was going to marry him. So they had settled it; difference of age seemed to make no obstacle in their eyes: it was to be so.

It must be admitted that appearances did not wholly discountenance this idea; Madame seemed so bent on retaining his services, so oblivious of her former protégé, Pillule. She made, too, such a point of personally receiving his visits, and was so unfailingly cheerful, blithe, and benignant in her manner to him. Moreover, she paid, about this time, marked attention to dress: the morning déshabille, the nightcap and shawl, were discarded; Dr. John's early visits always found her with auburn braids all nicely arranged, silk dress trimly fitted on, neat laced brodequins in lieu of slippers: in short, the whole toilette complete as a model, and fresh as a flower. I scarcely think, however, that her intention in this went further than just to show a very handsome man that she was not quite a plain woman: and plain she was not. Without beauty of figure or elegance of form, she pleased. Without youth and its gay graces, she cheered. One never tired of seeing her: she was never monotonous, or insipid, or colourless, or flat. Her unfaded hair, her eye with its temperate blue light, her cheek with its wholesome fruit-like bloom—these things pleased in moderation, but with constancy.

Had she, indeed, floating visions of adopting Dr. John as a husband, taking him to her well-furnished home, endowing him with her savings, which were said to amount to a moderate competency, and making him comfortable for the rest of his life? Did Dr. John suspect her of such visions? I have met him coming out of her presence with a mischievous half-smile about his lips, and in his eyes a look as of masculine vanity elate and tickled. With all his good looks and good nature, he was not perfect; he must have been very imperfect if he roguishly encouraged aims he never intended to be successful. But did he not intend them to be successful? People said he had no money, that he was wholly dependent upon his profession. Madame—though perhaps some fourteen years his senior—was yet the sort of woman never to grow old, never to wither, never to break down. They certainly were on good terms. *He* perhaps was not in love; but how many people ever *do* love, or at least marry for love, in this world? We waited the end.

For what *he* waited I do not know, nor for what he watched; but the peculiarity of his manner, his expectant, vigilant, absorbed, eager look, never wore off: it rather intensified. He had never been quite within the compass of my penetration, and I think he ranged farther and farther beyond it.

One morning little Georgette had been more feverish and consequently more peevish; she was crying, and would not be pacified. I thought a particular draught ordered disagreed with her, and I doubted whether it ought to be continued; I waited impatiently for the doctor's coming in order to consult him.

The door-bell rung, he was admitted—I felt sure of this, for I heard his voice addressing the portresse. It was his custom to mount straight to the nursery, taking about three degrees of the staircase at once, and coming upon us like a cheerful surprise. Five minutes elapsed—ten—and I saw and heard nothing of him. What could he be doing? Possibly waiting in the corridor below. Little Georgette still piped her plaintive wail, appealing to me by her familiar term, "Minnie, Minnie, me very poorly!" till my heart ached. I descended to ascertain why he did not come. The corridor was empty. Whither was he vanished? Was he with Madame in the salle à manger? Impossible: I had left her but a short time since, dressing in her own chamber. I listened. Three pupils were just then hard at work practising in three proximate rooms—the dining-room and the greater and lesser drawing-rooms, between which and the corridor there was but the portresse's cabinet communicating with the salons, and intended originally for a boudoir. Farther off, at a fourth instrument in the oratory, a whole class of a dozen or more were taking

a singing lesson, and just then joining in a "barcarole" (I think they called it), whereof I yet remember these words "fraîchë brisë" and "Venisë." Under these circumstances, what could I hear? A great deal, certainly; had it only been to the purpose.

Yes; I heard a giddy treble laugh in the above-mentioned little cabinet, close by the door of which I stood—that door half-unclosed; a man's voice in a soft, deep, pleading tone, uttered some words, whereof I only caught the adjuration, "For God's sake!" Then, after a second's pause, forth issued Dr. John, his eye full shining, but not with either joy or triumph; his fair English cheek high-coloured; a baffled, tortured, anxious, and yet a tender meaning on his brow.

The open door served me as a screen; but had I been full in his way, I believe he would have passed without seeing me. Some mortification, some strong vexation had hold of his soul: or rather, to write my impressions now as I received them at the time, I should say some sorrow, some sense of injustice. I did not so much think his pride was hurt, as that his affections had been wounded—cruelly wounded, it seemed to me. But who was the torturer? What being in the house had him so much in her power? Madame I believed to be in her chamber; the room whence he had stepped was dedicated to the portresse's sole use; and she, Rosine Matou, an unprincipled though pretty little French grisette, airy, fickle, dressy, vain, and mercenary—it was not, surely, to *her* hand he owed the ordeal through which he seemed to have passed?

But while I pondered, her voice, clear, though somewhat sharp, broke out in a lightsome French song, trilling through the door still ajar: I glanced in, doubting my senses. There at the table she sat in a smart dress of "jaconas rose," trimming a tiny blond cap: not a living thing save herself was in the room, except indeed some gold fish in a glass globe, some flowers in pots, and a broad July sunbeam.

Here was a problem: but I must go upstairs to ask about the medicine.

Dr. John sat in a chair at Georgette's bedside; Madame stood before him; the little patient had been examined and soothed, and now lay composed in her crib. Madame Beck, as I entered, was discussing the physician's own health, remarking on some real or fancied change in his looks, charging him with over-work, and recommending rest and change of air. He listened good-naturedly, but with laughing indifference, telling her that she was "trop bonne," and that he felt perfectly well. Madame appealed to me—Dr. John following her movement with a slow glance which seemed to express languid surprise at reference being made to a quarter so insignificant.

"What do you think, Miss Lucie?" asked Madame. "Is he not paler and thinner?"

It was very seldom that I uttered more than monosyllables in Dr. John's presence; he was the kind of person with whom I was likely ever to remain the neutral, passive thing he thought me. Now, however, I took license to answer in a phrase: and a phrase I purposely made quite significant.

"He looks ill at this moment; but perhaps it is owing to some temporary cause: Dr. John may have been vexed or harassed." I cannot tell how he took this speech, as I never sought his face for information. Georgette here began to ask me in her broken English if she might have a glass of *eau sucrée*. I answered her in English. For the first time, I fancy, he noticed that I spoke his language; hitherto he had always taken me for a foreigner, addressing me as "Mademoiselle," and giving in French the requisite directions about the children's treatment. He seemed on the point of making a remark, but thinking better of it, held his tongue.

Madame recommended advising him; he shook his head laughing, rose and bid her good morning, with courtesy, but still with the regardless air of one whom too much unsolicited attention was surfeiting and spoiling.

When he was gone, Madame dropped into the chair he had just left; she rested her chin in her hand; all that was animated and amiable vanished from her face: she looked stony and stern, almost mortified and morose. She sighed; a single, but

a deep sigh. A loud bell rang for morning school. She got up; as she passed a dressing-table with a glass upon it, she looked at her reflected image. One single white hair streaked her nut-brown tresses; she plucked it out with a shudder. In the full summer daylight, her face, though it still had the colour, could plainly be seen to have lost the texture of youth; and then, where were youth's contours? Ah, Madame! wise as you were, even *you* knew weakness. Never had I pitied Madame before, but my heart softened towards her, when she turned darkly from the glass. A calamity had come upon her. That hag Disappointment was greeting her with a grisly "All-hail," and her soul rejected the intimacy.

But Rosine! My bewilderment there surpasses description. I embraced five opportunities of passing her cabinet that day, with a view to contemplating her charms, and finding out the secret of their influence. She was pretty, young, and wore a well-made dress. All very good points, and, I suppose, amply sufficient to account, in any philosophic mind, for any amount of agony and distraction in a young man like Dr. John. Still, I could not help forming half a wish that the said doctor were my brother; or at least that he had a sister or a mother who would kindly sermonise him. I say *half* a wish; I broke it, and flung it away before it became a whole one, discovering in good time its exquisite folly. "Somebody," I argued "might as well sermonise Madame about her young physician: and what good would that do?"

I believe Madame sermonised herself. She did not behave weakly, or make herself in any shape ridiculous. It is true she had neither strong feelings to overcome, nor tender feelings by which to be miserably pained. It is true likewise that she had an important avocation, a real business to fill her time, divert her thoughts, and divide her interest. It is especially true that she possessed a genuine good sense which is not given to all women nor to all men; and by dint of these combined advantages she behaved wisely—she behaved well. Brava! once more, Madame Beck. I saw you matched against an Apollyon of a predilection; you fought a good fight, and you overcame!

Chapter XII

THE CASKET

BEHIND the house at the Rue Fossette there was a garden—large, considering that it lay in the heart of a city, and to my recollection at this day it seems pleasant: but time, like distance, lends to certain scenes an influence so softening; and where all is stone around, blank wall and hot pavement, how precious seems one shrub, how lovely an enclosed and planted spot of ground!

There went a tradition that Madame Beck's house had in old days been a convent. That in years gone by—how long gone by I cannot tell, but I think some centuries—before the city had overspread this quarter, and when it was tilled ground and avenue, and such deep and leafy seclusion as ought to embosom a religious house—that something had happened on this site which, rousing fear and inflicting horror, had left to the place the inheritance of a ghost story. A vague tale went of a black and white nun, sometimes, on some night or nights of the year, seen in some part of this vicinage. The ghost must have been built some ages ago, for there were houses all round now; but certain convent-relics, in the shape of old and huge fruit-trees, yet consecrated the spot; and, at the foot of one—a Methuselah of a pear-tree dead, all but a few boughs which still faithfully renewed their perfumed snow in spring, and their honey-sweet pendants in autumn—you saw, in scraping away the mossy earth between the half-bared roots, a glimpse of slab, smooth, hard, and black. The legend went, unconfirmed and unaccredited, but still propagated, that this was the portal of a vault, imprisoning deep beneath that ground, on whose

surface grass grew and flowers bloomed, the bones of a girl whom a monkish conclave of the drear middle ages had here buried alive for some sin against her vow. Her shadow it was that tremblers had feared, through long generations after her poor frame was dust; her black robe and white veil that, for timid eyes, moonlight and shade had mocked, as they fluctuated in the night-wind through the garden-thicket.

Independently of romantic rubbish, however, that old garden had its charms. On summer mornings I used to rise early, to enjoy them alone; on summer evenings, to linger solitary, to keep tryst with the rising moon, or taste one kiss of the evening breeze, or fancy rather than feel the freshness of dew descending. The turf was verdant, the gravelled walks were white; sun-bright nasturtiums clustered beautiful about the roots of the doddered orchard giants. There was a large berceau, above which spread the shade of an acacia; there was a smaller, more sequestered bower, nestled in the vines which ran all along a high and grey wall, and gathered their tendrils in a knot of beauty, and hung their clusters in loving profusion about the favoured spot where jasmine and ivy met and married them.

Doubtless at high noon, in the broad, vulgar middle of the day, when Madame Beck's large school turned out rampant, and externes and pensionnaires were spread abroad, vying with the denizens of the boys' college close at hand, in the brazen exercise of their lungs and limbs—doubtless *then* the garden was a trite, trodden-down place enough. But at sunset, or the hour of salut, when the externes were gone home, and the boarders quiet at their studies; pleasant was it then to stray down the peaceful alleys, and hear the bells of St. Jean Baptiste peal out with their sweet, soft, exalted sound.

I was walking thus one evening, and had been detained farther within the verge of twilight than usual, by the still-deepening calm, the mellow coolness, the fragrant breathing with which flowers no sunshine could win now answered the persuasion of the dew. I saw by a light in the oratory window that the Catholic household were then gathered to evening prayer—a rite from attendance on which I now and then, as a Protestant, exempted myself.

"One moment longer," whispered solitude and the summer moon, "stay with us: all is truly quiet now; for another quarter of an hour your presence will not be missed: the day's heat and bustle have tired you; enjoy these precious minutes."

The windowless backs of houses built in this garden, and in particular the whole of one side, was skirted by the rear of a long line of premises—being the boarding-houses of the neighbouring college. This rear, however, was all blank stone, with the exception of certain attic loopholes high up, opening from the sleeping-rooms of the women-servants, and also one casement in a lower storey said to mark the chamber or study of a master. But, though thus secure, an alley, which ran parallel with the very high wall on that side the garden, was forbidden to be entered by the pupils. It was called indeed "l'allée défendue," and any girl setting foot there would have rendered herself liable to as severe a penalty as the mild rules of Madame Beck's establishment permitted. Teachers might indeed go there with impunity; but as the walk was narrow, and the neglected shrubs were grown very thick and close on each side, weaving overhead a roof of branch and leaf which the sun's rays penetrated but in rare chequers, this alley was seldom entered even during day, and after dusk was carefully shunned.

From the first I was tempted to make an exception to this rule of avoidance: the seclusion, the very gloom of the walk attracted me. For a long time the fear of seeming singular scared me away; but by degrees, as people became accustomed to me and my habits, and to such shades of peculiarity as were engrained in my nature—shades, certainly not striking enough to interest, and perhaps not prominent enough to offend, but born in and with me, and no more to be parted with than my identity—by slow degrees I became a frequenter of this strait and narrow path. I made myself gardener of some tintless flowers that grew between its closely-

ranked shrubs; I cleared away the relics of past autumns, choking up a rustic seat at the far end. Borrowing of Goton, the cuisinière, a pail of water and a scrubbing-brush, I made this seat clean. Madame saw me at work and smiled approbation: whether sincerely or not I don't know; but she *seemed* sincere.

"Voyez-vous!" cried she, "comme elle est propre cette demoiselle Lucie! Vous aimez donc cette allée, Meess?"

"Yes," I said, "it is quiet and shady."

"C'est juste," cried she, with an air of bonté; and she kindly recommended me to confine myself to it as much as I chose, saying, that as I was not charged with the surveillance, I need not trouble myself to walk with the pupils: only I might permit her children to come there, to talk English with me.

On the night in question, I was sitting on the hidden seat reclaimed from fungi and mould, listening to what seemed the far-off sounds of the city. Far off, in truth, they were not: this school was in the city's centre; hence, it was but five minutes' walk to the park, scarce ten to buildings of palatial splendour. Quite near were wide streets brightly lit, teeming at this moment with life: carriages were rolling through them to balls or to the opera. The same hour which tolled curfew for our convent, which extinguished each lamp, and dropped the curtain round each couch, rang for the gay city about us the summons in festal enjoyment. Of this contrast I thought not, however: gay instincts my nature had few; ball or opera I had never seen; and though often I had heard them described, and even wished to see them, it was not the wish of one who hopes to partake of pleasure if she could only reach it—who feels fitted to shine in some bright distant sphere, could she but thither win her way; it was no yearning to attain, no hunger to taste; only the calm desire to look on a new thing.

A moon was in the sky, not a full moon, but a young crescent. I saw her through a space in the boughs overhead. She and the stars, visible beside her, were no strangers where all else was strange: my childhood knew them. I had seen that golden sign with the dark globe in its curve leaning back on azure beside an old thorn at the top of an old field, in Old England, in long past days, just as it now leaned back beside a stately spire in this continental capital.

Oh, my childhood! I had feelings: passive as I lived, little as I spoke, cold as I looked, when I thought of past days, I *could* feel. About the present, it was better to be stoical; about the future—such a future as mine—to be dead. And in catalepsy and a dead trance, I studiously held the quick of my nature.

At that time, I well remember whatever could excite—certain accidents of the weather, for instance, were almost dreaded by me, because they woke the being I was always lulling, and stirred up a craving cry I could not satisfy. One night a thunderstorm broke; a sort of hurricane shook us in our beds: the Catholics rose in panic and prayed to their saints. As for me, the tempest took hold of me with tyranny: I was roughly roused and obliged to live. I got up and dressed myself, and creeping outside the casement close by my bed, sat on its ledge, with my feet on the roof of a lower adjoining building. It was wet, it was wild, it was pitch-dark. Within the dormitory they gathered round the night-lamp in consternation, praying loud. I could not go in: too resistless was the delight of staying with the wild hour, black and full of thunder, pealing out such an ode as language never delivered to man—too terribly glorious, the spectacle of clouds, split and pierced by white and blinding bolts.

I did long, achingly, then and for four-and-twenty hours afterwards, for something to fetch me out of my present existence, and lead me upwards and onwards. This longing, and all of a similar kind, it was necessary to knock on the head; which I did, figuratively, after the manner of Jael to Sisera, driving a nail through their temples. Unlike Sisera, they did not die: they were but transiently stunned, and at intervals would turn on the nail with a rebellious wrench: then did the temples bleed, and the brain thrill to its core.

To-night, I was not so mutinous, nor so miserable. My Sisera lay quiet in the tent, slumbering; and if his pain ached through his slumbers, something like an angel—the idea!—knelt near, dropping balm on the soothed temples, holding before the sealed eyes a magic glass, of which the sweet, solemn visions were repeated in dreams, and shedding a reflex from her moonlight wings and robe over the transfixed sleeper, over the tent threshold, over all the landscape lying without. Jael, the stern woman, sat apart, relenting somewhat over her captive; but more prone to dwell on the faithful expectation of Heber coming home. By which words I mean that the cool peace and dewy sweetness of the night filled me with a mood of hope: not hope on any definite point, but a general sense of encouragement and heart-ease.

Should not such a mood, so sweet, so tranquil, so unwonted, have been the harbinger of good? Alas, no good came of it! Presently the rude Real burst coarsely in—all evil, grovelling and repellent as she too often is.

Amid the intense stillness of that pile of stone overlooking the walk, the trees, the high wall, I heard a sound; a casement (all the windows here are casements, opening on hinges) creaked. Ere I had time to look up and mark where, in which storey, or by whom unclosed, a tree overhead shook, as if struck by a missile; some object dropped prone at my feet.

Nine was striking by St. Jean Baptiste's clock; day was fading, but it was not dark: the crescent-moon aided little, but the deep gilding of that point in heaven where the sun beamed last, and the crystalline clearness of a wide space above sustained the summer twilight; even in my dark walk I could, by approaching an opening, have managed to read print of a small type. Easy was it to see then that the missile was a box, a small box of white and coloured ivory; its loose lid opened in my hand; violets lay within, violets smothering a closely folded bit of pink paper, a note, superscribed, "Pour la robe grise." I wore indeed a dress of French grey.

Good. Was this a billet-doux? A thing I had heard of, but hitherto had not had the honour of seeing or handling. Was it this sort of commodity I held between my finger and thumb at this moment?

Scarcely: I did not dream it for a moment. Suitor or admirer my very thoughts had not conceived. All the teachers had dreams of some lover; one (but she was naturally of a credulous turn) believed in a future husband. All the pupils above fourteen knew of some prospective bridegroom; two or three were already affianced by their parents, and had been so from childhood: but into the realm of feelings and hopes which such prospects open, my speculations, far less my presumptions, had never once had warrant to intrude. If the other teachers went into town, or took a walk on the boulevards, or only attended mass, they were very certain (according to the accounts brought back) to meet with some individual of the "opposite sex," whose rapt, earnest gaze assured them of their power to strike and to attract. I can't say that my experience tallied with theirs in this respect. I went to church and I took walks, and am very well convinced that nobody minded me. There was not a girl or woman in the Rue Fossette who could not, and did not testify to having received an admiring beam from our young doctor's blue eyes at one time or other. I am obliged, however humbling it may sound, to except myself: as far as I was concerned, those blue eyes were guiltless, and calm as the sky, to whose tint theirs seemed akin. So it came to pass that I heard the others talk, wondered often at their gaiety, security and self-satisfaction, but did not trouble myself to look up and gaze along the path they seemed so certain of treading. This then was no billet-doux; and it was in settled conviction to the contrary that I quietly opened it. Thus it ran—I translate:

"Angel of my dreams! A thousand, thousand thanks for the promise kept: scarcely did I venture to hope its fulfilment. I believed you, indeed, to be half in jest; and then you seemed to think the enterprise beset with such danger—the hour so untimely, the alley so strictly secluded—often, you said, haunted by that dragon, the English

teacher—une véritable bégueule Britannique à ce que vous dites—espèce de monstre, brusque et rude comme un vieux caporal de grenadiers, et revêche comme une religieuse'' (the reader will excuse my modesty in allowing this flattering sketch of my amiable self to retain the slight veil of the original tongue). ''You are aware,'' went on this precious effusion, ''that little Gustave, on account of his illness, has been removed to a master's chamber—that favoured chamber, whose lattice overlooks your prison-ground. There, I, the best uncle in the world, am admitted to visit him. How tremblingly I approached the window and glanced into your Eden—an Eden for me, though a desert for you!—how I feared to behold vacancy, or the dragon aforesaid! How my heart palpitated with delight when, through apertures in the envious boughs, I at once caught the gleam of your graceful straw-hat, and the waving of your grey dress—dress that I should recognise amongst a thousand. But why, my angel, will you not look up? Cruel, to deny me one ray of those adorable eyes!—how a single glance would have revived me! I write this in fiery haste: while the physician examines Gustave, I snatch an opportunity to enclose it in a small casket together with a bouquet of flowers, the sweetest that blow—yet less sweet than thee, my Peri—my all-charming! ever thine—thou well knowest whom!''

''I wish I did know whom,'' was my comment; and the wish bore even closer reference to the person addressed in this choice document, than to the writer thereof. Perhaps it was from the fiancé of one of the engaged pupils; and, in that case, there was no great harm done or intended—only a small irregularity. Several of the girls, the majority, indeed, had brothers or cousins at the neighbouring college. But, ''la robe grise, le chapeau de paille,'' here surely was a clue—a very confusing one. The straw-hat was an ordinary garden head-screen, common to a score besides myself. The grey dress hardly gave more definite indication. Madame Beck herself ordinarily wore a grey dress just now; another teacher, and three of the pensionnaires, had had grey dresses purchased of the same shade and fabric as mine: it was a sort of every-day wear which happened at that time to be in vogue.

Meanwhile, as I pondered, I knew I must go in. Lights, moving in the dormitory, announced that prayers were over, and the pupils going to bed. Another half-hour and all doors would be locked—all lights extinguished. The front door yet stood open, to admit into the heated house the coolness of the summer night; from the portresse's cabinet close by shone a lamp, showing the long vestibule with the two-leaved drawing-room doors on one side, the great street-door closing the vista.

All at once, quick rang the bell—quick, but not loud—a cautious tinkle—a sort of warning metal whisper. Rosine darted from her cabinet and ran to open. The person she admitted stood with her two minutes in parley: there seemed a demur, a delay. Rosine came to the garden door, lamp in hand; she stood on the steps, lifting her lamp, looking round vaguely.

''Quel conte!'' she cried, with a coquettish laugh. ''Personne n'y a été.''

''Let me pass,'' pleaded a voice I knew: ''I ask but five minutes''; and a familiar shape, tall and grand (as we of the Rue Fossette all thought it), issued from the house, and strode down amongst the beds and walks. It was sacrilege—the intrusion of a man into that spot, at that hour; but he knew himself privileged, and perhaps he trusted to the friendly night. He wandered down the alleys, looking on this side and on that—he was lost in the shrubs, trampling flowers and breaking branches in his search—he penetratcd at last the ''forbidden walk.'' There I met him, like some ghost, I suppose.

''Dr. John! it is found.''

He did not ask by whom, for with his quick eye he perceived that I held it in my hand.

''Do not betray her,'' he said, looking at me as if I were indeed a dragon.

''Were I ever so disposed to treachery, I cannot betray what I do not know,'' was my answer. ''Read the note, and you will see how little it reveals.''

"Perhaps you have read it," I thought to myself; and yet I could not believe he wrote it: that could hardly be his style: besides, I was fool enough to think there would be a degree of hardship in his calling me such names. His own look vindicated him; he grew hot, and coloured as he read.

"This is indeed too much: this is cruel, this is humiliating," were the words that fell from him. I thought it *was* cruel when I saw his countenance so moved. No matter whether he was to blame or not; somebody, it seemed to me, must be more to blame.

"What shall you do about it?" he inquired of me. "Shall you tell Madame Beck what you have found, and cause a stir—an esclandre?"

I thought I ought to tell, and said so; adding that I did not believe there would be either stir or esclandre: Madame was much too prudent to make a noise about an affair of that sort connected with her establishment.

He stood looking down and meditating. He was both too proud and too honourable to entreat my secrecy on a point which duty evidently commanded me to communicate. I wished to do right, yet loathed to grieve or injure him. Just then Rosine glanced out through the open door; she could not see us, though between the trees I could plainly see her: her dress was grey, like mine. This circumstance, taken in connection with prior transactions, suggested to me that perhaps the case, however deplorable, was one in which I was under no obligation whatever to concern myself. Accordingly, I said—

"If you can assure me that none of Madame Beck's pupils are implicated in this business, I shall be very happy to stand aloof from all interference. Take the casket, the bouquet, and the billet; for my part, I gladly forget the whole affair."

"Look there!" he whispered suddenly, as his hand closed on what I offered, and at the same time he pointed through the boughs.

I looked. Behold Madame, in shawl, wrapping-gown, and slippers, softly descending the steps, and stealing like a cat round the garden: in two minutes she would have been upon Dr. John. If *she* were like a cat, however, *he* quite as much resembled a leopard: nothing could be lighter than his tread when he chose. He watched, and as she turned a corner, he took the garden at two noiseless bounds. She reappeared, and he was gone. Rosine helped him, instantly interposing the door between him and his huntress. I, too, might have got away, but I preferred to meet Madame openly.

Though it was my frequent and well-known custom to spend twilight in the garden, yet, never till now, had I remained so late. Full sure was I that Madame had missed—was come in search of me, and designed now to pounce on the defaulter unawares. I expected a reprimand. No. Madame was all goodness. She tendered not even a remonstrance; she testified no shade of surprise. With that consummate tact of hers in which I believe she was never surpassed by living thing, she even professed merely to have issued forth to taste "la brise du soir."

"Quelle belle nuit!" cried she, looking up at the stars—the moon was now gone down behind the broad tower of Jean Baptiste. "Qu'il fait bon! que l'air est frais!"

And, instead of sending me in, she detained me to take a few turns with her down the principal alley. When at last we both re-entered, she leaned affably on my shoulder by way of support in mounting the front-door steps at parting, her cheek was presented to my lips, and "Bon soir, ma bonne amie; dormez bien!" was her kindly adieu for the night.

I caught myself smiling as I lay awake and thoughtful on my couch—smiling at Madame. The unction, the suavity of her behaviour offered, for one who knew her, a sure token that suspicion of some kind was busy in her brain. From some aperture or summit of observation, through parted bough or open window, she had doubtless caught a glimpse, remote or near, deceptive or instructive, of that night's transactions. Finely accomplished as she was in the art of surveillance, it was next to impossible that a casket could be thrown into her garden, or an interloper could

cross her walks to seek it, without that she, in shaken branch, passing shade, unwonted footfall, or stilly murmur (and though Dr. John had spoken very low in the few words he dropped me, yet the hum of his man's voice pervaded, I thought, the whole conventual ground)—without, I say, that she should have caught intimation of things extraordinary transpiring on her premises. *What* things, she might by no means see, or at that time be able to discover; but a delicious little ravelled plot lay tempting her to disentanglement; and in the midst, folded round and round in cobwebs, had she not secured "Meess Lucie," clumsily involved, like the foolish fly she was?

Chapter XIII

A SNEEZE OUT OF SEASON

I HAD occasion to smile—nay, to laugh, at Madame again, within the space of four-and-twenty hours after the little scene treated of in the last chapter.

Villette owns a climate as variable, though not so humid, as that of any English town. A night of high wind followed upon that soft sunset, and all the next day was one of dry storm—dark, beclouded, yet rainless,—the streets were dim with sand and dust, whirled from the boulevards. I know not that even lovely weather would have tempted me to spend the evening-time of study and recreation where I had spent it yesterday. My alley, and, indeed, all the walks and shrubs in the garden, had acquired a new, but not a pleasant interest; their seclusion was now become precarious; their calm insecure. That casement which rained billets had vulgarised the once dear nook it overlooked; and elsewhere, the eyes of the flowers had gained vision, and the knots in the tree-boles listened like secret ears. Some plants there were, indeed, trodden down by Dr. John in his search, and his hasty and heedless progress, which I wished to prop up, water, and revive; some footmarks, too, he had left on the beds: but these, in spite of the strong wind, I found a moment's leisure to efface very early in the morning, ere common eyes had discovered them. With a pensive sort of content I sat down to my desk and my German, while the pupils settled to their evening lessons, and the other teachers took up their needlework.

The scene of the "étude du soir" was always the refectory, a much smaller apartment than any of the three classes or schoolrooms; for here none, save the boarders, were ever admitted, and these numbered only a score. Two lamps hung from the ceiling over the two tables; these were lit at dusk, and their kindling was the signal for school-books being set aside, a grave demeanour assumed, general silence enforced, and then commenced "la lecture pieuse." This said "lecture pieuse" was, I soon found, mainly designed as a wholesome mortification of the Intellect, a useful humiliation of the Reason; and such a dose for Common Sense as she might digest at her leisure, and thrive on as she best could.

The book brought out (it was never changed, but when finished recommenced) was a venerable volume, old as the hills—grey as the Hôtel de Ville.

I would have given two francs for the chance of getting that book once into my hands, turning over the sacred yellow leaves, ascertaining the title, and perusing with my own eyes the enormous figments which, as an unworthy heretic, it was only permitted me to drink in with my bewildered ears. This book contained legends of the saints. Good God! (I speak the words reverently) what legends they were. What gasconading rascals those saints must have been, if they first boasted these exploits or invented these miracles. These legends, however, were no more than monkish extravagances, over which one laughed inwardly; there were, besides, priestly matters, and the priest-craft of the book was far worse than its monkery.

The ears burned on each side of my head as I listened, perforce, to tales of moral martyrdom inflicted by Rome; the dread boasts of confessors, who had wickedly abused their office, trampling to deep degradation high-born ladies, making of countesses and princesses the most tormented slaves under the sun. Stories like that of Conrad and Elizabeth of Hungary recurred again and again, with all its dreadful viciousness, sickening tyranny and black impiety: tales that were nightmares of oppression, privation, and agony.

I sat out this "lecture pieuse" for some nights as well as I could, and as quietly too; only once breaking off the points of my scissors by involuntarily sticking them somewhat deep in the worm-eaten board of the table before me. But, at last, it made me so burning hot, and my temples, and my heart, and my wrist throbbed so fast, and my sleep afterwards was so broken with excitement, that I could sit no longer. Prudence recommended henceforward a swift clearance of my person from the place, the moment that guilty old book was brought out. No Mause Headrigg ever felt a stronger call to take up her testimony against Sergeant Bothwell, than I—to speak my mind in this matter of the popish "lecture pieuse." However, I did manage somehow to curb and rein in; and though always, as soon as Rosine came to light the lamps, I shot from the room quickly, yet also I did it quietly; seizing that vantage moment given by the little bustle before the dead silence, and vanishing whilst the boarders put their books away.

When I vanished, it was into darkness; candles were not allowed to be carried about, and the teacher who forsook the refectory had only the unlit hall, schoolroom, or bedroom, as a refuge. In winter I sought the long "classes," and paced them fast to keep myself warm—fortunate if the moon shone, and if there were only stars, soon reconciled to their dim gleam, or even to the total eclipse of their absence. In summer it was never quite dark, and then I went upstairs to my own quarter of the long dormitory, opened my own casement (that chamber was lit by five casements large as great doors), and leaning out, looked forth upon the city beyond the garden, and listened to band-music from the park or the palace-square, thinking meantime my own thoughts, living my own life, in my own still, shadow-world.

This evening, fugitive as usual before the Pope and his works, I mounted the staircase, approached the dormitory, and quietly opened the door, which was always kept carefully shut, and which, like every other door in this house, revolved noiselessly on well-oiled hinges. Before I *saw*, I *felt* that life was in the great room, usually void: not that there was either stir or breath, or rustle of sound, but Vacuum lacked, Solitude was not at home. All the white beds—the "lits d'ange," as they were poetically termed—lay visible at a glance; all were empty: no sleeper reposed therein. The sound of a drawer cautiously slid out struck my ear; stepping a little to one side, my vision took a free range, unimpeded by falling curtains. I now commanded my own bed and my own toilet, with a locked work-box upon it, and locked drawers underneath.

Very good. A dumpy, motherly, little body, in decent shawl and the cleanest of possible nightcaps, stood before this toilet, hard at work, apparently doing me the kindness of "tidying out" the "meuble." Open stood the lid of the work-box, open the top drawer; duly and impartially was each succeeding drawer opened in turn: not an article of their contents but was lifted and unfolded, not a paper but was glanced over, not a little box but was unlidded; and beautiful was the adroitness, exemplary the care with which the search was accomplished. Madame wrought at it like a true star, "unhasting yet unresting." I will not deny that it was with a secret glee I watched her. Had I been a gentleman I believe Madame would have found favour in my eyes, she was so handy, neat, thorough in all she did: some people's movements provoke the soul by their loose awkwardness, hers satisfied by their trim compactness. I stood, in short, fascinated; but it was necessary to make an effort to break this spell: a retreat must be beaten. The searcher might

have turned and caught me; there would have been nothing for it then but a scene, and she and I would have had to come all at once, with a sudden clash, to a thorough knowledge of each other: down would have gone conventionalities, away swept disguises, and *I* should have looked into her eyes, and *she* into mine—we should have known that we could work together no more, and parted in this life for ever.

Where was the use of tempting such a catastrophe? I was not angry, and had no wish in the world to leave her. I could hardly get another employer whose yoke would be so light and so easy of carriage; and truly, I liked Madame for her capital sense, whatever I might think of her principles: as to her system, it did me no harm; she might work me with it to her heart's content: nothing would come of the operation. Loverless and inexpectant of love, I was as safe from spies in my heart-poverty, as the beggar from thieves in his destitution of purse. I turned, then, and fled; descending the stairs with progress as swift and soundless as that of the spider, which at the same instant ran down the bannister.

How I laughed when I reached the schoolroom. I knew now she had certainly seen Dr. John in the garden; I knew what her thoughts were. The spectacle of a suspicious nature so far misled by its own inventions, tickled me much. Yet as the laugh died, a kind of wrath smote me, and then bitterness followed: it was the rock struck, and Meribah's waters gushing out. I never had felt so strange and contradictory an inward tumult as I felt for an hour that evening: soreness and laughter, and fire, and grief, shared my heart between them. I cried hot tears: not because Madame mistrusted me—I did not care twopence for her mistrust—but for other reasons. Complicated, disquieting thoughts broke up the whole repose of my nature. However, that turmoil subsided: next day I was again Lucy Snowe.

On revisiting my drawers, I found them all securely locked; the closest subsequent examination could not discover change or apparent disturbance in the position of one object. My few dresses were folded as I had left them; a certain little bunch of white violets that had been once silently presented to me by a stranger (a stranger to me, for we had never exchanged words), and which I had dried and kept for its sweet perfume between the folds of my best dress, lay there unstirred; my black silk scarf, my lace chemisette and collars were unrumpled. Had she creased one solitary article, I own I should have felt much greater difficulty in forgiving her; but finding all straight and orderly, I said "Let bygones be bygones. I am unharmed: why should I bear malice?"

A thing there was which puzzled myself, and I sought in my brain a key to that riddle almost as sedulously as Madame had sought a guide to useful knowledge in my toilet drawers. How was it that Dr. John, if he had not been accessory to the dropping of that casket into the garden, should have known that it *was* dropped, and appeared so promptly on the spot to seek it? So strong was the wish to clear up this point that I began to entertain this daring suggestion—

"Why may I not, in case I should ever have the opportunity, ask Dr. John himself to explain this coincidence?"

And so long as Dr. John was absent, I really believed I had courage to test him with such a question.

Little Georgette was now convalescent; and her physician accordingly made his visits very rare: indeed, he would have ceased them altogether, had not Madame insisted on his giving an occasional call till the child should be quite well.

She came into the nursery one evening just after I had listened to Georgette's lisped and broken prayer, and had put her to bed. Taking the little one's hand, she said—

"Cette enfant a toujours un peu de fièvre." And presently afterwards, looking at me with a quicker glance than was habitual to her quiet eye, "Le Docteur John l'a-t-il vue dernièrement? Non, n'est ce pas?"

Of course she knew this better than any other person in the house. "Well," she continued, "I am going out, pour faire quelques courses en fiacre. I shall call on Dr. John, and send him to the child. I will that he sees her this evening; her cheeks are flushed, her pulse is quick: *you* will receive him—for my part, I shall be from home."

Now the child was well enough, only warm with the warmth of July; it was scarcely less needful to send for a priest to administer extreme unction than for a doctor to prescribe a dose; also Madame rarely made "courses," as she called them, in the evening: moreover, this was the first time she had chosen to absent herself on the occasion of a visit from Dr. John. The whole arrangement indicated some plan; this I saw, but without the least anxiety. "Ha! ha! Madame," laughed Lightheart the Beggar, "your crafty wits are on the wrong tack."

She departed, attired very smartly, in a shawl of price, and a certain *chapeau vert tendre*—hazardous, as to its tint, for any complexion less fresh than her own, but, to her, not unbecoming. I wondered what she intended: whether she really would send Dr. John or not; or whether indeed he would come: he might be engaged.

Madame had charged me not to let Georgette sleep till the doctor came; I had therefore sufficient occupation in telling her nursery tales and palavering the little language for her benefit. I affected Georgette; she was a sensitive and a loving child: to hold her in my lap, or carry her in my arms, was to me a treat. To-night she would have me lay my head on the pillow of her crib; she even put her little arms round my neck. Her clasp, and the nestling action with which she pressed her cheek to mine, made me almost cry with a tender pain. Feeling of no kind abounded in that house; this pure little drop from a pure little source was too sweet: it penetrated deep, and subdued the heart, and sent a gush to the eyes.

Half-an-hour or an hour passed; Georgette murmured in her soft lisp that she was growing sleepy. "And you *shall* sleep," thought I, "malgré maman and médecin, if they are not here in ten minutes."

Hark! There was a ring, and there the tread, astonishing the staircase by the fleetness with which it left the steps behind. Rosine introduced Dr. John, and, with a freedom of manner not altogether peculiar to herself, but characteristic of the domestics of Villette generally, she stayed to hear what he had to say. Madame's presence would have awed her back to her own realm of the vestibule and the cabinet—for mine, or that of any other teacher or pupil, she cared not a jot. Smart, trim, and pert, she stood, a hand in each pocket of her gay grisette apron, eyeing Dr. John with no more fear or shyness than if he had been a picture instead of a living gentleman.

"Le marmot n'a rien n'est ce pas?" said she, indicating Georgette with a jerk of her chin.

"Pas beaucoup," was the answer, as the doctor hastily scribbled with his pencil some harmless prescription.

"Eh bien!" pursued Rosine, approaching him quite near while he put up his pencil. "And the box—did you get it? Monsieur went off like a coup de vent the other night; I had not time to ask him."

"I found it: yes."

"And who threw it, then?" continued Rosine, speaking quite freely the very words I should so much have wished to say, but had no address or courage to bring it out: how short some people make the road to a point which, for others, seems unattainable!

"That may be my secret," rejoined Dr. John briefly but with no sort of hauteur: he seemed quite to understand the Rosine or grisette character.

"Mais enfin," continued she, nothing abashed, "monsieur knew it was thrown, since he came to seek it—how did he know?"

"I was attending a little patient in the college near," said he, "and saw it dropped out of his chamber window, and so came to pick it up."

How simple the whole explanation! The note had alluded to a physician as then examining "Gustave."

"Ah ça!" pursued Rosine, "il n'y a donc rien là-dessous: pas de mystère, pas d'amourette, par exemple?"

"Pas plus que sur ma main," responded the doctor, showing his palm.

"Quel dommage!" responded the grisette: "et moi—à qui tout cela commencait à donner des idées."

"Vraiment! vous en êtes pour vos frais," was the doctor's cool rejoinder.

She pouted. The doctor could not help laughing at the sort of "moue" she made: when he laughed, he had something peculiarly good-natured and genial in his look. I saw his hand incline to his pocket.

"How many times have you opened the door for me within this last month?" he asked.

"Monsieur ought to have kept count of that," said Rosine, quite readily.

"As if I had not something better to do!" rejoined he; but I saw him give her a piece of gold, which she took unscrupulously, and then danced off to answer the door-bell, ringing just now every five minutes, as the various servants came to fetch the half-boarders.

The reader must not think too hardly of Rosine; on the whole, she was not a bad sort of person, and had no idea there could be any disgrace in grasping at whatever she could get, or any effrontery in chattering like a pie to the best gentleman in Christendom.

I had learned something from the above scene besides what concerned the ivory box: viz., that not on the robe de jaconas, pink or grey, nor yet on the frilled and pocketed apron, lay the blame of breaking Dr. John's heart: these items of array were obviously guiltless as Georgette's little blue tunic. So much the better. But who then was the culprit? What was the ground—what the origin—what the perfect explanation of the whole business? Some points had been cleared, but how many yet remained obscure as night!

"However," I said to myself, "it is no affair of yours": and turning from the face on which I had been unconsciously dwelling with a questioning gaze, I looked through the window which commanded the garden below. Dr. John, meantime, standing by the bedside, was slowly drawing on his gloves and watching his little patient, as her eyes closed and her rosy lips parted in coming sleep. I waited till he should depart as usual, with a quick bow and scarce articulate "good-night." Just as he took his hat, my eyes, fixed on the tall houses bounding the garden, saw the one lattice, already commemorated, cautiously open; forth from the aperture projected a hand and a white handkerchief; both waved. I know not whether the signal was answered from some viewless quarter of our own dwelling; but immediately after there fluttered from the lattice a falling object, white and light—billet the second, of course.

"There!" I ejaculated involuntarily.

"Where?" asked Dr. John with energy, making direct for the window. "What is it?"

"They have gone and done it again," was my reply. "A handkerchief waved and something fell": and I pointed to the lattice, now closed and looking hypocritically blank.

"Go at once; pick it up and bring it here," was his prompt direction; adding, "nobody will take notice of *you*: *I* should be seen."

Straight I went. After some little search, I found a folded paper, lodged on the lower branch of a shrub; I seized and brought it direct to Dr. John. This time, I believe not even Rosine saw me.

He instantly tore the billet into small pieces, without reading it.

"It is not in the least *her* fault, you must remember," he said, looking at me.

"*Whose* fault?" I asked. "*Who* is it?"

"You don't yet know, then?"

"Not in the least."

"Have you no guess?"

"None."

"If I knew you better, I might be tempted to risk some confidence, and thus secure you as guardian over a most innocent and excellent, but somewhat inexperienced being."

"As a duenna?" I asked.

"Yes," said he abstractedly. "What snares are round her!" he added musingly: and now, certainly for the first time, he examined my face, anxious, doubtless, to see if any kindly expression there would warrant him in recommending to my care and indulgence some ethereal creature, against whom powers of darkness were plotting. I felt no particular vocation to undertake the surveillance of ethereal creatures; but recalling the scene at the bureau, it seemed to me that I owed *him* a good turn: if I *could* help him then I would, and it lay not with me to decide how. With as little reluctance as might be, I intimated that "I was willing to do what I could towards taking care of any person in whom he might be interested."

"I am no farther interested than as a spectator," said he, with a modesty, admirable, as I thought, to witness. "I happen to be acquainted with the rather worthless character of the person who, from the house opposite, has now twice invaded the sanctity of this place; I have also met in society the object at whom these vulgar attempts are aimed. Her exquisite superiority and innate refinement ought, one would think, to scare impertinence from her very idea. It is not so, however; and innocent, unsuspicious as she is, I would guard her from evil if I could. In person, however, I can do nothing: I cannot come near her"—he paused.

"Well, I am willing to help you," said I, "only tell me how." And busily, in my own mind, I ran over the list of our inmates, seeking this paragon, this pearl of great price, this gem without flaw. "It must be Madame," I concluded. "*She* only, amongst us all, has the art even to *seem* superior: but as to being unsuspicious, inexperienced, etc., Dr. John need not distract himself about that. However, this is just his whim, and I will not contradict him; he shall be humoured: his angel shall be an angel."

"Just notify the quarter to which my care is to be directed," I continued gravely: chuckling, however, to myself over the thought of being set to chaperon Madame Beck or any of her pupils.

Now Dr. John had a fine set of nerves, and he at once felt by instinct, what no more coarsely constituted mind would have detected; namely, that I was a little amused at him. The colour rose to his cheek; with half a smile he turned and took his hat—he was going. My heart smote me.

"I will—I will help you," said I eagerly. "I will do what you wish. I will watch over your angel: I will take care of her, only tell me who she is."

"But you *must* know," said he then with earnestness, yet speaking very low. "So spotless, so good, so unspeakably beautiful! impossible that one house should contain two like her. I allude, of course"——

Here the latch of Madame Beck's chamber-door (opening into the nursery) gave a sudden click, as if the hand holding it had been slightly convulsed; there was the suppressed explosion of an irrepressible sneeze. These little accidents will happen to the best of us. Madame—excellent woman! was then on duty. She had come home quietly, stolen upstairs on tip-toe; she was in her chamber. If she had not sneezed, she would have heard all, and so should I; but that unlucky sternutation routed Dr. John. While he stood aghast, she came forward alert, composed, in the best yet most tranquil spirits: no novice to her habits but would have thought she had just come in, and scouted the idea of her ear having been glued to the key-hole for at least ten minutes. She affected to sneeze again, declared she was "enrhumée," and then proceeded volubly to recount her "courses en fiacre." The prayer-bell rang, and I left her with the doctor.

Chapter XIV

THE FÊTE

As soon as Georgette was well, Madame sent her away into the country. I was sorry; I loved the child, and her loss made me poorer than before. But I must not complain. I lived in a house full of robust life; I might have had companions, and I chose solitude. Each of the teachers in turn made me overtures of special intimacy; I tried them all. One I found to be an honest woman, but a narrow thinker, a coarse feeler, and an egotist. The second was a Parisienne, externally refined—at heart corrupt—without a creed, without a principle, without an affection: having penetrated the outward crust of decorum in this character, you found a slough beneath. She had a wonderful passion for presents; and, in this point, the third teacher—a person otherwise characterless and insignificant—closely resembled her. This last-named had also one other distinctive property—that of avarice. In her reigned the love of money for its own sake. The sight of a piece of gold would bring into her eyes a green glisten, singular to witness. She once, as a mark of high favour, took me upstairs, and, opening a secret door, showed me a hoard—a mass of coarse, large coin—about fifteen guineas, in five-franc pieces. She loved this hoard as a bird loves its eggs. These were her savings. She would come and talk to me about them with an infatuated and persevering dotage, strange to behold in a person not yet twenty-five.

The Parisienne, on the other hand, was prodigal and profligate (in disposition, that is: as to action, I do not know). That latter quality showed its snake-head to me but once, peeping out very cautiously. A curious kind of reptile it seemed, judging from the glimpse I got; its novelty whetted my curiosity: if it would have come out boldly, perhaps I might philosophically have stood my ground, and coolly surveyed the long thing from forked tongue to scaly tail-tip; but it merely rustled in the leaves of a bad novel; and, on encountering a hasty and ill-advised demonstration of wrath, recoiled and vanished, hissing. She hated me from that day.

This Parisienne was always in debt; her salary being anticipated, not only in dress, but in perfumes, cosmetics, confectionery, and condiments. What a cold, callous epicure she was in all things! I see her now. Thin in face and figure, sallow in complexion, regular in features, with perfect teeth, lips like a thread, a large, prominent chin, a well-opened, but frozen eye, of light at once craving and ingrate. She mortally hated work, and loved what she called pleasure; being an insipid, heartless, brainless dissipation of time.

Madame Beck knew this woman's character perfectly well. She once talked to me about her, with an odd mixture of discrimination, indifference, and antipathy. I asked why she kept her in the establishment. She answered plainly, "because it suited her interest to do so"; and pointed out a fact I had already noticed, namely, that Mademoiselle St. Pierre possessed, in an almost unique degree, the power of keeping order amongst her undisciplined ranks of scholars. A certain petrifying influence accompanied and surrounded her: without passion, noise, or violence, she held them in check as a breezeless frost-air might still a brawling stream. She was of little use as far as communication of knowledge went, but for strict surveillance and maintenance of rules she was invaluable. "Je sais bien qu'elle n'a pas de principes, ni, peutêtre, de mœurs," admitted Madame frankly; but added with philosophy, "son maintien en classe est toujours convenable et rempli même d'une certaine dignité: c'est tout ce qu'il faut. Ni les élèves ni les parents ne regardent plus loin; ni, par conséquent, moi non plus."

A strange, frolicsome, noisy little world was this school: great pains were taken to hide chains with flowers: a subtle essence of Romanism pervaded every arrangement: large sensual indulgence (so to speak) was permitted by way of counterpoise to jealous spiritual restraint. Each mind was being reared in slavery; but, to prevent reflection from dwelling on this fact, every pretext for physical recreation was seized and made the most of. There, as elsewhere, the CHURCH strove to bring up her children robust in body, feeble in soul, fat, ruddy, hale, joyous, ignorant, unthinking, unquestioning. "Eat, drink, and live!" she says. "Look after your bodies; leave your souls to me. I hold their cure—guide their course: I guarantee their final fate." A bargain, in which every true Catholic deems himself a gainer. Lucifer just offers the same terms: "All this power will I give thee, and the glory of it; for that is delivered unto me, and to whomsoever I will I give it. If thou, therefore, wilt worship me, all shall be thine!"

About this time—in the ripest glow of summer—Madame Beck's house became as merry a place as a school could well be. All day long the broad folding-doors and the two-leaved casements stood wide open: settled sunshine seemed naturalised in the atmosphere; clouds were far off, sailing away beyond sea, resting, no doubt, round islands such as England—that dear land of mists—but withdrawn wholly from the drier continent. We lived far more in the garden than under a roof: classes were held, and meals partaken of, in the "grand berceau." Moreover, there was a note of holiday preparation, which almost turned freedom into license. The autumnal long vacation was but two months distant; but before that, a great day— an important ceremony—none other than the fête of Madame—awaited celebration.

The conduct of this fête devolved chiefly on Mademoiselle St. Pierre; Madame herself being supposed to stand aloof, disinterestedly unconscious of what might be going forward in her honour. Especially, she never knew, never in the least suspected, that a subscription was annually levied on the whole school for the purchase of a handsome present. The polite tact of the reader will please to leave out of the account a brief, secret consultation on this point in Madame's own chamber.

"What will you have this year?" was asked by her Parisian lieutenant.

"Oh, no matter! Let it alone. Let the poor children keep their francs." And Madame looked benign and modest.

The St. Pierre would here protrude her chin; she knew Madame by heart; she always called her airs of bonté—"des grimaces." She never even professed to respect them one instant.

"Vite!" she would say coldly. "Name the article. Shall it be jewellery or porcelain, haberdashery or silver?"

"Eh bien! Deux ou trois cuillers et autant de fourchettes en argent."

And the result was a handsome case, containing 300 francs' worth of plate.

The programme of the fête-day's proceedings comprised: Presentation of plate, collation in the garden, dramatic performance (with pupils and teachers for actors), a dance and supper. Very gorgeous seemed the effect of the whole to me, as I well remember. Zélie St. Pierre understood these things, and managed them ably.

The play was the main point: a month's previous drilling being there required. The choice, too, of the actors required knowledge and care; then came lessons in elocution, in attitude, and then the fatigue of countless rehearsals. For all this, as may well be supposed, St. Pierre did not suffice: other management, other accomplishments than hers were requisite here. They were supplied in the person of a master—M. Paul Emanuel, professor of literature. It was never my lot to be present at the histrionic lessons of M. Paul, but I often saw him as he crossed the "carré" (a square hall between the dwelling-house and school house). I heard him, too, in the warm evenings, lecturing with open doors, and his name, with anecdotes of him, resounded in one's ears from all sides. Especially our former acquaintance, Miss Ginevra Fanshawe, who had been selected to take a prominent part in the

play—used, in bestowing upon me a large portion of her leisure, to lard her discourse with frequent allusions to his sayings and doings. She esteemed him hideously plain, and used to profess herself frightened almost into hysterics at the sound of his step or voice. A dark little man he certainly was; pungent and austere. Even to me he seemed a harsh apparition, with his close-shorn, black head, his broad, sallow brow, his thin cheek, his wide and quivering nostril, his thorough glance, and hurried bearing. Irritable he was; one heard that, as he apostrophised with vehemence the awkward squad under his orders. Sometimes he would break out on these raw amateur actresses with a passion of impatience at their falseness of conception, their coldness of emotion, their feebleness of delivery. "Écoutez!" he would cry; and then his voice rang through the premises like a trumpet; and when, mimicking it, came the small pipe of a Ginevra, a Mathilde, or a Blanche, one understood why a hollow groan of scorn, or a fierce hiss of rage, rewarded the tame echo.

"Vous n'êtes donc que des poupées?" I heard him thunder. "Vous n'avez pas de passions—vous autres? Vous ne sentez donc rien? Votre chair est de neige, votre sang de glace? Moi, je veux que tout cela s'allume, qu'il ait une vie, une âme!"

Vain resolve! And when he at last found it *was* vain, he suddenly broke the whole business down. Hitherto he had been teaching them a grand tragedy; he tore the tragedy in morsels, and came next day with a compact little comic trifle. To this they took more kindly; he presently knocked it all into their smooth round pates.

Mademoiselle St. Pierre always presided at M. Emanuel's lessons, and I was told that the polish of her manner, her seeming attention, her tact and grace, impressed that gentleman very favourably. She had, indeed, the art of pleasing, for a given time, whom she would; but the feeling would not last: in an hour it was dried like dew, vanished like gossamer.

The day preceding Madame's fête was as much a holiday as the fête itself. It was devoted to clearing out, cleaning, arranging and decorating the three schoolrooms. All within doors was the gayest bustle; neither upstairs nor down could a quiet, isolated person find rest for the sole of her foot; accordingly, for my part, I took refuge in the garden. The whole day did I wander or sit there alone, finding warmth in the sun, shelter among the trees, and a sort of companionship in my own thoughts. I well remember that I exchanged but two sentences that day with any living being: not that I felt solitary; I was glad to be quiet. For a looker-on, it sufficed to pass through the rooms once or twice, observe what changes were being wrought, how a green-room and a dressing-room were being contrived, a little stage with scenery erected, how M. Paul Emanuel, in conjunction with Mademoiselle St. Pierre, was directing all, and how an eager band of pupils, amongst them Ginevra Fanshawe, were working gaily under his control.

The great day arrived. The sun rose hot and unclouded and hot and unclouded it burned on till evening. All the doors and all the windows were set open, which gave a pleasant sense of summer freedom—and freedom the most complete seemed indeed the order of the day. Teachers and pupils descended to breakfast in dressing-gowns and curl-papers: anticipating "avec délices" the toilette of the evening, they seemed to take a pleasure in indulging that forenoon in a luxury of slovenliness; like aldermen fasting in preparation for a feast. About nine o'clock A.M., an important functionary, the "coiffeur," arrived. Sacrilegious to state, he fixed his headquarters in the oratory, and there, in presence of "bénitier," candle, and crucifix, solemnised the mysteries of his art. Each girl was summoned in turn to pass through his hands; emerging from them with head as smooth as a shell, intersected by faultless white lines, and wreathed about with Grecian plaits that shone as if lacquered. I took my turn with the rest, and could hardly believe what the glass said when I applied to it for information afterwards; the lavished garlandry of woven brown hair amazed me—I feared it was not all my own, and it required several convincing pulls to

give assurance to the contrary. I then acknowledged in the coiffeur a first-rate artist—one who certainly made the most of indifferent materials.

The oratory closed, the dormitory became the scene of ablutions, arrayings and bedizenings curiously elaborate. To me it was, and ever must be an enigma, how they contrived to spend so much time in doing so little. The operation seemed close, intricate, prolonged: the result simple. A clear white muslin dress, a blue sash (the Virgin's colours), a pair of white, or straw-colour kid gloves—such was the gala uniform, to the assumption whereof that houseful of teachers and pupils devoted three mortal hours. But though simple, it must be allowed the array was perfect—perfect in fashion, fit, and freshness; every head being also dressed with exquisite nicety, and a certain compact taste—suiting the full, firm comeliness of Labassecourien contours, though too stiff for any more flowing and flexible style of beauty—the general effect was, on the whole, commendable.

In beholding this diaphanous and snowy mass, I well remember feeling myself to be a mere shadowy spot on a field of light; the courage was not in me to put on a transparent white dress: something thin I must wear—the weather and rooms being too hot to give substantial fabrics suffrance, so I had sought through a dozen shops till I lit upon a crape-like material of purple-grey—the colour, in short, of dun mist, lying on a moor in bloom. My "tailleuse" had kindly made it as well as she could: because, as she judiciously observed, it was "si triste—si peu voyant," care in the fashion was the more imperative: it was well she took this view of the matter, for I had no flower, no jewel to relieve it: and, what was more, I had no natural rose of complexion.

We become oblivious of these deficiencies in the uniform routine of daily drudgery, but they *will* force upon us their unwelcome blank on those bright occasions when beauty should shine.

However, in this same gown of shadow, I felt at home and at ease; an advantage I should not have enjoyed in anything more brilliant or striking. Madame Beck, too, kept me in countenance; her dress was almost as quiet as mine, except that she wore a bracelet, and a large brooch bright with gold and fine stones. We chanced to meet on the stairs, and she gave me a nod and smile of approbation. Not that she thought I was looking well—a point unlikely to engage her interest—but she considered me dressed "convenablement," "décemment," and la Convenance et la Décence were the two calm deities of Madame's worship. She even paused, laid on my shoulder her gloved hand, holding an embroidered and perfumed hand-kerchief, and confided to my ear a sarcasm on the other teachers (whom she had just been complimenting to their faces). "Nothing so absurd," she said, "as for des femmes mûres 'to dress themselves like girls of fifteen'—quant à la St. Pierre, elle a l'air d'une vieille coquette qui fait l'ingénue."

Being dressed at least a couple of hours before anybody else, I felt a pleasure in betaking myself—not to the garden, where servants were busy propping up long tables, placing seats, and spreading cloths in readiness for the collation—but to the schoolrooms, now empty, quiet, cool, and clean; their walls fresh stained, their plank floors fresh scoured, and scarce dry; flowers fresh gathered adorning the recesses in pots, and draperies, fresh hung, beautifying the great windows.

Withdrawing to the first classe, a smaller and neater room than the others, and taking from the glazed bookcase, of which I kept the key, a volume whose title promised some interest, I sat down to read. The glass-door of this classe, or schoolroom, opened into the large berceau; acacia-boughs caressed its panes, as they stretched across to meet a rose-bush blooming by the opposite lintel: in this rose-bush bees murmured busy and happy. I commenced reading. Just as the stilly hum, the embowering shade, the warm, lonely calm of my retreat were beginning to steal meaning from the page, vision from my eyes, and to lure me along the track of reverie, down into some deep dell of dreamland—just then, the sharpest

ring of the street-door bell to which that much-tried instrument had ever thrilled, snatched me back to consciousness.

Now the bell had been ringing all the morning, as workmen, or servants, or coiffeurs, or tailleuses, went and came on their several errands. Moreover, there was good reason to expect it would ring all the afternoon, since about one hundred externes were yet to arrive in carriages or fiacres: nor could it be expected to rest during the evening, when parents and friends would gather thronging to the play. Under these circumstances, a ring—even a sharp ring—was a matter of course: yet this particular peal had an accent of its own, which chased my dream, and startled my book from my knee.

I was stooping to pick up this last, when—firm, fast, straight—right on through vestibule—along corridor, across carré, through first division, second division, grand salle—strode a step, quick, regular, intent. The closed door of the first classe—my sanctuary—offered no obstacle; it burst open, and a paletôt and a bonnet grec filled the void; also two eyes first vaguely struck upon, and then hungrily dived into me.

"C'est cela!" said a voice. "Je la connais; c'est l'Anglaise. Tant pis. Tout Anglaise, et, par conséquent, toute bégueule qu'elle soit—elle fera mon affaire, ou je saurai pourquoi."

Then, with a certain stern politeness (I suppose he thought I had not caught the drift of his previous uncivil mutterings), and in a jargon the most execrable that ever was heard, "Meess——, play you must: I am planted there."

"What can I do for you, M. Paul Emanuel?" I inquired: for M. Paul Emanuel it was, and in a state of no little excitement.

"Play you must. I will not have you shrink, or frown, or make the prude. I read your skull that night you came; I see your moyens: play you can: play you must."

"But how, M. Paul? What do you mean?"

"There is no time to be lost," he went on, now speaking in French; "and let us thrust to the wall all reluctance, all excuses, all minauderies. You must take a part."

"In the vaudeville?"

"In the vaudeville. You have said it."

I gasped, horror-struck. *What* did the little man mean?

"Listen!" he said. "The case shall be stated, and you shall then answer me Yes or No; and according to your answer shall I ever after estimate you."

The scarce-suppressed impetus of a most irritable nature glowed in his cheek, fed with sharp shafts his glances, a nature—the injudicious, the mawkish, the hesitating, the sullen, the affected, above all, the unyielding, might quickly render violent and implacable. Silence and attention was the best balm to apply: I listened.

"The whole matter is going to fail," he began. "Louise Vanderkelkov has fallen ill—at least so her ridiculous mother asserts; for my part, I feel sure she might play if she would: it is only good-will that lacks. She was charged with a rôle, as you know, or do *not* know—it is equal: without that rôle the play is stopped. There are now but a few hours in which to learn it: not a girl in this school would hear reason, and accept the task. Forsooth, it is not an interesting, not an amiable, part; their vile amour-propre—that base quality of which women have so much—would revolt from it. Englishwomen are either the best or the worst of their sex. Dieu sait que je les déteste comme la peste, ordinairement" (this between his recreant teeth). "I apply to an Englishwoman to rescue me. What is her answer—Yes, or No?"

A thousand objections rushed into my mind. The foreign language, the limited time, the public display. . . . Inclination recoiled, Ability faltered, Self-respect (that "vile quality") trembled. "Non, non, non!" said all these; but looking up at M. Paul, and seeing in his vexed, fiery, and searching eye, a sort of appeal behind all its menace, my lips dropped the word "oui." For a moment his rigid countenance relaxed with a quiver of content: quickly bent up again, however, he went on—

"Vite à l'ouvrage! Here is the book; here is your rôle: read." And I read. He did not commend; at some passages he scowled and stamped. He gave me a lesson: I diligently imitated. It was a disagreeable part—a man's—an empty-headed fop's. One could put into it neither heart nor soul: I hated it. The play—a mere trifle— ran chiefly on the efforts of a brace of rivals to gain the hand of a fair coquette. One lover was called the "Ours," a good and gallant but unpolished man, a sort of diamond in the rough; the other was a butterfly, a talker, and a traitor: and I was to be the butterfly, talker, and traitor.

I did my best—which was bad, I know: it provoked M. Paul; he fumed. Putting both hands to the work, I endeavoured to do better than my best; I presume he gave me credit for good intentions; he professed to be partially content. "Ça ira!" he cried; and as voices began sounding from the garden, and white dresses fluttering among the trees, he added: "You must withdraw: you must be alone to learn this. Come with me."

Without being allowed time or power to deliberate, I found myself in the same breath convoyed along as in a species of whirlwind, up stairs, up two pair of stairs, nay, actually up three (for this fiery little man seemed as by instinct to know his way everywhere); to the solitary and lofty attic was I borne, put in and locked in, the key being in the door, and that key he took with him and vanished.

The attic was no pleasant place: I believe he did not know how unpleasant it was, or he never would have locked me in with so little ceremony. In this summer weather, it was hot as Africa; as in winter, it was always cold as Greenland. Boxes and lumber filled it; old dresses draped its unstained wall—cobwebs its unswept ceiling. Well was it known to be tenanted by rats, by black beetles, and by cock- roaches—nay, rumour affirmed that the ghostly Nun of the garden had once been seen here. A partial darkness obscured one end, across which, as for deeper mystery, an old russet curtain was drawn, by way of screen to a sombre band of winter cloaks, pendant each from its pin—like a malefactor from his gibbet. From amongst these cloaks, and behind that curtain, the Nun was said to issue. I did not believe this, nor was I troubled by apprehension thereof; but I saw a very dark and large rat, with a long tail, come gliding out from that squalid alcove; and, moreover, my eye fell on many a black beetle, dotting the floor. These objects discomposed me more, perhaps, than it would be wise to say, as also did the dust, lumber, and stifling heat of the place. The last inconvenience would soon have become intolerable, had I not found means to open and prop up the skylight, thus admitting some freshness. Underneath this aperture I pushed a large empty chest, and having mounted upon it a smaller box, and wiped from both the dust, I gathered my dress (my best, the reader must remember, and therefore a legitimate object of care) fastidiously around me, ascended this species of extempore throne, and being seated, commenced the acquisition of my task; while I learned, not forgetting to keep a sharp look-out on the black beetles and cockroaches, of which, more even, I believe, than of the rats, I sat in mortal dread.

My impression at first was that I had undertaken what it really was impossible to perform, and I simply resolved to do my best and be resigned to fail. I soon found, however, that one part in so short a piece was not more than memory could master at a few hours' notice. I learned and learned on, first in a whisper, and then aloud. Perfectly secure from human audience, I acted my part before the garret- vermin. Entering into its emptiness, frivolity, and falsehood, with a spirit inspired by scorn and impatience, I took my revenge on this "fat," by making him as fatuitous as I possibly could.

In this exercise the afternoon passed: day began to glide into evening; and I, who had eaten nothing since breakfast, grew excessively hungry. Now I thought of the collation, which doubtless they were just then devouring in the garden far below. (I had seen in the vestibule a basketful of small "pâtés à la crème," than which nothing in the whole range of cookery seemed to me better.) A pâté,

or a square of cake, it seemed to me would come very apropos; and as my relish
for those dainties increased, it began to appear somewhat hard that I should pass
my holiday fasting and in prison. Remote as was the attic from the street-door and
vestibule, yet the ever-tinkling bell was faintly audible here; and also the ceaseless
roll of wheels on the tormented pavement. I knew that the house and garden were
thronged, and that all was gay and glad below; here it began to grow dusk: the
beetles were fading from my sight; I trembled lest they should steal on me a march,
mount my throne unseen, and, unsuspected, invade my skirts. Impatient and ap-
prehensive, I recommenced the rehearsal of my part merely to kill time. Just as I
was concluding, the long-delayed rattle of the key in the lock came to my ear—
no unwelcome sound. M. Paul (I could just see through the dusk that it _was_ M.
Paul, for light enough still lingered to show the velvet blackness of his close-shorn
head, and the sallow ivory of his brow) looked in.

"Brava!" cried he, holding the door open and remaining at the threshold. "J'ai
tout entendu. C'est assez bien. Encore!"

A moment I hesitated.

"Encore!" said he sternly. "Et point de grimaces! A bas la timidité!"

Again I went through the part, but not half so well as I had spoken it alone.

"Enfin, elle sait," said he, half dissatisfied, "and one cannot be fastidious or
exacting under the circumstances." Then he added, "You may yet have twenty
minutes for preparation: au revoir!" And he was going.

"Monsieur," I called out, taking courage.

"Eh bien. Qu'est ce que c'est, Mademoiselle?"

"J'ai bien faim."

"Comment, vous avez faim! Et la collation?"

"I know nothing about it. I have not seen it, shut up here."

"Ah! C'est vrai," cried he.

In a moment my throne was abdicated, the attic evacuated; an inverse repetition
of the impetus which had brought me up into the attic, instantly took me down—
down—down to the very kitchen. I thought I should have gone to the cellar. The
cook was imperatively ordered to produce food, and I, as imperatively, was commanded
to eat. To my great joy this food was limited to coffee and cake: I had feared wine
and sweets, which I did not like. How he guessed that I should like a "petit pâté
à la crème" I cannot tell; but he went out and procured me one from some quarter.
With considerable willingness I ate and drank, keeping the "petit pâté" till the
last, as a bonne bouche. M. Paul superintended my repast, and almost forced upon
me more than I could swallow.

"A la bonne heure," he cried, when I had signified that I really could take no
more, and, with uplifted hands, implored to be spared the additional roll on which
he had just spread butter. "You will set me down as a species of tyrant and
Bluebeard, starving women in a garret; whereas, after all, I am no such thing. Now,
Mademoiselle, do you feel courage and strength to appear?"

I said I thought I did; though, in truth, I was perfectly confused, and could hardly
tell how I felt: but this little man was of the order of beings who must not be
opposed, unless you possessed an all-dominant force sufficient to crush him at
once.

"Come then," said he, offering his hand.

I gave him mine, and he set off with a rapid walk, which obliged me to run at
his side in order to keep pace. In the carré he stopped a moment; it was lit with
large lamps; the wide doors of the classes were open, and so were the equally wide
garden-doors; orange-trees in tubs, and tall flowers in pots, ornamented these portals,
on each side; groups of ladies and gentlemen in evening dress stood and walked
amongst the flowers. Within, the long vista of the schoolrooms presented a thronging,
undulating, murmuring, waving, streaming multitude, all rose, and blue, and half

translucent white. There were lustres, burning overhead; far off there was a stage, a solemn green curtain, a row of footlights.

"N'est-ce pas que c'est beau?" demanded my companion.

I should have said it was, but my heart got up into my throat. M. Paul discovered this, and gave me a side-scowl and a little shake for my pains.

"I will do my best, but I wish it was over," said I; then I asked: "Are we to walk through that crowd?"

"By no means: I manage matters better: we pass through the garden—here."

In an instant we were out of doors: the cool, calm night revived me somewhat. It was moonless, but the reflex from the many glowing windows lit the court brightly, and even the alleys—dimly. Heaven was cloudless, and grand with the quiver of its living fires. How soft are the nights of the Continent! How bland, balmy, safe! No sea-fog; no chilling damp: mistless as noon, and fresh as morning.

Having crossed court and garden, we reached the glass door of the first classe. It stood open, like all other doors that night; we passed, and then I was ushered into a small cabinet, dividing the first classe from the grand salle. This cabinet dazzled me, it was so full of light: it deafened me, it was clamorous with voices: it stifled me, it was so hot, choking, thronged.

"De l'ordre; Du silence!" cried M. Paul. "Is this chaos?" he demanded; and there was a hush. With a dozen words, and as many gestures, he turned out half the persons present, and obliged the remnant to fall into rank. Those left were all in costume: they were the performers, and this was the green-room. M. Paul introduced me. All stared and some tittered. It was a surprise: they had not expected the Englishwoman would play in a vaudeville. Ginevra Fanshawe, beautifully dressed for her part, and looking fascinatingly pretty, turned on me a pair of eyes as round as beads. In the highest spirit, unperturbed by fear or bashfulness, delighted indeed at the thought of shining off before hundreds—my entrance seemed to transfix her with amazement in the midst of her joy. She would have exclaimed, but M. Paul held her and all the rest in check.

Having surveyed and criticised the whole troop, he turned to me.

"You, too, must be dressed for your part."

"Dressed—dressed like a man!" exclaimed Zélie St. Pierre, darting forwards; adding with officiousness, "I will dress her myself."

To be dressed like a man did not please, and would not suit me. I had consented to take a man's name and part; as to his dress—halte là! No. I would keep my own dress; come what might. M. Paul might storm, might rage: I would keep my own dress. I said so, with a voice as resolute in intent, as it was low, aud perhaps unsteady, in utterance.

He did not immediately storm or rage, as I fully thought he would: he stood silent. But Zélie again interposed.

"She will make a capital petit maître. Here are the garments, all—all complete: somewhat too large, but I will arrange all that. Come, chère amie—belle Anglaise!"

And she sneered, for I was not "belle." She seized my hand, she was drawing me away. M. Paul stood impassable—neutral.

"You must not resist," pursued St. Pierre—for resist I did. "You will spoil all, destroy the mirth of the piece, the enjoyment of the company, sacrifice everything to your amour-propre. This would be too bad—Monsieur will never permit this?"

She sought his eye. I watched, likewise, for a glance. He gave her one, and then he gave me one. "Stop!" he said slowly, arresting St. Pierre, who continued her efforts to drag me after her. Everybody awaited the decision. He was not angry, not irritated; I perceived that, and took heart.

"You do not like these clothes?" he asked, pointing to the masculine vestments.

"I don't object to some of them, but I won't have them all."

"How must it be, then? How accept a man's part, and go on the stage dressed as a woman? This is an amateur affair, it is true—a vaudeville de pensionnat; certain

modifications I might sanction, yet something you must have to announce you as of the nobler sex.''

''And I will, Monsieur; but it must be arranged in my own way: nobody must meddle; the things must not be forced upon me. Just let me dress myself.''

Monsieur, without another word, took the costume from St. Pierre, gave it to me, and permitted me to pass into the dressing-room. Once alone, I grew calm, and collectedly went to work. Retaining my woman's garb without the slightest retrenchment, I merely assumed, in addition, a little vest, a collar, and cravat, and a paletôt of small dimensions; the whole being the costume of a brother of one of the pupils. Having loosened my hair out of its braids, made up the long back hair close, and brushed the front hair to one side, I took my hat and gloves in my hand, and came out. M. Paul was waiting, and so were the others. He looked at me. ''That may pass in a pensionnat,'' he pronounced. Then added, not unkindly, ''Courage, mon ami! Un peu de sang froid—un peu d'aplomb, M. Lucien, et tout ira bien.''

St. Pierre sneered again, in her cold snaky manner.

I was irritable, because excited, and I could not help turning upon her and saying, that if she were not a lady and I a gentleman, I should feel disposed to call her out.

''After the play, after the play,'' said M. Paul. ''I will then divide my pair of pistols between you, and we will settle the dispute according to form: it will only be the old quarrel of France and England.''

But now the moment approached for the performance to commence. M. Paul, setting us before him, harangued us briefly like a general addressing soldiers about to charge. I don't know what he said, except that he recommended each to penetrate herself with a sense of her personal insignificance. God knows I thought this advice superfluous for some of us. A bell tinkled. I and two more were ushered on to the stage, The bell tinkled again. I had to speak the very first words.

''Do not look at the crowd, nor think of it,'' whispered M. Paul in my ear. ''Imagine yourself in the garret, acting to the rats.''

He vanished. The curtain drew up—shrivelled to the ceiling: the bright lights, the long room, the gay throng, burst upon us. I thought of the black beetles, the old boxes, the worm-eaten bureaux. I said my say badly; but I said it. That first speech was the difficulty; it revealed to me this fact, that it was not the crowd I feared so much as my own voice. Foreigners and strangers, the crowd were nothing to me. Nor did I think of them. When my tongue once got free, and my voice took its true pitch, and found its natural tone, I thought of nothing but the personage I represented—and of M. Paul, who was listening, watching, prompting in the side-scenes.

By-and-by, feeling the right power come—the spring demanded gush and rise inwardly—I became sufficiently composed to notice my fellow-actors. Some of them played very well; especially Ginevra Fanshawe, who had to coquette between two suitors, and managed admirably: in fact she was in her element. I observed that she once or twice threw a certain marked fondness and pointed partiality into her manner towards me—the fop. With such emphasis and animation did she favour me, such glances did she dart out into the listening and applauding crowd, that to me—who knew her—it presently became evident she was acting *at* some one; and I followed her eye, her smile, her gesture, and ere long discovered that she had at least singled out a handsome and distinguished aim for her shafts; full in the path of those arrows—taller than other spectators, and therefore more sure to receive them—stood, in attitude quiet but intent, a well-known form—that of Dr. John.

The spectacle seemed somehow suggestive. There was language in Dr. John's look, though I cannot tell what he said; it animated me: I drew out of it a history; I put my idea into the part I performed; I threw it into my wooing of Ginevra. In the ''Ours,'' or sincere lover, I saw Dr. John. Did I pity him, as erst? No, I hardened

my heart, rivalled and out-rivalled him. I knew myself but a fop, but where *he* was outcast *I* could please. Now I know I acted as if wishful and resolute to win and conquer. Ginevra seconded me; between us we half-changed the nature of the rôle, gilding it from top to toe. Between the acts M. Paul told us he knew not what possessed us, and half expostulated, "C'est peutêtre plus beau que votre modèle," said he, "mais ce n'est pas juste." I know not what possessed me either; but somehow, my longing was to eclipse the "Ours," *i.e.,* Dr. John. Ginevra was tender; how could I be otherwise than chivalric? Retaining the letter, I recklessly altered the spirit of the rôle. Without heart, without interest, I could not play it at all. It must be played—in went the yearned-for seasoning—thus flavoured, I played it with relish.

What I felt that night, and what I did, I no more expected to feel and do, than to be lifted in a trance to the seventh heaven. Cold, reluctant, apprehensive, I had accepted a part to please another: ere long, warming, becoming interested, taking courage, I acted to please myself. Yet the next day, when I thought it over, I quite disapproved of these amateur performances; and though glad that I had obliged M. Paul, and tried my own strength for once, I took a firm resolution never to be drawn into a similar affair. A keen relish for dramatic expression had revealed itself as part of my nature; to cherish and exercise this new-found faculty might gift me with a world of delight, but it would not do for a mere looker-on at life: the strength and longing must be put by; and I put them by, and fastened them in with the lock of a resolution which neither Time nor Temptation has since picked.

No sooner was the play over and *well* over, than the choleric and arbitrary M. Paul underwent a metamorphosis. His hour of managerial responsibility past, he at once laid aside his magisterial austerity; in a moment he stood amongst us, vivacious, kind, and social, shook hands with us all round, thanked us separately, and announced his determination that each of us should in turn be his partner in the coming ball. On his claiming my promise, I told him I did not dance. "For once I must," was the answer; and if I had not slipped aside and kept out of his way, he would have compelled me to this second performance. But I had acted enough for one evening; it was time I retired into myself and my ordinary life. My dun-coloured dress did well enough under a paletôt on the stage, but would not suit a waltz or a quadrille. Withdrawing to a quiet nook, whence unobserved I could observe—the ball, its splendours and its pleasures, passed before me as a spectacle.

Again, Ginevra Fanshawe was the belle, the fairest and the gayest present; she was selected to open the ball: very lovely she looked, very gracefully she danced, very joyously she smiled. Such scenes were her triumphs—she was the child of pleasure. Work or suffering found her listless and dejected, powerless and repining; but gaiety expanded her butterfly's wings, lit up their gold-dust and bright spots, made her flash like a gem, and flush like a flower. At all ordinary diet and plain beverage she would pout; but she fed on creams and ices like a humming-bird on honey-paste: sweet wine was her element, and sweet cake her daily bread. Ginevra lived her full life in a ball-room; elsewhere she drooped dispirited.

Think not, reader, that she thus bloomed and sparkled for the mere sake of M. Paul, her partner, or that she lavished her best graces that night for the edification of her companions only, or for that of the parents and grand-parents, who filled the carré and lined the ballroom; under circumstances so insipid and limited, with motives so chilly and vapid, Ginevra would scarce have deigned to walk one quadrille, and weariness and fretfulness would have replaced animation and good-humour, but she knew of a leaven in the otherwise heavy festal mass which lighted the whole; she tasted a condiment which gave it zest; she perceived reasons justifying the display of her choicest attractions.

In the ball-room, indeed, not a single male spectator was to be seen who was not married and a father—M. Paul excepted—that gentleman, too, being the sole creature of his sex permitted to lead out a pupil to the dance; and this exceptional

part was allowed him, partly as a matter of old-established custom (for he was a kinsman of Madame Beck's, and high in her confidence), partly because he would always have his own way aud do as he pleased, and partly because—wilful, passionate, partial, as he might be—he was the soul of honour, and might be trusted with a regiment of the fairest and purest, in perfect security that under his leadership they would come to no harm. Many of the girls—it may be noted in parenthesis—were not pure-minded at all, very much otherwise; but they no more dare betray their natural coarseness in M. Paul's presence, than they dare tread purposely on his corns, laugh in his face during a stormy apostrophe, or speak above their breath while some crisis of irritability was covering his human visage with the mask of an intelligent tiger. M. Paul, then, might dance with whom he would—and woe be to the interference which put him out of step.

Others there were admitted as spectators—with (seeming) reluctance, through prayers, by influence, under restriction, by special and difficult exercise of Madame Beck's gracious good nature, and whom she all the evening—with her own personal surveillance—kept far aloof at the remotest, dreariest, coldest, darkest side of the carré—a small, forlorn band of "jeunes gens"; these being all of the best families, grown-up sons of mothers present, and whose sisters were pupils in the school. The whole evening was Madame on duty beside these "jeunes gens"—attentive to them as a mother, but strict with them as a dragon. There was a sort of cordon sketched before them, which they wearied her with prayers to be permitted to pass, and just to revive themselves by one dance with that "belle blonde," or that "jolie brune," or "cette jeune fille magnifique aux cheveux noirs comme le jais."

"Taisez-vous!" Madame would reply, heroically and inexorably. "Vous ne passerez pas à moins que ce ne soit sur mon cadavre, et vous ne danserez qu'avec la nonnette du jardin" (alluding to the legend). And she majestically walked to and fro along their disconsolate and impatient line, like a little Bonaparte in a mouse-coloured silk gown.

Madame knew something of the world; Madame knew much of human nature. I don't think that another directress in Villette would have dared to admit a "jeune homme" within her walls; but Madame knew that by granting such admission, on an occasion like the present, a bold stroke might be struck, and a great point gained.

In the first place, the parents were made accomplices to the deed, for it was only through their mediation it was brought about. Secondly: the admission of these rattlesnakes, so fascinating and so dangerous, served to draw out Madame precisely in her strongest character—that of a first-rate "surveillante." Thirdly: their presence furnished a most piquant ingredient to the entertainment: the pupils knew it, and saw it, and the view of such golden apples shining afar off, animated them with a spirit no other circumstance could have kindled. The children's pleasure spread to the parents; life and mirth circulated quickly round the ball-room; the "jeunes gens" themselves, though restrained, were amused: for Madame never permitted them to feel dull—and thus Madame Beck's fête annually ensured a success unknown to the fête of any other directress in the land.

I observed that Dr. John was at first permitted to walk at large through the classes: there was about him a manly, responsible look, that redeemed his youth, and half-expiated his beauty; but as soon as the ball began, Madame ran up to him.

"Come, Wolf; come," said she, laughing: "you wear sheep's clothing, but you must quit the fold notwithstanding. Come; I have a fine menagerie of twenty here in the carré: let me place you amongst my collection."

"But first suffer me to have one dance with one pupil of my choice."

"Have you the face to ask such a thing? It is madness: it is impiety. Sortez, sortez, et au plus vite."

She drove him before her, and soon had him enclosed within the cordon.

Ginevra being, I suppose, tired with dancing, sought me out in my retreat. She threw herself on the bench beside me, and (a demonstration I could very well have dispensed with) cast her arms round my neck.

"Lucy Snowe! Lucy Snowe!" she cried in a somewhat sobbing voice, half hysterical.

"What in the world is the matter?" I drily said.

"How do I look—how do I look to-night?" she demanded.

"As usual," said I; "preposterously vain."

"Caustic creature! You never have a kind word for me; but in spite of you, and all other envious detractors, I know I am beautiful; I feel it, I see it—for there is a great looking-glass in the dressing-room, where I can view my shape from head to foot. Will you go with me now, and let us two stand before it?"

"I will, Miss Fanshawe: you shall be humoured even to the top of your bent."

The dressing-room was very near, and we stepped in. Putting her arm through mine, she drew me to the mirror. Without resistance, remonstrance, or remark, I stood and let her self-love have its feast and triumph: curious to see how much it could swallow—whether it was possible it could feed to satiety—whether any whisper of consideration for others could penetrate her heart, and moderate its vain-glorious exultation.

Not at all. She turned me and herself round; she viewed us both on all sides; she smiled, she waved her curls, she retouched her sash, she spread her dress, and finally, letting go my arm, and curtseying with mock respect, she said—

"I would not be you for a kingdom."

The remark was too naïve to rouse anger; I merely said—

"Very good."

"And what would *you* give to be ME?" she inquired.

"Not a bad sixpence—strange as it may sound," I replied. "You are but a poor creature."

"You don't think so in your heart."

"No; for in my heart you have not the outline of a place: I only occasionally turn you over in my brain."

"Well, but," said she, in an expostulatory tone, "just listen to the difference of our positions, and then see how happy am I, and how miserable are you."

"Go on; I listen."

"In the first place: I am the daughter of a gentleman of family, and though my father is not rich, I have expectations from an uncle. Then, I am just eighteen, the finest age possible. I have had a continental education, and though I can't spell, I have abundant accomplishments. I *am* pretty; *you* can't deny that; I may have as many admirers as I choose. This very night I have been breaking the hearts of two gentlemen, and it is the dying look I had from one of them just now which puts me in such spirits. I do so like to watch them turn red and pale, and scowl and dart fiery glances at each other, and languishing ones at me. There is *me*—happy ME; now for *you*, poor soul!

"I suppose you are nobody's daughter, since you took care of little children when you first came to Villette: you have no relations; you can't call yourself young at twenty-three; you have no attractive accomplishments—no beauty. As to admirers, you hardly know what they are; you can't even talk on the subject: you sit dumb when the other teachers quote their conquests. I believe you never were in love, and never will be; you don't know the feeling: and so much the better, for though you might have your own heart broken, no living heart will you ever break. Isn't it all true?"

"A good deal of it is true as gospel, and shrewd besides. There must be good in you, Ginevra, to speak so honestly; that snake, Zélie St. Pierre, could not utter what you have uttered. Still, Miss Fanshawe, hapless as I am, according to your showing, sixpence I would not give to purchase you, body and soul."

"Just because I am not clever, and that is all *you* think of. Nobody in the world but you cares for cleverness."

"On the contrary, I consider you *are* clever, in your way—very smart indeed. But you were talking of breaking hearts—that edifying amusement into the merits of which I don't quite enter: pray on whom does your vanity lead you to think you have done execution to-night?"

She approached her lips to my ear—"Isidore and Alfred de Hamal are both here," she whispered.

"Oh! they are? I should like to see them."

"There's a dear creature! your curiosity is roused at last. Follow me, I will point them out."

She proudly led the way—"But you cannot see them well from the classes," said she, turning, "Madame keeps them too far off. Let us cross the garden, enter by the corridor, and get close to them behind: we shall be scolded if we are seen, but never mind."

For once, I did not mind. Through the garden we went—penetrated into the corridor by a quiet private entrance, and approaching the carré, yet keeping in the corridor shade, commanded a near view of the band of "jeunes gens."

I believe I could have picked out the conquering De Hamal even undirected. He was a straight-nosed, very correct-featured little dandy. I say *little* dandy, though he was not beneath the middle standard in stature; but his lineaments were small, and so were his hands and feet; and he was pretty and smooth, and as trim as a doll: so nicely dressed, so nicely curled, so booted and gloved and cravated—he was charming indeed. I said so: "What a dear personage!" cried I, and commended Ginevra's taste warmly; and asked her what she thought De Hamal might have done with the precious fragments of that heart she had broken—whether he kept them in a scent-vial, and conserved them in otto of roses? I observed, too, with deep rapture of approbation, that the Colonel's hands were scarce larger than Miss Fanshawe's own, and suggested that this circumstance might be convenient, as he could wear her gloves at a pinch. On his dear curls, I told her I doted; and as to his low, Grecian brow, and exquisite classic headpiece, I confessed I had no language to do such perfections justice.

"And if he were your lover?" suggested the cruelly exultant Ginevra.

"Oh! heavens, what bliss!" said I; "but do not be inhuman, Miss Fanshawe: to put such thoughts into my head is like showing poor outcast Cain a far glimpse of Paradise."

"You like him, then?"

"As I like sweets, and jams, and comfits, and conservatory flowers."

Ginevra admired my taste, for all these things were her adoration; she could then readily credit that they were mine too.

"Now for Isidore," I went on. I own I felt still more curious to see him than his rival; but Ginevra was absorbed in the latter.

"Alfred was admitted here to-night," said she, "through the influence of his aunt, Madame le Baronne de Dorlodot; and now, having seen him, can you not understand why I have been in such spirits all the evening, and acted so well, and danced with such life, and why I am now happy as a queen? Dieu! Dieu! It was such good fun to glance first at him and then at the other, and madden them both."

"But the other—where is he? Show me Isidore."

"I don't like."

"Why not?"

"I am ashamed of him."

" For what reason?"

"Because—because—(in a whisper)—he has such—such whiskers, orange—red—there now!"

"The murder is out," I subjoined. "Never mind, show him all the same; I engage not to faint."

She looked round. Just then an English voice spoke behind her and me.

"You are both standing in a draught; you must leave this corridor."

"There is no draught, Dr. John," said I, turning.

"She takes cold so easily," he pursued, looking at Ginevra with extreme kindness. "She is delicate; she must be cared for: fetch her a shawl."

"Permit me to judge for myself," said Miss Fanshawe, with hauteur. "I want no shawl."

"Your dress is thin, you have been dancing, you are heated."

"Always preaching," retorted she; "always coddling and admonishing."

The answer Dr. John would have given did not come; that his heart was hurt became evident in his eye; darkened, and saddened, and pained, he turned a little aside, but was patient. I knew where there were plenty of shawls near at hand; I ran and fetched one.

"She shall wear this if I have strength to make her," said I, folding it well round her muslin dress, covering carefully her neck and arms. "Is that Isidore?" I asked in a somewhat fierce whisper.

She pushed up her lip, smiled, and nodded.

"Is *that* Isidore?" I repeated, giving her a shake: I could have given her a dozen.

"C'est lui-même," said she. "How coarse he is, compared with the Colonel-Count! And then—oh, ciel!—the whiskers!"

Dr. John now passed on.

"The Colonel-Count!" I echoed. "The doll—the puppet—the manikin—the poor inferior creature! A mere lackey for Dr. John: his valet, his foot-boy! Is it possible that fine generous gentleman—handsome as a vision—offers you his honourable hand and gallant heart, and promises to protect your flimsy person and wretchless mind through the storms and struggles of life—and you hang back—you scorn, you sting, you torture him! Have you power to do this? Who gave you that power? Where is it? Does it lie all in your beauty—your pink and white complexion, and your yellow hair? Does this bind his soul at your feet, and bend his neck under your yoke? Does this purchase for you his affection, his tenderness, his thoughts, his hopes, his interest, his noble, cordial love—and will you not have it? Do you scorn it? You are only dissembling: you are not in earnest; you love him; you long for him; but you trifle with his heart to make him more surely yours?"

"Bah! How you run on! I don't understand half you have said."

I had got her out into the garden ere this. I now set her down on a seat and told her she should not stir till she had avowed which she meant in the end to accept—the man or the monkey.

"Him you call the man," said she, "is bourgeois, sandy-haired, and answers to the name of John—cela suffit: je n'en veux pas. Colonel de Hamal is a gentleman of excellent connections, perfect manners, sweet appearance, with pale interesting face, and hair and eyes like an Italian. Then, too, he is the most delightful company possible—a man quite in my way; not sensible and serious like the other, but one with whom I can talk on equal terms—who does not plague and bore, and harass me with depths, and heights, and passions, and talents for which I have no taste. There now. Don't hold me so fast."

I slackened my grasp, and she darted off. I did not care to pursue her.

Somehow I could not avoid returning once more in the direction of the corridor to get another glimpse of Dr. John; but I met him on the garden-steps, standing where the light from a window fell broad. His well-proportioned figure was not to be mistaken, for I doubt whether there was another in that assemblage his equal. He carried his hat in his hand; his uncovered head, his face and fine brow were most handsome and manly. *His* features were not delicate, not slight like those of a woman, nor were they cold, frivolous, and feeble; though well cut, they were

not so chiselled, so frittered away, as to lose in power and significance what they gained in unmeaning symmetry. Much feeling spoke in them at times, and more sat silent in his eye. Such at least were my thoughts of him: to me he seemed all this. An inexpressible sense of wonder occupied me as I looked at this man, and reflected that *he* could be slighted.

It was not my intention to approach or address him in the garden, our terms of acquaintance not warranting such a step; I had only meant to view him in the crowd—myself unseen: coming upon him thus alone, I withdrew. But he was looking out for me, or rather for her who had been with me: therefore he descended the steps, and followed me down the alley.

"You know Miss Fanshawe? I have often wished to ask whether you knew her," said he.

"Yes: I know her."

"Intimately?"

"Quite as intimately as I wish."

"What have you done with her now?"

"Am I her keeper?" I felt inclined to ask; but I simply answered, "I have shaken her well, and would have shaken her better, but she escaped out of my hands and ran away."

"Would you favour me," he asked, "by watching over her this one evening, and observing that she does nothing imprudent—does not, for instance, run out into the night-air immediately after dancing?"

"I may, perhaps, look after her a little, since you wish it; but she likes her own way too well to submit readily to control."

"She is so young, so thoroughly artless," said he.

"To me she is an enigma," I responded.

"Is she?" he asked, much interested. "How?"

"It would be difficult to say how—difficult, at least, to tell *you* how."

"And why me?"

"I wonder she is not better pleased that you are so much her friend."

"But she has not the slightest idea how much I *am* her friend. That is precisely the point I cannot teach her. May I inquire did she ever speak of me to you?"

"Under the name of 'Isidore' she has talked about you often; but I must add that it is only within the last ten minutes I have discovered that you and 'Isidore' are identical. It is only, Dr. John, within that brief space of time I have learned that Ginevra Fanshawe is the person, under this roof, in whom you have long been interested—that she is the magnet which attracts you to the Rue Fossette, that for her sake you venture into this garden, and seek out caskets dropped by rivals."

"You know all?"

"I know so much."

"For more than a year I have been accustomed to meet her in society. Mrs. Cholmondeley, her friend, is an acquaintance of mine; thus I see her every Sunday. But you observed that under the name of 'Isidore' she often spoke of me: may I—without inviting you to a breach of confidence—inquire what was the tone, what the feeling of her remarks? I feel somewhat anxious to know, being a little tormented with uncertainty as to how I stand with her."

"Oh, she varies: she shifts and changes like the wind."

"Still, you can gather some general idea?"——

"I can," thought I, "but it would not do to communicate that general idea to you. Besides, if I said she did not love you, I know you would not believe me."

"You are silent," he pursued. "I suppose you have no good news to impart. No matter. If she feels for me positive coldness and aversion, it is a sign I do not deserve her."

"Do you doubt yourself? Do you consider yourself the inferior of Colonel de Hamal?"

"I love Miss Fanshawe far more than De Hamal loves any human being, and would care for and guard her better than he. Respecting De Hamal, I fear she is under an illusion; the man's character is known to me, all his antecedents, all his scrapes. He is not worthy of your beautiful young friend."

"My 'beautiful young friend' ought to know that, and to know or feel who is worthy of her," said I. "If her beauty or her brains will not serve her so far, she merits the sharp lesson of experience."

"Are you not a little severe?"

"I am excessively severe—more severe than I choose to show you. You should hear the strictures with which I favour 'my beautiful young friend,' only that you would be unutterably shocked at my want of tender considerateness for her delicate nature."

"She is so lovely, one cannot but be loving towards her. You—every woman older than herself, must feel for such a simple, innocent, girlish fairy a sort of motherly or elder-sisterly fondness. Graceful angel! Does not your heart yearn towards her when she pours into your ear her pure, childlike confidences? How you are privileged!" And he sighed.

"I cut short these confidences somewhat abruptly now and then," said I. "But excuse me, Dr. John, may I change the theme for one instant? What a god-like person is that De Hamal! What a nose on his face—perfect! Model one in putty or clay, you could not make a better or straighter, or neater; and then, such classic lips and chin—and his bearing—sublime."

"De Hamal is an unutterable puppy, besides being a very white-livered hero."

"You, Dr. John, and every man of a less refined mould than he, must feel for him a sort of admiring affection, such as Mars and the coarser deities may be supposed to have borne the young, graceful Apollo."

"An unprincipled, gambling, little jackanapes!" said Dr. John curtly, "whom, with one hand, I could lift up by the waistband any day, and lay low in the kennel if I liked."

"The sweet seraph!" said I. "What a cruel idea? Are you not a little severe, Dr. John?"

And now I paused. For the second time that night I was going beyond myself—venturing out of what I looked on as my natural habits—speaking in an unpremeditated, impulsive strain, which startled me strangely when I halted to reflect. On rising that morning, had I anticipated that before night I should have acted the part of a gay lover in a vaudeville: and an hour after, frankly discussed with Dr. John the question of his hapless suit, and rallied him on his illusions? I had no more presaged such feats than I had looked forward to an ascent in a balloon, or a voyage to Cape Horn.

The Doctor and I, having paced down the walk, were now returning; the reflex from the window again lit his face: he smiled, but his eye was melancholy. How I wished that he could feel heart's-ease! How I grieved that he brooded over pain, and pain from such a cause! He, with his great advantages, *he* to love in vain! I did not then know that the pensiveness of reverse is the best phase for some minds; nor did I reflect that some herbs, "though scentless when entire, yield fragrance when they're bruised."

"Do not be sorrowful, do not grieve," I broke out. "If there is in Ginevra one spark of worthiness of your affection, she will—she *must* feel devotion in return. Be cheerful, be hopeful, Dr. John. Who should hope, if not you?"

In return for this speech I got—what, it must be supposed, I deserved—a look of surprise: I thought also of some disapprobation. We parted, and I went into the house very chill. The clocks struck and the bells tolled midnight; people were leaving fast: the fête was over; the lamps were fading. In another hour all the dwelling-house, and all the pensionnat, were dark and hushed. I too was in bed, but not asleep. To me it was not easy to sleep after a day of such excitement.

Chapter XV

THE LONG VACATION

FOLLOWING Madame Beck's fête, with its three preceding weeks of relaxation, its brief twelve hours' burst of hilarity and dissipation, and its one subsequent day of utter languor, came a period of reaction; two months of real application, of close, hard study. These two months, being the last of the "année scolaire," were indeed the only genuine working months in the year. To them was procrastinated—into them concentrated, alike by professors, mistresses, and pupils—the main burden of preparation for the examinations preceding the distribution of prizes. Candidates for rewards had then to work in good earnest; masters and teachers had to set their shoulders to the wheel, to urge on the backward, and diligently aid and train the more promising. A showy demonstration—a telling exhibition—must be got up for public view, and all means were fair to this end.

I scarcely noted how the other teachers went to work; I had my own business to mind; and *my* task was not the least onerous, being to imbue some ninety sets of brains with a due tincture of what they considered a most complicated and difficult science, that of the English language; and to drill ninety tongues in what, for them, was an almost impossible pronunciation—the lisping and hissing dentals of the isles.

The examination-day arrived. Awful day! Prepared for with anxious care, dressed for with silent dispatch—nothing vaporous or fluttering now—no white gauze or azure streamers; the grave, close, compact was the order of the toilette. It seemed to me that I was this day especially doomed—the main burden and trial falling on me alone of all the female teachers. The others were not expected to examine in the studies they taught; the professor of literature, M. Paul, taking upon himself this duty. He, this school autocrat, gathered all and sundry reins into the hollow of his one hand; he irefully rejected any colleague; he would not have help. Madame herself, who evidently rather wished to undertake the examination in geography— her favourite study, which she taught well—was forced to succumb, and be subordinate to her despotic kinsman's direction. The whole staff of instructors, male and female, he set aside, and stood on the examiner's estrade alone. It irked him that he was forced to make one exception to this rule. He could not manage English: he was obliged to leave that branch of education in the English teacher's hands; which he did, not without a flash of naïve jealousy.

A constant crusade against the amour-propre of every human being but himself was the crotchet of this able, but fiery and grasping little man. He had a strong relish for public representation in his own person, but an extreme abhorrence of the like display in any other. He quelled, he kept down when he could; and when he could not, he fumed like a bottled storm.

On the evening preceding the examination-day I was walking in the garden, as were the other teachers and all the boarders. M. Emanuel joined me in the "allée défendue"; his cigar was at his lips; his paletôt—a most characteristic garment of no particular shape—hung dark and menacing; the tassel of his bonnet grec sternly shadowed his left temple; his black whiskers curled like those of a wrathful cat; his blue eye had a cloud in its glitter.

"Ainsi," he began, abruptly fronting and arresting me, "vouz allez trôner comme une reine; demain—trôner à mes côtés? Sans doute vous savourez d'avance les délices de l'autorité. Je crois voir en vous je ne sais quoi de rayonnante, petite ambitieuse!"

Now the fact was, he happened to be entirely mistaken. I did not—could not— estimate the admiration or the good opinion of to-morrow's audience at the same rate he did. Had that audience numbered as many personal friends and acquaintances for me, as for him, I know not how it might have been: I speak of the case as it

stood. On me school-triumphs shed but a cold lustre. I had wondered—and I wondered now—how it was that for him they seemed to shine as with hearth-warmth and hearth-glow. *He* cared for them perhaps too much; *I*, probably, too little. However, I had my own fancies as well as he. I liked, for instance, to see M. Emanuel jealous; it lit up his nature, and woke his spirit; it threw all sorts of queer lights and shadows over his dun face, and into his violet-azure eyes (he used to say that his black hair and blue eyes were "une de ses beautés"). There was a relish in his anger; it was artless, earnest, quite unreasonable, but never hypocritical. I uttered no disclaimer then of the complacency he attributed to me; I merely asked where the English examination came in—whether at the commencement or close of the day?

"I hesitate," said he, "whether at the very beginning, before many persons are come, and when your aspiring nature will not be gratified by a large audience, or quite at the close, when everybody is tired, and only a jaded and worn-out attention will be at your service."

"Que vous êtes dur, monsieur!" I said, affecting dejection.

"One ought to be 'dur' with you. You are one of those beings who must be *kept down*. I know you! I know you! Other people in this house see you pass, and think that a colourless shadow has gone by. As for me, I scrutinised your face once, and it sufficed."

"You are satisfied that you understand me?"

Without answering directly, he went on, "Were you not gratified when you succeeded in that vaudeville? I watched you and saw a passionate ardour for triumph in your physiognomy. What fire shot into the glance! Not mere light, but flame: je me tins pour averti."

"What feeling I had on that occasion, Monsieur—and pardon me, if I say, you immensely exaggerate both its quality and quantity—was quite abstract. I did not care for the vaudeville. I hated the part you assigned me. I had not the slightest sympathy with the audience below the stage. They are good people, doubtless, but do I know them? Are they anything to me? Can I care for being brought before their view again to-morrow? Will the examination be anything but a task to me— a task I wish well over?"

"Shall I take it out of your hands?"

"With all my heart; if you do not fear failure."

"But I should fail. I only know three phrases of English, and a few words: par exemple, de sonn, de mone, de stare—est ce bien dit? My opinion is that it would be better to give up the thing altogether: to have no English examination, eh?"

"If Madame consents; I consent."

"Heartily?"

"Very heartily."

He smoked his cigar in silence. He turned suddenly.

"Donnez-moi la main," said he, and the spite and jealousy melted out of his face, and a generous kindliness shone there instead.

"Come, we will not be rivals, we will be friends"; he pursued. "The examination shall take place, and I will choose a good moment; and instead of vexing and hindering, as I felt half-inclined ten minutes ago—for I have my malevolent moods: I always had from childhood—I will aid you sincerely. After all, you are solitary and a stranger, and have your way to make and your bread to earn; it may be well that you should become known. We will be friends: do you agree?"

"Out of my heart, Monsieur. I am glad of a friend. I like that better than a triumph."

"Pauvrette!" said he, and turned away and left the alley.

The examination passed over well; M. Paul was as good as his word, and did his best to make my part easy. The next day came the distribution of prizes; that

also passed; the school broke up; the pupils went home, and now began the long vacation.

That vacation! Shall I ever forget it? I think not. Madame Beck went, the first day of the holidays, to join her children at the seaside; all the three teachers had parents or friends with whom they took refuge; every professor quitted the city; some went to Paris, some to Boue-Marine; M. Paul set forth on a pilgrimage to Rome; the house was left quite empty, but for me, a servant, and a poor deformed and imbecile pupil, a sort of crétin, whom her stepmother in a distant province would not allow to return home.

My heart almost died within me; miserable longings strained its chords. How long were the September days! How silent, how lifeless! How vast and void seemed the desolate premises! How gloomy the forsaken garden—grey now with the dust of a town summer departed. Looking forward at the commencement of those eight weeks, I hardly knew how I was to live to the end. My spirits had long been gradually sinking; now that the prop of employment was withdrawn, they went down fast. Even to look forward was not to hope: the dumb future spoke no comfort, offered no promise, gave no inducement to bear present evil in reliance on future good. A sorrowful indifference to existence often pressed on me—a despairing resignation to reach betimes the end of all things earthly. Alas! When I had full leisure to look on life as life must be looked on by such as me, I found it but a hopeless desert: tawny sands, with no green fields, no palm-tree, no well in view. The hopes which are dear to youth, which bear it up and lead it on, I knew not and dared not know. If they knocked at my heart sometimes, an inhospitable bar to admission must be inwardly drawn. When they turned away thus rejected, tears sad enough sometimes flowed; but it could not be helped: I dared not give such guests lodging. So mortally did I fear the sin and weakness of presumption.

Religious reader, you will preach to me a long sermon about what I have just written, and so will you, moralist; and you, stern sage: you, stoic, will frown; you, cynic, sneer; you, epicure, laugh. Well, each and all, take it your own way. I aecept the sermon, frown, sneer, and laugh; perhaps you are all right: and perhaps, circumstanced like me, you would have been, like me, wrong. The first month was, indeed, a long, black, heavy month to me.

The crétin did not seem unhappy. I did my best to feed her well and keep her warm, and she only asked food and sunshine, or when that lacked, fire. Her weak faculties approved of inertion: her brain, her eyes, her ears, her heart slept content; they could not wake to work, so lethargy was their Paradise.

Three weeks of that vacation were hot, fair, and dry, but the fourth and fifth were tempestuous and wet. I do not know why that change in the atmosphere made a cruel impression on me, why the raging storm and beating rain crushed me with a deadlier paralysis than I had experienced while the air had remained serene; but so it was; and my nervous system could hardly support what it had for many days and nights to undergo in that huge empty house. How I used to pray to Heaven for consolation and support! With what dread force the conviction would grasp me that Fate was my permanent foe, never to be conciliated. I did not, in my heart, arraign the mercy or justice of God for this; I concluded it to be a part of His great plan that some must deeply suffer while they live, and I thrilled in the certainty that of this number I was one.

It was some relief when an aunt of the crétin, a kind old woman, came one day, and took away my strange, deformed companion. The hapless creature had been at times a heavy charge; I could not take her out beyond the garden, and I could not leave her a minute alone: for her poor mind, like her body, was warped: its propensity was to evil. A vague bent to mischief, an aimless malevolence, made constant vigilance indispensable. As she rarely spoke, and would sit for hours together moping and mowing and distorting her features with indescribable grimaces, it was more like being prisoned with some strange tameless animal, than associating

with a human being. Then there were personal attentions to be rendered which required the nerve of an hospital nurse; my resolution was so tried, it sometimes fell dead-sick. These duties should not have fallen on me; a servant, now absent, had rendered them hitherto, and in the hurry of holiday departure, no substitute to fill this office had been provided. This tax and trial were by no means the least I have known in life. Still, menial and distasteful as they were, my mental pain was far more wasting and wearing. Attendance on the crétin deprived me often of the power and inclination to swallow a meal, and sent me faint to the fresh air, and the well or fountain in the court. But this duty never wrung my heart, or brimmed my eyes, or scalded my cheek with tears hot as molten metal.

The crétin being gone, I was free to walk out. At first I lacked courage to venture very far from the Rue Fossette, but by degrees I sought the city gates, and passed them, and then went wandering away far along chaussées, through fields, beyond cemeteries, Catholic and Protestant, beyond farm-steads, to lanes and little woods, and I know not where. A goad thrust me on, a fever forbade me to rest; a want of companionship maintained in my soul the cravings of a most deadly famine. I often walked all day, through the burning noon and the arid afternoon, and the dusk evening, and came back with moonrise.

While wandering in solitude, I would sometimes picture the present probable position of others, my acquaintance. There was Madame Beck at a cheerful watering-place with her children, her mother, and a whole troop of friends who had sought the same scene of relaxation. Zélie St. Pierre was at Paris, with her relatives; the other teachers were at their homes. There was Ginevra Fanshawe, whom certain of her connections had carried on a pleasant tour southward. Ginevra seemed to me the happiest. She was on the route of beautiful scenery; these September suns shone for her on fertile plains, where harvest and vintage matured under their mellow beam. These gold and crystal moons rose on her vision over blue horizons waved in mountain lines.

But all this was nothing; I too felt those autumn suns and saw those harvest moons, and I almost wished to be covered in with earth and turf, deep out of their influence; for I could not live in their light, nor make them comrades, nor yield them affection. But Ginevra had a kind of spirit with her, empowered to give constant strength and comfort, to gladden daylight and embalm darkness; the best of the good genii that guard humanity curtained her with his wings, and canopied her head with his bending form. By True Love was Ginevra followed: never could she be alone. Was she insensible to this presence? It seemed to me impossible: I could not realise such deadness. I imagined her grateful in secret, loving now with reserve; but purposing one day to show how much she loved: I pictured her faithful hero half conscious of her coy fondness, and comforted by that consciousness: I conceived an electric chord of sympathy between them, a fine chain of mutual understanding, sustaining union through a separation of a hundred leagues—carrying, across mound and hollow, communication by prayer and wish. Ginevra gradually became with me a sort of heroine. One day, perceiving this growing illusion, I said, "I really believe my nerves are getting overstretched: my mind has suffered somewhat too much; a malady is growing upon it—what shall I do? How shall I keep well?"

Indeed there was no way to keep well under the circumstances. At last a day and night of peculiarly agonising depression were succeeded by physical illness—I took perforce to my bed. About this time the Indian summer closed and the equinoctial storms began; and for nine dark and wet days, of which the hours rushed on all turbulent, deaf, dishevelled—bewildered with sounding hurricane—I lay in a strange fever of the nerves and blood. Sleep went quite away. I used to rise in the night look round for her, beseech her earnestly to return. A rattle of the window, a cry of the blast only replied—Sleep never came!

I err. She came once, but in anger. Impatient of my importunity she brought with her an avenging dream. By the clock of St. Jean Baptiste, that dream remained scarce fifteen minutes—a brief space, but sufficing to wring my whole frame with unknown anguish; to confer a nameless experience that had the hue, the mien, the terror, the very tone of a visitation from eternity. Between twelve and one that night a cup was forced to my lips, black, strong, strange, drawn from no well, but filled up seething from a bottomless and boundless sea. Suffering, brewed in temporal or calculable measure, and mixed for mortal lips, tastes not as this suffering tasted. Having drank and woke, I thought all was over: the end come and past by. Trembling fearfully—as consciousness returned—ready to cry out on some fellow-creature to help me, only that I knew no fellow-creature was near enough to catch the wild summons—Goton in her far distant attic could not hear—I rose on my knees in bed. Some fearful hours went over me: indescribably was I torn, racked and oppressed in mind. Amidst the horrors of that dream I think the worst lay here. Methought the well-loved dead, who had loved *me* well in life, met me elsewhere, alienated: galled was my inmost spirit with an unutterable sense of despair about the future. Motive there was none why I should try to recover or wish to live; and yet quite unendurable was the pitiless and haughty voice in which Death challenged me to engage his unknown terrors. When I tried to pray I could only utter these words—

"From my youth up Thy terrors have I suffered with a troubled mind."

Most true was it.

On bringing me my tea next morning Goton urged me to call in a doctor. I would not: I thought no doctor could cure me.

One evening—and I was not delirious: I was in my sane mind—I got up, I dressed myself, weak and shaking. The solitude and the stillness of the long dormitory could not be borne any longer; the ghastly white beds were turning into spectres—the coronal of each became a death's head, huge and sun-bleached—dead dreams of an elder world and mightier race lay frozen in their wide gaping eyeholes. That evening more firmly than ever fastened into my soul the conviction that Fate was of stone, and Hope a false idol—blind, bloodless, and of granite core. I felt, too, that the trial God had appointed me was gaining its climax, and must now be turned by my own hands, hot, feeble, trembling as they were. It rained still, and blew; but with more clemency, I thought, than it had poured and raged all day. Twilight was falling, and I deemed its influence pitiful; from the lattice I saw coming night-clouds trailing low like banners drooping. It seemed to me that at this hour there was affection and sorrow in Heaven above for all pain suffered on earth beneath; the weight of my dreadful dream became alleviated—that insufferable thought of being no more loved—no more owned, half-yielded to hope of the contrary—I was sure this hope would shine clearer if I got out from under this house-roof, which was crushing as the slab of a tomb, and went outside the city to a certain quiet hill, a long way distant in the fields. Covered with a cloak (I could not be delirious, for I had sense and recollection to put on warm clothing), forth I set. The bells of a church arrested me in passing; they seemed to call me in to the "salut," and I went in. Any solemn rite, any spectacle of sincere worship, any opening for appeal to God was as welcome to me then as bread to one in extremity of want. I knelt down with others on the stone pavement. It was an old solemn church, its pervading gloom not gilded but purpled by light shed through stained glass.

Few worshippers were assembled, and, the "salut" over, half of them departed. I discovered soon that those left remained to confess. I did not stir. Carefully every door of the church was shut; a holy quiet sank upon, and a solemn shade gathered about us. After a space, breathless and spent in prayer, a penitent approached the confessional. I watched. She whispered her avowal; her shrift was whispered back; she returned consoled. Another went, and another. A pale lady, kneeling near me, said in a low, kind voice—

"Go you now, I am not quite prepared."

Mechanically obedient, I rose and went. I knew what I was about; my mind had run over the intent with lightning-speed. To take this step could not make me more wretched than I was; it might soothe me.

The priest within the confessional never turned his eyes to regard me; he only quietly inclined his ear to my lips. He might be a good man, but this duty had become to him a sort of form: he went through it with the phlegm of custom. I hesitated; of the formula of confession I was ignorant: instead of commencing them with the prelude usual, I said—

"Mon père, je suis Protestante."

He directly turned. He was not a native priest: of that class, the cast of physiognomy is, almost invariably, grovelling: I saw by his profile and brow he was a Frenchman; though grey and advanced in years, he did not, I think, lack feeling or intelligence. He inquired, not unkindly, why, being a Protestant, I came to him?

I said I was perishing for a word of advice or an accent of comfort. I had been living for some weeks quite alone; I had been ill; I had a pressure of affliction on my mind of which it would hardly any longer endure the weight.

"Was it a sin, a crime?" he inquired, somewhat startled.

I reassured him on this point, and, as well as I could, I showed him the mere outline of my experience.

He looked thoughtful, surprised, puzzled. "You take me unawares," said he. "I have not had such a case as yours before: ordinarily we know our routine, and are prepared; but this makes a great break in the common course of confession. I am hardly furnished with counsel fitting the circumstances."

Of course, I had not expected he would be; but the mere relief of communication in an ear which was human and sentient, yet consecrated—the mere pouring out of some portion of long accumulating, long pent-up pain into a vessel whence it could not be again diffused—had done me good. I was already solaced.

"Must I go, father?" I asked of him as he sat silent.

"My daughter," he said kindly—and I am sure he was a kind man: he had a compassionate eye—"for the present you had better go: but I assure you your words have struck me. Confession, like other things, is apt to become formal and trivial with habit. You have come and poured your heart out; a thing seldom done. I would fain think your case over, and take it with me to my oratory. Were you of our faith I should know what to say—a mind so tossed can find repose but in the bosom of retreat, and the punctual practice of piety. The world, it is well known, has no satisfaction for that class of natures. Holy men have bidden penitents like you to hasten their path upward by penance, self-denial, and difficult good works. Tears are given them here for meat and drink—bread of affliction and waters of affliction—their recompense comes hereafter. It is my own conviction that these impressions under which you are smarting are messengers from God to bring you back to the true Church. You were made for our faith: depend upon it our faith alone could heal and help you—Protestantism is altogether too dry, cold, prosaic for you. The further I look into this matter, the more plainly I see it is entirely out of the common order of things. On no account would I lose sight of you. Go, my daughter, for the present; but return to me again."

I rose and thanked him. I was withdrawing when he signed me to return.

"You must not come to this church," said he: "I see you are ill, and this church is too cold; you must come to my house: I live"——(and he gave me his address). "Be there to-morrow morning at ten."

In reply to this appointment, I only bowed; and pulling down my veil, and gathering round me my cloak, I glided away.

Did I, do you suppose, reader, contemplate venturing again within that worthy priest's reach? As soon should I have thought of walking into a Babylonish furnace. That priest had arms which could influence me: he was naturally kind, with a

sentimental French kindness, to whose softness I knew myself not wholly impervious. Without respecting some sorts of affection, there was hardly any sort having a fibre of root in reality, which I could rely on my force wholly to withstand. Had I gone to him, he would have shown me all that was tender, and comforting, and gentle, in the honest Popish superstition. Then he would have tried to kindle, blow and stir up in me the zeal of good works. I know not how it would all have ended. We all think ourselves strong in some points; we all know ourselves weak in many; the probabilities are that had I visited Numéro 10, Rue des Mages, at the hour and day appointed, I might just now, instead of writing this heretic narrative, be counting my beads in the cell of a certain Carmelite convent on the Boulevard of Crécy, in Villette. There was something of Fénelon about that benign old priest; and whatever most of his brethren may be, and whatever I may think of his Church and creed (and I like neither), of himself I must ever retain a grateful recollection. He was kind when I needed kindness; he did me good. May Heaven bless him!

Twilight had passed into night, and the lamps were lit in the streets ere I issued from that sombre church. To turn back was now become possible to me; the wild longing to breathe this October wind on the little hill far without the city walls had ceased to be an imperative impulse, and was softened into a wish with which Reason could cope: she put it down, and I turned, as I thought, to the Rue Fossette. But I had become involved in a part of the city with which I was not familiar; it was the old part, and full of narrow streets of picturesque, ancient, and mouldering houses. I was much too weak to be very collected, and I was still too careless of my own welfare and safety to be cautious; I grew embarrassed; I got immeshed in a network of turns unknown. I was lost and had no resolution to ask guidance of any passenger.

If the storm had lulled a little at sunset, it made up now for lost time. Strong and horizontal thundered the current of the wind from north-west to south-east; it brought rain like spray, and sometimes a sharp, hail-like shot; it was cold, and pierced me to the vitals. I bent my head to meet it, but it beat me back. My heart did not fail at all in this conflict; I only wished that I had wings and could ascend the gale, spread and repose my pinions on its strength, career in its course, sweep where it swept. While wishing this, I suddenly felt colder where before I was cold, and more powerless where before I was weak. I tried to reach the porch of a great building near, but the mass of frontage and the giant-spire turned black and vanished from my eyes. Instead of sinking on the steps as I intended, I seemed to pitch headlong down an abyss. I remember no more.

Chapter XVI

AULD LANG SYNE

WHERE my soul went during that swoon I cannot tell. Whatever she saw, or wherever she travelled in her trance on that strange night, she kept her own secret; never whispering a word to Memory, and baffling imagination by an indissoluble silence. She may have gone upward, and come in sight of her eternal home, hoping for leave to rest now, and deeming that her painful union with matter was at last dissolved. While she so deemed, an angel may have warned her away from heaven's threshold, and, guiding her weeping down, have bound her, once more, all shuddering and unwilling, to that poor frame, cold and wasted, of whose companionship she was grown more than weary.

I know she re-entered her prison with pain, with reluctance, with a moan and a long shiver. The divorced mates, Spirit and Substance, were hard to reunite: they greeted each other, not in an embrace, but a racking sort of struggle. The returning

sense of sight came upon me, red, as if it swam in blood; suspended hearing rushed back loud, like thunder; consciousness revived in fear: I sat up appalled, wondering into what region, amongst what strange beings I was waking. At first I knew nothing I looked on: a wall was not a wall—a lamp not a lamp. I should have understood what we call a ghost, as well as I did the commonest object: which is another way of intimating that all my eye rested on struck it as spectral. But the faculties soon settled each in his place; the life-machine presently resumed its wonted and regular working.

Still, I knew not where I was; only in time I saw I had been removed from the spot where I fell: I lay on no portico-step; night and tempest were excluded by walls, windows, and ceiling. Into some house I had been carried—but what house?

I could only think of the pensionnat in the Rue Fossette. Still half-dreaming, I tried hard to discover in what room they had put me; whether the great dormitory, or one of the little dormitories. I was puzzled, because I could not make the glimpses of furniture I saw accord with my knowledge of any of these apartments. The empty white beds were wanting, and the long line of large windows. "Surely," thought I, "it is not to Madame Beck's own chamber they have carried me!" And here my eye fell on an easy chair covered with blue damask. Other seats, cushioned to match, dawned on me by degrees; and at last I took in the complete fact of a pleasant parlour, with a wood fire on a clear-shining hearth, a carpet where arabesques of bright blue relieved a ground of shaded fawn; pale walls over which a slight but endless garland of azure forget-me-nots ran mazed and bewildered amongst myriad gold leaves and tendrils. A gilded mirror filled up the space between two windows, curtained amply with blue damask. In this mirror I saw myself laid, not in bed, but on a sofa. I looked spectral; my eyes larger and more hollow, my hair darker than was natural, by contrast with my thin and ashen face. It was obvious, not only from the furniture, but from the position of windows, doors, and fireplace, that this was an unknown room in an unknown house.

Hardly less plain was it that my brain was not yet settled; for, as I gazed at the blue arm-chair, it appeared to grow familiar; so did a certain scroll-couch, and not less so the round centre-table, with a blue covering, bordered with autumn-tinted foliage; and, above all, two little footstools with worked covers, and a small ebony-framed chair, of which the seat and back were also worked with groups of brilliant flowers on a dark ground.

Struck with these things, I explored further. Strange to say, old acquaintance were all about me, and "auld lang syne" smiled out of every nook. There were two oval miniatures over the mantelpiece, of which I knew by heart the pearls about the high and powdered "heads"; the velvets circling the white throats; the swell of the full muslin kerchiefs: the pattern of the lace sleeve-ruffles. Upon the mantel-shelf there were two china vases, some relics of a diminutive tea service, as smooth as enamel and as thin as egg-shell, and a white centre ornament, a classic group in alabaster, preserved under glass. Of all these things I could have told the peculiarities, numbered the flaws or cracks, like any clairvoyante. Above all, there was a pair of handscreens, with elaborate pencil-drawings finished like line engravings: these, my very eyes ached at beholding again, recalling hours when they had followed, stroke by stroke and touch by touch, a tedious, feeble, finical, school-girl pencil held in these fingers, now so skeleton-like.

Where was I? Not only in what spot of the world, but in what year of our Lord? For all these objects were of past days, and of a distant country. Ten years ago I bade them good-bye; since my fourteenth year they and I had never met. I gasped audibly, "Where am I?"

A shape hitherto unnoticed, stirred, rose, came forward: a shape inharmonious with the environment, serving only to complicate the riddle further. This was no more than a sort of native bonne, in a commonplace bonne's cap and print-dress. She spoke neither French nor English, and I could get no intelligence from her,

not understanding her phrases of dialect. But she bathed my temples and forehead with some cool and perfumed water, and then she heightened the cushion on which I reclined, made signs that I was not to speak, and resumed her post at the foot of the sofa.

She was busy knitting; her eyes thus drawn from me, I could gaze on her without interruption. I did mightily wonder how she came there, or what she could have to do among the scenes, or with the days of my girlhood. Still more I marvelled what those scenes and days could now have to do with me.

Too weak to scrutinise thoroughly the mystery, I tried to settle it by saying it was a mistake, a dream, a fever ft; and yet I knew there could be no mistake, and that I was not sleeping, and I believed I was sane. I wished the room had not been so well lighted, that I might not so clearly have seen the little pictures, the ornaments, the screens, the worked chair. All these objects, as well as the blue-damask furniture, were, in fact, precisely the same, in every minutest detail, with those I so well remembered, and with which I had been so thoroughly intimate, in the drawing-room of my godmother's house at Bretton. Methought the apartment only was changed, being of different proportions and dimensions.

I thought of Bedreddin Hassan, transported in his sleep from Cairo to the gates of Damascus. Had a Genius stooped his dark wing down the storm to whose stress I had succumbed, and gathering me from the church-steps, and "rising high into the air," as the eastern tale said, had he borne me over land and ocean, and laid me quietly down beside a hearth of Old England? But no; I knew the fire of that hearth burned before its Lares no more—it went out long ago, and the household gods had been carried elsewhere.

The bonne turned again to survey me, and seeing my eyes wide open, and, I suppose, deeming their expression perturbed and excited, she put down her knitting. I saw her busied for a moment at a little stand; she poured out water, and measured drops from a phial: glass in hand, she approached me. What dark-tinged draught might she now be offering? what Genii-elixir or Magi-distillation?

It was too late to inquire—I had swallowed it passively, and at once. A tide of quiet thought now came gently caressing my brain; softer and softer rose the flow, with tepid undulations smoother than balm. The pain of weakness left my limbs, my muscles slept. I lost power to move; but, losing at the same time wish, it was no privation. That kind bonne placed a screen between me and the lamp; I saw her rise to do this, but do not remember seeing her resume her place; in the interval between the two acts, I "fell on sleep."

At waking, lo! all was again changed. The light of high day surrounded me; not, indeed, a warm, summer light, but the leaden gloom of raw and blustering autumn. I felt sure now that I was in the pensionnat—sure by the beating rain on the casement; sure by the "wuther" of wind amongst trees, denoting a garden outside; sure by the chill, the whiteness, the solitude, amidst which I lay. I say *whiteness*—for the dimity curtains, dropped before a French bed, bounded my view.

I lifted them; I looked out. My eye, prepared to take in the range of a long, large, and white-washed chamber, blinked baffled, on encountering the limited area of a small cabinet—a cabinet with sea-green walls; also, instead of five wide and naked windows, there was one high lattice, shaded with muslin festoons: instead of two dozen little stands of painted wood, each holding a basin and a ewer, there was a toilette-table dressed, like a lady for a ball, in a white robe over a pink skirt; a polished and large glass crowned, and a pretty pin-cushion frilled with lace adorned it. This toilette, together with a small, low, green and white chintz arm-chair, a wash-stand topped with a marble slab, and supplied with utensils of pale green-ware, sufficiently furnished the tiny chamber.

Reader, I felt alarmed! Why? you will ask. What was there in this simple and somewhat pretty sleeping-closet to startle the most timid? Merely this—these articles

of furniture could not be real, solid arm-chairs, looking-glasses, and wash-stands—they must be the ghosts of such articles; or, if this were denied as too wild an hypothesis—and, confounded as I was, I *did* deny it—there remained but to conclude that I had myself passed into an abnormal state of mind: in short, that I was very ill and delirious; and even then, mine was the strangest figment with which delirium had ever harassed a victim.

I knew—I was obliged to know—the green chintz of that little chair; the little snug chair itself, the carved, shining-black, foliated frame of that glass; the smooth, milky-green of the china vessels on the stand; the very stand too, with its top of grey marble, splintered at one corner; all these I was compelled to recognise and to hail, as last night I had, perforce, recognised and hailed the rosewood, the drapery, the porcelain, of the drawing-room.

Bretton! Bretton! and ten years ago shone reflected in that mirror. And why did Bretton and my fourteenth year haunt me thus? Why, if they came at all, did they not return complete? Why hovered before my distempered vision the mere furniture, while the rooms and the locality were gone? As to that pin-cushion made of crimson satin, ornamented with gold beads and frilled with thread-lace, I had the same right to know it as to know the screens—I had made it myself. Rising with a start from the bed, I took the cushion in my hand, and examined it. There was the cipher "L. L. B." formed in gold beads, and surrounded with an oval wreath embroidered in white silk. These were the initials of my godmother's name—Louisa Lucy Bretton.

Am I in England? Am I at Bretton? I muttered; and hastily pulling up the blind with which the lattice was shrouded, I looked out to try and discover *where* I was; half-prepared to meet the calm, old, handsome buildings and clean grey pavement of St. Ann's Street, and to see at the end the towers of the minster: or, if otherwise, full expectant of a town view somewhere, a rue in Villette, if not a street in a pleasant and ancient English city.

I looked, on the contrary, through a frame of leafage, clustering round the high lattice, and forth thence to a grassy mead-like level, a lawn-terrace with trees rising from the lower ground beyond—high forest-trees, such as I had not seen for many a day. They were now groaning under the gale of October, and between their trunks I traced the line of an avenue, where yellow leaves lay in heaps and drifts, or were whirled singly before the sweeping west wind. Whatever landscape might lie further must have been flat, and these tall beeches shut it out. The place seemed secluded, and was to me quite strange: I did not know it at all.

Once more I lay down. My bed stood in a little alcove; on turning my face to the wall, the room with its bewildering accompaniments became excluded. Excluded? No! For as I arranged my position in this hope, behold, on the green space between the divided and looped-up curtains, hung a broad, gilded picture-frame enclosing a portrait. It was drawn—well drawn, though but a sketch—in water-colours; a head, a boy's head, fresh, life-like, speaking, and animated. It seemed a youth of sixteen, fair-complexioned with sanguine health in his cheek; hair long, not dark, and with a sunny sheen; penetrating eyes, an arch mouth, and a gay smile. On the whole a most pleasant face to look at, especially for those claiming a right to that youth's affections—parents, for instance, or sisters. Any romantic little school-girl might almost have loved it in its frame. Those eyes looked as if when somewhat older they would flash a lightning-response to love: I cannot tell whether they kept in store the steady-beaming shine of faith. For whatever sentiment met him in form too facile, his lips menaced, beautifully but surely, caprice and light esteem.

Striving to take each new discovery as quietly as I could, I whispered to myself—

"Ah! that portrait used to hang in the breakfast-room, over the mantelpiece: somewhat too high, as I thought. I well remember how I used to mount a music-stool for the purpose of unhooking it, holding it in my hand, and searching into

those bonny wells of eyes, whose glance under their hazel lashes seemed like a pencilled laugh; and well I liked to note the colouring of the cheek, and the expression of the mouth.'' I hardly believed fancy could improve on the curve of that mouth, or of the chin; even *my* ignorance knew that both were beautiful, and pondered perplexed over this doubt: ''How it was that what charmed so much, could at the same time so keenly pain?'' Once, by way of test, I took little Missy Home, and, lifting her in my arms, told her to look at the picture.

''Do you like it, Polly?'' I asked. She never answered, but gazed long, and at last a darkness went trembling through her sensitive eye, as she said, ''Put me down.'' So I put her down, saying to myself: ''The child feels it too.''

All these things do I now think over, adding, ''He had his faults, yet scarce ever was a finer nature; liberal, suave, impressible.'' My reflections closed in an audibly pronounced word, ''Graham!''

''Graham!'' echoed a sudden voice at the bedside. ''Do you want Graham?''

I looked. The plot was but thickening; the wonder but culminating. If it was strange to see that well-remembered pictured form on the wall, still stranger was it to turn and behold the equally well-remembered living form opposite—a woman, a lady, most real and substantial, tall, well-attired, wearing widow's silk, and such a cap as best became her matron and motherly braids of hair. Hers, too, was a good face; too marked, perhaps, now for beauty, but not for sense or character. She was little changed; something sterner, something more robust—but she was my godmother: still the distinct vision of Mrs. Bretton.

I kept quiet, yet internally *I* was much agitated: my pulse fluttered, and the blood left my cheek, which turned cold.

''Madam, where am I?'' I inquired.

''In a very safe asylum; well protected for the present; make your mind quite easy till you get a little better; you look ill this morning.''

''I am so entirely bewildered, I do not know whether I can trust my senses at all, or whether they are misleading me in every particular: but you speak English, do you not, madam?''

''I should think you might hear that: it would puzzle me to hold a long discourse in French.''

''You do not come from England?''

''I am lately arrived thence. Have you been long in this country? You seem to know my son?''

''Do I, madam? Perhaps I do. Your son—the picture there?''

''That is his portrait as a youth. While looking at it, you pronounced his name.''

''Graham Bretton?''

She nodded.

''I speak to Mrs. Bretton, formerly of Bretton, ——shire?''

''Quite right; and you, I am told, are an English teacher in a foreign school here: my son recognised you as such.''

''How was I found, madam, and by whom?''

''My son shall tell you that by-and-by,'' said she; ''but at present you are too confused and weak for conversation: try to eat some breakfast, and then sleep.''

Notwithstanding all I had undergone—the bodily fatigue, the perturbation of spirits, the exposure to weather—it seemed that I was better: the fever, the real malady which had oppressed my frame, was abating; for, whereas during the last nine days I had taken no solid food, and suffered from continual thirst, this morning, on breakfast being offered, I experienced a craving for nourishment: an inward faintness which caused me eagerly to taste the tea this lady offered, and to eat the morsel of dry toast she allowed in accompaniment. It was only a morsel, but it sufficed; keeping up my strength till some two or three hours afterwards, when the bonne brought me a little cup of broth and a biscuit.

As evening began to darken, and the ceaseless blast still blew wild and cold, and the rain streamed on, deluge-like, I grew weary—very weary of my bed. The room, though pretty, was small: I felt it confining; I longed for a change. The increasing chill and gathering gloom, too, depressed me; I wanted to see—to feel firelight. Besides, I kept thinking of the son of that tall matron: when should I see him? Certainly not till I left my room.

At last the bonne came to make my bed for the night. She prepared to wrap me in a blanket and place me in the little chintz chair; but, declining these attentions, I proceeded to dress myself. The business was just achieved, and I was sitting down to take breath, when Mrs. Bretton once more appeared.

"Dressed!" she exclaimed, smiling with that smile I so well knew—a pleasant smile, though not soft;—"You are quite better then? Quite strong—eh?"

She spoke to me so much as of old she used to speak that I almost fancied she was beginning to know me. There was the same sort of patronage in her voice and manner that, as a girl, I had always experienced from her—a patronage I yielded to and even liked; it was not founded on conventional grounds of superior wealth or station (in the last particular there had never been any inequality; her degree was mine); but on natural reasons of physical advantage: it was the shelter the tree gives the herb. I put a request without further ceremony.

"Do let me go downstairs, madam; I am so cold and dull here."

"I desire nothing better, if you are strong enough to bear the change," was her reply. "Come then; here is an arm." And she offered me hers: I took it, and we descended one flight of carpeted steps to a landing where a tall door, standing open, gave admission into the blue-damask room. How pleasant it was in its air of perfect domestic comfort! How warm in its amber lamp-light and vermilion fire-flush! To render the picture perfect, tea stood ready on the table—an English tea, whereof the whole shining service glanced at me familiarly; from the solid silver urn, of antique pattern, and the massive pot of the same metal, to the thin porcelain cups, dark with purple and gilding. I knew the very seed-cake of peculiar form, baked in a peculiar mould, which always had a place on the tea-table at Bretton. Graham liked it, and there it was as of yore—set before Graham's plate with the silver knife and fork beside it. Graham was then expected to tea: Graham was now, perhaps, in the house; ere many minutes I might see him.

"Sit down—sit down," said my conductress, as my step faltered a little in passing to the hearth. She seated me on the sofa, but I soon passed behind it, saying the fire was too hot; in its shade I found another seat which suited me better. Mrs. Bretton was never wont to make a fuss about any person or anything; without remonstrance she suffered me to have my own way. She made the tea, and she took up the newspaper. I liked to watch every action of my godmother; all her movements were so young; she must have been now above fifty, yet neither her sinews nor her spirit seemed yet touched by the rust of age. Though portly, she was alert, and though serene, she was at times impetuous—good health and an excellent temperament kept her green as in her spring.

While she read, I perceived she listened—listened for her son. She was not the woman ever to confess herself uneasy, but there was yet no lull in the weather, and if Graham were out in that hoarse wind—roaring still unsatisfied—I well knew his mother's heart would be out with him.

"Ten minutes behind his time," said she, looking at her watch; then, in another minute, a lifting of her eyes from the page, and a slight inclination of her head towards the door, denoted that she heard some sound. Presently her brow cleared; and then even my ear, less practised, caught the iron clash of a gate swung to, steps on gravel, lastly the door-bell. He was come. His mother filled the teapot from the urn, she drew nearer the hearth the stuffed and cushioned blue chair— her own chair by right, but I saw there was one who might with impunity usurp it. And when that *one* came up the stairs—which he soon did, after, I suppose,

some such attention to the toilet as the wild and wet night rendered necessary, and strode straight in—

"Is it you, Graham?" said his mother, hiding a glad smile and speaking curtly.

"Who else should it be, mamma?" demanded the Unpunctual, possessing himself irreverently of the abdicated throne.

"Don't you deserve cold tea, for being late?"

"I shall not get my deserts, for the urn sings cheerily."

"Wheel yourself to the table, lazy boy: no seat will serve you but mine; if you had one spark of a sense of propriety, you would always leave that chair for the Old Lady."

"So I should; only the dear Old Lady persists in leaving it for me. How is your patient, mamma?"

"Will she come forward and speak for herself?" said Mrs. Bretton, turning to my corner; and at this invitation, forward I came. Graham courteously rose up to meet me. He stood tall on the hearth, a figure justifying his mother's unconcealed pride.

"So you are come down," said he; "you must be better then—much better. I scarcely expected we should meet thus, or here. I was alarmed last night, and if I had not been forced to hurry away to a dying patient, I certainly would not have left you; but my mother herself is something of a doctress, and Martha an excellent nurse. I saw the case was a fainting-fit, not necessarily dangerous. What brought it on, I have yet to learn, and all particulars; meantime, I trust you really do feel better."

"Much better," I said calmly. "Much better, I thank you, Dr. John."

For, reader, this tall young man—this darling son—this host of mine—this Graham Bretton, *was* Dr. John: he, and no other; and, what is more, I ascertained this identity scarcely with surprise. What is more, when I heard Graham's step on the stairs, I knew what manner of figure would enter, and for whose aspect to prepare my eyes. The discovery was not of to-day, its dawn had penetrated my perceptions long since. Of course I remembered young Bretton well; and though ten years (from sixteen to twenty-six) may greatly change the boy as they mature him to the man, yet they could bring no such utter difference as would suffice wholly to blind my eyes, or baffle my memory. Dr. John Graham Bretton retained still an affinity to the youth of sixteen: he had his eyes; he had some of his features; to wit, all the excellently moulded lower half of the face; I found him out soon. I first recognised him on that occasion, noted several chapters back, when my unguardedly-fixed attention had drawn on me the mortification of an implied rebuke. Subsequent observation confirmed, in every point, that early surmise. I traced in the gesture, the port, and the habits of his manhood, all his boy's promise. I heard in his now deep tones the accent of former days. Certain turns of phrase, peculiar to him of old, were peculiar to him still; and so was many a trick of eye and lip, many a smile, many a sudden ray levelled from the irid, under his well-charactered brow.

To *say* anything on the subject, to *hint* at my discovery, had not suited my habits of thought, or assimilated with my system of feeling. On the contrary, I had preferred to keep the matter to myself. I liked entering his presence covered with a cloud he had not seen through, while he stood before me under a ray of special illumination, which shone all partial over his head, trembled about his feet, and cast light no farther.

Well I knew that to him it could make little difference, were I to come forward and announce "This is Lucy Snowe!" So I kept back in my teacher's place; and as he never asked my name, so I never gave it. He heard me called "Miss," and "Miss Lucy"; he never heard the surname, "Snowe." As to spontaneous recognition— though I, perhaps, was still less changed than he—the idea never approached his mind, and why should I suggest it?

During tea, Dr. John was kind, as it was his nature to be; that meal over, and the tray carried out, he made a cosy arrangement of the cushions in a corner of the sofa, and obliged me to settle amongst them. He and his mother also drew to the fire, and ere we had sat ten minutes, I caught the eye of the latter fastened steadily upon me. Women are certainly quicker in some things than men.

"Well," she exclaimed presently; "I have seldom seen a stronger likeness! Graham, have you observed it?"

"Observed what? What ails the Old Lady now? How you stare, mamma! One would think you had an attack of second sight."

"Tell me, Graham, of whom does that young lady remind you?" pointing to me.

"Mamma, you put her out of countenance. I often tell you abruptness is your fault; remember, too, that to you she is a stranger, and does not know your ways."

"Now, when she looks down; now, when she turns sideways, who is she like, Graham?"

"Indeed, mamma, since you propound the riddle, I think you ought to solve it!"

"And you have known her some time, you say—ever since you first began to attend the school in the Rue Fossette:—yet you never mentioned to me that singular resemblance!"

"I could not mention a thing of which I never thought, and which I do not now acknowledge. What *can* you mean?"

"Stupid boy! look at her."

Graham did look: but this was not to be endured; I saw how it must end, so I thought it best to anticipate.

"Dr. John," I said, "has had so much to do and think of, since he and I shook hands at our last parting in St. Ann's Street, that, while I readily found out Mr. Graham Bretton, some months ago, it never occurred to me as possible that he should recognise Lucy Snowe."

"Lucy Snowe! I thought so! I knew it!" cried Mrs. Bretton. And she at once stepped across the hearth and kissed me. Some ladies would, perhaps, have made a great bustle upon such a discovery, without being particularly glad of it; but it was not my godmother's habit to make a bustle, and she preferred all sentimental demonstrations in bas-relief. So she and I got over the surprise with few words and a single salute; yet I dare say she was pleased, and I know I was. While we renewed old acquaintance, Graham, sitting opposite, silently disposed of his paroxysm of astonishment.

"Mamma calls me a stupid boy, and I think I am so," at length he said; "for, upon my honour, often as I have seen you, I never once suspected this fact: and yet I perceive it all now. Lucy Snowe! To be sure! I recollect her perfectly, and there she sits; not a doubt of it. But," he added, "you surely have not known me as an old acquaintance all this time, and never mentioned it?"

"That I have," was my answer.

Dr. John commented not. I supposed he regarded my silence as eccentric, but he was indulgent in refraining from censure. I dare say, too, he would have deemed it impertinent to have interrogated me very closely, to have asked me the why and wherefore of my reserve; and, though he might feel a little curious, the importance of the case was by no means such as to tempt curiosity to infringe on discretion.

For my part, I just ventured to inquire whether he remembered the circumstance of my once looking at him very fixedly; for the slight annoyance he had betrayed on that occasion still lingered sore on my mind.

"I think I do!" said he: "I think I was even cross with you."

"You considered me a little bold, perhaps?" I inquired.

"Not at all. Only, shy and retiring as your general manner was, I wondered what personal or facial enormity in me proved so magnetic to your usually averted eyes."

"You see how it was now?"

"Perfectly."

And here Mrs. Bretton broke in with many, many questions about past times; and for her satisfaction I had to recur to gone-by troubles, to explain causes of seeming estrangement, to touch on single-handed conflict with Life, with Death, with Grief, with Fate. Dr. John listened, saying little. He and she then told me of changes they had known: even with them all had not gone smoothly, and fortune had retrenched her once abundant gifts. But so courageous a mother, with such a champion in her son, was well fitted to fight a good fight with the world, and to prevail ultimately. Dr. John himself was one of those on whose birth benign planets have certainly smiled. Adversity might set against him her most sullen front: he was the man to beat her down with smiles. Strong and cheerful, and firm and courteous; not rash, yet valiant; he was the aspirant to woo Destiny herself, and to win from her stone eyeballs a beam almost loving.

In the profession he had adopted, his success was now quite decided. Within the last three months he had taken this house (a small chateau, they told me, about half a league without the Porte de Crécy); this country site being chosen for the sake of his mother's health, with which town air did not now agree. Hither he had invited Mrs. Bretton, and she, on leaving England, had brought with her such residue furniture of the former St. Ann's Street mansion as she had thought fit to keep unsold. Hence my bewilderment at the phantoms of chairs, and the wraiths of looking-glasses, tea-urns, and teacups.

As the clock struck eleven, Dr. John stopped his mother.

"Miss Snowe must retire now," he said; "she is beginning to look very pale. To-morrow I will venture to put some questions respecting the cause of her loss of health. She is much changed indeed, since last July, when I saw her enact with no little spirit the part of a very killing fine gentleman. As to last night's catastrophe, I am sure thereby hangs a tale, but we will inquire no further this evening. Good-night, Miss Lucy."

And so he kindly led me to the door, and holding a wax candle, lighted me up the one flight of stairs.

When I had said my prayers, and when I was undressed and laid down, I felt that I still had friends. Friends, not professing vehement attachment, not offering the tender solace of well-matched and congenial relationship; on whom, therefore, but moderate demand of affection was to be made, of whom but moderate expectation formed; but towards whom my heart softened instinctively, and yearned with an importunate gratitude, which I entreated Reason betimes to check.

"Do not let me think of them too often, too much, too fondly," I implored. "let me be content with a temperate draught of this living stream: let me not run athirst, and apply passionately to its welcome waters: let me not imagine in them a sweeter taste than earth's fountains know. Oh! would to God I may be enabled to feel enough sustained by an occasional, amicable intercourse, rare, brief, unengrossing and tranquil: quite tranquil!"

Still repeating this word, I turned to my pillow; and, *still* repeating it, I steeped that pillow with tears.

Chapter XVII

LA TERRASSE

THESE struggles with the natural character, the strong native bent of the heart, may seem futile and fruitless, but in the end they do good. They tend, however slightly, to give the actions, the conduct, that turn which Reason approves, and which Feeling, perhaps, too often opposes: they certainly make a difference in the general

tenor of a life, and enable it to be better regulated, more equable, quieter on the surface; and it is on the surface only the common gaze will fall. As to what lies below, leave that with God. Man, your equal, weak as you, and not fit to be your judge, may be shut out thence: take it to your Maker—show Him the secrets of the spirit He gave—ask Him how you are to bear the pains He has appointed— kneel in His presence, and pray with faith for light in darkness, for strength in piteous weakness, for patience in extreme need. Certainly, at some hour, though perhaps not *your* hour, the waiting waters will stir; in *some* shape, though perhaps not the shape you dreamed, which your heart loved, and for which it bled, the healing herald will descend, the cripple and the blind, and the dumb, and the possessed, will be led to bathe. Herald, come quickly! Thousands lie round the pool, weeping and despairing, to see it, through slow years, stagnant. Long are the "times" of Heaven: the orbits of angel messengers seem wide to mortal vision; they may enring ages; the cycle of one departure and return may clasp unnumbered generations; and dust, kindling to brief suffering life, and, through pain, passing back to dust, may meanwhile perish out of memory again, and yet again. To how many maimed and mourning millions is the first and sole angel visitant, him easterns call Azrael.

I tried to get up next morning, but while I was dressing, and at intervals drinking cold water from the carafe on my washstand, with design to brace up that trembling weakness which made dressing so difficult, in came Mrs. Bretton.

"Here is an absurdity!" was her morning accost. "Not so," she added, and dealing with me at once in her own brusque, energetic fashion—that fashion which I used formerly to enjoy seeing applied to her son, and by him vigorously resisted— in two minutes she consigned me captive to the French bed.

"There you lie till afternoon," said she. "My boy left orders before he went out that such should be the case, and I can assure you my son is master, and must be obeyed. Presently you shall have breakfast."

Presently she brought that meal—brought it with her own active hands—not leaving me to servants. She seated herself on the bed while I ate. Now it is not everybody, even amongst our respected friends and esteemed acquaintance, whom we like to have near us, whom we like to watch us, to wait on us, to approach us with the proximity of a nurse to a patient. It is not every friend whose eye is a light in a sick-room, whose presence is there a solace: but all this was Mrs. Bretton to me; all this she had ever been. Food or drink never pleased me so well as when it came through her hands. I do not remember the occasion when her entrance into a room had not made that room cheerier. Our natures own predilections and antipathies alike strange. There are people from whom we secretly shrink, whom we would personally avoid, though reason confesses that they are good people: there are others with faults of temper, etc., evident enough, beside whom we live content, as if the air about them did us good. My godmother's lively black eye and clear brunette cheek, her warm, prompt hand, her self-reliant mood, her decided bearing, were all beneficial to me as the atmosphere of some salubrious climate. Her son used to call her "the old lady"; it filled me with pleasant wonder to note how the alacrity and power of five-and-twenty still breathed from her and around her.

"I would bring my work here," she said, as she took from me the emptied tea-cup, "and sit with you the whole day, if that overbearing John Graham had not put his veto upon such a proceeding. 'Now mamma,' he said, when he went out, 'take notice, you are not to knock up your god-daughter with gossip,' and he particularly desired me to keep close to my own quarters, and spare you my fine company. He says, Lucy, he thinks you have had a nervous fever, judging from your look,—is that so?"

I replied that I did not quite know what my ailment had been, but that I had certainly suffered a good deal, especially in mind. Further, on this subject, I did not consider it advisable to dwell, for the details of what I had undergone belonged

to a portion of my existence in which I never expected my godmother to take a share. Into what a new region would such a confidence have led that hale, serene nature! The difference between her and me might be figured by that between the stately ship cruising safe on smooth seas, with its full complement of crew, a captain gay and brave, and venturous and provident; and the life-boat, which most days of the year lies dry and solitary in an old, dark boat-house, only putting to sea when the billows run high in rough weather, when cloud encounters water, when danger and death divide between them the rule of the great deep. No, the *Louisa Bretton* never was out of harbour on such a night, and in such a scene: her crew could not conceive it; so the half-drowned life-boat man keeps his own counsel, and spins no yarns.

She left me, and I lay in bed content: it was good of Graham to remember me before he went out.

My day was lonely, but the prospect of coming evening abridged and cheered it. Then, too, I felt weak, and rest seemed welcome; and after the morning hours were gone by,—those hours which always bring, even to the necessarily unoccupied, a sense of business to be done, of tasks waiting fulfilment, a vague impression of obligation to be employed—when this stirring time was past, and the silent descent of afternoon hushed housemaid steps on the stairs and in the chambers, I then passed into a dreamy mood, not unpleasant.

My calm little room seemed somehow like a cave in the sea. There was no colour about it, except that white and pale green, suggestive of foam and deep water; the blanched cornice was adorned with shell-shaped ornaments, and there were white mouldings like dolphins in the ceiling-angles. Even that one touch of colour visible in the red satin pincushion bore affinity to coral; even that dark, shining glass might have mirrored a mermaid. When I closed my eyes, I heard a gale, subsiding at last, bearing upon the house-front like a setting swell upon a rock-base. I heard it drawn and withdrawn far, far off, like a tide retiring from a shore of the upper world—a world so high above that the rush of its largest waves, the dash of its fiercest breakers, could sound down in this submarine home, only like murmurs and a lullaby.

Amidst these dreams came evening, and then Martha brought a light; with her aid I was quickly dressed, and stronger now than in the morning, I made my way down to the blue saloon unassisted.

Dr. John, it appears, had concluded his round of professional calls earlier than usual; his form was the first object that met my eyes as I entered the parlour; he stood in that window-recess opposite the door, reading the close type of a newspaper by such dull light as closing day yet gave. The fire shone clear, but the lamp stood on the table unlit, and tea was not yet brought up.

As to Mrs. Bretton, my active godmother—who, I afterwards found, had been out in the open air all day—lay half-reclined in her deep-cushioned chair, actually lost in a nap. Her son seeing me, came forward. I noticed that he trod carefully, not to wake the sleeper; he also spoke low: his mellow voice never had any sharpness in it; modulated as at present, it was calculated rather to soothe than startle slumber.

"This is a quiet little chateau," he observed, after inviting me to sit near the casement, "I don't know whether you may have noticed it in your walks: though, indeed, from the chaussée it is not visible; just a mile beyond the Porte de Crécy, you turn down a lane which soon becomes an avenue, and that leads you on, through meadow and shade, to the very door of this house. It is not a modern place, but built somewhat in the old style of the Basse-Ville. It is rather a manoir than a chateau; they call it 'La Terrasse,' because its front rises from a broad turfed walk, whence steps lead down a grassy slope to the avenue. See yonder! The moon rises: she looks well through the tree boles."

Where, indeed, does the moon not look well? What is the scene, confined or expansive, which her orb does not hallow? Rosy or fiery, she mounted now above

a not distant bank; even while we watched her flushed ascent, she cleared to gold, and in very brief space, floated up stainless into a now calm sky. Did moonlight soften or sadden Dr. Bretton? Did it touch him with romance? I think it did. Albeit of no sighing mood, he sighed in watching it: sighed to himself quietly. No need to ponder the cause or the course of that sigh; I knew it was wakened by beauty: I knew it pursued Ginevra. Knowing this, the idea pressed upon me that it was in some sort my duty to speak the name he meditated. Of course he was ready for the subject: I saw in his countenance a teeming plenitude of comment, question, and interest; a pressure of language and sentiment, only checked, I thought, by sense of embarrassment how to begin. To spare him this embarrassment was my best, indeed my sole use. I had but to utter the idol's name, and love's tender litany would flow out. I had just found a fitting phrase: "You know that Miss Fanshawe is gone on a tour with the Cholmondeleys," and was opening my lips to speak to it, when he scattered my plans by introducing another theme.

"The frst thing this morning," said he, putting his sentiment in his pocket, turning from the moon, and sitting down, "I went to the Rue Fossette, and told the cuisinière that you were safe and in good hands. Do you know that I actually found that she had not yet discovered your absence from the house: she thought you safe in the great dormitory. With what care you must have been waited on!"

"Oh! all that is very conceivable," said I. "Goton could do nothing for me but bring me a little tisane and a crust of bread, and I had rejected both so often during the past week, that the good woman got tired of useless journeys from the dwelling-house kitchen to the school dormitory, and only came once a day at noon to make my bed. Believe, however, that she is a good-natured creature, and would have been delighted to cook me cotelettes de mouton, if I could have eaten them."

"What did Madame Beck mean by leaving you alone?"

"Madame Beck could not foresee that I should fall ill."

"Your nervous system bore a good share of the suffering?"

"I am not quite sure what my nervous system is, but I was dreadfully low-spirited."

"Which disables me from helping you by pill or potion. Medicine can give nobody good spirits. My art halts at the threshold of hypochondria: she just looks in and sees a chamber of torture, but can neither say nor do much. Cheerful society would be of use; you should be as little alone as possible; you should take plenty of exercise."

Acquiescence and a pause followed these remarks. They sounded all right, I thought, and bore the safe sanction of custom, and the well-worn stamp of use.

"Miss Snowe," recommenced Dr. John—my health, nervous system included, being now, somewhat to my relief, discussed and done with—"is it permitted me to ask what your religion is? Are you a Catholic?"

I looked up in some surprise—"A Catholic? No! Why suggest such an idea?"

"The manner in which you were consigned to me last night made me doubt."

"I consigned to you? But indeed, I forget. It yet remains for me to learn how I fell into your hands."

"Why, under circumstances that puzzled me. I had been in attendance all day yesterday on a case of singularly interesting and critical character; the disease being rare, and its treatment doubtful: I saw a similar and still finer case in a hospital in Paris; but that will not interest you. At last a mitigation of the patient's most urgent symptoms (acute pain is one of its accompaniments) liberated me, and I set out homeward. My shortest way lay through the Basse-Ville, and as the night was excessively dark, wild, and wet, I took it. In riding past an old church belonging to a community of Béguines, I saw by a lamp burning over the porch or deep arch of the entrance, a priest lifting some object in his arms. The lamp was bright enough to reveal the priest's features clearly, and I recognised him; he was a man I have often met by the sick beds of both rich and poor: and chiefly the latter. He is, I

think, a good old man, far better than most of his class in this country; superior, indeed, in every way, better informed, as well as more devoted to duty. Our eyes met; he called on me to stop: what he supported was a woman, fainting or dying. I alighted.

" 'This person is one of your countrywomen,' he said: 'save her, if she is not dead.'

"My countrywoman, on examination, turned out to be the English teacher at Madame Beck's pensionnat. She was perfectly unconscious, perfectly bloodless, and nearly cold.

"What does it all mean?" was my inquiry.

"He communicated a curious account; that you had been to him that evening at confessional; that your exhausted and suffering appearance, coupled with some things you had said"——

"Things I had said? I wonder what things!"

"Awful crimes, no doubt; but he did not tell me what: there you know, the seal of the confessional checked his garrulity, and my curiosity. Your confidences, however, had not made an enemy of the good father; it seems he was so struck, and felt so sorry that you should be out on such a night alone, that he had esteemed it a Christian duty to watch you when you quitted the church, and so to manage as not to lose sight of you, till you should have reached home. Perhaps the worthy man might, half unconsciously, have blent in this proceeding some little of the subtilty of his class: it might have been his resolve to learn the locality of your home—did you impart that in your confession?"

"I did not: on the contrary, I carefully avoided the shadow of any indication: and as to my confession, Dr. John, I suppose you will think me mad for taking such a step, but I could not help it: I suppose it was all the fault of what you call my 'nervous system.' I cannot put the case into words, but my days and nights were grown intolerable: a cruel sense of desolation pained my mind: a feeling that would make its way, rush out, or kill me—like (and this you will understand, Dr. John) the current which passes through the heart, and which, if aneurism or any other morbid cause obstructs its natural channels, seeks abnormal outlet. I wanted companionship, I wanted friendship, I wanted counsel. I could find none of these in closet or chamber, so I went and sought them in church and confessional. As to what I said, it was no confidence, no narrative. I have done nothing wrong: my life has not been active enough for any dark deed, either of romance or reality: all I poured out was a dreary, desperate complaint."

"Lucy, you ought to travel for about six months: why, your calm nature is growing quite excitable! Confound Madame Beck! Has the little buxom widow no bowels, to condemn her best teacher to solitary confinement?"

"It was not Madame Beck's fault," said I; "it is no living being's fault, and I won't hear any one blamed."

"Who is in the wrong, then, Lucy?"

"Me—Dr. John—me; and a great abstraction on whose wide shoulders I like to lay the mountains of blame they were sculptured to bear: me and Fate."

" 'Me' must take better care in future," said Dr. John—smiling, I suppose, at my bad grammar.

"Change of air—change of scene; those are my prescriptions," pursued the practical young doctor. "But to return to our muttons, Lucy. As yet, Père Silas, with all his tact (they say he is a Jesuit), is no wiser than you choose him to be; for, instead of returning to the Rue Fossette, your fevered wanderings—there must have been high fever"——

"No, Dr. John: the fever took its turn that night—now, don't make out that I was delirious, for I know differently."

"Good! you were as collected as myself at this moment, no doubt! Your wanderings had taken an opposite direction to the pensionnat. Near the Béguinage, amidst the

stress of flood and gust, and in the perplexity of darkness, you had swooned and fallen. The priest came to your succour, and the physician, as we have seen, supervened. Between us we procured a fiacre and brought you here. Père Silas, old as he is, would carry you upstairs, and lay you on that couch himself. He would certainly have remained with you till suspended animation had been restored: and so should I, but, at that juncture, a hurried messenger arrived from the dying patient I had scarcely left—the last duties were called for—the physician's last visit and the priest's last rite; extreme unction could not be deferred. Père Silas and myself departed together, my mother was spending the evening abroad; we gave you in charge to Martha, leaving directions, which it seems she followed successfully. Now, are you a Catholic?''

"Not yet," said I, with a smile. "And never let Père Silas know where I live, or he will try to convert me; but give him my best and truest thanks when you see him, and if ever I get rich I will send him money for his charities. See, Dr. John, your mother wakes; you ought to ring for tea.''

Which he did; and, as Mrs. Bretton sat up—astonished and indignant at herself for the indulgence to which she had succumbed, and fully prepared to deny that she had slept at all—her son came gaily to the attack—

"Hushaby, mamma! Sleep again. You look the picture of innocence in your slumbers.''

"My slumbers, John Graham! What are you talking about? You know I never *do* sleep by day: it was the slightest doze possible.''

"Exactly! a seraph's gentle lapse—a fairy's dream. Mamma, under such circumstances, you always remind me of Titania.''

"That is because you, yourself, are so like Bottom.''

"Miss Snowe—did you ever hear anything like mamma's wit? She is a most sprightly woman for her size and age.''

"Keep your compliments to yourself, sir, and do not neglect your own size: which seems to me a good deal on the increase. Lucy, has he not rather the air of an incipient John Bull? He used to be slender as an eel, and now I fancy in him a sort of heavy dragoon bent—a beef-eater tendency. Graham, take notice! If you grow fat I disown you.''

"As if you could not sooner disown your own personality! I am indispensable to the old lady's happiness, Lucy. She would pine away in green and yellow melancholy if she had not my six feet of iniquity to scold. It keeps her lively—it maintains the wholesome ferment of her spirits.''

The two were now standing opposite to each other, one on each side the fireplace; their words were not very fond, but their mutual looks atoned for verbal deficiencies. At least, the best treasure of Mrs. Bretton's life was certainly casketed in her son's bosom; her dearest pulse throbbed in his heart. As to him, of course another love shared his feelings with filial love; and, no doubt, as the new passion was the latest born, so he assigned it in his emotions Benjamin's portion. Ginevra! Ginevra! Did Mrs. Bretton yet know at whose feet her own young idol had laid his homage? Would she approve that choice? I could not tell; but I could well guess that if she knew Miss Fanshawe's conduct towards Graham: her alternations between coldness and coaxing, and repulse and allurement; if she could at all suspect the pain with which she had tried him; if she could have seen, as I had seen, his fine spirits subdued and harassed, his inferior preferred before him, his subordinate made the instrument of his humiliation—*then* Mrs. Bretton would have pronounced Ginevra imbecile, or perverted, or both. Well—I thought so too.

That second evening passed as sweetly as the first—*more* sweetly indeed: we enjoyed a smoother interchange of thought: old troubles were not reverted to, acquaintance was better cemented; I felt happier, easier, more at home. That night—instead of crying myself asleep—I went down to dreamland by a pathway bordered with pleasant thoughts.

Chapter XVIII

WE QUARREL

DURING the first days of my stay at the terrace, Graham never took a seat near me, or in his frequent pacing of the room approached the quarter where I sat, or looked preoccupied, or more grave than usual, but I thought of Miss Fanshawe and expected her name to leap from his lips. I kept my ear and mind in perpetual readiness for the tender theme; my patience was ordered to be permanently under arms, and my sympathy desired to keep its cornucopia replenished and ready for outpouring. At last, and after a little inward struggle which I saw and respected, he one day launched into the topic. It was introduced delicately; anonymously as it were.

"Your friend is spending her vacation in travelling, I hear?"

"Friend, forsooth!" thought I to myself: but it would not do to contradict; he must have his own way; I must own the soft impeachment: friend let it be. Still, by way of experiment, I could not help asking whom he meant?

He had taken a seat at my work-table; he now laid hands on a reel of thread, which he proceeded recklessly to unwind.

"Ginevra—Miss Fanshawe, has accompanied the Cholmondeleys on a tour through the south of France?"

"She has."

"Do you and she correspond?"

"It will astonish you to hear that I never once thought of making application for that privilege."

"You have seen letters of her writing?"

"Yes; several to her uncle."

"They will not be deficient in wit and naïveté; there is so much sparkle, and so little art in her soul?"

"She writes comprehensively enough when she writes to M. de Bassompierre: he who runs may read." (In fact, Ginevra's epistles to her wealthy kinsman were commonly business documents, unequivocal applications for cash.)

"And her handwriting? It must be pretty, light, ladylike, I should think?"

It was, and I said so.

"I verily believe that all she does is well done," said Dr. John; and as I seemed in no hurry to chime in with this remark, he added—"You, who know her, could you name a point in which she is deficient?"

"She does some things very well." ("Flirtation amongst the rest," subjoined I, in thought.)

"When do you suppose she will return to town?" he soon inquired.

"Pardon me, Dr. John, I must explain. You honour me too much in ascribing to me a degree of intimacy with Miss Fanshawe I have not the felicity to enjoy. I have never been the depositary of her plans and secrets. You will find her particular friends in another sphere than mine: amongst the Cholmondeleys, for instance."

He actually thought I was stung with a kind of jealous pain similar to his own! "Excuse her," he said; "judge her indulgently; the glitter of fashion misleads her, but she will soon find out that these people are hollow, and will return to you with augmented attachment and confirmed trust. I know something of the Cholmondeleys: superficial, showy, selfish people; depend on it, at heart Ginevra values you beyond a score of such."

"You are very kind," I said briefly. A disclaimer of the sentiments attributed to me burned on my lips, but I extinguished the flame. I submitted to be looked upon as the humiliated, cast-off, and now pining confidante of the distinguished Miss Fanshawe: but, reader, it was a hard submission.

"Yet, you see," continued Graham, "while I comfort *you*, I cannot take the same consolation to myself; I cannot hope she will do me justice. De Hamal is most worthless, yet I fear he pleases her: wretched delusion!"

My patience really gave way, and without notice: all at once. I suppose illness and weakness had worn it and made it brittle.

"Dr. Bretton," I broke out, "there is no delusion like your own. On all points but one you are a man, frank, healthful, right-thinking, clear-sighted: on this exceptional point you are but a slave. I declare, where Miss Fanshawe is concerned, you merit no respect; nor have you mine."

I got up, and left the room very much excited.

This little scene took place in the morning; I had to meet him again in the evening, and then I saw I had done mischief. He was not made of common clay, not put together out of vulgar materials; while the outlines of his nature had been shaped with breadth and vigour, the details embraced workmanship of almost feminine delicacy: finer, much finer, than you could be prepared to meet with; than you could believe inherent in him, even after years of acquaintance. Indeed, till some over-sharp contact with his nerves had betrayed, by its effects, their acute sensibility, this elaborate construction must be ignored; and the more especially because the sympathetic faculty was not prominent in him: to feel, and to seize quickly another's feelings, are separate properties; a few constructions possess both, some neither. Dr. John had the one in exquisite perfection; and because I have admitted that he was not endowed with the other in equal degree, the reader will considerately refrain from passing to an extreme, and pronouncing him *un*-sympathising, unfeeling: on the contrary, he was a kind, generous man. Make your need known, his hand was open. Put your grief into words, he turned no deaf ear. Expect refinements of perception, miracles of intuition, and realise disappointment. This night, when Dr. John entered the room, and met the evening lamp, I saw well and at one glance his whole mechanism.

To one who had named him "slave," and, on any point, banned him from respect, he must now have peculiar feelings. That the epithet was well applied, and the ban just, might be; he put forth no denial that it was so: his mind even candidly revolved that unmanning possibility. He sought in this accusation the cause of that ill-success which had got so galling a hold on his mental peace. Amid the worry of a self-condemnatory soliloquy, his demeanour seemed grave, perhaps cold, both to me and his mother. And yet there was no bad feeling, no malice, no rancour, no littleness in his countenance, beautiful with a man's best beauty, even in its depression. When I placed his chair at the table, which I hastened to do, anticipating the servant, and when I handed him his tea, which I did with trembling care, he said—

"Thank you, Lucy," in as kindly a tone of his full, pleasant voice as ever my ear welcomed.

For my part, there was only one plan to be pursued; I must expiate my culpable vehemence, or I must not sleep that night. This would not do at all; I could not stand it: I made no pretence of capacity to wage war on this footing. School solitude, conventual silence and stagnation, anything seemed preferable to living embroiled with Dr. John. As to Ginevra, she might take the silver wings of a dove, or any other fowl that flies, and mount straight up to the highest place, among the highest stars, where her lover's highest flight of fancy chose to fix the constellation of her charms: never more be it mine to dispute the arrangement. Long I tried to catch his eye. Again and again that eye just met mine; but, having nothing to say, it withdrew and I was baffled. After tea, he sat, sad and quiet, reading a book. I wished I could have dared to go and sit near him, but it seemed that if I ventured to take that step, he would infallibly evince hostility and indignation. I longed to speak out, and I dared not whisper. His mother left the room; then, moved by insupportable regret, I just murmured the words,

"Dr. Bretton."

He looked up from his book; his eyes were not cold or malevolent, his mouth was not cynical; he was ready and willing to hear what I might have to say: his spirit was of vintage too mellow and generous to sour in one thunder-clap.

"Dr. Bretton, forgive my hasty words: *do, do* forgive them."

He smiled that moment I spoke. "Perhaps I deserved them, Lucy. If you don't respect me, I am sure it is because I am not respectable. I fear, I am an awkward fool: I must manage badly in some way, for where I wish to please, it seems I don't please."

"Of that you cannot be sure; and even if such be the case, is it the fault of your character or of another's perceptions? But now, let me unsay what I said in anger. In one thing, and in all things, I deeply respect you. If you think scarcely enough of yourself, and too much of others, what is that but an excellence?"

"Can I think too much of Ginevra?"

"*I* believe you may; *you* believe you can't. Let us agree to differ. Let me be pardoned; that is what I ask."

"Do you think I cherish ill-will for one warm word?"

"I see you do not and cannot; but just say, 'Lucy, I forgive you!' Say that, to ease me of the heart-ache."

"Put away your heart-ache, as I will put away mine; for you wounded me a little, Lucy. Now, when the pain is gone, I more than forgive: I feel grateful, as to a sincere well-wisher."

"I *am* your sincere well-wisher: you are right."

Thus our quarrel ended.

Reader, if, in the course of this work, you find that my opinion of Dr. John undergoes modifcation, excuse the seeming inconsistency. I give the feeling as at the time I felt it; I describe the view of character as it appeared when discovered.

He showed the fineness of his nature by being kinder to me after that misunderstanding than before. Nay, the very incident which, by my theory, must in some degree estrange me and him, changed, indeed, somewhat our relations; but not in the sense I painfully anticipated. An invisible, but a cold something, very slight, very transparent, but very chill: a sort of screen of ice had hitherto, all through our two lives, glazed the medium through which we exchanged intercourse. Those few warm words, though only warm with anger, breathed on that frail frost-work of reserve; about this time, it gave note of dissolution. I think from that day, so long as we continued friends, he never in discourse stood on topics of ceremony with me. He seemed to know that if he would but talk about himself, and about that in which he was most interested, my expectation would always be answered, my wish always satisfied. It follows as a matter of course, that I continued to hear much of "Ginevra."

"Ginevra!" He thought her so fair, so good; he spoke so lovingly of her charms, her sweetness, her innocence, that, in spite of my plain prose knowledge of the reality, a kind of reflected glow began to settle on her idea, even for me. Still, reader, I am free to confess that he often talked nonsense; but I strove to be unfailingly patient with him. I had had my lesson: I had learned how severe for me was the pain of crossing, or grieving, or disappointing him. In a strange and new sense, I grew most selfish, and quite powerless to deny myself the delight of indulging his mood, and being pliant to his will. He still seemed to me most absurd when he obstinately doubted, and desponded about his power to win in the end Miss Fanshawe's preference. The fancy became rooted in my own mind more stubbornly than ever, that she was only coquetting to goad him, and that, at heart, she coveted every one of his words and looks. Sometimes he harassed me, in spite of my resolution to bear and hear; in the midst of the indescribable gall-honey pleasure of thus bearing and hearing, he strnck so on the flint of what firmness I owned, that it emitted fire once and again. I chanced to assert one day, with a view

to stilling his impatience, that in my own mind, I felt positive Miss Fanshawe *must* intend eventually to accept him.

"Positive! It was easy to say so, but had I any grounds for such assurance?"

"The best grounds."

"Now, Lucy, *do* tell me what!"

"You know them as well as I; and, knowing them, Dr. John, it really amazes me that you should not repose the frankest confidence in her fidelity. To doubt, under the circumstances, is almost to insult."

"Now you are beginning to speak fast, and to breathe short; but speak a little faster and breathe a little shorter, till you have given an explanation—a full explanation: I must have it."

"You shall, Dr. John. In some cases, you are a lavish, generous man: you are a worshipper ever ready with the votive offering: should Père Silas ever convert *you*, you will give him abundance of alms for his poor, you will supply his altar with tapers, and the shrine of your favourite saint you will do your best to enrich: Ginevra, Dr. John"——

"Hush!" said he, "don't go on."

"Hush! I will *not*: and go on I *will*: Ginevra has had her hands filled from your hands more times than I can count. You have sought for her the costliest flowers; you have busied your brain in devising gifts the most delicate: such, one would have thought, as only a woman could have imagined; and in addition, Miss Fanshawe owns a set of ornaments, to purchase which your generosity must have verged on extravagance."

The modesty Ginevra herself had never evinced in this matter, now flushed all over the face of her admirer.

"Nonsense!" he said, destructively snipping a skein of silk with my scissors. "I offered them to please myself: I felt she did me a favour in accepting them."

"She did more than a favour, Dr. John; she pledged her very honour that she would make you some return; and if she cannot pay you in affection, she ought to hand out a business-like equivalent, in the shape of some rouleaux of gold pieces."

"But you don't understand her; she is far too disinterested to care for my gifts, and too simple-minded to know their value."

I laughed out: I had heard her adjudge to every jewel its price; and well I knew money-embarrassment, money-schemes, money's worth, and endeavours to realise supplies, had, young as she was, furnished the most frequent, and the favourite stimulus of her thoughts for years.

He pursued. "You should have seen her whenever I have laid on her lap some trifle; so cool, so unmoved: no eagerness to take, not even pleasure in contemplating. Just from amiable reluctance to grieve me, she would permit the bouquet to lie beside her, and perhaps consent to bear it away. Or, if I achieved the fastening of a bracelet on her ivory arm, however pretty the trinket might be (and I always carefully chose what seemed to *me* pretty, and what of course was not valueless), the glitter never dazzled her bright eyes: she would hardly cast one look on my gift."

"Then, of course, not valuing it, she would unloose, and return it to you?"

"No; for such a repulse she was too good-natured. She would consent to seem to forget what I had done, and retain the offering with lady-like quiet and easy oblivion. Under such circumstances, how can a man build on acceptance of his presents as a favourable symptom? For my part, were I to offer her all I have, and she to take it, such is her incapacity to be swayed by sordid considerations, I should not venture to believe the transaction advanced me one step."

"Dr. John," I began, "Love is blind!" but just then a blue, subtle ray sped sideways from Dr. John's eye: it reminded me of old days, it reminded me of his picture: it half led me to think that part, at least, of his professed persuasion of Miss Fanshawe's naïveté was assumed; it led me dubiously to conjecture that

perhaps, in spite of his passion for her beauty, his appreciation of her foibles might possibly be less mistaken, more clear-sighted, than from his general language was presumable. After all it might be only a chance look, or at best, the token of a merely momentary impression. Chance or intentional, real or imaginary, it closed the conversation.

Chapter XIX

THE CLEOPATRA

MY stay at La Terrasse was prolonged a fortnight beyond the close of the vacation. Mrs. Bretton's kind management procured me this respite. Her son having one day delivered the dictum that "Lucy was not yet strong enough to go back to that den of a pensionnat," she at once drove over to the Rue Fossette, had an interview with the directress, and procured the indulgence, on the plea of prolonged rest and change being necessary to perfect recovery. Hereupon, however, followed an attention I could very well have dispensed with, viz., a polite call from Madame Beck.

That lady—one fine day—actually came out in a fiacre as far as the chateau. I suppose she had resolved within herself to see what manner of place Dr. John inhabited. Apparently, the pleasant site and neat interior surpassed her expectations; she eulogised all she saw, pronounced the blue salon "une pièce magnifique," profusely congratulated me on the acquisition of friends, "tellement dignes, aimables, et respectables," turned also a neat compliment in my favour, and, upon Dr. John coming in, ran up to him with the utmost buoyancy, opening at the same time such a fire of rapid language, all sparkling with felicitations and protestations about his "chateau,"—"madame sa mère, la digne chatelaine": also his looks; which, indeed, were very flourishing, and at the moment additionally embellished by the good-natured but amused smile with which he always listened to Madame's fluent and florid French. In short, Madame shone in her very best phase that day, and came in and went out quite a living catherine-wheel of compliments, delight, and affability. Half-purposely, and half to ask some question about school-business, I followed her to the carriage, and looked in after she was seated and the door closed. In that brief fraction of time what a change had been wrought! An instant ago, all sparkles and jests, she now sat sterner than a judge and graver than a sage! Strange little woman!

I went back and teased Dr. John about Madame's devotion to him. How he laughed! What fun shone in his eyes as he recalled some of her fine speeches, and repeated them, imitating her voluble delivery! He had an acute sense of humour, and was the finest company in the world—when he could forget Miss Fanshawe.

To "sit in sunshine calm and sweet" is said to be excellent for weak people; it gives them vital force. When little Georgette Beck was recovering from her illness, I used to take her in my arms and walk with her in the garden by the hour together, beneath a certain wall hung with grapes, which the southern sun was ripening; that sun cherished her little pale frame quite as effectually as it mellowed and swelled the clustering fruit.

There are human tempers, bland, glowing, and genial, within whose influence it is as good for the poor in spirit to live, as it is for the feeble in frame to bask in the glow of noon. Of the number of these choice natures were certainly both Dr. Bretton's and his mother's. They liked to communicate happiness, as some like to occasion misery; they did it instinctively; without fuss, and apparently with little consciousness; the means to give pleasure rose spontaneously in their minds. Every day while I stayed with them, some little plan was proposed which resulted in

beneficial enjoyment. Fully occupied as was Dr. John's time, he still made it in his way to accompany us in each brief excursion. I can hardly tell how he managed his engagements; they were numerous, yet by dint of system, he classed them in an order which left him a daily period of liberty. I often saw him hard-worked, yet seldom over-driven, and never irritated, confused, or oppressed. What he did was accomplished with the ease and grace of all-sufficing strength; with the bountiful cheerfulness of high and unbroken energies. Under his guidance I saw, in that one happy fortnight, more of Villette, its environs, and its inhabitants, than I had seen in the whole eight months of my previous residence. He took me to places of interest in the town, of whose names I had not before so much as heard; with willingness and spirit he communicated much noteworthy information. He never seemed to think it a trouble to talk to me, and, I am sure, it was never a task to me to listen. It was not his way to treat subjects coldly and vaguely; he rarely generalised, never prosed. He seemed to like nice details almost as much as I liked them myself: he seemed observant of character: and not superficially observant, either. These points gave the quality of interest to his discourse; and the fact of his speaking direct from his own resources, and not borrowing or stealing from books—here a dry fact, and there a trite phrase, and elsewhere a hackneyed opinion—ensured a freshness, as welcome as it was rare. Before my eyes, too, his disposition seemed to unfold another phase; to pass to a fresh day: to rise in new and nobler dawn.

His mother possessed a good development of benevolence, but he owned a better and larger. I found, on accompanying him to the Basse-Ville—the poor and crowded quarter of the city—that his errands there were as much those of the philanthropist as the physician. I understood presently that—cheerfully, habitually, and in single-minded unconsciousness of any special merit distinguishing his deeds—he was achieving, amongst a very wretched population, a world of active good. The lower orders liked him well; his poor patients in the hospitals welcomed him with a sort of enthusiasm.

But stop—I must not, from the faithful narrator, degenerate into the partial eulogist. Well, full well, do I know that Dr. John was not perfect, any more than I am perfect. Human fallibility leavened him throughout; there was no hour, and scarcely a moment of the time I spent with him, that in act, or speech, or look, he did not betray something that was not of a god. A god could not have the cruel vanity of Dr. John, nor his some-time levity. No immortal could have resembled him in his occasional temporary oblivion of all but the present—in his passing passion for that present; shown not coarsely, by devoting it to material indulgence, but selfishly, by extracting from it whatever it could yield of nutriment to his masculine self-love: his delight was to feed that ravenous sentiment, without thought of the price of provender, or care for the cost of keeping it sleek and high-pampered.

The reader is requested to note a seeming contradiction in the two views which have been given of Graham Bretton—the public and private—the outdoor and the indoor view. In the first, the public, he is shown oblivious of self; as modest in the display of his energies, as earnest in their exercise. In the second, the fireside picture, there is expressed consciousness of what he has and what he is; pleasure in homage, some recklessness in exciting, some vanity in receiving the same. Both portraits are correct.

It was hardly possible to oblige Dr. John quietly and in secret. When you thought that the fabrication of some trifle dedicated to his use had been achieved unnoticed, and that, like other men, he would use it when placed ready for his use, and never ask whence it came, he amazed you by a smilingly-uttered observation or two proving that his eye had been on the work from commencement to close: that he had noted the design, traced its progress, and marked its completion. It pleased him to be thus served, and he let his pleasure beam in his eye and play about his mouth.

This would have been all very well, if he had not added to such kindly and unobtrusive evidence a certain wilfulness in discharging what he called debts. When his mother worked for him, he paid her by showering about her his bright animal spirits, with even more affluence than his gay, taunting, teasing, loving wont. If Lucy Snowe were discovered to have put her hand to such work, he planned, in recompense, some pleasant recreation.

I often felt amazed at his perfect knowledge of Villette; a knowledge not merely confined to its open streets, but penetrating to all its galleries, salles, and cabinets: of every door which shut in an object worth seeing, of every museum, of every hall, sacred to art or science, he seemed to possess the "Open! Sesame." I never had a head for science, but an ignorant, blind, fond instinct inclined me to art. I liked to visit the picture galleries, and I dearly liked to be left there alone. In company, a wretched idiosyncracy forbade me to see much or to feel anything. In unfamiliar company, where it was necessary to maintain a flow of talk on the subjects in presence, half-an-hour would knock me up, with a combined pressure of physical lassitude and entire mental incapacity. I never yet saw the well-reared child, much less the educated adult, who could not put me to shame by the sustained intelligence of its demeanour under the ordeal of a conversable, sociable visitation of pictures, historical sights or buildings, or any lions of public interest. Dr. Bretton was a cicerone after my own heart; he would take me betimes, ere the galleries were filled, leave me there for two or three hours, and call for me when his own engagements were discharged. Meantime, I was happy; happy, not always in admiring, but in examining, questioning, and forming conclusions. In the commencement of these visits, there was some misunderstanding and consequent struggle between Will and Power. The former faculty exacted approbation of that which it was considered orthodox to admire; the latter groaned forth its utter inability to pay the tax; it was then self-sneered at, spurred up, goaded on to refine its taste, and whet its zest. The more it was chidden, however, the more it wouldn't praise. Discovering gradually that a wonderful sense of fatigue resulted from these conscientious efforts, I began to reflect whether I might not dispense with that great labour, and concluded eventually that I might, and so sank supine into a luxury of calm before ninety-nine out of a hundred of the exhibited frames.

It seemed to me that an original and good picture was just as scarce as an original and good book; nor did I, in the end, tremble to say to myself, standing before certain chefs d'œuvre bearing great names, "These are not a whit like nature. Nature's daylight never had that colour: never was made so turbid, either by storm or cloud, as it is laid out there, under a sky of indigo: and that indigo is not ether; and those dark weeds plastered upon it are not trees." Several very well-executed and complacent-looking fat women struck me as by no means the goddesses they appeared to consider themselves. Many scores of marvellously-finished little Flemish pictures, and also of sketches, excellent for fashion-books, displaying varied costumes in the handsomest materials, gave evidence of laudable industry whimsically applied. And yet there were fragments of truth here and there which satisfied the conscience, and gleams of light that cheered the vision. Nature's power here broke through in a mountain snow-storm; and there her glory in a sunny southern day. An expression in this portrait proved clear insight into character; a face in that historical painting, by its vivid filial likeness, startingly reminded you that genius gave it birth. These exceptions I loved: they grew dear as friends.

One day, at a quiet early hour, I found myself nearly alone in a certain gallery, wherein one particular picture of portentous size, set up in the best light, having a cordon of protection stretched before it, and a cushioned bench duly set in front for the accommodation of worshipping connoisseurs, who, having gazed themselves off their feet, might be fain to complete the business sitting: this picture, I say, seemed to consider itself the queen of the collection.

It represented a woman, considerably larger, I thought, than the life. I calculated that this lady, put into a scale of magnitude suitable for the reception of a commodity of bulk, would infallibly turn from fourteen to sixteen stone. She was, indeed, extremely well fed: very much butcher's meat—to say nothing of bread, vegetables, and liquids—must she have consumed to attain that breadth and height, that wealth of muscle, that affluence of flesh. She lay half-reclined on a couch: why, it would be difficult to say; broad daylight blazed round her: she appeared in hearty health, strong enough to do the work of two plain cooks; she could not plead a weak spine; she ought to have been standing, or at least sitting bolt upright. She had no business to lounge away the noon on a sofa. She ought likewise to have worn decent garments; a gown covering her properly, which was not the case: out of abundance of material— seven-and-twenty yards, I should say, of drapery—she managed to make inefficient raiment. Then, for the wretched untidiness surrounding her, there could be no excuse. Pots and pans—perhaps I ought to say vases and goblets—were rolled here and there on the foreground; a perfect rubbish of flowers was mixed amongst them, and an absurd and disorderly mass of curtain upholstery smothered the couch and cumbered the floor. On referring to the catalogue, I found that this notable production bore name "Cleopatra."

Well, I was sitting wondering at it (as the bench was there, I thought I might as well take advantage of its accommodation), and thinking that while some of the details—as roses, gold cups, jewels, etc., were very prettily painted, it was on the whole an enormous piece of claptrap; the room, almost vacant when I entered, began to fill. Scarcely noticing this circumstance (as, indeed, it did not matter to me) I retained my seat, rather to rest myself than with a view to studying this huge, dark-complexioned gipsy-queen; of whom, indeed, I soon tired, and betook myself for refreshment to the contemplation of some exquisite little pictures of still life: wild-flowers, wild fruit, mossy wood-nests, casketing eggs that looked like pearls seen through clear green sea-water; all hung modestly beneath that coarse and preposterous canvas.

Suddenly a light tap visited my shoulder. Starting, turning, I met a face bent to encounter mine; a frowning, almost a shocked face it was.

"Que faites vous ici?" said a voice.

"Mais, monsieur, je m'amuse."

"Vous vous amusez! et à quoi, s'il vous plait? Mais d'abord, faites-moi le plaisir de vous lever; prenez mon bras, et allons de l'autre côté."

I did precisely as I was bid. M. Paul Emanuel (it was he), returned from Rome, and now a travelled man, was not likely to be less tolerant of insubordination now, than before this added distinction laurelled his temples.

"Permit me to conduct you to your party," said he, as he crossed the room.

"I have no party."

"You are not alone?"

"Yes, monsieur."

"Did you come here unaccompanied?"

"No monsieur. Dr. Bretton brought me here."

"Dr. Bretton and Madame his mother, of course?"

"No; only Dr. Bretton."

"And he told you to look at *that* picture?"

"By no means; I found it out for myself."

M. Paul's hair was shorn close as raven down, or I think it would have bristled on his head. Beginning now to perceive his drift, I had a certain pleasure in keeping cool, and working him up.

"Astounding insular audacity," cried the professor. "Singulières femmes que ces Anglaises!"

"What is the matter, monsieur?"

"Matter! How dare you, a young person, sit coolly down with the self-possession of a garçon, and look at *that* picture?''

"It is a very ugly picture, but I cannot at all see why I should not look at it."

"Bon! bon! Speak no more of it. But you ought not to be here alone."

"If, however, I have no society—no *party,* as you say? And then, what does it signify whether I am alone, or accompanied? Nobody meddles with me."

"Taisez-vous, et asseyez-vous là—là!'' Setting down a chair with emphasis in a particularly dull corner, before a series of most specially dreary cadres.

"Mais, monsieur."

"Mais, mademoiselle, asseyez-vous, et ne bougez pas—entendez-vous? jusqu'à ce qu'on vienne vous chercher, ou que je vous donne la permission."

"Quel triste coin!'' cried I, "et quelles laids tableaux!''

And "laids,'' indeed, they were; being a set of four denominated in the catalogue "La vie d'une femme.'' They were painted rather in a remarkable style—flat, dead, pale, and formal. The first represented a "Jeune Fille,'' coming out of a church-door, a missal in her hand, her dress very prim, her eyes cast down, her mouth pursed up—the image of a most villainous little precocious she-hypocrite. The second, a "Mariée'' with a long white veil, kneeling at a prie-dieu in her chamber, holding her hands plastered together, finger to finger, and showing the whites of her eyes in a most exasperating manner. The third, a "Jeune Mère,'' hanging disconsolate over a clayey and puffy baby with a face like an unwholesome full moon. The fourth, a "Veuve,'' being a black woman, holding by the hand a black little girl, and the twain studiously surveying an elegant French monument, set up in a corner of some Père la Chaise. All these four "Anges'' were grim and grey as burglars, and cold and vapid as ghosts. What women to live with! insincere, ill-humoured, bloodless, brainless nonentities! As bad in their way as the indolent gipsy-giantess, the Cleopatra, in hers.

It was impossible to keep one's attention long confined to these masterpieces, and so, by degrees, I veered round, and surveyed the gallery.

A perfect crowd of spectators was by this time gathered round the Lioness, from whose vicinage I had been banished; nearly half this crowd were ladies, but M. Paul afterwards told me, these were "des dames,'' and it was quite proper for them to contemplate what no "demoiselle'' ought to glance at. I assured him plainly I could not agree in this doctrine, and did not see the sense of it; whereupon, with his usual absolutism, he merely requested my silence, and also, in the same breath, denounced my mingled rashness and ignorance. A more despotic little man than M. Paul never filled a professor's chair. I noticed, by the way, that he looked at the picture himself quite at his ease, and for a very long while: he did not, however, neglect to glance from time to time my way, in order, I suppose, to make sure that I was obeying orders, and not breaking bounds. By-and-by, he again accosted me.

"Had I not been ill?'' he wished to know: "he understood I had.''

"Yes, but I was now quite well.''

"Where had I spent the vacation?''

"Chiefly in the Rue Fossette; partly with Madame Bretton.''

"He had heard that I was left alone in the Rue Fossette; was that so?''

"Not quite alone: Marie Broc (the *crétin*) was with me.''

He shrugged his shoulders; varied and contradictory expressions played rapidly over his countenance. Marie Broc was well known to M. Paul; he never gave a lesson in the third division (containing the least advanced pupils), that she did not occasion in him a sharp conflict between antagonistic impressions. Her personal appearance, her repulsive manners, her often unmanageable disposition, irritated his temper, and inspired him with strong antipathy; a feeling he was too apt to conceive when his taste was offended or his will thwarted. On the other hand, her misfortunes constituted a strong claim on his forbearance and compassion—such a claim as it was not in his nature to deny; hence resulted, almost daily, drawn battles

between impatience and disgust on the one hand, pity and a sense of justice on the other; in which, to his credit be it said, it was very seldom that the former feelings prevailed: when they did, however, M. Paul showed a phase of character which had its terrors. His passions were strong, his aversions and attachments alike vivid; the force he exerted in holding both in check by no means mitigated an observer's sense of their vehemence. With such tendencies, it may well be supposed he often excited in ordinary minds fear and dislike; yet it was an error to fear him: nothing drove him so nearly frantic as the tremor of an apprehensive and distrustful spirit; nothing soothed him like confidence tempered with gentleness. To evince these sentiments, however, required a thorough comprehension of his nature; and his nature was of an order rarely comprehended.

"How did you get on with Marie Broc?" he asked, after some minutes' silence.

"Monsieur, I did my best; but it was terrible to be alone with her!"

"You have, then, a weak heart! You lack courage; and perhaps charity. Yours are not the qualities which might constitute a Sister of Mercy."

[He was a religious little man, in his way: the self-denying and self-sacrificing part of the Catholic religion commanded the homage of his soul.]

"I don't know, indeed: I took as good care of her as I could; but when her aunt came to fetch her away, it was a great relief."

"Ah! you are an egotist. There are women who have nursed hospitals-full of similar unfortunates. You could not do that?"

"Could Monsieur do it himself?"

"Women who are worthy the name ought infinitely to surpass our coarse, fallible, self-indulgent sex, in the power to perform such duties."

"I washed her, I kept her clean, I fed her, I tried to amuse her; but she made mouths at me instead of speaking."

"You think you did great things?"

"No; but as great as I *could* do."

"Then limited are your powers, for in tending one idiot you fell sick."

"Not with that, monsieur; I had a nervous fever: my mind was ill."

"Vraiment! Vous valez peu de chose. You are not cast in an heroic mould; your courage will not avail to sustain you in solitude; it merely gives you the temerity to gaze with sang-froid at pictures of Cleopatra."

It would have been easy to show anger at the teasing, hostile tone of the little man. I have never been angry with him yet, however, and had no present disposition to begin.

"Cleopatra!" I repeated quietly. "Monsieur, too, has been looking at Cleopatra; what does he think of her?"

"Cela ne vaut rien," he responded. "Une femme superbe—une taille d'impératrice, des formes de Junon, mais une personne dont je ne voudrais ni pour femme, ni pour fille, ni pour sœur. Aussi vous ne jeterez plus un seul coup d'œil de sa côté."

"But I have looked at her a great many times while Monsieur has been talking: I can see her quite well from this corner."

"Turn to the wall and study your four pictures of a woman's life."

"Excuse me, M. Paul; they are too hideous: but if you admire them, allow me to vacate my seat and leave you to their contemplation."

"Mademoiselle," he said, grimacing a half-smile, or what he intended for a smile, though it was but a grim and hurried manifestation, "you nurslings of Protestantism astonish me. You unguarded Englishwomen walk calmly amidst red-hot ploughshares and escape burning. I believe, if some of you were thrown into Nebuchadnezzar's hottest furnace you would issue forth untraversed by the smell of fire."

"Will Monsieur have the goodness to move an inch to one side?"

"How! At what are you gazing now? You are not recognising an acquaintance amongst that group of jeunes gens?"

"I think so—yes, I see there a person I know."

In fact, I had caught a glimpse of a head too pretty to belong to any other than the redoubted Colonel de Hamal. What a very finished, highly polished little pate it was! What a figure, so trim and natty! What womanish feet and hands! How daintily he held a glass to one of his optics! with what admiration he gazed upon the Cleopatra! and then, how engagingly he tittered and whispered a friend at his elbow! Oh, the man of sense! Oh, the refined gentleman of superior taste and tact! I observed him for about ten minutes, and perceived that he was exceedingly taken with this dusk and portly Venus of the Nile. So much was I interested in his bearing, so absorbed in divining his character by his looks and movements, I temporarily forgot M. Paul; in the interim a group came between that gentleman and me; or possibly his scruples might have received another and worse shock from my present abstraction, causing him to withdraw voluntarily: at any rate, when I again looked round, he was gone.

My eye, pursuant of the search, met not him, but another and dissimilar figure, well seen amidst the crowd, for the height as well as the port lent each its distinction. This way came Dr. John, in visage, in shape, in hue, as unlike the dark, acerb, and caustic little professor as the fruit of the Hesperides might be unlike the sloe in the wild thicket; as the high-couraged but tractable Arabian is unlike the rude and stubborn "Sheltie." He was looking for me, but had not yet explored the corner where the schoolmaster had just put me. I remained quiet; yet another minute I would watch.

He approached De Hamal; he paused near him; I thought he had a pleasure in looking over his head; Dr. Bretton, too, gazed on the Cleopatra. I doubt if it were to his taste: he did not simper like the little Count; his mouth looked fastidious, his eye cool; without demonstration he stepped aside, leaving room for others to approach. I saw now that he was waiting, and, rising, I joined him.

We took one turn round the gallery; with Graham it was very pleasant to take such a turn. I always liked dearly to hear what he had to say about either pictures or books; because, without pretending to be a connoisseur, he always spoke his thought, and that was sure to be fresh: very often it was also just and pithy. It was pleasant also to tell him some things be did not know—he listened so kindly, so teachably; unformalised by scruples lest so to bend his bright handsome head, to gather a woman's rather obscure and stammering explanation, should imperil the dignity of his manhood. And when he communicated information in return, it was with a lucid intelligence that left all his words clear graven on the memory; no explanation of his giving, no fact of his narrating, did I ever forget.

As we left the gallery, I asked him what he thought of the Cleopatra (after making him laugh by telling him how Professor Emanuel had sent me to the right-about, and taking him to see the sweet series of pictures recommended to my attention).

"Pooh!" said he, "my mother is a better-looking woman. I heard some French fops, yonder, designating her as 'le type du voluptueux'; if so, I can only say, 'le voluptueux' is little to my liking. Compare that mulatto with Ginevra!"

Chapter XX

THE CONCERT

ONE morning, Mrs. Bretton, coming promptly into my room, desired me to open my drawers and show her my dresses; which I did, without a word.

"That will do," said she, when she had turned them over. "You must have a new one."

She went out. She returned presently with a dressmaker. She had me measured. "I mean," said she, "to follow my own taste, and to have my own way in this little matter."

Two days after came home—a pink dress!

"That is not for me," I said hurriedly, feeling that I would almost as soon clothe myself in the costume of a Chinese lady of rank.

"We shall see whether it is for you or not," rejoined my godmother; adding with her resistless decision, "Mark my words. You will wear it this very evening."

I thought I should not; I thought no human force should avail to put me into it. A pink dress! I knew it not. It knew me not. I had not proved it.

My godmother went on to decree that I was to go with her and Graham to a concert that same night: which concert, she explained, was a grand affair to be held in the large salle, or hall, of the principal musical society. The most advanced of the pupils of the Conservatoire were to perform: it was to be followed by a lottery "au bénéfice des pauvres"; and to crown all, the King, Queen, and Prince of Labassecour were to be present. Graham, in sending tickets, had enjoined attention to costume as a compliment due to royalty; he also recommended punctual readiness by seven o'clock.

About six, I was ushered upstairs. Without any force at all, I found myself led and influenced by another's will, unconsulted, unpersuaded, quietly over-ruled. In short, the pink dress went on, softened by some drapery of black lace. I was pronounced to be en grande tenue, and requested to look in the glass. I did so with some fear and trembling; with more fear and trembling, I turned away. Seven o'clock struck; Dr. Bretton was come; my godmother and I went down. *She* was clad in brown velvet; as I walked in her shadow, how I envied her those folds of grave, dark majesty! Graham stood in the drawing-room doorway.

"I *do* hope he will not think I have been decking myself out to draw attention," was my uneasy aspiration.

"Here, Lucy, are some flowers," said he, giving me a bouquet. He took no further notice of my dress than was conveyed in a kind smile and satisfied nod, which calmed at once my sense of shame and fear of ridicule. For the rest, the dress was made with extreme simplicity, guiltless of flounce or furbelow; it was but the light fabric and bright tint which scared me, and since Graham found in it nothing absurd, my own eye consented soon to become reconciled.

I suppose people who go every night to places of public amusement, can hardly enter into the fresh gala feeling with which an opera or a concert is enjoyed by those for whom it is a rarity. I am not sure that I expected great pleasure from the concert, having but a very vague notion of its nature, but I liked the drive there well. The snug comfort of the close carriage on a cold though fine night, the pleasure of setting out with companions so cheerful and friendly, the sight of the stars glinting fitfully through the trees as we rolled along the avenue; then the freer burst of the night-sky when we issued forth to the open chaussée, the passage through the city gates, the lights there burning, the guards there posted, the pretence of inspection to which we there submitted, and which amused us so much—all these small matters had for me, in their novelty, a peculiarly exhilarating charm. How much of it lay in the atmosphere of friendship diffused about me, I know not: Dr. John and his mother were both in their finest mood, contending animatedly with each other the whole way, and as frankly kind to me as if I had been of their kin.

Our way lay through some of the best streets of Villette, streets brightly lit, and far more lively now than at high noon. How brilliant seemed the shops! How glad, gay, and abundant flowed the tide of life along the broad pavement! While I looked, the thought of the Rue Fossette came across me—of the walled-in garden and school-house, and of the dark, vast "classes," where, as at this very hour, it was my wont to wander all solitary, gazing at the stars through the high, blindless

windows, and listening to the distant voice of the reader in the refectory, monotonously exercised upon the "lecture pieuse." Thus must I soon again listen and wander; and this shadow of the future stole with timely sobriety across the radiant present.

By this time we had got into a current of carriages all tending in one direction, and soon the front of a great illuminated building blazed before us. Of what I should see within this building, I had, as before intimated, but an imperfect idea; for no place of public entertainment had it ever been my lot to enter yet.

We alighted under a portico where there was a great bustle and a great crowd, but I do not distinctly remember further details, until I found myself mounting a majestic staircase wide and easy of ascent, deeply and softly carpeted with crimson, leading up to great doors closed solemnly, and whose panels were also crimson-clothed.

I hardly noticed by what magic these doors were made to roll back—Dr. John managed these points; roll back they did, however, and within was disclosed a hall—grand, wide, and high, whose sweeping circular walls, and domed hollow ceiling, seemed to me all dead gold (thus with nice art was it stained), relieved by cornicing, fluting, and garlandry, either bright, like gold burnished, or snow-white, like alabaster, or white and gold mingled in wreaths of gilded leaves and spotless lilies: wherever drapery hung, wherever carpets were spread, or cushions placed, the sole colour employed was deep crimson. Pendant from the dome, flamed a mass that dazzled me—a mass, I thought, of rock-crystal, sparkling with facets, streaming with drops, ablaze with stars, and gorgeously tinged with dews of gems dissolved, or fragments of rainbows shivered. It was only the chandelier, reader, but for me it seemed the work of eastern genii: I almost looked to see if a huge, dark, cloudy hand—that of the Slave of the Lamp—were not hovering in the lustrous and perfumed atmosphere of the cupola, guarding its wondrous treasure.

We moved on—I was not at all conscious whither—but at some turn we suddenly encountered another party approaching from the opposite direction. I just now see that group, as it flashed upon me for one moment. A handsome middle-aged lady in dark velvet; a gentleman who might be her son—the best face, the finest figure, I thought, I had ever seen; a third person in a pink dress and black lace mantle.

I noted them all—the third person as well as the other two—and for the fraction of a moment believed them all strangers, thus receiving an impartial impression of their appearance. But the impression was hardly felt and not fixed, before the consciousness that I faced a great mirror, filling a compartment between two pillars, dispelled it: the party was our own party. Thus for the first, and perhaps only time in my life, I enjoyed the "giftie" of seeing myself as others see me. No need to dwell on the result. It brought a jar of discord, a pang of regret; it was not flattering, yet, after all, I ought to be thankful; it might have been worse.

At last, we were seated in places commanding a good general view of that vast and dazzling, but warm and cheerful hall. Already it was filled, and filled with a spendid assemblage. I do not know that the women were very beautiful, but their dresses were so perfect; and foreigners, even such as are ungraceful in domestic privacy, seem to possess the art of appearing graceful in public: however blunt and boisterous those every-day and home movements connected with peignoir and papillotes, there is a slide, a bend, a carriage of the head and arms, a mien of the mouth and eyes, kept nicely in reserve for gala use—always brought out with the grande toilette, and duly put on with the parure.

Some fine forms there were here and there, models of a peculiar style of beauty; a style, I think, never seen in England: a solid, firm-set, sculptural style. These shapes have no angles: a caryatid in marble is almost as flexible; a Phidian goddess is not more perfect in a certain still and stately sort. They have such features as the Dutch painters give to their madonnas: low-country classic features, regular but round, straight but stolid; and for their depth of expressionless calm, of passionless peace, a polar snow-field could alone offer a type. Women of this order need no

ornament, and they seldom wear any; the smooth hair, closely braided, supplies a sufficient contrast to the smoother cheek and brow; the dress cannot be too simple; the rounded arm and perfect neck require neither bracelet nor chain.

With one of these beauties I once had the honour and rapture to be perfectly acquainted: the inert force of the deep, settled love she bore herself, was wonderful; it could only be surpassed by her proud impotency to care for any other living thing. Of blood, her cool veins conducted no flow; placid lymph filled and almost obstructed her arteries.

Such a Juno as I have described sat full in our view—a sort of mark for all eyes, and quite conscious that so she was, but proof to the magnetic influence of gaze or glance: cold, rounded, blonde, and beauteous as the white column, capitalled with gilding, which rose at her side.

Observing that Dr. John's attention was much drawn towards her, I entreated him in a low voice "for the love of heaven to shield well his heart. You need not fall in love with *that* lady," I said, "because, I tell you beforehand, you might die at her feet, and she would not love you again."

"Very well," said he, "and how do you know that the spectacle of her grand insensibility might not with me be the strongest stimulus to homage? The sting of desperation is, I think, a wonderful irritant to my emotions: but (shrugging his shoulders) you know nothing about these things; I'll address myself to my mother. Mamma, I'm in a dangerous way.

"As if that interested me!" said Mrs. Bretton.

"Alas! the cruelty of my lot!" responded her son. "Never man had a more unsentimental mother than mine: she never seems to think that such a calamity can befall her as a daughter-in-law."

"If I don't, it is not for want of having that same calamity held over my head: you have threatened me with it for the last ten years. 'Mamma, I am going to be married soon!' was the cry before you were well out of jackets."

"But, mother, one of these days it will be realised. All of a sudden, when you think you are most secure, I shall go forth like Jacob or Esau, or any other patriarch, and take me a wife: perhaps of these which are of the daughters of the land."

"At your peril, John Graham! that is all."

"This mother of mine means me to be an old bachelor. What a jealous old lady it is! But now just look at that splendid creature in the pale blue satin dress, and hair of paler brown, with 'reflets satinés' as those of her robe. Would you not feel proud, mamma, if I were to bring that goddess home some day, and introduce her to you as Mrs. Bretton, junior?"

"You will bring no goddess to La Terrasse: that little chateau will not contain two mistresses; especially if the second be of the height, bulk and circumference of that mighty doll in wood and wax, and kid and satin."

"Mamma, she would fill your blue chair so admirably!"

"Fill my chair! I defy the foreign usurper! a rueful chair should it be for her: but hush, John Graham! Hold your tongue, and use your eyes."

During the above skirmish, the hall, which, I had thought, seemed full at the entrance, continued to admit party after party, until the semicircle before the stage presented one dense mass of heads, sloping from floor to ceiling. The stage, too, or rather the wide temporary platform, larger than any stage, desert half-an-hour since, was now overflowing with life; round two grand pianos, placed about the centre, a white flock of young girls, the pupils of the Conservatoire, had noiselessly poured. I had noticed their gathering, while Graham and his mother were engaged in discussing the belle in blue satin, and had watched with interest the process of arraying and marshalling them. Two gentlemen, in each of whom I recognised an acquaintance, officered this virgin troop. One, an artistic-looking man, bearded, and with long hair, was a noted pianiste, and also the first music-teacher in Villette; he attended twice a week at Madame Beck's pensionnat, to give lessons to the few

pupils whose parents were rich enough to allow their daughters the privilege of his instruction; his name was M. Josef Emanuel, and he was half-brother to M. Paul: which potent personage was now visible in the person of the second gentleman.

M. Paul amused me; I smiled to myself as I watched him, he seemed so thoroughly in his element—standing conspicuous in presence of a wide and grand assemblage, arranging, restraining, over-awing about one hundred young ladies. He was, too, so perfectly in earnest—so energetic, so intent, and, above all, so absolute: and yet what business had he there? What had he to do with music or the Conservatoire— he who could hardly distinguish one note from another? I knew that it was his love of display and authority which had brought him there—a love not offensive, only because so naïve. It presently became obvious that his brother, M. Josef, was as much under his control as were the girls themselves. Never was such a little hawk of a man as that M. Paul! Ere long, some noted singers and musicians dawned upon the platform: as these stars rose, the comet-like professor set. Insufferable to him were all notorieties and celebrities: where he could not out-shine, he fled.

And now all was prepared: but one compartment of the hall waited to be filled— a compartment covered with crimson, like the grand staircase and doors, furnished with stuffed and cushioned benches, ranged on each side of two regal chairs, placed solemnly under a canopy.

A signal was given, the doors rolled back, the assembly stood up, the orchestra burst out, and, to the welcome of a choral burst, enter the King, the Queen, the Court of Labassecour.

Till then, I had never set eyes on living king or queen; it may consequently be conjectured how I strained my powers of vision to take in these specimens of European royalty. By whomsoever majesty is beheld for the first time, there will always be experienced a vague surprise bordering on disappointment, that the same does not appear seated, en permanence, on a throne, bonneted with a crown, and furnished, as to the hand, with a sceptre. Looking out for a king and queen, and seeing only a middle-aged soldier and a rather young lady, I felt half cheated, half pleased.

Well do I recall that King—a man of fifty, a little bowed, a little grey: there was no face in all that assembly which resembled his. I had never read, never been told anything of his nature or his habits; and at first the strong hieroglyphics graven as with iron stylet on his brow, round his eyes, beside his mouth, puzzled and baffled instinct. Ere long, however, if I did not *know*, at least I *felt*, the meaning of those characters written without hand. There sat a silent sufferer—a nervous, melancholy man. Those eyes had looked on the visits of a certain ghost—had long waited the comings and goings of that strangest spectre, Hypochondria. Perhaps he saw her now on that stage, over against him, amidst all that brilliant throng. Hypochondria has that wont, to rise in the midst of thousands—dark as Doom, pale as Malady, and well-nigh strong as Death. Her comrade and victim thinks to be happy one moment—"Not so," says she; "I come." And she freezes the blood in his heart, and beclouds the light in his eye.

Some might say it was the foreign crown pressing the King's brows which bent them to that peculiar and painful fold; some might quote the effects of early bereavement. Something there might be of both these; but these are embittered by that darkest foe of humanity—constitutional melancholy. The Queen, his wife, knew this: it seemed to me, the reflection of her husband's grief lay, a subduing shadow, on her own benignant face. A mild, thoughtful, graceful woman that princess seemed; not beautiful, not at all like the women of solid charms and marble feelings described a page or two since. Hers was a somewhat slender shape; her features, though distinguished enough, were too suggestive of reigning dynasties and royal lines to give unqualified pleasure. The expression clothing that profile was agreeable in the present instance; but you could not avoid connecting it with remembered effigies, where similar lines appeared, under phase ignoble; feeble, or

sensual, or cunning, as the case might be. The Queen's eye, however, was her own; and pity, goodness, sweet sympathy, blessed it with divinest light. She moved no sovereign, but a lady—kind, loving, elegant. Her little son, the Prince of Labassecour, and young Duc de Dindonneau, accompanied her: he leaned on his mother's knee; and, ever and anon, in the course of that evening, I saw her observant of the monarch at her side, conscious of his beclouded abstraction, and desirous to rouse him from it by drawing his attention to their son. She often bent her head to listen to the boy's remarks, and would then smilingly repeat them to his sire. The moody King started, listened, smiled, but invariably relapsed as soon as his good angel ceased speaking. Full mournful and significant was that spectacle! Not the less so because, both for the aristocracy and the honest bourgeoisie of Labassecour, its peculiarity seemed to be wholly invisible: I could not discover that one soul present was either struck or touched.

With the King and Queen had entered their court, comprising two or three foreign ambassadors; and with them came the élite of the foreigners then resident in Villette, These took possession of the crimson benches; the ladies were seated; most of the men remained standing: their sable rank, lining the background, looked like a dark foil to the splendour displayed in front. Nor was this splendour without varying light and shade and gradation: the middle distance was filled with matrons in velvets and satins, in plumes and gems; the benches in the foreground, to the Queen's right hand, seemed devoted exclusively to young girls, the flower—perhaps, I should rather say, the bud—of Villette aristocracy. Here were no jewels, no head-dresses, no velvet pile or silken sheen: purity, simplicity, and aërial grace reigned in that virgin band. Young heads simply braided, and fair forms—I was going to write *sylph* forms, but that would have been quite untrue: several of these "jeunes filles," who had not numbered more than sixteen or seventeen years, boasted contours as robust and solid as those of a stout Englishwoman of five-and-twenty—robed in white, or pale rose, or placid blue, suggested thoughts of heaven and angels. I knew a couple, at least, of these "rose et blanches" specimens of humanity. Here was a pair of Madame Beck's late pupils—Mesdemoiselles Mathilde and Angelique: pupils, who, during their last year at school, ought to have been in the first class, but whose brains never got them beyond the second division. In English they had been under my own charge, and hard work it was to get them to translate rationally a page of *The Vicar of Wakefield*. Also during three months I had one of them for my vis-à-vis at table, and the quantity of household bread, butter, and stewed fruit she would habitually consume at "second déjeuner" was a real world's wonder— to be exceeded only by the fact of her actually pocketing slices she could not eat. Here be truths—wholesome truths, too.

I knew another of these seraphs—the prettiest, or, at any rate, the least demure and hypocritical-looking of the lot: she was seated by the daughter of an English peer, also an honest, though haughty-looking girl: both had entered in the suite of the British embassy. She (*i.e.*, my acquaintance) had a slight pliant figure, not at all like the forms of the foreign damsels; her hair, too, was not close-braided, like a shell or a skull-cap of satin; it looked *like* hair, and waved from her head, long, curled, and flowing. She chatted away volubly, and seemed full of a light-headed sort of satisfaction with herself and her position. I did not look at Dr. Bretton; but I knew that he, too, saw Ginevra Fanshawe: he had become so quiet, he answered so briefly his mother's remarks, he so often suppressed a sigh. Why should he sigh? He had confessed a taste for the pursuit of love under difficulties; here was full gratification for that taste. His lady-love beamed upon him from a sphere above his own: he could not come near her; he was not certain that he could win from her a look. I watched to see if she would so far favour him. Our seat was not far from the crimson benches; we must inevitably be seen thence, by eyes so quick and roving as Miss Fanshawe's, and very soon those optics of hers were upon us: at least, upon Dr. and Mrs. Bretton. I kept rather in the shade and out of sight,

not wishing to be immediately recognised: she looked quite steadily at Dr. John, and then she raised a glass to examine his mother; a minute or two afterwards she laughingly whispered her neighbour; upon the performance commencing, her rambling attention was attracted to the platform.

On the concert I need not dwell; the reader would not care to have my impressions thereanent: and, indeed, it would not be worth while to record them, as they were the impressions of an ignorance crasse. The young ladies of the Conservatoire, being very much frightened, made rather a tremulous exhibition on the two grand pianos. M. Josef Emanuel stood by them while they played; but he had not the tact or influence of his kinsman, who, under similar circumstances, would certainly have *compelled* pupils of his to demean themselves with heroism and self-possession. M. Paul would have placed the hysteric débutantes between two fires—terror of the audience, and terror of himself—and would have inspired them with the courage of desperation, by making the latter terror incomparably the greater: M. Josef could not do this.

Following the white muslin pianistes, came a fine, full-grown, sulky lady in white satin. She sang. Her singing just affected me like the tricks of a conjuror: I wondered how she did it; how she made her voice run up and down, and cut such marvellous capers; but a simple Scotch melody, played by a rude street minstrel, has often moved me more deeply.

Afterwards stepped forth a gentleman, who, bending his body a good deal in the direction of the King and Queen, and frequently approaching his white gloved hand to the region of his heart, vented a bitter outcry against a certain "fausse Isabelle." I thought he seemed especially to solicit the Queen's sympathy; but, unless I am egregiously mistaken, her Majesty lent her attention rather with the calm of courtesy than the earnestness of interest. This gentleman's state of mind was very harrowing, and I was glad when he wound up his musical exposition of the same.

Some rousing choruses struck me as the best part of the evening's entertainment. There were present deputies from all the best provincial choral societies; genuine, barrel-shaped, native Labassecouriens. These worthies gave voice without mincing the matter: their hearty exertions had at least this good result—the ear drank thence a satisfying sense of power.

Through the whole performance—timid instrumental duets, conceited vocal solos, sonorous, brass-lunged choruses—my attention gave but one eye and one ear to the stage, the other being permanently retained in the service of Dr. Bretton: I could not forget him, nor cease to question how he was feeling, what he was thinking, whether he was amused or the contrary. At last he spoke.

"And how do you like it all, Lucy? You are very quiet," he said, in his own cheerful tone.

"I am quiet," I said, "because I am so very, *very* much interested: not merely with the music, but with everything about me."

He then proceeded to make some further remarks, with so much equanimity and composure that I began to think he had really not seen what I had seen, and I whispered—

"Miss Fanshawe is here: have you noticed her?"

"Oh, yes! and I observed that you noticed her too."

"Is she come with Mrs. Cholmondeley, do you think?"

"Mrs. Cholmondeley is there with a very grand party. Yes; Ginevra was in *her* train; and Mrs. Cholmondeley was in Lady ——'s train, who was in the Queen's train. If this were not one of the compact little minor European courts, whose very formalities are little more imposing than familiarities, and whose gala grandeur is but homeliness in Sunday array, it would sound all very fine."

"Ginevra saw you, I think?"

"So do I think so. I have had my eye on her several times since you withdrew yours; and I have had the honour of witnessing a little spectacle which you were spared."

I did not ask what; I waited voluntary information, which was presently given.

"Miss Fanshawe," he said, "has a companion with her—a lady of rank. I happen to know Lady Sara by sight; her noble mother has called me in professionally. She is a proud girl, but not in the least insolent, and I doubt whether Ginevra will have gained ground in her estimation by making a butt of her neighbours."

"What neighbours?"

"Merely myself and my mother. As to me, it is all very natural: nothing, I suppose, can be fairer game than the young bourgeois doctor; but my mother! I never saw her ridiculed before. Do you know, the curling lip, and sarcastically levelled glass thus directed, gave me a most curious sensation."

"Think nothing of it, Dr. John: it is not worth while. If Ginevra were in a giddy mood, as she is eminently to-night, she would make no scruple at laughing at that mild, pensive Queen, or that melancholy King. She is not actuated by malevolence, but sheer, heedless folly. To a feather-brained school-girl nothing is sacred."

"But you forget: I have not been accustomed to look on Miss Fanshawe in the light of a feather-brained school-girl. Was she not my divinity—the angel of my career?"

"Hem! There was your mistake."

"To speak the honest truth, without any false rant or assumed romance, there actually was a moment, six months ago, when I thought her divine. Do you remember our conversation about the presents? I was not quite open with you in discussing that subject: the warmth with which you took it up amused me. By way of having the full benefit of your lights, I allowed you to think me more in the dark than I really was. It was that test of the presents which first proved Ginevra mortal. Still her beauty retained its fascination: three days—three hours ago, I was very much her slave. As she passed me to-night, triumphant in beauty, my emotions did her homage: but for one luckless sneer, I should yet be the humblest of her servants. She might have scoffed at *me,* and, while wounding, she would not soon have alienated me: through myself, she could not in ten years have done what, in a moment, she has done through my mother."

He held his peace awhile. Never before had I seen so much fire and so little sunshine in Dr. John's blue eye, as just now.

"Lucy," he recommenced, "look well at my mother, and say, without fear or favour, in what light she now appears to you."

"As she always does—an English, middle-class gentlewoman; well, though gravely dressed, habitually independent of pretence, constitutionally composed and cheerful."

"So she seems to me—bless her! The merry may laugh *with* mamma, but the weak only will laugh *at* her. She shall not be ridiculed, with my consent, at least; nor without my—my scorn—my antipathy—my"——

He stopped: and it was time—for he was getting excited—more it seemed than the occasion warranted. I did not then know that he had witnessed double cause for dissatisfaction with Miss Fanshawe. The glow of his complexion, the expansion of his nostril, the bold curve which disdain gave his well-cut under-lip, showed him in a new and striking phase. Yet the rare passion of the constitutionally suave and serene, is not a pleasant spectacle; nor did I like the sort of vindictive thrill which passed through his strong young frame.

"Do I frighten you, Lucy?" he asked.

"I cannot tell why you are so very angry."

"For this reason," he muttered in my ear. "Ginevra is neither a pure angel nor a pure-minded woman."

"Nonsense! you exaggerate: she has no great harm in her."

"Too much for me. *I* can see where *you* are blind. Now dismiss the subject. Let me amuse myself by teasing mamma: I will assert that she is flagging. Mamma, pray rouse yourself."

"John, I will certainly rouse you if you are not better conducted. Will you and Lucy be silent, that I may hear the singing?"

They were then thundering in a chorus, under cover of which all the previous dialogue had taken place.

"*You* hear the singing, mamma! Now, I will wager my studs, which are genuine, against your paste brooch"——

"My paste brooch, Graham? Profane boy! you know that it is a stone of value."

"Oh! that is one of your superstitions: you were cheated in the business."

"I am cheated in fewer things than you imagine. How do you happen to be acquainted with young ladies of the court, John? I have observed two of them pay you no small attention during the last half-hour."

"I wish you would not observe them."

"Why not? Because one of them satirically levels her eye-glass at me? She is a pretty, silly girl: but are you apprehensive that her titter will discomfit the old lady?"

"The sensible, admirable old lady! Mother, you are better to me than ten wives yet."

"Don't be demonstrative, John, or I shall faint, and you will have to carry me out; and if that burden were laid upon you, you would reverse your last speech, and exclaim, 'Mother, ten wives could hardly be worse to me than you are!' "

The concert over, the Lottery "au bénéfice des pauvres" came next: the interval between was one of general relaxation, and the pleasantest imaginable stir and commotion. The white flock was cleared from the platform; a busy throng of gentlemen crowded it instead, making arrangements for the drawing; and amongst these—the busiest of all—re-appeared that certain well-known form, not tall but active, alive with the energy and movement of three tall men. How M. Paul did work! How he issued directions, and, at the same time, set his own shoulder to the wheel! Half-a-dozen assistants were at his back to remove the pianos, etc.; no matter, he must add to their strength his own. The redundancy of his alertness was half-vexing, half-ludicrous: in my mind I both disapproved and derided most of this fuss. Yet, in the midst of prejudice and annoyance, I could not, while watching, avoid perceiving a certain not disagreeable naïveté in all he did and said; nor could I be blind to certain vigorous characteristics of his physiognomy, rendered conspicuous now by the contrast with a throng of tamer faces: the deep, intent keenness of his eye, the power of his forehead, pale, broad, and full—the mobility of his most flexible mouth. He lacked the calm of force, but its movement and its fire he signally possessed.

Meantime the whole hall was in a stir; most people rose and remained standing, for a change; some walked about, all talked and laughed. The crimson compartment presented a peculiarly animated scene. The long cloud of gentlemen breaking into fragments, mixed with the rainbow line of ladies; two or three officer-like men approached the King and conversed with him. The Queen, leaving her chair, glided along the rank of young ladies, who all stood up as she passed; and to each in turn I saw her vouchsafe some token of kindness—a gracious word, look, or smile. To the two pretty English girls, Lady Sara and Ginevra Fanshawe, she addressed several sentences; as she left them, both, and especially the latter, seemed to glow all over with gratification. They were afterwards accosted by several ladies, and a little circle of gentlemen gathered round them; amongst these—the nearest to Ginevra—stood the Count de Hamal.

"This room is stiflingly hot," said Dr. Bretton, rising with sudden impatience. "Lucy—mother—will you come a moment to the fresh air?"

"Go with him, Lucy," said Mrs. Bretton, "I would rather keep my seat."

Willingly would I have kept mine also, but Graham's desire must take precedence of my own; I accompanied him.

We found the night-air keen; or at least I did: he did not seem to feel it; but it was very still, and the star-sown sky spread cloudless. I was wrapped in a fur shawl. We took some turns on the pavement; in passing under a lamp, Graham encountered my eye.

"You look pensive, Lucy: is it on my account?"

"I was only fearing that you were grieved."

"Not at all: so be of good cheer—as I am. Whenever I die, Lucy, my persuasion is that it will not be of heart-complaint. I may be stung, I may seem to droop for a time, but no pain or malady of sentiment has yet gone through my whole system. You have always seen me cheerful at home?"

"Generally."

"I am glad she laughed at my mother. I would not give the old lady for a dozen beauties. That sneer did me all the good in the world. Thank you, Miss Fanshawe!" And he lifted his hat from his waved locks, and made a mock reverence.

"Yes," he said, "I thank her. She has made me feel that nine parts in ten of my heart have always been sound as a bell, and the tenth bled from a mere puncture: a lancet-prick that will heal in a trice."

"You are angry just now, heated and indignant; you will think and feel differently to-morrow."

"*I* heated and indignant! You don't know me. On the contrary, the heat is gone: I am as cool as the night—which, by the way, may be too cool for you. We will go back."

"Dr. John, this is a sudden change."

"Not it: or if it be, there are good reasons for it—two good reasons: I have told you one. But now let us re-enter."

We did not easily regain our seats; the lottery was begun, and all was excited confusion; crowds blocked the sort of corridor along which we had to pass: it was necessary to pause for a time. Happening to glance round—indeed I half fancied I heard my name pronounced—I saw quite near, the ubiquitous, the inevitable M. Paul. He was looking at me gravely and intently: at me, or rather at my pink dress—sardonic comment on which gleamed in his eye. Now it was his habit to indulge in strictures on the dress, both of the teachers and pupils, at Madame Beck's—a habit which the former, at least, held to be an offensive impertinence: as yet I had not suffered from it—my sombre daily attire not being calculated to attract notice. I was in no mood to permit any new encroachment to-night: rather than accept his banter, I would ignore his presence, and accordingly steadily turned my face to the sleeve of Dr. John's coat; finding in that same black sleeve a prospect more redolent of pleasure and comfort, more genial, more friendly, I thought, than was offered by the dark little Professor's unlovely visage. Dr. John seemed unconsciously to sanction the preference by looking down and saying in his kind voice—

"Ay, keep close to my side, Lucy: these crowding burghers are no respecters of persons."

I could not, however, be true to myself. Yielding to some influence, mesmeric or otherwise—an influence unwelcome, displeasing, but effective—I again glanced round to see if M. Paul was gone. No, there he stood on the same spot, looking still, but with a changed eye; he had penetrated my thought, and read my wish to shun him. The mocking but not ill-humoured gaze was turned to a swarthy frown, and when I bowed with a view to reconciliation, I got only the stiffest and sternest of nods in return.

"Whom have you made angry, Lucy?" whispered Dr. Bretton, smiling. "Who is that savage-looking friend of yours?"

"One of the professors at Madame Beck's: a very cross little man."

"He looks mighty cross just now: what have you done to him? What is it all about? Ah, Lucy, Lucy! tell me the meaning of this."

"No mystery, I assure you. M. Emanuel is very exigeant, and because I looked at your coat sleeve, instead of curtseying and dipping to him, he thinks I have failed in respect."

"The little"——began Dr. John: I know not what more he would have added, for at that moment I was nearly thrown down amongst the feet of the crowd. M. Paul had rudely pushed past, and was elbowing his way with such utter disregard to the convenience and security of all around, that a very uncomfortable pressure was the consequence.

"I think he is what he himself would call 'méchant,' " said Dr. Bretton. I thought so, too.

Slowly and with difficulty we made our way along the passage, and at last regained our seats. The drawing of the lottery lasted nearly an hour; it was an animating and amusing scene; and as we each held tickets, we shared in the alternations of hope and fear raised by each turn of the wheel. Two little girls, of five and six years old, drew the numbers: and the prizes were duly proclaimed from the platform. These prizes were numerous, though of small value. It so fell out that Dr. John and I each gained one: mine was a cigar-case, his a lady's head-dress—a most airy sort of blue and silver turban, with a streamer of plumage on one side, like a snowy cloud. He was excessively anxious to make an exchange: but I could not be brought to hear reason, and to this day I keep my cigar-case; it serves, when I look at it, to remind me of old times, and one happy evening.

Dr. John, for his part, held his turban at arm's length between his finger and thumb, and looked at it with a mixture of reverence and embarrassment highly provocative of laughter. The contemplation over, he was about coolly to deposit the delicate fabric on the ground between his feet; he seemed to have no shadow of an idea of the treatment or stowage it ought to receive: if his mother had not come to the rescue, I think he would finally have crushed it under his arm like an opera hat; she restored it to the bandbox whence it had issued.

Graham was quite cheerful all the evening, and his cheerfulness seemed natural and unforced. His demeanour, his look, is not easily described; there was something in it peculiar, and, in its way, original. I read in it no common mastery of the passions, and a fund of deep and healthy strength which, without any exhausting effort, bore down Disappointment and extracted her fang. His manner now reminded me of qualities I had noticed in him when professionally engaged amongst the poor, the guilty, and the suffering, in the Basse-Ville: he looked at once determined, enduring, and sweet-tempered. Who could help liking him? *He* betrayed no weakness which harassed all your feelings with considerations as to how its faltering must be propped; from *him* broke no irritability which startled calm and quenched mirth; *his* lips let fall no caustic that burned to the bone; *his* eye shot no morose shafts that went cold, and rusty, and venomed through your heart: beside him was rest and refuge—around him, fostering sunshine.

And yet he had neither forgiven nor forgotten Miss Fanshawe. Once angered, I doubt if Dr. Bretton were to be soon propitiated—once alienated, whether he were ever to be reclaimed. He looked at her more than once; not stealthily or humbly, but with a movement of hardy, open observation. De Hamal was now a fixture beside her; Mrs. Cholmondeley sat near, and they and she were wholly absorbed in the discourse, mirth, and excitement, with which the crimson seats were as much astir as any plebeian part of the hall. In the course of some apparently animated discussion, Ginevra once or twice lifted her hand and arm; a handsome bracelet gleamed upon the latter. I saw that its gleam flickered in Dr. John's eye—quickening therein a derisive, ireful sparkle: he laughed—

"I think," he said, "I will lay my turban on my wonted altar of offerings; there, at any rate, it would be certain to find favour: no grisette has a more facile faculty of acceptance. Strange! for after all, I know she is a girl of family."

"But you don't know her education, Dr. John," said I. "Tossed about all her life from one foreign school to another, she may justly proffer the plea of ignorance in extenuation of most of her faults. And then, from what she says, I believe her father and mother were brought up much as she has been brought up."

"I always understood she had no fortune; and once I had pleasure in the thought," said he.

"She tells me," I answered, "that they are poor at home; she always speaks quite candidly on such points: you never find her lying, as these foreigners will often lie. Her parents have a large family: they occupy such a station and possess such connections as, in their opinion, demand display; stringent necessity of circumstances and inherent thoughtlessness of disposition combined, have engendered reckless unscrupulousness as to how they obtain the means of sustaining a good appearance. This is the state of things, and the only state of things she has seen from childhood upwards."

"I believe it—and I thought to mould her to something better: but, Lucy, to speak the plain truth, I have felt a new thing to-night, in looking at her and De Hamal. I felt it before noticing the impertinence directed at my mother. I saw a look interchanged between them immediately after their entrance which threw a most unwelcome light on my mind."

"How do you mean? You have been long aware of the flirtation they keep up?"

"Ay, flirtation! That might be an innocent girlish wile to lure on the true lover; but what I refer to was not flirtation: it was a look marking mutual and secret understanding—it was neither girlish nor innocent. No woman, were she as beautiful as Aphrodite, who could give or receive such a glance, shall ever be sought in marriage by me: I would rather wed a paysanne in a short petticoat and high cap—and be sure that she was honest."

I could not help smiling. I felt sure he now exaggerated the case: Ginevra, I was certain, was honest enough, with all her giddiness. I told him so. He shook his head, and said he would not be the man to trust her with his honour.

"The only thing," said I, "with which you may safely trust her. She would unscrupulously damage a husband's purse and property, recklessly try his patience and temper: I don't think she would breathe, or let another breathe, on his honour."

"You are becoming her advocate," said he. "Do you wish me to resume my old chains?"

"No: I am glad to see you free, and trust that free you will long remain. Yet be, at the same time, just."

"I am so: just as Rhadamanthus, Lucy. When once I am thoroughly estranged, I cannot help being severe. But look: the King and Queen are rising. I like that Queen: she has a sweet countenance. Mamma, too, is excessively tired; we shall never get the old lady home if we stay longer."

"I tired, John?" cried Mrs. Bretton, looking at least as animated and as wide-awake as her son, "I would undertake to sit you out yet: leave us both here till morning, and we should see which would look the most jaded by sunrise."

"I should not like to try the experiment; for, in truth mamma, you are the most unfading of evergreens and the freshest of matrons. It must then be on the plea of your son's delicate nerves and fragile constitution that I found a petition for our speedy adjournment."

"Indolent young man! You wish you were in bed, no doubt; and I suppose you must be humoured. There is Lucy, too, looking quite done up. For shame, Lucy! At your age, a week of evenings out would not have made me a shade paler. Come away, both of you; and you may laugh at the old lady as much as you please, but, for my part, I shall take charge of the bandbox and turban."

Which she did accordingly. I offered to relieve her, but was shaken off with kindly contempt: my godmother opined that I had enough to do to take care of myself. Not standing on ceremony now, in the midst of the gay "confusion worse confounded" succeeding to the King and Queen's departure, Mrs. Bretton preceded us, and promptly made us a lane through the crowd. Graham followed, apostrophising his mother as the most flourishing grisette it had ever been his good fortune to see charged with carriage of a bandbox; he also desired me to mark her affection for the sky-blue turban, and announced his conviction that she intended one day to wear it.

The night was now very cold and very dark, but with little delay we found the carriage. Soon we were packed in it, as warm and snug as at a fireside; and the drive home was, I think, still pleasanter than the drive to the concert. Pleasant it was, even though the coachman—having spent in the shop of a "marchand de vin" a portion of the time we passed at the concert—drove us along the dark and solitary chaussée far past the turn leading down to La Terrasse; we, who were occupied in talking and laughing, not noticing the aberration till, at last, Mrs. Bretton intimated that though she had always thought the chateau a retired spot, she did not know it was situated at the world's end, as she declared seemed now to be the case, for she believed we had been an hour and a half en route, and had not yet taken the turn down the avenue.

Then Graham looked out, and perceiving only dim-spread fields, with unfamiliar rows of pollards and limes ranged along their else invisible sunk-fences, began to conjecture how matters were, and calling a halt and descending, he mounted the box and took the reins himself. Thanks to him, we arrived safe at home about an hour and a half beyond our time.

Martha had not forgotten us; a cheerful fire was burning, and a neat supper spread in the dining-room: we were glad of both. The winter dawn was actually breaking before we gained our chambers. I took off my pink dress and lace mantle with happier feelings than I had experienced in putting them on. Not all, perhaps, who had shone brightly arrayed at that concert could say the same; for not all had been satisfied with friendship—with its calm comfort and modest hope.

Chapter XXI

REACTION

YET three days, and then I must go back to the pensionnat. I almost numbered the moments of these days upon the clock; fain would I have retarded their flight; but they glided by while I watched them: they were already gone while I yet feared their departure.

"Lucy will not leave us to-day," said Mrs. Bretton, coaxingly, at breakfast; "she knows we can procure a second respite."

"I would not ask for one if I might have it for a word," said I. "I long to get the good-bye over, and to be settled in the Rue Fossette again. I must go this morning: I must go directly; my trunk is packed and corded."

It appeared, however, that my going depended upon Graham; he had said he would accompany me, and it so fell out that he was engaged all day, and only returned home at dusk. Then ensued a little combat of words. Mrs. Bretton and her son pressed me to remain one night more. I could have cried, so irritated and eager was I to be gone. I longed to leave them as the criminal on the scaffold longs for the axe to descend: that is, I wished the pang over. How much I wished it, they could not tell. On these points, mine was a state of mind out of their experience.

It was dark when Dr. John handed me from the carriage at Madame Beck's door. The lamp above was lit; it rained a November drizzle, as it had rained all day: the

lamplight gleamed on the wet pavement. Just such a night was it as that on which, not a year ago, I had first stopped at this very threshold; just similar was the scene. I remembered the very shapes of the paving-stones which I had noted with idle eye, while, with a thick-beating heart, I waited the unclosing of that door at which I stood—a solitary and a suppliant. On that night, too, I had briefly met him who now stood with me. Had I ever reminded him of that rencontre, or explained it? I had not, nor ever felt the inclination to do so: it was a pleasant thought, laid by in my own mind, and best kept there.

Graham rung the bell. The door was instantly opened, for it was just that period of the evening when the half-boarders took their departure—consequently, Rosine was on the alert.

"Don't come in," said I to him; but he stepped a moment into the well-lighted vestibule. I had not wished him to see that "the water stood in my eyes," for his was too kind a nature ever to be needlessly shown such signs of sorrow. He always wished to heal—to relieve—when, physician as he was, neither cure nor alleviation were, perhaps, in his power.

"Keep up your courage, Lucy. Think of my mother and myself as true friends. We will not forget you."

"Nor will I forget you, Dr. John."

My trunk was now brought in. We had shaken hands; he had turned to go, but he was not satisfied: he had not done or said enough to content his generous impulses.

"Lucy,"—stepping after me—"shall you feel very solitary here?"

"At first I shall."

"Well, my mother will soon call to see you; and, meantime, I'll tell you what I'll do. I'll write—just any cheerful nonsense that comes into my head—shall I?"

"Good, gallant heart!" thought I to myself; but I shook my head, smiling, and said, "Never think of it: impose on yourself no such task. *You* write to *me*!—you'll not have time."

"Oh! I will find or make time. Good-bye!"

He was gone. The heavy door crashed to: the axe had fallen—the pang was experienced.

Allowing myself no time to think or feel—swallowing tears as if they had been wine—I passed to Madame's sitting-room to pay the necessary visit of ceremony and respect. She received me with perfectly well-acted cordiality—was even demonstrative, though brief, in her welcome. In ten minutes I was dismissed. From the salle-à-manger I proceeded to the refectory, where pupils and teachers were now assembled for evening study: again I had a welcome, and one not, I think, quite hollow. That over, I was free to repair to the dormitory.

"And will Graham really write?" I questioned, as I sank tired on the edge of the bed.

Reason, coming stealthily up to me through the twilight of that long, dim chamber, whispered sedately—

"He may write once. So kind is his nature, it may stimulate him for once to make the effort. But it *cannot* be continued—it *may* not be repeated. Great were that folly which should build on such a promise—insane that credulity which should mistake the transitory rain-pool, holding in its hollow one draught, for the perennial spring yielding the supply of seasons.

I bent my head: I sat thinking an hour longer. Reason still whispered me, laying on my shoulder a withered hand, and frostily touching my ear with the chill blue lips of eld.

"If," muttered she, "if he *should* write, what then? Do you meditate pleasure in replying? Ah, fool! I warn you! Brief be your answer. Hope no delight of heart—no indulgence of intellect: grant no expansion to feeling—give holiday to no single faculty: dally with no friendly exchange: foster no genial inter-communion"——

"But I have talked to Graham, and you did not chide," I pleaded.

"No," said she, "I needed not. Talk for you is good discipline. You converse imperfectly. While you speak, there can be no oblivion of inferiority—no encouragement to delusion: pain, privation, penury stamp your language"——

"But," I again broke in, "where the bodily presence is weak and the speech contemptible, surely there cannot be error in making written language the medium of better utterance than faltering lips can achieve?"

Reason only answered, "At your peril you cherish that idea, or suffer its influence to animate any writing of yours!"

"But if I feel, may I *never* express?"

"*Never!*" declared Reason.

I groaned under her bitter sternness. Never—never—oh, hard word! This hag, this Reason, would not let me look up, or smile, or hope: she could not rest unless I were altogether crushed, cowed, broken-in, and broken-down. According to her, I was born only to work for a piece of bread, to await the pains of death, and steadily through all life to despond. Reason might be right; yet no wonder we are glad at times to defy her, to rush from under her rod and give a truant hour to Imagination—*her* soft, bright foe, *our* sweet Help, our divine Hope. We shall and must break bounds at intervals, despite the terrible revenge that awaits our return. Reason is vindictive as a devil: for me she was always envenomed as a step-mother. If I have obeyed her it has chiefly been with the obedience of fear, not of love. Long ago I should have died of her ill-usage: her stint, her chill, her barren board, her icy bed, her savage, ceaseless blows; but for that kinder Power who holds my secret and sworn allegiance. Often has Reason turned me out by night, in midwinter, on cold snow, flinging for sustenance the gnawed bone dogs had forsaken: sternly has she vowed her stores held nothing more for me—harshly denied my right to ask better things. . . . Then, looking up, have I seen in the sky a head amidst circling stars, of which the midmost and the brightest lent a ray sympathetic and attent. A spirit, softer and better than Human Reason, has descended with quiet flight to the waste—bringing all round her a sphere of air borrowed of eternal summer; bringing perfume of flowers which cannot fade—fragrance of trees whose fruit is life; bringing breezes pure from a world whose day needs no sun to lighten it. My hunger has this good angel appeased with food, sweet, and strange, gathered amongst gleaning angels, garnering their dew-white harvest in the first fresh hour of a heavenly day; tenderly has she assuaged the insufferable tears which weep away life itself—kindly given rest to deadly weariness—generously lent hope and impulse to paralysed despair. Divine, compassionate, succourable influence! When I bend the knee to other than God, it shall be at thy white and winged feet, beautiful on mountain or on plain. Temples have been reared to the Sun—altars dedicated to the Moon. Oh, greater glory! To thee neither hands build, nor lips consecrate: but hearts, through ages, are faithful to thy worship. A dwelling thou hast, too wide for walls, too high for dome—a temple whose floors are space—rites whose mysteries transpire in presence, to the kindling, the harmony of worlds!

Sovereign complete! thou hadst, for endurance, thy great army of martyrs; for achievement, thy chosen band of worthies. Deity unquestioned, thine essence foils decay!

This daughter of Heaven remembered me to-night; she saw me weep, and she came with comfort: "Sleep," she said. "Sleep, sweetly—I gild thy dreams!"

She kept her word, and watched me through a night's rest; but at dawn Reason relieved the guard. I awoke with a sort of start; the rain was dashing against the panes, and the wind uttering a peevish cry at intervals; the night-lamp was dying on the black circular stand in the middle of the dormitory: day had already broken. How I pity those whom mental pain stuns instead of rousing! This morning the pang of waking snatched me out of bed like a hand with a giant's grip. How quickly I dressed in the cold of the raw dawn! How deeply I drank of the ice-cold water

in my carafe! This was always my cordial, to which, like other dram-drinkers, I had eager recourse when unsettled by chagrin.

Ere long the bell rang its réveillée to the whole school. Being dressed, I descended alone to the refectory, where the stove was lit and the air was warm; through the rest of the house it was cold, with the nipping severity of a continental winter: though now but the beginning of November, a north wind had thus early brought a wintry blight over Europe. I remember the black stoves pleased me little when I first came; but now I began to associate with them a sense of comfort, and liked them, as in England we like a fireside.

Sitting down before this dark comforter, I presently fell into a deep argument with myself on life and its chances, on destiny and her decrees. My mind, calmer and stronger now than last night, made for itself some imperious rules, prohibiting under deadly penalties all weak retrospect of happiness past; commanding a patient journeying through the wilderness of the present, enjoining a reliance on faith—a watching of the cloud and pillar which subdue while they guide, and awe while they illumine—hushing the impulse to fond idolatry, checking the longing outlook for a far-off promised land whose rivers are, perhaps, never to be reached save in dying dreams, whose sweet pastures are to be viewed but from the desolate and sepulchral summit of a Nebo.

By degrees, a composite feeling of blended strength and pain wound itself wirily round my heart, sustained, or at least restrained, its throbbings, and made me fit for the day's work. I lifted my head.

As I said before, I was sitting near the stove, let into the wall between the refectory and the carré, and thus sufficing to heat both apartments. Piercing the same wall, and close beside the stove, was a window, looking also into the carré; as I looked up a cap-tassel, a brow, two eyes, filled a pane of that window; the fixed gaze of those two eyes hit right against my own glance: they were watching me. I had not till that moment known that tears were on my cheek, but I felt them now.

This was a strange house, where no corner was sacred from intrusion, where not a tear could be shed, nor a thought pondered, but a spy was at hand to note and to divine. And this new, this outdoor, this male spy, what business had brought him to the premises at this unwonted hour? What possible right had he to intrude on me thus? No other professor would have dared to cross the carré, before the class-bell rang. M. Emanuel took no account of hours nor of classes; there was some book of reference in the first class library which he had occasion to consult; he had come to seek it: on his way he passed the refectory. It was very much his habit to wear eyes before, behind, and on each side of him: he had seen me through the little window—he now opened the refectory door, and there he stood.

"Mademoiselle, vous êtes triste."

"Monsieur, j'en ai bien le droit."

"Vous êtes malade de cœur et d'humeur," he pursued. "You are at once mournful and mutinous. I see on your cheek two tears which I know are hot as two sparks, and salt as two crystals of the sea. While I speak you eye me strangely. Shall I tell you of what I am reminded while watching you?"

"Monsieur, I shall be called away to prayers shortly; my time for conversation is very scant and brief at this hour—excuse"——

"I excuse everything," he interrupted; "my mood is so meek, neither rebuff nor, perhaps, insult could ruffle it. You remind me, then, of a young she wild creature, new caught, untamed, viewing with a mixture of fire and fear the first entrance of the breaker-in."

Unwarrantable accost!—rash and rude if addressed to a pupil; to a teacher inadmissible. He thought to provoke a warm reply; I had seen him vex the passionate to explosion before now. In me his malice should find no gratification; I sat silent.

"You look," said he, "like one who would snatch at a draught of sweet poison, and spurn wholesome bitters with disgust."

"Indeed, I never liked bitters; nor do I believe them wholesome. And to whatever is sweet, be it poison or food, you cannot, at least, deny its own delicious quality— sweetness. Better, perhaps, to die quickly a pleasant death, than drag on long a charmless life."

"Yet," said he, "you should take your bitter dose duly and daily, if I had the power to administer it; and, as to the well-beloved poison, I would, perhaps, break the very cup which held it."

I sharply turned my head away, partly because his presence utterly displeased me, and partly because I wished to shun questions: lest, in my present mood, the effort of answering should overmaster self-command.

"Come," said he, more softly, "tell me the truth—you grieve at being parted from friends—is it not so?"

The insinuating softness was not more acceptable than the inquisitorial curiosity. I was silent. He came into the room, sat down on the bench about two yards from me, and persevered long, and, for him, patiently, in attempts to draw me into conversation—attempts necessarily unavailing, because I *could* not talk. At last I entreated to be let alone. In uttering the request, my voice faltered, my head sank on my arms and the table. I wept bitterly, though quietly. He sat a while longer. I did not look up nor speak, till the closing door and his retreating step told me that he was gone. These tears proved a relief.

I had time to bathe my eyes before breakfast, and I suppose I appeared at that meal as serene as any other person: not, however, quite as jocund-looking as the young lady who placed herself in the seat opposite mine, fixed on me a pair of somewhat small eyes twinkling gleefully, and frankly stretched across the table a white hand to be shaken. Miss Fanshawe's travels, gaieties, and flirtations agreed with her mightily; she had become quite plump, her cheeks looked as round as apples. I had seen her last in elegant evening attire. I don't know that she looked less charming now in her school-dress, a kind of careless peignoir of a dark-blue material, dimly and dingily plaided with black. I even think this dusky wrapper gave her charms a triumph; enhancing by contrast the fairness of her skin, the freshness of her bloom, the golden beauty of her tresses.

"I am glad you are come back, Timon," said she. Timon was one of her dozen names for me. "You don't know how often I have wanted you in this dismal hole."

"Oh, have you? Then, of course, if you wanted me, you have something for me to do: stockings to mend, perhaps." I never gave Ginevra a minute's or a farthing's credit for disinterestedness.

"Crabbed and crusty as ever!" said she. "I expected as much: it would not be you if you did not snub one. But now, come, grandmother, I hope you like coffee as much, and pistolets as little as ever: are you disposed to barter?"

"Take your own way."

This way consisted in a habit she had of making me convenient. She did not like the morning cup of coffee; its school brewage not being strong or sweet enough to suit her palate; and she had an excellent appetite, like any other healthy schoolgirl, for the morning pistolets or rolls, which were new-baked and very good, and of which a certain allowance was served to each. This allowance being more than I needed, I gave half to Ginevra; never varying in my preference, though many others used to covet the superfluity; and she in return would sometimes give me a portion of her coffee. This morning I was glad of the draught; hunger I had none, and with thirst I was parched. I don't know why I chose to give my bread rather to Ginevra than to another; nor why, if two had to share the convenience of one drinking-vessel, as sometimes happened—for instance, when we took a long walk into the country, and halted for refreshment at a farm—I always contrived that she should be my convive, and rather liked to let her take the lion's share, whether of the

white beer, the sweet wine, or the new milk: so it was, however, and she knew it; and, therefore. while we wrangled daily, we were never alienated.

After breakfast my custom was to withdraw to the first classe, and sit and read, or think (oftenest the latter) there alone, till the nine o'clock bell threw open all doors, admitted the gathered rush of externes and demi-pensionnaires, and gave the signal for entrance on that bustle and business to which, till five p.m., there was no relax.

I was just seated this morning, when a tap came to the door.

"Pardon, mademoiselle," said a pensionnaire, entering gently; and having taken from her desk some necessary book or paper, she withdrew on tip-toe, murmuring as she passed me, "Que mademoiselle est appliquée!"

Appliquée, indeed! The means of application were spread before me, but I was doing nothing; and had done nothing, and meant to do nothing. Thus does the world give us credit for merits we have not. Madame Beck herself deemed me a regular bas-bleu, and often and solemnly used to warn me not to study too much, lest "the blood should all go to my head." Indeed, everybody in the Rue Fossette held a superstition that "Meess Lucie" was learned; with the notable exception of M. Emanuel, who, by means peculiar to himself and quite inscrutable to me, had obtained a not inaccurate inkling of my real qualifications, and used to take quiet opportunities of chuckling in my ear his malign glee over their scant measure. For my part, I never troubled myself about this penury. I dearly liked to think my own thoughts; I had great pleasure in reading a few books, but not many: preferring always those on whose style or sentiment the writer's individual nature was plainly stamped; flagging inevitably over characterless books, however clever and meritorious: perceiving well that, as far as my own mind was concerned, God had limited its powers and its action—thankful, I trust, for the gift bestowed, but unambitious of higher endowments, not restlessly eager after higher culture.

The polite pupil was scarcely gone, when, unceremoniously, without tap, in burst a second intruder. Had I been blind I should have known who this was. A constitutional reserve of manner had by this time told with wholesome and, for me commodious effect, on the manners of my co-inmates; rarely did I now suffer from rude or intrusive treatment. When I first came, it would happen once and again that a blunt German would clap me on the shoulder, and ask me to run a race; or a riotous Labassecourienne seize me by the arm and drag me towards the playground: urgent proposals to take a swing at the "Pas de Géant," or to join in a certain romping hide-and-seek game called "Un, deux, trois," were formerly also of hourly occurrence; but all these little attentions had ceased some time ago—ceased, too, without my finding it necessary to be at the trouble of point-blank cutting them short. I had now no familiar demonstration to dread or endure, save from one quarter; and as that was English, I could bear it. Ginevra Fanshawe made no scruple of—at times— catching me as I was crossing the carré, whirling me round in a compulsory waltz, and heartily enjoying the mental and physical discomfiture her proceeding induced. Ginevra Fanshawe it was who now broke in upon "my learned leisure." She carried a huge music-book under her arm.

"Go to your practising," said I to her at once: "away with you to the little salon!"

"Not till I have had a talk with you, chère amie. I know where you have been spending your vacation, and how you have commenced sacrificing to the graces, and enjoying life like any other belle. I saw you at the concert the other night, dressed, actually, like anybody else. Who is your tailleuse?"

"Tittle-tattle: how prettily it begins! My tailleuse!—a fiddlestick! Come, sheer off, Ginevra. I really don't want your company."

"But when I want yours so much, ange farouche, what does a little reluctance on your part signify? Dieu merci! we know how to manœuvre with our gifted compatriote—the learned 'ourse Britannique.' And so, Ourson, you know Isidore?"

"I know John Bretton."

"Oh, hush! (putting her fingers in her ears) you crack my tympanums with your rude Anglicisms. But, how is our well-beloved John? Do tell me about him. The poor man must be in a sad way. What did he say to my behaviour the other night? Wasn't I cruel?"

"Do you think I noticed you?"

"It was a delightful evening. Oh, that divine De Hamal! And then to watch the other sulking and dying in the distance; and the old lady—my future mamma-in-law! But I am afraid I and Lady Sara were a little rude in quizzing her."

"Lady Sara never quizzed her at all; and for what *you* did, don't make yourself in the least uneasy: Mrs. Bretton will survive *your* sneer."

"She may: old ladies are tough; but that poor son of hers! Do tell me what he said: I saw he was terribly cut up."

"He said you looked as if at heart you were already Madame de Hamal."

"Did he?" she cried with delight. "He noticed that? How charming! I thought he would be mad with jealousy!"

"Ginevra, have you seriously done with Dr. Bretton? Do you want him to give you up?"

"Oh! you know he *can't* do that: but wasn't he mad?"

"Quite mad," I assented; "as mad as a March hare."

"Well, and how *ever* did you get him home?"

"How *ever*, indeed! Have you no pity on his poor mother and me? Fancy us holding him tight down in the carriage, and he raving between us, fit to drive everybody delirious. The very coachman went wrong, somehow, and we lost our way."

"You don't say so? You are laughing at me. Now, Lucy Snowe"——

"I assure you it is fact—and fact, also, that Dr. Bretton would *not* stay in the carriage: he broke from us, and *would* ride outside."

"And afterwards?"

"Afterwards—when he *did* reach home—the scene transcends description."

"Oh, but describe it—you know it is such fun!"

"Fun for *you*, Miss Fanshawe! but (with stern gravity) you know the proverb— 'What is sport to one may be death to another.' "

"Go on, there's a darling Timon."

"Conscientiously, I cannot, unless you assure me you have some heart."

"I have—such an immensity, you don't know!"

"Good! In that case, you will be able to conceive Dr. Graham Bretton rejecting his supper in the first instance—the chicken, the sweet-bread prepared for his refreshment, left on the table untouched. Then——but it is of no use dwelling at length on the harrowing details. Suffice it to say, that never, in the most stormy fits and moments of his infancy, had his mother such work to tuck the sheets about him as she had that night."

"He wouldn't lie still?"

"He wouldn't lie still: there it was. The sheets might be tucked in, but the thing was to keep them tucked in."

"And what did he say?"

"Say! Can't you imagine him demanding his divine Ginevra, anathematising that demon, De Hamal—raving about golden locks, blue eyes, white arms, glittering bracelets?"

"No, did he? He saw the bracelet?"

"Saw the bracelet? Yes, as plain as I saw it: and, perhaps, for the first time, he saw also the brand-mark with which its pressure has encircled your arm. Ginevra (rising, and changing my tone), come, we will have an end of this. Go away to your practising." And I opened the door.

"But you have not told me all."

"You had better not wait until I *do* tell you all. Such extra communicativeness could give you no pleasure. March!"

"Cross thing!" said she; but she obeyed: and, indeed, the first classe was my territory, and she could not there legally resist a notice of quittance from me.

Yet, to speak the truth, never had I been less dissatisfied with her than I was then. There was pleasure in thinking of the contrast between the reality and my description—to remember Dr. John enjoying the drive home, eating his supper with relish, and retiring to rest with Christian composure. It was only when I saw him really unhappy that I felt really vexed with the fair, frail cause of his suffering.

A fortnight passed; I was getting once more inured to the harness of school, and lapsing from the passionate pain of change to the palsy of custom. One afternoon, in crossing the carré, on my way to the first classe, where l was expected to assist at a lesson of "style and literature," l saw, standing by one of the long and large windows, Rosine, the portress. Her attitude, as usual, was quite nonchalante. She always "stood at ease"; one of her hands rested in her apron-pocket, the other at this moment held to her eyes a letter, whereof Mademoiselle coolly perused the address, and deliberately studied the seal.

A letter! The shape of a letter similar to that had haunted my brain in its very core for seven days past. I had dreamed of a letter last night. Strong magnetism drew me to that letter now; yet, whether I should have ventured to demand of Rosine so much as a glance at that white envelope, with the spot of red wax in the middle, I know not. No; I think I should have sneaked past in terror of a rebuff from Disappointment: my heart throbbed now as if I already heard the tramp of her approach. Nervous mistake! It was the rapid step of the Professor of Literature measuring the corridor. I fled before him. Could I but be seated quietly at my desk before his arrival, with the class under my orders all in disciplined readiness, he would, perhaps, exempt me from notice; but, if caught lingering in the carré, I should be sure to come in for a special harangue. I had time to get seated, to enforce perfect silence, to take out my work, and to commence it amidst the profoundest and best-trained hush, ere M. Emanuel entered with his vehement burst of latch and panel, and his deep, redundant bow, prophetic of choler.

As usual, he broke upon us like a clap of thunder; but instead of flashing lightning-wise from the door to the estrade, his career halted midway at my desk. Setting his face towards me and the window, his back to the pupils and the room, he gave me a look—such a look as might have licensed me to stand straight up and demand what he meant—a look of scowling distrust.

"Voilà! pour vous," said he, drawing his hand from his waistcoat, and placing on my desk a letter—the very letter I had seen in Rosine's hand—the letter whose face of enamelled white and single Cyclop's-eye of vermilion red had printed themselves so clear and perfect on the retina of an inward vision. I knew it, I felt it to be the letter of my hope, the fruition of my wish, the release from my doubt, the ransom from my terror. This letter M. Paul, with his unwarrantably interfering habits, had taken from the portress, and now delivered it himself.

I might have been angry, but had not a second for the sensation. Yes: I held in my hand not a slight note, but an envelope which must, at least, contain a sheet: it felt, not flimsy, but firm, substantial, satisfying. And here was the direction, "Miss Lucy Snowe," in a clean, clear, equal, decided hand; and here was the seal, round, full, deftly dropped by untremulous fingers, stamped with the well-cut impress of initials, "J. G. B." I experienced a happy feeling—a glad emotion which went warm to my heart, and ran lively through all my veins. For once a hope was realised. I held in my hand a morsel of real solid joy: not a dream, not an image of the brain, not one of those shadowy chances imagination pictures, and on which humanity starves but cannot live; not a mess of that manna I drearily eulogised a while ago—which, indeed, at first melts on the lips with an unspeakable

and preternatural sweetness, but which, in the end, our souls full surely loathe; longing deliriously for natural and earth-grown food, wildly praying Heaven's Spirits to reclaim their own spirit-dew and essence—an aliment divine, but for mortals deadly. It was neither sweet hail nor small coriander-seed—neither slight wafer nor luscious honey, I had lighted on; it was the wild, savoury mess of the hunter, nourishing and salubrious meat, forest-fed or desert-reared, fresh, healthful, and life-sustaining. It was what the old dying patriarch demanded of his son Esau, promising in requital the blessing of his last breath. It was a godsend; and I inwardly thanked the God who had vouchsafed it. Outwardly, I only thanked man, crying, "Thank you, thank you, monsieur!"

Monsieur curled his lip, gave me a vicious glance of the eye, and strode to his estrade. M. Paul was not at all a good little man, though he had good points.

Did I read my letter there and then? Did I consume the venison at once and with haste, as if Esau's shaft flew every day?

I knew better. The cover with its address—the seal, with its three clear letters— was bounty and abundance for the present. I stole from the room, I procured the key of the great dormitory which was kept locked by day. I went to my bureau; with a sort of haste and trembling lest Madame should creep upstairs and spy me, I opened a drawer, unlocked a box, and took out a case, and—having feasted my eyes with one more look, and approached the seal with a mixture of awe and shame and delight, to my lips—I folded the untasted treasure, yet all fair and inviolate, in silver paper, committed it to the case, shut up box and drawer, reclosed, relocked the dormitory and returned to class, feeling as if fairy tales were true and fairy gifts no dream. Strange, sweet insanity! And this letter, the source of my joy, I had not yet read: did not yet know the number of its lines.

When I re-entered the schoolroom, behold M. Paul raging like a pestilence! Some pupil had not spoken audibly or distinctly enough to suit his ear and taste, and now she and others were weeping, and he was raving from his estrade, almost livid. Curious to mention, as I appeared, he fell on me.

"Was I the mistress of these girls? Did I profess to teach them the conduct befitting ladies?—and did I permit and, he doubted not, encourage them to strangle their mother-tongue in their throats, to mince and mash it between their teeth, as if they had some base cause to be ashamed of the words they uttered? Was this modesty? He knew better. It was a vile pseudo sentiment—the offspring or the forerunner of evil. Rather than submit to this mopping and mowing, this mincing and grimacing, this grinding of a noble tongue, this general affectation and sickening stubbornness of the pupils of the first class, he would throw them up for a set of insupportable petites maîtresses, and confine himself to teaching the A B C to the babies of the third division."

What could I say to all this? Really nothing: and I hoped he would allow me to be silent. The storm recommenced.

"Every answer to his queries was then refused? It seemed to be considered in *that* place—that conceited boudoir of a first class, with its pretentious book-cases, its green-baized desks, its rubbish of flower-stands, its trash of framed pictures and maps, and its foreign surveillante, forsooth!—it seemed to be the fashion to think *there* that the Professor of Literature was not worthy of a reply! These were new ideas; imported, he did not doubt, straight from 'la Grande Bretaigne': they savoured of island insolence and arrogance."

Lull the second—the girls, not one of whom was ever known to weep a tear for the rebukes of any other master, now all melting like snow-statues before the intemperate heat of M. Emanuel: I, not yet much shaken, sitting down, and venturing to resume my work.

Something—either in my continued silence or in the movement of my hand, stitching—transported M. Emanuel beyond the last boundary of patience; he actually

sprang from his estrade. The stove stood near my desk, he attacked it; the little iron door was nearly dashed from its hinges, the fuel was made to fly.

"Est-ce que vous avez l'intention de m'insulter?" said he to me, in a low, furious voice, as he thus outraged, under pretence of arranging, the fire.

It was time to soothe him a little if possible.

"Mais, monsieur," said I, "I would not insult you for the world. I remember too well that you once said we should be friends."

I did not intend my voice to falter, but it did; more, I think, through the agitation of late delight than in any spasm of present fear. Still there certainly was something in M. Paul's anger—a kind of passion of emotion—that specially tended to draw tears. I was not unhappy, not much afraid, yet I wept.

"Allons, allons!" said he presently, looking round and seeing the deluge universal. "Decidedly I am a monster and a ruffian. I have only one pocket-handkerchief," he added, "but if I had twenty, I would offer you each one. Your teacher shall be your representative. Here, Miss Lucy."

And he took forth and held out to me a clean silk handkerchief. Now a person who did not know M. Paul, who was unused to him and his impulses, would naturally have bungled at this offer—declined accepting the same—etcetera. But I too plainly felt this would never do: the slightest hesitation would have been fatal to the incipient treaty of peace. I rose and met the handkerchief half-way, received it with decorum, wiped therewith my eyes, and, resuming my seat, and retaining the flag of truce in my hand and on my lap, took especial care during the remainder of the lesson to touch neither needle nor thimble, scissors nor muslin. Many a jealous glance did M. Paul cast at these implements; he hated them mortally, considering sewing a source of distraction from the attention due to himself. A very eloquent lesson he gave, and very kind and friendly was he to the close. Ere he had done, the clouds were dispersed and the sun shining out—tears were exchanged for smiles.

In quitting the room he paused once more at my desk.

"And your letter?" said he, this time not quite fiercely.

"I have not yet read it, Monsieur."

"Ah! it is too good to read at once; you save it, as when I was a boy, I used to save a peach whose bloom was very ripe?"

The guess came so near the truth, I could not prevent a suddenly rising warmth in my face from revealing as much.

"You promise yourself a pleasant moment," said he, "in reading that letter; you will open it when alone—n'est ce pas? Ah! a smile answers. Well, well! one should not be too harsh; 'la jeunesse n'a qu'un temps.' "

"Monsieur, monsieur!" I cried or rather whispered after him, as he turned to go, "do not leave me under a mistake. This is merely a friend's letter. Without reading it, I can vouch for that."

"Je conçois, je conçois: on sait ce que c'est qu'un ami. Bon jour, mademoiselle!"

"But, monsieur, here is your handkerchief."

"Keep it, keep it, till the letter is read, then bring it me; I shall read the billet's tenor in your eyes."

When he was gone, the pupils having already poured out of the schoolroom into the berceau, and thence into the garden and court to take their customary recreation before the five o'clock dinner, I stood a moment thinking, and absently twisting the handkerchief round my arm. For some reason—gladdened, I think, by a sudden return of the golden glimmer of childhood, roused by an unwonted renewal of its buoyancy, made merry by the liberty of the closing hour, and, above all, solaced at heart by the joyous consciousness of that treasure in the case, box, drawer upstairs,—I fell to playing with the handkerchief as if it were a ball, casting it into the air and catching it as it fell. The game was stopped by another hand than mine—

a hand emerging from a paletôt-sleeve and stretched over my shoulder; it caught the extemporised plaything and bore it away with these sullen words—

"Je vois bien que vous vous moquez de moi et de mes effets."

Really that little man was dreadful: a mere sprite of caprice and ubiquity: one never knew either his whim or his whereabout.

Chapter XXII

THE LETTER

WHEN all was still in the house; when dinner was over and the noisy recreation-hour past; when darkness had set in, and the quiet lamp of study was lit in the refectory; when the externes were gone home, the clashing door and clamorous bell hushed for the evening; when Madame was safely settled in the salle à manger in company with her mother and some friends; I then glided to the kitchen, begged a bougie for one half-hour for a particular occasion, found acceptance of my petition at the hands of my friend Goton, who answered—"Mais certainement, chou-chou, vous en aurez deux, si vous voulez." And, light in hand, I mounted noiseless to the dormitory.

Great was my chagrin to find in that apartment a pupil gone to bed indisposed,—greater when I recognised amid the muslin nightcap borders, the "figure chiffonée" of Mistress Ginevra Fanshawe; supine at this moment, it is true—but certain to wake and overwhelm me with chatter when the interruption would be least acceptable: indeed, as I watched her, a slight twinkling of the eyelids warned me that the present appearance of repose might be but a ruse, assumed to cover sly vigilance over "Timon's" movements; she was not to be trusted. And I had so wished to be alone, just to read my precious letter in peace.

Well, I must go to the classes. Having sought and found my prize in its casket, I descended. Ill-luck pursued me. The classes were undergoing sweeping and purification by candlelight, according to hebdomadal custom: benches were piled on desks, the air was dim with dust, damp coffee-grounds (used by Labassecourien housemaids instead of tea-leaves) darkened the floor; all was hopeless confusion. Baffled, but not beaten, I withdrew, bent as resolutely as ever on finding solitude *somewhere*.

Taking the key whereof I knew the repository, I mounted three staircases in succession, reached a dark, narrow, silent landing, opened a worm-eaten door, and dived into the deep, black, cold garret. Here none would follow me—none interrupt—not Madame herself. I shut the garret-door; I placed my light on a doddered and mouldy chest of drawers; I put on a shawl, for the air was ice-cold; I took my letter, trembling with sweet impatience; I broke its seal.

"Will it be long—will it be short?" thought I, passing my hand across my eyes to dissipate the silvery dimness of a suave, south wind shower.

It was long.

"Will it be cool?—will it be kind?"

It was kind.

To my checked, bridled, disciplined expectation, it seemed very kind: to my longing and famished thought it seemed, perhaps, kinder than it was.

So little had I hoped, so much had I feared; there was a fulness of delight in this taste of fruition—such, perhaps, as many a human being passes through life without ever knowing. The poor English teacher in the frosty garret, reading by a dim candle guttering in the wintry air, a letter simply good-natured—nothing more; though that good-nature then seemed to me godlike—was happier than most queens in palaces.

Of course, happiness of such shallow origin could be but brief; yet, while it lasted, it was genuine and exquisite: a bubble—but a sweet bubble—of real honey-dew. Dr. John had written to me at length; he had written to me with pleasure; he had written in benignant mood, dwelling with sunny satisfaction on scenes that had passed before his eyes and mine,—on places we had visited together—on conversations we had held—on all the little subject-matter, in short, of the last few halcyon weeks. But the cordial core of the delight was, a conviction the blithe, genial language generously imparted, that it had been poured out not merely to content *me* but to gratify *himself*. A gratifcation he might never more desire, never more seek—an hypothesis in every point of view approaching the certain; but *that* concerned the future. This present moment had no pain, no blot, no want; full, pure, perfect, it deeply blessed me. A passing seraph seemed to have rested beside me, leaned towards my heart, and reposed on its throb a softening, cooling, healing, hallowing wing. Dr. John, you pained me afterwards: forgiven be every ill—freely forgiven—for the sake of that one dear remembered good!

Are there wicked things, not human, which envy human bliss? Are there evil influences haunting the air, and poisoning it for man? What was near me?

Something in that vast solitary garret sounded strangely. Most surely and certainly I heard, as it seemed, a stealthy foot on that floor: a sort of gliding out from the direction of the black recess haunted by the malefactor cloaks. I turned: my light was dim; the room was long—but as I live! I saw in the middle of that ghostly chamber a figure all black or white; the skirts straight, narrow, black; the head bandaged, veiled, white.

Say what you will, reader—tell me I was nervous or mad; affirm that I was unsettled by the excitement of that letter; declare that I dreamed; this I vow—I saw there—in that room—on that night—an image like—A NUN.

I cried out; I sickened. Had the shape approached me I might have swooned. It receded: I made for the door. How I descended all the stairs I know not. By instinct I shunned the refectory, and shaped my course to Madame's sitting-room: I burst in. I said—

"There is something in the grenier: I have been there: I saw something. Go and look at it, all of you!"

I said, "All of you!" for the room seemed to me full of people, though in truth there were but four present: Madame Beck; her mother, Madame Kint, who was out of health, and now staying with her on a visit; her brother, M. Victor Kint, and another gentleman: who, when I entered the room, was conversing with the old lady, and had his back towards the door.

My mortal fear and faintness must have made me deadly pale. I felt cold and shaking. They all rose in consternation; they surrounded me. I urged them to go to the grenier; the sight of the gentlemen did me good and gave me courage: it seemed as if there were some help and hope, with men at hand. I turned to the door, beckoning them to follow. They wanted to stop me, but I said they must come this way: they must see what I had seen—something strange, standing in the middle of the garret. And now I remembered my letter, left on the drawers with the light. This precious letter! Flesh or spirit must be defied for its sake. I flew upstairs, hastening the faster as I knew I was followed: they were obliged to come.

Lo! when I reached the garret-door, all within was dark as a pit: the light was out. Happily some one—Madame, I think, with her usual calm sense—had brought a lamp from the room; speedily, therefore, as they came up, a ray pierced the opaque blackness. There stood the bougie quenched on the drawers; but where was the letter? And I looked for *that* now, and not for the nun.

"My letter! my letter!" I panted and plained, almost beside myself. I groped on the floor, wringing my hands wildly. Cruel, cruel doom! To have my bit of comfort preternaturally snatched from me ere I had well tasted its virtue!

I don't know what the others were doing; I could not watch them, they asked me questions I did not answer; they ransacked all corners; they prattled about this and that disarrangement of cloaks, a breach or crack in the skylight—I know not what. "Something or somebody has been here," was sagely averred.

"Oh! they have taken my letter!" cried the grovelling, groping monomaniac.

"What letter, Lucy? My dear girl, what letter?" asked a known voice in my ear. Could I believe that ear? No: and I looked up. Could I trust my eyes? Had I recognised the tone? Did I now look on the face of the writer of that very letter? Was this gentleman near me in this dim garret, John Graham—Dr. Bretton himself?

Yes: it was. He had been called in that very evening to prescribe for some access of illness in old Madame Kint; he was the second gentleman present in the salle-à-manger when I entered.

"Was it *my* letter, Lucy?"

"Your own: yours—the letter you wrote to me. I had come here to read it quietly. I could not find another spot where it was possible to have it to myself. I had saved it all day—never opened it till this evening: it was scarcely glanced over: I *cannot bear* to lose it. Oh, my letter!"

"Hush! don't cry and distress yourself so cruelly. What is it worth? Hush! Come out of this cold room; they are going to send for the police now to examine further: we need not stay here—come, we will go down."

A warm hand, taking my cold fingers, led me down to a room where there was a fire. Dr. John and I sat before the stove. He talked to me and soothed me with unutterable goodness, promising me twenty letters for the one lost. If there are words and wrongs like knives, whose deep-inflicted lacerations never heal—cutting injuries and insults of serrated and poison-dripping edge—so, too, there are consolations of tone too fine for the ear not fondly and for ever to retain their echo: caressing kindnesses—loved, lingered over through a whole life, recalled with unfaded tenderness, and answering the call with undimmed shine out of that raven cloud foreshadowing Death himself. I have been told since that Dr. Bretton was not nearly so perfect as I thought him: that his actual character lacked the depth, height, compass, and endurance it possessed in my creed. I don't know: he was as good to me as the well is to the parched wayfarer—as the sun to the shivering jailbird. I remember him heroic. Heroic at this moment will I hold him to be.

He asked me, smiling, why I cared for his letter so very much. I thought, but did not say, that I prized it like the blood in my veins. I only answered that I had so few letters to care for.

"I am sure you did not read it," said he; "or you would think nothing of it!"

"I read it, but only once. I want to read it again. I am sorry it is lost." And I could not help weeping afresh.

"Lucy, Lucy, my poor little god-sister (if there be such a relationship), here—*here* is your letter. Why is it not better worth such tears, and such tenderly exaggerating faith?"

Curious characteristic manœuvre! His quick eye had seen the letter on the floor where I sought it; his hand, as quick, had snatched it up. He had hidden it in his waistcoat pocket. If my trouble had wrought with a whit less stress and reality, I doubt whether he would ever have acknowledged or restored it. Tears of temperature one degree cooler than those I shed would only have amused Dr. John.

Pleasure at regaining made me forget merited reproach for the teasing torment; my joy was great; it could not be concealed: yet I think it broke out more in countenance than language. I said little.

"Are you satisfied now?" asked Dr. John.

I replied that I was—satisfied and happy.

"Well then," he proceeded, "how do you feel physically? Are you growing calmer? Not much; for you tremble like a leaf still."

It seemed to me, however, that I was sufficiently calm; at least I felt no longer terrified. I expressed myself composed.

"You are able, consequently, to tell me what you saw? Your account was quite vague, do you know? You looked white as the wall; but you only spoke of 'something,' not defining *what*. Was it a man? Was it an animal? *What* was it?"

"I never will tell exactly what I saw," said I, "unless some one else sees it too, and then I will give corroborative testimony; but otherwise I shall be discredited and accused of dreaming."

"Tell me," said Dr. Bretton; "I will hear it in my professional character: I look on you now from a professional point of view, and I read, perhaps, all you would conceal—in your eye, which is curiously vivid and restless: in your cheek, which the blood has forsaken; in your hand, which you cannot steady. Come, Lucy, speak and tell me."

"You would laugh"——

"If you don't tell me you shall have no more letters."

"You are laughing now."

"I will again take away that single epistle: being mine, I think I have a right to reclaim it."

I felt raillery in his words: it made me grave and quiet; but I folded up the letter and covered it from sight.

"You may hide it, but I can possess it any moment I choose. You don't know my skill in sleight of hand: I might practise as a conjuror if I liked. Mamma says sometimes, too, that I have an harmonising property of tongue and eye; but you never saw that in me—did you, Lucy?"

"Indeed—indeed—when you were a mere boy I used to see both: far more then than now—for now you are strong, and strength dispenses with subtlety. But still, Dr. John, you have what they call in this country 'un air fin,' that nobody can mistake. Madame Beck saw it, and"——

"And liked it," said he, laughing, "because she has it herself. But, Lucy—give me that letter—you don't really care for it."

To this provocative speech I made no answer. Graham in mirthful mood must not be humoured too far. Just now there was a new sort of smile playing about his lips—very sweet, but it grieved me somehow—a new sort of light sparkling in his eyes: not hostile, but not reassuring. I rose to go—I bid him good-night a little sadly.

His sensitiveness—that peculiar, apprehensive, detective faculty of his—felt in a moment the unspoken complaint—the scarce-thought reproach. He asked quietly if I was offended. I shook my head as implying a negative.

"Permit me then to speak a little seriously to you before you go. You are in a highly nervous state. I feel sure from what is apparent in your look and manner, however well-controlled, that whilst alone this evening in that dismal, perishing, sepulchral garret—that dungeon under the leads, smelling of damp and mould, rank with phthisis and catarrh: a place you never ought to enter—that you saw, or *thought* you saw, some appearance peculiarly calculated to impress the imagination. I know that you *are* not, nor ever were, subject to material terrors, fears of robbers, etc.—I am not so sure that a visitation, bearing a spectral character, would not shake your very mind. Be calm now. This is all a matter of the nerves, I see: but just specify the vision."

"You will tell nobody?"

"Nobody—most certainly. You may trust me as implicitly as you did Père Silas. Indeed, the doctor is perhaps the safer confessor of the two, though he has not grey hair."

"You will not laugh?"

"Perhaps I may, to do you good: but not in scorn. Lucy, I feel as a friend towards you, though your timid nature is slow to trust."

He now looked like a friend: that indescribable smile and sparkle were gone; those formidable arched curves of lip, nostril, eyebrow, were depressed; repose marked his attitude—attention sobered his aspect. Won to confidence, I told him exactly what I had seen: ere now I had narrated to him the legend of the house— whiling away with that narrative an hour of a certain mild October afternoon, when he and I rode through Bois l'Etang.

He sat and thought, and while he thought we heard them all coming downstairs.

"Are they going to interrupt?" said he, glancing at the door with an annoyed expression.

"They will not come here," I answered; for we were in the little salon where Madame never sat in the evening, and where it was by mere chance that heat was still lingering in the stove. They passed the door and went on to the salle à manger.

"Now," he pursued, "they will talk about thieves, burglars, and so on: let them do so—mind you say nothing, and keep your resolution of describing your nun to nobody. She may appear to you again: don't start."

"You think then," I said, with secret horror, "she came out of my brain, and is now gone in there, and may glide out again at an hour and a day when I look not for her?"

"I think it a case of spectral illusion: I fear, following on and resulting from long-continued mental conflict."

"Oh, Dr. John—I shudder at the thought of being liable to such an illusion! It seemed so real. Is there no cure?—no preventive?"

"Happiness is the cure—a cheerful mind the preventive: cultivate both."

No mockery in this world ever sounds to me so hollow as that of being told to *cultivate* happiness. What does such advice mean? Happiness is not a potato, to be planted in mould, and tilled with manure. Happiness is a glory shining far down upon us out of Heaven. She is a divine dew which the soul, on certain of its summer mornings, feels dropping upon it from the amaranth bloom and golden fruitage of Paradise.

"Cultivate happiness!" I said briefly to the Doctor: "do *you* cultivate happiness? How do you manage?"

"I am a cheerful fellow by nature: and then ill-luck has never dogged me. Adversity gave me and my mother one passing scowl and brush, but we defied her, or rather laughed at her, and she went by."

"There is no cultivation in all this."

"I do not give way to melancholy."

"Yes: I have seen you subdued by that feeling."

"About Ginevra Fanshawe—eh?"

"Did she not sometimes make you miserable?"

"Pooh! stuff! nonsense! You see I am better now."

If a laughing eye with a lively light, and a face bright with beaming and healthy energy, could attest that he was better, better he certainly was.

"You do not look much amiss, or greatly out of condition," I allowed.

"And why, Lucy, can't you look and feel as I do—buoyant, courageous, and fit to defy all the nuns and flirts in Christendom? I would give gold on the spot just to see you snap your fingers. Try the manœuvre."

"If I were to bring Miss Fanshawe into your presence just now?"

"I vow, Lucy, she should not move me: or, she should move me but by one thing—true, yes, and passionate love. I would accord forgiveness at no less a price."

"Indeed! a smile of hers would have been a fortune to you a while since."

"Transformed, Lucy: transformed! Remember, you once called me a slave! but I am a free man now!"

He stood up: in the port of his head, the carriage of his figure, in his beaming eye and mien there revealed itself a liberty which was more than ease—a mood which was disdain of his past bondage.

"Miss Fanshawe," he pursued, "has led me through a phase of feeling which is over: I have entered another condition, and am now much disposed to exact love for love—passion for passion—and good measure of it, too."

"Ah, Doctor! Doctor! you said it was your nature to pursue Love under difficulties— to be charmed by a proud insensibility!"

He laughed, and answered, "My nature varies: the mood of one hour is sometimes the mockery of the next. Well, Lucy" (drawing on his gloves), "will the nun come again to-night, think you?"

"I don't think she will."

"Give her my compliments, if she does—Dr. John's compliments—and entreat her to have the goodness to wait a visit from him. Lucy, was she a pretty nun? Had she a pretty face? You have not told me that yet; and *that* is the really important point."

"She had a white cloth over her face," said I, "but her eyes glittered."

"Confusion to her goblin trappings!" cried he irreverently: "but at least she had handsome eyes—bright and soft."

"Cold and fixed," was the reply.

"No, no, we'll none of her: she shall not haunt you, Lucy. Give her that shake of the hand if she comes again. Will she stand *that*, do you think?"

I thought it too kind and cordial for a ghost to stand: and so was the smile which matched it, and accompanied his "Good-night."

And had there been anything in the garret? What did they discover? I believe, on the closest examination, their discoveries amounted to very little. They talked, at first, of the cloaks being disturbed; but Madame Beck told me afterwards she thought they hung much as usual: and as for the broken pane in the skylight, she affirmed that aperture was rarely without one or more panes broken or cracked: and besides, a heavy hail-storm had fallen a few days ago. Madame questioned me very closely as to what I had seen, but I only described an obscure figure clothed in black: I took care not to breathe the word "nun," certain that this word would at once suggest to her mind an idea of romance and unreality. She charged me to say nothing on the subject to any servant, pupil, or teacher, and highly recommended my discretion in coming to her private salle-à-manger, instead of carrying the tale of horror to the school refectory. Thus the subject dropped. I was left secretly and sadly to wonder, in my own mind, whether that strange thing was of this world, or of a realm beyond the grave; or whether indeed it was only the child of malady, and I of that malady the prey.

Chapter XXIII

VASHTI

To wonder sadly, did I say? No: a new influence began to act upon my life, and sadness, for a certain space, was held at bay. Conceive a dell, deep-hollowed in forest secrecy; it lies in dimness and mist: its turf is dank, its herbage pale and humid. A storm or an axe makes a wide gap amongst the oak-trees; the breeze sweeps in; the sun looks down; the sad, cold dell becomes a deep cup of lustre; high summer pours her blue glory and her golden light out of that beauteous sky, which till now the starved hollow never saw.

A new creed became mine—a belief in happiness.

It was three weeks since the adventure of the garret, and I possessed in that case, box, drawer upstairs, casketed with that first letter, four companions like to it, traced by the same fine pen, sealed with the same clear seal, full of the same vital comfort. Vital comfort it seemed to me then: I read them in after years; they were kind letters enough—pleasing letters, because composed by one well pleased; in the two last there were three or four closing lines half-gay, half-tender, "by *feeling* touched, but not subdued." Time, dear reader, mellowed them to a beverage of this mild quality; but when I first tasted their elixir, fresh from the fount so honoured, it seemed juice of a divine vintage: a draught which Hebe might fill, and the very gods approve.

Does the reader, remembering what was said some pages back, care to ask how I answered these letters: whether under the dry, stinting check of Reason, or according to the full, liberal impulse of Feeling?

To speak truth, I compromised matters: I served two masters: I bowed down in the house of Rimmon, and lifted the heart at another shrine. I wrote to these letters two answers—one for my own relief, the other for Graham's perusal.

To begin with: Feeling and I turned Reason out of doors, drew against her bar and bolt, then we sat down, spread our paper, dipped in the ink an eager pen, and, with deep enjoyment, poured out our sincere heart. When we had done—when two sheets were covered with the language of a strongly-adherent affection, a rooted and active gratitude—(once for all, in this parenthesis, I disclaim, with the utmost scorn, every sneaking suspicion of what are called "warmer feelings": women do not entertain these "warmer feelings" where, from the commencement, through the whole progress of an acquaintance, they have never once been cheated of the conviction that to do so would be to commit a mortal absurdity: nobody ever launches into Love unless he has seen or dreamed the rising of Hope's star over Love's troubled waters)—when, then, I had given expression to a closely clinging and deeply-honouring attachment—an attachment that wanted to attract to itself and take to its own lot all that was painful in the destiny of its object; that would, if it could, have absorbed and conducted away all storms and lightnings from an existence viewed with a passion of solicitude—then, just at that moment, the doors of my heart would shake, bolt and bar would yield, Reason would leap in vigorous and revengeful, snatch the full sheets, read, sneer, erase, tear up, re-write, fold, seal, direct, and send a terse, curt missive of a page. She did right.

I did not live on letters only: I was visited, I was looked after; once a week I was taken out to La Terrasse; always I was made much of. Dr. Bretton failed not to tell me *why* he was so kind: "To keep away the nun," he said; "he was determined to dispute with her her prey. He had taken," he declared, "a thorough dislike to her, chiefly on account of that white face-cloth and those cold grey eyes: the moment he heard of those odious particulars," he affirmed, "consummate disgust had incited him to oppose her; he was determined to try whether he or she was the cleverer, and he only wished she would once more look in upon me when he was present": but *that* she never did. In short, he regarded me scientifically in the light of a patient, and at once exercised his professional skill, and gratified his natural benevolence, by a course of cordial and attentive treatment.

One evening, the first in December, I was walking by myself in the carré; it was six o'clock; the classe doors were closed; but within, the pupils, rampant in the licence of evening recreation, were counterfeiting a miniature chaos. The carré was quite dark, except a red light shining under and about the stove; the wide glass-doors and the long windows were frosted over; a crystal sparkle of starlight, here and there spangling this blanched winter veil, and breaking with scattered brilliance the paleness of its embroidery, proved it a clear night, though moonless. That I should dare to remain thus alone in darkness showed that my nerves were regaining a healthy tone: I thought of the nun, but hardly feared her; though the staircase was behind me, leading up, through blind, black night, from landing to landing,

to the haunted grenier. Yet I own my heart quaked, my pulse leaped, when I suddenly heard breathing and rustling, and turning, saw in the deep shadow of the steps a deeper shadow still—a shape that moved and descended. It paused a while at the classe door, and then it glided before me. Simultaneously came a clangour of the distant door-bell. Life-like sounds bring life-like feelings: this shape was too round and low for my gaunt nun: it was only Madame Beck on duty.

"Mademoiselle Lucy!" cried Rosine, bursting in, lamp in hand, from the corridor, "On est là pour vous au salon."

Madame saw me, I saw Madame, Rosine saw us both: there was no mutual recognition. I made straight for the salon. There I found what I own I anticipated I should find—Dr. Bretton; but he was in evening dress.

"The carriage is at the door," said he; "my mother has sent it to take you to the theatre; she was going herself, but an arrival has prevented her: she immediately said, 'Take Lucy in my place.' Will you go?"

"Just now? I am not dressed," cried I, glancing despairingly at my dark merino.

"You have half-an-hour to dress. I should have given you notice, but I only determined on going since five o'clock, when I heard there was to be a genuine régal in the presence of a great actress."

And he mentioned a name that thrilled me—a name that, in those days, could thrill Europe. It is hushed now: its once restless echoes are all still: she who bore it went years ago to her rest: night and oblivion long since closed above her; but *then* her day—a day of Sirius—stood at its full height, light, and fervour.

"I'll go; I will be ready in ten minutes," I vowed. And away I flew, never once checked, reader, by the thought which perhaps at this moment checks you: namely, that to go anywhere with Graham and without Mrs. Bretton could be objectionable. I could not have conceived, much less have expressed to Graham, such thought—such scruple—without risk of exciting a tyrannous self-contempt; of kindling an inward fire of shame so quenchless, and so devouring, that I think it would soon have licked up the very life in my veins. Besides, my godmother, knowing her son, and knowing me, would as soon have thought of chaperoning a sister with a brother, as of keeping anxious guard over our incomings and outgoings.

The present was no occasion for showy array; my dun mist crape would suffice, and I sought the same in the great oak-wardrobe in the dormitory, where hung no less than forty dresses. But there had been changes and reforms, and some innovating hand had pruned this same crowded wardrobe, and carried divers garments to the grenier—my crape amongst the rest. I must fetch it. I got the key, and went aloft fearless, almost thoughtless. I unlocked the door, I plunged in. The reader may believe it or not, but when I thus suddenly entered that garret was not wholly dark as it should have been; from one point there shone a solemn light, like a star, but broader. So plainly it shone, that it revealed the deep alcove with a portion of the tarnished scarlet curtain drawn over it. Instantly, silently, before my eyes, it vanished; so did the curtain and alcove: all that end of the garret became black as night. I ventured no research; I had not time nor will; snatching my dress, which hung on the wall, happily near the door, I rushed out, relocked the door with convulsed haste, and darted downwards to the dormitory.

But I trembled too much to dress myself: impossible to arrange hair or fasten hooks-and-eyes with such fingers, so I called Rosine and bribed her to help me. Rosine liked a bribe, so she did her best, smoothed and plaited my hair as well as a coiffeur would have done, placed the lace collar mathematically straight, tied the neck ribbon accurately—in short, did her work like the neat-handed Phillis she could be when she chose. Having given me my handkerchief and gloves, she took the candle and lighted me downstairs. After all, I had forgotten my shawl; she ran back to fetch it; and I stood with Dr. John in the vestibule, waiting.

"What is this, Lucy?" said he, looking down at me narrowly. "Here is the old excitement. Ha! the nun again?"

But I utterly denied the charge; I was vexed to be suspected of a second illusion. He was sceptical.

"She has been, as sure as I live," said he; "her figure crossing your eyes leaves on them a peculiar gleam and expression not to be mistaken."

"She has *not* been," I persisted: for, indeed, I could deny her apparition with truth.

"The old symptoms are there," he affirmed; "a particular, pale, and what the Scotch call a 'raised' look."

He was so obstinate, I thought it better to tell him what I really *had* seen. Of course with him it was held to be another effect of the same cause: it was all optical illusion—nervous malady, and so on. Not one bit did I believe him; but I dared not contradict: doctors are so self-opinionated, so immovable in their dry, materialist views.

Rosine brought the shawl, and I was bundled into the carriage.

The theatre was full—crammed to its roof: royal and noble were there: palace and hotel had emptied their inmates into those tiers so thronged and so hushed. Deeply did I feel myself privileged in having a place before that stage; I longed to see a being of whose powers I had heard reports which made me conceive peculiar anticipations. I wondered if she would justify her renown: with strange curiosity, with feelings severe and austere, yet of riveted interest, I waited. She was a study of such nature as had not encountered my eyes yet: a great and new planet she was: but in what shape? I waited her rising.

She rose at nine that December night; above the horizon I saw her come. She could shine yet with pale grandeur and steady might; but that star verged already on its judgment day. Seen near, it was a chaos—hollow, half-consumed: an orb perished or perishing—half lava, half glow.

I had heard this woman termed "plain," and I expected bony harshness and grimness—something large, angular, sallow. What I saw was the shadow of a royal Vashti: a queen, fair as the day once, turned pale now like twilight, and wasted like wax in flame.

For a while—a long while—I thought it was only a woman, though a unique woman, who moved in might and grace before this multitude. By-and-by I recognised my mistake. Behold! I found upon her something neither of woman nor of man: in each of her eyes sat a devil. These evil forces bore her through the tragedy, kept up her feeble strength—for she was but a frail creature; and as the action rose and the stir deepened, how wildly they shook her with their passions of the pit! They wrote HELL on her straight, haughty brow. They tuned her voice to the note of torment. They writhed her regal face to a demoniac mask. Hate and Murder and Madness incarnate she stood.

It was a marvellous sight: a mighty revelation.

It was a spectacle low, horrible, immoral.

Swordsmen thrust through, and dying in their blood on the arena sand; bulls goring horses disembowelled, made a meeker vision for the public—a milder condiment for a people's palate—than Vashti torn by seven devils: devils which cried sore and rent the tenement they haunted, but still refused to be exorcised.

Suffering had struck that stage empress; and she stood before her audience neither yielding to, nor enduring, nor, in finite measure, resenting it: she stood locked in struggle, rigid in resistance. She stood, not dressed, but draped in pale antique folds, long and regular like sculpture. A background and entourage and flooring of deepest crimson threw her out, white like alabaster—like silver: rather, be it said, like Death.

Where was the artist of the Cleopatra? Let him come and sit down and study this different vision. Let him seek here the mighty brawn, the muscle, the abounding blood, the full-fed flesh he worshipped: let all materialists draw nigh and look on.

I have said that she does not *resent* her grief. No; the weakness of that word would make it a lie. To her, what hurts becomes immediately embodied: she looks on it as a thing that can be attacked, worried down, torn in shreds. Scarcely a substance herself, she grapples to conflict with abstractions. Before calamity she is a tigress; she rends her woes, shivers them in convulsed abhorrence. Pain, for her, has no result in good; tears water no harvest of wisdom; on sickness, on death itself, she looks with the eye of a rebel. Wicked, perhaps, she is, but also she is strong: and her strength has conquered Beauty, has overcome Grace, and bound both at her side, captives peerlessly fair, and docile as fair. Even in the uttermost frenzy of energy is each mænad movement royally, imperially, incedingly upborne. Her hair, flying loose in revel or war, is still an angel's hair, and glorious under a halo. Fallen, insurgent, banished, she remembers the heaven where she rebelled. Heaven's light, following her exile, pierces its confines, and discloses their forlorn remoteness.

Place now the Cleopatra, or any other slug, before her as an obstacle, and see her cut through the pulpy mass as the scimitar of Saladin clove the down cushion. Let Paul Peter Rubens wake from the dead, let him rise out of his cerements, and bring into this presence all the army of his fat women: the magian power or prophet-virtue gifting that slight rod of Moses could, at one waft, release and re-mingle a sea spell-parted, whelming the heavy host with the down-rush of overthrown sea ramparts.

Vashti was not good, I was told; and I have said she did not look good: though a spirit, she was a spirit out of Tophet. Well, if so much of unholy force can arise from below, may not an equal efflux of sacred essence descend one day from above?

What thought Dr. Graham of this being?

For long intervals I forgot to look how he demeaned himself, or to question what he thought. The strong magnetism of genius drew my heart out of its wonted orbit; the sunflower turned from the south to a fierce light, not solar—a rushing, red, cometary light—hot on vision and to sensation. I had seen acting before, but never anything like this: never anything which astonished Hope and hushed Desire; which outstripped Impulse and paled Conception; which, instead of merely irritating imagination with the thought of what *might* be done, at the same time fevering the nerves because it was *not* done, disclosed power like a deep, swollen winter river thundering in cataract, and bearing the soul, like a leaf, on the steep and steely sweep of its descent.

Miss Fanshawe, with her usual ripeness of judgment, pronounced Dr. Bretton a serious, impassioned man, too grave and too impressible. Not in such light did I ever see him: no such faults could I lay to his charge. His natural attitude was not the meditative, nor his natural mood the sentimental; *impressionable* he was as dimpling water, but, almost as water, *unimpressible:* the breeze, the sun, moved him—metal could not grave, nor fire brand.

Dr. John *could* think and think well, but he was rather a man of action than of thought; he *could* feel, and feel vividly in his way, but his heart had no chord for enthusiasm: to bright, soft, sweet influences his eyes and lips gave bright, soft, sweet welcome, beautiful to see as dyes of rose and silver, pearl and purple, embuing summer clouds; for what belonged to storm, what was wild and intense, dangerous, sudden, and flaming, he had no sympathy, and held with it no communion. When I took time and regained inclination to glance at him, it amused and enlightened me to discover that he was watching that sinister and sovereign Vashti, not with wonder, nor worship, nor yet dismay, but simply with intense curiosity. Her agony did not pain him, her wild moan—worse than a shriek—did not much move him; her fury revolted him somewhat, but not to the point of horror. Cool young Briton! The pale cliffs of his own England do not look down on the tides of the Channel more calmly than he watched the Pythian inspiration of that night.

Looking at his face, I longed to know his exact opinions, and at last I put a question tending to elicit them. At the sound of my voice he awoke as if out of a dream; for he had been thinking, and very intently thinking, his own thoughts, after his own manner. "How did he like Vashti?" I wished to know.

"Hm-m-m," was the first scarce articulate but expressive answer; and then such a strange smile went wandering round his lips, a smile so critical, so almost callous! I suppose that for natures of that order his sympathies *were* callous. In a few terse phrases he told me his opinion of, and feeling towards, the actress: he judged her as a woman, not an artist: it was a branding judgment.

That night was already marked in my book of life, not with white, but with a deep-red cross. But I had not done with it yet; and other memoranda were destined to be set down in characters of tint indelible.

Towards midnight, when the deepening tragedy blackened to the death scene, and all held their breath, and even Graham bit his under lip, and knit his brow, and sat still and struck—when the whole theatre was hushed, when the vision of all eyes centred in one point, when all ears listened towards one quarter—nothing being seen but the white form sunk on a seat, quivering in conflict with her last, her worst-hated, her visibly-conquering foe—nothing heard but her throes, her gaspings, breathing yet of mutiny, panting still defiance; when, as it seemed, an inordinate will, convulsing a perishing mortal frame, bent it to battle with doom and death, fought every inch of ground, sold every drop of blood, resisted to the latest the rape of every faculty, *would* see, *would* hear, *would* breathe, *would* live, up to, within, well-nigh *beyond* the moment when death says to all sense and all being—

"Thus far and no farther!"

Just then a stir, pregnant with omen, rustled behind the scenes—feet ran, voices spoke. What was it? demanded the whole house. A flame, a smell of smoke replied.

"Fire!" rang through the gallery. "Fire!" was repeated, re-echoed, yelled forth: and then, and faster than pen can set it down, came panic, rushing, crushing—a blind, selfish, cruel chaos.

And Dr. John? Reader, I see him yet, with his look of comely courage and cordial calm.

"Lucy will sit still, I know," said he, glancing down at me with the same serene goodness, the same repose of firmness that I have seen in him when sitting at his side amid the secure peace of his mother's hearth. Yes, thus adjured, I think I would have sat still under a rocking crag: but, indeed, to sit still in actual circumstances was my instinct; and at the price of my very life I would not have moved to give him trouble, thwart his will, or make demands on his attention. We were in the stalls, and for a few minutes there was a most terrible, ruthless pressure about us.

"How terrified are the women!" said he; "but if the men were not almost equally so, order might be maintained. This is a sorry scene: I see fifty selfish brutes at this moment, each of whom, if I were near, I could conscientiously knock down. I see some women braver than some men. There is one yonder—good God!"

While Graham was speaking, a young girl who had been very quietly and steadily clinging to a gentleman before us, was suddenly struck from her protector's arms by a big butcherly intruder, and hurled under the feet of the crowd. Scarce two seconds lasted her disappearance. Graham rushed forwards; he and the gentleman, a powerful man though grey-haired, united their strength to thrust back the throng; her head and long hair fell back over his shoulder: she seemed unconscious.

"Trust her with me; I am a medical man," said Dr. John.

"If you have no lady with you, be it so," was the answer. "Hold her, and I will force a passage: we must get her to the air." "I have a lady," said Graham; "but she will be neither hindrance nor incumbrance."

He summoned me with his eye: we were separated. Resolute, however, to rejoin him, I penetrated the living barrier, creeping under where I could not get between or over.

"Fasten on me, and don't leave go," he said; and I obeyed him.

Our pioneer proved strong and adroit; he opened the dense mass like a wedge; with patience and toil he at last bored through the flesh-and-blood rock—so solid, hot, and suffocating—and brought us to the fresh, freezing night.

"You are an Englishman!" said he, turning shortly on Dr. Bretton, when we got into the street.

"An Englishman. And I speak to a countryman?" was the reply.

"Right. Be good enough to stand here two minutes, whilst I find my carriage."

"Papa, I am not hurt," said a girlish voice; "am I with papa?"

"You are with a friend, and your father is close at hand."

"Tell him I am not hurt, except just in my shoulder. Oh, my shoulder! They trod just here."

"Dislocation, perhaps!" muttered the Doctor: "let us hope there is no worse injury done. Lucy, lend a hand one instant."

And I assisted while he made some arrangement of drapery and position for the ease of his suffering burden. She suppressed a moan, and lay in his arms quietly and patiently.

"She is very light," said Graham, "like a child!" and he asked in my ear, "Is she a child, Lucy? Did you notice her age?"

"I am not a child—I am a person of seventeen," responded the patient, demurely and with dignity. Then, directly after—

"Tell papa to come, I get anxious."

The carriage drove up; her father relieved Graham; but in the exchange from one bearer to another she was hurt, and moaned again.

"My darling!" said the father tenderly; then turning to Graham, "You said, sir, you are a medical man?"

"I am: Dr. Bretton of La Terrasse."

"Good. Will you step into my carriage?"

"My own carriage is here: I will seek it, and accompany you."

"Be pleased, then, to follow us." And he named his address: "The Hôtel Crécy, in the Rue Crécy."

We followed; the carriage drove fast; myself and Graham were silent. This seemed like an adventure.

Some little time being lost in seeking our own equipage, we reached the hotel perhaps about ten minutes after these strangers. It was an hotel in the foreign sense: a collection of dwelling-houses, not an inn—a vast, lofty pile, with a huge arch to its street-door, leading through a vaulted covered way into a square all built round.

We alighted, passed up a wide, handsome public staircase, and stopped at Numéro 2 on the second landing; the first floor comprising the abode of I know not what "prince Russe," as Graham informed me. On ringing the bell at a second great door, we were admitted to a suite of very handsome apartments. Announced by a servant in livery, we entered a drawing-room whose hearth glowed with an English fire, and whose walls gleamed with foreign mirrors. Near the hearth appeared a little group: a slight form sunk in a deep arm-chair, one or two women busy about it, the iron-grey gentleman anxiously looking on.

"Where is Harriet? I wish Harriet would come to me," said the girlish voice faintly.

"Where is Mrs. Hurst?" demanded the gentleman impatiently and somewhat sternly of the man-servant who had admitted us.

"I am sorry to say she is gone out of town, sir; my young lady gave her leave till to-morrow."

"Yes—I did—I did. She is gone to see her sister; I said she might go: I remember now," interposed the young lady; "but I am so sorry, for Manon and Louison cannot understand a word I say, and they hurt me without meaning to do so."

Dr. John and the gentleman now interchanged greetings: and while they passed a few minutes in consultation, I approached the easy-chair, and seeing what the faint and sinking girl wished to have done, I did it for her.

I was still occupied in the arrangement, when Graham drew near; he was no less skilled in surgery than medicine, and, on examination, found that no further advice than his own was necessary to the treatment of the present case. He ordered her to be carried to her chamber, and whispered to me—

"Go with the women, Lucy; they seem but dull; you can at least direct their movements, and thus spare her some pain. She must be touched very tenderly."

The chamber was a room shadowy with pale-blue hangings, vaporous with curtainings and veilings of muslin; the bed seemed to me like snow-drift and mist—spotless, soft, and gauzy. Making the women stand apart, I undressed their mistress, without their well-meaning but clumsy aid. I was not in a sufficiently collected mood to note with separate distinctness every detail of the attire I removed, but I received a general impression of refinement, delicacy, and perfect personal cultivation; which, in a period of afterthought, offered in my reflections a singular contrast to notes retained of Miss Ginevra Fanshawe's appointments.

The girl was herself a small delicate creature, but made like a model. As I folded back her plentiful yet fine hair, so shining and soft, and so exquisitely tended, I had under my observation a young, pale, weary, but high-bred face. The brow was smooth and clear; the eyebrows were distinct but soft, and melting to a mere trace at the temples; the eyes were a rich gift of nature—fine and full, large, deep, seeming to hold dominion over the slighter subordinate features—capable, probably, of much significance at another hour and under other circumstances than the present, but now languid and suffering. Her skin was perfectly fair, the neck and hands veined finely like the petals of a flower; a thin glazing of the ice of pride polished this delicate exterior, and her lip wore a curl—I doubt not inherent and unconscious, but which, if I had seen it first with the accompaniments of health and state, would have struck me as unwarranted, and proving in the little lady a quite mistaken view of life and her own consequence.

Her demeanour under the doctor's hands at first excited a smile; it was not puerile—rather, on the whole, patient and firm—but yet, once or twice, she addressed him with suddenness and sharpness, saying that he hurt her, and must contrive to give her less pain; I saw her large eyes, too, settle on his face like the solemn eyes of some pretty wondering child. I know not whether Graham felt this examination: if he did, he was cautious not to check or discomfort it by any retaliatory look. I think he performed his work with extreme care and gentleness, sparing her what pain he could; and she acknowledged as much, when he had done, by the words—

"Thank you, Doctor, and good-night," very gratefully pronounced: as she uttered them, however, it was with a repetition of the serious, direct gaze, I thought, peculiar in its gravity and intentness.

The injuries, it seems, were not dangerous: an assurance which her father received with a smile that almost made one his friend—it was so glad and gratified. He now expressed his obligations to Graham with as much earnestness as was befitting an Englishman addressing one who has served him, but is yet a stranger; he also begged him to call the next day.

"Papa," said a voice from the veiled couch, "thank the lady, too; is she there?"

I opened the curtain with a smile, and looked in at her. She lay now at comparative ease; she looked pretty, though pale; her face was delicately designed, and if at first sight it appeared proud, I believe custom might prove it to be soft.

"I thank the lady very sincerely," said her father: "I fancy she has been very good to my child. I think we scarcely dare tell Mrs. Hurst who has been her substitute and done her work; she will feel at once ashamed and jealous."

And thus, in the most friendly spirit, parting greetings were interchanged; and refreshment having been hospitably offered, but by us, as it was late, refused, we withdrew from the Hôtel Crécy.

On our way back we repassed the theatre. All was silence and darkness: the roaring, rushing crowd all vanished and gone—the lamps, as well as the incipient fire, extinct and forgotten. Next morning's papers explained that it was but some loose drapery on which a spark had fallen, and which had blazed up and been quenched in a moment.

Chapter XXIV

M. DE BASSOMPIERRE

THOSE who live in retirement, whose lives have fallen amid the seclusion of schools or of other walled-in and guarded dwellings, are liable to be suddenly and for a long while dropped out of the memory of their friends, the denizens of a freer world. Unaccountably, perhaps, and close upon some space of unusually frequent intercourse—some congeries of rather exciting little circumstances, whose natural sequel would rather seem to be the quickening than the suspension of communication—there falls a stilly pause, a wordless silence, a long blank of oblivion. Unbroken always is this blank; alike entire and unexplained. The letter, the message, once frequent, are cut off; the visit, formerly periodical, ceases to occur; the book, paper, or other token that indicated remembrance, comes no more.

Always there are excellent reasons for these lapses, if the hermit but knew them. Though he is stagnant in his cell, his connections without are whirling in the very vortex of life. That void interval which passes for him so slowly that the very clocks seem at a stand, and the wingless hours plod by in the likeness of tired tramps prone to rest at milestones—that same interval, perhaps, teems with events, and pants with hurry for his friends.

The hermit—if he be a sensible hermit—will swallow his own thoughts, and lock up his own emotions during these weeks of inward winter. He will know that Destiny designed him to imitate, on occasion, the dormouse, and he will be conformable; make a tidy ball of himself, creep into a hole of life's wall, and submit decently to the drift which blows in and soon blocks him up, preserving him in ice for the season.

Let him say, "It is quite right: it ought to be so, since so it is." And, perhaps, one day his snow sepulchre will open, spring's softness will return, the sun and the south wind will reach him; the budding of hedges, and carolling of birds, and singing of liberated streams will call him to kindly resurrection. *Perhaps* this may be the case, perhaps not: the frost may get into his heart and never thaw more; when spring comes, a crow or a pie may pick out of the wall only his dormouse-bones. Well, even in that case, all will be right: it is to be supposed he knew from the first he was mortal, and must one day go the way of all flesh, "As well soon as syne."

Following that eventful evening at the theatre, came for me seven weeks as bare as seven sheets of blank paper: no word was written on one of them; not a visit, not a token.

About the middle of that time I entertained fancies that something had happened to my friends at La Terrasse. The mid-blank is always a beclouded point for the solitary: his nerves ache with the strain of long expectancy; the doubts hitherto

repelled gather now to a mass and—strong in accumulation—roll back upon him with a force which savours of vindictiveness. Night, too, becomes an unkindly time, and sleep and his nature cannot agree; strange starts and struggles harass his couch; the sinister band of bad dreams, with horror of calamity, and sick dread of entire desertion at their head, join the league against him. Poor wretch! He does his best to bear up, but he is a poor, pallid, wasting wretch, despite that best.

Towards the last of these long seven weeks I admitted, what through the other six I had jealously excluded—the conviction that these blanks were inevitable; the result of circumstances, the fiat of fate, a part of my life's lot, and—above all—a matter about whose origin no question must ever be asked, for whose painful sequence no murmur ever uttered. Of course I did not blame myself for suffering: I thank God I had a truer sense of justice than to fall into any imbecile extravagance of self-accusation; and as to blaming others for silence, in my reason I well knew them blameless, and in my heart acknowledged them so: but it was a rough and heavy road to travel, and I longed for better days.

I tried different expedients to sustain and fill existence: I commenced an elaborate piece of lace-work, I studied German pretty hard, I undertook a course of regular reading of the driest and thickest books in the library; in all my efforts I was as orthodox as I knew how to be. Was there error somewhere? Very likely. I only know the result was as if I had gnawed a file to satisfy hunger, or drank brine to quench thirst.

My hour of torment was the post-hour. Unfortunately, I knew it too well, and tried as vainly as assiduously to cheat myself of that knowledge; dreading the rack of expectation, and the sick collapse of disappointment which daily preceded and followed upon that well-recognised ring.

I suppose animals kept in cages, and so scantily fed as to be always upon the verge of famine, await their food as I awaited a letter. Oh!—to speak truth, and drop that tone of a false calm which, long to sustain, outwears nature's endurance—I underwent in those seven weeks bitter fears and pains, strange inward trials, miserable defections of hope, intolerable encroachments of despair. This last came so near me sometimes that her breath went right through me. I used to feel it like a baleful air or sigh, penetrate deep, and make motion pause at my heart, or proceed only under unspeakable oppression. The letter—the well-beloved letter—would not come; and it was all of sweetness in life I had to look for.

In the very extremity of want, I had recourse again, and yet again, to the little packet in the case—the five letters. How splendid that month seemed whose skies had beheld the rising of these five stars! It was always at night I visited them, and not daring to ask every evening for a candle in the kitchen, I bought a wax taper and matches to light it, and at the study-hour stole up to the dormitory and feasted on my crust from the Barmecide's loaf. It did not nourish me: I pined on it, and got as thin as a shadow: otherwise I was not ill.

Reading there somewhat late one evening, and feeling that the power to read was leaving me—for the letters from incessant perusal were losing all sap and significance: my gold was withering to leaves before my eyes, and I was sorrowing over the disillusion—suddenly a quick tripping foot ran up the stairs. I knew Ginevra Fanshawe's step: she had dined in town that afternoon; she was now returned, and would come here to replace her shawl, etc., in the wardrobe.

Yes: in she came, dressed in bright silk, with her shawl falling from her shoulders, and her curls, half-uncurled in the damp of night, drooping careless and heavy upon her neck. I had hardly time to re-casket my treasures and lock them up when she was at my side: her humour seemed none of the best.

"It has been a stupid evening: they are stupid people," she began.

"Who? Mrs. Cholmondeley? I thought you always found her house charming?"

"I have not been to Mrs. Cholmondeley's."

"Indeed! Have you made new acquaintance?"

"My uncle De Bassompierre is come."

"Your uncle De Bassompierre! Are you not glad?—I thought he was a favourite."

"You thought wrong: the man is odious; I hate him."

"Because he is a foreigner? or for what other reason of equal weight?"

"He is not a foreigner. The man is English enough, goodness knows; and had an English name till three or four years ago; but his mother was a foreigner, a De Bassompierre, and some of her family are dead, and have left him estates, a title, and this name: he is quite a great man now."

"Do you hate him for that reason?"

"Don't I know what mamma says about him? He is not my own uncle, but married mamma's sister. Mamma detests him; she says he killed Aunt Ginevra with unkindness: he looks like a bear. Such a dismal evening!" she went on. "I'll go no more to his big hotel. Fancy me walking into a room alone, and a great man fifty years old coming forwards, and after a few minutes' conversation actually turning his back upon me, and then abruptly going out of the room. Such odd ways! I dare say his conscience smote him, for they all say at home I am the picture of Aunt Ginevra. Mamma often declares the likeness is quite ridiculous."

"Were you the only visitor?"

"The only visitor? Yes, then there was missy, my cousin: little spoiled, pampered thing."

"M. de Bassompierre has a daughter?"

"Yes, yes: don't tease one with questions. Oh, dear! I am so tired."

She yawned. Throwing herself without ceremony on my bed, she added, "It seems Mademoiselle was nearly crushed to a jelly in a hubbub at the theatre some weeks ago."

"Ah! indeed. And they live at a large hotel in the Rue Crécy?"

"Justement. How do *you* know?"

"I have been there."

"Oh, you have? Really! You go everywhere in these days. I suppose Mother Bretton took you. She and Esculapius have the entrée of the De Bassompierre apartments: it seems 'my son John' attended missy on the occasion of her accident— Accident? Bah! All affectation! I don't think she was squeezed more than she richly deserves for her airs. And now there is quite an intimacy struck up: I heard something about 'auld lang syne,' and what not. Oh, how stupid they all were!"

"*All!* You said you were the only visitor."

"Did I? You see one forgets to particularise an old woman and her boy."

"Dr. and Mrs. Bretton were at M. de Bassompierre's this evening?"

"Ay, ay! as large as life; and missy played the hostess. What a conceited doll it is!"

Soured and listless, Miss Fanshawe was beginning to disclose the causes of her prostrate condition. There had been a retrenchment of incense, a diversion or a total withholding of homage and attention: coquetry had failed of effect, vanity had undergone mortification. She lay fuming in the vapours.

"Is Miss de Bassompierre quite well now?" I asked.

"As well as you or I, no doubt; but she is an affected little thing, and gave herself invalid airs to attract medical notice. And to see the old dowager making her recline on a couch, and 'my son John' prohibiting excitement, etcetera—faugh! the scene was quite sickening."

"It would not have been so if the object of attention had been changed: if you had taken Miss de Bassompierre's place ."

"Indeed! I hate 'my son John.' "

" 'My son John!'—whom do you indicate by that name? Dr. Bretton's mother never calls him so."

"Then she ought. A clownish, bearish John he is."

"You violate the truth in saying so; and as the whole of my patience is now spun off the distaff, I peremptorily desire you to rise from that bed, and vacate this room."

"Passionate thing! Your face is the colour of a coquelicot. I wonder what always makes you so mighty testy à l'endroit du gros Jean? 'John Anderson, my jo, John!' Oh, the distinguished name!"

Thrilling with exasperation, to which it would have been sheer folly to have given vent—for there was no contending with that unsubstantial feather, that mealy-winged moth—I extinguished my taper, locked my bureau, and left her, since she would not leave me. Small-beer as she was, she had turned insufferably acid.

The morrow was Thursday and a half-holiday. Breakfast was over; I had withdrawn to the first classe. The dreaded hour, the post-hour, was nearing, and I sat waiting it, much as a ghost-seer might wait his spectre. Less than ever was a letter probable; still, strive as I would, I could not forget that it was possible. As the moments lessened, a restlessness and fear almost beyond the average assailed me. It was a day of winter east wind, and I had now for some time entered into that dreary fellowship with the winds and their changes, so little known, so incomprehensible to the healthy. The north and east owned a terrific influence, making all pain more poignant, all sorrow sadder. The south could calm, the west sometimes cheer: unless, indeed, they brought on their wings the burden of thunder-clouds, under the weight and warmth of which all energy died.

Bitter and dark as was this January day, I remember leaving the classe and running down without bonnet to the bottom of the long garden, and then lingering amongst the stripped shrubs, in the forlorn hope that the postman's ring might occur while I was out of hearing, and I might thus be spared the thrill which some particular nerve or nerves, almost gnawed through with the unremitting tooth of a fixed idea, were becoming wholly unfit to support. I lingered as long as I dared without fear of attracting attention by my absence. I muffled my head in my apron, and stopped my ears in terror of the torturing clang, sure to be followed by such blank silence, such barren vacuum for me. At last I ventured to re-enter the first classe, where, as it was not yet nine o'clock, no pupils had been admitted. The first thing seen was a white object on my black desk, a white, flat object. The post had, indeed, arrived; by me unheard. Rosine had visited my cell, and, like some angel, had left behind her a bright token of her presence. That shining thing on the desk was indeed a letter, a real letter; I saw so much at the distance of three yards, and as I had but one correspondent on earth, from that one it must come. He remembered me yet. How deep a pulse of gratitude sent new life through my heart!

Drawing near, bending and looking on the letter, in trembling but almost certain hope of seeing a known hand, it was my lot to find, on the contrary, an autograph for the moment deemed unknown—a pale, female scrawl, instead of a firm, masculine character. I then thought fate was *too* hard for me, and I said audibly, "This is cruel."

But I got over that pain also. Life is still life, whatever its pangs: our eyes and ears and their use remain with us, though the prospect of what pleases be wholly withdrawn, and the sound of what consoles be quite silenced.

I opened the billet: by this time I had recognised the handwriting as perfectly familiar. It was dated "La Terrasse," and it ran thus:—

> "DEAR LUCY—It occurs to me to inquire what you have been doing
> with yourself for the last month or two? Not that I suspect you would
> have the least difficulty in giving an account of your proceedings. I dare
> say you have been just as busy and as happy as ourselves at La Terrasse.
> As to Graham, his professional connection extends daily: he is so much
> sought after, so much engaged, that I tell him he will grow quite conceited.
> Like a right good mother as I am, I do my best to keep him down: no

flattery does he get from me, as you know. And yet, Lucy, he is a fine fellow; his mother's heart dances at the sight of him. After being hurried here and there the whole day, and passing the ordeal of fifty sorts of tempers, and combating a hundred caprices, and sometimes witnessing cruel sufferings—perhaps, occasionally, as I tell him, inflicting them— at night he still comes home to me in such kindly, pleasant mood, that, really, I seem to live in a sort of moral antipodes, and on these January evenings my day rises when other people's night sets in.

"Still he needs keeping in order, and correcting, and repressing, and I do him that good service; but the boy is so elastic there is no such thing as vexing him thoroughly. When I think I have at last driven him to the sullens, he turns on me with jokes for retaliation: but you know him and all his iniquities, and I am but an elderly simpleton to make him the subject of this epistle.

"As for me, I have had my old Bretton agent here on a visit, and have been plunged over head and ears in business matters. I do so wish to regain for Graham at least some part of what his father left him. He laughs to scorn my anxiety on this point, bidding me look and see how he can provide for himself and me too, and asking what the old lady can possibly want that she has not; hinting about sky-blue turbans; accusing me of an ambition to wear diamonds, keep livery servants, have an hotel, and lead the fashion amongst the English clan in Villette.

"Talking of sky-blue turbans, I wish you had been with us the other evening. He had come in really tired; and after I had given him his tea, he threw himself into my chair with his customary presumption. To my great delight, he dropped asleep. (You know how he teases me about being drowsy; I, who never, by any chance, close an eye by daylight.) While he slept, I thought he looked very bonnie, Lucy: fool as I am to be proud of him; but who can help it? Show me his peer. Look where I will, I see nothing like him in Villette. Well, I took it into my head to play him a trick: so I brought out the sky-blue turban, and handling it with gingerly precaution, I managed to invest his brows with this grand adornment. I assure you it did not at all misbecome him; he looked quite Eastern, except that he is so fair. Nobody, however, can accuse him of having red hair *now*—it is genuine chestnut—a dark, glossy chestnut; and when I put my large Cashmere about him, there was as fine a young bey, dey, or pacha improvised as you would wish to see.

"It was good entertainment; but only half-enjoyed, since I was alone: *you* should have been there.

"In due time my lord awoke: the looking-glass above the fireplace soon intimated to him his plight: as you may imagine, I now live under threat and dread of vengeance.

"But to come to the gist of my letter. I know Thursday is a half-holiday in the Rue Fossette: be ready, then, by five in the afternoon, at which hour I will send the carriage to take you out to La Terrasse. Be sure to come: you may meet some old acquaintance. Good-bye, my wise, dear, grave little god-daughter.—Very truly yours,

"LOUISA BRETTON."

Now, a letter like that sets one to rights! I might still be sad after reading that letter, but I was more composed; not exactly cheered, perhaps, but relieved. My friends, at least, were well and happy: no accident had occurred to Graham; no illness had seized his mother—calamities that had so long been my dream and thought. Their feelings for me too were—as they had been. Yet, how strange it was to look on Mrs. Bretton's seven weeks and contrast them with my seven weeks!

Also, how very wise it is in people placed in an exceptional position to hold their tongues and not rashly declare how such position galls them! The world can understand well enough the process of perishing for want of food: perhaps few persons can enter into or follow out that of going mad from solitary confinement. They see the long-buried prisoner disinterred, a maniac or an idiot!—how his senses left him—how his nerves, first inflamed, underwent nameless agony, and then sunk to palsy—is a subject too intricate for examination, too abstract for popular comprehension. Speak of it! you might almost as well stand up in a European market-place and propound dark sayings in that language and mood wherein Nebuchadnezzar, the imperial hypochondriac, communed with his baffled Chaldeans. And long, long may the minds to whom such themes are no mystery—by whom their bearings are sympathetically seized—be few in number, and rare of rencounter. Long may it be generally thought that physical privations alone merit compassion, and that the rest is a figment. When the world was younger and haler than now, moral trials were a deeper mystery still: perhaps in all the land of Israel there was but one Saul—certainly but one David to soothe or comprehend him.

The keen, still cold of the morning was succeeded, later in the day, by a sharp breathing from Russian wastes: the cold zone sighed over the temperate zone, and froze it fast. A heavy firmament, dull, and thick with snow, sailed up from the north, and settled over expectant Europe. Towards afternoon began the descent. I feared no carriage would come, the white tempest raged so dense and wild. But trust my godmother! Once having asked, she would have her guest. About six o'clock I was lifted from the carriage over the already blocked-up front steps of the chateau, and put in at the door of La Terrasse.

Running through the vestibule, and upstairs to the drawing-room, there I found Mrs. Bretton—a summer-day in her own person. Had I been twice as cold as I was, her kind kiss and cordial clasp would have warmed me. Inured now for so long a time to rooms with bare boards, black benches, desks, and stoves, the blue saloon seemed to me gorgeous. In its Christmas-like fire alone there was a clear and crimson splendour which quite dazzled me.

When my godmother had held my hand for a little while, and chatted with me, and scolded me for having become thinner than when she last saw me, she professed to discover that the snow-wind had disordered my hair, and sent me upstairs to make it neat and remove my shawl.

Repairing to my own little sea-green room, there also I found a bright fire, and candles too were lit: a tall wax-light stood on each side the great looking-glass: but between the candles, and before the glass, appeared something dressing itself—an airy, fairy thing—small, slight, white—a winter spirit.

I declare for one moment I thought of Graham and his spectral illusions. With distrustful eye I noted the details of this new vision. It wore white, sprinkled slightly with drops of scarlet; its girdle was red; it had something in its hair leafy,—yet shining—a little wreath, with an evergreen gloss. Spectral or not, here truly was nothing frightful, and I advanced.

Turning quick upon me, a large eye, under long lashes, flashed over me, the intruder: the lashes were as dark as long, and they softened with their pencilling the orb they guarded.

"Ah! you are come!" she breathed out, in a soft, quiet voice, and she smiled slowly, and gazed intently.

I knew her now. Having only once seen that sort of face, with that cast of fine and delicate featuring, I could not but know her.

"Miss de Bassompierre," I pronounced.

"No," was the reply, "not Miss de Bassompierre for *you*." I did not inquire who then she might be, but waited voluntary information.

"You are changed, but still you are yourself," she said, approaching nearer. "I remember you well—your countenance, the colour of your hair, the outline of your face . . ."

I had moved to the fire, and she stood opposite, and gazed into me; and as she gazed, her face became gradually more and more expressive of thought and feeling, till at last a dimness quenched her clear vision.

"It makes me almost cry to look so far back," said she; "but as to being sorry, or sentimental, don't think it: on the contrary, I am quite pleased and glad."

Interested, yet altogether at fault, I knew not what to say. At last I stammered, "I think I never met you till that night, some weeks ago, when you were hurt . . .?"

She smiled. "You have forgotten then that I have sat on your knee, been lifted in your arms, even shared your pillow? You no longer remember the night when I came crying, like a naughty little child as I was, to your bedside, and you took me in? You have no memory for the comfort and protection by which you soothed an acute distress? Go back to Bretton. Remember Mr. Home."

At last I saw it all. "And you are little Polly?"

"I am Paulina Mary Home de Bassompierre."

How time can change! Little Polly wore in her pale, small features, her fairy symmetry, her varying expression, a certain promise of interest and grace; but Paulina Mary was become beautiful—not with the beauty that strikes the eye like a rose—orbed, ruddy, and replete; not with the plump, and pink, and flaxen attributes of her blonde cousin Ginevra; but her seventeen years had brought her a refined and tender charm which did not lie in complexion, though hers was fair and clear; nor in outline, though her features were sweet, and her limbs perfectly turned; but, I think, rather in a subdued glow from the soul outward. This was not an opaque vase, of material however costly, but a lamp chastely lucent, guarding from extinction, yet not hiding from worship, a flame vital and vestal. In speaking of her attractions, I would not exaggerate language; but, indeed, they seemed to me very real and engaging. What though all was on a small scale, it was the perfume which gave this white violet distinction, and made it superior to the broadest camellia—the fullest dahlia that ever bloomed.

"Ah! and you remember the old time at Bretton?"

"Better," she said, "better, perhaps, than you. I remember it with minute distinctness: not only the time, but the days of the time, and the hours of the days."

"You must have forgotten some things?"

"Very little, I imagine."

"You were then a little creature of quick feelings: you must, long ere this, have outgrown the impressions with which joy and grief, affection and bereavement, stamped your mind ten years ago?"

"You think I have forgotten whom I liked, and in what degree I liked them when a child?"

"The sharpness must be gone—the point, the poignancy—the deep imprint must be softened away and effaced?"

"I have a good memory for those days."

She looked as if she had. Her eyes were the eyes of one who can remember; one whose childhood does not fade like a dream, nor whose youth vanish like a sunbeam. She would not take life, loosely and incoherently, in parts, and let one season slip as she entered on another: she would retain and add; often review from the commencement, and so grow in harmony and consistency as she grew in years. Still I could not quite admit the conviction that *all* the pictures which now crowded upon me were vivid and visible to her. Her fond attachments, her sports and contests with a well-loved playmate, the patient, true devotion of her child's heart, her fears, her delicate reserves, her little trials, the last piercing pain of separation. . . . I retraced these things, and shook my head incredulous. She persisted. "The child of seven years lives yet in the girl of seventeen," said she.

"You used to be excessively fond of Mrs. Bretton," I remarked, intending to test her. She set me right at once.

"Not *excessively* fond," said she; "I liked her: I respected her, as I should do now: she seems to me very little altered."

"She is not much changed," I assented.

We were silent a few minutes. Glancing round the room, she said—

"There are several things here that used to be at Bretton. I remember that pincushion and that looking-glass."

Evidently she was not deceived in her estimate of her own memory; not, at least, so far.

"You think, then, you would have known Mrs. Bretton?" I went on.

"I perfectly remembered her; the turn of her features, her olive complexion and black hair, her height, her walk, her voice."

"Dr. Bretton, of course," I pursued, "would be out of the question: and, indeed, as I saw your first interview with him, I am aware that he appeared to you as a stranger."

"That first night I was puzzled," she answered.

"How did the recognition between him and your father come about?"

"They exchanged cards. The names Graham Bretton and Home de Bassompierre gave rise to questions and explanations. That was on the second day; but before then I was beginning to know something."

"How—know something?"

"Why," she said, "how strange it is that most people seem so slow to feel the truth—not to see, but *feel*! When Dr. Bretton had visited me a few times, and sat near and talked to me; when I had observed the look in his eyes, the expression about his mouth, the form of his chin, the carriage of his head, and all that we *do* observe in persons who approach us—how could I avoid being led by association to think of Graham Bretton? Graham was slighter than he, and not grown so tall, and had a smoother face, and longer and lighter hair, and spoke—not so deeply— more like a girl; but yet *he* is Graham, just as *I* am little Polly, or you are Lucy Snowe."

I thought the same, but I wondered to find my thoughts hers: there are certain things in which we so rarely meet with our double that it seems a miracle when that chance befalls.

"You and Graham were once playmates."

"And do you remember that?" she questioned in her turn.

"No doubt he will remember it also," said I.

"I have not asked him: few things would surprise me so much as to find that he did. I suppose his disposition is still gay and careless?"

"Was it so formerly? Did it so strike you? Do you thus remember him?"

"I scarcely remember him in any other light. Sometimes he was studious; sometimes he was merry: but whether busy with his books or disposed to play, it was chiefly the books or game he thought of; not much heeding those with whom he read or amused himself."

"Yet to you he was partial."

"Partial to me? Oh, no! he had other playmates—his schoolfellows; I was of little consequence to him, except on Sundays: yes, he was kind on Sundays. I remember walking with him hand in hand to St. Mary's, and his finding the places in my prayer-book; and how good and still he was on Sunday evenings! So mild for such a proud, lively boy; so patient with all my blunders in reading; and so wonderfully to be depended on, for he never spent those evenings from home. I had a constant fear that he would accept some invitation and forsake us; but he never did, nor seemed ever to wish to do it. Thus, of course, it can be no more. I suppose Sunday will now be Dr. Bretton's dining-out day . . .?"

"Children, come down!" here called Mrs. Bretton from below. Paulina would still have lingered, but I inclined to descend: we went down.

Chapter XXV
THE LITTLE COUNTESS

CHEERFUL as my godmother naturally was, and entertaining as, for our sakes, she made a point of being, there was no true enjoyment that evening at La Terrasse, till, through the wild howl of the winter night, were heard the signal sounds of arrival. How often, while women and girls sit warm at snug firesides, their hearts and imaginations are doomed to divorce from the comfort surrounding their persons, forced out by night to wander through dark ways, to dare stress of weather, to contend with the snow-blast, to wait at lonely gates and stiles in wildest storms, watching and listening to see and hear the father, the son, the husband coming home.

Father and son came at last to the chateau: for the Count de Bassompierre that night accompanied Dr. Bretton. I know not which of our trio heard the horses first; the asperity, the violence of the weather warranted our running down into the hall to meet and greet the two riders as they came in; but they warned us to keep our distance: both were white—two mountains of snow; and indeed Mrs. Bretton, seeing their condition, ordered them instantly to the kitchen; prohibiting them, at their peril, from setting foot on her carpeted staircase till they had severally put off that mask of old Christmas they now affected. Into the kitchen, however, we could not help following them; it was a large old Dutch kitchen, picturesque and pleasant. The little white Countess danced in a circle about her equally white sire, clapping her hands and crying—

"Papa, papa, you look like an enormous Polar bear."

The bear shook himself, and the little sprite fled far from the frozen shower. Back she came, however, laughing, and eager to aid in removing the arctic disguise. The Count, at last issuing from his dreadnought, threatened to overwhelm her with it as an avalanche.

"Come, then," said she, bending to invite the fall, and when it was playfully advanced above her head, bounding out of reach like some little chamois.

Her movements had the supple softness, the velvet grace of a kitten; her laugh was clearer than the ring of silver and crystal; as she took her sire's cold hands and rubbed them, and stood on tiptoe to reach his lips for a kiss, there seemed to shine round her a halo of loving delight. The grave and reverend signior looked down on her as men *do* look on what is the apple of their eye.

"Mrs. Bretton," said he: "what am I to do with this daughter or daughterling of mine? She neither grows in wisdom nor in stature. Don't you find her pretty nearly as much the child as she was ten years ago?"

"She cannot be more the child than this great boy of mine," said Mrs. Bretton, who was in conflict with her son about some change of dress she deemed advisable, and which he resisted. He stood leaning against the Dutch dresser, laughing and keeping her at arm's length.

"Come, mamma," said he, "by way of compromise, and to secure for us inward as well as outward warmth, let us have a Christmas wassail-cup, and toast Old England here, on the hearth."

So, while the Count stood by the fire, and Paulina Mary still danced to and fro—happy in the liberty of the wide hall-like kitchen—Mrs. Bretton herself instructed Martha to spice and heat the wassail-bowl, and, pouring the draught into a Bretton flagon, it was served round, steaming hot, by means of a small silver vessel, which I recognised as Graham's christening-cup.

"Here's to Auld Lang Syne!" said the Count; holding the glancing cup on high. Then, looking at Mrs. Bretton—

> "We twa ha' paidlet i' the burn
> Fra morning sun till dine,
> But seas between us braid ha' roared
> Sin' auld lang syne.

> "And surely ye'll be your pint-stoup,
> And surely I'll be mine;
> And we'll taste a cup o' kindness
> For auld lang syne."

"Scotch! Scotch!" cried Paulina; "papa is talking Scotch: and Scotch he is, partly. We are Home and De Bassompierre, Caledonian and Gallic."

"And is that a Scotch reel you are dancing, you Highland fairy?" asked her father. "Mrs. Bretton, there will be a green ring growing up in the middle of your kitchen shortly. I would not answer for her being quite cannie: she is a strange little mortal."

"Tell Lucy to dance with me, papa; there is Lucy Snowe."

Mr. Home (there was still quite as much about him of plain Mr. Home as of proud Count de Bassompierre) held his hand out to me, saying kindly, "he remembered me well; and, even had his own memory been less trustworthy, my name was so often on his daughter's lips, and he had listened to so many long tales about me, I should seem like an old acquaintance."

Every one now had tasted the wassail-cup except Paulina, whose pas de fée, ou de fantaisie, nobody thought of interrupting to offer so profanatory a draught; but she was not to be overlooked, nor baulked of her mortal privileges.

"Let me taste," said she to Graham, as he was putting the cup on the shelf of the dresser out of her reach.

Mrs. Bretton and Mr. Home were now engaged in conversation. Dr. John had not been unobservant of the fairy's dance; he had watched it, and he had liked it. To say nothing of the softness and beauty of the movements, eminently grateful to his grace-loving eye, that ease in his mother's house charmed him, for it set *him* at ease: again she seemed a child for him—again, almost his playmate. I wondered how he would speak to her; I had not yet seen him address her; his first words proved that the old days of "little Polly" had been recalled to his mind by this evening's childlike light-heartedness.

"Your ladyship wishes for the tankard?"

"I think I said so. I think I intimated as much."

"Couldn't consent to a step of the kind on any account. Sorry for it, but couldn't do it."

"Why? I am quite well now: it can't break my collar-bone again, or dislocate my shoulder. Is it wine?"

"No; nor dew."

"I don't want dew; I don't like dew: but what is it?"

"Ale—strong ale—old October; brewed, perhaps, when I was born."

"It must be curious: is it good?"

"Excessively good."

And he took it down, administered to himself a second dose of this mighty elixir, expressed in his mischievous eyes extreme contentment with the same, and solemnly replaced the cup on the shelf.

"I should like a little," said Paulina, looking up; "I never had any 'old October'; is it sweet?"

"Perilously sweet," said Graham.

She continued to look up exactly with the countenance of a child that longs for some prohibited dainty. At last the doctor relented, took it down, and indulged himself in the gratification of letting her taste from his hand; his eyes, always expressive in the revelation of pleasurable feelings, luminously and smilingly avowed that it *was* a gratification; and he prolonged it by so regulating the position of the cup that only a drop at a time could reach the rosy, sipping lips by which its brim was courted.

"A little more—a little more," said she, petulantly touching his hand with the forefinger, to make him incline the cup more generously and yieldingly. "It smells of spice and sugar, but I can't taste it; your wrist is so stiff, and you are so stingy."

He indulged her, whispering, however, with gravity—"Don't tell my mother or Lucy: they wouldn't approve."

"Nor do I," said she, passing into another tone and manner as soon as she had fairly assayed the beverage, just as if it had acted upon her like some disenchanting draught, undoing the work of a wizard: "I find it anything but sweet; it is bitter and hot, and takes away my breath. Your 'old October' was only desirable while forbidden. Thank you, no more."

And with a slight bend—careless, but as graceful as her dance—she glided from him and rejoined her father.

I think she had spoken truth: the child of seven was in the girl of seventeen.

Graham looked after her a little baffled, a little puzzled; his eye was on her a good deal during the rest of the evening, but she did not seem to notice him.

As we ascended to the drawing-room for tea, she took her father's arm: her natural place seemed to be at his side; her eyes and her ears were dedicated to him. He and Mrs. Bretton were the chief talkers of our little party, and Paulina was their best listener, attending closely to all that was said, prompting the repetition of this or that trait or adventure.

"And where were you at such a time, papa? And what did you say then? And tell Mrs. Bretton what happened on that occasion." Thus she drew him out.

She did not again yield to any effervescence of glee; the infantine sparkle was exhaled for the night: she was soft, thoughtful, and docile. It was pretty to see her bid good-night; her manner to Graham was touched with dignity: in her very slight smile and quiet bow spoke the Countess, and Graham could not but look grave, and bend responsive. I saw he hardly knew how to blend together in his ideas the dancing fairy and delicate dame.

Next day, when we were all assembled round the breakfast table, shivering and fresh from the morning's chill ablutions, Mrs. Bretton pronounced a decree that nobody, who was not forced by dire necessity, should quit her house that day.

Indeed, egress seemed next to impossible; the drift darkened the lower panes of the casement, and on looking out, one saw the sky and air vexed and dim, the wind and snow in angry conflict. There was no fall now, but what had already descended was torn up from the earth, whirled round by brief shrieking gusts, and cast into a hundred fantastic forms.

The Countess seconded Mrs. Bretton.

"Papa shall not go out," said she, placing a seat for herself beside her father's arm-chair. "I will look after him. You won't go into town, will you, papa?"

"Ay and No," was the answer. "If you and Mrs. Bretton are *very* good to me, Polly—kind, you know, and attentive; if you pet me in a very nice manner, and make much of me, I may possibly be induced to wait an hour after breakfast and see whether the razor-edged wind settles. But, you see, you give me no breakfast; you offer me nothing: you let me starve."

"Quick! please, Mrs. Bretton, and pour out the coffee," entreated Paulina, "whilst I take care of the Count de Bassompierre in other respects: since he grew into a Count, he has needed *so* much attention."

She separated and prepared a roll.

"There, papa, are your 'pistolets' charged," said she. "And there is some marmalade, just the same sort of marmalade we used to have at Bretton, and which you said was as good as if it had been conserved in Scotland"——

"And which your little ladyship used to beg for my boy—do you remember that?" interposed Mrs. Bretton. "Have you forgotten how you would come to my elbow and touch my sleeve with the whisper, 'Please, ma'am, something good for Graham—a little marmalade, or honey, or jam'?"

"No, mamma," broke in Dr. John, laughing, yet reddening; "it surely was not so: I could not have cared for these things."

"Did he or did he not, Paulina?"

"He liked them," asserted Paulina.

"Never blush for it, John," said Mr. Home encouragingly. "I like them myself yet, and always did. And Polly showed her sense in catering for a friend's material comforts: it was I who put her into the way of such good manners—nor do I let her forget them. Polly, offer me a small slice of that tongue."

"There, papa: but remember you are only waited upon with this assiduity on condition of being persuadable and reconciling yourself to La Terrasse for the day."

"Mrs. Bretton," said the Count, "I want to get rid of my daughter—to send her to school. Do you know of any good school?"

"There is Lucy's place—Madame Beck's."

"Miss Snowe is in a school?"

"I am a teacher," I said, and was rather glad of the opportunity of saying this. For a little while I had been feeling as if placed in a false position. Mrs. Bretton and son knew my circumstances; but the Count and his daughter did not. They might choose to vary by some shades their hitherto cordial manner towards me, when aware of my grade in society. I spoke them readily: but a swarm of thoughts I had not anticipated nor invoked rose dim at the words, making me sigh involuntarily. Mr. Home did not lift his eyes from his breakfast-plate for about two minutes, nor did he speak; perhaps he had not caught the words—perhaps he thought that on a confession of that nature politeness would interdict comment: the Scotch are proverbially proud; and homely as was Mr. Home in look, simple in habits and tastes, I have all along intimated that he was not without his share of the national quality. Was his a pseudo-pride? was it real dignity? I leave the question undecided in its wide sense. Where it concerned me individually I can only answer: then, and always, he showed himself a true-hearted gentleman.

By nature he was a feeler and a thinker; over his emotions and his reflections spread a mellowing of melancholy; more than a mellowing: in trouble and bereavement it became a cloud. He did not know much about Lucy Snowe; what he knew, he did not very accurately comprehend: indeed, his misconceptions of my character often made me smile; but he saw my walk in life lay rather on the shady side of the hill; he gave me credit for doing my endeavour to keep the course honestly straight; he would have helped me if he could: having no opportunity of helping, he still wished me well. When he did look at me, his eye was kind; when he did speak, his voice was benevolent.

"Yours," said he, "is an arduous calling. I wish you health and strength to win in it—success."

His fair little daughter did not take the information quite so composedly: she fixed on me a pair of eyes wide with wonder—almost with dismay.

"Are you a teacher?" cried she. Then, having paused on the unpalatable idea, "Well, I never knew what you were, nor ever thought of asking: for me, you were always Lucy Snowe."

"And what am I now?" I could not forbear inquiring.

"Yourself, of course. But do you really teach here, in Villette?"

"I really do."

"And do you like it?"

"Not always."

"And why do you go on with it?"

Her father looked at, and, I feared, was going to check her; but he only said, "Proceed, Polly, proceed with that catechism—prove yourself the little wiseacre you are. If Miss Snowe were to blush and look confused, I should have to bid you hold your tongue; and you and I would sit out the present meal in some disgrace; but she only smiles, so push her hard, multiply the cross-questions. Well, Miss Snowe, why do you go on with it?"

"Chiefly, I fear, for the sake of the money I get."

"Not then from motives of pure philanthropy? Polly and I were clinging to that hypothesis as the most lenient way of accounting for your eccentricity."

"No—no, sir. Rather for the roof of shelter I am thus enabled to keep over my head; and for the comfort of mind it gives me to think that while I can work for myself, I am spared the pain of being a burden to anybody."

"Papa, say what you will, I pity Lucy."

"Take up that pity, Miss de Bassompierre; take it up in both hands, as you might a little callow gosling squattering out of bounds without leave; put it back in the warm nest of a heart whence it issued, and receive in your ear this whisper—If my Polly ever came to know by experience the uncertain nature of this world's goods, I should like her to act as Lucy acts: to work for herself, that she might burden neither kith nor kin."

"Yes, papa," said she, pensively and tractably. "But poor Lucy! I thought she was a rich lady, and had rich friends."

"You thought like a little simpleton. *I* never thought so. When I had time to consider Lucy's manner and aspect, which was not often, I saw she was one who had to guard and not be guarded; to act and not be served: and this lot has, I imagine, helped her to an experience for which, if she live long enough to realise its full benefit, she may yet bless Providence. But this school," he pursued, changing his tone from grave to gay: "Would Madame Beck admit my Polly, do you think, Miss Lucy?"

I said there needed but to try Madame; it would soon be seen: she was fond of English pupils. "If you, sir," I added, "will but take Miss de Bassompierre in your carriage this very afternoon, I think I can answer for it that Rosine, the portress, will not be very slow in answering your ring; and Madame, I am sure, will put on her best pair of gloves to come into the salon to receive you."

"In that case," responded Mr. Home, "I see no sort of necessity there is for delay. Mrs. Hurst can send what she calls her young lady's 'things' after her; Polly can settle down to her horn-book before night; and you, Miss Lucy, I trust, will not disdain to cast an occasional eye upon her, and let me know, from time to time, how she gets on. I hope you approve of the arrangement, Countess de Bassompierre?"

The Countess hemmed and hesitated. "I thought," said she, "I thought I had finished my education"——

"That only proves how much we may be mistaken in our thoughts: I hold a far different opinion, as most of these will who have been auditors of your profound knowledge of life this morning. Ah, my little girl, thou hast much to learn; and papa ought to have taught thee more than he has done! Come, there is nothing for it but to try Madame Beck; and the weather seems settling, and I have finished my breakfast"——

"But, papa!"

"Well?"

"I see an obstacle."

"I don't at all."

"It is enormous, papa; it can never be got over; it is as large as you in your greatcoat, and the snowdrift on the top."

"And, like that snowdrift, capable of melting?"

"No! it is of too, too solid flesh: it is just your own self. Miss Lucy, warn Madame Beck not to listen to any overtures about taking me, because in the end it would turn out that she would have to take papa too: as he is so teasing, I will just tell tales about him. Mrs. Bretton and all of you listen: About five years ago, when I was twelve years old, he took it into his head that he was spoiling me; that I was growing unfitted for the world, and I don't know what, and nothing would serve or satisfy him but I must go to school. I cried, and so on; but M. de Bassompierre proved hard-hearted, quite firm and flinty, and to school I went. What was the result? In the most admirable manner, papa came to school likewise; every other day he called to see me. Madame Aigredoux grumbled, but it was of no use; and so, at last, papa and I were both, in a manner, expelled. Lucy can just tell Madame Beck this little trait: it is only fair to let her know what she has to expect."

Mrs. Bretton asked Mr. Home what he had to say in answer to this statement. As he made no defence, judgment was given against him, and Paulina triumphed.

But she had other moods besides the arch and naïve. After breakfast, when the two elders withdrew—I suppose to talk over certain of Mrs. Bretton's business matters—and the Countess, Dr. Bretton, and I were for a short time alone together, all the child left her; with us, more nearly her companions in age, she rose at once to the little lady: her very face seemed to alter; that play of feature and candour of look which, when she spoke to her father, made it quite dimpled and round, yielded to an aspect more thoughtful, and lines distincter and less mobile.

No doubt Graham noted the change as well as I. He stood for some minutes near the window, looking out at the snow; presently he approached the hearth, and entered into conversation, but not quite with his usual ease: fit topics did not seem to rise to his lips; he chose them fastidiously, hesitatingly, and consequently infelicitously: he spoke vaguely of Villette—its inhabitants, its notable sights and buildings. He was answered by Miss de Bassompierre in quite womanly sort; with intelligence, with a manner not indeed wholly disindividualised: a tone, a glance, a gesture, here and there, rather animated and quick than measured and stately, still recalled little Polly; but yet there was so fine and even a polish, so calm and courteous a grace, gilding and sustaining these peculiarities, that a less sensitive man than Graham would not have ventured to seize upon them as vantage points leading to franker intimacy.

Yet while Dr. Bretton continued subdued, and, for him, sedate, he was still observant. Not one of those petty impulses and natural breaks escaped him. He did not miss one characteristic movement, one hesitation in language, or one lisp in utterance. At times, in speaking fast, she still lisped; but coloured whenever such lapse occurred, and in a painstaking, conscientious manner, quite as amusing as the slight error, repeated the word more distinctly.

Whenever she did this, Dr. Bretton smiled. Gradually, as they conversed, the restraint on each side slackened: might the conference have but been prolonged, I believe it would soon have become genial: already to Paulina's lip and cheek returned the wreathing, dimpling smile; she lisped once, and forgot to correct herself. And Dr. John, I know not how *he* changed, but change he did. He did not grow gayer—no raillery, no levity sparkled across his aspect—but his position seemed to become one of more pleasure to himself, and he spoke his augmented comfort in readier language, in tones more suave. Ten years ago this pair had always found abundance to say to each other; the intervening decade had not narrowed the experience or impoverished the intelligence of either: besides, there are certain natures of which the mutual influence is such that the more they say, the more they have to say. For these, out of association grows adhesion, and out of adhesion amalgamation.

Graham, however, must go: his was a profession whose claims had neither to be ignored nor deferred. He left the room: but before he could leave the house

there was a return. I am sure he came back—not for the paper, or card in his desk, which formed his ostensible errand—but to assure himself, by one more glance, that Paulina's aspect was really such as memory was bearing away: that he had not been viewing her somehow by a partial, artificial light, and making a fond mistake. No! he found the impression true—rather, indeed, he gained than lost by this return: he took away with him a parting look—shy, but very soft—as beautiful, as innocent, as any little fawn could lift out of its cover of fern, or any lamb from its meadow-bed.

Being left alone, Paulina and I kept silence for some time; we both took out some work, and plied a mute and diligent task. The whitewood work-box of old days was now replaced by one inlaid with precious mosaic, and furnished with implements of gold; the tiny and trembling fingers that could scarce guide the needle, though tiny still, were now swift and skilful: but there was the same busy knitting of the brow, the same little dainty mannerisms, the same quick turns and movements—now to replace a stray tress, and anon to shake from the silken skirt some imaginary atom of dust—some clinging fibre of thread.

That morning I was disposed for silence: the austere fury of the winter day had on me an awing, hushing influence. That passion of January, so white and so bloodless, was not yet spent: the storm had raved itself hoarse, but seemed no nearer exhaustion. Had Ginevra Fanshawe been my companion in that drawing-room, she would not have suffered me to muse and listen undisturbed. The presence just gone from us would have been her theme; and how she would have rung the changes on one topic! how she would have pursued and pestered me with questions and surmises—worried and oppressed me with comments and confidences I did not want, and longed to avoid.

Paulina Mary cast once or twice towards me a quiet but penetrating glance of her dark, full eye; her lips half opened, as if to the impulse of coming utterance: but she saw and delicately respected my inclination for silence.

"This will not hold long," I thought to myself; for I was not accustomed to find in women or girls any power of self-control, or strength of self-denial. As far as I knew them, the chance of a gossip about their usually trivial secrets, their often very washy and paltry feelings, was a treat not to be readily forgone.

The little Countess promised an exception: she sewed till she was tired of sewing, and then she took a book.

As chance would have it, she had sought it in Dr. Bretton's own compartment of the bookcase; and it proved to be an old Bretton book—some illustrated work of natural history. Often had I seen her standing at Graham's side, resting that volume on his knee, and reading to his tuition; and, when the lesson was over, begging, as a treat, that he would tell her all about the pictures. I watched her keenly: here was a true test of that memory she had boasted: would her recollections now be faithful?

Faithful? It could not be doubted. As she turned the leaves, over her face passed gleam after gleam of expression, the least intelligent of which was a full greeting to the Past. And then she turned to the title-page, and looked at the name written in the schoolboy hand. She looked at it long; nor was she satisfied with merely looking; she gently passed over the characters the tips of her fingers, accompanying the action with an unconscious but tender smile, which converted the touch into a caress. Paulina loved the Past; but the peculiarity of this little scene was that she *said* nothing: she could feel without pouring out her feelings in a flux of words.

She now occupied herself at the bookcase for nearly an hour; taking down volume after volume, and renewing her acquaintance with each. This done, she seated herself on a low stool, rested her cheek on her hand, and thought, and still was mute.

The sound of the front door opened below, a rush of cold wind, and her father's voice speaking to Mrs. Bretton in the hall, startled her at last. She sprang up: she was downstairs in one second.

"Papa! papa! you are not going out?"

"My pet; I must go into town."

"But it is too—*too* cold, papa."

And then I heard M. de Bassompierre showing to her how he was well provided against the weather; and how he was going to have the carriage, and to be quite snugly sheltered; and, in short, proving that she need not fear for his comfort.

"But you will promise to come back here this evening before it is quite dark—you and Dr. Bretton, both in the carriage? It is not fit to ride."

"Well, if I see the Doctor, I will tell him a lady has laid on him her commands to take care of his precious health and come home early under my escort."

"Yes, you must say a lady; and he will think it is his mother, and be obedient. And, papa, mind to come soon, for I *shall* watch and listen."

The door closed, and the carriage rolled softly through the snow; and back returned the Countess, pensive and anxious.

She *did* listen, and watch, when evening closed; but it was in stillest sort: walking the drawing-room with quite noiseless step. She checked at intervals her velvet march; inclined her ear, and consulted the night sounds: I should rather say, the night silence; for now, at last, the wind was fallen. The sky, relieved of its avalanche, lay naked and pale: through the barren boughs of the avenue we could see it well, and note also the polar splendour of the new-year moon—an orb white as a world of ice. Nor was it late when we saw also the return of the carriage.

Paulina had no dance of welcome for this evening. It was with a sort of gravity that she took immediate possession of her father as he entered the room; but she at once made him her entire property, led him to the seat of her choice, and, while softly showering round him honeyed words of commendation for being so good and coming home so soon, you would have thought it was entirely by the power of her little hands he was put into his chair, and settled and arranged; for the strong man seemed to take pleasure in wholly yielding himself to this dominion—potent only by love.

Graham did not appear till some minutes after the Count. Paulina half turned when his step was heard: they spoke, but only a word or two; their fingers met a moment, but obviously with slight contact. Paulina remained beside her father; Graham threw himself into a seat on the other side of the room.

It was well that Mrs. Bretton and Mr. Home had a great deal to say to each other—almost an inexhaustible fund of discourse in old recollections; otherwise, I think, our party would have been but a still one that evening.

After tea, Paulina's quick needle and pretty golden thimble were busily plied by the lamplight, but her tongue rested, and her eyes seemed reluctant to raise often their lids so smooth and so full-fringed. Graham, too, must have been tired with his day's work: he listened dutifully to his elders and betters, said very little himself, and followed with his eye the gilded glance of Paulina's thimble, as if it had been some bright moth on the wing, or the golden head of some darting little yellow serpent.

Chapter XXVI

A BURIAL

FROM this date my life did not want variety; I went out a good deal, with the entire consent of Madame Beck, who perfectly approved the grade of my acquaintance.

That worthy directress had never from the first treated me otherwise than with respect; and when she found that I was liable to frequent invitations from a chateau and a great hotel, respect improved into distinction.

Not that she was fulsome about it: Madame, in all things worldly, was in nothing weak; there was measure and sense in her hottest pursuit of self-interest, calm and considerateness in her closest clutch of gain; without, then, laying herself open to my contempt as a time-server and a toady, she marked with tact that she was pleased people connected with her establishment should frequent such associates as must cultivate and elevate, rather than those who might deteriorate and depress. She never praised either me or my friends; only once when she was sitting in the sun in the garden, a cup of coffee at her elbow and the *Gazette* in her hand, looking very comfortable, and I came up and asked leave of absence for the evening, she delivered herself in this gracious sort:—

"Oui, oui, ma bonne amie: je vous donne la permission de cœur et de gré. Votre travail dans ma maison a toujours été admirable, rempli de zèle et de discrétion: vous avez bien le droit de vous amuser. Sortez donc tant que vous voudrez. Quant à votre choix de connaissances, j'en suis contente; c'est sage, digne, louable."

She closed her lips, and resumed the *Gazette*.

The reader will not too gravely regard the little circumstance that about this time the triply-enclosed packet of five letters temporarily disappeared from my bureau. Blank dismay was naturally my first sensation on making the discovery; but in a moment I took heart of grace.

"Patience!" whispered I to myself. "Let me say nothing, but wait peaceably; they will come back again."

And they did come back: they had only been on a short visit to Madame's chamber; having passed their examination, they came back duly and truly: I found them all right the next day.

I wonder what she thought of my correspondence? What estimate did she form of Dr. John Bretton's epistolary powers? In what light did the often very pithy thoughts, the generally sound, and sometimes original, opinions set, without pretension, in an easily-flowing, spirited style, appear to her? How did she like that genial, half-humorous vein, which to me gave such delight? What did she think of the few kind words scattered here and there—not thickly, as the diamonds were scattered in the valley of Sindbad, but sparely, as those gems lie in unfabled beds? Oh, Madame Beck! how seemed these things to you?

I think in Madame Beck's eyes the five letters found a certain favour. One day after she had *borrowed* them of me (in speaking of so suave a little woman, one ought to use suave terms), I caught her examining me with a steady contemplative gaze, a little puzzled, but not at all malevolent. It was during that brief space between lessons, when the pupils turned out into the court for a quarter of an hour's recreation; she and I remained in the first classe alone: when I met her eye, her thoughts forced themselves partially through her lips.

"Il y a," said she, "quelquechose de bien remarquable dans le caractère Anglais."

"How, Madame?"

She gave a little laugh, repeating the word "how" in English.

"Je ne saurais vous dire 'how'; mais, enfin, les Anglais ont des idées à eux, en amitié, en amour, en tout. Mais au moins il n'est pas besoin de les surveiller," she added, getting up and trotting away like the compact little pony she was.

"Then I hope," murmured I to myself, "you will graciously let alone my letters for the future."

Alas! something came rushing into my eyes, dimming utterly their vision, blotting from sight the schoolroom, the garden, the bright winter sun, as I remembered that never more would letters such as she had read come to me. I had seen the last of them. That goodly river, on whose banks I had sojourned, of whose waves a few

reviving drops had trickled to my lips, was bending to another course: it was leaving my little hut and field forlorn and sand-dry, pouring its wealth of waters far away. The change was right, just, natural; not a word could be said: but I loved my Rhine, my Nile; I had almost worshipped my Ganges, and I grieved that the grand tide should roll estranged, should vanish like a false mirage. Though stoical, I was not quite a Stoic; drops streamed fast on my hands, on my desk: I wept one sultry shower, heavy and brief.

But soon I said to myself, "The Hope I am bemoaning suffered and made me suffer much: it did not die till it was full time; following an agony so lingering, death ought to be welcome."

Welcome I endeavoured to make it. Indeed, long pain had made patience a habit. In the end I closed the eyes of my dead, covered its face, and composed its limbs with great calm.

The letters, however, must be put away, out of sight: people who have undergone bereavement always jealously gather together and lock away mementos: it is not supportable to be stabbed to the heart each moment by sharp revival of regret.

One vacant holiday afternoon (the Thursday), going to my treasure with intent to consider its final disposal, I perceived—and this time with a strong impulse of displeasure—that it had been again tampered with: the packet was there, indeed, but the ribbon which secured it had been untied and retied; and by other symptoms I knew that my drawer had been visited.

This was a little too much. Madame Beck herself was the soul of discretion, besides having as strong a brain and sound a judgment as ever furnished a human head; that she should know the contents of my casket was not pleasant, but might be borne. Little Jesuit inquisitress as she was, she could see things in a true light, and understand them in an unperverted sense; but the idea that she had ventured to communicate information thus gained to others; that she had, perhaps, amused herself with a companion over documents in my eyes most sacred, shocked me cruelly. Yet that such was the case I now saw reason to fear; I even guessed her confidant. Her kinsman, M. Paul Emanuel, had spent yesterday evening with her: she was much in the habit of consulting him, and of discussing with him matters she broached to no one else. This very morning, in class, that gentleman had favoured me with a glance which he seemed to have borrowed from Vashti, the actress; I had not at the moment comprehended that blue, yet lurid, flash out of his angry eye, but I read its meaning now. *He*, I believed, was not apt to regard what concerned me from a fair point of view, nor to judge me with tolerance and candour: I had always found him severe and suspicious: the thought that these letters, mere friendly letters as they were, had fallen once, and might fall again, into his hands, jarred my very soul.

What should I do to prevent this? In what corner of this strange house was it possible to find security or secrecy? Where could a key be a safeguard, or a padlock a barrier?

In the grenier? No, I did not like the grenier. Besides, most of the boxes and drawers there were mouldering, and did not lock. Rats, too, gnawed their way through the decayed wood; and mice made nests amongst the litter of their contents: my dear letters (most dear still, though Ichabod was written on their covers) might be consumed by vermin; certainly the writing would soon become obliterated by damp. No; the grenier would not do—but where then!

While pondering this problem, I sat in the dormitory window-seat. It was a fine frosty afternoon; the winter sun, already setting, gleamed pale on the tops of the garden-shrubs in the "allée défendue." One great old pear-tree—the nun's pear-tree—stood up, a tall Dryad skeleton, grey, gaunt, and stripped. A thought struck me—one of those queer fantastic thoughts that will sometimes strike solitary people. I put on my bonnet, cloak and furs, and went out into the city.

Bending my steps to the old historical quarter of the town, whose hoary and overshadowed precincts I always sought by instinct in melancholy moods, I wandered on from street to street, till, having crossed a half-deserted "place" or square, I found myself before a sort of broker's shop; an ancient place, full of ancient things.

What I wanted was a metal box which might be soldered, or a thick glass jar or bottle which might be stoppered or sealed hermetically. Amongst miscellaneous heaps I found and purchased the latter article.

I then made a little roll of my letters, wrapped them in oiled silk, bound them with twine, and, having put them in the bottle, got the old Jew broker to stopper, seal, and make it airtight. While obeying my directions, he glanced at me now and then suspiciously from under his frost-white eyelashes. I believe he thought there was some evil deed on hand. In all this I had a dreary something—not pleasure—but a sad, lonely satisfaction. The impulse under which I acted, the mood controlling me, were similar to the impulse and the mood which had induced me to visit the confessional. With quick walking I regained the pensionnat just at dark, and in time for dinner.

At seven o'clock the moon rose. At half-past seven, when the pupils and teachers were at study, and Madame Beck was with her mother and children in the salle-à-manger, when the half-boarders were all gone home, and Rosine had left the vestibule, and all was still—I shawled myself, and, taking the sealed jar, stole out through the first classe door into the berceau, and thence into the "allée défendue."

Methusaleh, the pear-tree, stood at the farther end of this walk, near my seat: he rose up, dim and grey, above the lower shrubs around him. Now Methusaleh, though so very old, was of sound timber still; only there was a hole, or rather a deep hollow, near his root. I knew there was such a hollow, hidden partly by ivy and creepers growing thick round; and there I meditated hiding my treasure. But I was not only going to hide a treasure—I meant also to bury a grief. That grief over which I had lately been weeping, as I wrapped it in its winding-sheet, must be interred.

Well, I cleared away the ivy, and found the hole; it was large enough to receive the jar, and I thrust it deep in. In a tool-shed at the bottom of the garden lay the relics of building-materials left by masons lately employed to repair a part of the premises. I fetched thence a slate and some mortar, put the slate on the hollow, secured it with cement, covered the whole with black mould, and finally replaced the ivy. This done, I rested, leaning against the tree; lingering, like any other mourner, beside a newly-sodded grave.

The air of the night was very still, but dim with a peculiar mist, which changed the moonlight into a luminous haze. In this air, or this mist, there was some quality— electrical, perhaps—which acted in strange sort upon me. I felt then as I had felt a year ago in England—on a night when the aurora borealis was streaming and sweeping round heaven, when, belated in lonely fields, I had paused to watch that mustering of an army with banners—that quivering of serried lances—that swift ascent of messengers from below the north star to the dark, high keystone of heaven's arch. I felt, not happy, far otherwise, but strong with reinforced strength.

If life be a war, it seemed my destiny to conduct it single-handed. I pondered now how to break up my winter-quarters—to leave an encampment where food and forage failed. Perhaps, to effect this change, another pitched battle must be fought with fortune; if so, I had a mind to the encounter: too poor to lose, God might destine me to gain. But what road was open—what plan available?

On this question I was still pausing, when the moon, so dim hitherto, seemed to shine out somewhat brighter: a ray gleamed even white before me, and a shadow became distinct and marked. I looked more narrowly, to make out the cause of this well-defined contrast appearing a little suddenly in the obscure alley: whiter and blacker it grew on my eye: it took shape with instantaneous transformation. I stood about three yards from a tall, sable-robed, snowy-veiled woman.

Five minutes passed. I neither fled nor shrieked. She was there still. I spoke. "Who are you? and why do you come to me?"

She stood mute. She had no face—no features: all below her brow was masked with a white cloth; but she had eyes, and they viewed me.

I felt, if not brave, yet a little desperate; and desperation will often suffice to fill the post and do the work of courage. I advanced one step. I stretched out my hand, for I meant to touch her. She seemed to recede. I drew nearer: her recession, still silent, became swift. A mass of shrubs, full-leaved evergreens, laurel and dense yew, intervened between me and what I followed. Having passed that obstacle, I looked and saw nothing. I waited. I said, "If you have any errand to men, come back and deliver it." Nothing spoke or reappeared.

This time there was no Dr. John to whom to have recourse: there was no one to whom I dared whisper the words "I have again seen the nun."

Paulina Mary sought my frequent presence in the Rue Crécy. In the old Bretton days, though she had never professed herself fond of me, my society had soon become to her a sort of unconscious necessary. I used to notice that if I withdrew to my room, she would speedily come trotting after me and, opening the door and peeping in, say, with her little peremptory accent—

"Come down. Why do you sit here by yourself? You must come into the parlour."

In the same spirit she urged me now—

"Leave the Rue Fossette," she said, "and come and live with us. Papa would give you far more than Madame Beck gives you."

Mr. Home himself offered me a handsome sum—thrice my present salary—if I would accept the office of companion to his daughter. I declined. I think I should have declined had I been poorer than I was, and with scantier fund of resource, more stinted narrowness of future prospect. I had not that vocation. I could teach; I could give lessons; but to be either a private governess or a companion was unnatural to me. Rather than fill the former post in any great house, I would deliberately have taken a housemaid's place, bought a strong pair of gloves, swept bedrooms and staircases, and cleaned stoves and locks, in peace and independence. Rather than be a companion, I would have made shirts and starved.

I was no bright lady's shadow—not Miss de Bassompierre's. Overcast enough it was my nature often to be; of a subdued habit I was: but the dimness and depression must both be voluntary—such as kept me docile at my desk in the midst of my now well-accustomed pupils in Madame Beck's first classe; or alone at my own bedside in her dormitory, or in the alley and seat which were called mine in her garden: my qualifications were not convertible, nor adaptable; they could not be made the foil of any gem, the adjunct of any beauty, the appendage of any greatness in Christendom. Madame Beck and I, without assimilating, understood each other well. I was not *her* companion, nor her children's governess; she left me free: she tied me to nothing—not to herself—not even to her interests: once, when she had for a fortnight been called from home by a near relation's illness, and on her return, all anxious and full of care about her establishment lest something in her absence should have gone wrong—finding that matters had proceeded much as usual, and that there was no evidence of glaring neglect—she made each of the teachers a present, in acknowledgment of steadiness. To my bedside she came at twelve o'clock at night, and told me she had no present for me. "I must make fidelity advantageous to the St. Pierre," said she; "if I attempt to make it advantageous to you, there will arise misunderstanding between us—perhaps separation. One thing, however, I *can* do to please you—leave you alone with your liberty: c'est ce que je ferai."

She kept her word. Every slight shackle she had ever laid on me, she, from that time, with quiet hand removed. Thus I had pleasure in voluntarily respecting her rules: gratification in devoting double time, in taking double pains with the pupils she committed to my charge.

As to Mary de Bassompierre, I visited her with pleasure, though I would not live with her. My visits soon taught me that it was unlikely even my occasional and voluntary society would long be indispensable to her. M. de Bassompierre, for his part, seemed impervious to this conjecture, blind to this possibility; unconscious as any child to the signs, the likelihoods; the fitful beginnings of what, when it drew to an end, he might not approve.

Whether or not he would cordially approve, I used to speculate. Difficult to say. He was much taken up with scientific interests; keen, intent, and somewhat oppugnant in what concerned his favourite pursuits, but unsuspicious and trustful in the ordinary affairs of life. From all I could gather, he seemed to regard his ''daughterling'' as still but a child, and probably had not yet admitted the notion that others might look on her in a different light: he would speak of what should be done when ''Polly'' was a woman, when she should be grown up; and ''Polly,'' standing beside his chair, would sometimes smile and take his honoured head between her little hands, and kiss his iron-grey locks; and, at other times, she would pout and toss her curls: but she never said, ''Papa, I *am* grown up.''

She had different moods for different people. With her father she really was still a child, or child-like, affectionate, merry and playful. With me she was serious, and as womanly as thought and feeling could make her. With Mrs. Bretton she was docile and reliant, but not expansive. With Graham she was shy, at present very shy; at moments she tried to be cold; on occasion she endeavoured to shun him. His step made her start; his entrance hushed her; when he spoke her answers failed of fluency; when he took leave, she remained self-vexed and disconcerted. Even her father noticed this demeanour in her.

''My little Polly,'' he said once, ''you live too retired a life; if you grow to be a woman with these shy manners, you will hardly be fitted for society. You really make quite a stranger of Dr. Bretton: how is this? Don't you remember that, as a little girl, you used to be rather partial to him?''

''*Rather,* papa,'' echoed she, with her slightly dry, yet gentle and simple tone.

''And you don't like him now? What has he done?''

''Nothing. Y-e-s, I like him a little; but we are grown strange to each other.''

''Then rub it off, Polly: rub the rust and strangeness off. Talk away when he is here, and have no fear of him.''

''*He* does not talk much. Is he afraid of me, do you think, papa?''

''Oh, to be sure, what man would not be afraid of such a little silent lady?''

''Then tell him some day not to mind my being silent. Say that it is my way, and that I have no unfriendly intention.''

''Your way, you little chatterbox? So far from being your way, it is only your whim!''

''Well, I'll improve, papa.''

And very pretty was the grace with which, the next day, she tried to keep her word. I saw her make the effort to converse affably with Dr. John on general topics. The attention called into her guest's face a pleasurable glow; he met her with caution, and replied to her in his softest tones, as if there was a kind of gossamer happiness hanging in the air which he feared to disturb by drawing too deep a breath. Certainly, in her timid yet earnest advance to friendship, it could not be denied that there was a most exquisite and fairy charm.

When the Doctor was gone, she approached her father's chair.

''Did I keep my word, papa? Did I behave better?''

''My Polly behaved like a queen. I shall become quite proud of her if this improvement continues. By-and-by we shall see her receiving my guests with quite a calm, grand manner. Miss Lucy and I will have to look about us, and polish up all our best airs and graces lest we should be thrown into the shade. Still, Polly, there is a little flutter, a little tendency to stammer now and then, and even to lisp as you lisped when you were six years old.''

"No, papa," interrupted she indignantly, "that can't be true."

"I appeal to Miss Lucy. Did she not, in answering Dr. Bretton's question as to whether she had ever seen the palace of the Prince of Bois l'Etang, say 'yeth,' she had been there 'theveral' times?"

"Papa, you are satirical, you are méchant! I can pronounce all the letters of the alphabet as clearly as you can. But tell me this: you are very particular in making me be civil to Dr. Bretton—do you like him yourself?"

"To be sure: for old acquaintance' sake I like him: then he is a very good son to his mother; besides being a kind-hearted fellow and clever in his profession: yes, the callant is well enough."

"*Callant!* Ah, Scotchman! Papa, is it the Edinburgh or the Aberdeen accent you have?"

"Both, my pet, both: and doubtless the Glaswegian into the bargain: it is that which enables me to speak French so well: a gude Scots tongue always succeeds well at the French."

"*The* French! Scotch again: incorrigible papa. You, too, need schooling."

"Well, Polly, you must persuade Miss Snowe to undertake both you and me; to make you steady and womanly, and me refined and classical."

The light in which M. de Bassompierre evidently regarded "Miss Snowe," used to occasion me much inward edification. What contradictory attributes of character we sometimes find ascribed to us, according to the eye with which we are viewed! Madame Beck esteemed me learned and blue; Miss Fanshawe, caustic, ironic, and cynical; Mr. Home, a model teacher, the essence of the sedate and discreet: somewhat conventional, perhaps, too strict, limited, and scrupulous, but still the pink and pattern of governess-correctness; whilst another person, Professor Paul Emanuel to wit, never lost an opportunity of intimating his opinion that mine was rather a fiery and rash nature—adventurous, indocile, and audacious. I smiled at them all. If any one knew me it was little Paulina Mary.

As I would not be Paulina's nominal and paid companion, genial and harmonious as I began to find her intercourse, she persuaded me to join her in some study, as a regular and settled means of sustaining communication: she proposed the German language, which, like myself, she found difficult of mastery. We agreed to take our lessons in the Rue Crécy of the same mistress; this arrangement threw us together for some hours of every week. M. de Bassompierre seemed quite pleased: it perfectly met his approbation that Madame Minerva Gravity should associate a portion of her leisure with that of his fair and dear child.

That other self-elected judge of mine, the professor in the Rue Fossette, discovering by some surreptitious spying means that I was no longer so stationary as hitherto, but went out regularly at certain hours of certain days, took it upon himself to place me under surveillance. People said M. Emanuel had been brought up amongst Jesuits. I should more readily have accredited this report had his manœuvres been better masked. As it was, I doubted it. Never was a more undisguised schemer, a franker, looser intriguer. He would analyse his own machinations: elaborately contrive plots, and forthwith indulge in explanatory boasts of their skill. I know not whether I was more amused or provoked by his stepping up to me one morning and whispering solemnly that he "had his eye on me: *he* at least would discharge the duty of a friend, and not leave me entirely to my own devices. My proceedings seemed at present very unsettled: he did not know what to make of them: he thought his cousin Beck very much to blame in suffering this sort of fluttering inconsistency in a teacher attached to her house. What had a person devoted to a serious calling, that of education, to do with Counts and Countesses, hotels and chateaux? To him I seemed altogether 'en l'air.' On his faith, he believed I went out six days in the seven."

I said, "Monsieur exaggerated. I certainly had enjoyed the advantage of a little change lately, but not before it had become necessary; and the privilege was by no means exercised in excess."

"Necessary! How was it necessary? I was well enough, he supposed? Change necessary? He would recommend me to look at the Catholic 'religieuses,' and study *their* lives. *They* asked no change."

I am no judge of what expression crossed my face when he thus spoke, but it was one which provoked him: he accused me of being reckless, worldly, and epicurean; ambitious of greatness, and feverishly athirst for the pomps and vanities of life. It seems I had no "dévouement," no "récueillement" in my character; no spirit of grace, faith, sacrifice or self-abasement. Feeling the inutility of answering these charges, I mutely continued the correction of a pile of English exercises.

"He could see in me nothing Christian: like many other Protestants, I revelled in the pride and self-will of paganism."

I slightly turned from him, nestling still closer under the wing of silence.

A vague sound grumbled between his teeth; it could not surely be a "juron": he was too religious for that; but I am certain I heard the word "sacré." Grievous to relate, the same word was repeated, with the unequivocal addition of "mille" something, when I passed him about two hours afterwards in the corridor, prepared to go and take my German lesson in the Rue Crécy. Never was a better little man, in some points, than M. Paul: never, in others, a more waspish little despot.

Our German mistress, Fraülein Anna Braun, was a worthy, hearty woman of about forty-five; she ought, perhaps, to have lived in the days of Queen Elizabeth, as she habitually consumed for her first and second breakfasts beer and beef: also, her direct and downright Deutsch nature seemed to suffer a sensation of cruel restraint from what she called our English reserve; though we thought we were very cordial with her: but we did not slap her on the shoulder, and if we consented to kiss her cheek, it was done quietly, and without any explosive smack. These omissions oppressed and depressed her considerably; still, on the whole, we got on very well. Accustomed to instruct foreign girls, who hardly ever will think and study for themselves—who have no idea of grappling with a difficulty, and overcoming it by a dint of reflection or application—our progress, which in truth was very leisurely, seemed to astound her. In her eyes we were a pair of glacial prodigies, cold, proud, and preternatural.

The young Countess *was* a little proud, a little fastidious: and perhaps, with her native delicacy and beauty, she had a right to these feelings; but I think it was a total mistake to ascribe them to me. I never evaded the morning salute, which Paulina would slip when she could; nor was a certain little manner of still disdain a weapon known in my armoury of defence; whereas, Paulina always kept it clear, fine, and bright, and any rough German sally called forth at once its steely glisten.

Honest Anna Braun, in some measure, felt this difference; and while she half-feared, half-worshipped Paulina, as a sort of dainty nymph—an Undine—she took refuge with me as being all mortal, and of easier mood.

A book we liked well to read and translate was Schiller's Ballads; Paulina soon learned to read them beautifully; the Fraülein would listen to her with a broad smile of pleasure, and say her voice sounded like music. She translated them, too, with a facile flow of language, and in a strain of kindred and poetic fervour: her cheek would flush, her lips tremblingly smile, her beauteous eyes kindle or melt as she went on. She learnt the best by heart, and would often recite them when we were alone together. One she liked well was "Des Mädchens Klage": that is, she liked well to repeat the words, she found plaintive melody in the sound; the sense she would criticise. She murmured, as we sat over the fire one evening—

Du Heilige, rufe dein Kind zurück
Ich habe genossen das irdische Glück,
Ich habe gelebt und geliebet!

"Lived and loved!" said she, "is that the summit of earthly happiness, the end of life—to love? I don't think it is. It may be the extreme of mortal misery, it may be sheer waste of time, and fruitless torture of feeling. If Schiller had said to *be* loved, he might have come nearer the truth. Is not that another thing, Lucy, to be loved?"

"I suppose it may be: but why consider the subject? What is love to you? What do you know about it?"

She crimsoned, half in irritation, half in shame.

"Now, Lucy," she said, "I won't take that from you. It may be well for papa to look on me as a baby: I rather prefer that he should thus view me; but *you* know and shall learn to acknowledge that I am verging on my nineteenth year."

"No matter if it were your twenty-ninth; we will anticipate no feelings by discussion and conversation: we will not talk about love."

"Indeed, indeed!" said she—all in hurry and heat—"you may think to check and hold me in as much as you please; but I *have* talked about it, and heard about it too; and a great deal and lately, and disagreeably and detrimentally: and in a way you wouldn't approve."

And the vexed, triumphant, pretty, naughty being laughed. I could not discern what she meant, and I would not ask her: I was nonplussed. Seeing, however, the utmost innocence in her countenance—combined with some transient perverseness and petulance—I said at last,—

"Who talks to you disagreeably and detrimentally on such matters? Who that has near access to you would dare to do it?"

"Lucy," replied she more softly, "it is a person who makes me miserable sometimes; and I wish she would keep away—I don't want her."

"But who, Paulina, can it be? You puzzle me much."

"It is—it is my cousin Ginevra. Every time she has leave to visit Mrs. Cholmondeley she calls here, and whenever she finds me alone she begins to talk about her admirers. Love, indeed! You should hear all she has to say about love."

"Oh, I have heard it," said I, quite coolly; "and on the whole, perhaps it is as well you should have heard it too: it is not to be regretted, it is all right. Yet, surely, Ginevra's mind cannot influence yours. You can look over both her head and her heart."

"She does influence me very much. She has the art of disturbing my happiness and unsettling my opinions. She hurts me through the feelings and people dearest to me."

"What does she say, Paulina? Give me some idea. There may be counteraction of the damage done."

"The people I have longest and most esteemed are degraded by her. She does not spare Mrs. Bretton—she does not spare . . . Graham."

"No, I dare say: and how does she mix up these with her sentiment and her . . . *love*? She does mix them, I suppose?"

"Lucy, she is insolent; and, I believe, false. You know Dr. Bretton. We both know him. He may be careless and proud: but when was he ever mean or slavish? Day after day she shows him to me kneeling at her feet, pursuing her like her shadow, she repulsing him with insult, and he imploring her with infatuation. Lucy, is it true? Is any of it true?"

"It may be true that he once thought her handsome: does she give him out as still her suitor?"

"She says she might marry him any day: he only waits her consent."

"It is these tales which have caused that reserve in your manner towards Graham which your father noticed?"

"They have certainly made me all doubtful about his character. As Ginevra speaks, they do not carry with them the sound of unmixed truth: I believe she exaggerates—perhaps invents—but I want to know how far."

"Suppose we bring Miss Fanshawe to some proof. Give her an opportunity of displaying the power she boasts."

"I could do that to-morrow. Papa has asked some gentlemen to dinner, all savants. Graham, who papa is beginning to discover is a savant too—skilled, they say, in more than one branch of science—is among the number. Now I should be miserable to sit at table unsupported, amidst such a party. I could not talk to Messieurs A—— and Z——, the Parisian Academicians: all my new credit for manner would be put in peril. You and Mrs. Bretton must come for my sake; Ginevra, at a word, will join you."

"Yes; then I will carry a message of invitation, and she shall have the chance of justifying her character for veracity."

Chapter XXVII

THE HÔTEL CRÉCY

THE morrow turned out a more lively and busy day than we—or than I, at least—had anticipated. It seems it was the birthday of one of the young princes of Labassecour—the eldest, I think, the Duc de Dindonneau—and a general holiday was given in his honour at the schools, and especially at the principal "Athénée," or college. The youth of that institution had also concocted and were to present a loyal address; for which purpose they were to be assembled in the public building where the yearly examinations were conducted, and the prizes distributed. After the ceremony of presentation, an oration, or "discours," was to follow from one of the professors.

Several of M. de Bassompierre's friends—the savants—being more or less connected with the Athénée, they were expected to attend on this occasion; together with the worshipful municipality of Villette, M. le Chevalier Staas, the burgomaster, and the parents and kinsfolk of the Athenians in general. M. de Bassompierre was engaged by his friends to accompany them; his fair daughter would, of course, be of the party, and she wrote a little note to Ginevra and myself, bidding us come early that we might join her.

As Miss Fanshawe and I were dressing in the dormitory of the Rue Fossette, she (Miss F.) suddenly burst into a laugh.

"What now?" I asked; for she had suspended the operation of arranging her attire, and was gazing at me.

"It seems so odd," she replied, with her usual half-honest, half-insolent unreserve, "that you and I should now be so much on a level, visiting in the same sphere; having the same connections."

"Why, yes," said I; "I had not much respect for the connections you chiefly frequented awhile ago: Mrs. Cholmondeley and Co. would never have suited me at all."

"Who *are* you, Miss Snowe?" she inquired, in a tone of such undisguised and unsophisticated curiosity as made me laugh in my turn.

"You used to call yourself a nursery-governess; when you first came here you really had the care of the children in this house: I have seen you carry little Georgette in your arms like a bonne—few governesses would have condescended so far—and now Madame Beck treats you with more courtesy than she treats the Parisienne, St. Pierre; and that proud chit, my cousin, makes you her bosom friend!"

"Wonderful!" I agreed, much amused at her mystification. "Who am I indeed? Perhaps a personage in disguise. Pity I don't look the character."

"I wonder you are not more flattered by all this," she went on; "you take it with strange composure. If you really are the nobody I once thought you, you must be a cool hand."

"The nobody you once thought me!" I repeated, and my face grew a little hot; but I would not be angry: of what importance was a school-girl's crude use of the terms nobody and somebody? I confined myself, therefore, to the remark that I had merely met with civility; and asked what she saw in civility to throw the recipient into a fever of confusion.

"One can't help wondering at some things," she persisted.

"Wondering at marvels of your own manufacture. Are you ready at last?"

"Yes; let me take your arm."

"I would rather not: we will walk side by side."

When she took my arm, she always leaned upon me her whole weight; and, as I was not a gentleman, or her lover, I did not like it.

"There again!" she cried. "I thought, by offering to take your arm, to intimate approbation of your dress and general appearance: I meant it as a compliment."

"You did? You meant, in short, to express that you are not ashamed to be seen in the street with me? That if Mrs. Cholmondeley should be fondling her lap-dog at some window, or Colonel de Hamal picking his teeth in a balcony, and should catch a glimpse of us, you would not quite blush for your companion?"

"Yes," said she, with that directness which was her best point—which gave an honest plainness to her very fibs when she told them—which was, in short, the salt, the sole preservative ingredient of a character otherwise not formed to keep.

I delegated the trouble of commenting on this "yes" to my countenance; or, rather, my under-lip voluntarily anticipated my tongue: of course, reverence and solemnity were not the feelings expressed in the look I gave her.

"Scornful, sneering creature!" she went on, as we crossed a great square, and entered the quiet, pleasant park, our nearest way to the Rue Crécy. "Nobody in this world was ever such a Turk to me as you are!"

"You bring it on yourself: let me alone: have the sense to be quiet: I will let you alone."

"As if one *could* let you alone, when you are so peculiar and so mysterious!"

"The mystery and peculiarity being entirely the conception of your own brain— maggots—neither more nor less, be so good as to keep them out of my sight."

"But *are* you anybody?" persevered she, pushing her hand, in spite of me, under my arm; and that arm pressed itself with inhospitable closeness against my side, by way of keeping out the intruder.

"Yes," I said, "I am a rising character: once an old lady's companion, then a nursery-governess, now a school-teacher."

"Do—*do* tell me who you are! I'll not repeat it," she urged, adhering with ludicrous tenacity to the wise notion of an incognito she had got hold of; and she squeezed the arm of which she had now obtained full possession, and coaxed and conjured till I was obliged to pause in the park to laugh. Throughout our walk she rang the most fanciful changes on this theme; proving, by her obstinate credulity, or incredulity, her incapacity to conceive how any person not bolstered up by birth or wealth, not supported by some consciousness of name or connection, could maintain an attitude of reasonable integrity. As for me, it quite sufficed to my mental tranquillity that I was known where it imported that known I should be; the rest sat on me easily: pedigree, social position, and recondite intellectual acquisition, occupied about the same space and place in my interests and thoughts; they were my third-class lodgers—to whom could be assigned only the small sitting-room and the little back bedroom: even if the dining and drawing-rooms stood empty, I never confessed it to them, as thinking minor accommodations better suited to their

circumstances. The world, I soon learned, held a different estimate: and I make no doubt the world is very right in its view, yet believe also that I am not quite wrong in mine.

There are people whom a lowered position degrades morally, to whom loss of connection costs loss of self-respect: are not these justified in placing the highest value on that station and association which is their safeguard from debasement? If a man feels that he would become contemptible in his own eyes were it generally known that his ancestry were simple and not gentle, poor and not rich, workers and not capitalists, would it be right severely to blame him for keeping these fatal facts out of sight—for starting, trembling, quailing at the chance which threatens exposure? The longer we live, the more our experience widens; the less prone are we to judge our neighbour's conduct, to question the world's wisdom: wherever an accumulation of small defences is found, whether surrounding the prude's virtue or the man of the world's respectability, there, be sure, it is needed.

We reached the Hôtel Crécy; Paulina was ready; Mrs. Bretton was with her; and, under her escort and that of M. de Bassompierre, we were soon conducted to the place of assembly, and seated in good seats, at a convenient distance from the Tribune. The youth of the Athénée were marshalled before us, the municipality and their bourgmestre were in places of honour, the young princes, with their tutors, occupied a conspicuous position, and the body of the building was crowded with the aristocracy and first burghers of the town.

Concerning the identity of the professor by whom the "discours" was to be delivered I had as yet entertained neither care nor question. Some vague expectation I had that a savant would stand up and deliver a formal speech, half dogmatism to the Athenians, half flattery to the princes.

The Tribune was yet empty when we entered, but in ten minutes after it was filled; suddenly, in a second of time, a head, chest, and arms grew above the crimson desk. This head I knew: its colour, shape, port, expression, were familiar both to me and Miss Fanshawe; the blackness and closeness of cranium, the amplitude and paleness of brow, the blueness and fire of glance, were details so domesticated in the memory, and so knit with many a whimsical association, as almost by this their sudden apparition to tickle fancy to a laugh. Indeed, I confess, for my part, I did laugh till I was warm; but then I bent my head, and made my handkerchief and a lowered veil the sole confidants of my mirth.

I think I was glad to see M. Paul; I think it was rather pleasant than otherwise to behold him set up there, fierce and frank, dark and candid, testy and fearless, as when regnant on his estrade in class. His presence was such a surprise: I had not once thought of expecting him, though I knew he filled the chair of Belles Lettres in the college. With *him* in that Tribune, I felt sure that neither formalism nor flattery would be our doom; but for what was vouchsafed us, for what was poured suddenly, rapidly, continuously on our heads—I own I was not prepared.

He spoke to the princes, the nobles, the magistrates, and the burghers, with just the same ease, with almost the same pointed, choleric earnestness, with which he was wont to harangue the three divisions of the Rue Fossette. The collegians he addressed, not as schoolboys, but as future citizens and embryo patriots. The times which have since come on Europe had not been foretold yet, and M. Emanuel's spirit seemed new to me. Who would have thought the flat and fat soil of Labassecour could yield political convictions and national feelings such as were now strongly expressed? Of the bearing of his opinions I need here give no special indication; yet it may be permitted me to say that I believed the little man not more earnest than right in what he said: with all his fire he was severe and sensible; he trampled Utopian theories under his heel; he rejected wild dreams with scorn; but when he looked in the face of tyranny—oh, then there opened a light in his eye worth seeing; and when he spoke of injustice, his voice gave no uncertain sound, but reminded me rather of the band-trumpet, ringing at twilight from the park.

I do not think his audience were generally susceptible of sharing his flame in its purity; but some of the college youth caught fire as he eloquently told them what should be their path and endeavour in their country's and in Europe's future. They gave him a long, loud, ringing cheer as he concluded; with all his fierceness, he was their favourite professor.

As our party left the hall, he stood at the entrance; he saw and knew me, and lifted his hat; he offered his hand in passing, and uttered the words "Qu'en dîtes vous?''—question eminently characteristic and reminding me, even in this his moment of triumph, of that inquisitive restlessness, that absence of what I considered desirable self-control, which were amongst his faults. He should not have cared just then to ask what I thought, or what anybody thought; but he *did* care, and he was too natural to conceal, too impulsive to repress his wish.

Well! if I blamed his over-eagerness, I liked his naïveté. I would have praised him: I had plenty of praise in my heart; but, alas! no words on my lips. Who *has* words at the right moment? I stammered some lame expressions; but was truly glad when other people, coming up with profuse congratulations, covered my deficiency by their redundancy.

A gentleman introduced him to M. de Bassompierre: and the Count, who had likewise been highly gratified, asked him to join his friends (for the most part M. Emanuel's likewise), and to dine with them at the Hôtel Crécy. He declined dinner, for be was a man always somewhat shy at meeting the advances of the wealthy: there was a strength of sturdy independence in the stringing of his sinews— not obtrusive, but pleasant enough to discover as one advanced in knowledge of his character; he promised, however, to step in with his friend, M. A——, a French Academician, in the course of the evening.

At dinner that day, Ginevra and Paulina each looked, in her own way, very beautiful; the former, perhaps, boasted the advantage in material charms, but the latter shone pre-eminent for attractions more subtle and spiritual: for light and eloquence of eye, for grace of mien, for winning variety of expression. Ginevra's dress of deep crimson relieved well her light curls, and harmonised with her rose-like bloom. Paulina's attire—in fashion close, though faultlessly neat, but in texture clear and white—made the eye grateful for the delicate life of her complexion, for the soft animation of her countenance, for the tender depth of her eyes, for the brown shadow and bounteous flow of her hair—darker than that of her Saxon cousin, as were also her eyebrows, her eyelashes, her full irids, and large mobile pupils—Nature having traced all these details slightly, and with a careless hand, in Miss Fanshawe's case, and in Miss de Bassompierre's wrought them to a high and delicate finish.

Paulina was awed by the savants, but not quite to mutism: she conversed modestly, diffidently; not without effort, but with so true a sweetness, so fine and penetrating a sense, that her father more than once suspended his own discourse to listen and fixed on her an eye of proud delight. It was a polite Frenchman, M. Z——, a very learned, but quite a courtly man, who had drawn her into discourse. I was charmed with her French; it was faultless—the structure correct, the idioms true, the accent pure; Ginevra, who had lived half her life on the Continent, could do nothing like it: not that words ever failed Miss Fanshawe, but real accuracy and purity she neither possessed, nor in any number of years would acquire. Here, too, M. de Bassompierre was gratified; for, on the point of language, he was critical.

Another listener and observer there was; one who, detained by some exigency of his profession, had come in late to dinner. Both ladies were quietly scanned by Dr. Bretton, at the moment of taking his seat at the table; and that guarded survey was more than once renewed. His arrival roused Miss Fanshawe, who had hitherto appeared listless: she now became smiling and complacent, talked—though what she said was rarely to the purpose—or rather, was of a purpose somewhat mortifyingly below the standard of the occasion. Her light, disconnected prattle might have

gratified Graham once; perhaps it pleased him still: perhaps it was only fancy which suggested the thought that, while his eye was filled and his ear fed, his taste, his keen zest, his lively intelligence, were not equally consulted and regaled. It is certain that, restless and exacting as seemed the demand on his attention, he yielded courteously all that was required: his manner showed neither pique nor coldness: Ginevra was his neighbour, and to her, during dinner, he almost exclusively confined his notice. She appeared satisfied, and passed to the drawing-room in very good spirits.

Yet, no sooner had we reached that place of refuge, than she again became flat and listless: throwing herself on a couch, she denounced both the "discours" and the dinner as stupid affairs, and inquired of her cousin how she could hear such a set of prosaic "gros-bonnets" as her father gathered about him. The moment the gentlemen were heard to move, her railings ceased: she started up, flew to the piano, and dashed at it with spirit. Dr. Bretton entering, one of the first, took up his station beside her. I thought he would not long maintain that post: there was a position near the hearth to which I expected to see him attracted: this position he only scanned with his eye; while *he* looked, others drew in. The grace and mind of Paulina charmed those thoughtful Frenchmen: the fineness of her beauty, the soft courtesy of her manner, her immature but real and inbred tact pleased their national taste; they clustered about her, not indeed to talk science, which would have rendered her dumb, but to touch on many subjects in letters, in arts, in actual life, on which it soon appeared that she had both read and reflected. I listened. I am sure that though Graham stood aloof, he listened too: his hearing as well as his vision was very fine, quick, discriminating. I knew he gathered the conversation; I felt that the mode in which it was sustained suited him exquisitely—pleased him almost to pain.

In Paulina there was more force, both of feeling and character than most people thought—than Graham himself imagined—than she would ever show to those who did not wish to see it. To speak truth, reader, there is no excellent beauty, no accomplished grace, no reliable refinement, without strength as excellent, as complete, as trustworthy. As well might you look for good fruit and blossom on a rootless and sapless tree as for charms that will endure in a feeble and relaxed nature. For a little while the blooming semblance of beauty may flourish round weakness; but it cannot bear a blast: it soon fades, even in serenest sunshine. Graham would have started had any suggestive spirit whispered of the sinew and the stamina sustaining that delicate nature; but I who had known her as a child, knew or guessed by what a good and strong root her graces held to the firm soil of reality.

While Dr. Bretton listened, and waited an opening in the magic circle, his glance, restlessly sweeping the room at intervals, lighted by chance on me, where I sat in a quiet nook not far from my godmother and M. de Bassompierre, who, as usual, were engaged in what Mr. Home called "a two-handed crack": what the Count would have interpreted as a tête-à-tête. Graham smiled recognition, crossed the room, asked me how I was, told me I looked pale. I also had my own smile at my own thought: it was now about three months since Dr. John had spoken to me—a lapse of which he was not even conscious. He sat down, and became silent. His wish was rather to look than converse. Ginevra and Paulina were now opposite to him: he could gaze his fill: he surveyed both forms—studied both faces.

Several new guests, ladies as well as gentlemen, had entered the room since dinner, dropping in for the evening conversation; and amongst the gentlemen, I may incidentally observe, I had already noticed by glimpses a severe, dark, professorial outline, hovering aloof in an inner salon, seen only in vista. M. Emanuel knew many of the gentlemen present, but I think was a stranger to most of the ladies, excepting myself; in looking towards the hearth, he could not but see me, and naturally made a movement to approach; seeing, however, Dr. Bretton also, he changed his mind and held back. If that had been all, there would have been no

cause for quarrel; but not satisfied with holding back, he puckered up his eyebrows, protruded his lip, and looked so ugly that I averted my eyes from the displeasing spectacle. M. Josef Emanuel had arrived, as well as his austere brother, and at this very moment was relieving Ginevra at the piano. What a master-touch succeeded her school-girl jingle! In what grand, grateful tones the instrument acknowledged the hand of the true artist!

"Lucy," began Dr. Bretton, breaking silence and smiling, as Ginevra glided before him, casting a glance as she passed by, "Miss Fanshawe is certainly a fine girl."

Of course I assented.

"Is there," he pursued, "another in the room as lovely?"

"I think there is not another as handsome."

"I agree with you, Lucy: you and I do often agree in opinion, in taste, I think; or at least in judgment."

"Do we?" I said, somewhat doubtfully.

"I believe if you had been a boy, Lucy, instead of a girl—my mother's godson instead of her god-daughter, we should have been good friends: our opinions would have melted into each other."

He had assumed a bantering air: a light, half-caressing, half-ironic, shone aslant in his eye. Ah, Graham! I have given more than one solitary moment to thoughts and calculations of your estimate of Lucy Snowe: was it always kind or just? Had Lucy been intrinsically the same, but possessing the additional advantages of wealth and station, would your manner to her, your value for her, have been quite what they actually were? And yet by these questions I would not seriously infer blame. No; you might sadden and trouble me sometimes; but then mine was a soon-depressed, an easily-deranged temperament—it fell if a cloud crossed the sun. Perhaps before the eye of severe equity I should stand more at fault than you.

Trying, then, to keep down the unreasonable pain which thrilled my heart on thus being made to feel that while Graham could devote to others the most grave and earnest, the manliest interest, he had no more than light raillery for Lucy, the friend of lang syne, I inquired calmly—

"On what points are we so closely in accordance?"

"We each have an observant faculty. You, perhaps, don't give me credit for the possession; yet I have it."

"But you were speaking of tastes: we may see the same objects, yet estimate them differently?"

"Let us bring it to the test. Of course, you cannot but render homage to the merits of Miss Fanshawe: now, what do you think of others in the room?—my mother, for instance; or the lions yonder, Messieurs A—— and Z——; or, let us say, that pale little lady, Miss de Bassompierre?"

"You know what I think of your mother. I have not thought of Messieurs A—— and Z——."

"And the other?"

"I think she is, as you say, a pale little lady—pale, certainly, just now, when she is fatigued with over-excitement."

"You don't remember her as a child?"

"I wonder, sometimes, whether you do."

"I had forgotten her; but it is noticeable that circumstances, persons, even words and looks, that had slipped your memory may, under certain conditions, certain aspects of your own or another's mind, revive."

"That is possible enough."

"Yet," he continued, "the revival is imperfect—needs confirmation, partakes so much of the dim character of a dream, or of the airy one of a fancy, that the testimony of a witness becomes necessary for corroboration. Were you not a guest

at Bretton ten years ago, when Mr. Home brought his little girl, whom we then called 'little Polly,' to stay with mamma?''

"I was there the night she came, and also the morning she went away.''

"Rather a peculiar child, was she not? I wonder how I treated her. Was I fond of children in those days? Was there anything gracious or kindly about me—great, reckless schoolboy as I was? But you don't recollect me, of course?''

"You have seen your own picture at La Terrasse. It is like you personally. In manner, you were almost the same yesterday as to-day.''

"But, Lucy, how is that? Such an oracle really whets my curiosity. What am I to-day? What was I the yesterday of ten years back?''

"Gracious to whatever pleased you—unkindly or cruel to nothing.''

"There you are wrong; I think I was almost a brute to *you,* for instance.''

"A brute! No, Graham: I should never have patiently endured brutality.''

"*This,* however, I *do* remember: quiet Lucy Snowe tasted nothing of my grace.''

"As little of your cruelty.''

"Why, had I been Nero himself, I could not have tormented a being inoffensive as a shadow.''

I smiled; but I also hushed a groan. Oh!—I just wished he would let me alone—cease allusion to me. These epithets—these attributes I put from me. His "quiet Lucy Snowe,'' his "inoffensive shadow,'' I gave him back; not with scorn, but with extreme weariness: theirs was the coldness and the pressure of lead; let him whelm me with no such weight. Happily, he was soon on another theme.

"On what terms were 'little Polly' and I? Unless my recollections deceive me, we were not foes''——

"You speak very vaguely. Do you think little Polly's memory not more definite?''

"Oh! we don't talk of 'little Polly' *now.* Pray say Miss de Bassompierre; and, of course, such a stately personage remembers nothing of Bretton. Look at her large eyes, Lucy; can they read a word in the page of memory? Are they the same which I used to direct to a horn-book? She does not know that I partly taught her to read.''

"In the Bible on Sunday nights?''

"She has a calm, delicate, rather fine profile now: once what a little restless, anxious countenance was hers! What a thing is a child's preference—what a bubble! Would you believe it? that lady was fond of me!''

"I think she was in some measure fond of you,'' said I moderately.

"You don't remember then? *I* had forgotten; but I remember *now.* She liked me the best of whatever there was at Bretton.''

"You thought so.''

"I quite well recall it. I wish I could tell her all I recall, or rather, I wish some one, *you* for instance, would go behind and whisper it all in her ear, and I could have the delight—here, as I sit—of watching her look under the intelligence. Could you manage that, think you, Lucy, and make me ever grateful?''

"Could I manage to make you ever grateful?'' said I. "No, *I could not.*'' And I felt my fingers work and my hands interlock: I felt, too, an inward courage, warm and resistant. In this matter I was not disposed to gratify Dr. John: not at all. With now welcome force, I realised his entire misapprehension of my character and nature. He wanted always to give me a rôle not mine. Nature and I opposed him. He did not at all guess what I felt: he did not read my eyes, or face, or gestures; though, I doubt not, all spoke. Leaning towards me coaxingly, he said softly, "*Do* content me, Lucy.''

And I would have contented, or, at least, I would clearly have enlightened him, and taught him well never again to expect of me the part of officious soubrette in a love drama; when, following his soft, eager murmur, meeting almost his pleading, mellow—"*Do* content me, Lucy!'' a sharp hiss pierced my ear on the other side.

"Petite chatte, doucerette, coquette!" sibilated the sudden boa-constrictor; "vous avez l'air bien triste, soumise, rêveuse, mais vous ne l'êtes pas: c'est moi qui vous le dis: Sauvage! la flamme à l'âme, l'éclair aux yeux!"

"Oui; j'ai la flamme à l'âme, et je dois l'avoir!" retorted I, turning in just wrath; but Professor Emanuel had hissed his insult and was gone.

The worst of the matter was that Dr. Bretton, whose ears, as I have said, were quick and fine, caught every word of this apostrophe; he put his handkerchief to his face, and laughed till he shook.

"Well done, Lucy," cried he; "capital! petite chatte, petite coquette! Oh, I must tell my mother! Is it true, Lucy, or half-true? I believe it is: you redden to the colour of Miss Fanshawe's gown. And really, by my word, now I examine him, that is the same little man who was so savage with you at the concert: the very same, and in his soul he is frantic at this moment because he sees me laughing. Oh! I must tease him."

And Graham, yielding to his bent for mischief, laughed, jested, and whispered on till I could bear no more, and my eyes filled.

Suddenly he was sobered: a vacant space appeared near Miss de Bassompierre; the circle surrounding her seemed about to dissolve. This movement was instantly caught by Graham's eye—ever-vigilant, even while laughing; he rose, took his courage in both hands, crossed the room, and made the advantage his own. Dr. John, throughout his whole life, was a man of luck—a man of success. And why? Because he had the eye to see his opportunity, the heart to prompt to well-timed action, the nerve to consummate a perfect work. And no tyrant-passion dragged him back; no enthusiasms, no foibles encumbered his way. How well he looked at this very moment! When Paulina looked up as he reached her side, her glance mingled at once with an encountering glance, animated, yet modest; his colour, as he spoke to her, became half a blush, half a glow. He stood in her presence brave and bashful: subdued and unobtrusive, yet decided in his purpose and devoted in his ardour. I gathered all this by one view. I did not prolong my observation—time failed me, had inclination served: the night wore late; Ginevra and I ought already to have been in the Rue Fossette. I rose, and bade good-night to my godmother and M. de Bassompierre.

I know not whether Professor Emanuel had noticed my reluctant acceptance of Dr. Bretton's badinage, or whether he perceived that I was pained, and that on the whole the evening had not been one flow of exultant enjoyment for the volatile, pleasure-loving Mademoiselle Lucie; but, as I was leaving the room, he stepped up and inquired whether I had any one to attend me to the Rue Fossette. The Professor *now* spoke politely, and even deferentially, and he looked apologetic and repentant; but I could not recognise his civility at a word, nor meet his contrition with crude premature oblivion. Never hitherto had I felt seriously disposed to resent his brusqueries or freeze before his fierceness; what he had said to-night, however, I considered unwarranted: my extreme disapprobation of the proceeding must be marked, however slightly. I merely said—

"I am provided with attendance."

Which was true, as Ginevra and I were to be sent home in the carriage; and I passed him with the sliding obeisance with which he was wont to be saluted in classe by pupils crossing his estrade.

Having sought my shawl, I returned to the vestibule. M. Emanuel stood there as if waiting. He observed that the night was fine.

"Is it?" I said, with a tone and manner whose consummate chariness and frostiness I could not but applaud. It was so seldom I could properly act out my own resolution to be reserved and cool where I had been grieved or hurt, that I felt almost proud of this one successful effort. That "Is it?" sounded just like the manner of other people. I had heard hundreds of such little minced, docked, dry phrases from the pursed-up coral lips of a score of self-possessed, self-sufficing misses and mes-

demoiselles. That M. Paul would not stand any prolonged experience of this sort of dialogue I knew; but he certainly merited a sample of the curt and arid. I believe he thought so himself, for he took the dose quietly. He looked at my shawl, and objected to its lightness. I decidedly told him it was as heavy as I wished. Receding aloof and standing apart, I leaned on the banister of the stairs, folded my shawl about me, and fixed my eyes on a dreary religious painting darkening the wall.

Ginevra was long in coming: tedious seemed her loitering. M. Paul was still there; my ear expected from his lips an angry tone. He came nearer. "Now for another hiss!" thought I; had not the action been too uncivil I could have stopped my ears with my fingers in terror of the thrill. Nothing happens as we expect: listen for a coo or a murmur; it is then you will hear a cry of prey or pain. Await a piercing shriek, an angry threat, and welcome an amicable greeting, a low kind whisper. M. Paul spoke gently—

"Friends," said he, "do not quarrel for a word. Tell me, was it I or ce grand fat d'Anglais" (so he profanely denominated Dr. Bretton), "who made your eyes so humid, and your cheeks so hot as they are even now?"

"I am not conscious of you, monsieur, or of any other having excited such emotion as you indicate," was my answer; and in giving it, I again surpassed my usual self, and achieved a neat, frosty falsehood.

"But what did I say?" he pursued, "tell me; I was angry. I have forgotten my words; what were they?"

"Such as it is best to forget!" said I, still quite calm and chill.

"Then it was *my* words which wounded you? Consider them unsaid: permit my retractation; accord my pardon."

"I am not angry, monsieur."

"Then you are worse than angry—grieved. Forgive me, Miss Lucy."

"M. Emanuel, I *do* forgive you."

"Let us hear you say, in the voice natural to you, and not in that alien tone, 'Mon ami, je vous pardonne.' "

He made me smile. Who could help smiling at his wistfulness, his simplicity, his earnestness?

"Bon!" he cried; "Voilà que le jour va poindre! Dîtes donc, mon ami."

"Monsieur Paul, je vous pardonne."

"I will have no Monsieur: speak the other word, or I shall not believe you sincere: another effort—mon ami, or else in English—my friend!"

Now, "my friend" had rather another sound and significancy than "mon ami"; it did not breathe the same sense of domestic and intimate affection: "mon ami" I could *not* say to M. Paul; "my friend" I could and did say without difficulty. This distinction existed not for him, however, and he was quite satisfied with the English phrase. He smiled. You should have seen him smile, reader; and you should have marked the difference between his countenance now and that he wore half-an-hour ago. I cannot affirm that I have ever witnessed the smile of pleasure, or content, or kindness round M. Paul's lips or in his eyes before. The ironic, the sarcastic, the disdainful, the passionately exultant, I had hundreds of times seen him express by what he called a smile, but any illuminated sign of milder or warmer feelings struck me as wholly new in his visage. It changed it as from a mask to a face: the deep lines left his features; the very complexion seemed clearer and fresher; that swart, sallow, southern darkness which spoke his Spanish blood became displaced by a lighter hue. I know not that I have ever seen in any other human face an equal metamorphosis from a similar cause. He now took me to the carriage: at the same moment M. de Bassompierre came out with his niece.

In a pretty humour was Mistress Fanshawe; she had found the evening a grand failure: completely upset as to temper, she gave way to the most uncontrolled moroseness as soon as we were seated, and the carriage-door closed. Her invectives against Dr. Bretton had something venomous in them. Having found herself impotent

either to charm or sting him, hatred was her only resource; and this hatred she expressed in terms so unmeasured and proportion so monstrous, that, after listening for a while with assumed stoicism, my outraged sense of justice at last and suddenly caught fire. An explosion ensued: for I could be passionate too; especially with my present fair but faulty associate, who never failed to stir the worst dregs of me. It was well that the carriage-wheels made a tremendous rattle over the flinty Choseville pavement, for I can assure the reader there was neither dead silence nor calm discussion within the vehicle. Half in earnest, half in seeming, I made it my business to storm down Ginevra. She had set out rampant from the Rue Crécy; it was necessary to tame her before we reached the Rue Fossette: to this end it was indispensable to show up her sterling value and high deserts; and this must be done in language of which the fidelity and homeliness might challenge comparison with the compliments of a John Knox to a Mary Stuart. This was the right discipline for Ginevra; it suited her. I am quite sure she went to bed that night all the better and more settled in mind and mood, and slept all the more sweetly for having undergone a sound moral drubbing.

Chapter XXVIII

THE WATCHGUARD

M. PAUL EMANUEL owned an acute sensitiveness to the annoyance of interruption, from whatsoever cause occurring, during his lessons: to pass through the classe under such circumstances was considered by the teachers and pupils of the school, individually and collectively, to be as much as a woman's or girl's life was worth.

Madame Beck herself, if forced to the enterprise, would "skurry" through, retrenching her skirts, and carefully coasting the formidable estrade, like a ship dreading breakers. As to Rosine, the portress—on whom, every half-hour, devolved the fearful duty of fetching pupils out of the very heart of one or other of the divisions to take their music lessons in the oratory, the great or little salon, the salle-à-manger, or some other piano-station—she would, upon her second or third attempt, frequently become almost tongue-tied from excess of consternation—a sentiment inspired by the unspeakable looks levelled at her through a pair of dart-dealing spectacles.

One morning I was sitting in the carré, at work upon a piece of embroidery which one of the pupils had commenced but delayed to finish, and while my fingers wrought at the frame, my ears regaled themselves with listening to the crescendos and cadences of a voice haranguing in the neighbouring classe, in tones that waxed momentarily more unquiet, more ominously varied. There was a good strong partition-wall between me and the gathering storm, as well as a facile means of flight through the glass door to the court, in case it swept this way; so I am afraid I derived more amusement than alarm from these thickening symptoms. Poor Rosine was not safe: four times that blessed morning had she made the passage of peril; and now, for the fifth time, it became her dangerous duty to snatch, as it were, a brand from the burning—a pupil from under M. Paul's nose.

"Mon Dieu! mon Dieu!" cried she. "Que vais-je devenir? Monsieur va me tuer, je suis sûre; car il est d'une colère!"

Nerved by the courage of desperation, she opened the door.

"Mademoiselle La Malle au piano!" was her cry. Ere she could make good her retreat, or quite close the door, this voice uttered itself—

"Dès ce moment!—la classe est défendue. La première qui ouvrira cette porte, ou passera par cette division, sera pendue—fût-ce Madame Beck elle-même!"

Ten minutes had not succeeded the promulgation of this decree when Rosine's French pantoufles were again heard shuffling along the corridor.

"Mademoiselle," said she, "I would not for a five-franc piece go into that classe again just now: Monsieur's lunettes are really terrible; and here is a commissionaire come with a message from the Athénée. I have told Madame Beck I dare not deliver it, and she says I am to charge you with it."

"Me? No, that is rather too bad! It is not in my line of duty. Come, come, Rosine! bear your own burden. Be brave—charge once more!"

"I, Mademoiselle?—impossible! Five times I have crossed him this day. Madame must really hire a gendarme for this service. Ouf! Je n'en puis plus!"

"Bah! you are only a coward. What is the message?"

"Precisely of the kind with which Monsieur least likes to be pestered: an urgent summons to go directly to the Athénée, as there is an official visitor—inspector— I know not what—arrived, and Monsieur *must* meet him: you know how he hates a *must*."

Yes, I knew well enough. The restive little man detested spur or curb: against whatever was urgent or obligatory, he was sure to revolt. However, I accepted the responsibility—not, certainly, without fear, but fear blent with other sentiments, curiosity amongst them. I opened the door, I entered, I closed it behind me as quickly and quietly as a rather unsteady hand would permit; for to be slow or bustling, to rattle a latch, or leave a door gaping wide, were aggravations of crime often more disastrous in result than the main crime itself. There I stood then, and there he sat; his humour was visibly bad—almost at its worst; he had been giving a lesson in arithmetic—for he gave lessons on any and every subject that struck his fancy—and arithmetic being a dry subject, invariably disagreed with him: not a pupil but trembled when he spoke of figures. He sat, bent above his desk: to look up at the sound of an entrance, at the occurrence of a direct breach of his will and law, was an effort he could not for the moment bring himself to make. It was quite as well: I thus gained time to walk up the long classe; and it suited my idiosyncrasy far better to encounter the near burst of anger like his than to bear its menace at a distance.

At his estrade I paused, just in front; of course I was not worthy of immediate attention: he proceeded with his lesson. Disdain would not do: he must hear and he must answer my message.

Not being quite tall enough to lift my head over his desk, elevated upon the estrade, and thus suffering eclipse in my present position, I ventured to peep round, with the design, at first, of merely getting a better view of his face, which had struck me when I entered as bearing a close and picturesque resemblance to that of a black and sallow tiger. Twice did I enjoy this side view with impunity, advancing and receding unseen; the third time my eye had scarce dawned beyond the obscuration of the desk, when it was caught and transfixed through its very pupil—transfixed by the lunettes. Rosine was right; these utensils had in them a blank and immutable terror, beyond the mobile wrath of the wearer's own unglazed eyes.

I now found the advantage of proximity: these short-sighted lunettes were useless for the inspection of a criminal under Monsieur's nose; accordingly, he doffed them, and he and I stood on more equal terms.

I am glad I was not really much afraid of him—that, indeed, close in his presence, I felt no terror at all; for upon his demanding cord and gibbet to execute the sentence recently pronounced, I was able to furnish him with a needleful of embroidering thread with such accommodating civility as could not but allay some portion at least of his surplus irritation. Of course I did not parade this courtesy before public view: I merely handed the thread round the angle of the desk, and attached it, ready noosed, to the barred back of the Professor's chair.

"Que me voulez-vous?" said he, in a growl of which the music was wholly confined to his chest and throat, for he kept his teeth clenched, and seemed registering

to himself an inward vow that nothing earthly should wring from him a smile. My answer commenced uncompromisingly—

"Monsieur," I said, "je veux l'impossible, des choses inouïes"; and thinking it best not to mince matters, but to administer the "douche" with decision, in a low but quick voice I delivered the Athenian message, floridly exaggerating its urgency.

Of course, he would not hear a word of it. "He would not go; he would not leave his present class, let all the officials of Villette send for him. He would not put himself an inch out of his way at the bidding of king, cabinet, and chambers together."

I knew, however, that he *must* go; that, talk as he would, both his duty and interest commanded an immediate and literal compliance with the summons: I stood, therefore, waiting in silence, as if he had not yet spoken. He asked what more I wanted.

"Only Monsieur's answer to deliver to the commissionaire."

He waved an impatient negative.

I ventured to stretch my hand to the bonnet-grec which lay in grim repose on the window-sill. He followed this daring movement with his eye, no doubt in mixed pity and amazement at its presumption.

"Ah!" he muttered, "if it came to that—if Miss Lucy meddled with his bonnet-grec—she might just put it on herself, turn garçon for the occasion, and benevolently go to the Athénée in his stead."

With great respect I laid the bonnet on the desk, where its tassel seemed to give me an awful nod.

"I'll write a note of apology—that will do!" said he, still bent on evasion.

Knowing well it would *not* do, I gently pushed the bonnet towards his hand. Thus impelled, it slid down the polished slope of the varnished and unbaized desk, carried before it the light steel-framed lunettes, and, fearful to relate, they fell to the estrade. A score of times ere now had I seen them fall and receive no damage—*this* time, as Lucy Snowe's hapless luck would have it, they so fell that each clear pebble became a shivered and shapeless star.

Now, indeed, dismay seized me—dismay and regret. I knew the value of these lunettes: M. Paul's sight was peculiar, not easily fitted, and these glasses suited him. I had heard him call them his treasures: as I picked them up, cracked and worthless, my hand trembled. Frightened through all my nerves I was to see the mischief I had done, but I think I was even more sorry than afraid. For some seconds I dared not look the bereaved Professor in the face; he was the first to speak.

"Là!" said he: "me voilà veuf de mes lunettes! I think Mademoiselle Lucy will now confess that the cord and gallows are amply earned; she trembles in anticipation of her doom. Ah, traitress! traitress! You are resolved to have me quite blind and helpless in your hands!"

I lifted my eyes: his face, instead of being irate, lowering, and furrowed, was overflowing with the smile, coloured with the bloom I had seen brightening it that evening at the Hôtel Crécy. He was not angry—not even grieved. For the real injury he showed himself full of clemency; under the real provocation, patient as a saint. This event, which seemed so untoward—which I thought had ruined at once my chance of successful persuasion—proved my best help. Difficult of management so long as I had done him no harm, he became graciously pliant as soon as I stood in his presence a conscious and contrite offender.

Still gently railing at me as "une forte femme—une Anglaise terrible—une petite casse-tout"—he declared that he dared not but obey one who had given such an instance of her dangerous prowess; it was absolutely like the "grand Empereur" smashing the vase to inspire dismay. So, at last, crowning himself with his bonnet-grec, and taking his ruined lunettes from my hand with a clasp of kind pardon and

encouragement, he made his bow, and went off to the Athénée in first-rate humour and spirits.

After all this amiability, the reader will be sorry for my sake to hear that I was quarrelling with M. Paul again before night; yet so it was, and I could not help it.

It was his occasional custom—and a very laudable, acceptable custom, too—to arrive of an evening, always à l'improviste, unannounced, burst in on the silent hour of study, establish a sudden despotism over us and our occupations, cause books to be put away, work-bags to be brought, and, drawing forth a single thick volume, or a handful of pamphlets, substitute for the besotted "lecture pieuse," drawled by a sleepy pupil, some tragedy made grand by grand reading, ardent by fiery action—some drama, whereof, for my part, I rarely studied the intrinsic merit; for M. Emanuel made it a vessel for an outpouring, and filled it with his native verve and passion like a cup with a vital brewage. Or else he would flash through our conventional darkness a reflex of a brighter world, show us a glimpse of the current literature of the day, read us passages from some enchanting tale, or the last witty feuilleton which had awakened laughter in the salons of Paris; taking care always to expunge with the severest hand, whether from tragedy, melodrama, tale, or essay, whatever passage, phrase, or word could be deemed unsuited to an audience of "jeunes filles." I noticed more than once, that where retrenchment without substitute would have left unmeaning vacancy, or introduced weakness, he could, and did, improvise whole paragraphs, no less vigorous than irreproachable: the dialogue—the description—he engrafted was often far better than that he pruned away.

Well, on the evening in question, we were sitting silent as nuns in a "retreat," the pupils studying, the teachers working. I remember my work; it was a slight matter of fancy, and it rather interested me; it had a purpose; I was not doing it merely to kill time; I meant it when finished as a gift; and the occasion of presentation being near, haste was requisite, and my fingers were busy.

We heard the sharp bell-peal which we all knew; then the rapid step familiar to each ear: the words "Voilà Monsieur!" had scarcely broken simultaneously from every lip, when the two-leaved door split (as split it always did for his admission—such a slow word as "open" is inefficient to describe his movements), and he stood in the midst of us.

There were two study tables, both long and flanked with benches; over the centre of each hung a lamp; beneath this lamp, on either side the table, sat a teacher; the girls were arranged to the right hand and the left; the eldest and most studious nearest the lamps or tropics; the idlers and little ones towards the north and south poles. Monsieur's habit was politely to hand a chair to some teacher, generally Zélie St. Pierre, the senior mistress; then to take her vacated seat; and thus avail himself of the full beam of Cancer or Capricorn, which, owing to his near sight, he needed.

As usual, Zélie rose with alacrity, smiling to the whole extent of her mouth, and the full display of her upper and under rows of teeth—that strange smile which passes from ear to ear, and is marked only by a sharp thin curve, which fails to spread over the countenance, and neither dimples the cheek nor lights the eye. I suppose Monsieur did not see her, or he had taken a whim that he would not notice her, for he was as capricious as women are said to be; then his lunettes (he had got another pair) served him as an excuse for all sorts of little oversights and shortcomings. Whatever might be his reason, he passed by Zélie, came to the other side of the table, and before I could start up to clear the way, whispered, "Ne bougez pas," and established himself between me and Miss Fanshawe, who always would be my neighbour, and have her elbow in my side, however often I declared to her—

"Ginevra, I wish you were at Jericho."

It was easy to say, "Ne bougez pas"; but how could I help it? I must make him room, and I must request the pupils to recede that *I* might recede. It was very well for Ginevra to be gummed to me, "keeping herself warm," as she said, on the winter evenings, and harassing my very heart with her fidgetings and pokings, obliging me, indeed, sometimes to put an artful pin in my girdle by way of protection against her elbow; but I suppose M. Emanuel was not to be subjected to the same kind of treatment, so I swept away my working materials to clear space for his book, and withdrew myself to make room for his person; not, however, leaving more than a yard of interval, just what any reasonable man would have regarded as a convenient, respectful allowance of bench. But M. Emanuel never *was* reasonable; flint and tinder that he was, he struck and took fire directly.

"Vous ne voulez pas de moi pour voisin," he growled: "vous vous donnez des airs de caste; vous me traitez en paria," he scowled. "Soit! je vais arranger la chose!" And he set to work.

"Levez vous toutes, mesdemoiselles!" cried he.

The girls rose. He made them all file off to the other table. He then placed me at one extremity of the long bench, and having duly and carefully brought me my work-basket, silk, scissors, all my implements, he fixed himself quite at the other end.

At this arrangement, highly absurd as it was, not a soul in the room dared to laugh; luckless for the giggler would have been the giggle. As for me, I took it with entire coolness. There I sat, isolated and cut off from human intercourse; I sat and minded my work, and was quiet, and not at all unhappy.

"Est-ce assez de distance?" he demanded.

"Monsieur en est l'arbitre," said I.

"Vous savez bien que non. C'est vous qui avez créé ce vide immense: moi je n'y ai pas mis la main."

And with this assertion he commenced the reading.

For his misfortune he had chosen a French translation of what he called "un drame de Williams Shackspire; le faux dieu," he further announced, "de ces sots païens, les Anglais." How far otherwise he would have characterised him had his temper not been upset, I scarcely need intimate.

Of course, the translation being French was very inefficient; nor did I make any particular effort to conceal the contempt which some of its forlorn lapses were calculated to excite. Not that it behoved or beseemed me to *say* anything; but one can occasionally *look* the opinion it is forbidden to embody in words. Monsieur's lunettes being on the alert, he gleaned up every stray look; I don't think he lost one: the consequence was, his eyes soon discarded a screen that their blaze might sparkle free, and he waxed hotter at the north pole to which he had voluntarily exiled himself than, considering the general temperature of the room, it would have been reasonable to become under the vertical ray of Cancer itself.

The reading over, it appeared problematic whether he would depart with his anger unexpressed, or whether he would give it vent. Suppression was not much in his habits; but still, what had been done to him definite enough to afford matter for overt reproof? I had not uttered a sound, and could not justly be deemed amenable to reprimand or penalty for having permitted a slightly freer action than usual to the muscles about my eyes and mouth.

The supper, consisting of bread and milk diluted with tepid water, was brought in. In respectful consideration of the Professor's presence, the rolls and glasses were allowed to stand instead of being immediately handed round.

"Take your supper, ladies," said he, seeming to be occupied in making marginal notes to his "Williams Shackspire." They took it. I also accepted a roll and glass, but being now more than ever interested in my work, I kept my seat of punishment, and wrought while I munched my bread and sipped my beverage, the whole with easy sang-froid, with a certain snugness of composure, indeed, scarcely in my

habits, and pleasantly novel to my feelings. It seemed as if the presence of a nature so restless, chafing, thorny as that of M. Paul absorbed all feverish and unsettling influences like a magnet, and left me none but such as were placid and harmonious.

He rose. "Will he go away without saying another word?" Yes; he turned to the door.

No: he *re*-turned on his steps; but only, perhaps, to take his pencil-case, which had been left on the table.

He took it—shut the pencil in and out, broke its point against the wood, re-cut and pocketed it, and . . . walked promptly up to me.

The girls and teachers gathered round the other table were talking pretty freely: they always talked at meals; and, from the constant habit of speaking fast and loud at such times, did not now subdue their voices much.

M. Paul came and stood behind me. He asked at what I was working; and I said I was making a watchguard.

He asked, "For whom?" And I answered, "For a gentleman—one of my friends."

M. Paul stooped down and proceeded—as novel-writers say, and, as was literally true in his case—to "hiss" into my ear some poignant words.

He said that, of all the women he knew, I was the one who could make herself the most consummately unpleasant: I was she with whom it was least possible to live on friendly terms. I had a "caractère intraitable," and perverse to a miracle. How I managed it, or what possessed me, he, for his part, did not know; but with whatever pacific and amicable intentions a person accosted me—crac! I turned concord to discord, good-will to enmity. He was sure, he—M. Paul—wished me well enough; he had never done me any harm that he knew of; he might, at least, he supposed, claim a right to be regarded as a neutral acquaintance, guiltless of hostile sentiments: yet, how I behaved to him! With what pungent vivacities—what an impetus of mutiny—what a "fougue" of injustice!

Here I could not avoid opening my eyes somewhat wide, and even slipping in a slight interjectional observation—

"Vivacities? Impetus? Fougue? I didn't know . . ."

"Chut! à l'instant! There! there I went—vive comme la poudre!" He was sorry—he was very sorry: for my sake he grieved over the hapless peculiarity. This "emportement," this "chaleur"—generous, perhaps, but excessive—would yet, he feared, do me a mischief. It was a pity: I was not—he believed, in his soul—wholly without good qualities; and would I but hear reason, and be more sedate, more sober, less "en l'air," less "coquette," less taken by show, less prone to set an undue value on outside excellence—to make much of the attentions of people remarkable chiefly for so many feet of stature, "des couleurs de poupée," "un nez plus ou moins bien fait," and an enormous amount of fatuity—I might yet prove an useful, perhaps an exemplary character. But, as it was——And here the little man's voice was for a minute choked.

I would have looked up at him, or held out my hand, or said a soothing word; but I was afraid, if I stirred, I should either laugh or cry; so odd, in all this, was the mixture of the touching and the absurd.

I thought he had nearly done: but no; he sat down that he might go on at his ease.

"While he, M. Paul, was on these painful topics, he would dare my anger for the sake of my good, and would venture to refer to a change he had noticed in my dress. He was free to confess that when he first knew me—or, rather, was in the habit of catching a passing glimpse of me from time to time—I satisfied him on this point; the gravity, the austere simplicity, obvious in this particular, were such as to inspire the highest hopes for my best interests. What fatal influence had impelled me lately to introduce flowers under the brim of my bonnet, to wear 'des cols brodés,' and even to appear on one occasion in a *scarlet gown*—he might indeed conjecture, but, for the present, would not openly declare."

Again I interrupted, and this time not without an accent at once indignant and horror-struck.

"Scarlet, Monsieur Paul? It was not scarlet! It was pink, and pale pink, too: and further subdued by black lace."

"Pink or scarlet, yellow or crimson, pea-green or sky-blue; it was all one: these were all flaunting, giddy colours; and as to the lace I talked of, *that* was but a 'colifichet de plus.' '' And he sighed over my degeneracy. "He could not, he was sorry to say, be so particular on this theme as he could wish: not possessing the exact names of these 'babioles,' he might run into small verbal errors which would not fail to lay him open to my sarcasm, and excite my unhappily sudden and passionate disposition. He would merely say, in general terms—and in these general terms he knew he was correct—that my costume had of late assumed 'des façons mondaines,' which it wounded him to see."

What "façons mondaines" he discovered in my present winter merino and plain white collar, I own it puzzled me to guess: and when I asked him, he said it was all made with too much attention to effect—and besides, "had I not a bow of ribbon at my neck?"

"And if you condemn a bow of ribbon for a lady, monsieur, you would necessarily disapprove of a thing like this for a gentleman?"—holding up my bright little chainlet of silk and gold. His sole reply was a groan—I suppose over my levity.

After sitting some minutes in silence, and watching the progress of the chain, at which I now wrought more assiduously than ever, he inquired—

"Whether what he had just said would have the effect of making me entirely detest him?"

I hardly remember what answer I made, or how it came about; I don't think I spoke at all, but I know we managed to bid good-night on friendly terms: and, even after M. Paul had reached the door, he turned back just to explain "that he would not be understood to speak in entire condemnation of the scarlet dress" ("Pink! pink!" I threw in); "that he had no intention to deny it the merit of *looking* rather well" (the fact was, M. Emanuel's taste in colours decidedly leaned to the brilliant); "only he wished to counsel me, whenever I wore it, to do so in the same spirit as if its material were 'bure,' and its hue 'gris de poussière.' ''

"And the flowers under my bonnet, monsieur?" I asked. "They are very little ones"——

"Keep them little, then," said he. "Permit them not to become full-blown."

"And the bow, monsieur—the bit of ribbon?"

"Va pour le ruban!" was the propitious answer!

And so we settled it.

"Well done, Lucy Snowe!" cried I to myself; "you have come in for a pretty lecture—brought on yourself a 'rude savon,' and all through your wicked fondness for worldly vanities! Who would have thought it? You deemed yourself a melancholy sobersides enough! Miss Fanshawe there regards you as a second Diogenes. M. de Bassompierre, the other day, politely turned the conversation when it ran on the wild gifts of the actress Vashti, because, as he kindly said, 'Miss Snowe looked uncomfortable.' Dr. John Bretton knows you only as 'quiet Lucy'—'a creature inoffensive as a shadow'; he has said, and you have heard him say it: 'Lucy's disadvantages spring from over-gravity in tastes and manner—want of colour in character and costume.' Such are your own and your friends' impressions; and behold! there starts up a little man, differing diametrically from all these, roundly charging you with being too airy and cheery—too volatile and versatile—too flowery and coloury. This harsh little man—this pitiless censor—gathers up all your poor scattered sins of vanity, your luckless chiffon of rose colour, your small fringe of a wreath, your small scrap of ribbon, your silly bit of lace, and calls you to account for the lot, and for each item. You are well habituated to be passed by as a shadow

in Life's sunshine: it is a new thing to see one testily lifting his hand to screen his
eyes because you tease him with an obtrusive ray.''

Chapter XXIX

MONSIEUR'S FÊTE

I was up the next morning an hour before daybreak, and finished my guard, kneeling
on the dormitory floor beside the centre stand for the benefit of such expiring
glimmer as the night-lamp afforded in its last watch.

All my materials—my whole stock of beads and silk—were used up before the
chain assumed the length and richness I wished; I had wrought it double, as I knew,
by the rule of contraries, that to suit the particular taste whose gratification was in
view an effective appearance was quite indispensable. As a finish to the ornament,
a little gold clasp was needed; fortunately I possessed it in the fastening of my sole
necklace; I duly detached and re-attached it, then coiled compactly the completed
guard, and enclosed it in a small box I had bought for its brilliancy, made of some
tropic shell of the colour called ''nacarat,'' and decked with a little coronal of
sparkling blue stones. Within the lid of the box I carefully graved with my scissors'
point certain initials.

The reader will, perhaps, remember the description of Madame Beck's fête; nor
will he have forgotten that at each anniversary a handsome present was subscribed
for and offered by the school. The observance of this day was a distinction accorded
to none but Madame, and, in a modified form, to her kinsman and counsellor, M.
Emanuel. In the latter case it was an honour spontaneously awarded, not plotted
and contrived beforehand, and offered an additional proof, amongst many others,
of the estimation in which—despite his partialities, prejudices, and irritabilities—
the professor of literature was held by his pupils. No article of value was offered
to him: he distinctly gave it to be understood that he would accept neither plate
nor jewellery. Yet he liked a slight tribute; the cost, the money-value, did not touch
him: a diamond ring, a gold snuff-box, presented with pomp, would have pleased
him less than a flower, or a drawing, offered simply and with sincere feelings.
Such was his nature. He was a man, not wise in his generation, yet could he claim
a filial sympathy with ''the dayspring on high.''

M. Paul's fête fell on the first of March and a Thursday. It proved a fine sunny
day, and being likewise the morning on which it was customary to attend mass;
being also otherwise distinguished by the half-holiday which permitted the privilege
of walking out, shopping, or paying visits in the afternon: these combined considerations
induced a general smartness and freshness of dress. Clean collars were in vogue;
the ordinary dingy woollen classe-dress was exchanged for something lighter and
clearer. Mademoiselle Zélie St. Pierre, on this particular Thursday, even assumed
a ''robe de soie,'' deemed in economical Labassecour an article of hazardous
splendour and luxury; nay, it was remarked that she sent for a ''coiffeur'' to dress
her hair that morning; there were pupils acute enough to discover that she had
bedewed her handkerchief and her hands with a new and fashionable perfume. Poor
Zélie! It was much her wont to declare about this time that she was tired to death
of a life of seclusion and labour: that she longed to have the means and leisure for
relaxation: to have some one to work for her—a husband who would pay her debts
(she was woefully encumbered with debt), supply her wardrobe, and leave her at
liberty, as she said, to ''goûter un peu les plaisirs.'' It had long been rumoured
that her eye was upon M. Emanuel. Monsieur Emanuel's eye was certainly often
upon her. He would sit and watch her perseveringly for minutes together. I have

seen him give her a quarter of an hour's gaze while the class was silently composing
and he sat throned on his estrade unoccupied. Conscious always of this basilisk
attention, she would writhe under it, half-flattered, half-puzzled, and Monsieur
would follow her sensations, sometimes looking appallingly acute; for in some cases
he had the terrible unerring penetration of instinct, and pierced in its hiding-place
the last lurking thought of the heart, and discerned under florid veilings the bare,
barren places of the spirit: yes, and its perverted tendencies, and its hidden false
curves—all that men and women would not have known—the twisted spine, the
malformed limb that was born with them, and far worse, the stain or disfigurement
they have perhaps brought on themselves. No calamity so accursed but M. Emanuel
could pity and forgive, if it were acknowledged candidly; but where his questioning
eyes met dishonest denial—where his ruthless researches found deceitful concealment—
oh, then, he could be cruel, and I thought wicked! he would exultantly snatch the
screen from poor shrinking wretches, passionately hurry them to the summit of the
mount of exposure, and there show them all naked, all false—poor living lies—
the spawn of that horrid Truth which cannot be looked on unveiled. He thought he
did justice; for my part I doubt whether man has a right to do such justice on man:
more than once in these his visitations I have felt compelled to give tears to his
victims, and not spared ire and keen reproach to himself. He deserved it; but it
was more difficult to shake him in his firm conviction that the work was righteous
and needed.

Breakfast being over and mass attended, the school-bell rang and the rooms filled:
a very pretty spectacle was presented in classe. Pupils and teachers sat neatly
arrayed, orderly and expectant, each bearing in her hand the bouquet of felicitation—
the prettiest spring flowers, all fresh, and filling the air with their fragrance: I only
had no bouquet. I like to see flowers growing, but when they are gathered, they
cease to please. I look on them as things rootless and perishable; their likeness to
life makes me sad. I never offer flowers to those I love; I never wish to receive
them from hands dear to me. Mademoiselle St. Pierre marked my empty hands—
she could not believe I had been so remiss; with avidity her eye roved over and
round me: surely I must have some solitary symbolic flower somewhere: some
small knot of violets, something to win myself praise for taste, commendation for
ingenuity. The unimaginative "Anglaise" proved better than the Parisienne's fears:
she sat literally unprovided, as bare of bloom or leaf as the winter tree. This
ascertained, Zélie smiled, well pleased.

"How wisely you have acted to keep your money, Miss Lucie," she said: "silly
I have gone and thrown away two francs on a bouquet of hot-house flowers!"

And she showed with pride her splendid nosegay.

But hush! a step: *the* step. It came prompt, as usual, but with a promptitude, we
felt disposed to flatter ourselves, inspired by other feelings than mere excitability
of nerve and vehemence of intent. We thought our Professor's "footfall" (to speak
romantically) had in it a friendly promise this morning; and so it had.

He entered in a mood which made him as good as a new sunbeam to the already
well-lit first classe. The morning light playing amongst our plants and, laughing
on our walls, caught an added lustre from M. Paul's all-benignant salute. Like a
true Frenchman (though I don't know why I should say so, for he was of strain
neither French nor Labassecourien), he had dressed for the "situation" and the
occasion. Not by the vague folds, sinister and conspirator-like, of his soot-dark
paletôt were the outlines of his person obscured; on the contrary, his figure (such
as it was, I don't boast of it) was well set off by a civilised coat and a silken vest
quite pretty to behold. The defiant and pagan bonnet-grec had vanished: bare-headed
he came upon us, carrying a Christian hat in his gloved hand. The little man looked
well, very well; there was a clearness of amity in his blue eye, and a glow of good
feeling on his dark complexion, which passed perfectly in the place of beauty: one
really did not care to observe that his nose, though far from small, was of no

particular shape, his cheek thin, his brow marked and square, his mouth no rosebud: one accepted him as he was, and felt his presence the reverse of damping or insignificant.

He passed to his desk; he placed on the same his hat and gloves. "Bon jour, mes amies," said he, in a tone that somehow made amends to some amongst us for many a sharp snap and savage snarl: not a jocund, good-fellow tone, still less an unctuous priestly accent, but a voice he had belonging to himself—a voice used when his heart passed the words to his lips. That same heart *did* speak sometimes; though an irritable, it was not an ossified organ; in its core was a place tender beyond a man's tenderness; a place that humbled him to little children, that bound him to girls and women: to whom, rebel as he would, he could not disown his affinity, nor quite deny that, on the whole, he was better with them than with his own sex.

"We all wish Monsieur a good day, and present to him our congratulations on the anniversary of his fête," said Mademoiselle Zélie constituting herself spokeswoman of the assembly; and advancing with no more twists of affectation than were with her indispensable to the achievement of motion, she laid her costly bouquet before him. He bowed over it.

The long train of offerings followed: all the pupils, sweeping past with the gliding step foreigners practise, left their tributes as they went by. Each girl so dexterously adjusted her separate gift that when the last bouquet was laid on the desk it formed the apex to a blooming pyramid—a pyramid blooming, spreading, and towering with such exuberance as, in the end, to eclipse the hero behind it. This ceremony over, seats were resumed, and we sat in dead silence, expectant of a speech.

I suppose five minutes might have elapsed, and the hush remained unbroken; ten—and there was no sound.

Many present began, doubtless, to wonder for what Monsieur waited: as well they might. Voiceless and viewless, stirless and wordless, he kept his station behind the pile of flowers.

At last there issued forth a voice, rather deep, as if it spoke out of a hollow— "Est-ce là tout?"

Mademoiselle Zélie looked round.

"You have all presented your bouquets?" inquired she of the pupils.

Yes; they had all given their nosegays, from the eldest to the youngest, from the tallest to the most diminutive. The senior mistress signified as much.

"Est-ce là tout?" was reiterated in an intonation which, deep before, had now descended some notes lower.

"Monsieur," said Mademoiselle St. Pierre rising, and this time speaking with her own sweet smile, "I have the honour to tell you that, with a single exception, every person in classe has offered her bouquet. For Meess Lucie, Monsieur will kindly make allowance; as a foreigner she probably did not know our customs, or did not appreciate their significance. Meess Lucie has regarded this ceremony as too frivolous to be honoured by her observance."

"Famous!" I muttered between my teeth: "you are no bad speaker, Zélie, when you begin."

The answer vouchsafed to Mademoiselle St. Pierre from the estrade was given in the gesticulation of a hand from behind his pyramid. This manual action seemed to deprecate words, to enjoin silence.

A form ere long followed the hand. Monsieur emerged from his eclipse; and producing himself on the front of his estrade, and gazing straight and fixedly before him at a vast "mappe-monde" covering the wall opposite, he demanded a third time, and now in really tragic tones—

"Est-ce là tout?"

I might yet have made all right by stepping forwards and slipping into his hand the ruddy little shell-box I at that moment held tight in my own. It was what I had

fully purposed to do; but, first, the comic side of Monsieur's behaviour had tempted me to delay, and now, Mademoiselle St. Pierre's affected interference provoked contumacity. The reader not having hitherto had any cause to ascribe to Miss Snowe's character the most distant pretensions to perfection, will be scarcely surprised to learn that she felt too perverse to defend herself from any imputation the Parisienne might choose to insinuate: and besides, M. Paul was so tragic, and took my defection so seriously, he deserved to be vexed. I kept, then, both my box and my countenance, and sat insensate as any stone.

"It is well!" dropped at length from the lips of M. Paul; and having uttered this phrase, the shadow of some great paroxysm—the swell of wrath, scorn, resolve—passed over his brow, rippled his lips, and lined his cheeks. Gulping down all further comment, he launched into his customary "discours."

I can't at all remember what this "discours" was; I did not listen to it: the gulping-down process, the abrupt dismissal of his mortification or vexation, had given me a sensation which half-counteracted the ludicrous effect of the reiterated "Est-ce là tout?"

Towards the close of the speech there came a pleasing diversion; my attention was again amusingly arrested.

Owing to some little accidental movement—I think I dropped my thimble on the floor, and in stooping to regain it, hit the crown of my head against the sharp corner of my desk; which casualties (exasperating to me, by rights, if to anybody) naturally made a slight bustle—M. Paul became irritated, and dismissing his forced equanimity, and casting to the winds that dignity and self-control with which he never cared long to encumber himself, he broke forth into the strain best caculated to give him ease.

I don't know how, in the progress of his "discours," he had contrived to cross the Channel and land on British ground; but there I found him when I began to listen.

Casting a quick cynical glance round the room—a glance which scathed, or was intended to scathe, as it crossed me—he fell with fury upon "les Anglaises."

Never have I heard English women handled as M. Paul that morning handled them: he spared nothing—neither their minds, morals, manners, nor personal appearance. I specially remember his abuse of their tall stature, their long necks, their thin arms, their slovenly dress, their pedantic education, their impious scepticism(!), their insufferable pride, their pretentious virtue: over which he ground his teeth malignantly, and looked as if, had he dared, he would have said singular things. Oh! he was spiteful, acrid, savage; and, as a natural consequence, detestably ugly.

"Little wicked venomous man!" thought I; "am I going to harass myself with fears of displeasing *you,* or hurting *your* feelings? No, indeed; you shall be indifferent to me, as the shabbiest bouquet in your pyramid."

I grieve to say I could not quite carry out this resolution. For some time the abuse of England and the English found and left me stolid: I bore it some fifteen minutes stoically enough; but this hissing cockatrice was determined to sting, and he said such things at last—fastening not only upon our women, but upon our greatest names and best men; sullying the shield of Britannia, and dabbling the Union Jack in mud—that I *was* stung. With vicious relish he brought up the most spicy current continental historical falsehoods—than which nothing can be conceived more offensive. Zélie, and the whole class, became one grin of vindictive delight; for it is curious to discover how these clowns of Labassecour secretly hate England. At last I struck a sharp stroke on my desk, opened my lips, and let loose this cry—

"Vive l'Angleterre, l'Histoire et les Héros! A bas la France, la Fiction et les Faquins!"

The class was struck of a heap. I suppose they thought me mad. The Professor put up his handkerchief, and fiendishly smiled into its folds. Little monster of

malice! He now thought he had got the victory, since he had made me angry. In a second he became good-humoured. With great blandness he resumed the subject of his flowers; talked poetically and symbolically of their sweetness, perfume, purity, etcetera; made Frenchified comparisons between the "jeunes filles" and the sweet blossoms before him; paid Mademoiselle St. Pierre a very full-blown compliment on the superiority of her bouquet; and ended by announcing that the first really fine, mild, and balmy morning in spring he intended to take the whole class out to breakfast in the country. "Such of the class, at least" he added, with emphasis, "as he could count amongst the number of his friends."

"Donc je n'y serai pas," declared I involuntarily.

"Soit!" was his response, and, gathering his flowers in his arms, he flashed out of classe; while I, consigning my work, scissors, thimble, and the neglected little box to my desk, swept upstairs. I don't know whether *he* felt hot and angry, but I am free to confess that *I* did.

Yet with a strange evanescent anger. I had not sat an hour on the edge of my bed, picturing and repicturing his look, manner, words, ere I smiled at the whole scene. A little pang of regret I underwent that the box had not been offered. I had meant to gratify him. Fate would not have it so.

In the course of the afternoon, remembering that desks in classe were by no means inviolate repositories, and thinking that it was as well to secure the box, on account of the initials in the lid, P. C. D. E., for Paul Carl (or Carlos) David Emanuel—such was his full name—these foreigners must always have a string of baptismals—I descended to the schoolroom.

It slept in holiday repose. The day-pupils were all gone home, the boarders were out walking, the teachers, except the surveillante of the week, were in town, visiting or shopping; the suite of divisions was vacant; so was the grand salle, with its huge solemn globe hanging in the midst, its pair of many-branched chandeliers, and its horizontal grand piano closed, silent, enjoying its mid-week Sabbath. I rather wondered to find the first classe door ajar; this room being usually locked when empty, and being then inaccessible to any save Madame Beck and myself, who possessed a duplicate key. I wondered still more, on approaching, to hear a vague movement as of life—a step, a chair stirred, a sound like the opening of a desk.

"It is only Madame Beck doing inspection duty," was the conclusion following a moment's reflection. The partially-opened door gave opportunity for assurance on this point. I looked. Behold! not the inspecting garb of Madame Beck—the shawl and the clean cap—but the coat, and the close-shorn, dark head of a man. This person occupied my chair; his olive hand held my desk open, his nose was lost to view amongst my papers. His back was towards me, but there could not be a moment's question about identity. Already was the attire of ceremony discarded: the cherished and ink-stained paletôt was resumed; the perverse bonnet-grec lay on the floor, as if just dropped from the hand, culpably busy.

Now I knew, and I had long known, that that hand of M. Emanuel's was on the most intimate terms with my desk; that it raised and lowered the lid, ransacked and arranged the contents, almost as familiarly as my own. The fact was not dubious, nor did he wish it to be so: he left signs of each visit palpable and unmistakable; hitherto, however, I had never caught him in the act: watch as I would, I could not detect the hours and moments of his coming. I saw the brownies' work in exercises left overnight full of faults, and found next morning carefully corrected: I profited by his capricious good-will in loans full welcome and refreshing. Between a sallow dictionary and worn-out grammar would magically grow a fresh interesting new work, or a classic, mellow and sweet in its ripe age. Out of my work-basket would laughingly peep a romance, under it would lurk the pamphlet, the magazine, whence last evening's reading had been extracted. Impossible to doubt the source whence these treasures flowed: had there been no other indication, one condemning and traitor peculiarity common to them all, settled the question—*they smelt of*

cigars. This was very shocking, of course: *I* thought so at first, and used to open the window with some bustle, to air my desk, and with fastidious finger and thumb to hold the peccant brochures forth to the purifying breeze. I was cured of that formality suddenly. Monsieur caught me at it one day, understood the inference, instantly relieved my hand of its burden, and, in another moment, would have thrust the same into the glowing stove. It chanced to be a book, on the perusal of which I was bent; so for once I proved as decided and quicker than himself; recaptured the spoil, and—having saved this volume—never hazarded a second. With all this, I had never yet been able to arrest in his visits the freakish, friendly, cigar-loving phantom.

But now at last I had him: there he was—the very brownie himself; and there, curling from his lips, was the pale blue breath of his Indian darling: he was smoking into my desk: it might well betray him. Provoked at this particular, and yet pleased to surprise him—pleased, that is, with the mixed feeling of the housewife who discovers at last her strange elfin ally busy in the dairy at the untimely churn—I softly stole forward, stood behind him, bent with precaution over his shoulder.

My heart smote me to see that—after this morning's hostility, after my seeming remissness, after the puncture experienced by his feelings, and the ruffling undergone by his temper—he, all-willing to forget and forgive, had brought me a couple of handsome volumes, of which the title and authorship were guarantees for interest. Now, as he sat bending above the desk, he was stirring up its contents; but with gentle and careful hand; disarranging indeed, but not harming. My heart smote me: as I bent over him, as he sat unconscious, doing me what good he could, and I daresay not feeling towards me unkindly, my morning's anger quite melted: I did not dislike Professor Emanuel.

I think he heard me breathe. He turned suddenly: his temperament was nervous, yet he never started, and seldom changed colour; there was something hardy about him.

"I thought you were gone into town with the other teachers," said he, taking a grim grip of his self-possession, which half-escaped him—"It is as well you are not. Do you think I care for being caught? Not I. I often visit your desk."

"Monsieur, I know it."

"You find a brochure or tome now and then; but you don't read them, because they have passed under this?"—touching his cigar.

"They have, and are no better for the process; but I read them."

"Without pleasure?"

"Monsieur must not be contradicted."

"Do you like them, or any of them?—are they acceptable?"

"Monsieur has seen me reading them a hundred times, and knows I have not so many recreations as to undervalue those he provides."

"I mean well; and, if you see that I mean well, and derive some little amusement from my efforts, why can we not be friends?"

"A fatalist would say—because we cannot."

"This morning," he continued, "I awoke in a bright mood, and came into classe happy; you spoiled my day."

"No, monsieur, only an hour or two of it, and that unintentionally."

"Unintentionally! No. It was my fête-day; everybody wished me happiness but you. The little children of the third division gave each her knot of violets, lisped each her congratulation: you—nothing. Not a bud, leaf, whisper—not a glance. Was this unintentional?"

"I meant no harm."

"Then you really did not know our custom? You were unprepared? You would willingly have laid out a few centimes on a flower to give me pleasure had you been aware that it was expected? Say so, and all is forgotten, and the pain soothed."

"I *did* know that it was expected: I *was* prepared; yet I laid out no centimes on flowers."

"It is well—you do right to be honest. I should almost have hated you had you flattered and lied. Better declare at once—'Paul Carl Emanuel—je te déteste, mon garçon!'—than smile an interest, look an affection, and be false and cold at heart. False and cold I don't think you are; but you have made a great mistake in life, that I believe: I think your judgment is warped—that you are indifferent where you ought to be grateful—and perhaps devoted and infatuated where you ought to be cool as your name. Don't suppose that I wish you to have a passion for me, mademoiselle; Dieu vous en garde! What do you start for? Because I said passion? Well, I say it again. There is such a word, and there is such a thing—though not within these walls, thank Heaven! You are no child that one should not speak of what exists; but I only uttered the word—the thing, I assure you, is alien to my whole life and views. It died in the past—in the present it lies buried—its grave is deep-dug, well-heaped, and many winters old: in the future there will be a resurrection, as I believe to my soul's consolation; but all will then be changed—form and feeling: the mortal will have put on immortality—it will rise, not for earth, but heaven. All I say to *you*, Miss Lucy Snowe, is—that you ought to treat Professor Paul Emanuel decently."

I could not and did not contradict such a sentiment.

"Tell me," he pursued, "when it is *your* fête-day, and I will not grudge a few centimes for a small offering."

"You will be like me, monsieur: this cost more than a few centimes, and I did not grudge its price."

And taking from the open desk the little box, I put it into his hand.

"It lay ready in my lap this morning," I continued; "and if Monsieur had been rather more patient, and Mademoiselle St. Pierre less interfering—perhaps I should say, too, if *I* had been calmer and wiser—I should have given it then."

He looked at the box: I saw its clear warm tint and bright azure circlet pleased his eyes. I told him to open it.

"My initials!" said he, indicating the letters in the lid. "Who told you I was called Carl David?"

"A little bird, monsieur."

"Does it fly from me to you? Then one can tie a message under its wing when needful."

He took out the chain—a trifle indeed as to value, but glossy with silk and sparkling with beads. He liked that too—admired it artlessly, like a child.

"For me?"

"Yes, for you."

"This is the thing you were working at last night?"

"The same."

"You finished it this morning?"

"I did."

"You commenced it with the intention that it should be mine?"

"Undoubtedly."

"And offered on my fête-day?"

"Yes."

"This purpose continued as you wove it?"

Again I assented.

"Then it is not necessary that I should cut out any portion—saying, this part is not mine: it was plaited under the idea and for the adornment of another?"

"By no means. It is neither necessary, nor would it be just."

"This object is *all* mine?"

"That object is yours entirely."

Straightway Monsieur opened his paletôt, arranged the guard splendidly across his chest, displaying as much and suppressing as little as he could: for he had no notion of concealing what he admired and thought decorative. As to the box, he pronounced it a superb bonbonnière—he was fond of bon-bons, by the way—and as he always liked to share with others what pleased himself, he would give his "dragées" as freely as he lent his books. Amongst the kind brownie's gifts left in my desk I forgot to enumerate many a paper of chocolate comfits. His tastes in these matters were southern, and what we think infantine. His simple lunch consisted frequently of a brioche, which, as often as not, he shared with some child of the third division.

"A présent c'est un fait accompli," said he, readjusting his paletôt; and we had no more words on the subject. After looking over the two volumes he had brought, and cutting away some pages with his pen-knife (he generally pruned before lending his books, especially if they were novels, and sometimes I was a little provoked at the severity of his censorship, the retrenchments interrupting the narrative), he rose, politely touched his bonnet-grec, and bade me a civil good day.

"We are friends now," thought I, "till the next time we quarrel."

We *might* have quarrelled again that very same evening, but, wonderful to relate! failed, for once, to make the most of our opportunity.

Contrary to all expectation, M. Paul arrived at the study hour. Having seen so much of him in the morning, we did not look for his presence at night. No sooner were we seated at lessons, however, than he appeared. I own I was glad to see him, so glad that I could not help greeting his arrival with a smile; and when he made his way to the same seat about which so serious a misunderstanding had formerly arisen, I took good care not to make too much room for him; he watched with a jealous, side-long look to see whether I shrank away, but I did not, though the bench was a little crowded. I was losing the early impulse to recoil from M. Paul. Habituated to the paletôt and bonnet-grec, the neighbourhood of these garments seemed no longer uncomfortable or very formidable. I did not now sit restrained, "asphyxiée" (as he used to say) at his side; I stirred when I wished to stir, coughed when it was necessary, even yawned when I was tired—did, in short, what I pleased, blindly reliant upon his indulgence. Nor did my temerity, this evening at least, meet the punishment it perhaps merited; he was both indulgent and good-natured; not a cross glance shot from his eyes, not a hasty word left his lips. Till the very close of the evening, he did not indeed address me at all, yet I felt, somehow, that he was full of friendliness. Silence is of different kinds, and breathes different meanings; no words could inspire a pleasanter content than did M. Paul's wordless presence. When the tray came in, and the bustle of supper commenced, he just said, as he retired, that he wished me a good night and sweet dreams; and a good night and sweet dreams I had.

Chapter XXX

M. PAUL

YET the reader is advised not to be in any hurry with his kindly conclusions, or to suppose, with an over-hasty charity, that from that day M. Paul became a changed character—easy to live with, and no longer apt to flash danger and discomfort round him.

No; he was naturally a little man of unreasonable moods. When over-wrought, which he often was, he became acutely irritable; and, besides, his veins were dark with a livid belladonna tincture, the essence of jealousy. I do not mean merely the tender jealousy of the heart, but that sterner, narrower sentiment whose seat is in the head.

I used to think, as I sat looking at M. Paul, while he was knitting his brow or protruding his lip over some exercise of mine, which had not as many faults as he wished '(for he liked me to commit faults: a knot of blunders was sweet to him as a cluster of nuts), that he had points of resemblance to Napoleon Bonaparte. I think so still.

In a shameless disregard of magnanimity, he resembled the great Emperor. M. Paul would have quarrelled with twenty learned women, would have unblushingly carried on a system of petty bickering and recrimination with a whole capital of coteries, never troubling himself about loss or lack of dignity. He would have exiled fifty Madame de Staëls, if they had annoyed, offended, outrivalled, or opposed him.

I well remember a hot episode of his with a certain Madame Panache—a lady temporarily employed by Madame Beck to give lessons in history. She was clever— that is, she knew a good deal; and, besides, thoroughly possessed the art of making the most of what she knew; of words and confidence she held unlimited command. Her personal appearance was far from destitute of advantages; I believe many people would have pronounced her "a fine woman"; and yet there were points in her robust and ample attractions, as well as in her bustling and demonstrative presence, which, it appeared, the nice and capricious tastes of M. Paul could not away with. The sound of her voice, echoing through the carré, would put him into a strange taking; her long, free step—almost stride—along the corridor would often make him snatch up his papers and decamp on the instant.

With malicious intent he bethought himself, one day, to intrude on her class; as quick as lightning he gathered her method of instruction; it differed from a pet plan of his own. With little ceremony, and less courtesy, he pointed out what he termed her errors. Whether he expected submission and attention, I know not; he met an acrid opposition, accompanied by a round reprimand for his certainly unjustifiable interference.

Instead of withdrawing with dignity, as he might still have done, he threw down the gauntlet of defiance. Madame Panache, bellicose as a Penthesilea, picked it up in a minute. She snapped her fingers in the intermeddler's face; she rushed upon him with a storm of words. M. Emanuel was eloquent; but Madame Panache was voluble. A system of fierce antagonism ensued. Instead of laughing in his sleeve at his fair foe, with all her sore amour-propre and loud self-assertion, M. Paul detested her with intense seriousness; he honoured her with his earnest fury; he pursued her vindictively and implacably, refusing to rest peacably in his bed, to derive due benefit from his meals, or even serenely to relish his cigar, till she was fairly rooted out of the establishment. The Professor conquered, but I cannot say that the laurels of this victory shadowed gracefully his temples. Once I ventured to hint as much. To my great surprise he allowed that I might be right, but averred that when brought into contact with either men or women of the coarse, self-complacent quality whereof Madame Panache was a specimen he had no control over his own passions; an unspeakable and active aversion impelled him to a war of extermination.

Three months afterwards, hearing that his vanquished foe had met with reverses, and was likely to be really distressed for want of employment, he forgot his hatred, and, alike active in good and evil, he moved heaven and earth till he found her a place. Upon her coming to make up former differences, and thank him for his recent kindness, the old voice—a little loud—the old manner—a little forward— so acted upon him that in ten minutes he started up and bowed her, or rather himself, out of the room, in a transport of nervous irritation.

To pursue a somewhat audacious parallel, in a love of power, in an eager grasp after supremacy, M. Emanuel was like Bonaparte. He was a man not always to be submitted to. Sometimes it was needful to resist; it was right to stand still, to look

up into his eyes and tell him that his requirements went beyond reason—that his absolutism verged on tyranny.

The dawnings, the frst developments of peculiar talent appearing within his range, and under his rule, curiously excited, even disturbed him. He watched its struggle into life with a scowl; he held back his hand—perhaps said, "Come on if you have strength," but would not aid the birth.

When the pang and peril of the first conflict were over, when the breath of life was drawn, when he saw the lungs expand and contract, when he felt the heart beat and discovered life in the eye, he did not yet offer to foster.

"Prove yourself true ere I cherish you," was his ordinance; and how difficult he made that proof! What thorns and briars, what flints, he strewed in the path of feet not inured to rough travel! He watched tearlessly ordeals that he exacted should be passed through fearlessly. He followed footprints that, as they approached the bourne, were sometimes marked in blood—followed them grimly, holding the austerest police-watch over the pain-pressed pilgrim. And when at last he allowed a rest, before slumber might close the eyelids, he opened those same lids wide, with pitiless finger and thumb, and gazed deep through the pupil and the irids into the brain, into the heart, to search if Vanity, or Pride, or Falsehood, in any of its subtlest forms, was discoverable in the furthest recess of existence. If, at last, he let the neophyte sleep, it was but a moment; he woke him suddenly up to apply new tests: he sent him on irksome errands when he was staggering with weariness; he tried the temper, the sense, and the health; and it was only when every severest test had been applied and endured, when the most corrosive aquafortis had been used, and failed to tarnish the ore, that he admitted it genuine and, still in clouded silence, stamped it with his deep brand of approval.

I speak not ignorant of these evils.

Till the date at which the last chapter closes M. Paul had not been my professor—he had not given me lessons, but about that time, accidentally hearing me one day acknowledge an ignorance of some branch of education (I think it was arithmetic), which would have disgraced a charity-schoolboy, as he very truly remarked, he took me in hand, examined me first, found me, I need not say, abundantly deficient, gave me some books and appointed me some tasks.

He did this at first with pleasure, indeed with unconcealed exultation, condescending to say that he believed I was "bonne et pas trop faible" (*i.e.*, well enough disposed, and not wholly destitute of parts), but, owing he supposed to adverse circumstances, "as yet in a state of wretchedly imperfect mental development."

The beginning of all effort has indeed with me been marked by a preternatural imbecility. I never could, even in forming a common acquaintance, assert or prove a claim to average quickness. A depressing and difficult passage has prefaced every new page I have turned in life.

So long as this passage lasted, M. Paul was very kind, very good, very forbearing; he saw the sharp pain inflicted, and felt the weighty humiliation imposed by my own sense of incapacity; and words can hardly do justice to his tenderness and helpfulness. His own eyes would moisten when tears of shame and effort clouded mine; burdened as he was with work, he would steal half his brief space of recreation to give to me.

But, strange grief! when that heavy and overcast dawn began at last to yield to day; when my faculties began to struggle themselves free, and my time of energy and fulfilment came; when I voluntarily doubled, trebled, quadrupled the tasks he set, to please him as I thought, his kindness became sternness; the light changed in his eyes from a beam to a spark; he fretted, he opposed, he curbed me imperiously; the more I did, the harder I worked, the less he seemed content. Sarcasms of which the severity amazed and puzzled me, harassed my ears; then flowed out the bitterest innuendoes against the "pride of intellect." I was vaguely threatened with I know not what doom if I ever trespassed the limits proper to my sex, and conceived a

contraband appetite for unfeminine knowledge. Alas! I had no such appetite. What I loved, it joyed me by any effort to content: but the noble hunger for science in the abstract—the godlike thirst after discovery—these feelings were known to me but by briefest flashes.

Yet, when M. Paul sneered at me, I wanted to possess them more fully: his injustice stirred in me ambitious wishes—it imparted a strong stimulus—it gave wings to aspiration.

In the beginning, before I had penetrated to motives, that uncomprehended sneer of his made my heart ache, but by-and-by it only warmed the blood in my veins, and sent added action to my pulses. Whatever my powers—feminine or the contrary— God had given them, and I felt resolute to be ashamed of no faculty of His bestowal.

The combat was very sharp for a time. I seemed to have lost M. Paul's affection; he treated me strangely. In his most unjust moments he would insinuate that I had deceived him when I appeared what he called "faible"—that is, incompetent; he said I had feigned a false incapacity. Again, he would turn suddenly round and accuse me of the most far-fetched imitations and impossible plagiarisms, asserting that I had extracted the pith out of books I had not so much as heard of—and over the perusal of which I should infallibly have fallen down in a sleep as deep as that of Eutychus.

Once, upon his preferring such an accusation, I turned upon him—I rose against him. Gathering an armful of his books out of my desk, I filled my apron and poured them in a heap upon his estrade at his feet.

"Take them away, M. Paul," I said, "and teach me no more. I never asked to be made learned, and you compel me to feel very profoundly that learning is not happiness."

And returning to my desk, I laid my head on my arms, nor would I speak to him for two days afterwards. He pained and chagrined me. His affection had been very sweet and dear—a pleasure new and incomparable: now that this seemed withdrawn, I cared not for his lessons.

The books, however, were not taken away; they were all restored with careful hand to their places, and he came as usual to teach me. He made his peace somehow— too readily, perhaps; I ought to have stood out longer, but when he looked kind and good, and held out his hand with amity, memory refused to reproduce with due force his oppressive moments. And then, reconcilement is always sweet!

On a certain morning a message came from my godmother, inviting me to attend some notable lecture to be delivered in the same public rooms before described. Dr. John had brought the message himself, and delivered it verbally to Rosine, who had not scrupled to follow the steps of M. Emanuel, then passing to the first classe, and, in his presence, stand "carrément" before my desk, hand in apron-pocket, and rehearse the same, saucily and aloud, concluding with the words—

"Qu'il est vraiment beau, mademoiselle, ce jeune docteur! Quels yeux—quel regard! Tenez! J'en ai le cœur tout ému!"

When she was gone, my professor demanded of me why I suffered "cette fille effrontée, cette créature sans pudeur," to address me in such terms.

I had no pacifying answer to give. The terms were precisely such as Rosine—a young lady in whose skull the organs of reverence and reserve were not largely developed—was in the constant habit of using. Besides, what she said about the young doctor was true enough. Graham *was* handsome; he *had* fine eyes and a thrilling glance. An observance to that effect actually formed itself into sound on my lips.

"Elle ne dit que la vérité," I said.

"Ah! vous trouvez?"

"Mais, sans doute."

The lesson to which we had that day to submit was such as to make us very glad when it terminated. At its close, the released pupils rushed out half-trembling, half-

exultant. I, too, was going. A mandate to remain arrested me. I muttered that I wanted some fresh air sadly—the stove was in a glow, the classe over-heated. An inexorable voice merely recommended silence; and this salamander—for whom no room ever seemed too hot—sitting down between my desk and the stove—a situation in which he ought to have felt broiled, but did not—proceeded to confront me with—a Greek quotation!

In M. Emanuel's soul rankled a chronic suspicion that I knew both Greek and Latin. As monkeys are said to have the power of speech if they would but use it, and are reported to conceal this faculty in fear of its being turned to their detriment, so to me was ascribed a fund of knowledge which I was supposed criminally and craftily to conceal. The privileges of a "classical education," it was insinuated, had been mine; on flowers of Hymettus I had revelled; a golden store, hived in memory, now silently sustained my efforts, and privily nurtured my wits.

A hundred expedients did M. Paul employ to surprise my secret—to wheedle, to threaten, to startle it out of me. Sometimes he placed Greek and Latin books in my way, and then watched me, as Joan of Arc's jailers tempted her with the warrior's accoutrements, and lay in wait for the issue. Again he quoted I know not what authors and passages, and while rolling out their sweet and sounding lines (the classic tones fell musically from his lips—for he had a good voice—remarkable for compass, modulation, and matchless expression), he would fix on me a vigilant, piercing, and often malicious eye. It was evident he sometimes expected great demonstrations; they never occurred, however; not comprehending, of course, I could neither be charmed nor annoyed.

Baffled—almost angry—he still clung to his fixed idea; my susceptibilities were pronounced marble—my face a mask. It appeared as if he could not be brought to accept the homely truth, and take me for what I was: men, and women too, must have delusion of some sort; if not made ready to their hand, they will invent exaggeration for themselves.

At moments I *did* wish that his suspicions had been better founded. There were times when I would have given my right hand to possess the treasures he ascribed to me. He deserved condign punishment for his testy crotchets. I could have gloried in bringing home to him his worst apprehensions astoundingly realised. I could have exulted to burst on his vision, confront and confound his lunettes, one blaze of acquirements. Oh! why did nobody undertake to make me clever while I was young enough to learn, that I might, by one grand, sudden, inhuman revelation— one cold, cruel, overwhelming triumph—have for ever crushed the mocking spirit out of Paul Carl David Emanuel!

Alas! no such feat was in my power. To-day, as usual, his quotations fell ineffectual: he soon shifted his ground.

"Women of intellect" was the next theme: here he was at home. A "woman of intellect," it appeared, was a sort of *lusus naturae,* a luckless accident, a thing for which there was neither place nor use in creation, wanted neither as wife nor worker. Beauty anticipated her in the first office. He believed in his soul that lovely, placid, and passive feminine mediocrity was the only pillow on which manly thought and sense could find rest for its aching temples; and as to work, male mind alone could work to any good practical result—hein?

This "hein?" was a note of interrogation intended to draw from me contradiction or objection. However, I only said—

"Cela ne me regarde pas: je ne m'en soucie pas": and presently added—"May I go, monsieur? They have rung the bell for the second déjeuner" (*i.e.,* luncheon).

"What of that? You are not hungry?"

"Indeed I was," I said; "I had had nothing since breakfast, at seven, and should have nothing till dinner, at five, if I missed this bell."

"Well, he was in the same plight, but I might share with him."

And he broke in two the brioche intended for his own refreshment, and gave me half. Truly his bark was worse than his bite; but the really formidable attack was yet to come. While eating his cake, I could not forbear expressing my secret wish that I really knew all of which he accused me.

"Did I sincerely feel myself to be an ignoramus?" he asked, in a softened tone.

If I had replied meekly by an unqualified affirmative, I believe he would have stretched out his hand and we should have been friends on the spot, but I answered—

"Not exactly. I am ignorant, monsieur, in the knowledge you ascribe to me, but I *sometimes*, not *always*, feel a knowledge of my own."

"What did I mean?" he inquired sharply.

Unable to answer this question in a breath, I evaded it by change of subject. He had now finished his half of the brioche: feeling sure that on so trifling a fragment he could not have satisfied his appetite, as indeed I had not appeased mine, and inhaling the fragrance of baked apples afar from the refectory, I ventured to inquire whether he did not also perceive that agreeable odour. He confessed that he did. I said if he would let me out by the garden-door, and permit me just to run across the court, I would fetch him a plateful; and added that I believed they were excellent, as Goton had a very good method of baking, or rather stewing fruit, putting in a little spice, sugar, and a glass or two of vin blanc—might I go?

"Petite gourmande!" said he, smiling, "I have not forgotten how pleased you were with the pâté à la crème I once gave you, and you know very well, at this moment, that to fetch the apples for me will be the same as getting them for yourself. Go, then, but come back quickly."

And at last he liberated me on parole. My own plan was to go and return with speed and good faith, to put the plate in at the door, and then to vanish incontinent, leaving all consequences for future settlement.

That intolerably keen instinct of his seemed to have anticipated my scheme; he met me at the threshold, hurried me into the room, and fixed me in a minute in my former seat. Taking the plate of fruit from my hand, he divided the portion intended only for himself, and ordered me to eat my share. I complied with no good grace, and vexed, I suppose, by my reluctance, he opened a masked and dangerous battery. All he had yet said, I could count as mere sound and fury, signifying nothing: not so of the present attack.

It consisted in an unreasonable proposition with which he had before afflicted me: namely, that on the next public examination day I should engage—foreigner as I was—to take my place on the first form of first class pupils, and with them improvise a composition in French, on any subject any spectator might dictate, without benefit of grammar or lexicon.

I knew what the result of such an experiment would be. I, to whom nature had denied the impromptu faculty; who, in public, was by nature a cypher; whose time of mental activity, even when alone, was not under the meridian sun; who needed the fresh silence of morning, or the recluse peace of evening, to win from the Creative Impulse one evidence of his presence, one proof of his force; I, with whom that Impulse was the most intractable, the most capricious, the most maddening of masters (him before me always excepted)—a deity which sometimes, under circumstances apparently propitious, would not speak when questioned, would not hear when appealed to, would not, when sought, be found; but would stand, all cold, all indurated, all granite, a dark Baal with carven lips and blank eyeballs, and breast like the stone face of a tomb; and again, suddenly, at some turn, some sound, some long-trembling sob of the wind, at some rushing past of an unseen stream of electricity, the irrational demon would wake unsolicited, would stir strangely alive, would rush from its pedestal like a perturbed Dagon, calling to its votary for a sacrifice, whatever the hour—to its victim for some blood or some breath, whatever the circumstance or scene—rousing its priest, treacherously promising vaticination,

perhaps filling its temple with a strange hum of oracles, but sure to give half the significance to fateful winds, and grudging to the desperate listener even a miserable remnant—yielding it sordidly, as though each word had been a drop of the deathless ichor of its own dark veins. And this tyrant I was to compel into bondage, and make it improvise a theme, on a school estrade, between a Mathilde and a Coralie, under the eye of a Madame Beck, for the pleasure and to the inspiration of a bourgeois of Labassecour!

Upon this argument M. Paul and I did battle more than once—strong battle, with confused noise of demand and rejection, exaction and repulse.

On this particular day I was soundly rated. "The obstinacy of my whole sex," it seems, was concentrated in me: I had an "orgueil de diable." I feared to fail, forsooth? What did it matter whether I failed or not? Who was I that I should not fail, like my betters? It would do me good to fail. He wanted to see me worsted (I knew he did), and one minute he paused to take breath.

"Would I speak now, and be tractable?"

"Never would I be tractable in this matter. Law itself should not compel me. I would pay a fine, or undergo an imprisonment, rather than write for a show and to order, perched up on a platform."

"Could softer motives influence me? Would I yield for friendship's sake?"

"Not a whit, not a hair-breadth. No form of friendship under the sun had a right to exact such a concession. No true friendship would harass me thus."

He supposed then (with a sneer—M. Paul could sneer supremely, curling his lip, opening his nostrils, contracting his eyelids)—he supposed there was but one form of appeal to which I would listen, and of that form it was not for him to make use.

"Under certain persuasions, from certain quarters, je vous vois d'ici," said he, "eagerly subscribing to the sacrifice, passionately arming for the effort."

"Making a simpleton, a warning, and an example of myself before a hundred and fifty of the 'papas' and 'mammas' of Villette."

And here, losing patience, I broke out afresh with a cry that I wanted to be liberated—to get out into the air—I was almost in a fever.

"Chut," said the inexorable, "this was a mere pretext to run away; *he* was not hot, with the stove close at his back; how could I suffer, thoroughly screened by his person?"

"I did not understand his constitution. I knew nothing of the natural history of salamanders. For my own part, I was a phlegmatic islander, and sitting in an oven did not agree with me; at least, might I step to the well and get a glass of water— the sweet apples had made me thirsty?"

"If that was all, he would do my errand."

He went to fetch the water. Of course, with a door only on the latch behind me, I lost not my opportunity. Ere his return, his half-worried prey had escaped.

Chapter XXXI

THE DRYAD

THE spring was advancing, and the weather had turned suddenly warm. This change of temperature brought with it for me, as probably for many others, temporary decrease of strength. Slight exertion at this time left me overcome with fatigue— sleepless nights entailed languid days.

One Sunday afternoon, having walked the distance of half a league to the Protestant church, I came back weary and exhausted; and taking refuge in my solitary sanctuary,

the first classe, I was glad to sit down, and to make of my desk a pillow for my arms and head.

Awhile I listened to the lullaby of bees humming in the berceau, and watched, through the glass door and the tender, lightly-strewn spring foliage, Madame Beck and a gay party of friends, whom she had entertained that day at dinner after morning-mass, walking in the centre alley under orchard boughs dressed at this season in blossom, and wearing a colouring as pure and warm as mountain-snow at sunrise.

My principal attraction towards this group of guests lay, I remember, in one figure—that of a handsome young girl whom I had seen before as a visitor at Madame Beck's, and of whom I had been vaguely told that she was a "filleule," or god-daughter, of M. Emanuel's, and that between her mother, or aunt, or some other female relation of hers, and the Professor—had existed of old a special friendship. M. Paul was not of the holiday band to-day, but I had seen this young girl with him ere now, and as far as distant observation could enable me to judge, she seemed to enjoy him with the frank ease of a ward with an indulgent guardian. I had seen her run up to him, put her arm through his, and hang upon him. Once, when she did so, a curious sensation had struck through me—a disagreeable anticipatory sensation—one of the family of presentiments, I suppose—but I refused to analyse or dwell upon it. While watching this girl, Mademoiselle Sauveur by name, and following the gleam of her bright silk robe (she was always richly dressed, for she was said to be wealthy) through the flowers and glancing leaves of tender emerald, my eyes became dazzled—they closed; my lassitude, the warmth of the day, the hum of bees and birds, all lulled me, and at last I slept.

Two hours stole over me. Ere I woke, the sun had declined out of sight behind the towering houses, the garden and the room were grey, bees had gone homeward, and the flowers were closing; the party of guests, too, had vanished; each alley was void.

On waking, I felt much at ease—not chill, as I ought to have been after sitting so still for at least two hours; my cheek and arms were not benumbed by pressure against the hard desk. No wonder. Instead of the bare wood on which I had laid them, I found a thick shawl, carefully folded, substituted for support, and another shawl (both taken from the corridor where such things hung) wrapped warmly round me.

Who had done this? Who was my friend? Which of the teachers? Which of the pupils? None, except St. Pierre, was inimical to me; but which of them had the art, the thought, the habit, of benefiting thus tenderly? Which of them had a step so quiet, a hand so gentle, but I should have heard or felt her if she had approached or touched me in a day-sleep?

As to Ginevra Fanshawe, that bright young creature was not gentle at all, and would certainly have pulled me out of my chair, if she had meddled in the matter, I said at last: "It is Madame Beck's doing; she has come in, seen me asleep, and thought I might take cold. She considers me a useful machine, answering well the purpose for which it was hired; so would not have me needlessly injured. And now," methought, "I'll take a walk; the evening is fresh, and not very chill."

So I opened the glass door and stepped into the berceau.

I went to my own alley: had it been dark, or even dusk, I should have hardly ventured there, for I had not yet forgotten the curious illusion of vision (if illusion it were) experienced in that place some months ago. But a ray of the setting sun burnished the grey crown of Jean Baptiste; nor had all the birds of the garden yet vanished into their nests amongst the tufted shrubs and thick wall-ivy. I paced up and down, thinking almost the same thoughts I had pondered that night when I buried my glass jar—how I should make some advance in life, take another step towards an independent position; for this train of reflection, though not lately pursued, had never by me been wholly abandoned; and whenever a certain eye was

averted from me, and a certain countenance grew dark with unkindness and injustice, into that track of speculation did I at once strike; so that, little by little, I had laid half a plan.

"Living costs little," said I to myself, "in this economical town of Villette, where people are more sensible than I understand they are in dear old England—infinitely less worried about appearance, and less emulous of display—where nobody is in the least ashamed to be quite as homely and saving as he finds convenient. House rent, in a prudently chosen situation, need not be high. When I shall have saved one thousand francs, I will take a tenement with one large room and two or three smaller ones, furnish the first with a few benches and desks, a black tableau, an estrade for myself; upon it a chair and table, with a sponge and some white chalks; begin with taking day pupils, and so work my way upwards. Madame Beck's commencement was—as I have often heard her say—from no higher starting-point, and where is she now? All these premises and this garden are hers, bought with her money; she has a competency already secured for old age, and a flourishing establishment under her direction which will furnish a career for her children.

"Courage, Lucy Snowe! With self-denial and economy now, and steady exertion by-and-by, an object in life need not fail you. Venture not to complain that such an object is too selfish, too limited, and lacks interest; be content to labour for independence until you have proved, by winning that prize, your right to look higher. But afterwards, is there nothing more for me in life—no true home—nothing to be dearer to me than myself, and by its paramount preciousness to draw from me better things than I care to culture for myself only? Nothing at whose feet I can willingly lay down the whole burden of human egotism, and gloriously take up the nobler charge of labouring and living for others? I suppose, Lucy Snowe, the orb of your life is not to be so rounded: for you the crescent-phase must suffice. Very good. I see a huge mass of my fellow-creatures in no better circumstances. I see that a great many men, and more women, hold their span of life on conditions of denial and privation. I find no reason why I should be of the few favoured. I believe in some blending of hope and sunshine sweetening the worst lots. I believe that this life is not all; neither the beginning nor the end. I believe while I tremble; I trust while I weep."

So this subject is done with. It is right to look our life-accounts bravely in the face now and then, and settle them honestly. And he is a poor self-swindler who lies to himself while he reckons the items, and sets down under the head happiness that which is misery. Call anguish—anguish, and despair—despair; write both down in strong characters with resolute pen: you will the better pay your debt to Doom. Falsify; insert "privilege" where you should have written "pain"; and see if your mighty creditor will allow the fraud to pass, or accept the coin with which you would cheat him. Offer to the strongest—if the darkest angel of God's host—water, when he has asked blood—will he take it? Not a whole pale sea for one red drop. I settled another account.

Pausing before Methusaleh—the giant and patriarch of the garden—and leaning my brow against his knotty trunk, my foot rested on the stone sealing the small sepulchre at his root; and I recalled the passage of feeling therein buried; I recalled Dr. John; my warm affection for him; my faith in his excellence; my delight in his grace. What was become of that curious one-sided friendship which was half marble and half life; only on one hand truth, and on the other perhaps a jest?

Was this feeling dead? I do not know, but it was buried. Sometimes I thought the tomb unquiet, and dreamed strangely of disturbed earth, and of hair, still golden and living, obtruded through coffin-chinks.

Had I been too hasty? I used to ask myself; and this question would occur with a cruel sharpness after some brief chance interview with Dr. John. He had still such kind looks, such a warm hand; his voice still kept so pleasant a tone for my name; I never liked "Lucy" so well as when he uttered it. But I learned in time

that this benignity, this cordiality, this music, belonged in no shape to me: it was a part of himself; it was the honey of his temper: it was the balm of his mellow mood; he imparted it, as the ripe fruit rewards with sweetness the rifling bee; he diffused it about him, as sweet plants shed their perfume. Does the nectarine love either the bee or bird it feeds? Is the sweet-briar enamoured of the air?

"Good night, Dr. John; you are good, you are beautiful, but you are not mine. Good night, and God bless you!"

Thus I closed my musings. "Good night" left my lips in sound; I heard the words spoken, and then I heard an echo—quite close.

"Good night, mademoiselle; or, rather, good evening—the sun is scarce set; I hope you slept well?"

I started, but was only discomposed a moment; I knew the voice and speaker.

"Slept, monsieur! When? where?"

"You may well inquire when—where. It seems you turn day into night, and choose a desk for a pillow; rather hard lodging?"

"It was softened for me, monsieur, while I slept. That unseen, gift-bringing thing which haunts my desk remembered me. No matter how I fell asleep; I awoke pillowed and covered."

"Did the shawls keep you warm?"

"Very warm. Do you ask thanks for them?"

"No. You looked pale in your slumbers; are you home-sick?"

"To be home-sick one must have a home, which I have not."

"Then you have more need of a careful friend. I scarcely know any one, Miss Lucy, who needs a friend more absolutely than you; your very faults imperatively require it. You want so much checking, regulating, and keeping down."

This idea of "keeping down" never left M. Paul's head; the most habitual subjugation would, in my case, have failed to relieve him of it. No matter; what did it signify? I listened to him, and did not trouble myself to be too submissive; his occupation would have been gone had I left him nothing to "keep down."

"You need watching, and watching over," he pursued; "and it is well for you that I see this, and do my best to discharge both duties. I watch you and others pretty closely, pretty constantly, nearer and oftener than you or they think. Do you see that window with a light in it?"

He pointed to a lattice in one of the college boarding-houses.

"That," said he, "is a room I have hired, nominally for a study—virtually for a post of observation. There I sit and read for hours together: it is my way—my taste. My book is this garden; its contents are human nature—female human nature. I know you all by heart. Ah! I know you well—St. Pierre, the Parisienne—cette maîtresse-femme, my cousin Beck herself."

"It is not right, monsieur."

"Comment? it is not right? By whose creed? Does some dogma of Calvin or Luther condemn it? What is that to me? I am no Protestant. My rich father (for, though I have known poverty, and once starved for a year in a garret in Rome— starved wretchedly, often on a meal a day, and sometimes not that—yet I was born to wealth)—my rich father was a good Catholic; and he gave me a priest and a Jesuit for a tutor. I retain his lessons; and to what discoveries, grand Dieu! have they not aided me!"

"Discoveries made by stealth seem to me dishonourable discoveries."

"Puritaine! I doubt it not. You see how my Jesuit's system works. You know the St. Pierre?"

"Partially."

He laughed "You say right—'*partially*'; whereas *I* know her *thoroughly*; there is the difference. She played before me the amiable; offered me patte de velours; caressed, flattered, fawned on me. Now, I am accessible to a woman's flattery— accessible against my reason. Though never pretty, she was—when I first knew

her—young, or knew how to look young. Like all her countrywomen, she had the art of dressing—she had a certain cool, easy, social assurance which spared me the pain of embarrassment''——

''Monsieur, that must have been unnecessary. I never saw you embarrassed in my life.''

''Mademoiselle, you know little of me; I can be embarrassed as a petite pensionnaire; there is a fund of modesty and diffidence in my nature''——

''Monsieur, I never saw it.''

''Mademoiselle, it is there. You ought to have seen it.''

''Monsieur, I have observed you in public—on platforms, in tribunes, before titles and crowned heads—and you were as easy as you are in the third division.''

''Mademoiselle, neither titles nor crowned heads excite my modesty; and publicity is very much my element. I like it well, and breathe in it quite freely; but—but—in short, here is the sentiment brought into action, at this very moment; however, I disdain to be worsted by it. If, mademoiselle, I were a marrying man (which I am not; and you may spare yourself the trouble of any sneer you may be contemplating at the thought), and found it necessary to ask a lady whether she could look upon me in the light of a future husband, then would it be proved that I am as I say—modest.''

I quite believed him now; and, in believing, I honoured him with a sincerity of esteem which made my heart ache.

''As to the St. Pierre,'' he went on, recovering himself, for his voice had altered a little, ''she once intended to be Madame Emanuel; and I don't know whither I might have been led but for yonder little lattice with the light. Ah, magic lattice! what miracles of discovery hast thou wrought! Yes,'' he pursued, ''I have seen her rancours, her vanities, her levities—not only here, but elsewhere: I have witnessed what bucklers me against all her arts: I am safe from poor Zélie.''

''And my pupils,'' he presently recommenced, ''those blondes jeunes filles—so mild and meek—I have seen the most reserved romp like boys: the demurest snatch grapes from the walls, shake pears from the trees. When the English teacher came, I saw her, marked her early preference for this alley, noted her taste for seclusion, watched her well, long before she and I came to speaking terms; do you recollect my once coming silently and offering you a little knot of white violets when we were strangers?''

''I recollect it. I dried the violets, kept them, and have them still.''

''It pleased me when you took them peacefully and promptly, without prudery—that sentiment which I ever dread to excite, and which, when it is revealed in eye or gesture, I vindictively detest. To return. Not only did _I_ watch you, but often—especially at eventide—another guardian angel was noiselessly hovering near: night after night my cousin Beck has stolen down yonder steps, and glidingly pursued your movements when you did not see her.''

''But, monsieur, you could not from the distance of that window see what passed in this garden at night?''

''By moonlight I possibly might with a glass—I use a glass—but the garden itself is open to me. In the shed, at the bottom, there is a door leading into a court, which communicates with the college; of that door I possess the key, and thus come and go at pleasure. This afternoon I came through it, and found you asleep in classe; again this evening I have availed myself of the same entrance.''

I could not help saying, ''If you were a wicked, designing man, how terrible would all this be!''

His attention seemed incapable of being arrested by this view of the subject: he lit his cigar, and while he puffed it, leaning against a tree, and looking at me in a cool, amused way he had when his humour was tranquil, I thought proper to go on sermonising him: he often lectured me by the hour together—I did not see why

I should not speak my mind for once. So I told him my impressions concerning his Jesuit system.

"The knowledge it brings you is bought too dear, monsieur; this coming and going by stealth degrades your own dignity."

"My dignity!" he cried, laughing; "when did you ever see me trouble my head about my dignity? It is you, Miss Lucy, who are 'digne.' How often, in your high insular presence, have I taken a pleasure in trampling upon what you are pleased to call my dignity; tearing it, scattering it to the winds, in those mad transports you witness with such hauteur, and which I know you think very like the ravings of a third-rate London actor."

"Monsieur, I tell you every glance you cast from that lattice is a wrong done to the best part of your own nature. To study the human heart thus is to banquet secretly and sacrilegiously on Eve's apples. I wish you were a Protestant."

Indifferent to the wish, he smoked on. After a space of smiling yet thoughtful silence, he said, rather suddenly—

"I have seen other things."

Taking the weed from his lips, he threw the remnant amongst the shrubs, where, for a moment, it lay glowing in the gloom.

"Look at it," said he: "is not that spark like an eye watching you and me?"

He took a turn down the walk; presently returning, he went on—"I have seen, Miss Lucy, things to me unaccountable, that have made me watch all night for a solution, and I have not yet found it."

The tone was peculiar; my veins thrilled; he saw me shiver.

"Are you afraid? Whether it is of my words or that red jealous eye just winking itself out?"

"I am cold; the night grows dark and late, and the air is changed; it is time to go in."

"It is little past eight, but you shall go in soon. Answer me only this question."

Yet he paused ere he put it. The garden was truly growing dark; dusk had come on with clouds, and drops of rain began to patter through the trees. I hoped he would feel this, but, for the moment, he seemed too much absorbed to be sensible of the change.

"Mademoiselle, do you Protestants believe in the supernatural?"

"There is a difference of theory and belief on this point amongst Protestants as amongst other sects," I answered. "Why, monsieur, do you ask such a question?"

"Why do you shrink and speak so faintly? Are you superstitious?"

"I am constitutionally nervous. I dislike the discussion of such subjects. I dislike it the more because"——

"You believe?"

"No: but it has happened to me to experience impressions"——

"Since you came here?"

"Yes; not many months ago."

"Here?—in this house?"

"Yes."

"Bon! I am glad of it. I knew it, somehow, before you told me. I was conscious of rapport between you and myself. You are patient, and I am choleric; you are quiet and pale, and I am tanned and fiery; you are a strict Protestant, and I am a sort of lay Jesuit: but we are alike—there is affinity between us. Do you see it, mademoiselle, when you look in the glass? Do you observe that your forehead is shaped like mine—that your eyes are cut like mine? Do you hear that you have some of my tones of voice? Do you know that you have many of my looks? I perceive all this, and believe that you were born under my star! Yes, you were born under my star! Tremble! for where that is the case with mortals, the threads of their destinies are difficult to disentangle; knottings and catchings occur—sudden

breaks leave damage in the web. But these 'impressions,' as you say, with English caution. I, too, have had my 'impressions.' ''

"Monsieur, tell me them."

"I desire no better, and intend no less. You know the legend of this house and garden?''

"I know it. Yes. They say that hundreds of years ago a nun was buried here alive at the foot of this very tree, beneath the ground which now bears us."

"And that in former days a nun's ghost used to come and go here."

"Monsieur, what if it comes and goes here still?"

"Something comes and goes here: there is a shape frequenting this house by night, different to any forms that show themselves by day. I have indisputably seen a something, more than once; and to me its conventual weeds were a strange sight, saying more than they can do to any other living being. A nun!''

"Monsieur, I, too, have seen it."

"I anticipated that. Whether this nun be flesh and blood, or something that remains when blood is dried and flesh is wasted, her business is as much with you as with me probably. Well, I mean to make it out; it has baffled me so far, but I mean to follow up the mystery. I mean''——

Instead of telling what he meant, he raised his head suddenly; I made the same movement in the same instant; we both looked to one point—the high tree shadowing the great berceau, and resting some of its boughs on the roof of the first classe. There had been a strange and inexplicable sound from that quarter, as if the arms of that tree had swayed of their own motion, and its weight of foliage had rushed and crushed against the massive trunk. Yes; there scarce stirred a breeze, and that heavy tree was convulsed, whilst the feathery shrubs stood still. For some minutes amongst the wood and leafage a rending and heaving went on. Dark as it was, it seemed to me that something more solid than either night-shadow or branch-shadow blackened out of the boles. At last the struggle ceased. What birth succeeded this travail? What Dryad was born of these throes? We watched fixedly. A sudden bell rang in the house—the prayer-bell. Instantly into our alley there came, out of the berceau, an apparition, all black and white. With a sort of angry rush—close, close past our faces—swept swiftly the very NUN herself! Never had I seen her so clearly. She looked tall of stature, and fierce of gesture. As she went, the wind rose sobbing; the rain poured wild and cold; the whole night seemed to feel her.

Chapter XXXII

THE FIRST LETTER

WHERE, it becomes time to inquire, was Paulina Mary? How fared my intercourse with the sumptuous Hôtel Crécy? That intercourse had, for an interval, been suspended by absence; M. and Miss de Bassompierre had been travelling, dividing some weeks between the provinces and capital of France. Chance apprised me of their return very shortly after it took place.

I was walking one mild afternoon on a quiet boulevard, wandering slowly on, enjoying the benign April sun and some thoughts not unpleasing, when I saw before me a group of riders, stopping as if they had just encountered, and exchanging greetings in the midst of the broad, smooth, linden-bordered path; on one side a middle-aged gentleman and young lady, on the other a young and handsome man. Very graceful was the lady's mien, choice her appointments, delicate and stately her whole aspect. Still, as I looked, I felt they were known to me, and, drawing a little nearer, I fully recognised them all; the Count Home de Bassompierre, his daughter, and Dr. Graham Bretton.

How animated was Graham's face! How true, how warm, yet how retiring the joy it expressed! This was the state of things, this the combination of circumstances, at once to attract and enchain, to subdue and excite Dr. John. The pearl he admired was in itself of great price and truest purity, but he was not the man who, in appreciating the gem, could forget its setting. Had he seen Paulina with the same youth, beauty, and grace, but on foot, alone, unguarded, and in simple attire, a dependent, a worker, a demi-grisette, he would have thought her a pretty little creature, and would have loved with his eye her movements and her mien, but it required other than this to conquer him as he was now vanquished, to bring him safe under dominion as now, without loss, and even with gain to his manly honour—one saw that he was reduced; there was about Dr. John all the man of the world; to satisfy himself did not suffice; society must approve—the world must admire what he did, or he counted his measures false and futile. In his victrix he required all that was here visible—the imprint of high cultivation, the consecration of a careful and authoritative protection, the adjuncts that Fashion decrees, Wealth purchases, and Taste adjusts; for these conditions his spirit stipulated ere it surrendered: they were here to the utmost fulfilled; and now, proud, impassioned, yet fearing, he did homage to Paulina as his sovereign. As for her, the smile of feeling, rather than of conscious power, slept soft in her eyes.

They parted. He passed me at speed, hardly feeling the earth be skimmed, and seeing nothing on either hand. He looked very handsome; mettle and purpose were roused in him fully.

"Papa, there is Lucy!" cried a musical, friendly voice. "Lucy, dear Lucy—*do* come here!"

I hastened to her. She threw back her veil, and stooped from her saddle to kiss me.

"I was coming to see you to-morrow," said she; "but now to-morrow you will come and see me."

She named the hour, and I promised compliance.

The morrow's evening found me with her—she and I shut into her own room. I had not seen her since that occasion when her claims were brought into comparison with those of Ginevra Fanshawe, and had so signally prevailed; she had much to tell me of her travels in the interval. A most animated, rapid speaker was she in such a tête-à-tête, a most lively describer; yet, with her artless diction and clear soft voice, she never seemed to speak too fast or to say too much. My own attention, I think, would not soon have flagged, but by-and-by she herself seemed to need some change of subject; she hastened to wind up the narrative briefly. Yet why she terminated with so concise an abridgment did not immediately appear; silence followed—a restless silence, not without symptoms of abstraction. Then, turning to me, in a diffident, half-appealing voice—

"Lucy"——

"Well, I am at your side."

"Is my cousin Ginevra still at Madame Beck's?"

"Your cousin is still there; you must be longing to see her."

"No—not much."

"You want to invite her to spend another evening?"

"No. . . . I suppose she still talks about being married?"

"Not to anyone you care for."

"But of course she still thinks of Dr. Bretton? She cannot have changed her mind on that point, because it was so fixed two months ago."

"Why, you know, it does not matter. You saw the terms on which they stood."

"There was a little misunderstanding that evening, certainly; does she seem unhappy?"

"Not she. To change the subject. Have you heard or seen nothing of or from Graham during your absence?"

"Papa had letters from him once or twice about business, I think. He undertook the management of some affair which required attention while we were away. Dr. Bretton seems to respect papa, and to have pleasure in obliging him."

"Yes: you met him yesterday on the boulevard; you would be able to judge from his aspect that his friends need not be painfully anxious about his health?"

"Papa seems to have thought with you. I could not help smiling. He is not particularly observant, you know, because he is often thinking of other things than what pass before his eyes; but he said, as Dr. Bretton rode away, 'Really, it does a man good to see the spirit and energy of that boy.' He called Dr. Bretton a boy; I believe he almost thinks him so, just as he thinks me a little girl; he was not speaking to me, but dropped that remark to himself. Lucy . . ."

Again fell the appealing accent, and at the same instant she left her chair and came and sat on the stool at my feet.

I liked her. It is not a declaration I have often made concerning my acquaintance in the course of this book: the reader will bear with it for once. Intimate intercourse, close inspection, disclosed in Paulina only what was delicate, intelligent, and sincere; therefore my regard for her lay deep. An admiration more superficial might have been more demonstrative; mine, however, was quiet.

"What have you to ask of Lucy?" said I; "be brave, and speak out."

But there was no courage in her eye; as it met mine, it fell; and there was no coolness on her cheek—not a transient surface-blush, but a gathering inward excitement raised its tint and its temperature.

"Lucy, I *do* wish to know your thoughts of Dr. Bretton. Do, *do* give me your real opinion of his character, his disposition."

"His character stands high, and deservedly high."

"And his disposition? Tell me about his disposition," she urged; "you know him well."

"I know him pretty well."

"You know his home side. You have seen him with his mother; speak of him as a son."

"He is a fine-hearted son; his mother's comfort and hope, her pride and pleasure."

She held my hand between hers, and at each favourable word gave it a little caressing stroke.

"In what other way is he good, Lucy?"

"Dr. Bretton is benevolent—humanely disposed towards all his race. Dr. Bretton would have benignity for the lowest savage or the worst criminal."

"I heard some gentlemen, some of papa's friends, who were talking about him, say the same. They say many of the poor patients at the hospitals, who tremble before some pitiless and selfish surgeons, welcome him."

"They are right; I have witnessed as much. He once took me over a hospital; I saw how he was received: your father's friends are right."

The softest gratitude animated her eye as she lifted it a moment. She had yet more to say, but seemed hesitating about time and place. Dusk was beginning to reign; her parlour fire already glowed with twilight ruddiness; but I thought she wished the room dimmer, the hour later.

"How quiet and secluded we feel here!" I remarked, to reassure her.

"Do we? Yes; it is a still evening, and I shall not be called down to tea; papa is dining out."

Still holding my hand, she played with the fingers unconsciously, dressed them now in her own rings, and now circled them with a twine of her beautiful hair; she patted the palm against her hot cheek, and at last, having cleared a voice that was naturally liquid as a lark's, she said—"You must think it rather strange that I should talk so much about Dr. Bretton, ask so many questions, take such an interest, but"——

"Not at all strange; perfectly natural; you like him."

"And if I did," said she, with slight quickness, "is that a reason why I should talk? I suppose you think me weak, like my cousin Ginevra?"

"If I thought you one whit like Madame Ginevra, I would not sit here waiting for your communications. I would get up, walk at my ease about the room, and anticipate all you had to say by a round lecture. Go on."

"I mean to go on," retorted she; "what else do you suppose I mean to do?" And she looked and spoke—the little Polly of Bretton—petulant, sensitive. "If," said she emphatically, "if I liked Dr. John till I was fit to die for liking him, that alone could not license me to be otherwise than dumb—dumb as the grave—dumb as you, Lucy Snowe—you know it—and you know you would despise me if I failed in self-control, and whined about some rickety liking that was all on my side."

"It is true I little respect women or girls who are loquacious either in boasting the triumphs, or bemoaning the mortifications, of feelings. But as to *you*, Paulina, speak, for I earnestly wish to hear you. Tell me all it will give you pleasure or relief to tell: I ask no more."

"Do you care for me, Lucy?"

"Yes, I do, Paulina."

"And I love you. I had an odd content in being with you even when I was a little, troublesome, disobedient girl: it was charming to me then to lavish on you my naughtiness and whims. Now you are acceptable to me, and I like to talk with and trust you. So listen, Lucy."

And she settled herself, resting against my arm—resting gently, not with honest Mistress Fanshawe's fatiguing and selfish weight.

"A few minutes since you asked whether we had not heard from Graham during our absence, and I said there were two letters for papa on business; this was true, but I did not tell you all."

"You evaded?"

"I shuffled and equivocated, you know. However, I am going to speak the truth now; it is getting darker; one can talk at one's ease. Papa often lets me open the letter bag and give him out the contents. One morning, about three weeks ago, you don't know how surprised I was to find, amongst a dozen letters for M. de Bassompierre, a note addressed to Miss de Bassompierre. I spied it at once, amidst all the rest; the handwriting was not strange; it attracted me directly. I was going to say 'Papa, here is another letter from Dr. Bretton'; but the 'Miss' struck me mute. I actually never received a letter from a gentleman before. Ought I to have shown it to papa, and let him open it and read it first? I could not for my life, Lucy. I know so well papa's ideas about me: he forgets my age; he thinks I am a mere school-girl; he is not aware that other people see I am grown up as tall as I shall be; so, with a curious mixture of feelings, some of them self-reproachful, and some so fluttering and strong, I cannot describe them, I gave papa his twelve letters— his herd of possessions—and kept back my one, my ewe-lamb. It lay in my lap during breakfast, looking up at me with an inexplicable meaning, making me feel myself a thing double-existent—a child to that dear papa, but no more a child to myself. After breakfast I carried my letter upstairs, and having secured myself by turning the key in the door, I began to study the outside of my treasure: it was some minutes before I could get over the direction and penetrate the seal; one does not take a strong place of this kind by instant storm—one sits down awhile before it, as beleaguers say. Graham's hand is like himself, Lucy, and so is his seal—all clear, firm, and rounded—no slovenly splash of wax—a full, solid, steady drop— a distinct impress; no pointed turns harshly pricking the optic nerve, but a clean, mellow, pleasant, manuscript, that soothes you as you read. It is like his face— just like the chiselling of his features: do you know his autograph?"

"I have seen it: go on."

"The seal was too beautiful to be broken, so I cut it round with my scissors. On the point of reading the letter at last, I once more drew back voluntarily; it was

too soon yet to drink that draught—the sparkle in the cup was so beautiful—I would watch it yet a minute. Then I remembered all at once that I had not said my prayers that morning. Having heard papa go down to breakfast a little earlier than usual, I had been afraid of keeping him waiting, and had hastened to join him as soon as dressed, thinking no harm to put off prayers till afterwards. Some people would say I ought to have served God first and then man; but I don't think heaven could be jealous of anything I might do for papa. I believe I am superstitious. A voice seemed now to say that another feeling than filial affection was in question—to urge me to pray before I dared to read what I so longed to read—to deny myself yet a moment, and remember first a great duty. I have had these impulses ever since I can remember. I put the letter down and said my prayers, adding, at the end, a strong entreaty that whatever happened I might not be tempted or led to cause papa any sorrow, and might never, in caring for others, neglect him. The very thought of such a possibility so pierced my heart that it made me cry. But still, Lucy, I felt that in time papa would have to be taught the truth, managed, and induced to hear reason.

"I read the letter. Lucy, life is said to be all disappointment. *I* was not disappointed. Ere I read, and while I read, my heart did more than throb—it trembled fast—every quiver seemed like the pant of an animal athirst laid down at a well and drinking; and the well proved quite full, gloriously clear; it rose up munificently of its own impulse; I saw the sun through its gush, and not a mote, Lucy, no moss, no insect, no atom in the thrice-refined golden gurgle.

"Life," she went on, "is said to be full of pain to some. I have read biographies where the wayfarer seemed to journey on from suffering to suffering; where Hope flew before him fast, never alighting so near, or lingering so long, as to give his hand a chance of one realising grasp. I have read of those who sowed in tears, and whose harvest, so far from being reaped in joy, perished by untimely blight, or was borne off by sudden whirlwind; and, alas! some of these met the winter with empty garners, and died of utter want in the darkest and coldest of the year."

"Was it their fault, Paulina, that they of whom you speak thus died?"

"Not always their fault. Some of them were good endeavouring people. I am not endeavouring, nor actively good, yet God has caused me to grow in sun, due moisture, and safe protection, sheltered, fostered, taught by my dear father; and now—now—another comes. Graham loves me."

For some minutes we both paused on this climax.

"Does your father know?" I inquired, in a low voice.

"Graham spoke with deep respect of papa, but implied that he dared not approach that quarter as yet; he must first prove his worth: he added that he must have some light respecting myself and my own feelings ere he ventured to risk a step in the matter elsewhere."

"How did you reply?"

"I replied briefly, but I did not repulse him. Yet I almost trembled for fear of making the answer too cordial: Graham's tastes are so fastidious. I wrote it three times—chastening and subduing the phrases at every rescript; at last, having confected it till it seemed to me to resemble a morsel of ice flavoured with ever so slight a zest of fruit or sugar, I ventured to seal and despatch it."

"Excellent, Paulina! Your instinct is fine; you understand Dr. Bretton."

"But how must I manage about papa? There I am still in pain."

"Do not manage at all. Wait now. Only maintain no further correspondence till your father knows all, and gives his sanction."

"Will he ever give it?"

"Time will show. Wait."

"Dr. Bretton wrote one other letter, deeply grateful for my calm, brief note; but I anticipated your advice by saying that while my sentiments continued the same, I could not, without my father's knowledge, write again."

"You acted as you ought to have done; so Dr. Bretton will feel: it will increase his pride in you, his love for you, if either be capable of increase. Paulina, that gentle hoar-frost of yours, surrounding so much pure, fine flame, is a priceless privilege of nature."

"You see I feel Graham's disposition," said she. "I feel that no delicacy can be too exquisite for his treatment."

"It is perfectly proved that you comprehend him, and then—whatever Dr. Bretton's disposition, were he one who expected to be more nearly met—you would still act truthfully, openly, tenderly, with your father."

"Lucy, I trust I shall thus act always. Oh, it will be pain to wake papa from his dream, and tell him I am no more a little girl!"

"Be in no hurry to do so, Paulina. Leave the revelation to Time and your kind Fate. I also have noticed the gentleness of her cares for you: doubt not she will benignantly order the circumstances, and fitly appoint the hour. Yes; I have thought over your life just as you have yourself thought it over; I have made comparisons like those to which you adverted. We know not the future, but the past has been propitious.

"As a child I feared for you; nothing that has life was ever more susceptible than your nature in infancy: under harshness or neglect, neither your outward nor your inward self would have ripened to what they now are. Much pain, much fear, much struggle, would have troubled the very lines of your features, broken their regularity, would have harassed your nerves into the fever of habitual irritation: you would have lost in health and cheerfulness, in grace and sweetness. Providence has protected and cultured you, not only for your own sake, but I believe for Graham's. His star, too, was fortunate: to develop fully the best of his nature, a companion like you was needed: there you are, ready. You must be united. I knew it the first day I saw you together at La Terrasse. In all that mutually concerns you and Graham there seems to me promise, plan, harmony. I do not think the sunny youth of either will prove the forerunner of stormy age. I think it is deemed good that you two should live in peace and be happy—not as angels, but as few are happy amongst mortals. Some lives *are* thus blessed; it is God's will: it is the attesting trace and lingering evidence of Eden. Other lives run from the first another course. Other travellers encounter weather fitful and gusty, wild and variable—breast adverse winds, are belated and overtaken by the early closing winter night. Neither can this happen without the sanction of God; and I know that, amidst His boundless works, is somewhere stored the secret of this last fate's justice: I know that His treasures contain the proof as the promise of its mercy."

Chapter XXXIII

M. PAUL KEEPS HIS PROMISE

ON the first of May, we had all—*i.e.*, the twenty boarders and the four teachers—notice to rise at five o'clock of the morning, to be dressed and ready by six, to put ourselves under the command of M. le Professeur Emanuel, who was to head our march forth from Villette, for it was on this day he proposed to fulfil his promise of taking us to breakfast in the country. I, indeed, as the reader may perhaps remember, had not had the honour of an invitation when this excursion was first projected—rather the contrary; but on my now making allusion to this fact, and wishing to know how it was to be, my ear received a pull, of which I did not venture to challenge the repetition by raising further difficulties.

"Je vous conseille de vous faire prier," said M. Emanuel, imperially menacing the other ear. One Napoleonic compliment, however, was enough, so I made up my mind to be of the party.

The morning broke calm as summer, with singing of birds in the garden, and a light dew-mist that promised heat. We all said it would be warm, and we all felt pleasure in folding away heavy garments, and in assuming the attire suiting a sunny season. The clean fresh print dress, and the light straw bonnet, each made and trimmed as the French workwoman alone can make and trim, so as to unite the utterly unpretending with the perfectly becoming, was the rule of costume. Nobody flaunted in faded silk; nobody wore a second-hand best article.

At six the bell rang merrily, and we poured down the staircase, through the carré, along the corridor, into the vestibule. There stood our Professor, wearing, not his savage-looking paletôt and severe bonnet-grec, but a young-looking belted blouse and cheerful straw hat. He had for us all the kindest good-morrow, and most of us for him had a thanksgiving smile. We were marshalled in order and soon started.

The streets were yet quiet, and the boulevards were fresh and peaceful as fields. I believe we were very happy as we walked along. This chief of ours had the secret of giving a certain impetus to happiness when he would; just as, in an opposite mood, he could give a thrill to fear.

He did not lead nor follow us, but walked along the line, giving a word to every one, talking much to his favourites, and not wholly neglecting even those he disliked. It was rather my wish, for a reason I had, to keep slightly aloof from notice, and being paired with Ginevra Fanshawe, bearing on my arm the dear pressure of that angel's not unsubstantial limb—(she continued in excellent case, and I can assure the reader it was no trifling business to bear the burden of her loveliness; many a time in the course of that warm day I wished to goodness there had been less of the charming commodity)—however, having her, as I said, I tried to make her useful by interposing her always between myself and M. Paul, shifting my place, according as I heard him coming up to the right hand or the left. My private motive for this manœuvre might be traced to the circumstance of the new print dress I wore being pink in colour—a fact which, under our present convoy, made me feel something as I have felt when, clad in a shawl with a red border, necessitated to traverse a meadow where pastured a bull.

For awhile the shifting system, together with some modifications in the arrangement of a black silk scarf, answered my purpose; but, by-and-by, he found out that, whether he came to this side or to that, Miss Fanshawe was still his neighbour. The course of acquaintance between Ginevra and him had never run so smooth that his temper did not undergo a certain crisping process whenever he heard her English accent: nothing in their dispositions fitted; they jarred if they came in contact; he held her empty and affected; she deemed him bearish, meddling, repellent.

At last, when he had changed his place for about the sixth time, finding still the same untoward result to the experiment—he thrust his head forward, settled his eyes on mine, and demanded with impatience—

"Qu'est ce que c'est? Vous me jouez des tours?"

The words were hardly out of his mouth, however, ere, with his customary quickness, he seized the root of this proceeding: in vain I shook out the long fringe, and spread forth the broad end of my scarf. "A—h—h! c'est la robe rose!" broke from his lips, affecting me very much like the sudden and irate low of some lord of the meadow.

"It is only cotton," I alleged hurriedly; "and cheaper, and washes better than any other colour."

"Et Mademoiselle Lucy est coquette comme dix Parisiennes," he answered. "A-t-on jamais vu une Anglaise pareille. Regardez plutôt son chapeau, et ses gants, et ses brodequins!" These articles of dress were just like what my companions wore; certainly not one whit smarter—perhaps rather plainer than most—but Monsieur had now got hold of his text, and I began to chafe under the expected sermon. It went off, however, as mildly as the menace of a storm sometimes passes on a

summer day. I got but one flash of sheet lightning in the shape of a single bantering smile from his eyes; and then he said—

"Courage—à vrai dire je ne suis pas fâché, peutêtre même suis-je content qu'on s'est fait si belle pour ma petite fête."

"Mais ma robe n'est pas belle, monsieur—elle n'est que propre."

"J'aime la propreté," said he. In short, he was not to be dissatisfied; the sun of good humour was to triumph on this auspicious morning; it consumed scudding clouds ere they sullied its disk.

And now we were in the country, amongst what they called "les bois et les petits sentiers." These woods and lanes a month later would offer but a dusty and doubtful seclusion: now, however, in their May greenness and morning repose, they looked very pleasant.

We reached a certain well, planted round, in the taste of Labassecour, with an orderly circle of lime-trees: here a halt was called; on the green swell of ground surrounding this well we were ordered to be seated, Monsieur taking his place in our midst, and suffering us to gather in a knot round him. Those who liked him more than they feared, came close, and these were chiefly little ones; those who feared him more than they liked, kept somewhat aloof; those in whom much affection had given, even to what remained of fear, a pleasurable zest, observed the greatest distance.

He began to tell us a story. Well could he narrate: in such a diction as children love, and learned men emulate; a diction simple in its strength, and strong in its simplicity. There were beautiful touches in that little tale; sweet glimpses of feeling and hues of description that, while I listened, sunk into my mind, and since have never faded. He tinted a twilight scene—I hold it in memory still—such a picture I have never looked on from artist's pencil.

I have said that, for myself, I had no impromptu faculty; and perhaps that very deficiency made me marvel the more at one who possessed it in perfection. M. Emanuel was not a man to write books; but I have heard him lavish, with careless, unconscious prodigality, such mental wealth as books seldom boast; his mind was indeed my library, and whenever it was opened to me, I entered bliss. Intellectually imperfect as I was, I could read little; there were few bound and printed volumes that did not weary me—whose perusal did not fag and blind—but his tones of thought were collyrium to the spirit's eyes; over their contents, inward sight grew clear and strong. I used to think what a delight it would be for one who loved him better than he loved himself, to gather and store up those handfuls of gold-dust so recklessly flung to heaven's winds.

His story done, he approached the little knoll where I and Ginevra sat apart. In his usual mode of demanding an opinion (he had not reticence to wait till it was voluntarily offered) he asked—

"Were you interested?"

According to my wonted undemonstrative fashion, I simply answered—

"Yes."

"Was it good?"

"Very good."

"Yet I could not write that down," said he.

"Why not, monsieur?"

"I hate the mechanical labour; I hate to stoop and sit still. I could dictate it, though, with pleasure to an amanuensis who suited me. Would Mademoiselle Lucy write for me if I asked her?"

"Monsieur would be too quick; he would urge me, and be angry if my pen did not keep pace with his lips."

"Try some day; let us see the monster I can make of myself under the circumstances. But just now, there is no question of dictation; I mean to make you useful in another office. Do you see yonder farm-house?"

"Surrounded with trees? Yes."

"There we are to breakfast; and while the good fermière makes the café au lait in a caldron, you and five others, whom I shall select, will spread with butter half a hundred rolls."

Having formed his troop into line once more, he marched us straight on the farm, which, on seeing our force, surrendered without capitulation.

Clean knives and plates, and fresh butter being provided, half-a-dozen of us, chosen by our Professor, set to work under his directions, to prepare for breakfast a huge basket of rolls with which the baker had been ordered to provision the farm, in anticipation of our coming. Coffee and chocolate were already made hot; cream and new-laid eggs were added to the treat, and M. Emanuel, always generous, would have given a large order for "jambon" and "confitures" in addition, but that some of us, who presumed perhaps upon our influence, insisted that it would be a most reckless waste of victual. He railed at us for our pains, terming us "des ménagères avares"; but we let him talk, and managed the economy of the repast our own way.

With what a pleasant countenance he stood on the farm-kitchen hearth looking on! He was a man whom it made happy to see others happy; he liked to have movement, animation, abundance and enjoyment round him. We asked where he would sit. He told us we knew well he was our slave, and we his tyrants, and that he dared not so much as choose a chair without our leave; so we set him the farmer's great chair at the head of the long table, and put him into it.

Well might we like him, with all his passions and hurricanes, when he could be so benignant and docile at times, as he was just now. Indeed, at the worst, it was only his nerves that were irritable, not his temper that was radically bad; soothe, comprehend, comfort him, and he was a lamb; he would not harm a fly. Only to the very stupid, perverse, or unsympathising, was he in the slightest degree dangerous.

Mindful always of his religion, he made the youngest of the party say a little prayer before we began breakfast, crossing himself as devotedly as a woman. I had never seen him pray before, or make that pious sign; he did it so simply, with such childlike faith, I could not help smiling pleasurably as I watched; his eyes met my smile; he just stretched out his hand, saying—

"Donnez-moi la main! I see we worship the same God, in the same spirit, though by different rites."

Most of M. Emanuel's brother professors were emancipated free-thinkers, infidels, atheists; and many of them men whose lives would not bear scrutiny: he was more like a knight of old, religious in his way, and of spotless fame. Innocent childhood, beautiful youth, were safe at his side. He had vivid passions, keen feelings, but his pure honour and his artless piety were the strong charm that kept the lions couchant.

That breakfast was a merry meal, and the merriment was not mere vacant chatter: M. Paul originated, led, controlled, and heightened it; his social, lively temper played unfettered and unclouded; surrounded only by women and children, there was nothing to cross and thwart him; he had his own way, and a pleasant way it was.

The meal over, the party were free to run and play in the meadows: a few stayed to help the farmer's wife to put away her earthenware. M. Paul called me from among these to come out and sit near him under a tree—whence he could view the troop gambolling over a wide pasture—and read to him whilst he took his cigar. He sat on a rustic bench, and I at the tree-root. While I read (a pocket-classic—a Corneille—I did not like it, but he did, finding therein beauties I never could be brought to perceive), he listened with a sweetness of calm the more impressive from the impetuosity of his general nature; the deepest happiness filled his blue eye and smoothed his broad forehead. I, too, was happy—happy with the bright day, happier with his presence, happiest with his kindness.

He asked, by-and-by, if I would not rather run to my companions than sit there? I said no; I felt content to be where he was. He asked whether, if I were his sister, I should always be content to stay with a brother such as he. I said I believed I should; and I felt it. Again, he inquired whether, if he were to leave Villette, and go far away, I should be sorry; and I dropped Corneille, and made no reply.

"Petite sœur," said he: "how long could you remember me if we were separated?"

"That, monsieur, I can never tell, because I do not know how long it will be before I shall cease to remember everything earthly."

"If I were to go beyond seas for two—three—five years, should you welcome me on my return?"

"Monsieur, how could I live in the interval?"

"Pourtant j'ai été pour vous bien dur, bien exigeant."

I hid my face with the book, for it was covered with tears. I asked him why he talked so; and he said he would talk so no more, and cheered me again with the kindest encouragement. Still, the gentleness with which he treated me during the rest of the day went somehow to my heart. It was too tender. It was mournful. I would rather he had been abrupt, whimsical, and irate as was his wont.

When hot noon arrived—for the day turned out as we had anticipated, glowing as June—our shepherd collected his sheep from the pasture, and proceeded to lead us all softly home. But we had a whole league to walk, thus far from Villette was the farm where we had breakfasted; the children, especially, were tired with their play: the spirits of most flagged at the prospect of this mid-day walk over chaussées flinty, glaring, and dusty. This state of things had been foreseen and provided for. Just beyond the boundary of the farm we met two spacious vehicles coming to fetch us—such conveyances as are hired out purposely for the accommodation of school-parties; here, with good management, room was found for all, and in another hour M. Paul made safe consignment of his charge at the Rue Fossette. It had been a pleasant day; it would have been perfect, but for the breathing of melancholy which had dimmed its sunshine a moment.

That tarnish was renewed the same evening.

Just about sunset, I saw M. Emanuel come out of the front-door, accompanied by Madame Beck. They paced the centre alley for nearly an hour, talking earnestly: he—looking grave, yet restless; she—wearing an amazed, expostulatory, dissuasive air.

I wondered what was under discussion; and when Madame Beck re-entered the house as it darkened, leaving her kinsman Paul yet lingering in the garden, I said to myself—

"He called me 'petite sœur' this morning. If he were really my brother, how I should like to go to him just now, and ask what it is that presses on his mind. See how he leans against that tree, with his arms crossed and his brow bent. He wants consolation, I know: Madame does not console: she only remonstrates. What now"——

Starting from quiescence to action, M. Paul came striding erect and quick down the garden. The carré doors were yet open: I thought he was probably going to water the orange-trees in the tubs, after his occasional custom; on reaching the court, however, he took an abrupt turn and made for the berceau and the first classe glass door. There in that first classe I was, thence I had been watching him; but there I could not find courage to await his approach. He had turned so suddenly, he strode so fast, he looked so strange; the coward within me grew pale, shrank, and—not waiting to listen to reason, and hearing the shrubs crush and the gravel crunch to his advance—she was gone on the wings of panic.

Nor did I pause till I had taken sanctuary in the oratory, now empty. Listening there with beating pulses, and an unaccountable, undefined apprehension, I heard him pass through all the schoolrooms, clashing the doors impatiently as he went;

I heard him invade the refectory, which the "lecture pieuse" was now holding under hallowed constraint; I heard him pronounce these words—

"Où est Mademoiselle Lucie?"

And just as, summoning my courage, I was preparing to go down and do what, after all, I most wished to do in the world—viz., meet him—the wiry voice of St. Pierre replied glibly and falsely, "Elle est au lit." And he passed, with the stamp of vexation, into the corridor. There Madame Beck met, captured, chid, convoyed to the street-door, and finally dismissed him.

As that street-door closed, a sudden amazement at my own perverse proceeding struck like a blow upon me. I felt from the first it was me he wanted—me he was seeking—and had not I wanted him too? What, then, had carried me away? What had rapt me beyond his reach? He had something to tell: he was going to tell me that something: my ear strained its nerve to hear it, and I had made the confidence impossible. Yearning to listen and console, while I thought audience and solace beyond hope's reach—no sooner did opportunity suddenly and fully arrive, than I evaded it as I would have evaded the levelled shaft of mortality.

Well, my insane inconsistency had its reward. Instead of the comfort, the certain satisfaction I might have won—could I but have put choking panic down, and stood firm two minutes—here was dead blank, dark doubt, and drear suspense.

I took my wages to my pillow, and passed the night counting them.

Chapter XXXIV

MALEVOLA

MADAME BECK called me on Thursday afternoon, and asked whether I had any occupation to hinder me from going into town and executing some little commissions for her at the shops.

Being disengaged, and placing myself at her service, I was presently furnished with a list of the wools, silks, embroidering thread, etcetera, wanted in the pupils' work, and having equipped myself in a manner suiting the threatening aspect of a cloudy and sultry day, I was just drawing the spring-bolt of the street-door, in act to issue forth, when Madame's voice again summoned me to the salle-à-manger.

"Pardon, Meess Lucie!" cried she, in the seeming haste of an impromptu thought, "I have just recollected one more errand for you, if your good-nature will not deem itself over-burdened?"

Of course I "confounded myself" in asseverations to the contrary; and Madame, running into the little salon, brought thence a pretty basket, filled with fine hothouse fruit, rosy, perfect and tempting, reposing amongst the dark green, wax-like leaves and pale yellow stars of I know not what exotic plant.

"There," she said, "it is not heavy, and will not shame your neat toilette, as if it were a household, servant-like detail. Do me the favour to leave this little basket at the house of Madame Walravens, with my felicitations on her fête. She lives down in the old town, Numéro 3, Rue des Mages. I fear you will find the walk rather long, but you have the whole afternoon before you, and do not hurry; if you are not back in time for dinner, I will order a portion to be saved, or Goton, with whom you are a favourite, will have pleasure in tossing up some trifle for your especial benefit. You shall not be forgotten, ma bonne Meess. And oh! please!" (calling me back once more) "be sure to insist on seeing Madame Walravens herself, and giving the basket into her own hands, in order that there may be no mistake, for she is rather a punctilious personage. Adieu! Au revoir!"

And at last I got away. The shop commissions took some time to execute, that choosing and matching of silks and wools being always a tedious business, but at

last I got through my list. The patterns for the slippers, the bell-ropes, the cabas were selected—the slides and tassels for the purses chosen—the whole "tripotage," in short, was of my mind; nothing but the fruit and the felicitations remained to be attended to.

I rather liked the prospect of a long walk, deep into the old and grim Basse-Ville; and I liked it no worse because the evening sky, over the city, was settling into a mass of black-blue metal, heated at the rim, and inflaming slowly to a heavy red.

I fear a high wind, because storm demands that exertion of strength and use of action I always yield with pain; but the sullen downfall, the thick snow descent, or dark rush of rain, ask only resignation—the quiet abandonment of garments and person to be drenched. In return, it sweeps a great capital clean before you; it makes you a quiet path through broad, grand streets: it petrifies a living city as if by eastern enchantment; it transforms a Villette into a Tadmor. Let, then, the rains fall, and the floods descend—only I must first get rid of this basket of fruit.

An unknown clock from an unknown tower (Jean Baptiste's voice was now too distant to be audible) was tolling the third quarter past five when I reached that street and house whereof Madame Beck had given me the address. It was no street at all; it seemed rather to be part of a square: it was quiet, grass grew between the broad grey flags, the houses were large and looked very old—behind them rose the appearance of trees, indicating gardens at the back. Antiquity brooded above this region, business was banished thence. Rich men had once possessed this quarter, and once Grandeur had made her seat here. That church, whose dark, half-ruinous turrets overlooked the square, was the venerable and formerly opulent shrine of the Magi. But wealth and greatness had long since stretched their gilded pinions and fled hence, leaving these their ancient nests, perhaps to house Penury for a time, or perhaps to stand cold and empty, mouldering untenanted in the course of winters.

As I crossed this deserted "place," on whose pavement drops almost as large as a five-franc piece were now slowly darkening, I saw, in its whole expanse, no symptom or evidence of life except what was given in the figure of an infirm old priest, who went past bending and propped on a staff—the type of eld and decay.

He had issued from the very house to which I was directed; and when I paused before the door just closed after him, and rang the bell, he turned to look at me. Nor did he soon avert his gaze; perhaps he thought me, with my basket of summer fruit, and my lack of the dignity age confers, an incongruous figure in such a scene. I know, had a young ruddy-faced bonne opened the door to admit me, I should have thought such a one little in harmony with her dwelling; but when I found myself confronted by a very old woman, wearing a very antique peasant costume, a cap alike hideous and costly, with long flaps of native lace, a petticoat and jacket of cloth, and sabots more like little boats than shoes, it seemed all right, and soothingly in character.

The expression of her face was not quite so soothing as the cut of her costume; anything more cantankerous I have seldom seen; she would scarcely reply to my inquiry after Madame Walravens; I believe she would have snatched the basket of fruit from my hand, had not the old priest, hobbling up, checked her, and himself lent an ear to the message with which I was charged.

His apparent deafness rendered it a little difficult to make him fully understand that I must see Madame Walravens, and consign the fruit into her own hands. At last, however, he comprehended the fact that such were my orders, and that duty enjoined their literal fulfilment. Addressing the aged bonne, not in French, but in the aboriginal tongue of Labassecour, he persuaded her, at last, to let me cross the inhospitable threshold, and himself escorting me upstairs, I was ushered into a sort of salon, and there left.

The room was large, and had a fine old ceiling and almost church-like windows of coloured glass; but it was desolate, and in the shadow of a coming storm looked

strangely lowering. Within opened a smaller room; there, however, the blind of the single casement was closed; through the deep gloom few details of furniture were apparent. These few I amused myself by puzzling to make out; and, in particular, I was attracted by the outline of a picture on the wall.

By-and-by the picture seemed to give way: to my bewilderment, it shook, it sunk, it rolled back into nothing: its vanishing left an opening arched, leading into an arched passage, with a mystic winding stair; both passage and stair were of cold stone, uncarpeted and unpainted. Down this donjon stair descended a tap, tap like a stick; soon there fell on the steps a shadow, and last of all, I was aware of a substance.

Yet, was it actual substance, this appearance approaching me? this obstruction, partially darkening the arch?

It drew near, and I saw it well. I began to comprehend where I was. Well might this old square be named quarter of the Magi—well might the three towers, overlooking it, own for godfathers three mystic sages of a dead and dark art. Hoar enchantment here prevailed; a spell had opened for me elfland—that cell-like room, that vanishing picture, that arch and passage, and stair of stone, were all parts of a fairy tale. Distincter even than scenic details stood the chief figure—Cunegonde, the sorceress! Malevola, the evil fairy. How was she?

She might be three feet high, but she had no shape; her skinny hands rested upon each other, and pressed the gold knob of a wand-like ivory staff. Her face was large, set, not upon her shoulders, but before her breast; she seemed to have no neck; I should have said there were a hundred years in her features, and more perhaps in her eyes—her malign, unfriendly eyes, with thick grey brows above, and livid lids all round. How severely they viewed me, with a sort of dull displeasure!

This being wore a gown of brocade, dyed bright blue, full tinted as the gentianella flower, and covered with satin foliage in a large pattern; over the gown a costly shawl, gorgeously bordered, and so large for her that its many-coloured fringe swept the floor. But her chief points were her jewels: she had long, clear earrings, blazing with a lustre which could not be borrowed or false; she had rings on her skeleton hands, with thick gold hoops and stones—purple, green, and blood-red. Hunchbacked, dwarfish, and doting, she was adorned like a barbarian queen.

"Que me voulez-vous?" said she hoarsely, with the voice rather of male than of female old age; and, indeed, a silver beard bristled her chin.

I delivered my basket and my message.

"Is that all?" she demanded.

"It is all," said I.

"Truly, it was well worth while," she answered. "Return to Madame Beck, and tell her I can buy fruit when I want it, et quant à ses félicitations, je m'en moque!" And this courteous dame turned her back.

Just as she turned a peal of thunder broke, and a flash of lightning blazed broad over salon and boudoir. The tale of magic seemed to proceed with due accompaniment of the elements. The wanderer, decoyed into the enchanted castle, heard rising, outside, the spell-wakened tempest.

What, in all this, was I to think of Madame Beck? She owned strange acquaintance; she offered messages and gifts at an unique shrine, and inauspicious seemed the bearing of the uncouth thing she worshipped. There went that sullen Sidonia, tottering and trembling like palsy incarnate, tapping her ivory staff on the mosaic parquet, and muttering venomously as she vanished.

Down washed the rain, deep lowered the welkin; the clouds, ruddy a while ago, had now, through all their blackness, turned deadly pale, as if in terror. Notwithstanding my late boast about not fearing a shower, I hardly liked to go out under this waterspout. Then the gleams of lightning were very fierce, the thunder crashed very near; this storm had gathered immediately above Villette; it seemed to have burst at the zenith; rushed down prone; the forked, slant bolts pierced athwart

vertical torrents; red zig-zags interlaced a descent blanched as white metal: and all broke from a sky heavily black in its swollen abundance.

Leaving Madame Walraven's inhospitable salon, I betook myself to her cold staircase; there was a seat on the landing—there I waited. Somebody came gliding along the gallery just above; it was the old priest.

"Indeed Mademoiselle shall not sit there," said he. "It would displeasure our benefactor if he knew a stranger was so treated in this house."

And he begged me so earnestly to return to the salon, that, without discourtesy, I could not but comply. The smaller room was better furnished and more habitable than the larger; thither he introduced me. Partially withdrawing the blind, he disclosed what seemed more like an oratory than a boudoir, a very solemn little chamber, looking as if it were a place rather dedicated to relics and remembrance than designed for present use and comfort.

The good father sat down, as if to keep me company; but instead of conversing, he took out a book, fastened on the page his eyes, and employed his lips in whispering what sounded like a prayer or litany. A yellow electric light from the sky gilded his bald head; his figure remained in shape—deep and purple; he sat still as sculpture; he seemed to forget me for his prayers; he only looked up when a fiercer bolt, or a harsher, closer rattle told of nearing danger; even then, it was not in fear, but in seeming awe, he raised his eyes. I too was awestruck; being, however, under no pressure of slavish terror, my thoughts and observations were free.

To speak truth, I was beginning to fancy that the old priest resembled that Père Silas before whom I had knelt in the church of the Béguinage. The idea was vague, for I had seen my confessor only in the dusk and in profile, yet still I seemed to trace a likeness: I thought also I recognised the voice. While I watched him, he betrayed, by one lifted look, that he felt my scrutiny; I turned to note the room; that too had its half mystic interest.

Beside a cross of curiously carved old ivory, yellow with time, and sloped above a dark-red prie-dieu, furnished duly with rich missal and ebon rosary, hung the picture whose dim outline had drawn my eyes before—the picture which moved, fell away with the wall, and let in phantoms. Imperfectly seen, I had taken it for a Madonna; revealed by clearer light it proved to be a woman's portrait in a nun's dress. The face, though not beautiful, was pleasing; pale, young, and shaded with the dejection of grief or ill-health. I say again it was not beautiful; it was not even intellectual; its very amiability was the amiability of a weak frame, inactive passions, acquiescent habits: yet I looked long at that picture, and could not choose but look.

The old priest, who at first had seemed to me so deaf and infirm, must yet have retained his faculties in tolerable preservation; absorbed in his book as he appeared, without once lifting his head, or, as far as I knew, turning his eyes, he perceived the point towards which my attention was drawn, and, in a slow distinct voice, dropped concerning it these four observations.

"She was much beloved.

"She gave herself to God.

"She died young.

"She is still remembered, still wept."

"By that aged lady, Madame Walravens?" I inquired, fancying that I had discovered in the incurable grief of bereavement a key to that same aged lady's desperate ill-humour.

The father shook his head with half a smile.

"No, no," said he; "a grand-dame's affection for her children's children may be great, and her sorrow for their loss lively; but it is only the affianced lover, to whom Fate, Faith, and Death have trebly denied the bliss of union, who mourns what he has lost as Justine Marie is still mourned."

I thought the father rather wished to be questioned, and therefore I inquired who had lost and who still mourned "Justine Marie." I got, in reply, quite a litte romantic narrative, told not unimpressively, with the accompaniment of the now subsiding storm. I am bound to say it might have been made much more truly impressive if there had been less French, Rousseaulike sentimentalising and wire-drawing and rather more healthful carelessness of effect. But the worthy father was obviously a Frenchman born and bred (I became more and more persuaded of his resemblance to my confessor)—he was a true son of Rome; when he did lift his eyes, he looked at me out of their corners with more and sharper subtlety than, one would have thought, could survive the wear and tear of seventy years. Yet, I believe, he was a good old man.

The hero of his tale was some former pupil of his whom he now called his benefactor, and who, it appears, had loved this pale Justine Marie, the daughter of rich parents, at a time when his own worldly prospects were such as to justify his aspiring to a well-dowered hand. The pupil's father—once a rich banker—had failed, died, and left behind him only debts and destitution. The son was then forbidden to think of Marie; especially that old witch of a grand-dame I had seen, Madame Walravens, opposed the match with all the violence of a temper which deformity made sometimes demoniac. The mild Marie had neither the treachery to be false, nor the force to be quite staunch to her lover; she gave up her first suitor, but, refusing to accept a second with a heavier purse, withdrew to a convent, and there died in her noviciate.

Lasting anguish, it seems, had taken possession of the faithful heart which worshipped her, and the truth of that love and grief had been shown in a manner which touched even me as I listened.

Some years after Justine Marie's death, ruin had come on her house too; her father, by nominal calling a jeweller, but who also dealt a good deal on the Bourse, had been concerned in some financial transactions which entailed exposure and ruinous fines. He died of grief for the loss, and shame for the infamy. His old hunchbacked mother and his bereaved wife were left penniless, and might have died too of want; but their lost daughter's once despised yet most true-hearted suitor, hearing of the condition of these ladies, came with singular devotedness to the rescue. He took on their insolent pride the revenge of the purest charity—housing, caring for, befriending them so as no son could have done it more tenderly and efficiently. The mother—on the whole a good woman—died blessing him; the strange, godless, loveless misanthrope grandmother lived still, entirely supported by this self-sacrificing man. She, who had been the bane of his life, blighting his hope, and awarding him, for love and domestic happiness, long mourning and cheerless solitude, he treated with the respect a good son might offer a kind mother. He had brought her to this house, "and," continued the priest, while genuine tears rose to his eyes, "here, too, he shelters me, his old tutor, and Agnes, a superannuated servant of his father's family. To our sustenance, and to other charities, I know he devotes three parts of his income, keeping only the fourth to provide himself with bread and the most modest accommodations. By this arrangement he had rendered it impossible to himself ever to marry: he had given himself to God and to his angel-bride as much as if he were a priest like me."

The father had wiped away his tears before he uttered these last words, and in pronouncing them he for one instant raised his eyes to mine. I caught this glance, despite its veiled character; the momentary gleam shot a meaning which struck me. These Romanists are strange beings. Such a one among them—whom you know no more than the last Inca of Peru, or the first Emperor of China—knows you and all your concerns; and has his reasons for saying to you so and so, when you simply thought the communication sprang impromptu from the instant's impulse: his plan in bringing it about that you shall come on such a day, to such a place, under such and such circumstances, when the whole arrangement seems to your crude apprehension

the ordinance of chance, or the sequel of exigency. Madame Beck's suddenly recollected message and present, my artless embassy to the Place of Magi, the old priest accidentally descending the steps and crossing the square, his interposition on my behalf with the bonne who would have sent me away, his reappearance on the staircase, my introduction to this room, the portrait, the narrative so affably volunteered—all these little incidents, taken as they fell out, seemed each independent of its successor; a handful of loose beads: but threaded through by that quick-shot and crafty glance of a Jesuit-eye, they dropped pendant in a long string, like that rosary on the prie-dieu. Where lay the link of junction, where the little clasp of this monastic necklace? I saw or felt union, but could not yet find the spot, or detect the means of connection.

Perhaps the musing-fit into which I had by this time fallen appeared somewhat suspicious in its abstraction; he gently interrupted—

"Mademoiselle," said he, "I trust you have not far to go through these inundated streets?"

"More than half a league."

"You live"——

"In the Rue Fossette."

"Not" (with animation), "not at the pensionnat of Madame Beck?"

"The same."

"Donc" (clapping his hands), "donc, vous devez connaître mon noble élève, mon Paul?"

"Monsieur Paul Emanuel, Professor of Literature?"

"He, and none other."

A brief silence fell. The spring of junction seemed suddenly to have become palpable; I felt it yield to pressure.

"Was it of M. Paul you have been speaking?" I presently inquired. "Was he your pupil and the benefactor of Madame Walravens?"

"Yes, and of Agnes, the old servant; and moreover" (with a certain emphasis), "he was and *is* the lover, true, constant and eternal, of that saint in heaven—Justine Marie."

"And who, father, are *you*?" I continued, and though I accentuated the question, its utterance was well-nigh superfluous; I was ere this quite prepared for the answer which actually came.

"I, daughter, am Père Silas; that unworthy son of Holy Church whom you once honoured with a noble and touching confidence, showing me the core of a heart and the inner shrine of a mind whereof, in solemn truth, I coveted the direction in behalf of the only true faith. Nor have I for a day lost sight of you, nor for an hour failed to take in you a rooted interest. Passed under the discipline of Rome, moulded by her high training, inoculated with her salutary doctrines, inspired by the zeal she alone gives—I realise what then might be your spiritual rank, your practical value; and I envy Heresy her prey."

This struck me as a special state of things—I half-realised myself in that condition also; passed under discipline, moulded, trained, inoculated, and so on. "Not so," thought I, but I restrained deprecation and sat quietly enough.

"I suppose M. Paul does not live here?" I resumed, pursuing a theme which I thought more to the purpose than any wild renegade dreams.

"No; he only comes occasionally to worship his beloved saint, to make his confession to me, and to pay his respects to her he calls his mother. His own lodging consists but of two rooms: he has no servant, and yet he will not suffer Madame Walravens to dispose of those splendid jewels with which you see her adorned, and in which she takes a puerile pride as the ornaments of her youth, and the last relics of her son the jeweller's wealth."

"How often," murmured I to myself, "has this man, this M. Emanuel, seemed to me to lack magnanimity in trifles, yet how great he is in great things!"

I own I did not reckon amongst the proofs of his greatness either the act of confession or the saint-worship.

"How long is it since that lady died?" I inquired, looking at Justine Marie.

"Twenty years. She was somewhat older than M. Emanuel; he was then very young, for he is not much beyond forty."

"Does he yet weep her?"

"His heart will weep her always: the essence of Emanuel's nature is—constancy."

This was said with marked emphasis.

And now the sun broke out pallid and waterish; the rain yet fell, but there was no more tempest: that hot firmament had cloven and poured out its lightnings. A longer delay would scarce leave daylight for my return, so I rose, thanked the father for his hospitality and his tale, was benignantly answered by a "pax vobiscum," which I made kindly welcome, because it seemed uttered with a true benevolence; but I liked less the mystic phrase accompanying it—

"Daughter, you *shall* be what you *shall* be!" an oracle that made me shrug my shoulders as soon as I had got outside the door. Few of us know what we are to come to certainly, but for all that had happened yet, I had good hopes of living and dying a sober-minded Protestant: there was a hollowness within and a flourish around "Holy Church" which tempted me but moderately. I went on my way pondering many things. Whatever Romanism may be, there are good Romanists: this man Emanuel seemed of the best; touched with superstition, influenced by priestcraft, yet wondrous for fond faith, for pious devotion, for sacrifice of self, for charity unbounded. It remained to see how Rome, by her agents, handled such qualities; whether she cherished them for their own sake and for God's, or put them out to usury and made booty of the interest.

By the time I reached home it was sundown. Goton had kindly saved me a portion of dinner; which indeed I needed. She called me into the little cabinet to partake of it, and there Madame Beck soon made her appearance, bringing me a glass of wine.

"Well," began she, chuckling, "and what sort of a reception did Madame Walravens give you? Elle est drôle, n'est ce pas?"

I told her what had passed, delivering verbatim the courteous message with which I had been charged.

"Oh la singuliére petite bossue!" laughed she: "Et figurez-vous qu'elle me déteste, parcequ'elle me croit amoureuse de mon cousin Paul; ce petit devot qui n'ose pas bouger, à moins que son confesseur ne lui donne la permission! Au reste" (she went on), "if he wanted to marry ever so much—soit moi, soit une autre—he could not do it—he has too large a family already on his hands; Mère Walravens, Père Silas, Dame Agnes, and a whole troop of nameless paupers. There never was a man like him for laying on himself burdens greater than he can bear, voluntarily incurring needless responsibilities. Besides, he harbours a romantic idea about some pale-faced Marie Justine—personnage assez niaise à ce que je pense" (such was Madame's irreverent remark), "who has been an angel in heaven, or elsewhere, this score of years, and to whom he means to go, free from all earthly ties, pure comme un lis à ce qu'il dit. Oh, you would laugh could you but know half M. Emanuel's crotchets and eccentricities! But I hinder you from taking refreshment, ma bonne Mees, which you must need; eat your supper, drink your wine, oubliez les anges, les bossues, et surtout, les Professeurs—et bon soir!"

Chapter XXXV
FRATERNITY

"Oubliez les Professeurs." So said Madame Beck. Madame Beck was a wise woman, but she should not have uttered those words. To do so was a mistake. That

night she should have left me calm—not excited, indifferent, not interested, isolated in my own estimation and that of others—not connected, even in idea, with this second person whom I was to forget.

Forget him? Ah! they took a sage plan to make me forget him—the wiseheads! They showed me how good he was; they made of my dear little man a stainless little hero. And then they had prated about his manner of loving. What means had I, before this day, of being certain whether he could love at all or not?

I had known him jealous, suspicious; I had seen about him certain tendernesses, fitfulnesses—a softness which came like a warm air, and a ruth which passed like early dew, dried in the heat of his irritabilities: *this* was all I had seen. And they, Père Silas and Modeste Maria Beck (that these two wrought in concert I could not doubt) opened up the adytum of his heart—showed me one grand love, the child of this southern nature's youth, born so strong and perfect that it had laughed at Death himself, despised his mean rape of matter, clung to immortal spirit, and, in victory and faith, had watched beside a tomb twenty years.

This had been done—not idly: this was not a mere hollow indulgence of sentiment; he had proven his fidelity by the consecration of his best energies to an unselfish purpose, and attested it by limitless personal sacrifices: for those once dear to her he prized—he had laid down vengeance and taken up a cross.

Now, as for Justine Marie, I knew what she was as well as if I had seen her. I knew she was well enough; there were girls like her in Madame Beck's school—phlegmatics—pale, slow, inert, but kind-natured, neutral of evil, undistinguished for good.

If she wore angel's wings, I knew whose poet-fancy conferred them. If her forehead shone luminous with the reflex of a halo, I knew in the fire of whose irids that circlet of holy flame had generation.

Was I then to be frightened by Justine Marie? Was the picture of a pale dead nun to rise, an eternal barrier? And what of the charities which absorbed his worldly goods? What of his heart sworn to virginity?

Madame Beck—Père Silas—you should not have suggested these questions. They were at once the deepest puzzle, the strongest obstruction, and the keenest stimulus I had ever felt. For a week of nights and days I fell asleep—I dreamt and I woke upon these two questions. In the whole world there was no answer to them, except where one dark little man stood, sat, walked, lectured, under the headpiece of a bandit bonnet-grec, and within the girth of a sorry paletôt, much be-inked and no little a-dust.

After that visit to the Rue des Mages, I *did* want to see him again. I felt as if—knowing what I now knew—his countenance would offer a page more lucid, more interesting than ever; I felt a longing to trace in it the imprint of that primitive devotedness, the signs of that half-knightly, half-saintly chivalry which the priest's narrative imputed to his nature. He had become my Christian hero: under that character I wanted to view him.

Nor was opportunity slow to favour; my new impressions underwent her test the next day. Yes: I was granted an interview with my "Christian hero"—an interview not very heroic, or sentimental, or biblical, but lively enough in its way.

About three o'clock of the afternoon, the peace of the first classe—safely established, as it seemed, under the serene sway of Madame Beck, who, *in propriâ personâ,* was giving one of her orderly and useful lessons—this peace, I say, suffered a sudden fracture by the wild inburst of a paletôt.

Nobody at the moment was quieter than myself. Eased of responsibility by Madame Beck's presence, soothed by her uniform tones, pleased and edified with her clear exposition of the subject in hand (for she taught well), I sat bent over my desk drawing—that is, copying an elaborate line engraving, tediously working up my copy to the finish of the original, for that was my practical notion of art; and, strange to say, I took extreme pleasure in the labour, and could even produce

curiously finical Chinese facsimiles of steel or mezzotint plates—things about as valuable as so many achievements in worsted-work, but I thought pretty well of them in those days.

What was the matter? My drawing, my pencils, my precious copy, gathered in one crushed-up handful, perished from before my sight; I myself appeared to be shaken or emptied out of my chair as a solitary and withered nutmeg might be emptied out of a spice-box by an excited cook. That chair and my desk, seized by the wild paletôt, one under each sleeve, were borne afar; in a second, I followed the furniture; in two minutes they and I were fixed in the centre of the grande salle—a vast adjoining room, seldom used save for dancing and choral singing-lessons—fixed with an emphasis which seemed to prohibit the remotest hope of our ever being permitted to stir thence again.

Having partially collected my scared wits, I found myself in the presence of two men, gentlemen, I suppose I should say—one dark, the other light—one having a stiff, half-military air, and wearing a braided surtout; the other partaking, in garb and bearing, more of the careless aspect of the student or artist class: both flourishing in full magnificence of moustaches, whiskers, and imperial. M. Emanuel stood a little apart from these; his countenance and eyes expressed strong choler; he held forth his hand with his tribune gesture.

"Mademoiselle," said he, "your business is to prove to these gentlemen that I am no liar. You will answer to the best of your ability such questions as they shall put. You will also write on such theme as they shall select. In their eyes, it appears, I hold the position of an unprincipled impostor. I write essays; and, with deliberate forgery, sign to them my pupils' names, and boast of them as their work. You will disprove this charge."

Grand Ciel! Here was the show-trial, so long evaded, come on me like a thunder-clap. These two fine, braided, moustachioed, sneering personages were none other than dandy professors of the college—Messieurs Boissec and Rochemorte—a pair of cold-blooded fops and pedants, sceptics and scoffers. It seems that M. Paul had been rashly exhibiting something I had written—something he had never once praised, or even mentioned, in my hearing, and which I deemed forgotten. The essay was not remarkable at all; it only *seemed* remarkable, compared with the average productions of foreign school-girls; in an English establishment it would have passed scarce noticed. Messieurs Boissec and Rochemorte had thought proper to question its genuineness, and insinuate a cheat; I was now to bear my testimony to the truth, and to be put to the torture of their examination.

A memorable scene ensued.

They began with classics. A dead blank. They went on to French history. I hardly knew Mérovée from Pharamond. They tried me in various 'ologies, and still only got a shake of the head, and an unchanging "Je n'en sais rien."

After an expressive pause, they proceeded to matters of general information, broaching one or two subjects which I knew pretty well, and on which I had often reflected. M. Emanuel, who had hitherto stood looking on, dark as the winter solstice, brightened up somewhat; he thought I should now show myself at least no fool.

He learned his error. Though answers to the questions surged up fast, my mind filling like a rising well, ideas were there, but not words. I either *could* not or *would* not speak—I am not sure which: partly, I think my nerves had got wrong, and partly my humour was crossed.

I heard one of my examiners—he of the braided surtout—whisper to his co-professor: "Est-elle donc idiote?"

"Yes," I thought, "an idiot she is, and always will be, for such as you."

But I suffered—suffered cruelly; I saw the damps gather on M. Paul's brow, and his eyes spoke a passionate yet sad reproach. He would not believe in my total lack of popular cleverness; he thought I *could* be prompt if I *would*.

At last, to relieve him, the professors, and myself, I stammered out—

"Gentlemen, you had better let me go; you will get no good of me; as you say, I am an idiot."

I wish I could have spoken with calm and dignity, or I wish my sense had sufficed to make me hold my tongue: that traitor tongue tripped, faltered. Beholding the judges cast on M. Emanuel a hard look of triumph, and hearing the distressed tremor of my own voice, out I burst in a fit of choking tears. The emotion was far more of anger than grief; had I been a man and strong, I could have challenged that pair on the spot—but it *was* emotion, and I would rather have been scourged than betrayed it.

The incapables! Could they not see at once the crude hand of a novice in that composition they called a forgery? The subject was classical. When Paul dictated the trait on which the essay was to turn, I heard it for the first time; the matter was new to me, and I had no material for its treatment. But I got books, read up the facts, laboriously constructed a skeleton out of the dry bones of the real, and then clothed them, and tried to breathe into them life, and in this last aim I had pleasure. With me it was a difficult and anxious time till my facts were found, selected, and properly jointed; nor could I rest from research and effort till I was satisfied of correct anatomy; the strength of my inward repugnance to the idea of flaw or falsity sometimes enabled me to shun egregious blunders; but the knowledge was not there in my head, ready and mellow; it had not been sown in Spring, grown in Summer, harvested in Autumn, and garnered through Winter; whatever I wanted I must go out and gather fresh; glean of wild herbs my lap full, and shred them green into the pot. Messieurs Boissec and Rochemorte did not perceive this. They mistook my work for the work of a ripe scholar.

They would not yet let me go: I must sit down and write before them. As I dipped my pen in the ink with a shaking hand, and surveyed the white paper with eyes half-blinded and overflowing, one of my judges began mincingly to apologise for the pain he caused.

"Nous agissons dans l'intérêt de la verité. Nous ne voulons pas vous blesser," said he.

Scorn gave me nerve. I only answered—

"Dictate, monsieur."

Rochemorte named this theme: "Human Justice."

Human Justice! What was I to make of it? Blank, cold abstraction, unsuggestive to me of one inspiring idea; and there stood M. Emanuel, sad as Saul and stern as Joab, and there triumphed his accusers.

At these two I looked. I was gathering my courage to tell them that I would neither write nor speak another word for their satisfaction, that their theme did not suit, nor their presence inspire me, and that, notwithstanding, whoever threw the shadow of a doubt on M. Emanuel's honour, outraged that truth of which they had announced themselves the champions: I *meant* to utter all this, I say, when suddenly, a light darted on memory.

Those two faces looking out of the forest of long hair, moustache, and whisker—those two cold yet bold, trustless yet presumptuous visages—were the same faces, the very same that, projected in full gaslight from behind the pillars of a portico, had half frightened me to death on the night of my desolate arrival in Villette. These, I felt morally certain, were the very heroes who had driven a friendless foreigner beyond her reckoning and her strength, chased her breathless over a whole quarter of the town.

"Pious mentors!" thought I. "Pure guides for youth! If 'Human Justice' were what she ought to be, you two would scarce hold your present post, or enjoy your present credit."

An idea once seized, I fell to work. "Human Justice" rushed before me in novel guise, a red, random beldame with arms akimbo. I saw her in her house, the den

of confusion: servants called to her for orders or help which she did not give; beggars stood at her door waiting and starving unnoticed; a swarm of children, sick and quarrelsome, crawled round her feet and yelled in her ears appeals for notice, sympathy, cure, redress. The honest woman cared for none of these things. She had a warm seat of her own by the fire, she had her own solace in a short black pipe, and a bottle of Mrs. Sweeny's soothing syrup; she smoked and she sipped and she enjoyed her paradise, and whenever a cry of the suffering souls about her pierced her ears too keenly—my jolly dame seized the poker or the hearth-brush: if the offender was weak, wronged, and sickly, she effectually settled him: if he was strong, lively, and violent, she only menaced, then plunged her hand into her deep pouch, and flung a liberal shower of sugar-plums.

Such was the sketch of "Human Justice," scratched hurriedly on paper, and placed at the service of Messrs. Boissec and Rochemorte. M. Emanuel read it over my shoulder. Waiting no comment, I curtseyed to the trio and withdrew.

After school that day, M. Paul and I again met. Of course the meeting did not at first run smooth; there was a crow to pluck with him; that forced examination could not be immediately digested. A crabbed dialogue terminated in my being called "une petite moqueuse et sans-cœur," and in Monsieur's temporary departure.

Not wishing him to go quite away, only desiring he should feel that such a transport as he had that day given way to could not be indulged with perfect impunity, I was not sorry to see him, soon after, gardening in the berceau. He approached the glass door; I drew near also. We spoke of some flowers growing round it. By-and-by Monsieur laid down his spade; by-and-by he recommenced conversation, passed to other subjects, and at last touched a point of interest.

Conscious that his proceeding of that day was specially open to a charge of extravagance, M. Paul half apologised; he half regretted, too, the fitfulness of his moods at all times, yet he hinted that some allowance ought to be made for him. "But," said he, "I can hardly expect it at your hands, Miss Lucy; you know neither me, nor my position, nor my history."

His history. I took up the word at once; I pursued the idea.

"No, monsieur," I rejoined. "Of course, as you say, I know neither your history, nor your position, nor your sacrifices, nor any of your sorrows, or trials, or affections, or fidelities. Oh, no! I know nothing about you; you are for me altogether a stranger."

"Hein?" he murmured, arching his brows in surprise.

"You know, monsieur, I only see you in classe—stern, dogmatic, hasty, imperious. I only hear of you in town as active and wilful, quick to originate, hasty to lead, but slow to persuade, and hard to bend. A man like you, without ties, can have no attachments; without dependents, no duties. All we, with whom you come in contact, are machines, which you thrust here and there, inconsiderate of their feelings. You seek your recreations in public, by the light of the evening chandelier; this school and yonder college are your workshops, where you fabricate the ware called pupils. I don't so much as know where you live; it is natural to take it for granted that you have no home, and need none."

"I am judged," said he. "Your opinion of me is just what I thought it was. For you I am neither a man nor a Christian. You see me void of affection and religion, unattached by friend or family, unpiloted by principle or faith. It is well, mademoiselle, such is our reward in this life."

"You are a philosopher, monsieur; a cynic philosopher" (and I looked at his paletôt, of which he straightway brushed the dim sleeve with his hand), "despising the foibles of humanity—above its luxuries—independent of its comforts."

"Et vous, mademoiselle; vous êtes proprette et douillette et affreusement insensible, par-dessus le marché."

"But in short, monsieur, now I think of it, you *must* live somewhere? Do tell me where; and what establishment of servants do you keep?"

With a fearful projection of the under lip, implying an impetus of scorn the most decided, he broke out—

"Je vis dans un trou! I inhabit a den, miss—a cavern, where you would not put your dainty nose. Once, with base shame of speaking the whole truth, I talked about my 'study' in that college: know now that this 'study' is my whole abode; my chamber is there and my drawing-room. As for my 'establishment of servants' " (mimicking my voice), "they number ten; les voilà."

And he grimly spread, close under my eyes, his ten fingers.

"I black my boots," pursued he savagely. "I brush my paletôt."

"No, monsieur, it is too plain; you never do that," was my parenthesis.

"Je fais mon lit et mon ménage; I seek my dinner in a restaurant; my supper takes care of itself; I pass days laborious and loveless; nights long and lonely; I am ferocious, and bearded, and monkish; and nothing now living in this world loves me, except some old hearts worn like my own, and some few beings, impoverished, suffering, poor in purse and in spirit, whom the kingdoms of this world own not, but to whom a will and testament not to be disputed has bequeathed the kingdom of heaven."

"Ah, monsieur; but I know!"

"What do you know? many things, I verily believe; yet not me, Lucy!"

"I know that you have a pleasant old house in a pleasant old square of the Basse-Ville—why don't you go and live there?"

"Hein?" muttered he again.

"I liked it much, monsieur; with the steps ascending to the door, the grey flags in front, the nodding trees behind—real trees, not shrubs—trees dark, high, and of old growth. And the boudoir-oratoire—you should make that room your study; it is so quiet and solemn."

He eyed me closely; he half-smiled, half-coloured. "Where did you pick up all that? Who told you?" he asked.

"Nobody told me. Did I dream it, monsieur, do you think?"

"Can I enter into your visions? Can I guess a woman's waking thoughts, much less her sleeping fantasies?"

"If I dreamt it, I saw in my dream human beings as well as a house. I saw a priest, old, bent, and grey, and a domestic—old, too, and picturesque; and a lady, splendid but strange; her head would scarce reach to my elbow—her magnificence might ransom a duke. She wore a gown bright as lapis-lazuli—a shawl worth a thousand francs: she was decked with ornaments so brilliant, I never saw any with such a beautiful sparkle; but her figure looked as if it had been broken in two and bent double: she seemed to have outlived the common years of humanity, and to have attained those which are only labour and sorrow. She was become morose—almost malevolent; yet *somebody*, it appears, cared for her in her infirmities—somebody forgave her trespasses, hoping to have his trespasses forgiven. They lived together, these three people—the mistress, the chaplain, the servant—all old, all feeble, all sheltered under one kind wing."

He covered with his hand the upper part of his face, but did not conceal his mouth, where I saw hovering an expression I liked.

"I see you have entered into my secrets," said he, "but how was it done?"

So I told him how—the commission on which I had been sent, the storm which had detained me, the abruptness of the lady, the kindness of the priest. "As I sat waiting for the rain to cease, Père Silas whiled away the time with a story," I said.

"A story! What story? Père Silas is no romancist."

"Shall I tell Monsieur the tale?"

"Yes: begin at the beginning. Let me hear some of Miss Lucy's French—her best or her worst—I don't much care which: let us have a good poignée of barbarisms, and a bounteous dose of the insular accent."

"Monsieur is not going to be gratified by a tale of ambitious proportions, and the spectacle of the narrator sticking fast in the midst. But I will tell him the title—'The Priest's Pupil.' "

"Pah!" said he, the swarthy flush again dyeing his dark cheek. "The good old father could not have chosen a worse subject: it is his weak point. But what of 'The Priest's Pupil'?"

"Oh! many things."

"You may as well define *what* things. I mean to know."

"There was the pupil's youth, the pupil's manhood—his avarice, his ingratitude, his implacability, his inconstancy. Such a bad pupil, monsieur!—so thankless, cold-hearted, unchivalrous, unforgiving!"

"Et puis?" said he, taking a cigar.

"Et puis," I pursued, "he underwent calamities which one did not pity—bore them in a spirit one did not admire—endured wrongs for which one felt no sympathy; finally took the unchristian revenge of heaping coals of fire on his adversary's head."

"You have not told me all," said he.

"Nearly all, I think: I have indicated the heads of Père Silas's chapters."

"You have forgotten one—that which touched on the pupil's lack of affection—on his hard, cold, monkish heart."

"True; I remember now. Père Silas *did* say that his vocation was almost that of a priest—that his life was considered consecrated."

"By what bonds or duties?"

"By the ties of the past and the charities of the present."

"You have, then, the whole situation?"

"I have now told Monsieur all that was told me."

Some meditative minutes passed.

"Now, Mademoiselle Lucy, look at me, and with that truth which I believe you never knowingly violate, answer me one question. Raise your eyes; rest them on mine; have no hesitation; fear not to trust me—I am a man to be trusted."

I raised my eyes.

"Knowing me thoroughly now—all my antecedents, all my responsibilities—having long known my faults, can you and I still be friends?"

"If Monsieur wants a friend in me, I shall be glad to have a friend in him."

"But a close friend I mean—intimate and real—kindred in all but blood? Will Miss Lucy be the sister of a very poor, fettered, burdened, encumbered man?"

I could not answer him in words, yet I suppose I *did* answer him; he took my hand, which found comfort in the shelter of his. *His* friendship was not a doubtful, wavering benefit—a cold, distant hope—a sentiment so brittle as not to bear the weight of a finger: I at once felt (or *thought* I felt) its support like that of some rock.

"When I talk of friendship, I mean *true* friendship," he repeated emphatically; and I could hardly believe that words so earnest had blessed my ear; I hardly could credit the reality of that kind, anxious look he gave. If he *really* wished for my confidence and regard, and *really* would give me his—why, it seemed to me that life could offer nothing more or better. In that case, I was become strong and rich: in a moment I was made substantially happy. To ascertain the fact, to fix and seal it, I asked—

"Is Monsieur quite serious? Does he really think he needs me, and can take an interest in me as a sister?"

"Surely, surely," said he; "a lonely man like me, who has no sister, must be but too glad to find in some woman's heart a sister's pure affection."

"And dare I rely on Monsieur's regard? Dare I speak to him when I am so inclined?"

"My little sister must make her own experiments," said he; "I will give no promises. She must tease and try her wayward brother till she has drilled him into what she wishes. After all, he is no inductile material in some hands."

While he spoke, the tone of his voice, the light of his now affectionate eye, gave me such a pleasure as, certainly, I had never felt. I envied no girl her lover, no bride her bridegroom, no wife her husband; I was content with this my voluntary, self-offering friend. If he would but prove reliable, and he *looked* reliable, what, beyond his friendship, could I ever covet? But, if all melted like a dream, as once before had happened——

"Qu'est-ce donc? What is it?" said he, as this thought threw its weight on my heart, its shadow on my countenance. I told him; and after a moment's pause, and a thoughtful smile, he showed me how an equal fear—lest I should weary of him, a man of moods so difficult and fitful—had haunted his mind for more than one day, or one month.

On hearing this, a quiet courage cheered me. I ventured a word of reassurance. That word was not only tolerated; its repetition was courted. I grew quite happy—strangely happy—in making him secure, content, tranquil. Yesterday, I could not have believed that earth held, or life afforded, moments like the few I was now passing. Countless times it had been my lot to watch apprehended sorrow close darkly in; but to see unhoped-for happiness take form, find place, and grow more real as the seconds sped, was indeed a new experience.

"Lucy," said M. Paul, speaking low and still holding my hand, "did you see a picture in the boudoir of the old house?"

"I did; a picture painted on a panel."

"The portrait of a nun?"

"Yes."

"You heard her history?"

"Yes."

"You remember what we saw that night in the berceau?"

"I shall never forget it."

"You did not connect the two ideas; that would be folly?"

"I thought of the apparition when I saw the portrait," said I; which was true enough.

"You did not, nor will you fancy," pursued he, "that a saint in heaven perturbs herself with rivalries of earth? Protestants are rarely superstitious; these morbid fancies will not beset *you*?"

"I know not what to think of this matter; but I believe a perfectly natural solution of the seeming mystery will one day be arrived at."

"Doubtless, doubtless. Besides, no good living woman—much less a pure, happy spirit—would trouble amity like ours—n'est-il pas vrai?"

Ere I could answer, Fifine Beck burst in, rosy and abrupt, calling out that I was wanted. Her mother was going into town to call on some English family, who had applied for a prospectus: my services were needed as interpreter. The interruption was not unseasonable: sufficient for the day is always the evil; for this hour, its good sufficed. Yet I should have liked to ask M. Paul whether the "morbid fancies," against which he warned me, wrought in his own brain.

Chapter XXXVI

THE APPLE OF DISCORD

BESIDES Fifine Beck's mother, another power had a word to say to M. Paul and me before that covenant of friendship could be ratified. We were under the surveillance

of a sleepless eye: Rome watched jealously her son through that mystic lattice at which I had knelt once, and to which M. Emanuel drew nigh month by month—the sliding panel of the confessional.

"Why were you so glad to be friends with M. Paul?" asks the reader. "Had he not long been a friend to you? Had he not given proof on proof of a certain partiality in his feelings?"

Yes, he had; but still I liked to hear him say so earnestly—that he was my close, true friend; I liked his modest doubts, his tender deference—that trust which longed to rest, and was grateful when taught how. He had called me "sister." It was well. Yes; he might call me what he pleased, so long as he confided in me. I was willing to be his sister, on condition that he did not invite me to fill that relation to some future wife of his; and tacitly vowed as he was to celibacy, of this dilemma there seemed little danger.

Through most of the succeeding night I pondered that evening's interview. I wanted much the morning to break, and then listened for the bell to ring; and, after rising and dressing, I deemed prayers and breakfast slow, and all the hours lingering till that arrived at last which brought me the lesson of literature. My wish was to get a more thorough comprehension of this fraternal alliance: to note with how much of the brother he would demean himself when we met again; to prove how much of the sister was in my own feelings; to discover whether I could summon a sister's courage, and he a brother's frankness.

He came. Life is so constructed that the event does not, cannot, will not match the expectation. That whole day he never accosted me. His lesson was given rather more quietly than usual, more mildly, and also more gravely. He was fatherly to his pupils, but he was not brotherly to me. Ere he left the classe, I expected a smile, if not a word; I got neither: to my portion fell one nod—hurried, shy.

This distance, I argued, is accidental—it is involuntary; patience, and it will vanish. It vanished not; it continued for days; it increased. I suppressed my surprise, and swallowed whatever other feelings began to surge.

Well might I ask when he offered fraternity—"Dare I rely on you?" Well might he, doubtless knowing himself, withhold all pledge. True, he had bid me make my own experiments—tease and try him. Vain injunction! Privilege nominal and unavailable. Some women might use it! Nothing in my powers or instinct placed me amongst this brave band. Left alone, I was passive; repulsed, I withdrew; forgotten—my lips would not utter, nor my eyes dart a reminder. It seemed there had been an error somewhere in my calculations, and I waited for time to disclose it.

But the day came when, as usual, he was to give me a lesson. One evening in seven he had long generously bestowed on me, devoting it to the examination of what had been done in various studies during the past week, and to the preparation of work for the week in prospect. On these occasions my schoolroom was anywhere, wherever the pupils and the other teachers happened to be, or in their close vicinage, very often in the large second division, where it was easy to choose a quiet nook when the crowding day-pupils were absent, and the few boarders gathered in a knot about the surveillante's estrade.

On the customary evening, hearing the customary hour strike, I collected my books and papers, my pen and ink, and sought the large division.

In classe there was no one, and it lay all in cool deep shadow: but through the open double doors was seen the carré, filled with pupils aud with light; over hall and figures blushed the westering sun. It blushed so ruddily and vividly, that the hues of the walls and the variegated tints of the dresses seemed all fused in one warm glow. The girls were seated, working or studying; in the midst of their circle stood M. Emanuel, speaking good-humouredly to a teacher. His dark paletôt, his jetty hair, were tinged with many a reflex of crimson; his Spanish face, when he turned it momentarily, answered the sun's animated kiss with an animated smile. I took my place at a desk.

The orange-trees, and several plants full and bright with bloom, basked also in the sun's laughing bounty; they had partaken it the whole day, and now asked water. M. Emanuel had a taste for gardening; he liked to tend and foster plants. I used to think that working amongst shrubs with a spade or a watering-pot soothed his nerves; it was a recreation to which he often had recourse; and now he looked to the orange-trees, the geraniums, the gorgeous cactuses, and revived them all with the refreshment their drought needed. His lips meantime sustained his precious cigar, that (for him) first necessary and prime luxury of life; its blue wreaths curled prettily enough amongst the flowers, and in the evening light. He spoke no more to the pupils nor to the mistresses, but gave many an endearing word to a small spanieless (if one may coin a word) that nominally belonged to the house, but virtually owned him as master, being fonder of him than any inmate. A delicate, silky, loving, and lovable little doggie she was, trotting at his side, looking with expressive, attached eyes into his face: and whenever he dropped his bonnet-grec or his handkerchief, which he occasionally did in play, crouching beside it with the air of a miniature lion guarding a kingdom's flag.

There were many plants, and as the amateur gardener fetched all the water from the well in the court with his own active hands, his work spun on to some length. The great school-clock ticked on. Another hour struck. The carré and the youthful group lost the illusion of sunset. Day was drooping. My lesson, I perceived, must to-night be very short; but the orange trees, the cactuses, the camellias were all served now. Was it my turn?

Alas! in the garden were more plants to be looked after,—favourite rose-bushes, certain choice flowers; little Sylvie's glad bark and whine followed the receding paletôt down the alleys. I put up some of my books; I should not want them all; I sat and thought and waited, involuntarily deprecating the creeping invasion of twilight.

Sylvie, gaily frisking, emerged into view once more, heralding the returning paletôt; the watering-pot was deposited beside the well; it had fulfilled its office; how glad I was! Monsieur washed his hands in a little stone bowl. There was no longer time for a lesson now; ere long the prayer-bell must ring; but still we should meet; he would speak: a chance would be offered of reading in his eyes the riddle of his shyness. His ablutions over, he stood, slowly rearranging his cuffs, looking at the horn of a young moon, set pale in the opal sky, and glimmering faint on the oriel of Jean Baptiste. Sylvie watched the mood contemplative; its stillness irked her; she whined and jumped to break it. He looked down.

"Petite exigeante," said he; "you must not be forgotten one moment, it seems."

He stopped, lifted her in his arms, sauntered across the court within a yard of the line of windows near one of which I sat: he sauntered lingeringly, fondling the spaniel in his bosom, calling her tender names in a tender voice. On the front-door steps he turned; once again he looked at the moon, at the grey cathedral, over the remoter spires and house-roofs fading into a blue sea of night-mist; he tasted the sweet breath of dusk, and noted the folded bloom of the garden; he suddenly looked round; a keen beam out of his eye rased the white façade of the classes, swept the long line of croisées. I think he bowed; if he did, I had no time to return the courtesy. In a moment he was gone; the moonlit threshold lay pale and shadowless before the closed front-door.

Gathering in my arms all that was spread on the desk before me, I carried back the unused heap to its place in the third classe. The prayer-bell rang; I obeyed its summons.

The morrow would not restore him to the Rue Fossette, that day being devoted entirely to his college. I got through my teaching; I got over the intermediate hours; I saw evening approaching, and armed myself for its heavy ennuis. Whether it was worse to stay with my co-inmates or to sit alone I had not considered; I naturally took up the latter alternative; if there was a hope of comfort for any moment, the

heart or head of no human being in this house could yield it; only under the lid of my desk could it harbour, nestling between the leaves of some book, gilding a pencil-point, the nib of a pen, or tinging the black fluid in that ink-glass. With a heavy heart I opened my desk-lid; with a weary hand I turned up its contents.

One by one, well-accustomed books, volumes sewn in familiar covers, were taken out and put back hopeless; they had no charm; they could not comfort. Is this something new, this pamphlet in lilac? I had not seen it before, and I rearranged my desk this very day—this very afternoon; the tract must have been introduced within the last hour, while we were at dinner.

I opened it. What was it? What would it say to me?

It was neither tale nor poem, neither essay nor history; it neither sung, nor related, nor discussed. It was a theological work; it preached and it persuaded.

I lent to it my ear very willingly, for, small as it was, it possessed its own spell, and bound my attention at once. It preached Romanism; it persuaded to conversion. The voice of that sly little book was a honeyed voice; its accents were all unction and balm. Here roared no utterance of Rome's thunders, no blasting of the breath of her displeasure. The Protestant was to turn Papist, not so much in fear of the heretic's hell, as on account of the comfort, the indulgence, the tenderness Holy Church offered: far be from her to threaten or to coerce; her wish was to guide and win. *She* persecute? Oh dear no! not on any account!

This meek volume was not addressed to the hardened and worldly; it was not even strong meat for the strong: it was milk for babes; the mild effluence of a mother's love towards her tenderest and her youngest; intended wholly and solely for those whose head is to be reached through the heart. Its appeal was not to intellect; it sought to win the affectionate through their affections, the sympathising through their sympathies: St. Vincent de Paul, gathering his orphans about him, never spoke more sweetly.

I remember one capital inducement to apostacy was held out in the fact that the Catholic who had lost dear friends by death could enjoy the unspeakable solace of praying them out of purgatory. The writer did not touch on the firmer peace of those whose belief dispenses with purgatory altogether: but I thought of this, and, on the whole, preferred the latter doctrine as the most consolatory.

The little book amused and did not painfully displease me. It was a canting, sentimental, shallow little book, yet something about it cheered my gloom and made me smile; I was amused with the gambols of this unlicked wolf-cub muffled in the fleece, and mimicking the bleat of a guileless lamb. Portions of it reminded me of certain Wesleyan Methodist tracts I had once read when a child; they were flavoured with about the same seasoning of excitation to fanaticism. He that had written it was no bad man, and while perpetually betraying the trained cunning— the cloven hoof of his system—I should pause before accusing himself of insincerity. His judgment, however, wanted surgical props; it was rickety.

I smiled then over this dose of maternal tenderness coming from the ruddy old lady of the Seven Hills; smiled, too, at my own disinclination, not to say disability, to meet these melting favours. Glancing at the title-page, I found the name of "Père Silas." A flyleaf bore in small but clear and well-known pencil characters: "From P. C. D. E. to L—y." And when I saw this I laughed: but not in my former spirit. I was revived.

A mortal bewilderment cleared suddenly from my head and vision; the solution of the Sphinx-riddle was won; the conjunction of those two names, Père Silas and Paul Emanuel, gave the key to all. The penitent had been with his director; permitted to withhold nothing; suffered to keep no corner of his heart sacred to God and to himself; the whole narrative of our late interview had been drawn from him; he had avowed the covenant of fraternity, and spoken of his adopted sister. How could such a covenant, such adoption, be sanctioned by the Church? Fraternal communion with a heretic! I seemed to hear Père Silas annulling the unholy pact; warning his

penitent of its perils; entreating, enjoining reserve, nay, by the authority of his office, and in the name and by the memory of all M. Emanuel held most dear and sacred, commanding the enforcement of that new system whose frost had pierced to the marrow of my bones.

These may not seem pleasant hypotheses; yet, by comparison, they were welcome. The vision of a ghostly troubler hovering in the background was as nothing, matched with the fear of spontaneous change arising in M. Paul himself.

At this distance of time, I cannot be sure how far the above conjectures were self-suggested: or in what measure they owed their origin and confirmation to another quarter. Help was not wanting.

This evening there was no bright sunset: west and east were one cloud; no summer night-mist, blue, yet rose-tinged, softened the distance: a clammy fog from the marshes crept grey round Villette. To-night the watering-pot might rest in its niche by the well: a small rain had been drizzling all the afternoon, and still it fell fast and quietly. This was no weather for rambling in the wet alleys under the dripping trees; and I started to hear Sylvie's sudden bark in the garden—her bark of welcome. Surely she was not accompanied; and yet this glad, quick bark was never uttered save in homage to one presence.

Through the glass door and the arching berceau I commanded the deep vista of the allée défendue: thither rushed Sylvie, glistening through its gloom like a white guelder-rose. She ran to and fro, whining, springing, harassing little birds amongst the bushes. I watched five minutes; no fulfilment followed the omen. I returned to my books; Sylvie's sharp bark suddenly ceased. Again I looked up. She was standing not many yards distant, wagging her white, feathery tail as fast as the muscle would work, and intently watching the operations of a spade plied fast by an indefatigable hand. There was M. Emanuel, bent over the soil, digging in the wet mould amongst the rain-laden and streaming shrubs, working as hard as if his day's pittance were yet to earn by the literal sweat of his brow.

In this sign I read a ruffled mood. He would dig thus in frozen snow on the coldest winter day when urged inwardly by painful emotion, whether of nervous excitation or sad thoughts of self-reproach. He would dig by the hour, with knit brow and set teeth, nor once lift his head or open his lips.

Sylvie watched till she was tired. Again scampering devious, bounding here, rushing there, snuffing and sniffing everywhere; she at last discovered me in classe. Instantly she flew barking at the panes, as if to urge me forth to share her pleasure or her master's toil; she had seen me occasionally walking in that alley with M. Paul; and I doubt not considered it my duty to join him now, wet as it was.

She made such a bustle that M. Paul at last looked up, and of course perceived why and at whom she barked. He whistled to call her off; she only barked the louder. She seemed quite bent upon having the glass door opened. Tired, I suppose, with her importunity, he threw down his spade, approached, and pushed the door ajar. Sylvie burst in all impetuous, sprang to my lap, and with her paws at my neck, and her little nose and tongue somewhat overpoweringly busy about my face, mouth, and eyes, flourished her bushy tail over the desk, and scattered books and papers far and wide.

M. Emanuel advanced to still the clamour and repair the disarrangement. Having gathered up the books, he captured Sylvie, and stowed her away under his paletôt, where she nestled as quiet as a mouse, her head just peeping forth. She was very tiny, and had the prettiest little innocent face, the silkiest long ears, the finest dark eyes in the world. I never saw her but I thought of Paulina de Bassompierre: forgive the association, reader, it *would* occur.

M. Paul petted and patted her; the endearments she received were not to be wondered at; she invited affection by her beauty and her vivacious life.

While caressing the spaniel, his eye roved over the papers and books just replaced; it settled on the religious tract. His lips moved; he half checked the impulse to

speak. What! had he promised never to address me more? If so, his better nature pronounced the vow "more honoured in the breach than in the observance," for with a second effort, he spoke—

"You have not yet read the brochure, I presume? Is it not sufficiently inviting?" I replied that I had read it.

He waited, as if wishing me to give an opinion upon it unasked. Unasked, however, I was in no mood to do or say anything. If any concessions were to be made—if any advances were demanded—that was the affair of the very docile pupil of Père Silas, not mine. His eye settled upon me gently; there was mildness at the moment in its blue ray—there was solicitude—a shade of pathos; there were meanings composite and contrasted—reproach melting into remorse. At the moment probably he would have been glad to see something emotional in me. I could not show it. In another minute, however, I should have betrayed confusion, had I not bethought myself to take some quill-pens from my desk and begin soberly to mend them.

I knew that action would give a turn to his mood. He never liked to see me mend pens; my knife was always dull-edged—my hand, too, was unskilful; I hacked and chipped. On this occasion I cut my own finger—half on purpose. I wanted to restore him to his natural state, to set him at his ease, to get him to chide.

"Maladroit!" he cried at last, "she will make mincemeat of her hands."

He put Sylvie down, making her lie quiet beside his bonnet-grec, and, depriving me of the pens and penknife, proceeded to slice, nib, and point with the accuracy and celerity of a machine.

"Did I like the little book?" he now inquired.

Suppressing a yawn, I said I hardly knew.

"Had it moved me?"

"I thought it had made me a little sleepy."

(After a pause.) "Allons donc! It was of no use taking that tone with him. Bad as I was—and he should be sorry to have to name all my faults at a breath—God and nature had given me 'trop de sensibilité et de sympathie' not to be profoundly affected by an appeal so touching."

"Indeed!" I responded, rousing myself quickly, "I was not affected at all—not a whit."

And in proof, I drew from my pocket a perfectly dry handkerchief, still clean and in its folds.

Hereupon I was made the object of a string of strictures rather piquant than polite. I listened with zest. After those two days of unnatural silence, it was better than music to hear M. Paul haranguing again just in his old fashion. I listened, and meantime solaced myself and Sylvie with the contents of a bonbonnière which M. Emanuel's gifts kept well supplied with chocolate comfits. It pleased him to see even a small matter from his hand duly appreciated. He looked at me and the spaniel while we shared the spoil; he put up his penknife. Touching my hand with the bundle of new-cut quills, he said—

"Dites-donc, petite sœur—speak frankly—what have you thought of me during the last two days?"

But of this question I would take no manner of notice; its purport made my eyes fill. I caressed Sylvie assiduously. M. Paul, leaning over the desk, bent towards me—

"I called myself your brother," he said: "I hardly know what I am—brother—friend—I cannot tell. I know I think of you—I feel I wish you well—but I must check myself; you are to be feared. My best friends point out danger, and whisper caution."

"You do right to listen to your friends. By all means be cautious."

"It is your religion—your strange, self-reliant, invulnerable creed, whose influence seems to clothe you in I know not what unblessed panoply. You are good—Père Silas calls you good, and loves you—but your terrible, proud, earnest Protestantism,

there is the danger. It expresses itself by your eye at times; and again, it gives you certain tones and certain gestures that make my flesh creep. You are not demonstrative, and yet, just now—when you handled that tract—my God! I thought Lucifer smiled.''

''Certainly I don't respect that tract—what then?''

''Not respect that tract? But it is the pure essence of faith, love, charity! I thought it would touch you: in its gentleness, I trusted that it could not fail. I laid it in your desk with a prayer. I must indeed be a sinner: Heaven will not hear the petitions that come warmest from my heart. You scorn my little offering. Oh, cela me fait mal!''

''Monsieur, I don't scorn it—at least, not as your gift. Monsieur, sit down; listen to me. I am not a heathen, I am not hard-hearted, I am not unchristian, I am not dangerous, as they tell you; I would not trouble your faith; you believe in God and Christ and the Bible, and so do I.''

''But *do* you believe in the Bible? Do you receive Revelation? What limits are there to the wild, careless daring of your country and sect? Père Silas dropped dark hints.''

By dint of persuasion, I made him half define these hints; they amounted to crafty Jesuit slanders. That night M. Paul and I talked seriously and closely. He pleaded, he argued. *I* could not argue—a fortunate incapacity: it needed but triumphant, logical opposition to effect all the director wished to be effected; but I could talk in my own way—the way M. Paul was used to—and of which he could follow the meanderings and fill the hiatus, and pardon the strange stammerings, strange to him no longer. At ease with him, I could defend my creed and faith in my own fashion; in some degree I could lull his prejudices. He was not satisfied when he went away, hardly was he appeased; but he was made thoroughly to feel that Protestants were not necessarily the irreverent pagans his director had insinuated; he was made to comprehend something of their mode of honouring the Light, the Life, the Word; he was enabled partly to perceive that, while their veneration for things venerable was not quite like that cultivated in his Church, it had its own, perhaps, deeper power—its own more solemn awe.

I found that Père Silas (himself, I must repeat, not a bad man, though the advocate of a bad cause) had darkly stigmatised Protestants in general, and myself by inference, with strange names, had ascribed to us strange ''isms''; Monsieur Emanuel revealed all this in his frank fashion, which knew not secretiveness, looking at me as he spoke with a kind, earnest fear, almost trembling lest there should be truth in the charges. Père Silas, it seems, had closely watched me, had ascertained that I went by turns, and indiscriminately, to the three Protestant chapels of Villette— the French, German, and English—*id est,* the Presbyterian, Lutheran, Episcopalian. Such liberality argued in the Father's eyes profound indifference—who tolerates all, he reasoned, can be attached to none. Now, it happened that I had often secretly wondered at the minute and unimportant character of the differences between these three sects—at the unity and identity of their vital doctrines: I saw nothing to hinder them from being one day fused into one grand Holy Alliance, and I respected them all, though I thought that in each there were faults of form, incumbrances, and trivialities. Just what I thought, that did I tell M. Emanuel, and explained to him that my own last appeal, the guide to which I looked, and the teacher which I owned, must always be the Bible itself, rather than any sect, of whatever name or nation.

He left me soothed, yet full of solicitude, breathing a wish, as strong as a prayer, that if I were wrong, Heaven would lead me right. I heard, poured forth on the threshold, some fervid murmurings, to ''Marie, Reine du Ciel,'' some deep aspiration that *his* hope might yet be *mine*.

Strange! I had no such feverish wish to turn him from the faith of his fathers. I thought Romanism wrong, a great mixed image of gold and clay; but it seemed to

me that *this* Romanist held the purer elements of his creed with an innocency of heart which God must love.

The preceding conversation passed between eight and nine o'clock of the evening in a school-room of the quiet Rue Fossette opening on a sequestered garden. Probably about the same, or a somewhat later hour of the succeeding evening, its echoes, collected by holy obedience, were breathed verbatim in an attent ear, at the panel of a confessional, in the hoary church of the Magi. It ensued that Père Silas paid a visit to Madame Beck, and stirred by I know not what mixture of motives, persuaded her to let him undertake for a time the Englishwoman's spiritual direction.

Hereupon I was put through a course of reading—that is, I just glanced at the books lent me; they were too little in my way to be thoroughly read, marked, learned, or inwardly digested. And besides, I had a book upstairs, under my pillow, whereof certain chapters satisfied my needs in the article of spiritual lore, furnishing such precept and example as, to my heart's core, I was convinced could not be improved on.

Then Père Silas showed me the fair side of Rome, her good works, and bade me judge the tree by its fruits.

In answer, I felt and I avowed that these works were *not* the fruits of Rome; they were but her abundant blossoming, but the fair promise she showed the world. That bloom, when set, savoured not of charity; the apple full formed was ignorance, abasement, and bigotry. Out of men's afflictions and affections were forged the rivets of their servitude. Poverty was fed and clothed and sheltered to bind it by obligation to "the Church"; orphanage was reared and educated that it might grow up in the fold of "the Church"; sickness was tended that it might die after the formula and in the ordinance of "the Church"; and men were overwrought, and women most murderously sacrificed, and all laid down a world God made pleasant for His creatures' good, and took up a cross, monstrous in its galling weight, that they might serve Rome, prove her sanctity, confirm her power, and spread the reign of her tyrant "Church."

For man's good was little done; for God's glory, less. A thousand ways were opened with pain, with blood-sweats, with lavishing of life; mountains were cloven through their breasts and rocks were split to their base; and all for what? That a Priesthood might march straight on and straight upward to an all-dominating eminence, whence they might at last stretch the sceptre of their Moloch "Church."

It will not be. God is not with Rome, and, were human sorrows still for the Son of God, would He not mourn over her cruelties and ambitions, as once He mourned over the crimes and woes of doomed Jerusalem?

Oh, lovers of power! Oh, mitred aspirants for this world's kingdoms! an hour will come, even to you, when it will be well for your hearts—pausing faint at each broken beat—that there is a Mercy beyond human compassions, a Love stronger than this strong death which even you must face, and before it fall; a Charity more potent than any sin, even yours; a Pity which redeems worlds—nay, absolves Priests.

My third temptation was held out in the pomp of Rome—the glory of her kingdom. I was taken to the churches on solemn occasions—days of fête and state; I was shown the Papal ritual and ceremonial. I looked at it.

Many people—men and women—no doubt far my superiors in a thousand ways, have felt this display impressive, have declared that though their Reason protested, their Imagination was subjugated. I cannot say the same. Neither full procession, nor high mass, nor swarming tapers, nor swinging censers, nor ecclesiastical millinery, nor celestial jewellery, touched my imagination a whit. What I saw struck me as tawdry, not grand; as grossly material, not poetically spiritual.

This I did not tell Père Silas; he was old, he looked venerable; through every abortive experiment, under every repeated disappointment, he remained personally

kind to me, and I felt tender of hurting his feelings. But on the evening of a certain day, when, from the balcony of a great house, I had been made to witness a huge mingled procession of the Church and the army—priests with relics, and soldiers with weapons, an obese and aged archbishop, habited in cambric and lace, looking strangely like a grey daw in a bird-of-paradise plumage, and a band of young girls fantastically robed and garlanded—*then* I spoke my mind to M. Paul.

"I did not like it," I told him. "I did not respect such ceremonies; I wished to see no more."

And having relieved my conscience by this declaration, I was able to go on, and, speaking more currently and clearly than my wont, to show him that I had a mind to keep to my reformed creed; the more I saw of Popery the closer I clung to Protestantism; doubtless there were errors in every Church, but I now perceived by contrast how severely pure was my own, compared with her whose painted and meretricious face had been unveiled for my admiration. I told him how we kept fewer forms between us and God; retaining, indeed, no more than, perhaps, the nature of mankind in the mass rendered necessary for due observance. I told him I could not look on flowers and tinsel, on wax-lights and embroidery, at such times and under such circumstances as should be devoted to lifting the secret vision to Him whose home is Infinity, and His being—Eternity. That when I thought of sin and sorrow, of earthly corruption, mortal depravity, weighty temporal woe—I could not care for chanting priests or mumming officials; that when the pain of existence and the terrors of dissolution pressed before me—when the mighty hope and measureless doubt of the future arose in view—*then,* even the scientific strain, or the prayer in a language learned and dead, harassed with hindrance a heart which only longed to cry—

"God be merciful to me, a sinner!"

When I had so spoken, so declared my faith, and so widely severed myself from him I addressed—then, at last, came a tone accordant, an echo responsive, one sweet chord of harmony in two conflicting spirits.

"Whatever say priests or controversialists," murmured M. Emanuel, "God is good, and loves all the sincere. Believe, then, what you can; believe it as you can; one prayer, at least, we have in common; I also cry—'O Dieu, sois appaisé envers moi qui suis pécheur!' "

He leaned on the back of my chair. After some thought he again spoke—

"How seem in the eyes of that God who made all firmaments, from whose nostrils issued whatever of life is here, or in the stars, shining yonder—how seem the differences of man? But as Time is not for God, nor Space, so neither is Measure, nor Comparison. We abase ourselves in our littleness, and we do right; yet it may be that the constancy of one heart, the truth and faith of one mind according to the light He has appointed, import as much to Him as the just motion of satellites about their planets, of planets about their suns, of suns around that mighty unseen centre incomprehensible, irrealisable, with strange mental effort only divined.

"God guide us all! God bless you, Lucy!"

Chapter XXXVII

SUNSHINE

IT was very well for Paulina to decline further correspondence with Graham till her father had sanctioned the intercourse. But Dr. Bretton could not live within a league of the Hôtel Crécy and not contrive to visit there often. Both lovers meant at first, I believe, to be distant; they kept their intention so far as demonstrative courtship went, but in feeling they soon drew very near.

All that was best in Graham sought Paulina; whatever in him was noble, awoke, and grew in her presence. With his past admiration of Miss Fanshawe, I suppose his intellect had little to do, but his whole intellect, and his highest tastes, came in question now. These, like all his faculties, were active, eager for nutriment, and alive to gratification when it came.

I cannot say that Paulina designedly led him to talk of books, or formally proposed to herself for a moment the task of winning him to reflection, or planned the improvement of his mind, or so much as fancied his mind could in any one respect be improved. She thought him very perfect; it was Graham himself who, at first by the merest chance, mentioned some book he had been reading, and when in her response sounded a welcome harmony of sympathies, something pleasant to his soul, he talked on, more and better perhaps than he had ever talked before on such subjects. She listened with delight, and answered with animation. In each successive answer, Graham heard a music waxing finer and finer to his sense; in each he found a suggestive, persuasive, magic accent that opened a scarce-known treasure-house within, showed him unsuspected power in his own mind, and what was better, latent goodness in his heart. Each liked the way in which the other talked; the voice, the diction, the expression pleased; each keenly relished the flavour of the other's wit; they met each other's meaning with strange quickness, their thoughts often matched like carefully chosen pearls. Graham had wealth of mirth by nature; Paulina possessed no such inherent flow of animal spirits—unstimulated, she inclined to be thoughtful and pensive—but now she seemed merry as a lark; in her lover's genial presence, she glanced like some soft glad light. How beautiful she grew in her happiness I can hardly express, but I wondered to see her. As to that gentle ice of hers—that reserve on which she had depended; where was it now? Ah! Graham would not bear it; he brought with him a generous influence that soon thawed the timid, self-imposed restriction. Now were the old Bretton days talked over; perhaps brokenly at first, with a sort of smiling diffidence, then with opening candour and still growing confidence. Graham had made for himself a better opportunity than he had wished me to give; he had earned independence of the collateral help that disobliging Lucy had refused; all his reminiscences of "little Polly" found their proper expression in his own pleasant tones, by his own kind and handsome lips; how much better than if suggested by me.

More than once when we were alone, Paulina would tell me how wonderful and curious it was to discover the richness and accuracy of his memory in this matter. How, while he was looking at her, recollections would seem to be suddenly quickened in his mind. He reminded her that she had once gathered his head in her arms, caressed his leonine graces, and cried out, "Graham, I *do* like you!" He told her how she would set a footstool beside him, and climb by its aid to his knee. At this day he said he could recall the sensation of her little hands smoothing his cheek, or burying themselves in his thick mane. He remembered the touch of her small forefinger, placed half tremblingly, half curiously, in the cleft in his chin, the lisp, the look with which she would name it "a pretty dimple," then seek his eyes and question why they pierced so, telling him he had a "nice, strange face; far nicer, far stranger, than either his mamma or Lucy Snowe."

"Child as I was," remarked Paulina, "I wondered how I dared be so venturous. To me he seems now all sacred, his locks are inaccessible, and Lucy, I feel a sort of fear when I look at his firm, marble chin, at his straight Greek features. Women are called beautiful, Lucy; he is not like a woman, therefore I suppose he is not beautiful, but what is he then? Do other people see him with my eyes? Do *you* admire him?"

"I'll tell you what I do, Paulina," was once my answer to her many questions. "*I never see him*. I looked at him twice or thrice about a year ago, before he recognised me, and then I shut my eyes; and if he were to cross their balls twelve

times between each day's sunset and sunrise, except from memory, I should hardly know what shape had gone by.''

"Lucy, what do you mean?'' said she, under her breath.

"I mean that I value vision, and dread being struck stone blind.'' It was best to answer her strongly at once, and to silence for ever the tender, passionate confidences which left her lips sweet honey, and sometimes dropped in my ear—molten lead. To me she commented no more on her lover's beauty.

Yet speak of him she would; sometimes shyly in quiet, brief phrases; sometimes with a tenderness of cadence, and music of voice exquisite in itself; but which chafed me at times miserably; and then, I know, I gave her stern looks and words; but cloudless happiness had dazzled her native clear sight, and she only thought Lucy—fitful.

"Spartan girl! Proud Lucy!'' she would say, smiling at me. "Graham says you are the most peculiar, capricious little woman he knows; but yet you are excellent; we both think so.''

"You both think you know not what,'' said I. "Have the goodness to make me as little the subject of your mutual talk and thoughts as possible. I have my sort of life apart from yours.''

"But ours, Lucy, is a beautiful life, or it will be; and you shall share it.''

"I shall share no man's or woman's life in this world, as you understand sharing. I think I have one friend of my own, but am not sure; and till I *am* sure, I live solitary.''

"But solitude is sadness.''

"Yes; it is sadness. Life, however, has worse than that. Deeper than melancholy lies heart-break.''

"Lucy, I wonder if anybody will ever comprehend you altogether?''

There is, in lovers, a certain infatuation of egotism; they will have a witness of their happiness, cost that witness what it may. Paulina had forbidden letters, yet Dr. Bretton wrote; she had resolved against correspondence, yet she answered, were it only to chide. She showed me these letters; with something of the spoiled child's wilfulness, and of the heiress's imperiousness, she *made* me read them. As I read Graham's, I scarce wondered at her exaction, and understood her pride: they were fine letters—manly and fond—modest and gallant. Hers must have appeared to him beautiful. They had not been written to show her talents; still less, I think, to express her love. On the contrary, it appeared that she had proposed to herself the task of hiding that feeling, and bridling her lover's ardour. But how could such letters serve such a purpose? Graham was become dear as her life; he drew her like a powerful magnet. For her there was influence unspeakable in all he uttered, wrote, thought, or looked. With this unconfessed confession her letters glowed; it kindled them, from greeting to adieu.

"I wish papa knew; I *do* wish papa knew!'' began now to be her anxious murmur. "I wish, and yet I fear. I can hardly keep Graham back from telling him. There is nothing I long for more than to have this affair settled—to speak out candidly; and yet I dread the crisis. I know, I am certain, papa will be angry at the first; I fear he will dislike me almost; it will seem to him an untoward business; it will be a surprise, a shock: I can hardly foresee its whole effect on him.''

The fact was—her father, long calm, was beginning to be a little stirred: long blind on one point, an importunate light was beginning to trespass on his eye.

To *her,* he said nothing; but when she was not looking at, or perhaps thinking of him, I saw him gaze and meditate on her.

One evening—Paulina was in her dressing-room, writing, I believe, to Graham; she had left me in the library, reading—M. de Bassompierre came in; he sat down: I was about to withdraw; he requested me to remain—gently, yet in a manner which showed he wished compliance. He had taken his seat near the window, at a distance

from me; he opened a desk; he took from it what looked like a memorandum-book; of this book he studied a certain entry for several minutes.

"Miss Snowe," said he, laying it down, "do you know my little girl's age?"

"About eighteen, is it not, sir?"

"It seems so. This old pocket-book tells me she was born on the 5th of May, in the year 18—, eighteen years ago. It is strange; I had lost the just reckoning of her age. I thought of her as twelve—fourteen—an indefinite date; but she seemed a child."

"She is about eighteen," I repeated. "She is grown up; she will be no taller."

"My little jewel!" said M. de Bassompierre, in a tone which penetrated like some of his daughter's accents.

He sat very thoughtful.

"Sir, don't grieve," I said; for I knew his feelings, utterly unspoken as they were.

"She is the only pearl I have," he said; "and now others will find out that she is pure and of price: they will covet her."

I made no answer. Graham Bretton had dined with us that day; he had shone both in converse and looks: I know not what pride of bloom embellished his aspect and mellowed his intercourse. Under the stimulus of a high hope, something had unfolded in his whole manner which compelled attention. I think he had purposed on that day to indicate the origin of his endeavours, and the aim of his ambition. M. de Bassompierre had found himself forced, in a manner, to descry the direction and catch the character of his homage. Slow in remarking, he was logical in reasoning: having once seized the thread, it had guided him through a long labyrinth.

"Where is she?" he asked.

"She is upstairs."

"What is she doing?"

"She is writing."

"She writes, does she? Does she receive letters?"

"None but such as she can show me. And—sir—she—*they* have long wanted to consult you."

"Pshaw! They don't think of me—an old father! I am in the way."

"Ah, M. de Bassompierre—not so—that can't be! But Paulina must speak for herself; and Dr. Bretton, too, must be his own advocate."

"It is a little late. Matters are advanced, it seems."

"Sir, till you approve, nothing is done—only they love each other."

"Only!"

Invested by fate with the part of confidante and mediator, I was obliged to go on—

"Hundreds of times has Dr. Bretton been on the point of appealing to you, sir; but, with all his high courage, he fears you mortally."

"He may well—he may well fear me. He has touched the best thing I have. Had he but let her alone, she would have remained a child for years yet. So. Are they engaged?"

"They could not become engaged without your permission."

"It is well for you, Miss Snowe, to talk and think with that propriety which always characterises you; but this matter is a grief to me; my little girl was all I had: I have no more daughters and no son; Bretton might as well have looked elsewhere; there are scores of rich and pretty women who would not, I dare say, dislike him: he has looks, and conduct, and connection. Would nothing serve him but my Polly?"

"If he had never seen your 'Polly,' others might and would have pleased him—your niece, Miss Fanshawe, for instance."

"Ah! I would have given him Ginevra with all my heart; but Polly!—I can't let him have her. No—I can't. He is not her equal," he affirmed, rather gruffly. "In

what particular is he her match? They talk of fortune! I am not an avaricious or interested man, but the world thinks of these things—and Polly will be rich.''

"Yes, that is known,'' said I: "all Villette knows her as an heiress.''

"Do they talk of my little girl in that light?''

"They do, sir.''

He fell into deep thought. I ventured to say—

"Would you, sir, think any one Paulina's match? Would you prefer any other to Dr. Bretton? Do you think higher rank or more wealth would make much difference in your feelings towards a future son-in-law?''

"You touch me there,'' said he.

"Look at the aristocracy of Villette—you would not like them, sir?''

"I should not—never a duc, baron, or vicomte of the lot.''

"I am told many of these persons think about her, sir,'' I went on, gaining courage on finding that I met attention rather than repulse. "Other suitors will come, therefore, if Dr. Bretton is refused. Wherever you go, I suppose, aspirants will not be wanting. Independent of heiress-ship, it appears to me that Paulina charms most of those who see her.''

"Does she? How? My little girl is not thought a beauty?''

"Sir, Miss de Bassompierre is very beautiful.''

"Nonsense!—begging your pardon, Miss Snowe, but I think you are too partial. *I* like Polly: I like all her ways and all her looks—but then I am her father; and even *I* never thought about beauty. She is amusing, fairy-like, interesting to me— you must be mistaken in supposing her handsome?''

"She attracts, sir: she would attract without the advantages of your wealth and position.''

"My wealth and position! Are these any bait to Graham? If I thought so''——

"Dr. Bretton knows these points perfectly, as you may be sure, M. de Bassompierre, and values them as any gentleman would—as *you* would yourself under the same circumstances—but they are not his baits. He loves your daughter very much; he feels her finest qualities, and they influence him worthily.''

"What! has my little pet 'fine qualities'?''

"Ah, sir! did you observe her that evening when so many men of eminence and learning dined here?''

"I certainly was rather struck and surprised with her manner that day; its womanliness made me smile.''

"And did you see those accomplished Frenchmen gather round her in the drawing-room?''

"I did; but I thought it was by way of relaxation—as one might amuse oneself with a pretty infant.''

"Sir, she demeaned herself with distinction; and I heard the French gentlemen say she was 'pétrie d'esprit et de graces.' Dr. Bretton thought the same.''

"She is a good, dear child, that is certain; and I *do* believe she has some character. When I think of it, I was once ill: Polly nursed me; they thought I should die; she, I recollect, grew at once stronger and tenderer as I grew worse in health. And as I recovered, what a sunbeam she was in my sick-room! Yes; she played about my chair as noiselessly and as cheerful as light. And now she is sought in marriage! I don't want to part with her,'' said he, and he groaned.

"You have known Dr. and Mrs. Bretton so long,'' I suggested, "it would be less like separation to give her to him than to another.''

He reflected rather gloomily.

"True. I have long known Louisa Bretton,'' he murmured. "She and I are indeed old, old friends; a sweet, kind girl she was when she was young. You talk of beauty, Miss Snowe! *she* was handsome, if you will—tall, straight, and blooming— not the mere child or elf my Polly seems to me: at eighteen, Louisa had a carriage

and stature fit for a princess. She is a comely and a good woman now. The lad is like her; I have always thought so, and favoured and wished him well. Now he repays me by this robbery! My little treasure used to love her old father dearly and truly. It is all over now, doubtless—I am an incumbrance.''

The door opened—his ''little treasure'' came in. She was dressed, so to speak, in evening beauty; that animation which sometimes comes with the close of day warmed her eye and cheek; a tinge of summer crimson heightened her complexion; her curls fell full and long on her lily neck; her white dress suited the heat of June. Thinking me alone, she had brought in her hand the letter just written—brought it folded but unsealed. I was to read it. When she saw her father, her tripping step faltered a little, paused a moment—the colour in her cheek flowed rosy over her whole face.

''Polly,'' said M. de Bassompierre, in a low voice, with a grave smile, ''do you blush at seeing papa? That is something new.

''I don't blush—I never *do* blush,'' affirmed she, while another eddy from the heart sent up its scarlet. ''But I thought you were in the dining-room, and I wanted Lucy.''

''You thought I was with John Graham Bretton, I suppose? But he has just been called out: he will be back soon, Polly. He can post your letter for you; it will save Matthieu a 'course,' as he calls it.''

''I don't post letters,'' said she, rather pettishly.

''What do you do with them, then?—come here and tell me.''

Both her mind and gesture seemed to hesitate a second—to say, ''Shall I come?''—but she approached.

''How long is it since you became a letter-writer, Polly? It only seems yesterday when you were at your pot-hooks, labouring away absolutely with both hands at the pen.''

''Papa, they are not letters to send to the post in your letter-bag; they are only notes, which I give now and then into the person's hands, just to satisfy.''

''The person! That means Miss Snowe, I suppose?''

''No, papa—not Lucy.''

''Who then? Perhaps Mrs. Bretton?''

''No, papa—not Mrs. Bretton.''

''Who, then, my little daughter? Tell papa the truth.''

''Oh, papa!'' she cried with earnestness, ''I will—I *will* tell you the truth—all the truth; I am glad to tell you—glad, though I tremble.''

She *did* tremble: growing excitement, kindling feeling, and also gathering courage shook her.

''I hate to hide my actions from you, papa. I fear you and love you above everything but God. Read the letter; look at the address.''

She laid it on his knee. He took it up and read it through; his hand shaking, his eyes glistening meantime.

He re-folded it, and viewed the writer with a strange, tender, mournful amaze.

''Can *she* write so—the little thing that stood at my knee but yesterday? Can she feel so?''

''Papa, is it wrong? Does it pain you?''

''There is nothing wrong in it, my innocent little Mary; but it pains me.''

''But, papa, listen! You shall not be pained by me. I would give up everything—almost'' (correcting herself); ''I would die rather than make you unhappy; that would be too wicked!''

She shuddered.

''Does the letter not please you? Must it not go? Must it be torn? It shall, for your sake, if you order it.''

''I order nothing.''

"Order something, papa; express your wish; only don't hurt, don't grieve Graham. I cannot, *cannot* bear that. I love you, papa; but I love Graham, too, because—because—it is impossible to help it."

"This splendid Graham is a young scamp, Polly—that is my present notion of him: it will surprise you to hear that, for my part, I do not love him one whit. Ah! years ago I saw something in that lad's eye I never quite fathomed—something his mother has not—a depth which warned a man not to wade into that stream too far; now, suddenly, I find myself taken over the crown of the head."

"Papa, you don't—you have not fallen in; you are safe on the bank; you can do as you please; your power is despotic; you can shut me up in a convent, and break Graham's heart to-morrow, if you choose to be so cruel. Now autocrat, now czar, will you do this?"

"Off with him to Siberia, red whiskers and all; I say, I don't like him, Polly, and I wonder that you should."

"Papa," said she, "do you know you are very naughty? I never saw you look so disagreeable, so unjust, so almost vindictive before. There is an expression in your face which does not belong to you."

"Off with him!" pursued Mr. Home, who certainly did look sorely crossed and annoyed—even a little bitter; "but, I suppose, if he went, Polly would pack a bundle and run after him: her heart is fairly won—won, and weaned from her old father."

"Papa, I say it is naughty, it is decidedly wrong, to talk in that way. I am *not* weaned from you, and no human being and no mortal influence *can* wean me."

"Be married, Polly! Espouse the red whiskers. Cease to be a daughter; go and be a wife!"

"Red whiskers! I wonder what you mean, papa. You should take care of prejudice. You sometimes say to me that all the Scotch, your countrymen, are the victims of prejudice. It is proved now, I think, when no distinction is to be made between red and deep nut-brown."

"Leave the prejudiced old Scotchman; go away."

She stood looking at him a minute. She wanted to show firmness, superiority to taunts: knowing her father's character, guessing his new foibles, she had expected the sort of scene which was now transpiring; it did not take her by surprise, and she desired to let it pass with dignity, reliant upon reaction. Her dignity stood her in no stead. Suddenly her soul melted in her eyes; she fell on his neck—

"I won't leave you, papa: I'll never leave you. I won't pain you! I'll never pain you!" was her cry.

"My lamb! my treasure!" murmured the loving though rugged sire. He said no more for the moment; indeed, those two words were hoarse.

The room was now darkening. I heard a movement, a step without. Thinking it might be a servant coming with candles, I gently opened, to prevent intrusion. In the ante-room stood no servant: a tall gentleman was placing his hat on the table, drawing off his gloves slowly—lingering, waiting, it seemed to me. He called me neither by sign nor word; yet his eye said—

"Lucy, come here." And I went.

Over his face a smile flowed, while he looked down on me; no temper, save his own, would have expressed by a smile the sort of agitation which now fevered him.

"M. de Bassompierre is there—is he not?" he inquired, pointing to the library. "Yes."

"He noticed me at dinner? He understood me?"

"Yes, Graham."

"I am brought up for judgment, then, and so is *she*?"

"Mr. Home" (we now and always continued to term him Mr. Home at times) "is talking to his daughter."

"Ha! These are sharp moments, Lucy!"

He was quite stirred up; his young hand trembled; a vital (I was going to write *mortal,* but such words ill apply to one all living like him)—a vital suspense now held, now hurried, his breath: in all this trouble his smile never faded.

"Is he *very* angry, Lucy?"

"*She* is very faithful, Graham."

"What will be done unto me?"

"Graham, your star must be fortunate."

"Must it? Kind prophet! So cheered, I should be a faint heart indeed to quail. I think I find all women faithful, Lucy. I ought to love them, and I do. My mother is good; *she* is divine; and *you* are true as steel. Are you not?"

"Yes, Graham."

"Then give me thy hand, my little god-sister: it is a friendly little hand to me, and always has been. And now for the great venture. God be with the right. Lucy, say Amen!"

He turned, and waited till I said "Amen!"—which I did to please him: the old charm, in doing as he bid me, came back. I wished him success; and successful I knew he would be. He was born victor, as some are born vanquished.

"Follow me!" he said; and I followed him into Mr. Home's presence.

"Sir," he asked, "what is my sentence?"

The father looked at him: the daughter kept her face hid.

"Well, Bretton," said Mr. Home, "you have given me the usual reward of hospitality. I entertained you; you have taken my best. I was always glad to see you; you were glad to see the one precious thing I had. You spoke me fair; and, meantime, I will not say you *robbed* me, but I am bereaved, and what I have lost, *you,* it seems, have won."

"Sir, I cannot repent."

"Repent! Not you! You triumph, no doubt; John Graham, you descended partly from a Highlander and a chief, and there is a trace of the Celt in all you look, speak, and think. You have his cunning and his charm. The red——(Well then, Polly, the *fair)* hair, the tongue of guile, the brain of wile, are all come down by inheritance."

"Sir, I *feel* honest enough," said Graham; and a genuine English blush covered his face with its warm witness of sincerity. "And yet," he added, "I won't deny that in some respects you accuse me justly. In your presence I have always had a thought which I dared not show you. I did truly regard you as the possessor of the most valuable thing the world owns for me. I wished for it; I tried for it. Sir, I ask for it now."

"John, you ask much."

"Very much, sir. It must come from your generosity, as a gift; from your justice, as a reward. I can never earn it."

"Ay! Listen to the Highland tongue!" said Mr. Home. "Look up, Polly! Answer this 'braw wooer'; send him away."

She looked up. She shyly glanced at her eager, handsome suitor. She gazed tenderly on her furrowed sire.

"Papa, I love you both," said she; "I can take care of you both. I need not send Graham away—he can live here; he will be no inconvenience," she alleged with that simplicity of phraseology which at times was wont to make both her father and Graham smile. They smiled now.

"He will be a prodigious inconvenience to me," still persisted Mr. Home. "I don't want him, Polly, he is too tall; he is in my way. Tell him to march."

"You will get used to him, papa. He seemed exceedingly tall to me at first— like a tower when I looked up at him; but, on the whole, I would rather not have him otherwise."

"I object to him altogether, Polly: I can do without a son-in-law. I should never have requested the best man in the land to stand to me in that relation. Dismiss this gentleman."

"But he has known you so long, papa, and suits you so well."

"Suits *me,* forsooth! Yes; he has pretended to make my opinions and tastes his own. He has humoured me for good reasons. I think, Polly, you and I will bid him good-bye."

"Till to-morrow only. Shake hands with Graham, papa."

"No: I think not: I am not friends with him. Don't think to coax me between you."

"Indeed, indeed, you *are* friends. Graham, stretch out your right hand. Papa, put out yours. Now, let them touch. Papa, don't be stiff; close your fingers; be pliant—there! But that is not a clasp—it is a grasp! Papa, you grasp like a vise. You crush Graham's hand to the bone; you hurt him!"

He must have hurt him; for he wore a massive ring, set round with brilliants, of which the sharp facets cut into Graham's flesh and drew blood: but pain only made Dr. John laugh, as anxiety had made him smile.

"Come with me into my study," at last said Mr. Home to the Doctor. They went. Their intercourse was not long, but I suppose it was conclusive. The suitor had to undergo an interrogatory and a scrutiny on many things. Whether Dr. Bretton was at times guileful in look and language or not, there was a sound foundation below. His answers, I understood afterwards, evinced both wisdom and integrity. He had managed his affairs well. He had struggled through entanglements; his fortunes were in the way of retrieval; he proved himself in a position to marry.

Once more the father and lover appeared in the library. M. de Bassompierre shut the door; he pointed to his daughter.

"Take her," he said. "Take her, John Bretton: and may God deal with you as you deal with her!"

Not long after perhaps a fortnight, I saw three persons, Count de Bassompierre, his daughter, and Dr. Graham Bretton, sitting on one seat, under a low-spreading and umbrageous tree, in the grounds of the palace at Bois l'Etang. They had come thither to enjoy a summer evening: outside the magnificent gates their carriage waited to take them home: the green sweeps of turf spread round them quiet and dim; the palace rose at a distance, white as a crag on Pentelicus; the evening star shone above it; a forest of flowering shrubs embalmed the climate of this spot; the hour was still and sweet; the scene, but for this group, was solitary.

Paulina sat between the two gentlemen: while they conversed, her little hands were busy at some work; I thought at first she was binding a nosegay. No; with the tiny pair of scissors, glittering in her lap, she had severed spoils from each manly head beside her, and was now occupied in plaiting together the grey lock and the golden wave. The plait woven—no silk-thread being at hand to bind it—a tress of her own hair was made to serve that purpose; she tied it like a knot, prisoned it in a locket, and laid it on her heart.

"Now," said she, "there is an amulet made which has virtue to keep you two always friends. You can never quarrel so long as I wear this."

An amulet was indeed made, a spell framed which rendered enmity impossible. She was become a bond to both, an influence over each, a mutual concord. From them she drew her happiness, and what she borrowed, she, with interest, gave back.

Is there, indeed, such happiness on earth? I asked, as I watched the father, the daughter, the future husband, now united—all blessed and blessing.

Yes; it is so. Without any colouring of romance, or any exaggeration of fancy, it is so. Some real lives do—for some certain days or years—actually anticipate the happiness of heaven; and, I believe, if such perfect happiness is once felt by

good people (to the wicked it never comes), its sweet effect is never wholly lost. Whatever trials follow, whatever pains of sickness or shades of death, the glory precedent still shines through, cheering the keen anguish, and tinging the deep cloud.

I will go farther. I *do* believe there are some human beings so born, so reared, so guided from a soft cradle to a calm and late grave, that no excessive suffering penetrates their lot, and no tempestuous blackness overcasts their journey. And often these are not pampered, selfish beings, but Nature's elect, harmonious and benign; men and women mild with charity, kind agents of God's kind attributes.

Let me not delay the happy truth. Graham Bretton and Paulina de Bassompierre were married, and such an agent did Dr. Bretton prove. He did not with time degenerate; his faults decayed, his virtues ripened; he rose in intellectual refinement, he won in moral profit: all dregs filtered away, the clear wine settled bright and tranquil. Bright, too, was the destiny of his sweet wife. She kept her husband's love, she aided in his progress—of his happiness she was the corner-stone.

This pair was blessed indeed, for years brought them, with great prosperity, great goodness: they imparted with open hand, yet wisely. Doubtless they knew crosses, disappointments, difficulties; but these were well borne. More than once, too, they had to look on Him whose face flesh scarce can see and live: they had to pay their tribute to the King of Terrors. In the fulness of years, M. de Bassompierre was taken: in ripe old age departed Louisa Bretton. Once even there rose a cry in their halls, of Rachel weeping for her children; but others sprang healthy and blooming to replace the lost: Dr. Bretton saw himself live again in a son who inherited his looks and his disposition; he had stately daughters, too, like himself: these children he reared with a suave, yet firm hand; they grew up according to inheritance and nurture.

In short, I do but speak the truth when I say that these two lives of Graham and Paulina were blessed, like that of Jacob's favoured son, with "blessings of Heaven above, blessings of the deep that lies under." It was so, for God saw that it was good.

Chapter XXXVIII

CLOUD

BUT it is not so for all. What then? His will be done, as done it surely will be, whether we humble ourselves to resignation or not. The impulse of creation forwards it; the strength of powers, seen and unseen, has its fulfilment in charge. Proof of a life to come must be given. In fire and in blood, if needful, must that proof be written. In fire and in blood do we trace the record throughout nature. In fire and in blood does it cross our own experience. Sufferer, faint not through terror of this burning evidence. Tired wayfarer, gird up thy loins; look upward, march onward. Pilgrims and brother mourners, join in friendly company. Dark through the wilderness of this world stretches the way for most of us: equal and steady be our tread; be our cross our banner. For staff we have His promise, whose "word is tried, whose way perfect": for present hope His providence, "who gives the shield of salvation, whose gentleness makes great"; for final home His bosom, who "dwells in the height of Heaven"; for crowning prize a glory exceeding and eternal. Let us so run that we may obtain: let us endure hardness as good soldiers; let us finish our course, and keep the faith, reliant in the issue to come off more than conquerors: "Art thou not from everlasting mine Holy One? WE SHALL NOT DIE!"

On a Thursday morning we were all assembled in classe, waiting for the lesson of literature. The hour was come; we expected the master.

The pupils of the first classe sat very still; the cleanly-written compositions prepared since the last lesson lay ready before them, neatly tied with ribbon, waiting to be gathered by the hand of the Professor as he made his rapid round of the desks. The month was July, the morning fine, the glass door stood ajar, through it played a fresh breeze, and plants, growing at the lintel, waved, bent, looked in, seeming to whisper tidings.

M. Emanuel was not always quite punctual; we scarcely wondered at his being a little late, but we wondered when the door at last opened and, instead of him with his swiftness and his fire, there came quietly upon us the cautious Madame Beck.

She approached M. Paul's desk; she stood before it; she drew round her the light shawl covering her shoulders; beginning to speak in low, yet firm tones, and with a fixed gaze, she said—

"This morning there will be no lesson of literature."

The second paragraph of her address followed, after about two minutes' pause.

"It is probable the lessons will be suspended for a week. I shall require at least that space of time to find an efficient substitute for M. Emanuel. Meanwhile, it shall be our study to fill the blanks usefully.

"Your Professor, ladies," she went on, "intends, if possible, duly to take leave of you. At the present moment he has not leisure for that ceremony. He is preparing for a long voyage. A very sudden and urgent summons of duty calls him to a great distance. He has decided to leave Europe for an indefinite time. Perhaps he may tell you more himself. Ladies, instead of the usual lesson with M. Emanuel, you will, this morning, read English with Mademoiselle Lucy."

She bent her head courteously, drew closer the folds of her shawl, and passed from the classe.

A great silence fell: then a murmur went round the room: I believe some pupils wept.

Some time elapsed. The noise, the whispering, the occasional sobbing increased. I became conscious of a relaxation of discipline, a sort of growing disorder, as if my girls felt that vigilance was withdrawn, and that surveillance had virtually left the classe. Habit and the sense of duty enabled me to rally quickly, to rise in my usual way, to speak in my usual tone, to enjoin, and finally to establish quiet. I made the English reading long and close. I kept them at it the whole morning. I remember feeling a sentiment of impatience towards the pupils who sobbed. Indeed, their emotion was not of much value; it was only an hysteric agitation. I told them so unsparingly. I half ridiculed them. I was severe. The truth was, I could not do with their tears, or that gasping sound; I could not bear it. A rather weak-minded, low-spirited pupil kept it up when the others had done; relentless necessity obliged and assisted me so to accost her that she dared not carry on the demonstration, that she was forced to conquer the convulsion.

That girl would have had a right to hate me, except that, when school was over and her companions departing, I ordered her to stay, and when they were gone, I did what I had never done to one among them before—pressed her to my heart and kissed her cheek. But, this impulse yielded to, I speedily put her out of the classe, for, upon that poignant strain, she wept more bitterly than ever.

I filled with occupation every minute of that day, and should have liked to sit up all night if I might have kept a candle burning; the night, however, proved a bad one, and left bad effects, preparing me ill for the next day's ordeal of insufferable gossip. Of course this news fell under general discussion. Some little reserve had accompanied the first surprise: that soon wore off; every mouth opened; every tongue wagged; teachers, pupils, the very servants, mouthed the name of "Emanuel." He, whose connection with the school was contemporary with its commencement, thus suddenly to withdraw! All felt it strange.

They talked so much, so long, so often, that, out of the very multitude of their words and rumours, grew at last some intelligence. About the third day I heard it said that he was to sail in a week; then—that he was bound for the West Indies. I looked at Madame Beck's face, and into her eyes, for disproof or confirmation of this report; I perused her all over for information, but no part of her disclosed more than what was unperturbed and commonplace.

"This secession was an immense loss to her," she alleged. "She did not know how she should fill up the vacancy. She was so used to her kinsman, he had become her right hand; what should she do without him? She had opposed the step, but M. Paul had convinced her it was his duty."

She said all this in public, in classe, at the dinner-table, speaking audibly to Zélie St. Pierre.

"Why was it his duty?" I could have asked her that. I had impulses to take hold of her suddenly, as she calmly passed me in classe, to stretch out my hand and grasp her fast, and say, "Stop. Let us hear the conclusion of the whole matter. *Why* is it his duty to go into banishment?" But Madame always addressed some other teacher, and never looked at me, never seemed conscious I could have a care in the question.

The week wore on. Nothing more was said about M. Emanuel coming to bid us good-bye; and none seemed anxious for his coming; none questioned whether or not he would come; none betrayed torment lest he should depart silent and unseen; incessantly did they talk, and never, in all their talk, touched on this vital point. As to Madame, she of course could see him, and say to him as much as she pleased. What should *she* care whether or not he appeared in the schoolroom?

The week consumed. We were told that he was going on such a day, that his destination was "Basseterre in Guadaloupe": the business which called him abroad related to a friend's interest; not his own: I thought as much.

"Basseterre in Guadaloupe." I had little sleep about this time, but whenever I *did* slumber, it followed infallibly that I was quickly roused with a start, while the words "Basseterre," "Guadaloupe," seemed pronounced over my pillow, or ran athwart the darkness round and before me, in zig-zag characters of red or violet light.

For what I felt there was no help, and how could I help feeling? M. Emanuel had been very kind to me of late days; he had been growing hourly better and kinder. It was now a month since we had settled the theological difference, and in all that time there had been no quarrel. Nor had our peace been the cold daughter of divorce; we had not lived aloof; he had come oftener, he had talked with me more than before; he had spent hours with me, with temper soothed, with eye content, with manner home-like and mild. Kind subjects of conversation had grown between us; he had inquired into my plans of life, and I had communicated them; the school project pleased him; he made me repeat it more than once, though he called it an Alnaschar dream. The jar was over; the mutual understanding was settling and fixing; feelings of union and hope made themselves profoundly felt in the heart; affection and deep esteem and dawning trust had each fastened its bond.

What quiet lessons I had about this time! No more taunts on my "intellect," no more menaces of grating public shows! How sweetly, for the jealous gibe and the more jealous, half-passionate eulogy, were substituted a mute, indulgent help, a fond guidance, and a tender forbearance which forgave but never praised. There were times when he would sit for many minutes and not speak at all; and when dusk or duty brought separation, he would leave with words like these: "Il est doux, le repos! Il est précieux, le calme bonheur!"

One evening, not ten short days since, he joined me whilst walking in my alley. He took my hand. I looked up in his face. I thought he meant to arrest my attention.

"Bonne petite amie!" said he softly; "douce consolatrice!" But through his touch, and with his words, a new feeling and a strange thought found a course.

Could it be that he was becoming more than a friend or brother? Did his look speak a kindness beyond fraternity or amity?

His eloquent look had more to say, his hand drew me forward, his interpreting lips stirred. No. Not now. Here into the twilight alley broke an interruption: it came dual and ominous: we faced two bodeful forms—a woman's and a priest's—Madame Beck and Père Silas.

The aspect of the latter I shall never forget. On the first impulse it expressed a Jean-Jacques sensibility, stirred by the signs of affection just surprised; then, immediately, darkened over it the jaundice of ecclesiastical jealousy. He spoke to *me* with unction. He looked on his pupil with sternness. As to Madame Beck, she, of course, saw nothing—nothing; though her kinsman retained in her presence the hand of the heretic foreigner, not suffering withdrawal, but clasping it close and fast.

Following these incidents, that sudden announcement of departure had struck me at first as incredible. Indeed, it was only frequent repetition, and the credence of the hundred and fifty minds round me, which forced on me its full acceptance. As to that week of suspense, with its blank yet burning days, which brought from him no word of explanation—I remember, but I cannot describe its passage.

The last day broke. Now would he visit us. Now he would come and speak his farewell, or he would vanish mute, and be seen by us nevermore.

This alternative seemed to be present in the mind of not a living creature in that school. All rose at the usual hour; all breakfasted as usual; all, without reference to or apparent thought of their late Professor, betook themselves with wonted phlegm to their ordinary duties.

So oblivious was the house, so tame, so trained its proceedings, so inexpectant its aspect—I scarce knew how to breathe in an atmosphere thus stagnant, thus smothering. Would no one lend me a voice? Had no one a wish, no one a word, no one a prayer to which I could say—Amen?

I had seen them unanimous in demand for the merest trifle—a treat, a holiday, a lesson's remission; they could not, they *would* not now band to besiege Madame Beck, and insist on a last interview with a master who had certainly been loved, at least by some—loved as *they* could love—but, oh! what *is* the love of the multitude?

I knew where he lived: I knew where he was to be heard of, or communicated with; the distance was scarce a stone's-throw: had it been in the next room—unsummoned, I could make no use of my knowledge. To follow, to seek out, to remind, to recall—for these things I had no faculty.

M. Emanuel might have passed within reach of my arm: had he passed silent and unnoticing, silent and stirless should I have suffered him to go by.

Morning wasted. Afternoon came, and I thought all was over. My heart trembled in its place. My blood was troubled in its current. I was quite sick, and hardly knew how to keep at my post or do my work. Yet the little world round me plodded on indifferent; all seemed jocund, free of care, or fear, or thought: the very pupils who, seven days since, had wept hysterically at a startling piece of news, appeared quite to have forgotten the news, its import, and their emotion.

A little before five o'clock, the hour of dismissal, Madame Beck sent for me to her chamber, to read over and translate some English letter she had received, and to write for her the answer. Before settling to this work, I observed that she softly closed the two doors of her chamber; she even shut and fastened the casement, though it was a hot day and free circulation of air was usually regarded by her as indispensable. Why this precaution? A keen suspicion, an almost fierce distrust, suggested such question. Did she want to exclude sound? What sound?

I listened as I had never listened before: I listened like the evening and winter wolf, snuffing the snow, scenting prey, and hearing far off the traveller's tramp. Yet I could both listen and write. About the middle of the letter I heard—what

checked my pen—a tread in the vestibule. No door-bell had rung; Rosine—acting doubtless by orders—had anticipated such réveillée. Madame saw me halt. She coughed, made a bustle, spoke louder. The tread had passed on to the classes.

"Proceed," said Madame; but my hand was fettered, my ear enchained, my thoughts were carried off captive.

The classes formed another building; the hall parted them from the dwelling-house: despite distance and partition, I heard the sudden stir of numbers, a whole division rising at once.

"They are putting away work," said Madame.

It was indeed the hour to put away work, but why that sudden hush—that instant quell of the tumult?

"Wait, Madame—I will see what it is."

And I put down my pen and left her. Left her? No: she would not be left: powerless to detain me, she rose and followed, close as my shadow. I turned on the last step of the stair—

"Are you coming, too?" I asked.

"Yes," said she; meeting my glance with a peculiar aspect—a look clouded yet resolute. We proceeded then, not togeter, but she walked in my steps.

He was come. Entering the first classe, I saw him. There once more appeared the form most familiar. I doubt not they had tried to keep him away, but he was come.

The girls stood in a semicircle; he was passing round, giving his farewells, pressing each hand, touching with his lips each cheek. This last ceremony foreign custom permitted at such a parting—so solemn, to last so long.

I felt it hard that Madame Beck should dog me thus; following and watching me close; my neck and shoulder shrunk in fever under her breath; I became terribly goaded.

He was approaching; the semicircle was almost travelled round; he came to the last pupil; he turned. But Madame was before me; she had stepped out suddenly; she seemed to magnify her proportions and amplify her drapery; she eclipsed me; I was hid. She knew my weakness and deficiency; she could calculate the degree of moral paralysis—the total default of self-assertion—with which, in a crisis, I could be struck. She hastened to her kinsman, she broke upon him volubly, she mastered his attention, she hurried him to the door—the glass door opening on the garden. I think he looked round; could I have but caught his eye, courage, I think, would have rushed in to aid feeling, and there would have been a charge and perhaps a rescue; but already the room was all confusion, the semicircle broken into groups, my figure was lost among thirty more conspicuous. Madame had her will; yes, she got him away, and he had not seen me; he thought me absent. Five o'clock struck, the loud dismissal bell rang, the school separated, the room emptied.

There seems, to my memory, an entire darkness and distraction in some certain minutes I then passed alone—a grief inexpressible over a loss unendurable. *What* should I do; oh! *what* should I do; when all my life's hope was thus torn by the roots out of my riven, outraged heart?

What I *should* have done, I know not, when a little child—the least child in the school—broke with its simplicity and its unconsciousness into the raging yet silent centre of that inward conflict.

"Mademoiselle," lisped the treble voice, "I am to give you that. M. Paul said I was to seek you all over the house, from the grenier to the cellar, and when I found you, to give you that."

And the child delivered a note; the little dove dropped on my knee its olive-leaf plucked off. I found neither address nor name, only these words—

"It was not my intention to take leave of you when I said good-bye to the rest, but I hoped to see you in classe. I was disappointed. The interview is deferred. Be ready for me. Ere I sail, I must see you at leisure, and speak with you at length.

Be ready; my moments are numbered, and, just now, monopolised; besides, I have a private business on hand which I will not share with any, nor communicate—even to you.—PAUL.''

''Be ready!'' Then it must be this evening: was he not to go on the morrow? Yes; of that point I was certain. I had seen the date of his vessel's departure advertised. Oh! *I* would be ready, but could that longed-for meeting really be achieved? the time was so short, the schemers seemed so watchful, so active, so hostile; the way of access appeared strait as a gully, deep as a chasm—Apollyon straddled across it, breathing flames. Could my Greatheart overcome? Could my guide reach me?

Who might tell? Yet I began to take some courage, some comfort; it seemed to me that I felt a pulse of his heart beating yet true to the whole throb of mine.

I waited my champion. Apollyon came trailing his Hell behind him. I think if Eternity held torment, its form would not be fiery rack, nor its nature despair. I think that on a certain day amongst those days which never dawned, and will not set, an angel entered Hades—stood, shone, smiled, delivered a prophecy of conditional pardon, kindled a doubtful hope of bliss to come, not now, but at a day and hour unlooked for, revealed in his own glory and grandeur the height and compass of his promise: spoke thus—then towering, became a star, and vanished into his own Heaven. His legacy was suspense—a worse boon than despair.

All that evening I waited, trusting in the dove-sent olive-leaf, yet in the midst of my trust terribly fearing. My fear pressed heavy. Cold and peculiar, I knew it for the partner of a rarely-belied presentiment. The first hours seemed long and slow; in spirit I clung to the flying skirts of the last. They passed like drift cloud—like the rack scudding before a storm.

They passed. All the long hot summer day burned away like a Yule-log; the crimson of its close perished; I was left bent among the cool blue shades, over the pale and ashen gleams of its night.

Prayers were over; it was bed-time; my co-inmates were all retired. I still remained in the gloomy first classe, forgetting, or at least disregarding, rules I had never forgotten or disregarded before.

How long I paced that classe I cannot tell; I must have been afoot many hours; mechanically had I moved aside benches and desks, and had made for myself a path down its length. There I walked, and there, when certain that the whole household were abed and quite out of hearing—there I at last wept. Reliant on Night, confiding in Solitude, I kept my tears chained, my sobs longer; they heaved my heart; they tore their way. In this house, what grief could be sacred?

Soon after eleven o'clock—a very late hour in the Rue Fossette—the door unclosed—quietly but not stealthily; a lamp's flame invaded the moonlight; Madame Beck entered, with the same composed air as if coming on an ordinary occasion, at an ordinary season. Instead of at once addressing me, she went to her desk, took her keys, and seemed to seek something: she loitered over this feigned search long, too long. She was calm, too calm; my mood scarce endured the pretence; driven beyond common range, two hours since I had left behind me wonted respects and fears. Led by a touch, and ruled by a word, under usual circumstances, no yoke could now be borne, no curb obeyed.

''It is more than time for retirement,'' said Madame: ''the rule of the house has already been transgressed too long.''

Madame met no answer: I did not check my walk; when she came in my way, I put her out of it.

''Let me persuade you to calm, Meess; let me lead you to your chamber,'' said she, trying to speak softly.

''No!'' I said; ''neither you nor another shall persuade or lead me.''

''Your bed shall be warmed. Goton is sitting up still. She shall make you comfortable: she shall give you a sedative.''

"Madame," I broke out, "you are a sensualist. Under all your serenity, your peace, and your decorum, you are an undenied sensualist. Make your own bed warm and soft; take sedatives and meats, and drinks spiced and sweet, as much as you will. If you have any sorrow or disappointment—and, perhaps, you have—nay, I *know* you have—seek your own palliatives in your own chosen resources. Leave me, however. *Leave me,* I say!"

"I must send another to watch you, Meess: I must send Goton."

"I forbid it. Let me alone. Keep your hand off me, and my life, and my troubles. O Madame! in *your* hand there is both chill and poison. You envenom and you paralyse."

"What have I done, Meess? You must not marry Paul. He cannot marry."

"Dog in the manger!" I said: for I knew she secretly wanted him, and had always wanted him. She called him "insupportable": she railed at him for a "dévot"; she did not love, but she wanted to marry that she might bind him to her interest. Deep into some of Madame's secrets I had entered—I know not how: by an intuition or an inspiration which came to me—I know not whence. In the course of living with her, too, I had slowly learned that, unless with an inferior, she must ever be a rival. She was *my* rival, heart and soul, though secretly, under the smoothest bearing, and utterly unknown to all save her and myself.

Two minutes I stood over Madame, feeling that the whole woman was in my power, because in some moods, such as the present—in some stimulated states of perception, like that of this instant—her habitual disguise, her mask, and her domino were to me a mere network reticulated with holes; and I saw underneath a being heartless, self-indulgent, and ignoble. She quietly retreated from me: meek and self-possessed, though very uneasy, she said, "If I would not be persuaded to take rest, she must reluctantly leave me." Which she did incontinent, perhaps even more glad to get away than I was to see her vanish.

This was the sole flash-eliciting, truth-extorting rencontre which ever occurred between me and Madame Beck: this short night scene was never repeated. It did not one whit change her manner to me. I do not know that she revenged it. I do not know that she hated me the worse for my fell candour. I think she bucklered herself with the secret philosophy of her strong mind, and resolved to forget what it irked her to remember. I know that to the end of our mutual lives there occurred no repetition of, no allusion to, that fiery passage.

That night passed: all nights—even the starless night before dissolution—must wear away. About six o'clock, the hour which called up the household, I went out to the court, and washed my face in its cold, fresh well-water. Entering by the carré, a piece of mirror-glass, set in an oaken cabinet, repeated my image. It said I was changed: my cheeks and lips were sodden white, my eyes were glassy, and my eyelids swollen and purple.

On rejoining my companions, I knew they all looked at me—my heart seemed discovered to them: I believed myself self-betrayed. Hideously certain did it seem that the very youngest of the school must guess why and for whom I despaired.

Isabelle, the child whom I had once nursed in sickness, approached me. Would she, too, mock me?

"Que vous êtes pâle! Vous êtes donc bien malade, mademoiselle!" said she, putting her finger in her mouth, and staring with a wistful stupidity which at the moment seemed to me more beautiful than the keenest intelligence.

Isabelle did not long stand alone in the recommendation of ignorance: before the day was over, I gathered cause of gratitude towards the whole blind household. The multitude have something else to do than to read hearts and interpret dark sayings. Who wills, may keep his own counsel—be his own secret's sovereign. In the course of that day proof met me on proof, not only that the cause of my present sorrow was unguessed, but that my whole inner life for the last six months was still mine only. It was not known—it had not been noted—that I held in peculiar

value one life among all lives. Gossip had passed me by; curiosity had looked me over; both subtle influences, hovering always round, had never become centred upon me. A given organisation may live in a full fever-hospital and escape typhus. M. Emanuel had come and gone: I had been taught and sought; in season and out of season he had called me, and I had obeyed him: "M. Paul wants Miss Lucy"— "Miss Lucy is with M. Paul"—such had been the perpetual bulletin; and nobody commented, far less condemned. Nobody hinted, nobody jested.

Madame Beck read the riddle: none else resolved it. What I now suffered was called illness—a headache: I accepted the baptism.

But what bodily illness was ever like this pain? This certainty that he was gone without a farewell—this cruel conviction that fate and pursing furies—a woman's envy and a priest's bigotry—would suffer me to see him no more? What wonder that the second evening found me like the first—untamed, tortured, again pacing a solitary room in an unalterable passion of silent desolation?

Madame Beck did not herself summon me to bed that night—she did not come near me: she sent Ginevra Fanshawe—a more efficient agent for the purpose she could not have employed. Ginevra's first words—"Is your headache very bad to-night?" (for Ginevra, like the rest, thought I had a headache—an intolerable headache which made me frightfully white in the face, and insanely restless in the foot)— her first words, I say, inspired the impulse to flee anywhere so that it were only out of reach. And soon, what followed—plaints about her own headaches—completed the business.

I went upstairs. Presently I was in my bed—my miserable bed—haunted with quick scorpions. I had not been laid down five minutes, when another emissary arrived: Goton came, bringing me something to drink. I was consumed with thirst.— I drank eagerly; the beverage was sweet, but I tasted a drug.

"Madame says it will make you sleep, chou-chou," said Goton, as she received back the emptied cup.

Ah! the sedative had been administered. In fact, they had given me a strong opiate. I was to be held quiet for one night.

The household came to bed, the night light was lit, the dormitory hushed. Sleep soon reigned: over those pillows sleep won an easy supremacy: contented sovereign over heads and hearts which did not ache—he passed by the unquiet.

The drug wrought. I know not whether Madame had over-charged or under-charged the dose; its result was not that she intended. Instead of stupor, came excitement. I became alive to new thought—to reverie peculiar in colouring. A gathering call ran among the faculties, their bugles sang, their trumpets rang an untimely summons. Imagination was roused from her rest, and she came forth impetuous and venturous. With scorn she looked on Matter, her mate—

"Rise!" she said; "Sluggard! this night I will have *my* will; nor shalt thou prevail."

"Look forth and view the night!" was her cry; and when I lifted the heavy blind from the casement close at hand—with her own royal gesture, she showed me a moon supreme, in an element deep and splendid.

To my gasping senses she made the glimmering gloom, the narrow limits, the oppressive heat of the dormitory, intolerable. She lured me to leave this den and follow her forth into dew, coolness, and glory.

She brought upon me a strange vision of Villette at midnight. Especially she showed the park, the summer-park, with its long alleys all silent, lone, and safe; among these lay a huge stone basin—that basin I knew, and beside which I had often stood—deep-set in the tree-shadows, brimming with cool water, clear, with a green, leafy, rushy bed. What of all this? The park-gates were shut up, locked, sentinelled: the place could not be entered.

Could it not? A point worth considering; and while revolving it, I mechanically dressed. Utterly incapable of sleeping or lying still—excited from head to foot—what could I do better than dress?

The gates were locked, soldiers set before them: was there, then, no admission to the park?

The other day, in walking past, I had seen, without then attending to the circumstance, a gap in the paling—one stake broken down: I now saw this gap again in recollection—saw it very plainly—the narrow, irregular aperture visible between the stems of the lindens, planted orderly as a colonnade. A man could not have made his way through that aperture, nor could a stout woman, perhaps not Madame Beck; but I thought I might: I fancied I should like to try, and once within, at this hour the whole park would be mine—the moonlit, midnight park!

How soundly the dormitory slept! What deep slumbers! What quiet breathing! How very still the whole large house! What was the time? I felt restless to know. There stood a clock in the classe below: what hindered me from venturing down to consult it! By such a moon, its large white face and jet black figures must be vividly distinct.

As for hindrance to this step, there offered not so much as a creaking hinge or a clicking latch. On these hot July nights close air could not be tolerated, and the chamber-door stood wide open. Will the dormitory planks sustain my tread untraitorous? Yes. I know wherever a board is loose, and will avoid it. The oak staircase creaks somewhat as I descend, but not much—I am in the carré.

The great classe doors are close shut: they are bolted. On the other hand, the entrance to the corridor stands open. The classes seem to my thought great dreary jails, buried far back beyond thoroughfares, and for me, filled with spectral and intolerable Memories, laid miserable amongst their straw and their manacles. The corridor offers a cheerful vista, leading to the high vestibule which opens direct upon the street.

Hush!—the clock strikes. Ghostly deep as is the stillness of this convent, it is only eleven. While my ear follows in silence the hum of the last stroke, I catch faintly from the built-out capital a sound like bells or like a band—a sound where sweetness, where victory, where mourning blend. Oh, to approach this music nearer, to listen to it alone by the rushy basin! Let me go—oh, let me go! What hinders, what does not aid freedom?

There, in the corridor, hangs my garden costume, my large hat, my shawl. There is no lock on the huge, heavy, porte-cochère; there is no key to seek: it fastens with a sort of spring-bolt, not to be opened from the outside, but which, from within, may be noiselessly withdrawn. Can I manage it? It yields to my hand, yields with propitious facility. I wonder as that portal seems almost spontaneously to unclose—I wonder as I cross the threshold and step on the paved street, wonder at the strange ease with which this prison has been forced. It seems as if I had been pioneered invisibly, as if some dissolving force had gone before me: for myself, I have scarce made an effort.

Quiet Rue Fossette! I find on this pavement that wanderer-wooing summer night of which I mused; I see its moon over me; I feel its dew in the air. But here I cannot stay; I am still too near old haunts: so close under the dungeon, I can hear the prisoners moan. This solemn peace is not what I seek, it is not what I can bear: to me the face of that sky bears the aspect of a world's death. The park also will be calm—I know, a mortal serenity prevails everywhere—yet let me seek the park.

I took a route well known, and went up towards the palatial and royal Haute-Ville; thence the music I had heard certainly floated; it was hushed now, but it might re-waken. I went on: neither band nor bell-music came to meet me; another sound replaced it, a sound like a strong tide, a great flow, deepening as I proceeded. Light broke, movement gathered, chimes pealed—to what was I coming? Entering

on the level of a Grande Place, I found myself, with the suddenness of magic, plunged amidst a gay, living, joyous crowd.

Villette is one blaze, one broad illumination; the whole world seems abroad; moonlight and heaven are banished: the town, by her own flambeaux, beholds her own splendour—gay dresses, grand equipages, fine horses and gallant riders throng the bright streets. I see even scores of masks. It is a strange scene, stranger than dreams. But where is the park?—I ought to be near it. In the midst of this glare the park must be shadowy and calm—*there*, at least, are neither torches, lamps, nor crowd?

I was asking this question when an open carriage passed me filled with known faces. Through the deep throng it could pass but slowly; the spirited horses fretted in their curbed ardour. I saw the occupants of that carriage well: me they could not see, or, at least, not know, folded close in my large shawl, screened with my straw hat (in that motley crowd no dress was noticeably strange). I saw the Count de Bassompierre; I saw my godmother, handsomely apparelled, comely and cheerful; I saw, too, Paulina Mary, compassed with the triple halo of her beauty, her youth, and her happiness. In looking on her countenance of joy, and eyes of festal light, one scarce remembered to note the gala elegance of what she wore; I know only that the drapery floating about her was all white and light and bridal: seated opposite to her I saw Graham Bretton; it was in looking up at him her aspect had caught its lustre—the light repeated in *her* eyes beamed first out of his.

It gave me strange pleasure to follow these friends viewlessly and I *did* follow them, as I thought, to the park. I watched them alight (carriages were inadmissible) amidst new and unanticipated splendours. Lo! the iron gateway, between the stone columns, was spanned by a flaming arch built of massed stars; and, following them cautiously beneath that arch, where were they, and where was I?

In a land of enchantment, a garden most gorgeous, a plain sprinkled with coloured meteors, a forest with sparks of purple and ruby and golden fire gemming the foliage; a region, not of trees and shadow, but of strangest architectural wealth—of altar and of temple, of pyramid, obelisk, and sphinx; incredible to say, the wonders and the symbols of Egypt teemed throughout the park of Villette.

No matter that in five minutes the secret was mine—the key of the mystery picked up, and its illusion unveiled—no matter that I quickly recognised the material of these solemn fragments—the timber, the paint, and the pasteboard—these inevitable discoveries failed to quite destroy the charm, or undermine the marvel of that night. No matter that I now seized the explanation of the whole great fête—a fête of which the conventual Rue Fossette had not tasted, though it had opened at dawn that morning, and was still in full vigour near midnight.

In past days there had been, said history, an awful crisis in the fate of Labassecour, involving I know not what peril to the rights and liberties of her gallant citizens. Rumours of wars there had been, if not wars themselves; a kind of struggling in the streets—a bustle, a running to and fro, some rearing of barricades, some burgher-rioting, some calling out of troops, much interchange of brickbats, and even a little of shot. Tradition held that patriots had fallen: in the old Basse-Ville was shown an enclosure, solemnly built in and set apart, holding, it was said, the sacred bones of martyrs. Be this as it may, a certain day in the year was still kept as a festival in honour of the said patriots and martyrs of somewhat apocryphal memory—the morning being given to a solemn Te Deum in St. Jean Baptiste, the evening devoted to spectacles, decorations, and illuminations, such as these I now saw.

While looking up at the image of a white ibis fixed on a column—while fathoming the deep, torch-lit perspective of an avenue, at the close of which was couched a sphinx—I lost sight of the party which, from the middle of the great square, I had followed—or, rather, they vanished like a group of apparitions. On this whole scene was impressed a dream-like character: every shape was wavering, every movement floating, every voice echo-like—half-mocking, half-uncertain. Paulina and her friends

being gone, I scarce could avouch that I had really seen them; nor did I miss them as guides through the chaos, far less regret them as protectors amidst the night.

That festal night would have been safe for a very child. Half the peasantry had come in from the outlying environs of Villette, and the decent burghers were all abroad and around, dressed in their best. My straw hat passed amidst cap and jacket, short petticoat and long calico mantle, without, perhaps, attracting a glance; I only took the precaution to bind down the broad leaf gipsy-wise, with a supplementary ribbon—and then I felt safe as if masked.

Safe I passed down the avenues—safe I mixed with the crowd where it was deepest. To be still was not in my power, nor quietly to observe. I took a revel of the scene; I drank the elastic night-air—the swell of sound, the dubious light, now flashing, now fading. As to Happiness or Hope, they and I had shaken hands, but just now—I scorned Despair.

My vague aim, as I went, was to find the stone basin, with its clear depth and green lining: of that coolness and verdure I thought, with the passionate thirst of unconscious fever. Amidst the glare, and hurry, and throng, and noise, I still secretly and chiefly longed to come on that circular mirror of crystal, and surprise the moon glassing therein her pearly front.

I knew my route, yet it seemed as if I was hindered from pursuing it direct: now a sight, and now a sound, called me aside, luring me down this alley and down that. Already I saw the thick-planted trees which framed this tremulous and rippled glass, when, choiring out of a glade to the right, broke such a sound as I thought might be heard if Heaven were to open—such a sound, perhaps, as *was* heard above the plain of Bethlehem on the night of glad tidings.

The song, the sweet music, rose afar, but rushing swiftly on fast-strengthening pinions—there swept through these shades so full a storm of harmonies that, had no tree been near against which to lean, I think I must have dropped. Voices were there, it seemed to me, unnumbered; instruments varied and countless—bugle, horn, and trumpet I knew. The effect was as a sea breaking into song with all its waves.

The swaying tide swept this way, and then it fell back, and I followed its retreat. It led me towards a Byzantine building—a sort of kiosk near the park's centre. Round about stood crowded thousands, gathered to a grand concert in the open air. What I had heard was, I think, a wild Jäger chorus; the night, the space, the scene, and my own mood had but enhanced the sounds and their impression.

Here were assembled ladies, looking by this light most beautiful: some of their dresses were gauzy, and some had the sheen of satin; the flowers and the blond trembled, and the veils waved about their decorated bonnets, as that host-like chorus, with its greatly-gathering sound, sundered the air above them. Most of these ladies occupied the little light park-chairs, and behind and beside them stood guardian gentlemen. The outer ranks of the crowd were made up of citizens, plebeians and police.

In this outer rank I took my place. I rather liked to find myself the silent, unknown, consequently unaccosted neighbour of the short petticoat and the sabot; and only the distant gazer at the silk robe, the velvet mantle, and the plumed chapeau. Amidst so much life and joy, too, it suited me to be alone—quite alone. Having neither wish nor power to force my way through a mass so close-packed, my station was on the farthest confines, where, indeed, I might hear, but could see little.

"Mademoiselle is not well placed," said a voice at my elbow. Who dared accost *me*, a being in a mood so little social? I turned rather to repel than to reply. I saw a man—a burgher—an entire stranger, as I deemed him for one moment, but the next recognised in him a certain tradesman—a bookseller, whose shop furnished the Rue Fossette with its books and stationery; a man notorious in our pensionnat for the excessive brittleness of his temper, and frequent snappishness of his manner, even to us, his principal customers: but whom, for my solitary self, I had ever been disposed to like, and had always found civil, sometimes kind; once, in aiding me

about some troublesome little exchange of foreign money, he had done me a service. He was an intelligent man; under his asperity, he was a good-hearted man; the thought had sometimes crossed me that a part of his nature bore affinity to a part of M. Emanuel's (whom he knew well, and whom I had often seen sitting on Miret's counter, turning over the current month's publications); and it was in this affinity I read the explanation of that conciliatory feeling with which I instinctively regarded him.

Strange to say, this man knew me under my straw-hat and closely-folded shawl; and, though I deprecated the effort, he insisted on making a way for me through the crowd, and finding me a better situation. He carried his disinterested civility further; and, from some quarter, procured me a chair. Once and again I have found that the most cross-grained are by no means the worst of mankind; nor the humblest in station the least polished in feeling. This man, in his courtesy, seemed to find nothing strange in my being here alone; only a reason for extending to me, as far as he could, a retiring, yet efficient attention. Having secured me a place and a seat, he withdrew without asking a question, without obtruding a remark, without adding a superfluous word. No wonder that Professor Emanuel liked to take his cigar and his lounge and to read his feuilleton in M. Miret's shop—the two must have suited.

I had not been seated five minutes, ere I became aware that chance and my worthy burgher friend had brought me once more within view of a familiar and domestic group. Right before me sat the Brettons and De Bassompierres. Within reach of my hand—had I chosen to extend it—sat a figure like a fairy-queen, whose array lilies and their leaves seemed to have suggested; whatever was not spotless white being forest-green. My godmother, too, sat so near, that, had I leaned forward, my breath might have stirred the ribbon of her bonnet. They were too near; having been just recognised by a comparative stranger, I felt uneasy at this close vicinage of intimate acquaintance.

It made me quite start when Mrs. Bretton, turning to Mr. Home, and speaking out of a kind impulse of memory, said—"I wonder what my steady little Lucy would say to all this if she were here? I wish we had brought her, she would have enjoyed it much."

"So she would, so she would, in her grave sensible fashion; it is a pity but we had asked her," rejoined the kind gentleman; and added, "I like to see her so quietly pleased; so little moved, yet so content."

Dear were they both to me, dear are they to this day in their remembered benevolence. Little knew they the rack of pain which had driven Lucy almost into fever, and brought her out, guideless and reckless, urged and drugged to the brink of frenzy. I had half a mind to bend over the elder's shoulders, and answer their goodness with the thanks of my eyes. M. de Bassompierre did not well know *me*, but I knew *him*, and honoured and admired his nature, with all its plain sincerity, its warm affection, and unconscious enthusiasm. Possibly I might have spoken, but just then Graham turned; he turned with one of his stately firm movements, so different from those of a sharp-tempered undersized man: there was behind him a throng a hundred ranks deep; there were thousands to meet his eye and divide its scrutiny—why then did he concentrate all on me—oppressing me with the whole force of that full, blue, steadfast orb? Why, if he *would* look, did not one glance satisfy him? why did he turn on his chair, rest his elbow on its back, and study me leisurely? He could not see my face, I held it down: surely, he *could* not recognise me: I stooped, I turned, I *would* not be known. He rose, by some means he contrived to approach, in two minutes he would have had my secret: my identity would have been grasped between his never tyrannous but always powerful hands. There was but one way to evade or to check him. I implied, by a sort of supplicatory gesture, that it was my prayer to be let alone; after that, had he persisted, he would perhaps have seen the spectacle of Lucy incensed: not all that was grand, or good,

or kind in him (and Lucy felt the full amount) should have kept her quite tame, or absolutely inoffensive and shadowlike. He looked, but he desisted. He shook his handsome head, but he was mute. He resumed his seat, nor did he again turn or disturb me by a glance, except indeed for one single instant, when a look, rather solicitous than curious, stole my way—speaking what somehow stilled my heart like "the south-wind quieting the earth." Graham's thoughts of me were not entirely those of a frozen indifference, after all. I believe in that goodly mansion, his heart, he kept one little place under the skylights where Lucy might have entertainment if she chose to call. It was not so handsome as the chambers where he lodged his male friends; it was not like the hall where he accommodated his philanthropy, or the library where he treasured his science, still less did it resemble the pavilion where his marriage feast was splendidly spread; yet, gradually, by long and equal kindness, he proved to me that he kept one little closet, over the door of which was written "Lucy's Room." I kept a place for him, too—a place of which I never took the measure, either by rule or compass: I think it was like the tent of Peri-Banou. All my life long I carried it folded in the hollow of my hand—yet, released from that hold and constriction, I know not but its innate capacity for expanse might have magnified it into a tabernacle for a host.

Forbearing as he was to-night, I could not stay in this proximity; this dangerous place and seat must be given up: I watched my opportunity, rose, and stole away. He might think, he might even believe that Lucy was contained within that shawl, and sheltered under that hat: he never could be certain, for he did not see my face.

Surely the spirit of restlessness was by this time appeased? Had I not had enough of adventure? Did I not begin to flag, quail, and wish for safety under a roof? Not so. I still loathed my bed in the school dormitory more than words can express: I clung to whatever could distract thought. Somehow I felt, too, that the night's drama was but begun, that the prologue was scarce spoken: throughout this woody and turfy theatre reigned a shadow of mystery; actors and incidents unlooked for waited behind the scenes: I thought so: foreboding told me as much.

Straying at random, obeying the push of every chance elbow, I was brought to a quarter where trees planted in clusters, or towering singly, broke up somewhat the dense backing of the crowd, and gave it a more scattered character. These confines were far from the music, and somewhat aloof even from the lamps, but there was sound enough to soothe, and with that full, high moon lamps were scarce needed. Here had chiefly settled family groups, burgher-parents; some of them, late as was the hour, actually surrounded by their children, with whom it had not been thought advisable to venture into the closer throng.

Three fine tall trees growing close, almost twined stem within stem, lifted a thick canopy of shade above a green knoll, crowned with a seat—a seat which might have held several, yet it seemed abandoned to one, the remaining members of the fortunate party in possession of this site standing dutifully round; yet amongst this reverend circle was a lady, holding by the hand a little girl.

When I caught sight of this little girl, she was twisting herself round on her heel, swinging from the conductress's hand, flinging herself from side to side with wanton and fantastic gyrations. These perverse movements arrested my attention, they struck me as of a character fearfully familiar. On close inspection, no less so appeared the child's equipment; the lilac silk pelisse, the small swansdown boa, the white bonnet—the whole holiday toilette, in short, was the gala garb of a cherub but too well known, of that tadpole Désirée Beck—and Désirée Beck it was—she, or an imp in her likeness.

I might have taken this discovery as a thunder-clap, but such hyberbole would have been premature; discovery was destined to rise more than one degree ere it reached its climax.

On whose hand could the amiable Désirée swing thus selfishly, whose glove could she tear thus recklessly, whose arm thus strain with impunity, or on the

borders of whose dress thus turn and trample insolently, if not the hand, glove, arm, and robe of her lady-mother? And there, in an Indian shawl and a pale-green crape bonnet—there, fresh, portly, blithe, and pleasant—there stood Madame Beck.

Curious! I had certainly deemed Madame in her bed, and Désirée in her crib, at this blessed minute, sleeping, both of them, the sleep of the just, within the sacred walls, amidst the profound seclusion of the Rue Fossette. Most certainly also they did not picture "Meess Lucie" otherwise engaged; and here we all three were taking our "ébats" in the fête-blazing park at midnight!

The fact was, Madame was only acting according to her quite justifiable wont. I remembered now I had heard it said among the teachers—though without at the time particularly noticing the gossip—that often, when we thought Madame in her chamber, sleeping, she was gone, full-dressed, to take her pleasure at operas, or plays, or balls. Madame had no sort of taste for a monastic life, and took care— largely, though discreetly—to season her existence with a relish of the world.

Half-a-dozen gentlemen of her friends stood about her. Amongst these I was not slow to recognise two or three. There was her brother, M. Victor Kint: there was another person, moustached and with long hair—a calm, taciturn man, but whose traits bore a stamp and a semblance I could not mark unmoved. Amidst reserve and phlegm, amidst contrasts of character and of countenance, something there still was which recalled a face—mobile, fervent, feeling—a face changeable, now clouded, and now alight—a face from my world taken away, for my eyes lost, but where my best spring-hours of life had alternated in shadow and in glow; that face where I had often seen movements so near the signs of genius that why there did not shine fully out the undoubted fire, the thing, the spirit and the secret itself, I could never tell. Yes—this Josef Emanuel—this man of peace—reminded me of his ardent brother.

Besides Messieurs Victor and Josef, I knew another of this party. This third person stood behind and in the shade, his attitude too was stooping, yet his dress and bald white head made him the most conspicuous figure of the group. He was an ecclesiastic: he was Père Silas. Do not fancy, reader, that there was any inconsistency in the priest's presence at this fête. This was not considered a show of Vanity Fair, but a commemoration of patriotic sacrifice. The Church patronised it, even with ostentation. There were troops of priests in the park that night.

Père Silas stooped over the seat with its single occupant, the rustic bench and that which sat upon it: a strange mass it was—bearing no shape, yet magnificent. You saw, indeed, the outline of a face and features, but these were so cadaverous and so strangely placed, you could almost have fancied a head severed from its trunk and flung at random on a pile of rich merchandise. The distant lamp-rays glanced on clear pendants, on broad rings; neither the chasteness of moonlight, nor the distance of the torches, could quite subdue the gorgeous dyes of the drapery. Hail, Madame Walravens! I think you looked more witch-like than ever. And presently the good lady proved that she was indeed no corpse or ghost, but a harsh and hardy old woman; for, upon some aggravation in the clamorous petition of Désirée Beck to her mother, to go to the kiosk and take sweetmeats, the hunchback suddenly fetched her a resounding rap with her gold-knobbed cane.

There, then, were Madame Walravens, Madame Beck, Père Silas—the whole conjuration, the secret junta. The sight of them thus assembled did me good. I cannot say that I felt weak before them, or abashed, or dismayed. They outnumbered me and I was worsted and under their feet; but, as yet, I was not dead.

Chapter XXXIX

OLD AND NEW ACQUAINTANCE

FASCINATED as by a basilisk with three heads, I could not leave this clique; the ground near them seemed to hold my feet. The canopy of entwined trees held out

shadow, the night whispered a pledge of protection, and an officious lamp flashed just one beam to show me an obscure, safe seat, and then vanished. Let me now briefly tell the reader all that, during the past dark fortnight, I have been silently gathering from Rumour respecting the origin and the object of M. Emanuel's departure. The tale is short and not new: its alpha is Mammon, and its omega Interest.

If Madame Walravens was hideous as a Hindoo idol, she seemed also to possess, in the estimation of these her votaries, an idol's consequence. The fact was, she had been rich—very rich; and though, for the present, without the command of money, she was likely one day to be rich again. At Basseterre, in Guadaloupe, she possessed a large estate, received in dowry on her marriage sixty years ago, sequestered since her husband's failure; but now, it was supposed, cleared of claim, and, if duly looked after by a competent agent of integrity, considered capable of being made, in a few years, largely productive.

Père Silas took an interest in this prospective improvement for the sake of religion and the Church, whereof Magloire Walravens was a devout daughter. Madame Beck, distantly related to the hunchback and knowing her to be without family of her own, had long brooded over contingencies with a mother's calculating forethought, and, harshly treated as she was by Madame Walravens, never ceased to court her for interest's sake. Madame Beck and the priest were thus for money reasons equally and sincerely interested in the nursing of the West Indian estate.

But the distance was great, and the climate hazardous. The competent and upright agent wanted must be a devoted man. Just such a man had Madame Walravens retained for twenty years in her service, blighting his life, and then living on him, like an old fungus; such a man had Père Silas trained, taught, and bound to him by the ties of gratitude, habit, and belief. Such a man Madame Beck knew, and could in some measure influence. "My pupil," said Père Silas, "if he remain in Europe, runs risk of apostacy, for he has become entangled with a heretic." Madame Beck made also her private comment, and preferred in her own breast her secret reason for desiring expatriation. The thing she could not obtain, she desired not another to win: rather would she destroy it. As to Madame Walravens, she wanted her money and her land, and knew Paul, if he liked, could make the best and faithfullest steward: so the three self-seekers banded and beset the one unselfish. They reasoned, they appealed, they implored; on his mercy they cast themselves, into his hands they confidingly thrust their interests. They asked but two or three years of devotion—after that, he should live for himself: one of the number, perhaps, wished that in the meantime he might die.

No living being ever humbly laid his advantage at M. Emanuel's feet, or confidingly put it into his hands, that he spurned the trust or repulsed the repository. What might be his private pain or inward reluctance to leave Europe—what his calculations for his own future—none asked, or knew, or reported. All this was a blank to me. His conferences with his confessor I might guess; the part duty and religion were made to play in the persuasions used, I might conjecture. He was gone, and had made no sign. There my knowledge closed.

With my head bent, and my forehead resting on my hands, I sat amidst grouped tree-stems and branching brushwood. Whatever talk passed amongst my neighbours, I might hear if I would; I was near enough; but for some time there was scarce motive to attend. They gossiped about the dresses, the music, the illuminations, the fine night. I listened to hear them say, "It is calm weather for *his* voyage; the *Antigua*" (his ship) "will sail prosperously." No such remark fell; neither the *Antigua,* nor her course, nor her passenger were named.

Perhaps the light chat scarcely interested old Madame Walravens more than it did me; she appeared restless, turning her head now to this side, now that, looking through the trees, and among the crowd, as if expectant of an arrival and impatient of delay. "Où sont-ils? Pourquoi ne viennent-ils?" I heard her mutter more than once; and at last, as if determined to have an answer to her question—which hitherto none seemed to mind, she spoke aloud this phrase—a phrase brief enough, simple enough, but it sent a shock through me—

"Messieurs et mesdames," said she, "où donc est Justine Marie?"

"Justine Marie!" What was this? Justine Marie—the dead nun—where was she? Why, in her grave, Madame Walravens—what can you want with her? You shall go to her, but she shall not come to you.

Thus *I* should have answered, had the response lain with me, but nobody seemed to be of my mind; nobody seemed surprised, startled, or at a loss. The quietest commonplace answer met the strange, the dead-disturbing, the Witch-of-Endor query of the hunchback.

"Justine Marie," said one, "is coming; she is in the kiosk; she will be here presently."

Out of this question and reply sprang a change in the chat—chat it still remained—easy, desultory, familiar gossip. Hint, allusion, comment, went round the circle, but all so broken, so dependent on references to persons not named, or circumstances not defined, that, listen as intently as I would—and I *did* listen *now* with a fated interest—I could make out no more than that some scheme was on foot in which this ghostly Justine Marie—dead or alive—was concerned. This family junta seemed grasping at her somehow, for some reason; there seemed question of a marriage, of a fortune, for whom I could not quite make out—perhaps for Victor Kint, perhaps for Josef Emanuel—both were bachelors. Once I thought the hints and jests rained upon a young fair-haired foreigner of the party, whom they called Heinrich Mühler. Amidst all the badinage Madame Walravens still obtruded from time to time hoarse, cross-grained speeches; her impatience being diverted only by an implacable surveillance of Désirée, who could not stir but the old woman menaced her with her staff.

"La voilà!" suddenly cried one of the gentlemen, "voilà Justine Marie qui arrive!"

This moment was for me peculiar. I called up to memory the pictured nun on the panel; present to my mind was the sad love-story; I saw in thought the vision of the garret, the apparition of the alley, the strange birth of the berceau: I underwent a presentiment of discovery, a strong conviction of coming disclosure. Ah! when imagination once runs riot where do we stop? What winter tree so bare and branchless—what wayside, hedge-munching animal so humble, that Fancy, a passing cloud, and a struggling moonbeam will not clothe it in spirituality, and make of it a phantom?

With solemn force pressed on my heart, the expectation of mystery breaking up: hitherto I had seen this spectre only through a glass darkly; now was I to behold it face to face. I leaned forward; I looked.

"She comes!" cried Josef Emanuel.

The circle opened as if opening to admit a new and welcome member. At this instant a torch chanced to be carried past; its blaze aided the pale moon in doing justice to the crisis, in lighting to perfection the dénouement pressing on. Surely those near me must have felt some little of the anxiety I felt, in degree so unmeted. Of that group the coolest must have "held his breath for a time!" As for me, my life stood still.

It is over. The moment and the nun are come. The crisis and the revelation are passed by.

The flambeau glares still within a yard, held up in a park-keeper's hand; its long eager tongue of flame almost licks the figure of the Expected—there—where she

stands full in my sight! What is she like? What does she wear? How does she look? Who is she?

There are many masks in the Park to-night, and as the hour wears late, so strange a feeling of revelry and mystery begins to spread abroad that scarce would you discredit me, reader, were I to say that she is like the nun of the attic, that she wears black skirts and white head-clothes, that she looks the resurrection of the flesh, and that she is a risen ghost.

All falsities—all figments! We will not deal in this gear. Let us be honest, and cut, as heretofore, from the homely web of truth.

Homely, though, is an ill-chosen word. What I see is not precisely homely. A girl of Villette stands there—a girl fresh from her pensionnat. She is very comely, with the beauty indigenous to this country. She looks well-nourished, fair, and fat of flesh. Her cheeks are round, her eyes good; her hair is abundant. She is handsomely dressed. She is not alone; her escort consists of three persons—two being elderly; these she addresses as "Mon Oncle" and "Ma Tante." She laughs, she chats; good-humoured, buxom, and blooming, she looks at all points the bourgeoise belle.

So much for "Justine Marie;" so much for ghosts and mystery: not that this last was solved—this girl certainly is not my nun; what I saw in the garret and garden must have been taller by a span.

We have looked at the city belle; we have cursorily glanced at the respectable old uncle and aunt. Have we a stray glance to give to the third member of this company? Can we spare him a moment's notice? We ought to distinguish him so far, reader; he has claims on us; we do not now meet him for the first time. I clasped my hands very hard, and I drew my breath very deep: I held in the cry, I devoured the ejaculation, I forbade the start, I spoke and I stirred no more than a stone; but I knew what I looked on; through the dimness left in my eyes by many nights' weeping, I knew him. They said he was to sail by the *Antigua.* Madame Beck said so. She lied, or she had uttered what was once truth, and failed to contradict it when it became false. The *Antigua* was gone, and there stood Paul Emanuel.

Was I glad? A huge load left me. Was it a fact to warrant joy? I know not. Ask first what were the circumstances attendant on this respite? How far did this delay concern *me?* Were there not those whom it might touch more nearly?

After all, who may this young girl, this Justine Marie, be? Not a stranger, reader; she is known to me by sight; she visits at the Rue Fossette: she is often of Madame Beck's Sunday parties. She is a relation of both the Becks and Walravens; she derives her baptismal name from the sainted nun who would have been her aunt had she lived; her patronymic is Sauveur; she is an heiress and an orphan, and M. Emanuel is her guardian; some say her godfather. The family junta wish this heiress to be married to one of their band—which is it? Vital question—which is it?

I felt very glad now that the drug administered in the sweet draught had filled me with a possession which made bed and chamber intolerable. I always, through my whole life, liked to penetrate to the real truth; I like seeking the goddess in her temple, and handling the veil, and daring the dread glance. O Titaness among deities! The covered outline of thine aspect sickens often through its uncertainty, but define to us one trait, show us one lineament, clear in awful sincerity; we may gasp in untold terror, but with that gasp we drink in a breath of thy divinity; our heart shakes, and its currents sway like rivers lifted by earthquake, but we have swallowed strength. To see and know the worst is to take from Fear her main advantage.

The Walravens' party, augmented in numbers, now became very gay. The gentlemen fetched refreshments from the kiosk, all sat down on the turf under the trees; they drank healths and sentiments: they laughed, they jested. M. Emanuel underwent some raillery, half good-humoured, half, I thought, malicious, especially on Madame

Beck's part. I soon gathered that his voyage had been temporarily deferred of his own will, without the concurrence, even against the advice, of his friends; he had let the *Antigua* go, and had taken his berth in the *Paul et Virginie,* appointed to sail a fortnight later. It was his reason for this resolve which they teased him to assign, and which he would only vaguely indicate as "the settlement of a little piece of business which he had set his heart upon." What *was* this business? Nobody knew. Yes, there was one who seemed partly, at least, in his confidence; a meaning look passed between him and Justine Marie. "La petite va m'aider—n'est ce pas?" said he. The answer was prompt enough, God knows!

"Mais oui, je vous aiderai de tout mon cœur. Vous ferez de moi tout ce que vous voudrez, mon parrain."

And this dear "parrain" took her hand and lifted it to his grateful lips. Upon which demonstration, I saw the light-complexioned young Teuton, Heinrich Mühler, grow restless, as if he did not like it. He even grumbled a few words, whereat M. Emanuel actually laughed in his face, and with the ruthless triumph of the assured conqueror, he drew his ward nearer to him.

M. Emanuel was indeed very joyous that night. He seemed not one whit subdued by the change of scene and action impending. He was the true life of the party; a little despotic perhaps, determined to be chief in mirth as well as in labour, yet from moment to moment proving indisputably his right of leadership. His was the wittiest word, the pleasantest anecdote, the frankest laugh. Restlessly active, after his manner, he multiplied himself to wait on all; but oh! I saw which was his favourite. I saw at whose feet he lay on the turf, I saw whom he folded carefully from the night air, whom he tended, watched, and cherished as the apple of his eye.

Still hint and raillery flew thick, and still I gathered that while M. Paul should be absent, working for others, these others, not quite ungrateful, would guard for him the treasure he left in Europe. Let him bring them an Indian fortune: they would give him in return a young bride and a rich inheritance. As for the saintly consecration, the vow of constancy, that was forgotten: the blooming and charming Present prevailed over the Past; and, at length, his nun was indeed buried.

Thus it must be. The revelation was indeed come. Presentiment had not been mistaken in her impulse: there is a kind of presentiment which never *is* mistaken; it was I who had for a moment miscalculated; not seeing the true bearing of the oracle, I had thought she muttered of vision when, in truth, her prediction touched reality.

I might have paused longer upon what I saw; I might have deliberated ere I drew inferences. Some, perhaps, would have held the premises doubtful, the proofs insufficient: some slow sceptics would have incredulously examined ere they conclusively accepted the project of a marriage between a poor and unselfish man of forty and his wealthy ward of eighteen; but far from me such shifts and palliatives, far from me such temporary evasion of the actual, such coward fleeing from the dread, the swift-footed, the all-overtaking Fact, such feeble suspense of submission to her the sole sovereign, such paltering and faltering resistance to the Power whose errand is to march conquering and to conquer, such traitor defection from the TRUTH.

No. I hastened to accept the whole plan. I extended my grasp and took it all in. I gathered it to me with a sort of rage of haste, and folded it round me, as the soldier struck on the field folds his colours about his breast. I invoked Conviction to nail upon me the certainty, abhorred while embraced, to fix it with the strongest spikes her strongest strokes could drive; and when the iron had entered well my soul, I stood up, as I thought, renovated.

In my infatuation I said, "Truth, you are a good mistress to your faithful servants! While a Lie pressed me, how I suffered! Even when the Falsehood was still sweet, still flattering to the fancy, and warm to the feelings, it wasted me with hourly torment. The persuasion that affection was won could not be divorced from the

dread that, by another turn of the wheel, it might be lost. Truth stripped away Falsehood, and Flattery, and Expectancy, and here I stand—free!''

Nothing remained now but to take my freedom to my chamber, to carry it with me to my bed and see what I could make of it. The play was not yet, indeed, quite played out. I might have waited and watched longer that love scene under the trees, that sylvan courtship. Had there been nothing of love in the demonstration, my Fancy in this hour was so generous, so creative, she could have modelled for it the most salient lineaments, and given it the deepest life and highest colour of passion. But I *would* not look; I had fixed my resolve, but I would not violate my nature. And then—something tore me so cruelly under my shawl, something so dug into my side, a vulture so strong in beak and talon, I must be alone to grapple with it. I think I never felt jealousy till now. This was not like enduring the endearments of Dr. John and Paulina, against which, while I sealed my eyes and my ears, while I withdrew thence my thoughts, my sense of harmony still acknowledged in it a charm. This was an outrage. The love born of beauty was not mine: I had nothing in common with it: I could not dare to meddle with it, but another love, venturing diffidently into life after long acquaintance, furnace-tried by pain, stamped by constancy, consolidated by affection's pure and durable alloy, submitted by intellect to intellect's own tests, and finally wrought up, by his own process, to his own unflawed completeness, this Love that laughed at Passion, his fast frenzies and his hot and hurried extinction, in *this* Love I had a vested interest; and for whatever tended either to its culture or its destruction I could not view impassibly.

I turned from the group of trees and the ''merrie companie'' in its shade. Midnight was long past: the concert was over, the crowds were thinning. I followed the ebb. Leaving the radiant park and well-lit Haute-Ville (still well lit, this it seems was to be a ''nuit blanche'' in Villette), I sought the dim lower quarter.

Dim I should not say, for the beauty of moonlight—forgotten in the park—here once more flowed in upon perception. High she rode, and calm and stainlessly she shone. The music and the mirth of the fête, the fire and bright hues of those lamps had outdone and outshone her for an hour, but now again her glory and her silence triumphed. The rival lamps were dying: she held her course like a white fate. Drum, trumpet, bugle had uttered their clangour, and were forgotten; with pencil-ray she wrote on heaven and on earth records for archives everlasting. She and those stars seemed to me at once the types and witnesses of truth all regnant. The night-sky lit her reign: like its slow-wheeling progress, advanced her victory—that onward movement which has been, and is, and will be from eternity to eternity.

These oil-twinkling streets are very still: I like them for their lowliness and peace. Homeward-bound burghers pass me now and then, but these companies are pedestrian, make little noise, and are soon gone. So well do I love Villette under her present aspect, not willingly would I re-enter under a roof, but that I am bent on pursuing my strange adventure to a successful close, and quietly regaining my bed in the great dormitory before Madame Beck comes home.

Only one street lies between me and the Rue Fossette; as I enter it, for the first time, the sound of a carriage tears up the deep peace of this quarter. It comes this way—comes very fast. How loud sounds its rattle on the paved path! The street is narrow, and I keep carefully to the causeway. The carriage thunders past, but what do I see, or fancy I see, as it rushes by? Surely something white fluttered from that window—surely a hand waved a handkerchief. Was that signal meant for me? Am I known? Who could recognise me? That is not M. de Bassompierre's carriage, nor Mrs. Bretton's; and besides, neither the Hôtel Crécy nor the chateau of La Terrasse lies in that direction. Well, I have no time for conjecture; I must hurry home.

Gaining the Rue Fossette, reaching the pensionnat, all there was still; no fiacre had yet arrived with Madame and Désirée. I had left the great door ajar; should

I find it thus? Perhaps the wind or some other accident may have thrown it to with sufficient force to start the spring-bolt? In that case, hopeless became admission; my adventure must issue in catastrophe. I lightly pushed the heavy leaf; would it yield?

Yes. As soundless, as unresisting as if some propitious genius had waited on a sesame-charm in the vestibule within. Entering with bated breath, quietly making all fast, shoelessly mounting the staircase, I sought the dormitory, and reached my couch.

Ay! I reached it, and once more drew a free inspiration. The next moment, I almost shrieked—almost, but not quite, thank Heaven!

Throughout the dormitory, throughout the house, there reigned at this hour the stillness of death. All slept, and in such hush it seemed that none dreamed. Stretched on the nineteen beds lay nineteen forms, at full length and motionless. On mine— the twentieth couch—nothing *ought* to have lain: had left it void, and void should have found it. What, then, do I see between the half-drawn curtains? What dark, usurping shape, supine, long, and strange? Is it a robber who has made his way through the open street-door, and lies there in wait? It looks very black, I think it looks—not human. Can it be a wandering dog that has come in from the street and crept and nestled hither? Will it spring, will it leap out if I approach! Approach I must. Courage! One step!—

My head reeled, for by the faint night lamp I saw stretched on my bed the old phantom—the NUN.

A cry at this moment might have ruined me. Be the spectacle what it might, I could afford neither consternation, scream, nor swoon. Besides, I was not overcome. Tempered by late incidents, my nerves disdained hysteria. Warm from illuminations, and music, and thronging thousands, thoroughly lashed up by a new scourge, I defied spectra. In a moment, without exclamation, I had rushed on the haunted couch; nothing leaped out, or sprung, or stirred; all the movement was mine, so was all the life, the reality, the substance, the force; as my instinct felt. I tore her up—the incubus! I held her on high—the goblin! I shook her loose—the mystery! And down she fell—down all around me—down in shreds and fragments—and I trode upon her.

Here again—behold the branchless tree, the unstabled Rosinante; the film of cloud, the flicker of moonshine. The long nun proved a long bolster dressed in a long black stole, and artfully invested with a white veil. The garments in very truth, strange as it may seem, were genuine nun's garments, and by some hand they had been disposed with a view to illusion. Whence came these vestments? Who contrived this artifice? These questions still remained. To the head-bandage was pinned a slip of paper: it bore in pencil these mocking words—"The nun of the attic bequeaths to Lucy Snowe her wardrobe. She will be seen in the Rue Fossette no more."

And what and who was she that had haunted me? She I had actually seen three times? Not a woman of my acquaintance had the stature of that ghost. She was not of female height. Not to any man I knew could the machination, for a moment, be attributed.

Still mystified beyond expression, but as thoroughly, as suddenly, relieved from all sense of the spectral and unearthly; scorning also to wear out my brain with the fret of a trivial though insoluble riddle, I just bundled together stole, veil, and bandages, thrust them beneath my pillow, lay down, listened till I heard the wheels of Madame's home-returning fiacre, then turned, and worn out by many nights' vigils, conquered too, perhaps, by the now reacting narcotic, I deeply slept.

Chapter XL

THE HAPPY PAIR

THE day succeeding this remarkable midsummer night proved no common day. I do not mean that it brought signs in heaven above, or portents on the earth beneath; nor do I allude to meteorological phenomena, to storm, flood, or whirlwind. On the contrary: the sun rose jocund, with a July face. Morning decked her beauty with rubies, and so filled her lap with roses that they fell from her in showers, making her path blush: the Hours woke fresh as nymphs, and emptying on the early hills their dew-vials, they stepped out dismantled of vapour: shadowless, azure, and glorious, they led the sun's steeds on a burning and unclouded course.

In short, it was as fine a day as the finest summer could boast: but I doubt whether I was not the sole inhabitant of the Rue Fossette who cared or remembered to note this pleasant fact. Another thought busied all other heads; a thought, indeed, which had its share in my meditations; but this master consideration, not possessing for me so entire a novelty, so overwhelming a suddenness, especially so dense a mystery, as it offered to the majority of my co-speculators thereon, left me somewhat more open than the rest to any collateral observation or impression.

Still, while walking in the garden, feeling the sunshine and marking the blooming and growing plants, I pondered the same subject the whole house discussed.

What subject?

Merely this. When matins came to be said, there was a place vacant in the first rank of boarders. When breakfast was served, there remained a coffee-cup unclaimed. When the housemaid made the beds, she found in one, a bolster laid lengthwise, clad in a cap and nightgown; and when Ginevra Fanshawe's music-mistress came early, as usual, to give the morning lesson, that accomplished and promising young person, her pupil, failed utterly to be forthcoming.

High and low was Miss Fanshawe sought; through length and breadth was the house ransacked; vainly; not a trace, not an indication, not so much as a scrap of a billet rewarded the search; the nymph was vanished, engulfed in the past night, like a shooting star swallowed up by darkness.

Deep was the dismay of surveillante teachers, deeper the horror of the defaulting directress. Never had I seen Madame Beck so pale or so appalled. Here was a blow struck at her tender part, her weak side; here was damage done to her interest. How, too, had the untoward event happened? By what outlet had the fugitive taken wing? Not a casement was found unfastened, not a pane of glass broken; all the doors were bolted secure. Never to this day has Madame Beck obtained satisfaction on this point, nor indeed has anybody else concerned, save and excepting one, Lucy Snowe, who could not forget how, to facilitate a certain enterprise, a certain great door had been drawn softly to its lintel, closed, indeed, but neither bolted nor secure. The thundering carriage-and-pair encountered were now likewise recalled, as well as that puzzling signal, the waved handkerchief.

From these premises, and one or two others, inaccessible to any but myself, I could draw but one inference. It was a case of elopement. Morally certain on this head, and seeing Madame Beck's profound embarrassment, I at last communicated my conviction. Having alluded to M. de Hamal's suit, I found, as I expected, that Madame Beck was perfectly au fait to that affair. She had long since discussed it with Mrs. Cholmondeley, and laid her own responsibility in the business on that lady's shoulders. To Mrs. Cholmondeley and M. de Bassompierre she now had recourse.

We found that the Hôtel Crécy was already alive to what had happened. Ginevra had written to her cousin Paulina, vaguely signifying hymeneal intentions; communications had been received from the family of De Hamal; M. de Bassompierre was on the track of the fugitives. He overtook them too late.

In the course of the week, the post brought me a note. I may as well transcribe it; it contains explanation on more than one point:

"DEAR OLD TIM (short for Timon),—I am off, you see—gone like a shot. Alfred and I intended to be married in this way almost from the first; we never meant to be spliced in the humdrum way of other people; Alfred has too much spirit for that, and so have I—Dieu merci! Do you know, Alfred, who used to call you 'the dragon,' has seen so much of you during the last few months, that he begins to feel quite friendly towards you. He hopes you won't miss him now that he has gone; he begs to apologise for any little trouble he may have given you. He is afraid he rather inconvenienced you once when he came upon you in the grenier, just as you were reading a letter seemingly of the most special interest; but he could not resist the temptation to give you a start, you appeared so wonderfully taken up with your correspondent. En revanche, he says you once frightened him by rushing in for a dress or a shawl, or some other chiffon, at the moment when he had struck a light, and was going to take a quiet whiff of his cigar while waiting for me.

"Do you begin to comprehend by this time that M. le Comte de Hamal was the nun of the attic, and that he came to see your humble servant? I will tell you how he managed it. You know he has the entrée of the Athénée, where two or three of his nephews, the sons of his eldest sister, Madame de Melcy, are students. You know the court of the Athénée is on the other side of the high wall bounding your walk, the allée défendue. Alfred can climb as well as he can dance or fence; his amusement was to make the escalade of our pensionnat by mounting, first the wall, then—by the aid of that high tree overspreading the grand berceau, and resting some of its boughs on the roof of the lower buildings of our premises—he managed to scale the first classe and the grand salle. One night, by the way, he fell out of this tree, tore down some of the branches, nearly broke his own neck, and after all, in running away, got a terrible fright, and was nearly caught by two people, Madame Beck and M. Emanuel, he thinks, walking in the alley. From the grand salle the ascent is not difficult to the highest block of building, finishing in the great garret. The skylight, you know, is, day and night, left half open for air; and by the skylight he entered. Nearly a year ago I chanced to tell him our legend of the nun; that suggested his romantic idea of the spectral disguise, which I think you must allow he has very cleverly carried out.

"But for the nun's black gown and white veil, he would have been caught again and again both by you and that tiger-Jesuit, M. Paul. He thinks you both capital ghost-seers, and very brave. What I wonder at is rather your secretiveness than your courage. How could you endure the visitations of that long spectre, time after time, without crying out, telling everybody, and rousing the whole house and neighbourhood?

"Oh, and how did you like the nun as a bed-fellow? *I* dressed her up: didn't I do it well? Did you shriek when you saw her? *I* should have gone mad; but then you have such nerves—real iron and bend leather! I believe you feel nothing. You haven't the same sensitiveness that a person of my constitution has. You seem to me insensible both to pain and fear and grief. You are a real old Diogenes.

"Well, dear grandmother! and are you not mightily angry at my moonlight flitting and runaway match? I assure you it is excellent fun, and I did it partly to spite that minx Paulina and that bear Dr. John: to show them that, with all their airs, I could get married as well as they. M. de

Bassompierre was at first in a strange fume with Alfred; he threatened
a prosecution for 'détournement de mineur,' and I know not what; he
was so abominably in earnest, that I found myself forced to do a little
bit of the melodramatic—go down on my knees, sob, cry, drench three
pocket-handkerchiefs. Of course, 'mon oncle' soon gave in; indeed,
where was the use of making a fuss? I am married, and that's all about
it. He still says our marriage is not legal, because I am not of age,
forsooth! As if that made any difference! I am just as much married as
if I were a hundred. However, we are to be married again, and I am to
have a trousseau, and Mrs. Cholmondeley is going to superintend it; and
there are some hopes that M. de Bassompierre will give us a decent
portion, which will be very convenient, as dear Alfred has nothing but
his nobility, native and hereditary, and his pay. I only wish uncle would
do things unconditionally, in a generous, gentlemanlike fashion; he is so
disagreeable as to make the dowry depend on Alfred's giving his written
promise that he will never touch cards or dice from the day it is paid
down. They accuse my angel of a tendency to play: I don't know anything
about that, but I *do* know he is a dear, adorable creature.

"I cannot sufficiently extol the genius with which De Hamal managed
our flight. How clever in him to select the night of the fête, when
Madame (for he knows her habits), as he said, would infallibly be absent
at the concert in the park. I suppose *you* must have gone with her. I
watched you rise and leave the dormitory about eleven o'clock. How
you returned alone, and on foot, I cannot conjecture. That surely was
you we met in the narrow old Rue St. Jean? Did you see me wave my
handkerchief from the carriage window?

"Adieu! Rejoice in my good luck: congratulate me on my supreme
happiness, and believe me, dear cynic and misanthrope, yours, in the
best of health and spirits,

"GINEVRA LAURA DE HAMAL,
née FANSHAWE.

"*P.S.*—Remember, I am a countess now. Papa, mamma, and the girls
at home will be delighted to hear that. 'My daughter, the Countess! My
sister, the Countess!' Bravo! Sounds rather better than Mrs. John Bretton,
hein?"

In winding up Mistress Fanshawe's memoirs, the reader will no doubt expect to
hear that she came finally to bitter expiation of her youthful levities. Of course, a
large share of suffering lies in reserve for her future.

A few words will embody my further knowledge respecting her.

I saw her towards the close of her honeymoon. She called on Madame Beck,
and sent for me into the salon. She rushed into my arms laughing. She looked very
blooming and beautiful: her curls were longer, her cheeks rosier than ever: her
white bonnet and her Flanders veil, her orange flowers and her bride's dress, became
her mightily.

"I have got my portion!" she cried at once (Ginevra ever stuck to the substantial;
I always thought there was a good trading element in her composition, much as
she scorned the "bourgeoise"); "and Uncle de Bassompierre is quite reconciled.
I don't mind his calling Alfred a 'nincompoop'—that's only his coarse Scotch
breeding; and I believe Paulina envies me, and Dr. John is wild with jealousy—
fit to blow his brains out—and I'm so happy! I really think I've hardly anything
left to wish for—unless it be a carriage and a hotel, and, oh! I must introduce you
to 'mon mari.' Alfred, come here!"

And Alfred appeared from the inner salon, where he was talking to Madame Beck, receiving the blended felicitations and reprimands of that lady. I was presented under my various names: the Dragon, Diogenes, and Timon. The young Colonel was very polite. He made me a prettily-turned, neatly-worded apology about the ghost visits, etc., concluding with saying that "the best excuse for all his iniquities stood there!" pointing to his bride.

And then the bride sent him back to Madame Beck, and she took me to herself, and proceeded literally to suffocate me with her unrestrained spirits, her girlish, giddy, wild nonsense. She showed her ring exultingly; she called herself Madame la Comtesse de Hamal, and asked how it sounded, a score of times. I said very little. I gave her only the crust and rind of my nature. No matter: she expected of me nothing better—she knew me too well to look for compliment—my dry gibes pleased her well enough, and the more impassible and prosaic my mien, the more merrily she laughed.

Soon after his marriage, M. de Hamal was persuaded to leave the army as the surest way of weaning him from certain unprofitable associates and habits; a post of attaché was procured for him, and he and his young wife went abroad. I thought she would forget me now, but she did not. For many years she kept up a capricious, fitful sort of correspondence. During the first year or two it was only of herself and Alfred she wrote; then Alfred faded in the background; herself and a certain newcomer prevailed; one Alfred Fanshawe de Bassompierre de Hamal began to reign in his father's stead. There were great boastings about this personage, extravagant amplifications upon miracles of precocity, mixed with vehement objurgations against the phlegmatic incredulity with which I received them. I didn't know "what it was to be a mother": "unfeeling thing that I was, the sensibilities of the maternal heart were Greek and Hebrew to me," and so on. In due course of nature this young gentleman took his degrees in teething, measles, hooping-cough: that was a terrible time for me—the mamma's letters became a perfect shout of affliction; never woman was so put upon by calamity: never human being stood in such need of sympathy. I was frightened at first, and wrote back pathetically; but I soon found out there was more cry than wool in the business and relapsed into my natural cruel insensibility. As to the youthful sufferer, he weathered each storm like a hero. Five times was that youth "in articulo mortis," and five times did he miraculously revive.

In the course of years there arose ominous murmurings against Alfred the First; M. de Bassompierre had to be appealed to, debts had to be paid, some of them of that dismal and dingy order called "debts of honour"; ignoble plaints and difficulties became frequent. Under every cloud, no matter what its nature, Ginevra, as of old, called out lustily for sympathy and aid. She had no notion of meeting any distress single-handed. In some shape, from some quarter or other, she was pretty sure to obtain her will, and so she got on—fighting the battle of life by proxy, and, on the whole, suffering as little as any human being I have ever known.

Chapter XLI

FAUBOURG CLOTILDE

Must I, ere I close, render some account of that Freedom and Renovation which I won on the fête-night? Must I tell how I and the two stalwart companions I brought home from the illuminated park bore the test of intimate acquaintance?

I tried them the very next day. They had boasted their strength loudly when they reclaimed me from love and its bondage, but upon my demanding deeds, not words, some evidence of better comfort, some experience of a relieved life—Freedom excused himself, as for the present, impoverished and disabled to assist; and Renovation never spoke; he had died in the night suddenly.

I had nothing left for it then but to trust secretly that conjecture might have hurried me too fast and too far, to sustain the oppressive hour by reminders of the distorting and discolouring magic of jealousy. After a short and vain struggle, I found myself brought back captive to the old rack of suspense, tied down and strained anew.

Shall I yet see him before he goes? Will he bear me in mind? Does he purpose to come? Will this day—will the next hour bring him? or must I again assay that corroding pain of long attent—that rude agony of rupture at the close, that mute, mortal wrench, which, in at once uprooting hope and doubt, shakes life; while the hand that does the violence cannot be caressed to pity because absence interposes her barrier?

It was the Feast of the Assumption; no school was held. The boarders and teachers, after attending mass in the morning, were gone a long walk into the country to take their goûter, or afternoon meal, at some farm-house. I did not go with them, for now but two days remained ere the *Paul et Virginie* must sail, and I was clinging to my last chance, as the living waif of a wreck clings to his last raft or cable.

There was some joiners' work to do in the first classe, some bench or desk to repair; holidays were often turned to account for the performance of these operations, which could not be executed when the rooms were filled with pupils. As I sat solitary, purposing to adjourn to the garden and leave the coast clear, but too listless to fulfil my own intent, I heard the workmen coming.

Foreign artisans and servants do everything by couples: I believe it would take two Labassecourien carpenters to drive a nail. While tying on my bonnet, which had hitherto hung by its ribbons from my idle hand, I vaguely and momentarily wondered to hear the step of but one "ouvrier." I noted, too—as captives in dungeons find sometimes dreary leisure to note the merest trifles—that this man wore shoes, and not sabots: I concluded that it must be the master-carpenter, coming to inspect before he sent his journeymen. I threw round me my scarf. He advanced; he opened the door; my back was towards it; I felt a little thrill—a curious sensation, too quick and transient to be analysed. I turned, I stood in the supposed master-artisan's presence: looking towards the doorway, I saw it filled with a figure, and my eyes printed upon my brain the picture of M. Paul.

Hundreds of the prayers with which we weary Heaven bring to the suppliant no fulfilment. Once haply in life one golden gift falls prone in the lap—one boon full and bright, perfect from Fruition's mint.

M. Emanuel wore the dress in which he probably purposed to travel—a surtout, guarded with velvet; I thought him prepared for instant departure, and yet I had understood that two days were yet to run before the ship sailed. He looked well and cheerful. He looked kind and benign: he came in with eagerness; he was close to me in one second; he was all amity. It might be his bridegroom mood which thus brightened him. Whatever the cause, I could not meet his sunshine with cloud. If this were my last moment with him, I would not waste it in forced, unnatural distance. I loved him well—too well not to smite out of my path even Jealousy herself, when she would have obstructed a kind farewell. A cordial word from his lips, or a gentle look from his eyes, would do me good, for all the span of life that remained to me; it would be comfort in the last strait of loneliness; I would take it—I would taste the elixir, and pride should not spill the cup.

The interview would be short, of course: he would say to me just what he had said to each of the assembled pupils; he would take and hold my hand two minutes; he would touch my cheek with his lips for the first, last, only time—and then—no more. Then, indeed, the final parting, then the wide separation, the great gulf I could not pass to go to him—across which, haply, he would not glance to remember me.

He took my hand in one of his, with the other he put back my bonnet; he looked into my face, his luminous smile went out, his lips expressed something almost

like the wordless language of a mother who finds a child greatly and unexpectedly changed, broken with illness, or worn out by want. A check supervened.

"Paul, Paul!" said a woman's hurried voice behind, "Paul, come into the salon; I have yet a great many things to say to you—conversation for the whole day—and so has Victor; and Josef is here. Come, Paul, come to your friends."

Madame Beck, brought to the spot by vigilance or an inscrutable instinct, pressed so near she almost thrust herself between me and M. Emanuel. "Come, Paul!" she reiterated, her eye grazing me with its hard ray like a steel stylet. She pushed against her kinsman. I thought he receded; I thought he would go. Pierced deeper than I could endure, made now to feel what defied suppression, I cried—

"My heart will break!"

What I felt seemed literal heart-break; but the seal of another fountain yielded under the strain: one breath from M. Paul, the whisper, "Trust me!" lifted a load, opened an outlet. With many a deep sob, with thrilling, with icy shiver, with strong trembling, and yet with relief—I wept.

"Leave her to me; it is a crisis: I will give her a cordial, and it will pass," said the calm Madame Beck.

To be left to her and her cordial seemed to me something like being left to the poisoner and her bowl. When M. Paul answered deeply, harshly, and briefly—

"Laissez-moi!" in the grim sound I felt a music strange, strong, but life-giving.

"Laissez-moi!" he repeated, his nostrils opening, and his facial muscles all quivering as he spoke.

"But this will never do," said Madame, with sternness. More sternly rejoined her kinsman—

"Sortez d'ici!"

"I will send for Père Silas; on the spot I will send for him," she threatened pertinaciously.

"Femme!" cried the Professor, not now in his deep tones, but in his highest and most excited key, "Femme! sortez à l'instant!"

He was roused, and I loved him in his wrath with a passion beyond what I had yet felt.

"What you do is wrong," pursued Madame; "it is an act characteristic of men of your unreliable, imaginative temperament; a step impulsive, injudicious, inconsistent—a proceeding vexatious, and not estimable in the view of persons of steadier and more resolute character."

"You know not what I have of steady and resolute in me," said he, "but you shall see; the event shall teach you. Modeste," he continued, less fiercely, "be gentle, be pitying, be a woman; look at this poor face, and relent. You know I am your friend, and the friend of your friends; in spite of your taunts, you well and deeply know I may be trusted. Of sacrificing myself I made no difficulty, but my heart is pained by what I see; it *must* have and give solace. *Leave me!*"

This time, in the "*leave me*," there was an intonation so bitter, and so imperative, I wondered that even Madame Beck herself could for one moment delay obedience; but she stood firm; she gazed upon him dauntless: she met his eye, forbidding and fixed as stone. She was opening her lips to retort; I saw over all M. Paul's face a quick rising light and fire; I can hardly tell how he managed the movement; it did not seem violent; it kept the form of courtesy; he gave his hand; it scarce touched her, I thought; she ran, she whirled from the room; she was gone, and the door shut, in one second.

The flash of passion was all over very soon. He smiled as he told me to wipe my eyes; he waited quietly till I was calm, dropping from time to time a stilling, solacing word. Ere long I sat beside him once more myself—reassured, not desperate, nor yet desolate; not friendless, not hopeless, not sick of life and seeking death.

"It made you very sad then to lose your friend?" said he.

"It kills me to be forgotten, monsieur," I said. "All these weary days I have not heard from you one word, and I was crushed with the possibility, growing to certainty, that you would depart without saying farewell!"

"Must I tell you what I told Modeste Beck—that you do not know me? Must I show and teach you my character? You *will* have proof that I can be a firm friend? Without clear proof this hand will not lie still in mine, it will not trust my shoulder as a safe stay? Good. The proof is ready. I come to justify myself."

"Say anything, teach anything, prove anything, monsieur: I can listen now."

"Then, in the first place, you must go out with me a good distance into the town. I came on purpose to fetch you."

Without questioning his meaning, or sounding his plan, or offering the semblance of an objection, I retied my bonnet: I was ready.

The route he took was by the boulevards: he several times made me sit down on the seats stationed under the lime-trees; he did not ask if I was tired, but looked and drew his own conclusions.

"All these weary days," said he, repeating my words with a gentle, kindly mimicry of my voice and foreign accent not new from his lips, and of which the playful banter never wounded, not even when coupled, as it often was, with the assertion that, however I might *write* his language, I *spoke* and always should speak it imperfectly and hesitatingly. " 'All these weary days' I have not for one hour forgotten you. Faithful women err in this, that they think themselves the sole faithful of God's creatures. On a very fervent and living truth to myself I too till lately scarce dared count, from any quarter; but—look at me."

I lifted my happy eyes: they *were* happy now, or they would have been no interpreters of my heart.

"Well," said he, after some seconds' scrutiny, "there is no denying that signature: Constancy wrote it: her pen is of iron. Was the record painful?"

"Severely painful," I said, with truth. "Withdraw her hand, monsieur; I can bear its inscribing force no more."

"Elle est toute pâle," said he, speaking to himself; "cette figure là me fait mal."

"Ah! I am not pleasant to look at"——

I could not help saying this; the words came unbidden: I never remember the time when I had not a haunting dread of what might be the degree of my outward deficiency; this dread pressed me at the moment with special force.

A great softness passed upon his countenance; his violet eyes grew suffused and glistening under their deep Spanish lashes; he started up: "Let us walk on."

"Do I displease your eyes *much*?" I took courage to urge: the point had its vital import for me.

He stopped, and gave me a short, strong answer; an answer which silenced, subdued, yet profoundly satisfied. Ever after that I knew what I was for *him*; and what I might be for the rest of the world, I ceased painfully to care. Was it weak to lay so much stress on an opinion about appearance? I fear it might be; I fear it was; but in that case I must avow no light share of weakness. I must own a great fear of displeasing—a strong wish moderately to please M. Paul.

Whither we rambled I scarce knew. Our walk was long, yet seemed short; the path was pleasant, the day lovely, M. Emanuel talked of his voyage—he thought of staying away three years. On his return from Guadaloupe, he looked forward to release from liabilities and a clear course; and what did I purpose doing in the interval of his absence? he asked. I had talked once, he reminded me, of trying to be independent and keeping a little school of my own: had I dropped the idea?

"Indeed I had not: I was doing my best to save what would enable me to put it in practice."

"He did not like leaving me in the Rue Fossette; he feared I should miss him there too much—I should feel desolate—I should grow sad?"——

This was certain; but I promised to do my best to endure.

"Still," said he, speaking low, "there is another objection to your present residence. I should wish to write to you sometimes: it would not be well to have any uncertainty about the safe transmission of letters; and in the Rue Fossette—— in short, our Catholic discipline in certain matters—though justifiable and expedient— might possibly, under peculiar circumstances, become liable to misapplication— perhaps abuse."

"But if you write," said I, "I *must* have your letters; and I *will* have them: ten directors, twenty directresses, shall not keep them from me. I am a Protestant: I will not bear that kind of discipline: monsieur, I *will not*."

"Doucement—doucement," rejoined he: "we will contrive a plan; we have our resources; soyez tranquille."

So speaking, he paused.

We were now returning from the long walk. We had reached the middle of a clean faubourg, where the houses were small, but looked pleasant. It was before the white door-step of a very neat abode that M. Paul had halted.

"I call here," said he.

He did not knock, but taking from his pocket a key, he opened and entered at once. Ushering me in, he shut the door behind us. No servant appeared. The vestibule was small, like the house, but freshly and tastefully painted; its vista closed in a French window with vines trained about the panes, tendrils and green leaves kissing the glass. Silence reigned in this dwelling.

Opening an inner door, M. Paul disclosed a parlour, or salon—very tiny but, I thought, very pretty. Its delicate walls were tinged like a blush; its floor was waxed; a square of brilliant carpet covered its centre; its small round table shone like the mirror over its hearth; there was a little couch, a little chiffonière the half-open, crimson-silk door of which showed porcelain on the shelves; there was a French clock, a lamp; there were ornaments in biscuit china; the recess of the single ample window was filled with a green stand bearing three green flower-pots, each filled with a fine plant glowing in bloom; in one corner appeared a guéridon with a marble top, and upon it a work-box and a glass filled with violets in water. The lattice of this room was open; the outer air breathing through gave freshness, the sweet violets lent fragrance.

"Pretty, pretty place!" said I. M. Paul smiled to see me so pleased.

"Must we sit down here and wait?" I asked in a whisper, half awed by the deep pervading hush.

"We will first peep into one or two other nooks of this nutshell," he replied.

"Dare you take the freedom of going all over the house?" I inquired.

"Yes, I dare," said he quietly.

He led the way. I was shown a little kitchen with a little stove and oven, with few but bright brasses, two chairs and a table. A small cupboard held a diminutive but commodious set of earthenware.

"There is a coffee service of china in the salon," said M. Paul, as I looked at the six green and white dinner-plates, the four dishes, the cups and jugs to match.

Conducted up the narrow but clean staircase, I was permitted a glimpse of two pretty cabinets of sleeping-rooms; finally, I was once more led below, and we halted with a certain ceremony before a larger door than had yet been opened.

Producing a second key, M. Emanuel adjusted it to the lock of this door. He opened, put me in before him.

"Voici!" he cried.

I found myself in a good-sized apartment, scrupulously clean, though bare, compared with those I had hitherto seen. The well-scoured boards were carpetless; it contained two rows of green benches and desks, with an alley down the centre, terminating in an estrade, a teacher's chair and table; behind them a tableau. On

the walls hung two maps; in the windows flowered a few hardy plants; in short, here was a miniature classe—complete, neat, pleasant.

"It is a school then?" said I. "Who keeps it? I never heard of an establishment in this faubourg."

"Will you have the goodness to accept of a few prospectuses for distribution in behalf of a friend of mine?" asked he, taking from his surtout-pocket some quires of these documents, and putting them into my hand. I looked, I read—printed in fair characters—"Externat de demoiselles. Numéro 7, Faubourg Clotilde. Directrice, Mademoiselle Lucy Snowe."

And what did I say to M. Paul Emanuel?

Certain junctures of our lives must always be difficult of recall to memory. Certain points, crises, certain feelings, joys, griefs, and amazements, when reviewed, must strike us as things wildered and whirling, dim as a wheel fast spun.

I can no more remember the thoughts or the words of the ten minutes succeeding this disclosure than I can retrace the experience of my earliest year of life: and yet the first thing distinct to me is the consciousness that I was speaking very fast, repeating over and over again—

"Did you do this, M. Paul? Is this your house? Did you furnish it? Did you get these papers printed? Do you mean me? Am I the directress? Is there another Lucy Snowe? Tell me: say something."

But he would not speak. His pleased silence, his laughing down-look, his attitude, are visible to me now.

"How is it? I must know all—*all*," I cried.

The packet of papers fell on the floor. He had extended his hand, and I had fastened thereon, oblivious of all else.

"Ah! you said I had forgotten you all these weary days," said he. "Poor old Emanuel! These are the thanks he gets for trudging about three mortal weeks from house-painter to upholsterer, from cabinetmaker to charwoman. Lucy and Lucy's cot, the sole thoughts in his head!"

I hardly knew what to do. I first caressed the soft velvet on his cuff, and then I stroked the hand it surrounded, It was his foresight, his goodness, his silent, strong, effective goodness, that overpowered me by their proved reality. It was the assurance of his sleepless interest which broke on me like a light from heaven; it was his— I will dare to say it—his fond, tender look which now shook me indescribably. In the midst of all I forced myself to look at the practical.

"The trouble!" I cried, "and the cost! Had you money, M. Paul?"

"Plenty of money!" said he heartily. "The disposal of my large teaching connection put me in possession of a handsome sum: with part of it I determined to give myself the richest treat that I *have* known or *shall* know. I like this. I have reckoned on this hour day and night lately. I would not come near you, because I would not forestall it. Reserve is neither my virtue nor my vice. If I had put myself into your power, and you had begun with your questions of look and lip—Where have you been, M. Paul? What have you been doing? What is your mystery?—my solitary first and last secret would presently have unravelled itself in your lap. Now," he pursued, "you shall live here and have a school; you shall employ yourself while I am away; you shall think of me sometimes; you shall mind your health and happiness for my sake, and when I come back"——

There he left a blank.

I promised to do all he told me. I promised to work hard and willingly. "I will be your faithful steward," I said; "I trust at your coming the account will be ready. Monsieur, monsieur, you are *too* good!"

In such inadequate language my feelings struggled for expression: they could not get it; speech, brittle and unmalleable, and cold as ice, dissolved or shivered in the effort. He watched me still; he gently raised his hand to stroke my hair; it touched

my lips in passing; I pressed it close, I paid it tribute. He was my king; royal for me had been that hand's bounty; to offer homage was both a joy and a duty.

The afternoon hours were over, and the stiller time of evening shaded the quiet faubourg. M. Paul claimed my hospitality; occupied and afoot since morning, he needed refreshment; he said I should offer him chocolate in my pretty gold and white china service. He went out and ordered what was needful from the restaurant; he placed the small guéridon and two chairs in the balcony outside the French window under the screening vines. With what shy joy I accepted my part as hostess, arranged the salver, served the benefactor-guest!

This balcony was in the rear of the house, the gardens of the faubourg were round us, fields extended beyond. The air was still, mild, and fresh. Above the poplars, the laurels, the cypresses, and the roses, looked up a moon so lovely and so halcyon, the heart trembled under her smile; a star shone subject beside her, with the unemulous ray of pure love. In a large garden near us, a jet rose from a well, and a pale statue leaned over the play of waters.

M. Paul talked to me. His voice was so modulated that it mixed harmonious with the silver whisper, the gush, the musical sigh, in which light breeze, fountain, and foliage intoned their lulling vesper.

Happy hour—stay one moment! droop those plumes, rest those wings; incline to mine that brow of Heaven! White Angel! let thy light linger; leave its reflection on succeeding clouds; bequeath its cheer to that time which needs a ray in retrospect!

Our meal was simple: the chocolate, the rolls, the plate of fresh summer fruit, cherries and strawberries bedded in green leaves, formed the whole; but it was what we both liked better than a feast, and I took a delight inexpressible in tending M. Paul. I asked him whether his friends, Père Silas and Madame Beck, knew what he had done—whether they had seen my house?

"Mon amie," said he, "none knows what I have done save you and myself: the pleasure is consecrated to us two, unshared and unprofaned. To speak truth, there has been to me in this matter a refinement of enjoyment I would not make vulgar by communication. Besides" (smiling), "I wanted to prove to Miss Lucy that I *could* keep a secret. How often has she taunted me with lack of dignified reserve and needful caution! How many times has she saucily insinuated that all my affairs are the secret of Polichinelle!"

This was true enough: I had not spared him on this point, nor perhaps on any other that was assailable. Magnificent-minded, grand-hearted, dear, faulty little man. You deserved candour, and from me always had it.

Continuing my queries, I asked to whom the house belonged, who was my landlord, the amount of my rent. He instantly gave me these particulars in writing; he had foreseen and prepared all things.

The house was not M. Paul's—that I guessed; he was hardly the man to become a proprietor; I more than suspected in him a lamentable absence of the saving faculty; he could get, but not keep; he needed a treasurer. The tenement, then, belonged to a citizen in the Basse-Ville—a man of substance, M. Paul said; he startled me by adding: "a friend of yours, Miss Lucy, a person who has a most respectful regard for you." And, to my pleasant surprise, I found the landlord was none other than M. Miret, the short-tempered and kind-hearted bookseller, who had so kindly found me a seat that eventful night in the park. It seems M. Miret was in his station rich as well as much respected, and possessed several houses in this faubourg; the rent was moderate, scarce half of what it would have been for a house of equal size near the centre of Villette.

"And then," observed M. Paul, "should Fortune not favour you, though I think she will, I have the satisfaction to think you are in good hands; M. Miret will not be extortionate: the first year's rent you have already in your savings; afterwards Miss Lucy must trust God and herself. But now, what will you do for pupils?"

"I must distribute my prospectuses."

"Right! By way of losing no time, I gave one to M. Miret yesterday. Should you object to beginning with three petites bourgeoises, the Demoiselles Miret? They are at your service."

"Monsieur, you forget nothing; you are wonderful. Object? It would become me indeed to object! I suppose I hardly expect at the outset to number aristocrats in my little day-school; I care not if they never come. l shall be proud to receive M. Miret's daughters."

"Besides these," pursued he, "another pupil offers, who will come daily to take lessons in English; and as she is rich, she will pay handsomely. I mean my god-daughter and ward, Justine Marie Sauveur."

What is in a name?—what in three words? Till this moment I had listened with living joy—I had answered with gleeful quickness; a name froze me; three words struck me mute. The effect could not be hidden, and indeed I scarce tried to hide it.

"What now?" said M. Paul.

"Nothing."

"Nothing! Your countenance changes; your colour and your very eyes fade. Nothing! You must be ill; you have some suffering; tell me what?"

I had nothing to tell.

He drew his chair nearer. He did not grow vexed, though I continued silent and icy. He tried to win a word: he entreated with perseverance, he waited with patience.

"Justine Marie is a good girl," said he, "docile and amiable; not quick—but you will like her."

"I think not. I think she must not come here." Such was my speech.

"Do you wish to puzzle me? Do you know her? But, in truth, there *is* something. Again you are pale as that statue. Rely on Paul Carlos: tell him the grief."

His chair touched mine; his hand, quietly advanced, turned me towards him. "Do you know Justine Marie?" said he again.

The name re-pronounced by his lips overcame me unaccountably. It did not prostrate—no, it stirred me up, running with haste and heat through my veins—recalling an hour of quick pain, many days and nights of heart-sickness. Near me as he now sat, strongly and closely as he had long twined his life in mine—far as had progressed, and near as was achieved our minds' and affections' assimilation—the very suggestion of interference, of heart-separation, could be heard only with a fermenting excitement, an impetuous throe, a disdainful resolve, an ire, a resistance of which no human eye or cheek could hide the flame, nor any truth-accustomed human tongue curb the cry.

"I want to tell you something," I said; "I want to tell you all."

"Speak, Lucy; come near; speak. Who prizes you, if I do not? Who is your friend, if not Emanuel? Speak?"

I spoke. All escaped from my lips. I lacked not words now; fast I narrated; fluent I told my tale; it streamed on my tongue. I went back to the night in the park; I mentioned the medicated draught—why it was given—its goading effect—how it had torn rest from under my head, shaken me from my couch, carried me abroad with the lure of a vivid yet solemn fancy—a summer night solitude on turf, under trees, near a deep, cool lakelet. I told the scene realised; the crowd, the masques, the music, the lamps, the splendours, the guns booming afar, the bells sounding on high. All I had encountered I detailed, all I had recognised, heard, and seen; how I had beheld and watched himself; how I listened, how much heard, what conjectured; the whole history, in brief, summoned to his confidence, rushed thither truthful, literal, ardent, bitter.

Still as I narrated, instead of checking, he incited me to proceed; he spurred me by the gesture, the smile, the half-word. Before I had half done, he held both my hands, he consulted my eyes with a most piercing glance: there was something in

his face which tended neither to calm nor to put me down; he forgot his own doctrine, he forsook his own system of repression when I most challenged its exercise. I think I deserved strong reproof; but when have we our deserts? I merited severity; he looked indulgence. To my very self I seemed imperious and unreasonable, for I forbade Justine Marie my door and roof; he smiled, betraying delight. Warm, jealous, and haughty, I knew not till now that my nature had such a mood; he gathered me near his heart. I was full of faults: he took them and me all home. For the moment of utmost mutiny, he reserved the one deep spell of peace. These words caressed my ear—

"Lucy, take my love. One day share my life. Be my dearest, first on earth."

We walked back to the Rue Fossette by moonlight—such moonlight as fell on Eden—shining through the shades of the Great Garden, and haply gilding a path glorious for a step divine—a Presence nameless. Once in their lives some men and women go back to these first fresh days of our great Sire and Mother—taste that grand morning's dew—bathe in its sunrise.

In the course of the walk I was told how Justine Marie Sauveur had always been regarded with the affection proper to a daughter—how, with M. Paul's consent, she had been affianced for months to one Heinrich Mühler, a wealthy young German merchant, and was to be married in the course of a year. Some of M. Emanuel's relations and connections would, indeed, it seems, have liked him to marry her with a view to securing her fortune in the family; but to himself the scheme was repugnant, and the idea totally inadmissible.

We reached Madame Beck's door. Jean Baptiste's clock tolled nine. At this hour, in this house, eighteen months since, had this man at my side bent before me, looked into my face and eyes, and arbitered my destiny. This very evening he had again stooped, gazed, and decreed. How different the look—how far otherwise the fate!

He deemed me born under his star: he seemed to have spread over me its beam like a banner. Once—unknown and unloved, I held him harsh and strange; the low stature, the wiry make, the angles, the darkness, the manner, displeased me. Now, penetrated with his influence, and living by his affection, having his worth by intellect, and his goodness by heart—I preferred him before all humanity.

We parted: he gave me his pledge, and then his farewell. We parted: the next day—he sailed.

Chapter XLII

FINIS

MAN cannot prophesy. Love is no oracle. Fear sometimes imagines a vain thing. Those years of absence! How had I sickened over their anticipation! The woe they must bring seemed certain as death. I knew the nature of their course: I never had doubt how it would harrow as it went. The Juggernaut on his car towered there a grim load. Seeing him draw nigh, burying his broad wheels in the oppressed soil— I, the prostrate votary—felt beforehand the annihilating craunch.

Strange to say—strange, yet true, and owning many parallels in life's experience— that anticipatory craunch proved all—yes—nearly *all* the torture. The great Juggernaut, in his great chariot, drew on lofty, loud, and sullen. He passed quietly, like a shadow sweeping the sky at noon. Nothing but a chilling dimness was seen or felt. I looked up. Chariot and demon charioteer were gone by; the votary still lived.

M. Emanuel was away three years. Reader, they were the three happiest years of my life. Do you scout the paradox? Listen.

I commenced my school; I worked—I worked hard. I deemed myself the steward of his property, and determined, God willing, to render a good account. Pupils

came—burghers at first—a higher class ere long. About the middle of the second year an unexpected chance threw into my hands an additional hundred pounds: one day I received from England a letter containing that sum. It came from Mr. Marchmont, the cousin and heir of my dear and dead mistress. He was just recovering from a dangerous illness; the money was a peace-offering to his conscience, reproaching him in the matter of, I know not what, papers or memoranda found after his kinswoman's death—naming or recommending Lucy Snowe. Mrs. Barrett had given him my address. How far his conscience had been sinned against I never inquired. I asked no questions, but took the cash and made it useful.

With this hundred pounds I ventured to take the house adjoining mine. I would not leave that which M. Paul had chosen, in which he had left and where he expected again to find me. My externat became a pensionnat; that also prospered.

The secret of my success did not lie so much in myself, in any endowment, any power of mine, as in a new state of circumstances, a wonderfully changed life, a relieved heart. The spring which moved my energies lay far away beyond seas, in an Indian isle. At parting, I had been left a legacy; such a thought for the present, such a hope for the future, such a motive for a persevering, a laborious, an enterprising, a patient and a brave course—I *could* not flag. Few things shook me now; few things had importance to vex, intimidate, or depress me: most things pleased— mere trifles had a charm.

Do not think that this genial flame sustained itself, or lived wholly on a bequeathed hope or a parting promise. A generous provider supplied bounteous fuel. I was spared all chill, all stint; I was not suffered to fear penury; I was not tried with suspense. By every vessel he wrote; he wrote as he gave and as he loved, in full- handed, full-hearted plenitude. He wrote because he liked to write; he did not abridge, because he cared not to abridge. He sat down, he took pen and paper, because he loved Lucy and had much to say to her; because he was faithful and thoughtful, because he was tender and true. There was no sham and no cheat, and no hollow unreal in him. Apology never dropped her slippery oil on his lips—never proffered, by his pen, her coward feints and paltry nullities: he would give neither a stone, nor an excuse—neither a scorpion, nor a disappointment; his letters were real food that nourished, living water that refreshed.

And was I grateful? God knows! I believe that scarce a living being so remembered, so sustained, dealt with in kind so constant, honourable and noble, could be otherwise than grateful to the death.

Adherent to his own religion (in him was not the stuff of which is made the facile apostate), he freely left me my pure faith. He did not tease nor tempt. He said—

"Remain a Protestant. My little English Puritan, I love Protestantism in you. I own its severe charm. There is something in its ritual I cannot receive myself, but it is the sole creed for 'Lucy.' "

All Rome could not put into him bigotry, nor the Propaganda itself make him a real Jesuit. He was born honest, and not false—artless, and not cunning—a free man, and not a slave. His tenderness had rendered him ductile in a priest's hands, his affection, his devotedness, his sincere pious enthusiasm blinded his kind eyes sometimes, made him abandon justice to himself to do the work of craft, and serve the ends of selfishness; but these are faults so rare to find, so costly to their owner to indulge, we scarce know whether they will not one day be reckoned amongst the jewels.

And now the three years are past: M. Emanuel's return is fixed. It is Autumn; he is to be with me ere the mists of November come. My school flourishes, my house is ready: I have made him a little library, filled its shelves with the books he left in my care: I have cultivated out of love for him (I was naturally no florist)

the plants he preferred, and some of them are yet in bloom. I thought I loved him when he went away; I love him now in another degree; he is more my own.

The sun passes the equinox; the days shorten, the leaves grow sere; but—he is coming.

Frosts appear at night; November has sent his fogs in advance; the wind takes its autumn moan; but—he is coming.

The skies hang full and dark—a rack sails from the west; the clouds cast themselves into strange forms—arches and broad radiations; there rise resplendent mornings—glorious, royal, purple as monarch in his state; the heavens are one flame; so wild are they, they rival battle at its thickest—so bloody, they shame Victory in her pride. I know some signs of the sky; I have noted them ever since childhood. God, watch that sail! Oh! guard it!

The wind shifts to the west. Peace, peace, Banshee—"keening" at every window! It will rise—it will swell—it shrieks out long: wander as I may through the house this night, I cannot lull the blast. The advancing hours make it strong: by midnight, all sleepless watchers hear and fear a wild south-west storm.

That storm roared frenzied for seven days. It did not cease till the Atlantic was strewn with wrecks: it did not lull till the deeps had gorged their full of sustenance. Not till the destroying angel of tempest had achieved his perfect work would he fold the wings whose waft was thunder—the tremor of whose plumes was storm.

Peace, be still! Oh! a thousand weepers, praying in agony on waiting shores, listened for that voice, but it was not uttered—not uttered till, when the hush came, some could not feel it: till, when the sun returned, his light was night to some!

Here pause: pause at once. There is enough said. Trouble no quiet, kind heart; leave sunny imaginations hope. Let it be theirs to conceive the delight of joy born again fresh out of great terror, the rapture of rescue from peril, the wondrous reprieve from dread, the fruition of return. Let them picture union and a happy succeeding life.

Madame Beck prospered all the days of her life; so did Père Silas; Madame Walravens fulfilled her ninetieth year before she died. Farewell.

The Professor

by Charlotte Brontë

Chapter I

INTRODUCTORY

THE other day, in looking over my papers, I found in my desk the following copy of a letter, sent by me a year since to an old school acquaintance:

"DEAR CHARLES,—I think when you and I were at Eton together, we were neither of us what could be called popular characters: you were a sarcastic, observant, shrewd, cold-blooded creature: my own portrait I will not attempt to draw, but I cannot recollect that it was a strikingly attractive one—can you? What animal magnetism drew thee and me together I know not; certainly I never experienced anything of the Pylades and Orestes sentiment for you, and I have reason to believe that you, on your part, were equally free from all romantic regard to me. Still, out of school hours we walked and talked continually together; when the theme of conversation was our companions or our masters, we understood each other, and when I recurred to some sentiment of affection, some vague love of an excellent or beautiful object, whether in animate or inanimate nature, your sardonic coldness did not move me. I felt myself superior to that check *then* as I do *now*.

"It is a long time since I wrote to you, and a still longer time since I saw you. Chancing to take up a newspaper of your county the other day, my eye fell upon your name. I began to think of old times; to run over the events which have transpired since we separated; and I sat down and commenced this letter. What you have been doing I know not; but you shall hear, if you choose to listen, how the world has wagged with me.

"First, after leaving Eton, I had an interview with my maternal uncles, Lord Tynedale and the Hon. John Seacombe. They asked me if I would enter the Church, and my uncle the nobleman offered me the living of Seacombe, which is in his gift, if I would; then my other uncle, Mr. Seacombe, hinted that when I became rector of Seacombe-cum-Scaife, I might perhaps be allowed to take, as mistress of my house and head of my parish, one of my six cousins, his daughters, all of whom I greatly dislike.

"I declined both the Church and matrimony. A good clergyman is a good thing, but I should have made a very bad one. As to the wife— oh, how like a nightmare is the thought of being bound for life to one of my cousins! No doubt they are accomplished and pretty; but not an accomplishment, not a charm of theirs, touches a chord in my bosom. To think of passing the winter evenings by the parlour fireside of Seacombe Rectory alone with one of them—for instance, the large and well-modelled

statue, Sarah—no; I should be a bad husband, under such circumstances, as well as a bad clergyman.

"When I had declined my uncles' offers they asked me 'what I intended to do?' I said I should reflect. They reminded me that I had no fortune, and no expectation of any, and, after a considerable pause, Lord Tynedale demanded sternly, 'Whether I had thoughts of following my father's steps and engaging in trade?' Now I had no thought of the sort. I do not think that my turn of mind qualifies me to make a good tradesman; my taste, my ambition does not lie in that way; but such was the scorn expressed in Lord Tynedale's countenance as he pronounced the word *trade*—such the contemptuous sarcasm of his tone—that I was instantly decided. My father was but a name to me, yet that name I did not like to hear mentioned with a sneer to my very face. I answered then, with haste and warmth, 'I cannot do better than follow in my father's steps; yes, I will be a tradesman.' My uncles did not remonstrate; they and I parted with mutual disgust. In reviewing this transaction, I find that I was quite right to shake off the burden of Tynedale's patronage, but a fool to offer my shoulders instantly for the reception of another burden— one which might be more intolerable, and which certainly was yet untried.

"I wrote instantly to Edward—you know Edward—my only brother, ten years my senior, married to a rich mill-owner's daughter, and now possessor of the mill and business which was my father's before he failed. You are aware that my father—once reckoned a Crœsus of wealth— became bankrupt a short time previous to his death, and that my mother lived in destitution for some six months after him, unhelped by her aristocratical brothers, whom she had mortally offended by her union with Crimsworth, the ——shire manufacturer. At the end of the six months she brought me into the world, and then herself left it, without, I should think, much regret, as it contained little hope or comfort for her.

"My father's relations took charge of Edward, as they did of me, till I was nine years old. At that period it chanced that the representation of an important borough in our county fell vacant; Mr. Seacombe stood for it. My uncle Crimsworth, an astute mercantile man, took the opportunity of writing a fierce letter to the candidate, stating that if he and Lord Tynedale did not consent to do something towards the support of their sister's orphan children, he would expose their relentless and malignant conduct towards that sister, and do his best to turn the circumstances against Mr. Seacombe's election. That gentleman and Lord T. knew well enough that the Crimsworths were an unscrupulous and determined race; they knew also that they had influence in the borough of X——; and, making a virtue of necessity, they consented to defray the expenses of my education. I was sent to Eton, where I remained ten years, during which space of time Edward and I never met. He, when he grew up, entered into trade, and pursued his calling with such diligence, ability, and success, that now, in his thirtieth year, he was fast making a fortune. Of this I was apprised by the occasional short letters I received from him, some three or four times a year; which said letters never concluded without some expression of determined enmity against the house of Sea- combe, and some reproach to me for living, as he said, on the bounty of that house. At first, while still in boyhood, I could not understand why, as I had no parents, I should not be indebted to my uncles Tynedale and Seacombe for my education; but as I grew up, and heard by degrees of the persevering hostility, the hatred till death evinced by them against my father—of the sufferings of my mother—of all the wrongs, in short,

of our house—then did I conceive shame of the dependence in which I lived, and form a resolution no more to take bread from hands which had refused to minister to the necessities of my dying mother. It was by these feelings I was influenced when I refused the Rectory of Seacombe, and the union with one of my patrician cousins.

"An irreparable breach thus being effected between my uncles and myself, I wrote to Edward; told him what had occurred, and informed him of my intention to follow his steps and be a tradesman. I asked, moreover, if he could give me employment. His answer expressed no approbation of my conduct, but he said I might come down to ——shire, if I liked, and he would 'see what could be done in the way of furnishing me with work.' I repressed all—even *mental* comment on his note—packed my trunk and carpet-bag, and started for the North directly.

"After two days' travelling (railroads were not then in existence) I arrived, one wet October afternoon, in the town of X——. I had always understood that Edward lived in this town, but on inquiry I found that it was only Mr. Crimsworth's mill and warehouse which were situated in the smoky atmosphere of Bigben Close; his *residence* lay four miles out, in the country.

"It was late in the evening when I alighted at the gates of the habitation designated to me as my brother's. As I advanced up the avenue, I could see through the shades of twilight, and the dark gloomy mists which deepened those shades, that the house was large, and the grounds surrounding it sufficiently spacious. I paused a moment on the lawn in front, and leaning my back against a tall tree which rose in the centre, I gazed with interest on the exterior of Crimsworth Hall.

" 'Edward is rich,' thought I to myself. 'I believed him to be doing well—but I did not know he was master of a mansion like this.' Cutting short all marvelling, speculation, conjecture, etc., I advanced to the front door and rang. A man-servant opened it—I announced myself—he relieved me of my wet cloak and carpet-bag, and ushered me into a room furnished as a library, where there was a bright fire and candles burning on the table; he informed me that his master was not yet returned from X—— market, but that he would certainly be at home in the course of half-an-hour.

"Being left to myself, I took the stuffed easy-chair, covered with red morocco, which stood by the fireside, and while my eyes watched the flames dart from the glowing coals, and the cinders fall at intervals on the hearth, my mind busied itself in conjectures concerning the meeting about to take place. Amidst much that was doubtful in the subject of these conjectures, there was one thing tolerably certain—I was in no danger of encountering severe disappointment; from this, the moderation of my expectations guaranteed me. I anticipated no overflowings of fraternal tenderness: Edward's letters had always been such as to prevent the engendering or harbouring of delusions of this sort. Still, as I sat awaiting his arrival, I felt eager—very eager—I cannot tell you why; my hand, so utterly a stranger to the grasp of a kindred hand, clenched itself to repress the tremor with which impatience would fain have shaken it.

"I thought of my uncles; and as I was engaged in wondering whether Edward's indifference would equal the cold disdain I had always experienced from them, I heard the avenue gates open: wheels approached the house; Mr. Crimsworth was arrived; and after the lapse of some minutes, and a brief dialogue between himself and his servant in the hall, his tread drew near the library door—that tread alone announced the master of the house.

"I still retained some confused recollection of Edward as he was ten years ago—a tall, wiry, raw youth; *now*, as I rose from my seat and turned towards the library door, I saw a fine-looking and powerful man, light-complexioned, well-made, and of athletic proportions; the first glance made me aware of an air of promptitude and sharpness, shown as well in his movements as in his port, his eye, and the general expression of his face. He greeted me with brevity, and, in the moment of shaking hands, scanned me from head to foot; he took his seat in the morocco-covered arm-chair, and motioned me to another seat.

" 'I expected you would have called at the counting-house in the Close,' said he; and his voice, I noticed, had an abrupt accent, probably habitual to him; he spoke also with a guttural northern tone, which sounded harsh in my ears, accustomed to the silvery utterance of the South.

" 'The landlord of the inn, where the coach stopped, directed me here,' said I. 'I doubted at first the accuracy of his information, not being aware that you had such a residence as this.'

" 'Oh, it is all right!' he replied, 'only I was kept half-an-hour behind time, waiting for you—that is all. I thought you must be coming by the eight o'clock coach.'

"I expressed regret that he had had to wait; he made no answer, but stirred the fire, as if to cover a movement of impatience; then he scanned me again.

"I felt an inward satisfaction that I had not, in the first moment of meeting, betrayed any warmth, any enthusiasm; that I had saluted this man with a quiet and steady phlegm.

" 'Have you quite broken with Tynedale and Seacombe?' he asked hastily.

" 'I do not think I shall have any further communication with them; my refusal of their proposals will, I fancy, operate as a barrier against all future intercourse.'

" 'Why,' said he, 'I may as well remind you at the very outset of our connection, that "no man can serve two masters." Acquaintance with Lord Tynedale will be incompatible with assistance from me.' There was a kind of gratuitous menace in his eye as he looked at me in finishing this observation.

"Feeling no disposition to reply to him, I contented myself with an inward speculation on the differences which exist in the constitution of men's minds. I do not know what inference Mr. Crimsworth drew from my silence—whether he considered it a symptom of contumacity or an evidence of my being cowed by his peremptory manner. After a long and hard stare at me, he rose sharply from his seat.

" 'To-morrow,' said he, 'I shall call your attention to some other points; but now it is supper time, and Mrs. Crimsworth is probably waiting; will you come?'

"He strode from the room, and I followed. In crossing the hall, I wondered what Mrs. Crimsworth might be. 'Is she,' thought I, 'as alien to what I like as Tynedale, Seacombe, the Misses Seacombe—as the affectionate relative now striding before me? or is she better than these? Shall I, in conversing with her, feel free to show something of my real nature; or——' Further conjectures were arrested by my entrance into the dining-room.

"A lamp burning under a shade of ground-glass, showed a handsome apartment, wainscoted with oak; supper was laid on the table; by the fireplace, standing as if waiting our entrance, appeared a lady; she was

young, tall, and well-shaped; her dress was handsome and fashionable; so much my first glance sufficed to ascertain. A gay salutation passed between her and Mr. Crimsworth; she chid him, half playfully, half poutingly, for being late; her voice (I always take voices into the account in judging of character) was lively—it indicated, I thought, good animal spirits. Mr. Crimsworth soon checked her animated scolding with a kiss—a kiss that still told of the bridegroom (they had not yet been married a year); she took her seat at the supper-table in first-rate spirits. Perceiving me, she begged my pardon for not noticing me before, and then shook hands with me, as ladies do when a flow of good-humour disposes them to be cheerful to all, even the most indifferent of their acquaintance. It was now further obvious to me that she had a good complexion, and features sufficiently marked but agreeable; her hair was red—quite red. She and Edward talked much, always in a vein of playful contention; she was vexed, or pretended to be vexed, that he had that day driven a vicious horse in the gig, and he made light of her fears. Sometimes she appealed to me.

" 'Now, Mr. William, isn't it absurd in Edward to talk so? He says he will drive Jack, and no other horse, and the brute has thrown him twice already.'

"She spoke with a kind of lisp, not disagreeable, but childish. I soon saw also that there was more than girlish—a somewhat infantine expression in her by no means small features; this lisp and expression were, I have no doubt, a charm in Edward's eyes, and would be so to those of most men, but they were not to mine. I sought her eye, desirous to read there the intelligence which I could not discern in her face or hear in her conversation; it was merry, rather small; by turns I saw vivacity, vanity, coquetry, look out through its irid, but I watched in vain for a glimpse of soul. I am no Oriental; white necks, carmine lips and cheeks, clusters of bright curls, do not suffice for me without that Promethean spark which will live after the roses and lilies are faded, the burnished hair grown grey. In sunshine, in prosperity, the flowers are very well; but how many wet days are there in life—November seasons of disaster, when a man's hearth and home would be cold indeed, without the clear, cheering gleam of intellect.

"Having perused the fair page of Mrs. Crimsworth's face, a deep, involuntary sigh announced my disappointment; she took it as a homage to her beauty, and Edward, who was evidently proud of his rich and handsome young wife, threw on me a glance—half ridicule, half ire.

"I turned from them both, and gazing wearily round the room, I saw two pictures set in the oak panelling—one on each side the mantelpiece. Ceasing to take part in the bantering conversation that flowed on between Mr. and Mrs. Crimsworth, I bent my thoughts to the examination of these pictures. They were portraits—a lady and a gentleman, both costumed in the fashion of twenty years ago. The gentleman was in the shade. I could not see him well. The lady had the benefit of a full beam from the softly shaded lamp. I presently recognised her; I had seen this picture before in childhood; it was my mother; that and the compainion picture being the only heirlooms saved out of the sale of my father's property.

"The face, I remembered, had pleased me as a boy, but *then* I did not understand it; *now* I knew how rare that class of face is in the world, and I appreciated keenly its thoughtful, yet gentle expression. The serious grey eye possessed for me a strong charm, as did certain lines in the features indicative of most true and tender feeling. I was sorry it was only a picture.

"I soon left Mr. and Mrs. Crimsworth to themselves; a servant conducted me to my bedroom; in closing my chamber door, I shut out all intruders— you, Charles, as well as the rest.—Good-bye for the present.

WILLIAM CRIMSWORTH."

To this letter I never got an answer; before my old friend received it, he had accepted a government appointment in one of the colonies, and was already on his way to the scene of his official labours. What has become of him since, I know not.

The leisure time I have at command, and which I intended to employ for his private benefit, I shall now dedicate to that of the public at large. My narrative is not exciting, and above all, not marvellous; but it may interest some individuals, who, having toiled in the same vocation as myself, will find in my experience frequent reflections of their own. The above letter will serve as an introduction. I now proceed.

Chapter II

A FINE October morning succeeded to the foggy evening that had witnessed my first introduction to Crimsworth Hall. I was early up and walking in the large park- like meadow surrounding the house. The autumn sun rising over the ——shire hills, disclosed a pleasant country; woods brown and mellow varied the fields from which the harvest had been lately carried; a river, gliding between the woods, caught on its surface the somewhat cold gleam of the October sun and sky; at frequent intervals along the banks of the river, tall, cylindrical chimneys, almost like slender round towers, indicated the factories which the trees half concealed; here and there mansions, similar to Crimsworth Hall, occupied agreeable sites on the hillside; the country wore, on the whole, a cheerful, active, fertile look. Steam, trade, machinery, had long banished from it all romance and seclusion. At a distance of five miles, a valley, opening between the low hills, held in its cups the great town of X——. A dense, permanent vapour brooded over this locality—there lay Edward's "Concern."

I forced my eye to scrutinise this prospect, I forced my mind to dwell on it for a time, and when I found that it communicated no pleasurable emotion to my heart—that it stirred in me none of the hopes a man ought to feel, when he sees laid before him the scene of his life's career—I said to myself "William, you are a rebel against circumstances; you are a fool, and know not what you want; you have chosen trade and you shall be a tradesman. Look!" I continued mentally— "Look at the sooty smoke in that hollow, and know that there is your post! There you cannot dream, you cannot speculate and theorise—there you shall out and work!"

Thus self-schooled, I returned to the house. My brother was in the breakfast- room. I met him collectedly—I could not meet him cheerfully; he was standing on the rug, his back to the fire—how much did I read in the expression of his eye as my glance encountered his, when I advanced to bid him good morning; how much that was contradictory to my nature! He said "Good morning" abruptly and nodded, and then he snatched, rather than took, a newspaper from the table, and began to read it with the air of a master who seizes a pretext to escape the bore of conversing with an underling. It was well I had taken a resolution to endure for a time, or his

manner would have gone far to render insupportable the disgust I had just been endeavouring to subdue. I looked at him: I measured his robust frame and powerful proportions; I saw my own reflection in the mirror over the mantelpiece; I amused myself with comparing the two pictures. In face I resembled him, though I was not so handsome; my features were less regular; I had a darker eye, and a broader brow—in form I was greatly inferior—thinner, slighter, not so tall. As an animal, Edward excelled me far; should he prove as paramount in mind as in person I must be a slave—for I must expect from him no lion-like generosity to one weaker than himself; his cold, avaricious eye, his stern, forbidding manner told me he would not spare. Had I then force of mind to cope with him? I did not know; I had never been tried.

Mrs. Crimsworth's entrance diverted my thoughts for a moment. She looked well, dressed in white, her face and her attire shining in morning and bridal freshness. I addressed her with the degree of ease her last night's careless gaiety seemed to warrant, but she replied with coolness and restraint: her husband had tutored her; she was not to be too familiar with his clerk.

As soon as breakfast was over Mr. Crimsworth intimated to me that they were bringing the gig round to the door, and that in five minutes he should expect me to be ready to go down with him to X——. I did not keep him waiting; we were soon dashing at a rapid rate along the road. The horse he drove was the same vicious animal about which Mrs. Crimsworth had expressed her fears the night before. Once or twice Jack seemed disposed to turn restive, but a vigorous and determined application of the whip from the ruthless hand of his master soon compelled him to submission, and Edward's dilated nostril expressed his triumph in the result of the contest; he scarcely spoke to me during the whole of the brief drive, only opening his lips at intervals to damn his horse.

X—— was all stir and bustle when we entered it; we left the clean streets where there were dwelling-houses and shops, churches, and public buildings; we left all these, and turned down to a region of mills and warehouses; thence we passed through two massive gates into a great paved yard, and we were in Bigben Close, and the mill was before us, vomiting soot from its long chimney, and quivering through its thick brick walls with the commotion of its iron bowels. Workpeople were passing to and fro; a waggon was being laden with pieces. Mr. Crimsworth looked from side to side, and seemed at one glance to comprehend all that was going on; he alighted, and leaving his horse and gig to the care of a man who hastened to take the reins from his hand, he bid me follow him to the counting-house. We entered it; a very different place from the parlours of Crimsworth Hall—a place for business, with a bare, planked floor, a safe, two high desks and stools, and some chairs. A person was seated at one of the desks, who took off his square cap when Mr. Crimsworth entered, and in an instant was again absorbed in his occupation of writing or calculating—I know not which.

Mr. Crimsworth, having removed his mackintosh, sat down by the fire. I remained standing near the hearth; he said presently:

"Steighton, you may leave the room; I have some business to transact with this gentleman. Come back when you hear the bell."

The individual at the desk rose and departed, closing the door as he went out. Mr. Crimsworth stirred the fire, then folded his arms, and sat a moment thinking, his lips compressed, his brow knit. I had nothing to do but to watch him—how well his features were cut! what a handsome man he was! Whence, then, came that air of contraction—that now narrow and hard aspect on his forehead, in all his lineaments?

Turning to me he began abruptly:

"You are come down to ——shire to learn to be a tradesman?"

"Yes, I am."

"Have you made up your mind on the point? Let me know that at once."

"Yes."

"Well, I am not bound to help you, but I have a place here vacant, if you are qualified for it. I will take you on trial. What can you do? Do you know anything besides that useless trash of college learning—Greek, Latin, and so forth?"

"I have studied mathematics."

"Stuff! I dare say you have."

"I can read and write French and German."

"Hum!" He reflected a moment, then opening a drawer in a desk near him took out a letter, and gave it to me.

"Can you read that?" he asked.

It was a German commercial letter; I translated it; I could not tell whether he was gratified or not—his countenance remained fixed.

"It is well," he said, after a pause, "that you are acquainted with something useful, something that may enable you to earn your board and lodging: since you know French and German, I will take you as second clerk to manage the foreign correspondence of the house. I shall give you a good salary—£90 a year—and now," he continued, raising his voice, "hear once for all what I have to say about our relationship, and all that sort of humbug! I must have no nonsense on that point; it would never suit me. I shall excuse you nothing on the plea of being my brother; if I find you stupid, negligent, dissipated, idle, or possessed of any faults detrimental to the interests of the house, I shall dismiss you as I would any other clerk. Ninety pounds a year are good wages, and I expect to have the full value of my money out of you; remember, too, that things are on a practical footing in my establishment—business-like habits, feelings, and ideas, suit me best. Do you understand?"

"Partly," I replied. "I suppose you mean that I am to do my work for my wages; not to expect favour from you, and not to depend on you for any help but what I earn; that suits me exactly, and on these terms I will consent to be your clerk."

I turned on my heel, and walked to the window; this time I did not consult his face to learn his opinion: what it was I did not know, nor did I then care. After a silence of some minutes he recommenced:

"You perhaps expect to be accommodated with apartments at Crimsworth Hall, and to go and come with me in the gig. I wish you, however, to be aware that such an arrangement would be quite inconvenient to me. I like to have the seat in my gig at liberty for any gentleman whom for business reasons I may wish to take down to the hall for a night or so. You will seek out lodgings in X——."

Quitting the window, I walked back to the hearth.

"Of course I shall seek out lodgings in X——," I answered. "It would not suit me either to lodge at Crimsworth Hall."

My tone was quiet. I always speak quietly. Yet Mr. Crimsworth's blue eye became incensed; he took his revenge rather oddly. Turning to me he said bluntly:

"You are poor enough, I suppose; how do you expect to live till your quarter's salary becomes due?"

"I shall get on," said I.

"How do you expect to live?" he repeated in a louder voice.

"As I can, Mr. Crimsworth."

"Get into debt at your peril! that's all," he answered. "For aught I know you may have extravagant aristocratic habits: if you have, drop them; I tolerate nothing of the sort here, and I will never give you a shilling extra, whatever liabilities you may incur—mind that."

"Yes, Mr. Crimsworth, you will find I have a good memory."

I said no more. I did not think the time was come for much parley. I had an instinctive feeling that it would be folly to let one's temper effervesce often with such a man as Edward. I said to myself, "I will place my cup under this continual dropping; it shall stand there still and steady; when full, it will run over of itself—

meantime patience. Two things are certain. I am capable of performing the work Mr. Crimsworth has set me; I can earn my wages conscientiously, and those wages are sufficient to enable me to live. As to the fact of my brother assuming towards me the bearing of a proud, harsh master, the fault is his, not mine; and shall his injustice, his bad feeling, turn me at once aside from the path I have chosen? No; at least, ere I deviate, I will advance far enough to see whither my career tends. As yet I am only pressing in at the entrance—a strait gate enough; it ought to have a good terminus.'' While I thus reasoned, Mr. Crimsworth rang a bell; his first clerk, the individual dismissed previously to our conference, re-entered.

"Mr. Steighton," said he, "show Mr. William the letters from Voss Brothers, and give him English copies of the answers; he will translate them."

Mr. Steighton, a man of about thirty-five, with a face at once sly and heavy, hastened to execute this order; he laid the letters on the desk, and I was soon seated at it, and engaged in rendering the English answers into German. A sentiment of keen pleasure accompanied this first effort to earn my own living—a sentiment neither poisoned nor weakened by the presence of the taskmaster, who stood and watched me for some time as I wrote. I thought he was trying to read my character, but I felt as secure against his scrutiny as if I had had on a casque with the visor down—or rather I showed him my countenance with the confidence that one would show an unlearned man a letter written in Greek; he might see lines, and trace characters, but he could make nothing of them; my nature was not his nature, and its signs were to him like the words of an unknown tongue. Ere long he turned away abruptly, as if baffled, and left the counting-house; he returned to it but twice in the course of that day; each time he mixed and swallowed a glass of brandy-and-water, the materials for making which he extracted from a cupboard on one side of the fireplace; having glanced at my translations—he could read both French and German—he went out again in silence.

Chapter III

I SERVED Edward as his second clerk faithfully, punctually, diligently. What was given me to do I had the power and the determination to do well. Mr. Crimsworth watched sharply for defects, but found none; he set Timothy Steighton, his favourite and head man, to watch also. Tim was baffled; I was as exact as himself, and quicker. Mr. Crimsworth made inquiries as to how I lived, whether I got into debt—no, my accounts with my landlady were always straight. I had hired small lodgings, which I contrived to pay for out of a slender fund—the accumulated savings of my Eton pocket-money; for as it had ever been abhorrent to my nature to ask pecuniary assistance, I had early acquired habits of self-denying economy; husbanding my monthly allowance with anxious care, in order to obviate the danger of being forced, in some moment of future exigency, to beg additional aid. I remember many called me miser at the time, and I used to couple the reproach with this consolation— better to be misunderstood now than repulsed hereafter. At this day I had my reward; I had had it before, when on parting with my irritated uncles one of them threw down on the table before me a £5 note, which I was able to leave there, saying that my travelling expenses were already provided for. Mr. Crimsworth employed Tim to find out whether my landlady had any complaint to make on the score of my morals; she answered that she believed I was a very religious man, and asked him, in her turn, if he thought I had any intention of going into the Church some day; for, she said, she had had young curates to lodge in her house who were nothing equal to me for steadiness and quietness. Tim was "a religious man" himself; indeed, he was "a joined Methodist," which did not (be it understood)

prevent him from being at the same time an engrained rascal, and he came away much posed at hearing this account of my piety. Having imparted it to Mr. Crimsworth, that gentleman who himself frequented no place of worship, and owned no God but Mammon, turned the information into a weapon of attack against the equability of my temper. He commenced a series of covert sneers, of which I did not at first perceive the drift, till my landlady happened to relate the conversation she had had with Mr. Steighton; this enlightened me; afterwards I came to the counting-house prepared, and managed to receive the mill-owner's blasphemous sarcasms, when next levelled at me, on a buckler of impenetrable indifference. Ere long he tired of wasting his ammunition on a statue, but he did not throw away the shafts—he only kept them quiet in his quiver.

Once during my clerkship I had an invitation to Crimsworth Hall; it was on the occasion of a large party given in honour of the master's birthday; he had always been accustomed to invite his clerks on similar anniversaries, and could not well pass me over; I was, however, kept strictly in the background. Mrs. Crimsworth, elegantly dressed in satin and lace, blooming in youth and health, vouchsafed me no more notice than was expressed by a distant move; Crimsworth, of course, never spoke to me; I was introduced to none of the band of young ladies, who, enveloped in silvery clouds of white gauze and muslin, sat in array against me on the opposite side of a long and large room; in fact, I was fairly isolated, and could but contemplate the shining ones from afar, and when weary of such a dazzling scene, turn for a change to the consideration of the carpet pattern. Mr. Crimsworth, standing on the rug, his elbow supported by the marble mantelpiece, and about him a group of very pretty girls, with whom he conversed gaily—Mr. Crimsworth, thus placed, glanced at me; I looked weary, solitary, kept down like some desolate tutor or governess; he was satisfied.

Dancing began; I should have liked well enough to be introduced to some pleasing and intelligent girl, and to have freedom and opportunity to show that I could both feel and communicate the pleasure of social intercourse—that I was not, in short, a block, or a piece of furniture, but an acting, thinking, sentient man. Many smiling faces and graceful figures glided past me, but the smiles were lavished on other eyes, the figures sustained by other hands than mine. I turned away tantalised, left the dancers, and wandered into the oak-panelled dining-room. No fibre of sympathy united me to any living thing in this house; I looked for and found my mother's picture. I took a wax-taper from a stand, and held it up. I gazed long, earnestly; my heart grew to the image. My mother, I perceived, had bequeathed to me much of her features and countenance—her forehead, her eyes, her complexion. No regular beauty pleases egotistical human beings so much as a softened and refined likeness of themselves; for this reason, fathers regard with complacency the lineaments of their daughters' faces, where frequently their own similitude is found flatteringly associated with softness of hue and delicacy of outline. I was just wondering how that picture, to me so interesting, would strike an impartial spectator, when a voice close behind me pronounced the words:

"Humph! there's some sense in that face."

I turned; at my elbow stood a tall man, young, though probably five or six years older than I—in other respects of an appearance the opposite to commonplace; though just now, as I am not disposed to paint his portrait in detail, the reader must be content with the silhouette I have just thrown off; it was all I myself saw of him for the moment. I did not investigate the colour of his eyebrows, nor of his eyes either; I saw his stature, and the outline of his shape; I saw, too, his fastidious-looking *retroussé* nose; these observations, few in number, and general in character (the last excepted), sufficed, for they enabled me to recognise him.

"Good evening, Mr. Hunsden," muttered I with a bow, and then, like a shy noodle as I was, I began moving away—and why? Simply because Mr. Hunsden was a manufacturer and a mill-owner, and I was only a clerk, and my instinct

propelled me from my superior. I had frequently seen Hunsden in Bigben Close, where he came almost weekly to transact business with Mr. Crimsworth, but I had never spoken to him, nor he to me, and I owed him a sort of involuntary grudge, because he had more than once been the tacit witness of insults offered by Edward to me. I had the conviction that he could only regard me as a poor-spirited slave, wherefore I now went about to shun his presence and eschew his conversation.

"Where are you going?" asked he, as I edged off sideways. I had already noticed that Mr. Hunsden indulged in abrupt forms of speech, and I perversely said to myself:

"He thinks he may speak as he likes to a poor clerk; but my mood is not, perhaps, so supple as he deems it, and his rough freedom pleases me not at all."

I made some slight reply, rather indifferent than courteous, and continued to move away. He coolly planted himself in my path.

"Stay here awhile," said he: "it is so hot in the dancing-room; besides, you don't dance; you have not had a partner to-night."

He was right, and as he spoke neither his look, tone, nor manner displeased me; my *amour-propre* was propitiated; he had not addressed me out of condescension, but because, having repaired to the cool dining-room for refreshment, he now wanted some one to talk to, by way of temporary amusement. I hate to be condescended to, but I like well enough to oblige; I stayed.

"That is a good picture," he continued, recurring to the portrait.

"Do you consider the face pretty?" I asked.

"Pretty! no—how can it be pretty, with sunk eyes and hollow cheeks? but it is peculiar; it seems to think. You could have a talk with that woman, if she were alive, on other subjects than dress, visiting, and compliments."

I agreed with him, but did not say so. He went on.

"Not that I admire a head of that sort; it wants character and force; there's too much of the sen-si-tive (so he articulated it, curling his lip at the same time) in that mouth; besides, there is Aristocrat written on the brow and defined in the figure; I hate your aristocrats."

"You think, then, Mr. Hunsden, that patrician descent may be read in a distinctive cast of form and features?"

"Patrician descent be hanged! Who doubts that your lordlings may have their 'distinctive cast of form and features' as much as we ——shire tradesmen have ours? But which is the best? Not theirs assuredly. As to their women, it is a little different: they cultivate beauty from childhood upwards, and may by care and training attain to a certain degree of excellence in that point, just like the Oriental Odalisques. Yet even this superiority is doubtful. Compare the figure in that frame with Mrs. Edward Crimsworth—which is the finer animal?"

I replied quietly: "Compare yourself and Mr. Edward Crimsworth, Mr. Hunsden."

"Oh, Crimsworth is better filled up than I am, I know; besides, he has a straight nose, arched eyebrows, and all that: but these advantages—if they are advantages— he did not inherit from his mother, the patrician, but from his father, old Crimsworth, who, *my* father says, was as veritable a ——shire blue-dyer as ever put indigo in a vat; yet withal the handsomest man in the three Ridings. It is you, William, who are the aristocrat of your family, and you are not as fine a fellow as your plebeian brother by a long chalk."

There was something in Mr. Hunsden's point-blank mode of speech which rather pleased me than otherwise, because it set me at my ease. I continued the conversation with a degree of interest.

"How do you happen to know that I am Mr. Crimsworth's brother? I thought you and everybody else looked upon me only in the light of a poor clerk."

"Well, and so we do; and what are you but a poor clerk? You do Crimsworth's work, and he gives you wages—shabby wages they are, too."

I was silent. Hunsden's language now bordered on the impertinent, still his manner did not offend me in the least—it only piqued my curiosity; I wanted him to go on, which he did in a little while.

"This world is an absurd one," said he.

"Why so, Mr. Hunsden?"

"I wonder you should ask: you are yourself a strong proof of the absurdity I allude to."

I was determined he should explain himself of his own accord, without my pressing him so to do—so I resumed my silence.

"Is it your intention to become a tradesman?" he inquired presently.

"It was my serious intention three months ago."

"Humph! the more fool you—you look like a tradesman! What a practical business-like face you have!"

"My face is as the Lord made it, Mr. Hunsden."

"The Lord never made either your face or head for X——. What good can your bumps of ideality, comparison, self-esteem, conscientiousness, do you here? But if you like Bigben Close, stay there; it's your own affair, not mine."

"Perhaps I have no choice."

"Well I care nought about it—it will make little difference to me what you do or where you go; but I'm cool now—I want to dance again; and I see such a fine girl sitting in the corner of the sofa there by her mamma; see if I don't get her for a partner in a jiffy! There's Waddy—Sam Waddy, making up to her; won't I cut him out?"

And Mr. Hunsden strode away. I watched him through the open folding-doors; he outstripped Waddy, applied for the hand of the fine girl, and led her off triumphant. She was a tall, well-made, full-formed, dashingly-dressed young woman, much in the style of Mrs. E. Crimsworth; Hunsden whirled her through the waltz with spirit; he kept at her side during the remainder of the evening, and I read in her animated and gratified countenance that he succeeded in making himself perfectly agreeable. The mamma too (a stout person in a turban—Mrs. Lupton by name) looked well pleased; prophetic visions probably flattered her inward eye. The Hunsdens were of an old stem; and scornful as Yorke (such was my late interlocutor's name) professed to be of the advantages of birth, in his secret heart he well knew and fully appreciated the distinction his ancient, if not high lineage, conferred on him in a mushroom-place like X——, concerning whose inhabitants it was proverbially said, that not one in a thousand knew his own grandfather. Moreover, the Hunsdens, once rich, were still independent; and report affirmed that Yorke bade fair, by his success in business, to restore to pristine prosperity the partially decayed fortunes of his house. These circumstances considered, Mrs. Lupton's broad face might well wear a smile of complacency as she contemplated the heir of Hunsden Wood occupied in paying assiduous court to her darling Sarah Martha. I, however, whose observations being less anxious, were likely to be more accurate, soon saw that the grounds for maternal self-congratulation were slight indeed; the gentleman appeared to me much more desirous of making, than susceptible of receiving an impression. I know not what it was in Mr. Hunsden that, as I watched him (I had nothing better to do), suggested to me, every now and then, the idea of a foreigner. In form and features he might be pronounced English, though even there one caught a dash of something Gallic; but he had no English shyness: he had learnt somewhere, somehow, the art of setting himself quite at his ease, and of allowing no insular timidity to intervene as a barrier between him and his convenience or pleasure. Refinement he did not affect, yet vulgar he could not be called; he was not odd—no quiz—yet he resembled no one else I had ever seen before; his general bearing intimated complete, sovereign satisfaction with himself; yet, at times, an indescribable shade passed like an eclipse over his countenance, and seemed to me like the sign of a sudden and strong inward doubt of himself, his words and actions—an energetic

discontent at his life or his social position, his future prospects or his mental attainments—I know not which; perhaps after all it might only be a bilious caprice.

Chapter IV

No man likes to acknowledge that he has made a mistake in the choice of his profession, and every man, worthy of the name, will row long against wind and tide before he allows himself to cry out, "I am baffled!" and submits to be floated passively back to land. From the first week of my residence in X—— I felt my occupation irksome. The thing itself—the work of copying and translating business-letters—was a dry and tedious task enough, but had that been all, I should long have borne with the nuisance; I am not of an impatient nature, and influenced by the double desire of getting my living and justifying to myself and others the resolution I had taken to become a tradesman, I should have endured in silence the rust and cramp of my best faculties; I should not have whispered, even inwardly, that I longed for liberty; I should have pent in every sigh by which my heart might have ventured to intimate its distress under the closeness, smoke, monotony, and joyless tumult of Bigben Close, and its panting desire for freer and fresher scenes; I should have set up the image of Duty, the fetish of Perseverance, in my small bedroom at Mrs. King's lodgings, and they two should have been my household gods, from which my darling, my cherished-in-secret Imagination, the tender and the mighty, should never, either by softness or strength, have severed me. But this was not all; the antipathy which had sprung up between myself and my employer striking deeper root and spreading denser shade daily, excluded me from every glimpse of the sunshine of life; and I began to feel like a plant growing in humid darkness out of the slimy walls of a well.

Antipathy is the only word which can express the feeling Edward Crimsworth had for me—a feeling, in a great measure, involuntary, and which was liable to be excited by even the most trifling movement, look, or word of mine. My southern accent annoyed him; the degree of education evinced in my language irritated him; my punctuality, industry, and accuracy, fixed his dislike, and gave it the high flavour and poignant relish of envy; he feared that I too should one day make a successful tradesman. Had I been in anything inferior to him, he would not have hated me so thoroughly, but I knew all that he knew, and, what was worse, he suspected that I kept the padlock of silence on mental wealth in which he was no sharer. If he could have once placed me in a ridiculous or mortifying position, he would have forgiven me much, but I was guarded by three faculties—Caution, Tact, Observation; and prowling and prying as was Edward's malignity, it could never baffle the lynx-eyes of these, my natural sentinels. Day by day did his malice watch my tact, hoping it would sleep, and prepared to steal snake-like on its slumber; but tact, if it be genuine, never sleeps.

I had received my first quarter's wages, and was returning to my lodgings, possessed heart and soul with the pleasant feeling that the master who had paid me grudged every penny of that hard-earned pittance—(I had long ceased to regard Mr. Crimsworth as my brother—he was a hard, grinding master; he wished to be an inexorable tyrant: that was all). Thoughts, not varied but strong, occupied my mind; two voices spoke within me; again and again they uttered the same monotonous phrases. One said: "William, your life is intolerable." The other: "What can you do to alter it?" I walked fast, for it was a cold, frosty night in January; as I approached my lodgings, I turned from a general view of my affairs to the particular speculation as to whether my fire would be out; looking towards the window of my sitting-room, I saw no cheering red gleam.

"That slut of a servant has neglected it as usual," said I, "and I shall see nothing but pale ashes if I go in; it is a fine starlight night—I will walk a little farther."

It *was* a fine night, and the streets were dry and even clean for X——; there was a crescent curve of moonlight to be seen by the parish church tower, and hundreds of stars shone keenly bright in all quarters of the sky.

Unconsciously I steered my course towards the country; I had got into Grove Street, and began to feel the pleasure of seeing dim trees at the extremity, round a suburban house, when a person leaning over the iron gate of one of the small gardens which front the neat dwelling-houses in this street, addressed me as I was hurrying with quick stride past.

"What the deuce is the hurry? Just so must Lot have left Sodom, when he expected fire to pour down upon it out of burning brass clouds."

I stopped short, and looked towards the speaker. I smelt the fragrance, and saw the red spark of a cigar; the dusk outline of a man, too, bent towards me over the wicket.

"You see I am meditating in the field at eventide," continued this shade. "God knows it's cool work! especially as instead of Rebecca on a camel's hump, with bracelets on her arms and a ring in her nose, Fate sends me only a counting-house clerk, in a grey tweed wrapper."

The voice was familiar to me—its second utterance enabled me to seize the speaker's identity.

"Mr. Hunsden! good evening."

"Good evening, indeed! yes, but you would have passed me without recognition if I had not been so civil as to speak first."

"I did not know you."

"A famous excuse! You ought to have known me; I knew you, though you were going ahead like a steam-engine. Are the police after you?"

"It wouldn't be worth their while; I'm not of consequence enough to attract them."

"Alas, poor shepherd! Alack and well-a-day! What a theme for regret, and how down in the mouth you must be, judging from the sound of your voice! But since you're not running from the police, from whom are you running? the devil?"

"On the contrary, I am going post to him."

"That is well—you're just in luck: this is Tuesday evening; there are scores of market gigs and carts returning to Dinneford to-night; and he, or some of his, have a seat in all regularly; so, if you'll step in and sit half-an-hour in my bachelor's parlour, you may catch him as he passes without much trouble. I think though you'd better let him alone to-night, he'll have so many customers to serve; Tuesday is his busy day in X—— and Dinneford; come in, at all events."

He swung the wicket open as he spoke.

"Do you really wish me to go in?" I asked.

"As you please—I'm alone; your company for an hour or two would be agreeable to me; but, if you don't choose to favour me so far, I'll not press the point. I hate to bore any one."

It suited me to accept the invitation as it suited Hunsden to give it. I passed through the gate, and followed him to the front door, which he opened; thence we traversed a passage, and entered his parlour; the door being shut, he pointed me to an arm-chair by the hearth; I sat down, and glanced round me.

It was a comfortable room, at once snug and handsome; the bright grate was filled with a genuine ——shire fire, red, clear, and generous, no penurious South-of-England embers heaped in the corner of a grate. On the table a shaded lamp diffused around a soft, pleasant, and equal light; the furniture was almost luxurious for a young bachelor, comprising a couch and two very easy chairs; book-shelves filled the recesses on each side of the mantelpiece; they were well furnished, and arranged with perfect order. The neatness of the room suited my taste; I hate irregular

and slovenly habits. From what I saw I concluded that Hunsden's ideas on that point corresponded with my own. While he removed from the centre-table to the sideboard a few pamphlets and periodicals, I ran my eye along the shelves of the book-case nearest me. French and German works predominated, the old French dramatists, sundry modern authors, Thiers, Villemain, Paul de Kock, George Sand, Eugène Sue; in German—Goethe, Schiller, Zschokke, Jean Paul Richter; in English there were works on Political Economy. I examined no further, for Mr. Hunsden himself recalled my attention.

"You shall have something," said he, "for you ought to feel disposed for refreshment after walking nobody knows how far on such a Canadian night as this; but it shall not be brandy-and-water, and it shall not be a bottle of port, nor ditto of sherry. I keep no such poison. I have Rheinwein for my own drinking, and you may choose between that and coffee."

Here again Hunsden suited me: if there was one generally received practice I abhorred more than another, it was the habitual imbibing of spirits and strong wines. I had, however, no fancy for his acid German nectar, but I liked coffee, so I responded:

"Give me some coffee, Mr. Hunsden."

I perceived my answer pleased him; he had doubtless expected to see a chilling effect produced by his steady announcement that he would give me neither wine nor spirits; he just shot one searching glance at my face to ascertain whether my cordiality was genuine or a mere feint of politeness. I smiled, because I quite understood him; and while I honoured his conscientious firmness, I was amused at his mistrust; he seemed satisfied, rang the bell, and ordered coffee, which was presently brought; for himself, a bunch of grapes and half a pint of something sour sufficed. My coffee was excellent; I told him so, and expressed the shuddering pity with which his anchorite fare inspired me. He did not answer, and I scarcely think heard my remark. At that moment one of those momentary eclipses I before alluded to had come over his face, extinguishing his smile, and replacing, by an abstracted and alienated look, the customarily shrewd, bantering glance of his eye. I employed the interval of silence in a rapid scrutiny of his physiognomy. I had never observed him closely before; and, as my sight is very short, I had gathered only a vague, general idea of his appearance; I was surprised now, on examination, to perceive how small, and even feminine, were his lineaments; his tall figure, long and dark locks, his voice and general bearing, had impressed me with the notion of something powerful and massive; not at all:—my own features were cast in a harsher and squarer mould than his. I discerned that there would be contrasts between his inward and outward man; contentions, too; for I suspected his soul had more of will and ambition than his body had of fibre and muscle. Perhaps, in these incompatibilities of the "physique" with the "morale," lay the secret of that fitful gloom; he *would* but *could* not, and the athletic mind scowled scorn on its more fragile companion. As to his good looks, I should have liked to have a woman's opinion on that subject; it seemed to me that his face might produce the same effect on a lady that a very piquant and interesting, though scarcely pretty, female face would on a man. I have mentioned his dark locks—they were brushed sideways above a white and sufficiently expansive forehead; his cheek had a rather hectic freshness; his features might have done well on canvas, but indifferently in marble: they were plastic; character had set a stamp upon each; expression re-cast them at her pleasure, and strange metamorphoses she wrought, giving him now the mien of a morose bull, and anon that of an arch and mischievous girl; more frequently, the two semblances were blent, and a queer, composite countenance they made.

Starting from his silent fit, he began:

"William! what a fool you are to live in those dismal lodgings of Mrs. King's, when you might take rooms here in Grove Street, and have a garden like me!"

"I should be too far from the mill."

"What of that? It would do you good to walk there and back two or three times a day; besides, are you such a fossil that you never wish to see a flower or a green leaf?"

"I am no fossil."

"What are you then? You sit at that desk in Crimsworth's counting-house day by day and week by week, scraping with a pen on paper, just like an automaton; you never get up; you never say you are tired; you never ask for a holiday; you never take change or relaxation; you give way to no excess of an evening; you neither keep wild company, nor indulge in strong drink."

"Do you, Mr. Hunsden?"

"Don't think to pose me with short questions; your case and mine are diametrically different, and it is nonsense attempting to draw a parallel. I say, that when a man endures patiently what ought to be unendurable, he is a fossil."

"Whence do you acquire a knowledge of my patience?"

"Why, man, do you suppose you are a mystery! The other night you seemed surprised at my knowing to what family you belonged; now you find subject for wonderment in my calling you patient. What do you think I do with my eyes and ears? I've been in your counting-house more than once when Crimsworth has treated you like a dog; called for a book, for instance, and when you gave him the wrong one, or what he chose to consider the wrong one, flung it back almost in your face; desired you to shut or open the door as if you had been his flunkey; to say nothing of your position at the party about a month ago, where you had neither place nor partner, but hovered about like a poor, shabby hanger-on; and how patient you were under each and all of these circumstances!"

"Well, Mr. Hunsden, what then?"

"I can hardly tell you what then; the conclusion to be drawn as to your character depends upon the nature of the motives which guide your conduct; if you are patient because you expect to make something eventually out of Crimsworth, notwithstanding his tyranny, or perhaps by means of it, you are what the world calls an interested and mercenary, but may be a very wise fellow; if you are patient because you think it a duty to meet insult with submission, you are an essential sap, and in no shape the man for my money; if you are patient because your nature is phlegmatic, flat, inexcitable, and that you cannot get up to the pitch of resistance, why, God made you to be crushed; and lie down by all means, and lie flat, and let Juggernaut ride well over you."

Mr. Hunsden's eloquence was not, it will be perceived, of the smooth and oily order. As he spoke, he pleased me ill. I seemed to recognise in him one of those characters who, sensitive enough themselves, are selfishly relentless towards the sensitiveness of others. Moreover, though he was neither like Crimsworth nor Lord Tynedale, yet he was acrid, and, I suspected, overbearing in his way: there was a tone of despotism in the urgency of the very reproaches by which he aimed at goading the oppressed into rebellion against the oppressor. Looking at him still more fixedly than I had yet done, I saw written in his eye and mien a resolution to arrogate to himself a freedom so unlimited that it might often trench on the just liberty of his neighbours. I rapidly ran over these thoughts, and then I laughed a low and involuntary laugh, moved thereto by a slight inward revelation of the inconsistency of man. It was as I thought: Hunsden had expected me to take with calm his incorrect and offensive surmises, his bitter and haughty taunts; and himself was chafed by a laugh, scarce louder than a whisper.

His brow darkened, his thin nostril dilated a little.

"Yes," he began, "I told you that you were an aristocrat, and who but an aristocrat would laugh such a laugh as that, and look such a look? A laugh frigidly jeering; a look lazily mutinous; gentlemanlike irony, patrician resentment. What a nobleman you would have made, William Crimsworth! You are cut out for one; pity Fortune has baulked Nature! Look at the features, figure, even to the hands—

distinction all over—ugly distinction! Now, if you'd only an estate and a mansion, and a park, and a title, how you could play the exclusive, maintain the rights of your class, train your tenantry in habits of respect to the peerage, oppose at every step the advancing power of the people, support your rotten order, and be ready for its sake to wade knee-deep in churls' blood; as it is, you've no power; you can do nothing; you're wrecked and stranded on the shores of commerce; forced into collision with practical men, with whom you cannot cope, for *you'll never be a tradesman.*"

The first part of Hunsden's speech moved me not at all, or, if it did, it was only to wonder at the perversion into which prejudice had twisted his judgment of my character; the concluding sentence, however, not only moved, but shook me; the blow it gave was a severe one, because Truth wielded the weapon. If I smiled now, it was only in disdain of myself.

Hunsden saw his advantage; he followed it up.

"You'll make nothing by trade," continued he; "nothing more than the crust of dry bread and the draught of fair water on which you now live; your only chance of getting a competency lies in marrying a rich widow, or running away with an heiress."

"I leave such shifts to be put in practice by those who devise them," said I, rising.

"And even that is hopeless," he went on coolly. "What widow would have you? Much less, what heiress? You're not bold and venturesome enough for the one, nor handsome and fascinating enough for the other. You think perhaps you look intelligent and polished; carry your intellect and refinement to market, and tell me in a private note what price is bid for them."

Mr. Hunsden had taken his tone for the night; the string he struck was out of tune, he would finger no other. Averse to discord, of which I had enough every day and all day long, I concluded, at last, that silence and solitude were preferable to jarring converse; I bade him good-night.

"What! Are you going, lad? Well, good-night: you'll find the door." And he sat still in front of the fire, while I left the room and the house. I had got a good way on my return to my lodgings before I found out that I was walking very fast, and breathing very hard, and that my nails were almost stuck into the palms of my clenched hands, and that my teeth were set fast; on making this discovery, I relaxed both my pace, fists, and jaws, but I could not so soon cause the regrets rushing rapidly through my mind to slacken their tide. Why did I make myself a tradesman? Why did I enter Hunsden's house this evening? Why, at dawn tomorrow, must I repair to Crimsworth's mill? All that night did I ask myself these questions, and all that night fiercely demanded of my soul an answer. I got no sleep; my head burned, my feet froze; at last the factory bells rang, and I sprang from my bed with other slaves.

Chapter V

THERE is a climax to everything, to every state of feeling as well as to every position in life. I turned this truism over in my mind as, in the frosty dawn of a January morning, I hurried down the steep and now icy street which descended from Mrs. King's to the Close. The factory workpeople had preceded me by nearly an hour, and the mill was all lighted up and in full operation when I reached it. I repaired to my post in the counting-house as usual; the fire there, but just lit, as yet only smoked; Steighton was not yet arrived. I shut the door and sat down at the desk; my hands, recently washed in half-frozen water, were still numb; I could not write

till they had regained vitality, so I went on thinking, and still the theme of my thoughts was the "climax." Self-dissatisfaction troubled exceedingly the current of my meditations.

"Come, William Crimsworth," said my conscience, or whatever it is that within ourselves takes ourselves to task: "Come, get a clear notion of what you would have, or what you would not have. You talk of a climax; pray, has your endurance reached its climax? It is not four months old. What a fine resolute fellow you imagined yourself to be when you told Tynedale you would tread in your father's steps, and a pretty treading you are likely to make of it. How well you like X——! Just at this moment how redolent of pleasant associations are its streets, its shops, its warehouses, its factories! How the prospect of this day cheers you! Letter-copying till noon, solitary dinner at your lodgings, letter-copying till evening, solitude; for you neither find pleasure in Brown's, nor Smith's, nor Nicholl's, nor Eccle's company; and as to Hunsden, you fancied there was pleasure to be derived from his society—he! he! how did you like the taste you had of him last night? was it sweet? Yet he is a talented, an original-minded man, and even he does not like you; your self-respect defies you to like him; he has always seen you to disadvantage; he always will see you to disadvantage; your positions are unequal, and were they on the same level your minds could not assimilate; never hope, then, to gather the honey of friendship out of that thorn-guarded plant. Hollo, Crimsworth! where are your thoughts tending? You leave the recollection of Hunsden as a bee would a rock, as a bird a desert; and your aspirations spread eager wings towards a land of visions where, now in advancing daylight—in X—— daylight—you dare to dream of congeniality, repose, union. Those three you will never meet in this world; they are angels. The souls of just men made perfect may encounter them in heaven, but your soul will never be made perfect. Eight o'clock strikes! your hands are thawed, get to work!"

"Work? why should I work?" said I sullenly: "I cannot please though I toil like a slave." "Work, work!" reiterated the inward voice. "I may work, it will do no good," I growled; but nevertheless I drew out a packet of letters and commenced my task—task thankless and bitter as that of the Israelite crawling over the sun-baked fields of Egypt in search of straw and stubble wherewith to accomplish his tale of bricks.

About ten o'clock I heard Mr. Crimsworth's gig turn into the yard, and in a minute or two he entered the counting-house. It was his custom to glance his eye at Steighton and myself, to hang up his mackintosh, stand a minute with his back to the fire, and then walk out. To-day he did not deviate from his usual habits; the only difference was that when he looked at me, his brow, instead of being merely hard, was surly; his eye, instead of being cold, was fierce. He studied me a minute or two longer than usual, but went out in silence.

Twelve o'clock arrived; the bell rang for a suspension of labour; the workpeople went off to their dinners; Steighton, too, departed, desiring me to lock the counting-house door, and take the key with me. I was tying up a bundle of papers, and putting them in their place, preparatory to closing my desk, when Crimsworth reappeared at the door, and entering closed it behind him.

"You'll stay here a minute," said he, in a deep, brutal voice, while his nostrils distended and his eye shot a spark of sinister fire.

Alone with Edward I remembered our relationship and remembering that forgot the difference of position; I put away deference and careful forms of speech; I answered with simple brevity.

"It is time to go home," I said, turning the key in my desk.

"You'll stay here," he reiterated. "And take your hand off that key! leave it in the lock!"

"Why!" asked I. "What cause is there for changing my usual plans?"

"Do as I order," was the answer, "and no questions! You are my servant, obey me! What have you been about——!" He was going on in the same breath, when an abrupt pause anuounced that rage had for the moment got the better of articulation.

"You may look, if you wish to know," I replied. "There is the open desk, there are the papers."

"Confound your insolence! What have you been about?"

"Your work, and have done it well."

"Hypocrite and twaddler! Smooth-faced, sniveling grease-horn!" (this last term is, I believe, purely ——shire, and alludes to the horn of black, rancid whale-oil, usually to be seen suspended to cart wheels, and employed for greasing the same.)

"Come, Edward Crimsworth, enough of this. It is time you and I wound up accounts. I have now given your service three months' trial, and I find it the most nauseous slavery under the sun. Seek another clerk. I stay no longer."

"What! do you dare to give me notice? Stop at least for your wages." He took down the heavy gig whip hanging beside his mackintosh.

I permitted myself to laugh with a degree of scorn I took no pains to temper or hide. His fury boiled up, and when he had sworn half-a-dozen vulgar, impious oaths, without, however, venturing to lift the whip, he continued:

"I've found you out and know you thoroughly, you mean, whining lickspittle! What have you been saying all over X—— about me? Answer me that!"

"You? I have neither inclination nor temptation to talk about you."

"You lie! It is your practice to talk about me: it is your constant habit to make public complaint of the treatment you receive at my hands. You have gone and told it far and near that I give you low wages and knock you about like a dog. I wish you were a dog! I'd set-to this minute, and never stir from the spot till I'd cut every strip of flesh from your bones with this whip."

He flourished his tool. The end of the lash just touched my forehead. A warm excited thrill ran through my veins, my blood seemed to give a bound, and then raced fast and hot along its channels. I got up nimbly, came round to where he stood, and faced him.

"Down with your whip!" said I, "and explain this instant what you mean."

"Sirrah! to whom are you speaking?"

"To you. There is no one else present, I think. You say I have been calumniating you—complaining of your low wages and bad treatment. Give your grounds for these assertions."

Crimsworth had no dignity, and when I sternly demanded an explanation, he gave one in a loud, scolding voice.

"Grounds! you shall have them; and turn to the light that I may see your brazen face blush black, when you hear yourself proved to be a liar and a hypocrite. At a public meeting in the Town Hall yesterday, I had the pleasure of hearing myself insulted by the speaker opposed to me in the question under discussion, by allusions to my private affairs; by cant about monsters without natural affection, family despots, and such trash; and when I rose to answer, I was met by a shout from the filthy mob, where the mention of your name enabled me at once to detect the quarter in which this base attack had originated. When I looked round, I saw that treacherous villain, Hunsden, acting as fugleman. I detected you in close conversation with Hunsden at my house a month ago, and I know that you were at Hunsden's rooms last night. Deny it if you dare."

"Oh, I shall not deny it! And if Hunsden hounded on the people to hiss you, he did quite right. You deserve popular execration; for a worse man, a harder master, a more brutal brother than you are has seldom existed."

"Sirrah! sirrah!" reiterated Crimsworth: and to complete his apostrophe, he cracked the whip straight over my head.

A minute sufficed to wrest if from him, break it in two pieces, and throw it under the grate. He made a headlong rush at me, which I evaded, and said:

"Touch me, and I'll have you up before the nearest magistrate."

Men like Crimsworth if firmly and calmly resisted, always abate something of their exorbitant insolence; he had no mind to be brought before a magistrate, and I suppose he saw I meant what I said. After an odd and long stare at me, at once bull-like and amazed, he seemed to bethink himself that, after all, his money gave him sufficient superiority over a beggar like me, and that he had in his hands a surer and more dignified mode of revenge than the somewhat hazardous one of personal chastisement.

"Take your hat," said he. "Take what belongs to you, and go out at that door; get away to your parish, you pauper: beg, steal, starve, get transported, do what you like; but at your peril venture again into my sight! If ever I hear of your setting foot on an inch of ground belonging to me, I'll hire a man to cane you."

"It is not likely you'll have the chance; once off your premises, what temptation can I have to return to them? I leave a prison, I leave a tyrant; I leave what is worse than the worst that can lie before me, so no fear of my coming back."

"Go, or I'll make you!" exclaimed Crimsworth.

I walked deliberately to my desk, took out such of its contents as were my own property, put them in my pocket, locked the desk, and placed the key on the top.

"What are you abstracting from that desk?" demanded the mill-owner. "Leave all behind in its place, or I'll send for a policeman to search you."

"Look sharp about it, then," said I, and I took down my hat, drew on my gloves, and walked leisurely out of the counting-house—walked out of it to enter it no more.

I recollect that when the mill-bell rang the dinner hour, before Mr. Crimsworth entered, and the scene above related took place, I had had rather a sharp appetite, and had been waiting somewhat impatiently to hear the signal of feeding time. I forgot it now, however; the images of potatoes and roast mutton were effaced from my mind by the stir and tumult which the transaction of the last half-hour had there excited. I only thought of walking, that the action of my muscles might harmonise with the action of my nerves; and walk I did, fast and far. How could I do otherwise? A load was lifted off my heart; I felt light and liberated. I had got away from Bigben Close without a breach of resolution; without injury to my self-respect. I had not forced circumstances; circumstances had freed me. Life was again open to me; no longer was its horizon limited by the high black wall surrounding Crimsworth's mill. Two hours had elapsed before my sensations had so far subsided as to leave me calm enough to remark for what wider and clearer boundaries I had exchanged that sooty girdle. When I did look up, lo! straight before me lay Grovetown, a village of villas about five miles out of X——. The short winter day, as I perceived from the far-declined sun, was already approaching its close; a chill frost-mist was rising from the river on which X—— stands, and along whose banks the road I had taken lay; it dimmed the earth, but did not obscure the clear icy blue of the January sky. There was a great stillness near and far; the time of the day favoured tranquillity, as the people were all employed within doors, the hour of evening release from the factories not being yet arrived; a sound of full-flowing water alone pervaded the air, for the river was deep and abundant, swelled by the melting of a late snow. I stood awhile, leaning over a wall; and looking down at the current: I watched the rapid rush of its waves. I desired memory to take a clear and permanent impression of the scene, and treasure it for future years. Grovetown Church clock struck four; looking up, I beheld the last of that day's sun, glinting red through the leafless boughs of some very old oak trees surrounding the church—its light coloured and characterised the picture as I wished. I paused yet a moment, till the sweet, slow sound of the bell had quite died out of the air; then ear, eye, and feeling satisfied, I quitted the wall and once more turned my face towards X——.

Chapter VI

I RE-ENTERED the town a hungry man; the dinner I had forgotten recurred seductively to my recollection; and it was with a quick step and sharp appetite I ascended the narrow street leading to my lodgings. It was dark when I opened the front door and walked into the house. I wondered how my fire would be; the night was cold, and I shuddered at the prospect of a grate full of sparkless cinders. To my joyful surprise, I found, on entering my sitting-room, a good fire and a clean hearth. I had hardly noticed this phenomenon, when I became aware of another subject for wonderment; the chair I usually occupied near the hearth was already filled; a person sat there with his arms folded on his chest, and his legs stretched out on the rug. Short-sighted as I am, doubtful as was the gleam of the firelight, a moment's examination enabled me to recognise in this person my acquaintance, Mr. Hunsden. I could not of course be much pleased to see him, considering the manner in which I had parted from him the night before, and as I walked to the hearth, stirred the fire, and said coolly, "Good evening," my demeanour evinced as little cordiality as I felt; yet I wondered in my own mind what had brought him there; and I wondered, also, what motives had induced him to interfere so actively between me and Edward; it was to him, it appeared, that I owed my welcome dismissal. Still I could not bring myself to ask him questions, to show any eagerness of curiosity; if he chose to explain, he might, but the explanation should be a perfectly voluntary one on his part; I thought he was entering upon it.

"You owe me a debt of gratitude," were his first words.

"Do I?" said I; "I hope it is not a large one, for I am much too poor to charge myself with heavy liabilities of any kind."

"Then declare yourself bankrupt at once, for this liability is a ton weight at least. When I came in I found your fire out, aud I had it lit again, and made that sulky drab of a servant stay and blow at it with the bellows till it had burnt up properly; now, say 'Thank you!' "

"Not till I have had something to eat; I can thank nobody while I am so famished."

I rang the bell and ordered tea and some cold meat.

"Cold meat!" exclaimed Hunsden, as the servant closed the door, "what a glutton you are, man! Meat with tea! you'll die of eating too much."

"No, Mr. Hunsden, I shall not." I felt a necessity for contradicting him; I was irritated with hunger, and irritated at seeing him there, and irritated at the continued roughness of his manner.

"It is over-eating that makes you so ill-tempered," said he.

"How do you know?" I demanded. "It is like you to give a pragmatical opinion without being acquainted with any of the circumstances of the case; I have had no dinner."

What I said was petulant and snappish enough, and Hunsden only replied by looking in my face and laughing.

"Poor thing!" he whined, after a pause. "It has had no dinner, has it? What! I suppose its master would not let it come home. Did Crimsworth order you to fast by way of punishment, William?"

"No, Mr. Hunsden." Fortunately, at this sulky juncture, tea was brought in, and I fell to upon some bread and butter and cold beef directly. Having cleared a plateful, I became so far humanised as to intimate to Mr. Hunsden "that he need not sit there staring, but might come to the table and do as I did, if he liked."

"But I don't like in the least," said he, and therewith he summoned the servant by a fresh pull of the bell-rope, and intimated a desire to have a glass of toast-and-water. "And some more coal," he added; "Mr. Crimsworth shall keep a good fire while I stay."

His orders being executed, he wheeled his chair round to the table, so as to be opposite me.

"Well," he proceeded. "You are out of work, I suppose."

"Yes," said I; and not disposed to show the satisfaction I felt on this point, I, yielding to the whim of the moment, took up the subject as though I considered myself aggrieved rather than benefited by what had been done. "Yes—thanks to you, I am. Crimsworth turned me off at a minute's notice, owing to some interference of yours at a public meeting, I understand."

"Ah! what! he mentioned that? He observed me signalling the lads, did he? What had he to say about his friend Hunsden—anything sweet?"

"He called you a treacherous villain."

"Oh, he hardly knows me yet! I'm one of those shy people who don't come out all at once, and he is only just beginning to make my acquaintance, but he'll find I've some good qualities—excellent ones! The Hunsdens were always unrivalled at tracking a rascal; a downright, dishonourable villain is their natural prey—they could not keep off him wherever they met him; you used the word pragmatical just now—that word is the property of our family; it has been applied to us from generation to generation; we have fine noses for abuses; we scent a scoundrel a mile off; we are reformers born, radical reformers; and it was impossible for me to live in the same town with Crimsworth, to come into weekly contact with him, to witness some of his conduct to you (for whom personally I care nothing; I only consider the brutal injustice with which he violated your natural claim to equality)— I say it was impossible for me to be thus situated and not feel the angel or the demon of my race at work within me. I followed my instinct, opposed a tyrant, and broke a chain."

Now this speech interested me much, both because it brought out Hunsden's character, and because it explained his motives; it interested me so much that I forgot to reply to it, and sat silent, pondering over a throng of ideas it had suggested.

"Are you grateful to me?" he asked presently.

In fact I was grateful, or almost so, and I believe I half liked him at the moment, notwithstanding his proviso that what he had done was not out of regard for me. But human nature is perverse. Impossible to answer his blunt question in the affirmative, so I disclaimed all tendency to gratitude, and advised him, if he expected any reward for his championship, to look for it in a better world, as he was not likely to meet it here. In reply he termed me "a dry-hearted aristocratic scamp," whereupon I again charged him with having taken the bread out of my mouth.

"Your bread was dirty, man!" cried Hunsden—"dirty and unwholesome! It came through the hands of a tyrant, for I tell you Crimsworth is a tyrant,—a tyrant to his workpeople, a tyrant to his clerks, and will some day be a tyrant to his wife."

"Nonsense! bread is bread, and a salary is a salary. I've lost mine, and through your means."

"There's sense in what you say, after all," rejoined Hunsden. "I must say I am rather agreeably surprised to hear you make so practical an observation as that last. I had imagined now, from my previous observation of your character, that the sentimental delight you would have taken in your newly regained liberty would, for a while at least, have effaced all ideas of forethought and prudence. I think better of you for looking steadily to the needful."

"Looking steadily to the needful! How can I do otherwise? I must live, and to live I must have what you call 'the needful,' which I can only get by working. I repeat it, you have taken my work from me."

"What do you mean to do?" pursued Hunsden coolly. "You have influential relations; I suppose they'll soon provide you with another place."

"Influential relations? Who? I should like to know their names!"

"The Seacombes."

"Stuff! I have cut them."

Hunsden looked at me incredulously,

"I have," said I, "and that definitively."

"You must mean they have cut you, William."

"As you please. They offered me their patronage on condition of my entering the Church; I declined both the terms and the recompense; I withdrew from my cold uncles, and preferred throwing myself into my elder brother's arms, from whose affectionate embrace I am now torn by the cruel intermeddling of a stranger—of yourself, in short."

I could not repress a half-smile as I said this; a similar demi-manifestation of feeling appeared at the same moment on Hunsden's lips.

"Oh, I see!" said he, looking into my eyes, and it was evident he *did* see right down into my heart. Having sat a minute or two with his chin resting on his hand, diligently occupied in the continued perusal of my countenance, he went on:

"Seriously, have you then nothing to expect from the Seacombes?"

"Yes, rejection and repulsion. Why do you ask me twice? How can hands stained with the ink of a counting-house, soiled with the grease of a wool-warehouse, ever again be permitted to come into contact with aristocratic palms?"

"There would be a difficulty, no doubt; still you are such a complete Seacombe in appearance, feature, language, almost manner, I wonder they should disown you."

"They have disowned me; so talk no more about it."

"Do you regret it, William?"

"No."

"Why not, lad?"

"Because they are not people with whom I could ever have had any sympathy."

"I say you are one of them."

"That merely proves that you know nothing at all about it; I am my mother's son, but not my uncles' nephew."

"Still—one of your uncles is a lord, though rather an obscure and not a very wealthy one, and the other a right honourable: you should consider worldly interest."

"Nonsense, Mr. Hunsden. You know or may know that even had I desired to be submissive to my uncles, I could not have stooped with a good enough grace ever to have won their favour. I should have sacrificed my own comfort and not have gained their patronage in return."

"Very likely—so you calculated your wisest plan was to follow your own devices at once?"

"Exactly. I must follow my own devices—I must till the day of my death; because I can neither comprehend, adopt, nor work out those of other people."

Hunsden yawned. "Well," said he, "in all this, I see but one thing clearly—that is, that the whole affair is no business of mine." He stretched himself and again yawned. "I wonder what time it is," he went on: "I have an appointment for seven o'clock."

"Three quarters past six by my watch."

"Well, then, I'll go." He got up. "You'll not meddle with trade again?" said he, leaning his elbow on the mantelpiece.

"No; I think not."

"You would be a fool if you did. Probably, after all, you'll think better of your uncle's proposal and go into the Church."

"A singular regeneration must take place in my whole inner and outer man before I do that. A good clergyman is one of the best of men."

"Indeed! Do you think so?" interrupted Hunsden scoffingly.

"I do, and no mistake. But I have not the peculiar points which go to make a good clergyman; and rather than adopt a profession for which I have no vocation, I would endure extremities of hardship from poverty."

"You're a mighty difficult customer to suit. You won't be a tradesman or a parson; you can't be a lawyer, or a doctor, or a gentleman, because you've no money. I'd recommend you to travel."

"What! without money?"

"You must travel in search of money, man. You can speak French—with a vile English accent, no doubt—still, you can speak it. Go on to the Continent, and see what will turn up for you there."

"God knows I should like to go!" exclaimed I, with involuntary ardour.

"Go! what the deuce hinders you? You may get to Brussels, for instance, for five or six pounds, if you know how to manage with economy."

"Necessity would teach me if I didn't."

"Go, then, and let your wits make a way for you when you get there. I know Brussels almost as well as I know X——, and I am sure it would suit such a one as you better than London."

"But occupation, Mr. Hunsden! I must go where occupation is to be had; and how could I get recommendation, or introduction, or employment at Brussels?"

"There speaks the origin of caution. You hate to advance a step before you know every inch of the way. You haven't a sheet of paper and a pen and ink?"

"I hope so," and I produced writing materials with alacrity; for I guessed what he was going to do. He sat down, wrote a few lines, folded, sealed, and addressed a letter, and held it out to me.

"There, Prudence, there's a pioneer to hew down the first rough difficulties of your path. I know well enough, lad, you are not one of those who will run their neck into a noose without seeing how they are to get it out again, and you're right there. A reckless man is my aversion, and nothing should ever persuade me to meddle with the concerns of such a one. Those who are reckless for themselves are generally ten times more so for their friends."

"This is a letter of introduction, I suppose?" said I, taking the epistle.

"Yes. With that in your pocket you will run no risk of finding yourself in a state of absolute destitution, which, I know, you will regard as a degradation—so should I, for that matter. The person to whom you will present it generally has two or three respectable places depending upon his recommendation."

"That will just suit me," said I.

"Well, and where's your gratitude?" demanded Mr. Hunsden; "don't you know how to say 'Thank you'?"

"I've fifteen pounds and a watch, which my godmother, whom I never saw, gave me eighteen years ago," was my rather irrelevant answer; and I further avowed myself a happy man, and professed that I did not envy any being in Christendom.

"And your gratitude?"

"I shall be off presently, Mr. Hunsden—to-morrow, if all be well: I'll not stay a day longer in X—— than I'm obliged."

"Very good—but it will be decent to make due acknowledgment for the assistance you have received; be quick! It is just going to strike seven: I am waiting to be thanked."

"Just stand out of the way, will you, Mr. Hunsden: I want a key there is on the corner of the mantelpiece. I'll pack my portmanteau before I go to bed."

The house clock struck seven.

"The lad is a heathen," said Hunsden, and taking his hat from the sideboard, he left the room, laughing to himself. I had half an inclination to follow him: I really intended to leave X—— the next morning, and should certainly not have another opportunity of bidding him good-bye. The front door banged to.

"Let him go," said I, "we shall meet again some day."

Chapter VII

READER, perhaps you were never in Belgium? Haply you don't know the physiognomy of the country? You have not its lineaments defined upon your memory, as I have them on mine?

Three—nay four—pictures line the four-walled cell where are stored for me the records of the past. First, Eton. All in that picture is in far perspective, receding, diminutive; but freshly coloured, green, dewy, with a spring sky, piled with glittering yet showery clouds; for my childhood was not all sunshine—it had its overcast, its cold, its stormy hours. Second, X——, huge, dingy; the canvas cracked and smoked; a yellow sky, sooty clouds; no sun, no azure; the verdure of the suburbs blighted and sullied—a very dreary scene.

Third, Belgium; and I will pause before this landscape. As to the fourth, a curtain covers it, which I may hereafter withdraw, or may not, as suits my convenience and capacity. At any rate, for the present it must hang undisturbed. Belgium! name unromantic and unpoetic, yet name that whenever uttered has in my ear a sound, in my heart an echo, such as no other assemblage of syllables, however sweet or classic, can produce. Belgium! I repeat the word, now as I sit alone near midnight. It stirs my world of the past like a summons to resurrection; the graves unclose, the dead are raised; thoughts, feelings, memories that slept, are seen by me ascending from the clods—haloed most of them—but while I gaze on their vapoury forms, and strive to ascertain definitely their outline, the sound which wakened them dies, and they sink, each and all, like a light wreath of mist, absorbed in the mould, recalled to urns, resealed in monuments. Farewell, luminous phantoms!

This is Belgium, reader. Look! don't call the picture a flat or a dull one—it was neither flat nor dull to me when I first beheld it. When I left Ostend on a mild February morning, and found myself on the road to Brussels, nothing could look vapid to me. My sense of enjoyment possessed an edge whetted to the finest, untouched, keen, exquisite. I was young; I had good health; pleasure I had never met; no indulgence of hers had enervated or sated one faculty of my nature. Liberty I clasped in my arms for the first time, and the influence of her smile and embrace revived my life like the sun and the west wind. Yes, at that epoch I felt like a morning traveller who doubts not that from the hill he is ascending he shall behold a glorious sunrise; what if the track be straight, steep, and stony? he sees it not; his eyes are fixed on that summit, flushed already, flushed and gilded, and having gained it he is certain of the scene beyond. He knows that the sun will face him, that his chariot is even now coming over the eastern horizon, and that the herald breeze he feels on his cheek is opening for the god's career a clear, vast path of azure, amidst clouds soft as pearl and warm as flame. Difficulty and toil were to be my lot, but sustained by energy, drawn on by hopes as bright as vague, I deemed such a lot no hardship. I mounted now the hill in shade; there were pebbles, inequalities, briars in my path, but my eyes were fixed on the crimson peak above; my imagination was with the refulgent firmament beyond, and I thought nothing of the stones turning under my feet, or of the thorns scratching my face and hands.

I gazed often, and always with delight, from the window of the diligence (these, be it remembered, were not the days of trains and railroads). Well! and what did I see? I will tell you faithfully. Green, reedy swamps; fields fertile, but flat, cultivated in patches that made them look like magnified kitchen-gardens; belts of cut trees, formal as pollard willows, skirting the horizon; narrow canals, gliding slow by the roadside; painted Flemish farm-houses; some very dirty hovels; a grey, dead sky; wet road, wet fields, wet house-tops: not a beautiful, scarcely a picturesque object met my eye along the whole route; yet to me, all was beautiful, all was more than picturesque. It continued fair so long as daylight lasted, though the moisture

of many preceding damp days had sodden the whole country; as it grew dark, however, the rain recommenced, and it was through streaming and starless darkness my eye caught the first gleam of the lights of Brussels. I saw little of the city but its lights that night. Having alighted from the diligence, a fiacre conveyed me to the Hôtel de ——, where I had been advised by a fellow-traveller to put up; having eaten a traveller's supper, I retired to bed, and slept a traveller's sleep.

Next morning I awoke from prolonged and sound repose with the impression that I was yet in X——, and perceiving it to be broad daylight I started up, imagining that I had overslept myself and should be behind time at the counting-house. The momentary and painful sense of restraint vanished before the revived and reviving consciousness of freedom, as, throwing back the white curtains of my bed, I looked forth into a wide, lofty, foreign chamber; how different from the small and dingy, though not uncomfortable, apartment I had occupied for a night or two at a respectable inn in London while waiting for the sailing of the packet! Yet far be it from me to profane the memory of that little dingy room! It, too, is dear to my soul; for there, as I lay in quiet and darkness, I first heard the great bell of St. Paul's telling London it was midnight, and well do I recall the deep, deliberate tones, so full charged with colossal phlegm and force. From the small, narrow window of that room, I first saw *the* dome, looming through a London mist. I suppose the sensations, stirred by those first sounds, first sights, are felt but once; treasure them, Memory; seal them in urns, and keep them in safe niches! Well—I rose. Travellers talk of the apartments in foreign dwellings being bare and uncomfortable; I thought my chamber looked stately and cheerful. It had such large windows—*croisées* that opened like doors, with such broad, clear panes of glass; such a great looking-glass stood on my dressing-table —such a fine mirror glittered over the mantelpiece—the painted floor looked so clean and glossy; when I had dressed and was descending the stairs, the broad marble steps almost awed me, and so did the lofty hall into which they conducted. On the first landing I met a Flemish house-maid: she had wooden shoes, a short red petticoat, a printed cotton bedgown, her face was broad, her physiognomy eminently stupid; when I spoke to her in French, she answered me in Flemish, with an air the reverse of civil; yet I thought her charming; if she was not pretty or polite, she was, I conceived, very picturesque; she reminded me of the female figures in certain Dutch paintings I had seen in other years at Seacombe Hall.

I repaired to the public room; that, too, was very large and very lofty, and warmed by a stove; the floor was black, and the stove was black, and most of the furniture was black; yet I never experienced a freer sense of exhilaration than when I sat down at a very long, black table (covered, however, in part by a white cloth), and, having ordered breakfast, began to pour out my coffee from a little black coffee-pot. The stove might be dismal-looking to some eyes, not to mine, but it was indisputably very warm, and there were two gentlemen seated by it talking in French; impossible to follow their rapid utterance, or comprehend much of the purport of what they said—yet French, in the mouths of Frenchmen, or Belgians (I was not then sensible of the horrors of the Belgian accent) was as music to my ears. One of these gentlemen presently discerned me to be an Englishman—no doubt from the fashion in which I addressed the waiter; for I would persist in speaking French in my execrable South-of-England style, though the man understood English. The gentleman, after looking towards me once or twice, politely accosted me in very good English; I remember I wished to God that I could speak French as well; his fluency and correct pronunciation impressed me for the first time with a due notion of the cosmopolitan character of the capital I was in; it was my first experience of that skill in living languages I afterwards found to be so general in Brussels.

I lingered over my breakfast as long as I could; while it was there on the table, and while that stranger continued talking to me, I was a free, independent traveller; but at last the things were removed, the two gentlemen left the room; suddenly the

illusion ceased, reality and business came back. I, a bondsman just released from the yoke, freed for one week from twenty-one years of constraint, must, of necessity, resume the fetters of dependency. Hardly had I tasted the delight of being without a master when duty issued her stern mandate: "Go forth and seek another service." I never linger over a painful and necessary task; I never take pleasure before business, it is not in my nature to do so; impossible to enjoy a leisurely walk over the city, though I perceived the morning was very fine, until I had first presented Mr. Hunsden's letter of introduction, and got fairly on to the track of a new situation. Wrenching my mind from liberty and delight, I seized my hat and forced my reluctant body out of the Hotel de —— into the foreign street.

It was a fine day, but I would not look at the blue sky or at the stately houses round me; my mind was bent on one thing, finding out "Mr. Brown, Numéro —, Rue Royale," for so my letter was addressed. By dint of inquiry I succeeded; I stood at last at the desired door, knocked, asked for Mr. Brown, and was admitted.

Being shown into a small breakfast-room, I found myself in the presence of an elderly gentleman—very grave, business-like, and respectable-looking. I presented Mr. Hunsden's letter; he received me very civilly. After a little desultory conversation he asked me if there was anything in which his advice or experience could be of use. I said, "Yes," and then proceeded to tell him that I was not a gentleman of fortune, travelling for pleasure, but an ex-counting-house clerk, who wanted employment of some kind, and that immediately too. He replied that as a friend of Mr. Hunsden's he would be willing to assist me as well as he could. After some meditation he named a place in a mercantile house at Liège, and another in a bookseller's shop at Louvain.

"Clerk and shopman!" murmured I to myself. "No." I shook my head. I had tried the high stool; I hated it; I believed there were other occupations that would suit me better; besides, I did not wish to leave Brussels.

"I know of no place in Brussels," answered Mr. Brown, "unless indeed you were disposed to turn your attention to teaching. I am acquainted with the director of a large establishmeut who is in want of a professor of English and Latin."

I thought two minutes, then I seized the idea eagerly.

"The very thing, sir!" said I.

"But," asked he, "do you understand French well enough to teach Belgian boys English?"

Fortunately I could answer this question in the affirmative; having studied French under a Frenchman, I could speak the language intelligibly though not fluently. I could also read it well, and write it decently.

"Then," pursued Mr. Brown, "I think I can promise you the place, for Monsieur Pelet will not refuse a professor recommended by me; but come here again at five o'clock this afternoon, and I will introduce you to him."

The word "professor" struck me. "I am not a professor," said I.

"Oh," returned Mr. Brown, "professor, here in Belgium, means a teacher, that is all."

My conscience thus quieted, I thanked Mr. Brown, and, for the present, withdrew. This time I stepped out into the street with a relieved heart; the task I had imposed on myself for that day was executed. I might now take some hours of holiday. I felt free to look up. For the first time I remarked the sparkling clearness of the air, the deep blue of the sky, the gay clean aspect of the white-washed or painted houses; I saw what a fine street was the Rue Royale, and, walking leisurely along its broad pavement, I continued to survey its stately hotels, till the palisades, the gates, the trees of the park appearing in sight, offered to my eye a new attraction. I remember, before entering the park, I stood a while to contemplate the statue of General Belliard, and then I advanced to the top of the great staircase just beyond, and I looked down into a narrow back street, which I afterwards learnt was called the Rue d'Isabelle. I well recollect that my eye rested on the green door of a rather

large house opposite, where, on a brass plate, was inscribed, "Pensionnat de Demoiselles." Pensionnat! The word excited an uneasy sensation in my mind; it seemed to speak of restraint. Some of the demoiselles, externats no doubt, were at that moment issuing from the door—I looked for a pretty face amongst them, but their close, little French bonnets hid their features; in a moment they were gone.

I had traversed a good deal of Brussels before five o'clock arrived, but punctually as that hour struck I was again in the Rue Royale. Re-admitted to Mr. Brown's breakfast-room, I found him, as before, seated at the table, and he was not alone—a gentleman stood by the hearth. Two words of introduction designated him as my future master. "M. Pelet, Mr. Crimsworth; Mr. Crimsworth, M. Pelet." A bow on each side finished the ceremony. I don't know what sort of a bow I made; an ordinary one, I suppose, for I was in a tranquil, commonplace frame of mind; I felt none of the agitation which had troubled my first interview with Edward Crimsworth. M. Pelet's bow was extremely polite, yet not theatrical, scarcely French; he and I were presently seated opposite to each other. In a pleasing voice, low, and, out of consideration to my foreign ears, very distinct and deliberate, M. Pelet intimated that he had just been receiving from "le respectable M. Brown" an account of my attainments and character, which relieved him from all scruple as to the propriety of engaging me as professor of English and Latin in his establishment; nevertheless, for form's sake, he would put a few questions to test my powers. He did, and expressed in flattering terms his satisfaction at my answers. The subject of salary next came on; it was fixed at one thousand francs per annum, besides board and lodging. "And in addition," suggested M. Pelet, "as there will be some hours in each day during which your services will not be required in my establishment, you may, in time, obtain employment in other seminaries, and thus turn your vacant moments to profitable account."

I thought this very kind, and indeed I found afterwards that the terms on which M. Pelet had engaged me were really liberal for Brussels; instruction being extremely cheap there on account of the number of teachers. It was further arranged that I should be installed in my new post the very next day, after which M. Pelet and I parted.

Well, and what was he like? and what were my impressions concerning him? He was a man of about forty years of age, of middle size, and rather emaciated figure; his face was pale, his cheeks were sunk, and his eyes hollow; his features were pleasing and regular, they had a French turn (for M. Pelet was no Fleming, but a Frenchman both by birth and parentage), yet the degree of harshness inseparable from Gallic lineaments was, in his case, softened by a mild blue eye, and a melancholy, almost suffering, expression of countenance; his physiognomy was "fine et spirituelle." I use two French words because they define better than any English terms the species of intelligence with which his features were imbued. He was altogether an interesting and prepossessing personage. I wondered only at the utter absence of all the ordinary characteristics of his profession, and almost feared he could not be stern and resolute enough for a schoolmaster. Externally at least M. Pelet presented an absolute contrast to my late master, Edward Crimsworth.

Influenced by the impression I had received of his gentleness, I was a good deal surprised when, on arriving the next day at my new employer's house, and being admitted to a first view of what was to be the sphere of my future labours, namely, the large, lofty, and well-lighted schoolrooms, I beheld a numerous assemblage of pupils, boys of course, whose collective appearance showed all the signs of a full, flourishing, and well-disciplined seminary. As I traversed the classes in company with M. Pelet a profound silence reigned on all sides, and if by chance a murmur or a whisper arose, one glance from the pensive eye of this most gentle pedagogue stilled it instantly. It was astonishing, I thought, how so mild a check could prove so effectual. When I had perambulated the length and breadth of the classes, M. Pelet turned and said to me:

"Would you object to taking the boys as they are, and testing their proficiency in English?"

The proposal was unexpected. I had thought I should have been allowed at least a day to prepare; but it is a bad omen to commence any career by hesitation, so I just stepped to the professor's desk near which we stood, and faced the circle of my pupils. I took a moment to collect my thoughts, and likewise to frame in French the sentence by which I proposed to open business. I made it as short as possible:

"Messieurs, prenez vos livres de lecture."

"Anglais ou Français, Monsieur?" demanded a thick-set, moon-faced young Flamand in a blouse. The answer was fortunately easy:

"Anglais."

I determined to give myself as little trouble as possible in this lesson; it would not do yet to trust my unpractised tongue with the delivery of explanations; my accent and idiom would be too open to the criticisms of the young gentlemen before me, relative to whom I felt already it would be necessary at once to take up an advantageous position, and I proceeded to employ means accordingly.

"Commencez!" cried I, when they had all produced their books. The moon-faced youth (by name Jules Vanderkelkov, as I afterwards learnt) took the first sentence. The "livre de lecture" was the "Vicar of Wakefield," much used in foreign schools because it is supposed to contain prime samples of conversational English; it might, however, have been a Runic scroll for any resemblance the words, as enunciated by Jules, bore to the language in ordinary use amongst the natives of Great Britain. My God! how he did snuffle, snort, and wheeze! All he said was said in his throat and nose, for it is thus the Flamands speak, but I heard him to the end of his paragraph without proffering a word of correction, whereat he looked vastly self-complacent, convinced, no doubt, that he had acquainted himself like a real born and bred "Anglais." In the same unmoved silence I listened to a dozen in rotation, and when the twelfth had concluded with splutter, hiss, and mumble, I solemnly laid down the book.

"Arrêtez!" said I. There was a pause, during which I regarded them all with a steady and somewhat stern gaze; a dog, if stared at hard enough and long enough, will show symptoms of embarrassment, and so at length did my bench of Belgians. Perceiving that some of the faces before me were beginning to look sullen, and others ashamed, I slowly joined my hands, and ejaculated in a deep "voix de poitrine":

"Comme c'est affreux!"

They looked at each other, pouted, coloured, swung their heels; they were not pleased, I saw, but they were impressed, and in the way I wished them to be. Having thus taken them down a peg in their self-conceit, the next step was to raise myself in their estimation; not a very easy thing, considering that I hardly dared to speak for fear of betraying my own deficiencies.

"Écoutez, Messieurs!" said I, and I endeavoured to throw into my accents the compassionate tone of a superior being, who, touched by the extremity of the helplessness, which at first only excited his scorn, deigns at length to bestow aid. I then began at the very beginning of the "Vicar of Wakefield," and read, in a slow, distinct voice, some twenty pages, they all the while sitting mute and listening with fixed attention; by the time I had done nearly an hour had elapsed. I then rose and said:

"C'est assez pour aujourd'hui, Messieurs; demain nous recommencerons, et j'espère que tout ira bien."

With this oracular sentence I bowed, and in company with M. Pelet quitted the schoolroom.

"C'est bien! c'est très bien!" said my principal as we entered his parlour. "Je vois que Monsieur a de l'adresse; cela me plaît, car, dans l'instruction, l'adresse fait tout autant que le savoir."

From the parlour M. Pelet conducted me to my apartment, my "chambre," as Monsieur said with a certain air of complacency. It was a very small room, with an excessively small bed, but M. Pelet gave me to understand that I was to occupy it quite alone, which was of course a great comfort. Yet, though so limited in dimensions, it had two windows. Light not being taxed in Belgium, the people never grudge its admission into their houses; just here, however, this observation is not very *apropos,* for one of these windows was boarded up; the open window looked into the boys' playground. I glanced at the other, as wondering what aspect it would present if disencumbered of the boards. M. Pelet read, I suppose, the expression of my eye; he explained:

"La fenêtre fermée donne sur un jardin appartenant à un pensionnat de demoiselles," said he, "et les convenances exigent—enfin, vous comprenez—n'est-ce pas, Monsieur?"

"Oui, oui," was my reply, and I looked of course quite satisfied; but when M. Pelet had retired and closed the door after him, the first thing I did was to scrutinise closely the nailed boards, hoping to find some chink or crevice which I might enlarge, and so get a peep at the consecrated ground. My researches were vain, for the boards were well joined and strongly nailed. It is astonishing how disappointed I felt. I thought it would have been so pleasant to have looked out upon a garden planted with flowers and trees, so amusing to have watched the demoiselles at their play; to have studied female character in a variety of phases, myself the while sheltered from view by a modest muslin curtain, whereas owing doubtless to the absurd scruples of some old duenna of a directress, I had now only the option of looking at a bare gravelled court, with an enormous "pas de géant" in the middle, and the monotonous walls and windows of a boys' school-house round. Not only then, but many a time after, especially in moments of weariness and low spirits, did I look with dissatisfied eyes on that most tantalising board, longing to tear it away and get a glimpse of the green region which I imagined to lie beyond. I knew a tree grew close up to the window, for though there were as yet no leaves to rustle, I often heard at night the tapping of branches against the panes. In the daytime, when I listened attentively, I could hear, even through the boards, the voices of the demoiselles in their hours of recreation, and, to speak the honest truth, my sentimental reflections were occasionally a trifle disarranged by the not quite silvery, in fact the too often brazen sounds, which, rising from the unseen paradise below, penetrated clamorously into my solitude. Not to mince matters, it really seemed to me a doubtful case whether the lungs of Mdlle. Reuter's girls or those of M. Pelet's boys were the strongest, and when it came to shrieking the girls indisputably beat the boys hollow. I forgot to say, by-the-bye, that Reuter was the name of the old lady who had had my window boarded up. I say old, for such I, of course, concluded her to be, judging from her cautious, chaperon-like proceedings; besides, nobody ever spoke of her as young. I remember I was very much amused when I first heard her Christian name; it was Zoraïde—Mademoiselle Zoraïde Reuter. But the continental nations do allow themselves vagaries in the choice of names, such as we sober English never run into. I think, indeed, we have too limited a list to choose from.

Meantime my path was gradually growing smooth before me. I, in a few weeks, conquered the teasing difficulties inseparable from the commencement of almost every career. Ere long I had acquired as much facility in speaking French as set me at my ease with my pupils; and as I had encountered them on a right footing at the very beginning, and continued tenaciously to retain the advantage I had early gained, they never attempted mutiny, which circumstance, all who are in any degree acquainted with the ongoings of Belgian schools, and who know the relation in which professors and pupils too frequently stand towards each other in those establishments, will consider an important and uncommon one. Before concluding

this chapter I will say a word on the system I pursued with regard to my classes: my experience may possibly be of use to others.

It did not require very keen observation to detect the character of the youth of Brabant, but it needed a certain degree of tact to adapt one's measures to their capacity. Their intellectual faculties were generally weak, their animal propensities strong; thus there was at once an impotence and a kind of inert force in their natures; they were dull, but they were also singularly stubborn, heavy as lead and, like lead, most difficult to move. Such being the case, it would have been truly absurd to exact from them much in the way of mental exertion; having short memories, dense intelligence, feeble reflective powers, they recoiled with repugnance from any occupation that demanded close study or deep thought. Had the abhorred effort been extorted from them by injudicious and arbitrary measures on the part of the Professor, they would have resisted as obstinately, as clamorously, as desperate swine; and, though not brave singly, they were relentless acting *en masse*.

I understood that before my arrival in M. Pelet's establishment, the combined insubordination of the pupils had effected the dismissal of more than one English master. It was necessary then to exact only the most moderate application from natures so little qualified to apply—to assist, in every practicable way, understandings so opaque and contracted—to be ever gentle, considerate, yielding even, to a certain point, with dispositions so irrationally perverse; but, having reached that culminating point of indulgence, you must fix your foot, plant it, root it in rock—become immutable as the towers of Ste. Gudule; for a step—but half a step farther, and you would plunge headlong into the gulf of imbecility; there lodged, you would speedily receive proofs of Flemish gratitude and magnanimity in showers of Brabant saliva and handfuls of Low Country mud. You might smooth to the utmost the path of learning, remove every pebble from the track; but then you must finally insist with decision on the pupil taking your arm and allowing himself to be led quietly along the prepared road. When I had brought down my lesson to the lowest level of my dullest pupil's capacity—when I had shown myself the mildest, the most tolerant of masters—a word of impertinence, a movement of disobedience, changed me at once into a despot. I offered them but one alternative—submission and acknowledgment of error, or ignominious expulsion. This system answered, and my influence, by degrees, became established on a firm basis. "The boy is father to the man," it is said; and so I often thought when I looked at my boys and remembered the political history of their ancestors. Pelet's school was merely an epitome of the Belgian nation.

Chapter VIII

AND Pelet himself ? How did I continue to like him? Oh, extremely well! Nothing could be more smooth, gentlemanlike, and even friendly, than his demeanour to me. I had to endure from him neither cold neglect, irritating interference, nor pretentious assumption of superiority. I fear, however, two poor, hard-worked Belgian ushers in the establishment could not have said as much; to them the director's manner was invariably dry, stern, and cool. I believe he perceived once or twice that I was a little shocked at the difference he made between them and me, and accounted for it by saying, with a quiet sarcastic smile:

"Ce ne sont que des Flamands—allez!"

And then he took his cigar gently from his lips and spat on the painted floor of the room in which we were sitting. Flamands certainly they were, and both had the true Flamand physiognomy, where intellectual inferiority is marked in lines none can mistake; still they were men, and, in the main, honest men; and I could

not see why their being aboriginals of the flat, dull soil should serve as a pretext for treating them with perpetual severity and contempt. This idea of injustice somewhat poisoned the pleasure I might otherwise have derived from Pelet's soft affable manner to myself. Certainly it was agreeable, when the day's work was over, to find one's employer an intelligent and cheerful companion; and if he was sometimes a little sarcastic and sometimes a little too insinuating, and if I did discover that his mildness was more a matter of appearance than of reality—if I did occasionally suspect the existence of flint or steel under an external covering of velvet—still we are none of us perfect; and weary as I was of the atmosphere of brutality and insolence in which I had constantly lived at X——, I had no inclination now, on casting anchor in calmer regions, to institute at once a prying search after defects that were scrupulously withdrawn and carefully veiled from my view. I was willing to take Pelet for what he seemed—to believe him benevolent and friendly until some untoward event should prove him otherwise. He was not married, and I soon perceived he had all a Frenchman's, all a Parisian's notions about matrimony and women. I suspected a degree of laxity in his code of morals, there was something so cold and *blasé* in his tone whenever he alluded to what he called "le beau sexe"; but he was too gentlemanlike to intrude topics I did not invite, and as he was really intelligent and really fond of intellectual subjects of discourse, he and I always found enough to talk about, without seeking themes in the mire. I hated his fashion of mentioning love; I abhorred, from my soul, mere licentiousness. He felt the difference of our notions, and, by mutual consent, we kept off ground debatable.

Pelet's house was kept and his kitchen managed by his mother, a real old French-woman; she had been handsome—at least she told me so, and I strove to believe her; she was now ugly, as only continental old women can be; perhaps, though, her style of dress made her look uglier than she really was. Indoors she would go about without cap, her grey hair strangely dishevelled; then, when at home, she seldom wore a gown—only a shabby cotton camisole; shoes, too, were strangers to her feet, and in lieu of them she sported roomy slippers, trodden down at the heels. On the other hand, whenever it was her pleasure to appear abroad, as on Sundays and fête-days, she would put on some very brilliant-coloured dress, usually of thin texture, a silk bonnet with a wreath of flowers, and a very fine shawl. She was not, in the main, an ill-natured old woman, but an incessant and most indiscreet talker; she kept chiefly in and about the kitchen, and seemed rather to avoid her son's august presence; of him, indeed, she evidently stood in awe. When he reproved her, his reproofs were bitter and unsparing; but he seldom gave himself that trouble.

Madame Pelet had her own society, her own circle of chosen visitors, who, however, I seldom saw, as she generally entertained them in what she called her "cabinet," a small den of a place adjoining the kitchen, and descending into it by one or two steps. On these steps, by-the-bye, I have not unfrequently seen Madame Pelet seated with a trencher on her knee, engaged in the threefold employment of eating her dinner, gossiping with her favourite servant, the house-maid, and scolding her antagonist, the cook; she never dined, and seldom indeed took any meal with her son; and as to showing her face at the boys' table, that was quite out of the question. These details will sound very odd in English ears, but Belgium is not England, and its ways are not our ways.

Madame Pelet's habits of life, then, being taken into consideration, I was a good deal surprised when, one Thursday evening (Thursday was always a half-holiday), as I was sitting all alone in my apartment, correcting a huge pile of English and Latin exercises, a servant tapped at the door, and, on its being opened, presented Madame Pelet's compliments, and she would be happy to see me to take my "goûter" (a meal which answers to our English "tea") with her in the dining-room.

"Plaît-il?" said I, for I thought I must have misunderstood, the message and invitation were so unusual; the same words were repeated. I accepted, of course, and as I descended the stairs, I wondered what whim had entered the old lady's brain; her son was out—gone to pass the evening at the Salle of the Grande Harmonie or some other club of which he was a member. Just as I laid my hand on the handle of the dining-room door, a queer idea glanced across my mind.

"Surely she's not going to make love to me," said I. "I've heard of old French-women doing odd things in that line; and the goûter? They generally begin such affairs with eating and drinking, I believe."

There was a fearful dismay in this suggestion of my excited imagination, and if I had allowed myself time to dwell upon it, I should no doubt have cut there and then, rushed back to my chamber, and bolted myself in; but whenever a danger or a horror is veiled with uncertainty, the primary wish of the mind is to ascertain first the naked truth, reserving the expedient of flight for the moment when its dread anticipation shall be realised. I turned the door-handle, and in an instant had crossed the fatal threshold, closed the door behind me, and stood in the presence of Madame Pelet.

Gracious heavens! The first view of her seemed to confirm my worst apprehensions. There she sat, dressed out in a light green muslin gown, on her head a lace cap with flourishing red roses in the frill; her table was carefully spread; there were fruit, cakes, and coffee, with a bottle of something—I did not know what. Already the cold sweat started on my brow, already I glanced back over my shoulder at the closed door, when, to my unspeakable relief, my eye, wandering wildly in the direction of the stove, rested upon a second figure, seated in a large fauteuil beside it. This was a woman, too, and, moreover, an old woman, and as fat and as rubicund as Madame Pelet was meagre and yellow; her attire was likewise very fine, and spring flowers of different hues circled in a bright wreath the crown of her violet-coloured velvet bonnet.

I had only time to make these general observations when Madame Pelet, coming forward with what she intended should be a graceful and elastic step, thus accosted me:

"Monsieur is indeed most obliging to quit his books, his studies, at the request of an insignificant person like me—will Monsieur complete his kindness by allowing me to present him to my dear friend Madame Reuter, who resides in the neighbouring house—the young ladies' school."

"Ah!" thought I, "I knew she was old," and I bowed and took my seat. Madame Reuter placed herself at the table opposite to me.

"How do you like Belgium, Monsieur?" asked she, in an accent of the broadest Bruxellois. I could now well distinguish the difference between the fine and pure Parisian utterance of M. Pelet, for instance, and the guttural enunciation of the Flamands. I answered politely, and then wondered how so coarse and clumsy an old woman as the one before me should be at the head of a ladies' seminary, which I had always heard spoken of in terms of high commendation. In truth there was something to wonder at. Madame Reuter looked more like a joyous, free-living old Flemish fermière, or even a maîtresse d'auberge, than a staid, grave, rigid directrice de pensionnat. In general the continental, or at least the Belgian old women permit themselves a licence of manners, speech, and aspect, such as our venerable grand-dames would recoil from as absolutely disreputable, and Madame Reuter's jolly face bore evidence that she was no exception to the rule of her country; there was a twinkle and leer in her left eye; her right she kept habitually half shut, which I thought very odd indeed. After several vain attempts to comprehend the motives of these two droll old creatures for inviting me to join them at their goûter, I at last fairly gave it up, and resigning myself to inevitable mystification, I sat and looked first at one, then at the other, taking care meantime to do justice to the confitures, cakes, and coffee, with which they amply supplied me. They, too, ate,

and that with no delicate appetite, and having demolished a large portion of the solids, they proposed a "petit verre." I declined. Not so Mesdames Pelet and Reuter; each mixed herself what I thought rather a stiff tumbler of punch, and placing it on a stand near the stove, they drew up their chairs to that convenience, and invited me to do the same. I obeyed; and being seated fairly between them, I was thus addressed first by Madame Pelet, then by Madame Reuter.

"We will now speak of business," said Madame Pelet, and she went on to make an elaborate speech, which, being interpreted, was to the effect that she had asked for the pleasure of my company that evening in order to give her friend Madame Reuter an opportunity of broaching an important proposal, which might turn out greatly to my advantage.

"Pourvu que vous soyez sage," said Madame Reuter, "et à vrai dire, vous en avez bien l'air. Take one drop of the punch" (or ponche, as she pronounced it); "it is an agreeable and wholesome beverage after a full meal."

I bowed, but again declined it. She went on:

"I feel," said she, after a solemn sip: "I feel profoundly the importance of the commission with which my dear daughter has entrusted me, for you are aware, Monsieur, that it is my daughter who directs the establishment in the next house?"

"Ah! I thought it was yourself, Madame." Though, indeed, at that moment I recollected that it was called Mademoiselle, not Madame Reuter's pensionnat.

"I! Oh, no! I manage the house and look after the servants, as my friend Madame Pelet does for Monsieur her son—nothing more. Ah! you thought I gave lessons in class—did you?"

And she laughed loud and long, as though the idea tickled her fancy amazingly.

"Madame is in the wrong to laugh," I observed; "if she does not give lessons, I am sure it is not because she cannot"; and I whipped out a white pocket-handkerchief and wafted it, with a French grace, past my nose, bowing at the same time.

"Quel charmant jeune homme!" murmured Madame Pelet in a low voice. Madame Reuter, being less sentimental, as she was Flamand and not French, only laughed again.

"You are a dangerous person, I fear," said she; "if you can forge compliments at that rate, Zoraïde will positively be afraid of you; but if you are good, I will keep your secret, and not tell her how well you can flatter. Now, listen what sort of a proposal she makes to you. She has heard that you are an excellent professor, and as she wishes to get the very best masters for her school (car Zoraïde fait tout comme une reine, c'est une véritable maîtresse-femme), she has commissioned me to step over this afternoon, and sound Madame Pelet as to the possibility of engaging you. Zoraïde is a wary general; she never advances without first examining well her ground. I don't think she would be pleased if she knew I had already disclosed her intentions to you; she did not order me to go so far, but I thought there would be no harm in letting you into the secret, and Madame Pelet was of the same opinion. Take care, however, you don't betray either of us to Zoraïde—to my daughter, I mean; she is so discreet and circumspect herself, she cannot understand that one should find a pleasure in gossiping a little——"

"C'est absolument comme mon fils!" cried Madame Pelet.

"All the world is so changed since our girlhood!" rejoined the other: "young people have such old heads now. But to return, Monsieur. Madame Pelet will mention the subject of your giving lessons in my daughter's establishment to her son, and he will speak to you; and then to-morrow, you will step over to our house, and ask to see my daughter, and you will introduce the subject as if the first intimation of it had reached you from M. Pelet himself, and be sure you never mention my name, for I would not displease Zoraïde on any account."

"Bien, bien!" interrupted I—for all this chatter and circumlocution began to bore me very much; "I will consult M. Pelet, and the thing shall be settled as you desire. Good evening, Mesdames—I am infinitely obliged to you."

"Comment! vous vous en allez déjá?" exclaimed Madame Pelet.

"Prenez encore quelquechose, Monsieur; une pomme cuite, des biscuits, encore une tasse de café?"

"Merci, merci, Madame—au revoir." And I backed at last out of the apartment.

Having regained my own room, I set myself to turn over in my mind the incident of the evening. It seemed a queer affair altogether, and queerly managed; the two old women had made quite a little intricate mess of it; still I found that the uppermost feeling in my mind on the subject was one of satisfaction. In the first place it would be a change to give lessons in another seminary, and then to teach young ladies would be an occupation so interesting—to be admitted at all into a ladies' boarding-school would be an incident so new in my life. Besides, thought I, as I glanced at the boarded window, "I shall now at last see the mysterious garden: I shall gaze both on the angels and their Eden."

Chapter IX

M. PELET could not of course object to the proposal made by Mdlle. Reuter; permission to accept such additional employment, should it offer, having formed an article of the terms on which he had engaged me. It was, therefore, arranged in the course of next day that I should be at liberty to give lessons in Mdlle. Reuter's establishment four afternoons in every week.

When evening came I prepared to step over in order to seek a conference with Mademoiselle herself on the subject; I had not had time to pay the visit before, having been all day closely occupied in class. I remember very well that before quitting my chamber, I held a brief debate with myself as to whether I should change my ordinary attire for something smarter. At last I concluded it would be a waste of labour. "Doubtless," thought I, "she is some stiff old maid; for though the daughter of Madame Reuter, she may well number upwards of forty winters; besides, if it were otherwise, if she be both young and pretty, I am not handsome, and no dressing can make me so, therefore I'll go as I am." And off I started, cursorily glancing sideways as I passed the toilet-table, surmounted by a looking-glass: a thin irregular face I saw, with sunk, dark eyes under a large, square forehead, complexion destitute of bloom or attraction; something young, but not youthful, no object to win a lady's love, no butt for the shafts of Cupid.

I was soon at the entrance of the pensionnat, in a moment I had pulled the bell; in another moment the door was opened, and within appeared a passage paved alternately with black and white marble; the walls were painted in imitation of marble also; and at the far end opened a glass door, through which I saw shrubs and a grass-plat, looking pleasant in the sunshine of the mild spring evening—for it was now the middle of April.

This, then, was my first glimpse of *the* garden; but I had not time to look long, the portress, after having answered in the affirmative my question as to whether her mistress was at home, opened the folding-doors of a room to the left, and having ushered me in, closed them behind me. I found myself in a salon with a very well-painted, highly varnished floor; chairs and sofas covered with white draperies, a green porcelain stove, walls hung with pictures in gilt frames, a gilt pendule and other ornaments on the mantelpiece, a large lustre pendent from the centre of the ceiling, mirrors, consoles, muslin curtains, and a handsome centre table completed the inventory of furniture. All looked extremely clean and glittering, but the general effect would have been somewhat chilling had not a second large pair of folding-doors, standing wide open, and disclosing another and smaller salon, more snugly furnished, offered some relief to the eye. This room was carpeted,

and therein was a piano, a couch, a chiffonnière—above all, it contained a lofty window with a crimson curtain, which, being undrawn, afforded another glimpse of the garden, through the large, clear panes, round which some leaves of ivy, some tendrils of vine were trained.

"Monsieur Creemsvort, n'est ce pas?" said a voice behind me; and, starting involuntarily, I turned. I had been so taken up with the contemplation of the pretty little salon that I had not noticed the entrance of a person into the larger room. It was, however, Mdlle. Reuter who now addressed me, and stood close beside me; and when I had bowed with instantaneously recovered sang-froid—for I am not easily embarrassed—I commenced the conversation by remarking on the pleasant aspect of her little cabinet, and the advantage she had over M. Pelet in possessing a garden.

"Yes," she said, "she often thought so"; and added, "it is my garden, Monsieur, which makes me retain this house, otherwise I should probably have removed to larger and more commodious premises long since; but you see I could not take my garden with me, and I should scarcely find one so large and pleasant anywhere else in town."

I approved her judgment.

"But you have not seen it yet," said she, rising; "come to the window and take a better view." I followed her; she opened the sash, and leaning out I saw in full the enclosed demesne which had hitherto been to me an unknown region. It was a long, not very broad strip of cultured ground, with an alley bordered by enormous old fruit trees down the middle; there was a sort of lawn, a parterre of rose-trees, some flower-borders, and, on the far side, a thickly planted copse of lilacs, laburnums, and acacias. It looked pleasant, to me—very pleasant, so long a time had elapsed since I had seen a garden of any sort. But it was not only on Mdlle. Reuter's garden that my eyes dwelt; when I had taken a view of her well-trimmed beds and budding shrubberies, I allowed my glance to come back to herself, nor did I hastily withdraw it.

I had thought to see a tall, meagre, yellow, conventual image in black, with a close white cap, bandaged under the chin like a nun's head-gear; whereas, there stood by me a little and roundly formed woman, who might indeed be older than I, but was still young; she could not, I thought, be more than six or seven and twenty; she was as fair as a fair Englishwoman; she had no cap; her hair was nut-brown, and she wore it in curls; pretty her features were not, nor very soft, nor very regular, but neither were they in any degree plain, and I already saw cause to deem them expressive. What was their predominant cast? Was it sagacity?—sense? Yes, I thought so; but I could scarcely as yet be sure. I discovered, however, that there was a certain serenity of eye, and freshness of complexion, most pleasing to behold. The colour on her cheek was like the bloom on a good apple, which is as sound at the core as it is red on the rind.

Mdlle. Reuter and I entered upon business. She said she was not absolutely certain of the wisdom of the step she was about to take, because I was so young, and parents might possibly object to a professor like me for their daughters: "But it is often well to act on one's own judgment," said she, "and to lead parents, rather than be led by them. The fitness of a professor is not a matter of age; and, from what I have heard, and from what I observe myself, I would much rather trust you than M. Ledru, the music-master, who is a married man of near fifty."

I remarked that I hoped she would find me worthy of her good opinion; that if I knew myself, I was incapable of betraying any confidence reposed in me. "Du reste," said she, "the surveillance will be strictly attended to." And then she proceeded to discuss the subject of terms. She was very cautious, quite on her guard; she did not absolutely bargain, but she warily sounded me to find out what my expectations might be; and when she could not get me to name a sum, she reasoned and reasoned with a fluent yet quiet circumlocution of speech, and at last

nailed me down to five hundred francs per annum—not too much, but I agreed. Before the negotiation was completed, it began to grow a little dusk. I did not hasten it, for I liked well enough to sit and hear her talk; I was amused with the sort of business talent she displayed. Edward could not have shown himself more practical, though he might have evinced more coarseness and urgency; and then she had so many reasons, so many explanations; and, after all, she succeeded in proving herself quite disinterested and even liberal. At last she concluded, she could say no more, because, as I acquiesced in all things, there was no further ground for the exercise of her parts of speech. I was obliged to rise. I would rather have sat a little longer; what had I to return to but my small empty room? And my eyes had a pleasure in looking at Mdlle. Reuter, especially now, when the twilight softened her features a little, and, in the doubtful dusk, I could fancy her forehead as open as it was really elevated, her mouth touched with turns of sweetness as well as defined in lines of sense. When I rose to go, I held out my hand, on purpose, though I knew it was contrary to the etiquette of foreign habits; she smiled, and said:

"Ah! c'est comme tous les Anglais," but gave me her hand very kindly.

"It is the privilege of my country, Mademoiselle," said I; "and, remember, I shall always claim it."

She laughed a little, quite good-naturedly, and with the sort of tranquillity obvious in all she did—a tranquillity which soothed and suited me singularly, at least I thought so that evening. Brussels seemed a very pleasant place to me when I got out again into the street, and it appeared as if some cheerful, eventful, upward-tending career were even then opening to me, on that selfsame mild, still April night. So impressionable a being is man, or at least such a man as I was in those days.

Chapter X

NEXT day the morning hours seemed to pass very slowly at M. Pelet's; I wanted the afternoon to come that I might go again to the neighbouring pensionnat and give my first lesson within its pleasant precincts; for pleasant they appeared to me. At noon the hour of recreation arrived; at one o'clock we had lunch; this got on the time, and at last Ste. Gudule's deep bell, tolling slowly two, marked the moment for which I had been waiting.

At the foot of the narrow back-stairs that descended from my room, I met M. Pelet.

"Comme vous avez l'air rayonnant!" said he. "Je ne vous ai jamais vu aussi gai. Que s'est-il donc passé?"

"Apparemment que j'aime les changements," replied I.

"Ah! je comprends—c'est cela—soyez sage seulement. Vous êtes bien jeune—trop jeune pour le rôle que vous allez jouer; il faut prendre garde—savez-vous?"

"Mais quel danger y a-t-il?"

"Je n'en sais rien—ne vous laissez pas aller à de vives impressions—voilà tout."

I laughed: a sentiment of exquisite pleasure played over my nerves at the thought that "vives impressions" were likely to be created; it was the deadness, the sameness of life's daily ongoings that had hitherto been my bane; my blouse-clad élèves in the boys' seminary never stirred in me any "vives impressions," except it might be occasionally some of anger. I broke from M. Pelet, and as I strode down the passage he followed me with one of his laughs—a very French, rakish, mocking sound.

Again I stood at the neighbouring door, and soon was re-admitted into the cheerful passage with its clear dove-colour imitation marble walls. I followed the portress, and descending a step, and making a turn, I found myself in a sort of corridor; a side-door opened, Mdlle. Reuter's little figure, as graceful as it was plump, appeared. I could now see her dress in full daylight; a neat, simple mousseline-laine gown fitted her compact round shape to perfection—delicate little collar and manchettes of lace, trim Parisian brodequins showed her neck, wrists, and feet, to complete advantage; but how grave was her face as she came suddenly upon me! Solicitude and business were in her eye—on her forehead; she looked almost stern. Her "Bon jour, Monsieur," was quite polite, but so orderly, so commonplace, it spread directly a cool, damp towel over my "vives impressions." The servant turned back when her mistress appeared, and I walked slowly along the corridor, side by side with Mdlle. Reuter.

"Monsieur will give a lesson in the first class to-day," said she; "dictation or reading will perhaps be the best thing to begin with, for those are the easiest forms of communicating instruction in a foreign language; and, at the first, a master naturally feels a little unsettled."

She was quite right, as I had found from experience; it only remained for me to acquiesce. We proceeded now in silence. The corridor terminated in a hall, large, lofty, and square; a glass door on one side showed within a long narrow refectory, with tables, an armoire, and two lamps; it was empty; large glass doors, in front, opened on the playground and garden; a broad staircase ascended spirally on the opposite side; the remaining wall showed a pair of great folding-doors, now closed, and admitting, doubtless, to the classes.

Mdlle. Reuter turned her eye laterally on me, to ascertain, probably, whether I was collected enough to be ushered into her sanctum sanctorum. I suppose she judged me to be in a tolerable state of self-government, for she opened the door, and I followed her through. A rustling sound of uprising greeted our entrance; without looking to the right or left, I walked straight up the lane between two sets of benches and desks, and took possession of the empty chair and isolated desk raised on an estrade, of one step high, so as to command one division; the other division being under the surveillance of a maîtresse similarly elevated. At the back of the estrade, and attached to a movable partition dividing this schoolroom from another beyond, was a large tableau of wood painted black and varnished; a thick crayon of white chalk lay on my desk for the convenience of elucidating any grammatical or verbal obscurity which might occur in my lessons by writing it upon the tableau; a wet sponge appeared beside the chalk, to enable me to efface the marks when they had served the purpose intended.

I carefully and deliberately made these observations before allowing myself to take one glance at the benches before me; having handled the crayon, looked back at the tableau, fingered the sponge in order to ascertain that it was in a right state of moisture, I found myself cool enough to admit of looking calmly up and gazing deliberately round me.

And first I observed that Mdlle. Reuter had already glided away, she was nowhere visible; a maîtresse or teacher, the one who occupied the corresponding estrade to my own, alone remained to keep guard over me; she was a little in the shade, and, with my short sight, I could only see that she was of a thin bony figure and rather tallowy complexion, and that her attitude, as she sat, partook equally of listlessness and affectation. More obvious, more prominent, shone on by the full light of the large window, were the occupants of the benches just before me, of whom some were girls of fourteen, fifteen, sixteen, some young women from eighteen (as it appeared to me) up to twenty; the most modest attire, the simplest fashion of wearing the hair, were apparent in all; and good features, ruddy, blooming complexions, large and brilliant eyes, forms full, even to solidity, seemed to abound. I did not

bear the first view like a stoic; I was dazzled, my eyes fell, and in a voice somewhat too low I murmured:

"Prenez vos cahiers de dictée, Mesdemoiselles."

Not so had I bid the boys at Pelet's take their reading-books. A rustle followed, and an opening of desks; behind the lifted lids which momentarily screened the heads bent down to search for exercise books, I heard tittering and whispers.

"Eulalie, je suis prête à pâmer de rire," observed one.

"Comme il a rougi en parlant!"

"Oui, c'est un véritable blanc-bec."

"Tais-toi, Hortense—il nous écoute."

And now the lids sank and the heads reappeared; I had marked three, the whisperers, and I did not scruple to take a very steady look at them as they emerged from their temporary eclipse. It is astonishing what ease and courage their little phrases of flippancy had given me; the idea by which I had been awed was that the youthful beings before me, with their dark nun-like robes and softly braided hair, were a kind of half-angels. The light titter, the giddy whisper, had already in some measure relieved my mind of that fond and oppressive fancy. The three I allude to were just in front, within half a yard of my estrade, and were among the most womanly-looking present. Their names I knew afterwards, and may as well mention now; they were Eulalie, Hortense, Caroline. Eulalie was tall, and very finely shaped: she was fair, and her features were those of a Low Country Madonna; many a "figure de Vierge" have I seen in Dutch pictures exactly resembling hers; there were no angles in her shape or in her face, all was curve and roundness—neither thought, sentiment, nor passion disturbed by line or flush the equality of her pale, clear skin; her noble bust heaved with her regular breathing, her eyes moved a little—by these evidences of life alone could I have distinguished her from some large handsome figure moulded in wax. Hortense was of middle size and stout, her form was ungraceful, her face striking, more alive and brilliant than Eulalie's, her hair was dark brown, her complexion richly coloured; there were frolic and mischief in her eye: consistency and good sense she might possess, but none of her features betokened those qualities.

Caroline was little, though evidently full-grown; raven-black hair, very dark eyes, absolutely regular features, with a colourless olive complexion, clear as to the face and sallow about the neck, formed in her that assemblage of points whose union many persons regard as the perfection of beauty. How, with the tintless pallor of her skin aud the classic straightness of her lineaments, she managed to look sensual, I don't know. I think her lips and eyes contrived the affair between them, and the result left no uncertainty on the beholder's mind. She was sensual now, and in ten years' time she would be coarse—promise plain was written in her face of much future folly.

If I looked at these girls with little scruple, they looked at me with still less. Eulalie raised her unmoved eye to mine, and seemed to expect, passively but securely, an impromptu tribute to her majestic charms. Hortense regarded me boldly, and giggled at the same time, while she said, with an air of impudent freedom, "Dictez-nous quelquechose de facile pour commencer, Monsieur."

Caroline shook her loose ringlets of abundant but somewhat coarse hair over her rolling black eyes; parting her lips, as full as those of a hot-blooded Maroon, she showed her well-set teeth sparkling between them, and treated me at the same time to a smile "de sa façon." Beautiful as Pauline Borghese, she looked at the moment scarcely purer than Lucrèce de Borgia. Caroline was of noble family. I heard her lady-mother's character afterwards, and then I ceased to wonder at the precocious accomplishments of the daughter. These three, I at once saw, deemed themselves the queens of the school, and conceived that by their splendour they threw all the rest into the shade. In less than five minutes they had thus revealed to me their

characters, and in less than five minutes I had buckled on a breast-plate of steely indifference, and let down a visor of impassible austerity.

"Take your pens and commence writing," said I, in as dry and trite a voice as if I had been addressing only Jules Vanderkelkov and Co.

The dictée now commenced. My three belles interrupted me perpetually with little silly questions and uncalled-for remarks, to some of which I made no answer, and to others replied very quietly and briefly.

"Comment dit-on point et virgule en Anglais, Monsieur?"

"Semi-colon, Mademoiselle."

"Semi-collong? Ah, comme c'est drôle!" (giggle.)

"J'ai une si mauvaise plume—impossible d'écrire!"

"Mais, Monsieur—je ne sais pas suivre—vous allez si vîte."

"Je n'ai rien compris, moi!"

Here a general murmur arose, and the teacher, opening her lips for the first time, ejaculated:

"Silence, Mesdemoiselles!"

No silence followed—on the contrary, the three ladies in front began to talk more loudly.

"C'est si difficile, l'Anglaise!"

"Je déteste la dictée."

"Quel ennui d'écrire quelquechose que l'on ne comprend pas!"

Some of those behind laughed: a degree of confusion began to pervade the class; it was necessary to take prompt measures.

"Donnez-moi votre cahier," said I to Eulalie in an abrupt tone; and bending over, I took it before she had time to give it.

"Et vous, Mademoiselle—donnez-moi le vôtre," continued I, more mildly, addressing a little pale, plain-looking girl who sat in the first row of the other division, and whom I had remarked as being at once the ugliest and the most attentive in the room; she rose up, walked over to me, and delivered her book with a grave, modest curtsey. I glanced over the two dictations; Eulalie's was slurred, blotted, and full of silly mistakes—Sylvie's (such was the name of the ugly little girl) was clearly written, it contained no error against sense, and but few faults of orthography. I coolly read aloud both exercises, marking the faults—then I looked at Eulalie—

"C'est honteux!" said I, and I deliberately tore her dictation in four parts, and presented her with the fragments. I returned Sylvie her book with a smile, saying:

"C'est bien—je suis content de vous."

Sylvie looked calmly pleased, Eulalie swelled like an incensed turkey, but the mutiny was quelled: the conceited coquetry and futile flirtation of the first bench were exchanged for a taciturn sullenness, much more convenient to me, and the rest of my lesson passed without interruption.

A bell clanging out in the yard announced the moment for the cessation of school labours. I heard our own bell at the same time, and that of a certain public college immediately after. Order dissolved instantly; up started every pupil. I hastened to seize my hat, bow to the maîtresse, and quit the room before the tide of externats should pour from the inner class, where I knew near a hundred were prisoned, and whose rising tumult I already heard.

I had scarcely crossed the hall and gained the corridor, when Mdlle. Reuter came again upon me.

"Step in here a moment," said she, and she held open the door of the side room from whence she had issued on my arrival; it was a salle-à-manger, as appeared from the beaufet and the armoire vitrée, filled with glass and china, which formed part of its furniture. Ere she had closed the door on me and herself, the corridor was already filled with day-pupils, tearing down their cloaks, bonnets, and cabas from the wooden pegs on which they were suspended; the shrill voice of a maîtresse

was heard at intervals vainly endeavouring to enforce some sort of order; vainly, I say: discipline there was none in these rough ranks, and yet this was considered one of the best conducted schools in Brussels.

"Well, you have given your first lesson," began Mdlle. Reuter in the most calm, equable voice, as though quite unconscious of the chaos from which we were separated only by a single wall.

"Were you satisfied with your pupils, or did any circumstance in their conduct give you cause for complaint? Conceal nothing from me, repose in me entire confidence."

Happily, I felt in myself complete power to manage my pupils without aid; the enchantment, the golden haze which had dazzled my perspicuity at first, had been a good deal dissipated. I cannot say I was chagrined or downcast by the contrast which the reality of a pensionnat de demoiselles presented to my vague ideal of the same community; I was only enlightened and amused; consequently, I felt in no disposition to complain to Mdlle. Reuter, and I received her considerate invitation to confidence with a smile.

"A thousand thanks, Mademoiselle, all has gone very smoothly."

She looked more than doubtful.

"Et les trois demoiselles du premier banc?" said she.

"Ah! tout va au mieux!" was my answer, and Mdlle. Reuter ceased to question me; but her eye—not large, not brilliant, not melting, or kindling, but astute, penetrating, practical, showed she was even with me; it let out a momentary gleam, which said plainly, "Be as close as you like, I am not dependent on your candour; what you would conceal I already know."

By a transition so quiet as to be scarcely perceptible, the directress's manner changed; the anxious business-air passed from her face, and she began chatting about the weather and the town, and asking in neighbourly wise after M. and Madame Pelet. I answered all her little questions; she prolonged her talk, I went on following its many little windings; she sat so long, said so much, varied so often the topics of discourse, that it was not difficult to perceive she had a particular aim in thus detaining me. Her mere words could have afforded no clue to this aim, but her countenance aided; while her lips uttered only affable commonplaces, her eyes reverted continually to my face. Her glances were not given in full, but out of the corners, so quietly, so stealthily, yet I think I lost not one. I watched her as keenly as she watched me; I perceived soon that she was feeling after my real character; she was searching for salient points and weak points, and eccentric points; she was applying now this test, now that, hoping in the end to find some chink, some niche, where she could put in her little firm foot and stand upon my neck—mistress of my nature. Do not mistake me, reader, it was no amorous influence she wished to gain—at that time it was only the power of the politician to which she aspired; I was now installed as a professor in her establishment, and she wanted to know where her mind was superior to mine—by what feeling or opinion she could lead me.

I enjoyed the game much, and did not hasten its conclusion; sometimes I gave her hopes, beginning a sentence rather weakly, when her shrewd eye would light up—she thought she had me; having led her a little way, I delighted to turn round and finish with sound, hard sense, whereat her countenance would fall. At last a servant entered to announce dinner: the conflict being thus necessarily terminated, we parted without having gained any advantage on either side: Mdlle. Reuter had not even given me an opportunity of attacking her with feeling, and I had managed to baffle her little schemes of craft. It was a regular drawn battle. I again held out my hand when I left the room, she gave me hers; it was a small and white hand, but how cool! I met her eye too in full—obliging her to give me a straightforward look; this last test went against me: it left her as it found her—moderate, temperate, tranquil; me it disappointed.

"I am growing wiser," thought I, as I walked back to M. Pelet's. "Look at this little woman; is she like the women of novelists and romancers? To read of female character as depicted in Poetry and Fiction, one would think it was made up of sentiment, either for good or bad—here is a specimen, and a most sensible and respectable specimen too, whose staple ingredient is abstract reason. No Talleyrand was ever more passionless than Zoraïde Reuter!" So I thought then; I found afterwards that blunt susceptibilities are very consistent with strong propensities.

Chapter XI

I HAD indeed had a very long talk with the crafty little politician, and on regaining my quarters, I found that dinner was half over. To be late at meals was against a standing rule of the establishment, and had it been one of the Flemish ushers who thus entered after the removal of the soup and the commencement of the first course, M. Pelet would probably have greeted him with a public rebuke, and would certainly have mulcted him both of soup and fish; as it was, that polite though partial gentleman only shook his head, and as I took my place, unrolled my napkin, and said my heretical grace to myself, he civilly despatched a servant to the kitchen, to bring me a plate of "purée aux carottes" (for this was a maigre-day), and before sending away the first course, reserved for me a portion of the stock-fish of which it consisted. Dinner being over, the boys rushed out for their evening play; Kint and Vandam (the two ushers) of course followed them. Poor fellows! if they had not looked so very heavy, so very soulless, so very indifferent to all things in heaven above or in the earth beneath, I could have pitied them greatly for the obligation they were under to trail after those rough lads everywhere and at all times; even as it was, I felt disposed to scout myself as a privileged prig when I turned to ascend to my chamber, sure to find there, if not enjoyment, at least liberty; but this evening (as had often happened before) I was to be still further distinguished.

"Eh bien, mauvais sujet!" said the voice of M. Pelet behind me, as I set my foot on the first step of the stair, "où allez-vous? Venez à la salle-à-manger, que je vous gronde un peu."

"I beg pardon, Monsieur," said I, as I followed him to his private sitting-room, "for having returned so late—it was not my fault."

"That is just what I want to know," rejoined M. Pelet, as he ushered me into the comfortable parlour with a good wood-fire—for the stove had now been removed for the season. Having rung the bell he ordered "Coffee for two," and presently he and I were seated, almost in English comfort, one on each side of the hearth, a little round table between us, with a coffee-pot, a sugar-basin, and two large white china cups. While M. Pelet employed himself in choosing a cigar from a box, my thoughts reverted to the two outcast ushers, whose voices I could hear even now crying hoarsely for order in the playground.

"C'est une grande responsabilité, que la surveillance," observed I.

"Plaît-il?" said M. Pelet.

I remarked that I thought Messieurs Vandam and Kint must sometimes be a little fatigued with their labours.

"Des bêtes de somme,—des bêtes de somme," murmured scornfully the director. Meantime I offered him his cup of coffee.

"Servez-vous, mon garçon," said he blandly, when I had put a couple of huge lumps of continental sugar into his cup. "And now tell me why you stayed so long at Mdlle. Reuter's. I know that lessons conclude, in her establishment as in mine, at four o'clock, and when you returned it was past five."

"Mademoiselle wished to speak with me, Monsieur."

"Indeed! on what subject? if one may ask."

"Mademoiselle talked about nothing, Monsieur."

"A fertile topic! And did she discourse thereon in the schoolroom, before the pupils?"

"No; like you, Monsieur, she asked me to walk into her parlour."

"And Madame Reuter—the old duenna—my mother's gossip, was there, of course?"

"No, Monsieur; I had the honour of being quite alone with Mademoiselle."

"C'est joli—cela," observed M. Pelet, and he smiled and looked into the fire.

"Honi soit qui mal y pense," murmured I significantly.

"Je connais un peu ma petite voisine—voyez-vous."

"In that case, Monsieur will be able to aid me in finding out what was Mademoiselle's reason for making me sit before her sofa one mortal hour, listening to the most copious and fluent dissertation on the merest frivolities."

"She was sounding your character.

"I thought so, Monsieur."

"Did she find out your weak point?"

"What is my weak point?"

"Why the sentimental. Any woman sinking her shaft deep enough, will at last reach a fathomless spring of sensibility in thy breast, Crimsworth."

I felt the blood stir about my heart and rise warm to my cheek.

"Some women might, Monsieur."

"Is Mdlle. Reuter of the number? Come, speak frankly, mon fils; elle est encore jeune, plus âgée que toi peut-être, mais juste assez pour unir la tendresse d'une petite maman à l'amour d'une épouse dévouée; n'est-ce pas que cela t'irait supérieurement?"

"No, Monsieur; I should like my wife to be my wife, and not half my mother."

"She is then a little too old for you?"

"No, Monsieur, not a day too old if she suited me in other things."

"In what does she not suit you, William? She is personally agreeable, is she not?"

"Very; her hair and complexion are just what I admire; and her turn of form, though quite Belgian, is full of grace."

"Bravo! and her face? her features? How do you like them?"

"A little harsh, especially her mouth."

"Ah, yes! her mouth," said M. Pelet, and he chuckled inwardly. "There is character about her mouth—firmness—but she has a very pleasant smile; don't you think so?"

"Rather crafty."

"True, but that expression of craft is owing to her eyebrows; have you remarked her eyebrows?"

I answered that I had not.

"You have not seen her looking down then?" said he.

"No."

"It is a treat, notwithstanding. Observe her when she has some knitting, or some other woman's work in hand, and sits the image of peace, calmly intent on her needles and her silk, some discussion meantime going on around her, in the course of which peculiarities of character are being developed, or important interests canvassed; she takes no part in it; her humble, feminine mind is wholly with her knitting; none of her features move; she neither presumes to smile approval, nor frown disapprobation; her little hands assiduously ply their unpretending task; if she can only get this purse finished, or this bonnet-grec completed, it is enough for her. If gentlemen approach her chair, a deeper quiescence, a meeker modesty settles on her features, and clothes her general mien; observe then her eyebrows, et dîtes-moi s'il n'y a pas du chat dans l'un et du renard dans l'autre."

"I will take careful notice the first opportunity," said I.

"And then," continued M. Pelet, "the eyelid will flicker, the light-coloured lashes be lifted a second, and a blue eye, glancing out from under the screen, will take its brief, sly, searching survey, and retreat again."

I smiled and so did Pelet, and after a few minutes' silence, I asked:

"Will she ever marry, do you think?"

"Marry! Will birds pair? Of course it is both her intention and resolution to marry when she finds a suitable match, and no one is better aware than herself of the sort of impression she is capable of producing; no one likes better to captivate in a quiet way. I am mistaken if she will not yet leave the print of her stealing steps on thy heart, Crimsworth."

"Of her steps? Confound it, no! My heart is not a plank to be walked on."

"But the soft touch of a patte de velours will do it no harm."

"She offers me no patte de velours; she is all form and reserve with me."

"That to begin with; let respect be the foundation, affection the first floor, love the superstructure; Mdlle. Reuter is a skilful architect."

"And interest, M. Pelet—interest. Will not Mademoiselle consider that point?"

"Yes, yes, no doubt; it will be the cement between every stone. And now we have discussed the directress, what of the pupils? N'y-a-t-il pas de belles études parmi ces jeunes têtes?"

"Studies of character? Yes; curious ones, at least, I imagine; but one cannot divine much from a first interview."

"Ah, you affect discretion; but tell me now, were you not a little abashed before those blooming young creatures?"

"At first, yes; but I rallied and got through with all due sang-froid."

"I don't believe you."

"It is true, notwithstanding. At first I thought them angels, but they did not leave me long under that delusion; three of the eldest and handsomest undertook the task of setting me right, and they managed so cleverly that in five minutes I knew *them*, at least, for what they were—three arrant coquettes."

"Je les connais!" exclaimed M. Pelet, "Elles sont toujours au premier rang à l'église et à la promenade; une blonde superbe, une jolie espiègle, une belle brune."

"Exactly."

"Lovely creatures all of them—heads for artists; what a group they would make, taken together! Eulalie (I know their names), with her smooth braided hair and calm ivory brow. Hortense, with her rich chestnut locks so luxuriantly knotted, plaited, twisted, as if she did not know how to dispose of all their abundance, with her vermilion lips, damask cheek, and roguish laughing eye. And Caroline de Blémont! Ah, there is beauty! beauty in perfection. What a cloud of sable curls about the face of a houri! What fascinating lips! What glorious black eyes! Your Byron would have worshipped her, and you—you cold, frigid islander!—you played the austere, the insensible in the presence of an Aphrodite so exquisite?"

I might have laughed at the director's enthusiasm had I believed it real, but there was something in his tone which indicated got-up raptures. I felt he was only affecting fervour in order to put me off my guard, to induce me to come out in return, so I scarcely even smiled. He went on:

"Confess, William, do not the mere good looks of Zoraïde Reuter appear dowdyish and commonplace compared with the splendid charms of some of her pupils?"

The question discomposed me, but I now felt plainly that my principal was endeavouring (for reasons best known to himself—at that time I could not fathom them) to excite ideas and wishes in my mind alien to what was right and honourable. The iniquity of the instigation proved its antidote, and when he further added:

"Each of these three beautiful girls will have a handsome fortune; and with a little address, a gentlemanlike, intelligent young fellow like you might make himself master of the hand, heart, and purse of any one of the trio."

I replied by a look and an interrogative "Monsieur?" which startled him.

He laughed a forced laugh, affirmed that he had only been joking, and demanded whether I could possibly have thought him in earnest. Just then the bell rang; the play-hour was over; it was an evening on which M. Pelet was accustomed to read passages from the drama and the belles lettres to his pupils. He did not wait for my answer, but rising, left the room, humming as he went some gay strain of Béranger's.

Chapter XII

DAILY, as I continued my attendance at the seminary of Mdlle. Reuter, did I find fresh occasions to compare the ideal with the real. What had I known of female character previously to my arrival at Brussels? Precious little. And what was my notion of it? Something vague, slight, gauzy, glittering; now when I came in contact with it I found it to be a palpable substance enough; very hard too sometimes, and often heavy; there was metal in it, both lead and iron.

Let the idealists, the dreamers about earthly angels and human flowers, just look here while I open my portfolio and show them a sketch or two, pencilled after nature. I took these sketches in the second-class schoolroom of Mdlle. Reuter's establishment, where about a hundred specimens of the genus "jeune fille" collected together, offered a fertile variety of subject. A miscellaneous assortment they were, differing both in caste and country; as I sat on my estrade and glanced over the long range of desks, I had under my eye French, English, Belgians, Austrians, and Prussians. The majority belonged to the class bourgeois; but there were many countesses, there were the daughters of two generals, and of several colonels, captains, and government employés; these ladies sat side by side with young females destined to be demoiselles de magasins, and with some Flamandes, genuine aborigines of the country. In dress all were nearly similar, and in manners there was small difference; exceptions there were to the general rule, but the majority gave the tone to the establishment, and that tone was rough, boisterous, marked by a point-blank disregard of all forbearance towards each other or their teachers; an eager pursuit by each individual of her own interest and convenience; and a coarse indifference to the interest and convenience of every one else. Most of them could lie with audacity when it appeared advantageous to do so. All understood the art of speaking fair when a point was to be gained, and could with consummate skill and at a moment's notice turn the cold shoulder the instant civility ceased to be profitable. Very little open quarrelling ever took place amongst them; but backbiting and talebearing were universal. Close friendships were forbidden by the rules of the school, and no one girl seemed to cultivate more regard for another than was just necessary to secure a companion when solitude would have been irksome. They were each and all supposed to have been reared in utter unconsciousness of vice. The precautions used to keep them ignorant, if not innocent, were innumerable. How was it, then, that scarcely one of those girls having attained the age of fourteen could look a man in the face with modesty and propriety? An air of bold, impudent flirtation, or a loose, silly leer, was sure to answer the most ordinary glance from a masculine eye. I know nothing of the arcana of the Roman Catholic religion, and I am not a bigot in matters of theology, but I suspect the root of this precocious impurity, so obvious, so general in Popish countries, is to be found in the discipline, if not the doctrines of the Church of Rome. I record what I have seen: these girls

belonged to what are called the respectable ranks of society; they had all been carefully brought up, yet was the mass of them mentally depraved. So much for the general view: now for one or two selected specimens.

The first picture is a full length of Aurelia Koslow, a German frâulein, or rather a half-breed between German and Russian. She is eighteen years of age, and has been sent to Brussels to finish her education; she is of middle size, stiffly made, body long, legs short, bust much developed but not compactly moulded, waist disproportionately compressed by an inhumanly braced corset, dress carefully arranged, large feet tortured into small bottines, head small, hair smoothed, braided, oiled, and gummed to perfection; very low forehead, very diminutive and vindictive grey eyes, somewhat Tartar features, rather flat nose, rather high cheek-bones, yet the ensemble not positively ugly; tolerably good complexion. So much for person. As to mind, deplorably ignorant and ill-informed; incapable of writing or speaking correctly even German, her native tongue, a dunce in French, and her attempts at learning English a mere farce, yet she has been at school twelve years; but as she invariably gets her exercises, of every description, done by a fellow pupil, and reads her lessons off a book concealed in her lap, it is not wonderful that her progress has been so snail-like. I do not know what Aurelia's daily habits of life are, because I have not the opportunity of observing her at all times; but from what I see of the state of her desk, books, and papers, I should say she is slovenly and even dirty; her outward dress, as I have said, is well attended to, but in passing behind her bench, I have remarked that her neck is grey for want of washing, and her hair, so glossy with gum and grease, is not such as one feels tempted to pass the hand over, much less to run the fingers through. Aurelia's conduct in class, at least when I am present, is something extraordinary, considered as an index of girlish innocence. The moment I enter the room, she nudges her next neighbour and indulges in a half-suppressed laugh. As I take my seat on the estrade, she fixes her eye on me; she seems resolved to attract, and, if possible, monopolise my notice: to this end she launches at me all sorts of looks, languishing, provoking, leering, laughing. As I am found quite proof against this sort of artillery—for we scorn what, unasked, is lavishly offered—she has recourse to the expedient of making noises; sometimes she sighs, sometimes groans, sometimes utters inarticulate sounds, for which language has no name. If, in walking up the schoolroom, I pass near her, she puts out her foot that it may touch mine; if I do not happen to observe the manœuvre, and my boot comes in contact with her brodequin, she affects to fall into convulsions of suppressed laughter; if I notice the snare and avoid it, she expresses her mortification in sullen muttering, where I hear myself abused in bad French, pronounced with an intolerable Low German accent.

Not far from Mdlle. Koslow sits another young lady, by name Adèle Dronsart: this is a Belgian, rather low of stature, in form heavy, with broad waist, short neck and limbs, good red and white complexion, features well chiselled and regular, well-cut eyes of a clear brown colour, light brown hair, good teeth, age not much above fifteen, but as full-grown as a stout young Englishwoman of twenty. This portrait gives the idea of a somewhat dumpy but good-looking damsel, does it not? Well, when I looked along the row of young heads, my eye generally stopped at this of Adèle's; her gaze was ever waiting for mine, and it frequently succeeded in arresting it. She was an unnatural-looking being—so young, fresh, blooming, yet so Gorgon-like. Suspicion, sullen ill-temper were on her forehead, vicious propensities in her eyes, envy and panther-like deceit about her mouth. In general she sat very still; her massive shape looked as if it could not bend much, nor did her large head—so broad at the base, so narrow towards the top—seem made to turn readily on her short neck. She had but two varieties of expression; the prevalent one a forbidding, dissatisfied scowl, varied sometimes by a most pernicious and perfidious smile. She was shunned by her fellow-pupils, for, bad as many of them were, few were as bad as she.

Aurelia and Adèle were in the first division of the second class; the second division was headed by a pensionnaire named Juanna Trista. This girl was of mixed Belgian and Spanish origin; her Flemish mother was dead, her Catalonian father was a merchant residing in the —— Isles, where Juanna had been born and whence she was sent to Europe to be educated. I wonder that any one, looking at that girl's head and countenance, would have received her under their roof. She had precisely the same shape of skull as Pope Alexander the Sixth; her organs of benevolence, veneration, conscientiousness, adhesiveness, were singularly small, those of self-esteem, firmness, destructiveness, combativeness, preposterously large; her head sloped up in the penthouse shape, was contracted about the forehead, and prominent behind; she had rather good, though large and marked features; her temperament was fibrous and bilious, her complexion pale and dark, hair and eyes black, form angular and rigid but proportionate, age fifteen.

Juanna was not very thin, but she had a gaunt visage, and her "regard" was fierce and hungry; narrow as was her brow, it presented space enough for the legible graving of two words, Mutiny and Hate; in some one of her other lineaments—I think the eye—cowardice had also its distinct cipher. Mdlle. Trista thought fit to trouble my first lessons with a coarse work-day sort of turbulence; she made noises with her mouth like a horse, she ejected her saliva, she uttered brutal expressions; behind and below her were seated a band of very vulgar, inferior-looking Flamandes, including two or three examples of that deformity of person and imbecility of intellect whose frequency in the Low Countries would seem to furnish proof that the climate is such as to induce degeneracy of the human mind and body; these, I soon found, were completely under her influence, and with their aid she got up and sustained a swinish tumult, which I was constrained at last to quell by ordering her and two of her tools to rise from their seats, and, having kept them standing five minutes, turning them bodily out of the schoolroom; the accomplices into a large place adjoining called the grande salle; the principal into a cabinet, of which I closed the door and pocketed the key. This judgment I executed in the presence of Mdlle. Reuter, who looked much aghast at beholding so decided a proceeding— the most severe that had ever been ventured on in her establishment. Her look of affright I answered with one of composure, and finally with a smile, which perhaps flattered, and certainly soothed her. Juanna Trista remained in Europe long enough to repay, by malevolence and ingratitude, all who had ever done her a good turn; and she then went to join her father in the —— Isles, exulting in the thought that she should there have slaves, whom, as she said, she could kick and strike at will.

These three pictures are from the life. I possess others, as marked and as little agreeable, but I will spare my reader the exhibition of them.

Doubtless it will be thought that I ought now, by way of contrast, to show something charming; some gentle virgin head, circled with a halo, some sweet personification of innocence, clasping the dove of peace to her bosom. No: I saw nothing of the sort, and therefore cannot portray it. The pupil in the school possessing the happiest disposition was a young girl from the country, Louise Path; she was sufficiently benevolent and obliging, but not well taught nor well mannered; moreover, the plague-spot of dissimulation was in her also; honour and principle were unknown to her, she had scarcely heard their names. The least exceptionable pupil was the poor little Sylvie I have mentioned once before. Sylvie was gentle in manners, intelligent in mind; she was even sincere, as far as her religion would permit her to be so, but her physical organisation was defective; weak health stunted her growth and chilled her spirits, and then, destined as she was for the cloister, her whole soul was warped to a conventual bias, and in the tame, trained subjection of her manner, one read that she had already prepared herself for her future course of life, by giving up her independence of thought and action into the hands of some despotic confessor. She permitted herself no original opinion, no preference of companion or employment; in everything she was guided by another. With a pale,

passive, automaton air, she went about all day long doing what she was bid; never what she liked, or what, from innate conviction, she thought it right to do. The poor little future religieuse had been early taught to make the dictates of her own reason and conscience quite subordinate to the will of her spiritual director. She was the model pupil of Mdlle. Reuter's establishment; pale, blighted image, where life lingered feebly, but whence the soul had been conjured by Romish wizardcraft!

A few English pupils there were in this school, and these might be divided into two classes. 1st. The continental English—the daughters chiefly of broken adventurers, whom debt or dishonour had driven from their own country. These poor girls had never known the advantages of settled homes, decorous example, or honest Protestant education; resident a few months now in one Catholic school, now in another, as their parents wandered from land to land—from France to Germany, from Germany to Belgium—they had picked up some scanty instructions, many bad habits, losing every notion even of the first elements of religion and morals, and acquiring an imbecile indifference to every sentiment that can elevate humanity; they were distinguishable by an habitual look of sullen dejection, the result of crushed self-respect and constant browbeating from their Popish fellow-pupils, who hated them as English, and scorned them as heretics.

The second class were British English. Of these I did not encounter half-a-dozen during the whole time of my attendance at the seminary; their characteristics were clean but careless dress, ill-arranged hair (compared with the tight and trim foreigners), erect carriage, flexible figures, white and taper hands, features more irregular, but also more intellectual than those of the Belgians, grave and modest countenances, a general air of native propriety and decency; by this last circumstance alone I could at a glance distinguish the daughter of Albion and nursling of Protestantism from the foster-child of Rome, the *protégée* of Jesuitry: proud, too, was the aspect of these British girls; at once envied and ridiculed by their continental associates, they warded off insult with austere civility, and met hate with mute disdain; they eschewed company-keeping, and in the midst of numbers seemed to dwell isolated.

The teachers presiding over this mixed multitude were three in number, all French—their names Mdlles. Zéphyrine, Pélagie, and Suzette; the two last were commonplace personages enough; their look was ordinary, their manner was ordinary, their temper was ordinary, their thoughts, feelings, and views were all ordinary— were I to write a chapter on the subject I could not elucidate it further. Zéphyrine was somewhat more distinguished in appearance and deportment than Pélagie and Suzette, but in character a genuine Parisian coquette, perfidious, mercenary, and dry-hearted. A fourth maîtresse I sometimes saw who seemed to come daily to teach needlework, or netting, or lace-mending, or some such flimsy art; but of her I never had more than a passing glimpse, as she sat in the carré, with her frames and some dozen of the elder pupils about her, consequently I had no opportunity of studying her character, or even of observing her person much; the latter, I remarked, had a very girlish air for a maîtresse, otherwise it was not striking; of character I should think she possessed but little, as her pupils seemed constantly "en revolte" against her authority. She did not reside in the house; her name, I think, was Mdlle. Henri.

Amidst this assemblage of all that was insignificant and defective, much that was vicious and repulsive (by that last epithet many would have described the two or three stiff, silent, decently behaved, ill-dressed British girls), the sensible, sagacious, affable directress shone like a steady star over a marsh full of Jack-o'-lanterns; profoundly aware of her superiority, she derived an inward bliss from that consciousness which sustained her under all the care and responsibility inseparable from her position; it kept her temper calm, her brow smooth, her manner tranquil. She liked— as who would not?—on entering the schoolroom, to feel that her sole presence sufficed to diffuse that order and quiet which all the remonstrances, and even

commands, of her underlings frequently failed to enforce; she liked to stand in comparison, or rather contrast, with those who surrounded her, and to know that in personal as well as mental advantages, she bore away the undisputed palm of preference—(the three teachers were all plain). Her pupils she managed with such indulgence and address, taking always on herself the office of recompenser and eulogist, and abandoning to her subalterns every invidious task of blame and punishment, that they all regarded her with deference, if not with affection; her teachers did not love her, but they submitted because they were her inferiors in everything; the various masters who attended her school were each and all in some way or other under her influence: over one she had acquired power by her skilful management of his bad temper; over another by little attentions to his petty caprices; a third she had subdued by flattery; a fourth—a timid man—she kept in awe by a sort of austere decision of mien; me, she still watched, still tried by the most ingenious tests— she roved round me, baffled, yet persevering; I believe she thought I was like a smooth and bare precipice, which offered neither jutting stone nor tree-root, nor tuft of grass to aid the climber. Now she flattered with exquisite tact, now she moralised, now she tried how far I was accessible to mercenary motives, then she disported on the brink of affection—knowing that some men are won by weakness— anon, she talked excellent sense, aware that others have the folly to admire judgment. I found it at once pleasant and easy to evade all these efforts; it was sweet, when she thought me nearly won, to turn round and to smile in her very eyes, half scornfully, and then to witness her scarcely veiled, though mute mortification. Still she persevered, and at last, I am bound to confess it, her finger, essaying, proving every atom of the casket, touched its secret spring, and for a moment the lid sprung open; she laid her hand on the jewel within; whether she stole and broke it, or whether the lid shut again with a snap on her fingers, read on, and you shall know.

It happened that I came one day to give a lesson when I was indisposed; I had a bad cold and a cough; two hours' incessant talking left me very hoarse and tired; as I quitted the schoolroom, and was passing along the corridor, I met Mdlle. Reuter; she remarked, with an anxious air, that I looked very pale and tired. "Yes," I said, "I was fatigued"; and then, with increased interest, she rejoined, "You shall not go away till you have had some refreshment." She persuaded me to step into the parlour, and was very kind and gentle while I stayed. The next day she was kinder still; she came herself into the class to see that the windows were closed, and that there was no draught; she exhorted me with friendly earnestness not to over-exert myself; when I went away, she gave me her hand unasked, and I could not but mark, by a respectful and gentle pressure, that I was sensible of the favour, and grateful for it. My modest demonstration kindled a little merry smile on her countenance; I thought her almost charming. During the remainder of the evening, my mind was full of impatience for the afternoon of the next day to arrive, that I might see her again.

I was not disappointed, for she sat in the class during the whole of my subsequent lesson, and often looked at me almost with affection. At four o'clock she accompanied me out of the schoolroom, asking with solicitude after my health, then scolding me sweetly because I spoke too loud and gave myself too much trouble; I stopped at the glass door which led into the garden, to hear her lecture to the end; the door was open; it was a very fine day, and while I listened to the soothing reprimand, I looked at the sunshine and flowers, and felt very happy. The day-scholars began to pour from the schoolrooms into the passage.

"Will you go into the garden a minute or two," asked she, "till they are gone?" I descended the steps without answering, but I looked back as much as to say: "You will come with me?"

In another minute I and the directress were walking side by side down the alley bordered with fruit-trees, whose white blossoms were then in full blow as well as their tender green leaves. The sky was blue, the air still, the May afternoon was

full of brightness and fragrance. Released from the stifling class, surrounded with flowers and foliage, with a pleasing, smiling, affable woman at my side—how did I feel? Why, very enviably. It seemed as if the romantic visions my imagination had suggested of this garden, while it was yet hidden from me by the jealous boards, were more than realised; and, when a turn in the alley shut out the view of the house, and some tall shrubs excluded M. Pelet's mansion, and screened us momentarily from the other houses, rising amphitheatre-like round this green spot, I gave my arm to Mdlle. Reuter, and led her to a garden-chair, nestled under some lilacs near. She sat down; I took my place at her side. She went on talking to me with that ease which communicates ease, and, as I listened, a revelation dawned in my mind that I was on the brink of falling in love. The dinner-bell rang, both at her house and M. Pelet's; we were obliged to part; I detained her a moment as she was moving away.

"I want something," said I.

"What?" asked Zoraïde naïvely.

"Only a flower."

"Gather it then—or two, or twenty, if you like."

"No—one will do—but you must gather it, and give it to me."

"What a caprice!" she exclaimed, but she raised herself on her tiptoes, and, plucking a beautiful branch of lilac, offered it to me with grace. I took it, and went away, satisfied for the present, and hopeful for the future.

Certainly that May day was a lovely one, and it closed in moonlight night of summer warmth and serenity. I remember this well; for, having sat up late that evening, correcting devoirs, and feeling weary and a little oppressed with the closeness of my small room, I opened the often-mentioned boarded window, whose boards, however, I had persuaded old Madame Pelet to have removed since I had filled the post of professor in the pensionnat de demoiselles, as, from that time, it was no longer "inconvenant" for me to overlook my own pupils at their sports. I sat down in the window-seat, rested my arm on the sill, and leaned out: above me was the clear-obscure of a cloudless night sky—splendid moonlight subdued the tremulous sparkle of the stars—below lay the garden, varied with silvery lustre and deep shade, and all fresh with dew—a grateful perfume exhaled from the closed blossoms of the fruit-trees—not a leaf stirred, the night was breezeless. My window looked directly down upon a certain walk of Mdlle. Reuter's garden, called "l'allée défendue," so named because the pupils were forbidden to enter it on account of its proximity to the boys' school. It was here that the lilacs and laburnums grew especially thick; this was the most sheltered nook in the enclosure, its shrubs screened the garden-chair where that afternoon I had sat with the young directress. I need not say that my thoughts were chiefly with her as I leaned from the lattice, and let my eye roam, now over the walks and borders of the garden, now along the many-windowed front of the house which rose white beyond the masses of foliage. I wondered in what part of the building was situated her apartment; and a single light, shining through the persiennes of one croisée, seemed to direct me to it.

"She watches late," thought I, "for it must be now near midnight. She is a fascinating little woman," I continued in voiceless soliloquy; "her image forms a pleasant picture in memory; I know she is not what the world calls pretty—no matter, there is harmony in her aspect, and I like it; her brown hair, her blue eye, the freshness of her cheek, the whiteness of her neck, all suit my taste. Then I respect her talent; the idea of marrying a doll or a fool was always abhorrent to me: I know that a pretty doll, a fair fool, might do well enough for the honeymoon; but when passion cooled, how dreadful to find a lump of wax and wood laid in my bosom, a half-idiot clasped in my arms, and to remember that I had made of this my equal—nay, my idol—to know that I must pass the rest of my dreary life with a creature incapable of understanding what I said, of appreciating what I

thought, or of sympathising with what I felt! Now, Zoraïde Reuter,'' thought I, ''has tact, 'caractère,' judgment, discretion; has she heart? What a good, simple little smile played about her lips when she gave me the branch of lilacs! I have thought her crafty, dissembling, interested sometimes, it is true; but may not much that looks like cunning and dissimulation in her conduct be only the efforts made by a bland temper to traverse quietly perplexing difficulties? And as to interest, she wishes to make her way in the world, no doubt, and who can blame her? Even if she be truly deficient in sound principle, is it not rather her misfortune than her fault? She has been brought up a Catholic: had she been born an Englishwoman, and reared a Protestant, might she not have added straight integrity to all her other excellences? Supposing she were to marry an English and Protestant husband, would she not, rational, sensible as she is, quickly acknowledge the superiority of right over expediency, honesty over policy? It would be worth a man's while to try the experiment; to-morrow I will renew my observations. She knows that I watch her: how calm she is under scrutiny! it seems rather to gratify than annoy her.'' Here a strain of music stole in upon my monologue, and suspended it; it was a bugle, very skilfully played, in the neighbourhood of the park, I thought, or on the Place Royale. So sweet were the tones, so subduing their effect at that hour, in the midst of silence and under the quiet reign of moonlight, I ceased to think, that I might listen more intently. The strain retreated, its sound waxed fainter and was soon gone: my ear prepared to repose on the absolute hush of midnight once more. No. What murmur was that which, low, and yet near and approaching nearer, frustrated the expectation of total silence? It was some one conversing—yes, evidently, an audible, though subdued voice spoke in the garden immediately below me. Another answered: the first voice was that of a man, the second that of a woman; and a man and a woman I saw coming slowly down the alley. Their forms were at first in shade, I could but discern a dusk outline of each, but a ray of moonlight met them at the termination of the walk, when they were under my very nose, and revealed very plainly, very unequivocally, Mdlle. Zoraïde Reuter, arm-in-arm, or hand-in-hand (I forget which), with my principal, confidant, and counsellor, M. François Pelet. And M. Pelet was saying:

''À quand donc le jour des noces, ma bien-aimée?''

And Mdlle. Reuter answered:

''Mais, François, tu sais bien qu'il me serait impossible de me marier avant les vacances.''

''June, July, August, a whole quarter!'' exclaimed the director. ''How can I wait so long?—I who am ready, even now, to expire at your feet with impatience!''

''Ah! if you die, the whole affair will be settled without any trouble about notaries and contracts; I shall have only to order a slight mourning dress, which will be much sooner prepared than the nuptial trousseau.''

''Cruel Zoraïde! you laugh at the distress of one who loves you so devotedly as I do: my torment is your sport; you scruple not to stretch my soul on the rack of jealousy; for, deny it as you will, I am certain you have cast encouraging glances on that school-boy, Crimsworth; he has presumed to fall in love, which he dared not have done unless you had given him room to hope.''

''What do you say, François? Do you say Crimsworth is in love with me?''

''Over head and ears.''

''Has he told you so?''

''No—but I see it in his face: he blushes whenever your name is mentioned.''

A little laugh of exulting coquetry announced Mdlle. Reuter's gratification at this piece of intelligence (which was a lie, by-the-bye—I had never been so far gone as that, after all). M. Pelet proceeded to ask what she intended to do with me, intimating pretty plainly, and not very gallantly, that it was nonsense for her to think of taking such a ''blanc-bec'' as a husband, since she must be at least ten years older than I (was she then thirty-two? I should not have thought it). I heard

her disclaim any intentions on the subject—the director, however, still pressed her to give a definite answer.

"François," said she, "you are jealous," and still she laughed; then, as if suddenly recollecting that this coquetry was not consistent with the character for modest dignity she wished to establish, she proceeded, in a demure voice: "Truly, my dear François, I will not deny that this young Englishman may have made some attempts to ingratiate himself with me; but, so far from giving him any encouragement, I have always treated him with as much reserve as it was possible to combine with civility; affianced as I am to you, I would give no man false hopes; believe me, dear friend."

Still Pelet uttered murmurs of distrust—so I judged, at least, from her reply.

"What folly? How could I prefer an unknown foreigner to you? And then—not to flatter your vanity—Crimsworth could not bear comparison with you either physically or mentally; he is not a handsome man at all; some may call him gentlemanlike and intelligent-looking, but for my part——"

The rest of the sentence was lost in the distance as the pair, rising from the chair in which they had been seated, moved away. I waited their return, but soon the opening and shutting of a door informed me that they had re-entered the house; I listened a little longer, all was perfectly still; I listened more than a hour—at last I heard M. Pelet come in and ascend to his chamber. Glancing once more towards the long front of the garden-house, I perceived that its solitary light was at length extinguished; so, for a time, was my faith in love and friendship. I went to bed, but something feverish and fiery had got into my veins which prevented me from sleeping much that night.

Chapter XIII

NEXT morning I rose with the dawn, and having dressed myself and stood half-an-hour, my elbow leaning on the chest of drawers, considering what means I should adopt to restore my spirits, fagged with sleeplessness, to their ordinary tone—for I had no intention of getting up a scene with M. Pelet, reproaching him with perfidy, sending him a challenge, or performing other gambadoes of the sort—I hit at last on the expedient of walking out in the cool of the morning to a neighbouring establishment of baths, and treating myself to a bracing plunge. The remedy produced the desired effect. I came back at seven o'clock steadied and invigorated, and was able to greet M. Pelet, when he entered to breakfast, with an unchanged and tranquil countenance; even a cordial offering of the hand and the flattering appellation of "mon fils," pronounced in that caressing tone with which Monsieur had, of late days especially, been accustomed to address me, did not elicit any external sign of the feeling which, though subdued, still glowed at my heart. Not that I nursed vengeance—no; but the sense of insult and treachery lived in me like a kindling, though as yet smothered coal. God knows I am not by nature vindictive; I would not hurt a man because I can no longer trust or like him; but neither my reason nor feelings are of the vacillating order—they are not of that sand-like sort where impressions, if soon made, are as soon effaced. Once convinced that my friend's disposition is incompatible with my own, once assured that he is indelibly stained with certain defects obnoxious to my principles, and I dissolve the connection. I did so with Edward. As to Pelet, the discovery was yet new: should I act thus with him? It was the question I placed before my mind as I stirred my cup of coffee with a half-pistolet (we never had spoons), Pelet meantime being seated opposite, his pallid face looking as knowing and more haggard than usual, his blue eye turned, now sternly on his boys and ushers, and now graciously on me.

"Circumstances must guide me," said I; and meeting Pelet's false glance and insinuating smile, I thanked heaven that I had last night opened my window and read by the light of a full moon the true meaning of that guileful countenance. I felt half his master, because the reality of his nature was now known to me; smile and flatter as he would, I saw his soul lurk behind his smile, and heard in every one of his smooth phrases a voice interpreting their treacherous import.

But Zoraïde Reuter? Of course her defection had cut me to the quick? That sting must have gone too deep for any consolations of philosophy to be available in curing its smart? Not at all. The night fever over, I looked about for balm to that wound also, and found some nearer home than at Gilead. Reason was my physician; she began by proving that the prize I had missed was of little value: she admitted that, physically, Zoraïde might have suited me, but affirmed that our souls were not in harmony, and that discord must have resulted from the union of her mind with mine. She then insisted on the suppression of all repining, and commanded me rather to rejoice that I had escaped a snare. Her medicament did me good. I felt its strengthening effect when I met the directress the next day; its stringent operation on the nerves suffered no trembling, no faltering; it enabled me to face her with firmness, to pass her with ease. She had held out her hand to me—that I did not choose to see. She had greeted me with a charming smile—it fell on my heart like light on stone. I passed on to the estrade, she followed me; her eye, fastened on my face, demanded of every feature the meaning of my changed and careless manner. "I will give her an answer," thought I; and, meeting her gaze full, arresting, fixing her glance, I shot into her eyes, from my own, a look where there was no respect, no love, no tenderness, no gallantry; where the strictest analysis could detect nothing but scorn, hardihood, irony. I made her bear it, and feel it; her steady countenance did not change, but her colour rose, and she approached me as if fascinated. She stepped on to the estrade, and stood close by my side; she had nothing to say. I would not relieve her embarrassment, and negligently turned over the leaves of a book.

"I hope you feel quite recovered to-day," at last she said, in a low tone.

"And I, Mademoiselle, hope that you took no cold last night in consequence of your late walk in the garden."

Quick enough of comprehension, she understood me directly; her face became a little blanched—a very little—but no muscle in her rather marked features moved; and, calm and self-possessed, she retired from the estrade, taking her seat quietly at a little distance, and occupying herself with netting a purse. I proceeded to give my lesson; it was a "Composition," *i.e.*, I dictated certain general questions, of which the pupils were to compose the answers from memory, access to books being forbidden. While Mdlle. Eulalie, Hortense, Caroline, etc., were pondering over the string of rather abstruse grammatical interrogatories I had propounded, I was at liberty to employ the vacant half hour in further observing the directress herself. The green silk purse was progressing fast in her hands; her eyes were bent upon it; her attitude, as she sat netting within two yards of me, was still yet guarded; in her whole person were expressed at once, and with equal clearness, vigilance and repose—a rare union! Looking at her, I was forced, as I had often been before, to offer her good sense, her wondrous self-control, the tribute of involuntary admiration. She had felt that I had withdrawn from her my esteem; she had seen contempt and coldness in my eye, and to her, who coveted the approbation of all around her, who thirsted after universal good opinion, such discovery must have been an acute wound. I had witnessed its effect in the momentary pallor of her cheek—cheek unused to vary; yet how quickly, by dint of self-control, had she recovered her composure! With what quiet dignity she now sat, almost at my side, sustained by her sound and vigorous sense; no trembling in her somewhat lengthened, though shrewd upper lip, no coward shame on her austere forehead!

"There is metal there," I said, as I gazed. "Would that there were fire also, living ardour to make the steel glow—then I could love her."

Presently I discovered that she knew I was watching her, for she stirred not, she lifted not her crafty eyelid; she had glanced down from her netting to her small foot, peeping from the soft folds of her purple merino gown; thence her eye reverted to her hand, ivory white, with a bright garnet ring on the forefinger, and a light frill of lace round the wrist; with a scarcely perceptible movement she turned her head, causing her nut-brown curls to wave gracefully. In these slight signs I read that the wish of her heart, the design of her brain, was to lure back the game she had scared. A little incident gave her the opportunity of addressing me again.

While all was silence in the class—silence, but for the rustling of copy-books and the travelling of pens over their pages—a leaf of the large folding-door, opening from the hall, unclosed, admitting a pupil who, after making a hasty obeisance, ensconced herself with some appearance of trepidation, probably occasioned by her entering so late, in a vacant seat at the desk nearest the door. Being seated, she proceeded, still with an air of hurry and embarrassment, to open her cabas, to take out her books; and, while I was waiting for her to look up, in order to make out her identity—for, shortsighted as I was, I had not recognised her at her entrance—Mdlle. Reuter, leaving her chair, approached the estrade.

"Monsieur Creemsvort," said she, in a whisper: for when the schoolrooms were silent, the directress always moved with velvet tread, and spoke in the most subdued key, enforcing order and stillness fully as much by example as precept: "Monsieur Creemsvort, that young person, who has just entered, wishes to have the advantage of taking lessons with you in English; she is not a pupil of the house; she is, indeed, in one sense, a teacher, for she gives instruction in lace-mending, and in little varieties of ornamental needlework. She very properly proposes to qualify herself for a higher department in education, and has asked permission to attend your lessons, in order to perfect her knowledge of English, in which language she has, I believe, already made some progress; of course it is my wish to aid her in an effort so praiseworthy; you will permit her then to benefit by your instruction—n'est-ce pas, Monsieur?" And Mdlle. Reuter's eyes were raised to mine with a look at once naïve, benign, and beseeching.

I replied, "Of course," very laconically, almost abruptly.

"Another word," she said, with softness: "Mdlle. Henri has not received a regular education; perhaps her natural talents are not of the highest order: but I can assure you of the excellence of her intentions, and even of the amiability of her disposition. Monsieur will then, I am sure, have the goodness to be considerate with her at first, and not expose her backwardness, her inevitable deficiencies, before the young ladies, who, in a sense, are her pupils. Will Monsieur Creemsvort favour me by attending to this hint?" I nodded. She continued with subdued earnestness:

"Pardon me, Monsieur, if I venture to add that what I have just said is of importance to the poor girl; she already experiences great difficulty in impressing these giddy young things with a due degree of deference for her authority, and should that difficulty be increased by new discoveries of her incapacity, she might find her position in my establishment too painful to be retained; a circumstance I should much regret for her sake, as she can ill afford to lose the profits of her occupation here."

Mdlle. Reuter possessed marvellous tact; but tact the most exquisite, unsupported by sincerity, will sometimes fail of its effect; thus, on this occasion, the longer she preached about the necessity of being indulgent to the governess-pupil, the more impatient I felt as I listened. I discerned so clearly that while her professed motive was a wish to aid the dull, though well-meaning Mdlle. Henri, her real one was no other than a design to impress me with an idea of her own exalted goodness and tender considerateness; so having again hastily nodded assent to her remarks,

I obviated their renewal by suddenly demanding the compositions, in a sharp accent, and stepping from the estrade, I proceeded to collect them. As I passed the governess-pupil, I said to her:

"You have come in too late to receive a lesson to-day; try to be more punctual, next time."

I was behind her, and could not read in her face the effect of my not very civil speech. Probably I should not have troubled myself to do so, had I been full in front; but I observed that she immediately began to slip her books into her cabas again; and presently, after I had returned to the estrade, while I was arranging the mass of compositions, I heard the folding-door again open and close; and, on looking up, I perceived her place vacant. I thought to myself, "She will consider her first attempt at taking a lesson in English something of a failure"; and I wondered whether she had departed in the sulks, or whether stupidity had induced her to take my words too literally, or finally, whether my irritable tone had wounded her feelings. The last notion I dismissed almost as soon as I had conceived it, for not having seen any appearance of sensitiveness in any human face since my arrival in Belgium, I had begun to regard it almost as a fabulous quality. Whether her physiognomy announced it I could not tell, for her speedy exit had allowed me no time to ascertain the circumstance. I had, indeed, on two or three previous occasions, caught a passing view of her (as I believe has been mentioned before); but I had never stopped to scrutinise either her face or person, and had but the most vague idea of her general appearance. Just as I had finished rolling up the compositions, the four o'clock bell rang; with my accustomed alertness in obeying that signal, I grasped my hat and evacuated the premises.

Chapter XIV

If I was punctual in quitting Mdlle. Reuter's domicile, I was at least equally punctual in arriving there; I came the next day at five minutes before two, and on reaching the schoolroom door, before I opened it, I heard a rapid, gabbling sound, which warned me that the "prière du midi" was not yet concluded. I waited the termination thereof; it would have been impious to intrude my heretical presence during its progress. How the repeater of the prayer did cackle and splutter! I never before or since heard language enounced with such steam-engine haste. "Notre Père qui êtes au ciel" went off like a shot; then followed an address to Marie "vierge céleste, reine des anges, maison d'or, tour d'ivoire!" and then an invocation to the saint of the day; and then down they all sat, and the solemn (?) rite was over; and I entered, flinging the door wide and striding in fast, as it was my wont to do now; for I had found that in entering with aplomb, and mounting the estrade with emphasis, consisted the grand secret of ensuring immediate silence. The folding-doors between the two classes, opened for the prayer, were instantly closed; a maîtresse, work-box in hand, took her seat at her appropriate desk; the pupils sat still with their pens and books before them; my three beauties in the van, now well humbled by a demeanour of consistent coolness, sat erect with their hands folded quietly on their knees; they had given up giggling and whispering to each other, and no longer ventured to utter pert speeches in my presence; they now only talked to me occasionally with their eyes, by means of which organs they could still, however, say very audacious and coquettish things. Had affection, goodness, modesty, real talent, ever employed those bright orbs as interpreters, I do not think I could have refrained from giving a kind and encouraging, perhaps an ardent reply now and then; but as it was, I found pleasure in answering the glance of vanity with the gaze of stoicism. Youthful, fair, brilliant, as were many of my pupils, I can

truly say that in me they never saw any other bearing than such as an austere, though just guardian, might have observed towards them. If any doubt the accuracy of this assertion, as inferring more conscientious self-denial or Scipio-like self-control than they feel disposed to give me credit for, let them take into consideration the following circumstances, which, while detracting from my merit, justify my veracity.

Know, O incredulous reader! that a master stands in a somewhat different relation towards a pretty, light-headed, probably ignorant girl, to that occupied by a partner at a ball, or a gallant on the promenade. A professor does not meet his pupil to see her dressed in satin and muslin, with hair perfumed and curled, neck scarcely shaded by aërial lace, round white arms circled with bracelets, feet dressed for the gliding dance. It is not his business to whirl her through the waltz, to feed her with compliments, to heighten her beauty by the flush of gratified vanity. Neither does he encounter her on the smooth-rolled, tree-shaded Boulevard, in the green and sunny park, whither she repairs clad in her becoming walking dress, her scarf thrown with grace over her shoulders, her little bonnet scarcely screening her curls, the red rose under its brim adding a new tint to the softer rose on her cheek: her face and eyes, too, illumined with smiles, perhaps as transient as the sunshine of the gala-day, but also quite as brilliant; it is not his office to walk by her side, to listen to her lively chat, to carry her parasol, scarcely larger than a broad green leaf, to lead in a ribbon her Blenheim spaniel or Italian greyhound. No. he finds her in the schoolroom, plainly dressed, with books before her. Owing to her education or her nature books are to her a nuisance, and she opens them with aversion, yet her teacher must instil into her mind the contents of these books; that mind resists the admission of grave information, it recoils, it grows restive, sullen tempers are shown, disfiguring frowns spoil the symmetry of the face, sometimes coarse gestures banish grace from the deportment, while muttered expressions, redolent of native and ineradicable vulgarity, desecrate the sweetness of the voice. Where the temperament is serene though the intellect be sluggish, an unconquerable dulness opposes every effort to instruct. Where there is cunning but not energy, dissimulation, falsehood, a thousand schemes and tricks are put in play to evade the necessity of application; in short, to the tutor, female youth, female charms, are like tapestry hangings, of which the wrong side is continually turned towards him; and even when he sees the smooth, neat external surface he so well knows what knots, long stitches, and jagged ends are behind that he has scarce a temptation to admire too fondly the seemly forms and bright colours exposed to general view.

Our likings are regulated by our circumstances. The artist prefers a hilly country because it is picturesque; the engineer a flat one because it is convenient; the man of pleasure likes what he calls "a fine woman"—she suits him; the fashionable young gentleman admires the fashionable young lady—she is of his kind; the toil-worn, fagged, probably irritable tutor, blind almost to beauty, insensible to airs and graces, glories chiefly in certain mental qualities: application, love of knowledge, natural capacity, docility, truthfulness, gratefulness are the charms that attract his notice and win his regard. These he seeks, but seldom meets; these if by chance he finds, he would fain retain for ever, and when separation deprives him of them he feels as if some ruthless hand had snatched from him his only ewe-lamb. Such being the case, and the case it is, my readers will agree with me that there was nothing either very meritorious or very marvellous in the integrity and moderation of my conduct at Mdlle. Reuter's pensionnat de demoiselles.

My first business this afternoon consisted in reading the list of places for the month, determined by the relative correctness of the compositions given the preceding day. The list was headed, as usual, by the name of Sylvie, that plain, quiet little girl I have described before as being at once the best and ugliest pupil in the establishment; the second place had fallen to the lot of a certain Léonie Ledru, diminutive, sharp-featured, and parchment-skinned creature of quick wits, frail

conscience, and indurated feelings; a lawyer-like thing, of whom I used to say that, had she been a boy, she would have made a model of an unprincipled, clever attorney. Then came Eulalie, the proud beauty, the Juno of the school, whom six long years of drilling in the simple grammar of the English language had compelled, despite the stiff phlegm of her intellect, to acquire a mechanical acquaintance with most of its rules. No smile, no trace of pleasure or satisfaction appeared in Sylvie's nun-like and passive face as she heard her name read first. I always felt saddened by the sight of that poor girl's absolute quiescence on all occasions, and it was my custom to look at her, to address her, as seldom as possible; her extreme docility, her assiduous perseverance, would have recommended her warmly to my good opinion; her modesty, her intelligence, would have induced me to feel most kindly— most affectionately towards her, notwithstanding the almost ghastly plainness of her features, the disproportion of her form, the corpse-like lack of animation in her countenance, had I not been aware that every friendly word, every kindly action, would be reported by her to her confessor, and by him misinterpreted and poisoned. Once I laid my hand on her head in token of approbation; I thought Sylvie was going to smile, her dim eye almost kindled; but, presently, she shrank from me; I was a man and a heretic; she, poor child! a destined nun and devoted Catholic; thus a fourfold wall of separation divided her mind from mine. A pert smirk, and a hard glance of triumph, was Léonie's method of testifying her gratification; Eulalie looked sullen and envious—she had hoped to be first. Hortense and Caroline exchanged a reckless grimace on hearing their names read out somewhere near the bottom of the list; the brand of mental inferiority was considered by them as no disgrace, their hopes for the future being based solely on their personal attractions.

This affair arranged, the regular lesson followed. During a brief interval, employed by the pupils in ruling their books, my eye, ranging carelessly over the benches, observed, for the first time, that the farthest seat in the farthest row—a seat usually vacant—was again filled by the new scholar, the Mdlle. Henri so ostentatiously recommended to me by the directress. To-day I had on my spectacles; her appearance, therefore, was clear to me at the first glance; I had not to puzzle over it. She looked young; yet, had I been required to name her exact age, I should have been somewhat nonplussed: the slightness of her figure might have suited seventeen; a certain anxious and preoccupied expression of face seemed the indication of riper years. She was dressed, like all the rest, in a dark stuff gown and a white collar; her features were dissimilar to any there, not so rounded, more defined, yet scarcely regular. The shape of her head too was different, the superior part more developed, the base considerably less. I felt assured, at first sight, that she was not a Belgian; her complexion, her countenance, her lineaments, her figure, were all distinct from theirs, and, evidently, the type of another race—of a race less gifted with fulness of flesh and plenitude of blood; less jocund, material, unthinking. When I first cast my eyes on her, she sat looking fixedly down, her chin resting on her hand, and she did not change her attitude till I commenced the lesson. None of the Belgian girls would have retained one position, and that a reflective one, for the same length of time. Yet, having intimated that her appearance was peculiar, as being unlike that of her Flemish companions, I have little more to say respecting it; I can pronounce no encomiums on her beauty, for she was not beautiful; nor offer condolence on her plainness, for neither was she plain; a careworn character of forehead, and a corresponding moulding of the mouth, struck me with a sentiment resembling surprise, but these traits would probably have passed unnoticed by any less crotchety observer.

Now, reader, though I have spent more than a page in describing Mdlle. Henri, I know well enough that I have left on your mind's eye no distinct picture of her; I have not painted her complexion, nor her eyes, nor her hair, nor even drawn the outline of her shape. You cannot tell whether her nose was aquiline or retroussé, whether her chin was long or short, her face square or oval; nor could I the first

day, and it is not my intention to communicate to you at once a knowledge I myself gained by little and little.

I gave a short exercise which they all wrote down. I saw the new pupil was puzzled at first with the novelty of the form and language; once or twice she looked at me with a sort of painful solicitude, as not comprehending at all what I meant; then she was not ready when the others were, she could not write her phrases so fast as they did; I would not help her, I went on relentless. She looked at me; her eye said most plainly, "I cannot follow you." I disregarded the appeal, and, carelessly leaning back in my chair, glancing from time to time with a *nonchalant* air out of the window, I dictated a little faster. On looking towards her again, I perceived her face clouded with embarrassment, but she was still writing on most diligently; I paused a few seconds; she employed the interval in hurriedly re-perusing what she had written, and shame and discomfiture were apparent in her countenance; she evidently found she had made great nonsense of it. In ten minutes more the dictation was complete, and, having allowed a brief space in which to correct it, I took their books; it was with a reluctant hand Mdlle. Henri gave up hers, but, having once yielded it to my possession, she composed her anxious face, as if, for the present, she had resolved to dismiss regret, and had made up her mind to be thought unprecedentedly stupid. Glancing over her exercise, I found that several lines had been omitted, but what was written contained very few faults; I instantly inscribed "Bon" at the bottom of the page, and returned it to her; she smiled, at first incredulously, then as if reassured, but did not lift her eyes; she could look at me, it seemed, when perplexed and bewildered, but not when gratified; I thought that scarcely fair.

Chapter XV

SOME time elapsed before I again gave a lesson in the first class; the holiday of Whitsuntide occupied three days, and on the fourth it was the turn of the second division to receive my instructions. As I made the transit of the carré, I observed, as usual, the band of sewers surrounding Mdlle. Henri; there were only about a dozen of them, but they made as much noise as might have sufficed for fifty; they seemed very little under her control; three or four at once assailed her with importunate requirements; she looked harassed, she demanded silence, but in vain. She saw me, and I read in her eye pain that a stranger should witness the insubordination of her pupils; she seemed to entreat order—her prayers were useless; then I remarked that she compressed her lips and contracted her brow; and her countenance, if I read it correctly, said: "I have done my best; I seem to merit blame notwithstanding; blame me then who will." I passed on; as I closed the schoolroom door, I heard her say, suddenly and sharply, addressing one of the eldest and most turbulent of the lot:

"Amélie Müllenberg, ask me no question, and request of me no assistance, for a week to come; during that space of time I will neither speak to you nor help you."

The words were uttered with emphasis—nay, with vehemence—and a comparative silence followed; whether the calm was permanent, I know not; two doors now closed between me and the carré.

Next day was appropriated to the first class; on my arrival, I found the directress seated, as usual, in a chair between the two estrades, and before her was standing Mdlle. Henri, in an attitude (as it seemed to me) of somewhat reluctant attention. The directress was knitting and talking at the same time. Amidst the hum of a large schoolroom, it was easy so to speak in the ear of one person, as to be heard by

that person alone, and it was thus Mdlle. Reuter parleyed with her teacher. The face of the latter was a little flushed, not a little troubled; there was vexation in it, whence resulting I know not, for the directress looked very placid indeed; she could not be scolding in such gentle whispers, and with so equable a mien; no, it was presently proved that her discourse had been of the most friendly tendency, for I heard the closing words:

"C'est assez, ma bonne amie; à present je ne veux pas vous retenir davantage."

Without reply, Mdlle. Henri turned away: dissatisfaction was plainly evinced in her face, and a smile, slight and brief, but bitter, distrustful, and, I thought, scornful, curled her lip as she took her place in the class; it was a secret, involuntary smile, which lasted but a second; an air of depression succeeded, chased away presently by one of attention and interest, when I gave the word for all the pupils to take their reading-books. In general I hated the reading-lesson, it was such a torture to the ear to listen to their uncouth mouthing of my native tongue, and no effort of example or precept on my part ever seemed to effect the slightest improvement in their accent. To-day, each, in her appropriate key, lisped, stuttered, mumbled, and jabbered as usual; about fifteen had racked me in turn, and my auricular nerve was expecting with resignation the discords of the sixteenth, when a full, though low voice, read out, in clear correct English:

"On his way to Perth, the king was met by a Highland woman, calling herself a prophetess; she stood at the side of the ferry by which he was about to travel to the north, and cried with a loud voice, 'My lord the king, if you pass this water you will never return again alive!' "—(*Vide* the *History of Scotland*).

I looked up in amazement; the voice was a voice of Albion; the accent was pure and silvery; it only wanted firmness, and assurance, to be the counterpart of what any well-educated lady in Essex or Middlesex might have enounced, yet the speaker or reader was no other than Mdlle. Henri, in whose grave, joyless face I saw no mark of consciousness that she had performed any extraordinary feat. No one else evinced surprise either. Mdlle. Reuter knitted away assiduously; I was aware, however, that at the conclusion of the paragraph, she had lifted her eyelid and honoured me with a glance sideways; she did not know the full excellency of the teacher's style of reading, but she perceived that her accent was not that of the others, and wanted to discover what I thought; I masked my visage with indifference, and ordered the next girl to proceed.

When the lesson was over, I took advantage of the confusion caused by breaking up, to approach Mdlle. Henri; she was standing near the window, and retired as I advanced; she thought I wanted to look out, and did not imagine that I could have anything to say to her. I took her exercise-book out of her hand; as I turned over the leaves I addressed her:

"You have had lessons in English before?" I asked.

"No, sir."

"No! you read it well; you have been in England?"

"Oh, no!" with some animation.

"You have been in English families?"

Still the answer was "No." Here my eye, resting on the flyleaf of the book, saw written "Frances Evans Henri."

"Your name?" I asked.

"Yes, sir."

My interrogations were cut short; I heard a little rustling behind me, and close at my back was the directress, professing to be examining the interior of a desk.

"Mademoiselle," said she, looking up and addressing the teacher, "will you have the goodness to go and stand in the corridor, while the young ladies are putting on their things, and try to keep some order?"

Mdlle. Henri obeyed.

"What splendid weather!" observed the directress cheerfully, glancing at the same time from the window. I assented and was withdrawing. "What of your new pupil, Monsieur?" continued she, following my retreating steps. "Is she likely to make progress in English?"

"Indeed I can hardly judge. She possesses a pretty good accent; of her real knowledge of the language I have as yet had no opportunity of forming an opinion."

"And her natural capacity, Monsieur? I have had my fears about that: can you relieve me by an assurance at least of its average power?"

"I see no reason to doubt its average power, Mademoiselle, but really I scarcely know her, and have not had time to study the calibre of her capacity. I wish you a very good afternoon."

She still pursued me. "You will observe, Monsieur, and tell me what you think; I could so much better rely on your opinion than on my own; women cannot judge of these things as men can, and excuse my pertinacity, Monsieur, but it is natural I should feel interested about this poor little girl (pauvre petite); she has scarcely any relations, her own efforts are all she has to look to, her acquirements must be her sole fortune; her present position has once been mine, or nearly so; it is then but natural I should sympathise with her; and sometimes, when I see the difficulty she has in managing pupils, I feel quite chagrined. I doubt not she does her best, her intentions are excellent; but, Monsieur, she wants tact and firmness. I have talked to her on the subject, but I am not fluent, and probably did not express myself with clearness; she never appears to comprehend me. Now, would you occasionally, when you see an opportunity, slip in a word of advice to her on the subject; men have so much more influence than women have—they argue so much more logically than we do; and you, Monsieur, in particular, have so paramount a power of making yourself obeyed; a word of advice from you could not but do her good; even if she were sullen and headstrong (which I hope she is not), she would scarcely refuse to listen to you; for my own part, I can truly say that I never attend one of your lessons without deriving benefit from witnessing your management of the pupils. The other masters are a constant source of anxiety to me; they cannot impress the young ladies with sentiments of respect, nor restrain the levity natural to youth: in you, Monsieur, I feel the most absolute confidence; try then to put this poor child into the way of controlling our giddy, high-spirited Brabantoises. But, Monsieur, I would add one word more; don't alarm her *amour propre;* beware of inflicting a wound there. I reluctantly admit that in that particular she is blamably— some would say ridiculously—susceptible. I fear I have touched this sore point inadvertently, and she cannot get over it."

During the greater part of this harangue my hand was on the lock of the outer door; I now turned it.

"Au revoir, Mademoiselle," said I, and I escaped. I saw the directress's stock of words was yet far from exhausted. She looked after me, she would fain have detained me longer. Her manner towards me had been altered ever since I had begun to treat her with hardness and indifference: she almost cringed to me on every occasion; she consulted my countenance incessantly, and beset me with innumerable little officious attentions. Servility creates despotism. This slavish homage, instead of softening my heart, only pampered whatever was stern and exacting in its mood. The very circumstance of her hovering round me like a fascinated bird, seemed to transform me into a rigid pillar of stone; her flatteries irritated my scorn, her blandishments confirmed my reserve. At times I wondered what she meant by giving herself such trouble to win me, when the more profitable Pelet was already in her nets, and when, too, she was aware that I possessed her secret, for I had not scrupled to tell her as much: but the fact is that as it was her nature to doubt the reality and undervalue the worth of modesty, affection, disin- terestedness—to regard these qualities as foibles of character—so it was equally her tendency to consider pride, hardness, selfishness, as proofs of strength. She

would trample on the neck of humility, she would kneel at the feet of disdain; she would meet tenderness with secret contempt, indifference she would woo with ceaseless assiduities. Benevolence, devotedness, enthusiasm, were her antipathies; for dissimulation and self-interest she had a preference—they were real wisdom in her eyes; moral and physical degradation, mental and bodily inferiority, she regarded with indulgence; they were foils capable of being turned to good account as set-offs for her own endowments. To violence, injustice, tyranny, she succumbed—they were her natural masters; she had no propensity to hate, no impulse to resist them; the indignation their behests awake in some hearts was unknown in hers. From all this it resulted that the false and selfish called her wise, the vulgar and debased termed her charitable, the insolent and unjust dubbed her amiable, the conscientious and benevolent generally at first accepted as valid her claim to be considered one of themselves; but ere long the plating of pretension wore off, the real material appeared below, and they laid her aside as a deception.

Chapter XVI

In the course of another fortnight I had seen sufficient of Frances Evans Henri, to enable me to form a more definite opinion of her character. I found her possessed in a somewhat remarkable degree of at least two good points, viz., perseverance and a sense of duty; I found she was really capable of applying to study, of contending with difficulties. At first I offered her the same help which I had always found it necessary to confer on the others; I began with unloosing for her each knotty point, but I soon discovered that such help was regarded by my new pupil as degrading; she recoiled from it with a certain proud impatience. Hereupon I appointed her long lessons, and left her to solve alone any perplexities they might present. She set to the task with serious ardour, and having quickly accomplished one labour, eagerly demanded more. So much for her perseverance; as to her sense of duty, it evinced itself thus: she liked to learn, but hated to teach; her progress as a pupil depended upon herself, and I saw that on herself she could calculate with certainty; her success as a teacher rested partly, perhaps chiefly, upon the will of others; it cost her a most painful effort to enter into conflict with this foreign will, to endeavour to bend it into subjection to her own; for in what regarded people in general the action of her will was impeded by many scruples; it was as unembarrassed as strong where her own affairs were concerned, and to it she could at any time subject her inclination, if that inclination went counter to her convictions of right; yet when called upon to wrestle with the propensities, the habits, the faults of others, of children especially, who are deaf to reason, and, for the most part, insensate to persuasion, her will sometimes almost refused to act; then came in the sense of duty, and forced the reluctant will into operation. A wasteful expense of energy and labour was frequently the consequence; Frances toiled for and with her pupils like a drudge, but it was long ere her conscientious exertions were rewarded by anything like docility on their part, because they saw that they had power over her, inasmuch as by resisting her painful attempts to convince, persuade, control—by forcing her to the employment of coercive measures—they could inflict upon her exquisite suffering. Human beings—human children especially—seldom deny themselves the pleasure of exercising a power which they are conscious of possessing, even though that power consist only in a capacity to make others wretched; a pupil whose sensations are duller than those of his instructor, while his nerves are tougher and his bodily strength perhaps greater, has an immense advantage over that instructor, and he will generally use it relentlessly, because the very young, very healthy, very thoughtless, know neither how to sympathise nor how to spare. Frances, I fear,

suffered much; a continual weight seemed to oppress her spirits; I have said she did not live in the house, and whether in her own abode, wherever that might be, she wore the same pre-occupied, unsmiling, sorrowfully resolved air that always shaded her features under the roof of Mdlle. Reuter, I could not tell.

One day I gave, as a devoir, the trite little anecdote of Alfred tending cakes in the herdsman's hut, to be related with amplifications. A singular affair most of the pupils made of it; brevity was what they had chiefly studied; the majority of the narratives were perfectly unintelligible; those of Sylvie and Léonie Ledru alone pretended to anything like sense and connection. Eulalie, indeed, had hit upon a clever expedient for at once ensuring accuracy and saving trouble; she had obtained access somehow to an abridged history of England, and had copied the anecdote out fair. I wrote on the margin of her production "Stupid and deceitful," and then tore it down the middle.

Last in the pile of single-leaved devoirs, I found one of several sheets neatly written out and stitched together; I knew the hand, and scarcely needed the evidence of the signature "Frances Evans Henri" to confirm my conjecture as to the writer's identity.

Night was my usual time for correcting devoirs, and my own room the usual scene of such task—task most onerous hitherto; and it seemed strange to me to feel rising within me an incipient sense of interest, as I snuffed the candle and addressed myself to the perusal of the poor teacher's manuscript.

"Now," thought I, "I shall see a glimpse of what she really is; I shall get an idea of the nature and extent of her powers; not that she can be expected to express herself well in a foreign tongue, but still, if she has any mind, here will be a reflection of it."

The narrative commenced by a description of a Saxon peasant's hut, situated within the confines of a great, leafless, winter forest; it represented an evening in December; flakes of snow were falling, and the herdsman foretold a heavy storm; he summoned his wife to aid him in collecting their flock, roaming far away on the pastoral banks of the Thone; he warns her that it will be late ere they return. The good woman is reluctant to quit her occupation of baking cakes for the evening meal; but acknowledging the primary importance of securing the herds and flocks, she puts on her sheep-skin mantle; and, addressing a stranger who rests half reclined on a bed of rushes near the hearth, bids him mind the bread till her return.

"Take care, young man," she continues, "that you fasten the door well after us; and, above all, open to none in our absence; whatever sound you hear, stir not, and look not out. The night will soon fall; this forest is most wild and lonely; strange noises are often heard therein after sunset; wolves haunt these glades, and Danish warriors infest the country; worse things are talked of; you might chance to hear, as it were, a child cry, and on opening the door to afford it succour, a great black bull, or a shadowy goblin dog, might rush over the threshold; or, more awful still, if something flapped, as with wings, against the lattice, and then a raven or a white dove flew in and settled on the hearth, such a visitor would be a sure sign of misfortune to the house; therefore, heed my advice, and lift the latchet for nothing."

Her husband calls her away, both depart. The stranger, left alone, listens awhile to the muffled snow-wind, the remote, swollen sound of the river, and then he speaks.

"It is Christmas Eve," says he, "I mark the date; here I sit alone on a rude couch of rushes, sheltered by the thatch of a herdsman's hut; I, whose inheritance was a kingdom owe my night's harbourage to a poor serf; my throne is usurped, my crown presses the brow of an invader; I have no friends; my troops wander broken in the hills of Wales; reckless robbers spoil my country; my subjects lie prostrate, their breasts crushed by the heel of the brutal Dane. Fate! thou hast done thy worst, and now thou standest before me resting thy hand on thy blunted blade.

Ay; I see thine eye confront mine and demand why I still live, why I still hope. Pagan demon, I credit not thine omnipotence, and so cannot succumb to thy power. My God, whose Son, as on this night, took on Him the form of man, and for man vouchsafed to suffer and bleed, controls thy hand, and without His behest thou canst not strike a stroke. My God is sinless, eternal, all-wise—in Him is my trust; and though stripped and crushed by thee—though naked, desolate, void of resource— I do not despair, I cannot despair: were the lance of Guthrum now wet with my blood, I should not despair. I watch, I toil, I pray; Jehovah, in his own time, will aid.''

I need not continue the quotation; the whole devoir was in the same strain. There were errors of orthography, there were foreign idioms, there were some faults of construction, there were verbs irregular transformed into verbs regular; it was mostly made up, as the above example shows, of short and somewhat rude sentences, and the style stood in great need of polish and sustained dignity; yet such as it was, I had hitherto seen nothing like it in the course of my professional experience. The girl's mind had conceived a picture of the hut, of the two peasants, of the crownless king; she had imagined the wintry forest, she had recalled the old Saxon ghost-legends, she had appreciated Alfred's courage under calamity, she had remembered his Christian education, and had shown him, with the rooted confidence of those primitive days, relying on the scriptural Jehovah for aid against the mythological Destiny. This she had done without a hint from me: I had given the subject, but not said a word about the manner of treating it.

"I will find, or make, an opportunity of speaking to her," I said to myself as I rolled the devoir up; "I will learn what she has of English in her besides the name of Frances Evans; she is no novice in the language, that is evident, yet she told me she had neither been in England, nor taken lessons in English, nor lived in English families."

In the course of my next lesson, I made a report of the other devoirs, dealing out praise and blame in very small retail parcels, according to my custom, for there was no use in blaming severely, and high encomiums were rarely merited. I said nothing of Mdlle. Henri's exercise, and, spectacles on nose, I endeavoured to decipher in her countenance her sentiments at the omission. I wanted to find out whether in her existed a consciousness of her own talents. "If she thinks she did a clever thing in composing that devoir, she will now look mortified," thought I. Grave as usual, almost sombre, was her face: as usual, her eyes were fastened on the cahier open before her; there was something, I thought, of expectation in her attitude, as I concluded a brief review of the last devoir, and when, casting it from me and rubbing my hands, I bade them take their grammars, some slight change did pass over her air and mien, as though she now relinquished a faint prospect of pleasant excitement; she had been waiting for something to be discussed in which she had a degree of interest; the discussion was not to come on, so expectation sank back, shrunk, and sad, but attention, promptly filling up the void, repaired in a moment the transient collapse of feature; still, I felt, rather than saw, during the whole course of the lesson, that a hope had been wrenched from her, and that if she did not show distress, it was because she would not.

At four o'clock, when the bell rang and the room was in immediate tumult, instead of taking my hat and starting from the estrade, I sat still a moment. I looked at Frances, she was putting her books into her cabas; having fastened the button, she raised her head; encountering my eye, she made a quiet, respectful obeisance, as bidding good afternoon, and was turning to depart.

"Come here," said I, lifting my finger at the same time. She hesitated; she could not hear the words amidst the uproar now pervading both schoolrooms; I repeated the sign; she approached; again she paused within half a yard of the estrade, and looked shy, and still doubtful whether she had mistaken my meaning.

"Step up," I said, speaking with decision. It is the only way of dealing with diffident, easily embarrassed characters, and with some slight manual aid I presently got her placed just where I wanted her to be, that is, between my desk and the window, where she was screened from the rush of the second division, and where no one could sneak behind her to listen.

"Take a seat," I said, placing a tabouret: and I made her sit down. I knew what I was doing would be considered a very strange thing, and, what was more, I did not care. Frances knew it also, and, I fear, by an appearance of agitation and trembling, that she cared much. I drew from my pocket the rolled-up devoir.

"This is yours, I suppose?" said I, addressing her in English, for I now felt sure she could speak English.

"Yes," she answered distinctly; and as I unrolled it and laid it out flat on the desk before her with my hand upon it, and a pencil in that hand, I saw her moved, and, as it were, kindled; her depression beamed as a cloud might behind which the sun is burning.

"This devoir has numerous faults," said I. "It will take you some years of careful study before you are in a condition to write English with absolute correctness. Attend: I will point out some principal defects." And I went through it carefully, noting every error, and demonstrating why they were errors, and how the words or phrases ought to have been written. In the course of this sobering process she became calm. I now went on:

"As to the substance of your devoir, Mdlle. Henri, it has surprised me: I perused it with pleasure, because I saw in it some proofs of taste and fancy. Taste and fancy are not the highest gifts of the human mind, but such as they are you possess them—not probably in a paramount degree, but in a degree beyond what the majority can boast. You may then take courage; cultivate the faculties that God and nature have bestowed on you, and do not fear in any crisis of suffering, under any pressure of injustice, to derive free and full consolation from the consciousness of their strength and rarity."

"Strength and rarity!" I repeated to myself; "ay, the words are probably true," for on looking up, I saw the sun had dissevered its screening cloud, her countenance was transfigured, a smile shone in her eyes—a smile almost triumphant; it seemed to say:

"I am glad you have been forced to discover so much of my nature; you need not so carefully moderate your language. Do you think I am myself a stranger to myself? What you tell me in terms so qualified, I have known fully from a child."

She did say this as plainly as a frank and flashing glance could, but in a moment the glow of her complexion, the radiance of her aspect, had subsided; if strongly conscious of her talents, she was equally conscious of her harassing defects, and the remembrance of these obliterated for a single second, now reviving with sudden force, at once subdued the too vivid characters in which her sense of her powers had been expressed. So quick was the revulsion of feeling, I had not time to check her triumph by reproof; ere I could contract my brows to a frown she had become serious and almost mournful-looking.

"Thank you, sir," said she, rising. There was gratitude both in her voice and in the look with which she accompanied it. It was time, indeed, for our conference to terminate; for, when I glanced around, behold all the boarders (the day-scholars had departed) were congregated within a yard or two of my desk, and stood staring with eyes and mouths wide open: the three maîtresses formed a whispering knot in one corner, and, close to my elbow, was the directress, sitting on a low chair, calmly clipping the tassels of her finished purse.

Chapter XVII

AFTER all I had profited but imperfectly by the opportunity I had so boldly achieved of speaking to Mdlle. Henri; it was my intention to ask her how she came to be possessed of two English baptismal names, Frances and Evans, in addition to her French suruame, also whence she derived her good accent. I had forgotten both points, or, rather, our colloquy had been so brief that I had not had time to bring them forward; moreover, I had not half tested her powers of speaking English; all I had drawn from her in that language were the words "Yes," and "Thank you, sir." "No matter," I reflected. "What has been left incomplete now, shall be finished another day." Nor did I fail to keep the promise thus made to myself. It was difficult to get even a few words of particular conversation with one pupil among so many; but, according to the old proverb, "Where there is a will, there is a way"; and again and again I managed to find an opportunity for exchanging a few words with Mdlle. Henri, regardless that envy stared and detraction whispered whenever I approached her.

"Your book an instant." Such was the mode in which I often began these brief dialogues; the time was always just at the conclusion of the lesson; and motioning to her to rise, I installed myself in her place, allowing her to stand deferentially at my side; for I esteemed it wise and right in her case to enforce strictly all forms ordinarily in use between master and pupil; the rather because I perceived that in proportion as my manner grew austere and magisterial, hers became easy and self-possessed—an odd contradiction, doubtless, to the ordinary effect in such cases; but so it was.

"A pencil," said I, holding out my hand without looking at her. (I am now about to sketch a brief report of the first of these conferences.) She gave me one, and while I underlined some errors in a grammatical exercise she had written, I observed:

"You are not a native of Belgium?"

"No."

"Nor of France?"

"No."

"Where, then, is your birthplace?"

"I was born at Geneva."

"You don't call Frances and Evans Swiss names, I presume?"

"No, sir; they are English names."

"Just so; and is it the custom of the Genevese to give their children English appellatives?"

"Non, Monsieur; mais——"

"Speak English, if you please."

"Mais——"

"English——"

"But" (slowly and with embarrassment) "my parents were not all the two Genevese."

"Say *both*, instead of 'all the two,' Mademoiselle."

"Not *both* Swiss: my mother was English."

"Ah! and of English extraction?"

"Yes—her ancestors were all English."

"And your father?"

"He was Swiss."

"What besides? What was his profession?"

"Ecclesiastic—pastor—he had a church."

"Since your mother is an Englishwoman, why do you not speak English with more facility?"

"Maman est morte, il y a dix ans."

"And you do homage to her memory by forgetting her language. Have the goodness to put French out of your mind so long as I converse with you—keep to English."

"C'est si difficile, Monsieur, quand on n'en a plus l'habitude."

"You had the habitude formerly, I suppose? Now answer me in your mother tongue."

"Yes, sir, I spoke the English more than the French when I was a child."

"Why do you not speak it now?"

"Because I have no English friends."

"You live with your father, I suppose?"

"My father is dead."

"You have brothers and sisters?"

"Not one."

"Do you live alone?"

"No—I have an aunt—ma tante Julienne."

"Your father's sister?"

"Justement, Monsieur."

"Is that English?"

"No—but I forget——"

"For which, Mademoiselle, if you were a child, I should certainly devise some slight punishment; at your age—you must be two or three and twenty, I should think?"

"Pas encore, Monsieur—en un mois j'aurai dix-neuf ans."

"Well, nineteen is a mature age, and, having attained it, you ought to be so solicitous for your own improvement, that it should not be needful for a master to remind you twice of the expediency of your speaking English whenever practicable."

To this wise speech I received no answer; and, when I looked up, my pupil was smiling to herself a much-meaning, though not very gay smile; it seemed to say, "He talks of he knows not what": it said this so plainly, that I determined to request information on the point concerning which my ignorance seemed to be thus tacitly affirmed.

"Are you solicitous for your own improvement?"

"Rather."

"How do you prove it, Mademoiselle?"

An odd question, and bluntly put; it excited a second smile.

"Why, Monsieur, I am not inattentive—am I? I learn my lessons well——"

"Oh, a child can do that! and what more do you do?"

"What more can I do?"

"Oh, certainly, not much; but you are a teacher, are you not, as well as a pupil?"

"Yes."

"You teach lace-mending?"

"Yes."

"A dull, stupid occupation; do you like it?"

"No—it is tedious."

"Why do you pursue it? Why do you not rather teach history, geography, grammar, even arithmetic?"

"Is Monsieur certain that I am myself thoroughly acquainted with these studies?"

"I don't know; you ought to be at your age."

"But I never was at school, Monsieur——"

"Indeed! What then were your friends—what was your aunt about? She is very much to blame."

"No, Monsieur, no—my aunt is good—she is not to blame—she does what she can; she lodges and nourishes me" (I report Mdlle. Henri's phrases literally, and it was thus she translated from the French). "She is not rich; she has only an annuity of twelve hundred francs, and it would be impossible for her to send me to school."

"Rather," thought I to myself on hearing this, but I continued, in the dogmatical tone I had adopted:

"It is sad, however, that you should be brought up in ignorance of the most ordinary branches of education; had you known something of history and grammar you might, by degrees, have relinquished your lace-mending drudgery, and risen in the world."

"It is what I mean to do."

"How? By a knowledge of English alone? That will not suffice; no respectable family will receive a governess whose whole stock of knowledge consists in a familiarity with one foreign language."

"Monsieur, I know other things."

"Yes, yes, you can work with Berlin wools, and embroider handkerchiefs and collars—that will do little for you."

Mdlle. Henri's lips were unclosed to answer, but she checked herself, as thinking the discussion had been sufficiently pursued, and remained silent.

"Speak," I continued impatiently; "I never like the appearance of acquiescence when the reality is not there: and you had a contradiction at your tongue's end."

"Monsieur, I have had many lessons both in grammar, history, geography, and arithmetic. I have gone through a course of each study."

"Bravo! but how did you manage it, since your aunt could not afford to send you to school?"

"By lace-mending; by the thing Monsieur despises so much."

"Truly! And now, Mademoiselle, it will be a good exercise for you to explain to me in English how such a result was produced by such means."

"Monsieur, I begged my aunt to have me taught lace-mending soon after we came to Brussels, because I knew it was a métier, a trade which was easily learnt, and by which I could earn some money very soon. I learnt it in a few days, and I quickly got work, for all the Brussels ladies have old lace—very precious—which must be mended all the times it is washed. I earned money a little, and this money I gave for lessons in the studies I have mentioned; some of it I spent in buying books, English books especially; soon I shall try to find a place of governess, or school-teacher, when I can write and speak English well; but it will be difficult, because those who know I have been a lace-mender will despise me, as the pupils here despise me. Pourtant j'ai mon projet," she added in a lower tone.

"What is it?"

"I will go and live in England; I will teach French there."

The words were pronounced emphatically. She said "England" as you might suppose an Israelite of Moses' days would have said Canaan.

"Have you a wish to see England?"

"Yes, and an intention."

And here a voice, the voice of the directress, interposed:

"Mademoiselle Henri, je crois qu'il va pleuvoir; vous feriez bien, ma bonne amie, de retourner chez vous tout de suite."

In silence, without a word of thanks for this officious warning, Mdlle. Henri collected her books; she moved to me respectfully, endeavoured to move to her superior, thought the endeavour was almost a failure, for her head seemed as if it would not bend, and thus departed.

Where there is one grain of perseverance or wilfulness in the composition, trifling obstacles are ever known rather to stimulate than discourage. Mdlle. Reuter might as well have spared herself the trouble of giving that intimation about the weather

(by-the-bye, her prediction was falsified by the event—it did not rain that evening). At the close of the next lesson I was again at Mdlle. Henri's desk. Thus did I accost her:

"What is your idea of England, Mademoiselle? Why do you wish to go there?"

Accustomed by this time to the calculated abruptness of my manner, it no longer discomposed or surprised her, and she answered with only so much of hesitation as was rendered inevitable by the difficulty she experienced in improvising the translation of her thoughts from French to English.

"England is something unique, as I have heard and read; my idea of it is vague, and I want to go there to render my idea clear, definite."

"Hum! How much of England do you suppose you could see if you went there in the capacity of a teacher? A strange notion you must have of getting a clear and definite idea of a country! All you could see of Great Britain would be the interior of a school, or at most of one or two private dwellings."

"It would be an English school; they would be English dwellings."

"Indisputably; but what then? What would be the value of observations made on a scale so narrow?"

"Monsieur, might not one learn something by analogy? An—échantillon—a—a sample often serves to give an idea of the whole; besides, narrow and wide are words comparative, are they not? All my life would perhaps seem narrow in your eyes—all the life of a—that little animal subterranean—une taupe—comment dit-on?"

"Mole."

"Yes—a mole, which lives underground, would seem narrow even to me."

"Well, Mademoiselle—what then? Proceed."

"Mais, Monsieur, vous me comprenez."

"Not in the least; have the goodness to explain."

"Why, Monsieur, it is just so. In Switzerland I have done but little, learnt but little, and seen but little; my life there was in a circle; I walked the same round every day; I could not get out of it; had I rested—remained there even till my death, I should never have enlarged it, because I am poor and not skilful, I have not great acquirements; when I was quite tired of this round, I begged my aunt to go to Brussels; my existence is no larger here, because I am no richer or higher; I walk in as narrow a limit, but the scene is changed; it would change again if I went to England. I knew something of the bourgeois of Geneva, now I know something of the bourgeois of Brussels; if I went to London, I should know something of the bourgeois of London. Can you make any sense out of what I say, Monsieur, or is it all obscure?"

"I see, I see—now let us advert to another subject; you propose to devote your life to teaching, and you are a most unsuccessful teacher; you cannot keep your pupils in order."

A flush of painful confusion was the result of this harsh remark; she bent her head to the desk, but soon raising it, replied:

"Monsieur, I am not a skilful teacher, it is true, but practice improves; besides, I work under difficulties; here I only teach sewing, I can show no power in sewing, no superiority—it is a subordinate art; then I have no associates in this house, I am isolated; I am too a heretic, which deprives me of influence."

"And in England you would be a foreigner; that too would deprive you of influence, and would effectually separate you from all round you; in England you would have as few connections, as little importance as you have here."

"But I should be learning something; for the rest, there are probably difficulties for such as I everywhere, and if I must contend, and perhaps be conquered, I would rather submit to English pride than to Flemish coarseness; besides, Monsieur——"

She stopped—not evidently from any difficulty in finding words to express herself, but because discretion seemed to say, "You have said enough."

"Finish your phrase," I urged.

"Besides, Monsieur, I long to live once more among Protestants; they are more honest than Catholics; a Romish school is a building with porous walls, a hollow floor, a false ceiling; every room in this house, Monsieur, has eye-holes and ear-holes, and what the house is, the inhabitants are, very treacherous; they all think it lawful to tell lies; they all call it politeness to profess friendship where they feel hatred."

"All?" said I; "you mean the pupils—the mere children—inexperienced, giddy things, who have not learnt to distinguish the difference between right and wrong?"

"On the contrary, Monsieur—the children are the most sincere; they have not yet had time to become accomplished in duplicity; they will tell lies, but they do it inartificially, and you know they are lying; but the grown-up people are very false; they deceive strangers, they deceive each other——"

A servant here entered:

"Mdlle. Henri—Mdlle. Reuter vous prie de vouloir bien conduire la petite de Dorlodot chez elle, elle vous attend dans le cabinet de Rosalie la portière—c'est que sa bonne n'est pas venue la chercher—voyez-vous."

"Eh bien! est-ce que je suis sa bonne—moi?" demanded Mdlle. Henri; then smiling, with that same bitter, derisive smile I had seen on her lips once before, she hastily rose and made her exit.

Chapter XVIII

THE young Anglo-Swiss evidently derived both pleasure and profit from the study of her mother-tongue. In teaching her I did not, of course, confine myself to the ordinary school routine; I made instruction in English a channel for instruction in literature. I prescribed to her a course of reading; she had a little selection of English classics, a few of which had been left her by her mother, and the others she had purchased with her own penny-fee. I lent her some more modern works; all these she read with avidity, giving me, in writing, a clear summary of each work when she had perused it. Composition, too, she delighted in. Such occupation seemed the very breath of her nostrils, and soon her improved productions wrung from me the avowal that those qualities in her I had termed taste and fancy ought rather to have been denominated judgment and imagination. When I intimated so much, which I did as usual in dry and stinted phrase, I looked for the radiant and exulting smile my one word of eulogy had elicited before; but Frances coloured. If she did smile, it was very softly and shyly; and instead of looking up to me with a conquering glance, her eyes rested on my hand, which, stretched over her shoulder, was writing some directions with a pencil on the margin of her book.

"Well, are you pleased that I am satisfied with your progress?" I asked.

"Yes," said she slowly, gently, the blush that had half subsided returning.

"But I do not say enough, I suppose?" I continued. "My praises are too cool?"

She made no answer, and, I thought, looked a little sad. I divined her thoughts, and should much have liked to have responded to them, had it been expedient so to do. She was not now very ambitious of my admiration—not eagerly desirous of dazzling me; a little affection—ever so little—pleased her better than all the panegyrics in the world. Feeling this, I stood a good while behind her, writing on the margin of her book. I could hardly quit my station or relinquish my occupation; something retained me bending there, my head very near hers, and my hand near hers too, but the margin of a copy-book is not an illimitable space—so, doubtless, the

directress thought; and she took occasion to walk past in order to ascertain by what art I prolonged so disproportionately the period necessary for filling it. I was obliged to go. Distasteful effort—to leave what we most prefer!

Frances did not become pale or feeble in consequence of her sedentary employment; perhaps the stimulus it communicated to her mind counterbalanced the inaction it imposed on her body. She changed, indeed, changed obviously and rapidly; but it was for the better. When I first saw her, her countenance was sunless, her complexion colourless: she looked like one who had no source of enjoyment, no store of bliss anywhere in the world; now the cloud had passed from her mien, leaving space for the dawn of hope and interest, and those feelings rose like a clear morning, animating what had been depressed, tinting what had been pale. Her eyes, whose colour I had not at first known, so dim were they with repressed tears, so shadowed with ceaseless dejection, now, lit by a ray of the sunshine that cheered her heart, revealed irids of bright hazel—irids large and full, screened with long lashes; and pupils instinct with fire. That look of wan emaciation which anxiety or low spirits often communicates to a thoughtful, thin face, rather long than round, having vanished from hers; a clearness of skin almost bloom, and a plumpness almost embonpoint, softened the decided lines of her features. Her figure shared in this beneficial change; it became rounder, and as the harmony of her form was complete and her stature of the graceful middle height, one did not regret (or at least *I* did not regret) the absence of confirmed fulness, in contours, still slight, though compact, elegant, flexible—the exquisite turning of waist, wrist, hand, foot, and ankle satisfied completely my notions of symmetry, and allowed a lightness and freedom of movement which corresponded with my ideas of grace.

Thus improved, thus wakened to life, Mdlle. Henri began to take a new footing in the school; her mental power, manifested gradually but steadily, ere long extorted recognition even from the envious; and when the young and healthy saw that she could smile brightly, converse gaily, move with vivacity and alertness, they acknowledged in her a sisterhood of youth and health, and tolerated her as of their kind accordingly.

To speak truth, I watched this change much as a gardener watches the growth of a precious plant, and I contributed to it too, even as the said gardener contributes to the development of his favourite. To me it was not difficult to discover how I could best foster my pupil, cherish her starved feelings, and induce the outward manifestation of that inward vigour which sunless drought and blighting blast had hitherto forbidden to expand. Constancy of attention—a kindness as mute as watchful, always standing by her, cloaked in the rough garb of austerity, and making its real nature known only by a rare glance of interest, or a cordial and gentle word; real respect masked with seeming imperiousness, directing, urging her actions, yet helping her too, and that with devoted care: these were the means I used, for these means best suited Frances' feelings, as susceptible as deep-vibrating—her nature at once proud and shy.

The benefits of my system became apparent also in her altered demeanour as a teacher; she now took her place amongst her pupils with an air of spirit and firmness which assured them at once that she meant to be obeyed—and obeyed she was. They felt they had lost their power over her. If any girl had rebelled, she would no longer have taken her rebellion to heart; she possessed a source of comfort they could not drain, a pillar of support they could not overthrow: formerly, when insulted, she wept; now, she smiled.

The public reading of one of her devoirs achieved the revelation of her talents to all and sundry; I remember the subject—it was an emigrant's letter to his friends at home. It opened with simplicity; some natural and graphic touches disclosed to the reader the scene of virgin forest and great, New-World river—barren of sail and flag—amidst which the epistle was supposed to be indited. The difficulties and dangers that attend a settler's life were hinted at; and in the few words said on that

subject, Mdlle. Henri failed not to render audible the voice of resolve, patience, endeavour. The disasters which had driven him from his native country were alluded to; stainless honour, inflexible independence, indestructible self-respect there took the word. Past days were spoken of; the grief of parting, the regrets of absence, were touched upon; feeling, forcible and fine, breathed eloquent in every period. At the close, consolation was suggested; religious faith became there the speaker, and she spoke well.

The devoir was powerfully written in language at once chaste and choice, in a style nerved with vigour and graced with harmony.

Mdlle. Reuter was quite sufficiently acquainted with English to understand it when read or spoken in her presence, though she could neither speak nor write it herself. During the perusal of this devoir, she sat placidly busy, her eyes and fingers occupied with the formation of a "rivière," or open-work hem round a cambric handkerchief; she said nothing, and her face and forehead, clothed with a mask of purely negative expression, were as blank of comment as her lips. As neither surprise, pleasure, approbation, nor interest were evinced in her countenance, so no more were disdain, envy, annoyance, weariness; if that inscrutable mien said anything, it was simply this:

"The matter is too trite to excite an emotion, or call forth an opinion."

As soon as I had done, a hum rose; several of the pupils, pressing round Mdlle. Henri, began to beset her with compliments; the composed voice of the directress was now heard:

"Young ladies, such of you as have cloaks and umbrellas will hasten to return home before the shower becomes heavier" (it was raining a little), "the remainder will wait till their respective servants arrive to fetch them." And the school dispersed, for it was four o'clock.

"Monsieur, a word," said Mdlle. Reuter, stepping on to the estrade, and signifying, by a movement of the hand, that she wished me to relinquish, for an instant, the castor I had clutched.

"Mademoiselle, I am at your service."

"Monsieur, it is of course an excellent plan to encourage effort in young people by making conspicuous the progress of any particularly industrious pupil; but do you not think that in the present instance, Mdlle. Henri can hardly be considered as a concurrent with the other pupils? She is older than most of them, and has had advantages of an exclusive nature for acquiring a knowledge of English; on the other hand, her sphere of life is somewhat beneath theirs; under these circumstances, a public distinction, conferred upon Mdlle. Henri, may be the means of suggesting comparisons, and exciting feelings such as would be far from advantageous to the individual forming their object. The interest I take in Mdlle. Henri's real welfare makes me desirous of screening her from annoyances of this sort; besides, Monsieur, as I have before hinted to you, the sentiment of *amour-propre* has a somewhat marked preponderance in her character; celebrity has a tendency to foster this sentiment, and in her it should be rather repressed—she rather needs keeping down than bringing forward; and then I think, Monsieur—it appears to me that ambition, *literary* ambition especially, is not a feeling to be cherished in the mind of a woman: would not Mdlle. Henri be much safer and happier if taught to believe that in the quiet discharge of social duties consists her real vocation, than if stimulated to aspire after applause and publicity? She may never marry; scanty as are her resources, obscure as are her connections, uncertain as is her health (for I think her consumptive, her mother died of that complaint), it is more than probable she never will; I do not see how she can rise to a position, whence such a step would be possible; but even in celibacy it would be better for her to retain the character and habits of a respectable decorous female."

"Indisputably, Mademoiselle," was my answer. "Your opinion admits of no doubt"; and, fearful of the harangue being renewed, I retreated under cover of that cordial sentence of assent.

At the date of a fortnight after the little incident noted above, I find it recorded in my diary that a hiatus occurred in Mdlle. Henri's usually regular attendance in class. The first day or two I wondered at her absence, but did not like to ask an explanation of it; I thought indeed some chance word might be dropped which would afford me the information I wished to obtain, without my running the risk of exciting silly smiles and gossiping whispers by demanding it. But when a week passed and the seat at the desk near the door still remained vacant, and when no allusion was made to the circumstance by any individual of the class—when, on the contrary, I found that all observed a marked silence on the point—I determined, *coûte que coûte,* to break the ice of this silly reserve. I selected Sylvie as my informant, because from her I knew that I should at least get a sensible answer, unaccompanied by wriggle, titter, or other flourish of folly.

"Où donc est Mdlle. Henri?" I said one day as I returned an exercise-book I had been examining.

"Elle est partie, Monsieur."

"Partie! et pour combien de temps? Quand reviendra-t-elle?"

"Elle est partie pour toujours, Monsieur; elle ne reviendra plus."

"Ah!" was my involuntary exclamation; then after a pause:

"En êtes-vous bien sûre, Sylvie?"

"Oui, oui, Monsieur, Mademoiselle la directrice nous l'a dit elle-même il y a deux ou trois jours."

And I could pursue my inquiries no further; time, place, and circumstances forbade my adding another word. I could neither comment on what had been said, nor demand further particulars. A question as to the reason of the teacher's departure, as to whether it had been voluntary or otherwise, was indeed on my lips, but I suppressed it—there were listeners all round. An hour after, in passing Sylvie in the corridor as she was putting on her bonnet, I stopped short and asked:

"Sylvie, do you know Mdlle. Henri's address? I have some books of hers," I added carelessly, "and I should wish to send them to her."

"No, Monsieur," replied Sylvie; "but perhaps Rosalie, the portress, will be able to give it you."

Rosalie's cabinet was just at hand; I stepped in and repeated the inquiry. Rosalie— a smart French grisette—looked up from her work with a knowing smile, precisely the sort of smile I had been so desirous to avoid exciting. Her answer was prepared; she knew nothing whatever of Mdlle. Henri's address—had never known it. Turning from her with impatience—for I believed she lied and was hired to lie—I almost knocked down some one who had been standing at my back; it was the directress. My abrupt movement made her recoil two or three steps. I was obliged to apologise, which I did more concisely than politely. No man likes to be dogged, and in the very irritable mood in which I then was the sight of Mdlle. Reuter thoroughly incensed me. At the moment I turned her countenance looked hard, dark, and inquisitive; her eyes were bent upon me with an expression of almost hungry curiosity. I had scarcely caught this phase of physiognomy ere it had vanished; a bland smile played on her features; my harsh apology was received with good-humoured facility.

"Oh, don't mention it, Monsieur; you only touched my hair with your elbow; it is no worse, only a little dishevelled." She shook it back, and passing her fingers through her curls, loosened them into more numerous and flowing ringlets. Then she went on with vivacity:

"Rosalie, I was coming to tell you to go instantly and close the windows of the salon; the wind is rising, and the muslin curtains will be covered with dust."

Rosalie departed. "Now," thought I, "this will not do; Mdlle. Reuter thinks her meanness in eavesdropping is screened by her art in devising a pretext, whereas the muslin curtains she speaks of are not more transparent than this same pretext." An impulse came over me to thrust the flimsy screen aside, and confront her craft boldly with a word or two of plain truth. "The rough-shod foot treads most firmly on slippery ground," thought I; so I began:

"Mademoiselle Henri has left your establishment—been dismissed, I presume?"

"Ah, I wished to have a little conversation with you, Monsieur," replied the directress, with the most natural and affable air in the world; "but we cannot talk quietly here; will Monsieur step into the garden a minute?" And she preceded me, stepping out through the glass-door I have before mentioned.

"There," said she, when we had reached the centre of the middle alley, and when the foliage of shrubs and trees, now in their summer pride, closing behind and around us, shut out the view of the house, and thus imparted a sense of seclusion even to this little plot of ground in the very core of a capital.

"There, one feels quiet and free when there are only pear-trees and rose-bushes about one; I dare say you, like me, Monsieur, are sometimes tired of being eternally in the midst of life; of having human faces always round you, human eyes always upon you, human voices always in your ear. I am sure I often wish intensely for liberty to spend a whole month in the country at some little farmhouse, bien gentille, bien propre, tout entourée de champs et de bois; quelle vie charmante que la vie champêtre! N'est-ce pas, Monsieur!"

"Cela dépend, Mademoiselle."

"Que le vent est bon et frais!" continued the directress; and she was right there, for it was a south wind, soft and sweet. I carried my hat in my hand, and this gentle breeze, passing through my hair, soothed my temples like balm. Its refreshing effect, however, penetrated no deeper than the mere surface of the frame; for as I walked by the side of Mdlle. Reuter, my heart was still hot within me, and while I was musing the fire burned; then spake I with my tongue:

"I understaud Mdlle. Henri is gone from hence, and will not return?"

"Ah, true! I meant to have named the subject to you some days ago, but my time is so completely taken up, I cannot do half the things I wish: have you never experienced what it is, Monsieur, to find the day too short by twelve hours for your numerous duties?"

"Not often. Mdlle. Henri's departure was not voluntary, I presume? If it had been, she would certainly have given me some intimation of it, being my pupil."

"Oh, did she not tell you? that was strange; for my part, I never thought of adverting to the subject; when one has so many things to attend to, one is apt to forget little incidents that are not of primary importance."

"You consider Mdlle. Henri's dismission, then, as a very insignificant event?"

"Dismission? Ah! she was not dismissed; I can say with truth, Monsieur, that since I became the head of this establishment no master or teacher has ever been *dismissed* from it."

"Yet some have left it, Mademoiselle?"

"Many; I have found it necessary to change frequently—a change of instructors is often beneficial to the interests of a school; it gives life and variety to the proceedings; it amuses the pupils, and suggests to the parents the idea of exertion and progress."

"Yet when you are tired of a professor, or maîtresse, you scruple to dismiss them?"

"No need to have recourse to such extreme measures, I assure you. Allons, Monsieur le professeur—asseyons-nous; je vais vous donner une petite leçon dans votre état d'instituteur." (I wish I might write all she said to me in French—it loses sadly by being translated into English.) We had now reached *the* garden-chair; the directress sat down, and signed to me to sit by her, but I only rested my knee

on the seat, and stood leaning my head and arm against the embowering branch of
a huge laburnum, whose golden flowers, blent with the dusky green leaves of a
lilac-bush, formed a mixed arch of shade and sunshine over the retreat. Mdlle.
Reuter sat silent a moment; some novel movements were evidently working in her
mind, and they showed their nature on her astute brow; she was meditating some
chef d'œuvre of policy. Convinced by several months' experience that the affectation
of virtues she did not possess was unavailing to ensnare me—aware that I had read
her real nature, and would believe nothing of the character she gave out as being
hers—she had determined, at last, to try a new key, and see if the lock of my heart
would yield to that; a little audacity, a word of truth, a glimpse of the real. "Yes,
I will try," was her inward resolve; and then her blue eye glittered upon me—it
did not flash—nothing of flame ever kindled in its temperate gleam.

"Monsieur fears to sit by me?" she inquired playfully.

"I have no wish to usurp Pelet's place," I answered, for I had got the habit of
speaking to her bluntly—a habit begun in anger, but continued because I saw that,
instead of offending, it fascinated her. She cast down her eyes, and drooped her
eyelids; she sighed uneasily; she turned with an anxious gesture, as if she would
give me the idea of a bird that flutters in its cage, and would fain fly from its jail
and jailer, and seek its natural mate and pleasant nest.

"Well—and your lesson?" I demanded briefly.

"Ah!" she exclaimed, recovering herself, "you are so young, so frank and
fearless, so talented, so impatient of imbecility, so disdainful of vulgarity, you need
a lesson; here it is then: far more is to be done in this world by dexterity than by
strength; but, perhaps, you knew that before, for there is delicacy as well as power
in your character—policy, as well as pride!"

"Go on," said I; and I could hardly help smiling, the flattery was so piquant,
so finely seasoned. She caught the prohibited smile, though I passed my hand over
my mouth to conceal it; and again she made room for me to sit beside her. I shook
my head, though temptation penetrated to my senses at the moment, and once more
I told her to go on.

"Well, then, if ever you are at the head of a large establishment, dismiss nobody.
To speak truth, Monsieur (and to you I will speak truth), I despise people who are
always making rows, blustering, sending off one to the right, and another to the
left, urging and hurrying circumstances. I'll tell you what I like best to do, Monsieur,
shall I?" She looked up again; she had compounded her glance well this time—
much archness, more deference, a spicy dash of coquetry, an unveiled consciousness
of capacity. I nodded; she treated me like the great Mogul; so I became the great
Mogul as far as she was concerned.

"I like, Monsieur, to take my knitting in my hands, and to sit quietly down in
my chair; circumstances defile past me; I watch their march; so long as they follow
the course I wish, I say nothing, and do nothing; I don't clap my hands, and cry
out 'Bravo! How lucky I am!' to attract the attention and envy of my neighbours—
I am merely passive; but when events fall out ill—when circumstances become
adverse—I watch very vigilantly; I knit on still, and still I hold my tongue; but
every now and then, Monsieur, I just put my toe out—so—and give the rebellious
circumstance a little secret push, without noise, which sends it the way I wish, and
I am successful after all, and nobody has seen my expedient. So, when teachers
or masters become troublesome and inefficient—when, in short, the interests of the
school would suffer from their retaining their places—I mind my knitting, events
progress, circumstances glide past; I see one which, if pushed ever so little awry,
will render untenable the post I wish to have vacated—the deed is done—the
stumbling-block removed—and no one saw me: I have not made an enemy, I am
rid of an incumbrance."

A moment since, and I thought her alluring; this speech concluded, I looked on
her with distaste. "Just like you," was my cold answer. "And in this way you

have ousted Mdlle. Henri? You wanted her office, therefore you rendered it intolerable to her?''

"Not at all, Monsieur, I was merely anxious about Mdlle. Henri's health: no, your moral sight is clear and piercing, but there you have failed to discover the truth. I took—I have always taken a real interest in Mdlle. Henri's welfare; I did not like her going out in all weathers; I thought it would be more advantageous for her to obtain a permanent situation; besides, I considered her now qualified to do something more than teach sewing. I reasoned with her; left the decision to herself; she saw the correctness of my views, and adopted them.''

"Excellent! and now, Mademoiselle, you will have the goodness to give me her address.''

"Her address!'' and a sombre and stony change came over the mien of the directress. "Her address? Ah!—well—I wish I could oblige you, Monsieur, but I cannot, and I will tell you why; whenever I myself asked her for her address, she always evaded the inquiry. I thought—I may be wrong—but I *thought* her motive for doing so, was a natural, though mistaken reluctance to introduce me to some, probably, very poor abode; her means were narrow, her origin obscure; she lives somewhere, doubtless, in the 'basse-ville.' ''

"I'll not lose sight of my best pupil yet," said I, "though she were born of beggars and lodged in a cellar; for the rest, it is absurd to make a bugbear of her origin to me—I happen to know that she was a Swiss pastor's daughter, neither more nor less; and, as to her narrow means, I care nothing for the poverty of her purse so long as her heart overflows with affluence.''

"Your sentiments are perfectly noble, Monsieur," said the directress, affecting to suppress a yawn; her sprightliness was now extinct, her temporary candour shut up; the little, red-coloured, piratical-looking pennon of audacity she had allowed to float a minute in the air, was furled, and the broad, sober-hued flag of dissimulation again hung low over the citadel. I did not like her thus, so I cut short the *téte-à-téte* and departed.

Chapter XIX

NOVELISTS should never allow themselves to weary of the study of real life. If they observed this duty conscientiously, they would give us fewer pictures chequered with vivid contrasts of light and shade; they would seldom elevate their heroes and heroines to the heights of rapture—still seldomer sink them to the depths of despair; for if we rarely taste the fulness of joy in this life, we yet more rarely savour the acid bitterness of hopeless anguish; unless, indeed, we have plunged like beasts into sensual indulgence, abused, strained, stimulated, again overstrained, and, at last, destroyed our faculties for enjoyment; then, truly, we may find ourselves without support, robbed of hope. Our agony is great, and how can it end? We have broken the spring of our powers; life must be all suffering—too feeble to conceive faith—death must be darkness—God, spirits, religion can have no place in our collapsed minds, where linger only hideous and polluting recollections of vice, and time brings us on to the brink of the grave, and dissolution flings us in—a rag eaten through and through with disease, wrung together with pain, stamped into the churchyard sod by the inexorable heel of despair.

But the man of regular life and rational mind never despairs. He loses his property—it is a blow—he staggers a moment; then, his energies, roused by the smart, are at work to seek a remedy; activity soon mitigates regret. Sickness affects him; he takes patience—endures what he cannot cure. Acute pain racks him; his writhing limbs know not where to find rest; he leans on Hope's anchors. Death

takes from him what he loves; roots up, and tears violently away the stem round which his affections were twined—a dark, dismal time, a frightful wrench—but some morning Religion looks into his desolate house with sunrise, and says, that in another world, another life, he shall meet his kindred again. She speaks of that world as a place unsullied by sin—of that life, as an era unembittered by suffering; she mightily strengthens her consolation by connecting with it two ideas—which mortals cannot comprehend, but on which they love to repose—Eternity, Immortality; and the mind of the mourner, being filled with an image, faint yet glorious, of heavenly hills all light and peace—of a spirit resting there in bliss—of a day when his spirit shall also alight there, free and disembodied—of a reunion perfected by love, purified from fear—he takes courage—goes out to encounter the necessities and discharge the duties of life; and, though sadness may never lift her burden from his mind, Hope will enable him to support it.

Well—and what suggested all this? and what is the inference to be drawn therefrom? What suggested it, is the circumstance of my best pupil—my treasure—being snatched from my hands, and put away out of my reach; the inference to be drawn from it is—that, being a steady reasonable man, I did not allow the resentment, disappointment, and grief, engendered in my mind by this evil chance, to grow there to any monstrous size; nor did I allow them to monopolise the whole space of my heart; I pent them, on the contrary, in one strait and secret nook. In the day-time, too, when I was about my duties, I put them on the silent system; and it was only after I had closed the door of my chamber at night that I somewhat relaxed my severity towards these morose nurslings, and allowed vent to their language of murmurs; then, in revenge, they sat on my pillow, haunted my bed, and kept me awake with their long, midnight cry.

A week passed. I had said nothing more to Mdlle. Reuter. I had been calm in my demeanour to her, though stony cold and hard. When I looked at her, it was with the glance fitting to be bestowed on one who I knew had consulted jealousy as an adviser, and employed treachery as an instrument—the glance of quiet disdain and rooted distrust. On Saturday evening, ere I left the house, I stept into the *salle-à-manger,* where she was sitting alone, and, placing myself before her, I asked, with the same tranquil tone and manner that I should have used had I put the question for the first time:

"Mademoiselle, will you have the goodness to give me the address of Frances Evans Henri?"

A little surprised, but not disconcerted, she smilingly disclaimed any knowledge of that address, adding, "Monsieur has perhaps forgotten that I explained all about that circumstance before—a week ago?"

"Mademoiselle," I continued, "you would greatly oblige me by directing me to that young person's abode."

She seemed somewhat puzzled; and, at last, looking up with an admirably coun-terfeited air of naïveté, she demanded, "Does Monsieur think I am telling an untruth?"

Still avoiding to give her a direct answer, I said, "It is not then your intention, Mademoiselle, to oblige me in this particular?"

"But, Monsieur, how can I tell you what I do not know?"

"Very well; I understand you perfectly, Mademoiselle, and now I have only two or three words to say. This is the last week in July; in another month the vacation will commence; have the goodness to avail yourself of the leisure it will afford you to look out for another English master—at the close of August, I shall be under the necessity of resigning my post in your establishment."

I did not wait for her comments on this announcement, but bowed and immediately withdrew.

That same evening, soon after dinner, a servant brought me a small packet; it was directed in a hand I knew, but had not hoped so soon to see again; being in

my own apartment and alone, there was nothing to prevent my immediately opening it; it contained four five-franc pieces, and a note in English.

> "MONSIEUR,—I came to Mdlle. Reuter's house yesterday, at the time when I knew you would be just about finishing your lesson, and I asked if I might go into the schoolroom and speak to you. Mdlle. Reuter came out and said you were already gone; it had not yet struck four, so I thought she must be mistaken, but concluded it would be vain to call another day on the same errand. In one sense a note will do as well—it will wrap up the twenty francs, the price of the lessons I have received from you; and if it will not fully express the thanks I owe you in addition— if it will not bid you good-bye as I could wish to have done—if it will not tell you, as I long to do, how sorry I am that I shall probably never see you more—why, spoken words would hardly be more adequate to the task. Had I seen you, I should probably have stammered out something feeble and unsatisfactory—something belying my feelings rather than explaining them; so it is perhaps as well that I was denied admission to your presence. You often remarked, Monsieur, that my devoirs dwelt a great deal on fortitude in bearing grief—you said I introduced that theme too often: I find indeed that it is much easier to write about a severe duty than to perform it, for I am oppressed when I see and feel to what a reverse fate has condemned me; you were kind to me, Monsieur—very kind; I am afflicted—I am heartbroken to be quite separated from you; soon I shall have no friend on earth. But it is useless troubling you with my distresses. What claim have I on your sympathy? None: I will then say no more.—Farewell, Monsieur.
>
> "F. E. HENRI."

I put up the note in my pocket-book. I slipped the five-franc pieces into my purse—then I took a turn through my narrow chamber.

"Mdlle. Reuter talked about her poverty," said I, "and she is poor; yet she pays her debts and more. I have not yet given her a quarter's lessons, and she has sent me a quarter's due. I wonder of what she deprived herself to scrape together the twenty francs—I wonder what sort of a place she has to live in, and what sort of a woman her aunt is, and whether she is likely to get employment to supply the place she has lost. No doubt she will have to trudge about long enough from school to school, to inquire here, and apply there—be rejected in this place, disappointed in that. Many an evening she'll go to her bed tired and unsuccessful. And the directress would not let her in to bid me good-bye? I might not have the chance of standing with her for a few minutes at a window in the schoolroom and exchanging some half-dozen of sentences—getting to know where she lived—putting matters in train for having all things arranged to my mind? No address on the note"—I continued, drawing it again from the pocket-book and examining it on each side of the two leaves: "women are women, that is certain, and always do business like women; men mechanically put a date and address to their communications. And these five-franc pieces?"—(I hauled them forth from my purse)—"if she had offered me them herself instead of tying them up with a thread of green silk in a kind of Lilliputian packet, I could have thrust them back into her little hand, and shut up the small, taper fingers over them—so—and compelled her shame, her pride, her shyness, all to yield to a little bit of determined Will—now where is she? How can I get at her?"

Opening my chamber door I walked down into the kitchen.

"Who brought the packet?" I asked of the servant who had delivered it to me.

"Un petit commissionaire, Monsieur."

"Did he say anything?"

"Rien."

And I wended my way up the back-stairs, wondrously the wiser for my inquiries.

"No matter," said I to myself, as I again closed the door. "No matter—I'll seek her through Brussels."

And I did. I sought her day by day whenever I had a moment's leisure, for four weeks; I sought her on Sundays all day long; I sought her on the Boulevards, in the Allée Verte, in the Park; I sought her in Ste. Gudule and St. Jacques; I sought her in the two Protestant chapels; I attended these latter at the German, French, and English services not doubting that I should meet her at one of them. All my researches were absolutely fruitless; my security on the last point was proved by the event to be equally groundless with my other calculations. I stood at the door of each chapel after the service, and waited till every individual had come out, scrutinising every gown draping a slender form, peering under every bonnet covering a young head. In vain; I saw girlish figures pass me, drawing their black scarfs over their sloping shoulders, but none of them had the exact turn and air of Mdlle. Henri's; I saw pale and thoughtful faces "encadrées" in bands of brown hair, but I never found her forehead, her eyes, her eyebrows. All the features of all the faces I met seemed frittered away, because my eye failed to recognise the peculiarities it was bent upon; an ample space of brow and a large, dark, and serious eye, with a fine but decided line of eyebrow traced above.

"She has probably left Brussels—perhaps is gone to England, as she said she would," muttered I inwardly, as on the afternoon of the fourth Sunday, I turned from the door of the chapel-royal which the door-keeper had just closed and locked, and followed in the wake of the last of the congregation, now dispersed and dispersing over the square. I had soon outwalked the couples of English gentlemen and ladies. (Gracious goodness! why don't they dress better? My eye is yet filled with visions of the high-flounced, slovenly, and tumbled dresses in costly silk and satin, of the large unbecoming collars in expensive lace: of the ill-cut coats and strangely fashioned pantaloons which every Sunday, at the English service, filled the choirs of the chapel-royal, and after it, issuing forth into the square, came into disadvantageous contrast with freshly and trimly attired foreign figures, hastening to attend salut at the church of Coburg.) I had passed these pairs of Britons, and the groups of pretty English children, and the British footmen and waiting-maids; I had crossed the Place Royale, and got into the Rue Royale, thence I had diverged into the Rue de Louvain—an old and quiet street. I remember that, feeling a little hungry, and not desiring to go back and take my share of the "goûter," now on the refectory-table at Pelet's—to wit, pistolets and water—I stepped into a baker's and refreshed myself on a *couc* (?)—it is a Flemish word, I don't know how to spell it—*à Corinthe*—*anglicè*, a currant bun—and a cup of coffee; and then I strolled on towards the Porte de Louvain. Very soon I was out of the city, and slowly mounting the hill, which ascends from the gate; I took my time, for the afternoon, though cloudy, was very sultry, and not a breeze stirred to refresh the atmosphere. No inhabitant of Brussels need wander far to search for solitude; let him but move half a league from his own city and he will find her brooding still and blank over the wide fields, so drear though so fertile, spread out treeless and trackless round the capital of Brabant. Having gained the summit of the hill, and having stood and looked long over the cultured but lifeless campaign, I felt a wish to quit the high road, which I had hitherto followed, and get in among those tilled grounds—fertile as the beds of a Brobdignagian kitchen-garden—spreading far and wide even to the boundaries of the horizon, where, from a dusk green, distance changed them to a sullen blue, and confused their tints with those of the livid and thunderous-looking sky. Accordingly I turned up a by-path to the right; I had not followed it far ere it brought me, as I expected, into the fields, amidst which, just before me, stretched a long and lofty white wall enclosing, as it seemed from the

foliage showing above, some thickly planted nursery of yew and cypress, for of that species were the branches resting on the pale parapets, and crowding gloomily about a massive cross, planted doubtless on a central eminence and extending its arms, which seemed of black marble, over the summits of those sinister trees. I approached, wondering to what house this well-protected garden appertained; I turned the angle of the wall, thinking to see some stately residence; I was close upon great iron gates; there was a hut serving for a lodge near, but I had no occasion to apply for the key—the gates were open; I pushed one leaf back—rain had rusted its hinges, for it groaned dolefully as they revolved. Thick planting embowered the entrance. Passing up the avenue, I saw objects on each hand which, in their own mute language of inscription and sign, explained clearly to what abode I had made my way. This was the house appointed for all living; crosses, monuments, and garlands of everlastings announced, "The Protestant Cemetery, outside the gate of Louvain."

The place was large enough to afford half-an-hour's strolling without the monotony of treading continually the same path; and, for those who love to peruse the annals of graveyards, here was variety of inscription enough to occupy the attention for double or treble that space of time. Hither people of many kindreds, tongues, and nations, had brought their dead for interment; and here, on pages of stone, of marble, and of brass, were written names, dates, last tributes of pomp or love, in English, in French, in German, and Latin. Here the Englishman had erected a marble monument over the remains of his Mary Smith or Jane Brown, and inscribed it only with her name. There the French widower had shaded the grave of his Elmire or Célestine with a brilliant thicket of roses, amidst which a little tablet rising, bore an equally bright testimony to her countless virtues. Every nation, tribe, and kindred, mourned after its own fashion; and how soundless was the mourning of all! My own tread, though slow and upon smooth-rolled paths, seemed to startle, because it formed the sole break to a silence otherwise total. Not only the winds, but the very fitful, wandering airs, were that afternoon, as by common consent, all fallen asleep in their various quarters; the north was hushed, the south silent, the east sobbed not, nor did the west whisper. The clouds in heaven were condensed and dull, but apparently quite motionless. Under the trees of this cemetery nestled a warm breathless gloom, out of which the cypresses stood up straight and mute, above which the willows hung low and still; where the flowers, as languid as fair, waited listless for night dew or thunder-shower; where the tombs, and those they hid, lay impassible to sun or shadow, to rain or drought.

Importuned by the sound of my own footsteps, I turned off upon the turf, and slowly advanced to a grove of yews; I saw something stir among the stems; I thought it might be a broken branch swinging, my short-sighted vision had caught no form, only a sense of motion; but the dusky shade passed on, appearing and disappearing at the openings in the avenue. I soon discerned it was a living thing, and a human thing; and, drawing nearer, I perceived it was a woman, pacing slowly to and fro, and evidently deeming herself alone as I had deemed myself alone, and meditating as I had been meditating. Ere long she returned to a seat which I fancy she had but just quitted, or I should have caught sight of her before. It was in a nook, screened by a clump of trees; there was the white wall before her, and a little stone set up against the wall, and, at the foot of the stone, was an allotment of turf freshly turned up, a new-made grave. I put on my spectacles, and passed softly close behind her; glancing at the inscription on the stone, I read, "Julienne Henri, died at Brussels, aged sixty. August 10th, 18—." Having perused the inscription, I looked down at the form sitting bent thoughtful just under my eyes, unconscious of the vicinity of any living thing; it was a slim, youthful figure in mourning apparel of the plainest black stuff, with a little simple, black crape bonnet; I felt, as well as saw, who it was; and, moving neither hand nor foot, I stood some moments enjoying the security of conviction. I had sought her for a month, and had never discovered

one of her traces—never met a hope, or seized a chance of encountering her anywhere. I had been forced to loosen my grasp on expectation; and, but an hour ago, had sunk slackly under the discouraging thought that the current of life, and the impulse of destiny, had swept her for ever from my reach; and, behold, while bending suddenly earthward beneath the pressure of despondency—while following with my eyes the track of sorrow on the turf of a graveyard—here was my lost jewel dropped on the tear-fed herbage, nestling in the mossy and mouldy roots of yew-trees.

Frances sat very quiet, her elbow on her knee, and her head on her hand. I knew she could retain a thinking attitude a long time without change; at last, a tear fell; she had been looking at the name on the stone before her, and her heart had no doubt endured one of those constrictions with which the desolate living, regretting the dead, are, at times, so sorely oppressed. Many tears rolled down, which she wiped away, again and again, with her handkerchief: some distressed sobs escaped her, and then, the paroxysm over, she sat quiet as before. I put my hand gently on her shoulder; no need further to prepare her, for she was neither hysterical nor liable to fainting fits; a sudden push, indeed, might have startled her, but the contact of my quiet touch merely woke attention as I wished; and, though she turned quickly, yet so lightning-swift is thought—in some minds especially—I believe the wonder of what—the consciousness of who it was that thus stole unawares on her solitude, had passed through her brain, and flashed into her heart, even before she had effected that hasty movement; at least, Amazement had hardly opened her eyes and raised them to mine, ere Recognition informed their irids with most speaking brightness. Nervous surprise had hardly discomposed her features ere a sentiment of most vivid joy shone clear and warm on her whole countenance. I had hardly time to observe that she was wasted and pale, ere called to feel a responsive inward pleasure by the sense of most full and exquisite pleasure glowing in the animated flush, and shining in the expansive light, now diffused over my pupil's face. It was the summer sun flashing out after the heavy summer shower; and what fertilises more rapidly than that beam, burning almost like fire in its ardour?

I hate boldness—that boldness which is of the brassy brow and insensate nerves; but I love the courage of the strong heart, the fervour of the generous blood; I loved with passion the light of Frances Evans' clear hazel eye when it did not fear to look straight into mine; I loved the tones with which she uttered the words:

"Mon maître! mon maître!"

I loved the movement with which she confided her hand to my hand; I loved her as she stood there, penniless and parentless; for a sensualist charmless, for me a treasure—my best object of sympathy on earth, thinking such thoughts as I thought, feeling such feelings as I felt; my ideal of the shrine in which to seal my stores of love; personification of discretion and forethought, of diligence and perseverance, of self-denial and self-control—those guardians, those trusty keepers of the gift I longed to confer on her—the gift of all my affections; model of truth and honour, of independence and conscientiousness—those refiners and sustainers of an honest life; silent possessor of a well of tenderness, of a flame, as genial as still, as pure as quenchless, of natural feeling, natural passion—those sources of refreshment and comfort to the sanctuary of home. I knew how quietly and how deeply the well bubbled in her heart; I knew how the more dangerous flame burned safely under the eye of reason; I had seen when the fire shot up a moment high and vivid, when the accelerated heat troubled life's current in its channels; I had seen reason reduce the rebel, and humble its blaze to embers. I had confidence in Frances Evans; I had respect for her, and as I drew her arm through mine, and led her out of the cemetery, I felt I had another sentiment, as strong as confidence, as firm as respect, more fervid than either—that of love.

"Well, my pupil," said I, as the ominous-sounding gate swung to behind us—
"Well, I have found you again: a month's search has seemed long, and I little
thought to have discovered my lost sheep straying amongst graves."

Never had I addressed her but as "Mademoiselle," before, and to speak thus
was to take up a tone new to both her and me. Her answer apprised me that this
language ruffled none of her feelings, woke no discord in her heart:

"Mon maître," she said, "have you troubled yourself to seek me? I little
imagined you would think much of my absence, but I grieved bitterly to be taken
away from you. I was sorry for that circumstance when heavier troubles ought to
have made me forget it."

"Your aunt is dead?"

"Yes a fortnight since, and she died full of regret, which I could not chase from
her mind; she kept repeating, even during the last night of her existence, 'Frances,
you will be so lonely when I am gone, so friendless': she wished too that she could
have been buried in Switzerland, and it was I who persuaded her in her old age to
leave the banks of Lake Leman, and to come, only as it seems, to die, in this flat
region of Flanders. Willingly would I have observed her last wish, and taken her
remains back to our own country, but that was impossible; I was forced to lay her
here."

"She was ill but a short time, I presume?"

"But three weeks. When she began to sink I asked Mdlle. Reuter's leave to stay
with her and wait on her; I readily got leave."

"Do you return to the pensionnat?" I demanded hastily.

"Monsieur, when I had been at home a week Mdlle. Reuter called one evening,
just after I had got my aunt to bed; she went into her room to speak to her, and
was extremely civil and affable, as she always is; afterwards she came and sat with
me a long time, and just as she rose to go away, she said: 'Mademoiselle, I shall
not soon cease to regret your departure from my establishment, though indeed it
is true that you have taught your class of pupils so well that they are all quite
accomplished in the little works you manage so skilfully, and have not the slightest
need of further instruction; my second teacher must in future supply your place,
with regard to the younger pupils, as well as she can, though she is indeed an
inferior artiste to you, and doubtless it will be your part now to assume a higher
position in your calling; I am sure you will everywhere find schools and families
willing to profit by your talents.' And then she paid me my last quarter's salary.
I asked, as Mademoiselle would no doubt think, very bluntly, if she designed to
discharge me from the establishment. She smiled at my inelegance of speech, and
answered that 'our connection as employer and employed was certainly dissolved,
but that she hoped still to retain the pleasure of my acquaintance; she should always
be happy to see me as a friend'; and then she said something about the excellent
condition of the streets, and the long continuance of fine weather, and went away
quite cheerful."

I laughed inwardly; all this was so like the directress—so like what I had expected
and guessed of her conduct; and then the exposure and proof of her lie, unconsciously
afforded by Frances: "She had frequently applied for Mdlle. Henri's address,"
forsooth; "Mdlle. Henri had always evaded giving it," etc., etc., and here I found
her a visitor at the very house of whose locality she had professed absolute ignorance!

Any comments I might have intended to make on my pupil's communication,
were checked by the plashing of large rain drops on our faces and on the path, and
by the muttering of a distant but coming storm. The warning obvious in stagnant
air and leaden sky had already induced me to take the road leading back to Brussels,
and now I hastened my own steps and those of my companion, and, as our way
lay down hill, we got on rapidly. There was an interval after the fall of the first
broad drops before heavy rain came on; in the meantime we had passed through
the Porte de Louvain, and were again in the city.

"Where do you live?" I asked; "I will see you safe home."

"Rue Notre Dame aux Neiges," answered Frances.

It was not far from the Rue de Louvain, and we stood on the doorsteps of the house we sought ere the clouds, severing with loud peal and shattered cataract of lightning, emptied their livid folds in a torrent, heavy, prone, and broad.

"Come in! come in!" said Frances, as, after putting her into the house, I paused ere I followed: the word decided me; I stepped across the threshold, shut the door on the rushing, flashing, whitening storm, and followed her upstairs to her apartments. Neither she nor I were wet; a projection over the door had warded off the straight-descending flood; none but the first large drops had touched our garments; one minute more and we should not have had a dry thread on us.

Stepping over a little mat of green wool, I found myself in a small room with a painted floor and a square of green carpet in the middle; the articles of furniture were few, but all bright and exquisitely clean; order reigned through its narrow limits—such order as it soothed my punctilious soul to behold. And I had hesitated to enter the abode, because I apprehended after all that Mdlle. Reuter's hint about its extreme poverty might be too well founded, and I feared to embarrass the lace-mender by entering her lodgings unawares! Poor the place might be; poor truly it was; but its neatness was better than elegance, and had but a bright little fire shone on that clean hearth, I should have deemed it more attractive than a palace. No fire was there, however, and no fuel laid ready to light; the lace-mender was unable to allow herself that indulgence, especially now when, deprived by death of her sole relative, she had only her own unaided exertions to rely on. Frances went into an inner room to take off her bonnet, and she came out a model of frugal neatness, with her well-fitting black stuff dress, so accurately defining her elegant bust and taper waist, with her spotless white collar turned back from a fair and shapely neck, with her plenteous brown hair arranged in smooth bands on her temples, and in a large Grecian plait behind: ornaments she had none—neither brooch, ring, nor ribbon; she did well enough without them—perfection of fit, proportion of form, grace of carriage, agreeably supplied their place. Her eye, as she re-entered the small sitting-room, instantly sought mine, which was just then lingering on the hearth; I knew she read at once the sort of inward ruth and pitying pain which the chill vacancy of that hearth stirred in my soul: quick to penetrate, quick to determine, and quicker to put in practice, she had in a moment tied a holland apron round her waist; then she disappeared, and reappeared with a basket; it had a cover; she opened it, and produced wood and coal; deftly and compactly she arranged them in the grate.

"It is her whole stock, and she will exhaust it out of hospitality," thought I.

"What are you going to do?" I asked: "not surely to light a fire this hot evening? I shall be smothered."

"Indeed, Monsieur, I feel it very chilly since the rain began; besides, I must boil the water for my tea, for I take tea on Sundays; you will be obliged to try and bear the heat."

She had struck a light; the wood was already in a blaze; and truly, when contrasted with the darkness, the wild tumult of the tempest without, that peaceful glow which began to beam on the now animated hearth, seemed very cheering. A low, purring sound, from some quarter, announced that another being, besides myself, was pleased with the change; a black cat, roused by the light from its sleep on a little cushioned foot-stool, came and rubbed its head against Frances' gown as she knelt; she caressed it, saying it had been a favourite with her "pauvre tante Julienne."

The fire being lit, the hearth swept, and a small kettle of a very antique pattern, such as I thought I remembered to have seen in old farmhouses in England, placed over the now ruddy flame, Frances' hands were washed, and her apron removed in an instant; then she opened a cupboard, and took out a tea-tray, on which she had soon arranged a china tea-equipage, whose pattern, shape, and size, denoted

a remote antiquity; a little, old-fashioned silver spoon was deposited in each saucer; and a pair of silver tongs, equally old-fashioned, were laid on the sugar-basin; from the cupboard, too, was produced a tiny silver cream-ewer, not larger than an egg-shell. While making these preparations, she chanced to look up, and, reading curiosity in my eyes, she smiled and asked:

"Is this like England, Monsieur?"

"Like the England of a hundred years ago," I replied.

"Is it truly? Well, everything on this tray is at least a hundred years old: these cups, these spoons, this ewer, are all heirlooms; my great-grandmother left them to my grandmother, she to my mother, and my mother brought them with her from England to Switzerland, and left them to me; and, ever since I was a little girl, I have thought I should like to carry them back to England, whence they came."

She put some pistolets on the table; she made the tea, as foreigners do make tea—*i.e.*, at the rate of a teaspoonful to half-a-dozen cups; she placed me a chair, and as I took it, she asked, with a sort of exultation:

"Will it make you think yourself at home for a moment?"

"If I had a home in England, I believe it would recall it," I answered; and, in truth, there was a sort of illusion in seeing the fair-complexioned English-looking girl presiding at the English meal, and speaking in the English lauguage.

"You have then no home?" was her remark.

"None, nor ever have had. If ever I possess a home, it must be of my own making, and the task is yet to begin." And, as I spoke, a pang, new to me, shot across my heart: it was a pang of mortification at the humility of my position, and the inadequacy of my means; while with that pang was born a strong desire to do more, earn more, be more, possess more; and in the increased possessions, my roused and eager spirit panted to include the home I had never had, the wife I inwardly vowed to win.

Frances' tea was little better than hot water, sugar, and milk; and her pistolets, with which she could not offer me butter, were sweet to my palate as manna.

The repast over, and the treasured plate and porcelain being washed and put by, the bright table rubbed still brighter, "le chat de ma tante Julienne" also being fed with provisions brought forth on a plate for its special use, a few stray cinders, and a scattering of ashes too, being swept from the hearth, Frances at last sat down; and then, as she took a chair opposite to me, she betrayed, for the first time, a little embarrassment; and no wonder, for indeed I had unconsciously watched her rather too closely, followed all her steps and all her movements a little too perseveringly with my eyes, for she mesmerised me by the grace and alertness of her action— by the deft, cleanly, and even decorative effect resulting from each touch of her slight and fine fingers; and when, at last, she subsided to stillness, the intelligence of her face seemed beauty to me, and I dwelt on it accordingly. Her colour, however, rising, rather than settling with repose, and her eyes remaining downcast, though I kept waiting for the lids to be raised that I might drink a ray of the light I loved— a light where fire dissolved in softness, where affection tempered penetration, where, just now at least, pleasure played with thought—this expectation not being gratified, I began at last to suspect that I had probably myself to blame for the disappointment; I must cease gazing, and begin talking, if I wished to break the spell under which she now sat motionless; so recollecting the composing effect which an authoritative tone and manner had ever been wont to produce on her, I said:

"Get one of your English books, Mademoiselle, for the rain yet falls heavily, and will probably detain me half-an-hour longer."

Released, and set at ease, up she rose, got her book, and accepted at once the chair I placed for her at my side. She had selected "Paradise Lost" from her shelf of classics, thinking, I suppose, the religious character of the book best adapted it to Sunday; I told her to begin at the beginning, and while she read Milton's invocation to that heavenly muse, who on the "secret top of Oreb or Sinai" had

taught the Hebrew shepherd how in the womb of chaos, the conception of a world had originated and ripened, I enjoyed, undisturbed, the treble pleasure of having her near me, hearing the sound of her voice—a sound sweet and satisfying in my ear—and looking, by intervals, at her face: of this last privilege, I chiefly availed myself when I found fault with an intonation, a pause, or an emphasis; as long as I dogmatised, I might also gaze, without exciting too warm a flush.

"Enough," said I, when she had gone through some half-dozen pages (a work of time with her, for she read slowly and paused even to ask and receive information)— "enough; and now the rain is ceasing, and I must soon go." For indeed, at that moment, looking towards the window, I saw it all blue; the thunder-clouds were broken and scattered, and the setting August sun sent a gleam like the reflection of rubies through the lattice. I got up; I drew on my gloves.

"You have not yet found another situation to supply the place of that from which you were dismissed by Mdlle. Reuter?"

"No, Monsieur; I have made inquiries everywhere, but they all ask me for references; and to speak truth, I do not like to apply to the directress, because I consider she acted neither justly nor honourably towards me; she used underhand means to set my pupils against me, and thereby render me unhappy while I held my place in her establishment, and she eventually deprived me of it by a masked and hypocritical manœuvre, pretending that she was acting for my good, but really snatching from me my chief means of subsistence, at a crisis when not only my own life, but that of another, depended on my exertions: of her I will never more ask a favour."

"How, then, do you propose to get on? How do you live now?"

"I have still my lace-mending trade; with care it will keep me from starvation, and I doubt not by dint of exertion to get better employment yet; it is only a fortnight since I began to try; my courage or hopes are by no means worn out yet."

"And if you get what you wish, what then? what are your ultimate views?"

"To save enough to cross the channel: I always look to England as my Canaan."

"Well, well—ere long I shall pay you another visit; good evening now," and I left her rather abruptly; I had much ado to resist a strong inward impulse, urging me to take a warmer, more expressive leave: what so natural as to fold her for a moment in a close embrace, to imprint one kiss on her cheek or forehead? I was not unreasonable—that was all I wanted; satisfied in that point, I could go away content; and Reason denied me even this; she ordered me to turn my eyes from her face, and my steps from her apartment—to quit her as dryly and coldly as I would have quitted old Madame Pelet. I obeyed, but I swore rancorously to be avenged one day. "I'll earn a right to do as I please in this matter, or I'll die in the contest. I have one object before me now—to get that Genevese girl for my wife; and my wife she shall be—that is, provided she has as much, or half as much regard for her master as he has for her. And would she be so docile, so smiling, so happy under my instructions if she had not? Would she sit at my side when I dictated or corrected, with such a still, contented, halcyon mien?" For I had ever remarked, that however sad or harassed her countenance might be when I entered a room, yet after I had been near her, spoken to her a few words, given her some directions, uttered perhaps some reproofs, she would, all at once, nestle into a nook of happiness, and look up serene and revived. The reproofs suited her best of all: while I scolded she would chip away with her pen-knife at a pencil or pen; fidgetting a little, pouting a little, defending herself by monosyllables, and when I deprived her of the pen or pencil, fearing it would be all cut away, and when I interdicted even the monosyllabic defence, for the purpose of working up the subdued excitement a little higher, she would at last raise her eyes and give me a certain glance, sweetened with gaiety, and pointed with defiance, which, to speak truth, thrilled me as nothing had ever done, and made me, in a fashion (though happily she did not know it), her subject

if not her slave. After such little scenes her spirits would maintain their flow, often for some hours, and, as I remarked before, her health therefrom took a sustenance and vigour which, previous to the event of her aunt's death and her dismissal, had almost recreated her whole frame.

It has taken me several minutes to write these last sentences; but I had thought all their purport during the brief interval of descending the stairs from Frances' room. Just as I was opening the outer door, I remembered the twenty francs which I had not restored; I paused: impossible to carry them away with me; difficult to force them back on their original owner; I had now seen her in her own humble abode, witnessed the dignity of her poverty, the pride of order, the fastidious care of conservatism, obvious in the arrangement and economy of her little home; I was sure she would not suffer herself to be excused paying her debts; I was certain the favour of indemnity would be accepted from no hand, perhaps least of all from mine: yet these four five-franc pieces were a burden to my self-respect, and I must get rid of them. An expedient—a clumsy one no doubt, but the best I could devise—suggested itself to me. I darted up the stairs, knocked, re-entered the room as if in haste:

"Mademoiselle, I have forgotten one of my gloves; I must have left it here."

She instantly rose to seek it; as she turned her back, I—being now at the hearth—noiselessly lifted a little vase, one of a set of china ornaments, as old-fashioned as the tea-cups—slipped the money under it, then saying—"Oh, here is my glove! I had dropped it within the fender; good evening, Mademoiselle," I made my second exit.

Brief as my impromptu return had been, it had afforded me time to pick up a heart-ache; I remarked that Frances had already removed the red embers of her cheerful little fire from the grate: forced to calculate every item; to save in every detail, she had instantly on my departure retrenched a luxury too expensive to be enjoyed alone.

"I am glad it is not yet winter," thought I; "but in two months more come the winds and rains of November; would to God that before then I could earn the right, and the power, to shovel coals into that grate *ad libitum*!"

Already the pavement was drying; a balmy and fresh breeze stirred the air, purified by lightning; I left the West behind me, where spread a sky like opal; azure immingled with crimson: the enlarged sun, glorious in Tyrian tints, dipped his brim already; stepping, as I was, eastward, I faced a vast bank of clouds, but also I had before me the arch of an even rainbow; a perfect rainbow—high, wide, vivid. I looked long; my eye drank in the scene, and I suppose my brain must have absorbed it; for that night, after lying awake in pleasant fever a long time, watching the silent sheet-lightning, which still played among the retreating clouds, and flashed silvery over the stars, I at last fell asleep; and then in a dream were reproduced the setting sun, the bank of clouds, the mighty rainbow. I stood, methought, on a terrace; I leaned over a parapeted wall; there was space below me, depth I could not fathom, but hearing an endless dash of waves, I believed it to be the sea; sea spread to the horizon; sea of changeful green and intense blue: all was soft in the distance; all vapour-veiled. A spark of gold glistened on the line between water and air, floated up, approached, enlarged, changed; the object hung midway between heaven and earth, under the arch of the rainbow; the soft but dusk clouds diffused behind. It hovered as on wings; pearly, fleecy, gleaming air streamed like raiment round it; light, tinted with carnation, coloured what seemed face and limbs; a large star shone with still lustre on an angel's forehead; an uplifted arm and hand, glancing like a ray, pointed to the bow overhead, and a voice in my heart whispered: "Hope smiles on Effort!"

Chapter XX

A COMPETENCY was what I wanted; a competency it was now my aim and resolve to secure: but never had I been farther from the mark. With August the school-year (l'année scolaire) closed, the examinations concluded, the prizes were adjudged, the schools dispersed, the gates of all colleges, the doors of all pensionnats shut, not to be reopened till the beginning or middle of October. The last day of August was at hand, and what was my position? Had I advanced a step since the commencement of the past quarter? On the contrary, I had receded one. By renouncing my engagement as English master in Mdlle. Reuter's establishment, I had voluntarily cut off £20 from my yearly income; I had diminished my £60 per annum to £40, and even that sum I now held by a very precarious tenure.

It is some time since I made any reference to M. Pelet. The moonlight walk is, I think, the last incident recorded in this narrative where that gentleman cuts any conspicuous figure: the fact is, since that event, a change had come over the spirit of our intercourse. He, indeed, ignorant that the still hour, a cloudless moon, and an open lattice, had revealed to me the secret of his selfish love and false friendship, would have continued smooth and complacent as ever; but I grew spiny as a porcupine, and inflexible as a blackthorn cudgel; I never had a smile for his raillery, never a moment for his society; his invitations to take coffee with him in his parlour were invariably rejected, and very stiffly and sternly rejected too; his jesting allusions to the directress (which he still continued) were heard with a grim calm very different from the petulant pleasure they were formerly wont to excite. For a long time Pelet bore with my frigid demeanour very patiently; he even increased his attentions; but finding that even a cringing politeness failed to thaw or move me, he at last altered too; in his turn he cooled; his invitations ceased; his countenance became suspicious and overcast, and I read in the perplexed yet brooding aspect of his brow, a constant examination and comparison of premises, and an anxious endeavour to draw thence some explanatory inference. Ere long, I fancy, he succeeded, for he was not without penetration; perhaps, too, Mdlle. Zoraïde might have aided him in the solution of the enigma; at any rate I soon found that the uncertainty of doubt had vanished from his manner; renouncing all pretence of friendship and cordiality, he adopted a reserved, formal, but still scrupulously polite deportment. This was the point to which I had wished to bring him, and I was now again comparatively at my ease. I did not, it is true, like my position in his house; but being freed from the annoyance of false professions and double-dealing I could endure it, especially as no heroic sentiment of hatred or jealousy of the director distracted my philosophical soul; he had not, I found, wounded me in a very tender point, the wound was so soon and so radically healed, leaving only a sense of contempt for the treacherous fashion in which it had been inflicted, and a lasting mistrust of the hand which I had detected attempting to stab me in the dark.

This state of things continued till about the middle of July, and then there was a little change; Pelet came home one night, an hour after his usual time, in a state of unequivocal intoxication, a thing anomalous with him; for if he had some of the worst faults of his countrymen, he had also one at least of their virtues, *i.e.*, sobriety. So drunk, however, was he upon this occasion, that after having roused the whole establishment (except the pupils, whose dormitory being over the classes in a building apart from the dwelling-house, was consequently out of the reach of disturbance) by violently ringing the hall-bell and ordering lunch to be brought in immediately, for he imagined it was noon, whereas the city bells had just tolled midnight; after having furiously rated the servants for their want of punctuality, and gone near to chastise his poor old mother, who advised him to go to bed, he began raving dreadfully about "le maudit Anglais, Creemsvort." I had not yet

retired; some German books I had got hold of had kept me up late; I heard the uproar below, and could distinguish the director's voice exalted in a manner as appalling as it was unusual. Opening my door a little, I became aware of a demand on his part for "Creemsvort" to be brought down to him that he might cut his throat on the hall-table and wash his honour, which he affirmed to be in a dirty condition, in infernal British blood. "He is either mad or drunk," thought I, "and in either case the old woman and the servants will be the better of a man's assistance," so I descended straight to the hall. I found him staggering about, his eyes in a fine frenzy rolling—a pretty sight he was, a just medium between the fool and the lunatic.

"Come, M. Pelet," said I, "you had better go to bed," and I took hold of his arm. His excitement, of course, increased greatly at sight and touch of the individual for whose blood he had been making application: he struggled and struck with fury—but a drunken man is no match for a sober one; and, even in his normal state, Pelet's worn-out frame could not have stood against my sound one. I got him upstairs, and, in process of time, to bed. During the operation he did not fail to utter communications which, though broken, had a sense in them; while stigmatising me as the treacherous spawn of a perfidious country, he, in the same breath, anathematised Zoraïde Reuter; he termed her "femme sotte et vicieuse," who, in a fit of lewd caprice, had thrown herself away on an unprincipled adventurer; directing the point of the last appellation by a furious blow, obliquely aimed at me. I left him in the act of bounding elastically out of the bed into which I had tucked him; but, as I took the precaution of turning the key in the door behind me, I retired to my own room, assured of his safe custody till the morning, and free to draw undisturbed conclusions from the scene I had just witnessed.

Now, it was precisely about this time that the directress, stung by my coldness, bewitched by my scorn, and excited by the preference she suspected me of cherishing for another, had fallen into a snare of her own laying—was herself caught in the meshes of the very passion with which she wished to entangle me. Conscious of the state of things in that quarter, I gathered, from the condition in which I saw my employer, that his lady-love had betrayed the alienation of her affections— inclinations, rather, I would say; affection is a word at once too warm and too pure for the subject—had let him see that the cavity of her hollow heart, emptied of his image, was now occupied by that of his usher. It was not without some surprise that I found myself obliged to entertain this view of the case; Pelet, with his old-established school, was so convenient, so profitable a match—Zoraïde was so calculating, so interested a woman—I wondered mere personal preference could, in her mind, have prevailed for a moment over worldly advantage: yet, it was evident, from what Pelet said, that, not only had she repulsed him, but had even let slip expressions of partiality for me. One of his drunken exclamations was, "And the jade doats on your youth, you raw blockhead! and talks of your noble deportment, as she calls your accursed English formality—and your pure morals, forsooth! des mœurs de Caton a-t-elle dit—sotte!" Hers, I thought, must be a curious soul, where, in spite of a strong, natural tendency to estimate unduly advantages of wealth and station, the sardonic disdain of a fortuneless subordinate had wrought a deeper impression than could be imprinted by the most flattering assiduities of a prosperous *chef d'institution*. I smiled inwardly; and strange to say, though my *amour-propre* was excited not disagreeably by the conquest, my better feelings remained untouched. Next day, when I saw the directress, and when she made an excuse to meet me in the corridor, and besought my notice by a demeanour and look subdued to Helot humility, I could not love, I could scarcely pity her. To answer briefly and dryly some interesting inquiry about my health—to pass her by with a stern bow—was all I could; her presence and manner had then, and for some time previously and consequently, a singular effect upon me: they sealed up all that was good, elicited all that was noxious in my nature; sometimes they enervated

my senses, but they always hardened my heart. I was aware of the detriment done, and quarrelled with myself for the change. I had ever hated a tyrant; and, behold, the possession of a slave, self-given, went near to transform me into what I abhorred! There was at once a sort of low gratification in receiving this luscious incense from an attractive and still young worshipper; and an irritating sense of degradation in the very experience of the pleasure. When she stole about me with the soft step of a slave, I felt at once barbarous and sensual as a pasha. I endured her homage sometimes; sometimes I rebuked it. My indifference or harshness served equally to increase the evil I desired to check.

"Que le dédain lui sied bien!" I once overheard her say to her mother: "il est beau comme Apollon quand il sourit de son air hautain."

And the jolly old dame laughed, and said she thought her daughter was bewitched, for I had no point of a handsome man about me, except being straight and without deformity. "Pour moi," she continued, "il me fait tout l'effet d'un chat-huant, avec ses bésicles."

Worthy old girl! I could have gone and kissed her had she not been a little too old, too fat, and too red-faced; her sensible, truthful words seemed so wholesome contrasted with the morbid illusions of her daughter.

When Pelet awoke on the morning after his frenzy fit, he retained no recollection of what had happened the previous night, and his mother fortunately had the discretion to refrain from informing him that I had been a witness of his degradation. He did not again have recourse to wine for curing his griefs, but even in his sober mood he soon showed that the iron of jealousy had entered into his soul. A thorough Frenchman, the national characteristic of ferocity had not been omitted by nature in compounding the ingredients of his character; it had appeared first in his access of drunken wrath, when some of his demonstrations of hatred to my person were of a truly fiendish character, and now it was more covertly betrayed by momentary contractions of the features, and flashes of fierceness in his light blue eyes, when their glance chanced to encounter mine. He absolutely avoided speaking to me; I was now spared even the falsehood of his politeness. In this state of our mutual relations, my soul rebelled, sometimes almost ungovernably, against living in the house and discharging the service of such a man; but who is free from the constraint of circumstances? At that time, I was not: I used to rise each morning eager to shake off his yoke, and go out with my portmanteau under my arm, if a beggar, at least a freeman; and in the evening, when I came back from the pensionnat de demoiselles, a certain pleasant voice in my ear; a certain face, so intelligent, yet so docile, so reflective, yet so soft, in my eyes; a certain cast of character, at once proud and pliant, sensitive and sagacious, serious and ardent, in my head; a certain tone of feeling, fervid and modest, refined and practical, pure and powerful, delighting and troubling my memory—visions of new ties I longed to contract, of new duties I longed to undertake, had taken the rover and the rebel out of me, and had shown endurance of my hated lot in the light of a Spartan virtue.

But Pelet's fury subsided; a fortnight sufficed for its rise, progress, and extinction: in that space of time the dismissal of the obnoxious teacher had been effected in the neighbouring house, and in the same interval I had declared my resolution to follow and find out my pupil, and upon my application for her address being refused, I had summarily resigned my own post. This last act seemed at once to restore Mdlle. Reuter to her senses; her sagacity, her judgment, so long misled by a fascinating delusion, struck again into the right track the moment that delusion vanished. By the right track, I do not mean the steep and difficult path of principle— in that path she never trod; but the plain highway of common sense, from which she had of late widely diverged. When there she carefully sought, and having found, industriously pursued the trail of her old suitor, M. Pelet. She soon overtook him. What arts she employed to soothe and blind him I know not, but she succeeded both in allaying his wrath, and hoodwinking his discernment, as was soon proved

by the alteration in his mien and manner; she must have managed to convince him that I neither was, nor ever had been, a rival of his, for the fortnight of fury against me terminated in a fit of exceeding graciousness and amenity, not unmixed with a dash of exulting self-complacency, more ludicrous than irritating. Pelet's bachelor's life had been passed in proper French style with due disregard to moral restraint, and I thought his married life promised to be very French also. He often boasted to me what a terror he had been to certain husbands of his acquaintance; I perceived it would not now be difficult to pay him back in his own coin.

The crisis drew on. No sooner had the holidays commenced than note of preparation for some momentous event sounded through all the premises of Pelet; painters, polishers, and upholsterers were immediately set to work, and there was talk of "la chambre de Madame," "le salon de Madame." Not deeming it probable that the old duenna at present graced with that title in our house, had inspired her son with such enthusiasm of filial piety, as to induce him to fit up apartments expressly for her use, I concluded, in common with the cook, the two housemaids, and the kitchen-scullion, that a new and more juvenile Madame was destined to be the tenant of these gay chambers.

Presently official announcement of the coming event was put forth. In another week's time M. François Pelet, directeur, and Mdlle. Zoraïde Reuter, directrice, were to be joined together in the bonds of matrimony. Monsieur, in person, heralded the fact to me; terminating his communication by an obliging expression of his desire that I should continue, as heretofore, his ablest assistant and most trusted friend; and a proposition to raise my salary by an additional two hundred francs per annum. I thanked him, gave no conclusive answer at the time, and, when he had left me, threw off my blouse, put on my coat, and set out on a long walk outside the Porte de Flandre, in order, as I thought, to cool my blood, calm my nerves, and shake my disarranged ideas into some order. In fact, I had just received what was virtually my dismissal. I could not conceal, I did not desire to conceal from myself the conviction that, being now certain that Mdlle. Reuter was destined to become Madame Pelet, it would not do for me to remain a dependent dweller in the house which was soon to be hers. Her present demeanour towards me was deficient neither in dignity nor propriety; but I knew her former feeling was unchanged. Decorum now repressed, and Policy masked it, but Opportunity would be too strong for either of these—Temptation would shiver their restraints.

I was no pope—I could not boast infallibility: in short, if I stayed, the probability was that, in three months' time, a practical modern French novel would be in full process of concoction under the roof of the unsuspecting Pelet. Now, modern French novels are not to my taste, either practically or theoretically. Limited as had yet been my experience of life, I had once had the opportunity of contemplating, near at hand, an example of the results produced by a course of interesting and romantic domestic treachery. No golden halo of fiction was about this example, I saw it bare and real, and it was very loathsome. I saw a mind degraded by the practice of mean subterfuge, by the habit of perfidious deception, and a body depraved by the infectious influence of the vice-polluted soul. I had suffered much from the forced and prolonged view of this spectacle; those sufferings I did not now regret, for their simple recollection acted as a most wholesome antidote to temptation. They had inscribed on my reason the conviction that unlawful pleasure, trenching on another's rights, is delusive and envenomed pleasure—its hollowness disappoints at the time, its poison cruelly tortures afterwards, its effects deprave for ever.

From all this resulted the conclusion that I must leave Pelet's, and that instantly; "but," said Prudence, "you know not where to go, nor how to live"; and then the dream of true love came over me: Frances Henri seemed to stand at my side; her slender waist to invite my arm; her hand to court my hand; I felt it was made to nestle in mine; I could not relinquish my right to it, nor could I withdraw my eyes for ever from hers, where I saw so much happiness, such a correspondence

of heart with heart; over whose expression I had such influence; where I could kindle bliss, infuse awe, stir deep delight, rouse sparkling spirit, and sometimes waken pleasurable dread. My hopes to win and possess, my resolutions to work and rise, rose in array against me; and here I was about to plunge into the gulf of absolute destitution; "and all this," suggested an inward voice, "because you fear an evil which may never happen!" "It will happen; you *know* it will," answered that stubborn monitor, Conscience. "Do what you feel is right; obey me, and even in the sloughs of want I will plant for you firm footing." And then, as I walked fast along the road, there rose upon me a strange, inly-felt idea of some Great Being, unseen, but all-present, who in His beneficence desired only my welfare, and now watched the struggle of good and evil in my heart, and waited to see whether I should obey His voice, heard in the whispers of my conscience, or lend an ear to the sophisms by which His enemy and mine—the Spirit of Evil—sought to lead me astray. Rough and steep was the path indicated by divine suggestion; mossy and declining the green way along which Temptation strewed flowers; but whereas, methought, the Deity of Love, the Friend of all that exists, would smile well-pleased were I to gird up my loins and address myself to the rude ascent; so, on the other hand, each inclination to the velvet declivity seemed to kindle a gleam of triumph on the brow of the man-hating, God-defying demon. Sharp and short I turned round; fast I retraced my steps; in half-an-hour I was again at M. Pelet's: I sought him in his study; brief parley, concise explanation sufficed; my manner proved that I was resolved; he, perhaps, at heart approved my decision. After twenty minutes' conversation, I re-entered my own room, self-deprived of the means of living, self-sentenced to leave my present home, with the short notice of a week in which to provide another.

Chapter XXI

DIRECTLY as I closed the door, I saw laid on the table two letters; my first thought was, that they were notes of invitation from the friends of some of my pupils; I had received such marks of attention occasionally, and with me, who had no friends, correspondence of more interest was out of the question; the postman's arrival had never yet been an event of interest to me since I came to Brussels. I laid my hand carelessly on the documents, and coldly and slowly glancing at them, I prepared to break the seals; my eye was arrested and my hand too; I saw what excited me, as if I had found a vivid picture where I expected only to discover a blank page: on one cover was an English postmark; on the other, a lady's clear, fine autograph; the last I opened first:

"MONSIEUR,—I found out what you had done the very morning after your visit to me; you might be sure I should dust the china every day; and, as no one but you had been in my room for a week, and as fairy-money is not current in Brussels, I could not doubt who left the twenty francs on the chimney-piece. I thought I heard you stir the vase when I was stooping to look for your glove under the table, and I wondered you should imagine it had got into such a little cup. Now, Monsieur, the money is not mine, and I shall not keep it; I will not send it in this note because it might be lost—besides, it is heavy; but I will restore it to you the first time I see you, and you must make no difficulties about taking it; because, in the first place, I am sure, Monsieur, you can understand that one likes to pay one's debts; that it is satisfactory to owe no man anything; and, in the second place, I can now very well afford to be

honest, as I am provided with a situation. This last circumstance is, indeed, the reason of my writing to you, for it is pleasant to communicate good news; and, in these days, I have only my master to whom I can tell anything.

"A week ago, Monsieur, I was sent for by a Mrs. Wharton, an English lady; her eldest daughter was going to be married, and some rich relation having made her a present of a veil and dress in costly old lace, as precious, they said, almost as jewels, but a little damaged by time, I was commissioned to put them in repair. I had to do it at the house; they gave me, besides, some embroidery to complete, and nearly a week elapsed before I had finished everything. While I worked, Miss Wharton often came into the room and sat with me, and so did Mrs. Wharton; they made me talk English; asked how I had learned to speak it so well; then they inquired what I knew besides—what books I had read; soon they seemed to make a sort of wonder of me, considering me no doubt as a learned grisette. One afternoon, Mrs. Wharton brought in a Parisian lady to test the accuracy of my knowledge of French; the result of it was that, owing probably in a great degree to the mother's and daughter's good-humour about the marriage, which inclined them to do beneficent deeds, and partly, I think, because they are naturally benevolent people, they decided that the wish I had expressed to do something more than mend lace was a very legitimate one, and the same day they took me in their carriage to Mrs. D.'s, who is the directress of the first English school at Brussels. It seems she happened to be in want of a French lady to give lessons in geography, history, grammar, and composition, in the French language. Mrs. Wharton recommended me very warmly; and, as two of her younger daughters are pupils in the house, her patronage availed to get me the place. It was settled that I am to attend six hours daily (for, happily, it was not required that I should live in the house; I should have been sorry to leave my lodgings), and, for this, Mrs. D. will give me twelve hundred francs per annum.

"You see, therefore, Monsieur, that I am now rich; richer almost than I ever hoped to be: I feel thankful for it, especially as my sight was beginning to be injured by constant working at fine lace; and I was getting, too, very weary of sitting up late at nights, and yet not being able to find time for reading or study. I began to fear that I should fall ill, and be unable to pay my way; this fear is now, in a great measure, removed; and, in truth, Monsieur, I am very grateful to God for the relief; and I feel it necessary, almost, to speak of my happiness to some one who is kind-hearted enough to derive joy from seeing others joyful. I could not, therefore, resist the temptation of writing to you; I argued with myself it is very pleasant for me to write, and it will not be exactly painful, though it may be tiresome to Monsieur to read. Do not be too angry with my circumlocution and inelegancies of expression, and believe me your attached pupil,

"F. E. HENRI."

Having read this letter, I mused on its contents for a few moments—whether with sentiments pleasurable or otherwise I will hereafter note—and then took up the other. It was directed in a hand to me unknown—small, and rather neat; neither masculine nor exactly feminine; the seal bore a coat of arms, concerning which I could only decipher that it was not that of the Seacombe family, consequently the epistle could be from none of my almost forgotten, and certainly quite forgetting

patrician relations. From whom, then, was it? I removed the envelope: the note folded within ran as follows:

> "I have no doubt in the world that you are doing well in that greasy Flanders; living probably on the fat of the unctuous land; sitting like a black-haired, tawny-skinned, long-nosed Israelite by the flesh-pots of Egypt; or like a rascally son of Levi near the brass cauldrons of the sanctuary, and every now and then plunging in a consecrated hook, and drawing out of the sea of broth the fattest of heave-shoulders and the fleshiest of wave-breasts. I know this, because you never write to any one in England. Thankless dog that you are! I, by the sovereign efficacy of my recommendation, got you the place where you are now living in clover, and yet not a word of gratitude, or even acknowledgment, have you ever offered in return; but I am coming to see you, and small conception can you, with your addled aristocratic brains, form of the sort of moral kicking I have, ready packed in my carpet-bag, destined to be presented to you immediately on my arrival.
>
> "Meantime I know all about your affairs, and have just got information, by Brown's last letter, that you are said to be on the point of forming an advantageous match with a pursy, little Belgian schoolmistress—a Mdlle. Zénobie, or some such name. Won't I have a look at her when I come over? And this you may rely on: if she pleases my taste, or if I think it worth while in a pecuniary point of view, I'll pounce on your prize and bear her away triumphant in spite of your teeth. Yet I don't like dumpies either, and Brown says she is little and stout—the better fitted for a wiry, starved-looking chap like you.
>
> "Be on the look-out, for you know neither the day nor hour when your —— (I don't wish to blaspheme, so I'll leave a blank) cometh.— Yours truly,

<div align="center">

"Hunsden Yorke Hunsden."

</div>

"Humph!" said I; and ere I laid the letter down, I again glanced at the small, neat handwriting, not a bit like that of a mercantile man, nor, indeed, of any man except Hunsden himself. They talk of affinities between the autograph and the character: what affinity was there here? I recalled the writer's peculiar face and certain traits I suspected, rather than knew, to appertain to his nature, and I answered, "A great deal."

Hunsden, then, was coming to Brussels, and coming I knew not when; coming charged with the expectation of finding me on the summit of prosperity, about to be married, to step into a warm nest, to lie comfortably down by the side of a snug, well-fed little mate.

"I wish him joy of the fidelity of the picture he has painted," thought I. "What will he say when, instead of a pair of plump turtle-doves, billing and cooing in a bower of roses, he finds a single lean cormorant, standing mateless and shelterless on poverty's bleak cliff? Oh, confound him! Let him come, and let him laugh at the contrast between rumour and fact. Were he the devil himself, instead of being merely very like him, I'd not condescend to get out of his way, or to forge a smile or a cheerful word wherewith to avert his sarcasm."

Then I recurred to the other letter: that struck a chord whose sound I could not deaden by thrusting my fingers into my ears, for it vibrated within; and though its swell might be exquisite music, its cadence was a groan.

That Frances was relieved from the pressure of want, that the curse of excessive labour was taken off her, filled me with happiness; that her first thought in prosperity should be to augment her joy by sharing it with me, met and satisfied the wish of

my heart. Two results of her letter were then pleasant, sweet as two draughts of nectar; but applying my lips for the third time to the cup, and they were excoriated as with vinegar and gall.

Two persons whose desires are moderate may live well enough in Brussels on an income which would scarcely afford a respectable maintenance for one in London: and that, not because the necessaries of life are so much dearer in the latter capital, or taxes so much higher than in the former, but because the English surpass in folly all the nations on God's earth, and are more abject slaves to custom, to opinion, to the desire to keep up a certain appearance, than the Italians are to priestcraft, the French to vain-glory, the Russians to their Czar, or the Germans to black beer. I have seen a degree of sense in the modest arrangement of one homely Belgian household, that might put to shame the elegance, the superfluities, the luxuries, the strained refinements of a hundred genteel English mansions. In Belgium, provided you can make money, you may save it; this is scarcely possible in England; ostentation there lavishes in a month what industry has earned in a year. More shame to all classes in that most bountiful and beggarly country for their servile following of Fashion; I could write a chapter or two on this subject, but must forbear, at least for the present. Had I retained my £60 per annum I could, now that Frances was in possession of £50, have gone straight to her this very evening, and spoken out the words which, repressed, kept fretting my heart with fever; our united income would, as we should have managed it, have sufficed well for our mutual support; since we lived in a country where economy was not confounded with meanness, where frugality in dress, food, and furniture, was not synonymous with vulgarity in these various points. But the placeless usher, bare of resource, and unsupported by connections, must not think of this; such a sentiment as love, such a word as marriage, were misplaced in his heart, and on his lips. Now for the first time did I truly feel what it was to be poor; now did the sacrifice I had made in casting from me the means of living put on a new aspect; instead of a correct, just, honourable act, it seemed a deed at once light and fanatical; I took several turns in my room, under the goading influence of most poignant remorse; I walked a quarter of an hour from the wall to the window; and at the window, self-reproach seemed to face me; at the wall, self-disdain: all at once out spoke Conscience:

"Down, stupid tormentors!" cried she; "the man has done his duty; you shall not bait him thus by thoughts of what might have been; he relinquished a temporary and contingent good to avoid a permanent and certain evil; he did well. Let him reflect now, and when your blinding dust and deafening hum subside, he will discover a path."

I sat down; I propped my forehead on both my hands; I thought and thought an hour—two hours; vainly. I seemed like one sealed in a subterranean vault, who gazes at utter blackness; at blackness ensured by yard-thick stone walls around, and by piles of building above, expecting light to penetrate through granite, and through cement firm as granite. But there are chinks, or there may be chinks, in the best adjusted masonry; there was a chink in my cavernous cell; for, eventually, I saw, or seemed to see, a ray—pallid, indeed, and cold, and doubtful, but still a ray, for it showed that narrow path which conscience had promised. After two, three hours' torturing research in brain and memory, I disinterred certain remains of circumstances, and conceived a hope that by putting them together an expedient might be framed, and a resource discovered. The circumstances were briefly these:

Some three months ago M. Pelet had, on the occasion of his fête, given the boys a treat, which treat consisted in a party of pleasure to a certain place of public resort in the outskirts of Brussels, of which I do not at this moment remember the name, but near it were several of those lakelets called étangs; and there was one étang, larger than the rest, where on holidays people were accustomed to amuse themselves by rowing round it in little boats. The boys having eaten an unlimited quantity of "gaufres," and drunk several bottles of Louvain beer, amid the shades

of a garden made and provided for such crams, petitioned the director for leave to take a row on the étang. Half-a-dozen of the eldest succeeded in obtaining leave, and I was commissioned to accompany them as surveillant. Among the half-dozen happened to be a certain Jean Baptiste Vandenhuten, a most ponderous young Flamand, not tall, but even now, at the early age of sixteen, possessing a breadth and depth of personal development truly national. It chanced that Jean was the first lad to step into the boat; he stumbled, rolled to one side, the boat revolted at his weight and capsized. Vandenhuten sank like lead, rose, sank again. My coat and waistcoat were off in an instant; I had not been brought up at Eton and boated and bathed and swam there ten long years for nothing; it was a natural and easy act for me to leap to the rescue. The lads and the boatmen yelled; they thought there would be two deaths by drowning instead of one; but as Jean rose the third time, I clutched him by one leg and the collar, and in three minutes more both he and I were safe landed. To speak heaven's truth, my merit in the action was small indeed, for I had run no risk, and subsequently did not even catch cold from the wetting: but when M. and Madame Vandenhuten, of whom Jean Baptiste was the sole hope, came to hear of the exploit, they seemed to think I had evinced a bravery and devotion which no thanks could sufficiently repay. Madame, in particular, was "certain I must have dearly loved their sweet son, or I would not thus have hazarded my own life to save his." Monsieur, an honest-looking, though phlegmatic man, said very little, but he would not suffer me to leave the room, till I had promised that in case I ever stood in need of help I would, by applying to him, give him a chance of discharging the obligation under which he affirmed I had laid him. These words, then, were my glimmer of light; it was here I found my sole outlet; and in truth, though the cold light roused, it did not cheer me; nor did the outlet seem such as I should like to pass through. Right I had none to M. Vandenhuten's good offices; it was not on the ground of merit I could apply to him; no, I must stand on that of necessity: I had no work; I wanted work; my best chance of obtaining it lay in securing his recommendation. This I knew could be had by asking for it; not to ask, because the request revolted my pride and contradicted my habits, would, I felt, be an indulgence of false and indolent fastidiousness. I might repent the omission all my life; I would not then be guilty of it.

That evening I went to M. Vandenhuten's; but I had bent the bow and adjusted the shaft in vain; the string broke. I rang the bell at the great door (it was a large, handsome house in an expensive part of the town); a manservant opened; I asked for M. Vandenhuten; M. Vandenhuten and family were all out of town—gone to Ostend—did not know when they would be back. I left my card, and retraced my steps.

Chapter XXII

A week is gone; *le jour des noces* arrived; the marriage was solemnised at St. Jacques; Mdlle. Zoraïde became Madame Pelet *née* Reuter; and, in about an hour after this transformation, "the happy pair," as newspapers phrase it, were on their way to Paris; where, according to previous arrangement, the honeymoon was to be spent. The next day I quitted the pensionnat. Myself and my chattels (some books and clothes) were soon transferred to a modest lodging I had hired in a street not far off. In half-an-hour my clothes were arranged in a commode, my books on a shelf, and the "flitting" was effected. I should not have been unhappy that day had not one pang tortured me—a longing to go to the Rue Notre Dame aux Neiges, resisted, yet irritated by an inward resolve to avoid that street till such time as the mist of doubt should clear from my prospects.

It was a sweet September evening—very mild, very still; I had nothing to do; at that hour I knew Frances would be equally released from occupation; I thought she might possibly be wishing for her master, I knew I wished for my pupil. Imagination began with her low whispers, infusing into my soul the soft tale of pleasures that might be.

"You will find her reading or writing," said she; "you can take your seat at her side; you need not startle her peace by undue excitement; you need not embarrass her manner by unusual action or language. Be as you always are; look over what she has written; listen while she reads; chide her, or quietly approve; you know the efect of either system; you know her smile when pleased, you know the play of her looks when roused; you have the secret of awakening what expression you will, and you can choose amongst that pleasant variety. With you she will sit silent as long as it suits you to talk alone; you can hold her under a potent spell: intelligent as she is, eloquent as she can be, you can seal her lips, and veil her bright countenance with diffidence; yet, you know, she is not all monotonous mildness; you have seen, with a sort of strange pleasure, revolt, scorn, austerity, bitterness, lay energetic claim to a place in her feelings and physiognomy; you know that few could rule her as you do; you know she might break, but never bend under the hand of Tyranny and Injustice, but Reason and Affection can guide her by a sign. Try their influence now. Go—they are not passions; you may handle them safely."

"I will *not* go," was my answer to the sweet temptress. "A man is master of himself to a certain point, but not beyond it. Could I seek Frances to-night, could I sit with her alone in a quiet room, and address her only in the language of Reason and Affection?"

"No," was the brief, fervent reply of that Love which had conquered and now controlled me.

Time seemed to stagnate; the sun would not go down; my watch ticked, but I thought the hands were paralysed.

"What a hot evening!" I cried, throwing open the lattice; for, indeed, I had seldom felt so feverish. Hearing a step ascending the common stair, I wondered whether the "locataire," now mounting to his apartments, were as unsettled in mind and condition as I was, or whether he lived in the calm of certain resources, and in the freedom of unfettered feelings. What! was he coming in person to solve the problem hardly proposed in inaudible thought? He had actually knocked at the door—at *my* door; a smart, prompt rap; and, almost before I could invite him in, he was over the threshold, and had closed the door behind him.

"And how are you?" asked an indifferent, quiet voice, in the English language; while my visitor, without any sort of bustle or introduction, put his hat on the table, and his gloves into his hat, and drawing the only arm-chair the room afforded a little forward, seated himself tranquilly therein.

"Can't you speak?" he inquired in a few moments, in a tone whose nonchalance seemed to intimate that it was much the same thing whether I answered or not. The fact is, I found it desirable to have recourse to my good friends "les bésicles"; not exactly to ascertain the identity of my visitor—for I already knew him, confound his impudence! but to see how he looked—to get a clear notion of his mien and countenance. I wiped the glasses very deliberately, and put them on quite as deliberately; adjusting them so as not to hurt the bridge of my nose, or get entangled in my short tufts of dun hair. I was sitting in the window-seat, with my back to the light, and I had him *vis-à-vis*; a position he would much rather have had reversed; for, at any time, he preferred scrutinising to being scrutinised. Yes, it was *he*, and no mistake, with his six feet of length arranged in a sitting attitude; with his dark travelling surtout with its velvet collar, his grey pantaloons, his black stock, and *his* face, the most original one Nature ever modelled, yet the least obtrusively so; not one feature that could be termed marked or odd, yet the effect of the whole

unique. There is no use in attempting to describe what is indescribable. Being in no hurry to address him, I sat and stared at my ease.

"Oh, that's your game—is it?" said he at last. "Well, we'll see which is soonest tired." And he slowly drew out a fine cigar-case, picked one to his taste, lit it, took a book from the shelf convenient to his hand, then leaning back, proceeded to smoke and read as tranquilly as if he had been in his own room, in Grove Street, X——shire, England. I knew he was capable of continuing in that attitude till midnight, if he conceived the whim, so I rose, and taking the book from his hand, I said:

"You did not ask for it, and you shall not have it."

"It is silly and dull," he observed, "so I have not lost much"; then the spell being broken, he went on. "I thought you lived at Pelet's. I went there this afternoon, expecting to be starved to death by sitting in a boarding-school drawing room, and they told me you were gone, had departed this morning; you had left your address behind you though, which I wondered at: it was a more practical and sensible precaution than I should have imagined you capable of. Why did you leave?"

"Because M. Pelet has just married the lady whom you and Mr. Brown assigned to me as my wife."

"Oh, indeed!" replied Hunsden, with a short laugh; "so you've lost both your wife and your place?"

"Precisely so."

I saw him give a quick, covert glance all round my room; he marked its narrow limits, its scanty furniture: in an instant he had comprehended the state of matters— had absolved me from the crime of prosperity. A curious effect this discovery wrought in his strange mind: I am morally certain that if he had found me installed in a handsome parlour, lounging on a soft couch, with a pretty, wealthy wife at my side, he would have hated me; a brief, cold, haughty visit, would in such a case have been the extreme limit of his civilities, and never would he have come near me more, so long as the tide of fortune bore me smoothly on its surface; but the painted furniture, the bare walls, the cheerless solitude of my room relaxed his rigid pride, and I know not what softening change had taken place both in his voice and look ere he spoke again.

"You have got another place?"

"No."

"You are in the way of getting one?"

"No."

"That is bad; have you applied to Brown?"

"No, indeed."

"You had better; he often has it in his power to give useful information in such matters."

"He served me once very well; I have no claim on him, and am not in the humour to bother him again."

"Oh, if you're bashful, and dread being intrusive, you need only commission me. I shall see him to-night; I can put in a word."

"I beg you will not, Mr. Hunsden; I am in your debt already; you did me an important service when I was at X——; got me out of a den where I was dying: that service I have never repaid, and at present I decline positively adding another item to the account."

"If the wind sits that way, I'm satisfied. I thought my unexampled generosity in turning you out of that accursed counting-house would be duly appreciated some day: 'Cast your bread on the waters, and it shall be found after many days,' say the Scriptures. Yes, that's right, lad—make much of me—I'm a nonpareil: there's nothing like me in the common herd. In the meantime, to put all humbug aside and talk sense for a few moments, you would be greatly the better of a situation,

and what is more, you are a fool if you refuse to take one from any hand that offers it.''

"Very well, Mr. Hunsden; now you have settled that point, talk of something else. What news from X——?''

"I have not settled that point, or at least there is another to settle before we get to X——. Is this Miss Zénobie'' ("Zoraïde,'' interposed I)—"well, Zoraïde—is she really married to Pelet?''

"I tell you yes—and if you don't believe me, go and ask the curé of St. Jacques.''

"And your heart is broken?''

"I am not aware that it is; it feels all right—beats as usual.''

"Then your feelings are less superfine than I took them to be; you must be a coarse, callous character, to bear such a thwack without staggering under it.''

"Staggering under it? What the deuce is there to stagger under in the circumstance of a Belgian schoolmistress marrying a French schoolmaster? The progeny will doubtless be a strange hybrid race; but that's their look-out—not mine.''

"He indulges in scurrilous jests, and the bride was his affianced one!''

"Who said so?''

"Brown.''

"I'll tell you what, Hunsden—Brown is an old gossip.''

"He is; but in the meantime, if his gossip be founded on less than fact—if you took no particular interest in Miss Zoraïde—why, O youthful pedagogue! did you leave your place in consequence of her becoming Madame Pelet?''

"Because''—I felt my face grow a little hot; "because—in short, Mr. Hunsden, I decline answering any more questions,'' and I plunged my hands deep in my breeches' pockets.

Hunsden triumphed, his eyes—his laugh announced victory.

"What the deuce are you laughing at, Mr. Hunsden?''

"At your exemplary composure. Well, lad, I'll not bore you; I see how it is: Zoraïde has jilted you—married some one richer, as any sensible woman would have done if she had had the chance.''

I made no reply—I let him think so, not feeling inclined to enter into an explanation of the real state of things, and as little to forge a false account; but it was not easy to blind Hunsden; my very silence, instead of convincing him that he had hit the truth, seemed to render him doubtful about it; he went on:

"I suppose the affair has been conducted as such affairs always are amongst rational people: you offered her your youth and your talents—such as they are—in exchange for her position and money: I don't suppose you took appearance or what is called *love*, into the account—for I understand she is older than you, and Brown says, rather sensible-looking than beautiful. She, having then no chance of making a better bargain, was at first inclined to come to terms with you, but Pelet—the head of a flourishing school—stepped in with a higher bid; she accepted, and he has got her: a correct transaction—perfectly so—business-like and legitimate. And now we'll talk of something else.''

"Do,'' said I, very glad to dismiss the topic, and especially glad to have baffled the sagacity of my cross-questioner—if, indeed, I had baffled it; for though his words now led away from the dangerous point, his eyes, keen and watchful, seemed still pre-occupied with the former idea.

"You want to hear news from X——? And what interest can you have in X——? You left no friends there, for you made none. Nobody ever asks after you—neither man nor woman; and if I mention your name in company, the men look as if I had spoken of Prester John; and the women sneer covertly. Our X——belles must have disliked you. How did you excite their displeasure?''

"I don't know. I seldom spoke to them—they were nothing to me. I considered them only as something to be glanced at from a distance; their dresses and faces were often pleasing enough to the eye: but I could not understand their conversation,

nor even read their countenances. When I caught snatches of what they said, I could never make much of it; and the play of their lips and eyes did not help me at all.''

''That was your fault, not theirs. There are sensible, as well as handsome women in X——; women it is worth any man's while to talk to, and with whom I can talk with pleasure: but you had and have no pleasant address; there is nothing in you to induce a woman to be affable. I have remarked you sitting near the door in a room full of company, bent on hearing, not on speaking; on observing, not on entertaining; looking frigidly shy at the commencement of a party, confusingly vigilant about the middle, and insultingly weary towards the end. Is that the way, do you think, ever to communicate pleasure or excite interest? No; and if you are generally unpopular, it is because you deserve to be so.''

''Content!'' I ejaculated.

''No, you are not content; you see beauty always turning its back on you; you are mortified and then you sneer. I verily believe all that is desirable on earth—wealth, reputation, love—will for ever to you be the ripe grapes on the high trellis: you'll look up at them; they will tantalise in you the lust of the eye; but they are out of reach: you have not the address to fetch a ladder, and you'll go away calling them sour.''

Cutting as these words might have been under some circumstances, they drew no blood now. My life was changed; my experience had been varied since I left X——, but Hunsden could not know this; he had seen me only in the character of Mr. Crimsworth's clerk—a dependent amongst wealthy strangers, meeting disdain with a hard front, conscious of an unsocial and unattractive exterior, refusing to sue for notice which I was sure would be withheld, declining to evince an admiration which I knew would be scorned as worthless. He could not be aware that since then youth and loveliness had been to me everyday objects; that I had studied them at leisure and closely, and had seen the plain texture of truth under the embroidery of appearance; nor could he, keen-sighted as he was, penetrate into my heart, search my brain, and read my peculiar sympathies and antipathies; he had not known me long enough, or well enough, to perceive how low my feelings would ebb under some influences, powerful over most minds; how high, how fast they would flow under other influences, that perhaps acted with the more intense force on me, because they acted on me alone. Neither could he suspect for an instant the history of my communications with Mdlle. Reuter; secret to him and to all others was the tale of her strange infatuation; her blandishments, her wiles had been seen but by me, and to me only were they known; but they had changed me, for they had proved that I *could* impress. A sweeter secret nestled deeper in my heart; one full of tenderness and as full of strength; it took the sting out of Hunsden's sarcasm; it kept me unbent by shame, and unstirred by wrath. But of all this I could say nothing—nothing decisive at least; uncertainty sealed my lips, and during the interval of silence by which alone I replied to Mr. Hunsden, I made up my mind to be for the present wholly misjudged by him, and misjudged I was; he thought he had been rather too hard upon me, and that I was crushed by the weight of his upbraidings; so to reassure me he said, doubtless I should mend some day; I was only at the beginning of life yet; and since happily I was not quite without sense, every false step I made would be a good lesson.

Just then I turned my face a little to the light; the approach of twilight, and my position in the window-seat, had, for the last ten minutes, prevented him from studying my countenance; as I moved, however, he caught an expression which he thus interpreted:

''Confound it! How doggedly self-approving the lad looks! I thought he was fit to die with shame, and there he sits grinning smiles, as good as to say, 'Let the world wag as it will, I've the philosopher's stone in my waist-coat pocket, and the elixir of life in my cupboard; I'm independent of both Fate and Fortune!' ''

"Hunsden—you spoke of grapes; I was thinking of a fruit I like better than your X—— hot-house grapes—an unique fruit, growing wild, which I have marked as my own, and hope one day to gather and taste. It is of no use your offering me the draught of bitterness, or threatening me with death by thirst: I have the anticipation of sweetness on my palate; the hope of freshness on my lips; I can reject the unsavoury, and endure the exhausting."

"For how long?"

"Till the next opportunity for effort; and as the prize of success will be a treasure after my own heart, I'll bring a bull's strength to the struggle."

"Bad luck crushes bulls as easily as bullaces; and, I believe, the fury dogs you: you were born with a wooden spoon in your mouth, depend on it."

"I believe you; and I mean to make my wooden spoon do the work of some people's silver ladles; grasped firmly, and handled nimbly, even a wooden spoon will shovel up broth."

Hunsden rose: "I see," said he; "I suppose you're one of those who develop best unwatched, and act best unaided—work your own way. Now, I'll go." And, without another word, he was going; at the door he turned:

"Crimsworth Hall is sold," said he.

"Sold!" was my echo.

"Yes; you know, of course, that your brother failed three months ago?"

"What! Edward Crimsworth?"

"Precisely; and his wife went home to her father's; when affairs went awry, his temper sympathised with them; he used her ill; I told you he would be a tyrant to her some day; as to him——"

"Ay, as to him—what is become of him?"

"Nothing extraordinary—don't be alarmed; he put himself under the protection of the court, compounded with his creditors—tenpence in the pound; in six weeks set up again, coaxed back his wife, and is flourishing like a green bay-tree."

"And Crimsworth Hall—was the furniture sold too?"

"Everything—from the grand piano down to the rolling-pin."

"And the contents of the oak dining-room—were they sold?"

"Of course; why should the sofas and chairs of that room be held more sacred than those of any other?"

"And the pictures?"

"What pictures? Crimsworth had no special collection that I know of—he did not profess to be an amateur."

"There were two portraits, one on each side the mantelpiece; you cannot have forgotten them, Mr. Hunsden; you once noticed that of the lady——"

"Oh, I know! the thin-faced gentlewoman with a shawl put on like drapery.— Why, as a matter of course, it would be sold among the other things. If you had been rich, you might have bought it, for I remember you said it represented your mother: you see what it is to be without a sou."

I did. "But surely," I thought to myself, "I shall not always be so poverty-stricken; I may one day buy it back yet.—Who purchased it? do you know?" I asked.

"How is it likely? I never inquired who purchased anything; there spoke the unpractical man—to imagine all the world is interested in what interests himself! Now, good-night—I'm off for Germany to-morrow morning; I shall be back in six weeks, and possibly I may call and see you again; I wonder whether you'll be still out of place!" he laughed, as mockingly, as heartlessly as Mephistopheles, and so laughing, vanished.

Some people, however indifferent they may become after a considerable space of absence, always contrive to leave a pleasant impression just at parting; not so Hunsden; a conference with him affected one like a draught of Peruvian bark; it

seemed a concentration of the specially harsh, stringent, bitter; whether, like bark, it invigorated, I scarcely knew.

A ruffled mind makes a restless pillow; I slept little on the night after this interview; towards morning I began to doze, but hardly had my slumber become sleep, when I was roused from it by hearing a noise in my sitting-room to which my bedroom adjoined—a step, and a shoving of furniture; the movement lasted barely two minutes; with the closing of the door it ceased. I listened; not a mouse stirred; perhaps I had dreamt it; perhaps a *locataire* had made a mistake, and entered my apartment instead of his own. It was yet but five o'clock; neither I nor the day were wide awake; I turned, and was soon unconscious. When I did rise, about two hours later, I had forgotten the circumstance; the first thing I saw, however, on quitting my chamber, recalled it; just pushed in at the door of my sitting-room, and still standing on end, was a wooden packing-case—a rough deal affair, wide but shallow; a porter had doubtless shoved it forward, but seeing no occupant of the room, had left it at the entrance.

"That is none of mine," thought I, approaching; "it must be meant for somebody else." I stopped to examine the address:

"Wm. Crimsworth, Esq., No —, —— St., Brussels."

I was puzzled, but concluding that the best way to obtain information was to ask within, I cut the cords and opened the case. Green baize enveloped its contents, sewn carefully at the sides; I ripped the pack-thread with my pen-knife, and still, as the seam gave way, glimpses of gilding appeared through the widening interstices. Boards and baize being at length removed, I lifted from the case a large picture, in a magnificent frame; leaning it against a chair, in a position where the light from the window fell favourably upon it, I stepped back—already I had mounted my spectacles. A portrait-painter's sky (the most sombre and threatening of welkins), and distant trees of a conventional depth of hue, raised in full relief a pale, pensive-looking female face, shadowed with soft dark hair, almost blending with the equally dark clouds; large, solemn eyes looked reflectively into mine; a thin cheek rested on a delicate little hand; a shawl, artistically draped, half hid, half showed a slight figure. A listener (had there been one) might have heard me, after ten minutes' silent gazing, utter the word "Mother!" I might have said more—but with me, the first word uttered aloud in soliloquy rouses consciousness; it reminds me that only crazy people talk to themselves, and then I think out my monologue, instead of speaking it. I had thought a long while, and a long while had contemplated the intelligence, the sweetness, and—alas! the sadness also of those fine, grey eyes, the mental power of that forehead, and the rare sensibility of that serious mouth, when my glance, travelling downwards, fell on a narrow billet, stuck in the corner of the picture, between the frame and the canvas. Then I first asked, "Who sent this picture? Who sent this picture? Who thought of me, saved it out of the wreck of Crimsworth Hall, and now commits it to the care of its natural keeper?" I took the note from its niche; thus it spoke:

> "There is a sort of stupid pleasure in giving a child sweets, a fool his bells, a dog a bone. You are repaid by seeing the child besmear his face with sugar; by witnessing how the fool's ecstasy makes a greater fool of him than ever; by watching the dog's nature come out over his bone. In giving William Crimsworth his mother's picture, I give him sweets, bells, and bone all in one; what grieves me is, that I cannot behold the result; I would have added five shillings more to my bid if the auctioneer could only have promised me that pleasure.
>
> "H.Y.H.

"*P.S.*—You said last night you positively declined adding another item to your account with me; don't you think I've saved you that trouble?"

I muffled the picture in its green baize covering, restored it to the case, and having transported the whole concern to my bedroom, put it out of sight under my bed. My pleasure was now poisoned by pungent pain; I determined to look no more till I could look at my ease. If Hunsden had come in at that moment, I should have said to him, "I owe you nothing, Hunsden—not a fraction of a farthing: you have paid yourself in taunts."

Too anxious to remain any longer quiescent, I had no sooner breakfasted, than I repaired once more to M. Vandenhuten's, scarcely hoping to find him at home; for a week had barely elapsed since my first call: but fancying I might be able to glean information as to the time when his return was expected. A better result awaited me than I had anticipated, for though the family were yet at Ostend, M. Vandenhuten had come over to Brussels on business for the day. He received me with the quiet kindness of a sincere though not excitable man. I had not sat five minutes alone with him in his bureau, before I became aware of a sense of ease in his presence, such as I rarely experienced with strangers. I was surprised at my own composure, for, after all, I had come on business to me exceedingly painful—that of soliciting a favour. I asked on what basis the calm rested—I feared it might be deceptive. Ere long I caught a glimpse of the ground, and at once I felt assured of its solidity; I knew where it was.

M. Vandenhuten was rich, respected, and influential; I, poor, despised, and powerless; so we stood to the world at large as members of the world's society; but to each other, as a pair of human beings, our positions were reversed. The Dutchman (he was not Flamand, but pure Hollandais) was slow, cool, of rather dense intelligence, though sound and accurate judgment; the Englishman far more nervous, active, quicker both to plan and to practise, to conceive and to realise. The Dutchman was benevolent, the Englishman susceptible; in short our characters dovetailed, but my mind having more fire and action than his, instinctively assumed and kept the predominance.

This point settled, and my position well ascertained, I addressed him on the subject of my affairs with that genuine frankness which full confidence can alone inspire. It was a pleasure to him to be so appealed to; he thanked me for giving him this opportunity of using a little exertion in my behalf. I went on to explain to him that my wish was not so much to be helped, as to be put into the way of helping myself; of him I did not want exertion—that was to be my part—but only information and recommendation. Soon after I rose to go. He held out his hand at parting—an action of greater significance with foreigners than with Englishmen. As I exchanged a smile with him, I thought the benevolence of his truthful face was better than the intelligence of my own. Characters of my order experience a balm-like solace in the contact of such souls as animated the honest breast of Victor Vandenhuten.

The next fortnight was a period of many alternations; my existence during its lapse resembled a sky of one of those autumnal nights which are specially haunted by meteors and falling stars. Hopes and fears, expectations and disappointments, descended in glancing showers from zenith to horizon; but all were transient, and darkness followed swift each vanishing apparition. M. Vandenhuten aided me faithfully; he set me on the track of several places, and himself made efforts to secure them for me; but for a long time solicitation and recommendation were vain—the door either shut in my face when I was about to walk in, or another candidate, entering before me, rendered my further advance useless. Feverish and roused, no disappointment arrested me; defeat following fast on defeat served as stimulants to will. I forgot fastidiousness, conquered reserve, thrust pride from me:

I asked, I persevered, I remonstrated, I dunned. It is so that openings are forced into the guarded circle where Fortune sits dealing favours round. My perseverance made me known; my importunity made me remarked. I was inquired about; my former pupils' parents, gathering the reports of their children, heard me spoken of as talented, and they echoed the word: the sound, bandied about at random, came at last to ears which, but for its universality, it might never have reached; and at the very crisis when I had tried my last effort and knew not what to do, Fortune looked in at me one morning, as I sat in drear and almost desperate deliberation on my bedstead, nodded with the familiarity of an old acquaintance—though God knows I had never met her before—and threw a prize into my lap.

In the second week of October, 18—, I got the appointment of English professor to all the classes of —— College, Brussels, with a salary of three thousand francs per annum; and the certainty of being able, by dint of the reputation and publicity accompanying the position, to make as much more by private lessons. The official notice, which communicated this information, mentioned also that it was the strong recommendation of M. Vandenhuten, négociant, which had turned the scale of choice in my favour.

No sooner had I read the announcement than I hurried to M. Vandenhuten's bureau, pushed the document under his nose, and when he had perused it, took both his hands, and thanked him with unrestrained vivacity. My vivid words and emphatic gesture moved his Dutch calm to unwonted sensation. He said he was happy—glad to have served me; but he had done nothing meriting such thanks. He had not laid out a centime—only scratched a few words on a sheet of paper.

Again I repeated to him:

"You have made me quite happy, and in a way that suits me; I do not feel an obligation irksome, conferred by your kind hand; I do not feel disposed to shun you because you have done me a favour; from this day you must consent to admit me to your intimate acquaintance, for I shall hereafter recur again and again to the pleasure of your society."

"Ainsi soit-il," was the reply, accompanied by a smile of benignant content. I went away with its sunshine in my heart.

Chapter XXIII

IT was two o'clock when I returned to my lodgings; my dinner, just brought in from a neighbouring hotel, smoked on the table; I sat down thinking to eat—had the plate been heaped with potsherds and broken glass, instead of boiled beef and haricots, I could not have made a more signal failure: appetite had forsaken me. Impatient of seeing food which I could not taste, I put it all aside into a cupboard, and then demanded, "What shall I do till evening?" for before six P.M. it would be vain to seek the Rue Notre Dame aux Neiges; its inhabitant (for me it had but one) was detained by her vocation elsewhere. I walked in the streets of Brussels, and I walked in my own room from two o'clock till six; never once in that space of time did I sit down. I was in my chamber when the last-named hour struck; I had just bathed my face and feverish hands, and was standing near the glass; my cheek was crimson, my eye was flame, still all my features looked quite settled and calm. Descending swiftly the stair and stepping out, I was glad to see Twilight drawing on in clouds; such shade to me was like a grateful screen, and the chill of latter Autumn, breathing in a fitful wind from the north-west, met me as a refreshing coolness. Still I saw it was cold to others, for the women I passed were wrapped in shawls and the men had their coats buttoned close.

When are we quite happy? Was I so then? No; an urgent and growing dread worried my nerves, and worried them since the first moment good tidings had reached me. How was Frances? It was ten weeks since I had seen her, six since I had heard from her, or of her. I had answered her letter by a brief note, friendly but calm, in which no mention of continued correspondence or further visits was made. At that hour my bark hung on the topmost curl of a wave of fate, and I knew not on what shoal the onward rush of the billow might hurl it; I would not then attach her destiny to mine by the slightest thread; if doomed to split on the rock, or run aground on the sand-bank, I was resolved no other vessel should share my disaster; but six weeks was a long time; and could it be that she was still well and doing well? Were not all sages agreed in declaring that happiness finds no climax on earth? Dared I think that but half a street now divided me from the full cup of contentment—the draught drawn from waters said to flow only in heaven?

I was at the door; I entered the quiet house; I mounted the stairs; the lobby was void and still, all the doors closed; I looked for the neat green mat; it lay duly in its place.

"Signal of hope!" I said, and advanced. "But I will be a little calmer; 1 am not going to rush in, and get up a scene directly." Forcibly staying my eager step, I paused on the mat.

"What an absolute hush! Is she in? Is anybody in?" I demanded to myself. A little tinkle, as of cinders falling from a grate, replied; a movement—a fire was gently stirred; and the slight rustle of life continuing, a step paced equably backwards and forwards, backwards and forwards, in the apartment. Fascinated, I stood, more fixedly fascinated when a voice rewarded the attention of my strained ear—so low, so self-addressed, I never fancied the speaker otherwise than alone; solitude might speak thus in a desert, or in the hall of a forsaken house.

> *"And ne'er but once, my son," he said,*
> *"Was yon dark cavern trod;*
> *In persecution's iron days,*
> *When the land was left by God.*
> *From Bewley's bog, with slaughter red,*
> *A wanderer hither drew;*
> *And oft he stopp'd and turn'd his head,*
> *As by fits the night-winds blew.*
> *For trampling round by Cheviot-edge*
> *Were heard the troopers keen;*
> *And frequent from the Whitelaw ridge*
> *The death-shot flash'd between," etc., etc.,*

The old Scotch ballad was partly recited, then dropt; a pause ensued; then another strain followed, in French, of which the purport, translated, ran as follows:

> *I gave, at first, attention close;*
> *Then interest warm ensued;*
> *From interest, as improvement rose*
> *Succeeded gratitude.*
>
> *Obedience was no effort soon,*
> *And labour was no pain;*
> *If tired, a word, a glance alone*
> *Would give me strength again.*
>
> *From others of the studious band,*
> *Ere long he singled me;*

> *But only by more close demand,*
> *And sterner urgency.*
>
> *The task he from another took,*
> *From me he did reject;*
> *He would no slight omission brook,*
> *And suffer no defect.*
>
> *If my companions went astray,*
> *He scarce their wanderings blam'd;*
> *If I but falter'd in the way,*
> *His anger fiercely flam'd."*

Something stirred in an adjoining chamber; it would not do to be surprised eavesdropping; I tapped hastily and as hastily entered. Frances was just before me; she had been walking slowly in her room, and her step was checked by my advent: Twilight only was with her, and tranquil, ruddy Firelight; to these sisters, the Bright and the Dark, she had been speaking, ere I entered, in poetry. Sir Walter Scott's voice, to her a foreign, far-off sound, a mountain echo, had uttered itself in the first stanzas; the second, I thought, from the style and the substance, was the language of her own heart. Her face was grave, its expression concentrated; she bent on me an unsmiling eye—an eye just returning from abstraction, just awaking from dreams: well-arranged was her simple attire, smooth her dark hair, orderly her tranquil room; but what—with her thoughtful look, her serious self-reliance, her bent to meditation and happy inspiration—what had she to do with love? "Nothing," was the answer of her own sad, though gentle countenance; it seemed to say, "I must cultivate fortitude and cling to poetry; one is to be my support and the other my solace through life. Human affections do not bloom, nor do human passions glow for me." Other women have such thoughts. Frances, had she been as desolate as she deemed, would not have been worse off than thousands of her sex. Look at the rigid and formal race of old maids—the race whom all despise; they have fed themselves, from youth upwards, on maxims of resignation and endurance. Many of them get ossified with the dry diet; self-control is so continually their thought, so perpetually their object, that at last it absorbs the softer and more agreeable qualities of their nature; and they die mere models of austerity, fashioned out of a little parchment and much bone. Anatomists will tell you that there is a heart in the withered old maid's carcase—the same as in that of any cherished wife or proud mother in the land. Can this be so? I really don't know; but feel inclined to doubt it.

I came forward, bade Frances "good evening," and took my seat. The chair I had chosen was one she had probably just left; it stood by a little table where were her open desk and papers. I know not whether she had fully recognised me at first, but she did so now; and in a voice, soft but quiet, she returned my greeting. I had shown no eagerness; she took her cue from me, and evinced no surprise. We met as we had always met, as master and pupil—nothing more. I proceeded to handle the papers; Frances, observant and serviceable, stepped into an inner room, brought a candle, lit it, placed it by me; then drew the curtain over the lattice, and having added a little fresh fuel to the already bright fire, she drew a second chair to the table and sat down at my right hand, a little removed. The paper on the top was a translation of some grave French author into English, but underneath lay a sheet with stanzas; on this I laid hands. Frances half rose, made a movement to recover the captured spoil, saying, that was nothing—a mere copy of verses. I put by resistance with the decision I knew she never long opposed; but on this occasion her fingers had fastened on the paper. I had quietly to unloose them; their hold dissolved to my touch; her hand shrunk away; my own would fain have followed

it, but for the present I forbade such impulse. The first page of the sheet was occupied with the lines I had overheard; the sequel was not exactly the writer's own experience, but a composition by portions of that experience suggested. Thus while egotism was avoided, the fancy was exercised, and the heart satisfied. I translate as before, and my translation is nearly literal; it continued thus:

> *When sickness stay'd awhile my course,*
> *He seem'd impatient still,*
> *Because his pupil's flagging force*
> *Could not obey his will.*
>
> *One day when summoned to the bed*
> *Where pain and I did strive,*
> *I heard him, as he bent his head,*
> *Say, "God, she* must *revive!"*
>
> *I felt his hand, with gentle stress*
> *A moment laid on mine,*
> *And wished to mark my consciousness*
> *By some responsive sign.*
>
> *But pow'rless then to speak or move,*
> *I only felt, within,*
> *The sense of Hope, the strength of Love*
> *Their healing work begin.*
>
> *And as he from the room withdrew,*
> *My heart his steps pursued;*
> *I long'd to prove, by efforts new,*
> *My speechless gratitude.*
>
> *When once again I took my place,*
> *Long vacant, in the class,*
> *Th' unfrequent smile across his face*
> *Did for one moment pass.*
>
> *The lessons done; the signal made*
> *Of glad release and play,*
> *He, as he passed, an instant stay'd*
> *One kindly word to say.*
>
> *"Jane, till to-morrow you are free*
> *From tedious task and rule;*
> *This afternoon I must not see*
> *That yet pale face in school.*
>
> *"Seek in the garden-shades a seat,*
> *Far from the play-ground din;*
> *The sun is warm, the air is sweet;*
> *Stay till I call you in."*
>
> *A long and pleasant afternoon*
> *I passed in those green bowers;*
> *All silent, tranquil, and alone*
> *With birds, and bees, and flowers.*

Yet, when my master's voice I heard
Call, from the window, "Jane!"
I entered, joyful, at the word,
The busy house again.

He, in the hall, paced up and down;
He paused as I passed by;
His forehead stern relaxed its frown;
He raised his deep-set eye.

"Not quite so pale," he murmured low;
"Now, Jane, go rest awhile."
And as I smiled, his smoothened brow
Returned as glad a smile.

My perfect health restored, he took
His mien austere again;
And, as before, he would not brook
The slightest fault from Jane.

The longest task, the hardest theme
Fell to my share as erst,
And still I toiled to place my name
In every study first.

He yet begrudged and stinted praise,
But I had learnt to read
The secret meaning of his face,
And that was my best meed.

Even when his hasty temper spoke
In tones that sorrow stirred,
My grief was lulled as soon as woke
By some relenting word.

And when he lent some precious book,
Or gave some fragrant flower,
I did not quail to Envy's look,
Upheld by Pleasure's power.

At last our school ranks took their ground,
The hard-fought field I won:
The prize, a laurel-wreath, was bound
My throbbing forehead on.

Low at my master's knee I bent,
The offered crown to meet;
Its green leaves through my temples sent
A thrill as wild as sweet.

The strong pulse of Ambition struck
In every vein I owned;
At the same instant, bleeding broke
A secret, inward wound.

> The hour of triumph was to me
> The hour of sorrow sore;
> A day hence I must cross the sea,
> Ne'er to recross it more.
>
> An hour hence, in my master's room
> I with him sat alone,
> And told him what a dreary gloom
> O'er joy had parting thrown.
>
> He little said; the time was brief,
> The ship was soon to sail,
> And while I sobbed in bitter grief,
> My master but looked pale.
>
> They called in haste; he bade me go,
> Then snatched me back again:
> He held me fast and murmured low,
> "Why will they part us, Jane?
>
> "Were you not happy in my care?
> Did I not faithful prove?
> Will others to my darling bear
> As true, as deep a love?
>
> "O God, watch o'er my foster child:
> O guard her gentle head!
> When winds are high and tempests wild,
> Protection round her spread!
>
> "They call again; leave then my breast;
> Quit thy true shelter, Jane;
> But when deceived, repulsed, opprest,
> Come home to me again!"

I read—then dreamily made marks on the margin with my pencil; thinking all the while of other things; thinking that "Jane" was now at my side: no child, but a girl of nineteen; and she might be mine, so my heart affirmed; Poverty's curse was taken off me; Envy and Jealousy were far away, and unapprised of this our quiet meeting; the frost of the Master's manner might melt; I felt the thaw coming fast, whether I would or not; no further need for the eye to practise a hard look, for the brow to compress its expanse into a stern fold: it was now permitted to suffer the outward revelation of the inward glow—to seek, demand, elicit an answering ardour. While musing thus, I thought that the grass on Hermon never drank the fresh dews of sunset more gratefully than my feelings drank the bliss of this hour.

Frances rose as if restless; she passed before me to stir the fire, which did not want stirring; she lifted and put down the little ornaments on the mantelpiece; her dress waved within a yard of me; slight, straight, and elegant, she stood erect on the hearth.

There are impulses we can control; but there are others which control us, because they attain us with a tiger-leap, and are our masters ere we have seen them. Perhaps, though, such impulses are seldom altogether bad; perhaps Reason, by a process as brief as quiet, a process that is finished ere felt, has ascertained the sanity of the deed Instinct meditates, and feels justified in remaining passive while it is performed. I know I did not reason, I did not plan or intend, yet, whereas one moment I was

sitting solus on the chair near the table, the next, I held Frances on my knee, placed there with sharpness and decision, and retained with exceeding tenacity.

"Monsieur!" cried Frances, and was still: not another word escaped her lips; sorely confounded she seemed during the lapse of the first few moments; but the amazement soon subsided; terror did not succeed, nor fury: after all, she was only a little nearer than she had ever been before to one she habitually respected and trusted; embarrassment might have impelled her to contend, but self-respect checked resistance where resistance was useless.

"Frances, how much regard have you for me?" was my demand. No answer; the situation was yet too new and surprising to permit speech. On this consideration, I compelled myself for some seconds to tolerate her silence, though impatient of it: presently, I repeated the same question—probably, not in the calmest of tones; she looked at me; my face, doubtless, was no model of composure, my eyes no still wells of tranquillity.

"Do speak," I urged; and a very low, hurried, yet still arch voice said:

"Monsieur, vous me faîtes mal; de grâce lâchez un peu ma main droite."

In truth I became aware that I was holding the said "main droite" in a somewhat ruthless grasp: I did as desired; and, for the third time, asked more gently:

"Frances, how much regard have you for me?"

"Mon maître, j'en ai beaucoup," was the truthful rejoinder.

"Frances, have you enough to give yourself to me as my wife?—to accept me as your husband?"

I felt the agitation of the heart, I saw "the purple light of love" cast its glowing reflection on cheeks, temples, neck; I desired to consult the eye, but sheltering lash and lid forbade.

"Monsieur," said the soft voice at last,—"Monsieur désire savoir si je consens—si—enfin, si je veux me marier avec lui?"

"Justement."

"Monsieur sera-t-il aussi bon mari qu'il a été bon maître?"

"I will try, Frances."

A pause; then with a new, yet still subdued inflection of the voice—an inflection which provoked while it pleased me—accompanied, too, by a "sourire à la fois fin et timide" in perfect harmony with the tone:

"C'est à dire, Monsieur sera toujours un peu entêté, exigeant, volontaire——"

"Have I been so, Frances?"

"Mais oui; vous le savez bien."

"Have I been nothing else?"

"Mais oui; vous avez été mon meilleur ami."

"And what, Frances, are you to me?"

"Votre dévouée élève, qui vous aime de tout son cœur."

"Will my pupil consent to pass her life with me? Speak English now, Frances."

Some moments were taken for reflection; the answer, pronounced slowly, ran thus:

"You have always made me happy; I like to hear you speak; I like to see you; I like to be near you; I believe you are very good, and very superior; I know you are stern to those who are careless and idle, but you are kind, very kind to the attentive and industrious, even if they are not clever. Master, I should be *glad* to live with you always"; and she made a sort of movement, as if she would have clung to me, but restraining herself she only added with earnest emphasis—"Master, I consent to pass my life with you."

"Very well, Frances."

I drew her a little nearer to my heart; I took a first kiss from her lips, thereby sealing the compact, now framed between us; afterwards she and I were silent, nor was our silence brief. Frances' thoughts, during this interval, I know not, nor did

I attempt to guess them; I was not occupied in searching her countenance, nor in otherwise troubling her composure. The peace I felt, I wished her to feel; my arm, it is true, still detained her; but with a restraint that was gentle enough, so long as no opposition tightened it. My gaze was on the red fire; my heart was measuring its own content; it sounded and sounded, and found the depth fathomless.

"Monsieur," at last said my quiet companion, as stirless in her happiness as a mouse in its terror. Even now in speaking she scarcely lifted her head.

"Well, Frances?" I like unexaggerated intercourse; it is not my way to overpower with amorous epithets, any more than to worry with selfishly importunate caresses.

"Monsieur est raisonnable, n'est-ce pas?"

"Yes; especially when I am requested to be so in English: but why do you ask me? You see nothing vehement or obtrusive in my manner; am I not tranquil enough?"

"Ce n'est pas cela"—began Frances.

"English!" I reminded her.

"Well, Monsieur, I wished merely to say, that I should like, of course, to retain my employment of teaching. You will teach still, I suppose, Monsieur?"

"Oh yes! It is all I have to depend on."

"Bon!—I mean good. Thus we shall have both the same profession. I like that; and my efforts to get on will be as unrestrained as yours—will they not, Monsieur?"

"You are laying plans to be independent of me," said I.

"Yes, Monsieur; I must be no incumbrance to you—no burden in any way."

"But, Frances, I have not yet told you what my prospects are. I have left M. Pelet's; and after nearly a month's seeking, I have got another place, with a salary of three thousand francs a year, which I can easily double by a little additional exertion. Thus you see it would be useless for you to fag yourself by going out to give lessons; on six thousand francs you and I can live, and live well."

Frances seemed to consider. There is something flattering to man's strength, something consonant to his honourable pride in the idea of becoming the providence of what he loves—feeding and clothing it, as God does the lilies of the field. So, to decide her resolution, I went on:

"Life has been painful and laborious enough to you so far, Frances; you require complete rest; your twelve hundred francs would not form a very important addition to our income, and what sacrifice of comfort to earn it! Relinquish your labours: you must be weary, and let me have the happiness of giving you rest."

I am not sure whether Frances had accorded due attention to my harangue; instead of answering me with her usual respectful promptitude, she only sighed and said:

"How rich you are, Monsieur!" and then she stirred uneasy in my arms. "Three thousand francs!" she murmured, "while I get only twelve hundred!" She went on faster. "However, it must be so for the present; and, Monsieur, were you not saying something about my giving up my place? Oh no! I shall hold it fast"; and her little fingers emphatically tightened on mine.

"Think of my marrying you to be kept by you, Monsieur! I could not do it; and how dull my days would be! You would be away teaching in close, noisy schoolrooms, from morning till evening, and I should be lingering at home, unemployed and solitary; I should get depressed and sullen, and you would soon tire of me."

"Frances, you could read and study—two things you like so well."

"Monsieur, I could not; I like a contemplative life, but I like an active better; I must act in some way, and act with you. I have taken notice, Monsieur, that people who are only in each other's company for amusement, never really like each other so well, or esteem each other so highly, as those who work together, and perhaps suffer together."

"You speak God's truth," said I at last, "and you shall have your own way, for it is the best way. Now, as a reward for such ready consent, give me a voluntary kiss."

After some hesitation, natural to a novice in the art of kissing, she brought her lips into very shy and gentle contact with my forehead; I took the small gift as a loan, and repaid it promptly, and with generous interest.

I know not whether Frances was really much altered since the time I first saw her; but, as I looked at her now, I felt that she was singularly changed for me; the sad eye, the pale cheek, the dejected and joyless countenance I remembered as her early attributes, were quite gone, and now I saw a face dressed in graces; smile, dimple, and rosy tint, rounded its contours and brightened its hues. I had been accustomed to nurse a flattering idea that my strong attachment to her proved some particular perspicacity in my nature; she was not handsome, she was not rich, she was not even accomplished, yet was she my life's treasure; I must then be a man of peculiar discernment. To-night my eyes opened on the mistake I had made; I began to suspect that it was only my tastes which were unique, not my power of discovering and appreciating the superiority of moral worth over physical charms. For me Frances had physical charms: in her there was no deformity to get over; none of those prominent defects of eyes, teeth, complexion, shape, which hold at bay the admiration of the boldest male champions of intellect (for women can love a downright ugly man if he be but talented); had she been either "édentée, myope, rugueuse, ou bossue," my feelings towards her might still have been kindly, but they could never have been impassioned; I had affection for the poor little misshapen Sylvie, but for her I could never have had love. It is true Frances' mental points had been the first to interest me, and they still retained the strongest hold on my preference; but I liked the graces of her person too. I derived a pleasure, purely material, from contemplating the clearness of her brown eyes, the fairness of her fine skin, the purity of her well-set teeth, the proportion of her delicate form; and that pleasure I could ill have dispensed with. It appeared, then, that I too was a sensualist, in my temperate and fastidious way.

Now, reader, during the last two pages I have been giving you honey fresh from flowers, but you must not live entirely on food so luscious; taste then a little gall—just a drop, by way of change.

At a somewhat late hour I returned to my lodgings: having temporarily forgotten that man had any such coarse cares as those of eating and drinking, I went to bed fasting. I had been excited and in action all day, and had tasted no food since eight that morning; besides, for a fortnight past, I had known no rest either of body or mind; the last few hours had been a sweet delirium, it would not subside now, and till long after midnight broke with troubled ecstasy the rest I so much needed. At last I dozed, but not for long; it was yet quite dark when I awoke, and my waking was like that of Job when a spirit passed before his face, and like him, "the hair of my flesh stood up." I might continue the parallel, for in truth, though I saw nothing, yet "a thing was secretly brought unto me, and mine ear received a little thereof; there was silence, and I heard a voice," saying—"In the midst of life we are in death."

That sound, and the sensation of chill anguish accompanying it, many would have regarded as supernatural; but I recognised it at once as the effect of reaction. Man is ever clogged with his mortality, and it was my mortal nature which now faltered and plained; my nerves, which jarred and gave a false sound, because the soul, of late rushing headlong to an aim, had overstrained the body's comparative weakness. A horror of great darkness fell upon me; I felt my chamber invaded by one I had known formerly, but had thought for ever departed. I was temporarily a prey to hypochondria.

She had been my acquaintance, nay, my guest, once before in boyhood; I had entertained her at bed and board for a year; for that space of time I had her to myself in secret; she lay with me, she ate with me, she walked out with me, showing me nooks in woods, hollows in hills, where we could sit together, and where she could drop her drear veil over me, and so hide sky and sun, grass and green tree;

taking me entirely to her death-cold bosom, and holding me with arms of bone. What tales she would tell me at such hours! What songs she would recite in my ears! How she would discourse to me of her own country—the grave—and again and again promise to conduct me there ere long; and, drawing me to the very brink of a black, sullen river, show me, on the other side, shores unequal with mound, monument, and tablet, standing up in a glimmer more hoary than moonlight. "Necropolis!" she would whisper, pointing to the pale piles, and add, "It contains a mansion prepared for you."

But my boyhood was lonely, parentless; uncheered by brother or sister; and there was no marvel that, just as I rose to youth, a sorceress, finding me lost in vague mental wanderings, with many affections and few objects, glowing aspirations and gloomy prospects, strong desires and slender hopes, should lift up her illusive lamp to me in the distance, and lure me to her vaulted home of horrors. No wonder her spells *then* had power; but *now*, when my course was widening, my prospect brightening; when my affections had found a rest; when my desires, folding wings, weary with long flight, had just alighted on the very lap of fruition, and nestled there warm, content, under the caress of a soft hand—why did hypochondria accost me now?

I repulsed her as one would a dreaded and ghastly concubine coming to embitter a husband's heart toward his young bride; in vain; she kept her sway over me for that night and the next day, and eight succeeding days. Afterwards, my spirits began slowly to recover their tone; my appetite returned, and in a fortnight I was well. I had gone about as usual all the time, and had said nothing to anybody of what I felt; but I was glad when the evil spirit departed from me, and I could again seek Frances, and sit at her side, freed from the dreadful tyranny of my demon.

Chapter XXIV

ONE fine, frosty Sunday in November, Frances and I took a long walk; we made the tour of the city by the Boulevards; and, afterwards, Frances being a little tired, we sat down on one of those wayside seats placed under the trees, at intervals, for the accommodation of the weary. Frances was telling me about Switzerland; the subject animated her; and I was just thinking that her eyes spoke full as eloquently as her tongue, when she stopped and remarked:

"Monsieur, there is a gentleman who knows you."

I looked up; three fashionably dressed men were just then passing—Englishmen, I knew by their air and gait as well as by their features: in the tallest of the two I at once recognised Mr. Hunsden; he was in the act of lifting his hat to Frances; afterwards, he made a grimace at me, and passed on.

"Who is he?"

"A person I knew in England."

"Why did he bow to me? He does not know me."

"Yes, he does know you, in his way."

"How, Monsieur?" (She still called me "Monsieur"; I could not persuade her to adopt any more familiar term.)

"Did you not read the expression of his eyes?"

"Of his eyes? No. What did they say?"

"To you they said, 'How do you do, Wilhelmina Crimsworth?' To me, 'So you have found your counterpart at last; there she sits, the female of your kind!' "

"Monsieur, you could not read all that in his eyes; he was so soon gone."

"I read that and more, Frances; I read that he will probably call on me this evening, or on some future occasion shortly; and I have no doubt he will insist on being introduced to you; shall I bring him to your rooms?"

"If you please, Monsieur—I have no objection; I think indeed, I should rather like to see him nearer; he looks so original."

As I had anticipated, Mr. Hunsden came that evening. The first thing he said was:

"You need not begin boasting, Monsieur le Professeur; I know about your appointment to —— College, and all that; Brown has told me." Then he intimated that he had returned from Germany but a day or two since; afterwards, he abruptly demanded whether that was Madame Pelet-Reuter with whom he had seen me on the Boulevards. I was going to utter a rather emphatic negative, but on second thoughts I checked myself, and, seeming to assent, asked what he thought of her?

"As to her, I'll come back to that directly; but first I've a word for you. I see you are a scoundrel; you've no business to be promenading about with another man's wife. I thought you had sounder sense than to get mixed up in foreign hodge-podge of this sort."

"But the lady?"

"She's too good for you evidently; she is like you, but somewhat better than you—no beauty, though; yet when she rose (for I looked back to see you both walk away) I thought her figure and carriage good. These foreigners understand grace. What the devil has she done with Pelet? She has not been married to him three months—he must be a spoon!"

I would not let the mistake go too far; I did not like it much.

"Pelet? How your head runs on Mons. and Madame Pelet! You are always talking about them. I wish to the gods you had wed Mdlle. Zoraïde yourself!"

"Was that young gentlewoman not Mdlle. Zoraïde?"

"No; nor Madame Zoraïde either."

"Why did you tell a lie, then?"

"I told no lie; but you are in such a hurry. She is a pupil of mine—a Swiss girl."

"And of course you are going to be married to her? Don't deny that."

"Married! I think I shall—if Fate spares us both ten weeks longer. That is my little wild strawberry, Hunsden, whose sweetness made me careless of your hot-house grapes."

"Stop! No boasting—no heroics; I won't bear them. What is she? To what *caste* does she belong?"

I smiled. Hunsden unconsciously laid stress on the word *caste*, and, in fact, republican, lord-hater as he was, Hunsden was as proud of his old ——shire blood, of his descent and family standing, respectable and respected through long generations back, as any peer in the realm of his Norman race and Conquest-dated title. Hunsden would as little have thought of taking a wife from a *caste* inferior to his own, as a Stanley would think of mating with a Cobden. I enjoyed the surprise I should give; I enjoyed the triumph of my practice over his theory; and leaning over the table, and uttering the words slowly but with repressed glee, I said concisely:

"She is a lace-mender."

Hunsden examined me. He did not *say* he was surprised, but surprised he was; he had his own notions of good breeding. I saw he suspected I was going to take some very rash step; but repressing declamation or remonstrance, he only answered:

"Well, you are the best judge of your own affairs. A lace-mender may make a good wife as well as a lady; but of course you have taken care to ascertain thoroughly that since she has not education, fortune, or station, she is well furnished with such natural qualities as you think most likely to conduce to your happiness. Has she many relations?"

"None in Brussels."

"That is better. Relations are often the real evil in such cases. I cannot but think that a train of inferior connections would have been a bore to you to your life's end."

After sitting in silence a little while longer, Hunsden rose, and was quietly bidding me good evening; the polite, considerate manner in which he offered me his hand (a thing he had never done before), convinced me that he thought I had made a terrible fool of myself; and that, ruined and thrown away as I was, it was no time for sarcasm or cynicism, or indeed for anything but indulgence and forbearance.

"Good-night, William," he said, in a really soft voice, while his face looked benevolently compassionate. "Good-night, lad. I wish you and your future wife much prosperity, and I hope she will satisfy your fastidious soul."

I had much ado to refrain from laughing as I beheld the magnanimous pity of his mien; maintaining, however, a grave air, I said:

"I thought you would have liked to have seen Mdlle. Henri?"

"Oh that is the name? Yes—if it would be convenient, I should like to see her—but——" he hesitated.

"Well?"

"I should on no account wish to intrude."

"Come, then," said I. We set out. Hunsden no doubt regarded me as a rash, imprudent man, thus to show my poor little grisette sweetheart, in her poor little unfurnished grenier; but he prepared to act the real gentleman, having, in fact, the kernel of that character, under the harsh husk it pleased him to wear by way of mental mackintosh. He talked affably, and even gently, as we went along the street; he had never been so civil to me in his life. We reached the house, entered, ascended the stair; on gaining the lobby, Hunsden turned to mount a narrower stair which led to a higher storey; I saw his mind was bent on the attics.

"Here, Mr. Hunsden," said I quietly, tapping at Frances' door. He turned; in his genuine politeness he was a little disconcerted at having made the mistake; his eye reverted to the green mat, but he said nothing.

We walked in, and Frances rose from her seat near the table to receive us; her mourning attire gave her a recluse, rather conventual, but withal very distinguished look; its grave simplicity added nothing to beauty, but much to dignity; the finish of the white collar and manchettes sufficed for a relief to the merino gown of solemn black; ornament was forsworn. Frances curtsied with sedate grace, looking, as she always did, when one first accosted her, more a woman to respect than to love; I introduced Mr. Hunsden, and she expressed her happiness at making his acquaintance in French. The pure and polished accent, the low yet sweet and rather full voice, produced their effect immediately; Hunsden spoke French in reply; I had not heard him speak that language before; he managed it very well. I retired to the window-seat; Mr. Hunsden, at his hostess's invitation, occupied a chair near the hearth; from my position I could see them both, and the room too, at a glance. The room was so clean and bright, it looked like a little polished cabinet; a glass filled with flowers in the centre of the table, a fresh rose in each china cup on the mantelpiece gave it an air of *fête*. Frances was serious, and Mr. Hunsden subdued, but both mutually polite; they got on at the French swimmingly: ordinary topics were discussed with great state and decorum; I thought I had never seen two such models of propriety, for Hunsden (thanks to the constraint of the foreign tongue) was obliged to shape his phrases, and measure his sentences, with a care that forbade any eccentricity. At last England was mentioned, and Frances proceeded to ask questions. Animated by degrees, she began to change, just as a grave night-sky changes at the approach of sunrise: first it seemed as if her forehead cleared, then her eyes glittered, her features relaxed, and became quite mobile; her subdued complexion grew warm and transparent; to me she now looked pretty: before she had only looked ladylike.

She had many things to say to the Englishman just fresh from his island country, and she urged him with an enthusiasm of curiosity, which ere long thawed Hunsden's

reserve as fire thaws a congealed viper. I use this not very flattering comparison because he vividly reminded me of a snake waking from torpor, as he erected his tall form, reared his head, before a little declined, and putting back his hair from his broad Saxon forehead, showed unshaded the gleam of almost savage satire which his interlocutor's tone of eagerness and look of ardour had sufficed at once to kindle in his soul and elicit from his eyes: he was himself as Frances was herself, and in none but his own language would he now address her.

"You understand English?" was the prefatory question.

"A little."

"Well, then, you shall have plenty of it; and first, I see you've not much more sense than some others of my acquaintance" (indicating me with his thumb), "or else you'd never turn rabid about that dirty little country called England; for rabid, I see you are; I read Anglophobia in your looks, and hear it in your words. Why, Mademoiselle, is it possible, that anybody with a grain of rationality should feel enthusiasm about a mere name, and that name England? I thought you were a lady-abbess five minutes ago, and respected you accordingly; and now I see you are a sort of Swiss sibyl, with high Tory and high Church principles!"

"England is your country?" asked Frances.

"Yes."

"And you don't like it?"

"I'd be sorry to like it! A little corrupt, venal, lord-and-king-cursed nation, full of mucky pride (as they say in ——shire), and helpless pauperism; rotten with abuses, worm-eaten with prejudices!"

"You might say so of almost every state; there are abuses and prejudices everywhere, and I thought fewer in England than in other countries."

"Come to England and see. Come to Birmingham and Manchester; come to St. Giles' in London, and get a practical notion of how our system works. Examine the footprints of our august aristocracy; see how they walk in blood, crushing hearts as they go. Just put your head in at English cottage doors; get a glimpse of Famine crouched torpid on black hearthstones; of Disease lying bare on beds without coverlets, of Infamy wantoning viciously with Ignorance, though indeed Luxury is her favourite paramour, and princely halls are dearer to her than thatched hovels——"

"I was not thinking of the wretchedness and vice in England; I was thinking of the good side—of what is elevated in your character as a nation."

"There is no good side—none at least of which you can have any knowledge; for you cannot appreciate the efforts of science: narrowness of education, and obscurity of position quite incapacitate you from understanding these points; and as to historical and poetical associations, I will not insult you, Mademoiselle, by supposing that you alluded to such humbug."

"But I did partly."

Hunsden laughed—his laugh of unmitigated scorn.

"I did, Mr. Hunsden. Are you of the number of those to whom such associations give no pleasure?"

"Mademoiselle, what is an association? I never saw one. What is its length, breadth, weight, value—ay, *value*? What price will it bring in the market?"

"Your portrait, to any one who loved you, would, for the sake of association, be without price."

That inscrutable Hunsden heard this remark and felt it rather acutely, too, somewhere; for he coloured—a thing not unusual with him, when hit unawares on a tender point. A sort of trouble momentarily darkened his eye, and I believe he filled up the transient pause succeeding his antagonist's home thrust, by a wish that some one did love him as he would like to be loved—some one whose love he could unreservedly return.

The lady pursued her temporary advantage.

"If your world is a world without associations, Mr. Hunsden, I no longer wonder that you hate England so. I don't clearly know what Paradise is, and what angels are; yet taking it to be the most glorious region I can conceive, and angels the most elevated existences—if one of them—if Abdiel the faithful himself" (she was thinking of Milton) "were suddenly stripped of the faculty of association, I think he would soon rush forth from 'the ever-during gates,' leave heaven, and seek what he had lost in hell. Yes, in the very hell from which he turned 'with retorted scorn.' "

Frances' tone in saying this was as marked as her language, and it was when the word "hell" twanged off from her lips, with a somewhat startling emphasis, that Hunsden deigned to bestow one slight glance of admiration. He liked something strong, whether in man or woman; he liked whatever dared to clear conventional limits. He had never before heard a lady say "hell" with that uncompromising sort of accent, and the sound pleased him from a lady's lips; he would fain have had Frances to strike the string again, but it was not in her way. The display of eccentric vigour never gave her pleasure, and it only sounded in her voice or flashed in her countenance when extraordinary circumstances—and those generally painful—forced it out of the depths where it burned latent. To me, once or twice, she had, in intimate conversation, uttered venturous thoughts in nervous language; but when the hour of such manifestation was past, I could not recall it; it came of itself and of itself departed. Hunsden's excitations she put by soon with a smile, and recurring to the theme of disputation, said:

"Since England is nothing, why do the continental nations respect her so?"

"I should have thought no child would have asked that question," replied Hunsden, who never at any time gave information without reproving for stupidity those who asked it of him. "If you had been my pupil, as I suppose you once had the misfortune to be that of a deplorable character not a hundred miles off, I would have put you in the corner for such a confession of ignorance. Why, Mademoiselle, can't you see that it is our *gold* which buys us French politeness German good-will, and Swiss servility?" And he sneered diabolically.

"Swiss!" said Frances, catching the word "servility." "Do you call my countrymen servile?" And she started up. I could not suppress a low laugh; there was ire in her glance and defiance in her attitude. "Do you abuse Switzerland to me, Mr. Hunsden? Do you think I have no associations? Do you calculate that I am prepared to dwell only on what vice and degradation may be found in Alpine villages, and to leave quite out of my heart the social greatness of my countrymen, and our blood-earned freedom, and the natural glories of our mountains? You're mistaken—you're mistaken."

"Social greatness? Call it what you will, your countrymen are sensible fellows; they make a marketable article of what to you is an abstract idea; they have, ere this, sold their social greatness and also their blood-earned freedom to be the servants of foreign kings."

"You never were in Switzerland?"

"Yes—I have been there twice."

"You know nothing of it."

"I do."

"And you say the Swiss are mercenary, as a parrot says 'Poor Poll,' or as the Belgians here say the English are not brave, or as the French accuse them of being perfidious: there is no justice in your dictums."

"There is truth."

"I tell you, Mr. Hunsden, you are a more unpractical man than I am an unpractical woman, for you don't acknowledge what really exists; you want to annihilate individual patriotism and national greatness as an atheist would annihilate God and his own soul, by denying their existence."

''Where are you flying to? You are off at a tangent—I thought we were talking about the mercenary nature of the Swiss.''

''We were—and if you proved to me that the Swiss are mercenary to-morrow (which you cannot do) I should love Switzerland still.''

''You would be mad, then—mad as a March hare—to indulge in a passion for millions of shiploads of soil, timber, snow and ice.''

''Not so mad as you who love nothing.''

''There's a method in my madness: there's none in yours.''

''Your method is to squeeze the sap out of creation and make manure of the refuse, by way of turning it to what you call use.''

''You cannot reason at all,'' said Hunsden; ''there is no logic in you.''

''Better to be without logic than without feeling,'' retorted Frances, who was now passing backwards and forwards from her cupboard to the table, intent, if not on hospitable thoughts, at least on hospitable deeds, for she was laying the cloth, and putting plates, knives and forks thereon.

''Is that a hit at me, Mademoiselle? Do you suppose I am without feeling?''

''I suppose you are always interfering with your own feelings, and those of other people, and dogmatising about the irrationality of this, that, and the other sentiment, and then ordering it to be suppressed because you imagine it to be inconsistent with logic.''

''I do right.''

Frances had stepped out of sight into a sort of little pantry; she soon reappeared.

''You do right? Indeed, no! You are much mistaken if you think so. Just be so good as to let me get to the fire, Mr. Hunsden: I have something to cook.'' (An interval occupied in settling a casserole on the fire; then, while she stirred its contents:) ''Right! as if it were right to crush any pleasurable sentiment that God has given to man, especially any sentiment that, like patriotism, spreads man's selfishness in wider circles'' (fire stirred, dish put down before it).

''Were you born in Switzerland?''

''I should think so, or else why should I call it my country?''

''And where did you get your English features and figure?''

''I am English, too; half the blood in my veins is English; thus I have a right to a double power of patriotism, possessing an interest in two noble, free, and fortunate countries.''

''You had an English mother?''

''Yes, yes; and you, I suppose, had a mother from the moon or from Utopia, since not a nation in Europe has a claim on your interest?''

''On the contrary, I'm a universal patriot, if you could understand me rightly: my country is the world.''

''Sympathies so widely diffused must be very shallow: will you have the goodness to come to table? Monsieur'' (to me, who appeared to be now absorbed in reading by moonlight)—''Monsieur, supper is served.''

This was said in quite a different voice to that in which she had been bandying phrases with Mr. Hunsden—not so short, graver and softer.

''Frances, what do you mean by preparing supper? we had no intention of staying.''

''Ah, Monsieur, but you have stayed, and supper is prepared; you have only the alternative of eating it.''

The meal was a foreign one, of course; it consisted in two small but tasty dishes of meat prepared with skill and served with nicety; a salad and ''fromage français,'' completed it. The business of eating interposed a brief truce between the belligerents, but no sooner was supper disposed of than they were at it again. The fresh subject of dispute ran on the spirit of religious intolerance, which Mr. Hunsden affirmed to exist strongly in Switzerland, notwithstanding the professed attachment of the Swiss to freedom. Here Frances had greatly the worst of it, not only because she

was unskilled to argue, but because her own real opinions on the point in question happened to coincide pretty nearly with Mr. Hunsden's, and she only contradicted him out of opposition. At the last she gave in, confessing that she thought as he thought, but bidding him take notice that she did not consider herself beaten.

"No more did the French at Waterloo," said Hunsden.

"There is no comparison between the cases," rejoined Frances; "mine was a sham fight."

"Sham or real, it's up with you."

"No; though I have neither logic nor wealth of words, yet in a case where my opinion really differed from yours, I would adhere to it when I had not another word to say in its defence; you should be baffled by dumb determination. You speak of Waterloo; your Wellington ought to have been conquered there, according to Napoleon; but he persevered in spite of the laws of war, and was victorious in defiance of military tactics. I would do as he did."

"I'll be bound for it you would; probably you have some of the same sort of stubborn stuff in you."

"I should be sorry if I had not; he and Tell were brothers, and I'd scorn the Swiss, man or woman, who had none of the much-enduring nature of our heroic William in his soul."

"If Tell was like Wellington, he was an ass."

"Does not *ass* mean *baudet*?" asked Frances, turning to me.

"No, no," replied I, "it means an *esprit-fort*; and now," I continued, as I saw that fresh occasion of strife was brewing between these two, "it is high time to go."

Hunsden rose. "Good-bye," said he to Frances; "I shall be off for this glorious England to-morrow, and it may be twelve months or more before I come to Brussels again; whenever I do come I'll seek you out, and you shall see if I don't find means to make you fiercer than a dragon. You've done pretty well this evening, but next interview you shall challenge me outright. Meantime you're doomed to become Mrs. William Crimsworth, I suppose; poor young lady! but you have a spark of spirit; cherish it, and give the Professor the full benefit thereof."

"Are you married, Mr. Hunsden?" asked Frances suddenly.

"No. I should have thought you might have guessed I was a Benedict by my look."

"Well, whenever you marry don't take a wife out of Switzerland; for if you begin blaspheming Helvetia, and cursing the cantons—above all, if you mention the word *ass* in the same breath with the name Tell (for ass *is* baudet, I know; though Monsieur is pleased to translate it *esprit-fort*) your mountain maid will some night smother her Breton-bretonnant, even as your own Shakespeare's Othello smothered Desdemona."

"I am warned," said Hunsden; "and so are you, lad" (nodding to me). "I hope yet to hear of a travesty of the Moor and his gentle lady, in which the parts shall be reversed according to the plan just sketched—you, however, being in my nightcap. Farewell, Mademoiselle!" He bowed on her hand, absolutely like Sir Charles Grandison on that of Harriet Byron; adding—"Death from such fingers would not be without charms."

"Mon Dieu!" murmured Frances, opening her large eyes and lifting her distinctly arched brows; "c'est qu'il fait des compliments! je ne m'y suis pas attendu." She smiled, half in ire, half in mirth, curtsied with foreign grace, and so they parted.

No sooner had we got into the street than Hunsden collared me.

"And that is your lace-mender?" said he; "and you reckon you have done a fine, magnanimous thing in offering to marry her? You, a scion of Seacombe, have proved your disdain of social distinctions by taking up with an *ouvrière*! And I pitied the fellow, thinking his feelings had misled him, and that he had hurt himself by contracting a low match!"

"Just let go my collar, Hunsden."

On the contrary, he swayed me to and fro; so I grappled him round the waist. It was dark; the street lonely and lampless. We had then a tug for it; and after we had both rolled on the pavement, and with difficulty picked ourselves up, we agreed to walk on more soberly.

"Yes, that's my lace-mender," said I; "and she is to be mine for life—God willing."

"God is not willing—you can't suppose it; what business have you to be suited so well with a partner? And she treats you with a sort of respect, too, and says, 'Monsieur,' and modulates her tone in addressing you, actually, as if you were something superior! She could not evince more deference to such a one as I, were she favoured by fortune to the supreme extent of being my choice instead of yours."

"Hunsden, you're a puppy. But you've only seen the title page of my happiness; you don't know the tale that follows; you cannot conceive the interest and sweet variety and thrilling excitement of the narrative."

Hunsden—speaking low and deep, for we had now entered a busier street— desired me to hold my peace, threatening to do something dreadful if I stimulated his wrath further by boasting. I laughed till my sides ached. We soon reached his hotel; before he entered it, he said:

"Don't be vainglorious. Your lace-mender is too good for you, but not good enough for me; neither physically nor morally does she come up to my ideal of a woman. No; I dream of something far beyond that pale-faced, excitable little Helvetian (by-the-bye, she has infinitely more of the nervous, mobile Parisienne in her than of the robust 'jungfrau'). Your Mdlle. Henri is in person chétive, in mind sans caractère, compared with the queen of my visions. You, indeed, may put up with that minois chiffonné; but when I marry I must have straighter and more harmonious features, to say nothing of a nobler and better developed shape than that perverse, ill-shriven child can boast."

"Bribe a seraph to fetch you a coal of fire from heaven, if you will," said I, "and with it kindle life in the tallest, fattest, most boneless, fullest-blooded of Rubens' painted women—leave me only my Alpine peri, and I'll not envy you."

With a simultaneous movement, each turned his back on the other. Neither said "God bless you"; yet on the morrow the sea was to roll between us.

Chapter XXV

IN two months more Frances had fulfilled the time of mourning for her aunt. One January morning—the first of the new year holidays—I went in a fiacre, accompanied only by M. Vandenhuten, to the Rue Notre Dame aux Neiges, and having alighted alone and walked upstairs, I found Frances apparently waiting for me, dressed in a style scarcely appropriate to that cold, bright, frosty day. Never till now had I seen her attired in any other than black or sad-coloured stuff; and there she stood by the window, clad all in white, and white of a most diaphanous texture; her array was very simple, to be sure, but it looked imposing and festal because it was so clear, full, and floating; a veil shadowed her head, and hung below her knee; a little wreath of pink flowers fastened it to her thickly tressed Grecian plait, and thence it fell softly on each side of her face. Singular to state, she was, or had been crying; when I asked her if she were ready, she said "Yes, Monsieur," with something very like a checked sob; and when I took a shawl, which lay on the table, and folded it round her, not only did tear after tear course unbidden down her cheek, but she shook to my ministration like a reed. I said I was sorry to see her in such low spirits, and requested to be allowed an insight into the origin thereof.

She only said, "It was impossible to help it," and then voluntarily, though hurriedly, putting her hand into mine, accompanied me out of the room, and ran downstairs with a quick, uncertain step, like one who was eager to get some formidable piece of business over. I put her into the fiacre, M. Vandenhuten received her, and seated her beside himself; we drove all together to the Protestant chapel, went through a certain service in the Common Prayer Book, and she and I came out married. M. Vanderhuten had given the bride away.

We took no bridal trip; our modesty, screened by the peaceful obscurity of our station, and the pleasant isolation of our circumstances, did not exact that additional precaution. We repaired at once to a small house I had taken in the faubourg nearest to that part of the city where the scene of our avocations lay.

Three or four hours after the wedding ceremony, Frances, divested of her bridal snow, and attired in a pretty lilac gown of warmer materials, a piquant black silk apron, and a lace collar with some finishing decoration of lilac ribbon, was kneeling on the carpet of a neatly furnished though not spacious parlour, arranging on the shelves of a chiffonière some books, which I handed to her from the table. It was snowing fast out of doors; the afternoon had turned out wild and cold; the leaden sky seemed full of drifts, and the street was already ankle-deep in the white downfall. Our fire burned bright, our new habitation looked brilliantly clean and fresh, the furniture was all arranged, and there were but some articles of glass, china, books, etc., to put in order. Frances found in this business occupation till teatime, and then, after I had distinctly instructed her how to make a cup of tea in rational English style, and after she had got over the dismay occasioned by seeing such an extravagant amount of material put into the pot, she administered to me a proper British repast, at which there wanted neither candles nor urn, firelight nor comfort.

Our week's holiday glided by, and we re-addressed ourselves to labour. Both my wife and I began in good earnest with the notion that we were working people, destined to earn our bread by exertion, and that of the most assiduous kind. Our days were thoroughly occupied; we used to part every morning at eight o'clock, and not meet again till five P.M.; but into what sweet rest did the turmoil of each busy day decline! Looking down the vista of memory, I see the evenings passed in that little parlour like a long string of rubies circling the dusk brow of the past. Unvaried were they as each cut gem, and like each gem brilliant and burning.

A year and a half passed. One morning (it was a *fête*, and we had the day to ourselves) Frances said to me, with a suddenness peculiar to her when she had been thinking long on a subject, and at last, having come to a conclusion, wished to test its soundness by the touchstone of my judgment:

"I don't work enough."

"What now?" demanded I, looking up from my coffee, which I had been deliberately stirring, while enjoying, in anticipation, a walk I proposed to take with Frances, that fine summer day (it was June), to a certain farmhouse in the country, where we were to dine. "What now?" and I saw at once, in the serious ardour of her face, a project of vital importance.

"I am not satisfied," returned she: "you are now earning eight thousand francs a year" (it was true; my efforts, punctuality, the fame of my pupils' progress, the publicity of my station, had so far helped me on), "while I am still at my miserable twelve hundred francs. I *can* do better, and I *will*."

"You work as long and as diligently as I do, Frances."

"Yes, Monsieur, but I am not working in the right way, and I am convinced of it."

"You wish to change—you have a plan for progress in your mind; go and put on your bonnet; and, while we take our walk, you shall tell me of it."

"Yes, Monsieur."

She went—as docile as a well-trained child; she was a curious mixture of tractability and firmness; I sat thinking about her, and wondering what her plan could be, when she re-entered.

"Monsieur, I have given Minnie" (our bonne) "leave to go out too, as it is so very fine; so will you be kind enough to lock the door, and take the key with you?"

"Kiss me, Mrs. Crimsworth," was my not very apposite reply; but she looked so engaging in her light summer dress and little cottage bonnet, and her manner in speaking to me was then, as always, so unaffectedly and suavely respectful, that my heart expanded at the sight of her, and a kiss seemed necessary to content its importunity.

"There, Monsieur."

"Why do you always call me 'Monsieur'? Say, 'William.' "

"I cannot pronounce your W; besides, 'Monsieur' belongs to you; I like it best."

Minnie having departed in clean cap and smart shawl we, too, set out, leaving the house solitary and silent—silent, at least, but for the ticking of the clock. We were soon clear of Brussels; the fields received us, and then the lanes, remote from carriage-resounding *chaussées*. Ere long we came upon a nook, so rural, green, and secluded, it might have been a spot in some pastoral English province; a bank of short and mossy grass, under a hawthorn, offered a seat too tempting to be declined; we took it, and when we had admired and examined some English-looking wildflowers growing at our feet, I recalled Frances' attention and my own to the topic touched on at breakfast.

"What was her plan?" A natural one—the next step to be mounted by us, or, at least, by her, if she wanted to rise in her profession. She proposed to begin a school. We already had the means for commencing on a careful scale, having lived greatly within our income. We possessed, too, by this time, an extensive and eligible connection, in the sense advantageous to our business; for, though our circle of visiting acquaintance continued as limited as ever, we were now widely known in schools and families as teachers. When Frances had developed her plan, she intimated, in some closing sentences, her hopes for the future. If we only had good health and tolerable success, we might, she was sure, in time realise an independency; and that, perhaps, before we were too old to enjoy it; then both she and I would rest; and what was to hinder us from going to live in England? England was still her Promised Land.

I put no obstacle in her way; raised no objection; I knew she was not one who could live quiescent and inactive, or even comparatively inactive. Duties she must have to fulfil, and important duties; work to do—and exciting, absorbing, profitable work; strong faculties stirred in her frame, and they demanded full nourishment, free exercise: mine was not the hand ever to starve or cramp them; no, I delighted in offering them sustenance, and in clearing them wider space for action.

"You have conceived a plan, Frances," said I, "and a good plan; execute it; you have my free consent, and wherever and whenever my assistance is wanted, ask and you shall have."

Frances' eye thanked me almost with tears; just a sparkle or two, soon brushed away; she possessed herself of my hand too, and held it for some time very close clasped in both her own, but she said no more than "Thank you, Monsieur."

We passed a divine day, and came home late, lighted by a full summer moon.

Ten years rushed now upon me with dusty, vibrating, unresting wings; years of bustle, action, unslacked endeavour; years in which I and my wife, having launched ourselves in the full career of progress, as progress whirls on in European capitals, scarcely knew repose, were strangers to amusement, never thought of indulgence, and yet, as our course ran side by side, as we marched hand in hand, we neither murmured, repented, nor faltered. Hope indeed cheered us; health kept us up; harmony of thought and deed smoothed many difficulties, and finally, success bestowed every now and then encouraging reward on diligence. Our school became

one of the most popular in Brussels, and as by degrees we raised our terms and elevated our system of education, our choice of pupils grew more select, and at length included the children of the best families in Belgium. We had too an excellent connection in England, first opened by the unsolicited recommendation of Mr. Hunsden, who having been over, and having abused me for my prosperity in set terms, went back, and soon after sent a leash of young ——shire heiresses—his cousins; as he said, "to be polished off by Mrs. Crimsworth."

As to this same Mrs. Crimsworth, in one sense she was become another woman, though in another she remained unchanged. So different was she under different circumstances, I seemed to possess two wives. The faculties of her nature, already disclosed when I married her, remained fresh and fair; but other faculties shot up strong, branched out broad, and quite altered the external character of the plant. Firmness, activity, and enterprise, covered with grave foliage, poetic feeling and fervour; but these flowers were still there, preserved pure and dewy under the umbrage of later growth and hardier nature: perhaps I only in the world knew the secret of their existence, but to me they were ever ready to yield an exquisite fragrance and present a beauty as chaste as radiant.

In the daytime my house and establishment were conducted by Madame the directress, a stately and elegant woman, bearing much anxious thought on her large brow; much calculated dignity in her serious mien: immediately after breakfast I used to part with this lady; I went to my college, she to her schoolroom; returning for an hour in the course of the day, I found her always in class, intently occupied; silence, industry, observance, attending on her presence. When not actually teaching, she was overlooking and guiding by eye and gesture; she then appeared vigilant and solicitous. When communicating instruction, her aspect was more animated; she seemed to feel a certain enjoyment in the occupation. The language in which she addressed her pupils, though simple and unpretending, was never trite or dry; she did not speak from routine formulas—she made her own phrases as she went on, and very nervous and impressive phrases they frequently were; often, when elucidating favourite points of history, or geography, she would wax genuinely eloquent in her earnestness. Her pupils, or at least the elder and more intelligent amongst them, recognised well the language of a superior mind; they felt too, and some of them received the impression of elevated sentiments; there was little fondling between mistress and girls, but some of Frances' pupils in time learnt to love her sincerely, all of them beheld her with respect; her general demeanour towards them was serious; sometimes benignant when they pleased her with their progress and attention, always scrupulously refined and considerate. In cases where reproof or punishment was called for she was usually forbearing enough; but if any took advantage of that forbearance, which sometimes happened, a sharp, sudden, and lightning-like severity taught the culprit the extent of the mistake committed. Sometimes a gleam of tenderness softened her eyes and manner, but this was rare; only when a pupil was sick, or when it pined after home, or in the case of some little motherless child, or of one much poorer than its companions, whose scanty wardrobe and mean appointments brought on it the contempt of the jewelled young countesses and silk-clad misses. Over such feeble fledglings the directress spread a wing of kindliest protection: it was to their bedside she came at night to tuck them warmly in; it was after them she looked in winter to see that they always had a comfortable seat by the stove; it was they who by turns were summoned to the salon to receive some little dole of cake or fruit—to sit on a footstool at the fireside—to enjoy home comforts, and almost home liberty, for an evening together—to be spoken to gently and softly, comforted, encouraged, cherished—and when bedtime came, dismissed with a kiss of true tenderness. As to Julia and Georgiana G——, daughters of an English baronet, as to Mdlle. Mathilde de ——, heiress of a Belgian count, and sundry other children of patrician race, the directress was careful of them as of the others, anxious for their progress, as for that of the rest—but it never seemed to

enter her head to distinguish them by a mark of preference; one girl of noble blood she loved dearly—a young Irish baroness—Lady Catherine ——; but it was for her enthusiastic heart and clever head, for her generosity and her genius, the title and rank went for nothing.

My afternoons were spent also in college, with the exception of an hour that my wife daily exacted of me for her establishment, and with which she would not dispense. She said that I must spend that time amongst her pupils to learn their characters, to be *au courant* with everything that was passing in the house, to become interested in what interested her, to be able to give her my opinion on knotty points when she required it, and this she did constantly, never allowing my interest in the pupils to fall asleep, and never making any change of importance without my cognisance and consent. She delighted to sit by me when I gave my lessons (lessons in literature), her hands folded on her knee, the most fixedly attentive of any present. She rarely addressed me in class; when she did it was with an air of marked deference; it was her pleasure, her joy to make me still the master in all things.

At six o'clock P.M. my daily labours ceased. I then came home, for my home was my heaven; ever at that hour, as I entered our private sitting-room, the lady directress vanished from before my eyes, and Frances Henri, my own little lace-mender, was magically restored to my arms; much disappointed she would have been if her master had not been as constant to the tryste as herself, and if his truthful kiss had not been prompt to answer her soft, "Bon soir, Monsieur."

Talk French to me she would, and many a punishment she has had for her wilfulness. I fear the choice of chastisement must have been injudicious, for instead of correcting the fault, it seemed to encourage its renewal. Our evenings were our own; that recreation was necessary to refresh our strength for the due discharge of our duties; sometimes we spent them all in conversation, and my young Genevese, now that she was thoroughly accustomed to her English professor, now that she loved him too absolutely to fear him much, reposed in him a confidence so unlimited that topics of conversation could no more be wanting with him than subjects for communion with her own heart. In those moments, happy as a bird with its mate, she would show me what she had of vivacity, of mirth, of originality in her well-dowered nature. She would show, too, some stores of raillery, of "malice," and would vex, tease, pique me sometimes about what she called my "bizarreries anglaises," my "caprices insulaires," with a wild and witty wickedness that made a perfect white demon of her while it lasted. This was rare, however, and the elfish freak was always short: sometimes when driven a little hard in the war of words—for her tongue did ample justice to the pith, the point, the delicacy of her native French, in which language she always attacked me—I used to turn upon her with my old decision, and arrest bodily the sprite that teased me. Vain idea! no sooner had I grasped hand or arm than the elf was gone; the provocative smile quenched in the expressive brown eyes, and a ray of gentle homage shone under the lids in its place. I had seized a mere vexing fairy, and found a submissive and supplicating little mortal woman in my arms. Then I made her get a book, and read English to me for an hour by way of penance. I frequently dosed her with Wordsworth in this way, and Wordsworth steadied her soon; she had a difficulty in comprehending his deep, serene, and sober mind; his language, too, was not facile to her; she had to ask questions, to sue for explanations, to be like a child and a novice, and to acknowledge me as her senior and director. Her instinct instantly penetrated and possessed the meaning of more ardent and imaginative writers. Byron excited her; Scott she loved; Wordsworth only she puzzled at, wondered over, and hesitated to pronounce an opinion upon.

But whether she read to me, or talked with me; whether she teased me in French, or entreated me in English; whether she jested with wit, or inquired with deference; narrated with interest or listened with attention; whether she smiled *at* me or *on*

me, always at nine o'clock I was left—abandoned. She would extricate herself from my arms, quit my side, take her lamp, and be gone. Her mission was upstairs; I have followed her sometimes and watched her. First she opened the door of the dortoir (the pupils' chamber), noiselessly she glided up the long room between the two rows of white beds, surveyed all the sleepers; if any were wakeful, especially if any were sad, spoke to them and soothed them; stood some minutes to ascertain that all was safe and tranquil; trimmed the watch-light which burned in the apartment all night, then withdrew, closing the door behind her without sound. Thence she glided to our own chamber; it had a little cabinet within; this she sought; there, too, appeared a bed, but one, and that a very small one; her face (the night I followed and observed her) changed as she approached this tiny couch; from grave it warmed to earnest; she shaded with one hand the lamp she held in the other; she bent above the pillow and hung over a child asleep; its slumber (that evening at least, and usually, I believe) was sound and calm; no tear wet its dark eyelashes; no fever heated its round cheek; no ill dream discomposed its budding features. Frances gazed, she did not smile, and yet the deepest delight filled, flushed her face; feeling, pleasurable, powerful, worked in her whole frame, which still was motionless. I saw, indeed, her heart heave, her lips were a little apart, her breathing grew somewhat hurried; the child smiled; then at last the mother smiled too, and said in low soliloquy, "God bless my little son!" She stooped closer over him, breathed the softest of kisses on his brow, covered his minute hand with hers, and at last started up and came away. I regained the parlour before her. Entering it two minutes later she said quietly as she put down her extinguished lamp:

"Victor rests well: he smiled in his sleep; he has your smile, Monsieur."

The said Victor was of course her own boy, born in the third year of our marriage: his Christian name had been given in honour of M. Vandenhuten, who continued always our trusty and well-beloved friend.

Frances was then a good and dear wife to me, because I was to her a good, just, and faithful husband. What she would have been had she married a harsh, envious, careless man—a profligate, a prodigal, a drunkard, or a tyrant—is another question, and one which I once propounded to her. Her answer, given after some reflection, was:

"I should have tried to endure the evil or cure it for a while; and when I found it intolerable and incurable, I should have left my torturer suddenly and silently."

"And if law or might had forced you back again?"

"What, to a drunkard, a profligate, a selfish spendthrift, an unjust fool?"

"Yes."

"I would have gone back; again assured myself whether or not his vice and my misery were capable of remedy; and if not, have left him again."

"And if again forced to return, and compelled to abide?"

"I don't know," she said hastily. "Why do you ask me, Monsieur?"

I would have an answer, because I saw a strange kind of spirit in her eye, whose voice I determined to waken.

"Monsieur, if a wife's nature loathes that of the man she is wedded to, marriage must be slavery. Against slavery all right thinkers revolt, and though torture be the price of resistance, torture must be dared: though the only road to freedom lie through the gates of death, those gates must be passed; for freedom is indispensable. Then, Monsieur, I would resist as far as my strength permitted; when that strength failed I should be sure of a refuge. Death would certainly screen me both from bad laws and their consequences."

"Voluntary death, Frances?"

"No, Monsieur. I'd have courage to live out every throe of anguish fate assigned me, and principle to contend for justice and liberty to the last."

"I see you would have made no patient Grizzle. And now, supposing fate had merely assigned you the lot of an old maid, what then? How would you have liked celibacy?"

"Not much, certainly. An old maid's life must doubtless be void and vapid— her heart strained and empty. Had I been an old maid I should have spent existence in efforts to fill the void and ease the aching. I should have probably failed and died weary and disappointed, despised and of no account, like other single women. But I'm not an old maid," she added quickly, "I should have been, though, but for my master. I should never have suited any man but Professor Crimsworth—no other gentleman, French, English, or Belgian, would have thought me amiable or handsome; and I doubt whether I should have cared for the approbation of many others, if I could have obtained it. Now, I have been Professor Crimsworth's wife eight years, and what is he in my eyes? Is he honourable, beloved——" She stopped, her voice was cut off, her eyes suddenly suffused. She and I were standing side by side; she threw her arms round me, and strained me to her heart with passionate earnestness: the energy of her whole being glowed in her dark and then dilated eye, and crimsoned her animated cheek; her look and movement were like inspiration; in one there was such a flash, in the other such a power. Half-an-hour afterwards, when she had become calm, I asked where all that wild vigour was gone which had transformed her erewhile and made her glance so thrilling and ardent—her action so rapid and strong. She looked down, smiling softly and passively:

"I cannot tell where it is gone, Monsieur," said she; "but I know that, whenever it is wanted, it will come back again."

Behold us now at the close of the ten years, and we have realised an independency. The rapidity with which we attained this end had its origin in three reasons: Firstly, we worked so hard for it; secondly, we had no incumbrances to delay success; thirdly, as soon as we had capital to invest, two well-skilled counsellors, one in Belgium, one in England, viz., Vandenhuten and Hunsden, gave us each a word of advice as to the sort of investment to be chosen. The suggestion made was judicious; and, being promptly acted on, the result proved gainful—I need not say how gainful; I communicated details to Messrs. Vandenhuten and Hunsden; nobody else can be interested in hearing them.

Accounts being wound up, and our professional connection disposed of, we both agreed that, as Mammon was not our master, nor his service that in which we desired to spend our lives; as our desires were temperate, and our habits unostentatious, we had now abundance to live on—abundance to leave our boy; and should besides always have a balance on hand, which, properly managed by right sympathy and unselfish activity, might help philanthropy in her enterprises, and put solace into the hand of charity.

To England we now resolved to take wing; we arrived there safely; Frances realised the dream of her lifetime. We spent a whole summer and autumn in travelling from end to end of the British Islands, and afterwards passed a winter in London. Then we thought it high time to fix our residence. My heart yearned towards my native county of ——shire; and it is in ——shire I now live; it is in the library of my own home I am now writing. That home lies amid a sequestered and rather hilly region, thirty miles removed from X——; a region whose verdure the smoke of mills has not yet sullied, whose waters still run pure, whose swells of moorland preserve in some ferny glens that lie between them the very primal wildness of nature, her moss, her bracken, her blue-bells, her scents of reed and heather, her free and fresh breezes. My house is a picturesque and not too spacious dwelling, with low and long windows, a trellised and leaf-veiled porch over the front door, just now, on this summer evening, looking like an arch of roses and ivy. The garden is chiefly laid out in lawn, formed of the sod of the hills, with herbage short and soft as moss, full of its own peculiar flowers, tiny and starlike, imbedded in the minute embroidery of their fine foliage. At the bottom of the

sloping garden there is a wicket, which opens upon a lane as green as the lawn, very long, shady, and little frequented; on the turf of this lane generally appear the first daisies of spring—whence its name—Daisy Lane; serving also as a distinction to the house.

It terminates (the lane I mean) in a valley full of wood; which wood—chiefly oak and beech—spreads shadowy about the vicinage of a very old mansion, one of the Elizabethan structures, much larger, as well as more antique than Daisy Lane, the property and residence of an individual familiar both to me and to the reader. Yes, in Hunsden Wood—for so are those glades and that grey building, with many gables and more chimneys, named—abides Yorke Hunsden, still unmarried; never, I suppose, having yet found his ideal, though I know at least a score of young ladies within a circuit of forty miles, who would be willing to assist him in the search.

The estate fell to him by the death of his father, five years since; he has given up trade, after having made by it sufficient to pay off some incumbrances by which the family heritage was burdened. I say he abides here, but I do not think he is resident above five months out of the twelve; he wanders from land to land, and spends some part of each winter in town: he frequently brings visitors with him when he comes to ——shire, and these visitors are often foreigners; sometimes he has a German metaphysician, sometimes a French savant; he had once a dissatisfied and savage-looking Italian, who neither sang nor played, and of whom Frances affirmed that he had "tout l'air d'un conspirateur."

What English guests Hunsden invites, are all either men of Birmingham or Manchester—hard men, seemingly knit up in one thought, whose talk is of free trade. The foreign visitors, too, are politicians; they take a wider theme—European progress—the spread of liberal sentiments over the Continent; on their mental tablets, the names of Russia, Austria, and the Pope, are inscribed in red ink. I have heard some of them talk vigorous sense—yea, I have been present at polyglot discussions in the old, oak-lined dining-room at Hunsden Wood, where a singular insight was given of the sentiments entertained by resolute minds respecting old northern despotisms, and old southern superstitions; also, I have heard much twaddle, enounced chiefly in French and Deutsch, but let that pass. Hunsden himself tolerated the drivelling theorists; with the practical men he seemed leagued hand and heart.

When Hunsden is staying alone at the Wood (which seldom happens) he generally finds his way two or three times a week to Daisy Lane. He has a philanthropic motive for coming to smoke his cigar in our porch on summer evenings; he says he does it to kill the earwigs amongst the roses, with which insects, but for his benevolent fumigations, he intimates we should certainly be overrun. On wet days, too, we are almost sure to see him; according to him, it gets on time to work me into lunacy by treading on my mental corns, or to force from Mrs. Crimsworth revelations of the dragon within her, by insulting the memory of Hofer and Tell.

We also go frequently to Hunsden Wood, and both I and Frances relish a visit there highly. If there are other guests, their characters are an interesting study; their conversation is exciting and strange; the absence of all local narrowness both in the host and his chosen society gives a metropolitan, almost a cosmopolitan freedom and largeness to the talk. Hunsden himself is a polite man in his own house; he has, when he chooses to employ it, an inexhaustible power of entertaining guests; his very mansion too is interesting, the rooms look storied, the passages legendary, the low-ceiled chambers, with their long rows of diamond-paned lattices, have an old-world, haunted air; in his travels he has collected stores of articles of *vertu,* which are well and tastefully disposed in his panelled or tapestried rooms: I have seen there one or two pictures, and one or two pieces of statuary which many an aristocratic connoisseur might have envied.

When I and Frances have dined and spent an evening with Hunsden, he often walks home with us. His wood is large, and some of the timber is old and of huge

growth. There are winding ways in it which, pursued through glade and brake, make the walk back to Daisy Lane a somewhat long one. Many a time, when we have had the benefit of a full moon, and when the night has been mild and balmy, when, moreover, a certain nightingale has been singing, and a certain stream, hid in alders, has lent the song a soft accompaniment, the remote church-bell of the one hamlet in a district of ten miles, has tolled midnight ere the lord of the wood left us at our porch. Free-flowing was his talk at such hours, and far more quiet and gentle than in the daytime and before numbers. He would then forget politics and discussion, and would dwell on the past times of his house, on his family history, on himself and his own feelings—subjects each and all invested with a peculiar zest, for they were each and all unique. One glorious night in June, after I had been taunting him about his ideal bride and asking him when she would come and graft her foreign beauty on the old Hunsden oak, he answered suddenly:

"You call her ideal; but see, here is her shadow; and there cannot be a shadow without a substance."

He had led us from the depth of the "winding way" into a glade from whence the beeches withdrew, leaving it open to the sky; an unclouded moon poured her light into this glade, and Hunsden held out under her beam an ivory miniature.

Frances, with eagerness examined it first; then she gave it to me—still, however, pushing her little face close to mine, and seeking in my eyes what I thought of the portrait. I thought it represented a very handsome and very individual-looking female face, with, as he had once said, "straight and harmonious features." It was dark; the hair, raven-black, swept not only from the brow, but from the temples—seemed thrust away carelessly, as if such beauty dispensed with, nay, despised arrangement. The Italian eye looked straight into you, and an independent, determined eye it was; the mouth was as firm as fine; the chin ditto. On the back of the miniature was gilded "Lucia."

"That is a real head," was my conclusion.

Hunsden smiled.

"I think so," he replied. "All was real in Lucia."

"And she was somebody you would have liked to marry—but could not?"

"I should certainly have liked to marry her, and that I *have* not done so is a proof that I *could* not."

He repossessed himself of the miniature, now again in Frances' hand, and put it away.

"What do *you* think of it?" he asked of my wife, as he buttoned his coat over it.

"I am sure Lucia once wore chains and broke them," was the strange answer. "I do not mean matrimonial chains," she added, correcting herself, as if she feared misinterpretation, "but social chains of some sort. The face is that of one who has made an effort, and a successful and triumphant effort, to wrest some vigorous and valued faculty from insupportable constraint; and when Lucia's faculty got free, I am certain it spread wide pinions and carried her higher than——" She hesitated.

"Than what?" demanded Hunsden.

"Than 'les convenances' permitted you to follow."

"I think you grow spiteful—impertinent."

"Lucia has trodden the stage," continued Frances. "You never seriously thought of marrying her; you admitted her originality, her fearlessness, her energy of body and mind: you delighted in her talent, whatever that was, whether song, dance, or dramatic representation; you worshipped her beauty, which was of the sort after your own heart: but I am sure she filled a sphere from whence you would never have thought of taking a wife."

"Ingenious," remarked Hunsden; "whether true or not is another question. Meantime, don't you feel your little lamp of a spirit wax very pale, beside such a girandole as Lucia's?"

"Yes."

"Candid, at least; and the Professor will soon be dissatisfied with the dim light you give?"

"Will you, Monsieur?"

"My sight was always too weak to endure a blaze, Frances," and we had now reached the wicket.

I said, a few pages back, that this is a sweet summer evening; it is—there has been a series of lovely days, and this is the loveliest; the hay is just carried from my fields, its perfume still lingers in the air. Frances proposed to me, an hour or two since, to take tea out on the lawn; I see the round table, loaded with china, placed under a certain beech; Hunsden is expected—nay, I hear he is come—there is his voice, laying down the law on some point with authority; that of Frances replies; she opposes him of course. They are disputing about Victor, of whom Hunsden affirms that his mother is making a milksop. Mrs. Crimsworth retaliates:

Better a thousand times he should be a milksop than what he, Hunsden, calls "a fine lad": and moreover she says that if Hunsden were to become a fixture in the neighbourhood, and were not a mere comet, coming and going, no one knows how, when, where, or why, she should be quite uneasy till she had got Victor away to a school at least a hundred miles off; for that with his mutinous maxims and unpractical dogmas, he would ruin a score of children.

I have a word to say of Victor ere I shut this manuscript in my desk—but it must be a brief one, for I hear the tinkle of silver on porcelain.

Victor is as little of a pretty child as I am of a handsome man, or his mother of a fine woman; he is pale and spare, with large eyes, as dark as those of Frances, and as deeply set as mine. His shape is symmetrical enough, but slight; his health is good. I never saw a child smile less than he does, nor one who knits such a formidable brow when sitting over a book that interests him, or while listening to tales of adventure, peril, or wonder, narrated by his mother, Hunsden, or myself. But though still, he is not unhappy—though serious, not morose; he has a susceptibility to pleasurable sensations almost too keen, for it amounts to enthusiasm. He learned to read in the old-fashioned way out of a spelling-book at his mother's knee, and as he got on without driving by that method, she thought it unnecessary to buy him ivory letters, or to try any of the other inducements to learning now deemed indispensable. When he could read, he became a glutton of books, and is so still. His toys have been few, and he has never wanted more. For those he possesses, he seems to have contracted a partiality amounting to affection; this feeling, directed towards one or two living animals of the house, strengthens almost to a passion.

Mr. Hunsden gave him a mastiff cub, which he called Yorke, after the donor; it grew to a superb dog, whose fierceness, however, was much modified by the companionship and caresses of its young master. He would go nowhere, do nothing without Yorke; Yorke lay at his feet while he learned his lessons, played with him in the garden, walked with him in the lane and wood, sat near his chair at meals, was fed always by his own hand, was the first thing he sought in the morning, the last he left at night. Yorke accompanied Mr. Hunsden one day to X——, and was bitten in the street by a dog in a rabid state. As soon as Hunsden had brought him home, and had informed me of the circumstance, I went into the yard and shot him where he lay licking his wound: he was dead in an instant; he had not seen me level the gun; I stood behind him. I had scarcely been ten minutes in the house, when my ear was struck with sounds of anguish: I repaired to the yard once more, for they proceeded thence. Victor was kneeling beside his dead mastiff, bent over it, embracing its bull-like neck, and lost in a passion of the wildest woe; he saw me.

"O papa, I'll never forgive you! I'll never forgive you!" was his exclamation. "You shot Yorke—I saw it from the window. I never believed you could be so cruel—I can love you no more!"

I had much ado to explain to him, with a steady voice, the stern necessity of the deed; he still, with that inconsolable and bitter accent which I cannot render, but which pierced my heart, repeated:

"He might have been cured—you should have tried—you should have burnt the wound with a hot iron, or covered it with caustic. You gave no time; and now it is too late—he is dead!"

He sank fairly down on the senseless carcase; I waited patiently a long while, till his grief had somewhat exhausted him; and then I lifted him in my arms and carried him to his mother, sure that she would comfort him best. She had witnessed the whole scene from a window; she would not come out for fear of increasing my difficulties by her emotion, but she was ready now to receive him. She took him to her kind heart, and on to her gentle lap; consoled him but with her lips, her eyes, her soft embrace, for some time; and then, when his sobs diminished, told him that Yorke had felt no pain in dying, and that if he had been left to expire naturally, his end would have been most horrible; above all, she told him that I was not cruel (for that idea seemed to give exquisite pain to poor Victor), that it was my affection for Yorke and him which had made me act so, and that I was now almost heart-broken to see him weep thus bitterly.

Victor would have been no true son of his father, had these considerations, these reasons, breathed in so low, so sweet a tone—married to caresses so benign, so tender—to looks so inspired with pitying sympathy—produced no effect on him. They did produce an effect: he grew calmer, rested his face on her shoulder, and lay still in her arms. Looking up, shortly, he asked his mother to tell him over again what she had said about Yorke having suffered no pain, and my not being cruel; the balmy words being repeated, he again pillowed his cheek on her breast, and was again tranquil.

Some hours after, he came to me in my library, asked if I forgave him, and desired to be reconciled. I drew the lad to my side, and there I kept him a good while, and had much talk with him, in the course of which he disclosed many points of feeling and thought I approved of in my son. I found, it is true, few elements of the "good fellow" or the "fine fellow" in him; scant sparkles of the spirit which loves to flash over the wine-cup, or which kindles the passions to a destroying fire; but I saw in the soil of his heart healthy and swelling germs of compassion, affection, fidelity. I discovered in the garden of his intellect a rich growth of wholesome principles—reason, justice, moral courage, promised, if not blighted, a fertile bearing. So I bestowed on his large forehead, and on his cheek— still pale with tears—a proud and contented kiss, and sent him away comforted. Yet I saw him the next day laid on the mound under which Yorke had been buried, his face covered with his hands; he was melancholy for some weeks, and more than a year elapsed before he would listen to any proposal of having another dog.

Victor learns fast. He must soon go to Eton, where, I suspect, his first year or two will be utter wretchedness: to leave me, his mother, and his home, will give his heart an agonised wrench; then, the fagging will not suit him—but emulation, thirst after knowledge, the glory of success, will stir and reward him in time. Meantime, I feel in myself a strong repugnance to fix the hour which will uproot my sole olive branch, and transplant it far from me; and, when I speak to Frances on the subject, I am heard with a kind of patient pain, as though I alluded to some fearful operation, at which her nature shudders, but from which her fortitude will not permit her to recoil. The step must, however, be taken, and it *shall* be; for, though Frances will not make a milksop of her son, she will accustom him to a style of treatment, a forbearance, a congenial tenderness, he will meet with from none else. She sees, as I also see, a something in Victor's temper—a kind of electrical ardour and power—which emits, now and then, ominous sparks; Hunsden calls it his spirit, and says it should not be curbed. I call it the leaven of the offending Adam, and consider that it should be, if not *whipped* out of him, at least soundly

disciplined; and that he will be cheap of any amount of either bodily or mental suffering which will ground him radically in the art of self-control. Frances gives this *something* in her son's marked character no name; but when it appears in the grinding of his teeth, in the glittering of his eye, in the fierce revolt of feeling against disappointment, mischance, sudden sorrow, or supposed injustice, she folds him to her breast, or takes him to walk with her alone in the wood; then she reasons with him like any philosopher, and to reason Victor is ever accessible; then she looks at him with eyes of love, and by love Victor can be infallibly subjugated; but will reason or love be the weapons with which in future the world will meet his violence? Oh, no! for that flash in his black eye—for that cloud on his bonny brow—for that compression of his statuesque lips, the lad will some day get blows instead of blandishments—kicks instead of kisses; then for the fit of mute fury which will sicken his body and madden his soul; then for the ordeal of merited and salutary suffering, out of which he will come (I trust) a wiser and a better man.

I see him now; he stands by Hunsden, who is seated on the lawn under the beech; Hunsden's hand rests on the boy's collar, and he is instilling God knows what principles into his ear. Victor looks well just now, for he listens with a sort of smiling interest; he never looks so like his mother as when he smiles—pity the sunshine breaks out so rarely! Victor has a preference for Hunsden, full as strong as I deem desirable, being considerably more potent, decided, and indiscriminating, than any I ever entertained for that personage myself. Frances, too, regards it with a sort of unexpressed anxiety; while her son leans on Hunsden's knee, or rests against his shoulder, she roves with restless movement round, like a dove guarding its young from a hovering hawk; she says she wishes Hunsden had children of his own, for then he would better know the danger of inciting their pride and indulging their foibles.

Frances approaches my library window; puts aside the honeysuckle which half covers it, and tells me tea is ready; seeing that I continue busy she enters the room, comes near me quietly, and puts her hand on my shoulder.

"Monsieur est trop appliqué."

"I shall soon have done."

She draws a chair near, and sits down to wait till I have finished; her presence is as pleasant to my mind as the perfume of the fresh hay and spicy flowers, as the glow of the western sun, as the repose of the midsummer eve are to my senses.

But Hunsden comes; I hear his step, and there he is, bending through the lattice, from which he has thrust away the woodbine with unsparing hand, disturbing two bees and a butterfly.

"Crimsworth! I say Crimsworth, take that pen out of his hand, mistress, and make him lift up his head."

"Well, Hunsden? I hear you——"

"I was at X—— yesterday! your brother Ned is getting richer than Crœsus by railway speculations; they call him in the Piece Hall a stag of ten; and I have heard from Brown. M. and Madame Vandenhuten and Jean Baptiste talk of coming to see you next month. He mentions the Pelets too; he says their domestic harmony is not the finest in the world, but in business they are doing 'on ne peut mieux,' which circumstance he concludes will be a sufficient consolation to both for any little crosses in the affections. Why don't you invite the Pelets to ——shire, Crimsworth? I should so like to see your first flame, Zoraïde. Mistress, don't be jealous, but he loved that lady to distraction; I know it for a fact. Brown says she weighs twelve stones now; you see what you've lost, Mr. Professor. Now, Monsieur and Madame, if you don't come to tea, Victor and I will begin without you."

"Papa, come!"